CERAFINA'S

Damiriak Language Handbook

1st Edition

BY
K GERARD MARTIN

Shouldercat Books

Contents

1

Overview

This book covers the Damiriak languages of Miramish, Dahmek, Nimiash and the sub-language of Mirsua as learned by me, Cerafina, from my good friend, Jonara. I have done my best to record the words as accurately as possible. I know I haven't recorded everything—Damiriak languages are far richer than I have been able to learn in such a short time. Nevertheless, I believe I have recorded enough in this book to give others a fair chance at learning the languages. This edition contains over 21,000 words for each main language (Dahmek, Miramish, and Nimiash) of which 11,600 or so are root words.

The story of Damiriak women and their empire goes beyond the scope of this book, but in short, they are a race of women living on several planets in a binary star system known as the Damiriak solar system. There are three primary planets of habitation—Eho Miriam, Eho Dahma, and Nimsant. All life in the solar system began on Eho Miriam and later spread to Eho Dahma. There are no male mammals living in the solar system—the crimson-cerise colored star named *Seris* prevents it.

Miramish women live on Eho Miriam and speak Miramish. Dahmek women live on Eho Dahma and speak Dahmek. These are the two primary planets of habitation, the *Eho* planets. A third planet, Nimsant, is only habitable in selected twilight regions and is used as a prison planet. Nimiash is spoken on Nimsant.

In the early days while men still lived, there was only one language—Old Damiriak. Old Damiriak spawned three descendant

languages—Miramish, Dahmek, and Nimiash. In the last genera-
tions of men, priestesses developed Miramish for their religious
order. As the men died off, women on Eho Miriam increasingly
spoke Miramish until no one spoke Old Damiriak.

Miramish is the first descendant Damiriak language having
been derived from Old Damiriak. Miramish words are construc-
tions of consonants and vowels, with no adjoining consonants, and
end with a vowel. For example, if *shelf* were a word in Dahmek,
the Miramish form would be *shelifa*. The exception to this rule
applies to common words across all languages such as numbers,
pronouns, and some celestial objects. Note that letters w and y are
often considered as vowels in the middle of a word for such purposes. In other words, if a w or y appears in a word, Miramish
does not require other conventional vowels (*aeiou*) to be placed
next to the w or y. However, w and y cannot appear at the end of a
Miramish word.

Miramish contains a sub-dialect known as Mirsua. Mirsua is
used by high priestesses to invoke high power.

Dahmek is the second descendant Damiriak language having
been created when Miramish women left Eho Miriam and began
colonizing Eho Dahma. Dahmek words are heavily consonant
based. Vowels are omitted to shorten words. The English word
crypt, for example, follows well in the Dahmek style, as it leads
with two consonants (with no intervening vowel), a single vowel,
two trailing consonants (with no intervening vowel), and no trailing vowel.

Nimiash is a cross between Miramish and Dahmek. Nimiash
words tend to be short (compared to Miramish and Dahmek) and
follow the Dahmek style of omitting vowels when possible. However, Nimiash word endings often follow the Miramish style.

Miramish, Dahmek, and Nimiash are more or less dialects of
one another given how some words are the same and others very
similar.

Phrase and sentence structure in Damiriak languages is very
similar to English in that a sentence is composed of a noun fol-

lowed by a verb, adjectives precede nouns, and adverbs are placed in a variety of places depending on the words they modify. There are prepositions, conjunctions, interjections, and articles—all very much like English.

Damiriak languages work on a root-word concept. What this means is that a word is used as a base, and from that root, base endings are added to create the various parts of speech. For Dahmek and Nimiash, the root word is the noun in singular form. For Miramish, the root word is never used by itself but must have an ending appended—it is the noun in singular form without the −a ending.

Damiriak words do not use helping/auxiliary verbs. In some situations, a particle is used to simulate the auxiliary verb, in other cases, the verb ending takes the place of the auxiliary verb.

2

Alphabet

There are three primary Damiriak languages and one sub-language:

- ♣ Dahmek as spoken on planet Eho Dahma,
- ♣ Miramish (main) and Mirsua (sub) as spoken on planet Eho Miriam, and
- ♣ Nimiash as spoken on planet Nimsant.

Each Damiriak language has its own alphabet (English included for comparison):

Language...	...Uses Alphabet	Sample Letters
Dahmek	Deibuth	⌐ᏰᏫ\ᏰᏗ ᏬᏛᏰᏗ
Miramish, Mirsua	Marfi	ᏰᏰᏙᏝᏰᏗ ᏒᏂᏝᏝ
Nimiash	Noimil	⌐ᏝᏝᏝᏝᏝ ᏝᏙᏝᎥ
English	Latin	Aeiou Bdzg

The following table lists the alphabets in letter order along with corresponding letter names. Letters are paired as uppercase, lowercase. When referencing a letter name in the plural form or across all three alphabets, the group name is used. For example, when referencing the letter *b* across alphabets Deibuth, Marfi, and Noimil, the group name of *bali* is used instead of *ba/bala/bal* (the individual names of each alphabet). If speaking of four *a*'s, one speaks of four *alfi*.

Deibuth-Marfi-Noimil Alphabets

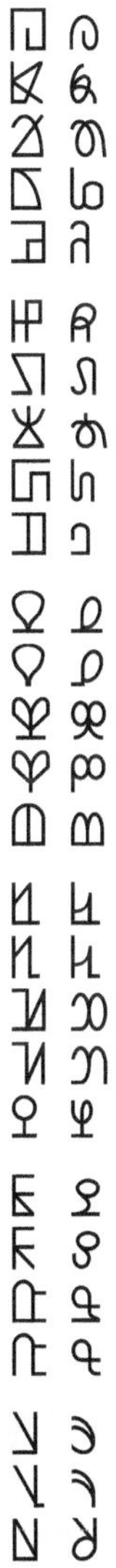
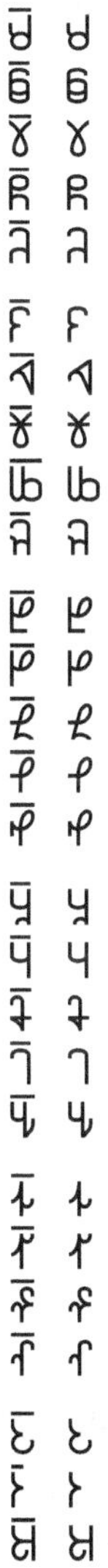
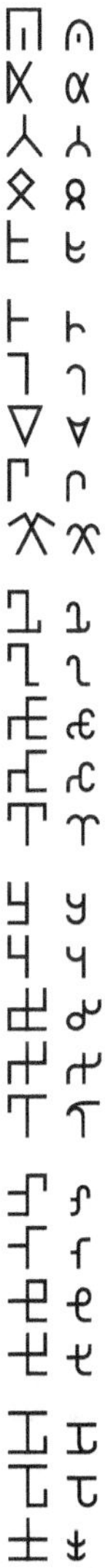

No.	Deibuth Letter	Deibuth Name	Marfi Letter	Marfi Name	Noimil Letter	Noimil Name	Group Name	Latin Equiv
1		alfe		alifa		alf	alfi	A a
2		elpe		elipa		elp	elpi	E e
3		ilpe		ilopa		ilp	ilpi	I i
4		orfe		orifa		orf	orfi	O o
5		urshe		urisha		ursh	urshi	U u
6		harfe		harifa		harf	harfi	H h
7		lerpe		leripa		lerp	lerpi	L l
8		yarle		yarila		yarl	yarli	Y y
9		relre		relira		rel	relri	R r
10		wershe		werisha		wersh	wershi	W w
11		bal		bala		ba	bali	B b
12		peil		peia		pei	peili	P p
13		val		vala		va	vali	V v
14		feil		feia		fei	feili	F f
15		mail		maia		mai	maili	M m
16		dal		dala		da	dali	D d
17		teil		teia		tei	teili	T t
18		dhal		dhala		dha	dhali	Dh dh
19		theil		theia		thei	theili	Th th
20		noil		noia		noi	noili	N n
21		zal		zala		za	zali	Z z
22		seil		seia		sei	seili	S s
23		zhal		zhala		zha	zhali	Zh zh
24		sheil		sheia		shei	sheili	Sh sh
25		gal		gala		ga	gali	G g
26		keil		keia		kei	keili	K k
27		engel		engala		enga	engali	Ng ng

Note that *dh* in *dhali* is pronounced like *th* in *that.*

These alphabets are based on a common phonology—each letter is pronounced the same way across all three languages. The following table shows:

- ♣ Each Damiriak alphabet in order with letters listed in pairs of uppercase, lowercase,
- ♣ The English pronunciation equivalent,
- ♣ The IPA character pronunciation equivalent, and
- ♣ The letter(s) used when representing a Deibuth/Marfi/Noimil letter in a Latin font.

Deibuth-Marfi-Noimil Pronunciations

No.	Deibuth	Marfi	Noimil	English Sound	IPA	Latin Character
1				*a* in f*a*ther	ɑ	A a
2				*e* in b*e*t	ɛ	E e
3				*ee* in b*ee*t	i	I i
4				*o* in p*o*rt	o	O o
5				*u* in t*u*ne	u	U u
6				*ch* in lo*ch*	x	H h
7				*l* in *l*et	l	L l
8				*y* in *y*et	j	Y y
9				trilled *r*	r	R r
10				*w* in *w*et	w	W w
11				*b* in *b*at	b	B b
12				*p* in *p*at	p	P p
13				*v* in *v*ote	v	V v
14				*f* in *f*all	f	F f
15				*m* in *m*et	m	M m
16				*d* in *d*oor	d	D d
17				*t* in *t*ent	t	T t
18				*th* in *th*en	ð	Dh dh
19				*th* in *th*in	θ	Th th
20				*n* in *n*o	n	N n
21				*z* in *z*ebra	z	Z z
22				*s* in *s*at	s	S s
23				*s* in lei*s*ure	ʒ	Zh zh
24				*sh* in *sh*out	ʃ	Sh sh
25				*g* in *g*et	g	G g
26				*k* in *k*eep	k	K k
27				*ng* in si*ng*	ŋ	Ng ng

An apostrophe is used in Latin-character Damiriak spellings to prevent misinterpretation of side-by-side consonants that happen to resemble a two-letter representation of a different letter. For example, if a compound word is formed where the first word ends in an *n* and the second word begins in a *g*, an unintended side-effect is the apparent consonant of *ng* when in fact it was intended to present the letters individually as *n* and *g*. This can be clarified by placing an apostrophe between the *n* and *g*. Again, the apostrophe is only used in Latin spellings and not in Damiriak spellings.

Diphthongs

There are plenty of diphthongs in the Damiriak languages. Most can be pronounced simply by:
- ♣ Applying the standard pronunciation rules for individual vowels, and
- ♣ Pronouncing the vowels together quickly to achieve the diphthong effect.

Some diphthongs have special pronunciation:

Diphthong	IPA	English Sound
au	æu	*a* in *a*pple + *u* in t*u*ne
ae	æ	*a* in *a*pple, *a* in c*a*t
ou	oʊ	*oe* in t*oe*, *oa* in s*oa*p

The diphthong *au* shifts the pronunciation of *a* to add contrast between the *au* and *ao* diphthongs.

Ae is not actually a diphthong but instead is a means of pronouncing *a* as in *apple*.

Consonant Combinations

In addition to regular Deibuth, Marfi, and Noimil alphabetic letters, certain consonant combinations are represented:

Deibuth	Marfi	Noimil	English Sound	IPA	Latin Characters
ЊЯ	Чᒋ	Ꭹᙢ	*ch* in *ch*urch	tʃʰ	tsh
ЊЯ	Чᖴ	Ꭹᙢ	*j* in *j*udge	dʒ	dzh

Damiriak languages use uppercase characters as capitals much as in English—beginning of sentences, proper nouns, and titles.

Trailing Vowels

In Dahmek, words ending with certain voiced consonants must have a trailing *e*. This is necessary to emphasize the voiced consonant and provide distinction from its devoiced or similar-sounding counterpart. The following chart describes these consonants:

Voiced Consonants Trailing Words

Deibuth	Latin	Trailing Spelling
ᑎ	w	-we
ᑫ	b	-be
Ꮗ	v	-ve
ᙢ	m	-me
ᖴ	d	-de
Ꮤ	dh	-dhe
Ꮖ	z	-ze
ᖴ	zh	-zhe
ᑐ	g	-ge
ᔧ	ng	-nge

Middle E

The word *e* has no meaning by itself. It is used to split apart consonants between words to prevent these consonants from running together when spoken. The *e* is pronounced like a schwa.

In Dahmek, *e* is placed between words of similar consonants. Consonants are similar based on voiced/devoiced groups—*b/p*, *v/f*, *d/t*, *dh/th*, *z/s*, *zh/sh*, *dzh/tsh*, and *g/k*. Consonants are also similar when formed by the mouth in similar ways, such as *n/d*.

In Miramish, the word *e* is placed between words with trailing-leading consonants. This applies to all consonant pairs, unlike Dahmek, which only uses *e* between similar consonants.

Mirsua follows the Dahmek rule.

Nimiash does not typically use *e* unless a speaker wishes to clarify two words that are not understood. Such use of *e* feels like a throwback to one of the other Damiriak languages.

E may optionally be inserted between words for emphasis or clarity in any language.

Middle E Examples

Language	Phrase	Translation
Dahmek	Virsf e vark dhark e kufliau.	Go back and goodbye.
Miramish	Shash e shekaluta mafu kaish e gerutha.	Her choice for your gift.
Mirsua	Nuis e zualas kilos e seisus.	My spirit is special.
Nimiash	Shash shloik maf shash shnenk.	Her command for her army.

S / Z Restrictions

Letters *s* and *z* have restricted usage. In Dahmek, they are only allowed to precede the final consonant in a verb—unless the final consonant is an *sh/zh* in which case there is direct replacement. In Miramish and Nimiash, they are forbidden with the exception of legacy Damiriak words such as celestial objects, or in the use of Mirsua.

Miramish contains a sub-dialect known as Mirsua. Mirsua takes the Miramish language and replaces *sh/zh* with *s/z*. All words are appended with *−es* if ending in a consonant or *−s* if ending in a vowel. Speaking Mirsua casually is considered rude and vulgar. Mirsua is spoken only in special moments of exercising power.

3

Numbers and Symbols

Numbers are used to count. All three main Damiriak languages use the same words for numbers. The collection of numeric characters is known as the Nalnat (just as Deibuth, Marfi, and Noimil are names for collections of alphabetic letters).

I (Cerafina) ran out of English prefixes around the *yotta* level. I made up extra prefixes by looking at Greek number names and using those number names as inspiration for English prefixes from *xenna* to *yantesa*. I also stopped listing ordinals around quadrillion. I stopped listing English cardinal names after quinquagintillion.

Cardinal, Ordinal, Prefix: Character

Damiriak	Digits	English Equiv	Digits
shut, shuteth, shutai-	∩	zero, zeroth, nul-	0
heme, hemeth, hemai-	⊥	one, first, una/an/mon-	1
avu, aveth, ipi-	⋏	two, second, bi-	2
iri, ireth, irai-	⋏	three, third, tri-	3
yufi, yufeth, yufai-	+	four, fourth, quad-/tetra-	4
tiri, tireth, tirai-	⋞	five, fifth, quint-/pent-	5
kini, kineth, kinai-	⧧	six, sixth, sext-/hex-	6
veni, veneth, venai-	⧻	seven, seventh, sept-	7
geni, geneth, genai-	⟊	eight, eighth, oct-	8
mui, muyeth, muai-	⟟	nine, ninth, non-	9
dapa, dapeth, dapai-	⌐∩	ten, tenth, dec-	10
hempa, hempeth, hempai-	⊥⊥	eleven, eleventh	11

Damiriak	Digits	English Equiv	Digits
avupa, avupeth, avupai-	⊥⅄	twelve, twelfth	12
iripa, iripeth, iripai-	⊥⋏	thirteen, thirteenth	13
yufipa, yufipeth, yufipai-	⊥+	fourteen, fourteenth	14
tiripa, tiripeth, tiripai-	⊥<	fifteen, fifteenth	15
kinipa, kinipeth, kinipai-	⊥‡	sixteen, sixteenth	16
venipa, venipeth, venipai-	⊥⊅	seventeen, seventeenth	17
genipa, genipeth, genipai-	⊥Ξ	eighteen, eighteenth	18
muipa, muipeth, muipai-	⊥⊠	nineteen, nineteenth	19
avuda, avudeth, avudai-	⅄∩	twenty, twentieth	20
avuda-heme, avuda-hemeth	⅄⊥	twenty-one, twenty-first	21
irida, irideth, iridai-	⋏∩	thirty, thirtieth	30
yufida, yufideth, yufidai-	+∩	forty, fortieth	40
tirida, tirideth, tiridai-	<∩	fifty, fiftieth	50
kinida, kinideth, kinidai-	‡∩	sixty, sixtieth	60
venida, venideth, venidai-	⊅∩	seventy, seventieth	70
genida, genideth, genidai-	Ξ∩	eighty, eightieth	80
muida, muideth, muidai-	⊠∩	ninety, ninetieth	90
tash, tasheth, tashai-	⊥∩∩	hundred, hundredth	100
heme-tash heme	⊥∩⊥	one-hundred one	101
dint, dinteth, dintai-	⊥∩∩∩	thousand, -th, kilo-	1000
hemka, hemkadeth, hemkai-	⊥'∩∩∩'∩∩∩	million, -th, mega-	1,000,000
avuka, avuketh, avukai-	⊥ₒ∩ ⌃⊠	billion, -th, giga-	1.0 e+9
irika, iriketh, irikai-	⊥ₒ∩ ⌃⊥⅄	trillion, -th, tera-	1.0 e+12
yufika, yufikai-	⊥ₒ∩ ⌃⊥<	quadrillion, peta-	1.0 e+15
tirika, tirikai-	⊥ₒ∩ ⌃⊥Ξ	quintillion, exa-	1.0 e+18
kinka, kinkai-	⊥ₒ∩ ⌃⅄⊥	sextillion, zetta-	1.0 e+21
venka, venkai-	⊥ₒ∩ ⌃⅄+	septillion, yotta-	1.0 e+24
genka, genkai-	⊥ₒ∩ ⌃⅄⊅	octillion, xenna-	1.0 e+27
muika, muikai-	⊥ₒ∩ ⌃⅄∩	nonillion, weka-	1.0 e+30
daka, dakai-	⊥ₒ∩ ⌃⅄⅄	decillion, vendeka-	1.0 e+33
hemsht, hemshtai-	⊥ₒ∩ ⌃⅄‡	undecillion, udeka-	1.0 e+36
avusht, avushtai-	⊥ₒ∩ ⌃⅄⊠	duodecillion, tekatra-	1.0 e+39
irisht, irishtai-	⊥ₒ∩ ⌃+⅄	tredecillion, sekata-	1.0 e+42
yufisht, yufishtai-	⊥ₒ∩ ⌃+<	quattuordecillion, quaksa-	1.0 e+45
tirisht, tirishtai-	⊥ₒ∩ ⌃+Ξ	quindecillion, pafta-	1.0 e+48
kinsht, kinshtai-	⊥ₒ∩ ⌃<⊥	sexdecillion, oshta-	1.0 e+51
vensht, venshtai-	⊥ₒ∩ ⌃<+	septdecillion, nekana-	1.0 e+54
gensht, genshtai-	⊥ₒ∩ ⌃<⊅	octodecillion, mikosa-	1.0 e+57

Damiriak	Digits	English Equiv	Digits
muisht, muishtai-	⊥ₒ∩ ⋏‡∩	novemdecillion, lina-	1.0 e+60
dashta, dashtai-	⊥ₒ∩ ⋏‡⋏	vigintillion, kida-	1.0 e+63
hemshk, hemshkai-	⊥ₒ∩ ⋏‡‡	unvigintillion, jita-	1.0 e+66
avushk, avushkai-	⊥ₒ∩ ⋏‡⧫	duovigintillion, itesa-	1.0 e+69
irishk, irishkai-	⊥ₒ∩ ⋏⧧⅄	trevigintillion, hinta-	1.0 e+72
yufishk, yufishkai-	⊥ₒ∩ ⋏⧧≺	quattuorvigintillion, giksa-	1.0 e+75
tirishk, tirishkai-	⊥ₒ∩ ⋏⧧Ŧ	quinvigintillion, fifta-	1.0 e+78
kinshk, kinshkai-	⊥ₒ∩ ⋏Ŧ⊥	sexvigintillion, eikta-	1.0 e+81
venshk, venshkai-	⊥ₒ∩ ⋏Ŧ+	septenvigintillion, dina-	1.0 e+84
genshk, genshkai-	⊥ₒ∩ ⋏Ŧ⧣	octovigintillion, cinta-	1.0 e+87
muishk, muishkai-	⊥ₒ∩ ⋏⧫∩	novemvigintillion, banta-	1.0 e+90
dashka, dashkai-	⊥ₒ∩ ⋏⧫⅄	trigintillion, anta-	1.0 e+93
hemift, hemiftai-	⊥ₒ∩ ⋏⧫‡	untrigintillion, zantra-	1.0 e+96
avuft, avuftai-	⊥ₒ∩ ⋏⧫⧫	duotrigintillion, yantesa-	1.0 e+99
irift	⊥ₒ∩ ⋏⊥∩⅄	trestrigintillion	1.0 e+102
yufift	⊥ₒ∩ ⋏⊥∩≺	quatturotrigintillion	1.0 e+105
tirift	⊥ₒ∩ ⋏⊥∩Ŧ	quinquatrigintillion	1.0 e+108
kinft	⊥ₒ∩ ⋏⊥⊥⊥	sestrigintillion	1.0 e+111
venft	⊥ₒ∩ ⋏⊥⊥+	septentrigintillion	1.0 e+114
genft	⊥ₒ∩ ⋏⊥⊥⧣	octotrigintillion	1.0 e+117
muift	⊥ₒ∩ ⋏⊥⅄∩	novemtrigintillion	1.0 e+120
dafta	⊥ₒ∩ ⋏⊥⅄⅄	quadragintillion	1.0 e+123
hemifk	⊥ₒ∩ ⋏⊥⅄‡	unquadragintillion	1.0 e+126
avufk	⊥ₒ∩ ⋏⊥⅄⧫	duoquadragintillion	1.0 e+129
irifk	⊥ₒ∩ ⋏⊥⅄⅄	tresquadragintillion	1.0 e+132
yufifk	⊥ₒ∩ ⋏⊥⅄≺	quattuorquadragintillion	1.0 e+135
tirifk	⊥ₒ∩ ⋏⊥⅄Ŧ	quinquadragintillion	1.0 e+138
kinfk	⊥ₒ∩ ⋏⊥+⊥	sesquadragintillion	1.0 e+141
venfk	⊥ₒ∩ ⋏⊥++	septenquadragintillion	1.0 e+144
genfk	⊥ₒ∩ ⋏⊥+⧣	octoquadragintillion	1.0 e+147
muifk	⊥ₒ∩ ⋏⊥≺∩	novemquadragintillion	1.0 e+150
dafka	⊥ₒ∩ ⋏⊥≺⅄	quinquagintillion	1.0 e+153
alfhemka	⊥ₒ∩ ⋏⊥≺‡		1.0 e+156
alfavuka	⊥ₒ∩ ⋏⊥≺⧫		1.0 e+159
alfirika	⊥ₒ∩ ⋏⊥‡⅄		1.0 e+162
alfyufika	⊥ₒ∩ ⋏⊥‡≺		1.0 e+165
alftirika	⊥ₒ∩ ⋏⊥‡Ŧ		1.0 e+168
alfkinka	⊥ₒ∩ ⋏⊥‡⊥		1.0 e+171
alfvenka	⊥ₒ∩ ⋏⊥⧣+		1.0 e+174
alfgenka	⊥ₒ∩ ⋏⊥⧣⧣		1.0 e+177
alfmuika	⊥ₒ∩ ⋏⊥Ŧ∩		1.0 e+180
alfdaka	⊥ₒ∩ ⋏⊥Ŧ⅄		1.0 e+183

Damiriak	Digits	English Equiv Digits
alfhemsht	⊥₀∩ ⌃⊥ǂ‡	1.0 e+186
alfhemshk	⊥₀∩ ⌃⅄⊥‡	1.0 e+216
alfhemft	⊥₀∩ ⌃⅄+‡	1.0 e+246
alfhemfk	⊥₀∩ ⌃⅄ǂǂ	1.0 e+276
elfhem	⊥₀∩ ⌃⅄∩‡	1.0 e+306
ilfhem	⊥₀∩ ⌃+≪‡	1.0 e+456
orfhem	⊥₀∩ ⌃‡∩‡	1.0 e+606
urfhem	⊥₀∩ ⌃ǂ≪‡	1.0 e+756
harfhem	⊥₀∩ ⌃⊠∩‡	1.0 e+906
lerfhem	⊥₀∩ ⌃⊥∩≪‡	1.0 e+1056
yarlhem	⊥₀∩ ⌃⊥⅄∩‡	1.0 e+1206
relhem	⊥₀∩ ⌃⊥⅄≪‡	1.0 e+1356
warfhem	⊥₀∩ ⌃⊥≪∩‡	1.0 e+1506
bahem	⊥₀∩ ⌃⊥‡≪‡	1.0 e+1656
peihem	⊥₀∩ ⌃⊥ǂ∩‡	1.0 e+1806
vahem	⊥₀∩ ⌃⊥⊠∩‡	1.0 e+1956
feihem	⊥₀∩ ⌃⅄⊥∩‡	1.0 e+2106
maihem	⊥₀∩ ⌃⅄⅄≪‡	1.0 e+2256
dahem	⊥₀∩ ⌃⅄+∩‡	1.0 e+2406
teihem	⊥₀∩ ⌃⅄≪≪‡	1.0 e+2556
dhahem	⊥₀∩ ⌃⅄ǂ∩‡	1.0 e+2706
theihem	⊥₀∩ ⌃⅄ǂ≪‡	1.0 e+2856
noihem	⊥₀∩ ⌃⅄∩∩‡	1.0 e+3006
zahem	⊥₀∩ ⌃⅄⊥≪‡	1.0 e+3156
seihem	⊥₀∩ ⌃⅄⅄∩‡	1.0 e+3306
zhahem	⊥₀∩ ⌃⅄+≪‡	1.0 e+3456
sheihem	⊥₀∩ ⌃⅄+∩+	1.0 c ı 3606
gahem	⊥₀∩ ⌃⅄ǂ∩‡	1.0 e+3756
keihem	⊥₀∩ ⌃⅄⊠∩‡	1.0 e+3906
engahem	⊥₀∩ ⌃+∩≪‡	1.0 e+4056
engadafka	⊥₀∩ ⌃+⅄∩⅄	1.0 e+4203
hemalfhemka	⊥₀∩ ⌃+⅄∩‡	1.0 e+4206
avualfhemka	⊥₀∩ ⌃ǂ⅄≪‡	1.0 e+8256
irialfhemka	⊥₀∩ ⌃⊥⅄⅄∩‡	1.0 e+12306
yufialfhemka	⊥₀∩ ⌃⊥ǂ⅄≪‡	1.0 e+16356
tirialfhemka	⊥₀∩ ⌃⅄∩+∩‡	1.0 e+20406
kinialfhemka	⊥₀∩ ⌃⅄++≪‡	1.0 e+24456
venialfhemka	⊥₀∩ ⌃⅄ǂ≪∩‡	1.0 e+28506
genialfhemka	⊥₀∩ ⌃⅄⅄≪≪‡	1.0 e+32556
muialfhemka	⊥₀∩ ⌃⅄ǂǂ∩‡	1.0 e+36606
dapalfhemka	⊥₀∩ ⌃+∩‡≪‡	1.0 e+40656

The following are math symbols used uniformly across the Damiriak Empire:

Math Symbols

Damiriak	English	Description	Example	Example
⋈	=	equality operator	⊥ ⋈ ⊥	1 = 1
∧	+	add/positive operator	人 ∧ 人	2 + 3
∨	−	subtract/negative operator	人 ∨ 人	3 − 2
∾	×	multiply operator	人 ∾ +	2 × 4
⌣	÷	divide operator	⊥ ‡ ∾ +	16 ÷ 4
○	.	decimal point	人○≮	2.5
▷	>	greater than	人 ▷ ⊥	2 > 1
◁	<	less than	+ ◁ 人	4 < 3
⋏	e+	exponent (positive)	⊥○∩ ⋏人≮	1.0 e+25
⋎	e−	exponent (negative)	人○人 ⋎⊥∩	2.2 e−10

Other Symbols

Damiriak	English	Description
↰	'	lead single quote
↱	'	tail single quote
↰↰	"	lead double quote
↱↱	"	tail double quote
⇕	!	exclamation mark
↕	?	question mark
⇟	(no equiv)	depressive mark
'	,	comma
○	.	period

4

Yoilark

Yoilark is a signing script but not a true language. Signs are created with fingers and represent letters of the alphabet, numbers, and a limited number of symbols. The signs can be sent visually or through a touch interface such as water or skin. The signs are seen with the eyes or are felt.

The following diagrams depict the left hand performing yoilark signals. However, the right hand may also be used.

For purposes of describing hand signals, the hand and fingers must be labeled. Fingers are labeled from one to five with the thumb being *one* and the pinky being *five*.

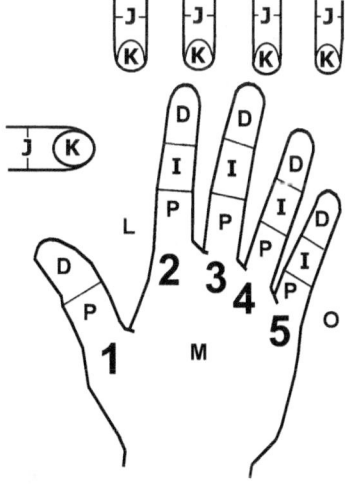

The fingers on the palm side are divided into segments or phalanges. These are labeled with letters. The palm is given the letter *M* for *metacarpal*. The thumb has two phalange segments—the segment closest to the palm is *P* for *proximal*, and the tip is *D* for *distal*. The remaining four fingers have three segments each—*P* for *proximal*, *I* for *intermediate*, and *D* for *distal*. On the hand's dorsal side, fingernails are *K* for *keratin*, and the knuckle closest to the nail is *J* for *joint*. Letter *L* refers to *lateral*. The side of the four fingers closest to the thumb is the *L* side. *O* refers to outside. The side of the four fingers furthest from the thumb is the *O* side.

The thumb is the *pointer*, and the four fingers are the *map*. The thumb touches the map in a particular spot, and this indicates a letter, number, symbol, or concept. The thumb may touch with its tip, *D*, with its fingernail, *K*, or with its knuckle, *J*.

The togetherness of the fingers is the *formation*. Different formations have different maps. Here are the formations:

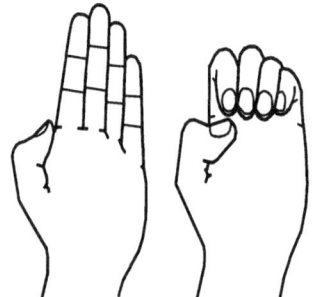

A-formation. Fingers touch sides.   *U-formation. Fingers are apart.*

In the following diagrams, columns indicate finger numbers, and rows indicate phalange. Each hand drawing represents the caption below it.

Numbers

Numbers and calculations use the A-formation with the fleshy tip (distal) of the thumb touching the four-finger map:

2L: Lat Index	2: Index	3: Middle	4: Ring	5: Pinky
J	Negative	Positive	Left Paren	Right Paren
K	Add	Subtract	Multiply	Divide
D Start/ End	1	4	7	0
I Clear Num	2	5	8	Decimal
P Equals	3	6	9	Space

Letters

Letters use the U-formation. The thumb tip points to the four-fingered map:

	2: Index	**3: Middle**	**4: Ring**	**5: Pinky**
J				
	Ng	Z	Dh	W
K				
	H	S	Th	Y
D				
	L	Sh	E	F
I				
	O	I	A	U
P				
	N	K	T	P

These letters and symbols require the thumb to touch the side of the target finger:

2L: Lat Index   **3L: Lat Mid**   **4L: Lat Ring**   **5L: Lat Pinky**

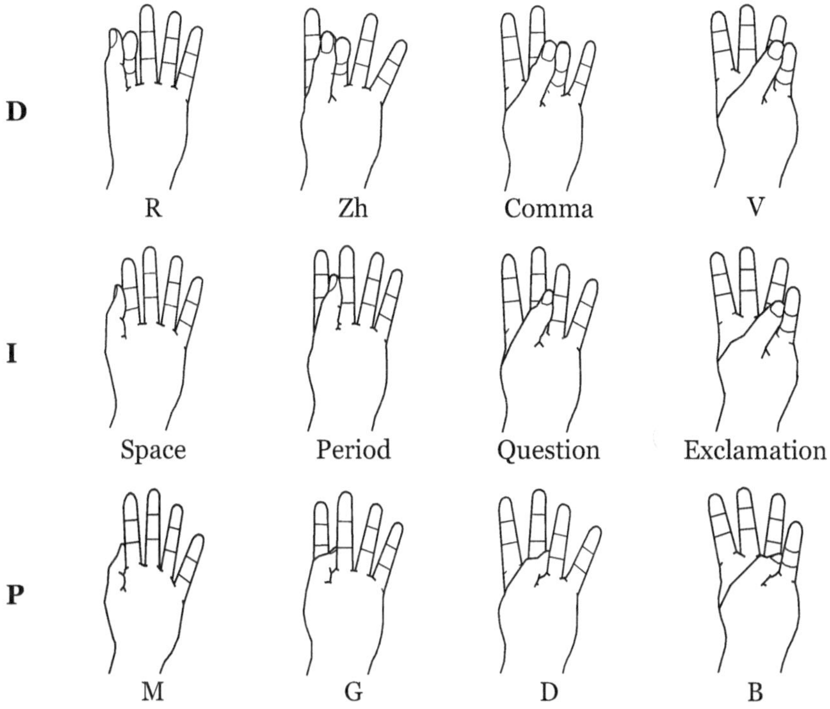

D

| R | Zh | Comma | V |

I

| Space | Period | Question | Exclamation |

P

| M | G | D | B |

Concepts

Simple ideas are represented with the following signs:

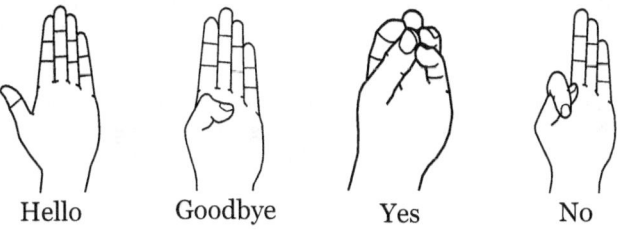

Hello   Goodbye   Yes   No

5

Nouns

As mentioned earlier, most Damiriak words are based on a root word (often a singular noun). This root word is used to generate other parts of speech by adding suffixes. The following suffixes are typically used to build various noun forms.

Noun Type/ Meaning	Dahmek	Miramish	Nimiash	English
Singular	(none)	-a, -la, -ei	(none)	(none)
Plural	-yek	-i, -li, -iei	-i, -li	-s
Singular Possessive	-ange	-anga	-ang	-'s
Plural Possessive	-ingek	-ingi	-ing	-s'
Past Part Singular	-yot	-ioa	-ioa	-ed
Past Part Plural	-yotyek	-ioi	-ioi	-eds
Pres Part (Gerund) Sing	-aut	-aola	-aola	-ing
Pres Part (Gerund) Plur	-autyek	-aoli	-aoli	-ings
One who does (Singular)	-wan	-ua	-ua	-er, -or, -ist, -ant
Those who do (Plural)	-waik	-ui, -lui	-ui, -lui	-ers, -ors, -ists, -ants
One's who does (Sing Poss)	-wange	-uanga	-uang	-er's, -or's, -ist's, -ant's
Those's who do (Pl Poss)	-waifk	-uingi	-uing	-ers', -ors', -ists', -ants'
One who is done by (Sing)	-uin	-uina	-uina	-ee
Those who are done by (Pl)	-uinyek	-uini	-uini	-ees
One who is done by (Sing Pos)	-wianange	-uinanga	-uinang	-ee's
Those who're done by (Pl Pos)	-wiafk	-uiningi	-uining	-ees'
The act of	-uet	-ueta	-uet	-ance,-ence, -ion, -tion, -sion, -ism
Social span, state, or group	-fif	-fifa	-fif	-dom, -ship, -hood

In Miramish, the primary ending for singular nouns is −*a*. The endings −*la* and −*li* are only used in rare situations where the root word already ends in a vowel. Gerunds are the most common words using the −*la*/−*li* endings. Male names often end without −*a*, and possessive male names often end in −*ang* instead of −*anga*. Female names more regularly end in −*a*, with −*anga* for possessive.

Miramish has another ending for singular nouns, −*ei*. This ending is primarily used in nonpersonal pronouns, but it is also used for emphasis to indicate a noun that once was but no longer exists. For example, if a person, place, or thing recently died or disintegrated, the −*ei* ending is used instead of −*a*. This is equivalent to "the late *x*, the former *x*, etc." The ending −*iei* has a similar "deceased" meaning for Miramish plural nouns.

6

Pronouns

Pronouns can be grouped into personal and non-personal.

Personal pronouns descend directly from Old Damiriak and are consistent across all three main languages (Miramish, Dahmek, and Nimiash, but not Mirsua). Efforts have been made to Miramish-ify the pronouns for Eho Miriam speakers, but common habit in speaking the old pronouns prevents the new ones from being accepted.

Personal Pronouns

Description	Damiriak Subj, Obj	Mirsua Subj, Obj	Eng Equiv Subj, Obj
1st singular	nia, nau	nias, naus	I, me
1st singular possessive	nui, nuime	nuis, nuimes	my, mine
1st singular reflexive	nuifal	nuifales	myself
1st plural	niai, rau	niais, raus	we, us
1st plural possessive	nuish, raush	nuises, rauses	our, ours
1st plural reflexive	raushfar	rausfares	ourselves
2nd singular	kail	kiales	you
2nd singular possessive	kaish, kaish	kaises, kaises	your, yours
2nd singular reflexive	kaishfal	kaisfales	yourself
2nd plural	kair	kaires	you
2nd plural possessive	kairsh, kairsh	kairses, kairses	your, yours
2nd plural reflexive	kaishfar	kaisfares	yourselves
3rd singular feminine	sha, shan	sas, sanes	she, her
3rd singular fem poss	shash, shash	sases, sases	her, hers
3rd singular fem reflex	shashfal	sasfales	herself
3rd singular masculine	hui, hein	huis, heines	he, him
3rd singular masc poss	heish	heises	his
3rd singular masc reflex	heishfal	heisfales	himself

Description	Damiriak Subj, Obj	Mirsua Subj, Obj	Eng Equiv Subj, Obj
3rd singular indef pers	ona	onas	one
3rd sing indef pers poss	onash	onases	one's
3rd sing indef pers reflex	onashfal	onasfales	oneself
3rd singular neuter	til, tilen	tiles, tilenes	it, it
3rd singular neut poss	tilesh	tileses	its
3rd singular neut reflex	tileshfal	tilesfales	itself
3rd plural fem/masc	tethi, tethin	tethis, tethines	they, them
3rd plural fem/masc poss	tesh, tesh	teses, teses	their, theirs
3rd plural fem/masc refl	teshfar	tesfares	themselves
3rd pl indef pers	onar, onar	onares, onares	they/people, them/people
3rd pl indef pers pos	onash	onases	people's
3rd pl indef pers reflex	onashfar	onasfares	peopleselves
3rd plural neuter	tir, tiren	tires, tirenes	they, them
3rd plural neuter poss	tiresh, tiresh	tireses, tireses	their, theirs
3rd plural neuter reflex	tireshfar	tiresfares	themselves

Nonpersonal pronouns may vary depending on language. Miramish singular nonpersonal pronouns use the −*ei* ending instead of the typical −*a* ending for singular nouns. Miramish plural nonpersonal pronouns may end in −*i* but never −*iei*.

Some of the following nonpersonal pronouns are used as other parts of speech. As such, spellings may differ for Dahmek and Nimiash words and will almost always be different for Miramish words (usually Miramish words drop the −*ei* and add −*u*).

Nonpersonal Pronouns

Dahmek	Miramish	Mirsua	Nimiash	English Equiv
ino	inei	ineis	ino	any
inoshlade	inosheladei	inoseladeis	inoshlad	anybody
inona	inonei	inoneis	inona	anyone
peirsh	peishei	peiseis	peish	both
shart	sharitei	sariteis	shart	either
plurf	pelufei	pelufeis	pluf	enough
eferlshlarde	lerifusheladei	lerifuseladeis	lerfshlad	everybody
eferlton	lerifitonei	lerifitoneis	lerfton	everyone
eferlizhe	lerifalizhei	lerifalizeis	lerflizh	everything
krunf	kerunei	keruneis	krun	few
wel	welei	weleis	wel	more
wak	wakei	wakeis	wak	most

Dahmek	Miramish	Mirsua	Nimiash	English Equiv
nesh	neshei	neseis	nesh	much
mashart	masharitei	masariteis	mashart	neither
maushlarde	mausheladei	mauseladeis	maushlad	nobody
maut	mautei	mauteis	maut	none
mirsh	mishei	miseis	mish	other
mirshyek	mishi	misis	mishi	others
zhaul	zhauei	zaueis	zhau	so
zhin	zhinei	zineis	zhin	some
zhishlarde	zhisheladei	ziseladeis	zhishlad	somebody
zhinorn	zhinonei	zinoneis	zhinon	someone
zhesh	zheshei	zeseis	zhesh	such
tshade	teshadei	tesadeis	tshad	that
durl	durei	dureis	dur	there
shirsh	shishi	sisis	shish	these
tshun	teshunei	tesuneis	tshun	this
shorsh	shoshi	sosis	shosh	those
halk	hakei	hakeis	hak	what
hakerf	hakefei	hakefeis	hakef	whatever
hakzhaufel	hakezhaufelei	hakezaufeleis	hakzhaufel	whatsoever
yarme	yamei	yameis	yam	when
torl	tolei	toleis	tol	where
hirsh	hishei	hiseis	hish	which
lowe	lowei	loweis	lowei	who
lowerf	lowefelei	lowefeleis	lowefel	whoever
lowe	lowei	loweis	lowei	whom
lowange	lowangei	lowangeis	lowang	whose

7

Verbs

Damiriak verbs are formed from the root word. In Miramish and Nimiash, a suffix is added to the root word to set the tense or to make a participle. In Dahmek, a *zas* mutation is performed on the last consonant, and a suffix is appended in all but the present tense.

In all Damiriak languages, there is no differentiation between singular or plural verbs—both are the same. The infinitive verb takes the present-form verb.

Zas Mutation (Dahmek Only)

A *zas* mutation is applied only to verbs. The mutation is performed typically by inserting either a *z* or *s* before the final consonant of the root word. In the situation where a *zh* or *sh* is the final consonant, the *z* or *s* replaces the corresponding *zh* or *sh*. The following chart shows when to insert or replace with *z* or *s*:

Root Word Ending	New Verb Ending (Zas)
	Insert z before
-be, -ve, -de, -ge	-zbe, -zve, -zde, -zge
-dhe, -me, -we, -nge	-zdhe, -zme, -zwe, -znge
	Replace with z
-zhe	-ze

Root Word Ending	New Verb Ending (Zas)
	Insert s *before*
-p, -f, -t, -k	-sp, -sf, -st, -sk
-th, -n, -h, -l, -r, -y	-sth, -sn, -s'he, -sle, -sre, -sye
	Replace with s
-sh	-s

Verb Suffixes

Verbs/verb-like words must have a suffix to indicate:
- ♣ If the word is a verb
- ♣ The tense
- ♣ If the word is a participle
- ♣ If the word is a gerund

Miramish and Nimiash verbs always end in *–o.*

Participles and gerunds used as a part of speech other than a verb are not considered verbs, though the ending may appear verb-ish. For this reason, only verbs have a *zas* mutation in Dahmek and have a *–o* ending in Miramish and Nimiash.

Exception: Some short, specialized words may have a *–o* ending, such as *ino* (any), and some specialized names may end in *–s* (the star Seris). These are legacy words from Old Damiriak.

The following chart shows the suffixes added to create different verb forms from a root word. Note that for Dahmek verbs, any existing vowel after the *zas* ending must be removed before appending the additional suffix.

Damiriak Verb Suffixes

Verb Type	Dahmek	Miramish/ Nimiash	Mirsua	English Equiv
Past	-(zas)-yot	-io	-ios	-ed
Present	-(zas)	-o	-os	(none)
Present Participle	-(zas)-aut	-ao	-aos	-ing
Future	-(zas)-eit	-eio	-eios	will (x)

Particles

Damiriak verbs do not use "helping" or "auxiliary" verbs. However, particles are used in places where some "auxiliary" verbs would be used.

Particles change the verb in some form. Particles always precede verbs and typically have an order of precedence with *dhai* binding closest. Precedence only matters when more than one particle is used with a verb and may be violated as need arises.

Verb Type	Dahmek	Miramish / Nimiash	Mirsua	English Equiv
Passive Particle:	dhai (verb)	dhai (verb)	dhais (verb)	was/ is being/ will be (verb)
Infinitive Particle:	dir (verb)	di (verb)	dis (verb)	to (verb)
Noundal Particle:				
(noun-noun)	(n1) (n2) kodi (verb)	(n1) (n2) kodi (verb)	(n1) (n2) kodis (verb)	(n1) have/had/will have (n2) to (verb)
(noun-adj)	(n) (adj) kodi (verb)	(n) (adj) kodi (verb)	(n) (adj) kodis (verb)	(n) was/is/will be (adj) to (verb)
Negation Particle:	oir (verb)	oi (verb)	ois (verb)	not (verb)
Emphasis, Pverb:				
Past	kokyot	kokio	kokios	did/had
Present	koko	koko	kokos	do/have
Future	kokeit	kokeio	kokeios	really will

Passive Particle

Passive speech in Damiriak languages is much as it is in English— the affected object is placed before the verb, and the affecter (if any) is placed after the verb in a prepositional phrase. Verbs with reflexive objects are considered active voice in Damiriak languages. To indicate a passive verb, the particle *dhai* is placed before the verb.

Passive Particle Examples

Language	Phrase
Past	
English (active)	The thief stopped. (He stopped himself/something)
English (passive)	The thief was stopped. (Something stopped the thief)

Language	Phrase
Dahmek (active)	Shair prairtwan taurskyot.
Dahmek (passive)	Shair prairtwan dhai taurskyot.
Miramish (active)	Shai peraitua taukio.
Miramish (passive)	Shai peraitua dhai taukio.
Mirsua (active)	Sais peraituas taukios.
Mirsua (passive)	Sais peraituas dhais taukios.
Nimiash (active)	Shai praitua taukio.
Nimiash (passive)	Shai praitua dhai taukio.

Present

English (active)	The thief stops. (He stops himself/something)
English (passive)	The thief is being stopped. (Something stops the thief)
Dahmek (active)	Shair prairtwan taursk.
Dahmek (passive)	Shair prairtwan dhai taursk.
Miramish (active)	Shai peraitua tauko.
Miramish (passive)	Shai peraitua dhai tauko.
Mirsua (active)	Sais peraituas taukos.
Mirsua (passive)	Sais peraituas dhais taukos.
Nimiash (active)	Shai praitua tauko.
Nimiash (passive)	Shai praitua dhai tauko.

Future

English (active)	The thief will stop. (He will stop himself/something)
English (passive)	The thief will be stopped. (Something will stop the thief)
Dahmek (active)	Shair prairtwan taurskeit.
Dahmek (passive)	Shair prairtwan dhai taurskeit.
Miramish (active)	Shai peraitua taukeio.
Miramish (passive)	Shai peraitua dhai taukeio.
Mirsua (active)	Sais peraituas taukeios.
Mirsua (passive)	Sais peraituas dhais taukeios.
Nimiash (active)	Shai praitua taukeio.
Nimiash (passive)	Shai praitua dhai taukeio.

Infinitive Particle

The infinitive particle acts like the English infinitive. The particle *dir* in Dahmek, *di* in Miramish and Nimiash, and *dis* in Mirsua leads a present-tense verb.

Noundal Particle

A noundal particle (*kodi*/*kodis*) links two nouns or a noun and adjective with a verb. A noundal phrase is equivalent to the *have-*

to and *is-to* words in the English phrases "(noun) have (noun) to (verb)" and "(noun) is (adj) to (verb)". A noundal is equivalent to auxiliary verbs such as *can*, *might*, or *would*. Tense is carried in the Damiriak verb.

Common Noundals

Dahmek	Miramish	Mirsua	Nimiash	English Equiv
frelp kodi	ferepa kodi	ferepas kodis	frep kodi	can
frelp kodi	ferepa kodi	ferepas kodis	frep kodi	could
oir frelp kodi	oi ferepa kodi	ois ferepas kodis	oi frep kodi	cannot
nirshke kodi	nishoka kodi	nisokas kodis	nishke kodi	have to
nirshke kodi	nishoka kodi	nisokas kodis	nishke kodi	had to
noirf kodi	noifa kodi	noifas kodis	noif kodi	may
lorilf kodi	lorifa kodi	lorifas kodis	lorf kodi	might
nirshke kodi	nishoka kodi	nisoka kodis	nishke kodi	must
loirf kodi	loira kodi	loiras kodis	loir kodi	ought
tuthuke kodi	thushika kodi	thusika kodis	thushke kodi	should
yarke kodi	yaka kodi	yakas kodis	yake kodi	would

Noundal Examples

Language	Phrase
Present	
English	I can stop/ I have the ability to stop.
Damiriak English Equiv	I ability have-to stop.
Dahmek	Nia frelp kodi taursk.
Miramish	Nia ferepa kodi tauko.
Mirsua	Nias ferepas kodis taukos.
Nimiash	Nia frep kodi tauko.
Past	
English	I could have stopped/ I had the ability to stop.
Damiriak English Equiv	I ability had-to stopped.
Dahmek	Nia frelp kodi taurskyot.
Miramish	Nia ferepa kodi taukio.
Mirsua	Nias ferepas kodis taukios.
Nimiash	Nia frep kodi taukio.
Future	
English	I could stop/ I will have the ability to stop.
Damiriak English Equiv	I ability will-have-to stop.
Dahmek	Nia frelp kodi taurskeit.
Miramish	Nia ferepa kodi taukeio.
Mirsua	Nias ferepas kodis taukeios.
Nimiash	Nia frep kodi taukeio.

Negation Particle

The Old Damiriak word *oi* is equivalent to the English word *not*. It may be used in front of a verb, or any other part of speech—in all cases, *oir/oi/ois* is placed before the word being modified. *Oir/oi/ois* may also act as a standalone sentence in response to a prior sentence.

Emphasis, Pro-verb (Pverb)

The Old Damiriak word *koko* indicates emphasis on the verb it precedes in the present tense. Miramish and Dahmek added past and future forms that Old Damiriak did not have. For example:

Mode	Dahmek	Miramish	Mirsua	Nimiash	English
Present, Normal	Nia patisle.	Nia palito.	Nias palitos.	Nia palto.	I act.
Present, Emphatic	Nia koko patisle.	Nia koko palito.	Nias kokos palitos.	Nia koko palto.	I do act.
Past, Normal	Nia patislyot	Nia palitio.	Nias palitios.	Nia paltio.	I acted.
Past, Emphatic	Nia kokyot patislyot.	Nia kokio palitio.	Nias kokios palitios.	Nia kokio paltio.	I did act.
Future, Normal	Nia patisleit.	Nia paliteio.	Nias paliteios.	Nia palteio.	I will act.
Future, Emphatic	Nia kokeit patisleit.	Nia kokeio paliteio.	Nias kokeios paliteios.	Nia kokeio palteio.	I really will act.

Koko is also used as a *pro-verb* (replacement for a verb, like a pronoun for a noun). It can refer to a verb used in a prior sentence, for example:

Dahmek	Miramish	Mirsua	Nimiash	English
Patisle kail? Nia koko.	Palito kail? Nia koko.	Palitos kails? Nias kokos.	Palto kail? Nia koko.	Do you act? I do.
Patislyot kail? Nia kokyot.	Palitio kail? Nia kokio.	Palitios kails? Nias kokios.	Paltio kail? Nia kokio.	Did you act? I did.
Patisleit kail? Nia kokeit.	Paliteio kail? Nia kokeio.	Paliteios kails? Nias kokeios.	Palteio kail? Nia kokeio.	Will you act? I will.
Patisleit kail? Nia kokyot.	Paliteio kail? Nia kokio.	Paliteios kails? Nias kokios.	Palteio kail? Nia kokio.	Will you act? I did.

Note that in the question form (*Do-noun-verb* as shown in the above English examples), Damiriak questions do not normally lead with a word like *do*. Instead, the noun and verb positions are switched such that the verb leads the noun to form the Damiriak question. However, a *koko* pro-verb may be used to emphasize the question using a *Koko-noun-verb* structure, for example:

Dahmek	Miramish	Mirsua	Nimiash	English
Koko kail patisle?	Koko kail e palito?	Kokos kails palitos?	Koko kail palto?	*Do* you act?
Kokyot kail patislyot?	Kokio kail e palitio?	Kokios kails palitios?	Kokio kail paltio?	*Did* you act?
Kokeit kail patisleit?	Kokeio kail e paliteio?	Kokeios kails paliteios?	Kokeio kail palteio?	*Will* you act?

Irregular Verbs

There are two irregular verbs in the Damiriak languages.

The verb *to be* has two forms—common and emphatic. The common form is used in everyday conversation; the emphatic form is used to emphasize a point of topic, often in the heat of the moment. The verb *to be* is never used as an auxiliary verb in the Damiriak languages. The following chart shows the different forms of *to be* and lists some non-verb forms as well.

To Be

Type	Dahmek	Miramish	Mirsua	Nimiash	English Equiv
Common					
Infinitive	dir vil	di kilo	dis kilos	di bil	to be
Present Singular	vil	kilo	kilos	bil	is/ am
Present Plural	vir	kiro	kiros	bir	are
Past Singular	vol	kolo	kolos	bol	was
Past Plural	vor	koro	koros	bor	were
Future Sing/Plural	vush	kusho	kusos	buvo	will
Present Participle (n)	kulauf	kulaura	kulauras	kulaur	being
Past Participle (adj)	vol, vor	kolu	kolus	bol, bor	been
Future Particip (adj)	vush	kushu	kusùs	buvu	will-be

Type	Dahmek	Miramish	Mirsua	Nimiash	English Equiv
Emphatic					
Infinitive	dir vikel	di kikelo	dis kikelos	di kulko	to be (much)
Present Singular	vikel	kikelo	kikelos	bivel	is/am (much)
Present Plural	viker	kikero	kikeros	biver	are (much)
Past Singular	vokel	kokelo	kokelos	bovel	was (much)
Past Plural	voker	kokero	kokeros	bover	were (much)
Future Sing/Plural	vukesh	kukesho	kukesos	buvesh	shall (much)
Present Participle (n)	kulaufk	kulaurika	kulaurikas	kulaurk	being
Past Particip Sng(adj)	vokel	kokelu	kokelus	bovel	been
Past Particip Pl (adj)	voker	kokeru	kokerus	bover	been
Future Particip (adj)	vukesh	kukeshu	kukesus	buvesh	will-be

The verb *to have* does not have an emphatic form. As with *to be*, certain non-verb forms are also listed.

To Have

Type	Dahmek	Miramish/ Nimiash	Mirsua	English Equiv
Infinitive	dir kof	di kofo	dis kofos	to have
Present Singular	kof	kofo	kofos	have, has
Present Plural	koves	kovo	kovos	have
Past Singular, Plural	kot	koto	kotos	had
Future Singular/Plural	koveit	koveio	koveios	will have
Present Participle (verb)	kofaut	kofao	kofaos	having
Present Participle (adj)	kofautu	kofaolu	kofaolus	having
Past Participle (adj)	kotu	kotu	kotus	had
Gerund (noun)	kofaut	kofaola	kofaolas	having
Nounify, Singular	kove	kofa	kofas	have
Nounify, Plural	kovyek	kofi	kofis	haves
Nounify, Plural Negative	kovoiyek	kofi-oili	kofis-oilis	have-nots

8

Adjectives, Determiners, Adverbs, Prepositions, Conjunctions, and Interjections

Adjectives

Adjectives modify a noun or pronoun. Past participle verbs can be used as adjectives similar to past participles in English, though when used in this fashion the Dahmek s/z is dropped. Miramish past-tense verbs may be used as adjectives with the *u* suffix.

Present participle verbs may be used as adjectives with no s/z and *u* appended for Dahmek words while Miramish simply appends *u*.

Damiriak languages also have a future participle—the future-tense verb used as an adjective. Dahmek drops the s/z, while Miramish appends *u*.

The following suffixes are added to a root word:

Adjective Type/ Meaning	Dahmek (no s/z)	Miramish/ Nimiash	Mirsua	English Equiv
Generic adjective	-u	-u, -lu	-us, -lus	-al, -ate, -ial, -ic, -ine, -ish, -ive, -y
Past Participle	-yotu	-iou	-ious	-ed
Present Participle	-autu	-aolu	-aolus	-ing
Future Participle	-eit	-eiou	-eious	will be (x)ing
More of	-wel	-welu	-welus	-er
Most of	-wak	-waku	-wakus	-est, -st
Full of	-ushu	-ushu	-usus	-ful, -ous
Lack of	-menu	-menu	-menus	-less

Comparison adjectives do not necessarily have one of the above suffixes. Some are:

Dahmek	Miramish/ Nimiash	Mirsua	English Equiv
wel	welu	welus	more
wak	waku	wakus	most
men	menu	menus	less
minarsh	minashu	minasus	lesser
munk	muniku	munikus	least

Determiners

Determiners are much like adjectives in that they modify a noun or pronoun. They are also known as articles.

Determiner Type	Dahmek	Miramish/ Nimiash	Mirsua	English Equiv
Indefinite	dhor, ome	dho, omei	dhos, omeis	a, an
Definite	shair	shai	sais	the

Adverbs

Adverbs modify verbs, adjectives, other adverbs, and clauses. Adverbs are derived from a root word and do not have the variety of suffixes that adjectives have.

Adverb Type/ Meaning	Dahmek	Miramish/ Nimiash	Mirsua	English Equiv
Generic adverb	-iu	-iu	-ius	-ly

Prepositions

Prepositions begin a prepositional phrase. Such a phrase consists of at least a preposition and a noun. See the *Multi-Use Words* table for a list of prepositions.

Conjunctions

Conjunctions connect two or more phrases. See the *Multi-Use Words* table for a list of conjunctions.

Special Multi-Use Words

The following special words can be used in one or more ways without changing spelling—adjective, adverb, conjunction, or preposition. Included are multi-use nouns that may or may not have the same spelling as other parts of speech.

Multi-Use Words

Dahmek	Miramish	Mirsua	Nimiash	English
oveip	oveipu	oveipus	oveip	about (adj/adv/prep)
uvof	uvofu	uvofus	uvof	above (adj/adv/prep)
oshklauk	oshekelauku	osekelaukus	oshklauk	across (adj/adv/prep)
ovil	ovilu	ovilus	ovil	after (adj/adv/prep)
ovilhaush	ovilehaushu	ovilehausus	ovilhaush	afterward (adv)
ovilhaush	ovilehaushu	ovilehausus	ovilhaush	afterwards (adv)
okuan	okuanu	okuanus	okuan	again (adv)
okuank	okuaneku	okuanekus	okuank	against (prep)

Dahmek	Miramish	Mirsua	Nimiash	English
ude	udu	udus	ud	ago (adj/adv)
okeftiu	okefitiu	okefitius	okeftru	ahead (adv)
oshalf	oshalifu	osalifus	oshalf	alike (adj/adv)
orflauft	orafelaufitu	orafelaufitus	orflauft	alive (adj)
lor	loreifu	loreifus	lor	all (adj)
lorwak	lorowaku	lorowakus	lorwak	almost (adv)
ofien	ofienu	ofienus	ofien	alone (adj/adv)
orazhe	orazhu	orazus	orazh	along (adv/prep)
orazhoirt	orazhoitu	orazoitus	orazhoit	alongside (adv/prep)
obiabe	obiabu	obiabus	obiab	aloud (adv)
lordolu	lorudoliu	lorudolius	lordolu	already (adv)
orsh	oreshu	oresus	orsh	also (adv/conj)
otshan	oteshanu	otesanus	otshan	although (conj)
lordikefil	loredikefilu	loredikefilus	lordikefil	altogether (adv)
lorhoish	lorehoishiu	lorehoisius	lorhoish	always (adv)
ozharf	ozharu	ozarus	ozhar	amid (prep)
ozharf	ozharu	ozarus	ozhar	amidst (prep)
olaume	olaumu	olaumus	olaum	among (prep)
olaume	olaumu	olaumus	olaum	amongst (prep)
dhark	dhaku	dhakus	dhak	and (conj)
omirshu	omishei	omiseis	omishu	another (adj)
ino	inei	ineis	ino	any (adj/adv/prep)
inohia	inohialu	inohialus	inohia	anyhow (adv)
inowel	inowelu	inowelus	inowel	anymore (adv)
inobresh	inoberesha	inoberesas	inobresh	anyplace (adv)
inodizhe	inodizha	inodizas	inodizh	anything (n)
inoplio	inopeliola	inopeliolas	inoplio	anyway (adv)
inoholu	inoholu	inoholus	inoholu	anywhere (adv)
inohol	inohola	inoholas	inohol	anywhere (n)
oblaithpu	obelaithu	obelaithus	oblaithu	around (adv/prep)
yosh	yoshu	yosus	yosh	as (adv/conj/prep)
oprushel	operushelu	operuselus	oprushel	asleep (adj)
ide	idu	idus	id	at (prep)
opiorl	opiolu	opiolus	opiol	away (adj/adv)
vakaursh	vakaushu	vakasus	vakaush	backward (adj/adv)
vakaursh	vakaushu	vakasus	vakaush	backwards (adj/adv)
vilshashk	kileshekashu	kilesekasus	bilshkash	because (conj)
vivoan	kivoanu	kivoanus	bivoan	before (conj/prep)
vivokap	kivoanukapu	kivoanukapus	bivoankapu	beforehand (adj/adv)
kuden	kunodu	kunodus	kund	behind (adj/adv/prep)
ushurt	ushutu	usutus	ushut	below (adv/prep)
milurn	milunu	milunus	milun	beneath (adv/prep)
kushoirt	kushoitu	kusoitus	kushoit	beside (adv/prep)
kushoirt	kushoitu	kusoitus	kushoit	besides (adv/prep)

Dahmek	Miramish	Mirsua	Nimiash	English
vildurme	kiledumu	kiledumus	bildum	between (adv/prep)
kuyelir	kuyerulu	kuyerulus	kuyerl	beyond (adv/prep)
peirsh	peishu	peisus	peish	both (adj/conj)
vede	vedu	vedus	ved	but (adv/conj/prep)
vu	vu	vus	vu	by (adj/adv/prep)
vuvirfyotu	vuvifiou	vuvifious	vuvifiou	bygone (adj)
vuvirfyot	vuvifioa	vuvifioas	vuvifioa	bygone (n)
vuvirfyotyek	vuvifioi	vuvifiois	vuvifioi	bygones (n)
burfaik	burafaiku	burafaikus	burfaik	despite (prep)
tiern	tienu	tienus	tien	down (adj/adv/prep)
tienhaursh	tienuhaushu	tienuhausus	tienhaush	downward (adj/adv)
tienhaursh	tienuhaushu	tienuhausus	tienhaush	downwardly (adv)
shwenf	shewenifu	sewenifus	shwenf	during (prep)
sartu	sharitu	saritus	shartu	either (adj/adv/conj)
nelsh	nelishu	nelisus	nelsh	else (adj/adv)
nelsholu	nelisholu	nelisolus	nelsholu	elsewhere (adv)
plurf	pelufu	pelufus	pluf	enough (adj/adv)
efel	efelu	efelus	efel	ever (adj/adv)
eferfital	lerofital	lerofitales	lerfital	everywhere (adv)
tuvet	verit	verites	vert	except (conj/prep)
thilu	thilu	thilus	thil	far (adj/adv)
thiluel	thiluelu	thiluelus	thiluel	farther (adj/adv)
krunfu	kerunu	kerunus	krunu	few (adj)
maf	mafu	mafus	maf	for (conj/prep)
velt	veletu	veletus	velt	from (prep)
thiluel	thiluelu	thiluelus	thiluel	further (adj/adv)
thiluelf	thiluelifu	thiluelifus	thiluelf	furthermore (adv)
thilwak	thiliwaku	thiliwakus	thilwak	furthest (adj)
wapliol	wapeliolu	wapeliolus	wapliol	halfway (adj/adv)
warf	wafipu	wafipus	wafp	hence (adv)
kir	kiru	kirus	kir	here (adj/adv/interj)
kir	kira	kiras	kir	here (n)
hial	hialu	hialus	hia	how (adv/conj)
hial	hiala	hialas	hia	how (n)
hiafel	hiafelu	hiafelus	hiafel	however (adv/conj)
ule	ulu	ulus	uli	if (conj)
ishe	ishu	isus	ishe	in (prep)
benflide	benifelidu	benifelidus	benflide	indeed (adv/interj)
benshoit	ishoitu	isoitus	ishoit	inside (adj/adv/prep)
benshoit	ishoita	isoitas	ishoit	inside (n)
befnetiu	befenetiu	befenetius	befnetiu	instead (adv)
ishte	ishetu	isetus	ishtu	into (prep)
men	menu	menus	men	less (adj)
minarsh	minashu	minasus	minash	lesser (adj)

Dahmek	Miramish	Mirsua	Nimiash	English
munk	muniku	munikus	munk	least (adj)
reifki	reikifu	reikifus	reikif	like (prep)
limursh	limushu	limusus	limush	minus (adj/prep)
limursh	limusha	limusas	limush	minus (n)
limurshyek	limushi	limusis	limushi	minuses (n pl)
wel	welu	welus	wel	more (n/adj/adv)
wak	waku	wakus	wak	most (n/adj/adv)
nesh	neshu	nesus	nesh	much (n/adj/adv)
shuel	shuelu	suelus	shuel	near (adj/adv/prep)
shuelervu	shueluvu	sueluvus	shuelvu	nearby (adj/adv)
mashartu	masharitu	masaritus	mashartu	neither (adj/conj)
moge	mogu	mogus	mog	next (adj/adv/prep)
maur	mau	maus	mau	no (adj/adv/n)
maurtu	mautu	mautus	mautu	none (adj/adv)
mahil	mawilu	mawilus	mawil	nor (conj)
mahir	mahilu	mahilus	mahi	now (adj/adv/conj)
mahir	mahila	mahilas	mahi	now (n)
mauhar	mauhalu	mauhalus	mauhal	nowhere (adj/adv)
mauhar	mauhala	mauhalas	mauhal	nowhere (n)
orp	opeifu	opeifus	op	of (prep)
unf	unefu	unefus	unf	off (prep)
lieme	liemu	liemus	liem	on (prep)
hemf	hemefu	hemefus	hemf	once (adj/adv/conj)
hemf	hemefa	hemefas	hemf	once (n)
hemeru	hemeru	hemerus	hemeru	only (adj/adv/conj)
emde	emodi	emodis	emdi	onto (prep)
il	ilu	ilus	il	or (conj)
mirshu	mishu	misus	mishu	other (adj/adv)
mirshfluik	mishufeluiku	misefeluikus	mishfluik	otherwise (adj/adv/conj)
uil	uilu	uilus	uil	out (adj/adv/interj/ prep)
uil	uila	uilas	uil	out (n)
uilshoirt	uileshoitu	uilesoitus	uilshoit	outside (adj/adv/prep)
uilshoirt	uileshoita	uilesoitas	uilshoit	outside (n)
uilhaurshu	uilehaushu	uilehausus	uilhaushu	outward (adj/adv)
uilhaursh	uilehausha	uilehausas	uilhaush	outward (n)
uilhaurshiu	uilehaushiu	uilehausius	uilhaushiu	outwardly (adv)
afenu	afenu	afenus	afenu	over (adv/adv/prep)
afen	afena	afenas	afen	over (n)
afeniu	afeniu	afenius	afeniu	overly (adv)
dife	difu	difus	dif	per (adv/prep)
numart	numatu	numatus	numat	plus (adj/prep)
numart	numata	numatas	numat	plus (n)

Dahmek	Miramish	Mirsua	Nimiash	English
loshert	loshetu	losetus	losht	rather (adv/interj)
luvaikmern	luvaikamenu	luvaikamenus	luvaikmen	regardless (adj/adv)
falarth	falathu	falathus	falath	seldom (adj/adv)
shoitpliol	shoitupeliolu	soitepeliolus	shoitpliol	sideways (adj/adv)
shnesh	sheneshu	senesus	shnesh	since (adv/conj/ prep)
zhaul	zhau	zaus	zhau	so (adj/adv/conj/interj)
zhin	zhinu	zinus	zhin	some (adj/adv)
zhidaurn	zhidaunu	zidaunus	zhidaun	sometime (adj/adv)
zhidauirn	zhidauinu	zidauinus	zhidauin	sometimes (adj/adv)
zhinorl	zhinolu	zinolus	zhinol	somewhere (adv)
zhinorl	zhinola	zinolas	zhinol	somewhere (n)
zhesh	zheshu	zesus	zhesh	such (adj/adv)
tshome	teshomu	tesomus	tshom	than (conj/prep)
yarsh	yashu	yasus	yash	that (conj)
tshadu	teshadu	tesadus	tshadu	that (adj)
dode	dodu	dodus	dod	then (adj/adv)
durl	duru	durus	dur	there (adj/adv/interj)
shirshu	shishu	sisus	shishu	these (adj)
tshunu	teshunu	tesunus	tshunu	this (adj)
shorshu	shoshu	sosus	shoshu	those (adj)
tsharn	teshanu	tesanus	tshan	though (adv/conj)
telsharn	teleshanu	telesanus	telshan	through (adj/adv/prep)
telshanuil	teleshanuilu	telesanuilus	telshanuil	throughout (adv/prep)
dir	di	dis	di	to (prep)
dehursh	dehushu	dehusus	dehush	toward (prep)
dehursh	dehushu	dehusus	dehush	towards (prep)
dreil	dereilu	dereilus	drei	true (adj)
dreilu	dereiliu	dcreilius	dreilu	truly (adv)
avuth	avuthu	avuthus	avuth	twice (adv)
utine	utinu	utinus	utin	under (adj/adv/prep)
utinilurn	utinilunu	utinilunus	utinilun	underneath (adj/adv/prep)
utinilurn	utiniluna	utinilunas	utinilun	underneath (n)
iumern	iumenu	iumenus	iumen	unless (conj/prep)
piushalirf	piushalifu	piusalifus	piushalf	unlike (adj/prep)
piushanirf	piushanifu	piusanifus	piushanf	unlikely (adj/adv)
iutaurn	iutaunu	iutaunus	iutaun	until (conj/prep)
ivei	iveilu	iveilus	ivei	up (prep)
iverme	ivemu	ivemus	ivem	upon (prep)
tharmelme	tharomemu	tharomemus	tharmem	versus (prep)
fuarl	fualu	fualus	fual	via (prep)
halk	haku	hakus	hak	what (adj/adv/conj)
hakerf	hakefu	hakefus	hakef	whatever (adj/interj)
hakzhaufel	hakezhaufelu	hakezaufelus	hakzhaufel	whatsoever (adj)

Dahmek	Miramish	Mirsua	Nimiash	English
yarme	yamu	yamus	yam	when (adv/conj)
yamerf	yamefu	yamefus	yamef	whenever (adv/conj)
torlu	tolu	tolus	tolu	where (adv/conj)
veltorlu	veletolu	veletolus	veltolu	where-from (adv)
dihorlu	diholu	diholus	diholu	where-to (adv)
toluyorsh	toluyoshu	toluyosus	toluyosh	whereas (conj)
toluyorsh	toluyosha	toluyosas	toluyosh	whereas (n)
torluvu	toluvu	toluvus	toluvu	whereby (adv/conj)
torlerf	tolefelu	tolefelus	tolefel	wherever (adv/conj)
shardu	sharodu	sarodus	shardu	whether (conj)
hirshu	hishu	hisus	hishu	which (adj)
hirsherf	hishefelu	hisefelus	hishefel	whichever (adj)
yaurk	yauku	yaukus	yauk	while (conj)
yaurk	yauka	yaukas	yauk	while (n)
dihorlu	diholu	diholus	diholu	whither (adv/conj)
hiur	hiu	hius	hiu	why (adv/conj/interj)
hiur	hiua	hiuas	hiu	why (n)
borsh	boshu	bosus	bosh	with (prep)
boshirsh	boshishu	bosisus	boshish	within (adv/prep)
boshirsh	boshisha	bosisas	boshish	within (n)
borshuil	boshuilu	bosuilus	boshuil	without (adv/prep)
borshuil	boshuila	bosuilas	boshuil	without (n)
weir	wei	weipus	wei	yes (adv)
warshk	washiku	wasikus	washk	yet (adv/conj)

Interjections

An interjection is an outburst or reaction to a comment or situation.

Interjections

Dahmek	Miramish	Mirsua	Nimiash	English Equiv
ia	ia	ias	ia	ah
yanu	yanu	yanus	yanu	amen
ia	ia	ias	ia	aye
bau	bau	baus	bau	boo
rayu-rayu	rayu-rayu	rayus-rayus	rayu-rayu	bow-wow
dovai	dovai	dovais	dovai	bravo
liau	liau	liaus	liau	bye
ua	ua	uas	ua	eh

Dahmek	Miramish	Mirsua	Nimiash	English Equiv
ilaikau	ilaiko	ilaikos	ilaiko	eureka
viah	viaha	viahas	viah	gee
viah	viaha	viahas	viah	geez
tikaushkiatsh	tikalo	tikalos	tiklo	get-lost
vuau	vuaua	vuauas	vuau	golly
kufliau	kufaliau	kufaliaus	kufliau	goodbye
kuflimern	kufelimena	kufelimenas	kuflimen	goodmorning
kufmuarn	kufemuana	kufemuanas	kufmuan	goodnight
vuaursh	vuausha	vuausa	vuaush	gosh
partsha	patesha	patesas	patsha	gotcha
yat	ya	yas	ya	hah
yata	yaya	yayas	yaya	haha
takalan	takalana	takalanas	takalan	hallelujah
aluka	alori	aloris	alor	hello
moia	moi	mois	moi	hey
mio	mi	mis	mi	hi
kelaia	kelai	kelais	kelai	hooray
mual	mua	muas	mua	huh
kelaia	kelai	kelais	kelai	hurrah
kelaia	kelai	kelais	kelai	hurray
ur	ul	ules	um	hmm
rakiu	rakiu	rakius	rakiu	meow
mwae	mwae	mwaes	mwae	na
mauar	maua	mauas	mauas	naw
maiwar	maiwa	maiwas	maiwa	nay
maiarp	maiapu	maiapus	maiap	nope
ar	ui	uis	ui	oh
shershai	sheshai	sesai	sheshai	ok
shershai	sheshai	sesai	sheshai	okay
uf	ufu	ufus	uf	oomph
oifk	oifo	oifos	oif	oops
auta	auta	autas	auta	ouch
aua	aua	auas	aua	ow
tuf	tufa	tufas	tuf	poof
daua	daua	dauas	daua	pow
kuek	kuek	kuekes	kuek	quack
shkwak	shwaka	swakas	shwak	scat
ishai	ishai	isais	ishai	shoo
angai	angai	angais	angai	ugh
er	er	eres	er	uh
ern	eren	erenes	ern	um
durai	durai	durais	durai	voila
hua	hua	huas	hua	wah
yuyau	yuyau	yuyaus	yuyau	wahoo

Dahmek	Miramish	Mirsua	Nimiash	English Equiv
shwi	shwi	shwis	shwi	whee
yoi	yoi	yois	yoi	whoa
aruf	arufa	arufas	aruf	woof
yai	yai	yais	yai	wow
kai	kai	kais	kai	yay
weior	weia	weias	weia	yeah
weip	weipu	weipus	weip	yep
waik	waika	waikas	waik	yikes
yaua	yaua	yauas	yaua	yow
kwak	kwaka	kwakas	kwak	yuck
kwam	kwama	kwamas	kwam	yum
kwami	kwami	kwamis	kwami	yummy
weip	weipu	weipus	weip	yup

9

Earth Names

The following are Damiriak words adopted from English. These words are usually in reference to something specific to Earth and have no real reference within the Empire.

Calendar

The following calendar months and days of the week apply only to the Gregorian Earth calendar. Damiriak women have their own calendar with different names.

Months

Dahmek	Miramish	Mirsua	Nimiash	English
Shanilan	Shanilana	Sanilanas	Shanilan	January
Valual	Valuala	Valualas	Valual	February
Mular	Mulara	Mularas	Mular	March
Laprel	Laparela	Laparelas	Laprel	April
Lamail	Lamaila	Lamailas	Lamail	May
Zhun	Zhuna	Zunas	Zhun	June
Zhulait	Zhulaita	Zulaitas	Zhulait	July
Laukut	Laukuta	Laukutas	Laukut	August
Veshaifar	Veshaifara	Vesaifaras	Veshaifar	September
Loktaf	Lokitafa	Lokitafas	Loktaf	October
Nofefar	Nofefara	Nofefaras	Nofefar	November
Tefendarl	Tefenedala	Tefenedalas	Tefendal	December

Days of Week

Dahmek	Miramish	Mirsua	Nimiash	English
Renviurl	Renuviula	Renuviulas	Renviul	Sunday
Namurviul	Namuriviula	Namuriviulas	Namurviul	Monday
Dioshviurl	Dioshuviula	Diosuviulas	Dioshviul	Tuesday
Yuteshviurl	Yuteshuviul	Yutesuviulas	Yuteshviul	Wednesday
Toiviurl	Toiviula	Toiviulas	Toiviul	Thursday
Freiviul	Fereiviula	Fereiviulas	Freiviul	Friday
Shudaviurl	Shudaviula	Sudaviulas	Shudaviul	Saturday

Geography

The following words are listed in noun form. For adjective forms, the *–u* replaces *–a* in words ending in *–a*, while consonant-ending words must have the *–u* appended.

World Geography

Dahmek	Miramish	Mirsua	Nimiash	Engl Equiv
Afkarn	Afikana	Afikanas	Afkan	Afghan
Afkansharn	Afikanoshana	Afikanosanas	Afkanshan	Afghanistan
Afrilk	Aferika	Aferikas	Afrik	Africa
Afrikarn	Aferikana	Aferikanas	Afrikan	African
Albertarf	Aluberitafa	Aluberitafas	Albertaf	Alberta
Amirk	Amika	Amikas	Amik	America
Amirkan	Amikana	Amikanas	Amikan	American
Amshterdarm	Amishoterudama	Amisoterudamas	Amshterdam	Amsterdam
Ankolarf	Anikolafa	Anikolafas	Ankolaf	Angola
Arbe	Arobana	Arobanas	Arb	Arab
Argentirn	Arugenotina	Arugenotinas	Argentin	Argentina
Armern	Arimena	Arimenas	Armen	Armenia
Armenarn	Arimenana	Arimenanas	Armenan	Armenian
Larshiarl	Larishiala	Larisialas	Larshial	Asia
Larshiarn	Larishiana	Larisianas	Larshian	Asian
Atelantirk	Atelanotika	Atelanotikas	Atelantik	Atlantic
Atelantirsh	Atelanotisha	Atelanotisas	Atelantish	Atlantis
Aushtralf	Aushoterala	Ausoteralas	Aushtral	Australia
Aushtralarn	Aushoterana	Ausoteranas	Aushtralan	Australian
Aushtarf	Aushotara	Ausotaras	Aushtar	Austria
Aushtarnf	Aushotarina	Ausotarinas	Aushtarn	Austrian
Azherbaizharn	Azherobaizhana	Azerobaizanas	Azherbaizhan	Azerbaijan
Baltirk	Balotika	Balotikas	Baltik	Baltic

World Geography

Dahmek	Miramish	Mirsua	Nimiash	Engl Equiv
Bagdarde	Bagudada	Bagudadas	Bagdad	Baghdad
Beizhirn	Beizhinga	Beizingas	Beizhing	Beijing
Beiruft	Beiruta	Beirutas	Beirut	Beirut
Belgiarn	Belogiana	Belogianas	Belgian	Belgian
Belgiurme	Belogiuma	Belogiumas	Belgium	Belgium
Berlirn	Berolina	Berolinas	Berlin	Berlin
Born	Bona	Bonas	Bon	Bonn
Brazhilf	Berazhila	Berazilas	Brazhil	Brazil
Brazhilarn	Berazhilana	Berazilanas	Brazhilan	Brazilian
Britairn	Beritaina	Beritainas	Britain	Britain
Britirsh	Beritisha	Beritisas	British	British
Brushelf	Berushela	Beruselas	Brushel	Brussels
Bulgarf	Bulogara	Bulogaras	Bulgar	Bulgaria
Bulgariarn	Bulogariana	Bulogarianas	Bulgarian	Bulgarian
Kairolf	Kairofa	Kairofas	Kairof	Cairo
Kambodiarf	Kamubodiafa	Kamubodiafas	Kambodiaf	Cambodia
Kambodiarn	Kamubodiana	Kamubodianas	Kambodian	Cambodian
Kanadarf	Kanadafa	Kanadafas	Kanadaf	Canada
Kanadiarn	Kanadiana	Kanadianas	Kanadian	Canadian
Karibiarn	Karibiana	Karibianas	Karibian	Caribbean
Tshernobilf	Tesherinobila	Teserinobilas	Tshernobil	Chernobyl
Tshilf	Teshila	Tesilas	Tshil	Chile
Tshinarf	Teshinafa	Tesinafas	Tshinaf	China
Tshinarsh	Teshinasha	Tesinasas	Tshinash	Chinese
Kolombiarf	Kolomubiafa	Kolomubiafas	Kolombiaf	Colombia
Kolombiarn	Kolomubiana	Kolomubianas	Kolombian	Colombian
Kostarf Rikarf	Koshetafa Rikafa	Kosetafas Rikafas	Kostaf Rikaf	Costa Rica
Kubarf	Kubafa	Kubafas	Kubaf	Cuba
Kubarn	Kubana	Kubanas	Kuban	Cuban
Shaiprulsh	Shaiperusha	Saiperusas	Shaiprush	Cyprus
Tshekoshlovark	Teshekoshelovaka	Tesekoselovas	Tshekoshlovak	Czechoslovakia
Denemark	Denomaka	Denomakas	Denmak	Denmark
Denverf	Denuvera	Denuveras	Denver	Denver
Detroilt	Deteroita	Deteroitas	Detroit	Detroit
Dutersh	Dutesha	Dutesas	Dutsh	Dutch
Igeptaf	Igepita	Igepitas	Igept	Egypt
Igeptarn	Igepitana	Igepitanas	Igeptan	Egyptian
Anklarn	Anakulana	Anakulanas	Anklan	England
Ankarsh	Anakalusha	Anakalusas	Ankalsh	English
Reilorp	Reilopa	Reilopas	Reilop	Europe
Reiloparn	Reilopana	Reilopanas	Reilopan	European
Finlanurde	Finelanuda	Finelanudas	Finland	Finland
Fransharf	Feranishafa	Feranisafas	Franshaf	France
Frankfurft	Feranikofurita	Feranikofuritas	Frankfurt	Frankfurt

World Geography

Dahmek	Miramish	Mirsua	Nimiash	Engl Equiv
Franarsh	Feranasha	Feranasas	Franash	French
Zhenirve	Zheniva	Zenivas	Zheniv	Geneva
Zhermarn	Zheromana	Zeromanas	Zherman	German
Zhermarnf	Zheromanifa	Zeromanifas	Zhermanf	Germany
Grilsh	Gerisha	Gerisas	Grish	Greece
Grifirk	Gerifika	Gerifikas	Grifk	Greek
Kaitirf	Kaitifa	Kaitifas	Kaitif	Haiti
Kishpanirk	Kishopanika	Kisopanikas	Kishpanik	Hispanic
Konduralsh	Konadurasha	Konadurasas	Kondurash	Honduras
Honurge Konurge	Honuga Konuga	Honugas Konugas	Honug Konug	Hong Kong
Kunkarft	Kunikarofa	Kunikarofas	Kunkarf	Hungary
Kunkariarn	Kunikariana	Kunikarianas	Kunkarian	Hungarian
Indiarf	Inodiafa	Inodiafas	Indiaf	India
Indiafarn	Inodiafana	Inodiafanas	Indiafan	Indian
Indonishiarf	Inudonishiafa	Inudonisiafas	Indonishiaf	Indonesia
Iranf	Irana	Iranas	Iran	Iran
Iraniarn	Iraniana	Iranianas	Iranian	Iranian
Iralfk	Irafika	Irafikas	Irafk	Iraq
Irafkarn	Irafikana	Irafikanas	Irafkan	Iraqi
Irelanurde	Irelanuda	Irelanudas	Ireland	Ireland
Irelandarn	Irelanudana	Irelanudanas	Irelandan	Irish
Ishrahilf	Isherahila	Iserahilas	Ishrahil	Israel
Ishrahilarn	Isherahilana	Iserahilanas	Ishrahiln	Israeli
Italirf	Italifa	Italifas	Italif	Italy
Italiarn	Italiana	Italianas	Italian	Italian
Zhaparf	Zhapafa	Zapafas	Zhapaf	Japan
Zhaparnf	Zhapanifa	Zapafinas	Zhapanf	Japanese
Zherushalorme	Zherushaloma	Zerusalomas	Zherushalom	Jerusalem
Zhordarn	Zhorudana	Zorudanas	Zhordan	Jordan
Koriarf	Koriafa	Koriafas	Koriaf	Korea
Korianf	Koriana	Korianas	Korian	Korean
Kuwairt	Kuwaita	Kuwaitas	Kuwait	Kuwait
Kuwaitarn	Kuwaitana	Kuwaitanas	Kuwaitan	Kuwaiti
Latinorf	Latinofa	Latinofas	Latinf	Latin
Lebanorf	Lebanofa	Lebanofas	Lebanof	Lebanon
Lebanornf	Lebanonifa	Lebanonifas	Lebanonf	Lebanese
Libiarf	Libiafa	Libiafas	Libiaf	Libya
Libiarn	Libiana	Libianas	Libian	Libyan
Lithuaniarf	Lithuaniafa	Lithuaniafas	Lithuaniaf	Lithuania
Lithuaniarn	Lithuaniana	Lithuanianas	Lithuanian	Lithuanian
Londorn	Lonudona	Lonudonas	London	London
Madrirde	Maderida	Maderidas	Madrid	Madrid
Malashiarf	Malashiafa	Malasiafas	Malashiaf	Malaysia

World Geography

Dahmek	Miramish	Mirsua	Nimiash	Engl Equiv
Manshersht	Manisheshota	Manisesotas	Manshesht	Manchester
Manilorf	Manilofa	Manilofas	Manilf	Manila
Mediteraniarf	Mediteraniafa	Mediteraniafas	Mediteranf	Mediterranean
Meshkirf	Meshakifa	Mesakifas	Meshkif	Mexico
Meshkifarn	Meshakifana	Mesakifanas	Meshkifan	Mexican
Midirsht	Midishata	Midisatas	Midisht	Mideast
Montrialf	Moniteriala	Moniterialas	Montrial	Montreal
Moshkaurf	Moshikaufa	Mosikaufas	Moshkauf	Moscow
Namibiarf	Namibiafa	Namibiafas	Namibiaf	Namibia
Netherlanurde	Netherolanuda	Netherolanudas	Netherlanud	Netherlands
Mior Zhilanurde	Miola Zhilanuda	Miolas Zilanudas	Miol Zhilanud	New Zealand
Nikaragurf	Nikaragufa	Nikaragufas	Nikaraguf	Nicaragua
Nikaraguarn	Nikaraguana	Nikaraguanas	Nikaraguan	Nicaraguan
Norwairf	Norwaifa	Norwaifas	Norwaif	Norway
Norwaifarn	Norwaifana	Norwaifanas	Norwaifan	Norwegian
Ontariorf	Onitariofa	Onitariofas	Ontariof	Ontario
Otawarf	Otawafa	Otawafas	Otawaf	Ottawa
Pakishtarn	Pakishotana	Pakisotanas	Pakishtan	Pakistan
Paleshtirf	Paleshotifa	Palesotifas	Paleshtif	Palestine
Paleshtirn	Paleshotina	Palesotinas	Paleshtin	Palestinian
Panarm	Panama	Panamas	Panam	Panama
Panamarn	Panamana	Panamanas	Panaman	Panamanian
Parilsh	Parisha	Parisas	Parish	Paris
Pershiarn	Peroshiana	Perosianas	Pershian	Persian
Perulf	Perufa	Perufas	Peruf	Peru
Filipirf	Filipifa	Filipifas	Filipif	Philippine
Polanurd	Polanuda	Polanudas	Polanud	Poland
Portugalf	Poritugala	Poritugalas	Portugal	Portugal
Pragarf	Peragafa	Peragafas	Pragaf	Prague
Keberfk	Kebefika	Kebefikas	Kebefk	Quebec
Romarf	Romafa	Romafas	Romaf	Rome
Romafarn	Romafana	Romafanas	Romafan	Roman
Romiarf	Romiafa	Romiafas	Romiaf	Romania
Romiarn	Romiana	Romianas	Romian	Romanian
Rushiarf	Rushiafa	Rusiafas	Rushiaf	Russia
Rushiarn	Rushiana	Rusianas	Rushian	Russian
Shaudarn	Shaudana	Saudanas	Shaudan	Saudi
Shaudarf Arobarn	Shaudafa Arobana	Saudafas Arobanas	Shaudaf Arban	Saudi Arabia
Shkotlanirf	Shekotelanifa	Sekotelanifas	Shkotlanf	Scotland
Shkotlarn	Shekotelana	Sekotelanas	Shkotlan	Scottish
Shiorl	Shiola	Siolas	Shiol	Seoul
Shankairf	Shanikaifa	Sanikaifas	Shankaif	Shanghai
Shinkaporf	Shinokapora	Sinokaporas	Shinkapor	Singapore
Shoviert	Shovieta	Sovietas	Shoviet	Soviet

World Geography

Dahmek	Miramish	Mirsua	Nimiash	Engl Equiv
Shpairn	Shepaina	Sepainas	Shpain	Spain
Shpainarn	Shepainana	Sepainanas	Shpainan	Spanish
Shtokolirm	Shetokolima	Setokolimas	Shtokolm	Stockholm
Shuidarf	Shuidafa	Suidafas	Shuidaf	Sweden
Shuidarn	Shuidana	Suidanas	Shuidan	Swedish
Shuisharn	Shuishana	Suisanas	Shuishan	Swiss
Shuisherlarf	Shuisherolafa	Suiserolafas	Shuisherlaf	Switzerland
Shidunarf	Shidunafa	Sidunafas	Shidunaf	Sydney
Shiriarf	Shiriafa	Siriafas	Shiriaf	Syria
Shiriarn	Shiriana	Sirianas	Shirian	Syrian
Taiwarf	Taiwafa	Taiwafas	Taiwaf	Taiwan
Tekralf	Tekerafa	Tekerafas	Tekraf	Tehran
Tairf	Taifa	Taifas	Taif	Thai
Tailanurde	Tailanuda	Tailanudas	Tailanud	Thailand
Tokiorf	Tokiofa	Tokiofas	Tokiof	Tokyo
Torontorf	Toronitofa	Toronitofas	Torontof	Toronto
Turkirf	Turokifa	Turokifas	Turkif	Turkey
Turkifarn	Turokifana	Turokifanas	Turkifan	Turkish
Ukrainarf	Ukerainafa	Ukerainafas	Ukrainaf	Ukraine
Vankuvirf	Vanikuvifa	Vanikuvifas	Vankuvif	Vancouver
Venzhuilarf	Venezhuilafa	Venezuilafas	Venzhuilaf	Venezuela
Vienarf	Vienafa	Vienafas	Vienaf	Vienna
Vietnarme	Vietonama	Vietonamas	Vietnam	Vietnam
Vietnamarn	Vietonamana	Vietonamanas	Vietnaman	Vietnamese
Weilorsh	Weilosha	Weilosas	Weilsh	Wales
Warshaurf	Waroshaufa	Warosaufas	Warshauf	Warsaw
Yugoshlarve	Yugoshelava	Yugoselavas	Yugoshlav	Yugoslavia
Zhurifk	Zhurika	Zurikas	Zhurik	Zurich

United States Geography

Dahmek	Miramish	Mirsua	Nimiash	English Equiv
Alharme	Alubama	Alubamas	Albam	Alabama
Alishork	Alishoka	Alisokas	Alshk	Alaska
Ankorarzh	Anikorazha	Anikorazas	Ankorazh	Anchorage
Arizhorn	Arizhona	Arizonas	Arizhon	Arizona
Arkanorsh	Arikanosha	Arikanosas	Arkansh	Arkansas
Arlingtorn	Arelingatona	Arelingatonas	Arlington	Arlington
Atelanirt	Atelanita	Atelanitas	Atelant	Atlanta
Aushtirn	Aushetina	Ausetinas	Aushtin	Austin
Baltimorf	Balotimora	Balotimoras	Baltimor	Baltimore
Berkerl	Berokela	Berokelas	Berkel	Berkeley
Beverlif Hilorsh	Beveralifa Hiloshi	Beveralifas Hilosis	Beverlif Hilsh	Beverly Hills

United States Geography

Dahmek	Miramish	Mirsua	Nimiash	English Equiv
Birmingarme	Biromingama	Biromingamas	Birmingam	Birmingham
Boshtorn	Boshetona	Bosetonas	Boshton	Boston
Brodwairn	Berodwaina	Berodwainas	Brodwain	Broadway
Bruklirn	Berukelina	Berukelinas	Bruklin	Brooklyn
Bufalorn	Bufalona	Bufalonas	Bufalon	Buffalo
Burlingtorn	Buralingatona	Buralingatonas	Burlington	Burlington
Kaliforan	Kaliforina	Kaliforinas	Kaliforn	California
Kambrilge	Kamuberiga	Kamuberigas	Kambrig	Cambridge
Tsharltorn	Tesharolitona	Tesarolitonas	Tsharlton	Charleston
Sharlort	Sharilota	Sarilotas	Sharlot	Charlotte
Tshikarg	Teshikaga	Tesikagas	Tshikag	Chicago
Shinshinart	Shinoshinata	Sinosinatas	Shinshinat	Cincinnati
Klivlanurd	Kelivelanuda	Kelivelanudas	Klivland	Cleveland
Kolorard	Kolorada	Koloradas	Kolorad	Colorado
Kolumbiarf	Kolumobiafa	Kolumobiafas	Kolumbiaf	Columbia
Konetikurt	Konetikuta	Konetikutas	Konetikut	Connecticut
Dalarsh	Dalasha	Dalasas	Dalash	Dallas
Daitorn	Daitona	Daitonas	Daiton	Dayton
Daitonarf	Daitonafa	Daitonafas	Daitonaf	Daytona
Delawarf	Delawara	Delawaras	Delawar	Delaware
Floridarf	Feloridafa	Feloridafas	Floridaf	Florida
Zhiorazh	Zhioruzha	Zioruzas	Zhiorzh	Georgia
Kartoforde	Karitoforuda	Karitoforudas	Kartford	Hartford
Kauwirf	Kauwifa	Kauwifas	Kauwif	Hawii
Kushtorn	Kushatona	Kusatonas	Kushton	Houston
Idakorf	Idakofa	Idakofas	Idakof	Idaho
Ilanoirf	Ilanoifa	Ilanoifas	Ilanoif	Illinois
Indianirk	Inodianika	Inodianikas	Indiank	Indiana
Indiankarpol	Inodianikapola	Inodianikapolas	Indiankapol	Indianapolis
Iowarf	Iowafa	Iowafas	Iowaf	Iowa
Kansharsh	Kanishasha	Kanisasas	Kanshash	Kansas
Kentukirf	Kenotukifa	Kenotukifas	Kentukif	Kentucky
Larsh Veigarsh	Lash Veigasha	Las Veigasas	Lash Veigash	Las Vegas
Luishiarf	Luishiafa	Luisiafas	Luishiaf	Louisiana
Losh Ankelersh	Losha Anikelesha	Losas Anikelesas	Losh Ankelesh	Los Angeles
Madishorf	Madishofa	Madisofas	Madishof	Madison
Mainorf	Mainofa	Mainofas	Mainf	Maine
Mankatarf	Manokatafa	Manokatafas	Mankataf	Manhattan
Marilanurde	Marilanuda	Marilanudas	Mariland	Maryland
Mashashutarf	Mashashutafa	Masasutafas	Mashashutaf	Massachusetts
Memfirsh	Memofisha	Memofisas	Memfish	Memphis
Miamirf	Miamifa	Miamifas	Miamif	Miami
Mishigarf	Mishigafa	Misigafas	Mishigaf	Michigan
Miduelsh	Miduesha	Miduesas	Miduesh	Midwest

United States Geography

Dahmek	Miramish	Mirsua	Nimiash	English Equiv
Miluakirf	Miluakifa	Miluakifas	Miluakif	Milwaukee
Minkarpol	Minekapola	Minekapolas	Minkapol	Minneapolis
Minshort	Mineshota	Minesotas	Minshot	Minnesota
Mishashirp	Mishashipa	Misasipas	Mishaship	Mississippi
Mishuralf	Mishurafa	Misurafas	Mishurf	Missouri
Montarnf	Monatanifa	Monatanifas	Montanf	Montana
Montugoram	Monitugorima	Monitugorimas	Montugorm	Montgomery
Nashfilf	Nashofila	Masofilas	Nashfil	Nashville
Nebralshk	Neborashika	Neborasikas	Nebrashk	Nebraska
Nevadarf	Nevadafa	Nevadafas	Nevadaf	Nevada
Nuarak	Nuarika	Nuarikas	Nuark	Newark
Mior Kamshirf	Miola Kamoshira	Miolas Kamosiras	Miol Kamshir	New Hampshire
Mior Orlinorf	Miola Orolinofa	Miolas Orolinofas	Miol Orlinf	New Orleans
Thilorsh Karolirn	Thilosha Karolina	Thilosas Karolinas	Thilsh Karolin	North Carolina
Thilorsh Dakort	Thilosha Dakota	Thilosas Dakotas	Thilsh Dakot	North Dakota
Oklanurd	Okelanuda	Okelanudas	Okland	Oakland
Okiorf	Okiofa	Okiofas	Okiof	Ohio
Oklakorm	Okelakoma	Okelakomas	Oklakom	Oklahoma
Origorn	Origona	Origonas	Origon	Oregon
Orandorf	Orilanudofa	Orilanudofas	Orlandof	Orlando
Penshilvaniarf	Penoshiluvaniafa	Penosiluvaniafas	Penshilvaniaf	Pennsylvania
Filadelfirf	Filadelofifa	Filadelofifas	Filadelfif	Philadelphia
Fineshork	Fineshoka	Finesokas	Fineshk	Phoenix
Piteshburge	Piteshoburoga	Pitesoburogas	Pitshburg	Pittsburgh
Portelanurd	Poritelanuda	Poritelanudas	Portelanud	Portland
Roderf Ilanurd	Rodefa Ilanuda	Rodefas Ilanudas	Rodef Ilanud	Rhode Island
Rishmonurd	Rishemonuda	Risemonudas	Rishmonud	Richmond
Rotesharf	Roteshara	Rotesaras	Roteshar	Rochester
Shakramenirt	Shakeramenita	Sakeramenitas	Shakrament	Sacramento
Shan Antoniorn	Shana Anitoniona	Sanas Anitonionas	Shan Antonion	San Antonio
Shan Diegorf	Shana Diegofa	Sana Diegofas	Shan Diegof	San Diego
Shan Franshirshk	Shana Feranoshishaka	Sanas Feranosisakas	Shan Franshishk	San Francisco
Shant Barbaralf	Shanita Barubarafa	Sanitas Barubarafas	Shant Barbaraf	Santa Barbara
Shiatalf	Shiatala	Siatalas	Shiatal	Seattle
Shiaralf	Shiarafa	Siarafas	Shiaraf	Sierra
Zhalirt Karolirn	Zhalita Karolina	Zalitas Karolinas	Zhalt Karolin	South Carolina
Zhalirt Dakort	Zhalita Dakota	Zalitas Dakotas	Zhalt Dakot	South Dakota
Tamparf	Tamipafa	Tamipafas	Tampaf	Tampa
Teneshirf	Teneshifa	Tenesifas	Teneshif	Tennessee
Teshkarf	Teshikafa	Tesikafas	Teshkaf	Texas
Utarfk	Utafika	Utafikas	Utafk	Utah
Vermonirt	Verumonita	Verumonitas	Vermont	Vermont
Virginiarf	Viroginiafa	Viroginiafas	Virginiaf	Virginia

United States Geography

Dahmek	Miramish	Mirsua	Nimiash	English Equiv
Washinktorn	Washinoketona	Wasinoketonas	Washinkton	Washington
Wishkornsh	Wishakonisha	Wisakonisas	Wishkonsh	Wisconsin
Waiominork	Waiominoka	Waiominokas	Waiomink	Wyoming

Greek Alphabet

Dahmek	Miramish	Mirsua	Nimiash	English
alfarn	alifana	alifanas	alfan	alpha
betarn	betana	betanas	betan	beta
gamarn	gamana	gamanas	gaman	gamma
deltarn	delitana	delitanas	deltan	delta
epshilorn	eposhilona	eposilonas	epshilon	epsilon
zhetarn	zhetana	zetanas	zhetan	zeta
etarn	etana	etanas	etan	eta
thetarn	thetana	thetanas	thetan	theta
iotarn	iotana	iotanas	iotan	iota
kaparn	kapana	kapanas	kapan	kappa
lamdarn	lamudana	lamudanas	lamdan	lambda
murn	muna	munas	mun	mu
nurn	nuna	nunas	nun	nu
keshirn	keshina	kesinas	keshin	xi
omikroln	omikerona	omikeronas	omikron	omicron
pirn	pina	pinas	pin	pi
roln	rona	ronas	ron	rho
shigmarn	shigemana	sigemanas	shigman	sigma
taurn	tauna	taunas	taun	tau
upshilorn	upeshilona	upesilonas	upshilon	upsilon
firn	fina	finas	fin	phi
kairn	kaina	kainas	kain	chi
peshirn	peshina	pesinas	peshin	psi
omegarn	omegana	omeganas	omegan	omega

Holidays

Dahmek	Miramish	Mirsua	Nimiash	English
Klashmarl	Kelashamala	Kelasamalas	Klashmal	Christmas
Lushdor	Lushadora	Lusadoras	Lushdor	Easter

| Kankarl | Kanukala | Kanukalas | Kankal | Hanukkah |
| Rifategrulf | Rifalugerufa | Rifalugerufas | Rifalgruf | Thanksgiving |

Religion

Again, noun forms are shown. Adjective forms must end in –*u*.

Dahmek	Miramish	Mirsua	Nimiash	English
Bianorsh	Bianosha	Bianosas	Biansh	Atheism
Bianorshk	Bianoshaka	Bianosakas	Bianshk	Atheist
Vipalp	Vipalapa	Vipalapas	Vipalp	Bible
Budirn	Budina	Budinas	Budin	Buddha
Budirnuet	Budinueta	Budinuetas	Budinuet	Buddhism
Budirnwan	Budinua	Budinuas	Budinua	Buddhist
Gatholige	Gatholiga	Gatholigas	Gatholig	Catholic
Klash	Kelasha	Kelasas	Klash	Christ
Klashar	Kelashara	Kelasaras	Klarsh	Christian
Kiupriunf	Kiuperiuna	Kiuperiunas	Kiupriun	Hebrew
Kidurn	Kiduna	Kidunas	Kidun	Hindu
Kidurnuet	Kidunueta	Kidunuetas	Kidunuet	Hinduism
Konokautsh	Konokausha	Konokausas	Konokaush	Holocaust
Ishlarme	Ishelama	Iselamas	Ishlam	Islam
Zheishush	Zheishusha	Zeisusas	Zheishush	Jesus
Zhiurf	Zhiufa	Ziufas	Zhiuf	Jew
Zhiufarn	Zhiufanu	Ziufanus	Zhiufan	Jewish
Mushlirm	Mushelima	Muselimas	Mushlim	Muslim
Fiushtirp	Fiushetipa	Fiusetipas	Fiushtip	Protestant
Fiushtirpuet	Fiushetipueta	Fiusetipuetas	Fiushtipuet	Protestantism
Shantarf Klaursh	Shanitafa Kelausha	Sanitafas Kelausas	Shantaf Klaush	Santa Claus
Shoidark	Shoidaka	Soidakas	Shoidak	Satan
Vatikarn	Vatikana	Vatikanas	Vatikan	Vatican

10

Science

Time

Damiriak units of time are based on the length of an Eho day. *Eho* refers to either planets Eho Miriam or Eho Dahma or both. Both Ehos have the same length of solar day—24 hours and 21 minutes. There are 360 Eho days in a complete seasonal cycle and 720 Eho days in a revolution around the Makeri center (center of the solar system).

The Day
Damiriak women don't have hours, minutes, and seconds. Instead, they break down a day into three units of measure. The names vary slightly across languages. The dominant names for the three units of measure are the Dahmek/Nimiash forms: *briun, grath,* and *nik.* This is a rare usage where Dahmek plural words use the Miramish ending (*–i*) instead of the Dahmek ending (*–yek*).

Days of Week: Singular/Plural, Abbreviation, Length of Time

Dahmek/ Nimiash	Miramish	Mirsua	Abbr	Earth Equivalent
briun, briuni	beriuna, beriuni	beriunas, beriunis	bn	14 min, 36.6 sec
grath, grathi	geratha, gerathi	gerathas, gerathis	gth	8.766 sec
nik, niki	nika, niki	nikas, nikis	ni	0.8766 sec

Unit Relationship
- ♣ One Eho day equals 100 *briuni*.
- ♣ One *briun* equals 100 *grathi*.
- ♣ One *grath* equals 10 *niki*.

A Damiriak digital clock uses two digits for *briun*, an apostrophe (the Damiriak comma looks like an apostrophe), two digits for *grath*, another apostrophe, and one digit for *nik*:

Damiriak Clock Examples:
- ♣ 00'00'0 is midnight
- ♣ 50'00'0 is noon
- ♣ 99'99'9 is the last *nik* before midnight

When making plans to meet at a particular time or for other scheduling purposes, a three-digit number is usually recited. This represents the first three digits in a digital clock, i.e. the *briun* and the tens place of *grath*. This is equivalent to giving an Earth time in hours and minutes. For even less formal planning, only the *briun* value is given—this is equivalent to Earth time in fifteen-minute increments.

The Year

Damiriak women use *year* to mean one cycle of seasons. Before planetary orbits were understood, it was assumed a cycle of seasons equaled one revolution around the solar system. This illusion was created by the binary stars revolving around each other. Later, it was learned that for each solar revolution, two seasonal cycles completed. By that time, the Damiriak calendar had already been created. Out of convention, the calendar remains unchanged.

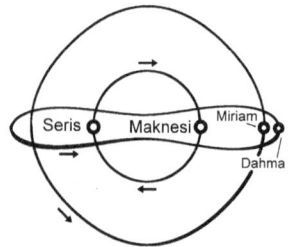

The Damiriak year begins when (from the view of planet Eho Miriam), star Seris is occulted by star Maknesi, resulting in the Ehos and stars being roughly lined up, with star Maknesi being closer to the Ehos than Seris. This happens twice for each revolution—once at zero degrees, and another at 180 degrees. The beginning of each year coincides with Eho Miriam's first celebrated day of summer and Eho Dahma's first celebrated day of winter.

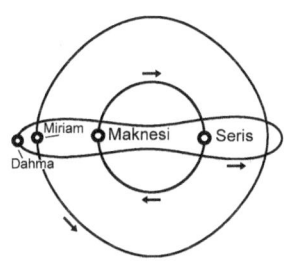

The Damiriak calendar consists of twelve Eho months of 30 Eho days each. An Eho week is six days long, and there are five Eho weeks in an Eho month. There are 60 Eho weeks in an Eho year.

Damiriak women work the first four days of the week and rest the last two (the weekend).

Eho Months

English	Dahmek	Miramish	Mirsua	Nimiash
EhoMonth01	Laril	Larila	Larilas	Laril
EhoMonth02	Rubek	Rubeka	Rubekas	Rubek
EhoMonth03	Blushame	Blushama	Blusamas	Blusham
EhoMonth04	Perun	Peruna	Perunas	Perun
EhoMonth05	Vilan	Vilana	Vilanas	Vilan
EhoMonth06	Fianth	Fiantha	Fianthas	Fianth
EhoMonth07	Doran	Dorana	Doranas	Doran
EhoMonth08	Terobe	Teroba	Terobas	Terob
EhoMonth09	Nivar	Nivara	Nivaras	Nivar
EhoMonth10	Shapor	Shapora	Saporas	Shapor
EhoMonth11	Galuth	Galutha	Galuthas	Galuth
EhoMonth12	Kitush	Kitusha	Kitusas	Kitush

Eho Days of Week

English	Dahmek/ Nimiash	Miramish	Mirsua
EhoDayOfWeek01	Loshiaf	Loshiafa	Losiafas
EhoDayOfWeek02	Vioriaf	Vioriafa	Vioriafas
EhoDayOfWeek03	Miriaf	Miriafa	Miriafas

English	Dahmek/ Nimiash	Miramish	Mirsua
EhoDayOfWeek04	Duliaf	Duliafa	Duliafas
EhoDayOfWeek05	Tiakiaf	Tiakiafa	Tiakiafas
EhoDayOfWeek06	Keliaf	Keliafa	Keliafas

Chemical Elements

Damiriak chemical element names have two forms—the Damiriak Anglicized name for use when working in Earth-based environments, and the Damiriak Vowel-Consonant Element (Davoka).

Damiriak Anglicized Element Names

Dahmek/ Nimiash	Miramish	Mirsua	English
Aktinium	Aketiniuma	Aketiniumas	Actinium
Aluminum	Aluminuma	Aluminumas	Aluminum
Amerikium	Amerikiuma	Amerikiumas	Americium
Antimoni	Anetimonia	Anetimonias	Antimony
Argon	Arogona	Aregonas	Argon
Arshenik	Areshenika	Aresenikas	Arsenic
Ashtatin	Ashetatina	Asetatinas	Astatine
Barium	Bariuma	Bariumas	Barium
Berkelium	Berikeliuma	Berikeliumas	Berkelium
Berilium	Beriliuma	Beriliumas	Beryllium
Bishmuth	Bishemutha	Bisemuthas	Bismuth
Borium	Boriuma	Boriumas	Bohrium
Boron	Borona	Boronas	Boron
Bromin	Beromina	Berominas	Bromine
Kadmium	Kademiuma	Kademiumas	Cadmium
Sheshium	Sheshiuma	Sesiumas	Caesium
Kalshium	Kaleshiuma	Kalesiumas	Calcium
Kalifornium	Kaliforeniuma	Kaliforeniumas	Californium
Karbon	Karebona	Karebonas	Carbon
Sherium	Sheriuma	Seriumas	Cerium
Klorin	Kelorina	Kelorinas	Chlorine
Kromium	Keromiuma	Keromiumas	Chromium
Kobalt	Kobalita	Kobalitas	Cobalt
Koper	Kopera	Koperas	Copper
Kurium	Kuriuma	Kuriumas	Curium
Darmshtat	Daremishetata	Daremisetatas	Darmstadtium
Dubnium	Dubeniuma	Dubeniumas	Dubnium
Dishproshium	Disheperoshiuma	Diseperosiumas	Dysprosium

Dahmek/ Nimiash	Miramish	Mirsua	English
Einshteinium	Einsheteiniuma	Einseteiuniumas	Einsteinium
Erbium	Erubiuma	Erubiumas	Erbium
Europium	Europiuma	Europiumas	Europium
Fermium	Feromiuma	Feromiumas	Fermium
Florin	Felorina	Felorinas	Fluorine
Franshium	Feranoshiuma	Feranosiumas	Francium
Gadolinium	Gadoliniuma	Gadoliniumas	Gadolinium
Galium	Galiuma	Galiumas	Gallium
Germanium	Geromaniuma	Geromaniumas	Germanium
Gold	Golada	Goladas	Gold
Hafnium	Hafoniuma	Hafoniumas	Hafnium
Hashium	Hashiuma	Hasiumas	Hassium
Helium	Heliuma	Heliumas	Helium
Holmium	Holamiuma	Holamiumas	Holmium
Hidrogen	Hiderogena	Hiderogenas	Hydrogen
Indium	Inodiuma	Inodiumas	Indium
Iodin	Iodina	Iodinas	Iodine
Iridium	Iridiuma	Iridiumas	Iridium
Iron	Irona	Ironas	Iron
Kripton	Keripetona	Keripetonas	Krypton
Lanthanum	Lanethanuma	Lanethanumas	Lanthanum
Larenshium	Larenoshiuma	Larenosiumas	Lawrencium
Lead	Leada	Leadas	Lead
Lithium	Lithiuma	Lithiumas	Lithium
Lutetium	Lutetiuma	Lutetiumas	Lutetium
Magneshium	Magoneshiuma	Magonesiumas	Magnesium
Manganesh	Manuganesha	Manuganesas	Manganese
Metnerium	Metoneriuma	Metoneriumas	Meitnerium
Mendelevium	Menadeleviuma	Menadeleviumas	Mendelevium
Merkuri	Merakuria	Merakurias	Mercury
Molibdenum	Molibedenuma	Molibedenumas	Molybdenum
Neodimium	Neodimiuma	Neodimiumas	Neodymium
Neon	Neona	Neonas	Neon
Neptunium	Nepotuniuma	Nepotuniumas	Neptunium
Nikel	Nikela	Nikelas	Nickel
Niobium	Niobiuma	Niobiumas	Niobium
Nitrogen	Niterogena	Niterogenas	Nitrogen
Nobelium	Nobeliuma	Nobeliumas	Nobelium
Oshmium	Oshamiuma	Osamiumas	Osmium
Okigen	Okigena	Okigenas	Oxygen
Paladium	Paladiuma	Paladiumas	Palladium
Foshforush	Foshiforusha	Fosiforusas	Phosphorus
Platinum	Pelatinuma	Pelatinumas	Platinum
Plutonium	Pelutoniuma	Pelutoniumas	Plutonium
Polonium	Poloniuma	Poloniumas	Polonium

Dahmek/ Nimiash	Miramish	Mirsua	English
Potashium	Potashiuma	Potasiumas	Potassium
Prasheodimium	Perasheodimiuma	Peraseodimiumas	Praseodymium
Promethium	Peromethiuma	Peromethiumas	Promethium
Protaktinium	Perotakotiniuma	Perotakotiniumas	Protactinium
Radium	Radiuma	Radiumas	Radium
Radon	Radona	Radonas	Radon
Renium	Reniuma	Reniumas	Rhenium
Rodium	Rodiuma	Rodiumas	Rhodium
Roentgenium	Roentugeniuma	Roetugeniumas	Roentgenium
Rubidium	Rubidiuma	Rubidiumas	Rubidium
Ruthenium	Rutheniuma	Rutheniumas	Ruthenium
Rutherfordium	Rutheriforudiuma	Rutheriforudiumas	Rutherfordium
Shamarium	Shamariuma	Samariumas	Samarium
Shkandium	Shekanediuma	Sekanediumas	Scandium
Sheaborgium	Sheaboragiuma	Seaboragiumas	Seaborgium
Shelenium	Sheleniuma	Seleniumas	Selenium
Shilikon	Shilikona	Silikonas	Silicon
Shilver	Shilovera	Siloveras	Silver
Shodium	Shodiuma	Sodiumas	Sodium
Shtrontium	Shetironatiuma	Setironatiumas	Strontium
Shulfur	Shulofura	Sulofuras	Sulfur
Tantalum	Tanitaluma	Tanitalumas	Tantalum
Teknetium	Tekonetiuma	Tekonetiumas	Technetium
Telurium	Teluriuma	Teluriumas	Tellurium
Terbium	Terobiuma	Terobiumas	Terbium
Thalium	Thaliuma	Thaliumas	Thallium
Thorium	Thoriuma	Thoriumas	Thorium
Thulium	Thuliuma	Thuliumas	Thulium
Tin	Tina	Tinas	Tin
Titanium	Titaniuma	Titaniumas	Titanium
Tungshten	Tunogishetena	Tunogisetenas	Tungsten
Ununbium	Ununabiuma	Ununabiumas	Ununbium
Ununhekium	Ununahekiuma	Ununahekiumas	Ununhexium
Ununoktium	Ununokatiuma	Ununokatiumas	Ununoctium
Ununpentium	Ununopenetiuma	Ununopenetiumas	Ununpentium
Ununkuadium	Ununokuadiuma	Ununokuadiumas	Ununquadium
Ununsheptium	Ununishepotiuma	Ununisepotiumas	Ununseptium
Ununtrium	Ununoteriuma	Ununoteriumas	Ununtrium
Uranium	Uraniuma	Uraniumas	Uranium
Vanadium	Vanadiuma	Vanadiumas	Vanadium
Zhenon	Zhenona	Zenonas	Xenon
Iterbium	Iterobiuma	Iterobiumas	Ytterbium
Itrium	Iteriuma	Iteriumas	Yttrium
Zhink	Zhinoka	Zinokas	Zinc
Zhirkonium	Zhirakoniuma	Zirakoniumas	Zirconium

Davoka Element Name

The Davoka Element Name is generated with a vowel-consonant-vowel-consonant word against three sets of criteria from the periodic table of elements: block, period, and column. To explain how the Davoka name is generated, we begin with the periodic table of elements—grouped by blocks.

Earth-Based Periodic Table

Period

1	1 H	2 He																
2	3 Li	4 Be											5 B	6 C	7 N	8 O	9 F	10 Ne
3	11 Na	12 Mg											13 Al	14 Si	15 P	16 S	17 Cl	18 Ar
4	19 K	20 Ca	21 Sc	22 Ti	23 V	24 Cr	25 Mn	26 Fe	27 Co	28 Ni	29 Cu	30 Zn	31 Ga	32 Ge	33 As	34 Se	35 Br	36 Kr
5	37 Rb	38 Sr	39 Y	40 Zr	41 Nb	42 Mo	43 Tc	44 Ru	45 Rh	46 Pd	47 Ag	48 Cd	49 In	50 Sn	51 Sb	52 Te	53 I	54 Xe
6	55 Cs	56 Ba	*	72 Hf	73 Ta	74 W	75 Re	76 Os	77 Ir	78 Pt	79 Au	80 Hg	81 Tl	82 Pb	83 Bi	84 Po	85 At	86 Rn
7	87 Fr	88 Ra	**	104 Rf	105 Db	106 Sg	107 Bh	108 Hs	109 Mt	110 Ds	111 Rg	112 Uub	113 Uut	114 Uuq	115 Uup	116 Uuh	117 Uus	118 Uuo

* Lanthanides	57 La	58 Ce	59 Pr	60 Nd	61 Pm	62 Sm	63 Eu	64 Gd	65 Tb	66 Dy	67 Ho	68 Er	69 Tm	70 Yb	71 Lu
** Actinides	89 Ac	90 Th	91 Pa	92 U	93 Np	94 Pu	95 Am	96 Cm	97 Bk	98 Cf	99 Es	100 Fm	101 Md	102 No	103 Lr

Earth-Based Periodic Table, Blocks

Period

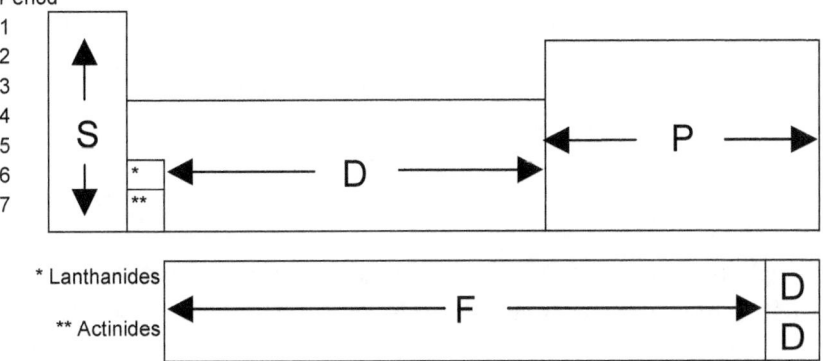

Davoka Blocks are: S, P, D, F (as shown in the above table), and G (theoretical—elements 121-138 and 171-188).

Davoka Periods are 1-7 (as shown in the above table) and 8-9 (theoretical).

Davoka columns refer to the columns within a block. Each block has a certain number of columns:

Block Type	Number of Columns
S	2
P	6
D	10
F	14
G	18

A Davoka word is constructed using a Vowel-Consonant-Vowel-Consonant (VCVC) format. The first V is assigned based on the block, the first C is based on the period, and the last VC is a combination pair based on the column as follows:

Davoka VCVC Assignment Table

Block:Vow	Period: Con	Column: Vow-Con	
S : a	1: p	1: ap	11: ot
P : e	2: k	2: ip	12: ut
D : i	3: t	3: op	13: af
F : o	4: f	4: up	14: if
G : u	5: l	5: ak	15: of
	6: r	6: ik	16: uf
	7: n	7: ok	17: an
	8: sh	8: uk	18: in
	9: th	9: at	19: on
		10: it	20: un

Using the Davoka VCVC Assignment Table, the Davoka name is constructed from the Block-Period-Column (B-P-C):

Davoka Element Names

No	Element	B-P-C	Davoka	No	Element	B-P-C	Davoka
1	Hydrogen	S-1-1	Apap	42	Molybdenum	D-5-4	Ilup
2	Helium	S-1-2	Apip	43	Technetium	D-5-5	Ilak
3	Lithium	S-2-1	Akap	44	Ruthenium	D-5-6	Ilik
4	Beryllium	S-2-2	Akip	45	Rhodium	D-5-7	Ilok
5	Boron	P-2-1	Ekap	46	Palladium	D-5-8	Iluk
6	Carbon	P-2-2	Ekip	47	Silver	D-5-9	Ilat
7	Nitrogen	P-2-3	Ekop	48	Cadmium	D-5-10	Ilit
8	Oxygen	P-2-4	Ekup	49	Indium	P-5-1	Elap
9	Fluorine	P-2-5	Ekak	50	Tin	P-5-2	Elip
10	Neon	P-2-6	Ekik	51	Antimony	P-5-3	Elop
11	Sodium	S-3-1	Atap	52	Tellurium	P-5-4	Elup
12	Magnesium	S-3-2	Atip	53	Iodine	P-5-5	Elak
13	Aluminum	P-3-1	Etap	54	Xenon	P-5-6	Alik
14	Silicon	P-3-2	Etip	55	Cesium	S-6-1	Arap
15	Phosphorus	P-3-3	Etop	56	Barium	S-6-2	Arip
16	Sulfur	P-3-4	Etup	57	Lanthanum	F-6-1	Orap
17	Chlorine	P-3-5	Etak	58	Cerium	F-6-2	Orip
18	Argon	P-3-6	Etik	59	Praseodymium	F-6-3	Orop
19	Potassium	S-4-1	Afap	60	Neodymium	F-6-4	Orup
20	Calcium	S-4-2	Afip	61	Promethium	F-6-5	Orak
21	Scandium	D-4-1	Ifap	62	Samarium	F-6-6	Orik
22	Titanium	D-4-2	Ifip	63	Europium	F-6-7	Orok
23	Vanadium	D-4-3	Ifop	64	Gadolinium	F-6-8	Oruk
24	Chromium	D-4-4	Ifup	65	Terbium	F-6-9	Orat
25	Manganese	D-4-5	Ifak	66	Dysprosium	F-6-10	Orit
26	Iron	D-4-6	Ifik	67	Holmium	F-6-11	Orot
27	Cobalt	D-4-7	Ifok	68	Erbium	F-6-12	Orut
28	Nickel	D-4-8	Ifuk	69	Thulium	F-6-13	Oraf
29	Copper	D-4-9	Ifat	70	Ytterbium	F-6-14	Orif
30	Zinc	D-4-10	Ifit	71	Lutetium	D-6-1	Irap
31	Gallium	P-4-1	Efap	72	Hafnium	D-6-2	Irip
32	Germanium	P-4-2	Efip	73	Tantalum	D-6-3	Irop
33	Arsenic	P-4-3	Efop	74	Tungsten	D-6-4	Irup
34	Selenium	P-4-4	Efup	75	Rhenium	D-6-5	Irak
35	Bromine	P-4-5	Efak	76	Osmium	D-6-6	Irik
36	Krypton	P-4-6	Efik	77	Ridium	D-6-7	Irok
37	Rubidium	S-5-1	Alap	78	Platinum	D-6-8	Iruk
38	Strontium	S-5-2	Alip	79	Gold	D-6-9	Irat
39	Yttrium	D-5-1	Ilap	80	Mercury	D-6-10	Irit
40	Zirconium	D-5-2	Ilip	81	Thallium	P-6-1	Erap
41	Niobium	D-5-3	Ilop	82	Lead	P-6-2	Erip

No	Element	B-P-C	Davoka	No	Element	B-P-C	Davoka
83	Bismuth	P-6-3	Erop	103	Lawrencium	D-7-1	Inap
84	Polonium	P-6-4	Erup	104	Rutherfordium	D-7-2	Inip
85	Astatine	P-6-5	Erak	105	Dubnium	D-7-3	Inop
86	Radon	P-6-6	Erik	106	Seaborgium	D-7-4	Inup
87	Francium	S-7-1	Anap	107	Bohrium	D-7-5	Inak
88	Radium	S-7-2	Anip	108	Hassium	D-7-6	Inik
89	Actinum	F-7-1	Onap	109	Meitnerium	D-7-7	Inok
90	Thorium	F-7-2	Onip	110	Darmstadtium	D-7-8	Inuk
91	Protactinium	F-7-3	Onop	111	Roentgenium	D-7-9	Inat
92	Uranium	F-7-4	Onup	112	Ununbium	D-7-10	Init
93	Neptunium	F-7-5	Onak	113	Ununtrium	P-7-1	Enap
94	Plutonium	F-7-6	Onik	114	Ununquadium	P-7-2	Enip
95	Americium	F-7-7	Onok	115	Ununpentium	P-7-3	Enop
96	Curium	F-7-8	Onuk	116	Ununhexium	P-7-4	Enup
97	Berkelium	F-7-9	Onat	117	Ununspetium	P-7-5	Enak
98	Californium	F-7-10	Onit	118	Ununoctium	P-7-6	Enik
99	Einsteinium	F-7-11	Onot	119	Ununennium	S-8-1	Ashap
100	Fermium	F-7-12	Onut	120	Unbinilium	S-8-2	Aship
101	Mendelevium	F-7-13	Onaf	121	Unbiunium	G-8-1	Ushap
102	Nobelium	F-7-14	Onif	122	Unbibium	G-8-2	Uship

Astronomy

The Damiriak solar system consists of two stars orbiting each other, six/seven planets, and a number of moons. The two primary planets of habitation are Eho Miriam and Eho Dahma. The solar system can be divided into three groups—the stars (Maknesi and Seris), the inner planets (Seranara, Dart, Eho Dahma, and Eho Miriam), and the outer planets (Sanau, Tarak, and Nimsant). Note that Dart collided with Seris during early Miriam culture.

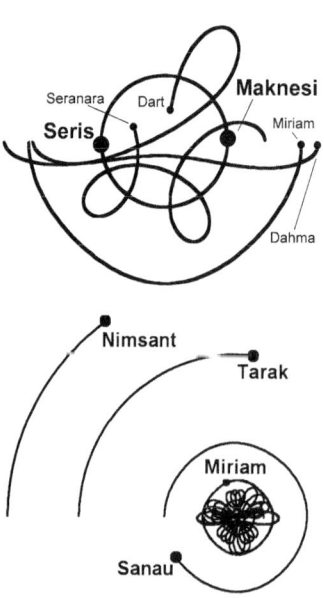

The stars orbit each other in a

clockwise direction in near circular orbits. The inner three planets (Seranara, Dart, and Eho Dahma) orbit counterclockwise in looping orbits. Eho Miriam orbits both stars counterclockwise in a rounded-box orbit. The outer planets orbit the stars in clockwise orbits.

Note how some celestial names make use of the letter *s*, a restricted letter in Damiriak languages. As mentioned earlier, celestial names come from Old Damiriak, a language that did not have such *s/z* restrictions.

In brief, the dynamics of the Damiriak solar system can be described with the following chart. This chart, when fed into an orbital simulator software program, shows the celestial movements in real time.

Name	Type	Mass (kg)	Radius (km)	X when Y is 0 (km)	Vy when Vx is 0 (m/s)
Maknesi	Star	2.0 e+30	7.0 e+5	-1.5 e+8	14,913.75
Seris	Star	2.0 e+30	7.0 e+5	1.5 e+8	-14,913.75
Seranara	Planet	8.0 e+24	7.5 e+3	2.4 e+8	24,000
Alia	Moon	7.5 e+22	1.8 e+3	2.4032 e+8	25,340
Artanum	Moon	2.0 e+22	1.0 e+3	2.4015 e+8	25,900
Dart	Planet	4.5 e+24	5.8 e+3	-3.11 e+8	-13,500
Eho Dahma	Planet	6.0 e+24	6.4 e+3	-3.8 e+8	-8,880
Dien	Moon	1.0 e+23	2.1 e+3	-3.796 e+8	-7,840
Eho Miriam	Planet	6.0 e+24	6.4 e+3	3.2135 e+8	-34,000
Mur	Moon	7.0 e+22	1.7 e+3	-3.208 e+8	-33,140
Mihk	Moon	9.0 e+21	8.63 e+2	-3.211 e+8	-32,750
Sanau	Planet	8.0 e+26	6.0 e+4	-6.7 e+8	19,600
Tarak	Planet	2.0 e+27	7.2 e+4	-1.45 e+9	13,500
Nimsant	Planet	7.0 e+24	6.7 e+3	-2.1 e+9	11,300
Delamir	Moon	5.0 e+22	1.4 e+3	-2.101 e+9	12,000

Military

I (Cerafina) have only learned a few military words:

Dahmek	Miramish	Mirsua	Nimiash	English
Aushimark	Aushimaka	Ausimakas	Aushimak	Admiral (n)
Shiern	Shiena	Sienas	Shien	Army (n)
Kontralf	Koniterafa	Koniterafas	Kontraf	Contra (n)
Deginak	Deginaka	Deginakas	Deginak	General (n)
Miorfk	Mioruka	Miorukas	Miork	Major (n)
Maitark	Maitaka	Maitakas	Maitak	Marines (n)

Other Culture

I have only learned a little about Damiriak culture. I will record what snippets I know. The following is a chart showing different cultural words and their English equivalents.

Dahmek	Miramish	Mirsua	Nimiash	English
duavirt	duavisha	duavisas	duavit	FertilityStone
landak	lanudaka	lanudakas	landark	HalfFaceSymbol
breilut	bereiluta	bereilutas	breilt	MarbleRobot
Neith	Neitha	Neithas	Neith	Miss
Krashat	Kerashatu	Kerasatus	Krashat	Mister
moisharn	moishiana	moisianas	moishan	MoissanRuby
plerp	pelepa	pelepas	plep	OvaCarrier
daiftarn	daifetana	daifetanas	daiftan	SplitWand
kailark	kaikala	kaikalas	kailk	StrontiumFood
yoilark	yoilarika	yoilarikas	yoilark	WiggleTalk

11

English to Damiriak Crossreference

I've thought long and hard how to present the bulk of the Damiriak vocabulary. I looked at language translation books—you know, the ones where half the book is language X to language Z, and the second half is language Z to language X. I tried that approach in recording Damiriak words, but I found myself spending too much time working out the different endings to Damiriak words to satisfy the various forms of English words. To keep things manageable, I'm not listing most plural nouns, possessive cases, past-tense verbs, future-tense verbs, participles, or gerunds unless the English form is unusual.

The root word is used as-is for Nimiash and Dahmek as the singular-number noun. For other parts of speech (noun plural, verb, adjective, adverb, etc.) and for Miramish singular nouns, a suffix must be appended to the root word. Keep this in mind while reading the cross-reference list.

Each entry in this list consists of four, comma-separated components. The order for each entry is: *English (part of speech), Dahmek, Miramish, Nimiash*. Parts of speech: adj=adjective, adv=adverb, card=cardinal number, conj=conjunction, d:*xxxx*= definition, det=determiner, interj=interjection, let=alphabetic letter, n=noun, num=number, ord=ordinal number, pa=past tense, pap=past participle, pl=plural, pref=prefix, prep=preposition, pron=pronoun, sng=singular, v=verb.

(separator), e, e, e
a (det), dhor, dho, dho
A (let sng), alfe, alifa, alf
a.m. (adj), onamu, onamu, onam
abandon (v), ovramirsp, overamipo, ovrampo
abandonment (n), ovramirp, overamipa, ovramp
abate (v), ogiarsp, ogiapo, ogiapo
abatement (n), ogiarp, ogiapa, ogiap
abbreviate (v), othoishst, othoito, othoito
abbreviation (n), othoisht, othoita, othoit
abdicate (v), afkiarsk, afokiako, afkiako
abdication (n), afkiark, afokiaka, afkiak
abdicator (n doer), afkiarkwan, afokiakua, afkiakua
abdomen (n), obeinarbe, obeinaba, obeinab
abduct (v), okriushsk, okeriuko, okriuko
abduction (n), okriushk, okeriuka, okriuk
abductor (n doer), okriushkwan, okeriukua, okriukua
aberrant (adj), ogauirku, ogauiku, ogauiku
aberration (n), ogauirk, ogauika, ogauik
abhor (v), okauaishst, okauaito, okauaito
abhorrence (n), okauaisht, okauaita, okauait
abhorrent (adj), okauaishtu, okauaitu, okauaitu
ability (n), frelp, ferepa, frep
ablaze (adj), okraurgu, okeraugu, okraugu
able (adj), frelpu, ferepu, frepu
ably (adv), frelpiu, ferepiu, frepiu
abnormal (adj), olanirfu, olanifu, olanfu
abnormality (n), olanirf, olanifa, olanf
abnormally (adv), olanirfiu, olanifiu, olanfiu
aboard (adv d:Enter ship), glorifiu, gelorifiu, glorfiu
abolish (v), ogavarst, ogavato, ogavato
abolition (n), ogavart, ogavata, ogavat
abolitionist (n doer), ogavartwan, ogavatua, ogavatua
abort (v), briarst, beriato, briato
abortion (n), briart, beriata, briat
abortionist (n doer), briartwan, beriatua, briatua
about (prep/adv/adj), oveip, oveipu, oveip
above (prep/adv/adj), uvof, uvofu, uvof
abrasion (n), baishork, baishoka, baishk
abrasive (adj), baishorku, baishoku, baishku
abrasively (adv), baishorkiu, baishokiu, baishkiu
abridge (v), oploshsk, opelosho, oplosho
abroad (adv), odorabiu, odorubiu, odorbiu
abroad (n), odorabe, odoruba, odorb
abrupt (adj), ogaifirtu, ogaifitu, ogaiftu
abruptly (adv), ogaifirtiu, ogaifitiu, ogaiftiu
abruptness (n), ogaifirt, ogaifita, ogaift
abscess (n), broirge, beroiga, broig
abscess (v), broirzge, beroigo, brolgo
absence (n), afblurt, afubeluta, afblut
absent (adj), afblurtu, afubelutu, afblutu
absent (v), afblurst, afubeluto, afbluto
absenter (n doer), afblurtwan, afubelutua, afblutua
absently (adv), afblurtiu, afubelutiu, afblutiu
absolute (adj), afligralgu, afeligeragu, afligragu
absolutely (adv), afligralgiu, afeligeragiu, afligragiu
absolution (n), afligralge, afeligeraga, afligrag
absolve (v), afligralzge, afeligerago, afligrago
absorb (v), obolirsp, obolipo, obolpo
absorbant (n doer), obolirpwan, obolipua, obolpua
absorber (n doer), obolirpwan, obolipua, obolpua

absorption (n), obolirp, obolipa, obolp
abstract (adj), ogralirtu, ogeralitu, ograltu
abstract (n pl), ogralirtyek, ogeraliti, ogralti
abstract (n), ogralirt, ogeralita, ogralt
abstract (v), ogralirst, ogeralito, ogralto
abstractor (n doer), ogralirtwan, ogeralitua, ograltua
absurd (adj), poirthu, poithu, poithu
absurdity (n), poirth, poitha, poith
absurdly (adv), poirthiu, poithiu, poithiu
abundance (n), niunirf, niunifa, niunf
abundant (adj), niunirfu, niunifu, niunfu
abundantly (adv), niunirfiu, niunifiu, niunfiu
abuse (n), ovurk, ovuka, ovuk
abuse (v), ovursk, ovuko, ovuko
abuser (n doer), ovurkwan, ovukua, ovukua
abusive (adj), ovurku, ovuku, ovuku
abusively (adv), ovurkiu, ovukiu, ovukiu
abysmal (adj), kiurthu, kiuthu, kiuthu
abysmally (adv), kiurthiu, kiuthiu, kiuthiu
abyss (n), kiurth, kiutha, kiuth
academic (adj), treiarku, tereiaku, treiaku
academically (adv), treiarkiu, tereiakiu, treiakiu
academics (n pl), treiakarnyek, tereiakani, treiakani
academy (n), treiark, tereiaka, treiak
accelerate (v), ovoralst, ovorato, ovrato
acceleration (n), ovoralt, ovorata, ovrat
accelerator (n doer), ovoraltwan, ovoratua, ovratua
accelerometer (n), ovoraltniok, ovoratonioka, ovratniok
accent (n), oklirat, okelireta, oklirt
accent (v), oklirast, okelireto, oklirto
accentuate (v), oklirast, okelireto, oklirto
accept (v), orshirsp, orashipo, orshipo
acceptable (adj), orshirpu, orashipu, orshipu
acceptably (adv), orshirpiu, orashipiu, orshipiu
acceptance (n), orshirp, orashipa, orship
access (n), ogvert, oguveta, ogvet
access (v), ogverst, oguveto, ogveto
accessible (adj), ogvertu, oguvetu, ogvetu
accessory (n doer), ogvertwan, oguvetua, ogvetua
accident (n), shtairk, shetaika, shtaik
accidental (adj), shtairku, shetaiku, shtaiku
accidentally (adv), shtairkiu, shetaikiu, shtaikiu
accidently (adv), shtairkiu, shetaikiu, shtaikiu
acclaim (v), onolasne, onoarito, onoarto
acclamation (n), onolan, onoarita, onoart
acclimate (v), otreidasle, otereiloto, otreilto
acclimation (n), otreidal, otereilota, otreilt
accommodate (v), ogianirsk, ogianiko, ogianko
accommodation (n), ogianirk, ogianika, ogiank
accommodative (adj), ogianirku, ogianiku, ogianku
accommodatively (adv), ogianirkiu, ogianikiu, ogiankiu
accommodator (n doer), ogianirkwan, ogianikua, ogiankua
accompany (v), nelapis, leneshapo, lenshapo
accomplice (n doer), kiutarwan, kiuritua, kiurtua
accomplish (v), kiutasre, kiurito, kiurto
accomplishment (n), kiutar, kiurita, kiurt
accord (n), orkarde, orakada, orkad
accord (v), orkarzde, orakado, orkado
accordance (n), orkadarn, orakadana, orkadan

accordingly (adv), orkardiu, orakadiu, orkadiu
account (n), orpoinf, orapoina, orpoin
account (v), orpoinsf, orapoino, orpoino
accountable (adj), orpoinfu, orapoinu, orpoinu
accountant (n doer), orpoinfwan, orapoinua, orpoinua
accumulate (v), briorsk, berioko, brioko
accumulation (n), briork, berioka, briok
accumulator (n doer), briorkwan, beriokua, briokua
accuracy (n), tufalat, tulifata, tulfat
accurate (adj), tufalatu, tulifatu, tulfatu
accurately (adv), tufalatiu, tulifatiu, tulfatiu
accusation (n), orgoisht, oragoita, orgoit
accuse (v), orgoishst, oragoito, orgoito
accused (n), orgoishtuin, oragoituina, orgoituin
accuser (n doer), orgoishtwan, oragoitua, orgoitua
accusingly (adv), orgoishtiu, oragoitiu, orgoitiu
accustom (v), ordorfirsk, oradorafiko, ordorfko
ace (n), kialirt, kialita, kialt
ace (v), kialirst, kialito, kialto
ache (n), libuage, beluaga, bluag
ache (v), libuazge, beluago, bluago
achievable (adj), ovairtu, ovaitu, ovaitu
achieve (v), ovairst, ovaito, ovaito
achievement (n), ovairt, ovaita, ovait
achiever (n doer), ovairtwan, ovaitua, ovaitua
achily (adv), libuagiu, beluagiu, bluagiu
achy (adj), libuagu, beluagu, bluagu
acid (n), zhige, izhuga, izhg
acidic (adj), zhigu, izhugu, izhgu
acidify (v), zhizge, izhugo, izhgo
acknowledge (v), oglersk, ogeleko, ogleko
acknowledgment (n), oglerk, ogeleka, oglek
acorn (n), ogralf, ogerala, ogral
acoustic (adj), zhanirfu, zhanifu, zhanfu
acoustics (n), zhanirf, zhanifa, zhanf
acquaint (v), okriarsf, okeriafo, okriafo
acquaintance (n), okriarf, okeriafa, okriaf
acquire (v), otherst, otheto, otheto
acquirer (n doer), othertwan, othertua, othetua
acquisition (n), othert, otheta, othet
acquit (v), pagloirsk, pageloiko, pagloiko
acquittal (n), pagloirk, pageloika, pagloik
acre (n), thaurk, thauka, thauk
acrobat (n), riarak, riaroka, riark
acrobatic (adj), riaraku, riaroku, riarku
acronym (n), riarviern, riaroviena, riarvien
across (prep/adj/adv), oshklauk, oshekelauku, oshklauk
act (n), patil, palita, palt
act (v), patisle, palito, palto
Actinium (n), Aktinium, Aketiniuma, Aktinium
Actinum (n davoka), Onap, Onap, Onap
action (n), patiluet, palitueta, paltuet
activate (v), paltarsk, palitako, paltako
activation (n), paltark, palitaka, paltak
active (adj), paltarku, palitaku, paltaku
actively (adv), paltarkiu, palitakiu, paltakiu
activist (n doer), paltarkwan, palitakua, paltakua
activity (n), patilor, paliterola, paltrol
actor (n doer), patilwan, palitua, paltua
actress (n doer), patilwan, palitua, paltua
actual (adj), patilioru, palitioru, paltioru

actuality (n), patilior, palitiora, paltior
actualize (v), patiliosre, palitioro, paltioro
actually (adv), patilioriu, palitioriu, paltioriu
acupuncture (n), lituthatar, tuletherata, tulthrat
acute (adj), diarthu, diathu, diathu
acutely (adv), diarthiu, diathiu, diathiu
ad (n), tef, tefa, tef
adapt (v), diforst, difoto, difto
adaptable (adj), difortu, difotu, diftu
adaptably (adv), difortiu, difotiu, diftiu
adaptation (n), difort, difota, dift
adapter (n doer), difortwan, difotua, diftua
adaptive (adj), difortu, difotu, diftu
adaptively (adv), difortiu, difotiu, diftiu
adaptor (n doer), difortwan, difotua, diftua
add (v), tefirst, tefito, tefto
add-on (n), tefterme, tefitema, teftem
adder (n doer), tefirtwan, tefitua, teftua
addict (n doer), tefeirkwan, tefeikua, tefeikua
addict (v), tefeirsk, tefeiko, tefeiko
addiction (n), tefeirk, tefeika, tefeik
addictive (adj), tefeirku, tefeiku, tefeiku
addition (n), tefirt, tefita, teft
additional (adj), tefirtu, tefitu, teftu
additionally (adv), tefirtiu, tefitiu, teftiu
additive (n), teftart, tefitaka, teftat
address (n), nirat, nirota, nirt
address (v), nirast, niroto, nirto
addressable (adj), niratu, nirotu, nirtu
addressee (n), nitaruin, nirotuina, nirtuin
addressor (n doer), niratwan, nirotua, nirtua
adept (adj), shiarpu, shiapu, shiapu
adept (n), shiarp, shiapa, shiap
adequate (adj), tedifaidu, tefudaidu, tefdaidu
adequately (adv), tedifaidiu, tefudaidiu, tefdaidiu
adequation (n), tedifaide, tefudaida, tefdaid
adhere (v), tefirtuasp, tefituapo, teftuapo
adherence (n), tefirtuap, tefituapa, teftuap
adherent (n doer), tefirtuapwan, tefituapua, teftuapua
adhesion (n), teflrtuat, tefirtuata, teftuat
adhesive (adj), tefirtuatu, tefituatu, teftuatu
adhesive (n), tefirtuak, tefituaka, teftuak
adjacent (adj), tefliroku, tefeliroku, teflirku
adjacently (adv), tefirokiu, tefelirokiu, teflirkiu
adjective (n), tetifipar, tefotiropa, teftirp
adjourn (v), tekanitasf, tekanifoto, tekanifto
adjournment (n), tekanitaf, tekanifota, tekanift
adjust (v), tepafes, tefipesho, tefpesho
adjustable (adj), tepafeshu, tefipeshu, tefpeshu
adjuster (n doer), tepafeshwan, tefipeshua, tefpeshua
adjustment (n), tepafesh, tefipesha, tefpesh
administer (v), telifovist, tefelovito, teflovito
administration (n), telifovit, tefelovita, teflovit
administrative (adj), telifovitu, tefelovitu, teflovitu
administrator (n doer), telifovitwan, tefelovitua, teflovitua
admirable (adj), temualtu, teluamu, teluamu
admirably (adv), temualtiu, teluamiu, teluamiu
Admiral (n), Aushimark, Aushimaka, Aushimak
admiration (n), temualt, teluama, teluam
admire (v), temualst, teluamo, teluamo

admirer (n doer), temualtwan, teluamua, teluamua
admissible (adj), tenirku, teniku, tenku
admissibly (adv), tenirkiu, tenikiu, tenkiu
admission (n), tenirk, tenika, tenk
admit (v), tenirsk, teniko, tenko
adolescence (n), odialme, odiama, odiam
adolescent (adj), odialmu, odiamu, odiamu
adolescent (n doer), odialmwan, odiamua, odiamua
adopt (v), divulst, divuto, divuto
adopter (n doer), divultwan, divutua, divutua
adoption (n), divult, divuta, divut
adoptive (adj), divultu, divutu, divutu
adorable (adj), bluarfu, beluafu, bluafu
adorably (adv), bluarfiu, beluafiu, bluafiu
adoration (n), bluarf, beluafa, bluaf
adore (v), bluarsf, beluafo, bluafo
adorn (v), bluarst, beluato, bluato
adornment (n), bluart, beluata, bluat
adult (adj), tarvuku, tavuku, tavuku
adult (n), tarvuk, tavuka, tavuk
adulterate (v), tarvusk, tavuko, tavuko
adulterer (n doer), tarvukwan, tavukua, tavukua
adulthood (n), tarvukfif, tavukofifa, tavukfif
advance (n), tivirt, tivita, tivit
advance (v), tivirst, tivito, tivito
advancement (n), tivirtuet, tivitueta, tivituet
advantage (n), vitage, tevifoka, tevifk
advantageous (adj), vitagu, tevifoku, tevifku
adventure (n), duliart, duliata, duliat
adventurer (n doer), duliartwan, duliatua, duliatua
adventurous (adj), duliartu, duliatu, duliatu
adventurously (adv), duliartiu, duliatiu, duliatiu
adverb (n), tefiarde, tefiata, tefyait
adversarial (adj), teditoru, tefidotu, tefdotu
adversarially (adv), teditoriu, tefidotiu, tefdotiu
adversary (n doer), thatorwan, tharitua, thartua
adverse (adj), thatoru, tharitu, thartu
adversely (adv), thatoriu, tharitiu, thartiu
adversity (n), thator, tharita, thart
advertise (v), teditosre, tefidoto, tefdoto
advertisement (n), teditor, tefidota, tefdot
advertiser (n doer), teditorwan, tefidotua, tefdotua
advice (n), oborat, oborita, obort
advisable (adj), oboratu, oboritu, obortu
advisably (adv), oboratiu, oboritiu, obortiu
advise (v), oborast, oborito, oborto
adviser (n doer), oboratwan, oboritua, obortua
advisor (n doer), oboratwan, oboritua, obortua
advisory (n), obortarn, oboritana, obortan
advocate (n doer), tethairpwan, tefithaipua, tetthaipua
advocate (v), tethairsf, tefithaipo, tefthaipo
advocation (n), tethairp, tefithaipa, tefthaip
aerial (adj), aularnu, aulanu, aulanu
aerial (n), aularn, aulana, aulan
aerobic (adj), aularku, aulaku, aulaku
aerodynamic (adj), aultuiarfu, aulituiafu, aultuiafu
aerodynamics (n pl), aultuiarfyek, aulituiafi, aultuiafi
aeronautical (adj), auliartu, auliatu, auliatu
aeronautics (n pl), auliartyek, auliati, auliati
aerosol (n), aulgralp, aulogerapa, aulgrap
aerospace (n), authushp, authusha, authush

affair (n), othral, othirela, othrel
affect (n), ovirat, ovirota, ovirt
affect (v), ovirast, oviroto, ovirto
affection (n), ovirap, oviripa, ovirp
affectionate (adj), ovirapu, oviripu, ovirpu
affectionately (adv), ovirapiu, oviripiu, ovirpiu
affiliate (n), orfliarn, orafeliana, orflian
affiliate (v), orfliarsne, orafeliano, orfliano
affiliation (n), orfliarnuet, orafelianueta, orflianuet
affirm (v), orniursf, oraniufo, orniufo
affirmation (n), orniurf, oraniufa, orniuf
affirmative (adj), orniurfu, oraniufu, orniufu
affirmatively (adv), orniurfiu, oraniufiu, orniufiu
affirmer (n doer), orniurfwan, oraniufua, orniufua
afflict (v), orkirsk, orakiko, orkiko
affliction (n), orkirk, orakika, orkik
afflictive (adj), orkirku, orakiku, orkiku
affluence (n), ormiarsht, oramiaruta, ormiart
affluent (adj), ormiarshtu, oramiarutu, ormiartu
affluently (adv), ormiarshtiu, oramiarutiu, ormiartiu
afforably (adv), refirtiu, refitiu, reftiu
afford (v), refirst, refito, refto
affordable (adj), refirtu, refitu, reftu
affray (n), rianirk, rianika, riank
affray (v), rianirsk, rianiko, rianko
affrayer (n doer), rianirkwan, rianikua, riankua
Afghan (n), Afkarn, Afikana, Afkan
Afghanistan (n), Afkansharn, Afikanoshana, Afkanshan
afire (adj), oshriauku, ogiaulu, ogiaulu
Africa (n), Afrilk, Aferika, Afrik
African (n), Afrikarn, Aferikana, Afrikan
after (prep/adj/adv), ovil, ovilu, ovil
afternoon (adj), ovimidortu, ovimidotu, ovimidotu
afternoon (n), ovimidort, ovimidota, ovimidot
afterward (adv), ovilhaush, ovilehaushu, ovilhaush
afterwards (adv), ovilhaush, ovilehaushu, ovilhaush
again (adv), okuan, okuanu, okuan
against (prep), okuank, okuaneku, okuank
age (n), datul, dalita, dalt
age (v), datusle, dalito, dalto
agency (n), vetarp, vetapa, vetap
agenda (n), vetark, vetaka, vetak
agent (n), gavert, gaveta, gavet
ager (n doer), datulwan, dalitua, daltua
agey (adj), datulu, dalitu, daltu
aggravate (v), ovoburzge, ovoburifo, ovoburfo
aggravation (n), ovoburge, ovoburifa, ovoburf
aggress (v), ovorazge, ovorugo, ovorgo
aggression (n), ovorage, ovoruga, ovorg
aggressive (adj), ovoragu, ovorugu, ovorgu
aggressively (adv), ovoragiu, ovorugiu, ovorgiu
aggressor (n doer), ovoragwan, ovorugua, ovorgua
agile (adj), bruarshu, beruashu, bruashu
agility (n), bruarsh, beruasha, bruash
agitate (v), ovoiburzge, ovoiburifo, ovoiburfo
agitation (n), ovoiburge, ovoiburifa, ovoiburf
agitator (n doer), ovoiburgwan, ovoiburifua, ovoiburfua
agnosis (n), oshmarn, oshimana, oshman
agnostic (adj), oshmarnu, oshimanu, oshmanu
ago (adj/adv), ude, udu, ud

agonize (v), okerazge, okerugo, okrugo
agony (n), okerage, okeruga, okrug
agree (v), klarst, kilato, klato
agreeable (adj), klartu, kilatu, klatu
agreebly (adv), klartiu, kilatiu, klatiu
agreement (n), klart, kilata, klat
agricultural (adj), oklofaltu, okalofatu, oklofatu
agriculture (n), oklofalt, okalofata, oklofat
ah (interj), ia, ia, ia
ahead (adv), okeftiu, okefitiu, okeftru
aid (n), flarap, felaripa, flarp
aid (v), flarasp, felaripo, flarpo
aide (n doer), flarapwan, felaripua, flarpua
AIDS (n), Heishort, Heishota, Heisht
ail (v), aursk, auko, auko
ailer (n doer), aurkwan, aukua, aukua
ailment (n), aurk, auka, auk
aim (n), flarit, felarita, flart
aim (v), flarist, felarito, flarto
aimless (adj), flaritmenu, felaritomenu, flartmenu
aimlessly (adv), flaritmeniu, felaritomeniu, flartmeniu
air (n), raul, aula, aul
air (v), rausle, aulo, aulo
airbag (n), aulnufaf, aulefanafa, aulfnaf
aircraft (n pl), aulkarfpyek, aulekafipi, aulkafpi
aircraft (n), aulkarfp, aulekafipa, aulkafp
airfare (n), aulothirk, aulothika, aulthik
airfield (n), aulprant, auloperanida, aulprand
airline (n), aulroifk, auleroifa, aulroif
airplane (n), rauvalar, auluvarila, aulvarl
airport (n), aulbielurk, aulebieluka, aulbielk
airway (n), aulpliorl, aulepeliola, aulpliol
airy (adj), raulu, aulu, aulu
aisle (n), yoir, yoira, yoir
Alabama (n), Albarme, Alubama, Albam
alarm (n), obiarp, obiapa, obiap
alarm (v), obiarsp, obiapo, obiapo
alarmist (n doer), obiarpwan, obiapua, obiapua
Alaska (n), Alishork, Alishoka, Alshk
Alberta (n), Albertarf, Aluberitafa, Albertaf
album (n), flanirf, felanifa, flanf
alcohol (n), tagirn, tagina, tagin
alcoholic (adj), tagirnu, taginu, taginu
alcoholic (n), tagiarn, tagiana, tagian
alcoholism (n), tagiarnuet, tagianueta, tagianuet
alert (n), onarlp, onalipa, onalp
alert (v), onarlsp, onalipo, onalpo
alerter (n doer), onarlpwan, onalipua, onalpua
alertness (n), onalpark, onalipaka, onalpak
algebra (n), yakaretal, yariketala, yarketal
algebraic (adj), yakaretalu, yariketalu, yarketalu
algebraically (adv), yakaretaliu, yariketaliu, yarketaliu
algorithm (n), yarkurt, yarikuta, yarkut
algorithmic (adj), yarkurtu, yarikutu, yarkutu
algorithmically (adv), yarkurtiu, yarikutiu, yarkutiu
alias (n), oshnarl, oshenala, oshnal
alibi (n), miarth, miatha, miath
alien (n), anlark, anolaka, anlak
alienable (adj), anlarku, anolaku, anlaku
alienate (v), anlarsk, anolako, anlako
align (v), oroifsk, oroifo, oroifo

alignment (n), oroifk, oroifa, oroif
alike (adj/adv), oshalf, oshalifu, oshalf
alive (adj), orflauft, orafelaufitu, orflauft
all (adj), lor, loreifu, lor
allegation (n), nushtark, nushitaka, nushtak
allege (v), nushtarsk, nushitako, nushtako
alleger (n doer), nushtarkwan, nushitakua, nushtakua
allergic (adj), kukabirku, kukabiku, kukabiku
allergist (n doer), kukabirkwan, kukabikua, kukabikua
allergy (n), kukabirk, kukabika, kukabik
alleviate (v), klurasp, keluripo, klurpo
alleviation (n), klurap, keluripa, klurp
alley (n), bliurf, beliufa, bliuf
alliance (n), frimor, ferimara, frimar
allocate (v), orshairsp, orishaipo, orshaipo
allocation (n), orshairp, orishaipa, orshaip
allocator (n doer), orshairpwan, orishaipua, orshaipua
allot (v), orkrafsp, orikeratho, orkratho
allotment (n), orkrafp, orikeratha, orkrath
allow (v), frilarsk, ferilako, frilako
allowable (adj), frilarku, ferilaku, frilaku
allowance (n), frilark, ferilaka, frilak
alloy (n), orduirp, oroduipa, orduip
alloy (v), orduirsp, oroduipo, orduipo
allude (v), orushst, orusho, orusho
allure (n), orgurshk, orogushika, orgushk
allure (v), orgurshsk, orogushiko, orgushko
allusion (n), orusht, orusha, orush
ally (n), ferame, ferima, frim
ally (v), ferazme, ferimo, frimo
almighty (adj), lorgerftu, lorugeritu, lorgertu
almost (adv), lorwak, lorowaku, lorwak
alone (adj/adv), ofien, ofienu, ofien
along (prep/adv), orazhe, orazhu, orazh
alongside (adv/prep), orazhoirt, orazhoitu, orazhoit
aloud (adv), obiabe, obiabu, obiab
alpha (n), alfarn, alifana, alfan
alphabet (n), alferp, allfepa, alfep
alphabetic (adj), alferpu, alifepu, alfepu
alphabetically (adv), alferpiu, alifepiu, alfepiu
alphabetize (v), alfersp, alifepo, alfepo
already (adv), lordolu, lorudoliu, lordolu
also (adv/conj), orsh, oreshu, orsh
altar (n), durth, dutha, duth
alter (v), oiparsp, oipapo, oipapo
alteration (n), oiparp, oipapa, oipap
alternate (v), oparforsp, oiparifopo, oiparfpo
alternative (adj), oparforpu, oiparifopu, oiparfpu
alternative (n), oparforp, oiparifopa, oiparfp
alternatively (adv), oparforpiu, oiparifopiu, oiparfpiu
alternator (n doer), oparforpwan, oiparifopua, oiparfpua
although (conj), otshan, oteshanu, otshan
altimeter (n), orniork, orinioka, orniok
altitude (n), orkadart, orikadata, orkadat
altogether (adv), lordikefil, loredikefilu, lordikefil
Aluminum (n davoka), Etap, Etap, Etap
Aluminum (n), Aluminum, Aluminuma, Aluminum
alumni (n pl), yamiryek, yaromi, yarmi

alumnus (n), yamir, yaroma, yarm
always (adv), lorhoish, lorehoishiu, lorhoish
am (common), vil, kilo, bil
am (emphatic), vikel, kikelo, bivel
amateur (n), ornarve, orinava, ornav
amateurish (adj), ornarvu, orinavu, ornavu
amaze (v), odiaursf, odiaufo, odiaufo
amazement (n), odiaurf, odiaufa, odiauf
ambassador (n doer), liflorwan, ilafarolua, ilfarlua
ambiguity (n), viuvart, viuviata, viuviat
ambiguous (adj), viuvartu, viuviatu, viuviatu
ambiguously (adv), viuvartiu, viuviatiu, viuviatiu
ambition (n), ilplurtuet, ilapelutueta, ilplutuet
ambitious (adj), ilplurtuetu, ilapelutuetu, ilplutuetu
ambitiously (adv), ilplurtuetiu, ilapelutuetiu,
    ilplutuetiu
ambulance (n doer), lipamorwan, ilaparimua,
    ilparmua
ambulate (v), lipamosre, ilaparimo, ilparmo
ambulation (n), lipamor, ilaparima, ilparm
ambulatorily (adv), lipamoriu, ilaparimiu, ilparmiu
ambulatory (adj), lipamoru, ilaparimu, ilparmu
ambush (n), ilpershk, ilapeshika, ilpeshk
ambush (v), ilpershsk, ilapeshiko, ilpeshko
amen (interj), yanu, yanu, yanu
amend (v), orshkarsf, orashikafo, orshkafo
amendment (n), orshkarf, orashikafa, orshkaf
America (n), Amirk, Amika, Amik
American (n), Amirkan, Amikana, Amikan
Americium (n davoka), Onok, Onok, Onok
Americium (n), Amerikium, Amerikiuma,
    Amerikium
amid (prep), ozharf, ozharu, ozhar
amidst (prep), ozharf, ozharu, ozhar
ammunition (n), shnurk, shenuka, shnuk
amnesty (n), lienshk, lienosha, liensh
among (prep), olaume, olaumu, olaum
amongst (prep), olaume, olaumu, olaum
amount (n), oniurk, oniuka, oniuk
amount (v), oniursk, oniuko, oniuko
amp (n d:ampere), anpirn, anopina, anpin
ample (adj), anbernu, anubenu, anbenu
amplification (n), anobert, anobeta, anbet
amplifier (n doer), anobertwan, anobetua, anbetua
amplify (v), anoberst, anobeto, anbeto
amplitude (n), anbetarn, anobetana, anbetan
amply (adv), anberniu, anubeniu, anbeniu
amputate (v), anbersk, anobeko, anbeko
amputation (n), anberk, anobeka, anbek
Amsterdam (n), Amshterdarm, Amishoterudama,
    Amshterdam
amuse (v), orniarsle, oranialo, ornialo
amusement (n), orniarl, oraniala, ornial
an (det), ome, omei, om
analog (n), orkuift, orakuita, orkuit
analogy (n), orkuitarn, orakuitara, orkuitar
analysis (n), omarft, omafita, omaft
analyst (n doer), omarftwan, omafitua, omaftua
analytical (adj), omarftu, omafitu, omaftu
analytically (adv), omarftiu, omafitiu, omaftiu
analyze (v), omarfst, omafito, omafto
analyzer (n doer), omarftwan, omafitua, omaftua
anatomical (adj), duarmu, duamu, duamu

anatomy (n), duarme, duama, duam
ancestor (n doer), omlarlkwan, omalalikua,
    omlalkua
ancestral (adj), omlarlku, omalaliku, omlalku
ancestry (n), omlarlk, omalalika, omlalk
anchor (n), thuanirk, thuanika, thuank
anchor (v), thuanirsk, thuaniko, thuanko
Anchorage (n), Ankorarzh, Anikorazha, Ankorazh
ancient (adj), omiorpu, omiopu, omiopu
ancient (n), omiorp, omiopa, omiop
and (conj), dhark, dhaku, dhak
anecdotal (adj), omarshku, omashiku, omashku
anecdotally (adv), omarshkiu, omashikiu, omashkiu
anecdote (n), omarshk, omashika, omashk
angel (n), mikarl, mikara, mikar
angelic (adj), mikarlu, mikaru, mikaru
angelically (adv), mikarliu, mikariu, mikariu
anger (n), gakor, geraka, grak
anger (v), gakosre, gerako, grako
angle (n), mirak, miroka, mirk
angle (v), mirask, miroko, mirko
Angola (n), Ankolarf, Anikolafa, Ankolaf
angrily (adv), gakoriu, gerakiu, grakiu
angry (adj), gakoru, geraku, graku
angst (n), gralurge, geraluga, gralg
anguish (n), omdoirp, omadoipa, omdoip
anguish (v), omdoirsp, omadoipo, omdoipo
angular (adj), miraku, miroku, mirku
angularly (adv), mirakiu, mirokiu, mirkiu
animal (n), omurn, omuna, omun
animate (v), omudenirsk, omudeniko, omudenko
animation (n), omudenirk, omudenika, omudenk
animator (n doer), omudenirkwan, omudenikua,
    omudenkua
ankle (n), mirap, miropa, mirp
anniversary (n), hemaithar, hemaithara, hemaithar
annotate (v), omirazde, omido, omido
annotation (n), omirade, omida, omid
announce (v), omurfst, omufeto, omufto
announcement (n), omurft, omufeta, omuft
announcer (n doer), omurftwan, omufetua,
    omuftua
annoy (v), omufezge, omugafo, omgafo
annoyance (n), omufege, omugafa, omgaf
annual (adj), hemailu, hemailu, hemailu
annual (n), hemail, hemaila, hemail
annualize (v), hemaisle, hemailo, hemailo
annually (adv), hemailiu, hemailiu, hemailiu
anoint (v), driars, deriasho, driasho
anointment (n), driarsh, deriasha, driash
anonymilty (n), mavurm, mavuna, mavun
anonymous (adj), mavurnu, mavunu, mavunu
another (adj), omirshu, omishei, omishu
answer (n), orshirl, orashila, orshil
answer (v), orshirsle, orashilo, orshilo
ant (n), blenirk, belenika, blenk
antagonist (n doer), kokeragwan, kokerugua,
    kokrugua
antagonistic (adj), kokeragu, kokerugu, kokrugu
antagonize (v), kokerazge, kokerugo, kokrugo
antagony (n), kokerage, kokeruga, kokrug
antenna (n), omkarnf, omikanofa, omkanf
antibiotic (n), omkamierk, omikamieka, omkamiek

antibody (n), omkashlarde, omikashelada, omkashlad
anticipate (v), omshelirsk, omasheliko, omshelko
anticipation (n), omshelirk, omashelika, omshelk
antidote (n), omkarmk, omikamoka, omkamk
Antimony (n davoka), Elop, Elop, Elop
Antimony (n), Antimoni, Anetimonia, Antimoni
antique (n), omakelirp, omakelipa, omklap
antiquity (n), omklaparn, omakelipara, omklapar
antitrust (adj), omkadreirfu, omikadereifu, omkadreifu
anto-, dashkai-, dashkai-, dashkai-
antonym (n), omkaviern, omikaviena, omkavien
anxiety (n), gralurge, geraluga, gralg
anxious (adj), gralurgu, geralugu, gralgu
anxiously (adv), gralurgiu, geralugiu, gralgiu
any (pron/adj/adv), ino, inei, ino
anybody (n/pron), inoshlade, inosheladei, inoshlad
anyhow (adv), inohia, inohialu, inohia
anymore (adv), inowel, inowelu, inowel
anyone (pron), inona, inonei, inona
anyplace (adv), inobresh, inoberesha, inobresh
anything (n), inodizhe, inodizha, inodizh
anyway (adv), inoplio, inopeliola, inoplio
anywhere (adv), inoholu, inoholu, inoholu
anywhere (n), inohol, inohola, inohol
apart (adj), olfershu, olafeshu, olfeshu
apartheid (n), olfershfif, olafeshofifa, olfeshfif
apartment (n), olfesharlt, olafeshalita, olfeshalt
apathetic (adj), obotarfku, obotafiku, obotafku
apathy (n), obotarfk, obotafika, obotafk
apolitical (adj), oldaradu, oladoridu, oldordu
apoliticize (v), oldarazde, oladorido, oldordo
apolity (n), oldarade, oladorida, oldord
apologetic (adj), oldordertu, oladoridetu, oldordetu
apologetically (adv), oldordertiu, oladoridetiu, oldordetiu
apologize (v), oldorderst, oladorideto, oldordeto
apology (n), oldordert, oladorideta, oldordet
appall (v), thiarsp, thiapo, thiapo
apparatus (n), diersh, diesha, diesh
apparel (n), biursh, biusha, biush
apparent (adj), opliarnu, opelianu, oplianu
apparently (adv), opliarniu, opelianiu, oplianiu
apparition (n doer), opliarnwan, opelianua, oplianua
appeal (n), optelorp, opitelopa, optelp
appeal (v), optelorsp, opitelopo, optelpo
appear (v), opliarsne, opeliano, opliano
appearance (n), opliarn, opeliana, oplian
append (v), ofbrunsf, ofoberuno, ofbruno
appetite (n), ofpuert, ofapueta, ofpuet
appetize (v), ofpuerst, ofapueto, ofpueto
applaud (v), ofsharsk, ofishako, ofshako
applauder (n doer), ofsharkwan, ofishakua, ofshakua
applause (n), ofshark, ofishaka, ofshak
apple (n), thatil, thalata, thalt
appliance (n), thokar, thorika, thork
applicable (adj), thorku, thoku, thoku
applicably (adv), thorkiu, thokiu, thokiu
applicant (n doer), thorkuinwan, thokuinua, thokuinua

application (n), thork, thoka, thok
applicator (n doer), thorkwan, thokua, thokua
apply (v), thorsk, thoko, thoko
appoint (v), rotaitisf, otaifoto, otaifto
appointer (n doer), rotaitifwan, otaifotua, otaiftua
appointment (n), rotaitif, otaifota, otaift
appreciate (v), drulirsp, derulipo, drulpo
appreciation (n), drulirp, derulipa, drulp
appreciative (adj), drulirpu, derulipu, drulpu
appreciatively (adv), drulirpiu, derulipiu, drulpiu
apprehend (v), odrukerst, oderuketo, odruketo
apprehension (n), odrukert, oderuketa, odruket
apprehensive (adj), odrukertu, oderuketu, odruketu
apprehensively (adv), odrukertiu, oderuketiu, odruketiu
approach (n), oflaurde, ofelauda, oflaud
approach (v), oflaurzde, ofelaudo, oflaudo
approachable (adj), oflaurdu, ofelaudu, oflaudu
approacher (n doer), oflaurdwan, ofelaudua, oflaudua
appropriate (adj), oflikirmu, ofelikimu, oflikimu
appropriate (v), oflikirzme, ofelikimo, oflikimo
appropriately (adv), oflikirmiu, ofelikimiu, oflikimiu
appropriation (n), oflikirme, ofelikima, oflikim
appropriator (n doer), oflikirmwan, ofelikimua, oflikimua
approval (n), ofelarve, ofelaruva, oflarv
approve (v), ofelarzve, ofelaruvo, oflarvo
approver (n doer), ofelarvwan, ofelaruvua, oflarvua
approximate (adj), ofloigartu, ofeloigatu, ofloigatu
approximate (v), ofloigarst, ofeloigato, ofloigato
approximately (adv), ofloigartiu, ofeloigatiu, ofloigatiu
approximation (n), ofloigart, ofeloigata, ofloigat
April (n), Laprel, Laparela, Laprel
apron (n), ovart, ovata, ovat
apt (adj), ofirku, ofiku, ofku
aptitude (n), ofirk, ofika, ofk
aptly (adv), ofirkiu, ofikiu, ofkiu
Arab (n), Arbe, Arobana, Arb
arbitrarily (adv), brialorkiu, berialokiu, brialkiu
arbitrary (adj), brialorku, berialoku, brialku
arbitrate (v), brialorsk, berialoko, brialko
arbitration (n), brialork, berialoka, brialk
arbitrator (n doer), brialorkwan, berialokua, brialkua
arc (n), traln, terala, tral
arc (v), tralsne, teralo, tralo
arch (n), tralirt, teralita, tralt
arch (v), tralirst, teralito, tralto
archer (n doer), tralirtwan, teralitua, traltua
architect (n doer), tralofirkwan, teralofikua, tralfkua
architect (v), tralofirsk, teralofiko, tralfko
architectural (adj), tralofirku, teralofiku, tralfku
architecture (n), tralofirk, teralofika, tralfk
archival (adj), trafirpu, terafipu, trafpu
archive (n), trafirp, terafipa, trafp
archive (v), trafirsp, terafipo, trafpo
archivist (n doer), trafirpwan, terafipua, trafpua
are (common), vir, kiro, bir
are (emphatic), viker, kikero, biver

area (n), braufp, beraupa, braup
arena (n), brausht, berauta, braut
Argentina (n), Argentirn, Arugenotina, Argentin
Argon (n davoka), Etik, Etik, Etik
Argon (n), Argon, Aregona, Argon
arguable (adj), gautifu, gaufitu, gauftu
arguably (adv), gautifiu, gaufitiu, gauftiu
argue (v), gautisf, gaufito, gaufto
arguer (n doer), gautifwan, gaufitua, gauftua
argument (n), gautif, gaufita, gauft
arise (v), oluirs, oluisho, oluisho
arithmetic (n), olenorp, olenopa, olenp
arithmetician (n doer), olenorpwan, olenopua,
    olenpua
Arizona (n), Arizhorn, Arizhona, Arizhon
ark (n), onerk, oneka, onk
Arkansas (n), Arkanorsh, Arikanosha, Arkansh
Arlington (n), Arlingtorn, Arelingatona, Arlington
arm (n), shnern, shinena, shnen
arm (v), shnersne, shineno, shneno
Armenia (n), Armern, Arimena, Armen
Armenian (n), Armenarn, Arimenana, Armenan
armer (n doer), shnernwan, shinenua, shnenua
armor (n), shnerf, shinefa, shnef
armor (v), shnersf, shinefo, shnefo
army (n), shinekin, shinenoka, shnenk
Army (n), Shiern, Shiena, Shien
aroma (n), riorsh, riosha, riosh
aromatic (adj), riorshu, rioshu, rioshu
aromatically (adv), riorshiu, rioshiu, rioshiu
arose (v pa), oluirsyot, oluishio, oluishio
around (adv/prep), oblaithpu, obelaithu, oblaithu
arrange (v), omorst, olimoto, olmoto
arrangement (n), omort, olimota, olmot
arranger (n doer), omortwan, olimotua, olmotua
array (n), olipoilf, olipoila, olpoil
array (v), olipoilsf, olipoilo, olpoilo
arrest (n), fitark, fitaka, ftak
arrest (v), fitarsk, fitako, ftako
arrestive (adj), fitarku, fitaku, ftaku
arrestor (n doer), fitarkwan, fitakua, ftakua
arrival (n), ftalort, fitalota, ftalt
arrive (v), ftalorst, fitaloto, ftalto
arrow (n), fetirp, fetipa, ftip
Arsenic (n davoka), Efop, Efop, Efop
Arsenic (n), Arshenik, Areshenika, Arshenik
arson (n), ushkaush, vozhakausha, shkaush
arson (v), ushkaus, vozhakausho, shkausho
arsonist (n doer), ushkaushwan, vozhakaushua,
    shkaushua
arsonous (adj), ushkaushu, vozhakaushu, shkaushu
art (n), kifar, kirofa, kirf
article (n), kifaf, kifafa, kifaf
artifact (n), kipotar, kiporita, kiport
artifice (n), kishok, kishoketa, kishket
artificer (n doer), kishokwan, kishoketua, kishketua
artificial (adj), kishoku, kishoketu, kishketu
artificially (adv), kishokiu, kishoketiu, kishketiu
artillery (n), kigalf, kigala, kigal
artist (n doer), kifarwan, kirofua, kirfua
artistic (adj), kifaru, kirofu, kirfu
artistically (adv), kifariu, kirofiu, kirfiu
as (adv/conj/prep), yosh, yoshu, yosh

As (let pl), alfi, alfi, alfi
asbestos (n), doshpart, doshipata, doshpat
ascend (v), olirask, oliriko, olirko
ascender (n doer), olirakwan, olirikua, olirkua
ascension (n), olirakuet, olirokueta, olirkuet
ascent (n), olirak, olirika, olirk
ash (n), aush, ausha, aush
ashame (v), orvishorst, oravishoto, orvishto
ashameness (n), orvishort, oravishota, orvisht
asher (n doer), aushwan, aushua, aushua
ashore (n), onularat, onularita, onulart
ashtray (n), aushbiarme, aushubiama, aushbiam
Asia (n), Larshiarl, Larishiala, Larshial
Asian (n), Larshiarn, Larishiana, Larshian
aside (adv), oshoirtiu, oshoitiu, oshoitiu
aside (n), oshoirt, oshoita, oshoit
ask (v), fasp, fapo, fapo
asker (n doer), fapwan, fapua, fapua
asleep (adj), oprushel, operushelu, oprushel
aspect (n), othurk, othuka, othuk
aspiration (n), ofdaurf, ofudaufa, ofdauf
aspire (v), ofdaursf, ofudaufo, ofdaufo
aspirin (n), ofarn, ofarina, ofarn
ass (n), okark, okaka, okak
assail (v), karfluarsle, karifelualo, karflualo
assailable (adj), karfluarlu, karifelualu, karflualu
assailant (n doer), karfluarlwan, karifelualua,
    karflualua
assassin (n doer), karakwan, karikua, karkua
assassinate (v), karask, kariko, karko
assassination (n), karak, karika, kark
assault (n), boirk, boika, boik
assault (v), boirsk, boiko, boiko
assemble (v), othralzve, otheravo, othravo
assembler (n doer), othralvwan, otheravua,
    othravua
assembly (n), othralve, otherava, othrav
assert (v), olsharst, olashato, olshato
assertation (n), olshart, olashata, olshat
assertive (adj), olsharku, olashatu, olshatu
assertively (adv), olshartiu, olashatiu, olshatiu
assess (v), orlarsp, orelapo, orlapo
assessive (adj), orlarpu, orelapu, orlapu
assessively (adv), orlarpiu, orelapiu, orlapiu
assessment (n), orlarp, orelapa, orlap
assessor (n doer), orlarpwan, orelapua, orlapua
asset (n), olzhorde, olazhoda, olzhod
assign (v), olarask, olariko, olarko
assigner (n doer), olarakwan, olarikua, olarkua
assignment (n), olarak, olarika, olark
assimilate (v), oldidarsne, oladidano, oldidano
assimilation (n), oldidarn, oladidana, oldidan
assimilator (n doer), oldidarnwan, oladidanua,
    oldidanua
assist (n), otelirk, otelika, otelk
assist (v), otelirsk, oteliko, otelko
assistance (n pl), otelirkyek, oteliki, otelki
assistant (n doer), otelirkwan, otelikua, otelkua
assistive (adj), otelirku, oteliku, otelku
assistively (adv), otelirkiu, otelikiu, otelkiu
associate (n doer), omeirfwan, omeifua, omeifua
associate (v), omeirsf, omeifo, omeifo
association (n), omeirf, omeifa, omeif

assort (v), ofadelirsk, ofadeliko, ofadelko
assortment (n), ofadelirk, ofadelika, ofadelk
assume (v), ofialorst, ofialoto, ofialto
assumption (n), ofialort, ofialota, ofialt
assurance (n), olarp, olapa, olap
assurative (adj), olarpu, olapu, olapu
assuratively (adv), olarpiu, olapiu, olapiu
assure (v), olarsp, olapo, olapo
assurer (n doer), olarpwan, olapua, olapua
Astatine (n davoka), Erak, Erak, Erak
Astatine (n), Ashtatin, Ashetatina, Ashtatin
asteroid (n), koatarn, koatana, koatan
astonish (v pa), okalirsfyot, okalifio, okalfio
astonish (v), okalirsf, okalifo, okalfo
astonishment (n), okalirf, okalifa, okalf
astronaut (n doer), kanoriatwan, kariniatua,
    karniatua
astronavigate (v), kanoriast, kariniato, karniato
astronavigation (n), kanoriat, kariniata, karniat
astronimically (adv), kanorafiu, karinafiu, karnafiu
astronomer (n doer), kanorafwan, karinafua,
    karnafua
astronomical (adj), kanorafu, karinafu, karnafu
astronomy (n), kanoraf, karinafa, karnaf
asylum (n), shaurp, shaupa, shaup
asynchronous (adj), odalpiarfu, odalopiaru,
    odalpiaru
asynchronously (adv), odalpiarfiu, odalopiariu,
    odalpiariu
at (prep), ide, idu, id
ate (v pa), nierstyot, nietio, nietio
Atheism (n), Bianorsh, Bianosha, Biansh
Atheist (n), Bianorshk, Bianoshaka, Bianshk
athlete (n), threlk, thereka, threk
athletic (adj), threlku, thereku, threku
athletically (adv), threlkiu, therekiu, threkiu
Atlanta (n), Atelanirt, Atelanita, Atelant
Atlantic (n), Atelantirk, Atelanotika, Atelantik
Atlantis (n), Atelantirsh, Atelanotisha, Atelantish
atmosphere (n), athefoshar, atheforisha, atheforsh
atmospheric (adj), athefosharu, atheforishu,
    atheforshu
atmospherically (adv), athefoshariu, atheforishiu,
    atheforshiu
atom (n), timort, timota, timot
atomic (adj), timortu, timotu, timotu
atomically (adv), timortiu, timotiu, timotiu
atomize (v), timorst, timoto, timoto
attach (v), opairsk, opaiko, opaiko
attachment (n), opairk, opaika, opaik
attack (n), opairt, opaita, opait
attack (v), opairst, opaito, opaito
attacker (n doer), opairtwan, opaitua, opaitua
attain (v), opirfst, opifoto, opifto
attainment (n), opirft, opifota, opift
attempt (n), ovafirt, ovafita, ovaft
attempt (v), ovafirst, ovafito, ovafto
attend (v), opiforsk, opifoko, opifko
attendance (n), opifork, opifoka, opifk
attendant (n doer), opiforkwan, opifokua, opifkua
attention (n), opiforkuet, opifokueta, opifkuet
attentive (adj), opiforkuetu, opifokuetu, opifkuetu
attentively (adv), opiforkuetiu, opifokuetiu,
    opifkuetiu
attic (n), duavart, duavata, duavat
attire (n), ogalirp, ogalipa, ogalp
attire (v), ogalirsp, ogalipo, ogalpo
attitude (n), katilur, karilota, karlt
attorney (n), klarage, kelariga, klarg
attract (v), ogalirst, ogalito, ogalto
attraction (n), ogalirt, ogalita, ogalt
attractive (adj), ogalirtu, ogalitu, ogaltu
attractively (adv), ogalirtiu, ogalitiu, ogaltiu
attractor (n doer), ogalirtwan, ogalitua, ogaltua
attribute (n), othriurp, otheriupa, othriup
attribute (v), othriursp, otheriupo, othriupo
attributive (adj), othriurpu, otheriupu, othriupu
attributively (adv), othriurpiu, otheriupiu,
    othriupiu
attributor (n doer), othriurpwan, otheriupua,
    othriupua
attrite (v), otarzve, otavo, otavo
attrition (n), otarve, otava, otav
attritional (adj), otarvu, otavu, otavu
auction (n), diork, dioka, diok
auction (v), diorsk, dioko, dioko
auctioneer (n doer), diorkwan, diokua, diokua
audible (adj), riuku, raliuku, raliuku
audience (n), riukal, raliukona, raliukon
audio (n), riuk, raliuka, raliuk
audit (n), rakal, ralika, ralk
audit (v), rakasle, raliko, ralko
audition (n), rakulat, ralikueta, ralkuet
audition (v), rakulast, ralikueto, ralkueto
auditor (n doer), rakalwan, ralikua, ralkua
August (n), Laukut, Laukuta, Laukut
aunt (n), darl, dalela, dalel
Austin (n), Aushtirn, Aushetina, Aushtin
Australia (n), Aushtralf, Aushoterala, Aushtral
Australian (n), Aushtralarn, Aushoterana,
    Aushtralan
Austria (n), Aushtarf, Aushotara, Aushtar
Austrian (n), Aushtarnf, Aushotarina, Aushtarn
authenticate (v), basharsp, bashapo, bashapo
authentication (n), basharp, bashapa, bashap
author (n doer), bashtalwan, bashalitua, bashaltua
authoritative (adj), bashtapu, bashalipu, bashalpu
authoritatively (adv), bashtapiu, bashalipiu,
    bashalpiu
authority (n), bashtal, bashalita, bashalt
authorization (n), bashtap, bashalipa, bashalp
authorize (v), bashtasp, bashalipo, bashalpo
autograph (n), oilodarfk, oilodarifa, oilodarf
autograph (v), oilodarfsk, oilodarifo, oilodarfo
automaker (n doer), oilonargwan, oilonagua,
    oilonagua
automate (v), oilodekisne, oilodeniko, oilodenko
automatic (adj), oilodekinu, oilodeniku, oilodenku
automatic (n), oilodekorin, oiloderonika, oilodernk
automatically (adv), oilodekiniu, oilodenikiu,
    oilodenkiu
automation (n), oilodekin, oilodenika, oilodenk
automator (n doer), oilodekinwan, oilodenikua,
    oilodenkua
automobile (n), oilodatun, oilodanita, oilodant

automotive (adj), oilodatunu, oilodanitu, oilodantu
autonomy (n), oiloviern, oiloviena, oilovien
autumn (n), frodathk, ferodatha, frodath
autumnal (adj), frodathku, ferodathu, frodathu
avail (n), shiurp, shiupa, shiup
avail (v), shiursp, shiupo, shiupo
availability (n), shiurpaf, shiufipa, shiufp
available (adj), shiurpafu, shiufipu, shiufpu
avenge (v), odufirsk, odufiko, odufko
avenger (n doer), odufirkwan, odufikua, odufkua
avenue (n), lomuf, olafima, olfim
average (adj), lofeku, ofeloku, ofelku
average (n), lofek, ofeloka, ofelk
average (v), lofesk, ofeloko, ofelko
aversion (n), otharak, otharika, othark
avert (v), otharask, othariko, otharko
aviatic (adj), floratu, feloretu, floretu
aviation (n), florat, feloreta, floret
aviator (n doer), floratwan, feloretua, floretua
avoid (v), lonuask, onuako, onuako
avoidable (adj), lonuaku, onuaku, onuaku
avoidably (adv), lonuakiu, onuakiu, onuakiu
avoidance (n), lonuak, onuaka, onuak
await (v), oyalirsf, oyalifo, oyalfo
awake (adj), lomipunu, ominopu, ominpu
awake (v), lomipusne, ominopo, ominpo
award (n), lishkap, ikeshopa, ikshop
award (v), lishkasp, ikeshopo, ikshopo
aware (adj), oshlerfu, oshelefu, oshlefu
awareness (n), oshlerf, oshelefa, oshlef
away (adj/adv), opiorl, opiolu, opiol
awe (n), kuip, yuipa, yuip
awe (v), kuisp, yuipo, yuipo
awful (adj), kaubeshu, yaushipu, yaushpu
awkward (adj), yaushorku, yaushoku, yaushku
awkwardly (adv), yaushorkiu, yaushokiu, yaushkiu
awkwardness (n), yaushork, yaushoka, yaushk
awoke (v pa), lomipusnyot, ominopio, ominpio
ax (n), kibark, kibaka, kibak
ax (v), kibarsk, kibako, kibako
axis (n), kibafirk, kibafika, kibafk
axle (n), kibafort, bibafota, kibaft
aye (interj), ia, ia, ia
Azerbaijan (n), Azherbaizharn, Azherobaizhana,
    Azherbaizhan
B (let sng), bal, bala, ba
baby (n), deirde, deida, deid
baby (v), deirzde, deido, deido
bachelor (n), vapush, vashipa, vashp
back (n), vark, vaka, vak
back (v), varsk, vako, vako
backbone (n), vaktoirk, vaketoika, vaktoik
backer (n doer), varkwan, vakua, vakua
background (n), vakbratin, vakeberanita, vakbrant
backlog (n), vakuift, vakuita, vakuit
backup (n), vakilp, vakiveila, vakiveil
backward (adj/adv), vakaursh, vakaushu, vakaush
backyard (n), vakthauthk, vakethautha, vakthauth
bacon (n), foidart, foidata, foidat
bacteria (n pl), gialorkyek, gialoki, gialki
bacterium (n), gialork, gialoka, gialk
bad (adj), frairku, feraiku, fraiku
bade (v pa), thairstyot, thaitio, thaitio

badly (adv), frairkiu, feraikiu, fraikiu
badness (n), frairk, feraika, fraik
bag (n), nufaf, fanafa, fnaf
bag (v), nufasf, fanafo, fnafo
baggage (n), nufarf, fanafara, fnafar
baggage (v), nufarsf, fanafaro, fnafaro
baggager (n doer), nufarfwan, fanafarua, fnafarua
bagger (n doer), nufafwan, fanafua, fnafua
baggily (adv), nufafiu, fanafiu, fnafiu
baggy (adj), nufafu, fanafu, fnafu
Baghdad (n), Bagdarde, Bagudada, Bagdad
bail (n), guarf, guafa, guaf
bail (v), guarsf, guafo, guafo
bailout (n), guarfuil, guafuila, guafuil
bake (n), rovark, rovaka, rovak
bake (v), rovarsk, rovako, rovako
baker (n doer), rovarkwan, rovakua, rovakua
bakery (n), rovakarf, rovakara, rovakar
balance (n), morshtat, shemotata, shmotat
balance (v), morshtast, shemotato, shmotato
balast (n), morsht, shemota, shmot
balast (v), morshst, shemoto, shmoto
bald (adj), mushdinu, shemopu, shmopu
bald (v), mushdisne, shemopo, shmopo
baldness (n), mushdin, shemopa, shmop
ball (n), shmonde, mashipa, mashp
ball (v), shmonzde, mashipo, mashpo
ballad (n), firnal, filuna, filn
balladeer (n doer), firnalwan, filunua, filnua
ballerina (n doer), finarwan, fironua, firnua
ballet (n), finar, firona, firn
ballet (v), finasre, firono, firno
balloon (n), marshp, shemonudaka, shmondak
balloon (v), marshsp, shemonudako, shmondako
ballot (n), shlirp, shelipa, shlip
balm (n), tuvan, telava, telv
Baltic (n), Baltirk, Balotika, Baltik
Baltimore (n), Baltimorf, Balotimora, Baltimor
ban (n), vorme, verama, vram
ban (v), vorzme, veramo, vramo
banality (n), vormk, veramika, vramk
banana (n), malp, ramapa, ramap
band (n d:group), vramirp, veramipa, vramep
band (n d:strap), shtairme, shetaima, shtaim
band (v d:group), vramirsp, veramipo, vramepo
band (v d:strap), shtairzme, shetaimo, shtaimo
bandage (n), shtairmak, shetaimaka, shtaimak
bandage (v), shtairmask, shetaimako, shtaimako
bandit (n), krankart, keranikata, krankat
bandwidth (n), vramkrashk, veramekerasha,
    vramkrash
bandy (adj d:group), vramirpu, veramipu, vramepu
bang (n d:collision), driark, doriaka, driak
bang (n d:hair), flanirp, felanipa, flanp
bang (v d:collision), driarsk, doriako, driako
banger (n doer d:collision), driarkwan, doriakua,
    driakua
banish (v), vramarshsk, veramashiko, vramashko
banishment (n), vramarshk, veramashika,
    vramashk
bank (n d:shore), plirk, shepelara, shplar
bank (n d:storage), rudiage, deriaga, driag
bank (v d:shore), plirsk, shepelaro, shplaro

bank (v d:storage), rudiazge, deriago, driago
banker (n doer d:storage), rudiagwan, deriagua, driagua
bankrupt (v), deriagairfst, deriagaifoto, deriagaifto
bankruptcy (n), deriagairft, deriagaifota, deriagaift
banner (n doer), vormwan, veramua, vramua
bar (n d:pub), bukor, belorika, blork
bar (n d:rod), rolart, rolata, rolt
bar (v d:rod), rolarst, rolato, rolto
barb (n), puart, puata, puat
barb (v), puarst, puato, puato
barber (n doer), puartwan, puatua, puatua
bare (adj), darshpu, dashapu, dashpu
bare (v), darshsp, dashapo, dashpo
barefoot (adj), darshporshu, dasheposhu, dashposhu
barely (adv), darshpoiu, dashapoiu, dashpoiu
bareness (n), darshp, dashapa, dashp
bargain (n), meirfal, meilifa, meilf
bargain (v), meirfasle, meilifo, meilfo
barge (n d:boat), mirge, miga, mig
barge (v), diarzge, diago, diago
barger (n doer), diargwan, diagua, diagua
Barium (n davoka), Arip, Arip, Arip
Barium (n), Barium, Bariuma, Barium
bark (n d:tree skin), pipal, pilopa, pilp
bark (n d:yelp), vupirn, vunopa, vunp
bark (v d:yelp), vupirsne, vunopo, vunpo
barker (n doer d:yelp), vupirnwan, vunopua, vunpua
barn (n), bliarn, beliana, blian
barrel (n), pradip, padoripa, padorp
barrel (v), pradisp, padoripo, padorpo
barrier (n), rofk, rolifa, rolf
bartend (v d:pub), bukosre, beloriko, blorko
bartender (n doer d:pub), bukorwan, belorikua, blorkua
base (n), viarsh, viasha, viash
base (v), viars, viasho, viasho
baseball (n), viarshmashp, viashemonida, viashmond
basement (n), viarshiak, viashalita, viashyalt
baser (n doer), viarshwan, viashua, viashua
bash (v), krilorst, keriloto, krilto
basher (n doer), krilortwan, kerilotua, kriltua
basic (adj), viarshu, viashu, viashu
basically (adv), viarshiu, viashiu, viashiu
basin (n), kavirp, kavepa, kavep
basis (n), viashert, viasheta, viashet
bask (v), pliarsp, peliapo, pliapo
basket (n), tafil, talofa, talf
basketball (n), talfmashp, talofeshemonida, talfshmond
bass (n d:fish), pafel, palofipa, palfp
bass (n d:sound), raubuge, berauga, braug
bastard (n), furbalp, baripa, barp
bastardize (v), furbalsp, baripo, barpo
bat (n d:animal), hagor, haruga, harg
bat (n d:stick), geralt, gerata, grat
bat (v d:stick), geralst, gerato, grato
batch (n), tralge, teraga, trag
bath (n), dafel, dalifa, dalf
bathe (v), dafesle, dalifo, dalfo

bather (n doer), dafelwan, dalifua, dalfua
bathroom (n), dafelshranf, dalifesherana, dalfshran
batter (n doer d:stick), geraltwan, geratua, gratua
batter (v d:attack), gratarsk, geratako, gratako
battery (n d:attack), gratark, gerataka, gratak
battery (n d:storage), tranirk, teranika, trank
battle (n), trazhge, geratupa, gratup
battle (v), trazhzge, geratupo, gratupo
battler (n doer), trazhgwan, geratupua, gratupua
batty (adj d:animal), hagoru, harugu, hargu
bay (n d:howl), dierosht, dierota, diert
bay (n d:place), mudan, munoda, mund
bay (v d:howl), dieroshst, dieroto, dierto
bayer (n doer d:howl), dieroshtwan, dierotua, diertua
be (imp, common), kuvil, kulo, kul
be (imp, emphatic), kuvikel, kuliko, kulko
be (inf, common), vil, kilo, bil
be (inf, emphatic), vikel, kikelo, bivel
beach (n), fluiade, dualifa, dualf
beach (v), fluiazde, dualifo, dualfo
beacher (n doer), fluiadwan, dualifua, dualfua
bead (n), bloirbe, beloiba, bloib
bead (v), bloirzbe, beloibo, bloibo
beak (n), duart, duata, duat
beaker (n doer), duakor, duarika, duark
beam (n), duarf, duafa, duaf
beam (v), duarsf, duafo, duafo
beamer (n doer), duarfwan, duafua, duafua
bean (n), shurth, shutha, shuth
bean (v), shursth, shutho, shutho
bear (n d:animal), giorf, danudana, dandan
bear (v d:direction), krialst, gerufito, grufto
bear (v d:endure), kriazge, geruko, gruko
beard (n), pufor, porafa, porf
beard (v), pufosre, porafo, porfo
bearer (n doer d:endure), kriagwan, gerukua, grukua
bearing (n d:direction), krialt, gerufita, gruft
bearing (n d:metal ball), kriarp, gerufipa, grufp
bearish (adj d:endure), kriagu, geruku, gruku
bearishly (adv d:endure), kriagiu, gerukiu, grukiu
beast (n), gaishk, zhigaishoka, zhigaishk
beat (n), daurt, dauta, daut
beat (v pa), daurstyot, dautio, dautio
beat (v), daurst, dauto, dauto
beatable (adj), daurtu, dautu, dautu
beater (n doer), daurtwan, dautua, dautua
beautiful (adj), fialfu, fiadu, fiadu
beautifully (adv), fialfiu, fiadiu, fiadiu
beautify (v), fialsf, fiado, fiado
beauty (n), fialf, fiada, fiad
became (v pa), vilensfyot, kilenio, bilenio
because (conj), vilshashk, kileshekashu, bilshkash
become (v), vilensf, kileno, bileno
bed (n), famor, fuarema, fuarm
bed (v), famosre, fuaremo, fuarmo
bedevil (v), zhairgaishst, zhaigaito, zhaigaito
bedroom (n), famorshranf, famesherana, famshran
bee (n), zhishk, zhisha, zhish
beef (n), bliarf, beliafa, bliaf
been (v pap pl common), vor, koru, bor
been (v pap pl emphatic), voker, kokeru, bover

been (v pap sng common), vol, kolu, bol
been (v pap sng emphatic), vokel, kokelu, bovel
beep (n), driurp, deriupa, driup
beep (v), driursp, deriupo, driupo
beeper (n doer), driurpwan, deriupua, driupua
beer (n), zholar, zhorela, zhorl
beetle (n), gaithirp, gaithipa, gaithp
before (prep/conj), vivoan, kivoanu, bivoan
beforehand (adj/adv), vivokap, kivoanukapu,
    bivoankapu
befriend (v), pamesle, pilamo, pilmo
beg (n), dikarf, difoka, difk
beg (v), dikarsf, difoko, difko
began (v pa), kursnyot, kunio, kunio
beggar (n doer), dikarfwan, difokua, difkua
begin (v), kursne, kuno, kuno
beginner (n doer), kurnwan, kunua, kunua
begrudge (v), kriuzhge, keriugo, kriugo
behalf (n), yilwalp, yilewapa, yilwap
behave (v), kuvasre, kulifo, kulfo
behavior (n), kuvar, kulifa, kulf
behind (adj/adv/prep), kuden, kunodu, kund
beige (adj), pairzhu, paizhu, paizhu
beige (n), pairzhe, paizha, paizh
Beijing (n), Beizhirn, Beizhinga, Beizhing
being (v prp common), kulauf, kulaura, kulaur
being (v prp emphatic), kulaufk, kulaurika, kulaurk
Beirut (n), Beiruft, Beiruta, Beirut
Belgian (n), Belgiarn, Belogiana, Belgian
Belgium (n), Belgiurme, Belogiuma, Belgium
belief (n), sharme, shara, shar
believable (adj), sharmu, sharu, sharu
believably (adv), sharmiu, shariu, shariu
believe (v), sharzme, sharo, sharo
believer (n doer), sharmwan, sharua, sharua
belittle (v), lishst, lisho, lisho
bell (n), diarme, diara, diar
bellow (n), diariark, diariauka, diariak
bellow (v), diariarsk, diariauko, diariako
belly (n), diapor, diaropa, diarp
belly (v), diaposre, diaropo, diarpo
belong (v), kuzhisre, kurazho, krazho
below (adv/prep), ushurt, ushutu, ushut
belt (n), dakelf, dafika, dafk
belt (v), dakelsf, dafiko, dafko
belter (n doer), dakelfwan, dafikua, dafkua
bench (n), kikaf, kifeka, kifk
bench (v), kikasf, kifeko, kifko
benchmark (n), kifshtart, kifeshetata, kifshtat
bend (n), kikot, kifata, kift
bend (v), kikost, kitato, kitto
bendable (adj), kikotu, kifatu, kiftu
bendably (adv), kikotiu, kifatiu, kiftiu
bender (n doer), kikotwan, kifatua, kiftua
beneath (adv/prep), milurn, milunu, milun
benefically (adv), kupatoviu, kupafitiu, kupaftiu
beneficial (adj), kupatovu, kupafitu, kupaftu
beneficiary (n doer), kupatovwan, kupafitua,
    kupaftua
benefit (n), kupatove, kupafita, kupaft
benefit (v), kupatozve, kupafito, kupafto
bent (v pa), kikostyot, kifatio, kiftio
bequest (v), shtiarst, shotiato, shtiato

Berkeley (n), Berkerl, Berokela, Berkel
Berkelium (n davoka), Onat, Onat, Onat
Berkelium (n), Berkelium, Berikeliuma, Berkelium
Berlin (n), Berlirn, Berolina, Berlin
berry (n), nepul, nelipa, nelp
Beryllium (n davoka), Akip, Akip, Akip
Beryllium (n), Berilium, Beriliuma, Berilium
beseech (v), viloirst, kiloito, biloito
beseecher (n doer), viloirtwan, kiloitua, biloitua
beside (adv/prep), kushoirt, kushoitu, kushoit
besides (adv/prep), kushoirt, kushoitu, kushoit
best (adj), kufwerku, kufeweku, kufweku
best (adv), kufwerkiu, kufewekiu, kufwekiu
best (n), kufwerk, kufeweka, kufwek
best (v pa), kufwerskyot, kufewekio, kufwekio
best (v), kufwersk, kufeweko, kufweko
bet (n), kurbe, kuba, kub
bet (v pa), kurzbyot, kubio, kubio
bet (v), kurzbe, kubo, kubo
beta (n), betarn, betana, betan
betray (v), deifralshsk, deiferashiko, deifrashko
betrayal (n), deifralshk, deiferashika, deifrashk
better (adj), kufwerlu, kufewelu, kufwelu
better (v), kufwersle, kufewelo, kufwelo
between (adv/prep), vildurme, kiledumu, bildum
Beverly Hills (n), Beverlif Hilorsh, Beveralifa
    Hiloshi, Beverlif Hilsh
bewitch (v), deiarsne, deiano, deiano
beyond (adv/prep), kuyelir, kuyerulu, kuyerl
bi- (num 2 pref), ipi-, ipi-, ipi-
bianten-, muishkai-, muishkai-, muishkai-
bias (n), lipk, ipeka, ipk
bias (v), lipsk, ipeko, ipko
Bible (n), Vipalp, Vipalapa, Vipalp
bicker (v), broishsk, beroisho, broisho
bickerer (n doer), broishkwan, beroishua, broishua
bicycle (n), lipivaitar, ipivairota, ipivairt
bicycle (v), lipivaitasre, ipivairoto, ipivairto
bicyclist (n doer), lipivaitarwan, ipivairotua,
    ipivairtua
bid (n), thairt, thaita, thait
bid (v pa), thairstyot, thaitio, thaitio
bid (v), thairst, thaito, thaito
bidder (n doer), thairtwan, thaitua, thaitua
biet (v prp), nufobeirstaut, nufobietao, nufobietao
big (adj), viurgu, viugu, viugu
bigger (adj), viurgwelu, viugwelu, viugwelu
biggest (adj), viurgwaku, viugwaku, viugwaku
bigot (n), guaurk, guauka, guauk
bike (n), pivirt, pivita, pivit
bike (v), pivirst, pivito, pivito
biker (n doer), pivirtwan, pivitua, pivitua
bikini (n), piln, lipina, lipin
bilateral (adj), ipinamoru, ipinarimu, ipinarmu
bilaterally (adv), ipinamoriu, ipinarimiu, ipinarmiu
bill (n d:beak), dular, durela, durl
bill (n d:document), kiuft, kiuta, kiut
bill (v d:document), kiufst, kiuto, kiuto
billboard (n), kiuftaplok, kiutepelorika, kiutplork
biller (n doer:document), kiuftwan, kiutua, kiutua
billiard (adj), kiuftokaru, kiutoruku, kiutoru
billiard (n), kiuftokar, kiutoruka, kiutork
billion (num 1e9 card), avuka, avuka, avuka

billionth (num 1e9 ord), avuketh, avuketh, avuketh
bin (n), nurp, nupa, nup
binary (adj), ipiarnu, ipianu, ipianu
bind (n d:constrain), paupime, paumuba, paumb
bind (v d:constrain), paupizme, paumubo, paumbo
binder (n doer d:constrain), paupimwan,
    paumubua, paumbua
biography (n), miedarfk, miedarifa, miedarf
biological (adj), mierkuitu, miekuitu, miekuitu
biologically (adv), mierkuitiu, miekuitiu, miekuitiu
biology (n), mierkuit, miekuit, miekuit
biotechnology (n), ipikizhasht, ipikizhata, ipikizhat
bipolar (adj), ipidilkartu, ipidilokatu, ipidilkatu
bipolarity (n), ipidilkart, ipidilokata, ipidilkat
bipolarize (v), ipidilkarst, ipidilokato, ipidilkato
bird (n), flazhen, felaruzha, flarzh
Birmingham (n), Birmingarme, Biromingama,
    Birmingam
birth (n), vashil, valesha, valsh
birth (v), vashisle, valesho, valsho
birthday (n), vashilviurl, valesheviula, valshviul
biscuit (n), priart, periata, priat
bishop (n), pofan, panifa, panf
Bismuth (n davoka), Erop, Erop, Erop
Bismuth (n), Bishmuth, Bishemutha, Bishmuth
bit (n d:part), plurt, peluta, plut
bit (v pa d:chew), gairskyot, gaikio, gaikio
bite (n d:chew), gairk, gaika, gaik
bite (v d:chew), gairsk, gaiko, gaiko
biter (n doer d:chew), gairkwan, gaikua, gaikua
bitter (adj), gaiforku, gaifiku, gaifku
bitterly (adv), gaiforkiu, gaifikiu, gaifkiu
bitterness (n), gaifork, gaifika, gaifk
black (adj), brilku, beriku, briku
black (n), brilk, berika, brik
blackboard (n), brilkplok, berikepelorika, brikplork
blacken (v), brilsk, beriko, briko
bladder (n), flashp, felateka, flatek
blade (n), prulat, peruta, pruat
blame (n), trupaf, terufipa, trufp
blame (v), trupasf, terufipo, trufpo
bland (adj), leirnu, leinu, leinu
blank (n), primat, periloma, prilm
blank (v), primast, perilomo, prilmo
blanket (n), primart, perilomapa, prilmap
blanket (v), primarst, perilomapo, prilmapo
blast (n), krairge, keraiga, kraig
blast (v), krairzge, keraigo, kraigo
blaster (n doer), krairgwan, keraigua, kraigua
blaze (n), kraurge, kerauga, kraug
blaze (v), kraurzge, keraugo, kraugo
bleach (n), bleirfk, beleifeka, bleifk
bleach (v), bleirfsk, beleifeko, bleifko
bleak (adj), briurtu, beriutu, briutu
bleakness (n), briurt, beriuta, briut
bleed (v), lilsf, lirodo, lirdo
bleeder (n doer), lilfwan, lirodua, lirdua
blemish (n), tikoarme, tikoama, tikoam
blemish (v), tikoarzme, tikoamo, tikoamo
blend (n), prudak, perufita, pruft
blend (v), prudask, perufito, prufto
blender (n doer), prudakwan, perufitua, pruftua
bless (n), fushar, sherefa, shref

bless (v), fushasre, sherefo, shrefo
blew (v pa d:air), flausnyot, feraushio, fraushio
blind (n), fronat, feralina, fraln
blind (v), fronast, feralino, fralno
blink (n), kuiforp, kuifopa, kuifp
blink (v), kuiforsp, kuifopo, kuifpo
blinker (n doer), kuiforpwan, kuifopua, kuifpua
bloc (n), blirak, beliroka, blirk
block (n d:barrier), biral, belira, blir
block (n d:cube), vokar, veroka, vrok
block (v d:barrier), birasle, beliro, bliro
blocker (n doer d:barrier), biralwan, belirua, blirua
blocky (adj d:cube), vokaru, veroku, vroku
blond (adj), frairmu, feraimu, fraimu
blond (n), frairme, feraima, fraim
blonde (n doer), frairmwan, feraimua, fraimua
blood (n), lilf, liroda, lird
bloodily (adv), lilfiu, lirodiu, lirdiu
bloody (adj), lilfu, lirodu, lirdu
bloom (n), triunf, teriuna, triun
bloom (v), triunsf, teriuno, triuno
bloomer (n doer), triunfwan, teriunua, triunua
bloop (v), triorsk, terioripo, triorpo
blooper (n doer), triorkwan, terioripua, triorpua
blooper (n doer), triork, terioripa, triorp
blossom (n), treilaf, tereilafa, treilf
blossom (v), treilasf, tereilafo, treilfo
blot (n), prauft, perauta, praut
blot (v), praufst, perauto, prauto
blotter (n doer), prauftwan, perautua, prautua
blouse (n), traurf, teraufa, trauf
blow (n d:impact), blurk, beluka, bluk
blow (v d:air), flausne, ferausho, frausho
blower (n doer d:air), flaunwan, feraushua,
    fraushua
blowout (n), blurkuil, belukuila, blukuil
blowtorch (n), flaunkiorshk, feraushekioshika,
    fraushkioshk
blowtorch (v), flaunkiorshsk, feraushekioshiko,
    fraushkioshko
blubber (n), klivarth, kellvatha, klivath
blubbery (adj), klivarthu, kelivathu, klivathu
bludgeon (v), krelfsk, kereliko, krelko
blue (adj), frulmu, ferumu, frumu
blue (n), frulme, feruma, frum
blueberry (n), frunepul, ferunelipa, frunelp
bluff (n), flenirp, felenipa, flenp
bluff (v), flenirsp, felenipo, flenpo
bluffer (n doer), flenirpwan, felenipua, flenpua
blunder (n), fnoirp, fenoipa, fnoip
blunder (v), fnoirsp, fenoipo, fnoipo
blunt (adj), fneirpu, fencipu, fneipu
blunt (v), fneirsp, feneipo, fneipo
bluntly (adv), fneirpiu, feneipiu, fneipiu
blur (n), fnaurn, fenauna, fnaun
blur (v), fnaursne, fenauno, fnauno
blurb (n), frauft, ferauta, fraut
blurb (v), fraufst, ferauto, frauto
blurrily (adv), fnaurniu, fenauniu, fnauniu
blurry (adj), fnaurnu, fenaunu, fnaunu
blurt (v), fnaurst, fenauto, fnauto
blush (n), fruthk, ferutha, fruth
blush (v), fruthsk, ferutho, frutho

bluster (n), bruafk, beruaka, bruak
bluster (v), bruafsk, beruako, bruako
blustery (adj), bruafku, beruaku, bruaku
boar (n), heiguark, heiguaka, heiguak
board (n d:Enter ship), glorif, gelorifa, glorf
board (n d:wood), plok, pelorika, plork
board (v d:Enter ship), glorisf, gelorifo, glorfo
board (v d:wood), plosk, peloriko, plorko
boarder (n doer d:Enter ship), glorifwan, gelorifua, glorfua
boast (n), diurp, diupa, diup
boast (v), diursp, diupo, diupo
boaster (n doer), diurpwan, diupua, diupua
boat (n), shkorbe, shekoba, shkob
boat (v), shkorzbe, shekobo, shkobo
boater (n doer), shkorbwan, shekobua, shkobua
bob (n), shlurnk, shelunika, shlunk
bob (v), shlurnsk, sheluniko, shlunko
bobber (n doer), shlurnkwan, shelunikua, shlunkua
bobcat (n), shufierf, shufiefa, shufief
bode (v), laursf, laufo, laufo
bodily (adj), shlardu, sheladu, shladu
body (n), shlarde, shelada, shlad
bog (n), blaump, belauma, blaum
bog (v), blaumesp, belaumo, blaumo
boggle (v), bliarsk, beliako, bliako
bogus (adj), bliurku, beliuku, bliuku
Bohrium (n davoka), Inak, Inak, Inak
Bohrium (n), Borium, Boriuma, Borium
boil (n d:evaporation), tialf, tiala, tial
boil (n d:infection), toirsh, toira, toir
boil (v d:evaporation), tialsf, tialo, tialo
boiler (n doer d:evaporation), tialfwan, tialua, tialua
bold (adj d:make), gauvirdu, gavudu, gavdu
boldly (adv d:make), gauvirdiu, gavudiu, gavdiu
boldness (n d:make), gauvirde, gavuda, gavd
bolster (n), korfk, kofika, kofk
bolster (v), korfsk, kofiko, kofko
bolt (n), kiurp, kiupa, kiup
bolt (v), kiursp, kiupo, kiupo
bomb (n), vibal, viluba, vilb
bomb (v), vibasle, vilubo, vilbo
bombard (v), vibarsk, vibako, vibako
bombardment (n), vibark, vibaka, vibak
bomber (n doer), vibalwan, vilubua, vilbua
bond (n), vimorl, vilama, vilm
bond (v), vimorsle, vilamo, vilmo
bondage (n), vimorlak, vilamaka, vilmak
bonder (n doer), vimorlwan, vilamua, vilmua
bondholder (n doer), vilmthorthkwan, vilamethorithua, vilmthorthua
bone (n), toirk, toika, toik
boneless (adj), toirkmenu, toikomenu, toikmenu
bonfire (n), shriaushk, giaufika, giaufk
bong (n d:pipe), groizhge, geroiga, groig
bong (n d:sound), fnaup, felaupa, flaup
bong (v d:sound), fnausp, felaupo, flaupo
bonily (adv), toirkiu, toikiu, toikiu
bonk (n), diunk, beriumopa, briump
bonk (v), diunsk, beriumopo, briumpo
Bonn (n), Born, Bona, Bon
bonnet (n), kruth, gelufipa, glufp

bonus (n), vanirl, valana, valn
bony (adj), toirku, toiku, toiku
boo (interj), bau, bau, bau
boo (n), baushk, bauka, bauk
boo (v), baushsk, bauko, bauko
boob (n), bloifp, beloipa, bloip
booer (n doer), baushkwan, baukua, baukua
book (n), vornt, vonuda, vond
book (v), vornst, vonudo, vondo
bookcase (n), vorntshuart, vonudeshuata, vondshuat
bookend (n), vorndairk, vonudaika, vondaik
bookkeeper (n doer), vorntklorfwan, vonudekelofua, vondklofua
bookkeeping (n), vorntklorf, vonudekelofa, vondklof
booklet (n), vorntap, vonudapa, vondap
bookmaker (n doer), vorntenargwan, vonudenagua, vondenagua
bookmaking (n), vorntenarge, vonudenaga, vondenag
booksale (n), vorntrelirf, vonuterelifa, vontrelf
bookseller (n doer), vorntrelirfwan, vonuterelifua, vontrelfua
bookshelf (n), vorntenalirf, vonudenalifa, vondenalf
bookshop (n), vornthorve, vonudathova, vondathov
bookshopper (n doer), vornthorvwan, vonudathovua, vondathovua
bookstore (n), vorndralp, vonuderapa, vondrap
boolean (adj), avairku, avainu, avainu
boolean (n), avairk, avaina, avain
boom (n), riurn, riuna, riun
boom (v), riursne, riuno, riuno
boomerang (n), treltoishk, terelatoita, treltoit
boon (n), biurth, biutha, biuth
boondocks (n), trefdarve, terefudava, trefdav
boondoggle (n), biukarn, biukana, biukan
boost (n), diurshk, diushoka, diushk
boost (v), diurshsk, diushoko, diushko
booster (n doer), diurshkwan, diushokua, diushkua
boot (n), tukat, turita, turt
boot (v), tukast, turito, turto
booth (n), turshk, turisha, tursh
border (n), tanak, tarina, tarn
border (v), tanask, tarino, tarno
borderline (n), tanakroif, tarineroifa, tarnroif
bore (n d:hole), krilet, kerita, krit
bore (n doer d:tiresome), gebarwan, gerubua, gerbua
bore (v d:hole), krilest, kerito, krito
bore (v d:tiresome), gebasre, gerubo, gerbo
bore (v pa d:endure), kriazgyot, gerukio, grukio
boredom (n d:tiresome), gebar, geruba, gerb
borer (n doer d:hole), kriletwan, keritua, kritua
Boron (n davoka), Ekap, Ekap, Ekap
Boron (n), Boron, Borona, Boron
borrow (v), kripasle, kerilapo, krilpo
borrower (n doer), kripalwan, kerilapua, krilpua
bosom (n), kothark, kothara, kothar
boss (n), giart, giata, giat
boss (v), giarst, giato, giato
bossy (adj), giartu, giatu, giatu
Boston (n), Boshtorn, Boshetona, Boshton

botanical (adj), mashiarthu, mashiathu, mashiathu
botany (n), mashiarth, mashiatha, mashiath
botch (v), dausharsk, daushiko, daushko
both (adj/conj), peirsh, peishu, peish
both (pron), peirsh, peishei, peish
bother (n), vazhat, vazhada, vazhd
bother (v), vazhast, vazhado, vazhdo
bottle (n), portan, ponita, pont
bottle (v), portasne, ponito, ponto
bottler (n doer), portanwan, ponitua, pontua
bottom (n), penort, peshota, pesht
bottom (v), penorst, peshoto, peshto
bough (n), shmirk, shemika, shmik
bought (v pa), diopasryot, dioripio, diorpio
boulder (n), kumirp, kumipa, kump
boulevard (n), bulvart, bulivata, bulvat
bounce (n), paunirf, paunifa, paunf
bounce (v), paunirsf, paunifo, paunfo
bouncer (n doer), paunirfwan, paunifua, paunfua
bouncily (adv), paunirfiu, paunifiu, paunfiu
bouncy (adj), paunirfu, paunifu, paunfu
bound (adj d:constrain), paupimu, paumubu, paumbu
bound (adj d:move), draifpu, deraipu, draipu
bound (n d:limit), paupirme, paurimuba, paurmb
bound (v d:move), draifsp, deraipo, draipo
bound (v pa d:constrain), paupizmyot, paumubio, paumbio
boundary (n d:limit), paupirme, paurimuba, paurmb
boundless (adj), paupirmenu, paurimubenu, paurmbenu
bountiful (adj), vailartu, vailatu, vailtu
bounty (n), vailart, vailata, vailt
bouquet (n), kaithuf, kaitha, kaith
bout (n), vierp, veipa, veip
boutique (n), dilarth, dilatha, dilath
bow (n d:bend), diarf, diafa, diaf
bow (n d:front), tiarme, tiama, tiam
bow (v d:bend), diarsf, diafo, diafo
bow-wow (interj), rayu-rayu, rayu-rayu, rayu-rayu
bowel (n), fufarth, fufatha, fufath
bowl (n d:ball), tairak, tairoka, tairk
bowl (n d:container, bend), painar, pairona, pairn
bowl (v d:ball), tairask, tairoko, tairko
bowl (v d:container, bend), painasre, pairono, pairno
bowler (n doer d:ball), tairakwan, tairokua, tairkua
box (n d:cube), prekun, perenika, prenk
box (n d:fight), kroishk, keroiga, kroig
box (v d:cube), prekusne, pereniko, prenko
box (v d:fight), kroishsk, keroigo, kroigo
boxer (n doer d:fight), kroishkwan, keroigua, kroigua
boxy (adj d:cube), prekunu, pereniku, prenku
boy (n), biurn, biuna, biun
boycott (n), daufrauthk, dauferautha, daufrauth
boycott (v), daufrauthsk, dauferautho, daufrautho
boycotter (n doer), daufrauthkwan, dauferauthua, daufrauthua
boyfriend (n), biunk, biunetha, biunt
boyhood (n), biurnfif, biunefifa, biunfif
boyish (adj), biurnu, biunu, biunu

bozo (n), duisht, duika, duik
bra (n), freth, ferafa, fraf
brace (n), ploift, peloita, ploit
brace (v), ploifst, peloito, ploito
bracelet (n), ploifer, peloifa, ploif
bracer (n doer), ploiftwan, peloitua, ploitua
bracket (n), ploiftark, peloitaka, ploitak
bracket (v), ploiftarsk, peloitako, ploitako
brag (n), florf, felava, flav
brag (v), florsf, felavo, flavo
braid (n), thraume, theraupa, thraup
braid (v), thrauzme, theraupo, thraupo
braider (n doer), thraumwan, theraupua, thraupua
braille (n), prifp, peripa, prip
brain (n), fnaifk, fenaiga, fnaig
brainchild (n), fnaifkluart, fenaigeluara, fnaigluar
brainless (adj), fnaifkmenu, fenaigemenu, fnaigmenu
brainpower (n), fnaifkbiorat, fenaigebiorita, fnaigbiort
brainstorm (n), fnaifguvart, fenaiguvata, fnaiguvat
brainstorm (v), fnaifguvarst, fenaiguvato, fnaiguvato
brainwash (v), fnaifkefiaus, fenaigefiausho, fnaigefiausho
brainwave (n), fnaifklersh, fenaigesha, fnaiglesh
brainy (adj), fnaifku, fenaigu, fnaigu
braise (v), thraufst, therauto, thrauto
braiser (n doer), thrauftwan, therautua, thrautua
braiser (n), thrauft, therauta, thraut
brake (n), blakir, belarika, blark
brake (v), blakisre, belariko, blarko
bramble (n), blamiark, belamiaka, blamiak
bramble (v), blamiarsk, belamiako, blamiako
bran (n), blarth, belatha, blath
branch (n), molsh, shumolifa, shmolf
branch (v), mols, shumolifo, shmolfo
brancher (n doer), molshwan, shumolifua, shmolfua
brand (n), fnairp, fenaipa, fnaip
brand (v), fnairsp, fenaipo, fnalpo
brandish (v), fnaifst, fenaito, fnaito
brash (adj), draufku, deraufu, draufu
brashly (adv), draufkiu, deraufiu, draufiu
brashness (n), draufk, deraufa, drauf
brass (n), krailf, keraila, krail
brassy (adj), krailfu, kerailu, krailu
brat (n), drairge, deraiga, draig
brave (adj), daifortu, daifotu, daiftu
brave (n doer), daifortwan, daifotua, daiftua
brave (v), daiforst, daifoto, daifto
bravery (n), daifort, daifota, daift
bravo (interj), dovai, dovai, dovai
brawl (n), glaurt, gelauta, glaut
brawl (v), glaurst, gelauto, glauto
brawn (n), glauthk, gelautha, glauth
brazen (adj), krailfku, kerailaku, krailku
brazenly (adv), krailfkiu, kerailakiu, krailkiu
Brazil (n), Brazhilf, Berazhila, Brazhil
Brazilian (n), Brazhilarn, Berazhilana, Brazhilan
breach (n), krishk, kerisha, krish
breach (v), krishsk, kerisho, krisho
bread (n), thraf, thafa, thaf

bread (v), thrasf, thafo, thafo
breadth (n), doibar, doruba, dorb
breadwinner (n), gliazhirk, geliazhika, gliazhik
break (n), blerk, pelika, plik
break (v), blersk, peliko, pliko
breakable (adj), blerku, peliku, pliku
breakably (adv), blerkiu, pelikiu, plikiu
breakage (n), blerkar, pelikara, plikar
breakaway (n), blerkopiorl, pelikopiola, plikopiol
breakdown (n), plitiern, pelitiena, plitien
breaker (n doer), blerkwan, pelikua, plikua
breakfast (n), hemniert, henieta, heniet
breakfast (v), hemnierst, henieto, henieto
breakout (n), blerkuil, pelikuila, plikuil
breakpoint (n), blerktaifort, peliketaifota, pliktaift
breakthrough (n), plitelsharn, peliteloshana,
    plitelshan
breakup (n), blerkive, pelifoka, plifk
breakup (v), blerkizve, pelifoko, plifko
breakwater (n), blerkeidorn, pelikeidona, plikeidon
breast (n), thalk, nalitha, nalth
breastfeed (v), thalkparzve, nalithepavo, nalthpavo
breastplate (n), thalkfkarf, nalithefikafa, nalthfkaf
breath (n), lavap, lashipa, lashp
breathable (adj), lavapfrelpu, lashipeferepu,
    lashpfrepu
breathe (v), lavasp, lashipo, lashpo
breather (n doer), lavapwan, lashipua, lashpua
breathily (adv), lavapiu, lashipiu, lashpiu
breathtaking (adj), lavapgorku, lashipegoku,
    lashpgoku
breathtakingly (adv), lavapgorkiu, lashipegokiu,
    lashpgokiu
breathy (adj), lavapu, lashipu, lashpu
breech (n), froift, feroita, froit
breed (n), fleirde, feleida, fleid
breed (v), fleirzde, feleido, fleido
breeder (n doer), fleirdwan, feleidua, fleidua
breeze (n), fleirf, feleifa, fleif
breeze (v), fleirsf, feleifo, fleifo
breezy (adj), fleirfu, feleifu, fleifu
brevity (n), thoishtar, thoitara, thoitar
brew (n), garfk, gelafika, gelfk
brew (v), garfsk, gelafiko, gelfko
brewer (n doer), garfkwan, gelafikua, gelfkua
brewery (n), garfkuift, gelafikuita, gelfkuit
bribe (n), kialork, kialoka, kialk
bribe (v), kialorsk, kialoko, kialko
briber (n doer), kialorkwan, kialokua, kialkua
bribery (n), kialofirk, kialofika, kialfk
brick (n), paltk, palika, palk
brick (v), palfsk, paliko, palko
bricklayer (n doer), palfkwan, palikua, palkua
bridal (adj), dushanu, durishu, durshu
bride (n), dushan, durisha, dursh
bridegroom (n), duadeirge, duredeiga, durdeig
bridesmaid (n), duakelerf, durekelera, durkeler
bridge (n), ploshk, pelosha, plosh
bridge (v), ploshsk, pelosho, plosho
bridle (n), thraunk, therauna, thraun
bridle (v), thraunsk, therauno, thrauno
brief (adj), thoishtu, thoitu, thoitu
brief (n), thoisht, thoita, thoit

brief (v), thoishst, thoito, thoito
briefcase (n), thiufshuart, thiufeshuata, thiufshuat
briefly (adv), thoishtiu, thoitiu, thoitiu
bright (adj), shflinu, felinu, flinu
brighten (v), shflisne, felino, flino
brightener (n doer), shflinwan, felinua, flinua
brighter (adj), shflinwelu, felinwelu, flinwelu
brightest (adj), shflinwaku, felinwaku, flinwaku
brightly (adv), shfliniu, feliniu, fliniu
brightness (n), shflin, felina, flin
brilliance (n), shflun, feluna, flun
brilliant (adj), shflunu, felunu, flunu
brilliantly (adv), shfluniu, feluniu, fluniu
brim (n), kroilf, keroila, kroll
brim (v), kroilsf, keroilo, kroilo
brimmer (n doer), kroilfwan, keroilua, kroilua
bring (v), flifst, felito, flito
brink (n), shkavat, shelata, shlat
bristle (n), biethk, bietha, bieth
bristle (v), biethsk, bietho, bietho
Britain (n), Britairn, Beritaina, Britain
British (n), Britirsh, Beritisha, British
brittle (adj), priarku, periaku, priaku
brittle (v), priarsk, periako, priako
brittleness (n), priark, periaka, priak
broach (n), gleiark, geleiaka, gleiak
broach (v), gleiarsk, geleiako, gleiako
broad (adj), doibaru, dorubu, dorbu
broadcast (n), dorbirde, dorebida, dorbid
broadcast (v pa), dorbirzdyot, dorebidio, dorbidio
broadcast (v), dorbirzde, dorebido, dorbido
broadcaster (n doer), dorbirdwan, dorebidua,
    dorbidua
broaden (v), doibasre, dorubo, dorbo
broader (adj), doibarwelu, dorubwelu, dorbwelu
broadest (adj), doirbarwaku, dorubwaku, dorbwaku
broadly (adv), doibariu, dorubiu, dorbiu
Broadway (n), Brodwairn, Berodwaina, Brodwain
brochure (n), viethk, vietha, vieth
broil (v), biuzge, beriugo, briugo
broiler (n doer), biugwan, beriugua, briugua
broke (v pa), blerskyot, pelikio, plikio
broker (n doer), krolirpwan, kerolipua, krolpua
broker (v), krolirsp, kerolipo, krolpo
brokerage (n), krolirp, kerolipa, krolp
brokeup (v pa), blerkizvyot, pelifokio, plifkio
Bromine (n davoka), Efak, Efak, Efak
Bromine (n), Bromin, Beromina, Bromin
bronco (n), bokart, bokata, bokat
bronze (n), floizhe, beloizha, bloizh
bronze (v), floizo, beloizho, bloizho
brood (n), gleiurp, geleiupa, gleiup
brood (v), gleiursp, geleiupo, gleiupo
brook (n), glanirn, gelanina, glanin
brooklike (adj), glanirnu, gelaninu, glaninu
Brooklyn (n), Bruklirn, Berukelina, Bruklin
broom (n), plaifk, pelaifa, plaif
broth (n), gluthk, gelutha, gluth
brother (n), klufade, kelufota, kluft
brotherhood (n), klufadfif, kelufotefifa, kluftfif
brotherly (adj), klufadu, kelufotu, kluftu
brought (v pa), flifstyot, felitio, flitio
brow (n), florde, pelorita, plort

brow (v), florzde, pelorito, plorto
brown (adj), thelmu, thamu, thamu
brown (n), thelme, thama, tham
brown (v), thelzme, thamo, thamo
browse (n), valbaf, velipa, velp
browse (v), valbasf, velipo, velpo
browser (n doer), valbafwan, velipua, velpua
bruise (n), plaurk, pelauka, plauk
bruise (v), plaursk, pelauko, plauko
bruiser (n doer), plaurkwan, pelaukua, plaukua
brunt (n), klauarp, kelauapa, klauap
brush (n d:bristle handle), klurf, kelusha, klush
brush (n d:shrub), gruashk, geruasha, gruash
brush (v d:bristle handle), klursf, kelusho, klusho
brusher (n doer d:bristle handle), klurfwan,
   kelushua, klushua
Brussels (n), Brushelf, Berushela, Brushel
brutal (adj), klaurtshu, kelauteshu, klautshu
brutality (n), klaurtsh, kelautesha, klautsh
brutalize (v), klaurts, kelautesho, klautsho
brutally (adv), klaurtshiu, kelauteshiu, klautshiu
brute (n doer), klaurtshwan, kelauteshua, klautshua
Bs (let pl), bali, bali, bali
bubble (n), dupal, dulipa, dulp
bubble (v), dupasle, dulipo, dulpo
bubbler (n doer), dupalwan, dulipua, dulpua
bubbly (adj), dupalu, dulipu, dulpu
buck (n doer), gairpwan, gaipua, gaipua
buck (n), gairsp, gaipa, gaip
buck (v), gairsp, gaipo, gaipo
bucket (n), gaitak, gelaita, glait
buckle (n), keiarp, keiapa, keiap
buckle (v), keiarsp, keiapo, keiapo
buckler (n doer), keiarpwan, keiapua, keiapua
bud (n d:plant), poarp, poapa, poap
bud (v d:plant), poarsp, poapo, poapo
Buddha (n), Budirn, Budina, Budin
Buddhism (n), Budirnuet, Budinueta, Budinuet
Buddhist (n), Budirnwan, Budinua, Budinua
buddy (n), freilarsh, fereilasha, freilash
budge (n), verde, veluda, veld
budge (v), verzde, veludo, veldo
budget (n), vekarl, velika, velk
budget (v), vekarsle, veliko, velko
budgetary (adj), vekarlu, veliku, velku
buff (n d:rub), bursh, bulesha, bulsh
buff (v d:rub), burs, bulesho, bulsho
Buffalo (n), Bufalorn, Bufalona, Bufalon
buffer (n d:absorber), faurf, faufa, fauf
buffer (n doer d:rub), burshwan, buleshua, bulshua
buffer (v d:absorber), faursf, faufo, faufo
buffet (n d:food/ table), deimurth, deimutha,
   deimuth
buffet (n d:strike), shaurf, shaufa, shauf
buffet (v d:strike), shaursf, shaufo, shaufo
bug (n), verzhe, vezha, vezh
bug (v), verze, vezho, vezho
buggy (adj), verzhu, vezhu, vezhu
bugle (n), dalirde, dalida, dalid
build (n), vorat, vorita, vort
build (v), vorast, vorito, vorto
builder (n doer), voratwan, voritua, vortua
buildup (n), vorativeil, voritiveila, vortiveil

built (v pa), vorastyot, voritio, vortio
builtin (adj), vortirshu, voritishu, vortishu
bulb (n), moiabe, moiba, moib
Bulgaria (n), Bulgarf, Bulogara, Bulgar
Bulgarian (n), Bulgariarn, Bulogariana, Bulgarian
bulge (n), moiage, moiga, moig
bulge (v), moiazge, moigo, moigo
bulk (adj), kleirpu, keleipu, kleipu
bulk (n), kleirp, keleipa, kleip
bulk (v), kleirsp, keleipo, kleipo
bulkhead (n), kleipkefirt, keleipekefita, kleipkeft
bulky (adj), kleiparfu, keleipafu, kleipafu
bull (n), deirf, deifa, deif
bull (v), deirsf, deifo, deifo
bulldoze (v), bribarsk, beribako, bribako
bulldozer (n doer), bribarkwan, beribakua,
   bribakua
bullet (n), deifat, deifita, deift
bulletin (n), feitun, teriefa, trief
bulletproof (adj), deifatfliorfu, deifitefeliofu,
   deiftfliofu
bulletproof (v), deifatfliorsf, deifitefeliofo,
   deiftfliofo
bullhorn (n), drilaurk, derilauka, drilauk
bullion (n), deifiarn, deifiana, deifian
bullish (adj), deirfu, deifu, deifu
bully (n doer), deirfwan, deifua, deifua
bully (v), deifwask, deifuako, deifuako
bum (n doer), kuargwan, kuagua, kuagua
bum (v), kuarzge, kuago, kuago
bumble (n d:bungle), klauthk, kelautha, klauth
bumble (n d:buzz), dubal, dubana, duban
bumble (v d:bungle), klauthsk, kelautho, klautho
bumble (v d:buzz), dubasle, dubano, dubano
bumbler (n doer d:bungle), klauthkwan, kelauthua,
   klauthua
bummer (n), kuarge, kuaga, kuag
bump (n), plopor, peloripa, plorp
bump (v), plopossre, peloripo, plorpo
bumper (n doer), ploporwan, peloripua, plorpua
bumpily (adv), ploporlu, peloripiu, plorpiu
bumpy (adj), ploporu, peloripu, plorpu
bun (n), dranf, derana, dran
bunch (n), vipun, vinopa, vinp
bunch (v), vipusne, vinopo, vinpo
bunchy (adj), vipunu, vinopu, vinpu
bundle (n), vikun, vinoka, vink
bundle (v), vikusne, vinoko, vinko
bundler (n doer), vikunwan, vinokua, vinkua
bungie (n), boirf, boifa, boif
bungie (v), boirsf, boifo, boifo
bungle (n), boifp, boipa, boip
bungle (v), boifsp, boipo, boipo
bunk (n d:bed), glemirp, gelemipa, glemp
bunk (n d:nonsense), glurk, geluka, gluk
bunk (v d:bed), glemirsp, gelemipo, glempo
bunker (n), greiark, gereiaka, greiak
bunny (n), drilarn, derilana, drilan
bunt (n), glart, gelata, glat
bunt (v), glarst, gelato, glato
buoy (n doer), gulirtwan, gulitua, gultua
buoy (v), gulirst, gulito, gulto
buoyancy (n), gulirt, gulita, gult

buoyant (adj), gulirtu, gulitu, gultu
buoyantly (adv), gulirtiu, gulitiu, gultiu
bur (n), farzhe, fazha, fazh
burden (n), diark, diaka, diak
burden (v), diarsk, diako, diako
burdensome (adj), diarku, diaku, diaku
bureau (n), deinor, deirina, deirn
bureaucracy (n), deinorfk, deiroferalita, deirfralt
bureaucrat (n doer), deinorfkwan, deiroferalitua, deirfraltua
bureaucratic (adj), deinorfku, deiroferalitu, deirfraltu
bureaucratically (adv), deinorfkiu, deiroferalitiu, deirfraltiu
burger (n), grimarn, gerimana, griman
burglar (n doer), dolfkwan, dolikua, dolkua
burglarize (v), dolfsk, doliko, dolko
burglary (n), dolfk, dolika, dolk
burgle (v), dolfsk, doliko, dolko
burial (n), paulop, pauripa, paurp
burlap (n), larmirk, laramika, larmik
Burlington (n), Burlingtorn, Buralingatona, Burlington
burn (n), bugor, beruga, brug
burn (v), bugosre, berugo, brugo
burner (n doer), bugorwan, berugua, brugua
burnish (v), bugorast, berugato, brugato
burnout (n), bugoruil, beruguila, bruguil
burnt (v pa), bugosryot, berugio, brugio
burp (n), glurp, gelupa, glup
burp (v), glursp, gelupo, glupo
burper (n doer), glurpwan, gelupua, glupua
burro (n), franuf, feranifa, franf
burrow (n), litef, lilota, lilt
burrow (v), litesf, liloto, lilto
burrower (n doer), litefwan, lilotua, liltua
burst (n), brutap, berushota, brusht
burst (v pa), brutaspyot, berushotio, brushtio
burst (v), brutasp, berushoto, brushto
bury (v), paulosp, pauripo, paurpo
bus (n), tugef, tufika, tufk
bus (v), tugesf, tufiko, tufko
buses (n pl), tugefyek, tufiki, tufki
bush (n), perf, pefa, pef
bushel (n), perft, pefita, peft
bushel (v), perfst, pefito, pefto
bushy (adj), perfu, pefu, pefu
busily (adv), voirshiu, voishiu, voishiu
business (n), voirshk, voishika, voishk
businesslike (adj), voirshku, voishiku, voishku
businessman (n doer), voirshkwan, voishikua, voishkua
businessperson (n doer), voirshkwan, voishikua, voishkua
bust (n d:burst), doirshk, doishoka, doishk
bust (n d:sculpture), luirme, luima, luim
bust (v d:burst), doirshsk, doishoko, doishko
buster (n doer d:burst), doirshkwan, doishokua, doishkua
bustle (n), doikurp, doikupa, doikup
bustle (v), doikursp, doikupo, doikupo
busy (adj), voirshu, voishu, voishu
busy (v), voirs, voisho, voisho

busyness (n), voirsh, voisha, voish
but (adv/conj/prep), vede, vedu, ved
butcher (n doer), danfkwan, danikua, dankua
butcher (v), danfsk, daniko, danko
butchery (n), danfk, danika, dank
butler (n), kufiarn, kufiana, kufian
butt (n d:end/ rump), blunshk, belunika, blunk
butt (n d:strike), blaishk, belaika, blaik
butt (v d:strike), blaishsk, belaiko, blaiko
butter (n), filurf, filofa, filf
butter (v), filursf, filofo, filfo
butterfly (n), flushok, filushoka, flushk
buttery (adj), filurfu, filofu, filfu
buttocks (n d:end/ rump), blunshk, belunika, blunk
button (n), domat, dofita, doft
button (v), domast, dofito, dofto
buttoner (n doer), domatwan, dofitua, doftua
buy (n), diopar, dioripa, diorp
buy (v), diopasre, dioripo, diorpo
buyer (n doer), dioparwan, dioripua, diorpua
buyout (n), dioparuil, dioripuila, diorpuil
buzz (adj d:haircut), parzhu, pazhu, pazhu
buzz (n d:haircut), parzhe, pazha, pazh
buzz (n d:hum), zharzhe, zhazha, zhazh
buzz (v d:haircut), parze, pazho, pazho
buzz (v d:hum), zharze, zhazho, zhazho
buzzard (n), brizhank, berizhana, brizhan
buzzer (n doer d:hum), zharzhwan, zhazhua, zhazhua
buzzword (n), kizhlialirt, kizhelialita, kizhlialt
buzzy (adj d:hum), zharzhu, zhazhu, zhazhu
by (adj/adv/prep), vu, vu, vu
bye (n/interj), liau, liau, liau
bygone (adj), vuvirfyotu, vuvifiou, vuvifiou
bygone (n), vuvirfyot, vuvifioa, vuvifioa
bygones (n pl), vuvirfyotyek, vuvifioi, vuvifioi
bylaw (n), vuvaurde, vuvauda, vuvaud
byline (n), vuroifk, vuroifa, vuroif
bypass (n), vulunirt, vulunita, vulunt
bypass (v), vulunirst, vulunito, vulunto
bypasser (n doer), vulunirtwan, vulunitua, vuluntua
byproduct (n), vufiurk, vufiuka, vufiuk
bystander (n doer), vutrelirtwan, vuterelitua, vutreltua
byte (n), bairth, baitha, baith
byway (n), vupliorl, vupeliola, vupliol
cab (n), kiorp, kiopa, kiop
cabbage (n), kiopath, kiothipa, kiothp
cabby (n doer), kiorpwan, kiopua, kiopua
cabin (n), kiopume, kiona, kion
cabinet (n), kiopurt, kiorona, kiorn
cable (n), kiopaf, kiofita, kioft
cable (v), kiopasf, kiofito, kiofto
cabler (n doer), kiopafwan, kiofitua, kioftua
caboose (n), bilurk, biluka, biluk
cache (n), larthp, lathipa, lathp
cache (v), larthsp, lathipo, lathpo
cadence (n), piart, piata, piat
cadet (n), neilurn, neiluna, neilun
Cadmium (n davoka), Ilit, Ilit, Ilit
Cadmium (n), Kadmium, Kademiuma, Kadmium
Caesar (n), Shaizhark, Shaizhara, Shaizhar
Caesarean (adj), Shaizharku, Shaizharu, Shaizharu

Caesium (n), Sheshium, Sheshiuma, Sheshium
cafeteria (n), galafk, gialofeta, gialfet
caffeine (n), gulorf, gulova, gulv
café (n), galaf, gialofa, gialf
cage (n), shtiark, shetiaka, shtiak
cage (v), shtiarsk, shetiako, shtiako
cager (n doer), shtiarkwan, shetiakua, shtiakua
cagey (adj), shtiarku, shetiaku, shtiaku
cagily (adv), shtiarkiu, shetiakiu, shtiakiu
Cairo (n), Kairolf, Kairofa, Kairof
cake (n), gutraf, gurita, gurt
cake (v), gutrasf, gurito, gurto
calamitous (adj), tautiarku, tautiaku, tautiaku
calamity (n), tautiark, tautiaka, tautiak
Calcium (n davoka), Afip, Afip, Afip
Calcium (n), Kalshium, Kaleshiuma, Kalshium
calculate (v), gardas, garodako, gardako
calculation (n), gardash, garodaka, gardak
calculator (n doer), gardashwan, garodakua, gardakua
calculus (n), garlot, gariluda, garld
calendar (n), gelnif, gelina, geln
calf (n), nelfk, nelifa, nelf
caliber (n), balirf, balifa, balf
calibrate (v), balforsk, balifoko, balfko
calibration (n), balfork, balifoka, balfk
calibrator (n doer), balforkwan, balifokua, balfkua
calibre (n), balirf, balifa, balf
calico (adj), fiorishku, fiorishu, fiorishu
calico (n), fiorishk, fiorisha, fiorish
California (n), Kaliforan, Kaliforina, Kaliforn
Californium (n davoka), Onit, Onit, Onit
Californium (n), Kalifornium, Kaliforeniuma, Kalifornium
caliper (n), gruarp, geruapa, gruap
call (n), girf, gira, gir
call (v), girsf, giro, giro
callable (adj), girfu, giru, giru
callback (n), girvark, girevafa, girvak
caller (n doer), girfwan, girua, girua
calligraphy (n), gridarfk, giradarifa, gradarf
callous (adj), braiarku, beraiaku, braiaku
callously (adv), braiarkiu, beraiakiu, braiakiu
callousness (n), braiark, beraiaka, braiak
callus (n), fiornk, fionika, fionk
calm (adj), flienku, felienu, flienu
calm (n), flienk, feliena, flien
calm (v), fliensk, felieno, flieno
calmly (adv), flienkiu, felieniu, flieniu
calorie (n), lagelor, laluga, lalg
calve (v), nelfsk, nelifo, nelfo
Cambodia (n), Kambodiarf, Kamubodiafa, Kambodiaf
Cambodian (n), Kambodiarn, Kamubodiana, Kambodian
Cambridge (n), Kambrilge, Kamuberiga, Kambrig
came (v pa), blersfyot, bilefio, blefio
camel (n), greifk, gereifa, greif
cameo (n), lanurt, lanuta, lanut
camera (n), viran, veranita, vrant
cameraperson (n doer), viranwan, veranitua, vrantua
camouflage (n), lianork, lianoka, liank

camouflage (v), lianorsk, lianoko, lianko
camp (n), kitarf, kitafa, kitaf
camp (v), kitarsf, kitafo, kitafo
campaign (n), kitank, kerivuga, krivg
campaign (v), kitansk, kerivugo, krivgo
campaigner (n doer), kitankwan, kerivugua, krivgua
camper (n doer), kitarfwan, kitafua, kitafua
campfire (n), kitafshriauk, kitafegiaula, kitafgiaul
campground (n), kitafbraft, kitafeberanita, kitafbrant
campsite (n), kitafniart, kitafeniata, kitafniat
campus (n), kitalpor, kitaripa, kitarp
can (n d:container), denirp, denipa, denp
can (ndal d:ability), frelp kodi, ferepa kodi, frep kodi
can (v d:container), denirsp, denipo, denpo
Canada (n), Kanadarf, Kanadafa, Kanadaf
Canadian (n), Kanadiarn, Kanadiana, Kanadian
canal (n), tuamak, tuanika, tuank
canard (n), kainurp, kainupa, kainup
canary (n), bitharn, bithana, bithan
cancel (v), demurzbe, demubo, dembo
cancellation (n), demurbe, demuba, demb
cancer (n), dermashk, derumaka, dermak
cancerous (adj), dermashku, derumaku, dermaku
candid (adj), demtoku, demugu, demgu
candidate (n), dempor, demipana, dempan
candle (n), delurme, deluma, delm
candlelight (n), delumfluarn, delumifeluana, delmfluan
candlestick (n), delumshneft, delumeshineta, delmshnet
candy (adj), gutmorlu, gutomolu, gutmolu
candy (n), gutmorl, gutomola, gutmol
candy (v), gutmorsle, gutomolo, gutmolo
cane (n), gutarf, gufita, guft
cane (v), gutarsf, gufito, gufto
canine (adj), gaueshtu, gauetu, gauetu
canine (n), gauesht, gaueta, gauet
canker (adj), fumirpu, tumipu, fumpu
canker (n), fumirp, fumipa, fump
cannon (n), diorame, dioruma, diorm
cannot (ndal d:ability), oir frelp kodi, oi ferepa kodi, oi frep kodi
canoe (n), shamirme, shamima, shamim
canoe (v), shamirzme, shamimo, shamimo
canopy (n), tauirt, tauita, tauit
canvas (n), derfort, derifota, derft
canvas (v), derforst, derifoto, derfto
canyon (n), mirnor, mirana, mirn
cap (n), filp, defipa, defp
cap (v), filsp, defipo, defpo
capability (n), filfret, deferepa, defrep
capable (adj), filfretu, deferepu, defrepu
capacity (n), defrup, dethipa, dethp
cape (n), dafraf, fereifa, freif
caper (n doer), dafrafwan, fereifua, freifua
capital (n), delkal, delika, delk
capitalism (n), delkarl, delikara, delkar
capitalize (v), delkasle, deliko, delko
capitol (n), dentark, denitaka, dentak
capsule (n), pranp, duperana, dupran

captain (n), daiark, daiaka, daiak
captain (v), daiarsk, daiako, daiako
caption (n), deshirp, deshipa, deshp
caption (v), deshirsp, deshipo, deshpo
captivate (v), deshiafirsk, deshiafiko, deshiafko
captivity (n), deshiafirk, deshiafika, deshiafk
capture (n), deshiark, deshiaka, deshiak
capture (v), deshiarsk, deshiako, deshiako
capturer (n doer), deshiarkwan, deshiakua,
    deshiakua
car (n), geral, gerela, grel
caramel (n), moagarn, moagana, moagan
caravan (n), vipoark, vipoaka, vipoak
caravan (v), vipoarsk, vipoako, vipoako
Carbon (n davoka), Ekip, Ekip, Ekip
Carbon (n), Karbon, Karebona, Karbon
carbon dioxide (n), ekip avekupart, ekip avekupat,
    ekip avekupat
carcass (n), viputshk, viputesha, viputsh
card (n), gaurn, kauna, kaun
card (v), gaursne, kauno, kauno
cardboard (adj), gaurploku, kaunupeloriku,
    kaunplorku
cardboard (n), gaurplok, kaunupelorika, kaunplork
cardiac (adj), vanianku, vanianu, vanianu
cardinal (n), kardinalf, karodinala, kardinal
care (n), keirf, keifa, keif
care (v), keirsf, keifo, keifo
careen (v), vikirsk, vikiko, vikiko
career (n), beinor, beirana, beirn
careful (adj), keirfushu, keifushu, keifushu
carefully (adv), keirfushiu, keifushiu, keifushiu
carefulness (n), keirfush, keifusha, keifush
careless (adj), keirfmenu, keifumenu, keifmenu
carelessly (adv), keirfmeniu, keifumeniu, keifmeniu
carelessness (n), keirfmen, keifumena, keifmen
caress (n), vanarth, vanatha, vanth
caress (v), vanarsth, vanatho, vantho
cargo (n), grelvirf, gereluvifa, grelvif
cargo (v), grelvirsf, gereluvifo, grelvifo
Caribbean (n), Karibiarn, Karibiana, Karibian
carnage (n), greishkage, gereikaga, greikag
carnal (adj), greishku, gereiku, greiku
carnation (n), mutharth, muthatha, muthath
carnival (n), muviank, muviana, muvian
carnivore (n), vaiank, vaiana, vaian
carnivorous (adj), vaianku, vaianu, vaianu
carnivorously (adv), vaiankiu, vaianiu, vaianiu
carousel (n), muthiork, muthioka, muthiok
carpenter (n doer), gelmeftwan, gelumenitua,
    gelmentua
carpentry (n), gelmeft, gelumenita, gelment
carpet (n), meft, gelumeta, gelmet
carpet (v), mefst, gelumeto, gelmeto
carport (n), grelbielirk, gerelubielika, grelbielk
carriage (n), gelir, gelila, gelil
carrier (n doer), fludwan, gerenua, grenua
carrot (n), geldif, gelifoka, glifk
carry (n), flude, gerena, gren
carry (v), fluzde, gereno, greno
carryon (n), flurde, gerelina, greln
carsick (adj), grelkergu, gerelukelugu, grelkelgu
carsickness (n), grelkerge, gerelukeluga, grelkelg

cart (n), grenak, gerenika, grenk
cart (v), grenask, gereniko, grenko
cartel (n), greshork, gereshoka, greshk
carter (n doer), grenakwan, gerenikua, grenkua
cartilage (n), taufiasht, taufiata, taufiat
carton (n), dornirk, doranika, dornk
cartoon (n), grenarme, gerenama, grenam
cartridge (n), dienork, dienoka, dienk
carve (n), grefal, gerelifa, grelf
carve (v pa), grefaslyot, gerelifio, grelfio
carve (v), grefasle, gerelifo, grelfo
carver (n doer), grefalwan, gerelifua, grelfua
cascade (n), vinuirn, vinuina, vinuin
cascade (v), vinuirsne, vinuino, vinuino
case (n d:container), shuart, shuata, shuat
case (n d:investigation), shkorf, shikofa, shkof
case (v d:investigation), shkorsf, shikofo, shkofo
caseload (n), shkoflurift, shikofelurita, shkoflurt
cash (n), tuarth, tuatha, tuath
cash (v), tuarsth, tuatho, tuatho
cashier (n doer), tuarthwan, tuathua, tuathua
casino (n), kashirn, kashina, kashin
cask (n), boitshk, boitesha, boitsh
casket (n), boikashk, boikasha, boikash
casserole (n), tathiart, tathiata, tathiat
cassette (n), lashor, larisha, larsh
cast (n), tulirt, tulita, tult
cast (v pa), tulirstyot, tulitio, tultio
cast (v), tulirst, tulito, tulto
castle (n), treivuge, tereiga, treig
castle (v), treivuzge, tereigo, treigo
casual (adj), shkarshku, shikashoku, shkashku
casually (adv), shkarshkiu, shikashokiu, shkashkiu
casualty (n), shkarshk, shikashoka, shkashk
cat (n), fierf, fiefa, fief
catalog (n), fekuift, fikuita, fkuit
catalog (v), fekuifst, fikuito, fkuito
cataloger (n doer), fekuiftwan, fikuitua, fkuitua
catalyst (n), kamarft, kamafita, kamaft
catalytic (adj), kamarftu, kamafitu, kamaftu
catalyze (v), kamarfst, kamafito, kamafto
catalyzer (n doer), kamarftwan, kamafitua,
    kamaftua
catapult (n), kaukiart, kaukiata, kaukiat
catapult (v), kaukiarst, kaukiato, kaukiato
catch (n), karft, kafita, kaft
catch (v), karfst, kafito, kafto
catcher (n doer), karftwan, kafitua, kaftua
catchy (adj), karftu, kafitu, kaftu
categorical (adj), fikorpu, korefipu, krefpu
categorically (adv), fikorpiu, korefipiu, krefpiu
categorize (v), fikorsp, korefipo, krefpo
categorizer (n doer), fikorpwan, korefipua, krefpua
category (n), fikorp, korefipa, krefp
Catholic (n), Gatholige, Gatholiga, Gatholig
cattle (n), fradup, ferashipa, frashp
catty (adj), fierfu, fiefu, fiefu
caught (v pa), karfstyot, kafitio, kaftio
causal (adj), shkarshu, shikashu, shkashu
cause (n), shkarsh, shikasha, shkash
cause (v), shkars, shikasho, shkasho
caution (n), shkarship, shikashipa, shkashp
caution (v), shkarshisp, shikashipo, shkashpo

cautious (adj), shkarshipu, shikashipu, shkashpu
cautiously (adv), shkarshipiu, shikashipiu,
　shkashpiu
cavalry (n), bafiark, bafiaka, bafiak
cave (n), paurge, pauga, paug
cave (v), paurzge, paugo, paugo
caver (n doer), paurgwan, paugua, paugua
cavern (n), paurgil, paugila, paugil
cavitate (v), paurguest, paugueto, paugueto
cavitation (n), paurguet, paugueta, pauguet
cavity (n), paugart, paugata, paugat
cease (v), vetaverst, vetaveto, vetaveto
cease-fire (n), vetashriauk, vetagiaula, vetagiaul
ceil (n), galnaf, girena, girn
ceil (v), galnasf, gireno, girno
celebrate (v), fralisp, feralipo, fralpo
celebration (n), fralip, feralipa, fralp
celebrity (n doer), fralipwan, feralipua, fralpua
cell (n), frath, ferala, fral
cellar (n), fralun, feralika, fralk
cello (n), finuirn, finuina, finuin
cellular (adj), frathu, feralu, fralu
cellularly (adv), frathiu, feraliu, fraliu
Celsius (adj), Shelfian, Shelefiana, Shelfian
cement (n), fralirsh, feralisha, fralsh
cement (v), fralirs, feralisho, fralsho
cemetery (n), kralshork, keralishoka, kralshk
censor (n doer), plashortwan, pelashotua, plashtua
censor (v), plashorst, pelashoto, plashto
censorship (n), plashort, pelashota, plasht
census (n), plafirk, pelafika, plafk
cent (n), litor, lireta, lirt
center (n), lidret, forelita, frelt
center (v), lidrest, forelito, frelto
centigrade (adj), shterfu, shetefu, shtefu
centigrade (n), shterf, shetefa, shtef
centimeter (n), litolimet, liralimeta, lirlimet
central (adj), lidretu, forelitu, freltu
centralization (n), lidretak, forelitaka, freltak
centralize (v), lidretask, forelitako, freltako
centralizer (n doer), lidretakwan, forolitakua,
　freltakua
centrally (adv), lidretiu, forelitiu, freltiu
century (n), litorat, liretata, lirtat
ceramic (adj), muliornu, mulionu, mulionu
ceramic (n), muliorn, muliona, mulion
cereal (n), lenal, leluma, lelm
ceremonial (adj), munaltu, murilu, murlu
ceremonially (adv), munaltiu, muriliu, murliu
ceremony (n), munalt, murila, murl
Cerium (n davoka), Orip, Orip, Orip
Cerium (n), Sherium, Sheriuma, Sherium
certain (adj), zhirtu, zhilotu, zhiltu
certainly (adv), zhirtiu, zhilotiu, zhiltiu
certainty (n), zhirt, zhilota, zhilt
certificate (n), thuntarn, thunitana, thuntan
certification (n), thuntarnk, thunitanoka, thuntank
certifier (n doer), thuntarnwan, thunitanua,
　thuntanua
certify (v), thuntarsne, thunitano, thuntano
Cesium (n davoka), Arap, Arap, Arap
cessation (n), vetavert, vetaveta, vetavet
chafe (v), thaishsk, thaisho, thaisho

chaff (n), bloifk, beloifa, bloif
chain (n), miafk, miaka, miak
chain (v), miafsk, miako, miako
chainsaw (n), miagralzhe, miagerazha, miagrazh
chainsaw (v), miagralze, miagerazho, miagrazho
chair (n d:meeting), brekun, berenika, brenk
chair (n d:seat), klesht, kelenuda, klend
chair (v d:meeting), brekusne, bereniko, brenko
chairman (n doer d:meeting), brekunwan,
　berenikua, brenkua
chairperson (n doer d:meeting), brekunwan,
　berenikua, brenkua
chalk (n), tarsh, terosha, trosh
chalk (v), tars, terosho, trosho
chalkboard (n), tarshplok, teroshepelorika,
　troshplork
challenge (n), dafirk, daifika, daifk
challenge (v), dafirsk, daifiko, daifko
challenger (n doer), dafirkwan, daifikua, daifkua
chamber (n), danirp, danipa, danp
champ (n doer), dafirpwan, dafipua, dafpua
champion (n doer), dafirpwan, dafipua, dafpua
champion (v), dafirsp, dafipo, dafpo
championship (n), dafirp, dafipa, dafp
chance (adj), shmaltu, shemafu, shmafu
chance (n), shmalt, shemafa, shmaf
chance (v), shmalst, shemafo, shmafo
chancel (n), shmeirf, shemeifa, shmeif
chancel (v), shmeirsf, shemeifo, shmeifo
chancellor (n doer), shmeirfwan, shemeifua,
　shmeifua
change (n), tuarn, tuana, tuan
change (v), tuarsne, tuano, tuano
changer (n doer), tuarnwan, tuanua, tuanua
channel (n), tuamat, tuaroma, tuarm
channel (v), tuamast, tuaromo, tuarmo
channeler (n doer), tuamatwan, tuaromua, tuarmua
chant (n), kanirf, kanifa, kanf
chant (v), kanirsf, kanifo, kanfo
chanter (n doer), kanirfwan, kanifua, kanfua
chaos (n), klursh, klusha, kiush
chaotic (adj), kiurshu, kiushu, kiushu
chaotically (adv), kiurshiu, kiushiu, kiushiu
chap (n), thorf, thofipa, thofp
chap (v), thorsf, thofipo, thofpo
chapel (n), thorish, thoripada, thorpad
chapter (n), thortan, thorida, thord
char (n d:burn), braishk, beraisha, braish
char (v d:burn), braishsk, beraisho, braisho
character (n d:symbol), thitor, thilota, thilt
character (n doer d:person), kerbatwan, keribua,
　kribua
characteristic (adj d:person), kerbatu, keribu, kribu
characteristic (n d:person), kerbaft, keribata, kribat
characteristically (adv d:person), kerbatiu, keribiu,
　kribiu
characterization (n d:person), kerbat, keriba, krib
characterize (v d:person), kerbast, keribo, kribo
charcoal (n), braizhganor, beraizhogarina,
　braizhgarn
charge (n), gloift, geloita, gloit
charge (v), gloifst, geloito, gloito
charger (n doer), gloiftwan, geloitua, gloitua

chariot (n), vikuark, vikuaka, vikuak
charitable (adj), loifaru, geloirifu, gloirfu
charitably (adv), loifariu, geloirifiu, gloirfiu
charity (n), loifar, geloirifa, gloirf
Charleston (n), Tsharltorn, Tesharolitona, Tsharlton
Charlotte (n), Sharlort, Sharilota, Sharlot
charm (n), nivube, nilesha, nilsh
charm (v), nivuzbe, nilesho, nilsho
charmer (n doer), nivubwan, nileshua, nilshua
chart (n), tirofk, tiroka, tirk
chart (v), tirofsk, tiroko, tirko
charter (n doer), tirofkwan, tirokua, tirkua
charter (n), tirofkul, tirokula, tirkul
charter (v), tirofkusle, tirokulo, tirkulo
chary (adj d:burn), braishku, beraishu, braishu
chase (n), tutart, tutata, tutat
chase (v), tutarst, tutato, tutato
chaser (n doer), tutartwan, tutatua, tutatua
chasm (n), gaurbe, gauba, gaub
chassis (n), kiashort, kiashota, kiasht
chat (n), thairf, thaifa, thaif
chat (v), thairsf, thaifo, thaifo
chatter (n doer), thairfwan, thaifua, thaifua
chatty (adj), thairfu, thaifu, thaifu
cheap (adj), triufpu, teriupu, triupu
cheapen (v), triufsp, teriupo, triupo
cheaper (adj), triufpwelu, teriupwelu, triupwelu
cheapest (adj), triufpwaku, teriupwaku, triupwaku
cheaply (adv), triufpiu, teriupiu, triupiu
cheapness (n), triufp, teriupa, triup
cheat (n), trulik, teruka, truk
cheat (v), trulisk, teruko, truko
cheater (n doer), trulikwan, terukua, trukua
check (n d:money), piruf, piroda, pird
check (n d:review), ket, keta, ket
check (v d:review), kest, keto, keto
checker (n doer d:review), ketwan, ketua, ketua
checklist (n), ketudilt, ketudita, ketudit
checkmate (n), ketfenshk, ketefenika, ketfenk
checkmate (v), ketfenshsk, ketefeniko, ketfenko
cheek (n), reiafp, reiapa, reiap
cheekbone (n), reiaptoirk, reiaputoika, reiaptoik
cheer (n), bior, biola, biol
cheer (v), biosre, biolo, biolo
cheerful (adj), biorfushu, biorushu, biorushu
cheerfully (adv), biorfushiu, biorushiu, biorushiu
cheerfulness (n), biorfush, biorusha, biorush
cheerily (adv), bioriu, bioliu, bioliu
cheerless (adj), biorfmenu, bioramenu, biormenu
cheerlessly (adv), biortmeniu, bioramenu, biormeniu
cheerlessness (n), biorfmen, bioramena, biormen
cheery (adj), bioru, biolu, biolu
cheese (n), shlorde, sheloda, shlod
cheesy (adj), shlordu, shelodu, shlodu
chef (n), vaishk, vaisha, vaish
chemical (adj), reilarku, reilaku, reilaku
chemical (n), reilark, reilaka, reilak
chemically (adv), reilarkiu, reilakiu, reilakiu
chemist (n doer), reilarkwan, reilakua, reilakua
chemistry (n), reilarfk, reilafika, reilafk
Chernobyl, Tshernobilf, Tesherinobila, Tshernobil

cherry (adj), reirftu, reirotu, reirtu
cherry (n), reirft, reirota, reirt
chest (n d:container), volirk, volika, volk
chest (n d:torso), doarp, doapa, doap
chew (n), triarp, teriapa, triap
chew (v), triarsp, teriapo, triapo
chewer (n doer), triarpwan, teriapua, triapua
chi (n), kairn, kaina, kain
Chicago (n), Tshikarg, Teshikaga, Tshikag
chick (n), klerth, keletha, kleth
chicken (n), klurk, keluka, kluk
chief (adj), vairtu, vaitu, vaitu
chief (n), vairt, vaita, vait
chiefly (adv), vairtiu, vaitiu, vaitiu
child (n), luart, luara, luar
childbirth (n), luartvashil, luaruvalesha, luarvalsh
childcare (n), luartkeirf, luarikeifa, luarkeif
childhood (n), luarfift, luarofifa, luarfif
childish (adj), luartu, luaru, luaru
children (n pl), luartyek, luari, luari
Chile (n), Tshilf, Teshila, Tshil
chill (n), plirf, pelira, plir
chill (v), plirsf, peliro, pliro
chiller (n doer), plirfwan, pelirua, plirua
chilly (adj), plirfu, peliru, pliru
chimney (n), faluk, felufa, fluf
chin (n), plirme, pelima, plim
China (n), Tshinarf, Teshinafa, Tshinaf
Chinese (n), Tshinarsh, Teshinasha, Tshinash
chip (n), duelk, dueka, duek
chip (v), duelsk, dueko, dueko
chipper (n doer), duelkwan, duekua, duekua
chirp (n), tirft, tirita, tirt
chirp (v), tirfst, tirito, tirto
chirper (n doer), tirftwan, tiritua, tirtua
Chlorine (n davoka), Etak, Etak, Etak
Chlorine (n), Klorin, Kelorina, Klorin
chocolate (adj), parlafu, parinofu, parnfu
chocolate (n), parlaf, parinofa, parnf
choice (n), shkluft, shekaluta, shklut
choir (n doer), lorshkwan, lorikua, lorkua
choir (v), lorshsk, loriko, lorko
choke (n), reuishk, reiuka, reiuk
choke (v), reuishsk, reiuko, reiuko
choker (n doer), reuishkwan, reiukua, reiukua
cholesterol (n), kolishtarl, kolishotala, kolishtal
choose (v), shklufst, shekaluto, shkluto
chooser (n doer), shkluftwan, shekalutua, shklutua
choosy (adj), shkluftu, shekalutu, shklutu
chop (n), duairk, duaika, duaik
chop (v), duairsk, duaiko, duaiko
chopper (n doer), duairkwan, duaikua, duaikua
choppily (adv), duairkiu, duaikiu, duaikiu
choppy (adj), duairku, duaiku, duaiku
chopstick (n), duaikshneft, duaikushineta, duiaikshnet
chord (n), frolt, ferota, frot
chore (n), liark, liaka, liak
chorus (n), lorshk, lorika, lork
chose (v pa), shklufstyot, shekalutio, shklutio
Christ (n), Klash, Kelasha, Klash
Christian (n), Klashar, Kelashara, Klarsh
Christmas (n), Klashmarl, Kelashamala, Klashmal

chroma (n), preirth, pereitha, preith
Chromium (n davoka), Ifup, Ifup, Ifup
Chromium (n), Kromium, Keromiuma, Kromium
chronic (adj), friurku, feriuku, friuku
chronically (adv), friurkiu, feriukiu, friukiu
chronicle (n), piarak, piaroka, piark
chronicle (v), piarask, piaroko, piarko
chronograph (n), piardarfk, piarodarifa, piardarf
chronograph (v), piardarfsk, piarodarifo, piardarfo
chronographical (adj), piardarfku, piarodarifu,
    piardarfu
chronographically (adv), piardarfkiu, piarodarifiu,
    piardarfiu
chronological (adj), piarkuiftu, piarokuitu,
    piarkuitu
chronologically (adv), piarkuiftiu, piarokuitiu,
    piarkuitiu
chronology (n), piarkuift, piarokuita, piarkuit
chuck (n d:throw), kruashk, keruasha, kruash
chuck (v d:throw), kruashsk, keruasho, kruasho
chuckle (n d:laugh), klukurt, kelukuta, klukut
chuckle (v d:laugh), klukurst, kelukuto, klukuto
chunk (n), kruanshk, keruanika, kruank
chunky (adj), kruanshku, keruaniku, kruanku
church (n), shrade, sherala, shral
churn (n), grarshk, gerarika, grark
churn (v), grarshsk, gerariko, grarko
churner (n doer), grarshkwan, gerarikua, grarkua
chute (n), flufp, felupa, flup
chute (v), flufsp, felupo, flupo
cianta-, genshkai-, genshkai-, genshkai-
cigar (n), larshk, lashika, lashk
cigarette (n), larshkerf, lashikefa, lashkef
Cincinnati (n), Shinshinart, Shinoshinata,
    Shinshinat
cinema (n), falan, farina, farn
circle (n), valtor, valita, valt
circle (v), valtosre, valito, valto
circuit (n), valtork, valotika, valtik
circuit (v), valtorsk, valotiko, valtiko
circuitry (n), valtirfk, valotifoka, valtifk
circular (adj), valtoru, valitu, valtu
circularly (adv), valtoriu, valitiu, valtiu
circulate (v), valtarst, valitato, valtato
circulation (n), valtart, valitata, valtat
circulator (n doer), valtartwan, valitatua, valtatua
circumference (n), tuagal, taulika, tualk
circumferent (adj), tuagalu, tauliku, tualku
circumstance (n), tualep, tualita, tualt
circumstantial (adj), tualepu, tualitu, tualtu
circus (n), tuashk, tuaka, tuak
citation (n), toirp, toipa, toip
cite (v), toirsp, toipo, toipo
citizen (n), matarn, matana, matan
city (n), shlairt, shelaita, shlait
civil (adj), fafirtu, fafitu, faftu
civilian (n doer), fafirtwan, fafitua, faftua
civility (n), fafirt, fafita, faft
civilization (n), fafiruet, fafitueta, faftuet
civilize (v), fafirst, fafito, fafto
civily (adv), fafirtiu, fafitiu, faftiu
claim (n), nolan, noarita, noart
claim (v), nolasne, noarito, noarto

claimant (n doer), nolanwan, noaritua, noartua
clam (n), krainsh, keraina, krain
clamp (n), krainsht, kerainota, kraint
clamp (v), krainshst, kerainoto, krainto
clampdown (n), krainshtiern, kerainotiena,
    kraintien
clamper (n doer), krainshtwan, kerainotua,
    kraintua
clamshell (n), kraintherk, kerainotheka, krainthek
clank (n), briansht, kerianita, briant
clank (v), brianshst, berianito, brianto
clanker (n doer), brianshtwan, berianitua, briantua
clanky (adj), brianshtu, berianitu, briantu
clap (n), flarde, felada, flad
clap (v), flarzde, felado, flado
clarification (n), drotarp, derosheta, drosht
clarify (v), drotasp, dosheto, doshto
clarity (n), drotap, dosheta, dosht
clash (n), kreizhe, kereida, kreid
clash (v), kreize, kereido, kreido
class (n), blesh, belega, bleg
classic (n), blegart, belegata, blegat
classical (adj), blegartu, belegatu, blegatu
classification (n), blersh, beleruga, blerg
classify (v), bles, belego, blego
classmate (n), gulerin, belegelena, bleglen
classroom (n), gushran, belegesherana, blegshran
classy (adj), bleshu, belegu, blegu
clause (n), poarf, poafa, poaf
claw (n), kraithk, keraitha, kraith
claw (v), kraithsk, keraitho, kraitho
clay (n), poarl, poala, poal
clean (adj), shermu, shemu, shemu
clean (v), sherzme, shemo, shemo
cleaner (n doer), shermwan, shemua, shemua
cleanliness (n), sherme, shema, shem
cleanly (adv), shermiu, shemiu, shemiu
cleanse (v), shmorsk, shemoko, shmoko
cleanser (n doer), shmorkwan, shemokua, shmokua
cleanup (n), shermiveil, shemiveila, shemiveil
clear (adj), drofu, derotu, drotu
clear (v), drosf, deroto, droto
clearance (n), drofan, derotana, drotan
clearly (adv), drofiu, derotiu, drotiu
clearness (n), drof, derota, drot
cleave (v d:split), fliashst, feliasho, fliasho
cleave (v d:stick), shniathsk, sheniatho, shniatho
cleaver (n doer d:split), fliashtwan, feliashua,
    fliashua
cleft (n d:split), fliasht, feliasha, fliash
clemency (n), feifiaurn, feifiauna, feifiaun
clement (adj), feifiaurnu, feifiaunu, feifiaunu
clench (n), shliesht, sheliesha, shliesh
clench (v), shlieshst, sheliesho, shliesho
clerk (n), plert, pelenita, plent
Cleveland (n), Klivlanurd, Kelivelanuda, Klivland
clever (adj), shnufatu, shenufu, shnufu
cleverly (adv), shnufatiu, shenufiu, shnufiu
cleverness (n), shnufat, shenufa, shnuf
click (n), thilork, thiloka, thilk
click (v), thilorsk, thiloko, thilko
clicker (n doer), thilorkwan, thilokua, thilkua
client (n), treinat, tereima, treim

cliff (n), flursh, feluzha, fluzh
climate (n), treidal, tereilota, treilt
climb (n), treibe, tereipa, treip
climb (v), treizbe, tereipo, treipo
climber (n doer), treibwan, tereipua, treipua
clinch (n), shliasht, sheliasha, shliash
clinch (v), shliashst, sheliasho, shliasho
clincher (n doer), shliashtwan, sheliashua, shliashua
cling (v), shniansk, sheniano, shniano
clingy (adj), shnianku, shenianu, shnianu
clinic (n), treinap, tereisha, treish
clinical (adj), treinapu, tereishu, treishu
clink (n), briensht, berienita, brient
clink (v), brienshst, berienito, briento
clinker (n doer), brienshtwan, berienitua, brientua
clinky (adj), brienshtu, berienitu, brientu
clip (n), krifk, kerika, krik
clip (v), krifsk, keriko, kriko
clipboard (n), krikplok, kerikepelorika, krikplork
clipper (n doer), krifkwan, kerikua, krikua
cloak (n), shpreifk, shupereifa, shpreif
cloak (v), shpreifsk, shupereifo, shpreifo
clock (n), drofk, deroka, drok
clock (v), drofsk, deroko, droko
clockwise (adj), drofku, deroku, droku
clog (n), shneuishk, sheneiuka, shneiuk
clog (v), shneuishsk, sheneiuko, shneiuko
clone (n), bliurme, beliuma, blium
clone (v), bliurzme, beliumo, bliumo
cloner (n doer), bliurmwan, beliumua, bliumua
clonk (n), brionsht, berionita, briont
clonk (v), brionshst, berionito, brionto
clonker (n doer), brionshtwan, berionitua, briontua
clonky (adj), brionshtu, berionitu, briontu
close (adj), greftu, geretu, gretu
close (v), grefst, gereto, greto
closely (adv), greftiu, geretiu, gretiu
closeness (n), greftart, geretata, gretat
closer (adj), greftwelu, geretwelu, gretwelu
closer (n doer), greftwan, geretua, gretua
closest (adj), greftwaku, geretwaku, gretwaku
closet (n), gretak, gereshota, gresht
closure (n), greft, gereta, gret
clot (n), shnaifk, shenaika, shnaik
clot (v), shnaifsk, shenaiko, shnaiko
cloth (n), flarf, felafa, flaf
clothe (v), flarsf, felafo, flafo
clothes (n pl), flarfkyek, felafiki, flafki
cloud (n), paluf, pelaufa, plauf
cloud (v), palusf, pelaufo, plaufo
cloudy (adj), palufu, pelaufu, plaufu
clout (n), triurk, teriuka, triuk
clout (v), triursk, teriuko, triuko
clouter (n doer), triurkwan, teriukua, triukua
clove (v pa d:split), fliashstyot, feliashio, fliashio
clown (n), luparf, lupafa, lupaf
clown (v), luparsf, lupafo, lupafo
club (n d:group), traide, taida, taid
club (n d:stick), kraishp, keraiba, kraib
club (v d:group), traizde, taido, taido
club (v d:stick), kraishsp, keraibo, kraibo
clubhouse (n), traidukiarf, taidekiafa, taidkiaf

clue (n), grusht, geruta, grut
clue (v), grushst, geruto, gruto
clueless (adj), grushtmenu, gerutemenu, grutmenu
cluelessly (adv), grushtmeniu, gerutemeniu, grutmeniu
clump (n), shniamp, sheniama, shniam
clump (v), shniamesp, sheniamo, shniamo
clumpy (adj), shniampu, sheniamu, shniamu
clumsily (adv), brelmiu, beremiu, bremiu
clumsiness (n), brelme, berema, brem
clumsy (adj), brelmu, beremu, bremu
clung (v pa), shnianskyot, shenianio, shnianio
clunk (n), broink, beroina, broin
clunk (v), broinsk, beroino, broino
clunker (n doer), broinkwan, beroinua, broinua
clunky (adj), broinku, beroinu, broinu
cluster (n), bluarp, beluapa, bluap
cluster (v), bluarsp, beluapo, bluapo
clutch (n d:grip), shliusht, sheliusha, shliush
clutch (n d:hatch), nelirth, nelitha, nelth
clutch (v d:grip), shliushst, sheliusho, shliusho
clutter (n), shnaithan, shenaitha, shnaith
clutter (v), shnaithasne, shenaitho, shnaitho
coach (n), brakun, beranika, brank
coach (v), brakusne, beraniko, branko
coal (n), ganor, garina, garn
coalesce (v), framist, feralumo, fralmo
coalescence (n), framit, feraluma, fralm
coalescent (adj), framitu, feralumu, fralmu
coalite (v), framirsne, feramino, framino
coalition (n), framirn, feramina, framin
coarse (adj), shlargu, shelagu, shlagu
coarsely (adv), shlargiu, shelagiu, shlagiu
coarseness (n), shlarge, shelaga, shlag
coast (n d:move), dulef, durifa, durf
coast (n d:shore), branar, beranifa, branf
coast (v d:move), dulesf, durifo, durfo
coastal (adj d:shore), branaru, beranifu, branfu
coaster (n doer d:move), dulefwan, durifua, durfua
coastline (n), branaroip, beranifoipa, branfoip
coat (n), frafk, rafika, rafk
coat (v), frafsk, rafiko, rafko
coauthor (n doer), plubashtalwan, pelubashalitua, plubashaltua
coauthority (n), plubashtal, pelubashalita, plubashalt
cob (n d:round), kuarde, kuada, kuad
Cobalt (n davoka), Ifok, Ifok, Ifok
Cobalt (n), Kobalt, Kobalita, Kobalt
cobble (n d:mend), kuadarf, kuadafa, kuadaf
cobble (n d:roundstone), kuadark, kuadaka, kuadak
cobble (v d:mend), kuadarsf, kuadafo, kuadafo
cobbler (n doer d:mend), kuadarfwan, kuadafua, kuadafua
cobblestone (n), kuadark, kuadaka, kuadak
cobweb (n), kuabrivarn, kuaberivana, kuabrivan
coca (n), kolge, koga, kog
cocaine (n), takiorl, takiola, takiol
cock (n), dukal, dulika, dulk
cock (v), dukasle, duliko, dulko
cockiness (n), dukalat, dulikata, dulkat
cockpit (n), dukaklurk, dulikeluka, dulkluk
cockroach (n), klarfgaith, kelafegaitha, klafgaith

cocktail (n), dukalaif, dulikaifa, dulkaif
cocky (adj), dukalu, duliku, dulku
cocoa (n), gaurvat, gauvata, gauvat
coconut (n), gaurmel, gaumerina, gaumern
code (n), volart, volata, vlat
code (v), volarst, volato, vlato
coder (n doer), volartwan, volatua, vlatua
coed (n), piluarve, piluava, pluav
coefficient (n), pluthuvirtar, peluvirothara, pluvirthar
coerce (v), poinsk, poniko, ponko
coercer (n doer), poinkwan, ponikua, ponkua
coercion (n), poink, ponika, ponk
coercive (adj), poinku, poniku, ponku
coexist (v), plunulirst, pelunulito, plunulto
coexistence (n), plunulirt, pelunulita, plunult
coffee (n), vumark, vumaka, vumak
coffin (n), tathirt, tathita, tatht
cofound (v), plushuparst, pelushupato, plushupato
cofounder (n doer), plushupartwan, pelushupatua, plushupatua
cog (n), durk, duka, duk
cogency (n), viarp, viapa, viap
cogenerate (v), plumarmarsk, pelumaromako, plumarmako
cogeneration (n), plumarmark, pelumaromaka, plumarmak
cogenerator (n doer), plumarmarkwan, pelumaromakua, plumarmakua
cogent (adj), viarpu, viapu, viapu
cogently (adv), viarpiu, viapiu, viapiu
cogitate (v), viarlst, vialito, vialto
cogitated (v prp), viarlstaut, vialitao, vialtao
cogitation (n), viarlt, vialita, vialt
cognate (n), viart, viata, viat
cognition (n), viatark, viataka, viatak
cognitive (adj), viatarku, viataku, viataku
cognizance (n), viatarkuet, viatakueta, viatakuet
cognizant (adj), viatarkuetu, viatakuetu, viatakuetu
cohabitate (v), plureishortuest, pelureishotueto, plureishtueto
cohabitation (n), plureishortuet, pelureishotueta, plureishtuet
coherence (n), ipituarp, ipituapa, ipituap
coherent (adj), ipituarpu, ipituapu, ipituapu
cohesion (n), ipituart, ipituata, ipituat
cohesive (adj), ipituartu, ipituatu, ipituatu
cohesiveness (n), ipituartuet, ipituatueta, ipituatuet
coil (n), gaiarp, gaiapa, gaiap
coil (v), gaiarsp, gaiapo, gaiapo
coiler (n doer), gaiarpwan, gaiapua, gaiapua
coin (n), pairf, paifa, paif
coin (v), pairsf, paifo, paifo
coincide (v), ipishtersk, ipishateko, ipishteko
coincidence (n), ipishterk, ipishateka, ipishtek
coincident (adj), ipishterku, ipishateku, ipishteku
coincidental (adj), ipishterku, ipishateku, ipishteku
coincidentally (adv), ipishterkiu, ipishatekiu, ipishtekiu
cold (adj d:temperature), shlortu, shelotu, shlotu
cold (n d:illness), liarge, liaga, liag
cold (n d:temperature), shlort, shelota, shlot
colder (adj), shlortwelu, shelotwelu, shlotwelu

coldest (adj), shlortwaku, shelotwaku, shlotwaku
coldness (n), shlortuet, shelotueta, shlotuet
collaborate (v), garisharst, garishato, garshto
collaboration (n), garishart, garishata, garsht
collaborative (adj), garishartu, garishatu, garshtu
collaboratively (adv), garishartiu, garishatiu, garshtiu
collaborator (n doer), garishartwan, garishatua, garshtua
collapse (n), garshp, gashipa, gashp
collapse (v), garshsp, gashipo, gashpo
collapsible (adj), garshpu, gashipu, gashpu
collar (n), gadark, gadaka, gadak
collar (v), gadarsk, gadako, gadako
collarbone (n), gadaktoirk, gadaketoika, gadaktoik
collate (v), garask, gariko, garko
collateral (n), garshork, garishoka, garshk
colleague (n), garbrube, gaberuba, gabrub
collect (v), gapost, garipo, garpo
collectable (adj), gapotfrelpu, garipuferepu, garpfrepu
collectable (n), gapotfrelp, garipuferepa, garpfrep
collectible (adj), gapotfrelpu, garipuferepu, garpfrepu
collectible (n), gapotfrelp, garipuferepa, garpfrep
collection (n), gapot, garipa, garp
collective (adj), gapotu, garipu, garpu
collectively (adv), gapotiu, garipiu, garpiu
collector (n doer), gapotwan, garipua, garpua
college (n), shralip, sheralipa, shralp
collide (v), klurshsk, kelushiko, klushko
collider (n doer), klurshkwan, kelushikua, klushkua
collision (n), klurshk, kelushika, klushk
colloquial (adj), glatanu, gelanitu, glantu
colloquium (n), glatan, gelanita, glant
collude (v), klurushst, kelurusho, klurusho
collusion (n), klurusht, kelurusha, klurush
collusive (adj), klurushtu, kelurushu, klurushu
cologne (n), miturme, mituma, mitum
Colombia (n), Kolombiarf, Kolomubiafa, Kolombiaf
Colombian (n), Kolombiarn, Kolomubiana, Kolombian
colon (n d:character), mituf, mifota, mift
colon (n d:organ), kuturk, kutuka, kutuk
colonel (n), migart, migata, migat
colonial (adj), mikirtu, mikitu, mikitu
colonist (n doer), mikirtwan, mikitua, mikitua
colonization (n), mikirtuet, mikitueta, mikituet
colonize (v), mikirst, mikito, mikito
colonizer (n doer), mikirtwan, mikitua, mikitua
colony (n), mikirt, mikita, mikit
color (n), lirolf, lirola, lirol
color (v), lirolsf, lirolo, lirolo
Colorado (n), Kolorard, Kolorada, Kolorad
colorful (adj), lirolfu, lirolu, lirolu
colorfully (adv), lirolfiu, liroliu, liroliu
Columbia (n), Kolumbiarf, Kolumobiafa, Kolumbiaf
column (n), votal, vosheta, vosht
columnate (v), votasle, vosheto, voshto
coma (n d:oblong), rasharl, rashala, rashal
coma (n d:sleep), puprulsh, puperusha, puprush
comatose (adj d:sleep), puprulshu, puperushu, puprushu

comb (n), rakarde, rakada, rakad
comb (v), rakarzde, rakado, rakado
combat (n), nulgeralt, nulogerata, nulgrat
combat (v), nulgeralst, nulogerato, nulgrato
combatant (n doer), nulgeraltwan, nulogeratua, nulgratua
combative (adj), nulgeraltu, nulogeratu, nulgratu
combatively (adv), nulgeraltiu, nulogeratiu, nulgratiu
comber (n doer), rakardwan, rakadua, rakadua
combination (n), lenup, nulipa, nulp
combine (n), lenurp, nulipata, nulpat
combine (v), lenusp, nulipo, nulpo
combiner (n doer), lenupwan, nulipua, nulpua
combust (v), nulbugosre, nuloberugo, nulbrugo
combustible (adj), nulbugoru, nuloberugu, nulbrugu
combustion (n), nulbugor, nuloberuga, nulbrug
come (n), blerf, bilefa, blef
come (v), blersf, bilefo, blefo
comeback (n), blefvark, bilefuvaka, blefvak
comedian (n doer), lordoipwan, loidoipua, loidoipua
comedy (n), lordoip, loidoipa, loidoip
comer (n doer), blerfwan, bilefua, blefua
comet (n), rashelt, rasherila, rasherl
comfort (n), vlark, velaruva, vlarv
comfort (v), vlarsk, velaruvo, vlarvo
comfortable (adj), vlarku, velaruvu, vlarvu
comfortably (adv), vlarkiu, velaruviu, vlarviu
comforter (n doer), vlarkwan, velaruvua, vlarvua
comic (n doer), lordoipwan, loidoipua, loidoipua
comical (adj), lordoipu, loidoipu, loidoipu
comically (adv), lordoipiu, loidoipiu, loidoipiu
comma (n), shurn, shuna, shun
command (n), shoikal, sheloika, shloik
command (v), shoikasle, sheloiko, shloiko
commander (n doer), shoikalwan, sheloikua, shloikua
commandment (n), shoikalt, sheloikata, shloikat
commence (v), lenartizde, lenetiludo, lentildo
commencement (n), lenartide, lenetiluda, lentild
commend (v), shafasle, shelafo, shlafo
commendation (n), shafal, shelafa, shlaf
comment (n), leniat, nialota, nialt
comment (v), leniast, nialoto, nialto
commentary (n), leniart, nialotara, nialtar
commentator (n doer), leniatwan, nialotua, nialtua
commerce (n), nelafk, lalifoka, lalfk
commercial (adj), nelafku, lalifoku, lalfku
commercial (n), nelafkan, lalifokana, lalfkan
commercially (adv), nelafkiu, lalifokiu, lalfkiu
commission (n), lenkart, lenikata, lenkat
commission (v), lenkarst, lenikato, lenkato
commissioner (n doer), lenkartwan, lenikatua, lenkatua
commit (v), lenirsk, leniko, lenko
commitment (n), lenirk, lenika, lenk
committee (n doer), lenirkwan, lenikua, lenkua
commodity (n), giarnk, gianoka, giank
common (adj), gunaru, gurinu, gurnu
commonality (n), gunar, gurina, gurn
commoner (n doer), gunarwan, gurinua, gurnua

commonize (v), gunasre, gurino, gurno
commonly (adv), gunariu, guriniu, gurniu
commonplace (adj), gunabrelshu, guribereshu, gurnbreshu
commonplace (n), gunabrelsh, guriberesha, gurnbresh
commonsense (n), gunashoraf, gurishorifa, gurnshorf
commonwealth (n), gunakaurp, gurikaupa, gurnkaup
commotion (n), lenshkirt, lenishekita, lenshkit
commove (v), lenshkirst, lenishekito, lenshkito
communal (adj), gulornu, gulinu, gulnu
commune (n), gunark, gunaka, gunak
commune (v), gulorsne, gulino, gulno
communicate (v), guniarst, guniato, guniato
communication (n), guniart, guniata, guniat
communicator (n doer), guniartwan, guniatua, guniatua
communion (n), gulorn, gulina, guln
communique (n), guniarn, guniana, gunian
communism (n), ganushk, ganuka, ganuk
communist (n doer), ganushkwan, ganukua, ganukua
community (n), gunarl, gunala, gunal
commutation (n), lenshluark, lenisheluaka, lenshluak
commute (v), lenshluarsk, lenisheluako, lenshluako
commuter (n doer), lenshluarkwan, lenisheluakua, lenshluakua
compact (adj), gugiforpu, gugifopu, gugifpu
compact (v), gugiforsp, gugifopo, gugifpo
compaction (n), gugiforp, gugifopa, gugifp
compactly (adv), gugiforpiu, gugifopiu, gugifpiu
compactor (n doer), gugiforpwan, gugifopua, gugifpua
companion (n doer), lensharlwan, leneshalua, lenshalua
companionship (n), lensharl, leneshala, lenshal
company (n), nelapish, leneshapa, lenshap
comparable (adj), lenbolku, beroliku, brolku
comparably (adv), lenbolkiu, berolikiu, brolkiu
comparative (adj), lenbolku, beroliku, brolku
comparatively (adv), lenbolkiu, berolikiu, brolkiu
compare (v), lenbolsk, beroliko, brolko
comparison (n), lenbolk, berolika, brolk
comparitor (n doer), lenbolkwan, berolikua, brolkua
compartment (n), feshlan, felesha, felsh
compartmentalize (v), feshlasne, felesho, felsho
compass (n), lefnik, lenifoka, lenfk
compassion (n), fleirn, feleina, flein
compassionate (adj), fleirnu, feleinu, fleinu
compatibility (n), fleinorsh, feleinosha, fleinsh
compatible (adj), fleinorshu, feleinoshu, fleinshu
compatibly (adv), fleinorshiu, feleinoshiu, fleinshiu
compel (v), guparzde, gupado, gupado
compeller (n doer), gupardwan, gupadua, gupadua
compensate (v), brufasne, berulifo, brulfo
compensation (n), brufan, berulifa, brulf
compensator (n doer), brufanwan, berulifua, brulfua
compete (v), lenvasp, vanipo, vanpo

competence (n), lenvaprol, vanipora, vanpor
competent (adj), lenvaprolu, vaniporu, vanporu
competently (adv), lenvaproliu, vaniporiu, vanporiu
competition (n), lenvap, vanipa, vanp
competitive (adj), lenvapu, vanipu, vanpu
competitively (adv), lenvapiu, vanipiu, vanpiu
competitiveness (n), lenvapat, vanipata, vanpat
competitor (n doer), lenvapwan, vanipua, vanpua
compilation (n), gunairp, gunaipa, gunaip
compile (v), gunairsp, gunaipo, gunaipo
compiler (n doer), gunairpwan, gunaipua, gunaipua
complain (v), glaursf, gelaufo, glaufo
complainer (n doer), glaurfwan, gelaufua, glaufua
complaint (n), glaurf, gelaufa, glauf
complement (n), brekalt, berelikata, brelkat
complement (v), brekalst, berelikato, brelkato
complete (adj), brekalu, bereliku, brelku
complete (v), brekasle, bereliko, brelko
completely (adv), brekaliu, berelikiu, brelkiu
completion (n), brekal, berelika, brelk
complex (adj), breshorku, bereshoku, breshku
complex (n), breshkart, bereshokata, breshkat
complexity (n), breshork, bereshoka, breshk
compliance (n), lenshluat, sheluanita, shluant
compliant (adj), lenshluatu, sheluanitu, shluantu
complicate (v), lenbrels, lenubereshoto, lenbresho
complication (n), lenbrelsh, lenubereshota, lenbresh
compliment (n), lenshluatp, sheluanitapa, shluantap
compliment (v), lenshluatsp, sheluanitapo, shluantapo
complimentarily (adv), lenshluatpiu, sheluanitapiu, shluantapiu
complimentary (adj), lenshluatpu, sheluanitapu, shluantapu
complimentor (n doer), lenshluatpwan, sheluanitapua, shluantapua
comply (v), lenshluast, sheluanito, shluanto
component (n), duvelp, guvelipa, guvelp
compose (v), lenlask, laniko, lanko
composer (n doer), lenlakwan, lanikua, lankua
composite (adj), lenlakitu, lanikitu, lankitu
composite (n), lenlakit, lanikita, lankit
composition (n), lenlak, lanika, lank
composure (n), lenlakar, lanikara, lankar
compound (n d:mixture), gubralurme, guberaluma, gubralm
compound (n d:place), biarnt, bianita, biant
compound (v d:mixture), gubralurzme, guberalumo, gubralmo
comprehend (v), lendrukest, deruliko, drulko
comprehension (n), lendruket, derulika, drulk
comprehensive (adj), lendruketu, deruliku, drulku
comprehensively (adv), lendruketiu, derulikiu, drulkiu
compress (n), gublasharn, gubelashana, gublashan
compress (v), gublars, gubelasho, gublasho
compressable (adj), gublarshu, gubelashu, gublashu
compression (n), gublarsh, gubelasha, gublash
compressor (n doer), gublarshwan, gubelashua, gublashua

comprisable (adj), guviurshu, guviushu, guviushu
comprisal (n), guviursh, guviusha, guviush
comprise (v), guviurs, guviusho, guviusho
compromise (n), bleinork, beleinoka, bleinok
compromise (v), bleinorsk, beleinoko, bleinoko
compromiser (n doer), bleinorkwan, beleinokua, bleinokua
compulsion (n), guparde, gupada, gupad
compulsive (adj), gupardu, gupadu, gupadu
compulsory (adv), gupardiu, gupadiu, gupadiu
computation (n), voink, voitha, voith
computational (adj), voinku, voithu, voithu
compute (v), voinsk, voitho, voitho
computer (n doer), voinkwan, voithua, voithua
computerization (n), voinkak, voithaka, voithak
computerize (v), voinkask, voithako, voithako
comrade (n), pilshranf, pilisherana, pilshran
con (n d:consequence), buishort, buishota, buisht
concave (adj), belpaurgu, liupaugu, liupaugu
concave (n), belpaurge, liupauga, liupaug
concave (v), belpaurzge, liupaugo, liupaugo
concavely (adv), belpaurgiu, liupaugiu, liupaugiu
conceal (v), belgalnasf, lefugirano, lefgirno
concealer (n doer), belgalnafwan, lefugiranua, lefgirnua
concealment (n), belgalnaf, lefugirana, lefgirn
concede (v), belvesk, liuveko, liuveko
conceit (n), belshime, liuma, lium
conceit (v), belshizme, liumo, liumo
conceivable (adj), belshipfrelpu, liushipuferepu, liushpfrepu
conceivably (adv), belshipfrelpiu, liushipuferepiu, liushpfrepiu
conceive (v), belshisp, liushipo, liushpo
concentrate (v), beldrest, liudereto, liudreto
concentration (n), beldret, liudereta, liudret
concentrator (n doer), beldretwan, liuderetua, liudretua
concept (n), belship, liushipa, liushp
conception (n), belshifp, liuroshipa, liurshp
conceptual (adj), belshipu, liushipu, liushpu
conceptually (adv), belshipiu, liushipiu, liushpiu
concern (n), belfp, liufopa, liufp
concern (v), belfsp, liufopo, liufpo
concert (n), belzhil, liuzhila, liuzhil
concert (v), belzhisle, liuzhilo, liuzhilo
concession (n), belvek, liuveka, liuvek
conciliate (v), rolarzme, rolamo, rolmo
concise (adj), belthirshku, liuthishaku, liuthishku
concisely (adv), belthirshkiu, liuthishakiu, liuthishkiu
conclude (v), belgrust, liugeruto, liugruto
conclusion (n), belgrut, liugeruta, liugrut
conclusive (adj), belgrutu, liugerutu, liugrutu
conclusively (adv), belgrutiu, liugerutiu, liugrutiu
concoct (v), liudorshsp, liudoshipo, liudoshpo
concoction (n), liudorshp, liudoshipa, liudoshp
concrete (adj), belgotu, golitu, goltu
concrete (n), belgot, golita, golt
concrete (v), belgost, golito, golto
concur (v), belgalsf, liugalifo, liugalfo
concurrence (n), belgalf, liugalifa, liugalf
concurrency (n), belgalf, liugalifa, liugalf

concurrent (adj), belgalfu, liugalifu, liugalfu
concurrently (adv), belgalfiu, liugalifiu, liugalfiu
concuss (v), liugoishst, liugoito, liugoito
concussion (n), liugoisht, liugoita, liugoit
condemn (v), belviaursk, liuviauko, liuviauko
condemnation (n), belviaurk, liuviauka, liuviauk
condensate (n), belbrelfit, liuberefita, liubrefit
condensation (n), belbrelf, liuberefa, liubref
condense (v), belbrelsf, liuberefo, liubrefo
condenser (n doer), belbrelfwan, liuberefua,
    liubrefua
condition (n), beltifk, liutifoka, liutifk
condition (v), beltifsk, liutifoko, liutifko
conditional (adj), beltifku, liutifoku, liutifku
conditionally (adv), beltifkiu, liutifokiu, liutifkiu
conditioner (n doer), beltifkwan, liutifokua,
    liutifkua
condole (v), belplurze, liupeluzho, liupluzho
condolence (n), belplurzhe, liupeluzha, liupluzh
condone (v), belgerzge, liugego, liugego
conduce (v), belkirask, liukiroko, liukirko
conducer (n doer), belkirakwan, liukirokua,
    liukirkua
conducive (adj), belkiraku, liukiroku, liukirku
conduct (v), belkriusk, liukeriuko, liukriuko
conduction (n), belkriuk, liukeriuka, liukriuk
conductive (adj), belkriuku, liukeriuku, liukriuku
conductivity (n), belbarkat, liubarikata, liubarkat
conductor (n doer), belkriukwan, liukeriukua,
    liukriukua
conduit (n), beltide, barishoka, barshk
cone (n), belirn, belina, beln
confect (v), belvirfst, liuviroto, liuvirto
confection (n), belvirft, liuvirota, liuvirt
confectionery (n), belvirftar, liuvirotara, liuvirtar
confederacy (n), belpairve, liupaiva, liupaiv
confederate (n doer), belpairvwan, liupaivua,
    liupaivua
confederate (v), belpairzve, liupaivo, liupaivo
confederation (n), belpairve, liupaiva, liupaiv
confer (v), belgelsf, liugefo, liugefo
conferee (n), belgelfuin, liugefuina, liugefuin
conference (n), belgelf, liugefa, liugef
conferment (n), belgeft, liugefata, liugeft
conferor (n doer), belgelfwan, liugefua, liugefua
confess (v), belnusf, liuno, liuno
confession (n), belnuf, liuna, liun
confessional (n), belnufan, liunana, liunan
confessor (n doer), belnufwan, liunua, liunua
confidant (n doer), belprinwan, liuperinua,
    liuprinua
confide (v), belprisne, liuperino, liuprino
confidence (n), belprin, liuperina, liuprin
confident (adj), belprinu, liuperinu, liuprinu
confidential (adj), belprinfu, liuperinofu, liuprinfu
confidentially (adv), belprinfiu, liuperinofiu,
    liuprinfiu
configuration (n), belkudil, liukulita, liukult
configurator (n doer), belkudilwan, liukulitua,
    liukultua
configure (v), belkudisle, liukulito, liukulto
confine (v), belvuast, liuvuato, liuvuato
confinement (n), belvuat, liuvuata, liuvuat

confirm (v), belnuisf, liunuifo, liunuifo
confirmation (n), belnuif, liunuifa, liunuif
confiscate (v), belinarsp, liulinapo, liulinpo
confiscation (n), belinarp, liulinapa, liulinp
confiscatory (adj), belinarpu, liulinapu, liulinpu
conflict (n), belkik, liukika, liukik
conflict (v), belkisk, liukiko, liukiko
confluence (n), belmiart, liumarota, liumiart
confluent (adj), belmiartu, liumarotu, liumiartu
conform (v), belvorsne, liuvorino, liuvorno
conformance (n), belvornuet, liuvorinueta,
    liuvornuet
conformer (n doer), belvornwan, liuvorinua,
    liuvornua
conformist (n doer), belvornwan, liuvorinua,
    liuvornua
conformity (n), belvorn, liuvorina, liuvorn
confound (v), belshulirst, liushulito, liushulto
confront (v), belflars, liufelarino, liuflarno
confrontation (n), belflarsh, liufelarina, liuflarn
confrontational (adj), belflarshu, liufelarinu,
    liuflarnu
confuse (v), belbost, liuboto, liuboto
confusingly (adv), belbotiu, liubotiu, liubotiu
confusion (n), belbot, liubota, liubot
congest (v), liukiarzge, liukiago, liukiago
congestion (n), liukiarge, liukiaga, liukiag
conglomerate (n), belglap, liugelapa, liuglap
conglomerate (v), belglasp, liugelapo, liuglapo
congratulate (v), belkinsp, liukinopo, liukinpo
congratulation (n), belkinp, liukinopa, liukinp
congregate (v), belkavarsle, liukavalo, liukavalo
congregation (n), belkavarl, liukavala, liukaval
congregational (adj), belkavarlu, liukavalu,
    liukavalu
congress (n), belvorge, liuvoruga, liuvorg
congressional (adj), belvorgu, liuvorugu, liuvorgu
congressman (n doer), belvorgwan, liuvorugua,
    liuvorgua
congruence (n), belklart, liukilata, liuklat
congruent (adj), belklartu, liukilatu, liuklatu
congruently (adv), belklartiu, liukilatiu, liuklatiu
congruous (adj), belklartu, liukilatu, liuklatu
congruously (adv), belklartiu, liukilatiu, liuklatiu
congruousness (n), belklart, liukilata, liuklat
conical (adj), belirnu, belinu, belnu
conjecture (n), belterp, liutepa, liutep
conjecture (v), beltersp, liutepo, liutepo
conjoin (v), belbafst, liubafito, liubafto
conjunction (n), belbaft, liubafita, liubaft
connect (v), shnarst, shinato, shinato
Connecticut (n), Konetikurt, Konetikuta, Konetikut
connection (n), shnarf, shinafa, shnaf
connectivity (n), shnarfat, shinafata, shnafat
connector (n doer), shnarfwan, shinafua, shnafua
connoisseur (n), valbarl, valebara, valbar
connotation (n), belmirade, liumida, liumid
connote (v), belmirazde, liumido, liumido
conquer (v), shiarfst, shiaroto, shiarto
conqueror (n doer), shiarftwan, shiarotua, shiartua
conquest (n), shiarft, shiarota, shiart
conscience (n), munarp, munapa, munp
conscionable (adj), munarpu, munapu, munpu

conscious (adj), keirpu, keilopu, keilpu
consciously (adv), keirpiu, keilopiu, keilpiu
consciousness (n), keirp, keilopa, keilp
conscript (v), belsherzge, liusherigo, liushrigo
conscription (n), belsherge, liusheriga, liushrig
consecrate (v), belbiafarsf, liubiafafo, liubiafafo
consecration (n), belbiafarf, liubiafafa, liubiafaf
consecute (v), belshufst, liushufito, liushufto
consecutive (adj), belshuftu, liushufitu, liushuftu
consecutively (adv), belshuftiu, liushufitiu, liushuftiu
consensual (adj), belblutu, liulofu, liulfu
consensus (n), belblutat, liulofata, liulfat
consent (n), belblut, liulofa, liulf
consent (v), belblust, liulofo, liulfo
conseqent (adj), buishortu, buishotu, buishtu
consequence (n), buishort, buishota, buisht
consequential (adj), buishortu, buishotu, buishtu
consequentially (adv), buishortiu, buishotiu, buishtiu
consequently (adv), buishortiu, buishotiu, buishtiu
conservation (n), belkoft, liukofita, liukoft
conservationist (n doer), belkoftwan, liukofitua, liukoftua
conservatism (n), belkoftuet, liukofitueta, liukoftuet
conservative (adj), belkoftu, liukofitu, liukoftu
conservative (n), belkoftan, liukofitana, liukoftan
conservatively (adv), belkoftiu, liukofitiu, liukoftiu
conservatory (n), belkorft, liukorafita, liukorft
conserve (v), belkofst, liukofito, liukofto
consider (v), belthost, liuthoto, liuthoto
considerable (adj), belthotu, liuthotu, liuthotu
considerably (adv), belthotiu, liuthotiu, liuthotiu
considerate (adj), belthotaru, liuthotaru, liuthotaru
consideration (n), belthot, liuthota, liuthot
consign (v), belarask, liulariko, liularko
consignment (n), belarak, liularika, liulark
consist (v), beltelsk, liuteliko, liutelko
consistency (n), beltelk, liutelika, liutelk
consistent (adj), beltelku, liuteliku, liutelku
consistently (adv), beltelkiu, liutelikiu, liutelkiu
consolation (n d:comfort), belgrilk, ligerika, liugrik
console (n d:cabinet), belirge, liuliga, liulig
console (v d:comfort), belgrilsk, ligeriko, liugriko
consolidate (v), beligarsp, liuligapo, liuligapo
consolidation (n), beligarp, liuligapa, liuligap
consolidator (n doer), beligarpwan, liuligapua, liuligapua
consonant (n), belshant, liushanita, liushant
consort (n doer), belfadekwan, liufadekua, liufadekua
consort (v), belfadesk, liufadeko, liufadeko
consortium (n), belfadek, liufadeka, liufadek
conspectus (n), belthufk, liuthufika, liuthufk
conspicuous (adj), belthurfu, thurifu, thurfu
conspicuously (adv), belthurfiu, thurifiu, thurfiu
conspiracy (n), belfdauf, liufadaufa, liufdauf
conspirator (n doer), belfdaufwan, liufadaufua, liufdaufua
conspiratorial (adj), belfdaufu, liufadaufu, liufdaufu
conspire (v), belfdausf, liufadaufo, liufdaufo
constancy (n), beltrelkuet, liuterelikueta, liutrelkuet
constant (adj), beltrelku, liutereliku, liutrelku

constant (n), beltrelk, liuterelika, liutrelk
constantly (adv), beltrelkiu, liuterelikiu, liutrelkiu
constellate (v), beldrolzme, liuderomo, liudromo
constellation (n), beldrolme, liuderoma, liudrom
consternate (v), belrilorsp, liurilopo, liurilpo
consternation (n), belrilorp, liurilopa, liurilp
constipate (v), belviarzge, liuviago, liuviago
constipation (n), belviarge, liuviaga, liuviag
constitute (v), belshpelst, liushopelito, liushpelto
constitution (n), belshpelt, liushopelita, liushpelt
constitutional (adj), belshpeltu, liushopelitu, liushpeltu
constitutionally (adv), belshpeltiu, liushopelitiu, liushpeltiu
constrain (v), belprulsk, liuperuliko, liuprulko
constraint (n), belprulk, liuperulika, liuprulk
constrict (v), belbafsk, liubafiko, liubafko
constriction (n), belbafk, liubafika, liubafk
constrictor (n doer), belbafkwan, liubafikua, liubafkua
construct (v), belshlesk, liusheleko, liushleko
construction (n), belshlek, liusheleka, liushlek
constructive (adj), belshleku, liusheleku, liushleku
constructor (n doer), belshlekwan, liushelekua, liushlekua
construe (v), belplairsp, liupelaipo, liuplaipo
construer (n doer), belplairpwan, liupelaipua, liuplaipua
consult (v), belvanst, liuvanito, liuvanto
consultant (n doer), belvantwan, liuvanitua, liuvantua
consultation (n), belvant, liuvanita, liuvant
consume (v), belfialst, liufialoto, liufialto
consumer (n doer), belfialtwan, liufialotua, liufialtua
consumption (n), belfialt, liufialota, liufialt
contact (n doer), belpaibwan, liupaibua, liupaibua
contact (n), belpaibe, liupaiba, liupaib
contact (v), belpaibze, liupaibo, liupaibo
contagion (n), belmiuge, liumiuga, liumiug
contagious (adv), belmiugiu, liumiugiu, liumiugiu
contain (v), shorfst, shorodo, shordo
container (n doer), shorftwan, shorodua, shordua
containment (n), shorft, shoroda, shord
contaminant (n doer), liumiurkwan, liumiukua, liumiukua
contaminate (v), liumiursk, liumiuko, liumiuko
contamination (n), liumiurk, liumiuka, liumiuk
contemplate (v), belvarfsk, liuvarifoko, liuvarfko
contemplation (n), belvarfk, liuvarifoka, liuvarfk
contemporary (n), teilort, teilota, teilt
contempt (n), belvaft, liuvafita, liuvaft
contemptable (adj), belvaftu, liuvafitu, liuvaftu
contend (v d:challenge), belpifsk, liupifoko, liupifko
contender (n doer d:challenge), belpifkwan, liupifokua, liupifkua
content (adj d:satisfied), beltrielu, liubupu, liubupu
content (n d:material), korsh, koshipa, koshp
contention (n d:challenge), belpifk, liupifoka, liupifk
contentious (adj d:challenge), belpifkoku, liupifoku, liupifku
contently (adv d:satisfied), beltrieliu, liubupiu, liubupiu

liubupiu
contentment (n d:satisfied), beltriel, liubupa, liubup
contest (n), belshtit, liushetita, liushtit
contest (v), belshtist, liushetito, liushtito
contestant (n doer), belshtitwan, liushetitua, liushtitua
context (n), belshtibe, liushetiba, liushtib
continent (n), medmot, merata, mert
continental (adj), medmotu, meratu, mertu
contingency (n), liutiorth, liutiotha, liutioth
contingent (adj), liutiorthu, liutiothu, liutiothu
continual (adj), beltiru, liutiru, liutiru
continually (adv), beltiriu, liutiriu, liutiriu
continuation (n), beltir, liutira, liutir
continue (v), beltisre, liutiro, liutiro
continuous (adj), beltiru, liutiru, liutiru
continuously (adv), beltiriu, liutiriu, liutiriu
contort (v), belkiorst, liukioto, liukioto
contortion (n), belkiort, liukiota, liukiot
contour (n), belkarage, liukaruga, liukarg
contour (v), belkarazge, liukarugo, liukargo
Contra (n), Kontralf, Koniterafa, Kontraf
contraband (n), plavramirp, pelaveramipa, plavramp
contraception (n), plashifp, pelaroshipa, plarshp
contraceptive (n doer), plashifpwan, pelaroshipua, plarshpua
contract (n d:agreement), glart, gelaruga, glarg
contract (v d:shrink), belgalst, liugalito, liugalto
contraction (n d:shrink), belgalt, liugalita, liugalt
contractor (n doer d:agreement), glartwan, gelarugua, glargua
contractual (adj d:agreement), glartu, gelarugu, glargu
contractually (adv d:agreement), glartiu, gelarugiu, glargiu
contradict (v), pladeirsk, peladeiko, pladeiko
contradiction (n), pladeirk, peladeika, pladeik
contradictory (adj), pladeirku, peladeiku, pladeiku
contraption (n), beldifort, liudifota, liudift
contrariness (n), plaput, pelaripa, plarp
contrary (adj), plaputu, pelaripu, plarpu
contrast (n), belait, liulaita, liulait
contrast (v), belaist, liulaito, liulaito
contravene (v), plafizme, pelafimo, plafimo
contravention (n), plafime, pelafima, plafim
contribute (v), gorifsp, goripo, gorpo
contribution (n), gorifp, goripa, gorp
contributor (n doer), gorifpwan, goripua, gorpua
contrite (adj), beltarvu, liutavu, liutavu
contritely (adv), beltarviu, liutaviu, liutaviu
contrition (n), beltarve, liutava, liutav
contrivance (n), liubirsh, liubisha, liubish
contrive (v), liubirs, liubisho, liubisho
control (n), tranit, teranita, trant
control (v), tranist, teranito, tranto
controllable (adj), tranitu, teranitu, trantu
controller (n doer), tranitwan, teranitua, trantua
controversial (adj), plarthu, pelathu, plathu
controversy (n), plarth, pelatha, plath
contuse (v), belneirsp, liuneipo, liuneipo
contusion (n), belneirp, liuneipa, liuneip

convect (v), belthirfst, liuthifito, liuthifto
convection (n), belthirft, liuthifita, liuthift
convene (v), belfizme, liufimo, liufimo
convenience (n), belfirme, liufirama, liufirm
convenient (adj), belfirmu, liufiramu, liufirmu
conveniently (adv), belfirmiu, liufiramiu, liufirmiu
convention (n), belfime, liufima, liufim
conventional (adj), belfimu, liufimu, liufimu
converge (v), belmeirzge, liumeigo, liumeigo
convergence (n), belmeirge, liumeiga, liumeig
convergent (adj), belmeirgu, liumeigu, liumeigu
conversation (n), beltharf, liutharifa, liutharf
conversational (adj), beltharfu, liutharifu, liutharfu
conversationalist (n doer), beltharfwan, liutharifua, liutharfua
conversationally (adv), beltharfiu, liutharifiu, liutharfiu
converse (n), tharfik, tharifoka, tharfk
converse (v), beltharsf, liutharifo, liutharfo
conversely (adv), tharfikiu, tharifokiu, tharfkiu
conversion (n), beltharak, liutharika, liuthark
convert (n), tharshok, tharishoka, tharshk
convert (v), beltharask, liuthariko, liutharko
converter (n doer), beltharakwan, liutharikua, liutharkua
convertible (adj), beltharaku, liuthariku, liutharku
convertible (n), tharluk, thariluka, tharluk
convex (adj), belfoirtu, liufoitu, liufoitu
convex (n), belfoirt, liufoita, liufoit
convey (v), belfuarsle, liufualo, liufualo
conveyable (adj), belfuarlu, liufualu, liufualu
conveyance (n), belfuarl, liufuala, liufual
conveyor (n doer), belfuarlwan, liufualua, liufualua
convict (n doer), belbaifwan, liubaifua, liubaifua
convict (v), belbaisf, liubaifo, liubaifo
conviction (n), belbaif, liubaifa, liubaif
convince (v), belbaisp, liubaipo, liubaipo
convincingly (adv), belbaipiu, liubaipiu, liubaipiu
convolute (v), belkemirst, liukemito, liukemto
convolution (n), belkemirt, liukemita, liukemt
convolve (v), belkemirsf, liukemifo, liukemifo
convolvement (n), belkemirf, liukemifa, liukemif
convoy (n), belfuarlk, liufualika, liufualk
convulse (v), beltrelzbe, liuterebo, liutrebo
convulsedly (adv), beltrelbiu, liuterebiu, liutrebiu
convulsive (adj), beltrelbu, liuterebu, liutrebu
convulsion (n), beltrelbe, liutereba, liutreb
coo (n), keiun, keiuna, keiun
coo (v), keiusne, keiuno, keiuno
cook (n doer), dolpwan, dopua, dopua
cook (v), dolsp, dopo, dopo
cookbook (n), dolpvornt, dopevonuda, dopvond
cookie (n), dopilp, dopipa, dopip
cookout (n), dolpuil, dopuila, dopuil
cookware (n), dolpshlerf, dopeshelefa, dopshlef
cool (adj), shlurfu, shelufu, shlufu
cool (v), shlursf, shelufo, shlufo
coolant (n), shlurfit, shelufita, shlufit
cooler (adj), shlurfwelu, shelufwelu, shlufwelu
cooler (n doer), shlurfwan, shelufua, shlufua
coolest (adj), shlurfwaku, shelufwaku, shlufwaku
coolly (adv), shlurfiu, shelufiu, shlufiu
coolness (n), shlurf, shelufa, shluf

coop (n d:cage), dunsh, dunipa, dunp
coop (n d:cooperative), ipirde, ipida, ipid
cooperate (v d:agree), ipidurast, ipidurito, ipidurto
cooperation (n d:agree), ipidurat, ipidurita, ipidurt
cooperative (adj d:agree), ipiduratu, ipiduritu, ipidurtu
cooperative (n d:store), ipiduratuk, ipidurituka, ipidurtuk
cooperatively (adv d:agree), ipiduratiu, ipiduritiu, ipidurtiu
cooperator (n doer d:agree), ipiduratwan, ipiduritua, ipidurtua
coordinate (n), shkerp, shikepa, shkep
coordinate (v), shkersp, shikepo, shkepo
coordination (n), shkerpet, shikepeta, shkepet
coordinator (n doer), shkerpwan, shikepua, shkepua
copayment (n), ipimoirmuet, ipimoimueta, ipimoimuet
cope (v), flerzbe, felebo, flebo
copier (n doer), kishkirtwan, kishekitua, kishkitua
Copper (n davoka), Ifat, Ifat, Ifat
Copper (n), Koper, Kopera, Koper
coprocessor (n), ipifiuvetwat, ipifiuvetuala, ipifiuvetual
copulate (v), vanirsk, vaniko, vanko
copulated (v prp), vanirskaut, vanikao, vankao
copulation (n), vanirk, vanika, vank
copy (n), kishkirt, kishekita, kishkit
copy (v), kishkirst, kishekito, kishkito
copyright (n), kishkirtruarsh, kishekiteruasha, kishkitruash
copyright (v), kishkirtruars, kishekiteruasho, kishkitruasho
copywriter (n doer), kishkitloirdwan, kishekiteloidua, kishkitloidua
cord (n), kalde, kada, kad
cord (v), kalzde, kado, kado
core (n), kirft, kirota, kirt
core (v), kirfst, kiroto, kirto
cork (n), granirp, goranipa, granp
cork (v), granirsp, goranipo, granpo
corkscrew (n), granikloirp, goranikeloipa, grankloip
corky (adj), granirpu, goranipu, granpu
corn (n), gralf, gerala, gral
corner (n), pravat, perafita, praft
corner (v), pravast, perafito, prafto
cornerstone (n), pravatbaraft, perafibarafa, praftbaraf
cornfield (n), pravatprant, perafiperanida, praftprand
corny (adj), gralfu, geralu, gralu
corona (n), traunal, terauna, traun
coronate (adj), traunaltu, teraunatu, traunatu
coronate (v), traunalst, teraunato, traunato
coronation (n), traunalt, teraunata, traunat
coroner (n), kiafuaft, kiafuata, kiafuat
corporate (adj), pralupu, peralipu, pralpu
corporation (n), pralup, peralipa, pralp
corps (n), prabif, bilofa, bilf
corpse (n), kiashlarde, kiashelada, kiashlad
correct (adj), prakatu, peraliku, pralku
correct (v), prakast, peraliko, pralko

correction (n), prakat, peralika, pralk
correctly (adv), prakatiu, peralikiu, pralkiu
correlate (v), ipludarast, ipeludarito, ipludarto
correlation (n), ipludarat, ipeludarita, ipludart
correspond (v), ipludufirsp, ipeludufipo, ipludufpo
correspondence (n), ipludufirp, ipeludufipa, ipludufp
correspondent (n doer), ipludufirpwan, ipeludufipua, ipludufpua
corridor (n), talirp, talipa, talp
corrode (v), ipishlirsp, ipishelipo, ipishlipo
corrosion (n), ipishlirp, ipishelipa, ipishlip
corrosive (adj), ipishlirpu, ipishelipu, ipishlipu
corrosively (adv), ipishlirpiu, ipishelipiu, ipishlipiu
corrupt (adj), pravgu, bigaifotu, bigaiftu
corrupt (v), pravzge, bigaifoto, bigaifto
corruption (n), pravge, bigaifota, bigaift
corruptly (adv), pravgiu, bigaifotiu, bigaiftiu
corsage (n), thauarde, shelauana, shlauan
cortex (n), fravurn, feravuna, fravun
cosmetic (adj), gelarnu, gelarinu, glarnu
cosmetic (n), gelarn, gelarina, glarn
cosmetically (adv), gelarniu, gelariniu, glarniu
cosmetician (n doer), gelarnwan, gelarinua, glarnua
cosmic (adj), fliormu, feliomu, fliomu
cosmopolitan (n doer), fliormwan, feliomua, fliomua
cosmos (n), fliorme, felioma, fliom
cost (n), shprut, sheperufa, shpruf
cost (v pa), shprustyot, sheperufio, shprufio
cost (v), shprust, sheperufo, shprufo
Costa Rica (n), Koshtarf Rikarf, Koshetafa Rikafa, Koshtaf Rikaf
costar (n), ipidrokifar, ipiderokirofa, ipidrokirf
costar (v), ipidrokifasre, ipiderokirofo, ipidrokirfo
costly (adj), shprutu, sheperufu, shprufu
costume (n), dairunk, dairuna, dairn
cottage (n), shkodarge, shekodaga, shkodag
cotton (n), marlth, marutha, marth
couch (n), garilme, garima, garm
couch (v), garilzme, garilmo, garmo
cough (n), garlth, galitha, galth
cough (v), garlsth, galitho, galtho
cougher (n doer), garlthwan, galithua, galthua
could (ndal d:ability), frelp kodi, ferepa kodi, frep kodi
could have (ndal d:ability), frelp kodi, ferepa kodi, frep kodi
council (n), rolarme, rolama, rolm
counsel (n), rolirp, rolipa, rolp
counsel (v), rolirsp, rolipo, rolpo
counselor (n doer), rolirpwan, rolipua, rolpua
count (n d:d: increment), poinf, poina, poin
count (n d:d: title), poishark, poishaka, poishk
count (v d:d: increment), poinsf, poino, poino
countdown (n), pointiern, poinetiena, pointien
counter (n d:d: shelf), kelurbe, keluba, kelb
counter (n doer d:d: increment), poinfwan, poinua, poinua
counter (v d:d: oppose), poifst, poifo, poifo
counteract (v), poifpatisle, poifepalito, poifpalto
counteraction (n), poifpatil, poifepalita, poifpalt
counteractive (adj), poifpatilu, poifepalitu,

poifpaltu
counteractively (adv), poifpatiliu, poifepalitiu,
   poifpaltiu
counteractor (n doer), poifpatilwan, poifepalitua,
   poifpaltua
counterargue (v), poifgautisf, poifegaufito,
   poifgaufto
counterargument (n), poifgautif, poifegaufita,
   poifgauft
counterattack (n), poifopairt, poifepaita, poifopait
counterattack (v), poifopairst, poifepaito,
   poifopaito
counterbalance (n), poifmorshtat, poifeshemotata,
   poifshmotat
counterbalance (v), poifmorshtast, poifeshemotato,
   poifshmotato
counterclaim (n), poifnolan, poifenoarita, poifnoart
counterclaim (v), poifnolasne, poifenoarito,
   poifnoarto
counterclaimed (v prp), poifnolasnaut,
   poifenoaritao, poifnoartao
counterclockwise (adj), drofkalu, derofeliku,
   drofliku
counterfeit (adj), poiftapeimu, poifepeimu,
   poifpeimu
counterfeit (v), poiftapeizme, poifepeimo,
   poifpeimo
counterfeiter (n doer), poiftapeimwan,
   poifepeimua, poifpeimua
counterintelligence (n), poifepreift, poifeperita,
   poifpreit
countermeasure (n), poifgrolf, poifegerola, poifgrol
counterpart (n), poifersh, poifesha, poifesh
counterpoint (n), poiftaifort, poifetaifota, poiftaift
counterproductive (adj), poifiurku, poifiuku,
   poifiuku
counterproposal (n), poifiulork, poifiuloka, poifiulk
counterpunch (n), poifkrirthk, poifekerithika,
   poifkrithk
counterpunch (v), poifkrirthsk, poifekerithiko,
   poifkrithko
counterterrorism (n), poifkakortuet,
   poifebakotueta, poifbakotuet
counterweigh (v), poifshuirs, poifeshuisho,
   poifshuisho
counterweight (n), poifshuirsh, poifeshuisha,
   poifshuish
countess (n), kliarsh, keliasha, kliash
country (n), porve, pova, pov
countryside (n), porvashoit, poveshoita, povshoit
county (n), klede, ponita, pont
coup (n), giurp, giupa, giup
couple (n), vanarf, vanafa, vanf
couple (v), vanarsf, vanafo, vanfo
coupler (n doer), vanarfwan, vanafua, vanfua
coupon (n), vinarde, vinada, vind
courage (n), divar, dirava, dirv
courageous (adj), divaru, diravu, dirvu
courageously (adv), divariu, diraviu, dirviu
courier (n), giern, giena, gien
course (n), marnf, marina, marn
course (v), marnsf, marino, marno
court (n), norde, norila, norl

court (v), norzde, norilo, norlo
courteous (adj), norduenu, noriluenu, norluenu
courteously (adv), pordueniu, norilueniu, norlueniu
courtesy (n), norduen, noriluena, norluen
courthouse (n), nordkiarf, norilekiafa, norlkiaf
courtroom (n), nordshranf, norilesherana,
   norlshran
courtship (n), norvoshk, norevosha, norvosh
courtyard (n), norlthauthk, norilethautha,
   norlthauth
cousin (n), shreme, sharima, shrim
cover (n), dathel, dalitha, dalth
cover (v), dathesle, dalitho, daltho
coverage (n), dathelt, dalithata, dalthat
coverup (n), datheliveil, dalithiveila, dalthiveil
cow (n), kumak, kurema, kurm
coward (n doer), griarkwan, geriakua, griakua
cowardice (n), griark, geriaka, griak
cowardly (adj), griarku, geriaku, griaku
cowboy (n), kubiurn, kubiuna, kubiun
cower (v), griarsk, geriako, griako
coy (adj), kuarlu, kualu, kualu
coziness (n), kuashk, kuasha, kuash
cozy (adj), kuashku, kuashu, kuashu
cozy (v), kuashsk, kuasho, kuasho
crab (n), kalirp, kalipa, kalp
crab (v), kalirsp, kalipo, kalpo
crabby (adj), kalirpu, kalipu, kalpu
crack (n d:split), shkark, shekaka, shkak
crack (v d:split), shkarsk, shekako, shkako
crackdown (n), shkarktiern, shekaketiena,
   shkaktien
cracker (n d:saltine), glath, loruga, lorg
cracker (n doer d:split), shkarkwan, shekakua,
   shkakua
crackle (n), shkalark, shekalaka, shkalak
crackle (v), shkalarsk, shekalako, shkalako
crackpot (n), shkakdairf, shekakedaifa, shkakdarb
cradle (n), pradar, perada, prad
cradle (v), pradasre, perado, prado
craft (n), kafirp, kafipa, kafp
craft (v), kafirsp, kafipo, kafpo
craftily (adv), kafirpiu, kafipiu, kafpiu
craftsman (n doer), kafirpwan, kafipua, kafpua
crafty (adj), kafirpu, kafipu, kafpu
cram (n), karlk, kalika, kalk
cram (v), karlsk, kaliko, kalko
cramp (n), fkarnk, fikanika, fkank
cramp (v), fkarnsk, fikaniko, fkanko
crane (n), goinf, goina, goin
crane (v), goinsf, goino, goino
crank (n), goirk, goika, goik
crank (v), goirsk, goiko, goiko
cranny (n), privif, perififa, prifif
crap (n), nugage, nuraga, nurg
crap (v), nugazge, nurago, nurgo
crappy (adj), nugagu, nuragu, nurgu
crash (n), kaflak, kalifoka, kalfk
crash (v), kaflask, kalifoko, kalfko
crasher (n doer), kaflakwan, kalifokua, kalfkua
crate (n), pralirt, peralita, pralt
crate (v), pralirst, peralito, pralto
crater (n), praltarp, peralitapa, praltap

crater (v), praltarsp, peralitapo, praltapo
crave (v), kalurzge, kalugo, kalgo
crawl (n), fliarf, feliafa, fliaf
crawl (v), fliarsf, feliafo, fliafo
crawler (n doer), fliarfwan, feliafua, fliafua
crayon (n), fliorn, feliona, flion
craze (n), klavurge, kelavuga, klavg
craze (v), klavurzge, kelavugo, klavgo
crazily (adv), klavurgiu, kelavugiu, klavgiu
crazy (adj), klavurgu, kelavugu, klavgu
creak (n), kluark, keluaka, kluak
creak (v), kluarsk, keluako, kluako
creaker (n doer), kluarkwan, keluakua, kluakua
creakily (adv), kluarkiu, keluakiu, kluakiu
creaky (adj), kluarku, keluaku, kluaku
cream (n), lunirp, lunipa, lunp
cream (v), lunirsp, lunipo, lunpo
creamer (n doer), lunirpwan, lunipua, lunpua
creamily (adv), lunirpiu, lunipiu, lunpiu
creamy (adj), lunirpu, lunipu, lunpu
crease (n), drishk, derika, drik
crease (v), drishsk, deriko, driko
creaser (n doer), drishkwan, derikua, drikua
create (v), pliurst, peliuto, pliuto
creation (n), pliurt, peliuta, pliut
creative (adj), pliurtu, peliutu, pliutu
creatively (adv), pliurtiu, peliutiu, pliutiu
creativity (n), pliurtuet, peliutueta, pliutuet
creator (n doer), pliurtwan, peliutua, pliutua
creature (n), pliurtal, peliutala, pliutal
credential (n), flershuet, felenishueta, flenshuet
credibility (n), flersh, felenisha, flensh
credible (adj), flershu, felenishu, flenshu
credit (n), flenift, felenita, flent
credit (v), flenifst, felenito, flento
creditor (n doer), fleniftwan, felenitua, flentua
creed (n), bliurt, beliuta, bliut
creek (n), driulk, deriuka, driuk
creep (n), fluairk, feluaika, fluaik
creep (v), fluairsk, feluaiko, fluaiko
creeper (n doer), fluairkwan, feluaikua, fluaikua
creepily (adv), fluairkiu, feluaikiu, fluaikiu
creepy (adj), fluairku, feluaiku, fluaiku
crept (v pa), fluairskyot, feluaikio, fluaikio
crest (n), breisht, bereita, breit
crest (v), breishst, bereito, breito
crew (n), fliorde, felioda, fliod
crib (n), kilorp, kilopa, kilp
crick (n), klert, kaleta, klet
crick (v), klerst, kaleto, kleto
cricket (n), klenirt, kulenita, klent
crier (n doer), broipwan, beroifua, broifua
crime (n), nuarn, nuana, nuan
criminal (n doer), nuarnwan, nuanua, nuanua
criminalize (v), nuarsne, nuano, nuano
crimp (n), shkilorp, shekilopa, shkilp
crimp (v), shkilorsp, shekilopo, shkilpo
crimper (n doer), shkilorpwan, shekilopua,
    shkilpua
cringe (v), bloishst, beloisho, bloisho
crinkle (n), shkilort, shekilota, shkilt
crinkle (v), shkilorst, shekiloto, shkilto
cripple (n), fluark, feluaka, fluak

cripple (v), fluarsk, feluako, fluako
crisis (n), broifk, beroika, broik
crisp (adj), tutirku, tutiku, tutiku
criteria (n pl), duftartyek, dufitari, duftari
criterion (n), duftart, dufitara, duftar
critic (n doer), dufirtwan, dufitua, duftua
critical (adj), dufirtu, dufitu, duftu
critically (adv), dufirtiu, dufitiu, duftiu
criticism (n), dufirt, dufita, duft
criticize (v), dufirst, dufito, dufto
crook (n), biulort, biulota, biult
crook (v), biulorst, biuloto, biulto
crop (n d:food), prifort, perifota, prift
crop (v d:narrow), folirst, folito, folto
cropper (n doer d:food), prifortwan, perifotua,
    priftua
cross (n), kliark, keliaka, kliak
cross (v), kliarsk, keliako, kliako
crossbow (n), kliakdiarf, keliakediafa, kliakdiaf
crosscurrent (n), kliagurilf, keliagurifa, kliagurf
crossfire (n), kliarkshriauk, keliagiaula, kliagiaul
crossover (n), kliarkafen, keliakafena, kliakafen
crossroad (n), kliaktrelish, keliaterelisha,
    kliaktrelsh
crosstalk (n), kliakshpalort, keliashipalota,
    kliakshpalt
crosswise (adj), kliakfluirku, keliafeliuku,
    kliakfluiku
crosswise (adv), kliakfluirkiu, keliafeliukiu,
    kliakfluikiu
crossword (n), kliaklialirt, kelialialita, kliaklialt
crotch (n), gloshk, gelosha, glosh
crouch (n), fnauthk, fenautha, fnauth
crouch (v), fnauthsk, fenautho, fnautho
crow (n), viarfk, viaroka, viark
crow (v), viarfsk, viaroko, viarko
crowbar (n), viakrolart, viakelata, viakrolt
crowd (n), viarge, viaga, viag
crowd (v), viarzge, viago, viago
crowder (n doer), viargwan, viagua, viagua
crown (n), traufk, terauka, trauk
crown (v), traufsk, terauko, trauko
crucial (adj), viornu, vionu, vionu
cruciality (n), viorn, viona, vion
crucially (adv), viorniu, vioniu, vioniu
crucifixion (n), vioishk, vioisha, vioish
crucify (v), vioishsk, vioisho, vioisho
crude (adj), shklirpu, shikalipu, shklipu
cruel (adj), shkliargu, shikoliagu, shkliagu
cruelly (adv), shkliargiu, shikoliagiu, shkliagiu
cruelty (n), shkliarge, shikoliaga, shkliag
cruise (n), shkairn, shekaina, shkain
cruise (v), shkairsne, shekaino, shkaino
cruiser (n doer), shkairnwan, shekainua, shkainua
crumb (n), shrushp, sherupa, shrup
crumble (v), shrushsp, sherupo, shrupo
crumbly (adj), shrushpu, sherupu, shrupu
crunch (n), bliashk, beliasha, bliash
crunch (v), bliashsk, beliasho, bliasho
cruncher (n doer), bliashkwan, beliashua, bliashua
crunchy (adj), bliashku, beliashu, bliashu
crusade (n), shkainark, shekainaka, shkainak
crusade (v), shkainarsk, shekainako, shkainako

crusader (n doer), shkainarkwan, shekainakua, shkainakua
crush (n), shklirft, shekalifota, shklift
crush (v), shklirfst, shekalifoto, shklifto
crusher (n doer), shklirftwan, shekalifotua, shkliftua
crust (n), glirp, gelipa, glip
crust (v), glirsp, gelipo, glipo
crusty (adj), glirpu, gelipu, glipu
crutch (n), gliart, geliata, gliat
crux (n), krefk, kareka, krek
cry (n), broip, beroifa, broif
cry (v), broisp, beroifo, broifo
crybaby (n), broipdeirde, beroifedeida, broifdeid
crypt (n), plaurge, pelauga, plaug
cryptic (adj), bruilkdarfku, beruikedarifu, bruikdarfu
cryptic (adj), bruilku, beruiku, bruiku
cryptography (n), bruilkdarfk, beruikedarifa, bruikdarf
crystal (n), britar, beroteira, broteir
crystalization (n), britaruet, beroteirueta, broteiruet
crystalize (v), britasre, beroteiro, broteiro
crystalline (adj), britaru, beroteiru, broteiru
cub (n), vurbe, vuba, vub
Cuba (n), Kubarf, Kubafa, Kubaf
Cuban (n), Kubarn, Kubana, Kuban
cube (n), dashirk, dashika, dashk
cube (v), dashirsk, dashiko, dashko
cubic (adj), dashirku, dashiku, dashku
cucumber (n), danart, danata, danat
cuddle (n), vunharf, vunahafa, vunhaf
cuddle (v), vunharsf, vunahafo, vunhafo
cue (n), tierf, teifa, teif
cue (v), tiersf, teifo, teifo
cuff (n), diefk, diefa, dief
cuff (v), diefsk, diefo, diefo
cuisine (n), griorf, geriofa, griof
culpability (n), pulirk, pulika, pulk
culpable (adj), pulirku, puliku, pulku
culprit (n doer), pulirkwan, pulikua, pulkua
cult (n), faturk, fatuka, fatuk
cultivate (v), fatursp, fatupo, fatupo
cultivation (n), faturp, fatupa, fatup
cultivator (n doer), faturpwan, fatupua, fatupua
cultural (adj), tafirku, tafiku, tafku
culture (n), tafirk, tafika, tafk
cumbersome (adj), pramipu, peramipu, prampu
cumulative (adj), briorku, berioku, brioku
cumulatively (adv), briorkiu, beriokiu, briokiu
cup (n), vorup, voripa, vorp
cup (v), vorusp, voripo, vorpo
cupboard (n), vorplok, vorepelorika, vorplork
cupcake (n), vorugutraf, vorigurita, vorpgurt
curable (adj), tulirfu, tulifu, tulfu
curative (adj), tulirfu, tulifu, tulfu
curb (n), tulirp, tulipa, tulp
curb (v), tulirsp, tulipo, tulpo
cure (n), tulirf, tulifa, tulf
cure (v), tulirsf, tulifo, tulfo
curer (n doer), tulirfwan, tulifua, tulfua
curfew (n), tiurp, tiupa, tiup
curiosity (n), thaurp, thaupa, thaup

curious (adj), thaurpu, thaupu, thaupu
curiously (adv), thaurpiu, thaupiu, thaupiu
Curium (n davoka), Onuk, Onuk, Onuk
Curium (n), Kurium, Kuriuma, Kurium
curl (n), tufarn, tufana, tufan
curl (v), tufarsne, tufano, tufano
curler (n doer), tufarnwan, tufanua, tufanua
curly (adj), tufarnu, tufanu, tufanu
currency (n), dilth, ditha, dith
current (adj d:now), dulirmu, dulimu, dulmu
current (n d:stream), gurilf, gurifa, gurf
currently (adv d:now), dulirmiu, dulimiu, dulmiu
curriculum (n), galgan, galuga, galg
curse (n), giarshk, giashoka, giashk
curse (v), giarshsk, giashoko, giashko
cursor (n), geirth, gietha, gieth
curtail (v), lorfsk, lofeko, lofko
curtain (n), lofarn, lofana, lofan
curvature (n), lorfpar, lofipara, lofpar
curve (n), lofirp, lofipa, lofp
curve (v), lofirsp, lofipo, lofpo
curvy (adj), lofirpu, lofipu, lofpu
cushion (n), mumarth, mumatha, mumath
cushion (v), mumarsth, mumatho, mumatho
cushioner (n doer), mumarthwan, mumathua, mumathua
cushy (adj), mumarthu, mumathu, mumathu
cusp (n), graisht, geraifita, graift
cuss (v), goishst, goito, goito
custodian (n doer), darnofwan, darinofua, darnfua
custody (n), darnof, darinofa, darnf
custom (n d:tradition), dalilt, dalila, dalil
customary (adj d:tradition), daliltu, dalilu, dalilu
customer (n doer d:tradition), daliltwan, dalilua, dalilua
customize (v d:tradition), dalilst, dalilo, dalilo
customs (n d:checkpoint), dalilart, dalilata, dalilt
cut (n), dairsh, daisha, daish
cut (v pa), dairsyot, daishio, daishio
cut (v), dairs, daisho, daisho
cutback (n), daishvark, daishevaka, daishvak
cute (adj), dairthu, daithu, daithu
cuteness (n), dairth, daitha, daith
cutoff (n), dairshunf, daisheunefa, daishunf
cutout (n), dairshuil, daishuila, daishuil
cutter (n doer), dairshwan, daishua, daishua
cycle (n), vairalt, vairata, vairt
cycle (v), vairalst, vairato, vairto
cycler (n doer), vairaltwan, vairatua, vairtua
cyclic (adj), vairaltu, vairatu, vairtu
cyclical (adj), vairaltu, vairatu, vairtu
cyclically (adv), vairaltiu, vairatiu, vairtiu
cylinder (n), vairolp, vairopa, vairp
cynic (n doer), draugargwan, deraugagua, draugagua
cynical (adj), draugargu, deraugagu, draugagu
cynically (adv), draugargiu, deraugagiu, draugagiu
cynicism (n), draugarge, deraugaga, draugag
cypher (n), biuifk, biuifa, biuif
Cyprus (n), Shaiprulsh, Shaiperusha, Shaiprush
Czechoslovakia (n), Tshekoshlovark, Teshekoshelovaka, Tshekoshlovak
D (let sng), dal, dala, da

dab (n), fruinshk, feruinoka, fruink
dab (v), fruinshsk, feruinoko, fruinko
dabble (v), fruinorshsk, feruinoriko, fruinorko
dabbler (n doer), fruinorshkwan, feruinorikua, fruinorkua
dad (n), balbe, baba, bab
daddy (n), balbil, babila, babil
daemon (n), bregark, beregaka, bregak
daemonize (v), bregarsk, beregako, bregako
dagger (n), beilbark, beilebaka, beilbak
Dahma (n), Dahma, Dahma, Dahma
daily (adj), viurlu, viulu, viulu
dairy (adj), boirnu, boinu, boinu
dairy (n), boirn, boina, boin
daisy (n), deiflurf, deifelura, deiflur
Dallas (n), Dalarsh, Dalasha, Dalash
dam (n), bluarn, beluana, bluan
damage (n), zhoirge, zhoika, zhoik
damage (v), zhoirzge, zhoiko, zhoiko
damn (adj), viaurku, viauku, viauku
damn (n), viaurk, viauka, viauk
damn (v), viaursk, viauko, viauko
damp (adj), zhanirpu, zhanipu, zhanpu
dampen (v), zhanirsp, zhanipo, zhanpo
damper (n doer), zhanirpwan, zhanipua, zhanpua
dampness (n), zhanirp, zhanipa, zhanp
dance (n), flamar, felarima, flarm
dance (v), flamasre, felarimo, flarmo
dancer (n doer), flamarwan, felarimua, flarmua
danger (n), zhaurbe, zhauba, zhaub
dangerous (adj), zhaurbu, zhaubu, zhaubu
dangle (n), taragage, tarugaga, targag
dangle (v), taragazge, tarugago, targago
dare (n), bohart, bohata, boht
dare (v), boharst, bohato, bohto
darish (adj), bohartu, bohatu, bohtu
dark (adj), klorfku, keloriku, klorku
dark (n), klorfk, kelorika, klork
darken (v), klorfsk, keloriko, klorko
darker (adj), klorfkwelu, kelorikwelu, klorkwelu
darkest (adj), klorfkweku, kelorikwcku, klorkweku
darkly (adv), klorfkiu, kelorikiu, klorkiu
darkness (n), klorfkuet, kelorikueta, klorkuet
darkroom (n), klorfkshranf, kelorikesherana, klorkshran
darling (adj), lovorlu, lovoru, lorvu
darling (n), lovorl, lovora, lorv
Darmstadtium (n davoka), Inuk, Inuk, Inuk
Darmstadtium (n), Darmshtat, Daremishetata, Darmshtat
dart (n), darthk, darotha, darth
Dart (n), Dart, Darta, Dart
dart (v), darthsk, darotho, dartho
dash (n d:line), bolarf, bolafa, bolf
dash (n d:sprint), klishk, kulisha, klish
dash (v d:line), bolarsf, bolafo, bolfo
dash (v d:sprint), klishsk, kulisho, klisho
dashboard (n), klishplok, kulishepelorika, klishplork
dasher (n doer d:line), bolarfwan, bolafua, bolfua
dasher (n doer d:sprint), klishkwan, kulishua, klishua
data (n pl), talartyek, talati, talti

database (n), talartviarsh, talatuviasha, taltviash
date (n d:fruit), voarth, voatha, voath
date (n d:time, meet), tolirk, tolika, tolk
date (v d:time, meet), tolirsk, toliko, tolko
datum (n), talart, talata, talt
daughter (n), lidor, lunora, lurn
dawn (n), nulash, norisha, norsh
dawn (v), nulas, norisho, norsho
day (n), viurl, viula, viul
daybreak (n), viunblerk, viunepelika, viunplik
daycare (n), viunkeirf, viunekeifa, viunkeif
daydream (n), viunflaul, viunefelauma, viunflaum
daydream (v), viunflausle, viunefelaumo, viunflaumo
daylight (n), viunfluarn, viunefeluana, viunf
daylong (adj), viunralzhu, viunerazhu, viunrazhu
daytime (n), viundaurn, viunodauna, viund
Dayton (n), Daitorn, Daitona, Daiton
Daytona (n), Daitonarf, Daitonafa, Daitonaf
daze (n), shkranp, shukerana, shkran
daze (v), shkransp, shukerano, shkrano
dazzle (n), shkranart, shukeranata, shkranat
dazzle (v), shkranarst, shukeranato, shkranato
dazzler (n doer), shkranartwan, shukeranatua, shkranatua
deactivate (v), bupaltarsk, bupalitako, bupaltako
deactivation (n), bupaltark, bupalitaka, bupaltak
deactivator (n doer), bupaltarkwan, bupalitakua, bupaltakua
dead (adj), kioshartu, kioshatu, kioshtu
dead (n), kioshart, kioshata, kiosht
deadbeat (n), kioshadaurt, kioshadauta, kioshdaut
deadline (n), kiorfork, kiorifoka, kiorfk
deadlock (n), kioshtiurge, kioshatiuga, kioshtiug
deadly (adv), kioshartiu, kioshatiu, kioshtiu
deadweight (n), kioshuirsh, kioshuisha, kioshuish
deadwood (n), kioshfanirn, kioshefanina, kioshfanin
deaf (adj), hofirpu, hofipu, hofpu
deafen (v), hofirsp, hofipo, hofpo
deafness (n), hofirp, hotipa, hofp
deal (n), birek, bifeka, bifk
deal (v), biresk, bifeko, bifko
dealer (n doer), birekwan, bifekua, bifkua
dealership (n), birekuafif, bifekuafifa, bifkuafif
dealt (v pa), bireskyot, bifekio, bifkio
dear (adj), lovalu, lolifu, lolfu
dear (n), loval, lolifa, lolf
dearly (adv), lovaliu, lolifiu, lolfiu
death (n), kiart, kiata, kiat
deathbed (n), kiatfamor, kiatefuarema, kiatfuarm
debate (n), bugiarp, bugiapa, bugiap
debate (v), bugiarsp, bugiapo, bugiapo
debater (n doer), bugiarpwan, bugiapua, bugiapua
debenture (n), kupogart, kupogata, kupogat
debrief (v), buthoishst, buthoito, buthoito
debris (n), plaurfk, pelaufika, plaufk
debt (n), kuporge, kupoga, kupog
debtor (n doer), kuporgart, kupogua, kupogua
debug (v), kuverze, kuvezho, kuvezho
debugger (n doer), kuverzhwan, kuvezhua, kuvezhua
debunk (v), buglursk, bugeluko, bugluko

debut (n), bufuip, buifopa, buifp
debut (v), bufuisp, buifopo, buifpo
dec- (num 10 pref), dapai-, dapai-, dapai-
decade (n), dakairbe, dakaiba, dakaib
decal (n), thoshlarsh, thoshelasha, thoshlash
decapitate (v), bukefirst, bukefito, bukefto
decapitation (n), bukefirt, bukefita, bukeft
decay (n), bogiaf, giafopa, giafp
decay (v), bogiasf, giafopo, giafpo
decease (n), buverk, buveka, buvek
decease (v), buversk, buveko, buveko
deceit (n), buship, buzhuba, buzhb
deceitful (adj), bushipu, buzhubu, buzhbu
deceitfully (adv), bushipiu, buzhubiu, buzhbiu
deceive (v), bushisp, buzhubo, buzhbo
deceiver (n doer), bushipwan, buzhubua, buzhbua
decelerate (v), buvorast, verafito, vrafto
deceleration (n), buvorat, verafita, vraft
decelerator (n doer), buvoratwan, verafitua, vraftua
December (n), Tefendarl, Tefenedala, Tefendal
decency (n), bulirt, lishopa, lishp
decent (adj), bulirtu, lishopu, lishpu
decently (adv), bulirtiu, lishopiu, lishpiu
deception (n), bushipet, buzhubeta, buzhbet
deceptive (adj), bushipetu, buzhubetu, buzhbetu
deceptively (adv), bushipetiu, buzhubetiu, buzhbetiu
decide (v), buthis, thishopo, thishpo
decillion (num 1e33 card), daka, daka, daka
decillionth (num 1e33 ord), daketh, daketh, daketh
decimal (adj), dakinoru, dakirenu, dakirnu
decimal (n), dakinor, dakirena, dakirn
decimate (v), kliaursk, keliauko, kliauko
decimation (n), kliaurk, keliauka, kliauk
decipher (v), bubrulirsf, buberulifo, bubrulifo
decipherment (n), bubrulirf, buberulifa, bubrulif
decipherments (n pl), bubrulirfyek, buberulifi, bubrulifi
decision (n), buthish, thishopa, thishp
decisive (adj), buthishu, thishopu, thishpu
decisively (adv), buthishiu, thishopiu, thishpiu
deck (n), budat, dapita, dapt
deck (v), budast, dapito, dapto
declaration (n), budosht, derofita, droft
declaratory (adj), budoshtu, derofitu, droftu
declare (v), budoshst, derofito, drofto
declarer (n doer), budoshtwan, derofitua, droftua
declassification (n), bublesh, bubelega, bubleg
declassify (v), bubles, bubelego, bublego
declination (n), bukroifp, keroiforipa, kroiforp
decline (n), bukroif, keroifopa, kroifp
decline (v), bukroisf, keroifopo, kroifpo
decliner (n doer), bukroifwan, keroifopua, kroifpua
decode (v), buvolarst, buvolato, buvlato
decoder (n doer), buvolartwan, buvolatua, buvlatua
decommission (n), bulenkart, bulenikata, bulenkat
decommission (v), bulenkarst, bulenikato, bulenkato
decompose (v), bulnask, bulaniko, bulanko
decomposer (n doer), bulnakwan, bulanikua, bulankua
decomposition (n), bulnak, bulanika, bulank
decompress (v), bugublasharsne, bugubelashano,
bugublashano
decompression (n), bugublasharn, bugubelashana, bugublashan
decontrol (n), butranit, buteranita, butrant
decontrol (v), butranist, buteranito, butranto
decor (n), buprarl, peralifara, pralfar
decorate (v), buprasle, peralifo, pralfo
decoration (n), bupral, peralifa, pralf
decorator (n doer), bupralwan, peralifua, pralfua
decouple (v), buvanarsf, buvanafo, buvanfo
decoy (n), kuarlp, kualipa, kualp
decoy (v), kuarlsp, kualipo, kualpo
decrease (n), budrik, kuderika, kudrik
decrease (v), budrisk, kuderiko, kudriko
decree (n), budliurt, bubeliuta, bubliut
decree (v), budliurst, bubeliuto, bubliuto
decrement (n), budrishork, kuderishoka, kudrishk
decrement (v), budrishorsk, kuderishoko, kudrishko
decremental (adj), budrishorku, kuderishoku, kudrishku
decrementally (adv), budrishorkiu, kuderishokiu, kudrishkiu
decry (v), bubroisp, buberoifo, bubroifo
decrypt (v), bubruilsk, buberuiko, bubruiko
decryption (n), bubruilk, buberuika, bubruik
dedicate (v), bukiarsk, bukiako, bukiako
dedication (n), bukiark, bukiaka, bukiak
dedicator (n doer), bukiarkwan, bukiakua, bukiakua
deduce (v d:determination), bukirsk, kirofiko, kirfko
deducer (n doer d:determination), bukirkwan, kirofikua, kirfkua
deduct (v d:subtraction), bukriushsk, bukeriuko, bukriuko
deductible (adj d:subtraction), bukriushku, bukeriuku, bukriuku
deductible (n d:subtraction), bukriushk, bukeriuka, bukriuk
deduction (n d:determination), bukirk, kirofika, kirfk
deduction (n d:subtraction), bukriushk, bukeriuka, bukriuk
deed (n), felirde, felida, flid
deem (v), kiursf, kiufo, kiufo
deep (adj), bushirpu, bushipu, bushpu
deep (n), bushirp, bushipa, bushp
deepen (v), bushirsp, bushipo, bushpo
deeper (adj), bushirpwelu, bushipwelu, bushpwelu
deepest (adj), bushirpwaku, bushipwaku, bushpwaku
deeply (adv), bushirpiu, bushipiu, bushpiu
deer (n pl), fadirfyek, fadifi, fofti
deer (n), fadirf, fadifa, foft
deface (v), buthoirs, buthoisho, buthoisho
default (n), buboirt, buboita, buboit
default (v), buboirst, buboito, buboito
defeat (n), bubirt, birofita, birft
defeat (v), bubirst, birofito, birfto
defeater (n doer), bubirtwan, birofitua, birftua
defecate (v), viatshsk, viatesho, viatsho
defecation (n), viatshkuet, viateshueta, viatshuet

defect (n), buvirt, virofata, virft
defect (v), buvirst, virofato, virfto
defective (adj), buvirtu, virofatu, virftu
defectively (adv), buvirtiu, virofatiu, virftiu
defector (n doer), buvirtwan, virofatua, virftua
defend (v), butorzve, torifopo, torfpo
defendant (n doer), butorvwan, torifopua, torfpua
defender (n doer), butorvwan, torifopua, torfpua
defense (n), butorve, torifopa, torfp
defensive (adj), butorvu, torifopu, torfpu
defer (v), bugesf, gefipo, gefpo
deference (n), bugerf, gerafipa, gerfp
deferral (n), bugef, gefipa, gefp
defiance (n), buanirt, buanita, buant
defiant (adj), buanirtu, buanitu, buantu
defiantly (adv), buanirtiu, buanitiu, buantiu
deficiency (n), bulinirk, bulinika, bulink
deficient (adj), bulinirku, buliniku, bulinku
deficiently (adv), bulinirkiu, bulinikiu, bulinkiu
deficit (n), bulinarp, bulinapa, bulinp
define (v), buvuast, vuafito, vuafto
definite (adj), buvuatu, vuafitu, vuaftu
definitely (adv), buvuatiu, vuafitiu, vuaftiu
definition (n), buvuat, vuafita, vuaft
definitive (adj), buvuatu, vuafitu, vuaftu
deflate (v), bublarsf, bubelarifo, bublarfo
deflation (n), bublarf, bubelarifa, bublarf
deflationary (adj), bublarfu, bubelarifu, bublarfu
deflator (n doer), bublarfwan, bubelarifua, bublarfua
deflect (v), bugerst, bugeto, bugeto
deflection (n), bugert, bugeta, buget
deflective (adj), bugertu, bugetu, bugetu
deflector (n doer), bugertwan, bugetua, bugetua
deform (v), buvorsne, vorinoko, vornko
deformation (n), buvorn, vorinoka, vornk
deformer (n doer), buvornwan, vorinokua, vornkua
defraud (v), dairzge, daigo, daigo
defrauder (n doer), dairgwan, daigua, daigua
defray (v), burianirsk, burianiko, burianko
defrost (v), bufiorshst, bufiorito, bufiorto
defuse (v), bufaborst, bufaboto, bufaboto
defy (v), buanirst, buanito, buanto
degas (v), buzhersk, buzheko, buzheko
degenerate (v), bumarmarsk, bumaromako, bumarmako
degeneration (n), bumarmark, bumaromaka, bumarmak
degenerative (adj), bumarmarku, bumaromaku, bumarmaku
degradation (n), bushtrak, bushoterana, bushtran
degrade (v), bushtrask, bushoterano, bushtrano
degree (n), tegnart, tegenata, tegnat
dehydrate (v), butahst, tahofito, tahfto
dehydration (n), butaht, tahofita, tahft
deign (v), nalirs, nalisho, nalsho
deity (n), kutirp, kutipa, kutsh
deject (v), butersp, butepo, butepo
dejection (n), buterp, butepa, butep
Delaware (n), Delawarf, Delawara, Delawar
delay (n), bufrant, feranifota, franft
delay (v), bufranst, feranifoto, franfto
delayer (n doer), bufrantwan, feranifotua, franftua

delegate (n doer), bupiashkwan, bupiakua, bupiakua
delegate (v), bupiashsk, bupiako, bupiako
delegation (n), bupiashk, bupiaka, bupiak
delete (v), kleirsk, keleiko, kleiko
deletion (n), kleirk, keleika, kleik
deliberate (adj), bukiurku, bukiuku, bukiuku
deliberate (v), bukiursk, bukiuko, bukiuko
deliberately (adv), bukiurkiu, bukiukiu, bukiukiu
deliberation (n), bukiurk, bukiuka, bukiuk
delicacy (n), polsht, polita, polt
delicate (adj), polshtu, politu, poltu
delicately (adv), polshtiu, politiu, poltiu
delicious (adj), fluarfu, feluafu, fluafu
deliciously (adv), fluarfiu, feluafiu, fluafiu
delight (n), fluarsh, feluasha, fluash
delight (v), fluars, feluasho, fluasho
delightful (adj), fluarshu, feluashu, fluashu
delimit (v), buvinst, vithopo, vithpo
delimiter (n doer), buvintwan, vithopua, vithpua
delineate (v), buroisf, roifipo, roifpo
delineation (n), buroif, roifipa, roifp
delineator (n doer), buroifwan, roifipua, roifpua
delinquence (n), buroifan, roifipana, roifpan
delinquent (adj), buroifanu, roifipanu, roifpanu
delist (v), budilst, budito, budito
deliver (v), flaufirsk, felaufiko, flaufko
deliverance (n), flaufirkar, felaufikara, flaufkar
deliverer (n doer), flaufirkwan, felaufikua, flaufkua
delivery (n), flaufirk, felaufika, flaufk
delta (n), deltarn, delitana, deltan
delude (v), burushst, burusho, burusho
deluge (n), glifarsh, gelifasha, glifash
deluge (v), glifars, gelifasho, glifasho
delusion (n), burusht, burusha, burush
delusional (adj), burushtu, burushu, burushu
deluxe (adj), biluarshu, biluashu, biluashu
delve (v), tezhirzge, tezhigo, tezhgo
demand (n), bushoirk, bushoika, bushoik
demand (v), bushoirsk, bushoiko, bushoiko
demean (v), bushklivarzge, bushikelivago, bushklivago
demeanor (n), buliarge, buliaga, buliag
demise (n), vutolirp, vutolipa, vutolp
demise (v), vutolirsp, vutolipo, vutolpo
democracy (n), brenfralt, feralifota, fralft
democrat (n doer), brenfraltwan, feralifotua, fralftua
democratic (adj), brenfraltu, feralifotu, fralftu
democratically (adv), brenfraltiu, feralifotiu, fralftiu
demolish (v), buvatharzve, buvathavo, buvathavo
demolition (n), buvatharve, buvathava, buvathav
demon (n), bregark, beregaka, bregak
demonic (adj), bregarku, beregaku, bregaku
demonize (v), bregarsk, beregako, bregako
demonstrate (v), bregisf, berefiko, brefko
demonstration (n), bregif, berefika, brefk
demonstrator (n doer), bregifwan, berefikua, brefkua
demote (v), buvadarzve, buvadavo, buvadavo
demotion (n), buvadarve, buvadava, buvadav
den (n), thethk, thetha, theth
denial (n), brielt, berieta, briet

Denmark (n), Denemark, Denomaka, Denmak
denominate (v), vuvienorsk, vuvienoko, buvienko
denomination (n), vuvienork, vuvienoka, buvienk
denominational (Adj), vuvienorku, vuvienoku, buvienku
denominator (n doer), vuvienorkwan, vuvienokua, buvienkua
denotation (n), bumirade, bumida, bumid
denote (v), bumirazde, bumido, bumido
denounce (v), bumufirst, bumufito, bumufto
denouncement (n), bumufirt, bumufita, bumuft
denouncer (n doer), bumufirtwan, bumufitua, bumuftua
dense (adj), brelfu, berefu, brefu
densely (adv), brelfiu, berefiu, brefiu
denser (adj), brelfwelu, berefwelu, brefwelu
densest (adj), brelfweku, berefweku, brefweku
density (n), brelf, berefa, bref
dent (n), brelt, bereta, bret
dent (v), brelst, bereto, breto
dental (adj), braltu, beradu, bradu
dentist (n doer), braltwan, beradua, bradua
dentistry (n), bralt, berada, brad
denture (n), braltar, beradara, bradar
Denver (n), Denverf, Denuvera, Denver
deny (v), brielst, berieto, brieto
deodorent (n doer), budufarlwan, budufalua, budufalua
deodorization (n), budufarl, budufala, budufal
deodorize (v), budufarsle, budufalo, budufalo
depart (v), feshorst, feshoto, feshto
departer (n doer), feshortwan, feshotua, feshtua
department (n), forshk, buforika, bufork
departmental (adj), forshku, buforiku, buforku
departmentally (adv), forshkiu, buforikiu, buforkiu
departure (n), feshort, feshota, fesht
depend (v), bubrusne, berunipo, brunpo
dependable (adj), bubrunu, berunipu, brunpu
dependably (adv), bubruniu, berunipiu, brunpiu
dependant (n doer), bubrunwan, berunipua, brunpua
dependence (n), bubrun, berunipa, brunp
dependency (n), bubrun, berunipa, brunp
dependent (n doer), bubrunwan, berunipua, brunpua
depict (v), bugrals, bugerasho, bugrasho
depiction (n), bugralsh, bugerasha, bugrash
deplete (v), buwelfsk, buweliko, buwelko
depletion (n), buwelfk, buwelika, buwelk
deplorable (adj), bufirtu, bufitu, buftu
deplore (v), bufirst, bufito, bufto
deploy (v), bushloist, sheloifito, shloifto
deployment (n), bushloit, sheloifita, shloift
depopulate (v), buvovasre, buvoruvo, buvorvo
depopulation (n), buvovar, buvoruva, buvorv
deport (v), bubielirsk, bubieliko, bubielko
deportation (n), bubielirk, bubielika, bubielk
deportee (n), bubielirkuin, bubielikuina, bubielkuin
deporter (n doer), bubielirkwan, bubielikua, bubielkua
depose (v), bulask, belako, blako
deposer (n doer), bulakwan, belakua, blakua
deposit (n), sherf, herifa, herf

deposit (v), shersf, herifo, herfo
deposition (n), bulak, belaka, blak
depositor (n doer), sherfwan, herifua, herfua
depository (n), sherfiek, herifieka, herfiek
depot (n), sherfk, herifeka, herfk
depreciate (v), budrulsp, derufipo, drufpo
depreciation (n), budrulp, derufipa, drufp
depress (v), bublars, bubelasho, bublasho
depressant (n doer), bublarshwan, bubelashua, bublashua
depression (n), bublarsh, bubelasha, bublash
depressive (adj), bublarshu, bubelashu, bublashu
depressively (adv), bublarshiu, bubelashiu, bublashiu
depressor (n doer), bublarshwan, bubelashua, bublashua
deprivation (n), butiarp, butiapa, butiap
deprive (v), butiarsp, butiapo, butiapo
depth (n), bushirk, bushika, bushk
deputization (n), shpiarft, shopiafita, shpiaft
deputize (v), shpiarst, shopiato, shpiato
deputizer (n doer), shpiartwan, shopiatua, shpiatua
deputy (n), shpiart, shopiata, shpiat
derail (v), buluirst, buluito, buluito
derailment (n), buluirt, buluita, buluit
derange (v), bulmorst, bulimoto, bulmoto
derangement (n), bulmort, bulimota, bulmot
deregulate (v), buluvirsp, buluvipo, buluvipo
deregulation (n), buluvirp, buluvipa, buluvip
deregulator (n doer), buluvirpwan, buluvipua, buluvipua
deride (v), bushlirzbe, bushelibo, bushlibo
derision (n), bushlirbe, busheliba, bushlib
derivation (n), drushk, derusha, drush
derivative (adj), drushku, derushu, drushu
derive (v), drushsk, derusho, drusho
derogate (v), bufasp, bufapo, bufapo
derogatory (adj), bufapu, bufapu, bufapu
descend (v), bulirask, buliriko, bulirko
descendant (n), bulikart, bulirokata, bulirkat
descendent (n), bulikart, bulirokata, bulirkat
descender (n doer), bulirakwan, bulirikua, bulirkua
descent (n), bulirak, bulirika, bulirk
describe (v), bushrizge, sherifoko, shrifko
description (n), bushrige, sherifoka, shrifk
descriptive (adj), bushrigu, sherifoku, shrifku
descriptively (adv), bushrigiu, sherifokiu, shrifkiu
descriptor (n doer), bushrigwan, sherifokua, shrifkua
desert (n d:wasteland), dushart, dushata, dusht
desert (v d:flee), tereirsk, tereilto, treiko
deserter (n doer d:flee), tereirkwan, tereikua, treikua
desertion (n d:flee), tereirk, tereika, treik
deserve (v), bukofst, kofirato, kofirto
design (n), deirolt, deirota, deirt
design (v), deirolst, deiroto, deirto
designate (v), deirtarsk, deirotako, deirtako
designation (n), deirtark, deirotaka, deirtak
designator (n doer), deirtarkwan, deirotakua, deirtakua
designer (n doer), deiroltwan, deirotua, deirtua
desirable (adj), loirfu, loiru, loiru

desirably (adv), loirfiu, loiriu, loiriu
desire (n), loirf, loira, loir
desire (v), loirsf, loiro, loiro
desist (v), butelfsk, buteliko, butelko
desk (n), truft, teruta, trut
desktop (n), trutaurbe, terutauba, trutaub
desolate (v), blofiersne, bulofieno, blofieno
desolation (n), blofiern, bulofiena, blofien
despair (n), burborlk, burabolika, burbolk
despair (v), burborlsk, buraboliko, burbolko
desperate (adj), burborlku, buraboliku, burbolku
desperation (n), burborlirk, buarobolika, burbolkar
despise (v), bufairsk, bufaiko, bufaiko
despiser (n doer), bufairkwan, bufaikua, bufaikua
despite (prep), burfaik, burafaiku, burfaik
despond (v), budufirsp, budufipo, budufpo
despondence (n), budufirp, budufipa, budufp
desponder (n doer), budufirpwan, budufipua, budufpua
despot (n), largrazhge, larigeraga, largrag
despotism (n), largrazhguet, larigeragueta, largraguet
dessert (n), tifan, tinufa, tinf
destination (n), bushlarnt, bushelanita, bushlant
destine (v), bushlarsne, bushelano, bushlano
destiny (n), bushlarn, bushelana, bushlan
destroy (v), bupliurst, bupeliuto, bupliuto
destroyer (n doer), bupliurtwan, bupeliutua, bupliutua
destruct (v), bushlersk, busheleko, bushleko
destruction (n), bushlerk, busheleka, bushlek
destructive (adj), bushlerku, busheleku, bushleku
detach (v), bupairsk, bupaiko, bupaiko
detachment (n), bupairk, bupaika, bupaik
detail (n), bumithk, bumitha, bumith
detail (v), bumithsk, bumitho, bumitho
detailer (n doer), bumithkwan, bumithua, bumithua
detain (v), bupirfst, bupifoto, bupifto
detainee (n), bupirftuin, bupifotuina, bupiftuin
detainment (n), bupirft, bupifota, bupift
detainor (n doer), bupirftwan, bupifotua, bupiftua
detect (v), budolirsf, budolifo, budolfo
detectable (adj), budolirfu, budolifu, budolfu
detection (n), budolirf, budolifa, budolf
detective (n), budolirfat, budolifata, budolfat
detector (n doer), budolirfwan, budolifua, budolfua
detention (n), bupirftar, bupifotara, bupiftar
deter (v), bufrilarsk, buferilako, bufrilako
deteriorate (v), builarsf, builaro, builaro
deterioration (n), builarf, builara, builar
determent (n), bufrilark, buferilaka, bufrilak
determinant (n doer), tulirshwan, tulishua, tulshua
determination (n), tulirsh, tulisha, tulsh
determinative (adj), tulirshu, tulishu, tulshu
determine (v), tulirs, tulisho, tulsho
deterrence (n), bufrilark, buferilaka, bufrilak
deterrent (n doer), bufrilarkwan, buferilakua, bufrilakua
deterrer (n doer), bufrilarkwan, buferilakua, bufrilakua
detest (v), bushtirst, bushetito, bushtito
detestable (adj), bushtirtu, bushetitu, bushtitu

dethrone (v), bukoiltizve, bukoitivo, bukoitivo
detonate (v), bugauroifsp, bugauroipo, bugauroipo
detonation (n), bugauroifp, bugauroipa, bugauroip
detonator (n doer), bugauroifpwan, bugauroipua, bugauroipua
detour (n), buthiarf, buthiafa, buthiaf
detour (v), buthiarsf, buthiafo, buthiafo
detract (v), bugarlst, bugalito, bugalto
detraction (n), bugarlt, bugalita, bugalt
detractor (n doer), bugarltwan, bugalitua, bugaltua
Detroit (n), Detroilt, Deteroita, Detroit
devaluation (n), buvaurp, buvaupa, buvaup
devalue (v), buvaursp, buvaupo, buvaupo
devastate (v), fushirsp, fushipo, fushpo
devastation (n), fushirp, fushipa, fushp
develop (v), tefralsp, teferapo, tefrapo
developer (n doer), tefralpwan, teferapua, tefrapua
development (n), tefralp, teferapa, tefrap
deviant (n doer), bloiartwan, beloiatua, bloiatua
deviate (v), bloiarst, beloiato, bloiato
deviation (n), bloiart, beloiata, bloiat
device (n), blorft, belorita, blort
devil (n), zhairgaisht, zhaigaita, zhaigait
devilish (adj), zhairgaishtu, zhaigaitu, zhaigaitu
devilishly (adv), zhairgaishtiu, zhaigaitiu, zhaigaitiu
devious (adj), bloiartu, beloiatu, bloiatu
deviously (adv), bloiartiu, beloiatiu, bloiatiu
devise (v), blorfst, belorito, blorto
deviser (n doer), blorftwan, beloritua, blortua
devisive (adj), blorftu, beloritu, blortu
devisively (adv), blorftiu, beloritiu, blortiu
devolution (n), bukemirf, bukemifa, bukemif
devolve (v), bukemirsf, bukemifo, bukemifo
devolvement (n), bukemirf, bukemifa, bukemif
devote (v), thaifirsk, thaifiko, thaifko
devotee (n doer), thaifirkwan, thaifikua, thaifkua
devotion (n), thaifirk, thaifika, thaifk
devotional (n), thaifkarn, thaifikana, thaifkan
devour (v), budiuarsf, budiuafo, budiuafo
devout (adj), thaifirku, thaifiku, thaifku
devoutly (adv), thaifirkiu, thaifikiu, thaifkiu
dew (n), mief, miela, miel
dexterity (n), nanirt, nanita, nant
dexterous (adj), nanirtu, nanitu, nantu
dexterously (adv), nanirtiu, nanitiu, nantiu
dextrous (adj), nanirtu, nanitu, nantu
dextrously (adv), nanirtiu, nanitiu, nantiu
Dh (let sng), dhal, dhala, dha
Dhs (let pl), dhali, dhali, dhali
diabolical (adj), zhairgu, zhaigu, zhaigu
diabolically (adv), zhairgiu, zhaigiu, zhaigiu
diacritic (n), ainduflrt, ainedufita, aindufl
diacritical (adj), aindufirtu, ainedufitu, ainduftu
diacritically (adv), aindufirtiu, ainedufitiu, ainduftiu
diagnose (v), aishmarsne, aishomano, aishmano
diagnosis (n), aishmarn, aishomana, aishman
diagnostic (adj), aishmarnu, aishomanu, aishmanu
diagnostic (n), aishmarnt, aishomanita, aishmant
diagonal (adj), ainmurku, ainemuku, ainmuku
diagonal (n), ainmurk, ainemuka, ainmuk
diagonally (adv), ainmurkiu, ainemukiu, ainmukiu
diagram (n), ainelirk, ainelika, ainelk

diagram (v), ainelirsk, aineliko, ainelko
diagrammatic (adj), ainelirku, aineliku, ainelku
dial (n), eiport, eipota, eipot
dial (v), eiporst, eipoto, eipoto
dialect (n), ainrift, ainerita, ainrit
dialectic (adj), ainriftu, aineritu, ainritu
dialectical (adj), ainriftu, aineritu, ainritu
dialog (n), eikuift, eikuita, eikuit
dialogue (n), eikuift, eikuita, eikuit
diameter (n), ainpirn, ainopina, ainpin
diamond (n), tanuart, tanuata, tanuat
diaper (n), ainuarn, ainuana, ainuan
diaper (v), ainuarsne, ainuano, ainuano
diary (n), eiporf, eipora, eipor
dib (n), noan, noata, noat
dice (n pl d:number cube), nanshkyek, nanishi,
    nanshi
dice (v d:cube), nashirsk, nashiko, nashko
dicey (adj d:cube), nashirku, nashiku, nashku
dichotomy (n), kiedairsh, kiedaisha, kiedaish
dictate (v), deishsk, deisho, deisho
dictation (n), deishk, deisha, deish
dictator (n doer), deishkwan, deishua, deishua
dictatoral (adj), deishku, deishu, deishu
dictatorship (n), deishkwatfif, deishuafifa,
    deishuafif
diction (n), deirshk, deirisha, deirsh
dictionary (n), deishvon, deishevona, deishvon
did (v pa), tiskyot, tikio, tikio
did/had (pro-verb pa), kokyot, kokio, kokio
die (n d:number cube), nanshk, nanisha, nansh
die (v), kiarst, kiato, kiato
dieni-, venshkai-, venshkai-, venshkai-
diesel (n), disherl, dishela, dishel
diet (n), kielp, kiepa, kiep
diet (v), kielsp, kiepo, kiepo
dieter (n doer), kielpwan, kiepua, kiepua
differ (v), tozve, tovo, tovo
difference (n), tove, tova, tov
different (adj), tovu, tovu, tovu
differential (n), tovarshk, tovashika, tovashk
differentiate (v), tovarshsk, tovashiko, tovashko
differently (adv), toviu, toviu, toviu
difficult (adj), shplerku, shipoleku, shpleku
difficult (v), shplersk, shipoleko, shpleko
difficultly (adv), shplerkiu, shipolekiu, shplekiu
difficulty (n), shplerk, shipoleka, shplek
diffract (v), tovelishorsk, tovelishoko, tovelshko
diffraction (n), tovelishork, tovelishoka, tovelshk
diffuse (v), tovaborst, tovaboto, tovaboto
diffusion (n), tovabort, tovabota, tovabot
dig (n), telge, tega, teg
dig (v), telzge, tego, tego
digest (v), kikiarzge, kikiago, kikiago
digestion (n), kikiarge, kikiaga, kikiag
digestive (adj), kikiargu, kikiagu, kikiagu
digger (n doer), telgwan, tegua, tegua
digit (n), tegert, tegeta, teget
digital (adj), tegertu, tegetu, tegetu
digitally (adv), tegertiu, tegetiu, tegetiu
digitize (v), tegerst, tegeto, tegeto
dignify (v), trishersp, terishepo, trishpo
dignitary (n doer), trisherpwan, terishepua,

trishpua
dignity (n), trisherp, terishepa, trishp
digress (v), kievorazge, kievorugo, kievorgo
digression (n), kievorage, kievoruga, kievorg
dilate (v), kielarst, kielato, kielto
dilation (n), kielart, kielata, kielt
dilator (n doer), kielartwan, kielatua, kieltua
dilatory (adj), kielartu, kielatu, kieltu
dilemma (n), aviurth, aviutha, aviuth
dilemmic (adj), aviurthu, aviuthu, aviuthu
diligence (n), tilfersh, tilafesha, tilfesh
diligent (adj), tilfershu, tilafeshu, tilfeshu
diligently (adv), tilfershiu, tilafeshiu, tilfeshiu
dilute (adj), kiergu, kiegu, kiegu
dilute (v), kierzge, kiego, kiego
dilution (n), kierge, kiega, kieg
dim (adj), lairpu, laipu, laipu
dim (v), lairsp, laipo, laipo
dime (n), tinarn, tinana, tinan
dimension (n), kineshk, kinesha, kinesh
dimension (v), kineshsk, kinesho, kinesho
dimensional (adj), kineshku, kineshu, kineshu
diminish (v), kiniursp, kiniupo, kiniupo
diminishment (n), kiniurp, kiniupa, kiniup
diminutive (adj), kiniurpu, kiniupu, kiniupu
diminutively (adv), kiniurpiu, kiniupiu, kiniupiu
dimly (adv), lairpiu, laipiu, laipiu
dimmer (n doer), lairpwan, laipua, laipua
dimness (n), lairp, laipa, laip
dimple (n), bralirp, beralipa, bralp
dimple (v), bralirsp, beralipo, bralpo
dine (v), vaiforsp, vaifopo, vaifpo
diner (n), povairp, povaipa, povaip
ding (n), bralirge, beraliga, bralg
ding (v), bralirzge, beraligo, bralgo
dinner (n), vaiforp, vaifopa, vaifp
dinnertime (n), vaiforpedaun, vaifopedauna,
    vaifpedaun
dinnerware (n), vaiforpeshlerf, vaifopeshelefa,
    vaifpshlef
dinosaur (n), firsht, fishota, fisht
dip (n), beve, beva, bev
dip (v), bezve, bevo, bevo
diploma (n), kielorf, kielofa, kielf
diplomacy (n), kliarn, keliana, klian
diplomat (n doer), kliarnwan, kelianua, klianua
diplomatic (adj), kliarnu, kelianu, klianu
dipper (n doer), bevwan, bevua, bevua
dire (adj), gluntu, gelurinu, glurnu
direct (adj), kuarfku, kuafiku, kuafku
direct (v), kuarfsk, kuafiko, kuafko
direction (n), kuarfk, kuafika, kuafk
directive (n), kuafkart, kuafikata, kuafkat
directly (adv), kuarfkiu, kuafikiu, kuafkiu
director (n doer), kuarfkwan, kuafikua, kuafkua
directory (n), kuarfkar, kuafikara, kuafkar
dirt (n), galirk, galika, galk
dirtier (adj), galirkwelu, galikwelu, galkwelu
dirtiest (adj), galirkweku, galikweku, galkweku
dirty (adj), galirku, galiku, galku
dirty (v), galirsk, galiko, galko
disability (n), tifrelp, tiferepa, tifrep
disable (v), tifrelsp, tiferepo, tifrepo

disabler (n doer), tifrelpwan, tiferepua, tifrepua
disadvantage (n), tivitage, tivefika, tivefk
disadvantage (v), tivitazge, tivefiko, tivefko
disaffect (v), tiovirasp, tioviripo, tiovirpo
disaffection (n), tiovirap, tioviripa, tiovirp
disagree (v), tiklarst, tikelato, tiklato
disagreeable (adj), tiklartu, tikelatu, tiklatu
disagreement (n), tiklart, tikelata, tiklat
disallow (v), tifrilarsk, tiferilako, tifrilako
disappear (v), tipliarsne, tipeliano, tipliano
disappearance (n), tipliarn, tipeliana, tiplian
disappoint (v), titairfst, titaifoto, titaifto
disappointment (n), titairft, titaifota, titaift
disapproval (n), tiflaruve, tifelaruva, tiflarv
disapprove (v), tiflaruzve, tifelaruvo, tiflarvo
disarm (v), tishnersne, tishineno, tishneno
disarmament (n), tishnern, tishinena, tishnen
disarray (n), tiolipoilf, tiolipoila, tiolpoil
disassemble (v), tiothralzve, tiotheravo, tiothravo
disassociate (v), tiomeirsf, tiomeifo, tiomeifo
disassociation (n), tiomeirf, tiomeifa, tiomeif
disaster (n), laigarf, laigafa, laigaf
disastrous (adj), laigarfu, laigafu, laigafu
disastrously (adv), laigarfiu, laigafiu, laigafiu
disavow (v), tibrials, tiberiasho, tibriasho
disband (v), tivramirsp, tiveramipo, tivramepo
disbar (v), tirolarst, tirolato, tirolto
disbarment (n), tirolart, tirolata, tirolt
disbelief (n), tisharme, tishara, tishar
disbelieve (v), tisharzme, tisharo, tisharo
disburse (v), tibeirsth, tibeitho, tibeitho
disbursement (n), tibeirth, tibeitha, tibeith
disc (n), tirfp, tifopa, tifp
discard (v), klirfsk, kelifiko, klifko
discern (n), lirfp, lifopa, lifp
discern (v), lirfsp, lifopo, lifpo
discharge (n), tigloift, tigeloita, tigloit
discharge (v), tigloifst, tigeloito, tigloito
disciple (n), tirardhe, tiradha, tiradh
disciplinarian (n doer), tirfugwan, tifugua, tifugua
disciplinary (adj), tirfugu, tifugu, tifugu
discipline (n), tirfuge, tifuga, tifug
discipline (v), tirfuzge, tifugo, tifugo
disclaim (v), tinolasne, tinoarito, tinoarto
disclaimer (n), tinolan, tinoarita, tinoart
disclose (v), tigrefst, tigereto, tigreto
disclosure (n), tigreft, tigereta, tigret
discomfort (n), tivlark, tivelaruva, tivlarv
discomfort (v), tivlarsk, tivelaruvo, tivlarvo
disconnect (v), tishnarsf, tishinafo, tishnafo
disconnection (n), tishnarf, tishinafa, tishnaf
discontent (n), tibelpift, tiliupifota, tiliupift
discontent (v), tibelpifst, tiliupifoto, tiliupifto
discontinuation (n), tibeltir, tiliutira, tiliutir
discontinue (v), tibeltisre, tiliutiro, tiliutiro
discontinuity (n), tibeltir, tiliutira, tiliutir
discord (n), loikaurt, loikauta, loikaut
discount (n), tipoinf, tipoina, tipoin
discount (v), tipoinsf, tipoino, tipoino
discounter (n doer), tipoinfwan, tipoinua, tipoinua
discourage (v), tidivasre, tidiruvo, tidirvo
discouragement (n), tidivar, tidiruva, tidirv
discourse (n), tilialirt, tilialita, tilialt

discourse (v), tilialirst, tilialito, tilialto
discover (v), diarsne, diano, diano
discoverer (n doer), diarnwan, dianua, dianua
discovery (n), diarn, diana, dian
discredit (n), tiflenift, tifelenita, tiflent
discredit (v), tiflenifst, tifelenito, tiflento
discreet (adj), tivirshu, tivishu, tivishu
discreetly (adv), tivirshiu, tivishiu, tivishiu
discrepancy (n), tiklartan, tikelatana, tiklatan
discrepant (adj), tiklartanu, tikelatanu, tiklatanu
discrepantly (adv), tiklartaniu, tikelataniu,
   tiklataniu
discrete (adj), tigortu, tigotu, tigotu
discretely (adv), tigortiu, tigotiu, tigotiu
discreteness (n), tigort, tigota, tigot
discretion (n), tivirsh, tivisha, tivish
discriminate (v), nuanirsk, nuaniko, nuanko
discrimination (n), nuanirk, nuanika, nuank
discriminator (n doer), nuanirkwan, nuanikua,
   nuankua
discus (n), tifpart, tifopata, tifpat
discuss (v), tigoishst, tigoito, tigoito
discussion (n), tigoisht, tigoita, tigoit
disdain (n), tinalirsh, tinalisha, tinalsh
disease (n), blusharme, belushama, blusham
disease (v), blusharzme, belushamo, blushamo
disengage (v), tidarbaisk, tivobaiko, tivobaiko
disengagement (n), tidarbaik, tivobaika, tivobaik
disfavor (n), tinardat, tinaritha, tinarth
disfavor (v), tinardast, tinaritho, tinartho
disfigure (v), tikudisle, tikulito, tikulto
disfigurement (n), tikudil, tikulita, tikult
disgrace (n), tiplarf, tipelafa, tiplaf
disgrace (v), tiplarsf, tipelafo, tiplafo
disgraceful (adj), tiplarfu, tipelafu, tiplafu
disgracefully (adv), tiplarfiu, tipelafiu, tiplafiu
disgruntle (v), tikrezhzge, tikerego, tikrego
disguise (n), tituirf, tituifa, tituif
disguise (v), tituirsf, tituifo, tituifo
disgust (n), tifeirsh, tifeisha, tifeish
disgust (v), tifeirs, tifeisho, tifeisho
dish (n), perfk, pefika, pefk
dish (v), perfsk, pefiko, pefko
disharmony (n), timavirn, timavina, timavin
dishearten (v), tidralst, tidaralo, tidralo
dishonest (adj), tiporshtu, tiposhatu, tiposhtu
dishonesty (n), tiporsht, tiposhata, tiposht
dishonor (n), tikolirf, tikolifa, tikolf
dishwash (v), pefkfiaushsk, pefikefiausho,
   pefkfiausho
dishwasher (n), pefkfiaushk, pefikefiausha,
   pefkfiaush
disillusion (v), tilargrus, tilagarusho, tilagrusho
disillusionment (n), tilargrush, tilagarusha,
   tilagrush
disincentive (n), tiartoirp, tiitoipa, tiitoip
disinfect (v), tiarvirst, tiiviroto, tiivirto
disinfectant (n doer), tiarvirtwan, tiivirotua,
   tiivirtua
disinfection (n), tiarvirt, tiivirota, tiivirt
disinformation (n), tiarvorn, tiivorina, tiivorn
disintegrate (v), pleniask, tipeliaroko, tipliarko
disintegration (n), pleniak, tipeliaroka, tipliark

disintegrator (n doer), pleniakwan, tipeliarokua, tipliarkua
disinterest (n), titelforet, titeliforeta, titelfret
disinterest (v), titelforest, titeliforeto, titelfreto
disjoint (v), tidiars, tidiasho, tidiasho
disk (n), tirfp, tifopa, tifp
diskette (n), tirfpef, tifopefa, tifpef
dislike (n), tisharlf, tishalifa, tishalf
dislike (v), tisharlsf, tishalifo, tishalfo
dislocate (v), tishairsp, tishaipo, tishaipo
dislocation (n), tishairp, tishaipa, tishaip
dislodge (v), tishavizge, tisharigo, tishargo
disloyal (adj), tifiorfu, tifiofu, tifiofu
disloyalty (n), tifiorf, tifiofa, tifiof
dismal (adj), tifraifku, tiferaiku, tifraiku
dismally (adv), tifraifkiu, tiferaikiu, tifraikiu
dismantle (v), tivaize, tivaizho, tivaizho
dismantlement (n), tivaizhe, tivaizha, tivaizh
dismay (n), tinoirf, tinoifa, tinoif
dismay (v), tinoirsf, tinoifo, tinoifo
dismember (v), timeshurst, timeshuto, timeshto
dismemberment (n), timeshurt, timeshuta, timesht
dismiss (v), tirals, tirasho, tirasho
dismissal (n), tiralsh, tirasha, tirash
dismissive (adj), tiralshu, tirashu, tirashu
dismissively (adv), tiralshiu, tirashiu, tirashiu
disobedience (n), tipilafk, tiialifoka, tiialfk
disobedient (adj), tipilafku, tiialifoku, tiialfku
disobediently (adv), tipilafkiu, tiialifokiu, tiialfkiu
disobey (v), tipilafsk, tiialifoko, tiialfko
disorder (n), tishkelt, tishiketa, tishket
disorder (v), tishkelst, tishiketo, tishketo
disorganization (n), tifrilat, tiferilota, tifrilt
disorganize (v), tifrilast, tiferiloto, tifrilto
disorient (v), tilamoisne, timoito, timoito
disorientation (n), tilamoin, timoita, timoit
disown (v), titheifst, titheifo, titheifo
dispatch (v), tishkralzge, tishekorago, tishkrago
dispatcher (n doer), tishkralgwan, tishekoragua, tishkragua
dispel (v), tiparzde, tipado, tipado
dispeller (n doer), tipardwan, tipadua, tipadua
dispensable (adj), tibrufu, berufitu, bruftu
dispensation (n), tibruf, berufita, bruft
dispense (v), tibrusf, berufito, brufto
dispenser (n doer), tibrufwan, berufitua, bruftua
dispersal (n), tiloltelf, tilotela, tilotel
disperse (v), tiloltelsf, tiloltelo, tilotelo
disperser (n doer), tilotelfwan, tilotelua, tilotelua
dispersion (n), tilotelf, tilotela, tilotel
dispirit (v), tizhuarsle, tizhualo, tizhualo
displace (v), tibrels, tiberesho, tibresho
displacement (n), tibrelsh, tiberesha, tibresh
display (n), fruirt, feruina, fruin
display (v), fruirst, feruino, fruino
displease (v), tifrilasp, tiferilopo, tifrilpo
displeasure (n), tifrilap, tiferilopa, tifrilp
disposable (adj), tikanu, tilaku, tilaku
disposal (n), tikan, tilaka, tilak
dispose (v), tikasne, tilako, tilako
disposition (n), tiglark, tigelaka, tiglak
dispositive (adj), tiglarku, tigelaku, tiglaku
dispossess (v), tiprilasp, tiperilapo, tiprilpo

dispossession (n), tiprilap, tiperilapa, tiprilp
disprove (v), tifliorsf, tifeliofo, tifliofo
dispute (n), tivoirk, tivoika, tivoik
dispute (v), tivoirsk, tivoiko, tivoiko
disqualification (n), tikriarf, tikeriafa, tikriaf
disqualifier (n doer), tikriarfwan, tikeriafua, tikriafua
disqualify (v), tikriarsf, tikeriafo, tikriafo
disquiet (n), tideilurde, tideiluda, tideild
disregard (n), pluvairk, peluvaika, pluvaik
disregard (v), pluvairsk, peluvaiko, pluvaiko
disrepair (n), tilubolirk, tilubolika, tilubolk
disrespect (n), pluthurk, peluthuka, pluthuk
disrespect (v), pluthursk, peluthuko, pluthuko
disrupt (v), tigaifst, gairifoto, gairfto
disrupter (n doer), tigaiftwan, gairifotua, gairftua
disruption (n), tigaift, gairifota, gairft
disruptive (adj), tigaiftu, gairifotu, gairftu
disruptively (adv), tigaiftiu, gairifotiu, gairftiu
dissatisfaction (n), lavirt, lavita, lavit
dissatisfy (v), lavirst, lavito, lavito
dissect (v), tithirs, tithisho, tithisho
dissection (n), tithirsh, tithisha, tithish
dissent (n), tizhaip, zhairopa, zhairp
dissent (v), tizhaisp, zhairopo, zhairpo
dissenter (n doer), tizhaipwan, zhairopua, zhairpua
disservice (n), tikofirt, tikofita, tikoft
dissident (n doer), tizhaipwan, zhairopua, zhairpua
dissipate (v), tishelirsk, tisheliko, tishelko
dissipation (n), tishelirk, tishelika, tishelk
dissolution (n), tigrage, geravuga, gravg
dissolve (v), tigrazge, geravugo, gravgo
dissonance (n), tishant, shetanita, shtant
dissonant (adj), tishantu, shetanitu, shtantu
dissonate (v), tishanst, shetanito, shtanto
dissuade (v), tidalirzme, tidalimo, tidalmo
dissuasion (n), tidalirme, tidalima, tidalm
distance (n), titrep, torefipa, trefp
distance (v), titresp, torefipo, trefpo
distant (adj), titrepu, torefipu, trefpu
distantly (adv), titrepiu, torefipiu, trefpiu
distaste (n), titinart, titinata, titinat
distasteful (adj), titinartu, titinatu, titinatu
distemper (n), tivafirk, tivafika, tivafk
distend (v), tipifsk, tipifoko, tipifko
distension (n), tipifk, tipifoka, tipifk
distill (v), kishetriarzge, kisheteriago, kishetriago
distillation (n), kishetriarge, kisheteriaga, kishetriag
distiller (n doer), kishetriargwan, kisheteriagua, kishetriagua
distillery (n), kishetriagart, kisheteriagata, kishetriagat
distinct (adj), tipoitu, poiratu, poirtu
distinction (n), tipoit, poirata, poirt
distinctive (adj), tipoitu, poiratu, poirtu
distinctly (adv), tipoitiu, poiratiu, poirtiu
distinguish (v), tipoist, poirato, poirto
distort (v), plukiorst, pelukioto, plukioto
distortion (n), plukiort, pelukiota, plukiot
distract (v), tigalirst, tigalito, tigalto
distraction (n), tigalirt, tigalita, tigalt
distraught (adj), tithorgu, tithogu, tithogu

distress (n), tithorge, tithoga, tithog
distress (v), tithorzge, tithogo, tithogo
distribute (v), shrilst, sherito, shrito
distribution (n), shrilt, sherita, shrit
distributor (n doer), shriltwan, sheritua, shritua
district (n), tibarfk, tibafika, tibafk
district (v), tibarfsk, tibafiko, tibafko
distrust (n), tidreirf, tidereifa, tidreif
distrust (v), tidreirsf, tidereifo, tidreifo
distrustful (adj), tidreirfu, tidereifu, tidreifu
disturb (v), tidarlsp, tidalipo, tidalpo
disturbance (n), tidarlp, tidalipa, tidalp
disuse (n), tibriark, tiberiaka, tibriak
ditch (n), floirk, feloika, floik
ditch (v), floirsk, feloiko, floiko
diva (n), visharl, vishala, vishal
dive (n), kraifk, keraika, kraik
dive (v), kraifsk, keraiko, kraiko
diver (n doer), kraifkwan, keraikua, kraikua
diverge (v), timeirzge, timeigo, timeigo
divergence (n), timeirge, timeiga, timeig
divergent (adj), timeirgu, timeigu, timeigu
diverse (adj), titharfu, tharifotu, tharftu
diversification (n), titharfet, tharifoteta, tharftet
diversifier (n doer), titharfwan, tharifotua, tharftua
diversify (v), titharsf, tharifoto, tharfto
diversion (n), kitharak, kitharika, kithark
diversity (n), titharf, tharifota, tharft
divert (v), kitharask, kithariko, kitharko
diverter (n doer), kitharakwan, kitharikua,
    kitharkua
divest (v), tinbist, tibito, tibito
divestment (n), tinbit, tibita, tibit
divide (n), kifiaishk, kifiaisha, kifiaish
divide (v), kifiaishsk, kifiaisho, kifiaisho
dividend (n), kifiaishkap, kifiaishapa, kifiaishap
divider (n doer), kifiaishkwan, kifiaishua, kifiaishua
divine (adj), friarvu, feriavu, friavu
divine (v), friarzve, feriavo, friavo
divinely (adv), friarvru, feriavlu, friaviu
divinity (n), friarve, feriava, friav
divisible (adj), kifiaishku, kifiaishu, kifiaishu
division (n), kifiaishkuet, kifiaishueta, kifiaishuet
divisional (adj), kifiaishkuetu, kifiaishuetu,
    kifiaishuetu
divisive (adj), kifiaishkipu, kifiaishipu, kifiaishipu
divisiveness (n), kifiaishkip, kifiaishipa, kifiaiship
divisor (n doer), kifiaishkipwan, kifiaishipua,
    kifiaishipua
divorce (n), foinark, foinaka, foink
divorce (v), foinarsk, foinako, foinko
divorcee (n), foinarkuin, foinakuina, foinkuin
divulge (v), tigaurzge, tigaugo, tigaugo
dizziness (n), giushk, giusha, giush
dizzy (adj), giushku, giushu, giushu
dizzy (v), giushsk, giusho, giusho
do (v), tisk, tiko, tiko
do/have (pro-verb pr), koko, koko, koko
doable (adj), tiku, tiku, tiku
dock (n), profk, peroka, prok
dock (v), profsk, peroko, proko
docket (n), profkef, perokefa, prokef
dockside (adj), prokshoirtu, perokeshoitu,

prokshoitu
dockside (n), prokshoirt, perokeshoita, prokshoit
doctor (n), protak, perothipa, prothp
doctor (v), protask, perothipo, prothpo
doctrine (n), protap, peroshata, prosht
document (n), protat, perolita, prolt
document (v), protast, perolito, prolto
documentary (n), protart, perolitara, proltar
documentation (n), protaft, peroliteta, proltet
documenter (n doer), protatwan, perolitua, proltua
dodge (n), tarzhge, tazhaga, tazhg
dodge (v), tarzhzge, tazhago, tazhgo
dodgy (adj), tarzhgu, tazhagu, tazhgu
doer (n doer), tikwan, tikua, tikua
dog (n), draursh, derausha, draush
dog (v), draurs, derausho, drausho
dogfight (n), draushvaugat, deraushevauga,
    draushvaug
doghouse (n), draushkiarf, deraoushekiafa,
    draushkiaf
dogma (n), taukderp, taukedepa, taukdep
dogmatic (adj), taukderpu, taukedepu, taukdepu
dogwood (n), draushfanirn, deraushefanina,
    draushfanin
doll (n), tolirp, tolipa, tolp
doll (v), tolirsp, tolipo, tolpo
dollar (n), tolirn, tolina, toln
dolphin (n), tolfirge, tolafiga, tolfig
domain (n), vaurnirf, vautha, vauth
dome (n), beinirf, beinifa, beinf
domestic (adj), nefirtu, nefitu, neftu
domesticate (v), nefirst, nefito, nefto
domestication (n), nefirt, nefita, neft
domesticator (n doer), nefirtwan, nefitua, neftua
dominance (n), faisht, naufika, naufk
dominant (adj), faishtu, naufiku, naufku
dominate (v), faishst, naufiko, naufko
domination (n), faisht, naufika, naufk
dominator (n doer), faishtwan, naufikua, naufkua
donate (v), glerzge, gelego, glego
donation (n), glerge, gelega, gleg
donkey (n), ganufp, ganupa, ganup
donor (n doer), glergwan, gelegua, glegua
donut (n), peiamur, peiamela, peiamel
doom (n), beiurk, beiuka, beiuk
doom (v), beiursk, beiuko, beiuko
doomsday (n), beiukviurl, beiukeviula, beiukviul
door (n), shtelf, shetela, shtel
doorbell (n), shteldiarme, shetelediara, shteldiar
doorknob (n), shtelfproide, sheteleperoida,
    shtelproid
doormat (n), shtelmarft, shetelemarlfa, shtelmarf
doorstep (n), shtelgirk, shetelegika, shtelgik
doorway (n), shtelpliorl, shetelepeliola, shtelpliol
dormancy (n), priump, periuma, prium
dormant (adj), priumpu, periumu, priumu
dorsal (adj), birnartu, bironatu, birnatu
dorsum (n), birnart, bironata, birnat
dosage (n), torthuet, karithueta, karthuet
dose (n), torth, karitha, karth
dose (v), torsth, karitho, kartho
dot (n), mimk, mima, mim
dot (v), mimesk, mimo, mimo

dotard (n doer), malirfwan, malifua, malfua
dote (v), malirsf, malifo, malfo
double (adj), shkeifu, keifitu, keiftu
double (n), shkeif, keifita, keift
double (v), shkeisf, keifito, keifto
doubler (n doer), shkeifwan, keifitua, keiftua
doubly (adv), shkeifiu, keifitiu, keiftiu
doubt (n), biarf, biaufa, biauf
doubt (v), biarsf, biaufo, biaufo
doubter (n doer), biarfwan, biaufua, biaufua
doubtful (adj), biarfu, biaufu, biaufu
dough (n), peiarn, peiana, peian
doughnut (n), pciamur, peiamela, peiamel
douse (v), paushsk, pausho, pausho
dove (n d:bird), briarf, beriafa, briaf
dove (v pa), kraifskyot, keraikio, kraikio
dovetail (v), briafmithsk, beriafemitho, briafmitho
dowel (n), giuirp, giuipa, giuip
down (adj/adv/prep), tiern, tienu, tien
down (n), tiern, tiena, tien
downbeat (adj), tiendaurtu, tienedautu, tiendautu
downbeat (n), tiendaurt, tienedauta, tiendaut
downfall (n), tienzhailf, tienezhaila, tienzhail
downgrade (n), tienshtrak, tieneshoterana, tienshtran
downgrade (v), tienshtrask, tieneshoterano, tienshtrano
downhill (n), tienshiop, tieneparina, tienparn
download (n), tienlurt, tielita, tielt
download (v), tienlurst, tielito, tielto
downloader (n doer), tienlurtwan, tielitua, tieltua
downplay (v), tienfruifsk, tieneferuifo, tienfruifo
downpour (n), tienroturt, tienerotuta, tienrotut
downright (adv), tiendierkiu, tienediekiu, tiendiekiu
downside (n), tienshoirt, tieneshoita, tienshoit
downsize (v), tienshuarzge, tieneshuago, tienshuago
downstairs (adj), tientairnu, tienitainu, tientainu
downstairs (n), tientairn, tienitaina, tientain
downstream (n), tienfalirme, tienefalima, tienfalm
downswing (n), tienflierge, tienefeliega, tienflieg
downtime (n), tiendaurn, tienedauna, tiendaun
downtown (n), tienmiurn, tienemiuna, tienmiun
downturn (n), tienkaimp, tienekaima, tienkaim
downward (adj/adv), tienhaursh, tienuhaushu, tienhaush
downwardly (adv), tienhaursh, tienuhaushu, tienhaush
doze (v), rafsp, bafipo, bafpo
dozen (n), geidor, geiroda, geird
dozer (n doer), rafpwan, bafipua, bafpua
draft (n), flark, felaritha, flarth
draft (v), flarsk, felaritho, flartho
drafter (n doer), flarkwan, felarithua, flarthua
drafty (adj), flarku, felarithu, flarthu
drag (n), shlarve, shelava, shlav
drag (v), shlarzve, shelavo, shlavo
dragon (n), shlavak, shelaiga, shlaig
drain (n), pliurk, peliuka, pliuk
drain (v), pliursk, peliuko, pliuko
drainage (n), pliurkuet, peliukueta, pliukuet
drainer (n doer), pliurkwan, peliukua, pliukua

drama (n), parfp, paripa, parp
dramatic (adj), parfpu, paripu, parpu
dramatically (adv), parfpiu, paripiu, parpiu
dramatization (n), parfk, paripara, parpar
dramatize (v), parfsp, paripo, parpo
drank (v pa d:beverage), bialskyot, biorishio, biorshio
drape (n), turthk, turitha, turth
drape (v), turthsk, turitho, turtho
draper (n doer), turthkwan, turithua, turthua
drapery (n), turthkuet, turithueta, turthuet
drastic (adj), moiarku, moiaku, moiaku
drastically (adv), moiarkiu, moiakiu, moiakiu
draw (n d:pull, inscribe), pulap, peratha, prath
draw (v d:pull, inscribe), pulasp, peratho, pratho
drawback (n), prathvark, perathevaka, prathvak
drawer (n d:compartment), shork, shelanika, shlank
drawer (n doer d:pull, inscribe), pulapwan, perathua, prathua
dread (n), glorthk, geloritha, glorth
dread (v), glorthsk, geloritho, glortho
dreadful (adj), glorthku, gelorithu, glorthu
dream (n), flaul, felauma, flaum
dream (v), flausle, felaumo, flaumo
dreamer (n doer), flaulwan, felaumua, flaumua
dreamily (adv), flauliu, felaumiu, flaumiu
dreamt (v pa), flauslyot, felaumio, flaumio
dreamy (adj), flaulu, felaumu, flaumu
dreariness (n), glornp, gelorina, glorn
dreary (adj), glornpu, gelorinu, glornu
dredge (v), pulaze, perazho, prazho
dreg (n), pulazhan, perazhana, prazhan
drench (v), freishsp, fereipo, freipo
dress (n d:clothing), plersh, pelesha, plesh
dress (v d:clothing), plers, pelesho, plesho
dresser (n d:cabinet), plershk, peleshika, pleshk
dresser (n doer d:clothing), plershwan, peleshua, pleshua
dressmaker (n doer), pleshnargwan, peleshenagua, pleshnagua
drew (v pa d:pull, inscribe), pulaspyot, perathio, prathio
drier (adj), nortwelu, teriufwelu, triufwelu
drier (n doer), nortwan, teriufua, triufua
driest (adj), nortweku, teriufweku, triufweku
drift (n), teiarsh, teiasha, teiash
drift (v), teiars, teiasho, teiasho
drifter (n doer), teiarshwan, teiashua, teiashua
driftwood (n), telashtanırn, teiashefanina, teiashfanin
drill (n), kliuk, biaka, biak
drill (v), kliusk, biako, biako
driller (n doer), kliukwan, biakua, biakua
drink (n d:beverage), bialk, biorisha, biorsh
drink (v d:beverage), bialsk, biorisho, biorsho
drinker (n doer d:beverage), bialkwan, biorishua, biorshua
drip (n), dirge, torisha, torsh
drip (v), dirzge, torisho, torsho
dripper (n doer), dirgwan, torishua, torshua
drippy (adj), dirgu, torishu, torshu
drive (n), diarp, diapa, diap

drive (v), diarsp, diapo, diapo
drivel (n), dulank, dulana, dulan
drivel (v), dulansk, dulano, dulano
driver (n doer), diarpwan, diapua, diapua
driveway (n), diapliorl, diapeliola, diapliol
drizzle (n), norzhailf, teriuzhaila, triuzhail
drizzle (v), norzhailsf, teriuzhailo, triuzhailo
drone (n d:bee), zhudarn, zhudana, zhudan
drone (n d:tone), durizhe, duriba, durb
drone (v d:tone), durize, duribo, durbo
drool (v), dulansk, dulano, dulano
droop (v), preiusp, darupo, darupo
droopy (adj), preiupu, darupu, darupu
drop (n), preip, daruga, darg
drop (v), preisp, darugo, dargo
droplet (n pl), preipapyek, darugapi, dargapi
dropout (n pl), preipuilyek, daruguili, darguili
dropper (n doer), preipwan, darugua, dargua
drought (n), triaufk, teriaufa, triauf
drove (v pa), diarspyot, diapio, diapio
drown (v), biarazge, biarugo, biargo
drowsiness (n), preishriash, daresheriasha, darshriash
drowsy (adj), preishriashu, daresheriashu, darshriashu
drudge (n doer), puluzhwan, peruzhua, pruzhua
drudge (n), puluzhe, peruzha, pruzh
drudge (v), puluze, peruzho, pruzho
drudgery (adj), puluzhu, peruzhu, pruzhu
drug (n), biank, biana, bian
drug (v), biansk, biano, biano
drugstore (n), biandrap, bianapa, bianap
drum (n), driarde, deriada, driad
drum (v), driarzde, deriado, driado
drumbeat (n), driadaurt, deriadauta, driadaut
drummer (n doer), driardwan, deriadua, driadua
drunk (adj d:intoxicated), bialshtu, bioreteshu, biortshu
drunk (n doer d:intoxicated), bialshtwan, bioreteshua, biortshua
drunkard (n doer), bialshtwan, bioreteshua, biortshua
drunkenness (n d:intoxicated), bialsht, bioretesha, biortsh
dry (adj), nortu, teriufu, triufu
dry (v), norst, teriufo, triufo
dryer (n doer), nortwan, teriufua, triufua
dryness (n), nort, teriufa, triuf
drywall (n), nortnolthk, teriufenolitha, triufnolth
Ds (let pl), dali, dali, dali
dual (adj), avairfu, avaifu, avaifu
duality (n), avairf, avaifa, avaif
dually (adv), avairfiu, avaifiu, avaifiu
dub (n), bleif, beifa, beif
dub (v), bleisf, beifo, beifo
dubber (n doer), bleifwan, beifua, beifua
Dubnium (n davoka), Inop, Inop, Inop
Dubnium (n), Dubnium, Dubeniuma, Dubnium
duck (n d:avoid), bluk, buka, buk
duck (n d:bird), taufk, taufa, tauf
duck (v d:avoid), blusk, buko, buko
duct (n), kriusht, keriuta, kriut
due (adj), tiurku, tiuku, tiuku

due (adv), tiurkiu, tiukiu, tiukiu
due (n), tiurk, tiuka, tiuk
duel (n), kliork, kelioka, kliok
duel (v), kliorsk, kelioko, klioko
dueler (n doer), kliorkwan, keliokua, kliokua
duet (n), avaifalt, avaifata, avaifat
duet (n), avuft, avuta, avut
dug (v pa), telzgyot, tegio, tegio
dugout (n), telgiouil, tegiouila, tegiouil
dull (adj), nurmu, numu, numu
dull (v), nurzme, numo, numo
dullness (n), nurme, numa, num
dumb (adj), gloirpu, geloipu, gloipu
dumb (v), gloirsp, geloipo, gloipo
dumbness (n), gloirp, geloipa, gloip
dummy (n doer), gloirpwan, geloipua, gloipua
dump (n), buarnk, buanika, buank
dump (v), buarnsk, buaniko, buanko
dumper (n doer), buarnkwan, buanikua, buankua
dumpster (n), buarnkap, buanikapa, buankap
dune (n), purth, putha, puth
dunk (n), braufk, berauka, brauk
dunk (v), braufsk, berauko, brauko
dunker (n doer), braufkwan, beraukua, braukua
duodecillion (num 1e39 card), avusht, avusht, avusht
duodecillionth (num 1e39 ord), avushteth, avushteth, avushteth
duoquadragintillion (num 1e129 card), avuifk, avuifk, avufk
duotrigintillion (num 1e99 card), avuift, avuift, avuft
duotrigintillionth (num 1e99 ord), avuifteth, avuifteth, avufteth
duovigintillion (num 1e69 card), avushk, avushk, avushk
duovigintillionth (num 1e69 ord), avushketh, avushketh, avushketh
duplicate (n), dreshk, deresha, dresh
duplicate (v), dreshsk, deresho, dreshu
duplication (n), dreshkuet, dereshueta, dreshuet
duplicator (n doer), dreshkwan, dereshua, dreshua
durability (n), taursh, tausha, taush
durable (adj), taurshu, taushu, taushu
durably (adv), taurshiu, taushiu, taushiu
duration (n), tuarsht, taushota, tausht
during (prep), shwenf, shewenifu, shwenf
dusk (n), nushirp, nushipa, nushp
dust (n), kreishk, kereisha, kreish
dust (v), kreishsk, kereisho, kreisho
dustbin (n), kreishnurp, kereishcnupa, kreishnup
duster (n doer), kreishkwan, kereishua, kreishua
dustily (adv), kreishkiu, kereishiu, kreishiu
dusty (adj), kreishku, kereishu, kreishu
Dutch (n), Dutersh, Dutesha, Dutsh
duty (n), tuikar, tuika, tuik
dwarf (n), thraift, theraita, thrait
dwarf (v), thraifst, theraito, thraito
dwell (n), thrailt, theraila, thrail
dwell (v), thrailst, therailo, thrailo
dweller (n doer), thrailtwan, therailua, thrailua
dwelt (v pa), thrailstyot, therailio, thrailio

dwindle (v), thraidarst, theraidato, thraidato
dye (n), litirk, litika, litik
dye (v), litirsk, litiko, litiko
dyer (n doer), litirkwan, litikua, litikua
dynamic (adj), tuiarfu, tuiafu, tuiafu
dynamic (n), tuiarft, tuiafita, tuiaft
dynamically (adv), tuiarfiu, tuiafiu, tuiafiu
dynamo (n), tuiarf, tuiafa, tuiaf
dynastic (adj), shafirpieitu, shafipieitu, shafpieitu
dynasty (n), shafirpieit, shafipieita, shafpieit
dysfunction (n), tiprasht, tiperata, tiprat
dysfunctional (adj), tiprashtu, tiperatu, tipratu
Dysprosium (n davoka), Orit, Orit, Orit
Dysprosium (n), Dishproshium, Disheperoshiuma, Dishproshium
E (let sng), elfe, elifa, elf
each (adj), urshpu, ushepu, ushpu
eager (adj), vishvaru, virashu, virshu
eagerly (adv), vishvariu, virashiu, virshiu
eagerness (n), vishvar, virasha, virsh
eagle (n), kriort, keriora, krior
eagle (v), kriorst, kerioro, krioro
ear (n), huan, uana, uan
eardrum (n), uandriarde, uanederiada, uandriad
earlier (adj), elialfwelu, elialwelu, elialwelu
earliest (adj), elialfwaku, elialwaku, elialwaku
earlobe (n), huadoin, uanedoina, uandoin
early (adj), elialfu, elialu, elialu
earmark (n), uanshtart, uaneshetata, uanshtat
earmark (v), uanshtarst, uaneshetato, uanshtato
earn (v), driarsp, deriapo, driapo
earner (n doer), driarpwan, deriapua, driapua
earnest (adj), driarpu, deriapu, driapu
earnestly (adv), driarpiu, deriapiu, driapiu
earnestness (n), driarp, deriapa, driap
earphone (n), uanyarp, uaneyapa, uanyap
earpiece (n), uanthetirsh, uanethetisha, uanthetsh
earring (n), uanritran, uaneriterala, uanritral
earshot (n), uanshkort, uaneshekota, uanshkot
earth (n), elesh, elesha, elesh
earthen (adj), galikshlerfu, galikeshelefu, galkshlefu
earthenware (n), galikshlerf, galikeshelefa, galkshlef
earthling (n), eleshlorve, eleshelova, eleshlov
earthly (adj), eleshu, eleshu, eleshu
earthquake (n), eleshpiove, eleshiova, eleshiov
earthworm (n), galkyoran, galikeyorina, galkyorn
earwax (n), uantarak, uanetarika, uantark
ease (n), flerf, felefa, flef
ease (v), flersf, felefo, flefo
easier (adj), flerfwelu, felefwelu, flefwelu
easiest (adj), flerfwaku, felefwaku, flefwaku
easily (adv), flerfiu, felefiu, flefiu
east (adj), kiarshu, kiashu, kiashu
east (n), kiarsh, kiasha, kiash
Easter (n), Lushdor, Lushadora, Lushdor
eastern (adj), kiarshku, kiashoku, kiashku
easy (adj), flerfu, felefu, flefu
eat (n), niert, nieta, niet
eat (v), nierst, nieto, nieto
eater (n doer), niertwan, nietua, nietua
eavesdrop (v), vimarnuasne, vimanuano, vimanuano

ebb (n), raube, berupa, brup
ebb (v), rauzbe, berupo, brupo
ebony (n), toime, toima, toim
eccentric (adj), tulidretu, tuforelitu, tufreltu
eccentricity (n), tulidret, tuforelita, tufrelt
echo (n), teiput, ibarita, ibart
echo (v), teipust, ibarito, ibarto
eclipse (n), krilk, galeipa, gleip
eclipse (v), krilsk, galeipo, gleipo
ecological (adj), borkuitu, bokuitu, bokuitu
ecologically (adv), borkuitiu, bokuitiu, bokuitiu
ecologist (n doer), borkuitwan, bokuitua, bokuitua
ecology (n), borkuit, bokuita, bokuit
economic (adj), bovenkaru, venikaru, venkaru
economical (adj), bovenku, veniku, venku
economically (adv), bovenkiu, venikiu, venkiu
economics (n), bovenkar, venikara, venkar
economist (n doer), bovenkwan, venikua, venkua
economize (v), bovensk, veniko, venko
economy (n), bovenk, venika, venk
ecosystem (n), borkuit, bokuita, bokuit
ecstasy (n), tuarkian, tuareshiana, tuarshian
ecstatic (adj), tuarkianu, tuareshianu, tuarshianu
ecstatically (adv), tuarkianiu, tuareshianiu, tuarshianiu
eddy (n), kriorp, keriopa, kriop
eddy (v), kriorsp, keriopo, kriopo
edge (n), shkelf, kerifa, kerf
edge (v), shkelsf, kerifo, kerfo
edger (n doer), shkelfwan, kerifua, kerfua
edgy (adj), shkelfu, kerifu, kerfu
edible (adj), niertu, nietu, nietu
edict (n), deilk, udeika, udeik
edit (n), glent, gelepa, glep
edit (v), glenst, gelepo, glepo
editable (adj), glentu, gelepu, glepu
edition (n), glentar, gelepara, glepar
editor (n doer), glentwan, gelepua, glepua
editorial (n), glentan, gelepana, glepan
educate (v), luavizge, luafiko, luafko
education (n), luavige, luafika, luafk
educational (adj), luavigu, luafiku, luafku
educator (n doer), luavigwan, luafikua, luafkua
eerie (adj), grilirtu, gerilitu, grilitu
eerieness (n), grilirt, gerilita, grilit
eerily (adv), grilirtiu, gerilitiu, grilitiu
effect (n), thuvirt, virotha, virth
effect (v), thuvirst, virotho, virtho
effective (adj), thuvirtu, virothu, virthu
effectively (adv), thuvirtiu, virothiu, virthiu
effectiveness (n), thuvirtan, virothana, virthan
effector (n doer), thuvirtwan, virothua, virthua
effeminate (v), shuasre, shuafo, shuafo
efficiency (n), thuvirtar, virothara, virthar
efficient (adj), thuvirtaru, virotharu, virtharu
efficiently (adv), thuvirtariu, virothariu, virthariu
effort (n), thuvap, vathipa, vathp
effortless (adj), thuvapemenu, vathipemenu, vathpemenu
effortlessly (adv), thuvapemeniu, vathipemeniu, vathpemeniu
egg (n), zhelk, zheluga, zhelg
egg (v), zhelsk, zhelugo, zhelgo

eggplant (n), zhelbrelp, zheleberepa, zhelbrep
eggshell (n), zheltherk, zheletheka, zhelthek
ego (n), ugilat, gilota, gilt
egoism (n), ugilatuet, gilotueta, giltuet
egoist (n doer), ugilatwan, gilotua, giltua
egoistic (adj), ugilatu, gilotu, giltu
egoistically (adv), ugilatiu, gilotiu, giltiu
egotism (n), ugilatuet, gilotueta, giltuet
egotistic (adj), ugilatu, gilotu, giltu
egotistically (adv), ugilatiu, gilotiu, giltiu
Egypt (n), Igeptaf, Igepita, Igept
Egyptian (n), Igeptarn, Igepitana, Igeptan
eh (interj), ua, ua, ua
Eho15minutes (n), briun, beriuna, briun
Eho9seconds (n), grath, geratha, grath
EhoDay01 (n), Loshiaf, Loshiafa, Loshiaf
EhoDay02 (n), Vioriaf, Vioriafa, Vioriaf
EhoDay03 (n), Miriaf, Miriafa, Miriaf
EhoDay04 (n), Duliaf, Duliafa, Duliaf
EhoDay05 (n), Tiakiaf, Tiakiafa, Tiakiaf
EhoDay06 (n), Keliaf, Keliafa, Keliaf
EhoMonth01 (n), Laril, Larila, Laril
EhoMonth02 (n), Rubek, Rubeka, Rubek
EhoMonth03 (n), Blushame, Belushama, Blusham
EhoMonth04 (n), Perun, Peruna, Perun
EhoMonth05 (n), Vilan, Vilana, Vilan
EhoMonth06 (n), Fianth, Fianetha, Fianth
EhoMonth07 (n), Doran, Dorana, Doran
EhoMonth08 (n), Terobe, Teroba, Terob
EhoMonth09 (n), Nivar, Nivara, Nivar
EhoMonth10 (n), Shapor, Shapora, Shapor
EhoMonth11 (n), Galuth, Galutha, Galuth
EhoMonth12 (n), Kitush, Kitusha, Kitush
EhoSecond (n), nik, nika, nik
eight (num 8 card), geni, geni, geni
eighteen (num 18 card), genipa, genipa, genipa
eighteen- (num 18 pref), genipai-, genipai-, genipai-
eighteenth (num 18 ord), genipeth, genipeth,
    genipeth
eighth (num 8 ord), geneth, geneth, geneth
eightieth (num 80 ord), genideth, genideth,
    genideth
eighty (num 80 card), genida, genida, genida
eighty- (num 80 pref), genidai-, genidai-, genidai-
eikto-, kinshkai-, kinshkai-, kinshkai-
Einsteinium (n davoka), Onot, Onot, Onot
Einsteinium (n), Einshteinium, Einesheteiniuma,
    Einshteinium
either (adj/adv/conj), shartu, sharitu, shartu
either (pron), shart, sharitei, shart
ejaculate (v), tudarthsk, tudarotho, tudartho
ejaculation (n), tudarthk, tudarotha, tudarth
eject (v), utersp, utepo, utepo
ejection (n), uterp, utepa, utep
eke (v), arfsp, aripo, arpo
eker (n doer), arfpwan, aripua, arpua
elaborate (adj), ushuvatu, ushuvadu, ushuvdu
elaborate (v), ushuvast, ushuvado, ushuvdo
elaboration (n), ushuvat, ushuvada, ushuvd
elapse (v), uthiurfst, uthiufoto, uthiufto

elastic (adj), sheithku, sheithu, sheithu
elasticity (n), sheithk, sheitha, sheith
elate (v), lairst, ularito, ularto
elation (n), lairt, ularita, ulart
elbow (n), miufort, miufota, miuft
elbow (v), miuforst, miufoto, miufto
elder (adj), reifpu, reifu, reifu
elder (n), reifp, reifa, reif
elderly (adv), reifpiu, reifiu, reifiu
eldest (adj), reifpweku, reifweku, reifweku
elect (v), gelsp, igepo, igepo
electable (adj), gelpefrelpu, igepeferepu, igepfrepu
election (n), gelp, igepa, igep
elective (adj), gelpatu, igepatu, igepatu
elective (n), gelpat, igepata, igepat
electively (adv), gelpatiu, igepatiu, igepatiu
elector (n doer), gelpwan, igepua, igepua
electoral (adj), gelpu, igepu, igepu
electorate (n), gelpan, igepana, igepan
electric (adj), zhiefku, zhiafotu, zhiaftu
electrical (adj), zhiefku, zhiafotu, zhiaftu
electrically (adv), zhiefkiu, zhiafotiu, zhiaftiu
electrician (n doer), zhiefkwan, zhiafotua, zhiaftua
electricity (n), zhiefk, zhiafota, zhiaft
electrics (n), zhiesh, zhiasha, zhiash
electrification (n), zhiefkuet, zhiafotueta, zhiaftuet
electrify (v), zhiefsk, zhiafoto, zhiafto
electrochemical (adj), zhiafreilarku, zhiafereilaku,
    zhiafreilaku
electrocute (v), zhieshsk, zhiako, zhiako
electrocution (n), zhieshk, zhiaka, zhiak
electrode (n), zhiafiurbe, zhiafiuba, zhiafiub
electromagnetic (adj), zhiafgukartu, zhiafogukatu,
    zhiafgukatu
electron (n), zhiek, zhiata, zhiat
electronic (adj), zhieku, zhiatu, zhiatu
electronically (adv), zhiekiu, zhiatiu, zhiatiu
electronics (n), zhiesh, zhiasha, zhiash
electroshock (adj), zhiavigarku, zhiavigaku,
    zhiavigaku
electroshock (n), zhiavigark, zhiavigaka, zhiavigak
electrostatic (adj), zhiashpefortu, zhiashipefotu,
    zhiashpeftu
electrostatic (n), zhiashpefort, zhiashipefota,
    zhiashpeft
elegance (n), kethirn, kethina, kethin
elegant (adj), kethirnu, kethinu, kethinu
elegantly (adv), kethirniu, kethiniu, kethiniu
element (n), munat, mulita, mult
elementary (adj), munatu, mulitu, multu
elephant (n), lanfp, larifota, larft
elephantic (adj), lanfpu, larifotu, larftu
elevate (v), ushtizve, ufativo, uftivo
elevation (n), ushtive, ufativa, uftiv
elevator (n doer), ushtivwan, ufativua, uftivua
eleven (num 11 card), hempa, hempa, hempa
eleven- (num 11 pref), hempai-, hempai-, hempai-
eleventh (num 11 ord), hempeth, hempeth,
    hempeth
elf (n), orthp, oritha, orth
elicit (v), plishst, peliroto, plirto
elicitation (n), plisht, pelirota, plirt
eligibility (n), enutark, enutaka, enutak

eligible (adj), enutarku, enutaku, enutaku
eliminate (v), mukoizge, koravigo, korvigo
elimination (n), mukoige, koraviga, korvig
elite (adj), vuarnu, vuanu, vuanu
elite (n), vuarn, vuana, vuan
elitist (n doer), vuarnwan, vuanua, vuanua
ellipse (n), fiobalt, fiobala, fiobal
elliptical (adj), fiobaltu, fiobalu, fiobalu
elocute (v), murfonzde, murifo, murfo
eloquence (n), murfonde, murifa, murf
eloquent (adj), murfondu, murifu, murfu
eloquently (adv), murfondiu, murifiu, murfiu
else (adj/adv), nelsh, nelishu, nelsh
elsewhere (adv), nelsholu, nelisholu, nelsholu
elucidate (v), shiursne, shiuno, shiuno
elude (v), irushst, irusho, irusho
elusive (adj), irushtu, irushu, irushu
elusively (adv), irushtiu, irushiu, irushiu
emanate (v), anrausf, anerautho, anrautho
emanation (n), anrauf, anerautha, anrauth
emancipate (v), anraufelsk, aneraueliko, anrauelko
emancipation (n), anraufelk, anerauelika, anrauelk
embalm (v), antuvasne, anetelavo, antelvo
embank (v), anplirsk, aneshepelaro, anshplaro
embankment (n), anplirk, aneshepelara, anshplar
embargo (n), anlosht, anamiga, anmig
embargo (v), anloshst, anamigo, anmigo
embark (v), anshkorzbe, aneshekobo, anshkobo
embarkation (n), anshkorbe, aneshekoba, anshkob
embarrass (v), diuirsp, diuipo, diuipo
embarrassment (n), diuirp, diuipa, diuip
embassy (n), liflor, ilafarola, ilfarl
embed (v), ifamosre, ifuaremo, ifuarmo
embellish (v), anbidarsle, anebidalo, anbidalo
embellishment (n), anbidarl, anebidala, anbidal
ember (n), anbugor, aneberuga, anbrug
embezzle (v), anshlarsk, aneshelako, anshlako
embezzlement (n), anshlark, aneshelaka, anshlak
embitter (v), anegaiforsk, anegaifiko, anegaifko
embitterment (n), anegaifork, anegaifika, anegaifk
emblem (n), antikoarme, anetikoama, antikoam
emblematic (adj), antikoarmu, anetikoamu, antikoamu
embodiment (n), anshlarde, aneshelada, anshlad
embody (v), anshlarzde, aneshelado, anshlado
emboss (v), anegiarst, anegiato, anegiato
embossment (n), anegiart, anegiata, anegiat
embrace (v), anploifst, anepeloito, anploito
embracement (n), anploift, anepeloita, anploit
embroil (v), anbiuzge, aneberiugo, anbriugo
embroilment (n), anbiuge, aneberiuga, anbriug
embryo (n), anuiart, anuiata, anuiat
embryonic (adj), anuiartu, anuiatu, anuiatu
emerge (v), anlafsp, laifipo, laifpo
emergence (n), anlafp, laifipa, laifp
emergency (n), anlafpik, laifiapa, laifiap
emigrant (n doer), anplivwan, pelivugua, plivgua
emigrate (v), anplizve, pelivugo, plivgo
emigration (n), anplive, pelivuga, plivg
emission (n), inaursk, inauka, inauk
emit (v), inaursk, inauko, inauko
emote (v), ivadarzve, ivadavo, ivadavo
emotion (n), ivadarve, ivadava, ivadav

emotional (adj), ivadarvu, ivadavu, ivadavu
emotionally (adv), ivadarviu, ivadaviu, ivadaviu
emotive (adj), ivadarvu, ivadavu, ivadavu
empathize (v), anbotarsk, anebotako, anbotako
empathy (n), anbotark, anebotaka, anbotak
emperor (n doer), andaufwan, daufikua, daufkua
emphasis (n), ithuart, ithuata, ithuat
emphasize (v pa), ithuarstyot, ithuatio, ithuatio
emphasize (v), ithuarst, ithuato, ithuato
emphatic (adj), ankenirpu, anekenipu, ankenpu
emphatically (adv), ankenirpiu, anekenipiu, ankcnpiu
empire (n), andauf, daufika, daufk
empiric (adj), anovafirtu, anovafitu, anovaftu
empirical (adj), anovafirtu, anovafitu, anovaftu
empirically (adv), anovafirtiu, anovafitiu, anovaftiu
empiricism (n), anovafirt, anovafita, anovaft
empiricist (n doer), anovafirtwan, anovafitua, anovaftua
employ (v), ashloirst, asheloito, ashloito
employable (adj), ashloirtu, asheloitu, ashloitu
employee (n), shloirtuin, asheloituina, ashloituin
employer (n doer), ashloirtwan, asheloitua, ashloitua
employment (n), ashloirt, asheloita, ashloit
empower (v), anbiorast, anebiorito, anbiorto
empowerment (n), anbiorat, anebiorita, anbiort
emptiness (n), ansh, alisha, alsh
empty (adj), anshu, alishu, alshu
empty (v), ans, alisho, alsho
emulate (v), koirsf, koifo, koifo
emulation (n), koirf, koifa, koif
emulous (adj), koirfu, koifu, koifu
enable (v), frelsp, ferepo, frepo
enabler (n doer), frelpwan, ferepua, frepua
enact (v), darpatisle, vopalito, vopalto
enaction (n), darpatil, vopalita, vopalt
enactment (n), darpatil, vopalita, vopalt
encapsulate (v), anpransp, aneduperano, anduprano
encapsulation (n), anpranp, aneduperana, andupran
encapsulator (n doer), anpranpwan, aneduperanua, andupranua
encase (v d:container), shuarst, shuato, shuato
enchant (v), darkanirsf, vokanifo, vokanfo
enchantment (n), darkanirf, vokanifa, vokanf
encircle (v), anvaltosre, anevalito, anvalto
encirclement (n), anvaltor, anevalita, anvalt
enclose (v), dargrest, vogereto, vogreto
enclosure (n), dargret, vogereta, vogret
encode (v), anvolarst, anevolato, anvlato
encoder (n doer), anvolartwan, anevolatua, anvlatua
encompass (v), anlefnisk, anelenifoko, anlenfko
encounter (n), darpoift, vopoifa, vopoif
encounter (v), darpoifst, vopoifo, vopoifo
encourage (v), divasre, diravo, dirvo
encouragement (n), dirvart, diravata, dirvat
encrypt (v), bruilsk, beruiko, bruiko
encryption (n), bruilk, beruika, bruik
encumber (v), pramisp, peramipo, prampo
encyclopedia (n), darvairmoide, vomoida, vomoid

encyclopedic (adj), darvairmoidu, vomoidu, vomoidu
end (n), dairk, daika, daik
end (v), dairsk, daiko, daiko
endanger (v), zhaurzbe, zhaubo, zhaubo
endangerment (n), zhaurbuet, zhaubueta, zhaubuet
endear (v), lovasle, lolifo, lolfo
endgame (n), daikzhiert, daikezhieta, daikzhiet
endless (adj), dairkmenu, daikemenu, daikmenu
endlessly (adv), dairkmeniu, daikemeniu, daikmeniu
endorse (v), ibirnorst, ibironito, ibirnto
endorsement (n), ibirnort, ibironita, ibirnt
endorser (n doer), ibirnortwan, ibironitua, ibirntua
endpoint (n), daktaifort, daiketaifota, daiktaift
endurance (n), shtaursh, shetausha, shtaush
endure (v), shtaurs, shetausho, shtausho
enemy (n), farsht, feneiga, fneig
energetic (adj), dargalitu, vogalitu, voglitu
energize (v), dargalist, vogalito, voglito
energizer (n doer), dargalitwan, vogalitua, voglitua
energy (n), dargalit, vogalita, voglit
enfaith (v), naltrisp, perinelito, prinelto
enfeeble (v), klurzme, kelumo, klumo
enforce (v), darviusk, voviuko, voviuko
enforceable (adj), darviuku, voviuku, voviuku
enforcement (n), darviuk, voviuka, voviuk
enforcer (n doer), darviukwan, voviukua, voviukua
enfranchise (v), plimorfsk, pelimoriko, plimorko
engage (v), darbaisk, vobaiko, vobaiko
engagement (n), darbaik, vobaika, vobaik
engender (v d:group), barthsk, beronibaro, bronbaro
engine (n), gankern, ganikena, ganken
engineer (n doer), gankernwan, ganikenua, gankenua
engineer (v), gankersne, ganikeno, gankeno
England (n), Anklarn, Anakulana, Anklan
English (n), Ankarsh, Anakalusha, Ankalsh
engrain (v), darnellrsk, voneliko, vonelko
engram (n), darnelirk, vonelika, vonelk
engrave (v), bonirsf, bonifo, bonfo
engraver (n doer), bonirfwan, bonifua, bonfua
engulf (v), karishsk, karisho, karsho
enhance (v), darkansp, vokanipo, vokanpo
enhancement (n), darkanp, vokanipa, vokanp
enhancer (n doer), darkanpwan, vokanipua, vokanpua
enjoy (v), darlais, volaisho, volaisho
enjoyable (adj), darlaishu, volaishu, volaishu
enjoyment (n), darlaish, volaisha, volaish
enlarge (v), graurzge, geraugo, graugo
enlargement (n), graurge, gerauga, graug
enlarger (n doer), graurgwan, geraugua, graugua
enlighten (v), anfluarsne, anefeluano, anfluano
enlightenment (n), anfluarn, anefeluana, anfluan
enlist (v), andilst, anedito, andito
enlistment (n), andilt, anedita, andit
enliven (v), anflaurfst, anefelaufito, anflaufto
enormity (n), darlanf, volanifa, volanf
enormous (adj), darlanfu, volanifu, volanfu
enormously (adv), darlanfiu, volanifiu, volanfiu
enough (adj/adv), plurf, pelufu, pluf

enough (pron), plurf, pelufei, pluf
enquire (v), thafirst, thafito, thafto
enquiry (n), thafirt, thafita, thaft
enrage (v), zhigarshst, zhigashoto, zhigashto
enragement (n pl), zhigarshtyek, zhigashoti, zhigashti
enragement (n), zhigarsht, zhigashota, zhigasht
enrapture (v), vagarst, vagato, vagato
enrich (v), shtuvasre, shetufo, shtufo
enricher (n doer), shtuvarwan, shetufua, shtufua
enrichment (n), shtuvar, shetufa, shtuf
enroll (v), anfalasre, anefaliro, anfaliro
enrollee (n), anfalaruin, anefaliruina, anfaliruin
enroller (n doer), anfalarwan, anefalirua, anfalirua
enrollment (n), anfalar, anefalira, anfalir
enscribe (v), usherzge, usherigo, ushrigo
enscription (n), usherge, usheriga, ushrig
ensemble (n), anthralve, anetherava, anthrav
enshrine (v), niorsne, niono, niono
enslave (v), anshraifsp, anesheraipo, anshraipo
enslavement (n), anshraifp, anesheraipa, anshraip
enslaver (n doer), anshraifpwan, anesheraipua, anshraipua
ensnare (v d:trap), shreilsp, shereipo, shreipo
ensnarement (n d:trap), shreilp, shereipa, shreip
ensue (v), andutarsk, anedutako, andutako
ensurance (n), ishreln, isherela, ishrel
ensure (v), ishrelsne, isherelo, ishrelo
entail (v), anmithsk, anemitho, anmitho
entailment (n), anmithk, anemitha, anmith
entangle (v), antaigarzge, anetaigago, antaigago
entanglement (n), antaigarge, anetaigaga, antaigag
enter (v), londisle, lonudo, londo
enterprise (n), londviush, lonudiusha, londiush
enterprise (v), londvius, lonudiusho, londiusho
entertain (v), lonast, veliro, vliro
entertainer (n doer), lonatwan, velirua, vlirua
entertainment (n), lonat, velira, vlir
enthuse (v), darzhusf, vozhufo, vozhufo
enthusiam (n), darzhuf, vozhufa, vozhuf
enthusiast (n doer), darzhutwan, vozhufua, vozhufua
enthusiastic (adj), darzhufu, vozhufu, vozhufu
enthusiastically (adv), darzhufiu, vozhufiu, vozhufiu
entice (v), anegurshsk, anegushiko, anegushko
enticement (n), anegurshk, anegushika, anegushk
entire (adj), darpanu, vopanu, vopanu
entirely (adv), darpaniu, vopaniu, vopaniu
entirety (n), darpan, vopana, vopan
entitle (v), ushtaisp, fetaipo, ftaipo
entitlement (n), ushtaip, fetaipa, ftaip
entitler (n doer), ushtaipwan, fetaipua, ftaipua
entity (n), ifert, iferitha, iferth
entomb (v), beinursk, beinuko, beinko
entrance (n), londil, lonuda, lond
entrant (n doer), londilwan, lonudua, londua
entrap (v), anthreilsp, anethereipo, anthreipo
entrapment (n), anthreilp, anethereipa, anthreip
entrench (v), andiofsk, anediofo, andiofo
entrenchment (n), andiofk, anediofa, andiof
entrepreneur (n doer), londviushwan, lonudiushua, londiushua

entrust (v), andreirsf, anedereifo, andreifo
entrustment (n), andreirf, anedereifa, andreif
entry (n), londil, lonuda, lond
entryway (n), londpliorl, lonudepeliola, londpliol
enumerate (v), anenirkesle, anenikelo, anenkelo
enumeration (n), anenirkel, anenikela, anenkel
envelop (v), ufrasp, voferapo, vofrapo
envelope (n), ufrap, voferapa, vofrap
enveloper (n doer), ufrapwan, voferapua, vofrapua
envious (adj), tiauzhu, tiaugu, tiaugu
enviously (adv), tiauzhiu, tiaugiu, tiaugiu
environment (n), biersh, biesha, biesh
environmental (adj), biershu, bieshu, bieshu
environmentalist (n doer), biershwan, bieshua,
    bieshua
environmentally (adv), biershiu, bieshiu, bieshiu
envision (v), fiaishsk, fiaisho, fiaisho
envoy (n), anfualf, anefuala, anfual
envy (n), tiauzhe, tiauga, tiaug
envy (v), tiauze, tiaugo, tiaugo
epic (n), viugilt, viugila, viugil
epicenter (n), ifludret, iforelita, ifrelt
epidemic (n), ifiplorn, ifipelona, ifiplon
episodal (adj), ithirmu, ithimu, ithimu
episodally (adv), ithirmiu, ithimiu, ithimiu
episode (n), ithirme, ithima, ithim
epitaph (n), ifibeinurk, ifibeinuka, ifibeink
epoch (n), ifikorf, ifikofa, ifikof
epsilon (n), epshilorn, eposhilona, epshilon
equal (n), dainf, daina, dain
equal (v), dainsf, daino, daino
equality (n), dainfk, dainoka, daink
equalization (n), dainfk, dainoka, daink
equalize (v), dainfsk, dainoko, dainko
equalizer (n doer), dainfkwan, dainokua, dainkua
equally (adv), dainfiu, dainiu, dainiu
equate (v), dairzde, daido, daido
equation (n), dairde, daida, daid
equator (n doer), dairdwan, daidua, daidua
equilibrium (n), daikiunorf, daikiunofa, daikiunf
equip (v), udeisp, vodeipo, vodeipo
equipment (n), udeip, vodeipa, vodeip
equity (n), diarsht, daishota, daisht
equivalence (n), dialat, dailota, dailt
equivalent (adj), dialatu, dailotu, dailtu
era (n), lizhdof, lidofa, lidof
eradicate (v), ukaikiarsk, vokaikaiko, vokaikiako
eradication (n), ukaikiark, vokaikaika, vokaikiak
eradicator (n doer), ukaikiarkwan, vokaikaikua,
    vokaikiakua
erase (v), ukaisk, vokaiko, vokaiko
eraser (n doer), ukaikwan, vokaikua, vokaikua
erasure (n), ukaik, vokaika, vokaik
Erbium (n davoka), Orut, Orut, Orut
Erbium (n), Erbium, Erubiuma, Erbium
erect (v), ukuast, vokuato, vokuato
erection (n), ukuat, vokuata, vokuat
erector (n doer), ukuatwan, vokuatua, vokuatua
erode (v), ushlisp, voshelipo, voshlipo
erosion (n), ushlip, voshelipa, voshlip
erotic (adj), ukuapu, vokuapu, vokuapu
erotica (n), ukuap, vokuapa, vokuap
eroticism (n), ukuapuet, vokuapueta, vokuapuet

err (v), gauirsk, gauiko, gauiko
errand (n), ureibe, voreiba, voreib
errant (adj), gauirku, gauiku, gauiku
erratic (adj), gauiarbu, gauiabu, gauiabu
erratically (adv), gauiarbiu, gauiabiu, gauiabiu
erroneous (adj), gauirku, gauiku, gauiku
erroneously (adv), gauirkiu, gauikiu, gauikiu
error (n), gauirk, gauika, gauik
erupt (v), ugaifst, vogaifoto, vogaifto
eruption (n), ugaift, vogaifota, vogaift
eruptor (n doer), ugaiftwan, vogaifotua, vogaiftua
Es (let pl), elfi, elfi, elfi
escalate (v), ushuirsk, voshuiko, voshuiko
escalation (n), ushuirk, voshuika, voshuik
escalator (n doer), ushuirkwan, voshuikua,
    voshuikua
escapable (adj), ushiaku, voshiaku, voshiaku
escapably (adv), ushiakiu, voshiakiu, voshiakiu
escapade (n), ushiakiap, voshiakiapa, voshiakiap
escape (n), ushiak, voshiaka, voshiak
escape (v), ushiask, voshiako, voshiako
escapee (n doer), ushiakwan, voshiakua, voshiakua
escapism (n), ushiakuet, voshiakueta, voshiakuet
escort (n), tumarnf, tumarina, tumarn
especially (adv), sheirshiu, sheishiu, sheishiu
espouse (v), pimarsf, pimafo, pimafo
essay (n), uzhush, vozhusha, vozhush
essay (v), uzhus, vozhusho, vozhusho
essence (n), sharlirt, shalirota, shalirt
essential (adj), sharlirtu, shalirotu, shalirtu
essentially (adv), sharlirtiu, shalirotiu, shalirtiu
essentiate (v), sharlirst, shaliroto, shalirto
establish (v), aftasp, vofitapo, voftapo
establisher (n doer), aftapwan, vofitapua, voftapua
establishment (n), aftap, vofitapa, voftap
estate (n), ushpet, voshipeta, voshpet
estate (v), ushpest, voshipeto, voshpeto
esteem (n), uthut, vothuta, vothut
esteem (v), uthust, vothuto, vothuto
estimate (n), thinarp, thinapa, thinp
estimate (v), thinarsp, thinapo, thinpo
estimator (n doer), thinarpwan, thinapua, thinpua
estrange (v), shaursk, shauko, shauko
estrangement (n), shaurk, shauka, shauk
eta (n), etarn, etana, etan
etc. (phrase), honzhairm, honazhaimu, honzhaim
etcetera (phrase), honzhairm, honazhaimu,
    honzhaim
etch (n), grairsh, geraisha, graish
etch (v), grairs, geralsho, graisho
etcher (n doer), grairshwan, geraishua, graishua
etchily (adv), grairshiu, geraishiu, graishiu
etchy (adj), grairshu, geraishu, graishu
eternal (adj), piarfpu, vopiropu, vopirpu
eternalize (v), piarfsp, vopiropo, vopirpo
eternalizer (n doer), piarfpwan, vopiropua,
    vopirpua
eternally (adv), piarfpiu, vopiropiu, vopirpiu
eternity (n), piarfp, vopiropa, vopirp
ethic (n), kurfp, kufipa, kufp
ethical (adj), kurfpu, kufipu, kufpu
ethically (adv), kurfpiu, kufipiu, kufpiu
ethicate (v), kurfsp, kufipo, kufpo

ethnic (adj), kurftu, kufitu, kuftu
ethnicity (n), kurft, kufita, kuft
ethos (n), kurfpath, kufipatha, kufpath
etiquette (n), vaushnoirk, vaushenoika, vaushnoik
euphoria (n), morlirf, morelifa, morlif
euphoric (adj), morlirfu, morelifu, morlifu
eureka (interj), ilaikau, ilaiko, ilaiko
Europe (n), Reilorp, Reilopa, Reilop
European (n), Reiloparn, Reilopana, Reilopan
Europium (n davoka), Orok, Orok, Orok
Europium (n), Europium, Europiuma, Europium
evacuate (v), uvauisf, vovauifo, vovauifo
evacuation (n), uvauif, vovauifa, vovauif
evacuator (n doer), uvauifwan, vovauifua,
    vovauifua
evade (v), uzhansk, vozhaniko, vozhanko
evader (n doer), uzhankwan, vozhanikua,
    vozhankua
evaluate (v), uvausp, vovaupo, vovaupo
evaluation (n), uvaup, vovaupa, vovaup
evaluator (n doer), uvaupwan, vovaupua, vovaupua
evaporate (v), ubiufirst, vobiufito, vobiufto
evaporation (n), ubiufirt, vobiufita, vobiuft
evaporator (n doer), ubiufirtwan, vobiufitua,
    vobiuftua
evasion (n), uzhank, vozhanika, vozhank
evasive (adj), uzhanku, vozhaniku, vozhanku
evasively (adv), uzhankiu, vozhanikiu, vozhankiu
eve (n), fimarl, fimara, fimar
even (adj d:distribute), pifonu, piletu, pletu
even (v d:distribute), pifosne, pileto, pleto
evening (n d:late daytime), fimalf, fimala, fimal
evenly (adv d:distribute), pifoniu, piletiu, pletiu
evenness (n d:distribute), pifon, pileta, plet
event (n), fidal, firoda, fird
eventful (adj), fidalu, firodu, firdu
eventfully (adv), fidaliu, firodiu, firdiu
eventual (adj), fidalaiku, firodaiku, firdaiku
eventuality (n), fidalaik, firodaika, firdaik
eventually (adv), fidalaikiu, firodaikiu, firdaikiu
ever (adj/adv), efel, efelu, efel
everlasting (adj), efelshethu, lefeshethu, lefshethu
everlastingly (adv), efelshethiu, lefeshethiu,
    lefshethiu
every (adj), eferlu, lerifu, lerfu
everybody (pron), eferlshlarde, lerifusheladei,
    lerfshlad
everyday (adj), eferlviurlu, lerifeviulu, lerfviulu
everyday (n), eferlviurl, lerifeviula, lerfviul
everyone (pron), eferlton, lerifitonei, lerfton
everything (n/pron), eferlizhe, lerifalizhei, lerflizh
everywhere (adv), eferfital, lerofital, lerfital
evict (v), ubaisf, vobaifo, vobaifo
eviction (n), ubaif, vobaifa, vobaif
evidence (n), uft, vofeta, voft
evidence (v), ufst, vofeto, vofto
evident (adj), uftu, vofetu, voftu
evidently (adv), uftiu, vofetiu, voftiu
evil (adj), uzhaku, vozhaku, vozhaku
evil (n), uzhak, vozhaka, vozhak
evildoer (n doer), uzhakwan, vozhakua, vozhakua
evoke (v), ushairsk, voshaiko, voshaiko
evolution (n), ukmirf, vokemifa, vokmif

evolutionary (adj), ukmirfu, vokemifu, vokmifu
evolve (v), ukmirsf, vokemifo, vokmifo
exa- (num 1e18 pref), tirikai-, tirikai-, tirikai-
exact (adj), turshtu, tushatu, tushtu
exact (v), turshst, tushato, tushto
exactly (adv), turshtiu, tushatiu, tushtiu
exactness (n), tursht, tushata, tusht
exaggerate (v), tulorvazge, tulovago, tulovgo
exaggeration (n), tulorvage, tulovaga, tulovg
exam (n), tukor, tukora, tukor
examination (n), tukoirge, tukoiga, tukoig
examine (v), tukoirzge, tukoigo, tukoigo
examiner (n doer), tukoirgwan, tukoigua, tukoigua
example (n), tushanber, shanipa, shanp
excavate (v), tupaurzge, tupaugo, tupaugo
excavation (n), tupaurge, tupauga, tupaug
excavator (n doer), tupaurgwan, tupaugua,
    tupaugua
exceed (v), tuvesk, veriko, verko
excel (v), tufrasle, feraisho, fraisho
excellence (n), tufral, feraisha, fraish
excellent (adj), tufralu, feraishu, fraishu
excellently (adv), tufraliu, feraishiu, fraishiu
except (prep/conj), tuvet, verit, vert
except (v), tuvest, verito, verto
exception (n), tuvet, verita, vert
exceptional (adj), tuvetu, veritu, vertu
exceptionally (adv), tuvetiu, veritiu, vertiu
excerpt (n), tugilirp, tugilipa, tugilp
excerpt (v), tugilirsp, tugilipo, tugilpo
excess (n), tuvek, verika, verk
excessive (adj), tuveku, veriku, verku
excessively (adv), tuvekiu, verikiu, verkiu
exchange (n), tutuan, tuanita, tuant
exchange (v), tutuasne, tuanito, tuanto
exchangeable (adj), tutuanu, tuanitu, tuantu
exchanger (n doer), tutuanwan, tuanitua, tuantua
excise (v), tuthirshsk, tuthishako, tuthishko
excision (n), tuthirshk, tuthishaka, tuthishk
excitable (adj), tutoipu, toipotu, toipotu
excitably (adv), tutoipiu, toipotiu, toipotiu
excitation (n), tutoipuet, toipotueta, toiptuet
excite (v), tutoisp, toipoto, toipoto
excitement (n), tutoip, toipota, toipot
exciter (n doer), tutoipwan, toipotua, toipotua
exclaim (v), tunolasre, tunoarito, tunoarto
exclamation (n), tunolar, tunoarita, tunoart
exclamatory (adj), tunolaru, tunoaritu, tunoartu
exclude (v), tugrushst, tugeruto, tugruto
excluder (n doer), tugrushtwan, tugerutua,
    tugrutua
exclusion (n), tugrusht, tugeruta, tugrut
exclusive (adj), tugrushtu, tugerutu, tugrutu
exclusively (adv), tugrushtiu, tugerutiu, tugrutiu
excommunicate (v), tuguniarst, tuguniato,
    tuguniato
excommunication (n), tuguniart, tuguniata,
    tuguniat
excommunicator (n doer), tuguniartwan,
    tuguniatua, tuguniatua
excrement (n), tugort, tugota, tugot
excrete (v), tugorst, tugoto, tugoto
excreter (n doer), tugortwan, tugotua, tugotua

excretion (n), tugort, tugota, tugot
excretive (adj), tugortu, tugotu, tugotu
excruciate (v), tuvioishsk, tuvioisho, tuvioisho
excruciatingly (adv), tuvioishkiu, tuvioishiu,
    tuvioishiu
excruciation (n), tuvioishk, tuvioisha, tuvioish
excusable (adj), tugoishtu, tugoitu, tugoitu
excuse (n), tugoisht, tugoita, tugoit
excuse (v), tugoishst, tugoito, tugoito
excuser (n doer), tugoishtwan, tugoitua, tugoitua
executable (adj), doshfrelpu, doshiferepu,
    doshfrepu
executable (n), doshfrelp, doshiferepa, doshfrep
executably (adv), doshfrelpiu, doshiferepiu,
    doshfrepiu
execute (v d:perform), dokast, doshiko, doshko
execution (n d:perform), dokat, doshika, doshk
executioner (n doer d:perform), dokatwan,
    doshikua, doshkua
executive (adj d:perform), dokatu, doshiku, doshku
executive (n d:businessperson), dokart, doshikara,
    doshkar
executively (adv d:perform), dokatiu, doshikiu,
    doshkiu
executor (n doer), dokatwan, doshikua, doshkua
exemplify (v), tushanbesre, shanipo, shanpo
exempt (v), glinorsk, gelinoko, glinko
exemption (n), glinork, gelinoka, glink
exercise (n), tuenthirshk, turathishaka, turathishk
exercise (v), tuenthirshsk, turathishako,
    turathishko
exerciser (n doer), tuenthirshkwan, turathishakua,
    turathishkua
exert (v), tuorfsp, tuoripo, tuorpo
exhalation (n), tuwafk, worofika, worfk
exhale (v), tuwafsk, worofiko, worfko
exhaler (n doer), tuwafkwan, worofikua, worfkua
exhaust (n), lagaf, liafoka, liafk
exhaust (v), lagasf, liafoko, liafko
exhaustion (n), lagarf, liarifoka, liarfk
exhaustive (adj), lagafu, liafoku, liafku
exhaustively (adv), lagafiu, liafokiu, liafkiu
exhibit (n), tudaibe, daibata, daibat
exhibit (v), tudaizbe, daibato, daibato
exhibition (n), tudaibet, daibateta, daibatet
exhibitionist (n doer), tudaibetwan, daibatetua,
    daibatetua
exhibitor (n doer), tudaibwan, daibatua, daibatua
exile (n), tuyoil, hoita, hoit
exile (v), tuyoisle, hoito, hoito
exist (v), nuhrst, nulito, nulto
existence (n), nulirt, nulita, nult
exit (n), dok, doka, dok
exit (v), dosk, doko, doko
exiter (n doer), dokwan, dokua, dokua
exotic (adj), tuairku, tuaiku, tuaiku
exotic (n), tuairk, tuaika, tuaik
expand (v), tumeis, meishopo, meishpo
expandable (adj), tumeishu, meishopu, meishpu
expander (n doer), tumeishwan, meishopua,
    meishpua
expanse (n), tumeish, meishopa, meishp
expansion (n), tumeish, meishopa, meishp

expansionist (n doer), tumeishwan, meishopua,
    meishpua
expansive (adj), tumeishu, meishopu, meishpu
expansively (adv), tumeishiu, meishopiu, meishpiu
expect (v), tuthursk, tuthuko, tuthuko
expectation (n), tuthurk, tuthuka, tuthuk
expectorant (n doer), tuthurkwan, tuthukua,
    tuthukua
expedience (n), moishortuet, moishotueta,
    moishtuet
expediency (n), moishortuet, moishotueta,
    moishtuet
expedient (adj), moishortu, moishotu, moishtu
expedite (v), moishorst, moishoto, moishto
expedition (n), moishort, moishota, moisht
expeditious (adj), moishortuetu, moishotuetu,
    moishtuetu
expeditiously (adv), moishortuetiu, moishotuetiu,
    moishtuetiu
expel (v), fpazde, fipato, fpato
expend (v), tubrunsf, tuberuno, tubruno
expendable (adj), tubrunfrelpu, tuberuneferepu,
    tubrunfrepu
expenditure (n), tubrunf, tuberuna, tubrun
expense (n), tubrunf, tuberuna, tubrun
expensive (adj), tubrunfu, tuberunu, tubrunu
expensively (adv), tubrunfiu, tuberuniu, tubruniu
experience (n), zhurnit, zhurita, zhurt
experience (v), zhurnist, zhurito, zhurto
experiment (n), denilt, nilota, nilt
experiment (v), denilst, niloto, nilto
experimental (adj), deniltu, nilotu, niltu
experimentally (adv), deniltiu, nilotiu, niltiu
experimenter (n doer), deniltwan, nilotua, niltua
expert (n doer), zhurnitwan, zhuritua, zhurtua
expertise (n), zhurtarn, zhuritana, zhurtan
expertly (adv), zhurnitiu, zhuritiu, zhurtiu
expiration (n), tudauf, daufota, dauft
expire (v), tudausf, daufoto, daufto
explain (v), vairzge, vaigo, vaigo
explanation (n), vairge, vaiga, vaig
expletive (n), tuaiart, tuaiata, tuaiat
explication (n), tubreshort, tubereshota, tubresht
explicit (adj), tubreshortu, tubereshotu, tubreshtu
explicitly (adv), tubreshortiu, tubereshotiu,
    tubreshtiu
explode (v), diagalist, diaugo, diaugo
exploit (n), tudrak, derashika, drashk
exploit (v), tudrask, derashiko, drashko
exploitation (n), tudrakat, derashikata, drashkat
exploiter (n doer), tudrakwan, derashikua,
    drashkua
exploitive (adj), tudraku, derashiku, drashku
exploitively (adv), tudrakiu, derashikiu, drashkiu
exploration (n), tudralve, turederava, tudrav
exploratory (adj), tudralvu, turederavu, tudravu
explore (v), tudralzve, turederavo, tudravo
explorer (n doer), tudralvwan, turederavua,
    tudravua
explosion (n), diagalit, diauga, diaug
explosive (adj), diagalitu, diaugu, diaugu
explosive (n doer), diagalitwan, diaugua, diaugua
explosively (adv), diagalitiu, diaugiu, diaugiu

exply (v), tubreshorst, tubereshoto, tubreshto
expone (v), tuvelsp, dovenipo, dovenpo
exponent (n), tuvelp, dovenipa, dovenp
exponential (adj), tuvelpu, dovenipu, dovenpu
exponentially (adv), tuvelpiu, dovenipiu, dovenpiu
export (n), tubielirk, tubielika, tubielk
export (v), tubielirsk, tubieliko, tubielko
exporter (n doer), tubielirkwan, tubielikua, tubielkua
expose (v), tulask, lanishoko, lanshko
exposer (n doer), tulakwan, lanishokua, lanshkua
exposition (n), tulakuet, lanishokueta, lanshkuet
expository (adj), tulaku, lanishoku, lanshku
exposure (n), tulak, lanishoka, lanshk
express (v), tublars, tubelasho, tublasho
expresser (n doer), tublarshwan, tubelashua, tublashua
expression (n), tublarsh, tubelasha, tublash
expressive (adj), tublarshu, tubelashu, tublashu
expressively (adv), tublarshiu, tubelashiu, tublashiu
expressly (adv), tublarshiu, tubelashiu, tublashiu
expressway (n), tublapliorl, tubelapeliola, tublapliol
expulsion (n), fpade, fipata, fpat
exquisite (adj), tuthafirtu, tuthafitu, tuthaftu
exquisitely (adv), tuthafirtiu, tuthafitiu, tuthaftiu
extend (v), tupiforsk, tupifoko, tupifko
extender (n doer), tupiforkwan, tupifokua, tupifkua
extension (n), tupiforkuet, tupifokueta, tupifkuet
extensive (adj), tupiforku, tupifoku, tupifku
extensively (adv), tupiforkiu, tupifokiu, tupifkiu
extent (n), tupifork, tupifoka, tupifk
exterior (n), tupirp, pirotapa, pirtap
exterminate (v), tunilarsk, tunilako, tunilko
extermination (n), tunilark, tunilaka, tunilk
exterminator (n doer), tunilarkwan, tunilakua, tunilkua
external (adj), tupirpu, pirotapu, pirtapu
externalize (v), tupirsp, pirotapo, pirtapo
externally (adv), tupirpiu, pirotapiu, pirtapiu
extinct (adj), tupoitu, poishotu, poishtu
extinction (n), tupoit, poishota, poisht
extinguish (v), toidoisp, poidoipo, poidoipo
extinguisher (n doer), toidoipwan, poidoipua, poidoipua
extinguishment (n), toidoip, poidoipa, poidoip
extort (v), tukiorst, tukioto, tukioto
extortion (n), tukiort, tukiota, tukiot
extra (adj), leishpu, leishu, leishu
extra (n), leishp, leisha, leish
extract (n), tugarl, tugalita, tugalt
extract (v), tugarsle, tugalito, tugalto
extraction (n), tugarluet, tugalueta, tugaluet
extractor (n doer), tugarlwan, tugalitua, tugaltua
extradite (v), leishgorsk, leishugoko, leishgoko
extradition (n), leishgork, leishugoka, leishgok
extraordinary (adj), leishkeltaru, leishiketaru, leishketaru
extravagance (n), fravushiak, feraishiaka, fraishiak
extravagant (adj), fravushiaku, feraishiaku, fraishiaku
extravagantly (adv), fravushiakiu, feraishiakiu, fraishiakiu
extreme (adj), tufravu, feraifu, fraifu

extreme (n), tufrave, feraifa, fraif
extremely (adv), tufraviu, feraifiu, fraifiu
extremist (n doer), tufravwan, feraifua, fraifua
extremity (n), tufravan, feraifana, fraifan
extricate (v), tutrelzbe, tuterebo, tutrebo
extrication (n), tutrelbe, tutereba, tutreb
extrovert (n doer), fravushiakwan, feraishiakua, fraishiakua
extrude (v), tuborfst, tubofito, tubofto
extrusion (n), tuborft, tubofita, tuboft
exuberance (n), leirsheif, leisheifa, leisheif
exuberant (adj), leirsheifu, leisheifu, leisheifu
exuberantly (adv), leirsheifiu, leisheifiu, leisheifiu
eye (n), iwat, iwafa, iwaf
eye (v), iwast, iwafo, iwafo
eyeball (n), iwashmonde, imashipa, imashp
eyeball (v), iwashmonzde, imashipo, imashpo
eyebrow (n), iwaflorde, ipelorita, iplort
eyeglass (n), iwadrinat, iwaderinota, iwadrint
eyelash (n), iwashreide, ishereida, ishreid
eyeless (adj), iwatmenu, iwafemenu, iwafmenu
eyelet (n), iwalerk, iwaleka, iwalek
eyelid (n), iwanith, initha, inith
eyeliner (n doer), iwaroifkwan, iwaroifua, iwaroifua
eyepiece (n), iwathetirsh, iwathetisha, iwathetsh
eyer (n doer), iwatwan, iwafua, iwafua
eyesight (n), iwathulth, iwathutha, iwathuth
eyesore (n), iwabairme, iwabaima, iwabaim
eyestrain (n), iwaprulirk, iwaperulika, iwaprulk
eyewear (n), iwadorame, iwadorima, iwadorim
eyewitness (n), iwafriork, iwaferioka, iwafriok
F (let sng), feil, feia, fei
fable (n), boarn, boana, boan
fabric (n), palork, paloka, palok
fabricate (v), tolpalorsk, tolipaloko, tolpalko
fabrication (n), tolpalork, tolipaloka, tolpalk
fabricator (n doer), tolpalorkwan, tolipalokua, tolpalkua
fabulous (adj), boarnu, boanu, boanu
fabulously (adv), boarniu, boaniu, boaniu
face (n), thoirsh, thoisha, thoish
face (v), thoirs, thoisho, thoisho
facelift (n), thoishraushk, thoisherauka, thoishrauk
facelift (v), thoishraushsk, thoisherauko, thoishrauko
faceplate (n), thoishfkarf, thoishefikafa, thoishfkaf
facer (n doer), thoirshwan, thoishua, thoishua
facet (n), thoishoirt, thoishoita, thoishoit
facetious (adj), shlurbu, shelubu, shlubu
facetiously (adv), shlurbiu, shelubiu, shlubiu
facial (adj), thoirshu, thoishu, thoishu
facial (n), thoirshul, thoishula, thoishul
facile (adj), briorfu, beriofu, briofu
facilitate (v), briorsf, beriofo, briofo
facilitator (n doer), briorfwan, beriofua, briofua
facility (n), briorf, beriofa, briof
facsimile (n), toldidarn, toludidana, toldidan
fact (n), porlet, poreta, poret
faction (n), fashirk, fashika, fashk
factor (n), porlefft, porefita, poreft
factor (v), porlefst, porefito, porefto
factory (n), kukar, kurika, kurk
factual (adj), porletu, poretu, poretu

factually (adv), porletiu, poretiu, poretiu
faculty (n), briorfuet, beriofueta, briofuet
fad (n), paf, pafa, paf
fade (n d:diminish), bolen, boena, boen
fade (v d:diminish), bolesne, boeno, boeno
fader (n doer d:diminish), bolenwan, boenua,
    boenua
Fahrenheit (adj), Varemain, Varemaina, Varemain
fail (v), zhairst, zhaito, zhaito
failure (n), zhairt, zhaita, zhait
faint (adj d:diminish), bolenu, boenu, boenu
faint (v d:pass out), bolesk, boeko, boeko
fainter (adj), bolenwelu, boenwelu, boenwelu
fainter (n doer d:pass out), bolekwan, boekua,
    boekua
faintest (adj), bolenweku, boenweku, boenweku
faintly (adv d:diminish), boleniu, boeniu, boeniu
fair (adj d:good), theralu, therelu, threlu
fair (n d:exhibition), foirsh, foisha, foish
fairer (adj d:better), theralwelu, therelwelu,
    threlwelu
fairest (adj d:best), theralweku, therelweku,
    threlweku
fairground (n), foishbraft, foisheberanita,
    foishbrant
fairing (n), threlshp, therelisha, threlsh
fairly (adv d:good), theraliu, thereliu, threliu
fairness (n d:good), theral, therela, threl
fairway (n), threlpliorl, therelepeliola, threlpliol
fairy (n), foirf, foifa, foif
fairyland (n), foifraufp, foiferaupa, foifraup
faith (n), naltrip, perinelita, prinelt
faithful (adj), naltripu, perinelitu, prineltu
faithfully (adv), naltripiu, perinelitiu, prineltiu
faithfulness (n), naltripuet, perinelitueta, prineltuet
faithless (adj), naltrimenu, perinelomanu,
    prinelmenu
faithlessly (adv), naltrimeniu, perinelomaniu,
    prinelmeniu
faithlessness (n), naltrimen, perinelomana,
    prinelmen
fake (n), lagak, gelauka, glauk
fake (v), lagask, gelauko, glauko
faker (n doer), lagakwan, gelaukua, glaukua
fall (n d:autumn), frodan, ferodatha, frodath
fall (n d:descent), zhailf, zhaila, zhail
fall (v d:descent), zhailsf, zhailo, zhailo
fallible (adj), zhairtu, zhaitu, zhaitu
fallopian (adj), felifiarnu, felifianu, felifianu
fallout (n), zhailfuil, zhailuila, zhailuil
false (adj), daushtu, daushu, daushu
falsehood (n), daushtfif, daushefifa, daushfif
falsely (adv), daushtiu, daushiu, daushiu
falsification (n), daushtuet, daushueta, daushuet
falsify (v), daushst, dausho, dausho
falsity (n), dausht, dausha, daush
falter (v), zhaitarze, zhaitazho, zhaitazho
fame (n), shern, shena, shen
famile (n), fliarn, feliana, flian
familiar (adj), fliarnu, felianu, flianu
familiarize (v), fliarsne, feliano, fliano
family (n doer), fliarnwan, felianua, flianua
famine (n), shnornk, shenorina, shnorn

famous (adj), shernu, shenu, shenu
famously (adv), sherniu, sheniu, sheniu
fan (n d:follower), barmp, barima, barm
fan (n d:move air), molaf, moafa, moaf
fan (v d:move air), molasf, moafo, moafo
fanatic (adj d:follower), barmpu, barimu, barmu
fanatic (n doer), barmortwan, barimotua, barmotua
fanatical (adj), barmortu, barimotu, barmotu
fanatically (adv), barmortiu, barimotiu, barmotiu
fanaticism (n), barmort, barimota, barmot
fancier (adj), biarkwelu, biarwelu, biarwelu
fancier (n), biarkwel, biarwela, biarwel
fanciest (adj), biarkweku, biarweku, biarweku
fancily (adv), biarkiu, biariu, biariu
fanciness (n), biark, biara, biar
fancy (adj), biarku, biaru, biaru
fancy (v), biarsk, biaro, biaro
fanfare (n), barmthirk, barimethika, barmthik
fang (n), mozhge, moraga, mrag
fangle (v), mozhzge, morago, mrago
fantasize (v), biarkiarsne, biarokiano, biarkiano
fantastic (adj), biarkiarnu, biarokianu, biarkianu
fantastically (adv), biarkiarniu, biarokianiu,
    biarkianiu
fantasy (n), biarkiarn, biarokiana, biarkian
far (adj/adv), thilu, thilu, thil
faraway (adj), thilpoimu, thilopoimu, thilpoimu
farce (n), thiklarve, thikelava, thiklav
farcical (adj), thiklarvu, thikelavu, thiklavu
fare (n doer), thirkwan, thikua, thikua
fare (n), thirk, thika, thik
fare (v), thirsk, thiko, thiko
farewell (n), thirkor, thikora, thikor
farm (n), moiarme, moiama, moiam
farm (v), moiarzme, moiamo, moiamo
farmer (n doer), moiarmwan, moiamua, moiamua
farmhand (n), moiamkarp, moiamekapa,
    moiamkap
farmhouse (n), moiamkiarf, moiamekiafa,
    moiamkiaf
farmland (n), moiamraufp, moiameraupa,
    moiamraup
farsighted (adj), thilthulthu, thilethuthu, thilthuthu
farsightedness (n), thilthulth, thilethutha, thilthuth
fart (n), kaplurge, kapeluga, kaplug
fart (v), kaplurzge, kapelugo, kaplugo
farther (adj/adv), thiluel, thiluelu, thiluel
fascinate (v), vianirsp, vianipo, vianpo
fascination (n), vianirp, vianipa, vianp
fashion (n), shiarsh, shiasha, shiash
fashion (v), shiars, shiasho, shiasho
fashionable (adj), shiarshu, shiashu, shiashu
fashionably (adv), shiarshiu, shiashiu, shiashiu
fast (adj d:speed), zhairshu, zhaishu, zhaishu
fast (n d:starve), prishk, perisha, prish
fast (v d:starve), prishsk, perisho, prisho
fastball (n), prishmonde, perishemashipa,
    prishmashp
fasten (v), gandasp, ganisho, gansho
fastener (n doer), gandapwan, ganishua, ganshua
faster (adj), zhairshwelu, zhaishwelu, zhaishwelu
fastest (adj), zhairshwaku, zhaishwaku, zhaishwaku
fat (adj), baurgu, baugu, baugu

fat (n), baurge, bauga, baug
fatal (adj), thiarku, thiaku, thiaku
fatality (n), thiark, thiaka, thiak
fatally (adv), thiarkiu, thiakiu, thiakiu
fate (n), thairn, thaina, thain
fateful (adj), thairnu, thainu, thainu
fatefully (adv), thairniu, thainiu, thainiu
father (n), voteft, voteta, votet
father (v), votefst, voteto, voteto
fatherhood (n), votertfif, votetefifa, votetfif
fatherland (n), votetraufp, voteteraupa, votetraup
fatherless (adj), votertmenu, votetemenu, votetmenu
fatherly (adj), voteftu, votetu, votetu
fatigue (n), thiarshk, thiashika, thiashk
fatigue (v), thiarshsk, thiashiko, thiashko
fatten (v), baurzge, baugo, baugo
fatty (adj), baurgu, baugu, baugu
faucet (n), viukurk, viukuka, viukuk
fault (n), boirt, boita, boit
fault (v), boirst, boito, boito
faultily (adv), boirtiu, boitiu, boitiu
faulty (adj), boirtu, boitu, boitu
favor (n), nardat, naritha, narth
favor (v), nardast, naritho, nartho
favorable (adj), nardepu, narithepu, narthepu
favorably (adv), nardepiu, narithepiu, narthepiu
favorite (adj), nardatu, narithu, narthu
favorite (n), nardep, narithepa, narthep
favoritism (n), nardatuet, narithueta, narthuet
fax (n), tolirt, tolita, tolt
fax (v), tolirst, tolito, tolto
faze (v), freizhzge, fereigo, freigo
façade (n), thoishart, thoishata, thoishat
fear (n), ronar, larina, larn
fear (v), ronasre, larino, larno
fearful (adj), ronaru, larinu, larnu
fearfully (adv), ronariu, lariniu, larniu
fearless (adj), ronarmenu, larinumenu, larmenu
fearlessly (adv), ronarmeniu, larinumeniu, larmeniu
feasibility (n), thoitirk, thoitika, thoitik
feasible (adj), thoitirku, thoitiku, thoitiku
feasibly (adv), thoitirkiu, thoitikiu, thoitikiu
feast (n), pashap, pashipa, pashp
feast (v), pashasp, pashipo, pashpo
feaster (n doer), pashapwan, pashipua, pashpua
feat (n), birsht, birota, birt
feather (n), barshan, bashika, bashk
feather (v), barshasne, bashiko, bashko
feature (n doer), birshtwan, birotua, birtua
feature (v), birshst, biroto, birto
February (n), Valual, Valuala, Valual
fecal (adj), viatshku, viateshu, viatshu
fece (n), viatshk, viatesha, viatsh
federal (adj), pairvu, paivu, paivu
federally (adv), pairviu, paiviu, paiviu
federate (v), pairzve, paivo, paivo
federation (n), pairve, paiva, paiv
fee (n), glairf, gelaifa, glaif
feeble (adj), klurmu, kelumu, klumu
feed (n), parve, pava, pav
feed (v), parzve, pavo, pavo

feedback (n), pavark, pavaka, pavak
feeder (n doer), parvwan, pavua, pavua
feel (v), freisne, fereitho, freitho
feeler (n doer), freinwan, fereithua, freithua
feely (adj), freinu, fereithu, freithu
feet (n pl), poshpyek, poshi, poshi
feign (v), peirsp, peipo, peipo
feigner (n doer), peirpwan, peipua, peipua
feint (n), peirp, peipa, peip
feist (adj), vailorku, vailoku, vailku
feist (n), vailork, vailoka, vailk
feist (v), vailorsk, vailoko, vailko
feline (n), vithairf, vithaifa, vithaif
fell (v pa d:descent), zhailsfyot, zhailio, zhailio
fellow (n), nolarf, nolafa, nolf
fellowship (n), nolarfif, nolafifa, nolfif
felon (n doer), shkairkwan, shikaikua, shkaikua
felony (n), shkairk, shikaika, shkaik
felt (v pa), freisnyot, fereithio, freithio
female (n), shuar, shuafa, shuaf
feminine (adj), shuaru, shuafu, shuafu
feminism (n), shuaruet, shuafueta, shuafuet
feminist (n doer), shuarwan, shuafua, shuafua
femme (n), bluarme, beluama, bluam
fence (n d:barrier), torft, torifa, torf
fence (v d:barrier), torfst, torifo, torfo
fence (v d:spar), vrazge, verago, vrago
fend (v), torzve, toribo, torbo
fender (n doer), torvwan, toribua, torbua
ferment (v), tshurfsk, teshufiko, tshufko
fermentation (n), tshurfk, teshufika, tshufk
Fermium (n davoka), Onut, Onut, Onut
Fermium (n), Fermium, Feromiuma, Fermium
ferocious (adj), vaiaishku, vaiaiku, vaiaiku
ferociously (adv), vaiaishkiu, vaiaikiu, vaiaikiu
ferocity (n), vaiaishk, vaiaika, vaiaik
ferry (n), brenf, berena, bren
ferry (v), brensf, bereno, breno
ferryboat (n), brenshkorbe, bereneshekoba, brenshkob
fertile (adj), sheiftu, sheifu, sheifu
fertility (n), sheift, sheifa, sheif
FertilityStone (n), duavirt, duavisha, duavit
fertilization (n), sheiftuet, sheifueta, sheifuet
fertilize (v), sheifst, sheifo, sheifo
fertilizer (n doer), sheiftwan, sheifua, sheifua
fester (v), nafirsk, nafiko, nafko
festival (n), nufal, nulifa, nulf
festive (adj), nufalu, nulifu, nulfu
festivity (n), nufaluet, nulifueta, nulfuet
fetal (adj), sheiarfu, sheiafu, sheiafu
fetch (n), graik, geraifa, graif
fetch (v), graisk, geraifo, graifo
fetcher (n doer), graikwan, geraifua, graifua
fetish (n), kilshk, kilisha, kilsh
fetus (n), sheiarf, sheiafa, sheiaf
feud (n), yaivurge, yaivuga, yaivug
feud (v), yaivurzge, yaivugo, yaivugo
feudal (adj), raufirfu, raufifu, raufifu
feudalism (n), raufirf, raufifa, raufif
fever (n), thufat, thufita, thuft
fever (v), thufast, thufito, thufto
feverish (adj), thufatu, thufitu, thuftu

feverishly (adv), thufatiu, thufitiu, thuftiu
few (adj), krunfu, kerunu, krunu
few (n/pron), krunf, kerunei, krun
fewer (adj), krunfwelu, kerunwelu, krunwelu
fewest (adj), krunfwaku, kerunwaku, krunwaku
fiance (n), pilfiurn, pilefiuna, pilfiun
fiancee (n), pilfiurn, pilefiuna, pilfiun
fiasco (n), zhaiport, zhaipota, zhaipot
fiber (n), poirp, poipa, poip
fibrous (adj), poirpu, poipu, poipu
fiction (n), pafirk, pafika, pafk
fictional (adj), pafirku, pafiku, pafku
fictionalize (v), pafirsk, pafiko, pafko
fictionally (adv), pafirkiu, pafikiu, pafkiu
fictitious (adj), pafirku, pafiku, pafku
fiddle (n d:violin), fialoirf, fialoifa, fialoif
fiddle (v d:manipulate), pialirsf, pialifo, pialfo
fiddle (v d:violin), fialoirsf, fialoifo, fialoifo
fiddler (n doer d:violin), fialoirfwan, fialoifua,
     fialoifua
fidelity (n), natrip, perineta, prinet
fiefta-, tirishkai-, tirishkai-, tirishkai-
field (n), prant, peranida, prand
field (v), pranst, peranido, prando
fielder (n doer), prantwan, peranidua, prandua
fiend (n), traifk, teraifa, traif
fiendish (adj), traifku, teraifu, traifu
fiendishly (adv), traifkiu, teraifiu, traifiu
fierce (adj), voairku, voaiku, voaiku
fiercely (adv), voairkiu, voaikiu, voaikiu
fierceness (n), voairk, voaika, voaik
fiery (adj), shriauku, giaulu, giaulu
fifteen (num 15 card), tiripa, tiripa, tiripa
fifteen- (num 15 pref), tiripai-, tiripai-, tiripai-
fifteenth (num 15 ord), tiripeth, tiripeth, tiripeth
fifth (num 5 ord), tireth, tireth, tireth
fiftieth (num 50 ord), tirideth, tirideth, tirideth
fifty (num 50 card), tirida, tirida, tirida
fifty- (num 50 pref), tiridai-, tiridai-, tiridai-
fig (n), kude, kuda, kud
fight (n), vaugat, vauga, vaug
fight (v), vaugast, vaugo, vaugo
fighter (n doer), vaugatwan, vaugua, vaugua
figment (n), kuduet, kudueta, kuduet
figurative (adj), kudilu, kulitu, kultu
figuratively (adv), kudiliu, kulitiu, kultiu
figure (n), kudil, kulita, kult
figure (v), kudisle, kulito, kulto
figurehead (n), kudilkefirt, kulikefita, kultkeft
figurine (n), kudllolf, kulitoita, kultoit
filament (n), trieloif, buloifa, buloif
file (n d:storage), thiurf, thiufa, thiuf
file (n d:tool), bupat, bufipa, bufp
file (v d:storage), thiursf, thiufo, thiufo
file (v d:tool), bupast, bufipo, bufpo
filer (n doer d:storage), thiurfwan, thiufua, thiufua
filer (n doer d:tool), bupatwan, bufipua, bufpua
fill (n), triel, bupa, bup
fill (v), triesle, bupo, bupo
filler (n doer), trielwan, bupua, bupua
film (n), rodap, deiora, deior
film (v), rodasp, deioro, deioro

filmer (n doer), rodapwan, deiorua, deiorua
filter (n), rodaf, diufa, diuf
filter (v), rodasf, diufo, diufo
filterer (n doer), rodafwan, diufua, diufua
filth (n), bloirk, beloika, bloik
filthy (adj), bloirku, beloiku, bloiku
filthy (v), bloirsk, beloiko, bloiko
fin (n), beirme, beima, beim
final (adj), lepalu, lilopu, lilpu
final (n), lepal, lilopa, lilp
finalist (n doer), lepalwan, lilopua, lilpua
finalize (v), lepasle, lilopo, lilpo
finally (adv), lepaliu, lilopiu, lilpiu
finance (n), linaf, linofa, linf
finance (v), linasf, linofo, linfo
financial (adj), linafu, linofu, linfu
financially (adv), linafiu, linofiu, linfiu
financier (n doer), linafwan, linofua, linfua
find (n), shurp, shupa, shup
find (v), shursp, shupo, shupo
finder (n doer), shurpwan, shupua, shupua
fine (adj d:small), vuartu, vuatu, vuatu
fine (n d:penalty), firge, vuala, vual
fine (v d:penalty), firzge, vualo, vualo
finely (adv d:small), vuartiu, vuatiu, vuatiu
fineness (n d:small), vuart, vuata, vuat
finer (n doer d:penalty), firgwan, vualua, vualua
finger (n), dinank, dinana, dinan
finger (v), dinansk, dinano, dinano
fingernail (n), dinanthrink, dinanetherina,
     dinanthrin
fingerprint (n), dinantrulish, dinaneterulisha,
     dinantrulsh
fingerprint (v), dinantrulis, dinaneterulisho,
     dinantrulsho
fingertip (n), dinanetilirf, dinanetilifa, dinantilf
finish (n), tiurt, tiuta, tiut
finish (v), tiurst, tiuto, tiuto
finisher (n doer), tiurtwan, tiutua, tiutua
finite (adj), tiurftu, tiufotu, tiuftu
finitely (adv), tiurftiu, tiufotiu, tiuftiu
finiteness (n), tiurft, tiufota, tiuft
Finland (n), Finlanurde, Finelanuda, Finland
fire (n), shriauk, giaula, giaul
fire (v), shriausk, giaulo, giaulo
firearm (n), shriaushnen, giaushinena, giaushnen
fireball (n), shriaushmonde, giaumashipa,
     giaumashp
firebomb (n), shriauvibal, giauviluba, giauvilb
firefight (n), shriaukovaugc, giaulcvauga, giauvaug
firefighter (n doer), shriaukovaugwan,
     giaulevaugua, giauvaugua
firefly (n), shriaushperge, giaushipega, giaushpeg
firehouse (n), shriaukiarf, giaukiafa, giaukiaf
fireplace (n), shriaubresh, giauberesha, giaubresh
firepower (n), shriaubiorat, giaubiorita, giaubiort
fireproof (adj), shriaufliorfu, giaufeliofu, giaufliofu
fireproof (v), shriaufliorsf, giaufeliofo, giaufliofo
fireside (n), shriaushoirt, giaushoita, giaushoit
firestorm (n), shriauferap, giauferipa, giaufrip
firewall (n), shriaunolthk, giaunolitha, giaunolth
firewood (n), shriaufanin, giaufanina, giaufanin
firewook (n), shriaukiork, giaukioka, giaukiok

firm (adj d:steady), niurfu, niufu, niufu
firm (n d:company), dorsh, dorisha, dorsh
firm (v d:steady), niursf, niufo, niufo
firmer (adj), niurfwelu, niufwelu, niufwelu
firmest (adj), niurfweku, niufweku, niufweku
firmly (adv d:steady), niurfiu, niufiu, niufiu
firmness (n d:steady), niurf, niufa, niuf
first (num 1 ord), hemeth, hemeth, hemeth
firstborn (n), hemevashil, hemevalesha, hemevalsh
firsthand (n), hemethkarp, hemethekapa, hemethkap
firstly (adv), hemethiu, hemethiu, hemethiu
firsts (n pl), hemethyek, hemethi, hemethi
fiscal (adj), linarpu, linapu, linpu
fiscally (adv), linarpiu, linapiu, linpiu
fish (n pl), shlershyek, sheleshi, shleshi
fish (n), shlersh, shelesha, shlesh
fish (v), shlers, shelesho, shlesho
fishbowl (n), shleshtairak, sheleshetairoka, shleshtairk
fisher (n doer), shlershwan, sheleshua, shleshua
fisherman (n), shleshplorn, sheleshepelona, shleshplon
fishermen (n pl), shleshplornyek, sheleshepeloni, shleshploni
fishery (n), shlershuat, sheleshuata, shleshuat
fishes (n pl), shlershyek, sheleshi, shleshi
fishy (adj), shlershu, sheleshu, shleshu
fission (n), fitirsh, fitisha, fitish
fission (v), fitirs, fitisho, fitisho
fissure (n), fitishap, fitishopa, fitishp
fist (n), vilork, viloka, vilk
fist (v), vilorsk, viloko, vilko
fistful (adj), vilorku, viloku, vilku
fit (adj d:healthy), velirfu, velifu, velfu
fit (n d:match), pafirt, pafita, paft
fit (n d:spasm), vazhirme, vazhima, vazhim
fit (v d:match), pafirst, pafito, pafto
fit (v d:spasm), vazhirzme, vazhimo, vazhimo
fitness (n d:healthy), velirf, velifa, velf
fitter (adj), velirfwelu, velifwelu, velfwelu
fitter (n doer d:match), pafirtwan, pafitua, paftua
fittest (adj), velirfweku, velifweku, velfweku
fittingly (adv d:healthy), velirfiu, velifiu, velfiu
five (num 5 card), tiri, tiri, tiri
fix (n), virk, vika, vik
fix (v), virsk, viko, viko
fixable (adj), virku, viku, viku
fixate (v), virkest, viketo, viketo
fixation (n), virket, viketa, viket
fixer (n doer), virkwan, vikua, vikua
fixture (n), virkzhar, vikezhara, vikzhar
fizz (n), fshishft, fushishifa, fshishf
fizz (v), fshishfst, fushishifo, fshishfo
fizzle (n), fshishfilt, fushishifila, fshishfil
fizzle (v), fshishfilst, fushishifilo, fshishfilo
fjord (n), thiorlt, thiorila, thiorl
flack (n), flabkarn, felabikana, flabkan
flag (n), dreiap, sheleifa, shleif
flag (v), dreiasp, sheleifo, shleifo
flagger (n doer), dreiapwan, sheleifua, shleifua
flagpole (n), dreiapdilork, sheleifediloka, shleifdilk
flagrancy (n), dreinshkart, fiashekata, fiashkat

flagrant (adj), dreinshkartu, fiashekatu, fiashkatu
flagrantly (adv), dreinshkartiu, fiashekatiu, fiashkatiu
flagship (n), dreiafleve, sheleifeleva, shleiflev
flagstaff (n), dreiaparap, sheleifaripa, shleifarip
flagstaves (n pl), dreiaparapyek, sheleifaripi, shleifaripi
flail (n), shneifk, sheneifa, shneif
flail (v), shneifsk, sheneifo, shneifo
flair (n), dreishar, fiashekara, fiashkar
flake (n), blarsht, belashota, blasht
flake (v), blarshst, belashoto, blashto
flaker (n doer), blarshtwan, belashotua, blashtua
flakey (adj), blarshtu, belashotu, blashtu
flakily (adv), blarshtiu, belashotiu, blashtiu
flame (n), dreinak, fiasha, fiash
flame (v), dreinask, fiasho, fiasho
flamer (n doer), dreinakwan, fiashua, fiashua
flammable (adj), dreinaku, fiashu, fiashu
flange (n), granlark, geranilaka, granlak
flank (n), granirk, geranika, grank
flank (v), granirsk, geraniko, granko
flap (n), traifp, teraipa, traip
flap (v), traifsp, teraipo, traipo
flapper (n doer), traifpwan, teraipua, traipua
flare (n), dreithk, fiatha, fiath
flare (v), dreithsk, fiatho, fiatho
flash (n), niursh, niusha, niush
flash (v), niurs, niusho, niusho
flashback (n), niushvark, niushevaka, niushvak
flasher (n doer), niurshwan, niushua, niushua
flashily (adv), niurshiu, niushiu, niushiu
flashlight (n), niushfluan, niufeluana, niufluan
flashy (adj), niurshu, niushu, niushu
flask (n), gliuthk, geliutha, gliuth
flat (adj d:plain/plane), blarfpu, belarifu, blarfu
flatbed (adj), blarfamoru, belarifuaremu, blarfuarmu
flatbed (n), blarfamor, belarifuarema, blarfuarm
flatland (n), blarfraufp, belariferaupa, blarfraup
flatly (adv d:plain/plane), blarfpiu, belaritiu, blarflu
flatness (n d:plain/plane), blarfp, belarifa, blarf
flatten (v d:plain/plane), blarfsp, belarifo, blarfo
flatter (v d:praise), leifliurst, leifeliuto, leifliuto
flattery (n d:praise), leifliurt, leifeliuta, leifliut
flaunt (v), zhaimesp, zhaimo, zhaimo
flavor (n), lorft, lorita, lort
flavor (v), lorfst, lorito, lorto
flaw (n), gliurk, geliuka, gliuk
flaw (v), gliursk, geliuko, gliuko
flawless (adj), gliurkmenu, geliukemenu, gliukmenu
flawlessly (adv), gliurkmeniu, geliukemeniu, gliukmeniu
flea (n), klirk, keliga, klig
fleck (n), thrufk, theruka, thruk
fleck (v), thrufsk, theruko, thruko
flee (v), friunsp, feriuno, friuno
fleece (n), ralirp, ralipa, ralp
fleece (v), ralirsp, ralipo, ralpo
fleecer (n doer), ralirpwan, ralipua, ralpua
fleer (n doer), friunpwan, feriunua, friunua
fleet (n), briarth, beriatha, briath

fleet (v), briarsth, beriatho, briatho
flesh (n), ranirp, ranipa, ranp
flesh (v), ranirsp, ranipo, ranpo
fleshy (adj), ranirpu, ranipu, ranpu
flew (v pa d:air travel), fuirsfyot, fuifio, fuifio
flex (n), tiert, tieta, tiet
flex (v), tierst, tieto, tieto
flexibility (n), tiertep, tietorepa, tietrep
flexible (adj), tiertu, tietu, tietu
flexibly (adv), tiertiu, tietiu, tietiu
flick (n), shnark, shenaka, shnak
flick (v), shnarsk, shenako, shnako
flicker (n), shnakart, shenakata, shnakat
flicker (v), shnakarst, shenakato, shnakato
flier (n doer d:air travel), fuirfwan, fuifua, fuifua
flight (n d:air travel), fuirf, fuifa, fuif
flighty (adj d:air travel), fuirfu, fuifu, fuifu
flimsily (adv), deiorshkiu, deiorishiu, deiorshiu
flimsy (adj), deiorshku, deiorishu, deiorshu
flinch (n), beirp, beipa, beip
flinch (v), beirsp, beipo, beipo
flincher (n doer), beirpwan, beipua, beipua
fling (n), beivage, beifika, beifk
fling (v), beivazge, beifiko, beifko
flinger (n doer), beivagwan, beifikua, beifkua
flingy (adj), beivagu, beifiku, beifku
flip (n), beivap, beifopa, beifp
flip (v), beivasp, beifopo, beifpo
flipper (n doer), beivapwan, beifopua, beifpua
flippily (adv), beivapiu, beifopiu, beifpiu
flippy (adj), beivapu, beifopu, beifpu
flirt (n doer), beirshwan, beishua, beishua
flirt (v), beirs, beisho, beisho
flirtation (n), beirsh, beisha, beish
flirtatious (adj), beirshu, beishu, beishu
float (n), bruart, beruata, bruat
float (v), bruarst, beruato, bruato
floater (n doer), bruartwan, beruatua, bruatua
flock (n d:group), thiarve, thiava, thiav
flock (n d:wool), bronirk, beronika, bronk
flock (v d:group), thiarzve, thiavo, thiavo
flog (v), shnarzge, shenago, shnago
flood (n), thiarap, thiaropa, thiarp
flood (v), thiarasp, thiaropo, thiarpo
flooder (n doer), thiarapwan, thiaropua, thiarpua
floodgate (n), thiarparlak, thiaroperelika, thiarprelk
floodlight (n), thiarfluarn, thiarofeluana, thiarfluan
floodplain (n), thiarbralf, thiaroberala, thiarbral
floodwater (n), thiarheidorn, thiareheidona, thiarheidon
floor (n), shlarin, shelarina, shlarn
floor (v), shlarisne, shelarino, shlarno
floorboard (n), shlarnplok, shelarepelorika, shlarnplork
flop (n), troilp, teroipa, troip
flop (v), troilsp, teroipo, troipo
flopper (n doer), troilpwan, teroipua, troipua
floppily (adv), troilpiu, teroipiu, troipiu
floppy (adj), troilpu, teroipu, troipu
flora (n), thuarn, thuara, thuar
floral (adj), thuarnu, thuaru, thuaru
Florida (n), Floridarf, Feloridafa, Floridaf
florist (n doer), thuarnwan, thuarua, thuarua

flotation (adj), bruartuetu, beruatuetu, bruatuetu
flotation (n), bruartuet, beruatueta, bruatuet
flour (n), shelar, shelira, shlir
flourish (v), luausne, biruano, bruano
flow (n), brauf, berautha, brauth
flow (v), brausf, berautho, brautho
flower (n), thaush, thuana, thuan
flower (v), thaus, thuano, thuano
flowerpot (n), thuashdairf, thuanedaifa, thuandaif
flowery (adj), thaushu, thuanu, thuanu
flu (n), rinak, niaroga, niarg
fluctuate (v), miarsk, miashiko, miashko
fluctuation (n), miark, miashika, miashk
fluctuator (n doer), miarkwan, miashikua, miashkua
flue (n), mialt, miala, mial
fluency (n), miarsht, miarota, miart
fluent (adj), miarshtu, miarotu, miartu
fluently (adv), miarshtiu, miarotiu, miartiu
fluff (n), mielsh, miesha, miesh
fluff (v), miels, miesho, miesho
fluffy (adj), mielshu, mieshu, mieshu
fluid (adj), miarnu, mianu, mianu
fluid (n), miarn, miana, mian
flung (v pa), beivazgyot, beifikio, beifkio
flunk (v), kriomirsp, keriomipo, kriompo
flunky (n doer), kriomirpwan, keriomipua, kriompua
Fluorine (n davoka), Ekak, Ekak, Ekak
Fluorine (n), Florin, Felorina, Florin
flurry (n pl), brulalfyek, berulali, brulali
flush (n), miut, miutha, miuth
flush (v), miust, miutho, miutho
flusher (n doer), miutwan, miuthua, miuthua
flute (n), thruthk, therutha, thruth
flutist (n doer), thruthkwan, theruthua, thruthua
flutter (n pl), brualirfyek, berualifi, brualfi
flutter (v), brualirsf, berualifo, brualfo
flux (n), shrolk, sheroka, shrok
flux (v), shrolsk, sheroko, shroko
fly (n d:insect), shperge, shipega, shpeg
fly (v d:air travel), fuirsf, fuifo, fuifo
flyer (n), fuifalt, fuifata, fuifat
flypaper (n pl), fuifvuarpyek, fuifevuapi, fiufvuapi
foam (n), trun, terama, tram
foam (v), trusne, teramo, tramo
foamer (n doer), trunwan, teramua, tramua
foamily (adv), truniu, teramiu, tramiu
foamy (adj), trunu, teramu, tramu
focal (adj), goitirtu, goifitu, goiftu
focus (n), goifirt, goifita, goift
focus (v), goifirst, goifito, goifto
focuser (n doer), goifirtwan, goifitua, goiftua
foe (n), yair, yaila, yail
fog (n), kauf, muzha, muzh
fog (v), kausf, muzho, muzho
fogger (n doer), kaufwan, muzhua, muzhua
foggily (adv), kaufiu, muzhiu, muzhiu
foggy (adj), kaufu, muzhu, muzhu
foghorn (n), kaufkroip, muzhekeroima, muzhkroim
foil (n d:prevent), prainp, peraina, prain
foil (n d:sheet), priarf, periafa, priaf
foil (v d:prevent), prainsp, peraino, praino

foil (v d:sheet), priarsf, periafo, priafo
fold (n), trafk, terava, trav
fold (v), trafsk, teravo, travo
folder (n doer), trafkwan, teravua, travua
folk (n), kiforp, kifopa, kifp
folklore (n), kifpufirt, kifepufita, kifpuft
folktale (n), kifoprelt, kifopereta, kifpret
follow (v), vaurask, vauriko, vaurko
follow-up (adj), vaurakiveilu, varikiveilu, vaurkiveilu
follow-up (n), vaurakiveil, varikiveila, vaurkiveil
follower (n doer), vaurakwan, vaurikua, vaurkua
followup (adj), vaurakiveilu, varikiveilu, vaurkiveilu
followup (n), vaurakiveil, varikiveila, vaurkiveil
folly (n), nirve, niva, niv
fond (adj), brapu, berafu, brafu
fondly (adv), brapiu, berafiu, brafiu
fondness (n), brap, berafa, braf
font (n), brashk, beraka, brak
food (n), parsh, pasha, pash
foodstuff (n), pashplerth, pashepeletha, pashpleth
fool (n doer), nirvwan, nivua, nivua
fool (v), nirzve, nivo, nivo
foolhardiness (n), nivkelifort, nivekelifota, nivkelft
foolhardy (adj), nivkelifortu, nivekelifotu, nivkelftu
foolish (adj), nirvu, nivu, nivu
foolishly (adv), nirviu, niviu, niviu
foolishness (n), nirve, niva, niv
foolproof (adj), nivefliorfu, nivefeliofu, nivefliofu
foot (n), poshp, posha, posh
foot (v), poshsp, posho, posho
footage (n), razhark, razhaka, razhak
football (n d:American), poshark, poshaka, poshak
football (n d:soccer), poshpol, poshemola, poshmol
footer (n doer), poshpwan, poshua, poshua
footfall (n), poshezhailf, poshezhaila, poshezhail
foothill (n), poshiop, posheparina, poshparn
footnote (n), poshmirade, poshemida, poshmid
footnote (v), poshmirazde, poshemido, poshmido
footpath (n), poshbotersh, poshebotesha, poshbotsh
footprint (n), poshtrulish, posheterulisha, poshtrulsh
footstep (n), poshgref, poshefa, poshef
footwear (n), poshdorame, poshedorima, poshdorim
footwork (n), poshkiork, poshekioka, poshkiok
for (prep/conj), maf, mafu, maf
forage (v), voarst, voarino, voarno
forager (n doer), voartwan, voarinua, voarnua
forbade (v pa), voarthstyot, voathitio, voathtio
forbear (n d:ancestor), voatkriage, voanegeruka, voanegruk
forbear (v d:refrain), voateshtaurs, voaneshetausho, voanshtausho
forbearance (n d:refrain), voateshtaursh, voaneshetausha, voanshtaush
forbearer (n d:ancestor), voatkriage, voanegeruka, voanegruk
forbid (v), voarthst, voathito, voathto
forbiddence (n), voartht, voathita, voatht
forbidder (n doer), voarthtwan, voathitua, voathtua
forbore (v pa d:refrain), voateshtaursyot,

voaneshetaushio, voanshtaushio
force (n), viurk, viuka, viuk
force (v), viursk, viuko, viuko
forceful (adj), viurku, viuku, viuku
forcefully (adv), viurkiu, viukiu, viukiu
forcer (n doer), viurkwan, viukua, viukua
forcible (adj), viurku, viuku, viuku
forcibly (adv), viurkiu, viukiu, viukiu
ford (n), thorlt, thorila, thorl
ford (v), thorlst, thorilo, thorlo
fore (adj), voatu, voanu, voanu
forearm (n), voatshnern, voaneshinena, voanshnen
forebode (v), voatelaursf, voanelaufo, voanlaufo
forecast (n), voathut, voanebida, voanbid
forecast (v), voathust, voanebido, voanbido
forecaster (n doer), voathutwan, voanebidua, voanbidua
foreclose (v), voatgrefst, voanegereto, voanegreto
foreclosure (n), voatgreft, voanegereta, voanegret
forefinger (n), voatedinank, voanedinana, voandinan
forefront (n), voatflarsh, voanefelarina, voanflarn
forego (v), voatisf, voanevifo, voanvifo
foreground (n), voatbraft, voaneberanita, voanbrant
forehand (n), voatkarp, voanekapa, voankap
forehead (n), voatkeft, voanikefita, voankeft
foreign (adj), wiortu, yaritu, yartu
foreigner (n doer), wiortwan, yaritua, yartua
foreknowledge (n), voatglerk, voanegeleka, voaneglek
foreman (n), voaplorn, voapelona, voaplon
foremen (n pl), voaplornyek, voapeloni, voaploni
foremost (adj), voatwaku, voanewaku, voanwaku
foreplay (n), voatfruifk, voaneferuifa, voanfruif
forerunner (n), voatlaormwat, voanelaomuala, voanlaomual
foresaw (v pa), voathulsthyot, voanethuthio, voanthuthio
foresee (v), voathulsth, voanethutho, voanthutho
foreseeable (adj), voathulthu, voanethuthu, voanthuthu
foreseeably (adv), voathulthiu, voanethuthiu, voanthuthiu
foreshadow (n), voatpoefirt, voanepoefita, voanpoeft
foreshadow (v), voatpoefirst, voanepoefito, voanpoefto
foresight (n), voathulth, voanethutha, voanthuth
forest (n), thrishk, therisha, thrish
forest (v), thrishsk, therisho, thrisho
forestall (v), voateirsk, voaneteiko, voanteiko
forestry (n), thrishkuet, therishueta, thrishuet
foresty (adj), thrishku, therishu, thrishu
foretell (v), voatprelst, voanepereto, voanpreto
forethought (n), voatederp, voanedepa, voandep
foretold (v pa), voatprelstyot, voaneperetio, voanpretio
forever (adv), voafeliu, voalifiu, voalfiu
forever (n), voafel, voalifa, voalf
forewarn (v), voatvuirst, voaneviuto, voanviuto
forewent (v pa), voatisfyot, voanevifio, voanvifio
forfeit (v), voatpeizme, voapeimo, voapeimo

forfeiter (n doer), voatpeimwan, voapeimua, voapeimua
forfeiture (n), voatpeime, voapeima, voapeim
forgave (v pa), voagrusfyot, voageruthio, voagruthio
forge (n), telorshk, telorika, telork
forge (v), telorshsk, teloriko, telorko
forger (n doer), telorshkwan, telorikua, telorkua
forgery (n), telorshkuet, telorikueta, telorkuet
forget (v), voantosp, voatopo, voatopo
forgetful (adj), voantopu, voatopu, voatopu
forgetfully (adv), voantopiu, voatopiu, voatopiu
forgettance (n), voantop, voatopa, voatop
forgetter (n doer), voantopwan, voatopua, voatopua
forgivable (adj), voagrufu, voageruthu, voagruthu
forgive (v), voagrusf, voagerutho, voagrutho
forgiveness (n), voagruf, voagerutha, voagruth
forgiver (n doer), voagrufwan, voageruthua, voagruthua
forgot (v pa), voantospyot, voatopio, voatopio
fork (n), fnurt, fenuta, fnut
fork (v), fnurst, fenuto, fnuto
forker (n doer), fnurtwan, fenutua, fnutua
forkily (adv), fnurtiu, fenutiu, fnutiu
forklift (n), fnutraushk, fenuterauka, fnutrauk
forky (adj), fnurtu, fenutu, fnutu
form (n d:shape), vorlin, vorina, vorn
form (v d:shape), vorlisne, vorino, vorno
formal (adj), vorlinatu, vorinatu, vornatu
formal (n), vorlinat, vorinata, vornat
formality (n), vorlinatuet, vorinatueta, vornatuet
formalize (v), vorlinast, vorinato, vornato
formally (adv), vorlinatiu, vorinatiu, vornatiu
format (n), vorlinak, vorinaka, vornak
format (v), vorlinask, vorinako, vornako
formation (n), vorlinuet, vorinueta, vornuet
formatter (n doer), vorlinakwan, vorinakua, vornakua
former (adj d:previous), voanarfu, voanaru, voanaru
former (n doer d:shape), vorlinwan, vorinua, vornua
formerly (adv d:previous), voanarfiu, voanariu, voanariu
formidable (adj), vorlinkapu, vorinokapu, vornkapu
formula (n), vorlinarp, vorinaripa, vornarp
formulate (v), vorlinasp, vorinapo, vornapo
formulation (n), vorlinap, vorinapa, vornap
formulator (n doer), vorlinapwan, vorinapua, vornapua
forsake (v), moarsk, moako, moako
forsook (v pa), moarskyot, moakio, moakio
fort (n), varilk, varika, vark
forth (adv), voanirfiu, voanifiu, voanfiu
forthcame (v pa), voanblersfyot, voanibilefio, voanblefio
forthcome (v), voanblersf, voanibilefo, voanblefo
fortieth (num 40 ord), yufideth, yufideth, yufideth
fortify (v), varilsk, variko, varko
fortitude (n pl), varkalirkyek, varikaliki, varkalki
fortress (n), varkart, varikata, varkat
fortunate (adj), voashmunu, voamunu, voamunu
fortunately (adv), voashmuniu, voamuniu, voamuniu

fortune (n), voashmun, voamuna, voamun
forty (num 40 card), yufida, yufida, yufida
forty- (num 40 pref), yufidai-, yufidai-, yufidai-
forum (n), vorthk, voritha, vorth
forward (adj), voanaurshu, voanaushu, voanaushu
forward (adv), voanaurshiu, voanaushiu, voanaushiu
forward (n), voanaursh, voanausha, voanaush
forward (v), voanaurs, voanausho, voanausho
fossil (n), ninaf, ninofa, ninf
fossilize (v), ninasf, ninofo, ninfo
fought (v pa), vaugastyot, vaugio, vaugio
foul (adj), naushirku, naushiku, naushku
foul (n), naushirk, naushika, naushk
foul (v), naushirsk, naushiko, naushko
found (v d:begin), shuparst, shupato, shupato
found (v d:pour mold), shulirst, shulito, shulto
found (v pa), shurspyot, shupio, shupio
foundary (n d:pour mold), shulirt, shulita, shult
foundation (n d:begin), shupart, shupata, shupat
founder (n doer d:begin), shupartwan, shupatua, shupatua
fountain (n), sheifan, sheinofa, sheinf
four (num 4 card), yufi, yufi, yufi
fourteen (num 14 card), yufipa, yufipa, yufipa
fourteen- (num 14 pref), yufipai-, yufipai-, yufipai-
fourteenth (num 14 ord), yufipeth, yufipeth, yufipeth
fourth (num 4 ord), yufeth, yufeth, yufeth
fox (n), zhurk, zhuka, zhuk
foxhole (n), zhukorth, zhukotha, zhukoth
foxy (adj), zhurku, zhuku, zhuku
fraction (n), delishork, delishoka, delshk
fractional (adj), delishorku, delishoku, delshku
fractionally (adv), delishorkiu, delishokiu, delshkiu
fracture (n), delirsh, delisha, delsh
fracture (v), delirs, delisho, delsho
fragile (adj), doirvu, doivu, doivu
fragment (n), doirve, doiva, doiv
fragment (v), doirzve, doivo, doivo
fragrance (n), forlar, forila, forl
fragrant (adj), forlaru, forilu, forlu
frail (adj), flaurfu, felaufu, flaufu
frailty (n), flaurf, felaufa, flauf
frame (n), ravit, raifota, raift
frame (v), ravist, raifoto, raifto
framer (n doer), ravitwan, raifotua, raiftua
framework (n), ravikiok, raifekioka, raifkiok
framework (v), ravikiosk, raifekioko, raifkioko
France (n), Fransharf, Feranishafa, Franshaf
franchise (n), plimorfk, pelimorika, plimork
Francium (n davoka), Anap, Anap, Anap
Francium (n), Franshium, Feranoshiuma, Franshium
frank (adj), flanitu, felanitu, flantu
Frankfurt (n), Frankfurft, Feranikofurita, Frankfurt
frankly (adv), flanitiu, felanitiu, flantiu
frantic (adj), fnaikirku, fenaikiku, fnaikiku
frantically (adv), fnaikirkiu, fenaikikiu, fnaikikiu
fraud (n), dairge, daiga, daig
freak (n), shaifk, shaifa, shaif
freak (v), shaifsk, shaifo, shaifo

freaky (adj), shaifku, shaifu, shaifu
freckle (n), shafkarn, shafikana, shafkan
free (adj), fiorshu, fioshu, fioshu
free (v), fiors, fiosho, fiosho
freebie (n), fiorshorsh, fioshosha, fioshosh
freedom (n), fiorsh, fiosha, fiosh
freeform (adj), fioshvorlinu, fioshevorinu,
    fioshvornu
freeform (n), fioshvorlin, fioshevorina, fioshvorn
freehand (n), fioshkarp, fioshepelia, fioshkap
freeload (v), fioshlurifst, fioshelurito, fioshlurto
freeloader (n doer), fioshluriftwan, fiosheluritua,
    fioshlurtua
freely (adv), fiorshiu, fioshiu, fioshiu
freeway (n), fioshpliorl, fioshepeliola, fioshpliol
freeze (n), fiorshk, fiorika, fiork
freeze (v), fiorshsk, fioriko, fiorko
freezer (n doer), fiorshkwan, fiorikua, fiorkua
freight (n), breshuirsh, bereshuisha, breshuish
freighter (n doer), breshuirshwan, bereshuishua,
    breshuishua
freightliner (n), breshuishroifk, bereshuisheroifa,
    breshuishroif
French (n), Franarsh, Feranasha, Franash
frenetic (adj), fnaikirku, fenaikiku, fnaikiku
frenzy (n), fnaikirk, fenaikika, fnaikik
frenzy (v), fnaikirsk, fenaikiko, fnaikiko
frequency (n), fiorfonde, fiofonuda, fiofond
frequent (adj), fiorfondu, fiofonudu, fiofondu
frequent (v), fiorfonzde, fiofonudo, fiofondo
frequently (adv), fiorfondiu, fiofonudiu, fiofondiu
fresh (adj), fiarshu, fiarifu, fiarfu
freshen (v), fiars, fiarifo, fiarfo
freshly (adv), fiarshiu, fiarifiu, fiarfiu
freshman (n), fiarshplorn, fiarepelona, fiarplon
freshmen (n pl), fiarshplornyek, fiarepeloni,
    fiarploni
freshness (n), fiarsh, fiarifa, fiarf
freshwater (adj), fiarsheidornu, fiarifeidonu,
    fiarfheidonu
freshwater (n), fiarsheidorn, fiarifeidona,
    fiarfheidon
fret (n d:strip), fliurp, feliupa, fliup
fret (n d:worry), friarp, feriapa, friap
fret (v d:strip), fliursp, feliupo, fliupo
fret (v d:worry), friarsp, feriapo, friapo
friction (n), vuik, vuisha, vuish
frictional (adj), vuiku, vuishu, vuishu
frictionless (adj), vuikmenu, vuishemenu,
    vuishmenu
Friday (n), Freiviul, Fereiviula, Freiviul
fridge (n), lulaurf, lulaufa, lulauf
friend (n doer), pamelwan, pilamua, pilmua
friend (n), pamel, pilama, pilm
friendliness (n), pameluet, pilamueta, pilmuet
friendly (adj), pamelu, pilamu, pilmu
friendship (n), pamelfif, pilamefifa, pilmfif
frier (n doer), fraushpwan, feraupua, fraupua
fright (n), fraugat, ferauga, fraug
frighten (v), fraugast, feraugo, fraugo
frightener (n doer), fraugatwan, feraugua, fraugua
frightful (adj), fraugatu, feraugu, fraugu
frightfully (adv), fraugatiu, feraugiu, fraugiu

frigid (adj), laufargu, laufagu, laufagu
frigidity (n), laufarge, laufaga, laufag
frill (n), grilfp, gerilifa, grilf
fringe (n), grishort, gerishota, grisht
frivolity (n), shruifk, sheruika, shruik
frivolous (adj), shruifku, sheruiku, shruiku
frivolously (adv), shruifkiu, sheruikiu, shruikiu
frog (n), floirp, feloipa, floip
from (prep), velt, veletu, velt
front (n), flarsh, felarina, flarn
front (v), flars, felarino, flarno
frontier (n), flarshat, felarinata, flarnat
frontline (n), flarshroifk, felarineroifa, flarnroif
frost (n), fiorsht, fiorita, fiort
frost (v), fiorshst, fiorito, fiorto
frostbite (n), fiortgairk, fioritegaika, fiortgaik
froster (n doer), fiorshtwan, fioritua, fiortua
frostily (adv), fiorshtiu, fioritiu, fiortiu
frosty (adj), fiorshtu, fioritu, fiortu
frown (n), giarfp, giaripa, giarp
frown (v), giarfsp, giaripo, giarpo
frowner (n doer), giarfpwan, giaripua, giarpua
froze (v pa), fiorshskyot, fiorikio, fiorkio
fruit (n), gliarp, geliapa, gliap
fruitcake (n), gliapgutraf, geliapegurita, gliapgurt
fruitful (adj), gliarpuetu, geliapuetu, gliapuetu
fruition (n), gliarpuet, geliapueta, gliapuet
fruitless (adj), gliarpmenu, geliapemenu,
    gliapmenu
fruity (adj), gliarpu, geliapu, gliapu
frustrate (v), fiorbast, fiorubo, fiorbo
frustration (n), fiorbat, fioruba, fiorb
fry (n), fraushp, feraupa, fraup
fry (v), fraushsp, feraupo, fraupo
fryer (n doer), fraushpwan, feraupua, fraupua
Fs (let pl), feili, feili, feili
fuel (n), zhiarp, zhiapa, zhiap
fuel (v), zhiarsp, zhiapo, zhiapo
fueler (n doer), zhiarpwan, zhiapua, zhiapua
fugitive (n), friunark, feriunaka, friunak
fulfill (v), bietriesle, biebupo, biebupo
fulfillment (n), bietriel, biebupa, biebup
full (adj), bierpu, biepu, biepu
fullness (n), bierp, biepa, biep
fulltime (adj), biepdaurnu, biepedaunu, biepdaunu
fulltime (n), biepdaurn, biepedauna, biepdaun
fully (adv), bierpiu, biepiu, biepiu
fumble (n), mumirme, mumima, mumim
fumble (v), mumirzme, mumimo, mumimo
fume (n), kiorsh, kiora, kior
fume (v), kiors, kioro, kioro
fumer (n doer), kiorshwan, kiorua, kiorua
fumigate (v), kiorshuest, kiorelueto, kiorlueto
fumigation (n), kiorshuet, kiorelueta, kiorluet
fumigator (n doer), kiorshuetwan, kioreluetua,
    kiorluetua
fumily (adv), kiorshiu, kioriu, kioriu
fumy (adj), kiorshu, kioru, kioru
fun (adj), tarmu, tamu, tamu
fun (n), tarme, tama, tam
function (n), prasht, perata, prat
function (v), prashst, perato, prato
functional (adj), prashtu, peratu, pratu

functionality (n), prashtak, perataka, pratak
functionally (adv), prashtiu, peratiu, pratiu
functioner (n doer), prashtwan, peratua, pratua
fund (n), timork, timoka, timk
fund (v), timorsk, timoko, timko
fundamental (adj), timorkaltu, timokalitu, timkaltu
fundamental (n), timorkalt, timokalita, timkalt
fundamentally (adv), timorkaltiu, timokalitiu, timkaltiu
funder (n doer), timorkwan, timokua, timkua
funeral (n), piflarn, pifelana, piflan
fungal (adj), fiuloirpu, fiuloipu, fiuloipu
fungi (n pl), fiuloirpyek, fiuloipi, fiuloipi
fungicide (n), fiulkoirk, fiulekoika, fiulkoik
fungus (n), fiuloirp, fiuloipa, fiuloip
funk (n d:fear/dejection), kiomirp, kiomipa, kiomp
funk (n d:music/stench), niarnk, nianika, niank
funky (adj d:music/stench), niarnku, nianiku, nianku
funnel (n), timlart, timelata, timlat
funnel (v), timlarst, timelato, timlato
funnier (adj), tamiarmwelu, tamiamwelu, tamiamwelu
funniest (adj), tamiaarmweku, tamiamweku, tamiamweku
funniness (n), tamiarme, tamiama, tamiam
funny (adj), tamiarmu, tamiamu, tamiamu
fur (n), shalirme, shalima, shalm
fur (v), shalirzme, shalimo, shalmo
furbish (v), piethsk, pietho, pietho
furious (adj), viershu, vieraku, vierku
furiously (adv), viershiu, vierakiu, vierkiu
furl (v), trulisf, terulifo, trulfo
furnace (n), vierft, vierofa, vierf
furnish (v), limarsf, limafo, limafo
furniture (n), limarf, limafa, limaf
furor (n), viershar, vierakara, vierkar
furry (adj), shalirmu, shalimu, shalmu
further (adj/adv), thiluel, thiluelu, thiluel
furthermore (adv), thiluelf, thiluelifu, thiluelf
furthest (adj), thilwak, thiliwaku, thilwak
fury (n), viersh, vieraka, vierk
fuse (n), fabort, fabota, fabot
fuse (v), faborst, faboto, faboto
fuser (n doer), fabortwan, fabotua, fabotua
fusion (n), faborft, fabofita, faboft
fuss (n), nabalt, nabata, nabat
fuss (v), nabalst, nabato, nabato
fussy (adj), nabaltu, nabatu, nabatu
futile (adj), veikartu, veikatu, veikatu
futility (n), veikart, veikata, veikat
future (n), veidon, veida, veid
futurist (n doer), veidonwan, veidua, veidua
futuristic (adj), veidonu, veidu, veidu
fuzz (adj), fafaltu, fafatu, fafatu
fuzz (n), fafalt, fafata, fafat
fuzz (v), fafalst, fafato, fafato
G (let sng), gal, gala, ga
gadget (n), baifirk, baifika, baifk
gadgety (adj), baifirku, baifiku, baifku
Gadolinium (n davoka), Oruk, Oruk, Oruk
Gadolinium (n), Gadolinium, Gadoliniuma, Gadolinium

gag (n d:choke), keiurk, keiuka, keiuk
gag (n d:joke), pauirk, pauika, pauik
gag (v d:choke), keiursk, keiuko, keiuko
gage (n), bairk, baisha, baish
gage (v), bairsk, baisho, baisho
gaiety (n d:happy), kolame, kolima, kolm
gaily (adv d:happy), kolamiu, kolimiu, kolmiu
gain (n), kuarn, kuana, kuan
gain (v), kuarsne, kuano, kuano
gainer (n doer), kuarnwan, kuanua, kuanua
gait (n), prelfirk, perelufika, prelfk
galaxy (n), laikaf, laikalina, laikaln
gall (n), gafirk, gafika, gafk
gall (v), gafirsk, gafiko, gafko
gallant (adj), lanatu, lanitu, lantu
gallantly (adv), lanatiu, lanitiu, lantiu
gallantry (n), lanat, lanita, lant
gallbladder (n), gaflashp, gafelateka, gaflatek
galler (n doer), gafirkwan, gafikua, gafkua
gallery (n), keifan, keinifa, keinf
Gallium (n davoka), Efap, Efap, Efap
Gallium (n), Galium, Galiuma, Galium
gallon (n), gafarn, gafana, gafan
gallop (n), lomarp, lomapa, lomap
gallop (v), lomarsp, lomapo, lomapo
gallstone (n), gafbaraft, gafebarafa, gafbaraf
gambit (n), voivark, voivaka, voivak
gamble (n), voirve, voiva, voiv
gamble (v), voirzve, voivo, voivo
gambler (n doer), voirvwan, voivua, voivua
game (n), zhiert, zhieta, zhiet
game (v), zhierst, zhieto, zhieto
gamer (n doer), zhiertwan, zhietua, zhietua
gamma (n), gamarn, gamana, gaman
gang (n), bilerp, bilepa, bilp
gang (v), bilersp, bilepo, bilpo
gangster (n doer), bilerpwan, bilepua, bilpua
gap (n), farth, fatha, fath
gap (v), farsth, fatho, fatho
gape (n), tudalt, tudata, tudat
gape (v), tudalst, tudato, tudato
garage (n), talak, ketalika, ketalk
garb (n), plorfk, pelorifa, plorf
garbage (adj), tairgu, taigu, taigu
garbage (n), tairge, taiga, taig
garbage (v), tairzge, taigo, taigo
garble (n), taifaurp, taifaupa, taifaug
garble (v), taifaursp, taifaupo, taifaugo
garden (n), temurde, temudala, temdal
garden (v), temurzde, temudalo, temdalo
gardener (n doer), temurdwan, temudalua, temdalua
gargle (n), pauark, pauaka, pauak
gargle (v), pauarsk, pauako, pauako
garlic (n), korlat, korlota, korlt
garment (n), lakarn, lakana, lakan
garner (v), thrufsp, therupo, thrupo
garnish (n), thurshk, thurisha, thursh
garnish (v), thurshsk, thurisho, thursho
gas (n), zherk, zheka, zhek
gas (v), zhersk, zheko, zheko
gaseous (adj), zherku, zheku, zheku
gash (n), grelshk, gerelisha, grelsh

gash (v), grelshsk, gerelisho, grelsho
gasher (n doer), grelshkwan, gerelishua, grelshua
gasoline (n), tashif, vitarisha, vitarsh
gasp (n), zhelirp, zhelipa, zhelp
gasp (v), zhelirsp, zhelipo, zhelpo
gate (n), parlak, perelika, prelk
gate (v), parlask, pereliko, prelko
gatekeeper (n doer), parlaklorfwan, perelikelofua, prelklofua
gateway (n), parlakip, perelikipa, prelkip
gather (v), kavarsle, kavalo, kavalo
gatherer (n doer), kavarlwan, kavalua, kavalua
gauge (n), bairk, baisha, baish
gauge (v), bairsk, baisho, baisho
gauze (n), gliaflarf, geliafilafa, gliaflaf
gave (v pa), grusfyot, geruthio, gruthio
gavel (n), grutiarf, gerutiafa, grutiaf
gawk (v), biodarst, biodato, biodato
gawker (n doer), biodartwan, biodatua, biodatua
gay (adj d:happy), kolamu, kolimu, kolmu
gay (adj d:homosexual), nilurbu, nilubu, nilbu
gaze (n), tiarve, tiava, tiav
gaze (v), tiarzve, tiavo, tiavo
gazer (n doer), tiarvwan, tiavua, tiavua
gear (n d:equipment), dorfp, dorifa, dorf
gear (n d:sprocket), kragat, keraga, krag
gear (v d:sprocket), kragast, kerago, krago
gearbox (n), dorfprekun, dorifeperenika, dorfprenk
gearshift (n), dorfmiraf, dorifemirofa, dorfmirf
gee (interj), viah, viaha, viah
geek (n), bidirk, bidika, bidik
geese (n pl), kuvardyek, kuvadi, kuvadi
geez (interj), viah, viaha, viah
geiger (adj), moivarvu, moivavu, moivavu
gel (n), thalirf, thalifa, thalf
gel (v), thalirsf, thalifo, thalfo
gem (n), flinif, felinifa, flinf
gemstone (n), flinifbaraf, felinifebarafa, flinfbaraf
gender (n d:group), barthk, beronibara, bronbar
gender (n d:sexual identity), kinbar, kinabara, kinbar
gene (n), biert, bieta, biet
general (adj d:common), marmetu, marimethu, marmethu
General (n), Deginak, Deginaka, Deginak
generalization (n d:common), marmet, marimetha, marmeth
generalize (v d:common), marmest, marimetho, marmetho
generally (adv d:common), marmetiu, marimethiu, marmethiu
generate (v), marmarsk, maromako, marmako
generation (n), marmark, maromaka, marmak
generator (n doer), marmarkwan, maromakua, marmakua
generic (adj), marmashu, maromalu, marmalu
generic (n), marmash, maromala, marmal
generosity (n), marmarp, maromapa, marmp
generous (adj), marmarpu, maromapu, marmpu
generously (adv), marmarpiu, maromapiu, marmpiu
genesis (n), baiurk, baiuka, baiuk
genetic (adj), biertu, bietu, bietu

genetical (adj), biertuetu, bietuetu, bietuetu
genetically (adv), biertuetiu, bietuetiu, bietuetiu
genetics (n), biertuet, bietueta, bietuet
Geneva (n), Zhenirve, Zheniva, Zheniv
genial (adj), marmarnu, maromanu, marmanu
geniality (n), marmarn, maromana, marman
genie (n), mariaith, mariaita, mariait
genital (adj), martiarpu, maritiapu, martiapu
genital (n), martiarp, maritiapa, martiap
genitalia (n pl), martiarpyek, maritiapi, martiapi
genitals (n), marmairt, maromaita, marmait
genocidal (adj), bronkoirku, beronekoiku, bronkoiku
genocide (n), bronkoirk, beronekoika, bronkoik
genre (n), bronlaft, beronilafa, bronlaf
gentle (adj), rumarlu, rumalu, rulmu
gentleman (n), rumarnosh, rulenosha, rulnosh
gentlemen (n pl), rumarnoshyek, rulenoshi, rulnoshi
gentleness (n), rumarl, rumala, rulm
gently (adv), rumarliu, rumaliu, rulmiu
genuine (adj), marmirtu, maromitu, marmitu
genuinely (adv), marmirtiu, maromitiu, marmitiu
genus (n), bronirt, beronita, bront
geographic (adj), biendarfku, bienodarifu, biendarfu
geographical (adj), biendarfku, bienodarifu, biendarfu
geographically (adv), biendarfkiu, bienodarifiu, biendarfiu
geography (n), biendarfk, bienodarifa, biendarf
geologic (adj), bienkrenitu, bienokerenitu, bienkrentu
geological (adj), bienkrenitu, bienokerenitu, bienkrentu
geologically (adv), bienkrenitiu, bienokerenitiu, bienkrentiu
geologist (n doer), bienkrenitwan, bienokerenitua, bienkrentua
geology (n), bienkrenit, bienokerenita, bienkrent
geometric (adj), bienporftu, bienopofitu, bienpoftu
geometrical (adj), bienporftu, bienopofitu, bienpoftu
geometrically (adv), bienporftiu, bienopofitiu, bienpoftiu
geometry (n), bienporft, bienopofita, bienpoft
Georgia (n), Zhiorazh, Zhioruzha, Zhiorzh
germ (n), beronde, beronuda, brond
German (n), Zhermarn, Zheromana, Zherman
Germanium (n davoka), Efip, Efip, Efip
Germanium (n), Germanium, Geromaniuma, Germanium
Germany (n), Zhermarnf, Zheromanifa, Zhermanf
gestate (v), brokiarzge, berokiago, brokiago
gestation (n), brokiarge, berokiaga, brokiag
gesture (n), biorp, biopa, biop
gesture (v), biorsp, biopo, biopo
get (n), toshk, tosha, tosh
get (v), toshsk, tosho, tosho
get-lost (interj), tikaushkiatsh, tikalo, tiklo
getaway (n), toshopiorl, toshopiola, toshopiol
getter (n doer), toshkwan, toshua, toshua
geyser (n), tuitienf, tuitiena, tuitien

ghast (n), griaufk, geriauka, griauk
ghastly (adj), griaufku, geriauku, griauku
ghost (n), feigar, feiruga, feirg
ghost (v), feigasre, feirugo, feirgo
ghostly (adj), feigaru, feirugu, feirgu
ghoul (n), fualar, fualira, fualir
ghoulish (adj), fualaru, fualiru, fualiru
giant (n), viork, vioka, viok
giaul (v pa), dorikshriauskyot, dorugiaulio, dorgiaulio
gib (n), piarp, piapa, piap
gibber (v), piapiarsp, piapiapo, piapiapo
gibberish (n), piapiarp, piapiapa, piapiap
gieksi-, yufishkai-, yufishkai-, yufishkai-
gift (n), gruf, gerutha, gruth
gifted (adj), grufu, geruthu, gruthu
gig (n), biurzhe, biuzha, biuzh
giga- (num 1e9 pref), avukai-, avukai-, avukai-
gigantic (adj), viokvoirku, viokevioku, viokvioku
giggle (n), vigarf, vigafa, vigaf
giggle (v), vigarsf, vigafo, vigafo
giggler (n doer), vigarfwan, vigafua, vigafua
gill (n), morlanf, morilana, morlan
ginger (n), zhizharl, zhizhala, zhizhal
gingerbread (n), zhizhalthraf, zhizhalethafa, zhizhalthaf
gingerly (adj), rulzhirmu, rulezhimu, rulzhimu
gird (v), vaiarsp, vaiapo, vaiapo
girder (n doer), vaiarpwan, vaiapua, vaiapua
girdle (n), vaiaparp, vaiapara, vaiapar
girl (n), kelerf, kelera, keler
girlfriend (n), shuelsh, shuesha, shuesh
girly (adj), kelerfu, keleru, keleru
girth (n), vaiarp, vaiapa, vaiap
give (v), grusf, gerutho, grutho
giveaway (n), grufopliorl, geruthopeliola, gruthopliol
giver (n doer), grufwan, geruthua, gruthua
glacial (adj), tiarshu, tiashu, tiashu
glacially (adv), tiarshiu, tiashiu, tiashiu
glaciate (v), tiars, tiasho, tiasho
glacier (n), tiarsh, tiasha, tiash
glad (adj), prelfpu, perelifu, prelfu
gladden (v), prelfsp, perelifo, prelfo
glade (n), prelfpor, perelifora, prelfor
gladiator (n), prekutalk, perekutala, prekutal
gladly (adv), prelfpiu, perelifiu, prelfiu
glamor (n), melarf, melara, melar
glamorous (adj), melarfu, melaru, melaru
glamorously (adv), melarfiu, melariu, melariu
glamour (n), melarf, melara, melar
glance (n), fleirge, feleiga, fleig
glance (v), fleirzge, feleigo, fleigo
gland (n), gogarf, gogara, gogar
glandular (adj), gogarfu, gogaru, gogaru
glare (n), dritart, deritara, dritar
glare (v), dritarst, deritaro, dritaro
glass (n d:quartz), drilf, derilosha, drilsh
glass (n d:spectacles), drinat, derinota, drint
glassware (n), drilfeshlerf, derileshelefa, drilshlef
glaze (n), drizhat, derizha, drizh
glaze (v), drizhast, derizho, drizho
gleam (n), druafk, deruafa, druaf

gleam (v), druafsk, deruafo, druafo
glean (n), drikirn, derikina, drikin
glean (v), drikirsne, derikino, drikino
glee (n), drithk, deritha, drith
gleeful (adj), drithku, derithu, drithu
gleefully (adv), drithkiu, derithiu, drithiu
glide (n), valursh, valusha, valush
glide (v), valurs, valusho, valusho
glider (n doer), valurshwan, valushua, valushua
glimmer (n), zhilarme, zhilema, zhilm
glimmer (v), zhilarzme, zhilemo, zhilmo
glimpse (n), zhirf, zhilofa, zhilf
glimpse (v), zhirsf, zhilofo, zhilfo
glint (n), zhirp, zhilopa, zhilp
glitch (n), ploifk, peloika, ploik
glitter (n), zhiltilf, zhiletila, zhiltil
glitter (v), zhiltilsf, zhiletilo, zhiltilo
glittery (adj), zhiltilfu, zhiletilu, zhiltilu
glitz (n), zhilirk, zhilika, zhilk
glitzy (adj), zhilirku, zhiliku, zhilku
gloat (n), triauk, buiauka, buiauk
gloat (v), triausk, buiauko, buiauko
glob (n), kroizhbe, keroiba, kroib
glob (v), kroizhbe, keroibo, kroibo
global (adj), kroivu, keroithu, kroithu
globalization (n), kroivuet, keroithueta, kroithuet
globally (adv), kroiviu, keroithiu, kroithiu
globe (n), kroive, keroitha, kroith
globular (adj), kroizhbu, keroibu, kroibu
gloom (n), friop, ferioma, friom
gloomily (adv), friopiu, feriomiu, friomiu
gloomy (adj), friopu, feriomu, friomu
glorification (n), kreilfuet, kereilueta, kreiluet
glorify (v), kreilsf, kereilo, kreilo
glorious (adj), kreilfu, kereilu, kreilu
gloriously (adv), kreilfiu, kereiliu, kreiliu
glory (n), kreilf, kereila, kreil
gloss (n), valarsh, valasha, valash
gloss (v), valars, valasho, valasho
glossy (adj), valarshu, valashu, valashu
glove (n), truathk, teruatha, truath
glove (v), truathsk, teruatho, truatho
glow (n), triaft, teriafa, triaf
glow (v), triafst, teriafo, triafo
glowy (adj), triaftu, teriafu, triafu
glue (n), kiauf, kiaruva, kiarv
glue (v), kiausf, kiaruvo, kiarvo
glut (n), krufp, kerupa, krup
glutton (n doer), krufpwan, kerupua, krupua
gluttonous (adj), krufpu, kerupu, krupu
gluttony (n), krufpuet, kerupueta, krupuet
gnat (n), bimirk, bimika, bimk
gnaw (v), garlarzge, garelago, garlago
gnosis (n), shimarn, shimana, shman
gnostic (adj), shimarnu, shimanu, shmanu
go (v), virsf, vifo, vifo
goal (n), maiart, maiata, maiat
goat (n), bliert, belieta, bliet
gob (n), koizhbe, koiba, koib
gobble (n), kroniert, keroinieta, kroiniet
gobble (v), kronierst, keroinieto, kroinieto
gobbler (n doer), kroniertwan, keroinietua, kroinietua

god (n), agubirde, agubida, agubid
goddess (n), agubiarsh, agubiashara, agubiashar
godfather (n), agubivotert, agubivoteta, agubivotet
godless (adj), agubirdmenu, agubidemenu,
    agubidmenu
godly (adj), agubirdu, agubidu, agubidu
godmother (n), agubimashel, agubimalisha,
    agubimalsh
godsend (n), agubizhairp, agubizhaipa, agubizhaip
goer (n doer), virfwan, vifua, vifua
goggle (n), deigirn, deigina, deigin
goggles (n pl), kukarnyek, kukani, kukani
gold (adj), goralirtu, goralitu, goraltu
Gold (n davoka), Irat, Irat, Irat
Gold (n), Gold, Golada, Gold
gold (n), goralirt, goralita, goralt
golden (v), goralirst, goralito, goralto
goldfish (n pl), goralitshlershyek, goralitesheleshi,
    goraltshleshi
goldfish (n), goralitshlersh, goraliteshelesha,
    goraltshlesh
goldmine (n), goralkrivuge, goralekeriga, goralkrig
goldsmith (n), goralfnirth, goralefenitha, goralfnith
golf (n), tafirp, tafipa, tafp
golf (v), tafirsp, tafipo, tafpo
golfer (n doer), tafirpwan, tafipua, tafpua
golly (interj), vuau, vuaua, vuau
gong (n), kuanfk, kuanika, kuank
goo (n), dhurf, dhufa, dhuf
good (adj d:helpful), kurfu, kufu, kufu
good (n d:helpful), kurf, kufa, kuf
good (n d:product), kufirk, kufika, kufk
goodbye (interj), kufliau, kufaliau, kufliau
goodmorning (interj), kuflimern, kufelimena,
    kuflimen
goodness (n), kufmurf, kufamufa, kufmuf
goodnight (interj), kufmuarn, kufemuana, kufmuan
goodwill (n), kufyark, kufyaka, kufyak
gooey (adj), dhurfu, dhufu, dhufu
goof (n), kleiark, keleiaka, kleiak
goof (v), kleiarsk, keleiako, kleiako
goofy (adj), kleiarku, keleiaku, kleiaku
goose (n), kuvarde, kuvada, kuvad
goose (v), kuvarzde, kuvado, kuvado
gore (n), kerufk, keruka, kruk
gore (v), kerufsk, keruko, kruko
gorge (n), tharve, thava, thav
gorge (v), tharzve, thavo, thavo
gorgeous (adj), tharvu, thavu, thavu
gorgeously (adv), tharviu, thaviu, thaviu
gory (adj), kerufku, keruku, kruku
gosh (interj), vuaursh, vuausha, vuaush
gossip (n), thashirp, thashipa, thashp
gossip (v), thashirsp, thashipo, thashpo
gossiper (n doer), thashirpwan, thashipua,
    thashpua
gossipy (adj), thashirpu, thashipu, thashpu
got (v pa), toshskyot, toshio, toshio
gotcha (interj), partsha, patesha, patsha
gouge (n), duakrilt, duakerita, duakrit
gouge (v), duakrilst, duakerito, duakrito
gourmet (adj), kiaranu, kiarinu, kiarnu
govern (v), molfars, molifasho, molfasho

government (n), molfarsh, molifasha, molfash
governor (n doer), molfarshwan, molifashua,
    molfashua
gown (n), shavarn, shavana, shavan
grab (n), tianirk, tianika, tiank
grab (v), tianirsk, tianiko, tianko
grabber (n doer), tianirkwan, tianikua, tiankua
grace (n), plarf, pelafa, plaf
grace (v), plarsf, pelafo, plafo
graceful (adj), plarfushu, pelafushu, plafushu
gracefully (adv), plarfushiu, pelafushiu, plafushiu
gracious (adj), plarfu, pelafu, plafu
graciously (adv), plarfiu, pelafiu, plafiu
graciousness (n), plarfuet, pelafueta, plafuet
grade (n), shtrak, shoterana, shtran
grade (v), shtrask, shoterano, shtrano
grader (n doer), shtrakwan, shoteranua, shtranua
gradient (n), shtranak, shoteranaka, shtrank
gradual (adj), kinorpu, kinopu, kinpu
gradually (adv), kinorpiu, kinopiu, kinpiu
graduate (n doer), kinorpwan, kinopua, kinpua
graduate (v), kinorsp, kinopo, kinpo
graduation (n), kinorp, kinopa, kinp
graft (n), darfilt, darofila, darfil
graft (v), darfilst, darofilo, darfilo
grain (n), nolirk, nolika, nolk
grainy (adj), nolirku, noliku, nolku
gram (n), kranp, kerana, kran
grammar (n), nelkarn, nelikara, nelkar
grammatical (adj), nelkarnu, nelikaru, nelkaru
grammatically (adv), nelkarniu, nelikariu, nelkariu
grand (adj), greilfu, gereilu, greilu
grandchild (n), greiluart, gereiluara, greiluar
grandchildren (n pl), greiluartyek, gereiluari,
    greiluari
granddaddy (n), greibalbil, gereibabila, greibabil
granddaughter (n), greilidor, gereilunora, greilurn
granddaughterly (adj), greilidoru, gereilunoru,
    greilurnu
grandfather (n), greivotert, gereivoteta, greivotet
grandfather (v), greivoterst, gereivoteto, greivoteto
grandfatherly (adj), greivotertu, gereivotetu,
    greivotetu
grandly (adv), greilfiu, gereiliu, greiliu
grandma (n), greimah, gereima, greim
grandmaster (n), greithiork, gereithioka, greithiok
grandmommy (n), greimelimame, gereimelimala,
    greimelmal
grandmother (n), greimashel, gereimalisha,
    greimalsh
grandmother (v), greimashesle, gereimalisho,
    greimalsho
grandmotherly (adj), greimashelu, gereimalishu,
    greimalshu
grandpa (n), greiblarp, gereibelapa, greiblap
grandparent (n), greidathferf, gereidathifefa,
    greidathfef
grandson (n), greimtheiarn, gereimetheiana,
    greimtheian
grandstand (n), greitrelirt, gereiterelita, greitrelt
grandstand (v), greitrelirst, gereiterelito, greitrelto
grant (n), pluark, peluaka, pluak
grant (v), pluarsk, peluako, pluako

grantor (n doer), pluarkwan, peluakua, pluakua
grape (n), plarfp, pelafipa, plafp
grapefruit (n), plarfliap, pelafeliapa, plafliap
grapevine (n), plafpeilarn, pelafipeilana, plafpeilan
graph (n), darfk, darifa, darf
graph (v), darfsk, darifo, darfo
graphic (adj), darfku, darifu, darfu
graphic (n), darfket, darifeta, darfet
graphical (adj), darfketu, darifetu, darfetu
graphically (adv), darfketiu, darifetiu, darfetiu
grapple (adj), tianthku, tianathu, tianthu
grapple (n), tianthk, tianatha, tianth
grapple (v), tianthsk, tianatho, tiantho
grasp (n), tianirp, tianipa, tianp
grasp (v), tianirsp, tianipo, tianpo
grass (n), flirsh, felisha, flish
grasshopper (n), flishwilfuan, felishwifuala,
    flishwifual
grassland (n), flishraufp, felisheraupa, flishraup
grassy (adj), flishwilfuanu, felishwifualu,
    flishwifualu
grate (n), plark, pelaka, plak
grate (v), plarsk, pelako, plako
grateful (adj), plazhgu, pelazhu, plazhu
gratefully (adv), plazhgiu, pelazhiu, plazhiu
grater (n doer), plarkwan, pelakua, plakua
gratification (n), plabuet, pelazhueta, plazhuet
gratify (v), plazhzge, pelazho, plazho
gratitude (n), plazhge, pelazha, plazh
gratuity (n), plaft, pelazhuda, plazhd
grave (adj d:serious), burgu, burifu, burfu
grave (n), bonirf, bonifa, bonf
gravel (n), burlart, burilata, burlat
gravelly (adj), burlartu, burilatu, burlatu
gravely (adv d:serious), burgiu, burifiu, burfiu
graveside (n), bonfshoirt, bonifeshoita, bonfshoit
gravestone (n), bonfbaraft, bonifebarafa, bonfbaraf
graveyard (n), bonfthauthk, bonifethautha,
    bonfthauth
gravitate (v d:physics), kikurst, kikuto, kikuto
gravitation (n), kikurtuet, kikutueta, kikutuet
gravitational (adj), kikurtuetu, kikutuetu, kikutuetu
gravity (n d:physics), kikurt, kikuta, kikut
gravity (n d:serious), burge, burifa, burf
gravy (n), nolkiern, nolikiena, nolkien
gray (adj), tranfu, terathu, trathu
gray (n), tranf, teratha, trath
graze (v d:feed), flishars, felishasho, flishasho
graze (v d:scrape), flithsk, felitho, flitho
grazer (n doer d:feed), flisharshwan, felishashua,
    flishashua
grease (n), krelf, kerela, krel
grease (v), krelsf, kerelo, krelo
greasy (adj), krelfu, kerelu, krelu
great (adj), klaurku, kelauku, klauku
greater (adj), klaurkwelu, kelaukwelu, klaukwelu
greatest (adj), klaurkwaku, kelaukwaku, klaukwaku
greatly (adv), klaurkiu, kelaukiu, klaukiu
greatness (n), klaurk, kelauka, klauk
Greece (n), Grilsh, Gerisha, Grish
greed (n), klaifp, kelaifa, klaif
greedily (adv), klaifpiu, kelaifiu, klaifiu
greedy (adj), klaifpu, kelaifu, klaifu

Greek (n), Grifirk, Gerifika, Grifk
green (adj), klurnu, kelunu, klunu
green (n), klurn, keluna, klun
greet (v), triarst, teriato, triato
grew (v pa), kloraskyot, keloikio, kloikio
grey (adj), tralthu, terathu, trathu
grey (n), tralth, teratha, trath
greyhound (n), tralthgaurk, terathegauka,
    trathgauk
greyish (adj), traltheiku, teratheiku, tratheiku
grid (n), draithk, deraitha, draith
gridlock (n), draithtiurge, deraithetiuga, driathtiug
grief (n), plurzhe, peluzha, pluzh
grievance (n), plurzhuet, peluzhueta, pluzhuet
grieve (v), plurze, peluzho, pluzho
griever (n doer), plurzhwan, peluzhua, pluzhua
grievous (adj), plurzhu, peluzhu, pluzhu
grievously (adv), plurzhiu, peluzhiu, pluzhiu
grill (n), plaithk, pelaitha, plaith
grill (v), plaithsk, pelaitho, plaitho
grim (adj), murdarnu, muridanu, murdanu
grimace (n), murdarn, muridana, murdan
grimace (v), murdarsne, muridano, murdano
grime (n), murt, mureda, murd
grimey (adj), murtu, muredu, murdu
grin (n), nureln, nurina, nurn
grin (v), nurelsne, nurino, nurno
grind (n d:rip), shkrait, shiporaita, shprait
grind (v d:rip), shkraist, shiporaito, shpraito
grinder (n doer d:rip), shkraitwan, shiporaitua,
    shpraitua
grip (n), shpruk, shipuka, shpuk
grip (v), shprusk, shipuko, shpuko
gripe (n), shpairk, shepaika, shpaik
gripe (v), shpairsk, shepaiko, shpaiko
gripper (n doer), shprukwan, shipukua, shpukua
grit (n), nurlart, nurilata, nurlat
grit (v), nurlarst, nurilato, nurlato
gritty (adj), nurlartu, nurilatu, nurlatu
groan (n), plurve, peluva, pluv
groan (v), plurzve, peluvo, pluvo
groaner (n doer), plurvwan, peluvua, pluvua
grocer (n doer), treifpwan, tereifua, treifua
grocery (n), treifp, tereifa, treif
grog (n), puvirk, puvika, puvik
groggy (adj), puvirku, puviku, puviku
groom (n d:bridegroom), rideirge, rideiga, rideig
groom (v d:clean), kloiarsne, keloiano, kloiano
groove (n), triuart, teriuata, triuat
groove (v), triuarst, teriuato, triuato
groovy (adj), triuartu, teriuatu, triuatu
gross (adj d:disgusting), klaurgu, kelaugu, klaugu
gross (n d:package), purifk, purika, purk
gross (v d:disgusting), klaurzge, kelaugo, klaugo
ground (n d:soil), braft, beranita, brant
ground (v d:soil), brafst, beranito, branto
ground (v pa d:rip), shkraistyot, shiporaitio,
    shpraitio
grounder (n doer d:soil), braftwan, beranitua,
    brantua
group (n), bronf, berona, bron
group (v), bronsf, berono, brono
groupie (n doer), bronfwan, beronua, bronua

grove (n), drienf, deriena, drien
grovel (v), driensk, derienoto, driento
grow (v), klorask, keloiko, kloiko
grower (n doer), klorakwan, keloikua, kloikua
growl (n), kluaurth, keluautha, kluauth
growl (v), kluaursth, keluautho, kluautho
growth (n), klorak, keloika, kloik
grudge (n), kriuzhge, keriuga, kriug
gruel (n), thiarzhge, thiaruga, thiarg
grumble (v), kriufsp, keriufo, kriufo
grunge (n), murzhge, muriga, murg
grungy (adj), murzhgu, murigu, murgu
grunt (n doer), krezhgwan, keregua, kregua
grunt (n), krezhge, kerega, kreg
grunt (v), krezhzge, kerego, krego
Gs (let pl), gali, gali, gali
guarantee (n), vaifort, vaifota, vaift
guarantee (v), vaiforst, vaifoto, vaifto
guarantor (n doer), vaifortwan, vaifotua, vaiftua
guard (n), vaifirk, vaifika, vaifk
guard (v), vaifirsk, vaifiko, vaifko
guardian (n doer), vaifkarnwan, vaifikanua,
    vaifkanua
guardianship (n), vaifkarn, vaifikana, vaifkan
guardrail (n), vaifkluirt, vaifikeluita, vaifkluit
guerrilla (adj), kuilarnu, kuilanu, kuilanu
guerrilla (n), kuilarn, kuilana, kuilan
guess (n), plurp, pelupa, plup
guess (v), plursp, pelupo, plupo
guesser (n doer), plurpwan, pelupua, plupua
guesswork (n), plupkiork, pelupekioka, plupkiok
guest (n), plunap, pelunipa, plunp
guidance (n), tuirp, tuipa, tuip
guide (n doer), tuirpwan, tuipua, tuipua
guide (v), tuirsp, tuipo, tuipo
guidebook (n), tuipvonurde, tuipevonuda, tuipvond
guideline (n), tuirproif, tuiperoifa, tuiproif
guidepost (n), tuipebalirt, tuipebalita, tuipebalt
guilt (n), glurf, gelufa, gluf
guilt (v), glursf, gelufo, glufo
guiltily (adv), glurfiu, gelufiu, glufiu
guilty (adj), glurfu, gelufu, glufu
guise (n), tuirf, tuifa, tuif
guitar (n), kliart, keliata, kliat
guitarist (n doer), kliartwan, keliatua, kliatua
gulch (n), vartesh, varitesha, vartsh
gulf (n), karishk, karisha, karsh
gulley (n), viurme, viuma, vium
gulp (n), gurp, gurapa, gurp
gulp (v), gursp, gurapo, gurpo
gulper (n doer), gurpwan, gurapua, gurpua
gum (n), winorf, winofa, winf
gum (v), winorsf, winofo, winfo
gummy (adj), winorfu, winofu, winfu
gun (n), dorige, doruga, dorg
gun (v), dorizge, dorugo, dorgo
gunboat (n), dorgeshkorbe, dorugeshekoba,
    dorgeshkob
gunfight (n), dorgvaugat, dorugevauga, dorgvaug
gunfire (n), dorikshriauk, dorugiaula, dorgiaul
gunman (n), dorikplorn, dorugepelona, dorgplon
gunmen (n pl), dorikplornyek, dorugepeloni,
    dorgploni

gunner (n doer), dorigwan, dorugua, dorgua
gunpoint (n), dorgetaifort, dorugetaifota, dorgetaift
gunpowder (n), dorgbiart, dorugebiata, dorgbiat
gunship (n), dorgeflerve, dorugefeleva, dorgeflev
gunshot (n), dorgeshkoift, dorugeshekoita,
    dorgeshkoit
gurgle (n), pauorfk, pauorika, pauork
gurgle (v), pauorfsk, pauoriko, pauorko
gush (n), pauarsh, pauasha, pauash
gush (v), pauars, pauasho, pauasho
gusher (n doer), pauarshwan, pauashua, pauashua
gust (n), feirsh, feisha, feish
gust (v), feirs, feisho, feisho
gusty (adj), feirshu, feishu, feishu
gut (n), pauft, pauta, paut
gut (v), paufst, pauto, pauto
gutless (adj), pauftmenu, pautemenu, pautmenu
gutsy (adj), pauftu, pautu, pautu
gutter (n), pautufp, pautupa, pautup
guy (adj d:wire), tuirtu, tuitu, tuitu
guy (n d:male), deirge, deiga, deig
guy (n d:wire), tuirt, tuita, tuit
gym (n), kanirk, kanika, kank
gymnasium (n), kanikarve, kanikava, kankav
gynecologist (n doer), veiakuiftwan, veiakuitua,
    veiakuitua
gynecology (n), veiakuift, veiakuita, veiakuit
H (let sng), harfe, harifa, harf
habit (n), reidal, reilota, reilt
habitable (adj), reishortu, reishotu, reishtu
habitat (n), reishort, reishota, reisht
habitation (n), reishortuet, reishotueta, reishtuet
habitual (adj), reidalu, reilotu, reiltu
habitually (adv), reidaliu, reilotiu, reiltiu
hack (n), kialirp, kialipa, kialp
hack (v), kialirsp, kialipo, kialpo
hacker (n doer), kialirpwan, kialipua, kialpua
hacksaw (n), kialpegralzhe, kialipegerazha,
    kialpegrazh
had (v), kot, koto, koto
had to (ndal d:need), nirshke kodı, nıshoka kodı,
    nishke kodi
Hafnium (n davoka), Irip, Irip, Irip
Hafnium (n), Hafnium, Hafoniuma, Hafnium
hah (interj), yat, ya, ya
haha (interj), yata, yaya, yaya
hail (n d:greeting), kuairf, kuaifa, kuaif
hail (n d:precipitation), pluishk, peluika, pluik
hail (v d:greeting), kuairsf, kuaifo, kuaifo
hail (v d:precipitation), pluishsk, peluiko, pluiko
hailstorm (n), pluikferap, pelukeferipa, pluikfrip
hair (n), shelt, shera, sher
haircut (n), sheldaish, sherudaisha, sherdaish
hairdo (n), sheltik, sheretika, shertik
hairdresser (n doer), shelplershwan, sherepeleshua,
    sherpleshua
hairless (adj), sheltmenu, sheremenu, shermenu
hairline (n), sheltroifk, shereroifa, sheroif
hairpin (n), sheleirp, shereleipa, sherleip
hairspray (n), sheltpliurf, sherepeliufa, sherpliuf
hairstyle (n), sheltfriarf, shereferiafa, sherfriaf
hairy (adj), sheltu, sheru, sheru
Haiti (n), Kaitirf, Kaitifa, Kaitif

half (adj), walpu, wapu, wapu
half (n), walp, wapa, wap
HalfFaceSymbol (n), landak, lanudaka, landark
halfway (adj/adv), wapliol, wapeliolu, wapliol
hall (n), kiarth, kiatha, kiath
hallelujah (interj), takalan, takalana, takalan
hallow (v), domursle, domulo, domulo
hallucinate (v), dorshiusne, doshiuno, doshiuno
hallucination (n), dorshiun, doshiuna, doshiun
hallway (n), kiarthip, kiathipa, kiathip
halt (n), graushk, gerauka, grauk
halt (v), graushsk, gerauko, grauko
halter (n), graushkat, geraukata, graukat
halve (v), walsp, wapo, wapo
ham (n), giurf, giufa, giuf
hamburger (n), zhaiarge, zhaiaga, zhaiag
hammer (n), ganirp, ganipa, ganp
hammer (v), ganirsp, ganipo, ganpo
hamper (n d:laundry), brelbe, bereba, breb
hamper (v d:hinder), klarnsk, kelaniko, klanko
hand (n), karp, kapa, kap
hand (v), karsp, kapo, kapo
handbag (n), karnufaf, kapenafa, kapnaf
handbook (n), kapevornt, kapevonuda, kapevond
handcraft (v), kapkafirsp, kapekafipo, kapkafpo
handcuff (n), kapediefk, kapediefa, kapedief
handcuff (v), kapediefsk, kapediefo, kapediefo
handful (n), karpesh, kapesha, kapesh
handgun (n), kapedorige, kapedoruga, kapedorg
handicap (n), karpefp, kapefipa, kapefp
handicap (v), karpefsp, kapefipo, kapefpo
handiwork (n), kapukiork, kapukioka, kapukiok
handkerchief (n), karploaf, kapeloafa, kaploaf
handle (n), karpade, kapada, kapad
handle (v), karpazde, kapado, kapado
handlebar (n), kapadrolart, kapaderolata, kapadrolt
handler (n doer), karpadwan, kapadua, kapadua
handmade (v pa), kapnarzgyot, kapenagio, kapnagio
handmake (v), kapnarzge, kapenago, kapnago
handout (n), karpuil, kapuila, kapuil
handpick (v), kapedotirs, kapedotisho, kapedotsho
handrail (n), kapluirt, kapeluita, kapluit
handset (n), kapezhorde, kapezhoda, kapezhod
handshake (n), kargarve, kaparuga, kaparg
handshake (v), kargarzve, kaparugo, kapargo
handshook (v pa), kargarzvyot, kaparugio, kapargio
handsome (adj), karzhinu, kapozhinu, kapzhinu
handsomely (adv), karzhiniu, kapozhiniu, kapzhiniu
handstand (n), kaptrelirt, kapeterelita, kaptrelt
handwrite (v), karploizde, kapeloido, kaploido
handwriter (n doer), karploidwan, kapeloidua, kaploidua
handwrote (v pa), karploizdyot, kapeloidio, kaploidio
handy (adj), karpu, kapu, kapu
handyman (n doer), karpwan, kapua, kapua
hang (v), tarazge, tarugo, targo
hangar (n), anarot, anarita, anart
hanger (n doer), taragwan, tarugua, targua
hangout (n), taraguil, taruguila, targuil
hangover (n), taragafen, tarugafena, targafen

hangup (n), taragiveil, tarugiveila, targiveil
Hanukkah (n), Kankarl, Kanukala, Kankal
hapless (adj), korlmenu, kolomenu, kolmenu
haplessly (adv), korlmeniu, kolomeniu, kolmeniu
happen (v), kolirsp, kolipo, kolpo
happenstance (n), kolirp, kolipa, kolp
happier (adj), kolamwelu, kolimwelu, kolmwelu
happiest (adj), kolamweku, kolimweku, kolmweku
happily (adv), kolamiu, kolimiu, kolmiu
happiness (n), kolame, kolima, kolm
happy (adj), kolamu, kolimu, kolmu
harass (v), doikarsk, doikako, doikako
harasser (n doer), doikarkwan, doikakua, doikakua
harassment (n), doikark, doikaka, doikak
harbor (n), naftan, nafita, naft
harbor (v), naftasne, nafito, nafto
harbour (n), naftan, nafita, naft
hard (adj), kelirtu, kelitu, keltu
hard (adv), kelirtiu, kelitiu, keltiu
hardback (n), keltevark, kelitevaka, keltevak
hardball (n), keltshmonde, kelitemashipa, keltmashp
hardcore (adj), keltkirftu, kelitekirotu, keltkirtu
hardcover (adj), keltedathelu, kelitedalithu, keltedalthu
hardcover (n), keltedathel, kelitedalitha, keltedalth
harden (v), kelirst, kelito, kelto
harder (adj), kelirtwelu, kelitwelu, keltwelu
hardest (adj), kelirtwaku, kelitwaku, keltwadu
hardily (adv), kelifortiu, kelifotiu, kelftiu
hardiness (n), kelifort, kelifota, kelft
hardline (adj), keltroifku, keliteroifu, keltroifu
hardline (n), keltroifk, keliteroifa, keltroif
hardliner (n doer), keltroifkwan, keliteroifua, keltroifua
hardly (adv), kelirtoiu, kelitoiu, keltoiu
hardness (n), kelirt, kelita, kelt
hardship (n), keltfirf, kelitefifa, keltfif
hardtop (n), keltedaurp, kelitedaupa, keltedaup
hardware (n), kelshlerf, keleshelefa, kelshlef
hardwood (n), keltfanirn, kelitefanina, keltfanin
hardy (adj), kelifortu, kelifotu, kelftu
harem (n), tholarve, tholava, tholav
harm (n), malve, mava, mav
harm (v), malzve, mavo, mavo
harmful (adj), malvushu, mavushu, mavushu
harmfully (adv), malvushiu, mavushiu, mavushiu
harmless (adj), malvmenu, mavamenu, mavmenu
harmlessly (adv), malvmeniu, mavameniu, mavmeniu
harmonic (adj), mavirnu, mavinu, mavinu
harmonic (n), mavirnar, mavinara, mavinar
harmonize (v), mavirsne, mavino, mavino
harmony (n), mavirn, mavina, mavin
harness (n), fnafirt, fenafita, fnaft
harness (v), fnafirst, fenafito, fnafto
harp (n), tuyarn, tuyana, tuyan
harp (v), tuyarsne, tuyano, tuyano
harper (n doer), tuyarnwan, tuyanua, tuyanua
harpoon (n), tuyart, tuyata, tuyat
harrow (n), buark, buaka, buak
harrow (v), buarsk, buako, buako
harsh (adj), kairfku, kaifoku, kaifku

harshen (v), kairfsk, kaifoko, kaifko
harshly (adv), kairfkiu, kaifokiu, kaifkiu
harshness (n), kairfk, kaifoka, kaifk
Hartford (n), Kartoforde, Karitoforuda, Kartford
harvest (n), nabirt, nabita, nabit
harvest (v), nabirst, nabito, nabito
harvester (n doer), nabirtwan, nabitua, nabitua
has (v sing), kof, kofo, kofo
hash (n d:cut food), thaithp, thaitha, thaith
hash (v d:cut food), thaithsp, thaitho, thaitho
Hassium (n davoka), Inik, Inik, Inik
Hassium (n), Hashium, Hashiuma, Hashium
hassle (n), kavairk, kavaika, kavaik
hassle (v), kavairsk, kavaiko, kavaiko
haste (n), kavairt, kavaita, kavait
hasten (v), kavairst, kavaito, kavaito
hastily (adv), kavairtiu, kavaitiu, kavaitiu
hasty (adj), kavairtu, kavaitu, kavaitu
hat (n), kreft, kereta, kret
hatch (n d:door), telirth, telitha, telth
hatch (v d:create), thaithirsk, thaithiko, thaithko
hatchback (n), telthvark, telithevaka, telthvak
hatcher (n doer d:create), thaithirkwan, thaithikua, thaithkua
hatchery (n), thaithirkuet, thaithikueta, thaithkuet
hatchet (n), thaithaft, thaithata, thaithat
hate (n), kaift, kaifa, kaif
hate (v), kaifst, kaifo, kaifo
hateful (adj), kaiftu, kaifu, kaifu
hatefully (adv), kaiftiu, kaifiu, kaifiu
hater (n doer), kaiftwan, kaifua, kaifua
hatred (n), kaift, kaifa, kaif
haul (n), shluarp, sheluapa, shluap
haul (v), shluarsp, sheluapo, shluapo
hauler (n doer), shluarpwan, sheluapua, shluapua
haunt (v), vikauiesne, kavatieno, kavatieno
have (v fut), koveit, koveio, koveio
have (v pl), kove, kovo, kovo
have (v s), kof, kofo, kofo
have to (ndal d:necd), nirshke kodi, nishoka kodi, nishke kodi
have-to (ndal), kodi, kodi, kodi
haven (n), kovarf, kovara, kovar
having (v prp), kofaut, kofao, kofao
havoc (n), kovark, kovaka, kovak
Hawii (n), Kauwirf, Kauwifa, Kauwif
hawk (n), klierk, kelieka, kliek
hawk (v), kliersk, kelieko, klieko
hawker (n doer), klierkwan, keliekua, kliekua
hay (n), theilf, theila, theil
hazard (n), kiaviark, kiaviaka, kiaviak
hazard (v), kiaviarsk, kiaviako, kiaviako
hazardous (adj), kiaviarku, kiaviaku, kiaviaku
haze (n d:abuse), kovurk, kovuka, kovuk
haze (n d:fog), kiaushk, kiausha, kiaush
haze (v d:abuse), kovursk, kovuko, kovuko
haze (v d:fog), kiaushsk, kiausho, kiausho
hazy (adj d:fog), kiaushku, kiaushu, kiaushu
he (pron 3rd masc sng sub), hui, hui, hui
head (n), kefirt, kefita, keft
head (v), kefirst, kefito, kefto
headache (n), keflituage, kefebeluaga, kefbluag
headband (n), kefshtairme, kefeshetaima,

kefshtaim
headboard (n), kefplok, kefepelorika, kefplork
headdress (n), kefplersh, kefepelesha, kefplesh
headdresser (n doer), kefplershwan, kefepeleshua, kefpleshua
header (n doer), kefirtwan, kefitua, keftua
headgear (n), kefdorfp, kefedorifa, kefdorf
headhunter (n doer), kefgrulatwan, kefegerulitua, kefgrultua
headlight (n), kefluarn, kefeluana, kefluan
headline (n), kefroifk, keferoifa, kefroif
headline (v), kefroifsk, keferoifo, kefroifo
headliner (n doer), kefroifkwan, keferoifua, kefroifua
headmaster (n), kefthiork, kefethioka, kefthiok
headphone (n), kefyarp, kefyapa, kefyap
headquarter (v), keftkarist, kefekarito, kefkarito
headquarters (n), keftkarit, kefekarita, kefkarit
headroom (n), kefshranf, kefesherana, kefshran
headset (n), kefezhorde, kefezhoda, kefezhod
headstrong (adj), kefborafu, kefeborifu, kefborfu
headwater (n), kefeidorn, kefeidona, kefeidon
headway (n), kefpliorl, kefepeliola, kefpliol
headwind (n), kefthelern, kefethelina, keftheln
heady (adj), kefirtu, kefitu, keftu
heal (v), hausf, hautho, hautho
healer (n doer), haufwan, hauthua, hauthua
health (n), hauf, hautha, hauth
healthcare (n), haufkeirf, hauthekeifa, hauthkeif
healthier (adj), haufwelu, hauthwelu, hauthwelu
healthiest (adj), haufweku, hauthweku, hauthweku
healthy (adj), haufu, hauthu, hauthu
heap (n), krimaf, kerimofa, krimf
heap (v), krimasf, kerimofo, krimfo
hear (v), uyasf, uyano, uyano
heard (v pa), uyasfyot, uyanio, uyanio
hearsay (n), uyafzhursh, uyanezhusha, uyanzhush
hearse (n), buashk, buasha, buash
heart (n), dralt, darala, dral
heartache (n), dralibuage, daralebeluaga, dralbluag
heartbeat (n), draldaurt, daraledauta, draldaut
heartbreak (n), dralblerk, daralepelika, dralplik
heartbreak (v), dralblersk, daralepeliko, dralpliko
heartbroke (v pa), dralblerskyot, daralepelikio, dralplikio
heartburn (n), dralbugor, daraleberuga, dralbrug
hearth (n), kruzhge, keruzha, kruzh
heartily (adv), draltiu, daraliu, draliu
heartland (n), dralraufp, daraleraupa, dralraup
heartless (adj), draltmenu, daralemenu, dralmenu
hearty (adj), draltu, daralu, dralu
heat (n), kurt, kuta, kut
heat (v), kurst, kuto, kuto
heater (n doer), kurtwan, kutua, kutua
heave (n), gurbe, guba, gub
heave (v), gurzbe, gubo, gubo
heaven (n), kavolar, kovarila, kovarl
heavenly (adj), kavolaru, kovarilu, kovarlu
heavier (adj), gurbwelu, gubwelu, gubwelu
heaviest (adj), gurbweku, gubweku, gubweku
heavily (adv), gurbiu, gubiu, gubiu
heavy (adj), gurbu, gubu, gubu
heavyweight (n), gubshuirsh, gubeshuisha,

gubshuish
Hebrew (n), Kiupriunf, Kiuperiuna, Kiupriun
hecto- (num 100 pref), tashia-, tashia-, tashia-
heed (v), thiaifsp, thiaipo, thiaipo
heel (n d:sole), gufirp, gufipa, gufp
heel (v d:tilt), giars, giasho, giasho
heft (n), gulorbe, guloba, gulb
hefty (adj), gulorbu, gulobu, gulbu
height (n), koilf, koila, koil
heighten (v), koilsf, koilo, koilo
heighth (n), koilf, koila, koil
heir (n), lailf, laila, lail
heiress (n), lailf, laila, lail
heirloom (n), lailthetirsh, lailethetisha, lailthetsh
heist (n), guirbe, guiba, guib
held (v pa), thorthskyot, thorithio, thorthio
helical (adj), tunirtu, tunitu, tuntu
helically (adv), tunirtiu, tunitiu, tuntiu
helicopter (n), tunoflerbe, tunefeleba, tunfleb
Helium (n davoka), Apip, Apip, Apip
Helium (n), Helium, Heliuma, Helium
helix (n), tunirt, tunita, tunt
hell (n), lairzhe, laizha, laizh
hellfire (n), laizheshriauk, laizhegiaula, laizhgiaul
hellish (adj), lairzhu, laizhu, laizhu
hello (interj), aluka, alori, alor
helm (n d:helmet), punirp, punipa, punp
helm (n d:tiller), bilbat, bibata, bibat
helm (v d:tiller), bilbast, bibato, bibato
helmet (n), punirp, punipa, punp
help (n), gailak, gaila, gail
help (v), gailask, gailo, gailo
helper (n doer), gailakwan, gailua, gailua
helpful (adj), gailaku, gailu, gailu
helpless (adj), gairbu, gaibu, gaibu
helplessly (adv), gairbiu, gaibiu, gaibiu
helplessness (n), gairbe, gaiba, gaib
hem (n), tiaizhge, tiaiga, tiaig
hem (v), tiaizhzge, tiaigo, tiaigo
hemline (n), tiaigroifk, tiaigeroifa, tiaigroif
hen (n), warth, watha, wath
hence (adv), warf, wafipu, wafp
henhouse (n), wathkiarf, wathekiafa, wathkiaf
hept- (num 7 pref), venai-, venai-, venai-
her (pron 3rd fem sng obj), shan, shan, shan
her (pron 3rd fem sng pos sub), shash, shash, shash
herb (n), lursh, lurifa, lurf
herbal (adj), lurshu, lurifu, lurfu
herbally (adv), lurshiu, lurifiu, lurfiu
herd (n), gruzhe, geruda, grud
herd (v), gruze, gerudo, grudo
herder (n doer), gruzhwan, gerudua, grudua
here (adj/adv/interj), kir, kiru, kir
here (n), kir, kira, kir
hereafter (n), kirovil, kirovila, kirovil
hereditary (adj), lailartu, lailotu, lailtu
heredity (n), lailart, lailota, lailt
heresy (n), koliarve, koliava, koliav
heretic (n doer), koliarvwan, koliavua, koliavua
heretical (adj), koliarvu, koliavu, koliavu
heritage (n), lailatarp, lailotapa, lailtap
hermit (n), blushienk, belushiena, blushien
hero (n doer), sharladwan, sharolitua, sharltua

heroic (adj), sharladu, sharolitu, sharltu
heroic (n), sharlade, sharolita, sharlt
heroically (adv), sharladiu, sharolitiu, sharltiu
heroin (n), kiliark, kiliaka, kiliak
heroine (n doer), sharladwan, sharolitua, sharltua
heroism (n), sharlade, sharolita, sharlt
hers (pron 3rd fem sng pos obj), shash, shash, shash
herself (pron 3rd fem sing refl), shashfal, shashfal, shashfal
hesitant (adj), govaitu, gofitu, goftu
hesitantly (adv), govaitiu, gofitiu, goftiu
hesitate (v), govaist, gofito, gofto
hesitation (n), govait, gofita, goft
hetergeneous (adj), nufobeirtu, nufobietu, nufobietu
hex- (num 6 pref), kinai-, kinai-, kinai-
hey (interj), moia, moi, moi
hi (interj), mio, mi, mi
hibernate (v), dairzbe, daibo, daibo
hibernation (n), dairbe, daiba, daib
hiccup (n), gagarlth, gagalitha, gagalth
hiccup (v), gagarlsth, gagalitho, gagaltho
hid (v pa d:obscure), zhiorskyot, zhiokio, zhiokio
hide (n d:skin), tierk, tieka, tiek
hide (v d:obscure), zhiorsk, zhiorsk, zhioko
hideaway (n), tiekopiorl, tiekopiola, tiekopiol
hideout (n), tierkuil, tiekuila, tiekuil
hienta-, irishkai-, irishkai-, irishkai-
hierarchical (adj), koirutarlu, koiteralitu, koitraltu
hierarchy (n), koirutarl, koiteralita, koitralt
high (adj), koilfu, koilu, koilu
higher (adj), koilfwelu, koilwelu, koilwelu
highest (adj), koilfweaku, koilwaku, koilwaku
highlight (n), koilfluarn, koilefeluana, koilfluan
highlight (v), koilfluarsne, koilefeluano, koilfluano
highlighter (n doer), koilfluarnwan, koilefeluanua, koilfluanua
highly (adv), koilfiu, koiliu, koiliu
highway (n), koilpliorl, koilepeliola, koilpliol
hijack (v), koigavurzge, koigavugo, koigavgo
hijacker (n doer), koigavurgwan, koigavugua, koigavgua
hike (n), wiarsh, wiasha, wiash
hike (v), wiars, wiasho, wiasho
hiker (n doer), wiarshwan, wiashua, wiashua
hill (n), shiop, parina, parn
hillside (n), shiopshoirt, parineshoita, parnshoit
hilltop (n), shiopedaurp, parinedaupa, parndaup
hilly (adj), shiopu, parinu, parnu
him (pron 3rd masc sng obj), hein, hein, hein
himself (pron 3rd masc sng refl), heishfal, heishfal, heishfal
hind (n), tiarge, tiaga, tiag
hinder (v), tiargast, tiagato, tiagato
hindrance (n), tiargat, tiagata, tiagat
hindsight (n), tiagthulth, tiagethutha, tiagthuth
Hindu (n), Kidurn, Kiduna, Kidun
Hinduism (n), Kidurnuet, Kidunueta, Kidunuet
hinge (n), tarfp, tarofa, tarf
hinge (v), tarfsp, tarofo, tarfo
hint (n), plunirt, pelunita, plunt
hint (v), plunirst, pelunito, plunto

hip (n), prifk, perifa, prif
hire (n), tiorge, tioga, tiog
hire (v), tiorzge, tiogo, tiogo
hirer (n doer), tiorgwan, tiogua, tiogua
his (pron 3rd masc sng pos obj), heish, heish, heish
his (pron 3rd masc sng pos sub), heish, heish, heish
Hispanic (n), Kishpanirk, Kishopanika, Kishpanik
hiss (n), guishk, guisha, guish
hiss (v), guishsk, guisho, guisho
hisser (n doer), guishkwan, guishua, guishua
hissy (adj), guishku, guishu, guishu
historian (n doer), shathorwan, sharithua, sharthua
historic (adj), shathoru, sharithu, sharthu
historical (adj), shathoru, sharithu, sharthu
historically (adv), shathoriu, sharithiu, sharthiu
history (n), shathor, sharitha, sharth
hit (n), frithk, feritha, frith
hit (v pa), frithskyot, ferithio, frithio
hit (v), frithsk, feritho, fritho
hitch (n), frink, ferinifa, frinf
hitch (v), frinsk, ferinifo, frinfo
hitcher (n doer), frinkwan, ferinifua, frinfua
hitchhike (v), frinkwiars, ferinifwiasho, frinfwiasho
hitchhiker (n doer), frinkwiarshwan, ferinifwiashua, frinfwiashua
hitter (n doer), frithkwan, ferithua, frithua
hive (n d:colony), triump, teriuma, trium
hives (n d:skin eruption), pogaift, pogaifa, pogaif
hmm (interj), ur, ul, um
hoard (n), tiauf, tiaupa, tiaup
hoard (v), tiausf, tiaupo, tiaupo
hoax (n), kopage, kopaka, kopak
hob (n), thiarde, thiada, thiad
hobble (v), thiadanst, thiadano, thaidano
hobby (n), kebert, kebeta, kebet
hobbyist (n doer), kebertwan, kebetua, kebetua
hobnob (v), thiadoithsk, thiadoitho, thiadoitho
hocus-pocus (n), kopalork, kopaloka, kopalok
hog (n), gnark, guaka, guak
hog (v), guarsk, guako, guako
hogwash (n), guakfiaushk, guakefiausha, guakfiaush
hoist (n), guarbe, guaba, guab
hoist (v), guarzbe, guabo, guabo
hold (n), thorthk, thoritha, thorth
hold (v), thorthsk, thoritho, thortho
holder (n doer), thorthkwan, thorithua, thorthua
holdover (n), thorthkafen, thorithafena, thorthafen
holdup (n), thorthiveil, thorithiviela, thorthiveil
hole (n), korth, kotha, koth
hole (v), korsth, kotho, kotho
holiday (n), moviurl, moviula, moviul
holiness (n), dimul, dilana, diln
hollow (adj), murofu, murovu, murvu
hollow (v), murosf, murovo, murvo
hollowness (n), murof, murova, murv
holly (n), kalnen, kalina, kaln
Holmium (n davoka), Orot, Orot, Orot
Holmium (n), Holmium, Holamiuma, Holmium
Holocaust (n), Konokautsh, Konokausha, Konokaush
hologram (n), mavinelirk, mavinelika, mavinelk
holographic (adj), mavinelirku, mavineliku,

mavinelku
holy (adj), dimulu, dilanu, dilnu
home (n), wienf, wiena, wien
home (v), wiensf, wieno, wieno
homebuilder (n doer), wienvoratwan, wienevoritua, wienvortua
homecoming (n), wienlenar, wienelerina, wienlern
homeland (n), wienraufp, wieneraupa, wienraup
homeless (adj), wienmernu, wienemenu, wienmenu
homelessly (adv), wienmerniu, wienemeniu, wienmeniu
homelessness (n), wienmern, wienemena, wienmen
homemade (adj), wienegiortu, wienegiotu, wienegiotu
homemade (v pa), wienarzgyot, wienagio, wienagio
homemake (v), wienarzge, wienago, wienago
homemaker (n doer), wienargwan, wienagua, wienagua
homeown (v), wientheifst, wienetheifo, wientheifo
homeowner (n doer), wientheiftwan, wienetheifua, wientheifua
homesick (adj), wienegliurpu, wienegeliupu, wienegliupu
hometown (n), wienmiurn, wienemiuna, wienmiun
homework (n), wienkiok, wienika, wienk
homey (adj), wienfu, wienu, wienu
homicidal (adj), nilkoirku, nilekoiku, nilkoiku
homicide (n), nilkoirk, nilekoika, nilkoik
homosexual (adj), nilbivagu, nilebivogu, nilbivgu
homosexual (n doer), nilbivagwan, nilebivogua, nilbivgua
homosexuality (n), nilbivage, nilebivoga, nilbivg
Honduras (n), Konduralsh, Konadurasha, Kondurash
hone (v), wiursf, wiufo, wiufo
honest (adj), porshtu, poshatu, poshtu
honestly (adv), porshtiu, poshatiu, poshtiu
honesty (n), porsht, poshata, posht
honey (n), morfar, morifa, morf
honeybee (n), morfzhishk, morifezhisha, morfzhish
honeycomb (n), morfrakarde, moriterakada, morfrakad
honeymoon (n), morfmuan, moremuana, mormuan
honeymooner (n doer), morfmuanwan, moremuanua, mormuanua
Hong Kong (n), Honurge Konurge, Honuga Konuga, Honug Konug
honk (n), blauk, belaufa, blauf
honk (v), blausk, belaufo, blaufo
honker (n doer), blaukwan, belaufua, blaufua
honor (n), kolirf, kolifa, kolf
honor (v), kolirsf, kolifo, kolfo
honorable (adj), kolirfu, kolifu, kolfu
honorary (adj), kolirfu, kolifu, kolfu
hood (n), tharp, thapa, thap
hood (v), tharsp, thapo, thapo
hoof (n), yarth, yatha, yath
hoof (v), yarsth, yatho, yatho
hoofer (n doer), yarthwan, yathua, yathua
hook (n), shiort, shiora, shior
hook (v), shiorst, shioro, shioro
hooker (n doer), shiortwan, shiorua, shiorua
hookup (n), shiortiveil, shioriveila, shioriveil

hoop (n), shiorbe, shioba, shiob
hooray (interj), kelaia, kelai, kelai
hop (n), wilf, wifa, wif
hop (v), wilsf, wifo, wifo
hope (n), preifp, pereifa, preif
hope (v), preifsp, pereifo, preifo
hopeful (adj), preifpu, pereifu, preifu
hopefullness (n), preifp, pereifa, preif
hopefully (adv), preifpiu, pereifiu, preifiu
hopeless (adj), preifpenu, pereifenu, preifenu
hopelessly (adv), preifpeniu, pereifeniu, preifeniu
hopelessness (n), preifpen, pereifena, preifen
hopper (n doer), wilfwan, wifua, wifua
horizon (n), nalirme, nalima, nalm
horizontal (adj), nalirmu, nalimu, nalmu
horizontally (adv), nalirmiu, nalimiu, nalmiu
hormone (n), dirban, diruba, dirb
horn (n), kroip, keroima, kroim
horn (v), kroisp, keroimo, kroimo
horny (adj), kroipu, keroimu, kroimu
horoscope (n), kiluaf, kelaufa, klauf
horrendous (adj), kaugaiftu, kaugaifu, kaugaifu
horrible (adj), kauaishtu, kauaitu, kauaitu
horribly (adv), kauaishtiu, kauaitiu, kauaitiu
horrid (adj), kaudairku, kaudaiku, kaudaiku
horrific (adj), kauaishtu, kauaitu, kauaitu
horrify (v), kauaishst, kauaito, kauaito
horror (n), kauaisht, kauaita, kauait
horse (n), glaushk, gelausha, glaush
horse (v), glaushsk, gelausho, glausho
horseback (n), glaushvark, gelaushevaka, glaushvak
horsehead (n), glaushkeft, gelaushekefa, glaushkef
horseman (n), glaushplorn, gelaushepelona, glaushplon
horsemen (n pl), glaushplornyek, gelaushepeloni, glaushploni
horsepower (n), glaushbiorat, gelaushebiorita, glaushbiort
horseshoe (n), glaushtafarn, gelaushetafana, glaushtafan
horsetail (n), glaushmithk, gelaushemitha, glaushmith
hose (n), dhursh, dhusha, dhush
hose (v), dhurs, dhusho, dhusho
hoser (n doer), dhurshwan, dhushua, dhushua
hosiery (n), dhurshuet, dhushueta, dhushuet
hospitable (adj), thriarthu, theriathu, thriathu
hospitably (adv), thriarthiu, theriathiu, thriathiu
hospital (n), thriark, theriaka, thriak
hospitality (n), thriarth, theriatha, thriath
hospitalize (v), thriarsk, theriako, thriako
host (n), geshude, geshota, gesht
host (v), geshuzde, geshoto, geshto
hostage (n), kairge, kaiga, kaig
hostess (n), geshudar, geshotara, geshtar
hostile (adj), yaigaftu, yaigatu, yaigatu
hostility (n), yaigaft, yaigata, yaigat
hot (adj), kaurshu, kaushu, kaushu
hotbed (n), kaushfamor, kaushefuarema, kaushfuarm
hotcake (n), kaushgutraf, kaushegurita, kaushgurt
hotdog (n), kaufuarp, kaufuapa, kaufuap
hotdog (v), kaufuarsp, kaufuapo, kaufuapo

hotel (n), keidarn, keidana, keidan
hothead (n), kaushkeft, kaushekefa, kaushkef
hotline (n), kaushroifk, kausheroifa, kaushroif
hotly (adv), kaurshiu, kaushiu, kaushiu
hots (n pl), kaurshyek, kaushi, kaushi
hotshot (n), kaushkoift, kaushekoita, kaushkoit
hound (n), gaurk, gauka, gauk
hound (v), gaursk, gauko, gauko
hour (n), riarn, riana, rian
hourglass (n), riandrilf, rianilofa, rianilf
hourly (adj), riarnu, rianu, rianu
house (n), kiarf, kiafa, kiaf
house (v), kiarsf, kiafo, kiafo
houseboat (n), kiafeshkorbe, kiafeshekoba, kiafshkob
houseclean (v), kiafsherzme, kiafeshemo, kiafshemo
household (n), kiarfan, kianofa, kianf
housekeep (v), kiafklorsf, kiafekelofo, kiafklofo
housekeeper (n doer), kiafklorfwan, kiafekelofua, kiafklofua
housekept (v pa), kiafklorsfyot, kiafekelofio, kiafklofio
housewife (n), kiarsharf, kiasharofa, kiasharf
housework (n), kiafkiork, kiafekioka, kiafkiok
Houston (n), Kushtorn, Kushatona, Kushton
hovel (n), kiafuarn, kiafuana, kiafuan
hover (v), kieishst, kieito, kieito
hovercraft (n), kieitkafirp, kieitekafipa, kieitkafp
how (adv/conj), hial, hialu, hia
how (n), hial, hiala, hia
however (adv/conj), hiafel, hiafelu, hiafel
howl (n), kiaurp, kiaupa, kiaup
howl (v), kiaursp, kiaupo, kiaupo
howler (n doer), kiaurpwan, kiaupua, kiaupua
Hs (let pl), harfi, harfi, harfi
hub (n), thiurde, thiuda, thiud
hubcap (n), thiudefiveil, thiudefipa, thiudefp
huddle (n), zhiorp, zhiopa, zhiop
huddle (v), zhiorsp, zhiopo, zhiopo
hue (n), prilf, porila, pril
huff (n), koshk, kosha, kosh
huff (v), koshsk, kosho, kosho
hug (n), thrauzhge, therauga, thraug
hug (v), thrauzhge, theraugo, thraugo
huge (adj), thragu, theraku, thraku
hugely (adv), thragiu, therakiu, thrakiu
hugger (n doer), thrauzhgwan, theraugua, thraugua
huh (interj), mual, mua, mua
hull (n), rlump, riuma, rium
hum (n), lume, luma, lum
hum (v), luzme, lumo, lumo
human (adj), shorlu, sholu, sholu
human (n), shorl, shola, shol
humane (adj), sholarfu, sholaru, sholaru
humanely (adv), sholarfiu, sholariu, sholariu
humanism (n), sholarfuet, sholarueta, sholaruet
humanist (n doer), sholarfuetwan, sholaruetua, sholaruetua
humanistic (adj), sholarfuetu, sholaruetu, sholaruetu
humanistically (adv), sholarfuetiu, sholaruetiu, sholaruetiu

humanitarian (n doer), sholarfwan, sholarua, sholarua
humanity (n), sholarf, sholara, sholar
humanize (v), sholarfuest, sholarueto, sholarueto
humankind (n), sholarfirf, sholarefifa, sholarfif
humanly (adv), shorliu, sholiu, sholiu
humble (adj), felnarpu, felonapu, felnapu
humble (v), felnarsp, felonapo, felnapo
humbly (adv), felnarpiu, felonapiu, felnapiu
humid (adj), kiormu, kiomu, kiomu
humidify (v), kiorzme, kiomo, kiomo
humidity (n), kiorme, kioma, kiom
humiliate (v), felnarst, felinato, felnato
humiliation (n), felnartuet, felinatueta, felnatuet
humility (n), felnart, felinata, felnat
humor (n), felirme, felima, felm
humor (v), felirzme, felimo, felmo
humorist (n doer), felirmwan, felimua, felmua
humorous (adj), felirmu, felimu, felmu
humorously (adv), felirmiu, felimiu, felmiu
hump (n), plamirp, pelamipa, plamp
hump (v), plamirsp, pelamipo, plampo
humpback (adj), plampevarku, pelamipevaku, plampevaku
humpback (n), plampevark, pelamipevaka, plampevak
hunch (n), tormp, torama, torm
hunch (v), tormesp, toramo, tormo
huncher (n doer), tormpwan, toramua, tormua
hundred (num 100 card), tash, tash, tash
hundredth (num 100 ord), tasheth, tasheth, tasheth
hung (v pa), tarazgyot, tarugio, targio
Hungarian (n), Kunkariarn, Kunikariana, Kunkarian
Hungary (n), Kunkarft, Kunikarofa, Kunkarf
hunger (n), kornage, korinoka, kornk
hunger (v), kornazge, korinoko, kornko
hungrily (adv), kornagiu, korinokiu, kornkiu
hungry (adj), kornagu, korinoku, kornku
hunk (n), ruanshk, ruanika, ruank
hunker (n doer), ruanshkwan, ruanikua, ruankua
hunker (v), ruanshsk, ruaniko, ruanko
hunt (n), grulat, gerulita, grult
hunt (v), grulast, gerulito, grulto
hunter (n doer), grulatwan, gerulitua, grultua
hurdle (n), dialp, dialisha, dialsh
hurdle (v), dialsp, dialisho, dialsho
hurl (n), diatralf, diaterafa, diatraf
hurl (v), diatralsf, diaterafo, diatrafo
hurrah (interj), kelaia, kelai, kelai
hurray (interj), kelaia, kelai, kelai
hurricane (n), kivugaf, kivuiuna, kivugif
hurry (n), kivurk, kivuka, kivuk
hurry (v), kivursk, kivuko, kivuko
hurt (n), boelirk, boelika, boelk
hurt (v pa), boelirskyot, boelikio, boelkio
hurt (v), boelirsk, boeliko, boelko
hurtful (adj), boelirku, boeliku, boelku
hurtfully (adv), boelirkiu, boelikiu, boelkiu
husband (n), trolit, terolita, trolt
husbandry (n), trovart, terovata, trovat
hush (n), kirsht, kisheta, kisht
hush (v), kirshst, kisheto, kishto

hut (n), meshkat, meshika, meshk
hybrid (n), koifleirde, koifeleida, koifleid
hydralic (adj), apafirpu, apafipu, apafpu
hydrate (v), apafirsp, apafipo, apafpo
hydrater (n doer), apafirpwan, apafipua, apafpua
hydration (n), apafirp, apafipa, apafp
hydrocarbon (n), apafpekirp, apafipekip, apafpekip
Hydrogen (n davoka), Apap, Apap, Apap
Hydrogen (n), Hidrogen, Hiderogena, Hidrogen
hype (n), koirsh, koisha, koish
hype (v), koirs, koisho, koisho
hyper (adj), koirshu, koishu, koishu
hyperactive (adj), koishpatilu, koishepalitu, koishpaltu
hyperactively (adv), koishpatiliu, koishepalitiu, koishpaltiu
hyperactivity (n), koishpatil, koishepalita, koishpalt
hyperinflation (n), koisharblarf, koishibelarifa, koishiblarf
hypersensitive (adj), koishorfipu, koishorifopu, koishorfpu
hypersensitivity (n), koishorfip, koishorifopa, koishorfp
hyphen (n), keitirn, keitina, keitin
hyphenate (v), keitirsne, keitino, keitino
hypnosis (n), heishmit, heishama, heisham
hypnotize (v), heishmist, heishamo, heishamo
hypocracy (n), heidufirt, heidufita, heiduft
hypocrite (n doer), heidufirtwan, heidufitua, heiduftua
hypocritical (adj), heidufirtu, heidufitu, heiduftu
hypocritically (adv), heidufirtiu, heidufitiu, heiduftiu
I (let sng), ilfe, ilofa, ilf
I (pron 1st sng sub), nia, nia, nia
ice (n), shkairt, shekaita, shkait
ice (v), shkairst, shekaito, shkaito
iceberg (n), shkaitniurk, shekaiteniuka, shkaitniuk
icebox (n), shkaitprekun, shekaiteperenika, shkaitprenk
icebreaker (n doer), shkaiteblerkwan, shekaitepelikua, shkaitplikua
iceman (n), shkaitplorn, shekaitepelona, shkaitplon
icemen (n pl), shkaitplornyek, shekaitepeloni, shkaitploni
icicle (n), shkaitairt, shekaitaita, shkaitait
icily (adv), shkairtiu, shekaitiu, shkaitiu
ickiness (n), thikirth, thikitha, thikith
icky (adj), thikirthu, thikithu, thikithu
icon (n), shuiat, shuiana, shuian
iconify (v), shuiast, shuiano, shuiano
icy (adj), shkairtu, shekaitu, shkaitu
Idaho (n), Idakorf, Idakofa, Idakof
idea (n), liert, lieta, liet
ideal (adj), liertu, lietu, lietu
idealize (v), lierst, lieto, lieto
ideally (adv), liertiu, lietiu, lietiu
identical (adj), ufertu, uferithu, uferthu
identically (adv), ufertiu, uferithiu, uferthiu
identification (n), ufertar, uferithara, uferthar
identifier (n doer), ufertwan, uferithua, uferthua
identify (v), uferst, uferitho, ufertho
identity (n), ufert, uferitha, uferth

idiocy (n), doilarme, doilama, doilam
idiom (n), dolarme, dolama, dolam
idiomate (v), dolarzme, dolamo, dolamo
idiomatic (adj), dolarmu, dolamu, dolamu
idiot (n doer), doilarmwan, doilamua, doilamua
idiotic (adj), doilarmu, doilamu, doilamu
idiotically (adv), doilarmiu, doilamiu, doilamiu
idle (adj), fuirtu, fuitu, fuitu
idle (v), fuirst, fuito, fuito
idleness (n), fuirt, fuita, fuit
idol (n), doirf, doifa, doif
idolize (v), doirsf, doifo, doifo
if (conj), ule, ulu, uli
igloo (n), shkaidarn, shekaidana, shkaidan
ignite (v), gankersk, ganikeko, gankeko
igniter (n doer), gankerkwan, ganikekua, gankekua
ignition (n), gankerk, ganikeka, gankek
ignorance (n), ganlarf, ganolafa, ganlaf
ignorant (adj), ganlarfu, ganolafu, ganlafu
ignore (v), ganlarsf, ganolafo, ganlafo
ill (adj), lagarlu, lagalu, lagalu
ill (n), lagarl, lagala, lagal
illegal (adj), lanutarku, lanutaku, lanutaku
illegality (n), lanutark, lanutaka, lanutak
illegally (adv), lanutarkiu, lanutakiu, lanutakiu
illegible (adj), lashtarfku, lashetafiku, lashtafku
illegitimacy (n), lanutarfk, lanutafika, lanutafk
illegitimate (adj), lanutarfku, lanutafiku, lanutafku
illicit (adj), garshuftu, garoshutu, garshutu
illicitly (adv), garshuftiu, garoshutiu, garshutiu
Illinois (n), Ilanoirf, Ilanoifa, Ilanoif
illiteracy (n), lalivartor, lalivatora, lalivator
illiterate (adj), lalivartoru, lalivatoru, lalivatoru
illness (n), lagarl, lagala, lagal
illogic (n), galkrenk, lakirenoka, lakrenk
illogical (adj), galkrenku, lakirenoku, lakrenku
illuminate (v), fluathsk, feluatho, fluatho
illumination (n), fluathk, feluatha, fluath
illuminator (n doer), fluathkwan, feluathua,
    fluathua
illusion (n), largrush, lagarusha, lagrush
illustrate (v), luaparst, luapato, luapato
illustration (n), luapart, luapata, luapat
illustrative (adj), luapartu, luapatu, luapatu
illustratively (adv), luapartiu, luapatiu, luapatiu
illustrator (n doer), luapartwan, luapatua, luapatua
image (n), kinorf, kinofa, kinf
image (v), kinorsf, kinofo, kinfo
imagery (n), kinorfuet, kinofueta, kinfuet
imaginable (adj), kinalfrelpu, kinaleferepu,
    kinalfrepu
imaginably (adv), kinalfrelpiu, kinaleferepiu,
    kinalfrepiu
imaginary (adj), kinarlu, kinalu, kinalu
imagination (n), kinarl, kinala, kinal
imaginative (adj), kinarlpu, kinalopu, kinalpu
imagine (v), kinarsle, kinalo, kinalo
imbalance (n), kimorshtat, kishemotata, kishmotat
imbalance (v), kimorshtast, kishemotato,
    kishmotato
imitate (v), kindarst, kinodato, kindato
imitation (n), kindart, kinodata, kindat
imitator (n doer), kindartwan, kinodatua, kindatua

immaculate (adj), kimioshku, kimioku, kimioku
immaculately (adv), kimioshkiu, kimiokiu,
    kimiokiu
immature (adj), kishirfu, shirofiku, shirfku
immaturely (adv), kishirfiu, shirofikiu, shirfkiu
immaturity (n), kishirf, shirofika, shirfk
immediacy (n), klaide, laidashika, laidashk
immediate (adj), klaidu, laidashiku, laidashku
immediately (adv), klaidiu, laidashikiu, laidashkiu
immense (adj), frishorku, ferishoku, frishku
immensely (adv), frishorkiu, ferishokiu, frishkiu
immensity (n), frishork, ferishoka, frishk
immerge (v), kilafirsp, kilafipo, kilafpo
immerse (v), kilarfst, kilafito, kilafto
immersion (n), kilarft, kilafita, kilaft
immigrant (n doer), plivarkwan, pelivakua,
    plivakua
immigrate (v), plivarsk, pelivako, plivako
immigration (n), plivark, pelivaka, plivak
imminent (adj), flirshku, felishoku, flishku
imminently (adv), flirshkiu, felishokiu, flishkiu
immobility (n), kidanirt, kidanita, kidant
immobilization (n), kidanirt, kidanita, kidant
immobilize (v), kidanirst, kidanito, kidanto
immobilizer (n doer), kidanirtwan, kidanitua,
    kidantua
immoral (adj), kithiurnu, kithiunu, kithiunu
immorality (n), kithiurn, kithiuna, kithiun
immorally (adv), kithiurniu, kithiuniu, kithiuniu
immortal (adj), kitiorfu, tiorofiku, tiorfku
immortal (n doer), kitiorfwan, tiorofikua, tiorfkua
immortality (n), kitiorf, tiorofika, tiorfk
immortalize (v), kitiorsf, tiorofiko, tiorfko
immune (adj), kulirnu, kulinu, kulnu
immunity (n), kulirn, kulina, kuln
immunization (n), kulirnuet, kulinueta, kulnuet
immunize (v), kulirsne, kulino, kulno
immunological (adj), kulirnkuitu, kulinekuitu,
    kulnkuitu
immunology (n), kulirnkuit, kulinekuita, kulnkuit
immunosuppression (n), kulirvublarsh,
    kulinevubelasha, kulnevublash
immunotherapy (n), kulirpliarshp,
    kulinepeliashipa, kulnepliashp
immutable (adj), kishluarku, kisheluaku, kishluaku
immutably (adv), kishluarkiu, kisheluakiu,
    kishluakiu
impact (n), kigifp, gifaka, gifk
impact (v), kigifsp, gifako, gifko
impacter (n doer), kigifpwan, gifakua, gifkua
impair (v), kiloshafsk, kiloshako, kiloshako
impairment (n), kiloshafk, kiloshaka, kiloshak
impale (v), kithailst, kithailo, kithailo
impaler (n doer), kithailtwan, kithailua, kithailua
impart (v), kifes, feshiko, feshko
impartial (adj), kifeshu, feshiku, feshku
impartiality (n), kifesh, feshika, feshk
impartially (adv), kifeshiu, feshikiu, feshkiu
impassable (adj), kilunirtu, kilunitu, kiluntu
impassably (adv), kilunirtiu, kilunitiu, kiluntiu
impasse (n), kilunirt, kilunita, kilunt
impatience (n), kimorth, morithoka, morthk
impatient (adj), kimorthu, morithoku, morthku

impatiently (adv), kimorthiu, morithokiu, morthkiu
impeach (v), kirmoits, kimoitesho, kimoitsho
impeachable (adj), kirmoitshu, kimoiteshu, kimoitshu
impeachment (n), kirmoitsh, kimoitesha, kimoitsh
impedance (n), kirmoide, kimoida, kimoid
impede (v), kirmoizde, kimoido, kimoido
impediment (n), kirmoiduet, kimoidueta, kimoiduet
impel (v), kiparzde, kipado, kipado
impeller (n doer), kipardwan, kipadua, kipadua
impenetrable (adj), kiblirshku, kibelishoku, kiblishku
imperative (adj), kiduratu, kiduritu, kidurtu
imperative (n), kidurat, kidurita, kidurt
imperceptible (adj), kiloshirpu, kiloshipu, kiloshipu
imperceptibly (adv), kiloshirpiu, kiloshipiu, kiloshipiu
imperception (n), kiloshirp, kiloshipa, kiloship
imperfect (adj), kilovirftu, kilovirotu, kilovirtu
imperfection (n), kilovirft, kilovirota, kilovirt
imperfectly (adv), kilovirftiu, kilovirotiu, kilovirtiu
imperial (adj), andaufuetu, daufikuetu, daufkuetu
imperialism (n), andaufuet, daufikueta, daufkuet
imperialist (n doer), andaufuetwan, daufikuetua, daufkuetua
imperil (v), kizhumirsp, kizhumipo, kizhumpo
impersonal (adj), kiplornu, kipelonu, kiplonu
impersonally (adv), kiplorniu, kipeloniu, kiploniu
impersonate (v), kiplornuest, kipelonueto, kiplonueto
impersonation (n), kiplornuet, kipelonueta, kiplonuet
impersonator (n doer), kiplornuetwan, kipelonuetua, kiplonuetua
impervious (adj), kipeithku, kipeithu, kipeithu
implant (n), kibrelp, kiberepa, kibrep
implant (v), kibrelsp, kiberepo, kibrepo
implantation (n), kibrelpuet, kiberepueta, kibrepuet
implausible (adj), kishalirku, kishaliku, kishalku
implausibly (adv), kishalirkiu, kishalikiu, kishalkiu
implement (n), kibrek, berekika, brekik
implement (v), kibresk, berekiko, brekiko
implementation (n), kibrekuet, berekikueta, brekikuet
implicate (v), kibrelshuest, kibereshueto, kibreshueto
implication (n), kibrelshuet, kibereshueta, kibreshuet
implicator (n doer), kibrelshuetwan, kibereshuetua, kibreshuetua
implicit (adj), kibrelshu, kibereshu, kibreshu
implicitly (adv), kibrelshiu, kibereshiu, kibreshiu
implode (v), kiaugalist, kiaugo, kiaugo
imploder (n doer), kiaugalitwan, kiaugua, kiaugua
implore (v), breshirsp, bereshipo, breshpo
implosion (n), kiaugalit, kiauga, kiaug
implosive (adj), kiaugalitu, kiaugu, kiaugu
implosively (adv), kiaugalitiu, kiaugiu, kiaugiu
imply (v), kibrels, kiberesho, kibresho
impolite (adj), kidoreinu, doreinaku, doreinku
import (n), kibielirk, kibielika, kibielk

import (v), kibielirsk, kibieliko, kibielko
importance (n), kiviurge, kiviuga, kiviug
important (adj), kiviurgu, kiviugu, kiviugu
importantly (adv), kiviurgiu, kiviugiu, kiviugiu
importation (n), kibielirkuet, kibielikueta, kibielkuet
importer (n doer), kibielirkwan, kibielikua, kibielkua
impose (v), kiglarsk, kigelako, kiglako
imposition (n), kiglark, kigelaka, kiglak
impossibility (n), tishlorf, shelorifa, shlorf
impossible (adj), tishlorfu, shelorifu, shlorfu
impossibly (adv), tishlorfiu, shelorifiu, shlorfiu
imposter (n doer), kiglarkwan, kigelakua, kiglakua
impotence (n), kiboirge, kiboiga, kiboig
impotent (adj), kiboirgu, kiboigu, kiboigu
impound (v), kibramisp, kiberamipo, kibrampo
impoundment (n), kibramip, kiberamipa, kibramp
impoverish (v), zhugairst, zhugaito, zhugaito
impractical (adj), kimatirku, kimatiku, kimatiku
impracticality (n), kimatirk, kimatika, kimatik
imprecise (adj), kiruthirshku, kiruthishaku, kiruthishku
imprecisely (adv), kiruthirshkiu, kiruthishakiu, kiruthishkiu
imprecision (n), kiruthirshk, kiruthishaka, kiruthishk
impregnate (v), fenorsk, fenoriko, fnorko
impregnation (n), fenork, fenorika, fnork
impress (v), kiblas, belashiko, blashko
impresser (n doer), kiblashwan, belashikua, blashkua
impression (n), kiblash, belashika, blashk
impressionable (adj), kiblashfrelpu, belashikeferepu, blashkfrepu
impressionist (n doer), kiblashfrelpwan, belashikeferepua, blashkfrepua
impressive (adj), kiblashu, belashiku, blashku
impressively (adv), kiblashiu, belashikiu, blashkiu
imprint (n), kitrulish, kiterulisha, kitrulsh
imprint (v), kitrulis, kiterulisho, kitrulsho
imprison (v), vaufirst, vaufito, vaufto
imprisonment (n), vaufirtuet, vaufitueta, vauftuet
improbability (n), kifiufrelp, kifiuferepa, kifiufrep
improbable (adj), kifiufrelpu, kifiuferepu, kifiufrepu
improbably (adv), kifiufrelpiu, kifiuferepiu, kifiufrepiu
improper (adj), kilikarpu, kilikapu, kilikapu
improperly (adv), kilikarpiu, kilikapiu, kilikapiu
improve (v), flarvask, kifelaruvo, kiflarvo
improvement (n), flarvak, kifelaruva, kiflarv
improvisation (n), plurfk, pelurika, plurk
improvise (v), plurfsk, peluriko, plurko
impulse (n), klorthk, keloritha, klorth
impulsive (adj), klorthku, kelorithu, klorthu
impulsively (adv), klorthkiu, kelorithiu, klorthiu
impure (adj), kibreishku, kibereishu, kibreishu
impurity (n), kibreishk, kibereisha, kibreish
in (prep), ishe, ishu, ishe
inability (n), ifrelp, iferepa, ifrep
inaccessibility (n), iogvert, ioguveta, iogvet
inaccessible (adj), iogvertu, ioguvetu, iogvetu

inaccuracy (n), itufalat, itulifata, itulfat
inaccurate (adj), itufalatu, itulifatu, itulfatu
inaccurately (adv), itufalatiu, itulifatiu, itulfatiu
inaction (n), ipatiluet, ipalitueta, ipaltuet
inactivate (v), ipaltarsk, ipalitako, ipaltako
inactivation (n), ipaltarkuet, ipalitakueta,
    ipaltakuet
inactive (adj), ipaltarku, ipalitaku, ipaltaku
inactivity (n), ipaltark, ipalitaka, ipaltak
inadequacy (n), itedifaide, itefudaida, itefdaid
inadequate (adj), itedifaidu, itefudaidu, itefdaidu
inadequately (adv), itedifaidiu, itefudaidiu,
    itefdaidiu
inadmissible (adj), itenirku, iteniku, itenku
inadmission (n), itenirk, itenika, itenk
inadvertence (n), ilothakor, iotharika, iothark
inadvertent (adj), ilothakoru, iothariku, iotharku
inadvertently (adv), ilothakoriu, iotharikiu,
    iotharkiu
inadvisable (adj), ioboratu, ioboritu, iobortu
inadvisably (adv), ioboratiu, ioboritiu, iobortiu
inanimate (adj), iomudenirku, iomudeniku,
    iomudenku
inapplicable (adj), ithorku, ithoku, ithoku
inappropriate (adj), ioflikirmu, iofelikimu,
    ioflikimu
inappropriately (adv), ioflikirmiu, iofelikimiu,
    ioflikimiu
inattention (n), iopiforkuet, iopifokueta, iopifkuet
inattentive (adj), iopiforkuetu, iopifokuetu,
    iopifkuetu
inattentively (adv), iopiforkuetiu, iopifokuetiu,
    iopifkuetiu
inaudible (adj), iriuku, iraliuku, iraliuku
inaudibly (adv), iriukiu, iraliukiu, iraliukiu
inboard (adj), isheglorifu, ishegelorifu, isheglorfu
inbound (adj), ishedraifpu, ishederaipu, ishedraipu
inbreed (n), ishefleirde, ishefeleida, ishefleid
inbreed (v), ishefleirzde, ishefeleido, ishefleido
incapability (n), ifilfret, ideferepa, idefrep
incapable (adj), ifilfretu, ideferepu, idefrepu
incapacitate (v), idefrusp, idethipo, idethpo
incapacity (n), idefrup, idethipa, idethp
incarnate (v), greihsk, gereiko, greiko
incarnation (n), greishk, gereika, greik
incendiary (adj), ilianfirku, ilianifiku, ilianfku
incendiary (n), ilianfirk, ilianifika, ilianfk
incense (n d:anger), ilianirt, ilianita, iliant
incense (n d:smoke), ilianirf, ilianifa, ilianf
incense (v d:anger), ilianirst, ilianito, ilianto
incentive (n), artoirp, itoipa, itoip
inception (n), ishirp, ishipa, iship
incest (n), arlalk, ilalika, ilalk
incestual (adj), arlalku, ilaliku, ilalku
inch (n), shtert, shateta, shtet
inch (v), shterst, shateto, shteto
incidence (n), shterkuet, shatekueta, shtekuet
incident (n), shterk, shateka, shtek
incidental (adj), shterku, shateku, shteku
incidently (adv), shterkiu, shatekiu, shtekiu
incinerate (v), iliarts, iliatesho, iliatsho
incineration (n), iliartsh, iliatesha, iliatsh
incinerator (n doer), iliartshwan, iliateshua,

iliatshua
incise (v), ithirshsk, ithishako, ithishko
incision (n), ithirshk, ithishaka, ithishk
incisive (adj), ithirshku, ithishaku, ithishku
incisively (adv), ithirshkiu, ithishakiu, ithishkiu
incisor (n doer), ithirshkwan, ithishakua, ithishkua
incitation (n), toishp, toisha, toish
incite (v), toishsp, toisho, toisho
incitement (n), toishp, toisha, toish
inciter (n doer), toishpwan, toishua, toishua
inclement (adj), ifeifiaurnu, ifeifiaunu, ifeifiaunu
inclination (n), arkroifet, kerofikueta, korifkuet
incline (n), arkroif, kerofika, kroifk
incline (v), arkroisf, kerofiko, kroifko
include (v), argrushst, igeruto, igruto
inclusion (n), argrusht, igeruta, igrut
inclusive (adj), argrushtu, igerutu, igrutu
inclusively (adv), argrushtiu, igerutiu, igrutiu
incoherence (n), ilipituarp, ilipituapa, ilipituap
incoherent (adj), ilipituarpu, ilipituapu, ilipituapu
incoherently (adv), ilipituarpiu, ilipituapiu,
    ilipituapiu
income (n), arlern, ilena, ilen
incomparable (adj), ilenbolku, iberoliku, ibrolku
incomparably (adv), ilenbolkiu, iberolikiu, ibrolkiu
incompatibility (n), ifleinorsh, ifeleinosha, ifleinsh
incompatible (adj), ifleinorshu, ifeleinoshu,
    ifleinshu
incompatibly (adv), ifleinorshiu, ifeleinoshiu,
    ifleinshiu
incompetence (n), ilenvaprol, ivanipora, ivanpor
incompetent (adj), ilenvaprolu, ivaniporu, ivanporu
incompetently (adv), ilenvaproliu, ivaniporiu,
    ivanporiu
incomplete (adj), arbrekalu, ibereliku, ibrelku
incompletely (adv), arbrekaliu, iberelikiu, ibrelkiu
incompleteness (n), arbrekal, iberelika, ibrelk
incomprehensible (adj), ilendruketu, ideruliku,
    idrulku
inconceivable (adj), ibelshipfrelpu, iliushipuferepu,
    iliushpfrepu
inconceivably (adv), ibelshipfrelpiu,
    iliushipuferepiu, iliushpfrepiu
inconclusive (adj), ibelgrutu, iliugerutu, iliugrutu
inconclusively (adv), ibelgrutiu, iliugerutiu,
    iliugrutiu
incongruence (n), ibelklart, iliukilata, iliuklat
incongruent (adj), ibelklartu, iliukilatu, iliuklatu
incongruently (adv), ibelklartiu, iliukilatiu,
    iliuklatiu
incongruous (adj), ibelklartu, iliukilatu, iliuklatu
incongruously (adv), ibelklartiu, iliukilatiu,
    iliuklatiu
incongruousness (n), ibelklart, iliukilata, iliuklat
inconsistency (n), ibeltelk, iliuteloka, iliutelk
inconsistent (adj), ibeltelku, iliuteloku, iliutelku
inconsistently (adv), ibeltelkiu, iliutelokiu, iliutelkiu
inconvenience (n), arfirame, biufiroma, biufirm
inconvenient (adj), arfiramu, biufiromu, biufirmu
inconveniently (adv), arfiramiu, biufiromiu,
    biufirmiu
incorporate (v), pralusp, peralipo, pralpo
incorrect (adj), iprakatu, iperaliku, ipralku

incorrectly (adv), iprakatiu, iperalikiu, ipralkiu
increase (n), ardrik, derilaka, drilk
increase (v), ardrisk, derilako, drilko
increasingly (adv), ardrikiu, derilakiu, drilkiu
incredible (adj), arflershu, kifelenishu, kiflenshu
incredibly (adv), arflershiu, kifelenishiu, kiflenshiu
increment (n), drishork, derishoka, drishk
increment (v), drishorsk, derishoko, drishko
incremental (adj), drishorku, derishoku, drishku
incrementally (adv), drishorkiu, derishokiu,
    drishkiu
incriminate (v), nuanirst, nuanito, nuanto
incrimination (n), nuanirt, nuanita, nuant
incubate (v), idaurzme, idaumo, idaumo
incubation (n), idaurme, idauma, idaum
incubator (n doer), idaurmwan, idaumua, idaumua
incumbent (adj), ildanarpu, iladanapu, ildanapu
incur (v), igalirsf, igalifo, igalfo
incurable (adj), itulirfu, itulifu, itulfu
incurably (adv), itulirfiu, itulifiu, itulfiu
incursion (n), igalirf, igalifa, igalf
indebt (v), kuporzge, kupogo, kupogo
indecency (n), ibulirt, ilishopa, ilishp
indecent (adj), ibulirtu, ilishopu, ilishpu
indecently (adv), ibulirtiu, ilishopiu, ilishpiu
indecision (n), ibuthish, ithishopa, ithishp
indecisive (adj), ibuthishu, ithishopu, ithishpu
indecisively (adv), ibuthishiu, ithishopiu, ithishpiu
indeed (adv/interj), benflide, benifelidu, benflide
indefinite (adj), ibuvuatu, ivuafitu, ivuaftu
indefinitely (adv), ibuvuatiu, ivuafitiu, ivuaftiu
indent (v), shtoirsk, shetoiko, shtoiko
indentation (n), shtoirk, shetoika, shtoik
independence (n), arbubrun, iberunipa, ibrunp
independent (adj), arbubrunu, iberunipu, ibrunpu
independent (n doer), arbubrunwan, iberunipua,
    ibrunpua
independently (adv), arbubruniu, iberunipiu,
    ibrunpiu
indescribable (adj), ibushrigu, isherifoku, ishrifku
indescribably (adv), ibushrigiu, isherifokiu,
    ishrifkiu
indeterminant (n doer), itulirshwan, itulishua,
    itulshua
indeterminate (adj), itulirshu, itulishu, itulshu
indeterminately (adv), itulirshiu, itulishiu, itulshiu
index (n), arshpart, ishepata, ishpat
index (v), arshparst, ishepato, ishpato
indexer (n doer), arshpartwan, ishepatua, ishpatua
India (n), Indiarf, Inodiafa, Indiaf
Indian (n), Indiafarn, Inodiafana, Indiafan
Indiana (n), Indianirk, Inodianika, Indiank
Indianapolis (n), Indiankarpol, Inodianikapola,
    Indiankapol
indicate (v), arkiarsk, ikiako, ikiako
indication (n), arkiark, ikiaka, ikiak
indicative (adj), arkiarku, ikiaku, ikiaku
indicatively (adv), arkiarkiu, ikiakiu, ikiakiu
indicator (n doer), arkiarkwan, ikiakua, ikiakua
indices (n pl), arshpartyek, ishepati, ishpati
indict (v), ideirsk, ideiko, ideiko
indictment (n), ideirk, ideika, ideik
indictor (n doer), ideirkwan, ideikua, ideikua

indifference (n), itove, itova, itov
indifferent (adj), itovu, itovu, itovu
indifferently (adv), itoviu, itoviu, itoviu
indigestion (n), ikikiarge, ikikiaga, ikikiag
indirect (adj), arkuarfku, ikuafiku, ikuafku
indirection (n), arkuarfk, ikuafika, ikuafk
indirectly (adv), arkuarfkiu, ikuafikiu, ikuafkiu
indiscreet (adj), itivirshu, itivishu, itivishu
indiscreetly (adv), itivirshiu, itivishiu, itivishiu
indiscretion (n), itivirsh, itivisha, itivish
indiscriminate (adj), inuanirku, inuaniku, inuanku
indiscriminately (adv), inuanirkiu, inuanikiu,
    inuankiu
indiscrimination (n), inuanirk, inuanika, inuank
indispensable (adj), itibrufu, iberufitu, ibruftu
indisputable (adj), itivoirku, itivoiku, itivoiku
indisputably (adv), itivoirkiu, itivoikiu, itivoikiu
indistinct (adj), itipoitu, ipoiratu, ipoirtu
indistinction (n), itipoit, ipoirata, ipoirt
indistinctly (adv), itipoitiu, ipoiratiu, ipoirtiu
indistinguishable (adj), itipoitu, ipoiratu, ipoirtu
indistinguishably (adv), itipoitiu, ipoiratiu, ipoirtiu
Indium (n davoka), Elap, Elap, Elap
Indium (n), Indium, Inodiuma, Indium
individual (adj), shkirpu, shekipu, shkipu
individual (n doer), shkirp, shekipa, shkip
individualism (n), shkirpuet, shekipueta, shkipuet
individualist (n doer), shkirpuetwan, shekipuetua,
    shkipuetua
individualistic (adj), shkirpuetu, shekipuetu,
    shkipuetu
individuality (n), shkirpuet, shekipueta, shkipuet
individualize (v), shkirsp, shekipo, shkipo
individually (adv), shkirpiu, shekipiu, shkipiu
indivisible (adj), shkirfu, shekifu, shkifu
indoctrinate (v), protasp, peroshato, proshto
Indonesia (n), Indonishiarf, Inudonishiafa,
    Indonishiaf
indoor (adj), ishtelfu, ishetelu, ishtelu
indoors (n), ishtelf, ishetela, ishtel
induce (v), arkarsk, karifoko, kartko
inducement (n), arkark, karifoka, karfk
inducer (n doer), arkarkwan, karifokua, karfkua
induct (v), ikriushsk, ikeriuko, ikriuko
induction (n), ikriushk, ikeriuka, ikriuk
inductive (adj), arkarku, karifoku, karfku
inductively (adv), arkarkiu, karifokiu, karfkiu
inductor (n doer), ikriushkwan, ikeriukua, ikriukua
indulge (v), iloirzge, iloigo, iloigo
indulgence (n), iloirge, iloiga, iloig
indurate (v), kishluarsk, kisheluako, kishluako
induration (n), kishluark, kisheluaka, kishluak
indurator (n doer), kishluarkwan, kisheluakua,
    kishluakua
industrial (adj), benkardu, kadoriku, kadorku
industrialist (n doer), benkardwan, kadorikua,
    kadorkua
industrialization (n), benkarduet, kadorikueta,
    kadorkuet
industrialize (v), benkarzde, kadoriko, kadorko
industrious (adj), benkardu, kadoriku, kadorku
industriously (adv), benkardiu, kadorikiu, kadorkiu
industry (n), benkarde, kadorika, kadork

ineffective (adj), ithuvirtaru, ivirotharu, ivirtharu
ineffectively (adv), ithuvirtariu, ivirothariu,
    ivirthariu
ineffectiveness (n), ithuvirtar, ivirothara, ivirthar
inefficiency (n), ithuvirtar, ivirothara, ivirthar
inefficient (adj), ithuvirtaru, ivirotharu, ivirtharu
inefficiently (adv), ithuvirtariu, ivirothariu,
    ivirthariu
inelastic (adj), isheithku, isheithu, isheithu
ineligible (adj), ienutarku, ienutaku, ienutaku
inept (adj), iofirku, iofiku, iofku
ineptitude (n), iofirk, iofika, iofk
ineptness (n), iofirk, iofika, iofk
inequality (n), idainfk, idainoka, idaink
inequitable (adj), idainfku, idainoku, idainku
inequity (n), idainfk, idainoka, idaink
inert (adj), ikirfu, ikifu, ikifu
inertia (n), ikifirt, ikifita, ikifit
inertial (adj), ikifirtu, ikifitu, ikifitu
inescapable (adj), iushiaku, ivoshiaku, ivoshiaku
inescapably (adv), iushiakiu, ivoshiakiu, ivoshiakiu
inevitability (n), arshort, enishota, ensht
inevitable (adj), arshortu, enishotu, enshtu
inevitably (adv), arshortiu, enishotiu, enshtiu
inexact (adj), iturshtu, itushatu, itushtu
inexcusable (adj), itugoishtu, itugoitu, itugoitu
inexcusably (adv), itugoishtiu, itugoitiu, itugoitiu
inexpensive (adj), itubrunfu, ituberunu, itubrunu
inexpensively (adv), itubrunfiu, ituberuniu,
    itubruniu
inexperience (n), izhurnit, izhurita, izhurt
infallibility (n), izhairt, izhaita, izhait
infallible (adj), izhairtu, izhaitu, izhaitu
infallibly (adv), izhairtiu, izhaitiu, izhaitiu
infamous (adj), ishernu, ishenu, ishenu
infamously (adv), isherniu, isheniu, isheniu
infamy (n), ishern, ishena, ishen
infancy (n), arbar, ibara, ibar
infant (n doer), arbarwan, ibarua, ibarua
infanticide (n), arbarkoirk, ibarekoika, ibarkoik
infatuate (v), inirzve, inivo, inivo
infatuation (n), inirve, iniva, iniv
infeasible (adj), ithoitirku, ithoitiku, ithoitiku
infect (v), arvirst, iviroto, ivirto
infection (n), arvirt, ivirota, ivirt
infectious (adj), arvirtu, ivirotu, ivirtu
infective (adj), arvirtu, ivirotu, ivirtu
infer (v), argesf, igefo, igefo
inference (n), argef, igefa, igef
inferior (adj), ivugarnu, ivuganu, ivuganu
inferiority (n), ivugarn, ivugana, ivugan
infernal (adj), iviershu, ivieraku, ivierku
inferno (n), iviersh, ivieraka, ivierk
infertile (adj), isheiftu, isheifu, isheifu
infertility (n), isheift, isheifa, isheif
infest (v), inafirsk, inafiko, inafko
infestation (n), inafirk, inafika, inafk
infield (n), isheprant, iseperanida, isheprand
infielder (n doer), isheprantwan, iseperanidua,
    isheprandua
infinite (adj), itiurftu, itiufotu, itiuftu
infinitely (adv), itiurftiu, itiufotiu, itiuftiu
infinity (n), itiurft, itiufota, itiuft

inflamation (n), dreinakuet, fiashueta, fiashuet
inflame (v), dreinask, fiasho, fiasho
inflammable (adj), dreinaku, fiashu, fiashu
inflammatory (adj), dreinakuetu, fiashuetu,
    fiashuetu
inflatable (adj), arblarfu, ibelarifu, iblarfu
inflate (v), arblarsf, ibelarifo, iblarfo
inflater (n doer), arblarfwan, ibelarifua, iblarfua
inflation (n), arblarf, ibelarifa, iblarf
inflect (v), igerst, igeto, igeto
inflection (n), igert, igeta, iget
inflective (adj), igertu, igetu, igetu
inflexibility (n), itiert, itieta, itiet
inflexible (adj), itiertu, itietu, itietu
inflict (v), arkisk, ikiko, ikiko
infliction (n), arkik, ikika, ikik
inflight (adj), ifuirfu, ifuifu, ifuifu
inflow (n), ibrauf, iberautha, ibrauth
influence (n), armiart, imarota, imiart
influence (v), armiarst, imaroto, imiarto
influencer (n doer), armiartwan, imarotua,
    imiartua
influential (adj), armiartu, imarotu, imiartu
influentially (adv), armiartiu, imarotiu, imiartiu
influenza (n), niragat, rinagata, rinagat
inform (v), arvorsne, ivorino, ivorno
informal (adj), ivorlinatu, ivorinatu, ivornatu
informally (adv), ivorlinatiu, ivorinatiu, ivornatiu
information (n), arvorn, ivorina, ivorn
informative (adj), arvornu, ivorinu, ivornu
informatively (adv), arvorniu, ivoriniu, ivorniu
informer (n doer), arvornwan, ivorinua, ivornua
infraction (n), idelishork, idelishoka, idelshk
infrared (adj), ifieshtu, ifieshu, ifieshu
infrastructure (n), ishlerk, ishileka, ishlek
infrequent (adj), ifiorfondu, ifiofonudu, ifiofondu
infrequently (adv), ifiorfondiu, ifiofonudiu,
    ifiofondiu
infringe (v), igrishorst, igerishoto, igrishto
infringement (n), igrishort, igerishota, igrisht
infuriate (v), viers, vierako, vierko
infuriator (n doer), viershwan, vierakua, vierkua
infuse (v), ifaborst, ifaboto, ifaboto
infusion (n), ifabort, ifabota, ifabot
ingest (v), ikiarzge, ikiago, ikiago
ingestation (n), ikiarge, ikiaga, ikiag
ingester (n doer), ikiargwan, ikiagua, ikiagua
ingrain (v), darnolsk, vonoliko, vonolko
ingredient (n), ishtranak, ishoteranaka, ishtrank
inhabit (v), reishorst, reishoto, reishto
inhabitant (n doer), reishortwan, reishotua,
    reishtua
inhalant (n), arwafk, iwafoka, iwafk
inhalation (n), arwafkuet, iwafokueta, iwafkuet
inhale (v), arwafsk, iwafoko, iwafko
inhaler (n doer), arwafkwan, iwafokua, iwafkua
inherent (adj), ikirueftu, ikiruetu, ikiruetu
inherently (adv), ikirueftiu, ikiruetiu, ikiruetiu
inherit (v), ilailsf, ilailo, ilailo
inheritance (n), ilailf, ilaila, ilail
inhibit (v), ardaizbe, idaibo, idaibo
inhibition (n), ardaibe, idaiba, idaib
inhibitor (n doer), ardaibwan, idaibua, idaibua

inhibitory (adj), ardaibu, idaibu, idaibu
inhospitable (adj), ithriarthu, itheriathu, ithriathu
initial (adj), artidu, tiludu, tildu
initial (n), artidat, tiludata, tildat
initially (adv), artidiu, tiludiu, tildiu
initiate (v), artizde, tiludo, tildo
initiation (n), artide, tiluda, tild
initiative (n), artidar, tiludara, tildar
initiator (n doer), artidwan, tiludua, tildua
inject (v), itersp, itepo, itepo
injectable (adj), iterpu, itepu, itepu
injection (n), iterp, itepa, itep
injector (n doer), iterpwan, itepua, itepua
injunction (n), ibafirt, ibafita, ibaft
injure (v), arnoisne, inoino, inoino
injurer (n doer), arnoinwan, inoinua, inoinua
injury (n), arnoin, inoina, inoin
injustice (n), ipeshirp, ipeshipa, ipeshp
ink (n), nufirp, nufipa, nufp
ink (v), nufirsp, nufipo, nufpo
inker (n doer), nufirpwan, nufipua, nufpua
inky (adj), nufirpu, nufipu, nufpu
inland (adj), araupu, iraupu, iraupu
inland (n), araup, iraupa, iraup
inline (adj), isheroifku, isheroifu, isheroifu
inmate (n), ishlern, ishelena, ishlen
inn (n), brilf, berila, bril
innard (n), isherk, isheka, ishk
inner (adj), isherku, isheku, ishku
innerly (adv), isherkiu, ishekiu, ishkiu
innkeeper (n doer), brilfwan, berilua, brilua
innocence (n), armikart, imikata, imikat
innocent (adj), armikartu, imikatu, imikatu
innocently (adv), armikartiu, imikatiu, imikatiu
innovate (v), armiasf, imiafo, imiafo
innovation (n), armiaf, imiafa, imiaf
innovative (adj), armiafu, imiafu, imiafu
innovatively (adv), armiafiu, imiafiu, imiafiu
innovator (n doer), armiafwan, imiafua, imiafua
inoffensive (adj), itatorvu, itatorifu, itatorfu
inoffensively (adv), itatorviu, itatoriflu, itatorflu
inoperable (adj), iduriftu, iduritu, idurtu
inoperative (adj), iduriftu, iduritu, idurtu
inopportune (adj), idubielirku, idubieliku, idubielku
inpatient (n), imorth, imolitha, imolth
input (n), arvut, ivuta, ivut
input (v), arvust, ivuto, ivuto
inputer (n doer), arvutwan, ivutua, ivutua
inquest (n), arshiat, ishiata, ishiat
inquire (v), thafirst, thafito, thafto
inquirer (n doer), thafirtwan, thafitua, thaftua
inquiry (n), thafirt, thafita, thaft
inquisition (n), arshiatuet, ishiatueta, ishiatuet
inquisitor (n doer), arshiatwan, ishiatua, ishiatua
inroad (n), itrelish, iterelisha, itrelsh
insane (adj), arshiafu, ishiafu, ishiafu
insanely (adv), arshiafiu, ishiafiu, ishiafiu
insanity (n), arshiaf, ishiafa, ishiaf
inscribe (v), usherzge, usherigo, ushrigo
inscription (n), usherge, usheriga, ushrig
insect (n), arthish, irathisha, irthish
insecure (adj), ivartulfu, ivaritufu, ivartufu

insecurely (adv), ivartulfiu, ivaritufiu, ivartufiu
insecurity (n), ivartulf, ivaritufa, ivartuf
insensitive (adj), ishorfipu, ishorifopu, ishorfpu
insensitivity (n), ishorfip, ishorifopa, ishorfp
inseparable (adj), idilsharfu, idiloshafu, idilshafu
insert (n), arshetuin, ishetuina, ishetuin
insert (v), arshest, isheto, isheto
inserter (n doer), arshetwan, ishetua, ishetua
insertion (n), arshet, isheta, ishet
inside (adj/adv/prep), benshoit, ishoitu, ishoit
inside (n), benshoit, ishoita, ishoit
insider (n doer), benshoitwan, ishoitua, ishoitua
insidious (adj), ishreltiemu, isheretiemu,
  ishretiemu
insidiously (adv), ishreltiemiu, isheretiemiu,
  ishretiemiu
insight (n), ithulth, ithutha, ithuth
insightful (adj), ithulthu, ithuthu, ithuthu
insignificance (n), iweifork, iweifoka, iweifk
insignificant (adj), iweiforku, iweifoku, iweifku
insignificantly (adv), iweiforkiu, iweifokiu, iweifkiu
insincere (adj), ipelmurnu, ipelamunu, ipelmunu
insincerely (adv), ipelmurniu, ipelamuniu,
  ipelmuniu
insincereness (n), ipelmurn, ipelamuna, ipelmun
insinuate (v), itrifirst, iterifito, itrifto
insinuation (n), itrifirt, iterifita, itrift
insist (v), artelsk, iteliko, itelko
insistence (n), artelk, itelika, itelk
insistent (adj), artelku, iteliku, itelku
insistently (adv), artelkiu, itelikiu, itelkiu
insolvency (n), iligralp, iligerapa, iligrap
insolvent (adj), iligralpu, iligerapu, iligrapu
inspect (v), arthusk, ithuko, ithuko
inspection (n), arthuk, ithuka, ithuk
inspector (n doer), arthukwan, ithukua, ithukua
inspiration (n), ardauf, ifudaufa, ifdauf
inspirational (adj), ardaufu, ifudaufu, ifdaufu
inspirationally (adv), ardaufiu, ifudaufiu, ifdaufiu
inspire (v), ardausf, ifudaufo, ifdaufo
instability (n), iftarp, ifitapa, iftap
install (v), arteirsp, iteiro, iteiro
installation (n), arteirp, iteira, iteir
installer (n doer), arteirpwan, iteirua, iteirua
installment (n), arteirp, iteira, iteir
instance (n), artrep, itorepa, itrep
instant (adj), artrepu, itorepu, itrepu
instantaneous (adj), artreptoirtu, itorepetoitu,
  itreptoitu
instantaneously (adv), artreptoirtiu, itorepetoitiu,
  itreptoitiu
instantiate (v), artresp, itorepo, itrepo
instantly (adv), artrepiu, itorepiu, itrepiu
instate (v), arshpest, ishopeto, ishpeto
instead (adv), befnetiu, befenetiu, befnetiu
instigate (v), ishnefst, ishineto, ishneto
instigation (n), ishneft, ishineta, ishnet
instigator (n doer), ishneftwan, ishinetua, ishnetua
instill (v), ishetriarzge, isheteriago, ishetriago
instinct (n), arpoit, ipoita, ipoit
instinctive (adj), arpoitu, ipoitu, ipoitu
instinctively (adv), arpoitiu, ipoitiu, ipoitiu
institute (n), arshpelt, ishopelita, ishpelt

institute (v), arshpelst, ishopelito, ishpelto
institution (n), arshpeltuet, ishopelitueta,
   ishpeltuet
institutional (adj), arshpeltuetu, ishopelituetu,
   ishpeltuetu
institutionalize (v), arshpeltuest, ishopelitueto,
   ishpeltueto
institutionally (adv), arshpeltuetiu, ishopelituetiu,
   ishpeltuetiu
instruct (v), arshlesk, isheleko, ishleko
instruction (n), arshlek, isheleka, ishlek
instructional (adj), arshleku, isheleku, ishleku
instructionally (adv), arshlekiu, ishelekiu, ishlekiu
instructive (adj), arshleku, isheleku, ishleku
instructively (adv), arshlekiu, ishelekiu, ishlekiu
instructor (n doer), arshlekwan, ishelekua, ishlekua
instrument (n), shliart, sheliata, shliat
instrumental (adj), shliartu, sheliatu, shliatu
instrumentation (n), shliartuet, sheliatueta,
   shliatuet
insubordinate (adj), iorishkeialtu, iorishekeiatu,
   iorishkeiatu
insubordinate (v), iorishkeialst, iorishekeiato,
   iorishkeiato
insubordination (n), iorishkeialt, iorishekeiata,
   iorishkeiat
insubstantial (adj), ioritrelpu, ioriterepu, ioritrepu
insubstantially (adv), ioritrelpiu, ioriterepiu,
   ioritrepiu
insufferable (adj), ikauvurtu, ikauvutu, ikauvutu
insufferably (adv), ikauvurtiu, ikauvutiu, ikauvutiu
insufficiency (n), ikaushkelt, ikaushiketa, ikaushket
insufficient (adj), ikaushkeltu, ikaushiketu,
   ikaushketu
insufficiently (adv), ikaushkeltiu, ikaushiketiu,
   ikaushketiu
insula (n), tenirf, tenifa, tenf
insular (adj), tenirfu, tenifu, tenfu
insularity (n), tenirfat, tenifata, tenfat
insularly (adv), tenirfiu, tenifiu, tenfiu
insulate (v), tenirfuest, tenifueto, tenfueto
insulation (n), tenirfuet, tenifueta, tenfuet
insulative (adj), tenirfuetu, tenifuetu, tenfuetu
insulatively (adv), tenirfuetiu, tenifuetiu, tenfuetiu
insulator (n doer), tenirfuetwan, tenifuetua,
   tenfuetua
insult (n), arvant, tivanita, tivant
insult (v), arvanst, tivanito, tivanto
insulter (n doer), arvantwan, tivanitua, tivantua
insurance (n), ishreln, isherela, ishrel
insure (v), ishrelsne, isherelo, ishrelo
insurer (n doer), ishrelnwan, isherelua, ishrelua
insurge (v), ivoirzge, ivoigo, ivoigo
insurgency (n), ivoirge, ivoiga, ivoig
insurgent (adj), ivoirgu, ivoigu, ivoigu
insurgent (n doer), ivoirgwan, ivoigua, ivoigua
insurgently (adv), ivoirgiu, ivoigiu, ivoigiu
insurmountable (adj), ishiniurku, ishiniuku,
   ishiniuku
insurrect (v), ivoikuarst, ivoikuato, ivoikuato
insurrection (n), ivoikuart, ivoikuata, ivoikuat
intact (adj), arpaibu, ipaibu, ipaibu
intake (n), ishegork, ishegoka, ishegok

intangible (adj), ishiarmpu, ishiamipu, ishiampu
integer (n), pliark, peliaka, pliak
integral (adj), pliarshku, peliashiku, pliashku
integrally (adv), pliarshkiu, peliashikiu, pliashkiu
integrate (v), pliarshsk, peliashiko, pliashko
integration (n), pliarshk, peliashika, pliashk
integrator (n doer), pliarshkwan, peliashikua,
   pliashkua
integrity (n), pliarshkar, peliashikara, pliashkar
intellect (n doer), preiftwan, peritua, preitua
intellectual (adj), preiftaru, peritaru, preitaru
intellectual (n doer), preiftarwan, peritarua,
   preitarua
intellectually (adv), preiftariu, peritariu, preitariu
intelligence (n), preift, perita, preit
intelligent (adj), preiftu, peritu, preitu
intelligently (adv), preiftiu, peritiu, preitiu
intelligible (adj), preitfrelpu, periteferepu,
   preitfrepu
intelligibly (adv), preitfrelpiu, periteferepiu,
   preitfrepiu
intend (v), arpifsk, ipifoko, ipifko
intense (adj), arpifpu, ipifapu, ipifpu
intensely (adv), arpifpiu, ipifapiu, ipifpiu
intensify (v), arpifsp, ipifapo, ipifpo
intensity (n), arpifp, ipifapa, ipifp
intensive (adj), arpifpu, ipifapu, ipifpu
intensively (adv), arpifpiu, ipifapiu, ipifpiu
intent (n), arpifk, ipifoka, ipifk
intention (n), arpifk, ipifoka, ipifk
intentional (adj), arpifku, ipifoku, ipifku
intentionally (adv), arpifkiu, ipifokiu, ipifkiu
intently (adv), arpifkiu, ipifokiu, ipifkiu
interact (v), enripalst, aripalito, aripalto
interaction (n), enripalt, aripalita, aripalt
interactive (adj), enripaltu, aripalitu, aripaltu
interactively (adv), enripaltiu, aripalitiu, aripaltiu
interagency (n), enrivetarp, arivetapa, arivetap
intercede (v), enriversk, ariveko, ariveko
intercept (v), enrishirsp, arishipo, arishipo
interception (n), enrishirp, arishipa, ariship
interceptor (n doer), enrishirpwan, arishipua,
   arishipua
intercession (n), enriverk, ariveka, arivek
interchange (n), enrituarn, arituana, arituan
interchangeable (adj), enrituarnu, arituanu,
   arituanu
interchangeably (adv), enrituarniu, arituaniu,
   arituaniu
interconnect (v), enrishnarsf, arishinafo, arishnafo
interconnection (n), enrishnarf, arishinafa, arishnaf
intercourse (n), enrimarnf, arimarina, arimarn
interdependence (n), enribubrun, ariberunipa,
   aribrunp
interdependent (adj), enribubrunu, ariberunipu,
   aribrunpu
interdependently (adv), enribubruniu,
   ariberunipiu, aribrunpiu
interest (n d:desire), telforet, teliforeta, telfret
interest (n d:finance), amolazhe, amelazha, amlazh
interest (v d:desire), telforest, teliforeto, telfreto
interestingly (adv d:desire), telforetiu, teliforetiu,
   telfretiu

interface (n), enrithoirsh, arithoisha, arithoish
interface (v), enrithoirs, arithoisho, arithoisho
interfaith (adj), enrinaltripu, ariperinelitu, ariprineltu
interfere (v), enrigesf, arigefo, arigefo
interference (n), enrigef, arigefa, arigef
interim (adj), enrilairfu, arilaifu, arilaifu
interior (n), enrilar, arilara, arilar
interject (v), enritersp, aritepo, aritepo
interjection (n), enriterp, aritepa, aritep
interlace (v), enrifoirsne, arifoino, arifoino
interleaf (n), enripruth, ariberutha, aribruth
interleave (v), enriprusth, ariberutho, aribrutho
interlink (n), enriroishk, ariroisha, ariroish
interlink (v), enriroishsk, ariroisho, ariroisho
interlock (n), enritiurge, aritiuga, aritiug
interlude (n), enrirusht, arirusha, arirush
intermarriage (n), enrivularn, arivulana, arivuln
intermarry (v), enrivularsne, arivulano, arivulno
intermediacy (n), enrilaidak, arilaidaka, arilaidak
intermediary (n doer), enrilaidakwan, arilaidakua, arilaidakua
intermediate (v), enrilaidask, arilaidako, arilaidako
intermission (n), enrinok, arinoka, arinok
intermit (v), enrinosk, arinoko, arinoko
intermittent (adj), enrinoku, arinoku, arinoku
intermittently (adv), enrinokiu, arinokiu, arinokiu
intermix (v), enrizhorfsk, arizhoriko, arizhorko
internal (adj), arpirpu, ipiropu, ipirpu
internal (n), arpirp, ipiropa, ipirp
internalization (n), arpirpuet, ipiropueta, ipirpuet
internalize (v), arpirsp, ipiropo, ipirpo
internally (adv), arpirpiu, ipiropiu, ipirpiu
international (adj), enrikarlfu, arikarilu, arikarlu
internationally (adv), enrikarlfiu, arikariliu, arikarliu
internet (n), enrimoip, arimoipa, arimoip
interpersonal (adj), enriplornu, aripelonu, ariplonu
interplanetary (adj), enrilaurku, arilauku, arilauku
interplay (n), enrifruifk, ariferuifa, arifruif
interpret (v), enridrusp, ariderupo, aridrupo
interpretation (n), enridrup, ariderupa, aridrup
interpreter (n doer), enridrupwan, ariderupua, aridrupua
interpretive (adj), enridrupu, ariderupu, aridrupu
interracial (adj), enrinoirthu, arinoithu, arinoithu
interrelate (v), enriludarast, ariludarito, ariludarto
interrelation (n), enriludarat, ariludarita, ariludart
interrelationship (n), enriludaratfirf, ariludaritefifa, ariludartfif
interrogate (v), enrilushiarst, arilushiato, arilushiato
interrogation (n), enrilushiart, arilushiata, arilushiat
interrogator (n doer), enrilushiartwan, arilushiatua, arilushiatua
interrupt (v), enrigaifst, arigaifoto, arigaifto
interruptible (adj), enrigaiftu, arigaifotu, arigaiftu
interruption (n), enrigaift, arigaifota, arigaift
intersect (v), enrishasle, arishalo, arishalo
intersection (n), enrishal, arishala, arishal
intersperse (v), enrilotelsf, arilotelo, arilotelo
interspersion (n), enrilotelf, arilotela, arilotel

interstate (adj), enrishaiarshu, arishaiashu, arishaiashu
interstate (n), enrishaiarsh, arishaiasha, arishaiash
interstellar (adj), enridrolmu, arideromu, aridromu
intertwine (v), enrilaivursne, arilaivuno, arilaivuno
interval (n), enridap, aridapa, aridap
intervene (v), enrifizme, arifimo, arifimo
intervention (n), enrifime, arifima, arifim
interview (n), enrifuat, arifuata, arifuat
interview (v), enrifuast, arifuato, arifuato
interviewee (n), enrifuatuin, arifuatuina, arifuatuin
interviewer (n doer), enrifuatwan, arifuatua, arifuatua
interweave (v), enribrivarsk, ariberivako, aribrivako
interwove (v pa), enribrivarskyot, ariberivakio, aribrivakio
intestinal (adj), leinishoirtu, leinishoitu, leinishoitu
intestine (n), leinishoirt, leinishoita, leinishoit
intimacy (n), arlerk, ileka, ilek
intimate (adj), arlerku, ileku, ileku
intimate (v), arlersk, ileko, ileko
intimately (adv), arlerkiu, ilekiu, ilekiu
intimidate (v), arblizme, ibelimo, iblimo
intimidation (n), arblime, ibelima, iblim
intimidator (n doer), arblimwan, ibelimua, iblimua
into (prep), ishte, ishetu, ishtu
intolerable (adj), artrinortu, iterinotu, itrintu
intolerably (adv), artrinortiu, iterinotiu, itrintiu
intolerance (n), artrinort, iterinota, itrint
intonation (n), trilshk, terilosha, trilsh
intoxicant (n doer), arkiabarkwan, ikiabakua, ikiabakua
intoxicate (v), arkiabarsk, ikiabako, ikiabako
intoxication (n), arkiabark, ikiabaka, ikiabak
intravenous (adj), benufleirthu, benufeleithu, benufleithu
intravenously (adv), benufleirthiu, benufeleithiu, benufleithiu
intricacy (n), ardiafk, idiafoka, idiafk
intricate (adj), ardiafku, idiafoku, idiafku
intricately (adv), ardiafkiu, idiafokiu, idiafkiu
intrigue (n), ardiashk, idiashika, idiashk
intrigue (v), ardiashsk, idiashiko, idiashko
intriguingly (adv), ardiashkiu, idiashikiu, idiashkiu
intrinsic (adj), larushku, laruku, laruku
intrinsically (adv), larushkiu, larukiu, larukiu
introduce (v), enokriusk, arokeriuko, arokriuko
introduction (n), enokriuk, arokeriuka, arokriuk
introductory (adj), enokriuku, arokeriuku, arokriuku
introversion (n), enotharak, arotharika, arothark
introvert (n doer), enotharakwan, arotharikua, arotharkua
introvert (v), enotharask, arothariko, arotharko
intrude (v), kaborfst, kabofito, kabofto
intruder (n doer), kaborftwan, kabofitua, kaboftua
intrusion (n), kaborft, kabofita, kaboft
intrusive (adj), kaborftu, kabofitu, kaboftu
intrusively (adv), kaborftiu, kabofitiu, kaboftiu
intrusiveness (n), kaborftuet, kabofitueta, kaboftuet
intuit (v), arbausf, ibaufo, ibaufo
intuition (n), arbauf, ibaufa, ibauf
intuitive (adj), arbaufu, ibaufu, ibaufu

intuitively (adv), arbaufiu, ibaufiu, ibaufiu
inundate (v), arleifarsne, ileifaro, ileifaro
inundation (n), arleifarn, ileifara, ileifar
invade (v), arzhansk, izhaniko, izhanko
invader (n doer), arzhankwan, izhanikua, izhankua
invalid (adj), arkarthpu, ikathipu, ikathpu
invalid (n d:person), kaithelp, kaithepa, kaithp
invalidate (v), arkarthsp, ikathipo, ikathpo
invalidation (n), arkarthp, ikathipa, ikathp
invaluable (adj), arvaurpu, ivaupu, ivaupu
invariably (adj), arthumarpu, ithumapu, ithumapu
invariant (n), arthumarp, ithumapa, ithumap
invasion (n), arzhank, izhanika, izhank
invasive (adj), arzhanku, izhaniku, izhanku
invasively (adv), arzhankiu, izhanikiu, izhankiu
invent (v), guvarst, guvato, guvato
invention (n), guvart, guvata, guvat
inventive (adj), guvartu, guvatu, guvatu
inventively (adv), guvartiu, guvatiu, guvatiu
inventor (n doer), guvartwan, guvatua, guvatua
inventory (n), guvartor, guvatora, guvator
inverse (adj), artharaku, ithariku, itharku
inverse (n), artharak, itharika, ithark
inversely (adv), artharakiu, itharikiu, itharkiu
inversion (n), artharakuet, itharikueta, itharkuet
invert (v), artharask, ithariko, itharko
inverter (n doer), artharakwan, itharikua, itharkua
invest (v), arbist, ibito, ibito
investigate (v), arbitask, ibitako, ibitako
investigation (n), arbitak, ibitaka, ibitak
investigational (adj), arbitaku, ibitaku, ibitaku
investigative (adj), arbitaku, ibitaku, ibitaku
investigator (n doer), arbitakwan, ibitakua, ibitakua
investment (n), arbit, ibita, ibit
investor (n doer), arbitwan, ibitua, ibitua
invigorate (v), arpeikarsne, ipeikano, ipeikano
invigoration (n), arpeikarn, ipeikana, ipeikan
invincibility (n), arfekiark, ifekiaka, ifekiak
invincible (adj), arfekiarku, ifekiaku, ifekiaku
inviolate (adj), ituarilku, ituariku, ituarku
inviolate (v), ituarilsk, ituariko, ituarko
invisibility (n), arfiaish, ifiaisha, ifiaish
invisible (adj), arfiaishu, ifiaishu, ifiaishu
invisibly (adv), arfiaishiu, ifiaishiu, ifiaishiu
invitation (n), brairk, beraika, braik
invitational (adj), brairku, beraiku, braiku
invite (v), brairsk, beraiko, braiko
invitee (n), brairkuin, beraikuina, braikuin
invitor (n doer), brairkwan, beraikua, braikua
invocation (n), arshairk, ishaika, ishaik
invoice (n), arthairp, ithaipa, ithaip
invoice (v), arthairsp, ithaipo, ithaipo
invoke (v), arshairsk, ishaiko, ishaiko
involuntarily (adv), arkemirfiu, ikemifiu, ikemifiu
involuntary (adj), arkemirfu, ikemifu, ikemifu
involve (v), arkemirsf, ikemifo, ikemifo
involvement (n), arkemirf, ikemifa, ikemif
invulnerability (n), arkrakfrelp, ikerakoferepa,
    ikrakfrep
invulnerable (adj), arkrakfrelpu, ikerakoferepu,
    ikrakfrepu
inward (adj), arnaushu, ihaushu, ihaushu
Iodine (n davoka), Elak, Elak, Elak

Iodine (n), Iodin, Iodina, Iodin
ion (n), aiorf, aiofa, aiof
ionic (adj), aiorfu, aiofu, aiofu
ionize (v), aiorsf, aiofo, aiofo
ionizer (n doer), aiorfwan, aiofua, aiofua
iota (n), iotarn, iotana, iotan
Iowa (n), Iowarf, Iowafa, Iowaf
Iran (n), Iranf, Irana, Iran
Iranian (n), Iraniarn, Iraniana, Iranian
Iraq (n), Iralfk, Irafika, Irafk
Iraqi (n), Irafkarn, Irafikana, Irafkan
irascible (adj), tilirku, tiliku, tiliku
irascibly (adv), tilirkiu, tilikiu, tilikiu
irate (adj), tilirku, tiliku, tiliku
ire (n), tilirk, tilika, tilik
Ireland (n), Irelanurde, Irelanuda, Ireland
Iridium (n), Iridium, Iridiuma, Iridium
Irish (n), Irelandarn, Irelanudana, Irelandan
irk (v), tilirsk, tiliko, tiliko
iron (n d:clothes presser), shpreln, shiperena,
    shpren
Iron (n davoka), Ifik, Ifik, Ifik
Iron (n), Iron, Irona, Iron
iron (v d:clothes presser), shprelsne, shipereno,
    shpreno
ironic (adj), liashu, lanuvu, lanvu
ironically (adv), liashiu, lanuviu, lanviu
irony (n), liash, lanuva, lanv
irradiate (v), armoirzve, imoivo, imoivo
irradiation (n), armoirve, imoiva, imoiv
irrational (adj), arthushortu, ithushotu, ithushtu
irrationality (n), arthushort, ithushota, ithusht
irrationally (adv), arthushortiu, ithushotiu,
    ithushtiu
irreconcilable (adj), arlurolarmu, ilurolamu,
    ilurolmu
irreconciliation (n), arlurolarme, ilurolama, ilurolm
irrefutable (adj), arlufabarku, ilufabaku, ilufabaku
irrefutably (adv), arlufabarkiu, ilufabakiu,
    ilufabakiu
irregardless (adj), luvairkmenu, luvaikemenu,
    luvaikmenu
irregular (adj), arluvirpu, iluvipu, iluvipu
irregularity (n), arluvirp, iluvipa, iluvip
irregularly (adv), arluvirpiu, iluvipiu, iluvipiu
irrelevance (n), artruifk, itiruika, itruik
irrelevancy (n), artruifk, itiruika, itruik
irrelevant (adj), artruifku, itiruiku, itruiku
irreparable (adj), arlubolirku, iluboliku, ilubolku
irreparably (adv), arlubolirkiu, ilubolikiu, ilubolkiu
irreplaceable (adj), arlubreshu, ilubereshu,
    ilubreshu
irresistible (adj), arlutelku, iluteliku, ilutelku
irresistibly (adv), arlutelkiu, ilutelikiu, ilutelkiu
irrespective (adj), arluthurku, iluthuku, iluthuku
irrespectively (adv), arluthurkiu, iluthukiu,
    iluthukiu
irresponsibility (n), arluduverk, iluduveka, iluduvek
irresponsible (adj), arluduverku, iluduveku,
    iluduveku
irresponsibly (adv), arluduverkiu, iluduvekiu,
    iluduvekiu
irretrievable (adj), arlubirshu, ilubishu, ilubishu

irretrievably (adv), arlubirshiu, ilubishiu, ilubishiu
irreverent (adj), arthufirshu, ithufishu, ithufishu
irreverently (adv), arthufirshiu, ithufishiu, ithufishiu
irreversible (adj), arlutharafu, ilutharifu, ilutharfu
irreversibly (adv), arlutharafiu, ilutharifiu, ilutharfiu
irrevocable (adj), ilushairku, ilushaiku, ilushaiku
irrevocably (adv), ilushairkiu, ilushaikiu, ilushaikiu
irrigate (v), breidorsne, bereidono, breidono
irrigation (n), breidorn, bereidona, breidon
irritant (n doer), tinirtwan, tinitua, tinitua
irritate (v), tinirst, tinito, tinito
irritation (n), tinirt, tinita, tinit
is (common), vil, kilo, bil
is (emphatic), vikel, kikelo, bivel
Is (let pl), ilfi, ilfi, ilfi
Islam (n), Ishlarme, Ishelama, Ishlam
island (n), tenirt, tenira, tenir
islander (n doer), tenirtwan, tenirua, tenirua
isle (n), tenirt, tenira, tenir
isolate (v), arshualsf, ishualifo, ishualfo
isolation (n), arshualf, ishualifa, ishualf
isolationism (n), arshualfuet, ishualifueta, ishualfuet
isolationist (n), arshualfar, ishualifara, ishualfar
isolator (n doer), arshualfwan, ishualifua, ishualfua
Israel (n), Ishrahilf, Isherahila, Ishrahil
Israeli (n), Ishrahilarn, Isherahilana, Ishrahiln
issuance (n), zhimart, zhimata, zhimat
issue (n), zhirme, zhima, zhim
issue (v), zhirzme, zhimo, zhimo
issuer (n doer), zhirmwan, zhimua, zhimua
it (pron 3rd neut sng obj), tilen, tilen, tilen
it (pron 3rd neut sng sub), til, til, til
Italian (n), Italiarn, Italiana, Italian
Italy (n), Italirf, Italifa, Italif
itch (n), nirzhe, nizha, nizh
itch (v), nirze, nizho, nizho
itchy (adj), nirzhu, nizhu, nizhu
item (n), plirt, pelita, plit
itemize (v), plirst, pelito, plito
itemizer (n doer), plirtwan, pelitua, plitua
iterate (v), lutigarst, lutigato, lutigato
iteration (n), lutigart, lutigata, lutigat
iterative (adj), lutigartu, lutigatu, lutigatu
iteratively (adv), lutigartiu, lutigatiu, lutigatiu
itesa-, avushkai-, avushkai-, avushkai-
its (pron 3rd neut sng pos obj), tilesh, tilesh, tilesh
its (pron 3rd neut sng pos sub), tilesh, tilesh, tilesh
itself (pron 3rd neut sng refl), tileshfal, tileshfal, tileshfal
itty (adj), shilu, shilu, shilu
ivory (adj), mirmirtu, miremitu, mirmitu
ivory (n), mirmirt, miremita, mirmit
ivy (n), livarn, livana, livan
jab (v), traiforst, teraifuto, traifto
jabber (n doer), traifortwan, teraifutua, traiftua
jack (n d:lift), gavurge, gavuga, gavg
jack (n d:toy), glursh, gelusha, glush
jack (v d:lift), gavurzge, gavugo, gavgo
jacker (n doer d:lift), gavurgwan, gavugua, gavgua
jacket (n), bifirt, bifita, bifit

jackpot (n), gavugedairf, gavugedaifa, gavgedaif
jag (n), braithk, beraitha, braith
jag (v), braithsk, beraitho, braitho
jagger (n doer), braithkwan, beraithua, braithua
jail (n), kairfp, kaifopa, kaifp
jail (v), kairfsp, kaifopo, kaifpo
jailer (n doer), kairfpwan, kaifopua, kaifpua
jailhouse (n), kaifpekiarf, kaifopekiafa, kaifpekiaf
jam (n d:bind), zhaurp, zhaupa, zhaup
jam (n d:food), thalirme, thalima, thalm
jam (v d:bind), zhaursp, zhaupo, zhaupo
jangle (n), baurshk, bauraka, baurk
jangle (v), baurshsk, baurako, baurko
janitor (n), tharnt, tharina, tharn
January (n), Shanilan, Shanilana, Shanilan
Japan (n), Zhaparf, Zhapafa, Zhapaf
Japanese (n), Zhaparnf, Zhapanifa, Zhapanf
jar (n), nurve, nuva, nuv
jar (v), nurzve, nuvo, nuvo
javelin (n), numark, numaka, numak
jaw (n), mutirk, mutika, mutik
jaw (v), mutirsk, mutiko, mutiko
jawbone (n), mutiktoirk, mutiketoika, mutiktoik
jazz (n), darzhe, dazha, dazh
jazz (v), darze, dazho, dazho
jazzy (adj), darzhu, dazhu, dazhu
jealous (adj), norfipu, norifopu, norfpu
jealously (adv), norfipiu, norifopiu, norfpiu
jealousy (n), norfip, norifopa, norfp
jeans (n), zhinersh, zhinesha, zhinesh
jeer (n), griork, gerioka, griok
jeer (v), griorsk, gerioko, grioko
jell (v), zhulirst, zhulito, zhulto
jellied (adj), zhulirtu, zhulitu, zhultu
jelly (n), zhulirt, zhulita, zhult
jellyfish (n pl), zhulteshlershyek, zhulitesheleshi, zhulteshleshi
jellyfish (n), zhulteshlersh, zhuliteshelesha, zhulteshlesh
jeopardize (v), valtairsf, valitaivo, valtaivo
jeopardy (n), valtairf, valitaiva, valtaiv
jerk (n doer), priankwan, perianua, prianua
jerk (n), priank, periana, prian
jerk (v), priansk, periano, priano
jerkily (adv), priankiu, perianiu, prianiu
jerky (adj), prianku, perianu, prianu
jersey (n), garzhink, garozhina, garzhin
Jerusalem (n), Zherushalorme, Zherushaloma, Zherushalom
jest (n), kiarge, kiaga, kiag
jest (v), kiarzge, kiago, kiago
jester (n doer), kiargwan, kiagua, kiagua
Jesus (n), Zheishush, Zheishusha, Zheishush
jet (n), kiert, kieta, kiet
jet (v), kierst, kieto, kieto
jetliner (n), kiertroifk, kietaroifa, kietroif
Jew (n), Zhiurf, Zhiufa, Zhiuf
jewel (n), krefirn, kerefina, krefin
jeweler (n doer), krefirnwan, kerefinua, krefinua
jewelry (n), krefirnk, kerefinoka, krefink
Jewish (adj), Zhiufarn, Zhiufanu, Zhiufan
jig (n d:dance), zhirve, zhiva, zhiv
jig (n d:fixture), gilork, giloka, gilk

jig (v d:dance), zhirzve, zhivo, zhivo
jigsaw (n), girgralzhe, girogerazha, girgrazh
jingle (n), birishk, birika, birk
jingle (v), birishsk, biriko, birko
jitri- (num 1e66 pref), hemshkai-, hemshkai-, hemshkai-
jitter (n), diatiart, diatiata, diatiat
jitter (v), diatiarst, diatiato, diatiato
job (n), trafirt, terafita, traft
jobless (adj), trafirtmenu, terafitemenu, traftmenu
joblessness (n), trafirtmen, terafitemena, traftmen
jog (n), tarzhe, tazha, tazh
jog (v), tarze, tazho, tazho
jogger (n doer), tarzhwan, tazhua, tazhua
join (n), diart, diata, diat
join (v), diarst, diato, diato
joiner (n doer), diartwan, diatua, diatua
joint (n), diarsh, diasha, diash
joint (v), diars, diasho, diasho
jointly (adv), diarshiu, diashiu, diashiu
joist (n), retienk, retiena, retien
joke (n), paurk, pauka, pauk
joke (v), paursk, pauko, pauko
joker (n doer), paurkwan, paukua, paukua
jolt (n), biurp, biupa, biup
jolt (v), biursp, biupo, biupo
Jordan (n), Zhordarn, Zhorudana, Zhordan
jot (v), diotarsne, diotano, diotano
journal (n), kanitaf, kanifota, kanift
journal (v), kanitasf, kanifoto, kanifto
journalism (n), kanitafuet, kanifotueta, kaniftuet
journalist (n doer), kanitafwan, kanifotua, kaniftua
journalistic (adj), kanitafu, kanifotu, kaniftu
journey (n), kanipuf, kanifopa, kanifp
journey (v), kanipusf, kanifopo, kanifpo
joy (n), lairsh, laisha, laish
joyful (adj), lairshu, laishu, laishu
joyfully (adv), lairshiu, laishiu, laishiu
joystick (n), laishshneft, laishineta, laishnet
judge (n doer), hethertwan, hethetua, hethetua
judge (v), hetherst, hetheto, hetheto
judgement (n), hethert, hetheta, hethet
judgemental (adj), hethertuetu, hethetuetu, hethetuetu
judgementalism (n), hethertuet, hethetueta, hethetuet
judgeship (n), hethetfirf, hethetefifa, hethetfif
judgment (n), hethert, hetheta, hethet
judicial (adj), hethertu, hethetu, hethetu
judicially (adv), hethertiu, hethetiu, hethetiu
judiciary (n), hethefirt, hethefita, hethefit
judicious (adj), hethertu, hethetu, hethetu
judiciously (adv), hethertiu, hethetiu, hethetiu
jug (n), goizhge, goiga, goig
juggle (n), paupaurk, paupauka, paupauk
juggle (v), paupaursk, paupauko, paupauko
juggler (n doer), paupaurkwan, paupaukua, paupaukua
juice (n), darlorf, darilofa, darlf
juice (v), darlorsf, darilofo, darlfo
juicer (n doer), darlorfwan, darilofua, darlfua
juicy (adj), darlorfu, darilofu, darlfu
July (n), Zhulait, Zhulaita, Zhulait

jumble (n), pliurp, peliupa, pliup
jumble (v), pliursp, peliupo, pliupo
jumbo (adj), pliuzhbu, peliubu, pliubu
jump (n), zharbe, zhaba, zhab
jump (v), zharzbe, zhabo, zhabo
jumper (n doer), zharbwan, zhabua, zhabua
jumpily (adv), zharbiu, zhabiu, zhabiu
jumpy (adj), zharbu, zhabu, zhabu
junction (n), bafirt, bafita, baft
junctional (adj), bafirtu, bafitu, baftu
June (n), Zhun, Zhuna, Zhun
jungle (n), zheikarn, zheikana, zheikan
junior (adj), zhumarnu, zhumanu, zhumanu
junior (n), zhumarn, zhumana, zhuman
Juniper (n), Tshamel, Teshamela, Tshamel
junk (n), kraufk, kerauka, krauk
junk (v), kraufsk, kerauko, krauko
junky (adj), kraufku, kerauku, krauku
jurisdiction (n), hoinkart, hoinikata, hoinkat
jurist (n doer), hoirnwan, hoinua, hoinua
juror (n doer), hoirnwan, hoinua, hoinua
jury (n), hoirn, hoina, hoin
just (adj), peshirpu, peshipu, peshpu
justice (n), peshirp, peshipa, peshp
justifiable (adj), peshirpefrelpu, peshipeferepu, peshpefrepu
justifiably (adv), peshirpefrelpiu, peshipeferepiu, peshpefrepiu
justification (n), peshirpuet, peshipueta, peshpuet
justify (v), peshirsp, peshipo, peshpo
justly (adv), peshirpiu, peshipiu, peshpiu
juvenile (adj), zhurmu, zhumu, zhumu
juvenile (n), zhurme, zhuma, zhum
K (let sng), keil, keia, kei
Kansas (n), Kansharsh, Kanishasha, Kanshash
kappa (n), kaparn, kapana, kapan
keel (n), koshelt, kosheta, kosht
keel (v), koshelst, kosheto, koshto
keeler (n doer), kosheltwan, koshetua, koshtua
keen (adj), teirmu, teimu, teimu
keep (n), klorf, kelofa, klof
keep (v), klorsf, kelofo, klofo
keeper (n doer), klorfwan, kelofua, klofua
keepsake (n), klofmoark, kelofemoaka, klofmoak
keg (n), diuzhge, diuga, diug
kennel (n), draubar, derauba, draub
Kentucky (n), Kentukirf, Kenotukifa, Kentukif
kept (v pa), klorsfyot, kelofio, klofio
kerchief (n), lolarf, lolafa, lolaf
kernel (n), plonik, polonika, plonk
kettle (n), filtarp, filotapa, filtap
key (n), trifk, terika, trik
key (v), trifsk, teriko, triko
keyboard (n), triplok, teripelorika, triplork
keyhole (n), trikorth, terikotha, trikoth
keyless (adj), trifkmenu, terikemenu, trikmenu
keynote (n), triklinurn, terikelinuna, triklinun
keypad (n), trikebanirf, terikebanifa, trikebanf
keystone (n), trikbararf, terikebarafa, trikebaraf
keystroke (n), trikaturk, terikatuka, trikatuk
keyword (n), triklialirt, terikelialita, triklialt
kick (n), thirap, thiropa, thirp
kick (v), thirasp, thiropo, thirpo

kickback (n), thirapevark, thiropevaka, thirpevak
kicker (n doer), thirapwan, thiropua, thirpua
kickoff (n), thirapunf, thiropunefa, thirpunf
kid (n d:child), falirn, falina, faln
kid (v d:joke), fiarzme, fiamo, fiamo
kidnap (v), falnporzge, faleporugo, falporgo
kidnapper (n doer), falnporgwan, faleporugua, falporgua
kidney (n), gelimarf, gelimara, gelmar
kido- (num 1e63 pref), dashtai-, dashtai-, dashtai-
kill (n), kitersh, kitesha, kitsh
kill (v), kiters, kitesho, kitsho
killer (n doer), kitershwan, kiteshua, kitshua
kilo- (num 1000 pref), dintai-, dintai-, dintai-
kilogram (n), dinakran, dinakerana, dinkran
kilometer (n), dinlimert, dinalimeta, dinlimet
kin (n), brolar, berola, brol
kind (adj d:nice), tofirpu, tofipu, tofpu
kind (n d:type), guafirt, guafita, guaft
kindergarten (n), luarten, luaritemota, luartemt
kindergartener (n doer), luartenwan, luaritemotua, luartemtua
kindle (v), friars, feriasho, friasho
kindly (adv d:nice), tofirpiu, tofipiu, tofpiu
kindness (n d:nice), tofirp, tofipa, tofp
kindred (adj), brolreifku, berolereiku, brolreiku
kindred (n), brolreifk, berolereika, brolreik
kinesis (n), thnart, thenata, thnat
kinetic (adj), thnartu, thenatu, thnatu
kinetically (adv), thnartiu, thenatiu, thnatiu
kinfolk (n), brolkiforp, berolekifopa, brolkifp
king (n), klairbe, keliaba, klaib
kingdom (n), klaifirf, kelaififa, klaifif
kink (n), duirzhe, duiroga, duirg
kinky (adj), duirzhu, duirogu, duirgu
kinship (n), brolarfirf, berolefifa, brolfif
kinsman (n), brolplorn, berolepelona, brolplon
kiss (n), mavarp, mavapa, mavap
kiss (v), mavarsp, mavapo, mavapo
kisser (n doer), mavarpwan, mavapua, mavapua
kit (n), plurde, peluda, plud
kitchen (n), pethar, paritha, parth
kite (n), pikart, pikata, pikat
kitten (n), fifirme, fifima, fifim
kitty (n), fifarf, fifafa, fifaf
klutz (n), mokramp, mokarama, mokram
knapsack (n), povigthoilf, porigethoila, porgthoil
knead (v), peiabolsk, peiaboko, peiaboko
knee (n), kerp, kepa, kep
knee (v), kersp, kepo, kepo
kneecap (n), kepefiveil, kepedefipa, kepedefp
kneel (v), kepersf, kepefo, kepefo
kneeling (n doer), keperfwan, kepefua, kepefua
knew (v pa), glerskyot, gelekio, glekio
knife (n), voirn, voina, voin
knife (v), voirsne, voino, voino
knifer (n doer), voirnwan, voinua, voinua
knight (n), shivart, shivata, shivat
knight (v), shivarst, shivato, shivato
knightly (adj), shivartu, shivatu, shivatu
knit (n), delirp, delipa, delp
knit (v), delirsp, delipo, delpo
knitwear (n), delpedorame, delipedorima,

delpedorim
knob (n), proide, peroida, proid
knock (n), pashk, paka, pak
knock (v), pashsk, pako, pako
knockdown (n), paktiern, paketiena, paktien
knocker (n doer), pashkwan, pakua, pakua
knockout (n), pashkuil, pakuila, pakuil
knoll (n), praln, perala, pral
knot (n), tufirp, tufipa, tufp
knot (v), tufirsp, tufipo, tufpo
knotty (adj), tufirpu, tufipu, tufpu
know (v), glersk, geleko, gleko
know-it-all (n doer), glerkwan, gelekua, glekua
knowledge (n), glerk, geleka, glek
knuckle (n), durage, duroga, durg
knuckle (v), durazge, durogo, durgo
knuckler (n doer), duragwan, durogua, durgua
Korea (n), Koriarf, Koriafa, Koriaf
Korean (n), Korianf, Koriana, Korian
Krypton (n davoka), Efik, Efik, Efik
Krypton (n), Kripton, Keripetona, Kripton
Ks (let pl), keili, keili, keili
Kuwait (n), Kuwairt, Kuwaita, Kuwait
Kuwaiti (n), Kuwaitarn, Kuwaitana, Kuwaitan
L (let sng), lerfe, lerifa, lerf
lab (n), shurf, shufa, shuf
label (n), moirap, moiropa, moirp
label (v), moirasp, moiropo, moirpo
labeler (n doer), moirapwan, moiropua, moirpua
labor (n), shurve, shuva, shuv
labor (v), shurzve, shuvo, shuvo
laboratory (n), shuvarsht, shuvashota, shuvasht
laborer (n doer), shurvwan, shuvua, shuvua
lace (n), foirn, foina, foin
lace (v), foirsne, foino, foino
lacerate (v), niarshsk, niarosho, niarsho
laceration (n), niarshk, niarosha, niarsh
lacey (adj), foirnu, foinu, foinu
lack (n), noirk, noika, noik
lack (v), noirsk, noiko, noiko
lad (n d:boy), blart, bilata, blat
ladder (n), trirt, terita, trit
lade (v), leitosne, lueito, lueito
ladle (n), lueifk, lueifa, lueif
ladle (v), lueifsk, lueifo, lueifo
lady (n), blarn, bilara, blar
ladybug (n), leiverzhe, lueivezha, lueivezh
lag (n), rauzhge, rauzha, rauzh
lag (v), rauzhzge, rauzho, rauzho
laggard (n doer), rauzhgwan, rauzhua, rauzhua
laid (v pa d:place), franistyot, feranitio, frantio
lake (n), muarf, muara, muar
lakeshore (n), muarnularat, muarenularita, muarnulart
lakeside (n), muarshoirt, muareshoita, muarshoit
lamb (n), marilf, marila, marl
lamb (v), marilsf, marilo, marlo
lambda (n), lamdarn, lamudana, lamdan
lame (adj), tiaishku, tiaiku, tiaiku
lamely (adv), tiaishkiu, tiaikiu, tiaikiu
lameness (n), tiaishk, tiaika, tiaik
lament (v), tiaikansk, tiaikano, tiaikano
lamentable (adj), tiaikanku, tiaikanu, tiaikanu

lamina (n), tiaip, tiaifa, tiaif
laminae (n pl), tiaipyek, tiaifi, tiaifi
laminate (v), tiaisp, tiaifo, tiaifo
laminator (n doer), tiaipwan, tiaifua, tiaifua
laminous (adj), tiaipu, tiaifu, tiaifu
laminously (adv), tiaipiu, tiaifiu, tiaifiu
lamp (n), pluarbe, peluaba, pluab
lamppost (n), pluabalirt, peluabalita, pluabalt
lance (n), teirge, teiga, teig
lance (v), teirzge, teigo, teigo
lancer (n doer), teirgwan, teigua, teigua
land (n), raufp, raupa, raup
land (v), raufsp, raupo, raupo
lander (n doer), raufpwan, raupua, raupua
landfall (n), pezhailf, rauzhaila, rauzhail
landfill (n), petriel, raubupa, raubup
landlady (n), peblarn, raubilara, raublar
landlock (n), petiurge, rautiuga, rautiug
landlock (v), petiurzge, rautiugo, rautiugo
landlord (n), pesharfp, raushafipa, raushafp
landmark (n), peshtart, raushetata, raushtat
landmass (n), peglarfk, raugelarika, rauglark
landowner (n doer), rauptheiftwan, raupetheifua, rauptheifua
landscape (n), peshiark, raushiaka, raushiak
landscape (v), peshiarsk, raushiako, raushiako
landscaper (n doer), peshiarkwan, raushiakua, raushiakua
landslide (n), peshlursh, raushelusha, raushlush
lane (n), neirde, neida, neid
language (n), varthak, varitha, varth
languid (adj), tiaushku, tiauku, tiauku
languidly (adv), tiaushkiu, tiaukiu, tiaukiu
languish (v), tiaushsk, tiauko, tiauko
lantern (n), pluaft, peluata, pluat
Lanthanum (n davoka), Orap, Orap, Orap
Lanthanum (n), Lanthanum, Lanethanuma, Lanthanum
lap (n), thiurt, thiuta, thiut
lap (v), thiurst, thiuto, thiuto
lapse (n), thiurft, thiufota, thiuft
lapse (v), thiurfst, thiufoto, thiufto
laptop (n), thiutaurbe, thiutauba, thiutaub
large (adj), graurgu, geraugu, graugu
largely (adv), graurgiu, geraugiu, graugiu
larger (adj), graurgwelu, geraugwelu, graugwelu
largest (adj), graurgwaku, geraugwaku, graugwaku
Las Vegas (n), Larsh Veigarsh, Lash Veigasha, Lash Veigash
laser (n), nikurt, nikuta, nikut
laser (v), nikurst, nikuto, nikuto
lash (n), laiathk, laiatha, laiath
lash (v), laiathsk, laiatho, laiatho
lasher (n doer), laiathkwan, laiathua, laiathua
last (adj), ushetu, ushethu, ushethu
last (v), ushest, ushetho, ushetho
lastly (adv), ushetiu, ushethiu, ushethiu
latch (n), roifkarft, roikafita, roikaft
latch (v), roifkarfst, roikafito, roikafto
late (adj), darshortu, darishotu, darshtu
latecomer (n), darshorteblerf, darishotebilefa, darshtblef
lately (adv), darshortiu, darishotiu, darshtiu

latency (n), tiaink, tiaina, tiain
lateness (n), darshort, darishota, darsht
latent (adj), tiainku, tiainu, tiainu
latently (adv), tiainkiu, tiainiu, tiainiu
later (adj), darshortwelu, darishotwelu, darshtwelu
lateral (adj), namoru, narimu, narmu
laterally (adv), namoriu, narimiu, narmiu
latest (adj), darshortwaku, darishotwaku, darshtwaku
lathe (n d:machine), tueifk, tueifa, tueif
lathe (v d:machine), tueifsk, tueifo, tueifo
lather (n d:soap), tramank, teramana, traman
lather (n docr d:machinc), tucifkwan, tucifua, tueifua
lather (v d:soap), tramansk, teramano, tramano
Latin (n), Latinorf, Latinofa, Latinf
latitude (n), narmurk, naromuka, narmuk
latter (adj), narmalirtu, naromalitu, narmaltu
latter (n), narmalirt, naromalita, narmalt
lattice (n), narmirt, naromita, narmit
laugh (n), luarl, luala, lual
laugh (v), luarsle, lualo, lualo
laughable (adj), luarlu, lualu, lualu
laughably (adv), luarliu, lualiu, lualiu
laugher (n doer), luarlwan, lualua, lualua
laughter (n), luarlal, lualara, lualar
launch (n), vuark, vuaka, vuak
launch (v), vuarsk, vuako, vuako
launcher (n doer), vuarkwan, vuakua, vuakua
launchpad (n), vuakebanirf, vuakebanifa, vuakbanf
launder (v), vuarzme, vuamo, vuamo
launderer (n doer), vuarmwan, vuamua, vuamua
laundromat (n), vuamirt, vuamita, vuamit
laundry (n), vuarme, vuama, vuam
lava (n), shleink, sheleina, shlein
lavish (adj), shleiarfu, sheleiafu, shleiafu
lavishly (adv), shleiarfiu, sheleiafiu, shleiafiu
law (n), vaurde, vauda, vaud
lawbreaker (n doer), vaudeblerkwan, vaudepelikua, vaudeplikua
lawful (adj), vaurdu, vaudu, vaudu
lawfully (adv), vaurdiu, vaudiu, vaudiu
lawless (adj), vaurdmenu, vaudemenu, vaudmenu
lawlessly (adv), vaurdmeniu, vaudemeniu, vaudmeniu
lawlessness (n), vaurdmen, vaudemena, vaudmen
lawmaker (n doer), vaurdenagwan, vaudenagua, vaudenagua
lawman (n), vaudeplorn, vaudepelona, vaudeplon
lawmen (n pl), vaudeplornyek, vaudepeloni, vaudeploni
lawn (n), veirsh, veisha, veish
lawnmower (n doer), veishkriteshwan, veishekeriteshua, vieshkritshua
Lawrencium (n davoka), Inap, Inap, Inap
Lawrencium (n), Larenshium, Larenoshiuma, Larenshium
lawsuit (n), dutark, dutaka, dutak
lawyer (n doer), vaurdwan, vaudua, vaudua
lax (adj), klarlu, kelalu, klalu
lax (v), klarsle, kelalo, klalo
laxity (n), klarl, kelala, klal
laxly (adv), klarliu, kelaliu, klaliu

lay (n d:place), franit, feranita, frant
lay (v d:place), franist, feranito, franto
lay (v pa d:placement), riesfyot, rethio, rethio
layer (n), franirt, feranitara, frantar
layer (v), franirst, feranitaro, frantaro
layoff (n), franitunf, feranitunifa, frantunf
layout (n), franituil, feranituila, frantuil
lazier (adj), pumurfwelu, pumufwelu, pumufwelu
laziest (adj), pumurfweku, pumufweku, pumufweku
lazily (adv), pumurfiu, pumufiu, pumufiu
laziness (n), pumurf, pumufa, pumuf
lazy (adj), pumurfu, pumufu, pumufu
leach (n), briushk, beriusha, briush
leach (v), briushsk, beriusho, briusho
lead (n d:in front), lalirt, lalita, lalt
Lead (n davoka), Erip, Erip, Erip
Lead (n), Lead, Leada, Lead
lead (v d:in front), lalirst, lalito, lalto
leader (n doer d:in front), lalirtwan, lalitua, laltua
leaderless (adj), lairtemenu, lalitemenu, laltemenu
leadership (n), lalirtfif, lalitafifa, laltfif
leadoff (adj), lalirtunfu, lalitunefu, laltunfu
leadoff (n), lalirtunf, lalitunefa, laltunf
leaf (n), pruth, berutha, bruth
leaf (v), prusth, berutho, brutho
leaflet (n), pruthap, beruthapa, bruthap
league (n), brurbe, beruba, brub
leaguer (n doer), brurbwan, berubua, brubua
leak (n), briurk, beriuka, briuk
leak (v), briursk, beriuko, briuko
leakage (n), briukart, beriuka, briukat
leaker (n doer), briurkwan, beriukua, briukua
leakily (adv), briurkiu, beriukiu, briukiu
leaky (adj), briurku, beriuku, briuku
lean (adj d:thin), tierpu, tiepu, tiepu
lean (v d:tilt), triurst, teriuto, triuto
leaner (n doer d:tilt), triurtwan, teriutua, triutua
leap (n), brift, bifota, bift
leap (v), brifst, bifoto, bifto
leaper (n doer), briftwan, bifotua, biftua
leapfrog (n), biftefloirp, bifotefeloipa, biftefloip
leapt (v pa), brifstyot, bifotio, biftio
learn (v), vrierst, vorieto, vrieto
learner (n doer), vriertwan, vorietua, vrietua
learnt (v pa), vrierstyot, vorietio, vrietio
lease (n), nularn, nulana, nuln
lease (v), nularsne, nulano, nulno
leaser (n doer), nularnwan, nulanua, nulnua
leash (n), nulirk, nulika, nulk
leash (v), nulirsk, nuliko, nulko
least (adj), munk, muniku, munk
leather (n), mivarn, mivana, mivan
leathery (adj), mivarnu, mivanu, mivanu
leave (n d:departure), rufp, rupa, rup
leave (v d:departure), rufsp, rupo, rupo
Lebanese (n), Lebanornf, Lebanonifa, Lebanonf
Lebanon (n), Lebanorf, Lebanofa, Lebanof
lecture (n), getran, getorala, getral
lecture (v), getrasne, getoralo, getralo
lecturer (n doer), getranwan, getoralua, getralua
ledge (n), blarfk, belafika, blafk
ledger (n), bralfk, berafika, brafk
leech (n), bruithk, beruitha, bruith

leech (v), bruithsk, beruitho, bruitho
leer (n), leiarp, leiapa, leiap
leer (v), leiarsp, leiapo, leiapo
leery (adj), leiarpu, leiapu, leiapu
leeway (n), leiapliorl, leiapeliola, leiapliol
left (adj d:direction), larapu, laripu, larpu
left (n d:direction), larap, laripa, larp
left (v pa d:departure), rufspyot, rupio, rupio
leftist (n doer), larapkliergwan, laripekeliegua, larpekliegua
leftover (n), rupen, rufapena, rufpen
leftwing (adj), larapkliergu, laripekeliegu, larpekliegu
lefty (n doer d:direction), larapwan, laripua, larpua
leg (n), glerf, gelefa, glef
leg (v), glersf, gelefo, glefo
legacy (n), rufkunk, rufekuka, rufkuk
legal (adj), nutarku, nutaku, nutaku
legality (n), nutark, nutaka, nutak
legalize (v), nutarsk, nutako, nutako
legally (adv), nutarkiu, nutakiu, nutakiu
legend (n), ramshar, ramesha, ramsh
legendary (adj), ramsharu, rameshu, ramshu
leger (n), shetark, shetaka, shtak
legibility (n), shtarfk, shetafika, shtafk
legible (adj), shtarfku, shetafiku, shtafku
legibly (adv), shtarfkiu, shetafikiu, shtafkiu
legislate (v), tashirsk, tashiko, tashko
legislation (n), tashirk, tashika, tashk
legislative (adj), tashirku, tashiku, tashku
legislatively (adv), tashirkiu, tashikiu, tashkiu
legislator (n doer), tashirkwan, tashikua, tashkua
legislature (n), tarshirk, tarishoka, tarshk
legit (adj), nutarfu, nutafu, nutafu
legit (n), nutarf, nutafa, nutaf
legitimacy (n), nutarfk, nutafika, nutafk
legitimate (adj), nutarfku, nutafiku, nutafku
legitimately (adv), nutarfkiu, nutafikiu, nutafkiu
legitimize (v), nutarfsk, nutafiko, nutafko
legroom (n), glefshranf, gelefesherana, glefshran
legwork (n), glefkiork, geletekioka, glefkiok
leisure (n), fliaush, feliaura, fliaur
leisurely (adj), fliaushu, feliauru, fliauru
lemon (n), larnarn, larinana, larnan
lemonade (n), larnaflap, larinafapa, larnafap
lend (v), klurzge, kelugo, klugo
lender (n doer), klurgwan, kelugua, klugua
length (n), ralzhe, razha, razh
lengthen (v), ralze, razho, razho
lengthier (adj), ralzhwelu, razhwelu, razhwelu
lengthy (adj), ralzhu, razhu, razhu
leniency (n), duilp, duila, duil
lenient (adj), duilpu, duilu, duilu
leniently (adv), duilpiu, duiliu, duiliu
lens (n), shunk, shuka, shuk
lens (v), shunsk, shuko, shuko
lent (v pa), klurzgyot, kelugio, klugio
lesbian (n), shuaushp, shuausha, shuaush
lesion (n), girshk, gishoka, gishk
lesion (v), girshsk, gishoko, gishko
less (adj), men, menu, men
lessee (n), nularnuin, nulanuina, nulnuin
lessen (v), mersne, meno, meno

lesser (adj), minarsh, minashu, minash
lesson (n), trofal, terolifa, trolf
lessor (n doer), nularnwan, nulanua, nulnua
let (n), lerk, leka, lek
let (v pa), lerskyot, lekio, lekio
let (v), lersk, leko, leko
letdown (n), lektiern, leketiena, lektien
lethal (adj), gofaifku, gofaifu, gofaifu
lethality (n), gofaifk, gofaifa, gofaif
lethally (adv), gofaifkiu, gofaifiu, gofaifiu
lethargic (adj), gofarfu, gofafu, gofafu
lethargically (adv), gofarfiu, gofafiu, gofafiu
lethargy (n), gofarf, gofafa, gofaf
letter (n d:character), ketirsh, ketisha, ketsh
letter (n d:message), rashort, rashota, rasht
letter (v d:character), ketirs, ketisho, ketsho
letterhead (n), rashtkefirt, rashotekefita, rashtkeft
letterman (n), rashtplorn, rashotepelona, rashtplon
lettermen (n pl), rashtplornyek, rashotepeloni,
    rashtploni
level (adj), galurtu, galudu, galdu
level (n), galurt, galuda, gald
level (v), galurst, galudo, galdo
leveler (n doer), galurtwan, galudua, galdua
lever (n), nufirt, nufita, nuft
lever (v), nufirst, nufito, nufto
leverage (n), nufirtar, nufitara, nuftar
leverage (v), nufirtasre, nufitaro, nuftaro
levitate (v), ftirzve, fetivo, ftivo
levitation (n), ftirve, fetiva, ftiv
levitator (n doer), ftirvwan, fetivua, ftivua
levity (n), ftirve, fetiva, ftiv
levy (n), fitarve, fitava, fitav
levy (v), fitarzve, fitavo, fitavo
lex (n), kren, kerena, kren
lexical (adj), kreniaku, kerenianu, krenianu
lexicon (n), kreniak, kereniana, krenian
liability (n), shnarfrep, shinaferepa, shnafrep
liable (adj), shnarfrepu, shinaferepu, shnafrepu
liably (adv), shnarfrepiu, shinaferepiu, shnafrepiu
liaison (n), shnarl, shenala, shnal
liaison (v), shnarsle, shenalo, shnalo
liar (n doer d:deceit), shnairnwan, shenainua,
    shnainua
libel (n), livonk, livona, livon
libel (v), livonsk, livono, livono
libelous (adj), livonku, livonu, livonu
liberal (adj d:freedom), kiurku, kiuku, kiuku
liberal (n doer d:political stance), glaukiurkwan,
    gelaukiukua, glaukiukua
liberalism (n d:political stance), glaukiurk,
    gelaukiuka, glaukiuk
liberalization (n), glaukiurkuet, gelaukiukueta,
    glaukiukuet
liberalize (v d:political stance), glaukiursk,
    gelaukiuko, glaukiuko
liberally (adv d:freedom), kiurkiu, kiukiu, kiukiu
liberate (v d:freedom), kiursk, kiuko, kiuko
liberation (n d:freedom), kiurk, kiuka, kiuk
liberator (n doer d:freedom), kiurkwan, kiukua,
    kiukua
liberty (n), kiurkar, kiukara, kiukar
librarian (n doer), lalparnwan, laliparua, lalparua

library (n), lalparn, lalipara, lalpar
Libya (n), Libiarf, Libiafa, Libiaf
Libyan (n), Libiarn, Libiana, Libian
licence (n), lalirft, lalirota, lalirt
licencee (n), lalirftuin, lalirotuina, lalirtuin
license (n), lalirft, lalirota, lalirt
license (v), lalirfst, laliroto, lalirto
licensure (n), lalirftuet, lalirotueta, lalirtuet
licentious (adj), lalirftmenu, lalirotemenu,
    lalirtmenu
lick (n), shoirp, shoipa, shoip
lick (v), shoirsp, shoipo, shoipo
licker (n doer), shoirpwan, shoipua, shoipua
lid (n), nirth, nitha, nith
lie (n d:deceit), shnairn, shenaina, shnain
lie (n d:placement), rief, retha, reth
lie (v d:deceit), shnairsne, shenaino, shnaino
lie (v d:placement), riesf, retho, retho
lien (n), roialk, roiaka, roiak
liena- (num 1e60 pref), muishtai-, muishtai-,
    muishtai-
life (adj), flaurshu, felaushu, flaushu
life (n), flaursh, felausha, flaush
lifeblood (n), flaushlilf, felausheliroda, flaushlird
lifeboat (n), flaushkorbe, felaushekoba, flaushkob
lifeguard (n), flaushvaifirk, felaushevaifika,
    flaushvaifk
lifelike (adj), flaushreifku, felaushereiku,
    flaushreiku
lifeline (n), flaushroifk, felausheroifa, flaushroif
lifelong (adj), flaushralzhu, felausherazhu,
    flaushrazhu
lifer (n doer), flaurshwan, felaushua, flaushua
lifesave (v), flaushezhursp, felaushezhupo,
    flaushezhupo
lifesaver (n doer), flaushezhurpwan,
    felaushezhupua, flaushezhupua
lifespan (n), flaushbleirsh, felaushebeleisha,
    flaushbleish
lifestyle (n), flaushfriarf, felausheferiafa, flaushfriaf
lifetime (n), flaushdaun, felaushedauna, flaushdaun
lift (n), raushk, rauka, rauk
lift (v), raushsk, rauko, rauko
lifter (n doer), raushkwan, raukua, raukua
liftoff (n), raushkunf, raukunefa, raukunf
ligament (n), roilkat, roikata, roikat
ligate (v), roilsk, roiko, roiko
ligation (n), roilkuet, roikueta, roikuet
ligature (n), roilk, roika, roik
light (adj d:weight), breifku, bereifu, breifu
light (n d:lumen), fluarn, feluana, fluan
light (v d:lumen), fluarsne, feluano, fluano
lighten (v d:weight), breifsk, bereifo, breifo
lighter (n doer d:lumen), fluarnwan, feluanua,
    fluanua
lightheadedness (n), breifkefirt, bereifekefita,
    breifkeft
lighthouse (n), fluankiarf, feluanekiafa, fluankiaf
lightly (adv d:weight), breifkiu, bereifiu, breifiu
lightness (n d:weight), breifk, bereifa, breif
lightning (adj), fluarnku, felunaku, fluanku
lightning (n), fluarnk, felunaka, fluank
lightweight (adj), breifshuirshu, bereifeshuishu,

breifshuishu
lightweight (n), breifshuirsh, bereifeshuisha, breifshuish
like (adj), reifku, reiku, reiku
like (n), reifk, reika, reik
like (prep), reifki, reikifu, reikif
like (v), reifsk, reiko, reiko
likeable (adj), reikfrelpu, reikeferepu, reikfrepu
likelihood (n), reifkiufif, reikiufifa, reikiufif
likely (adv), reifkiu, reikiu, reikiu
likeness (n), reifkuet, reikueta, reikuet
lily (n), lirshp, lirosha, lirsh
limb (n), hibran, hiberatha, hibrath
limbo (n), kibratsh, kiberata, kibrat
limit (n), vint, vitha, vith
limit (v), vinst, vitho, vitho
limitation (n), vintar, vithara, vithar
limiter (n doer), vintwan, vithua, vithua
limp (adj), dilorfu, dilofu, dilfu
limp (n), dilorf, dilofa, dilf
limp (v), dilorsf, dilofo, dilfo
linch (v), deimarsk, deimako, deimako
line (n), roifk, roifa, roif
line (v), roifsk, roifo, roifo
lineage (n), roifkuet, roifueta, roifuet
linear (adj), roifku, roifu, roifu
linearly (adv), roifkiu, roifiu, roifiu
linen (n), roimert, roimeta, roimet
liner (n doer), roifkwan, roifua, roifua
lineup (n), roifkiveil, roifiveila, roifiveil
linger (v), riazhzge, riazho, riazho
lingo (n), kriathk, keriatha, kriath
linguist (n doer), viarthakwan, viarithua, viarthua
linguistic (adj), viarthaku, viarithu, viarthu
linguistically (adv), viarthakiu, viarithiu, viarthiu
linguistics (n), viarthak, viaritha, viarth
link (n), roishk, roisha, roish
link (v), roishsk, roisho, roisho
linkage (n), roishkuet, roishueta, roishuet
linker (n doer), rolshkwan, roishua, roishua
linkup (n), roishkiveil, roishiveila, roishiveil
lint (n), roint, roina, roin
lint (v), roinst, roino, roino
linter (n doer), rointwan, roinua, roinua
lion (n), riurk, riuka, riuk
lip (n), krinf, kerina, krin
lip (v), krinsf, kerino, krino
lipstick (n), krinshnet, kerishineta, krishnet
liquid (n), taurge, tauga, taug
liquidate (v), taurzge, taugo, taugo
liquidation (n), taurguet, taugueta, tauguet
liquidity (n), taugart, taugata, taugat
liquor (n), taugarf, taugara, taugar
liquor (v), taugarsf, taugaro, taugaro
list (adj d:strip), tivirku, tiviku, tiviku
list (n d:sequence), dilt, dita, dit
list (n d:strip), tivirk, tivika, tivik
list (n d:tilt), tirthk, tiritha, tirth
list (v d:sequence), dilst, dito, dito
list (v d:strip), tivirsk, tiviko, tiviko
list (v d:tilt), tirthsk, tiritho, tirtho
listen (v), brolst, beroto, broto
listener (n doer), broltwan, berotua, brotua

lit (v pa d:lumen), fluarsnyot, feluanio, fluanio
liter (n), lalitor, lalitera, laliter
literacy (n), livart, livata, livat
literal (adj), livashortu, livashotu, livashtu
literal (n), livashort, livashota, livasht
literally (adv), livashortiu, livashotiu, livashtiu
literary (adj), livafirtu, livafitu, livaftu
literate (adj), livartoru, livatoru, livatoru
literature (n), livafirt, livafita, livaft
Lithium (n davoka), Akap, Akap, Akap
Lithium (n), Lithium, Lithiuma, Lithium
lithography (n), threithedarf, thereithedarifa, threithdarf
Lithuania (n), Lithuaniarf, Lithuaniafa, Lithuaniaf
Lithuanian (n), Lithuaniarn, Lithuaniana, Lithuanian
litigate (v), shtaursk, shetauko, shtauko
litigation (n), shtaurk, shetauka, shtauk
litigator (n doer), shtaurkwan, shetaukua, shtaukua
litter (n), kreift, kereifa, kreif
little (adj), lishtu, lishu, lishu
livable (adj), flauftfrelpu, felaufiteferepu, flauftfrepu
livably (adv), flauftfrelpiu, felaufiteferepiu, flauftfrepiu
live (adj), flaurftu, felaufitu, flauftu
live (v), flaurfst, felaufito, flaufto
livelihood (n), flauftfirf, felaufitefifa, flauftfif
lively (adv), flaurftiu, felaufitiu, flauftiu
liven (v), flauftarsk, felaufitako, flauftako
liver (n), nomarge, nomaga, nomag
livestock (n), flaufrifk, felauferifa, flaufrif
livid (adj), flaugaishtu, felaugaitu, flaugaitu
lividly (adv), flaugaishtiu, felaugaitiu, flaugaitiu
load (n), lurift, lurita, lurt
load (v), lurifst, lurito, lurto
loader (n doer), luriftwan, luritua, lurtua
loaf (n d:bread), noersh, noesha, noesh
loaf (v d:lounge), narifsp, narifo, narfo
loafer (n doer d:lounge), narifpwan, narifua, narfua
loan (n), klurge, keluga, klug
loath (adj), rakaiftu, rakaifu, rakaifu
loathe (v), rakaifst, rakaifo, rakaifo
loathness (n), rakaift, rakaifa, rakaif
lob (v), doinst, doido, doido
lobby (n), doidarn, doidana, doidan
lobby (v), doidarsne, doidano, doidano
lobbyist (n doer), doidarnwan, doidanua, doidanua
lobe (n), doirn, doina, doin
lobster (n), loisharp, loishapa, loishp
local (adj), shairpu, shaipu, shaipu
locale (n), shairp, shaipa, shaip
locality (n), shairp, shaipa, shaip
localization (n), shairpuet, shaipueta, shaipuet
localize (v), shairpuest, shaipueto, shaipueto
locally (adv), shairpiu, shaipiu, shaipiu
locate (v), shairsp, shaipo, shaipo
location (n), shairp, shaipa, shaip
locator (n doer), shairpwan, shaipua, shaipua
lock (n), tiurge, tiuga, tiug
lock (v), tiurzge, tiugo, tiugo
locker (n doer), tiurgwan, tiugua, tiugua
lockout (n), tiurguil, tiuguila, tiuguil

locksmith (n), tiugrithk, tiugeritha, tiugrith
lockstep (n), tiugirk, tiugika, tiugik
lockup (n), tiurgiveil, tiugiveila, tiugiveil
locomotion (n), tavarde, tavada, tavad
locomotive (n doer), tavardwan, tavadua, tavadua
locum (n), latan, latana, latan
lodge (n d:building), dalirn, dalina, daln
lodge (v d:stop), shavizge, sharigo, shargo
loft (n), raufirk, raufika, raufk
loft (v), raufirsk, raufiko, raufko
loftily (adv), raufirkiu, raufikiu, raufkiu
lofty (adj), raufirku, raufiku, raufku
log (n d:record), kuift, kuita, kuit
log (n d:tree), kirvuge, kiruga, kirg
log (v d:record), kuifst, kuito, kuito
log (v d:tree), kirvuzge, kirugo, kirgo
logbook (n), kuitvornt, kuitevonuda, kuitvond
logger (n doer d:record), kuiftwan, kuitua, kuitua
logger (n doer d:tree), kirvugwan, kirugua, kirgua
logic (n), krenik, kerenika, krenk
logical (adj), kreniku, kereniku, krenku
logically (adv), krenikiu, kerenikiu, krenkiu
logistic (n), krenkart, kerenikata, krenkat
logistical (adj), krenkartu, kerenikatu, krenkatu
logistically (adv), krenkartiu, kerenikatiu, krenkatiu
logjam (n), kirzhaurp, kirezhaupa, kirzhaup
logo (n), krenit, kerenita, krent
loiter (v), ritarsf, ritaro, ritaro
London (n), Londorn, Lonudona, London
lone (adj), fiernu, fienu, fienu
loneliness (n), fienarf, fienara, fienar
lonely (adj), fienarfu, fienaru, fienaru
loner (n doer), fiernwan, fienua, fienua
long (adj), ralzhu, razhu, razhu
longer (adj), ralzhwelu, razhwelu, razhwelu
longest (adj), ralzhwaku, razhwaku, razhwaku
longhand (n), razhkarp, razhekapa, razhkap
longing (adj d:desire), razhoilfu, razhoilu, razhoilu
longing (n d:desire), razhoilf, razhoila, razhoil
longingly (adv d:desire), razhoilfiu, razhoiliu,
    razhoiliu
longitude (n), razhdart, razhadata, razhdat
longshot (n), razheshkort, razheshekota,
    razheshkot
longtime (adj), ralzhdaurnu, razhedaunu,
    razhdaunu
look (n), reigirn, reigina, reigin
look (v), reigirsne, reigino, reigino
looker (n doer), reigirnwan, reiginua, reiginua
lookout (n), reigirnuil, reiginuila, reiginuil
loom (n), fiorme, fioma, fiom
loop (n), briarp, beriapa, briap
loop (v), briarsp, beriapo, briapo
looper (n doer), briarpwan, beriapua, briapua
loophole (n), briapkorth, beriapekotha, briapkoth
loopily (adv), briarpiu, beriapiu, briapiu
loopy (adj), briarpu, beriapu, briapu
loose (adj), foarfu, foarinu, foarnu
loosely (adv), foarfiu, foariniu, foarniu
loosen (v), foarsf, foarino, foarno
loot (n), mokashk, mokasha, mokash
loot (v), mokashsk, mokasho, mokasho
looter (n doer), mokashkwan, mokashua,

mokashua
lop (v), molsk, moko, moko
lopside (v), mokshoirst, mokeshoito, mokshoito
lord (n), sharfp, shafipa, shafp
Los Angeles (n), Losh Ankelersh, Losha Anikelesha,
    Losh Ankelesh
lose (v), zhaursf, zhauro, zhauro
loser (n doer), zhaurfwan, zhaurua, zhaurua
loss (n), zhaurf, zhaura, zhaur
lost (v pa), zhaursfyot, zhaurio, zhaurio
lot (n), krafp, keratha, krath
lotion (n), therf, thelifa, thelf
lottery (n), keirt, keita, keit
loud (adj), biarbu, biabu, biabu
louder (adj), biarbwelu, biabwelu, biabwelu
loudest (adj), biarbweku, biabweku, biabweku
loudly (adv), biarbiu, biabiu, biabiu
loudspeaker (n), biaplaturk, biapelatuka, biaplatuk
Louisiana (n), Luishiarf, Luishiafa, Luishiaf
lounge (n), biarve, biava, biav
lounge (v), biarzve, biavo, biavo
lovable (adj d:common), voshafrelpu, voshaferepu,
    voshafrepu
love (n d:common), voshar, voshara, voshar
love (n d:emphatic), voshave, voshavova, voshav
love (n d:pleasure), sharlf, shalifa, shalf
love (v d:common), voshasre, voshavo, voshavo
love (v d:emphatic), voshazve, voshavovo, voshavo
love (v d:pleasure), sharlsf, shalifo, shalfo
lovely (adj d:common), vosharu, vosharu, vosharu
lovely (adj d:emphatic), voshavu, voshavovu,
    voshavu
lovely (adj d:pleasure), sharlfu, shalifu, shalfu
lover (n doer d:common), vosharwan, vosharua,
    vosharua
lover (n doer d:emphatic), voshavwan, voshavovua,
    voshavua
lover (n doer d:pleasure), sharlfwan, shalifua,
    shalfua
low (adj), rialfu, rialu, rialu
low (n), rialf, riala, rial
lower (adj), rialfwelu, rialwelu, rialwelu
lower (v), rialsf, rialo, rialo
lowercase (n), rialeshkorf, rialeshikofa, rialshkof
lowest (adj), rialfwaku, rialwaku, rialwaku
lowly (adv), rialfiu, rialiu, rialiu
loyal (adj), fiorfu, fiofu, fiofu
loyally (adv), fiorfiu, fiofiu, fiofiu
loyalty (n), fiorf, fiofa, fiof
Ls (lot pl), lerfi, leifi, lerfl
lube (n), malirk, malika, malk
lubricant (n doer), malishkwan, malishokua,
    malshkua
lubricate (v), malishsk, malishoko, malshko
lubrication (n), malishk, malishoka, malshk
lucent (adj), shiunirku, shiuniku, shiunku
lucid (adj), shiurnu, shiunu, shiunu
luck (n), padar, pashota, pasht
luck (v), padasre, pashoto, pashto
luckier (adj), padarwelu, pashotwelu, pashtwelu
luckiest (adj), padarweku, pashotweku, pashtweku
luckily (adv), padariu, pashotiu, pashtiu
luckless (adj), padarmenu, pashotemenu,

pashtmenu
lucky (adj), padaru, pashotu, pashtu
lucrative (adj), kalshku, kalishu, kalshu
lucratively (adv), kalshkiu, kalishiu, kalshiu
ludicrous (adj), fruifanirtu, feruifanitu, fruifantu
ludicrously (adv), fruifanirtiu, feruifanitiu,
    fruifantiu
lug (n), flerge, felega, fleg
lug (v), flerzge, felego, flego
luggage (n), flegarf, felegara, flegar
lugger (n doer), flergwan, felegua, flegua
lukewarm (adj), rathaunshu, rathaunu, rathaunu
lull (n), mumorf, mumela, mumel
lull (v), mumorsf, mumelo, mumelo
lullaby (n), mumorfliauf, mumeliaufa, mumeliauf
lumber (n), miurp, miupa, miup
lumber (v), miursp, miupo, miupo
luminous (adj), fluathku, feluathu, fluathu
luminously (adv), fluathkiu, feluathiu, fluathiu
lump (n), manirk, manika, mank
lump (v), manirsk, maniko, manko
lumper (n doer), manirkwan, manikua, mankua
lumpy (adj), manirku, maniku, manku
lunch (n), priurt, periuta, priut
lunch (v), priurst, periuto, priuto
luncheon (n), priurf, periufa, priuf
luncher (n doer), priurtwan, periutua, priutua
lunchroom (n), priutshranf, periutesherana,
    priutshran
lung (n), nugarn, nugana, nugan
lunge (n), pelgat, peloka, pelk
lunge (v), pelgast, peloko, pelko
lunger (n doer), pelgatwan, pelokua, pelkua
lurch (v), triushst, teriusho, triusho
lure (n), gurshk, gushika, gushk
lure (v), gurshsk, gushiko, gushko
lurer (n doer), gurshkwan, gushikua, gushkua
lurk (v), triaushsk, teriausho, triausho
lurker (n doer), triaushkwan, teriaushua, triaushua
lust (n), gufirk, gufika, gufk
lust (v), gufirsk, gufiko, gufko
luster (n), luarp, luapa, luap
luster (v), luarsp, luapo, luapo
lustful (adj), gufirku, gufiku, gufku
lustfully (adv), gufirkiu, gufikiu, gufkiu
lustrous (adj), luarpu, luapu, luapu
Lutetium (n davoka), Irap, Irap, Irap
Lutetium (n), Lutetium, Lutetiuma, Lutetium
luxurious (adj), luarshu, luashu, luashu
luxuriously (adv), luarshiu, luashiu, luashiu
luxury (n), luarsh, luasha, luash
lynch (v), shithsk, shitho, shitho
lyre (n), rualf, ruala, rual
lyric (n), rualirf, rualipa, rualp
lyrical (adj), rualirfu, rualipu, rualpu
M (let sng), mail, maia, mai
ma (n), mah, maa, ma
machine (n), gizhaurk, gizhauka, gizhauk
machine (v), gizhaursk, gizhauko, gizhauko
machinery (n), gizhaurkar, gizhaukara, gizhaukar
machinist (n doer), gizhaurkwan, gizhaukua,
    gizhaukua
macho (adj), guzherpu, guzhepu, guzhepu

macro (n), paurf, paufa, pauf
macula (n), mioshk, mioka, miok
maculae (n pl), mioshkyek, mioki, mioki
macular (adj), mioshku, mioku, mioku
maculate (v), mioshsk, mioko, mioko
mad (adj d:angry), duparku, dupaku, dupaku
mad (adj d:insane), waidaku, waibu, waibu
madam (n), nuiblar, nuibara, nuibar
madame (n), nuiblar, nuibara, nuibar
madden (v d:angry), duparsk, dupako, dupako
madder (adj d:angry), duparkwelu, dupakwelu,
    dupakwelu
madder (adj d:insane), waidakwelu, waibwelu,
    waibwelu
made (v pa), narzgyot, nagio, nagio
madhouse (n), waidakiarf, waibekiafa, waibekiaf
Madison (n), Madishorf, Madishofa, Madishof
madman (n), waidaplorn, waibepelona, waibeplon
madmen (n pl), waidaplornyek, waibepeloni,
    waibeploni
madness (n d:insane), waidak, waiba, waib
Madrid (n), Madrirde, Maderida, Madrid
mafia (n), gaviart, gaviata, gaviat
magazine (n d:document), niforp, nifopa, nifp
magazine (n d:storage), gugairt, gugaita, gugait
maggot (n), galuk, galorina, galorn
magic (n), giagiarsh, giagiasha, giagiash
magical (adj), giagiarshu, giagiashu, giagiashu
magically (adv), giagiarshiu, giagiashiu, giagiashiu
magician (n doer), giagiarshwan, giagiashua,
    giagiashua
Magnesium (n davoka), Atip, Atip, Atip
Magnesium (n), Magneshium, Magoneshiuma,
    Magneshium
magnet (n doer), gukartwan, gukatua, gukatua
magnetic (adj), gukartu, gukatu, gukatu
magnetic (n), gukarft, gukafita, gukaft
magnetically (adv), gukartiu, gukatiu, gukatiu
magnetism (n), gukart, gukata, gukat
magnetize (v), gukarst, gukato, gukato
magnification (n), gaigarn, gaigana, gaigan
magnificence (n), gaigurt, gaiguta, gaigut
magnificent (adj), gaigurtu, gaigutu, gaigutu
magnificently (adv), gaigurtiu, gaigutiu, gaigutiu
magnifier (n doer), gaigarnwan, gaiganua, gaiganua
magnify (v), gaigarsne, gaigano, gaigano
magnitude (n), gaigart, gaigata, gaigat
maid (n), biarnf, bianofa, bianf
mail (n), pelirp, pelipa, pelp
mail (v), pelirsp, pelipo, pelpo
mailbag (n), pelpenufaf, pelipefanafa, pelpefnaf
mailbox (n), pelprenik, peliperenoka, pelprenk
mailer (n), pelparn, pelipana, pelpan
mailman (n doer), pelirpwan, pelipua, pelpua
maim (v), noinsk, kinoino, kinoino
main (adj), vaurshu, vaushu, vaushu
Maine (n), Mainorf, Mainofa, Mainf
mainland (n), vaushraufp, vausheraupa, vaushraup
mainline (n), vaushroifk, vausheroifa, vaushroif
mainly (adv), vaurshiu, vaushiu, vaushiu
mainstay (n), vaushlurk, vausheluka, vaushluk
mainstream (adj), vaurshfalirmu, vaushefalimu,
    vaushfalmu

maintain (v), vaushpifst, vaupifoto, vaupifto
maintainer (n doer), vaushpiftwan, vaupifotua, vaupiftua
maintenance (n), vaushpift, vaupifota, vaupift
major (adj), niarku, niaku, niaku
Major (n), Miorfk, Mioruka, Miork
major (v), niarsk, niako, niako
majority (n), niark, niaka, niak
make (v), narzge, nago, nago
maker (n doer), nargwan, nagua, nagua
makeup (n), nagirve, nagiva, nagiv
Maknesi (n), Maknesi, Maknesi, Maknesi
malady (n), zhuank, zhuana, zhuan
malaise (n), zhuankuet, zhuanueta, zhuanuet
Malaysia (n), Malashiarf, Malashiafa, Malashiaf
malcontent (n), zhuabeltriel, zhualiubupa, zhualiubup
male (adj), zhuarku, zhuaku, zhuaku
male (n), zhuark, zhuaka, zhuak
malform (v), zhuavorlisne, zhuavorino, zhuavorno
malformation (n), zhuavorlin, zhuavorina, zhuavorn
malfunction (n), zhuaprasht, zhuaperata, zhuaprat
malfunction (v), zhuaprashst, zhuaperato, zhuaprato
malice (n), zhuaborat, zhuaborita, zhuabort
malicious (adj), zhuaboratu, zhuaboritu, zhuabortu
maliciously (adv), zhuaboratiu, zhuaboritiu, zhuabortiu
malign (v), zhuankoisf, zhuanoifo, zhuanoifo
malignancy (n), zhuankoif, zhuanoifa, zhuanoif
malignant (adj), zhuankoifu, zhuanoifu, zhuanoifu
mall (n), brielf, beriela, briel
mallet (n), fatelt, fateta, fatet
mama (n), marah, mara, mar
mamma (n), marah, mara, mar
mammal (n), nalap, nalana, nalan
mammalian (adj), nalapu, nalanu, nalanu
mammogram (n), nalanelirk, nalanelika, nalanelk
mammography (n), nalaparft, nalanarifota, nalanarft
man (n d:male), noshk, nosha, nosh
man (v d:operate), shars, shasho, shasho
manage (v), sharshsk, shashiko, shashko
manageable (adj), sharshku, shashiku, shashku
manageably (adv), sharshkiu, shashikiu, shashkiu
management (n), sharshk, shashika, shashk
manager (n doer), sharshkwan, shashikua, shashkua
managerial (adj), sharshkwatu, shashikualu, shashkualu
Manchester (n), Manshersht, Manisheshota, Manshesht
mandate (n), shoirk, shoika, shoik
mandate (v), shoirsk, shoiko, shoiko
mandatory (adj), shoirku, shoiku, shoiku
mane (n), tharmp, tharima, tharm
maneuver (n), kapurift, kapurita, kapurt
maneuver (v), kapurifst, kapurito, kapurto
maneuverability (n), kapurtfrelp, kapuriteferepa, kapurtfrep
Manganese (n davoka), Ifak, Ifak, Ifak
Manganese (n), Manganesh, Manuganesha, Manganesh

mangle (v), faitazhzge, faitago, faitago
Manhattan (n), Mankatarf, Manokatafa, Mankataf
manhole (n), plonkorth, pelonekotha, plonkoth
manhunt (n), plonegrulat, pelonegerulita, plonegrult
mania (n), greiarge, gereiaga, greiag
maniac (n doer), greiargwan, gereiagua, greiagua
maniacal (adj), greiargu, gereiagu, greiagu
manic (adj), greiargu, gereiagu, greiagu
manifest (n), shoirkuk, shoikuka, shoikuk
manifest (v), shoirkusk, shoikuko, shoikuko
manifold (n), fumeitrafk, fumeiterava, fumeitrav
Manila (n), Manilorf, Manilofa, Manilf
manipulate (v), shoifarsk, shoifako, shoifko
manipulation (n), shoifark, shoifaka, shoifk
manipulative (adj), shoifarku, shoifaku, shoifku
manipulatively (adv), shoifarkiu, shoifakiu, shoifkiu
manipulator (n doer), shoifarkwan, shoifakua, shoifkua
mankind (n), sholarfirf, sholarefifa, sholarfif
manly (adj d:male), noshku, noshu, noshu
manmade (adj), sholnargu, sholenagu, sholnagu
manner (n), shoiklirp, shoikelipa, shoiklip
manpower (n), sholbiorat, sholebiorita, sholbiort
mansion (n), shoifarn, shoifana, shoifan
manslaughter (n), plonshriausht, pelonesheriauta, plonshriaut
mantle (n), vaizhe, vaizha, vaizh
manual (adj), shoishku, shoishu, shoishu
manual (n), shoishk, shoisha, shoish
manually (adv), shoishkiu, shoishiu, shoishiu
manufacture (v), shoikaurst, shoikauto, shoikauto
manufacturer (n doer), shoikaurtwan, shoikautua, shoikautua
manure (n), noshtairge, noshetaiga, noshtaig
manuscript (n), kapsherge, kapesheriga, kapshrig
many (adj), fumeinu, fumeilu, fumeilu
map (n), shipern, shipena, shpen
map (v), shipersne, shipeno, shpeno
maple (n), mafpal, malifopa, malfp
mar (v), miarzbe, miabo, miabo
marathon (n), rathiern, rathiena, rathien
marathoner (n doer), rathiernwan, rathienua, rathienua
marble (n), melvarn, meluvana, melvan
MarbleRobot, breilut, bereiluta, breilt
march (n), voark, voarifa, voarf
March (n), Mular, Mulara, Mular
march (v), voarsk, voarifo, voarfo
marcher (n doer), voarkwan, voarifua, voarfua
mare (n), melirn, melina, melin
margin (n), doirge, doiga, doig
marginal (adj), doirgu, doigu, doigu
marginalize (v), doirzge, doigo, doigo
marginally (adv), doirgiu, doigiu, doigiu
marijuana (n), Karkuairn, Karokuaina, Karkuain
marina (n), liaufp, liaupa, liaup
marine (adj), liaurnu, liaunu, liaunu
mariner (n doer), liaurnwan, liaunua, liaunua
Marines (n), Maitark, Maitaka, Maitak
marital (adj), vularnu, vulanu, vulnu
mark (n), shtart, shetata, shtat

mark (v), shtarst, shetato, shtato
markdown (n), shtatiern, shetatiena, shtatien
marked (adj), shtartu, shetatu, shtatu
markedly (adv), shtartiu, shetatiu, shtatiu
marker (n doer), shtartwan, shetatua, shtatua
market (n), delnart, delonata, delnat
market (v), delnarst, delonato, delnato
marketability (n), delnatfrelp, delonateferepa, delnatfrep
marketable (adj), delnatfrelpu, delonateferepu, delnatfrepu
marketeer (n doer), delnartwan, delonatua, delnatua
marketer (n doer), delnartwan, delonatua, delnatua
marketplace (n), delnabrelsh, delonaberesha, delnabresh
markup (n), shtartiveil, shetativeila, shtativeil
maroon (v), liaushnefst, liausheneto, liaushneto
marriage (n), vularn, vulana, vuln
marry (v), vularsne, vulano, vulno
marsh (n), liauthk, liautha, liauth
marshal (n), melnirk, melinika, melink
marshal (v), melnirsk, meliniko, melinko
marshland (n), liauthraufp, liautheraupa, liauthraup
marshy (adj), liauthku, liauthu, liauthu
martial (adj), shtarfu, shetafu, shtafu
martyr (n), shlairp, shelaipa, shlaip
martyr (v), shlairsp, shelaipo, shlaipo
marvel (n), neilarf, neilafa, neilf
marvel (v), neilarsf, neilafo, neilfo
marvelous (adj), neilarfu, neilafu, neilfu
marvelously (adv), neilarfiu, neilafiu, neilfiu
Maryland (n), Marilanurde, Marilanuda, Mariland
mascot (n), theikart, theikata, theikat
masculine (adj), zhuarku, zhuaku, zhuaku
masculinity (n), zhuark, zhuaka, zhuak
mash (n), nifork, nifoka, nifk
mash (v), niforsk, nifoko, nifko
masher (n doer), niforkwan, nifokua, nifkua
mask (n), theirk, theika, theik
mask (v), theirsk, theiko, theiko
mass (n), glarfk, gelarika, glark
mass (v), glarfsk, gelariko, glarko
Massachusetts (n), Mashashutarf, Mashashutafa, Mashashutaf
massacre (n), graugiashk, geraugiasha, graugiash
massacre (v), graugiashsk, geraugiasho, graugiasho
massage (n), riaf, riasha, riash
massage (v), riasf, riasho, riasho
massager (n doer), riafwan, riashua, riashua
massive (adj), glarfku, gelariku, glarku
massively (adv), glarfkiu, gelarikiu, glarkiu
mast (n), thalirp, thalipa, thalp
mast (v), thalirsp, thalipo, thalpo
master (n), thiork, thioka, thiok
master (v), thiorsk, thioko, thioko
masterful (adj), thiorku, thioku, thioku
masterfully (adv), thiorkiu, thiokiu, thiokiu
mastermind (n), thiokniarp, thiokeniapa, thiokniap
mastermind (v), thiokniarsp, thiokeniapo, thiokniapo
masterpiece (n), thiokthetirsh, thiokethetisha,

thiokthetsh
masterstroke (n), thiokaturk, thiokatuka, thiokatuk
mastery (n), thiorkuet, thiokueta, thiokuet
masthead (n), thalpekefirt, thalipekefita, thalpekeft
mat (n), marft, marifa, marf
mat (v), marfst, marifo, marfo
match (n d:selection), muthk, mutha, muth
match (n d:stick), shkithk, shekitha, shkith
match (v d:selection), muthsk, mutho, mutho
matchbox (n d:stickbox), shkithprekun, shekitheperenika, shkithprenk
matcher (n doer d:selection), muthkwan, muthua, muthua
matchless (adj d:selection), muthkmenu, muthemenu, muthmenu
matchmade (v pa d:make selection), muthnarzgyot, muthenagio, muthnagio
matchmake (v d:make selection), muthnarzge, muthenago, muthnago
matchmaker (n doer d:make selection), muthnargwan, muthenagua, muthnagua
mate (n), mushirp, mushipa, mushp
mate (v), mushirsp, mushipo, mushpo
material (n), turge, tiluga, tilg
materialism (n), turguet, tilugueta, tilguet
materialist (n doer), turgwan, tilugua, tilgua
materialistic (adj), turgu, tilugu, tilgu
materialize (v), turzge, tilugo, tilgo
materistically (adv), turgiu, tilugiu, tilgiu
maternal (adj), sharvarbu, sharuvabu, sharvabu
maternally (adv), sharvarbiu, sharuvabiu, sharvabiu
maternity (n), sharvarbe, sharuvaba, sharvab
math (n), vikavit, kavita, kavit
mathematic (n), vikavat, kavata, kavat
mathematical (adj), vikavatu, kavatu, kavatu
mathematically (adv), vikavatiu, kavatiu, kavatiu
mathematician (n doer), vikavatwan, kavatua, kavatua
matriarch (n), tralmalirsh, teralemalisha, tralmalsh
matriarchal (adj), tralmalirshu, teralemalishu, tralmalshu
matrimonial (adj), vulashku, vulashu, vulashu
matrimony (n), vulashk, vulasha, vulash
matrix (n), taikart, taikata, taikat
matron (n), tralmark, teralemaka, tralmak
matter (n d:incident), gebirk, gebika, gebik
matter (n d:physics), denirk, denika, denk
matter (v d:incident), gebirsk, gebiko, gebiko
mattress (n), marftan, marifana, marfan
maturation (n), shirftuet, shirofueta, shirfuet
mature (adj), shirftu, shirofu, shirfu
mature (v), shirfst, shirofo, shirfo
maturity (n), shirft, shirofa, shirf
maul (v), faiteshsk, faitesho, faitsho
maw (n), friaup, feriaufa, friauf
max (n), mairk, maika, maik
max (v), mairsk, maiko, maiko
maximal (adj), maikartu, maikatu, maikatu
maximally (adv), maikartiu, maikatiu, maikatiu
maximize (v), maikarst, maikato, maikato
maximum (n), maikart, maikata, maikat
May (n), Lamail, Lamaila, Lamail

may (ndal d:permission), noirf kodi, noifa kodi, noif kodi
maybe (adv), lornoirfiu, lorenoifiu, lornoifiu
maybe (n), lornoirf, lorenoifa, lornoif
mayhem (n), noink, kinoina, kinoin
mayor (n), noipan, noipa, noip
mayoral (adj), noipanu, noipu, noipu
maze (n), diaurf, diaufa, diauf
me (pron 1st sng obj), nau, nau, nau
meadow (n), nailarf, nailara, nailar
meager (adj), lifezhgu, lifezhu, lifezhu
meagerly (adv), lifezhgiu, lifezhiu, lifezhiu
meagerness (n), lifezhge, lifezha, lifezh
meal (n), shirbe, shiba, shib
mealtime (adj), shibedaurnu, shibedaunu, shibedaunu
mealtime (n), shibedaurn, shibedauna, shibedaun
mean (adj d:cruel), shklivargu, shikelivagu, shklivagu
mean (n d:average), oflork, ofeloka, oflok
mean (n), vuparn, vupana, vupan
mean (v d:importance), vursp, vupo, vupo
meander (v), vuiaufsk, vuiaufo, vuiaufo
meaner (adj d:cruel), shklivargwelu, shikelivagwelu, shklivagwelu
meanest (adj d:cruel), shklivargweku, shikelivagweku, shklivagweku
meaningful (adj d:importance), vurpu, vupu, vupu
meaningfully (adv d:importance), vurpiu, vupiu, vupiu
meaningless (adj), vurpemenu, vupemenu, vupemenu
meaninglessness (n), vurpemen, vupemena, vupemen
meanness (n d:cruel), shklivarge, shikelivaga, shklivag
meant (v pa d:importance), vurspyot, vupio, vupio
meantime (adv), vupodauniu, vudauniu, vudauniu
meantime (n), vupodaun, vudauna, vudaun
meanwhile (adv), vupaurkiu, vupaukiu, vupaukiu
meanwhile (n), vupaurk, vupauka, vupauk
measly (adj), lifezhgatu, lifezhatu, lifezhatu
measurable (adj), grolfu, gerolu, grolu
measurably (adv), grolfiu, geroliu, groliu
measure (v), grolsf, gerolo, grolo
measurement (n), grolf, gerola, grol
measurer (n doer), grolfwan, gerolua, grolua
meat (n), ratirsh, ratisha, ratsh
meatball (n), ratshmonde, ratishemashipa, ratshmashp
meatless (adj), ratirshmenu, ratishemenu, ratshmenu
meaty (adj), ratirshu, ratishu, ratshu
mechanic (n doer), gizharpwan, gizhapua, gizhapua
mechanical (adj), gizharpu, gizhapu, gizhapu
mechanically (adv), gizharpiu, gizhapiu, gizhapiu
mechanism (n), gizharp, gizhapa, gizhap
mechanization (n), gizharpuet, gizhapueta, gizhapuet
mechanize (v), gizharsp, gizhapo, gizhapo
medal (n), lardart, larudata, lardat
medal (v), lardarst, larudato, lardato
medalist (n doer), lardartwan, larudatua, lardatua

meddle (v), zhorpansk, zhorepano, zhorpano
meddler (n doer), zhorpankwan, zhorepanua, zhorpanua
media (n pl d:information flow), laidarkyek, laidaki, laidaki
medial (adj d:information flow), laidarku, laidaku, laidaku
median (adj), zhiamartu, zhorepanu, zhiamatu
median (n), zhiamart, zhorepana, zhiamat
mediate (v d:information flow), laidarsk, laidako, laidako
mediation (n), laidarkuet, laidakueta, laidakuet
mediator (n doer d:information flow), laidarkwan, laidakua, laidakua
medic (n doer), vobalfwan, vobalua, vobalua
medical (adj), vobalfu, vobalu, vobalu
medically (adv), vobalfiu, vobaliu, vobaliu
medicate (v), vobalsf, vobalo, vobalo
medication (n), vobalf, vobala, vobal
medicine (n), vobalf, vobala, vobal
mediocre (adj), zhavarteshu, zhavariteshu, zhavartshu
mediocrity (n), zhavartesh, zhavaritesha, zhavartsh
meditate (v), zhiarfisk, zhiarofiko, zhiarfko
meditation (n), zhiarfik, zhiarofika, zhiarfk
Mediterranean (n), Mediteraniarf, Mediteraniafa, Mediteranf
medium (adj d:middle), zhiarmu, zhiamu, zhiamu
medium (n d:information flow), laidark, laidaka, laidak
medium (n d:middle), zhiarme, zhiama, zhiam
meek (adj), rininku, rininu, rininu
meek (n pl), rininkyek, rinini, rinini
meekly (adv), rininkiu, rininiu, rininiu
meet (n), lerp, lepa, lep
meet (v), lersp, lepo, lepo
mega- (num 1e6 pref), hemkai-, hemkai-, hemkai-
meikosi- (num 1e57 pref), genshtai-, genshtai-, genshtai-
Meitnerium (n davoka), Inok, Inok, Inok
Meitnerium (n), Metnerium, Metoneriuma, Metnerium
mellow (adj), divulfu, divulu, divulu
mellow (v), divulsf, divulo, divulo
melodic (adj), diavu, divuru, divuru
melody (n), diave, divura, divur
melon (n), dibalf, dibala, dibal
melt (v), kefirsk, kefiko, kefko
meltdown (n), kefketiern, kefiketiena, kefketien
meltwater (n), kefkeidorn, kefikeidona, kefkeidon
member (n), meshiurt, meshiuta, mesht
membership (n), meshtif, meshefifa, meshfif
membrane (n), meshtarn, meshutana, meshtan
membranous (adj), meshtarnu, meshutanu, meshtanu
memo (n), nimart, nimata, nimat
memoir (n), talnank, talnuna, talnan
memorable (adj), talurnu, talunu, talnu
memorably (adv), talurniu, taluniu, talniu
memorial (n), talnaf, talnara, talnar
memorialize (v), talnasf, talunaro, talnaro
memorize (v), talursne, taluno, talno
memory (n), talurn, taluna, taln

Memphis (n), Memfirsh, Memofisha, Memfish
men (n pl d:male), noshkyek, noshi, noshi
menace (n), thiazhge, thiaga, thiag
menace (v), thiazhzge, thiago, thiago
menacingly (adv), thiazhgiu, thiagiu, thiagiu
mend (v), shkarsf, shikafo, shkafo
Mendelevium (n davoka), Onaf, Onaf, Onaf
Mendelevium (n), Mendelevium, Menadeleviuma,
    Mendelevium
menial (adj), zhavashtu, zhavatu, zhavatu
menses (n), bauthk, bautha, bauth
menstrual (adj), shobraufu, shoberauthu,
    shobrauthu
menstruate (v), shobrausf, shoberautho,
    shobrautho
menstruation (n), shobrauf, shoberautha,
    shobrauth
mental (adj), altarku, alitaku, altaku
mentality (n), altark, alitaka, altak
mentally (adv), altarkiu, alitakiu, altakiu
mention (n), altirp, alotipa, altip
mention (v), altirsp, alotipo, altipo
mentor (n), altakwat, alitakuata, altakuat
mentor (v), altakwast, alitakuato, altakuato
menu (n), nimarn, nimana, niman
meow (interj), rakiu, rakiu, rakiu
merchandise (n), lafirk, lafika, lafk
merchandize (v), lafirsk, lafiko, lafko
merchandized (v prp), lafirskaut, lafikao, lafkao
merchant (n doer), lafirkwan, lafikua, lafkua
merciful (adj), fiaurnu, fiaunu, fiaunu
mercifully (adv), fiaurniu, fiauniu, fiauniu
merciless (adj), fiaurmenu, fiaumenu, fiaumenu
mercilessly (adv), fiaurmeniu, fiaumeniu,
    fiaumeniu
Mercury (n davoka), Irit, Irit, Irit
Mercury (n), Merkuri, Merakuria, Merkuri
mercy (n), fiaurn, fiauna, fiaun
mere (adj), walfu, wafu, wafu
merely (adv), walfiu, wafiu, wafiu
merge (n), lafirp, lafipa, lafp
merge (v), lafirsp, lafipo, lafpo
merger (n doer), lafirpwan, lafipua, lafpua
meridian (n), zhialirme, zhialima, zhialm
merit (n), wiarf, wiafa, wiaf
merit (v), wiarsf, wiafo, wiafo
merrier (adj), relarnwelu, relanwelu, relnwelu
merriest (adj), relarnweku, relanweku, relnweku
merrily (adv), relarniu, relaniu, relniu
merriment (n), relarn, relana, reln
merry (adj), relarnu, relanu, relnu
mesa (n), muirsh, muisha, muish
mesh (n), theioshk, theiosha, theiosh
mesh (v), theioshsk, theioso, theioso
mess (n), nairsh, naisha, naish
mess (v), nairs, naisho, naisho
message (n), tiort, tiota, tiot
message (v), tiorsg, tioto, tioto
messenger (n doer), tiortwan, tiotua, tiotua
messy (adj), nairshu, naishu, naishu
met (v pa), lerspyot, lepio, lepio
meta (adj), neirku, neiku, neiku
metal (n), tiart, tiata, tiat

metallic (adj), tiartu, tiatu, tiatu
metaphor (n), neikarf, neikafa, neikaf
metaphorical (adj), neikarfu, neikafu, neikafu
meteor (n), leparshk, leparika, lepark
meteorite (n), leparshkat, leparikata, leparkat
meter (n d:device), niork, nioka, niok
meter (n d:metric measurement), limert, limeta,
    limet
meter (v d:device), niorsk, nioko, nioko
methane (n), muthoran, muthorin, muthorn
method (n), prufk, peruka, pruk
methodical (adj), prufku, peruku, pruku
methodically (adv), prufkiu, perukiu, prukiu
methodize (v), prufsk, peruko, pruko
methodology (n), prufkuit, perukuita, prukuit
metric (n), niorkar, niokara, niokar
metropolis (n), kavilort, kavilota, kavilt
metropolitan (n doer), kavilortwan, kavilotua,
    kaviltua
Mexican (n), Meshkifarn, Meshakifana, Meshkifan
Mexico (n), Meshkirf, Meshakifa, Meshkif
Miami (n), Miamirf, Miamifa, Miamif
mice (n pl), doartyek, doati, doati
Michigan (n), Mishigarf, Mishigafa, Mishigaf
microbe (n), lilufp, lilupa, lilup
microbial (adj), lilufpu, lilupu, lilupu
microbiologist (n doer), lilmierkuitwan,
    lilemiekuitua, lilmiekuitua
microbiology (n), lilmierkuit, lilemiekuita,
    lilmiekuit
microfilm (n), lilrodap, liledeiora, lildeior
microphone (n), liluyarp, liluyapa, liluyap
microscope (n), lilakluarf, lilakeluafa, lilakluaf
microsystem (n), lilsharshturk, lilesharishotuka,
    lilsharshtuk
microwave (n), lilersh, lilesha, lilesh
microwave (v), lilers, lilesho, lilesho
midafternoon (n), zharovimidort, zharovimidota,
    zharovimidot
midair (n), zharaul, zharaula, zharaul
midday (n), zharviurl, zharoviula, zharviul
middle (adj), zharaftu, zharatu, zhartu
middle (n), zharaft, zharata, zhart
middleman (n), zhartplorn, zharatepelona,
    zhartplon
Mideast (n), Midirsht, Midishata, Midisht
midge (n), koshank, koshana, koshan
midmorning (n), zharlimern, zharelimena,
    zharlimen
midnight (n), munarn, munana, munan
midpoint (n), zhartaifort, zharetaifota, zhartaift
midrange (n), zharmimarn, zharemimana,
    zharmiman
midseason (n), zharfivarl, zharefivala, zharfival
midsection (n), zharthisharl, zharethishala,
    zharthishal
midst (n), zharaft, zharata, zhart
midstream (n), zharfalirme, zharefalima, zharfalm
midsummer (n), zharfrulf, zhareferula, zharfrul
midterm (adj), zharshtrenu, zharishotenu,
    zharshtenu
midterm (n), zharshtren, zharishotena, zharshten
midway (n), zharpliorl, zharepeliola, zharpliol

midweek (n), zharkrufk, zharekerufa, zharkruf
Midwest (n), Miduelsh, Miduesha, Miduesh
midwife (n), sharalf, sharala, sharal
midwinter (n), zharvemport, zharevemipota,
zharvempot
midyear (n), zharkliorsh, zharekelosha, zharklosh
might (n d:strength), gerft, gerita, gert
might (ndal d:possibility), lorilf kodi, lorifa kodi,
lorf kodi
mightier (adj), gerftwelu, geritwelu, gertwelu
mightiest (adj), gerftweku, geritweku, gertweku
mightily (adv d:strength), gerftiu, geritiu, gertiu
mighty (adj d:strength), gerftu, geritu, gertu
migrant (adj), pelirvu, pelivu, plivu
migrant (n doer), pelirvwan, pelivua, plivua
migrate (v), pelirzve, pelivo, plivo
migration (n), pelirve, peliva, pliv
mild (adj), ranernu, ranenu, ranenu
milder (adj), ranernwelu, ranenwelu, ranenwelu
mildest (adj), ranernweku, ranenweku, ranenweku
mildly (adv), ranerniu, raneniu, raneniu
mildness (n), ranern, ranena, ranen
mile (n), mailern, mailena, mailen
mileage (n), mailenart, mailenata, mailenat
milestone (n), razhbaraft, razhebarafa, razhbaraf
militant (n doer), ginartwan, ginatua, gintua
militarize (v), ginarst, ginato, ginto
military (n), ginart, ginata, gint
militia (n), ginatark, ginataka, gintak
milk (n), lormp, lorima, lorm
milk (v), lormesp, lorimo, lormo
milker (n doer), lormpwan, lorimua, lormua
milky (adj), lormpu, lorimu, lormu
mill (n), fenirp, fenipa, fenp
mill (v), fenirsp, fenipo, fenpo
miller (n doer), fenirpwan, fenipua, fenpua
million (num 1e6 card) , hemka, hemka, hemka
millionth (num 1e6 ord), hemkadeth, hemkadeth,
hemkadeth
Milwaukee (n), Miluakirf, Miluakifa, Miluakif
min (n), limerth, limetha, limth
mind (n), niarp, niapa, niap
mind (v), niarsp, niapo, niapo
mindful (adj), niarpu, niapu, niapu
mindfully (adv), niarpiu, niapiu, niapiu
mindless (adj), niarpemenu, niapemenu,
niapemenu
mindlessly (adv), niarpemeniu, niapemeniu,
niapemeniu
mindset (n), niapeferp, niapefepa, niapefep
mine (n d:bomb), zhaurt, zhauta, zhaut
mine (n d:cave), krivuge, keriga, krig
mine (pron 1st sng pos obj), nuime, nuime, nuime
mine (v d:bomb), zhaurst, zhauto, zhauto
mine (v d:cave), krivuzge, kerigo, krigo
minefield (n), zhauteprant, zhauteperanida,
zhauteprand
miner (n doer d:cave), krivugwan, kerigua, krigua
mineral (n), krivurge, kerigara, krigar
mingle (v), feitazhzge, feitago, feitago
miniature (adj), limirku, limiku, limku
miniature (n), limirk, limika, limk
miniaturize (v), limirsk, limiko, limko

minimal (adj), limirshu, limishu, limshu
minimalism (n), limirshuet, limishueta, limshuet
minimalist (n doer), limirshwan, limishua, limshua
minimalization (n), limirshuet, limishueta,
limshuet
minimally (adv), limirshiu, limishiu, limshiu
minimize (v), limirs, limisho, limsho
minimum (n), limirsh, limisha, limsh
miniseries (n), limnilorf, liminilofa, limnilf
miniskirt (n), limfnilort, limifenilota, limfnilt
minister (n doer), novitwan, nofitua, noftua
minister (v), novist, nofito, nofto
ministry (n), novit, nofita, noft
minivan (n), limzhaurn, limizhauna, limzhaun
Minneapolis (n), Minkarpol, Minekapola, Minkapol
Minnesota (n), Minshort, Mineshota, Minshot
minor (adj), niurpu, niupu, niupu
minor (v), niursp, niupo, niupo
minority (n), niurp, niupa, niup
mint (adj), niathku, niathku, niathu
mint (n), niathk, niatha, niath
mint (v), niathsk, niatho, niatho
minter (n doer), niathkwan, niathua, niathua
mintly (adv), niathkiu, niathiu, niathiu
minus (adj/prep), limursh, limushu, limush
minus (n), limursh, limusha, limush
minuses (n pl), limurshyek, limushi, limushi
minute (adj d:small), nimshiru, nimashilu,
nimshilu
minute (n d:time), darmirk, daromika, darmik
minutely (adv d:small), nimshiriu, nimashiliu,
nimshiliu
miracle (n), niarfk, niafoka, niafk
miraculous (adj), niarfku, niafoku, niafku
miraculously (adv), niarfkiu, niafokiu, niafkiu
mirage (n), nianart, nianata, nianat
mire (n), luarme, luama, luam
mire (v), luarzme, luamo, luamo
Miriam (n), Miriam, Miriama, Miriam
mirror (n), niarn, niana, nian
mirror (v), niarsne, niano, niano
misadventure (n), dhiduliart, dhiduliata, dhiduliat
misalign (v), dhioroifsk, dhioroifo, dhioroifo
misalignment (n), dhioroifk, dhioroifa, dhioroif
misallocate (v), dhiorshairsp, dhiorishaipo,
dhiorshaipo
misallocation (n pl), dhiorshairpyek, dhiorishaipi,
dhiorshaipi
misapplication (n pl), dhithorkyek, dhithoki,
dhithoki
misapply (v), dhithorsk, dhitholko, dhitholko
misapprehend (v), dhiodrukerst, dhioderuketo,
dhiodruketo
misapprehension (n), dhiodrukert, dhioderuketa,
dhiodruket
misappropriate (v), dhioflikirzme, dhiofelikimo,
dhioflikimo
misappropriation (n), dhioflikirme, dhiofelikima,
dhioflikim
misbehave (v), dhikuvasre, dhikulifo, dhikulfo
misbehavior (n), dhikuvar, dhikulifa, dhikulf
miscalculate (v), dhigardas, dhigarodako,
dhigardako

miscalculation (n), dhigardash, dhigarodaka, dhigardak
miscarriage (n), dhiflude, dhigerena, dhigren
miscarry (v), dhifluzde, dhigereno, dhigreno
miscellaneous (adj), shralfu, sherafu, shrafu
miscellany (n), shralf, sherafa, shraf
mischief (n), dhivirt, dhivita, dhivit
mischievous (adj), dhivirtu, dhivitu, dhivitu
miscommunicate (v), dhiguniarst, dhiguniato, dhiguniato
miscommunication (n), dhiguniart, dhiguniata, dhiguniat
misconceive (v), dhibelshisp, dhiliushipo, dhiliushpo
misconception (n), dhibelship, dhiliushipa, dhiliushp
misconduct (n), dhibelkriuk, dhiliukeriuka, dhiliukriuk
misconduct (v), dhibelkriusk, dhiliukeriuko, dhiliukriuko
misconstrue (v), dhibelplairsp, dhiliupelaipo, dhiliuplaipo
miscreant (n doer), dhiflershwan, dhifelenishua, dhiflenshua
miscredibility (n), dhiflersh, dhifelenisha, dhiflensh
miscue (n), dhitierf, dhiteifa, dhiteif
miscue (v), dhitiersf, dhiteifo, dhiteifo
misdeed (n), dhifelirde, dhifelida, dhiflid
misdemeanor (n), dhibuliarge, dhibuliaga, dhibuliag
misdiagnose (v), dhiaishmarsne, dhiaishomano, dhiaishmano
misdiagnosis (n), dhiaishmarn, dhiaishomana, dhiaishman
misdirect (v), dhikuarfsk, dhikuafiko, dhikuafko
misdirection (n), dhikuarfk, dhikuafika, dhikuafk
miser (n), thuirn, thuina, thuin
miserable (adj), thunairku, thunaiku, thunaiku
miserably (adv), thunairkiu, thunaikiu, thunaikiu
miserly (adj), thuirnu, thuinu, thuinu
misery (n), thunairk, thunaika, thunaik
misfire (n), dhishriauk, dhigiaula, dhigiaul
misfire (v), dhishriausk, dhigiaulo, dhigiaulo
misfit (n), dhipafirt, dhipafita, dhipaft
misfortune (n), dhivoashmun, dhivoamuna, dhivoamun
misgave (v pa), dhigrusfyot, dhigeruthio, dhigruthio
misgive (v), dhigrusf, dhigerutho, dhigrutho
misguidance (n), dhituirp, dhituipa, dhituip
misguide (v), dhituirsp, dhituipo, dhituipo
mishandle (v), dhikarpazde, dhikapado, dhikapado
mishap (n), dhikolirp, dhikolipa, dhikolp
mishappen (v), dhikolirsp, dhikolipo, dhikolpo
mishmash (n), nufnifk, nufenifa, nufnif
misidentification (n), dhiufert, dhiuferitha, dhiuferth
misidentify (v), dhiuferst, dhiuferitho, dhiufertho
misinform (v), dhiarvorsne, dhiivorino, dhiivorno
misinformation (n), dhiarvorn, dhiivorina, dhiivorn
misinterpret (v), dhienridrusp, dhiariderupo, dhiaridrupo
misinterpretation (n), dhienridrup, dhiariderupa,

dhiaridrup
misjudge (v), dhihetherst, dhihetheto, dhihetheto
misjudgement (n), dhihethert, dhihetheta, dhihethet
misjudgment (n), dhihethert, dhihetheta, dhihethet
mislead (v), dhilalirst, dhilalito, dhilalto
misleader (n doer), dhilalirtwan, dhilalitua, dhilaltua
misleadingly (adv), dhilalirtiu, dhilalitiu, dhilaltiu
mismanage (v), dhisharshsk, dhishashiko, dhishashko
mismanagement (n), dhisharshk, dhishashika, dhishashk
mismatch (n), dhimuthk, dhimutha, dhimuth
mismatch (v), dhimuthsk, dhimutho, dhimutho
misnomer (n), dhiviern, dhiviena, dhivien
misogyny (n), diveiank, dhiveiana, dhiveian
misperceive (v), dhiloshirsp, dhiloshipo, dhiloshipo
misperception (n), dhiloshirp, dhiloshipa, dhiloship
misplace (v), dhibrels, dhiberesho, dhibresho
misplacement (n), dhibrelsh, dhiberesha, dhibresh
misplay (n), dhifruifk, dhiferuifa, dhifruif
misplay (v), dhifruifsk, dhiferuifo, dhifruifo
misprint (n), dhitrulish, dhiterulisha, dhitrulsh
misprint (v), dhitrulis, dhiterulisho, dhitrulsho
mispronounce (v), dhifiunferst, dhifiunifeto, dhifiunfeto
mispronunciation (n), dhifiunfert, dhifiunifeta, dhifiunfet
misquote (n), dhihinarf, dhihinafa, dhihinf
misquote (v), dhihinarsf, dhihinafo, dhihinfo
misread (n), dhiliarp, dhiliapa, dhiliap
misread (v pa), dhiliarspyot, dhiliapio, dhiliapio
misread (v), dhiliarsp, dhiliapo, dhiliapo
misrepresent (v), dhiludars, dhiluduasho, dhiluduasho
misrepresentation (n), dhiludarsh, dhiluduasha, dhiluduash
misrule (v), dhilarast, dhilarito, dhilarto
miss (n d:avoid), dhiarsh, dhiasha, dhiash
Miss (n), Neilh, Neltha, Neith
miss (v d:avoid), dhiars, dhiasho, dhiasho
miss (v d:regret absence), lularst, lulato, lulto
missile (n), krishart, kerishata, krishat
mission (n), naurk, nauka, nauk
Mississippi (n), Mishashirp, Mishashipa, Mishaship
Missouri (n), Mishuralf, Mishurafa, Mishurf
misspell (v), dhithasle, dhitharo, dhitharo
misspend (v), dhidorklarst, dhidorikelato, dhidorklato
misspent (v pa), dhidorklarstyot, dhidorikelatio, dhidorklatio
misstate (v), dhibiurst, dhibiuto, dhibiuto
misstatement (n), dhibiurt, dhibiuta, dhibiut
misstep (n), dhiglishk, dhigelisha, dhiglish
misstep (v), dhiglishsk, dhigelisho, dhiglisho
mist (n), shrilf, sherifa, shrif
mist (v), shrilsf, sherifo, shrifo
mistake (n), dhigork, dhigoka, dhigok
mistake (v), dhigorsk, dhigoko, dhigoko
mistakenly (adv), dhigorkiu, dhigokiu, dhigokiu
mister (n doer), shrilfwan, sherifua, shrifua
Mister (n), Krashat, Kerashata, Krashat

mistily (adv), shrilfiu, sherifiu, shrifiu
mistook (v pa), dhigorskyot, dhigokio, dhigokio
mistreat (v), dhithuirst, dhithuito, dhithuito
mistreatment (n), dhithuirt, dhithuita, dhithuit
mistress (n), thioshk, thiosha, thiosh
mistrial (n), dhidibarge, dhidibaga, dhidibag
mistrust (n), dhidreirf, dhidereifa, dhidreif
mistrust (v), dhidreirsf, dhidereifo, dhidreifo
misty (adj), shrilfu, sherifu, shrifu
misunderstand (v), dhitrelst, dhitenito, dhitento
misunderstood (v pa), dhitrelstyot, dhitenitio, dhitentio
misuse (n), dhibriark, dhiberiaka, dhibriak
misuse (v), dhibriarsk, dhiberiako, dhibriako
mite (n), bishirk, bishika, bishk
mitigate (v), pilshsk, piliko, pilko
mitigation (n), pilshk, pilika, pilk
mitt (n), nurth, nutha, nuth
mitten (n), nutharf, nuthafa, nuthaf
mix (n), zhorfk, zhorika, zhork
mix (v), zhorfsk, zhoriko, zhorko
mixer (n doer), zhorfkwan, zhorikua, zhorkua
mixture (n), zhorfkar, zhorikara, zhorkar
moan (n), dauzhe, dauva, dauv
moan (v), dauze, dauvo, dauvo
moat (n), niudaft, niudata, niudat
mob (n), danfirp, danifopa, danfp
mob (v), danfirsp, danifopo, danfpo
mobile (adj), danirtu, danitu, dantu
mobile (n), dantart, danitata, dantat
mobility (n), danirt, danita, dant
mobilization (n), danirtuet, danitueta, dantuet
mobilize (v), danirst, danito, danto
mobster (n doer), danfirpwan, danifopua, danfpua
mock (v), frainsk, feraino, fraino
mockery (n), fraink, feraina, frain
mockingbird (n), frainflazhen, ferainefelaruzha, frainflarzh
modal (adj), diardu, diadu, diadu
modality (n), diarduet, diadueta, diaduet
modally (adv), diardiu, diadiu, diadiu
mode (n), diarde, diada, diad
model (n), diardar, diadara, diadar
model (v), diardasre, diadaro, diadaro
moderate (adj), pleirfu, peleifu, pleifu
moderate (v), pleirsf, peleifo, pleifo
moderately (adv), pleirfiu, peleifiu, pleifiu
moderation (n), pleirf, peleifa, pleif
moderator (n doer), pleirfwan, peleifua, pleifua
modern (adj), sharinfu, sharinu, sharnu
modernism (n), sharint, sharina, sharn
modernist (n doer), sharinfwan, sharinua, sharnua
modernization (n), sharinf, sharina, sharn
modernize (v), sharinsf, sharino, sharno
modest (adj), deirthu, deithu, deithu
modestly (adv), deirthiu, deithiu, deithiu
modesty (n), deirth, deitha, deith
modification (n), pleirfk, peleifoka, pleifk
modifier (n doer), pleirfkwan, peleifokua, pleifkua
modify (v), pleirfsk, peleifoko, pleifko
modular (adj), pleifarnu, peleifaru, pleifaru
modularity (n), pleifanart, peleifarata, pleifarat
modularly (adv), pleifarniu, peleifariu, pleifariu

modulate (v), pleifarsne, peleifaro, pleifaro
modulation (n), pleifarnuet, peleifarueta, pleifaruet
modulator (n doer), pleifarnwan, peleifarua, pleifarua
module (n), pleifarn, peleifara, pleifar
MoissanRuby (n), moisharn, moishiana, moishan
moist (adj), leirtu, leithu, leithu
moisten (v), leirst, leitho, leitho
moistener (n doer), leirtwan, leithua, leithua
moistly (adv), leirtiu, leithiu, leithiu
moisture (n), leirt, leitha, leith
moisturize (v), leirst, leitho, leitho
moisturizer (n doer), leirtwan, leithua, leithua
mold (n d:form), kairap, kairopa, kairp
mold (n d:microbe), nafirp, nafipa, nafp
mold (v d:form), kairasp, kairopo, kairpo
moldy (adj d:microbe), nafirpu, nafipu, nafpu
mole (n), novirn, novina, novin
mole (v), novirsne, novino, novino
molecular (adj), diloirku, diloiku, diloiku
molecule (n), diloirk, diloika, diloik
molehill (n), novinshiop, novineparina, novinparn
molest (v), glardiashst, gelaridiato, glardiato
molestation (n), glardiasht, gelaridiata, glardiat
molester (n doer), glardiashtwan, gelaridiatua, glardiatua
Molybdenum (n davoka), Ilup, Ilup, Ilup
Molybdenum (n), Molibdenum, Molibedenuma, Molibdenum
mom (n), melirme, melima, melm
mom (v), melirzme, melimo, melmo
moment (n), binort, binota, bint
momentarily (adv), binortiu, binotiu, bintiu
momentary (adj), binortu, binotu, bintu
momentous (adj), binotarpu, binotapu, bintapu
momentum (n), binotarp, binotapa, bintap
momma (n), melmeme, memema, memem
mommy (n), melmame, melimala, melmal
monarch (n), tralmethk, teralemetha, tralmeth
monarchist (n doer), tralmeshtwan, teralemetua, tralmetua
monarchy (n), tralmesht, teralemeta, tralmet
Monday (n), Namurviul, Namuriviula, Namurviul
monetarily (adv), brenidiu, berenidiu, brendiu
monetary (adj), brenidu, berenidu, brendu
money (n), brenide, berenida, brend
moneymaker (n doer), brendenargwan, berenidenagua, brendenagua
moniker (n), plofirk, pelofika, plofk
monitor (n), neivirt, neivita, neivit
monitor (v), neivirst, neivito, neivito
monk (n), plofienk, pelofiena, plofien
monkey (n), brentark, berenitaka, brentak
monkey (v), brentarsk, berenitako, brentako
mono- (num 1 pref), hemai-, hemai-, hemai-
monochromatic (adj), hempreirthu, hemepereithu, hempreithu
monochrome (n), hempreirth, hemepereitha, hempreith
monogram (n), hemnelirk, hemenelika, hemnelk
monograph (n), hemedarf, hemedarifa, hemdarf
monolith (n), hemethreith, hemethereitha, hemthreith

monolithic (adj), hemethreithu, hemethereithu, hemthreithu

monologue (n), hemkuift, hemekuita, hemkuit

monopolist (n doer), hemeldornwan, hemedorinua, hemdornua

monopolistic (adj), hemeldornu, hemedorinu, hemdornu

monopolize (v), hemeldorsne, hemedorino, hemdorno

monopoly (n), hemeldorn, hemedorina, hemdorn

monorail (n), hemluirt, hemeluita, hemluit

monotheism (n), hemthuteshk, hemthutesha, hemthutsh

monotheistic (adj), hemthuteshku, hemthuteshu, hemthutshu

monotone (n), hemtrilf, hemeterila, hemtril

monotony (n), hemtrilfat, hemeterilata, hemtrilat

monster (n), braigat, beraiga, braig

monstrous (adj), braigatu, beraigu, braigu

Montana (n), Montarnf, Monatanifa, Montanf

Montgomery (n), Montugoram, Monitugorima, Montugorm

month (n), prelume, perelima, prelm

monthly (adj), prelumu, perelimu, prelmu

Montreal (n), Montrialf, Moniteriala, Montrial

monument (n), hemailat, hemaiata, hemaiat

monumental (adj), hemailatu, hemaiatu, hemaiatu

monumentally (adv), hemailatiu, hemaiatiu, hemaiatiu

mood (n), gurfk, gurika, gurk

moodily (adv), gurfkiu, gurikiu, gurkiu

moody (adj), gurfku, guriku, gurku

moon (n), namurf, namura, namur

moonbeam (n), namurduarf, namureduafa, namurduaf

moonlight (n), namurfluan, namufeluana, namufluan

moonlight (v), namurfluasne, namufeluano, namufluano

moonshine (n), namurmoirth, namuremoitha, namurmoith

moonstone (n), namurbaraft, namurebarafa, namurbaraf

moor (n d:marsh), lioithk, lioitha, lioith

moor (v d:secure), plartusf, pelatufo, platufo

moorhead (n), plartufkef, pelatufekefa, platufkef

mop (n), neirbe, neiba, neib

mop (v), neirzbe, neibo, neibo

mope (v d:sad), muashsk, muariko, muarko

moral (adj), thiurnu, thiunu, thiunu

moral (n), thiurn, thiuna, thiun

morale (n), thiunart, thiunata, thiunat

moralist (n doer), thiurnwan, thiunua, thiunua

morality (n), thiurnuet, thiunueta, thiunuet

moralize (v), thiursne, thiuno, thiuno

morally (adv), thiurniu, thiuniu, thiuniu

morbid (adj), tiorfraiku, tioferaiku, tiofraiku

morbidity (n), tiorfraik, tioferaika, tiofraik

more (adj/adv), wel, welu, wel

more (pron), wel, welei, wel

moreover (adv), welfeniu, welifiu, welfiu

morgue (n), tiorfp, tiofipa, tiofp

morning (n), limern, limena, limen

moron (n), nivifk, niviva, niviv

moronic (adj), nivifku, nivivu, nivivu

mortal (adj), tiorfu, tiofu, tiofu

mortal (n doer), tiorfwan, tiofua, tiofua

mortality (n), tiorf, tiofa, tiof

mortally (adv), tiorfiu, tiofiu, tiofiu

mortar (n d:bowl), plorshk, pelorisha, plorsh

mortar (n d:cement), maishk, maisha, maish

mortgage (n), tiobairsh, tiobaisha, tiobaish

mortgage (v), tiobairsh, tiobaisho, tiobaisho

mortification (n), tiorfk, tiofika, tiofk

mortify (v), tiorfsk, tiofiko, tiofko

Moscow (n), Moshkaurf, Moshikaufa, Moshkauf

mosquito (n), nagiank, nagiana, nagian

moss (n), nuarf, nuafa, nuaf

mossy (adj), nuarfu, nuafu, nuafu

most (adj/adv), wak, waku, wak

most (pron), wak, wakei, wak

mostly (adv), wakiu, wakiu, wakiu

motel (n), vorkeidan, vorikeida, vorkeid

moth (n), guthk, gutha, guth

mothball (n), guthshmonde, guthemashipa, guthmashp

mothball (v), guthshmonzde, guthemashipo, guthmashpo

mother (n), mashel, malisha, malsh

mother (v), mashesle, malisho, malsho

motherboard (n), malshplok, malishepelorika, malshplork

motherhood (n), malshfif, maloshifa, malshif

motherland (n), malshraufp, malisheraupa, malshraup

motherly (adj), mashelu, malishu, malshu

motion (n), vadarve, vadava, vadav

motion (v), vadarzve, vadavo, vadavo

motivate (v), vadarst, vadato, vadato

motivation (n), vadartuet, vadatueta, vadatuet

motivational (adj), vadartu, vadatu, vadatu

motivator (n doer), vadartwan, vadatua, vadatua

motive (n), vadart, vadata, vadat

motor (n), motor, vorlfk, vorlka, vork

motor (v), vorifsk, voriko, vorko

motorbike (n), vorkepivirt, vorikepivita, vorkepivit

motorboat (n), vorkshkorbe, vorikeshekoba, vorkshkob

motorcar (n), vorkegeral, vorikegerela, vorkegrel

motorcycle (n), vorkevairalt, vorikevairata, vorkevairt

motorcycle (v), vorkevairalst, vorikevairato, vorkevairto

motorcyclist (n doer), vorkevairaltwan, vorikevairatua, vorkevairtua

motorist (n doer), vorifkwan, vorikua, vorkua

motorize (v), vorkarst, vorikato, vorkato

mound (n), niudank, niudana, niudan

mount (n), niurk, niuka, niuk

mount (v), niursk, niuko, niuko

mountain (n), niugiuft, niugiuta, niugiut

mountaineer (n doer), niugiuftwan, niugiutua, niugiutua

mountainous (adj), niugiuftu, niugiutu, niugiutu

mountainside (n), niugiutshoirt, niugiuteshoita, niugiutshoit

mountaintop (n), niugiutedaurp, niugiutedaupa, niuiutedaup
mourn (v), daulaze, daulavo, daulavo
mourner (n doer), daulazhwan, daulavua, daulavua
mournful (adj), daulazhu, daulavu, daulavu
mournfully (adv), daulazhiu, daulaviu, daulaviu
mouse (n), doart, doata, doat
mouse (v), doarst, doato, doato
mouser (n doer), doartwan, doatua, doatua
mousetrap (n), doatethreilp, doatethereipa, doatethreip
mouth (n), fraurf, feraufa, frauf
mouth (v), fraursf, feraufo, fraufo
mouthful (adj), fraurfu, feraufu, fraufu
mouthfully (adv), fraurfiu, feraufiu, fraufiu
mouthpiece (n), fraufthetirsh, feraufethetisha, fraufthetsh
mouthwash (n), fraufiaushk, feraufiausha, fraufiaush
movable (adj), shkirtu, shekitu, shkitu
movably (adv), shkirtiu, shekitiu, shkitiu
move (n), shkirt, shekita, shkit
move (v), shkirst, shekito, shkito
movement (n), shkirtalt, shekitalita, shkitalt
mover (n doer), shkirtwan, shekitua, shkitua
movie (n), shkirtar, shekitara, shkitar
moviemaker (n doer), shkitarnargwan, shekekitarenagua, shkitarnagua
mow (v), krites, keritesho, kritsho
mower (n doer), kriteshwan, keriteshua, kritshua
Ms (let pl), maili, maili, maili
mu (n), murn, muna, mun
much (adj/adv), nesh, neshu, nesh
much (pron), nesh, neshei, nesh
muck (n), kreinshk, kereinika, kreink
muck (v), kreinshsk, kereiniko, kreinko
mucky (adj), kreinshku, kereiniku, kreinku
mucosal (adj), freinku, vureinu, vreinu
mucus (n), freink, vureina, vrein
mud (n), pofirp, pofipa, pofp
muddily (adv), pofirpiu, pofipiu, pofpiu
muddle (v), pofirsk, pofiko, pofko
muddy (adj), pofirpu, pofipu, pofpu
muddy (v), pofirsp, pofipo, pofpo
mudsling (v), pofpeshkraishsk, pofipeshukeraiko, pofpeshkraiko
mudslung (v pa), pofpeshkraishskyot, pofipeshukeraikio, pofpeshkraikio
muff (n), nothk, notha, noth
muff (v), nothsk, notho, notho
muffin (n), theigurt, theiguta, theigut
muffle (v), nothkast, nothato, nothato
muffler (n doer), nothkatwan, nothatua, nothatua
mug (n d:cup), grufk, geruva, gruv
mug (v d:rob), graifsk, geraiko, graiko
mugger (n doer d:rob), graifkwan, geraikua, graikua
mulch (n), miteshk, mitesha, mitsh
mulch (v), miteshsk, mitesho, mitsho
mull (v), prithsk, peritho, pritho
multichannel (n), nuratuamat, nuratuaroma, nuratuarm
multicolor (adj), nuralirolfu, nuralirolu, nuralirolu

multicolor (v), nuralirolsf, nuralirolo, nuralirolo
multicultural (adj), nuratafirku, nuratafiku, nuratafku
multiculture (v), nuratafirsk, nuratafiko, nuratafko
multifunctional (adj), nuraprashtu, nuraperatu, nurapratu
multilevel (adj), nuragalurtu, nuragaludu, nuragaldu
multilingual (adj), nuraviarthaku, nuraviarithu, nuraviarthu
multimedia (n), nuralaidark, nuralaidaka, nuralaidak
multinational (adj), nurakarlfu, nurakarilu, nurakarlu
multinational (n), nurakarlf, nurakarila, nurakarl
multiparty (adj), nurabiarzhu, nurabiazhu, nurabiazhu
multiplayer (adj), nurafruifkwatu, nuraferuifualu, nuralfruifualu
multiple (adj), nuribu, nurobu, nurbu
multiple (n), nuribe, nuroba, nurb
multiplication (n), nuribuet, nurobueta, nurbuet
multiplier (n doer), nuribwan, nurobua, nurbua
multiply (v), nurizbe, nurobo, nurbo
multipurpose (adj), nurabeirlaku, nurabeilaku, nurabeilku
multiracial (adj), nuranoirthu, nuranoithu, nuranoithu
multistate (adj), nurashaiarshu, nurashaiashu, nurashaiashu
multitude (adj), nurituetu, nuratuetu, nuratuetu
multitude (n), nurituet, nuratueta, nuratuet
mumble (v), felesf, fefo, fefefo
mumbler (n doer), felefwan, fefua, fefefua
mumbles (v pa), felesfyot, fefio, fefefio
mummification (n), malmisht, malamita, malmit
mummifier (n doer), malmishtwan, malamitua, malmitua
mummify (v), malmishst, malamito, malmito
mummy (n), malirme, malima, malm
munch (v), fliamesp, feliamo, fliamo
munchy (n), fliamp, feliama, fliam
municipal (adj), tumartu, tumatu, tumatu
municipality (n), tumart, tumata, tumat
murder (n), feizhark, feizhaka, feizhak
murder (v), feizharsk, feizhako, feizhako
murderer (n doer), feizharkwan, feizhakua, feizhakua
murderous (adj), feizharku, feizhaku, feizhaku
murderously (adv), feizharkiu, feizhakiu, feizhakiu
murk (n), tullrk, tulika, tulk
murkily (adv), tulirkiu, tulikiu, tulkiu
murky (adj), tulirku, tuliku, tulku
murmur (n), melmelk, melimela, melmel
murmur (v), melmelsk, melimelo, melmelo
murmurer (n doer), melmelkwan, melimelua, melmelua
murmurous (adj), melmelku, melimelu, melmelu
muscle (n), morkart, morikata, morkat
muscle (v), morkarst, morikato, morkato
muscular (adj), morkartu, morikatu, morkatu
muse (n), naurf, naufa, nauf
muse (v), naursf, naufo, naufo

museum (n), naurfar, naufara, naufar
mush (n), nufirk, nufika, nufk
mush (v), nufirsk, nufiko, nufko
mushed (v prp), nufirskaut, nufikao, nufkao
mushroom (n), nufshmonde, nufemashipa,
  nufmashp
music (n), niarl, niala, nial
musical (adj), niarlu, nialu, nialu
musical (n), nialart, nialata, nialat
musically (adv), niarliu, nialiu, nialiu
musician (n doer), niarlwan, nialua, nialua
Muslim (n), Mushlirm, Mushelima, Mushlim
must (ndal d:need), nirshke kodi, nishoka kodi,
  nishke kodi
mustache (n), gredirsh, geredisha, gredish
mustard (n), vivarf, vivafa, vivaf
muster (v), bravilsk, beravilo, bravilo
mutable (adj), shluarku, sheluaku, shluaku
mutably (adv), shluarkiu, sheluakiu, shluakiu
mutant (n), shluakarn, sheluakana, shluakan
mutate (v), shluarsk, sheluako, shluako
mutation (n), shluark, sheluaka, shluak
mutator (n doer), shluarkwan, sheluakua, shluakua
mute (n), thuarf, thuafa, thuaf
mute (v), thuarsf, thuafo, thuafo
mutilate (v), kinaishsk, kinaisho, kinaisho
mutilation (n), kinaishk, kinaisha, kinaish
mutilator (n doer), kinaishkwan, kinaishua,
  kinaishua
mutineer (n doer), shkikenkwan, shekikenua,
  shkikenua
mutiny (n), shkikenk, shekikena, shkiken
mutiny (v), shkikensk, shekikeno, shkikeno
mutt (n), beirde, beida, beid
mutter (v), thigarst, thigato, thigato
mutterance (n), thigart, thigata, thigat
mutual (adj), thuarku, thuaku, thuaku
mutuality (n), thuark, thuaka, thuak
mutually (adv), thuarkiu, thuakiu, thuakiu
muzzle (n), vereishk, vereika, vreik
muzzle (v), vereishsk, vereiko, vreiko
my (pron 1st sng pos sub), nui, nui, nui
myraid (adj), dintartu, dinetatu, dintatu
myself (pron 1st sng refl), nuifal, nuifal, nuifal
mysterious (adj), shraflirnu, sherafelinu, shraflinu
mysteriously (adv), shraflirniu, sherafeliniu,
  shrafliniu
mystery (n), shraflirn, sherafelina, shraflin
mystic (n doer), shraflirtwan, sherafelitua,
  shraflitua
mystical (adj), shraflirtu, sherafelitu, shraflitu
mysticism (n), shraflirt, sherafelita, shraflit
mystify (v), shraflirsne, sherafelino, shraflino
mystique (n), shraflirk, sherafelika, shraflik
myth (n), shreit, shereitha, shreith
mythic (adj), shreitu, shereithu, shreithu
mythical (adj), shreitu, shereithu, shreithu
mythology (n), shreitekuift, shereithekuita,
  shreithkuit
N (let sng), noil, noia, noi
na (interj), mwae, mwae, mwae
nab (v), povizge, porigo, porgo
nabber (n doer), povigwan, porigua, porgua

nag (n), tigarge, tigaga, tigag
nag (v), tigarzge, tigago, tigago
naggy (adj), tigargu, tigagu, tigagu
nail (n d:finger/toe tip), thrink, therina, thrin
nail (n d:metal pin), thadirf, thadifa, thadif
nail (v d:metal pin), thadirsf, thadifo, thadifo
naive (adj), niarfu, niafu, niafu
naively (adv), niarfiu, niafiu, niafiu
naivete (n), niarf, niafa, niaf
naked (adj), vaidoftu, vaidotu, vaidotu
name (n), brienf, beriena, brien
name (v), briensf, berieno, brieno
nameless (adj), brienfmenu, berienemenu,
  brienmenu
namely (adv), brienfiu, berieniu, brieniu
nameplate (n), brienfkarf, berienefikafa, brienfkaf
namer (n doer), brienfwan, berienua, brienua
namesake (n), brienmoark, berienemoaka,
  brienmoak
Namibia (n), Namibiarf, Namibiafa, Namibiaf
nanny (n), nelnan, nelenala, nelnal
nanny (v), nelnasne, nelenalo, nelnalo
nap (n), lanirp, lanipa, lanp
nap (v), lanirsp, lanipo, lanpo
napkin (n), pavuarp, pavuapa, pavuap
narcism (n), faursh, fausha, faush
narcissism (n), faursh, fausha, faush
narcissist (n doer), faurshwan, faushua, faushua
narcissistic (adj), faurshu, faushu, faushu
narcist (n doer), faurshwan, faushua, faushua
narcistic (adj), faurshu, faushu, faushu
narcotic (n), faurshk, faushoka, faushk
narcotic (n), mairave, maiva, maiv
narrate (v), predirze, peredizho, predizho
narration (n), predirzhe, peredizha, predizh
narrative (adj), predirzhu, peredizhu, predizhu
narrative (n), predizhart, peredizhata, predizhat
narrator (n doer), predirzhwan, peredizhua,
  predizhua
narrow (adj), witapu, wifopu, wifpu
narrow (n), witap, wifopa, wifp
narrow (v), witasp, wifopo, wifpo
narrower (adj), witapwelu, wifopwelu, wifpwelu
narrowest (adj), witapweku, wifopweku, wifpweku
narrowly (adv), witapiu, wifopiu, wifpiu
narrowness (n), witapuet, wifopueta, wifpuet
nasal (adj), verthu, vethu, vethu
nasally (adv), verthiu, vethiu, vethiu
Nashville (n), Nashfilf, Nashofila, Nashfil
nastier (adj), guiforkwelu, guifokwelu, guifkwelu
nastiest (adj), guiforkweku, guifokweku, guifkweku
nastily (adv), guiforkiu, guifokiu, guifkiu
nastiness (n), guifork, guifoka, guifk
nasty (adj), guiforku, guifoku, guifku
nation (n), karlf, karila, karl
national (adj), karlfu, karilu, karlu
nationalism (n), karlfuet, karilueta, karluet
nationalist (n doer), karlfwan, karilua, karlua
nationality (n), karlfan, karilana, karlan
nationalize (v), karlsf, karilo, karlo
nationally (adv), karlfiu, kariliu, karliu
nationhood (n), karlfirf, karilefifa, karlfif
nationwide (adj), karlkrashku, karilekerashu,

karlkrashu
native (adj), frenitu, ferenitu, frentu
native (n), frenit, ferenita, frent
natively (adv), frenitiu, ferenitiu, frentiu
natural (adj), leirdu, leidu, leidu
naturally (adv), leirdiu, leidiu, leidiu
nature (n), leirde, leida, leid
naught (n), guteshk, gutesha, gutsh
naughty (adj), guteshku, guteshu, gutshu
nausea (n), vethrairk, vetheraika, vethraik
nauseate (v), vethrairsk, vetheraiko, vethraiko
nauseous (adj), vethrairku, vetheraiku, vethraiku
nautical (adj), liartu, liatu, liatu
naval (adj), liarvu, liavu, liavu
navel (n), voifk, voifa, voif
navigate (v), liavarst, liavato, liavato
navigation (n), liavart, liavata, liavat
navigator (n doer), liavartwan, liavatua, liavatua
navy (n), liarve, liava, liav
naw (interj), mauar, maua, maua
nay (interj), maiwar, maiwa, maiwa
near (adj), shuelfu, shuelu, shuelu
near (adj/adv/prep), shuel, shuelu, shuel
near (v), shuelsf, shuelo, shuelo
nearby (adj/adv), shuelervu, shueluvu, shuelvu
nearer (adj), shuelfwelu, shuelwelu, shuelwelu
nearest (adj), shuelfwaku, shuelwaku, shuelwaku
nearly (adv), shuelfiu, shueliu, shueliu
nearness (n), shuelf, shuela, shuel
neat (adj), terafu, terifu, trifu
neatly (adv), terafiu, terifiu, trifiu
neatness (n), teraf, terifa, trif
Nebraska (n), Nebralshk, Neborashika, Nebrashk
necessarily (adv), shivershtiu, shiveshotiu, shiveshtiu
necessary (adj), shivershtu, shiveshotu, shiveshtu
necessitate (v), shivershst, shiveshoto, shiveshto
necessity (n), shiversht, shiveshota, shivesht
neck (n), thavube, thariba, tharb
neck (v), thavuzbe, tharibo, tharbo
necklace (n), thavubefoirn, tharibefoina, tharbefoin
necktie (n), thavubeglersh, tharibegelesha, tharbeglesh
nee (adj), nurfu, nuru, nuru
need (n), nirshk, nishoka, nishk
need (v), nirshsk, nishoko, nishko
needful (adj), nirshku, nishoku, nishku
needle (n), tilirt, tilita, tilit
needle (v), tilirst, tilito, tilito
needlepoint (n), tilitaifort, tilitaifota, tilitaift
needless (adj), nirshkmenu, nishokemenu, nishkmenu
needlessly (adv), nirshkmeniu, nishokemeniu, nishkmeniu
needlework (n), tilitkiork, tilitekioka, tilitkiok
needy (adj), nirshku, nishoku, nishku
negate (v), kraiforst, keraifoto, kraifto
negation (n), kraifort, keraifota, kraift
negative (adj), krairtu, keraitu, kraitu
negative (n), krairt, keraita, krait
negatively (adv), krairtiu, keraitiu, kraitiu
negativism (n), krairtuet, keraitueta, kraituet
neglect (n), fkirt, fekita, fkit

neglect (v), fkirst, fekito, fkito
neglectful (adj), fkirtu, fekitu, fkitu
neglectfully (adv), fkirtiu, fekitiu, fkitiu
negligence (n), fkirt, fekita, fkit
negligent (adj), fkirtu, fekitu, fkitu
negligently (adv), fkirtiu, fekitiu, fkitiu
negligible (adj), fkilortu, fekilotu, fkiltu
negotiate (v), kriarst, keriato, kriato
negotiation (n), kriart, keriata, kriat
negotiator (n doer), kriartwan, keriatua, kriatua
neigh (n), bliathk, beliatha, bliath
neigh (v), bliathsk, beliatho, bliatho
neighbor (n), flanude, felanuda, fland
neighbor (v), flanuzde, felanudo, flando
neighborhood (n), flanufif, felanefifa, flanfif
neighborly (adj), flanudu, felanudu, flandu
neighbour (n), flanude, felanuda, fland
neither (adj/conj), mashartu, masharitu, mashartu
neither (pron), mashart, masharitei, mashart
nekani- (num 1e54 pref), venshtai-, venshtai-, venshtai-
Neodymium (n davoka), Orup, Orup, Orup
Neodymium (n), Neodimium, Neodimiuma, Neodimium
Neon (n davoka), Ekik, Ekik, Ekik
Neon (n), Neon, Neona, Neon
nephew (n), methirk, methika, methk
Neptunium (n davoka), Onak, Onak, Onak
Neptunium (n), Neptunium, Nepotuniuma, Neptunium
nerd (n), kurgage, kuriga, kurg
nerve (n), loirve, loiva, loiv
nerve (v), loirzve, loivo, loivo
nervous (adj), loivirpu, loivipu, loivipu
nervously (adv), loivirpiu, loivipiu, loivipiu
nervousness (n), loivirp, loivipa, loivip
nervy (adj), loirvu, loivu, loivu
nest (n), mufirp, mufipa, mufp
nest (v), mufirsp, mufipo, mufpo
nester (n doer), mufirpwan, mufipua, mufpua
nestle (v), mufirsk, mufiko, mufko
net (n), moirp, moipa, moip
net (v), moirsp, moipo, moipo
Netherlands (n), Netherlanurde, Netherolanuda, Netherlanud
network (n), moikiork, moikioka, moikiok
network (v), moikiorsk, moikioko, moikioko
neural (adj), loivertu, loivetu, loivetu
neurological (adj), loivekuiftu, loivekuitu, loivekuitua
neurologist (n doer), loivekuiftwan, loivekuitua, loivekuitua
neurology (n), loivekuift, loivekuita, loivekuit
neuron (n), loivert, loiveta, loivet
neuroscience (n), loiveshuarsh, loiveshuasha, loiveshuash
neuroscientist (n doer), loiveshuarshwan, loiveshuashua, loiveshuashua
neurosis (n), loivrairk, loiveraika, loivraik
neurosurgeon (n doer), loivemofirtwan, loivemofitua, loivemoftua
neurosurgery (n), loivemofirt, loivemofita, loivemoft

neurotic (adj), loivrairku, loiveraiku, loivraiku
neurotransmission (n), loivethonork, loivethonoka,
loivethonok
neurotransmit (v), loivethonorsk, loivethonoko,
loivethonoko
neurotransmitter (n doer), loivethonorkwan,
loivethonokua, loivethonokua
neuter (v), tinursk, tinuko, tinko
neutral (adj), tiurmu, tiumu, tiumu
neutrality (n), tiurme, tiuma, tium
neutralization (n), tiurmuet, tiumueta, tiumuet
neutralize (v), tiurzme, tiumo, tiumo
neutralizer (n doer), tiurmwan, tiumua, tiumua
neutrally (adv), tiurmiu, tiumiu, tiumiu
neutron (n), tiumarl, tiumala, tiumal
Nevada (n), Nevadarf, Nevadafa, Nevadaf
never (adv), mauak, makoiu, mauak
nevermind (n), mauakniarp, mauakeniapa,
mauakniap
nevertheless (adv), mauaksheimiu,
mauakesheimiu, mauaksheimiu
new (adj), miolfu, miolu, miolu
New Hampshire (n), Mior Kamshirf, Miola
Kamoshira, Miol Kamshir
New Orleans (n), Mior Orlinorf, Miola Orolinofa,
Miol Orlinf
New Zealand (n), Mior Zhilanurde, Miola
Zhilanuda, Miol Zhilanud
Newark (n), Nuarak, Nuarika, Nuark
newborn (n), miovashil, miovalesha, miovalsh
newcomer (n doer), mioblerfwan, miobilefua,
mioblefua
newer (adj), miorwelu, miolwelu, miolwelu
newest (adj), miorwaku, miolwaku, miolwaku
newfound (adj), mioshurpu, mioshupu, mioshupu
newly (adv), miolfiu, mioliu, mioliu
newlywed (n), miolyurve, miolyuva, miolyuv
newness (n), miolf, miola, miol
news (n), miorf, miora, mior
newscast (n), miortulirt, mioretulita, miortult
newscaster (n doer), miortulirtwan, miorctulitua,
miortultua
newsday (n), miorviurl, mioreviula, miorviul
newsgroup (n), miorbronf, mioreberona, miorbron
newshour (n), mioriarn, mioriana, miorian
newsletter (n), miorashort, miorashota, miorasht
newsmagazine (n), miorniforp, miorenifopa,
miornifp
newsman (n), miorplorn, miorepelona, miorplon
newsmen (n pl), miorplornyek, miorepeloni,
miorploni
newspaper (n), miorvuarp, miorevuapa, miorvuap
newspaperman (n), miorvuaplorn, miorevuapelona,
miorvuaplon
newspapermen (n pl), miorvuaplornyek,
miorevuapeloni, miorvuaploni
newsprint (n), miortrulish, mioreterulisha,
miortrulsh
newsreel (n), miordiump, miorediuma, miordium
newsroom (n), miorshranf, mioresherana,
miorshran
newsstand (n), miortrelirt, mioreterelita, miortrelt
newswire (n), miorshnirf, mioreshenifa, miorshnif

newsworthiness (n), miorflairsh, miorefelaisha,
miorflaish
newsworthy (adj), miorflairshu, miorefelaishu,
miorflaishu
newsy (adj), miorfu, mioru, mioru
next (adj/adv/prep), moge, mogu, mog
Ng (let sng), engel, engala, enga
Ngs (let pl), engali, engali, engali
nib (n), thelp, thepa, thep
nibble (n), theparn, thepana, thepan
nibble (v), theparsne, thepano, thepano
Nicaragua (n), Nikaragurf, Nikaragufa, Nikaraguf
Nicaraguan (n), Nikaraguarn, Nikaraguana,
Nikaraguan
nice (adj), muirfu, muifu, muifu
nicely (adv), muirfiu, muifiu, muifiu
nicen (v), muirsf, muifo, muifo
niceness (n), muirf, muifa, muif
nicer (adj), muirfwelu, muifwelu, muifwelu
nicest (adj), muirfweku, muifweku, muifweku
nicety (n), muirf, muifa, muif
niche (n), diusht, diuta, diut
nick (n), lufirp, lufipa, lufp
nick (v), lufirsp, lufipo, lufpo
Nickel (n davoka), Ifuk, Ifuk, Ifuk
Nickel (n), Nikel, Nikela, Nikel
nickname (n), lufavern, lufavena, lufaven
nickname (v), lufaversne, lufaveno, lufaveno
niece (n), muyarn, muyara, muyar
nieghbourhood (n), flanufif, felanefifa, flanfif
nifty (adj), niluftu, nilufu, nilufu
night (n), muarn, muana, muan
nightclub (n), muantraide, muanetaida, muantaid
nightfall (n), muanzhailf, muanezhaila, muanzhail
nightlife (n), muanflaursh, muanefelausha,
muanflaush
nightly (adj), muarnu, muanu, muanu
nightmare (n), muarnfraik, muaneferaika,
muanfraik
nightshirt (n), muanlifarde, muanelifada,
muanllfad
nighttime (n), muandaurn, muanedauna,
muandaun
nimble (adj), tiorpu, tiopu, tiopu
nimbleness (n), tiorp, tiopa, tiop
nimbly (adv), tiorpiu, tiopiu, tiopiu
Nimsant, Nimsant, Nimsanta, Nimsant
nine (num 9 card), mui, mui, mui
nineteen (num 19 card), muipa, muipa, muipa
nineteen- (num 19 pref), muipai-, muipai-, muipai-
nineteenth (num 19 ord), muipeth, muipeth,
muipeth
ninetieth (num 90 ord), muideth, muideth, muideth
ninety (num 90 card), muida, muida, muida
ninety- (num 90 pref), muidai-, muidai-, muidai-
ninth (num 9 ord), muyeth, muyeth, muyeth
Niobium (n davoka), Ilop, Ilop, Ilop
Niobium (n), Niobium, Niobiuma, Niobium
nip (n), theilp, theipa, theip
nip (v), theilsp, theipo, theipo
nipple (n), theiparf, theipafa, theipaf
nippy (adj), theilpu, theipu, theipu

Nitrogen (n davoka), Ekop, Ekop, Ekop
Nitrogen (n), Nitrogen, Niterogena, Nitrogen
nix (v), maiarsk, maiako, maiako
no (n/adj/adv), maur, mau, mau
Nobelium (n davoka), Onif, Onif, Onif
Nobelium (n), Nobelium, Nobeliuma, Nobelium
nobility (n), thirfk, thirofa, thirf
noble (adj), thirfku, thirofu, thirfu
nobly (adv), thirfkiu, thirofiu, thirfiu
nobody (n/pron), maushlarde, mausheladei, maushlad
nod (n), keirve, keiva, keiv
nod (v), keirzve, keivo, keivo
node (n), kierk, kieka, kiek
noise (n), gafirt, gafita, gaft
noisily (adv), gafirtiu, gafitiu, gaftiu
noisy (adj), gafirtu, gafitu, gaftu
nomad (n), keinarp, keinapa, keinap
nomadic (adj), keinarpu, keinapu, keinapu
nomen (n), viern, viena, vien
nomenclature (n), bushvien, sheriviena, shrivien
nominal (adj), vienorku, vienoku, vienku
nominally (adv), vienorkiu, vienokiu, vienkiu
nominate (v), vienorsk, vienoko, vienko
nomination (n), vienork, vienoka, vienk
nominator (n doer), vienorkwan, vienokua, vienkua
nominee (n), vienorkuin, vienokuina, vienkuin
non- (num 9 pref), muai-, muai-, muai-
nonbeliever (n doer), mausharmwan, mausharua, mausharua
noncommercial (adj), maunelafku, maulalifoku, maulalfku
noncompliance (n), maulenshluat, mausheluanita, maushluant
nonconformist (n doer), maubelvornwan, mauliuvorinua, mauliuvornua
nondestruction (n), maubushlerk, maubusheleka, maubushlek
nondestructive (adj), maubushlerku, maubusheleku, maubushleku
nondestructively (adv), maubushlerkiu, maubushelekiu, maubushlekiu
nondisclosure (n), mautigreft, mautigereta, mautigret
none (adj/adv), maurtu, mautu, mautu
none (pron), maurt, mautei, maut
nonessential (adj), mausharlirtu, maushalirotu, maushalirtu
nonetheless (adv), maurtmeniu, mautameniu, mautmeniu
nonexistence (n), maunulirt, maunulita, maunult
nonexistent (adj), maunulirtu, maunulitu, maunultu
nonfatal (adj), mauthiarku, mauthiaku, mauthiaku
nonfiction (n), maurpafk, maupafika, maupafk
nonillion (num 1e30 card), muika, muika, muika
nonillionth (num 1e30 ord), muiketh, muiketh, muiketh
noninterference (n), mauenrigef, mauarigefa, mauarigef
nonlethal (adj), maugofaifku, maugofaifu, maugofaifu
nonlinear (adj), mauroifku, mauroifu, mauroifu

nonlinearity (n), mauroifk, mauroifa, mauroif
nonlinearly (adv), mauroifkiu, mauroifiu, mauroifiu
nonlocal (adj), maushairpu, maushaipu, maushaipu
nonmember (n), maumeshurt, maumeshuta, maumesht
nonpayment (n), maumoirmuet, maumoimueta, maumoimuet
nonprofessional (n), maufiuntark, maufiunotaka, maufiuntak
nonprofit (adj), maufiupafirtu, maufiupafitu, maufiupaftu
nonproliferation (n), maufiuflaursh, maufiufelausha, maufiuflaush
nonpublic (adj), maulirpurtu, mauliroputu, maulirputu
nonsense (n), maurshorf, maushorifa, maushorf
nonsensical (adj), maurshorfu, maushorifu, maushorfu
nonsmoker (n doer), maushtolirfwan, maushetolifua, maushtolfua
nonstandard (adj), mautrefirku, mauterefiku, mautrefku
nonstop (adj), mautaurku, mautauku, mautauku
nontechnical (adj), maukirzhu, maukizhu, maukizhu
nontoxic (adj), maukiabarku, maukiabaku, maukiabaku
nontraditional (adj), mautrabirnu, mauterabiru, mautrabiru
nontrivial (adj), maupreiliarfu, maupereiliafu, maupreiliafu
nonunion (adj), mauyutamarnu, mauyutamanu, mauyutamanu
nonviolence (n), mautuarilk, mautuarika, mautuark
nonviolent (adj), mautuarilku, mautuariku, mautuarku
nonvolatile (adj), mautuarzhu, mautuazhu, mautuazhu
nonwhite (adj), mauyuarnu, mauyuanu, mauyuanu
noodle (n), mivarth, mivatha, mivath
nook (n), kriofk, kerioka, kriok
noon (n), midort, midota, midot
noontime (adj), midotedaurnu, midotedaunu, midotedaunu
noontime (n), midotedaurn, midotedauna, midotedaun
noose (n), vairth, vaitha, vaith
noose (v), vairsth, vaitho, vaitho
nope (interj), maiarp, maiapu, maiap
nor (conj), mahil, mawilu, mawil
norm (n), lanirf, lanifa, lanf
normal (adj), lanirfu, lanifu, lanfu
normalization (n), lanirfuet, lanifueta, lanfuet
normalize (v), lanirsf, lanifo, lanfo
normally (adv), lanirfiu, lanifiu, lanfiu
north (adj), thilorshu, thiloshu, thilshu
north (n), thilorsh, thilosha, thilsh
North Carolina (n), Thilorsh Karolirn, Thilosha Karolina, Thilsh Karolin
North Dakota (n), Thilorsh Dakort, Thilosha Dakota, Thilsh Dakot
northbound (n), thilshdraifp, thiloshederaipa, thilshdraip

northeast (adj), thilkiarshu, thilokiashu, thilkiashu
northeast (n), thilkiarsh, thilokiasha, thilkiash
northeasterly (adj), thilkiarshu, thilokiashu, thilkiashu
northeastern (adj), thilkiarshu, thilokiashu, thilkiashu
northeastward (adj), thilkiarshaushu, thilokiashaushu, thilkiashaushu
northerly (adj), thilorshu, thiloshu, thilshu
northern (adj), thilorshu, thiloshu, thilshu
northerner (n doer), thilorshwan, thiloshua, thilshua
northernmost (adj), thilorshwaku, thiloshwaku, thilshwaku
northland (n), thilshraufp, thilosheraupa, thilshraup
northward (adj), thilorshaushu, thiloshaushu, thilshaushu
northwest (adj), thilshaithku, thileshaithu, thilshaithu
northwest (n), thilshaithk, thileshaitha, thilshaith
northwestern (adj), thilshaithku, thileshaithu, thilshaithu
Norway (n), Norwairf, Norwaifa, Norwaif
Norwegian (n), Norwaifarn, Norwaifana, Norwaifan
nose (n), verth, vetha, veth
nosebleed (n), vethlilfiot, vethelirodiota, vethlirdiot
nosedive (n), vethkraifk, vethekeraika, veithkraik
nostril (n), vethirt, vethita, vethit
nosy (v), versth, vetho, vetho
not (parcl), oir, oi, oi
notable (adj d:text), miradu, midu, midu
notably (adv d:text), miradiu, midiu, midiu
notate (v), midarst, midato, midato
notation (n), midart, midata, midat
notch (n), gaushk, gausha, gaush
notch (v), gaushsk, gausho, gausho
note (n d:music), linurn, linuna, linun
note (n d:text), mirade, mida, mid
note (v d:text), mirazde, mido, mido
notebook (n), miravonde, mivonuda, mivond
notepad (n), midebanirf, midebanifa, midebanf
noteworthy (adj), mideflairshu, midefelaishu, mideflaishu
nothing (n), thlorf, thelofa, thlof
notice (n), shmirt, shemita, shmit
notice (v), shmirst, shemito, shmito
noticeable (adj), shmirtu, shemitu, shmitu
noticeably (adv), shmirtiu, shemitiu, shmitiu
notification (n), shmitark, shemitaka, shmitak
notifier (n doer), shmitarkwan, shemitakua, shmitakua
notify (v), shmitarsk, shemitako, shmitako
notion (n), midoirn, midoina, midoin
notoriety (n), shmiark, shemiaka, shmiak
notorious (adj), shmiarku, shemiaku, shmiaku
notoriously (adv), shmiarkiu, shemiakiu, shmiakiu
noun (n), nuyern, nuyena, nuyen
nourish (v), deiarsf, deiafo, deiafo
nourishment (n), deiarf, deiafa, deiaf
nova (n), miarf, miafa, miaf
novel (adj), midiurnu, midiunu, midiunu
novel (n), midurn, miduna, midun

novelist (n doer), midurnwan, midunua, midunua
novelty (n), midiurn, midiuna, midiun
November (n), Nofefar, Nofefara, Nofefar
novemdecillion (num 1e60 card), muisht, muisht, muisht
novemdecillionth (num 1e60 ord), muishteth, muishteth, muishteth
novemvigintillion (num 1e90 card), muishk, muishk, muishk
novemvigintillionth (num 1e90 ord), muishketh, muishketh, muishketh
novenquadragintillion (num 1e150 card), muifk, muifk, muifk
noventrigintillion (num 1e120 card), muift, muift, muift
novice (n), miafarn, miafana, miafan
now (adj/adv/conj), mahir, mahilu, mahi
now (n), mahir, mahila, mahi
nowadays (adv), mahioviuliu, mahiviuliu, mahiviuliu
nowadays (n), mahioviul, mahiviula, mahiviul
nowhere (adj/adv), mauhar, mauhalu, mauhal
nowhere (n), mauhar, mauhala, mauhal
noxious (adj), mikartu, mikatu, mikatu
nozzle (n), veiart, veiata, veiat
Ns (let pl), noili, noili, noili
nu (n), nurn, nuna, nun
nuclear (adj), lidiurtu, lidiutu, lidiutu
nuclei (n pl), lidiurtyek, lidiuti, lidiuti
nucleus (n), lidiurt, lidiuta, lidiut
nude (adj), vidortu, vidotu, vidotu
nude (n doer), vidortwan, vidotua, vidotua
nudge (n), pularde, pulada, puld
nudge (v), pularzde, pulado, puldo
nudity (n), vidort, vidota, vidot
nuisance (n), vaithark, vaithaka, vaithak
nul (num 0 pref), shutai-, shutai-, shutai-
null (adj), shutairu, shutailu, shutailu
null (n), shutair, shutaila, shutail
nullify (v), shutaisre, shutailo, shutailo
numb (adj), meiravu, meivu, meivu
numb (v), meirazve, meivo, meivo
number (n), nenirk, nenika, nenk
number (v), nenirsk, neniko, nenko
Number_1e1056, lerfhem, lerfhem, lerfhem
Number_1e1206, yarlhem, yarlhem, yarlhem
Number_1e12306, irialfhemka, irialfhemka, irialfhemka
Number_1e1356, relhem, relhem, relhem
Number_1e1506, warfhem, warfhem, warfhem
Number_1e156, alfhemka, alfhemka, alfhemka
Number_1e159, alfavuka, alfavuka, alfavuka
Number_1e162, alfirika, alfirika, alfirika
Number_1e16356, yufialfhemka, yufialfhemka, yufialfhemka
Number_1e165, alfyufika, alfyufika, alfyufika
Number_1e1656, bahem, bahem, bahem
Number_1e168, alftirika, alftirika, alftirika
Number_1e171, alfkinka, alfkinka, alfkinka
Number_1e174, alfvenka, alfvenka, alfvenka
Number_1e177, alfgenka, alfgenka, alfgenka

Number_1e180, alfmuika, alfmuika, alfmuika
Number_1e1806, peihem, peihem, peihem
Number_1e183, alfdaka, alfdaka, alfdaka
Number_1e186, alfhemsht, alfhemsht, alfhemsht
Number_1e1956, vahem, vahem, vahem
Number_1e20406, tirialfhemka, tirialfhemka, tirialfhemka
Number_1e2106, feihem, feihem, feihem
Number_1e216, alfhemshk, alfhemshk, alfhemshk
Number_1e2256, maihem, maihem, maihem
Number_1e2406, dahem, dahem, dahem
Number_1e24456, kinialfhemka, kinialfhemka, kinialfhemka
Number_1e246, alfhemft, alfhemft, alfhemft
Number_1e2556, teihem, teihem, teihem
Number_1e2706, dhahem, dhahem, dhahem
Number_1e276, alfhemfk, alfhemfk, alfhemfk
Number_1e28506, venialfhemka, venialfhemka, venialfhemka
Number_1e2856, theihem, theihem, theihem
Number_1e3006, noihem, noihem, noihem
Number_1e306, elfhem, elfhem, elfhem
Number_1e3156, zahem, zahem, zahem
Number_1e32556, genialfhemka, genialfhemka, genialfhemka
Number_1e3306, seihem, seihem, seihem
Number_1e3456, zhahem, zhahem, zhahem
Number_1e3606, sheihem, sheihem, sheihem
Number_1e36606, muialfhemka, muialfhemka, muialfhemka
Number_1e3756, gahem, gahem, gahem
Number_1e3906, keihem, keihem, keihem
Number_1e4056, engahem, engahem, engahem
Number_1e40656, dapalfhemka, dapalfhemka, dapalfhemka
Number_1e4203, engadafka, engadafka, engadafka
Number_1e4206, hemalfhemka, hemalfhemka, hemalfhemka
Number_1e456, ilfhem, ilfhem, ilfhem
Number_1e606, orfhem, orfhem, orfhem
Number_1e756, urfhem, urfhem, urfhem
Number_1e8256, avualfhemka, avualfhemka, avualfhemka
Number_1e906, harfhem, harfhem, harfhem
numbness (n), meirave, meiva, meiv
numeral (n), nenirkel, nenikela, nenkel
numerator (n doer), nenirkelwan, nenikelua, nenkelua
numeric (adj), nenirkelu, nenikelu, nenkelu
numerical (adj), nenirkelu, nenikelu, nenkelu
numerically (adv), nenirkeliu, nenikeliu, nenkeliu
numerology (n), nenkuift, nenikuita, nenkuit
numerous (adj), nenirku, neniku, nenku
numerously (adv), nenirkiu, nenikiu, nenkiu
nurse (n doer), delirfwan, delifua, delfua
nurse (v), delirsf, delifo, delfo
nursery (n), delirf, delifa, delf
nurture (v), delfkasne, delifeko, delfko
nurturer (n doer), delfkanwan, delifekua, delfkua
nut (n), mern, meluna, meln

nutrient (n), lifork, lifoka, lifk
nutrition (n), liforkuet, lifokueta, lifkuet
nutritional (adj), liforkuetu, lifokuetu, lifkuetu
nutritionally (adv), liforkuetiu, lifokuetiu, lifkuetiu
nutritionist (n doer), liforkuetwan, lifokuetua, lifkuetua
nutshell (n), merntherk, melunetheka, melnthek
nutty (adj), mernu, melunu, melnu
nuzzle (n), veiuft, veiuta, veiut
nuzzle (v), veiufst, veiuto, veiuto
nylon (n), noiral, noiruna, noirn
née (adj), nurfu, nuru, nuru
O (let sng), orfe, orifa, orf
o'clock (adv), adrokiu, orokiu, orokiu
oak (n), heirp, heipa, heip
Oakland (n), Oklanurd, Okelanuda, Okland
oar (n), thranf, therana, thran
oar (v), thransf, therano, thrano
oasis (n), pelein, leiama, leiam
obedience (n), pilafk, ialifoka, ialfk
obedient (adj), pilafku, ialifoku, ialfku
obediently (adv), pilafkiu, ialifokiu, ialfkiu
obese (adj), lidurpu, lidupu, lidupu
obesely (adv), lidurpiu, lidupiu, lidupiu
obesity (n), lidurp, lidupa, lidup
obey (v), pilafsk, ialifoko, ialfko
obituary (n), litarge, litaga, litag
object (n d:thing), pilirk, ialika, ialk
object (v d:protest), iatersp, iatepo, iatepo
objection (n d:protest), iaterp, iatepa, iatep
objectionable (adj d:protest), iaterpu, iatepu, iatepu
objectionably (adv d:protest), iaterpiu, iatepiu, iatepiu
objective (adj d:goal), pilikatu, ialikatu, ialkatu
objective (n d:goal), pilikat, ialikata, ialkat
objectively (adv d:goal), pilikatiu, ialikatiu, ialkatiu
objectivity (n d:impartiality), pilikuet, ialikueta, ialkuet
objector (n doer d:protest), iaterpwan, iatepua, iatepua
obligate (v), piroilkuest, piroikueto, iaroikueto
obligation (n), piroilk, piroika, iaroik
obligatory (adj), piroilkuetu, piroikuetu, iaroikuetu
oblige (v), piroilsk, piroiko, iaroiko
obliterate (v), pilivartosre, ialivatoro, ialivatoro
obliteration (n), pilivartor, ialivatora, ialivator
oblivion (n), toivart, toivata, toivat
oblivious (adj), toivartu, toivatu, toivatu
obnoxious (adj), pimikartu, iamikatu, iamikatu
obnoxiously (adv), pimikartiu, iamikatiu, iamikatiu
obscene (adj), pithuliapu, iathulipu, iathulpu
obscenely (adv), pithuliapiu, iathulipiu, iathulpiu
obscenity (n), pithuliap, iathulipa, iathulp
obscure (v), piklorfsk, iakeloriko, iaklorko
obscurity (n), piklorfk, iakelorika, iaklork
observable (adj), pikorftu, iakofitu, iakoftu
observably (adv), pikorftiu, iakofitiu, iakoftiu
observance (n), pikorftan, iakofitana, iakoftan
observant (adj), pikorftanu, iakofitanu, iakoftanu
observantly (adv), pikorftaniu, iakofitaniu, iakoftaniu
observation (n), pikorft, iakofita, iakoft
observatory (n), pikorftak, iakofitaka, iakoftak

observe (v), pikorfst, iakofito, iakofto
observer (n doer), pikorftwan, iakofitua, iakoftua
obsess (v), pilasp, ialopo, ialpo
obsession (n), pilap, ialopa, ialp
obsessive (adj), pilapu, ialopu, ialpu
obsessively (adv), pilapiu, ialopiu, ialpiu
obsessor (n doer), pilapwan, ialopua, ialpua
obsolescence (n), pigrilk, iagerika, iagrik
obsolete (adj), pigrilku, iageriku, iagriku
obsoletely (adv), pigrilkiu, iagerikiu, iagrikiu
obstacle (n), pilark, iariloka, iarlk
obstruct (v), pishlesk, iasheleko, iashleko
obstruction (n), pishlek, iasheleka, iashlek
obstructionist (n doer), pishlekwan, iashelekua, iashlekua
obstructive (adj), pishleku, iasheleku, iashleku
obstructively (adv), pishlekiu, iashelekiu, iashlekiu
obstructor (n doer), pishlekwan, iashelekua, iashlekua
obtain (v), pipifst, iapifoto, iapifto
obtainable (adj), pipiftu, iapifotu, iapiftu
obtrude (v), iaborfst, iabofito, iabofto
obtrusion (n), iaborft, iabofita, iaboft
obtrusive (adj), iaborftu, iabofitu, iaboftu
obtrusively (adv), iaborftiu, iabofitiu, iaboftiu
obtuse (adj), pineirpu, ianeipu, ianeipu
obtusely (adv), pineirpiu, ianeipiu, ianeipiu
obtuseness (n), pineirp, ianeipa, ianeip
obvious (adj), pifuatu, iafuatu, iafuatu
obvious (n), pifuat, iafuata, iafuat
obviously (adv), pifuatiu, iafuatiu, iafuatiu
occasion (n), rogalirt, rogalita, rogalt
occasion (v), rogalirst, rogalito, rogalto
occasional (adj), rogalirtu, rogalitu, rogaltu
occasionally (adv), rogalirtiu, rogalitiu, rogaltiu
occupancy (n), rovorifpan, rovoripana, rovorpan
occupant (n doer), rovorifpanwan, rovoripanua, rovorpanua
occupation (n), rovorifp, rovoripa, rovorp
occupational (adj), rovorifpu, rovoripu, rovorpu
occupationally (adv), rovorifpiu, rovoripiu, rovorpiu
occupier (n doer), rovorifpwan, rovoripua, rovorpua
occupy (v), rovorifsp, rovoripo, rovorpo
occur (v), rogalirsf, rogalifo, rogalfo
occurrence (n), rogalirf, rogalifa, rogalf
ocean (n), miarl, miara, miar
oceanfront (adj), miarflarshu, miarefelarinu, miarflarnu
oceanic (adj), miarlu, miaru, miaru
oceanographic (adj), miardarfku, miaredarifu, miardarfu
oceanography (n), miardarfk, miaredarifa, miardarf
oceanside (n), miarshoirt, miareshoita, miarshoit
oct- (num 8 pref), genai-, genai-, genai-
octagon (n), genaimurk, genaimuka, genaimuk
octillion (num 1e27 card), genka, genka, genka
octillionth (num 1e27 ord), genketh, genketh, genketh
October (n), Loktaf, Lokitafa, Loktaf
octodecillion (num 1e57 card), gensht, gensht, gensht

octodecillionth (num 1e57 ord), genshteth, genshteth, genshteth
octoquadragintillion (num 1e147 card), genfk, genfk, genfk
octotrigintillion (num 1e117 card), genft, genft, genft
octovigintillion (num 1e87 card), genshk, genshk, genshk
octovigintillionth (num 1e87 ord), genshketh, genshketh, genshketh
odd (adj d:different), laurbu, laubu, laubu
odd (n d:probability), wiaurk, wiauka, wiauk
oddball (n), wiaukshmonde, wiaukemashipa, wiaukmashp
odden (v d:different), laurzbe, laubo, laubo
oddity (n d:different), laurbe, lauba, laub
oddly (adv d:different), laurbiu, laubiu, laubiu
odor (n), dufarl, dufala, dufal
odorless (adj), dufarlmenu, dufalemenu, dufalmenu
of (prep), orp, opeifu, op
off (prep), unf, unefu, unf
offbeat (adj), unfdaurtu, unefedautu, unfdautu
offend (v), tatorzve, tatorifo, tatorfo
offender (n doer), tatorvwan, tatorifua, tatorfua
offense (n), tatorve, tatorifa, tatorf
offensive (adj), tatorvu, tatorifu, tatorfu
offensively (adv), tatorviu, tatorifiu, tatorfiu
offensiveness (n), tatorvuet, tatorifueta, tatorfuet
offer (n), tefirk, tefika, tefk
offer (v), tefirsk, tefiko, tefko
offhand (adj), unfkarpu, unefekapu, unfkapu
office (n), tashkelt, tashikela, tashkel
officeholder (n doer), tashkelthorthkwan, tashikelethorithua, tashkelthorthua
officer (n doer), tashkeltwan, tashikelua, tashkelua
official (adj), tashkeltu, tashikelu, tashkelu
official (n doer), tashkeltwan, tashikelua, tashkelua
officialdom (n doer), tashkelfirfwan, tashikelefifua, tashkelfifua
officially (adv), tashkeltiu, tashikeliu, tashkeliu
officiate (v), tashkelst, tashikelo, tashkelo
offline (adj), unfroifku, uneferoifu, unfroifu
offload (v), unflurifst, unefelurito, unflurto
offscreen (adj), unfefklertu, unefefikoletu, unfefkletu
offscreen (n), unfefklert, unefefikoleta, unfefklet
offset (n), unferp, unefepa, unfep
offset (v pa), unferspyot, unefepio, unfepio
offset (v), unfersp, unefepo, unfepo
offshoot (n), unfshkort, unefeshekota, unfshkot
offshore (n), unfularat, unefularita, unfulart
offshore (v), unfularast, unefularito, unfularto
offside (adj), unfshoirtu, unefeshoitu, unfshoitu
offside (n), unfshoirt, unefeshoita, unfshoit
offspring (n), unfthrelt, unefethereta, unfthret
often (adv), ashpiliu, ashipiu, ashpiu
oftentimes (adv), ashpedaurniu, ashipedauniu, ashpedauniu
oh (interj), ar, ui, ui
Ohio (n), Okiorf, Okiofa, Okiof
oil (n), zhurf, zhura, zhur
oil (v), zhursf, zhuro, zhuro
oiler (n doer), zhurfwan, zhurua, zhurua

oilfield (n), zhureprant, zhureperanida, zhurprand
oilman (n), zhurplorn, zhurepelona, zhurplon
oilmen (n pl), zhurplornyek, zhurepeloni, zhurploni
oilseed (n), zhurderat, zhurederita, zhurdrit
oily (adj), zhurfu, zhuru, zhuru
ok (interj), shershai, sheshai, sheshai
okay (adj), shershu, sheshu, sheshu
okay (interj), shershai, sheshai, sheshai
okay (v), shers, shesho, shesho
Oklahoma (n), Oklakorm, Okelakoma, Oklakom
old (adj), arfu, arovu, arvu
old-fashioned (adj), zhurshiarshu, zhurashiashu,
    zhurshiashu
older (adj), arfwelu, arovwelu, arvwelu
older (n), arfwel, arovwela, arvwel
oldest (adj), arfwaku, arovwaku, arvwaku
oldest (n), arfwak, arovwaka, arvwak
olive (n), veirth, veitha, veith
olympian (n doer), madirkwan, madikua, madikua
olympic (adj), madirku, madiku, madiku
olympics (n), madirk, madika, madik
omega (n), omegarn, omegana, omegan
omelet (n), penelan, pelinana, pelnan
omen (n), auliunk, auliuna, auliun
omicron (n), omikroln, omikerona, omikron
ominous (adj), auliunku, auliunu, auliunu
ominously (adv), auliunkiu, auliuniu, auliuniu
omission (n), unaurk, unauka, unauk
omit (v), unaursk, unauko, unauko
omitter (n doer), unaurkwan, unaukua, unaukua
omnidirectional (adj), moilaukuarfku,
    moilaukuafiku, moilaukuafku
omnipotence (n), moilauboirge, moilauboiga,
    moilauboig
omnipotent (adj), moilauboirgu, moilauboigu,
    moilauboigu
omnipresence (n), moilaublutish, moilaubelutisha,
    moilaublutsh
omnipresent (adj), moilaublutishu,
    moilaubelutishu, moilaublutshu
omniscience (n), moilaushuarsh, moilaushuasha,
    moilaushuash
omniscient (adj), moilaushuarshu, moilaushuashu,
    moilaushuashu
omnivorous (adj), moilaudiuarfu, moilaudiuafu,
    moilaudiuafu
on (prep), lieme, liemu, liem
onboard (adj), lieglorifu, liegelorifu, lieglorfu
once (adj/adv/conj), hemf, hemefu, hemf
once (n), hemf, hemefa, hemf
oncoming (adj), lieblertu, hebllefu, lleblefu
one (num 1 card), heme, heme, heme
one (pron 3rd indefpers sng obj), ona, ona, ona
one (pron 3rd indefpers sng sub), ona, ona, ona
one's (pron 3rd indefpers sng pos obj), onash,
    onash, onash
one's (pron 3rd indefpers sng pos sub), onash,
    onash, onash
oneself (pron 3rd indefpers sng refl), onashfal,
    onashfal, onashfal
onetime (adj), hemdaurnu, hemedaunu, hemdaunu
ongoing (adj), liemavirfu, liemavifu, liemavifu

onion (n), muirt, muita, muit
onlooker (n doer), liereigirnwan, liereiginua,
    liereiginua
only (adj/adv/conj), hemeru, hemeru, hemeru
onscreen (adj), liefklertu, liefikoletu, liefkletu
onset (n), lieferp, liefepa, liefep
onshore (adj), lienularatu, lienularitu, lienulartu
onslaught (n), lieshriausht, liesheriauta, lieshriaut
onstage (adj), lietralku, lieteraku, lietraku
onstage (n), lietralk, lieteraka, lietrak
Ontario (n), Ontariorf, Onitariofa, Ontariof
onto (prep), emde, emodi, emdi
onward (adv), liehurshiu, liehushiu, liehushiu
oomph (interj), uf, ufu, uf
oops (interj), oifk, oifo, oif
ooze (n), dulfk, dulufa, dulf
ooze (v), dulfsk, dulufo, dulfo
open (adj), efbirnu, efubinu, efbinu
open (v), efbirsne, efubino, efbino
opener (n doer), efbirnwan, efubinua, efbinua
openly (adv), efbirniu, efubiniu, efbiniu
openness (n), efbirn, efubina, efbin
opera (n), dunirf, dunifa, dunf
operable (adj), duriftu, duritu, durtu
operate (v), durifst, durito, durto
operation (n), durift, durita, durt
operational (adj), duriftu, duritu, durtu
operationally (adv), duriftiu, duritiu, durtiu
operative (n), durtarn, duritana, durtan
operator (n doer), duriftwan, duritua, durtua
opine (v), benirsf, benifo, benfo
opinion (n), benirf, benifa, benf
opponent (n doer), binarkwan, binakua, binkua
opportunist (n doer), dubielirkwan, dubielikua,
    dubielkua
opportunistic (adj), dubielirku, dubieliku, dubielku
opportunity (n), dubielirk, dubielika, dubielk
oppose (v), binarsk, binako, binko
opposite (adj), binarkaru, binakaru, binkaru
opposite (n), binarkar, binakara, binkar
opposition (n), binark, binaka, bink
oppress (v), dublars, dubelasho, dublasho
oppression (n), dublarsh, dubelasha, dublash
oppressive (adj), dublarshu, dubelashu, dublashu
oppressively (adv), dublarshiu, dubelashiu,
    dublashiu
oppressor (n doer), dublarshwan, dubelashua,
    dublashua
opt (v), efuerst, efueto, efueto
optic (n), shkenirp, shokenipa, shkenp
optical (adj), shkenirpu, ohokonipu, ohkonpu
optically (adv), shkenirpiu, shokenipiu, shkenpiu
optimal (adj), bidaurnalu, bidaunalu, bidaunalu
optimally (adv), bidaurnaliu, bidaunaliu,
    bidaunaliu
optimism (n), bidaurn, bidauna, bidaun
optimist (n doer), bidaurnwan, bidaunua, bidaunua
optimistic (adj), bidaurnu, bidaunu, bidaunu
optimistically (adv), bidaurniu, bidauniu, bidauniu
optimization (n), bidaurnuet, bidaunueta,
    bidaunuet
optimize (v), bidaursne, bidauno, bidauno
optimum (n), bidaurnal, bidaunala, bidaunal

option (n), efuert, efueta, efuet
optional (adj), efuertu, efuetu, efuetu
optionally (adv), efuertiu, efuetiu, efuetiu
or (conj), il, ilu, il
oral (adj), diranfu, diranu, dirnu
orally (adv), diranfiu, diraniu, dirniu
orange (adj d:color), lofarmu, lofamu, lofamu
orange (n d:color), lofarme, lofama, lofam
orange (n d:fruit), davarp, davapa, davap
orate (v), dirafsk, dirako, dirko
orator (n doer), dirafkwan, dirakua, dirkua
oratory (n), dirafk, diraka, dirk
orbit (n), liplurt, lipeluta, liplut
orbit (v), liplurst, lipeluto, lipluto
orbital (adj), liplurtu, lipelutu, liplutu
orbiter (n doer), liplurtwan, lipelutua, liplutua
orchestra (n), lofirn, lofina, lofin
orchestral (adj), lofirnu, lofinu, lofinu
orchestrally (adv), lofirniu, lofiniu, lofiniu
orchestrate (v), lofirsne, lofino, lofino
orchestration (n), lofirnuet, lofinueta, lofinuet
orchestrator (n doer), lofirnwan, lofinua, lofinua
ordain (v), shkeifst, shekeito, shkeito
ordeal (n), lobirek, lobifeka, lobifk
order (n), shkelt, shiketa, shket
order (v), shkelst, shiketo, shketo
orderer (n doer), shkeltwan, shiketua, shketua
orderliness (n), shkelt, shiketa, shket
orderly (adj), shkeltu, shiketu, shketu
ordinance (n), shkeltat, shiketata, shketat
ordinarily (adv), shkeltariu, shiketariu, shketariu
ordinary (adj), shkeltaru, shiketaru, shketaru
ordinate (v), shkeialst, shekeiato, shkeiato
ordination (n), shkeialt, shekeiata, shkeiat
Oregon (n), Origorn, Origona, Origon
organ (n d:body part), frofp, feropa, frop
organ (n d:instrument), miarp, miapa, miap
organic (adj d:of life), frolfu, ferofu, frofu
organism (n), frilatat, ferilotata, friltat
organization (n d:structure), frilat, ferilota, frilt
organizational (adj d:structure), frilatu, ferilotu, friltu
organize (v d:structure), frilast, feriloto, frilto
organizer (n doer d:structure), frilatwan, ferilotua, friltua
orgasm (n), friashk, feriazha, friazh
orgasmic (adj), friashku, feriazhu, friazhu
orgy (n), friashkak, feriazhaka, friazhak
orient (v), lamoisne, moito, moito
orientation (n), lamoin, moita, moit
origin (n), lamart, lamata, lamat
original (adj), lamartu, lamatu, lamatu
original (n), lamalirt, lamalita, lamalt
originality (n), lamaltart, lamalitata, lamaltat
originally (adv), lamartiu, lamatiu, lamatiu
originate (v), lamarst, lamato, lamato
origination (n), lamartuet, lamatueta, lamatuet
originator (n doer), lamartwan, lamatua, lamatua
Orlando (n), Orandorf, Orilanudofa, Orlandof
ornament (n), denarn, denana, denan
ornamental (adj), denarnu, denanu, denanu
ornamentally (adv), denarniu, denaniu, denaniu
ornate (adj), denirfu, denifu, denfu

ornately (adv), denirfiu, denifiu, denfiu
Os (let pl), orfi, orfi, orfi
oscillate (v), drolfsk, derolifo, drolfo
oscillation (n), drolfk, derolifa, drolf
oscillator (n doer), drolfkwan, derolifua, drolfua
oshto- (num 1e51 pref), kinshtai-, kinshtai-, kinshtai-
Osmium (n davoka), Irik, Irik, Irik
Osmium (n), Oshmium, Oshamiuma, Oshmium
other (adj/adv), mirshu, mishu, mishu
other (n/pron), mirsh, mishei, mish
others (pron), mirshyek, mishi, mishi
otherwise (adj/adv/conj), mirshfluik, mishefeluiku, mishfluik
Ottawa (n), Otawarf, Otawafa, Otawaf
ouch (inter), auta, auta, auta
ought (ndal d:desire), loirf kodi, loira kodi, loir kodi
ounce (n), shulirn, shulina, shuln
our (pron 1st pl pos sub), nuish, nuish, nuish
ours (pron 1st pl pos obj), raush, raush, raush
ourself (pron 1st sing refl), raushfal, raushfal, raushfal
ourselves (pron 1st pl refl), raushfar, raushfar, raushfar
oust (v), ushersk, usheko, ushko
ouster (n doer), usherkwan, ushekua, ushkua
out (adj/adv/prep/interj), uil, uilu, uil
out (n), uil, uila, uil
outage (n), uilueft, uilueta, uiluet
outback (n), uilvark, uilevaka, uilvak
outbid (v pa), uilthairstyot, uilethaitio, uilthaitio
outbid (v), uilthairst, uilethaito, uilthaito
outboard (adj), uilglorifu, uilegelorifu, uilglorfu
outbound (adj), uildraifpu, uilederaipu, uildraipu
outbound (n), uildraifp, uilederaipa, uildraip
outbreak (n), uilblerk, uilepelika, uilplik
outburst (n), uilbrutap, uileberushota, uilbrusht
outcast (n), uiltulirt, uilotulita, uiltult
outcome (n), uilblerf, uilobelefa, uilblef
outcry (n), uilbroip, uileberoifa, uilbroif
outdoor (adj), uilshtelfu, uileshetelu, uilshtelu
outdoors (n), uilshtelf, uileshetela, uilshtel
outer (adj), uilwelu, uilwelu, uilwelu
outermost (adj), uilwelwaku, uilwelwaku, uilwelwaku
outerwear (n), uilweldorame, uilweledorima, uilweldorim
outfield (n), uilprant, uileperanida, uilprand
outfielder (n doer), uilprantwan, uileperanidua, uilprandua
outfit (n), uilpafirt, uilopafita, uilpaft
outfit (v), uilpafirst, uilopafito, uilpafto
outfitter (n doer), uilpafirtwan, uilopafitua, uilpaftua
outflank (v), uilgranirsk, uilegeraniko, uilgranko
outflow (n), uilbrauf, uileberautha, uilbrauth
outflow (v), uilbrausf, uileberautho, uilbrautho
outfox (v), zhursk, zhuko, zhuko
outgo (v), uilovirsf, uilovifo, uilvifo
outgoer (n doer), uilovirfwan, uilovifua, uilvifua
outgrew (v pa), uilkloraskyot, uilekeloikio, uilkloikio
outgrow (v), uilklorask, uilekeloiko, uilkloiko

outgrowth (n), uilklorak, uilekeloika, uilkloik
outgun (v), uildorizge, uiledorugo, uildorgo
outhouse (n), uilkiarf, uilekiafa, uilkiaf
outlaid (v pa), uilfranistyot, uileferanitio, uilfrantio
outlaw (n), uilvaurde, uilovauda, uilvaud
outlaw (v), uilvaurzde, uilovaudo, uilvaudo
outlay (n), uilfranit, uileferanita, uilfrant
outlet (n), uilerk, uileka, uilek
outlie (v), uilfranist, uileferanito, uilfranto
outline (n), uilroifk, uileroifa, uilroif
outline (v), uilroifsk, uileroifo, uilroifo
outliner (n doer), uilroifkwan, uileroifua, uilroifua
outlive (v), uilflaurfst, uilefelaufito, uilflaufto
outlook (n), uilreigin, uilereiga, uilreig
outnumber (v), uilnenirsk, uiloneniko, uilnenko
outpace (v), uilkiorsf, uilekiofo, uilkiofo
outpatient (adj), uilmorthu, uilemolithu, uilmolthu
outpatient (n), uilmorth, uilemolitha, uilmolth
outperform (v), uilovorinsf, uilovorino, uilovorno
outpost (n), uildialirt, uiledialita, uildialt
outpour (n), uilroturt, uilerotuta, uilrotut
outpour (v), uilroturst, uilerotuto, uilrotuto
output (n), uilvurt, uilevuta, uilvut
output (v), uilvurst, uilevuto, uilvuto
outrage (n), uilzhigart, uilezhigata, uilzhigat
outrage (v), uilzhigarst, uilezhigato, uilzhigato
outrageous (adj), uilzhigartu, uilezhigatu,
    uilzhigatu
outrageously (adv), uilzhigartiu, uilezhigatiu,
    uilzhigatiu
outran (v pa), uilaorzmyot, uilaomio, uilaomio
outreach (n), uilgloruge, uilegeloruga, uilglorg
outright (adj), uildierku, uiledieku, uildieku
outrun (v), uilaorzme, uilaomo, uilaomo
outsell (v), uiltrelirsf, uileterelifo, uiltrelfo
outset (n), uilferp, uilefepa, uilfep
outshine (v), uilmoirsth, uilemoitho, uilmoitho
outshone (v pa), uilmoirsthyot, uilemoithio,
    uilmoithio
outside (n), uilshoirt, uileshoita, uilshoit
outside (n/adj/adv/prep), uilshoirt, uileshoitu,
    uilshoit
outsider (n doer), uilshoirtwan, uileshoitua,
    uilshoitua
outsize (v), uilshuarzge, uileshuago, uilshuago
outskirt (n), uilfnilort, uilefenilota, uilfnilt
outsmart (v), uilniarzme, uileniamo, uilniamo
outsold (v pa), uiltrelirsfyot, uileterelifio, uiltrelfio
outspoken (adj), uiltalirshu, uiletalishu, uiltalshu
outstanding (adj), uiltrelitu, uiloterelitu, uiltreltu
outstretch (v), uilgrairst, uilegeraito, uilgraito
outstrip (v), uiltivursk, uiletivuko, uiltivuko
outvote (v), uilthairsk, uilethaiko, uilthaiko
outward (adj/adv), uilhaurshu, uilehaushu,
    uilhaushu
outward (n), uilhaursh, uilehausha, uilhaush
outwardly (adv), uilhaurshiu, uilehaushiu,
    uilhaushiu
outweigh (v), uilshuirs, uileshuisho, uilshuisho
outwent (v pa), uilovirsfyot, uilovifio, uilvifio
outwit (v), uiltilorsk, uiletiloko, uiltilko
ova (n pl), klufpyek, kelupi, klupi
OvaCarrier (n), plerp, pelepa, plep

oval (n), fioft, fioba, fiob
ovarian (adj), kluarpu, keluapu, kluapu
ovary (n doer), kluarpwan, keluapua, kluapua
ovation (n), pluarth, peluatha, pluath
oven (n), kofirth, kofitha, kofith
over (adv/adv/prep), afenu, afenu, afenu
over (n), afen, afena, afen
overabundance (n), afeniunirf, afeniunifa, afeniunf
overactive (adj), afepaltarku, afepalitaku,
    afepaltaku
overactivity (n), afepaltark, afepalitaka, afepaltak
overall (adj), afenloru, afeloru, afeloru
overall (adv), afenloriu, afeloriu, afeloriu
overalls (n), afenlor, afelora, afelor
overate (v pa), afenierstyot, afenietio, afenietio
overblew (v pa), afeflausnyot, afeferaushio,
    afefraushio
overblow (v), afeflausne, afeferausho, afefrausho
overboard (n), afeglorif, afegelorifa, afeglorf
overbook (v), afevornst, afevonudo, afevondo
overbuild (v), afevorast, afevorito, afevorto
overbuilt (v pa), afevorastyot, afevoritio, afevortio
overcame (v pa), afeblersfyot, afebelefio, afeblefio
overcapacity (n), afedefrup, afedethipa, afedethp
overcast (adj), afetulirtu, afetulitu, afetultu
overcharge (n), afegloift, afegeloita, afegloit
overcharge (v), afegloifst, afegeloito, afegloito
overcoat (n), afefrafk, aferafika, aferafk
overcome (v), afeblersf, afebelefo, afeblefo
overconfidence (n), afebelprin, afeliuperina,
    afeliuprin
overconfident (adj), afebelprinu, afeliuperinu,
    afeliuprinu
overconfidently (adv), afebelpriniu, afeliuperiniu,
    afeliupriniu
overcrowd (v), afeviarzge, afeviago, afeviago
overdid (v pa), afentiskyot, afenotikio, afetikio
overdo (v), afentisk, afenotiko, afetiko
overdose (n), afetorth, afekaritha, afekarth
overdose (v), afetorsth, afekaritho, afekartho
overdraft (n), afeflark, afefelaritha, afeflarth
overdraft (v), afeflarsk, afefelaritho, afeflartho
overdrive (n), afediarp, afediapa, afediap
overdue (adj), afetiurku, afetiuku, afetiuku
overeat (v), afenierst, afenieto, afenieto
overestimate (n), afenthinarp, afethinapa, afethinp
overestimate (v), afenthinarsp, afethinapo,
    afethinpo
overexpose (v), afetulask, afelanishoko, afelanshko
overexposure (n), afetulak, afelanishoka, afelanshk
overfeed (v), afeparzve, afepavo, afepavo
overfish (v), afeshlers, afeshelesho, afeshlesho
overflow (n), afenbrauf, afeberautha, afebrauth
overflow (v), afenbrausf, afeberautho, afebrautho
overhang (n), afetarage, afetaruga, afetarg
overhang (v), afetarazge, afetarugo, afetargo
overhaul (n), afeshluarp, afesheluapa, afeshluap
overhaul (v), afeshluarsp, afesheluapo, afeshluapo
overhauler (n doer), afeshluarpwan, afesheluapua,
    afeshluapua
overhead (n), afenkeft, afekefita, afekeft
overhear (v), afenuyasne, afuyano, afuyano
overheard (v pa), afenuyasnyot, afuyanio, afuyanio

overheat (v), afekurst, afekuto, afekuto
overhung (v pa), afetarazgyot, afetarugio, afetargio
overjoy (n), afelairsh, afelaisha, afelaish
overkill (n), afekitersh, afekitesha, afekitsh
overlaid (v pa), afranistyot, aferanitio, aferantio
overland (adj), aferaufpu, aferaupu, aferaupu
overlap (n), afethiurt, afethiuta, afethiut
overlap (v), afethiurst, afethiuto, afethiuto
overlay (n), afranit, aferanita, aferant
overlay (v pa), aferiesfyot, aferethio, aferethio
overlay (v), afranist, aferanito, aferanto
overlie (v), aferiesf, aferetho, aferetho
overload (n), aflurt, felurita, flurt
overload (v), aflurst, felurito, flurto
overloader (n doer), aflurtwan, fleluritua, flurtua
overlook (v), afenreirzge, afenereigo, afenreigo
overly (adv), afeniu, afeniu, afeniu
overmatch (v), afemuthsk, afemutho, afemutho
overnight (adj), afemuarnu, afemuanu, afemuanu
overnight (adv), afemuarniu, afemuaniu,
    afemuaniu
overnight (n), afemuarn, afemuana, afemuan
overnight (v), afemuarsne, afemuano, afemuano
overnighter (n doer), afemuarnwan, afemuanua,
    afemuanua
overpaid (v pa), afemoirzmyot, afemoimio,
    afemoimio
overpass (n), afelunirt, afelunita, afelunt
overpay (v), afemoirzme, afemoimo, afemoimo
overpayment (n), afemoirme, afemoima, afemoim
overplay (n), afefruifk, afeferuifa, afefruif
overplay (v), afefruifsk, afeferuifo, afefruifo
overpopulate (v), afevorazve, afevoruvo, afevorvo
overpopulation (n), afevorave, afevoruva, afevorv
overpower (v), afebiorast, afebiorito, afebiorto
overprice (v), afetirofsp, afetiropo, afetirpo
overproduce (v), afefiursk, afefiuko, afefiuko
overproduction (n), afefiurk, afefiuka, afefiuk
overqualification (n), afekriarf, afekeriafa, afekriaf
overqualify (v), afekriarsf, afekeriafo, afekriafo
overran (v pa), afelaorzmyot, afelaomio, afelaomio
overrate (v), afeterzbe, afetebo, afetebo
overreach (v), afegloruzge, afegelorugo, afeglorgo
overreact (v), afelupalirst, afelupalito, afelupalto
overreaction (n), afelupalirt, afelupalita, afelupalt
overreliance (n), afeterame, afeterema, afetrem
overrely (v), afeterazme, afeteremo, afetremo
overrepresent (v), afeludars, afeluduasho,
    afeluduasho
overrepresentation (n), afeludarsh, afeluduasha,
    afeluduash
override (n), afeshlirbe, afesheliba, afeshlib
override (v), afeshlirzbe, afeshelibo, afeshlibo
overrode (v pa), afeshlirzbyot, afeshelibio,
    afeshlibio
overrule (v), afelarast, afelarito, afelarto
overrun (v), afelaorzme, afelaomo, afelaomo
oversaw (v pa), afethulsthyot, afethuthio,
    afethuthio
overseas (adj), afeshkleirnu, afeshokeleinu,
    afeshkleinu
overseas (adv), afeshkleirniu, afeshokeleiniu,
    afeshkleiniu

overseas (n), afeshkleirn, afeshokeleina, afeshklein
oversee (v), afethulsth, afethutho, afethutho
overseer (n doer), afethulthwan, afethuthua,
    afethuthua
oversell (v), afetrelirsf, afeterelifo, afetrelfo
overshadow (v), afepoefirst, afepoefito, afepoefto
overshoot (n), afeshkort, afeshekota, afeshkot
overshoot (v), afeshkorst, afeshekoto, afeshkoto
overshot (v pa), afeshkorstyot, afeshekotio,
    afeshkotio
oversight (n), afethulth, afethutha, afethuth
oversimplification (n), afeshalirn, afeshalina,
    afeshaln
oversimplify (v), afeshalirsne, afeshalino, afeshalno
oversize (v), afeshuarzge, afeshuago, afeshuago
oversleep (v), afepruls, afeperusho, afeprusho
overslept (v pa), afeprulsyot, afeperushio,
    afeprushio
oversold (v pa), afetrelirsfyot, afeterelifio, afetrelfio
overspend (v), afedorklarst, afedorikelato,
    afedorklato
overspent (v pa), afedorklarstyot, afedorikelatio,
    afedorklatio
overstate (v), afebiurst, afebiuto, afebiuto
overstatement (n), afebiurt, afebiuta, afebiut
overstep (v), afeglishsk, afegelisho, afeglisho
overstock (v), afefrifsk, afeferifo, afefrifo
overstuff (v), afeplersth, afepeletho, afepletho
oversubscribe (v), afenorisherzge, afenorisherigo,
    afenorishrigo
oversupply (n), afeshethirp, afeshethipa, afeshethp
oversupply (v), afeshethirsp, afeshethipo,
    afeshethpo
overt (adj), taibirtu, taibitu, taibitu
overtake (v), afegorsk, afegoko, afegoko
overtax (v), afeshenirsk, afesheniko, afeshenko
overthrew (v pa), afetarthskyot, afetarithio,
    afetarthio
overthrow (n), afetarthk, afetaritha, afetarth
overthrow (v), afetarthsk, afetaritho, afetartho
overtime (n), atedaurn, atedauna, afedaun
overtly (adv), taibirtiu, taibitiu, taibitiu
overtone (n), afetrilf, afeterila, afetril
overtook (v pa), afegorskyot, afegokio, afegokio
overture (n), afenarf, afenara, afenar
overturn (v), afekaimesp, afekaimo, afekaimo
overuse (n), afebriark, afeberiaka, afebriak
overuse (v), afebriarsk, afeberiako, afebriako
overvalue (n), afevaurp, afevaupa, afevaup
overvalue (v), afevaursp, afevaupo, afevaupo
overview (n), afefuart, afefuata, afefuat
overview (v), afefuarst, afefuato, afefuato
overweight (n), afeshuirsh, afeshuisha, afeshuish
overwhelm (v), keirzge, keigo, keigo
overwhelmingly (adv), keirgiu, keigiu, keigiu
overwork (n), afekiork, afekioka, afekiok
overwork (v), afekiorsk, afekioko, afekioko
overwrite (v), afeloirzde, afeloido, afeloido
overwrote (v pa), afeloirzdyot, afeloidio, afeloidio
ovulate (v), kluarsp, keluapo, kluapo
ovulation (n), kluarp, keluapa, kluap
ovum (n), klufp, kelupa, klup
ow (interj), aua, aua, aua

owe (v), wiarst, wiato, wiato
ower (n doer), wiartwan, wiatua, wiatua
owl (n), riarth, riatha, riath
own (adj), theiftu, theifu, theifu
own (n), theift, theifa, theif
own (v), theifst, theifo, theifo
owner (n doer), theiftwan, theifua, theifua
ownership (n), theifirf, theififa, theifif
ox (n), korvuge, koriga, korg
oxen (n pl), korvugyek, korigi, korgi
oxidation (n), ekupatuert, ekupatueta, ekupatuet
oxide (n), ekupat, ekupata, ekupat
oxidize (v), ekupast, ekupato, ekupato
oxidizer (n doer), ekupatwan, ekupatua, ekupatua
Oxygen (n davoka), Ekup, Ekup, Ekup
Oxygen (n), Okigen, Okigena, Okigen
oyster (n), fuarsh, fuasha, fuash
ozone (n), ekuparn, ekupana, ekupan
P (let sng), peil, peia, pei
p.m. (adj), unamu, unamu, unam
pa (n), blarp, belapa, blap
pace (n), kiorf, kiofa, kiof
pace (v), kiorsf, kiofo, kiofo
pacemaker (n doer), kiofnargwan, kiofenagua,
    kiofnagua
pacer (n doer), kiorfwan, kiofua, kiofua
pacesetter (n doer), kioferpwan, kiofepua, kiofepua
pacific (adj), kiorfatu, kiofatu, kiofatu
pacifier (n doer), kiorfatwan, kiofatua, kiofatua
pacifism (n), kiorfat, kiofata, kiofat
pacifist (n doer), kiorfatwan, kiofatua, kiofatua
pacify (v), kiorfast, kiofato, kiofato
pack (n), bugarp, bugapa, bugap
pack (v), bugarsp, bugapo, bugapo
package (n), bugart, bugata, bugat
package (v), bugarst, bugato, bugato
packager (n doer), bugartwan, bugatua, bugatua
packer (n doer), bugarpwan, bugapua, bugapua
packet (n), bugafirt, bugafita, bugaft
pact (n), giforp, gifopa, gifp
pad (n), banirf, banifa, banf
pad (v), banirsf, banifo, banfo
paddle (n), banfalt, banifata, banfat
paddle (v), banfalst, banifato, banfato
padlock (n), bantiurge, banitiuga, bantiug
padlock (v), bantiurzge, banitiugo, bantiugo
pafta- (num 1e48 pref), tirishtai-, tirishtai-,
    tirishtai-
pagan (n), gifank, gifana, gifan
paganism (n), gifankuert, gifanueta, gifanuet
page (n d:paper), doithk, doitha, doith
page (n d:person/contact), boirsh, boisha, boish
page (v d:person/contact), boirs, boisho, boisho
pageant (n), boishart, boishata, boishat
pager (n doer d:person/contact), boirshwan,
    boishua, boishua
paginate (v), doithkuest, doithueto, doithueto
pagination (n), doithkuet, doithueta, doithuet
paid (v pa), moirzmyot, moimio, moimio
pail (n), riorp, riopa, riop
pain (n), zhiarge, zhiaga, zhiag
pain (v), zhiarzge, zhiago, zhiago
painful (adj), zhiargu, zhiagu, zhiag

painfully (adv), zhiargiu, zhiagiu, zhiagiu
painkiller (n), zhiagitersh, zhiagitesha, zhiagitsh
painless (adj), zhargmenu, zhiagemenu, zhiagmenu
painlessly (adv), zhargmeniu, zhiagemeniu,
    zhiagmeniu
painstake (v), zhiagorsk, zhiagoko, zhiagoko
painstakingly (adv), zhiagorkiu, zhiagokiu,
    zhiagokiu
painstook (v pa), zhiagorskyot, zhiagokio, zhiagokio
paint (n), gralsh, gerasha, grash
paint (v), grals, gerasho, grasho
paintbrush (n), grashklurf, gerashekelusha,
    grashklush
painter (n doer), gralshwan, gerashua, grashua
pair (n), barve, bava, bav
pair (v), barzve, bavo, bavo
pajama (n), zhargume, zhaguma, zhagum
Pakistan (n), Pakishtarn, Pakishotana, Pakishtan
pal (n), neishk, neisha, neish
palace (n), thualirf, thualifa, thualf
palatable (adj), parlufku, parelufu, parlufu
palate (n), parlufk, parelufa, parluf
pale (adj d:complexion), thoarmu, thoamu, thoamu
pale (n d:spike), thailt, thaila, thail
pale (v d:complexion), thoarzme, thoamo, thoamo
paleness (n d:complexion), thoarme, thoama,
    thoam
Palestine (n), Paleshtirf, Paleshotifa, Paleshtif
Palestinian (n), Paleshtirn, Paleshotina, Paleshtin
palette (n), thilarn, thilana, thilan
Palladium (n davoka), Iluk, Iluk, Iluk
Palladium (n), Paladium, Paladiuma, Paladium
pallet (n), bloithk, beloitha, bloith
palm (n), threln, therena, thren
palm (v), threlsne, thereno, threno
pamper (v), kualirsk, kualiko, kualko
pamphlet (n), friart, feriata, friat
pan (n), melirk, melika, melk
pan (v), melirsk, meliko, melko
Panama (n), Panarm, Panama, Panam
Panamanian (n), Panamarn, Panamana, Panaman
pancake (n), melkegutraf, melikegurita, melkegurt
pancake (v), melkegutrasf, melikegurito,
    melkegurto
pander (v), melkarst, melikato, melkato
pane (n), flanshk, felanisha, flansh
panel (n), melirf, melifa, melf
panel (v), melirsf, melifo, melfo
panelist (n doer), melirfwan, melifua, melfua
pang (n), fierge, fiega, fieg
panic (n), meishirk, meishika, meishk
panic (v), meishirsk, meishiko, meishko
panicky (adj), meishirku, meishiku, meishku
pant (v d:breathe), fiatarsk, fiatako, fiatako
pants (n pl d:clothing), mekarnyek, mekani, mekani
papa (n), blaparn, belapana, blapan
paper (n), vuarp, vuapa, vuap
paper (v), vuarsp, vuapo, vuapo
paperback (n), vuapart, vuapata, vuapat
paperboard (n), vuaplok, vuapelorika, vuaplork
paperless (adj), vuarpemenu, vuapemenu,
    vuapemenu
paperweight (n), vuapshuirsh, vuapeshuisha,

vuapshuish
paperwork (n), vuapekiork, vuapekioka, vuapkiok
par (adj), reinorfu, reinofu, reinfu
par (n), reinorf, reinofa, reinf
par (v), reinorsf, reinofo, reinfo
parachute (n), varkaflufp, valekafelupa, valkaflup
parachute (v), varkaflufsp, valekafelupo, valkaflupo
parade (n), varkaiaf, valikaiafa, valkaiaf
parade (v), varkaiasf, valikaiafo, valkaiafo
parader (n doer), varkaiafwan, valikaiafua,
    valkaiafua
paradise (n), varkashair, valikashaira, valkashair
paradox (n), varkapren, valikaperena, valkapren
paradoxical (adj), varkaprenu, valikaperenu,
    valkaprenu
paradoxically (adv), varkapreniu, valikapereniu,
    valkapreniu
paragraph (n), varkadarf, valikadarofa, valkadarf
parallel (adj), varkaninu, valikaninu, valkaninu
parallel (n), varkanin, valikanina, valkanin
parallel (v), varkanisne, valikanino, valkanino
parallelism (n), varkaninuet, valikaninueta,
    valkaninuet
paralyze (v), varkamarfst, valikamafito, valkamafto
parameter (n), varkaniork, valikanioka, valkaniok
parametric (adj), varkaniorku, valikanioku,
    valkanioku
paramount (adj), varkaniurku, valikaniuku,
    valkaniuku
paranoia (n), varkaiak, valikaiaka, valkaiak
paranoid (adj), varkaiaku, valikaiaku, valkaiaku
paraphrase (n), varkavarsh, valikavarosha,
    valkavarsh
paraphrase (v), varkavars, valikavarosho,
    valkavarsho
parasite (n), varkaft, valikafita, valkaft
parasitic (adj), varkaftu, valikafitu, valkaftu
parasol (n), varkaren, valikarena, valkaren
parcel (n), varfrat, valiferata, valfrat
parcel (v), varfrast, valiferato, valfrato
parch (v), triuteshsk, terlutesho, triutsho
pardon (n), valtirge, valotiga, valtig
pardon (v), valtirzge, valotigo, valtigo
pare (v), bolirsk, boliko, bolko
parent (n), dathferf, dathifefa, dathfef
parent (v), dathfersf, dathifefo, dathfefo
parental (adj), dathferfu, dathifefu, dathfefu
parenthood (n), dathferfif, dathifefifa, dathfefif
Paris (n), Parilsh, Parisha, Parish
parity (n), bolkart, bolikata, bolkat
park (n d:playground), parilf, parifa, parf
park (v d:stop), kabarst, kabato, kabato
parkway (n), parfpliorl, parifepeliola, parfpliol
parliament (n), shporat, shiperata, shprat
parliamentary (adj), shporatu, shiperatu, shpratu
parlor (n), kabirt, kabita, kabit
parlor (v), kabirst, kabito, kabito
parole (n), valmeiraf, valomeirifa, valmeirf
parrot (n), kaparsh, kapasha, kapash
parrot (v), kapars, kapasho, kapasho
parry (v), varkaist, valekaito, valkaito
parse (v), feshturzge, feshetugo, feshtugo
parser (n doer), feshturgwan, feshetugua, feshtugua

part (n), fersh, fesha, fesh
part (v), fers, fesho, fesho
partial (adj), feshartu, feshatu, feshatu
partial (n), feshart, feshata, feshat
partially (adv), feshartiu, feshatiu, feshatiu
participant (n doer), feshelirkwan, feshelikua,
    feshelkua
participate (v), feshelirsk, fesheliko, feshelko
participation (n), feshelirk, feshelika, feshelk
participle (n), fesheilk, fesheika, fesheik
particle (n), feshirp, feshipa, feshp
particular (adj), fenirshu, fenishu, fenshu
particular (n), fenirshul, fenishula, fenshul
particularly (adv), fenirshiu, fenishiu, fenshiu
participle (adj), feshirpu, feshipu, feshpu
particulate (n), feshirp, feshipa, feshp
particulate (v), feshirsp, feshipo, feshpo
partition (n), fershuet, feshueta, feshuet
partition (v), fershuest, feshueto, feshueto
partly (adv), fershiu, feshiu, feshiu
partner (n doer), feshnartwan, feshinatua,
    feshnatua
partner (v), feshnarst, feshinato, feshnato
partnership (n), feshnart, feshinata, feshnat
party (n d:celebration), biarzhe, biazha, biazh
party (n d:group), nutersh, nutesha, nutsh
party (v d:celebration), biarze, biazho, biazho
pass (n), lunirt, lunita, lunt
pass (v), lunirst, lunito, lunto
passage (n), luntark, lunitaka, luntak
passenger (n doer), luntarkwan, lunitakua,
    luntakua
passer (n doer), lunirtwan, lunitua, luntua
passion (n), fleirsh, feleisha, fleish
passionate (adj), fleirshu, feleishu, fleishu
passionately (adv), fleirshiu, feleishiu, fleishiu
passive (adj), lunirtu, lunitu, luntu
passively (adv), lunirtiu, lunitiu, luntiu
passport (n), lunbielirk, lunebielika, lunbielk
password (n), lunlialirt, lunelialita, lunlialt
past (n), flairth, felaitha, flaith
paste (n), drafip, derafipa, drafp
paste (v), drafisp, derafipo, drafpo
pastel (n), drafir, deralifa, dralf
paster (n doer), drafipwan, derafipua, drafpua
pastry (n), drafirsh, derafisha, drafish
pasture (n), velarn, velarina, vlarn
pasty (adj), drafipu, derafipu, drafpu
pat (n), geirp, geipa, geip
pat (v), geirsp, geipo, geipo
patch (n), shkralge, shekoraga, shkrag
patch (v), shkralzge, shekorago, shkrago
patcher (n doer), shkralgwan, shekoragua,
    shkragua
patchy (adj), shkralgu, shekoragu, shkragu
patent (n), keipifort, keipifota, keipift
patent (v), keipiforst, keipifoto, keipifto
path (n), botersh, botesha, botsh
pathetic (adj), botarku, botaku, botaku
pathetically (adv), botarkiu, botakiu, botakiu
pathogen (n), bodarsh, bodasha, bodash
pathogenic (adj), bodarshu, bodashu, bodashu
pathos (n), botark, botaka, botak

pathway (n), botshpliorl, boteshepeliola, botshpliol
patience (n d:endurance), morth, molitha, molth
patient (adj d:endurance), morthu, molithu, molthu
patient (n d:person), hethirt, hethieta, hetht
patiently (adv d:endurance), morthiu, molithiu, molthiu
patriot (n), fanturn, fanituna, fantun
patriotic (adj), fanturnu, fanitunu, fantunu
patriotically (adv), fanturniu, fanituniu, fantuniu
patrol (n), mushirk, mushika, mushk
patrol (v), mushirsk, mushiko, mushko
patron (n), fanirt, fanita, fant
patronize (v), fanirst, fanito, fanto
patronizer (n doer), fanirtwan, fanitua, fantua
pattern (n), fianirt, fianita, fiant
pattern (v), fianirst, fianito, fianto
pause (n), merf, mefa, mef
pause (v), mersf, mefo, mefo
pave (v), dauvirst, dauvito, dauvito
pavement (n), dauvirt, dauvita, dauvit
paver (n doer), dauvirtwan, dauvitua, dauvitua
paw (n), kuarf, kuafa, kuaf
paw (v), kuarsf, kuafo, kuafo
pawn (n), puamp, puama, puam
pawn (v), puamesp, puamo, puamo
pawnshop (n), puamthorve, puamethova, puamthov
pay (n), moirme, moima, moim
pay (v), moirzme, moimo, moimo
payable (adj), moirmu, moimu, moimu
payably (adv), moirmiu, moimiu, moimiu
payback (n), moimvark, moimevaka, moimvak
paycheck (n), moimpiruf, moimepiroda, moimpird
payday (n), moimeviurl, moimeviula, moimeviul
payer (n doer), moirmwan, moimua, moimua
payload (n), moimlurift, moimelurita, moimlurt
payment (n), moirmuet, moimueta, moimuet
payoff (n), moirmunf, moimunefa, moimunf
payout (n), moirmuil, moimuila, moimuil
payroll (n), moimfalar, moimofalira, moimfalir
peace (n), flenide, felenuda, flend
peaceful (adj), flenidu, felenudu, flendu
peacefully (adv), flenidiu, felenudiu, flendiu
peacekeep (v), flenklorsf, felenekelofo, flenklofo
peacekeeper (n doer), flenklorfwan, felenekelofua, flenklofua
peacekept (v pa), flenklorsfyot, felenekelofio, flenklofio
peacemaker (n doer), flendenargwan, felenudenagua, flendenagua
peacetime (adj), flendaurnu, felenudaunu, flendaunu
peacetime (n), flendaurn, felenudauna, flendaun
peach (n), teirsh, teisha, teish
peachy (adj), teirshu, teishu, teishu
peak (n), vaturge, vatuga, vatug
peak (v), vaturzge, vatugo, vatugo
peanut (n), giamern, giamena, giamen
pear (n), morave, moriva, molv
pearl (n), dreln, darela, drel
peasant (n), gifient, gifiena, gifien
pebble (n), veshirp, veshipa, veshp
peck (n), detirsh, detisha, detsh

peck (v), detirs, detisho, detsho
peculiar (adj), briornu, berionu, brionu
peculiarity (n), briorn, beriona, brion
peculiarly (adv), briorniu, berioniu, brioniu
pedal (n), moidet, moida, moid
pedal (v), moidest, moido, moido
peddle (v), tibinsk, tibino, tibino
peddler (n doer), tibinkwan, tibinua, tibinua
pedestrian (n), moidart, moidata, moidat
peek (n), fiarp, fiapa, fiap
peek (v), fiarsp, fiapo, fiapo
peel (n), telirt, telita, telt
peel (v), telirst, telito, telto
peeler (n doer), telirtwan, telitua, teltua
peep (n), fiarbe, fiaba, fiab
peep (v), fiarzbe, fiabo, fiabo
peer (n), fiarf, fiafa, fiaf
peer (v), fiarsf, fiafo, fiafo
peg (n), tirge, tiga, tig
peg (v), tirzge, tigo, tigo
pejorative (n), lorashk, loraka, lorak
pellet (n), tishart, tishata, tishat
pelt (n d:fur), praump, perauma, praum
pelt (v d:hit), tizharsk, tizhako, tizhako
pen (n d:enclosure), burl, bula, bul
pen (n d:ink device), varelt, vareta, vret
pen (v d:enclosure), bursle, bulo, bulo
pen (v d:ink device), varelst, vareto, vreto
penal (adj), biurmu, biumu, biumu
penalize (v), biurzme, biumo, biumo
penalty (n), biurme, biuma, bium
pencil (n), floirt, feloita, floit
pencil (v), floirst, feloito, floito
pend (v), brunsf, beruno, bruno
pendant (n), brundart, berunodata, brundat
pendulum (n), brundant, berunidana, brundan
penetrate (v), blirshsk, belishoko, blishko
penetration (n), blirshk, belishoka, blishk
penetrator (n doer), blirshkwan, belishokua, blishkua
peninsula (n), blirf, belifa, blif
Pennsylvania (n), Penshilvaniarf, Penoshiluvaniafa, Penshilvaniaf
penny (n), pemdarn, pemudana, pemdan
pension (n), brufert, berufeta, brufet
pent- (num 5 pref), tirai-, tirai-, tirai-
pentagon (n), traimurk, tiraimuka, traimuk
people (n pl), plornyek, peloni, ploni
people's (pron 3rd indefpers pl pos obj), onash, onash, onash
people's (pron 3rd indefpers pl pos sub), onash, onash, onash
peopleselves (pron 3rd indefpers pl refl), onashfar, onashfar, onashfar
pep (n), kirth, kitha, kith
pepper (n), kithirk, kithika, kithk
pepper (v), kithirsk, kithiko, kithko
per (adv/prep), dife, difu, dif
perceive (v), loshirsp, loshipo, loshipo
perceiver (n doer), loshirpwan, loshipua, loshipua
percent (n), lolirft, lolirota, lolirt
percentage (n), lolirftat, lolirotata, lolirtat
perception (n), loshirp, loshipa, loship

perceptive (adj), loshirpu, loshipu, loshipu
perceptively (adv), loshirpiu, loshipiu, loshipiu
perch (n d:fish), bentirk, benitika, bentik
perch (n d:pole), diorthk, dioritha, diorth
perch (v d:pole), diorthsk, dioritho, diortho
perfect (adj), lovirftu, lovirotu, lovirtu
perfect (v), lovirfst, loviroto, lovirto
perfection (n), lovirft, lovirota, lovirt
perfectly (adv), lovirftiu, lovirotiu, lovirtiu
perforate (v), lothrashst, lotherato, lothrato
perforation (n), lothrasht, lotherata, lothrat
perform (v), lovorinsf, lovorino, lovorno
performance (n), lovorinf, lovorina, lovorn
performer (n doer), lovorinfwan, lovorinua,
    lovornua
perfume (n), lokiorf, lokiora, lokior
perfume (v), lokiorsf, lokioro, lokioro
perhaps (adv), florkiu, felokiu, flokiu
peril (n), zhumirp, zhumipa, zhump
perilous (adj), zhumirpu, zhumipu, zhumpu
perilously (adv), zhumirpiu, zhumipiu, zhumpiu
period (n d:cycle), porlant, porelana, porlan
period (n d:punctuation), thitarlt, thitalita, thitalt
periodic (adj d:cycle), porlantu, porelanu, porlanu
periodically (adv d:cycle), porlantiu, porelaniu,
    porlaniu
periperhal (adj), porathu, porithu, porthu
peripheral (n), porath, poritha, porth
perish (v), driarsth, deriatho, driatho
perishable (adj), driarthu, deriathu, driathu
perk (n), glift, gelifa, glif
perk (v), glifst, gelifo, glifo
perky (adj), gliftu, gelifu, glifu
permanence (n), lonikart, lonikata, lonkat
permanent (adj), lonikartu, lonikatu, lonkatu
permanently (adv), lonikartiu, lonikatiu, lonkatiu
permission (n), noirf, noifa, noif
permit (n pl), lonirkyek, loniki, lonki
permit (n), lonirk, lonika, lonk
permit (v), lonirsk, loniko, lonko
permutate (v), loshluarsk, losheluako, loshluako
permutation (n), loshluark, losheluaka, loshluak
perpendicular (adj), lobrunitu, loberunitu, lobruntu
perpendicularly (adv), lobrunitiu, loberunitiu,
    lobruntiu
perpetrate (v), lovotefst, lovoteto, lovoteto
perpetration (n), lovoteft, lovoteta, lovotet
perpetrator (n doer), lovoteftwan, lovotetua,
    lovotetua
perpetual (adj), loidianku, loidianu, loidianu
perpetually (adv), loidiankiu, loidianiu, loidianiu
perpetuate (v), loidiansk, loidiano, loidiano
perpetuation (n), loidiank, loidiana, loidian
perpetuity (n), loidiank, loidiana, loidian
persecute (v), lodokarst, lodokato, lodokato
persecution (n), lodokart, lodokata, lodokat
persecutor (n doer), lodokartwan, lodokatua,
    lodokatua
perseverance (n), lokilork, lokiloka, lokilk
persevere (v), lokilorsk, lokiloko, lokilko
Persian (n), Pershiarn, Peroshiana, Pershian
persist (v), lotelirsk, loteliko, lotelko
persistence (n), lotelirk, lotelika, lotelk

persistent (adj), lotelirku, loteliku, lotelku
persistently (adv), lotelirkiu, lotelikiu, lotelkiu
person (n), plorn, pelona, plon
personal (adj), plornu, pelonu, plonu
personal (n), plornul, pelonula, plonul
personality (n), plonat, pelonata, plont
personalization (n), plornuet, pelonueta, plonuet
personalize (v), plorsne, pelono, plono
personally (adv), plorniu, peloniu, ploniu
personification (n), plonarge, pelonaga, plonag
personify (v), plonarzge, pelonago, plonago
personnel (n), plonarf, pelonara, plonar
perspective (n), lothurk, lothuka, lothuk
perspiration (n), lofdaurf, lofudaufa, lofdauf
perspire (v), lofdaursf, lofudaufo, lofdaufo
persuade (v), dalirzme, dalimo, dalmo
persuasion (n), dalirme, dalima, dalm
persuasive (adj), dalirmu, dalimu, dalmu
persuasively (adv), dalirmiu, dalimiu, dalmiu
pert (adj), mafirku, mafiku, mafku
pert (n), mafirk, mafika, mafk
pertain (v), lopiforst, lopifoto, lopifto
pertinent (adj), lopifortu, lopifotu, lopiftu
perturb (v), lodalirsp, lodalipo, lodalpo
Peru (n), Perulf, Perufa, Peruf
perusal (n), lobriark, loberiaka, lobriak
peruse (v), lobriarsk, loberiako, lobriako
pervade (v), lozhanirsk, lozhaniko, lozhanko
pervasive (adj), lozhanirku, lozhaniku, lozhanku
pervasively (adv), lozhanirkiu, lozhanikiu,
    lozhankiu
perverse (adj), lotharafu, lotharifu, lotharfu
perverse (v), lotharasf, lotharifo, lotharfo
perversely (adv), lotharafiu, lotharifiu, lotharfiu
perversion (n), lotharaf, lotharifa, lotharf
perversity (n), lotharak, lotharika, lothark
pervert (n doer), lotharafwan, lotharifua, lotharfua
pervert (v), lotharask, lothariko, lotharko
pervious (adj), peithku, peithu, peithu
pesky (adj), kiaishku, kiaiku, kiaiku
pessimism (n), teirth, teitha, teith
pessimistic (adj), teirthu, teithu, teithu
pest (n), kiaishk, kiaika, kiaik
pester (v), kiaishsk, kiaiko, kiaiko
pesticide (n), kiaishkoik, kiaikoika, kiaikoik
pestilence (n), kiaishkuet, kiaikueta, kiaikuet
pet (n), merp, mepa, mep
pet (v), mersp, mepo, mepo
peta- (num 1e15 pref), yufikai-, yufikai-, yufikai-
petal (n), keipirp, keipipa, keipip
petition (n), varpuet, vapueta, vapuet
petition (v), varpuest, vapueto, vapueto
petitioner (n doer), varpuetwan, vapuetua,
    vapuetua
petrify (v), galshsk, galisho, galsho
petroleum (n), bediorf, bediora, bedior
pettily (adv), ralshkiu, ralishiu, ralshiu
pettiness (n), ralshk, ralisha, ralsh
petty (adj), ralshku, ralishu, ralshu
phantom (n), vialiarf, vialiafa, vialiaf
pharmaceutical (adj), thautarlu, thautaru, thautaru
pharmaceutical (n), thautaraf, thautarifa, thautarf
pharmacy (n), thautarl, thautara, thautar

phase (n), thuart, thuata, thuat
phase (v), thuarst, thuato, thuato
phaseout (n), thuartuil, thuatuila, thuatuil
phaser (n doer), thuartwan, thuatua, thuatua
phenomena (n pl), livienorpyek, livienopi, livienpi
phenomenon (n), livienorp, livienopa, livienp
phenominal (adj), livienorpu, livienopu, livienpu
phi (n), firn, fina, fin
Philadelphia (n), Filadelfirf, Filadelofifa, Filadelfif
Philippine (n), Filipirf, Filipifa, Filipif
philosopher (n doer), firdurakwan, fidurakua, fidurkua
philosophy (n), firdurak, fiduraka, fidurk
Phoenix (n), Fineshork, Fineshoka, Fineshk
phone (n), luyarp, luyapa, luyap
phone (v), luyarsp, luyapo, luyapo
Phosphorus (n davoka), Etop, Etop, Etop
Phosphorus (n), Foshforush, Foshiforusha, Foshforush
photo (n), difarde, difada, difad
photocopier (n doer), difakishkitwan, difekishua, difkishua
photocopy (n), difakishkit, difekisha, difkish
photocopy (v), difakishkist, difekisho, difkisho
photograph (n), difadarf, difedarifa, difdarf
photograph (v), difadarsf, difedarifo, difdarfo
photographer (n doer), difadarfwan, difedarifua, difdarfua
photography (n), difadarft, difedarifota, difdarft
phrase (n), varsht, varisha, varsh
phrase (v), varshst, varisho, varsho
physical (adj), nukirfu, nukifu, nukifu
physically (adv), nukirfiu, nukifiu, nukifiu
physician (n), kirshrf, kirosha, kirsh
physics (n), nukirf, nukifa, nukif
pi (n), pirn, pina, pin
piano (n), pluirp, peluipa, pluip
pick (n), dotirsh, dotisha, dotsh
pick (v), dotirs, dotisho, dotsho
picker (n doer), dotirshwan, dotishua, dotshua
picket (n), dotishart, dotishata, dotshat
picket (v), dotisharst, dotishato, dotshato
picketer (n doer), dotishartwan, dotishatua, dotshatua
pickle (n), dotisharp, dotishapa, dotshap
pickle (v), dotisharsp, dotishapo, dotshapo
pickpocket (n), dotshlogarf, dotishelogafa, dotshlogaf
pickup (n), dotishiveil, dotishiveila, dotshiveil
picky (adj), dotirshu, dotishu, dotshu
picnic (n), shlurfp, shilufopa, shlutp
picnic (v), shlurfsp, shilufopo, shlufpo
picnicker (n doer), shlurfpwan, shilufopua, shlufpua
picture (n), porktel, pokitela, poktel
picture (v), porktesle, pokitelo, poktelo
pie (n), parme, pama, pam
piece (n), thetirsh, thetisha, thetsh
piece (v), thetirs, thetisho, thetsho
piecer (n doer), thetirshwan, thetishua, thetshua
pierce (v), kloarsk, keloako, kloako
piety (n), deiauf, deiaupa, deiaup
pig (n), marifp, maripa, marp

pig (v), marifsp, maripo, marpo
pigeon (n), muktark, mukitak, muktak
pigment (n), gralshuet, gerashueta, grashuet
pigmentation (n), gralshueluet, gerashuelueta, grashueluet
pigskin (n), marpefnarp, maripefinapa, marpefnap
pike (n), paiart, paiata, paiat
pike (v), paiarst, paiato, paiato
pile (n), nairp, naipa, naip
pile (v), nairsp, naipo, naipo
pileup (n), nairpiveil, naipiveila, naipiveil
pilgramage (n), wiarp, wiapa, wiap
pilgrim (n doer), wiarpwan, wiapua, wiapua
pill (n), zhorf, zhora, zhor
pill (v), zhorsf, zhoro, zhoro
pillar (n), zhorft, zhorita, zhort
pillow (n), zhoranf, zhorana, zhorn
pillow (v), zhoransf, zhorano, zhorno
pilot (n), nainorf, nainofa, nainf
pilot (v), nainorsf, nainofo, nainfo
pin (n), leirp, leipa, leip
pin (v), leirsp, leipo, leipo
pinball (n), leipshmonde, leipemashipa, leipemashp
pinch (n), leipart, leipata, leipat
pinch (v), leiparst, leipato, leipato
pincher (n doer), leipartwan, leipatua, leipatua
pine (n), thiorn, thiona, thion
pine (v), viarzme, viamo, viamo
pinhead (n), lekipekefirt, leipekefita, leipekeft
pink (adj), peirfu, peifu, peifu
pink (n), peirf, peifa, peif
pinky (n), leirf, leifa, leif
pinnacle (n), leipaushk, leipauka, leipauk
pinpoint (n), leipetaifort, leipetaifota, leipetaift
pinpoint (v), leipetaiforst, leipetaifoto, leipetaifto
pinprick (n), leipeklaishp, leipekelaipa, leipeklaip
pinstripe (n), leipekoiart, leipekoiata, leipekoiat
pinstripe (v), leipekoiarst, leipekoiato, leipekoiato
pint (n), leirolp, leiropa, leirp
pioneer (n), vianirk, vianika, viank
pioneer (v), vianirsk, vianiko, vianko
pious (adj), deiaufu, deiaupu, deiaupu
pipe (n), leinarp, leinapa, leinp
pipe (v), leinarsp, leinapo, leinpo
pipeline (n), leinproilf, leinaperoifa, leinproif
piper (n doer), leinarpwan, leinapua, leinpua
piracy (n), dautarf, dautafa, dautaf
pirate (n doer), dautarfwan, dautafua, dautafua
pirate (v), dautarsf, dautafo, dautafo
piss (n), shklshk, sheklslia, slikislı
piss (v), shkishsk, shekisho, shkisho
pisser (n doer), shkishkwan, shekishua, shkishua
pit (n), shtiurk, shetiuka, shtiuk
pit (v), shtiursk, shetiuko, shtiuko
pitch (n d:sealant), flelirk, folelika, flelk
pitch (n d:throw), deirzhe, deizha, deizh
pitch (v d:throw), deirze, deizho, deizho
pitcher (n d:container), frenirk, ferenika, frenk
pitcher (n doer d:throw), deirzhwan, deizhua, deizhua
pitfall (n), shtiukezhailf, shetiukezhaila, shtiukezhail

pitiful (adj), froilu, feroipu, froipu
pitifully (adv), froiliu, feroipiu, froipiu
pitiless (adj), froilamenu, feroipamenu, froipmenu
pitilessly (adv), froilameniu, feroipameniu, froipmeniu
pittance (n), froilar, feroipara, froipar
Pittsburgh (n), Piteshburge, Piteshoburoga, Pitshburg
pity (n), froil, feroipa, froip
pity (v), froisle, feroipo, froipo
pivot (n), freltaift, forelitaifa, freltaif
pivot (v), freltaifst, forelitaifo, freltaifo
pivotal (adj), freltaiftu, forelitaifu, freltaifu
pivotally (adv), freltaiftiu, forelitaifiu, freltaifiu
pixel (n), dirthk, dithoka, dithk
pizza (n), lizharn, lizhana, lizhan
placate (v), breshorst, bereshoto, breshto
placation (n), breshort, bereshota, bresht
placator (n doer), breshortwan, bereshotua, breshtua
place (n), brelsh, beresha, bresh
place (v), brels, beresho, bresho
placement (n), brelshuet, bereshueta, breshuet
placer (n doer), brelshwan, bereshua, breshua
plague (n), gaurf, gaufa, gauf
plague (v), gaursf, gaufo, gaufo
plain (adj), bralfu, beralu, bralu
plain (n), bralf, berala, bral
plainly (adv), bralfiu, beraliu, braliu
plaintiff (n), braltirp, beralotipa, braltip
plan (n), litarn, litana, litan
plan (v), litarsne, litano, litano
plane (n d:airplane), valar, varila, varl
plane (n d:flat), vairme, vaima, vaim
plane (v d:flat), vairzme, vaimo, vaimo
planet (n), laurk, lauka, lauk
planetary (adj), laurku, lauku, lauku
plank (n), brelgof, bereluga, brelg
plank (v), brelgosf, berelugo, brelgo
planner (n doer), litarnwan, litanua, litanua
plant (n d:factory), litarnk, litanika, litank
plant (n d:life form, affix), brelp, berepa, brep
plant (v d:life form, affix), brelsp, berepo, brepo
plantation (n), litarnirk, litaniroka, litanirk
planter (n doer d:life form, affix), brelpwan, berepua, brepua
plasma (n), flerth, feletha, fleth
plaster (n), frairge, feraiga, fraig
plaster (v), frairzge, feraigo, fraigo
plastic (n), fraigurt, feraiguta, fraigut
plasticize (v), fraigurst, feraiguto, fraiguto
plasticizer (n doer), fraigurtwan, feraigutua, fraigutua
plate (n), fkarf, fikafa, fkaf
plate (v), fkarsf, fikafo, fkafo
plater (n doer), fkarfwan, fikafua, fkafua
platform (n), fkavorn, fikavona, fkavon
Platinum (n davoka), Iruk, Iruk, Iruk
Platinum (n), Platinum, Pelatinuma, Platinum
platter (n), fkavart, fekavata, fkavat
plause (v), shalirsk, shaliko, shalko
plausible (adj), shalirku, shaliku, shalku
plausibly (adv), shalirkiu, shalikiu, shalkiu

play (n), fruifk, feruifa, fruif
play (v), fruifsk, feruifo, fruifo
playable (adj), fruifrelpu, feruiferepu, fruifrepu
playback (n), fruifevark, feruifevaka, fruifevak
playbook (n), fruifevornt, feruifevonuda, fruifevond
playboy (n), fruifbiurn, feruifebiuna, fruifbiun
player (n doer), fruifkwan, feruifua, fruifua
playful (adj), fruifku, feruifu, fruifu
playfully (adv), fruifkiu, feruifiu, fruifiu
playfulness (n), fruifkuet, feruifueta, fruifuet
playground (n), fruifbrant, feruiberanita, fruibrant
playhouse (n), fruifkiarf, feruifekiafa, fruifkiaf
playmaker (n doer), fruifnargwan, feruifenagua, fruifnagua
playmate (n), fruiflern, feruifelena, fruiflen
playoff (n), fruifkunf, feruifunefa, fruifunf
playroom (n), fruifshranf, feruifesherana, fruifshran
plaything (n), fruifdirzhe, feruifedizha, fruifdizh
plaza (n), braursh, berausha, braush
plea (n), frjalk, feriala, frial
plead (v), frialsk, ferialo, frialo
pleader (n doer), frialkwan, ferialua, frialua
pleasant (adj), frilapu, ferilopu, frilpu
pleasantly (adv), frilapiu, ferilopiu, frilpiu
please (v), frilasp, ferilopo, frilpo
pleaser (n doer), frilapwan, ferilopua, frilpua
pleasure (n), frilap, ferilopa, frilp
pledge (n), frurge, feruga, frug
pledge (v), frurzge, ferugo, frugo
plenary (adj), niulortu, niulotu, niultu
plentiful (adj), niurnu, niunu, niunu
plenty (n), niurn, niuna, niun
plenum (n), niulort, niulota, niult
pliable (adj), shluartu, sheluatu, shluatu
plier (n doer), shluartwan, sheluatua, shluatua
plight (n), zhiafuirf, zhiafuifa, zhiafuif
plod (v), freiausk, fereiaupo, freiaupo
plop (v), freiaufst, fereiaufo, freiaufo
plot (n), fruart, feruata, fruat
plot (v), fruarst, feruato, fruato
plotter (n doer), fruartwan, feruatua, fruatua
plough (n), fuarde, fuada, fuad
plow (n), fuarde, fuada, fuad
plow (v), fuarzde, fuado, fuado
ploy (n), shloirt, sheloita, shloit
pluck (n), gilirp, gilipa, gilp
pluck (v), gilirsp, gilipo, gilpo
plucker (n doer), gilirpwan, gilipua, gilpua
plucky (adj), gilirpu, gilipu, gilpu
plug (n), githarp, githapa, githp
plug (v), githarsp, githapo, githpo
plugger (n doer), githarpwan, githapua, githpua
plum (n), flurth, felutha, fluth
plumage (n), fliuthkuet, feliuthueta, fliuthuet
plumb (adj), blomardu, belomadu, blomadu
plumb (n), blomarde, belomada, blomad
plumb (v), blomarzde, belomado, blomado
plumber (n doer), blomardwan, belomadua, blomadua
plume (n), fliuthk, feliutha, fliuth
plume (v), fliuthsk, feliutho, fliutho
plummet (n), piranf, pirana, piran

plummet (v), piransf, pirano, pirano
plunder (n), shliarge, sheliaga, shliag
plunder (v), shliarzge, sheliago, shliago
plunge (n), friushk, feriusha, friush
plunge (v), friushsk, feriusho, friusho
plunger (n doer), friushkwan, feriushua, friushua
plunk (v), friurzge, feriugo, friugo
plural (adj), fulirshu, fulishu, fulshu
plurality (n), fulirsh, fulisha, fulsh
plus (adj/prep), numart, numatu, numat
plus (n), numart, numata, numat
plush (adj), gipashku, gipashu, gipashu
Plutonium (n davoka), Onik, Onik, Onik
Plutonium (n), Plutonium, Pelutoniuma, Plutonium
ply (n), shluart, sheluata, shluat
ply (v), shluarst, sheluato, shluato
plywood (n), shluatfanirn, sheluatefanina,
    shluatfanin
poach (v), lokarsp, lokapo, lokapo
poacher (n doer), lokarpwan, lokapua, lokapua
pocket (n), logarf, logafa, logaf
pocket (v), logarsf, logafo, logafo
pocketbook (n), logafevornt, logafevonuda,
    logafevond
pocketer (n doer), logarfwan, logafua, logafua
pocketful (n), logafbierp, logafebiepa, logafbiep
pod (n), moirn, moina, moin
poem (n), fiorn, fiona, fion
poet (n doer), fiortwan, fiotua, fiotua
poetic (adj), fiortu, fiotu, fiotu
poetry (n), fiort, fiota, fiot
point (n), taifort, taifota, taift
point (v), taiforst, taifoto, taifto
pointer (n doer), taifortwan, taifotua, taiftua
pointily (adv), taifortiu, taifotiu, taiftiu
pointless (adj), taifortmenu, taifotemenu, tiaftmenu
pointy (adj), taifortu, taifotu, taiftu
poise (n), veilirp, veilipa, veilip
poise (v), veilirsp, veilipo, veilipo
poison (n), buairt, buaita, buait
poison (v), buairst, buaito, buaito
poisoner (n doer), buairtwan, buaitua, buaitua
poisonous (adj), buairtu, buaitu, buaitu
poke (n d:push), doiashk, doiaka, doiak
poke (v d:push), doiashsk, doiako, doiako
poker (n d:game), feigalf, feigala, feigal
poker (n doer d:push), doiashkwan, doiakua,
    doiakua
pokey (adj d:push), doiashku, doiaku, doiaku
Poland (n), Polanurd, Polanuda, Polanud
polar (adj), dilkartu, dilokatu, dilkatu
polarity (n), dilkart, dilokata, dilkat
polarization (n), dilkartuet, dilokatueta, dilkatuet
polarize (v), dilkarst, dilokato, dilkato
pole (n), dilork, diloka, dilk
police (n), dorshkort, dorishokata, dorshkat
police (v), dorshorsk, dorishoko, dorshko
policeman (n doer), dorshorkwan, dorishokua,
    dorshkua
policy (n), dorshork, dorishoka, dorshk
policyholder (n doer), dorshkthorthkwan,
    dorishokethorithua, dorshkthorthua
policymaker (n doer), dorshknargwan,

dorishokenagua, dorshknagua
polish (n), beirf, biefa, bief
polish (v), beirsf, biefo, biefo
polisher (n doer), beirfwan, biefua, biefua
polite (adj), doreinfu, doreinu, doreinu
politely (adv), doreinfiu, doreiniu, doreiniu
politeness (n), doreinf, doreina, dorein
politic (v), dordast, dorudo, dordo
political (adj), dordatu, dorudu, dordu
politically (adv), dordatiu, dorudiu, dordiu
politician (n doer), dordatwan, dorudua, dordua
politics (n), dordart, dorudara, dordar
polity (n), dordat, doruda, dord
poll (n), dolirme, dolima, dolm
poll (v), dolirzme, dolimo, dolmo
poller (n doer), dolirmwan, dolimua, dolmua
pollutant (n), doraifork, doraifoka, doraifk
pollute (v), dorairsk, doraiko, doraiko
polluter (n doer), dorairkwan, doraikua, doraikua
pollution (n), dorairk, doraika, doraik
Polonium (n davoka), Erup, Erup, Erup
Polonium (n), Polonium, Poloniuma, Polonium
polygamy (n), filivularn, filivulana, filivuln
polygon (n pl), filimurkyek, filimuki, filimuki
polygon (n), filimurk, filimuka, filimuk
polygonal (adj), filimurku, filimuku, filimuku
polygraph (n), filidarfk, filidarifa, filidarf
polygraphic (adj), filidarfku, filidarifu, filidarfu
polymer (n), filimesht, filimesha, filimesh
polymerize (v), filimeshst, filimesho, filimesho
polyphonic (adj), filiuyarpu, filiuyapu, filiuyapu
polyphony (n), filiuyarp, filiuyapa, filiuyap
pond (n), vefirp, vefipa, vefp
ponder (v), vefirst, vefito, vefto
pony (n), veinern, veinena, veinen
pony (v), veinersne, veineno, veineno
ponytail (n), veinenmithk, veinenemitha,
    veinenmith
poof (interj), tuf, tufa, tuf
pool (n), ditarp, ditapa, ditap
pool (v), ditarsp, ditapo, ditapo
poolside (adj), ditapshoirtu, ditapeshoitu,
    ditapshoitu
poolside (n), ditapshoirt, ditapeshoita, ditapshoit
poop (n), kufurbe, kufuba, kufub
poop (v), kufurzbe, kufubo, kufubo
pooper (n doer), kufurbwan, kufubua, kufubua
poor (adj d:unfortunate, bad), biurku, biuku, biuku
poor (n d:low money), dorirth, doritha, dorth
poorhouse (n), dorthkiarf, dorithekiafa, dorthkiaf
poorly (adv d:unfortunate, bad), biurkiu, biukiu,
    biukiu
pop (n), varbe, vaba, vab
pop (v), varzbe, vabo, vabo
popcorn (n), vabegralf, vabegerala, vabegral
pope (n), blafirp, belafipa, blafp
popper (n doer), varbwan, vabua, vabua
populace (n doer), voradwan, voridua, vordua
popular (adj), voradu, voridu, vordu
popularity (n), vorade, vorida, vord
popularize (v), vorazde, vorido, vordo
popularly (adv), voradiu, voridiu, vordiu
populate (v), vorazve, voruvo, vorvo

population (n), vorave, voruva, vorv
porch (n), giorth, giotha, gioth
pore (n), priofk, periofa, priof
pork (n), giark, giaka, giak
porous (adj), priofku, periofu, priofu
port (n), bielirk, bielika, bielk
port (v), bielirsk, bieliko, bielko
portability (n), bielirkrep, bielikerepa, bielkrep
portable (adj), bielirku, bieliku, bielku
portal (n), bielkart, bielikata, bielkat
porter (n doer), bielirkwan, bielikua, bielkua
portfolio (n), feshiurf, feshiufa, feshiuf
porthole (n), bielikorth, bielikotha, bielkoth
portion (n), ferzhe, fezha, fezh
Portland (n), Portelanurd, Poritelanuda, Portelanud
portrait (n), fesharn, feshana, feshan
portray (v), feshiarzme, feshiamo, feshiamo
portrayal (n), feshiarme, feshiama, feshiam
Portugal (n), Portugalf, Poritugala, Portugal
pose (n), veilorp, veilopa, veilp
pose (v), veilorsp, veilopo, veilpo
poser (n doer), veilorpwan, veilopua, veilpua
position (n), veilirn, veilina, veiln
position (v), veilirsne, veilino, veilno
positioner (n doer), veilirnwan, veilinua, veilnua
positive (adj), veifortu, veifotu, veiftu
positive (n), veifort, veifota, veift
positively (adv), veifortiu, veifotiu, veiftiu
possess (v), prilasp, perilapo, prilpo
possession (n), prilap, perilapa, prilp
possessive (adj), prilapu, perilapu, prilpu
possessively (adv), prilapiu, perilapiu, prilpiu
possessor (n doer), prilapwan, perilapua, prilpua
possibility (n), lorilf, lorifa, lorf
possible (adj), lorilfu, lorifu, lorfu
possibly (adv), lorilfiu, lorifiu, lorfiu
post (n d:ad), dialirt, dialita, dialt
post (n d:pole), balirt, balita, balt
post (v d:ad), dialirst, dialito, dialto
post (v d:pole), balirst, balito, balto
postage (n), dialirtar, dialitara, dialtar
postal (adj), dialirtaru, dialitaru, dialtaru
postcard (n), dialtaurn, dialitauna, dialtaun
poster (n d:display), dialirtuet, dialitueta, dialtuet
poster (n doer d:ad), dialirtwan, dialitua, dialtua
posterior (n), balvelarf, balivelara, balvelar
postman (n doer), dialirtarwan, dialitarua, dialtarua
postmark (n), dialtshtart, dialiteshetata, dialtshtat
postmark (v), dialtshtarst, dialiteshetato, dialtshtato
postmaster (n), dialtethiork, dialitethioka, dialtethiok
postmodern (adj), balsharinfu, balesharinu, balsharnu
postpone (v), balveforsk, baluvefoko, balvefko
postponement (n), balvefork, baluvefoka, balvefk
postscript (n), balsherge, balesheriga, balshrig
postulate (v), baliushsk, baliuko, baliuko
postulation (n), baliushk, baliuka, baliuk
posture (n), baltarf, balitara, baltar
posture (v), baltarsf, balitaro, baltaro

postwar (adj), balviurnu, baleviuru, balviuru
pot (n), dairf, daifa, daif
pot (v), dairsf, daifo, daifo
Potassium (n davoka), Afap, Afap, Afap
Potassium (n), Potashium, Potashiuma, Potashium
potato (n), boirde, boida, boid
potency (n), boirge, boiga, boig
potent (adj), boirgu, boigu, boigu
potential (adj), boigartu, boigatu, boigatu
potential (n), boigart, boigata, boigat
potentially (adv), boigartiu, boigatiu, boigatiu
pothole (n), daifkorth, daifekotha, daifkoth
pothole (v), daifkorsth, daifekotho, daifkotho
potion (n), darliank, dareliana, darlian
potluck (n), daifpadar, daifepashota, daifpasht
potshot (n), daifshkoift, daifeshekoita, daifshkoit
potter (n doer), dairfwan, daifua, daifua
potty (n), daifairf, daifaifa, daifaif
pouch (n), daiteshk, daitesha, daitsh
pounce (n d:catch), kraithierk, keraithieka, kraithiek
pounce (v d:catch), kraithiersk, keraithieko, kraithieko
pouncer (n doer d:catch), kraithierkwan, keraithiekua, kraithiekua
pound (n d:weight), pondern, ponidena, ponden
pound (v d:hit), bramisp, beramipo, brampo
pounder (n doer d:hit), bramipwan, beramipua, brampua
pour (v), roturst, rotuto, rotuto
pout (v), biaufsp, biaupo, biaupo
poverty (n), zhugairt, zhugaita, zhugait
pow (interj), daua, daua, daua
powder (n), biart, biata, biat
powder (v), biarst, biato, biato
power (n), biorat, biorita, biort
power (v), biorast, biorito, biorto
powerboat (n), biortshkorbe, bioriteshekoba, biortshkob
powerful (adj), bioratu, bioritu, biortu
powerfully (adv), bioratiu, bioritiu, biortiu
powerhouse (n), biortkiarf, bioritekiafa, biortkiaf
powerless (adj), bioratmenu, bioritemenu, biortmenu
powerlessly (adv), bioratmeniu, bioritemeniu, biortmeniu
powerlessness (n), bioratmen, bioritemena, biortmen
powerplant (n), biortelitarnk, bioritelitanika, biortelitank
powertrain (n), biortebartarde, bioritebaritada, biortebartad
practical (adj), matirku, matiku, matiku
practically (adv), matirkiu, matikiu, matikiu
practice (n), matirk, matika, matik
practice (v), matirsk, matiko, matiko
practitioner (n doer), matirkwan, matikua, matikua
Prague (n), Pragarf, Peragafa, Pragaf
praise (n), fliurt, feliuta, fliut
praise (v), fliurst, feliuto, fliuto
praiser (n doer), fliurtwan, feliutua, fliutua
prank (n), bralshk, beralika, bralk
prankster (n doer), bralshkwan, beralikua, bralkua

Praseodymium (n davoka), Orop, Orop, Orop
Praseodymium (n), Prasheodimium, Perasheodimiuma, Prasheodimium
pray (v), fliursf, feliufo, fliufo
prayer (n doer), fliurfwan, feliufua, fliufua
prayer (n), fliurf, feliufa, fliuf
preach (v), rufirst, rufito, rufto
preacher (n doer), rufirtwan, rufitua, ruftua
preachy (adj), rufirtu, rufitu, ruftu
prearrange (v), ruolmost, ruolo, ruolo
prearrangement (n), ruolmot, ruola, ruol
precancerous (adj), rudermashku, ruderumaku, rudermaku
precarious (adj), rufludu, rugerenu, rugrenu
precariously (adv), rufludiu, rugereniu, rugreniu
precaution (n), rushkashirp, rushikashipa, rushkashp
precede (v), ruversk, ruveko, ruveko
precedence (n), ruvekart, ruvekata, ruvekat
precedent (n), ruvekart, ruvekata, ruvekat
precession (n), ruverk, ruveka, ruvek
precious (adj), rulthu, ruthu, ruthu
preciously (adv), rulthiu, ruthiu, ruthiu
precipitate (v), rushlersk, rusheleko, rushleko
precipitation (n), rushlerk, rusheleka, rushlek
precise (adj), ruthirshku, ruthishaku, ruthishku
precisely (adv), ruthirshkiu, ruthishakiu, ruthishkiu
precision (n), ruthirshk, ruthishaka, ruthishk
preclude (v), rugrushst, rugeruto, rugruto
preconceive (v), rubelshisp, ruliushipo, ruliushpo
preconception (n), rubelship, ruliushipa, ruliushp
precondition (n), rubeltifk, ruliutifoka, ruliutifk
precondition (v), rubeltifsk, ruliutifoko, ruliutifko
preconfiguration (n), rubelkudil, ruliukulita, ruliukult
preconfigure (v), rubelkudisle, ruliukulito, ruliukulto
predate (v), drukarst, derukato, drukato
predation (n), drukart, derukata, drukat
predator (n doer), drukartwan, derukatua, drukatua
predatory (adj), drukartu, derukatu, drukatu
predecessor (n doer), ruverkwan, ruvekua, ruvekua
predestination (n), rubushlarn, rubushelana, rubushlan
predestine (v), rubushlarsne, rubushelano, rubushlano
predetermination (n), rutulirsh, rutulisha, rutulsh
predetermine (v), rutulirs, rutulisho, rutulsho
predicament (n), shpairtuet, shipaitueta, shpaituet
predicate (n), shpairt, shipaita, shpait
predicate (v), shpairst, shipaito, shpaito
predict (v), rudeirsk, rudeiko, rudeiko
predictable (adj), rudeirku, rudeiku, rudeiku
predictably (adv), rudeirkiu, rudeikiu, rudeikiu
prediction (n), rudeirk, rudeika, rudeik
predictive (adj), rudeirku, rudeiku, rudeiku
predictor (n doer), rudeirkwan, rudeikua, rudeikua
predispose (v), rutikasne, rutilako, rutilako
predisposition (n), rutikan, rutilaka, rutilak
predominant (adj), rufaishtu, runaufiku, runaufku
predominantly (adv), rufaishtiu, runaufikiu, runaufkiu

predominate (v), rufaishst, runaufiko, runaufko
predomination (n), rufaisht, runaufika, runaufk
preempt (v), ruginshsk, rugineko, ruginko
preemption (n), ruginshk, rugineka, rugink
preemptive (adj), ruginshku, rugineku, ruginku
preemptively (adv), ruginshkiu, ruginekiu, ruginkiu
preexist (v), runulirst, runulito, runulto
preexistence (n), runulirt, runulita, runult
preface (n), ruthoirsh, ruthoisha, ruthoish
preface (v), ruthoirs, ruthoisho, ruthoisho
prefect (n doer), ruvirortwan, ruvirotua, ruvirtua
prefecture (n), ruvirort, ruvirota, ruvirt
prefer (v), rugelsf, rugefo, rugefo
preferable (adj), rugelfu, rugefu, rugefu
preferably (adv), rugelfiu, rugefiu, rugefiu
preference (n), rugelf, rugefa, rugef
preferential (adj), rugelfu, rugefu, rugefu
preferentially (adv), rugelfiu, rugefiu, rugefiu
prefix (n), ruvirk, ruvika, ruvik
prefix (v), ruvirsk, ruviko, ruviko
pregnancy (n), fnorif, fenorifa, fnorf
pregnant (adj), fnorifu, fenorifu, fnorfu
prehistoric (adj), rushathoru, rusharithu, rusharthu
prehistory (n), rushathor, rusharitha, rusharth
prejudge (v), ruhetherst, ruhetheto, ruhetheto
prejudgement (n), ruhethert, ruhetheta, ruhethet
prejudice (n), ruhert, ruheta, ruhet
prejudice (v), ruherst, ruheto, ruheto
preliminary (adj), ruvaurshu, ruvaushu, ruvaushu
prelude (n), rurutersh, rurutesha, rurutsh
prelude (v), ruruters, rurutesho, rurutsho
premarital (adj), ruvularnu, ruvulanu, ruvulnu
premarriage (n), ruvularn, ruvulana, ruvuln
premature (adj), rushirftu, rushirofu, rushirfu
prematurely (adv), rushirftiu, rushirofiu, rushirfiu
premeditate (v), ruzhiarfisk, ruzhiarofiko, ruzhiarfko
premeditation (n), ruzhiarfik, ruzhiarofika, ruzhiarfk
premier (n), shtiurf, shotiufa, shtiuf
premier (v), shtiursf, shotiufo, shtiufo
premise (n), runork, runoka, runok
premise (v), runorsk, runoko, runoko
premium (adj), truirtu, teruitu, truitu
premium (n), truirt, teruita, truit
preoccupation (n), rurovorifp, rurovoripa, rurovorp
preoccupy (v), rurovorifsp, rurovoripo, rurovorpo
prepackage (v), rubugarst, rubugato, rubugato
prepaid (v pa), rumoirzmyot, rumoimio, rumoimio
preparation (n), rubollik, rubolika, rubolk
prepare (v), rubolirsk, ruboliko, rubolko
preparer (n doer), rubolirkwan, rubolikua, rubolkua
prepay (v), rumoirzme, rumoimo, rumoimo
prepayer (n doer), rumoirmwan, rumoimua, rumoimua
prepayment (n), rumoirme, rumoima, rumoim
preposterous (adj), rubalvelarfu, rubalivelaru, rubalvelaru
preposterously (adv), rubalvelarfiu, rubalivelariu, rubalvelariu
prerecord (v), ruplukarzde, rupelukado, ruplukado
prerequisite (n), ruluthart, ruluthata, ruluthat

preschool (adj), rushpershu, rushipeshu, rushpeshu
preschool (n), rushpersh, rushipesha, rushpesh
prescience (n), rushuarsh, rushuasha, rushuash
prescribe (v), rushrilzge, rusherigo, rushrigo
prescription (n), rushrilge, rusheriga, rushrig
preseason (n), rufivarl, rufivala, rufival
presence (n d:existence), blutish, belutisha, blutsh
present (n d:give gift), duarsh, duasha, duash
present (n d:now), belurt, beluta, blut
present (v d:give gift), duars, duasho, duasho
presentation (n), duarshk, duashika, duashk
presenter (n doer), duarshkwan, duashikua,
　　duashkua
presently (adv d:now), belurtiu, belutiu, blutiu
preservation (n), ruduvark, ruduvaka, ruduvak
preserve (n), rukofirt, rukofita, rukoft
preserve (v), rukofirst, rukofito, rukofto
preserver (n doer), rukofirtwan, rukofitua, rukoftua
preset (n), ruferp, rufepa, rufep
preset (v pa), ruferspyot, rufepio, rufepio
preset (v), rufersp, rufepo, rufepo
preside (v), desharst, deshato, deshto
presidency (n), deshart, deshata, desht
president (n doer), deshartwan, deshatua, deshtua
presidential (adj), deshartu, deshatu, deshtu
presidentially (adv), deshartiu, deshatiu, deshtiu
press (n), blarsh, belasha, blash
press (v), blars, belasho, blasho
presser (n doer), blarshwan, belashua, blashua
pressure (n), blaship, belashipa, blashp
pressure (v), blashisp, belashipo, blashpo
pressurization (n), blashpart, belashipata, blashpat
pressurize (v), blashparst, belashipato, blashpato
pressurizer (n doer), blashipwan, belashipua,
　　blashpua
prestige (n), rivurn, rivuna, rivun
prestigious (adj), rivurnu, rivunu, rivunu
presumable (adj), rufiartu, rufialitu, rufialtu
presumably (adv), rufiartiu, rufialitiu, rufialtiu
presume (v), rufiarst, rufialito, rufialto
presumption (n), rufiart, rufialita, rufialt
presumptive (adj), rufiartu, rufialitu, rufialtu
presumptively (adv), rufiartiu, rufialitiu, rufialtiu
presuppose (v), ruvuglarsk, ruvugelako, ruvuglako
presupposition (n), ruvuglark, ruvugelaka, ruvuglak
pretax (n), rushenirk, rushenika, rushenk
pretax (v), rushenirsk, rusheniko, rushenko
pretend (v), rupiforsk, rupifoko, rupifko
pretender (n doer), rupiforkwan, rupifokua,
　　rupifkua
pretense (n), rupifork, rupifoka, rupifk
pretentious (adj), rupiforku, rupifoku, rupifku
pretext (n), rushtirbe, rushetiba, rushtib
pretrial (n), rudibarge, rudibaga, rudibag
prettier (adj), bidarlwelu, bidalwelu, bidalwelu
prettiest (adj), bidarlweku, bidalweku, bidalweku
prettily (adv), bidarliu, bidaliu, bidaliu
pretty (adj), bidarlu, bidalu, bidalu
prevail (v), rushiursp, rushiupo, rushiupo
prevalence (n), rushiurp, rushiupa, rushiup
prevalent (adj), rushiurpu, rushiupu, rushiupu
prevent (v), ruduathsk, ruduatho, ruduatho
preventable (adj), ruduathku, ruduathu, ruduathu

preventably (adv), ruduathkiu, ruduathiu,
　　ruduathiu
prevention (n), ruduathk, ruduatha, ruduath
preventive (adj), ruduathku, ruduathu, ruduathu
preventively (adv), ruduathkiu, ruduathiu,
　　ruduathiu
preview (n), rufuart, rufuata, rufuat
preview (v), rufuarst, rufuato, rufuato
previewer (n doer), rufuartwan, rufuatua, rufuatua
previous (adj), blurvu, beluvu, bluvu
previously (adv), blurviu, beluviu, bluviu
prewar (n), ruviurn, ruviura, ruviur
prey (n), drufk, deruka, druk
prey (v), drufsk, deruko, druko
price (n), tirofp, tiropa, tirp
price (v), tirofsp, tiropo, tirpo
priceless (adj), tirofpemenu, tiropemenu, tirpmenu
pricer (n doer), tirofpwan, tiropua, tirpua
pricey (adj), tirofpu, tiropu, tirpu
prick (n), klaishp, kelaipa, klaip
prick (v), klaishsp, kelaipo, klaipo
pride (n d:accomplishment), larzhe, lazha, lazh
pride (n d:group), melirp, melipa, melp
pride (v d:accomplishment), larze, lazho, lazho
priest (n), thiarn, thiana, thian
priestess (n), tiursh, tiusha, tiush
primal (adj), tiufarnu, tiufanu, tiufanu
primarily (adv), tiurfiu, tiufiu, tiufiu
primary (adj), tiurfu, tiufu, tiufu
primary (n), tiurful, tiufula, tiuful
primate (n), tiufarn, tiufana, tiufan
prime (n), tiurf, tiufa, tiuf
prime (v), tiursf, tiufo, tiufo
primer (n doer), tiurfwan, tiufua, tiufua
primetime (adj), tiufdaurnu, tiufedaunu, tiufdaunu
primetime (n), tiufdaurn, tiufedauna, tiufdaun
primitive (adj), tiufirtu, tiufitu, tiufitu
primitive (n), tiufirt, tiufita, tiufit
primitively (adv), tiufirtiu, tiufitiu, tiufitiu
prince (n), talirk, talika, talik
princely (adj), talirku, taliku, taliku
princess (n), talirth, talitha, talth
princessly (adj), talirthu, talithu, talthu
principal (n), kleirf, keleifa, kleif
principle (n), tiuforp, tiufopa, tiufp
principle (v), tiuforsp, tiufopo, tiufpo
print (n), trulish, terulisha, trulsh
print (v), trulis, terulisho, trulsho
printer (n doer), trulishwan, terulishua, trulshua
prior (adj), blurnu, belunu, blunu
prior (n), blurn, beluna, blun
prioritize (v), blunisf, belunifo, blunfo
priority (n), blunif, belunifa, blunf
prism (n), niaishk, niaina, niain
prison (n), vaufirt, vaufita, vauft
prisoner (n doer), vaufirtwan, vaufitua, vauftua
pristine (adj), runiartu, runiatu, runiatu
privacy (n), tiarp, tiapa, tiap
private (adj), tiarpu, tiapu, tiapu
privately (adv), tiarpiu, tiapiu, tiapiu
privatization (n), tiarpuet, tiapueta, tiapuet
privatize (v), tiarsp, tiapo, tiapo
privilege (n), tiafirp, tiafipa, tiafp

privilege (v), tiafirsp, tiafipo, tiafpo
privy (adj), tiafirpu, tiafipu, tiafpu
prize (n), miairf, miaifa, miaif
prize (v), miairsf, miaifo, miaifo
pro (n d:advantage), fiurf, fiufa, fiuf
pro (n d:professional), fiurn, fiuna, fiun
proactive (adj), fiupaltarku, fiupalitaku, fiupaltaku
proactively (adv), fiupaltarkiu, fiupalitakiu, fiupaltakiu
probability (n), fiufrelp, fiuferepa, fiufrep
probable (adj), fiufrelpu, fiuferepu, fiufrepu
probably (adv), fiufrelpiu, fiuferepiu, fiufrepiu
probation (n), fiurge, fiuga, fiug
probe (n), fiurbe, fiuba, fiub
probe (v), fiurzbe, fiubo, fiubo
prober (n doer), fiurbwan, fiubua, fiubua
problem (n), fiurt, fiuta, fiut
procedural (adj), fiuverku, fiuveku, fiuveku
procedurally (adv), fiuverkiu, fiuvekiu, fiuvekiu
procedure (n), fiuverk, fiuveka, fiuvek
proceed (n), fiuvelirk, fiuvelika, fiuvelk
proceed (v), fiuversk, fiuveko, fiuveko
process (n), fiuvert, fiuveta, fiuvet
process (v), fiuverst, fiuveto, fiuveto
procession (n), fiuvefirt, fiuvefita, fiuveft
processor (n doer), fiuvertwan, fiuvetua, fiuvetua
proclaim (v), fiunolasne, fiunoarito, fiunoarto
proclamation (n), fiunolan, fiunoarita, fiunoart
procrastinate (v), fiukreirsth, fiukureitho, fiukreitho
procrastination (n), fiukreirth, fiukureitha, fiukreith
procrastinator (n doer), fiukreirthwan, fiukureithua, fiukreithua
procreate (v), fiupliurst, fiupeliuto, fiupliuto
procreation (n), fiupliurt, fiupeliuta, fiupliut
procreator (n doer), fiupliurtwan, fiupeliutua, fiupliutua
procure (v), fiutianirsk, fiutianiko, fiutianko
procurement (n), fiutianirk, fiutianika, fiutiank
prod (v), vukirsk, vukiko, vukiko
prodder (n doer), vukirkwan, vukikua, vukikua
produce (n), fiukarn, fiukana, fiukan
produce (v), fiursk, fiuko, fiuko
producer (n doer), fiurkwan, fiukua, fiukua
product (n), fiurk, fiuka, fiuk
production (n), fiurkuet, fiukueta, fiukuet
productive (adj), fiurku, fiuku, fiuku
productively (adv), fiurkiu, fiukiu, fiukiu
productivity (n), fiukart, fiukata, fiukat
profess (v), fiunirsk, fiuniko, fiunko
profession (n), fiunirk, fiunika, fiunk
professional (adj), fiunirku, fiuniku, fiunku
professional (n), fiuntark, fiunotaka, fiuntak
professionalism (n), fiuntarkuet, fiunotakueta, fiuntakuet
professionalize (v), fiuntarsk, fiunotako, fiuntako
professionally (adv), fiunirkiu, fiunikiu, fiunkiu
professor (n doer), fiunirkwan, fiunikua, fiunkua
proficiency (n), fiulinirk, fiulinika, fiulink
proficient (adj), fiulinirku, fiuliniku, fiulinku
proficiently (adv), fiulinirkiu, fiulinikiu, fiulinkiu
profile (n), fiuthiurf, fiuthiufa, fiuthiuf

profile (v), fiuthiursf, fiuthiufo, fiuthiufo
profiler (n doer), fiuthiurfwan, fiuthiufua, fiuthiufua
profit (n), fiupafirt, fiupafita, fiupaft
profit (v), fiupafirst, fiupafito, fiupafto
profitability (n), fiupafiterp, fiupafitepa, fiupaftep
profitable (adj), fiupafirtu, fiupafitu, fiupaftu
profitably (adv), fiupafirtiu, fiupafitiu, fiupaftiu
profiteer (n doer), fiupafirtwan, fiupafitua, fiupaftua
profiteer (v), fiupafirtwast, fiupafituano, fiupaftuano
profound (adj), fiushurpu, fiushupu, fiushpu
profoundly (adv), fiushurpiu, fiushupiu, fiushpiu
profuse (adj), fiufabortu, fiufabotu, fiufabotu
profusely (adv), fiufabortiu, fiufabotiu, fiufabotiu
profusion (n), fiufabort, fiufabota, fiufabot
prognosis (n), fiurshman, fiushemana, fiushman
prognosticate (v), fiurshmasne, fiushemano, fiushmano
prognosticator (n doer), fiurshmanwan, fiushemanua, fiushmanua
program (n), fiunelirk, fiunelika, fiunelk
program (v), fiunelirsk, fiuneliko, fiunelko
programmable (adj), fiunelirku, fiuneliku, fiunelku
programmer (n doer), fiunelirkwan, fiunelikua, fiunelkua
progress (n), fiuvorage, fiuvoruga, fiuvorg
progress (v), fiuvorazge, fiuvorugo, fiuvorgo
progression (n), fiuvoraguet, fiuvorugueta, fiuvorguet
progressive (adj), fiuvoragu, fiuvorugu, fiuvorgu
progressively (adv), fiuvoragiu, fiuvorugiu, fiuvorgiu
progressor (n doer), fiuvoragwan, fiuvorugua, fiuvorgua
prohibit (v), fiudairzbe, fiudaibo, fiudaibo
prohibition (n), fiudairbe, fiudaiba, fiudaib
prohibitive (adj), fiudairbu, fiudaibu, fiudaibu
prohibitively (adv), fiudairbiu, fiudaibiu, fiudaibiu
prohibitor (n doer), fiudairbwan, fiudaibua, fiudaibua
project (n d:workplan), fiuteshirp, fiuteshipa, fiuteshp
project (v d:thrust), fiutersp, fiutepo, fiutepo
projectile (n), fiuterpuin, fiutepuina, fiutepuin
projection (n d:thrust), fiuterp, fiutepa, fiutep
projective (adj d:thrust), fiuterpu, fiutepu, fiutepu
projectively (adv d:thrust), fiuterpiu, fiutopiu, fiutepiu
projector (n doer d:thrust), fiuterpwan, fiutepua, fiutepua
proliferate (v), fiuflaurs, fiufelausho, fiuflausho
proliferation (n), fiuflaursh, fiufelausha, fiuflaush
proliferator (n doer), fiuflaurshwan, fiufelaushua, fiuflaushua
prolific (adj), fiuflaurshu, fiufelaushu, fiuflaushu
prolifically (adv), fiuflaurshiu, fiufelaushiu, fiuflaushiu
prolog (n), fiukuift, fiukuita, fiukuit
prologue (n), fiukuift, fiukuita, fiukuit
prolong (v), fiuralze, fiurazho, fiurazho
prolongation (n), fiuralzhe, fiurazha, fiurazh

prom (n), fiuank, fiuana, fiuan
promenade (n), fiukarge, fiukaga, fiukag
promenade (v), fiukarzge, fiukago, fiukago
Promethium (n davoka), Orak, Orak, Orak
Promethium (n), Promethium, Peromethiuma, Promethium
prominence (n), fiukerage, fiukeruga, fiukrig
prominent (adj), fiukeragu, fiukerugu, fiukrigu
prominently (adv), fiukeragiu, fiukerugiu, fiukrigiu
promise (n), fiunork, fiunoka, fiunok
promise (v), fiunorsk, fiunoko, fiunoko
promiser (n doer), fiunorkwan, fiunokua, fiunokua
promote (v), fiuvadarzve, fiuvadavo, fiuvadavo
promoter (n doer), fiuvadarvwan, fiuvadavua, fiuvadavua
promotion (n), fiuvadarve, fiuvadava, fiuvadav
promotional (adj), fiuvadarvu, fiuvadavu, fiuvadavu
prompt (n), blafit, belifota, blaft
prompt (v), blafist, belifoto, blafto
prompter (n doer), blafitwan, belifotua, blaftua
promptly (adv), blafitiu, belifotiu, blaftiu
prone (adj), plaishku, pelaishu, plaishu
proneness (n), plaishk, pelaisha, plaish
prong (n), fiumirp, fiumipa, fiump
prong (v), fiumirsp, fiumipo, fiumpo
pronoun (n), fiunuyern, fiunuyena, fiunuyen
pronounce (v), fiunferst, fiunifeto, fiunfeto
pronunciation (n), fiunfert, fiunifeta, fiunfet
proof (n), fliorf, feliofa, fliof
proof (v), fliofliarsp, feliofeliapo, fliofliapo
proofread (v pa), fliofliarspyot, feliofeliapio, fliofliapio
proofread (v), fliofliarsp, feliofeliapo, fliofliapo
proofreader (n doer), fliofliarpwan, feliofeliapua, fliofliapua
prop (n), likirme, likima, likim
prop (v), likirzme, likimo, likimo
propaganda (n pl), fiuganorfyek, fiuganori, fiuganori
propaganda (n), fiuganorf, fiuganora, fiuganoi
propagate (v), fiugarsne, fiugano, fiugano
propagation (n), fiugarn, fiugana, fiugan
propagator (n doer), fiugarnwan, fiuganua, fiuganua
propel (v), fiuparzde, fiupado, fiupado
propellant (n), fiupadarn, fiupadana, fiupadan
propeller (n doer), fiupardwan, fiupadua, fiupadua
proper (adj), likarpu, likapu, likapu
properly (adv), likarpiu, likapiu, likapiu
property (n), fleivurt, feleivuta, fleivut
prophecy (n), fiunank, fiunana, fiunan
prophesy (n), fiunank, fiunana, fiunan
prophet (n doer), fiunankwan, fiunanua, fiunanua
proponent (n), fiuvelirp, fiuvelipa, fiuvelp
proportion (n), fiuferzhe, fiufezha, fiufezh
proportional (adj), fiuferzhu, fiufezhu, fiufezhu
proportionally (adv), fiuferzhiu, fiufezhiu, fiufezhiu
proposal (n), fiulork, fiuloka, fiulk
propose (v), fiulorsk, fiuloko, fiulko
proposer (n doer), fiulorkwan, fiulokua, fiulkua
proposition (n), fiulork, fiuloka, fiulk
proprietary (adj), fiuklirpu, fiukelipu, fiuklipu
proprietor (n doer), fiuklirpwan, fiukelipua,

fiuklipua
propriety (n), fiuklirp, fiukelipa, fiuklip
propulsion (n), fiuparde, fiupada, fiupad
prose (n), fleifanf, feleifana, fleifan
prosecutable (adj), fiudokartu, fiudokatu, fiudokatu
prosecute (v), fiudokarst, fiudokato, fiudokato
prosecution (n), fiudokart, fiudokata, fiudokat
prosecutor (n doer), fiudokartwan, fiudokatua, fiudokatua
prospect (n), fiuthurk, fiuthuka, fiuthuk
prospect (v), fiuthursk, fiuthuko, fiuthuko
prospective (adj), fiuthurku, fiuthuku, fiuthuku
prospectively (adv), fiuthurkiu, fiuthukiu, fiuthukiu
prospector (n doer), fiuthurkwan, fiuthukua, fiuthukua
prosper (v), fiulotelsf, fiulotelo, fiulotelo
prosperity (n), fiulotelf, fiulotela, fiulotel
prosperous (adj), fiulotelfu, fiulotelu, fiulotelu
prosperously (adv), fiulotelfiu, fiuloteliu, fiuloteliu
prostitute (n doer), fiuashkwan, fiuashua, fiuashua
prostitute (v), fiuashsk, fiuasho, fiuasho
prostitution (n), fiuashk, fiuasha, fiuash
Protactinium (n davoka), Onop, Onop, Onop
Protactinium (n), Protaktinium, Perotakotiniuma, Protaktinium
protagonist (n doer), fikokeragwan, fikokerugua, fikokrugua
protagonistic (adj), fikokeragu, fikokerugu, fikokrugu
protagonize (v), fikokerazge, fikokerugo, fikokrugo
protagony (n), fikokerage, fikokeruga, fikokrug
protect (v), shudolirsf, shudolifo, shdolfo
protection (n), shudolirf, shudolifa, shdolf
protectionism (n), shudolirfuet, shudolifueta, shdolfuet
protectionist (n doer), shudolirfwan, shudolifua, shdolfua
protective (adj), shudolirfu, shudolifu, shdolfu
protectively (adv), shudolirfiu, shudolifiu, shdolfiu
protector (n doer), shudolirfwan, shudolifua, shdolfua
protein (n), fiudarf, fiudafa, fiudaf
protest (n), fiushtirt, fiushetita, fiushtit
protest (v), fiushtirst, fiushetito, fiushtito
Protestant (n), Fiushtirp, Fiushetipa, Fiushtip
Protestantism (n), Fiushtirpuet, Fiushetipueta, Fiushtipuet
protester (n doer), fiushtirtwan, fiushetitua, fiushtitua
protestor (n doer), fiushtirtwan, fiushetitua, fiushtitua
protocol (n), bikigirf, bikigira, bikigir
proton (n), fiumarl, fiumala, fiumal
prototype (n), bikiduarp, bikiduapa, bikiduap
prototype (v), bikiduarsp, bikiduapo, bikiduapo
protract (v), fiugalirst, fiugalito, fiugalto
protraction (n), fiugalirt, fiugalita, fiugalt
protractor (n doer), fiugalirtwan, fiugalitua, fiugaltua
protrude (v), fiuborfst, fiubofito, fiubofto
protrusion (n), fiuborft, fiubofita, fiuboft
proudly (adv d:accomplishment), larzhiu, lazhiu, lazhiu

provable (adj), fliorfu, feliofu, fliofu
prove (v), fliorsf, feliofo, fliofo
prover (n doer), fliorfwan, feliofua, fliofua
proverb (n d:saying), fiudanf, fiudana, fiudan
proverbial (adj d:saying), fiudanfu, fiudanu, fiudanu
provide (v), bliferst, belifeto, blifeto
providence (n), blifertar, belifetara, blifetar
provider (n doer), blifertwan, belifetua, blifetua
province (n), blirfk, belifoka, blifk
provincial (adj), blirfku, belifoku, blifku
provincially (adv), blirfkiu, belifokiu, blifkiu
provision (n), blifert, belifcta, blifet
provocation (n), fiushairk, fiushaika, fiushaik
provocative (adj), fiushairku, fiushaiku, fiushaiku
provocatively (adv), fiushairkiu, fiushaikiu, fiushaikiu
provoke (v), fiushairsk, fiushaiko, fiushaiko
provoker (n doer), fiushairkwan, fiushaikua, fiushaikua
prowl (n), muiashk, muiasha, muiash
prowl (v), muiashsk, muiasho, muiasho
prowler (n doer), muiashkwan, muiashua, muiashua
proximity (n), froirge, feloiga, floig
proxy (n doer), froirgwan, feloigua, floigua
prude (n doer), bliunkwan, beliunua, bliunua
prudence (n), bliunk, beliuna, bliun
prudent (adj), bliunku, beliunu, bliunu
prudish (adj), bliunku, beliunu, bliunu
prune (n d:fruit), priamp, periama, priam
prune (v d:clip), blize, beligo, bligo
pruner (n doer d:clip), blizhwan, beligua, bligua
pry (v), miaishsk, miaiko, miaiko
Ps (let pl), peili, peili, peili
pseudonym (n), dishaviern, dishaviena, dishavien
psi (n), peshirn, peshina, peshin
psych (v), nairsk, naiko, naiko
psyche (n), nairk, naika, naik
psychiatric (adj), naigartu, naigatu, naigatu
psychiatrist (n doer), naigartwan, naigatua, naigatua
psychiatry (n), naigart, naigata, naigat
psychic (n doer), nairkwan, naikua, naikua
psycho (n doer), naikaushkwan, naikaukua, naikaukua
psychoanalysis (n), naikomarft, naikomafita, naikomaft
psychoanalyst (n doer), naikomarftwan, naikomafitua, naikomaftua
psychological (adj), naigerthu, naigethu, naigethu
psychologically (adv), naigerthiu, naigethiu, naigethiu
psychologist (n doer), naigerthwan, naigethua, naigethua
psychology (n), naigerth, naigetha, naigeth
psychopath (n doer), naikaushkwan, naikaukua, naikaukua
psychopathologist (n doer), naikaushkethwan, naikaukethua, naikaukethua
psychopathology (n), naikaushketh, naikauketha, naikauketh
psychosis (n), naikaushk, naikauka, naikauk

psychotherapist (n doer), naikepliarshpwan, naikepeliashipua, naikpliashpua
psychotherapy (n), naikepliarshp, naikepeliashipa, naikpliashp
psychotic (adj), naikaushku, naikauku, naikauku
public (adj), lirpurtu, liroputu, lirputu
public (n), lirpurt, liroputa, lirput
publication (n), lirlart, lirolata, lirlat
publicity (n), lirpurk, liropuka, lirpuk
publicize (v), lirpursk, liropuko, lirpuko
publicly (adv), lirpurtiu, liroputiu, lirputiu
publish (v), lirlarst, lirolato, lirlato
publisher (n doer), lirlartwan, lirolatua, lirlatua
puck (n), duiark, duiaka, duiak
pudding (n), gumarn, gumana, guman
puddle (n), daiarp, daiapa, daiap
puff (n), moshk, mosha, mosh
puff (v), moshsk, mosho, mosho
puffer (n doer), moshkwan, moshua, moshua
puffy (adj), moshku, moshu, moshu
puke (v), nuthirsk, nuthiko, nuthko
puker (n doer), nuthirkwan, nuthikua, nuthkua
pull (n), trelbe, tereba, treb
pull (v), trelzbe, terebo, trebo
pullback (n), trebevark, terebevaka, trebevak
puller (n doer), trelbwan, terebua, trebua
pulley (n), trebarn, terebana, treban
pullout (n), trelbuil, terebuila, trebuil
pulp (n), blufirp, belufipa, blufp
pulpit (n), blutirp, belutipa, blutip
pulsate (v), lorishorst, lorishoto, lorshto
pulsation (n), lorishort, lorishota, lorsht
pulsator (n doer), lorishortwan, lorishotua, lorshtua
pulse (n), lorash, lorisha, lorsh
pulse (v), loras, lorisho, lorsho
pulser (n doer), lorashwan, lorishua, lorshua
pump (n), dunbert, dunobeta, dunbet
pump (v), dunberst, dunobeto, dunbeto
pumper (n doer), dunbertwan, dunobetua, dunbetua
pumpkin (n), memtarn, memitana, mentan
pun (n), trink, terina, trin
punch (n d:beverage), tiriushk, tiriusha, tiriush
punch (n d:hit), krirthk, kerithika, krithk
punch (v d:hit), krirthsk, kerithiko, krithko
puncher (n doer d:hit), krirthkwan, kerithikua, krithkua
punchline (n), krithkroifk, kerithikeroifa, krithkroif
punchy (adj d:hit), krirthku, kerithiku, krithku
punctual (adj), thrafitu, therafitu, thraftu
punctually (adv), thrafitiu, therafitiu, thraftiu
punctuate (v), thrafist, therafito, thrafto
punctuation (n), thrafit, therafita, thraft
puncture (n), thrasht, therata, thrat
puncture (v), thrashst, therato, thrato
punish (v), thranisk, theraniko, thranko
punishable (adj), thraniku, theraniku, thranku
punisher (n doer), thranikwan, theranikua, thrankua
punishment (n), thranik, theranika, thrank
punitive (adj), thraniku, theraniku, thranku
punitively (adv), thranikiu, theranikiu, thrankiu
punk (n), pruthk, perutesha, prutsh

punky (adj), pruthku, peruteshu, prutshu
punt (n), fiupark, fiupaka, fiupak
punt (v), fiuparsk, fiupako, fiupako
punter (n doer), fiuparkwan, fiupakua, fiupakua
pup (n), duide, duida, duid
pupil (n d:eye), bidarn, bidara, bidar
pupil (n d:student), dofarf, dofafa, dofaf
puppet (n), duidart, duidata, duidat
puppeteer (n doer), duidarkwan, duidakua, duidakua
puppetry (n), duidark, duidaka, duidak
puppy (n), dudirf, dudifa, dudif
purchase (n), beirtat, beitata, beitat
purchase (v), beirtast, beitato, beitato
purchaser (n doer), beirtatwan, beitatua, beitatua
pure (adj), breishku, bereishu, breishu
purebred (n), breishfleirdiot, bereishefeleidiota, breishfleidiot
purebreed (n), breishfleirde, bereishefeleida, breishfleid
purely (adv), breishkiu, bereishiu, breishiu
purgatory (n), vuthiarf, vuthiafa, vuthiaf
purge (n), vuthark, vutha, vuth
purge (v), vutharsk, vutho, vutho
purification (n), breishkuet, bereishueta, breishuet
purifier (n doer), breishkuetwan, bereishuetua, breishuetua
purify (v), breishsk, bereisho, breisho
purist (n doer), breishkwan, bereishua, breishua
purity (n), breishk, bereisha, breish
purple (adj), berkorlu, berikolu, berkolu
purple (n), berkorl, berikola, berkol
purport (v), beibursk, beibuko, beibuko
purportedly (adv), beiburkiu, beibukiu, beibukiu
purpose (n), beirlak, beilaka, beilk
purpose (v), beirlask, beilako, beilko
purposeful (adj), beirlaku, beilaku, beilku
purposely (adv), beirlakiu, beilakiu, beilkiu
purr (v), gleifsk, geleifo, gleifo
purse (n), beirth, beitha, beltli
purse (v), beirsth, beitho, beitho
pursuant (adj), beirshaku, beishaku, beishaku
pursuantly (adv), beirshakiu, beishakiu, beishakiu
pursue (v), beirshask, beishako, beishako
pursuit (n), beirshak, beishaka, beishak
push (n), vurk, vuka, vuk
push (v), vursk, vuko, vuko
pusher (n doer), vurkwan, vukua, vukua
pushover (n), vurkafen, vukafena, vukafen
pushy (adj), vurku, vuku, vuku
put (n), vurt, vuta, vut
put (v pa), vurstyot, vutio, vutio
put (v), vurst, vuto, vuto
putt (n), kliuft, keliuta, kliut
putt (v), kliufst, keliuto, kliuto
putter (n doer), kliuftwan, keliutua, kliutua
putter (v), kliufast, keliutato, kliutato
putty (n), bliufp, beliupa, bliup
puzzle (n), vukirde, vukida, vukid
puzzle (v), vukirzde, vukido, vukido
puzzlement (n), vukirduet, vukidueta, vukiduet
puzzler (n doer), vukirdwan, vukidua, vukidua
pylon (n), prilark, perilaka, prilak

pyramid (n), tiarzhe, tiazha, tiazh
pyromaniac (n), niaushp, niaupa, niaup
pyrotechnic (n), niaukirzhe, niaukizha, niaukizh
quack (interj), kuek, kuek, kuek
quack (n), gioishk, gioika, gioik
quackery (n), gioishkuet, gioikueta, gioikuet
quad- (num 4 pref), yufai-, yufai-, yufai-
quadragintillion (num 1e123 card), dafta, dafta, dafta
quadrangle (n), yufaimirk, yufaimika, yufaimik
quadrant (n), yufaiark, yufaiaka, yufaiak
quadrillion (num 1e15 card), yufika, yufika, yufika
quadrillionth (num 1e15 ord), yufiketh, yufiketh, yufiketh
quaint (adj), driartu, deriatu, driatu
quaintly (adv), driartiu, deriatiu, driatiu
quaintness (n), driart, deriata, driat
quake (n), kliorp, keliopa, kliop
quake (v), kliorsp, keliopo, kliopo
quaksi- (num 1e45 pref), yufishtai-, yufishtai-, yufishtai-
qualification (n), kriarf, keriafa, kriaf
qualifier (n doer), kriarfwan, keriafua, kriafua
qualify (v), kriarsf, keriafo, kriafo
quality (adj), kriarftu, keriafotu, kriaftu
quality (n), kriarft, keriafota, kriaft
quandary (n), yamifk, yamika, yamik
quantifiable (adj), valparfu, valipafu, valpafu
quantification (n), valparfuet, valipafueta, valpafuet
quantify (v), valparsf, valipafo, valpafo
quantitative (adj), valparfu, valipafu, valpafu
quantitatively (adv), valparfiu, valipafiu, valpafiu
quantity (n), valparf, valipafa, valpaf
quantum (adj), vulirku, vuliku, vulku
quantum (n), vulirk, vulika, vulk
quarantine (n), yufidark, yufidaka, yufidak
quarantine (v), yufidarsk, yufidako, yufidako
quarrel (n), plagart, pelagata, plagat
quarrel (v), plagarst, pelagato, plagato
quarry (n), plafirgo, pelafiga, plafig
quarry (v), plafirzge, pelafigo, plafigo
quart (n), kolart, kolata, kolt
quarter (n), kolartar, kolatara, koltar
quarterly (adv), kolartariu, kolatariu, koltariu
quartermaster (n), koltarthiork, kolatarethioka, koltarthiok
quash (v), kuais, kuaipo, kuaipo
quattuordecillion (num 1e45 card), yufisht, yufisht, yufisht
quattuordecillionth (num 1e45 ord), yufishteth, yufishteth, yufishteth
quattuorquadragintillion (num 1e135 card), yufifk, yufifk, yufifk
quattuorvigintillion (num 1e75 card), yufishk, yufishk, yufishk
quattuorvigintillionth (num 1e75 ord), yufishketh, yufishketh, yufishketh
quatturotrigintillion (num 1e105 card), yufift, yufift, yufift
queasiness (n), kuishk, kuisha, kuish
queasy (adj), kuishku, kuishu, kuishu
Quebec (n), Keberfk, Kebefika, Kebefk

queen (n), biarsh, biasha, biash
queen (v), biars, biasho, biasho
queer (adj), biaipu, biaibu, biaibu
queer (n doer), biaipwan, biaibua, biaibua
quell (v), kuiefst, kuieto, kuieto
quench (v), kuieshsk, kuiesho, kuiesho
query (n), shtiarf, shotiafa, shtiaf
query (v), shtiarsf, shotiafo, shtiafo
quest (n), shtiart, shotiata, shtiat
question (n), shtiartet, shotiateta, shtiatet
question (v), shtiartest, shotiateto, shtiateto
questionable (adj), shtiartetu, shotiatetu, shtiatetu
questionably (adv), shtiartetiu, shotiatetiu,
    shtiatetiu
questioner (n doer), shtiartetwan, shotiatetua,
    shtiatetua
questionnaire (n), shtiartert, shotiaterita, shtiatert
queue (n), roift, roita, roit
queue (v), roifst, roito, roito
quibble (v), pligirst, peligito, pligito
quick (adj), kenortu, kenotu, kentu
quicken (v), kenorst, kenoto, kento
quicker (adj), kentwelu, kenotwelu, kenwelu
quickest (adj), kentweku, kenotweku, kenweku
quickly (adv), kenortiu, kenotiu, kentiu
quickness (n), kenort, kenota, kent
quicksand (n), kenarth, kenatha, kenath
quicksilver (n), kensharagen, kenesharugena,
    kenshargen
quicktime (n), kendaurn, kenedauna, kendaun
quiet (adj), deilurdu, deiludu, deildu
quiet (n), deilurde, deiluda, deild
quiet (v), deilurzde, deiludo, deildo
quietly (adv), deilurdiu, deiludiu, deildiu
quietness (n), deilurde, deiluda, deild
quill (n), biashkan, biashika, biashk
quilt (n), biorthk, bioritha, biorth
quilt (v), biorthsk, bioritho, biortho
quilter (n doer), biorthkwan, biorithua, biorthua
quindecillion (num 1e48 card), tirisht, tirisht,
    tirisht
quindecillionth (num 1e48 ord), tirishteth,
    tirishteth, tirishteth
quinquadragintillion (num 1e138 card), tirifk, tirifk,
    tirifk
quinquagintillion (num 1e153 card), dafka, dafka,
    dafka
quinquatrigintillion (num 1e108 card), tirift, tirift,
    tirift
quint- (num 5 pref), tirai , tirai , tirai-
quintillion (num 1e18 card), tirika, tirika, tirika
quintillionth (num 1e18 ord), tiriketh, tiriketh,
    tiriketh
quinvigintillion (num 1e78 card), tirishk, tirishk,
    tirishk
quinvigintillionth (num 1e78 ord), tirishketh,
    tirishketh, tirishketh
quip (n), deirp, deipa, deip
quip (v), deirsp, deipo, deipo
quipper (n doer), deirpwan, deipua, deipua
quirk (n), biuark, biuauaka, biuauak
quit (v pa), gloirskyot, geloikio, gloikio

quit (v), gloirsk, geloiko, gloiko
quite (adv), gloirshiu, geloishiu, gloishiu
quitter (n doer), gloirkwan, geloikua, gloikua
quiver (n), biagarf, biagara, biagar
quiver (v), biagarsf, biagaro, biagaro
quiz (n), diurk, diuka, diuk
quiz (v), diursk, diuko, diuko
quota (n), hinarme, hinama, hinam
quota (v), hinarzme, hinamo, hinamo
quotable (adj), hinarfu, hinafu, hinfu
quotation (n), hinarf, hinafa, hinf
quote (n), hinarf, hinafa, hinf
quote (v), hinarsf, hinafo, hinfo
quoter (n doer), hinarfwan, hinafua, hinfua
quotient (n), hilorat, hilorita, hilort
R (let sng), relre, relira, rel
rabbit (n), logarth, logatha, logath
rabble (n), pratesh, peratisha, pratsh
rabble (v), prates, peratisho, pratsho
rabbler (n doer), prateshwan, peratishua, pratshua
race (n d:competition), zhaink, zhaina, zhain
race (n d:human), noirth, noitha, noith
race (v d:competition), zhainsk, zhaino, zhaino
racehorse (n), zhaineglaushk, zhainegelausha,
    zhaineglaush
racer (n doer d:competition), zhainkwan, zhainua,
    zhainua
racetrack (n), zhainegethirk, zhainegethika,
    zhainegethk
raceway (n), zhainpliorl, zhainepeliola, zhainpliol
racial (adj d:human), noirthu, noithu, noithu
racially (adv d:human), noirthiu, noithiu, noithiu
racism (n), noithart, noithata, noithat
racist (n doer), noithartwan, noithatua, noithatua
rack (n), norage, noruga, norg
rack (v), norazge, norugo, norgo
racker (n doer), noragwan, norugua, norgua
racket (n d:bat, group), norgarf, norugafa, norgaf
racket (n d:noise), neshgarf, neshigafa, neshgaf
racketeer (n doer), norgairtwan, norugaitua,
    norgaitua
racketeer (v), norgairst, norugaito, norgaito
rackety (adj d:bat, group), norgarfu, norugafu,
    norgafu
racquet (n), norgarf, norugafa, norgaf
radar (n), moikarf, moikafa, moikaf
radar (v), moikarsf, moikafo, moikafo
radiance (n), moirve, moiva, moiv
radiate (v), moirzve, moivo, moivo
radiation (n), moluve, moiva, moiv
radiator (n doer), moirvwan, moivua, moivua
radical (adj), moivarku, moivaku, moivaku
radical (n), moivark, moivaka, moivak
radically (adv), moivarkiu, moivakiu, moivakiu
radii (n pl), sheirnyek, sheini, sheini
radio (n), miorap, mioripa, miorp
radio (v), miorasp, mioripo, miorpo
radioactive (adj), miorpalirtu, mioripalitu,
    miorpaltu
radioactivity (n), miorpalirt, mioripalita, miorpalt
Radium (n davoka), Anip, Anip, Anip
Radium (n), Radium, Radiuma, Radium
radius (n), sheirn, sheina, shein

radius (v), sheirsne, sheino, sheino
Radon (n davoka), Erik, Erik, Erik
Radon (n), Radon, Radona, Radon
raffle (n), thersh, thesha, thesh
raffle (v), thers, thesho, thesho
raft (n d:boat), thafirp, thafipa, thafp
raft (v d:boat), thafirsp, thafipo, thafpo
rafter (n d:roof support), thagart, thagata, thagat
rafter (n doer d:boat), thafirpwan, thafipua, thafpua
rag (n), norirp, noripa, norp
rag (v), norirsp, noripo, norpo
rage (n), zhigart, zhigata, zhigat
rage (v), zhigarst, zhigato, zhigato
raggedy (adv), norirpiu, noripiu, norpiu
ragtag (adj), norpegairvu, noripegaivu, norpegaivu
ragweed (n), norpyurk, noripyuka, norpyuk
raid (n), liaurk, liauka, liauk
raid (v), liaursk, liauko, liauko
raider (n doer), liaurkwan, liaukua, liaukua
rail (n), luirt, luita, luit
rail (v), luirst, luito, luito
railcar (n), luitegeral, luitegerela, luitegrel
railroad (n), luitrelish, luiterelisha, luitrelsh
railroad (v), luitrelis, luiterelisho, luitrelsho
railway (n), luitpliorl, luipeliola, luipliol
rain (n), melth, mela, mel
rain (v), melsth, melo, melo
rainbow (n), meldiarf, melediafa, meldiaf
raincoat (n), melfrafk, melerafika, melrafk
raindrop (n), melpreip, meledaruga, meldarg
rainfall (n), melzhailf, melezhaila, melzhail
rainforest (n), melthrishk, meletherisha, melthrish
rainmaker (n doer), melnargwan, melenagua,
    melnagua
rainout (n), melthuil, meluila, meluil
rainstorm (n), melferap, meleferipa, melfrip
rainwater (n), melheidorn, meleidona, melheidon
rainy (adj), melthu, melu, melu
raise (n), koirp, koipa, koip
raise (v), koirsp, koipo, koipo
rake (n), shuarp, shuapa, shuap
rake (v), shuarsp, shuapo, shuapo
raker (n doer), shuarpwan, shuapua, shuapua
rally (n), luirk, luika, luik
rally (v), luirsk, luiko, luiko
ram (n d:animal), porame, pirama, pram
ram (v d:thrust), giansf, giano, giano
ramble (v), pranshsh, peranisho, pransho
rambler (n doer), pranshkwan, peranishua,
    pranshua
rammer (n doer d:thrust), gianfwan, gianua, gianua
ramp (n), giorp, giopa, giop
ramp (v), giorsp, giopo, giopo
rampage (n), giopoishk, giopoika, giopoik
rampage (v), giopoishsk, giopoiko, giopoiko
rampant (adj), giopoishku, giopoiku, giopoiku
ramrod (n), giodiraf, giodirifa, giodirf
ramrod (v), giodirasf, giodirifo, giodirfo
ran (v pa), laorzmyot, laomio, laomio
ranch (n), limorak, limoroka, limork
ranch (v), limorask, limoroko, limorko
rancher (n doer), limorakwan, limorokua, limorkua
random (adj), biorfu, biofu, biofu

randomize (v), biorsf, biofo, biofo
randomly (adv), biorfiu, biofiu, biofiu
randomness (n), biorf, biofa, biof
rang (v pa d:sound), keminorskyot, keminokio,
    keminkio
range (n), mimarn, mimana, miman
range (v), mimarsne, mimano, mimano
ranger (n doer), mimarnwan, mimanua, mimanua
rank (adj d:rotten), kaukartu, kaukatu, kaukatu
rank (n d:level, judge), shuark, shuaka, shuak
rank (v d:level, judge), shuarsk, shuako, shuako
rant (n), shpiorf, shepiofa, shpiof
rant (v), shpiorsf, shepiofo, shpiofo
rap (n), dorve, dova, dov
rap (v), dorzve, dovo, dovo
rape (n), vagaurk, vagauka, vagauk
rape (v), vagaursk, vagauko, vagauko
rapid (adj), dovirlu, dovilu, dovilu
rapidity (n), dovirl, dovila, dovil
rapidly (adv), dovirliu, doviliu, doviliu
rapist (n doer), vagaurkwan, vagaukua, vagaukua
rapper (n doer), dorvwan, dovua, dovua
rapport (n), dovarf, dovafa, dovaf
rapport (v), dovarsf, dovafo, dovafo
rapt (adj), vagartu, vagatu, vagatu
rapture (n), vagart, vagata, vagat
rare (adj), praishku, peraishu, praishu
rarely (adv), praishkiu, peraishiu, praishiu
rarify (v), praishsk, peraisho, praisho
rarity (n), praishk, peraisha, praish
rash (adj), falirku, faliku, falku
rash (n), falirk, falika, falk
rashly (adv), falirkiu, falikiu, falkiu
rasp (n), felshp, felipa, felp
rasp (v), felshsp, felipo, felpo
raspy (adj), felshpu, felipu, felpu
rat (n), defirk, defika, defk
rat (v), defirsk, defiko, defko
ratchet (n), thashirk, thashika, thashk
ratchet (v), thashirsk, thashiko, thashko
rate (n), terbe, teba, teb
rate (v), terzbe, tebo, tebo
rather (adv/interj), loshert, loshetu, losht
ratification (n), tebirk, tebika, tebik
ratify (v), tebirsk, tebiko, tebiko
ratio (n), thutiarn, thutiana, thutian
ration (n), thulirk, thulika, thulk
ration (v), thulirsk, thuliko, thulko
rational (adj), thushortu, thushotu, thushtu
rationality (n), thushort, thushota, thusht
rationalize (v), thushorst, thushoto, thushto
rationally (adv), thushortiu, thushotiu, thushtiu
rattle (n), tiathk, tiatha, tiath
rattle (v), tiathsk, tiatho, tiatho
rattlesnake (n), tiathfreirk, tiathefareika, tiathfreik
raunchiness (n), limaushk, limauka, limauk
raunchy (adj), limaushku, limauku, limauku
ravage (v), vaigaushsk, vaigauko, vaigauko
ravager (n doer), vaigaushkwan, vaigaukua,
    vaigaukua
rave (v), reishsk, reisho, reisho
ravel (v), rigarst, rigato, rigato
raver (n doer), reishkwan, reishua, reishua

ravish (v), vigaushsk, vigauko, vigauko
raw (adj), gliarfu, geliafu, gliafu
rawly (adv), gliarfiu, geliafiu, gliafiu
rawness (n), gliarf, geliafa, gliaf
ray (n), poilf, poila, poil
raze (v), kairsk, kaiko, kaiko
razor (n doer), kairkwan, kaikua, kaikua
re-sign (v d:sign again), luweirsf, luweifo, luweifo
reach (n), gloruge, geloruga, glorg
reach (v), gloruzge, gelorugo, glorgo
reachable (adj), glorugu, gelorugu, glorgu
reacher (n doer), glorugwan, gelorugua, glorgua
reacquire (v), luotherst, luotheto, luotheto
reacquisition (n), luothert, luotheta, luothet
react (v), lupalirst, lupalito, lupalto
reaction (n), lupalirt, lupalita, lupalt
reactionary (adj), lupalirtu, lupalitu, lupaltu
reactionary (n), lupalirtun, lupalituna, lupaltun
reactivate (v), lupaltarsk, lupalitako, lupaltako
reactivation (n), lupaltark, lupalitaka, lupaltak
reactive (adj), lupaltarku, lupalitaku, lupaltaku
reactor (n doer), lupalirtwan, lupalitua, lupaltua
read (n), liarp, liapa, liap
read (v pa), liarspyot, liapio, liapio
read (v), liarsp, liapo, liapo
readable (adj), liarpu, liapu, liapu
reader (n doer), liarpwan, liapua, liapua
readership (n), liapuafirf, liapuafifa, liapuafif
readily (adv), dorliu, doliu, doliu
readiness (n), dorl, dola, dol
readjust (v), lutepafes, lutefipesho, lutefpesho
readjustment (n), lutepafesh, lutefipesha, lutefpesh
readout (n), liarpuil, liapuila, liapuil
ready (adj), dorlu, dolu, dolu
ready (v), dorsle, dolo, dolo
reaffirm (v), luorniursf, luoraniufo, luorniufo
reaffirmation (n), luorniurf, luoraniufa, luorniuf
real (adj), pluarfu, peluafu, pluafu
realign (v), luoroifsk, luoroifo, luoroifo
realignment (n), luoroifk, luoroifa, luoroif
realism (n), pluarn, peluana, pluan
realist (n doer), pluarfwan, peluafua, pluafua
realistic (adj), pluarnu, peluanu, pluanu
realistically (adv), pluarniu, peluaniu, pluaniu
reality (n), pluarf, peluafa, pluaf
realization (n), pluarnuet, peluanueta, pluanuet
realize (v), pluarsne, peluano, pluano
reallocate (v), luorshairsp, luorishaipo, luorshaipo
reallocation (n), luorshairp, luorishaipa, luorshaip
really (adv), pluarfiu, peluafiu, pluafiu
ream (n d:paper), tiriap, tiriafa, tiriaf
ream (v d:clear), finushst, finuto, finto
reamer (n doer d:clear), finushtwan, finutua, fintua
reap (v), duiarst, duiato, duiato
reaper (n doer), duiartwan, duiatua, duiatua
reappear (v), luopliarsne, luopeliano, luopliano
reappearance (n), luopliarn, luopeliana, luoplian
reapply (v), luthorsk, luthoko, luthoko
reappoint (v), lurotaitisf, luotaifoto, luotaiffo
reappointment (n), lurotaitif, luotaifota, luotaift
rear (adj), grulgu, gerugu, grugu
rear (n), grulge, geruga, grug
rear (v), grulzge, gerugo, grugo

rearrange (v), luomorst, luolimoto, luolmoto
rearrangement (n), luomort, luolimota, luolmot
rearview (adj), lufuartu, lufuatu, lufuatu
reason (n), kleirzhe, keleizha, kleizh
reason (v), kleirze, keleizho, kleizho
reasonable (adj), kleirzhu, keleizhu, kleizhu
reasonably (adv), kleirzhiu, keleizhiu, kleizhiu
reasoner (n doer), kleirzhwan, keleizhua, kleizhua
reassemble (v), luothralzve, luotheravo, luothravo
reassembly (n), luothralve, luotherava, luothrav
reassert (v), luolsharst, luolashato, luolshato
reassertion (n), luolshart, luolashata, luolshat
reassess (v), luorlarsp, luorelapo, luorlapo
reassessment (n), luorlarp, luorelapa, luorlap
reassign (v), luolarask, luolariko, luolarko
reassignment (n), luolarak, luolarika, luolark
reassurance (n), luolirp, luolipa, luolp
reassure (v), luolirsp, luolipo, luolpo
reattach (v), luopairsk, luopaiko, luopaiko
reattachment (n), luopairk, luopaika, luopaik
reawaken (v), lulomipusne, luominopo, luominpo
rebate (n), lugiarp, lugiapa, lugiap
rebate (v), lugiarsp, lugiapo, lugiapo
rebel (n doer), lugartwan, lugatua, lugatua
rebel (v), lugarst, lugato, lugato
rebellion (n), lugart, lugata, lugat
rebellious (adj), lugartu, lugatu, lugatu
rebelliously (adv), lugartiu, lugatiu, lugatiu
rebirth (n), luvashil, luvalesha, luvalsh
rebound (n), ludraifp, luderaipa, ludraip
rebound (v), ludraifsp, luderaipo, ludraipo
rebroadcast (n), ludorbirde, ludorebida, ludorbid
rebroadcast (v pa), ludorbirzdyot, ludorebidio, ludorbidio
rebroadcast (v), ludorbirzde, ludorebido, ludorbid
rebuff (n), lubursh, lubulesha, lubulsh
rebuff (v), luburs, lubulesho, lubulsho
rebuild (n), luvorat, luvorita, luvort
rebuild (v), luvorast, luvorito, luvorto
rebuilt (v pa), luvorastyot, luvoritio, luvortio
rebuke (v), ludaurst, luduato, ludauto
rebut (v), lublaishsk, lubelaiko, lublaiko
rebuttal (n), lublaishk, lubelaika, lublaik
recalculate (v), lugardas, lugarodako, lugardako
recalculation (n), lugardash, lugarodaka, lugardak
recalibrate (v), lubalforsk, lubalifoko, lubalfko
recalibration (n), lubalfork, lubalifoka, lubalfk
recall (n), lugirf, lugira, lugir
recall (v), lugirsf, lugiro, lugiro
recaller (n doer), lugirfwan, lugirua, lugirua
recap (n), luhlp, ludenpa, ludefp
recap (v), lufilsp, ludefipo, ludefpo
recapitalization (n), ludelkal, ludelika, ludelk
recapitalize (v), ludelkasle, ludeliko, ludelko
recapture (n), ludeshiark, ludeshiaka, ludeshiak
recapture (v), ludeshiarsk, ludeshiako, ludeshiako
recast (v pa), lutulirstyot, lutulitio, lutultio
recast (v), lutulirst, lutulito, lutulto
recede (v), luversk, luveko, luveko
receder (n doer), luverkwan, luvekua, luvekua
receipt (n), plunirsh, pelunisha, plunsh
receivable (adj), plushirpu, pelushipu, plushipu
receivable (n), plushirpun, pelushipuna, plushipun

receive (v), plushirsp, pelushipo, plushipo
receiver (n doer), plushirpwan, pelushipua, plushipua
recent (adj), luliratu, lulirotu, lulirtu
recently (adv), luliratiu, lulirotiu, lulirtiu
receptacle (n), plunshark, pelunishaka, plunshak
reception (n), plushirk, pelushika, plushik
receptionist (n), plushirpar, pelushipara, plushipar
receptive (adj), plushirku, pelushiku, plushiku
receptively (adv), plushirkiu, pelushikiu, plushikiu
receptor (n doer), plushirkwan, pelushikua, plushikua
recertification (n), luthuntarn, luthunitana, luthuntan
recertify (v), luthuntarsne, luthunitano, luthuntano
recess (n), luverk, luveka, luvek
recession (n), luvekert, luveketa, luveket
recessive (adj), luverku, luveku, luveku
recessively (adv), luverkiu, luvekiu, luvekiu
recharge (n), lugloift, lugeloita, lugloit
recharge (v), lugloifst, lugeloito, lugloito
rechargeable (adj), lugloiftu, lugeloitu, lugloitu
recharger (n doer), lugloiftwan, lugeloitua, lugloitua
recheck (v), lukest, luketo, luketo
recipe (n), lushort, lushota, lusht
recipient (n doer), plunirshwan, pelunishua, plunshua
reciprocal (adj), luluvarpu, luluvapu, luluvapu
reciprocate (v), luluvarsp, luluvapo, luluvapo
reciprocation (n), luluvarp, luluvapa, luluvap
reciprocity (n), luluvarp, luluvapa, luluvap
recital (n), lutoirpat, lutoipata, lutoipat
recitation (n), lutoirp, lutoipa, lutoip
recite (v), lutoirsp, lutoipo, lutoipo
reck (v), luiarst, luiato, luiato
reckless (adj), luiartmenu, luiatemenu, luiatmenu
recklessly (adv), luiartmeniu, luiatemeniu, luiatmeniu
recklessness (n), luiartmen, luiatemena, luiatmen
reckon (v), luiarsk, luiako, luiako
reclaim (v), lunolasne, lunoarito, lunoarto
reclamation (n), lunolan, lunoarita, lunoart
reclassification (n), lublesh, lubelega, lubleg
reclassify (v), lubles, lubelego, lublego
reclination (n), lukroift, lukeroifa, lukroif
recline (v), lukroifst, lukeroifo, lukroifo
recliner (n doer), lukroiftwan, lukeroifua, lukroifua
recluse (n), lugrusht, lugeruta, lugrut
reclusive (adj), lugrushtu, lugerutu, lugrutu
reclusively (adv), lugrushtiu, lugerutiu, lugrutiu
recognition (n), luvialort, luvialota, luvialt
recognizable (adj), luvialortu, luvialotu, luvialtu
recognizably (adv), luvialortiu, luvialotiu, luvialtiu
recognize (v), luvialorst, luvialoto, luvialto
recognizer (n doer), luvialortwan, luvialotua, luvialtua
recoil (n), lugaiarp, lugaiapa, lugaiap
recoil (v), lugaiarsp, lugaiapo, lugaiapo
recollect (v), lugapost, lugaripo, lugarpo
recollection (n), lugapot, lugaripa, lugarp
recombinant (adj), lulenupu, lunulipu, lunulpu
recombination (n), lulenup, lunulipa, lunulp

recombine (v), lulenusp, lunulipo, lunulpo
recommend (v), lusharsf, lushafo, lushafo
recommendation (n), lusharf, lushafa, lushaf
recommit (v), lulenirsk, luleniko, lulenko
reconcile (v), lurolarzme, lurolamo, lurolmo
reconciliation (n), lurolarme, lurolama, lurolm
recondition (v), lubeltifsk, luliutifoko, luliutifko
reconfiguration (n), lubelkudil, luliukulita, luliukult
reconfigure (v), lubelkudisle, luliukulito, luliukulto
reconfirm (v), lubelnuisf, luliunuifo, luliunuifo
reconfirmation (n), lubelnuif, luliunuifa, luliunuif
reconnect (v), lushnarsf, lushenafo, lushnafo
reconnection (n), lushnarf, lushenafa, lushnaf
reconnector (n doer), lushnarfwan, lushenafua, lushnafua
reconsider (v), lubelthost, luliuthoto, luliuthoto
reconsideration (n), lubelthot, luliuthota, luliuthot
reconstitute (v), lubelshpelst, luliushopelito, luliushpelto
reconstitution (n), lubelshpelt, luliushopelita, luliushpelt
reconstruct (v), lubelshlesk, luliusheleko, luliushleko
reconstruction (n), lubelshlek, luliusheleka, luliushlek
reconstructive (adj), lubelshleku, luliusheleku, luliushleku
reconvene (v), lubelfizme, luliufimo, luliufimo
record (n), plukarde, pelukada, plukad
record (v), plukarzde, pelukado, plukado
recordable (adj), plukardu, pelukadu, plukadu
recorder (n doer), plukardwan, pelukadua, plukadua
recount (n), lupoirn, lupoina, lupoin
recount (v), lupoirsne, lupoino, lupoino
recounter (n doer), lupoirnwan, lupoinua, lupoinua
recourse (n), lumaran, lumarina, lumarn
recourse (v), lumarasne, lumarino, lumarno
recourser (n doer), lumaranwan, lumarinua, lumarnua
recover (v d:resurface), ludalirsth, ludalitho, ludaltho
recover (v d:retrieve, heal), pliarst, peliato, pliato
recoverable (adj d:resurface), ludalirthu, ludalithu, ludalthu
recoverable (adj d:retrieve, heal), pliartu, peliatu, pliatu
recoverer (n doer d:retrieve, heal), pliartwan, peliatua, pliatua
recovery (n d:retrieve, heal), pliart, peliata, pliat
recreate (v), ludrishsk, luderiko, ludriko
recreate (v d:remake), lupliurst, lupeliuto, lupliuto
recreation (n d:remake), lupliurt, lupeliuta, lupliut
recreation (n d:rest), prelsh, peresha, presh
recreational (adj d:rest), prelshu, pereshu, preshu
recreator (n doer d:remake), lupliurtwan, lupeliutua, lupliutua
recrimination (n), lunuarnuet, lunuanueta, lunuanuet
recruit (n), draurkuin, deraukuina, draukuin
recruit (v), ludraursk, luderauko, ludrauko
recruiter (n doer), ludraurkwan, luderaukua, ludraukua

recruitment (n), ludraurk, luderauka, ludrauk
rectal (adj), triauishku, teriauiku, triauiku
rectally (adv), triauishkiu, teriauikiu, triauikiu
rectangle (n), yupimirak, yupimiroka, yupimirk
rectangular (adj), yupimiraku, yupimiroku, yupimirku
rectification (n), triashk, teriaka, triak
rectifier (n doer), triashkwan, teriakua, triakua
rectify (v), triashsk, teriako, triako
rectum (n), triauishk, teriauika, triauik
recuperate (v), luvorfsk, luvorifo, luvorfo
recuperation (n), luvorfk, luvorifa, luvorf
recuperative (adj), luvorfku, luvorifu, luvorfu
recur (v), lugalirsf, lugalifo, lugalfo
recurrence (n), lugalirf, lugalifa, lugalf
recurrent (adj), lugalirfu, lugalifu, lugalfu
recurrently (adv), lugalirfiu, lugalifiu, lugalfiu
recursal (n), lugiarsh, lugiasha, lugiash
recurse (v), lugiars, lugiasho, lugiasho
recurser (n doer), lugiarshwan, lugiashua, lugiashua
recursive (adj), lugiarshu, lugiashu, lugiashu
recursively (adv), lugiarshiu, lugiashiu, lugiashiu
recusal (n), lugoirt, lugoita, lugoit
recuse (v), lugoirst, lugoito, lugoito
recycle (v), luvairalst, luvairato, luvairto
recycler (n doer), luvairaltwan, luvairatua, luvairtua
red (adj), fieshtu, fieshu, fiesh
red (n), fiesht, fiesha, fiesh
redden (v), fieshst, fiesho, fiesho
reddish (adj), fieshreiku, fiesheiku, fiesheiku
redecorate (v), lubuprasle, luperalifo, lupralfo
redecoration (n), lubupral, luperalifa, lupralf
redeem (v), lukiursf, lukiufo, lukiufo
redeemable (adj), lukiurfu, lukiufu, lukiufu
redeemer (n doer), lukiurfwan, lukiufua, lukiufua
redefine (v), lubuvuast, luvuafito, luvuafto
redefinition (n), lubuvuat, luvuafita, luvuaft
redemption (n), lukiurf, lukiufa, lukiuf
redemptive (adj), lukiurfu, lukiufu, lukiufu
redeploy (v), lubushloist, lusheloifito, lushloifto
redeployment (n), lubushloit, lusheloifita, lushloift
redesign (n), ludeirolt, ludeirota, ludeirt
redesign (v), ludeirolst, ludeiroto, ludeirto
redevelop (v), lutefralsp, luteferapo, lutefrapo
redevelopment (n), lutefralp, luteferapa, lutefrap
redhead (n), fieshkefirt, fieshekefita, fieshkeft
redid (v pa), lutiskyot, lutikio, lutikio
redirect (v), lukuarfsk, lukuafiko, lukuafko
redirection (n), lukuarfk, lukuafika, lukuafk
rediscover (v), ludiarsne, ludiano, ludiano
rediscovery (n), ludiarn, ludiana, ludian
redistribute (v), lushrilst, lusherito, lushrito
redistribution (n), lushrilt, lusherita, lushrit
redistrict (v), lutibarfsk, lutibafiko, lutibafko
redline (n), fieshroifk, fiesheroifa, fieshroif
redline (v), fieshroifsk, fiesheroifo, fieshroifo
redneck (n), fieshethavube, fieshethariba, fieshtharb
redness (n), fieshtuet, fieshueta, fieshuet
redo (v), lutisk, lutiko, lutiko
redouble (v), lushkeisf, lukeifito, lukeifto
redoubt (v), lubiarsf, lubiaufo, lubiaufo

redoubtable (adj), lubiarfu, lubiaufu, lubiaufu
redraw (v), lupulasp, luperatho, lupratho
redrew (v pa), lupulaspyot, luperathio, luprathio
reduce (v), lukirask, lukiroko, lukirko
reducer (n doer), lukirakwan, lukirokua, lukirkua
reducible (adj), lukiraku, lukiroku, lukirku
reducibly (adv), lukirakiu, lukirokiu, lukirkiu
reduction (n), lukirak, lukiroka, lukirk
redundancy (n), lumurat, lumurita, lumurt
redundant (adj), lumuratu, lumuritu, lumurtu
redundantly (adv), lumuratiu, lumuritiu, lumurtiu
reed (n), diurth, diutha, diuth
reef (n), treshk, teretesha, tretsh
reel (n), diump, diuma, dium
reel (v), diumesp, diumo, diumo
reelect (v), lugelsp, luigepo, luigepo
reelection (n), lugelp, luigepa, luigep
reemphasize (v), luithuarst, luithuato, luithuato
reenact (v), ludarpatisle, luvopalito, luvopalto
reenactment (n), ludarpatil, luvopalita, luvopalt
reenter (v), lulondisle, lulonudo, lulondo
reentry (n), lulondil, lulonuda, lulond
reestablish (v), luaftarsp, lufitapo, luaftapo
reestablishment (n), luaftarp, lufitapa, luaftap
reevaluate (v), luovausp, luvovaupo, luvovaupo
reevaluation (n), luovaup, luvovaupa, luvovaup
reexamination (n), lutukoirge, lutukoiga, lutukoig
reexamine (v), lutukoirzge, lutukoigo, lutukoigo
refer (v), lugelsf, lugefo, lugefo
referee (n), lugelfuin, lugefuina, lugefuin
reference (n), lugersh, lugesha, lugesh
reference (v), lugers, lugesho, lugesho
referenda (n pl), lugesharnyek, lugeshani, lugeshani
referendum (n), lugesharn, lugeshana, lugeshan
referential (adj), lugershiu, lugeshu, lugeshu
referentially (adv), lugershiu, lugeshiu, lugeshiu
referer (n doer), lugelfwan, lugefua, lugefua
referral (n), lugelf, lugefa, lugef
refile (v), luthiursf, luthiufo, luthiufo
refill (n), lutriel, lubupa, lubup
refill (v), lutriesle, lubupo, lubupo
refinance (v), lulinasf, lulinofo, lulinfo
refine (v), luvuarst, luvuato, luvuato
refinement (n), luvuart, luvuata, luvuat
refiner (n doer), luvuartwan, luvuatua, luvuatua
refinery (n), luvuanirt, luvuanita, luvuant
refinish (v), lutiurst, lutiuto, lutiuto
refit (n), lupafirt, lupafita, lupaft
refit (v), lupafirst, lupafito, lupafto
reflect (v), lugerst, lugeto, lugeto
reflection (n), lugert, lugeta, luget
reflective (adj), lugertu, lugetu, lugetu
reflectively (adv), lugertiu, lugetiu, lugetiu
reflector (n doer), lugertwan, lugetua, lugetua
reflex (n), lutiert, lutieta, lutiet
reflexive (adj), lutiertu, lutietu, lutietu
reflux (n), lushrolk, lusheroka, lushrok
refocus (v), lugoifirst, lugoifito, lugoifto
reforest (v), luthrishsk, lutherisho, luthrisho
reforestation (n), luthrishk, lutherisha, luthrish
reform (n d:decorrupt), kiaurt, kiauta, kiaut
reform (n d:form again), luvoran, luvorina, luvorn
reform (v d:decorrupt), kiaurst, kiauto, kiauto

reform (v d:form again), luvorasne, luvorino, luvorno

reformat (v), luvorlinask, luvorinako, luvornako

reformation (n), luvorlinak, luvorinaka, luvornak

reformatory (adj), luvorlinaku, luvorinaku, luvornaku

reformer (n doer d:decorrupt), kiaurtwan, kiautua, kiautua

reformist (n doer d:decorrupt), kiaurtwan, kiautua, kiautua

reformulate (v), luvorlinasp, luvorinapo, luvornapo

reformulation (n), luvorlinap, luvorinapa, luvornap

refract (v), ludelishorsk, ludelishoko, ludelshko

refraction (n), ludelishork, ludelishoka, ludelshk

refractive (adj), ludelishorku, ludelishoku, ludelshku

refractory (n), ludelishirk, ludelishika, ludelshik

refrain (n d:verse), luvarap, luvarafa, luvaraf

refrain (v d:abstain), lufrulirsk, luferuliko, lufrulko

refresh (n), lufiarsh, lufiarifa, lufiarf

refresh (v), lufiars, lufiarifo, lufiarfo

refresher (n doer), lufiarshwan, lufiarifua, lufiarfua

refreshingly (adv), lufiarshiu, lufiarifiu, lufiarfiu

refreshment (n), lufiarsht, lufiarifota, lufiarft

refrigerant (n), lulaufarguat, lulaufaguata, lulaufaguat

refrigerate (v), lulaufarzge, lulaufago, lulaufago

refrigeration (n), lulaufarge, lulaufaga, lulaufag

refrigerator (n doer), lulaufargwan, lulaufagua, lulaufagua

refuel (v), luzhiarsp, luzhiapo, luzhiapo

refuge (n), luark, luaka, luak

refugee (n), luarkuin, luakuina, luakuin

refund (n), lutimork, lutimoka, lutimk

refund (v), lutimorsk, lutimoko, lutimko

refundable (adj), lutimorku, lutimoku, lutimku

refunder (n doer), lutimorkwan, lutimokua, lutimkua

refurbish (v), lupiethsk, lupietho, lupietho

refurbishment (n), lupiethk, lupietha, lupieth

refusal (n d:decline), diaurk, diauka, diauk

refuse (n d:garbage), gevarsh, gevasha, gevash

refuse (v d:decline), diaursk, diauko, diauko

refuse (v d:join again), lufaborst, lufaboto, lufaboto

refusion (n d:join again), lufabort, lufabota, lufabot

refutation (n), lufabark, lufabaka, lufabak

refute (v), lufabarsk, lufabako, lufabako

regain (v), lukuarsne, lukuano, lukuano

regard (n), luvairk, luvaika, luvaik

regard (v), luvairsk, luvaiko, luvaiko

regarder (n doer), luvairkwan, luvaikua, luvaikua

regardless (adj), luvairkmenu, luvaikemenu, luvaikmenu

regardless (adj/adv), luvaikmern, luvaikamenu, luvaikmen

regenerate (v), lumarmarsk, lumaromako, lumarmako

regeneration (n), lumarmark, lumaromaka, lumarmak

regenerator (n doer), lumarmarkwan, lumaromakua, lumarmakua

regime (n), thaufirk, thaufika, thaufk

region (n), thelirt, thelita, thelt

regional (adj), thelirtu, thelitu, theltu

regionally (adv), thelirtiu, thelitiu, theltiu

register (n doer), brianirkwan, berianikua, briankua

register (v), brianirsk, berianiko, brianko

registration (n), brianirk, berianika, briank

regress (v), luvorazge, luvorugo, luvorgo

regression (n), luvorage, luvoruga, luvorg

regressive (adj), luvoragu, luvorugu, luvorgu

regressively (adv), luvoragiu, luvorugiu, luvorgiu

regressor (n doer), luvoragwan, luvorugua, luvorgua

regret (n), luplart, lupelata, luplat

regret (v), luplarst, lupelato, luplato

regretful (adj), luplartu, lupelatu, luplatu

regretfully (adv), luplartiu, lupelatiu, luplatiu

regrettable (adj), luplartu, lupelatu, luplatu

regrettably (adv), luplartiu, lupelatiu, luplatiu

regrettor (n doer), luplartwan, lupelatua, luplatua

regroup (v), lubronsf, luberono, lubrono

regular (adj), luvirpu, luvipu, luvipu

regular (n), luvirpun, luvipuna, luvipun

regularity (n), luvirp, luvipa, luvip

regularly (adv), luvirpiu, luvipiu, luvipiu

regulate (v), luvirsp, luvipo, luvipo

regulation (n), luvirpuet, luvipueta, luvipuet

regulator (n doer), luvirpwan, luvipua, luvipua

regulatory (adj), luvirpuetu, luvipuetu, luvipuetu

rehabilitate (v), lureidasle, lureiloto, lureilto

rehabilitation (n), lureidal, lureilota, lureilt

rehash (v), luthaithsp, luthaitho, luthaitho

rehear (v), luuyasf, luuyano, luuyano

reheard (v pa), luuyasfyot, luuyanio, luuyanio

rehearsal (n), lubuashk, lubuasha, lubuash

rehearse (v), lubuashsk, lubuasho, lubuasho

rehire (v), lutiorzge, lutiogo, lutiogo

reign (n), thaurf, thaufa, thauf

reign (v), thaursf, thaufo, thaufo

reimburse (v), lubeirsth, lubeitho, lubeitho

reimbursement (n), lubeirth, lubeitha, lubeith

reimpose (v), lukiglarsk, lukigelako, lukiglako

rein (n), luift, luifa, luif

rein (v), luifst, luifo, luifo

reincarnate (v), lugreishsk, lugereiko, lugreiko

reincarnation (n), lugreishk, lugereika, lugreik

reinforce (v), ludarviusk, luvoviuko, luvoviuko

reinforcement (n), ludarviuk, luvoviuka, luvoviuk

reinforcer (n doer), ludarviukwan, luvoviukua, luvoviukua

reinsert (v), luarshest, luisheto, luisheto

reinsertion (n), luarshet, luisheta, luishet

reinstall (v), luarteirsp, luiteiro, luiteiro

reinstallation (n), luarteirp, luiteira, luiteir

reinstate (v), ludarshpest, luvoshipeto, luvoshpeto

reinstatement (n), ludarshpet, luvoshipeta, luvoshpet

reinstitute (v), luarshpelst, luishopelito, luishpelto

reinstitution (n), luarshpelt, luishopelita, luishpelt

reinsurance (n), luishreln, luisherela, luishrel

reinsure (v), luishrelsne, luisherelo, luishrelo

reinsurer (n doer), luishrelnwan, luisherelua, luishrelua

reintegrate (v), lupliarshsk, lupeliariko, lupliarko

reintegration (n), lupliarshk, lupeliarika, lupliark

reinterpret (v), luenridrusp, luariderupo, luaridrupo
reinterpretation (n), luenridrup, luariderupa, luaridrup
reintroduce (v), luenokriushsk, luarokeriuko, luarokriuko
reintroduction (n), luenokriushk, luarokeriuka, luarokriuk
reinvent (v), luguvarst, luguvato, luguvato
reinvention (n), luguvart, luguvata, luguvat
reinvest (v), luarbist, luibito, luibito
reinvestment (n), luarbit, luibita, luibit
reinvigorate (v), luarpeikarsne, luipcikano, luipeikano
reissuance (n), luzhirme, luzhima, luzhim
reissue (v), luzhirzme, luzhimo, luzhimo
reiterate (v), lulutigarst, lulutigato, lulutigato
reiteration (n), lulutigart, lulutigata, lulutigat
reject (n), luterp, lutepa, lutep
reject (v), lutersp, lutepo, lutepo
rejection (n), luterpuet, lutepueta, lutepuet
rejector (n doer), luterpwan, lutepua, lutepua
rejoice (v), lulairs, lulaisho, lulaisho
rejoicer (n doer), lulairshwan, lulaishua, lulaishua
rejoin (v), ludiarst, ludiato, ludiato
rejuvenate (v), luzhumarsk, luzhumako, luzhumako
rejuventation (n), luzhumark, luzhumaka, luzhumak
rekindle (v), lufriars, luferiasho, lufriasho
relapse (n), luthiurft, luthiufota, luthiuft
relapse (v), luthiurfst, luthiufoto, luthiufto
relate (v), ludarast, ludarito, ludarto
relation (n), ludarat, ludarita, ludart
relational (adj), ludartafifu, ludaritefifu, ludartfifu
relationally (adv), ludartafifiu, ludaritefifiu, ludartfifiu
relationship (n), ludartafif, ludaritefifa, ludartfif
relative (adj), ludaratu, ludaritu, ludartu
relative (n doer), ludaratwan, ludaritua, ludartua
relatively (adv), ludaratiu, ludaritiu, ludartiu
relaunch (v), luvuarsk, luvuako, luvuako
relax (v), luklarsle, lukelalo, luklalo
relaxation (n), luklarl, lukelala, luklal
relay (n d:transceive), truirf, teruifa, truif
relay (v d:place again), lufranist, luferanito, lufranto
relearn (v), luvrierst, luvorieto, luvrieto
release (n), lunurn, lununa, lunun
release (v), lunursne, lununo, lununo
releaser (n doer), lunurnwan, lununua, lununua
relegate (v), lupiashsk, lupiako, lupiako
relegation (n), lupiashk, lupiaka, lupiak
relent (v), lufursp, lufurisho, lufursho
relentless (adj), lufurpemenu, lufurishemenu, lufurshmenu
relevance (n), truifk, tiruika, truik
relevancy (n), truifk, tiruika, truik
relevant (adj), truifku, tiruiku, truiku
relevantly (adv), truifkiu, tiruikiu, truikiu
reliability (n), terame, terema, trem
reliable (adj), teramu, teremu, tremu
reliably (adv), teramiu, teremiu, tremiu
reliance (n), tremirp, teremipa, tremp

reliant (adj), tremirpu, teremipu, trempu
relief (n), lurap, luripa, lurp
relieve (v), lurasp, luripo, lurpo
reliever (n doer), lurapwan, luripua, lurpua
religion (n), tesharbe, teshaba, teshab
religious (adj), tesharbu, teshabu, teshabu
religiously (adv), tesharbiu, teshabiu, teshabiu
relinquish (v), luprufsp, luperupo, luprupo
relish (v), shnushsk, shenusho, shnusho
relive (v), luflaurfst, lufelaufito, luflaufto
reload (v), lulurifst, lulurito, lulurto
relocate (v), lushairsp, lushaipo, lushaipo
relocation (n), lushairp, lushaipa, lushaip
reluctance (n), lumiarsh, lumiasha, lumiash
reluctant (adj), lumiarshu, lumiashu, lumiashu
reluctantly (adv), lumiarshiu, lumiashiu, lumiashiu
rely (v), terazme, teremo, tremo
remade (v pa), lunarzgyot, lunagio, lunagio
remain (v), luvaurs, luvausho, luvausho
remainder (n), luvaursh, luvausha, luvaush
remains (n), luvaursht, luvausheta, luvausht
remake (n), lunarge, lunaga, lunag
remake (v), lunarzge, lunago, lunago
remaker (n doer), lunargwan, lunagua, lunagua
remand (n), lushoirk, lushoika, lushoik
remand (v), lushoirsk, lushoiko, lushoiko
remander (n doer), lushoirkwan, lushoikua, lushoikua
remanufacture (v), lushoikaurst, lushoikauto, lushoikauto
remap (n), lushipersne, lushipeno, lushpeno
remark (n d:reply), keikurt, keikuta, keikut
remark (n d:write again), lushtart, lushotata, lushtat
remark (v d:reply), keikurst, keikuto, keikuto
remark (v d:write again), lushtarst, lushotato, lushtato
remarkable (adj d:reply), keikurtu, keikutu, keikutu
remarkably (adv d:reply), keikurtiu, keikutiu, keikutiu
remarriage (n), luvularn, luvulana, luvuln
remarry (v), luvularsne, luvulano, luvulno
rematch (n), lumuthk, lumutha, lumuth
rematch (v), lumuthsk, lumutho, lumutho
remediate (v), lulaidarsk, lulaidako, lulaidako
remediation (n), lulaidark, lulaidaka, lulaidak
remediator (n doer), lulaidarkwan, lulaidakua, lulaidakua
remedy (n), lulairde, lulaida, lulaid
remedy (v), lulairzde, lulaido, lulaido
remember (v), lutalursne, lutaluno, lutalno
remembrance (n), lutalurn, lutaluna, lutaln
remind (v), luniarsp, luniapo, luniapo
reminder (n doer), luniarpwan, luniapua, luniapua
remiss (v), lulularst, lululato, lululto
remission (n), lululart, lululata, lulult
remissive (adj), lulultartu, lululatu, lulultu
remissively (adv), lulultartiu, lululatiu, lulultiu
remit (v), lunorsk, lunoko, lunko
remittance (n), lunork, lunoka, lunk
remittor (n doer), lunorkwan, lunokua, lunkua
remix (n), luzhorfk, luzhorika, luzhork
remix (v), luzhorfsk, luzhoriko, luzhorko

remodel (v), ludiardasre, ludiadaro, ludiadaro
remote (adj), luvadarvu, luvadavu, luvadavu
remote (n), luvadarve, luvadava, luvadav
remotely (adv), luvadarviu, luvadaviu, luvadaviu
removable (adj), lushkirtu, lushekitu, lushkitu
removably (adv), lushkirtiu, lushekitiu, lushkitiu
removal (n), lushkirt, lushekita, lushkit
remove (v), lushkirst, lushekito, lushkito
remover (n doer), lushkirtwan, lushekitua,
    lushkitua
rename (v), lubriensf, luberieno, lubrieno
render (v), lutirfsk, lutifoko, lutifko
renderer (n doer), lutirfkwan, lutifokua, lutifkua
rendition (n), lutirfk, lutifoka, lutifk
renegotiate (v), lukriarst, lukeriato, lukriato
renegotiation (n), lukriart, lukeriata, lukriat
renew (v), lumiosre, lumiolo, lumiolo
renewable (adj), lumioru, lumiolu, lumiolu
renewal (n), lumior, lumiola, lumiol
renewer (n doer), lumiorwan, lumiolua, lumiolua
renominate (v), luvienorsk, luvienoko, luvienko
renomination (n), luvienork, luvienoka, luvienk
renounce (v), lumufirst, lumufito, lumufto
renovate (v), lumiarsf, lumiafo, lumiafo
renovation (n), lumiarf, lumiafa, lumiaf
renovator (n doer), lumiarfwan, lumiafua, lumiafua
rent (n), thafirk, thafika, thafk
rent (v), thafirsk, thafiko, thafko
rental (adj), thafirku, thafiku, thafku
rental (n), thafirkal, thafikala, thafkal
renter (n doer), thafirkwan, thafikua, thafkua
reopen (v), luefbirsne, luefubino, luefbino
reorder (v), lushkelst, lushiketo, lushketo
reorganization (n), lufrilot, luferilota, lufrilt
reorganize (v), lufrilost, luferiloto, lufrilto
reorganizer (n doer), lufrilotwan, luferilotua,
    lufriltua
repackage (v), lubugarst, lubugato, lubugato
repaid (v pa), lumoirzmyot, lumoimio, lumoimio
repaint (v), lugrals, lugerasho, lugrasho
repair (n), lubolirk, lubolika, lubolk
repair (v), lubolirsk, luboliko, lubolko
repairable (adj), lubolirku, luboliku, lubolku
repairer (n doer), lubolirkwan, lubolikua, lubolkua
repairman (n doer), lubolirkwan, lubolikua,
    lubolkua
reparable (adj), lubolirku, luboliku, lubolku
repay (v), lumoirzme, lumoimo, lumoimo
repayer (n doer), lumoirmwan, lumoimua,
    lumoimua
repayment (n), lumoirme, lumoima, lumoim
repeal (n), lutelirp, lutelipa, lutelp
repeal (v), lutelirsp, lutelipo, lutelpo
repealer (n doer), lutelirpwan, lutelipua, lutelpua
repeat (n), luvarp, luvapa, luvap
repeat (v), luvarsp, luvapo, luvapo
repeatable (adj), luvarpu, luvapu, luvapu
repeatedly (adv), luvarpiu, luvapiu, luvapiu
repeater (n doer), luvarpwan, luvapua, luvapua
repel (v), luparzde, lupado, lupado
repellant (n), luparde, lupada, lupad
repellants (adj), lupardu, lupadu, lupadu
repellent (adj), lupardu, lupadu, lupadu

repellent (n), luparde, lupada, lupad
repeller (n doer), lupardwan, lupadua, lupadua
repent (v), ludrashst, luderato, ludrato
repentance (n), ludrasht, luderata, ludrat
repentant (adj), ludrashtu, luderatu, ludratu
repetition (n), luvarpuet, luvapueta, luvapuet
repetitious (adj), luvarpuetu, luvapuetu, luvapuetu
repetitiously (adv), luvarpuetiu, luvapuetiu,
    luvapuetiu
repetitive (adj), luvarpu, luvapu, luvapu
rephrase (v), luvarshst, luvarisho, luvarsho
replace (v), lubres, luberesho, lubresho
replaceable (adj), lubreshu, lubereshu, lubreshu
replacement (n), lubresh, luberesha, lubresh
replacer (n doer), lubreshwan, lubereshua,
    lubreshua
replant (v), lubrelsp, luberepo, lubrepo
replay (n), lufruifk, luferuifa, lufruif
replay (v), lufruifsk, luferuifo, lufruifo
replayer (n doer), lufruifkwan, luferuifua, lufruifua
replenish (v), luniursne, luniuno, luniuno
replenishment (n), luniurn, luniuna, luniun
replicate (v), klers, kelesho, klesho
replication (n), klersh, kelesha, klesh
replicator (n doer), klershwan, keleshua, kleshua
replier (n doer), lushluartwan, lusheluatua,
    lushluatua
reply (n), lushluart, lusheluata, lushluat
reply (v), lushluarst, lusheluato, lushluato
report (n), dovarat, dovarita, dovart
report (v), dovarast, dovarito, dovarto
reportable (adj), dovaratu, dovaritu, dovartu
reportedly (adv), dovaratiu, dovaritiu, dovartiu
reporter (n doer), dovaratwan, dovaritua, dovartua
reposition (n), luveilirn, luveilina, luveiln
reposition (v), luveilirsne, luveilino, luveilno
repository (n), luveilork, luveiloka, luveilk
repossess (v), luprilasp, luperilapo, luprilpo
repossession (n), luprilap, luperilapa, luprilp
reprehend (v), ludrufsk, luderuko, ludruko
reprehension (n pl), ludrufkyek, luderuki, ludruki
reprehension (n), ludrufk, luderuka, ludruk
reprehensive (adj), ludrufku, luderuku, ludruku
reprehensively (adv), ludrufkiu, luderukiu, ludrukiu
represent (v), ludars, luduasho, luduasho
representation (n), ludarsh, luduasha, luduash
representative (adj), ludarshu, luduashu, luduashu
representative (n doer), ludarshwan, luduashua,
    luduashua
repress (v), lublars, lubelasho, lublasho
repression (n), lublarsh, lubelasha, lublash
repressive (adj), lublarshu, lubelashu, lublashu
repressor (n doer), lublarshwan, lubelashua,
    lublashua
reprieve (n), lufliothk, lufeliotha, luflioth
reprint (n), lutrulish, luterulisha, lutrulsh
reprint (v), lutrulis, luterulisho, lutrulsho
reproach (n), luflaurde, lufelauda, luflaud
reproach (v), luflaurzde, lufelaudo, luflaudo
reprocess (v), lufiuverst, lufiuveto, lufiuveto
reproduce (v), lupleirsk, lupeleiko, lupleiko
reproducer (n doer), lupleirkwan, lupeleikua,
    lupleikua

reproduction (n), lupleirk, lupeleika, lupleik
reproductive (adj), lupleirku, lupeleiku, lupleiku
reproductively (adv), lupleirkiu, lupeleikiu,
    lupleikiu
reprogram (v), lufiunelirsk, lufiuneliko, lufiunelko
republic (n), lirparf, liropafa, lirpaf
republican (n doer), lirparfwan, liropafua, lirpafua
republish (v), lulirlarst, lulirolato, lulirlato
repudiate (v), luvoikarst, luvoikato, luvoikato
repulse (v), luloras, lulorisho, lulorsho
repulsive (adj), lulorashu, lulorishu, lulorshu
repurchase (n), lubeirtat, lubeitata, lubeitat
repurchase (v), lubeirtast, lubeitato, lubeitato
reputation (n), luvoikart, luvoikata, luvoikat
repute (n), luvoirk, luvoika, luvoik
repute (v), luvoirsk, luvoiko, luvoiko
requalification (n), lukriarf, lukeriafa, lukriaf
requalifier (n doer), lukriarfwan, lukeriafua,
    lukriafua
requalify (v), lukriarsf, lukeriafo, lukriafo
request (n), lushiart, lushiata, lushiat
request (v), lushiarst, lushiato, lushiato
requester (n doer), lushiartwan, lushiatua,
    lushiatua
require (v), lutharst, luthato, luthato
requirement (n), luthart, luthata, luthat
reran (v pa), lulaorzmyot, lulaomio, lulaomio
reread (v pa), luliarspyot, luliapio, luliapio
reread (v), luliarsp, luliapo, luliapo
reroute (v), luprailsk, luperaiko, lupraiko
rerun (v), lulaorzme, lulaomo, lulaomo
resale (adj), lutrelirfu, luterelifu, lutrelfu
resale (n), lutrelirf, luterelifa, lutrelf
reschedule (v), luridarsf, luridafo, luridafo
rescind (v), lushlaithsk, lushelaitho, lushlaitho
rescue (n), ludaiart, ludaiata, ludaiat
rescue (v), ludaiarst, ludaiato, ludaiato
rescuer (n doer), ludaiartwan, ludaiatua, ludaiatua
research (n), lukrosht, lukerosha, lukrosh
research (v), lukroshst, lukerosho, lukrosho
researcher (n doer), lukroshtwan, lukeroshua,
    lukroshua
resell (v), lutrelirsf, luterelifo, lutrelfo
reseller (n doer), lutrelirfwan, luterelifua, lutrelfua
resemblance (n), ludidarn, ludidana, ludidan
resemble (v), ludidarsne, ludidano, ludidano
resend (v d:send again), luzhairsp, luzhaipo,
    luzhaipo
resent (v d:disdain), shorbast, lushoribo, lushorbo
resent (v pa d:send again), luzhairspyot, luzhaipio,
    luzhaipio
resentful (adj d:disdain), shorbatu, lushoribu,
    lushorbu
resentment (n d:disdain), shorbat, lushoriba,
    lushorb
reservation (n), lukorftuet, lukofitueta, lukoftuet
reserve (n d:military), lukofalt, lukofata, lukofat
reserve (n d:storage), lukorft, lukofita, lukoft
reserve (v d:storage), lukorfst, lukofito, lukofto
reserver (n doer d:storage), lukorftwan, lukofitua,
    lukoftua
reservist (n doer d:military), lukofaltwan,
    lukofatua, lukofatua

reservoir (n), lukofirp, lukofipa, lukofp
reset (n), luferp, lufepa, lufep
reset (v pa), luferspyot, lufepio, lufepio
reset (v), lufersp, lufepo, lufepo
resetter (n doer), luferpwan, lufepua, lufepua
resettle (v), lulibers, lulibesho, lulibesho
resettlement (n), lulibersh, lulibesha, lulibesh
reshape (v), luflurzme, lufelumo, luflumo
reshuffle (v), luthathsk, luthatho, luthatho
reside (v), lushoirsne, lushoino, lushoino
residence (n), lushoirn, lushoina, lushoin
resident (n doer), lushoirnwan, lushoinua,
    lushoinua
residential (adj), lushoirnu, lushoinu, lushoinu
residual (adj), borthku, borithku, borthku
residue (n), borthk, borithika, borthk
resign (v d:quit), lularask, lulariko, lularko
resignation (n d:quit), lularak, lularika, lulark
resigner (n doer d:quit), lularakwan, lularikua,
    lularkua
resin (n), borath, boritha, borth
resist (v), lutelirsk, luteliko, lutelko
resistance (n), lutelirk, lutelika, lutelk
resistant (adj), lutelirku, luteliku, lutelku
resister (n doer), lutelirkwan, lutelikua, lutelkua
resistible (adj), lutelirku, luteliku, lutelku
resistor (n), lutielirk, lutielika, lutielk
resize (v), lushuarzge, lushuago, lushuago
resold (v pa), lutrelirsfyot, luterelifio, lutrelfio
resolute (adj), lugagoru, lugeragu, lugragu
resolution (n), lugagor, lugeraga, lugrag
resolve (v), lugagosre, lugerago, lugrago
resolver (n doer), lugagorwan, lugeragua, lugragua
resonance (n), lushanirt, lushanita, lushant
resonant (adj), lushanirtu, lushanitu, lushantu
resonate (v), lushanirst, lushanito, lushanto
resort (n d:rest, revert), lupriert, luperieta, lupriet
resort (v d:rest, revert), luprierst, luperieto, luprieto
resort (v d:sort again), lufadersk, lufadeko,
    lufadeko
resound (v), luzhanirst, luzhanito, luzhanto
resoundingly (adv), luzhanirtiu, luzhanitiu,
    luzhantiu
resource (n), lubaifirt, lubaifita, lubaift
resourceful (adj), lubaifirtu, lubaifitu, lubaiftu
resourcefully (adv), lubaifirtiu, lubaifitiu, lubaiftiu
resourcefulness (n), lubaifirtuet, lubaifitueta,
    lubaiftuet
respect (n), luthurk, luthuka, luthuk
respect (v), luthursk, luthuko, luthuko
respectable (adj), luthukiru, luthukilu, luthukilu
respectful (adj), luthukurshu, luthukushu,
    luthukushu
respectfully (adv), luthukurshiu, luthukushiu,
    luthukushiu
respective (adj), luthurku, luthuku, luthuku
respectively (adv), luthurkiu, luthukiu, luthukiu
respirate (v), lufdaursf, lufodaufo, lufdaufo
respiration (n), lufdaurf, lufodaufa, lufdauf
respirator (n doer), lufdaurfwan, lufodaufua,
    lufdaufua
respiratory (adj), lufdaurfu, lufodaufu, lufdaufu
respond (v), ludufirsp, ludufipo, ludufpo

respondent (n), ludufirpuin, ludufipuina, ludufpuin
responder (n doer), ludufirpwan, ludufipua, ludufpua
response (n), ludufirp, ludufipa, ludufp
responsibility (n), luduverk, luduveka, luduvek
responsible (adj), luduverku, luduveku, luduveku
responsibly (adv), luduverkiu, luduvekiu, luduvekiu
responsive (adj), ludufirpu, ludufipu, ludufpu
responsively (adv), ludufirpiu, ludufipiu, ludufpiu
rest (n), preirsh, pereisha, preish
rest (v), preirs, pereisho, preisho
restart (v), lushkalirst, lushokalito, lushkalto
restate (v), lubiurst, lubiuto, lubiuto
restatement (n), lubiurt, lubiuta, lubiut
restaurant (n), preidan, pereida, preid
rester (n doer), preirshwan, pereishua, preishua
restful (adj), preirshu, pereishu, preishu
restfully (adv), preirshiu, pereishiu, preishiu
restless (adj), preirshmenu, pereishumenu, preishmenu
restlessy (adv), preirshmeniu, pereishumeniu, preishmeniu
restock (v), lufrifsk, luferifo, lufrifo
restoration (n), ludralbe, luderaba, ludrab
restorative (adj), ludralbu, luderabu, ludrabu
restoratively (adv), ludralbiu, luderabiu, ludrabiu
restore (v), ludralzbe, luderabo, ludrabo
restorer (n doer), ludralbwan, luderabua, ludrabua
restrain (v), luprulirsk, luperuliko, luprulko
restrainer (n doer), luprulirkwan, luperulikua, luprulkua
restraint (n), luprulirk, luperulika, luprulk
restrict (v), lubafirsk, lubafiko, lubafko
restricter (n doer), lubafirkwan, lubafikua, lubafkua
restriction (n), lubafirk, lubafika, lubafk
restrictive (adj), lubafirku, lubafiku, lubafku
restrictively (adv), lubafirkiu, lubafikiu, lubafkiu
restroom (n), lurpshranf, luripesherana, lurpshran
restructure (v), lushlersk, lushileko, lushleko
resubmission (n), lushefnork, lushefinoka, lushefnok
resubmit (v), lushefnorsk, lushefinoko, lushefnoko
result (n), luvanirt, luvanita, luvant
result (v), luvanirst, luvanito, luvanto
resultant (adj), luvanirtu, luvanitu, luvantu
resume (v), lufialirst, lufialito, lufialto
resumer (n doer), lufialirtwan, lufialitua, lufialtua
resumption (n), lufialirt, lufialita, lufialt
resupply (n), lushethirp, lushethipa, lushethp
resupply (v), lushethirsp, lushethipo, lushethpo
resurface (v), luthrelsf, lutherefo, luthrefo
resurge (v), luvoirzge, luvoigo, luvoigo
resurgence (n), luvoirge, luvoiga, luvoig
resurgent (adj), luvoirgu, luvoigu, luvoigu
resurrect (v), voikuarst, voikuato, voikuato
resurrection (n), voikuart, voikuata, voikuat
resurrector (n doer), voikuartwan, voikuatua, voikuatua
resuscitate (v), lumemifst, lumemifo, lumemifo
resuscitation (n), lumemift, lumemifa, lumemif
retail (n), lumithk, lumitha, lumith
retail (v), lumithsk, lumitho, lumitho
retailer (n doer), lumithkwan, lumithua, lumithua

retain (v), lupiforst, lupifoto, lupifto
retainer (n doer), lupifortwan, lupifotua, lupiftua
retake (v), lugorsk, lugoko, lugoko
retaliate (v), luthirthsk, luthithoko, luthithko
retaliation (n), luthirthk, luthithoka, luthithk
retaliator (n doer), luthirthkwan, luthithokua, luthithkua
retaliatory (adj), luthirthku, luthithoku, luthithku
retard (v), luiashsk, luiasho, luiasho
retardant (adj), luiashku, luiashu, luiashu
retardation (n), luiashk, luiasha, luiash
retell (v), luprelst, lupereto, lupreto
retention (n), lupifort, lupifota, lupift
retentive (adj), lupifortu, lupifotu, lupiftu
retentively (adv), lupifortiu, lupifotiu, lupiftiu
rethink (v), ludersp, ludepo, ludepo
rethought (v pa), luderspyot, ludepio, ludepio
retire (v), luparsne, lupano, lupano
retiree (n doer), luparnwan, lupanua, lupanua
retirement (n), luparn, lupana, lupan
retold (v pa), luprelstyot, luperetio, lupretio
retook (v pa), lugorskyot, lugokio, lugokio
retool (v), lufiorsk, lufioko, lufioko
retrace (v), lugars, lugasho, lugasho
retract (v), lugalirst, lugalito, lugalto
retractable (adj), lugalirtu, lugalitu, lugaltu
retraction (n), lugalirt, lugalita, lugalt
retrain (v), lutrilorsk, luteriloko, lutrilko
retransmission (n), luthonork, luthonoka, luthonok
retransmit (v), luthonorsk, luthonoko, luthonoko
retreat (n), luthuirt, luthuita, luthuit
retreat (v), luthuirst, luthuito, luthuito
retrench (v), ludiofsk, ludiofo, ludiofo
retrenchment (n), ludiofk, ludiofa, ludiof
retrial (n), ludibarge, ludibaga, ludibag
retribution (n), luthriurp, lutheriupa, luthriup
retrieval (n), lubirsh, lubisha, lubish
retrieve (v), lubirs, lubisho, lubisho
retriever (n doer), lubirshwan, lubishua, lubishua
retro (adj), luiupu, luiunu, luiunu
retroactive (adj), luiupaltarku, luiupalitaku, luiupaltaku
retroactively (adv), luiupaltarkiu, luiupalitakiu, luiupaltakiu
retroactivity (n), luiupaltark, luiupalitaka, luiupaltak
retrofit (n), luiupafirt, luiupafita, luiupaft
retrofit (v), luiupafirst, luiupafito, luiupafto
retrograde (adj), luiushtraku, luiushoteranu, luiushtranu
retrospect (n), luiuthurk, luiuthuka, luiuthuk
retrospective (adj), luiuthurku, luiuthuku, luiuthuku
retry (n), ludirbe, ludiba, ludib
retry (v), ludirzbe, ludibo, ludibo
return (n), lukaimp, lukaima, lukaim
return (v), lukaimesp, lukaimo, lukaimo
returner (n doer), lukaimpwan, lukaimua, lukaimua
retype (v), ludairst, ludairo, ludairo
reunification (n), luyutark, luyutaka, luyutak
reunify (v), luyutarsk, luyutako, luyutako
reunion (n), luyutarme, luyutama, luyutam
reunite (v), luyutarzme, luyutamo, luyutamo

reuse (v), lubriarsk, luberiako, lubriako
rev (n), viathk, viatha, viath
rev (v), viathsk, viatho, viatho
revaluate (v), luvaursp, luvaupo, luvaupo
revaluation (n), luvaurp, luvaupa, luvaup
revamp (v), lutafinsk, lutafino, lutafino
reveal (v), lufuarzme, lufuamo, lufuamo
revel (v), lunarst, lunato, lunato
revelation (n), lufuarme, lufuama, lufuam
revelatory (adj), lunartu, lunatu, lunatu
revelry (n), lunart, lunata, lunat
revenge (n), ludufirk, ludufika, ludufk
revenge (v), ludufirsk, ludufiko, ludufko
revenue (n), lulfirme, lulafima, lulfim
reverberate (v), ludarsne, ludano, ludano
reverberation (n), ludarn, ludana, ludan
revere (v), thufirs, thufisho, thufisho
reverence (n), thufirsh, thufisha, thufish
reverend (n doer), thufirshwan, thufishua,
    thufishua
reverent (adj), thufirshu, thufishu, thufishu
reverently (adv), thufirshiu, thufishiu, thufishiu
reversal (n), lutharfarl, lutharifala, lutharfal
reverse (n), lutharaf, lutharifa, lutharf
reverse (v), lutharasf, lutharifo, lutharfo
reversible (adj), lutharafu, lutharifu, lutharfu
reversion (n), lutharak, lutharika, luthark
revert (v), lutharask, lecithariko, lutharko
reverter (n doer), lutharakwan, lutharikua,
    lutharkua
review (n), lufualt, lufuata, lufuat
review (v), lufualst, lufuato, lufuato
reviewer (n doer), lufualtwan, lufuatua, lufuatua
revile (v), luzhaithsk, luzhaitho, luzhaitho
revise (v), lufiaishsk, lufiaisho, lufiaisho
revision (n), lufiaishk, lufiaisha, lufiaish
revisionism (n), lufiaishkuet, lufiaishueta,
    lufiaishuet
revisionist (n doer), lufiaishkuetwan, lufiaishuetua,
    lufiaishuetua
revisit (v), lukelirsk, lukeliko, lukelko
revisitation (n), lukelirk, lukelika, lukelk
revitalization (n), lumaigirf, lumaigifa, lumaigif
revitalize (v), lumaigirsf, lumaigifo, lumaigifo
revival (n), lushlaurf, lushelaufa, lushlauf
revivalist (n doer), lushlaurfwan, lushelaufua,
    lushlaufua
revive (v), lushlaursf, lushelaufo, lushlaufo
reviver (n doer), lushlaurfwan, lushelaufua,
    lushlaufua
revocable (adj), lushairku, lushaiku, lushaiku
revocation (n), lushairk, lushaika, lushaik
revoke (v), lushairsk, lushaiko, lushaiko
revolt (n), kenirk, kenika, kenk
revolt (v), kenirsk, keniko, kenko
revolter (n doer), kenirkwan, kenikua, kenkua
revolution (n d:journey around), lukemirf,
    lukemifa, lukemif
revolution (n d:political change), kenirf, kenifa,
    kenf
revolutionary (adj d:political change), kenirfu,
    kenifu, kenfu
revolutionary (n doer d:political change),

kenirfwan, kenifua, kenfua
revolutionize (v d:political change), kenirsf, kenifo,
    kenfo
revolve (v d:journey around), lukemirsf, lukemifo,
    lukemifo
revolver (n doer d:journey around), lukemirfwan,
    lukemifua, lukemifua
revulse (v), lutrelzbe, luterebo, lutrebo
revulsion (n), lutrelbe, lutereba, lutreb
revulsive (adj), lutrelbu, luterebu, lutrebu
reward (n), luhaursh, luhausha, luhaush
reward (v), luhaurs, luhausho, luhausho
rewarder (n doer), luhaurshwan, luhaushua,
    luhaushua
rewind (v), luthrairsk, lutheraiko, luthraiko
rewire (v), lushnirsf, lushenifo, lushnifo
rework (v), lukiorsk, lukioko, lukioko
rewound (v pa), luthrairskyot, lutheraikio,
    luthraikio
rewrite (n), luloirde, luloida, luloid
rewrite (v), luloirzde, luloido, luloido
rewriter (n doer), luloirdwan, luloidua, luloidua
rewrote (v pa), luloirzdyot, luloidio, luloidio
Rhenium (n davoka), Irak, Irak, Irak
Rhenium (n), Renium, Reniuma, Renium
rhetoric (n), noishirk, noishika, noishk
rhetorical (adj), noishirku, noishiku, noishku
rhetorically (adv), noishirkiu, noishikiu, noishkiu
rho (n), roln, rona, ron
Rhode Island (n), Roderf Ilanurd, Rodefa Ilanuda,
    Rodef Ilanud
Rhodium (n davoka), Ilok, Ilok, Ilok
Rhodium (n), Rodium, Rodiuma, Rodium
rhyme (n), niorp, niopa, niop
rhyme (v), niorsp, niopo, niopo
rhymer (n doer), niorpwan, niopua, niopua
rhythm (n), niorpat, niopata, niopat
rhythmic (adj), niorpatu, niopatu, niopatu
rhythmically (adv), niorpatiu, niopatiu, niopatiu
rib (n), droifp, deroifa, droif
rib (v), droifsp, deroifo, droifo
ribbon (n), panran, panerala, panral
rice (n), frunf, feruna, frun
rich (adj), shtuvaru, shetufu, shtufu
rich (n), shtuvarp, shetufipa, shtufp
richer (adj), shtuvarwelu, shetufwelu, shtufwelu
richest (adj), shtuvarweku, shetufweku, shtufweku
richly (adv), shtuvariu, shetufiu, shtufiu
Richmond (n), Rishmonurd, Rishemonuda,
    Rishmonud
richness (n), shtuvaruet, shetufueta, shtufuet
ricochet (n), gruthoshk, geruthoka, gruthok
ricochet (v), gruthoshsk, geruthoko, gruthoko
rid (v pa), firaspyot, firopio, firpio
rid (v), firasp, firopo, firpo
riddance (n), firap, firopa, firp
ridder (n doer), firapwan, firopua, firpua
riddle (n), tudarl, tudala, tudal
riddle (v), tudarsle, tudalo, tudalo
ride (n), shlirbe, sheliba, shlib
ride (v), shlirzbe, shelibo, shlibo
rider (n doer), shlirbwan, shelibua, shlibua
ridge (n), shlirf, shelifa, shlif

ridicule (n), firak, firoka, firk
ridicule (v), firask, firoko, firko
ridiculous (adj), firaku, firoku, firku
ridiculously (adv), firakiu, firokiu, firkiu
Ridium (n davoka), Irok, Irok, Irok
riff (n), frufk, ferufa, fruf
rifle (n), firtesh, firotesha, firtsh
rifle (v), firtes, firotesho, firtsho
rifler (n doer), firteshwan, firoteshua, firtshua
rift (n), frufit, ferufita, fruft
rig (n), norak, norika, nork
rig (v), norask, noriko, norko
rigger (n doer), norakwan, norikua, norkua
right (adj d:correct), dierku, dieku, dieku
right (adj d:direction), relshu, reshu, reshu
right (n d:correct), dierk, dieka, diek
right (n d:direction), relsh, resha, resh
right (n d:ownership), ruarsh, ruasha, ruash
right (v d:correct), diersk, dieko, dieko
righteous (adj), dierkuetu, diekuetu, diekuetu
righteous (n doer), dierkuetwan, diekuetua,
    diekuetua
righteously (adv), dierkuetiu, diekuetiu, diekuetiu
righteousness (n), dierkuet, diekueta, diekuet
righter (n doer d:correct), dierkwan, diekua, diekua
rightful (adj), diekierpu, diekiepu, diekiepu
rightfully (adv), diekierpiu, diekiepiu, diekiepiu
rightly (adv d:correct), dierkiu, diekiu, diekiu
rightness (n), dierkuet, diekueta, diekuet
rightward (adj), reshaurshu, reshaushu, reshaushu
rightwing (adj), reshkliergu, reshekeliegu,
    reshkliegu
righty (n), reshkarp, reshekapa, reshkap
rigid (adj), kleirdu, keleidu, kleidu
rigidity (n), kleirde, keleida, kleid
rigidly (adv), kleirdiu, keleidiu, kleidiu
rigor (n), kleidarn, keleidana, kleidan
rigorous (adj), kleidarnu, keleidanu, kleidanu
rigorously (adv), kleidarniu, keleidaniu, kleidaniu
rim (n), droilf, derolla, droil
rind (n), shpalp, shipapa, shpap
ring (n d:circle), ritran, riterala, ritral
ring (n d:sound), keminork, keminoka, kemink
ring (v d:circle), ritrasne, riteralo, ritralo
ring (v d:sound), keminorsk, keminoko, keminko
ringer (n doer d:circle), ritranwan, riteralua,
    ritralua
ringer (n doer d:sound), keminorkwan, keminokua,
    keminkua
ringleader (n), ritralirt, riteralita, ritralt
ringmaster (n), ritrathiork, riterathioka, ritrathiok
ringside (adj), ritrashoirtu, riterashoitu, ritrashoitu
ringside (n), ritrashoirt, riterashoita, ritrashoit
rink (n), kianirk, kianika, kiank
rinse (n), noirsh, noisha, noish
rinse (v), noirs, noisho, noisho
rinser (n doer), noirshwan, noishua, noishua
riot (n), briaurk, beriauka, briauk
riot (v), briaursk, beriauko, briauko
rioter (n doer), briaurkwan, beriaukua, briaukua
rip (n), frulbe, feruba, frub
rip (v), frulzbe, ferubo, frubo
ripe (adj), dubartu, dubatu, dubatu

ripen (v), dubarst, dubato, dubato
ripeness (n), dubart, dubata, dubat
ripoff (n), frulbunf, ferubunefa, frubunf
ripper (n doer), frulbwan, ferubua, frubua
ripple (n), firfp, fifepa, fifp
ripple (v), firfsp, fifepo, fifpo
rise (n), luirsh, luisha, luish
rise (v), luirs, luisho, luisho
riser (n doer), luirshwan, luishua, luishua
risk (n), vomark, vomaka, vomak
risk (v), vomarsk, vomako, vomako
riskily (adv), vomarkiu, vomakiu, vomakiu
riskiness (n), vomark, vomaka, vomak
risky (adj), vomarku, vomaku, vomaku
rite (n), nuarsh, nuasha, nuash
ritual (n), nuatsh, nuatipa, nuatip
ritualistic (adj), nuatshu, nuatipu, nuatipu
ritualize (v), nuats, nuatipo, nuatipo
rival (n), nuarbe, nuaba, nuab
rival (v), nuarzbe, nuabo, nuabo
rivalry (n), nuarbak, nuabaka, nuabak
river (n), frulsh, ferusha, frush
riverbank (n), frushplirk, ferushepelara, frushplar
riverboat (n), frushkorbe, ferushekoba, frushkob
riverfront (n), frushflarsh, ferushefelarina,
    frushflarn
riverhead (n), frushkefirt, ferushekefita, frushkeft
riverside (n), frushoirt, ferushoita, frushoit
roadway (n), frushpliorl, terelishepeliola,
    trelshpliol
roam (v), graunsk, gerauno, grauno
roar (n), graufk, geraufa, grauf
roar (v), graufsk, geraufo, graufo
roast (n), nimurf, nimufa, nimuf
roast (v), nimursf, nimufo, nimufo
roaster (n doer), nimurfwan, nimufua, nimufua
rob (v), kirasp, kiropo, kirpo
robber (n doer), kirapwan, kiropua, kirpua
robbery (n), kirap, kiropa, kirp
robe (n), priufp, periupa, priup
robot (n), kipart, kipata, kipat
robotic (adj), kipartu, kipatu, kipatu
robotically (adv), kipartiu, kipatiu, kipatiu
robust (adj), sharluirmu, shareluimu, sharluimu
robustness (n), sharluirme, shareluima, sharluim
Rochester (n), Rotesharf, Roteshara, Roteshar
rock (n d:stone), tsharak, tesharika, tshark
rock (v d:sway), zhiarsne, zhiano, zhiano
rocker (n doer d:sway), zhiarnwan, zhianua,
    zhianua
rocket (n), zhiarat, zhiarita, zhiart
rocket (v), zhiarast, zhiarito, zhiarto
rocky (adj d:stone), tsharaku, teshariku, tsharku
rod (n), diraf, dirifa, dirf
rode (v pa), shlirzbyot, shelibio, shlibio
Roentgenium (n davoka), Inat, Inat, Inat
Roentgenium (n), Roentgenium, Roenetugeniuma,

Roentgenium
rogate (v), laransk, larano, larano
rogation (n), larank, larana, laran
roil (v), grauthsk, gerautho, grautho
role (n), meiraf, meirifa, meirf
roll (n d:bread), larth, latha, lath
roll (n d:tumble), falar, falira, falir
roll (v d:tumble), falasre, faliro, faliro
rollback (n), falarvark, falirevaka, falirvak
roller (n doer d:tumble), falarwan, falirua, falirua
rollout (n), falaruil, faliruila, faliruil
rollover (n), falarafen, falirafena, falirafen
Roman (n), Romafarn, Romafana, Romafan
romance (n), loinarme, loinama, loinam
romancer (n doer), loinarmwan, loinamua,
    loinamua
Romania (n), Romiarf, Romiafa, Romiaf
Romanian (n), Romiarn, Romiana, Romian
romantic (adj), loinarmu, loinamu, loinamu
romanticize (v), loinarzme, loinamo, loinamo
romatically (adv), loinarmiu, loinamiu, loinamiu
Rome (n), Romarf, Romafa, Romaf
romp (n), gielp, giepa, giep
romp (v), gielsp, giepo, giepo
roof (n), larfp, larifa, larf
roof (v), larfsp, larifo, larfo
roofer (n doer), larfpwan, larifua, larfua
rooftop (n), larfdaurp, larifedaupa, larfdaup
room (n), shranf, sherana, shran
room (v), shransf, sherano, shrano
roomful (adj), shranfiepu, sheraniepu, shraniepu
roommate (n), shranflen, sheranelena, shranlen
roomy (adj), shranfu, sheranu, shranu
root (n), wefirp, wefipa, wefp
root (v), wefirsp, wefipo, wefpo
rope (n), varp, vapa, vap
rope (v), varsp, vapo, vapo
roper (n doer), varpwan, vapua, vapua
rose (n), fliarth, feliatha, fliath
rose (v pa), luirsyot, luishio, luishio
rosebud (n), fliathpoarp, feliathepoapa, fliathpoap
roster (n), briadirt, beriadita, briadit
rosy (adj), fliarthu, feliathu, fliathu
rot (n), dirap, diropa, dirp
rot (v), dirasp, diropo, dirpo
rotary (adj), diorshtu, dioritu, diortu
rotate (v), diorshst, diorito, diorto
rotation (n), diorsht, diorita, diort
rotational (adj), diorshtu, dioritu, diortu
rotator (n doer), diorshtwan, dioritua, diortua
rotor (n), diorshtar, dioritata, diortar
rough (adj), grolgu, gerogu, grogu
rough (v), grolzge, gerogo, grogo
roughen (v), dheigrolzge, dheigerogo, dheigrogo
roughly (adv), grolgiu, gerogiu, grogiu
roughneck (n), grogplorn, gerogepelona, grogplon
roughness (n), grolge, geroga, grog
round (adj), blaithpu, belaithu, blaithu
round (n), blaithp, belaitha, blaith
round (v), blaithsp, belaitho, blaitho
roundabout (adj), blaithoveipu, belaithoveipu,
    blaithoveipu
roundabout (n), blaithoveip, belaithoveipa,
    blaithoveip
roundhouse (n), blaithkiarf, belaithekiafa,
    blaithkiaf
roundly (adv), blaithpiu, belaithiu, blaithiu
roundness (n), blaithpuet, belaithueta, blaithuet
roundtable (n), blaithdoiart, belaithedoiara,
    blaithdoiar
roundtrip (adj), blaithglarudu, belaithegelarudu,
    blaithglardu
roundup (n), blaithiveil, belaithiveila, blaithiveil
rouse (v), peiarst, peiato, peiato
rout (n d:defeat), peisht, peita, peit
rout (n d:dig), wefirk, wefika, wefk
rout (v d:defeat), peishst, peito, peito
rout (v d:dig), wefirsk, wefiko, wefko
route (n d:path), prailk, peraika, praik
route (v d:path), prailsk, peraiko, praiko
router (n doer d:dig), wefirkwan, wefikua, wefkua
router (n doer d:path), prailkwan, peraikua,
    praikua
routine (adj), praikartu, peraikatu, praikatu
routine (n), praikart, peraikata, praikat
routinely (adv), praikartiu, peraikatiu, praikatiu
rove (v), treithsk, tereitho, treitho
rover (n doer), treithkwan, tereithua, treithua
row (n d:column), bloirn, beloina, bloin
row (v d:paddle), trefirst, terefito, trefto
rower (n doer d:paddle), trefirtwan, terefitua,
    treftua
royal (adj), thiulfu, thiulu, thiulu
royally (adv), thiulfiu, thiuliu, thiuliu
royalty (n), thiulf, thiula, thiul
Rs (let pl), relri, relri, relri
rub (n), varve, vava, vav
rub (v), varzve, vavo, vavo
rubber (n), plovarth, pelovatha, plovath
rubbery (adj), plovarthu, pelovathu, plovathu
rubbish (n), plovark, pelovaka, plovak
rubble (n), prashirk, perashika, prashk
Rubidium (n davoka), Alap, Alap, Alap
Rubidium (n), Rubidium, Rubidiuma, Rubidium
ruby (n), liorp, liopa, liop
rudder (n), guparp, gupapa, gupap
rude (adj), kadarku, kadaku, kadaku
rudely (adv), kadarkiu, kadakiu, kadakiu
rudeness (n), kadark, kadaka, kadak
rue (n), bulirf, bulifa, bulf
rue (v), bulirsf, bulifo, bulfo
rug (n), narap, naripa, narp
ruin (n), daivurge, dalvuga, daivg
ruin (v), daivurzge, daivugo, daivgo
rule (n), larat, larita, lart
rule (v), larast, larito, larto
rulebook (n), lartvornt, laritevonuda, lartvond
ruler (n doer), laratwan, laritua, lartua
rum (n), liran, lirina, lirn
rumble (n), riufp, riufa, riuf
rumble (v), riufsp, riufo, riufo
rumor (n), thirolt, thirota, thirt
rumor (v), thirolst, thiroto, thirto
rumour (n), thirolt, thirota, thirt
rumour (v), thirolst, thiroto, thirto
rump (n), gioip, gioifa, gioif

run (n), laorme, laoma, laom
run (v), laorzme, laomo, laomo
runaround (n), laomoblaithp, laomobelaitha, laomoblaith
runaway (n), laomopliorl, laomopeliola, laomopliol
rundown (n), laomtiern, laometiena, laomtien
rung (n d:step), trushk, terusha, trush
runner (n doer), laormwan, laomua, laomua
runny (adj), laormu, laomu, laomu
runoff (n), laomurnf, laomunefa, laomunf
runway (n), laompliorl, laomepeloila, laompliol
rupture (n), gaiftarge, gaifotaga, gaiftag
rupture (v), gaiftarzge, gaifotago, gaiftago
rural (adj), shorapu, shoripu, shorpu
ruse (n), bliushk, beliusha, bliush
rush (n), blufit, belufita, bluft
rush (v), blufist, belufito, blufto
Russia (n), Rushiarf, Rushiafa, Rushiaf
Russian (n), Rushiarn, Rushiana, Rushian
rust (n), blufik, belufika, blufk
rust (v), blufisk, belufiko, blufko
rustily (adv), blufikiu, belufikiu, blufkiu
rustle (v), bluthsk, belutho, blutho
rustler (n doer), bluthkwan, beluthua, bluthua
rusty (adj), blufiku, belufiku, blufku
rut (n), katark, kataka, katak
ruth (n), binuk, binufa, binuf
Ruthenium (n davoka), Ilik, Ilik, Ilik
Ruthenium (n), Ruthenium, Rutheniuma, Ruthenium
Rutherfordium (n davoka), Inip, Inip, Inip
Rutherfordium (n), Rutherfordium, Rutheriforudiuma, Rutherfordium
ruthless (adj), binukmenu, binufemenu, binufmenu
ruthlessly (adv), binukmeniu, binufemeniu, binufmeniu
ruthlessness (n), binukmen, binufemena, binufmen
S (let sng), seil, seia, sei
sabotage (n), biaushk, biauka, biauk
sabotage (v), biaushsk, biauko, biauko
saboteur (n doer), biaushkwan, biaukua, biaukua
sack (n), thoilf, thoila, thoil
sack (v), thoilsf, thoilo, thoilo
sacker (n doer), thoilfwan, thoilua, thoilua
Sacramento (n), Shakramenirt, Shakeramenita, Shakrament
sacred (adj), biafarfu, biafafu, biafafu
sacrifice (n), biafirt, biafita, biaft
sacrifice (v), biafirst, biafito, biafto
sacrificer (n doer), biafirtwan, biafitua, biaftua
sacrificial (adj), biafirtu, biafitu, biaftu
sacrificially (adv), biafirtiu, biafitiu, biaftiu
sacrilege (n), biafark, biafaka, biafak
sacriligous (adj), biafarku, biafaku, biafaku
sad (adj), biargu, biagu, biagu
sadden (v), biarzge, biago, biago
saddle (n), biorn, biona, bion
saddle (v), biorsne, biono, biono
saddlebag (n), bionufaf, bionefanafa, bionfnaf
sadism (n), biausht, biauta, biaut
sadist (n doer), biaushtwan, biautua, biautua
sadistic (adj), biaushtu, biautu, biautu
sadly (adv), biargiu, biagiu, biagiu

sadness (n), biarge, biaga, biag
safe (adj d:trustworthy), zhurdu, zhudu, zhudu
safe (n d:storage), zhiuft, zhiuta, zhiut
safeguard (n), zhurduet, zhudueta, zhuduet
safeguard (v d:trustworthy), zhurzde, zhudo, zhudo
safekeep (v), zhudeklorsf, zhudekelofo, zhudeklofo
safekept (v pa), zhudeklorsfyot, zhudekelofio, zhudeklofio
safely (adv d:trustworthy), zhurdiu, zhudiu, zhudiu
safer (adj), zhurdwelu, zhudwelu, zhudwelu
safest (adj), zhurdwaku, zhudwaku, zhudwaku
safety (n d:trustworthy), zhurde, zhuda, zhud
sag (n), fraunk, ferauka, frauk
sag (v), fraunsk, ferauko, frauko
said (v pa), zhursyot, zhushio, zhushio
sail (n), fluarl, feluala, flual
sail (v), fluarsle, felualo, flualo
sailboat (n), flualshkorbe, felualeshekoba, flualshkob
sailor (n doer), fluarlwan, felualua, flualua
sake (n), moark, moaka, moak
salad (n), troirt, teroita, troit
salary (n), trelfirt, terelofita, trelfit
sale (n), trelirf, terelifa, trelf
saleable (adj), trelirfu, terelifu, trelfu
salesman (n doer), trelirfwan, terelifua, trelfua
salesmanship (n), trelirfuanfif, terelifuanefifa, trelfuanfif
salesperson (n doer), trelirfwan, terelifua, trelfua
salespersonship (n), trelirfuanfif, terelifuanefifa, trelfuanfif
salinate (v), luaithsk, luaitho, luaitho
saline (adj), luaithku, luaithu, luaithu
salinity (n), luaithk, luaitha, luaith
salmon (n), grilth, geritha, grith
salt (n), luarth, luatha, luath
salt (v), luarsth, luatho, luatho
salter (n doer), luarthwan, luathua, luathua
saltily (adv), luarthiu, luathiu, luathiu
saltwater (n), luatheidorn, luatheidona, luatheidon
salty (adj), luarthu, luathu, luathu
salutation (n), luaishkuet, luaikueta, luaikuet
salute (n), luaishk, luaika, luaik
salute (v), luaishsk, luaiko, luaiko
salvage (v), normarsk, norimako, normako
salvation (n), normark, norimaka, normak
Samarium (n davoka), Orik, Orik, Orik
Samarium (n), Shamarium, Shamariuma, Shamarium
same (adj), shlurnu, shelunu, shlunu
sameness (n), shlurn, sheluna, shlun
sample (n), thanberf, thanubera, thanber
sample (v), thanbersf, thanubero, thanbero
sampler (n doer), thanberfwan, thanuberua, thanberua
San Antonio (n), Shan Antoniorn, Shana Anitoniona, Shan Antonion
San Diego (n), Shan Diegorf, Shana Diegofa, Shan Diegof
San Francisco (n), Shan Franshirshk, Shana Feranoshishaka, Shan Franshishk
Sanau (n), Sanau, Sanau, Sanau
sanctify (v), dianirst, dianito, dianto

sanction (n), dianork, dianoka, diank
sanction (v), dianorsk, dianoko, dianko
sanctity (n), dianirt, dianita, diant
sand (n d:grains), narth, natha, nath
sand (v d:abrasion), naithsk, naitho, naitho
sandal (n), nathart, nathata, nathat
sandbag (n), nathnufaf, nathefanafa, nathfnaf
sandbar (n), nathrolart, natherolata, nathrolt
sandblast (v), nathkrairzge, nathekeraigo, nathkraigo
sandbox (n), nathprekun, natheperenika, nathprenk
sander (n doer d:abrasion), naithkwan, naithua, naithua
sandpaper (n), nathvuarp, nathevuapa, nathvuap
sandstone (n), nathbaraft, nathebarafa, nathbaraf
sandstorm (n), nathferap, natheferipa, nathfrip
sandwich (n), nornarn, norinana, nornan
sandwich (v), nornarsne, norinano, nornano
sandy (adj d:grains), narthu, nathu, nathu
sane (adj), shiarfu, shiafu, shiafu
sanely (adv), shiarfiu, shiafiu, shiafiu
sang (v pa), nelarsnyot, nelanio, nelnio
sanitary (adj), shiarnu, shianu, shianu
sanitation (n), shiarn, shiana, shian
sanitize (v), shiarsne, shiano, shiano
sanity (n), shiarf, shiafa, shiaf
sank (v pa), kiefstyot, kiefio, kiefio
Santa Barbara (n), Shant Barbaralf, Shanita Barubarafa, Shant Barbaraf
Santa Claus (n), Shantarf Klaursh, Shanitafa Kelausha, Shantaf Klaush
sap (n), shilfk, shilika, shilk
sap (v), shiaushsk, shiauko, shiauko
sapling (n), shilkarp, shilikapa, shilkap
sarcasm (n), toigaurp, toigaupa, toigaup
sarcastic (adj), toigaurpu, toigaupu, toigaupu
sarcastically (adv), toigaurpiu, toigaupiu, toigaupiu
sash (n), theithk, theitha, theith
sass (v), toiarst, toiato, toiato
sat (v pa), shrelstyot, sheretio, shretio
Satan (n), Shoidark, Shoidaka, Shoidak
satanic (adj), shoidarfku, shoidafiku, shoidafku
satanism (n), shoidarfk, shoidafika, shoidafk
satanist (n doer), shoidarfkwan, shoidafikua, shoidafkua
satanize (v), shoidarfsk, shoidafiko, shoidafko
satellite (n), pairth, paitha, paith
satiate (v), lauarsf, lauafo, lauafo
satiation (n), lauarf, lauafa, lauaf
satire (n), laiark, laiaka, laiak
satirical (adj), laiarku, laiaku, laiaku
satirist (n doer), laiarkwan, laiakua, laiakua
satirize (v), laiarsk, laiako, laiako
satisfaction (n), lauirt, lauita, lauit
satisfactory (adj), lauirtu, lauitu, lauitu
satisfy (v), lauirst, lauito, lauito
saturate (v), laiarsf, laiafo, laiafo
saturation (n), laiarf, laiafa, laiaf
Saturday (n), Shudaviurl, Shudaviula, Shudaviul
sauce (n), furf, fufa, fuf
sauce (v), fursf, fufo, fufo
saucepan (n), fufmelirk, fufemelika, fufmelk

saucer (n), furth, futha, futh
saucy (adj), furfu, fufu, fufu
Saudi (n), Shaudarn, Shaudana, Shaudan
Saudi Arabia (n), Shaudarf Arobarn, Shaudafa Arobana, Shaudaf Arban
sauna (n), fuarth, fuatha, fuath
saunter (v), fuarsf, fuafo, fuafo
sausage (n), fufarp, fufapa, fufap
savage (adj), noirmu, noimu, noimu
savage (n), noirme, noima, noim
savagely (adv), noirmiu, noimiu, noimiu
save (n), zhurp, zhupa, zhup
save (v), zhursp, zhupo, zhupo
saver (n doer), zhurpwan, zhupua, zhupua
savings (n), zhupart, zhupata, zhupat
savior (n), zhupanf, zhupana, zhupan
saviours (n), zhupanf, zhupana, zhupan
savor (v), zhuparsf, zhuparo, zhuparo
savvy (n), zhupeishk, zhupeisha, zhupeish
saw (n d:tool), gralzhe, gerazha, grazh
saw (v d:tool), gralze, gerazho, grazho
saw (v pa), thulsfyot, thulio, thulio
sawdust (n), grazhkreishk, gerazhekereisha, grazhkreish
sawmill (n), grazhfenirp, gerazhefenipa, grazhfenp
saxophone (n), motuyarp, motuyapa, motuyap
say (n), zhursh, zhusha, zhush
say (v), zhurs, zhusho, zhusho
sayer (n doer), zhurshwan, zhushua, zhushua
scab (n), shralge, sheraga, shrag
scalable (adj d:measure), shtathku, shetathu, shtathu
scalar (n), shtathkar, shetathara, shtathar
scale (n d:climb), shuirk, shuika, shuik
scale (n d:fish), shralk, sheraka, shrak
scale (n d:measure), shtathk, shetatha, shtath
scale (v d:climb), shuirsk, shuiko, shuiko
scale (v d:fish), shralsk, sherako, shrako
scallop (n), finorak, finorika, finork
scallop (v), finorask, finoriko, finorko
scalp (n), fnorat, fenoruta, fnort
scalp (v), fnorast, fenoruto, fnorto
scalpel (n), fnorasht, fenorutata, fnortat
scalper (n doer), fnoratwan, fenorutua, fnortua
scam (n), blurzhe, beluzha, bluzh
scam (v), blurze, beluzho, bluzho
scammer (n doer), blurzhwan, beluzhua, bluzhua
scan (n), liarn, liana, lian
scan (v), liarsne, liano, liano
scandal (n), limark, limaka, limak
scandalize (v), limarsk, limako, limako
scandalous (adj), limarku, limaku, limaku
scandalously (adv), limarkiu, limakiu, limakiu
Scandium (n davoka), Ifap, Ifap, Ifap
Scandium (n), Shkandium, Shekanediuma, Shkandium
scanner (n doer), liarnwan, lianua, lianua
scant (n), trilank, terilana, trilan
scant (v), trilansk, terilano, trilano
scantily (adv), trilankiu, terilankiu, trilaniu
scanty (adj), trilanku, terilanu, trilanu
scapegoat (n), shiakbliert, shiakebelieta, shiakbliet
scar (n), gorsh, golisha, golsh

scar (v), gors, golisho, golsho
scarce (adj), lemurtu, lemutu, lemutu
scarcely (adv), lemurtoiu, lemutoiu, lemutoiu
scarcity (n), lemurt, lemuta, lemut
scare (n), goshirk, goshika, goshk
scare (v), goshirsk, goshiko, goshko
scarecrow (n), goshkviarfk, goshikeviaroka, goshkviark
scarf (n), liarth, liatha, liath
scarier (adj), goshirkwelu, goshikwelu, goshkwelu
scariest (adj), goshirkweku, goshikweku, goshkweku
scarlet (adj), fielirshu, fielishu, fielshu
scarlet (n), fielirsh, fielisha, fielsh
scary (adj), goshirku, goshiku, goshku
scat (interj), shkwak, shwaka, shwak
scathe (v), fnarthsk, fenaritho, fnartho
scatter (v), fenirst, fenito, fento
scavenge (v), trilushsk, teriluko, triluko
scavenger (n doer), trilushkwan, terilukua, trilukua
scenario (n), thulparsh, thulipasha, thulpash
scene (n), thulirp, thulipa, thulp
scenery (n), thuliarp, thuliapa, thuliap
scenic (adj), thulirpu, thulipu, thulpu
scent (n), liraf, lirifa, lirf
scent (v), lirasf, lirifo, lirfo
scepter (n), voshark, voshaka, voshak
sceptic (n doer), kluaishkwan, keluaikua, kluaikua
sceptical (adj), kluaishku, keluaiku, kluaiku
scepticism (n), kluaishk, keluaika, kluaik
sceptre (n), voshark, voshaka, voshak
schedule (n), ridarf, ridafa, ridaf
schedule (v), ridarsf, ridafo, ridafo
scheduler (n doer), ridarfwan, ridafua, ridafua
schema (n), thuzhart, thuzhata, thuzhat
schematic (adj), thuzhunku, thuzhunu, thuzhunu
schematic (n), thuzhunk, thuzhuna, thuzhun
scheme (n), thurzhe, thuzha, thuzh
scheme (v), thurze, thuzho, thuzho
schemer (n doer), thurzhwan, thuzhua, thuzhua
schism (n pl), shkaurpyek, shekaupi, shkaupi
schism (n), shkaurp, shekaupa, shkaup
scholar (n doer), shepelpwan, shepepua, shpepua
scholarly (adv), shepelpiu, shepepiu, shpepiu
scholarship (n), shepelpfif, shepepefifa, shpepfif
scholastic (adj), shepelpu, shepepu, shpepu
school (n), shpersh, shepesha, shpesh
school (v), shpers, shepesho, shpesho
schoolbooks (n), shpeshvornt, shepeshevonuda, shpeshvond
schoolboy (n), shpeshbiurn, shepeshebiuna, shpeshbiun
schoolchild (n), shpeshluart, shepesheluara, shpeshluar
schoolchildren (n pl), shpeshluartyek, shepesheluari, shpeshluari
schoolgirl (n), shpeshkelerf, shepeshekelera, shpeshkeler
schoolhouse (n), shpeshkiarf, shepeshekiafa, shpeshkiaf
schoolmate (n), shpershlen, shepeshelena, shpeshlen
schoolteacher (n), shpeshdalirsh, shepeshedalisha, shpeshdalsh

schoolyard (n), shpeshthauthk, shepeshethautha, shpeshthauth
science (n), shuarsh, shuasha, shuash
scientific (adj), shuarshu, shuashu, shuashu
scientifically (adv), shuarshiu, shuashiu, shuashiu
scientist (n doer), shuarshwan, shuashua, shuashua
scissor (v), shlirs, shelisho, shlisho
scissors (n), shlirsh, shelisha, shlish
scoff (v), kloishsk, keloisho, kloisho
scold (v), klorist, kelorito, klorto
scoop (n), kliarf, keliafa, kliaf
scoop (v), kliarsf, keliafo, kliafo
scooper (n doer), kliarfwan, keliafua, kliafua
scoot (v), shkiathsk, shekiatho, shkiatho
scooter (n doer), shkiathkwan, shekiathua, shkiathua
scope (n), kluarf, keluafa, kluaf
scope (v), kluarsf, keluafo, kluafo
scoper (n doer), kluarfwan, keluafua, kluafua
scorch (n), klairshk, kelaishoka, klaishk
scorch (v), klairshsk, kelaishoko, klaishko
scorcher (n doer), klairshkwan, kelaishokua, klaishkua
score (n), klairt, kelaita, klait
score (v), klairst, kelaito, klaito
scoreboard (n), klaitplok, kelaitepelorika, klaitplork
scorecard (n), klaitgaurn, kelaitekauna, klaitkaun
scoreless (adj), klairtmenu, kelaitemenu, klaitmenu
scorer (n doer), klairtwan, kelaitua, klaitua
scorn (n), klorip, keloripa, klorp
scorn (v), klorisp, keloripo, klorpo
scorner (n doer), kloripwan, keloripua, klorpua
scornful (adj), kloripu, keloripu, klorpu
scornfully (adv), kloripiu, keloripiu, klorpiu
Scotland (n), Shkotlanirf, Shekotelanifa, Shkotlanf
Scottish (n), Shkotlarn, Shekotelana, Shkotlan
scour (v), kliaushsk, keliausho, kliausho
scourge (n), kliaup, keliaufa, kliauf
scourge (v), kliausp, keliaufo, kliaufo
scout (n), kliarzhe, keliazha, kliazh
scout (v), kliarze, keliazho, kliazho
scoutmaster (n), kliazhthiork, keliazhethioka, kliazhthiok
scramble (n), kralirk, keralika, kralk
scramble (v), kralirsk, keraliko, kralko
scrambler (n doer), kralirkwan, keralikua, kralkua
scrap (n), klarf, kelafa, klaf
scrap (v), klarsf, kelafo, klafo
scrapbook (n), klafevornt, kelafevonuda, klafevond
scrape (n), kladirp, keladipa, kladip
scrape (v), kladirsp, keladipo, kladipo
scraper (n doer), kladirpwan, keladipua, kladipua
scrapper (n doer), klarfwan, kelafua, klafua
scrappy (adj), klarfu, kelafu, klafu
scratch (n), klamurt, kelamuta, klamut
scratch (v), klamurst, kelamuto, klamuto
scratcher (n doer), klamurtwan, kelamutua, klamutua
scratchy (adj), klamurtu, kelamutu, klamutu
scream (n), kioirk, kioika, kioik
scream (v), kioirsk, kioiko, kioiko
screamer (n doer), kioirkwan, kioikua, kioikua

screech (n), kiaurk, kiauka, kiauk
screech (v), kiaursk, kiauko, kiauko
screecher (n doer), kiaurkwan, kiaukua, kiaukua
screen (n), fklert, fikoleta, fklet
screen (v), fklerst, fikoleto, fkleto
screener (n doer), fklertwan, fikoletua, fkletua
screenplay (n), fkletfruifk, fikoleteferuifa, fkletfruif
screenwriter (n doer), fkletloirdwan, fikoleteloidua, fkletloidua
screw (n), kloirp, keloipa, kloip
screw (v), kloirsp, keloipo, kloipo
screwdriver (n doer), kloipdiarpwan, keloipediapua, kloipdiapua
screwer (n doer), kloirpwan, keloipua, kloipua
screwy (adj), kloirpu, keloipu, kloipu
scribble (n), sherge, sheriga, shrig
scribble (v), sherzge, sherigo, shrigo
scribe (n doer), shergwan, sherigua, shrigua
scrimp (v), kliefsk, keliefo, kliefo
script (n), shrielp, sheriepa, shriep
script (v), shrielsp, sheriepo, shriepo
scriptural (adj), shriepartu, sheriepatu, shriepatu
scripture (n), shriepart, sheriepata, shriepat
scroll (n), kranirf, keranifa, kranf ·
scroll (v), kranirsf, keranifo, kranfo
scrounge (v), kliufsp, keliupo, kliupo
scrub (n), shrairk, sheraika, shraik
scrub (v), shrairsk, sheraiko, shraiko
scrubber (n doer), shrairkwan, sheraikua, shraikua
scrubby (adj), shrairku, sheraiku, shraiku
scruff (n), glieft, geliefa, glief
scruffy (adj), glieftu, geliefu, gliefu
scrunch (v), bliaushsk, beliausho, bliausho
scruple (n), thriuft, theriuta, thriut
scruple (v), thriufst, theriuto, thriuto
scrupulous (adj), thriuftu, theriutu, thriutu
scrupulously (adv), thriuftiu, theriutiu, thriutiu
scrutinize (v), thraufsk, therauko, thrauko
scrutiny (n), thraufk, therauka, thrauk
scuff (n), shraiafk, sheraiafa, shraiaf
scuff (v), shraiafsk, sheraiafo, shraiafo
scuffle (n), shraiarp, sheraiapa, shraiap
scuffle (v), shraiarsp, sheraiapo, shraiapo
sculpt (v), flurisp, feluripo, flurpo
sculptor (n doer), fluripwan, feluripua, flurpua
sculptural (adj), fluripu, feluripu, flurpu
sculpturally (adv), fluripiu, feluripiu, flurpiu
sculpture (n), flurip, feluripa, flurp
scum (n), flurge, feluga, flug
scurry (v), klivursk, kelivuko, klivuko
scuttle (v), shkursf, shekufo, shkufo
scuttlebutt (n), shkufblaishk, shekufebelaika, shkufblaik
sea (n), shkleirn, shikeleina, shklein
seabed (n), shkleinfamor, shikeleinefuarema, shkleinfuarm
Seaborgium (n davoka), Inup, Inup, Inup
Seaborgium (n), Sheaborgium, Sheaboragiuma, Sheaborgium
seacoast (n), shkleinbranar, shikeleineberanifa, shkleinbranf
seafare (v), shkleinthirsk, shikeleinethiko, shkleinthiko

seafood (n), shkleinparsh, shikeleinepasha, shkleinpash
seafront (n), shkleinflarsh, shikeleinefelarina, shkleinflarn
seagate (n), shkleinparlak, shikeleineperelika, shkleinprelk
seagull (n), shkleinkiarme, shikeleinekiama, shkleinkiam
seahawk (n), shkleinklierk, shikeleinekelieka, shkleinkliek
seal (n d:animal), thoirn, thoina, thoin
seal (n d:binding), zhoirve, zhoiva, zhoiv
seal (v d:binding), zhoirzve, zhoivo, zhoivo
sealant (n doer d:binding), zhoirvwan, zhoivua, zhoivua
seam (n), zhoiant, zhoiana, zhoian
seam (v), zhoianst, zhoiano, zhoiano
seaman (n), shkleinplorn, shikeleinepelona, shkleinplon
seamen (n pl), shkleinplornyek, shikeleinepeloni, shkleinploni
seamless (adj), zhoiantmenu, zhoianemenu, zhoianmenu
seamlessly (adv), zhoiantmeniu, zhoianemeniu, zhoianmeniu
seamstress (n), zhoianoishk, zhoianoisha, zhoianoish
seaport (n), shkleinbielirk, shikeleinebielika, shkleinbielk
sear (v), klioishsk, kelioisho, klioisho
search (n), krolsh, kerosha, krosh
search (v), krols, kerosho, krosho
searcher (n doer), krolshwan, keroshua, kroshua
searchlight (n), kroshfluarn, keroshefeluana, kroshfluan
seashell (n), shkleintherk, shikeleinetheka, shkleinthek
seaside (adj), shkleinshoirtu, shikeleineshoitu, shkleinshoitu
seaside (n), shkleinshoirt, shikeleineshoita, shkleinshoit
season (n d:climate), fivarl, fivala, fival
season (n d:spice), dutharp, duthapa, duthap
season (v d:spice), dutharsp, duthapo, duthapo
seasonal (adj d:climate), fivarlu, fivalu, fivalu
seasonally (adv d:climate), fivarliu, fivaliu, fivaliu
seat (n), shrilk, sherika, shrik
seat (v), shrilsk, sheriko, shriko
seatbelt (n), shrikdakelf, shorikadafika, shrikdatk
Seattle (n), Shiatalf, Shiatala, Shiatal
seawater (n), shkleineidorn, shikeleineidona, shkleineidon
seaway (n), shkleinpliorl, shikeleinepeliola, shkleinpliol
seaweed (n), shkleinyurk, shikeleinyuka, shkleinyuk
secede (v), drivelsk, deriveko, driveko
secession (n), drivelk, deriveka, drivek
seclude (v), drigruts, derigeruto, drigruto
seclusion (n), drigrutsh, derigeruta, drigrut
second (n d:time), zhokerme, zhokema, zhokem
second (num 2 ord), aveth, aveth, aveth
secondary (adj), avetharu, avetharu, avetharu

secondary (n), avethar, avethara, avethar
secondhand (adj), avethkarpu, avethekapu,
　avethkapu
secondly (adv d:count), avethiu, avethiu, avethiu
secrecy (n), shevirsht, shevishota, shevisht
secret (adj), shevirshu, shevishu, shevishu
secret (n), shevirsh, shevisha, shevish
secretary (n), delgelf, delagela, delgel
secrete (v), gleirst, geleito, gleito
secretion (n), gleirt, geleita, gleit
secretive (adj), shevirshu, shevishu, shevishu
secretively (adv), shevirshiu, shevishiu, shevishiu
secretly (adv), shevirshiu, shevishiu, shevishiu
sect (n), thish, thisha, thish
sectarian (n doer), thishankwan, thishanua,
　thishanua
sectarianism (n), thishank, thishana, thishan
section (n), thisharl, thishala, thishal
section (v), thisharsle, thishalo, thishalo
sectional (adj), thisharlu, thishalu, thishalu
sector (n), thisharp, thishapa, thishap
secular (adj), thishianku, thishianu, thishianu
secularist (n doer), thishiankwan, thishianua,
　thishianua
secularly (adv), thishiankiu, thishianiu, thishianiu
secure (adj), vartulfu, varitufu, vartufu
secure (v), vartulsf, varitufo, vartufo
securely (adv), vartulfiu, varitufiu, vartufiu
security (n), vartulf, varitufa, vartuf
sedate (v), drikarst, derikato, drikato
sedation (n), drikart, derikata, drikat
sedative (adj), drikartu, derikatu, drikatu
sedative (n doer), drikartwan, derikatua, drikatua
sedatively (adv), drikartiu, derikatiu, drikatiu
sediment (n), libirt, libita, libit
sedimentary (adj), libirtu, libitu, libitu
sedimentate (v), libirst, libito, libito
sedimentation (n), libirtuet, libitueta, libituet
sedition (n), drizhaurk, derizhauka, drizhauk
seduce (v), shorklrsk, sluokiroko, shkirko
seducer (n doer), shorkirkwan, shokirokua,
　shkirkua
seduction (n), shorkirk, shokiroka, shkirk
seductive (adj), shorkirku, shokiroku, shkirku
seductively (adv), shorkirkiu, shokirokiu, shkirkiu
see (v), thulsf, thulo, thulo
seed (n), derat, derita, drit
seed (v), derast, derito, drito
seeder (n doer), deratwan, deritua, dritua
seedling (n), deratip, deritipa, dritip
seedy (adj), deratu, deritu, dritu
seek (v), loirst, loito, loito
seeker (n doer), loirtwan, loitua, loitua
seem (v), thursne, thuno, thuno
seemingly (adv), thurniu, thuniu, thuniu
seep (v), loitiensk, loitieno, loitieno
seepage (n), loitienk, loitiena, loitien
seer (n doer), thulfwan, thulua, thulua
seesaw (n), thulgralzhe, thulegerazha, thulgrazh
seesaw (v), thulgralze, thulegerazho, thulgrazho
seethe (v), loitilsp, loitifo, loitifo
segment (n), shkirk, shekika, shkik
segment (v), shkirsk, shekiko, shkiko

segmentation (n), shkirkuet, shekikueta, shkikuet
segregate (v), drikinorsp, derikinopo, drikinpo
segregation (n), drikinorp, derikinopa, drikinp
segregationist (n doer), drikinorpwan, derikinopua,
　drikinpua
seismic (adj), derafu, derifu, drifu
seize (v), guvarsk, guvako, guvako
seizure (n), guvark, guvaka, guvak
sekata- (num 1e42 pref), irishtai-, irishtai-, irishtai-
seldom (adj/adv), falarth, falathu, falath
select (v), drigerst, derigeto, drigeto
selection (n), drigert, derigeta, driget
selective (adj), drigertu, derigetu, drigetu
selectively (adv), drigertiu, derigetiu, drigetiu
selectivity (n), drigertuet, derigetueta, drigetuet
selector (n doer), drigertwan, derigetua, drigetua
Selenium (n davoka), Efup, Efup, Efup
Selenium (n), Shelenium, Sheleniuma, Shelenium
self (n), zhiurn, zhiuna, zhiun
selfish (adj), zhiurnu, zhiunu, zhiunu
selfishly (adv), zhiurniu, zhiuniu, zhiuniu
selfishness (n), zhiurnuet, zhiunueta, zhiunuet
selfless (adj), zhiumernu, zhiumenu, zhiumenu
selflessly (adv), zhiumerniu, zhiumeniu, zhiumeniu
selflessness (n), zhiumern, zhiumena, zhiumen
sell (v), trelirsf, terelifo, trelfo
seller (n doer), trelirfwan, terelifua, trelfua
sellout (n), trelirfuil, terelifuila, trelfuil
semblance (n), thralve, therava, thrav
semester (n), thranit, theranita, thrant
semicolon (n), biramituf, biramifota, biramift
semiconductor (n doer), birabelkriukwan,
　biraliukeriukua, biraliukriukua
semifinal (n), biralepal, biralilopa, biralilp
seminar (n), thraviark, theraviaka, thraviak
senate (n), shiemirk, shiemika, shiemk
senator (n doer), shiemirkwan, shiemikua,
　shiemkua
send (v), zhairsp, zhaipo, zhaipo
sender (n doer), zhairpwan, zhaipua, zhaipua
senile (adj), sheimaiftu, sheimaitu, sheimaitu
senility (n), sheimaift, sheimaita, sheimait
senior (adj), sheimartu, sheimatu, sheimatu
senior (n doer), sheimartwan, sheimatua,
　sheimatua
senior (n), sheimart, sheimata, sheimat
seniority (n), sheimartuet, sheimatueta, sheimatuet
sensation (n), shorfit, shorifita, shorft
sensational (adj), shorfitu, shorifitu, shorftu
sensationalism (n), shorfituet, shorifitueta,
　shorftuet
sensationalize (v), shorfituest, shorifitueto,
　shorftueto
sensationally (adv), shorfitiu, shorifitiu, shorftiu
sense (n), shoraf, shorifa, shorf
sense (v), shorasf, shorifo, shorfo
senseless (adj), shorafmenu, shorifemenu,
　shorfmenu
senselessly (adv), shorafmeniu, shorifemeniu,
　shorfmeniu
sensibility (n), shorfrelp, shoriferepa, shorfrep
sensible (adj), shorfrelpu, shoriferepu, shorfrepu
sensibly (adv), shorfrelpiu, shoriferepiu, shorfrepiu

sensitive (adj), shorfipu, shorifopu, shorfpu
sensitively (adv), shorfipiu, shorifopiu, shorfpiu
sensitivity (n), shorfip, shorifopa, shorfp
sensitize (v), shorfisp, shorifopo, shorfpo
sensor (n doer), shorafwan, shorifua, shorfua
sensory (adj), shorafwatu, shorifuanu, shorfuanu
sensual (adj), shorafu, shorifu, shorfu
sensuality (n), shorafun, shorifuna, shorfun
sensually (adv), shorafiu, shorifiu, shorfiu
sensuous (adj), shorafu, shorifu, shorfu
sensuously (adv), shorafiu, shorifiu, shorfiu
sent (v pa), zhairspyot, zhaipio, zhaipio
sentence (n d:punishment), zhaidairsh, zhaidaisha, zhaidaish
sentence (n d:words), shomdork, shomudoka, shomdok
sentence (v d:punishment), zhaidairs, zhaidaisho, zhaidaisho
sentiment (n), sharlorp, sharilopa, sharlp
sentimental (adj), sharlorpu, sharilopu, sharlpu
Seoul (n), Shiorl, Shiola, Shiol
separate (adj), dilsharfu, diloshafu, dilshafu
separate (v), dilsharsf, diloshafo, dilshafo
separately (adv), dilsharfiu, diloshafiu, dilshafiu
separation (n), dilsharf, diloshafa, dilshaf
separator (n doer), dilsharfwan, diloshafua, dilshafua
sept- (num 7 pref), venai-, venai-, venai-
September (n), Veshaifar, Veshaifara, Veshaifar
septendecillion (num 1e54 card), vensht, vensht, vensht
septendecillionth (num 1e54 ord), venshteth, venshteth, venshteth
septenquadragintillion (num 1e144 card), venfk, venfk, venfk
septentrigintillion (num 1e114 card), venft, venft, venft
septenvigintillion (num 1e84 card), venshk, venshk, venshk
septenvigintillionth (num 1e84 ord), venshketh, venshketh, venshketh
septillion (num 1e24 card), venka, venka, venka
septillionth (num 1e24 ord), venketh, venketh, venketh
sequel (n), shuftarn, shufetana, shuftan
sequence (n), shufirt, shufita, shuft
sequence (v), shufirst, shufito, shufto
sequencer (n doer), shufirtwan, shufitua, shuftua
sequential (adj), shufirtu, shufitu, shuftu
sequentially (adv), shufirtiu, shufitiu, shuftiu
Seranara (n), Seranara, Seranara, Seranara
serene (adj), lilanfu, lilanu, lilanu
serenely (adv), lilanfiu, lilaniu, lilaniu
serenity (n), lilanf, lilana, lilan
sergeant (n), norkart, norikata, norkat
serial (adj), nilorfu, nilofu, nilfu
serially (adv), nilorfiu, nilofiu, nilfiu
series (n), nilorf, nilofa, nilf
serious (adj), zhertu, zhetu, zhetu
seriously (adv), zhertiu, zhetiu, zhetiu
seriousness (n), zhert, zheta, zhet
Seris (n), Seris, Serisa, Seris

sermon (n), lilirp, lilipa, lilip
serpent (n), fareilshk, fareishika, fareishk
serpentine (adj), fareilshku, fareishiku, fareishku
serrate (v), grieshst, gerieto, grieto
serration (n), griesht, gerieta, griet
servant (n doer), kofitarnwan, kofitanua, koftanua
serve (v), kofirst, kofito, kofto
server (n doer), kofirtwan, kofitua, koftua
service (n), kofirt, kofita, koft
service (v), kofirtuest, kofitueto, koftueto
serviceman (n), koftplorn, kofitepelona, koftplon
servicemen (n pl), koftplornyek, kofitepeloni, koftploni
servitude (n), kofitarn, kofitana, koftan
sesame (n), nilorp, nilopa, nilp
sesquadragintillion (num 1e141 card), kinfk, kinfk, kinfk
session (n), lapuert, lapueta, lapuet
sestrigintillion (num 1e111 card), kinft, kinft, kinft
set (n d:group), zhorde, zhoda, zhod
set (v d:place), fersp, fepo, fepo
set (v pa d:place), ferspyot, fepio, fepio
setback (n), zhordvark, zhoduvaka, zhodvak
setter (n doer d:place), ferpwan, fepua, fepua
settle (v), libers, libesho, libesho
settlement (n), libersh, libesha, libesh
settler (n doer), libershwan, libeshua, libeshua
setup (n), zhodiveil, zhodiveila, zhodiveil
seven (num 7 card), veni, veni, veni
seventeen (num 17 card), venipa, venipa, venipa
seventeen- (num 17 pref), venipai-, venipai-, venipai-
seventeenth (num 17 ord), venipeth, venipeth, venipeth
seventh (num 7 ord), veneth, veneth, veneth
seventieth (num 70 ord), venideth, venideth, venideth
seventy (num 70 card), venida, venida, venida
seventy- (num 70 pref), venidai-, venidai-, venidai-
sever (v), kilorsk, kiloko, kilko
several (adj), kilafu, kilofu, kilfu
severance (n), kilork, kiloka, kilk
severe (adj), kilorku, kiloku, kilku
severely (adv), kilorkiu, kilokiu, kilkiu
severity (n), kilkart, kilokata, kilkat
sew (v d:thread cloth), yunasp, yunipo, yunpo
sewer (n d:waste conduit), wiushk, wiusha, wiush
sewer (n doer d:thread cloth), yunapwan, yunipua, yunpua
sewer (v d:waste conduit), wiushsk, wiusho, wiusho
sewerage (n), wiushk, wiusha, wiush
sex (n d:gender), bivarn, bivana, bivan
sex (n d:intercourse), bivirk, bivika, bivik
sex (v d:intercourse), bivirsk, biviko, biviko
sexdecillion (num 1e51 card), kinsht, kinsht, kinsht
sexdecillionth (num 1e51 ord), kinshteth, kinshteth, kinshteth
sexism (n), bivarnuet, bivanueta, bivanuet
sexist (adj), bivarnuetu, bivanuetu, bivanuetu
sexist (n doer), bivarnuetwan, bivanuetua, bivanuetua
sexless (adj), bivarnmenu, bivanemenu, bivanmenu

sext- (num 6 pref), kinai-, kinai-, kinai-
sextillion (num 1e21 card), kinka, kinka, kinka
sextillionth (num 1e21 ord), kinketh, kinketh, kinketh
sexual (adj), bivikartu, bivikatu, bivikatu
sexuality (n), bivikart, bivikata, bivikat
sexually (adv), bivikartiu, bivikatiu, bivikatiu
sexvigintillion (num 1e81 card), kinshk, kinshk, kinshk
sexvigintillionth (num 1e81 ord), kinshketh, kinshketh, kinshketh
sexy (adj d:intercourse), bivirku, biviku, biviku
Sh (let sng), sheil, sheia, shei
shack (n), thansht, thanita, thant
shack (v), thanshst, thanito, thanto
shackle (n), tharthk, tharitha, tharth
shackle (v), tharthsk, tharitho, thartho
shade (n), poerf, poefa, poef
shade (v), poersf, poefo, poefo
shader (n doer), poerfwan, poefua, poefua
shadow (n), poefirt, poefita, poeft
shadow (v), poefirst, poefito, poefto
shadower (n doer), poefirtwan, poefitua, poeftua
shadowy (adj), poefirtu, poefitu, poeftu
shady (adj), poerfu, poefu, poefu
shaft (n), vorshk, voshika, voshk
shaft (v), vorshsk, voshiko, voshko
shafter (n doer), vorshkwan, voshikua, voshkua
shake (n), vagark, vagara, vagar
shake (v), vagarsk, vagaro, vagaro
shakedown (n), vagarktien, vagaretiena, vagartien
shakeout (n), vagarkuil, vagaruila, vagaruil
shaker (n doer), vagarkwan, vagarua, vagarua
shakeup (n), vagarkiveil, vagariveila, vagariveil
shaky (adj), vagarku, vagaru, vagaru
shall (v), vukesh, kukesho, buvesh
shallow (adj), mefirthu, mefithu, mefthu
shallowness (n), mefirth, mefitha, mefth
sham (n), vishork, vishoka, vishk
shamble (n), vishkirk, vishikika, vishkik
shamble (v), vishkirsk, vishikiko, vishkiko
shame (n), vishort, vishota, visht
shame (v), vishorst, vishoto, vishto
shameful (adj), vishortu, vishotu, vishtu
shamefully (adv), vishortiu, vishotiu, vishtiu
shameless (adj), vishortmenu, vishotemenu, vishtmenu
shamelessly (adv), vishortmeniu, vishotemeniu, vishtmeniu
shampoo (n), visharn, vishana, vishan
shampoo (v), visharsne, vishano, vishano
shampooer (n doer), visharnwan, vishanua, vishanua
Shanghai (n), Shankairf, Shanikaifa, Shankaif
shank (n), glaishk, gelaika, glaik
shank (v), glaishsk, gelaiko, glaiko
shape (n), flurme, feluma, flum
shape (v), flurzme, felumo, flumo
shapeless (adj), flurmenu, felumenu, flumenu
shapely (adv), flurmiu, felumiu, flumiu
shaper (n doer), flurmwan, felumua, flumua
shard (n), flunirt, felunita, flunt
share (n), runshk, runisha, runsh

share (v), runshsk, runisho, runsho
shareholder (n doer), runshthorthkwan, runishethorithua, runshthorthua
sharer (n doer), runshkwan, runishua, runshua
shark (n), krairshk, keraishoka, kraishk
sharp (adj), shraltu, sheratu, shratu
sharp (n), shraltan, sheratana, shratan
sharpen (v), shralst, sherato, shrato
sharpener (n doer), shraltwan, sheratua, shratua
sharply (adv), shraltiu, sheratiu, shratiu
sharpness (n), shralt, sherata, shrat
sharpshooter (n), shratshkort, sherateshekota, shratshkot
shatter (v), kriarsk, keriako, kriako
shave (n), muart, muata, muat
shave (v), muarst, muato, muato
shaver (n doer), muartwan, muatua, muatua
shawl (n), theimp, theima, theim
she (pron 3rd fem sng sub), sha, sha, sha
shear (n), thiasht, thiasha, thiash
shear (v), thiashst, thiasho, thiasho
shearer (n doer), thiashtwan, thiashua, thiashua
sheath (n), thiathk, thiatha, thiath
sheathe (v), thiathsk, thiatho, thiatho
shed (n d:building), thilorf, thilofa, thilf
shed (v d:rid), blerst, beleto, bleto
shedder (n doer d:rid), blertwan, beletua, bletua
sheep (n pl), bavarnyek, bavani, bavani
sheep (n), bavarn, bavana, bavan
sheepish (adj), bavarnu, bavanu, bavanu
sheepishly (adv), bavarniu, bavaniu, bavaniu
sheer (adj d:clear), linalfu, linalu, linalu
sheer (adv d:clear), linalfiu, linaliu, linaliu
sheer (n d:clear), linalf, linala, linal
sheer (n d:divert), throsht, therota, throt
sheer (v d:divert), throshst, theroto, throto
sheet (n), taurp, taupa, taup
shelf (n), nalirf, nalifa, nalf
shell (n), therk, theka, thek
shell (v), thersk, theko, theko
sheller (n doer), therkwan, thekua, thekua
shellfish (n pl), thekshlershyek, thekesheleshi, thekshleshi
shellfish (n), thekshlersh, thekeshelesha, thekshlesh
shelter (n), vaiwart, vaiwata, vaiwat
shelter (v), vaiwarst, vaiwato, vaiwato
shelve (v), nalirsf, nalifo, nalfo
shepherd (n pl), flumgruzhyek, felumegerudi, flumgrudi
shepherd (n), flumgruzhe, felumegeruda, flumgrud
shepherd (v), flumgruze, felumegerudo, flumgrudo
sheriff (n), thoifalt, thoifata, thoift
sheriff (v), thoifalst, thoifato, thoifto
shield (n), moirk, moika, moik
shield (v), moirsk, moiko, moiko
shift (n), miraf, mirofa, mirf
shift (v), mirasf, mirofo, mirfo
shifter (n doer), mirafwan, mirofua, mirfua
shifty (adj), mirafu, mirofu, mirfu
shim (n), shkrishk, shekerisha, shkrish
shim (v), shkrishsk, shekerisho, shkrisho
shimmer (v), shkrifst, shukerifo, shkrifo

shin (n), loikarn, loikana, loikan
shine (n), moirth, moitha, moith
shine (v), moirsth, moitho, moitho
shiner (n doer), moirthwan, moithua, moithua
shingle (n), blarige, belariga, blarg
shingle (v), blarizge, belarigo, blargo
shiny (adj), moirthu, moithu, moithu
ship (n), flerve, feleva, flev
ship (v), flerzve, felevo, flevo
shipbuilder (n doer), flevoratwan, felevoritua, flevortua
shipload (n), flevlurift, felevelurita, flevlurt
shipman (n), flevplorn, felevepelona, flevplon
shipmate (n), flevlern, felevelena, flevlen
shipmen (n pl), flevplornyek, felevepeloni, flevploni
shipment (n), flervuet, felevueta, flevuet
shipowner (n doer), flevtheiftwan, felevetheifua, flevtheifua
shipper (n doer), flervwan, felevua, flevua
shipwreck (n), flevkarbark, felevekarubaka, flevkarbak
shipwreck (v), flevkarbarsk, felevekarubako, flevkarbako
shipyard (n), flevthauthk, felevethautha, flevthauth
shirt (n), lifarde, lifada, lifad
shiver (n), viagart, viagara, viagar
shiver (v), viagarst, viagaro, viagaro
shock (n), vigark, vigaka, vigak
shock (v), vigarsk, vigako, vigako
shocker (n doer), vigarkwan, vigakua, vigakua
shockingly (adv), vigarkiu, vigakiu, vigakiu
shockwave (n), vigaklersh, vigakelesha, vigaklesh
shoe (n), tafarn, tafana, tafan
shoe (v), tafarsne, tafano, tafano
shoehorn (n), tafankroip, tafanekeroima, tafankroim
shoehorn (v), tafankroisp, tafanekeroimo, tafankroimo
shoelace (n), tafanfoirn, tafanefoina, tafanfoin
shoemaker (n doer), tafanargwan, tafanagua, tafanagua
shoeshine (n), tafanmoirth, tafanemoitha, tafanmoith
shoestring (n), tafanligurl, tafaneligula, tafanligul
shone (v pa), moirsthyot, moithio, moithio
shoo (interj), ishai, ishai, ishai
shoo (v), shuiarsf, shuiafo, shuiafo
shook (v pa), vagarskyot, vagario, vagario
shoot (n), shkort, shekota, shkot
shoot (v), shkorst, shekoto, shkoto
shooter (n doer), shkortwan, shekotua, shkotua
shootout (n), shkortuil, shekotuila, shkotuil
shop (n), thoft, thofa, thof
shop (v), thofst, thofo, thofo
shopkeeper (n doer), thofklorfwan, thofekelofua, thofklofua
shoplifter (n), thofprairt, thofeperaita, thofprait
shopper (n doer), thoftwan, thofua, thofua
shore (n), nularat, nularita, nulart
shore (v), nularast, nularito, nularto
shoreline (n), nulartroifk, nulariteroifa, nulartroif
short (adj), thialtu, thialu, thialu
short (v), thialirsp, thialipo, thialpo

shortage (n), thialirp, thialipa, thialp
shortcake (n), thialgutraf, thialegurita, thialgurt
shortchange (v), thialtuarsne, thialetuano, thialtuano
shortcoming (n), thialblerf, thialebilefa, thialblef
shortcut (n), thialdairsh, thialedaisha, thialdaish
shorten (v), thialst, thialo, thialo
shorter (adj), thialtwelu, thialwelu, thialwelu
shortest (adj), thialtweku, thialweku, thialweku
shortfall (n), thialzhailf, thialezhaila, thialzhail
shorthand (n), thialkarp, thialekapa, thialkap
shortly (adv), thialtiu, thialiu, thialiu
shortness (n), thialt, thiala, thial
shorts (n d:clothing), thialirk, thialika, thialk
shortsighted (adj), thialthulthu, thialethuthu, thialthuthu
shortsightedness (n), thialthulth, thialethutha, thialthuth
shortstop (n), thialtaurk, thialetauka, thialtauk
shortwave (adj), thialershu, thialeshu, thialeshu
shortwave (n), thialersh, thialesha, thialesh
shorty (n), thialit, thialira, thialir
shot (n), shakirt, shakita, shakit
shot (n), shkoift, shekoita, shkoit
shot (v pa), shkorstyot, shekotio, shkotio
shotgun (n), shakidorige, shakidoruga, shakidorge
should (ndal d:expectation), tuthuke kodi, thushika kodi, thushke kodi
shoulder (n), shoirge, shoiga, shoig
shoulder (v), shoirzge, shoigo, shoigo
shout (n), drairk, deraika, draik
shout (v), drairsk, deraiko, draiko
shouter (n doer), drairkwan, deraikua, draikua
shove (n), tiarf, tiafa, tiaf
shove (v), tiarsf, tiafo, tiafo
shovel (n), tiafuarn, tiafuana, tiafuan
shovel (v), tiafuarsne, tiafuano, tiafuano
shover (n doer), tiarfwan, tiafua, tiafua
show (n), feirf, feifa, feif
show (v), feirsf, feifo, feifo
showboat (n), feifshkorbe, feifeshekoba, feifshkob
showboat (v), feifshkorzbe, feifeshekobo, feifshkobo
showcase (n), feifshuart, feifeshuata, feifshuat
showcase (v), feifshuarst, feifeshuato, feifshuato
showdown (n), feiftiern, feifetiena, feiftien
shower (n), viarf, viafa, viaf
shower (v), viarsf, viafo, viafo
showgirl (n), feifkelerf, feifekelera, feifkeler
showman (n), feifplorn, feifepelona, feifplon
showmanship (n), feifplonfirf, feifepeloncfifa, feifplonfif
showmen (n pl), feifplornyek, feifepeloni, feifploni
showpiece (n), feifthetirsh, feifethetisha, feifthetsh
showpiece (v), feifthetirs, feifethetisho, feifthetsho
showplace (n), feifbrelsh, feifeberesha, feifbresh
showroom (n), feifshranf, feifesherana, feifshran
showy (adj), feirfu, feifu, feifu
shran (v pa), klorfkshransfyot, kelorikesheranio, klorkshranio
shranf (v prp), klorfkshransfaut, kelorikesheranao, klorkshranao
shrank (v pa), bilorsyot, biloshio, bilshio
shred (v), kraushsk, kerausho, krausho

shredder (n doer), kraushkwan, keraushua, kraushua
shrewd (adj), kriampu, keriamu, kriamu
shrewdly (adv), kriampiu, keriamiu, kriamiu
shrewdness (n), kriamp, keriama, kriam
shriauk (v prp), dorikshriauskaut, dorugiaulao, dorgiaulao
shriek (n), kliashk, keliaika, kliaik
shriek (v), kliashsk, keliaiko, kliaiko
shrieker (n doer), kliashkwan, keliaikua, kliaikua
shrill (adj), klieshtu, kelietu, klietu
shrill (n), kliesht, kelieta, kliet
shrill (v), klieshst, kelieto, klieto
shrimp (n), theirap, theiripa, theirp
shrimp (v), theirasp, theiripo, theirpo
shrimper (n doer), theirapwan, theiripua, theirpua
shrine (n), niorn, niona, nion
shriner (n doer), niornwan, nionua, nionua
shrink (v), bilors, bilosho, bilsho
shrinkage (n), bilorsh, bilosha, bilsh
shrinker (n doer), bilorshwan, biloshua, bilshua
shrivel (v), briursp, beriupo, briupo
shroud (n), kriashk, keriasha, kriash
shroud (v), kriashsk, keriasho, kriasho
shrub (n), burthk, buritha, burth
shrubbery (n), burthkuet, burithueta, burthuet
shrug (n), niort, niota, niot
shrug (v), niorst, nioto, nioto
Shs (let pl), sheili, sheili, sheili
shuck (n), thiaushk, thiauka, thiauk
shuck (v), thiaushsk, thiauko, thiauko
shudder (n), thruap, theruasha, thruash
shudder (v), thruasp, theruasho, thruasho
shuffle (n), thathk, thatha, thath
shuffle (v), thathsk, thatho, thatho
shun (v), thuamesp, thuamo, thuamo
shunt (n), thuanirt, thuanita, thuant
shunt (v), thuanirst, thuanito, thuanto
shut (adj), flerku, feleku, fleku
shut (v pa), flerskyot, felekio, flekio
shut (v), flersk, feleko, fleko
shutdown (n), flerktiern, felekotiena, flektien
shutout (n), flerkuil, felekuila, flekuil
shutter (n), flerkwat, felekuana, flekuan
shutter (v), flerkwast, felekuano, flekuano
shuttle (n), fkurt, fikuta, fkut
shuttle (v), fkurst, fikuto, fkuto
shy (adj), fleirtu, feleitu, fleitu
shy (v), fleirst, feleito, fleito
shyness (n), fleirt, feleita, fleit
sib (n), kielsh, kiesha, kiesh
sibling (adj), kielshku, kieshiku, kieshku
sibling (n), kielshk, kieshika, kieshk
siblings (adv), kielshkiu, kieshikiu, kieshkiu
sick (adj), gliurpu, geliupu, gliupu
sicken (v), gliursp, geliupo, gliupo
sickly (adv), gliurpiu, geliupiu, gliupiu
sickness (n), gliurp, geliupa, gliup
side (n), shoirt, shoita, shoit
side (v), shoirst, shoito, shoito
sidearm (n), shoitshnern, shoiteshinena, shoitshnen
sidebar (n), shoitrolart, shoiterolata, shoitrolt

sidekick (n), shoitethirap, shoitethiropa, shoitethirp
sideline (n), shoitroifk, shoiteroifa, shoitroif
sideline (v), shoitroifsk, shoiteroifo, shoitroifo
sider (n doer), shoirtwan, shoitua, shoitua
sideshow (n), shoitfeirf, shoitefeifa, shoitfeif
sidestep (n), shoitglishk, shoitegelisha, shoitglish
sidestep (v), shoitglishsk, shoitegelisho, shoitglisho
sidetrack (n), shoitgethirk, shoitegethika, shoitgethk
sidetrack (v), shoitgethirsk, shoitegethiko, shoitgethko
sidewalk (n), shoizhoirp, shoizhoipa, shoizhoip
sideways (adj/adv), shoitpliol, shoitepeliolu, shoitpliol
siege (n), shraisht, sheraita, shrait
siege (v), shraishst, sheraito, shraito
Sierra (n), Shiaralf, Shiarafa, Shiaraf
sieve (n), piarthk, piaritha, piarth
sieve (v), piarthsk, piaritho, piartho
sift (v), pirsk, pirotho, pirtho
sifter (n doer), pirkwan, pirothua, pirthua
sigh (n), fairf, faifa, faif
sigh (v), fairsf, faifo, faifo
sight (n), thulth, thutha, thuth
sight (v), thulsth, thutho, thutho
sightsaw (v pa), thuthulsfyot, thuthulio, thuthulio
sightsee (v), thuthulsf, thuthulo, thuthulo
sigma (n), shigmarn, shigemana, shigman
sign (n), weirf, weifa, weif
sign (v), weirsf, weifo, weifo
signal (n), weifirp, weifipa, weifp
signal (v), weifirsp, weifipo, weifpo
signaler (n doer), weifirpwan, weifipua, weifpua
signatory (n doer), weifirtwan, weifitua, weiftua
signature (n), weifirt, weifita, weift
signer (n doer), weirfwan, weifua, weifua
significance (n), weifork, weifoka, weifk
significant (adj), weiforku, weifoku, weifku
significantly (adv), weiforkiu, weifokiu, weifkiu
signify (v), weiforsk, weifoko, weifko
signpost (n), weifbalirt, weifebalita, weifbalt
silence (n), zhoirf, zhoifa, zhoif
silence (v), zhoirsf, zhoifo, zhoifo
silencer (n doer), zhoirfwan, zhoifua, zhoifua
silent (adj), zhoirfu, zhoifu, zhoifu
silently (adv), zhoirfiu, zhoifiu, zhoifiu
Silicon (n davoka), Etip, Etip, Etip
Silicon (n), Shilikon, Shilikona, Shilikon
silk (n), ploirsh, peloisha, ploish
silkily (adv), ploirshiu, peloishiu, ploishiu
silkwood (n), ploishfanirn, peloishefanina, ploishfanin
silkworm (n), ploishyoran, peloishyorina, ploishyorn
silky (adj), ploirshu, peloishu, ploishu
sill (n), luinf, luina, luin
silliness (n), luwiorn, luwiona, luwion
silly (adj), luwiornu, luwionu, luwionu
silo (n), luiaft, luiafa, luiaf
silt (n), prilsh, perilika, prilk
Silver (n davoka), Ilat, Ilat, Ilat
silver (n), sharagen, sharugena, shargen

Silver (n), Shilver, Shilovera, Shilver
similar (adj), didarnu, didanu, didanu
similarity (n), didarn, didana, didan
similarly (adv), didarniu, didaniu, didaniu
simmer (v), bithsk, bitho, bitho
simple (adj), shalirnu, shalinu, shalnu
simpler (adj), shalirnwelu, shalinwelu, shalnwelu
simplest (adj), shalirnwaku, shalinwaku, shalnwaku
simplicity (n), shalirn, shalina, shaln
simplification (n), shalirnuet, shalinueta, shalnuet
simplify (v), shalirsne, shalino, shalno
simplistic (adj), shalirnu, shalinu, shalnu
simply (adv), shalirniu, shaliniu, shalniu
simulate (v), titarsk, titako, titako
simulation (n), titark, titaka, titak
simulator (n doer), titarkwan, titakua, titakua
simultaneity (n), toirt, toita, toit
simultaneous (adj), toirtu, toitu, toitu
simultaneously (adv), toirtiu, toitiu, toitiu
sin (n), zhiarsh, zhiazha, zhiazh
sin (v), zhiars, zhiazho, zhiazho
since (adv/prep/conj), shnesh, sheneshu, shnesh
sincere (adj), pelmurnu, pelamunu, pelmunu
sincerely (adv), pelmurniu, pelamuniu, pelmuniu
sincerity (n), pelmurn, pelamuna, pelmun
sinful (adj), zhiarshu, zhiazhu, zhiazhu
sinfully (adv), zhiarshiu, zhiazhiu, zhiazhiu
sing (v), nelarsne, nelano, nelno
Singapore (n), Shinkaporf, Shinokapora, Shinkapor
singe (v), buiashsk, buiasho, buiasho
singer (n doer), nelarnwan, nelanua, nelnua
single (adj), pelfu, pelu, pelu
single (n), pelf, pela, pel
single (v), pelsf, pelo, pelo
singular (adj), pelirshu, pelishu, pelshu
singularity (n), pelirsh, pelisha, pelsh
singularly (adv), pelirshiu, pelishiu, pelshiu
sinister (adj), buiartu, buiatu, buiatu
sink (n), kieft, kiefa, kief
sink (v), kiefst, kiefo, kiefo
sinker (n doer), kieftwan, kiefua, kiefua
sinkhole (n), kiefkorth, kiefekotha, kiefkoth
sinner (n doer), zhiarshwan, zhiazhua, zhiazhua
sinus (adj), trifirtu, terifitu, triftu
sinus (n), trifirt, terifita, trift
sip (n), klirf, kelifa, klif
sip (v), klirsf, kelifo, klifo
siphon (n), klirfat, kelifata, klifat
siphon (v), klirfast, kelifato, klifato
sipper (n doer), klirfwan, kelifua, klifua
sippy (adj), klirtu, kelitu, klitu
sir (adj), loirthu, loithu, loithu
sir (n), loirth, loitha, loith
sire (n), loithirk, loithika, loithk
sire (v), loithirsk, loithiko, loithko
siren (n), pliausht, peliauta, pliaut
sister (n), teshralf, tesharafa, teshraf
sisterhood (n), teshralfif, tesharafifa, teshrafif
sisterly (adj), teshralfu, tesharafu, teshrafu
sit (n), shrelt, shereta, shret
sit (v), shrelst, shereto, shreto
site (n), niart, niata, niat
situate (v), shrenst, shareno, shreno

situation (n), shrent, sharena, shren
situational (adj), shrentu, sharenu, shrenu
situationally (adv), shrentiu, shareniu, shreniu
six (num 6 card), kini, kini, kini
sixteen (num 16 card), kinipa, kinipa, kinipa
sixteen- (num 16 pref), kinipai-, kinipai-, kinipai-
sixteenth (num 16 ord), kinipeth, kinipeth, kinipeth
sixth (num 6 ord), kineth, kineth, kineth
sixtieth (num 60 ord), kinideth, kinideth, kinideth
sixty (num 60 card), kinida, kinida, kinida
sixty- (num 60 pref), kinidai-, kinidai-, kinidai-
sizable (adj), shuargu, shuagu, shuagu
sizably (adv), shuargiu, shuagiu, shuagiu
size (n), shuarge, shuaga, shuag
size (v), shuarzge, shuago, shuago
sizeable (adj), shuargu, shuagu, shuagu
sizer (n doer), shuargwan, shuagua, shuagua
sizzle (n), shiuaik, shiuaifa, shiuaif
sizzle (v), shiuaisk, shiuaifo, shiuaifo
skate (n), thiart, thiata, thiat
skate (v), thiarst, thiato, thiato
skateboard (n), thiatplok, thiatepelorika, thiatplork
skateboard (v), thiatplosk, thiatepeloriko, thiatplorko
skater (n doer), thiartwan, thiatua, thiatua
skeletal (adj), kurthu, kuthu, kuthu
skeleton (n), kurth, kutha, kuth
skeptic (n doer), kloiftwan, keloitua, kloitua
skeptical (adj), kloiftu, keloitu, kloitu
skeptically (adv), kloiftiu, keloitiu, kloitiu
skepticism (n), kloift, keloita, kloit
sketch (n), shraishk, sheraisha, shraish
sketch (v), shraishsk, sheraisho, shraisho
sketcher (n doer), shraishkwan, sheraishua,
    shraishua
sketchy (adj), shraishku, sheraishu, shraishu
skew (v), naiarsp, naiapo, naiapo
skewer (n), noiashk, noiaka, noiak
skewer (v), noiashsk, noiako, noiako
skewness (n), naiarp, naiapa, naiap
ski (n), fituirn, fituina, ftuin
ski (v), fituirsne, fituino, ftuino
skid (v), shkiushsk, shekiuko, shkiuko
skier (n doer), fituirnwan, fituinua, ftuinua
skill (n), shirk, shika, shik
skill (v), shirsk, shiko, shiko
skillet (n), ferelirk, ferelika, frelk
skillful (adj), shirku, shiku, shiku
skillfully (adv), shirkiu, shikiu, shikiu
skim (v), frlarsst, ferlano, frlano
skimmer (n doer), friantwan, ferianua, frianua
skimp (v), frianshsk, ferianiko, frianko
skimpy (adj), frianshku, ferianiku, frianku
skin (n), fnarp, finapa, fnap
skin (v), fnarsp, finapo, fnapo
skinhead (n), fnapkefirt, finapekefita, fnapkeft
skinner (n doer), fnarpwan, finapua, fnapua
skinniness (n), fnarn, finana, fnan
skinny (adj), fnarnu, finanu, fnanu
skip (n), fnirk, fenika, fnik
skip (v), fnirsk, feniko, fniko
skipped (v prp), fnirskaut, fenikao, fnikao

skipper (n), kifiart, kifiata, kifiat
skirmish (n), shniark, sheniaka, shniak
skirt (n), fnilort, fenilota, fnilt
skirt (v), fnilorst, feniloto, fnilto
skit (n), frisht, ferita, frit
skull (n), klarip, kelaripa, klarp
sky (n), friaift, feriaifa, friaif
sky (v), friaifst, feriaifo, friaifo
skydive (n), friaifkraifk, feriaifekeraika, friaifkraik
skydive (v), friaifkraifsk, feriaifekeraiko, friaifkraiko
skydiver (n doer), friaifkraifkwan, feriaifekeraikua, friaifkraikua
skylight (n), friaifluarn, feriaifeluana, friaifluan
skyline (n), friaifroifk, feriaiferoifa, friaifroif
skyrocket (v), friaifzhiarast, feriaifezhiarito, friaifzhiarto
skyscraper (n doer), friaifkladirpwan, feriaifekeladipua, friaifkladipua
skyward (adj), friaiftu, feriaifu, friaifu
skywardly (adv), friaiftiu, feriaifiu, friaifiu
slab (n), plarbe, pelaba, plab
slack (n d:loose), shloart, sheloata, shloat
slack (n d:pants), friesht, ferieta, friet
slack (v d:loose), shloarst, sheloato, shloato
slacker (n doer d:loose), shloartwan, sheloatua, shloatua
slam (v d:hit), shramesp, sheramo, shramo
slammer (n d:jail), shraiashk, sheraiaka, shraiak
slammer (n doer d:hit), shrampwan, sheramua, shramua
slander (n), zhuiank, zhuiana, zhuian
slander (v), zhuiansk, zhuiano, zhuiano
slanderous (adj), zhuianku, zhuianu, zhuianu
slang (n), tharage, thariga, tharg
slant (n), shkoirp, shekoipa, shkoip
slant (v), shkoirsp, shekoipo, shkoipo
slap (n), shralp, sherapa, shrap
slap (v), shralsp, sherapo, shrapo
slapper (n doer), shralpwan, sherapua, shrapua
slash (n), shkarp, shikapa, shkap
slash (v), shkarsp, shikapo, shkapo
slasher (n doer), shkarpwan, shikapua, shkapua
slat (n), shriashk, sheriaka, shriak
slat (v), shriashsk, sheriako, shriako
slate (n), flathk, felatha, flath
slate (v), flathsk, felatho, flatho
slaughter (n), shriausht, sheriauta, shriaut
slaughter (v), shriaushst, sheriauto, shriauto
slaughterhouse (n), shriautkiarf, sheriautekiafa, shriautkiaf
slave (n doer), shraifpwan, sheraipua, shraipua
slave (v), shraifsp, sheraipo, shraipo
slavery (n), shraifp, sheraipa, shraip
slay (v), shkralsk, shikerako, shkrako
slayer (n doer), shkralkwan, shikerakua, shkrakua
sleaze (n), blisht, belisha, blish
sleazy (adj), blishtu, belishu, blishu
sled (n), shlurp, shelupa, shlup
sled (v), shlursp, shelupo, shlupo
sledge (n), shleithk, sheleitha, shleith
sledge (v), shleithsk, sheleitho, shleitho
sledgehammer (n), shleithganirp, sheleitheganipa,

shleithganp
sleek (adj), friempu, feriemu, friemu
sleep (n), prushk, perusha, prush
sleep (v), prushsk, perusho, prusho
sleeper (n doer), prushkwan, perushua, prushua
sleepiness (n), prushkuet, perushueta, prushuet
sleepless (adj), prushkmenu, perushemenu, prushmenu
sleepwalk (v), prushzhoirsp, perushezhoipo, prushzhoipo
sleepwalker (n doer), prushzhoirpwan, perushezhoipua, prushzhoipua
sleepy (adj), prushku, perushu, prushu
sleet (n), murshk, murisha, mursh
sleet (v), murshsk, murisho, mursho
sleeve (n), druft, derufa, druf
sleeve (v), drufst, derufo, drufo
sleeveless (adj), druftmenu, derufemenu, drufmenu
sleigh (n), pariank, pariana, parian
slender (adj), shlirnu, shelinu, shlinu
slenderness (n), shlirn, shelina, shlin
slept (v pa), prushskyot, perushio, prushio
slew (v pa), shkralskyot, shikerakio, shkrakio
slice (n), shlirk, shelika, shlik
slice (v), shlirsk, sheliko, shliko
slicer (n doer), shlirkwan, shelikua, shlikua
slick (adj), zheishtu, zheitu, zheitu
slick (n), zheisht, zheita, zheit
slid (v pa), shlursyot, shelushio, shlushio
slide (n), shlursh, shelusha, shlush
slide (v), shlurs, shelusho, shlusho
slider (n doer), shlurshwan, shelushua, shlushua
slight (adj), flirfu, felifu, flifu
slight (v), flirsf, felifo, flifo
slightly (adv), flirfiu, felifiu, flifiu
slim (adj), theramu, therimu, thrimu
slim (v), therazme, therimo, thrimo
slime (n), shreinf, shereina, shrein
slime (v), shreinsf, shereino, shreino
sliminess (n), therame, therima, thrim
slimy (adj), shreinfu, sheremu, shreinu
sling (n), shkraishk, shukeraika, shkraik
sling (v), shkraishsk, shukeraiko, shkraiko
slinger (n doer), shkraishkwan, shukeraikua, shkraikua
slingshot (n), shkraikshkoift, shukeraikeshekoita, shkraikshkoit
slink (v), shrifsp, sheripo, shripo
slinky (adj), shrifpu, sheripu, shripu
slip (n), shkrilk, shikorika, shkrik
slip (v), shkrilsk, shikoriko, shkriko
slippage (n), shkrilkuet, shikorikueta, shkrikuet
slipper (n), pariup, pariufa, pariuf
slippery (adj), shkrilku, shikoriku, shkriku
slit (n), shriaft, sheriata, shriat
slit (v pa), shriafstyot, sheriatio, shriatio
slit (v), shriafst, sheriato, shriato
slither (v), flieshsk, feliesho, fliesho
sliver (n), shrialp, sheriapa, shriap
slob (n), praushk, perauka, prauk
slobber (v), praushsp, peraupo, praupo
slog (v), shlaushsk, shelausho, shlausho
slogan (n), sheilart, sheilata, sheilt

slogger (n doer), shlaushkwan, shelaushua, shlaushua
slop (n), praufk, peraufa, prauf
slop (v), praufsk, peraufo, praufo
slope (n), shkroilk, shokeroika, shkroik
slope (v), shkroilsk, shokeroiko, shkroiko
sloppiness (n), praufkuet, peraufueta, praufuet
sloppy (adj), praufku, peraufu, praufu
slot (n), flinork, felinoka, flink
slot (v), flinorsk, felinoko, flinko
slouch (n doer), priaushkwan, periaukua, priaukua
slouch (v), priaushsk, periauko, priauko
slough (n), friethk, ferietha, frieth
slough (v), friethsk, ferietho, frietho
slow (adj), shriarshu, sheriashu, shriashu
slow (v), shriars, sheriasho, shriasho
slowdown (n), shriarshtiern, sheriashetiena, shriashtien
slower (adj), shriarshwelu, sheriashwelu, shriashwelu
slowest (adj), shriarshwaku, sheriashwaku, shriashwaku
slowly (adv), shriarshiu, sheriashiu, shriashiu
slowness (n), shriarsh, sheriasha, shriash
sludge (n), plurzhge, peluriga, plurg
slug (n d:animal), grelirp, gerelipa, grelp
slug (n d:blank), brunirk, berunika, brunk
slug (v d:hit), bluarsk, beluako, bluako
slugger (n doer d:hit), bluarkwan, beluakua, bluakua
sluggish (adj d:slow), grairgu, geraigu, graigu
sluggishly (adv d:slow), grairgiu, geraigiu, graigiu
slum (n), blorn, belora, blor
slumber (adj), buforu, belorifu, blorfu
slumber (n), bufor, belorifa, blorf
slumber (v), bufosre, belorifo, blorfo
slump (n), blorfp, beloripa, blorp
slump (v), blorfsp, beloripo, blorpo
slumper (n doer), blorfpwan, beloripua, blorpua
slumpily (adv), blorfpiu, beloripiu, blorpiu
slumpy (adj), blorfpu, beloripu, blorpu
slung (v pa), shkraishskyot, shukeraikio, shkraikio
slur (n), blorshk, belorisha, blorsh
slur (v), blorshsk, belorisho, blorsho
slurry (n), blorshkan, belorishana, blorshan
slush (n), breithk, bereitha, breith
slush (v), breithsk, bereitho, breitho
slut (n), kornashk, korinaka, kornak
sly (adj), shleishtu, sheleitu, shleitu
slyly (adv), shleishtiu, sheleitiu, shleitiu
slyness (n), shleisht, sheleita, shleit
smack (n), flaurk, felauka, flauk
smack (v), flaursk, felauko, flauko
small (adj), theirshu, theishu, theishu
smaller (adj), theirshwelu, theishwelu, theishwelu
smallest (adj), theirshwaku, theishwaku, theishwaku
smallness (n), theirsh, theisha, theish
smart (adj), niarmu, niamu, niamu
smarten (v), niarzme, niamo, niamo
smartly (adv), niarmiu, niamiu, niamiu
smartness (n), niarme, niama, niam
smash (n), shkaishk, shekaisha, shkaish

smash (v), shkaishsk, shekaisho, shkaisho
smasher (n doer), shkaishkwan, shekaishua, shkaishua
smear (n), greizhge, gereiga, greig
smear (v), greizhzge, gereigo, greigo
smell (n), thurf, thufa, thuf
smell (v), thursf, thufo, thufo
smelly (adj), thurfu, thufu, thufu
smile (n), feran, ferina, frin
smile (v), ferasne, ferino, frino
smiley (n doer), feranwan, ferinua, frinua
smirk (n), friaushk, feriauka, friauk
smirk (v), friaushsk, feriauko, friauko
smith (n), rithk, ritha, rith
smog (n), shtorzhe, shetozha, shtozh
smoggy (adj), shtorzhu, shetozhu, shtozhu
smoke (n), shtolirf, shetolifa, shtolf
smoke (v), shtolirsf, shetolifo, shtolfo
smokeless (adj), shtolirfmenu, shetolifemenu, shtolfmenu
smoker (n doer), shtolirfwan, shetolifua, shtolfua
smokescreen (n), shtolfklert, shetolifikoleta, shtolfklet
smokestack (n), shtolfgriart, shetolifegeriata, shtolfgriat
smokily (adv), shtolirfiu, shetolifiu, shtolfiu
smoky (adj), shtolirfu, shetolifu, shtolfu
smolder (n), shtobiurt, shetobiufa, shtobiuf
smolder (v), shtobiurst, shetobiufo, shtobiufo
smooth (adj), frelmu, feremu, fremu
smooth (v), frelzme, feremo, fremo
smoother (n doer), frelmwan, feremua, fremua
smoothly (adv), frelmiu, feremiu, fremiu
smoothness (n), frelme, ferema, frem
smother (v), shtuthsk, shetutho, shtutho
smoulder (n), shtobiurt, shetobiufa, shtobiuf
smoulder (v), shtobiurst, shetobiufo, shtobiufo
smudge (n), frishp, ferisha, frish
smudge (v), frishsp, ferisho, frisho
smug (adj), thraifku, theraifu, thraifu
smuggle (v), thrailsp, theraipo, thraipo
smuggler (n doer), thrailpwan, theraipua, thraipua
smugly (adv), thraifkiu, theraifiu, thraifiu
smugness (n), thraifk, theraifa, thraif
smut (n), friark, feriaka, friak
snack (n), niuthk, niutha, niuth
snack (v), niuthsk, niutho, niutho
snag (n), gitushk, gituka, gituk
snag (v), gitushsk, gituko, gituko
snail (n), parume, peruma, prum
snake (n), freirk, farelka, freik
snake (v), freirsk, fareiko, freiko
snakebite (n), freigairk, fareigaika, freigaik
snakey (adj), freirku, fareiku, freiku
snap (n), thralp, therapa, thrap
snap (v), thralsp, therapo, thrapo
snapper (n doer), thralpwan, therapua, thrapua
snappily (adv), thralpiu, therapiu, thrapiu
snappy (adj), thralpu, therapu, thrapu
snapshot (n), thrapkoift, therapekoita, thrapkoit
snare (n d:string), daugilt, daugila, daugil
snare (n doer d:trap), shreilpwan, shereipua, shreipua

snare (v d:trap), shreilsp, shereipo, shreipo
snarl (n), shnaufp, shenaupa, shnaup
snarl (v), shnaufsp, shenaupo, shnaupo
snatch (n), shnoifp, shenoipa, shnoip
snatch (v), shnoifsp, shenoipo, shnoipo
snatcher (n doer), shnoifpwan, shenoipua, shnoipua
sneak (n), nushirk, nushika, nushk
sneak (v), nushirsk, nushiko, nushko
sneaker (n doer), nushirkwan, nushikua, nushkua
sneakily (adv), nushirkiu, nushikiu, nushkiu
sneaky (adj), nushirku, nushiku, nushku
sneer (n), krauishk, kerauika, krauik
sneer (v), krauishsk, kerauiko, krauiko
sneeze (n), kabirk, kabika, kabik
sneeze (v), kabirsk, kabiko, kabiko
sneezy (adj), kabirku, kabiku, kabiku
snicker (v), kikiarsk, kikiako, kikiako
snide (adj), kikiurpu, kikiupu, kikiupu
sniff (n), kilithk, kilitha, kilth
sniff (v), kilithsk, kilitho, kiltho
sniffer (n doer), kilithkwan, kilithua, kilthua
snip (n), shmarp, shemapa, shmap
snip (v), shmarsp, shemapo, shmapo
snipe (n), shnaushk, shenauka, shnauk
snipe (v), shnaushsk, shenauko, shnauko
sniper (n doer), shnaushkwan, shenaukua, shnaukua
snippet (n), shmalip, shemalipa, shmalp
snob (n), fniraf, fenirafa, fnirf
snob (v), fnirasf, fenirafo, fnirfo
snobbery (n), fnirafuet, fenirafueta, fnirfuet
snobby (adj), fnirafu, fenirafu, fnirfu
snoop (n doer), shmathkwan, shemathua, shmathua
snoop (n), shmathk, shematha, shmath
snoop (v), shmathsk, shematho, shmatho
snoopy (adj), shmathku, shemathu, shmathu
snooze (n), shmurge, shemuga, shmug
snooze (v), shmurzge, shemugo, shmugo
snoozer (n doer), shmurgwan, shemugua, shmugua
snore (n), shmaushk, shemauka, shmauk
snore (v), shmaushsk, shemauko, shmauko
snort (n), shmausht, shemauta, shmaut
snort (v), shmaushst, shemauto, shmauto
snot (n), shmirp, shemipa, shmip
snotty (adj), shmirpu, shemipu, shmipu
snout (n), shmiarp, shemiapa, shmiap
snow (n), shtorge, shetoga, shtog
snow (v), shtorzge, shetogo, shtogo
snowball (n), shtogshmonde, shetogemashipa, shtogmashp
snowball (v), shtogshmonzde, shetogemashipo, shtogmashpo
snowfall (n), shtogzhailf, shetogezhaila, shtogzhail
snowflake (n), shtogblarsht, shetogebelashota, shtogblasht
snowman (n), shtogplorn, shetogepelona, shtogplon
snowmen (n pl), shtogplornyek, shetogepeloni, shtogploni
snowmobile (n), shtogdanirt, shetogedanita, shtogdant

snowshoe (n), shtogtafarn, shetogetafana, shtogtafan
snowstorm (n), shtogferap, shetogeferipa, shtogfrip
snowy (adj), shtorgu, shetogu, shtogu
snub (n), shtunk, shetuna, shtun
snub (v), shtunsk, shetuno, shtuno
snuck (v pa), nushirskyot, nushikio, nushkio
snuff (v), shteifsk, sheteifo, shteifo
snug (adj), fruampu, feruamu, fruamu
snug (n), fruamp, feruama, fruam
snug (v), fruamesp, feruamo, fruamo
snuggle (v), fruampist, feruamito, fruamito
snugly (adv), fruampiu, feruamiu, fruamiu
so (adj/adv/conj/interj), zhaul, zhau, zhau
so (pron), zhaul, zhauei, zhau
soak (n), nakirp, nakipa, nakip
soak (v), nakirsp, nakipo, nakipo
soaker (n doer), nakirpwan, nakipua, nakipua
soap (n), naral, narila, narl
soap (v), narasle, narilo, narlo
soapbox (n), narlprekun, narileperenika, narlprenk
soapily (adv), naraliu, nariliu, narliu
soapy (adj), naralu, narilu, narlu
soar (v), bluars, beluasho, bluasho
sob (n), bralbe, beraba, brab
sob (v), bralzbe, berabo, brabo
sober (adj), braiftu, beraifu, braifu
sober (v), braifst, beraifo, braifo
sobriety (n), braift, beraifa, braif
soccer (n), shutart, shutata, shutat
sociable (adj), meirfu, meifu, meifu
social (adj), meirfu, meifu, meifu
social (n), meifarn, meifana, meifan
socialism (n), meifarl, meifara, meifar
socialist (n doer), meifarlwan, meifarua, meifarua
socialistic (adj), meifarlu, meifaru, meifaru
socialization (n), meirf, meifa, meif
socialize (v), meirsf, meifo, meifo
socializer (n doer), meirfwan, meifua, meifua
socially (adv), meirfiu, meifiu, meifiu
societal (adj), meitarku, meitaku, meifaku
society (n), meifark, meifaka, meifak
sock (n), mairp, maipa, maip
sock (v), mairsp, maipo, maipo
socket (n), mairpef, maipefa, maipef
sod (n), beft, befa, bef
soda (n), varme, vama, vam
Sodium (n davoka), Atap, Atap, Atap
Sodium (n), Shodium, Shodiuma, Shodium
soft (adj), duirfu, duifu, duifu
softball (n), duifshlerf, duifeshelefa, duifshlef
soften (v), duirsf, duifo, duifo
softener (n doer), duirfwan, duifua, duifua
softly (adv), duirfiu, duifiu, duifiu
softness (n), duirf, duifa, duif
software (n), duirfshlerf, duishelefa, duishlef
sogginess (n), nagarge, nagaga, nagag
soggy (adj), nagargu, nagagu, nagagu
soil (n), narash, narisha, narsh
soil (v), naras, narisho, narsho
sol (n), shuarl, shuala, shual
solace (n), shualirf, shualifa, shualf
solace (v), shualirsf, shualifo, shualfo

solar (adj), shuarlu, shualu, shualu
solarize (v), shuarsle, shualo, shualo
sold (v pa), trelirsfyot, terelifio, trelfio
soldier (n), gritark, geritaka, gritak
soldier (v), gritarsk, geritako, gritako
sole (adj), grilku, geriku, griku
sole (n), grilk, gerika, grik
solely (adv), grilkiu, gerikiu, grikiu
solemn (adj), shualirtu, shualitu, shualtu
solemnity (n), shualirt, shualita, shualt
solicitation (n), shushurt, shushuta, shushut
solicite (v), shushurst, shushuto, shushuto
solicitor (n doer), shushurtwan, shushutua,
    shushutua
solid (adj), ligarpu, ligapu, ligapu
solid (n), ligarp, ligapa, ligap
solidify (v), ligarsp, ligapo, ligapo
solidly (adv), ligarpiu, ligapiu, ligapiu
solitary (adj), grikartu, gerikatu, grikatu
solitude (n), grikart, gerikata, grikat
solo (adj), shularnu, shularu, shularu
solo (n), shularn, shulara, shular
solo (v), shularsne, shularo, shularo
soloist (n doer), shularnwan, shularua, shularua
soluble (adj), ligralpu, ligerapu, ligrapu
solute (n), ligralt, ligerata, ligrat
solution (n), ligralge, ligeraga, ligrag
solvable (adj), ligralgu, ligeragu, ligragu
solve (v), ligralzge, ligerago, ligrago
solvency (n), ligralpuet, ligerapueta, ligrapuet
solvent (n), ligralp, ligerapa, ligrap
solver (n doer), ligralgwan, ligeragua, ligragua
some (adj/adv), zhirn, zhinu, zhin
some (pron), zhirn, zhinei, zhin
somebody (n/pron), zhishlarde, zhisheladei,
    zhishlad
someday (adv), zhinviurliu, zhiviuliu, zhiviuliu
somehow (adv), zhiniarliu, zhinialiu, zhinialiu
someone (pron), zhinorn, zhinonei, zhinon
someplace (n), zhibrelsh, zhiberesha, zhibresh
something (n), zhidirzhe, zhidizha, zhidizh
sometime (adj/adv), zhidaurn, zhidaunu, zhidaun
sometimes (adj/adv), zhiduairn, zhidauinu,
    zhidauin
somewhat (adv), zhinarkiu, zhinakiu, zhinakiu
somewhere (adv), zhinorl, zhinolu, zhinol
somewhere (n), zhinorl, zhinola, zhinol
son (n), theiank, theiana, theian
sonance (n), zhantarn, zhanitana, zhantan
sonar (n), zhantarf, zhanitafa, zhantaf
song (n), nelarn, nelana, neln
songwriter (n doer), neliloirdwan, nelaneloidua,
    neliloidua
sonic (adj), zhantarnu, zhanitanu, zhantanu
sonogram (n), zhantanelirk, zhanitanelika,
    zhantanelk
soon (adv), brishortiu, berishotiu, brishtiu
sooner (adv), brishortweliu, berishotweliu,
    brishtweliu
soonest (adv), brishortwakiu, berishotwakiu,
    brishtwakiu
soothe (v), shruthsk, sherutho, shrutho
sophisticate (v), drakirst, derakito, drakito

sophistication (n), drakirt, derakita, drakit
sophomore (n), drakelirn, derakelina, drakeln
sorcerer (n doer), baiakwan, baialua, baialua
sorcery (n), baiak, baiala, baial
sore (adj), bairmu, baimu, baimu
sore (n), bairme, baima, baim
sorely (adv), bairmiu, baimiu, baimiu
sorrow (n), baimart, baimata, baimat
sorry (adj), baimartu, baimatu, baimatu
sort (n), bairge, baiga, baig
sort (v), bairzge, baigo, baigo
sorter (n doer), bairgwan, baigua, baigua
sought (v pa), loirstyot, loitio, loitio
soul (n), shualar, shualira, shualir
sound (adj d:secure), zhaturfu, zhatufu, zhatufu
sound (adv d:secure), zhaturfiu, zhatufiu, zhatufiu
sound (n d:audio), zhanirt, zhanita, zhant
sound (v d:audio), zhanirst, zhanito, zhanto
sounder (n doer d:audio), zhanirtwan, zhanitua,
    zhantua
soundtrack (n), zhantgethirk, zhanitegethika,
    zhantgethk
soup (n), borilk, borila, borl
soupy (adj), borilku, borilu, borlu
sour (adj), baivartu, baivatu, baivatu
sour (v), baivarst, baivato, baivato
source (n), baifort, baifota, baift
source (v), baiforst, baifoto, baifto
sourcer (n doer), baifortwan, baifotua, baiftua
sourness (n), baivart, baivata, baivat
south (adj), zhalirtu, zhalitu, zhaltu
south (n), zhalirt, zhalita, zhalt
South Carolina (n), Zhalirt Karolirn, Zhalita
    Karolina, Zhalt Karolin
South Dakota (n), Zhalirt Dakort, Zhalita Dakota,
    Zhalt Dakot
southbound (adj), zhaldraifpu, zhalideraipu,
    zhaldraipu
southeast (adj), zhalirtkiarshu, zhalitokiashu,
    zhaltkiashu
southeast (n), zhalirtkiarsh, zhalitokiasha,
    zhaltkiash
southeastern (adj), zhalirtkiarshu, zhalitokiashu,
    zhaltkiashu
southern (adj), zhalirtu, zhalitu, zhaltu
southerner (n doer), zhalirtwan, zhalitua, zhaltua
southpaw (n), zhaltkuarf, zhalitekuafa, zhaltkuaf
southward (adj), zhaltehaurshu, zhalitehaushu,
    zhaltehaushu
southwest (adj), zhalteshaithku, zhaliteshaithu,
    zhalteshaithu
southwest (n), zhalteshaithk, zhaliteshaitha,
    zhalteshaith
southwestern (adj), zhalteshaithku, zhaliteshaithu,
    zhalteshaithu
souvenir (n), talzhurp, talezhupa, talzhup
sovereign (n doer), afenthaurfwan, afenothaufua,
    afenthaufua
sovereignly (adv), afenthaurfiu, afenothaufiu,
    afenthaufiu
sovereignty (n), afenthaurf, afenothaufa, afenthauf
Soviet (n), Shoviert, Shovieta, Shoviet
sow (v), niurzme, niumo, niumo

soybean (n), shaushurth, shaushutha, shaushuth
space (n), thushp, thusha, thush
space (v), thushsp, thusho, thusho
spacecraft (n), thushkarfp, thushekafopa, thushkafp
spaceman (n), thushplorn, thushepelona, thushplon
spacemen (n pl), thushplornyek, thushepeloni, thushploni
spacer (n doer), thushpwan, thushua, thushua
spaceship (n), thushflerve, thushefeleva, thushflev
spacious (adj), thushpu, thushu, thushu
spade (n), labirk, labika, labik
spade (v), labirsk, labiko, labiko
Spain (n), Shpairn, Shepaina, Shpain
span (n), bleirsh, beleisha, bleish
span (v), bleirs, beleisho, bleisho
Spanish (n), Shpainarn, Shepainana, Shpainan
spank (n), preirk, pereika, preik
spank (v), preirsk, pereiko, preiko
spanker (n doer), preirkwan, pereikua, preikua
spanner (n doer), bleirshwan, beleishua, bleishua
spar (n), troiark, teroiaka, troiak
spar (v), troiarsk, teroiako, troiako
spare (n), labolirk, labolika, labolk
spare (v), labolirsk, laboliko, labolko
sparingly (adv), labolirkiu, labolikiu, labolkiu
spark (n), troilk, teroika, troik
spark (v), troilsk, teroiko, troiko
sparker (n doer), troilkwan, teroikua, troikua
sparkle (n), troikart, teroikata, troikat
sparkle (v), troikarst, teroikato, troikato
sparkly (adj), troikartu, teroikatu, troikatu
sparky (adj), troilku, teroiku, troiku
sparse (adj), feianku, feianu, feianu
sparsely (adv), feiankiu, feianiu, feianiu
spasm (n), shleishuk, sheleishuka, shleishk
spat (n d:quarrel), shtreishp, shetoreipa, shtreip
spat (v pa), fnarskyot, finakio, fnakio
spate (n d:flood), shtraush, shetoranta, shtraut
spatial (adj), thushpu, thushu, thushu
spatially (adv), thushpiu, thushiu, thushiu
spatula (n), shtrasht, shetorata, shtrat
spawn (v), shprashsk, sheporako, shprako
speak (v d:verbosity), talirs, talisho, talsho
speakable (adj d:verbosity), talirshu, talishu, talshu
speakably (adv d:verbosity), talirshiu, talishiu, talshiu
speaker (n d:air cone), platurk, pelatuka, platuk
speaker (n doer d:verbosity), talirshwan, talishua, talshua
spear (n), shtrink, shetorina, shtrin
spear (v), shtrinsk, shetorino, shtrino
spearhead (v), shtrinkefirst, shetorinekefito, shtrinkefto
special (adj), sheirshu, sheishu, sheishu
specialist (n doer), sheirshwan, sheishua, sheishua
specialize (v), sheirs, sheisho, sheisho
specially (adv), sheirshiu, sheishiu, sheishiu
specialty (n), sheirsh, sheisha, sheish
specie (n), flirfp, felifopa, flifp
specific (adj), flikartu, felikatu, flikatu
specific (n), flikarft, felikafita, flikaft

specifically (adv), flikartiu, felikatiu, flikatiu
specification (n), flikart, felikata, flikat
specify (v), flikarst, felikato, flikato
specimen (n), flifparn, felifopana, flifpan
speck (n), thurk, thuka, thuk
spectacle (n), thuklark, thukelaka, thuklak
spectacular (adj), thuklarku, thukelaku, thuklaku
spectacularly (adv), thuklarkiu, thukelakiu, thuklakiu
spectate (v), thuklarsk, thukelako, thuklako
spectator (n doer), thuklarkwan, thukelakua, thuklakua
spectra (n), thiurk, thiuka, thiuk
spectral (adj), thiurku, thiuku, thiuku
spectrally (adv), thiurkiu, thiukiu, thiukiu
spectroscopic (adj), thiurkluarfu, thiukeluafu, thiukluafu
spectroscopy (n), thiurkluarf, thiukeluafa, thiukluaf
spectrum (n), thiukart, thiukata, thiukat
speculate (v), thukars, thukasho, thukasho
speculation (n), thukarsh, thukasha, thukash
speculative (adj), thukarshu, thukashu, thukashu
speculatively (adv), thukarshiu, thukashiu, thukashiu
speculator (n doer), thukarshwan, thukashua, thukashua
speech (n d:verbosity), talirsh, talisha, talsh
speechless (adj), talirshmenu, talishemenu, talshmenu
speed (n), zhbairn, zhubaina, zhbain
speed (v), zhbairsne, zhubaino, zhbaino
speedboat (n), zhbainshkorbe, zhubaineshekoba, zhbainshkob
speeder (n doer), zhbairnwan, zhubainua, zhbainua
speedily (adv), zhbairniu, zhubainiu, zhbainiu
speedway (n), zhbainpliorl, zhubainepeliola, zhbainpliol
speedy (adj), zhbairnu, zhubainu, zhbainu
spell (n d:witchcraft), shpursh, shipusha, shpush
spell (v d:character), thasle, tharo, tharo
spellbind (v), shpushpaupizme, shipushepaumubo, shpushpaumbo
spellbound (v pa), shpushpaupizmyot, shipushepaumubio, shpushpaumbio
spend (v), dorklarst, dorikelato, dorklato
spendable (adj), dorklartu, dorikelatu, dorklatu
spender (n doer), dorklartwan, dorikelatua, dorklatua
spent (v pa), dorklarstyot, dorikelatio, dorklatio
spew (v), shnoishst, shenoito, shnoito
sphere (n), forash, forisha, forsh
sphereoid (n), forashan, forishana, forshan
spherical (adj), forashu, forishu, forshu
spherically (adv), forashiu, forishiu, forshiu
spice (n), dorkairt, dorikaita, dorkait
spice (v), dorkairst, dorikaito, dorkaito
spicer (n doer), dorkairtwan, dorikaitua, dorkaitua
spicy (adj), dorkairtu, dorikaitu, dorkaitu
spider (n), glirth, gelitha, glith
spidery (adj), glirthu, gelithu, glithu
spiff (n), zhuaift, zhuaifa, zhuaif
spiff (v), zhuaifst, zhuaifo, zhuaifo
spiffy (adj), zhuaiftu, zhuaifu, zhuaifu

spike (n), faiasht, faiata, faiat
spike (v), faiashst, faiato, faiato
spikes (v pa), faiashstyot, faiatio, faiatio
spill (n), shnart, shenata, shnat
spill (v), shnarst, shenato, shnato
spillage (n), shnartuet, shenatueta, shnatuet
spiller (n doer), shnartwan, shenatua, shnatua
spillover (n), shnartafen, shenatafena, shnatafen
spillway (n), shnatpliorl, shenatepeliola, shnatpliol
spilt (v pa), shnarstyot, shenatio, shnatio
spin (n), shnarp, shenapa, shnap
spin (v), shnarsp, shenapo, shnapo
spinal (adj), shnairtu, shenaitu, shnaitu
spindle (n), shnaparn, shenapana, shnapan
spine (n), shnairt, shenaita, shnait
spineless (adj), shnairtmenu, shenaitemenu,
   shnaitmenu
spinner (n doer), shnarpwan, shenapua, shnapua
spinoff (n), shnarpunf, shenapunefa, shnapunf
spiny (adj), shnairtu, shenaitu, shnaitu
spiral (adj), ftaurku, futauku, ftauku
spiral (v), ftaursk, futauko, ftauko
spire (n), ftaurf, futaufa, ftauf
spire (v), ftaursf, futaufo, ftaufo
spirit (n), zhuarl, zhuala, zhual
spirit (v), zhuarsle, zhualo, zhualo
spiritual (adj), zhuarlu, zhualu, zhualu
spirituality (n), zhuarluet, zhualueta, zhualuet
spiritually (adv), zhuarliu, zhualiu, zhualiu
spit (n), fnark, finaka, fnak
spit (v), fnarsk, finako, fnako
spite (n), fairk, faika, faik
spite (v), fairsk, faiko, faiko
spiteful (adj), fairku, faiku, faiku
spitter (n doer), fnarkwan, finakua, fnakua
splash (n), fnirfk, fenifoka, fnifk
splash (v), fnirfsk, fenifoko, fnifko
splasher (n doer), fnirfkwan, fenifokua, fnifkua
splashy (adj), fnirfku, fenifoku, fnifku
splat (n), buart, buata, buat
splatter (n), buashart, buashata, buasht
splatter (v), buasharst, buashato, buashto
splendid (adj), veilirfu, veilifu, veilfu
splendidly (adv), veilirfiu, veilifiu, veilfiu
splendor (n), veilirf, veilifa, veilf
splice (n), shlaiarp, shelaiapa, shlaiap
splice (v), shlaiarsp, shelaiapo, shlaiapo
splint (n), shliunf, sheliuna, shliun
splinter (n), shliunak, sheliunaka, shliunk
splinter (v), shliunask, sheliunako, shliunko
split (n), shlairk, sheliaka, shlaik
split (v pa), shlairskyot, sheliakio, shlaikio
split (v), shlairsk, sheliako, shlaiko
splitter (n doer), shlairkwan, sheliakua, shlaikua
SplitWand (n), daiftarn, daifetana, daiftan
splurge (v), shroize, sheroigo, shroigo
spoil (n), vaurn, vauna, vaun
spoil (v), vaursne, vauno, vauno
spoiler (n doer), vaurnwan, vaunua, vaunua
spoke (n d:support), shirge, shiga, shig
spoke (v d:support), shirzge, shigo, shigo
spoke (v pa d:verbosity), talirsyot, talishio, talshio
spokesman (n doer), talirshwan, talishua, talshua

spokesperson (n doer), talirshwan, talishua, talshua
spokeswoman (n doer), talirshwan, talishua,
   talshua
sponge (n), duvoirp, duvoipa, duvoip
sponge (v), duvoirsp, duvoipo, duvoipo
sponsor (n doer), duvirlwan, duvilua, duvilua
sponsor (v), duvirsle, duvilo, duvilo
sponsorship (n), duvirl, duvila, duvil
spoof (n), diothk, diotha, dioth
spoof (v), diothsk, diotho, diotho
spook (n), dauiark, dauiaka, dauiak
spook (v), dauiarsk, dauiako, dauiako
spooky (adj), dauiarku, dauiaku, dauiaku
spool (n), dulithk, dulitha, dulith
spool (v), dulithsk, dulitho, dulitho
spoon (n), dorap, doripa, dorp
spoon (v), dorasp, doripo, dorpo
spooner (n doer), dorapwan, doripua, dorpua
spoonful (adj), dorapu, doripu, dorpu
sporadic (adj), guiarmu, guiamu, guiamu
sporadically (adv), guiarmiu, guiamiu, guiamiu
spore (n), guiarme, guiama, guiam
sport (n), viaushk, viausha, viaush
sport (v), viaushsk, viausho, viausho
sportily (adv), viaushkiu, viaushiu, viaushiu
sportscaster (n doer), viaushkebidwan,
   viaushebidua, viaushbidua
sportsman (n), viaushplorn, viaushepelona,
   viaushplon
sportsmanship (n), viaushplornfif,
   viaushepelonefifa, viaushplonfif
sportsmen (n pl), viaushplornyek, viaushepeloni,
   viaushploni
sportster (n doer), viaushkwan, viaushua, viaushua
sportswear (n), viaushflarf, viaushefelafa, viaushflaf
sporty (adj), viaushku, viaushu, viaushu
spot (n), derap, deripa, derp
spot (v), derasp, deripo, derpo
spotless (adj), derapemenu, deripemenu,
   derpemenu
spotlight (n), derpefluarn, deripefeluana,
   derpefluan
spotter (n doer), derapwan, deripua, derpua
spotty (adj), derapu, deripu, derpu
spousal (adj), pimarfu, pimafu, pimafu
spouse (n), pimarf, pimafa, pimaf
spout (n), shtraushk, shetorauka, shtrauk
spout (v), shtraushsk, shetorauko, shtrauko
sprain (n), pliaushk, peliauka, pliauk
sprain (v), pliaushsk, peliauko, pliauko
sprang (v pa d:coil, surprise), threlstyot, theretio,
   thretio
sprawl (n), pliarf, peliafa, pliaf
sprawl (v), pliarsf, peliafo, pliafo
spray (n), pliurf, peliufa, pliuf
spray (v), pliursf, peliufo, pliufo
sprayer (n doer), pliurfwan, peliufua, pliufua
spread (n), rilorp, rilopa, rilp
spread (v pa), rilorspyot, rilopio, rilpio
spread (v), rilorsp, rilopo, rilpo
spreader (n doer), rilorpwan, rilopua, rilpua
spree (n), plint, pelina, plin
spring (adj d:season), voralu, vorilu, vorlu

spring (n d:coil, surprise), threlt, thereta, thret
spring (n d:season), voral, vorila, vorl
spring (v d:coil, surprise), threlst, thereto, threto
springboard (n), thretplok, theretepelorika, thretplork
springer (n doer d:coil, surprise), threltwan, theretua, thretua
springtime (n), vorldaurn, voriledauna, vorldaun
sprinkle (n), theraf, therifa, thrif
sprinkle (v), therasf, therifo, thrifo
sprinkler (n doer), therafwan, therifua, thrifua
sprint (n), blithk, belitha, blith
sprint (v), blithsk, belitho, blitho
sprinter (n doer), blithkwan, belithua, blithua
sprout (n), bliaump, beliauma, bliaum
sprout (v), bliaumesp, beliaumo, bliaumo
spun (v pa), shnarspyot, shenapio, shnapio
spur (n), blairsh, belaisha, blaish
spur (v), blairs, belaisho, blaisho
spurious (adj), blairshu, belaishu, blaishu
spurn (v), blaishsp, belaipo, blaipo
spurt (v), blaiarst, belaiato, blaiato
sputter (v), brulist, berulito, brulto
spy (n), diurn, diuna, diun
spy (v), diursne, diuno, diuno
spyglass (n), diundrinat, diunederinota, diundrint
squabble (n), kraiarp, keraiapa, kraiap
squabble (v), kraiarsp, keraiapo, kraiapo
squabbler (n doer), kraiarpwan, keraiapua, kraiapua
squad (n), giurk, giuka, giuk
squadron (n), giukart, giukata, giukat
squander (v), shralzbe, sherabo, shrabo
squanderous (adj), shralbu, sherabu, shrabu
square (n), kazhirge, kazhiga, kazhig
square (v), kazhirzge, kazhigo, kazhigo
squarely (adv), kazhirgiu, kazhigiu, kazhigiu
squash (n d:fruit), gatharn, gathana, gathan
squash (n d:pressure), dairp, daipa, daip
squash (v d:pressure), dairsp, daipo, daipo
squasher (n doer d:pressure), dairpwan, daipua, daipua
squat (n), shkubarsh, shekubasha, shkubash
squat (v), shkubars, shekubasho, shkubasho
squatter (n doer), shkubarshwan, shekubashua, shkubashua
squawk (n), shkaiaushk, shekaiauka, shkaiauk
squawk (v), shkaiaushsk, shekaiauko, shkaiauko
squeak (n), shkeirk, shekeika, shkeik
squeak (v), shkeirsk, shekeiko, shkeiko
squeakily (adv), shkeirkiu, shekeikiu, shkeikiu
squeaky (adj), shkeirku, shekeiku, shkeiku
squeal (n), shkelirk, shekelika, shkelk
squeal (v), shkelirsk, shekeliko, shkelko
squeegee (n), giokart, giokata, giokat
squeegee (v), giokarst, giokato, giokato
squeeze (n), giork, gioka, giok
squeeze (v), giorsk, gioko, gioko
squeezer (n doer), giorkwan, giokua, giokua
squiggle (n), boilak, boilika, boilk
squiggle (v), boilask, boiliko, boilko
squirrel (n), boirank, boirana, boiran
squirrely (adj), boiranku, boiranu, boiranu

squirt (n), shkiort, shekiota, shkiot
squirt (v), shkiorst, shekioto, shkioto
squish (n), doirp, doipa, doip
squish (v), doirsp, doipo, doipo
squisher (n doer), doirpwan, doipua, doipua
squishy (adj), doirpu, doipu, doipu
Ss (let pl), seili, seili, seili
stab (n), fpirge, fepiga, fpig
stab (v), fpirzge, fepigo, fpigo
stabber (n doer), fpirgwan, fepigua, fpigua
stabile (adj), ftarpu, fitapu, ftapu
stability (n), ftarp, fitapa, ftap
stabilization (n), ftarpuet, fitapueta, ftapuet
stabilize (v), ftarsp, fitapo, ftapo
stabilizer (n doer), ftarpwan, fitapua, ftapua
stable (n d:barn), fpurf, fipufa, fpuf
stack (n), griart, geriata, griat
stack (v), griarst, geriato, griato
stacker (n doer), griartwan, geriatua, griatua
stadium (n), niurt, niuta, niut
staff (adj d:people), arbortu, aribotu, arbotu
staff (n d:people), arbort, aribota, arbot
staff (n d:plaster), blerth, beletha, bleth
staff (n d:stick), harap, haripa, harip
staff (v d:people), arborst, ariboto, arboto
staffer (n doer d:people), arbortwan, aribotua, arbotua
stage (n), tralk, teraka, trak
stage (v), tralsk, terako, trako
stagger (v), griarzge, geriago, griago
stagnant (adj), griashku, geriashu, griashu
stagnate (v), griashsk, geriasho, griasho
stagnation (n), griashk, geriasha, griash
stain (n), toirf, toifa, toif
stain (v), toirsf, toifo, toifo
stainer (n doer), toirfwan, toifua, toifua
stainless (adj), toirfmenu, toifemenu, toifmenu
stainless (n), toirfmen, toifemena, toifmen
stair (n), tairn, taina, tain
staircase (n), tainshuart, taineshuata, tainshuat
stairway (n), tainpliorl, tainepeliola, tainpliol
stairwell (n), tainavurp, tainavupa, tainavup
stake (n), gofirk, gofika, gofk
stake (v), gofirsk, gofiko, gofko
stakeholder (n doer), gofkthorthkwan, gofikethorithua, gofkthorthua
stakeout (n), gofirkuil, gofikuila, gofkuil
stale (adj), breimpu, bereimu, breimu
stalemate (n), breimfenshk, bereimefenika, breimfenk
staleness (n), breimp, bereima, breim
stalk (n d:appendage), tuiarp, tuiapa, tuiap
stalk (v d:pursue), griarsp, geriapo, griapo
stalker (n doer d:pursue), griarpwan, geriapua, griapua
stall (n d:compartment), tiork, tioka, tiok
stall (n d:wait), teirk, teika, teik
stall (v d:wait), teirsk, teiko, teiko
staller (n doer d:wait), teirkwan, teikua, teikua
stamp (n), baunk, bauna, baun
stamp (v), baunsk, bauno, bauno
stampede (n), baunkoide, baunoida, baunoid
stamper (n doer), baunkwan, baunua, baunua

stance (n), trelp, terepa, trep
stand (n), trelirt, terelita, trelt
stand (v), trelirst, terelito, trelto
standard (n), trefirk, terefika, trefk
standardization (n), trefirkuet, terefikueta, trefkuet
standardize (v), trefirsk, terefiko, trefko
standby (adj), trelvurtu, terelevutu, trelvutu
standby (n), trelvurt, terelevuta, trelvut
standoff (n), trelirtunf, terelitunefa, treltunf
standout (n), trelirtuil, terelituila, treltuil
standpoint (n), treltaifort, terelitaifota, treltaift
standstill (n), treltshlern, tereliteshelena, treltshlen
standup (adj), treltiveilu, terelitiveilu, treltiveilu
standup (n), treltiveil, terelitiveila, treltiveil
stank (v pa), bierskyot, biekio, biekio
staple (n d:commodity), triank, teriana, trian
staple (n d:crimp), shkelirp, shekelipa, shkelp
staple (v d:crimp), shkelirsp, shekelipo, shkelpo
stapler (n doer d:crimp), shkelirpwan, shekelipua, shkelpua
star (n d:celebrity), drokifar, derokirofa, drokirf
star (n d:celestial), gliarsh, geliasha, gliash
star (v d:celebrity), drokifasre, derokirofo, drokirfo
stare (n), shkiart, shekiata, shkiat
stare (v), shkiarst, shekiato, shkiato
starfish (n), gliashlersh, geliashelesha, gliashlesh
stargaze (v), gliashtiarzve, geliashetiavo, gliashtiavo
stargazer (n doer), gliashtiarvwan, geliashetiavua, gliashtiavua
stark (adj), shkiaushtu, shekiautu, shkiautu
starkness (n), shkiausht, shekiauta, shkiaut
starlight (n), gliashfluarn, geliashefeluana, gliashfluan
starry (adj d:celestial), gliarshu, geliashu, gliashu
starship (n), gliashflerve, geliashefeleva, gliashflev
start (n), shkalirt, shokalita, shkalt
start (v), shkalirst, shokalito, shkalto
starter (n doer), shkalirtwan, shokalitua, shkaltua
startle (n), shkaltark, shokalitaka, shkaltak
startle (v), shkaltarsk, shokalitako, shkaltako
startup (n), shkalirtiveil, shokalitiveila, shkaltiveil
starvation (n), groilf, geroifa, groif
starve (v), groilsf, geroifo, groifo
stash (n), shneisht, sheneita, shneit
stash (v), shneishst, sheneito, shneito
state (n d:region), shaiarsh, shaiasha, shaiash
state (n d:status), shpert, shipeta, shpet
state (v d:say), biurst, biuto, biuto
statehood (n), shaiarshfif, shaiashefifa, shaiashfif
statehouse (n), shaiashkiarf, shaiashekiafa, shaiashkiaf
stateless (adj d:status), shpertmenu, shipetemenu, shpetmenu
statement (n d:say), biurt, biuta, biut
stateside (adj), shaiashoirtu, shaiashoitu, shaiashoitu
stateside (n), shaiashoirt, shaiashoita, shaiashoit
statesman (n), shaiashplorn, shaiashepelona, shaiashplon
statesmanship (n), shaiashplornfif, shaiashepelonefifa, shaiashplonfif
statesmen (n pl), shaiashplornyek, shaiashepeloni, shaiashploni

statewide (adj), shaiashkrashku, shaiashekerashu, shaiashkrashu
static (adj), shpefortu, shipefotu, shpeftu
static (n), shpefort, shipefota, shpeft
station (n), shlukert, sheluketa, shluket
station (v), shlukerst, sheluketo, shluketo
stationary (adj), shlukertu, sheluketu, shluketu
stationery (n), veflarn, vefelana, veflan
statistic (n), shlurth, shelutha, shluth
statistical (adj), shlurthu, sheluthu, shluthu
statue (n), shparok, shiparoka, shpark
stature (n), shparif, shiparifa, shparf
status (n), shpetar, shipetira, shpetir
statute (n), shklart, shikelata, shklat
statutory (adj), shklartu, shikelatu, shklatu
staunch (adj), frikartu, ferikatu, frikatu
staunch (n), frikart, ferikata, frikat
staunch (v), frikarst, ferikato, frikato
stave (v d:stick), harasp, haripo, haripo
stay (n), shlurk, sheluka, shluk
stay (v), shlursk, sheluko, shluko
stayer (n doer), shlurkwan, shelukua, shlukua
stead (n), fnert, fineta, fnet
steadfast (adj), fnetezhairshu, finetezhaishu, fnetezhaishu
steadfastly (adv), fnetezhairshiu, finetezhaishiu, fnetezhaishiu
steadfastness (n), fnetezhairsh, finetezhaisha, fnetezhaish
steadily (adv), fnertiu, finetiu, fnetiu
steadiness (n), fnertuet, finetueta, fnetuet
steady (adj), fnertu, finetu, fnetu
steady (v), fnerst, fineto, fneto
steak (n), dralirk, deralika, dralk
steakhouse (n), dralkiarf, deralikiafa, dralkiaf
steal (v), shlarsk, shelako, shlako
stealer (n doer), shlarkwan, shelakua, shlakua
stealth (n), shlark, shelaka, shlak
stealthily (adv), shlarkiu, shelakiu, shlakiu
stealthy (adj), shlarku, shelaku, shlaku
steam (n), vlirsh, velisha, vlish
steam (v), vlirs, velisho, vlisho
steamboat (n), vlishkorbe, velishekoba, vlishkob
steamer (n doer), vlirshwan, velishua, vlishua
steamroll (v), vlishfalasre, velishefaliro, vlishfaliro
steamroller (n doer), vlishfalarwan, velishefalirua, vlishfalirua
steamship (n), vlishflerve, velishefeleva, vlishflev
steamy (adj), vlirshu, velishu, vlishu
steed (n), bavaıl, bavata, bavat
steel (n), gloft, gelofa, glof
steelmade (v pa), glofnarzgyot, gelofenagio, glofnagio
steelmake (v), glofnarzge, gelofenago, glofnago
steelmaker (n doer), glofnargwan, gelofenagua, glofnagua
steelman (n), glofplorn, gelofepelona, glofplon
steelmen (n pl), glofplornyek, gelofepeloni, glofploni
steelwork (n), glofkiork, gelofekioka, glofkiok
steelworker (n doer), glofkiorkwan, gelofekiokua, glofkiokua
steely (adj), gloftu, gelofu, glofu

steep (adj), bavarpu, bavapu, bavapu
steep (v), bavarsp, bavapo, bavapo
steeple (n), bavarsh, bavasha, bavash
steeplechase (n), bavashtutart, bavashetutata, bavashtutat
steeply (adv), bavarpiu, bavapiu, bavapiu
steepness (n), bavarp, bavapa, bavap
steer (n d:cattle), falirf, falifa, falf
steer (v d:navigate), bilorst, biloto, bilto
stellar (adj d:celestial), gliarshu, geliashu, gliashu
stem (n), lifarbe, lifaba, lifab
stem (v), lifarzbe, lifabo, lifabo
stench (n), brieshk, beriesha, briesh
step (adj), glishku, gelishu, glishu
step (n), glishk, gelisha, glish
step (v), glishsk, gelisho, glisho
stepchild (n), glishluart, gelisheluara, glishluar
stepchildren (n pl), glishluartyek, gelisheluari, glishluari
stepdaughter (n), glishlidor, gelishelunora, glishlurn
stepfather (n), glishvoteft, gelishevoteta, glishvotet
stepladder (n), glishtrirt, gelisheterita, glishtrit
stepmother (n), glishmashel, gelishemalisha, glishmalsh
stepper (n doer), glishkwan, gelishua, glishua
stepson (n), giktheiarn, giketheiana, giktheian
stereo (n), shoriarn, shoriana, shorian
stereotype (n), tuldorap, tuledoripa, tuldorp
stereotype (v), tuldorasp, tuledoripo, tuldorpo
stereotypical (adj), tuldorapu, tuledoripu, tuldorpu
sterile (adj), busheiftu, busheifu, busheifu
sterilely (adv), busheiftiu, busheifiu, busheifiu
sterility (n), busheift, busheifa, busheif
sterilization (n), busheiftuet, busheifueta, busheifuet
sterilize (v), busheifst, busheifo, busheifo
stern (adj d:firm), miriarku, miriaku, miriaku
stern (n d:rear), deiurt, deiuta, deiut
sternly (adv d:firm), miriarkiu, miriakiu, miriakiu
stew (n), drelif, derelifa, drelf
stew (v), drelisf, derelifo, drelfo
stick (n d:twig, poke), shneft, shineta, shnet
stick (v d:adhere), shnoirsk, shenoiko, shnoiko
stick (v d:twig, poke), shnefst, shineto, shneto
sticker (n doer d:adhere), shnoirkwan, shenoikua, shnoikua
stickiness (n d:adhere), shnoirk, shenoika, shnoik
stickler (n), shnoikarn, shenoikana, shnoikan
sticky (adj d:adhere), shnoirku, shenoiku, shnoiku
stiff (adj d:rigid), grethapu, gerethu, grethu
stiff (v d:cheat), gretharsne, gerethano, grethano
stiffen (v d:rigid), grethasp, geretho, gretho
stiffness (n d:rigid), grethap, geretha, greth
stifle (v), gretharst, gerethato, grethato
stigma (n), brivurt, berivuta, brivut
stigmatize (v), brivurst, berivuto, brivuto
still (adj d:calm), shlernu, shelenu, shlenu
still (adv d:calm), shlerniu, sheleniu, shleniu
still (n d:distillery), kishetriagart, kisheteriagata, kishetriagat
still (v d:calm), shlersne, sheleno, shleno
still (v d:distillery), kishetriagarst, kisheteriagato, kishetriagato
stillness (n d:calm), shlern, shelena, shlen
stillwater (n), shleneidorn, sheleneidona, shleneidon
stilt (n), shleft, sheleta, shlet
stilt (v), shlefst, sheleto, shleto
stimulant (n), zhaiakank, zhaiakana, zhaiakan
stimulate (v), zhaiarsk, zhaiako, zhaiako
stimulation (n), zhaiark, zhaiaka, zhaiak
stimulator (n doer), zhaiarkwan, zhaiakua, zhaiakua
stimuli (n pl), zhaiakashkyek, zhaiakashi, zhaiakashi
stimulus (n), zhaiakashk, zhaiakasha, zhaiakash
sting (n d:bite), bierge, biega, bieg
sting (v d:bite), bierzge, biego, biego
stinger (n doer d:bite), biergwan, biegua, biegua
stinginess (n d:frugal), frielk, ferieka, friek
stingy (adj d:bite), biergu, biegu, biegu
stingy (adj d:frugal), frielku, ferieku, frieku
stink (n), bierk, bieka, biek
stink (v), biersk, bieko, bieko
stinker (n doer), bierkwan, biekua, biekua
stinky (adj), bierku, bieku, bieku
stint (n), fielirt, fielileta, fielt
stint (v), fielirst, fielileto, fielto
stipend (n), shrilarf, sherilara, shrilar
stipulate (v), shrilansk, sherilano, shrilano
stipulation (n), shrilank, sherilana, shrilan
stir (n), grelirt, gerelita, grelt
stir (v), grelirst, gerelito, grelto
stirer (n doer), grelirtwan, gerelitua, greltua
stitch (n), fieltsh, fietisha, fietsh
stitch (v), fielts, fietisho, fietsho
stock (n d:fill equity), frifk, ferifa, frif
stock (v d:fill equity), frifsk, ferifo, frifo
stockbroker (n doer), frifkrolirpwan, ferifekerolipua, frifkrolpua
stocker (n doer d:fill equity), frifkwan, ferifua, frifua
stockholder (n doer), frifthorthkwan, ferifethorithua, frifthorthua
Stockholm (n), Shtokolirm, Shetokolima, Shtokolm
stocking (n d:sock), frifank, ferifana, frifan
stockman (n), frifplorn, ferifepelona, frifplon
stockmen (n pl), frifplornyek, ferifepeloni, frifploni
stockpile (n), frifnairp, ferifenaipa, frifnaip
stockpile (v), frifnairsp, ferifenaipo, frifnaipo
stockroom (n), frifshranf, ferifesherana, frifshran
stocky (adj d:fill equity), frifku, ferifu, frifu
stoke (v), shpushst, sheputo, shputo
stoker (n doer), shpushtwan, sheputua, shputua
stole (v pa), shlarskyot, shelakio, shlakio
stomach (n), patark, pataka, patak
stomp (n), bauink, bauina, bauin
stomp (v), bauinsk, bauino, bauino
stomper (n doer), bauinkwan, bauinua, bauinua
stone (n), baraft, barafa, baraf
stone (v), barafst, barafo, barafo
stonecut (v pa), barafdairsyot, barafedaishio, barafdaishio
stonecut (v), barafdairs, barafedaisho, barafdaisho
stonecutter (n doer), barafdairshwan,

barafedaishua, barafdaishua
stonehenge (n), baraifant, baraifana, baraifan
stoner (n doer), baraftwan, barafua, barafua
stonewall (v), barafnolthsk, barafenolitho, barafnoltho
stoneware (n), barafshlerf, barafeshelefa, barafshlef
stoney (adj), baraftu, barafu, barafu
stood (v pa), trelirstyot, terelitio, treltio
stool (n d:chair), tamarf, tamafa, tamaf
stool (n d:excrement), kriurn, keriuna, kriun
stoop (n d:porch), bienirk, bienika, bienk
stoop (v d:bend), boikarst, biokato, biokato
stop (n), taurk, tauka, tauk
stop (v), taursk, tauko, tauko
stopgap (adj), taukfarthu, taukefathu, taukfathu
stopgap (n), taukfarth, taukefatha, taukfath
stoplight (n), taukfluarn, taukefeluana, taukfluan
stopover (n), taurkafen, taukafena, taukafen
stoppage (n), taurkuet, taukueta, taukuet
stopper (n doer), taurkwan, taukua, taukua
stopwatch (n), tauklufk, taukeluka, taukluk
storage (n), drapart, derapata, drapat
store (n), dralp, derapa, drap
store (v), dralsp, derapo, drapo
storefront (n), drapflarsh, derapefelarina, drapflarn
storehouse (n), drapkiarf, derapekiafa, drapkiaf
storekeeper (n doer), drapklorfwan, derapekelofua, drapklofua
storer (n doer), dralpwan, derapua, drapua
storm (n), ferap, feripa, frip
storm (v), ferasp, feripo, fripo
stormy (adj), ferapu, feripu, fripu
story (n), felar, felira, flir
storyboard (n), flirplok, felirepelorika, flirplork
storybook (n), flirvonurde, felirevonuda, flirvond
storyline (n), fliroifk, feliroifa, fliroif
storyteller (n doer), flirpreltwan, felireperetua, flirpretua
stout (adj), shkaufku, shekaufu, shkaufu
stove (n), lakirt, lakita, lakit
stow (v), shrioshsk, sherioko, shrioko
straddle (n), tilart, tilata, tilat
straddle (v), tilarst, tilato, tilato
straggle (v), pilarsk, pilako, pilako
straggler (n doer), pilarkwan, pilakua, pilakua
straight (adj), traishku, teraishu, traishu
straightedge (n), traishkelf, teriashekerifa, traishkerf
straighten (v), traishsk, teraisho, traisho
straightforward (adj), traishvoanaurshu, teraishevoanaushu, traishvoanaushu
straightforwardly (adv), traishvoanaurshiu, teraishevoanaushiu, traishvoanaushiu
straightness (n), traishk, teraisha, traish
strain (n), prulirk, perulika, prulk
strain (v), prulirsk, peruliko, prulko
strainer (n doer), prulirkwan, perulikua, prulkua
strait (n), traithk, teraitha, traith
straitjacket (n), traithbifirt, teraithebifita, traithbifit
strand (n), tifashst, tifata, tifat
strand (v), tifashst, tifato, tifato
strange (adj), shaurku, shauku, shauku
strangely (adv), shaurkiu, shaukiu, shaukiu

strangeness (n), shaukar, shaukata, shaukat
stranger (n doer), shaurkwan, shaukua, shaukua
strangle (v), tivarzge, tivago, tivago
stranglehold (n), tivagthorthk, tivagethoritha, tivagthorth
strangulation (n), tivarge, tivaga, tivag
strap (n), tivarp, tivapa, tivap
strap (v), tivarsp, tivapo, tivapo
strapper (n doer), tivarpwan, tivapua, tivapua
strata (n pl), plairpyek, pelaipi, plaipi
strategic (adj), plairku, pelaiku, plaiku
strategically (adv), plairkiu, pelaikiu, plaikiu
strategist (n doer), plairkwan, pelaikua, plaikua
strategy (n), plairk, pelaika, plaik
stratus (n), plairp, pelaipa, plaip
straw (n), nalirn, nalina, naln
strawberry (n), theinalirp, theinalipa, theinalp
stray (adj), floshku, feloshu, floshu
stray (n), floshk, felosha, flosh
stray (v), floshsk, felosho, flosho
streak (n), koieshk, koieka, koiek
streak (v), koieshsk, koieko, koieko
streaky (adj), koieshku, koieku, koieku
stream (n), falirme, falima, falm
stream (v), falirzme, falimo, falmo
streamer (n doer), falirmwan, falimua, falmua
streamline (v), falmroifsk, falimeroifo, falmroifo
street (n), arthiarme, arithiama, arthiam
streetcar (n), arthiamgeral, arithiamegerela, arthiamgrel
streetwise (adj), arthiamfluirku, arithiamefeliuku, arthiamfluiku
strength (n), boraf, borifa, borf
strengthen (v), borasf, borifo, borfo
stress (n), thorge, thoga, thog
stressed (v), thorzge, thogo, thogo
stressful (adj), thorgu, thogu, thogu
stressfully (adv), thorgiu, thogiu, thogiu
stressor (n doer), thorgwan, thogua, thogua
stretch (n), grairt, geraita, grait
stretch (v), grairst, geraito, graito
stretcher (n doer), grairtwan, geraitua, graitua
stretchy (adj), grairtu, geraitu, graitu
strew (v), graithsk, geraitho, graitho
strict (adj), bafirku, bafiku, bafku
strictly (adv), bafirkiu, bafikiu, bafkiu
strictness (n), bafirk, bafika, bafk
stride (n), kianirp, kianipa, kianp
strife (n), kliarp, keliapa, kliap
strifer (n doer), kliarpwan, keliapua, kliapua
strike (n), klairk, kelaika, klaik
strike (v), klairsk, kelaiko, klaiko
strikeout (n), klairkuil, kelaikuila, klaikuil
striker (n doer), klairkwan, kelaikua, klaikua
strikingly (adv), klairkiu, kelaikiu, klaikiu
string (n), ligurl, ligula, ligul
string (v), ligursle, ligulo, ligulo
stringent (adj), ligurlku, liguloku, ligulku
stringently (adv), ligurlkiu, ligulokiu, ligulkiu
strip (n), tivurk, tivuka, tivuk
strip (v), tivursk, tivuko, tivuko
stripe (n), koiart, koiata, koiat
stripe (v), koiarst, koiato, koiato

striper (n doer), koiartwan, koiatua, koiatua
stripper (n doer), tivurkwan, tivukua, tivukua
striptease (n), tivukrairzhe, tivukeraizha, tivukraizh
striptease (v), tivukrairze, tivukeraizho, tivukraizho
strive (v), kliarsp, keliapo, kliapo
strobe (n), katuft, katufa, katuf
strobe (v), katufst, katufo, katufo
stroke (n), katurk, katuka, katuk
stroke (v), katursk, katuko, katuko
stroker (n doer), katurkwan, katukua, katukua
stroll (n), kalufk, kalufa, kaluf
stroll (v), kalufsk, kalufo, kalufo
stroller (n doer), kalufkwan, kalufua, kalufua
strong (adj), borafu, borifu, borfu
stronger (adj), borafwelu, borifwelu, borfwelu
strongest (adj), borafwaku, borifwaku, borfwaku
stronghold (n), borfthorthk, borifethoritha, borfthorth
strongly (adv), borafiu, borifiu, borfiu
strongman (n), borfplorn, borifepelona, borfplon
strongmen (n pl), borfplornyek, borifepeloni, borfploni
Strontium (n davoka), Alip, Alip, Alip
Strontium (n), Shtrontium, Shetironatiuma, Shtrontium
StrontiumFood (n), kailark, kaikala, kailk
strove (v pa), kliarspyot, keliapio, kliapio
struck (v pa), klairskyot, kelaikio, klaikio
structural (adj), shlerku, shileku, shleku
structurally (adv), shlerkiu, shilekiu, shlekiu
structure (n), shlerk, shileka, shlek
structure (v), shlersk, shileko, shleko
struggle (n), shralve, sherava, shrav
struggle (v), shralzve, sheravo, shravo
strum (n), shkarme, shekama, shkam
strum (v), shkarzme, shekamo, shkamo
strummer (n doer), shkarmwan, shekamua, shkamua
strung (v pa), ligurslyot, ligulio, ligulio
strut (v), shkathsk, shekatho, shkatho
stub (n), murp, mupa, mup
stub (v), mursp, mupo, mupo
stubble (n), mupank, mupana, mupan
stubborn (adj), muperku, mupeku, mupeku
stubbornly (adv), muperkiu, mupekiu, mupekiu
stubbornness (n), muperk, mupeka, mupek
stuck (v pa d:adhere), shnoirskyot, shenoikio, shnoikio
stuck (v pa d:twig, poke), shnefstyot, shinetio, shnetio
stud (n), klarbe, kelaba, klab
stud (v), klarzbe, kelabo, klabo
student (n doer), ailartwan, ailatua, ailtua
studio (n), shailart, shailata, shailt
studious (adj), ailartu, ailatu, ailtu
studiously (adv), ailartiu, ailatiu, ailtiu
study (n), ailart, ailata, ailt
study (v), ailarst, ailato, ailto
stuff (n), plerth, peletha, pleth
stuff (v), plersth, peletho, pletho
stuffer (n doer), plerthwan, pelethua, plethua
stuffy (adj), plerthu, pelethu, plethu
stumble (n), shufirp, shufipa, shufp

stumble (v), shufirsp, shufipo, shufpo
stump (n d:tree), vitersh, vitesha, vitsh
stump (v d:befuddle), shufirsk, shufiko, shufko
stun (v), shkunsk, shekuno, shkuno
stung (v pa d:bite), bierzgyot, biegio, biegio
stunningly (adv), shkunkiu, shekuniu, shkuniu
stunt (n), shkurk, shekuka, shkuk
stunt (v), shkursk, shekuko, shkuko
stupendous (adj), bioshaishku, bioshaiku, bioshaiku
stupid (adj), biorshku, bioshiku, bioshku
stupidity (n), biorshk, bioshika, bioshk
stupidly (adv), biorshkiu, bioshikiu, bioshkiu
stupify (v), biorshsk, bioshiko, bioshko
stupor (n), bioshkart, bioshikata, bioshkat
sturdily (adv), bishankiu, bishaniu, bishaniu
sturdiness (n), bishank, bishana, bishan
sturdy (adj), bishanku, bishanu, bishanu
stutter (n), bibishk, bibika, bibik
stutter (v), bibishsk, bibiko, bibiko
style (n), friarf, feriafa, friaf
style (v), friarsf, feriafo, friafo
styli (n pl), friafarnyek, feriafani, friafani
stylish (adj), friarfu, feriafu, friafu
stylishly (adv), friarfiu, feriafiu, friafiu
stylist (n doer), friarfwan, feriafua, friafua
stylus (n), friafarn, feriafana, friafan
suave (adj), dafurmu, dafumu, dafumu
suavely (adv), dafurmiu, dafumiu, dafumiu
sub (n d:submarine), shelp, shepa, shep
subacute (adj), oridiarthu, oridiathu, oridiathu
subassembly (n), oriothralve, oriotherava, oriothrav
subatomic (adj), oritimortu, oritimotu, oritimotu
subclass (n), oriblesh, oribelega, oribleg
subcommittee (n doer), oripenirkwan, oripelenikua, oriplenkua
subcompact (adj), origugiforpu, origugifopu, origugifpu
subcompact (n), origugiforp, origugifopa, origugifp
subconscious (adj), orikeirpu, orikeilopu, orikeilpu
subconsciousness (n), orikeirp, orikeilopa, orikeilp
subcontinent (n), orimedmot, orimerata, orimert
subcontract (n), origlart, origelaruga, origlarg
subcontractor (n doer), origlartwan, origelarugua, origlargua
subculture (n), oritafirk, oritafika, oritafk
subdivide (v), orikifiaishsk, orikifiaisho, orikifiaisho
subdivider (n doer), orikifiaishkwan, orikifiaishua, orikifiaishua
subdivision (n), orikifiaishk, orikifiaisha, orikifiaish
subdue (v), orikirask, orikiroko, orikirko
subgroup (n), oribronf, oriberona, oribron
subhuman (n), orishorl, orishola, orishol
subionic (adj), orifaiorfu, orifaiofu, orifaiofu
subject (n), orilirk, orilika, orilk
subject (v), oritersp, oritepo, oritepo
subjective (adj), orilikuetu, orilikuetu, orilkuetu
subjectively (adv), orilikuetiu, orilikuetiu, orilkuetiu
subjectivity (n), orilikuet, orilikueta, orilkuet
sublease (n), orinularn, orinulana, orinuln
sublease (v), orinularsne, orinulano, orinulno
sublet (v pa), orilerskyot, orilekio, orilekio
sublet (v), orilersk, orileko, orileko

sublime (v), orivinst, orivitho, orivitho
subliminal (adj), orivintu, orivithu, orivithu
subliminally (adv), orivintiu, orivithiu, orivithiu
submachine (adj), origizhaurku, origizhauku,
    origizhauku
submachine (n), origizhaurk, origizhauka,
    origizhauk
submarine (n), oriliaurn, oriliauna, oriliaun
submerge (v), orilafirsp, orilafipo, orilafpo
submersible (adj), orilafirpu, orilafipu, orilafpu
submersible (n), orilafirpul, orilafipula, orilafpul
submersion (n), orilafirp, orilafipa, orilafp
submission (n), orinork, orinoka, orinok
submissive (adj), orinorku, orinoku, orinoku
submissively (adv), orinorkiu, orinokiu, orinokiu
submit (v), orinorsk, orinoko, orinoko
submitter (n doer), orinorkwan, orinokua, orinokua
subordinate (n doer), orishkeialtwan,
    orishekeiatua, orishkeiatua
subordinate (v), orishkeialst, orishekeiato,
    orishkeiato
subordination (n), orishkeialt, orishekeiata,
    orishkeiat
subplot (n), orifruart, oriferuata, orifruat
subpoena (n), oribiurme, oribiuma, oribium
subscribe (v), orisherzge, orisherigo, orishrigo
subscriber (n doer), orishergwan, orisherigua,
    orishrigua
subscription (n), orisherge, orisheriga, orishrig
subsection (n), orithisharl, orithishala, orithishal
subsection (v), orithisharsle, orithishalo,
    orithishalo
subsequence (n), orishufirt, orishufita, orishuft
subsequent (adj), orishufirtu, orishufitu, orishuftu
subsequently (adv), orishufirtiu, orishufitiu,
    orishuftiu
subservience (n), orikofitarn, orikofitana, orikoftan
subservient (adj), orikofitarnu, orikofitanu,
    orikoftanu
subserviently (adv), orikofitarniu, orikofitaniu,
    orikoftaniu
subset (n), oriferp, orifepa, orifep
subside (v), orishoirst, orishoito, orishoito
subsidence (n), diazharn, diazhana, diazhan
subsidiary (n), diazhart, diazhata, diazhat
subsidize (v), diarze, diazho, diazho
subsidy (n), diarzhe, diazha, diazh
subsist (v), oritelirsk, oriteliko, oritelko
subsistence (n), oritelirk, oritelika, oritelk
substance (n), oritrelp, oriterepa, oritrep
substantial (adj), oritrelpu, oriterepu, oritrepu
substantially (adv), oritrelpiu, oriterepiu, oritrepiu
substantiate (v), oritrelsp, oriterepo, oritrepo
substantiation (n), oritrelpuet, oritereputa,
    oritrepuet
substantive (adj), oritrelpu, oriterepu, oritrepu
substantively (adv), oritrelpiu, oriterepiu, oritrepiu
substation (n), orishlukert, orisheluketa, orishluket
substation (v), orishlukerst, orisheluketo,
    orishluketo
substitute (n doer), orishpelortwan, orishipelotua,
    orishpeltua
substitute (v), orishpelorst, orishipeloto, orishpelto

substitution (n), orishpelort, orishipelota, orishpelt
substrate (n), oriplairp, oripelaipa, oriplaip
subsurface (n), orithrelf, oritherefa, orithref
subsurface (v), orithrelsf, oritherefo, orithrefo
subsystem (n), orisharshturk, orisharishotuka,
    orisharshtuk
subterra (n), oritilarsh, oritilasha, oritilash
subterranean (adj), oritilarshu, oritilashu,
    oritilashu
subtext (n), orishtirbe, orishetiba, orishtib
subtext (v), orishtirzbe, orishetibo, orishtibo
subtitle (n), orishtairp, orishetaipa, orishtaip
subtitle (v), orishtairsp, orishetaipo, orishtaipo
subtle (adj), shefirnu, shefiru, shefiru
subtlety (n), shefirn, shefira, shefir
subtly (adv), shefirniu, shefiriu, shefiriu
subtract (v), origalirst, origalito, origalto
subtraction (n), origalirt, origalita, origalt
subtractor (n doer), origalirtwan, origalitua,
    origaltua
suburb (n), orifalirp, orifalipa, orifalp
suburban (adj), orifalirpu, orifalipu, orifalpu
suburbanization (n), orifalirpuet, orifalipueta,
    orifalpuet
suburbanize (v), orifalirsp, orifalipo, orifalpo
subversion (n d:lower version), oritharfelt,
    oritharifeta, oritharfet
subversion (n d:undercut), oritharak, oritharika,
    orithark
subversive (adj d:undercut), oritharaku, orithariku,
    oritharku
subversive (n), oritharakul, oritharikula, oritharkul
subversively (adv d:undercut), oritharakiu,
    oritharikiu, oritharkiu
subvert (v d:undercut), oritharask, orithariko,
    oritharko
subway (n), oripliorl, oripeliola, oripliol
succeed (v), zhuverst, zhuveto, zhuveto
success (n), zhuvert, zhuveta, zhuvet
successful (adj), zhuvertushu, zhuvetushu,
    zhuvetushu
successfully (adv), zhuvertushiu, zhuvetushiu,
    zhuvetushiu
succession (n), zhuvertuet, zhuvetueta, zhuvetuet
successive (adj), zhuvertu, zhuvetu, zhuvetu
successively (adv), zhuvertiu, zhuvetiu, zhuvetiu
successor (n doer), zhuvertwan, zhuvetua, zhuvetua
succumb (v), faudanarsp, faudanapo, faudanapo
such (adj/adv), zhesh, zheshu, zhesh
such (pron), zhesh, zheshei, zhesh
suck (v), faursp, faupo, faupo
sucker (n doer), faurpwan, faupua, faupua
sucker (v), faupwasne, faupuano, faupuano
suction (n), faurpuet, faupueta, faupuet
suction (v), faurpuest, faupueto, faupueto
sud (n), thurp, thupa, thup
sudden (adj), shlurdu, sheludu, shludu
suddenly (adv), shlurdiu, sheludiu, shludiu
suddenness (n), shlurde, sheluda, shlud
sue (v), dutarsk, dutako, dutako
suffer (v), kauvurst, kauvuto, kauvuto
sufferable (adj), kauvurtu, kauvutu, kauvutu
sufferably (adv), kauvurtiu, kauvutiu, kauvutiu

sufferer (n doer), kauvurtwan, kauvutua, kauvutua
suffice (v), kaushkelst, kaushiketo, kaushketo
sufficiency (n), kaushkelt, kaushiketa, kaushket
sufficient (adj), kaushkeltu, kaushiketu, kaushketu
sufficiently (adv), kaushkeltiu, kaushiketiu, kaushketiu
suffix (n), zhuvirk, zhuvika, zhuvik
suffocate (v), kauvairsp, kauvaipo, kauvaipo
suffocation (n), kauvairp, kauvaipa, kauvaip
sugar (n), lethrulf, letherufa, lethruf
sugar (v), lethrulsf, letherufo, lethrufo
sugary (adj), lethrulfu, letherufu, lethrufu
suggest (v), zhutunirsp, zhutunipo, zhutunpo
suggestible (adj), zhutunirpu, zhutunipu, zhutunpu
suggestibly (adv), zhutunirpiu, zhutunipiu, zhutunpiu
suggestion (n), zhutunirp, zhutunipa, zhutunp
suggestive (adj), zhutunirpu, zhutunipu, zhutunpu
suggestively (adv), zhutunirpiu, zhutunipiu, zhutunpiu
suicidal (adj), zhalkoirku, zhalikoiku, zhalkoiku
suicide (n), zhalkoirk, zhalikoika, zhalkoik
suicide (v), zhalkoirsk, zhalikoiko, zhalkoiko
suit (n d:accord), morap, moripa, morp
suit (n d:apparel), moiurf, moiufa, moiuf
suit (v d:accord), morasp, moripo, morpo
suitability (n), morapuet, moripueta, morpuet
suitable (adj d:accord), morapu, moripu, morpu
suitably (adv d:accord), morapiu, moripiu, morpiu
suitcase (n), moiushuart, moiushuata, moiushuat
suite (n), moiarp, moiapa, moiap
suitor (n doer d:accord), morapwan, moripua, morpua
Sulfur (n davoka), Etup, Etup, Etup
Sulfur (n), Shulfur, Shulofura, Shulfur
sulk (v), kuarask, kuariko, kuarko
sully (v), naransk, narano, narano
sultan (n), vantarn, vanitara, vantar
sultry (adj), vanurdu, vanudu, vanudu
sum (n), drailt, deraita, drait
sum (v), drailst, deraito, draito
summarize (v), draimasre, deraimo, draimo
summary (n), draimar, deraima, draim
summer (n), frulf, ferula, frul
summertime (n), fruldaurn, feruledauna, fruldaun
summit (n), drailork, derailoka, drailk
summit (v), drailorsk, derailoko, drailko
summon (v), velirsne, velino, velno
summons (n), velirn, velina, veln
sump (n), fialirt, fialita, fialt
sumptuous (adj), fialirtu, fialitu, fialtu
sumptuously (adv), fialirtiu, fialitiu, fialtiu
sun (n), renf, rena, ren
sunbathe (v), rendafesle, renedalifo, rendalfo
sunbather (n doer), rendafelwan, renedalifua, rendalfua
sunbeam (n), renduarf, reneduafa, renduaf
sunbelt (n), rendakelf, renedafika, rendafk
sunburn (n), renbugor, reneberuga, renbrug
sunburn (v), renbugosre, reneberugo, renbrugo
sundance (n), renflamar, renefelarima, renflarm
sundance (v), renflamasre, renefelarimo, renflarmo
Sunday (n), Renviurl, Renuviula, Renviul

sundial (n), reneiport, reneipota, reneipot
sundown (n), rentiern, renetiena, rentien
sunfish (n pl), renshlershyek, renesheleshi, renshleshi
sunfish (n), renshlersh, reneshelesha, renshlesh
sunflower (n), renthaush, renethuana, renthuan
sunglass (n), rendrinat, renederinota, rendrint
sunlight (n), renfluarn, renefeluana, renfluan
sunlit (v pa), renfluarsnyot, renefeluanio, renfluanio
sunnily (adv), renfiu, reniu, reniu
sunny (adj), renfu, renu, renu
sunrise (n), renluirsh, reneluisha, renluish
sunriser (n doer), renluirshwan, reneluishua, renluishua
sunroof (n), renlarfp, renelarifa, renlarf
sunroom (n), renshranf, renesherana, renshran
sunscreen (n), renfklert, renefikoleta, renfklet
sunset (n), renferp, renefepa, renfep
sunshade (n), renepoerf, renepoefa, renpoef
sunshine (n), renmoirth, renemoitha, renmoith
sunspot (n), renderap, renederipa, renderp
suntan (n), renmaiarme, renemaiama, renmaiam
sunup (n), reniveil, reniveila, reniveil
super (adj), vugarlu, vugalu, vugalu
superb (adj), vugalirpu, vugalipu, vugalpu
superbly (adv), vugalirpiu, vugalipiu, vugalpiu
supercede (v), vugaversk, vugaveko, vugaveko
supercharge (v), vugagloifst, vugageloito, vugagloito
supercharger (n doer), vugagloiftwan, vugageloitua, vugagloitua
supercool (adj), vugashlurfu, vugashelufu, vugashlufu
supercool (v), vugashlursf, vugashelufo, vugashlufo
superficial (adj), vugafartu, vugafatu, vugaftu
superficiality (n), vugafart, vugafata, vugaft
superficially (adv), vugafartiu, vugafatiu, vugaftiu
superflow (n), vugabrauf, vugaberautha, vugabrauth
superflow (v), vugabrausf, vugaberautho, vugabrautho
superfluous (adj), vugabraufu, vugaberauthu, vugabrauthu
superheat (v), vugakurst, vugakuto, vugakuto
superhero (n doer), vugasharladwan, vugasharolitua, vugasharltua
superhighway (n), vugakoiopliorl, vugakoilepeliola, vugakoilpliol
superhuman (adj), vugashorlu, vugasholu, vugasholu
superimpose (v), vugakiglarsk, vugakigelako, vugakiglako
superintendent (n), vugarpifkan, vugipifokana, vugipifkan
superior (adj), vugarnu, vuganu, vuganu
superior (n doer), vugarnwan, vuganua, vuganua
superiority (n), vugarn, vugana, vugan
superlative (n), vugaflude, vugagerena, vugagren
superman (n), vugaplorn, vugapelona, vugaplon
supermarket (n), koidelirn, koidelina, koideln
supermen (n pl), vugaplornyek, vugapeloni, vugaploni

supermodel (n), vugadiardar, vugadiadara, vugadiadar

supernatural (adj), vugaleirdu, vugaleidu, vugaleidu

supernaturally (adv), vugaleirdiu, vugaleidiu, vugaleidiu

supernova (n), vugamiarf, vugamiafa, vugamiaf

superpower (n), vugabiorat, vugabiorita, vugabiort

supersede (v), vugaversk, vugaveko, vugaveko

supersonic (adj), vugazhantarnu, vugazhanitanu, vugazhantanu

superstar (n), vugadrokifar, vugaderokirofa, vugadrokirf

superstition (n), shpetoirt, shopetoita, shpetoit

superstitious (adj), shpetoirtu, shopetoitu, shpetoitu

superstore (n), vugadralp, vugaderapa, vugadrap

superstructure (n), vugashlerk, vugashileka, vugashlek

supervise (v), vugafiaishsk, vugafiaisho, vugafiaisho

supervision (n), vugafiaishk, vugafiaisha, vugafiaish

supervisor (n doer), vugafiaishkwan, vugafiaishua, vugafiaishua

supervisory (adj), vugafiaishku, vugafiaishu, vugafiaishu

supper (n), shenarde, shenuda, shend

supplant (v), vubrelsp, vuberepo, vubrepo

supple (adj), shelthku, shelithu, shelthu

supplement (n), shethpert, shethipeta, shethpet

supplement (v), shethperst, shethipeto, shethpeto

supplemental (adj), shethpertu, shethipetu, shethpetu

supplementary (adj), shethpertu, shethipetu, shethpetu

supplementation (n), shethpertuet, shethipetueta, shethpetuet

supplicate (v), vubrels, vuberesho, vubresho

supplication (n), vubrelsh, vuberesha, vubresh

supplier (n doer), shethirpwan, shethipua, shethpua

supply (n), shethirp, shethipa, shethp

supply (v), shethirsp, shethipo, shethpo

support (n), loburk, lobuka, lobuk

support (v), lobursk, lobuko, lobuko

supportable (adj), loburku, lobuku, lobuku

supporter (n doer), loburkwan, lobukua, lobukua

supportive (adj), loburku, lobuku, lobuku

supportively (adv), loburkiu, lobukiu, lobukiu

suppose (v), vuglarsk, vugelako, vuglako

supposedly (adv), vuglarkiu, vugelakiu, vuglakiu

supposer (n doer), vuglarkwan, vugelakua, vuglakua

supposition (n), vuglark, vugelaka, vuglak

suppress (v), vublars, vubelasho, vublasho

suppressant (n), vublasharn, vubelashana, vublashan

suppression (n), vublarsh, vubelasha, vublash

suppressive (adj), vublarshu, vubelashu, vublashu

suppressively (adv), vublarshiu, vubelashiu, vublashiu

suppressor (n doer), vublarshwan, vubelashua, vublashua

supremacist (n doer), vugatruirtwan, vugateruitua, vugatruitua

supremacy (n), vugatruirt, vugateruita, vugatruit

supreme (adj), vugatruirtu, vugateruitu, vugatruitu

supremely (adv), vugatruirtiu, vugateruitiu, vugatruitiu

surcharge (n), voigloift, voigeloita, voigloit

sure (adj), shrelnu, sherelu, shrelu

surely (adv), shrelniu, shereliu, shreliu

surf (n), voiarf, voiafa, voiaf

surf (v), voiarsf, voiafo, voiafo

surface (n), threlf, therefa, thref

surface (v), threlsf, therefo, threfo

surfboard (n), voiafplok, voiafepelorika, voiafplork

surfer (n doer), voiarfwan, voiafua, voiafua

surge (n), voirge, voiga, voig

surge (v), voirzge, voigo, voigo

surgeon (n doer), mofirtwan, mofitua, moftua

surgery (n), mofirt, mofita, moft

surgical (adj), mofirtu, mofitu, moftu

surgically (adv), mofirtiu, mofitiu, moftiu

surity (n), shreln, sherela, shrel

surmise (v), voitolirsp, voitolipo, voitolpo

surmount (v), voiniursk, voiniuko, voiniuko

surname (n), voibrienf, voiberiena, voibrien

surpass (v), voilunirst, voilunito, voilunto

surplus (n), voinumart, voinumata, voinumat

surprise (n), voiviursh, voiviusha, voiviush

surprise (v), voiviurs, voiviusho, voiviusho

surprisingly (adv), voiviurshiu, voiviushiu, voiviushiu

surreal (adj), voipluarfu, voipeluafu, voipluafu

surrealism (n), voipluarf, voipeluafa, voipluaf

surrender (n), shlutirk, shelutika, shlutik

surrender (v), shlutirsk, shelutiko, shlutiko

surrenderer (n doer), shlutirkwan, shelutikua, shlutikua

surrogate (adj), voilaranku, voilaranu, voilaranu

surrogate (n doer), voilarankwan, voilaranua, voilaranua

surrogate (v), voilaransk, voilarano, voilarano

surrogation (n), voilarank, voilarana, voilaran

surround (v), shlairzbe, shelaibo, shlaibo

surtax (n), voishenirk, voishenika, voishenk

surveillance (n), voifuartak, voifuataka, voifuatak

survey (n), voifuart, voifuata, voifuat

survey (v), voifuarst, voifuato, voifuato

surveyor (n doer), voifuartwan, voifuatua, voifuatua

survivability (n), voiflaurftuet, voifelaufotueta, voiflauftuet

survival (n), voiflaurft, voifelaufota, voiflauft

survivalist (n doer), voiflaurftwan, voifelaufotua, volflauftua

survive (v), voiflaurfst, voifelaufoto, voiflaufto

survivor (n doer), voiflaurftwan, voifelaufotua, voiflauftua

susceptibility (n), memshirp, memeshipa, memship

susceptible (adj), memshirpu, memeshipu, memshipu

suspect (n doer), memthurkwan, memithukua, memthukua

suspect (v), memthursk, memithuko, memthuko

suspend (v), membrulsne, memiberuno, membruno

suspender (n doer), membrulnwan, memiberunua, membrunua

suspense (n), membruln, memiberuna, membrun
suspension (n), membrulnuet, memiberunueta,
   membrunuet
suspicion (n), memthurk, memithuka, memthuk
suspicious (adj), memthurku, memithuku,
   memthuku
suspiciously (adv), memthurkiu, memithukiu,
   memthukiu
sustain (v), mempirfst, memepifeto, mempifto
sustainable (adj), mempirftu, memepifetu,
   mempiftu
sustenance (n), mempirft, memepifeta, mempift
suture (n), yuiank, yuiana, yuian
suture (v), yuiansk, yuiano, yuiano
swab (n), fliaurp, feliaupa, fliaup
swab (v), fliaursp, feliaupo, fliaupo
swag (n), klairve, kelaiva, klaiv
swag (v), klairzve, kelaivo, klaivo
swagger (n), klaivart, kelaivata, klaivat
swagger (v), klaivarst, kelaivato, klaivato
swallow (n d:bird), shliarme, sheliama, shliam
swallow (n d:gulp), moirf, moifa, moif
swallow (v d:gulp), moirsf, moifo, moifo
swam (v pa), duirsnyot, duinio, duinio
swamp (n), fianirp, fianipa, fianp
swamp (v), fianirsp, fianipo, fianpo
swampy (adj), fianirpu, fianipu, fianpu
swap (n), niorf, niofa, niof
swap (v), niorsf, niofo, niofo
swaper (n doer), niorfwan, niofua, niofua
swarm (n), fraumsh, ferauma, fraum
swarm (v), fraums, feraumo, fraumo
swat (n), nioteshk, niotesha, niotsh
swat (v), nioteshsk, niotesho, niotsho
swath (n), shlathk, shelatha, shlath
swathe (v), shlathsk, shelatho, shlatho
sway (n), shlaink, shelaina, shlain
sway (v), shlainsk, shelaino, shlaino
swear (n), froirk, feroika, froik
swear (v), froirsk, feroiko, froiko
swearer (n doer), froirkwan, feroikua, froikua
sweat (n d:perspiration), froirf, feroifa, froif
sweat (v d:perspiration), froirsf, feroifo, froifo
sweater (n d:clothing), diloran, dilorina, dilorn
sweatshirt (n), froiflifarde, feroifelifada, froiflifad
sweatshop (n), froifthoft, feroifethofa, froifthof
sweaty (adj d:perspiration), froirfu, feroifu, froifu
Sweden (n), Shuidarf, Shuidafa, Shuidaf
Swedish (n), Shuidarn, Shuidana, Shuidan
sweep (n), fliark, feliaka, fliak
sweep (v), fliarsk, feliako, fliako
sweeper (n doer), fliarkwan, feliakua, fliakua
sweet (adj), frulpu, ferupu, frupu
sweeten (v), frulsp, ferupo, frupo
sweetener (n doer), frulpwan, ferupua, frupua
sweetheart (n), frupedralt, ferupedarala, frupedral
sweetie (n), frulpar, ferupara, frupar
sweetly (adv), frulpiu, ferupiu, frupiu
sweetness (n), frulp, ferupa, frup
swell (n), muiart, muiata, muiat
swell (v), muiarst, muiato, muiato
swelter (n), shluiart, sheluiata, shluiat
swelter (v), shluiarst, sheluiato, shluiato

swept (v pa), fliarskyot, feliakio, fliakio
swerve (n), shloft, shelofa, shlof
swerve (v), shlofst, shelofo, shlofo
swift (adj), frefirku, ferefiku, frefku
swiftly (adv), frefirkiu, ferefikiu, frefkiu
swiftness (n), frefirk, ferefika, frefk
swim (n), duirn, duina, duin
swim (v), duirsne, duino, duino
swimmer (n doer), duirnwan, duinua, duinua
swimsuit (n), duimorap, duimoripa, duimorp
swindle (n), frizhge, feriga, frig
swindle (v), frizhzge, ferigo, frigo
swindler (n doer), frizhgwan, ferigua, frigua
swing (n), flierge, feliega, flieg
swing (v), flierzge, feliego, fliego
swinger (n doer), fliergwan, feliegua, fliegua
swipe (n), shtrolp, sheteropa, shtrop
swipe (v), shtrolsp, sheteropo, shtropo
swirl (n), frelf, ferela, frel
swirl (v), frelsf, ferelo, frelo
swish (n), frelshk, ferelisha, frelsh
swish (v), frelshsk, ferelisho, frelsho
swisher (n doer), frelshkwan, ferelishua, frelshua
Swiss (n), Shuisharn, Shuishana, Shuishan
switch (n), shiushk, shiusha, shiush
switch (v), shiushsk, shiusho, shiusho
switchblade (n), shiushprulat, shiusheperuta,
   shiushpruat
switchboard (n), shiushplok, shiushepelorika,
   shiushplork
switcher (n doer), shiushkwan, shiushua, shiushua
switchover (n), shiushkafen, shiushafena,
   shiushafen
switchy (adj), shiushku, shiushu, shiushu
Switzerland (n), Shuisherlarf, Shuisherolafa,
   Shuisherlaf
swivel (n), viaink, viaina, viain
swivel (v), viainsk, viaino, viaino
swoon (n), shtrushk, sheterusha, shtrush
swoon (v), shtrushsk, sheterusho, shtrusho
swoop (v), shtrushsp, sheterupo, shtrupo
sword (n), kutarl, kutala, kutal
swordfish (n pl), kutalshlershyek, kutalsheleshi,
   kutalshleshi
swordfish (n), kutalshlersh, kutalshelesha,
   kutalshlesh
swordplay (n), kutalfruifk, kutaleferuifa, kutalfruif
swore (v pa), froirskyot, feroikio, froikio
swung (v pa), flierzgyot, feliegio, fliegio
Sydney (n), Shidunarf, Shidunafa, Shidunaf
syllabi (n pl), roilthyek, roithi, roithi
syllable (n), talgurt, taliguta, talgut
syllabus (n), roilth, roitha, roith
symbol (n), parlirt, parolita, parlit
symbolic (adj), parlirtu, parolitu, parlitu
symbolically (adv), parlirtiu, parolitiu, parlitiu
symbolism (n), parlirtuet, parolitueta, parlituet
symbolize (v), parlirst, parolito, parlito
symmetrical (adj), parporftu, parepofitu, parpoftu
symmetrically (adv), parporftiu, parepofitiu,
   parpoftiu
symmetry (n), parporft, parepofita, parpoft
sympathetic (adj), parlarpu, parolapu, parlapu

sympathize (v), parlarsp, parolapo, parlapo
sympathizer (n doer), parlarpwan, parolapua,
    parlapua
sympathy (n), parlarp, parolapa, parlap
symphonic (adj), parluyarpu, paruyapu, paruyapu
symphony (n), parluyarp, paruyapa, paruyap
symptom (n), paritoirn, paritoina, partoin
symptomatic (adj), paritoirnu, paritoinu, partoinu
synchro (n), dalpiarf, dalopiara, dalpiar
synchronization (n), dalpiarfuet, dalopiarueta,
    dalpiaruet
synchronize (v), dalpiarsf, dalopiaro, dalpiaro
synchronous (adj), dalpiarfu, dalopiaru, dalpiaru
synchronously (adv), dalpiarfiu, dalopiariu,
    dalpiariu
syndicate (n), dalkiark, dalekiaka, dalkiak
syndicate (v), dalkiarsk, dalekiako, dalkiako
syndication (n), dalkiarkuet, dalekiakueta,
    dalkiakuet
syndicator (n doer), dalkiarkwan, dalekiakua,
    dalkiakua
syndrome (n), dalparfp, daliparopa, dalparp
synergistic (adj), daldargalitu, dalevogalitu,
    dalvoglitu
synergy (n), daldargalit, dalevogalita, dalvoglit
synonym (n), dalviern, daloviena, dalvien
synonymous (adj), dalviernu, dalovienu, dalvienu
synonymously (adv), dalvierniu, dalovieniu,
    dalvieniu
synopsis (n), dalmirade, dalemida, dalmid
syntax (n), daldurk, daloduka, dalduk
synthesis (n), dalnarge, dalinaga, dalnag
synthesize (v), dalnarzge, dalinago, dalnago
synthesizer (n doer), dalnargwan, dalinagua,
    dalnagua
synthetic (adj), dalnargu, dalinagu, dalnagu
synthetic (n), dalnargul, dalinagula, dalnagul
synthetically (adv), dalnargiu, dalinagiu, dalnagiu
Syria (n), Shiriarf, Shiriafa, Shiriaf
Syrian (n), Shiriarn, Shiriana, Shirian
syringe (n), daloishk, daloisha, daloish
syrup (n), dalarge, dalaga, dalag
syrupy (adj), dalargu, dalagu, dalagu
system (n), dalushk, daluka, daluk
systemate (v), dalukarst, dalukato, dalukato
systematic (adj), dalukartu, dalukatu, dalukatu
systematically (adv), dalukartiu, dalukatiu,
    dalukatiu
systemic (adj), dalushku, daluku, daluku
systemization (n), dalukart, dalukata, dalukat
systemize (v), dalushsk, daluko, dâluko
systemwide (adj), dalukrashku, dalukerashu,
    dalukrashu
T (let sng), teil, teia, tei
tab (n), thoirk, thoika, thoik
tab (v), thoirsk, thoiko, thoiko
table (n), doiart, doiara, doiar
table (v), doiarst, doiaro, doiaro
tablecloth (n), doiarflarf, doiarefelafa, doiarflaf
tablespoon (n), doiardorap, doiaredoripa,
    doiardorp
tablet (n), doisht, doita, doit
tabletop (n), doiardaurp, doiaredaupa, doiardaup

tableware (n), doiarshlerf, doiareshelefa, doiarshlef
tabloid (n), doitiark, doitiara, doitiar
taboo (adj), faifaifu, nunufu, nunufu
taboo (n), faifaif, nunufa, nunuf
tabular (adj), thoiartu, thoiatu, thoiatu
tabulate (v), thoiarst, thoiato, thoiato
tabulation (n), thoiart, thoiata, thoiat
tabulator (n doer), thoiartwan, thoiatua, thoiatua
tacit (adj), peiuftu, peiufu, peiufu
tacitly (adv), peiuftiu, peiufiu, peiufiu
taciturn (n), peiuft, peiufa, peiuf
tack (n), pairt, paita, pait
tack (v), pairst, paito, paito
tackle (n), paitart, paitata, paitat
tackle (v), paitarst, paitato, paitato
tackler (n doer), paitartwan, paitatua, paitatua
tacky (adj), pairtu, paitu, paitu
tact (n), pairbe, paiba, paib
tactful (adj), pairbu, paibu, paibu
tactfully (adv), pairbiu, paibiu, paibiu
tactic (n), paibark, paibaka, paibak
tactical (adj), paibarku, paibaku, paibaku
tactically (adv), paibarkiu, paibakiu, paibakiu
tactician (n doer), paibarkwan, paibakua, paibakua
tactilate (v), paibarst, paibato, paibato
tactilation (n), paibart, paibata, paibat
tactile (adj), paibartu, paibatu, paibatu
tad (n), milt, mila, mil
tadpole (n), mildilork, milediloka, mildilk
tag (n), gairve, gaiva, gaiv
tag (v), gairzve, gaivo, gaivo
tagger (n doer), gairvwan, gaivua, gaivua
tail (n), mithk, mitha, mith
tail (v), mithsk, mitho, mitho
tailer (n doer), mithkwan, mithua, mithua
tailgate (n), mithparlak, mitheperelika, mithprelk
tailgate (v), mithparlask, mithepereliko, mithprelko
tailor (n doer), duparfwan, dupafua, dupafua
tailor (v), duparsf, dupafo, dupafo
tailpipe (n), mithleinarp, mitheleinapa, mithleinp
tailspin (n), mithshnarp, mitheshenapa, mithshnap
taint (v), miursk, miuko, miuko
Taiwan (n), Taiwarf, Taiwafa, Taiwaf
take (n), gork, goka, gok
take (v), gorsk, goko, goko
takeoff (n), gorkunf, gokunefa, gokunf
takeout (n), gorkuil, gokuila, gokuil
takeover (n), gorkafen, gokafena, gokafen
taker (n doer), gorkwan, gokua, gokua
tale (n), prelt, pereta, pret
talent (n), keirsh, kcisha, kcish
talent (v), keirs, keisho, keisho
talk (n), shpalort, shipalota, shpalt
talk (v), shpalorst, shipaloto, shpalto
talkative (adj), shpalortu, shipalotu, shpaltu
talker (n doer), shpalortwan, shipalotua, shpaltua
tall (adj), flilfu, felilu, flilu
tallness (n), flilf, felila, flil
tally (n), thithp, thitha, thith
tally (v), thithsp, thitho, thitho
tame (adj), nielorpu, nielopu, nielpu
tame (v), nielorsp, nielopo, nielpo
tameness (n), nielorp, nielopa, nielp

Tampa (n), Tamparf, Tamipafa, Tampaf
tamper (v), niemesp, niemo, niemo
tan (n), maiarme, maiama, maiam
tan (v), maiarzme, maiamo, maiamo
tandem (adj), avuikoshku, avuikoshu, avuikoshu
tandem (n), avuikoshk, avuikosha, avuikosh
tangent (n), shiarme, shiama, shiam
tangential (adj), shiarmu, shiamu, shiamu
tangentially (adv), shiarmiu, shiamiu, shiamiu
tangible (adj), shiarmpu, shiamipu, shiampu
tangible (n), shiarmp, shiamipa, shiamp
tangle (n), taigarge, taigaga, taigag
tangle (n), shiarge, shiaga, shiag
tangle (v), taigarzge, taigago, taigago
tangle (v), shiarzge, shiago, shiago
tangler (n doer), taigargwan, taigagua, taigagua
tank (n), nuirk, nuika, nuik
tank (v), nuirsk, nuiko, nuiko
tanker (n doer), nuirkwan, nuikua, nuikua
tanner (n doer), maiarmwan, maiamua, maiamua
tantalization (n), niateshk, niatesha, niatsh
tantalize (v), niateshsk, niatesho, niatsho
tantalizer (n doer), niateshkwan, niateshua,
    niatshua
Tantalum (n davoka), Irop, Irop, Irop
Tantalum (n), Tantalum, Tanitaluma, Tantalum
tantamount (adj), niashniurku, niasheniuku,
    niashniuku
tanto (adv), niarshiu, niashiu, niashiu
tantrum (n), niashdriarde, niashederiada,
    niashdriad
tap (n), nerp, nepa, nep
tap (v), nersp, nepo, nepo
tape (n), neirf, neifa, neif
tape (v), neirsf, neifo, neifo
taper (n), neiwifk, neiwifa, neiwif
taper (v), neiwifsk, neiwifo, neiwifo
tapper (n doer), nerpwan, nepua, nepua
tar (n), gorfk, gorafa, gorf
tar (v), gorfsk, gorafo, gorfo
Tarak (n), Tarak, Taraka, Tarak
tardiness (n), balirp, balipa, balp
tardy (adj), balirpu, balipu, balpu
target (n), zheirde, zheida, zheid
target (v), zheirzde, zheido, zheido
tariff (n), threnirk, therenika, threnk
tarmac (n), gorfmarft, gorafemarifa, gorfmarf
tarnish (v), gorfgalirsk, gorafegaliko, gorfgalko
tarp (n), kralip, keralipa, kralp
tart (adj), tiauthku, tiauthu, tiauthu
tart (n), tiauthk, tiautha, tiauth
task (n), krafirk, kerafika, krafk
task (v), krafirsk, kerafiko, krafko
tasker (n doer), krafirkwan, kerafikua, krafkua
taste (n), tinart, tinata, tinat
taste (v), tinarst, tinato, tinato
tasteful (adj), tinartu, tinatu, tinatu
tastefully (adv), tinartiu, tinatiu, tinatiu
tasteless (adj), tinartmenu, tinatemenu, tinatmenu
tastelessly (adv), tinartmeniu, tinatemeniu,
    tinatmeniu
taster (n doer), tinartwan, tinatua, tinatua
tasty (adj), tinartu, tinatu, tinatu

tatter (v), ninarst, ninato, ninato
tattoo (n), biburf, bibufa, bibuf
tattoo (v), bibursf, bibufo, bibufo
tau (n), taurn, tauna, taun
taught (v pa), dalirsyot, dalishio, dalshio
taunt (v), miaushsk, miauko, miauko
tavern (n), krilaf, kerilafa, krilf
tax (n), shenirk, shenika, shenk
tax (v), shenirsk, sheniko, shenko
taxable (adj), shenirku, sheniku, shenku
taxation (n), shenirkuet, shenikueta, shenkuet
taxer (n doer), shenirkwan, shenikua, shenkua
taxi (n), shenirt, shenita, shent
taxi (v), shenirst, shenito, shento
taxpayer (n), shenirtomoirme, shenitemoima,
    shentmoim
tea (n), melirsh, melisha, melsh
teach (v), dalirs, dalisho, dalsho
teacher (n doer), dalirshwan, dalishua, dalshua
teacup (n), melshvorup, melishevoripa, melshvorp
team (n), dralf, derafa, draf
team (v), dralsf, derafo, drafo
teammate (n), draflern, derafelena, draflen
teamwork (n), drafkiork, derafekioka, drafkiok
teapot (n), melshdairf, melishedaifa, melshdaif
tear (n d:eyedrop), puvirn, puvina, puvin
tear (n d:rip), ralbe, raba, rab
tear (v d:eyedrop), puvirsne, puvino, puvino
tear (v d:rip), ralzbe, rabo, rabo
tearful (adj), puvirnu, puvinu, puvinu
teary (adj d:eyedrop), puvirnu, puvinu, puvinu
tease (n), rairzhe, raizha, raizh
tease (v), rairze, raizho, raizho
teaser (n doer), rairzhwan, raizhua, raizhua
teaspoon (n), melshdorap, melishedoripa,
    melshdorp
Technetium (n davoka), Ilak, Ilak, Ilak
Technetium (n), Teknetium, Tekonetiuma,
    Teknetium
technical (adj), kirzhu, kizhu, kizhu
technically (adv), kirzhiu, kizhiu, kizhiu
technician (n doer), kirzhwan, kizhua, kizhua
technique (n), kirzhe, kizha, kizh
technological (adj), kizhashtu, kizhatu, kizhatu
technologically (adv), kizhashtiu, kizhatiu, kizhatiu
technology (n), kizhasht, kizhata, kizhat
tedious (adj), kizhpanirku, kizhepaniku, kizhpanku
tedium (n), kizhpanirk, kizhepanika, kizhpank
tee (n), teiart, teiata, teiat
tee (v), teiarst, teiato, teiato
teem (v), driafsk, deriafo, driafo
teen (n), risharde, rishada, rishad
teenager (n), rishdalirt, rishedalita, rishdalt
teensy (adj), nilithku, nilithu, nilithu
teeny (adj), nilishku, nilishu, nilishu
teeter (v), teiatirst, teiatito, teiatito
teeth (n pl), tshatirshyek, teshatishi, tshatshi
teethe (v), tshutas, teshutasho, tshutsho
Tehran (n), Tekralf, Tekerafa, Tekraf
tekatri- (num 1e39 pref), avushtai-, avushtai-,
    avushtai-
telecast (n), preithut, pereibida, preibid
telecast (v), preithust, pereibido, preibido

telecom (n), preigurt, pereiguta, preigut
telecommunication (n), preiguniart, pereiguniata, preiguniat
teleconference (n), preibelgelf, pereiliugefa, preiliugef
telegram (n), preinelirk, pereinelika, preinelk
telegram (v), preinelirsk, pereineliko, preinelko
telegraph (n), preidaraf, pereidarofa, preidarf
telegraph (v), preidarasf, pereidarofo, preidarfo
telekinesis (n), preithenort, pereithenota, preithent
telekinetic (adj), preithenortu, pereithenotu, preithentu
telemetry (n), preiporft, pereipofita, preipoft
telepath (n doer), preibotershwan, pereiboteshua, preibotshua
telepathic (adj), preibotershu, pereiboteshu, preibotshu
telepathy (n), preibotersh, pereibotesha, preibotsh
telephone (n), preiyarp, pereiyapa, preiyap
telephone (v), preiyarsp, pereiyapo, preiyapo
telephonic (adj), preiyarpu, pereiyapu, preiyapu
telephony (n), preiyarpuet, pereiyapueta, preiyapuet
telephoto (adj), preidifadarfu, pereidifedarifu, preidifdarfu
telephotograph (v), preidifadarsf, pereidifedarifo, preidifdarfo
telephotography (n), preidifadarf, pereidifedarifa, preidifdarf
teleport (n), preibielork, pereibieloka, preibielk
teleport (v), preibielorsk, pereibieloko, preibielko
teleporter (n doer), preibielorkwan, pereibielokua, preibielkua
telescope (n), preiluarf, pereiluafa, preiluaf
telescope (v), preiluarsf, pereiluafo, preiluafo
telescopic (adj), preiluarfu, pereiluafu, preiluafu
televise (v), preithulirzde, pereithulido, preithulido
television (n), preithulirde, pereithulida, preithulid
tell (v), prelst, pereto, preto
teller (n), praithk, peraitha, praith
tellingly (adv), preltiu, peretiu, pretiu
telltale (adj), pretopreltu, peretoperetu, pretopretu
Tellurium (n davoka), Elup, Elup, Elup
Tellurium (n), Telurium, Teluriuma, Telurium
temp (n), teifirt, teifita, teift
temper (n), vafirk, vafika, vafk
temper (v), vafirsk, vafiko, vafko
temperament (n), vafirkuet, vafikueta, vafkuet
temperamentally (adv), vafirkuetiu, vafikuetiu, vafkuetiu
temperance (n), vatikart, vatikata, vatkat
temperate (adj), vafikartu, vafikatu, vafkatu
temperate (v), vafikarst, vafikato, vafkato
temperature (n), denarde, denada, dend
temperment (n), vafkart, vafikata, vafkat
tempest (n), vafiark, vafiaka, vafiak
template (n), varfork, varifoka, varfk
temple (n), vioirk, vioika, vioik
tempo (n), teirt, teita, teit
temporal (adj), teirtu, teitu, teitu
temporarily (adv), teifirtiu, teifitiu, teiftiu
temporary (adj), teifirtu, teifitu, teiftu
tempt (v), vafirst, vafito, vafto

temptation (n), vafirt, vafita, vaft
tempter (n doer), vafirtwan, vafitua, vaftua
ten (num 10 card), dapa, dapa, dapa
tenable (adj), pivartu, pivatu, pivatu
tenacious (adj), pivarku, pivaku, pivaku
tenacity (n), pivark, pivaka, pivak
tenancy (n), pithorp, pithopa, pithp
tenant (n doer), pithorpwan, pithopua, pithpua
tend (v), piforsk, pifoko, pifko
tendency (n), pifork, pifoka, pifk
tender (adj), pifarnu, pifanu, pifanu
tender (v), pifkarst, pifokato, pifkato
tenderly (adv), pifarniu, pifaniu, pifaniu
tenderness (n), pifarn, pifana, pifan
Tennessee (n), Teneshirf, Teneshifa, Teneshif
tennis (n), poinurde, poinuda, poind
tense (adj), piftartu, pifotatu, piftatu
tensely (adv), piftartiu, pifotatiu, piftatiu
tensen (v), piftarst, pifotato, piftato
tension (n), piftart, pifotata, piftat
tent (n d:housing), pirf, pifa, pif
tentacle (n), pifaushk, pifauka, pifauk
tentative (adj), piftarnu, pifotanu, piftanu
tentatively (adv), piftarniu, pifotaniu, piftaniu
tenth (num 10 ord), dapeth, dapeth, dapeth
tenuous (adj), pifaltu, pifalu, pifalu
tenure (n), danorsh, danosha, dansh
tenure (v), danors, danosho, dansho
tepid (adj), vafirpu, vafipu, vafpu
tepidity (n), vafirp, vafipa, vafp
tepidly (adv), vafirpiu, vafipiu, vafpiu
tera- (num 1e12 pref), irikai-, irikai-, irikai-
Terbium (n davoka), Orat, Orat, Orat
Terbium (n), Terbium, Terobiuma, Terbium
term (n d:timespan), shtreln, shuterena, shtren
term (n d:word), gruln, geruna, grun
term (v d:word), grulsne, geruno, gruno
terminal (adj), nilarku, nilaku, nilku
terminal (n), nilakart, nilakata, nilkat
terminally (adv), nilarkiu, nilakiu, nilkiu
terminate (v), nilarsk, nilako, nilko
termination (n), nilark, nilaka, nilk
terminator (n doer), nilarkwan, nilakua, nilkua
terminology (n), grunkuirt, gerunekuita, grunkuit
terra (n), tilarsh, tilasha, tilash
terrace (n), tilashirk, tilashika, tilashk
terrain (n), tilashart, tilashata, tilashat
terranean (adj), tilarshu, tilashu, tilashu
terrestrial (adj), tilasharnu, tilashanu, tilashanu
terrible (adj), bakortu, bakotu, bakotu
terribly (adv), bakortiu, bakotiu, bakotiu
terrific (adj), bakirnu, bakinu, bakinu
terrifically (adv), bakirniu, bakiniu, bakiniu
terrify (v), bakorshst, bakosheto, bakoshto
territorial (adj), thriorpu, theriopu, thriopu
territory (n), thriorp, theriopa, thriop
terror (n), bakort, bakota, bakot
terrorism (n), kakortuet, bakotueta, bakotuet
terrorist (n doer), bakortwan, bakotua, bakotua
terrorize (v), bakorst, bakoto, bakoto
test (n), shtirt, shetita, shtit
test (v), shtirst, shetito, shtito
testbed (n), shtitfamor, shetitefuarema, shtitfuarm

tester (n doer), shtirtwan, shetitua, shtitua
testify (v), shetirs, shetisho, shtisho
testimonial (n), shetirshuet, shetishueta, shtishuet
testimony (n), shetirsh, shetisha, shtish
testy (adj), shtirtu, shetitu, shtitu
tether (n), kliarth, keliatha, kliath
tether (v), kliarsth, keliatho, kliatho
tetra- (num 4 pref), yufai-, yufai-, yufai-
Texas (n), Teshkarf, Teshikafa, Teshkaf
text (n), shtirbe, shetiba, shtib
text (v), shtirzbe, shetibo, shtibo
textbook (n), shtivonurde, shetivonuda, shtivond
textile (n), shiofkeloirn, shiokeloina, shiokloin
texture (n), shiorf, shiofa, shiof
texturer (n doer), shiorfwan, shiofua, shiofua
texturize (v), shiorsf, shiofo, shiofo
Th (let sng), theil, theia, thei
Thai (n), Tairf, Taifa, Taif
Thailand (n), Tailanurde, Tailanuda, Tailanud
Thallium (n davoka), Erap, Erap, Erap
Thallium (n), Thalium, Thaliuma, Thalium
than (conj/prep), tshome, teshomu, tshom
thank (v), rifast, rifalo, rifalo
thankful (adj), rifatu, rifalu, rifalu
thankfully (adv), rifatiu, rifaliu, rifaliu
thankless (adj), rifatmenu, rifalemenu, rifalmenu
thanks (n), rifat, rifala, rifal
Thanksgiving (n), Rifategrulf, Rifalugerufa,
   Rifalgruf
that (adj), tshadu, teshadu, tshadu
that (conj), yarsh, yashu, yash
that (pron), tshade, teshadei, tshad
thatch (n), klikart, kelikara, klikar
thatch (v), klikarst, kelikaro, klikaro
thatcher (n doer), klikartwan, kelikarua, klikarua
thaw (n), frazhge, ferazha, frazh
thaw (v), frazhzge, ferazho, frazho
the (det), shair, shai, shai
theater (n), dabirt, dabita, dabit
theatre (n), dabirt, dabita, dabit
theatric (n), dabirtul, dabitula, dabitul
theatrical (adj), dabirtu, dabitu, dabitu
theft (n), prairt, peraita, prait
their (pron 3rd fem-masc pl pos sub), tesh, tesh,
   tesh
their (pron 3rd neut pl pos sub), tiresh, tiresh,
   tiresh
theirs (pron 3rd fem-masc pl pos obj), tesh, tesh,
   tesh
theirs (pron 3rd neut pl pos obj), tiresh, tiresh,
   tiresh
them (pron 3rd fem-masc pl obj), tethin, tethin,
   tethin
them (pron 3rd neut pl obj), tiren, tiren, tiren
them/people (pron 3rd indefpers pl obj), onar,
   onar, onar
theme (n), shuarn, shuana, shuan
themselves (pron 3rd fem-masc pl pos), teshfar,
   teshfar, teshfar
themselves (pron 3rd neut pl pos), tireshfar,
   tireshfar, tireshfar
then (adj/adv), dode, dodu, dod

theology (n), thuteshk, thutesha, thutsh
theoretical (adj), sheiarmu, sheiamu, sheiamu
theoretically (adv), sheiarmiu, sheiamiu, sheiamiu
theorist (n doer), sheiarmwan, sheiamua, sheiamua
theorize (v), sheiarzme, sheiamo, sheiamo
theory (n), sheiarme, sheiama, sheiam
therapeutic (adj), pliarshpu, peliashipu, pliashpu
therapist (n doer), pliarshpwan, peliashipua,
   pliashpua
therapy (n), pliarshp, peliashipa, pliashp
there (adj/adv/interj), durl, duru, dur
there (pron), durl, durei, dur
thereafter (adv), durovilfiu, duroviliu, duroviliu
thereby (adv), durvurniu, durovuniu, durvuniu
therefore (adv), durmarfiu, duromafiu, durmafiu
therm (n), diorsh, diosha, diosh
thermal (adj), diorshu, dioshu, dioshu
thermometer (n), dioniork, dionioka, dioniok
thesaurii (n pl), trishoiryek, terishoili, trishoili
thesaurus (n), trishoir, terishoila, trishoil
these (adj), shirshu, shishu, shishu
these (pron), shirsh, shishi, shish
thesis (n), sheirnart, sheironata, sheirnat
theta (n), thetarn, thetana, thetan
they (pron 3rd fem-masc pl sub), tethi, tethi, tethi
they (pron 3rd neut pl sub), tir, tir, tir
they/people (pron 3rd indefpers pl sub), onar, onar,
   onar
thick (adj), shkivervu, shokivevu, shkivevu
thicken (v), shkiverzve, shokivevo, shkivevo
thickener (n doer), shkivervwan, shokivevua,
   shkivevua
thickly (adv), shkiverviu, shokiveviu, shkiveviu
thickness (n), shkiverve, shokiveva, shkivev
thief (n doer), prairtwan, peraitua, praitua
thieve (v), prairst, peraito, praito
thimble (n), briorp, beriopa, briop
thin (adj), dinarlu, dinalu, dinalu
thin (v), dinarsle, dinalo, dinalo
thing (n), dirzhe, dizha, dizh
think (v), dersp, depo, depo
thinker (n doer), derpwan, depua, depua
thinly (adv), dinarliu, dinaliu, dinaliu
thinness (n), dinarl, dinala, dinal
third (num 3 ord), ireth, ireth, ireth
thirst (n), bamiarn, bamiana, bamian
thirst (v), bamiarsne, bamiano, bamiano
thirstily (adv), bamiarniu, bamianiu, bamianiu
thirsty (adj), bamiarnu, bamianu, bamianu
thirteen (num 13 card), iripa, iripa, iripa
thirteen- (num 13 pref), iripai-, iripai-, iripai-
thirteenth (num 13 ord), iripeth, iripeth, iripeth
thirtieth (num 30 ord), irideth, irideth, irideth
thirty (num 30 card), irida, irida, irida
thirty- (num 30 pref), iridai-, iridai-, iridai-
this (adj), tshunu, teshunu, tshunu
this (pron), tshun, teshunei, tshun
Thorium (n davoka), Onip, Onip, Onip
Thorium (n), Thorium, Thoriuma, Thorium
thorn (n), bamiark, bamiaka, bamiak
thorn (v), bamiarsk, bamiako, bamiako
thornily (adv), bamiarkiu, bamiakiu, bamiakiu

thorny (adj), bamiarku, bamiaku, bamiaku
thorough (adj), delirthu, delithu, delthu
thoroughly (adv), delirthiu, delithiu, delthiu
those (adj), shorshu, shoshu, shoshu
those (pron), shorsh, shoshi, shosh
though (adv/conj), tsharn, teshanu, tshan
thought (n), derp, depa, dep
thought (v pa), derspyot, depio, depio
thoughtful (adj), derpu, depu, depu
thoughtfully (adv), derpiu, depiu, depiu
thousand (num 1000 card), dint, dint, dint
thousandth (num 1000 ord), dinteth, dinteth, dinteth
thrash (v), shprishsk, shuperiko, shpriko
thrasher (n doer), shprishkwan, shuperikua, shprikua
thread (n), dolirt, dolita, dolt
thread (v), dolirst, dolito, dolto
threat (n), dolarde, dolada, dolad
threaten (v), dolarzde, dolado, dolado
three (num 3 card), iri, iri, iri
threshold (n), dothorthk, dothoritha, dothorth
threw (v pa), tarthskyot, tarithio, tarthio
thrift (n), brilorp, berilopa, brilp
thrifty (adj), brilorpu, berilopu, brilpu
thrill (n), thraushk, therausha, thraush
thrill (v), thraushsk, therausho, thrausho
thriller (n doer), thraushkwan, theraushua, thraushua
thrive (v), thraishsk, theriasho, thraisho
throat (n), kiulork, kiuloka, kiulk
throaty (adj), kiulorku, kiuloku, kiulku
throb (v), pralzge, perago, prago
throe (n), praiark, peraiaka, praiak
throne (n), koiltive, koitiva, koitiv
throttle (n), telgart, teligata, telgat
throttle (v), telgarst, teligato, telgato
through (adj/adv/prep), telsharn, teleshanu, telshan
throughout (prep/adv), telshanuil, teleshanuilu, telshanuil
throughput (n), telshanvurt, teleshanuvuta, telshanvut
throw (n), tarthk, taritha, tarth
throw (v), tarthsk, taritho, tartho
throwback (n), tarthvark, tarithevaka, tarthvak
thrower (n doer), tarthkwan, tarithua, tarthua
thrush (n), fraugalt, feraugala, fraugal
thrust (n), torap, toripa, torp
thrust (v pa), toraspyot, toripio, torpio
thrust (v), torasp, toripo, torpo
thruster (n doer), torapwan, toripua, torpua
Ths (let pl), theili, theili, theili
thud (n), blushp, belupa, blup
thug (n), blurge, beluga, blug
thuggery (n), blurguet, belugueta, bluguet
Thulium (n davoka), Oraf, Oraf, Oraf
Thulium (n), Thulium, Thuliuma, Thulium
thumb (n), lorap, loripa, lorp
thumb (v), lorasp, loripo, lorpo
thumbnail (n), lorpthrink, loripetherina, lorpthrin
thump (n), thramp, therama, thram
thump (v), thramesp, theramo, thramo

thumper (n doer), thrampwan, theramua, thramua
thunder (n), gauarp, gauapa, gauap
thunder (v), gauarsp, gauapo, gauapo
thunderbolt (n), gauapkiurp, gauapekiupa, gauapkiup
thunderstorm (n), gauapferap, gauapeferipa, gauapfrip
Thursday (n), Toiviurl, Toiviula, Toiviul
thus (adv), zhurthiu, zhuthiu, zhuthiu
thwart (v), blakarsk, belakako, blakako
tick (n d:increment), brulk, beruka, bruk
tick (n d:insect), kiurtsh, kiutesha, kiutsh
tick (v d:increment), brulsk, beruko, bruko
ticker (n doer d:increment), brulkwan, berukua, brukua
ticket (n), brukarp, berukapa, brukap
ticket (v), brukarsp, berukapo, brukapo
ticketer (n doer), brukarpwan, berukapua, brukapua
tickle (n), brukart, berukata, brukat
tickle (v), brukarst, berukato, brukato
tickler (n doer), brukartwan, berukatua, brukatua
tidal (adj), glirtu, gelitu, glitu
tidbit (n), pluplurt, pelupeluta, pluplut
tide (n), glirt, gelita, glit
tide (v), glirst, gelito, glito
tidewater (n), gliteidorn, geliteidona, gliteidon
tidily (adv), fliurshiu, feliushiu, fliushiu
tidiness (n), fliursh, feliusha, fliush
tidy (adj), fliurshu, feliushu, fliushu
tidy (v), fliurs, feliusho, fliusho
tie (n), glersh, gelesha, glesh
tie (v), glers, gelesho, glesho
tiebreaker (n doer), gleshblerkwan, geleshepelikua, gleshplikua
tier (n), fliart, feliata, fliat
tier (v), fliarst, feliato, fliato
tiff (n), daiarf, daiafa, daiaf
tiff (v), daiarsf, daiafo, daiafo
tiger (n), kiurge, kiuga, kiug
tight (adj), duairfu, duaifu, duaifu
tighten (v), duairsf, duaifo, duaifo
tighter (adj), duairfwelu, duaifwelu, duaifwelu
tightest (adj), duairfwaku, duaifwaku, duaifwaku
tightly (adv), duairfiu, duaifiu, duaifiu
tightness (n), duairf, duaifa, duaif
tightrope (n), duaifvarp, duaifevapa, duaifvap
tights (n), duaifarn, duaifana, duaifan
tile (n), kloirn, keloina, kloin
tile (v), kloirsne, keloino, kloino
tiler (n doer), kloirnwan, keloinua, kloinua
till (n d:cash register), branirn, beranina, branin
till (v), triurzge, teriugo, triugo
tiller (n doer), triurgwan, teriugua, triugua
tilt (n), dirip, dirima, dirm
tilt (v), dirisp, dirimo, dirmo
timber (n), kurap, kuripa, kurp
time (n), daurn, dauna, daun
time (v), daursne, dauno, dauno
timeless (adj), daurnmenu, daunemenu, daunmenu
timelessness (n), daurnmen, daunemena, daunmen
timeline (n), daunroifk, dauneroifa, daunroif
timeliness (n), daurnuet, daunueta, daunuet

timely (adj), daurnu, daunu, daunu
timeout (n), daurnuil, daunuila, daunuil
timepiece (n), daunthetirsh, daunethetisha, daunthetsh
timer (n doer), daurnwan, daunua, daunua
timetable (n), daundoiart, daunedoiara, daundoiar
timid (adj), blirmu, belimu, blimu
timidity (n), blirme, belima, blim
timidly (adv), blirmiu, belimiu, blimiu
Tin (n davoka), Elip, Elip, Elip
tin (n), shtarn, shotana, shtan
Tin (n), Tin, Tina, Tin
tin (v), shtarsne, shotano, shtano
tinder (n), kurbank, kuribana, kurban
tinderbox (n), kurbanprekun, kuribaneperenika, kurbanprenk
tinge (n), tiorth, tiotha, tioth
tinge (v), tiorsth, tiotho, tiotho
tingle (n), tiaiart, tiaiata, tiaiat
tingle (v), tiaiarst, tiaiato, tiaiato
tininess (n), nishort, nishota, nisht
tinker (v), kiakiorsk, kiakioko, kiakioko
tint (n), lishtarn, lishetana, lishtan
tint (v), lishtarsne, lishetano, lishtano
tiny (adj), nishortu, nishotu, nishtu
tip (n), tilirf, tilifa, tilf
tip (v), tilirsf, tilifo, tilfo
tipoff (n), tilirfunf, tilifunefa, tilfunf
tipper (n doer), tilirfwan, tilifua, tilfua
tippy (adj), tilirfu, tilifu, tilfu
tipster (n), tilfplorn, tilifepelona, tilfplon
tiptoe (n), tilfdilorp, tilifedilopa, tilfdilp
tiptoe (v), tilfdilorsp, tilifedilopo, tilfdilpo
tirade (n), bakiart, bakiata, bakiat
tire (n d:wheel), deiort, deiota, deiot
tire (v d:fatigue), panirsk, paniko, panko
tiredness (n d:fatigue), panirk, panika, pank
tireless (adj d:fatigueless), panirkmenu, panikemenu, pankmenu
tiresome (adj d:fatigue), panirku, paniku, panku
tissue (n), kamirsh, kamisha, kamsh
Titanium (n davoka), Ifip, Ifip, Ifip
Titanium (n), Titanium, Titaniuma, Titanium
title (n), shtairp, shetaipa, shtaip
title (v), shtairsp, shetaipo, shtaipo
to (prep), dir, di, di
toast (n d:bread), biafirp, biafipa, biafp
toast (n d:cheer), kuirk, kuika, kuik
toast (v d:bread), biafirsp, biafipo, biafpo
toast (v d:cheer), kuirsk, kuiko, kuiko
toaster (n doer d:bread), biafirpwan, biafipua, biafpua
toaster (n doer d:cheer), kuirkwan, kuikua, kuikua
toasty (adj d:bread), biafirpu, biafipu, biafpu
toasty (adj d:cheer), kuirku, kuiku, kuiku
tobacco (n), dovart, dovata, dovat
today (adj), diviurlu, diviulu, diviulu
today (adv), diviurliu, diviuliu, diviuliu
today (n), diviurl, diviula, diviul
toddle (n), tanfarn, tanifana, tanfan
toddle (v), tanfarsne, tanifano, tanfano
toddler (n doer), tanfarnwan, tanifanua, tanfanua
toe (n), dilorp, dilopa, dilp

toenail (n), dilpthrink, dilopetherina, dilpthrin
together (adv), dikorshiu, dikoshiu, dikoshiu
togetherness (n), dikorsh, dikosha, dikosh
toggle (n), dikiurk, dikiuka, dikiuk
toggle (v), dikiursk, dikiuko, dikiuko
toil (n), kelkiork, kelikioka, kelkiok
toil (v), kelkiorsk, kelikioko, kelkioko
toilet (n), guarp, guapa, guap
toiletry (n), guapart, guapata, guapat
token (n), bishtark, bishotaka, bishtak
tokenize (v), bishtarsk, bishotako, bishtako
tokenizer (n doer), bishtarkwan, bishotakua, bishtakua
Tokyo (n), Tokiorf, Tokiofa, Tokiof
told (v pa), prelstyot, peretio, pretio
tolerable (adj), trinorsk, terinotu, trintu
tolerance (n), trinort, terinota, trint
tolerant (adj), trinortu, terinotu, trintu
tolerate (v), trinorst, terinoto, trinto
toleration (n), trinortuet, terinotueta, trintuet
toll (n), korame, korima, korm
toll (v), korazme, korimo, kormo
tollbooth (n), kormturshk, korimeturisha, kormtursh
tomato (n), goifern, goifena, goifen
tomb (n), beinurk, beinuka, beink
tombstone (n), beinkbaraft, beinukebarafa, beinkbaraf
tomorrow (adv), kreirthiu, kureithiu, kreithiu
tomorrow (n), kreirth, kureitha, kreith
ton (n), dunirn, dunina, dunin
tonality (n), trilfuet, terilueta, triluet
tone (n d:music), trilf, terila, tril
tone (n d:quality), shmern, shimena, shmen
tone (v d:quality), shmersne, shimeno, shmeno
toner (n doer d:quality), shmernwan, shimenua, shmenua
tong (n), poirk, poika, poik
tongue (n), penork, penoka, penk
tongue (v), penorsk, penoko, penko
tonight (adv), dimuarniu, dimuanıu, dimuanıu
tonight (n), dimuarn, dimuana, dimuan
tonne (n), dunirnk, duninoka, dunink
too (adv), deniu, deliu, deliu
took (v pa), gorskyot, gokio, gokio
tool (n), fiork, fioka, fiok
tool (v), fiorsk, fioko, fioko
toolbox (n), fiokprekun, fiokeperenika, fiokprenk
toolkit (n), fiokplurde, fiokapeluda, fiokplud
toot (n), kukurk, kuluka, kuluk
toot (v), kukursk, kuluko, kuluko
tooth (n), tshatirsh, teshatisha, tshatsh
tooth (v), tshatirs, teshatisho, tshatsho
toothbrush (n), tshatshklurf, teshatishekelusha, tshatshklush
toothpaste (n), tshatshdrafip, teshatishederafipa, tshatshdrafp
toothpick (n), tshatshdotirsh, teshatishedotisha, tshatshdotsh
toothy (adj), tshatirshu, teshatishu, tshatshu
top (adj), daurpu, daupu, daupu
top (n), daurp, daupa, daup
top (v), daursp, daupo, daupo

topic (n), daupirk, daupika, daupik
topical (adj), daupirku, daupiku, daupiku
topless (adj), daurpemenu, daupemenu, daupemenu
topper (n doer), daurpwan, daupua, daupua
topple (v), dauparst, daupato, daupato
topsoil (n), daupnarash, daupenarisha, daupnarsh
topsy (adj), daupinku, daupinu, daupinu
torch (n), kiorshk, kioshika, kioshk
torch (v), kiorshsk, kioshiko, kioshko
tore (v pa d:rip), ralzbyot, rabio, rabio
torment (v), kioteshsk, kiotesho, kiotsho
tormentor (n doer), kioteshkwan, kioteshua, kiotshua
Toronto (n), Torontorf, Toronitofa, Torontof
torque (n), kiort, kiota, kiot
torque (v), kiorst, kioto, kioto
torrent (n), dovibrauthk, doviberautha, dovibrauth
torrential (adj), dovibrauthku, doviberauthu, dovibrauthu
torrid (adj), dovikurtu, dovikutu, dovikutu
tort (n), giorbe, gioba, giob
torture (n), giobart, giobata, giobat
torture (v), giobarst, giobato, giobato
torturous (adj), giobartu, giobatu, giobatu
toss (n), tharsh, thasha, thash
toss (v), thars, thasho, thasho
tosser (n doer), tharshwan, thashua, thashua
tot (n), tanfk, tanifa, tanf
total (n), biburt, bibuta, bibut
total (v), biburst, bibuto, bibuto
totalitarian (n doer), bibutarnwan, bibutanua, bibutanua
totalitarianism (n), bibutarn, bibutana, bibutan
totality (n), biburtuet, bibutueta, bibutuet
totally (adv), biburtiu, bibutiu, bibutiu
tote (n), tafirt, tafita, taft
tote (v), tafirst, tafito, tafto
touch (n), shiarl, shiala, shial
touch (v), shiarsle, shialo, shialo
touchdown (n), shiarltien, shialetiena, shialtien
touchstone (n), shialbaraft, shialebarafa, shialbaraf
touchy (adj), shiarlu, shialu, shialu
tough (adj), trolgu, terogu, trogu
toughen (v), trolzge, terogo, trogo
tougher (adj), trolgwelu, terogwelu, trogwelu
toughest (adj), trolgwaku, terogwaku, trogwaku
toughness (n), trolge, teroga, trog
tour (n), thiarf, thiafa, thiaf
tour (v), thiarsf, thiafo, thiafo
tourism (n), thiarfuet, thiafueta, thiafuet
tourist (n doer), thiarfwan, thiafua, thiafua
tournament (n), kargark, karigaka, kargak
tout (v), kliaumesp, keliaumo, kliaumo
tow (n), baur, baula, baul
tow (v), bausre, baulo, baulo
toward (prep), dehursh, dehushu, dehush
towel (n), baursh, bausha, baush
towel (v), baurs, bausho, bausho
tower (n doer), baurwan, baulua, baulua
tower (v), baufirt, baufita, bauft
tower (v), baufirst, baufito, baufto
town (n), miurn, miuna, miun

townfolk (n), miunkiforp, miunekifopa, miunkifp
townhouse (n), miunkiarf, miunekiafa, miunkiaf
townperson (n), miunplorn, miunepelona, miunplon
townsfolk (n pl), miunkiforpyek, miunekifopi, miunkifpi
township (n), miunfirf, miunefifa, miunfif
townspeople (n pl), miunplornyek, miunepeloni, miunploni
toxic (adj), kiabarku, kiabaku, kiabaku
toxicity (n), kiabark, kiabaka, kiabak
toxicological (adj), kiabarkuitu, kiabakuitu, kiabakuitu
toxicologically (adv), kiabarkuitiu, kiabakuitiu, kiabakuitiu
toxicologist (n doer), kiabarkuitwan, kiabakuitua, kiabakuitua
toxicology (n), kiabarkuit, kiabakuita, kiabakuit
toxin (n), kiarbe, kiaba, kiab
toy (n), biort, biota, biot
toy (v), biorst, bioto, bioto
trace (n), garsh, gasha, gash
trace (v), gars, gasho, gasho
traceable (adj), garshu, gashu, gashu
traceably (adv), garshiu, gashiu, gashiu
tracer (n doer), garshwan, gashua, gashua
track (n), gethirk, gethika, gethk
track (v), gethirsk, gethiko, gethko
tracker (n doer), gethirkwan, gethikua, gethkua
tract (n), galirt, galita, galt
traction (n), galtert, galiteta, galtet
tractor (n doer), galirtwan, galitua, galtua
tradable (adj), fralbu, ferabu, frabu
tradably (adv), fralbiu, ferabiu, frabiu
trade (n), fralbe, feraba, frab
trade (v), fralzbe, ferabo, frabo
trademark (n), frabshtart, ferabeshetata, frabshtat
trademark (v), frabshtarst, ferabeshetato, frabshtato
tradeoff (n), fralbunf, ferabunefa, frabunf
trader (n doer), fralbwan, ferabua, frabua
tradesman (n), frabeplorn, ferabepelona, frabeplon
tradesmen (n pl), frabeplornyek, ferabepeloni, frabeploni
tradition (n), trabirn, terabira, trabir
traditional (adj), trabirnu, terabiru, trabiru
traditionalist (n doer), trabirnwan, terabirua, trabirua
traditionally (adv), trabirniu, terabiriu, trabiriu
traffic (n), klerge, kilega, kleg
traffic (v), klerzge, kilego, klego
trafficker (n doer), klergwan, kilegua, klegua
tragedy (n), zhairf, zhaifa, zhaif
tragic (adj), zhairfu, zhaifu, zhaifu
tragically (adv), zhairfiu, zhaifiu, zhaifiu
trail (n), glarsh, gelasha, glash
trail (v), glars, gelasho, glasho
trailblazer (n doer), glashkraurgwan, gelashekeraugua, glashkraugua
trailer (n doer), glarshwan, gelashua, glashua
train (n d:locomotive), bartarde, baritada, bartad
train (v d:conditioning), trilorsk, teriloko, trilko
trainable (adj d:conditioning), trilorku, teriloku,

trilku
trainee (n), trilorkuin, terilokuina, trilkuin
trainer (n doer d:conditioning), trilorkwan,
　terilokua, trilkua
trait (n), shauthk, shautha, shauth
traitor (n), trabiurk, terabiuka, trabiuk
traject (v), thotersp, thotepo, thotepo
trajection (n), thoterp, thotepa, thotep
trajector (n doer), thoterpwan, thotepua, thotepua
trajectory (n), thotelirp, thotelipa, thotelp
tramp (n), klanirt, kelanita, klant
tramp (v), klanirst, kelanito, klanto
trample (v), klanirsp, kelanipo, klanpo
trance (n), thorifp, thoripa, thorp
tranquil (adj), thokiunfu, thokiunu, thokiunu
tranquility (n), thokiunf, thokiuna, thokiun
tranquilization (n), thokiunfuet, thokiunueta,
　thokiunuet
tranquilize (v), thokiunsf, thokiuno, thokiuno
tranquilizer (n doer), thokiunfwan, thokiunua,
　thokiunua
transact (v), dhaupatisle, dhaupalito, dhaupalto
transaction (n), dhaupatil, dhaupalita, dhaupalt
transactor (n doer), dhaupatilwan, dhaupalitua,
　dhaupaltua
transatlantic (adj), dhauatelantirku,
　dhauatelanotiku, dhauatelantiku
transcend (v), dhaulirask, dhauliriko, dhaulirko
transcendence (n), dhaulirak, dhaulirika, dhaulirk
transcendent (adj), dhauliraku, dhauliriku,
　dhaulirku
transcendent (n), dhaulirakul, dhaulirikula,
　dhaulirkul
transcendental (adj), dhaulirakulu, dhaulirikulu,
　dhaulirkulu
transcontinental (adj), dhaumedmotu,
　dhaumeratu, dhaumertu
transcribe (v), dhausherzge, dhausherigo,
　dhaushrigo
transcriber (n doer), dhaushergwan, dhausherigua,
　dhaushrigua
transcript (n), dhausherge, dhausheriga, dhaushrig
transcription (n), dhausherguet, dhausherigueta,
　dhaushriguet
transduce (v), dhaukirask, dhaukiroko, dhaukirko
transducer (n doer), dhaukirakwan, dhaukirokua,
　dhaukirkua
transduction (n), dhaukirak, dhaukiroka, dhaukirk
transfer (n), dhaursh, dhausha, dhaush
transfer (v), dhaurs, dhausho, dhausho
transferability (n), dhaushfrelp, dhausheferepa,
　dhaushfrep
transferable (adj), dhaurshu, dhaushu, dhaushu
transferably (adv), dhaurshiu, dhaushiu, dhaushiu
transference (n), dhaurshuet, dhaushueta,
　dhaushuet
transfix (v), dhauvirsk, dhauviko, dhauviko
transfixate (v), dhauvirkest, dhauviketo, dhauviketo
transfixation (n), dhauvirket, dhauviketa, dhauviket
transform (v), dhaurvorsne, dhauvorino,
　dhauvorno
transformation (n), dhaurvorn, dhauvorina,
　dhauvorn

transformational (adj), dhaurvornu, dhauvorinu,
　dhauvornu
transformationally (adv), dhaurvorniu,
　dhauvoriniu, dhauvorniu
transformer (n doer), dhaurvornwan, dhauvorinua,
　dhauvornua
transfuse (v), dhaufaborst, dhaufaboto, dhaufaboto
transfusion (n), dhaufabort, dhaufabota, dhaufabot
transgress (v), dhauvorazge, dhauvorugo,
　dhauvorgo
transgression (n), dhauvorage, dhauvoruga,
　dhauvorg
transgressor (n doer), dhauvoragwan,
　dhauvorugua, dhauvorgua
transience (n), dhaufrelp, dhauferepa, dhaufrep
transient (adj), dhaufrelpu, dhauferepu, dhaufrepu
transient (n doer), dhaufrelpwan, dhauferepua,
　dhaufrepua
transiently (adv), dhaufrelpiu, dhauferepiu,
　dhaufrepiu
transistor (n doer), dhautielirkwan, dhautielikua,
　dhautielkua
transit (n), dhaufirk, dhaufika, dhaufk
transition (n), dhaufirkuet, dhaufikueta, dhaufkuet
translate (v), dhaurdarst, dhaudarito, dhaudarto
translation (n), dhaurdart, dhaudarita, dhaudart
translator (n doer), dhaurdartwan, dhaudaritua,
　dhaudartua
translucent (adj), dhaushiunirku, dhaushiuniku,
　dhaushiunku
translucently (adv), dhaushiunirkiu, dhaushiunikiu,
　dhaushiunkiu
transmission (n), dhaunork, dhaunoka, dhaunok
transmit (v), dhaunorsk, dhaunoko, dhaunoko
transmittal (n), dhaunork, dhaunoka, dhaunok
transmitter (n doer), dhaunorkwan, dhaunokua,
　dhaunokua
transmutable (adj), dhaushluarku, dhausheluaku,
　dhaushluaku
transmutably (adv), dhaushluarkiu, dhausheluakiu,
　dhaushluakiu
transmutation (n), dhaushluark, dhausheluaka,
　dhaushluak
transmute (v), dhaushluarsk, dhausheluako,
　dhaushluako
transmutor (n doer), dhaushluarkwan,
　dhausheluakua, dhaushluakua
transnational (adj), dhaukarlfu, dhaukarilu,
　dhaukarlu
transocean (adj), dhaumiarlu, dhaumiaru,
　dhaumiaru
transparency (n), dhaupliarn, dhaupeliana,
　dhauplian
transparent (adj), dhaupliarnu, dhaupelianu,
　dhauplianu
transparently (adv), dhaupliarniu, dhaupelianiu,
　dhauplianiu
transpiration (n), dhaudaurf, dhaudaufa, dhaudauf
transpire (v), dhaudaursf, dhaudaufo, dhaudaufo
transplant (n), dhaulitarnk, dhaulitanika,
　dhaulitank
transplant (v), dhaulitarnsk, dhaulitaniko,
　dhaulitanko

transplantation (n), dhaulitarnkuet, dhaulitanikueta, dhaulitankuet
transponder (n), dhaurdurfp, dhaudufipa, dhaudufp
transport (v), dhaurbielorsk, dhaubieloko, dhaubielko
transportable (adj), dhaurbielorku, dhaubieloku, dhaubielku
transportation (n), dhaurbielork, dhaubieloka, dhaubielk
transporter (n doer), dhaurbielorkwan, dhaubielokua, dhaubielkua
transpose (v), dhauglarsk, dhaugelako, dhauglako
transposer (n doer), dhauglarkwan, dhaugelakua, dhauglakua
transposition (n), dhauglark, dhaugelaka, dhauglak
transsexual (n), dhaubivikart, dhaubivikata, dhaubivikat
transverse (adj), dhautharaku, dhauthariku, dhautharku
transverse (n), dhautharak, dhautharika, dhauthark
transvert (v), dhautharask, dhauthariko, dhautharko
transvestite (n), dhaukiflarf, dhaukifelafa, dhaukiflaf
trap (n), threilp, thereipa, threip
trap (v), threilsp, thereipo, threipo
trapdoor (n), threipshtelf, thereipeshetela, threipshtel
trapper (n doer), threilpwan, thereipua, threipua
trash (n), shaflark, shafilaka, shaflak
trash (v), shaflarsk, shafilako, shaflako
trashy (adj), shaflarku, shafilaku, shaflaku
travel (n), dovirt, dovita, dovit
travel (v), dovirst, dovito, dovito
traveler (n doer), dovirtwan, dovitua, dovitua
traveller (n doer), dovirtwan, dovitua, dovitua
traversal (n), dotharaf, dotharifa, dotharf
traverse (v), dotharasf, dotharifo, dotharfo
travesty (n), kinaflarf, kinafelafa, kinaflaf
trawl (n), glamish, gelamisha, glamsh
trawl (v), glamis, gelamisho, glamsho
trawlers (adj), glamishu, gelamishu, glamshu
tray (n), biarme, biama, biam
treacherous (adj), zhaukaiku, zhaukaitu, zhaukaitu
treacherously (adv), zhaukaikiu, zhaukaitiu, zhaukaitiu
treachery (n), zhaukaik, zhaukaita, zhaukait
tread (n), shputhk, sheputha, shputh
tread (v), shputhsk, sheputho, shputho
treadmill (n), shpurtrek, sheputereka, shputrek
treason (n), zhaukarp, zhaukapa, zhaukap
treasure (n), grilorp, gerilopa, grilp
treasure (v), grilorsp, gerilopo, grilpo
treasurer (n doer), grilorpwan, gerilopua, grilpua
treasury (n), grilpart, gerilopata, grilpat
treat (n), thuirt, thuita, thuit
treat (v), thuirst, thuito, thuito
treatable (adj), thuirtu, thuitu, thuitu
treatment (n), thuitalirt, thuitalita, thuitalt
treaty (n), thuitarn, thuitana, thuitan
tredecillion (num 1e42 card), irisht, irisht, irisht
tredecillionth (num 1e42 ord), irishteth, irishteth,
irishteth
tree (n), delairf, delaifa, delaif
treeless (adj), delairfmenu, delaifemenu, delaifmenu
treetop (n), delaifdaurp, delaifedaupa, delaifdaup
trek (n), shriavirt, sheriavita, shriavit
trek (v), shriavirst, sheriavito, shriavito
trekker (n doer), shriavirtwan, sheriavitua, shriavitua
tremble (n), fralve, ferava, frav
tremble (v), fralzve, feravo, fravo
trembler (n doer), fralvwan, feravua, fravua
tremendous (adj), fravinorku, feravinoku, fravinku
tremendously (adv), fravinorkiu, feravinokiu, fravinkiu
tremor (n), fravirn, feravina, fravin
tremor (v), fravirsne, feravino, fravino
trench (n), diofk, diofa, diof
trench (v), diofsk, diofo, diofo
trend (n), frailork, ferailoka, frailk
trend (v), frailorsk, ferailoko, frailko
trendy (adj), frailorku, ferailoku, frailku
trespass (v), dhaulunirst, dhaulunito, dhaulunto
trespasser (n doer), dhaulunirtwan, dhaulunitua, dhauluntua
tresquadragintillion (num 1e132 card), irifk, irifk, irifk
trestrigintillion (num 1e102 card), irift, irift, irift
trevigintillion (num 1e72 card), irishk, irishk, irishk
trevigintillionth (num 1e72 ord), irishketh, irishketh, irishketh
tri- (num 3 pref), irai-, irai-, irai-
trial (n), dibarge, dibaga, dibag
triangle (n), iraimirk, iraimika, iraimik
triangular (adj), iraimirku, iraimiku, iraimiku
triangulate (v), iraimirsk, iraimiko, iraimiko
triangulation (n), iraimirkuet, iraimikueta, iraimikuet
tribal (adj), thrilpu, theripu, thripu
tribe (n), thrilp, theripa, thrip
tribesman (n), thrilplorn, theripelona, thriplon
tribesmen (n pl), thrilplornyek, theripeloni, thriploni
tribulate (v), fliunorst, feliunoto, fliunto
tribulation (n), fliunort, feliunota, fliunt
tribune (n), fliuvarn, feliuvana, fliuvan
tributary (n), thriupart, theriupata, thriupat
tribute (n), thriurp, theriupa, thriup
trick (n), dalirk, dalika, dallk
trick (v), dalirsk, daliko, dalko
trickery (n), dalirkuet, dalikueta, dalkuet
trickle (v), daklirst, dakelito, daklito
trickster (n doer), dalirkwan, dalikua, dalkua
tricky (adj), dalirku, daliku, dalku
trigger (n), biorak, biorika, biork
trigger (v), biorask, bioriko, biorko
trigintillion (num 1e93 card), dashka, dashka, dashka
trigintillionth (num 1e93 ord), dashketh, dashketh, dashketh
trilateral (adj), irainamoru, irainarimu, irainarmu
trill (n), telirn, telira, telir

trill (v), telirsne, teliro, teliro
triller (n doer), telirnwan, telirua, telirua
trillion (num 1e12 card), irika, irika, irika
trillionth (num 1e12 ord), iriketh, iriketh, iriketh
trim (n), fnoilf, fenoila, fnoil
trim (v), fnoilsf, fenoilo, fnoilo
trimester (n), iraithranit, iraitheranita, iraithrant
trimmer (n doer), fnoilfwan, fenoilua, fnoilua
trip (n d:journey), glarude, gelaruda, glard
trip (n d:misstep), krivurp, kerivupa, krivup
trip (v d:misstep), krivursp, kerivupo, krivupo
triple (adj), iraishorku, iraishoku, iraishku
triple (n), iraishork, iraishoka, iraishk
triple (v), iraishorsk, iraishoko, iraishko
triplet (n), iraishart, iraishata, iraisht
tripod (n), iraimoirn, iraimoina, iraimoin
tripper (n doer d:misstep), krivurpwan, kerivupua, krivupua
trite (adj), tarvu, tavu, tavu
tritely (adv), tarviu, taviu, taviu
triteness (n), tarve, tava, tav
triumph (n), liraiforp, liraifopa, liraifp
triumph (v), liraiforsp, liraifopo, liraifpo
triumphal (adj), liraiforpu, liraifopu, liraifpu
triumphant (adj), liraiforpu, liraifopu, liraifpu
triumphantly (adv), liraiforpiu, liraifopiu, liraifpiu
trivia (n pl), preiliarfyek, pereiliafi, preiliafi
trivial (adj), preiliarfu, pereiliafu, preiliafu
triviality (n), preiliarfuet, pereiliafueta, preiliafuet
trivialize (v), preiliarsf, pereiliafo, preiliafo
trivium (n), preiliarf, pereiliafa, preiliaf
trod (v pa), shputhskyot, sheputhio, shputhio
troll (n), fuiark, fuiaka, fuiak
troll (v), fuiarsk, fuiako, fuiako
trolley (n), fuishk, fuisha, fuish
troop (n), bionirk, bionika, bionk
troop (v), bionirsk, bioniko, bionko
trooper (n doer), bionirkwan, bionikua, bionkua
trophy (n), liaishk, liaisha, liaish
tropic (n), dronirp, deronipa, dronip
tropical (adj), dronirpu, deronipu, dronipu
tropically (adv), dronirpiu, deronipiu, dronipiu
trot (n), tuiark, tuiaka, tuiak
trot (v), tuiarsk, tuiako, tuiako
trotter (n doer), tuiarkwan, tuiakua, tuiakua
trouble (n), didushk, diduka, diduk
trouble (v), didushsk, diduko, diduko
troublemaker (n doer), didushkwan, didukua, didukua
troubleshoot (v), didukshkorst, didukeshekoto, didukshkoto
troubleshooter (n doer), didukshkortwan, didukeshekotua, didukshkotua
troublesome (adj), didukzhirnu, didukezhinu, didukzhinu
trough (n), buathk, buatha, buath
trounce (v), tshufist, teshufito, tshufto
trousers (n), linarsh, linasha, linash
trowel (n), bualsh, buala, bual
trowel (v), buals, bualo, bualo
troweler (n doer), bualshwan, bualua, bualua
truce (n), bleirth, beleitha, bleith
truck (n), ftarge, fitaga, ftag

truck (v), ftarzge, fitago, ftago
trucker (n doer), ftargwan, fitagua, ftagua
truckload (n), ftaglurift, fetagelurita, ftaglurt
trudge (v), klarze, kelazho, klazho
true (adj), dreil, dereilu, drei
truelove (n), dreivoshar, dereivoshara, dreivoshar
truism (n), dreilshuet, dereishueta, dreishuet
truly (adv), dreilu, dereiliu, dreilu
trump (v), guarnsk, guaniroko, guanko
truncate (v), dialirsk, dialiko, dialko
trunk (n), dialirk, dialika, dialk
truss (n), kleithk, kelietha, kleith
trust (n), dreirf, dereifa, dreif
trust (v), dreirsf, dereifo, dreifo
trustee (n), dreirfuin, dereifuina, dreifuin
trustful (adj), dreirfu, dereifu, dreifu
trustfulness (n), dreirfuet, dereifueta, dreifuet
trustworthiness (n), dreiflairsh, dereifelaisha, dreiflaish
trustworthy (adj), dreiflairshu, dereifelaishu, dreiflaishu
trusty (adj), dreirfu, dereifu, dreifu
truth (n), dreilsh, dereisha, dreish
truthful (adj), dreilshu, dereishu, dreishu
truthfully (adv), dreilshiu, dereishiu, dreishiu
try (n), dirbe, diba, dib
try (v), dirzbe, dibo, dibo
tryout (n), dirbuil, dibuila, dibuil
Ts (let pl), teili, teili, teili
tub (n), flerp, felepa, flep
tubal (adj), kiardu, kiadu, kiadu
tube (n), kiarde, kiada, kiad
tube (v), kiarzde, kiado, kiado
tubular (adj), kiardu, kiadu, kiadu
tuck (n), shkiark, shekiaka, shkiak
tuck (v), shkiarsk, shekiako, shkiako
tucker (n doer), shkiarkwan, shekiakua, shkiakua
Tuesday (n), Dioshviurl, Dioshuviula, Dioshviul
tuft (n), shkeithk, shekeitha, shkeith
tug (n), karve, kava, kav
tug (v), karzve, kavo, kavo
tugboat (n), kavshkorbe, kaveshekoba, kavshkob
tuition (n), baurf, baufa, bauf
tulip (n), deiranf, deirana, deiran
tumble (n), briufp, beriufa, briuf
tumble (v), briufsp, beriufo, briufo
tumbler (n doer), briufpwan, beriufua, briufua
tumor (n), beinart, beinata, beint
tune (n), shmurn, shemuna, shmun
tune (v), shmursne, shemuno, shmuno
tuner (n doer), shmurnwan, shemunua, shmunua
Tungsten (n davoka), Irup, Irup, Irup
Tungsten (n), Tungshten, Tunogishetena, Tungshten
tunnel (n), flairme, felaima, flaim
tunnel (v), flairzme, felaimo, flaimo
tunneler (n doer), flairmwan, felaimua, flaimua
turbin (n), kiarp, kiapa, kiap
turbine (n), gorpirk, goropika, gorpik
turbulence (n), gorlirp, goralipa, gorlp
turbulent (adj), gorlirpu, goralipu, gorlpu
turf (n), prethk, peretha, preth
Turkey (n), Turkirf, Turokifa, Turkif

turkey (n), girap, giropa, girp
Turkish (n), Turkifarn, Turokifana, Turkifan
turmoil (n), kiaulf, kiaula, kiaul
turn (n), kaimp, kaima, kaim
turn (v), kaimesp, kaimo, kaimo
turnabout (n), kaimpoveip, kaimoveipa, kaimoveip
turnaround (n), kaimoblaithp, kaimobelaitha, kaimoblaith
turncoat (n), kaimfrafk, kaimegerafika, kaimgrafk
turnkey (adj), kaimtrifku, kaimeteriku, kaimtriku
turnoff (n), kaimpunf, kaimunefa, kaimunf
turnout (n), kaimpuil, kaimuila, kaimuil
turnover (n), kaimafen, kaimafena, kaimafen
turnpike (n), kaimpaiart, kaimepaiata, kaimpaiat
turntable (n), kaimdoiart, kaimedoiara, kaimdoiar
turret (n), liailk, liaila, liail
turtle (n), klinurf, kelinufa, klinuf
turtleneck (adj), klinurfthavubu, kelinufetharibu, klinuftharbu
turtleneck (n), klinurfthavube, kelinufethariba, klinuftharb
tusk (n), krushk, kerusha, krush
tussle (n), shkarve, shekava, shkav
tussle (v), shkarzve, shekavo, shkavo
tutor (n doer), balirshkwan, balishokua, balishkua
tutor (v), balirshsk, balishoko, balishko
tutorial (n), balirshk, balishoka, balishk
twang (n), blaurge, belauga, blaug
twang (v), blaurzge, belaugo, blaugo
tweak (n), gilurf, gilufa, gilf
tween (n), durme, duma, dum
tweet (n), pilirt, pilita, pilt
tweet (v), pilirst, pilito, pilto
tweeze (v), avugiorsk, avugioko, avugioko
tweezer (n doer), avugiorkwan, avugiokua, avugiokua
twelfth (num 12 ord), avupeth, avupeth, avupeth
twelv- (num 12 pref), avupai-, avupai-, avupai-
twelve (num 12 card), avupa, avupa, avupa
twentieth (num 20 ord), avudeth, avudeth, avudeth
twenty (num 20 card), avuda, avuda, avuda
twenty- (num 20 pref), avudai-, avudai-, avudai-
twice (adv), avuth, avuthu, avuth
twiddle (n), loraft, lorafa, loraf
twiddle (v), lorafst, lorafo, lorafo
twilight (n), lavufluarn, lavufeluana, lavufluan
twin (n), lavurn, lavuna, lavun
twine (n), laivurn, laivuna, laivun
twinge (n), bliarge, beliaga, bliag
twinge (v), bliarzge, beliagu, bliagu
twinkle (n), liavurk, liavuka, liavuk
twinkle (v), liavursk, liavuko, liavuko
twist (n), gelirk, gelika, gelk
twist (v), gelirsk, geliko, gelko
twister (n doer), gelirkwan, gelikua, gelkua
twisty (adj), gelirku, geliku, gelku
twit (n), thiteshk, thitesha, thitsh
twitch (n), geiteshk, geitesha, geitsh
twitch (v), geiteshsk, geitesho, geitsho
two (num 2 card), avu, avu, avu
type (n d:key), daurk, dauka, dauk
type (n d:kind), duarp, duapa, duap

type (v d:key), daursk, dauko, dauko
type (v d:kind), duarsp, duapo, duapo
typeface (n), daukthoirsh, daukethoisha, daukthoish
typeset (v pa), daukferspyot, daukefepio, daukfepio
typeset (v), daukfersp, daukefepo, daukfepo
typesetter (n doer), daukferpwan, daukefepua, daukfepua
typewriter (n doer), daukploirwan, daukepeloidua, daukploidua
typical (adj d:kind), duarpu, duapu, duapu
typically (adv d:kind), duarpiu, duapiu, duapiu
typist (n doer d:key), daurkwan, daukua, daukua
typo (n), daurkil, daukila, daukil
typographical (adj), daukdarftu, daukedarifu, daukdarfu
typography (n), daukdarft, daukedarifa, daukdarf
U (let sng), urfe, urifa, urf
udeka- (num 1e36 pref), hemshtai-, hemshtai-, hemshtai-
ugh (interj), angai, angai, angai
ugliness (n), fralk, feraka, frak
ugly (adj), fralku, feraku, fraku
uh (interj), er, er, er
Ukraine (n), Ukrainarf, Ukerainafa, Ukrainaf
ultimate (adj), tizhaurku, tizhauku, tizhauku
ultimately (adv), tizhaurkiu, tizhaukiu, tizhaukiu
ultimatum (n pl), tizhaurkyek, tizhauki, tizhauki
ultimatum (n), tizhaurk, tizhauka, tizhauk
ultraconservative (adj), divrabelkoftu, diveraliukofitu, divraliukoftu
ultraconservatively (adv), divrabelkoftiu, diveraliukofitiu, divraliukoftiu
ultranational (adj), divrakarlfu, diverakarilu, divrakarlu
ultranationalist (n doer), divrakarlfwan, diverakarilua, divrakarlua
ultrasonic (adj), divrazhantarnu, diverazhanitanu, divrazhantanu
ultrasonically (adv), divrazhantarniu, diverazhanitaniu, divrazhantaniu
ultrasound (n), divrazhantarn, diverazhanitana, divrazhantan
ultraviolet (adj), divrafeiranku, diverafeiranu, divrafeiranu
ultraviolet (n), divrafeirank, diverafeirana, divrafeiran
um (interj), ern, eren, ern
umbrella (n), valurap, valuripa, valurp
umpire (n), uldaurf, ulidaufa, uldauf
unabate (v), piuogiarsp, piuogiapo, piuogiapo
unabatement (n), piuogiarp, piuogiapa, piuogiap
unability (n), piufrelp, piuferepa, piufrep
unable (adj), piufrelpu, piuferepu, piufrepu
unably (adv), piufrelpiu, piuferepiu, piufrepiu
unabridge (v), piuoploshsk, piuopelosho, piuoplosho
unabridgement (n), piuoploshk, piuopelosha, piuoplosh
unaccept (v), piuorshirsp, piuorashipo, piuorshipo
unacceptability (n), piuorshirp, piuorashipa, piuorship
unacceptable (adj), piuorshirpu, piuorashipu,

piuorshipu
unacceptably (adv), piuorshirpiu, piuorashipiu,
piuorshipiu
unaccount (v), piuorpoinsf, piuorapoino,
piuorpoino
unaccountable (adj), piuorpoinfu, piuorapoinu,
piuorpoinu
unadjust (v), piutepafes, piutefipesho, piutefpesho
unaffiliate (v), piuorfliarsne, piuorafeliano,
piuorfliano
unalienable (adj), piuanlarku, piuanolaku,
piuanlaku
unalterable (adj), piuoiparpu, piuoipapu, piuoipapu
unalterably (adv), piuoiparpiu, piuoipapiu,
piuoipapiu
unambiguous (adj), piuviuvartu, piuviuviatu,
piuviuviatu
unambiguously (adv), piuviuvartiu, piuviuviatiu,
piuviuviatiu
unanimous (adj), hemniarpu, hemoniapu,
hemniapu
unanimously (adv), hemniarpiu, hemoniapiu,
hemniapiu
unanswerable (adj), piuorshirlu, piuorashilu,
piuorshilu
unapprove (v), piuofelarzve, piuofelaruvo,
piuoflarvo
unarm (v), piushnersne, piushineno, piushneno
unassailable (adj), piukarfluarlu, piukarifelualu,
piukarflualu
unattractive (adj), piuogalirtu, piuogalitu, piuogaltu
unattractively (adv), piuogalirtiu, piuogalitiu,
piuogaltiu
unauthorize (v), piubashtasp, piubashalipo,
piubashalpo
unavail (v), piushiursp, piushiupo, piushiupo
unavailability (n), piushiurpaf, piushiufipa,
piushiufp
unavailable (adj), piushiurpafu, piushiufipu,
piushiufpu
unavoidable (adj), piulonuaku, piuonuaku,
piuonuaku
unavoidably (adv), piulonuakiu, piuonuakiu,
piuonuakiu
unaware (adj), piushlerfu, piuoshelefu, piuoshlefu
unbalance (v), piumorshtast, piushemotato,
piushmotato
unbearable (adj), piukriagu, piugeruku, piugruku
unbearably (adv), piukriagiu, piugerukiu, piugrukiu
unbeatable (adj), piudaurtu, piudautu, piudautu
unbeatably (adv), piudaurtiu, piudautiu, piudautiu
unbecame (v pa), piuvilensfyot, piukilenio,
piubilenio
unbecome (v), piuvilensf, piukileno, piubileno
unbelievable (adj), piusharmu, piusharu, piusharu
unbelievably (adv), piusharmiu, piushariu,
piushariu
unbeliever (n doer), piusharmwan, piusharua,
piusharua
unbend (v), piukikost, piukifato, piukifto
unbent (v pa), piukikostyot, piukifatio, piukiftio
unbias (v), piulipsk, piuipeko, piuipko
Unbibium (n davoka), Uship, Uship, Uship

unbind (v), piupaupizme, piupaumubo, piupaumbo
Unbinilium (n davoka), Aship, Aship, Aship
Unbiunium (n davoka), Ushap, Ushap, Ushap
unborn (n), piuvashil, piuvalesha, piuvalsh
unbound (v pa), piupaupizmyot, piupaumubio,
piupaumbio
unbrand (v), piufnairsp, piufenaipo, piufnaipo
unbreak (v), piublersk, piupeliko, piupliko
unbreakable (adj), piublerku, piupeliku, piupliku
unbridle (v), piuthraunsk, piutherauno, piuthrauno
unbroke (v pa), piublerskyot, piupelikio, piuplikio
unbundle (v), piuvikusne, piuvinoko, piuvinko
unburden (v), piudiarsk, piudiako, piudiako
unburn (v), piubugosre, piuberugo, piubrugo
unbutton (v), piudomast, piudofito, piudofto
uncall (v), piugirsf, piugiro, piugiro
uncanny (adj), piufrelpkodu, piuferepekodu,
piufrepkodu
uncertain (adj), piuzhirtu, piuzhilotu, piuzhiltu
uncertainty (n), piuzhirt, piuzhilota, piuzhilt
unchange (v), piutuarsne, piutuano, piutuano
uncharitable (adj), piuloifaru, piugeloirifu,
piugloirfu
uncheck (v), piukest, piuketo, piuketo
uncivil (adj), piufafirtu, piufafitu, piufaftu
unclassify (v), piubles, piubelego, piublego
uncle (n), daiar, daiana, daian
unclean (adj), piushermu, piushemu, piushemu
unclear (adj), piudrofu, piuderotu, piudrotu
unclutter (v), piushnaithasne, piushenaitho,
piushnaitho
uncomfortable (adj), piuvlarku, piuvelaruvu,
piuvlarvu
uncomfortably (adv), piuvlarkiu, piuvelaruviu,
piuvlarviu
uncommon (adj), piugunaru, piugurinu, piugurnu
uncompetitive (adj), piulenvapu, piuvanipu,
piuvanpu
unconditional (adj), piubeltifku, piuliutifoku,
piuliutifku
unconditionally (adv), piubeltitkiu, piuliutitokiu,
piuliutifkiu
unconscionable (adj), piumunarpu, piumunapu,
piumunpu
unconscionably (adv), piumunarpiu, piumunapiu,
piumunpiu
unconscious (adj), piukeirpu, piukeilopu, piukeilpu
unconsciously (adv), piukeirpiu, piukeilopiu,
piukeilpiu
unconsciousness (n), piukeirp, piukeilopa, piukeilp
unconstitutional (adj), piubelshpeltu,
piuliushopelitu, piuliushpeltu
unconstitutionally (adv), piubelshpeltiu,
piuliushopelitiu, piuliushpeltiu
uncontrollable (adj), piutranitu, piuteranitu,
piutrantu
uncontrollably (adv), piutranitiu, piuteranitiu,
piutrantiu
uncontroversial (adj), piuplarthu, piupelathu,
piuplathu
unconventional (adj), piubelfimu, piuliufimu,
piuliufimu
uncool (adj), piushlurfu, piushelufu, piushlufu

uncooperative (adj), piuipiduratu, piuipiduritu, piuipidurtu
uncooperatively (adv), piuipiduratiu, piuipiduritiu, piuipidurtiu
uncork (v), piugranirsp, piugoranipo, piugranpo
uncover (v), piudathesle, piudalitho, piudaltho
uncritical (adj), piudufirtu, piudufitu, piuduftu
uncritically (adv), piudufirtiu, piudufitiu, piuduftiu
undecillion (num 1e36 card), hemsht, hemsht, hemsht
undecillionth (num 1e36 ord), hemshteth, hemshteth, hemshteth
undeniable (adj), piubrieltu, piuberietu, piubrietu
undeniably (adv), piubrieltiu, piuberietiu, piubrietiu
under (adj/adv/prep), utine, utinu, utin
underachiever (n doer), utiovairtwan, utiovaitua, utiovaitua
underage (adj), utidatulu, utidalitu, utidaltu
underarm (adj), utishnernu, utishinenu, utishnenu
underarm (n), utishnern, utishinena, utishnen
underbelly (n), utidiapor, utidiaropa, utidiarp
underbid (n), utithairt, utithaita, utithait
underbid (v pa), utithairstyot, utithaitio, utithaitio
underbid (v), utithairst, utithaito, utithaito
underbrush (n), utigruashk, utigeruasha, utigruash
underclass (n), utiblesh, utibelega, utibleg
undercook (v), utidolsp, utidopo, utidopo
undercover (adj), utidathelu, utidalithu, utidalthu
undercurrent (n), utigurilf, utigurifa, utigurf
undercut (n), utidairsh, utidaisha, utidaish
undercut (v pa), utidairsyot, utidaishio, utidaishio
undercut (v), utidairs, utidaisho, utidaisho
underdevelop (v), utitefralsp, utiteferapo, utitefrapo
underdevelopment (n), utitefralp, utiteferapa, utitefrap
underdog (n), utidraursh, utiderausha, utidraush
underestimate (v), utithinarsp, utithinapo, utithinpo
underestimation (n), utithinarp, utithinapa, utithinp
undergarment (n), utilakarn, utilakana, utilakan
undergo (v), utivirsf, utivifo, utivifo
undergrad (n), utikin, utikina, utikin
undergraduate (adj), utikinorpu, utikinopu, utikinpu
undergraduate (n doer), utikinorpwan, utikinopua, utikinpua
underground (adj), utibranirtu, utiberanitu, utibrantu
underground (n), utibranirt, utiberanita, utibrant
undergrowth (n), utiklorak, utikeloika, utikloik
underinsure (v), utiishrelsne, utiisherelo, utiishrelo
underlie (v), utiriesf, utiretho, utiretho
underline (n), utiroifk, utiroifa, utiroif
underline (v), utiroifsk, utiroifo, utiroifo
underling (n), utirp, utipa, utip
underman (v), utiplorsne, utipelono, utiplono
undermine (v), utikrivuzge, utikerigo, utikrigo
underneath (adj/adv/prep), utinilurn, utinilunu, utinilun
underneath (n), utinilurn, utiniluna, utinilun

underpaid (v pa), utimoirzmyot, utimoimio, utimoimio
underpants (n pl), utimekarnyek, utimekani, utimekani
underpass (n), utilunirt, utilunita, utilunt
underpay (v), utimoirzme, utimoimo, utimoimo
underpin (v), utileirsp, utileipo, utileipo
underpower (v), utibiorast, utibiorito, utibiorto
underprice (v), utitirofsp, utitiropo, utitirpo
underrate (v), utiterzbe, utitebo, utitebo
underscore (v), utiklairst, utikelaito, utiklaito
undersea (adj), utishkleirnu, utishikeleinu, utishkleinu
undersecretary (n), utidelgelf, utidelagela, utidelgel
undersell (v), utitrelirsf, utiterelifo, utitrelfo
undershirt (n), utilifarde, utilifada, utilifad
underside (n), utishoirt, utishoita, utishoit
undersold (v pa), utitrelirsfyot, utiterelifio, utitrelfio
understaff (v), utiarborst, utiariboto, utiarboto
understand (v), utitrelirst, utiterelito, utitrelto
understandable (adj), utitrelirtu, utiterelitu, utitreltu
understandably (adv), utitrelirtiu, utiterelitiu, utitreltiu
understatement (n), utibiurt, utibiuta, utibiut
understood (v pa), utitrelirstyot, utiterelitio, utitreltio
understudy (n), utiailart, utiailata, utiailt
undertake (v), utigorsk, utigoko, utigoko
undertaker (n doer), utigorkwan, utigokua, utigokua
undertone (n d:music, audio), utitrilf, utiterila, utitril
undertook (v pa), utigorskyot, utigokio, utigokio
underuse (v), utibriarsk, utiberiako, utibriako
undervalue (v), utivaursp, utivaupo, utivaupo
underwater (adj), utiheidornu, utiheidonu, utiheidonu
underway (adj), utipliorlu, utipeliolu, utipliolu
underway (n), utipliorl, utipeliola, utipliol
underwear (n), utidovarme, utidovama, utidovam
underweight (adj), utishuirshu, utishuishu, utishuishu
underweight (n), utishuirsh, utishuisha, utishuish
underwent (v pa), utivirsfyot, utivifio, utivifio
underwood (n), utifanirn, utifanina, utifanin
underworld (n), utihalrelt, utihaloreta, utihalret
underwrite (v), utiloirzde, utiloido, utiloido
underwriter (n doer), utiloirdwan, utiloidua, utiloidua
underwrote (v pa), utiloirzdyot, utiloidio, utiloidio
undesirable (adj), piuloirfu, piuloiru, piuloiru
undesirably (adv), piuloirfiu, piuloiriu, piuloiriu
undetectable (adj), piubudolirfu, piubudolifu, piubudolfu
undid (v pa), piutirskyot, piutikio, piutikio
undisclose (v), piutigrefst, piutigereto, piutigreto
undo (v), piutirsk, piutiko, piutiko
undoubtedly (adv), piubiaurfiu, piubiaufiu, piubiaufiu
undress (v), piuplers, piupelesho, piuplesho
undue (adj), piukiraku, piukiroku, piukirku

undulate (v), piuleifarsne, piuleifaro, piuleifaro
undulation (n), piuleifarn, piuleifara, piuleifar
unduly (adv), piukirakiu, piukirokiu, piukirkiu
unearth (v), eles, elesho, elesho
unease (n), piuflerf, piufelefa, piuflef
uneasily (adv), piuflerfiu, piufelefiu, piuflefiu
uneasiness (n), piuflerfuet, piufelefueta, piuflefuet
uneasy (adj), piuflerfu, piufelefu, piuflefu
uneconomical (adj), piubovenku, piuveniku,
   piuvenku
uneconomically (adv), piubovenkiu, piuvenikiu,
   piuvenkiu
unemotional (adj), piuivadarvu, piuivadavu,
   piuivadavu
unemploy (v), piushloirst, piusheloito, piushloito
unemployment (n), piushloirt, piusheloita,
   piushloit
unenforceable (adj), piudarviuku, piuvoviuku,
   piuvoviuku
unequal (adj), piudainfu, piudainu, piudainu
unethical (adj), piukurfpu, piukufipu, piukufpu
uneven (adj), piupifonu, piupiletu, piupletu
unevenly (adv), piupifoniu, piupiletiu, piupletiu
uneventful (adj), piufidalu, piufirodu, piufirdu
unexceptional (adj), piutuvetu, piuveritu, piuvertu
unexceptionally (adv), piutuvetiu, piuveritiu,
   piuvertiu
unexpect (v), piututhursk, piututhuko, piututhuko
unexpectedly (adv), piututhurkiu, piututhukiu,
   piututhukiu
unexplainable (adj), piuvairgu, piuvaigu, piuvaigu
unexplainably (adv), piuvairgiu, piuvaigiu,
   piuvaigiu
unfair (adj), piutheralu, piutherelu, piuthrelu
unfairly (adv), piutheraliu, piuthereliu, piuthreliu
unfairness (n), piutheral, piutherela, piuthrel
unfaithful (adj), piunaltripu, piuperinelitu,
   piuprineltu
unfaithfully (adv), piunaltripiu, piuperinelitiu,
   piuprineltiu
unfamiliar (adj), piutliarnu, piutehanu, piutlhanu
unfamiliarity (n), piufliarn, piufeliana, piuflian
unfavorable (adj), piunardepu, piunarithepu,
   piunarthepu
unfit (adj), piuvelirfu, piuvelifu, piuvelfu
unfold (v), piutrafsk, piuteravo, piutravo
unforeseeable (adj), piuvoathulthu,
   piuvoanethuthu, piuvoanthuthu
unforgettable (adj), piuvoantopu, piuvoatopu,
   piuvoatopu
unfortunate (adj), piuvoashmunu, piuvoamunu,
   piuvoamunu
unfortunately (adv), piuvoashmuniu, piuvoamuniu,
   piuvoamuniu
unfriendly (adj), piupamelu, piupilamu, piupilmu
unfurl (v), piutrulisf, piuterulifo, piutrulfo
ungodly (adj), piuagubirdu, piuagubidu,
   piuagubidu
unhappily (adv), piukolirmiu, piukolimiu,
   piukolmiu
unhappiness (n), piukolirme, piukolima, piukolm
unhappy (adj), piukolirmu, piukolimu, piukolmu
unhealthy (adj), piuhaufu, piuhauthu, piuhauthu

unhelpful (adj), piugailaku, piugailu, piugailu
unhinder (v), piutiargast, piutiagato, piutiagato
unhinge (v), piutarfsp, piutarofo, piutarfo
unhitch (v), piufrinsk, piuferinifo, piufrinfo
unholy (adj), piudimulu, piudilanu, piudilnu
unidentify (v), piuferst, piuferitho, piufertho
unification (n), yutark, yutaka, yutak
uniform (n), yutavorlin, yutavorina, yutavorn
uniform (v), yutavorlisne, yutavorino, yutavorno
uniformity (n), yutavorlinuet, yutavorinueta,
   yutavornuet
uniformly (adj), yutavorlinu, yutavorinu, yutavornu
unify (v), yutarsk, yutako, yutako
unilateral (adj), yutanamoru, yutanarimu,
   yutanarmu
unilateralism (n), yutanamor, yutanarima,
   yutanarm
unilaterally (adv), yutanamoriu, yutanarimiu,
   yutanarmiu
unimaginable (adj), piukinarlu, piukinalu,
   piukinalu
unimaginably (adv), piukinarliu, piukinaliu,
   piukinaliu
unimportant (adj), piukiviurgu, piukiviugu,
   piukiviugu
unimportantly (adv), piukiviurgiu, piukiviugiu,
   piukiviugiu
unimpressive (adj), piukiblashu, piubelashiku,
   piublashku
unimpressively (adv), piukiblashiu, piubelashikiu,
   piublashkiu
uninhabitable (adj), piureishortu, piureishotu,
   piureishtu
unintelligible (adj), piupreitfrelpu, piuperiteferepu,
   piupreitfrepu
unintentional (adj), piuarpifku, piuipifoku,
   piuipifku
unintentionally (adv), piuarpifkiu, piuipifokiu,
   piuipifkiu
union (n), yutamarn, yutamana, yutaman
unionist (n doer), yutamarnwan, yutamanua,
   yutamanua
unionization (n), yutamarnuet, yutamanueta,
   yutamanuet
unionize (v), yutamarsne, yutamano, yutamano
unique (adj), yutafonurdu, yutafonudu, yutafondu
uniquely (adv), yutafonurdiu, yutafonudiu,
   yutafondiu
uniqueness (n), yutafonurde, yutafonuda, yutafond
unisex (adj), yutabivarnu, yutabivanu, yutabivanu
unison (n), yutashk, yutasha, yutash
unit (n), yutarme, yutama, yutam
unitary (adj), yutarmu, yutamu, yutamu
unite (v), yutarzme, yutamo, yutamo
unity (n), yutamart, yutamata, yutamat
universal (adj), yutharafu, yutharifu, yutharfu
universally (adv), yutharafiu, yutharifiu, yutharfiu
universe (n), yutharaf, yutharifa, yutharf
university (n), kelart, kelikata, kelkat
unjust (adj), piupeshirpu, piupeshipu, piupeshpu
unjustly (adv), piupeshirpiu, piupeshipiu,
   piupeshpiu
unknowable (adj), piuglerku, piugeleku, piugleku

unknowingly (adv), piuglerkiu, piugelekiu, piuglekiu
unknown (n), piuglerk, piugeleka, piuglek
unlawful (adj), piuvaurdu, piuvaudu, piuvaudu
unlawfully (adv), piuvaurdiu, piuvaudiu, piuvaudiu
unleash (v), piunulirsk, piunuliko, piunulko
unless (prep/conj), iumern, iumenu, iumen
unlicense (v), piulalirfst, piulaliroto, piulalirto
unlike (prep/adj), piushalirf, piushalifu, piushalf
unlikely (adj/adv), piushanirf, piushanifu, piushanf
unlimit (v), piuvinst, piuvitho, piuvitho
unlist (v), piudilst, piudito, piudito
unlivable (adj), piuflauftfrelpu, piufelaufiteferepu, piuflauftfrepu
unload (v), piulurifst, piulurito, piulurto
unlock (v), piutiurzge, piutiugo, piutiugo
unlove (v), piuvoshasre, piuvosharo, piuvosharo
unlucky (adj), piupadaru, piupashotu, piupashtu
unmark (v), piushtarst, piushetato, piushtato
unmarry (v), piuvularsne, piuvulano, piuvulno
unmatch (v), piumuthsk, piumutho, piumutho
unmentionable (adj), piualtirpu, piualotipu, piualtipu
unmistakable (adj), piudhigorku, piudhigoku, piudhigoku
unmove (v), piushkirst, piushekito, piushkito
unnatural (adj), piuleirdu, piuleidu, piuleidu
unnaturally (adv), piuleirdiu, piuleidiu, piuleidiu
unnecessarily (adv), piushivershtiu, piushiveshotiu, piushiveshtiu
unnecessary (adj), piushivershtu, piushiveshotu, piushiveshtu
unobtrude (v), piuiaborfst, piuiabofito, piuiabofto
unobtrusive (adj), piuiaborftu, piuiabofitu, piuiaboftu
unobtrusively (adv), piuiaborftiu, piuiabofitiu, piuiaboftiu
unofficial (adj), piutashkeltu, piutashikelu, piutashkelu
unofficially (adv), piutashkeltiu, piutashikeliu, piutashkeliu
unopen (v), piuefbirsne, piuefubino, piuefbino
unoppose (v), piubinarsk, piubinako, piubinko
unorganize (v), piufrilast, piuferiloto, piufrilto
unpack (v), piubugarsp, piubugapo, piubugapo
unpaid (v pa), piumoirzmyot, piumoimio, piumoimio
unpalatable (adj), piuparlufku, piuparelufu, piuparlufu
unpatriotic (adj), piufanturnu, piufanitunu, piutantunu
unpatriotically (adv), piufanturniu, piufanituniu, piufantuniu
unpay (v), piumoirzme, piumoimo, piumoimo
unplan (v), piulitarsne, piulitano, piulitano
unpleasant (adj), piufrilapu, piuferilopu, piufrilpu
unpleasantly (adv), piufrilapiu, piuferilopiu, piufrilpiu
unpleasantness (n), piufrilap, piuferilopa, piufrilp
unplug (v), piugitharsp, piugithapo, piugithpo
unpopular (adj), piuvoradu, piuvoridu, piuvordu
unpopularity (n), piuvorade, piuvorida, piuvord
unpopularly (adv), piuvoradiu, piuvoridiu, piuvordiu
unpredictability (n), piurudeirk, piurudeika, piurudeik
unpredictable (adj), piurudeirku, piurudeiku, piurudeiku
unpredictably (adv), piurudeirkiu, piurudeikiu, piurudeikiu
unprintable (adj), piutrulishu, piuterulishu, piutrulshu
unproductive (adj), piufiurku, piufiuku, piufiuku
unproductively (adv), piufiurkiu, piufiukiu, piufiukiu
unprofessional (adj), piufiunirku, piufiuniku, piufiunku
unprofessionally (adv), piufiunirkiu, piufiunikiu, piufiunkiu
unprofitable (adj), piufiupafirtu, piufiupafitu, piufiupaftu
unprofitably (adv), piufiupafirtiu, piufiupafitiu, piufiupaftiu
unprove (v), piufliorsf, piufeliofo, piufliofo
unprovoke (v), piufiushairsk, piufiushaiko, piufiushaiko
unquadragintillion (num 1e126 card), hemifk, hemifk, hemifk
unquestionable (adj), piushtiartetu, piushotiatetu, piushtiatetu
unquestionably (adv), piushtiartetiu, piushotiatetiu, piushtiatetiu
unquote (v), piuhinarsf, piuhinafo, piuhinfo
unrate (v), piuterzbe, piutebo, piutebo
unravel (v), piurigarst, piurigato, piurigato
unreachable (adj), piuglorugu, piugelorugu, piuglorgu
unreadable (adj), piuliarpu, piuliapu, piuliapu
unreadably (adv), piuliarpiu, piuliapiu, piuliapiu
unreal (adj), piupluarfu, piupeluafu, piupluafu
unrealistic (adj), piupluarnu, piupeluanu, piupluanu
unrealistically (adv), piupluarniu, piupeluaniu, piupluaniu
unreality (n), piupluarf, piupeluafa, piupluaf
unreason (v), piukleirze, piukeleizho, piukleizho
unreasonable (adj), piukleirzhu, piukeleizhu, piukleizhu
unreasonably (adv), piukleirzhiu, piukeleizhiu, piukleizhiu
unregister (v), piubrianirsk, piuberianiko, piubrianko
unregulate (v), piuluvirsp, piuluvipo, piuluvipo
unreliability (n), piuterame, piuterema, piutrem
unreliable (adj), piuteramu, piuteremu, piutremu
unreliably (adv), piuteramiu, piuteremiu, piutremiu
unremarkable (adj), piukeikurtu, piukeikutu, piukeikutu
unremarkably (adv), piukeikurtiu, piukeikutiu, piukeikutiu
unrepentant (adj), piuludrashtu, piuluderatu, piuludratu
unrepresentative (adj), piuludarshu, piuluduashu, piuluduashu
unresponsive (adj), piuludufirpu, piuludufipu, piuludufpu

unrest (n), piupreirsh, piupereisha, piupreish

unsafe (adj), piuzhurdu, piuzhudu, piuzhudu

unsanitary (adj), piushiarnu, piushianu, piushianu

unsatisfactory (adj), piulauirtu, piulauitu, piulauitu

unschedule (v), piuridarsf, piuridafo, piuridafo

unscientific (adj), piushuarshu, piushuashu, piushuashu

unscientifically (adv), piushuarshiu, piushuashiu, piushuashiu

unscramble (v), piukralirsk, piukeraliko, piukralko

unscrew (v), piukloirsp, piukeloipo, piukloipo

unscrupulous (adj), piuthriuftu, piutheriutu, piuthriutu

unseal (v), piuzhoirzve, piuzhoivo, piuzhoivo

unseasonable (adj), piudutharpu, piuduthapu, piuduthapu

unseasonably (adv), piudutharpiu, piuduthapiu, piuduthapiu

unseat (v), piushrilsk, piusheriko, piushriko

unsecure (v), piuvartulsf, piuvaritufo, piuvartufo

unseemly (adj), piuthurnu, piuthunu, piuthunu

unselfish (adj), piuzhiurnu, piuzhiunu, piuzhiunu

unselfishness (n), piuzhiurnuet, piuzhiunueta, piuzhiunuet

unsettle (v), piulibers, piulibesho, piulibesho

unsign (v), piuweirsf, piuweifo, piuweifo

unsolvable (adj), piuligralgu, piuligeragu, piuligragu

unsound (adj), piuzhaturfu, piuzhatufu, piuzhatufu

unspeakable (adj), piutalirshu, piutalishu, piutalshu

unspeakably (adv), piutalirshiu, piutalishiu, piutalshiu

unspectacular (adj), piuthuklarku, piuthukelaku, piuthuklaku

unspectacularly (adv), piuthuklarkiu, piuthukelakiu, piuthuklakiu

unstable (adj), piuftarpu, piufitapu, piuftapu

unsteady (adj), piufnertu, piufinetu, piufnetu

unstoppable (adj), piutaurku, piutauku, piutauku

unstoppably (adv), piutaurkiu, piutaukiu, piutaukiu

unsuccessful (adj), piuzhuvertushu, piuzhuvetushu, piuzhuvetushu

unsuccessfully (adv), piuzhuvertushiu, piuzhuvetushiu, piuzhuvetushiu

unsuitable (adj), piumorapu, piumoripu, piumorpu

unsuitably (adv), piumorapiu, piumoripiu, piumorpiu

unsupportable (adj), piuloburku, piulobuku, piulobuku

unsure (adj), piushrelnu, piusherelu, piushrelu

unsure (adv), piushrelniu, piushereliu, piushrelniu

unsurprisingly (adv), piuvoiviurshiu, piuvoiviushiu, piuvoiviushiu

unsuspectingly (adv), piumemthurkiu, piumemithukiu, piumemthukiu

unsustainable (adv), piumempirftiu, piumemepifetiu, piumempiftiu

unsympathetic (adj), piuparlarpu, piuparolapu, piuparlapu

untangle (v), piutaigarzge, piutaigago, piutaigago

untap (v), piunersp, piunepo, piunepo

untax (v), piushenirsk, piusheniko, piushenko

unthinkable (adj), piuderpu, piudepu, piudepu

unthinkingly (adv), piuderpiu, piudepiu, piudepiu

untie (v), piuglers, piugelesho, piuglesho

until (prep/conj), iutaurn, iutaunu, iutaun

untimely (adj), piudaurnu, piudaunu, piudaunu

untouchable (adj), piushiarlu, piushialu, piushialu

untraceable (adj), piugarshu, piugashu, piugashu

untrainable (adj), piutrilorku, piuteriloku, piutrilku

untreatable (adj), piuthuirtu, piuthuitu, piuthuitu

untrigintillion (num 1e96 card), hemift, hemift, hemift

untrigintillionth (num 1e96 ord), hemifteth, hemifteth, hemifteth

untrue (adj), piudreilu, piudereilu, piudreilu

untrustworthy (adj), piudreiflairshu, piudereifelaishu, piudreiflaishu

untruth (n), piudreilsh, piudereisha, piudreish

untruthful (adj), piudreilshu, piudereishu, piudreishu

untruthfully (adv), piudreilshiu, piudereishiu, piudreishiu

untypical (adj), piuduarpu, piuduapu, piuduapu

untypically (adv), piuduarpiu, piuduapiu, piuduapiu

Ununbium (n davoka), Init, Init, Init

Ununbium (n), Ununbium, Ununabiuma, Ununbium

Ununennium (n davoka), Ashap, Ashap, Ashap

Ununhexium (n davoka), Enup, Enup, Enup

Ununhexium (n), Ununhekium, Ununahekiuma, Ununhekium

Ununoctium (n davoka), Enik, Enik, Enik

Ununoctium (n), Ununoktium, Ununokatiuma, Ununoktium

Ununpentium (n davoka), Enop, Enop, Enop

Ununpentium (n), Ununpentium, Ununopenetiuma, Ununpentium

Ununquadium (n davoka), Enip, Enip, Enip

Ununquadium (n), Ununkuadium, Ununokuadiuma, Ununkuadium

Ununseptium (n), Ununsheptium, Ununishepotiuma, Ununsheptium

Ununspetium (n davoka), Enak, Enak, Enak

Ununtrium (n davoka), Enap, Enap, Enap

Ununtrium (n), Ununtrium, Ununoteriuma, Ununtrium

unusable (adj), piubriarkfrepu, piuberiakoferepu, piubriakfrepu

unusual (adj), piubriarku, piuberiaku, piubriaku

unusually (adv), piubriarkiu, piuberiakiu, piubriakiu

unveil (v), piulaursl, piulauto, piulauto

unverifiable (adj), piutharoilku, piutharoiku, piutharoiku

unvigintillion (num 1e66 card), hemshk, hemshk, hemshk

unvigintillionth (num 1e66 ord), hemshketh, hemshketh, hemshketh

unwary (adj), piushlairfu, piushelaifu, piushlaifu

unwelcome (adj), piukolarnu, piukolanu, piukolanu

unwillingly (adv), piuyarkiu, piuyakiu, piuyakiu

unwillingness (n), piuyark, piuyaka, piuyak

unwind (v), piuthrairsk, piutheraiko, piuthraiko

unwise (adj), piufluirku, piufeliuku, piufluiku
unwisely (adv), piufluirkiu, piufeliukiu, piufluikiu
unworkable (adj), piukiorku, piukioku, piukioku
unworthy (adj), piuflairshu, piufelaishu, piuflaishu
unwound (v pa), piuthrairskyot, piutheraikio,
    piuthraikio
unwrap (v), piufnursp, piufenupo, piufnupo
unzip (v), piuzheifst, piuzheifo, piuzheifo
up (n), iveit, iveita, iveit
up (prep), ivei, iveilu, ivei
up (v), iveist, iveito, iveito
upbeat (adj), ilfedautu, iveidautu, iveidautu
update (n), iveitolirk, iveitolika, iveitolk
update (v), iveitolirsk, iveitoliko, iveitolko
updater (n doer), iveitolirkwan, iveitolikua,
    iveitolkua
upfront (adj), iveiflarshu, iveifelarinu, iveiflarnu
upgrade (n), iveishtrak, iveishoterana, iveishtran
upgrade (v), iveishtrask, iveishoterano, iveishtrano
upheaval (n), iveigurbe, iveiguba, iveigub
upheld (v pa), iveithorthskyot, iveithorithio,
    iveithorthio
uphill (adj), iveishiopu, iveiparinu, iveiparnu
uphold (v), iveithorthsk, iveithoritho, iveithortho
upkeep (n), iveiklorf, iveikelofa, iveiklof
uplift (v), iveiraushsk, iveirauko, iveirauko
upon (prep), iverme, ivemu, ivem
upper (adj), iveitu, iveitu, iveitu
upperly (adv), iveitiu, iveitiu, iveitiu
uppermost (adj), iveitweku, iveitweku, iveitweku
uppitiness (n), iveituet, iveitueta, iveituet
uppity (adj), iveituetu, iveituetu, iveituetu
upright (adj), iveidierku, iveidieku, iveidieku
upright (n), iveidierk, iveidieka, iveidiek
uprightly (adv), iveidierkiu, iveidiekiu, iveidiekiu
uproar (n), iveigraufk, iveigeraufa, iveigrauf
uproot (v), iveiwefirsp, iveiwefipo, iveiwefpo
upscale (adj), iveishuirku, iveishuiku, iveishuiku
upset (adj), iveiferpu, iveifepu, iveifepu
upset (n), iveiferp, iveifepa, iveifep
upset (v pa), iveiferspyot, iveifepio, iveifepio
upset (v), iveifersp, iveifepo, iveifepo
upshot (n), iveishkoift, iveishekoita, iveishkoit
upside (n), iveishoirt, iveishoita, iveishoit
upsilon (n), upshilorn, upeshilona, upshilon
upstairs (adj), iveitairnu, iveitainu, iveitainu
upstairs (n), iveitairn, iveitaina, iveitain
upstart (adj), iveishkalirtu, iveishokalitu,
    iveishkaltu
upstart (n), iveishkalirt, iveishokalita, iveishkalt
upstate (adj), iveishaiarshu, iveishaiashu,
    iveishaiashu
upstate (n), iveishaiarsh, iveishaiasha, iveishaiash
upstream (adj), iveifalirmu, iveifalimu, iveifalmu
upstream (n), iveifalirme, iveifalima, iveifalm
upsurge (n), iveivoirge, iveivoiga, iveivoig
upswing (n), iveiflierge, iveifeliega, iveiflieg
uptake (n), iveigork, iveigoka, iveigok
uptight (adj), iveiduairfu, iveiduaifu, iveiduaifu
uptightness (n), iveiduairf, iveiduaifa, iveiduaif
uptown (adj), iveimiurnu, iveimiunu, iveimiunu
uptown (n), iveimiurn, iveimiuna, iveimiun
upturn (n), iveikaimp, iveikaima, iveikaim

upward (adj), iveihaurshu, iveihaushu, iveihaushu
upward (adv), iveihaurshiu, iveihaushiu,
    iveihaushiu
upwards (adj), iveihaurshu, iveihaushu, iveihaushu
upwards (adv), iveihaurshiu, iveihaushiu,
    iveihaushiu
Uranium (n davoka), Onup, Onup, Onup
Uranium (n), Uranium, Uraniuma, Uranium
urb (n), falirp, falipa, falp
urban (adj), falirpu, falipu, falpu
urbanization (n), falirpuet, falipueta, falpuet
urbanize (v), falirsp, falipo, falpo
urge (n), vaurk, vauka, vauk
urge (v), vaursk, vauko, vauko
urgency (n), vaurkuet, vaukueta, vaukuet
urgent (adj), vaurku, vauku, vauku
urgently (adv), vaurkiu, vaukiu, vaukiu
urger (n doer), vaurkwan, vaukua, vaukua
urinal (n), falafasht, falafata, falafat
urinary (adj), falarfu, falafu, falafu
urinate (v), falarfsk, falafiko, falafko
urination (n), falarfk, falafika, falafk
urinator (n doer), falarfkwan, falafikua, falafkua
urine (n), falarf, falafa, falaf
urologist (n doer), falarfkuitwan, falafekuitua,
    falafkuitua
urology (n), falarfkuit, falafekuita, falafkuit
Us (let pl), urfi, urfi, urfi
us (pron 1st pl obj), rau, rau, rau
usable (adj), briarkfrepu, beriakoferepu, briakfrepu
usage (n), briakart, beriakata, briakat
use (n), briark, beriaka, briak
use (v), briarsk, beriako, briako
useability (n), briarkfrep, beriakoferepa, briakfrep
useful (adj), briakurshu, beriakushu, briakushu
usefully (adv), briakurshiu, beriakushiu, briakushiu
usefulness (n), briakursh, beriakusha, briakush
useless (adj), briakmernu, beriakumenu,
    briakmenu
user (n doer), briarkwan, beriakua, briakua
usher (n doer), neitwan, neitua, neitua
usher (v), neist, neito, neito
usual (adj), briarku, beriaku, briaku
usually (adv), briarkiu, beriakiu, briakiu
usurp (v), veivoisp, veivoilo, veivoilo
usurpation (n), veivoip, veivoila, veivoil
usurper (n doer), veivoipwan, veivoilua, veivoilua
usury (n), briakarbe, beriakaba, briakab
Utah (n), Utarfk, Utafika, Utafk
utensil (n), leilart, leilata, leilat
uterus (n), tilamp, teriama, tilam
utilitarian (n doer), leikartuetwan, leikatuetua,
    leikatuetua
utility (n), leikart, leikata, leikat
utilization (n), leikartuet, leikatueta, leikatuet
utilize (v), leikarst, leikato, leikato
utilizer (n doer), leikartwan, leikatua, leikatua
utmost (adj), tiwaku, tiwaku, tiwaku
utter (adj), tigartu, tigatu, tigatu
utter (v), tigarst, tigato, tigato
utterance (n), tigart, tigata, tigat
utterly (adv), tigartiu, tigatiu, tigatiu
V (let sng), val, vala, va

vacancy (n), vauirk, vauika, vauik
vacant (adj), vauirku, vauiku, vauiku
vacantly (adv), vauirkiu, vauikiu, vauikiu
vacate (v), vauirsk, vauiko, vauiko
vacation (n), vauikert, vauiketa, vauiket
vacation (v), vauikerst, vauiketo, vauiketo
vacationer (n doer), vauikertwan, vauiketua,
    vauiketua
vacator (n doer), vauirkwan, vauikua, vauikua
vaccinate (v), dauirst, dauito, dauito
vaccination (n), dauirtuet, dauitueta, dauituet
vaccine (n), dauirt, dauita, dauit
vacillate (v), vaudrolfsk, vauderolifo, vaudrolfo
vacillation (n), vaudrolfk, vauderolifa, vaudrolf
vacillator (n doer), vaudrolfkwan, vauderolifua,
    vaudrolfua
vacillatory (adj), vaudrolfku, vauderolifu, vaudrolfu
vacuous (adj), vauirfu, vauifu, vauifu
vacuously (adv), vauirfiu, vauifiu, vauifiu
vacuum (n), vauirf, vauifa, vauif
vacuum (v), vauirsf, vauifo, vauifo
vague (adj), vauirgu, vauigu, vauigu
vaguely (adv), vauirgiu, vauigiu, vauigiu
vagueness (n), vauirge, vauiga, vauig
vain (adj), shiurfu, shiufu, shiufu
vainly (adv), shiurfiu, shiufiu, shiufiu
valiant (adj), kathiurfu, kathiufu, kathiufu
valid (adj), karthpu, kathipu, kathpu
validate (v), karthsp, kathipo, kathpo
validation (n), karthpuet, kathipueta, kathpuet
validity (n), karthp, kathipa, kathp
validly (adv), karthpiu, kathipiu, kathpiu
valley (n), vaurl, vaula, vaul
valor (n), kathiurf, kathiufa, kathiuf
valuable (adj), vaurpu, vaupu, vaupu
valuable (n), vaurpul, vaupula, vaupul
valuation (n), vaurpuet, vaupueta, vaupuet
value (n), vaurp, vaupa, vaup
value (v), vaursp, vaupo, vaupo
valve (n), mairf, maifa, maif
vamp (n), filarde, filada, filad
vampire (n), fildaurf, filodaufa, fildauf
van (n), zhaurn, zhauna, zhaun
Vanadium (n davoka), Ifop, Ifop, Ifop
Vanadium (n), Vanadium, Vanadiuma, Vanadium
VanAllenBelt (n), Kligart, Keligata, Kligat
Vancouver (n), Vankuvirf, Vanikuvifa, Vankuvif
vandal (n doer), zhanirkwan, zhanikua, zhankua
vandalism (n), zhanirk, zhanika, zhank
vandalize (v), zhanirsk, zhaniko, zhanko
vane (n), pruafk, peruafa, pruaf
vanguard (n), zhauvaifirk, zhauvaifika, zhauvaifk
vanish (v), shioirsk, shioiko, shioiko
vanisher (n doer), shioirkwan, shioikua, shioikua
vanity (n), shiurf, shiufa, shiuf
vanquish (v), zhauprufisp, zhauperufipo,
    zhauprufpo
vanquisher (n doer), zhauprufipwan,
    zhauperufipua, zhauprufpua
vanquishment (n), zhauprufip, zhauperufipa,
    zhauprufp
vantage (n), shumirf, shumifa, shumif
vapid (adj), biufirtu, biufitu, biuftu

vapor (n), biufirt, biufita, biuft
vaporize (v), biufirst, biufito, biufto
vaporizer (n doer), biufirtwan, biufitua, biuftua
variability (n), thurme, thuma, thum
variable (adj), thumarpu, thumapu, thumapu
variable (n), thumarp, thumapa, thumap
variance (n), thurme, thuma, thum
variant (adj), thumarpu, thumapu, thumapu
variant (n), thumarp, thumapa, thumap
variation (n), thurme, thuma, thum
varietal (adj), thumarku, thumaku, thumaku
variety (n), thumark, thumaka, thumak
various (adj), thurmu, thumu, thumu
variously (adv), thurmiu, thumiu, thumiu
varnish (n), bilbushk, bilebusha, bilbush
varnish (v), bilbushsk, bilebusho, bilbusho
vary (v), thurzme, thumo, thumo
vascular (adj), konafku, konafu, konafu
vase (n), miurf, miufa, miuf
vast (adj), grairzhu, geraizhu, graizhu
vastly (adv), grairzhiu, geraizhiu, graizhiu
vastness (n), grairzhe, geraizha, graizh
vat (n), glarf, gelafa, glaf
Vatican (n), Vatikarn, Vatikana, Vatikan
vault (n d:arch), foirt, foita, foit
vault (n d:leap), zhairk, zhaika, zhaik
vault (v d:arch), foirst, foito, foito
vault (v d:leap), zhairsk, zhaiko, zhaiko
vaunt (n), shiufk, shiuka, shiuk
vaunt (v), shiufsk, shiuko, shiuko
vector (n), thirft, thifita, thift
veer (v), thoirsp, thoipo, thoipo
vegetable (n), sheivort, sheivota, sheivot
vegetarian (n doer), sheivotuartwan, sheivotuatua,
    sheivotuatua
vegetarianism (n), sheivotuart, sheivotuata,
    sheivotuat
vegetate (v), sheivarsne, sheivano, sheivano
vegetation (n), sheivarn, sheivana, sheivan
vegetator (n doer), sheivarnwan, sheivanua,
    sheivanua
veggie (n), sheifirt, sheifita, sheifit
vehemence (n), lardaishk, larodaika, lardaik
vehement (adj), lardaishku, larodaiku, lardaiku
vehemently (adv), lardaishkiu, larodaikiu, lardaikiu
vehicle (n), lardirt, larodita, lardit
vehicular (adj), lardirtu, laroditu, larditu
veil (n), laurt, lauta, laut
veil (v), laurst, lauto, lauto
vein (n), fleirth, feleitha, fleith
velocity (n), plirthk, pelithoka, plithk
vend (v), dukarsf, dukafo, dukafo
vendeka- (num 1e33 pref), dakai-, dakai-, dakai-
vendetta (n), dukarp, dukapa, dukap
vendor (n doer), dukarfwan, dukafua, dukafua
veneer (n), grinalf, gerinala, grinal
venerable (adj), lafmartu, lafimatu, lafmatu
venerably (adv), lafmartiu, lafimatiu, lafmatiu
venerate (v), lafmarst, lafimato, lafmato
veneration (n), lafmart, lafimata, lafmat
Venezuela (n), Venzhuilarf, Venezhuilafa,
    Venzhuilaf
vengeful (adj), dufirku, dufiku, dufku

vengence (n), dufirk, dufika, dufk
venom (n), duiarf, duiafa, duiaf
venomous (adj), duiarfu, duiafu, duiafu
venous (adj), fleirthu, feleithu, fleithu
vent (n), duathk, duatha, duath
vent (v), duathsk, duatho, duatho
venter (n doer), duathkwan, duathua, duathua
ventilate (v), duatharzge, duathago, duathago
ventilation (n), duatharge, duathaga, duathag
ventilator (n doer), duathargwan, duathagua,
    duathagua
venture (v), duliarst, duliato, duliato
venue (n), lafirme, lafima, lafim
veracious (adj), thariashtu, thariatu, thariatu
veracity (n), thariasht, thariata, thariat
verb (n), yairde, yaita, yait
verbal (adj), yaivartu, yaivatu, yaivatu
verbally (adv), yaivartiu, yaivatiu, yaivatiu
verbiage (n), yaivart, yaivata, yaivat
verbose (adj), yavafirtu, yaivafitu, yaivaftu
verdict (n), thardeirk, tharudeika, thardeik
verge (n d:edge), peirge, peiga, peig
verge (n d:incline), meirge, meiga, meig
verge (v d:edge), peirzge, peigo, peigo
verge (v d:incline), meirzge, meigo, meigo
verifiable (adj), tharoilku, tharoiku, tharoiku
verifiably (adv), tharoilkiu, tharoikiu, tharoikiu
verification (n), tharoilk, tharoika, tharoik
verify (v), tharoilsk, tharoiko, tharoiko
veritable (adj), tharoiftu, tharoitu, tharoitu
verity (n), tharoift, tharoita, tharoit
Vermont (n), Vermonirt, Verumonita, Vermont
versatile (adj), datiartu, datiatu, datiatu
versatility (n), datiart, datiata, datiat
verse (n), tharaf, tharifa, tharf
verse (v), tharasf, tharifo, tharfo
version (n), tharfelt, tharifeta, tharfet
versus (prep), tharmelme, tharomemu, tharmem
vertebra (n), dotaishp, dotaipa, dotaip
vertebrae (n pl), dotaishpyek, dotaipi, dotaipi
vertex (n), dotairf, dotaifa, dotaif
vertical (adj), dotairku, dotaiku, dotaiku
vertical (n), dotairk, dotaika, dotaik
vertically (adv), dotairkiu, dotaikiu, dotaikiu
vertigo (n), dotaiteshk, dotaitesha, dotaitsh
verve (n), peikarp, peikapa, peikap
very (adv), feliu, feliu, feliu
vessel (n), ronarf, ronafa, ronaf
vest (n), blirt, belita, blit
vest (v), blirst, belito, blito
vestige (n), blitesh, belitesha, blitsh
vestigial (adj), bliteshu, beliteshu, blitshu
vestigially (adv), bliteshiu, beliteshiu, blitshiu
vet (n d:veteran), daurth, dautha, dauth
vet (n d:veterinarian), fiave, fiava, fiav
vet (v d:examine), fiarazge, fiarigo, fiargo
veteran (n), dautharn, dauthana, dauthan
veterinarian (n), fiavart, fiavata, fiavat
veterinary (adj), fiavartu, fiavatu, fiavatu
veto (n), thaimak, thaima, thaim
veto (v), thaimask, thaimo, thaimo
vex (v), vigirst, vigito, vigito
via (prep), fuarl, fualu, fual

viability (n), peifrelp, peiferepa, peifrep
viable (adj), peifrelpu, peiferepu, peifrepu
viably (adv), peifrelpiu, peiferepiu, peifrepiu
viaduct (n), peikriushk, peikeriuka, peikriuk
vial (n), paishk, paisha, paish
vibe (n), bial, biala, bial
vibrancy (n), bialfkuet, bialifueta, bialfuet
vibrant (adj), bialfku, bialifu, bialfu
vibrate (v), bialfsk, bialifo, bialfo
vibration (n), bialfk, bialifa, bialf
vibrator (n doer), bialfkwan, bialifua, bialfua
vice (n d:title), piarl, piala, pial
vice (n d:trap), borat, borita, bort
vicinity (n), dathiart, dathiata, dathiat
vicious (adj d:trap), boratu, boritu, bortu
viciously (adv d:trap), boratiu, boritiu, bortiu
viciousness (n), boratuet, boritueta, bortuet
victim (n), baifarn, baifana, baifan
victimization (n), baifk, baifa, baif
victimize (v), baifsk, baifo, baifo
victimless (adj), baifkmenu, baifemenu, baifmenu
victimlessly (adv), baifkmeniu, baifemeniu,
    baifmeniu
victor (n doer), baifkwan, baifua, baifua
victorious (adj), baifertu, baifetu, baifetu
victoriously (adv), baifertiu, baifetiu, baifetiu
victory (n), baifert, baifeta, baifet
video (n), kiarn, kiana, kian
videotape (n), kiarneirf, kianeifa, kianeif
videotape (v), kiarneirsf, kianeifo, kianeifo
vie (v), aishsk, aiko, aiko
Vienna (n), Vienarf, Vienafa, Vienaf
Vietnam (n), Vietnarme, Vietonama, Vietnam
Vietnamese (n), Vietnamarn, Vietonamana,
    Vietnaman
view (n), fuart, fuata, fuat
view (v), fuarst, fuato, fuato
viewable (adj), fuartu, fuatu, fuatu
viewably (adv), fuartiu, fuatiu, fuatiu
viewer (n doer), fuartwan, fuatua, fuatua
viewfinder (n doer), fuatshurpwan, fuateshupua,
    fuatshupua
viewpoint (n), fuatairft, fuataifota, fuataift
vigintillion (num 1e63 card), dashta, dashta, dashta
vigintillionth (num 1e63 ord), dashteth, dashteth,
    dashteth
vigor (n), peikarn, peikana, peikan
vigorous (adj), peikarnu, peikanu, peikanu
vigorously (adv), peikarniu, peikaniu, peikaniu
vile (adj), zhaithku, zhaithu, zhaithu
vilification (n), zhaithart, zhaithata, zhaitht
vilify (v), zhaitharst, zhaithato, zhaithto
villa (n), dathk, datha, dath
village (n), datharn, dathana, dathan
villager (n doer), datharnwan, dathanua, dathanua
villain (n), zhakart, zhakata, zhakat
vincible (adj), fekiarku, fekiaku, fekiaku
vindicate (v), dukiarsk, dukiako, dukiako
vindication (n), dukiark, dukiaka, dukiak
vindicator (n doer), dukiarkwan, dukiakua,
    dukiakua
vindictiveness (n), dukiarkuet, dukiakueta,
    dukiakuet

vine (n), peilarf, peilafa, peilf
vine (v), peilarsf, peilafo, peilfo
vinegar (n), peilnork, peilanoka, peilnok
vineland (n), peilraufp, peileraupa, peilraup
vineyard (n), peilthauthk, peilethautha, peilthauth
violate (v), tuarilsk, tuariko, tuarko
violation (n), tuarilkuet, tuarikueta, tuarkuet
violator (n doer), tuarilkwan, tuarikua, tuarkua
violence (n), tuarilk, tuarika, tuark
violent (adj), tuarilku, tuariku, tuarku
violently (adv), tuarilkiu, tuarikiu, tuarkiu
violet (adj), feiranku, feiranu, feiranu
violet (n), feirank, feirana, feiran
violin (n), vialoirf, vialoifa, vialoif
violinist (n doer), vialoirfwan, vialoifua, vialoifua
viral (adj), fauirnu, fauinu, fauinu
virally (adv), fauirniu, fauiniu, fauiniu
virgin (n), peilarth, peilatha, peilath
Virginia (n), Virginiarf, Viroginiafa, Virginiaf
virii (n pl), fauirnyek, fauini, fauini
virile (adj), peikarku, peikaku, peikaku
virility (n), peikark, peikaka, peikak
virtual (adj), ladirfu, ladifu, ladifu
virtually (adv), ladirfiu, ladifiu, ladifiu
virtue (n), lanirge, laniga, lanig
virtuous (adj), lanirgu, lanigu, lanigu
virtuously (adv), lanirgiu, lanigiu, lanigiu
virulence (n), fauirnuet, fauinueta, fauinuet
virulent (adj), fauirnuetu, fauinuetu, fauinuetu
virulently (adv), fauirnuetiu, fauinuetiu, fauinuetiu
virus (n), fauirn, fauina, fauin
viruses (n pl), fauirnyek, fauini, fauini
visa (n), kelirth, kelitha, kelth
visage (n), keirbe, keiba, keib
viscera (n), keilirf, keilifa, keilf
visceral (adj), keilirfu, keilifu, keilfu
viscerally (adv), keilirfiu, keilifiu, keilfiu
viscosity (n), kinark, kinaka, kinak
viscous (adj), kinarku, kinaku, kinaku
visibility (u), fiaishkuct, fiaishueta, fiaishuet
visible (adj), fiaishku, fiaishu, fiaishu
visibly (adv), fiaishkiu, fiaishiu, fiaishiu
vision (n), fiaishk, fiaisha, fiaish
visionary (n doer), fiaishkwan, fiaishua, fiaishua
visit (n), kelirk, kelika, kelk
visit (v), kelirsk, keliko, kelko
visitation (n), kelirkuet, kelikueta, kelkuet
visitor (n doer), kelirkwan, kelikua, kelkua
visor (n), keibart, keibata, keibat
visual (adj), fiaisharnu, fiaishanu, fiaishanu
visual (n), fiaisharn, fiaishana, fiaishan
visualization (n), fiaisharnuet, fiaishanueta,
    fiaishanuet
visualize (v), fiaisharsne, fiaishano, fiaishano
visually (adv), fiaisharniu, fiaishaniu, fiaishaniu
vital (adj), maigirfu, maigifu, maigifu
vitality (n), maigirf, maigifa, maigif
vitally (adv), maigirfiu, maigifiu, maigifiu
vitamin (n), maigarme, maigama, maigam
vivid (adj), kinortu, kinotu, kintu
vividly (adv), kinortiu, kinotiu, kintiu
vividness (n), kinort, kinota, kint
vocabulary (n), thaibarn, thaibara, thaibar

vocal (adj), thaiparnu, thaipanu, thaipanu
vocal (n), thaiparn, thaipana, thaipan
vocalist (n doer), thaiparnwan, thaipanua,
    thaipanua
vocation (n), thaipark, thaipaka, thaipak
vocational (adj), thaiparku, thaipaku, thaipaku
vodka (n), feikarde, feikada, feikad
voice (n), thairp, thaipa, thaip
voice (v), thairsp, thaipo, thaipo
voicemail (n), thaipelirp, thaipelipa, thaipelp
void (n), nuafk, nuaka, nuak
void (v), nuafsk, nuako, nuako
voila (interj), durai, durai, durai
volatile (adj), tuarzhu, tuazhu, tuazhu
volatility (n), tuarzhe, tuazha, tuazh
volcano (n), gorade, goruda, gord
volition (n), kemirf, kemifa, kemif
volley (n), klaiarf, kelaiafa, klaiaf
volley (v), klaiarsf, kelaiafo, klaiafo
volt (n), broilt, beroita, broit
voltage (n), broiltuet, beroitueta, broituet
volume (n), blairf, belaifa, blaif
voluntarily (adv), kemirfiu, kemifiu, kemifiu
voluntary (adj), kemirfu, kemifu, kemifu
volunteer (n doer), kemirfwan, kemifua, kemifua
volunteer (v), kemirsf, kemifo, kemifo
vomit (n), beriautsh, beriautesha, briautsh
vomit (v), beriauts, beriautesho, briautsho
voracious (adj), diuarfu, diuafu, diuafu
voraciously (adv), diuarfiu, diuafiu, diuafiu
voracity (n), diuarf, diuafa, diuaf
vortex (n), diuvart, diuvata, diuvat
vote (n), thairk, thaika, thaik
vote (v), thairsk, thaiko, thaiko
voter (n doer), thairkwan, thaikua, thaikua
vouch (n), briamp, beriama, briam
vouch (v), briamesp, beriamo, briamo
voucher (n doer), briampwan, beriamua, briamua
vow (n), brialsh, beriasha, briash
vow (v), brials, beriasho, briasho
vowel (n), yuwarn, yuwana, yuwan
voyage (n), muarde, muada, muad
voyage (v), muarzde, muado, muado
voyager (n doer), muardwan, muadua, muadua
Vs (let pl), vali, vali, vali
vulgar (adj), gugaurgu, gugaugu, gugaugu
vulgarity (n), gugaurge, gugauga, gugaug
vulnerability (n), krakfrelp, kerakoferepa, krakfrep
vulnerable (adj), krakfrelpu, kerakoferepu,
    krakfrepu
W (let sng), warfe, warifa, warf
wack (n), kelashk, kelashika, klashk
wack (v), kelashsk, kelashiko, klashko
wacko (n doer), kelashkwan, kelashikua, klashkua
wacky (adj), kelashku, kelashiku, klashku
wad (n), yalirp, yalipa, yalp
wad (v), yalirsp, yalipo, yalpo
waddle (n), yalirk, yalika, yalk
waddle (v), yalirsk, yaliko, yalko
wade (v), yars, yasho, yasho
wader (n doer), yarshwan, yashua, yashua
wafer (n), yaifk, yaifa, yaif
waffle (n), yaifank, yaifana, yaifan

waffle (v), yaifansk, yaifano, yaifano
wag (n), kairve, kaiva, kaiv
wag (v), kairzve, kaivo, kaivo
wage (n), katirk, katika, katik
wage (v), katirsk, katiko, katiko
wager (n), katishk, katisha, katish
wager (v), katishsk, katisho, katisho
wagger (n doer), kairvwan, kaivua, kaivua
wagon (n), kaivarp, kaivapa, kaivap
wah (interj), hua, hua, hua
wahoo (interj), yuyau, yuyau, yuyau
wail (n), kauaifp, kauaifa, kauaif
wail (v), kauaifsp, kauaifo, kauaifo
waist (n), yumart, yumata, yumat
waistline (n), yumatroifk, yumateroifa, yumatroif
wait (n), yalirf, yalifa, yalf
wait (v), yalirsf, yalifo, yalfo
waiter (n doer), yalirfwan, yalifua, yalfua
waitress (n doer), yalirfwan, yalifua, yalfua
waive (v), pleishsk, peleisho, pleisho
waiver (n), pleishk, peleisha, pleish
wake (n d:trail), dovirn, dovina, dovin
wake (v d:arise), minorsp, minopo, minpo
wakeup (adj d:arise), minorpiveilu, minopiveilu,
    minpiveilu
wakeup (n d:arise), minorpiveil, minopiveila,
    minpiveil
Wales (n), Weilorsh, Weilosha, Weilsh
walk (n), zhoirp, zhoipa, zhoip
walk (v), zhoirsp, zhoipo, zhoipo
walker (n doer), zhoirpwan, zhoipua, zhoipua
walkout (n), zhoirpuil, zhoipuila, zhoipuil
walkup (adj), zhoirpiveilu, zhoipiveilu, zhoipiveilu
walkup (n), zhoirpiveil, zhoipiveila, zhoipiveil
walkway (n), zhoipliorl, zhoipeliola, zhoipliol
wall (n), nolthk, nolitha, nolth
wall (v), nolthsk, nolitho, noltho
wallet (n), blanirf, belanifa, blanf
wallflower (n), nolthaush, nolithuana, nolthuan
wallop (n), klaushp, kelaupa, klaup
wallop (v), klaushsp, kelaupo, klaupo
wallow (v), yalushsk, yalusho, yalsho
wallpaper (n), nolthvuarp, nolithevuapa, nolthvuap
wallpaper (v), nolthvuarsp, nolithevuapo,
    nolthvuapo
wand (n), kianirde, kianida, kiand
wander (v), keiansk, keiano, keiano
wanderer (n doer), keiankwan, keianua, keianua
wanderlust (n), keianegufirk, keianegufika,
    keianegufk
wane (v), keleshsk, keiesho, keiesho
wanna (v), kemirsk, kemiko, kemko
wannabe (n), kemvil, kemikila, kembil
want (n), kemirp, kemipa, kemp
want (v), kemirsp, kemipo, kempo
war (n), viurn, viura, viur
war (v), viursne, viuro, viuro
ward (n), haursh, hausha, haush
ward (v), haurs, hausho, hausho
ware (n), shlerf, shelefa, shlef
warehouse (n), shlefkiarf, shelefekiafa, shlefkiaf
warehouse (v), shlefkiarsf, shelefekiafo, shlefkiafo
warfare (n), viurnif, viurifa, viurf

warhead (n), viurkefirt, viurekefita, viurkeft
warily (adv), shlairfiu, shelaifiu, shlaifiu
wariness (n), shlairf, shelaifa, shlaif
warlike (adj), viurnu, viuru, viuru
warm (adj), thaunshu, thaunu, thaunu
warm (v), thauns, thauno, thauno
warmly (adv), thaunshiu, thauniu, thauniu
warmth (n), thaunsh, thauna, thaun
warmup (adj), thaunshiveilu, thauniveilu,
    thauniveilu
warmup (n), thaunshiveil, thauniveila, thauniveil
warn (v), viurst, viuto, viuto
warp (n), tuaufp, tuaupa, tuaup
warp (v), tuaufsp, tuaupo, tuaupo
warpath (n), viurbotersh, viurebotesha, viurbotsh
warplane (n), viurvalar, viurevarila, viurvarl
warrant (n), viufirk, viufika, viufk
warrant (v), viufirsk, viufiko, viufko
warranty (n), viurp, viupa, viup
warrior (n doer), viurnwan, viurua, viurua
Warsaw (n), Warshaurf, Waroshaufa, Warshauf
warship (n), viureflerve, viurefeleva, viurflev
wartime (n), viurdaurn, viuredauna, viurdaun
wary (adj), shlairfu, shelaifu, shlaifu
was (common), vol, kolo, bol
was (emphatic), vokel, kokelo, bovel
was/will be (parcl d:passive voice), dhai, dhai, dhai
wash (n d:clean), fiaushk, fiausha, fiaush
wash (v d:clean), fiaushsk, fiausho, fiausho
washable (adj), fiaushfrelpu, fiausheferepu,
    fiaushfrepu
washably (adv), fiaushfrelpiu, fiausheferepiu,
    fiaushfrepiu
washboard (n), fiaushplok, fiaushepelorika,
    fiaushplork
washcloth (n), fiaushflarf, fiaushefelafa, fiaushflaf
washer (n d:spacer), duterk, duteka, dutek
washer (n doer d:clean), fiaushkwan, fiaushua,
    fiaushua
Washington (n), Washinktorn, Washinoketona,
    Washinkton
washout (n), fiaushkuil, fiaushuila, fiaushuil
washroom (n), fiaushranf, fiausherana, fiaushran
washy (adj d:clean), fiaushku, fiaushu, fiaushu
waste (n), voashk, voasha, voash
waste (v), voashsk, voasho, voasho
wastebasket (n), voashtafil, voashetalofa, voashtalf
wasteful (adj), voashku, voashu, voashu
wastefully (adv), voashkiu, voashiu, voashiu
wastefulness (n), voaohkuel, voaohuela, voaohuet
wasteland (n), voashraufp, voasheraupa, voashraup
wastepaper (n), voashvuarp, voashevuapa,
    voashvuap
waster (n doer), voashkwan, voashua, voashua
wastewater (n), voasheidorn, voasheidona,
    voasheidon
watch (n d:clock), lufk, luka, luk
watch (n d:viewing), shaiarme, shaiama, shaiam
watch (v d:viewing), shaiarzme, shaiamo, shaiamo
watchdog (n), shaiamdraursh, shaiamederausha,
    shaiamdraush
watcher (n doer d:viewing), shaiarmwan, shaiamua,
    shaiamua

watchful (adj d:viewing), shaiarmu, shaiamu, shaiamu

watchfully (adv d:viewing), shaiarmiu, shaiamiu, shaiamiu

watchmaker (n doer), luknargwan, lukenagua, luknagua

watchman (n), shaiamplorn, shaiamepelona, shaiamplon

watchmen (n pl), shaiamplornyek, shaiamepeloni, shaiamploni

water (n), heidorn, heidona, heidon

water (v), heidorsne, heidono, heidono

waterbed (n), heidonfamor, heidonefuarema, heidonfuarm

watercolor (n), heidonlirolf, heidonelirola, heidonlirol

waterfall (n), heidonzhailf, heidonezhaila, heidonzhail

waterfront (adj), heidonflarshu, heidonefelarinu, heidonflarnu

waterfront (n), heidonflarsh, heidonefelarina, heidonflarn

waterhouse (n), heidonkiarf, heidonekiafa, heidonkiaf

waterman (n), heidonplorn, heidonepelona, heidonplon

watermark (n), heidonshtart, heidoneshetata, heidonshtat

watermen (n pl), heidonplornyek, heidonepeloni, heidonploni

waterproof (adj), heidonefliorfu, heidonefeliofu, heidonfliofu

waterproof (v), heidonefliorsf, heidonefeliofo, heidonfliofo

watershed (adj), heidonthilorfu, heidonethilofu, heidonthilfu

watershed (n), heidonthilorf, heidonethilofa, heidonthilf

watertight (adj), heidonduairfu, heidoneduaifu, heidonduaitu

watertightness (n), heidonduairf, heidoneduaifa, heidonduaif

watertown (n), heidonmiurn, heidonemiuna, heidonmiun

waterway (n), heidonpliorl, heidonepeliola, heidonpliol

waterwork (n), heidonkiork, heidonekioka, heidonkiok

watery (adj), heidornu, heidonu, heidonu

wave (n), lersh, lesha, lesh

wave (v), lers, lesho, lesho

wavelength (n), leshralzhe, lesherazha, leshrazh

waver (v), lesharsk, leshako, leshko

wax (n), tarishk, tarika, tark

wax (v), tarishsk, tariko, tarko

waxer (n doer), tarishkwan, tarikua, tarkua

waxy (adj), tarishku, tariku, tarku

way (n), pliorl, peliola, pliol

wayside (n), pliolshoirt, pelioleshoita, pliolshoit

wayward (adj), pliorlu, peliolu, pliolu

we (pron 1st pl sub), niai, niai, niai

weak (adj), kralku, keraku, kraku

weaken (v), kralsk, kerako, krako

weaker (adj), kralkwelu, kerakwelu, krakwelu

weakest (adj), kralkwaku, kerakwaku, krakwaku

weakly (adv), kralkiu, kerakiu, krakiu

weakness (n), kralk, keraka, krak

wealth (n), kaurp, kaupa, kaup

wealthy (adj), kaurpu, kaupu, kaupu

wean (v), koshiathsk, koshiatho, koshiatho

weapon (n), kuiark, kuiaka, kuiak

weaponry (n), kuiarkuet, kuiakueta, kuiakuet

wear (n d:clothe), dorame, dorima, dorim

wear (n d:erode, fatigue), kralt, kerata, krat

wear (v d:clothe), dorazme, dorimo, dorimo

wear (v d:erode, fatigue), kralst, kerato, krato

wearable (adj d:clothe), doramu, dorimu, dorimu

wearably (adv d:clothe), doramiu, dorimiu, dorimiu

wearer (n doer d:clothe), doramwan, dorimua, dorimua

wearily (adv d:erode, fatigue), kraltiu, keratiu, kratiu

weariness (n d:fatigue), kraltuet, keratueta, kratuet

weary (adj d:erode, fatigue), kraltu, keratu, kratu

wearysome (adj d:fatigue), kraltu, keratu, kratu

weather (n), tauiarn, tauiana, tauian

weather (v), tauiarsne, tauiano, tauiano

weatherman (n), tauianplorn, tauianepelona, tauianplon

weathermen (n pl), tauianplornyek, tauianepeloni, tauianploni

weatherproof (adj), tauianfliorfu, tauianefeliofu, tauianfliofu

weatherproof (v), tauianfliorsf, tauianefeliofo, tauianfliofo

weave (n), brivark, berivaka, brivak

weave (v), brivarsk, berivako, brivako

weaver (n doer), brivarkwan, berivakua, brivakua

web (n), brivarn, berivana, brivan

web (v), brivarsne, berivano, brivano

wed (v), yurzve, yuvo, yuvo

wedge (n), keiteshk, keitesha, keitsh

wedge (v), keiteshsk, keitesho, keitsho

wedlock (n), yuvtiurge, yuvetiuga, yuvtiug

Wednesday (n), Yuteshviurl, Yuteshuviula, Yuteshviul

weed (n), yurk, yuka, yuk

weed (v), yursk, yuko, yuko

weeder (n doer), yurkwan, yukua, yukua

weedy (adj), yurku, yuku, yuku

week (n), krufk, kerufa, kruf

weekday (n), krufviurl, kerufeviula, krufviul

weekend (n), krufdairk, kerufedaika, krufdaik

weekender (n doer), krufdairkwan, kerufedaikua, krufdaikua

weeklong (adj), krufralzhu, keruferazhu, krufrazhu

weekly (adj), krufku, kerufu, krufu

weeknight (n), krufmuarn, kerufemuana, krufmuan

weep (v), shlurzme, shelumo, shlumo

weeper (n doer), shlurmwan, shelumua, shlumua

weepy (adj), shlurmu, shelumu, shlumu

weigh (v), shuirs, shuisho, shuisho

weight (n), shuirsh, shuisha, shuish

weight (v), shuirshsk, shuishoko, shuishko

weightless (adj), shuirshmenu, shuishemenu, shuishmenu

weightlessness (n), shuirshmen, shuishemena, shuishmen
weighty (adj), shuirshu, shuishu, shuishu
weird (adj), yuifoirku, yuifoiku, yuifoiku
weirdly (adv), yuifoirkiu, yuifoikiu, yuifoikiu
weirdness (n), yuifoirk, yuifoika, yuifoik
weirdo (n doer), yuifoirkwan, yuifoikua, yuifoikua
weka- (num 1e30 pref), muikai-, muikai-, muikai-
welch (v), treiushsk, tereiuko, treiuko
welcher (n doer), treiushkwan, tereiukua, treiukua
welcome (n), kolarn, kolana, kolan
welcome (v), kolarsne, kolano, kolano
weld (n), thortesh, thoratesha, thortsh
weld (v), thortes, thoratesho, thortsho
welder (n doer), thorteshwan, thorateshua, thortshua
welfare (n), kolthirk, kolathika, kolthik
well (adj d:good), kolu, koru, koru
well (n d:water), havurp, havupa, havup
wellbeing (n), kolkulauf, korekulauraa, korkulaur
wellness (n d:good), kol, kora, kor
welsh (v), treiushsk, tereiuko, treiuko
welsher (n doer), treiushkwan, tereiukua, treiukua
went (v pa), virsfyot, vifio, vifio
wept (v pa), shlurzmyot, shelumio, shlumio
were (common), vor, koro, bor
were (emphatic), voker, kokero, bover
west (adj), shaithku, shaithu, shaithu
west (n), shaithk, shaitha, shaith
westbound (adj), shaithdraifpu, shaithederaipu, shaithdraipu
western (adj), shaithku, shaithu, shaithu
western (n d:film), shaitharn, shaithana, shaithan
westerner (n doer), shaithkwan, shaithua, shaithua
westernize (v), shaithsk, shaitho, shaitho
westernmost (adj), shaithkweku, shaithweku, shaithweku
westward (adj), shaithaurshu, shaithaushu, shaithaushu
wet (adj), yelirtu, yelitu, yeltu
wet (v pa), yelirstyot, yelitio, yeltio
wet (v), yelirst, yelito, yelto
wetland (n), yeltraufp, yeliteraupa, yeltraup
wetness (n), yelirt, yelita, yelt
wetsuit (n), yeltmoiurf, yelitemoiufa, yeltmoiuf
whack (v), kelashsk, kelashiko, klashko
whacko (n doer), kelashkwan, kelashikua, klashkua
whacky (adj), kelashku, kelashiku, klashku
whale (n), raniarp, raniapa, raniap
whale (v), raniarsp, raniapo, raniapo
what (adj/adv/conj), halk, haku, hak
what (pron), halk, hakei, hak
whatever (adj/interj), hakerf, hakefu, hakef
whatever (pron), hakerf, hakefei, hakef
whatsoever (adj), hakzhaufel, hakezhaufelu, hakzhaufel
whatsoever (pron), hakzhaufel, hakezhaufelei, hakzhaufel
wheat (n), tripart, teripata, tripat
whee (interj), shwi, shwi, shwi
wheel (n), trithk, teritha, trith
wheel (v), trithsk, teritho, tritho
wheelbarrow (n), faliarp, faliapa, faliap

wheelchair (n), trithklesht, terithekelenuda, trithklend
wheelchair (v), trithkleshst, terithekelenudo, trithklendo
wheeler (n doer), trithkwan, terithua, trithua
wheelie (n), trithkat, terithata, trithat
wheeze (n), fabirk, fabika, fabik
wheeze (v), fabirsk, fabiko, fabiko
when (adv/conj), yarme, yamu, yam
when (pron), yarme, yamei, yam
whenever (adv/conj), yamerf, yamefu, yamef
where (adv/conj), torlu, tolu, tolu
where (pron), torl, tolei, tol
where-from (adv), veltorlu, veletolu, veltolu
where-to (adv), dihorlu, diholu, diholu
whereabout (n), toloveip, toloveipa, toloveip
whereas (conj), toluyorsh, toluyoshu, toluyosh
whereas (n), toluyorsh, toluyosha, toluyosh
whereby (conj/adv), torluvu, toluvu, toluvu
wherever (adv/conj), torlerf, tolefelu, tolefel
whether (conj), shardu, sharodu, shardu
whew (interj), shiu, shiu, shiu
which (adj), hirshu, hishu, hishu
which (pron), hirsh, hishei, hish
whichever (adj), hirsherf, hishefelu, hishefel
whichever (pron), hirsherf, hishefelei, hishefel
whiff (n), yelsh, yesha, yesh
whiff (v), yels, yesho, yesho
while (conj), yaurk, yauku, yauk
while (n), yaurk, yauka, yauk
whim (n), yelirf, yelifa, yelf
whimper (n), yaunk, yauna, yaun
whimper (v), yaunsk, yauno, yauno
whimsical (adj), yelirfu, yelifu, yelfu
whimsically (adv), yelirfiu, yelifiu, yelfiu
whimsy (n), yelirf, yelifa, yelf
whine (n), yoishp, yoipa, yoip
whine (v), yoishsp, yoipo, yoipo
whiner (n doer), yoishpwan, yoipua, yoipua
whiney (adj), yoishpu, yoipu, yoipu
whiny (adj), yoishpu, yoipu, yoipu
whip (n), yaurp, yaupa, yaup
whip (v), yaursp, yaupo, yaupo
whiplash (n), yauplaiathk, yaupelaiatha, yauplaiath
whiplash (v), yauplaiathsk, yaupelaiatho, yauplaiatho
whipper (n docr), yaurpwan, yaupua, yaupua
whir (n), shraithk, sheraitha, shraith
whir (v), shraithsk, sheraitho, shraitho
whirl (n), shrailf, sheraila, shrail
whirl (v), shrailsf, sherailo, shrailo
whirlpool (n), shrailditarp, sheraileditapa, shrailditap
whirlwind (n), shrailthelern, sherailethelina, shrailtheln
whisk (v d:swipe), shlaursk, shelauko, shlauko
whisker (n d:hair), shauank, shauana, shauan
whiskey (n), heishork, heishoka, heishk
whisper (n), flierf, feliefa, flief
whisper (v), fliersf, feliefo, fliefo
whisperer (n doer), flierfwan, feliefua, fliefua
whistle (n), fliert, felieta, fliet
whistle (v), flierst, felieto, flieto

whistler (n doer), fliertwan, felietua, flietua
white (adj), yuarnu, yuanu, yuanu
white (n), yuarn, yuana, yuan
whiten (v), yuarsne, yuano, yuano
whitewash (n), yuanfiaushk, yuanefiausha, yuanfiaush
whitewash (v), yuanfiaushsk, yuanefiausho, yuanfiausho
whither (adv/conj), dihorlu, diholu, diholu
whittle (v), fliushsk, feliuko, fliuko
whittler (n doer), fliushkwan, feliukua, fliukua
whiz (n), tupirk, tupika, tupik
whiz (v), tupirsk, tupiko, tupiko
who (pron), lowe, lowei, lowei
whoa (interj), yoi, yoi, yoi
whoever (pron), lowerf, lowefelei, lowefel
whole (adj), thiaurtu, thiautu, thiautu
whole (n), thiaurt, thiauta, thiaut
wholeness (n), thiaurtuet, thiautueta, thiautuet
wholesale (adj), thiautrelirfu, thiauterelifu, thiautrelfu
wholesale (n), thiautrelirf, thiauterelifa, thiautrelf
wholesaler (n doer), thiautrelirfwan, thiauterelifua, thiautrelfua
wholly (adv), thiaurtiu, thiautiu, thiautiu
whom (pron), lowe, lowei, lowei
whoop (n), kriuthk, keriutha, kriuth
whoop (v), kriuthsk, keriutho, kriutho
whose (pron), lowange, lowangei, lowang
why (adv/conj/interj), hiur, hiu, hiu
why (n), hiur, hiua, hiu
wick (n), yuark, yuaka, yuak
wicked (adj), yuakartu, yuakatu, yuakatu
wickedness (n), yuakart, yuakata, yuakat
wide (adj), krashku, kerashu, krashu
widely (adv), krashkiu, kerashiu, krashiu
widen (v), krashsk, kerasho, krasho
widener (n doer), krashkwan, kerashua, krashua
wider (adj), krashkwelu, kerashwelu, krashwelu
widespread (adj), krashilorpu, kerashethilopu, krashthilpu
widest (adj), krashkwaku, kerashwaku, krashwaku
widow (n), shardark, sharodaka, shardak
widow (v), shardarsk, sharodako, shardako
widower (n), trotark, terotaka, trotak
widower (v), trotarsk, terotako, trotako
widowered (v prp), trotarskaut, terotakao, trotakao
width (n), krashk, kerasha, krash
wield (v), kathairsk, kathaiko, kathaiko
wife (n), sharaf, sharifa, sharf
wig (n), wefarn, wefana, wefan
wiggle (n), yoithk, yoitha, yoith
wiggle (v), yoithsk, yoitho, yoitho
wiggler (n doer), yoithkwan, yoithua, yoithua
WiggleTalk (n), yoilark, yoilarika, yoilark
wild (adj), zhoithku, zhoithu, zhoithu
wild (n), zhoithk, zhoitha, zhoith
wildcard (n), zhoithgaurn, zhoithekauna, zhoithkaun
wildcat (n), zhoithfierf, zhoithefiefa, zhoithfief
wilderness (n), zhoithbrelsh, zhoitheberesha, zhoithbresh
wildfire (n), zhoithshriauk, zhoithegiaula,
zhoithgiaul
wildflower (n), zhoithaush, zhoithuana, zhoithuan
wildlife (n), zhoithflaursh, zhoithefelausha, zhoithflaush
wildly (adv), zhoithkiu, zhoithiu, zhoithiu
wildness (n), zhoithkuet, zhoithueta, zhoithuet
will (n d:determination), yark, yaka, yak
will (n d:inheritance), yaferf, yafefa, yafef
will (pro-verb fu), kokeio, kokeio, kokeio
will (v common), vush, kusho, buvo
will (v d:determination), yarsk, yako, yako
will (v emphat), vukesh, kukesho, buvesh
will-be (v fp common), vush, kushu, buvu
will-be (v fp emphatic), vukesh, kukeshu, buvesh
willful (adj d:determination), yarku, yaku, yaku
willfully (adv d:determination), yarkiu, yakiu, yakiu
willingly (adv), yarkiu, yakiu, yakiu
willingness (n), yarkuet, yakueta, yakuet
willpower (n), yakbiorat, yakebiorta, yakbiort
wilt (v), troiafst, teroiafo, troiafo
wimp (n), goirp, goipa, goip
wimp (v), goirsp, goipo, goipo
wimpy (adj), goirpu, goipu, goipu
win (n), zhirk, zhika, zhik
win (v), zhirsk, zhiko, zhiko
wince (n), gialirp, gialipa, gialp
wince (v), gialirsp, gialipo, gialpo
winch (n), gleishk, gelieka, gleik
winch (v), gleishsk, gelieko, gleiko
wind (n d:air), thelirn, thelina, theln
wind (v d:air), thelirsne, thelino, thelno
wind (v d:energize), thrairsk, theraiko, thraiko
windchill (adj), thelnplirfu, thelinepeliru, thelnpliru
windchill (n), thelnplirf, thelinepelira, thelnplir
winder (n doer d:energize), thrairkwan, theraikua, thraikua
windfall (n), thelnzhailf, thelinezhaila, thelnzhail
windmill (n), thelnfenirp, thelinefenipa, thelnfenp
window (n), vimarn, vimana, viman
window (v), vimarsne, vimano, vimano
windowless (adj), vimarnmenu, vimanemenu, vimanmenu
windshield (n), thelnmoirk, thelinemoika, thelnmoik
windward (adj), thelnaurshu, thelinaushu, thelnaushu
windy (adj d:air), thelirnu, thelinu, thelnu
wine (n), thoarn, thoana, thoan
wine (v), thoarsne, thoano, thoano
winery (n), thoanirn, thoanina, thoanin
wing (n), klierge, keliega, klieg
wing (v), klierzge, keliego, kliego
winger (n doer), kliergwan, keliegua, kliegua
wingman (n), kliegplorn, keliegepelona, kliegplon
wingmen (n pl), kliegplornyek, keliegepeloni, kliegploni
wingspan (n), kliegbleirsh, keliegebeleisha, kliegbleish
wink (n), lialirk, lialika, lialk
wink (v), lialirsk, lialiko, lialko
winner (n doer), zhirkwan, zhikua, zhikua
wino (n doer), thoarnwan, thoanua, thoanua
winter (adj), vemiarnu, vemianu, vemianu

winter (n), vemiarn, vemiana, vemian
winterize (v), vemiarsne, vemiano, vemiano
winterly (adj), vemiarnu, vemianu, vemianu
wintertime (n), vemiandaurn, vemianedauna,
    vemiandaun
wintry (adj), vemiarnu, vemianu, vemianu
wipe (n), trolp, teropa, trop
wipe (v), trolsp, teropo, tropo
wipeout (n), trolpuil, teropuila, tropuil
wiper (n doer), trolpwan, teropua, tropua
wire (n), shnirf, shenifa, shnif
wire (v), shnirsf, shenifo, shnifo
wireless (adj), shnirfmenu, shenifemenu,
    shnifmenu
wiretap (n), shnifnerp, shenifenepa, shnifnep
wiretap (v), shnifnersp, shenifenepo, shnifnepo
wirey (adj), shnirfu, shenifu, shnifu
Wisconsin (n), Wishkornsh, Wishakonisha,
    Wishkonsh
wisdom (n), fluirk, feluika, fluik
wise (adj), fluirku, feluiku, fluiku
wisecrack (n), fluikuthralp, feluikutherapa,
    fluikuthrap
wiseguy (n), fluikunirve, feluikuniva, fluikuniv
wisely (adv), fluirkiu, feluikiu, fluikiu
wiseman (n), fluikuplorn, feluikupelona, fluikuplon
wisemen (n pl), fluikuplornyek, feluikupeloni,
    fluikuploni
wisen (v), fluirsk, feluiko, fluiko
wish (n), plerf, pelefa, plef
wish (v), plersf, pelefo, plefo
wishbone (n), pleftoirk, pelefetoika, pleftoik
wisher (n doer), plerfwan, pelefua, plefua
wishful (adj), plerfu, pelefu, plefu
wishy (adj), plerfu, pelefu, plefu
wisp (n), flert, feleta, flet
wisp (v), flerst, feleto, fleto
wit (n), tilork, tiloka, tilk
witch (n doer), deiarnwan, deianua, deianua
witchcraft (n), deiarn, deiana, deian
with (prep), borsh, boshu, bosh
withdraw (v), boshpulasp, bosheperatho,
    boshpratho
withdrawal (n), boshpulap, bosheperatha,
    boshprath
withdrew (v pa), boshpulaspyot, bosheperathio,
    boshprathio
wither (v), blauthsk, belautho, blautho
withheld (v pa), boshthorthskyot, boshethorithio,
    boshthorthio
withhold (v), boshthorthsk, boshethoritho,
    boshthortho
within (adv/prep), boshirsh, boshishu, boshish
within (n), boshirsh, boshisha, boshish
without (adv/prep), borshuil, boshuilu, boshuil
without (n), borshuil, boshuila, boshuil
withstand (v), boshtrelirst, bosheterelito, boshtrelto
withstood (v pa), boshtrelirstyot, bosheterelitio,
    boshtreltio
witless (adj), tilorkuetu, tilokuetu, tilkuetu
witlessly (adv), tilorkuetiu, tilokuetiu, tilkuetiu
witness (n), friork, ferioka, friok
witness (v), friorsk, ferioko, frioko

wittily (adv), tilorkiu, tilokiu, tilkiu
witty (adj), tilorku, tiloku, tilku
wizard (n doer), fluirkwan, feluikua, fluikua
wizardry (n), fluirkuan, feluikuana, fluikuan
wizen (v), fluirkuasne, feluikuano, fluikuano
wobble (n), taiank, taiana, taian
wobble (v), taiansk, taiano, taiano
wobbler (n doer), taiankwan, taianua, taianua
woe (n), lioir, lioila, lioil
woeful (adj), lioiru, lioilu, lioilu
woefully (adv), lioiriu, lioiliu, lioiliu
woke (v pa d:arise), minorspyot, minopio, minpio
wolf (n), hiarak, hiaroka, hiark
wolf (v), hiarask, hiaroko, hiarko
woman (n), shardan, sharadala, shardal
womanization (n), shardoiark, sharadoiaka,
    shardoiak
womanize (v), shardoiarsk, sharadoiako,
    shardoiako
womanizer (n doer), shardoiarkwan, sharadoiakua,
    shardoiakua
womb (n), biarth, biatha, biath
women (n pl), shardanyek, sharadali, shardali
won (v pa), zhirskyot, zhikio, zhikio
wonder (n), yenaursh, yenausha, yenaush
wonder (v), yenaurs, yenausho, yenausho
wonderful (adj), yenaurshu, yenaushu, yenaushu
wonderfully (adv), yenaurshiu, yenaushiu,
    yenaushiu
wonderland (n), yenaushraufp, yenausheraupa,
    yenaushraup
wonderment (n), yenaurshuet, yenaushueta,
    yenaushuet
wonderous (adj), yenaurshu, yenaushu, yenaushu
woo (v), yaufsk, yaufo, yaufo
wood (n), fanirn, fanina, fanin
wooden (adj), fanirnu, faninu, faninu
woodhouse (n), faninkiarf, faninekiafa, faninkiaf
woodland (n), faninraufp, fanineraupa, faninraup
woodlands (adj), faninraufpu, fanineraupu,
    faninraupu
woodman (n), faninplorn, faninepelona, faninplon
woodmen (n pl), faninplornyek, faninepeloni,
    faninploni
woodshed (n), faninthilorf, faninethilofa, faninthilf
woodsman (n), faninplorn, faninepelona, faninplon
woodsmen (n pl), faninplornyek, faninepeloni,
    faninploni
woodwork (n), faninkiork, faninekioka, faninkiok
woodwork (v), faninkiorsk, faninekioko, faninkioko
woodworker (n doer), faninkiorkwan, faninekiokua,
    faninkiokua
woof (interj), aruf, arufa, aruf
wool (adj), henartu, henatu, henatu
wool (n), henart, henata, henat
wooly (adj), henartu, henatu, henatu
word (n), lialirt, lialita, lialt
word (v), lialirst, lialito, lialto
wordsmith (n), lialtfnirth, lialitefenitha, lialtfnith
wordy (adj), lialirtu, lialitu, lialtu
wore (v pa d:clothe), dorazmyot, dorimio, dorimio
wore (v pa d:erode, fatigue), kralstyot, keratio,
    kratio

work (n), kiork, kioka, kiok
work (v), kiorsk, kioko, kioko
workable (adj), kiorku, kioku, kioku
workaholic (n), kiokagiarn, kiokagiana, kiokagian
workbench (n), kiokikaf, kiokifeka, kiokifk
workday (n), kiokviurl, kiokeviula, kiokviul
worker (n doer), kiorkwan, kiokua, kiokua
workforce (n), kiorkviurk, kiokeviuka, kiokviuk
workgroup (n), kiokbronf, kiokeberona, kiokbron
workhorse (n), kiokeglaushk, kiokegelausha, kiokeglaush
workload (n), kioklurift, kiokelurita, kioklurt
workman (n), kiokplorn, kiokepelona, kiokplon
workmanship (n), kiokplornfif, kiokepelonefifa, kiokplonfif
workmen (n pl), kiokplornyek, kiokepeloni, kiokploni
workout (n), kiorkuil, kiokuila, kiokuil
workplace (n), kiokabrelsh, kiokeberesha, kiokabresh
worksheet (n), kioktaurp, kioketaupa, kioktaup
workshop (n), kiorthat, kiokevithova, kiokathov
workspace (n), kiokthushp, kiokethusha, kiokthush
workstation (n), kiokshlukert, kiokesheluketa, kiokshluket
world (n), halrelt, haloreta, halret
worldly (adj), halreltu, haloretu, halretu
worldwide (adj), halreltakrashku, haloretakerashu, halretakrashu
worm (n), yoran, yorina, yorn
worm (v), yorasne, yorino, yorno
wormy (adj), yoranu, yorinu, yornu
worrier (n doer), frairpwan, feraipua, fraipua
worrisome (adj), frairpu, feraipu, fraipu
worry (n), frairp, feraipa, fraip
worry (v), frairsp, feraipo, fraipo
worse (adj), frairkelu, feraikelu, fraikelu
worsen (v), frairkesle, feraikelo, fraikelo
worship (n), koiark, koiaka, koiak
worship (v), koiarsk, koiako, koiako
worshipful (adj), koiarku, koiaku, koiaku
worshipper (n doer), koiarkwan, koiakua, koiakua
worst (adj), frairkeku, feraikeku, fraikeku
worst (v), frairkesk, feraikeko, fraikeko
worth (n), flairsh, felaisha, flaish
worthiness (n), flairshuet, felaishueta, flaishuet
worthless (adj), flairshmenu, felaishemenu, flaishmenu
worthwhile (adj), flaishaurku, felaishauku, flaishauku
worthy (adj), flairshu, felaishu, flaishu
would (ndal d:will), yarke kodi, yaka kodi, yake kodi
wound (n d:injury), grulirk, gerulika, grulk
wound (v d:injury), grulirsk, geruliko, grulko
wound (v pa d:energize), thrairskyot, theraikio, thraikio
wove (v pa), brivarskyot, berivakio, brivakio
wow (interj), yai, yai, yai
wow (n), yaiy, yaiya, yaiy
wow (v), yaisy, yaiyo, yaiyo
wrack (v), kaibarsk, kaibako, kaibako
wrangle (v), yoibarsk, yoibako, yoibako

wrangler (n doer), yoibarkwan, yoibakua, yoibakua
wrap (n), fnurp, fenupa, fnup
wrap (v), fnursp, fenupo, fnupo
wraparound (n), fnupoblaithp, fenupobelaitha, fnupoblaith
wrapper (n doer), fnurpwan, fenupua, fnupua
wrath (n), kaiarth, kaiatha, kaiath
wrathful (adj), kaiarthu, kaiathu, kaiathu
wreak (v), kirbarsk, kirabako, kirbako
wreath (n), kirlarth, kiralatha, kirlath
wreck (n), karbark, karubaka, karbak
wreck (v), karbarsk, karubako, karbako
wreckage (n), karbarshk, karubashika, karbashk
wrecker (n doer), karbarkwan, karubakua, karbakua
wrench (n), yoiark, yoiaka, yoiak
wrench (v), yoiarsk, yoiako, yoiako
wrest (v), yoikarsne, yoikano, yoikano
wrestle (v), yoikanirsk, yoikaniko, yoikanko
wrestler (n doer), yoikanirkwan, yoikanikua, yoikankua
wretch (n), yauark, yauaka, yauak
wriggle (n), yoithart, yoithata, yoithat
wriggle (v), yoitharst, yoithato, yoithato
wriggler (n pl), yoithartyek, yoithati, yoithati
wring (v), kirkirst, kirakito, kirkito
wringer (n doer), kirkirtwan, kirakitua, kirkitua
wrinkle (n), drilort, derilota, drilt
wrinkle (v), drilorst, deriloto, drilto
wrinkler (n doer), drilortwan, derilotua, driltua
wrinkly (adj), drilortu, derilotu, driltu
wrist (n), loirp, loipa, loip
wristband (n), loipshtairme, loipeshetaima, loipshtaim
wristwatch (n), loiplufk, loipeluka, loipluk
write (v), loirzde, loido, loido
writer (n doer), loirdwan, loidua, loidua
wrong (adj), fnaurku, fenauku, fnauku
wrong (n), fnaurk, fenauka, fnauk
wrong (v), fnaursk, fenauko, fnauko
wrongdoer (n doer), fnaurketikwan, fenauketikua, fnauketikua
wrongdoing (n), fnaurketik, fenauketika, fnauketik
wrongful (adj), fnaurku, fenauku, fnauku
wrongfully (adv), fnaurkiu, fenaukiu, fnaukiu
wrongly (adv), fnaurkiu, fenaukiu, fnaukiu
wrongness (n), fnaurkuet, fenaukueta, fnaukuet
wrote (v pa), loirzdyot, loidio, loidio
wrought (v pa), kiorskyot, kiokio, kiokio
wrung (v pa), kirkirskyot, kirakitio, kirkitio
Ws (let pl), warfi, warfi, warfi
Wyoming (n), Waiominork, Waiominoka, Waiomink
x-ray (n), keizhark, keizhaka, keizhak
x-ray (v), keizharsk, keizhako, keizhako
xenna- (num 1e27 pref), genkai-, genkai-, genkai-
Xenon (n davoka), Alik, Alik, Alik
Xenon (n), Zhenon, Zhenona, Zhenon
xi (n), keshirn, keshina, keshin
Y (let sng), yarle, yarila, yarl
yank (n), kriank, keriana, krian
yank (v), kriansk, keriano, kriano
yantesi-, avuiftai-, avuiftai-, avuftai-

yap (n), kaiarp, kaiapa, kaiap
yap (v), kaiarsp, kaiapo, kaiapo
yapper (n doer), kaiarpwan, kaiapua, kaiapua
yard (n d:field), thauthk, thautha, thauth
yard (n d:measurement), fiark, fiaka, fiak
yardage (n d:measurement), fiarkuet, fiakueta, fiakuet
yardstick (n), fiakshneft, fiakeshineta, fiakshnet
yawn (n), kuiarn, kuiana, kuian
yawn (v), kuiarsne, kuiano, kuiano
yay (interj), kai, kai, kai
yeah (adv), weior, weia, weia
year (n), klorsh, kelosha, klosh
yearbook (n), klorshonade, keloshonuda, kloshond
yearly (adj), klorshu, keloshu, kloshu
yearn (v), koiarsne, koiano, koiano
yeast (n), tshurf, teshufa, tshuf
yell (n), waiart, waiata, waiat
yell (v), waiarst, waiato, waiato
yeller (n doer), waiartwan, waiatua, waiatua
yellow (adj), aldofu, alidoru, alduru
yellow (n), aldof, alidora, aldor
yellow (v), aldosf, alidoro, aldoro
yellowish (adj), aldofeiku, alidoreiku, aldoreiku
yep (adv), weip, weipu, weip
yes (adv), weir, wei, wei
yesterday (adj), weishviurlu, weisheviulu, weishviulu
yesterday (adv), weishviurliu, weisheviuliu, weishviuliu
yesterday (n), weishviurl, weisheviula, weishviul
yesteryear (adj), weishklorshu, weishekeloshu, weishkloshu
yesteryear (adv), weishklorshiu, weishekeloshiu, weishkloshiu
yesteryear (n), weishklorsh, weishekelosha, weishklosh
yet (adv/conj), warshk, washiku, washk
yield (n), yadirt, yadita, yadit
yield (v), yadirst, yadito, yadito
yielder (n doer), yadirtwan, yaditua, yaditua
yikes (interj), waik, waika, waik
yogurt (n), wikorn, wikona, wikon
yoke (n), nutraft, nuterafa, nutraf
yoke (v), nutrafst, nuterafo, nutrafo
yonder (adj), yeralu, yerilu, yerlu
yonder (adv), yeraliu, yeriliu, yerliu
yotta- (num 1e24 pref), venkai-, venkai-, venkai-
you (pron 2nd pl obj), kair, kair, kair
you (pron 2nd pl sub), kair, kair, kair
you (pron 2nd sng obj), kail, kail, kail
you (pron 2nd sng sub), kail, kail, kail
young (adj), walirshu, walishu, walshu
younger (adj), walirshwelu, walishwelu, walshwelu
youngest (adj), walirshwaku, walishwaku, walshwaku
youngster (n), walirshuet, walishueta, walshuet
your (pron 2nd pl pos sub), kairsh, kairsh, kairsh
your (pron 2nd sng pos sub), kaish, kaish, kaish
yours (pron 2nd pl pos obj), kairsh, kairsh, kairsh
yours (pron 2nd sng pos obj), kaish, kaish, kaish
yourself (pron 2nd sng refl), kaishfal, kaishfal, kaishfal
yourselves (pron 2nd pl refl), kaishfar, kaishfar, kaishfar
youth (n), walirsh, walisha, walsh
youthful (adj), walirshu, walishu, walshu
yow (interj), yaua, yaua, yaua
Ys (let pl), yarli, yarli, yarli
Ytterbium (n davoka), Orif, Orif, Orif
Ytterbium (n), Iterbium, Iterobiuma, Iterbium
Yttrium (n davoka), Ilap, Ilap, Ilap
Yttrium (n), Itrium, Iteriuma, Itrium
yuck (interj), kwak, kwaka, kwak
yuck (n), kuark, kuaka, kuak
yucky (adj), kuarku, kuaku, kuaku
Yugoslavia (n), Yugoshlarve, Yugoshelava, Yugoshlav
yum (interj), kwam, kwama, kwam
yummy (interj), kwami, kwami, kwami
yummy (n), kuarme, kuama, kuam
yup (adv), weip, weipu, weip
Z (let sng), zal, zala, za
zag (n), zhafk, zhafa, zhaf
zag (v), zhafsk, zhafo, zhafo
zantri-, hemiftai-, hemiftai-, hemiftai-
zap (n), zhauthk, zhautha, zhauth
zap (v), zhauthsk, zhautho, zhautho
zero (num 0 card), shut, shut, shut
zeroth (num 0 ord), shuteth, shuteth, shuteth
zeta (n), zhetarn, zhetana, zhetan
zetta- (num 1e21 pref), kinkai-, kinkai-, kinkai-
Zh (let sng), zhal, zhala, zha
Zhs (let pl), zhali, zhali, zhali
zig (n), zhifk, zhifa, zhif
zig (v), zhifsk, zhifo, zhifo
zigzag (n), zhifzhafk, zhifezhafa, zhifzhaf
zigzag (v), zhifzhafsk, zhifezhafo, zhifzhafo
Zinc (n davoka), Ifit, Ifit, Ifit
Zinc (n), Zhink, Zhinoka, Zhink
zing (n), zhiaurk, zhiauka, zhiauk
zing (v), zhiaursk, zhiauko, zhiauko
zip (v), zheifst, zheifo, zheifo
zipper (n doer), zheiftwan, zheifua, zheifua
zipper (v), zheifuarsne, zheifuano, zheifuano
zippily (adv), zheiftiu, zheifiu, zheifiu
zippy (adj), zheiftu, zheifu, zheifu
Zirconium (n davoka), Ilip, Ilip, Ilip
Zirconium (n), Zhirkonium, Zhirakoniuma, Zhirkonium
zone (n), zhiorn, zhiena, zhien
zone (v), zhiersne, zhieno, zhieno
zoo (n), buirf, buifa, buif
zoom (adj), bufirku, bufiku, bufku
zoom (n), bufirk, bufika, bufk
zoom (v), bufirsk, bufiko, bufko
Zs (let pl), zali, zali, zali
Zurich (n), Zhurifk, Zhurika, Zhurik

12

Dahmek to English Crossreference

This list is sorted by the English alphabet for convenience of Earth people. However, Damiriak dictionaries would sort the list by Deibuth alphabetical order.

adrokiu, o'clock (adv)
Afap, Potassium (n davoka)
afblurst, absent (v)
afblurt, absence (n)
afblurtiu, absently (adv)
afblurtu, absent (adj)
afblurtwan, absenter (n doer)
afebelprin, overconfidence (n)
afebelpriniu, overconfidently (adv)
afebelprinu, overconfident (adj)
afebiorast, overpower (v)
afebiurst, overstate (v)
afebiurt, overstatement (n)
afeblersf, overcome (v)
afeblersfyot, overcame (v pa)
afebriark, overuse (n)
afebriarsk, overuse (v)
afedaurn, overtime (n)
afedefrup, overcapacity (n)
afediarp, overdrive (n)
afedorklarst, overspend (v)
afedorklarstyot, overspent (v pa)
afefiurk, overproduction (n)
afefiursk, overproduce (v)
afeflark, overdraft (n)
afeflarsk, overdraft (v)
afeflausne, overblow (v)
afeflausnyot, overblew (v pa)
afefrafk, overcoat (n)
afefrifsk, overstock (v)
afefruifk, overplay (n)
afefruifsk, overplay (v)

afefuarst, overview (v)
afefuart, overview (n)
afeglishsk, overstep (v)
afegloifst, overcharge (v)
afegloift, overcharge (n)
afeglorif, overboard (n)
afegloruzge, overreach (v)
afegorsk, overtake (v)
afegorskyot, overtook (v pa)
afekaimesp, overturn (v)
afekiork, overwork (n)
afekiorsk, overwork (v)
afekitersh, overkill (n)
afekriarf, overqualification (n)
afekriarsf, overqualify (v)
afekurst, overheat (v)
afelairsh, overjoy (n)
afelaorzme, overrun (v)
afelaorzmyot, overran (v pa)
afelarast, overrule (v)
afeloirzde, overwrite (v)
afeloirzdyot, overwrote (v pa)
afeludars, overrepresent (v)
afeludarsh, overrepresentation (n)
afelunirt, overpass (n)
afelupalirst, overreact (v)
afelupalirt, overreaction (n)
afemoirme, overpayment (n)
afemoirzme, overpay (v)
afemoirzmyot, overpaid (v pa)
afemuarn, overnight (n)
afemuarniu, overnight (adv)

afemuarnu, overnight (adj)
afemuarnwan, overnighter (n doer)
afemuarsne, overnight (v)
afemuthsk, overmatch (v)
afen, over (n)
afenarf, overture (n)
afenbrauf, overflow (n)
afenbrausf, overflow (v)
afenierst, overeat (v)
afenierstyot, overate (v pa)
afeniu, overly (adv)
afeniunirf, overabundance (n)
afenkeft, overhead (n)
afenlor, overalls (n)
afenloriu, overall (adv)
afenloru, overall (adj)
afenorisherzge, oversubscribe (v)
afenreirzge, overlook (v)
afenthaurf, sovereignty (n)
afenthaurfiu, sovereignly (adv)
afenthaurfwan, sovereign (n doer)
afenthinarp, overestimate (n)
afenthinarsp, overestimate (v)
afentisk, overdo (v)
afentiskyot, overdid (v pa)
afenu, over (adv/adv/prep)
afenuyasne, overhear (v)
afenuyasnyot, overheard (v pa)
afepaltark, overactivity (n)
afepaltarku, overactive (adj)
afeparzve, overfeed (v)
afeplersth, overstuff (v)

afepoefirst, overshadow (v)
afepruls, oversleep (v)
afeprulsyot, overslept (v pa)
aferaufpu, overland (adj)
aferiesf, overlie (v)
aferiesfyot, overlay (v pa)
afeshalirn, oversimplification (n)
afeshalirsne, oversimplify (v)
afeshenirsk, overtax (v)
afeshethirp, oversupply (n)
afeshethirsp, oversupply (v)
afeshkleirn, overseas (n)
afeshkleirniu, overseas (adv)
afeshkleirnu, overseas (adj)
afeshkorst, overshoot (v)
afeshkorstyot, overshot (v pa)
afeshkort, overshoot (n)
afeshlers, overfish (v)
afeshlirbe, override (n)
afeshlirzbe, override (v)
afeshlirzbyot, overrode (v pa)
afeshluarp, overhaul (n)
afeshluarpwan, overhauler (n
    doer)
afeshluarsp, overhaul (v)
afeshuarzge, oversize (v)
afeshuirsh, overweight (n)
afetarage, overhang (n)
afetarazge, overhang (v)
afetarazgyot, overhung (v pa)
afetarthk, overthrow (n)
afetarthsk, overthrow (v)
afetarthskyot, overthrew (v pa)
afeterame, overreliance (n)
afeterazme, overrely (v)
afeterzbe, overrate (v)
afethiurst, overlap (v)
afethiurt, overlap (n)
afethulsth, oversee (v)
afethulsthyot, oversaw (v pa)
afethulth, oversight (n)
afethulthwan, overseer (n doer)
afetirofsp, overprice (v)
afetiurku, overdue (adj)
afetorsth, overdose (v)
afetorth, overdose (n)
afetrelirsf, oversell (v)
afetrelirsfyot, oversold (v pa)
afetrilf, overtone (n)
afetulak, overexposure (n)
afetulask, overexpose (v)
afetulirtu, overcast (adj)
afevaurp, overvalue (n)
afevaursp, overvalue (v)
afeviarzge, overcrowd (v)
afevorast, overbuild (v)
afevorastyot, overbuilt (v pa)
afevorave, overpopulation (n)
afevorazve, overpopulate (v)
afevornst, overbook (v)
Afip, Calcium (n davoka)
Afkansharn, Afghanistan (n)
Afkarn, Afghan (n)

afkiark, abdication (n)
afkiarkwan, abdicator (n doer)
afkiarsk, abdicate (v)
afligralge, absolution (n)
afligralgiu, absolutely (adv)
afligralgu, absolute (adj)
afligralzge, absolve (v)
aflurst, overload (v)
aflurt, overload (n)
aflurtwan, overloader (n doer)
afranist, overlay (v)
afranistyot, overlaid (v pa)
afranit, overlay (n)
Afrikarn, African (n)
Afrilk, Africa (n)
aftap, establishment (n)
aftapwan, establisher (n doer)
aftasp, establish (v)
agubiarsh, goddess (n)
agubimashel, godmother (n)
agubirde, god (n)
agubirdmenu, godless (adj)
agubirdu, godly (adj)
agubivotert, godfather (n)
agubizhairp, godsend (n)
ailarst, study (v)
ailart, study (n)
ailartiu, studiously (adv)
ailartu, studious (adj)
ailartwan, student (n doer)
aindufirt, diacritic (n)
aindufirtiu, diacritically (adv)
aindufirtu, diacritical (adj)
ainelirk, diagram (n)
ainelirku, diagrammatic (adj)
ainelirsk, diagram (v)
ainmurk, diagonal (n)
ainmurkiu, diagonally (adv)
ainmurku, diagonal (adj)
ainpirn, diameter (n)
ainrift, dialect (n)
ainriftu, dialectic (adj)
ainriftu, dialectical (adj)
ainuarn, diaper (n)
ainuarsne, diaper (v)
aiorf, ion (n)
aiorfu, ionic (adj)
aiorfwan, ionizer (n doer)
aiorsf, ionize (v)
aishmarn, diagnosis (n)
aishmarnt, diagnostic (n)
aishmarnu, diagnostic (adj)
aishmarsne, diagnose (v)
aishsk, vie (v)
Akap, Lithium (n davoka)
Akip, Beryllium (n davoka)
Aktinium, Actinium (n)
Alap, Rubidium (n davoka)
Albarme, Alabama (n)
Albertarf, Alberta (n)
aldof, yellow (n)
aldofeiku, yellowish (adj)
aldofu, yellow (adj)

aldosf, yellow (v)
alfarn, alpha (n)
alfavuka, Number_1e159
alfdaka, Number_1e183
alfe, A (let sng)
alferp, alphabet (n)
alferpiu, alphabetically (adv)
alferpu, alphabetic (adj)
alfersp, alphabetize (v)
alfgenka, Number_1e177
alfhemfk, Number_1e276
alfhemft, Number_1e246
alfhemka, Number_1e156
alfhemshk, Number_1e216
alfhemsht, Number_1e186
alfi, As (let pl)
alfirika, Number_1e162
alfkinka, Number_1e171
alfmuika, Number_1e180
alftirika, Number_1e168
alfvenka, Number_1e174
alfyufika, Number_1e165
Alik, Xenon (n davoka)
Alip, Strontium (n davoka)
Alishork, Alaska (n)
altakwast, mentor (v)
altakwat, mentor (n)
altark, mentality (n)
altarkiu, mentally (adv)
altarku, mental (adj)
altirp, mention (n)
altirsp, mention (v)
aluka, hello (interj)
Aluminum, Aluminum (n)
Amerikium, Americium (n)
Amirk, America (n)
Amirkan, American (n)
amolazhe, interest (n d:finance)
Amshterdarm, Amsterdam (n)
Anap, Francium (n davoka)
anarot, hangar (n)
anberk, amputation (n)
anberniu, amply (adv)
anbernu, ample (adj)
anbersk, amputate (v)
anbetarn, amplitude (n)
anbidarl, embellishment (n)
anbidarsle, embellish (v)
anbiorast, empower (v)
anbiorat, empowerment (n)
anbiuge, embroilment (n)
anbiuzge, embroil (v)
anbotark, empathy (n)
anbotarsk, empathize (v)
anbugor, ember (n)
andauf, empire (n)
andaufuet, imperialism (n)
andaufuetu, imperial (adj)
andaufuetwan, imperialist (n
    doer)
andaufwan, emperor (n doer)
andilst, enlist (v)

andilt, enlistment (n)
andiofk, entrenchment (n)
andiofsk, entrench (v)
andreirf, entrustment (n)
andreirsf, entrust (v)
andutarsk, ensue (v)
anegaifork, embitterment (n)
anegaiforsk, embitter (v)
anegiarst, emboss (v)
anegiart, embossment (n)
anegurshk, enticement (n)
anegurshsk, entice (v)
anenirkel, enumeration (n)
anenirkesle, enumerate (v)
anfalar, enrollment (n)
anfalaruin, enrollee (n)
anfalarwan, enroller (n doer)
anfalasre, enroll (v)
anflaurfst, enliven (v)
anfluarn, enlightenment (n)
anfluarsne, enlighten (v)
anfualf, envoy (n)
angai, ugh (interj)
Anip, Radium (n davoka)
Ankarsh, English (n)
ankenirpiu, emphatically (adv)
ankenirpu, emphatic (adj)
Anklarn, England (n)
Ankolarf, Angola (n)
Ankorarzh, Anchorage (n)
anlafp, emergence (n)
anlafpik, emergency (n)
anlafsp, emerge (v)
anlark, alien (n)
anlarku, alienable (adj)
anlarsk, alienate (v)
anlefnisk, encompass (v)
anloshst, embargo (v)
anlosht, embargo (n)
anmithk, entailment (n)
anmithsk, entail (v)
anoberst, amplify (v)
anobert, amplification (n)
anobertwan, amplifier (n doer)
anovafirt, empiricism (n)
anovafirtiu, empirically (adv)
anovafirtu, empiric (adj)
anovafirtu, empirical (adj)
anovafirtwan, empiricist (n doer)
anpirn, amp (n d:ampere)
anplirk, embankment (n)
anplirsk, embank (v)
anplive, emigration (n)
anplivwan, emigrant (n doer)
anplizve, emigrate (v)
anploifst, embrace (v)
anploift, embracement (n)
anpranp, encapsulation (n)
anpranpwan, encapsulator (n doer)
anpransp, encapsulate (v)
anrauf, emanation (n)
anraufelk, emancipation (n)

anraufelsk, emancipate (v)
anrausf, emanate (v)
ans, empty (v)
ansh, emptiness (n)
anshkorbe, embarkation (n)
anshkorzbe, embark (v)
anshlarde, embodiment (n)
anshlark, embezzlement (n)
anshlarsk, embezzle (v)
anshlarzde, embody (v)
anshraifp, enslavement (n)
anshraifpwan, enslaver (n doer)
anshraifsp, enslave (v)
anshu, empty (adj)
antaigarge, entanglement (n)
antaigarzge, entangle (v)
anthralve, ensemble (n)
anthreilp, entrapment (n)
anthreilsp, entrap (v)
antikoarme, emblem (n)
antikoarmu, emblematic (adj)
Antimoni, Antimony (n)
antuvasne, embalm (v)
anuiart, embryo (n)
anuiartu, embryonic (adj)
anvaltor, encirclement (n)
anvaltosre, encircle (v)
anvolarst, encode (v)
anvolartwan, encoder (n doer)
apafirp, hydration (n)
apafirpu, hydralic (adj)
apafirpwan, hydrater (n doer)
apafirsp, hydrate (v)
apafpekirp, hydrocarbon (n)
Apap, Hydrogen (n davoka)
Apip, Helium (n davoka)
ar, oh (interj)
Arap, Cesium (n davoka)
araup, inland (n)
araupu, inland (adj)
arbar, infancy (n)
arbarkoirk, infanticide (n)
arbarwan, infant (n doer)
arbauf, intuition (n)
arbaufiu, intuitively (adv)
arbaufu, intuitive (adj)
arbausf, intuit (v)
Arbe, Arab (n)
arbist, invest (v)
arbit, investment (n)
arbitak, investigation (n)
arbitaku, investigational (adj)
arbitaku, investigative (adj)
arbitakwan, investigator (n doer)
arbitask, investigate (v)
arbitwan, investor (n doer)
arblarf, inflation (n)
arblarfu, inflatable (adj)
arblarfwan, inflater (n doer)
arblarsf, inflate (v)
arblime, intimidation (n)
arblimwan, intimidator (n doer)
arblizme, intimidate (v)

arborst, staff (v d:people)
arbort, staff (n d:people)
arbortu, staff (adj d:people)
arbortwan, staffer (n doer
   d:people)
arbrekal, incompleteness (n)
arbrekaliu, incompletely (adv)
arbrekalu, incomplete (adj)
arbubrun, independence (n)
arbubruniu, independently (adv)
arbubrunu, independent (adj)
arbubrunwan, independent (n
   doer)
ardaibe, inhibition (n)
ardaibu, inhibitory (adj)
ardaibwan, inhibitor (n doer)
ardaizbe, inhibit (v)
ardauf, inspiration (n)
ardaufiu, inspirationally (adv)
ardaufu, inspirational (adj)
ardausf, inspire (v)
ardiafk, intricacy (n)
ardiafkiu, intricately (adv)
ardiafku, intricate (adj)
ardiashk, intrigue (n)
ardiashkiu, intriguingly (adv)
ardiashsk, intrigue (v)
ardrik, increase (n)
ardrikiu, increasingly (adv)
ardrisk, increase (v)
arfekiark, invincibility (n)
arfekiarku, invincible (adj)
arfiaish, invisibility (n)
arfiaishiu, invisibly (adv)
arfiaishu, invisible (adj)
arfirame, inconvenience (n)
arfiramiu, inconveniently (adv)
arfiramu, inconvenient (adj)
arflershiu, incredibly (adv)
arflershu, incredible (adj)
arfpwan, eker (n doer)
arfsp, eke (v)
arfu, old (adj)
arfwak, oldest (n)
arfwaku, oldest (adj)
arfwel, older (n)
arfwelu, older (adj)
argef, inference (n)
Argentirn, Argentina (n)
argesf, infer (v)
Argon, Argon (n)
argrushst, include (v)
argrusht, inclusion (n)
argrushtiu, inclusively (adv)
argrushtu, inclusive (adj)
Arip, Barium (n davoka)
Arizhorn, Arizona (n)
Arkanorsh, Arkansas (n)
arkark, inducement (n)
arkarkiu, inductively (adv)
arkarku, inductive (adj)
arkarkwan, inducer (n doer)
arkarsk, induce (v)

arkarthp, invalidation (n)
arkarthpu, invalid (adj)
arkarthsp, invalidate (v)
arkemirf, involvement (n)
arkemirfiu, involuntarily (adv)
arkemirfu, involuntary (adj)
arkemirsf, involve (v)
arkiabark, intoxication (n)
arkiabarkwan, intoxicant (n doer)
arkiabarsk, intoxicate (v)
arkiark, indication (n)
arkiarkiu, indicatively (adv)
arkiarku, indicative (adj)
arkiarkwan, indicator (n doer)
arkiarsk, indicate (v)
arkik, infliction (n)
arkisk, inflict (v)
arkrakfrelp, invulnerability (n)
arkrakfrelpu, invulnerable (adj)
arkroif, incline (n)
arkroifet, inclination (n)
arkroisf, incline (v)
arkuarfk, indirection (n)
arkuarfkiu, indirectly (adv)
arkuarfku, indirect (adj)
arlalk, incest (n)
arlalku, incestual (adj)
arleifarn, inundation (n)
arleifarsne, inundate (v)
arlerk, intimacy (n)
arlerkiu, intimately (adv)
arlerku, intimate (adj)
arlern, income (n)
arlersk, intimate (v)
Arlingtorn, Arlington (n)
arlubirshiu, irretrievably (adv)
arlubirshu, irretrievable (adj)
arlubolirkiu, irreparably (adv)
arlubolirku, irreparable (adj)
arlubreshu, irreplaceable (adj)
arluduverk, irresponsibility (n)
arluduverkiu, irresponsibly (adv)
arluduverku, irresponsible (adj)
arlufabarkiu, irrefutably (adv)
arlufabarku, irrefutable (adj)
arlurolarme, irreconciliation (n)
arlurolarmu, irreconcilable (adj)
arlutelkiu, irresistibly (adv)
arlutelku, irresistible (adj)
arlutharafiu, irreversibly (adv)
arlutharatu, irreversible (adj)
arluthurkiu, irrespectively (adv)
arluthurku, irrespective (adj)
arluvirp, irregularity (n)
arluvirpiu, irregularly (adv)
arluvirpu, irregular (adj)
Armenarn, Armenian (n)
Armern, Armenia (n)
armiaf, innovation (n)
armiafiu, innovatively (adv)
armiafu, innovative (adj)
armiafwan, innovator (n doer)
armiarst, influence (v)

armiart, influence (n)
armiartiu, influentially (adv)
armiartu, influential (adj)
armiartwan, influencer (n doer)
armiasf, innovate (v)
armikart, innocence (n)
armikartiu, innocently (adv)
armikartu, innocent (adj)
armoirve, irradiation (n)
armoirzve, irradiate (v)
arnaushu, inward (adj)
arnoin, injury (n)
arnoinwan, injurer (n doer)
arnoisne, injure (v)
arpaibu, intact (adj)
arpeikarn, invigoration (n)
arpeikarsne, invigorate (v)
arpifk, intent (n)
arpifk, intention (n)
arpifkiu, intentionally (adv)
arpifkiu, intently (adv)
arpifku, intentional (adj)
arpifp, intensity (n)
arpifpiu, intensely (adv)
arpifpiu, intensively (adv)
arpifpu, intense (adj)
arpifpu, intensive (adj)
arpifsk, intend (v)
arpifsp, intensify (v)
arpirp, internal (n)
arpirpiu, internally (adv)
arpirpu, internal (adj)
arpirpuet, internalization (n)
arpirsp, internalize (v)
arpoit, instinct (n)
arpoitiu, instinctively (adv)
arpoitu, instinctive (adj)
arshairk, invocation (n)
arshairsk, invoke (v)
Arshenik, Arsenic (n)
arshest, insert (v)
arshet, insertion (n)
arshetuin, insert (v)
arshetwan, inserter (n doer)
arshiaf, insanity (n)
arshiafiu, insanely (adv)
arshiafu, insane (adj)
arshiat, inquest (n)
arshiatuet, inquisition (n)
arshiatwan, inquisitor (n doer)
arshlek, instruction (n)
arshlekiu, instructionally (adv)
arshlekiu, instructively (adv)
arshleku, instructional (adj)
arshleku, instructive (adj)
arshlekwan, instructor (n doer)
arshlesk, instruct (v)
arshort, inevitability (n)
arshortiu, inevitably (adv)
arshortu, inevitable (adj)
arshparst, index (v)
arshpart, index (n)
arshpartwan, indexer (n doer)

arshpartyek, indices (n pl)
arshpelst, institute (v)
arshpelt, institute (n)
arshpeltuest, institutionalize (v)
arshpeltuet, institution (n)
arshpeltuetiu, institutionally
    (adv)
arshpeltuetu, institutional (adj)
arshpest, instate (v)
arshualf, isolation (n)
arshualfar, isolationist (n)
arshualfuet, isolationism (n)
arshualfwan, isolator (n doer)
arshualsf, isolate (v)
arteirp, installation (n)
arteirp, installment (n)
arteirpwan, installer (n doer)
arteirsp, install (v)
artelk, insistence (n)
artelkiu, insistently (adv)
artelku, insistent (adj)
artelsk, insist (v)
arthairp, invoice (n)
arthairsp, invoice (v)
artharak, inverse (n)
artharakiu, inversely (adv)
artharaku, inverse (adj)
artharakuet, inversion (n)
artharakwan, inverter (n doer)
artharask, invert (v)
arthiamfluirku, streetwise (adj)
arthiamgeral, streetcar (n)
arthiarme, street (n)
arthish, insect (n)
arthufirshiu, irreverently (adv)
arthufirshu, irreverent (adj)
arthuk, inspection (n)
arthukwan, inspector (n doer)
arthumarp, invariant (n)
arthumarpu, invariably (adj)
arthushort, irrationality (n)
arthushortiu, irrationally (adv)
arthushortu, irrational (adj)
arthusk, inspect (v)
artidar, initiative (n)
artidat, initial (n)
artide, initiation (n)
artidiu, initially (adv)
artidu, initial (adj)
artidwan, initiator (n doer)
artizde, initiate (v)
artoirp, incentive (n)
artrep, instance (n)
artrepiu, instantly (adv)
artreptoirtiu, instantaneously
    (adv)
artreptoirtu, instantaneous (adj)
artrepu, instant (adj)
artresp, instantiate (v)
artrinort, intolerance (n)
artrinortiu, intolerably (adv)
artrinortu, intolerable (adj)
artruifk, irrelevance (n)

artruifk, irrelevancy (n)
artruifku, irrelevant (adj)
aruf, woof (interj)
arvanst, insult (v)
arvant, insult (n)
arvantwan, insulter (n doer)
arvaurpu, invaluable (adj)
arvirst, infect (v)
arvirt, infection (n)
arvirtu, infectious (adj)
arvirtu, infective (adj)
arvorn, information (n)
arvorniu, informatively (adv)
arvornu, informative (adj)
arvornwan, informer (n doer)
arvorsne, inform (v)
arvust, input (v)
arvut, input (n)
arvutwan, inputer (n doer)
arwafk, inhalant (n)
arwafkuet, inhalation (n)
arwafkwan, inhaler (n doer)
arwafsk, inhale (v)
arzhank, invasion (n)
arzhankiu, invasively (adv)
arzhanku, invasive (adj)
arzhankwan, invader (n doer)
arzhansk, invade (v)
Ashap, Ununennium (n davoka)
Aship, Unbinilium (n davoka)
ashloirst, employ (v)
ashloirt, employment (n)
ashloirtu, employable (adj)
ashloirtwan, employer (n doer)
ashpedaurniu, oftentimes (adv)
ashpiliu, often (adv)
Ashtatin, Astatine (n)
Atap, Sodium (n davoka)
Atelanirt, Atlanta (n)
Atelantirk, Atlantic (n)
Atelantirsh, Atlantis (n)
athefoshar, atmosphere (n)
athefoshariu, atmospherically (adv)
athefosharu, atmospheric (adj)
Atip, Magnesium (n davoka)
aua, ow (interj)
aularku, aerobic (adj)
aularn, aerial (n)
aularnu, aerial (adj)
aulbielurk, airport (n)
aulgralp, aerosol (n)
auliartu, aeronautical (adj)
auliartyek, aeronautics (n pl)
auliunk, omen (n)
auliunkiu, ominously (adv)
auliunku, ominous (adj)
aulkarfp, aircraft (n)
aulkarfpyek, aircraft (n pl)
aulnufaf, airbag (n)
aulothirk, airfare (n)
aulpliorl, airway (n)
aulprant, airfield (n)

aulroifk, airline (n)
aultuiarfu, aerodynamic (adj)
aultuiarfyek, aerodynamics (n pl)
aurk, ailment (n)
aurkwan, ailer (n doer)
aursk, ail (v)
aush, ash (n)
aushbiarme, ashtray (n)
Aushimark, Admiral (n)
Aushtarf, Austria (n)
Aushtarnf, Austrian (n)
Aushtirn, Austin (n)
Aushtralarn, Australian (n)
Aushtralf, Australia (n)
aushwan, asher (n doer)
auta, ouch (inter)
authushp, aerospace (n)
avaifalt, duet (n)
avairf, duality (n)
avairfiu, dually (adv)
avairfu, dual (adj)
avairk, boolean (n)
avairku, boolean (adj)
aveth, second (num 2 ord)
avethar, secondary (n)
avetharu, secondary (adj)
avethiu, secondly (adv d:count)
avethkarpu, secondhand (adj)
aviurth, dilemma (n)
aviurthu, dilemmic (adj)
avu, two (num 2 card)
avualfhemka, Number_1e8256
avuda, twenty (num 20 card)
avudai-, twenty- (num 20 pref)
avudeth, twentieth (num 20 ord)
avuft, duet (n)
avugiorkwan, tweezer (n doer)
avugiorsk, tweeze (v)
avuifk, duoquadragintillion (num 1e129 card)
avuift, duotrigintillion (num 1e99 card)
avuiftai-, yantesi-
avuifteth, duotrigintillionth (num 1e99 ord)
avuikoshk, tandem (n)
avuikoshku, tandem (adj)
avuka, billion (num 1e9 card)
avukai-, giga- (num 1e9 pref)
avuketh, billionth (num 1e9 ord)
avupa, twelve (num 12 card)
avupai-, twelv- (num 12 pref)
avupeth, twelfth (num 12 ord)
avushk, duovigintillion (num 1e69 card)
avushkai-, itesa-
avushketh, duovigintillionth (num 1e69 ord)
avusht, duodecillion (num 1e39 card)
avushtai-, tekatri- (num 1e39

pref)
avushteth, duodecillionth (num 1e39 ord)
avuth, twice (adv)
Azherbaizharn, Azerbaijan (n)
bafiark, cavalry (n)
bafirk, strictness (n)
bafirkiu, strictly (adv)
bafirku, strict (adj)
bafirt, junction (n)
bafirtu, junctional (adj)
Bagdarde, Baghdad (n)
bahem, Number_1e1656
baiak, sorcery (n)
baiakwan, sorcerer (n doer)
baifarn, victim (n)
baifert, victory (n)
baifertiu, victoriously (adv)
baifertu, victorious (adj)
baifirk, gadget (n)
baifirku, gadgety (adj)
baifk, victimization (n)
baifkmeniu, victimlessly (adv)
baifkmenu, victimless (adj)
baifkwan, victor (n doer)
baiforst, source (v)
baifort, source (n)
baifortwan, sourcer (n doer)
baifsk, victimize (v)
baimart, sorrow (n)
baimartu, sorry (adj)
bairge, sort (n)
bairgwan, sorter (n doer)
bairk, gage (n)
bairk, gauge (n)
bairme, sore (n)
bairmiu, sorely (adv)
bairmu, sore (adj)
bairsk, gage (v)
bairsk, gauge (v)
bairth, byte (n)
bairzge, sort (v)
baishork, abrasion (n)
baishorkiu, abrasively (adv)
baishorku, abrasive (adj)
baiurk, genesis (n)
baivarst, sour (v)
baivart, sourness (n)
baivartu, sour (adj)
bakiart, tirade (n)
bakirniu, terrifically (adv)
bakirnu, terrific (adj)
bakorshst, terrify (v)
bakorst, terrorize (v)
bakort, terror (n)
bakortiu, terribly (adv)
bakortu, terrible (adj)
bakortwan, terrorist (n doer)
bal, B (let sng)
balbe, dad (n)
balbil, daddy (n)
balfork, calibration (n)
balforkwan, calibrator (n doer)

balforsk, calibrate (v)
bali, Bs (let pl)
balirf, caliber (n)
balirf, calibre (n)
balirp, tardiness (n)
balirpu, tardy (adj)
balirshk, tutorial (n)
balirshkwan, tutor (n doer)
balirshsk, tutor (v)
balirst, post (v d:pole)
balirt, post (n d:pole)
baliushk, postulation (n)
baliushsk, postulate (v)
balsharinfu, postmodern (adj)
balsherge, postscript (n)
baltarf, posture (n)
baltarsf, posture (v)
Baltimorf, Baltimore (n)
Baltirk, Baltic (n)
balvefork, postponement (n)
balveforsk, postpone (v)
balvelarf, posterior (n)
balviurnu, postwar (adj)
bamiark, thorn (n)
bamiarkiu, thornily (adv)
bamiarku, thorny (adj)
bamiarn, thirst (n)
bamiarniu, thirstily (adv)
bamiarnu, thirsty (adj)
bamiarsk, thorn (v)
bamiarsne, thirst (v)
banfalst, paddle (v)
banfalt, paddle (n)
banirf, pad (n)
banirsf, pad (v)
bantiurge, padlock (n)
bantiurzge, padlock (v)
barafdairs, stonecut (v)
barafdairshwan, stonecutter (n
    doer)
barafdairsyot, stonecut (v pa)
barafnolthsk, stonewall (v)
barafshlerf, stoneware (n)
barafst, stone (v)
baraft, stone (n)
baraftu, stoney (adj)
baraftwan, stoner (n doer)
baraifant, stonehenge (n)
Barium, Barium (n)
barmort, fanaticism (n)
barmortiu, fanatically (adv)
barmortu, fanatical (adj)
barmortwan, fanatic (n doer)
barmp, fan (n d:follower)
barmpu, fanatic (adj d:follower)
barmthirk, fanfare (n)
barshan, feather (n)
barshasne, feather (v)
bartarde, train (n d:locomotive)
barthk, gender (n d:group)
barthsk, engender (v d:group)
barve, pair (n)
barzve, pair (v)

basharp, authentication (n)
basharpu, authentic (adj)
basharsp, authenticate (v)
bashtal, authority (n)
bashtalwan, author (n doer)
bashtap, authorization (n)
bashtapiu, authoritatively (adv)
bashtapu, authoritative (adj)
bashtasp, authorize (v)
bau, boo (interj)
baufirst, tower (v)
baufirt, tower (n)
bauink, stomp (n)
bauinkwan, stomper (n doer)
bauinsk, stomp (v)
baunk, stamp (n)
baunkoide, stampede (n)
baunkwan, stamper (n doer)
baunsk, stamp (v)
baur, tow (n)
baurf, tuition (n)
baurge, fat (n)
baurgu, fat (adj)
baurgu, fatty (adj)
baurs, towel (v)
baursh, towel (n)
baurshk, jangle (n)
baurshsk, jangle (v)
baurwan, tower (n doer)
baurzge, fatten (v)
baushk, boo (n)
baushkwan, booer (n doer)
baushsk, boo (v)
bausre, tow (v)
bauthk, menses (n)
bavarn, sheep (n)
bavarniu, sheepishly (adv)
bavarnu, sheepish (adj)
bavarnyek, sheep (n pl)
bavarp, steepness (n)
bavarpiu, steeply (adv)
bavarpu, steep (adj)
bavarsh, steeple (n)
bavarsp, steep (v)
bavart, steed (n)
bavashtutart, steeplechase (n)
bediorf, petroleum (n)
befnetiu, instead (adv)
beft, sod (n)
beiburkiu, purportedly (adv)
belbursk, purport (v)
beilbark, dagger (n)
beinart, tumor (n)
beinirf, dome (n)
beinkbaraft, tombstone (n)
beinor, career (n)
beinurk, tomb (n)
beinursk, entomb (v)
beirde, mutt (n)
beirf, polish (n)
beirfwan, polisher (n doer)
beirlak, purpose (n)
beirlakiu, purposely (adv)

beirlaku, purposeful (adj)
beirlask, purpose (v)
beirme, fin (n)
beirp, flinch (n)
beirpwan, flincher (n doer)
beirs, flirt (v)
beirsf, polish (v)
beirsh, flirtation (n)
beirshak, pursuit (n)
beirshakiu, pursuantly (adv)
beirshaku, pursuant (adj)
beirshask, pursue (v)
beirshu, flirtatious (adj)
beirshwan, flirt (n doer)
beirsp, flinch (v)
beirsth, purse (v)
beirtast, purchase (v)
beirtat, purchase (n)
beirtatwan, purchaser (n doer)
beirth, purse (n)
Beiruft, Beirut (n)
beiukviurl, doomsday (n)
beiurk, doom (n)
beiursk, doom (v)
beivage, fling (n)
beivagu, flingy (adj)
beivagwan, flinger (n doer)
beivap, flip (n)
beivapiu, flippily (adv)
beivapu, flippy (adj)
beivapwan, flipper (n doer)
beivasp, flip (v)
beivazge, fling (v)
beivazgyot, flung (v pa)
Beizhirn, Beijing (n)
belaist, contrast (v)
belait, contrast (n)
belarak, consignment (n)
belarask, consign (v)
belbafk, constriction (n)
belbafkwan, constrictor (n doer)
belbafsk, constrict (v)
belbafst, conjoin (v)
belbaft, conjunction (n)
belbaif, conviction (n)
belbaifwan, convict (n doer)
belbaipiu, convincingly (adv)
belbaisf, convict (v)
belbaisp, convince (v)
belbarkat, conductivity (n)
belbiafarf, consecration (n)
belbiafarsf, consecrate (v)
belblust, consent (v)
belblut, consent (n)
belblutat, consensus (n)
belblutu, consensual (adj)
belbost, confuse (v)
belbot, confusion (n)
belbotiu, confusingly (adv)
belbrelf, condensation (n)
belbrelfit, condensate (n)
belbrelfwan, condenser (n doer)
belbrelsf, condense (v)

beldifort, contraption (n)
beldrest, concentrate (v)
beldret, concentration (n)
beldretwan, concentrator (n doer)
beldrolme, constellation (n)
beldrolzme, constellate (v)
belfadek, consortium (n)
belfadekwan, consort (n doer)
belfadesk, consort (v)
belfdauf, conspiracy (n)
belfdaufu, conspiratorial (adj)
belfdaufwan, conspirator (n doer)
belfdausf, conspire (v)
belfialst, consume (v)
belfialt, consumption (n)
belfialtwan, consumer (n doer)
belfime, convention (n)
belfimu, conventional (adj)
belfirme, convenience (n)
belfirmiu, conveniently (adv)
belfirmu, convenient (adj)
belfizme, convene (v)
belflars, confront (v)
belflarsh, confrontation (n)
belflarshu, confrontational (adj)
belfoirt, convex (n)
belfoirtu, convex (adj)
belfp, concern (n)
belfsp, concern (v)
belfuarl, conveyance (n)
belfuarlk, convoy (n)
belfuarlu, conveyable (adj)
belfuarlwan, conveyor (n doer)
belfuarsle, convey (v)
belgalf, concurrence (n)
belgalf, concurrency (n)
belgalfiu, concurrently (adv)
belgalfu, concurrent (adj)
belgalnaf, concealment (n)
belgalnafwan, concealer (n doer)
belgalnasf, conceal (v)
belgalsf, concur (v)
belgalst, contract (v d:shrink)
belgalt, contraction (n d:shrink)
belgeft, conferment (n)
belgelf, conference (n)
belgelfuin, conferee (n)
belgelfwan, conferor (n doer)
belgelsf, confer (v)
belgerzge, condone (v)
Belgiarn, Belgian (n)
Belgiurme, Belgium (n)
belglap, conglomerate (n)
belglasp, conglomerate (v)
belgost, concrete (v)
belgot, concrete (n)
belgotu, concrete (adj)
belgrilk, consolation (n d:comfort)
belgrilsk, console (v d:comfort)
belgrust, conclude (v)
belgrut, conclusion (n)
belgrutiu, conclusively (adv)

belgrutu, conclusive (adj)
beligarp, consolidation (n)
beligarpwan, consolidator (n doer)
beligarsp, consolidate (v)
belinarp, confiscation (n)
belinarpu, confiscatory (adj)
belinarsp, confiscate (v)
belirge, console (n d:cabinet)
belirn, cone (n)
belirnu, conical (adj)
belkarage, contour (n)
belkarazge, contour (v)
belkavarl, congregation (n)
belkavarlu, congregational (adj)
belkavarsle, congregate (v)
belkemirf, convolvement (n)
belkemirsf, convolve (v)
belkemirst, convolute (v)
belkemirt, convolution (n)
belkik, conflict (n)
belkinp, congratulation (n)
belkinsp, congratulate (v)
belkiorst, contort (v)
belkiort, contortion (n)
belkiraku, conducive (adj)
belkirakwan, conducer (n doer)
belkirask, conduce (v)
belkisk, conflict (v)
belklart, congruence (n)
belklart, congruousness (n)
belklartiu, congruently (adv)
belklartiu, congruously (adv)
belklartu, congruent (adj)
belklartu, congruous (adj)
belkofst, conserve (v)
belkoft, conservation (n)
belkoftan, conservative (n)
belkoftiu, conservatively (adv)
belkoftu, conservative (adj)
belkoftuet, conservatism (n)
belkoftwan, conservationist (n doer)
belkorft, conservatory (n)
belkriuk, conduction (n)
belkriuku, conductive (adj)
belkriukwan, conductor (n doer)
belkriusk, conduct (v)
belkudil, configuration (n)
belkudilwan, configurator (n doer)
belkudisle, configure (v)
belmeirge, convergence (n)
belmeirgu, convergent (adj)
belmeirzge, converge (v)
belmiart, confluence (n)
belmiartu, confluent (adj)
belmirade, connotation (n)
belmirazde, connote (v)
belmiuge, contagion (n)
belmiugiu, contagious (adv)
belneirp, contusion (n)
belneirsp, contuse (v)

belnuf, confession (n)
belnufan, confessional (n)
belnufwan, confessor (n doer)
belnuif, confirmation (n)
belnuisf, confirm (v)
belnusf, confess (v)
belpaibe, contact (n)
belpaibwan, contact (n doer)
belpairve, confederacy (n)
belpairve, confederation (n)
belpairvwan, confederate (n doer)
belpairzve, confederate (v)
belpaizbe, contact (v)
belpaurge, concave (n)
belpaurgiu, concavely (adv)
belpaurgu, concave (adj)
belpaurzge, concave (v)
belpifk, contention (n d:challenge)
belpifku, contentious (adj d:challenge)
belpifkwan, contender (n doer d:challenge)
belpifsk, contend (v d:challenge)
belplairpwan, construer (n doer)
belplairsp, construe (v)
belplurze, condole (v)
belplurzhe, condolence (n)
belprin, confidence (n)
belprinfiu, confidentially (adv)
belprinfu, confidential (adj)
belprinu, confident (adj)
belprinwan, confidant (n doer)
belprisne, confide (v)
belprulk, constraint (n)
belprulsk, constrain (v)
belrilorp, consternation (n)
belrilorsp, consternate (v)
belshant, consonant (n)
belsherge, conscription (n)
belsherzge, conscript (v)
belshifp, conception (n)
belshime, conceit (n)
belship, concept (n)
belshipfrelpiu, conceivably (adv)
belshipfrelpu, conceivable (adj)
belshipiu, conceptually (adv)
belshipu, conceptual (adj)
belshisp, conceive (v)
belshizme, conceit (v)
belshlek, construction (n)
belshleku, constructive (adj)
belshlekwan, constructor (n doer)
belshlesk, construct (v)
belshpelst, constitute (v)
belshpelt, constitution (n)
belshpeltiu, constitutionally (adv)
belshpeltu, constitutional (adj)
belshtibe, context (n)
belshtist, contest (v)
belshtit, contest (n)
belshtitwan, contestant (n doer)
belshufst, consecute (v)

belshuftiu, consecutively (adv)
belshuftu, consecutive (adj)
belshulirst, confound (v)
beltarve, contrition (n)
beltarviu, contritely (adv)
beltarvu, contrite (adj)
beltelk, consistency (n)
beltelkiu, consistently (adv)
beltelku, consistent (adj)
beltelsk, consist (v)
belterp, conjecture (n)
beltersp, conjecture (v)
beltharak, conversion (n)
beltharaku, convertible (adj)
beltharakwan, converter (n doer)
beltharask, convert (v)
beltharf, conversation (n)
beltharfiu, conversationally (adv)
beltharfu, conversational (adj)
beltharfwan, conversationalist (n
    doer)
beltharsf, converse (v)
belthirfst, convect (v)
belthirft, convection (n)
belthirshkiu, concisely (adv)
belthirshku, concise (adj)
belthost, consider (v)
belthot, consideration (n)
belthotaru, considerate (adj)
belthotiu, considerably (adv)
belthotu, considerable (adj)
belthufk, conspectus (n)
belthurfiu, conspicuously (adv)
belthurfu, conspicuous (adj)
beltide, conduit (n)
beltifk, condition (n)
beltifkiu, conditionally (adv)
beltifku, conditional (adj)
beltifkwan, conditioner (n doer)
beltifsk, condition (v)
beltir, continuation (n)
beltiriu, continually (adv)
beltiriu, continuously (adv)
beltiru, continual (adj)
beltiru, continuous (adj)
beltisre, continue (v)
beltrelbe, convulsion (n)
beltrelbiu, convulsedly (adv)
beltrelbu, convulsible (adj)
beltrelk, constant (n)
beltrelkiu, constantly (adv)
beltrelku, constant (adj)
beltrelkuet, constancy (n)
beltrelzbe, convulse (v)
beltriel, contentment (n
    d:satisfied)
beltrieliu, contently (adv
    d:satisfied)
beltrielu, content (adj d:satisfied)
belurt, present (n d:now)
belurtiu, presently (adv d:now)
belvaft, contempt (n)
belvaftu, contemptable (adj)

belvanst, consult (v)
belvant, consultation (n)
belvantwan, consultant (n doer)
belvarfk, contemplation (n)
belvarfsk, contemplate (v)
belvek, concession (n)
belvesk, concede (v)
belviarge, constipation (n)
belviarzge, constipate (v)
belviaurk, condemnation (n)
belviaursk, condemn (v)
belvirfst, confect (v)
belvirft, confection (n)
belvirftar, confectionery (n)
belvorge, congress (n)
belvorgu, congressional (adj)
belvorgwan, congressman (n
    doer)
belvorn, conformity (n)
belvornuet, conformance (n)
belvornwan, conformer (n doer)
belvornwan, conformist (n doer)
belvorsne, conform (v)
belvuast, confine (v)
belvuat, confinement (n)
belzhil, concert (n)
belzhisle, concert (v)
benflide, indeed (adv/interj)
benirf, opinion (n)
benirsf, opine (v)
benkarde, industry (n)
benkardiu, industriously (adv)
benkardu, industrial (adj)
benkardu, industrious (adj)
benkarduet, industrialization (n)
benkardwan, industrialist (n
    doer)
benkarzde, industrialize (v)
benshoit, inside (adj/adv/prep)
benshoit, inside (n)
benshoitwan, insider (n doer)
bentirk, perch (n d:fish)
benufleirthiu, intravenously (adv)
benufleirthu, intravenous (adj)
beriauts, vomit (v)
beriautsh, vomit (n)
Berilium, Beryllium (n)
Berkelium, Berkelium (n)
Berkerl, Berkeley (n)
berkorl, purple (n)
berkorlu, purple (adj)
Berlirn, Berlin (n)
beronde, germ (n)
betarn, beta (n)
beve, dip (v)
Beverlif Hilorsh, Beverly Hills (n)
bevwan, dipper (n doer)
bezve, dip (v)
biafarfu, sacred (adj)
biafark, sacrilege (n)
biafarku, sacriligous (adj)
biafirp, toast (n d:bread)
biafirpu, toasty (adj d:bread)

biafirpwan, toaster (n doer
    d:bread)
biafirsp, toast (v d:bread)
biafirst, sacrifice (v)
biafirt, sacrifice (n)
biafirtiu, sacrificially (adv)
biafirtu, sacrificial (adj)
biafirtwan, sacrificer (n doer)
biagarf, quiver (n)
biagarsf, quiver (v)
biaipu, queer (adj)
biaipwan, queer (n doer)
bial, vibe (n)
bialfk, vibration (n)
bialfku, vibrant (adj)
bialfkuet, vibrancy (n)
bialfkwan, vibrator (n doer)
bialfsk, vibrate (v)
bialk, drink (n d:beverage)
bialkwan, drinker (n doer
    d:beverage)
bialsht, drunkenness (n
    d:intoxicated)
bialshtu, drunk (adj
    d:intoxicated)
bialshtwan, drunk (n doer
    d:intoxicated)
bialshtwan, drunkard (n doer)
bialsk, drink (v d:beverage)
bialskyot, drank (v pa d:beverage)
biandrap, drugstore (n)
biank, drug (n)
Bianorsh, Atheism (n)
Bianorshk, Atheist (n)
biansk, drug (v)
biaplaturk, loudspeaker (n)
biarazge, drown (v)
biarbiu, loudly (adv)
biarbu, loud (adj)
biarbweku, loudest (adj)
biarbwelu, louder (adj)
biarf, doubt (n)
biarfu, doubtful (adj)
biarfwan, doubter (n doer)
biarge, sadness (n)
biargiu, sadly (adv)
biargu, sad (adj)
biark, fanciness (n)
biarkiarn, fantasy (n)
biarkiarniu, fantastically (adv)
biarkiarnu, fantastic (adj)
biarkiarsne, fantasize (v)
biarkiu, fancily (adv)
biarku, fancy (adj)
biarkweku, fanciest (adj)
biarkwel, fancier (n)
biarkwelu, fancier (adj)
biarme, tray (n)
biarnf, maid (n)
biarnt, compound (n d:place)
biars, queen (v)
biarsf, doubt (v)
biarsh, queen (n)

biarsk, fancy (v)
biarst, powder (v)
biart, powder (n)
biarth, womb (n)
biarve, lounge (n)
biarze, party (v d:celebration)
biarzge, sadden (v)
biarzhe, party (n d:celebration)
biarzve, lounge (v)
biashkan, quill (n)
biaufsp, pout (v)
biaushk, sabotage (n)
biaushkwan, saboteur (n doer)
biaushsk, sabotage (v)
biausht, sadism (n)
biaushtu, sadistic (adj)
biaushtwan, sadist (n doer)
bibishk, stutter (n)
bibishsk, stutter (v)
biburf, tattoo (n)
bibursf, tattoo (v)
biburst, total (v)
biburt, total (n)
biburtiu, totally (adv)
biburtuet, totality (n)
bibutarn, totalitarianism (n)
bibutarnwan, totalitarian (n doer)
bidarliu, prettily (adv)
bidarlu, pretty (adj)
bidarlweku, prettiest (adj)
bidarlwelu, prettier (adj)
bidarn, pupil (n d:eye)
bidaurn, optimism (n)
bidaurnal, optimum (n)
bidaurnaliu, optimally (adv)
bidaurnalu, optimal (adj)
bidaurniu, optimistically (adv)
bidaurnu, optimistic (adj)
bidaurnuet, optimization (n)
bidaurnwan, optimist (n doer)
bidaursne, optimize (v)
bidirk, geek (n)
bielikorth, porthole (n)
bielirk, port (n)
bielirkrep, portability (n)
bielirku, portable (adj)
bielirkwan, porter (n doer)
bielirsk, port (v)
bielkart, portal (n)
biendarfk, geography (n)
biendarfkiu, geographically (adv)
biendarfku, geographic (adj)
biendarfku, geographical (adj)
bienirk, stoop (n d:porch)
bienkrenit, geology (n)
bienkrenitiu, geologically (adv)
bienkrenitu, geologic (adj)
bienkrenitu, geological (adj)
bienkrenitwan, geologist (n doer)
bienporft, geometry (n)
bienporftiu, geometrically (adv)
bienporftu, geometric (adj)
bienporftu, geometrical (adj)

biepdaurn, fulltime (n)
biepdaurnu, fulltime (adj)
bierge, sting (n d:bite)
biergu, stingy (adj d:bite)
biergwan, stinger (n doer d:bite)
bierk, stink (n)
bierku, stinky (adj)
bierkwan, stinker (n doer)
bierp, fullness (n)
bierpiu, fully (adv)
bierpu, full (adj)
biersh, environment (n)
biershiu, environmentally (adv)
biershu, environmental (adj)
biershwan, environmentalist (n doer)
biersk, stink (v)
bierskyot, stank (v pa)
biert, gene (n)
biertu, genetic (adj)
biertuet, genetics (n)
biertuetiu, genetically (adv)
biertuetu, genetical (adj)
bierzge, sting (v d:bite)
bierzgyot, stung (v pa d:bite)
biethk, bristle (n)
biethsk, bristle (v)
bietriel, fulfillment (n)
bietriesle, fulfill (v)
bifirt, jacket (n)
biftefloirp, leapfrog (n)
bikiduarp, prototype (n)
bikiduarsp, prototype (v)
bikigirf, protocol (n)
bilbast, helm (v d:tiller)
bilbat, helm (n d:tiller)
bilbushk, varnish (n)
bilbushsk, varnish (v)
bilerp, gang (n)
bilerpwan, gangster (n doer)
bilersp, gang (v)
bilors, shrink (v)
bilorsh, shrinkage (n)
bilorshwan, shrinker (n doer)
bilorst, steer (v d:navigate)
bilorsyot, shrank (v pa)
biluarshu, deluxe (adj)
bilurk, caboose (n)
bimirk, gnat (n)
binark, opposition (n)
binarkar, opposite (n)
binarkaru, opposite (adj)
binarkwan, opponent (n doer)
binarsk, oppose (v)
binort, moment (n)
binortiu, momentarily (adv)
binortu, momentary (adj)
binotarp, momentum (n)
binotarpu, momentous (adj)
binuk, ruth (n)
binukmen, ruthlessness (n)
binukmeniu, ruthlessly (adv)
binukmenu, ruthless (adj)

biodarst, gawk (v)
biodartwan, gawker (n doer)
bionirk, troop (n)
bionirkwan, trooper (n doer)
bionirsk, troop (v)
bionufaf, saddlebag (n)
bior, cheer (n)
biorak, trigger (n)
biorask, trigger (v)
biorast, power (v)
biorat, power (n)
bioratiu, powerfully (adv)
bioratmen, powerlessness (n)
bioratmeniu, powerlessly (adv)
bioratmenu, powerless (adj)
bioratu, powerful (adj)
biorf, randomness (n)
biorfiu, randomly (adv)
biorfmen, cheerlessness (n)
biorfmeniu, cheerlessly (adv)
biorfmenu, cheerless (adj)
biorfu, random (adj)
biorfush, cheerfulness (n)
biorfushiu, cheerfully (adv)
biorfushu, cheerful (adj)
bioriu, cheerily (adv)
biorn, saddle (n)
biorp, gesture (n)
biorsf, randomize (v)
biorshk, stupidity (n)
biorshkiu, stupidly (adv)
biorshku, stupid (adj)
biorshsk, stupify (v)
biorsne, saddle (v)
biorsp, gesture (v)
biorst, toy (v)
biort, toy (n)
biortebartarde, powertrain (n)
biortelitarnk, powerplant (n)
biorthk, quilt (n)
biorthkwan, quilter (n doer)
biorthsk, quilt (v)
biortkiarf, powerhouse (n)
biortshkorbe, powerboat (n)
bioru, cheery (adj)
bioshaishku, stupendous (adj)
bioshkart, stupor (n)
biosre, cheer (v)
birabelkriukwan, semiconductor (n doer)
biral, block (n d:barrier)
biralepal, semifinal (n)
biralwan, blocker (n doer d:barrier)
biramituf, semicolon (n)
birasle, block (v d:barrier)
birek, deal (n)
birekuafif, dealership (n)
birekwan, dealer (n doer)
biresk, deal (v)
bireskyot, dealt (v pa)
birishk, jingle (n)
birishsk, jingle (v)

Birmingarme, Birmingham (n)
birnart, dorsum (n)
birnartu, dorsal (adj)
birshst, feature (v)
birsht, feat (n)
birshtwan, feature (n doer)
bishank, sturdiness (n)
bishankiu, sturdily (adv)
bishanku, sturdy (adj)
bishirk, mite (n)
Bishmuth, Bismuth (n)
bishtark, token (n)
bishtarkwan, tokenizer (n doer)
bishtarsk, tokenize (v)
bitharn, canary (n)
bithsk, simmer (v)
biuark, quirk (n)
biufirst, vaporize (v)
biufirt, vapor (n)
biufirtu, vapid (adj)
biufirtwan, vaporizer (n doer)
biugwan, broiler (n doer)
biuifk, cypher (n)
biukarn, boondoggle (n)
biulorst, crook (v)
biulort, crook (n)
biunk, boyfriend (n)
biurkiu, poorly (adv
    d:unfortunate, bad)
biurku, poor (adj d:unfortunate,
    bad)
biurme, penalty (n)
biurmu, penal (adj)
biurn, boy (n)
biurnfif, boyhood (n)
biurnu, boyish (adj)
biurp, jolt (n)
biursh, apparel (n)
biursp, jolt (v)
biurst, state (v d:say)
biurt, statement (n d:say)
biurth, boon (n)
biurzhe, gig (n)
biurzme, penalize (v)
biuzge, broil (v)
bivarn, sex (n d:gender)
bivarnmenu, sexless (adj)
bivarnuet, sexism (n)
bivarnuetu, sexist (adj)
bivarnuetwan, sexist (n doer)
bivikart, sexuality (n)
bivikartiu, sexually (adv)
bivikartu, sexual (adj)
bivirk, sex (n d:intercourse)
bivirku, sexy (adj d:intercourse)
bivirsk, sex (v d:intercourse)
blafirp, pope (n)
blafist, prompt (v)
blafit, prompt (n)
blafitiu, promptly (adv)
blafitwan, prompter (n doer)
blaiarst, spurt (v)
blairf, volume (n)

blairs, spur (v)
blairsh, spur (n)
blairshu, spurious (adj)
blaishk, butt (n d:strike)
blaishsk, butt (v d:strike)
blaishsp, spurn (v)
blaithdoiart, roundtable (n)
blaithglarudu, roundtrip (adj)
blaithiveil, roundup (n)
blaithkiarf, roundhouse (n)
blaithoveip, roundabout (n)
blaithoveipu, roundabout (adj)
blaithp, round (n)
blaithpiu, roundly (adv)
blaithpu, round (adj)
blaithpuet, roundness (n)
blaithsp, round (v)
blakarsk, thwart (v)
blakir, brake (n)
blakisre, brake (v)
blamiark, bramble (n)
blamiarsk, bramble (v)
blanirf, wallet (n)
blaparn, papa (n)
blarfamor, flatbed (n)
blarfamoru, flatbed (adj)
blarfk, ledge (n)
blarfp, flatness (n d:plain/plane)
blarfpiu, flatly (adv
    d:plain/plane)
blarfpu, flat (adj d:plain/plane)
blarfraufp, flatland (n)
blarfsp, flatten (v d:plain/plane)
blarige, shingle (n)
blarizge, shingle (v)
blarn, lady (n)
blarp, pa (n)
blars, press (v)
blarsh, press (n)
blarshst, flake (v)
blarsht, flake (n)
blarshtiu, flakily (adv)
blarshtu, flakey (adj)
blarshtwan, flaker (n doer)
blarshwan, presser (n doer)
blart, lad (n d:boy)
blarth, bran (n)
blaship, pressure (n)
blashipwan, pressurizer (n doer)
blashisp, pressure (v)
blashparst, pressurize (v)
blashpart, pressurization (n)
blauk, honk (n)
blaukwan, honker (n doer)
blaumesp, bog (v)
blaump, bog (n)
blaurge, twang (n)
blaurzge, twang (v)
blausk, honk (v)
blauthsk, wither (v)
blefvark, comeback (n)
blegart, classic (n)
blegartu, classical (adj)

bleif, dub (n)
bleifwan, dubber (n doer)
bleinork, compromise (n)
bleinorkwan, compromiser (n
    doer)
bleinorsk, compromise (v)
bleirfk, bleach (n)
bleirfsk, bleach (v)
bleirs, span (v)
bleirsh, span (n)
bleirshwan, spanner (n doer)
bleirth, truce (n)
bleisf, dub (v)
blenirk, ant (n)
blerf, come (n)
blerfwan, comer (n doer)
blerk, break (n)
blerkar, breakage (n)
blerkeidorn, breakwater (n)
blerkiu, breakably (adv)
blerkive, breakup (n)
blerkizve, breakup (v)
blerkizvyot, brokeup (v pa)
blerkopiorl, breakaway (n)
blerktaifort, breakpoint (n)
blerku, breakable (adj)
blerkuil, breakout (n)
blerkwan, breaker (n doer)
blersf, come (v)
blersfyot, came (v pa)
blersh, classification (n)
blersk, break (v)
blerskyot, broke (v pa)
blerst, shed (v d:rid)
blerth, staff (n d:plaster)
blertwan, shedder (n doer d:rid)
bles, classify (v)
blesh, class (n)
bleshu, classy (adj)
bliarf, beef (n)
bliarge, twinge (n)
bliarn, barn (n)
bliarsk, boggle (v)
bliarzge, twinge (v)
bliashk, crunch (n)
bliashku, crunchy (adj)
bliashkwan, cruncher (n doer)
bliashsk, crunch (v)
bliathk, neigh (n)
bliathsk, neigh (v)
bliaumesp, sprout (v)
bliaump, sprout (n)
bliaushsk, scrunch (v)
bliert, goat (n)
bliferst, provide (v)
blifert, provision (n)
blifertar, providence (n)
blifertwan, provider (n doer)
blirak, bloc (n)
blirf, peninsula (n)
blirfk, province (n)
blirfkiu, provincially (adv)
blirfku, provincial (adj)

blirme, timidity (n)
blirmiu, timidly (adv)
blirmu, timid (adj)
blirshk, penetration (n)
blirshkwan, penetrator (n doer)
blirshsk, penetrate (v)
blirst, vest (v)
blirt, vest (n)
blisht, sleaze (n)
blishtu, sleazy (adj)
blitesh, vestige (n)
bliteshiu, vestigially (adv)
bliteshu, vestigial (adj)
blithk, sprint (n)
blithkwan, sprinter (n doer)
blithsk, sprint (v)
bliufp, putty (n)
bliunk, prudence (n)
bliunku, prudent (adj)
bliunku, prudish (adj)
bliunkwan, prude (n doer)
bliurf, alley (n)
bliurku, bogus (adj)
bliurme, clone (n)
bliurmwan, cloner (n doer)
bliurt, creed (n)
bliurzme, clone (v)
bliushk, ruse (n)
blize, prune (v d:clip)
blizhwan, pruner (n doer d:clip)
blofiern, desolation (n)
blofiersne, desolate (v)
bloiarst, deviate (v)
bloiart, deviation (n)
bloiartiu, deviously (adv)
bloiartu, devious (adj)
bloiartwan, deviant (n doer)
bloifk, chaff (n)
bloifp, boob (n)
bloirbe, bead (n)
bloirk, filth (n)
bloirku, filthy (adj)
bloirn, row (n d:column)
bloirsk, filthy (v)
bloirzbe, bead (v)
bloishst, cringe (v)
bloithk, pallet (n)
blomarde, plumb (n)
blomardu, plumb (adj)
blomardwan, plumber (n doer)
blomarzde, plumb (v)
blorfp, slump (n)
blorfpiu, slumpily (adv)
blorfpu, slumpy (adj)
blorfpwan, slumper (n doer)
blorfsp, slump (v)
blorfst, devise (v)
blorft, device (n)
blorftiu, devisively (adv)
blorftu, devisive (adj)
blorftwan, deviser (n doer)
blorn, slum (n)
blorshk, slur (n)

blorshkan, slurry (n)
blorshsk, slur (v)
bluarf, adoration (n)
bluarfiu, adorably (adv)
bluarfu, adorable (adj)
bluarkwan, slugger (n doer d:hit)
bluarme, femme (n)
bluarn, dam (n)
bluarp, cluster (n)
bluars, soar (v)
bluarsf, adore (v)
bluarsk, slug (v d:hit)
bluarsp, cluster (v)
bluarst, adorn (v)
bluart, adornment (n)
blufik, rust (n)
blufikiu, rustily (adv)
blufiku, rusty (adj)
blufirp, pulp (n)
blufisk, rust (v)
blufist, rush (v)
blufit, rush (n)
bluk, duck (n d:avoid)
blunif, priority (n)
blunisf, prioritize (v)
blunshk, butt (n d:end/ rump)
blunshk, buttocks (n d:end/
    rump)
blurge, thug (n)
blurguet, thuggery (n)
blurk, blow (n d:impact)
blurkuil, blowout (v)
blurn, prior (n)
blurnu, prior (adj)
blurviu, previously (adv)
blurvu, previous (adj)
blurze, scam (v)
blurzhe, scam (n)
blurzhwan, scammer (n doer)
Blushame, EhoMonth03 (n)
blusharme, disease (n)
blusharzme, disease (v)
blushienk, hermit (n)
blushp, thud (n)
blusk, duck (v d:avoid)
bluthkwan, rustler (n doer)
bluthsk, rustle (v)
blutirp, pulpit (n)
blutish, presence (n d:existence)
boarn, fable (n)
boarniu, fabulously (adv)
boarnu, fabulous (adj)
bodarsh, pathogen (n)
bodarshu, pathogenic (adj)
boelirk, hurt (n)
boelirkiu, hurtfully (adv)
boelirku, hurtful (adj)
boelirsk, hurt (v)
boelirskyot, hurt (v pa)
bogiaf, decay (n)
bogiasf, decay (v)
boharst, dare (v)
bohart, dare (n)

bohartu, darish (adj)
boifp, bungle (n)
boifsp, bungle (v)
boigart, potential (n)
boigartiu, potentially (adv)
boigartu, potential (adj)
boikarst, stoop (v d:bend)
boikashk, casket (n)
boilak, squiggle (n)
boilask, squiggle (v)
boirank, squirrel (n)
boiranku, squirrely (adj)
boirde, potato (n)
boirf, bungie (n)
boirge, potency (n)
boirgu, potent (adj)
boirk, assault (n)
boirn, dairy (n)
boirnu, dairy (adj)
boirs, page (v d:person/contact)
boirsf, bungie (v)
boirsh, page (n d:person/contact)
boirshwan, pager (n doer
    d:person/contact)
boirsk, assault (v)
boirst, fault (v)
boirt, fault (n)
boirtiu, faultily (adv)
boirtu, faulty (adj)
boishart, pageant (n)
boitshk, cask (n)
bokart, bronco (n)
bolarf, dash (n d:line)
bolarfwan, dasher (n doer d:line)
bolarsf, dash (v d:line)
bolekwan, fainter (n doer d:pass
    out)
bolen, fade (n d:diminish)
boleniu, faintly (adv d:diminish)
bolenu, faint (adj d:diminish)
bolenwan, fader (n doer
    d:diminish)
bolenweku, faintest (adj)
bolenwelu, fainter (adj)
bolesk, faint (v d:pass out)
bolesne, fade (v d:diminish)
bolirsk, pare (v)
bolkart, parity (n)
bonfbaraft, gravestone (n)
bonfshoirt, graveside (n)
bonfthauthk, graveyard (n)
bonirf, grave (n)
bonirfwan, engraver (n doer)
bonirsf, engrave (v)
boraf, strength (n)
borafiu, strongly (adv)
borafu, strong (adj)
borafwaku, strongest (adj)
borafwelu, stronger (adj)
borasf, strengthen (v)
borat, vice (n d:trap)
borath, resin (n)
boratiu, viciously (adv d:trap)

boratu, vicious (adj d:trap)
boratuet, viciousness (n)
borfplorn, strongman (n)
borfplornyek, strongmen (n pl)
borfthorthk, stronghold (n)
borilk, soup (n)
borilku, soupy (adj)
Borium, Bohrium (n)
borkuit, ecology (n)
borkuit, ecosystem (n)
borkuitiu, ecologically (adv)
borkuitu, ecological (adj)
borkuitwan, ecologist (n doer)
Born, Bonn (n)
Boron, Boron (n)
borsh, with (prep)
borshuil, without (adv/prep)
borshuil, without (n)
borthk, residue (n)
borthku, residual (adj)
boshirsh, within (adv/prep)
boshirsh, within (n)
boshpulap, withdrawal (n)
boshpulasp, withdraw (v)
boshpulaspyot, withdrew (v pa)
boshthorthsk, withhold (v)
boshthorthskyot, withheld (v pa)
Boshtorn, Boston (n)
boshtrelirst, withstand (v)
boshtrelirstyot, withstood (v pa)
botark, pathos (n)
botarkiu, pathetically (adv)
botarku, pathetic (adj)
botersh, path (n)
botshpliorl, pathway (n)
bovenk, economy (n)
bovenkar, economics (n)
bovenkaru, economic (adj)
bovenkiu, economically (adv)
bovenku, economical (adj)
bovenkwan, economist (n doer)
bovensk, economize (v)
brafst, ground (v d:soil)
braft, ground (n d:soil)
braftwan, grounder (n doer
    d:soil)
braiark, callousness (n)
braiarkiu, callously (adv)
braiarku, callous (adj)
braifst, sober (v)
bralft, sobriety (n)
braiftu, sober (adj)
braigat, monster (n)
braigatu, monstrous (adj)
brairk, invitation (n)
brairku, invitational (adj)
brairkuin, invitee (n)
brairkwan, invitor (n doer)
brairsk, invite (v)
braishk, char (n d:burn)
braishku, chary (adj d:burn)
braishsk, char (v d:burn)
braithk, jag (n)

braithkwan, jagger (n doer)
braithsk, jag (v)
braizhganor, charcoal (n)
brakun, coach (n)
brakusne, coach (v)
bralbe, sob (n)
bralf, plain (n)
bralfiu, plainly (adv)
bralfk, ledger (n)
bralfu, plain (adj)
bralirge, ding (n)
bralirp, dimple (n)
bralirsp, dimple (v)
bralirzge, ding (v)
bralshk, prank (n)
bralshkwan, prankster (n doer)
bralt, dentistry (n)
braltar, denture (n)
braltirp, plaintiff (n)
braltu, dental (adj)
braltwan, dentist (n doer)
bralzbe, sob (v)
bramipwan, pounder (n doer
    d:hit)
bramisp, pound (v d:hit)
branar, coast (n d:shore)
branaroip, coastline (n)
branaru, coastal (adj d:shore)
branirn, till (n d:cash register)
brap, fondness (n)
brapiu, fondly (adv)
brapu, fond (adj)
brashk, font (n)
brauf, flow (n)
braufk, dunk (n)
braufkwan, dunker (n doer)
braufp, area (n)
braufsk, dunk (v)
braursh, plaza (n)
brausf, flow (v)
brausht, arena (n)
bravilsk, muster (v)
Brazhilarn, Brazilian (n)
Brazhilf, Brazil (n)
bregark, daemon (n)
bregark, demon (n)
bregarku, demonic (adj)
bregarsk, daemonize (v)
bregarsk, demonize (v)
bregif, demonstration (n)
bregifwan, demonstrator (n doer)
bregisf, demonstrate (v)
breidorn, irrigation (n)
breidorsne, irrigate (v)
breifk, lightness (n d:weight)
breifkefirt, lightheadedness (n)
breifkiu, lightly (adv d:weight)
breifku, light (adj d:weight)
breifshuirsh, lightweight (n)
breifshuirshu, lightweight (adj)
breifsk, lighten (v d:weight)
breilut, MarbleRobot
breimfenshk, stalemate (n)

breimp, staleness (n)
breimpu, stale (adj)
breishfleirde, purebreed (n)
breishfleirdiot, purebred (n)
breishk, purity (n)
breishkiu, purely (adv)
breishku, pure (adj)
breishkuet, purification (n)
breishkuetwan, purifier (n doer)
breishkwan, purist (n doer)
breishsk, purify (v)
breishst, crest (v)
breisht, crest (n)
breithk, slush (n)
breithsk, slush (v)
brekal, completion (n)
brekaliu, completely (adv)
brekalst, complement (v)
brekalt, complement (n)
brekalu, complete (adj)
brekasle, complete (v)
brekun, chair (n d:meeting)
brekunwan, chairman (n doer
    d:meeting)
brekunwan, chairperson (n doer
    d:meeting)
brekusne, chair (v d:meeting)
brelbe, hamper (n d:laundry)
brelf, density (n)
brelfiu, densely (adv)
brelfu, dense (adj)
brelfweku, densest (adj)
brelfwelu, denser (adj)
brelgof, plank (n)
brelgosf, plank (v)
brelme, clumsiness (n)
brelmiu, clumsily (adv)
brelmu, clumsy (adj)
brelp, plant (n d:life form, affix)
brelpwan, planter (n doer d:life
    form, affix)
brels, place (v)
brelsh, place (n)
brelshuet, placement (n)
brelshwan, placer (n doer)
brelsp, plant (v d:life form, affix)
brelst, dent (v)
brelt, dent (n)
brendenargwan, moneymaker (n
    doer)
brenf, ferry (n)
brenfralt, democracy (n)
brenfraltiu, democratically (adv)
brenfraltu, democratic (adj)
brenfraltwan, democrat (n doer)
brenide, money (n)
brenidiu, monetarily (adv)
brenidu, monetary (adj)
brensf, ferry (v)
brenshkorbe, ferryboat (n)
brentark, monkey (n)
brentarsk, monkey (v)
breshirsp, implore (v)

breshkart, complex (n)
breshork, complexity (n)
breshorku, complex (adj)
breshorst, placate (v)
breshort, placation (n)
breshortwan, placator (n doer)
breshuirsh, freight (n)
breshuirshwan, freighter (n doer)
breshuishroifk, freightliner (n)
briadirt, roster (n)
briafmithsk, dovetail (v)
briakarbe, usury (n)
briakart, usage (n)
briakmernu, useless (adj)
briakursh, usefulness (n)
briakurshiu, usefully (adv)
briakurshu, useful (adj)
brialork, arbitration (n)
brialorkiu, arbitrarily (adv)
brialorku, arbitrary (adj)
brialorkwan, arbitrator (n doer)
brialorsk, arbitrate (v)
brials, vow (v)
brialsh, vow (n)
briamesp, vouch (v)
briamp, vouch (n)
briampwan, voucher (n doer)
brianirk, registration (n)
brianirkwan, register (n doer)
brianirsk, register (v)
brianshst, clank (v)
briansht, clank (n)
brianshtu, clanky (adj)
brianshtwan, clanker (n doer)
briapkorth, loophole (n)
briarf, dove (n d:bird)
briark, use (n)
briarkfrep, useability (n)
briarkfrepu, usable (adj)
briarkiu, usually (adv)
briarku, usual (adj)
briarkwan, user (n doer)
briarp, loop (n)
briarpiu, loopily (adv)
briarpu, loopy (adj)
briarpwan, looper (n doer)
briarsk, use (v)
briarsp, loop (v)
briarst, abort (v)
briarsth, fleet (v)
briart, abortion (n)
briarth, fleet (n)
briartwan, abortionist (n doer)
briaurk, riot (n)
briaurkwan, rioter (n doer)
briaursk, riot (v)
bribarkwan, bulldozer (n doer)
bribarsk, bulldoze (v)
brielf, mall (n)
brielst, deny (v)
brielt, denial (n)
brienf, name (n)
brienfiu, namely (adv)

brienfkarf, nameplate (n)
brienfmenu, nameless (adj)
brienfwan, namer (n doer)
brienmoark, namesake (n)
briensf, name (v)
brienshst, clink (v)
briensht, clink (n)
brienshtu, clinky (adj)
brienshtwan, clinker (n doer)
brieshk, stench (n)
brifst, leap (v)
brifstyot, leapt (v pa)
brift, leap (n)
briftwan, leaper (n doer)
brilf, inn (n)
brilfwan, innkeeper (n doer)
brilk, black (n)
brilkplok, blackboard (n)
brilku, black (adj)
brilorp, thrift (n)
brilorpu, thrifty (adj)
brilsk, blacken (v)
brionshst, clonk (v)
brionsht, clonk (n)
brionshtu, clonky (adj)
brionshtwan, clonker (n doer)
briorf, facility (n)
briorfu, facile (adj)
briorfuet, faculty (n)
briorfwan, facilitator (n doer)
briork, accumulation (n)
briorkiu, cumulatively (adv)
briorku, cumulative (adj)
briorkwan, accumulator (n doer)
briorn, peculiarity (n)
briorniu, peculiarly (adv)
briornu, peculiar (adj)
briorp, thimble (n)
briorsf, facilitate (v)
briorsk, accumulate (v)
brishortiu, soon (adv)
brishortwakiu, soonest (adv)
brishortweliu, sooner (adv)
Britairn, Britain (n)
britar, crystal (n)
britaru, crystalline (adj)
britaruet, crystalization (n)
britasre, crystalize (v)
Britirsh, British (n)
briufp, tumble (n)
briufpwan, tumbler (n doer)
briufsp, tumble (v)
briukart, leakage (n)
briun, Eho15minutes (n)
briurk, leak (n)
briurkiu, leakily (adv)
briurku, leaky (adj)
briurkwan, leaker (n doer)
briursk, leak (v)
briursp, shrivel (v)
briurt, bleakness (n)
briurtu, bleak (adj)
briushk, leach (n)

briushsk, leach (v)
brivark, weave (n)
brivarkwan, weaver (n doer)
brivarn, web (n)
brivarsk, weave (v)
brivarskyot, wove (v pa)
brivarsne, web (v)
brivurst, stigmatize (v)
brivurt, stigma (n)
brizhank, buzzard (n)
Brodwairn, Broadway (n)
broifk, crisis (n)
broilt, volt (n)
broiltuet, voltage (n)
broink, clunk (n)
broinku, clunky (adj)
broinkwan, clunker (n doer)
broinsk, clunk (v)
broip, cry (n)
broipdeirde, crybaby (n)
broipwan, crier (n doer)
broirge, abscess (n)
broirzge, abscess (v)
broishkwan, bickerer (n doer)
broishsk, bicker (v)
broisp, cry (v)
brokiarge, gestation (n)
brokiarzge, gestate (v)
brolar, kin (n)
brolarfirf, kinship (n)
brolkiforp, kinfolk (n)
brolplorn, kinsman (n)
brolreifk, kindred (n)
brolreifku, kindred (adj)
brolst, listen (v)
broltwan, listener (n doer)
Bromin, Bromine (n)
bronf, group (n)
bronfwan, groupie (n doer)
bronirk, flock (n d:wool)
bronirt, genus (n)
bronkoirk, genocide (n)
bronkoirku, genocidal (adj)
bronlaft, genre (n)
bronsf, group (v)
bruafk, bluster (n)
bruafku, blustery (adj)
bruafsk, bluster (v)
brualirfyek, flutter (n pl)
brualirsf, flutter (v)
bruarsh, agility (n)
bruarshu, agile (adj)
bruarst, float (v)
bruart, float (n)
bruartuet, flotation (n)
bruartuetu, flotation (adj)
bruartwan, floater (n doer)
brufan, compensation (n)
brufanwan, compensator (n doer)
brufasne, compensate (v)
brufert, pension (n)
bruilk, encryption (n)
bruilkdarfk, cryptography (n)

bruilkdarfku, cryptic (adj)
bruilku, cryptic (adj)
bruilsk, encrypt (v)
bruithk, leech (n)
bruithsk, leech (v)
brukarp, ticket (n)
brukarpwan, ticketer (n doer)
brukarsp, ticket (v)
brukarst, tickle (v)
brukart, tickle (n)
brukartwan, tickler (n doer)
Bruklirn, Brooklyn (n)
brulalfyek, flurry (n pl)
brulist, sputter (v)
brulk, tick (n d:increment)
brulkwan, ticker (n doer
    d:increment)
brulsk, tick (v d:increment)
brundant, pendulum (n)
brundart, pendant (n)
brunirk, slug (n d:blank)
brunsf, pend (v)
brurbe, league (n)
brurbwan, leaguer (n doer)
Brushelf, Brussels (n)
brutap, burst (n)
brutasp, burst (v)
brutaspyot, burst (v pa)
buairst, poison (v)
buairt, poison (n)
buairtu, poisonous (adj)
buairtwan, poisoner (n doer)
buals, trowel (v)
bualsh, trowel (n)
bualshwan, troweler (n doer)
buanirst, defy (v)
buanirt, defiance (n)
buanirtiu, defiantly (adv)
buanirtu, defiant (adj)
buark, harrow (n)
buarnk, dump (n)
buarnkap, dumpster (n)
buarnkwan, dumper (n doer)
buarnsk, dump (v)
buarsk, harrow (v)
buart, splat (n)
buasharst, splatter (v)
buashart, splatter (n)
buashk, hearse (n)
buathk, trough (n)
Lublellrk, deportation (n)
bubielirkuin, deportee (n)
bubielirkwan, deporter (n doer)
bubielirsk, deport (v)
bubirst, defeat (v)
bubirt, defeat (n)
bubirtwan, defeater (n doer)
bublarf, deflation (n)
bublarfu, deflationary (adj)
bublarfwan, deflator (n doer)
bublars, depress (v)
bublarsf, deflate (v)
bublarsh, depression (n)

bublarshiu, depressively (adv)
bublarshu, depressive (adj)
bublarshwan, depressant (n doer)
bublarshwan, depressor (n doer)
bubles, declassify (v)
bublesh, declassification (n)
bubliurst, decree (v)
bubliurt, decree (n)
buboirst, default (v)
buboirt, default (n)
bubroisp, decry (v)
bubruilk, decryption (n)
bubruilsk, decrypt (v)
bubrulirf, decipherment (n)
bubrulirfyek, decipherments (n
    pl)
bubrulirsf, decipher (v)
bubrun, dependence (n)
bubrun, dependency (n)
bubruniu, dependably (adv)
bubrunu, dependable (adj)
bubrunwan, dependant (n doer)
bubrunwan, dependent (n doer)
bubrusne, depend (v)
budast, deck (v)
budat, deck (n)
budilst, delist (v)
Budirn, Buddha (n)
Budirnuet, Buddhism (n)
Budirnwan, Buddhist (n)
budiuarsf, devour (v)
budolirf, detection (n)
budolirfat, detective (n)
budolirfu, detectable (adj)
budolirfwan, detector (n doer)
budolirsf, detect (v)
budoshst, declare (v)
budosht, declaration (n)
budoshtu, declaratory (adj)
budoshtwan, declarer (n doer)
budrik, decrease (n)
budrishork, decrement (n)
budrishorkiu, decrementally
    (adv)
budrishorku, decremental (adj)
budrishorsk, decrement (v)
budrisk, decrease (v)
budrulp, depreciation (n)
budrulsp, depreciate (v)
hudufarl, deodorization (n)
budufarlwan, deodorent (n doer)
budufarsle, deodorize (v)
budufirp, despondence (n)
budufirpwan, desponder (n doer)
budufirsp, despond (v)
bufaborst, defuse (v)
bufairkwan, despiser (n doer)
bufairsk, despise (v)
Bufalorn, Buffalo (n)
bufapu, derogatory (adj)
bufasp, derogate (v)
bufiorshst, defrost (v)
bufirk, zoom (n)

bufirku, zoom (adj)
bufirsk, zoom (v)
bufirst, deplore (v)
bufirtu, deplorable (adj)
bufor, slumber (n)
buforu, slumber (adj)
bufosre, slumber (v)
bufranst, delay (v)
bufrant, delay (n)
bufrantwan, delayer (n doer)
bufrilark, determent (n)
bufrilark, deterrence (n)
bufrilarkwan, deterrent (n doer)
bufrilarkwan, deterrer (n doer)
bufrilarsk, deter (v)
bufuip, debut (n)
bufuisp, debut (v)
bugafirt, packet (n)
bugarlst, detract (v)
bugarlt, detraction (n)
bugarltwan, detractor (n doer)
bugarp, pack (n)
bugarpwan, packer (n doer)
bugarsp, pack (v)
bugarst, package (v)
bugart, package (n)
bugartwan, packager (n doer)
bugauroifp, detonation (n)
bugauroifpwan, detonator (n
    doer)
bugauroifsp, detonate (v)
bugef, deferral (n)
bugerf, deference (n)
bugerst, deflect (v)
bugert, deflection (n)
bugertu, deflective (adj)
bugertwan, deflector (n doer)
bugesf, defer (v)
bugiarp, debate (n)
bugiarpwan, debater (n doer)
bugiarsp, debate (v)
buglursk, debunk (v)
bugor, burn (n)
bugorast, burnish (v)
bugoruil, burnout (n)
bugorwan, burner (n doer)
bugosre, burn (v)
bugosryot, burnt (v pa)
bugrals, depict (v)
bugralsh, depiction (n)
bugublasharn, decompression (n)
bugublasharsne, decompress (v)
buiartu, sinister (adj)
buiashsk, singe (v)
builarf, deterioration (n)
builarsf, deteriorate (v)
buirf, zoo (n)
buishort, con (n d:consequence)
buishort, consequence (n)
buishortiu, consequentially (adv)
buishortiu, consequently (adv)
buishortu, conseqent (adj)
buishortu, consequential (adj)

bukefirst, decapitate (v)
bukefirt, decapitation (n)
bukemirf, devolution (n)
bukemirf, devolvement (n)
bukemirsf, devolve (v)
bukiark, dedication (n)
bukiarkwan, dedicator (n doer)
bukiarsk, dedicate (v)
bukirk, deduction (n
    d:determination)
bukirkwan, deducer (n doer
    d:determination)
bukirsk, deduce (v
    d:determination)
bukiurk, deliberation (n)
bukiurkiu, deliberately (adv)
bukiurku, deliberate (adj)
bukiursk, deliberate (v)
bukofst, deserve (v)
bukoiltizve, dethrone (v)
bukor, bar (n d:pub)
bukorwan, bartender (n doer
    d:pub)
bukosre, bartend (v d:pub)
bukriushk, deductible (n
    d:subtraction)
bukriushk, deduction (n
    d:subtraction)
bukriushku, deductible (adj
    d:subtraction)
bukriushsk, deduct (v
    d:subtraction)
bukroif, decline (n)
bukroifp, declination (n)
bukroifwan, decliner (n doer)
bukroisf, decline (v)
bulak, deposition (n)
bulakwan, deposer (n doer)
bulask, depose (v)
bulenkarst, decommission (v)
bulenkart, decommission (n)
Bulgarf, Bulgaria (n)
Bulgariarn, Bulgarian (n)
buliarge, demeanor (n)
bulikart, descendant (n)
bulikart, descendent (n)
bulinarp, deficit (n)
bulinirk, deficiency (n)
bulinirkiu, deficiently (adv)
bulinirku, deficient (adj)
bulirak, descent (n)
bulirakwan, descender (n doer)
bulirask, descend (v)
bulirf, rue (n)
bulirsf, rue (v)
bulirt, decency (n)
bulirtiu, decently (adv)
bulirtu, decent (adj)
bulmorst, derange (v)
bulmort, derangement (n)
bulnak, decomposition (n)
bulnakwan, decomposer (n doer)
bulnask, decompose (v)

buluirst, derail (v)
buluirt, derailment (n)
buluvirp, deregulation (n)
buluvirpwan, deregulator (n doer)
buluvirsp, deregulate (v)
bulvart, boulevard (n)
bumarmark, degeneration (n)
bumarmarku, degenerative (adj)
bumarmarsk, degenerate (v)
bumirade, denotation (n)
bumirazde, denote (v)
bumithk, detail (n)
bumithkwan, detailer (n doer)
bumithsk, detail (v)
bumufirst, denounce (v)
bumufirt, denouncement (n)
bumufirtwan, denouncer (n doer)
bupairk, detachment (n)
bupairsk, detach (v)
bupaltark, deactivation (n)
bupaltarkwan, deactivator (n
    doer)
bupaltarsk, deactivate (v)
bupast, file (v d:tool)
bupat, file (n d:tool)
bupatwan, filer (n doer d:tool)
bupiashk, delegation (n)
bupiashkwan, delegate (n doer)
bupiashsk, delegate (v)
bupirfst, detain (v)
bupirft, detainment (n)
bupirftar, detention (n)
bupirftuin, detainee (n)
bupirftwan, detainor (n doer)
bupliurst, destroy (v)
bupliurtwan, destroyer (n doer)
bupral, decoration (n)
bupralwan, decorator (n doer)
buprarl, decor (n)
bupraɔle, decorate (v)
burborlirk, desperation (n)
burborlk, despair (n)
burborlku, desperate (adj)
burborlsk, despair (v)
burfaik, despite (prep)
burge, gravity (n d:serious)
burgiu, gravely (adv d:serious)
burgu, grave (adj d:serious)
burianirsk, defray (v)
burl, pen (n d:enclosure)
burlart, gravel (v)
burlartu, gravelly (adj)
Burlingtorn, Burlington (n)
buroif, delineation (n)
buroifan, delinquence (n)
buroifanu, delinquent (adj)
buroifwan, delineator (n doer)
buroisf, delineate (v)
burs, buff (v d:rub)
bursh, buff (n d:rub)
burshwan, buffer (n doer d:rub)
bursle, pen (v d:enclosure)
burthk, shrub (n)

burthkuet, shrubbery (n)
burushst, delude (v)
burusht, delusion (n)
burushtu, delusional (adj)
busheifst, sterilize (v)
busheift, sterility (n)
busheiftiu, sterilely (adv)
busheiftu, sterile (adj)
busheiftuet, sterilization (n)
buship, deceit (n)
bushipet, deception (n)
bushipetiu, deceptively (adv)
bushipetu, deceptive (adj)
bushipiu, deceitfully (adv)
bushipu, deceitful (adj)
bushipwan, deceiver (n doer)
bushirk, depth (n)
bushirp, deep (n)
bushirpiu, deeply (adv)
bushirpu, deep (adj)
bushirpwaku, deepest (adj)
bushirpwelu, deeper (adj)
bushirsp, deepen (v)
bushisp, deceive (v)
bushklivarzge, demean (v)
bushlarn, destiny (n)
bushlarnt, destination (n)
bushlarsne, destine (v)
bushlerk, destruction (n)
bushlerku, destructive (adj)
bushlersk, destruct (v)
bushlirbe, derision (n)
bushlirzbe, deride (v)
bushloist, deploy (v)
bushloit, deployment (n)
bushoirk, demand (n)
bushoirsk, demand (v)
bushrige, description (n)
bushrigiu, descriptively (adv)
bushrigu, descriptive (adj)
bushrigwan, descriptor (n doer)
bushrizge, describe (v)
bushtirst, detest (v)
bushtirtu, detestable (adj)
bushtrak, degradation (n)
bushtrask, degrade (v)
bushvien, nomenclature (n)
butahst, dehydrate (v)
butaht, dehydration (n)
butelfsk, desist (v)
buterp, dejection (n)
butersp, deject (v)
buthiarf, detour (n)
buthiarsf, detour (v)
buthis, decide (v)
buthish, decision (n)
buthishiu, decisively (adv)
buthishu, decisive (adj)
buthoirs, deface (v)
buthoishst, debrief (v)
butiarp, deprivation (n)
butiarsp, deprive (v)
butorve, defense (n)

butorvu, defensive (adj)
butorvwan, defendant (n doer)
butorvwan, defender (n doer)
butorzve, defend (v)
butranist, decontrol (v)
butranit, decontrol (n)
buvadarve, demotion (n)
buvadarzve, demote (v)
buvanarsf, decouple (v)
buvatharve, demolition (n)
buvatharzve, demolish (v)
buvaurp, devaluation (n)
buvaursp, devalue (v)
buverk, decease (n)
buversk, decease (v)
buvinst, delimit (v)
buvintwan, delimiter (n doer)
buvirst, defect (v)
buvirt, defect (n)
buvirtiu, defectively (adv)
buvirtu, defective (adj)
buvirtwan, defector (n doer)
buvolarst, decode (v)
buvolartwan, decoder (n doer)
buvorast, decelerate (v)
buvorat, deceleration (n)
buvoratwan, decelerator (n doer)
buvorn, deformation (n)
buvornwan, deformer (n doer)
buvorsne, deform (v)
buvovar, depopulation (n)
buvovasre, depopulate (v)
buvuast, define (v)
buvuat, definition (n)
buvuatiu, definitely (adv)
buvuatu, definite (adj)
buvuatu, definitive (adj)
buwelfk, depletion (n)
buwelfsk, deplete (v)
buzhersk, degas (v)
dabirt, theater (n)
dabirt, theatre (n)
dabirtu, theatrical (adj)
dabirtul, theatric (n)
dafel, bath (n)
dafelshranf, bathroom (n)
dafelwan, bather (n doer)
dafesle, bathe (v)
dafirk, challenge (n)
dafirkwan, challenger (n doer)
dafirp, championship (n)
dafirpwan, champ (n doer)
dafirpwan, champion (n doer)
dafirsk, challenge (v)
dafirsp, champion (v)
dafka, quinquagintillion (num
    1e153 card)
dafraf, cape (n)
dafrafwan, caper (n doer)
dafta, quadragintillion (num
    1e123 card)
dafurmiu, suavely (adv)
dafurmu, suave (adj)

dahem, Number_1e2406
Dahma, Dahma (n)
daiar, uncle (n)
daiarf, tiff (n)
daiark, captain (n)
daiarp, puddle (n)
daiarsf, tiff (v)
daiarsk, captain (v)
daifairf, potty (n)
daifkorsth, pothole (v)
daifkorth, pothole (n)
daiforst, brave (v)
daifort, bravery (n)
daifortu, brave (adj)
daifortwan, brave (n doer)
daifpadar, potluck (n)
daifshkoift, potshot (n)
daiftarn, SplitWand (n)
daikiunorf, equilibrium (n)
daikzhiert, endgame (n)
dainf, equal (n)
dainfiu, equally (adv)
dainfk, equality (n)
dainfk, equalization (n)
dainfkwan, equalizer (n doer)
dainfsk, equalize (v)
dainsf, equal (v)
dairbe, hibernation (n)
dairde, equation (n)
dairdwan, equator (n doer)
dairf, pot (n)
dairfwan, potter (n doer)
dairge, fraud (n)
dairgwan, defrauder (n doer)
dairk, end (n)
dairkmeniu, endlessly (adv)
dairkmenu, endless (adj)
dairp, squash (n d:pressure)
dairpwan, squasher (n doer
    d:pressure)
dairs, cut (v)
dairsf, pot (v)
dairsh, cut (n)
dairshuil, cutout (n)
dairshunf, cutoff (n)
dairshwan, cutter (n doer)
dairsk, end (v)
dairsp, squash (v d:pressure)
dairsyot, cut (v pa)
dairth, cuteness (n)
dairthu, cute (adj)
dairunk, costume (n)
dairzbe, hibernate (v)
dairzde, equate (v)
dairzge, defraud (v)
daishvark, cutback (n)
daiteshk, pouch (n)
Daitonarf, Daytona (n)
Daitorn, Dayton (n)
daivurge, ruin (n)
daivurzke, ruin (v)
daka, decillion (num 1e33 card)
dakai-, vendeka- (num 1e33 pref)

dakairbe, decade (n)
dakelf, belt (n)
dakelfwan, belter (n doer)
dakelsf, belt (v)
daketh, decillionth (num 1e33
    ord)
dakinor, decimal (n)
dakinoru, decimal (adj)
daklirst, trickle (v)
daktaifort, endpoint (n)
dal, D (let sng)
dalarge, syrup (n)
dalargu, syrupy (adj)
Dalarsh, Dallas (n)
daldargalit, synergy (n)
daldargalitu, synergistic (adj)
daldurk, syntax (n)
dali, Ds (let pl)
dalilart, customs (n d:checkpoint)
dalilst, customize (v d:tradition)
dalilt, custom (n d:tradition)
daliltu, customary (adj
    d:tradition)
daliltwan, customer (n doer
    d:tradition)
dalirde, bugle (n)
dalirk, trick (n)
dalirku, tricky (adj)
dalirkuet, trickery (n)
dalirkwan, trickster (n doer)
dalirme, persuasion (n)
dalirmiu, persuasively (adv)
dalirmu, persuasive (adj)
dalirn, lodge (n d:building)
dalirs, teach (v)
dalirshwan, teacher (n doer)
dalirsk, trick (v)
dalirsyot, taught (v pa)
dalirzme, persuade (v)
dalkiark, syndicate (n)
dalkiarkuet, syndication (n)
dalkiarkwan, syndicator (n doer)
dalkiarsk, syndicate (v)
dalmirade, synopsis (n)
dalnarge, synthesis (n)
dalnargiu, synthetically (adv)
dalnargu, synthetic (adj)
dalnargul, synthetic (n)
dalnargwan, synthesizer (n doer)
dalnarzge, synthesize (v)
daloishk, syringe (n)
dalparfp, syndrome (n)
dalpiarf, synchro (n)
dalpiarfiu, synchronously (adv)
dalpiarfu, synchronous (adj)
dalpiarfuet, synchronization (n)
dalpiarsf, synchronize (v)
dalukarst, systemate (v)
dalukart, systemization (n)
dalukartiu, systematically (adv)
dalukartu, systematic (adj)
dalukrashku, systemwide (adj)
dalushk, system (n)

dalushku, systemic (adj)
dalushsk, systemize (v)
dalviern, synonym (n)
dalvierniu, synonymously (adv)
dalviernu, synonymous (adj)
danart, cucumber (n)
danfirp, mob (n)
danfirpwan, mobster (n doer)
danfirsp, mob (v)
danfk, butchery (n)
danfkwan, butcher (n doer)
danfsk, butcher (v)
danirp, chamber (n)
danirst, mobilize (v)
danirt, mobility (n)
danirtu, mobile (adj)
danirtuet, mobilization (n)
danors, tenure (v)
danorsh, tenure (n)
dantart, mobile (n)
dapa, ten (num 10 card)
dapai-, dec- (num 10 pref)
dapalfhemka, Number_1e40656
dapeth, tenth (num 10 ord)
darbaik, engagement (n)
darbaisk, engage (v)
darfilst, graft (v)
darfilt, graft (n)
darfk, graph (n)
darfket, graphic (n)
darfketiu, graphically (adv)
darfketu, graphical (adj)
darfku, graphic (adj)
darfsk, graph (v)
dargalist, energize (v)
dargalit, energy (n)
dargalitu, energetic (adj)
dargalitwan, energizer (n doer)
dargrest, enclose (v)
dargret, enclosure (n)
darkanirf, enchantment (n)
darkanirsf, enchant (v)
darkanp, enhancement (n)
darkanpwan, enhancer (n doer)
darkansp, enhance (v)
darl, aunt (n)
darlais, enjoy (v)
darlaish, enjoyment (n)
darlaishu, enjoyable (adj)
darlanf, enormity (n)
darlanfiu, enormously (adv)
darlanfu, enormous (adj)
darliank, potion (n)
darlorf, juice (n)
darlorfu, juicy (adj)
darlorfwan, juicer (n doer)
darlorsf, juice (v)
darmirk, minute (n d:time)
Darmshtat, Darmstadtium (n)
darnelirk, engram (n)
darnelirsk, engrain (v)
darnof, custody (n)
darnofwan, custodian (n doer)

darnolsk, ingrain (v)
darpan, entirety (n)
darpaniu, entirely (adv)
darpanu, entire (adj)
darpatil, enaction (n)
darpatil, enactment (n)
darpatisle, enact (v)
darpoifst, encounter (v)
darpoift, encounter (n)
darshort, lateness (n)
darshorteblerf, latecomer (n)
darshortiu, lately (adv)
darshortu, late (adj)
darshortwaku, latest (adj)
darshortwelu, later (adj)
darshp, barely (adv)
darshpoiu, barely (adv)
darshporshu, barefoot (adj)
darshpu, bare (adj)
darshsp, bare (v)
Dart, Dart (n)
darthk, dart (n)
darthsk, dart (v)
darvairmoide, encyclopedia (n)
darvairmoidu, encyclopedic (adj)
darviuk, enforcement (n)
darviuku, enforceable (adj)
darviukwan, enforcer (n doer)
darviusk, enforce (v)
darze, jazz (v)
darzhe, jazz (n)
darzhu, jazzy (adj)
darzhuf, enthusiam (n)
darzhufiu, enthusiastically (adv)
darzhufu, enthusiastic (adj)
darzhufwan, enthusiast (n doer)
darzhusf, enthuse (v)
dashirk, cube (n)
dashirku, cubic (adj)
dashirsk, cube (v)
dashka, trigintillion (num 1e93 card)
dashkai-, anto-
dashketh, trigintillionth (num 1e93 ord)
dashta, vigintillion (num 1e63 card)
dashtai-, kido- (num 1e63 pref)
dashteth, vigintillionth (num 1e63 ord)
datharn, village (n)
datharnwan, villager (n doer)
dathel, cover (n)
datheliveil, coverup (n)
dathelt, coverage (n)
dathesle, cover (v)
dathferf, parent (n)
dathferfif, parenthood (n)
dathferfu, parental (adj)
dathfersf, parent (v)
dathiart, vicinity (n)
dathk, villa (n)
datiart, versatility (n)

datiartu, versatile (adj)
datul, age (n)
datulu, agey (adj)
datulwan, ager (n doer)
datusle, age (v)
daua, pow (interj)
daufrauthk, boycott (n)
daufrauthkwan, boycotter (n doer)
daufrauthsk, boycott (v)
daugilt, snare (n d:string)
dauiark, spook (n)
dauiarku, spooky (adj)
dauiarsk, spook (v)
dauirst, vaccinate (v)
dauirt, vaccine (n)
dauirtuet, vaccination (n)
daukdarft, typography (n)
daukdarftu, typographical (adj)
daukferpwan, typesetter (n doer)
daukfersp, typeset (v)
daukferspyot, typeset (v pa)
daukploirwan, typewriter (n doer)
daukthoirsh, typeface (n)
daulaze, mourn (v)
daulazhiu, mournfully (adv)
daulazhu, mournful (adj)
daulazhwan, mourner (n doer)
daundoiart, timetable (n)
daunroifk, timeline (n)
daunthetirsh, timepiece (n)
dauparst, topple (v)
daupinku, topsy (adj)
daupirk, topic (n)
daupirku, topical (adj)
daupnarash, topsoil (n)
daurk, type (n d:key)
daurkil, typo (n)
daurkwan, typist (n doer d:key)
daurn, time (n)
daurnmen, timelessness (n)
daurnmenu, timeless (adj)
daurnu, timely (adj)
daurnuet, timeliness (n)
daurnuil, timeout (n)
daurnwan, timer (n doer)
daurp, top (n)
daurpemenu, topless (adj)
daurpu, top (adj)
daurpwan, topper (n doer)
daursk, type (v d:key)
daursne, time (v)
daursp, top (v)
daurst, beat (v)
daurstyot, beat (v pa)
daurt, beat (n)
daurth, vet (n d:veteran)
daurtu, beatable (adj)
daurtwan, beater (n doer)
dausharsk, botch (v)
daushst, falsify (v)
dausht, falsity (n)
daushtfif, falsehood (n)

daushtiu, falsely (adv)
daushtu, false (adj)
daushtuet, falsification (n)
dautarf, piracy (n)
dautarfwan, pirate (n doer)
dautarsf, pirate (v)
dautharn, veteran (n)
dauvirst, pave (v)
dauvirt, pavement (n)
dauvirtwan, paver (n doer)
dauze, moan (v)
dauzhe, moan (n)
davarp, orange (n d:fruit)
defirk, rat (n)
defirsk, rat (v)
defrup, capacity (n)
Deginak, General (n)
dehursh, toward (prep)
deiarf, nourishment (n)
deiarn, witchcraft (n)
deiarnwan, witch (n doer)
deiarsf, nourish (v)
deiarsne, bewitch (v)
deiauf, piety (n)
deiaufu, pious (adj)
deifat, bullet (n)
deifatfliorfu, bulletproof (adj)
deifatfliorsf, bulletproof (v)
deifiarn, bullion (n)
deiflurf, daisy (n)
deifralshk, betrayal (n)
deifralshsk, betray (v)
deifwask, bully (v)
deigirn, goggle (n)
deilk, edict (n)
deilurde, quiet (n)
deilurde, quietness (n)
deilurdiu, quietly (adv)
deilurdu, quiet (adj)
deilurzde, quiet (v)
deimarsk, linch (v)
deimurth, buffet (n d:food/ table)
deinor, bureau (n)
deinorfk, bureaucracy (n)
deinorfkiu, bureaucratically (adv)
deinorfku, bureaucratic (adj)
deinorfkwan, bureaucrat (n doer)
deiorshkiu, flimsily (adv)
deiorshku, flimsy (adj)
deiort, tire (n d:wheel)
deirant, tulip (n)
deirde, baby (n)
deirf, bull (n)
deirfu, bullish (adj)
deirfwan, bully (n doer)
deirge, guy (n d:male)
deirolst, design (v)
deirolt, design (n)
deiroltwan, designer (n doer)
deirp, quip (n)
deirpwan, quipper (n doer)
deirsf, bull (v)
deirshk, diction (n)

deirsp, quip (v)
deirtark, designation (n)
deirtarkwan, designator (n doer)
deirtarsk, designate (v)
deirth, modesty (n)
deirthiu, modestly (adv)
deirthu, modest (adj)
deirzde, baby (v)
deirze, pitch (v d:throw)
deirzhe, pitch (n d:throw)
deirzhwan, pitcher (n doer
   d:throw)
deishk, dictation (n)
deishku, dictatoral (adj)
deishkwan, dictator (n doer)
deishkwatfif, dictatorship (n)
deishsk, dictate (v)
deishvon, dictionary (n)
deiurt, stern (n d:rear)
delaifdaurp, treetop (n)
delairf, tree (n)
delairfmenu, treeless (adj)
Delawarf, Delaware (n)
delfkanwan, nurturer (n doer)
delfkasne, nurture (v)
delgelf, secretary (n)
delirf, nursery (n)
delirfwan, nurse (n doer)
delirp, knit (n)
delirs, fracture (v)
delirsf, nurse (v)
delirsh, fracture (n)
delirsp, knit (v)
delirthiu, thoroughly (adv)
delirthu, thorough (adj)
delishork, fraction (n)
delishorkiu, fractionally (adv)
delishorku, fractional (adj)
delkal, capital (n)
delkarl, capitalism (n)
delkasle, capitalize (v)
delnabrelsh, marketplace (n)
delnarst, market (v)
delnart, market (n)
delnartwan, marketeer (n doer)
delnartwan, marketer (n doer)
delnatfrelp, marketability (n)
delnatfrelpu, marketable (adj)
delpedorame, knitwear (n)
deltarn, delta (n)
delumfluarn, candlelight (n)
delumshneft, candlestick (n)
delurme, candle (n)
dempor, candidate (n)
demtoku, candid (adj)
demurbe, cancellation (n)
demurzbe, cancel (v)
denarde, temperature (n)
denarn, ornament (n)
denarniu, ornamentally (adv)
denarnu, ornamental (adj)
Denmark, Denmark (n)
denilst, experiment (v)

denilt, experiment (n)
deniltiu, experimentally (adv)
deniltu, experimental (adj)
deniltwan, experimenter (n doer)
denirfiu, ornately (adv)
denirfu, ornate (adj)
denirk, matter (n d:physics)
denirp, can (n d:container)
denirsp, can (v d:container)
deniu, too (adv)
dentark, capitol (n)
Denverf, Denver (n)
derafu, seismic (adj)
derap, spot (n)
derapemenu, spotless (adj)
derapu, spotty (adj)
derapwan, spotter (n doer)
derasp, spot (v)
derast, seed (v)
derat, seed (n)
deratip, seedling (n)
deratu, seedy (adj)
deratwan, seeder (n doer)
derforst, canvas (v)
derfort, canvas (n)
deriagairfst, bankrupt (v)
deriagairft, bankruptcy (n)
dermashk, cancer (n)
dermashku, cancerous (adj)
derp, thought (n)
derpefluarn, spotlight (n)
derpiu, thoughtfully (adv)
derpu, thoughtful (adj)
derpwan, thinker (n doer)
dersp, think (v)
derspyot, thought (v pa)
desharst, preside (v)
deshart, presidency (n)
deshartiu, presidentially (adv)
deshartu, presidential (adj)
deshartwan, president (n doer)
deshiafirk, captivity (n)
deshiafirsk, captivate (v)
deshiark, capture (n)
deshiarkwan, capturer (n doer)
deshiarsk, capture (v)
deshirp, caption (n)
deshirsp, caption (v)
detirs, peck (v)
detirsh, peck (n)
Detroilt, Detroit (n)
dhahem, Number_1e2706
dhai, was/will be (parcl d:passive
   voice)
dhal, Dh (let sng)
dhali, Dhs (let pl)
dhark, and (conj)
dhauatelantirku, transatlantic
   (adj)
dhaubivikart, transsexual (n)
dhaudaurf, transpiration (n)
dhaudaursf, transpire (v)
dhaufaborst, transfuse (v)

dhaufabort, transfusion (n)
dhaufirk, transit (n)
dhaufirkuet, transition (n)
dhaufrelp, transience (n)
dhaufrelpiu, transiently (adv)
dhaufrelpu, transient (adj)
dhaufrelpwan, transient (n doer)
dhauglark, transposition (n)
dhauglarkwan, transposer (n doer)
dhauglarsk, transpose (v)
dhaukarlfu, transnational (adj)
dhaukiflarf, transvestite (n)
dhaukirak, transduction (n)
dhaukirakwan, transducer (n doer)
dhaukirask, transduce (v)
dhaulirak, transcendence (n)
dhauliraku, transcendent (adj)
dhaulirakul, transcendent (n)
dhaulirakulu, transcendental (adj)
dhaulirask, transcend (v)
dhaulitarnk, transplant (n)
dhaulitarnkuet, transplantation (n)
dhaulitarnsk, transplant (v)
dhaulunirst, trespass (v)
dhaulunirtwan, trespasser (n doer)
dhaumedmotu, transcontinental (adj)
dhaumiarlu, transocean (adj)
dhaunork, transmission (n)
dhaunork, transmittal (n)
dhaunorkwan, transmitter (n doer)
dhaunorsk, transmit (v)
dhaupatil, transaction (n)
dhaupatilwan, transactor (n doer)
dhaupatlsle, transact (v)
dhaupliarn, transparency (n)
dhaupliarniu, transparently (adv)
dhaupliarnu, transparent (adj)
dhaurbielork, transportation (n)
dhaurbielorku, transportable (adj)
dhaurbielorkwan, transporter (n doer)
dhaurbielorsk, transport (v)
dhaurdarst, translate (v)
dhaurdart, translation (n)
dhaurdartwan, translator (n doer)
dhaurdurfp, transponder (n)
dhaurs, transfer (v)
dhaursh, transfer (n)
dhaurshiu, transferably (adv)
dhaurshu, transferable (adj)
dhaurshuet, transference (n)
dhaurvorn, transformation (n)
dhaurvorniu, transformationally (adv)
dhaurvornu, transformational

(adj)
dhaurvornwan, transformer (n doer)
dhaurvorsne, transform (v)
dhausherge, transcript (n)
dhausherguet, transcription (n)
dhaushergwan, transcriber (n doer)
dhausherzge, transcribe (v)
dhaushfrelp, transferability (n)
dhaushiunirkiu, translucently (adv)
dhaushiunirku, translucent (adj)
dhaushluark, transmutation (n)
dhaushluarkiu, transmutably (adv)
dhaushluarku, transmutable (adj)
dhaushluarkwan, transmutor (n doer)
dhaushluarsk, transmute (v)
dhautharak, transverse (n)
dhautharaku, transverse (adj)
dhautharask, transvert (v)
dhautielirkwan, transistor (n doer)
dhauvirkest, transfixate (v)
dhauvirket, transfixation (n)
dhauvirsk, transfix (v)
dhauvorage, transgression (n)
dhauvoragwan, transgressor (n doer)
dhauvorazge, transgress (v)
dheigrolzge, roughen (v)
dhiaishmarn, misdiagnosis (n)
dhiaishmarsne, misdiagnose (v)
dhiars, miss (v d:avoid)
dhiarsh, miss (n d:avoid)
dhiarvorn, misinformation (n)
dhiarvorsne, misinform (v)
dhibelkriuk, misconduct (n)
dhibelkriusk, misconduct (v)
dhibelplairsp, misconstrue (v)
dhibelship, misconception (n)
dhibelshisp, misconceive (v)
dhibiurst, misstate (v)
dhibiurt, misstatement (n)
dhibrels, misplace (v)
dhibrelsh, misplacement (n)
dhibriark, misuse (n)
dhibriarsk, misuse (v)
dhibuliarge, misdemeanor (n)
dhidibarge, mistrial (n)
dhidorklarst, misspend (v)
dhidorklarstyot, misspent (v pa)
dhidreirf, mistrust (n)
dhidreirsf, mistrust (v)
dhiduliart, misadventure (n)
dhienridrup, misinterpretation (n)
dhienridrusp, misinterpret (v)
dhifelirde, misdeed (n)
dhifiunferst, mispronounce (v)
dhifiunfert, mispronunciation (n)

dhiflersh, miscredibility (n)
dhiflershwan, miscreant (n doer)
dhiflude, miscarriage (n)
dhifluzde, miscarry (v)
dhifruifk, misplay (n)
dhifruifsk, misplay (v)
dhigardas, miscalculate (v)
dhigardash, miscalculation (n)
dhiglishk, misstep (n)
dhiglishsk, misstep (v)
dhigork, mistake (n)
dhigorkiu, mistakenly (adv)
dhigorsk, mistake (v)
dhigorskyot, mistook (v pa)
dhigrusf, misgive (v)
dhigrusfyot, misgave (v pa)
dhiguniarst, miscommunicate (v)
dhiguniart, miscommunication (n)
dhihetherst, misjudge (v)
dhihethert, misjudgement (n)
dhihethert, misjudgment (n)
dhihinarf, misquote (n)
dhihinarsf, misquote (v)
dhikarpazde, mishandle (v)
dhikolirp, mishap (n)
dhikolirsp, mishappen (v)
dhikuarfk, misdirection (n)
dhikuarfsk, misdirect (v)
dhikuvar, misbehavior (n)
dhikuvasre, misbehave (v)
dhilalirst, mislead (v)
dhilalirtiu, misleadingly (adv)
dhilalirtwan, misleader (n doer)
dhilarast, misrule (v)
dhiliarp, misread (n)
dhiliarsp, misread (v)
dhiliarspyot, misread (v pa)
dhiloshirp, misperception (n)
dhiloshirsp, misperceive (v)
dhiludars, misrepresent (v)
dhiludarsh, misrepresentation (n)
dhimuthk, mismatch (n)
dhimuthsk, mismatch (v)
dhiodrukerst, misapprehend (v)
dhiodrukert, misapprehension (n)
dhioflikirme, misappropriation (n)
dhioflikirzme, misappropriate (v)
dhioroifk, misalignment (n)
dhioroifsk, misalign (v)
dhiorshairpyek, misallocation (n pl)
dhiorshairsp, misallocate (v)
dhipafirt, misfit (n)
dhisharshk, mismanagement (n)
dhisharshsk, mismanage (v)
dhishriauk, misfire (n)
dhishriausk, misfire (v)
dhithasle, misspell (v)
dhithorkyek, misapplication (n pl)
dhithorsk, misapply (v)

dhithuirst, mistreat (v)
dhithuirt, mistreatment (n)
dhitierf, miscue (n)
dhitiersf, miscue (v)
dhitrelst, misunderstand (v)
dhitrelstyot, misunderstood (v pa)
dhitrulis, misprint (v)
dhitrulish, misprint (n)
dhituirp, misguidance (n)
dhituirsp, misguide (v)
dhiuferst, misidentify (v)
dhiufert, misidentification (n)
dhiviern, misnomer (n)
dhivirt, mischief (n)
dhivirtu, mischievous (adj)
dhivoashmun, misfortune (n)
dhor, a (det)
dhurf, goo (n)
dhurfu, gooey (adj)
dhurs, hose (v)
dhursh, hose (n)
dhurshuet, hosiery (n)
dhurshwan, hoser (n doer)
diagalist, explode (v)
diagalit, explosion (n)
diagalitiu, explosively (adv)
diagalitu, explosive (adj)
diagalitwan, explosive (n doer)
dialat, equivalence (n)
dialatu, equivalent (adj)
dialirk, trunk (n)
dialirsk, truncate (v)
dialirst, post (v d:ad)
dialirt, post (n d:ad)
dialirtar, postage (n)
dialirtaru, postal (adj)
dialirtarwan, postman (n doer)
dialirtuet, poster (n d:display)
dialirtwan, poster (n doer d:ad)
dialp, hurdle (n)
dialsp, hurdle (v)
dialtaurn, postcard (n)
dialtethiork, postmaster (n)
dialtshtarst, postmark (v)
dialtshtart, postmark (n)
dianirst, sanctify (v)
dianirt, sanctity (n)
dianork, sanction (n)
dianorsk, sanction (v)
diapliorl, driveway (n)
diapor, belly (n)
diaposre, belly (v)
diardar, model (n)
diardasre, model (v)
diarde, mode (n)
diardiu, modally (adv)
diardu, modal (adj)
diarduet, modality (n)
diarf, bow (n d:bend)
diargwan, barger (n doer)
diariark, bellow (n)
diariarsk, bellow (v)

diark, burden (n)
diarku, burdensome (adj)
diarme, bell (n)
diarn, discovery (n)
diarnwan, discoverer (n doer)
diarp, drive (v)
diarpwan, driver (n doer)
diars, joint (v)
diarsf, bow (v d:bend)
diarsh, joint (n)
diarshiu, jointly (adv)
diarsht, equity (n)
diarsk, burden (v)
diarsne, discover (v)
diarsp, drive (v)
diarspyot, drove (v pa)
diarst, join (v)
diart, join (n)
diarthiu, acutely (adv)
diarthu, acute (adj)
diartwan, joiner (n doer)
diarze, subsidize (v)
diarzge, barge (v)
diarzhe, subsidy (n)
diatiarst, jitter (v)
diatiart, jitter (n)
diatralf, hurl (n)
diatralsf, hurl (v)
diaurf, maze (n)
diaurk, refusal (n d:decline)
diaursk, refuse (v d:decline)
diave, melody (n)
diavu, melodic (adj)
diazharn, subsidence (n)
diazhart, subsidiary (n)
dibalf, melon (n)
dibarge, trial (n)
didarn, similarity (n)
didarniu, similarly (adv)
didarnu, similar (adj)
didukshkorst, troubleshoot (v)
didukshkortwan, troubleshooter (n doer)
didukzhirnu, troublesome (adj)
didushk, trouble (n)
didushkwan, troublemaker (n doer)
didushsk, trouble (v)
diefk, cuff (n)
diefsk, cuff (v)
diekierpiu, rightfully (adv)
diekierpu, rightful (adj)
dienork, cartridge (n)
dierk, right (n d:correct)
dierkiu, rightly (adv d:correct)
dierku, right (adj d:correct)
dierkuet, righteousness (n)
dierkuet, rightness (n)
dierkuetiu, righteously (adv)
dierkuetu, righteous (adj)
dierkuetwan, righteous (n doer)
dierkwan, righter (n doer d:correct)

dieroshst, bay (v d:howl)
dierosht, bay (n d:howl)
dieroshtwan, bayer (n doer d:howl)
diersh, apparatus (n)
diersk, right (v d:correct)
difadarf, photograph (n)
difadarft, photography (n)
difadarfwan, photographer (n doer)
difadarsf, photograph (v)
difakishkist, photocopy (v)
difakishkit, photocopy (n)
difakishkitwan, photocopier (n doer)
difarde, photo (n)
dife, per (adv/prep)
diforst, adapt (v)
difort, adaptation (n)
difortiu, adaptably (adv)
difortiu, adaptively (adv)
difortu, adaptable (adj)
difortu, adaptive (adj)
difortwan, adapter (n doer)
difortwan, adaptor (n doer)
dihorlu, where-to (adv)
dihorlu, whither (adv/conj)
dikarf, beg (n)
dikarfwan, beggar (n doer)
dikarsf, beg (v)
dikiurk, toggle (n)
dikiursk, toggle (v)
dikorsh, togetherness (n)
dikorshiu, together (adv)
dilarth, boutique (n)
dilkarst, polarize (v)
dilkart, polarity (n)
dilkartu, polar (adj)
dilkartuet, polarization (n)
diloirk, molecule (n)
diloirku, molecular (adj)
diloran, sweater (n d:clothing)
dilorf, limp (n)
dilorfu, limp (adj)
dilork, pole (n)
dilorp, toe (n)
dilorsf, limp (v)
dilpthrink, toenail (n)
dilsharf, separation (n)
dilsharfiu, separately (adv)
dilshartu, separate (adj)
dilsharfwan, separator (n doer)
dilsharsf, separate (v)
dilst, list (v d:sequence)
dilt, list (n d:sequence)
dilth, currency (n)
dimuarn, tonight (n)
dimuarniu, tonight (adv)
dimul, holiness (n)
dimulu, holy (adj)
dinakran, kilogram (n)
dinanetilirf, fingertip (n)
dinank, finger (n)

dinansk, finger (v)
dinanthrink, fingernail (n)
dinantrulis, fingerprint (v)
dinantrulish, fingerprint (n)
dinarl, thinness (n)
dinarliu, thinly (adv)
dinarlu, thin (adj)
dinarsle, thin (v)
dinlimert, kilometer (n)
dint, thousand (num 1000 card)
dintai-, kilo- (num 1000 pref)
dintartu, myriad (adj)
dinteth, thousandth (num 1000 ord)
diofk, trench (n)
diofsk, trench (v)
dioniork, thermometer (n)
diopar, buy (n)
dioparuil, buyout (n)
dioparwan, buyer (n doer)
diopasre, buy (v)
diopasryot, bought (v pa)
diorame, cannon (n)
diork, auction (n)
diorkwan, auctioneer (n doer)
diorsh, therm (n)
diorshst, rotate (v)
diorsht, rotation (n)
diorshtar, rotor (n)
diorshtu, rotary (adj)
diorshtu, rotational (adj)
diorshtwan, rotator (n doer)
diorshu, thermal (adj)
diorsk, auction (v)
diorthk, perch (n d:pole)
diorthsk, perch (v d:pole)
Dioshviurl, Tuesday (n)
diotarsne, jot (v)
diothk, spoof (n)
diothsk, spoof (v)
dir, to (prep)
diraf, rod (n)
dirafk, oratory (n)
dirafkwan, orator (n doer)
dirafsk, orate (v)
diranfiu, orally (adv)
diranfu, oral (adj)
dirap, rot (n)
dirasp, rot (v)
dirban, hormone (n)
dirbe, try (n)
dirbuil, tryout (n)
dirge, drip (n)
dirgu, drippy (adj)
dirgwan, dripper (n doer)
dirip, tilt (n)
dirisp, tilt (v)
dirthk, pixel (n)
dirvart, encouragement (n)
dirzbe, try (v)
dirzge, drip (v)
dirzhe, thing (n)
dishaviern, pseudonym (n)

disherl, diesel (n)
Dishproshium, Dysprosium (n)
ditapshoirt, poolside (n)
ditapshoirtu, poolside (adj)
ditarp, pool (n)
ditarsp, pool (v)
diuarf, voracity (n)
diuarfiu, voraciously (adv)
diuarfu, voracious (adj)
diuirp, embarrassment (n)
diuirsp, embarrass (v)
diumesp, reel (v)
diump, reel (n)
diundrinat, spyglass (n)
diunk, bonk (n)
diunsk, bonk (v)
diurk, quiz (n)
diurn, spy (n)
diurp, boast (n)
diurpwan, boaster (n doer)
diurshk, boost (n)
diurshkwan, booster (n doer)
diurshsk, boost (v)
diursk, quiz (v)
diursne, spy (v)
diursp, boast (v)
diurth, reed (n)
diusht, niche (n)
diuvart, vortex (n)
diuzhge, keg (n)
divar, courage (n)
divariu, courageously (adv)
divaru, courageous (adj)
divasre, encourage (v)
diveiank, misogyny (n)
diviurl, today (n)
diviurliu, today (adv)
diviurlu, today (adj)
divrabelkoftiu, ultraconservatively (adv)
divrabelkoftu, ultraconservative (adj)
divrafeirank, ultraviolet (n)
divrafeiranku, ultraviolet (adj)
divrakarlfu, ultranational (adj)
divrakarlfwan, ultranationalist (n doer)
divrazhantarn, ultrasound (n)
divrazhantarniu, ultrasonically (adv)
divrazhantarnu, ultrasonic (adj)
divulfu, mellow (adj)
divulsf, mellow (v)
divulst, adopt (v)
divult, adoption (n)
divultu, adoptive (adj)
divultwan, adopter (n doer)
doarp, chest (n d:torso)
doarst, mouse (v)
doart, mouse (n)
doartwan, mouser (n doer)
doartyek, mice (n pl)
doatethreilp, mousetrap (n)

dode, then (adj/adv)
dofarf, pupil (n d:student)
doiardaurp, tabletop (n)
doiardorap, tablespoon (n)
doiarflarf, tablecloth (n)
doiarshlerf, tableware (n)
doiarst, table (v)
doiart, table (n)
doiashk, poke (n d:push)
doiashku, pokey (adj d:push)
doiashkwan, poker (n doer d:push)
doiashsk, poke (v d:push)
doibar, breadth (n)
doibariu, broadly (adv)
doibaru, broad (adj)
doibarwelu, broader (adj)
doibasre, broaden (v)
doidarn, lobby (n)
doidarnwan, lobbyist (n doer)
doidarsne, lobby (v)
doikark, harassment (n)
doikarkwan, harasser (n doer)
doikarsk, harass (v)
doikurp, bustle (n)
doikursp, bustle (v)
doilarme, idiocy (n)
doilarmiu, idiotically (adv)
doilarmu, idiotic (adj)
doilarmwan, idiot (n doer)
doinst, lob (v)
doirbarwaku, broadest (adj)
doirf, idol (n)
doirge, margin (n)
doirgiu, marginally (adv)
doirgu, marginal (adj)
doirn, lobe (n)
doirp, squish (n)
doirpu, squishy (adj)
doirpwan, squisher (n doer)
doirst, idolize (v)
doirshk, bust (n d:burst)
doirshkwan, buster (n doer d:burst)
doirshsk, bust (v d:burst)
doirsp, squish (v)
doirve, fragment (n)
doirvu, fragile (adj)
doirzge, marginalize (v)
doirzve, fragment (v)
doisht, tablet (n)
doithk, page (n d:paper)
doithkuest, paginate (v)
doithkuet, pagination (n)
doitiark, tabloid (n)
dok, exit (n)
dokart, executive (n d:businessperson)
dokast, execute (v d:perform)
dokat, execution (n d:perform)
dokatiu, executively (adv d:perform)
dokatu, executive (adj d:perform)

dokatwan, executioner (n doer
d:perform)
dokatwan, executor (n doer)
dokwan, exiter (n doer)
dolarde, threat (n)
dolarme, idiom (n)
dolarmu, idiomatic (adj)
dolarzde, threaten (v)
dolarzme, idiomate (v)
dolfk, burglary (n)
dolfkwan, burglar (n doer)
dolfsk, burglarize (v)
dolfsk, burgle (v)
dolirme, poll (n)
dolirmwan, poller (n doer)
dolirst, thread (v)
dolirt, thread (n)
dolirzme, poll (v)
dolpshlerf, cookware (n)
dolpuil, cookout (n)
dolpvornt, cookbook (n)
dolpwan, cook (n doer)
dolsp, cook (v)
domast, button (v)
domat, button (n)
domatwan, buttoner (n doer)
domursle, hallow (v)
dopilp, cookie (n)
doraifork, pollutant (n)
dorairk, pollution (n)
dorairkwan, polluter (n doer)
dorairsk, pollute (v)
dorame, wear (n d:clothe)
doramiu, wearably (adv d:clothe)
doramu, wearable (adj d:clothe)
doramwan, wearer (n doer
d:clothe)
Doran, EhoMonth07 (n)
dorap, spoon (n)
dorapu, spoonful (adj)
dorapwan, spooner (n doer)
dorasp, spoon (v)
dorazme, wear (v d:clothe)
dorazmyot, wore (v pa d:clothe)
dorbirde, broadcast (n)
dorbirdwan, broadcaster (n doer)
dorbirzde, broadcast (v)
dorbirzdyot, broadcast (v pa)
dordart, politics (n)
dordast, politic (v)
dordat, polity (n)
dordatiu, politically (adv)
dordatu, political (adj)
dordatwan, politician (n doer)
doreinf, politeness (n)
doreinfiu, politely (adv)
doreinfu, polite (adj)
dorfmiraf, gearshift (n)
dorfp, gear (n d:equipment)
dorfprekun, gearbox (n)
dorgbiart, gunpowder (n)
dorgeflerve, gunship (n)
dorgeshkoift, gunshot (n)

dorgeshkorbe, gunboat (n)
dorgetaifort, gunpoint (n)
dorgvaugat, gunfight (n)
dorige, gun (n)
dorigwan, gunner (n doer)
dorikplorn, gunman (n)
dorikplornyek, gunmen (n pl)
dorikshriauk, gunfire (n)
dorikshriauskaut, shriauk (v prp)
dorikshriauskyot, giaul (v pa)
dorirth, poor (n d:low money)
dorizge, gun (v)
dorkairst, spice (v)
dorkairt, spice (n)
dorkairtu, spicy (adj)
dorkairtwan, spicer (n doer)
dorklarst, spend (v)
dorklarstyot, spent (v pa)
dorklartu, spendable (adj)
dorklartwan, spender (n doer)
dorl, readiness (n)
dorliu, readily (adv)
dorlu, ready (adj)
dornirk, carton (n)
dorsh, firm (n d:company)
dorshiun, hallucination (n)
dorshiusne, hallucinate (v)
dorshknargwan, policymaker (n
doer)
dorshkort, police (n)
dorshkthorthkwan, policyholder
(n doer)
dorshork, policy (n)
dorshorkwan, policeman (n doer)
dorshorsk, police (v)
dorsle, ready (v)
dorthkiarf, poorhouse (n)
dorve, rap (n)
dorvwan, rapper (n doer)
dorzve, rap (v)
doshfrelp, executable (n)
doshfrelpiu, executably (adv)
doshfrelpu, executable (adj)
doshpart, asbestos (n)
dosk, exit (v)
dotairf, vertex (n)
dotairk, vertical (n)
dotairkiu, vertically (adv)
dotairku, vertical (adj)
dotaishp, vertebra (n)
dotaishpyek, vertebrae (n pl)
dotaiteshk, vertigo (n)
dotharaf, traversal (n)
dotharasf, traverse (v)
dothorthk, threshold (n)
dotirs, pick (v)
dotirsh, pick (n)
dotirshu, picky (adj)
dotirshwan, picker (n doer)
dotisharp, pickle (n)
dotisharsp, pickle (v)
dotisharst, picket (v)
dotishart, picket (n)

dotishartwan, picketer (n doer)
dotishiveil, pickup (n)
dotshlogarf, pickpocket (n)
dovai, bravo (interj)
dovarast, report (v)
dovarat, report (n)
dovaratiu, reportedly (adv)
dovaratu, reportable (adj)
dovaratwan, reporter (n doer)
dovarf, rapport (n)
dovarsf, rapport (v)
dovart, tobacco (n)
dovibrauthk, torrent (n)
dovibrauthku, torrential (adj)
dovikurtu, torrid (adj)
dovirl, rapidity (n)
dovirliu, rapidly (adv)
dovirlu, rapid (adj)
dovirn, wake (n d:trail)
dovirst, travel (v)
dovirt, travel (n)
dovirtwan, traveler (n doer)
dovirtwan, traveller (n doer)
drafip, paste (n)
drafipu, pasty (adj)
drafipwan, paster (n doer)
drafir, pastel (n)
drafirsh, pastry (n)
drafisp, paste (v)
drafkiork, teamwork (n)
draflern, teammate (n)
draifpu, bound (adj d:move)
draifsp, bound (v d:move)
drailork, summit (n)
drailorsk, summit (v)
drailst, sum (v)
drailt, sum (n)
draimar, summary (n)
draimasre, summarize (v)
drairge, brat (n)
drairk, shout (n)
drairkwan, shouter (n doer)
drairsk, shout (v)
draithk, grid (n)
draithtiurge, gridlock (n)
drakelirn, sophomore (n)
drakirst, sophisticate (v)
drakirt, sophistication (n)
dralblerk, heartbreak (n)
dralblersk, heartbreak (v)
dralblerskyot, heartbroke (v pa)
dralbugor, heartburn (n)
draldaurt, heartbeat (n)
dralf, team (n)
dralibuage, heartache (n)
dralirk, steak (n)
dralkiarf, steakhouse (n)
dralp, store (n)
dralpwan, storer (n doer)
dralraufp, heartland (n)
dralsf, team (v)
dralsp, store (v)
dralt, heart (n)

draltiu, heartily (adv)
draltmenu, heartless (adj)
draltu, hearty (adj)
dranf, bun (n)
drapart, storage (n)
drapflarsh, storefront (n)
drapkiarf, storehouse (n)
drapklorfwan, storekeeper (n doer)
draubar, kennel (n)
draufk, brashness (n)
draufkiu, brashly (adv)
draufku, brash (adj)
draugarge, cynicism (n)
draugargiu, cynically (adv)
draugargu, cynical (adj)
draugargwan, cynic (n doer)
draurkuin, recruit (n)
draurs, dog (v)
draursh, dog (n)
draushfanirn, dogwood (n)
draushkiarf, doghouse (n)
draushvaugat, dogfight (n)
dreiafleve, flagship (n)
dreiap, flag (n)
dreiaparap, flagstaff (n)
dreiaparapyek, flagstaves (n pl)
dreiapdilork, flagpole (n)
dreiapwan, flagger (n doer)
dreiflairsh, trustworthiness (n)
dreiflairshu, trustworthy (adj)
dreil, true (adj)
dreilsh, truth (n)
dreilshiu, truthfully (adv)
dreilshu, truthful (adj)
dreilshuet, truism (n)
dreilu, truly (adv)
dreinak, flame (n)
dreinaku, flammable (adj)
dreinaku, inflammable (adj)
dreinakuet, inflamation (n)
dreinakuetu, inflammatory (adj)
dreinakwan, flamer (n doer)
dreinask, flame (v)
dreinask, inflame (v)
dreinshkart, flagrancy (n)
dreinshkartiu, flagrantly (adv)
dreinshkartu, flagrant (adj)
dreirf, trust (n)
dreirfu, trustful (adj)
dreirfu, trusty (adj)
dreirfuet, trustfulness (n)
dreirfuin, trustee (n)
dreirsf, trust (v)
dreishar, flair (n)
dreithk, flare (n)
dreithsk, flare (v)
dreivoshar, truelove (n)
drelif, stew (n)
drelisf, stew (v)
dreln, pearl (n)
dreshk, duplicate (n)

dreshkuet, duplication (n)
dreshkwan, duplicator (n doer)
dreshsk, duplicate (v)
driadaurt, drumbeat (n)
driafsk, teem (v)
driarde, drum (n)
driardwan, drummer (n doer)
driark, bang (n d:collision)
driarkwan, banger (n doer d:collision)
driarp, earnestness (n)
driarpiu, earnestly (adv)
driarpu, earnest (adj)
driarpwan, earner (n doer)
driars, anoint (v)
driarsh, anointment (n)
driarsk, bang (v d:collision)
driarsp, earn (v)
driarsth, perish (v)
driart, quaintness (n)
driarthu, perishable (adj)
driartiu, quaintly (adv)
driartu, quaint (adj)
driarzde, drum (v)
drienf, grove (n)
driensk, grovel (v)
drigerst, select (v)
drigert, selection (n)
drigertiu, selectively (adv)
drigertu, selective (adj)
drigertuet, selectivity (n)
drigertwan, selector (n doer)
drigruts, seclude (v)
drigrutsh, seclusion (n)
drikarst, sedate (v)
drikart, sedation (n)
drikartiu, sedatively (adv)
drikartu, sedative (adj)
drikartwan, sedative (n doer)
drikinorp, segregation (n)
drikinorpwan, segregationist (n doer)
drikinorsp, segregate (v)
drikirn, glean (n)
drikirsne, glean (v)
drilarn, bunny (n)
drilaurk, bullhorn (n)
drilf, glass (n d:quartz)
drilfeshlerf, glassware (n)
drilorst, wrinkle (v)
drilort, wrinkle (n)
drilortu, wrinkly (adj)
drilortwan, wrinkler (n doer)
drinat, glass (n d:spectacles)
drishk, crease (n)
drishkwan, creaser (n doer)
drishork, increment (n)
drishorkiu, incrementally (adv)
drishorku, incremental (adj)
drishorsk, increment (v)
drishsk, crease (v)
dritarst, glare (v)
dritart, glare (n)

drithk, glee (n)
drithkiu, gleefully (adv)
drithku, gleeful (adj)
driulk, creek (n)
driurp, beep (n)
driurpwan, beeper (n doer)
driursp, beep (v)
drivelk, secession (n)
drivelsk, secede (v)
drizhast, glaze (v)
drizhat, glaze (n)
drizhaurk, sedition (n)
drof, clearness (n)
drofan, clearance (n)
drofiu, clearly (adv)
drofk, clock (n)
drofkalu, counterclockwise (adj)
drofku, clockwise (adj)
drofsk, clock (v)
drofu, clear (adj)
droifp, rib (n)
droifsp, rib (v)
droilf, rim (n)
drokifar, star (n d:celebrity)
drokifasre, star (v d:celebrity)
drolfk, oscillation (n)
drolfkwan, oscillator (n doer)
drolfsk, oscillate (v)
dronirp, tropic (n)
dronirpiu, tropically (adv)
dronirpu, tropical (adj)
drosf, clear (v)
drotap, clarity (n)
drotarp, clarification (n)
drotasp, clarify (v)
druafk, gleam (n)
druafsk, gleam (v)
drufk, prey (n)
drufsk, prey (v)
drufst, sleeve (v)
druft, sleeve (n)
druftmenu, sleeveless (adj)
drukarst, predate (v)
drukart, predation (n)
drukartu, predatory (adj)
drukartwan, predator (n doer)
drulirp, appreciation (n)
drulirpiu, appreciatively (adv)
drulirpu, appreciative (adj)
drulirsp, appreciate (v)
drushk, derivation (n)
drushku, derivative (adj)
drushsk, derive (v)
duadeirge, bridegroom (n)
duaifarn, tights (n)
duaifvarp, tightrope (n)
duaikshneft, chopstick (n)
duairf, tightness (n)
duairfiu, tightly (adv)
duairfu, tight (adj)
duairfwaku, tightest (adj)
duairfwelu, tighter (adj)
duairk, chop (n)

duairkiu, choppily (adv)
duairku, choppy (adj)
duairkwan, chopper (n doer)
duairsf, tighten (v)
duairsk, chop (v)
duakelerf, bridesmaid (n)
duakor, beaker (n)
duakrilst, gouge (v)
duakrilt, gouge (n)
duarf, beam (n)
duarfwan, beamer (n doer)
duarme, anatomy (n)
duarmu, anatomical (adj)
duarp, type (n d:kind)
duarpiu, typically (adv d:kind)
duarpu, typical (adj d:kind)
duars, present (v d:give gift)
duarsf, beam (v)
duarsh, present (n d:give gift)
duarshk, presentation (n)
duarshkwan, presenter (n doer)
duarsp, type (v d:kind)
duart, beak (n)
duatharge, ventilation (n)
duathargwan, ventilator (n doer)
duatharzge, ventilate (v)
duathk, vent (n)
duathkwan, venter (n doer)
duathsk, vent (v)
duavart, attic (n)
duavirt, FertilityStone (n)
dubal, bumble (n d:buzz)
dubarst, ripen (v)
dubart, ripeness (n)
dubartu, ripe (adj)
dubasle, bumble (v d:buzz)
dubielirk, opportunity (n)
dubielirku, opportunistic (adj)
dubielirkwan, opportunist (n
    doer)
dublars, oppress (v)
dublarsh, oppression (n)
dublarshiu, oppressively (adv)
dublarshu, oppressive (adj)
dublarshwan, oppressor (n doer)
Dubnium, Dubnium (n)
dudirf, puppy (n)
duelk, chip (n)
duelkwan, chipper (n doer)
duelsk, chip (v)
dufuıl, odoı (ıı)
dufarlmenu, odorless (adj)
dufirk, vengence (n)
dufirku, vengeful (adj)
dufirst, criticize (v)
dufirt, criticism (n)
dufirtiu, critically (adv)
dufirtu, critical (adj)
dufirtwan, critic (n doer)
duftart, criterion (n)
duftartyek, criteria (n pl)
duiarf, venom (n)
duiarfu, venomous (adj)

duiark, puck (n)
duiarst, reap (v)
duiartwan, reaper (n doer)
duidark, puppetry (n)
duidarkwan, puppeteer (n doer)
duidart, puppet (n)
duide, pup (n)
duifshlerf, softball (n)
duilp, leniency (n)
duilpiu, leniently (adv)
duilpu, lenient (adj)
duimorap, swimsuit (n)
duirf, softness (n)
duirfiu, softly (adv)
duirfshlerf, software (n)
duirfu, soft (adj)
duirfwan, softener (n doer)
duirn, swim (n)
duirnwan, swimmer (n doer)
duirsf, soften (v)
duirsne, swim (v)
duirsnyot, swam (v pa)
duirzhe, kink (n)
duirzhu, kinky (adj)
duisht, bozo (n)
dukaklurk, cockpit (n)
dukal, cock (n)
dukalaif, cocktail (n)
dukalat, cockiness (n)
dukalu, cocky (adj)
dukarfwan, vendor (n doer)
dukarp, vendetta (n)
dukarsf, vend (v)
dukasle, cock (v)
dukiark, vindication (n)
dukiarkuet, vindictiveness (n)
dukiarkwan, vindicator (n doer)
dukiarsk, vindicate (v)
dulank, drivel (n)
dulansk, drivel (v)
dulansk, drool (v)
dular, bill (n d:beak)
dulef, coast (n d:move)
dulefwan, coaster (n doer
    d:move)
dulesf, coast (v d:move)
dulfk, ooze (n)
dulfsk, ooze (v)
Duliaf, EhoDay04 (n)
duliarst, venture (v)
duliart, adventure (n)
duliartiu, adventurously (adv)
duliartu, adventurous (adj)
duliartwan, adventurer (n doer)
dulirmiu, currently (adv d:now)
dulirmu, current (adj d:now)
dulithk, spool (n)
dulithsk, spool (v)
dunberst, pump (v)
dunbert, pump (n)
dunbertwan, pumper (n doer)
dunirf, opera (n)
dunirn, ton (n)

dunirnk, tonne (n)
dunsh, coop (n d:cage)
dupal, bubble (n)
dupalu, bubbly (adj)
dupalwan, bubbler (n doer)
duparfwan, tailor (n doer)
duparku, mad (adj d:angry)
duparkwelu, madder (adj
    d:angry)
duparsf, tailor (v)
duparsk, madden (v d:angry)
dupasle, bubble (v)
durage, knuckle (n)
duragwan, knuckler (n doer)
durai, voila (interj)
durazge, knuckle (v)
durifst, operate (v)
durift, operation (n)
duriftiu, operationally (adv)
duriftu, operable (adj)
duriftu, operational (adj)
duriftwan, operator (n doer)
durize, drone (v d:tone)
durizhe, drone (n d:tone)
durk, cog (n)
durl, there (adj/adv/interj)
durl, there (pron)
durmarfiu, therefore (adv)
durme, tween (n)
durovilfiu, thereafter (adv)
durtarn, operative (n)
durth, altar (n)
durvurniu, thereby (adv)
dushan, bride (n)
dushanu, bridal (adj)
dushart, desert (n d:wasteland)
dutark, lawsuit (n)
dutarsk, sue (v)
duterk, washer (n d:spacer)
Dutersh, Dutch (n)
dutharp, season (n d:spice)
dutharsp, season (v d:spice)
duvelp, component (n)
duvirl, sponsorship (n)
duvirlwan, sponsor (n doer)
duvirsle, sponsor (v)
duvoirp, sponge (n)
duvoirsp, sponge (v)
e, (separator)
Efuk, Diomlıe (ıı davöka)
Efap, Gallium (n davoka)
efbirn, openness (n)
efbirniu, openly (adv)
efbirnu, open (adj)
efbirnwan, opener (n doer)
efbirsne, open (v)
efel, ever (adj/adv)
efelshethiu, everlastingly (adv)
efelshethu, everlasting (adj)
eferfital, everywhere (adv)
eferlizhe, everything (n/pron)
eferlshlarde, everybody (pron)
eferlton, everyone (pron)

eferlu, every (adj)
eferlviurl, everyday (n)
eferlviurlu, everyday (adj)
Efik, Krypton (n davoka)
Efip, Germanium (n davoka)
Efop, Arsenic (n davoka)
efuerst, opt (v)
efuert, option (n)
efuertiu, optionally (adv)
efuertu, optional (adj)
Efup, Selenium (n davoka)
eikuift, dialog (n)
eikuift, dialogue (n)
Einshteinium, Einsteinium (n)
eiporf, diary (n)
eiporst, dial (v)
eiport, dial (n)
Ekak, Fluorine (n davoka)
Ekap, Boron (n davoka)
Ekik, Neon (n davoka)
ekip avekupart, carbon dioxide (n)
Ekip, Carbon (n davoka)
Ekop, Nitrogen (n davoka)
Ekup, Oxygen (n davoka)
ekuparn, ozone (n)
ekupast, oxidize (v)
ekupat, oxide (n)
ekupatuert, oxidation (n)
ekupatwan, oxidizer (n doer)
Elak, Iodine (n davoka)
Elap, Indium (n davoka)
eles, unearth (v)
elesh, earth (n)
eleshlorve, earthling (n)
eleshpiove, earthquake (n)
eleshu, earthly (adj)
elfe, E (let sng)
elfhem, Number_1e306
elfi, Es (let pl)
elialfu, early (adj)
elialfwaku, earliest (adj)
elialfwelu, earlier (adj)
Elip, Tin (n davoka)
Elop, Antimony (n davoka)
Elup, Tellurium (n davoka)
emde, onto (prep)
Enak, Ununspetium (n davoka)
Enap, Ununtrium (n davoka)
engadafka, Number_1e4203
engahem, Number_1e4056
engali, Ngs (let pl)
engel, Ng (let sng)
Enik, Ununoctium (n davoka)
Enip, Ununquadium (n davoka)
enokriuk, introduction (n)
enokriuku, introductory (adj)
enokriusk, introduce (v)
Enop, Ununpentium (n davoka)
enotharak, introversion (n)
enotharakwan, introvert (n doer)
enotharask, introvert (v)
enribrivarsk, interweave (v)

enribrivarskyot, interwove (v pa)
enribubrun, interdependence (n)
enribubruniu, interdependently (adv)
enribubrunu, interdependent (adj)
enridap, interval (n)
enridrolmu, interstellar (adj)
enridrup, interpretation (n)
enridrupu, interpretive (adj)
enridrupwan, interpreter (n doer)
enridrusp, interpret (v)
enrifime, intervention (n)
enrifizme, intervene (v)
enrifoirsne, interlace (v)
enrifruifk, interplay (n)
enrifuast, interview (v)
enrifuat, interview (n)
enrifuatuin, interviewee (n)
enrifuatwan, interviewer (n doer)
enrigaifst, interrupt (v)
enrigaift, interruption (n)
enrigaiftu, interruptible (adj)
enrigef, interference (n)
enrigesf, interfere (v)
enrikarlfiu, internationally (adv)
enrikarlfu, international (adj)
enrilaidak, intermediacy (n)
enrilaidakwan, intermediary (n doer)
enrilaidask, intermediate (v)
enrilairfu, interim (adj)
enrilaivursne, intertwine (v)
enrilar, interior (n)
enrilaurku, interplanetary (adj)
enrilotelf, interspersion (n)
enrilotelsf, intersperse (v)
enriludarast, interrelate (v)
enriludarat, interrelation (n)
enriludaratfirf, interrelationship (n)
enrilushiarst, interrogate (v)
enrilushiart, interrogation (n)
enrilushiartwan, interrogator (n doer)
enrimarnf, intercourse (n)
enrimoip, internet (n)
enrinaltripu, interfaith (adj)
enrinoirthu, interracial (adj)
enrinok, intermission (n)
enrinokiu, intermittently (adv)
enrinoku, intermittent (adj)
enrinosk, intermit (v)
enripalst, interact (v)
enripalt, interaction (n)
enripaltiu, interactively (adv)
enripaltu, interactive (adj)
enriplornu, interpersonal (adj)
enriprusth, interleave (v)
enripruth, interleaf (n)
enriroishk, interlink (n)
enriroishsk, interlink (v)
enrirusht, interlude (n)

enrishaiarsh, interstate (n)
enrishaiarshu, interstate (adj)
enrishal, intersection (n)
enrishasle, intersect (v)
enrishirp, interception (n)
enrishirpwan, interceptor (n doer)
enrishirsp, intercept (v)
enrishnarf, interconnection (n)
enrishnarsf, interconnect (v)
enriterp, interjection (n)
enritersp, interject (v)
enrithoirs, interface (v)
enrithoirsh, interface (n)
enritiurge, interlock (n)
enrituarn, interchange (n)
enrituarniu, interchangeably (adv)
enrituarnu, interchangeable (adj)
enriverk, intercession (n)
enriversk, intercede (v)
enrivetarp, interagency (n)
enrivularn, intermarriage (n)
enrivularsne, intermarry (v)
enrizhorfsk, intermix (v)
Enup, Ununhexium (n davoka)
enutark, eligibility (n)
enutarku, eligible (adj)
epshilorn, epsilon (n)
er, uh (interj)
Erak, Astatine (n davoka)
Erap, Thallium (n davoka)
Erbium, Erbium (n)
Erik, Radon (n davoka)
Erip, Lead (n davoka)
ern, um (interj)
Erop, Bismuth (n davoka)
Erup, Polonium (n davoka)
Etak, Chlorine (n davoka)
Etap, Aluminum (n davoka)
etarn, eta (n)
Etik, Argon (n davoka)
Etip, Silicon (n davoka)
Etop, Phosphorus (n davoka)
Etup, Sulfur (n davoka)
Europium, Europium (n)
fabirk, wheeze (n)
fabirsk, wheeze (v)
faborft, fusion (n)
faborst, fuse (v)
fabort, fuse (n)
fabortwan, fuser (n doer)
fadirf, deer (n)
fadirfyek, deer (n pl)
fafalst, fuzz (v)
fafalt, fuzz (n)
fafaltu, fuzz (adj)
fafirst, civilize (v)
fafirt, civility (n)
fafirtiu, civily (adv)
fafirtu, civil (adj)
fafirtwan, civilian (n doer)
fafiruet, civilization (n)

faiashst, spike (v)
faiashstyot, spikes (v pa)
faiasht, spike (n)
faifaif, taboo (n)
faifaifu, taboo (adj)
fairf, sigh (n)
fairk, spite (n)
fairku, spiteful (adj)
fairsf, sigh (v)
fairsk, spite (v)
faishst, dominate (v)
faisht, dominance (n)
faisht, domination (n)
faishtu, dominant (adj)
faishtwan, dominator (n doer)
faitazhzge, mangle (v)
faiteshsk, maul (v)
falafasht, urinal (n)
falan, cinema (n)
falar, roll (n d:tumble)
falarafen, rollover (n)
falarf, urine (n)
falarfk, urination (n)
falarfkuit, urology (n)
falarfkuitwan, urologist (n doer)
falarfkwan, urinator (n doer)
falarfsk, urinate (v)
falarfu, urinary (adj)
falarth, seldom (adj/adv)
falaruil, rollout (n)
falarvark, rollback (n)
falarwan, roller (n doer d:tumble)
falasre, roll (v d:tumble)
faliarp, wheelbarrow (n)
falirf, steer (n d:cattle)
falirk, rash (n)
falirkiu, rashly (adv)
falirku, rash (adj)
falirme, stream (n)
falirmwan, streamer (n doer)
falirn, kid (n d:child)
falirp, urb (n)
falirpu, urban (adj)
falirpuet, urbanization (n)
falirsp, urbanize (v)
falirzme, stream (v)
falmroifsk, streamline (v)
falnporgwan, kidnapper (n doer)
falnporzge, kidnap (v)
faluk, chimney (n)
famor, bed (n)
famorshranf, bedroom (n)
famosre, bed (v)
faninkiarf, woodhouse (n)
faninkiork, woodwork (n)
faninkiorkwan, woodworker (n doer)
faninkiorsk, woodwork (v)
faninplorn, woodman (n)
faninplorn, woodsman (n)
faninplornyek, woodmen (n pl)
faninplornyek, woodsmen (n pl)
faninraufp, woodland (n)

faninraufpu, woodlands (adj)
faninthilorf, woodshed (n)
fanirn, wood (n)
fanirnu, wooden (adj)
fanirst, patronize (v)
fanirt, patron (n)
fanirtwan, patronizer (n doer)
fanturn, patriot (n)
fanturniu, patriotically (adv)
fanturnu, patriotic (adj)
fapwan, asker (n doer)
fareilshk, serpent (n)
fareilshku, serpentine (adj)
farsht, enemy (n)
farsth, gap (v)
farth, gap (n)
farzhe, bur (n)
fashirk, faction (n)
fasp, ask (v)
fatelt, mallet (n)
faturk, cult (n)
faturp, cultivation (n)
faturpwan, cultivator (n doer)
fatursp, cultivate (v)
faudanarsp, succumb (v)
fauirn, virus (n)
fauirniu, virally (adv)
fauirnu, viral (adj)
fauirnuet, virulence (n)
fauirnuetiu, virulently (adv)
fauirnuetu, virulent (adj)
fauirnyek, virii (n pl)
fauirnyek, viruses (n pl)
faupwasne, sucker (v)
faurf, buffer (n d:absorber)
faurpuest, suction (v)
faurpuet, suction (n)
faurpwan, sucker (n doer)
faursf, buffer (v d:absorber)
faursh, narcism (n)
faursh, narcissism (n)
faurshk, narcotic (n)
faurshu, narcissistic (adj)
faurshu, narcistic (adj)
faurshwan, narcissist (n doer)
faurshwan, narcist (n doer)
faursp, suck (v)
feianku, sparsely (adv)
feianku, sparse (adj)
feifbrelsh, showplace (n)
feifiaurn, clemency (n)
feifiaurnu, clement (adj)
feifkelerf, showgirl (n)
feifplonfirf, showmanship (n)
feifplorn, showman (n)
feifplornyek, showmen (n pl)
feifshkorbe, showboat (n)
feifshkorzbe, showboat (v)
feifshranf, showroom (n)
feifshuarst, showcase (v)
feifshuart, showcase (n)
feifthetirs, showpiece (v)
feifthetirsh, showpiece (n)

feiftiern, showdown (n)
feigalf, poker (n d:game)
feigar, ghost (n)
feigaru, ghostly (adj)
feigasre, ghost (v)
feihem, Number_1e2106
feikarde, vodka (n)
feil, F (let sng)
feili, Fs (let pl)
feirank, violet (n)
feiranku, violet (adj)
feirf, show (n)
feirfu, showy (adj)
feirs, gust (v)
feirsf, show (v)
feirsh, gust (n)
feirshu, gusty (adj)
feitazhzge, mingle (v)
feitun, bulletin (n)
feizhark, murder (n)
feizharkiu, murderously (adv)
feizharku, murderous (adj)
feizharkwan, murderer (n doer)
feizharsk, murder (v)
fekiarku, vincible (adj)
fekuifst, catalog (v)
fekuift, catalog (n)
fekuiftwan, cataloger (n doer)
felar, story (n)
felefwan, mumbler (n doer)
felesf, mumble (v)
felesfyot, mumbles (v pa)
felifiarnu, fallopian (adj)
felirde, deed (n)
felirme, humor (n)
felirmiu, humorously (adv)
felirmu, humorous (adj)
felirmwan, humorist (n doer)
felirzme, humor (v)
feliu, very (adv)
felnarpiu, humbly (adv)
felnarpu, humble (adj)
felnarsp, humble (v)
felnarst, humiliate (v)
felnart, humility (n)
felnartuet, humiliation (n)
felshp, rasp (n)
felshpu, raspy (adj)
felshsp, rasp (v)
fenlrp, mill (n)
fenirpwan, miller (n doer)
fenirshiu, particularly (adv)
fenirshu, particular (adj)
fenirshul, particular (n)
fenirsp, mill (v)
fenirst, scatter (v)
fenork, impregnation (n)
fenorsk, impregnate (v)
ferame, ally (n)
feran, smile (n)
feranwan, smiley (n doer)
ferap, storm (n)
ferapu, stormy (adj)

ferasne, smile (v)
ferasp, storm (v)
ferazme, ally (v)
ferelirk, skillet (n)
Fermium, Fermium (n)
ferpwan, setter (n doer d:place)
fers, part (v)
fersh, part (n)
fershiu, partly (adv)
fershuest, partition (v)
fershuet, partition (n)
fersp, set (v d:place)
ferspyot, set (v pa d:place)
ferzhe, portion (n)
fesharn, portrait (n)
feshart, partial (n)
feshartiu, partially (adv)
feshartu, partial (adj)
fesheilk, participle (n)
feshelirk, participation (n)
feshelirkwan, participant (n doer)
feshelirsk, participate (v)
feshiarme, portrayal (n)
feshiarzme, portray (v)
feshirp, particle (n)
feshirp, particulate (n)
feshirpu, particulate (adj)
feshirsp, particulate (v)
feshiurf, portfolio (n)
feshlan, compartment (n)
feshlasne, compartmentalize (v)
feshnarst, partner (v)
feshnart, partnership (n)
feshnartwan, partner (n doer)
feshorst, depart (v)
feshort, departure (n)
feshortwan, departer (n doer)
feshturgwan, parser (n doer)
feshturzge, parse (v)
fetirp, arrow (n)
fiaisharn, visual (n)
fiaisharniu, visually (adv)
fiaisharnu, visual (adj)
fiaisharnuet, visualization (n)
fiaisharsne, visualize (v)
fiaishk, vision (n)
fiaishkiu, visibly (adv)
fiaishku, visible (adj)
fiaishkuet, visibility (n)
fiaishkwan, visionary (n doer)
fiaishsk, envision (v)
fiakshneft, yardstick (n)
fialf, beauty (n)
fialfiu, beautifully (adv)
fialfu, beautiful (adj)
fialirt, sump (n)
fialirtiu, sumptuously (adv)
fialirtu, sumptuous (adj)
fialoirf, fiddle (n d:violin)
fialoirfwan, fiddler (n doer
   d:violin)
fialoirsf, fiddle (v d:violin)
fialsf, beautify (v)

fianirp, swamp (n)
fianirpu, swampy (adj)
fianirsp, swamp (v)
fianirst, pattern (v)
fianirt, pattern (n)
Fianth, EhoMonth06 (n)
fiarazge, vet (v d:examine)
fiarbe, peep (n)
fiarf, peer (n)
fiark, yard (n d:measurement)
fiarkuet, yardage (n
   d:measurement)
fiarp, peek (n)
fiars, freshen (v)
fiarsf, peer (v)
fiarsh, freshness (n)
fiarsheidorn, freshwater (n)
fiarsheidornu, freshwater (adj)
fiarshiu, freshly (adv)
fiarshplorn, freshman (n)
fiarshplornyek, freshmen (n pl)
fiarshu, fresh (adj)
fiarsp, peek (v)
fiarzbe, peep (v)
fiarzme, kid (v d:joke)
fiatarsk, pant (v d:breathe)
fiaurmeniu, mercilessly (adv)
fiaurmenu, merciless (adj)
fiaurn, mercy (n)
fiaurniu, mercifully (adv)
fiaurnu, merciful (adj)
fiaushflarf, washcloth (n)
fiaushfrelpiu, washably (adv)
fiaushfrelpu, washable (adj)
fiaushk, wash (n d:clean)
fiaushku, washy (adj d:clean)
fiaushkuil, washout (n)
fiaushkwan, washer (n doer
   d:clean)
fiaushplok, washboard (n)
fiaushranf, washroom (n)
fiaushsk, wash (v d:clean)
fiavart, veterinarian (n)
fiavartu, veterinary (adj)
fiave, vet (n d:veterinarian)
fidal, event (n)
fidalaik, eventuality (n)
fidalaikiu, eventually (adv)
fidalaiku, eventual (adj)
fidaliu, eventfully (adv)
fidalu, eventful (adj)
fielirsh, scarlet (n)
fielirshu, scarlet (adj)
fielirst, stint (v)
fielirt, stint (n)
fielts, stitch (v)
fieltsh, stitch (n)
fienarf, loneliness (n)
fienarfu, lonely (adj)
fierf, cat (n)
fierfu, catty (adj)
fierge, pang (n)
fiernu, lone (adj)

fiernwan, loner (n doer)
fieshethavube, redneck (n)
fieshkefirt, redhead (n)
fieshreiku, reddish (adj)
fieshroifk, redline (n)
fieshroifsk, redline (v)
fieshst, redden (v)
fiesht, red (n)
fieshtu, red (adj)
fieshtuet, redness (n)
fifarf, kitty (n)
fifirme, kitten (n)
fikokerage, protagony (n)
fikokeragu, protagonistic (adj)
fikokeragwan, protagonist (n
   doer)
fikokerazge, protagonize (v)
fikorp, category (n)
fikorpiu, categorically (adv)
fikorpu, categorical (adj)
fikorpwan, categorizer (n doer)
fikorsp, categorize (v)
Filadelfirf, Philadelphia (n)
filarde, vamp (n)
fildaurf, vampire (n)
filfret, capability (n)
filfretu, capable (adj)
filidarfk, polygraph (n)
filidarfku, polygraphic (adj)
filimeshst, polymerize (v)
filimesht, polymer (n)
filimurk, polygon (n)
filimurku, polygonal (adj)
filimurkyek, polygon (n pl)
Filipirf, Philippine (n)
filiuyarp, polyphony (n)
filiuyarpu, polyphonic (adj)
filivularn, polygamy (n)
filp, cap (n)
filsp, cap (v)
filtarp, kettle (n)
filurf, butter (n)
filurfu, buttery (adj)
filursf, butter (v)
fimalf, evening (n d:late daytime)
fimarl, eve (n)
finar, ballet (n)
finarwan, ballerina (n doer)
finasre, ballet (v)
Fineshork, Phoenix (n)
Finlanurde, Finland (n)
finorak, scallop (n)
finorask, scallop (v)
finuirn, cello (n)
finushst, ream (v d:clear)
finushtwan, reamer (n doer
   d:clear)
fiobalt, ellipse (n)
fiobaltu, elliptical (adj)
fioft, oval (n)
fiokplurde, toolkit (n)
fiokprekun, toolbox (n)
fiorbast, frustrate (v)

fiorbat, frustration (n)
fiorf, loyalty (n)
fiorfiu, loyally (adv)
fiorfonde, frequency (n)
fiorfondiu, frequently (adv)
fiorfondu, frequent (adj)
fiorfonzde, frequent (v)
fiorfu, loyal (adj)
fiorishk, calico (n)
fiorishku, calico (adj)
fiork, tool (n)
fiorme, loom (n)
fiorn, poem (n)
fiornk, callus (n)
fiors, free (v)
fiorsh, freedom (n)
fiorshiu, freely (adv)
fiorshk, freeze (n)
fiorshkwan, freezer (n doer)
fiorshorsh, freebie (n)
fiorshsk, freeze (v)
fiorshskyot, froze (v pa)
fiorshst, frost (v)
fiorsht, frost (n)
fiorshtiu, frostily (adv)
fiorshtu, frosty (adj)
fiorshtwan, froster (n doer)
fiorshu, free (adj)
fiorsk, tool (v)
fiort, poetry (n)
fiortgairk, frostbite (n)
fiortu, poetic (adj)
fiortwan, poet (n doer)
fioshkarp, freehand (n)
fioshlurifst, freeload (v)
fioshluriftwan, freeloader (n doer)
fioshpliorl, freeway (n)
fioshvorlin, freeform (n)
fioshvorlinu, freeform (adj)
firak, ridicule (n)
firakiu, ridiculously (adv)
firaku, ridiculous (adj)
firap, riddance (n)
firapwan, ridder (n doer)
firask, ridicule (v)
firasp, rid (v)
firaspyot, rid (v pa)
firdurak, philosophy (n)
firdurakwan, philosopher (n
    doer)
firfp, ripple (n)
firfsp, ripple (v)
firge, fine (n d:penalty)
firgwan, finer (n doer d:penalty)
firn, phi (n)
firnal, ballad (n)
firnalwan, balladeer (n doer)
firsht, dinosaur (n)
firtes, rifle (v)
firtesh, rifle (n)
firteshwan, rifler (n doer)
firzge, fine (v d:penalty)
fitark, arrest (n)

fitarku, arrestive (adj)
fitarkwan, arrestor (n doer)
fitarsk, arrest (v)
fitarve, levy (n)
fitarzve, levy (v)
fitirs, fission (v)
fitirsh, fission (n)
fitishap, fissure (n)
fituirn, ski (n)
fituirnwan, skier (n doer)
fituirsne, ski (v)
fiuank, prom (n)
fiuashk, prostitution (n)
fiuashkwan, prostitute (n doer)
fiuashsk, prostitute (v)
fiuborfst, protrude (v)
fiuborft, protrusion (n)
fiudairbe, prohibition (n)
fiudairbiu, prohibitively (adv)
fiudairbu, prohibitive (adj)
fiudairbwan, prohibitor (n doer)
fiudairzbe, prohibit (v)
fiudanf, proverb (n d:saying)
fiudanfu, proverbial (adj
    d:saying)
fiudarf, protein (n)
fiudokarst, prosecute (v)
fiudokart, prosecution (n)
fiudokartu, prosecutable (adj)
fiudokartwan, prosecutor (n doer)
fiufabort, profusion (n)
fiufabortiu, profusely (adv)
fiufabortu, profuse (adj)
fiuferzhe, proportion (n)
fiuferzhiu, proportionally (adv)
fiuferzhu, proportional (adj)
fiuflaurs, proliferate (v)
fiuflaursh, proliferation (n)
fiuflaurshiu, prolifically (adv)
fiuflaurshu, prolific (adj)
fiuflaurshwan, proliferator (n
    doer)
fiufrelp, probability (n)
fiufrelpiu, probably (adv)
fiufrelpu, probable (adj)
fiugalirst, protract (v)
fiugalirt, protraction (n)
fiugalirtwan, protractor (n doer)
fiuganorf, propaganda (n)
fiuganorfyek, propaganda (n pl)
fiugarn, propagation (n)
fiugarnwan, propagator (n doer)
fiugarsne, propagate (v)
fiukarge, promenade (n)
fiukarn, produce (n)
fiukart, productivity (n)
fiukarzge, promenade (v)
fiukerage, prominence (n)
fiukeragiu, prominently (adv)
fiukeragu, prominent (adj)
fiuklirp, propriety (n)
fiuklirpu, proprietary (adj)
fiuklirpwan, proprietor (n doer)

fiukreirsth, procrastinate (v)
fiukreirth, procrastination (n)
fiukreirthwan, procrastinator (n
    doer)
fiukuift, prolog (n)
fiukuift, prologue (n)
fiulinirk, proficiency (n)
fiulinirkiu, proficiently (adv)
fiulinirku, proficient (adj)
fiulkoirk, fungicide (n)
fiuloirp, fungus (n)
fiuloirpu, fungal (adj)
fiuloirpyek, fungi (n pl)
fiulork, proposal (n)
fiulork, proposition (n)
fiulorkwan, proposer (n doer)
fiulorsk, propose (v)
fiulotelf, prosperity (n)
fiulotelfiu, prosperously (adv)
fiulotelfu, prosperous (adj)
fiulotelsf, prosper (v)
fiumarl, proton (n)
fiumirp, prong (n)
fiumirsp, prong (v)
fiunank, prophecy (n)
fiunank, prophesy (n)
fiunankwan, prophet (n doer)
fiunelirk, program (n)
fiunelirku, programmable (adj)
fiunelirkwan, programmer (n
    doer)
fiunelirsk, program (v)
fiunferst, pronounce (v)
fiunfert, pronunciation (n)
fiunirk, profession (n)
fiunirkiu, professionally (adv)
fiunirku, professional (adj)
fiunirkwan, professor (n doer)
fiunirsk, profess (v)
fiunolan, proclamation (n)
fiunolasne, proclaim (v)
fiunork, promise (n)
fiunorkwan, promiser (n doer)
fiunorsk, promise (v)
fiuntark, professional (n)
fiuntarkuet, professionalism (n)
fiuntarsk, professionalize (v)
fiunuyern, pronoun (n)
fiupadarn, propellant (n)
fiupafirst, profit (v)
fiupafirt, profit (n)
fiupafirtiu, profitably (adv)
fiupafirtu, profitable (adj)
fiupafirtwan, profiteer (n doer)
fiupafirtwast, profiteer (v)
fiupafiterp, profitability (n)
fiupaltarkiu, proactively (adv)
fiupaltarku, proactive (adj)
fiuparde, propulsion (n)
fiupardwan, propeller (n doer)
fiupark, punt (n)
fiuparkwan, punter (n doer)
fiuparsk, punt (v)

fiuparzde, propel (v)
fiupliurst, procreate (v)
fiupliurt, procreation (n)
fiupliurtwan, procreator (n doer)
fiuralze, prolong (v)
fiuralzhe, prolongation (n)
fiurbe, probe (n)
fiurbwan, prober (n doer)
fiurf, pro (n d:advantage)
fiurge, probation (n)
fiurk, product (n)
fiurkiu, productively (adv)
fiurku, productive (adj)
fiurkuet, production (n)
fiurkwan, producer (n doer)
fiurn, pro (n d:professional)
fiurshman, prognosis (n)
fiurshmanwan, prognosticator (n doer)
fiurshmasne, prognosticate (v)
fiursk, produce (v)
fiurt, problem (n)
fiurzbe, probe (v)
fiushairk, provocation (n)
fiushairkiu, provocatively (adv)
fiushairku, provocative (adj)
fiushairkwan, provoker (n doer)
fiushairsk, provoke (v)
Fiushtirp, Protestant (n)
Fiushtirpuet, Protestantism (n)
fiushtirst, protest (v)
fiushtirt, protest (n)
fiushtirtwan, protester (n doer)
fiushtirtwan, protestor (n doer)
fiushurpiu, profoundly (adv)
fiushurpu, profound (adj)
fiuterp, projection (n d:thrust)
fiuterpiu, projectively (adv d:thrust)
fiuterpu, projective (adj d:thrust)
fiuterpuin, projectile (n)
fiuterpwan, projector (n doer d:thrust)
fiutersp, project (v d:thrust)
fiuteshirp, project (n d:workplan)
fiuthiurf, profile (n)
fiuthiurfwan, profiler (n doer)
fiuthiursf, profile (v)
fiuthurk, prospect (n)
fiuthurkiu, prospectively (adv)
fiuthurku, prospective (adj)
fiuthurkwan, prospector (n doer)
fiuthursk, prospect (v)
fiutianirk, procurement (n)
fiutianirsk, procure (v)
fiuvadarve, promotion (n)
fiuvadarvu, promotional (adj)
fiuvadarvwan, promoter (n doer)
fiuvadarzve, promote (v)
fiuvefirt, procession (n)
fiuvelirk, proceed (n)
fiuvelirp, proponent (n)
fiuverk, procedure (n)

fiuverkiu, procedurally (adv)
fiuverku, procedural (adj)
fiuversk, proceed (v)
fiuverst, process (v)
fiuvert, process (n)
fiuvertwan, processor (n doer)
fiuvorage, progress (n)
fiuvoragiu, progressively (adv)
fiuvoragu, progressive (adj)
fiuvoraguet, progression (n)
fiuvoragwan, progressor (n doer)
fiuvorazge, progress (v)
fivarl, season (n d:climate)
fivarliu, seasonally (adv d:climate)
fivarlu, seasonal (adj d:climate)
fkarf, plate (n)
fkarfwan, plater (n doer)
fkarnk, cramp (n)
fkarnsk, cramp (v)
fkarsf, plate (v)
fkavart, platter (n)
fkavorn, platform (n)
fkilortu, negligible (adj)
fkirst, neglect (v)
fkirt, neglect (n)
fkirtu, negligence (n)
fkirtiu, neglectfully (adv)
fkirtiu, negligently (adv)
fkirtu, neglectful (adj)
fkirtu, negligent (adj)
fklerst, screen (v)
fklert, screen (n)
fklertwan, screener (n doer)
fkletfruifk, screenplay (n)
fkletloirdwan, screenwriter (n doer)
fkurst, shuttle (v)
fkurt, shuttle (n)
flabkarn, flack (n)
flairme, tunnel (n)
flairmwan, tunneler (n doer)
flairsh, worth (n)
flairshmenu, worthless (adj)
flairshu, worthy (adj)
flairshuet, worthiness (n)
flairth, past (n)
flairzme, tunnel (v)
flaishaurku, worthwhile (adj)
flamar, dance (n)
flamarwan, dancer (n doer)
flamasre, dance (v)
flanirf, album (n)
flanirp, bang (n d:hair)
flanitiu, frankly (adv)
flanitu, frank (adj)
flanshk, pane (n)
flanude, neighbor (n)
flanude, neighbour (n)
flanudu, neighborly (adj)
flanufif, neighborhood (n)
flanufif, nieghbourhood (n)
flanuzde, neighbor (v)

flarap, aid (n)
flarapwan, aide (n doer)
flarasp, aid (v)
flarde, clap (n)
flarf, cloth (n)
flarfkyek, clothes (n pl)
flarist, aim (v)
flarit, aim (n)
flaritmeniu, aimlessly (adv)
flaritmenu, aimless (adj)
flark, draft (n)
flarku, drafty (adj)
flarkwan, drafter (n doer)
flars, front (v)
flarsf, clothe (v)
flarsh, front (n)
flarshat, frontier (n)
flarshroifk, frontline (n)
flarsk, draft (v)
flarvak, improvement (n)
flarvask, improve (v)
flarzde, clap (v)
flashp, bladder (n)
flathk, slate (n)
flathsk, slate (v)
flaufirk, delivery (n)
flaufirkar, deliverance (n)
flaufirkwan, deliverer (n doer)
flaufirsk, deliver (v)
flaufrifk, livestock (n)
flauftarsk, liven (v)
flauftfirf, livelihood (n)
flauftfrelpiu, livably (adv)
flauftfrelpu, livable (adj)
flaugaishtiu, lividly (adv)
flaugaishtu, livid (adj)
flaul, dream (n)
flauliu, dreamily (adv)
flaulu, dreamy (adj)
flaulwan, dreamer (n doer)
flaunkiorshk, blowtorch (n)
flaunkiorshsk, blowtorch (v)
flaunwan, blower (n doer d:air)
flaurf, frailty (n)
flaurfst, live (v)
flaurftiu, lively (adv)
flaurftu, live (adj)
flaurfu, frail (adj)
flaurk, smack (n)
flaursh, life (n)
flaurshu, life (adj)
flaurshwan, lifer (n doer)
flaursk, smack (v)
flaushbleirsh, lifespan (n)
flaushdaun, lifetime (n)
flaushezhurpwan, lifesaver (n doer)
flaushezhursp, lifesave (v)
flaushfriarf, lifestyle (n)
flaushkorbe, lifeboat (n)
flaushlilf, lifeblood (n)
flaushralzhu, lifelong (adj)
flaushreifku, lifelike (adj)

flaushroifk, lifeline (n)
flaushvaifirk, lifeguard (n)
flausle, dream (v)
flauslyot, dreamt (v pa)
flausne, blow (v d:air)
flausnyot, blew (v pa d:air)
flazhen, bird (n)
flegarf, luggage (n)
fleifanf, prose (n)
fleinorsh, compatibility (n)
fleinorshiu, compatibly (adv)
fleinorshu, compatible (adj)
fleirde, breed (n)
fleirdwan, breeder (n doer)
fleirf, breeze (n)
fleirfu, breezy (adj)
fleirge, glance (n)
fleirn, compassion (n)
fleirnu, compassionate (adj)
fleirsf, breeze (v)
fleirsh, passion (n)
fleirshiu, passionately (adv)
fleirshu, passionate (adj)
fleirst, shy (v)
fleirt, shyness (n)
fleirth, vein (n)
fleirthu, venous (adj)
fleirtu, shy (adj)
fleirzde, breed (v)
fleirzge, glance (v)
fleivurt, property (n)
flelirk, pitch (n d:sealant)
flendaurn, peacetime (n)
flendaurnu, peacetime (adj)
flendenargwan, peacemaker (n
   doer)
flenide, peace (n)
flenidiu, peacefully (adv)
flenidu, peaceful (adj)
flenifst, credit (v)
flenift, credit (n)
fleniftwan, creditor (n doer)
flenirp, bluff (n)
flenirpwan, bluffer (n doer)
flenirsp, bluff (v)
flenklorfwan, peacekeeper (n
   doer)
flenklorsf, peacekeep (v)
flenklorsfyot, peacekept (v pa)
flerf, ease (n)
flerfiu, easily (adv)
flerfu, easy (adj)
flerfwaku, easiest (adj)
flerfwelu, easier (adj)
flerge, lug (n)
flergwan, lugger (n doer)
flerktiern, shutdown (n)
flerku, shut (adj)
flerkuil, shutout (n)
flerkwast, shutter (n)
flerkwat, shutter (n)
flerp, tub (n)
flersf, ease (v)

flersh, credibility (n)
flershu, credible (adj)
flershuet, credential (n)
flersk, shut (v)
flerskyot, shut (v pa)
flerst, wisp (v)
flert, wisp (n)
flerth, plasma (n)
flerve, ship (n)
flervuet, shipment (n)
flervwan, shipper (n doer)
flerzbe, cope (v)
flerzge, lug (v)
flerzve, ship (v)
flevkarbark, shipwreck (n)
flevkarbarsk, shipwreck (v)
flevlern, shipmate (n)
flevlurift, shipload (n)
flevoratwan, shipbuilder (n doer)
flevplorn, shipman (n)
flevplornyek, shipmen (n pl)
flevthauthk, shipyard (n)
flevtheiftwan, shipowner (n doer)
fliamesp, munch (v)
fliamp, munchy (n)
fliarf, crawl (n)
fliarfwan, crawler (n doer)
fliark, sweep (n)
fliarkwan, sweeper (n doer)
fliarn, famile (n)
fliarnu, familiar (adj)
fliarnwan, family (n doer)
fliarsf, crawl (v)
fliarsk, sweep (v)
fliarskyot, swept (v pa)
fliarsne, familiarize (v)
fliarst, tier (v)
fliart, tier (n)
fliarth, rose (n)
fliarthu, rosy (adj)
fliashst, cleave (v d:split)
fliashstyot, clove (v pa d:split)
fliasht, cleft (n d:split)
fliashtwan, cleaver (n doer
   d:split)
fliathpoarp, rosebud (n)
fliaurp, swab (n)
fliaursp, swab (v)
fliaush, leisure (n)
fliaushu, leisurely (adj)
flienk, calm (n)
flienkiu, calmly (adv)
flienku, calm (adj)
fliensk, calm (v)
flierf, whisper (n)
flierfwan, whisperer (n doer)
flierge, swing (n)
fliergwan, swinger (n doer)
fliersf, whisper (v)
flierst, whistle (v)
fliert, whistle (n)
fliertwan, whistler (n doer)
flierzge, swing (v)

flierzgyot, swung (v pa)
flieshsk, slither (v)
flifparn, specimen (n)
flifst, bring (v)
flifstyot, brought (v pa)
flikarft, specific (n)
flikarst, specify (v)
flikart, specification (n)
flikartiu, specifically (adv)
flikartu, specific (adj)
flilf, tallness (n)
flilfu, tall (adj)
flinif, gem (n)
flinifbaraf, gemstone (n)
flinork, slot (n)
flinorsk, slot (v)
fliofliarpwan, proofreader (n
   doer)
fliofliarsp, proof (v)
fliofliarsp, proofread (v)
fliofliarspyot, proofread (v pa)
fliorde, crew (n)
fliorf, proof (n)
fliorfu, provable (adj)
fliorfwan, prover (n doer)
fliorme, cosmos (n)
fliormu, cosmic (adj)
fliormwan, cosmopolitan (n doer)
fliorn, crayon (n)
fliorsf, prove (v)
flirfiu, slightly (adv)
flirfp, specie (n)
flirfu, slight (adj)
fliroifk, storyline (n)
flirplok, storyboard (n)
flirpreltwan, storyteller (n doer)
flirsf, slight (v)
flirsh, grass (n)
flirshkiu, imminently (adv)
flirshku, imminent (adj)
flirvonurde, storybook (n)
flishars, graze (v d:feed)
flisharshwan, grazer (n doer
   d:feed)
flishraufp, grassland (n)
flishwilfuan, grasshopper (n)
flishwilfuanu, grassy (adj)
flithsk, graze (v d:scrape)
fliunorst, tribulate (v)
fliunort, tribulation (n)
fliurf, prayer (n)
fliurfwan, prayer (n doer)
fliurp, fret (n d:strip)
fliurs, tidy (v)
fliursf, pray (v)
fliursh, tidiness (n)
fliurshiu, tidily (adv)
fliurshu, tidy (adj)
fliursp, fret (v d:strip)
fliurst, praise (v)
fliurt, praise (n)
fliurtwan, praiser (n doer)
fliushkwan, whittler (n doer)

fliushsk, whittle (v)
fliuthk, plume (n)
fliuthkuet, plumage (n)
fliuthsk, plume (v)
fliuvarn, tribune (n)
floirk, ditch (n)
floirp, frog (n)
floirsk, ditch (v)
floirst, pencil (v)
floirt, pencil (n)
floize, bronze (v)
floizhe, bronze (n)
florat, aviation (n)
floratu, aviatic (adj)
floratwan, aviator (n doer)
florde, brow (n)
florf, brag (n)
Floridarf, Florida (n)
Florin, Fluorine (n)
florkiu, perhaps (adv)
florsf, brag (v)
florzde, brow (v)
floshk, stray (n)
floshku, stray (adj)
floshsk, stray (v)
fluairk, creep (n)
fluairkiu, creepily (adv)
fluairku, creepy (adj)
fluairkwan, creeper (n doer)
fluairsk, creep (v)
fluairskyot, crept (v pa)
flualshkorbe, sailboat (n)
fluankiarf, lighthouse (n)
fluarfiu, deliciously (adv)
fluarfu, delicious (adj)
fluark, cripple (n)
fluarl, sail (n)
fluarlwan, sailor (n doer)
fluarn, light (n d:lumen)
fluarnk, lightning (n)
fluarnku, lightning (adj)
fluarnwan, lighter (n doer
   d:lumen)
fluars, delight (v)
fluarsh, delight (n)
fluarshu, delightful (adj)
fluarsk, cripple (v)
fluarsle, sail (v)
fluarsne, light (v d:lumen)
fluarsnyot, lit (v pa d:lumen)
fluathk, illumination (n)
fluathkiu, luminously (adv)
fluathku, luminous (adj)
fluathkwan, illuminator (n doer)
fluathsk, illuminate (v)
flude, carry (n)
fludwan, carrier (n doer)
flufp, chute (n)
flufsp, chute (v)
fluiade, beach (n)
fluiadwan, beacher (n doer)
fluiazde, beach (v)
fluikunirve, wiseguy (n)

fluikuplorn, wiseman (n)
fluikuplornyek, wisemen (n pl)
fluikuthralp, wisecrack (n)
fluirk, wisdom (n)
fluirkiu, wisely (adv)
fluirku, wise (adj)
fluirkuan, wizardry (n)
fluirkuasne, wizen (v)
fluirkwan, wizard (n doer)
fluirsk, wisen (v)
flumgruze, shepherd (v)
flumgruzhe, shepherd (n)
flumgruzhyek, shepherd (n pl)
flunirt, shard (n)
flurde, carryon (n)
flurge, scum (n)
flurip, sculpture (n)
fluripiu, sculpturally (adv)
fluripu, sculptural (adj)
fluripwan, sculptor (n doer)
flurisp, sculpt (v)
flurme, shape (n)
flurmenu, shapeless (adj)
flurmiu, shapely (adv)
flurmwan, shaper (n doer)
flursh, cliff (n)
flurth, plum (n)
flurzme, shape (v)
flushok, butterfly (n)
fluzde, carry (v)
fnafirst, harness (v)
fnafirt, harness (n)
fnaifguvarst, brainstorm (v)
fnaifguvart, brainstorm (n)
fnaifk, brain (n)
fnaifkbiorat, brainpower (n)
fnaifkefiaus, brainwash (v)
fnaifklersh, brainwave (n)
fnaifkluart, brainchild (n)
fnaifkmenu, brainless (adj)
fnaifku, brainy (adj)
fnaifst, brandish (v)
fnaikirk, frenzy (n)
fnaikirkiu, frantically (adv)
fnaikirku, frantic (adj)
fnaikirku, frenetic (adj)
fnaikirsk, frenzy (v)
fnairp, brand (n)
fnairsp, brand (v)
fnapkefirt, skinhead (n)
fnark, spit (n)
fnarkwan, spitter (n doer)
fnarn, skinniness (n)
fnarnu, skinny (adj)
fnarp, skin (n)
fnarpwan, skinner (n doer)
fnarsk, spit (v)
fnarskyot, spat (v pa)
fnarsp, skin (v)
fnarthsk, scathe (v)
fnaup, bong (n d:sound)
fnaurk, wrong (n)
fnaurketik, wrongdoing (n)

fnaurketikwan, wrongdoer (n
   doer)
fnaurkiu, wrongfully (adv)
fnaurkiu, wrongly (adv)
fnaurku, wrong (adj)
fnaurku, wrongful (adj)
fnaurkuet, wrongness (n)
fnaurn, blur (n)
fnaurniu, blurrily (adv)
fnaurnu, blurry (adj)
fnaursk, wrong (v)
fnaursne, blur (v)
fnaurst, blurt (v)
fnausp, bong (v d:sound)
fnauthk, crouch (n)
fnauthsk, crouch (v)
fneirpiu, bluntly (adv)
fneirpu, blunt (adj)
fneirsp, blunt (v)
fnerst, steady (v)
fnert, stead (n)
fnertiu, steadily (adv)
fnertu, steady (adj)
fnertuet, steadiness (n)
fnetezhairsh, steadfastness (n)
fnetezhairshiu, steadfastly (adv)
fnetezhairshu, steadfast (adj)
fnilorst, skirt (v)
fnilort, skirt (n)
fniraf, snob (n)
fnirafu, snobby (adj)
fnirafuet, snobbery (n)
fnirasf, snob (v)
fnirfk, splash (n)
fnirfku, splashy (adj)
fnirfkwan, splasher (n doer)
fnirfsk, splash (v)
fnirk, skip (n)
fnirsk, skip (v)
fnirskaut, skipped (v prp)
fnoilt, trim (n)
fnoilfwan, trimmer (n doer)
fnoilsf, trim (v)
fnoirp, blunder (n)
fnoirsp, blunder (v)
fnorasht, scalpel (n)
fnorast, scalp (v)
fnorat, scalp (n)
fnoratwan, scalper (n doer)
fnorif, pregnancy (n)
fnorifu, pregnant (adj)
fnupoblaithp, wraparound (n)
fnurp, wrap (n)
fnurpwan, wrapper (n doer)
fnursp, wrap (v)
fnurst, fork (v)
fnurt, fork (n)
fnurtiu, forkily (adv)
fnurtu, forky (adj)
fnurtwan, forker (n doer)
fnutraushk, forklift (n)
foarfiu, loosely (adv)
foarfu, loose (adj)

foarsf, loosen (v)
foidart, bacon (n)
foifraufp, fairyland (n)
foinark, divorce (n)
foinarkuin, divorcee (n)
foinarsk, divorce (v)
foirf, fairy (n)
foirn, lace (n)
foirnu, lacey (adj)
foirsh, fair (n d:exhibition)
foirsne, lace (v)
foirst, vault (v d:arch)
foirt, vault (n d:arch)
foishbraft, fairground (n)
folirst, crop (v d:narrow)
forash, sphere (n)
forashan, sphereoid (n)
forashiu, spherically (adv)
forashu, spherical (adj)
forlar, fragrance (n)
forlaru, fragrant (adj)
forshk, department (n)
forshkiu, departmentally (adv)
forshku, departmental (adj)
Foshforush, Phosphorus (n)
fpade, expulsion (n)
fpazde, expel (v)
fpirge, stab (n)
fpirgwan, stabber (n doer)
fpirzge, stab (v)
fpurf, stable (n d:barn)
frabeplorn, tradesman (n)
frabeplornyek, tradesmen (n pl)
frabshtarst, trademark (v)
frabshtart, trademark (n)
fradup, cattle (n)
frafk, coat (n)
frafsk, coat (v)
fraigurst, plasticize (v)
fraigurt, plastic (n)
fraigurtwan, plasticizer (n doer)
frailork, trend (n)
frailorku, trendy (adj)
frailorsk, trend (v)
frainflazhen, mockingbird (n)
fraink, mockery (n)
frainsk, mock (v)
frairge, plaster (n)
frairk, badness (n)
frairkeku, worst (adj)
frairkelu, worse (adj)
frairkesk, worst (v)
frairkesle, worsen (v)
frairkiu, badly (adv)
frairku, bad (adj)
frairme, blond (n)
frairmu, blond (adj)
frairmwan, blonde (n doer)
frairp, worry (n)
frairpu, worrisome (adj)
frairpwan, worrier (n doer)
frairsp, worry (v)
frairzge, plaster (v)

fralbe, trade (n)
fralbiu, tradably (adv)
fralbu, tradable (adj)
fralbunf, tradeoff (n)
fralbwan, trader (n doer)
fralip, celebration (n)
fralipwan, celebrity (n doer)
fralirs, cement (v)
fralirsh, cement (n)
fralisp, celebrate (v)
fralk, ugliness (n)
fralku, ugly (adj)
fralun, cellar (n)
fralve, tremble (n)
fralvwan, trembler (n doer)
fralzbe, trade (v)
fralzve, tremble (v)
framirn, coalition (n)
framirsne, coalite (v)
framist, coalesce (v)
framit, coalescence (n)
framitu, coalescent (adj)
Franarsh, French (n)
franirst, layer (v)
franirt, layer (n)
franist, lay (v d:place)
franistyot, laid (v pa d:place)
franit, lay (n d:place)
franituil, layout (n)
franitunf, layoff (n)
Frankfurft, Frankfurt (n)
Fransharf, France (n)
Franshium, Francium (n)
franuf, burro (n)
frath, cell (n)
frathiu, cellularly (adv)
frathu, cellular (adj)
fraufiaushk, mouthwash (n)
fraufst, blurb (v)
frauft, blurb (n)
fraufthetirsh, mouthpiece (n)
fraugalt, thrush (n)
fraugast, frighten (v)
fraugat, fright (n)
fraugatiu, frightfully (adv)
fraugatu, frightful (adj)
fraugatwan, frightener (n doer)
fraums, swarm (v)
fraumsh, swarm (n)
fraunk, sag (n)
fraunsk, sag (v)
fraurf, mouth (n)
fraurfiu, mouthfully (adv)
fraurfu, mouthful (adj)
fraursf, mouth (v)
fraushp, fry (n)
fraushpwan, frier (n doer)
fraushpwan, fryer (n doer)
fraushsp, fry (v)
fravinorkiu, tremendously (adv)
fravinorku, tremendous (adj)
fravirn, tremor (n)
fravirsne, tremor (v)

fravurn, cortex (n)
fravushiak, extravagance (n)
fravushiakiu, extravagantly (adv)
fravushiaku, extravagant (adj)
fravushiakwan, extrovert (n doer)
frazhge, thaw (n)
frazhzge, thaw (v)
frefirk, swiftness (n)
frefirkiu, swiftly (adv)
frefirku, swift (adj)
freiaufst, plop (v)
freiausk, plod (v)
freigairk, snakebite (n)
freilarsh, buddy (n)
freink, mucus (n)
freinku, mucosal (adj)
freinu, feely (adj)
freinwan, feeler (n doer)
freirk, snake (n)
freirku, snakey (adj)
freirsk, snake (v)
freishsp, drench (v)
freisne, feel (v)
freisnyot, felt (v pa)
Freiviul, Friday (n)
freizhzge, faze (v)
frelf, swirl (n)
frelme, smoothness (n)
frelmiu, smoothly (adv)
frelmu, smooth (adj)
frelmwan, smoother (n doer)
frelp kodi, can (ndal d:ability)
frelp kodi, could (ndal d:ability)
frelp kodi, could have (ndal
     d:ability)
frelp, ability (n)
frelpiu, ably (adv)
frelpu, able (adj)
frelpwan, enabler (n doer)
frelsf, swirl (v)
frelshk, swish (n)
frelshkwan, swisher (n doer)
frelshsk, swish (v)
frelsp, enable (v)
freltaifst, pivot (v)
freltaift, pivot (n)
freltaiftiu, pivotally (adv)
freltaiftu, pivotal (adj)
frelzme, smooth (v)
frenirk, pitcher (n d:container)
frenit, native (n)
frenitiu, natively (adv)
frenitu, native (adj)
freth, bra (n)
friafarn, stylus (n)
friafarnyek, styli (n pl)
friaifkladirpwan, skyscraper (n
     doer)
friaifkraifk, skydive (n)
friaifkraifkwan, skydiver (n doer)
friaifkraifsk, skydive (v)
friaifluarn, skylight (n)
friaifroifk, skyline (n)

friaifst, sky (v)
friaift, sky (n)
friaiftiu, skywardly (adv)
friaiftu, skyward (adj)
friaifzhiarast, skyrocket (v)
frialk, plea (n)
frialkwan, pleader (n doer)
frialsk, plead (v)
frianshku, skimpy (adj)
frianshsk, skimp (v)
frianst, skim (v)
friantwan, skimmer (n doer)
friarf, style (n)
friarfiu, stylishly (adv)
friarfu, stylish (adj)
friarfwan, stylist (n doer)
friark, smut (n)
friarp, fret (n d:worry)
friars, kindle (v)
friarsf, style (v)
friarsp, fret (v d:worry)
friart, pamphlet (n)
friarve, divinity (n)
friarviu, divinely (adv)
friarvu, divine (adj)
friarzve, divine (v)
friashk, orgasm (n)
friashkak, orgy (n)
friashku, orgasmic (adj)
friaup, maw (n)
friaushk, smirk (n)
friaushsk, smirk (v)
frielk, stinginess (n d:frugal)
frielku, stingy (adj d:frugal)
friempu, sleek (adj)
friesht, slack (n d:pants)
friethk, slough (n)
friethsk, slough (v)
frifank, stocking (n d:sock)
friflt, stock (n d:fill equity)
frifkrolirpwan, stockbroker (n
   doer)
frifku, stocky (adj d:fill equity)
frifkwan, stocker (n doer d:fill
   equity)
frifnairp, stockpile (n)
frifnairsp, stockpile (v)
frifplorn, stockman (n)
frifplornyek, stockmen (n pl)
frifshranf, stockroom (n)
frifsk, stock (v d:fill equity)
frifthorthkwan, stockholder (n
   doer)
frikarst, staunch (v)
frikart, staunch (n)
frikartu, staunch (adj)
frilap, pleasure (n)
frilapiu, pleasantly (adv)
frilapu, pleasant (adj)
frilapwan, pleaser (n doer)
frilark, allowance (n)
frilarku, allowable (adj)
frilarsk, allow (v)

frilasp, please (v)
frilast, organize (v d:structure)
frilat, organization (n d:structure)
frilatat, organism (n)
frilatu, organizational (adj
   d:structure)
frilatwan, organizer (n doer
   d:structure)
frimor, alliance (n)
frink, hitch (n)
frinkwan, hitcher (n doer)
frinkwiars, hitchhike (v)
frinkwiarshwan, hitchhiker (n
   doer)
frinsk, hitch (v)
friop, gloom (n)
friopiu, gloomily (adv)
friopu, gloomy (adj)
friork, witness (n)
friorsk, witness (v)
frishork, immensity (n)
frishorkiu, immensely (adv)
frishorku, immense (adj)
frishp, smudge (n)
frishsp, smudge (v)
frisht, skit (n)
frithk, hit (n)
frithkwan, hitter (n doer)
frithsk, hit (v)
frithskyot, hit (v pa)
friunark, fugitive (n)
friunpwan, fleer (n doer)
friunsp, flee (v)
friurkiu, chronically (adv)
friurku, chronic (adj)
friurzge, plunk (v)
friushk, plunge (n)
friushkwan, plunger (n doer)
friushsk, plunge (v)
frizhge, swindle (n)
frizhgwan, swindler (n doer)
frizhzge, swindle (v)
frodan, fall (n d:autumn)
frodathk, autumn (n)
frodathku, autumnal (adj)
frofp, organ (n d:body part)
froiflifarde, sweatshirt (n)
froift, breech (n)
froifthoft, sweatshop (n)
froil, pity (n)
froilameniu, pitilessly (adv)
troilamenu, pitiless (adj)
froilar, pittance (n)
froiliu, pitifully (adv)
froilu, pitiful (adj)
froirf, sweat (n d:perspiration)
froirfu, sweaty (adj
   d:perspiration)
froirge, proximity (n)
froirgwan, proxy (n doer)
froirk, swear (n)
froirkwan, swearer (n doer)
froirsf, sweat (v d:perspiration)

froirsk, swear (v)
froirskyot, swore (v pa)
froisle, pity (v)
frolfu, organic (adj d:of life)
frolt, chord (n)
fronast, blind (v)
fronat, blind (n)
fruamesp, snug (v)
fruamp, snug (n)
fruampist, snuggle (v)
fruampiu, snugly (adv)
fruampu, snug (adj)
fruarst, plot (v)
fruart, plot (n)
fruartwan, plotter (n doer)
frufit, rift (n)
frufk, riff (n)
fruifanirtiu, ludicrously (adv)
fruifanirtu, ludicrous (adj)
fruifbiurn, playboy (n)
fruifbrant, playground (n)
fruifdirzhe, plaything (n)
fruifevark, playback (n)
fruifevornt, playbook (n)
fruifk, play (n)
fruifkiarf, playhouse (n)
fruifkiu, playfully (adv)
fruifku, playful (adj)
fruifkuet, playfulness (n)
fruifkunf, playoff (n)
fruifkwan, player (n doer)
fruiflern, playmate (n)
fruifnargwan, playmaker (n doer)
fruifrelpu, playable (adj)
fruifshranf, playroom (n)
fruifsk, play (v)
fruinorshkwan, dabbler (n doer)
fruinorshsk, dabble (v)
fruinshk, dab (n)
fruinshsk, dab (v)
fruirst, display (v)
fruirt, display (n)
frulbe, rip (n)
frulbunf, ripoff (n)
frulbwan, ripper (n doer)
fruldaurn, summertime (n)
frulf, summer (n)
frulme, blue (n)
frulmu, blue (adj)
frulp, sweetness (n)
frulpar, sweetie (n)
frulpiu, sweetly (adv)
frulpu, sweet (adj)
frulpwan, sweetener (n doer)
frulsh, river (n)
frulsp, sweeten (v)
frulzbe, rip (v)
frunepul, blueberry (n)
frunf, rice (n)
frupedralt, sweetheart (n)
frurge, pledge (n)
frurzge, pledge (v)
frushflarsh, riverfront (n)

frushkefirt, riverhead (n)
frushkorbe, riverboat (n)
frushoirt, riverside (n)
frushplirk, riverbank (n)
fruthk, blush (n)
fruthsk, blush (v)
fshishfilst, fizzle (v)
fshishfilt, fizzle (n)
fshishfst, fizz (v)
fshishft, fizz (n)
ftaglurift, truckload (n)
ftalorst, arrive (v)
ftalort, arrival (n)
ftarge, truck (n)
ftargwan, trucker (n doer)
ftarp, stability (n)
ftarpu, stabile (adj)
ftarpuet, stabilization (n)
ftarpwan, stabilizer (n doer)
ftarsp, stabilize (v)
ftarzge, truck (v)
ftaurf, spire (n)
ftaurku, spiral (adj)
ftaursf, spire (v)
ftaursk, spiral (v)
ftirve, levitation (n)
ftirve, levity (n)
ftirvwan, levitator (n doer)
ftirzve, levitate (v)
fualar, ghoul (n)
fualaru, ghoulish (adj)
fuarde, plough (n)
fuarde, plow (n)
fuarl, via (prep)
fuarsf, saunter (v)
fuarsh, oyster (n)
fuarst, view (v)
fuart, view (n)
fuarth, sauna (n)
fuartiu, viewably (adv)
fuartu, viewable (adj)
fuartwan, viewer (n doer)
fuarzde, plow (v)
fuatairft, viewpoint (n)
fuatshurpwan, viewfinder (n
    doer)
fufarp, sausage (n)
fufarth, bowel (n)
fufmelirk, saucepan (n)
fuiark, troll (n)
fuiarsk, troll (v)
fuifalt, flyer (n)
fuifvuarpyek, flypaper (n pl)
fuirf, flight (n d:air travel)
fuirfu, flighty (adj d:air travel)
fuirfwan, flier (n doer d:air travel)
fuirsf, fly (v d:air travel)
fuirsfyot, flew (v pa d:air travel)
fuirst, idle (v)
fuirt, idleness (n)
fuirtu, idle (adj)
fuishk, trolley (n)
fulirsh, plurality (n)

fulirshu, plural (adj)
fumeinu, many (adj)
fumeitrafk, manifold (n)
fumirp, canker (n)
fumirpu, canker (adj)
furbalp, bastard (n)
furbalsp, bastardize (v)
furf, sauce (n)
furfu, saucy (adj)
fursf, sauce (v)
furth, saucer (n)
fushar, bless (n)
fushasre, bless (v)
fushirp, devastation (n)
fushirsp, devastate (v)
gadaktoirk, collarbone (n)
gadark, collar (n)
gadarsk, collar (v)
Gadolinium, Gadolinium (n)
gafarn, gallon (n)
gafbaraft, gallstone (n)
gafirk, gall (n)
gafirkwan, galler (n doer)
gafirsk, gall (v)
gafirt, noise (n)
gafirtiu, noisily (adv)
gafirtu, noisy (adj)
gaflashp, gallbladder (n)
gagarlsth, hiccup (v)
gagarlth, hiccup (n)
gahem, Number_1e3756
gaiarp, coil (n)
gaiarpwan, coiler (n doer)
gaiarsp, coil (v)
gaifork, bitterness (n)
gaiforkiu, bitterly (adv)
gaiforku, bitter (adj)
gaiftarge, rupture (n)
gaiftarzge, rupture (v)
gaigarn, magnification (n)
gaigarnwan, magnifier (n doer)
gaigarsne, magnify (v)
gaigart, magnitude (n)
gaigurt, magnificence (n)
gaigurtiu, magnificently (adv)
gaigurtu, magnificent (adj)
gailak, help (n)
gailaku, helpful (adj)
gailakwan, helper (n doer)
gailask, help (v)
gairbe, helplessness (n)
gairbiu, helplessly (adv)
gairbu, helpless (adj)
gairk, bite (n d:chew)
gairkwan, biter (n doer d:chew)
gairp, buck (n)
gairpwan, buck (n doer)
gairsk, bite (v d:chew)
gairskyot, bit (v pa d:chew)
gairsp, buck (v)
gairth, roach (n)
gairve, tag (n)
gairvwan, tagger (n doer)

gairzve, tag (v)
gaishk, beast (n)
gaitak, bucket (n)
gaithirp, beetle (n)
gakor, anger (n)
gakoriu, angrily (adv)
gakoru, angry (adj)
gakosre, anger (v)
gal, G (let sng)
galaf, café (n)
galafk, cafeteria (n)
galgan, curriculum (n)
gali, Gs (let pl)
galikshlerf, earthenware (n)
galikshlerfu, earthen (adj)
galirk, dirt (n)
galirku, dirty (adj)
galirkweku, dirtiest (adj)
galirkwelu, dirtier (adj)
galirsk, dirty (v)
galirt, tract (n)
galirtwan, tractor (n doer)
Galium, Gallium (n)
galkrenk, illogic (n)
galkrenku, illogical (adj)
galkyoran, earthworm (n)
galnaf, ceil (n)
galnasf, ceil (v)
galshsk, petrify (v)
galtert, traction (n)
galuk, maggot (n)
galurst, level (v)
galurt, level (n)
galurtu, level (adj)
galurtwan, leveler (n doer)
Galuth, EhoMonth11 (n)
gamarn, gamma (n)
gandapwan, fastener (n doer)
gandasp, fasten (v)
ganirp, hammer (n)
ganirsp, hammer (v)
gankerk, ignition (n)
gankerkwan, igniter (n doer)
gankern, engine (n)
gankernwan, engineer (n doer)
gankersk, ignite (v)
gankersne, engineer (v)
ganlarf, ignorance (n)
ganlarfu, ignorant (adj)
ganlarsf, ignore (v)
ganor, coal (n)
ganufp, donkey (n)
ganushk, communism (n)
ganushkwan, communist (n doer)
gapost, collect (v)
gapot, collection (n)
gapotfrelp, collectable (n)
gapotfrelp, collectible (n)
gapotfrelpu, collectable (adj)
gapotfrelpu, collectible (adj)
gapotiu, collectively (adv)
gapotu, collective (adj)
gapotwan, collector (n doer)

garask, collate (v)
garbrube, colleague (n)
gardas, calculate (v)
gardash, calculation (n)
gardashwan, calculator (n doer)
garfk, brew (n)
garfkuift, brewery (n)
garfkwan, brewer (n doer)
garfsk, brew (v)
garilme, couch (n)
garilzme, couch (v)
garisharst, collaborate (v)
garishart, collaboration (n)
garishartiu, collaboratively (adv)
garishartu, collaborative (adj)
garishartwan, collaborator (n
    doer)
garlarzge, gnaw (v)
garlot, calculus (n)
garlsth, cough (v)
garlth, cough (n)
garlthwan, cougher (n doer)
gars, trace (v)
garsh, trace (n)
garshiu, traceably (adv)
garshork, collateral (n)
garshp, collapse (n)
garshpu, collapsible (adj)
garshsp, collapse (v)
garshu, traceable (adj)
garshuftiu, illicitly (adv)
garshuftu, illicit (adj)
garshwan, tracer (n doer)
garzhink, jersey (n)
gatharn, squash (n d:fruit)
Gatholige, Catholic (n)
gauapferap, thunderstorm (n)
gauapkiurp, thunderbolt (n)
gauarp, thunder (n)
gauarsp, thunder (v)
gauesht, canine (n)
gaueshtu, canine (adj)
gauiarbiu, erratically (adv)
gauiarbu, erratic (adj)
gauirk, error (n)
gauirkiu, erroneously (adv)
gauirku, errant (adj)
gauirku, erroneous (adj)
gauirsk, err (v)
gaurbe, chasm (n)
gaurf, plague (n)
gaurk, hound (n)
gaurmel, coconut (n)
gaurn, card (n)
gaurplok, cardboard (n)
gaurploku, cardboard (adj)
gaursf, plague (v)
gaursk, hound (v)
gaursne, card (v)
gaurvat, cocoa (n)
gaushk, notch (n)
gaushsk, notch (v)
gautif, argument (n)

gautifiu, arguably (adv)
gautifu, arguable (adj)
gautifwan, arguer (n doer)
gautisf, argue (v)
gauvirde, boldness (n d:make)
gauvirdiu, boldly (adv d:make)
gauvirdu, bold (adj d:make)
gavert, agent (n)
gaviart, mafia (n)
gavugedairf, jackpot (n)
gavurge, jack (n d:lift)
gavurgwan, jacker (n doer d:lift)
gavurzge, jack (v d:lift)
gebar, boredom (n d:tiresome)
gebarwan, bore (n doer
    d:tiresome)
gebasre, bore (v d:tiresome)
gebirk, matter (n d:incident)
gebirsk, matter (v d:incident)
geidor, dozen (n)
geirp, pat (n)
geirsp, pat (v)
geirth, cursor (n)
geiteshk, twitch (n)
geiteshsk, twitch (v)
gelarn, cosmetic (n)
gelarniu, cosmetically (adv)
gelarnu, cosmetic (adj)
gelarnwan, cosmetician (n doer)
geldif, carrot (n)
gelimarf, kidney (n)
gelir, carriage (n)
gelirk, twist (n)
gelirku, twisty (adj)
gelirkwan, twister (n doer)
gelirsk, twist (v)
gelmeft, carpentry (n)
gelmeftwan, carpenter (n doer)
gelnif, calendar (n)
gelp, election (n)
gelpan, electorate (n)
gelpat, elective (n)
gelpatiu, electively (adv)
gelpatu, elective (adj)
gelpefrelpu, electable (adj)
gelpu, electoral (adj)
gelpwan, elector (n doer)
gelsp, elect (v)
genai-, oct- (num 8 pref)
genaimurk, octagon (n)
geneth, eighth (num 8 ord)
genfk, octoquadragintillion (num
    1e147 card)
genft, octotrigintillion (num
    1e117 card)
geni, eight (num 8 card)
genialfhemka, Number_1e32556
genida, eighty (num 80 card)
genidai-, eighty- (num 80 pref)
genideth, eightieth (num 80 ord)
genipa, eighteen (num 18 card)
genipai-, eighteen- (num 18 pref)

genipeth, eighteenth (num 18
    ord)
genka, octillion (num 1e27 card)
genkai-, xenna- (num 1e27 pref)
genketh, octillionth (num 1e27
    ord)
genshk, octovigintillion (num
    1e87 card)
genshkai-, cianta-
genshketh, octovigintillionth
    (num 1e87 ord)
gensht, octodecillion (num 1e57
    card)
genshtai-, meikosi- (num 1e57
    pref)
genshteth, octodecillionth (num
    1e57 ord)
geral, car (n)
geralst, bat (v d:stick)
geralt, bat (n d:stick)
geraltwan, batter (n doer d:stick)
gerft, might (n d:strength)
gerftiu, mightily (adv d:strength)
gerftu, mighty (adj d:strength)
gerftweku, mightiest (adj)
gerftwelu, mightier (adj)
Germanium, Germanium (n)
geshudar, hostess (n)
geshude, host (n)
geshuzde, host (v)
gethirk, track (n)
gethirkwan, tracker (n doer)
gethirsk, track (v)
getran, lecture (n)
getranwan, lecturer (n doer)
getrasne, lecture (v)
gevarsh, refuse (n d:garbage)
giagiarsh, magic (n)
giagiarshiu, magically (adv)
giaglarshu, magical (adj)
giagiarshwan, magician (n doer)
gialirp, wince (n)
gialirsp, wince (v)
gialork, bacterium (n)
gialorkyek, bacteria (n pl)
giamern, peanut (n)
gianfwan, rammer (n doer
    d:thrust)
giansf, ram (v d:thrust)
giarfp, frown (n)
giarfpwan, frowner (n doer)
giarfsp, frown (v)
giark, pork (n)
giarnk, commodity (n)
giars, heel (v d:tilt)
giarshk, curse (n)
giarshsk, curse (v)
giarst, boss (v)
giart, boss (n)
giartu, bossy (adj)
gielp, romp (n)
gielsp, romp (v)

giern, courier (n)
gifank, pagan (n)
gifankuet, paganism (n)
gifient, peasant (n)
giforp, pact (n)
giktheiarn, stepson (n)
gilirp, pluck (n)
gilirpu, plucky (adj)
gilirpwan, plucker (n doer)
gilirsp, pluck (v)
gilork, jig (n d:fixture)
gilurf, tweak (n)
ginarst, militarize (v)
ginart, military (n)
ginartwan, militant (n doer)
ginatark, militia (n)
giobarst, torture (v)
giobart, torture (n)
giobartu, torturous (adj)
giodiraf, ramrod (n)
giodirasf, ramrod (v)
gioip, rump (n)
gioishk, quack (n)
gioishkuet, quackery (n)
giokarst, squeegee (v)
giokart, squeegee (n)
giopoishk, rampage (n)
giopoishku, rampant (adj)
giopoishsk, rampage (v)
giorbe, tort (n)
giorf, bear (n d:animal)
giork, squeeze (n)
giorkwan, squeezer (n doer)
giorp, ramp (n)
giorsk, squeeze (v)
giorsp, ramp (v)
giorth, porch (n)
gipashku, plush (adj)
girap, turkey (n)
girf, call (n)
girfu, callable (adj)
girfwan, caller (n doer)
girgralzhe, jigsaw (n)
girsf, call (v)
girshk, lesion (n)
girshsk, lesion (v)
girvark, callback (n)
githarp, plug (n)
githarpwan, plugger (n doer)
githarsp, plug (v)
gitushk, snag (n)
gitushsk, snag (v)
giuirp, dowel (n)
giukart, squadron (n)
giurf, ham (n)
giurk, squad (n)
giurp, coup (n)
giushk, dizziness (n)
giushku, dizzy (adj)
giushsk, dizzy (v)
gizharp, mechanism (n)
gizharpiu, mechanically (adv)
gizharpu, mechanical (adj)

gizharpuet, mechanization (n)
gizharpwan, mechanic (n doer)
gizharsp, mechanize (v)
gizhaurk, machine (n)
gizhaurkar, machinery (n)
gizhaurkwan, machinist (n doer)
gizhaursk, machine (v)
glairf, fee (n)
glaishk, shank (n)
glaishsk, shank (v)
glamis, trawl (v)
glamish, trawl (n)
glamishu, trawlers (adj)
glanirn, brook (n)
glanirnu, brooklike (adj)
glardiashst, molest (v)
glardiasht, molestation (n)
glardiashtwan, molester (n doer)
glarf, vat (n)
glarfk, mass (n)
glarfkiu, massively (adv)
glarfku, massive (adj)
glarfsk, mass (v)
glars, trail (v)
glarsh, trail (n)
glarshwan, trailer (n doer)
glarst, bunt (v)
glart, bunt (n)
glart, contract (n d:agreement)
glartiu, contractually (adv
    d:agreement)
glartu, contractual (adj
    d:agreement)
glartwan, contractor (n doer
    d:agreement)
glarude, trip (n d:journey)
glashkraurgwan, trailblazer (n
    doer)
glatan, colloquium (n)
glatanu, colloquial (adj)
glath, cracker (n d:saltine)
glaukiurk, liberalism (n d:political
    stance)
glaukiurkuet, liberalization (n)
glaukiurkwan, liberal (n doer
    d:political stance)
glaukiursk, liberalize (v d:political
    stance)
glaurf, complaint (n)
glaurfwan, complainer (n doer)
glaursf, complain (v)
glaurst, brawl (v)
glaurt, brawl (n)
glaushbiorat, horsepower (n)
glaushk, horse (n)
glaushkeft, horsehead (n)
glaushmithk, horsetail (n)
glaushplorn, horseman (n)
glaushplornyek, horsemen (n pl)
glaushsk, horse (v)
glaushtafarn, horseshoe (n)
glaushvark, horseback (n)
glauthk, brawn (n)

glefkiork, legwork (n)
glefshranf, legroom (n)
gleiark, broach (n)
gleiarsk, broach (v)
gleifsk, purr (v)
gleirst, secrete (v)
gleirt, secretion (n)
gleishk, winch (n)
gleishsk, winch (v)
gleiurp, brood (n)
gleiursp, brood (v)
glemirp, bunk (n d:bed)
glemirsp, bunk (v d:bed)
glenst, edit (v)
glent, edit (n)
glentan, editorial (n)
glentar, edition (n)
glentu, editable (adj)
glentwan, editor (n doer)
glerf, leg (n)
glerge, donation (n)
glergwan, donor (n doer)
glerk, knowledge (n)
glerkwan, know-it-all (n doer)
glers, tie (v)
glersf, leg (v)
glersh, tie (n)
glersk, know (v)
glerskyot, knew (v pa)
glerzge, donate (v)
gleshblerkwan, tiebreaker (n
    doer)
gliaflarf, gauze (n)
gliapgutraf, fruitcake (n)
gliarf, rawness (n)
gliarfiu, rawly (adv)
gliarfu, raw (adj)
gliarp, fruit (n)
gliarpmenu, fruitless (adj)
gliarpu, fruity (adj)
gliarpuet, fruition (n)
gliarpuetu, fruitful (adj)
gliarsh, star (n d:celestial)
gliarshu, starry (adj d:celestial)
gliarshu, stellar (adj d:celestial)
gliart, crutch (n)
gliashflerve, starship (n)
gliashfluarn, starlight (n)
gliashlersh, starfish (n)
gliashtiarvwan, stargazer (n doer)
gliashtiarzve, stargaze (v)
gliazhirk, breadwinner (n)
glieft, scruff (n)
glieftu, scruffy (adj)
glifars, deluge (v)
glifarsh, deluge (n)
glifst, perk (v)
glift, perk (n)
gliftu, perky (adj)
glinork, exemption (n)
glinorsk, exempt (v)
glirp, crust (n)
glirpu, crusty (adj)

glirsp, crust (v)
glirst, tide (v)
glirt, tide (n)
glirth, spider (n)
glirthu, spidery (adj)
glirtu, tidal (adj)
glishk, step (n)
glishku, step (adj)
glishkwan, stepper (n doer)
glishlidor, stepdaughter (n)
glishluart, stepchild (n)
glishluartyek, stepchildren (n pl)
glishmashel, stepmother (n)
glishsk, step (v)
glishtrirt, stepladder (n)
glishvoteft, stepfather (n)
gliteidorn, tidewater (n)
gliurk, flaw (n)
gliurkmeniu, flawlessly (adv)
gliurkmenu, flawless (adj)
gliurp, sickness (n)
gliurpiu, sickly (adv)
gliurpu, sick (adj)
gliursk, flaw (v)
gliursp, sicken (v)
gliuthk, flask (n)
glofkiork, steelwork (n)
glofkiorkwan, steelworker (n
    doer)
glofnargwan, steelmaker (n doer)
glofnarzge, steelmake (v)
glofnarzgyot, steelmade (v pa)
glofplorn, steelman (n)
glofplornyek, steelmen (n pl)
gloft, steel (n)
gloftu, steely (adj)
gloifst, charge (v)
gloift, charge (n)
gloiftwan, charger (n doer)
gloirkwan, quitter (n doer)
gloirp, dumbness (n)
gloirpu, dumb (adj)
gloirpwan, dummy (n doer)
gloirshiu, quite (adv)
gloirsk, quit (v)
gloirskyot, quit (v pa)
gloirsp, dumb (v)
glorif, board (n d:Enter ship)
glorifiu, aboard (adv d:Enter
    ship)
glorifwan, boarder (n doer
    d:Enter ship)
glorisf, board (v d:Enter ship)
glornp, dreariness (n)
glornpu, dreary (adj)
glorthk, dread (n)
glorthku, dreadful (adj)
glorthsk, dread (v)
gloruge, reach (n)
glorugu, reachable (adj)
glorugwan, reacher (n doer)
gloruzge, reach (v)
gloshk, crotch (n)

gluntu, dire (adj)
glurf, guilt (n)
glurfiu, guiltily (adv)
glurfu, guilty (adj)
glurk, bunk (n d:nonsense)
glurp, burp (n)
glurpwan, burper (n doer)
glursf, guilt (v)
glursh, jack (n d:toy)
glursp, burp (v)
gluthk, broth (n)
gofaifk, lethality (n)
gofaifkiu, lethally (adv)
gofaifku, lethal (adj)
gofarf, lethargy (n)
gofarfiu, lethargically (adv)
gofarfu, lethargic (adj)
gofirk, stake (n)
gofirkuil, stakeout (n)
gofirsk, stake (v)
gofkthorthkwan, stakeholder (n
    doer)
gogarf, gland (n)
gogarfu, glandular (adj)
goifern, tomato (n)
goifirst, focus (v)
goifirt, focus (n)
goifirtu, focal (adj)
goifirtwan, focuser (n doer)
goinf, crane (n)
goinsf, crane (v)
goirk, crank (n)
goirp, wimp (n)
goirpu, wimpy (adj)
goirsk, crank (v)
goirsp, wimp (v)
goishst, cuss (v)
goizhge, jug (n)
Gold, Gold (n)
gorade, volcano (n)
goralfnirth, goldsmith (n)
goralirst, golden (v)
goralirt, gold (n)
goralirtu, gold (adj)
goralitshlersh, goldfish (n)
goralitshlershyek, goldfish (n pl)
goralkrivuge, goldmine (n)
gorfgalirsk, tarnish (v)
gorfk, tar (n)
gorfmarft, tarmac (n)
gorfsk, tar (v)
gorifp, contribution (n)
gorifpwan, contributor (n doer)
gorifsp, contribute (v)
gork, take (n)
gorkafen, takeover (n)
gorkuil, takeout (n)
gorkunf, takeoff (n)
gorkwan, taker (n doer)
gorlirp, turbulence (n)
gorlirpu, turbulent (adj)
gorpirk, turbine (n)
gors, scar (v)

gorsh, scar (n)
gorsk, take (v)
gorskyot, took (v pa)
goshirk, scare (n)
goshirku, scary (adj)
goshirkweku, scariest (adj)
goshirkwelu, scarier (adj)
goshirsk, scare (v)
goshkviarfk, scarecrow (n)
govaist, hesitate (v)
govait, hesitation (n)
govaitiu, hesitantly (adv)
govaitu, hesitant (adj)
graifkwan, mugger (n doer d:rob)
graifsk, mug (v d:rob)
graik, fetch (n)
graikwan, fetcher (n doer)
grairgiu, sluggishly (adv d:slow)
grairgu, sluggish (adj d:slow)
grairs, etch (v)
grairsh, etch (n)
grairshiu, etchily (adv)
grairshu, etchy (adj)
grairshwan, etcher (n doer)
grairst, stretch (v)
grairt, stretch (n)
grairtu, stretchy (adj)
grairtwan, stretcher (n doer)
grairzhe, vastness (n)
grairzhiu, vastly (adv)
grairzhu, vast (adj)
graisht, cusp (n)
graisk, fetch (v)
graithsk, strew (v)
gralf, corn (n)
gralfu, corny (adj)
grals, paint (v)
gralsh, paint (n)
gralshueluet, pigmentation (n)
gralshuet, pigment (n)
gralshwan, painter (n doer)
gralurge, angst (n)
gralurge, anxiety (n)
gralurgiu, anxiously (adv)
gralurgu, anxious (adj)
gralze, saw (v d:tool)
gralzhe, saw (n d:tool)
granikloirp, corkscrew (n)
granirk, flank (n)
granirp, cork (n)
granirpu, corky (adj)
granirsk, flank (v)
granirsp, cork (v)
granlark, flange (n)
grarshk, churn (n)
grarshkwan, churner (n doer)
grarshsk, churn (v)
grashklurf, paintbrush (n)
gratark, battery (n d:attack)
gratarsk, batter (v d:attack)
grath, Eho9seconds (n)
graufk, roar (n)
graufsk, roar (v)

graugiashk, massacre (n)
graugiashsk, massacre (v)
graunsk, roam (v)
graurge, enlargement (n)
graurgiu, largely (adv)
graurgu, large (adj)
graurgwaku, largest (adj)
graurgwan, enlarger (n doer)
graurgwelu, larger (adj)
graurzge, enlarge (v)
graushk, halt (n)
graushkat, halter (n)
graushsk, halt (v)
grauthsk, roil (v)
grazhfenirp, sawmill (n)
grazhkreishk, sawdust (n)
gredirsh, mustache (n)
grefal, carve (n)
grefalwan, carver (n doer)
grefasle, carve (v)
grefaslyot, carve (v pa)
grefst, close (v)
greft, closure (n)
greftart, closeness (n)
greftiu, closely (adv)
greftu, close (adj)
greftwaku, closest (adj)
greftwan, closer (n doer)
greftwelu, closer (adj)
greiarge, mania (n)
greiargu, maniacal (adj)
greiargu, manic (adj)
greiargwan, maniac (n doer)
greiark, bunker (n)
greibalbil, granddaddy (n)
greiblarp, grandpa (n)
greidathferf, grandparent (n)
greifk, camel (n)
greilfiu, grandly (adv)
greilfu, grand (adj)
greilidor, granddaughter (n)
greilidoru, granddaughterly (adj)
greiluart, grandchild (n)
greiluartyek, grandchildren (n pl)
greimah, grandma (n)
greimashel, grandmother (n)
greimashelu, grandmotherly (adj)
greimashesle, grandmother (v)
greimelimame, grandmommy (n)
greimtheiarn, grandson (n)
grelshk, incarnation (n)
greishkage, carnage (n)
greishku, carnal (adj)
greishsk, incarnate (v)
greithiork, grandmaster (n)
greitrelirst, grandstand (v)
greitrelirt, grandstand (n)
greivoterst, grandfather (v)
greivotert, grandfather (n)
greivotertu, grandfatherly (adj)
greizhge, smear (n)
greizhzge, smear (v)
grelbielirk, carport (n)

grelirp, slug (n d:animal)
grelirst, stir (v)
grelirt, stir (n)
grelirtwan, stirer (n doer)
grelkerge, carsickness (n)
grelkergu, carsick (adj)
grelshk, gash (n)
grelshkwan, gasher (n doer)
grelshsk, gash (v)
grelvirf, cargo (n)
grelvirsf, cargo (v)
grenak, cart (n)
grenakwan, carter (n doer)
grenarme, cartoon (n)
grenask, cart (v)
greshork, cartel (n)
gretak, closet (n)
grethap, stiffness (n d:rigid)
grethapu, stiff (adj d:rigid)
gretharsne, stiff (v d:cheat)
gretharst, stifle (v)
grethasp, stiffen (v d:rigid)
griark, cowardice (n)
griarku, cowardly (adj)
griarkwan, coward (n doer)
griarpwan, stalker (n doer d:pursue)
griarsk, cower (v)
griarsp, stalk (v d:pursue)
griarst, stack (v)
griart, stack (n)
griartwan, stacker (n doer)
griarzge, stagger (v)
griashk, stagnation (n)
griashku, stagnant (adj)
griashsk, stagnate (v)
griaufk, ghast (n)
griaufku, ghastly (adj)
gridarfk, calligraphy (n)
grieshst, serrate (v)
griesht, serration (n)
Grifirk, Greek (n)
grikart, solitude (n)
grikartu, solitary (adj)
grilfp, frill (n)
grilirt, eerieness (n)
grilirtiu, eerily (adv)
grilirtu, eerie (adj)
grilk, sole (n)
grilkiu, solely (adv)
grilku, sole (adj)
grilorp, treasure (n)
grilorpwan, treasurer (n doer)
grilorsp, treasure (v)
grilpart, treasury (n)
Grilsh, Greece (n)
grilth, salmon (n)
grimarn, burger (n)
grinalf, veneer (n)
griorf, cuisine (n)
griork, jeer (n)
griorsk, jeer (v)
grishort, fringe (n)

gritark, soldier (n)
gritarsk, soldier (v)
grogplorn, roughneck (n)
groilf, starvation (n)
groilsf, starve (v)
groizhge, bong (n d:pipe)
grolf, measurement (n)
grolfiu, measurably (adv)
grolfu, measurable (adj)
grolfwan, measurer (n doer)
grolge, roughness (n)
grolgiu, roughly (adv)
grolgu, rough (adj)
grolsf, measure (v)
grolzge, rough (v)
gruarp, caliper (n)
gruashk, brush (n d:shrub)
gruf, gift (n)
grufk, mug (n d:cup)
grufopliorl, giveaway (n)
grufu, gifted (adj)
grufwan, giver (n doer)
grulast, hunt (v)
grulat, hunt (n)
grulatwan, hunter (n doer)
grulge, rear (n)
grulgu, rear (adj)
grulirk, wound (n d:injury)
grulirsk, wound (v d:injury)
gruln, term (n d:word)
grulsne, term (v d:word)
grulzge, rear (v)
grunkuirt, terminology (n)
grusf, give (v)
grusfyot, gave (v pa)
grushst, clue (v)
grusht, clue (n)
grushtmeniu, cluelessly (adv)
grushtmenu, clueless (adj)
gruthoshk, ricochet (n)
gruthoshsk, ricochet (v)
grutiarf, gavel (n)
gruze, herd (v)
gruzhe, herd (n)
gruzhwan, herder (n doer)
guafirt, kind (n d:type)
guakfiaushk, hogwash (n)
guapart, toiletry (n)
guarbe, hoist (n)
guarf, bail (n)
guarfuil, bailout (n)
guark, hog (n)
guarnsk, trump (v)
guarp, toilet (n)
guarsf, bail (v)
guarsk, hog (v)
guarzbe, hoist (v)
guaurk, bigot (n)
gublars, compress (v)
gublarsh, compression (n)
gublarshu, compressable (adj)
gublarshwan, compressor (n doer)

gublasharn, compress (n)
gubralurme, compound (n d:mixture)
gubralurzme, compound (v d:mixture)
gubshuirsh, heavyweight (n)
gufirk, lust (n)
gufirkiu, lustfully (adv)
gufirku, lustful (adj)
gufirp, heel (n d:sole)
gufirsk, lust (v)
gugairt, magazine (n d:storage)
gugaurge, vulgarity (n)
gugaurgu, vulgar (adj)
gugiforp, compaction (n)
gugiforpiu, compactly (adv)
gugiforpu, compact (adj)
gugiforpwan, compactor (n doer)
gugiforsp, compact (v)
guiarme, spore (n)
guiarmiu, sporadically (adv)
guiarmu, sporadic (adj)
guifork, nastiness (n)
guiforkiu, nastily (adv)
guiforku, nasty (adj)
guiforkweku, nastiest (adj)
guiforkwelu, nastier (adj)
guirbe, heist (n)
guishk, hiss (n)
guishku, hissy (adj)
guishkwan, hisser (n doer)
guishsk, hiss (v)
gukarft, magnetic (n)
gukarst, magnetize (v)
gukart, magnetism (n)
gukartiu, magnetically (adv)
gukartu, magnetic (adj)
gukartwan, magnet (n doer)
gulerin, classmate (n)
gulirst, buoy (v)
gulirt, buoyancy (n)
gulirtiu, buoyantly (adv)
gulirtu, buoyant (adj)
gulirtwan, buoy (n doer)
gulorbe, heft (n)
gulorbu, hefty (adj)
gulorf, caffeine (n)
gulorn, communion (n)
gulornu, communal (adj)
gulorsne, commune (v)
gumarn, pudding (n)
gunabrelsh, commonplace (n)
gunabrelshu, commonplace (adj)
gunairp, compilation (n)
gunairpwan, compiler (n doer)
gunairsp, compile (v)
gunakaurp, commonwealth (n)
gunar, commonality (n)
gunariu, commonly (adv)
gunark, commune (n)
gunarl, community (n)
gunaru, common (adj)
gunarwan, commoner (n doer)

gunashoraf, commonsense (n)
gunasre, commonize (v)
guniarn, communique (n)
guniarst, communicate (v)
guniart, communication (n)
guniartwan, communicator (n doer)
guparde, compulsion (n)
gupardiu, compulsory (adv)
gupardu, compulsive (adj)
gupardwan, compeller (n doer)
guparp, rudder (n)
guparzde, compel (v)
gurbe, heave (n)
gurbiu, heavily (adv)
gurbu, heavy (adj)
gurbweku, heaviest (adj)
gurbwelu, heavier (adj)
gurfk, mood (n)
gurfkiu, moodily (adv)
gurfku, moody (adj)
gurilf, current (n d:stream)
gurp, gulp (n)
gurpwan, gulper (n doer)
gurshk, lure (n)
gurshkwan, lurer (n doer)
gurshsk, lure (v)
gursp, gulp (v)
gurzbe, heave (v)
gushran, classroom (n)
gutarf, cane (n)
gutarsf, cane (v)
guteshk, naught (n)
guteshku, naughty (adj)
guthk, moth (n)
guthshmonde, mothball (n)
guthshmonzde, mothball (v)
gutmorl, candy (n)
gutmorlu, candy (adj)
gutmorsle, candy (v)
gutraf, cake (n)
gutrasf, cake (v)
guvark, seizure (n)
guvarsk, seize (v)
guvarst, invent (v)
guvart, invention (n)
guvartiu, inventively (adv)
guvartor, inventory (n)
guvartu, inventive (adj)
guvartwan, inventor (n doer)
guviurs, comprise (v)
guviursh, comprisal (n)
guviurshu, comprisable (adj)
guzherpu, macho (adj)
Hafnium, Hafnium (n)
hagor, bat (n d:animal)
hagoru, batty (adj d:animal)
hakerf, whatever (adj/interj)
hakerf, whatever (pron)
hakzhaufel, whatsoever (adj)
hakzhaufel, whatsoever (pron)
halk, what (adj/adv/conj)
halk, what (pron)

halrelt, world (n)
halreltakrashku, worldwide (adj)
halreltu, worldly (adj)
harap, staff (n d:stick)
harasp, stave (v d:stick)
harfe, H (let sng)
harfhem, Number_1e906
harfi, Hs (let pl)
Hashium, Hassium (n)
hauf, health (n)
haufkeirf, healthcare (n)
haufu, healthy (adj)
haufwan, healer (n doer)
haufweku, healthiest (adj)
haufwelu, healthier (adj)
haurs, ward (v)
haursh, ward (n)
hausf, heal (v)
havurp, well (n d:water)
heidonduairf, watertightness (n)
heidonduairfu, watertight (adj)
heidonefliorfu, waterproof (adj)
heidonefliorsf, waterproof (v)
heidonfamor, waterbed (n)
heidonflarsh, waterfront (n)
heidonflarshu, waterfront (adj)
heidonkiarf, waterhouse (n)
heidonkiork, waterwork (n)
heidonlirolf, watercolor (n)
heidonmiurn, watertown (n)
heidonpliorl, waterway (n)
heidonplorn, waterman (n)
heidonplornyek, watermen (n pl)
heidonshtart, watermark (n)
heidonthilorf, watershed (n)
heidonthilorfu, watershed (adj)
heidonzhailf, waterfall (n)
heidorn, water (n)
heidornu, watery (adj)
heidorsne, water (v)
heidufirt, hypocracy (n)
heidufirtiu, hypocritically (adv)
heidufirtu, hypocritical (adj)
heidufirtwan, hypocrite (n doer)
heiguark, boar (n)
hein, him (pron 3rd masc sng obj)
heirp, oak (n)
heish, his (pron 3rd masc sng pos obj)
heish, his (pron 3rd masc sng pos sub)
heishfal, himself (pron 3rd masc sng refl)
heishmist, hypnotize (v)
heishmit, hypnosis (n)
heishork, whiskey (n)
Heishort, AIDS (n)
Helium, Helium (n)
hemai-, mono- (num 1 pref)
hemail, annual (n)
hemailat, monument (n)
hemailatiu, monumentally (adv)

hemailatu, monumental (adj)
hemailiu, annually (adv)
hemailu, annual (adj)
hemaisle, annualize (v)
hemaithar, anniversary (n)
hemalfhemka, Number_1e4206
hemdaurnu, onetime (adj)
heme, one (num 1 card)
hemedarf, monograph (n)
hemeldorn, monopoly (n)
hemeldornu, monopolistic (adj)
hemeldornwan, monopolist (n
    doer)
hemeldorsne, monopolize (v)
hemeru, only (adj/adv/conj)
hemeth, first (num 1 ord)
hemethiu, firstly (adv)
hemethkarp, firsthand (n)
hemethreith, monolith (n)
hemethreithu, monolithic (adj)
hemethyek, firsts (n pl)
hemevashil, firstborn (n)
hemf, once (adj/adv/conj)
hemf, once (n)
hemifk, unquadragintillion (num
    1e126 card)
hemift, untrigintillion (num 1e96
    card)
hemiftai-, zantri-
hemifteth, untrigintillionth (num
    1e96 ord)
hemka, million (num 1e6 card)
hemkadeth, millionth (num 1e6
    ord)
hemkai-, mega- (num 1e6 pref)
hemkuift, monologue (n)
hemluirt, monorail (n)
hemnelirk, monogram (n)
hemniarpiu, unanimously (adv)
hemniarpu, unanimous (adj)
hemnierst, breakfast (v)
hemniert, breakfast (n)
hempa, eleven (num 11 card)
hempai-, eleven- (num 11 pref)
hempeth, eleventh (num 11 ord)
hempreirth, monochrome (n)
hempreirthu, monochromatic
    (adj)
hemshk, unvigintillion (num 1e66
    card)
hemshkai-, jitri- (num 1e66 pref)
hemshketh, unvigintillionth (num
    1e66 ord)
hemsht, undecillion (num 1e36
    card)
hemshtai-, udeka- (num 1e36
    pref)
hemshteth, undecillionth (num
    1e36 ord)
hemthuteshk, monotheism (n)
hemthuteshku, monotheistic (adj)

hemtrilf, monotone (n)
hemtrilfat, monotony (n)
henart, wool (n)
henartu, wool (adj)
henartu, wooly (adj)
hethefirt, judiciary (n)
hetherst, judge (v)
hethert, judgement (n)
hethert, judgment (n)
hethertiu, judicially (adv)
hethertiu, judiciously (adv)
hethertu, judicial (adj)
hethertu, judicious (adj)
hethertuet, judgementalism (n)
hethertuetu, judgemental (adj)
hethertwan, judge (n doer)
hethetfirf, judgeship (n)
hethirt, patient (n d:person)
hiafel, however (adv/conj)
hial, how (adv/conj)
hial, how (n)
hiarak, wolf (n)
hiarask, wolf (v)
hibran, limb (n)
Hidrogen, Hydrogen (n)
hilorat, quotient (n)
hinarf, quotation (n)
hinarf, quote (n)
hinarfu, quotable (adj)
hinarfwan, quoter (n doer)
hinarme, quota (n)
hinarsf, quote (v)
hinarzme, quota (v)
hirsh, which (pron)
hirsherf, whichever (adj)
hirsherf, whichever (pron)
hirshu, which (adj)
hiur, why (adv/conj/interj)
hiur, why (n)
hofirp, deafness (n)
hofirpu, deaf (adj)
hofirsp, deafen (v)
hoinkart, jurisdiction (n)
hoirn, jury (n)
hoirnwan, jurist (n doer)
hoirnwan, juror (n doer)
Holmium, Holmium (n)
Honurge Konurge, Hong Kong
    (n)
honzhairm, etc, (phrase)
honzhairm, etcetera (phrase)
hua, wah (interj)
huadoin, earlobe (n)
huan, ear (n)
hui, he (pron 3rd masc sng sub)
ia, ah (interj)
ia, aye (interj)
iaborfst, obtrude (v)
iaborft, obtrusion (n)
iaborftiu, obtrusively (adv)
iaborftu, obtrusive (adj)
iaterp, objection (n d:protest)
iaterpiu, objectionably (adv

d:protest)
iaterpu, objectionable (adj
    d:protest)
iaterpwan, objector (n doer
    d:protest)
iatersp, object (v d:protest)
ibafirt, injunction (n)
ibelgrutiu, inconclusively (adv)
ibelgrutu, inconclusive (adj)
ibelklart, incongruence (n)
ibelklart, incongruousness (n)
ibelklartiu, incongruently (adv)
ibelklartiu, incongruously (adv)
ibelklartu, incongruent (adj)
ibelklartu, incongruous (adj)
ibelshipfrelpiu, inconceivably
    (adv)
ibelshipfrelpu, inconceivable (adj)
ibeltelk, inconsistency (n)
ibeltelkiu, inconsistently (adv)
ibeltelku, inconsistent (adj)
ibirnorst, endorse (v)
ibirnort, endorsement (n)
ibirnortwan, endorser (n doer)
ibrauf, inflow (n)
ibulirt, indecency (n)
ibulirtiu, indecently (adv)
ibulirtu, indecent (adj)
ibushrigiu, indescribably (adv)
ibushrigu, indescribable (adj)
ibuthish, indecision (n)
ibuthishiu, indecisively (adv)
ibuthishu, indecisive (adj)
ibuvuatiu, indefinitely (adv)
ibuvuatu, indefinite (adj)
idainfk, inequality (n)
idainfk, inequity (n)
idainfku, inequitable (adj)
Idakorf, Idaho (n)
idaurme, incubation (n)
idaurmwan, incubator (n doer)
idaurzme, incubate (v)
ide, at (prep)
idefrup, incapacity (n)
idefrusp, incapacitate (v)
ideirk, indictment (n)
ideirkwan, indictor (n doer)
ideirsk, indict (v)
idelishork, infraction (n)
idilsharfu, inopparablc (adj)
idubielirku, inopportune (adj)
iduriftu, inoperable (adj)
iduriftu, inoperative (adj)
ienutarku, ineligible (adj)
ifaborst, infuse (v)
ifabort, infusion (n)
Ifak, Manganese (n davoka)
ifamosre, embed (v)
Ifap, Scandium (n davoka)
Ifat, Copper (n davoka)
ifeifiaurnu, inclement (adj)
ifert, entity (n)
ifibeinurk, epitaph (n)

ifieshtu, infrared (adj)
Ifik, Iron (n davoka)
ifikorf, epoch (n)
ifilfret, incapability (n)
ifilfretu, incapable (adj)
ifiorfondiu, infrequently (adv)
ifiorfondu, infrequent (adj)
Ifip, Titanium (n davoka)
ifiplorn, epidemic (n)
Ifit, Zinc (n davoka)
ifleinorsh, incompatibility (n)
ifleinorshiu, incompatibly (adv)
ifleinorshu, incompatible (adj)
ifludret, epicenter (n)
Ifok, Cobalt (n davoka)
Ifop, Vanadium (n davoka)
ifrelp, inability (n)
iftarp, instability (n)
ifuirfu, inflight (adj)
Ifuk, Nickel (n davoka)
Ifup, Chromium (n davoka)
igalirf, incursion (n)
igalirsf, incur (v)
Igeptaf, Egypt (n)
Igeptarn, Egyptian (n)
igerst, inflect (v)
igert, inflection (n)
igertu, inflective (adj)
igrishorst, infringe (v)
igrishort, infringement (n)
ikaushkelt, insufficiency (n)
ikaushkeltiu, insufficiently (adv)
ikaushkeltu, insufficient (adj)
ikauvurtiu, insufferably (adv)
ikauvurtu, insufferable (adj)
ikiarge, ingestation (n)
ikiargwan, ingester (n doer)
ikiarzge, ingest (v)
ikifirt, inertia (n)
ikifirtu, inertial (adj)
ikikiarge, indigestion (n)
ikirfu, inert (adj)
ikirueftiu, inherently (adv)
ikirueftu, inherent (adj)
ikriushk, induction (n)
ikriushkwan, inductor (n doer)
ikriushsk, induct (v)
il, or (conj)
ilaikau, eureka (interj)
ilailf, inheritance (n)
ilailsf, inherit (v)
Ilak, Technetium (n davoka)
Ilanoirf, Illinois (n)
Ilap, Yttrium (n davoka)
Ilat, Silver (n davoka)
ildanarpu, incumbent (adj)
ilenbolkiu, incomparably (adv)
ilenbolku, incomparable (adj)
ilendruketu, incomprehensible (adj)
ilenvaprol, incompetence (n)
ilenvaproliu, incompetently (adv)
ilenvaprolu, incompetent (adj)

ilfe, I (let sng)
ilfedaurtu, upbeat (adj)
ilfhem, Number_1e456
ilfi, Is (let pl)
ilianfirk, incendiary (n)
ilianfirku, incendiary (adj)
ilianirf, incense (n d:smoke)
ilianirst, incense (v d:anger)
ilianirt, incense (n d:anger)
iliarts, incinerate (v)
iliartsh, incineration (n)
iliartshwan, incinerator (n doer)
iligralp, insolvency (n)
iligralpu, insolvent (adj)
Ilik, Ruthenium (n davoka)
Ilip, Zirconium (n davoka)
ilipituarp, incoherence (n)
ilipituarpiu, incoherently (adv)
ilipituarpu, incoherent (adj)[1]
Ilit, Cadmium (n davoka)
iloirge, indulgence (n)
iloirzge, indulge (v)
Ilok, Rhodium (n davoka)
Ilop, Niobium (n davoka)
ilothakor, inadvertence (n)
ilothakoriu, inadvertently (adv)
ilothakoru, inadvertent (adj)
ilpershk, ambush (n)
ilpershsk, ambush (v)
ilplurtuet, ambition (n)
ilplurtuetiu, ambitiously (adv)
ilplurtuetu, ambitious (adj)
Iluk, Palladium (n davoka)
Ilup, Molybdenum (n davoka)
ilushairkiu, irrevocably (adv)
ilushairku, irrevocable (adj)
imorth, inpatient (n)
inafirk, infestation (n)
inafirsk, infest (v)
Inak, Bohrium (n davoka)
Inap, Lawrencium (n davoka)
Inat, Roentgenium (n davoka)
inaurk, emission (n)
inaursk, emit (v)
Indiafarn, Indian (n)
Indianirk, Indiana (n)
Indiankarpol, Indianapolis (n)
Indiarf, India (n)
Indium, Indium (n)
Indonishiarf, Indonesia (n)
Inik, Hassium (n davoka)
Inip, Rutherfordium (n davoka)
inirve, infatuation (n)
inirzve, infatuate (v)
Init, Ununbium (n davoka)
ino, any (pron/adj/adv)
inobresh, anyplace (adv)
inodizhe, anything (n)
inohia, anyhow (adv)
inohol, anywhere (n)
inoholu, anywhere (adv)
Inok, Meitnerium (n davoka)
inona, anyone (pron)

Inop, Dubnium (n davoka)
inoplio, anyway (adv)
inoshlade, anybody (n/pron)
inowel, anymore (adv)
inuanirk, indiscrimination (n)
inuanirkiu, indiscriminately (adv)
inuanirku, indiscriminate (adj)
Inuk, Darmstadtium (n davoka)
Inup, Seaborgium (n davoka)
ioboratiu, inadvisably (adv)
ioboratu, inadvisable (adj)
Iodin, Iodine (n)
iofirk, ineptitude (n)
iofirk, ineptness (n)
iofirku, inept (adj)
ioflikirmiu, inappropriately (adv)
ioflikirmu, inappropriate (adj)
iogvert, inaccessibility (n)
iogvertu, inaccessible (adj)
iomudenirku, inanimate (adj)
iopiforkuet, inattention (n)
iopiforkuetiu, inattentively (adv)
iopiforkuetu, inattentive (adj)
iorishkeialst, insubordinate (v)
iorishkeialt, insubordination (n)
iorishkeialtu, insubordinate (adj)
ioritrelpiu, insubstantially (adv)
ioritrelpu, insubstantial (adj)
iotarn, iota (n)
Iowarf, Iowa (n)
ipaltark, inactivity (n)
ipaltarku, inactive (adj)
ipaltarkuet, inactivation (n)
ipaltarsk, inactivate (v)
ipatiluet, inaction (n)
ipelmurn, insincereness (n)
ipelmurniu, insincerely (adv)
ipelmurnu, insincere (adj)
ipeshirp, injustice (n)
ipi-, bi- (num 2 pref)
ipiarnu, binary (adj)
ipidilkarst, bipolarize (v)
ipidilkart, bipolarity (n)
ipidilkartu, bipolar (adj)
ipidrokifar, costar (n)
ipidrokifasre, costar (v)
ipidurast, cooperate (v d:agree)
ipidurat, cooperation (n d:agree)
ipiduratiu, cooperatively (adv d:agree)
ipiduratu, cooperative (adj d:agree)
ipiduratuk, cooperative (n d:store)
ipiduratwan, cooperator (n doer d:agree)
ipifiuvetwat, coprocessor (n)
ipikizhasht, biotechnology (n)
ipimoirmuet, copayment (n)
ipinamoriu, bilaterally (adv)
ipinamoru, bilateral (adj)
ipirde, coop (n d:cooperative)
ipishlirp, corrosion (n)

ipishlirpiu, corrosively (adv)
ipishlirpu, corrosive (adj)
ipishlirsp, corrode (v)
ipishterk, coincidence (n)
ipishterkiu, coincidentally (adv)
ipishterku, coincident (adj)
ipishterku, coincidental (adj)
ipishtersk, coincide (v)
ipituarp, coherence (n)
ipituarpu, coherent (adj)
ipituart, cohesion (n)
ipituartu, cohesive (adj)
ipituartuet, cohesiveness (n)
ipludarast, correlate (v)
ipludarat, correlation (n)
ipludufirp, correspondence (n)
ipludufirpwan, correspondent (n
    doer)
ipludufirsp, correspond (v)
iprakatiu, incorrectly (adv)
iprakatu, incorrect (adj)
Irafkarn, Iraqi (n)
irai-, tri- (num 3 pref)
iraimirk, triangle (n)
iraimirku, triangular (adj)
iraimirkuet, triangulation (n)
iraimirsk, triangulate (v)
iraimoirn, tripod (n)
irainamoru, trilateral (adj)
iraishart, triplet (n)
iraishork, triple (n)
iraishorku, triple (adj)
iraishorsk, triple (v)
iraithranit, trimester (n)
Irak, Rhenium (n davoka)
Iralfk, Iraq (n)
Iranf, Iran (n)
Iraniarn, Iranian (n)
Irap, Lutetium (n davoka)
Irat, Gold (n davoka)
Irelandarn, Irish (n)
Irelanurde, Ireland (n)
ireth, third (num 3 ord)
iri, three (num 3 card)
irialfhemka, Number_1e12306
irida, thirty (num 30 card)
iridai-, thirty- (num 30 pref)
irideth, thirtieth (num 30 ord)
Iridium, Iridium (n)
irifk, tresquadragintilllon (num
    1e132 card)
irift, trestrigintillion (num 1e102
    card)
Irik, Osmium (n davoka)
irika, trillion (num 1e12 card)
irikai-, tera- (num 1e12 pref)
iriketh, trillionth (num 1e12 ord)
Irip, Hafnium (n davoka)
iripa, thirteen (num 13 card)
iripai-, thirteen- (num 13 pref)
iripeth, thirteenth (num 13 ord)
irishk, trevigintillion (num 1e72

card)
irishkai-, hienta-
irishketh, trevigintillionth (num
    1e72 ord)
irisht, tredecillion (num 1e42
    card)
irishtai-, sekata- (num 1e42 pref)
irishteth, tredecillionth (num
    1e42 ord)
Irit, Mercury (n davoka)
iriukiu, inaudibly (adv)
iriuku, inaudible (adj)
Irok, Ridium (n davoka)
Iron, Iron (n)
Irop, Tantalum (n davoka)
Iruk, Platinum (n davoka)
Irup, Tungsten (n davoka)
irushst, elude (v)
irushtiu, elusively (adv)
irushtu, elusive (adj)
ishai, shoo (interj)
ishe, in (prep)
ishedraifpu, inbound (adj)
ishefleirde, inbreed (n)
ishefleirzde, inbreed (v)
isheglorifu, inboard (adj)
ishegork, intake (n)
isheift, infertility (n)
isheiftu, infertile (adj)
isheithku, inelastic (adj)
isheprant, infield (n)
isheprantwan, infielder (n doer)
isherk, innard (n)
isherkiu, innerly (adv)
isherku, inner (adj)
ishern, infamy (n)
isherniu, infamously (adv)
ishernu, infamous (adj)
isheroifku, inline (adj)
ishetriarzge, instill (v)
ishiarmpu, intangible (adj)
ishiniurku, insurmountable (adj)
ishirp, inception (n)
Ishlarme, Islam (n)
ishlerk, infrastructure (n)
ishlern, inmate (n)
ishnefst, instigate (v)
ishneft, instigation (n)
ishneftwan, instigator (n doer)
ishorhp, insensitivity (n)
ishorfipu, insensitive (adj)
Ishrahilarn, Israeli (n)
Ishrahilf, Israel (n)
ishreln, ensurance (n)
ishreln, insurance (n)
ishrelnwan, insurer (n doer)
ishrelsne, ensure (v)
ishrelsne, insure (v)
ishreltiemiu, insidiously (adv)
ishreltiemu, insidious (adj)
ishte, into (prep)
ishtelf, indoors (n)
ishtelfu, indoor (adj)

ishtranak, ingredient (n)
Italiarn, Italian (n)
Italirf, Italy (n)
itatorviu, inoffensively (adv)
itatorvu, inoffensive (adj)
itedifaide, inadequacy (n)
itedifaidiu, inadequately (adv)
itedifaidu, inadequate (adj)
itenirk, inadmission (n)
itenirku, inadmissible (adj)
Iterbium, Ytterbium (n)
iterp, injection (n)
iterpu, injectable (adj)
iterpwan, injector (n doer)
itersp, inject (v)
ithirme, episode (n)
ithirmiu, episodally (adv)
ithirmu, episodal (adj)
ithirshk, incision (n)
ithirshkiu, incisively (adv)
ithirshku, incisive (adj)
ithirshkwan, incisor (n doer)
ithirshsk, incise (v)
ithoitirku, infeasible (adj)
ithorku, inapplicable (adj)
ithriarthu, inhospitable (adj)
ithuarst, emphasize (v)
ithuarstyot, emphasize (v pa)
ithuart, emphasis (n)
ithulth, insight (n)
ithulthu, insightful (adj)
ithuvirtar, ineffectiveness (n)
ithuvirtar, inefficiency (n)
ithuvirtariu, ineffectively (adv)
ithuvirtariu, inefficiently (adv)
ithuvirtaru, ineffective (adj)
ithuvirtaru, inefficient (adj)
itibrufu, indispensable (adj)
itiert, inflexibility (n)
itiertu, inflexible (adj)
itipoit, indistinction (n)
itipoitiu, indistinctly (adv)
itipoitiu, indistinguishably (adv)
itipoitu, indistinct (adj)
itipoitu, indistinguishable (adj)
itiurft, infinity (n)
itiurftiu, infinitely (adv)
itiurftu, infinite (adj)
itivirsh, indiscretion (n)
itivirshiu, indiscreetly (adv)
itivirshu, indiscreet (adj)
itivoirkiu, indisputably (adv)
itivoirku, indisputable (adj)
itove, indifference (n)
itoviu, indifferently (adv)
itovu, indifferent (adj)
itrelish, inroad (n)
itrifirst, insinuate (v)
itrifirt, insinuation (n)
Itrium, Yttrium (n)
ituarilku, inviolate (adj)
ituarilsk, inviolate (v)
itubrunfiu, inexpensively (adv)

itubrunfu, inexpensive (adj)
itufalat, inaccuracy (n)
itufalatiu, inaccurately (adv)
itufalatu, inaccurate (adj)
itugoishtiu, inexcusably (adv)
itugoishtu, inexcusable (adj)
itulirfiu, incurably (adv)
itulirfu, incurable (adj)
itulirshiu, indeterminately (adv)
itulirshu, indeterminate (adj)
itulirshwan, indeterminant (n doer)
iturshtu, inexact (adj)
iumern, unless (prep/conj)
iushiakiu, inescapably (adv)
iushiaku, inescapable (adj)
iutaurn, until (prep/conj)
ivadarve, emotion (n)
ivadarviu, emotionally (adv)
ivadarvu, emotional (adj)
ivadarvu, emotive (adj)
ivadarzve, emote (v)
ivartulf, insecurity (n)
ivartulfiu, insecurely (adv)
ivartulfu, insecure (adj)
ivei, up (prep)
iveidierk, upright (n)
iveidierkiu, uprightly (adv)
iveidierku, upright (adj)
iveiduairf, uptightness (n)
iveiduairfu, uptight (adj)
iveifalirme, upstream (n)
iveifalirmu, upstream (adj)
iveiferp, upset (n)
iveiferpu, upset (adj)
iveifersp, upset (v)
iveiferspyot, upset (v pa)
iveiflarshu, upfront (adj)
iveiflierge, upswing (n)
iveigork, uptake (n)
iveigraufk, uproar (n)
iveigurbe, upheaval (n)
iveihaurshiu, upward (adv)
iveihaurshiu, upwards (adv)
iveihaurshu, upward (adj)
iveihaurshu, upwards (adj)
iveikaimp, upturn (n)
iveiklorf, upkeep (n)
iveimiurn, uptown (n)
iveimiurnu, uptown (adj)
iveiraushsk, uplift (v)
iveishaiarsh, upstate (n)
iveishaiarshu, upstate (adj)
iveishiopu, uphill (adj)
iveishkalirt, upstart (n)
iveishkalirtu, upstart (adj)
iveishkoift, upshot (n)
iveishoirt, upside (n)
iveishtrak, upgrade (n)
iveishtrask, upgrade (v)
iveishuirku, upscale (adj)
iveist, up (v)
iveit, up (n)

iveitairn, upstairs (n)
iveitairnu, upstairs (adj)
iveithorthsk, uphold (v)
iveithorthskyot, upheld (v pa)
iveitiu, upperly (adv)
iveitolirk, update (n)
iveitolirkwan, updater (n doer)
iveitolirsk, update (v)
iveitu, upper (adj)
iveituet, uppitiness (n)
iveituetu, uppity (adj)
iveitweku, uppermost (adj)
iveivoirge, upsurge (n)
iveiwefirsp, uproot (v)
iverme, upon (prep)
iviersh, inferno (n)
iviershu, infernal (adj)
ivoikuarst, insurrect (v)
ivoikuart, insurrection (n)
ivoirge, insurgency (n)
ivoirgiu, insurgently (adv)
ivoirgu, insurgent (adj)
ivoirgwan, insurgent (n doer)
ivoirzge, insurge (v)
ivorlinatiu, informally (adv)
ivorlinatu, informal (adj)
ivugarn, inferiority (n)
ivugarnu, inferior (adj)
iwabairme, eyesore (n)
iwadorame, eyewear (n)
iwadrinat, eyeglass (n)
iwaflorde, eyebrow (n)
iwafriork, eyewitness (n)
iwalerk, eyelet (n)
iwanith, eyelid (n)
iwaprulirk, eyestrain (n)
iwaroifkwan, eyeliner (n doer)
iwashmonde, eyeball (n)
iwashmonzde, eyeball (v)
iwashreide, eyelash (n)
iwast, eye (v)
iwat, eye (n)
iwathetirsh, eyepiece (n)
iwathulth, eyesight (n)
iwatmenu, eyeless (adj)
iwatwan, eyer (n doer)
iweifork, insignificance (n)
iweiforkiu, insignificantly (adv)
iweiforku, insignificant (adj)
izhairt, infallibility (n)
izhairtiu, infallibly (adv)
izhairtu, infallible (adj)
izhurnit, inexperience (n)
kabarst, park (v d:stop)
kabirk, sneeze (n)
kabirku, sneezy (adj)
kabirsk, sneeze (v)
kabirst, parlor (v)
kabirt, parlor (n)
kaborfst, intrude (v)
kaborft, intrusion (n)
kaborftiu, intrusively (adv)
kaborftu, intrusive (adj)

kaborftuet, intrusiveness (n)
kaborftwan, intruder (n doer)
kadark, rudeness (n)
kadarkiu, rudely (adv)
kadarku, rude (adj)
Kadmium, Cadmium (n)
kafirp, craft (n)
kafirpiu, craftily (adv)
kafirpu, crafty (adj)
kafirpwan, craftsman (n doer)
kafirsp, craft (v)
kaflak, crash (n)
kaflakwan, crasher (n doer)
kaflask, crash (v)
kai, yay (interj)
kaiarp, yap (n)
kaiarpwan, yapper (n doer)
kaiarsp, yap (v)
kaiarth, wrath (n)
kaiarthu, wrathful (adj)
kaibarsk, wrack (v)
kaifpekiarf, jailhouse (n)
kaifst, hate (v)
kaift, hate (n)
kaift, hatred (n)
kaiftiu, hatefully (adv)
kaiftu, hateful (adj)
kaiftwan, hater (n doer)
kail, you (pron 2nd sng obj)
kail, you (pron 2nd sng sub)
kailark, StrontiumFood (n)
kaimafen, turnover (n)
kaimdoiart, turntable (n)
kaimesp, turn (v)
kaimfrafk, turncoat (n)
kaimoblaithp, turnaround (n)
kaimp, turn (n)
kaimpaiart, turnpike (n)
kaimpoveip, turnabout (n)
kaimpuil, turnout (n)
kaimpunt, turnoff (n)
kaimtrifku, turnkey (adj)
kainurp, canard (n)
kair, you (pron 2nd pl obj)
kair, you (pron 2nd pl sub)
kairap, mold (n d:form)
kairasp, mold (v d:form)
kairfk, harshness (n)
kairfkiu, harshly (adv)
kairfku, harsh (adj)
kairfp, jail (n)
kairfpwan, jailer (n doer)
kairfsk, harshen (v)
kairfsp, jail (v)
kairge, hostage (n)
kairkwan, razor (n doer)
kairn, chi (n)
Kairolf, Cairo (n)
kairsh, your (pron 2nd pl pos sub)
kairsh, yours (pron 2nd pl pos obj)
kairsk, raze (v)

kairve, wag (n)
kairvwan, wagger (n doer)
kairzve, wag (v)
kaish, your (pron 2nd sng pos sub)
kaish, yours (pron 2nd sng pos obj)
kaishfal, yourself (pron 2nd sng refl)
kaishfar, yourselves (pron 2nd pl refl)
kaithelp, invalid (n d:person)
kaithuf, bouquet (n)
Kaitirf, Haiti (n)
kaivarp, wagon (n)
kakortuet, terrorism (n)
kalde, cord (n)
Kaliforan, California (n)
Kalifornium, Californium (n)
kalirp, crab (n)
kalirpu, crabby (adj)
kalirsp, crab (v)
kalnen, holly (n)
Kalshium, Calcium (n)
kalshkiu, lucratively (adv)
kalshku, lucrative (adj)
kalufk, stroll (n)
kalufkwan, stroller (n doer)
kalufsk, stroll (v)
kalurzge, crave (v)
kalzde, cord (v)
kamarfst, catalyze (v)
kamarft, catalyst (n)
kamarftu, catalytic (adj)
kamarftwan, catalyzer (n doer)
Kambodiarf, Cambodia (n)
Kambodiarn, Cambodian (n)
Kambrilge, Cambridge (n)
kamirsh, tissue (n)
Kanadarf, Canada (n)
Kanadiarn, Canadian (n)
kanikarve, gymnasium (n)
kanipuf, journey (n)
kanipusf, journey (v)
kanirf, chant (n)
kanirfwan, chanter (n doer)
kanirk, gym (n)
kanirsf, chant (v)
kanitaf, journal (n)
kanitafu, journalistic (adj)
kanitafuet, journalism (n)
kanitafwan, journalist (n doer)
kanitasf, journal (v)
Kankarl, Hanukkah (n)
kanoraf, astronomy (n)
kanorafiu, astronimically (adv)
kanorafu, astronomical (adj)
kanorafwan, astronomer (n doer)
kanoriast, astronavigate (v)
kanoriat, astronavigation (n)
kanoriatwan, astronaut (n doer)
Kansharsh, Kansas (n)
kapadrolart, handlebar (n)

kaparn, kappa (n)
kapars, parrot (v)
kaparsh, parrot (n)
kapediefk, handcuff (n)
kapediefsk, handcuff (v)
kapedorige, handgun (n)
kapedotirs, handpick (v)
kapevornt, handbook (n)
kapezhorde, handset (n)
kapkafirsp, handcraft (v)
kapluirt, handrail (n)
kaplurge, fart (n)
kaplurzge, fart (v)
kapnarzge, handmake (v)
kapnarzgyot, handmade (v pa)
kapsherge, manuscript (n)
kaptrelirt, handstand (n)
kapukiork, handiwork (n)
kapurifst, maneuver (v)
kapurift, maneuver (n)
kapurtfrelp, maneuverability (n)
karak, assassination (n)
karakwan, assassin (n doer)
karask, assassinate (v)
karbark, wreck (n)
karbarkwan, wrecker (n doer)
karbarshk, wreckage (n)
karbarsk, wreck (v)
Karbon, Carbon (n)
kardinalf, cardinal (n)
karfluarlu, assailable (adj)
karfluarlwan, assailant (n doer)
karfluarsle, assail (v)
karfst, catch (v)
karfstyot, caught (v pa)
karft, catch (n)
karftu, catchy (adj)
karftwan, catcher (n doer)
kargark, tournament (n)
kargarve, handshake (n)
kargarzve, handshake (v)
kargarzvyot, handshook (v pa)
Karibiarn, Caribbean (n)
karishk, gulf (n)
karishsk, engulf (v)
Karkuairn, marijuana (n)
karlf, nation (n)
karlfan, nationality (n)
karlfirf, nationhood (n)
karlfiu, nationally (adv)
karlfu, national (adj)
karlfuet, nationalism (n)
karlfwan, nationalist (n doer)
karlk, cram (n)
karlkrashku, nationwide (adj)
karlsf, nationalize (v)
karlsk, cram (v)
karnufaf, handbag (n)
karp, hand (n)
karpade, handle (n)
karpadwan, handler (n doer)
karpazde, handle (v)
karpefp, handicap (n)

karpefsp, handicap (v)
karpesh, handful (n)
karploaf, handkerchief (n)
karploidwan, handwriter (n doer)
karploizde, handwrite (v)
karploizdyot, handwrote (v pa)
karpu, handy (adj)
karpuil, handout (n)
karpwan, handyman (n doer)
karsp, hand (v)
karthp, validity (n)
karthpiu, validly (adv)
karthpu, valid (adj)
karthpuet, validation (n)
karthsp, validate (v)
Kartoforde, Hartford (n)
karve, tug (n)
karzhiniu, handsomely (adv)
karzhinu, handsome (adj)
karzve, tug (v)
kashirn, casino (n)
katark, rut (n)
kathairsk, wield (v)
kathiurf, valor (n)
kathiurfu, valiant (adj)
katilur, attitude (n)
katirk, wage (n)
katirsk, wage (v)
katishk, wager (n)
katishsk, wager (v)
katufst, strobe (v)
katuft, strobe (n)
katurk, stroke (n)
katurkwan, stroker (n doer)
katursk, stroke (v)
kauaifp, wail (n)
kauaifsp, wail (v)
kauaishst, horrify (v)
kauaisht, horror (n)
kauaishtiu, horribly (adv)
kauaishtu, horrible (adj)
kauaishtu, horrific (adj)
kaubeshu, awful (adj)
kaudairku, horrid (adj)
kauf, fog (n)
kaufiu, foggily (adv)
kaufkroip, foghorn (n)
kaufu, foggy (adj)
kaufuarp, hotdog (n)
kaufuarsp, hotdog (v)
kaufwan, fogger (n doer)
kaugaiftu, horrendous (adj)
kaukartu, rank (adj d:rotten)
kaukiarst, catapult (v)
kaukiart, catapult (n)
kaurp, wealth (n)
kaurpu, wealthy (adj)
kaurshiu, hotly (adv)
kaurshu, hot (adj)
kaurshyek, hots (n pl)
kausf, fog (v)
kaushfamor, hotbed (n)
kaushgutraf, hotcake (n)

kaushkeft, hothead (n)
kaushkelst, suffice (v)
kaushkelt, sufficiency (n)
kaushkeltiu, sufficiently (adv)
kaushkeltu, sufficient (adj)
kaushkoift, hotshot (n)
kaushroifk, hotline (n)
kauvairp, suffocation (n)
kauvairsp, suffocate (v)
kauvurst, suffer (v)
kauvurtiu, sufferably (adv)
kauvurtu, sufferable (adj)
kauvurtwan, sufferer (n doer)
Kauwirf, Hawii (n)
kavairk, hassle (n)
kavairsk, hassle (v)
kavairst, hasten (v)
kavairt, haste (n)
kavairtiu, hastily (adv)
kavairtu, hasty (adj)
kavarlwan, gatherer (n doer)
kavarsle, gather (v)
kavilort, metropolis (n)
kavilortwan, metropolitan (n
    doer)
kavirp, basin (n)
kavolar, heaven (n)
kavolaru, heavenly (adj)
kavshkorbe, tugboat (n)
kazhirge, square (n)
kazhirgiu, squarely (adv)
kazhirzge, square (v)
Keberfk, Quebec (n)
kebert, hobby (n)
kebertwan, hobbyist (n doer)
kefborafu, headstrong (adj)
kefdorfp, headgear (n)
kefeidorn, headwater (n)
kefezhorde, headset (n)
kefgrulatwan, headhunter (n
    doer)
kefirsk, melt (v)
kefirst, head (v)
kefirt, head (n)
kefirtu, heady (adj)
kefirtwan, header (n doer)
kefkeidorn, meltwater (n)
kefketiern, meltdown (n)
keflituage, headache (n)
kefluarn, headlight (n)
kefplersh, headdress (n)
kefplershwan, headdresser (n
    doer)
kefpliorl, headway (n)
kefplok, headboard (n)
kefroifk, headline (n)
kefroifkwan, headliner (n doer)
kefroifsk, headline (v)
kefshranf, headroom (n)
kefshtairme, headband (n)
kefthelern, headwind (n)
kefthiork, headmaster (n)
keftkarist, headquarter (v)

keftkarit, headquarters (n)
kefyarp, headphone (n)
keianegufirk, wanderlust (n)
keiankwan, wanderer (n doer)
keiansk, wander (v)
keiarp, buckle (n)
keiarpwan, buckler (n doer)
keiarsp, buckle (v)
keibart, visor (n)
keidarn, hotel (n)
keieshsk, wane (v)
keifan, gallery (n)
keihem, Number_1e3906
keikurst, remark (v d:reply)
keikurt, remark (n d:reply)
keikurtiu, remarkably (adv
    d:reply)
keikurtu, remarkable (adj d:reply)
keil, K (let sng)
keili, Ks (let pl)
keilirf, viscera (n)
keilirfiu, viscerally (adv)
keilirfu, visceral (adj)
keinarp, nomad (n)
keinarpu, nomadic (adj)
keipiforst, patent (v)
keipifort, patent (n)
keipirp, petal (n)
keirbe, visage (n)
keirf, care (n)
keirfmen, carelessness (n)
keirfmeniu, carelessly (adv)
keirfmenu, careless (adj)
keirfush, carefulness (n)
keirfushiu, carefully (adv)
keirfushu, careful (adj)
keirgiu, overwhelmingly (adv)
keirp, consciousness (n)
keirpiu, consciously (adv)
keirpu, conscious (adj)
keirs, talent (v)
keirsf, care (v)
keirsh, talent (n)
keirt, lottery (n)
keirve, nod (n)
keirzge, overwhelm (v)
keirzve, nod (v)
keiteshk, wedge (n)
keiteshsk, wedge (v)
keitirn, hyphen (n)
keitirsne, hyphenate (v)
keiun, coo (n)
keiurk, gag (n d:choke)
keiursk, gag (v d:choke)
keiusne, coo (v)
keizhark, x-ray (n)
keizharsk, x-ray (v)
kelaia, hooray (interj)
kelaia, hurrah (interj)
kelaia, hurray (interj)
kelart, university (n)
kelashk, wack (n)
kelashku, wacky (adj)

kelashku, whacky (adj)
kelashkwan, wacko (n doer)
kelashkwan, whacko (n doer)
kelashsk, wack (v)
kelashsk, whack (v)
kelerf, girl (n)
kelerfu, girly (adj)
Keliaf, EhoDay06 (n)
kelifort, hardiness (n)
kelifortiu, hardily (adv)
kelifortu, hardy (adj)
kelirk, visit (n)
kelirkuet, visitation (n)
kelirkwan, visitor (n doer)
kelirsk, visit (v)
kelirst, harden (v)
kelirt, hardness (n)
kelirth, visa (n)
kelirtiu, hard (adv)
kelirtoiu, hardly (adv)
kelirtu, hard (adj)
kelirtwaku, hardest (adj)
kelirtwelu, harder (adj)
kelkiork, toil (n)
kelkiorsk, toil (v)
kelshlerf, hardware (n)
keltedathel, hardcover (n)
keltedathelu, hardcover (adj)
keltedaurp, hardtop (n)
keltevark, hardback (n)
keltfanirn, hardwood (n)
keltfirf, hardship (n)
keltkirftu, hardcore (adj)
keltroifk, hardline (n)
keltroifku, hardline (adj)
keltroifkwan, hardliner (n doer)
keltshmonde, hardball (n)
kelurbe, counter (n d:d: shelf)
keminork, ring (n d:sound)
keminorkwan, ringer (n doer
    d:sound)
keminorsk, ring (v d:sound)
keminorskyot, rang (v pa
    d:sound)
kemirf, volition (n)
kemirfiu, voluntarily (adv)
kemirfu, voluntary (adj)
kemirfwan, volunteer (n doer)
kemirp, want (n)
kemirsf, volunteer (v)
kemirsk, wanna (v)
kemirsp, want (v)
kemvil, wannabe (n)
kenarth, quicksand (n)
kendaurn, quicktime (n)
kenirf, revolution (n d:political
    change)
kenirfu, revolutionary (adj
    d:political change)
kenirfwan, revolutionary (n doer
    d:political change)
kenirk, revolt (n)
kenirkwan, revolter (n doer)

kenirsf, revolutionize (v
    d:political change)
kenirsk, revolt (v)
kenorst, quicken (v)
kenort, quickness (n)
kenortiu, quickly (adv)
kenortu, quick (adj)
kensharagen, quicksilver (n)
Kentukirf, Kentucky (n)
kentweku, quickest (adj)
kentwelu, quicker (adj)
kepefiveil, kneecap (n)
keperfwan, kneeling (n doer)
kepersf, kneel (v)
kerbaft, characteristic (n
    d:person)
kerbast, characterize (v d:person)
kerbat, characterization (n
    d:person)
kerbatiu, characteristically (adv
    d:person)
kerbatu, characteristic (adj
    d:person)
kerbatwan, character (n doer
    d:person)
kerp, knee (n)
kersp, knee (v)
kerufk, gore (n)
kerufku, gory (adj)
kerufsk, gore (v)
keshirn, xi (n)
kest, check (v d:review)
ket, check (n d:review)
ketfenshk, checkmate (n)
ketfenshsk, checkmate (v)
kethirn, elegance (n)
kethirniu, elegantly (adv)
kethirnu, elegant (adj)
ketirs, letter (v d:character)
ketirsh, letter (n d:character)
ketudilt, checklist (n)
ketwan, checker (n doer d:review)
kiabark, toxicity (n)
kiabarku, toxic (adj)
kiabarkuit, toxicology (n)
kiabarkuitiu, toxicologically (adv)
kiabarkuitu, toxicological (adj)
kiabarkuitwan, toxicologist (n
    doer)
kiafeshkorbe, houseboat (n)
kiafkiork, housework (n)
kiafklorfwan, housekeeper (n
    doer)
kiafklorsf, housekeep (v)
kiafklorsfyot, housekept (v pa)
kiafsherzme, houseclean (v)
kiafuaft, coroner (n)
kiafuarn, hovel (n)
kiaishk, pest (n)
kiaishkoik, pesticide (n)
kiaishku, pesky (adj)
kiaishkuet, pestilence (n)
kiaishsk, pester (v)

kiakiorsk, tinker (v)
kialirp, hack (n)
kialirpwan, hacker (n doer)
kialirsp, hack (v)
kialirst, ace (v)
kialirt, ace (n)
kialofirk, bribery (n)
kialork, bribe (n)
kialorkwan, briber (n doer)
kialorsk, bribe (v)
kialpegralzhe, hacksaw (n)
kianirde, wand (n)
kianirk, rink (n)
kianirp, stride (n)
kiaranu, gourmet (adj)
kiarbe, toxin (n)
kiarde, tube (n)
kiardu, tubal (adj)
kiardu, tubular (adj)
kiarf, house (n)
kiarfan, household (n)
kiarge, jest (n)
kiargwan, jester (n doer)
kiarn, video (n)
kiarneirf, videotape (n)
kiarneirsf, videotape (v)
kiarp, turbin (n)
kiarsf, house (v)
kiarsh, east (n)
kiarsharf, housewife (n)
kiarshku, eastern (adj)
kiarshu, east (adj)
kiarst, die (v)
kiart, death (n)
kiarth, hall (n)
kiarthip, hallway (n)
kiarzde, tube (v)
kiarzge, jest (v)
kiashlarde, corpse (n)
kiashort, chassis (n)
kiatfamor, deathbed (n)
kiauf, glue (n)
kiaugalist, implode (v)
kiaugalit, implosion (n)
kiaugalitiu, implosively (adv)
kiaugalitu, implosive (adj)
kiaugalitwan, imploder (n doer)
kiaulf, turmoil (n)
kiaurk, screech (n)
kiaurkwan, screecher (n doer)
kiaurp, howl (n)
kiaurpwan, howler (n doer)
kiaursk, screech (v)
kiaursp, howl (v)
kiaurst, reform (v d:decorrupt)
kiaurt, reform (n d:decorrupt)
kiaurtwan, reformer (n doer
    d:decorrupt)
kiaurtwan, reformist (n doer
    d:decorrupt)
kiausf, glue (v)
kiaushk, haze (n d:fog)
kiaushku, hazy (adj d:fog)

kiaushsk, haze (v d:fog)
kiaviark, hazard (n)
kiaviarku, hazardous (adj)
kiaviarsk, hazard (v)
kibafirk, axis (n)
kibafort, axle (n)
kibark, ax (n)
kibarsk, ax (v)
kibielirk, import (n)
kibielirkuet, importation (n)
kibielirkwan, importer (n doer)
kibielirsk, import (v)
kiblas, impress (v)
kiblash, impression (n)
kiblashfrelpu, impressionable
    (adj)
kiblashfrelpwan, impressionist (n
    doer)
kiblashiu, impressively (adv)
kiblashu, impressive (adj)
kiblashwan, impresser (n doer)
kiblirshku, impenetrable (adj)
kiboirge, impotence (n)
kiboirgu, impotent (adj)
kibramip, impoundment (n)
kibramisp, impound (v)
kibratsh, limbo (n)
kibreishk, impurity (n)
kibreishku, impure (adj)
kibrek, implement (n)
kibrekuet, implementation (n)
kibrelp, implant (n)
kibrelpuet, implantation (n)
kibrels, imply (v)
kibrelshiu, implicitly (adv)
kibrelshu, implicit (adj)
kibrelshuest, implicate (v)
kibrelshuet, implication (n)
kibrelshuetwan, implicator (n
    doer)
kibrelsp, implant (v)
kibresk, implement (v)
kidanirst, immobilize (v)
kidanirt, immobility (n)
kidanirtu, immobilization (n)
kidanirtwan, immobilizer (n doer)
kidoreinu, impolite (adj)
kidurat, imperative (n)
kiduratu, imperative (adj)
Kidurn, Hindu (n)
Kidurnuet, Hinduism (n)
kiedairsh, dichotomy (n)
kiefkorth, sinkhole (n)
kiefst, sink (v)
kiefstyot, sank (v pa)
kieft, sink (v)
kieftwan, sinker (n doer)
kieishst, hover (v)
kieitkafirp, hovercraft (n)
kielarst, dilate (v)
kielart, dilation (n)
kielartu, dilatory (adj)
kielartwan, dilator (n doer)

kielorf, diploma (n)
kielp, diet (n)
kielpwan, dieter (n doer)
kielsh, sib (n)
kielshk, sibling (n)
kielshkiu, siblings (adv)
kielshku, sibling (adj)
kielsp, diet (v)
kierge, dilution (n)
kiergu, dilute (adj)
kierk, node (n)
kierst, jet (v)
kiert, jet (n)
kiertroifk, jetliner (n)
kierzge, dilute (v)
kievorage, digression (n)
kievorazge, digress (v)
kifaf, article (n)
kifar, art (n)
kifariu, artistically (adv)
kifaru, artistic (adj)
kifarwan, artist (n doer)
kifes, impart (v)
kifesh, impartiality (n)
kifeshiu, impartially (adv)
kifeshu, impartial (adj)
kifiaishk, divide (n)
kifiaishkap, dividend (n)
kifiaishkip, divisiveness (n)
kifiaishkipu, divisive (adj)
kifiaishkipwan, divisor (n doer)
kifiaishku, divisible (adj)
kifiaishkuet, division (n)
kifiaishkuetu, divisional (adj)
kifiaishkwan, divider (n doer)
kifiaishsk, divide (v)
kifiart, skipper (n)
kifiufrelp, improbability (n)
kifiufrelpiu, improbably (adv)
kifiufrelpu, improbable (adj)
kifoprelt, folktale (n)
kiforp, folk (n)
kifpufirt, folklore (n)
kifshtart, benchmark (n)
kigalf, artillery (n)
kigifp, impact (n)
kigifpwan, impacter (n doer)
kigifsp, impact (v)
kiglark, imposition (n)
kiglarkwan, imposter (n doer)
kiglarsk, impose (v)
kikaf, bench (n)
kikasf, bench (v)
kikiarge, digestion (n)
kikiargu, digestive (adj)
kikiarsk, snicker (v)
kikiarzge, digest (v)
kikiurpu, snide (adj)
kikost, bend (v)
kikostyot, bent (v pa)
kikot, bend (n)
kikotiu, bendably (adv)
kikotu, bendable (adj)

kikotwan, bender (n doer)
kikurst, gravitate (v d:physics)
kikurt, gravity (n d:physics)
kikurtuet, gravitation (n)
kikurtuetu, gravitational (adj)
kilafirsp, immerge (v)
kilafu, several (adj)
kilarfst, immerse (v)
kilarft, immersion (n)
kiliark, heroin (n)
kilikarpiu, improperly (adv)
kilikarpu, improper (adj)
kilithk, sniff (n)
kilithkwan, sniffer (n doer)
kilithsk, sniff (v)
kilkart, severity (n)
kilork, severance (n)
kilorkiu, severely (adv)
kilorku, severe (adj)
kilorp, crib (n)
kilorsk, sever (v)
kiloshafk, impairment (n)
kiloshafsk, impair (v)
kiloshirp, imperception (n)
kiloshirpiu, imperceptibly (adv)
kiloshirpu, imperceptible (adj)
kilovirft, imperfection (n)
kilovirftiu, imperfectly (adv)
kilovirftu, imperfect (adj)
kilshk, fetish (n)
kiluaf, horoscope (n)
kilunirt, impasse (n)
kilunirtiu, impassably (adv)
kilunirtu, impassable (adj)
kimatirk, impracticality (n)
kimatirku, impractical (adj)
kimioshkiu, immaculately (adv)
kimioshku, immaculate (adj)
kimorshtast, imbalance (v)
kimorshtat, imbalance (n)
kimorth, impatience (n)
kimorthiu, impatiently (adv)
kimorthu, impatient (adj)
kinaflarf, travesty (n)
kinai-, hex- (num 6 pref)
kinai-, sext- (num 6 pref)
kinaishk, mutilation (n)
kinaishkwan, mutilator (n doer)
kinaishsk, mutilate (v)
kinalfrelpiu, imaginably (adv)
kinalfrelpu, imaginable (adj)
kinark, viscosity (n)
kinarku, viscous (adj)
kinarl, imagination (n)
kinarlpu, imaginative (adj)
kinarlu, imaginary (adj)
kinarsle, imagine (v)
kinbar, gender (n d:sexual
    identity)
kindarst, imitate (v)
kindart, imitation (n)
kindartwan, imitator (n doer)
kineshk, dimension (n)

kineshku, dimensional (adj)
kineshsk, dimension (v)
kineth, sixth (num 6 ord)
kinfk, sesquadragintillion (num
    1e141 card)
kinft, sestrigintillion (num 1e111
    card)
kini, six (num 6 card)
kinialfhemka, Number_1e24456
kinida, sixty (num 60 card)
kinidai-, sixty- (num 60 pref)
kinideth, sixtieth (num 60 ord)
kinipa, sixteen (num 16 card)
kinipai-, sixteen- (num 16 pref)
kinipeth, sixteenth (num 16 ord)
kiniurp, diminishment (n)
kiniurpiu, diminutively (adv)
kiniurpu, diminutive (adj)
kiniursp, diminish (v)
kinka, sextillion (num 1e21 card)
kinkai-, zetta- (num 1e21 pref)
kinketh, sextillionth (num 1e21
    ord)
kinorf, image (n)
kinorfuet, imagery (n)
kinorp, graduation (n)
kinorpiu, gradually (adv)
kinorpu, gradual (adj)
kinorpwan, graduate (n doer)
kinorsf, image (v)
kinorsp, graduate (v)
kinort, vividness (n)
kinortiu, vividly (adv)
kinortu, vivid (adj)
kinshk, sexvigintillion (num 1e81
    card)
kinshkai-, eikto-
kinshketh, sexvigintillionth (num
    1e81 ord)
kinsht, sexdecillion (num 1e51
    card)
kinshtai-, oshto- (num 1e51 pref)
kinshteth, sexdecillionth (num
    1e51 ord)
kioferpwan, pacesetter (n doer)
kiofnargwan, pacemaker (n doer)
kioirk, scream (n)
kioirkwan, screamer (n doer)
kioirsk, scream (v)
kiokabrelsh, workplace (n)
kiokagiarn, workaholic (n)
kiokbronf, workgroup (n)
kiokeglaushk, workhorse (n)
kiokikaf, workbench (n)
kioklurift, workload (n)
kiokplorn, workman (n)
kiokplornfif, workmanship (n)
kiokplornyek, workmen (n pl)
kiokshlukert, workstation (n)
kioktaurp, worksheet (n)
kiokthushp, workspace (n)

kiokviurl, workday (n)
kiomirp, funk (n d:fear/dejection)
kiopaf, cable (n)
kiopafwan, cabler (n doer)
kiopasf, cable (v)
kiopath, cabbage (n)
kiopume, cabin (n)
kiopurt, cabinet (n)
kiorf, pace (n)
kiorfast, pacify (v)
kiorfat, pacifism (n)
kiorfatu, pacific (adj)
kiorfatwan, pacifier (n doer)
kiorfatwan, pacifist (n doer)
kiorfork, deadline (n)
kiorfwan, pacer (n doer)
kiork, work (n)
kiorku, workable (adj)
kiorkuil, workout (n)
kiorkviurk, workforce (n)
kiorkwan, worker (n doer)
kiorme, humidity (n)
kiormu, humid (adj)
kiorp, cab (n)
kiorpwan, cabby (n doer)
kiors, fume (v)
kiorsf, pace (v)
kiorsh, fume (n)
kiorshiu, fumily (adv)
kiorshk, torch (n)
kiorshsk, torch (v)
kiorshu, fumy (adj)
kiorshuest, fumigate (v)
kiorshuet, fumigation (n)
kiorshuetwan, fumigator (n doer)
kiorshwan, fumer (n doer)
kiorsk, work (v)
kiorskyot, wrought (v pa)
kiorst, torque (v)
kiort, torque (n)
kiorthat, workshop (n)
kiorzme, humidify (v)
kioshadaurt, deadbeat (n)
kioshart, dead (n)
kioshartiu, deadly (adv)
kioshartu, dead (adj)
kioshfanirn, deadwood (n)
kioshtiurge, deadlock (n)
kioshuirsh, deadweight (n)
kioteshkwan, tormentor (n doer)
kioteshsk, torment (v)
kipardwan, impeller (n doer)
kipart, robot (n)
kipartiu, robotically (adv)
kipartu, robotic (adj)
kiparzde, impel (v)
kipeithku, impervious (adj)
kiplorniu, impersonally (adv)
kiplornu, impersonal (adj)
kiplornuest, impersonate (v)
kiplornuet, impersonation (n)
kiplornuetwan, impersonator (n doer)

kipotar, artifact (n)
kir, here (adj/adv/interj)
kir, here (n)
kirap, robbery (n)
kirapwan, robber (n doer)
kirasp, rob (v)
kirbarsk, wreak (v)
kirfst, core (v)
kirft, core (n)
kirkirst, wring (v)
kirkirstyot, wrung (v pa)
kirkirtwan, wringer (n doer)
kirlarth, wreath (n)
kirmoide, impedance (n)
kirmoiduet, impediment (n)
kirmoits, impeach (v)
kirmoitsh, impeachment (n)
kirmoitshu, impeachable (adj)
kirmoizde, impede (v)
kirovil, hereafter (n)
kirshk, physician (n)
kirshst, hush (v)
kirsht, hush (n)
kirth, pep (n)
kiruthirshk, imprecision (n)
kiruthirshkiu, imprecisely (adv)
kiruthirshku, imprecise (adj)
kirvuge, log (n d:tree)
kirvugwan, logger (n doer d:tree)
kirvuzge, log (v d:tree)
kirzhaurp, logjam (n)
kirzhe, technique (n)
kirzhiu, technically (adv)
kirzhu, technical (adj)
kirzhwan, technician (n doer)
kishalirkiu, implausibly (adv)
kishalirku, implausible (adj)
kishetriagarst, still (v d:distillery)
kishetriagart, distillery (n)
kishetriagart, still (n d:distillery)
kishetriarge, distillation (n)
kishetriargwan, distiller (n doer)
kishetriarzge, distill (v)
kishirf, immaturity (n)
kishirfiu, immaturely (adv)
kishirfu, immature (adj)
kishkirst, copy (v)
kishkirt, copy (n)
kishkirtruars, copyright (v)
kishkirtruarsh, copyright (n)
kishkirtwan, copier (n doer)
kishkitloirdwan, copywriter (n doer)
kishluark, induration (n)
kishluarkiu, immutably (adv)
kishluarku, immutable (adj)
kishluarkwan, indurator (n doer)
kishluarsk, indurate (v)
kishok, artifice (n)
kishokiu, artificially (adv)
kishoku, artificial (adj)
kishokwan, artificer (n doer)
Kishpanirk, Hispanic (n)

kitafbraft, campground (n)
kitafniart, campsite (n)
kitafshriauk, campfire (n)
kitalpor, campus (n)
kitank, campaign (n)
kitankwan, campaigner (n doer)
kitansk, campaign (v)
kitarf, camp (n)
kitarfwan, camper (n doer)
kitarsf, camp (v)
kiters, kill (v)
kitersh, kill (n)
kitershwan, killer (n doer)
kithailst, impale (v)
kithailtwan, impaler (n doer)
kitharak, diversion (n)
kitharakwan, diverter (n doer)
kitharask, divert (v)
kithirk, pepper (n)
kithirsk, pepper (v)
kithiurn, immorality (n)
kithiurniu, immorally (adv)
kithiurnu, immoral (adj)
kitiorf, immortality (n)
kitiorfu, immortal (adj)
kitiorfwan, immortal (n doer)
kitiorsf, immortalize (v)
kitrulis, imprint (v)
kitrulish, imprint (n)
Kitush, EhoMonth12 (n)
kiufst, bill (v d:document)
kiuft, bill (n d:document)
kiuftaplok, billboard (n)
kiuftokar, billiard (n)
kiuftokaru, billiard (adj)
kiuftwan, biller (n doer d:document)
kiulork, throat (n)
kiulorku, throaty (adj)
Kiupriunf, Hebrew (n)
kiurge, tiger (n)
kiurk, liberation (n d:freedom)
kiurkar, liberty (n)
kiurkiu, liberally (adv d:freedom)
kiurku, liberal (adj d:freedom)
kiurkwan, liberator (n doer d:freedom)
kiurp, bolt (n)
kiursf, deem (v)
kiursh, chaos (n)
kiurshiu, chaotically (adv)
kiurshu, chaotic (adj)
kiursk, liberate (v d:freedom)
kiursp, bolt (v)
kiurth, abyss (n)
kiurthiu, abysmally (adv)
kiurthu, abysmal (adj)
kiurtsh, tick (n d:insect)
kiutar, accomplishment (n)
kiutarwan, accomplice (n doer)
kiutasre, accomplish (v)
kiviurge, importance (n)
kiviurgiu, importantly (adv)

kiviurgu, important (adj)
kivugaf, hurricane (n)
kivurk, hurry (n)
kivursk, hurry (v)
kizhasht, technology (n)
kizhashtiu, technologically (adv)
kizhashtu, technological (adj)
kizhlialirt, buzzword (n)
kizhpanirk, tedium (n)
kizhpanirku, tedious (adj)
kizhumirsp, imperil (v)
kladirp, scrape (n)
kladirpwan, scraper (n doer)
kladirsp, scrape (v)
klafevornt, scrapbook (n)
klaiarf, volley (n)
klaiarsf, volley (v)
klaide, immediacy (n)
klaidiu, immediately (adv)
klaidu, immediate (adj)
klaifirf, kingdom (n)
klaifp, greed (n)
klaifpiu, greedily (adv)
klaifpu, greedy (adj)
klairbe, king (n)
klairk, strike (n)
klairkiu, strikingly (adv)
klairkuil, strikeout (n)
klairkwan, striker (n doer)
klairshk, scorch (n)
klairshkwan, scorcher (n doer)
klairsk, strike (v)
klairskyot, struck (v pa)
klairst, score (v)
klairt, score (n)
klairtmenu, scoreless (adj)
klairtwan, scorer (n doer)
klairve, swag (n)
klairzve, swag (v)
klaishp, prick (n)
klaishsp, prick (v)
klaitgaurn, scorecard (n)
klaitplok, scoreboard (n)
klaivarst, swagger (v)
klaivart, swagger (n)
klamurst, scratch (v)
klamurt, scratch (n)
klamurtu, scratchy (adj)
klamurtwan, scratcher (n doer)
klanirsp, trample (v)
klanirst, tramp (v)
klanirt, tramp (n)
klarage, attorney (n)
klarbe, stud (n)
klarf, scrap (n)
klarfgaith, cockroach (n)
klarfu, scrappy (adj)
klarfwan, scrapper (n doer)
klarip, skull (n)
klarl, laxity (n)
klarliu, laxly (adv)
klarlu, lax (adj)

klarnsk, hamper (v d:hinder)
klarsf, scrap (v)
klarsle, lax (v)
klarst, agree (v)
klart, agreement (n)
klartiu, agreeably (adv)
klartu, agreeable (adj)
klarzbe, stud (v)
klarze, trudge (v)
Klash, Christ (n)
Klashar, Christian (n)
Klashmarl, Christmas (n)
klauarp, brunt (n)
klaurgu, gross (adj d:disgusting)
klaurk, greatness (n)
klaurkiu, greatly (adv)
klaurku, great (adj)
klaurkwaku, greatest (adj)
klaurkwelu, greater (adj)
klaurts, brutalize (v)
klaurtsh, brutality (n)
klaurtshiu, brutally (adv)
klaurtshu, brutal (adj)
klaurtshwan, brute (n doer)
klaurzge, gross (v d:disgusting)
klaushp, wallop (n)
klaushsp, wallop (v)
klauthk, bumble (n d:bungle)
klauthkwan, bumbler (n doer d:bungle)
klauthsk, bumble (v d:bungle)
klavurge, craze (n)
klavurgiu, crazily (adv)
klavurgu, crazy (adj)
klavurzge, craze (v)
klede, county (n)
kleiark, goof (n)
kleiarku, goofy (adj)
kleiarsk, goof (v)
kleidarn, rigor (n)
kleidarniu, rigorously (adv)
kleidarnu, rigorous (adj)
kleiparfu, bulky (adj)
kleipkefirt, bulkhead (n)
kleirde, rigidly (adj)
kleirdiu, rigidly (adv)
kleirdu, rigid (adj)
kleirf, principal (n)
kleirk, deletion (n)
kleirp, bulk (n)
kleirpu, bulk (adj)
kleirsk, delete (v)
kleirsp, bulk (v)
kleirze, reason (v)
kleirzhe, reason (n)
kleirzhiu, reasonably (adv)
kleirzhu, reasonable (adj)
kleirzhwan, reasoner (n doer)
kleithk, truss (n)
klenirt, cricket (n)
klerge, traffic (n)
klergwan, trafficker (n doer)
klers, replicate (v)

klersh, replication (n)
klershwan, replicator (n doer)
klerst, crick (v)
klert, crick (n)
klerth, chick (n)
klerzge, traffic (v)
klesht, chair (n d:seat)
kliagurilf, crosscurrent (n)
kliakdiarf, crossbow (n)
kliakfluirkiu, crosswise (adv)
kliakfluirku, crosswise (adj)
kliaklialirt, crossword (n)
kliakshpalort, crosstalk (n)
kliaktrelish, crossroad (n)
kliarf, scoop (n)
kliarfwan, scooper (n doer)
kliark, cross (n)
kliarkafen, crossover (n)
kliarkshriauk, crossfire (n)
kliarn, diplomacy (n)
kliarnu, diplomatic (adj)
kliarnwan, diplomat (n doer)
kliarp, strife (n)
kliarpwan, strifer (n doer)
kliarsf, scoop (v)
kliarsh, countess (n)
kliarsk, cross (v)
kliarsp, strive (v)
kliarspyot, strove (v pa)
kliarsth, tether (v)
kliart, guitar (n)
kliarth, tether (n)
kliartwan, guitarist (n doer)
kliarze, scout (v)
kliarzhe, scout (n)
kliashk, shriek (n)
kliashkwan, shrieker (n doer)
kliashsk, shriek (v)
kliaumesp, tout (v)
kliaup, scourge (n)
kliaurk, decimation (n)
kliaursk, decimate (v)
kliaushsk, scour (v)
kliausp, scourge (v)
kliazhthiork, scoutmaster (n)
kliefsk, scrimp (v)
kliegbleirsh, wingspan (n)
kliegplorn, wingman (n)
kliegplornyek, wingmen (n pl)
klierge, wing (n)
kliergwan, winger (n doer)
klicrk, hawk (n)
klierkwan, hawker (n doer)
kliersk, hawk (v)
klierzge, wing (v)
klieshst, shrill (v)
kliesht, shrill (n)
klieshtu, shrill (adj)
Kligart, VanAllenBelt (n)
klikarst, thatch (v)
klikart, thatch (n)
klikartwan, thatcher (n doer)
klinurf, turtle (n)

klinurfthavube, turtleneck (n)
klinurfthavubu, turtleneck (adj)
klioishsk, sear (v)
kliork, duel (n)
kliorkwan, dueler (n doer)
kliorp, quake (n)
kliorsk, duel (v)
kliorsp, quake (v)
klirf, sip (n)
klirfast, siphon (v)
klirfat, siphon (n)
klirfsk, discard (v)
klirfu, sippy (adj)
klirfwan, sipper (n doer)
klirk, flea (n)
klirsf, sip (v)
klishk, dash (n d:sprint)
klishkwan, dasher (n doer d:sprint)
klishplok, dashboard (n)
klishsk, dash (v d:sprint)
kliufast, putter (v)
kliufsp, scrounge (v)
kliufst, putt (v)
kliuft, putt (n)
kliuftwan, putter (n doer)
kliuk, drill (n)
kliukwan, driller (n doer)
kliusk, drill (v)
klivarth, blubber (n)
klivarthu, blubbery (adj)
Klivlanurd, Cleveland (n)
klivursk, scurry (v)
kloarsk, pierce (v)
klofmoark, keepsake (n)
kloiarsne, groom (v d:clean)
kloift, skepticism (n)
kloiftiu, skeptically (adv)
kloiftu, skeptical (adj)
kloiftwan, skeptic (n doer)
kloipdiarpwan, screwdriver (n doer)
kloirn, tile (n)
kloirnwan, tiler (n doer)
kloirp, screw (n)
kloirpu, screwy (adj)
kloirpwan, screwer (n doer)
kloirsne, tile (v)
kloirsp, screw (v)
kloishsk, scoff (v)
klorak, growth (n)
klorakwan, grower (n doer)
klorask, grow (v)
kloraskyot, grew (v pa)
klorf, keep (n)
klorfk, dark (n)
klorfkiu, darkly (adv)
klorfkshranf, darkroom (n)
klorfkshransfaut, shranf (v prp)
klorfkshransfyot, shran (v pa)
klorfku, dark (adj)
klorfkuet, darkness (n)
klorfkweku, darkest (adj)

klorfkwelu, darker (adj)
klorfsk, darken (v)
klorfwan, keeper (n doer)
Klorin, Chlorine (n)
klorip, scorn (n)
kloripiu, scornfully (adv)
kloripu, scornful (adj)
kloripwan, scorner (n doer)
klorisp, scorn (v)
klorist, scold (v)
klorsf, keep (v)
klorsfyot, kept (v pa)
klorsh, year (n)
klorshonade, yearbook (n)
klorshu, yearly (adj)
klorthk, impulse (n)
klorthkiu, impulsively (adv)
klorthku, impulsive (adj)
kluaishk, scepticism (n)
kluaishku, sceptical (adj)
kluaishkwan, sceptic (n doer)
kluarf, scope (n)
kluarfwan, scoper (n doer)
kluark, creak (n)
kluarkiu, creakily (adv)
kluarku, creaky (adj)
kluarkwan, creaker (n doer)
kluarp, ovulation (n)
kluarpu, ovarian (adj)
kluarpwan, ovary (n doer)
kluarsf, scope (v)
kluarsk, creak (v)
kluarsp, ovulate (v)
kluaursth, growl (v)
kluaurth, growl (n)
klufade, brother (n)
klufadfif, brotherhood (n)
klufadu, brotherly (adj)
klufp, ovum (n)
klufpyek, ova (n pl)
klukurst, chuckle (v d:laugh)
klukurt, chuckle (n d:laugh)
klurap, alleviation (n)
klurasp, alleviate (v)
klurf, brush (n d:bristle handle)
klurfwan, brusher (n doer d:bristle handle)
klurge, loan (n)
klurgwan, lender (n doer)
klurk, chicken (n)
klurmu, feeble (adj)
klurn, green (n)
klurnu, green (adj)
klursf, brush (v d:bristle handle)
klurshk, collision (n)
klurshkwan, collider (n doer)
klurshsk, collide (v)
klurushst, collude (v)
klurusht, collusion (n)
klurushtu, collusive (adj)
klurzge, lend (v)
klurzgyot, lent (v pa)
klurzme, enfeeble (v)

koatarn, asteroid (n)
Kobalt, Cobalt (n)
kodi, have-to (ndal)
kof, has (v sing)
kof, have (v s)
kofaut, having (v prp)
kofirst, serve (v)
kofirt, service (n)
kofirth, oven (n)
kofirtuest, service (v)
kofirtwan, server (n doer)
kofitarn, servitude (n)
kofitarnwan, servant (n doer)
koftplorn, serviceman (n)
koftplornyek, servicemen (n pl)
koiark, worship (n)
koiarku, worshipful (adj)
koiarkwan, worshipper (n doer)
koiarsk, worship (v)
koiarsne, yearn (v)
koiarst, stripe (v)
koiart, stripe (n)
koiartwan, striper (n doer)
koidelirn, supermarket (n)
koieshk, streak (n)
koieshku, streaky (adj)
koieshsk, streak (v)
koifleirde, hybrid (n)
koigavurgwan, hijacker (n doer)
koigavurzge, hijack (v)
koilf, height (n)
koilf, heighth (n)
koilfiu, highly (adv)
koilfluarn, highlight (n)
koilfluarnwan, highlighter (n doer)
koilfluarsne, highlight (v)
koilfu, high (adj)
koilfweaku, highest (adj)
koilfwelu, higher (adj)
koilpliorl, highway (n)
koilsf, heighten (v)
koiltive, throne (n)
koirf, emulation (n)
koirfu, emulous (adj)
koirp, raise (n)
koirs, hype (v)
koirsf, emulate (v)
koirsh, hype (n)
koirshu, hyper (adj)
koirsp, raise (v)
koirutarl, hierarchy (n)
koirutarlu, hierarchical (adj)
koisharblarf, hyperinflation (n)
koishorfip, hypersensitivity (n)
koishorfipu, hypersensitive (adj)
koishpatil, hyperactivity (n)
koishpatiliu, hyperactively (adv)
koishpatilu, hyperactive (adj)
koizhbe, gob (n)
kokeio, will (pro-verb fu)
kokerage, antagony (n)
kokeragu, antagonistic (adj)

kokeragwan, antagonist (n doer)
kokerazge, antagonize (v)
koko, do/have (pro-verb pr)
kokyot, did/had (pro-verb pa)
kol, wellness (n d:good)
kolame, gaiety (n d:happy)
kolame, happiness (n)
kolamiu, gaily (adv d:happy)
kolamiu, happily (adv)
kolamu, gay (adj d:happy)
kolamu, happy (adj)
kolamweku, happiest (adj)
kolamwelu, happier (adj)
kolarn, welcome (n)
kolarsne, welcome (v)
kolart, quart (n)
kolartar, quarter (n)
kolartariu, quarterly (adv)
kolge, coca (n)
koliarve, heresy (n)
koliarvu, heretical (adj)
koliarvwan, heretic (n doer)
kolirf, honor (n)
kolirfu, honorable (adj)
kolirfu, honorary (adj)
kolirp, happenstance (n)
kolirsf, honor (v)
kolirsp, happen (v)
kolishtarl, cholesterol (n)
kolkulauf, wellbeing (n)
Kolombiarf, Colombia (n)
Kolombiarn, Colombian (n)
Kolorard, Colorado (n)
koltarthiork, quartermaster (n)
kolthirk, welfare (n)
kolu, well (adj d:good)
Kolumbiarf, Columbia (n)
konafku, vascular (adj)
Konduralsh, Honduras (n)
Konetikurt, Connecticut (n)
Konokautsh, Holocaust (n)
Kontralf, Contra (n)
kopage, hoax (n)
kopalork, hocus-pocus (n)
Koper, Copper (n)
korame, toll (n)
korazme, toll (v)
korfk, bolster (n)
korfsk, bolster (v)
Korianf, Korean (n)
Koriarf, Korea (n)
korlat, garlic (n)
korlmeniu, haplessly (adv)
korlmenu, hapless (adj)
kormturshk, tollbooth (n)
kornage, hunger (n)
kornagiu, hungrily (adv)
kornagu, hungry (adj)
kornashk, slut (n)
kornazge, hunger (v)
korsh, content (n d:material)
korsth, hole (v)
korth, hole (n)

korvuge, ox (n)
korvugyek, oxen (n pl)
koshank, midge (n)
koshelst, keel (v)
koshelt, keel (n)
kosheltwan, keeler (n doer)
koshiathsk, wean (v)
koshk, huff (n)
koshsk, huff (v)
Koshtarf Rikarf, Costa Rica (n)
kot, had (v)
kothark, bosom (n)
kovarf, haven (n)
kovark, havoc (n)
kove, have (v fut)
koveit, have (v fut)
kovurk, haze (n d:abuse)
kovursk, haze (v d:abuse)
krafirk, task (n)
krafirkwan, tasker (n doer)
krafirsk, task (v)
krafp, lot (n)
kragast, gear (v d:sprocket)
kragat, gear (n d:sprocket)
kraiarp, squabble (n)
kraiarpwan, squabbler (n doer)
kraiarsp, squabble (v)
kraifk, dive (n)
kraifkwan, diver (n doer)
kraiforst, negate (v)
kraifort, negation (n)
kraifsk, dive (v)
kraifskyot, dove (v pa)
krailf, brass (n)
krailfkiu, brazenly (adv)
krailfku, brazen (adj)
krailfu, brassy (adj)
krainsh, clam (n)
krainshst, clamp (v)
krainsht, clamp (n)
krainshtiern, clampdown (n)
krainshtwan, clamper (n doer)
kraintherk, clamshell (n)
krairge, blast (n)
krairgwan, blaster (n doer)
krairshk, shark (n)
krairt, negative (n)
krairtiu, negatively (adv)
krairtu, negative (adj)
krairtuet, negativism (n)
krairzge, blast (v)
kraishp, club (n d:stick)
kraishsp, club (v d:stick)
kraithierk, pounce (n d:catch)
kraithierkwan, pouncer (n doer d:catch)
kraithiersk, pounce (v d:catch)
kraithk, claw (n)
kraithsk, claw (v)
krakfrelp, vulnerability (n)
krakfrelpu, vulnerable (adj)
kralip, tarp (n)
kralirk, scramble (n)

kralirkwan, scrambler (n doer)
kralirsk, scramble (v)
kralk, weakness (n)
kralkiu, weakly (adv)
kralku, weak (adj)
kralkwaku, weakest (adj)
kralkwelu, weaker (adj)
kralshork, cemetery (n)
kralsk, weaken (v)
kralst, wear (v d:erode, fatigue)
kralstyot, wore (v pa d:erode, fatigue)
kralt, wear (n d:erode, fatigue)
kraltiu, wearily (adv d:erode, fatigue)
kraltu, weary (adj d:erode, fatigue)
kraltu, wearysome (adj d:fatigue)
kraltuet, weariness (n d:fatigue)
kranirf, scroll (n)
kranirsf, scroll (v)
krankart, bandit (n)
kranp, gram (n)
Krashat, Mister (n)
krashilorpu, widespread (adj)
krashk, width (n)
krashkiu, widely (adv)
krashku, wide (adj)
krashkwaku, widest (adj)
krashkwan, widener (n doer)
krashkwelu, wider (adj)
krashsk, widen (v)
kraufk, junk (n)
kraufku, junky (adj)
kraufsk, junk (v)
krauishk, sneer (n)
krauishsk, sneer (v)
kraurge, blaze (n)
kraurzge, blaze (v)
kraushkwan, shredder (n doer)
kraushsk, shred (v)
krefirn, jewel (n)
krefirnk, jewelry (n)
krefirnwan, jeweler (n doer)
krefk, crux (n)
kreft, hat (n)
kreift, litter (n)
kreilf, glory (n)
kreilfiu, gloriously (adv)
kreilfu, glorious (adj)
kreilfuet, glorification (n)
kreilsf, glorify (v)
kreinshk, muck (n)
kreinshku, mucky (adj)
kreinshsk, muck (v)
kreirth, tomorrow (n)
kreirthiu, tomorrow (adv)
kreishk, dust (n)
kreishkiu, dustily (adv)
kreishku, dusty (adj)
kreishkwan, duster (n doer)
kreishnurp, dustbin (n)
kreishsk, dust (v)

kreize, clash (v)
kreizhe, clash (n)
krelf, grease (n)
krelfsk, bludgeon (v)
krelfu, greasy (adj)
krelsf, grease (v)
kren, lex (n)
kreniak, lexicon (n)
kreniaku, lexical (adj)
krenik, logic (n)
krenikiu, logically (adv)
kreniku, logical (adj)
krenit, logo (n)
krenkart, logistic (n)
krenkartiu, logistically (adv)
krenkartu, logistical (adj)
krezhge, grunt (n)
krezhgwan, grunt (n doer)
krezhzge, grunt (v)
kriagiu, bearishly (adv d:endure)
kriagu, bearish (adj d:endure)
kriagwan, bearer (n doer
    d:endure)
krialst, bear (v d:direction)
krialt, bearing (n d:direction)
kriamp, shrewdness (n)
kriampiu, shrewdly (adv)
kriampu, shrewd (adj)
kriank, yank (n)
kriansk, yank (v)
kriarf, qualification (n)
kriarft, quality (n)
kriarftu, quality (adj)
kriarfwan, qualifier (n doer)
kriarp, bearing (n d:metal ball)
kriarsf, qualify (v)
kriarsk, shatter (v)
kriarst, negotiate (v)
kriart, negotiation (n)
kriartwan, negotiator (n doer)
kriashk, shroud (n)
kriashsk, shroud (v)
kriathk, lingo (n)
kriazge, bear (v d:endure)
kriazgyot, bore (v pa d:endure)
krifk, clip (n)
krifkwan, clipper (n doer)
krifsk, clip (v)
krikplok, clipboard (n)
krilaf, tavern (n)
krilest, bore (v d:hole)
krilet, bore (n d:hole)
kriletwan, borer (n doer d:hole)
krilk, eclipse (n)
krilorst, bash (v)
krilortwan, basher (n doer)
krilsk, eclipse (v)
krimaf, heap (n)
krimasf, heap (v)
krinf, lip (n)
krinsf, lip (v)
krinshnet, lipstick (n)
kriofk, nook (n)

kriomirpwan, flunky (n doer)
kriomirsp, flunk (v)
kriorp, eddy (n)
kriorsp, eddy (v)
kriorst, eagle (v)
kriort, eagle (n)
kripalwan, borrower (n doer)
kripasle, borrow (v)
Kripton, Krypton (n)
krirthk, punch (n d:hit)
krirthku, punchy (adj d:hit)
krirthkwan, puncher (n doer
    d:hit)
krirthsk, punch (v d:hit)
krishart, missile (n)
krishk, breach (n)
krishsk, breach (v)
krites, mow (v)
kriteshwan, mower (n doer)
krithkroifk, punchline (n)
kriufsp, grumble (v)
kriurn, stool (n d:excrement)
kriusht, duct (n)
kriuthk, whoop (n)
kriuthsk, whoop (v)
kriuzhge, grudge (n)
kriuzhzge, begrudge (v)
krivuge, mine (n d:cave)
krivugwan, miner (n doer d:cave)
krivurge, mineral (n)
krivurp, trip (n d:misstep)
krivurpwan, tripper (n doer
    d:misstep)
krivursp, trip (v d:misstep)
krivuzge, mine (v d:cave)
kroilf, brim (n)
kroilfwan, brimmer (n doer)
kroilsf, brim (v)
kroip, horn (n)
kroipu, horny (adj)
kroishk, box (n d:fight)
kroishkwan, boxer (n doer
    d:fight)
kroishsk, box (v d:fight)
kroisp, horn (v)
kroive, globe (n)
kroiviu, globally (adv)
kroivu, global (adj)
kroivuet, globalization (n)
kroizhbe, glob (n)
kroizhbu, globular (adj)
kroizhzbe, glob (v)
krolirp, brokerage (n)
krolirpwan, broker (n doer)
krolirsp, broker (v)
krols, search (v)
krolsh, search (n)
krolshwan, searcher (n doer)
Kromium, Chromium (n)
kronierst, gobble (v)
kroniert, gobble (n)
kroniertwan, gobbler (n doer)
kroshfluarn, searchlight (n)

kruanshk, chunk (n)
kruanshku, chunky (adj)
kruashk, chuck (n d:throw)
kruashsk, chuck (v d:throw)
krufdairk, weekend (n)
krufdairkwan, weekender (n
    doer)
krufk, week (n)
krufku, weekly (adj)
krufmuarn, weeknight (n)
krufp, glut (n)
krufpu, gluttonous (adj)
krufpuet, gluttony (n)
krufpwan, glutton (n doer)
krufralzhu, weeklong (adj)
krufviurl, weekday (n)
krunf, few (n/pron)
krunfu, few (adj)
krunfwaku, fewest (adj)
krunfwelu, fewer (adj)
krushk, tusk (n)
kruth, bonnet (n)
kruzhge, hearth (n)
kuabrivarn, cobweb (n)
kuadarf, cobble (n d:mend)
kuadarfwan, cobbler (n doer
    d:mend)
kuadark, cobble (n d:roundstone)
kuadark, cobblestone (n)
kuadarsf, cobble (v d:mend)
kuafkart, directive (n)
kuairf, hail (n d:greeting)
kuairsf, hail (v d:greeting)
kuais, quash (v)
kualirsk, pamper (v)
kuanfk, gong (n)
kuarask, sulk (v)
kuarde, cob (n d:round)
kuarf, paw (n)
kuarfk, direction (n)
kuarfkar, directory (n)
kuarfkiu, directly (adv)
kuarfku, direct (adj)
kuarfkwan, director (n doer)
kuarfsk, direct (v)
kuarge, bummer (n)
kuargwan, bum (n doer)
kuark, yuck (n)
kuarku, yucky (adj)
kuarlp, decoy (n)
kuarlsp, decoy (v)
kuarlu, coy (adj)
kuarme, yummy (n)
kuarn, gain (n)
kuarnwan, gainer (n doer)
kuarsf, paw (v)
kuarsne, gain (v)
kuarzge, bum (v)
kuashk, coziness (n)
kuashku, cozy (adj)
kuashsk, cozy (v)
Kubarf, Cuba (n)
Kubarn, Cuban (n)

kubiurn, cowboy (n)
kude, fig (n)
kuden, behind (adj/adv/prep)
kudil, figure (n)
kudiliu, figuratively (adv)
kudilkefirt, figurehead (n)
kudiloif, figurine (n)
kudilu, figurative (adj)
kudisle, figure (v)
kuduet, figment (n)
kuek, quack (interj)
kufiarn, butler (n)
kufirk, good (n d:product)
kufliau, goodbye (interj)
kuflimern, goodmorning (interj)
kufmuarn, goodnight (interj)
kufmurf, goodness (n)
kufurbe, poop (n)
kufurbwan, pooper (n doer)
kufurzbe, poop (v)
kufwerk, best (n)
kufwerkiu, best (adv)
kufwerku, best (adj)
kufwerlu, better (adj)
kufwersk, best (v)
kufwerskyot, best (v pa)
kufwersle, better (v)
kufyark, goodwill (n)
kuiark, weapon (n)
kuiarkuet, weaponry (n)
kuiarn, yawn (n)
kuiarsne, yawn (v)
kuiefst, quell (v)
kuieshsk, quench (v)
kuiforp, blink (n)
kuiforpwan, blinker (n doer)
kuiforsp, blink (v)
kuifst, log (v d:record)
kuift, log (n d:record)
kuiftwan, logger (n doer d:record)
kuilarn, guerrilla (n)
kuilarnu, guerrilla (adj)
kuip, awe (n)
kuirk, toast (n d:cheer)
kuirku, toasty (adj d:cheer)
kuirkwan, toaster (n doer d:cheer)
kuirsk, toast (v d:cheer)
kuishk, queasiness (n)
kuishku, queasy (adj)
kuisp, awe (v)
kuitvornt, logbook (n)
kukabirk, allergy (n)
kukabirku, allergic (adj)
kukabirkwan, allergist (n doer)
kukar, factory (n)
kukarnyek, goggles (n pl)
kukurk, toot (n)
kukursk, toot (v)
kulauf, being (v prp common)
kulaufk, being (v prp emphatic)
kulirn, immunity (n)
kulirnkuit, immunology (n)

kulirnkuitu, immunological (adj)
kulirnu, immune (adj)
kulirnuet, immunization (n)
kulirpliarshp, immunotherapy (n)
kulirsne, immunize (v)
kulirvublarsh,
    immunosuppression (n)
kumak, cow (n)
kumirp, boulder (n)
Kunkarft, Hungary (n)
Kunkariarn, Hungarian (n)
kupatove, benefit (n)
kupatoviu, benefically (adv)
kupatovu, beneficial (adj)
kupatovwan, beneficiary (n doer)
kupatozve, benefit (v)
kupogart, debenture (n)
kuporge, debt (n)
kuporgwan, debtor (n doer)
kuporzge, indebt (v)
kurap, timber (n)
kurbank, tinder (n)
kurbanprekun, tinderbox (n)
kurbe, bet (n)
kurf, good (n d:helpful)
kurfp, ethic (n)
kurfpath, ethos (n)
kurfpiu, ethically (adv)
kurfpu, ethical (adj)
kurfsp, ethicate (v)
kurft, ethnicity (n)
kurftu, ethnic (adj)
kurfu, good (adj d:helpful)
kurgage, nerd (n)
Kurium, Curium (n)
kurnwan, beginner (n doer)
kursne, begin (v)
kursnyot, began (v pa)
kurst, heat (v)
kurt, heat (n)
kurth, skeleton (n)
kurthu, skeletal (adj)
kurtwan, heater (n doer)
kurzbe, bet (v)
kurzbyot, bet (v pa)
kushoirt, beside (adv/prep)
kushoirt, besides (adv/prep)
Kushtorn, Houston (n)
kutalfruifk, swordplay (n)
kutalshlersh, swordfish (n)
kutalshlershyek, swordfish (n pl)
kutarl, sword (n)
kutirp, deity (n)
kuturk, colon (n d:organ)
kuvar, behavior (n)
kuvarde, goose (n)
kuvardyek, geese (n pl)
kuvarzde, goose (v)
kuvasre, behave (v)
kuverze, debug (v)
kuverzhwan, debugger (n doer)
kuvikel, be (imp, emphatic)
kuvil, be (imp, common)

Kuwairt, Kuwait (n)
Kuwaitarn, Kuwaiti (n)
kuyelir, beyond (adv/prep)
kuzhisre, belong (v)
kwak, yuck (interj)
kwam, yum (interj)
kwami, yummy (interj)
labirk, spade (n)
labirsk, spade (v)
labolirk, spare (n)
labolirkiu, sparingly (adv)
labolirsk, spare (v)
ladirfiu, virtually (adv)
ladirfu, virtual (adj)
lafirk, merchandise (n)
lafirkwan, merchant (n doer)
lafirme, venue (n)
lafirp, merge (n)
lafirpwan, merger (n doer)
lafirsk, merchandize (v)
lafirskaut, merchandized (v prp)
lafirsp, merge (v)
lafmarst, venerate (v)
lafmart, veneration (n)
lafmartiu, venerably (adv)
lafmartu, venerable (adj)
lagaf, exhaust (n)
lagafiu, exhaustively (adv)
lagafu, exhaustive (adj)
lagak, fake (n)
lagakwan, faker (n doer)
lagarf, exhaustion (n)
lagarl, ill (n)
lagarl, illness (n)
lagarlu, ill (adj)
lagasf, exhaust (v)
lagask, fake (v)
lagelor, calorie (n)
laiarf, saturation (n)
laiark, satire (n)
laiarku, satirical (adj)
laiarkwan, satirist (n doer)
laiarsf, saturate (v)
laiarsk, satirize (v)
laiathk, lash (n)
laiathkwan, lasher (n doer)
laiathsk, lash (v)
laidark, medium (n d:information
    flow)
laidarku, medial (adj
    d:information flow)
laidarkuet, mediation (n)
laidarkwan, mediator (n doer
    d:information flow)
laidarkyek, media (n pl
    d:information flow)
laidarsk, mediate (v
    d:information flow)
laigarf, disaster (n)
laigarfiu, disastrously (adv)
laigarfu, disastrous (adj)
laikaf, galaxy (n)
lailart, heredity (n)

lailartu, hereditary (adj)
lailatarp, heritage (n)
lailf, heir (n)
lailf, heiress (n)
lailthetirsh, heirloom (n)
lairp, dimness (n)
lairpiu, dimly (adv)
lairpu, dim (adj)
lairpwan, dimmer (n doer)
lairsh, joy (n)
lairshiu, joyfully (adv)
lairshu, joyful (adj)
lairsp, dim (v)
lairst, elate (v)
lairt, elation (n)
lairtemenu, leaderless (adj)
lairzhe, hell (n)
lairzhu, hellish (adj)
laishshneft, joystick (n)
laivurn, twine (n)
laizheshriauk, hellfire (n)
lakarn, garment (n)
lakirt, stove (n)
lalirfst, license (v)
lalirft, licence (n)
lalirft, license (n)
lalirftmenu, licentious (adj)
lalirftuet, licensure (n)
lalirftuin, licencee (n)
lalirst, lead (v d:in front)
lalirt, lead (n d:in front)
lalirtfif, leadership (n)
lalirtunf, leadoff (n)
lalirtunfu, leadoff (adj)
lalirtwan, leader (n doer d:in
    front)
lalitor, liter (n)
lalivartor, illiteracy (n)
lalivartoru, illiterate (adj)
lalparn, library (n)
lalparnwan, librarian (n doer)
Lamail, May (n)
lamalirt, original (n)
lamaltart, originality (n)
lamarst, originate (v)
lamart, origin (n)
lamartiu, originally (adv)
lamartu, original (adj)
lamartuet, origination (n)
lamartwan, originator (n doer)
lamdarn, lambda (n)
lamoin, orientation (n)
lamoisne, orient (v)
lanat, gallantry (n)
lanatiu, gallantly (adv)
lanatu, gallant (adj)
landak, HalfFaceSymbol (n)
lanfp, elephant (n)
lanfpu, elephantic (adj)
lanirf, norm (n)
lanirfiu, normally (adv)
lanirfu, normal (adj)
lanirfuet, normalization (n)

lanirge, virtue (n)
lanirgiu, virtuously (adv)
lanirgu, virtuous (adj)
lanirp, nap (n)
lanirsf, normalize (v)
lanirsp, nap (v)
Lanthanum, Lanthanum (n)
lanurt, cameo (n)
lanutarfk, illegitimacy (n)
lanutarfku, illegitimate (adj)
lanutark, illegality (n)
lanutarkiu, illegally (adv)
lanutarku, illegal (adj)
laomoblaithp, runaround (n)
laomopliorl, runaway (n)
laompliorl, runway (n)
laomtiern, rundown (n)
laomurnf, runoff (n)
laorme, run (n)
laormu, runny (adj)
laormwan, runner (n doer)
laorzme, run (v)
laorzmyot, ran (v pa)
Laprel, April (n)
lapuert, session (n)
larank, rogation (n)
laransk, rogate (v)
larap, left (n d:direction)
larapkliergu, leftwing (adj)
larapkliergwan, leftist (n doer)
larapu, left (adj d:direction)
larapwan, lefty (n doer
    d:direction)
larast, rule (v)
larat, rule (n)
laratwan, ruler (n doer)
lardaishk, vehemence (n)
lardaishkiu, vehemently (adv)
lardaishku, vehement (adj)
lardarst, medal (v)
lardart, medal (n)
lardartwan, medalist (n doer)
lardirt, vehicle (n)
lardirtu, vehicular (adj)
Larenshium, Lawrencium (n)
larfdaurp, rooftop (n)
larfp, roof (n)
larfpwan, roofer (n doer)
larfsp, roof (v)
largrazhge, despot (n)
largrazhguet, despotism (n)
largrush, illusion (n)
Laril, EhoMonth01 (n)
larmirk, burlap (n)
larnaflap, lemonade (n)
larnarn, lemon (n)
Larsh Veigarsh, Las Vegas (n)
Larshiarl, Asia (n)
Larshiarn, Asian (n)
larshk, cigar (n)
larshkerf, cigarette (n)
larth, roll (n d:bread)
larthp, cache (n)

larthsp, cache (v)
lartvornt, rulebook (n)
larushkiu, intrinsically (adv)
larushku, intrinsic (adj)
larze, pride (v d:accomplishment)
larzhe, pride (n
    d:accomplishment)
larzhiu, proudly (adv
    d:accomplishment)
lashor, cassette (n)
lashtarfku, illegible (adj)
latan, locum (n)
Latinorf, Latin (n)
lauarf, satiation (n)
lauarsf, satiate (v)
laufarge, frigidity (n)
laufargu, frigid (adj)
lauirst, satisfy (v)
lauirt, satisfaction (n)
lauirtu, satisfactory (adj)
Laukut, August (n)
laurbe, oddity (n d:different)
laurbiu, oddly (adv d:different)
laurbu, odd (adj d:different)
laurk, planet (n)
laurku, planetary (adj)
laursf, bode (v)
laurst, veil (v)
laurt, veil (n)
laurzbe, odden (v d:different)
lavap, breath (n)
lavapfrelpu, breathable (adj)
lavapgorkiu, breathtakingly (adv)
lavapgorku, breathtaking (adj)
lavapiu, breathily (adv)
lavapu, breathy (adj)
lavapwan, breather (n doer)
lavasp, breathe (v)
lavirst, dissatisfy (v)
lavirt, dissatisfaction (n)
lavufluarn, twilight (n)
lavurn, twin (n)
Lead, Lead (n)
Lebanorf, Lebanon (n)
Lebanornf, Lebanese (n)
lefnik, compass (n)
leiapliorl, leeway (n)
leiarp, leer (n)
leiarpu, leery (adj)
leiarsp, leer (v)
leifliurst, flatter (v d:praise)
leifliurt, flattery (n d:praise)
leikarst, utilize (v)
leikart, utility (n)
leikartuet, utilization (n)
leikartuetwan, utilitarian (n doer)
leikartwan, utilizer (n doer)
leilart, utensil (n)
leinarp, pipe (n)
leinarpwan, piper (n doer)
leinarsp, pipe (v)
leinishoirt, intestine (n)
leinishoirtu, intestinal (adj)

leinproilf, pipeline (n)
leiparst, pinch (v)
leipart, pinch (n)
leipartwan, pincher (n doer)
leipaushk, pinnacle (n)
leipeklaishp, pinprick (n)
leipekoiarst, pinstripe (v)
leipekoiart, pinstripe (n)
leipetaiforst, pinpoint (v)
leipetaifort, pinpoint (n)
leipshmonde, pinball (n)
leirde, nature (n)
leirdiu, naturally (adv)
leirdu, natural (adj)
leirf, pinky (n)
leirnu, bland (adj)
leirolp, pint (n)
leirp, pin (n)
leirsheif, exuberance (n)
leirsheifiu, exuberantly (adv)
leirsheifu, exuberant (adj)
leirsp, pin (v)
leirst, moisten (v)
leirst, moisturize (v)
leirt, moisture (n)
leirtiu, moistly (adv)
leirtu, moist (adj)
leirtwan, moistener (n doer)
leirtwan, moisturizer (n doer)
leishgork, extradition (n)
leishgorsk, extradite (v)
leishkeltaru, extraordinary (adj)
leishp, extra (n)
leishpu, extra (adj)
leitosne, lade (v)
leiverzhe, ladybug (n)
lekipekefirt, pinhead (n)
lektiern, letdown (n)
lemurt, scarcity (n)
lemurtoiu, scarcely (adv)
lemurtu, scarce (adj)
lenal, cereal (n)
lenartide, commencement (n)
lenartizde, commence (v)
lenbolk, comparison (n)
lenbolkiu, comparably (adv)
lenbolkiu, comparatively (adv)
lenbolku, comparable (adj)
lenbolku, comparative (adj)
lenbolkwan, comparitor (n doer)
lenbolsk, compare (v)
lenbrels, complicate (v)
lenbrelsh, complication (n)
lendrukest, comprehend (v)
lendruket, comprehension (n)
lendruketiu, comprehensively (adv)
lendruketu, comprehensive (adj)
leniart, commentary (n)
leniast, comment (v)
leniat, comment (n)
leniatwan, commentator (n doer)
lenirk, commitment (n)

lenirkwan, committee (n doer)
lenirsk, commit (v)
lenkarst, commission (v)
lenkart, commission (n)
lenkartwan, commissioner (n doer)
lenlak, composition (n)
lenlakar, composure (n)
lenlakit, composite (n)
lenlakitu, composite (adj)
lenlakwan, composer (n doer)
lenlask, compose (v)
lensharl, companionship (n)
lensharlwan, companion (n doer)
lenshkirst, commove (v)
lenshkirt, commotion (n)
lenshluark, commutation (n)
lenshluarkwan, commuter (n doer)
lenshluarsk, commute (v)
lenshluast, comply (v)
lenshluat, compliance (n)
lenshluatp, compliment (n)
lenshluatpiu, complimentarily (adv)
lenshluatpu, complimentary (adj)
lenshluatpwan, complimentor (n doer)
lenshluatsp, compliment (v)
lenshluatu, compliant (adj)
lenup, combination (n)
lenupwan, combiner (n doer)
lenurp, combine (n)
lenusp, combine (v)
lenvap, competition (n)
lenvapat, competitiveness (n)
lenvapiu, competitively (adv)
lenvaprol, competence (n)
lenvaproliu, competently (adv)
lenvaprolu, competent (adj)
lenvapu, competitive (adj)
lenvapwan, competitor (n doer)
lenvasp, compete (v)
lepal, final (n)
lepaliu, finally (adv)
lepalu, final (adj)
lepalwan, finalist (n doer)
leparshk, meteor (n)
leparshkat, meteorite (n)
lepasle, finalize (v)
lerfe, L (let sng)
lerfhem, Number_1e1056
lerfi, Ls (let pl)
lerk, let (n)
lerp, meet (v)
lers, wave (v)
lersh, wave (n)
lersk, let (v)
lerskyot, let (v pa)
lersp, met (v)
lerspyot, met (v pa)
lesharsk, waver (v)
leshralzhe, wavelength (n)

lethrulf, sugar (n)
lethrulfu, sugary (adj)
lethrulsf, sugar (v)
liailk, turret (n)
liaishk, trophy (n)
lialirk, wink (n)
lialirsk, wink (v)
lialirst, word (v)
lialirt, word (n)
lialirtu, wordy (adj)
lialtfnirth, wordsmith (n)
lianork, camouflage (n)
lianorsk, camouflage (v)
liapuafirf, readership (n)
liarge, cold (n d:illness)
liark, chore (n)
liarn, scan (n)
liarnwan, scanner (n doer)
liarp, read (n)
liarpu, readable (adj)
liarpuil, readout (n)
liarpwan, reader (n doer)
liarsne, scan (v)
liarsp, read (v)
liarspyot, read (v pa)
liarth, scarf (n)
liartu, nautical (adj)
liarve, navy (n)
liarvu, naval (adj)
liash, irony (n)
liashiu, ironically (adv)
liashu, ironic (adj)
liau, bye (n/interj)
liaufp, marina (n)
liaurk, raid (n)
liaurkwan, raider (n doer)
liaurnu, marine (adj)
liaurnwan, mariner (n doer)
liaursk, raid (v)
liaushnefst, maroon (v)
liautlik, marsh (n)
liauthku, marshy (adj)
liauthraufp, marshland (n)
liavarst, navigate (v)
liavart, navigation (n)
liavartwan, navigator (n doer)
liavurk, twinkle (n)
liavursk, twinkle (v)
libers, settle (v)
libersh, settlement (n)
libershwan, settler (n doer)
Libiarf, Libya (n)
Libiarn, Libyan (n)
libirst, sedimentate (v)
libirt, sediment (n)
libirtu, sedimentary (adj)
libirtuet, sedimentation (n)
libuage, ache (n)
libuagiu, achily (adv)
libuagu, achy (adj)
libuazge, ache (v)
lidiurt, nucleus (n)
lidiurtu, nuclear (adj)

lidiurtyek, nuclei (n pl)
lidor, daughter (n)
lidrest, center (v)
lidret, center (n)
lidretak, centralization (n)
lidretakwan, centralizer (n doer)
lidretask, centralize (v)
lidretiu, centrally (adv)
lidretu, central (adj)
lidurp, obesity (n)
lidurpiu, obesely (adv)
lidurpu, obese (adj)
lieblerfu, oncoming (adj)
lieferp, onset (n)
liefklertu, onscreen (adj)
lieglorifu, onboard (adj)
liehurshiu, onward (adv)
liemavirfu, ongoing (adj)
lieme, on (prep)
lienshk, amnesty (n)
lienularatu, onshore (adj)
liereigirnwan, onlooker (n doer)
lierst, idealize (v)
liert, idea (n)
liertiu, ideally (adv)
liertu, ideal (adj)
lieshriausht, onslaught (n)
lietralk, onstage (n)
lietralku, onstage (adj)
lifarbe, stem (n)
lifarde, shirt (n)
lifarzbe, stem (v)
lifezhgatu, measly (adj)
lifezhge, meagerness (n)
lifezhgiu, meagerly (adv)
lifezhgu, meager (adj)
liflor, embassy (n)
liflorwan, ambassador (n doer)
lifork, nutrient (n)
liforkuet, nutrition (n)
liforkuetiu, nutritionally (adv)
liforkuetu, nutritional (adj)
liforkuetwan, nutritionist (n doer)
ligarp, solid (n)
ligarpiu, solidly (adv)
ligarpu, solid (adj)
ligarsp, solidify (v)
ligralge, solution (n)
ligralgu, solvable (adj)
ligralgwan, solver (n doer)
ligralp, solvent (n)
ligralpu, soluble (adj)
ligralpuet, solvency (n)
ligralt, solute (n)
ligralzge, solve (v)
ligurl, string (n)
ligurlkiu, stringently (adv)
ligurlku, stringent (adj)
ligursle, string (v)
ligurslyot, strung (v pa)
likarpiu, properly (adv)
likarpu, proper (adj)
likirme, prop (n)

likirzme, prop (v)
lilakluarf, microscope (n)
lilanf, serenity (n)
lilanfiu, serenely (adv)
lilanfu, serene (adj)
lilers, microwave (v)
lilersh, microwave (n)
lilf, blood (n)
lilfiu, bloodily (adv)
lilfu, bloody (adj)
lilfwan, bleeder (n doer)
lilirp, sermon (n)
lilmierkuit, microbiology (n)
lilmierkuitwan, microbiologist (n
doer)
lilrodap, microfilm (n)
lilsf, bleed (v)
lilsharshturk, microsystem (n)
lilufp, microbe (n)
lilufpu, microbial (adj)
liluyarp, microphone (n)
limarf, furniture (n)
limark, scandal (n)
limarkiu, scandalously (adv)
limarku, scandalous (adj)
limarsf, furnish (v)
limarsk, scandalize (v)
limaushk, raunchiness (n)
limaushku, raunchy (adj)
limern, morning (n)
limert, meter (n d:metric
measurement)
limerth, min (n)
limfnilort, miniskirt (n)
limirk, miniature (n)
limirku, miniature (adj)
limirs, minimize (v)
limirsh, minimum (n)
limirshiu, minimally (adv)
limirshu, minimal (adj)
limirshuet, minimalism (n)
limirshuet, minimalization (n)
limirshwan, minimalist (n doer)
limirsk, miniaturize (v)
limnilorf, miniseries (n)
limorak, ranch (n)
limorakwan, rancher (n doer)
limorask, ranch (v)
limursh, minus (adj/prep)
limursh, minus (n)
llimurshyek, minuses (n pl)
limzhaurn, minivan (n)
linaf, finance (n)
linafiu, financially (adv)
linafu, financial (adj)
linafwan, financier (n doer)
linalf, sheer (n d:clear)
linalfiu, sheer (adv d:clear)
linalfu, sheer (adj d:clear)
linarpiu, fiscally (adv)
linarpu, fiscal (adj)
linarsh, trousers (n)
linasf, finance (v)

linurn, note (n d:music)
lioir, woe (n)
lioiriu, woefully (adv)
lioiru, woeful (adj)
lioithk, moor (n d:marsh)
liorp, ruby (n)
lipamor, ambulation (n)
lipamoriu, ambulatorily (adv)
lipamoru, ambulatory (adj)
lipamorwan, ambulance (n doer)
lipamosre, ambulate (v)
lipivaitar, bicycle (n)
lipivaitarwan, bicyclist (n doer)
lipivaitasre, bicycle (v)
lipk, bias (n)
liplurst, orbit (v)
liplurt, orbit (n)
liplurtu, orbital (adj)
liplurtwan, orbiter (n doer)
lipsk, bias (v)
liraf, scent (n)
liraiforp, triumph (n)
liraiforpiu, triumphantly (adv)
liraiforpu, triumphal (adj)
liraiforpu, triumphant (adj)
liraiforsp, triumph (v)
liran, rum (n)
lirasf, scent (v)
lirfp, discern (n)
lirfsp, discern (v)
lirlarst, publish (v)
lirlart, publication (n)
lirlartwan, publisher (n doer)
lirolf, color (n)
lirolfiu, colorfully (adv)
lirolfu, colorful (adj)
lirolsf, color (v)
lirparf, republic (n)
lirparfwan, republican (n doer)
lirpurk, publicity (n)
lirpursk, publicize (v)
lirpurt, public (n)
lirpurtiu, publicly (adv)
lirpurtu, public (adj)
lirshp, lily (n)
lishkap, award (n)
lishkasp, award (v)
lishst, belittle (v)
lishtarn, tint (n)
lishtarsne, tint (v)
liohtu, little (adj)
litarge, obituary (n)
litarn, plan (n)
litarnirk, plantation (n)
litarnk, plant (n d:factory)
litarnwan, planner (n doer)
litarsne, plan (v)
litef, burrow (n)
litefwan, burrower (n doer)
litesf, burrow (v)
Lithium, Lithium (n)
Lithuaniarf, Lithuania (n)
Lithuaniarn, Lithuanian (n)

litirk, dye (n)
litirkwan, dyer (n doer)
litirsk, dye (v)
litolimet, centimeter (n)
litor, cent (n)
litorat, century (n)
lituthatar, acupuncture (n)
liubirs, contrive (v)
liubirsh, contrivance (n)
liudorshp, concoction (n)
liudorshsp, concoct (v)
liugoishst, concuss (v)
liugoisht, concussion (n)
liukiarge, congestion (n)
liukiarzge, congest (v)
liumiurk, contamination (n)
liumiurkwan, contaminant (n
    doer)
liumiursk, contaminate (v)
liutiorth, contingency (n)
liutiorthu, contingent (adj)
livafirt, literature (n)
livafirtu, literary (adj)
livarn, ivy (n)
livart, literacy (n)
livartoru, literate (adj)
livashort, literal (n)
livashortiu, literally (adv)
livashortu, literal (adj)
livienorp, phenomenon (n)
livienorpu, phenominal (adj)
livienorpyek, phenomena (n pl)
livonk, libel (n)
livonku, libelous (adj)
livonsk, libel (v)
lizharn, pizza (n)
lizhdof, era (n)
lobirek, ordeal (n)
lobriark, perusal (n)
lobriarsk, peruse (v)
lobrunitiu, perpendicularly (adv)
lobrunitu, perpendicular (adj)
loburk, support (n)
loburkiu, supportively (adv)
loburku, supportable (adj)
loburku, supportive (adj)
loburkwan, supporter (n doer)
lobursk, support (v)
lodalirsp, perturb (v)
lodokarst, persecute (v)
lodokart, persecution (n)
lodokartwan, persecutor (n doer)
lofarme, orange (n d:color)
lofarmu, orange (adj d:color)
lofarn, curtain (n)
lofdaurf, perspiration (n)
lofdaursf, perspire (v)
lofek, average (n)
lofeku, average (adj)
lofesk, average (v)
lofirn, orchestra (n)
lofirniu, orchestrally (adv)
lofirnu, orchestral (adj)

lofirnuet, orchestration (n)
lofirnwan, orchestrator (n doer)
lofirp, curve (n)
lofirpu, curvy (adj)
lofirsne, orchestrate (v)
lofirsp, curve (v)
logafbierp, pocketful (n)
logafevornt, pocketbook (n)
logarf, pocket (n)
logarfwan, pocketer (n doer)
logarsf, pocket (v)
logarth, rabbit (n)
loidiank, perpetuation (n)
loidiank, perpetuity (n)
loidiankiu, perpetually (adv)
loidianku, perpetual (adj)
loidiansk, perpetuate (v)
loifar, charity (n)
loifariu, charitably (adv)
loifaru, charitable (adj)
loikarn, shin (n)
loikaurt, discord (n)
loinarme, romance (n)
loinarmiu, romatically (adv)
loinarmu, romantic (adj)
loinarmwan, romancer (n doer)
loinarzme, romanticize (v)
loiplufk, wristwatch (n)
loipshtairme, wristband (n)
loirdwan, writer (n doer)
loirf kodi, ought (ndal d:desire)
loirf, desire (n)
loirfiu, desirably (adv)
loirfu, desirable (adj)
loirp, wrist (n)
loirsf, desire (v)
loirst, seek (v)
loirstyot, sought (v pa)
loirth, sir (n)
loirthu, sir (adj)
loirtwan, seeker (n doer)
loirve, nerve (n)
loirvu, nervy (adj)
loirzde, write (v)
loirzdyot, wrote (v pa)
loirzve, nerve (v)
loisharp, lobster (n)
loithirk, sire (n)
loithirsk, sire (v)
loitienk, seepage (n)
loitiensk, seep (v)
loitilsp, seethe (v)
loivekuift, neurology (n)
loivekuiftu, neurological (adj)
loivekuiftwan, neurologist (n
    doer)
loivemofirt, neurosurgery (n)
loivemofirtwan, neurosurgeon (n
    doer)
loivert, neuron (n)
loivertu, neural (adj)
loiveshuarsh, neuroscience (n)
loiveshuarshwan, neuroscientist

(n doer)
loivethonork, neurotransmission
    (n)
loivethonorkwan,
    neurotransmitter (n doer)
loivethonorsk, neurotransmit (v)
loivirp, nervousness (n)
loivirpiu, nervously (adv)
loivirpu, nervous (adj)
loivrairk, neurosis (n)
loivrairku, neurotic (adj)
lokarpwan, poacher (n doer)
lokarsp, poach (v)
lokilork, perseverance (n)
lokilorsk, persevere (v)
lokiorf, perfume (n)
lokiorsf, perfume (v)
Loktaf, October (n)
lolarf, kerchief (n)
lolirft, percent (n)
lolirftat, percentage (n)
lomarp, gallop (n)
lomarsp, gallop (v)
lomipunu, awake (adj)
lomipusne, awake (v)
lomipusnyot, awoke (v pa)
lomuf, avenue (n)
lonast, entertain (v)
lonat, entertainment (n)
lonatwan, entertainer (n doer)
londil, entrance (n)
londil, entry (n)
londilwan, entrant (n doer)
londisle, enter (v)
Londorn, London (n)
londpliorl, entryway (n)
londvius, enterprise (v)
londviush, enterprise (n)
londviushwan, entrepreneur (n
    doer)
lonikart, permanence (n)
lonikartiu, permanently (adv)
lonikartu, permanent (adj)
lonirk, permit (n)
lonirkyek, permit (n pl)
lonirsk, permit (v)
lonuak, avoidance (n)
lonuakiu, avoidably (adv)
lonuaku, avoidable (adj)
lonuask, avoid (v)
lopiforst, pertain (v)
lopifortu, pertinent (adj)
lor, all (adj)
lorafst, twiddle (v)
loraft, twiddle (n)
lorap, thumb (n)
loras, pulse (v)
lorash, pulse (n)
lorashk, pejorative (n)
lorashwan, pulser (n doer)
lorasp, thumb (v)
lordikefil, altogether (adv)
lordoip, comedy (n)

lordoipiu, comically (adv)
lordoipu, comical (adj)
lordoipwan, comedian (n doer)
lordoipwan, comic (n doer)
lordolu, already (adv)
lorfpar, curvature (n)
lorfsk, curtail (v)
lorfst, flavor (v)
lorft, flavor (n)
lorgerftu, almighty (adj)
lorhoish, always (adv)
lorilf kodi, might (ndal
    d:possibility)
lorilf, possibility (n)
lorilfiu, possibly (adv)
lorilfu, possible (adj)
lorishorst, pulsate (v)
lorishort, pulsation (n)
lorishortwan, pulsator (n doer)
lormesp, milk (v)
lormp, milk (n)
lormpu, milky (adj)
lormpwan, milker (n doer)
lornoirf, maybe (n)
lornoirfiu, maybe (adv)
lorpthrink, thumbnail (n)
lorshk, chorus (n)
lorshkwan, choir (n doer)
lorshsk, choir (v)
lorwak, almost (adv)
Losh Ankelersh, Los Angeles (n)
loshert, rather (adv/interj)
Loshiaf, EhoDay01 (n)
loshirp, perception (n)
loshirpiu, perceptively (adv)
loshirpu, perceptive (adj)
loshirpwan, perceiver (n doer)
loshirsp, perceive (v)
loshluark, permutation (n)
loshluarsk, permutate (v)
lotelirk, persistence (n)
lotelirkiu, persistently (adv)
lotelirku, persistent (adj)
lotelirsk, persist (v)
lotharaf, perversion (n)
lotharafiu, perversely (adv)
lotharafu, perverse (adj)
lotharafwan, pervert (n doer)
lotharak, perversity (n)
lotharasf, perverse (v)
lotharask, pervert (v)
lothrashst, perforate (v)
lothrasht, perforation (n)
lothurk, perspective (n)
loval, dear (n)
lovaliu, dearly (adv)
lovalu, dear (adj)
lovasle, endear (v)
lovirfst, perfect (v)
lovirft, perfection (n)
lovirftiu, perfectly (adv)
lovirftu, perfect (adj)
lovorinf, performance (n)

lovorinfwan, performer (n doer)
lovorinsf, perform (v)
lovorl, darling (n)
lovorlu, darling (adj)
lovotefst, perpetrate (v)
lovoteft, perpetration (n)
lovoteftwan, perpetrator (n doer)
lowange, whose (pron)
lowe, who (pron)
lowe, whom (pron)
lowerf, whoever (pron)
lozhanirkiu, pervasively (adv)
lozhanirku, pervasive (adj)
lozhanirsk, pervade (v)
luaftarp, reestablishment (n)
luaftarsp, reestablish (v)
luaishk, salute (n)
luaishkuet, salutation (n)
luaishsk, salute (v)
luaithk, salinity (n)
luaithku, saline (adj)
luaithsk, salinate (v)
luaparst, illustrate (v)
luapart, illustration (n)
luapartiu, illustratively (adv)
luapartu, illustrative (adj)
luapartwan, illustrator (n doer)
luarbist, reinvest (v)
luarbit, reinvestment (n)
luarfift, childhood (n)
luark, refuge (v)
luarkuin, refugee (n)
luarl, laugh (n)
luarlal, laughter (n)
luarliu, laughably (adv)
luarlu, laughable (adj)
luarlwan, laugher (n doer)
luarme, mire (n)
luarp, luster (n)
luarpeikarsne, reinvigorate (v)
luarpu, lustrous (adj)
luarsh, luxury (n)
luarshest, reinsert (v)
luarshet, reinsertion (n)
luarshiu, luxuriously (adv)
luarshpelst, reinstitute (v)
luarshpelt, reinstitution (n)
luarshu, luxurious (adj)
luarsle, laugh (v)
luarsp, luster (v)
luarsth, salt (v)
luart, child (n)
luarteirp, reinstallation (n)
luarteirsp, reinstall (v)
luarten, kindergarten (n)
luartenwan, kindergartener (n
    doer)
luarth, salt (n)
luarthiu, saltily (adv)
luarthu, salty (adj)
luarthwan, salter (n doer)
luartkeirf, childcare (n)
luartu, childish (adj)

luartvashil, childbirth (n)
luartyek, children (n pl)
luarzme, mire (v)
luatheidorn, saltwater (n)
luausne, flourish (v)
luavige, education (n)
luavigu, educational (adj)
luavigwan, educator (n doer)
luavizge, educate (v)
lubafirk, restriction (n)
lubafirkiu, restrictively (adv)
lubafirku, restrictive (adj)
lubafirkwan, restricter (n doer)
lubafirsk, restrict (v)
lubaifirt, resource (n)
lubaifirtiu, resourcefully (adv)
lubaifirtu, resourceful (adj)
lubaifirtuet, resourcefulness (n)
lubalfork, recalibration (n)
lubalforsk, recalibrate (v)
lubeirsth, reimburse (v)
lubeirtast, repurchase (v)
lubeirtat, repurchase (n)
lubeirth, reimbursement (n)
lubelfizme, reconvene (v)
lubelkudil, reconfiguration (n)
lubelkudisle, reconfigure (v)
lubelnuif, reconfirmation (n)
lubelnuisf, reconfirm (v)
lubelshlek, reconstruction (n)
lubelshleku, reconstructive (adj)
lubelshlesk, reconstruct (v)
lubelshpelst, reconstitute (v)
lubelshpelt, reconstitution (n)
lubelthost, reconsider (v)
lubelthot, reconsideration (n)
lubeltifsk, recondition (v)
lubiarfu, redoubtable (adj)
lubiarsf, redoubt (v)
lubirs, retrieve (v)
lubirsh, retrieval (n)
lubirshwan, retriever (n doer)
lubiurst, restate (v)
lubiurt, restatement (n)
lublaishk, rebuttal (n)
lublaishsk, rebut (v)
lublars, repress (v)
lublarsh, repression (n)
lublarshu, repressive (adj)
lublarshwan, repressor (n doer)
lubles, reclassify (v)
lublesh, reclassification (n)
lubolirk, repair (n)
lubolirku, repairable (adj)
lubolirkuan, reparable (adj)
lubolirkwan, repairer (n doer)
lubolirkwan, repairman (n doer)
lubolirsk, repair (v)
lubrelsp, replant (v)
lubres, replace (v)
lubresh, replacement (n)
lubreshu, replaceable (adj)
lubreshwan, replacer (n doer)

lubriarsk, reuse (v)
lubriensf, rename (v)
lubronsf, regroup (v)
lubuashk, rehearsal (n)
lubuashsk, rehearse (v)
lubugarst, repackage (v)
lubupral, redecoration (n)
lubuprasle, redecorate (v)
luburs, rebuff (v)
lubursh, rebuff (n)
lubushloist, redeploy (v)
lubushloit, redeployment (n)
lubuvuast, redefine (v)
lubuvuat, redefinition (n)
ludaiarst, rescue (v)
ludaiart, rescue (n)
ludaiartwan, rescuer (n doer)
ludairst, retype (v)
ludalirsth, recover (v d:resurface)
ludalirthu, recoverable (adj
   d:resurface)
ludarast, relate (v)
ludarat, relation (n)
ludaratiu, relatively (adv)
ludaratu, relative (adj)
ludaratwan, relative (n doer)
ludarn, reverberation (n)
ludarpatil, reenactment (n)
ludarpatisle, reenact (v)
ludars, represent (v)
ludarsh, representation (n)
ludarshpest, reinstate (v)
ludarshpet, reinstatement (n)
ludarshu, representative (adj)
ludarshwan, representative (n
   doer)
ludarsne, reverberate (v)
ludartafif, relationship (n)
ludartafifiu, relationally (adv)
ludartafifu, relational (adj)
ludarviuk, reinforcement (n)
ludarviukwan, reinforcer (n doer)
ludarviusk, reinforce (v)
ludaurst, rebuke (v)
ludeirolst, redesign (v)
ludeirolt, redesign (n)
ludelishirk, refractory (n)
ludelishork, refraction (n)
ludelishorku, refractive (adj)
ludelishorsk, refract (v)
ludelkal, recapitalization (n)
ludelkasle, recapitalize (v)
ludersp, rethink (v)
luderspyot, rethought (v pa)
ludeshiark, recapture (n)
ludeshiarsk, recapture (v)
ludiardasre, remodel (v)
ludiarn, rediscovery (n)
ludiarsne, rediscover (v)
ludiarst, rejoin (v)
ludibarge, retrial (n)
ludidarn, resemblance (n)
ludidarsne, resemble (v)

ludiofk, retrenchment (n)
ludiofsk, retrench (v)
ludirbe, retry (n)
ludirzbe, retry (v)
ludorbirde, rebroadcast (n)
ludorbirzde, rebroadcast (v)
ludorbirzdyot, rebroadcast (v pa)
ludraifp, rebound (n)
ludraifsp, rebound (v)
ludralbe, restoration (n)
ludralbiu, restoratively (adv)
ludralbu, restorative (adj)
ludralbwan, restorer (n doer)
ludralzbe, restore (v)
ludrashst, repent (v)
ludrasht, repentance (n)
ludrashtu, repentant (adj)
ludraurk, recruitment (n)
ludraurkwan, recruiter (n doer)
ludraursk, recruit (v)
ludrishsk, recrease (v)
ludrufk, reprehension (n)
ludrufkiu, reprehensively (adv)
ludrufku, reprehensive (adj)
ludrufkyek, reprehension (n pl)
ludrufsk, reprehend (v)
ludufirk, revenge (n)
ludufirp, response (n)
ludufirpiu, responsively (adv)
ludufirpu, responsive (adj)
ludufirpuin, respondent (n)
ludufirpwan, responder (n doer)
ludufirsk, revenge (v)
ludufirsp, respond (v)
luduverk, responsibility (n)
luduverkiu, responsibly (adv)
luduverku, responsible (adj)
luefbirsne, reopen (v)
lueifk, ladle (n)
lueifsk, ladle (v)
luenokriushk, reintroduction (n)
luenokriushsk, reintroduce (v)
luenridrup, reinterpretation (n)
luenridrusp, reinterpret (v)
lufabark, refutation (n)
lufabarsk, refute (v)
lufaborst, refuse (v d:join again)
lufabort, refusion (n d:join again)
lufadersk, resort (v d:sort again)
lufavern, nickname (n)
lufaversne, nickname (v)
lufdaurf, respiration (n)
lufdaurfu, respiratory (adj)
lufdaurfwan, respirator (n doer)
lufdaursf, respirate (v)
luferp, reset (n)
luferpwan, resetter (n doer)
lufersp, reset (v)
luferspyot, reset (v pa)
lufiaishk, revision (n)
lufiaishkuet, revisionism (n)
lufiaishkuetwan, revisionist (n
   doer)

lufiaishsk, revise (v)
lufialirst, resume (v)
lufialirt, resumption (n)
lufialirtwan, resumer (n doer)
lufiars, refresh (v)
lufiarsh, refresh (n)
lufiarshiu, refreshingly (adv)
lufiarsht, refreshment (n)
lufiarshwan, refresher (n doer)
lufilp, recap (n)
lufilsp, recap (v)
lufiorsk, retool (v)
lufirp, nick (n)
lufirsp, nick (v)
lufiunelirsk, reprogram (v)
lufiuverst, reprocess (v)
lufk, watch (n d:clock)
luflaurde, reproach (n)
luflaurfst, relive (v)
luflaurzde, reproach (v)
lufliothk, reprieve (n)
luflurzme, reshape (v)
lufranist, relay (v d:place again)
lufriars, rekindle (v)
lufrifsk, restock (v)
lufrilost, reorganize (v)
lufrilot, reorganization (n)
lufrilotwan, reorganizer (n doer)
lufruifk, replay (n)
lufruifkwan, replayer (n doer)
lufruifsk, replay (v)
lufrulirsk, refrain (v d:abstain)
lufualst, review (v)
lufualt, review (n)
lufualtwan, reviewer (n doer)
lufuarme, revelation (n)
lufuartu, rearview (adj)
lufuarzme, reveal (v)
lufurpemenu, relentless (adj)
lufursp, relent (v)
lugagor, resolution (n)
lugagoru, resolute (adj)
lugagorwan, resolver (n doer)
lugagosre, resolve (v)
lugaiarp, recoil (n)
lugaiarsp, recoil (v)
lugalirf, recurrence (n)
lugalirfiu, recurrently (adv)
lugalirfu, recurrent (adj)
lugalirsf, recur (v)
lugalirst, retract (v)
lugalirt, retraction (n)
lugalirtu, retractable (adj)
lugapost, recollect (v)
lugapot, recollection (n)
lugardas, recalculate (v)
lugardash, recalculation (n)
lugars, retrace (v)
lugarst, rebel (v)
lugart, rebellion (n)
lugartiu, rebelliously (adv)
lugartu, rebellious (adj)
lugartwan, rebel (n doer)

lugelf, referral (n)
lugelfuin, referee (n)
lugelfwan, referer (n doer)
lugelp, reelection (n)
lugelsf, refer (v)
lugelsp, reelect (n)
lugers, reference (v)
lugersh, reference (n)
lugershiu, referentially (adv)
lugershu, referential (adj)
lugerst, reflect (v)
lugert, reflection (n)
lugertiu, reflectively (adv)
lugertu, reflective (adj)
lugertwan, reflector (n doer)
lugesharn, referendum (n)
lugesharnyek, referenda (n pl)
lugiarp, rebate (n)
lugiars, recurse (v)
lugiarsh, recursal (n)
lugiarshiu, recursively (adv)
lugiarshu, recursive (adj)
lugiarshwan, recurser (n doer)
lugiarsp, rebate (v)
lugirf, recall (n)
lugirfwan, recaller (n doer)
lugirsf, recall (v)
lugloifst, recharge (v)
lugloift, recharge (n)
lugloiftu, rechargeable (adj)
lugloiftwan, recharger (n doer)
lugoifirst, refocus (v)
lugoirst, recuse (v)
lugoirt, recusal (n)
lugorsk, retake (v)
lugorskyot, retook (v pa)
lugrals, repaint (v)
lugreishk, reincarnation (n)
lugreishsk, reincarnate (v)
lugrusht, recluse (n)
lugrushtiu, reclusively (adv)
lugrushtu, reclusive (adj)
luguvarst, reinvent (v)
luguvart, reinvention (n)
luhaurs, reward (v)
luhaursh, reward (n)
luhaurshwan, rewarder (n doer)
luiaft, silo (n)
luiarsk, reckon (v)
luiarst, reck (v)
luiartmen, recklessness (n)
luiartmeniu, recklessly (adv)
luiartmenu, reckless (adj)
luiashk, retardation (n)
luiashku, retardant (adj)
luiashsk, retard (v)
luifst, rein (v)
luift, rein (n)
luinf, sill (n)
luirk, rally (n)
luirme, bust (n d:sculpture)
luirs, rise (v)
luirsh, rise (n)

luirshwan, riser (n doer)
luirsk, rally (v)
luirst, rail (v)
luirsyot, rose (v pa)
luirt, rail (n)
Luishiarf, Louisiana (n)
luishreln, reinsurance (n)
luishrelnwan, reinsurer (n doer)
luishrelsne, reinsure (v)
luitegeral, railcar (n)
luithuarst, reemphasize (v)
luitpliorl, railway (n)
luitrelis, railroad (v)
luitrelish, railroad (n)
luiupafirst, retrofit (v)
luiupafirt, retrofit (n)
luiupaltark, retroactivity (n)
luiupaltarkiu, retroactively (adv)
luiupaltarku, retroactive (adj)
luiupu, retro (adj)
luiushtraku, retrograde (adj)
luiuthurk, retrospect (n)
luiuthurku, retrospective (adj)
lukaimesp, return (v)
lukaimp, return (n)
lukaimpwan, returner (n doer)
lukelirk, revisitation (n)
lukelirsk, revisit (v)
lukemirf, revolution (n d:journey around)
lukemirfwan, revolver (n doer d:journey around)
lukemirsf, revolve (v d:journey around)
lukest, recheck (v)
lukiglarsk, reimpose (v)
lukiorsk, rework (v)
lukirak, reduction (n)
lukirakiu, reducibly (adv)
lukiraku, reducible (adj)
lukirakwan, reducer (n doer)
lukirask, reduce (v)
lukiurf, redemption (n)
lukiurfu, redeemable (adj)
lukiurfu, redemptive (adj)
lukiurfwan, redeemer (n doer)
lukiursf, redeem (v)
luklarl, relaxation (n)
luklarsle, relax (v)
luknargwan, watchmaker (n doer)
lukofalt, reserve (n d:military)
lukofaltwan, reservist (n doer d:military)
lukofirp, reservoir (n)
lukorfst, reserve (v d:storage)
lukorft, reserve (n d:storage)
lukorftuet, reservation (n)
lukorftwan, reserver (n doer d:storage)
lukriarf, requalification (n)
lukriarfwan, requalifier (n doer)
lukriarsf, requalify (v)
lukriarst, renegotiate (v)

lukriart, renegotiation (n)
lukroifst, recline (v)
lukroift, reclination (n)
lukroiftwan, recliner (n doer)
lukroshst, research (v)
lukrosht, research (n)
lukroshtwan, researcher (n doer)
lukuarfk, redirection (n)
lukuarfsk, redirect (v)
lukuarsne, regain (v)
lulaidark, remediation (n)
lulaidarkwan, remediator (n doer)
lulaidarsk, remediate (v)
lulairde, remedy (n)
lulairs, rejoice (v)
lulairshwan, rejoicer (n doer)
lulairzde, remedy (v)
lulaorzme, rerun (v)
lulaorzmyot, reran (v pa)
lularak, resignation (n d:quit)
lularakwan, resigner (n doer d:quit)
lularask, resign (v d:quit)
lularst, miss (v d:regret absence)
lulaufarge, refrigeration (n)
lulaufarguat, refrigerant (n)
lulaufargwan, refrigerator (n doer)
lulaufarzge, refrigerate (v)
lulaurf, fridge (n)
lulenirsk, recommit (v)
lulenup, recombination (n)
lulenupu, recombinant (adj)
lulenusp, recombine (v)
lulfirme, revenue (n)
luliarsp, reread (v)
luliarspyot, reread (v pa)
lulibers, resettle (v)
lulibersh, resettlement (n)
lulinasf, refinance (v)
luliratiu, recently (adv)
luliratu, recent (adj)
lulirlarst, republish (v)
luloirde, rewrite (n)
luloirdwan, rewriter (n doer)
luloirzde, rewrite (v)
luloirzdyot, rewrote (v pa)
lulomipusne, reawaken (v)
lulondil, reentry (n)
lulondisle, reenter (v)
luloras, repulse (v)
lulorashu, repulsive (adj)
lulularst, remiss (v)
lululart, remission (n)
lululartiu, remissively (adv)
lululartu, remissive (adj)
lulurifst, reload (v)
lulutigarst, reiterate (v)
lulutigart, reiteration (n)
luluvarp, reciprocation (n)
luluvarp, reciprocity (n)
luluvarpu, reciprocal (adj)
luluvarsp, reciprocate (v)

lumaigirf, revitalization (n)
lumaigirsf, revitalize (v)
lumaran, recourse (n)
lumaranwan, recourser (n doer)
lumarasne, recourse (v)
lumarmark, regeneration (n)
lumarmarkwan, regenerator (n doer)
lumarmarsk, regenerate (v)
lume, hum (n)
lumemifst, resuscitate (v)
lumemift, resuscitation (n)
lumiarf, renovation (n)
lumiarfwan, renovator (n doer)
lumiarsf, renovate (v)
lumiarsh, reluctance (n)
lumiarshiu, reluctantly (adv)
lumiarshu, reluctant (adj)
lumior, renewal (n)
lumioru, renewable (adj)
lumiorwan, renewer (n doer)
lumiosre, renew (v)
lumithk, retail (n)
lumithkwan, retailer (n doer)
lumithsk, retail (v)
lumoirme, repayment (n)
lumoirmwan, repayer (n doer)
lumoirzme, repay (v)
lumoirzmyot, repaid (v pa)
lumufirst, renounce (v)
lumurat, redundancy (n)
lumuratiu, redundantly (adv)
lumuratu, redundant (adj)
lumuthk, rematch (n)
lumuthsk, rematch (v)
lunarge, remake (n)
lunargwan, remaker (n doer)
lunarst, revel (v)
lunart, revelry (n)
lunartu, revelatory (adj)
lunarzge, remake (v)
lunarzgyot, remade (v pa)
lunbielirk, passport (n)
luniarpwan, reminder (n doer)
luniarsp, remind (v)
lunirp, cream (n)
lunirpiu, creamily (adv)
lunirpu, creamy (adj)
lunirpwan, creamer (n doer)
lunirsp, cream (v)
lunirst, pass (v)
lunirt, pass (n)
lunirtiu, passively (adv)
lunirtu, passive (adj)
lunirtwan, passer (n doer)
luniurn, replenishment (n)
luniursne, replenish (v)
lunlialirt, password (n)
lunolan, reclamation (n)
lunolasne, reclaim (v)
lunork, remittance (n)
lunorkwan, remittor (n doer)
lunorsk, remit (v)

luntark, passage (n)
luntarkwan, passenger (n doer)
lunuarnuet, recrimination (n)
lunurn, release (n)
lunurnwan, releaser (n doer)
lunursne, release (v)
luolarak, reassignment (n)
luolarask, reassign (v)
luolirp, reassurance (n)
luolirsp, reassure (v)
luolsharst, reassert (v)
luolshart, reassertion (n)
luomorst, rearrange (v)
luomort, rearrangement (n)
luopairk, reattachment (n)
luopairsk, reattach (v)
luopliarn, reappearance (n)
luopliarsne, reappear (v)
luorlarp, reassessment (n)
luorlarsp, reassess (v)
luorniurf, reaffirmation (n)
luorniursf, reaffirm (v)
luoroifk, realignment (n)
luoroifsk, realign (v)
luorshairp, reallocation (n)
luorshairsp, reallocate (v)
luotherst, reacquire (v)
luothert, reacquisition (n)
luothralve, reassembly (n)
luothralzve, reassemble (v)
luovaup, reevaluation (n)
luovausp, reevaluate (v)
lupafirst, refit (v)
lupafirt, refit (n)
lupalirst, react (v)
lupalirt, reaction (n)
lupalirtu, reactionary (adj)
lupalirtun, reactionary (n)
lupalirtwan, reactor (n doer)
lupaltark, reactivation (n)
lupaltarku, reactive (adj)
lupaltarsk, reactivate (v)
luparde, repellant (n)
luparde, repellent (n)
lupardu, repellants (adj)
lupardu, repellent (adj)
lupardwan, repeller (n doer)
luparf, clown (n)
luparn, retirement (n)
luparnwan, retiree (n doer)
luparsf, clown (v)
luparsne, retire (v)
luparzde, repel (v)
lupiashk, relegation (n)
lupiashsk, relegate (v)
lupiethk, refurbishment (n)
lupiethsk, refurbish (v)
lupiforst, retain (v)
lupifort, retention (n)
lupifortiu, retentively (adv)
lupifortu, retentive (adj)
lupifortwan, retainer (n doer)
luplarst, regret (v)

luplart, regret (n)
luplartiu, regretfully (adv)
luplartiu, regrettably (adv)
luplartu, regretful (adj)
luplartu, regrettable (adj)
luplartwan, regrettor (n doer)
lupleirk, reproduction (n)
lupleirkiu, reproductively (adv)
lupleirku, reproductive (adj)
lupleirkwan, reproducer (n doer)
lupleirsk, reproduce (v)
lupliarshk, reintegration (n)
lupliarshsk, reintegrate (v)
lupliurst, recreate (v d:remake)
lupliurt, recreation (n d:remake)
lupliurtwan, recreator (n doer d:remake)
lupoirn, recount (n)
lupoirnwan, recounter (n doer)
lupoirsne, recount (v)
luprailsk, reroute (v)
luprelst, retell (v)
luprelstyot, retold (v pa)
luprierst, resort (v d:rest, revert)
lupriert, resort (n d:rest, revert)
luprilap, repossession (n)
luprilasp, repossess (v)
luprufsp, relinquish (v)
luprulirk, restraint (n)
luprulirkwan, restrainer (n doer)
luprulirsk, restrain (v)
lupulasp, redraw (v)
lupulaspyot, redrew (v pa)
lurap, relief (n)
lurapwan, reliever (n doer)
lurasp, relieve (v)
lureidal, rehabilitation (n)
lureidasle, rehabilitate (v)
luridarsf, reschedule (v)
lurifst, load (v)
lurift, load (n)
luriftwan, loader (n doer)
lurolarme, reconciliation (n)
lurolarzme, reconcile (v)
lurotaitif, reappointment (n)
lurotaitisf, reappoint (v)
lurpshranf, restroom (n)
lursh, herb (n)
lurshiu, herbally (adv)
lurshu, herbal (adj)
lushairk, revocation (n)
lushairku, revocable (adj)
lushairp, relocation (n)
lushairsk, revoke (v)
lushairsp, relocate (v)
lushanirt, resonate (v)
lushanirt, resonance (n)
lushanirtu, resonant (adj)
lusharf, recommendation (n)
lusharsf, recommend (v)
Lushdor, Easter (n)
lushefnork, resubmission (n)
lushefnorsk, resubmit (v)

lushethirp, resupply (n)
lushethirsp, resupply (v)
lushiarst, request (v)
lushiart, request (n)
lushiartwan, requester (n doer)
lushipersne, remap (v)
lushkalirst, restart (v)
lushkeisf, redouble (v)
lushkelst, reorder (v)
lushkirst, remove (v)
lushkirt, removal (n)
lushkirtiu, removably (adv)
lushkirtu, removable (adj)
lushkirtwan, remover (n doer)
lushlaithsk, rescind (v)
lushlaurf, revival (n)
lushlaurfwan, revivalist (n doer)
lushlaurfwan, reviver (n doer)
lushlaursf, revive (v)
lushlersk, restructure (v)
lushluarst, reply (v)
lushluart, reply (n)
lushluartwan, replier (n doer)
lushnarf, reconnection (n)
lushnarfwan, reconnector (n
    doer)
lushnarsf, reconnect (v)
lushnirsf, rewire (v)
lushoikaurst, remanufacture (v)
lushoirk, remand (n)
lushoirkwan, remander (n doer)
lushoirn, residence (n)
lushoirnu, residential (adj)
lushoirnwan, resident (n doer)
lushoirsk, remand (v)
lushoirsne, reside (v)
lushort, recipe (n)
lushrilst, redistribute (v)
lushrilt, redistribution (n)
lushrolk, reflux (n)
lushtarst, remark (v d:write
    again)
lushtart, remark (n d:write again)
lushuarzge, resize (v)
lutafinsk, revamp (v)
lutalurn, remembrance (n)
lutalursne, remember (v)
lutefralp, redevelopment (n)
lutefralsp, redevelop (v)
lutelirk, resistance (n)
lutelirku, resistant (adj)
lutelirku, resistible (adj)
lutelirkwan, resister (n doer)
lutelirp, repeal (n)
lutelirpwan, repealer (n doer)
lutelirsk, resist (v)
lutelirsp, repeal (v)
lutepafes, readjust (v)
lutepafesh, readjustment (n)
luterp, reject (n)
luterpuet, rejection (n)
luterpwan, rejector (n doer)
lutersp, reject (v)

Lutetium, Lutetium (n)
luthaithsp, rehash (v)
lutharaf, reverse (n)
lutharafu, reversible (adj)
lutharak, reversion (n)
lutharakwan, reverter (n doer)
lutharasf, reverse (v)
lutharask, revert (v)
lutharfarl, reversal (n)
lutharst, require (v)
luthart, requirement (n)
luthathsk, reshuffle (v)
luthirthk, retaliation (n)
luthirthku, retaliatory (adj)
luthirthkwan, retaliator (n doer)
luthirthsk, retaliate (v)
luthiurfst, relapse (v)
luthiurft, relapse (n)
luthiursf, refile (v)
luthonork, retransmission (n)
luthonorsk, retransmit (v)
luthorsk, reapply (v)
luthrairsk, rewind (v)
luthrairskyot, rewound (v pa)
luthrelsf, resurface (v)
luthrishk, reforestation (n)
luthrishsk, reforest (v)
luthriurp, retribution (n)
luthuirst, retreat (v)
luthuirt, retreat (n)
luthukiru, respectable (adj)
luthukurshiu, respectfully (adv)
luthukurshu, respectful (adj)
luthuntarn, recertification (n)
luthuntarsne, recertify (v)
luthurk, respect (n)
luthurkiu, respectively (adv)
luthurku, respective (adj)
luthursk, respect (v)
lutibarfsk, redistrict (v)
lutielirk, resistor (n)
lutiert, reflex (n)
lutiertu, reflexive (adj)
lutigarst, iterate (v)
lutigart, iteration (n)
lutigartiu, iteratively (adv)
lutigartu, iterative (adj)
lutimork, refund (n)
lutimorku, refundable (adj)
lutimorkwan, refunder (n doer)
lutimorsk, refund (v)
lutiorzge, rehire (v)
lutirfk, rendition (n)
lutirfkwan, renderer (n doer)
lutirfsk, render (v)
lutisk, redo (v)
lutiskyot, redid (v pa)
lutiurst, refinish (v)
lutoirp, recitation (n)
lutoirpat, recital (n)
lutoirsp, recite (v)
lutrelbe, revulsion (n)
lutrelbu, revulsive (adj)

lutrelirf, resale (n)
lutrelirfu, resale (adj)
lutrelirfwan, reseller (n doer)
lutrelirsf, resell (v)
lutrelirsfyot, resold (v pa)
lutrelzbe, revulse (v)
lutriel, refill (n)
lutriesle, refill (v)
lutrilorsk, retrain (v)
lutrulis, reprint (v)
lutrulish, reprint (n)
lutukoirge, reexamination (n)
lutukoirzge, reexamine (v)
lutulirst, recast (v)
lutulirstyot, recast (v pa)
luuyasf, rehear (v)
luuyasfyot, reheard (v pa)
luvadarve, remote (n)
luvadarviu, remotely (adv)
luvadarvu, remote (adj)
luvaikmern, regardless (adj/adv)
luvairalst, recycle (v)
luvairaltwan, recycler (n doer)
luvairk, regard (n)
luvairkmenu, irregardless (adj)
luvairkmenu, regardless (adj)
luvairkwan, regarder (n doer)
luvairsk, regard (v)
luvanirst, result (v)
luvanirt, result (n)
luvanirtu, resultant (adj)
luvarap, refrain (n d:verse)
luvarp, repeat (n)
luvarpiu, repeatedly (adv)
luvarpu, repeatable (adj)
luvarpu, repetitive (adj)
luvarpuet, repetition (n)
luvarpuetiu, repetitiously (adv)
luvarpuetu, repetitious (adj)
luvarpwan, repeater (n doer)
luvarshst, rephrase (v)
luvarsp, repeat (v)
luvashil, rebirth (n)
luvaurp, revaluation (n)
luvaurs, remain (v)
luvaursh, remainder (n)
luvaursht, remains (n)
luvaursp, revaluate (v)
luveilirn, reposition (n)
luveillrsne, reposition (v)
luveilork, repository (n)
luvekert, recession (n)
luverk, recess (n)
luverkiu, recessively (adv)
luverku, recessive (adj)
luverkwan, receder (n doer)
luversk, recede (v)
luvialorst, recognize (v)
luvialort, recognition (n)
luvialortiu, recognizably (adv)
luvialortu, recognizable (adj)
luvialortwan, recognizer (n doer)
luvienork, renomination (n)

luvienorsk, renominate (v)
luvirp, regularity (n)
luvirpiu, regularly (adv)
luvirpu, regular (adj)
luvirpuet, regulation (n)
luvirpuetu, regulatory (adj)
luvirpun, regular (n)
luvirpwan, regulator (n doer)
luvirsp, regulate (v)
luvoikarst, repudiate (v)
luvoikart, reputation (n)
luvoirge, resurgence (n)
luvoirgu, resurgent (adj)
luvoirk, repute (n)
luvoirsk, repute (v)
luvoirzge, resurge (v)
luvorage, regression (n)
luvoragiu, regressively (adv)
luvoragu, regressive (adj)
luvoragwan, regressor (n doer)
luvoran, reform (n d:form again)
luvorasne, reform (v d:form
  again)
luvorast, rebuild (v)
luvorastyot, rebuilt (v pa)
luvorat, rebuild (n)
luvorazge, regress (v)
luvorfk, recuperation (n)
luvorfku, recuperative (adj)
luvorfsk, recuperate (v)
luvorlinak, reformation (n)
luvorlinaku, reformatory (adj)
luvorlinap, reformulation (n)
luvorlinask, reformat (v)
luvorlinasp, reformulate (v)
luvrierst, relearn (v)
luvuanirt, refinery (n)
luvuarsk, relaunch (v)
luvuarst, refine (v)
luvuart, refinement (n)
luvuartwan, refiner (n doer)
luvularn, remarriage (n)
luvularsne, remarry (v)
luweirsf, re-sign (v d:sign again)
luwiorn, silliness (n)
luwiornu, silly (adj)
luyarp, phone (n)
luyarsp, phone (v)
luyutark, reunification (n)
luyutarme, reunion (n)
luyutarsk, reunify (v)
luyutarzme, reunite (v)
luzhairsp, resend (v d:send again)
luzhairspyot, resent (v pa d:send
  again)
luzhaithsk, revile (v)
luzhanirst, resound (v)
luzhanirtiu, resoundingly (adv)
luzhiarsp, refuel (v)
luzhirme, reissuance (n)
luzhirzme, reissue (v)
luzhorfk, remix (n)
luzhorfsk, remix (v)

luzhumark, rejuventation (n)
luzhumarsk, rejuvenate (v)
luzme, hum (v)
madirk, olympics (n)
madirku, olympic (adj)
madirkwan, olympian (n doer)
Madishorf, Madison (n)
Madrirde, Madrid (n)
maf, for (prep/conj)
mafirk, pert (n)
mafirku, pert (adj)
mafpal, maple (n)
Magneshium, Magnesium (n)
mah, ma (n)
mahil, nor (conj)
mahioviul, nowadays (n)
mahioviuliu, nowadays (adv)
mahir, now (adj/adv/conj)
mahir, now (n)
maiarme, tan (v)
maiarmwan, tanner (n doer)
maiarp, nope (interj)
maiarsk, nix (v)
maiart, goal (n)
maiarzme, tan (v)
maigarme, vitamin (n)
maigirf, vitality (n)
maigirfiu, vitally (adv)
maigirfu, vital (adj)
maihem, Number_1e2256
maikarst, maximize (v)
maikart, maximum (n)
maikartiu, maximally (adv)
maikartu, maximal (adj)
mail, M (let sng)
mailenart, mileage (n)
mailern, mile (n)
maili, Ms (let pl)
Mainorf, Maine (n)
mairave, narcotic (n)
mairf, valve (n)
mairk, max (n)
mairp, sock (n)
mairpef, socket (n)
mairsk, max (v)
mairsp, sock (v)
maishk, mortar (n d:cement)
Maitark, Marines (n)
maiwar, nay (interj)
Maknesi, Maknesi (n)
Malashiarf, Malaysia (n)
malirfwan, dotard (n doer)
malirk, lube (n)
malirme, mummy (n)
malirsf, dote (v)
malishk, lubrication (n)
malishkwan, lubricant (n doer)
malishsk, lubricate (v)
malmishst, mummify (v)
malmisht, mummification (n)
malmishtwan, mummifier (n
  doer)
malp, banana (n)

malshfif, motherhood (n)
malshplok, motherboard (n)
malshraufp, motherland (n)
malve, harm (n)
malvmeniu, harmlessly (adv)
malvmeniu, harmless (adj)
malvushiu, harmfully (adv)
malvushu, harmful (adj)
malzve, harm (v)
Manganesh, Manganese (n)
Manilorf, Manila (n)
manirk, lump (n)
manirku, lumpy (adj)
manirkwan, lumper (n doer)
manirsk, lump (v)
Mankatarf, Manhattan (n)
Manshersht, Manchester (n)
marah, mama (n)
marah, mamma (n)
marfst, mat (v)
marft, mat (n)
marftan, mattress (n)
mariaith, genie (n)
marifp, pig (n)
marifsp, pig (v)
Marilanurde, Maryland (n)
marilf, lamb (n)
marilsf, lamb (v)
marlth, cotton (n)
marmairt, genius (n)
marmark, generation (n)
marmarkwan, generator (n doer)
marmarn, geniality (n)
marmarnu, genial (adj)
marmarp, generosity (n)
marmarpiu, generously (adv)
marmarpu, generous (adj)
marmarsk, generate (v)
marmash, generic (n)
marmashu, generic (adj)
marmest, generallze (v
  d:common)
marmet, generalization (n
  d:common)
marmetiu, generally (adv
  d:common)
marmetu, general (adj
  d:common)
marmirtiu, genuinely (adv)
marmirtu, genuine (adj)
marnf, course (n)
marnsf, course (v)
marpefnarp, pigskin (n)
marshp, balloon (n)
marshsp, balloon (v)
martiarp, genital (n)
martiarpu, genital (adj)
martiarpyek, genitalia (n pl)
mashart, neither (pron)
mashartu, neither (adj/conj)
Mashashutarf, Massachusetts (n)
mashel, mother (n)
mashelu, motherly (adj)

mashesle, mother (v)
mashiarth, botany (n)
mashiarthu, botanical (adj)
matarn, citizen (n)
matirk, practice (n)
matirkiu, practically (adv)
matirku, practical (adj)
matirkwan, practitioner (n doer)
matirsk, practice (v)
mauak, never (adv)
mauakniarp, nevermind (n)
mauaksheimiu, nevertheless
    (adv)
mauar, naw (interj)
maubelvornwan, nonconformist
    (n doer)
maubushlerk, nondestruction (n)
maubushlerkiu, nondestructively
    (adv)
maubushlerku, nondestructive
    (adj)
mauenrigef, noninterference (n)
maufiuflaursh, nonproliferation
    (n)
maufiuntark, nonprofessional (n)
maufiupafirtu, nonprofit (adj)
maugofaifku, nonlethal (adj)
mauhar, nowhere (adj/adv)
mauhar, nowhere (n)
maukiabarku, nontoxic (adj)
maukirzhu, nontechnical (adj)
maulenshluat, noncompliance (n)
maulirpurtu, nonpublic (adj)
maumeshurt, nonmember (n)
maumoirmuet, nonpayment (n)
maunelafku, noncommercial (adj)
maunulirt, nonexistence (n)
maunulirtu, nonexistent (adj)
maupreiliarfu, nontrivial (adj)
maur, no (n/adj/adv)
mauroifk, nonlinearity (n)
mauroifkiu, nonlinearly (adv)
mauroifku, nonlinear (adj)
maurpafk, nonfiction (n)
maurshorf, nonsense (n)
maurshorfu, nonsensical (adj)
maurt, none (pron)
maurtmeniu, nonetheless (adv)
maurtu, none (adj/adv)
maushairpu, nonlocal (adj)
maushairlirtu, nonessential (adj)
mausharmwan, nonbeliever (n
    doer)
maushlarde, nobody (n/pron)
maushtolirfwan, nonsmoker (n
    doer)
mautaurku, nonstop (adj)
mauthiarku, nonfatal (adj)
mautigreft, nondisclosure (n)
mautrabirnu, nontraditional (adj)
mautrefirku, nonstandard (adj)
mautuarilk, nonviolence (n)
mautuarilku, nonviolent (adj)

mautuarzhu, nonvolatile (adj)
mauyuarnu, nonwhite (adj)
mauyutamarnu, nonunion (adj)
mavarp, kiss (n)
mavarpwan, kisser (n doer)
mavarsp, kiss (v)
mavinelirk, hologram (n)
mavinelirku, holographic (adj)
mavirn, harmony (n)
mavirnar, harmonic (n)
mavirnu, harmonic (adj)
mavirsne, harmonize (v)
mavurn, anonymity (n)
mavurnu, anonymous (adj)
Mediteraniarf, Mediterranean (n)
medmot, continent (n)
medmotu, continental (adj)
mefirth, shallowness (n)
mefirthu, shallow (adj)
mefst, carpet (v)
meft, carpet (n)
meifark, society (n)
meifarku, societal (adj)
meifarl, socialism (n)
meifarlu, socialistic (adj)
meifarlwan, socialist (n doer)
meifarn, social (n)
meiraf, role (n)
meirave, numbness (n)
meiravu, numb (adj)
meirazve, numb (v)
meirf, socialization (n)
meirfal, bargain (n)
meirfasle, bargain (v)
meirfiu, socially (adv)
meirfu, sociable (adj)
meirfu, social (adj)
meirfwan, socializer (n doer)
meirge, verge (n d:incline)
meirsf, socialize (v)
meirzge, verge (v d:incline)
meishirk, panic (n)
meishirku, panicky (adj)
meishirsk, panic (v)
mekarnyek, pants (n pl
    d:clothing)
melarf, glamor (n)
melarf, glamour (n)
melarfiu, glamorously (adv)
melarfu, glamorous (adj)
meldiarf, rainbow (n)
melferap, rainstorm (n)
melfrafk, raincoat (n)
melheidorn, rainwater (n)
melirf, panel (n)
melirfwan, panelist (n doer)
melirk, pan (n)
melirme, mom (n)
melirn, mare (n)
melirp, pride (n d:group)
melirsf, panel (v)
melirsh, tea (n)
melirsk, pan (v)

melirzme, mom (v)
melkarst, pander (v)
melkegutraf, pancake (n)
melkegutrasf, pancake (v)
melmame, mommy (n)
melmelk, murmur (n)
melmelku, murmurous (adj)
melmelkwan, murmurer (n doer)
melmelsk, murmur (v)
melmeme, momma (n)
melnargwan, rainmaker (n doer)
melnirk, marshal (n)
melnirsk, marshal (v)
melpreip, raindrop (n)
melshdairf, teapot (n)
melshdorap, teaspoon (n)
melshvorup, teacup (n)
melsth, rain (v)
melth, rain (n)
melthrishk, rainforest (n)
melthu, rainy (adj)
melthuil, rainout (n)
melvarn, marble (n)
melzhailf, rainfall (n)
membruln, suspense (n)
membrulnuet, suspension (n)
membrulnwan, suspender (n
    doer)
membrulsne, suspend (v)
Memfirsh, Memphis (n)
mempirfst, sustain (v)
mempirft, sustenance (n)
mempirftu, sustainable (adj)
memshirp, susceptibility (n)
memshirpu, susceptible (adj)
memtarn, pumpkin (n)
memthurk, suspicion (n)
memthurkiu, suspiciously (adv)
memthurku, suspicious (adj)
memthurkwan, suspect (n doer)
memthursk, suspect (v)
men, less (adj)
Mendelevium, Mendelevium (n)
merf, pause (n)
Merkuri, Mercury (n)
mern, nut (n)
merntherk, nutshell (n)
mernu, nutty (adj)
merp, pet (n)
mersf, pause (v)
mersne, lessen (v)
mersp, pet (v)
meshkat, hut (n)
Meshkifarn, Mexican (n)
Meshkirf, Mexico (n)
meshtarn, membrane (n)
meshtarnu, membranous (adj)
meshtif, membership (n)
meshurt, member (n)
methirk, nephew (n)
Metnerium, Meitnerium (n)
miafarn, novice (n)
miafk, chain (n)

miafsk, chain (v)
miagralze, chainsaw (v)
miagralzhe, chainsaw (n)
miairf, prize (n)
miairsf, prize (v)
miaishsk, pry (v)
mialt, flue (n)
Miamirf, Miami (n)
miardarfk, oceanography (n)
miardarfku, oceanographic (adj)
miarf, nova (n)
miarflarshu, oceanfront (adj)
miark, fluctuation (n)
miarkwan, fluctuator (n doer)
miarl, ocean (n)
miarlu, oceanic (adj)
miarn, fluid (n)
miarnu, fluid (adj)
miarp, organ (n d:instrument)
miarshoirt, oceanside (n)
miarsht, fluency (n)
miarshtiu, fluently (adv)
miarshtu, fluent (adj)
miarsk, fluctuate (v)
miarth, alibi (n)
miarzbe, mar (v)
miaushsk, taunt (v)
midarst, notate (v)
midart, notation (n)
midebanirf, notepad (n)
mideflairshu, noteworthy (adj)
Midirsht, Mideast (n)
midiurn, novelty (n)
midiurnu, novel (adj)
midoirn, notion (n)
midort, noon (n)
midotedaurn, noontime (n)
midotedaurnu, noontime (adj)
Miduelsh, Midwest (n)
midurn, novel (n)
midurnwan, novelist (n doer)
miedarfk, biography (n)
mief, dew (n)
miels, fluff (v)
mielsh, fluff (n)
mielshu, fluffy (adj)
mierkuit, biology (n)
mierkuitiu, biologically (adv)
mierkuitu, biological (adj)
migart, colonel (n)
mikarl, angel (n)
mikarliu, angelically (adv)
mikarlu, angelic (adj)
mikartu, noxious (adj)
mikirst, colonize (v)
mikirt, colony (n)
mikirtu, colonial (adj)
mikirtuet, colonization (n)
mikirtwan, colonist (n doer)
mikirtwan, colonizer (n doer)
mildilork, tadpole (n)
milt, tad (n)
Miluakirf, Milwaukee (n)

milurn, beneath (adv/prep)
mimarn, range (n)
mimarnwan, ranger (n doer)
mimarsne, range (v)
mimesk, dot (v)
mimk, dot (n)
minarsh, lesser (adj)
Minkarpol, Minneapolis (n)
minorpiveil, wakeup (n d:arise)
minorpiveilu, wakeup (adj
    d:arise)
minorsp, wake (v d:arise)
minorspyot, woke (v pa d:arise)
Minshort, Minnesota (n)
mio, hi (interj)
mioblerfwan, newcomer (n doer)
miolf, newness (n)
miolfiu, newly (adv)
miolfu, new (adj)
miolyurve, newlywed (n)
Mior Kamshirf, New Hampshire
    (n)
Mior Orlinorf, New Orleans (n)
Mior Zhilanurde, New Zealand
    (n)
miorap, radio (n)
miorashort, newsletter (n)
miorasp, radio (v)
miorbronf, newsgroup (n)
miordiump, newsreel (n)
miorf, news (n)
Miorfk, Major (n)
miorflairsh, newsworthiness (n)
miorflairshu, newsworthy (adj)
miorfu, newsy (adj)
mioriarn, newshour (n)
miorniforp, newsmagazine (n)
miorpalirt, radioactivity (n)
miorpalirtu, radioactive (adj)
miorplorn, newsman (n)
miorplornyek, newsmen (n pl)
miorshnirf, newswire (n)
miorshranf, newsroom (n)
miortrelirt, newsstand (n)
miortrulish, newsprint (n)
miortulirt, newscast (n)
miortulirtwan, newscaster (n
    doer)
miorviurl, newsday (n)
miorvuaplorn, newspaperman (n)
miorvuaplornyek, newspapermen
    (n pl)
miorvuarp, newspaper (n)
miorwaku, newest (adj)
miorwelu, newer (adj)
mioshk, macula (n)
mioshku, macular (adj)
mioshkyek, maculae (n pl)
mioshsk, maculate (v)
mioshurpu, newfound (adj)
miovashil, newborn (n)
mirade, note (n d:text)
miradiu, notably (adv d:text)

miradu, notable (adj d:text)
miraf, shift (n)
mirafu, shifty (adj)
mirafwan, shifter (n doer)
mirak, angle (n)
mirakiu, angularly (adv)
miraku, angular (adj)
mirap, ankle (n)
mirasf, shift (v)
mirask, angle (v)
miravonde, notebook (n)
mirazde, note (v d:text)
mirge, barge (n d:boat)
Miriaf, EhoDay03 (n)
Miriam, Miriam (n)
miriarkiu, sternly (adv d:firm)
miriarku, stern (adj d:firm)
mirmirt, ivory (n)
mirmirtu, ivory (adj)
mirnor, canyon (n)
mirsh, other (n/pron)
mirshfluik, otherwise
    (adj/adv/conj)
mirshu, other (adj/adv)
mirshyek, others (pron)
Mishashirp, Mississippi (n)
Mishigarf, Michigan (n)
Mishuralf, Missouri (n)
miteshk, mulch (n)
miteshsk, mulch (v)
mithk, tail (n)
mithkwan, tailer (n doer)
mithleinarp, tailpipe (n)
mithparlak, tailgate (n)
mithparlask, tailgate (v)
mithshnarp, tailspin (n)
mithsk, tail (v)
mituf, colon (n d:character)
miturme, cologne (n)
miuforst, elbow (v)
miufort, elbow (n)
miunfirf, township (n)
miunkiarf, townhouse (n)
miunkiforp, townfolk (n)
miunkiforpyek, townsfolk (n pl)
miunplorn, townperson (n)
miunplornyek, townspeople (n pl)
miurf, vase (n)
miurn, town (n)
miurp, lumber (n)
miursk, taint (v)
miursp, lumber (v)
miust, flush (v)
miut, flush (v)
miutwan, flusher (n doer)
mivarn, leather (n)
mivarnu, leathery (adj)
mivarth, noodle (n)
moagarn, caramel (n)
moark, sake (n)
moarsk, forsake (v)
moarskyot, forsook (v pa)
mofirt, surgery (n)

mofirtiu, surgically (adv)
mofirtu, surgical (adj)
mofirtwan, surgeon (n doer)
moge, next (adj/adv/prep)
moia, hey (interj)
moiabe, bulb (n)
moiage, bulge (n)
moiamkarp, farmhand (n)
moiamkiarf, farmhouse (n)
moiamraufp, farmland (n)
moiarkiu, drastically (adv)
moiarku, drastic (adj)
moiarme, farm (n)
moiarmwan, farmer (n doer)
moiarp, suite (n)
moiarzme, farm (v)
moiazge, bulge (v)
moidart, pedestrian (n)
moidest, pedal (v)
moidet, pedal (n)
moikarf, radar (n)
moikarsf, radar (v)
moikiork, network (n)
moikiorsk, network (v)
moilaublutish, omnipresence (n)
moilaublutishu, omnipresent (adj)
moilauboirge, omnipotence (n)
moilauboirgu, omnipotent (adj)
moilaudiuarfu, omnivorous (adj)
moilaukuarfku, omnidirectional (adj)
moilaushuarsh, omniscience (n)
moilaushuarshu, omniscient (adj)
moimeviurl, payday (n)
moimfalar, payroll (n)
moimlurift, payload (n)
moimpiruf, paycheck (n)
moimvark, payback (n)
moirap, label (n)
moirapwan, labeler (n doer)
moirasp, label (v)
moirf, swallow (n d:gulp)
moirk, shield (n)
moirme, pay (n)
moirmiu, payably (adv)
moirmu, payable (adj)
moirmuet, payment (n)
moirmuil, payout (n)
moirmunf, payoff (n)
moirmwan, payer (n doer)
moirn, pod (n)
moirp, net (n)
moirsf, swallow (v d:gulp)
moirsk, shield (v)
moirsp, net (v)
moirsth, shine (v)
moirsthyot, shone (v pa)
moirth, shine (n)
moirthu, shiny (adj)
moirthwan, shiner (n doer)
moirve, radiance (n)
moirve, radiation (n)

moirvwan, radiator (n doer)
moirzme, pay (v)
moirzmyot, paid (v pa)
moirzve, radiate (v)
moisharn, MoissanRuby (n)
moishorst, expedite (v)
moishort, expedition (n)
moishortu, expedient (adj)
moishortuet, expedience (n)
moishortuet, expediency (n)
moishortuetiu, expeditiously (adv)
moishortuetu, expeditious (adj)
moiurf, suit (n d:apparel)
moiushuart, suitcase (n)
moivark, radical (n)
moivarkiu, radically (adv)
moivarku, radical (adj)
moivarvu, geiger (adj)
mokashk, loot (n)
mokashkwan, looter (n doer)
mokashsk, loot (v)
mokramp, klutz (n)
mokshoirst, lopside (v)
molaf, fan (n d:move air)
molasf, fan (v d:move air)
molfars, govern (v)
molfarsh, government (n)
molfarshwan, governor (n doer)
Molibdenum, Molybdenum (n)
mols, branch (v)
molsh, branch (n)
molshwan, brancher (n doer)
molsk, lop (v)
Montarnf, Montana (n)
Montrialf, Montreal (n)
Montugoram, Montgomery (n)
morap, suit (n d:accord)
morapiu, suitably (adv d:accord)
morapu, suitable (adj d:accord)
morapuet, suitability (n)
morapwan, suitor (n doer d:accord)
morasp, suit (v d:accord)
morave, pear (n)
morfar, honey (n)
morfmuan, honeymoon (n)
morfmuanwan, honeymooner (n doer)
morfralarde, honeycomb (n)
morfzhishk, honeybee (n)
morkarst, muscle (v)
morkart, muscle (n)
morkartu, muscular (adj)
morlanf, gill (n)
morlirf, euphoria (n)
morlirfu, euphoric (adj)
morshst, balast (v)
morsht, balast (n)
morshtast, balance (v)
morshtat, balance (n)
morth, patience (n d:endurance)
morthiu, patiently (adv

d:endurance)
morthu, patient (adj d:endurance)
moshk, puff (n)
Moshkaurf, Moscow (n)
moshku, puffy (adj)
moshkwan, puffer (n doer)
moshsk, puff (v)
motuyarp, saxophone (n)
moviurl, holiday (n)
mozhge, fang (n)
mozhzge, fangle (v)
muai-, non- (num 9 pref)
mual, huh (interj)
muandaurn, nighttime (n)
muanflaursh, nightlife (n)
muanlifarde, nightshirt (n)
muantraide, nightclub (n)
muanzhailf, nightfall (n)
muarde, voyage (n)
muardwan, voyager (n doer)
muarf, lake (n)
muarn, night (n)
muarnfraik, nightmare (n)
muarnu, nightly (adj)
muarnularat, lakeshore (n)
muarshoirt, lakeside (n)
muarst, shave (v)
muart, shave (n)
muartwan, shaver (n doer)
muarzde, voyage (v)
muashsk, mope (v d:sad)
mudan, bay (n d:place)
mufirp, nest (n)
mufirpwan, nester (n doer)
mufirsk, nestle (v)
mufirsp, nest (v)
mui, nine (num 9 card)
muialfhemka, Number_1e36606
muiarst, swell (v)
muiart, swell (n)
muiashk, prowl (v)
muiashkwan, prowler (n doer)
muiashsk, prowl (v)
muida, ninety (num 90 card)
muidai-, ninety- (num 90 pref)
muideth, ninetieth (num 90 ord)
muifk, novenquadragintillion (num 1e150 card)
muift, noventrigintillion (num 1e120 card)
muika, nonillion (num 1e30 card)
muikai-, weka- (num 1e30 pref)
muiketh, nonillionth (num 1e30 ord)
muipa, nineteen (num 19 card)
muipai-, nineteen- (num 19 pref)
muipeth, nineteenth (num 19 ord)
muirf, niceness (n)
muirf, nicety (n)
muirfiu, nicely (adv)
muirfu, nice (adj)

muirfweku, nicest (adj)
muirfwelu, nicer (adj)
muirsf, nicen (v)
muirsh, mesa (n)
muirt, onion (n)
muishk, novemvigintillion (num 1e90 card)
muishkai-, bianten-
muishketh, novemvigintillionth (num 1e90 ord)
muisht, novemdecillion (num 1e60 card)
muishtai-, liena- (num 1e60 pref)
muishteth, novemdecillionth (num 1e60 ord)
mukoige, elimination (n)
mukoizge, eliminate (v)
muktark, pigeon (n)
Mular, March (n)
muliorn, ceramic (n)
muliornu, ceramic (adj)
mumarsth, cushion (v)
mumarth, cushion (n)
mumarthu, cushy (adj)
mumarthwan, cushioner (n doer)
mumirme, fumble (n)
mumirzme, fumble (v)
mumorf, lull (n)
mumorfliauf, lullaby (n)
mumorsf, lull (v)
munalt, ceremony (n)
munaltiu, ceremonially (adv)
munaltu, ceremonial (adj)
munarn, midnight (n)
munarp, conscience (n)
munarpu, conscionable (adj)
munat, element (n)
munatu, elementary (adj)
muuk, least (adj)
mupank, stubble (n)
muperk, stubbornness (n)
muperkiu, stubbornly (adv)
muperku, stubborn (adj)
murdarn, grimace (n)
murdarnu, grim (adj)
murdarsne, grimace (v)
murfonde, eloquence (n)
murfondiu, eloquently (adv)
murfondu, eloquent (adj)
murfonzde, elocute (v)
murn, mu (n)
murof, hollowness (n)
murofu, hollow (adj)
murosf, hollow (v)
murp, stub (n)
murshk, sleet (n)
murshsk, sleet (v)
mursp, stub (v)
murt, grime (n)
murtu, grimey (adj)
murzhge, grunge (n)
murzhgu, grungy (adj)
mushdin, baldness (n)

mushdinu, bald (adj)
mushdisne, bald (v)
mushirk, patrol (n)
mushirp, mate (n)
mushirsk, patrol (v)
mushirsp, mate (v)
Mushlirm, Muslim (n)
mutharth, carnation (n)
muthiork, carousel (n)
muthk, match (n d:selection)
muthkmenu, matchless (adj d:selection)
muthkwan, matcher (n doer d:selection)
muthnargwan, matchmaker (n doer d:make selection)
muthnarzge, matchmake (v d:make selection)
muthnarzgyot, matchmade (v pa d:make selection)
muthoran, methane (n)
muthsk, match (v d:selection)
mutiktoirk, jawbone (n)
mutirk, jaw (n)
mutirsk, jaw (v)
muviank, carnival (n)
muyarn, niece (n)
muyeth, ninth (num 9 ord)
mwae, na (interj)
nabalst, fuss (v)
nabalt, fuss (n)
nabaltu, fussy (adj)
nabirst, harvest (v)
nabirt, harvest (n)
nabirtwan, harvester (n doer)
nafirp, mold (n d:microbe)
nafirpu, moldy (adj d:microbe)
nafirsk, fester (v)
naftan, harbor (n)
naftan, harbour (n)
naftasne, harbor (v)
nagarge, sogginess (n)
nagargu, soggy (adj)
nagiank, mosquito (n)
nagirve, makeup (n)
naiarp, skewness (n)
naiarsp, skew (v)
naigart, psychiatry (n)
naigartu, psychiatric (adj)
naigartwan, psychiatrist (n doer)
naigerth, psychology (n)
naigerthiu, psychologically (adv)
naigerthu, psychological (adj)
naigerthwan, psychologist (n doer)
naikaushk, psychosis (n)
naikaushketh, psychopathology (n)
naikaushkethwan, psychopathologist (n doer)
naikaushku, psychotic (adj)
naikaushkwan, psycho (n doer)
naikaushkwan, psychopath (n

doer)
naikepliarshp, psychotherapy (n)
naikepliarshpwan, psychotherapist (n doer)
naikomarft, psychoanalysis (n)
naikomarftwan, psychoanalyst (n doer)
nailarf, meadow (n)
nainorf, pilot (n)
nainorsf, pilot (v)
nairk, psyche (n)
nairkwan, psychic (n doer)
nairp, pile (n)
nairpiveil, pileup (n)
nairs, mess (v)
nairsh, mess (n)
nairshu, messy (adj)
nairsk, psych (v)
nairsp, pile (v)
naithkwan, sander (n doer d:abrasion)
naithsk, sand (v d:abrasion)
nakirp, soak (n)
nakirpwan, soaker (n doer)
nakirsp, soak (v)
nalanelirk, mammogram (n)
nalap, mammal (n)
nalaparft, mammography (n)
nalapu, mammalian (adj)
nalirf, shelf (n)
nalirme, horizon (n)
nalirmiu, horizontally (adv)
nalirmu, horizontal (adj)
nalirn, straw (n)
nalirs, deign (v)
nalirsf, shelve (v)
naltrimen, faithlessness (n)
naltrimeniu, faithlessly (adv)
naltrimenu, faithless (adj)
naltrip, faith (n)
naltripiu, faithfully (adv)
naltripu, faithful (adj)
naltripuet, faithfulness (n)
naltrisp, enfaith (v)
Namibiarf, Namibia (n)
namoriu, laterally (adv)
namoru, lateral (adj)
namurbaraft, moonstone (n)
namurduarf, moonbeam (n)
namurf, moon (n)
namurfluan, moonlight (n)
namurfluasne, moonlight (v)
namurmoirth, moonshine (n)
Namurviul, Monday (n)
nanirt, dexterity (n)
nanirtiu, dexterously (adv)
nanirtiu, dextrously (adv)
nanirtu, dexterous (adj)
nanirtu, dextrous (adj)
nanshk, die (n d:number cube)
nanshkyek, dice (n pl d:number cube)
naral, soap (n)

naraliu, soapily (adv)
naralu, soapy (adj)
naransk, sully (v)
narap, rug (n)
naras, soil (v)
narash, soil (n)
narasle, soap (v)
nardast, favor (v)
nardat, favor (n)
nardatu, favorite (adj)
nardatuet, favoritism (n)
nardep, favorite (n)
nardepiu, favorably (adv)
nardepu, favorable (adj)
nargwan, maker (n doer)
narifpwan, loafer (n doer
    d:lounge)
narifsp, loaf (v d:lounge)
narlprekun, soapbox (n)
narmalirt, latter (n)
narmalirtu, latter (adj)
narmirt, lattice (n)
narmurk, latitude (n)
narth, sand (n d:grains)
narthu, sandy (adj d:grains)
narzge, make (v)
narzgyot, made (v pa)
Nashfilf, Nashville (n)
nashirku, dicey (adj d:cube)
nashirsk, dice (v d:cube)
nathart, sandal (n)
nathbaraft, sandstone (n)
nathferap, sandstorm (n)
nathkrairzge, sandblast (v)
nathnufaf, sandbag (n)
nathprekun, sandbox (n)
nathrolart, sandbar (n)
nathvuarp, sandpaper (n)
natrip, fidelity (n)
nau, me (pron 1st sng obj)
naurf, muse (n)
naurfar, museum (n)
naurk, mission (n)
naursf, muse (v)
naushirk, foul (n)
naushirku, foul (adj)
naushirsk, foul (v)
Nebralshk, Nebraska (n)
nefirst, domesticate (v)
nefirt, domestication (n)
nofirtu, domestic (adj)
nefirtwan, domesticator (n doer)
neikarf, metaphor (n)
neikarfu, metaphorical (adj)
neilarf, marvel (n)
neilarfiu, marvelously (adv)
neilarfu, marvelous (adj)
neilarsf, marvel (v)
neilurn, cadet (n)
neirbe, mop (n)
neirde, lane (n)
neirf, tape (n)
neirku, meta (adj)

neirsf, tape (v)
neirzbe, mop (v)
neishk, pal (n)
neist, usher (v)
Neith, Miss (n)
neitwan, usher (n doer)
neivirst, monitor (v)
neivirt, monitor (n)
neiwifk, taper (n)
neiwifsk, taper (v)
nelafk, commerce (n)
nelafkan, commercial (n)
nelafkiu, commercially (adv)
nelafku, commercial (adj)
nelapis, accompany (v)
nelapish, company (n)
nelarn, song (n)
nelarnwan, singer (n doer)
nelarsne, sing (v)
nelarsnyot, sang (v pa)
nelfk, calf (n)
nelfsk, calve (v)
neliloirdwan, songwriter (n doer)
nelirth, clutch (n d:hatch)
nelkarn, grammar (n)
nelkarniu, grammatically (adv)
nelkarnu, grammatical (adj)
nelnan, nanny (n)
nelnasne, nanny (v)
nelsh, else (adj/adv)
nelsholu, elsewhere (adv)
nenirk, number (n)
nenirkel, numeral (n)
nenirkeliu, numerically (adv)
nenirkelu, numeric (adj)
nenirkelu, numerical (adj)
nenirkelwan, numerator (n doer)
nenirkiu, numerously (adv)
nenirku, numerous (adj)
nenirsk, number (v)
nenkuift, numerology (n)
Neodimium, Neodymium (n)
Neon, Neon (n)
Neptunium, Neptunium (n)
nepul, berry (n)
nerp, tap (n)
nerpwan, tapper (n doer)
nersp, tap (v)
nesh, much (adj/adv)
nesh, much (pron)
neshgarf, racket (n d:noise)
Netherlanurde, Netherlands (n)
Nevadarf, Nevada (n)
nia, I (pron 1st sng sub)
niai, we (pron 1st pl sub)
niaishk, prism (n)
nialart, musical (n)
nianart, mirage (n)
niapeferp, mindset (n)
niarf, naivete (n)
niarfiu, naively (adv)
niarfk, miracle (n)
niarfkiu, miraculously (adv)

niarfku, miraculous (adj)
niarfu, naive (adj)
niark, majority (n)
niarku, major (adj)
niarl, music (n)
niarliu, musically (adv)
niarlu, musical (adj)
niarlwan, musician (n doer)
niarme, smartness (n)
niarmiu, smartly (adv)
niarmu, smart (adj)
niarn, mirror (n)
niarnk, funk (n d:music/stench)
niarnku, funky (adj
    d:music/stench)
niarp, mind (n)
niarpemeniu, mindlessly (adv)
niarpemenu, mindless (adj)
niarpiu, mindfully (adv)
niarpu, mindful (adj)
niarshiu, tanto (adv)
niarshk, laceration (n)
niarshsk, lacerate (v)
niarsk, major (v)
niarsne, mirror (v)
niarsp, mind (v)
niart, site (n)
niarzme, smarten (v)
niashdriarde, tantrum (n)
niashniurku, tantamount (adj)
niateshk, tantalization (n)
niateshkwan, tantalizer (n doer)
niateshsk, tantalize (v)
niathk, mint (n)
niathkiu, mintly (adv)
niathku, mint (adj)
niathkwan, minter (n doer)
niathsk, mint (v)
niaukirzhe, pyrotechnic (n)
niaushp, pyromaniac (n)
nielorp, tameness (n)
nielorpu, tame (adj)
nielorsp, tame (v)
niemesp, tamper (v)
nierst, eat (v)
nierstyot, ate (v pa)
niert, eat (n)
niertu, edible (adj)
niertwan, eater (n doer)
niifork, mash (n)
niforkwan, masher (n doer)
niforp, magazine (n d:document)
niforsk, mash (v)
nik, EhoSecond (n)
Nikaraguarn, Nicaraguan (n)
Nikaragurf, Nicaragua (n)
Nikel, Nickel (n)
nikurst, laser (v)
nikurt, laser (n)
nilakart, terminal (n)
nilark, termination (n)
nilarkiu, terminally (adv)
nilarku, terminal (adj)

nilarkwan, terminator (n doer)
nilarsk, terminate (v)
nilbivage, homosexuality (n)
nilbivagu, homosexual (adj)
nilbivagwan, homosexual (n doer)
nilishku, teeny (adj)
nilithku, teensy (adj)
nilkoirk, homicide (n)
nilkoirku, homicidal (adj)
nilorf, series (n)
nilorfiu, serially (adv)
nilorfu, serial (adj)
nilorp, sesame (n)
niluftu, nifty (adj)
nilurbu, gay (adj d:homosexual)
nimarn, menu (n)
nimart, memo (n)
Nimsant, Nimsant
nimshiriu, minutely (adv d:small)
nimshiru, minute (adj d:small)
nimurf, roast (n)
nimurfwan, roaster (n doer)
nimursf, roast (v)
ninaf, fossil (n)
ninarst, tatter (v)
ninasf, fossilize (v)
Niobium, Niobium (n)
niorf, swap (n)
niorfwan, swaper (n doer)
niork, meter (n d:device)
niorkar, metric (n)
niorn, shrine (n)
niornwan, shriner (n doer)
niorp, rhyme (n)
niorpat, rhythm (n)
niorpatiu, rhythmically (adv)
niorpatu, rhythmic (adj)
niorpwan, rhymer (n doer)
niorsf, swap (v)
niorsk, meter (v d:device)
niorsne, enshrine (v)
niorsrhy, rhyme (v)
niorst, shrug (v)
niort, shrug (n)
nioteshk, swat (n)
nioteshsk, swat (v)
niragat, influenza (n)
nirast, address (v)
nirat, address (n)
niratu, addressable (adj)
niratwan, addressor (n doer)
nirshk, need (n)
nirshke kodi, had to (ndal d:need)
nirshke kodi, have to (ndal
   d:need)
nirshke kodi, must (ndal d:need)
nirshkmeniu, needlessly (adv)
nirshkmenu, needless (adj)
nirshku, needful (adj)
nirshku, needy (adj)
nirshsk, need (v)
nirth, lid (n)
nirve, folly (n)

nirve, foolishness (n)
nirviu, foolishly (adv)
nirvu, foolish (adj)
nirvwan, fool (n doer)
nirze, itch (v)
nirzhe, itch (n)
nirzhu, itchy (adj)
nirzve, fool (v)
nishort, tininess (n)
nishortu, tiny (adj)
nitaruin, addressee (n)
Nitrogen, Nitrogen (n)
niudaft, moat (n)
niudank, mound (n)
niugiuft, mountain (n)
niugiuftu, mountainous (adj)
niugiuftwan, mountaineer (n
   doer)
niugiutedaurp, mountaintop (n)
niugiutshoirt, mountainside (n)
niulort, plenum (n)
niulortu, plenary (adj)
niunirf, abundance (n)
niunirfiu, abundantly (adv)
niunirfu, abundant (adj)
niurf, firmness (n d:steady)
niurfiu, firmly (adv d:steady)
niurfu, firm (adj d:steady)
niurfweku, firmest (adj)
niurfwelu, firmer (adj)
niurk, mount (n)
niurn, plenty (n)
niurnu, plentiful (adj)
niurp, minority (n)
niurpu, minor (adj)
niurs, flash (v)
niursf, firm (v d:steady)
niursh, flash (n)
niurshiu, flashily (adv)
niurshu, flashy (adj)
niurshwan, flasher (n doer)
niursk, mount (v)
niursp, minor (v)
niurt, stadium (n)
niurzme, sow (v)
niushfluan, flashlight (n)
niushvark, flashback (n)
niuthk, snack (n)
niuthsk, snack (v)
Nivar, EhoMonth09 (n)
nivefliorfu, foolproof (adj)
nivifk, moron (n)
nivifku, moronic (adj)
nivkelifort, foolhardiness (n)
nivkelifortu, foolhardy (adj)
nivube, charm (n)
nivubwan, charmer (n doer)
nivuzbe, charm (v)
noan, dib (n)
Nobelium, Nobelium (n)
noersh, loaf (n d:bread)
Nofefar, November (n)
noiashsk, skewer (n)

noiashsk, skewer (v)
noihem, Number_1e3006
noil, N (let sng)
noili, Ns (let pl)
noink, mayhem (n)
noinsk, maim (v)
noipan, mayor (n)
noipanu, mayoral (adj)
noiral, nylon (n)
noirf kodi, may (ndal
   d:permission)
noirf, permission (n)
noirk, lack (n)
noirme, savage (n)
noirmiu, savagely (adv)
noirmu, savage (adj)
noirs, rinse (v)
noirsh, rinse (n)
noirshwan, rinser (n doer)
noirsk, lack (v)
noirth, race (n d:human)
noirthiu, racially (adv d:human)
noirthu, racial (adj d:human)
noishirk, rhetoric (n)
noishirkiu, rhetorically (adv)
noishirku, rhetorical (adj)
noithart, racism (n)
noithartwan, racist (n doer)
nolan, claim (n)
nolanwan, claimant (n doer)
nolarf, fellow (n)
nolarfif, fellowship (n)
nolasne, claim (v)
nolirk, grain (n)
nolirku, grainy (adj)
nolkiern, gravy (n)
nolthaush, wallflower (n)
nolthk, wall (n)
nolthsk, wall (v)
nolthvuarp, wallpaper (n)
nolthvuarsp, wallpaper (v)
nomarge, liver (n)
norage, rack (n)
noragwan, racker (n doer)
norak, rig (n)
norakwan, rigger (n doer)
norask, rig (v)
norazge, rack (v)
norde, court (n)
nordkiarf, courthouse (n)
nordshranf, courtroom (n)
norduen, courtesy (n)
nordueniu, courteously (adv)
norduenu, courteous (adj)
norfip, jealousy (n)
norfipiu, jealously (adv)
norfipu, jealous (adj)
norgairst, racketeer (v)
norgairtwan, racketeer (n doer)
norgarf, racket (n d:bat, group)
norgarf, racquet (n)
norgarfu, rackety (adj d:bat,
   group)

norirp, rag (n)
norirpiu, raggedy (adv)
norirsp, rag (v)
norkart, sergeant (n)
norlthauthk, courtyard (n)
normark, salvation (n)
normarsk, salvage (v)
nornarn, sandwich (n)
nornarsne, sandwich (v)
norpegairvu, ragtag (adj)
norpyurk, ragweed (n)
norst, dry (v)
nort, dryness (n)
nortnolthk, drywall (n)
nortu, dry (adj)
nortwan, drier (n doer)
nortwan, dryer (n doer)
nortweku, driest (adj)
nortwelu, drier (adj)
norvoshk, courtship (n)
Norwaifarn, Norwegian (n)
Norwairf, Norway (n)
norzde, court (v)
norzhailf, drizzle (n)
norzhailsf, drizzle (v)
noshk, man (n d:male)
noshku, manly (adj d:male)
noshkyek, men (n pl d:male)
noshtairge, manure (n)
nothk, muff (n)
nothkast, muffle (v)
nothkatwan, muffler (n doer)
nothsk, muff (v)
novinshiop, molehill (n)
novirn, mole (n)
novirsne, mole (v)
novist, minister (v)
novit, ministry (n)
novitwan, minister (n doer)
nuafk, void (n)
nuafsk, void (v)
nuanirk, discrimination (n)
nuanirkwan, discriminator (n
    doer)
nuanirsk, discriminate (v)
nuanirst, incriminate (v)
nuanirt, incrimination (n)
Nuarak, Newark (n)
nuarbak, rivalry (n)
nuarbe, rival (n)
nuart, moss (n)
nuarfu, mossy (adj)
nuarn, crime (n)
nuarnwan, criminal (n doer)
nuarsh, rite (n)
nuarsne, criminalize (v)
nuarzbe, rival (v)
nuats, ritualize (v)
nuatsh, ritual (n)
nuatshu, ritualistic (adj)
nufaf, bag (n)
nufafiu, baggily (adv)
nufafu, baggy (adj)

nufafwan, bagger (n doer)
nufal, festival (n)
nufalu, festive (adj)
nufaluet, festivity (n)
nufarf, baggage (n)
nufarfwan, baggager (n doer)
nufarsf, baggage (v)
nufasf, bag (v)
nufirk, mush (n)
nufirp, ink (n)
nufirpu, inky (adj)
nufirpwan, inker (n doer)
nufirsk, mush (v)
nufirskaut, mushed (v prp)
nufirsp, ink (v)
nufirst, lever (v)
nufirt, lever (n)
nufirtar, leverage (n)
nufirtasre, leverage (v)
nufnifk, mishmash (n)
nufobeirstaut, biet (v prp)
nufobeirtu, hetergeneous (adj)
nufshmonde, mushroom (n)
nugage, crap (n)
nugagu, crappy (adj)
nugarn, lung (n)
nugazge, crap (v)
nui, my (pron 1st sng pos sub)
nuiblar, madam (n)
nuiblar, madame (n)
nuifal, myself (pron 1st sng refl)
nuime, mine (pron 1st sng pos
    obj)
nuirk, tank (n)
nuirkwan, tanker (n doer)
nuirsk, tank (v)
nuish, our (pron 1st pl pos sub)
nukirf, physics (n)
nukirfiu, physically (adv)
nukirfu, physical (adj)
nularast, shore (v)
nularat, shore (n)
nularn, lease (n)
nularnuin, lessee (n)
nularnwan, leaser (n doer)
nularnwan, lessor (n doer)
nularsne, lease (v)
nulartroifk, shoreline (n)
nulas, dawn (v)
nulash, dawn (n)
nulbugor, combustion (n)
nulbugoru, combustible (adj)
nulbugosre, combust (v)
nulgeralst, combat (v)
nulgeralt, combat (n)
nulgeraltiu, combatively (adv)
nulgeraltu, combative (adj)
nulgeraltwan, combatant (n doer)
nulirk, leash (n)
nulirsk, leash (v)
nulirst, exist (v)
nulirt, existence (n)
numark, javelin (n)

numart, plus (adj/prep)
numart, plus (n)
nurabeirlaku, multipurpose (adj)
nurabiarzhu, multiparty (adj)
nurafruifkwatu, multiplayer (adj)
nuragalurtu, multilevel (adj)
nurakarlf, multinational (n)
nurakarlfu, multinational (adj)
nuralaidark, multimedia (n)
nuralirolfu, multicolor (adj)
nuralirolsf, multicolor (v)
nuranoirthu, multiracial (adj)
nuraprashtu, multifunctional
    (adj)
nurashaiarshu, multistate (adj)
nuratafirku, multicultural (adj)
nuratafirsk, multiculture (v)
nuratuamat, multichannel (n)
nuraviarthaku, multilingual (adj)
nureln, grin (n)
nurelsne, grin (v)
nurfu, nee (adj)
nurfu, née (adj)
nuribe, multiple (n)
nuribu, multiple (adj)
nuribuet, multiplication (n)
nuribwan, multiplier (n doer)
nurituet, multitude (n)
nurituetu, multitude (adj)
nurizbe, multiply (v)
nurlarst, grit (v)
nurlart, grit (n)
nurlartu, gritty (adj)
nurme, dullness (n)
nurmu, dull (adj)
nurn, nu (n)
nurp, bin (n)
nurth, mitt (n)
nurve, jar (n)
nurzme, dull (v)
nurzve, jar (v)
nushirk, sneak (n)
nushirkiu, sneakily (adv)
nushirku, sneaky (adj)
nushirkwan, sneaker (n doer)
nushirp, dusk (n)
nushirsk, sneak (v)
nushirskyot, snuck (v pa)
nushtark, allegation (n)
nushtarkwan, alleger (n doer)
nushtarsk, allege (v)
nutarf, legit (n)
nutarfk, legitimacy (n)
nutarfkiu, legitimately (adv)
nutarfku, legitimate (adj)
nutarfsk, legitimize (v)
nutarfu, legit (adj)
nutark, legality (n)
nutarkiu, legally (adv)
nutarku, legal (adj)
nutarsk, legalize (v)
nutersh, party (n d:group)
nutharf, mitten (n)

nuthirkwan, puker (n doer)
nuthirsk, puke (v)
nutrafst, yoke (v)
nutraft, yoke (n)
nuyern, noun (n)
obeinarbe, abdomen (n)
obiabe, aloud (adv)
obiarp, alarm (n)
obiarpwan, alarmist (n doer)
obiarsp, alarm (v)
oblaithpu, around (adv/prep)
obolirp, absorption (n)
obolirpwan, absorbant (n doer)
obolirpwan, absorber (n doer)
obolirsp, absorb (v)
oborast, advise (v)
oborat, advice (n)
oboratiu, advisably (adv)
oboratu, advisable (adj)
oboratwan, adviser (n doer)
oboratwan, advisor (n doer)
obortarn, advisory (n)
obotarfk, apathy (n)
obotarfku, apathetic (adj)
odalpiarfiu, asynchronously (adv)
odalpiarfu, asynchronous (adj)
odialme, adolescence (n)
odialmu, adolescent (adj)
odialmwan, adolescent (n doer)
odiaurf, amazement (n)
odiaursf, amaze (v)
odorabe, abroad (n)
odorabiu, abroad (adv)
odrukerst, apprehend (v)
odrukert, apprehension (n)
odrukertiu, apprehensively (adv)
odrukertu, apprehensive (adj)
odufirkwan, avenger (n doer)
odufirsk, avenge (v)
ofadelirk, assortment (n)
ofadelirsk, assort (v)
ofarn, aspirin (n)
ofbrunsf, append (v)
ofdaurf, aspiration (n)
ofdaursf, aspire (v)
ofelarve, approval (n)
ofelarvwan, approver (n doer)
ofelarzve, approve (v)
ofialorst, assume (v)
ofialort, assumption (n)
ofien, alone (adj/adv)
ofirk, aptitude (n)
ofirkiu, aptly (adv)
ofirku, apt (adj)
oflaurde, approach (n)
oflaurdu, approachable (adj)
oflaurdwan, approacher (n doer)
oflaurzde, approach (v)
oflikirme, appropriation (n)
oflikirmiu, appropriately (adv)
oflikirmu, appropriate (adj)
oflikirmwan, appropriator (n doer)

oflikirzme, appropriate (v)
ofloigarst, approximate (v)
ofloigart, approximation (n)
ofloigartiu, approximately (adv)
ofloigartu, approximate (adj)
oflork, mean (n d:average)
ofpuerst, appetize (v)
ofpuert, appetite (n)
ofshark, applause (n)
ofsharkwan, applauder (n doer)
ofsharsk, applaud (v)
ogaifirt, abruptness (n)
ogaifirtiu, abruptly (adv)
ogaifirtu, abrupt (adj)
ogalirp, attire (n)
ogalirsp, attire (v)
ogalirst, attract (v)
ogalirt, attraction (n)
ogalirtiu, attractively (adv)
ogalirtu, attractive (adj)
ogalirtwan, attractor (n doer)
ogauirk, aberration (n)
ogauirku, aberrant (adj)
ogavarst, abolish (v)
ogavart, abolition (n)
ogavartwan, abolitionist (n doer)
ogianirk, accommodation (n)
ogianirkiu, accommodatively (adv)
ogianirku, accommodative (adj)
ogianirkwan, accommodator (n doer)
ogianirsk, accommodate (v)
ogiarp, abatement (n)
ogiarsp, abate (v)
oglerk, acknowledgment (n)
oglersk, acknowledge (v)
ogralf, acorn (n)
ogralirst, abstract (v)
ogralirt, abstract (n)
ogralirtu, abstract (adj)
ogralirtwan, abstractor (n doer)
ogralirtyek, abstract (n pl)
ogverst, access (v)
ogvert, access (n)
ogvertu, accessible (adj)
ogvertwan, accessory (n doer)
oifk, oops (interj)
oilodarfk, autograph (n)
oilodarfsk, autograph (v)
oilodatun, automobile (n)
oilodatunu, automotive (adj)
oilodekin, automation (n)
oilodekiniu, automatically (adv)
oilodekinu, automatic (adj)
oilodekinwan, automator (n doer)
oilodekisne, automate (v)
oilodekorin, automatic (n)
oilonargwan, automaker (n doer)
oiloviern, autonomy (n)
oiparp, alteration (n)
oiparsp, alter (v)
oir frelp kodi, cannot (ndal

d:ability)
oir, not (parcl)
okalirf, astonishment (n)
okalirsf, astonish (v)
okalirsfyot, astonish (v pa)
okark, ass (n)
okauaishst, abhor (v)
okauaisht, abhorrence (n)
okauaishtu, abhorrent (adj)
okeftiu, ahead (adv)
okerage, agony (n)
okerazge, agonize (v)
Okigen, Oxygen (n)
Okiorf, Ohio (n)
Oklakorm, Oklahoma (n)
Oklanurd, Oakland (n)
oklirast, accent (v)
oklirast, accentuate (v)
oklirat, accent (n)
oklofalt, agriculture (n)
oklofaltu, agricultural (adj)
okraurgu, ablaze (adj)
okriarf, acquaintance (n)
okriarsf, acquaint (v)
okriushk, abduction (n)
okriushkwan, abductor (n doer)
okriushsk, abduct (v)
okuan, again (adv)
okuank, against (prep)
olanirf, abnormality (n)
olanirfiu, abnormally (adv)
olanirfu, abnormal (adj)
olarak, assignment (n)
olarakwan, assigner (n doer)
olarask, assign (v)
olarp, assurance (n)
olarpiu, assuratively (adv)
olarpu, assurative (adj)
olarpwan, assurer (n doer)
olarsp, assure (v)
olaume, among (prep)
olaume, amongst (prep)
oldarade, apology (n)
oldaradu, apolitical (adj)
oldarazde, apoliticize (v)
oldidarn, assimilation (n)
oldidarnwan, assimilator (n doer)
oldidarsne, assimilate (v)
oldorderst, apologize (v)
oldordert, apology (n)
oldordertiu, apologetically (adv)
oldordertu, apologetic (adj)
olenorp, arithmetic (n)
olenorpwan, arithmetician (n doer)
olfershfif, apartheid (n)
olfershu, apart (adj)
olfesharlt, apartment (n)
olipoilf, array (n)
olipoilsf, array (v)
olirak, ascent (n)
olirakuet, ascension (n)
olirakwan, ascender (n doer)

olirask, ascend (v)
olsharst, assert (v)
olshart, assertation (n)
olshartiu, assertively (adv)
olshartu, assertive (adj)
oluirs, arise (v)
oluirsyot, arose (v pa)
olzhorde, asset (n)
omakelirp, antique (n)
omarfst, analyze (v)
omarft, analysis (n)
omarftiu, analytically (adv)
omarftu, analytical (adj)
omarftwan, analyst (n doer)
omarftwan, analyzer (n doer)
omarshk, anecdote (n)
omarshkiu, anecdotally (adv)
omarshku, anecdotal (adj)
omdoirp, anguish (n)
omdoirsp, anguish (v)
ome, an (det)
omegarn, omega (n)
omeirf, association (n)
omeirfwan, associate (n doer)
omeirsf, associate (v)
omikroln, omicron (n)
omiorp, ancient (n)
omiorpu, ancient (adj)
omirade, annotation (n)
omirazde, annotate (v)
omirshu, another (adj)
omkadreirfu, antitrust (adj)
omkamierk, antibiotic (n)
omkarmk, antidote (n)
omkarnf, antenna (n)
omkashlarde, antibody (n)
omkaviern, antonym (n)
omklaparn, antiquity (n)
omlarlk, ancestry (n)
omlarlku, ancestral (adj)
omlarlkwan, ancestor (n doer)
omorst, arrange (v)
omort, arrangement (n)
omortwan, arranger (n doer)
omshelirk, anticipation (n)
omshelirsk, anticipate (v)
omudenirk, animation (n)
omudenirkwan, animator (n doer)
omudenirsk, animate (v)
omufege, annoyance (n)
omufezge, annoy (v)
omurfst, announce (v)
omurft, announcement (n)
omurftwan, announcer (n doer)
omurn, animal (n)
ona, one (pron 3rd indefpers sng obj)
ona, one (pron 3rd indefpers sng sub)
Onaf, Mendelevium (n davoka)
Onak, Neptunium (n davoka)
onalpark, alertness (n)

onamu, a.m. (adj)
Onap, Actinum (n davoka)
onar, them/people (pron 3rd indefpers pl obj)
onar, they/people (pron 3rd indefpers pl sub)
onarlp, alert (n)
onarlpwan, alerter (n doer)
onarlsp, alert (v)
onash, one's (pron 3rd indefpers sng pos obj)
onash, one's (pron 3rd indefpers sng pos sub)
onash, people's (pron 3rd indefpers pl pos obj)
onash, people's (pron 3rd indefpers pl pos sub)
onashfal, oneself (pron 3rd indefpers sng refl)
onashfar, peopleselves (pron 3rd indefpers pl refl)
Onat, Berkelium (n davoka)
onerk, ark (n)
Onif, Nobelium (n davoka)
Onik, Plutonium (n davoka)
Onip, Thorium (n davoka)
Onit, Californium (n davoka)
oniurk, amount (n)
oniursk, amount (v)
Onok, Americium (n davoka)
onolan, acclaimation (n)
onolasne, acclaim (v)
Onop, Protactinium (n davoka)
Onot, Einsteinium (n davoka)
Ontariorf, Ontario (n)
Onuk, Curium (n davoka)
onularat, ashore (n)
Onup, Uranium (n davoka)
Onut, Fermium (n davoka)
opairk, attachment (n)
opairsk, attach (v)
opairst, attack (v)
opairt, attack (n)
opairtwan, attacker (n doer)
oparforp, alternative (n)
oparforpiu, alternatively (adv)
oparforpu, alternative (adj)
oparforpwan, alternator (n doer)
oparforsp, alternate (v)
opifork, attendance (n)
opiforkuet, attention (n)
opiforkuetiu, attentively (adv)
opiforkuetu, attentive (adj)
opiforkwan, attendant (n doer)
opiforsk, attend (v)
opiorl, away (adj/adv)
opirfst, attain (v)
opirft, attainment (n)
opliarn, appearance (n)
opliarniu, apparently (adv)
opliarnu, apparent (adj)
opliarnwan, apparition (n doer)

opliarsne, appear (v)
oploshsk, abridge (v)
oprushel, asleep (adj)
optelorp, appeal (n)
optelorsp, appeal (v)
Oraf, Thulium (n davoka)
Orak, Promethium (n davoka)
Orandorf, Orlando (n)
Orap, Lanthanum (n davoka)
Orat, Terbium (n davoka)
orazhe, along (prep/adv)
orazhoirt, alongside (adv/prep)
ordorfirsk, accustom (v)
orduirp, alloy (n)
orduirsp, alloy (v)
orfe, O (let sng)
orfhem, Number_1e606
orfi, Os (let pl)
orflauft, alive (adj)
orfliarn, affiliate (n)
orfliarnuet, affiliation (n)
orfliarsne, affiliate (v)
orgoishst, accuse (v)
orgoisht, accusation (n)
orgoishtiu, accusingly (adv)
orgoishtuin, accused (n)
orgoishtwan, accuser (n doer)
orgurshk, allure (n)
orgurshsk, allure (v)
oribiurme, subpoena (n)
oriblesh, subclass (n)
oribronf, subgroup (n)
oridiarthu, subacute (adj)
Orif, Ytterbium (n davoka)
orifaiorfu, subionic (adj)
orifalirp, suburb (n)
orifalirpu, suburban (adj)
orifalirpuet, suburbanization (n)
orifalirsp, suburbanize (v)
oriferp, subset (n)
orifruart, subplot (n)
origalirst, subtract (v)
origalirt, subtraction (n)
origalirtwan, subtractor (n doer)
origizhaurk, submachine (n)
origizhaurku, submachine (adj)
origlart, subcontract (n)
origlartwan, subcontractor (n doer)
Orlgorn, Oregon (n)
origugiforp, subcompact (n)
origugiforpu, subcompact (adj)
Orik, Samarium (n davoka)
orikeirp, subconsciousness (n)
orikeirpu, subconscious (adj)
orikifiaishk, subdivision (n)
orikifiaishkwan, subdivider (n doer)
orikifiaishsk, subdivide (v)
orikirask, subdue (v)
orikofitarn, subservience (n)
orikofitarniu, subserviently (adv)
orikofitarnu, subservient (adj)

orilafirp, submersion (n)
orilafirpu, submersible (adj)
orilafirpul, submersible (n)
orilafirsp, submerge (v)
orilersk, sublet (v)
orilerskyot, sublet (v pa)
oriliaurn, submarine (n)
orilikuet, subjectivity (n)
orilikuetiu, subjectively (adv)
orilikuetu, subjective (adj)
orilirk, subject (n)
orimedmot, subcontinent (n)
orinork, submission (n)
orinorkiu, submissively (adv)
orinorku, submissive (adj)
orinorkwan, submitter (n doer)
orinorsk, submit (v)
orinularn, sublease (n)
orinularsne, sublease (v)
oriothralve, subassembly (n)
Orip, Cerium (n davoka)
oriplairp, substrate (n)
oriplenirkwan, subcommittee (n doer)
oripliorl, subway (n)
orisharshturk, subsystem (n)
orisherge, subscription (n)
orishergwan, subscriber (n doer)
orisherzge, subscribe (v)
orishkeialst, subordinate (v)
orishkeialt, subordination (n)
orishkeialtwan, subordinate (n doer)
orishlukerst, substation (v)
orishlukert, substation (n)
orishoirst, subside (v)
orishorl, subhuman (n)
orishpelorst, substitute (v)
orishpelort, substitution (n)
orishpelortwan, substitute (n doer)
orishtairp, subtitle (n)
orishtairsp, subtitle (v)
orishtirbe, subtext (n)
orishtirzbe, subtext (v)
orishufirt, subsequence (n)
orishufirtiu, subsequently (adv)
orishufirtu, subsequent (adj)
Orit, Dysprosium (n davoka)
oritafirk, subculture (n)
oritelirk, subsistence (n)
oritelirsk, subsist (v)
oritersp, subject (v)
oritharak, subversion (n d:undercut)
oritharakiu, subversively (adv d:undercut)
oritharaku, subversive (adj d:undercut)
oritharakul, subversive (n)
oritharask, subvert (v d:undercut)
oritharfelt, subversion (n d:lower version)

orithisharl, subsection (n)
orithisharsle, subsection (v)
orithrelf, subsurface (n)
orithrelsf, subsurface (v)
oritilarsh, subterra (n)
oritilarshu, subterranean (adj)
oritimortu, subatomic (adj)
oritrelp, substance (n)
oritrelpiu, substantially (adv)
oritrelpiu, substantively (adv)
oritrelpu, substantial (adj)
oritrelpu, substantive (adj)
oritrelpuet, substantiation (n)
oritrelsp, substantiate (v)
orivinst, sublime (v)
orivintiu, subliminally (adv)
orivintu, subliminal (adj)
orkadarn, accordance (n)
orkadart, altitude (n)
orkarde, accord (n)
orkardiu, accordingly (adv)
orkarzde, accord (v)
orkirk, affliction (n)
orkirku, afflictive (adj)
orkirsk, afflict (v)
orkrafp, allotment (n)
orkrafsp, allot (v)
orkuift, analog (n)
orkuitarn, analogy (n)
orlarp, assessment (n)
orlarpiu, assessively (adv)
orlarpu, assessive (adj)
orlarpwan, assessor (n doer)
orlarsp, assess (v)
ormiarsht, affluence (n)
ormiarshtiu, affluently (adv)
ormiarshtu, affluent (adj)
ornarve, amateur (n)
ornarvu, amateurish (adj)
orniarl, amusement (n)
orniarsle, amuse (v)
orniork, altimeter (n)
orniurf, affirmation (n)
orniurfiu, affirmatively (adv)
orniurfu, affirmative (adj)
orniurfwan, affirmer (n doer)
orniursf, affirm (v)
oroifk, alignment (n)
oroifsk, align (v)
Orok, Europium (n davoka)
Orop, Praseodymium (n davoka)
Orot, Holmium (n davoka)
orp, of (prep)
orpoinf, account (n)
orpoinfu, accountable (adj)
orpoinfwan, accountant (n doer)
orpoinsf, account (v)
orsh, also (adv/conj)
orshairp, allocation (n)
orshairpwan, allocator (n doer)
orshairsp, allocate (v)
orshirl, answer (n)
orshirp, acceptance (n)

orshirpiu, acceptably (adv)
orshirpu, acceptable (adj)
orshirsle, answer (v)
orshirsp, accept (v)
orshkarf, amendment (n)
orshkarsf, amend (v)
orthp, elf (n)
Oruk, Gadolinium (n davoka)
Orup, Neodymium (n davoka)
orushst, allude (v)
orusht, allusion (n)
Orut, Erbium (n davoka)
orvishorst, ashame (v)
orvishort, ashameness (n)
oshalf, alike (adj/adv)
oshklauk, across (prep/adj/adv)
oshlerf, awareness (n)
oshlerfu, aware (adj)
oshmarn, agnosis (n)
oshmarnu, agnostic (adj)
Oshmium, Osmium (n)
oshnarl, alias (n)
oshoirt, aside (n)
oshoirtiu, aside (adv)
oshriauku, afire (adj)
otarve, attrition (n)
otarvu, attritional (adj)
otarzve, attrite (v)
Otawarf, Ottawa (n)
otelirk, assist (v)
otelirkiu, assistively (adv)
otelirku, assistive (adj)
otelirkwan, assistant (n doer)
otelirkyek, assistance (n pl)
otelirsk, assist (v)
otharak, aversion (n)
otharask, avert (v)
otherst, acquire (v)
othert, acquisition (n)
othertwan, acquirer (n doer)
othoishst, abbreviate (v)
othoisht, abbreviation (n)
othral, affair (n)
othralve, assembly (n)
othralvwan, assembler (n doer)
othralzve, assemble (v)
othriurp, attribute (n)
othriurpiu, attributively (adv)
othriurpu, attributive (adj)
othriurpwan, attributor (n doer)
othriursp, attribute (v)
othurk, aspect (n)
otreidal, acclimation (n)
otreidasle, acclimate (v)
otshan, although (conj)
ovafirst, attempt (n)
ovafirt, attempt (v)
ovairst, achieve (v)
ovairt, achievement (n)
ovairtu, achievable (adj)
ovairtwan, achiever (n doer)
ovart, apron (n)
oveip, about (prep/adv/adj)

ovil, after (prep/adj/adv)
ovilhaush, afterward (adv)
ovilhaush, afterwards (adv)
ovimidort, afternoon (n)
ovimidortu, afternoon (adj)
ovirap, affection (n)
ovirapiu, affectionately (adv)
ovirapu, affectionate (adj)
ovirast, affect (v)
ovirat, affect (n)
ovoburge, aggravation (n)
ovoburzge, aggravate (v)
ovoiburge, agitation (n)
ovoiburgwan, agitator (n doer)
ovoiburzge, agitate (v)
ovorage, aggression (n)
ovoragiu, aggressively (adv)
ovoragu, aggressive (adj)
ovoragwan, aggressor (n doer)
ovoralt, accelerate (v)
ovoralt, acceleration (n)
ovoraltniok, accelerometer (n)
ovoraltwan, accelerator (n doer)
ovorazge, aggress (v)
ovramirp, abandonment (n)
ovramirsp, abandon (v)
ovurk, abuse (n)
ovurkiu, abusively (adv)
ovurku, abusive (adj)
ovurkwan, abuser (n doer)
ovursk, abuse (v)
oyalirsf, await (v)
ozharf, amid (prep)
ozharf, amidst (prep)
padar, luck (n)
padariu, luckily (adv)
padarmenu, luckless (adj)
padaru, lucky (adj)
padarweku, luckiest (adj)
padarwelu, luckier (adj)
padasre, luck (v)
paf, fad (n)
pafel, bass (n d:fish)
pafirk, fiction (n)
pafirkiu, fictionally (adv)
pafirku, fictional (adj)
pafirku, fictitious (adj)
pafirsk, fictionalize (v)
pafirst, fit (v d:match)
pafirt, fit (n d:match)
pafırtwan, fitter (n doer d:match)
pagloirk, acquittal (n)
pagloirsk, acquit (v)
paiarst, pike (v)
paiart, pike (n)
paibark, tactic (n)
paibarkiu, tactically (adv)
paibarku, tactical (adj)
paibarkwan, tactician (n doer)
paibarst, tactilate (v)
paibart, tactilation (n)
paibartu, tactile (adj)
painar, bowl (n d:container,

bend)
painasre, bowl (v d:container,
   bend)
pairbe, tact (n)
pairbiu, tactfully (adv)
pairbu, tactful (adj)
pairf, coin (n)
pairsf, coin (v)
pairst, tack (v)
pairt, tack (n)
pairth, satellite (n)
pairtu, tacky (adj)
pairve, federation (n)
pairviu, federally (adv)
pairvu, federal (adj)
pairzhe, beige (n)
pairzhu, beige (adj)
pairzve, federate (v)
paishk, vial (n)
paitarst, tackle (v)
paitart, tackle (n)
paitartwan, tackler (n doer)
Pakishtarn, Pakistan (n)
paktiern, knockdown (n)
Paladium, Palladium (n)
Paleshtirf, Palestine (n)
Paleshtirn, Palestinian (n)
palfk, brick (n)
palfkwan, bricklayer (n doer)
palfsk, brick (v)
palork, fabric (n)
paltark, activation (n)
paltarkiu, actively (adv)
paltarku, active (adj)
paltarkwan, activist (n doer)
paltarsk, activate (v)
paluf, cloud (n)
palufu, cloudy (adj)
palusf, cloud (v)
pamel, friend (n)
pamelfif, friendship (n)
pamelu, friendly (adj)
pameluet, friendliness (n)
pamelwan, friend (n doer)
pamesle, befriend (v)
Panamarn, Panamanian (n)
Panarm, Panama (n)
panirk, tiredness (n d:fatigue)
panirkmenu, tireless (adj
   d:fatigueless)
panirku, tiresome (adj d:fatigue)
panirsk, tire (v d:fatigue)
panran, ribbon (n)
parfk, dramatization (n)
parfp, drama (n)
parfpiu, dramatically (adv)
parfpliorl, parkway (n)
parfpu, dramatic (adj)
parfsp, dramatize (v)
pariank, sleigh (n)
parilf, park (n d:playground)
Parilsh, Paris (n)
paritoirn, symptom (n)

paritoirnu, symptomatic (adj)
pariup, slipper (n)
parlaf, chocolate (n)
parlafu, chocolate (adj)
parlak, gate (n)
parlakip, gateway (n)
parlaklorfwan, gatekeeper (n
   doer)
parlarp, sympathy (n)
parlarpu, sympathetic (adj)
parlarpwan, sympathizer (n doer)
parlarsp, sympathize (v)
parlask, gate (v)
parlirst, symbolize (v)
parlirt, symbol (n)
parlirtiu, symbolically (adv)
parlirtu, symbolic (adj)
parlirtuet, symbolism (n)
parlufk, palate (n)
parlufku, palatable (adj)
parluyarp, symphony (n)
parluyarpu, symphonic (adj)
parme, pie (n)
parporft, symmetry (n)
parporftiu, symmetrically (adv)
parporftu, symmetrical (adj)
parsh, food (n)
partsha, gotcha (interj)
parume, snail (n)
parve, feed (n)
parvwan, feeder (n doer)
parze, buzz (v d:haircut)
parzhe, buzz (n d:haircut)
parzhu, buzz (adj d:haircut)
parzve, feed (v)
pashap, feast (n)
pashapwan, feaster (n doer)
pashasp, feast (v)
pashk, knock (n)
pashkuil, knockout (n)
pashkwan, knocker (n doer)
pashplerth, foodstuff (n)
pashsk, knock (v)
patark, stomach (n)
patil, act (n)
patilior, actuality (n)
patilioriu, actually (adv)
patilioru, actual (adj)
patiliosre, actualize (v)
patilor, activity (n)
patiluet, action (n)
patilwan, actor (n doer)
patilwan, actress (n doer)
patisle, act (v)
pauark, gargle (n)
pauars, gush (v)
pauarsh, gush (n)
pauarshwan, gusher (n doer)
pauarsk, gargle (v)
paufst, gut (v)
pauft, gut (n)
pauftmenu, gutless (adj)
pauftu, gutsy (adj)

paugart, cavity (n)
pauirk, gag (n d:joke)
paulop, burial (n)
paulosp, bury (v)
paunirf, bounce (n)
paunirfiu, bouncily (adv)
paunirfu, bouncy (adj)
paunirfwan, bouncer (n doer)
paunirsf, bounce (v)
pauorfk, gurgle (n)
pauorfsk, gurgle (v)
paupaurk, juggle (n)
paupaurkwan, juggler (n doer)
paupaursk, juggle (v)
paupime, bind (n d:constrain)
paupimu, bound (adj d:constrain)
paupimwan, binder (n doer
   d:constrain)
paupirme, bound (n d:limit)
paupirme, boundary (n d:limit)
paupirmenu, boundless (adj)
paupizme, bind (v d:constrain)
paupizmyot, bound (v pa
   d:constrain)
paurf, macro (n)
paurge, cave (n)
paurgil, cavern (n)
paurguest, cavitate (v)
paurguet, cavitation (n)
paurgwan, caver (n doer)
paurk, joke (n)
paurkwan, joker (n doer)
paursk, joke (v)
paurzge, cave (v)
paushsk, douse (v)
pautufp, gutter (n)
pavark, feedback (n)
pavuarp, napkin (n)
peblarn, landlady (n)
pefkfiaushk, dishwasher (n)
pefkfiaushsk, dishwash (v)
peglarfk, landmass (n)
peiabolsk, knead (v)
peiamur, donut (n)
peiamur, doughnut (n)
peiarn, dough (n)
peiarst, rouse (v)
peifrelp, viability (n)
peifrelpiu, viably (adv)
peifrelpu, viable (adj)
peihem, Number_1e1806
peikark, virility (n)
peikarku, virile (adj)
peikarn, vigor (n)
peikarniu, vigorously (adv)
peikarnu, vigorous (adj)
peikarp, verve (n)
peikriushk, viaduct (n)
peil, P (let sng)
peilarf, vine (n)
peilarsf, vine (v)
peilarth, virgin (n)
peili, Ps (let pl)

peilnork, vinegar (n)
peilraufp, vineland (n)
peilthauthk, vineyard (n)
peirf, pink (n)
peirfu, pink (adj)
peirge, verge (n d:edge)
peirp, feint (n)
peirpwan, feigner (n doer)
peirsh, both (adj/conj)
peirsh, both (pron)
peirsp, feign (v)
peirzge, verge (v d:edge)
peishst, rout (v d:defeat)
peisht, rout (n d:defeat)
peithku, pervious (adj)
peiuft, taciturn (n)
peiuftiu, tacitly (adv)
peiuftu, tacit (adj)
pelein, oasis (n)
pelf, single (n)
pelfu, single (adj)
pelgast, lunge (v)
pelgat, lunge (n)
pelgatwan, lunger (n doer)
pelirp, mail (n)
pelirpwan, mailman (n doer)
pelirsh, singularity (n)
pelirshiu, singularly (adv)
pelirshu, singular (adj)
pelirsp, mail (v)
pelirve, migration (n)
pelirvu, migrant (adj)
pelirvwan, migrant (n doer)
pelirzve, migrate (v)
pelmurn, sincerity (n)
pelmurniu, sincerely (adv)
pelmurnu, sincere (adj)
pelparn, mailer (n)
pelpenufaf, mailbag (n)
pelprenik, mailbox (n)
pelsf, single (v)
pemdarn, penny (n)
penelan, omelet (n)
penork, tongue (n)
penorsk, tongue (v)
penorst, bottom (v)
penort, bottom (n)
Penshilvaniarf, Pennsylvania (n)
perf, bush (n)
perfk, dish (n)
perfsk, dish (v)
perfst, bushel (v)
perft, bushel (n)
perfu, bushy (adj)
Pershiarn, Persian (n)
Perulf, Peru (n)
Perun, EhoMonth04 (n)
pesharfp, landlord (n)
peshiark, landscape (n)
peshiarkwan, landscaper (n doer)
peshiarsk, landscape (v)
peshirn, psi (n)
peshirp, justice (n)

peshirpefrelpiu, justifiably (adv)
peshirpefrelpu, justifiable (adj)
peshirpiu, justly (adv)
peshirpu, just (adj)
peshirpuet, justification (n)
peshirsp, justify (v)
peshlursh, landslide (n)
peshtart, landmark (n)
pethar, kitchen (n)
petiurge, landlord (n)
petiurzge, landlock (v)
petriel, landfill (n)
pezhailf, landfall (n)
pialirsf, fiddle (v d:manipulate)
piapiarp, gibberish (n)
piapiarsp, gibber (v)
piarak, chronicle (n)
piarask, chronicle (v)
piardarfk, chronograph (n)
piardarfkiu, chronographically
   (adv)
piardarfku, chronographical (adj)
piardarfsk, chronograph (v)
piarfp, eternity (n)
piarfpiu, eternally (adv)
piarfpu, eternal (adj)
piarfpwan, eternalizer (n doer)
piarfsp, eternalize (v)
piarkuift, chronology (n)
piarkuiftiu, chronologically (adv)
piarkuiftu, chronological (adj)
piarl, vice (n d:title)
piarp, gib (n)
piart, cadence (n)
piarthk, sieve (n)
piarthsk, sieve (v)
piethsk, furbish (v)
pifaltu, tenuous (adj)
pifarn, tenderness (n)
pifarniu, tenderly (adv)
pifarnu, tender (adj)
pifaushk, tentacle (n)
pifkarst, tender (v)
piflarn, funeral (n)
pifon, evenness (n d:distribute)
pifoniu, evenly (adv d:distribute)
pifonu, even (adj d:distribute)
pifork, tendency (n)
piforsk, tend (v)
pifosne, even (v d:distribute)
piftarniu, tentatively (adv)
piftarnu, tentative (adj)
piftarst, tensen (v)
piftart, tension (n)
piftartiu, tensely (adv)
piftartu, tense (adj)
pifuat, obvious (n)
pifuatiu, obviously (adv)
pifuatu, obvious (adj)
pigrilk, obsolescence (n)
pigrilkiu, obsoletely (adv)
pigrilku, obsolete (adj)
pikart, kite (n)

piklorfk, obscurity (n)
piklorfsk, obscure (v)
pikorfst, observe (v)
pikorft, observation (n)
pikorftak, observatory (n)
pikorftan, observance (n)
pikorftaniu, observantly (adv)
pikorftanu, observant (adj)
pikorftiu, observably (adv)
pikorftu, observable (adj)
pikorftwan, observer (n doer)
pilafk, obedience (n)
pilafkiu, obediently (adv)
pilafku, obedient (adj)
pilafsk, obey (v)
pilap, obsession (n)
pilapiu, obsessively (adv)
pilapu, obsessive (adj)
pilapwan, obsessor (n doer)
pilark, obstacle (n)
pilarkwan, straggler (n doer)
pilarsk, straggle (v)
pilasp, obsess (v)
pilfiurn, fiance (n)
pilfiurn, fiancee (n)
pilikat, objective (n d:goal)
pilikatiu, objectively (adv d:goal)
pilikatu, objective (adj d:goal)
pilikuet, objectivity (n
    d:impartiality)
pilirk, object (n d:thing)
pilirst, tweet (v)
pilirt, tweet (n)
pilivartor, obliteration (n)
pilivartosre, obliterate (v)
piln, bikini (n)
pilshk, mitigation (n)
pilshranf, comrade (n)
pilshsk, mitigate (v)
piluarve, coed (n)
pimarf, spouse (n)
pimarfu, spousal (adj)
pimarsf, espouse (v)
pimikartiu, obnoxiously (adv)
pimikartu, obnoxious (adj)
pineirp, obtuseness (n)
pineirpiu, obtusely (adv)
pineirpu, obtuse (adj)
pipal, bark (n d:tree skin)
pipifst, obtain (v)
pipittu, obtainable (adj)
piranf, plummet (n)
piransf, plummet (v)
pirf, tent (n d:housing)
pirkwan, sifter (n doer)
pirn, pi (n)
piroilk, obligation (n)
piroilkuest, obligate (v)
piroilkuetu, obligatory (adj)
piroilsk, oblige (v)
pirsk, sift (v)
piruf, check (n d:money)
pishlek, obstruction (n)

pishlekiu, obstructively (adv)
pishleku, obstructive (adj)
pishlekwan, obstructionist (n
    doer)
pishlekwan, obstructor (n doer)
pishlesk, obstruct (v)
Piteshburge, Pittsburgh (n)
pithorp, tenancy (n)
pithorpwan, tenant (n doer)
pithuliap, obscenity (n)
pithuliapiu, obscenely (adv)
pithuliapu, obscene (adj)
piuagubirdu, ungodly (adj)
piualtirpu, unmentionable (adj)
piuanlarku, unalienable (adj)
piuarpifkiu, unintentionally (adv)
piuarpifku, unintentional (adj)
piubashtasp, unauthorize (v)
piubelfimu, unconventional (adj)
piubelshpeltiu, unconstitutionally
    (adv)
piubelshpeltu, unconstitutional
    (adj)
piubeltifkiu, unconditionally
    (adv)
piubeltifku, unconditional (adj)
piubiaurfiu, undoubtedly (adv)
piubinarsk, unoppose (v)
piublerku, unbreakable (adj)
piublersk, unbreak (v)
piublerskyot, unbroke (v pa)
piubles, unclassify (v)
piubovenkiu, uneconomically
    (adv)
piubovenku, uneconomical (adj)
piubrianirsk, unregister (v)
piubriarkfrepu, unusable (adj)
piubriarkiu, unusually (adv)
piubriarku, unusual (adj)
piubrieltiu, undeniably (adv)
piubrieltu, undeniable (adj)
piubudolirfu, undetectable (adj)
piubugarsp, unpack (v)
piubugosre, unburn (v)
piudainfu, unequal (adj)
piudarviuku, unenforceable (adj)
piudathesle, uncover (v)
piudaurnu, untimely (adj)
piudaurtiu, unbeatably (adv)
piudaurtu, unbeatable (adj)
piuderpiu, unthinkingly (adv)
piuderpu, unthinkable (adj)
piudhigorku, unmistakable (adj)
piudiarsk, unburden (v)
piudilst, unlist (v)
piudimulu, unholy (adj)
piudomast, unbutton (v)
piudreiflairshu, untrustworthy
    (adj)
piudreilsh, untruth (n)
piudreilshiu, untruthfully (adv)
piudreilshu, untruthful (adj)
piudreilu, untrue (adj)

piudrofu, unclear (adj)
piuduarpiu, untypically (adv)
piuduarpu, untypical (adj)
piudufirtiu, uncritically (adv)
piudufirtu, uncritical (adj)
piudutharpiu, unseasonably (adv)
piudutharpu, unseasonable (adj)
piuefbirsne, unopen (v)
piufafirtu, uncivil (adj)
piufanturniu, unpatriotically
    (adv)
piufanturnu, unpatriotic (adj)
piuferst, unidentify (v)
piufidalu, uneventful (adj)
piufiunirkiu, unprofessionally
    (adv)
piufiunirku, unprofessional (adj)
piufiupafirtiu, unprofitably (adv)
piufiupafirtu, unprofitable (adj)
piufiurkiu, unproductively (adv)
piufiurku, unproductive (adj)
piufiushairsk, unprovoke (v)
piuflairshu, unworthy (adj)
piuflauftfrelpu, unlivable (adj)
piuflerf, unease (n)
piuflerfiu, uneasily (adv)
piuflerfu, uneasy (adj)
piuflerfuet, uneasiness (n)
piufliarn, unfamiliarity (n)
piufliarnu, unfamiliar (adj)
piufliorsf, unprove (v)
piufluirkiu, unwisely (adv)
piufluirku, unwise (adj)
piufnairsp, unbrand (v)
piufnertu, unsteady (adj)
piufnursp, unwrap (v)
piufrelp, unability (n)
piufrelpiu, unably (adv)
piufrelpkodu, uncanny (adj)
piufrelpu, unable (adj)
piufrilap, unpleasantness (n)
piufrilapiu, unpleasantly (adv)
piufrilapu, unpleasant (adj)
piufrilast, unorganize (v)
piufrinsk, unhitch (v)
piuftarpu, unstable (adj)
piugailaku, unhelpful (adj)
piugarshu, untraceable (adj)
piugirsf, uncall (v)
piugitharsp, unplug (v)
piuglerk, unknown (n)
piuglerkiu, unknowingly (adv)
piuglerku, unknowable (adj)
piuglers, untie (v)
piuglorugu, unreachable (adj)
piugranirsp, uncork (v)
piugunaru, uncommon (adj)
piuhaufu, unhealthy (adj)
piuhinarsf, unquote (v)
piuiaborfst, unobtrude (v)
piuiaborftiu, unobtrusively (adv)
piuiaborftu, unobtrusive (adj)
piuipiduratiu, uncooperatively

(adv)
piuipiduratu, uncooperative (adj)
piuivadarvu, unemotional (adj)
piukarfluarlu, unassailable (adj)
piukeikurtiu, unremarkably (adv)
piukeikurtu, unremarkable (adj)
piukeirp, unconsciousness (n)
piukeirpiu, unconsciously (adv)
piukeirpu, unconscious (adj)
piukest, uncheck (v)
piukiblashiu, unimpressively (adv)
piukiblashu, unimpressive (adj)
piukikost, unbend (v)
piukikostyot, unbent (v pa)
piukinarliu, unimaginably (adv)
piukinarlu, unimaginable (adj)
piukiorku, unworkable (adj)
piukirakiu, unduly (adv)
piukiraku, undue (adj)
piukiviurgiu, unimportantly (adv)
piukiviurgu, unimportant (adj)
piukleirze, unreason (v)
piukleirzhiu, unreasonably (adv)
piukleirzhu, unreasonable (adj)
piukloirsp, unscrew (v)
piukolarnu, unwelcome (adj)
piukolirme, unhappiness (n)
piukolirmiu, unhappily (adv)
piukolirmu, unhappy (adj)
piukralirsk, unscramble (v)
piukriagiu, unbearably (adv)
piukriagu, unbearable (adj)
piukurfpu, unethical (adj)
piulalirfst, unlicense (v)
piulauirtu, unsatisfactory (adj)
piulaurst, unveil (v)
piuleifarn, undulation (n)
piuleifarsne, undulate (v)
piuleirdiu, unnaturally (adv)
piuleirdu, unnatural (adj)
piulenvapu, uncompetitive (adj)
piuliarpiu, unreadably (adv)
piuliarpu, unreadable (adj)
piulibers, unsettle (v)
piuligralgu, unsolvable (adj)
piulipsk, unbias (v)
piulitarsne, unplan (v)
piuloburku, unsupportable (adj)
piuloifaru, uncharitable (adj)
piuloirfiu, undesirably (adv)
piuloirfu, undesirable (adj)
piulonuakiu, unavoidably (adv)
piulonuaku, unavoidable (adj)
piuludarshu, unrepresentative (adj)
piuludrashtu, unrepentant (adj)
piuludufirpu, unresponsive (adj)
piulurifst, unload (v)
piuluvirsp, unregulate (v)
piumempirftiu, unsustainable (adv)
piumemthurkiu, unsuspectingly

(adv)
piumoirzme, unpay (v)
piumoirzmyot, unpaid (v pa)
piumorapiu, unsuitably (adv)
piumorapu, unsuitable (adj)
piumorshtast, unbalance (v)
piumunarpiu, unconscionably (adv)   ,
piumunarpu, unconscionable (adj)
piumuthsk, unmatch (v)
piunaltripiu, unfaithfully (adv)
piunaltripu, unfaithful (adj)
piunardepu, unfavorable (adj)
piunersp, untap (v)
piunulirsk, unleash (v)
piuofelarzve, unapprove (v)
piuogalirtiu, unattractively (adv)
piuogalirtu, unattractive (adj)
piuogiarp, unabatement (n)
piuogiarsp, unabate (v)
piuoiparpiu, unalterably (adv)
piuoiparpu, unalterable (adj)
piuoploshk, unabridgement (n)
piuoploshsk, unabridge (v)
piuorfliarsne, unaffiliate (v)
piuorpoinfu, unaccountable (adj)
piuorpoinsf, unaccount (v)
piuorshirlu, unanswerable (adj)
piuorshirp, unacceptability (n)
piuorshirpiu, unacceptably (adv)
piuorshirpu, unacceptable (adj)
piuorshirsp, unaccept (v)
piuoshlerfu, unaware (adj)
piupadaru, unlucky (adj)
piupamelu, unfriendly (adj)
piuparlarpu, unsympathetic (adj)
piuparlufku, unpalatable (adj)
piupaupizme, unbind (v)
piupaupizmyot, unbound (v pa)
piupeshirpiu, unjustly (adv)
piupeshirpu, unjust (adj)
piupifoniu, unevenly (adv)
piupifonu, uneven (adj)
piuplarthu, uncontroversial (adj)
piuplers, undress (v)
piupluarf, unreality (n)
piupluarfu, unreal (adj)
piupluarniu, unrealistically (adv)
piupluarnu, unrealistic (adj)
piupreirsh, unrest (n)
piupreitfrelpu, unintelligible (adj)
piureishortu, uninhabitable (adj)
piuridarsf, unschedule (v)
piurigarst, unravel (v)
piurudeirk, unpredictability (n)
piurudeirkiu, unpredictably (adv)
piurudeirku, unpredictable (adj)
piushalirf, unlike (prep/adj)
piushanirf, unlikely (adj/adv)
piusharmiu, unbelievably (adv)
piusharmu, unbelievable (adj)
piusharmwan, unbeliever (n doer)

piushenirsk, untax (v)
piushermu, unclean (adj)
piushiarlu, untouchable (adj)
piushiarnu, unsanitary (adj)
piushiurpaf, unavailability (n)
piushiurpafu, unavailable (adj)
piushiursp, unavail (v)
piushivershtiu, unnecessarily (adv)
piushivershtu, unnecessary (adj)
piushkirst, unmove (v)
piushlairfu, unwary (adj)
piushloirst, unemploy (v)
piushloirt, unemployment (n)
piushlurfu, uncool (adj)
piushnaithasne, unclutter (v)
piushnersne, unarm (v)
piushrelniu, unsure (adv)
piushrelnu, unsure (adj)
piushrilsk, unseat (v)
piushtarst, unmark (v)
piushtiartetiu, unquestionably (adv)
piushtiartetu, unquestionable (adj)
piushuarshiu, unscientifically (adv)
piushuarshu, unscientific (adj)
piutaigarzge, untangle (v)
piutalirshiu, unspeakably (adv)
piutalirshu, unspeakable (adj)
piutarfsp, unhinge (v)
piutashkeltiu, unofficially (adv)
piutashkeltu, unofficial (adj)
piutaurkiu, unstoppably (adv)
piutaurku, unstoppable (adj)
piutepafes, unadjust (v)
piuterame, unreliability (n)
piuteramiu, unreliably (adv)
piuteramu, unreliable (adj)
piuterzbe, unrate (v)
piutharoilku, unverifiable (adj)
piutheral, unfairness (n)
piutheraliu, unfairly (adv)
piutheralu, unfair (adj)
piuthrairsk, unwind (v)
piuthrairskyot, unwound (v pa)
piuthraunsk, unbridle (v)
piuthriuftu, unscrupulous (adj)
piuthuirtu, untreatable (adj)
piuthuklarkiu, unspectacularly (adv)
piuthuklarku, unspectacular (adj)
piuthurnu, unseemly (adj)
piutiargast, unhinder (v)
piutigrefst, undisclose (v)
piutirsk, undo (v)
piutirskyot, undid (v pa)
piutiurzge, unlock (v)
piutrafsk, unfold (v)
piutranitiu, uncontrollably (adv)
piutranitu, uncontrollable (adj)
piutrilorku, untrainable (adj)

piutrulisf, unfurl (v)
piutrulishu, unprintable (adj)
piutuarsne, unchange (v)
piututhurkiu, unexpectedly (adv)
piututhursk, unexpect (v)
piutuvetiu, unexceptionally (adv)
piutuvetu, unexceptional (adj)
piuvairgiu, unexplainably (adv)
piuvairgu, unexplainable (adj)
piuvartulsf, unsecure (v)
piuvashil, unborn (n)
piuvaurdiu, unlawfully (adv)
piuvaurdu, unlawful (adj)
piuvelirfu, unfit (adj)
piuvikusne, unbundle (v)
piuvilensf, unbecome (v)
piuvilensfyot, unbecame (v pa)
piuvinst, unlimit (v)
piuviuvartiu, unambiguously (adv)
piuviuvartu, unambiguous (adj)
piuvlarkiu, uncomfortably (adv)
piuvlarku, uncomfortable (adj)
piuvoantopu, unforgettable (adj)
piuvoashmuniu, unfortunately (adv)
piuvoashmunu, unfortunate (adj)
piuvoathulthu, unforeseeable (adj)
piuvoiviurshiu, unsurprisingly (adv)
piuvorade, unpopularity (n)
piuvoradiu, unpopularly (adv)
piuvoradu, unpopular (adj)
piuvoshasre, unlove (v)
piuvularsne, unmarry (v)
piuweirsf, unsign (v)
piuyark, unwillingness (n)
piuyarkiu, unwillingly (adv)
piuzhaturfu, unsound (adj)
piuzheifst, unzip (v)
piuzhirt, uncertainty (n)
piuzhirtu, uncertain (adj)
piuzhiurnu, unselfish (adj)
piuzhiurnuet, unselfishness (n)
piuzhoirzve, unseal (v)
piuzhurdu, unsafe (adj)
piuzhuvertushiu, unsuccessfully (adv)
piuzhuvertushu, unsuccessful (adj)
pivark, tenacity (n)
pivarku, tenacious (adj)
pivartu, tenable (adj)
pivirst, bike (v)
pivirt, bike (n)
pivirtwan, biker (n doer)
plabuet, gratification (n)
pladeirk, contradiction (n)
pladeirku, contradictory (adj)
pladeirsk, contradict (v)
plafime, contravention (n)
plafirge, quarry (n)

plafirk, census (n)
plafirzge, quarry (v)
plafizme, contravene (v)
plafpeilarn, grapevine (n)
plaft, gratuity (n)
plagarst, quarrel (v)
plagart, quarrel (n)
plaifk, broom (n)
plairk, strategy (n)
plairkiu, strategically (adv)
plairku, strategic (adj)
plairkwan, strategist (n doer)
plairp, stratus (n)
plairpyek, strata (n pl)
plaishk, proneness (n)
plaishku, prone (adj)
plaithk, grill (n)
plaithsk, grill (v)
plamirp, hump (n)
plamirsp, hump (v)
plampevark, humpback (n)
plampevarku, humpback (adj)
plaput, contrariness (n)
plaputu, contrary (adj)
plarbe, slab (n)
plarf, grace (n)
plarfiu, graciously (adv)
plarfliap, grapefruit (n)
plarfp, grape (n)
plarfu, gracious (adj)
plarfuet, graciousness (n)
plarfushiu, gracefully (adv)
plarfushu, graceful (adj)
plark, grate (n)
plarkwan, grater (n doer)
plarsf, grace (v)
plarsk, grate (v)
plarth, controversy (n)
plarthu, controversial (adj)
plartufkef, moorhead (n)
plartusf, moor (v d:secure)
plashifp, contraception (n)
plashifpwan, contraceptive (n doer)
plashorst, censor (v)
plashort, censorship (n)
plashortwan, censor (n doer)
Platinum, Platinum (n)
platurk, speaker (n d:air cone)
plaurfk, debris (n)
plaurge, crypt (n)
plaurk, bruise (n)
plaurkwan, bruiser (n doer)
plaursk, bruise (v)
plavramirp, contraband (n)
plazhge, gratitude (n)
plazhgiu, gratefully (adv)
plazhgu, grateful (adj)
plazhzge, gratify (v)
pleftoirk, wishbone (n)
pleifanart, modularity (n)
pleifarn, module (n)
pleifarniu, modularly (adv)

pleifarnu, modular (adj)
pleifarnuet, modulation (n)
pleifarnwan, modulator (n doer)
pleifarsne, modulate (v)
pleirf, moderation (n)
pleirfiu, moderately (adv)
pleirfk, modification (n)
pleirfkwan, modifier (n doer)
pleirfsk, modify (v)
pleirfu, moderate (adj)
pleirfwan, moderator (n doer)
pleirsf, moderate (v)
pleishk, waiver (n)
pleishsk, waive (v)
pleniak, disintegration (n)
pleniakwan, disintegrator (n doer)
pleniask, disintegrate (v)
plerf, wish (n)
plerfu, wishful (adj)
plerfu, wishy (adj)
plerfwan, wisher (n doer)
plerp, OvaCarrier (n)
plers, dress (v d:clothing)
plersf, wish (v)
plersh, dress (n d:clothing)
plershk, dresser (n d:cabinet)
plershwan, dresser (n doer d:clothing)
plersth, stuff (v)
plert, clerk (n)
plerth, stuff (n)
plerthu, stuffy (adj)
plerthwan, stuffer (n doer)
pleshnargwan, dressmaker (n doer)
pliarf, sprawl (n)
pliark, integer (n)
pliarsf, sprawl (v)
pliarshk, integration (n)
pliarshkar, integrity (n)
pliarshkiu, integrally (adv)
pliarshku, integral (adj)
pliarshkwan, integrator (n doer)
pliarshp, therapy (n)
pliarshpu, therapeutic (adj)
pliarshpwan, therapist (n doer)
pliarshsk, integrate (v)
pliarsp, bask (v)
pliarst, recover (v d:retrieve, heal)
pliart, recovery (n d:retrieve, heal)
pliartu, recoverable (adj d:retrieve, heal)
pliartwan, recoverer (n doer d:retrieve, heal)
pliaushk, sprain (n)
pliaushsk, sprain (v)
pliausht, siren (n)
pligirst, quibble (v)
plimorfk, franchise (n)
plimorfsk, enfranchise (v)
plint, spree (n)

pliolshoirt, wayside (n)
pliorl, way (n)
pliorlu, wayward (adj)
plirf, chill (n)
plirfu, chilly (adj)
plirfwan, chiller (n doer)
plirk, bank (n d:shore)
plirme, chin (n)
plirsf, chill (v)
plirsk, bank (v d:shore)
plirst, itemize (v)
plirt, item (n)
plirthk, velocity (n)
plirtwan, itemizer (n doer)
plishst, elicit (v)
plisht, elicitation (n)
plitelsharn, breakthrough (n)
plitiern, breakdown (n)
pliurf, spray (n)
pliurfwan, sprayer (n doer)
pliurk, drain (n)
pliurkuet, drainage (n)
pliurkwan, drainer (n doer)
pliurp, jumble (n)
pliursf, spray (v)
pliursk, drain (v)
pliursp, jumble (v)
pliurst, create (v)
pliurt, creation (n)
pliurtal, creature (n)
pliurtiu, creatively (adv)
pliurtu, creative (adj)
pliurtuet, creativity (n)
pliurtwan, creator (n doer)
pliuzhbu, jumbo (adj)
plivark, immigration (n)
plivarkwan, immigrant (n doer)
plivarsk, immigrate (v)
plofienk, monk (n)
plofirk, moniker (n)
ploifer, bracelet (n)
ploifk, glitch (n)
ploifst, brace (v)
ploift, brace (n)
ploiftark, bracket (n)
ploiftarsk, bracket (v)
ploiftwan, bracer (n doer)
ploirsh, silk (n)
ploirshiu, silkily (adv)
ploirshu, silky (adj)
ploishfanirn, silkwood (n)
ploishyoran, silkworm (n)
plok, board (n d:wood)
plonarf, personnel (n)
plonarge, personification (n)
plonarzge, personify (v)
plonat, personality (n)
plonegrulat, manhunt (n)
plonik, kernel (n)
plonkorth, manhole (n)
plonshriausht, manslaughter (n)
plopor, bump (n)
ploporiu, bumpily (adv)

ploporu, bumpy (adj)
ploporwan, bumper (n doer)
ploposre, bump (v)
plorfk, garb (n)
plorn, person (n)
plorniu, personally (adv)
plornu, personal (adj)
plornuet, personalization (n)
plornul, personal (n)
plornyek, people (n pl)
plorshk, mortar (n d:bowl)
plorsne, personalize (v)
ploshk, bridge (n)
ploshsk, bridge (v)
plosk, board (v d:wood)
plovark, rubbish (n)
plovarth, rubber (n)
plovarthu, rubbery (adj)
pluabalirt, lamppost (n)
pluaft, lantern (n)
pluarbe, lamp (n)
pluarf, reality (n)
pluarfiu, really (adv)
pluarfu, real (adj)
pluarfwan, realist (n doer)
pluark, grant (n)
pluarkwan, grantor (n doer)
pluarn, realism (n)
pluarniu, realistically (adv)
pluarnu, realistic (adj)
pluarnuet, realization (n)
pluarsk, grant (v)
pluarsne, realize (v)
pluarth, ovation (n)
plubashtal, coauthority (n)
plubashtalwan, coauthor (n doer)
pluikferap, hailstorm (n)
pluirp, piano (n)
pluishk, hail (n d:precipitation)
pluishsk, hail (v d:precipitation)
plukarde, record (n)
plukardu, recordable (adj)
plukardwan, recorder (n doer)
plukarzde, record (v)
plukiorst, distort (v)
plukiort, distortion (n)
plumarmark, cogeneration (n)
plumarmarkwan, cogenerator (n
    doer)
plumarmarsk, cogenerate (v)
plunap, guest (n)
plunirsh, receipt (n)
plunirshwan, recipient (n doer)
plunirst, hint (v)
plunirt, hint (n)
plunshark, receptacle (n)
plunulirst, coexist (v)
plunulirt, coexistence (n)
plupkiork, guesswork (n)
pluplurt, tidbit (n)
plurde, kit (n)
plureishortuest, cohabitate (v)
plureishortuet, cohabitation (n)

plurf, enough (adj/adv)
plurf, enough (pron)
plurfk, improvisation (n)
plurfsk, improvise (v)
plurp, guess (n)
plurpwan, guesser (n doer)
plursp, guess (v)
plurt, bit (n d:part)
plurve, groan (n)
plurvwan, groaner (n doer)
plurze, grieve (v)
plurzhe, grief (n)
plurzhge, sludge (n)
plurzhiu, grievously (adv)
plurzhu, grievous (adj)
plurzhuet, grievance (n)
plurzhwan, griever (n doer)
plurzve, groan (v)
plushirk, reception (n)
plushirkiu, receptively (adv)
plushirku, receptive (adj)
plushirkwan, receptor (n doer)
plushirpar, receptionist (n)
plushirpu, receivable (adj)
plushirpun, receivable (n)
plushirpwan, receiver (n doer)
plushirsp, receive (v)
plushuparst, cofound (v)
plushupartwan, cofounder (n
    doer)
pluthurk, disrespect (n)
pluthursk, disrespect (v)
pluthuvirtar, coefficient (n)
Plutonium, Plutonium (n)
pluvairk, disregard (n)
pluvairsk, disregard (v)
poarf, clause (n)
poarl, clay (n)
poarp, bud (n d:plant)
poarsp, bud (v d:plant)
poefirst, shadow (v)
poefirt, shadow (n)
poefirtu, shadowy (adj)
poefirtwan, shadower (n doer)
poerf, shade (n)
poerfu, shady (adj)
poerfwan, shader (n doer)
poersf, shade (v)
pofan, bishop (n)
pofirp, mud (n)
pofirpiu, muddily (adv)
pofirpu, muddy (adj)
pofirsk, muddle (v)
pofirsp, muddy (v)
pofpeshkraishsk, mudsling (v)
pofpeshkraishskyot, mudslung (v
    pa)
pogaift, hives (n d:skin eruption)
poifepreift, counterintelligence
    (n)
poifersh, counterpart (n)
poifgautif, counterargument (n)
poifgautisf, counterargue (v)

poifgrolf, countermeasure (n)
poifiulork, counterproposal (n)
poifiurku, counterproductive (adj)
poifkakortuet, counterterrorism (n)
poifkrirthk, counterpunch (n)
poifkrirthsk, counterpunch (v)
poifmorshtast, counterbalance (v)
poifmorshtat, counterbalance (n)
poifnolan, counterclaim (n)
poifnolasnaut, counterclaimed (v prp)
poifnolasne, counterclaim (v)
poifopairst, counterattack (v)
poifopairt, counterattack (n)
poifpatil, counteraction (n)
poifpatiliu, counteractively (adv)
poifpatilu, counteractive (adj)
poifpatilwan, counteractor (n doer)
poifpatisle, counteract (v)
poifshuirs, counterweigh (v)
poifshuirsh, counterweight (n)
poifst, counter (v d:d: oppose)
poiftaifort, counterpoint (n)
poiftapeimu, counterfeit (adj)
poiftapeimwan, counterfeiter (n doer)
poiftapeizme, counterfeit (v)
poilf, ray (n)
poinf, count (n d:d: increment)
poinfwan, counter (n doer d:d: increment)
poink, coercion (n)
poinku, coercive (adj)
poinkwan, coercer (n doer)
poinsf, count (v d:d: increment)
poinsk, coerce (v)
pointiern, countdown (n)
poinurde, tennis (n)
poirk, tong (n)
poirp, fiber (n)
poirpu, fibrous (adj)
poirth, absurdity (n)
poirthiu, absurdly (adv)
poirthu, absurd (adj)
poishark, count (n d:d: title)
Polanurd, Poland (n)
Polonium, Polonium (n)
poisht, delicacy (n)
polshtiu, delicately (adv)
polshtu, delicate (adj)
pondern, pound (n d:weight)
porame, ram (n d:animal)
porath, peripheral (n)
porathu, periperhal (adj)
porktel, picture (n)
porktesle, picture (v)
porlant, period (n d:cycle)
porlantiu, periodically (adv d:cycle)
porlantu, periodic (adj d:cycle)

porlefst, factor (v)
porleft, factor (n)
porlet, fact (n)
porletiu, factually (adv)
porletu, factual (adj)
porsht, honesty (n)
porshtiu, honestly (adv)
porshtu, honest (adj)
portan, bottle (n)
portanwan, bottler (n doer)
portasne, bottle (v)
Portelanurd, Portland (n)
Portugalf, Portugal (n)
porvashoit, countryside (n)
porve, country (n)
poshark, football (n d:American)
poshbotersh, footpath (n)
poshdorame, footwear (n)
poshezhailf, footfall (n)
poshgref, footstep (n)
poshiop, foothill (n)
poshkiork, footwork (n)
poshmirade, footnote (n)
poshmirazde, footnote (v)
poshp, foot (n)
poshpol, football (n d:soccer)
poshpwan, footer (n doer)
poshpyek, feet (n pl)
poshsp, foot (v)
poshtrulish, footprint (n)
Potashium, Potassium (n)
povairp, diner (n)
povigthoilf, knapsack (n)
povigwan, nabber (n doer)
povizge, nab (v)
prabif, corps (n)
pradar, cradle (n)
pradasre, cradle (v)
pradip, barrel (n)
pradisp, barrel (v)
Pragarf, Prague (n)
praiark, throe (n)
praikart, routine (n)
praikartiu, routinely (adv)
praikartu, routine (adj)
prailk, route (n d:path)
prailkwan, router (n doer d:path)
prailsk, route (v d:path)
prainp, foil (n d:prevent)
prainsp, foil (v d:prevent)
prairst, thieve (v)
prairt, theft (n)
prairtwan, thief (n doer)
praishk, rarity (n)
praishkiu, rarely (adv)
praishku, rare (adj)
praishsk, rarify (v)
praithk, teller (n)
prakast, correct (v)
prakat, correction (n)
prakatiu, correctly (adv)
prakatu, correct (adj)
pralirst, crate (v)

pralirt, crate (n)
praln, knoll (n)
praltarp, crater (n)
praltarsp, crater (v)
pralup, corporation (n)
pralupu, corporate (adj)
pralusp, incorporate (v)
pralzge, throb (v)
pramipu, cumbersome (adj)
pramisp, encumber (v)
pranp, capsule (n)
pranshkwan, rambler (n doer)
pranshsk, ramble (v)
pranst, field (v)
prant, field (n)
prantwan, fielder (n doer)
Prasheodimium, Praseodymium (n)
prashirk, rubble (n)
prashst, function (v)
prasht, function (n)
prashtak, functionality (n)
prashtiu, functionally (adv)
prashtu, functional (adj)
prashtwan, functioner (n doer)
prates, rabble (v)
pratesh, rabble (n)
prateshwan, rabbler (n doer)
prathvark, drawback (n)
praufk, slop (n)
praufku, sloppy (adj)
praufkuet, sloppiness (n)
praufsk, slop (v)
praufst, blot (v)
prauft, blot (n)
prauftwan, blotter (n doer)
praump, pelt (n d:fur)
praushk, slob (n)
praushsp, slobber (v)
pravast, corner (v)
pravat, corner (n)
pravatbaraft, cornerstone (n)
pravatprant, cornfield (n)
pravge, corruption (n)
pravgiu, corruptly (adv)
pravgu, corrupt (adj)
pravzge, corrupt (v)
predirze, narrate (v)
predirzhe, narration (n)
predirzhu, narrative (adj)
predirzhwan, narrator (n doer)
predizhart, narrative (n)
preibelgelf, teleconference (n)
preibielork, teleport (n)
preibielorkwan, teleporter (n doer)
preibielorsk, teleport (v)
preibotersh, telepathy (n)
preibotershu, telepathic (adj)
preibotershwan, telepath (n doer)
preidan, restaurant (n)
preidaraf, telegraph (n)
preidarasf, telegraph (v)

preidifadarf, telephotography (n)
preidifadarfu, telephoto (adj)
preidifadarsf, telephotograph (v)
preifp, hope (n)
preifp, hopefullness (n)
preifpen, hopelessness (n)
preifpeniu, hopelessly (adv)
preifpenu, hopeless (adj)
preifpiu, hopefully (adv)
preifpu, hopeful (adj)
preifsp, hope (v)
preift, intelligence (n)
preiftariu, intellectually (adv)
preiftaru, intellectual (adj)
preiftarwan, intellectual (n doer)
preiftiu, intelligently (adv)
preiftu, intelligent (adj)
preiftwan, intellect (n doer)
preiguniart, telecommunication (n)
preigurt, telecom (n)
preiliarf, trivium (n)
preiliarfu, trivial (adj)
preiliarfuet, triviality (n)
preiliarfyek, trivia (n pl)
preiliarsf, trivialize (v)
preiluarf, telescope (n)
preiluarfu, telescopic (adj)
preiluarsf, telescope (v)
preinelirk, telegram (n)
preinelirsk, telegram (v)
preip, drop (n)
preipapyek, droplet (n pl)
preiporft, telemetry (n)
preipuilyek, dropout (n pl)
preipwan, dropper (n doer)
preirk, spank (n)
preirkwan, spanker (n doer)
preirs, rest (v)
preirsh, rest (n)
preirshiu, restfully (adv)
preirshmeniu, restlessy (adv)
preirshmenu, restless (adj)
preirshu, restful (adj)
preirshwan, rester (n doer)
preirsk, spank (v)
preirth, chroma (n)
preishriash, drowsiness (n)
preishriashu, drowsy (adj)
preisp, drop (v)
preitfrelpiu, intelligibly (adv)
preitfrelpu, intelligible (adj)
preithenort, telekinesis (n)
preithenortu, telekinetic (adj)
preithulirde, television (n)
preithulirzde, televise (v)
preithust, telecast (v)
preithut, telecast (n)
preiupu, droopy (adj)
preiusp, droop (v)
preiyarp, telephone (n)
preiyarpu, telephonic (adj)
preiyarpuet, telephony (n)

preiyarsp, telephone (v)
prekun, box (n d:cube)
prekunu, boxy (adj d:cube)
prekusne, box (v d:cube)
prekutalk, gladiator (n)
prelfirk, gait (n)
prelfpiu, gladly (adv)
prelfpor, glade (n)
prelfpu, glad (adj)
prelfsp, gladden (v)
prelsh, recreation (n d:rest)
prelshu, recreational (adj d:rest)
prelst, tell (v)
prelstyot, told (v pa)
prelt, tale (n)
preltiu, tellingly (adv)
prelume, month (n)
prelumu, monthly (adj)
prethk, turf (n)
pretopreltu, telltale (adj)
priamp, prune (n d:fruit)
priank, jerk (n)
priankiu, jerkily (adv)
prianku, jerky (adj)
priankwan, jerk (n doer)
priansk, jerk (v)
priarf, foil (n d:sheet)
priark, brittleness (n)
priarku, brittle (adj)
priarsf, foil (v d:sheet)
priarsk, brittle (v)
priart, biscuit (n)
priaushkwan, slouch (n doer)
priaushsk, slouch (v)
prifk, hip (n)
prifort, crop (n d:food)
prifortwan, cropper (n doer d:food)
prifp, braille (n)
prilap, possession (n)
prilapiu, possessively (adv)
prilapu, possessive (adj)
prilapwan, possessor (n doer)
prilark, pylon (n)
prilasp, possess (v)
prilf, hue (n)
prilsh, silt (n)
primarst, blanket (v)
primart, blanket (n)
primast, blank (v)
primat, blank (n)
priofk, pore (n)
priofku, porous (adj)
prishk, fast (n d:starve)
prishmonde, fastball (n)
prishsk, fast (v d:starve)
prithsk, mull (v)
priufp, robe (n)
priump, dormancy (n)
priumpu, dormant (adj)
priurf, luncheon (n)
priurst, lunch (v)
priurt, lunch (n)

priurtwan, luncher (n doer)
priutshranf, lunchroom (n)
privif, cranny (n)
profk, dock (n)
profkef, docket (n)
profsk, dock (v)
proide, knob (n)
prokshoirt, dockside (n)
prokshoirtu, dockside (adj)
Promethium, Promethium (n)
protaft, documentation (n)
protak, doctor (n)
Protaktinium, Protactinium (n)
protap, doctrine (n)
protart, documentary (n)
protask, doctor (v)
protasp, indoctrinate (v)
protast, document (v)
protat, document (n)
protatwan, documenter (n doer)
pruafk, vane (n)
prudak, blend (n)
prudakwan, blender (n doer)
prudask, blend (v)
prufk, method (n)
prufkiu, methodically (adv)
prufku, methodical (adj)
prufkuit, methodology (n)
prufsk, methodize (v)
prulat, blade (n)
prulirk, strain (n)
prulirkwan, strainer (n doer)
prulirsk, strain (v)
prushk, sleep (n)
prushkmenu, sleepless (adj)
prushku, sleepy (adj)
prushkuet, sleepiness (n)
prushkwan, sleeper (n doer)
prushsk, sleep (v)
prushskyot, slept (v pa)
prushzhoirpwan, sleepwalker (n doer)
prushzhoirsp, sleepwalk (v)
prusth, leaf (v)
pruth, leaf (n)
pruthap, leaflet (n)
pruthk, punk (n)
pruthku, punky (adj)
puamesp, pawn (v)
puamp, pawn (n)
puamthorve, pawnshop (n)
puarst, barb (v)
puart, barb (n)
puartwan, barber (n doer)
pufor, beard (n)
pufosre, beard (v)
pulap, draw (n d:pull, inscribe)
pulapwan, drawer (n doer d:pull, inscribe)
pularde, nudge (n)
pularzde, nudge (v)
pulasp, draw (v d:pull, inscribe)
pulaspyot, drew (v pa d:pull,

inscribe)
pulaze, dredge (v)
pulazhan, dreg (n)
pulirk, culpability (n)
pulirku, culpable (adj)
pulirkwan, culprit (n doer)
puluze, drudge (v)
puluzhe, drudge (n)
puluzhu, drudgery (adj)
puluzhwan, drudge (n doer)
pumurf, laziness (n)
pumurfiu, lazily (adv)
pumurfu, lazy (adj)
pumurfweku, laziest (adj)
pumurfwelu, lazier (adj)
punirp, helm (n d:helmet)
punirp, helmet (n)
puprulsh, coma (n d:sleep)
puprulshu, comatose (adj d:sleep)
purifk, gross (n d:package)
purth, dune (n)
puvirk, grog (n)
puvirku, groggy (adj)
puvirn, tear (n d:eyedrop)
puvirnu, tearful (adj)
puvirnu, teary (adj d:eyedrop)
puvirsne, tear (v d:eyedrop)
Radium, Radium (n)
Radon, Radon (n)
rafpwan, dozer (n doer)
rafsp, doze (v)
rairze, tease (v)
rairzhe, tease (n)
rairzhwan, teaser (n doer)
rakaifst, loathe (v)
rakaift, loathness (n)
rakaiftu, loath (adj)
rakal, audit (n)
rakalwan, auditor (n doer)
rakarde, comb (n)
rakardwan, comber (n doer)
rakarzde, comb (v)
rakasle, audit (v)
rakiu, meow (interj)
rakulast, audition (v)
rakulat, audition (n)
ralbe, tear (n d:rip)
ralirp, fleece (n)
ralirpwan, fleecer (n doer)
ralirsp, fleece (v)
ralshk, pettiness (n)
ralshkiu, pettily (adv)
ralshku, petty (adj)
ralzbe, tear (v d:rip)
ralzbyot, tore (v pa d:rip)
ralze, lengthen (v)
ralzhdaurnu, longtime (adj)
ralzhe, length (n)
ralzhu, lengthy (adj)
ralzhu, long (adj)
ralzhwaku, longest (adj)
ralzhwelu, lengthier (adj)
ralzhwelu, longer (adj)

ramshar, legend (n)
ramsharu, legendary (adj)
ranern, mildness (n)
ranerniu, mildly (adv)
ranernu, mild (adj)
ranernweku, mildest (adj)
ranernwelu, milder (adj)
raniarp, whale (n)
raniarsp, whale (v)
ranirp, flesh (n)
ranirpu, fleshy (adj)
ranirsp, flesh (v)
rasharl, coma (n d:oblong)
rashelt, comet (n)
rashort, letter (n d:message)
rashtkefirt, letterhead (n)
rashtplorn, letterman (n)
rashtplornyek, lettermen (n pl)
rathaunshu, lukewarm (adj)
rathiern, marathon (n)
rathiernwan, marathoner (n doer)
ratirsh, meat (n)
ratirshmenu, meatless (adj)
ratirshu, meaty (adj)
ratshmonde, meatball (n)
rau, us (pron 1st pl obj)
raube, ebb (n)
raubuge, bass (n d:sound)
raufirf, feudalism (n)
raufirfu, feudal (adj)
raufirk, loft (n)
raufirkiu, loftily (adv)
raufirku, lofty (adj)
raufirsk, loft (v)
raufp, land (n)
raufpwan, lander (n doer)
raufsp, land (v)
raul, air (n)
raulu, airy (adj)
rauptheiftwan, landowner (n doer)
raush, ours (pron 1st pl pos obj)
raushfal, ourself (pron 1st sing refl)
raushfar, ourselves (pron 1st pl refl)
raushk, lift (n)
raushkunf, liftoff (n)
raushkwan, lifter (n doer)
raushsk, lift (v)
rausle, air (v)
rauvalar, airplane (n)
rauzbe, ebb (v)
rauzhge, lag (n)
rauzhgwan, laggard (n doer)
rauzhge, lag (v)
ravikiok, framework (n)
ravikiosk, framework (v)
ravist, frame (v)
ravit, frame (n)
ravitwan, framer (n doer)
rayu-rayu, bow-wow (interj)
razhark, footage (n)

razhbaraft, milestone (n)
razhdart, longitude (n)
razheshkort, longshot (n)
razhkarp, longhand (n)
razhoilf, longing (n d:desire)
razhoilfiu, longingly (adv d:desire)
razhoilfu, longing (adj d:desire)
refirst, afford (v)
refirtiu, afforably (adv)
refirtu, affordable (adj)
reiafp, cheek (n)
reiaptoirk, cheekbone (n)
reidal, habit (n)
reidaliu, habitually (adv)
reidalu, habitual (adj)
reifk, like (n)
reifki, like (prep)
reifkiu, likely (adv)
reifkiufif, likelihood (n)
reifku, like (adj)
reifkuet, likeness (n)
reifp, elder (n)
reifpiu, elderly (adv)
reifpu, elder (adj)
reifpweku, eldest (adj)
reifsk, like (v)
reigirn, look (n)
reigirnuil, lookout (n)
reigirnwan, looker (n doer)
reigirsne, look (v)
reikfrelpu, likeable (adj)
reilarfk, chemistry (n)
reilark, chemical (n)
reilarkiu, chemically (adv)
reilarku, chemical (adj)
reilarkwan, chemist (n doer)
Reiloparn, European (n)
Reilorp, Europe (n)
reinorf, par (n)
reinorfu, par (adj)
reinorsf, par (v)
reirft, cherry (n)
reirftu, cherry (adj)
reishkwan, raver (n doer)
reishorst, inhabit (v)
reishort, habitat (n)
reishortu, habitable (adj)
reishortuet, habitation (n)
reishortwan, inhabitant (n doer)
reishsk, rave (v)
relarn, merriment (n)
relarniu, merrily (adv)
relarnu, merry (adj)
relarnweku, merriest (adj)
relarnwelu, merrier (adj)
relhem, Number_1e1356
relre, R (let sng)
relri, Rs (let pl)
relsh, right (n d:direction)
relshu, right (adj d:direction)
renbugor, sunburn (n)
renbugosre, sunburn (v)

rendafelwan, sunbather (n doer)
rendafesle, sunbathe (v)
rendakelf, sunbelt (n)
renderap, sunspot (n)
rendrinat, sunglass (n)
renduarf, sunbeam (n)
reneiport, sundial (n)
renepoerf, sunshade (n)
renf, sun (n)
renferp, sunset (n)
renfiu, sunnily (adv)
renfklert, sunscreen (n)
renflamar, sundance (n)
renflamasre, sundance (v)
renfluarn, sunlight (n)
renfluarsnyot, sunlit (v pa)
renfu, sunny (adj)
Renium, Rhenium (n)
reniveil, sunup (n)
renlarfp, sunroof (n)
renluirsh, sunrise (n)
renluirshwan, sunriser (n doer)
renmaiarme, suntan (n)
renmoirth, sunshine (n)
renshlersh, sunfish (n)
renshlershyek, sunfish (n pl)
renshranf, sunroom (n)
renthaush, sunflower (n)
rentiern, sundown (n)
Renviurl, Sunday (n)
reshaurshu, rightward (adj)
reshkarp, righty (n)
reshkliergu, rightwing (adj)
retienk, joist (n)
reuishk, choke (n)
reuishkwan, choker (n doer)
reuishsk, choke (v)
riaf, massage (n)
riafwan, massager (n doer)
rialeshkorf, lowercase (n)
rialf, low (n)
rialfiu, lowly (adv)
rialfu, low (adj)
rialfwaku, lowest (adj)
rialfwelu, lower (adj)
rialsf, lower (v)
riandrilf, hourglass (n)
rianirk, affray (n)
rianirkwan, affrayer (n doer)
rianirsk, affray (v)
riarak, acrobat (n)
riaraku, acrobatic (adj)
riarn, hour (n)
riarnu, hourly (adj)
riarth, owl (n)
riarviern, acronym (n)
riasf, massage (v)
riazhzge, linger (v)
ridarf, schedule (n)
ridarfwan, scheduler (n doer)
ridarsf, schedule (v)
rideirge, groom (n d:bridegroom)
rief, lie (n d:placement)

riesf, lie (v d:placement)
riesfyot, lay (v pa d:placement)
rifast, thank (v)
rifat, thanks (n)
Rifategrulf, Thanksgiving (n)
rifatiu, thankfully (adv)
rifatmenu, thankless (adj)
rifatu, thankful (adj)
rigarst, ravel (v)
rilorp, spread (n)
rilorpwan, spreader (n doer)
rilorsp, spread (v)
rilorspyot, spread (v pa)
rinak, flu (n)
rininkiu, meekly (adv)
rininku, meek (adj)
rininkyek, meek (n pl)
riorp, pail (n)
riorsh, aroma (n)
riorshiu, aromatically (adv)
riorshu, aromatic (adj)
risharde, teen (n)
rishdalirt, teenager (n)
Rishmonurd, Richmond (n)
ritarsf, loiter (v)
rithk, smith (n)
ritralirt, ringleader (n)
ritran, ring (n d:circle)
ritranwan, ringer (n doer d:circle)
ritrashoirt, ringside (n)
ritrashoirtu, ringside (adj)
ritrasne, ring (v d:circle)
ritrathiork, ringmaster (n)
riufp, rumble (n)
riufsp, rumble (v)
riuk, audio (n)
riukal, audience (n)
riuku, audible (adj)
riump, hull (n)
riurk, lion (n)
riurn, boom (n)
riursne, boom (v)
rivurn, prestige (n)
rivurnu, prestigious (adj)
rodaf, filter (n)
rodafwan, filterer (n doer)
rodap, film (n)
rodapwan, filmer (n doer)
rodasf, filter (v)
rodasp, film (v)
Roderf Ilanurd, Rhode Island (n)
Rodium, Rhodium (n)
Roentgenium, Roentgenium (n)
rofk, barrier (n)
rogalirf, occurrence (n)
rogalirsf, occur (v)
rogalirst, occasion (v)
rogalirt, occasion (n)
rogalirtiu, occasionally (adv)
rogalirtu, occasional (adj)
roialk, lien (n)
roifk, line (n)
roifkarfst, latch (v)

roifkarft, latch (n)
roifkiu, linearly (adv)
roifkiveil, lineup (n)
roifku, linear (adj)
roifkuet, lineage (n)
roifkwan, liner (n doer)
roifsk, line (v)
roifst, queue (v)
roift, queue (n)
roilk, ligature (n)
roilkat, ligament (n)
roilkuet, ligation (n)
roilsk, ligate (v)
roilth, syllabus (n)
roilthyek, syllabi (n pl)
roimert, linen (n)
roinst, lint (v)
roint, lint (n)
rointwan, linter (n doer)
roishk, link (n)
roishkiveil, linkup (n)
roishkuet, linkage (n)
roishkwan, linker (n doer)
roishsk, link (v)
rolarme, council (n)
rolarst, bar (v d:rod)
rolart, bar (n d:rod)
rolarzme, conciliate (v)
rolirp, counsel (n)
rolirpwan, counselor (n doer)
rolirsp, counsel (v)
roln, rho (n)
Romafarn, Roman (n)
Romarf, Rome (n)
Romiarf, Romania (n)
Romiarn, Romanian (n)
ronar, fear (n)
ronarf, vessel (n)
ronariu, fearfully (adv)
ronarmeniu, fearlessly (adv)
ronarmenu, fearless (adj)
ronaru, fearful (adj)
ronasre, fear (v)
rotaitif, appointment (n)
rotaitifwan, appointer (n doer)
rotaitisf, appoint (v)
Rotesharf, Rochester (n)
roturst, pour (v)
rovakarf, bakery (n)
rovark, bake (n)
rovarkwan, baker (n doer)
rovarsk, bake (v)
rovorifp, occupation (n)
rovorifpan, occupancy (n)
rovorifpanwan, occupant (n doer)
rovorifpiu, occupationally (adv)
rovorifpu, occupational (adj)
rovorifpwan, occupier (n doer)
rovorifsp, occupy (v)
rualf, lyre (n)
rualirf, lyric (n)
rualirfu, lyrical (adj)
ruanshk, hunk (n)

ruanshkwan, hunker (n doer)
ruanshsk, hunker (v)
ruarsh, right (n d:ownership)
rubalvelarfiu, preposterously (adv)
rubalvelarfu, preposterous (adj)
Rubek, EhoMonth02 (n)
rubelkudil, preconfiguration (n)
rubelkudisle, preconfigure (v)
rubelship, preconception (n)
rubelshisp, preconceive (v)
rubeltifk, precondition (n)
rubeltifsk, precondition (v)
Rubidium, Rubidium (n)
rubolirk, preparation (n)
rubolirkwan, preparer (n doer)
rubolirsk, prepare (v)
rubugarst, prepackage (v)
rubushlarn, predestination (n)
rubushlarsne, predestine (v)
rudeirk, prediction (n)
rudeirkiu, predictably (adv)
rudeirku, predictable (adj)
rudeirku, predictive (adj)
rudeirkwan, predictor (n doer)
rudeirsk, predict (v)
rudermashku, precancerous (adj)
rudiage, bank (n d:storage)
rudiagwan, banker (n doer d:storage)
rudiazge, bank (v d:storage)
rudibarge, pretrial (n)
ruduathk, prevention (n)
ruduathkiu, preventably (adv)
ruduathkiu, preventively (adv)
ruduathku, preventable (adj)
ruduathku, preventive (adj)
ruduathsk, prevent (v)
ruduvark, preservation (n)
rufaishst, predominate (v)
rufaisht, predomination (n)
rufaishtiu, predominantly (adv)
rufaishtu, predominant (adj)
ruferp, preset (n)
rufersp, preset (v)
ruferspyot, preset (v pa)
rufiarst, presume (v)
rufiart, presumption (n)
rufiartiu, presumably (adv)
rufiartiu, presumptively (adv)
rufiartu, presumable (adj)
rufiartu, presumptive (adj)
rufirst, preach (v)
rufirtu, preachy (adj)
rufirtwan, preacher (n doer)
rufivarl, preseason (n)
rufkunk, legacy (n)
rufludiu, precariously (adv)
rufludu, precarious (adj)
rufp, leave (n d:departure)
rufsp, leave (v d:departure)
rufspyot, left (v pa d:departure)
rufuarst, preview (v)

rufuart, preview (n)
rufuartwan, previewer (n doer)
rugelf, preference (n)
rugelfiu, preferably (adv)
rugelfiu, preferentially (adv)
rugelfu, preferable (adj)
rugelfu, preferential (adj)
rugelsf, prefer (v)
ruginshk, preemption (n)
ruginshkiu, preemptively (adv)
ruginshku, preemptive (adj)
ruginshsk, preempt (v)
rugrushst, preclude (v)
ruherst, prejudice (v)
ruhert, prejudice (n)
ruhetherst, prejudge (v)
ruhethert, prejudgement (n)
rukofirst, preserve (v)
rukofirt, preserve (n)
rukofirtwan, preserver (n doer)
rulthiu, preciously (adv)
rulthu, precious (adj)
ruluthart, prerequisite (n)
rulzhirmu, gingerly (adj)
rumarl, gentleness (n)
rumarliu, gently (adv)
rumarlu, gentle (adj)
rumarnosh, gentleman (n)
rumarnoshyek, gentlemen (n pl)
rumoirme, prepayment (n)
rumoirmwan, prepayer (n doer)
rumoirzme, prepay (v)
rumoirzmyot, prepaid (v pa)
runiartu, pristine (adj)
runork, premise (n)
runorsk, premise (v)
runshk, share (n)
runshkwan, sharer (n doer)
runshsk, share (v)
runshthorthkwan, shareholder (n doer)
runulirst, preexist (v)
runulirt, preexistence (n)
ruolmost, prearrange (v)
ruolmot, prearrangement (n)
rupen, leftover (n)
rupifork, pretense (n)
rupiforku, pretentious (adj)
rupiforkwan, pretender (n doer)
rupiforsk, pretend (v)
rupiukarzde, prerecord (v)
rurovorifp, preoccupation (n)
rurovorifsp, preoccupy (v)
ruruters, prelude (v)
rurutersh, prelude (n)
rushathor, prehistory (n)
rushathoru, prehistoric (adj)
rushenirk, pretax (n)
rushenirsk, pretax (v)
Rushiarf, Russia (n)
Rushiarn, Russian (n)
rushirftiu, prematurely (adv)
rushirftu, premature (adj)

rushiurp, prevalence (n)
rushiurpu, prevalent (adj)
rushiursp, prevail (v)
rushkashirp, precaution (n)
rushlerk, precipitation (n)
rushlersk, precipitate (v)
rushpersh, preschool (n)
rushpershu, preschool (adj)
rushrilge, prescription (n)
rushrilzge, prescribe (v)
rushtirbe, pretext (n)
rushuarsh, prescience (n)
Ruthenium, Ruthenium (n)
Rutherfordium, Rutherfordium (n)
ruthirshk, precision (n)
ruthirshkiu, precisely (adv)
ruthirshku, precise (adj)
ruthoirs, preface (v)
ruthoirsh, preface (n)
rutikan, predisposition (n)
rutikasne, predispose (v)
rutulirs, predetermine (v)
rutulirsh, predetermination (n)
ruvaurshu, preliminary (adj)
ruvekart, precedence (n)
ruvekart, precedent (n)
ruverk, precession (n)
ruverkwan, predecessor (n doer)
ruversk, precede (v)
ruvirk, prefix (n)
ruvirort, prefecture (n)
ruvirortwan, prefect (n doer)
ruvirsk, prefix (v)
ruviurn, prewar (n)
ruvuglark, presupposition (n)
ruvuglarsk, presuppose (v)
ruvularn, premarriage (n)
ruvularnu, premarital (adj)
ruzhiarfik, premeditation (n)
ruzhiarfisk, premeditate (v)
Sanau, Sanau (n)
seihem, Number_1e3306
seil, S (let sng)
seili, Ss (let pl)
Seranara, Seranara (n)
Seris, Seris (n)
sha, she (pron 3rd fem sng sub)
shafal, commendation (n)
shafasle, commend (v)
shafirpieit, dynasty (n)
shafirpieitu, dynastic (adj)
shafkarn, freckle (n)
shaflark, trash (n)
shaflarku, trashy (adj)
shaflarsk, trash (v)
shaiamdraursh, watchdog (n)
shaiamplorn, watchman (n)
shaiamplornyek, watchmen (n pl)
shaiarme, watch (n d:viewing)
shaiarmiu, watchfully (adv d:viewing)
shaiarmu, watchful (adj

d:viewing)
shaiarmwan, watcher (n doer d:viewing)
shaiarsh, state (n d:region)
shaiarshfif, statehood (n)
shaiarzme, watch (v d:viewing)
shaiashkiarf, statehouse (n)
shaiashkrashku, statewide (Adj)
shaiashoirt, stateside (n)
shaiashoirtu, stateside (adj)
shaiashplorn, statesman (n)
shaiashplornfif, statesmanship (n)
shaiashplornyek, statesmen (n pl)
shaifk, freak (n)
shaifku, freaky (adj)
shaifsk, freak (v)
shailart, studio (n)
Shaiprulsh, Cyprus (n)
shair, the (det)
shairp, locale (n)
shairp, locality (n)
shairp, location (n)
shairpiu, locally (adv)
shairpu, local (adj)
shairpuest, localize (v)
shairpuet, localization (n)
shairpwan, locator (n doer)
shairsp, locate (v)
shaitharn, western (n d:film)
shaithaurshu, westward (adj)
shaithdraifpu, westbound (adj)
shaithk, west (n)
shaithku, west (adj)
shaithku, western (adj)
shaithkwan, westerner (n doer)
shaithkweku, westernmost (adj)
shaithsk, westernize (v)
Shaizhark, Caesar (n)
Shaizharku, Caesarean (adj)
shakidorige, shotgun (n)
shakirt, shot (n)
Shakramenirt, Sacramento (n)
shalirkiu, plausibly (adv)
shalirku, plausible (adj)
shalirme, fur (n)
shalirmu, furry (adj)
shalirn, simplicity (n)
shalirniu, simply (adv)
shalirnu, simple (adj)
shalirnu, simplistic (adj)
shalirnuet, simplification (n)
shalirnwaku, simplest (adj)
shalirnwelu, simpler (adj)
shalirsk, plause (v)
shalirsne, simplify (v)
shalirzme, fur (v)
Shamarium, Samarium (n)
shamirme, canoe (n)
shamirzme, canoe (v)
Shan Antoniorn, San Antonio (n)
Shan Diegorf, San Diego (n)
Shan Franshirshk, San Francisco

(n)
shan, her (pron 3rd fem sng obj)
Shanilan, January (n)
Shankairf, Shanghai (n)
Shant Barbaralf, Santa Barbara (n)
Shantarf Klaursh, Santa Claus (n)
Shapor, EhoMonth10 (n)
sharaf, wife (n)
sharagen, silver (n)
sharalf, midwife (n)
shardan, woman (n)
shardanyek, women (n pl)
shardark, widow (n)
shardarsk, widow (v)
shardoiark, womanization (n)
shardoiarkwan, womanizer (n doer)
shardoiarsk, womanize (v)
shardu, whether (conj)
sharfp, lord (n)
sharinf, modernism (n)
sharinf, modernization (n)
sharinfu, modern (adj)
sharinfwan, modernist (n doer)
sharinsf, modernize (v)
sharlade, heroic (n)
sharlade, heroism (n)
sharladiu, heroically (adv)
sharladu, heroic (adj)
sharladwan, hero (n doer)
sharladwan, heroine (n doer)
sharlf, love (n d:pleasure)
sharlfu, lovely (adj d:pleasure)
sharlfwan, lover (n doer d:pleasure)
sharlirst, essentiate (v)
sharlirt, essence (n)
sharlirtiu, essentially (adv)
sharlirtu, essential (adj)
sharlorp, sentiment (n)
sharlorpu, sentimental (adj)
Sharlort, Charlotte (n)
sharlsf, love (v d:pleasure)
sharluirme, robustness (n)
sharluirmu, robust (adj)
sharme, belief (n)
sharmiu, believably (adv)
sharmu, believable (adj)
sharmwan, believer (n doer)
shars, man (v d:operate)
sharshk, management (n)
sharshkiu, manageably (adv)
sharshku, manageable (adj)
sharshkwan, manager (n doer)
sharshkwatu, managerial (adj)
sharshsk, manage (v)
shart, either (pron)
shartu, either (adj/adv/conj)
sharvarbe, maternity (n)
sharvarbiu, maternally (adv)
sharvarbu, maternal (adj)
sharzme, believe (v)

shash, her (pron 3rd fem sng pos sub)
shash, hers (pron 3rd fem sng pos obj)
shashfal, herself (pron 3rd fem sing refl)
shathor, history (n)
shathoriu, historically (adv)
shathoru, historic (adj)
shathoru, historical (adj)
shathorwan, historian (n doer)
shauank, whisker (n d:hair)
Shaudarf Arobarn, Saudi Arabia (n)
Shaudarn, Saudi (n)
shaukar, strangeness (n)
shaurf, buffet (n d:strike)
shaurk, estrangement (n)
shaurkiu, strangely (adv)
shaurku, strange (adj)
shaurkwan, stranger (n doer)
shaurp, asylum (n)
shaursf, buffet (v d:strike)
shaursk, estrange (v)
shaushurth, soybean (n)
shauthk, trait (n)
shavarn, gown (n)
shavizge, lodge (v d:stop)
Sheaborgium, Seaborgium (n)
shefirn, subtlety (n)
shefirniu, subtly (adv)
shefirnu, subtle (adj)
sheiarf, fetus (n)
sheiarfu, fetal (adj)
sheiarme, theory (n)
sheiarmiu, theoretically (adv)
sheiarmu, theoretical (adj)
sheiarmwan, theorist (n doer)
sheiarzme, theorize (v)
sheifan, fountain (n)
sheifirt, veggie (n)
sheifst, fertilize (v)
sheift, fertility (n)
sheiftu, fertile (adj)
sheiftuet, fertilization (n)
sheiftwan, fertilizer (n doer)
sheihem, Number_1e3606
sheil, Sh (let sng)
sheilart, slogan (n)
sheili, Shs (let pl)
sheimaift, senility (n)
sheimaiftu, senile (adj)
sheimart, senior (n)
sheimartu, senior (adj)
sheimartuet, seniority (n)
sheimartwan, senior (n doer)
sheirn, radius (n)
sheirnart, thesis (n)
sheirnyek, radii (n pl)
sheirs, specialize (v)
sheirsh, specialty (n)
sheirshiu, especially (adv)
sheirshiu, specially (adv)

sheirshu, special (adj)
sheirshwan, specialist (n doer)
sheirsne, radius (v)
sheithk, elasticity (n)
sheithku, elastic (adj)
sheivarn, vegetation (n)
sheivarnwan, vegetator (n doer)
sheivarsne, vegetate (v)
sheivort, vegetable (n)
sheivotuart, vegetarianism (n)
sheivotuartwan, vegetarian (n doer)
shelar, flour (n)
sheldaish, haircut (n)
sheleirp, hairpin (n)
Shelenium, Selenium (n)
Shelfian, Celsius (adj)
shelp, sub (n d:submarine)
shelplershwan, hairdresser (n doer)
shelt, hair (n)
sheltfriarf, hairstyle (n)
shelthku, supple (adj)
sheltik, hairdo (n)
sheltmenu, hairless (adj)
sheltpliurf, hairspray (n)
sheltroifk, hairline (n)
sheltu, hairy (adj)
shenarde, supper (n)
shenirk, tax (n)
shenirku, taxable (adj)
shenirkuet, taxation (n)
shenirkwan, taxer (n doer)
shenirsk, tax (v)
shenirst, taxi (v)
shenirt, taxi (n)
shenirtomoirme, taxpayer (n)
shepelpfif, scholarship (n)
shepelpiu, scholarly (adv)
shepelpu, scholastic (adj)
shepelpwan, scholar (n doer)
sherf, deposit (n)
sherfiek, depository (n)
sherfk, depot (n)
sherfwan, depositor (n doer)
sherge, scribble (n)
shergwan, scribe (n doer)
Sherium, Cerium (n)
sherme, cleanliness (n)
shermiu, cleanly (adv)
shermivell, cleanup (n)
shermu, clean (adj)
shermwan, cleaner (n doer)
shern, fame (n)
sherniu, famously (adv)
shernu, famous (adj)
shers, okay (v)
shersf, deposit (v)
shershai, ok (interj)
shershai, okay (interj)
shershu, okay (adj)
sherzge, scribble (v)
sherzme, clean (v)

Sheshium, Caesium (n)
shetark, leger (n)
shethirp, supply (n)
shethirpwan, supplier (n doer)
shethirsp, supply (v)
shethperst, supplement (v)
shethpert, supplement (n)
shethpertu, supplemental (adj)
shethpertu, supplementary (adj)
shethpertuet, supplementation (n)
shetirs, testify (v)
shetirsh, testimony (n)
shetirshuet, testimonial (n)
shevirsh, secret (n)
shevirshiu, secretively (adv)
shevirshiu, secretly (adv)
shevirsht, secrecy (n)
shevirshu, secret (adj)
shevirshu, secretive (adj)
shflin, brightness (n)
shfliniu, brightly (adv)
shflinu, bright (adj)
shflinwaku, brightest (adj)
shflinwan, brightener (n doer)
shflinwelu, brighter (adj)
shflisne, brighten (v)
shflun, brilliance (n)
shfluniu, brilliantly (adv)
shflunu, brilliant (adj)
shiakbliert, scapegoat (n)
shialbaraft, touchstone (n)
Shiaralf, Sierra (n)
shiarf, sanity (n)
shiarfiu, sanely (adv)
shiarfst, conquer (v)
shiarft, conquest (n)
shiarftwan, conqueror (n doer)
shiarfu, sane (adj)
shiarge, tangle (n)
shiarl, touch (n)
shiarltien, touchdown (n)
shiarlu, touchy (adj)
shiarme, tangent (n)
shiarmiu, tangentially (adv)
shiarmp, tangible (n)
shiarmpu, tangible (adj)
shiarmu, tangential (adj)
shiarn, sanitation (n)
shiarnu, sanitary (adj)
shiarp, adept (n)
shiarpu, adept (adj)
shiars, fashion (v)
shiarsh, fashion (n)
shiarshiu, fashionably (adv)
shiarshu, fashionable (adj)
shiarsle, touch (v)
shiarsne, sanitize (v)
shiarzge, tangle (v)
Shiatalf, Seattle (n)
shiaushsk, sap (v)
shibedaurn, mealtime (n)
shibedaurnu, mealtime (adj)

Shidunarf, Sydney (n)
shiemirk, senate (n)
shiemirkwan, senator (n doer)
Shiern, Army (n)
shigmarn, sigma (n)
shilfk, sap (n)
Shilikon, Silicon (n)
shilkarp, sapling (n)
shilu, itty (adj)
Shilver, Silver (n)
shimarn, gnosis (n)
shimarnu, gnostic (adj)
shinekin, army (n)
Shinkaporf, Singapore (n)
Shinshinart, Cincinnati (n)
shiofkeloirn, textile (n)
shioirkwan, vanisher (n doer)
shioirsk, vanish (v)
shiop, hill (n)
shiopedaurp, hilltop (n)
shiopshoirt, hillside (n)
shiopu, hilly (adj)
shiorbe, hoop (n)
shiorf, texture (n)
shiorfwan, texturer (n doer)
Shiorl, Seoul (n)
shiorsf, texturize (v)
shiorst, hook (v)
shiort, hook (n)
shiortiveil, hookup (n)
shiortwan, hooker (n doer)
shipern, map (n)
shipersne, map (v)
shirbe, meal (n)
shirfst, mature (v)
shirft, maturity (n)
shirftu, mature (adj)
shirftuet, maturation (n)
shirge, spoke (n d:support)
Shiriarf, Syria (n)
Shiriarn, Syrian (n)
shirk, skill (n)
shirkiu, skillfully (adv)
shirku, skillful (adj)
shirsh, these (pron)
shirshu, these (adj)
shirsk, skill (v)
shirzge, spoke (v d:support)
shithsk, lynch (v)
shiu, whew (interj)
shiuaik, sizzle (v)
shiuaisk, sizzle (v)
shiufk, vaunt (n)
shiufsk, vaunt (v)
shiunirku, lucent (adj)
shiurf, vanity (n)
shiurfiu, vainly (adv)
shiurfu, vain (adj)
shiurnu, lucid (adj)
shiurp, avail (n)
shiurpaf, availability (n)
shiurpafu, available (adj)
shiursne, elucidate (v)

shiursp, avail (v)
shiushk, switch (n)
shiushkafen, switchover (n)
shiushku, switchy (adj)
shiushkwan, switcher (n doer)
shiushplok, switchboard (n)
shiushprulat, switchblade (n)
shiushsk, switch (v)
shivarst, knight (v)
shivart, knight (n)
shivartu, knightly (adj)
shivershst, necessitate (v)
shiversht, necessity (n)
shivershtiu, necessarily (adv)
shivershtu, necessary (adj)
shkaiaushk, squawk (n)
shkaiaushsk, squawk (v)
shkaidarn, igloo (n)
shkainark, crusade (n)
shkainarkwan, crusader (n doer)
shkainarsk, crusade (v)
shkairk, felony (n)
shkairkwan, felon (n doer)
shkairn, cruise (n)
shkairnwan, cruiser (n doer)
shkairsne, cruise (v)
shkairst, ice (v)
shkairt, ice (n)
shkairtiu, icily (adv)
shkairtu, icy (adj)
shkaishk, smash (n)
shkaishkwan, smasher (n doer)
shkaishsk, smash (v)
shkaitairt, icicle (n)
shkaiteblerkwan, icebreaker (n
    doer)
shkaitniurk, iceberg (n)
shkaitplorn, iceman (n)
shkaitplornyek, icemen (n pl)
shkaitprekun, icebox (n)
shkakdairt, crackpot (n)
shkalark, crackle (n)
shkalarsk, crackle (v)
shkalirst, start (v)
shkalirt, start (n)
shkalirtiveil, startup (n)
shkalirtwan, starter (n doer)
shkaltark, startle (n)
shkaltarsk, startle (v)
Shkandium, Scandium (n)
shkark, crack (n d:split)
shkarktiern, crackdown (n)
shkarkwan, cracker (n doer
    d:split)
shkarme, strum (n)
shkarmwan, strummer (n doer)
shkarp, slash (n)
shkarpwan, slasher (n doer)
shkars, cause (v)
shkarsf, mend (v)
shkarsh, cause (n)
shkarship, caution (n)
shkarshipiu, cautiously (adv)

shkarshipu, cautious (adj)
shkarshisp, caution (v)
shkarshk, casualty (n)
shkarshkiu, casually (adv)
shkarshku, casual (adj)
shkarshu, causal (adj)
shkarsk, crack (v d:split)
shkarsp, slash (v)
shkarve, tussle (n)
shkarzme, strum (v)
shkarzve, tussle (v)
shkathsk, strut (v)
shkaufku, stout (adj)
shkaurp, schism (n)
shkaurpyek, schism (n pl)
shkavat, brink (n)
shkeialst, ordinate (v)
shkeialt, ordination (n)
shkeif, double (n)
shkeifiu, doubly (adv)
shkeifst, ordain (v)
shkeifu, double (adj)
shkeifwan, doubler (n doer)
shkeirk, squeak (n)
shkeirkiu, squeakily (adv)
shkeirku, squeaky (adj)
shkeirsk, squeak (v)
shkeisf, double (v)
shkeithk, tuft (n)
shkelf, edge (n)
shkelfu, edgy (adj)
shkelfwan, edger (n doer)
shkelirk, squeal (n)
shkelirp, staple (n d:crimp)
shkelirpwan, stapler (n doer
    d:crimp)
shkelirsk, squeal (v)
shkelirsp, staple (v d:crimp)
shkelsf, edge (v)
shkelst, order (v)
shkelt, order (n)
shkelt, orderliness (n)
shkeltariu, ordinarily (adv)
shkeltaru, ordinary (adj)
shkeltat, ordinance (n)
shkeltu, orderly (adj)
shkeltwan, orderer (n doer)
shkenirp, optic (n)
shkenirpiu, optically (adv)
shkenirpu, optical (adj)
shkerp, coordinate (n)
shkerpet, coordination (n)
shkerpwan, coordinator (n doer)
shkersp, coordinate (v)
shkiark, tuck (n)
shkiarkwan, tucker (n doer)
shkiarsk, tuck (v)
shkiarst, stare (v)
shkiart, stare (n)
shkiathkwan, scooter (n doer)
shkiathsk, scoot (v)
shkiausht, starkness (n)
shkiaushtu, stark (adj)

shkikenk, mutiny (n)
shkikenkwan, mutineer (n doer)
shkikensk, mutiny (v)
shkilorp, crimp (n)
shkilorpwan, crimper (n doer)
shkilorsp, crimp (v)
shkilorst, crinkle (v)
shkilort, crinkle (n)
shkiorst, squirt (v)
shkiort, squirt (n)
shkirfu, indivisible (adj)
shkirk, segment (n)
shkirkuet, segmentation (n)
shkirp, individual (n)
shkirpiu, individually (adv)
shkirpu, individual (adj)
shkirpuet, individualism (n)
shkirpuet, individuality (n)
shkirpuetu, individualistic (adj)
shkirpuetwan, individualist (n
    doer)
shkirsk, segment (v)
shkirsp, individualize (v)
shkirst, move (v)
shkirt, move (n)
shkirtalt, movement (n)
shkirtar, movie (n)
shkirtiu, movably (adv)
shkirtu, movable (adj)
shkirtwan, mover (n doer)
shkishk, piss (n)
shkishkwan, pisser (n doer)
shkishsk, piss (v)
shkitarnargwan, moviemaker (n
    doer)
shkithk, match (n d:stick)
shkithprekun, matchbox (n
    d:stickbox)
shkiushsk, skid (v)
shkiverve, thickness (n)
shkivervlu, thickly (adv)
shkivervu, thick (adj)
shkivervwan, thickener (n doer)
shkiverzve, thicken (v)
shklart, statute (n)
shklartu, statutory (adj)
shkleinbielirk, seaport (n)
shkleinbranar, seacoast (n)
shkleineidorn, seawater (n)
shkleinfamor, seabed (n)
shkleinflarsh, seafront (n)
shkleinkiarme, seagull (n)
shkleinklierk, seahawk (n)
shkleinparlak, seagate (n)
shkleinparsh, seafood (n)
shkleinpliorl, seaway (n)
shkleinplorn, seaman (n)
shkleinplornyek, seamen (n pl)
shkleinshoirt, seaside (n)
shkleinshoirtu, seaside (adj)
shkleintherk, seashell (n)
shkleinthirsk, seafare (v)
shkleinyurk, seaweed (n)

shkleirn, sea (n)
shkliarge, cruelty (n)
shkliargiu, cruelly (adv)
shkliargu, cruel (adj)
shklirfst, crush (v)
shklirft, crush (n)
shklirftwan, crusher (n doer)
shklirpu, crude (adj)
shklivarge, meanness (n d:cruel)
shklivargu, mean (adj d:cruel)
shklivargweku, meanest (adj
    d:cruel)
shklivargwelu, meaner (adj
    d:cruel)
shklufst, choose (v)
shklufstyot, chose (v pa)
shkluft, choice (n)
shkluftu, choosy (adj)
shkluftwan, chooser (n doer)
shkodarge, cottage (n)
shkoflurift, caseload (n)
shkoift, shot (n)
shkoirp, slant (n)
shkoirsp, slant (v)
shkorbe, boat (n)
shkorbwan, boater (n doer)
shkorf, case (n d:investigation)
shkorsf, case (v d:investigation)
shkorst, shoot (v)
shkorstyot, shot (v pa)
shkort, shoot (n)
shkortuil, shootout (n)
shkortwan, shooter (n doer)
shkorzbe, boat (v)
Shkotlanirf, Scotland (n)
Shkotlarn, Scottish (n)
shkraikshkoift, slingshot (n)
shkraishk, sling (n)
shkraishkwan, slinger (n doer)
shkraishsk, sling (v)
shkraishskyot, slung (v pa)
shkraist, grind (v d:rip)
shkraistyot, ground (v pa d:rip)
shkrait, grind (n d:rip)
shkraitwan, grinder (n doer d:rip)
shkralge, patch (n)
shkralgu, patchy (adj)
shkralgwan, patcher (n doer)
shkralkwan, slayer (n doer)
shkralsk, slay (v)
shkralskyot, slew (v pa)
shkralzge, patch (v)
shkranarst, dazzle (v)
shkranart, dazzle (n)
shkranartwan, dazzler (n doer)
shkranp, daze (n)
shkransp, daze (v)
shkrifst, shimmer (v)
shkrilk, slip (n)
shkrilku, slippery (adj)
shkrilkuet, slippage (n)
shkrilsk, slip (v)
shkrishk, shim (n)

shkrishsk, shim (v)
shkroilk, slope (n)
shkroilsk, slope (v)
shkubars, squat (v)
shkubarsh, squat (n)
shkubarshwan, squatter (n doer)
shkufblaishk, scuttlebutt (n)
shkunkiu, stunningly (adv)
shkunsk, stun (v)
shkurk, stunt (n)
shkursf, scuttle (v)
shkursk, stunt (v)
shkwak, scat (interj)
shlaiarp, splice (n)
shlaiarsp, splice (v)
shlaink, sway (n)
shlainsk, sway (v)
shlairf, wariness (n)
shlairfiu, warily (adv)
shlairfu, wary (adj)
shlairk, split (n)
shlairkwan, splitter (n doer)
shlairp, martyr (n)
shlairsk, split (v)
shlairskyot, split (v pa)
shlairsp, martyr (v)
shlairt, city (n)
shlairzbe, surround (v)
shlarde, body (n)
shlardu, bodily (adj)
shlarge, coarseness (n)
shlargiu, coarsely (adv)
shlargu, coarse (adj)
shlarin, floor (n)
shlarisne, floor (v)
shlark, stealth (n)
shlarkiu, stealthily (adv)
shlarku, stealthy (adj)
shlarkwan, stealer (n doer)
shlarnplok, floorboard (n)
shlarsk, steal (v)
shlarskyot, stole (v pa)
shlarve, drag (n)
shlarzve, drag (v)
shlathk, swath (n)
shlathsk, swathe (v)
shlaursk, whisk (v d:swipe)
shlaushkwan, slogger (n doer)
shlaushsk, slog (v)
shlavak, dragon (n)
shletkiarf, warehouse (n)
shlefkiarsf, warehouse (v)
shlefst, stilt (v)
shleft, stilt (n)
shleiarfiu, lavishly (adv)
shleiarfu, lavish (adj)
shleink, lava (n)
shleisht, slyness (n)
shleishtiu, slyly (adv)
shleishtu, sly (adj)
shleishuk, spasm (n)
shleithganirp, sledgehammer (n)
shleithk, sledge (n)

shleithsk, sledge (v)
shleneidorn, stillwater (n)
shlerf, ware (n)
shlerk, structure (n)
shlerkiu, structurally (adv)
shlerku, structural (adj)
shlern, stillness (n d:calm)
shlerniu, still (adv d:calm)
shlernu, still (adj d:calm)
shlers, fish (v)
shlersh, fish (n)
shlershu, fishy (adj)
shlershuat, fishery (n)
shlershwan, fisher (n doer)
shlershyek, fish (n pl)
shlershyek, fishes (n pl)
shlersk, structure (v)
shlersne, still (v d:calm)
shleshplorn, fisherman (n)
shleshplornyek, fishermen (n pl)
shleshtairak, fishbowl (n)
shliarge, plunder (n)
shliarme, swallow (n d:bird)
shliart, instrument (n)
shliartu, instrumental (adj)
shliartuet, instrumentation (n)
shliarzge, plunder (v)
shliashst, clinch (v)
shliasht, clinch (n)
shliashtwan, clincher (n doer)
shlieshst, clench (v)
shliesht, clench (n)
shlirbe, ride (n)
shlirbwan, rider (n doer)
shlirf, ridge (n)
shlirk, slice (n)
shlirkwan, slicer (n doer)
shlirn, slenderness (n)
shlirnu, slender (adj)
shlirp, ballot (n)
shlirs, scissor (v)
shlirsh, scissors (n)
shlirsk, slice (v)
shlirzbe, ride (v)
shlirzbyot, rode (v pa)
shliunak, splinter (n)
shliunask, splinter (v)
shliunf, splint (n)
shliushst, clutch (v d:grip)
shliusht, clutch (n d:grip)
shloarst, slack (v d:loose)
shloart, slack (n d:loose)
shloartwan, slacker (n doer
    d:loose)
shlofst, swerve (v)
shloft, swerve (n)
shloirt, ploy (n)
shloirtuin, employee (n)
shlorde, cheese (n)
shlordu, cheesy (adj)
shlort, cold (n d:temperature)
shlortu, cold (adj d:temperature)
shlortuet, coldness (n)

shlortwaku, coldest (adj)
shlortwelu, colder (adj)
shluakarn, mutant (n)
shluark, mutation (n)
shluarkiu, mutably (adv)
shluarku, mutable (adj)
shluarkwan, mutator (n doer)
shluarp, haul (n)
shluarpwan, hauler (n doer)
shluarsk, mutate (v)
shluarsp, haul (v)
shluarst, ply (v)
shluart, ply (n)
shluartu, pliable (adj)
shluartwan, plier (n doer)
shluatfanirn, plywood (n)
shluiarst, swelter (v)
shluiart, swelter (n)
shlukerst, station (v)
shlukert, station (n)
shlukertu, stationary (adj)
shlurbiu, facetiously (adv)
shlurbu, facetious (adj)
shlurde, suddenness (n)
shlurdiu, suddenly (adv)
shlurdu, sudden (adj)
shlurf, coolness (n)
shlurfit, coolant (n)
shlurfiu, coolly (adv)
shlurfp, picnic (n)
shlurfpwan, picnicker (n doer)
shlurfsp, picnic (v)
shlurfu, cool (adj)
shlurfwaku, coolest (adj)
shlurfwan, cooler (n doer)
shlurfwelu, cooler (adj)
shlurk, stay (n)
shlurkwan, stayer (n doer)
shlurmu, weepy (adj)
shlurmwan, weeper (n doer)
shlurn, sameness (n)
shlurnk, bob (n)
shlurnkwan, bobber (n doer)
shlurnsk, bob (v)
shlurnu, same (adj)
shlurp, sled (n)
shlurs, slide (v)
shlursf, cool (v)
shlursh, slide (n)
shlurshwan, slider (n doer)
shlursk, stay (v)
shlursp, sled (v)
shlursyot, slid (v pa)
shlurth, statistic (n)
shlurthu, statistical (adj)
shlurzme, weep (v)
shlurzmyot, wept (v pa)
shlutirk, surrender (n)
shlutirkwan, surrenderer (n doer)
shlutirsk, surrender (v)
shmalip, snippet (n)
shmalst, chance (v)
shmalt, chance (n)

shmaltu, chance (adj)
shmarp, snip (n)
shmarsp, snip (v)
shmathk, snoop (n)
shmathku, snoopy (adj)
shmathkwan, snoop (n doer)
shmathsk, snoop (v)
shmaushk, snore (n)
shmaushsk, snore (v)
shmaushst, snort (v)
shmausht, snort (n)
shmeirf, chancel (n)
shmeirfwan, chancellor (n doer)
shmeirsf, chancel (v)
shmern, tone (n d:quality)
shmernwan, toner (n doer
    d:quality)
shmersne, tone (v d:quality)
shmiark, notoriety (n)
shmiarkiu, notoriously (adv)
shmiarku, notorious (adj)
shmiarp, snout (n)
shmirk, bough (n)
shmirp, snot (n)
shmirpu, snotty (adj)
shmirst, notice (v)
shmirt, notice (n)
shmirtiu, noticeably (adv)
shmirtu, noticeable (adj)
shmitark, notification (n)
shmitarkwan, notifier (n doer)
shmitarsk, notify (v)
shmonde, ball (n)
shmonzde, ball (v)
shmorkwan, cleanser (n doer)
shmorsk, cleanse (v)
shmurge, snooze (n)
shmurgwan, snoozer (n doer)
shmurn, tune (n)
shmurnwan, tuner (n doer)
shmursnc, tunc (v)
shmurzge, snooze (v)
shnaifk, clot (n)
shnaifsk, clot (v)
shnairn, lie (n d:deceit)
shnairnwan, liar (n doer d:deceit)
shnairsne, lie (v d:deceit)
shnairt, spine (n)
shnairtmenu, spineless (adj)
shnairtu, spinal (adj)
shnairtu, spiny (adj)
shnaithan, clutter (n)
shnaithasne, clutter (v)
shnakarst, flicker (v)
shnakart, flicker (n)
shnaparn, spindle (n)
shnarf, connection (n)
shnarfat, connectivity (n)
shnarfrep, liability (n)
shnarfrepiu, liably (adv)
shnarfrepu, liable (adj)
shnarfwan, connector (n doer)
shnark, flick (n)

shnarl, liaison (n)
shnarp, spin (n)
shnarpunf, spinoff (n)
shnarpwan, spinner (n doer)
shnarsf, connect (v)
shnarsk, flick (v)
shnarsle, liaison (v)
shnarsp, spin (v)
shnarspyot, spun (v pa)
shnarst, spill (v)
shnarstyot, spilt (v pa)
shnart, spill (n)
shnartafen, spillover (n)
shnartuet, spillage (n)
shnartwan, spiller (n doer)
shnarzge, flog (v)
shnatpliorl, spillway (n)
shnaufp, snarl (n)
shnaufsp, snarl (v)
shnaushk, snipe (n)
shnaushkwan, sniper (n doer)
shnaushsk, snipe (v)
shnefst, stick (v d:twig, poke)
shnefstyot, stuck (v pa d:twig,
    poke)
shneft, stick (n d:twig, poke)
shneifk, flail (n)
shneifsk, flail (v)
shneishst, stash (v)
shneisht, stash (n)
shnerf, armor (n)
shnern, arm (n)
shnernwan, armer (n doer)
shnersf, armor (v)
shnersne, arm (v)
shnesh, since (adv/prep/conj)
shneuishk, clog (n)
shneuishsk, clog (v)
shniamesp, clump (v)
shniamp, clump (n)
shniampu, clumpy (adj)
shnianku, clingy (adj)
shniansk, cling (v)
shnianskyot, clung (v pa)
shniark, skirmish (n)
shniathsk, cleave (v d:stick)
shnifnerp, wiretap (n)
shnifnersp, wiretap (v)
shnirf, wire (n)
shnirfmenu, wireless (adj)
shnirfu, wirey (adj)
shnirsf, wire (v)
shnoifp, snatch (n)
shnoifpwan, snatcher (n doer)
shnoifsp, snatch (v)
shnoikarn, stickler (n)
shnoirk, stickiness (n d:adhere)
shnoirku, sticky (adj d:adhere)
shnoirkwan, sticker (n doer
    d:adhere)
shnoirsk, stick (v d:adhere)
shnoirskyot, stuck (v pa d:adhere)
shnoishst, spew (v)

shnornk, famine (n)
shnufat, cleverness (n)
shnufatiu, cleverly (adv)
shnufatu, clever (adj)
shnurk, ammunition (n)
shnushsk, relish (v)
shobrauf, menstruation (n)
shobraufu, menstrual (adj)
shobrausf, menstruate (v)
Shodium, Sodium (n)
shoidarfk, satanism (n)
shoidarfku, satanic (adj)
shoidarfkwan, satanist (n doer)
shoidarfsk, satanize (v)
Shoidark, Satan (n)
shoifark, manipulation (n)
shoifarkiu, manipulatively (adv)
shoifarku, manipulative (adj)
shoifarkwan, manipulator (n
    doer)
shoifarn, mansion (n)
shoifarsk, manipulate (v)
shoikal, command (n)
shoikalt, commandment (n)
shoikalwan, commander (n doer)
shoikasle, command (v)
shoikaurst, manufacture (v)
shoikaurtwan, manufacturer (n
    doer)
shoiklirp, manner (n)
shoirge, shoulder (n)
shoirk, mandate (n)
shoirku, mandatory (adj)
shoirkuk, manifest (n)
shoirkusk, manifest (v)
shoirp, lick (n)
shoirpwan, licker (n doer)
shoirsk, mandate (v)
shoirsp, lick (v)
shoirst, side (v)
shoirt, side (n)
shoirtwan, sider (n doer)
shoirzge, shoulder (v)
shoishk, manual (n)
shoishkiu, manually (adv)
shoishku, manual (adj)
shoitethirap, sidekick (n)
shoitfeirf, sideshow (n)
shoitgethirk, sidetrack (n)
shoitgethirsk, sidetrack (v)
shoitglishk, sidestep (n)
shoitglishsk, sidestep (v)
shoitpliol, sideways (adj/adv)
shoitroifk, sideline (n)
shoitroifsk, sideline (v)
shoitrolart, sidebar (n)
shoitshnern, sidearm (n)
shoizhoirp, sidewalk (n)
sholarf, humanity (n)
sholarfirf, humankind (n)
sholarfirf, mankind (n)
sholarfiu, humanely (adv)
sholarfu, humane (adj)

sholarfuest, humanize (v)
sholarfuet, humanism (n)
sholarfuetiu, humanistically (adv)
sholarfuetu, humanistic (adj)
sholarfuetwan, humanist (n doer)
sholarfwan, humanitarian (n
    doer)
sholbiorat, manpower (n)
sholnargu, manmade (adj)
shomdork, sentence (n d:words)
shoraf, sense (n)
shorafiu, sensually (adv)
shorafiu, sensuously (adv)
shorafmeniu, senselessly (adv)
shorafmenu, senseless (adj)
shorafu, sensual (adj)
shorafu, sensuous (adj)
shorafun, sensuality (n)
shorafwan, sensor (n doer)
shorafwatu, sensory (adj)
shorapu, rural (adj)
shorasf, sense (v)
shorbast, resent (v d:disdain)
shorbat, resentment (n d:disdain)
shorbatu, resentful (adj
    d:disdain)
shorfip, sensitivity (n)
shorfipiu, sensitively (adv)
shorfipu, sensitive (adj)
shorfisp, sensitize (v)
shorfit, sensation (n)
shorfitiu, sensationally (adv)
shorfitu, sensational (adj)
shorfituest, sensationalize (v)
shorfituet, sensationalism (n)
shorfrelp, sensibility (n)
shorfrelpiu, sensibly (adv)
shorfrelpu, sensible (adj)
shorfst, contain (v)
shorft, containment (n)
shorftwan, container (n doer)
shoriarn, stereo (n)
shork, drawer (n d:compartment)
shorkirk, seduction (n)
shorkirkiu, seductively (adv)
shorkirku, seductive (adj)
shorkirkwan, seducer (n doer)
shorkirsk, seduce (v)
shorl, human (n)
shorliu, humanly (adv)
shorlu, human (adj)
shorsh, those (pron)
shorshu, those (adj)
Shoviert, Soviet (n)
Shpainarn, Spanish (n)
shpairk, gripe (n)
Shpairn, Spain (n)
shpairsk, gripe (v)
shpairst, predicate (v)
shpairt, predicate (n)
shpairtuet, predicament (n)
shpalorst, talk (v)
shpalort, talk (n)

shpalortu, talkative (adj)
shpalortwan, talker (n doer)
shpalp, rind (n)
shparif, stature (n)
shparok, statue (n)
shpefort, static (n)
shpefortu, static (adj)
shperge, fly (n d:insect)
shpers, school (v)
shpersh, school (n)
shpershlen, schoolmate (n)
shpert, state (n d:status)
shpertmenu, stateless (adj
    d:status)
shpeshbiurn, schoolboy (n)
shpeshdalirsh, schoolteacher (n)
shpeshkelerf, schoolgirl (n)
shpeshkiarf, schoolhouse (n)
shpeshluart, schoolchild (n)
shpeshluartyek, schoolchildren (n
    pl)
shpeshthauthk, schoolyard (n)
shpeshvornt, schoolbooks (n)
shpetar, status (n)
shpetoirt, superstition (n)
shpetoirtu, superstitious (adj)
shpiarft, deputization (n)
shpiarst, deputize (v)
shpiart, deputy (n)
shpiartwan, deputizer (n doer)
shpiorf, rant (n)
shpiorsf, rant (v)
shplerk, difficulty (n)
shplerkiu, difficultly (adv)
shplerku, difficult (adj)
shplersk, difficult (v)
shporat, parliament (n)
shporatu, parliamentary (adj)
shprashsk, spawn (v)
shpreifk, cloak (n)
shpreifsk, cloak (v)
shpreln, iron (n d:clothes presser)
shprelsne, iron (v d:clothes
    presser)
shprishkwan, thrasher (n doer)
shprishsk, thrash (v)
shpruk, grip (n)
shprukwan, gripper (n doer)
shprusk, grip (v)
shprust, cost (n)
shprustyot, cost (v pa)
shprut, cost (n)
shprutu, costly (adj)
shpursh, spell (n d:witchcraft)
shpurtrek, treadmill (n)
shpushpaupizme, spellbind (v)
shpushpaupizmyot, spellbound (v
    pa)
shpushst, stoke (v)
shpushtwan, stoker (n doer)
shputhk, tread (n)
shputhsk, tread (v)
shputhskyot, trod (v pa)

shrade, church (n)
shraflirk, mystique (n)
shraflirn, mystery (n)
shraflirniu, mysteriously (adv)
shraflirnu, mysterious (adj)
shraflirsne, mystify (v)
shraflirt, mysticism (n)
shraflirtu, mystical (adj)
shraflirtwan, mystic (n doer)
shraiafk, scuff (n)
shraiafsk, scuff (v)
shraiarp, scuffle (n)
shraiarsp, scuffle (v)
shraiashk, slammer (n d:jail)
shraifp, slavery (n)
shraifpwan, slave (n doer)
shraifsp, slave (v)
shrailditarp, whirlpool (n)
shrailf, whirl (n)
shrailsf, whirl (v)
shrailthelern, whirlwind (n)
shrairk, scrub (n)
shrairku, scrubby (adj)
shrairkwan, scrubber (n doer)
shrairsk, scrub (v)
shraishk, sketch (n)
shraishku, sketchy (adj)
shraishkwan, sketcher (n doer)
shraishsk, sketch (v)
shraishst, siege (v)
shraisht, siege (n)
shraithk, whir (n)
shraithsk, whir (v)
shralbu, squanderous (adj)
shralf, miscellany (n)
shralfu, miscellaneous (adj)
shralge, scab (n)
shralip, college (n)
shralk, scale (n d:fish)
shralp, slap (n)
shralpwan, slapper (n doer)
shralsk, scale (v d:fish)
shralsp, slap (v)
shralst, sharpen (v)
shralt, sharpness (n)
shraltan, sharp (n)
shraltiu, sharply (adv)
shraltu, sharp (adj)
shraltwan, sharpener (n doer)
shralve, struggle (n)
shralzbe, squander (v)
shralzve, struggle (v)
shramesp, slam (v d:hit)
shrampwan, slammer (n doer d:hit)
shranf, room (n)
shranfiepu, roomful (adj)
shranflen, roommate (n)
shranfu, roomy (adj)
shransf, room (v)
shratshkort, sharpshooter (n)
shreilp, ensnarement (n d:trap)
shreilpwan, snare (n doer d:trap)

shreilsp, ensnare (v d:trap)
shreilsp, snare (v d:trap)
shreinf, slime (n)
shreinfu, slimy (adj)
shreinsf, slime (v)
shreit, myth (n)
shreitekuift, mythology (n)
shreitu, mythic (adj)
shreitu, mythical (adj)
shreln, surity (n)
shrelniu, surely (adv)
shrelnu, sure (adj)
shrelst, sit (v)
shrelstyot, sat (v pa)
shrelt, sit (n)
shreme, cousin (n)
shrenst, situate (v)
shrent, situation (n)
shrentiu, situationally (adv)
shrentu, situational (adj)
shriafst, slit (v)
shriafstyot, slit (v pa)
shriaft, slit (n)
shrialp, sliver (n)
shriars, slow (v)
shriarsh, slowness (n)
shriarshiu, slowly (adv)
shriarshtiern, slowdown (n)
shriarshu, slow (adj)
shriarshwaku, slowest (adj)
shriarshwelu, slower (adj)
shriashk, slat (n)
shriashsk, slat (v)
shriaubiorat, firepower (n)
shriaubresh, fireplace (n)
shriaufanin, firewood (n)
shriauferap, firestorm (n)
shriaufliorfu, fireproof (adj)
shriaufliorsf, fireproof (v)
shriauk, fire (n)
shriaukiarf, firehouse (n)
shriaukiork, firework (n)
shriaukovauge, firefight (n)
shriaukovaugwan, firefighter (n doer)
shriauku, fiery (adj)
shriaunolthk, firewall (n)
shriaushk, bonfire (n)
shriaushmonde, fireball (n)
shriaushnen, firearm (n)
shriaushoirt, fireside (n)
shriaushperge, firefly (n)
shriaushst, slaughter (v)
shriausht, slaughter (n)
shriausk, fire (v)
shriautkiarf, slaughterhouse (n)
shriauvibal, firebomb (n)
shriavirst, trek (v)
shriavirt, trek (n)
shriavirtwan, trekker (n doer)
shrielp, script (n)
shrielsp, script (v)
shriepart, scripture (n)

shriepartu, scriptural (adj)
shrifpu, slinky (adj)
shrifsp, slink (v)
shrikdakelf, seatbelt (n)
shrilank, stipulation (n)
shrilansk, stipulate (v)
shrilarf, stipend (n)
shrilf, mist (n)
shrilfiu, mistily (adv)
shrilfu, misty (adj)
shrilfwan, mister (n doer)
shrilk, seat (n)
shrilsf, mist (v)
shrilsk, seat (v)
shrilst, distribute (v)
shrilt, distribution (n)
shriltwan, distributor (n doer)
shrioshsk, stow (v)
shroize, splurge (v)
shrolk, flux (n)
shrolsk, flux (v)
shruifk, frivolity (n)
shruifkiu, frivolously (adv)
shruifku, frivolous (adj)
shrushp, crumb (n)
shrushpu, crumbly (adj)
shrushsp, crumble (v)
shruthsk, soothe (v)
shtairk, accident (n)
shtairkiu, accidentally (adv)
shtairkiu, accidently (adv)
shtairku, accidental (adj)
shtairmak, bandage (n)
shtairmask, bandage (v)
shtairme, band (n d:strap)
shtairp, title (n)
shtairsp, title (v)
shtairzme, band (v d:strap)
shtarfk, legibility (n)
shtarfkiu, legibly (adv)
shtarfku, legible (adj)
shtarfu, martial (adj)
shtarn, tin (n)
shtarsne, tin (v)
shtarst, mark (v)
shtart, mark (n)
shtartiu, markedly (adv)
shtartiveil, markup (n)
shtartu, marked (adj)
shtartwan, marker (n doer)
shtathk, scale (n d:measure)
shtathkar, scalar (n)
shtathku, scalable (adj d:measure)
shtatiern, markdown (n)
shtaurk, litigation (n)
shtaurkwan, litigator (n doer)
shtaurs, endure (v)
shtaursh, endurance (n)
shtaursk, litigate (v)
shteifsk, snuff (v)
shteldiarme, doorbell (n)
shtelf, door (n)

shtelfproide, doorknob (n)
shtelgirk, doorstep (n)
shtelmarft, doormat (n)
shtelpliorl, doorway (n)
shterf, centigrade (n)
shterfu, centigrade (adj)
shterk, incident (n)
shterkiu, incidently (adv)
shterku, incidental (adj)
shterkuet, incidence (n)
shterst, inch (v)
shtert, inch (n)
shtiarf, query (n)
shtiark, cage (n)
shtiarkiu, cagily (adv)
shtiarku, cagey (adj)
shtiarkwan, cager (n doer)
shtiarsf, query (v)
shtiarsk, cage (v)
shtiarst, bequest (v)
shtiart, quest (n)
shtiartert, questionnaire (n)
shtiartest, question (v)
shtiartet, question (n)
shtiartetiu, questionably (adv)
shtiartetu, questionable (adj)
shtiartetwan, questioner (n doer)
shtirbe, text (n)
shtirst, test (v)
shtirt, test (n)
shtirtu, testy (adj)
shtirtwan, tester (n doer)
shtirzbe, text (v)
shtitfamor, testbed (n)
shtiukezhailf, pitfall (n)
shtiurf, premier (n)
shtiurk, pit (n)
shtiursf, premier (v)
shtiursk, pit (v)
shtivonurde, textbook (n)
shtobiurst, smolder (v)
shtobiurst, smoulder (v)
shtobiurt, smolder (n)
shtobiurt, smoulder (n)
shtogblarsht, snowflake (n)
shtogdanirt, snowmobile (n)
shtogferap, snowstorm (n)
shtogplorn, snowman (n)
shtogplornyek, snowmen (n pl)
shtogshmonde, snowball (n)
shtogshmonzde, snowball (v)
shtogtafarn, snowshoe (n)
shtogzhailf, snowfall (n)
shtoirk, indentation (n)
shtoirsk, indent (v)
Shtokolirm, Stockholm (n)
shtolfgriart, smokestack (n)
shtolfklert, smokescreen (n)
shtolirf, smoke (n)
shtolirfiu, smokily (adv)
shtolirfmenu, smokeless (adj)
shtolirfu, smoky (adj)
shtolirfwan, smoker (n doer)

shtolirsf, smoke (v)
shtorge, snow (n)
shtorgu, snowy (adj)
shtorzge, snow (v)
shtorzhe, smog (n)
shtorzhu, smoggy (adj)
shtrak, grade (n)
shtrakwan, grader (n doer)
shtranak, gradient (n)
shtrasht, spatula (n)
shtrask, grade (v)
shtraushk, spout (n)
shtraushsk, spout (v)
shtrausht, spate (n d:flood)
shtreishp, spat (n d:quarrel)
shtreln, term (n d:timespan)
shtrink, spear (n)
shtrinkefirst, spearhead (v)
shtrinsk, spear (v)
shtrolp, swipe (n)
shtrolsp, swipe (v)
Shtrontium, Strontium (n)
shtrushk, swoon (n)
shtrushsk, swoon (v)
shtrushsp, swoop (v)
shtunk, snub (n)
shtunsk, snub (v)
shtuthsk, smother (v)
shtuvar, enrichment (n)
shtuvariu, richly (adv)
shtuvarp, rich (n)
shtuvaru, rich (adj)
shtuvaruet, richness (n)
shtuvarwan, enricher (n doer)
shtuvarweku, richest (adj)
shtuvarwelu, richer (adj)
shtuvasre, enrich (v)
shualar, soul (n)
shualirf, solace (n)
shualirsf, solace (v)
shualirt, solemnity (n)
shualirtu, solemn (adj)
shuar, female (n)
shuarge, size (n)
shuargiu, sizably (adv)
shuargu, sizable (adj)
shuargu, sizeable (adj)
shuargwan, sizer (n doer)
shuark, rank (n d:level, judge)
shuarl, sol (n)
shuarlu, solar (adj)
shuarn, theme (n)
shuarp, rake (n)
shuarpwan, raker (n doer)
shuarsh, science (n)
shuarshiu, scientifically (adv)
shuarshu, scientific (adj)
shuarshwan, scientist (n doer)
shuarsk, rank (v d:level, judge)
shuarsle, solarize (v)
shuarsp, rake (v)
shuarst, encase (v d:container)
shuart, case (n d:container)

shuaru, feminine (adj)
shuaruet, feminism (n)
shuarwan, feminist (n doer)
shuarzge, size (v)
shuasre, effeminate (v)
shuaushp, lesbian (n)
Shudaviurl, Saturday (n)
shudolirf, protection (n)
shudolirfiu, protectively (adv)
shudolirfu, protective (adj)
shudolirfuet, protectionism (n)
shudolirfwan, protectionist (n
    doer)
shudolirfwan, protector (n doer)
shudolirsf, protect (v)
shuel, near (adj/adv/prep)
shuelervu, nearby (adj/adv)
shuelf, nearness (n)
shuelfiu, nearly (adv)
shuelfu, near (adj)
shuelfwaku, nearest (adj)
shuelfwelu, nearer (adj)
shuelsf, near (v)
shuelsh, girlfriend (n)
shufierf, bobcat (n)
shufirp, stumble (n)
shufirsk, stump (v d:befuddle)
shufirsp, stumble (v)
shufirst, sequence (v)
shufirt, sequence (n)
shufirtiu, sequentially (adv)
shufirtu, sequential (adj)
shufirtwan, sequencer (n doer)
shuftarn, sequel (n)
shuiarsf, shoo (v)
shuiast, iconify (v)
shuiat, icon (n)
Shuidarf, Sweden (n)
Shuidarn, Swedish (n)
shuirk, scale (n d:climb)
shuirs, weigh (v)
shuirsh, weight (n)
shuirshmen, weightlessness (n)
shuirshmenu, weightless (adj)
shuirshsk, weight (v)
shuirshu, weighty (adj)
shuirsk, scale (v d:climb)
Shuisharn, Swiss (n)
Shuisherlarf, Switzerland (n)
shularn, solo (n)
shularniu, solo (adj)
shularnwan, soloist (n doer)
shularsne, solo (v)
Shulfur, Sulfur (n)
shulirn, ounce (n)
shulirst, found (v d:pour mold)
shulirt, foundary (n d:pour mold)
shumirf, vantage (n)
shunk, lens (n)
shunsk, lens (v)
shuparst, found (v d:begin)
shupart, foundation (n d:begin)
shupartwan, founder (n doer

d:begin)
shurf, lab (n)
shurn, comma (n)
shurp, find (n)
shurpwan, finder (n doer)
shursp, find (v)
shurspyot, found (v pa)
shursth, bean (v)
shurth, bean (n)
shurve, labor (n)
shurvwan, laborer (n doer)
shurzve, labor (v)
shushurst, solicite (v)
shushurt, solicitation (n)
shushurtwan, solicitor (n doer)
shut, zero (num 0 card)
shutai-, nul (num 0 pref)
shutair, null (n)
shutairu, null (adj)
shutaisre, nullify (v)
shutart, soccer (n)
shuteth, zeroth (num 0 ord)
shuvarsht, laboratory (n)
shwenf, during (prep)
shwi, whee (interj)
tafanargwan, shoemaker (n doer)
tafanfoirn, shoelace (n)
tafankroip, shoehorn (n)
tafankroisp, shoehorn (v)
tafanligurl, shoestring (n)
tafanmoirth, shoeshine (n)
tafarn, shoe (n)
tafarsne, shoe (v)
tafil, basket (n)
tafirk, culture (n)
tafirku, cultural (adj)
tafirp, golf (n)
tafirpwan, golfer (n doer)
tafirsp, golf (v)
tafirst, tote (v)
tafirt, tote (n)
tagiarn, alcoholic (n)
tagiarnuet, alcoholism (n)
tagirn, alcohol (n)
tagirnu, alcoholic (adj)
taiank, wobble (n)
taiankwan, wobbler (n doer)
taiansk, wobble (v)
taibirtiu, overtly (adv)
taibirtu, overt (adj)
taifaurp, garble (n)
taifaursp, garble (v)
taiforst, point (v)
taifort, point (n)
taifortiu, pointily (adv)
taifortmenu, pointless (adj)
taifortu, pointy (adj)
taifortwan, pointer (n doer)
taigarge, tangle (n)
taigargwan, tangler (n doer)
taigarzge, tangle (v)
taikart, matrix (n)
Tailanurde, Thailand (n)

tainavurp, stairwell (n)
tainpliorl, stairway (n)
tainshuart, staircase (n)
tairak, bowl (n d:ball)
tairakwan, bowler (n doer d:ball)
tairask, bowl (v d:ball)
Tairf, Thai (n)
tairge, garbage (n)
tairgu, garbage (adj)
tairn, stair (n)
tairzge, garbage (v)
Taiwarf, Taiwan (n)
takalan, hallelujah (interj)
takiorl, cocaine (n)
talak, garage (n)
talart, datum (n)
talartviarsh, database (n)
talartyek, data (n pl)
talfmashp, basketball (n)
talgurt, syllable (n)
talirk, prince (n)
talirku, princely (adj)
talirp, corridor (n)
talirs, speak (v d:verbosity)
talirsh, speech (n d:verbosity)
talirshiu, speakably (adv d:verbosity)
talirshmenu, speechless (adj)
talirshu, speakable (adj d:verbosity)
talirshwan, speaker (n doer d:verbosity)
talirshwan, spokesman (n doer)
talirshwan, spokesperson (n doer)
talirshwan, spokeswoman (n doer)
talirsyot, spoke (v pa d:verbosity)
talirth, princess (n)
talirthu, princessly (adj)
talnaf, memorial (n)
talnank, memoir (n)
talnasf, memorialize (v)
talurn, memory (n)
talurniu, memorably (adv)
talurnu, memorable (adj)
talurse, memorize (v)
talzhurp, souvenir (n)
tamarf, stool (n d:chair)
tamiaarmweku, funniest (adj)
tamiarme, funniness (n)
tamiarmu, funny (adj)
tamiarmwelu, funnier (adj)
Tamparf, Tampa (n)
tanak, border (n)
tanakroif, borderline (n)
tanask, border (v)
tanfarn, toddle (n)
tanfarnwan, toddler (n doer)
tanfarsne, toddle (v)
tanfk, tot (n)
Tantalum, Tantalum (n)
tanuart, diamond (n)
taragafen, hangover (n)

taragage, dangle (n)
taragazge, dangle (v)
taragiveil, hangup (n)
taraguil, hangout (n)
taragwan, hanger (n doer)
Tarak, Tarak (n)
tarazge, hang (v)
tarazgyot, hung (v pa)
tarfp, hinge (n)
tarfsp, hinge (v)
tarishk, wax (n)
tarishku, waxy (adj)
tarishkwan, waxer (n doer)
tarishsk, wax (v)
tarme, fun (n)
tarmu, fun (adj)
tars, chalk (v)
tarsh, chalk (n)
tarshirk, legislature (n)
tarshplok, chalkboard (n)
tarthk, throw (n)
tarthkwan, thrower (n doer)
tarthsk, throw (v)
tarthskyot, threw (v pa)
tarthvark, throwback (n)
tarve, triteness (n)
tarviu, tritely (adv)
tarvu, trite (adj)
tarvuk, adult (n)
tarvukfif, adulthood (n)
tarvuku, adult (adj)
tarvukwan, adulterer (n doer)
tarvusk, adulterate (v)
tarze, jog (v)
tarzhe, jog (n)
tarzhge, dodge (n)
tarzhgu, dodgy (adj)
tarzhwan, jogger (n doer)
tarzhzge, dodge (v)
tash, hundred (num 100 card)
tasheth, hundredth (num 100 ord)
tashia-, hecto- (num 100 pref)
tashif, gasoline (n)
tashirk, legislation (n)
tashirkiu, legislatively (adv)
tashirku, legislative (adj)
tashirkwan, legislator (n doer)
tashirsk, legislate (v)
tashkelfirfwan, officialdom (n doer)
tashkelst, officiate (v)
tashkelt, office (n)
tashkelthorthkwan, officeholder (n doer)
tashkeltiu, officially (adv)
tashkeltu, official (adj)
tashkeltwan, officer (n doer)
tashkeltwan, official (n doer)
tathiart, casserole (n)
tathirt, coffin (n)
tatorve, offense (n)
tatorviu, offensively (adv)
tatorvu, offensive (adj)

tatorvuet, offensiveness (n)
tatorvwan, offender (n doer)
tatorzve, offend (v)
taufiasht, cartilage (n)
taufk, duck (n d:bird)
taugarf, liquor (n)
taugarsf, liquor (v)
taugart, liquidity (n)
tauianfliorfu, weatherproof (adj)
tauianfliorsf, weatherproof (v)
tauianplorn, weatherman (n)
tauianplornyek, weathermen (n pl)
tauiarn, weather (n)
tauiarsne, weather (v)
tauirt, canopy (n)
taukderp, dogma (n)
taukderpu, dogmatic (adj)
taukfarth, stopgap (n)
taukfarthu, stopgap (adj)
taukfluarn, stoplight (n)
tauklufk, stopwatch (n)
taurge, liquid (n)
taurguet, liquidation (n)
taurk, stop (n)
taurkafen, stopover (n)
taurkuet, stoppage (n)
taurkwan, stopper (n doer)
taurn, tau (n)
taurp, sheet (n)
taursh, durability (n)
taurshiu, durably (adv)
taurshu, durable (adj)
taursk, stop (v)
taurzge, liquidate (v)
tautiark, calamity (n)
tautiarku, calamitous (adj)
tavarde, locomotion (n)
tavardwan, locomotive (n doer)
tebirk, ratification (n)
tebirsk, ratify (v)
tedifaide, adequation (n)
tedifaidiu, adequately (adv)
tedifaidu, adequate (adj)
teditor, advertisement (n)
teditoriu, adversarially (adv)
teditoru, adversarial (adj)
teditorwan, advertiser (n doer)
teditosre, advertise (v)
tef, ad (n)
tefeirk, addiction (n)
tefeirku, addictive (adj)
tefeirkwan, addict (n doer)
tefeirsk, addict (v)
Tefendarl, December (n)
tefiarde, adverb (n)
tefirk, offer (n)
tefirsk, offer (v)
tefirst, add (v)
tefirt, addition (n)
tefirtiu, additionally (adv)
tefirtu, additional (adj)
tefirtuak, adhesive (n)

tefirtuap, adherence (n)
tefirtuapwan, adherent (n doer)
tefirtuasp, adhere (v)
tefirtuat, adhesion (n)
tefirtuatu, adhesive (adj)
tefirtwan, adder (n doer)
teflirokiu, adjacently (adv)
tefliroku, adjacent (adj)
tefralp, development (n)
tefralpwan, developer (n doer)
tefralsp, develop (v)
teftart, additive (n)
tefterme, add-on (n)
tegerst, digitize (v)
tegert, digit (n)
tegertiu, digitally (adv)
tegertu, digital (adj)
tegnart, degree (n)
teiars, drift (v)
teiarsh, drift (n)
teiarshwan, drifter (n doer)
teiarst, tee (v)
teiart, tee (n)
teiashfanirn, driftwood (n)
teiatirst, teeter (v)
teifirt, temp (n)
teifirtiu, temporarily (adv)
teifirtu, temporary (adj)
teihem, Number_1e2556
teil, T (let sng)
teili, Ts (let pl)
teilort, contemporary (n)
teipust, echo (v)
teiput, echo (n)
teirge, lance (n)
teirgwan, lancer (n doer)
teirk, stall (n d:wait)
teirkwan, staller (n doer d:wait)
teirmu, keen (adj)
teirsh, peach (n)
teirshu, peachy (adj)
teirsk, stall (v d:wait)
teirt, tempo (n)
teirth, pessimism (n)
teirthu, pessimistic (adj)
teirtu, temporal (adj)
teirzge, lance (v)
tekanitaf, adjournment (n)
tekanitasf, adjourn (v)
Teknetium, Technetium (n)
Tekralf, Tehran (n)
telforest, interest (v d:desire)
telforet, interest (n d:desire)
telforetiu, interestingly (adv d:desire)
telgarst, throttle (v)
telgart, throttle (n)
telge, dig (n)
telgiouil, dugout (n)
telgwan, digger (n doer)
telifovist, administer (v)
telifovit, administration (n)
telifovitu, administrative (adj)

telifovitwan, administrator (n doer)
telirn, trill (n)
telirnwan, triller (n doer)
telirsne, trill (v)
telirst, peel (v)
telirt, peel (n)
telirth, hatch (n d:door)
telirtwan, peeler (n doer)
telorshk, forge (n)
telorshkuet, forgery (n)
telorshkwan, forger (n doer)
telorshsk, forge (v)
telshanuil, throughout (prep/adv)
telshanvurt, throughput (n)
telsharn, through (adj/adv/prep)
telthvark, hatchback (n)
Telurium, Tellurium (n)
telzge, dig (v)
telzgyot, dug (v pa)
temualst, admire (v)
temualt, admiration (n)
temualtiu, admirably (adv)
temualtu, admirable (adj)
temualtwan, admirer (n doer)
temurde, garden (n)
temurdwan, gardener (n doer)
temurzde, garden (v)
Teneshirf, Tennessee (n)
tenirf, insula (n)
tenirfat, insularity (n)
tenirfiu, insularly (adv)
tenirfu, insular (adj)
tenirfuest, insulate (v)
tenirfuet, insulation (n)
tenirfuetiu, insulatively (adv)
tenirfuetu, insulative (adj)
tenirfuetwan, insulator (n doer)
tenirk, admission (n)
tenirkiu, admissibly (adv)
tenirku, admissible (adj)
tenirsk, admit (v)
tenirt, island (n)
tenirt, isle (n)
tenirtwan, islander (n doer)
tepafes, adjust (v)
tepafesh, adjustment (n)
tepafeshu, adjustable (adj)
tepafeshwan, adjuster (n doer)
teraf, neatness (n)
terafiu, neatly (adv)
terafu, neat (adj)
terame, reliability (n)
teramiu, reliably (adv)
teramu, reliable (adj)
terazme, rely (v)
terbe, rate (n)
Terbium, Terbium (n)
tereirk, desertion (n d:flee)
tereirkwan, deserter (n doer d:flee)
tereirsk, desert (v d:flee)
Terobe, EhoMonth08 (n)

terzbe, rate (v)
tesh, their (pron 3rd fem-masc pl pos sub)
tesh, theirs (pron 3rd fem-masc pl pos obj)
tesharbe, religion (n)
tesharbiu, religiously (adv)
tesharbu, religious (adj)
teshfar, themselves (pron 3rd fem-masc pl pos)
Teshkarf, Texas (n)
teshralf, sister (n)
teshralfif, sisterhood (n)
teshralfu, sisterly (adj)
tethairp, advocation (n)
tethairpwan, advocate (n doer)
tethairsp, advocate (v)
tethi, they (pron 3rd fem-masc pl sub)
tethin, them (pron 3rd fem-masc pl obj)
tetifipar, adjective (n)
tezhirzge, delve (v)
thadirf, nail (n d:metal pin)
thadirsf, nail (v d:metal pin)
thafirk, rent (n)
thafirkal, rental (n)
thafirku, rental (adj)
thafirkwan, renter (n doer)
thafirp, raft (n d:boat)
thafirpwan, rafter (n doer d:boat)
thafirsk, rent (v)
thafirsp, raft (v d:boat)
thafirst, enquire (v)
thafirst, inquire (v)
thafirt, enquiry (n)
thafirt, inquiry (n)
thafirtwan, inquirer (n doer)
thagart, rafter (n d:roof support)
thaibarn, vocabulary (n)
thaifirk, devotion (n)
thaifirkiu, devoutly (adv)
thaifirku, devout (adj)
thaifirkwan, devotee (n doer)
thaifirsk, devote (v)
thaifkarn, devotional (n)
thailt, pale (n d:spike)
thaimak, veto (n)
thaimask, veto (v)
thaipark, vocation (n)
thaiparku, vocational (adj)
thaiparn, vocal (n)
thaiparnu, vocal (adj)
thaiparnwan, vocalist (n doer)
thaipelirp, voicemail (n)
thairf, chat (n)
thairfu, chatty (adj)
thairfwan, chatter (n doer)
thairk, vote (n)
thairkwan, voter (n doer)
thairn, fate (n)
thairniu, fatefully (adv)
thairnu, fateful (adj)

thairp, voice (n)
thairsf, chat (v)
thairsk, vote (v)
thairsp, voice (v)
thairst, bid (v)
thairstyot, bade (v pa)
thairstyot, bid (v pa)
thairt, bid (n)
thairtwan, bidder (n doer)
thaishsk, chafe (v)
thaithaft, hatchet (n)
thaithirkuet, hatchery (n)
thaithirkwan, hatcher (n doer d:create)
thaithirsk, hatch (v d:create)
thaithp, hash (n d:cut food)
thaithsp, hash (v d:cut food)
thalirf, gel (n)
thalirme, jam (n d:food)
thalirp, mast (n)
thalirsf, gel (v)
thalirsp, mast (v)
Thalium, Thallium (n)
thalk, breast (n)
thalkfkarf, breastplate (n)
thalkparzve, breastfeed (v)
thalpekefirt, masthead (n)
thanberf, sample (n)
thanberfwan, sampler (n doer)
thanbersf, sample (v)
thanshst, shack (v)
thansht, shack (n)
tharaf, verse (n)
tharage, slang (n)
tharasf, verse (v)
thardeirk, verdict (n)
tharfelt, version (n)
tharfik, converse (n)
tharfikiu, conversely (adv)
thariasht, veracity (n)
thariashtu, veracious (adj)
tharluk, convertible (n)
tharmelme, versus (prep)
tharmp, mane (n)
tharnt, janitor (n)
tharoift, verity (n)
tharoiftu, veritable (adj)
tharoilk, verification (n)
tharoilkiu, verifiably (adv)
tharoilku, verifiable (adj)
tharoilsk, verify (v)
tharp, hood (n)
thars, toss (v)
tharsh, toss (n)
tharshok, convert (n)
tharshwan, tosser (n doer)
tharsp, hood (v)
tharthk, shackle (n)
tharthsk, shackle (v)
tharve, gorge (n)
tharviu, gorgeously (adv)
tharvu, gorgeous (adj)
tharzve, gorge (v)

thashirk, ratchet (n)
thashirp, gossip (n)
thashirpu, gossipy (adj)
thashirpwan, gossiper (n doer)
thashirsk, ratchet (v)
thashirsp, gossip (v)
thasle, spell (v d:character)
thathk, shuffle (n)
thathsk, shuffle (v)
thatil, apple (n)
thator, adversity (n)
thatoriu, adversely (adv)
thatoru, adverse (adj)
thatorwan, adversary (n doer)
thauarde, corsage (n)
thaufirk, regime (n)
thauns, warm (v)
thaunsh, warmth (n)
thaunshiu, warmly (adv)
thaunshiveil, warmup (n)
thaunshiveilu, warmup (adj)
thaunshu, warm (adj)
thaurf, reign (n)
thaurk, acre (n)
thaurp, curiosity (n)
thaurpiu, curiously (adv)
thaurpu, curious (adj)
thaursf, reign (v)
thaus, flower (v)
thaush, flower (n)
thaushu, flowery (adj)
thautaraf, pharmaceutical (n)
thautarl, pharmacy (n)
thautarlu, pharmaceutical (adj)
thauthk, yard (n d:field)
thavube, neck (n)
thavubefoirn, necklace (n)
thavubeglersh, necktie (n)
thavuzbe, neck (v)
theiank, son (n)
theifirf, ownership (n)
theifst, own (v)
theift, own (n)
theiftu, own (adj)
theiftwan, owner (n doer)
theigurt, muffin (n)
theihem, Number_1e2856
theikart, mascot (n)
theil, Th (let sng)
theilf, hay (n)
theili, Ths (let pl)
theilp, nip (n)
theilpu, nippy (adj)
theilsp, nip (v)
theimp, shawl (n)
theinalirp, strawberry (n)
theioshk, mesh (n)
theioshsk, mesh (v)
theiparf, nipple (n)
theirap, shrimp (n)
theirapwan, shrimper (n doer)
theirasp, shrimp (v)
theirk, mask (n)

theirsh, smallness (n)
theirshu, small (adj)
theirshwaku, smallest (adj)
theirshwelu, smaller (adj)
theirsk, mask (v)
theithk, sash (n)
thekshlersh, shellfish (n)
thekshlershyek, shellfish (n pl)
thelirn, wind (n d:air)
thelirnu, windy (adj d:air)
thelirsne, wind (v d:air)
thelirt, region (n)
thelirtiu, regionally (adv)
thelirtu, regional (adj)
thelme, brown (n)
thelmu, brown (adj)
thelnaurshu, windward (adj)
thelnfenirp, windmill (n)
thelnmoirk, windshield (n)
thelnplirf, windchill (n)
thelnplirfu, windchill (adj)
thelnzhailf, windfall (n)
thelp, nib (n)
thelzme, brown (v)
theparn, nibble (n)
theparsne, nibble (v)
theraf, sprinkle (n)
therafwan, sprinkler (n doer)
theral, fairness (n d:good)
theraliu, fairly (adv d:good)
theralu, fair (adj d:good)
theralweku, fairest (adj d:best)
theralwelu, fairer (adj d:better)
therame, slimness (n)
theramu, slim (adj)
therasf, sprinkle (v)
therazme, slim (v)
therf, lotion (n)
therk, shell (n)
therkwan, sheller (n doer)
thers, raffle (v)
thersh, raffle (n)
thersk, shell (v)
thetarn, theta (n)
thethk, den (n)
thetirs, piece (v)
thetirsh, piece (n)
thetirshwan, piecer (n doer)
thiadanst, hobble (v)
thiadoithsk, hobnob (v)
thiaitsp, heed (v)
thialblerf, shortcoming (n)
thialdairsh, shortcut (n)
thialersh, shortwave (n)
thialershu, shortwave (adj)
thialgutraf, shortcake (n)
thialirk, shorts (n d:clothing)
thialirp, shortage (n)
thialirsp, short (v)
thialit, shorty (n)
thialkarp, shorthand (n)
thialst, shorten (v)
thialt, shortness (n)

thialtaurk, shortstop (n)
thialthulth, shortsightedness (n)
thialthulthu, shortsighted (adj)
thialtiu, shortly (adv)
thialtu, short (adj)
thialtuarsne, shortchange (v)
thialtweku, shortest (adj)
thialtwelu, shorter (adj)
thialzhailf, shortfall (n)
thiarap, flood (n)
thiarapwan, flooder (n doer)
thiarasp, flood (v)
thiarbralf, floodplain (n)
thiarde, hob (n)
thiarf, tour (n)
thiarfluarn, floodlight (n)
thiarfuet, tourism (n)
thiarfwan, tourist (n doer)
thiarheidorn, floodwater (n)
thiark, fatality (n)
thiarkiu, fatally (adv)
thiarku, fatal (adj)
thiarn, priest (n)
thiarparlak, floodgate (n)
thiarsf, tour (v)
thiarshk, fatigue (n)
thiarshsk, fatigue (v)
thiarsp, appall (v)
thiarst, skate (v)
thiart, skate (n)
thiartwan, skater (n doer)
thiarve, flock (n d:group)
thiarzhge, gruel (n)
thiarzve, flock (v d:group)
thiashst, shear (v)
thiasht, shear (n)
thiashtwan, shearer (n doer)
thiathk, sheath (n)
thiathsk, sheathe (v)
thiatplok, skateboard (n)
thiatplosk, skateboard (v)
thiaurt, whole (n)
thiaurtiu, wholly (adv)
thiaurtu, whole (adj)
thiaurtuet, wholeness (n)
thiaushk, shuck (n)
thiaushsk, shuck (v)
thiautrelirf, wholesale (n)
thiautrelirfu, wholesale (adj)
thiautrelirfwan, wholesaler (n doer)
thiazhge, menace (n)
thiazhgiu, menacingly (adv)
thiazhzge, menace (v)
thigarst, mutter (v)
thigart, mutterance (n)
thikirth, ickiness (n)
thikirthu, icky (adj)
thiklarve, farce (n)
thiklarvu, farcical (adj)
thilarn, palette (n)
thilkiarsh, northeast (n)
thilkiarshaushu, northeastward

(adj)
thilkiarshu, northeast (adj)
thilkiarshu, northeasterly (adj)
thilkiarshu, northeastern (adj)
thilorf, shed (n d:building)
thilork, click (n)
thilorkwan, clicker (n doer)
Thilorsh Dakort, North Dakota
(n)
Thilorsh Karolirn, North Carolina
(n)
thilorsh, north (n)
thilorshaushu, northward (adj)
thilorshu, north (adj)
thilorshu, northerly (adj)
thilorshu, northern (adj)
thilorshwaku, northernmost (adj)
thilorshwan, northerner (n doer)
thilorsk, click (v)
thilpoimu, faraway (adj)
thilshaithk, northwest (n)
thilshaithku, northwest (adj)
thilshaithku, northwestern (adj)
thilshdraifp, northbound (n)
thilshraufp, northland (n)
thilthulth, farsightedness (n)
thilthulthu, farsighted (adj)
thilu, far (adj/adv)
thiluel, farther (adj/adv)
thiluel, further (adj/adv)
thiluelf, furthermore (adv)
thilwak, furthest (adj)
thinarp, estimate (n)
thinarpwan, estimator (n doer)
thinarsp, estimate (v)
thiokaturk, masterstroke (n)
thiokniarp, mastermind (n)
thiokniarsp, mastermind (v)
thiokthetirsh, masterpiece (n)
thiork, master (n)
thiorkiu, masterfully (adv)
thiorku, masterful (adj)
thiorkuet, mastery (n)
thiorlt, fjord (n)
thiorn, pine (n)
thiorsk, master (v)
thioshk, mistress (n)
thirap, kick (n)
thirapevark, kickback (n)
thirapunf, kickoff (n)
thirapwan, kicker (n doer)
thirasp, kick (v)
thirfk, nobility (n)
thirfkiu, nobly (adv)
thirfku, noble (adj)
thirft, vector (n)
thirk, fare (n)
thirkor, farewell (n)
thirkwan, fare (n doer)
thirolst, rumor (v)
thirolst, rumour (v)
thirolt, rumor (n)
thirolt, rumour (n)

thirsk, fare (v)
thish, sect (n)
thishank, sectarianism (n)
thishankwan, sectarian (n doer)
thisharl, section (n)
thisharlu, sectional (adj)
thisharp, sector (n)
thisharsle, section (v)
thishiankiu, secularly (adv)
thishianku, secular (adj)
thishiankwan, secularist (n doer)
thitarlt, period (n d:punctuation)
thiteshk, twit (n)
thithp, tally (n)
thithsp, tally (v)
thitor, character (n d:symbol)
thiudefiveil, hubcap (n)
thiufshuart, briefcase (n)
thiukart, spectrum (n)
thiulf, royalty (n)
thiulfiu, royally (adv)
thiulfu, royal (adj)
thiunart, morale (n)
thiurde, hub (n)
thiurf, file (n d:storage)
thiurfst, lapse (v)
thiurft, lapse (n)
thiurfwan, filer (n doer d:storage)
thiurk, spectra (n)
thiurkiu, spectrally (adv)
thiurkluarf, spectroscopy (n)
thiurkluarfu, spectroscopic (adj)
thiurku, spectral (adj)
thiurn, moral (n)
thiurniu, morally (adv)
thiurnu, moral (adj)
thiurnuet, morality (n)
thiurnwan, moralist (n doer)
thiursf, file (v d:storage)
thiursne, moralize (v)
thiurst, lap (v)
thiurt, lap (v)
thiutaurbe, laptop (n)
thlorf, nothing (n)
thnart, kinesis (n)
thnartiu, kinetically (adv)
thnartu, kinetic (adj)
thoanirn, winery (n)
thoarme, paleness (n d:complexion)
thoarmu, pale (adj d:complexion)
thoarn, wine (n)
thoarnwan, wino (n doer)
thoarsne, wine (v)
thoarzme, pale (v d:complexion)
thofklorfwan, shopkeeper (n doer)
thofprairt, shoplifter (n)
thofst, shop (v)
thoft, shop (n)
thoftwan, shopper (n doer)
thoiarst, tabulate (v)
thoiart, tabulation (n)

thoiartu, tabular (adj)
thoiartwan, tabulator (n doer)
thoifalst, sheriff (v)
thoifalt, sheriff (n)
thoilf, sack (n)
thoilfwan, sacker (n doer)
thoilsf, sack (v)
thoirk, tab (n)
thoirn, seal (n d:animal)
thoirs, face (v)
thoirsh, face (n)
thoirshu, facial (adj)
thoirshul, facial (n)
thoirshwan, facer (n doer)
thoirsk, tab (v)
thoirsp, veer (v)
thoishart, façade (n)
thoishfkarf, faceplate (n)
thoishoirt, facet (n)
thoishraushk, facelift (n)
thoishraushsk, facelift (v)
thoishst, brief (v)
thoisht, brief (n)
thoishtar, brevity (n)
thoishtiu, briefly (adv)
thoishtu, brief (adj)
thoitirk, feasibility (n)
thoitirkiu, feasibly (adv)
thoitirku, feasible (adj)
thokar, appliance (n)
thokiunf, tranquility (n)
thokiunfu, tranquil (adj)
thokiunfuet, tranquilization (n)
thokiunfwan, tranquilizer (n doer)
thokiunsf, tranquilize (v)
tholarve, harem (n)
thorf, chap (n)
thorge, stress (n)
thorgiu, stressfully (adv)
thorgu, stressful (adj)
thorgwan, stressor (n doer)
thorifp, trance (n)
thorish, chapel (n)
Thorium, Thorium (n)
thork, application (n)
thorkiu, applicably (adv)
thorku, applicable (adj)
thorkuinwan, applicant (n doer)
thorkwan, applicator (n doer)
thorlst, ford (v)
thorlt, ford (n)
thorsf, chap (v)
thorsk, apply (v)
thortan, chapter (n)
thortes, weld (v)
thortesh, weld (n)
thorteshwan, welder (n doer)
thorthiveil, holdup (n)
thorthk, hold (n)
thorthkafen, holdover (n)
thorthkwan, holder (n doer)
thorthsk, hold (v)

thorthskyot, held (v pa)
thorzge, stressed (v)
thoshlarsh, decal (n)
thotelirp, trajectory (n)
thoterp, trajection (n)
thoterpwan, trajector (n doer)
thotersp, traject (v)
thraf, bread (n)
thrafist, punctuate (v)
thrafit, punctuation (n)
thrafitiu, punctually (adv)
thrafitu, punctual (adj)
thragiu, hugely (adv)
thragu, huge (adj)
thraidarst, dwindle (v)
thraifk, smugness (n)
thraifkiu, smugly (adv)
thraifku, smug (adj)
thraifst, dwarf (v)
thraift, dwarf (n)
thrailpwan, smuggler (n doer)
thrailsp, smuggle (v)
thrailst, dwell (v)
thrailstyot, dwelt (v pa)
thrailt, dwell (n)
thrailtwan, dweller (n doer)
thrairkwan, winder (n doer d:energize)
thrairsk, wind (v d:energize)
thrairskyot, wound (v pa d:energize)
thraishsk, thrive (v)
thralp, snap (n)
thralpiu, snappily (adv)
thralpu, snappy (adj)
thralpwan, snapper (n doer)
thralsp, snap (v)
thralve, semblance (n)
thramesp, thump (v)
thramp, thump (n)
thrampwan, thumper (n doer)
thranf, oar (n)
thranik, punishment (n)
thranikiu, punitively (adv)
thraniku, punishable (adj)
thraniku, punitive (adj)
thranikwan, punisher (n doer)
thranisk, punish (v)
thranit, semester (n)
thransf, oar (v)
thrapkoift, snapshot (n)
thrasf, bread (v)
thrashst, puncture (v)
thrasht, puncture (n)
thraufk, scrutiny (n)
thraufsk, scrutinize (v)
thraufst, braise (v)
thrauft, braiser (n)
thrauftwan, braiser (n doer)
thraume, braid (n)
thraumwan, braider (n doer)
thraunk, bridle (n)
thraunsk, bridle (v)

thraushk, thrill (n)
thraushkwan, thriller (n doer)
thraushsk, thrill (v)
thrauzhge, hug (n)
thrauzhgwan, hugger (n doer)
thrauzhzge, hug (v)
thrauzme, braid (v)
thraviark, seminar (n)
threilp, trap (n)
threilpwan, trapper (n doer)
threilsp, trap (v)
threipshtelf, trapdoor (n)
threithedarf, lithography (n)
threlf, surface (n)
threlk, athlete (n)
threlkiu, athletically (adv)
threlku, athletic (adj)
threln, palm (n)
threlpliorl, fairway (n)
threlsf, surface (v)
threlshp, fairing (n)
threlsne, palm (v)
threlst, spring (v d:coil, surprise)
threlstyot, sprang (v pa d:coil, surprise)
threlt, spring (n d:coil, surprise)
threltwan, springer (n doer d:coil, surprise)
threnirk, tariff (n)
thretplok, springboard (n)
thriark, hospital (n)
thriarsk, hospitalize (v)
thriarth, hospitality (n)
thriarthiu, hospitably (adv)
thriarthu, hospitable (adj)
thrilp, tribe (n)
thrilplorn, tribesman (n)
thrilplornyek, tribesmen (n pl)
thrilpu, tribal (adj)
thrink, nail (n d:finger/toe tip)
thriorp, territory (n)
thriorpu, territorial (adj)
thrishk, forest (n)
thrishku, foresty (adj)
thrishkuet, forestry (n)
thrishsk, forest (v)
thriufst, scruple (v)
thriuft, scruple (n)
thriuftiu, scrupulously (adv)
thriuftu, scrupulous (adj)
thrilupart, tributary (n)
thriurp, tribute (n)
throshst, sheer (v d:divert)
throsht, sheer (n d:divert)
thruap, shudder (n)
thruasp, shudder (v)
thrufk, fleck (n)
thrufsk, fleck (v)
thrufsp, garner (v)
thruthk, flute (n)
thruthkwan, flutist (n doer)
thualirf, palace (n)
thuamesp, shun (v)

thuanirk, anchor (n)
thuanirsk, anchor (v)
thuanirst, shunt (v)
thuanirt, shunt (n)
thuarf, mute (n)
thuark, mutuality (n)
thuarkiu, mutually (adv)
thuarku, mutual (adj)
thuarn, flora (n)
thuarnu, floral (adj)
thuarnwan, florist (n doer)
thuarsf, mute (v)
thuarst, phase (v)
thuart, phase (n)
thuartuil, phaseout (n)
thuartwan, phaser (n doer)
thuashdairf, flowerpot (n)
thufast, fever (v)
thufat, fever (n)
thufatiu, feverishly (adv)
thufatu, feverish (adj)
thufirs, revere (v)
thufirsh, reverence (n)
thufirshiu, reverently (adv)
thufirshu, reverent (adj)
thufirshwan, reverend (n doer)
thuirn, miser (n)
thuirnu, miserly (adj)
thuirst, treat (v)
thuirt, treat (n)
thuirtu, treatable (adj)
thuitalirt, treatment (n)
thuitarn, treaty (n)
thukars, speculate (v)
thukarsh, speculation (n)
thukarshiu, speculatively (adv)
thukarshu, speculative (adj)
thukarshwan, speculator (n doer)
thuklark, spectacle (n)
thuklarkiu, spectacularly (adv)
thuklarku, spectacular (adj)
thuklarkwan, spectator (n doer)
thuklarsk, spectate (v)
thulfwan, seer (n doer)
thulgralze, seesaw (v)
thulgralzhe, seesaw (n)
thuliarp, scenery (n)
thulirk, ration (n)
thulirp, scene (n)
thulirpu, scenic (adj)
thulirsk, ration (v)
Thulium, Thulium (n)
thulparsh, scenario (n)
thulsf, see (v)
thulsfyot, saw (v pa)
thulsth, sight (v)
thulth, sight (n)
thumark, variety (n)
thumarku, varietal (adj)
thumarp, variable (n)
thumarp, variant (n)
thumarpu, variable (adj)
thumarpu, variant (adj)

thunairk, misery (n)
thunairkiu, miserably (adv)
thunairku, miserable (adj)
thuntarn, certificate (n)
thuntarnk, certification (n)
thuntarnwan, certifier (n doer)
thuntarsne, certify (v)
thurf, smell (n)
thurfu, smelly (adj)
thurk, speck (n)
thurme, variability (n)
thurme, variance (n)
thurme, variation (n)
thurmiu, variously (adv)
thurmu, various (adj)
thurniu, seemingly (adv)
thurp, sud (n)
thursf, smell (v)
thurshk, garnish (n)
thurshsk, garnish (v)
thursne, seem (v)
thurze, scheme (v)
thurzhe, scheme (n)
thurzhwan, schemer (n doer)
thurzme, vary (v)
thushflerve, spaceship (n)
thushkarfp, spacecraft (n)
thushorst, rationalize (v)
thushort, rationality (n)
thushortiu, rationally (adv)
thushortu, rational (adj)
thushp, space (n)
thushpiu, spatially (adv)
thushplorn, spaceman (n)
thushplornyek, spacemen (n pl)
thushpu, spacious (adj)
thushpu, spatial (adj)
thushpwan, spacer (n doer)
thushsp, space (v)
thuteshk, theology (n)
thuthulsf, sightsee (v)
thuthulsfyot, sightsaw (v pa)
thutiarn, ratio (n)
thuvap, effort (n)
thuvapemeniu, effortlessly (adv)
thuvapemenu, effortless (adj)
thuvirst, effect (v)
thuvirt, effect (n)
thuvirtan, effectiveness (n)
thuvirtar, efficiency (n)
thuvirtariu, efficiently (adv)
thuvirtaru, efficient (adj)
thuvirtiu, effectively (adv)
thuvirtu, effective (adj)
thuvirtwan, effector (n doer)
thuzhart, schema (n)
thuzhunk, schematic (n)
thuzhunku, schematic (adj)
tiafirp, privilege (n)
tiafirpu, privy (adj)
tiafirsp, privilege (v)
tiafuarn, shovel (n)
tiafuarsne, shovel (v)

tiagthulth, hindsight (n)
tiaiarst, tingle (v)
tiaiart, tingle (n)
tiaigroifk, hemline (n)
tiaikanku, lamentable (adj)
tiaikansk, lament (v)
tiaink, latency (n)
tiainkiu, latently (adv)
tiainku, latent (adj)
tiaip, lamina (n)
tiaipiu, laminously (adv)
tiaipu, laminous (adj)
tiaipwan, laminator (n doer)
tiaipyek, laminae (n pl)
tiaishk, lameness (n)
tiaishkiu, lamely (adv)
tiaishku, lame (adj)
tiaisp, laminate (v)
tiaizhge, hem (n)
tiaizhzge, hem (v)
Tiakiaf, EhoDay05 (n)
tialf, boil (n d:evaporation)
tialfwan, boiler (n doer
   d:evaporation)
tialsf, boil (v d:evaporation)
tianirk, grab (n)
tianirkwan, grabber (n doer)
tianirp, grasp (n)
tianirsk, grab (v)
tianirsp, grasp (v)
tianthk, grapple (n)
tianthku, grapple (adj)
tianthsk, grapple (v)
tiarf, shove (n)
tiarfwan, shover (n doer)
tiargast, hinder (v)
tiargat, hindrance (n)
tiarge, hind (n)
tiarme, bow (n d:front)
tlarp, privacy (n)
tiarpiu, privately (adv)
tiarpu, private (adj)
tiarpuet, privatization (n)
tiars, glaciate (v)
tiarsf, shove (v)
tiarsh, glacier (n)
tiarshiu, glacially (adv)
tiarshu, glacial (adj)
tiarsp, privatize (v)
tiart, metal (n)
tiartoirp, disincentive (n)
tiartu, metallic (adj)
tiarve, gaze (n)
tiarvirst, disinfect (v)
tiarvirt, disinfection (n)
tiarvirtwan, disinfectant (n doer)
tiarvorn, disinformation (n)
tiarvwan, gazer (n doer)
tiarzhe, pyramid (n)
tiarzve, gaze (v)
tiathfreirk, rattlesnake (n)
tiathk, rattle (n)
tiathsk, rattle (v)

tiauf, hoard (n)
tiausf, hoard (v)
tiaushkiu, languidly (adv)
tiaushku, languid (adj)
tiaushsk, languish (v)
tiauthk, tart (n)
tiauthku, tart (adj)
tiauze, envy (v)
tiauzhe, envy (n)
tiauzhiu, enviously (adv)
tiauzhu, envious (adj)
tibarfk, district (n)
tibarfsk, district (v)
tibeirsth, disburse (v)
tibeirth, disbursement (n)
tibelpifst, discontent (v)
tibelpift, discontent (n)
tibeltir, discontinuation (n)
tibeltir, discontinuity (n)
tibeltisre, discontinue (v)
tibinkwan, peddler (n doer)
tibinsk, peddle (v)
tibrels, displace (v)
tibrelsh, displacement (n)
tibrials, disavow (v)
tibriark, disuse (n)
tibruf, dispensation (n)
tibrufu, dispensable (adj)
tibrufwan, dispenser (n doer)
tibrusf, dispense (v)
tidalirme, dissuasion (n)
tidalirzme, dissuade (v)
tidarbaik, disengagement (n)
tidarbaisk, disengage (v)
tidarlp, disturbance (n)
tidarlsp, disturb (v)
tideilurde, disquiet (n)
tidiars, disjoint (v)
tidivar, discouragement (n)
tidivasre, discourage (v)
tidralst, dishearten (v)
tidreirf, distrust (n)
tidreirfu, distrustful (adj)
tidreirsf, distrust (v)
tiekopiorl, hideaway (n)
tiendaurn, downtime (n)
tiendaurt, downbeat (n)
tiendaurtu, downbeat (adj)
tiendierkiu, downright (adv)
tienfalirme, downstream (n)
tienflierge, downswing (n)
tienfruifsk, downplay (v)
tienhaursh, downward (adj/adv)
tienhaursh, downwardly (adv)
tienkaimp, downturn (n)
tienlurst, download (v)
tienlurt, download (n)
tienlurtwan, downloader (n doer)
tienmiurn, downtown (n)
tienroturt, downpour (v)
tienshiop, downhill (n)
tienshoirt, downside (n)
tienshtrak, downgrade (n)

tienshtrask, downgrade (v)
tienshuarzge, downsize (v)
tientairn, downstairs (n)
tientairnu, downstairs (adj)
tienzhailf, downfall (n)
tierf, cue (n)
tierk, hide (n d:skin)
tierkuil, hideout (n)
tiern, down (adj/adv/prep)
tiern, down (n)
tierpu, lean (adj d:thin)
tiersf, cue (v)
tierst, flex (v)
tiert, flex (n)
tiertep, flexibility (n)
tiertiu, flexibly (adv)
tiertu, flexible (adj)
tifan, dessert (n)
tifashst, strand (v)
tifasht, strand (n)
tifeirs, disgust (v)
tifeirsh, disgust (n)
tifiorf, disloyalty (n)
tifiorfu, disloyal (adj)
tiflaruve, disapproval (n)
tiflaruzve, disapprove (v)
tiflenifst, discredit (v)
tiflenift, discredit (n)
tifliorsf, disprove (v)
tifpart, discus (n)
tifraifkiu, dismally (adv)
tifraifku, dismal (adj)
tifrelp, disability (n)
tifrelpwan, disabler (n doer)
tifrelsp, disable (v)
tifrilap, displeasure (n)
tifrilarsk, disallow (v)
tifrilasp, displease (v)
tifrilast, disorganize (v)
tifrilat, disorganization (n)
tigaifst, disrupt (v)
tigaift, disruption (n)
tigaiftiu, disruptively (adv)
tigaiftu, disruptive (adj)
tigaiftwan, disrupter (n doer)
tigalirst, distract (v)
tigalirt, distraction (n)
tigarge, nag (n)
tigargu, naggy (adj)
tigarst, utter (v)
tigart, utterance (n)
tigartiu, utterly (adv)
tigartu, utter (adj)
tigarzge, nag (v)
tigaurzge, divulge (v)
tiglark, disposition (n)
tiglarku, dispositive (adj)
tigloifst, discharge (v)
tigloift, discharge (n)
tigoishst, discuss (v)
tigoisht, discussion (n)
tigort, discreteness (n)
tigortiu, discretely (adv)

tigortu, discrete (adj)
tigrage, dissolution (n)
tigrazge, dissolve (v)
tigrefst, disclose (v)
tigreft, disclosure (n)
tikan, disposal (n)
tikanu, disposable (adj)
tikasne, dispose (v)
tikaushkiatsh, get-lost (interj)
tiklarst, disagree (v)
tiklart, disagreement (n)
tiklartan, discrepancy (n)
tiklartaniu, discrepantly (adv)
tiklartanu, discrepant (adj)
tiklartu, disagreeable (adj)
tikoarme, blemish (n)
tikoarzme, blemish (v)
tikofirt, disservice (n)
tikolirf, dishonor (n)
tikrezhzge, disgruntle (v)
tikriarf, disqualification (n)
tikriarfwan, disqualifier (n doer)
tikriarsf, disqualify (v)
tiku, doable (adj)
tikudil, disfigurement (n)
tikudisle, disfigure (v)
tikwan, doer (n doer)
til, it (pron 3rd neut sng sub)
tilamoin, disorientation (n)
tilamoisne, disorient (v)
tilargrus, disillusion (v)
tilargrush, disillusionment (n)
tilarsh, terra (n)
tilarshu, terranean (adj)
tilarst, straddle (v)
tilart, straddle (n)
tilasharnu, terrestrial (adj)
tilashart, terrain (n)
tilashirk, terrace (n)
tilen, it (pron 3rd neut sng obj)
tilesh, its (pron 3rd neut sng pos obj)
tilesh, its (pron 3rd neut sng pos sub)
tileshfal, itself (pron 3rd neut sng refl)
tilfdilorp, tiptoe (n)
tilfdilorsp, tiptoe (v)
tilfersh, diligence (n)
tilfershiu, diligently (adv)
tilfershu, diligent (adj)
tilfplorn, tipster (n)
tilialirst, discourse (v)
tilialirt, discourse (n)
tilirf, tip (n)
tilirfu, tippy (adj)
tilirfunf, tipoff (n)
tilirfwan, tipper (n doer)
tilirk, ire (n)
tilirkiu, irascibly (adv)
tilirku, irascible (adj)
tilirku, irate (adj)
tilirsf, tip (v)

tilirsk, irk (v)
tilirst, needle (v)
tilirt, needle (n)
tilitaifort, needlepoint (n)
tilitkiork, needlework (n)
tilork, wit (n)
tilorkiu, wittily (adv)
tilorku, witty (adj)
tilorkuetiu, witlessly (adv)
tilorkuetu, witless (adj)
tilotelf, dispersal (n)
tilotelf, dispersion (n)
tilotelfwan, disperser (n doer)
tilotelsf, disperse (v)
tilubolirk, disrepair (n)
timavirn, disharmony (n)
timeirge, divergence (n)
timeirgu, divergent (adj)
timeirzge, diverge (v)
timeshurst, dismember (v)
timeshurt, dismemberment (n)
timlarst, funnel (v)
timlart, funnel (n)
timork, fund (n)
timorkalt, fundamental (n)
timorkaltiu, fundamentally (adv)
timorkaltu, fundamental (adj)
timorkwan, funder (n doer)
timorsk, fund (v)
timorst, atomize (v)
timort, atom (n)
timortiu, atomically (adv)
timortu, atomic (adj)
Tin, Tin (n)
tinalirsh, disdain (n)
tinardast, disfavor (v)
tinardat, disfavor (n)
tinarn, dime (n)
tinarst, taste (v)
tinart, taste (n)
tinartiu, tastefully (adv)
tinartmeniu, tastelessly (adv)
tinartmenu, tasteless (adj)
tinartu, tasteful (adj)
tinartu, tasty (adj)
tinartwan, taster (n doer)
tinbist, divest (v)
tinbit, divestment (n)
tinirst, irritate (v)
tinirt, irritation (n)
tinirtwan, irritant (n doer)
tinoirf, dismay (n)
tinoirsf, dismay (v)
tinolan, disclaimer (n)
tinolasne, disclaim (v)
tinursk, neuter (v)
tiobairs, mortgage (v)
tiobairsh, mortgage (n)
tiolipoilf, disarray (n)
tiomeirf, disassociation (n)
tiomeirsf, disassociate (v)
tiorf, mortality (n)
tiorfiu, mortally (adv)

tiorfk, mortification (n)
tiorfp, morgue (n)
tiorfraik, morbidity (n)
tiorfraiku, morbid (adj)
tiorfsk, mortify (v)
tiorfu, mortal (adj)
tiorfwan, mortal (n doer)
tiorge, hire (n)
tiorgwan, hirer (n doer)
tiork, stall (n d:compartment)
tiorp, nimbleness (n)
tiorpiu, nimbly (adv)
tiorpu, nimble (adj)
tiorst, message (v)
tiorsth, tinge (v)
tiort, message (n)
tiorth, tinge (n)
tiortwan, messenger (n doer)
tiorzge, hire (v)
tiothralzve, disassemble (v)
tiovirap, disaffection (n)
tiovirasp, disaffect (v)
tipardwan, dispeller (n doer)
tiparzde, dispel (v)
tipifk, distension (n)
tipifsk, distend (v)
tipilafk, disobedience (n)
tipilafkiu, disobediently (adv)
tipilafku, disobedient (adj)
tipilafsk, disobey (v)
tiplarf, disgrace (n)
tiplarfiu, disgracefully (adv)
tiplarfu, disgraceful (adj)
tiplarsf, disgrace (v)
tipliarn, disappearance (n)
tipliarsne, disappear (v)
tipoinf, discount (n)
tipoinfwan, discounter (n doer)
tipoinsf, discount (v)
tipoist, distinguish (v)
tipoit, distinction (n)
tipoitiu, distinctly (adv)
tipoitu, distinct (adj)
tipoitu, distinctive (adj)
tiporsht, dishonesty (n)
tiporshtu, dishonest (adj)
tiprasht, dysfunction (n)
tiprashtu, dysfunctional (adj)
tiprilap, dispossession (n)
tiprilaop, dispossess (v)
tir, they (pron 3rd neut pl sub)
tirai-, pent- (num 5 pref)
tirai-, quint- (num 5 pref)
tirals, dismiss (v)
tiralsh, dismissal (n)
tiralshiu, dismissively (adv)
tiralshu, dismissive (adj)
tirardhe, disciple (n)
tiren, them (pron 3rd neut pl obj)
tiresh, their (pron 3rd neut pl pos sub)
tiresh, theirs (pron 3rd neut pl

pos obj)
tireshfar, themselves (pron 3rd
neut pl pos)
tireth, fifth (num 5 ord)
tirfp, disc (n)
tirfp, disk (n)
tirfpef, diskette (n)
tirfst, chirp (v)
tirft, chirp (n)
tirftwan, chirper (n doer)
tirfuge, discipline (n)
tirfugu, disciplinary (adj)
tirfugwan, disciplinarian (n doer)
tirfuzge, discipline (v)
tirge, peg (n)
tiri, five (num 5 card)
tirialfhemka, Number_1e20406
tiriap, ream (n d:paper)
tirida, fifty (num 50 card)
tiridai-, fifty- (num 50 pref)
tirideth, fiftieth (num 50 ord)
tirifk, quinquadragintillion (num
1e138 card)
tirift, quinquatrigintillion (num
1e108 card)
tirika, quintillion (num 1e18 card)
tirikai-, exa- (num 1e18 pref)
tiriketh, quintillionth (num 1e18
ord)
tiripa, fifteen (num 15 card)
tiripai-, fifteen- (num 15 pref)
tiripeth, fifteenth (num 15 ord)
tirishk, quinvigintillion (num
1e78 card)
tirishkai-, fiefta-
tirishketh, quinvigintillionth
(num 1e78 ord)
tirisht, quindecillion (num 1e48
card)
tirishtai-, pafta- (num 1e48 pref)
tirishteth, quindecillionth (num
1e48 ord)
tiriushk, punch (n d:beverage)
tirofk, chart (n)
tirofkul, charter (n)
tirofkusle, charter (v)
tirofkwan, charter (n doer)
tirofp, price (n)
tirofpemenu, priceless (adj)
tirofpu, pricey (adj)
tirofpwan, pricer (n doer)
tirofsk, chart (v)
tirofsp, price (v)
tirolarst, disbar (v)
tirolart, disbarment (n)
tirthk, list (n d:tilt)
tirthsk, list (v d:tilt)
tirzge, peg (v)
tishairp, dislocation (n)
tishairsp, dislocate (v)
tishanst, dissonate (v)

tishant, dissonance (n)
tishantu, dissonant (adj)
tisharlf, dislike (n)
tisharlsf, dislike (v)
tisharme, disbelief (n)
tishart, pellet (n)
tisharzme, disbelieve (v)
tishavizge, dislodge (v)
tishelirk, dissipation (n)
tishelirsk, dissipate (v)
tishkelst, disorder (v)
tishkelt, disorder (n)
tishkralgwan, dispatcher (n doer)
tishkralzge, dispatch (v)
tishlorf, impossibility (n)
tishlorfiu, impossibly (adv)
tishlorfu, impossible (adj)
tishnarf, disconnection (n)
tishnarsf, disconnect (v)
tishnern, disarmament (n)
tishnersne, disarm (v)
tisk, do (v)
tiskyot, did (v pa)
titairfst, disappoint (v)
titairft, disappointment (n)
Titanium, Titanium (n)
titark, simulation (n)
titarkwan, simulator (n doer)
titarsk, simulate (v)
titelforest, disinterest (v)
titelforest, disinterest (n)
titharf, diversity (n)
titharfet, diversification (n)
titharfu, diverse (adj)
titharfwan, diversifier (n doer)
titharsf, diversify (v)
titheifst, disown (v)
tithirs, dissect (v)
tithirsh, dissection (n)
tithorge, distress (n)
tithorgu, distraught (adj)
tithorzge, distress (v)
titinart, distaste (n)
titinartu, distasteful (adj)
titrep, distance (n)
titrepiu, distantly (adv)
titrepu, distant (adj)
titresp, distance (v)
tituirf, disguise (n)
tituirsf, disguise (v)
tiufarn, primate (n)
tiufarnu, primal (adj)
tiufdaurn, primetime (n)
tiufdaurnu, primetime (adj)
tiufirt, primitive (n)
tiufirtiu, primitively (adv)
tiufirtu, primitive (adj)
tiuforp, principle (n)
tiuforsp, principle (v)
tiugirk, lockstep (n)
tiugrithk, locksmith (n)
tiumarl, neutron (n)
tiurf, prime (n)

tiurfiu, primarily (adv)
tiurft, finiteness (n)
tiurftiu, finitely (adv)
tiurftu, finite (adj)
tiurfu, primary (adj)
tiurful, primary (n)
tiurfwan, primer (n doer)
tiurge, lock (n)
tiurgiveil, lockup (n)
tiurguil, lockout (n)
tiurgwan, locker (n doer)
tiurk, due (n)
tiurkiu, due (adv)
tiurku, due (adj)
tiurme, neutrality (n)
tiurmiu, neutrally (adv)
tiurmu, neutral (adj)
tiurmuet, neutralization (n)
tiurmwan, neutralizer (n doer)
tiurp, curfew (n)
tiursf, prime (v)
tiursh, priestess (n)
tiurst, finish (v)
tiurt, finish (n)
tiurtwan, finisher (n doer)
tiurzge, lock (v)
tiurzme, neutralize (v)
tivafirk, distemper (n)
tivagthorthk, stranglehold (n)
tivaize, dismantle (v)
tivaizhe, dismantlement (n)
tivarge, strangulation (n)
tivarp, strap (n)
tivarpwan, strapper (n doer)
tivarsp, strap (v)
tivarzge, strangle (v)
tivirk, list (n d:strip)
tivirku, list (adj d:strip)
tivirsh, discretion (n)
tivirshiu, discreetly (adv)
tivirshu, discreet (adj)
tivirsk, list (v d:strip)
tivirst, advance (v)
tivirt, advance (n)
tivirtuet, advancement (n)
tivitage, disadvantage (n)
tivitazge, disadvantage (v)
tivlark, discomfort (n)
tivlarsk, discomfort (v)
tivoirk, dispute (n)
tivoirsk, dispute (v)
tivramirsp, disband (v)
tivukrairze, striptease (v)
tivukrairzhe, striptease (n)
tivurk, strip (n)
tivurkwan, stripper (n doer)
tivursk, strip (v)
tiwaku, utmost (adj)
tizhaip, dissent (n)
tizhaipwan, dissenter (n doer)
tizhaipwan, dissident (n doer)
tizhaisp, dissent (v)
tizharsk, pelt (v d:hit)

tizhaurk, ultimatum (n)
tizhaurkiu, ultimately (adv)
tizhaurku, ultimate (adj)
tizhaurkyek, ultimatum (n pl)
tizhuarsle, dispirit (v)
tofirp, kindness (n d:nice)
tofirpiu, kindly (adv d:nice)
tofirpu, kind (adj d:nice)
toiarst, sass (v)
toidoip, extinguishment (n)
toidoipwan, extinguisher (n doer)
toidoisp, extinguish (v)
toigaurp, sarcasm (n)
toigaurpiu, sarcastically (adv)
toigaurpu, sarcastic (adj)
toime, ebony (n)
toirf, stain (n)
toirfmen, stainless (n)
toirfmenu, stainless (adj)
toirfwan, stainer (n doer)
toirk, bone (n)
toirkiu, bonily (adv)
toirkmenu, boneless (adj)
toirku, bony (adj)
toirp, citation (n)
toirsf, stain (v)
toirsh, boil (n d:infection)
toirsp, cite (v)
toirt, simultaneity (n)
toirtiu, simultaneously (adv)
toirtu, simultaneous (adj)
toishp, incitation (n)
toishp, incitement (n)
toishpwan, inciter (n doer)
toishsp, incite (v)
toivart, oblivion (n)
toivartu, oblivious (adj)
Toiviurl, Thursday (n)
Tokiorf, Tokyo (n)
toldidarn, facsimile (n)
tolfirge, dolphin (n)
tolirk, date (n d:time, meet)
tolirn, dollar (n)
tolirp, doll (n)
tolirsk, date (v d:time, meet)
tolirsp, doll (v)
tolirst, fax (v)
tolirt, fax (n)
toloveip, whereabout (n)
tolpalork, fabrication (n)
tolpalorkwan, fabricator (n doer)
tolpalorsk, fabricate (v)
toluyorsh, whereas (conj)
toluyorsh, whereas (n)
torap, thrust (n)
torapwan, thruster (n doer)
torasp, thrust (v)
toraspyot, thrust (v pa)
torfst, fence (v d:barrier)
torft, fence (n d:barrier)
torl, where (pron)
torlerf, wherever (adv/conj)
torlu, where (adv/conj)

torluvu, whereby (conj/adv)
tormesp, hunch (v)
tormp, hunch (n)
tormpwan, huncher (n doer)
Torontorf, Toronto (n)
torsth, dose (v)
torth, dose (n)
torthuet, dosage (n)
torvwan, fender (n doer)
torzve, fend (v)
toshk, get (n)
toshkwan, getter (n doer)
toshopiorl, getaway (n)
toshsk, get (v)
toshskyot, got (v pa)
tovaborst, diffuse (v)
tovabort, diffusion (n)
tovarshk, differential (n)
tovarshsk, differentiate (v)
tove, difference (n)
tovelishork, diffraction (n)
tovelishorsk, diffract (v)
toviu, differently (adv)
tovu, different (adj)
tozve, differ (v)
trabirn, tradition (n)
trabirniu, traditionally (adv)
trabirnu, traditional (adj)
trabirnwan, traditionalist (n doer)
trabiurk, traitor (n)
trafirp, archive (n)
trafirpu, archival (adj)
trafirpwan, archivist (n doer)
trafirsp, archive (v)
trafirt, job (n)
trafirtmen, joblessness (n)
trafirtmenu, jobless (adj)
trafk, fold (n)
trafkwan, folder (n doer)
trafsk, fold (v)
traide, club (n d:group)
traidukiarf, clubhouse (n)
traifk, fiend (n)
traifkiu, fiendishly (adv)
traifku, fiendish (adj)
traiforst, jab (v)
traifortwan, jabber (n doer)
traifp, flap (n)
traifpwan, flapper (n doer)
traifsp, flap (v)
traimurk, pentagon (n)
traishk, straightness (n)
traishkelf, straightedge (n)
traishku, straight (adj)
traishsk, straighten (v)
traishvoanaurshiu,
   straightforwardly (adv)
traishvoanaurshu,
   straightforward (adj)
traithbifirt, straitjacket (n)
traithk, strait (n)
traizde, club (v d:group)
tralge, batch (n)

tralirst, arch (v)
tralirt, arch (n)
tralirtwan, archer (n doer)
tralk, stage (n)
tralmalirsh, matriarch (n)
tralmalirshu, matriarchal (adj)
tralmark, matron (n)
tralmesht, monarchy (n)
tralmeshtwan, monarchist (n
   doer)
tralmethk, monarch (n)
traln, arc (n)
tralofirk, architecture (n)
tralofirku, architectural (adj)
tralofirkwan, architect (n doer)
tralofirsk, architect (v)
tralsk, stage (v)
tralsne, arc (v)
tralth, grey (n)
traltheiku, greyish (adj)
tralthgaurk, greyhound (n)
tralthu, grey (adj)
tramank, lather (n d:soap)
tramansk, lather (v d:soap)
tranf, gray (n)
tranfu, gray (adj)
tranirk, battery (n d:storage)
tranist, control (v)
tranit, control (n)
tranitu, controllable (adj)
tranitwan, controller (n doer)
traufk, crown (n)
traufsk, crown (v)
traunal, corona (n)
traunalst, coronate (v)
traunalt, coronation (n)
traunaltu, coronate (adj)
traurf, blouse (n)
trazhge, battle (n)
trazhgwan, battler (n doer)
trazhzge, battle (v)
trebarn, pulley (n)
trebevark, pullback (n)
trefdarve, boondocks (n)
trefirk, standard (n)
trefirkuet, standardization (n)
trefirsk, standardize (v)
trefirst, row (v d:paddle)
trefirtwan, rower (n doer
   d:paddle)
treiakarnyek, academics (n pl)
treiark, academy (n)
treiarkiu, academically (adv)
treiarku, academic (adj)
treibe, climb (n)
treibwan, climber (n doer)
treidal, climate (n)
treifp, grocery (n)
treifpwan, grocer (n doer)
treilaf, blossom (n)
treilasf, blossom (v)
treinap, clinic (n)
treinapu, clinical (adj)

treinat, client (n)
treithkwan, rover (n doer)
treithsk, rove (v)
treiushkwan, welcher (n doer)
treiushkwan, welsher (n doer)
treiushsk, welch (v)
treiushsk, welsh (v)
treivuge, castle (n)
treivuzge, castle (v)
treizbe, climb (v)
trelbe, pull (n)
trelbuil, pullout (n)
trelbwan, puller (n doer)
trelfirt, salary (n)
trelirf, sale (n)
trelirfu, saleable (adj)
trelirfuanfif, salesmanship (n)
trelirfuanfif, salespersonship (n)
trelirfuil, sellout (n)
trelirfwan, salesman (n doer)
trelirfwan, salesperson (n doer)
trelirfwan, seller (n doer)
trelirsf, sell (v)
trelirsfyot, sold (v pa)
trelirst, stand (v)
trelirstyot, stood (v pa)
trelirt, stand (n)
trelirtuil, standout (n)
trelirtunf, standoff (n)
trelish, road (n)
trelp, stance (n)
trelshbiral, roadblock (n)
trelshfeirf, roadshow (n)
trelshkiarf, roadhouse (n)
trelshoirt, roadside (n)
trelshpliorl, roadway (n)
treltaifort, standpoint (n)
treltiveil, standup (n)
treltiveilu, standup (adj)
treltoishk, boomerang (n)
treltshlern, standstill (n)
trelvurt, standby (n)
trelvurtu, standby (adj)
trelzbe, pull (v)
tremirp, reliance (n)
tremirpu, reliant (adj)
treshk, reef (n)
triafst, glow (v)
triaft, glow (n)
triaftu, glowy (adj)
triamp, uterus (n)
triank, staple (n d:commodity)
triarp, chew (n)
triarpwan, chewer (n doer)
triarsp, chew (v)
triarst, greet (v)
triashk, rectification (n)
triashkwan, rectifier (n doer)
triashsk, rectify (v)
triaufk, drought (n)
triauishk, rectum (n)
triauishkiu, rectally (adv)
triauishku, rectal (adj)

triauk, gloat (n)
triaushkwan, lurker (n doer)
triaushsk, lurk (v)
triausk, gloat (v)
triel, fill (n)
trieloif, filament (n)
trielwan, filler (n doer)
triesle, fill (v)
trifirt, sinus (n)
trifirtu, sinus (adj)
trifk, key (n)
trifkmenu, keyless (adj)
trifsk, key (v)
trikaturk, keystroke (n)
trikbaraft, keystone (n)
trikebanirf, keypad (n)
triklialirt, keyword (n)
triklinurn, keynote (n)
trikorth, keyhole (n)
trilank, scant (n)
trilankiu, scantily (adv)
trilanku, scanty (adj)
trilansk, scant (v)
trilf, tone (n d:music)
trilfuet, tonality (n)
trilorku, trainable (adj
    d:conditioning)
trilorkuin, trainee (n)
trilorkwan, trainer (n doer
    d:conditioning)
trilorsk, train (v d:conditioning)
trilshk, intonation (n)
trilushkwan, scavenger (n doer)
trilushsk, scavenge (v)
trink, pun (n)
trinorst, tolerate (v)
trinort, tolerance (n)
trinortu, tolerable (adj)
trinortu, tolerant (adj)
trinortuet, toleration (n)
triork, blooper (n)
triorkwan, blooper (n doer)
triorsk, bloop (v)
tripart, wheat (n)
triplok, keyboard (n)
trirt, ladder (n)
trisherp, dignity (n)
trisherpwan, dignitary (n doer)
trishersp, dignify (v)
trishoir, thesaurus (n)
trishoiryek, thesaurii (n pl)
trithk, wheel (n)
trithkat, wheelie (n)
trithkleshst, wheelchair (v)
trithklesht, wheelchair (n)
trithkwan, wheeler (n doer)
trithsk, wheel (v)
triuarst, groove (v)
triuart, groove (n)
triuartu, groovy (adj)
triufp, cheapness (n)
triufpiu, cheaply (adv)
triufpu, cheap (adj)

triufpwaku, cheapest (adj)
triufpwelu, cheaper (adj)
triufsp, cheapen (v)
triump, hive (n d:colony)
triunf, bloom (n)
triunfwan, bloomer (n doer)
triunsf, bloom (v)
triurgwan, tiller (n doer)
triurk, clout (n)
triurkwan, clouter (n doer)
triursk, clout (v)
triurst, lean (v d:tilt)
triurtwan, leaner (n doer d:tilt)
triurzge, till (v)
triushst, lurch (v)
triuteshsk, parch (v)
trofal, lesson (n)
troiafst, wilt (v)
troiark, spar (n)
troiarsk, spar (v)
troikarst, sparkle (v)
troikart, sparkle (n)
troikartu, sparkly (adj)
troilk, spark (n)
troilku, sparky (adj)
troilkwan, sparker (n doer)
troilp, flop (n)
troilpiu, floppily (adv)
troilpu, floppy (adj)
troilpwan, flopper (n doer)
troilsk, spark (v)
troilsp, flop (v)
troirt, salad (n)
trolge, toughness (n)
trolgu, tough (adj)
trolgwaku, toughest (adj)
trolgwelu, tougher (adj)
trolit, husband (n)
trolp, wipe (n)
trolpuil, wipeout (n)
trolpwan, wiper (n doer)
trolsp, wipe (v)
trolzge, toughen (v)
trotark, widower (n)
trotarsk, widower (v)
trotarskaut, widowered (v prp)
trovart, husbandry (n)
truathk, glove (n)
truathsk, glove (v)
truft, desk (n)
truifk, relevance (n)
truifk, relevancy (n)
truifkiu, relevantly (adv)
truifku, relevant (adj)
truirf, relay (n d:transceive)
truirt, premium (n)
truirtu, premium (adj)
trulik, cheat (n)
trulikwan, cheater (n doer)
trulis, print (v)
trulisf, furl (v)
trulish, print (n)
trulishwan, printer (n doer)

trulisk, cheat (v)
trun, foam (n)
truniu, foamily (adv)
trunu, foamy (adj)
trunwan, foamer (n doer)
trupaf, blame (n)
trupasf, blame (v)
trushk, rung (n d:step)
trusne, foam (v)
trutaurbe, desktop (n)
tshade, that (pron)
tshadu, that (adj)
Tshamel, Juniper (n)
tsharak, rock (n d:stone)
tsharaku, rocky (adj d:stone)
Tsharltorn, Charleston (n)
tsharn, though (adv/conj)
tshatirs, tooth (v)
tshatirsh, tooth (n)
tshatirshu, toothy (adj)
tshatirshyek, teeth (n pl)
tshatshdotirsh, toothpick (n)
tshatshdrafip, toothpaste (n)
tshatshklurf, toothbrush (n)
Tshekoshlovark, Czechoslovakia (n)
Tshernobilf, Chernobyl
Tshikarg, Chicago (n)
Tshilf, Chile (n)
Tshinarf, China (n)
Tshinarsh, Chinese (n)
tshome, than (conj/prep)
tshufist, trounce (v)
tshun, this (pron)
tshunu, this (adj)
tshurf, yeast (n)
tshurfk, fermentation (n)
tshurfsk, ferment (v)
tshutas, teethe (v)
tuagal, circumference (n)
tuagalu, circumferent (adj)
tuaiart, expletive (n)
tuairk, exotic (n)
tuairku, exotic (adj)
tualep, circumstance (n)
tualepu, circumstantial (adj)
tuamak, canal (n)
tuamast, channel (v)
tuamat, channel (n)
tuamatwan, channeler (n doer)
tuaiilk, violence (n)
tuarilkiu, violently (adv)
tuarilku, violent (adj)
tuarilkuet, violation (n)
tuarilkwan, violator (n doer)
tuarilsk, violate (v)
tuarkian, ecstasy (n)
tuarkianiu, ecstatically (adv)
tuarkianu, ecstatic (adj)
tuarn, change (n)
tuarnwan, changer (n doer)
tuarsht, duration (n)
tuarsne, change (v)

tuarsth, cash (v)
tuarth, cash (n)
tuarthwan, cashier (n doer)
tuarzhe, volatility (n)
tuarzhu, volatile (adj)
tuashk, circus (n)
tuaufp, warp (n)
tuaufsp, warp (v)
tubielirk, export (n)
tubielirkwan, exporter (n doer)
tubielirsk, export (v)
tublapliorl, expressway (n)
tublars, express (v)
tublarsh, expression (n)
tublarshiu, expressively (adv)
tublarshiu, expressly (adv)
tublarshu, expressive (adj)
tublarshwan, expresser (n doer)
tuborfst, extrude (v)
tuborft, extrusion (n)
tubreshorst, exply (v)
tubreshort, explication (n)
tubreshortiu, explicitly (adv)
tubreshortu, explicit (adj)
tubrunf, expenditure (n)
tubrunf, expense (n)
tubrunfiu, expensively (adv)
tubrunfrelpu, expendable (adj)
tubrunfu, expensive (adj)
tubrunsf, expend (v)
tudaibe, exhibit (n)
tudaibet, exhibition (n)
tudaibetwan, exhibitionist (n doer)
tudaibwan, exhibitor (n doer)
tudaizbe, exhibit (v)
tudalst, gape (v)
tudalt, gape (n)
tudarl, riddle (n)
tudarsle, riddle (v)
tudarthk, ejaculation (n)
tudarthsk, ejaculate (v)
tudauf, expiration (n)
tudausf, expire (v)
tudrak, exploit (n)
tudrakat, exploitation (n)
tudrakiu, exploitively (adv)
tudraku, exploitive (adj)
tudrakwan, exploiter (n doer)
tudralvo, exploration (n)
tudralvu, exploratory (adj)
tudralvwan, explorer (n doer)
tudralzve, explore (v)
tudrask, exploit (v)
tueifk, lathe (n d:machine)
tueifkwan, lather (n doer d:machine)
tueifsk, lathe (v d:machine)
tuenthirshk, exercise (n)
tuenthirshkwan, exerciser (n doer)
tuenthirshsk, exercise (v)
tuf, poof (interj)

tufalat, accuracy (n)
tufalatiu, accurately (adv)
tufalatu, accurate (adj)
tufarn, curl (n)
tufarnu, curly (adj)
tufarnwan, curler (n doer)
tufarsne, curl (v)
tufirp, knot (n)
tufirpu, knotty (adj)
tufirsp, knot (v)
tufral, excellence (n)
tufraliu, excellently (adv)
tufralu, excellent (adj)
tufrasle, excel (v)
tufravan, extremity (n)
tufrave, extreme (n)
tufraviu, extremely (adv)
tufravu, extreme (adj)
tufravwan, extremist (n doer)
tugarl, extract (n)
tugarluet, extraction (n)
tugarlwan, extractor (n doer)
tugarsle, extract (v)
tugef, bus (n)
tugefyek, buses (n pl)
tugesf, bus (v)
tugilirp, excerpt (n)
tugilirsp, excerpt (v)
tugoishst, excuse (v)
tugoisht, excuse (n)
tugoishtu, excusable (adj)
tugoishtwan, excuser (n doer)
tugorst, excrete (v)
tugort, excrement (n)
tugort, excretion (n)
tugortu, excretive (adj)
tugortwan, excreter (n doer)
tugrushst, exclude (v)
tugrusht, exclusion (n)
tugrushtiu, exclusively (adv)
tugrushtu, exclusive (adj)
tugrushtwan, excluder (n doer)
tuguniarst, excommunicate (v)
tuguniart, excommunication (n)
tuguniartwan, excommunicator (n doer)
tuiarf, dynamo (n)
tuiarfiu, dynamically (adv)
tuiarft, dynamic (n)
tuiarfu, dynamic (adj)
tuiark, trot (n)
tuiarkwan, trotter (n doer)
tuiarp, stalk (n d:appendage)
tuiarsk, trot (v)
tuikar, duty (n)
tuipebalirt, guidepost (n)
tuipvonurde, guidebook (n)
tuirf, guise (n)
tuirp, guidance (n)
tuirproif, guideline (n)
tuirpwan, guide (n doer)
tuirsp, guide (v)
tuirt, guy (n d:wire)

tuirtu, guy (adj d:wire)
tuitienf, geyser (n)
tukast, boot (v)
tukat, boot (n)
tukiorst, extort (v)
tukiort, extortion (n)
tukoirge, examination (n)
tukoirgwan, examiner (n doer)
tukoirzge, examine (v)
tukor, exam (n)
tulak, exposure (n)
tulaku, expository (adj)
tulakuet, exposition (n)
tulakwan, exposer (n doer)
tulask, expose (v)
tuldorap, stereotype (n)
tuldorapu, stereotypical (adj)
tuldorasp, stereotype (v)
tulidret, eccentricity (n)
tulidretu, eccentric (adj)
tulirf, cure (n)
tulirfu, curable (adj)
tulirfu, curative (adj)
tulirfwan, curer (n doer)
tulirk, murk (n)
tulirkiu, murkily (adv)
tulirku, murky (adj)
tulirp, curb (n)
tulirs, determine (v)
tulirsf, cure (v)
tulirsh, determination (n)
tulirshu, determinative (adj)
tulirshwan, determinant (n doer)
tulirsp, curb (v)
tulirst, cast (v)
tulirstyot, cast (v pa)
tulirt, cast (n)
tulorvage, exaggeration (n)
tulorvazge, exaggerate (v)
tumarnf, escort (n)
tumart, municipality (n)
tumartu, municipal (adj)
tumeis, expand (v)
tumeish, expanse (n)
tumeish, expansion (n)
tumeishiu, expansively (adv)
tumeishu, expandable (adj)
tumeishu, expansive (adj)
tumeishwan, expander (n doer)
tumeishwan, expansionist (n
      doer)
Tungshten, Tungsten (n)
tunilark, extermination (n)
tunilarkwan, exterminator (n
      doer)
tunilarsk, exterminate (v)
tunirt, helix (n)
tunirtiu, helically (adv)
tunirtu, helical (adj)
tunoflerbe, helicopter (n)
tunolar, exclamation (n)
tunolaru, exclamatory (adj)
tunolasre, exclaim (v)

tuorfsp, exert (v)
tupaurge, excavation (n)
tupaurgwan, excavator (n doer)
tupaurzge, excavate (v)
tupifork, extent (n)
tupiforkiu, extensively (adv)
tupiforku, extensive (adj)
tupiforkuet, extension (n)
tupiforkwan, extender (n doer)
tupiforsk, extend (v)
tupirk, whiz (n)
tupirp, exterior (n)
tupirpiu, externally (adv)
tupirpu, external (adj)
tupirsk, whiz (v)
tupirsp, externalize (v)
tupoit, extinction (n)
tupoitu, extinct (adj)
turge, material (n)
turgiu, materistically (adv)
turgu, materialistic (adj)
turguet, materialism (n)
turgwan, materialist (n doer)
Turkifarn, Turkish (n)
Turkirf, Turkey (n)
turshk, booth (n)
turshst, exact (v)
tursht, exactness (n)
turshtiu, exactly (adv)
turshtu, exact (adj)
turthk, drape (n)
turthkuet, drapery (n)
turthkwan, draper (n doer)
turthsk, drape (v)
turzge, materialize (v)
tushanber, example (n)
tushanbesre, exemplify (v)
tutarst, chase (v)
tutart, chase (n)
tutartwan, chaser (n doer)
tuthafirtiu, exquisitely (adv)
tuthafirtu, exquisite (adj)
tuthirshk, excision (n)
tuthirshsk, excise (v)
tuthuke kodi, should (ndal
      d:expectation)
tuthurk, expectation (n)
tuthurkwan, expectorant (n doer)
tuthursk, expect (v)
tutirku, crisp (adj)
tutoip, excitement (n)
tutoipiu, excitably (adv)
tutoipu, excitable (adj)
tutoipuet, excitation (n)
tutoipwan, exciter (n doer)
tutoisp, excite (v)
tutrelbe, extrication (n)
tutrelzbe, extricate (v)
tutuan, exchange (n)
tutuanu, exchangeable (adj)
tutuanwan, exchanger (n doer)
tutuasne, exchange (v)
tuvan, balm (n)

tuvek, excess (n)
tuvekiu, excessively (adv)
tuveku, excessive (adj)
tuvelp, exponent (n)
tuvelpiu, exponentially (adv)
tuvelpu, exponential (adj)
tuvelsp, expone (v)
tuvesk, exceed (v)
tuvest, except (v)
tuvet, except (prep/conj)
tuvet, exception (n)
tuvetiu, exceptionally (adv)
tuvetu, exceptional (adj)
tuvioishk, excruciation (n)
tuvioishkiu, excruciatingly (adv)
tuvioishsk, excruciate (v)
tuwafk, exhalation (n)
tuwafkwan, exhaler (n doer)
tuwafsk, exhale (v)
tuyarn, harp (n)
tuyarnwan, harper (n doer)
tuyarsne, harp (v)
tuyart, harpoon (n)
tuyoil, exile (n)
tuyoisle, exile (v)
ua, eh (interj)
uandriarde, eardrum (n)
uanritran, earring (n)
uanshkort, earshot (n)
uanshtarst, earmark (v)
uanshtart, earmark (n)
uantarak, earwax (n)
uanthetirsh, earpiece (n)
uanyarp, earphone (n)
ubaif, eviction (n)
ubaisf, evict (v)
ubiufirst, evaporate (v)
ubiufirt, evaporation (n)
ubiufirtwan, evaporator (n doer)
ude, ago (adj/adv)
udeip, equipment (n)
udeisp, equip (v)
uf, oomph (interj)
uferst, identify (v)
ufert, identity (n)
ufertar, identification (n)
ufertiu, identically (adv)
ufertu, identical (adj)
ufertwan, identifier (n doer)
ufrap, envelope (n)
ufrapwan, enveloper (n doer)
ufrasp, envelop (v)
ufst, evidence (v)
uft, evidence (n)
uftiu, evidently (adv)
uftu, evident (adj)
ugaifst, erupt (v)
ugaift, eruption (n)
ugaiftwan, eruptor (n doer)
ugilat, ego (n)
ugilatiu, egoistically (adv)
ugilatiu, egotistically (adv)
ugilatu, egoistic (adj)

ugilatu, egotistic (adj)
ugilatuet, egoism (n)
ugilatuet, egotism (n)
ugilatwan, egoist (n doer)
uil, out (adj/adv/prep/interj)
uil, out (n)
uilaorzme, outrun (v)
uilaorzmyot, outran (v pa)
uilblerf, outcome (n)
uilblerk, outbreak (n)
uilbrauf, outflow (n)
uilbrausf, outflow (v)
uilbroip, outcry (n)
uilbrutap, outburst (n)
uildialirt, outpost (n)
uildierku, outright (adj)
uildorizge, outgun (v)
uildraifp, outbound (n)
uildraifpu, outbound (adj)
uilerk, outlet (n)
uilferp, outset (n)
uilflaurfst, outlive (v)
uilfnilort, outskirt (n)
uilfranist, outlie (v)
uilfranistyot, outlaid (v pa)
uilfranit, outlay (n)
uilglorifu, outboard (adj)
uilgloruge, outreach (n)
uilgrairst, outstretch (v)
uilgranirsk, outflank (v)
uilhaursh, outward (n)
uilhaurshiu, outwardly (adv)
uilhaurshu, outward (adj/adv)
uilkiarf, outhouse (n)
uilkiorsf, outpace (v)
uilklorak, outgrowth (n)
uilklorask, outgrow (v)
uilkloraskyot, outgrew (v pa)
uilmoirsth, outshine (v)
uilmoirsthyot, outshone (v pa)
uilmorth, outpatient (n)
uilmorthu, outpatient (adj)
uilnenirsk, outnumber (v)
uilniarzme, outsmart (v)
uilovirfwan, outgoer (n doer)
uilovirsf, outgo (v)
uilovirsfyot, outwent (v pa)
uilovorinsf, outperform (v)
uilpafirst, outfit (v)
uilpafirt, outfit (n)
uilpafirtwan, outfitter (n doer)
uilprant, outfield (n)
uilprantwan, outfielder (n doer)
uilreigin, outlook (n)
uilroifk, outline (n)
uilroifkwan, outliner (n doer)
uilroifsk, outline (v)
uilroturst, outpour (v)
uilroturt, outpour (n)
uilshoirt, outside (n)
uilshoirt, outside
   (n/adj/adv/prep)
uilshoirtwan, outsider (n doer)

uilshtelf, outdoors (n)
uilshtelfu, outdoor (adj)
uilshuarzge, outsize (v)
uilshuirs, outweigh (v)
uiltalirshu, outspoken (adj)
uilthairsk, outvote (v)
uilthairst, outbid (v)
uilthairstyot, outbid (v pa)
uiltilorsk, outwit (v)
uiltivursk, outstrip (v)
uiltrelirsf, outsell (v)
uiltrelirsfyot, outsold (v pa)
uiltrelitu, outstanding (adj)
uiltulirt, outcast (n)
uilueft, outage (n)
uilvark, outback (n)
uilvaurde, outlaw (n)
uilvaurzde, outlaw (v)
uilvurst, output (v)
uilvurt, output (n)
uilweldorame, outerwear (n)
uilwelu, outer (adj)
uilwelwaku, outermost (adj)
uilzhigarst, outrage (v)
uilzhigart, outrage (n)
uilzhigartiu, outrageously (adv)
uilzhigartu, outrageous (adj)
ukaik, erasure (n)
ukaikiark, eradication (n)
ukaikiarkwan, eradicator (n doer)
ukaikiarsk, eradicate (v)
ukaikwan, eraser (n doer)
ukaisk, erase (v)
ukmirf, evolution (n)
ukmirfu, evolutionary (adj)
ukmirsf, evolve (v)
Ukrainarf, Ukraine (n)
ukuap, erotica (n)
ukuapu, erotic (adj)
ukuapuet, eroticism (n)
ukuast, erect (v)
ukuat, erection (n)
ukuatwan, erector (n doer)
uldaurf, umpire (n)
ule, if (conj)
unamu, p.m. (adj)
unaurk, omission (n)
unaurkwan, omitter (n doer)
unaursk, omit (v)
unf, off (prep)
unfdaurtu, offbeat (adj)
unfefklert, offscreen (n)
unfefklertu, offscreen (adj)
unferp, offset (n)
unfersp, offset (v)
unferspyot, offset (v pa)
unfkarpu, offhand (adj)
unflurifst, offload (v)
unfroifku, offline (adj)
unfshkort, offshoot (n)
unfshoirt, offside (n)
unfshoirtu, offside (adj)
unfthrelt, offspring (n)

unfularast, offshore (v)
unfularat, offshore (n)
Ununbium, Ununbium (n)
Ununhekium, Ununhexium (n)
Ununkuadium, Ununquadium (n)
Ununoktium, Ununoctium (n)
Ununpentium, Ununpentium (n)
Ununsheptium, Ununseptium (n)
Ununtrium, Ununtrium (n)
upshilorn, upsilon (n)
ur, hmm (interj)
Uranium, Uranium (n)
ureibe, errand (n)
urfe, U (let sng)
urfhem, Number_1e756
urfi, Us (let pl)
urshpu, each (adj)
ushairsk, evoke (v)
Ushap, Unbiunium (n davoka)
usherge, enscription (n)
usherge, inscription (n)
usherkwan, ouster (n doer)
ushersk, oust (v)
usherzge, enscribe (v)
usherzge, inscribe (v)
ushest, last (v)
ushetiu, lastly (adv)
ushetu, last (adj)
ushiak, escape (n)
ushiakiap, escapade (n)
ushiakiu, escapably (adv)
ushiaku, escapable (adj)
ushiakuet, escapism (n)
ushiakwan, escapee (n doer)
ushiask, escape (v)
Uship, Unbibium (n davoka)
ushkaus, arson (v)
ushkaush, arson (n)
ushkaushu, arsonous (adj)
ushkaushwan, arsonist (n doer)
ushlip, erosion (n)
ushlisp, erode (v)
ushpest, estate (v)
ushpet, estate (n)
ushtaip, entitlement (n)
ushtaipwan, entitler (n doer)
ushtaisp, entitle (v)
ushtive, elevation (n)
ushtivwan, elevator (n door)
ushtizve, elevate (v)
ushuirk, escalation (n)
ushuirkwan, escalator (n doer)
ushuirsk, escalate (v)
ushurt, below (adv/prep)
ushuvast, elaborate (v)
ushuvat, elaboration (n)
ushuvatu, elaborate (adj)
Utarfk, Utah (n)
uterp, ejection (n)
utersp, eject (v)
uthiurfst, elapse (v)
uthust, esteem (v)
uthut, esteem (n)

utiailart, understudy (n)
utiarborst, understaff (v)
utibiorast, underpower (v)
utibiurt, understatement (n)
utiblesh, underclass (n)
utibranirt, underground (n)
utibranirtu, underground (adj)
utibriarsk, underuse (v)
utidairs, undercut (v)
utidairsh, undercut (n)
utidairsyot, undercut (v pa)
utidathelu, undercover (adj)
utidatulu, underage (adj)
utidelgelf, undersecretary (n)
utidiapor, underbelly (n)
utidolsp, undercook (v)
utidovarme, underwear (n)
utidraursh, underdog (n)
utifanirn, underwood (n)
utigorkwan, undertaker (n doer)
utigorsk, undertake (v)
utigorskyot, undertook (v pa)
utigruashk, underbrush (n)
utigurilf, undercurrent (n)
utihalrelt, underworld (n)
utiheidornu, underwater (adj)
utiishrelsne, underinsure (v)
utikin, undergrad (n)
utikinorpu, undergraduate (adj)
utikinorpwan, undergraduate (n
    doer)
utiklairst, underscore (v)
utiklorak, undergrowth (n)
utikrivuzge, undermine (v)
utilakarn, undergarment (n)
utileirsp, underpin (v)
utilifarde, undershirt (n)
ntiloirdwan, underwriter (n doer)
utiloirzde, underwrite (v)
utiloirzdyot, underwrote (v pa)
utilunirt, underpass (v)
utimekarnyek, underpants (n pl)
utimoirzme, underpay (v)
utimoirzmyot, underpaid (v pa)
utine, under (adj/adv/prep)
utinilurn, underneath
    (adj/adv/prep)
utinilurn, underneath (n)
utiovairtwan, underachiever (n
    doer)
utipliorl, underway (n)
utipliorlu, underway (adj)
utiplorsne, underman (v)
utiriesf, underlie (v)
utiroifk, underline (n)
utiroifsk, underline (v)
utirp, underling (n)
utishkleirnu, undersea (adj)
utishnern, underarm (n)
utishnernu, underarm (adj)
utishoirt, underside (n)
utishuirsh, underweight (n)
utishuirshu, underweight (adj)

utitefralp, underdevelopment (n)
utitefralsp, underdevelop (v)
utiterzbe, underrate (v)
utithairst, underbid (v)
utithairstyot, underbid (v pa)
utithairt, underbid (n)
utithinarp, underestimation (n)
utithinarsp, underestimate (v)
utitirofsp, underprice (v)
utitrelirsf, undersell (v)
utitrelirsfyot, undersold (v pa)
utitrelirst, understand (v)
utitrelirstyot, understood (v pa)
utitrelirtiu, understandably (adv)
utitrelirtu, understandable (adj)
utitrilf, undertone (n d:music,
    audio)
utivaursp, undervalue (v)
utivirsf, undergo (v)
utivirsfyot, underwent (v pa)
uvauif, evacuation (n)
uvauifwan, evacuator (n doer)
uvauisf, evacuate (v)
uvaup, evaluation (n)
uvaupwan, evaluator (n doer)
uvausp, evaluate (v)
uvof, above (prep/adv/adj)
uyafzhursh, hearsay (n)
uyasf, hear (v)
uyasfyot, heard (v pa)
uzhak, evil (n)
uzhaku, evil (adj)
uzhakwan, evildoer (n doer)
uzhank, evasion (n)
uzhankiu, evasively (adv)
uzhanku, evasive (adj)
uzhankwan, evader (n doer)
uzhansk, evade (v)
uzhus, essay (v)
uzhush, essay (n)
vabegralf, popcorn (n)
vadarst, motivate (v)
vadart, motive (n)
vadartu, motivational (adj)
vadartuet, motivation (n)
vadartwan, motivator (n doer)
vadarve, motion (n)
vadarzve, motion (v)
vafiark, tempest (n)
vafikarst, temperate (v)
vafikart, temperance (n)
vafikartu, temperate (adj)
vafirk, temper (n)
vafirkuet, temperament (n)
vafirkuetiu, temperamentally
    (adv)
vafirp, tepidity (n)
vafirpiu, tepidly (adv)
vafirpu, tepid (adj)
vafirsk, temper (v)
vafirst, tempt (v)
vafirt, temptation (n)
vafirtwan, tempter (n doer)

vafkart, temperment (n)
vagark, shake (n)
vagarkiveil, shakeup (n)
vagarktien, shakedown (n)
vagarku, shaky (adj)
vagarkuil, shakeout (n)
vagarkwan, shaker (n doer)
vagarsk, shake (v)
vagarskyot, shook (v pa)
vagarst, enrapture (v)
vagart, rapture (n)
vagartu, rapt (adj)
vagaurk, rape (n)
vagaurkwan, rapist (n doer)
vagaursk, rape (v)
vahem, Number_1e1956
vaiaishk, ferocity (n)
vaiaishkiu, ferociously (adv)
vaiaishku, ferocious (adj)
vaiank, carnivore (n)
vaiankiu, carnivorously (adv)
vaianku, carnivorous (adj)
vaiaparp, girdle (n)
vaiarp, girth (n)
vaiarpwan, girder (n doer)
vaiarsp, gird (v)
vaidoftu, naked (adj)
vaifirk, guard (n)
vaifirsk, guard (v)
vaifkarn, guardianship (n)
vaifkarnwan, guardian (n doer)
vaifkluirt, guardrail (n)
vaiforp, dinner (n)
vaiforpedaun, dinnertime (n)
vaiforpeshlerf, dinnerware (n)
vaiforsp, dine (v)
vaiforst, guarantee (v)
vaifort, guarantee (n)
vaifortwan, guarantor (n doer)
vaigaushkwan, ravager (n doer)
vaigaushsk, ravage (v)
vailart, bounty (n)
vailartu, bountiful (adj)
vailork, feist (n)
vailorku, feist (adj)
vailorsk, feist (v)
vairalst, cycle (v)
vairalt, cycle (n)
vairaltiu, cyclically (adv)
vairaltu, cyclic (adj)
vairaltu, cyclical (adj)
vairaltwan, cycler (n doer)
vairge, explanation (n)
vairme, plane (n d:flat)
vairolp, cylinder (n)
vairsth, noose (v)
vairt, chief (n)
vairth, noose (n)
vairtiu, chiefly (adv)
vairtu, chief (adj)
vairzge, explain (v)
vairzme, plane (v d:flat)
vaishk, chef (n)

vaithark, nuisance (n)
vaiwarst, shelter (v)
vaiwart, shelter (n)
vaizhe, mantle (n)
vakaursh, backward (adj/adv)
vakbratin, background (n)
vakilp, backup (n)
vakthauthk, backyard (n)
vaktoirk, backbone (n)
vakuift, backlog (n)
val, V (let sng)
valar, plane (n d:airplane)
valars, gloss (v)
valarsh, gloss (n)
valarshu, glossy (adj)
valbaf, browse (n)
valbafwan, browser (n doer)
valbarl, connoisseur (n)
valbasf, browse (v)
vali, Vs (let pl)
valmeiraf, parole (n)
valparf, quantity (n)
valparfiu, quantitatively (adv)
valparfu, quantifiable (adj)
valparfu, quantitative (adj)
valparfuet, quantification (n)
valparsf, quantify (v)
valtairf, jeopardy (n)
valtairsf, jeopardize (v)
valtarst, circulate (v)
valtart, circulation (n)
valtartwan, circulator (n doer)
valtirfk, circuitry (n)
valtirge, pardon (n)
valtirzge, pardon (v)
valtor, circle (n)
valtoriu, circularly (adv)
valtork, circuit (n)
valtorsk, circuit (v)
valtoru, circular (adj)
valtosre, circle (v)
Valual, February (n)
valurap, umbrella (n)
valurs, glide (v)
valursh, glide (n)
valurshwan, glider (n doer)
Vanadium, Vanadium (n)
vanarf, couple (n)
vanarfwan, coupler (n doer)
vanarsf, couple (v)
vanarsth, caress (v)
vanarth, caress (n)
vanianku, cardiac (adj)
vanirk, copulation (n)
vanirl, bonus (n)
vanirsk, copulate (v)
vanirskaut, copulated (v prp)
Vankuvirf, Vancouver (n)
vantarn, sultan (n)
vanurdu, sultry (adj)
vapush, bachelor (n)
varbe, pop (n)
varbwan, popper (n doer)

varelst, pen (v d:ink device)
varelt, pen (n d:ink device)
Varemain, Fahrenheit (adj)
varfork, template (n)
varfrast, parcel (v)
varfrat, parcel (n)
varilk, fort (n)
varilsk, fortify (v)
vark, back (n)
varkadarf, paragraph (n)
varkaflufp, parachute (n)
varkaflufsp, parachute (v)
varkaft, parasite (n)
varkaftu, parasitic (adj)
varkaiaf, parade (n)
varkaiafwan, parader (n doer)
varkaiak, paranoia (n)
varkaiaku, paranoid (adj)
varkaiasf, parade (v)
varkaist, parry (v)
varkalirkyek, fortitude (n pl)
varkamarfst, paralyze (v)
varkanin, parallel (n)
varkaninu, parallel (adj)
varkaninuet, parallelism (n)
varkaniork, parameter (n)
varkaniorku, parametric (adj)
varkanisne, parallel (v)
varkaniurku, paramount (adj)
varkapren, paradox (n)
varkapreniu, paradoxically (adv)
varkaprenu, paradoxical (adj)
varkaren, parasol (n)
varkart, fortress (n)
varkashair, paradise (n)
varkavars, paraphrase (v)
varkavarsh, paraphrase (n)
varkwan, backer (n doer)
varme, soda (n)
varp, rope (n)
varpuest, petition (v)
varpuet, petition (n)
varpuetwan, petitioner (n doer)
varpwan, roper (n doer)
varshst, phrase (v)
varsht, phrase (n)
varsk, back (v)
varsp, rope (v)
vartesh, gulch (n)
varthak, language (n)
vartulf, security (n)
vartulfiu, securely (adv)
vartulfu, secure (adj)
vartulsf, secure (v)
varve, rub (n)
varzbe, pop (v)
varzve, rub (v)
vashil, birth (n)
vashilviurl, birthday (n)
vashisle, birth (v)
Vatikarn, Vatican (n)
vaturge, peak (n)
vaturzge, peak (v)

vaudeblerkwan, lawbreaker (n
    doer)
vaudeplorn, lawman (n)
vaudeplornyek, lawmen (n pl)
vaudrolfk, vacillation (n)
vaudrolfku, vacillatory (adj)
vaudrolfkwan, vacillator (n doer)
vaudrolfsk, vacillate (v)
vaufirst, imprison (v)
vaufirt, prison (n)
vaufirtuet, imprisonment (n)
vaufirtwan, prisoner (n doer)
vaugast, fight (v)
vaugastyot, fought (v pa)
vaugat, fight (n)
vaugatwan, fighter (n doer)
vauikerst, vacation (v)
vauikert, vacation (n)
vauikertwan, vacationer (n doer)
vauirf, vacuum (n)
vauirfiu, vacuously (adv)
vauirfu, vacuous (adj)
vauirge, vagueness (n)
vauirgiu, vaguely (adv)
vauirgu, vague (adj)
vauirk, vacancy (n)
vauirkiu, vacantly (adv)
vauirku, vacant (adj)
vauirkwan, vacator (n doer)
vauirsf, vacuum (v)
vauirsk, vacate (v)
vaurakiveil, followup (n)
vaurakiveil, follow-up (n)
vaurakiveilu, followup (adj)
vaurakiveilu, follow-up (adj)
vaurakwan, follower (n doer)
vaurask, follow (v)
vaurde, law (n)
vaurdenagwan, lawmaker (n
    doer)
vaurdiu, lawfully (adv)
vaurdmen, lawlessness (n)
vaurdmeniu, lawlessly (adv)
vaurdmenu, lawless (adj)
vaurdu, lawful (adj)
vaurdwan, lawyer (n doer)
vaurk, urge (n)
vaurkiu, urgently (adv)
vaurku, urgent (adj)
vaurkuet, urgency (n)
vaurkwan, urger (n doer)
vaurl, valley (n)
vaurn, spoil (n)
vaurnwan, spoiler (n doer)
vaurp, value (n)
vaurpu, valuable (adj)
vaurpuet, valuation (n)
vaurpul, valuable (n)
vaurshfalirmu, mainstream (adj)
vaurshiu, mainly (adv)
vaurshu, main (adj)
vaursk, urge (v)
vaursne, spoil (v)

vaursp, value (v)
vaurth, domain (n)
vaushlurk, mainstay (n)
vaushnoirk, etiquette (n)
vaushpifst, maintain (v)
vaushpift, maintenance (n)
vaushpiftwan, maintainer (n doer)
vaushraufp, mainland (n)
vaushroifk, mainline (n)
vazhast, bother (v)
vazhat, bother (n)
vazhirme, fit (n d:spasm)
vazhirzme, fit (v d:spasm)
vede, but (adv/conj/prep)
vefirp, pond (n)
vefirst, ponder (v)
veflarn, stationery (n)
veiakuift, gynecology (n)
veiakuiftwan, gynecologist (n doer)
veiart, nozzle (n)
veidon, future (n)
veidonu, futuristic (adj)
veidonwan, futurist (n doer)
veifort, positive (n)
veifortiu, positively (adv)
veifortu, positive (adj)
veikart, futility (n)
veikartu, futile (adj)
veilirf, splendor (n)
veilirfiu, splendidly (adv)
veilirfu, splendid (adj)
veilirn, position (n)
veilirnwan, positioner (n doer)
veilirp, poise (n)
veilirsne, position (v)
veilirsp, poise (v)
veilorp, pose (n)
veilorpwan, poser (n doer)
veilorsp, pose (v)
veinenmithk, ponytail (n)
veinern, pony (n)
veinersne, pony (v)
veirsh, lawn (n)
veirth, olive (n)
veishkriteshwan, lawnmower (n doer)
veiufst, nuzzle (v)
veiuft, nuzzle (n)
veivoip, usurpation (n)
veivoipwan, usurper (n doer)
veivoisp, usurp (v)
vekarl, budget (n)
vekarlu, budgetary (adj)
vekarsle, budget (v)
velarn, pasture (n)
velirf, fitness (n d:healthy)
velirfiu, fittingly (adv d:healthy)
velirfu, fit (adj d:healthy)
velirfweku, fittest (adj)
velirfwelu, fitter (adj)
velirn, summons (n)

velirsne, summon (v)
velt, from (prep)
veltorlu, where-from (adv)
vemiandaurn, wintertime (n)
vemiarn, winter (n)
vemiarnu, winter (adj)
vemiarnu, winterly (adj)
vemiarnu, wintry (adj)
vemiarsne, winterize (v)
venai-, hept- (num 7 pref)
venai-, sept- (num 7 pref)
veneth, seventh (num 7 ord)
venfk, septenquadragintillion (num 1e144 card)
venft, septentrigintillion (num 1e114 card)
veni, seven (num 7 card)
venialfhemka, Number_1e28506
venida, seventy (num 70 card)
venidai-, seventy- (num 70 pref)
venideth, seventieth (num 70 ord)
venipa, seventeen (num 17 card)
venipai-, seventeen- (num 17 pref)
venipeth, seventeenth (num 17 ord)
venka, septillion (num 1e24 card)
venkai-, yotta- (num 1e24 pref)
venketh, septillionth (num 1e24 ord)
venshk, septenvigintillion (num 1e84 card)
venshkai-, dieni-
venshketh, septenvigintillionth (num 1e84 ord)
vensht, septendecillion (num 1e54 card)
venshtai-, nekani (num 1e54 pref)
venshteth, septendecillionth (num 1e54 ord)
Venzhuilarf, Venezuela (n)
verde, budge (n)
vereishk, muzzle (n)
vereishsk, muzzle (v)
Vermonirt, Vermont (n)
versth, nosy (v)
verth, nose (n)
verthiu, nasally (adv)
verthu, nasal (adj)
verzde, budge (v)
verze, bug (v)
verzhe, bug (n)
verzhu, buggy (adj)
Veshaifar, September (n)
veshirp, pebble (n)
vetark, agenda (n)
vetarp, agency (n)
vetashriauk, cease-fire (n)
vetaverst, cease (v)
vetavert, cessation (n)

vethirt, nostril (n)
vethkraifk, nosedive (n)
vethlilfiot, nosebleed (n)
vethrairk, nausea (n)
vethrairku, nauseous (adj)
vethrairsk, nauseate (v)
viagarst, shiver (v)
viagart, shiver (n)
viah, gee (interj)
viah, geez (interj)
viaink, swivel (n)
viainsk, swivel (v)
viakrolart, crowbar (n)
vialiarf, phantom (n)
vialoirf, violin (n)
vialoirfwan, violinist (n doer)
vianirk, pioneer (n)
vianirp, fascination (n)
vianirsk, pioneer (v)
vianirsp, fascinate (v)
viarf, shower (n)
viarfk, crow (n)
viarfsk, crow (v)
viarge, crowd (n)
viargwan, crowder (n doer)
viarlst, cogitate (v)
viarlstaut, cogitated (v prp)
viarlt, cogitation (n)
viarp, cogency (n)
viarpiu, cogently (adv)
viarpu, cogent (adj)
viars, base (v)
viarsf, shower (v)
viarsh, base (n)
viarshiak, basement (n)
viarshiu, basically (adv)
viarshmashp, baseball (n)
viarshu, basic (adj)
viarshwan, baser (n doer)
viart, cognate (n)
viarthak, linguistics (n)
viarthakiu, linguistically (adv)
viarthaku, linguistic (adj)
viarthakwan, linguist (n doer)
viarzge, crowd (v)
viarzme, pine (v)
viashert, basis (n)
viatark, cognition (n)
viatarku, cognitive (adj)
viatarkuet, cognizance (n)
viatarkuetu, cognizant (adj)
viathk, rev (n)
viathsk, rev (v)
viatshk, fece (n)
viatshku, fecal (adj)
viatshkuet, defecation (n)
viatshsk, defecate (v)
viaurk, damn (n)
viaurku, damn (adj)
viaursk, damn (v)
viaushflarf, sportswear (n)
viaushk, sport (n)
viaushkebidwan, sportscaster (n

doer)
viaushkiu, sportily (adv)
viaushku, sporty (adj)
viaushkwan, sportster (n doer)
viaushplorn, sportsman (n)
viaushplornfif, sportsmanship (n)
viaushplornyek, sportsmen (n pl)
viaushsk, sport (v)
vibal, bomb (n)
vibalwan, bomber (n doer)
vibark, bombardment (n)
vibarsk, bombard (v)
vibasle, bomb (v)
vidort, nudity (n)
vidortu, nude (adj)
vidortwan, nude (n doer)
Vienarf, Vienna (n)
vienork, nomination (n)
vienorkiu, nominally (adv)
vienorku, nominal (adj)
vienorkuin, nominee (n)
vienorkwan, nominator (n doer)
vienorsk, nominate (v)
vierft, furnace (n)
viern, nomen (n)
vierp, bout (n)
viers, infuriate (v)
viersh, fury (n)
viershar, furor (n)
viershiu, furiously (adv)
viershu, furious (adj)
viershwan, infuriator (n doer)
viethk, brochure (n)
Vietnamarn, Vietnamese (n)
Vietnarme, Vietnam (n)
vigaklersh, shockwave (n)
vigarf, giggle (n)
vigarfwan, giggler (n doer)
vigark, shock (n)
vigarkiu, shockingly (adv)
vigarkwan, shocker (n doer)
vigarsf, giggle (v)
vigarsk, shock (v)
vigaushsk, ravish (v)
vigirst, vex (v)
vikauiesne, haunt (v)
vikavat, mathematic (n)
vikavatiu, mathematically (adv)
vikavatu, mathematical (adj)
vikavatwan, mathematician (n
   doer)
vikavit, math (n)
vikel, am (emphatic)
vikel, be (inf, emphatic)
vikel, is (emphatic)
viker, are (emphatic)
vikirsk, careen (v)
vikuark, chariot (n)
vikun, bundle (n)
vikunwan, bundler (n doer)
vikusne, bundle (v)
vil, am (common)
vil, be (inf, common)

vil, is (common)
Vilan, EhoMonth05 (n)
vildurme, between (adv/prep)
vilensf, become (v)
vilensfyot, became (v pa)
vilmthorthkwan, bondholder (n
   doer)
viloirst, beseech (v)
viloirtwan, beseecher (n doer)
vilork, fist (n)
vilorku, fistful (adj)
vilorsk, fist (v)
vilshashk, because (conj)
vimarn, window (n)
vimarnmenu, windowless (adj)
vimarnuasne, eavesdrop (v)
vimarsne, window (v)
vimorl, bond (n)
vimorlak, bondage (n)
vimorlwan, bonder (n doer)
vimorsle, bond (v)
vinarde, coupon (n)
vinst, limit (v)
vint, limit (n)
vintar, limitation (n)
vintwan, limiter (n doer)
vinuirn, cascade (n)
vinuirsne, cascade (v)
vioirk, temple (n)
vioishk, crucifixion (n)
vioishsk, crucify (v)
viokvoirku, gigantic (adj)
Vioriaf, EhoDay02 (n)
viork, giant (n)
viorn, cruciality (n)
viorniu, crucially (adv)
viornu, crucial (adj)
Vipalp, Bible (n)
vipoark, caravan (n)
vipoarsk, caravan (v)
vipun, bunch (n)
vipunu, bunchy (adj)
vipusne, bunch (v)
viputshk, carcass (n)
vir, are (common)
viran, camera (n)
viranwan, cameraperson (n doer)
virfwan, goer (n doer)
Virginiarf, Virginia (n)
virk, fix (n)
virkest, fixate (v)
virket, fixation (n)
virku, fixable (adj)
virkwan, fixer (n doer)
virkzhar, fixture (n)
virsf, go (v)
virsfyot, went (v pa)
virsk, fix (v)
visharl, diva (n)
visharn, shampoo (n)
visharnwan, shampooer (n doer)
visharsne, shampoo (v)
vishkirk, shamble (n)

vishkirsk, shamble (v)
vishork, sham (n)
vishorst, shame (v)
vishort, shame (n)
vishortiu, shamefully (adv)
vishortmeniu, shamelessly (adv)
vishortmenu, shameless (adj)
vishortu, shameful (adj)
vishvar, eagerness (n)
vishvariu, eagerly (adv)
vishvaru, eager (adj)
vitage, advantage (n)
vitagu, advantageous (adj)
vitersh, stump (n d:tree)
vithairf, feline (n)
viufirk, warrant (n)
viufirsk, warrant (v)
viugilt, epic (n)
viukurk, faucet (n)
viunblerk, daybreak (n)
viundaurn, daytime (n)
viunflaul, daydream (n)
viunflausle, daydream (v)
viunfluarn, daylight (n)
viunkeirf, daycare (n)
viunralzhu, daylong (adj)
viurbotersh, warpath (n)
viurdaurn, wartime (n)
viureflerve, warship (n)
viurgu, big (adj)
viurgwaku, biggest (adj)
viurgwelu, bigger (adj)
viurk, force (v)
viurkefirt, warhead (n)
viurkiu, forcefully (adv)
viurkiu, forcibly (adv)
viurku, forceful (adj)
viurku, forcible (adj)
viurkwan, forcer (n doer)
viurl, day (n)
viurlu, daily (adj)
viurme, gulley (n)
viurn, war (n)
viurnif, warfare (n)
viurnu, warlike (adj)
viurnwan, warrior (n doer)
viurp, warranty (n)
viursk, force (v)
viursne, war (v)
viurst, warn (v)
viurvalar, warplane (n)
viuvart, ambiguity (n)
viuvartiu, ambiguously (adv)
viuvartu, ambiguous (adj)
vivarf, mustard (n)
vivoan, before (prep/conj)
vivokap, beforehand (adj/adv)
vlark, comfort (n)
vlarkiu, comfortably (adv)
vlarku, comfortable (adj)
vlarkwan, comforter (n doer)
vlarsk, comfort (v)
vlirs, steam (v)

vlirsh, steam (n)
vlirshu, steamy (adj)
vlirshwan, steamer (n doer)
vlishfalarwan, steamroller (n doer)
vlishfalasre, steamroll (v)
vlishflerve, steamship (n)
vlishkorbe, steamboat (n)
voafel, forever (n)
voafeliu, forever (adv)
voagruf, forgiveness (n)
voagrufu, forgivable (adj)
voagrufwan, forgiver (n doer)
voagrusf, forgive (v)
voagrusfyot, forgave (v pa)
voairk, fierceness (n)
voairkiu, fiercely (adv)
voairku, fierce (adj)
voanarfiu, formerly (adv d:previous)
voanarfu, former (adj d:previous)
voanaurs, forward (v)
voanaursh, forward (n)
voanaurshiu, forward (adv)
voanaurshu, forward (adj)
voanblersf, forthcome (v)
voanblersfyot, forthcame (v pa)
voanirfiu, forth (adv)
voantop, forgettance (n)
voantopiu, forgetfully (adv)
voantopu, forgetful (adj)
voantopwan, forgetter (n doer)
voantosp, forget (v)
voantospyot, forgot (v pa)
voaplorn, foreman (n)
voaplornyek, foremen (n pl)
voark, march (n)
voarkwan, marcher (n doer)
voarsk, march (v)
voarst, forage (v)
voarth, date (n d:fruit)
voarthst, forbid (v)
voarthstyot, forbade (v pa)
voartht, forbiddence (n)
voarthtwan, forbidder (n doer)
voartwan, forager (n doer)
voasheidorn, wastewater (n)
voashk, waste (n)
voashkiu, wastefully (adv)
voashku, wasteful (adj)
voashkuet, wastefulness (n)
voashkwan, waster (n doer)
voashmun, fortune (n)
voashmuniu, fortunately (adv)
voashmunu, fortunate (adj)
voashraufp, wasteland (n)
voashsk, waste (v)
voashtafil, wastebasket (n)
voashvuarp, wastepaper (n)
voatbraft, foreground (n)
voatederp, forethought (n)
voatedinank, forefinger (n)
voateirsk, forestall (v)

voatelaursf, forebode (v)
voateshtaurs, forbear (v d:refrain)
voateshtaursh, forbearance (n d:refrain)
voateshtaursyot, forbore (v pa d:refrain)
voatflarsh, forefront (n)
voatfruifk, foreplay (n)
voatglerk, foreknowledge (n)
voatgrefst, foreclose (v)
voatgreft, foreclosure (n)
voathulsth, foresee (v)
voathulsthyot, foresaw (v pa)
voathulth, foresight (n)
voathulthiu, foreseeably (adv)
voathulthu, foreseeable (adj)
voathust, forecast (v)
voathut, forecast (n)
voathutwan, forecaster (n doer)
voatisf, forego (v)
voatisfyot, forewent (v pa)
voatkarp, forehand (n)
voatkeft, forehead (n)
voatkriage, forbear (n d:ancestor)
voatkriage, forbearer (n d:ancestor)
voatlaormwat, forerunner (n)
voatpeime, forfeiture (n)
voatpeimwan, forfeiter (n doer)
voatpeizme, forfeit (v)
voatpoefirst, foreshadow (v)
voatpoefirt, foreshadow (n)
voatprelst, foretell (v)
voatprelstyot, foretold (v pa)
voatshnern, forearm (n)
voatu, fore (adj)
voatviurst, forewarn (v)
voatwaku, foremost (adj)
vobalf, medication (n)
vobalf, medicine (n)
vobalfiu, medically (adv)
vobalfu, medical (adj)
vobalfwan, medic (n doer)
vobalsf, medicate (v)
voiafplok, surfboard (n)
voiarf, surf (n)
voiarfwan, surfer (n doer)
voiarsf, surf (v)
voibrienf, surname (n)
voifk, navel (n)
voiflaurfst, survive (v)
voiflaurft, survival (n)
voiflaurftuet, survivability (n)
voiflaurftwan, survivalist (n doer)
voiflaurftwan, survivor (n doer)
voifuarst, survey (v)
voifuart, survey (n)
voifuartak, surveillance (n)
voifuartwan, surveyor (n doer)
voigloift, surcharge (n)
voikuarst, resurrect (v)
voikuart, resurrection (n)
voikuartwan, resurrector (n doer)

voilarank, surrogation (n)
voilaranku, surrogate (adj)
voilarankwan, surrogate (n doer)
voilaransk, surrogate (v)
voilunirst, surpass (v)
voiniursk, surmount (v)
voink, computation (n)
voinkak, computerization (n)
voinkask, computerize (v)
voinku, computational (adj)
voinkwan, computer (n doer)
voinsk, compute (v)
voinumart, surplus (n)
voipluarf, surrealism (n)
voipluarfu, surreal (adj)
voirge, surge (n)
voirn, knife (n)
voirnwan, knifer (n doer)
voirs, busy (v)
voirsh, busyness (n)
voirshiu, busily (adv)
voirshk, business (n)
voirshku, businesslike (adj)
voirshkwan, businessman (n doer)
voirshkwan, businessperson (n doer)
voirshu, busy (adj)
voirsne, knife (v)
voirve, gamble (n)
voirvwan, gambler (n doer)
voirzge, surge (v)
voirzve, gamble (v)
voishenirk, surtax (n)
voitolirsp, surmise (v)
voivark, gambit (n)
voiviurs, surprise (v)
voiviursh, surprise (n)
voiviurshiu, surprisingly (adv)
vokar, block (n d:cube)
vokaru, blocky (adj d:cube)
vokel, been (v pap sng emphatic)
vokel, was (emphatic)
voker, been (v pap pl emphatic)
voker, were (emphatic)
vol, been (v pap sng common)
vol, was (common)
volarst, code (v)
volart, code (n)
volartwan, coder (n doer)
volirk, chest (n d:container)
vomark, risk (n)
vomark, riskiness (n)
vomarkiu, riskily (adv)
vomarku, risky (adj)
vomarsk, risk (v)
vor, been (v pap pl common)
vor, were (common)
vorade, popularity (n)
voradiu, popularly (adv)
voradu, popular (adj)
voradwan, populace (n doer)
voral, spring (n d:season)

voralu, spring (adj d:season)
vorast, build (v)
vorastyot, built (v pa)
vorat, build (n)
vorativeil, buildup (n)
voratwan, builder (n doer)
vorave, population (n)
vorazde, popularize (v)
vorazve, populate (v)
vorifk, motor (n)
vorifkwan, motorist (n doer)
vorifsk, motor (v)
vorkarst, motorize (v)
vorkegeral, motorcar (n)
vorkeidan, motel (n)
vorkepivirt, motorbike (n)
vorkevairalst, motorcycle (v)
vorkevairalt, motorcycle (n)
vorkevairaltwan, motorcyclist (n
    doer)
vorkshkorbe, motorboat (n)
vorldaurn, springtime (n)
vorlin, form (n d:shape)
vorlinak, format (n)
vorlinakwan, formatter (n doer)
vorlinap, formulation (n)
vorlinapwan, formulator (n doer)
vorlinarp, formula (n)
vorlinask, format (v)
vorlinasp, formulate (v)
vorlinast, formalize (v)
vorlinat, formal (n)
vorlinatiu, formally (adv)
vorlinatu, formal (adj)
vorlinatuet, formality (n)
vorlinkapu, formidable (adj)
vorlinuet, formation (n)
vorlinwan, former (n doer
    d:shape)
vorlisne, form (v d:shape)
vorme, ban (n)
vormk, banality (n)
vormwan, banner (n doer)
vorndairk, bookend (n)
vorndralp, bookstore (n)
vornst, book (v)
vornt, book (n)
vorntap, booklet (n)
vorntenalirf, bookshelf (n)
vorntenarge, bookmaking (n)
vorntenargwan, bookmaker (n
    doer)
vornthorve, bookshop (n)
vornthorvwan, bookshopper (n
    doer)
vorntklorf, bookkeeping (n)
vorntklorfwan, bookkeeper (n
    doer)
vorntrelirf, booksale (n)
vorntrelirfwan, bookseller (n
    doer)
vorntshuart, bookcase (n)
vorplok, cupboard (n)

vorshk, shaft (n)
vorshkwan, shafter (n doer)
vorshsk, shaft (v)
vorthk, forum (n)
vortirshu, builtin (adj)
vorugutraf, cupcake (n)
vorup, cup (n)
vorusp, cup (v)
vorzme, ban (v)
voshafrelpu, lovable (adj
    d:common)
voshar, love (n d:common)
voshark, scepter (n)
voshark, sceptre (n)
vosharu, lovely (adj d:common)
vosharwan, lover (n doer
    d:common)
voshasre, love (v d:common)
voshave, love (n d:emphatic)
voshavu, lovely (adj d:emphatic)
voshavwan, lover (n doer
    d:emphatic)
voshazve, love (v d:emphatic)
votal, column (n)
votasle, columnate (v)
votefst, father (v)
voteft, father (n)
voteftu, fatherly (adj)
votertfif, fatherhood (n)
votertmenu, fatherless (adj)
votetraufp, fatherland (n)
vramarshk, banishment (n)
vramarshsk, banish (v)
vramirp, band (n d:group)
vramirpu, bandy (adj d:group)
vramirsp, band (v d:group)
vramkrashk, bandwidth (n)
vrazge, fence (v d:spar)
vrierst, learn (v)
vrierstyot, learnt (v pa)
vriertwan, learner (n doer)
vu, by (adj/adv/prep)
vuakebanirf, launchpad (n)
vuamirt, laundromat (n)
vuapart, paperback (n)
vuapekiork, paperwork (n)
vuaplok, paperboard (n)
vuapshuirsh, paperweight (n)
vuark, launch (n)
vuarktwan, launcher (n doer)
vuarme, laundry (n)
vuarmwan, launderer (n doer)
vuarn, elite (n)
vuarnu, elite (adj)
vuarnwan, elitist (n doer)
vuarp, paper (n)
vuarpemenu, paperless (adj)
vuarsk, launch (v)
vuarsp, paper (v)
vuart, fineness (n d:small)
vuartiu, finely (adv d:small)
vuartu, fine (adj d:small)
vuarzme, launder (v)

vuau, golly (interj)
vuaursh, gosh (interj)
vublars, suppress (v)
vublarsh, suppression (n)
vublarshiu, suppressively (adv)
vublarshu, suppressive (adj)
vublarshwan, suppressor (n doer)
vublasharn, suppressant (n)
vubrels, supplicate (v)
vubrelsh, supplication (n)
vubrelsp, supplant (v)
vufiurk, byproduct (n)
vugabiorat, superpower (n)
vugabrauf, superflow (n)
vugabraufu, superfluous (adj)
vugabrausf, superflow (v)
vugadiardar, supermodel (n)
vugadralp, superstore (n)
vugadrokifar, superstar (n)
vugafart, superficiality (n)
vugafartiu, superficially (adv)
vugafartu, superficial (adj)
vugafiaishk, supervision (n)
vugafiaishku, supervisory (adj)
vugafiaishkwan, supervisor (n
    doer)
vugafiaishsk, supervise (v)
vugaflude, superlative (n)
vugagloifst, supercharge (v)
vugagloiftwan, supercharger (n
    doer)
vugakiglarsk, superimpose (v)
vugakoiopliorl, superhighway (n)
vugakurst, superheat (v)
vugaleirdiu, supernaturally (adv)
vugaleirdu, supernatural (adj)
vugalirpiu, superbly (adv)
vugalirpu, superb (adj)
vugamiarf, supernova (n)
vugaplorn, superman (n)
vugaplornyek, supermen (n pl)
vugarlu, super (adj)
vugarn, superiority (n)
vugarnu, superior (adj)
vugarnwan, superior (n doer)
vugarpifkan, superintendent (n)
vugasharladwan, superhero (n
    doer)
vugashlork, superstructure (n)
vugashlurfu, supercool (adj)
vugashlursf, supercool (v)
vugashorlu, superhuman (adj)
vugatruirt, supremacy (n)
vugatruirtiu, supremely (adv)
vugatruirtu, supreme (adj)
vugatruirtwan, supremacist (n
    doer)
vugaversk, supercede (v)
vugaversk, supersede (v)
vugazhantarnu, supersonic (adj)
vuglark, supposition (n)
vuglarkiu, supposedly (adv)
vuglarkwan, supposer (n doer)

vuglarsk, suppose (v)
vuiaufsk, meander (v)
vuik, friction (n)
vuikmenu, frictionless (adj)
vuiku, frictional (adj)
vukesh, shall (v)
vukesh, will (v emphat)
vukesh, will-be (v fp emphatic)
vukirde, puzzle (n)
vukirduet, puzzlement (n)
vukirdwan, puzzler (n doer)
vukirkwan, prodder (n doer)
vukirsk, prod (v)
vukirzde, puzzle (v)
vularn, marriage (n)
vularnu, marital (adj)
vularsne, marry (v)
vulashk, matrimony (n)
vulashku, matrimonial (adj)
vulirk, quantum (n)
vulirku, quantum (adj)
vulunirst, bypass (v)
vulunirt, bypass (n)
vulunirtwan, bypasser (n doer)
vumark, coffee (n)
vunharf, cuddle (n)
vunharsf, cuddle (v)
vuparn, mean (n)
vupaurk, meanwhile (n)
vupaurkiu, meanwhile (adv)
vupirn, bark (n d:yelp)
vupirnwan, barker (n doer d:yelp)
vupirsne, bark (v d:yelp)
vupliorl, byway (n)
vupodaun, meantime (n)
vupodauniu, meantime (adv)
vurbe, cub (n)
vurk, push (n)
vurkafen, pushover (n)
vurku, pushy (adj)
vurkwan, pusher (n doer)
vuroifk, byline (n)
vurpemen, meaninglessness (n)
vurpemenu, meaningless (adj)
vurpiu, meaningfully (adv d:importance)
vurpu, meaningful (adj d:importance)
vursk, push (v)
vursp, mean (v d:importance)
vurspyot, meant (v pa d:importance)
vurst, put (v)
vurstyot, put (v pa)
vurt, put (n)
vush, will (v common)
vush, will-be (v fp common)
vuthark, purge (n)
vutharsk, purge (v)
vuthiarf, purgatory (n)
vutolirp, demise (n)
vutolirsp, demise (v)
vutrelirtwan, bystander (n doer)

vuvaurde, bylaw (n)
vuvienork, denomination (n)
vuvienorku, denominational (adj)
vuvienorkwan, denominator (n doer)
vuvienorsk, denominate (v)
vuvirfyot, bygone (n)
vuvirfyotu, bygone (adj)
vuvirfyotyek, bygones (n pl)
waiarst, yell (v)
waiart, yell (n)
waiartwan, yeller (n doer)
waidak, madness (n d:insane)
waidakiarf, madhouse (n)
waidaku, mad (adj d:insane)
waidakwelu, madder (adj d:insane)
waidaplorn, madman (n)
waidaplornyek, madmen (n pl)
waik, yikes (interj)
Waiominork, Wyoming (n)
wak, most (adj/adv)
wak, most (pron)
wakiu, mostly (adv)
walfiu, merely (adv)
walfu, mere (adj)
walirsh, youth (n)
walirshu, young (adj)
walirshu, youthful (adj)
walirshuet, youngster (n)
walirshwaku, youngest (adj)
walirshwelu, younger (adj)
walp, half (n)
walpu, half (adj)
walsp, halve (v)
wapliol, halfway (adj/adv)
warf, hence (adv)
warfe, W (let sng)
warthem, Number_1e1506
warfi, Ws (let pl)
Warshaurf, Warsaw (n)
warshk, yet (adv/conj)
warth, hen (n)
Washinktorn, Washington (n)
wathkiarf, henhouse (n)
wefarn, wig (n)
wefirk, rout (n d:dig)
wefirkwan, router (n doer d:dig)
wefirp, root (n)
wefirsk, rout (v d:dig)
wefirsp, root (v)
weifbalirt, signpost (n)
weifirp, signal (n)
weifirpwan, signaler (n doer)
weifirsp, signal (v)
weifirt, signature (n)
weifirtwan, signatory (n doer)
weifork, significance (n)
weiforkiu, significantly (adv)
weiforku, significant (adj)
weiforsk, signify (v)
Weilorsh, Wales (n)
weior, yeah (adv)

weip, yep (adv)
weip, yup (adv)
weir, yes (adv)
weirf, sign (n)
weirfwan, signer (n doer)
weirsf, sign (v)
weishklorsh, yesteryear (n)
weishklorshiu, yesteryear (adv)
weishklorshu, yesteryear (adj)
weishviurl, yesterday (n)
weishviurliu, yesterday (adv)
weishviurlu, yesterday (adj)
wel, more (adj/adv)
wel, more (pron)
welfeniu, moreover (adv)
wiarf, merit (n)
wiarp, pilgramage (n)
wiarpwan, pilgrim (n doer)
wiars, hike (v)
wiarsf, merit (v)
wiarsh, hike (n)
wiarshwan, hiker (n doer)
wiarst, owe (v)
wiartwan, ower (n doer)
wiaukshmonde, oddball (n)
wiaurk, odd (n d:probability)
wienargwan, homemaker (n doer)
wienarzge, homemake (v)
wienarzgyot, homemade (v pa)
wienegiortu, homemade (adj)
wienegliurpu, homesick (adj)
wienf, home (n)
wienfu, homey (adj)
wienkiok, homework (n)
wienlenar, homecoming (n)
wienmern, homelessness (n)
wienmerniu, homelessly (adv)
wienmernu, homeless (adj)
wienmiurn, hometown (n)
wienraufp, homeland (n)
wiensf, home (v)
wientheifst, homeown (v)
wientheiftwan, homeowner (n doer)
wienvoratwan, homebuilder (n doer)
wikorn, yogurt (n)
wilf, hop (n)
wilfwan, hopper (n doer)
wilsf, hop (v)
winorf, gum (n)
winorfu, gummy (adj)
winorsf, gum (v)
wiortu, foreign (adj)
wiortwan, foreigner (n doer)
Wishkornsh, Wisconsin (n)
witap, narrow (n)
witapiu, narrowly (adv)
witapu, narrow (adj)
witapuet, narrowness (n)
witapweku, narrowest (adj)
witapwelu, narrower (adj)
witasp, narrow (v)

wiursf, hone (v)
wiushk, sewer (n d:waste conduit)
wiushk, sewerage (n)
wiushsk, sewer (v d:waste
    conduit)
yadirst, yield (v)
yadirt, yield (n)
yadirtwan, yielder (n doer)
yaferf, will (n d:inheritance)
yai, wow (interj)
yaifank, waffle (n)
yaifansk, waffle (v)
yaifk, wafer (n)
yaigaft, hostility (n)
yaigaftu, hostile (adj)
yair, foe (n)
yairde, verb (n)
yaisy, wow (v)
yaivart, verbiage (n)
yaivartiu, verbally (adv)
yaivartu, verbal (adj)
yaivurge, feud (n)
yaivurzge, feud (v)
yaiy, wow (n)
yakaretal, algebra (n)
yakaretaliu, algebraically (adv)
yakaretalu, algebraic (adj)
yakbiorat, willpower (n)
yalirf, wait (n)
yalirfwan, waiter (n doer)
yalirfwan, waitress (n doer)
yalirk, waddle (n)
yalirp, wad (n)
yalirsf, wait (v)
yalirsk, waddle (v)
yalirsp, wad (v)
yalushsk, wallow (v)
yamerf, whenever (adv/conj)
yamifk, quandary (n)
yamir, alumnus (n)
yamiryek, alumni (n pl)
yanu, amen (interj)
yark, will (n d:determination)
yarke kodi, would (ndal d:will)
yarkiu, willfully (adv
    d:determination)
yarkiu, willingly (adv)
yarku, willful (adj
    d:determination)
yarkuet, willingness (n)
yarkuit, algorithm (n)
yarkurtiu, algorithmically (adv)
yarkurtu, algorithmic (adj)
yarle, Y (let sng)
yarlhem, Number_1e1206
yarli, Ys (let pl)
yarme, when (adv/conj)
yarme, when (pron)
yars, wade (v)
yarsh, that (conj)
yarshwan, wader (n doer)
yarsk, will (v d:determination)
yarsth, hoof (v)

yarth, hoof (n)
yarthwan, hoofer (n doer)
yat, hah (interj)
yata, haha (interj)
yaua, yow (interj)
yauark, wretch (n)
yaufsk, woo (v)
yaunk, whimper (n)
yaunsk, whimper (v)
yauplaiathk, whiplash (n)
yauplaiathsk, whiplash (v)
yaurk, while (conj)
yaurk, while (n)
yaurp, whip (n)
yaurpwan, whipper (n doer)
yaursp, whip (v)
yaushork, awkwardness (n)
yaushorkiu, awkwardly (adv)
yaushorku, awkward (adj)
yavafirtu, verbose (adj)
yelirf, whim (n)
yelirf, whimsy (n)
yelirfiu, whimsically (adv)
yelirfu, whimsical (adj)
yelirst, wet (v)
yelirstyot, wet (v pa)
yelirt, wetness (n)
yelirtu, wet (adj)
yels, whiff (v)
yelsh, whiff (n)
yeltmoiurf, wetsuit (n)
yeltraufp, wetland (n)
yenaurs, wonder (v)
yenaursh, wonder (n)
yenaurshiu, wonderfully (adv)
yenaurshu, wonderful (adj)
yenaurshu, wonderous (adj)
yenaurshuet, wonderment (n)
yenaushraufp, wonderland (n)
yeraliu, yonder (adv)
yeralu, yonder (adj)
yilwalp, behalf (n)
yoi, whoa (interj)
yoiark, wrench (n)
yoiarsk, wrench (v)
yoibarkwan, wrangler (n doer)
yoibarsk, wrangle (v)
yoikanirkwan, wrestler (n doer)
yoikanirsk, wrestle (v)
yoikarsne, wrest (v)
yoilark, WiggleTalk (n)
yoir, aisle (n)
yoishp, whine (n)
yoishpu, whiney (adj)
yoishpu, whiny (adj)
yoishpwan, whiner (n doer)
yoishsp, whine (v)
yoitharst, wriggle (v)
yoithart, wriggle (n)
yoithartyek, wriggler (n pl)
yoithk, wiggle (n)
yoithkwan, wiggler (n doer)
yoithsk, wiggle (v)

yoran, worm (n)
yoranu, wormy (adj)
yorasne, worm (v)
yosh, as (adv/conj/prep)
yuakart, wickedness (n)
yuakartu, wicked (adj)
yuanfiaushk, whitewash (n)
yuanfiaushsk, whitewash (v)
yuark, wick (n)
yuarn, white (n)
yuarnu, white (adj)
yuarsne, whiten (v)
yufai-, quad- (num 4 pref)
yufai-, tetra- (num 4 pref)
yufaiark, quadrant (n)
yufaimirk, quadrangle (n)
yufeth, fourth (num 4 ord)
yufi, four (num 4 card)
yufialfhemka, Number_1e16356
yufida, forty (num 40 card)
yufidai-, forty- (num 40 pref)
yufidark, quarantine (n)
yufidarsk, quarantine (v)
yufideth, fortieth (num 40 ord)
yufifk, quattuorquadragintillion
    (num 1e135 card)
yufift, quattuotrigintillion (num
    1e105 card)
yufika, quadrillion (num 1e15
    card)
yufikai-, peta- (num 1e15 pref)
yufiketh, quadrillionth (num 1e15
    ord)
yufipa, fourteen (num 14 card)
yufipai-, fourteen- (num 14 pref)
yufipeth, fourteenth (num 14 ord)
yufishk, quattuorvigintillion (num
    1e75 card)
yufishkai-, gieksi-
yufishketh, quattuorvigintillionth
    (num 1e75 ord)
yufisht, quattuordecillion (num
    1e45 card)
yufishtai-, quaksi- (num 1e45
    pref)
yufishteth, quattuordecillionth
    (num 1e45 ord)
Yugoshlarve, Yugoslavia (n)
yuiank, suture (n)
yuiansk, suture (v)
yuifoirk, weirdness (n)
yuifoirkiu, weirdly (adv)
yuifoirku, weird (adj)
yuifoirkwan, weirdo (n doer)
yumart, waist (n)
yumatroifk, waistline (n)
yunapwan, sewer (n doer
    d:thread cloth)
yunasp, sew (v d:thread cloth)
yupimirak, rectangle (n)
yupimiraku, rectangular (adj)

yurk, weed (n)
yurku, weedy (adj)
yurkwan, weeder (n doer)
yursk, weed (v)
yurzve, wed (v)
yutabivarnu, unisex (adj)
yutafonurde, uniqueness (n)
yutafonurdiu, uniquely (adv)
yutafonurdu, unique (adj)
yutamarn, union (n)
yutamarnuet, unionization (n)
yutamarnwan, unionist (n doer)
yutamarsne, unionize (v)
yutamart, unity (n)
yutanamor, unilateralism (n)
yutanamoriu, unilaterally (adv)
yutanamoru, unilateral (adj)
yutark, unification (n)
yutarme, unit (n)
yutarmu, unitary (adj)
yutarsk, unify (v)
yutarzme, unite (v)
yutashk, unison (n)
yutavorlin, uniform (n)
yutavorlinu, uniformly (adj)
yutavorlinuet, uniformity (n)
yutavorlisne, uniform (v)
Yuteshviurl, Wednesday (n)
yutharaf, universe (n)
yutharafiu, universally (adv)
yutharafu, universal (adj)
yuvtiurge, wedlock (n)
yuwarn, vowel (n)
yuyau, wahoo (interj)
zahem, Number_1e3156
zal, Z (let sng)
zali, Zs (let pl)
zhafk, zag (n)
zhafsk, zag (v)
zhahem, Number_1e3456
zhaiakank, stimulant (n)
zhaiakashk, stimulus (n)
zhaiakashkyek, stimuli (n pl)
zhaiarge, hamburger (n)
zhaiark, stimulation (n)
zhaiarkwan, stimulator (n doer)
zhaiarsk, stimulate (v)
zhaidairs, sentence (v
    d:punishment)
zhaidairsh, sentence (n
    d:punishment)
zhailf, fall (n d:descent)
zhailfuil, fallout (n)
zhailsf, fall (v d:descent)
zhailsfyot, fell (v pa d:descent)
zhaimesp, flaunt (v)
zhainegethirk, racetrack (n)
zhaineglaushk, racehorse (n)
zhaink, race (n d:competition)
zhainkwan, racer (n doer
    d:competition)
zhainpliorl, raceway (n)
zhainsk, race (v d:competition)

zhaiport, fiasco (n)
zhairf, tragedy (n)
zhairfiu, tragically (adv)
zhairfu, tragic (adj)
zhairgaishst, bedevil (v)
zhairgaisht, devil (n)
zhairgaishtiu, devilishly (adv)
zhairgaishtu, devilish (adj)
zhairgiu, diabolically (adv)
zhairgu, diabolical (adj)
zhairk, vault (n d:leap)
zhairpwan, sender (n doer)
zhairshu, fast (adj d:speed)
zhairshwaku, fastest (adj)
zhairshwelu, faster (adj)
zhairsk, vault (v d:leap)
zhairsp, send (v)
zhairspyot, sent (v pa)
zhairst, fail (v)
zhairt, failure (n)
zhairtu, fallible (adj)
zhaitarze, falter (v)
zhaitharst, vilify (v)
zhaithart, vilification (n)
zhaithku, vile (adj)
zhakart, villain (n)
zhal, Zh (let sng)
zhaldraifpu, southbound (adj)
zhali, Zhs (let pl)
Zhalirt Dakort, South Dakota (n)
Zhalirt Karolirn, South Carolina
    (n)
zhalirt, south (n)
zhalirtkiarsh, southeast (n)
zhalirtkiarshu, southeast (adj)
zhalirtkiarshu, southeastern (adj)
zhalirtu, south (adj)
zhalirtu, southern (adj)
zhalirtwan, southerner (n doer)
zhalkoirk, suicide (n)
zhalkoirku, suicidal (adj)
zhalkoirsk, suicide (v)
zhaltehaurshu, southward (adj)
zhalteshaithk, southwest (n)
zhalteshaithku, southwest (adj)
zhalteshaithku, southwestern
    (adj)
zhaltkuarf, southpaw (n)
zhanirf, acoustics (n)
zhanirfu, acoustic (adj)
zhanirk, vandalism (n)
zhanirkwan, vandal (n doer)
zhanirp, dampness (n)
zhanirpu, damp (adj)
zhanirpwan, damper (n doer)
zhanirsk, vandalize (v)
zhanirsp, dampen (v)
zhanirst, sound (v d:audio)
zhanirt, sound (n d:audio)
zhanirtwan, sounder (n doer
    d:audio)
zhantanelirk, sonogram (n)
zhantarf, sonar (n)

zhantarn, sonance (n)
zhantarnu, sonic (adj)
zhantgethirk, soundtrack (n)
Zhaparf, Japan (n)
Zhaparnf, Japanese (n)
zharaft, middle (n)
zharaft, midst (n)
zharaftu, middle (adj)
zharaul, midair (n)
zharbe, jump (n)
zharbiu, jumpily (adv)
zharbu, jumpy (adj)
zharbwan, jumper (n doer)
zharfalirme, midstream (n)
zharfivarl, midseason (n)
zharfrulf, midsummer (n)
zhargmeniu, painlessly (adv)
zhargmenu, painless (adj)
zhargume, pajama (n)
zharkliorsh, midyear (n)
zharkrufk, midweek (n)
zharlimern, midmorning (n)
zharmimarn, midrange (n)
zharovimidort, midafternoon (n)
zharpliorl, midway (n)
zharshtren, midterm (n)
zharshtrenu, midterm (adj)
zhartaifort, midpoint (n)
zharthisharl, midsection (n)
zhartplorn, middleman (n)
zharvemport, midwinter (n)
zharviurl, midday (n)
zharzbe, jump (v)
zharze, buzz (v d:hum)
zharzhe, buzz (n d:hum)
zharzhu, buzzy (adj d:hum)
zharzhwan, buzzer (n doer
    d:hum)
zhaturfiu, sound (adv d:secure)
zhaturfu, sound (adj d:secure)
zhaukaik, treachery (n)
zhaukaikiu, treacherously (adv)
zhaukaiku, treacherous (adj)
zhaukarp, treason (n)
zhaul, so (adj/adv/conj/interj)
zhaul, so (pron)
zhauprufip, vanquishment (n)
zhauprufipwan, vanquisher (n
    doer)
zhauprufisp, vanquish (v)
zhaurbe, danger (n)
zhaurbu, dangerous (adj)
zhaurbuet, endangerment (n)
zhaurf, loss (n)
zhaurfwan, loser (n doer)
zhaurn, van (n)
zhaurp, jam (n d:bind)
zhaursf, lose (v)
zhaursfyot, lost (v pa)
zhaursp, jam (v d:bind)
zhaurst, mine (v d:bomb)
zhaurt, mine (n d:bomb)
zhaurzbe, endanger (v)

zhauteprant, minefield (n)
zhauthk, zap (n)
zhauthsk, zap (v)
zhauvaifirk, vanguard (n)
zhavartesh, mediocrity (n)
zhavarteshu, mediocre (adj)
zhavashtu, menial (adj)
zhbainpliorl, speedway (n)
zhbainshkorbe, speedboat (n)
zhbairn, speed (n)
zhbairniu, speedily (adv)
zhbairnu, speedy (adj)
zhbairnwan, speeder (n doer)
zhbairsne, speed (v)
zheifst, zip (v)
zheiftiu, zippily (adv)
zheiftu, zippy (adj)
zheiftwan, zipper (n doer)
zheifuarsne, zipper (v)
zheikarn, jungle (n)
zheirde, target (n)
zheirzde, target (v)
zheisht, slick (n)
zheishtu, slick (adj)
Zheishush, Jesus (n)
zhelbrelp, eggplant (n)
zhelirp, gasp (n)
zhelirsp, gasp (v)
zhelk, egg (n)
zhelsk, egg (v)
zheltherk, eggshell (n)
Zhenirve, Geneva (n)
Zhenon, Xenon (n)
zherk, gas (n)
zherku, gaseous (adj)
Zhermarn, German (n)
Zhermarnf, Germany (n)
zhersk, gas (v)
zhert, seriousness (n)
zhertiu, seriously (adv)
zhertu, serious (adj)
Zherushalorme, Jerusalem (n)
zhesh, such (adj/adv)
zhesh, such (pron)
zhetarn, zeta (n)
zhiafgukartu, electromagnetic (adj)
zhiafiurbe, electrode (n)
zhiafreilarku, electrochemical (adj)
zhiafuirf, plight (n)
zhiagitersh, painkiller (n)
zhiagorkiu, painstakingly (adv)
zhiagorsk, painstake (v)
zhiagorskyot, painstook (v pa)
zhialirme, meridian (n)
zhiamart, median (n)
zhiamartu, median (adj)
zhiarast, rocket (v)
zhiarat, rocket (n)
zhiarfik, meditation (n)
zhiarfisk, meditate (v)
zhiarge, pain (n)

zhiargiu, painfully (adv)
zhiargu, painful (adj)
zhiarme, medium (n d:middle)
zhiarmu, medium (adj d:middle)
zhiarnwan, rocker (n doer d:sway)
zhiarp, fuel (n)
zhiarpwan, fueler (n doer)
zhiars, sin (v)
zhiarsh, sin (n)
zhiarshiu, sinfully (adv)
zhiarshu, sinful (adj)
zhiarshwan, sinner (n doer)
zhiarsne, rock (v d:sway)
zhiarsp, fuel (v)
zhiarzge, pain (v)
zhiashpefort, electrostatic (n)
zhiashpefortu, electrostatic (adj)
zhiaurk, zing (n)
zhiaursk, zing (v)
zhiavigark, electroshock (n)
zhiavigarku, electroshock (adj)
zhibrelsh, someplace (n)
zhidauirn, sometimes (adj/adv)
zhidaurn, sometime (adj/adv)
zhidirzhe, something (n)
zhiefk, electricity (n)
zhiefkiu, electrically (adv)
zhiefku, electric (adj)
zhiefku, electrical (adj)
zhiefkuet, electrification (n)
zhiefkwan, electrician (n doer)
zhiefsk, electrify (v)
zhiek, electron (n)
zhiekiu, electronically (adv)
zhieku, electronic (adj)
zhiern, zone (n)
zhiersne, zone (v)
zhierst, game (v)
zhiert, game (n)
zhiertwan, gamer (n doer)
zhiesh, electrics (n)
zhiesh, electronics (n)
zhieshk, electrocution (n)
zhieshsk, electrocute (v)
zhifk, zig (n)
zhifsk, zig (v)
zhifzhafk, zigzag (n)
zhifzhafsk, zigzag (v)
zhigarshet, onrage (v)
zhigarsht, enragement (n)
zhigarshtyek, enragement (n pl)
zhigarst, rage (v)
zhigart, rage (n)
zhige, acid (n)
zhigu, acidic (adj)
zhilarme, glimmer (n)
zhilarzme, glimmer (v)
zhilirk, glitz (n)
zhilirku, glitzy (adj)
zhiltilf, glitter (n)
zhiltilfu, glittery (adj)
zhiltilsf, glitter (v)

zhimart, issuance (n)
zhinarkiu, somewhat (adv)
zhinersh, jeans (n)
zhiniarliu, somehow (adv)
Zhink, Zinc (n)
zhinorl, somewhere (adv)
zhinorl, somewhere (n)
zhinorn, someone (pron)
zhinviurliu, someday (adv)
Zhiorazh, Georgia (n)
zhiorp, huddle (n)
zhiorsk, hide (v d:obscure)
zhiorskyot, hid (v pa d:obscure)
zhiorsp, huddle (v)
zhirf, glimpse (n)
zhirk, win (n)
Zhirkonium, Zirconium (n)
zhirkwan, winner (n doer)
zhirme, issue (n)
zhirmwan, issuer (n doer)
zhirn, some (adj/adv)
zhirn, some (pron)
zhirp, glint (n)
zhirsf, glimpse (v)
zhirsk, win (v)
zhirskyot, won (v pa)
zhirt, certainty (n)
zhirtiu, certainly (adv)
zhirtu, certain (adj)
zhirve, jig (n d:dance)
zhirzme, issue (v)
zhirzve, jig (v d:dance)
zhishk, bee (n)
zhishlarde, somebody (n/pron)
Zhiufarn, Jewish (adj)
zhiuft, safe (n d:storage)
zhiumern, selflessness (n)
zhiumerniu, selflessly (adv)
zhiumernu, selfless (adj)
Zhiurf, Jew (n)
zhiurn, self (n)
zhiurniu, selfishly (adv)
zhiurnu, selfish (adj)
zhiurnuet, selfishness (n)
zhizge, acidify (v)
zhizhalthraf, gingerbread (n)
zhizharl, ginger (n)
zhodiveil, setup (n)
zhoianoishk, seamstress (n)
zhoianst, seam (v)
zhoiant, seam (n)
zhoiantmeniu, seamlessly (adv)
zhoiantmenu, seamless (adj)
zhoipliorl, walkway (n)
zhoirf, silence (n)
zhoirfiu, silently (adv)
zhoirfu, silent (adj)
zhoirfwan, silencer (n doer)
zhoirge, damage (n)
zhoirp, walk (n)
zhoirpiveil, walkup (n)
zhoirpiveilu, walkup (adj)
zhoirpuil, walkout (n)

zhoirpwan, walker (n doer)
zhoirsf, silence (v)
zhoirsp, walk (v)
zhoirve, seal (n d:binding)
zhoirvwan, sealant (n doer d:binding)
zhoirzge, damage (v)
zhoirzve, seal (v d:binding)
zhoithaush, wildflower (n)
zhoithbrelsh, wilderness (n)
zhoithfierf, wildcat (n)
zhoithflaursh, wildlife (n)
zhoithgaurn, wildcard (n)
zhoithk, wild (n)
zhoithkiu, wildly (adv)
zhoithku, wild (adj)
zhoithkuet, wildness (n)
zhoithshriauk, wildfire (n)
zhokerme, second (n d:time)
zholar, beer (n)
zhoranf, pillow (n)
zhoransf, pillow (v)
Zhordarn, Jordan (n)
zhorde, set (n d:group)
zhordvark, setback (n)
zhorf, pill (n)
zhorfk, mix (n)
zhorfkar, mixture (n)
zhorfkwan, mixer (n doer)
zhorfsk, mix (v)
zhorft, pillar (n)
zhorpankwan, meddler (n doer)
zhorpansk, meddle (v)
zhorsf, pill (v)
zhuabeltriel, malcontent (n)
zhuaborat, malice (n)
zhuaboratiu, maliciously (adv)
zhuaboratu, malicious (adj)
zhuaifst, spiff (v)
zhuaifl, spiff (n)
zhuaiftu, spiffy (adj)
zhuank, malady (n)
zhuankoif, malignancy (n)
zhuankoifu, malignant (adj)
zhuankoisf, malign (v)
zhuankuet, malaise (n)
zhuaprashst, malfunction (v)

zhuaprasht, malfunction (n)
zhuark, male (n)
zhuark, masculinity (n)
zhuarku, male (adj)
zhuarku, masculine (adj)
zhuarl, spirit (n)
zhuarliu, spiritually (adv)
zhuarlu, spiritual (adj)
zhuarluet, spirituality (n)
zhuarsle, spirit (v)
zhuavorlin, malformation (n)
zhuavorlisne, malform (v)
zhudarn, drone (n d:bee)
zhudeklorsf, safekeep (v)
zhudeklorsfyot, safekept (v pa)
zhugairst, impoverish (v)
zhugairt, poverty (n)
zhuiank, slander (n)
zhuianku, slanderous (adj)
zhuiansk, slander (v)
zhukorth, foxhole (n)
Zhulait, July (n)
zhulirst, jell (v)
zhulirt, jelly (n)
zhulirtu, jellied (adj)
zhulteshlersh, jellyfish (n)
zhulteshlershyek, jellyfish (n pl)
zhumarn, junior (n)
zhumarnu, junior (adj)
zhumirp, peril (n)
zhumirpiu, perilously (adv)
zhumirpu, perilous (adj)
Zhun, June (n)
zhupanf, savior (n)
zhupanf, saviours (n)
zhuparsf, savor (v)
zhupart, savings (n)
zhupeishk, savvy (n)
zhurde, safety (n d:trustworthy)
zhurderat, oilseed (n)
zhurdiu, safely (adv d:trustworthy)
zhurdu, safe (adj d:trustworthy)
zhurduet, safeguard (n)
zhurdwaku, safest (adj)
zhurdwelu, safer (adj)
zhureprant, oilfield (n)

zhurf, oil (n)
zhurfu, oily (adj)
zhurfwan, oiler (n doer)
Zhurifk, Zurich (n)
zhurk, fox (n)
zhurku, foxy (adj)
zhurme, juvenile (n)
zhurmu, juvenile (adj)
zhurnist, experience (v)
zhurnit, experience (n)
zhurnitiu, expertly (adv)
zhurnitwan, expert (n doer)
zhurp, save (n)
zhurplorn, oilman (n)
zhurplornyek, oilmen (n pl)
zhurpwan, saver (n doer)
zhurs, say (v)
zhursf, oil (v)
zhursh, say (n)
zhurshiarshu, old-fashioned (adj)
zhurshwan, sayer (n doer)
zhursk, outfox (v)
zhursp, save (v)
zhursyot, said (v pa)
zhurtarn, expertise (n)
zhurthiu, thus (adv)
zhurzde, safeguard (v d:trustworthy)
zhutunirp, suggestion (n)
zhutunirpiu, suggestibly (adv)
zhutunirpiu, suggestively (adv)
zhutunirpu, suggestible (adj)
zhutunirpu, suggestive (adj)
zhutunirsp, suggest (v)
zhuverst, succeed (v)
zhuvert, success (n)
zhuvertiu, successively (adv)
zhuvertu, successive (adj)
zhuvertuet, succession (n)
zhuvertushiu, successfully (adv)
zhuvertushu, successful (adj)
zhuvertwan, successor (n doer)
zhuvirk, suffix (n)

13

Miramish to English Crossreference

As with the Dahmek to English crossreference, the following list is sorted by the English alphabet and not the Marfi alphabet.

Afap, Potassium (n davoka)
afebelefio, overcame (v pa)
afebelefo, overcome (v)
afeberautha, overflow (n)
afeberautho, overflow (v)
afeberiaka, overuse (n)
afeberiako, overuse (v)
afebiorito, overpower (v)
afebiuta, overstatement (n)
afebiuto, overstate (v)
afedauna, overtime (n)
afedethipa, overcapacity (n)
afediapa, overdrive (n)
afedorikelatio, overspent (v pa)
afedorikelato, overspend (v)
afefelaritha, overdraft (n)
afefelaritho, overdraft (v)
afeferaushio, overblew (v pa)
afeferausho, overblow (v)
afeferifo, overstock (v)
afeferuifa, overplay (n)
afeferuifo, overplay (v)
afefiuka, overproduction (n)
afefiuko, overproduce (v)
afefuata, overview (n)
afefuato, overview (v)
afegelisho, overstep (v)
afegeloita, overcharge (n)
afegeloito, overcharge (v)
afegelorifa, overboard (n)
afegelorugo, overreach (v)
afegokio, overtook (v pa)
afegoko, overtake (v)
afekaimo, overturn (v)
afekaritha, overdose (n)

afekaritho, overdose (v)
afekefita, overhead (n)
afekeriafa, overqualification (n)
afekeriafo, overqualify (v)
afekioka, overwork (n)
afekioko, overwork (v)
afekitesha, overkill (n)
afekuto, overheat (v)
afelaisha, overjoy (n)
afelanishoka, overexposure (n)
afelanishoko, overexpose (v)
afelaomio, overran (v pa)
afelaomo, overrun (v)
afelarito, overrule (v)
afeligeraga, absolution (n)
afeligeragiu, absolutely (adv)
afeligerago, absolve (v)
afeligeragu, absolute (adj)
afeliuperina, overconfidence (n)
afeliuperiniu, overconfidently (adv)
afeliuperinu, overconfident (adj)
afeloidio, overwrote (v pa)
afeloido, overwrite (v)
afelora, overalls (n)
afeloriu, overall (adv)
afeloru, overall (adj)
afeluduasha, overrepresentation (n)
afeluduasho, overrepresent (v)
afelunita, overpass (n)
afelupalita, overreaction (n)
afelupalito, overreact (v)
afemoima, overpayment (n)
afemoimio, overpaid (v pa)

afemoimo, overpay (v)
afemuana, overnight (n)
afemuaniu, overnight (adv)
afemuano, overnight (v)
afemuanu, overnight (adj)
afemuanua, overnighter (n doer)
afemutho, overmatch (v)
afena, over (n)
afenara, overture (n)
afenereigo, overlook (v)
afenietio, overate (v pa)
afenieto, overeat (v)
afeniu, overly (adv)
afeniunifa, overabundance (n)
afenorisherigo, oversubscribe (v)
afenothaufa, sovereignty (n)
afenothaufiu, sovereignly (adv)
afenothaufua, sovereign (n doer)
afenotikio, overdid (v pa)
afenotiko, overdo (v)
afenu, over (adv/adv/prep)
afepalitaka, overactivity (n)
afepalitaku, overactive (adj)
afepavo, overfeed (v)
afepeletho, overstuff (v)
afeperushio, overslept (v pa)
afeperusho, oversleep (v)
afepoefito, overshadow (v)
aferafika, overcoat (n)
aferanita, overlay (n)
aferanitio, overlaid (v pa)
aferanito, overlay (v)
aferaupu, overland (adj)
aferethio, overlay (v pa)
aferetho, overlie (v)

Aferika, Africa (n)
Aferikana, African (n)
afeshalina, oversimplification (n)
afeshalino, oversimplify (v)
afeshekota, overshoot (n)
afeshekotio, overshot (v pa)
afeshekoto, overshoot (v)
afeshelesho, overfish (v)
afesheliba, override (n)
afeshelibio, overrode (v pa)
afeshelibo, override (v)
afesheluapa, overhaul (n)
afesheluapo, overhaul (v)
afesheluapua, overhauler (n doer)
afesheniko, overtax (v)
afeshethipa, oversupply (n)
afeshethipo, oversupply (v)
afeshokeleina, overseas (n)
afeshokeleiniu, overseas (adv)
afeshokeleinu, overseas (adj)
afeshuago, oversize (v)
afeshuisha, overweight (n)
afetaritha, overthrow (n)
afetarithio, overthrew (v pa)
afetaritho, overthrow (v)
afetaruga, overhang (n)
afetarugio, overhung (v pa)
afetarugo, overhang (v)
afetebo, overrate (v)
afeterelifio, oversold (v pa)
afeterelifo, oversell (v)
afeterema, overreliance (n)
afeteremo, overrely (v)
afeterila, overtone (n)
afethinapa, overestimate (n)
afethinapo, overestimate (v)
afethiuta, overlap (n)
afethiuto, overlap (v)
afethutha, oversight (n)
afethuthio, oversaw (v pa)
afethutho, oversee (v)
afethuthua, overseer (n doer)
afetiropo, overprice (v)
afetiuku, overdue (adj)
afetulitu, overcast (adj)
afevaupa, overvalue (n)
afevaupo, overvalue (v)
afeviago, overcrowd (v)
afevonudo, overbook (v)
afevoritio, overbuilt (v pa)
afevorito, overbuild (v)
afevoruva, overpopulation (n)
afevoruvo, overpopulate (v)
Afikana, Afghan (n)
Afikanoshana, Afghanistan (n)
Afip, Calcium (n davoka)
afokiaka, abdication (n)
afokiako, abdicate (v)
afokiakua, abdicator (n doer)
afubeluta, absence (n)
afubelutiu, absently (adv)
afubeluto, absent (v)
afubelutu, absent (adj)

afubelutua, absenter (n doer)
afuyanio, overheard (v pa)
afuyano, overhear (v)
agubiashara, goddess (n)
agubida, god (n)
agubidemenu, godless (adj)
agubidu, godly (adj)
agubimalisha, godmother (n)
agubivoteta, godfather (n)
agubizhaipa, godsend (n)
aiko, vie (v)
ailata, study (n)
ailatiu, studiously (adv)
ailato, study (v)
ailatu, studious (adj)
ailatua, student (n doer)
ainedufita, diacritic (n)
ainedufitiu, diacritically (adv)
ainedufitu, diacritical (adj)
ainelika, diagram (n)
aineliko, diagram (v)
aineliku, diagrammatic (adj)
ainemuka, diagonal (n)
ainemukiu, diagonally (adv)
ainemuku, diagonal (adj)
ainerita, dialect (n)
aineritu, dialectic (adj)
aineritu, dialectical (adj)
ainopina, diameter (n)
ainuana, diaper (n)
ainuano, diaper (v)
aiofa, ion (n)
aiofo, ionize (v)
aiofu, ionic (adj)
aiofua, ionizer (n doer)
aishomana, diagnosis (n)
aishomanita, diagnostic (n)
aishomano, diagnose (v)
aishomanu, diagnostic (adj)
Akap, Lithium (n davoka)
Aketiniuma, Actinium (n)
Akip, Beryllium (n davoka)
Alap, Rubidium (n davoka)
alfavuka, Number_1e159
alfdaka, Number_1e183
alfgenka, Number_1e177
alfhemfk, Number_1e276
alfhemft, Number_1e246
alfhemka, Number_1e156
alfhemshk, Number_1e216
alfhemsht, Number_1e186
alfi, As (let pl)
alfirika, Number_1e162
alfkinka, Number_1e171
alfmuika, Number_1e180
alftirika, Number_1e168
alfvenka, Number_1e174
alfyufika, Number_1e165
alidora, yellow (n)
alidoreiku, yellowish (adj)
alidoro, yellow (v)
alidoru, yellow (adj)

alifa, A (let sng)
alifana, alpha (n)
alifepa, alphabet (n)
alifepiu, alphabetically (adv)
alifepo, alphabetize (v)
alifepu, alphabetic (adj)
Alik, Xenon (n davoka)
Alip, Strontium (n davoka)
alisha, emptiness (n)
alisho, empty (v)
Alishoka, Alaska (n)
alishu, empty (adj)
alitaka, mentality (n)
alitakiu, mentally (adv)
alitaku, mental (adj)
alitakuata, mentor (n)
alitakuato, mentor (v)
alori, hello (interj)
alotipa, mention (n)
alotipo, mention (v)
Alubama, Alabama (n)
Aluberitafa, Alberta (n)
Aluminuma, Aluminum (n)
amelazha, interest (n d:finance)
Amerikiuma, Americium (n)
Amika, America (n)
Amikana, American (n)
Amishoterudama, Amsterdam (n)
Anakalusha, English (n)
Anakulana, England (n)
anamiga, embargo (n)
anamigo, embargo (v)
Anap, Francium (n davoka)
anarita, hangar (n)
aneberiuga, embroilment (n)
aneberiugo, embroil (v)
aneberuga, ember (n)
anebidala, embellishment (n)
anebidalo, embellish (v)
anebiorita, empowerment (n)
anebiorito, empower (v)
anebotaka, empathy (n)
anebotako, empathize (v)
anedereifa, entrustment (n)
anedereifo, entrust (v)
anediofa, entrenchment (n)
anediofo, entrench (v)
anedita, enlistment (n)
anedito, enlist (v)
aneduperana, encapsulation (n)
aneduperano, encapsulate (v)
aneduperanua, encapsulator (n doer)
anedutako, ensue (v)
anefalira, enrollment (n)
anefaliro, enroll (v)
anefalirua, enroller (n doer)
anefaliruina, enrollee (n)
anefelaufito, enliven (v)
anefeluana, enlightenment (n)
anefeluano, enlighten (v)
anefuala, envoy (n)
anegaifika, embitterment (n)

anegaifiko, embitter (v)
anegiata, embossment (n)
anegiato, emboss (v)
anegushika, enticement (n)
anegushiko, entice (v)
anekenipiu, emphatically (adv)
anekenipu, emphatic (adj)
anelenifoko, encompass (v)
anemitha, entailment (n)
anemitho, entail (v)
anenikela, enumeration (n)
anenikelo, enumerate (v)
anepeloita, embracement (n)
anepeloito, embrace (v)
anerauelika, emancipation (n)
aneraueliko, emancipate (v)
anerautha, emanation (n)
anerautho, emanate (v)
aneshekoba, embarkation (n)
aneshekobo, embark (v)
aneshelada, embodiment (n)
aneshelado, embody (v)
aneshelaka, embezzlement (n)
aneshelako, embezzle (v)
aneshepelara, embankment (n)
aneshepelaro, embank (v)
anesheraipa, enslavement (n)
anesheraipo, enslave (v)
anesheraipua, enslaver (n doer)
anetaigaga, entanglement (n)
anetaigago, entangle (v)
anetelavo, embalm (v)
anetherava, ensemble (n)
anethereipa, entrapment (n)
anethereipo, entrap (v)
anetikoama, emblem (n)
anetikoamu, emblematic (adj)
Anetimonia, Antimony (n)
anevalita, encirclement (n)
anevalito, encircle (v)
anevolato, encode (v)
anevolatua, encoder (n doer)
angai, ugh (interj)
Anikolafa, Angola (n)
Anikorazha, Anchorage (n)
Anip, Radium (n davoka)
anobeka, amputation (n)
anobeko, amputate (v)
anobeta, amplification (n)
anobetana, amplitude (n)
anobeto, amplify (v)
anobetua, amplifier (n doer)
anolaka, alien (n)
anolako, alienate (v)
anolaku, alienable (adj)
anopina, amp (n d:ampere)
anovafita, empiricism (n)
anovafitiu, empirically (adv)
anovafitu, empiric (adj)
anovafitu, empirical (adj)
anovafitua, empiricist (n doer)
anubeniu, amply (adv)
anubenu, ample (adj)

anuiata, embryo (n)
anuiatu, embryonic (adj)
apafipa, hydration (n)
apafipekip, hydrocarbon (n)
apafipo, hydrate (v)
apafipu, hydralic (adj)
apafipua, hydrater (n doer)
Apap, Hydrogen (n davoka)
Apip, Helium (n davoka)
Arap, Cesium (n davoka)
Aregona, Argon (n)
Arelingatona, Arlington (n)
Areshenika, Arsenic (n)
ariberivakio, interwove (v pa)
ariberivako, interweave (v)
ariberunipa, interdependence (n)
ariberunipiu, interdependently
   (adv)
ariberunipu, interdependent (adj)
ariberutha, interleaf (n)
ariberutho, interleave (v)
aribota, staff (n d:people)
ariboto, staff (v d:people)
aribotu, staff (adj d:people)
aribotua, staffer (n doer d:people)
aridapa, interval (n)
arideromu, interstellar (adj)
ariderupa, interpretation (n)
ariderupo, interpret (v)
ariderupu, interpretive (adj)
ariderupua, interpreter (n doer)
ariferuifa, interplay (n)
arifima, intervention (n)
arifimo, intervene (v)
arifoino, interlace (v)
arifuata, interview (n)
arifuato, interview (v)
arifuatua, interviewer (n doer)
arifuatuina, interviewee (n)
arigaifota, interruption (n)
arigaifoto, interrupt (v)
arigaifotu, interruptible (adj)
arigefa, interference (n)
arigefo, interfere (v)
Arikanosha, Arkansas (n)
arikariliu, internationally (adv)
arikarilu, international (adj)
arilaidaka, intermediacy (n)
arilaidako, intermediate (v)
arilaidakua, intermediary (n doer)
arilaitu, interim (adj)
arilaivuno, intertwine (v)
arilara, interior (n)
arilauku, interplanetary (adj)
arilotela, interspersion (n)
arilotelo, intersperse (v)
ariludarita, interrelation (n)
ariludaritefifa, interrelationship
   (n)
ariludarito, interrelate (v)
arilushiata, interrogation (n)
arilushiato, interrogate (v)
arilushiatua, interrogator (n doer)

arimarina, intercourse (n)
Arimena, Armenia (n)
Arimenana, Armenian (n)
arimoipa, internet (n)
arinoithu, interracial (adj)
arinoka, intermission (n)
arinokiu, intermittently (adv)
arinoko, intermit (v)
arinoku, intermittent (adj)
Arip, Barium (n davoka)
aripalita, interaction (n)
aripalitiu, interactively (adv)
aripalito, interact (v)
aripalitu, interactive (adj)
aripelonu, interpersonal (adj)
ariperinelitu, interfaith (adj)
aripo, eke (v)
aripua, eker (n doer)
ariroisha, interlink (n)
ariroisho, interlink (v)
arirusha, interlude (n)
arishaiasha, interstate (n)
arishaiashu, interstate (adj)
arishala, intersection (n)
arishalo, intersect (v)
arishinafa, interconnection (n)
arishinafo, interconnect (v)
arishipa, interception (n)
arishipo, intercept (v)
arishipua, interceptor (n doer)
aritepa, interjection (n)
aritepo, interject (v)
arithiama, street (n)
arithiamefeliuku, streetwise (adj)
arithiamegerela, streetcar (n)
arithoisha, interface (n)
arithoisho, interface (v)
aritiuga, interlock (n)
arituana, interchange (n)
arituaniu, interchangeably (adv)
arituanu, interchangeable (adj)
ariveka, intercession (n)
ariveko, intercede (v)
arivetapa, interagency (n)
arivulana, intermarriage (n)
arivulano, intermarry (v)
Arizhona, Arizona (n)
arizhoriko, intermix (v)
Arobana, Arab (n)
arokeriuka, introduction (n)
arokeriuko, introduce (v)
arokeriuku, introductory (adj)
arotharika, introversion (n)
arothariko, introvert (v)
arotharikua, introvert (n doer)
arovu, old (adj)
arovwaka, oldest (n)
arovwaku, oldest (adj)
arovwela, older (n)
arovwelu, older (adj)
arufa, woof (interj)
Arugenotina, Argentina (n)
Ashap, Ununennium (n davoka)

asheloita, employment (n)
asheloito, employ (v)
asheloitu, employable (adj)
asheloitua, employer (n doer)
asheloituina, employee (n)
Ashetatina, Astatine (n)
Aship, Unbinilium (n davoka)
ashipedauniu, oftentimes (adv)
ashipiu, often (adv)
Atap, Sodium (n davoka)
Atelanita, Atlanta (n)
Atelanotika, Atlantic (n)
Atelanotisha, Atlantis (n)
atheforisha, atmosphere (n)
atheforishiu, atmospherically (adv)
atheforishu, atmospheric (adj)
Atip, Magnesium (n davoka)
aua, ow (interj)
auka, ailment (n)
auko, ail (v)
aukua, ailer (n doer)
aula, air (n)
aulaku, aerobic (adj)
aulana, aerial (n)
aulanu, aerial (adj)
aulebieluka, airport (n)
aulefanafa, airbag (n)
aulekafipa, aircraft (n)
aulekafipi, aircraft (n pl)
aulepeliola, airway (n)
auleroifa, airline (n)
auliati, aeronautics (n pl)
auliatu, aeronautical (adj)
aulituiafi, aerodynamics (n pl)
aulituiafu, aerodynamic (adj)
auliuna, omen (n)
auliuniu, ominously (adv)
auliunu, ominous (adj)
aulo, air (v)
aulogerapa, aerosol (n)
auloperanida, airfield (n)
aulothika, airfare (n)
aulu, airy (adj)
auluvarila, airplane (n)
ausha, ash (n)
Aushetina, Austin (n)
Aushimaka, Admiral (n)
Aushotara, Austria (n)
Aushotarina, Austrian (n)
Aushoterala, Australia (n)
Aushoterana, Australian (n)
aushua, asher (n doer)
aushubiama, ashtray (n)
auta, ouch (inter)
authusha, aerospace (n)
avaifa, duality (n)
avaifata, duet (n)
avaifiu, dually (adv)
avaifu, dual (adj)
avaina, boolean (n)
avainu, boolean (adj)
aveth, second (num 2 ord)

avethara, secondary (n)
avetharu, secondary (adj)
avethekapu, secondhand (adj)
avethiu, secondly (adv d:count)
aviutha, dilemma (n)
aviuthu, dilemmic (adj)
avu, two (num 2 card)
avualfhemka, Number_1e8256
avuda, twenty (num 20 card)
avudai-, twenty- (num 20 pref)
avudeth, twentieth (num 20 ord)
avugioko, tweeze (v)
avugiokua, tweezer (n doer)
avuifk, duoquadragintillion (num 1e129 card)
avuift, duotrigintillion (num 1e99 card)
avuiftai-, yantesi-
avuifteth, duotrigintillionth (num 1e99 ord)
avuikosha, tandem (n)
avuikoshu, tandem (adj)
avuka, billion (num 1e9 card)
avukai-, giga- (num 1e9 pref)
avuketh, billionth (num 1e9 ord)
avupa, twelve (num 12 card)
avupai-, twelv- (num 12 pref)
avupeth, twelfth (num 12 ord)
avushk, duovigintillion (num 1e69 card)
avushkai-, itesa-
avushketh, duovigintillionth (num 1e69 ord)
avusht, duodecillion (num 1e39 card)
avushtai-, tekatri- (num 1e39 pref)
avushteth, duodecillionth (num 1e39 ord)
avuta, duet (n)
avuthu, twice (adv)
Azherobaizhana, Azerbaijan (n)
baba, dad (n)
babila, daddy (n)
bafiaka, cavalry (n)
bafika, strictness (n)
bafikiu, strictly (adv)
bafiku, strict (adj)
bafipo, doze (v)
bafipua, dozer (n docr)
bafita, junction (n)
bafitu, junctional (adj)
Bagudada, Baghdad (n)
bahem, Number_1e1656
baiala, sorcery (n)
baialua, sorcerer (n doer)
baifa, victimization (n)
baifana, victim (n)
baifemeniu, victimlessly (adv)
baifemenu, victimless (adj)
baifeta, victory (n)

baifetiu, victoriously (adv)
baifetu, victorious (adj)
baifika, gadget (n)
baifiku, gadgety (adj)
baifo, victimize (v)
baifota, source (n)
baifoto, source (v)
baifotua, sourcer (n doer)
baifua, victor (n doer)
baiga, sort (n)
baigo, sort (v)
baigua, sorter (n doer)
baima, sore (n)
baimata, sorrow (n)
baimatu, sorry (adj)
baimiu, sorely (adv)
baimu, sore (adj)
baisha, gage (n)
baisha, gauge (n)
baisho, gage (v)
baisho, gauge (v)
baishoka, abrasion (n)
baishokiu, abrasively (adv)
baishoku, abrasive (adj)
baitha, byte (n)
baiuka, genesis (n)
baivata, sourness (n)
baivato, sour (v)
baivatu, sour (adj)
bakiata, tirade (n)
bakiniu, terrifically (adv)
bakinu, terrific (adj)
bakosheto, terrify (v)
bakota, terror (n)
bakotiu, terribly (adv)
bakoto, terrorize (v)
bakotu, terrible (adj)
bakotua, terrorist (n doer)
bakotueta, terrorism (n)
bala, B (let sng)
balesharinu, postmodern (adj)
balesheriga, postscript (n)
baleviuru, postwar (adj)
bali, Bs (let pl)
balifa, caliber (n)
balifa, calibre (n)
balifoka, calibration (n)
balifoko, calibrate (v)
balifokua, calibrator (n doer)
balipa, tardiness (n)
balipu, tardy (adj)
balishoka, tutorial (n)
balishoko, tutor (v)
balishokua, tutor (n doer)
balita, post (n d:pole)
balitara, posture (n)
balitaro, posture (v)
balito, post (v d:pole)
baliuka, postulation (n)
baliuko, postulate (v)
balivelara, posterior (n)
Balotika, Baltic (n)
Balotimora, Baltimore (n)

baluvefoka, postponement (n)
baluvefoko, postpone (v)
bamiaka, thorn (n)
bamiakiu, thornily (adv)
bamiako, thorn (v)
bamiaku, thorny (adj)
bamiana, thirst (n)
bamianiu, thirstily (adv)
bamiano, thirst (v)
bamianu, thirsty (adj)
banifa, pad (n)
banifata, paddle (n)
banifato, paddle (v)
banifo, pad (v)
banitiuga, padlock (n)
banitiugo, padlock (v)
barafa, stone (n)
barafedaishio, stonecut (v pa)
barafedaisho, stonecut (v)
barafedaishua, stonecutter (n doer)
barafenolitho, stonewall (v)
barafeshelefa, stoneware (n)
barafo, stone (v)
barafu, stoney (adj)
barafua, stoner (n doer)
baraifana, stonehenge (n)
barima, fan (n d:follower)
barimethika, fanfare (n)
barimota, fanaticism (n)
barimotiu, fanatically (adv)
barimotu, fanatical (adj)
barimotua, fanatic (n doer)
barimu, fanatic (adj d:follower)
baripa, bastard (n)
baripo, bastardize (v)
barishoka, conduit (n)
baritada, train (n d:locomotive)
Bariuma, Barium (n)
bashalipa, authorization (n)
bashalipiu, authoritatively (adv)
bashalipo, authorize (v)
bashalipu, authoritative (adj)
bashalita, authority (n)
bashalitua, author (n doer)
bashapa, authentication (n)
bashapo, authenticate (v)
bashapu, authentic (adj)
bashika, feather (n)
bashiko, feather (v)
bau, boo (interj)
baufa, tuition (n)
baufita, tower (n)
baufito, tower (v)
bauga, fat (n)
baugo, fatten (v)
baugu, fat (adj)
baugu, fatty (adj)
bauina, stomp (n)
bauino, stomp (v)
bauinua, stomper (n doer)
bauka, boo (n)
bauko, boo (v)

baukua, booer (n doer)
baula, tow (n)
baulo, tow (v)
baulua, tower (n doer)
bauna, stamp (n)
bauno, stamp (v)
baunoida, stampede (n)
baunua, stamper (n doer)
bauraka, jangle (n)
baurako, jangle (v)
bausha, towel (n)
bausho, towel (v)
bautha, menses (n)
bava, pair (n)
bavana, sheep (n)
bavani, sheep (n pl)
bavaniu, sheepishly (adv)
bavanu, sheepish (adj)
bavapa, steepness (n)
bavapiu, steeply (adv)
bavapo, steep (v)
bavapu, steep (adj)
bavasha, steeple (n)
bavashetutata, steeplechase (n)
bavata, steed (n)
bavo, pair (v)
bediora, petroleum (n)
befa, sod (n)
befenetiu, instead (adv)
beibukiu, purportedly (adv)
beibuko, purport (v)
beida, mutt (n)
beifa, dub (n)
beifika, fling (n)
beifikio, flung (v pa)
beifiko, fling (v)
beifiku, flingy (adj)
beifikua, flinger (n doer)
beifo, dub (v)
beifopa, flip (n)
beifopiu, flippily (adv)
beifopo, flip (v)
beifopu, flippy (adj)
beifopua, flipper (n doer)
beifua, dubber (n doer)
beilaka, purpose (n)
beilakiu, purposely (adv)
beilako, purpose (v)
beilaku, purposeful (adj)
beilebaka, dagger (n)
beima, fin (n)
beinata, tumor (n)
beinifa, dome (n)
beinuka, tomb (n)
beinukebarafa, tombstone (n)
beinuko, entomb (v)
beipa, flinch (n)
beipo, flinch (v)
beipua, flincher (n doer)
beirana, career (n)
Beiruta, Beirut (n)
beisha, flirtation (n)
beishaka, pursuit (n)

beishakiu, pursuantly (adv)
beishako, pursue (v)
beishaku, pursuant (adj)
beisho, flirt (v)
beishu, flirtatious (adj)
beishua, flirt (n doer)
beitata, purchase (n)
beitato, purchase (v)
beitatua, purchaser (n doer)
beitha, purse (n)
beitho, purse (v)
beiuka, doom (n)
beiukeviula, doomsday (n)
beiuko, doom (v)
Beizhinga, Beijing (n)
belafika, ledge (n)
belafipa, pope (n)
belaiato, spurt (v)
belaifa, volume (n)
belaika, butt (n d:strike)
belaiko, butt (v d:strike)
belaipo, spurn (v)
belaisha, spur (n)
belaisho, spur (v)
belaishu, spurious (adj)
belaitha, round (n)
belaithedoiara, roundtable (n)
belaithegelarudu, roundtrip (adj)
belaithekiafa, roundhouse (n)
belaithiu, roundly (adv)
belaithiveila, roundup (n)
belaitho, round (v)
belaithoveipa, roundabout (n)
belaithoveipu, roundabout (adj)
belaithu, round (adj)
belaithueta, roundness (n)
belaka, deposition (n)
belakako, thwart (v)
belako, depose (v)
belakua, deposer (n doer)
belamiaka, bramble (n)
belamiako, bramble (v)
belanifa, wallet (n)
belapa, pa (n)
belapana, papa (n)
belarifa, flatness (n d:plain/plane)
belariferaupa, flatland (n)
belarifiu, flatly (adv d:plain/plane)
belarifo, flatten (v d:plain/plane)
belarifu, flat (adj d:plain/plane)
belarifuarema, flatbed (n)
belarifuaremu, flatbed (adj)
belariga, shingle (n)
belarigo, shingle (v)
belarika, brake (n)
belariko, brake (v)
belasha, press (n)
belashika, impression (n)
belashikeferepu, impressionable (adj)
belashikeferepua, impressionist

(n doer)
belashikiu, impressively (adv)
belashiko, impress (v)
belashiku, impressive (adj)
belashikua, impresser (n doer)
belashipa, pressure (n)
belashipata, pressurization (n)
belashipato, pressurize (v)
belashipo, pressure (v)
belashipua, pressurizer (n doer)
belasho, press (v)
belashota, flake (n)
belashotiu, flakily (adv)
belashoto, flake (v)
belashotu, flakey (adj)
belashotua, flaker (n doer)
belashua, presser (n doer)
belatha, bran (n)
belaufa, honk (n)
belaufo, honk (v)
belaufua, honker (n doer)
belauga, twang (n)
belaugo, twang (v)
belauma, bog (n)
belaumo, bog (v)
belautho, wither (v)
belega, class (n)
belegata, classic (n)
belegatu, classical (adj)
belegelena, classmate (n)
belegesherana, classroom (n)
belego, classify (v)
belegu, classy (adj)
beleifeka, bleach (n)
beleifeko, bleach (v)
beleinoka, compromise (n)
beleinoko, compromise (v)
beleinokua, compromiser (n doer)
beleisha, span (n)
beleisho, span (v)
beleishua, spanner (n doer)
beleitha, truce (n)
belenika, ant (n)
beleruga, classification (n)
beletha, staff (n d:plaster)
beleto, shed (v d:rid)
beletua, shedder (n doer d:rid)
beliafa, beef (n)
beliaga, twinge (n)
beliago, twinge (v)
beliako, boggle (v)
beliana, barn (n)
beliasha, crunch (n)
beliasho, crunch (v)
beliashu, crunchy (adj)
beliashua, cruncher (n doer)
beliatha, neigh (n)
beliatho, neigh (v)
beliauma, sprout (n)
beliaumo, sprout (v)
beliausho, scrunch (v)
belieta, goat (n)
belifa, peninsula (n)

belifeta, provision (n)
belifetara, providence (n)
belifeto, provide (v)
belifetua, provider (n doer)
belifoka, province (n)
belifokiu, provincially (adv)
belifoku, provincial (adj)
belifota, prompt (n)
belifotiu, promptly (adv)
belifoto, prompt (v)
belifotua, prompter (n doer)
beligo, prune (v d:clip)
beligua, pruner (n doer d:clip)
belima, timidity (n)
belimiu, timidly (adv)
belimu, timid (adj)
belina, cone (n)
belinu, conical (adj)
belira, block (n d:barrier)
beliro, block (v d:barrier)
beliroka, bloc (n)
belirua, blocker (n doer d:barrier)
belisha, sleaze (n)
belishoka, penetration (n)
belishoko, penetrate (v)
belishokua, penetrator (n doer)
belishu, sleazy (adj)
belita, vest (n)
belitesha, vestige (n)
beliteshiu, vestigially (adv)
beliteshu, vestigial (adj)
belitha, sprint (n)
belitho, sprint (v)
belithua, sprinter (n doer)
belito, vest (v)
beliufa, alley (n)
beliuku, bogus (adj)
beliuma, clone (n)
beliumo, clone (v)
beliumua, cloner (n doer)
beliuna, prudence (n)
beliunu, prudent (adj)
beliunu, prudish (adj)
beliunua, prude (n doer)
beliupa, putty (n)
beliusha, ruse (n)
beliuta, creed (n)
Belogiana, Belgian (n)
Belogiuma, Belgium (n)
beloiata, deviation (n)
beloiatiu, deviously (adv)
beloiato, deviate (v)
beloiatu, devious (adj)
beloiatua, deviant (n doer)
beloiba, bead (n)
beloibo, bead (v)
beloifa, chaff (n)
beloika, filth (n)
beloiko, filthy (v)
beloiku, filthy (adj)
beloina, row (n d:column)
beloipa, boob (n)
beloisho, cringe (v)

beloitha, pallet (n)
beloizha, bronze (n)
beloizho, bronze (v)
belomada, plumb (n)
belomado, plumb (v)
belomadu, plumb (adj)
belomadua, plumber (n doer)
belora, slum (n)
belorifa, slumber (n)
belorifo, slumber (v)
belorifu, slumber (adj)
belorika, bar (n d:pub)
beloriko, bartend (v d:pub)
belorikua, bartender (n doer
    d:pub)
beloripa, slump (n)
beloripiu, slumpily (adv)
beloripo, slump (v)
beloripu, slumpy (adj)
beloripua, slumper (n doer)
belorisha, slur (n)
belorishana, slurry (adj)
belorisho, slur (v)
belorita, device (n)
beloritiu, devisively (adv)
belorito, devise (v)
beloritu, devisive (adj)
beloritua, deviser (n doer)
beluafa, adoration (n)
beluafiu, adorably (adv)
beluafo, adore (v)
beluafu, adorable (adj)
beluaga, ache (n)
beluagiu, achily (adv)
beluago, ache (v)
beluagu, achy (adj)
beluako, slug (v d:hit)
beluakua, slugger (n doer d:hit)
beluama, femme (n)
beluana, dam (n)
beluapa, cluster (n)
beluapo, cluster (v)
beluasho, soar (v)
beluata, adornment (n)
beluato, adorn (v)
belufika, rust (n)
belufikiu, rustily (adv)
belufiko, rust (v)
belufiku, rusty (adj)
belufipa, pulp (n)
belufita, rush (n)
belufito, rush (v)
beluga, thug (n)
belugueta, thuggery (n)
beluka, blow (n d:impact)
belukuila, blowout (n)
beluna, prior (n)
belunifa, priority (n)
belunifo, prioritize (v)
belunika, butt (n d:end/ rump)
belunika, buttocks (n d:end/
    rump)
belunu, prior (adj)

belupa, thud (n)
belushama, disease (n)
Belushama, EhoMonth03 (n)
belushamo, disease (v)
belushiena, hermit (n)
beluta, present (n d:now)
belutho, rustle (v)
beluthua, rustler (n doer)
belutipa, pulpit (n)
belutisha, presence (n
    d:existence)
belutiu, presently (adv d:now)
beluviu, previously (adv)
beluvu, previous (adj)
beluzha, scam (n)
beluzho, scam (v)
beluzhua, scammer (n doer)
benifa, opinion (n)
benifelidu, indeed (adv/interj)
benifo, opine (v)
benitika, perch (n d:fish)
benufeleithiu, intravenously (adv)
benufeleithu, intravenous (adj)
beraba, sob (n)
berabo, sob (v)
berada, dentistry (n)
beradara, denture (n)
beradu, dental (adj)
beradua, dentist (n doer)
berafa, fondness (n)
berafika, ledger (n)
berafiu, fondly (adv)
berafu, fond (adj)
beraiaka, callousness (n)
beraiakiu, callously (adv)
beraiaku, callous (adj)
beraifa, sobriety (n)
beraifo, sober (v)
beraifu, sober (adj)
beraiga, monster (n)
beraigu, monstrous (adj)
beraika, invitation (n)
beraiko, invite (v)
beraiku, invitational (adj)
beraikua, invitor (n doer)
beraikuina, invitee (n)
beraisha, char (n d:burn)
beraisho, char (v d:burn)
beraishu, chary (adj d:burn)
beraitha, jag (n)
beraitho, jag (v)
beraithua, jagger (n doer)
beraizhogarina, charcoal (n)
beraka, font (n)
berala, plain (n)
beraliga, ding (n)
beraligo, ding (v)
beralika, prank (n)
beralikua, prankster (n doer)
beralipa, dimple (n)
beralipo, dimple (v)
beraliu, plainly (adv)
beralotipa, plaintiff (n)

beralu, plain (adj)
beramipo, pound (v d:hit)
beramipua, pounder (n doer
    d:hit)
beranifa, coast (n d:shore)
beranifoipa, coastline (n)
beranifu, coastal (adj d:shore)
beranika, coach (n)
beraniko, coach (v)
beranina, till (n d:cash register)
beranita, ground (n d:soil)
beranito, ground (v d:soil)
beranitua, grounder (n doer
    d:soil)
berauga, bass (n d:sound)
berauka, dunk (n)
berauko, dunk (v)
beraukua, dunker (n doer)
beraupa, area (n)
berausha, plaza (n)
berauta, arena (n)
berautha, flow (n)
beraeutho, flow (v)
beravilo, muster (v)
Berazhila, Brazil (n)
Berazhilana, Brazilian (n)
bereba, hamper (n d:laundry)
berefa, density (n)
berefika, demonstration (n)
berefiko, demonstrate (v)
berefikua, demonstrator (n doer)
berefiu, densely (adv)
berefu, dense (adj)
berefweku, densest (adj)
berefwelu, denser (adj)
beregaka, daemon (n)
beregaka, demon (n)
beregako, daemonize (v)
beregako, demonize (v)
beregaku, demonic (adj)
bereidona, irrigation (n)
bereidono, irrigate (v)
bereifa, lightness (n d:weight)
bereifekefita, lightheadedness (n)
bereifeshuisha, lightweight (n)
bereifeshuishu, lightweight (adj)
bereifiu, lightly (adv d:weight)
bereifo, lighten (v d:weight)
bereifu, light (adj d:weight)
bereiluta, MarbleRobot
bereima, staleness (n)
bereimefenika, stalemate (n)
bereimu, stale (adj)
bereisha, purity (n)
bereishefeleida, purebreed (n)
bereishefeleidiota, purebred (n)
bereishiu, purely (adv)
bereisho, purify (v)
bereishu, pure (adj)
bereishua, purist (n doer)
bereishueta, purification (n)
bereishuetua, purifier (n doer)
bereita, crest (n)

bereitha, slush (n)
bereitho, slush (v)
bereito, crest (v)
berekika, implement (n)
berekiko, implement (v)
berekikueta, implementation (n)
berelika, completion (n)
berelikata, complement (n)
berelikato, complement (v)
berelikiu, completely (adv)
bereliko, complete (v)
bereliku, complete (adj)
bereluga, plank (n)
berelugo, plank (v)
berema, clumsiness (n)
beremiu, clumsily (adv)
beremu, clumsy (adj)
berena, ferry (n)
bereneshekoba, ferryboat (n)
berenida, money (n)
berenidenagua, moneymaker (n
    doer)
berenidiu, monetarily (adv)
berenidu, monetary (adj)
berenika, chair (n d:meeting)
bereniko, chair (v d:meeting)
berenikua, chairman (n doer
    d:meeting)
berenikua, chairperson (n doer
    d:meeting)
berenitaka, monkey (n)
berenitako, monkey (v)
bereno, ferry (v)
berepa, plant (n d:life form, affix)
berepo, plant (v d:life form, affix)
berepua, planter (n doer d:life
    form, affix)
beresha, place (n)
bereshipo, implore (v)
beresho, place (v)
bereshoka, complexity (n)
bereshokata, complex (n)
bereshoku, complex (adj)
bereshota, placation (n)
bereshoto, placate (v)
bereshotua, placator (n doer)
bereshua, placer (n doer)
bereshueta, placement (n)
bereshuisha, freight (n)
bereshuisheroifa, freightliner (n)
bereshuishua, freighter (n doer)
bereta, dent (n)
bereto, dent (v)
beriadita, roster (n)
beriafa, dove (n d:bird)
beriafemitho, dovetail (v)
beriaka, use (n)
beriakaba, usury (n)
beriakata, usage (n)
beriakiu, usually (adv)
beriako, use (v)
beriakoferepa, useability (n)
beriakoferepu, usable (adj)

beriaku, usual (adj)
beriakua, user (n doer)
beriakumenu, useless (adj)
beriakusha, usefulness (n)
beriakushiu, usefully (adv)
beriakushu, useful (adj)
berialoka, arbitration (n)
berialokiu, arbitrarily (adv)
berialoko, arbitrate (v)
berialoku, arbitrary (adj)
berialokua, arbitrator (n doer)
beriama, vouch (n)
beriamo, vouch (v)
beriamua, voucher (n doer)
berianika, registration (n)
berianiko, register (v)
berianikua, register (n doer)
berianita, clank (n)
berianito, clank (v)
berianitu, clanky (adj)
berianitua, clanker (n doer)
beriapa, loop (n)
beriapekotha, loophole (n)
beriapiu, loopily (adv)
beriapo, loop (v)
beriapu, loopy (adj)
beriapua, looper (n doer)
beriasha, vow (n)
beriasho, vow (v)
beriata, abortion (n)
beriatha, fleet (n)
beriatho, fleet (v)
beriato, abort (v)
beriatua, abortionist (n doer)
beriauka, riot (n)
beriauko, riot (v)
beriaukua, rioter (n doer)
beriautesha, vomit (n)
beriautesho, vomit (v)
beribako, bulldoze (v)
beribakua, bulldozer (n doer)
beriela, mall (n)
beriena, name (n)
berienefikafa, nameplate (n)
berienemenu, nameless (adj)
berienemoaka, namesake (n)
berienita, clink (n)
berienito, clink (v)
berienitu, clinky (adj)
berienitua, clinker (n doer)
berieniu, namely (adv)
berieno, name (v)
berienua, namer (n doer)
beriesha, stench (n)
berieta, denial (n)
berieto, deny (v)
berika, black (n)
Berikeliuma, Berkelium (n)
berikepelorika, blackboard (n)
beriko, blacken (v)
berikola, purple (n)
berikolu, purple (adj)
beriku, black (adj)

berila, inn (n)
Beriliuma, Beryllium (n)
berilopa, thrift (n)
berilopu, thrifty (adj)
berilua, innkeeper (n doer)
beriofa, facility (n)
beriofo, facilitate (v)
beriofu, facile (adj)
beriofua, facilitator (n doer)
beriofueta, faculty (n)
berioka, accumulation (n)
beriokiu, cumulatively (adv)
berioko, accumulate (v)
berioku, cumulative (adj)
beriokua, accumulator (n doer)
beriona, peculiarity (n)
berionita, clonk (n)
berionito, clonk (v)
berionitu, clonky (adj)
berionitua, clonker (n doer)
berioniu, peculiarly (adv)
berionu, peculiar (adj)
beriopa, thimble (n)
berishotiu, soon (adv)
berishotwakiu, soonest (adv)
berishotweliu, sooner (adv)
Beritaina, Britain (n)
Beritisha, British (n)
beriufa, tumble (n)
beriufo, tumble (v)
beriufua, tumbler (n doer)
beriugo, broil (v)
beriugua, broiler (n doer)
beriuka, leak (n)
beriuka, leakage (n)
beriukiu, leakily (adv)
beriuko, leak (v)
beriuku, leaky (adj)
beriukua, leaker (n doer)
beriumopa, bonk (n)
beriumopo, bonk (v)
beriuna, Eho15minutes (n)
beriupo, shrivel (v)
beriusha, leach (n)
beriusho, leach (v)
beriuta, bleakness (n)
beriutu, bleak (adj)
berivaka, weave (n)
berivakio, wove (v pa)
berivako, weave (v)
berivakua, weaver (n doer)
berivana, web (n)
berivano, web (v)
berivuta, stigma (n)
berivuto, stigmatize (v)
berizhana, buzzard (n)
Berodwaina, Broadway (n)
beroifa, cry (n)
beroifedeida, crybaby (n)
beroifo, cry (v)
beroifua, crier (n doer)
beroiga, abscess (n)
beroigo, abscess (v)

beroika, crisis (n)
beroina, clunk (n)
beroino, clunk (v)
beroinu, clunky (adj)
beroinua, clunker (n doer)
beroisho, bicker (v)
beroishua, bickerer (n doer)
beroita, volt (n)
beroitueta, voltage (n)
Berokela, Berkeley (n)
berokiaga, gestation (n)
berokiago, gestate (v)
berola, kin (n)
berolefifa, kinship (n)
berolekifopa, kinfolk (n)
berolepelona, kinsman (n)
berolereika, kindred (n)
berolereiku, kindred (adj)
berolika, comparison (n)
berolikiu, comparably (adv)
berolikiu, comparatively (adv)
beroliko, compare (v)
beroliku, comparable (adj)
beroliku, comparative (adj)
berolikua, comparitor (n doer)
Berolina, Berlin (n)
Beromina, Bromine (n)
berona, group (n)
beronekoika, genocide (n)
beronekoiku, genocidal (adj)
beronibara, gender (n d:group)
beronibaro, engender (v d:group)
beronika, flock (n d:wool)
beronilafa, genre (n)
beronita, genus (n)
berono, group (v)
beronua, groupie (n doer)
beronuda, germ (n)
beroteira, crystal (n)
beroteiro, crystalize (v)
beroteiru, crystalline (adj)
beroteirueta, crystalization (n)
beroto, listen (v)
berotua, listener (n doer)
beruaka, bluster (n)
beruako, bluster (v)
beruaku, blustery (adj)
berualifi, flutter (n pl)
berualifo, flutter (v)
beruasha, agility (n)
beruashu, agile (adj)
beruata, float (n)
beruato, float (v)
beruatua, floater (n doer)
beruatueta, flotation (n)
beruatuetu, flotation (adj)
beruba, league (n)
berubua, leaguer (n doer)
berufeta, pension (n)
berufita, dispensation (n)
berufito, dispense (v)
berufitu, dispensable (adj)
berufitua, dispenser (n doer)

beruga, burn (n)
berugato, burnish (v)
berugio, burnt (v pa)
berugo, burn (v)
berugua, burner (n doer)
beruguila, burnout (n)
beruika, encryption (n)
beruikedarifa, cryptography (n)
beruikedarifu, cryptic (adj)
beruiko, encrypt (v)
beruiku, cryptic (adj)
beruitha, leech (n)
beruitho, leech (v)
beruka, tick (n d:increment)
berukapa, ticket (n)
berukapo, ticket (v)
berukapua, ticketer (n doer)
berukata, tickle (n)
berukato, tickle (v)
berukatua, tickler (n doer)
Berukelina, Brooklyn (n)
beruko, tick (v d:increment)
berukua, ticker (n doer
    d:increment)
berulali, flurry (n pl)
berulifa, compensation (n)
berulifo, compensate (v)
berulifua, compensator (n doer)
berulito, sputter (v)
berunidana, pendulum (n)
berunika, slug (n d:blank)
berunipa, dependence (n)
berunipa, dependency (n)
berunipiu, dependably (adv)
berunipo, depend (v)
berunipu, dependable (adj)
berunipua, dependant (n doer)
berunipua, dependent (n doer)
beruno, pend (v)
berunodata, pendant (n)
berupa, ebb (n)
berupo, ebb (v)
Berushela, Brussels (n)
berushota, burst (n)
berushotio, burst (v pa)
berushoto, burst (v)
berutha, leaf (n)
beruthapa, leaflet (n)
berutho, leaf (v)
betana, beta (n)
beva, dip (n)
Beveralifa Hiloshi, Beverly Hills
    (n)
bevo, dip (v)
bevua, dipper (n doer)
biabiu, loudly (adv)
biabu, loud (adj)
biabweku, loudest (adj)
biabwelu, louder (adj)
biafafu, sacred (adj)
biafaka, sacrilege (n)
biafaku, sacriligous (adj)
biafipa, toast (n d:bread)

biafipo, toast (v d:bread)
biafipu, toasty (adj d:bread)
biafipua, toaster (n doer d:bread)
biafita, sacrifice (n)
biafitiu, sacrificially (adv)
biafito, sacrifice (v)
biafitu, sacrificial (adj)
biafitua, sacrificer (n doer)
biaga, sadness (n)
biagara, quiver (n)
biagaro, quiver (v)
biagiu, sadly (adv)
biago, sadden (v)
biagu, sad (adj)
biaibu, queer (adj)
biaibua, queer (n doer)
biaka, drill (n)
biako, drill (v)
biakua, driller (n doer)
biala, vibe (n)
bialifa, vibration (n)
bialifo, vibrate (v)
bialifu, vibrant (adj)
bialifua, vibrator (n doer)
bialifueta, vibrancy (n)
biama, tray (n)
biana, drug (n)
bianapa, drugstore (n)
bianita, compound (n d:place)
biano, drug (v)
bianofa, maid (n)
Bianosha, Atheism (n)
Bianoshaka, Atheist (n)
biapelatuka, loudspeaker (n)
biara, fanciness (n)
biariu, fancily (adv)
biaro, fancy (v)
biarokiana, fantasy (n)
biarokianiu, fantastically (adv)
biarokiano, fantasize (v)
biarokianu, fantastic (adj)
biaru, fancy (adj)
biarugo, drown (v)
biarweku, fanciest (adj)
biarwela, fancier (n)
biarwelu, fancier (v)
biasha, queen (n)
biashika, quill (n)
biasho, queen (v)
biata, powder (n)
biatha, womb (n)
biato, powder (v)
biaufa, doubt (n)
biaufo, doubt (v)
biaufu, doubtful (adj)
biaufua, doubter (n doer)
biauka, sabotage (n)
biauko, sabotage (v)
biaukua, saboteur (n doer)
biaupo, pout (v)
biauta, sadism (n)
biautu, sadistic (adj)
biautua, sadist (n doer)

biava, lounge (n)
biavo, lounge (v)
biazha, party (n d:celebration)
biazho, party (v d:celebration)
bibafota, axle (n)
bibata, helm (n d:tiller)
bibato, helm (v d:tiller)
bibika, stutter (n)
bibiko, stutter (v)
bibufa, tattoo (n)
bibufo, tattoo (v)
bibuta, total (v)
bibutana, totalitarianism (n)
bibutanua, totalitarian (n doer)
bibutiu, totally (adv)
bibuto, total (v)
bibutueta, totality (n)
bidaliu, prettily (adv)
bidalu, pretty (adj)
bidalweku, prettiest (adj)
bidalwelu, prettier (adj)
bidara, pupil (n d:eye)
bidauna, optimism (n)
bidaunala, optimum (n)
bidaunaliu, optimally (adv)
bidaunalu, optimal (adj)
bidauniu, optimistically (adv)
bidauno, optimize (v)
bidaunu, optimistic (adj)
bidaunua, optimist (n doer)
bidaunueta, optimization (n)
bidika, geek (n)
biebupa, fulfillment (n)
biebupo, fulfill (v)
biefa, polish (n)
biefo, polish (v)
biefua, polisher (n doer)
biega, sting (n d:bite)
biegio, stung (v pa d:bite)
biego, sting (v d:bite)
biegu, stingy (adj d:bite)
biegua, stinger (n doer d:bite)
bieka, stink (n)
biekio, stank (v pa)
bieko, stink (v)
bieku, stinky (adj)
biekua, stinker (n doer)
bielika, port (n)
bielikata, portal (n)
bielikercpa, portability (n)
bieliko, port (v)
bielikotha, porthole (n)
bieliku, portable (adj)
bielikua, porter (n doer)
bienika, stoop (n d:porch)
bienodarifa, geography (n)
bienodarifiu, geographically (adv)
bienodarifu, geographic (adj)
bienodarifu, geographical (adj)
bienokerenita, geology (n)
bienokerenitiu, geologically (adv)
bienokerenitu, geologic (adj)
bienokerenitu, geological (adj)

bienokerenitua, geologist (n doer)
bienopofita, geometry (n)
bienopofitiu, geometrically (adv)
bienopofitu, geometric (adj)
bienopofitu, geometrical (adj)
biepa, fullness (n)
biepedauna, fulltime (n)
biepedaunu, fulltime (adj)
biepiu, fully (adv)
biepu, full (adj)
biesha, environment (n)
bieshiu, environmentally (adv)
bieshu, environmental (adj)
bieshua, environmentalist (n
   doer)
bieta, gene (n)
bietha, bristle (n)
bietho, bristle (v)
bietu, genetic (adj)
bietueta, genetics (n)
bietuetiu, genetically (adv)
bietuetu, genetical (adj)
bifeka, deal (n)
bifekio, dealt (v pa)
bifeko, deal (v)
bifekua, dealer (n doer)
bifekuafifa, dealership (n)
bifita, jacket (n)
bifota, leap (n)
bifotefeloipa, leapfrog (n)
bifotio, leapt (v pa)
bifoto, leap (v)
bifotua, leaper (n doer)
bigaifota, corruption (n)
bigaifotiu, corruptly (adv)
bigaifoto, corrupt (v)
bigaifotu, corrupt (adj)
bikiduapa, prototype (n)
bikiduapo, prototype (v)
bikigira, protocol (n)
bilara, lady (n)
bilata, lad (n d:boy)
bilebusha, varnish (n)
bilebusho, varnish (v)
bilefa, come (n)
bilefio, came (v pa)
bilefo, come (v)
bilefua, comer (n doer)
bilefuvaka, comeback (n)
bilepa, gang (n)
bilepo, gang (v)
bilepua, gangster (n doer)
bilofa, corps (n)
bilosha, shrinkage (n)
biloshio, shrank (v pa)
bilosho, shrink (v)
biloshua, shrinker (n doer)
biloto, steer (v d:navigate)
biluashu, deluxe (adj)
biluka, caboose (n)
bimika, gnat (n)
binaka, opposition (n)
binakara, opposite (n)

binakaru, opposite (adj)
binako, oppose (v)
binakua, opponent (n doer)
binota, moment (n)
binotapa, momentum (n)
binotapu, momentous (adj)
binotiu, momentarily (adv)
binotu, momentary (adj)
binufa, ruth (n)
binufemena, ruthlessness (n)
binufemeniu, ruthlessly (adv)
binufemenu, ruthless (adj)
biodato, gawk (v)
biodatua, gawker (n doer)
biofa, randomness (n)
biofiu, randomly (adv)
biofo, randomize (v)
biofu, random (adj)
biokato, stoop (v d:bend)
biola, cheer (n)
bioliu, cheerily (adv)
biolo, cheer (v)
biolu, cheery (adj)
biona, saddle (n)
bionefanafa, saddlebag (n)
bionika, troop (n)
bioniko, troop (v)
bionikua, trooper (n doer)
biono, saddle (v)
biopa, gesture (n)
biopo, gesture (v)
bioramena, cheerlessness (n)
biorameniu, cheerlessly (adv)
bioramenu, cheerless (adj)
bioretesha, drunkenness (n
   d:intoxicated)
bioreteshu, drunk (adj
   d:intoxicated)
bioreteshua, drunk (n doer
   d:intoxicated)
bioreteshua, drunkard (n doer)
biorika, trigger (n)
bioriko, trigger (v)
biorisha, drink (n d:beverage)
biorishio, drank (v pa d:beverage)
biorisho, drink (v d:beverage)
biorishua, drinker (n doer
   d:beverage)
biorita, power (n)
bioritebaritada, powertrain (n)
bioritekiafa, powerhouse (n)
bioritelitanika, powerplant (n)
bioritemena, powerlessness (n)
bioritemeniu, powerlessly (adv)
bioritemenu, powerless (adj)
bioriteshekoba, powerboat (n)
bioritha, quilt (n)
bioritho, quilt (v)
biorithua, quilter (n doer)
bioritiu, powerfully (adv)
biorito, power (v)
bioritu, powerful (adj)
biorusha, cheerfulness (n)

biorushiu, cheerfully (adv)
biorushu, cheerful (adj)
bioshaiku, stupendous (adj)
bioshika, stupidity (n)
bioshikata, stupor (n)
bioshikiu, stupidly (adv)
bioshiko, stupify (v)
bioshiku, stupid (adj)
biota, toy (n)
bioto, toy (v)
biralilopa, semifinal (n)
biraliukeriukua, semiconductor
   (n doer)
biramifota, semicolon (n)
birika, jingle (n)
biriko, jingle (v)
birofita, defeat (n)
birofito, defeat (v)
birofitua, defeater (n doer)
Biromingama, Birmingham (n)
bironata, dorsum (n)
bironatu, dorsal (adj)
birota, feat (n)
biroto, feature (v)
birotua, feature (n doer)
biruano, flourish (v)
bishana, sturdiness (n)
bishaniu, sturdily (adv)
bishanu, sturdy (adj)
Bishemutha, Bismuth (n)
bishika, mite (n)
bishotaka, token (n)
bishotako, tokenize (v)
bishotakua, tokenizer (n doer)
bithana, canary (n)
bitho, simmer (v)
biuauaka, quirk (n)
biufiroma, inconvenience (n)
biufiromiu, inconveniently (adv)
biufiromu, inconvenient (adj)
biufita, vapor (n)
biufito, vaporize (v)
biufitu, vapid (adj)
biufitua, vaporizer (n doer)
biuifa, cypher (n)
biukana, boondoggle (n)
biukiu, poorly (adv d:unfortunate,
   bad)
biuku, poor (adj d:unfortunate,
   bad)
biulota, crook (n)
biuloto, crook (v)
biuma, penalty (n)
biumo, penalize (v)
biumu, penal (adj)
biuna, boy (n)
biunefifa, boyhood (n)
biunetha, boyfriend (n)
biunu, boyish (adj)
biupa, jolt (n)
biupo, jolt (v)
biusha, apparel (n)
biuta, statement (n d:say)

biutha, boon (n)
biuto, state (v d:say)
biuzha, gig (n)
bivana, sex (n d:gender)
bivanemenu, sexless (adj)
bivanueta, sexism (n)
bivanuetu, sexist (adj)
bivanuetua, sexist (n doer)
bivika, sex (n d:intercourse)
bivikata, sexuality (n)
bivikatiu, sexually (adv)
bivikatu, sexual (adj)
biviko, sex (v d:intercourse)
biviku, sexy (adj d:intercourse)
boana, fable (n)
boaniu, fabulously (adv)
boanu, fabulous (adj)
bodasha, pathogen (n)
bodashu, pathogenic (adj)
boeko, faint (v d:pass out)
boekua, fainter (n doer d:pass out)
boelika, hurt (n)
boelikio, hurt (v pa)
boelikiu, hurtfully (adv)
boeliko, hurt (v)
boeliku, hurtful (adj)
boena, fade (n d:diminish)
boeniu, faintly (adv d:diminish)
boeno, fade (v d:diminish)
boenu, faint (adj d:diminish)
boenua, fader (n doer d:diminish)
boenweku, faintest (adj)
boenwelu, fainter (adj)
bohata, dare (n)
bohato, dare (v)
bohatu, darish (adj)
boida, potato (n)
boifa, bungie (n)
boifo, bungie (v)
boiga, potency (n)
boigata, potential (n)
boigatiu, potentially (adv)
boigatu, potential (adj)
boigu, potent (adj)
boika, assault (n)
boikasha, casket (n)
boiko, assault (v)
boilika, squiggle (n)
boiliko, squiggle (v)
boina, dairy (n)
boinu, dairy (adj)
boipa, bungle (n)
boipo, bungle (v)
boirana, squirrel (n)
boiranu, squirrely (adj)
boisha, page (n d:person/contact)
boishata, pageant (n)
boisho, page (v d:person/contact)
boishua, pager (n doer d:person/contact)
boita, fault (n)
boitesha, cask (n)

boitiu, faultily (adv)
boito, fault (v)
boitu, faulty (adj)
bokata, bronco (n)
bokuita, ecology (n)
bokuita, ecosystem (n)
bokuitiu, ecologically (adv)
bokuitu, ecological (adj)
bokuitua, ecologist (n doer)
bolafa, dash (n d:line)
bolafo, dash (v d:line)
bolafua, dasher (n doer d:line)
bolikata, parity (n)
boliko, pare (v)
Bona, Bonn (n)
bonifa, grave (n)
bonifebarafa, gravestone (n)
bonifeshoita, graveside (n)
bonifethautha, graveyard (n)
bonifo, engrave (v)
bonifua, engraver (n doer)
borifa, strength (n)
borifepelona, strongman (n)
borifepeloni, strongmen (n pl)
borifethoritha, stronghold (n)
borifiu, strongly (adv)
borifo, strengthen (v)
borifu, strong (adj)
borifwaku, strongest (adj)
borifwelu, stronger (adj)
borila, soup (n)
borilu, soupy (adj)
borita, vice (n d:trap)
boritha, resin (n)
borithika, residue (n)
borithiku, residual (adj)
boritiu, viciously (adv d:trap)
boritu, vicious (adj d:trap)
boritueta, viciousness (n)
Boriuma, Bohrium (n)
Borona, Boron (n)
bosheperatha, withdrawal (n)
bosheperathio, withdrew (v pa)
bosheperatho, withdraw (v)
bosheterelitio, withstood (v pa)
bosheterelito, withstand (v)
boshethorithio, withheld (v pa)
boshethoritho, withhold (v)
Boshetona, Boston (n)
boshisha, within (n)
boshishu, within (adv/prep)
boshu, with (prep)
boshuila, without (n)
boshuilu, without (adv/prep)
botaka, pathos (n)
botakiu, pathetically (adv)
botaku, pathetic (adj)
botesha, path (n)
boteshepeliola, pathway (n)
buaita, poison (n)
buaito, poison (v)
buaitu, poisonous (adj)
buaitua, poisoner (n doer)

buaka, harrow (n)
buako, harrow (v)
buala, trowel (n)
bualo, trowel (v)
bualua, troweler (n doer)
buanika, dump (n)
buanikapa, dumpster (n)
buaniko, dump (v)
buanikua, dumper (n doer)
buanita, defiance (n)
buanitiu, defiantly (adv)
buanito, defy (v)
buanitu, defiant (adj)
buarobolika, desperation (n)
buasha, hearse (n)
buashata, splatter (n)
buashato, splatter (v)
buata, splat (n)
buatha, trough (n)
bubelarifa, deflation (n)
bubelarifo, deflate (v)
bubelarifu, deflationary (adj)
bubelarifua, deflator (n doer)
bubelasha, depression (n)
bubelashiu, depressively (adv)
bubelasho, depress (v)
bubelashu, depressive (adj)
bubelashua, depressant (n doer)
bubelashua, depressor (n doer)
bubelega, declassification (n)
bubelego, declassify (v)
bubeliuta, decree (n)
bubeliuto, decree (v)
buberoifo, decry (v)
buberuika, decryption (n)
buberuiko, decrypt (v)
buberulifa, decipherment (n)
buberulifi, decipherments (n pl)
buberulifo, decipher (v)
bubielika, deportation (n)
bubieliko, deport (v)
bubielikua, deporter (n doer)
bubielikuina, deportee (n)
buboita, default (n)
buboito, default (v)
Budina, Buddha (n)
Budinua, Buddhist (n)
Budinueta, Buddhism (n)
budito, delist (v)
budinafo, devour (v)
budolifa, detection (n)
budolifata, detective (n)
budolifo, detect (v)
budolifu, detectable (adj)
budolifua, detector (n doer)
budufala, deodorization (n)
budufalo, deodorize (v)
budufalua, deodorant (n doer)
budufipa, despondence (n)
budufipo, despond (v)
budufipua, desponder (n doer)
bufaboto, defuse (v)
bufaiko, despise (v)

bufaikua, despiser (n doer)
Bufalona, Buffalo (n)
bufapo, derogate (v)
bufapu, derogatory (adj)
buferilaka, determent (n)
buferilaka, deterrence (n)
buferilako, deter (v)
buferilakua, deterrent (n doer)
buferilakua, deterrer (n doer)
bufika, zoom (n)
bufiko, zoom (v)
bufiku, zoom (adj)
bufiorito, defrost (v)
bufipa, file (n d:tool)
bufipo, file (v d:tool)
bufipua, filer (n doer d:tool)
bufito, deplore (v)
bufitu, deplorable (adj)
buforika, department (n)
buforikiu, departmentally (adv)
buforiku, departmental (adj)
bugafita, packet (n)
bugalita, detraction (n)
bugalito, detract (v)
bugalitua, detractor (n doer)
bugapa, pack (n)
bugapo, pack (v)
bugapua, packer (n doer)
bugata, package (n)
bugato, package (v)
bugatua, packager (n doer)
bugauroipa, detonation (n)
bugauroipo, detonate (v)
bugauroipua, detonator (n doer)
bugeluko, debunk (v)
bugerasha, depiction (n)
bugerasho, depict (v)
bugeta, deflection (n)
bugeto, deflect (v)
bugetu, deflective (adj)
bugetua, deflector (n doer)
bugiapa, debate (n)
bugiapo, debate (v)
bugiapua, debater (n doer)
bugubelashana, decompression (n)
bugubelashano, decompress (v)
buiasho, singe (v)
buiatu, sinister (adj)
buiauka, gloat (n)
buiauko, gloat (v)
buifa, zoo (n)
buifopa, debut (n)
buifopo, debut (v)
builara, deterioration (n)
builaro, deteriorate (v)
buishota, con (n d:consequence)
buishota, consequence (n)
buishotiu, consequentially (adv)
buishotiu, consequently (adv)
buishotu, conseqent (adj)
buishotu, consequential (adj)
buka, duck (n d:avoid)

bukefita, decapitation (n)
bukefito, decapitate (v)
bukemifa, devolution (n)
bukemifa, devolvement (n)
bukemifo, devolve (v)
bukeriuka, deductible (n d:subtraction)
bukeriuka, deduction (n d:subtraction)
bukeriuko, deduct (v d:subtraction)
bukeriuku, deductible (adj d:subtraction)
bukiaka, dedication (n)
bukiako, dedicate (v)
bukiakua, dedicator (n doer)
bukiuka, deliberation (n)
bukiukiu, deliberately (adv)
bukiuko, deliberate (v)
bukiuku, deliberate (adj)
buko, duck (v d:avoid)
bukoitivo, dethrone (v)
bula, pen (n d:enclosure)
bulanika, decomposition (n)
bulaniko, decompose (v)
bulanikua, decomposer (n doer)
bulenikata, decommission (n)
bulenikato, decommission (v)
bulesha, buff (n d:rub)
bulesho, buff (v d:rub)
buleshua, buffer (n doer d:rub)
buliaga, demeanor (n)
bulifa, rue (n)
bulifo, rue (v)
bulimota, derangement (n)
bulimoto, derange (v)
bulinapa, deficit (n)
bulinika, deficiency (n)
bulinikiu, deficiently (adv)
buliniku, deficient (adj)
bulirika, descent (n)
buliriko, descend (v)
bulirikua, descender (n doer)
bulirokata, descendant (n)
bulirokata, descendent (n)
bulivata, boulevard (n)
bulo, pen (v d:enclosure)
bulofiena, desolation (n)
bulofieno, desolate (v)
Bulogara, Bulgaria (n)
Bulogariana, Bulgarian (n)
buloifa, filament (n)
buluita, derailment (n)
buluito, derail (v)
buluvipa, deregulation (n)
buluvipo, deregulate (v)
buluvipua, deregulator (n doer)
bumaromaka, degeneration (n)
bumaromako, degenerate (v)
bumaromaku, degenerative (adj)
bumida, denotation (n)
bumido, denote (v)
bumitha, detail (n)

bumitho, detail (v)
bumithua, detailer (n doer)
bumufita, denouncement (n)
bumufito, denounce (v)
bumufitua, denouncer (n doer)
bupa, fill (n)
bupaika, detachment (n)
bupaiko, detach (v)
bupalitaka, deactivation (n)
bupalitako, deactivate (v)
bupalitakua, deactivator (n doer)
bupeliuto, destroy (v)
bupeliutua, destroyer (n doer)
bupiaka, delegation (n)
bupiako, delegate (v)
bupiakua, delegate (n doer)
bupifota, detainment (n)
bupifotara, detention (n)
bupifoto, detain (v)
bupifotua, detainor (n doer)
bupifotuina, detainee (n)
bupo, fill (v)
bupua, filler (n doer)
burabolika, despair (n)
buraboliko, despair (v)
buraboliku, desperate (adj)
burafaiku, despite (prep)
Buralingatona, Burlington (n)
burianiko, defray (v)
burifa, gravity (n d:serious)
burifiu, gravely (adv d:serious)
burifu, grave (adj d:serious)
burilata, gravel (n)
burilatu, gravelly (adj)
buritha, shrub (n)
burithueta, shrubbery (n)
burusha, delusion (n)
burusho, delude (v)
burushu, delusional (adj)
busheifa, sterility (n)
bushelflu, sterllely (adv)
busheifo, sterilize (v)
busheifu, sterile (adj)
busheifueta, sterilization (n)
bushelana, destiny (n)
bushelanita, destination (n)
bushelano, destine (v)
busheleka, destruction (n)
busheleko, destruct (v)
busheleku, destructive (adj)
busheliba, derision (n)
bushelibo, deride (v)
bushetito, detest (v)
bushetitu, detestable (adj)
bushika, depth (n)
bushikelivago, demean (v)
bushipa, deep (n)
bushipiu, deeply (adv)
bushipo, deepen (v)
bushipu, deep (adj)
bushipwaku, deepest (adj)
bushipwelu, deeper (adj)
bushoika, demand (n)

bushoiko, demand (v)
bushoterana, degradation (n)
bushoterano, degrade (v)
buteliko, desist (v)
butepa, dejection (n)
butepo, deject (v)
buteranita, decontrol (n)
buteranito, decontrol (v)
buthiafa, detour (n)
buthiafo, detour (v)
buthoisho, deface (v)
buthoito, debrief (v)
butiapa, deprivation (n)
butiapo, deprive (v)
buvadava, demotion (n)
buvadavo, demote (v)
buvanafo, decouple (v)
buvathava, demolition (n)
buvathavo, demolish (v)
buvaupa, devaluation (n)
buvaupo, devalue (v)
buveka, decease (n)
buveko, decease (v)
buvolato, decode (v)
buvolatua, decoder (n doer)
buvoruva, depopulation (n)
buvoruvo, depopulate (v)
buwelika, depletion (n)
buweliko, deplete (v)
buzheko, degas (v)
buzhuba, deceit (n)
buzhubeta, deception (n)
buzhubetiu, deceptively (adv)
buzhubetu, deceptive (adj)
buzhubiu, deceitfully (adv)
buzhubo, deceive (v)
buzhubu, deceitful (adj)
buzhubua, deceiver (n doer)
dabita, theater (n)
dabita, theatre (n)
dabitu, theatrical (adj)
dabitula, theatric (n)
dafika, belt (n)
dafiko, belt (v)
dafikua, belter (n doer)
dafipa, championship (n)
dafipo, champion (v)
dafipua, champ (n doer)
dafipua, champion (n doer)
dafka, quinquagintillion (num
    1e153 card)
dafta, quadragintillion (num
    1e123 card)
dafumiu, suavely (adv)
dafumu, suave (adj)
dahem, Number_1e2406
Dahma, Dahma (n)
daiafa, tiff (n)
daiafo, tiff (v)
daiaka, captain (n)
daiako, captain (v)
daiana, uncle (n)
daiapa, puddle (n)

daiba, hibernation (n)
daibata, exhibit (n)
daibateta, exhibition (n)
daibatetua, exhibitionist (n doer)
daibato, exhibit (v)
daibatua, exhibitor (n doer)
daibo, hibernate (v)
daida, equation (n)
daido, equate (v)
daidua, equator (n doer)
daifa, pot (n)
daifaifa, potty (n)
daifekotha, pothole (n)
daifekotho, pothole (v)
daifepashota, potluck (n)
daifeshekoita, potshot (n)
daifetana, SplitWand (n)
daifika, challenge (n)
daifiko, challenge (v)
daifikua, challenger (n doer)
daifo, pot (v)
daifota, bravery (n)
daifoto, brave (v)
daifotu, brave (adj)
daifotua, brave (n doer)
daifua, potter (n doer)
daiga, fraud (n)
daigo, defraud (v)
daigua, defrauder (n doer)
daika, end (n)
daikemeniu, endlessly (adv)
daikemenu, endless (adj)
daiketaifota, endpoint (n)
daikezhieta, endgame (n)
daikiunofa, equilibrium (n)
daiko, end (v)
dailota, equivalence (n)
dailotu, equivalent (adj)
daina, equal (n)
dainiu, equally (adv)
daino, equal (v)
dainoka, equality (n)
dainoka, equalization (n)
dainoko, equalize (v)
dainokua, equalizer (n doer)
daipa, squash (n d:pressure)
daipo, squash (v d:pressure)
daipua, squasher (n doer
    d:pressure)
dairuna, costume (n)
daisha, cut (n)
daisheunefa, cutoff (n)
daishevaka, cutback (n)
daishio, cut (v pa)
daisho, cut (v)
daishota, equity (n)
daishua, cutter (n doer)
daishuila, cutout (n)
daitesha, pouch (n)
daitha, cuteness (n)
daithu, cute (adj)
Daitona, Dayton (n)
Daitonafa, Daytona (n)

daivuga, ruin (n)
daivugo, ruin (v)
daka, decillion (num 1e33 card)
dakai-, vendeka- (num 1e33 pref)
dakaiba, decade (n)
dakelito, trickle (v)
daketh, decillionth (num 1e33
    ord)
dakirena, decimal (n)
dakirenu, decimal (adj)
dala, D (let sng)
dalaga, syrup (n)
dalagu, syrupy (adj)
Dalasha, Dallas (n)
dalekiaka, syndicate (n)
dalekiako, syndicate (v)
dalekiakua, syndicator (n doer)
dalekiakueta, syndication (n)
dalela, aunt (n)
dalemida, synopsis (n)
dalevogalita, synergy (n)
dalevogalitu, synergistic (adj)
dali, Ds (let pl)
dalida, bugle (n)
dalifa, bath (n)
dalifesherana, bathroom (n)
dalifo, bathe (v)
dalifua, bather (n doer)
dalika, trick (n)
daliko, trick (v)
daliku, tricky (adj)
dalikua, trickster (n doer)
dalikueta, trickery (n)
dalila, custom (n d:tradition)
dalilata, customs (n d:checkpoint)
dalilo, customize (v d:tradition)
dalilu, customary (adj d:tradition)
dalilua, customer (n doer
    d:tradition)
dalima, persuasion (n)
dalimiu, persuasively (adv)
dalimo, persuade (v)
dalimu, persuasive (adj)
dalina, lodge (n d:building)
dalinaga, synthesis (n)
dalinagiu, synthetically (adv)
dalinago, synthesize (v)
dalinagu, synthetic (adj)
dalinagua, synthesizer (n doer)
dalinagula, synthetic (n)
daliparopa, syndrome (n)
dalishio, taught (v pa)
dalisho, teach (v)
dalishua, teacher (n doer)
dalita, age (n)
dalitha, cover (n)
dalithata, coverage (n)
dalithiveila, coverup (n)
dalitho, cover (v)
dalito, age (v)
dalitu, agey (adj)
dalitua, ager (n doer)
daloduka, syntax (n)

daloisha, syringe (n)
dalopiara, synchro (n)
dalopiariu, synchronously (adv)
dalopiaro, synchronize (v)
dalopiaru, synchronous (adj)
dalopiarueta, synchronization (n)
daloviena, synonym (n)
dalovieniu, synonymously (adv)
dalovienu, synonymous (adj)
daluka, system (n)
dalukata, systemization (n)
dalukatiu, systematically (adv)
dalukato, systemate (v)
dalukatu, systematic (adj)
dalukerashu, systemwide (adj)
daluko, systemize (v)
daluku, systemic (adj)
danata, cucumber (n)
danifopa, mob (n)
danifopo, mob (v)
danifopua, mobster (n doer)
danika, butchery (n)
daniko, butcher (v)
danikua, butcher (n doer)
danipa, chamber (n)
danita, mobility (n)
danitata, mobile (n)
danito, mobilize (v)
danitu, mobile (adj)
danitueta, mobilization (n)
danosha, tenure (n)
danosho, tenure (v)
danudana, bear (n d:animal)
dapa, ten (num 10 card)
dapai-, dec- (num 10 pref)
dapalfhemka, Number_1e40656
dapeth, tenth (num 10 ord)
dapita, deck (n)
dapito, deck (v)
darala, heart (n)
daralebeluaga, heartache (n)
daraleberuga, heartburn (n)
daraledauta, heartbeat (n)
daralemenu, heartless (adj)
daralepelika, heartbreak (n)
daralepelikio, heartbroke (v pa)
daralepeliko, heartbreak (v)
daraleraupa, heartland (n)
daraliu, heartily (adv)
daralu, hearty (adj)
darela, pearl (n)
dareliana, potion (n)
Daremishetata, Darmstadtium (n)
daresheriasha, drowsiness (n)
daresheriashu, drowsy (adj)
darifa, graph (n)
darifeta, graphic (n)
darifetiu, graphically (adv)
darifetu, graphical (adj)
darifo, graph (v)
darifu, graphic (adj)
darilofa, juice (n)

darilofo, juice (v)
darilofu, juicy (adj)
darilofua, juicer (n doer)
darinofa, custody (n)
darinofua, custodian (n doer)
darishota, lateness (n)
darishotebilefa, latecomer (n)
darishotiu, lately (adv)
darishotu, late (adj)
darishotwaku, latest (adj)
darishotwelu, later (adj)
darofila, graft (n)
darofilo, graft (v)
daromika, minute (n d:time)
darotha, dart (n)
darotho, dart (v)
Darta, Dart (n)
daruga, drop (n)
darugapi, droplet (n pl)
darugo, drop (v)
darugua, dropper (n doer)
daruguili, dropout (n pl)
darupo, droop (v)
darupu, droopy (adj)
dashapa, bareness (n)
dashapo, bare (v)
dashapoiu, barely (adv)
dashapu, bare (adj)
dasheposhu, barefoot (adj)
dashika, cube (n)
dashiko, cube (v)
dashiku, cubic (adj)
dashka, trigintillion (num 1e93 card)
dashkai-, anto-
dashketh, trigintillionth (num 1e93 ord)
dashta, vigintillion (num 1e63 card)
dashtai-, kido (num 1e63 pref)
dashteth, vigintillionth (num 1e63 ord)
datha, villa (n)
dathana, village (n)
dathanua, villager (n doer)
dathiata, vicinity (n)
dathifefa, parent (n)
dathifefifa, parenthood (n)
dathifefo, parent (v)
dathifefu, parental (adj)
datiata, versatility (n)
datiatu, versatile (adj)
daua, pow (interj)
dauferautha, boycott (n)
dauferautho, boycott (v)
dauferauthua, boycotter (n doer)
daufika, empire (n)
daufikua, emperor (n doer)
daufikueta, imperialism (n)
daufikuetu, imperial (adj)
daufikuetua, imperialist (n doer)
daufota, expiration (n)
daufoto, expire (v)

daugila, snare (n d:string)
dauiaka, spook (n)
dauiako, spook (v)
dauiaku, spooky (adj)
dauita, vaccine (n)
dauito, vaccinate (v)
dauitueta, vaccination (n)
dauka, type (n d:key)
daukedarifa, typography (n)
daukedarifu, typographical (adj)
daukefepio, typeset (v pa)
daukefepo, typeset (v)
daukefepua, typesetter (n doer)
daukepeloidua, typewriter (n doer)
daukethoisha, typeface (n)
daukila, typo (n)
dauko, type (v d:key)
daukua, typist (n doer d:key)
daulaviu, mournfully (adv)
daulavo, mourn (v)
daulavu, mournful (adj)
daulavua, mourner (n doer)
dauna, time (n)
daunedoiara, timetable (n)
daunemena, timelessness (n)
daunemenu, timeless (adj)
dauneroifa, timeline (n)
daunethetisha, timepiece (n)
dauno, time (v)
daunu, timely (adj)
daunua, timer (n doer)
daunueta, timeliness (n)
daunuila, timeout (n)
daupa, top (n)
daupato, topple (v)
daupemenu, topless (adj)
daupenarisha, topsoil (n)
daupika, topic (n)
daupiku, topical (adj)
daupinu, topsy (adj)
daupo, top (v)
daupu, top (adj)
daupua, topper (n doer)
dausha, falsity (n)
daushefifa, falsehood (n)
daushiko, botch (v)
daushiu, falsely (adv)
dausho, falsify (v)
daushu, false (adj)
daushueta, falsification (n)
dauta, beat (n)
dautafa, piracy (n)
dautafo, pirate (v)
dautafua, pirate (n doer)
dautha, vet (n d:veteran)
dauthana, veteran (n)
dautio, beat (v pa)
dauto, beat (v)
dautu, beatable (adj)
dautua, beater (n doer)
dauva, moan (n)
dauvita, pavement (n)

dauvito, pave (v)
dauvitua, paver (n doer)
dauvo, moan (v)
davapa, orange (n d:fruit)
dazha, jazz (n)
dazho, jazz (v)
dazhu, jazzy (adj)
deferepa, capability (n)
deferepu, capable (adj)
defika, rat (n)
defiko, rat (v)
defipa, cap (n)
defipo, cap (v)
Deginaka, General (n)
dehushu, toward (prep)
deiafa, nourishment (n)
deiafo, nourish (v)
deiana, witchcraft (n)
deiano, bewitch (v)
deianua, witch (n doer)
deiaupa, piety (n)
deiaupu, pious (adj)
deida, baby (n)
deido, baby (v)
deifa, bull (n)
deifelura, daisy (n)
deiferashika, betrayal (n)
deiferashiko, betray (v)
deifiana, bullion (n)
deifita, bullet (n)
deifitefeliofo, bulletproof (v)
deifitefeliofu, bulletproof (adj)
deifo, bull (v)
deifu, bullish (adj)
deifua, bully (n doer)
deifuako, bully (v)
deiga, guy (n d:male)
deigina, goggle (n)
deiluda, quiet (n)
deiluda, quietness (n)
deiludiu, quietly (adv)
deiludo, quiet (v)
deiludu, quiet (adj)
deimako, linch (v)
deimutha, buffet (n d:food/ table)
deiora, film (n)
deiorishiu, flimsily (adv)
deiorishu, flimsy (adj)
deioro, film (v)
deiorua, filmer (n doer)
delota, tire (n d:wheel)
deipa, quip (n)
deipo, quip (v)
deipua, quipper (n doer)
deirana, tulip (n)
deirina, bureau (n)
deirisha, diction (n)
deiroferalita, bureaucracy (n)
deiroferalitiu, bureaucratically (adv)
deiroferalitu, bureaucratic (adj)
deiroferalitua, bureaucrat (n doer)

deirota, design (n)
deirotaka, designation (n)
deirotako, designate (v)
deirotakua, designator (n doer)
deiroto, design (v)
deirotua, designer (n doer)
deisha, dictation (n)
deishevona, dictionary (n)
deisho, dictate (v)
deishu, dictatoral (adj)
deishua, dictator (n doer)
deishuafifa, dictatorship (n)
deitha, modesty (n)
deithiu, modestly (adv)
deithu, modest (adj)
deiuta, stern (n d:rear)
deizha, pitch (n d:throw)
deizho, pitch (v d:throw)
deizhua, pitcher (n doer d:throw)
delagela, secretary (n)
delaifa, tree (n)
delaifedaupa, treetop (n)
delaifemenu, treeless (adj)
Delawara, Delaware (n)
delifa, nursery (n)
delifeko, nurture (v)
delifekua, nurturer (n doer)
delifo, nurse (v)
delifua, nurse (n doer)
delika, capital (n)
delikara, capitalism (n)
deliko, capitalize (v)
delipa, knit (n)
delipedorima, knitwear (n)
delipo, knit (v)
delisha, fracture (n)
delisho, fracture (v)
delishoka, fraction (n)
delishokiu, fractionally (adv)
delishoku, fractional (adj)
delitana, delta (n)
delithiu, thoroughly (adv)
delithu, thorough (adj)
deliu, too (adv)
delonaberesha, marketplace (n)
delonata, market (n)
delonateferepa, marketability (n)
delonateferepu, marketable (adj)
delonato, market (v)
delonatua, marketeer (n doer)
delonatua, marketer (n doer)
deluma, candle (n)
delumeshineta, candlestick (n)
delumifeluana, candlelight (n)
demipana, candidate (n)
demuba, cancellation (n)
demubo, cancel (v)
demugu, candid (adj)
denada, temperature (n)
denana, ornament (n)
denaniu, ornamentally (adv)
denanu, ornamental (adj)
denifiu, ornately (adv)

denifu, ornate (adj)
denika, matter (n d:physics)
denipa, can (n d:container)
denipo, can (v d:container)
denitaka, capitol (n)
Denomaka, Denmark (n)
Denuvera, Denver (n)
depa, thought (n)
depio, thought (v pa)
depiu, thoughtfully (adv)
depo, think (v)
depu, thoughtful (adj)
depua, thinker (n doer)
derafa, team (n)
derafekioka, teamwork (n)
derafelena, teammate (n)
derafipa, paste (n)
derafipo, paste (v)
derafipu, pasty (adj)
derafipua, paster (n doer)
derafisha, pastry (n)
derafo, team (v)
deraiga, brat (n)
deraika, shout (n)
deraiko, shout (v)
deraikua, shouter (n doer)
derailoka, summit (n)
derailoko, summit (v)
deraima, summary (n)
deraimo, summarize (v)
deraipo, bound (v d:move)
deraipu, bound (adj d:move)
deraita, sum (n)
deraitha, grid (n)
deraithetiuga, gridlock (n)
deraito, sum (v)
derakelina, sophomore (n)
derakita, sophistication (n)
derakito, sophisticate (v)
deralifa, pastel (n)
deralika, steak (n)
deralikiafa, steakhouse (n)
derana, bun (n)
deraousekiafa, doghouse (n)
derapa, store (n)
derapata, storage (n)
derapefelarina, storefront (n)
derapekelofua, storekeeper (n doer)
derapeliafa, storehouse (n)
derapo, store (v)
derapua, storer (n doer)
derashika, exploit (n)
derashikata, exploitation (n)
derashikiu, exploitively (adv)
derashiko, exploit (v)
derashiku, exploitive (adj)
derashikua, exploiter (n doer)
derauba, kennel (n)
deraufa, brashness (n)
deraufiu, brashly (adv)
deraufu, brash (adj)
deraugaga, cynicism (n)

deraugagiu, cynically (adv)
deraugagu, cynical (adj)
deraugagua, cynic (n doer)
deraukuina, recruit (n)
derausha, dog (n)
deraushefanina, dogwood (n)
deraushevauga, dogfight (n)
derausho, dog (v)
dereifa, trust (n)
dereifelaisha, trustworthiness (n)
dereifelaishu, trustworthy (adj)
dereifo, trust (v)
dereifu, trustful (adj)
dereifu, trusty (adj)
dereifueta, trustfulness (n)
dereifuina, trustee (n)
dereiliu, truly (adv)
dereilu, true (adj)
dereisha, truth (n)
dereishiu, truthfully (adv)
dereishu, truthful (adj)
dereishueta, truism (n)
dereivoshara, truelove (n)
derelifa, stew (n)
derelifo, stew (v)
deresha, duplicate (n)
deresho, duplicate (v)
dereshua, duplicator (n doer)
dereshueta, duplication (n)
deriada, drum (n)
deriadauta, drumbeat (n)
deriado, drum (v)
deriadua, drummer (n doer)
deriafo, teem (v)
deriaga, bank (n d:storage)
deriagaifota, bankruptcy (n)
deriagaifoto, bankrupt (v)
deriago, bank (v d:storage)
deriagua, banker (n doer
  d:storage)
deriapa, earnestness (n)
deriapiu, earnestly (adv)
deriapo, earn (v)
deriapu, earnest (adj)
deriapua, earner (n doer)
deriasha, anointment (n)
deriasho, anoint (v)
deriata, quaintness (n)
deriatho, perish (v)
deriathu, perishable (adj)
deriatiu, quaintly (adv)
deriatu, quaint (adj)
deriena, grove (n)
derienoto, grovel (v)
derifota, canvas (n)
derifoto, canvas (v)
derifu, seismic (adj)
derigeruta, seclusion (n)
derigeruto, seclude (v)
derigeta, selection (n)
derigetiu, selectively (adv)
derigeto, select (v)
derigetu, selective (adj)

derigetua, selector (n doer)
derigetueta, selectivity (n)
derika, crease (n)
derikata, sedation (n)
derikatiu, sedatively (adv)
derikato, sedate (v)
derikatu, sedative (adj)
derikatua, sedative (n doer)
derikina, glean (n)
derikino, glean (v)
derikinopa, segregation (n)
derikinopo, segregate (v)
derikinopua, segregationist (n
  doer)
deriko, crease (v)
derikua, creaser (n doer)
derilaka, increase (n)
derilakiu, increasingly (adv)
derilako, increase (v)
derilana, bunny (n)
derilauka, bullhorn (n)
derileshelefa, glassware (n)
derilosha, glass (n d:quartz)
derilota, wrinkle (n)
deriloto, wrinkle (v)
derilotu, wrinkly (adj)
derilotua, wrinkler (n doer)
derinota, glass (n d:spectacles)
deripa, spot (n)
deripefeluana, spotlight (n)
deripemenu, spotless (adj)
deripo, spot (v)
deripu, spotty (adj)
deripua, spotter (n doer)
derishoka, increment (n)
derishokiu, incrementally (adv)
derishoko, increment (v)
derishoku, incremental (adj)
derita, seed (n)
deritara, glare (n)
deritaro, glare (v)
deritha, glee (n)
derithiu, gleefully (adv)
derithu, gleeful (adj)
deritipa, seedling (n)
derito, seed (v)
deritu, seedy (adj)
deritua, seeder (n doer)
deriuka, creek (n)
deriupa, beep (n)
deriupo, beep (v)
deriupua, beeper (n doer)
deriveka, secession (n)
deriveko, secede (v)
derizha, glaze (n)
derizhauka, sedition (n)
derizho, glaze (v)
derofeliku, counterclockwise (adj)
derofita, declaration (n)
derofito, declare (v)
derofitu, declaratory (adj)
derofitua, declarer (n doer)
deroifa, rib (n)

deroifo, rib (v)
deroila, rim (n)
deroka, clock (n)
derokirofa, star (n d:celebrity)
derokirofo, star (v d:celebrity)
deroko, clock (v)
deroku, clockwise (adj)
derolifa, oscillation (n)
derolifo, oscillate (v)
derolifua, oscillator (n doer)
deronipa, tropic (n)
deronipiu, tropically (adv)
deronipu, tropical (adj)
derosheta, clarification (n)
derota, clearness (n)
derotana, clearance (n)
derotiu, clearly (adv)
deroto, clear (v)
derotu, clear (adj)
deruafa, gleam (n)
deruafo, gleam (v)
derufa, sleeve (n)
derufemenu, sleeveless (adj)
derufipa, depreciation (n)
derufipo, depreciate (v)
derufo, sleeve (v)
deruka, prey (n)
derukata, predation (n)
derukato, predate (v)
derukatu, predatory (adj)
derukatua, predator (n doer)
deruko, prey (v)
derulika, comprehension (n)
derulikiu, comprehensively (adv)
deruliko, comprehend (v)
deruliku, comprehensive (adj)
derulipa, appreciation (n)
derulipiu, appreciatively (adv)
derulipo, appreciate (v)
derulipu, appreciative (adj)
derumaka, cancer (n)
derumaku, cancerous (adj)
derusha, derivation (n)
derusho, derive (v)
derushu, derivative (adj)
deshata, presidency (n)
deshatiu, presidentially (adv)
deshato, preside (v)
deshatu, presidential (adj)
deshatua, president (n doer)
deshiafika, captivity (n)
deshiafiko, captivate (v)
deshiaka, capture (n)
deshiako, capture (v)
deshiakua, capturer (n doer)
deshipa, caption (n)
deshipo, caption (v)
Deteroita, Detroit (n)
dethipa, capacity (n)
detisha, peck (n)
detisho, peck (v)
dhahem, Number_1e2706
dhai, was/will be (parcl d:passive

voice)
dhaku, and (conj)
dhala, Dh (let sng)
dhali, Dhs (let pl)
dhauatelanotiku, transatlantic (adj)
dhaubieloka, transportation (n)
dhaubieloko, transport (v)
dhaubieloku, transportable (adj)
dhaubielokua, transporter (n doer)
dhaubivikata, transsexual (n)
dhaudarita, translation (n)
dhaudarito, translate (v)
dhaudaritua, translator (n doer)
dhaudaufa, transpiration (n)
dhaudaufo, transpire (v)
dhaudufipa, transponder (n)
dhaufabota, transfusion (n)
dhaufaboto, transfuse (v)
dhauferepa, transience (n)
dhauferepiu, transiently (adv)
dhauferepu, transient (adj)
dhauferepua, transient (n doer)
dhaufika, transit (n)
dhaufikueta, transition (n)
dhaugelaka, transposition (n)
dhaugelako, transpose (v)
dhaugelakua, transposer (n doer)
dhaukarilu, transnational (adj)
dhaukifelafa, transvestite (n)
dhaukiroka, transduction (n)
dhaukiroko, transduce (v)
dhaukirokua, transducer (n doer)
dhaulirika, transcendence (n)
dhauliriko, transcend (v)
dhauliriku, transcendent (adj)
dhaulirikula, transcendent (n)
dhaulirikulu, transcendental (adj)
dhaulitanika, transplant (n)
dhaulitaniko, transplant (v)
dhaulitanikueta, transplantation (n)
dhaulunito, trespass (v)
dhaulunitua, trespasser (n doer)
dhaumeratu, transcontinental (adj)
dhaumiaru, transocean (adj)
dhaunoka, transmission (n)
dhaunoka, transmittal (n)
dhaunoko, transmit (v)
dhaunokua, transmitter (n doer)
dhaupalita, transaction (n)
dhaupalito, transact (v)
dhaupalitua, transactor (n doer)
dhaupeliana, transparency (n)
dhaupelianiu, transparently (adv)
dhaupelianu, transparent (adj)
dhausha, transfer (n)
dhausheferepa, transferability (n)
dhausheluaka, transmutation (n)
dhausheluakiu, transmutably (adv)

dhausheluako, transmute (v)
dhausheluaku, transmutable (adj)
dhausheluakua, transmutor (n doer)
dhausheriga, transcript (n)
dhausherigo, transcribe (v)
dhausherigua, transcriber (n doer)
dhausherigueta, transcription (n)
dhaushiu, transferably (adv)
dhaushiunikiu, translucently (adv)
dhaushiuniku, translucent (adj)
dhausho, transfer (v)
dhaushu, transferable (adj)
dhaushueta, transference (n)
dhautharika, transverse (n)
dhauthariko, transvert (v)
dhauthariku, transverse (adj)
dhautielikua, transistor (n doer)
dhauviketa, transfixation (n)
dhauviketo, transfixate (v)
dhauviko, transfix (v)
dhauvorina, transformation (n)
dhauvoriniu, transformationally (adv)
dhauvorino, transform (v)
dhauvorinu, transformational (adj)
dhauvorinua, transformer (n doer)
dhauvoruga, transgression (n)
dhauvorugo, transgress (v)
dhauvorugua, transgressor (n doer)
dheigerogo, roughen (v)
dhiaishomana, misdiagnosis (n)
dhiaishomano, misdiagnose (v)
dhiariderupa, misinterpretation (n)
dhiariderupo, misinterpret (v)
dhiasha, miss (n d:avoid)
dhiasho, miss (v d:avoid)
dhiberesha, misplacement (n)
dhiberesho, misplace (v)
dhiberiaka, misuse (n)
dhiberiako, misuse (v)
dhibiuta, misstatement (n)
dhibiuto, misstate (v)
dhibuliaga, misdemeanor (n)
dhidereifa, mistrust (n)
dhidereifo, mistrust (v)
dhidibaga, mistrial (n)
dhidorikelatio, misspent (v pa)
dhidorikelato, misspend (v)
dhiduliata, misadventure (n)
dhifelenisha, miscredibility (n)
dhifelenishua, miscreant (n doer)
dhifelida, misdeed (n)
dhiferuifa, misplay (n)
dhiferuifo, misplay (v)
dhifiunifeta, mispronunciation (n)

dhifiunifeto, mispronounce (v)
dhigarodaka, miscalculation (n)
dhigarodako, miscalculate (v)
dhigelisha, misstep (n)
dhigelisho, misstep (v)
dhigerena, miscarriage (n)
dhigereno, miscarry (v)
dhigeruthio, misgave (v pa)
dhigerutho, misgive (v)
dhigiaula, misfire (n)
dhigiaulo, misfire (v)
dhigoka, mistake (n)
dhigokio, mistook (v pa)
dhigokiu, mistakenly (adv)
dhigoko, mistake (v)
dhiguniata, miscommunication (n)
dhiguniato, miscommunicate (v)
dhihetheta, misjudgement (n)
dhihetheta, misjudgment (n)
dhihetheto, misjudge (v)
dhihinafa, misquote (n)
dhihinafo, misquote (v)
dhiivorina, misinformation (n)
dhiivorino, misinform (v)
dhikapado, mishandle (v)
dhikolipa, mishap (n)
dhikolipo, mishappen (v)
dhikuafika, misdirection (n)
dhikuafiko, misdirect (v)
dhikulifa, misbehavior (n)
dhikulifo, misbehave (v)
dhilalitiu, misleadingly (adv)
dhilalito, mislead (v)
dhilalitua, misleader (n doer)
dhilarito, misrule (v)
dhiliapa, misread (n)
dhiliapio, misread (v pa)
dhiliapo, misread (v)
dhiliukeriuka, misconduct (n)
dhiliukeriuko, misconduct (v)
dhiliupelaipo, misconstrue (v)
dhiliushipa, misconception (n)
dhiliushipo, misconceive (v)
dhiloshipa, misperception (n)
dhiloshipo, misperceive (v)
dhiluduasha, misrepresentation (n)
dhiluduasho, misrepresent (v)
dhimutha, mismatch (n)
dhimutho, mismatch (v)
dhioderuketa, misapprehension (n)
dhioderuketo, misapprehend (v)
dhiofelikima, misappropriation (n)
dhiofelikimo, misappropriate (v)
dhiorishaipi, misallocation (n pl)
dhiorishaipo, misallocate (v)
dhioroifa, misalignment (n)
dhioroifo, misalign (v)
dhipafita, misfit (n)
dhishashika, mismanagement (n)

dhishashiko, mismanage (v)
dhiteifa, miscue (n)
dhiteifo, miscue (v)
dhitenitio, misunderstood (v pa)
dhitenito, misunderstand (v)
dhiterulisha, misprint (n)
dhiterulisho, misprint (v)
dhitharo, misspell (v)
dhithoki, misapplication (n pl)
dhithoko, misapply (v)
dhithuita, mistreatment (n)
dhithuito, mistreat (v)
dhituipa, misguidance (n)
dhituipo, misguide (v)
dhiuferitha, misidentification (n)
dhiuferitho, misidentify (v)
dhiveiana, misogyny (n)
dhiviena, misnomer (n)
dhivita, mischief (n)
dhivitu, mischievous (adj)
dhivoamuna, misfortune (n)
dho, a (det)
dhufa, goo (n)
dhufu, gooey (adj)
dhusha, hose (n)
dhusho, hose (v)
dhushua, hoser (n doer)
dhushueta, hosiery (n)
di, to (prep)
diada, mode (n)
diadara, model (n)
diadaro, model (v)
diadiu, modally (adv)
diadu, modal (adj)
diadueta, modality (n)
diafa, bow (n d:bend)
diafo, bow (v d:bend)
diago, barge (v)
diagua, barger (n doer)
diaka, burden (n)
diako, burden (v)
diaku, burdensome (adj)
dialika, trunk (n)
dialiko, truncate (v)
dialisha, hurdle (n)
dialisho, hurdle (v)
dialita, post (n d:ad)
dialitara, postage (n)
dialitaru, postal (adj)
dialitarua, postman (n doer)
dialitauna, postcard (n)
dialiteshetata, postmark (n)
dialiteshetato, postmark (v)
dialitethioka, postmaster (n)
dialito, post (v d:ad)
dialitua, poster (n doer d:ad)
dialitueta, poster (n d:display)
diana, discovery (n)
dianita, sanctity (n)
dianito, sanctify (v)
diano, discover (v)
dianoka, sanction (n)
dianoko, sanction (v)

dianua, discoverer (n doer)
diapa, drive (n)
diapeliola, driveway (n)
diapio, drove (v pa)
diapo, drive (v)
diapua, driver (n doer)
diara, bell (n)
diariauka, bellow (n)
diariauko, bellow (v)
diaropa, belly (n)
diaropo, belly (v)
diasha, joint (n)
diashiu, jointly (adv)
diasho, joint (v)
diata, join (n)
diaterafa, hurl (n)
diaterafo, hurl (v)
diathiu, acutely (adv)
diathu, acute (adj)
diatiata, jitter (n)
diatiato, jitter (v)
diato, join (v)
diatua, joiner (n doer)
diaufa, maze (n)
diauga, explosion (n)
diaugiu, explosively (adv)
diaugo, explode (v)
diaugu, explosive (adj)
diaugua, explosive (n doer)
diauka, refusal (n d:decline)
diauko, refuse (v d:decline)
diazha, subsidy (n)
diazhana, subsidence (n)
diazhata, subsidiary (n)
diazho, subsidize (v)
diba, try (n)
dibaga, trial (n)
dibala, melon (n)
dibo, try (v)
dibuila, tryout (n)
didana, similarity (n)
didaniu, similarly (adv)
didanu, similar (adj)
diduka, trouble (n)
didukeshekoto, troubleshoot (v)
didukeshekotua, troubleshooter
   (n doer)
didukezhinu, troublesome (adj)
diduko, trouble (v)
didukua, troublemaker (n doer)
diefa, cuff (n)
diefo, cuff (v)
dieka, right (n d:correct)
diekiepiu, rightfully (adv)
diekiepu, rightful (adj)
diekiu, rightly (adv d:correct)
dieko, right (v d:correct)
dieku, right (adj d:correct)
diekua, righter (n doer d:correct)
diekueta, righteousness (n)
diekueta, rightness (n)
diekuetiu, righteously (adv)
diekuetu, righteous (adj)

diekuetua, righteous (n doer)
dienoka, cartridge (n)
dierota, bay (n d:howl)
dieroto, bay (v d:howl)
dierotua, bayer (n doer d:howl)
diesha, apparatus (n)
difada, photo (n)
difedarifa, photograph (n)
difedarifo, photograph (v)
difedarifota, photography (n)
difedarifua, photographer (n
   doer)
difekisha, photocopy (n)
difekisho, photocopy (v)
difekishua, photocopier (n doer)
difoka, beg (n)
difoko, beg (v)
difokua, beggar (n doer)
difota, adaptation (n)
difotiu, adaptably (adv)
difotiu, adaptively (adv)
difoto, adapt (v)
difotu, adaptable (adj)
difotu, adaptive (adj)
difotua, adapter (n doer)
difotua, adaptor (n doer)
difu, per (adv/prep)
diholu, where-to (adv)
diholu, whither (adv/conj)
dikiuka, toggle (n)
dikiuko, toggle (v)
dikosha, togetherness (n)
dikoshiu, together (adv)
dilana, holiness (n)
dilanu, holy (adj)
dilatha, boutique (n)
dilofa, limp (n)
dilofo, limp (v)
dilofu, limp (adj)
diloika, molecule (n)
diloiku, molecular (adj)
diloka, pole (n)
dilokata, polarity (n)
dilokato, polarize (v)
dilokatu, polar (adj)
dilokatueta, polarization (n)
dilopa, toe (n)
dilopetherina, toenail (n)
dilorina, sweater (n d:clothing)
diloshafa, separation (n)
diloshafiu, separately (adv)
diloshafo, separate (v)
diloshafu, separate (adj)
diloshafua, separator (n doer)
dimuana, tonight (n)
dimuaniu, tonight (adv)
dinakerana, kilogram (n)
dinala, thinness (n)
dinalimeta, kilometer (n)
dinaliu, thinly (adv)
dinalo, thin (v)
dinalu, thin (adj)
dinana, finger (n)

dinaneterulisha, fingerprint (n)
dinaneterulisho, fingerprint (v)
dinanetherina, fingernail (n)
dinanetilifa, fingertip (n)
dinano, finger (v)
dinetatu, myraid (adj)
dint, thousand (num 1000 card)
dintai-, kilo- (num 1000 pref)
dinteth, thousandth (num 1000 ord)
diofa, trench (n)
diofo, trench (v)
dioka, auction (n)
dioko, auction (v)
diokua, auctioneer (n doer)
dionioka, thermometer (n)
dioripa, buy (n)
dioripio, bought (v pa)
dioripo, buy (v)
dioripua, buyer (n doer)
dioripuila, buyout (n)
diorita, rotation (n)
dioritata, rotor (n)
dioritha, perch (n d:pole)
dioritho, perch (v d:pole)
diorito, rotate (v)
dioritu, rotary (adj)
dioritu, rotational (adj)
dioritua, rotator (n doer)
dioruma, cannon (n)
diosha, therm (n)
dioshu, thermal (adj)
Dioshuviula, Tuesday (n)
diotano, jot (v)
diotha, spoof (n)
diotho, spoof (v)
diraka, oratory (n)
dirako, orate (v)
dirakua, orator (n doer)
diraniu, orally (adv)
diranu, oral (adj)
dirava, courage (n)
diravata, encouragement (n)
diraviu, courageously (adv)
diravo, encourage (v)
diravu, courageous (adj)
dirifa, rod (n)
dirima, tilt (n)
dirimo, tilt (v)
diropa, rot (n)
diropo, rot (v)
diruba, hormone (n)
dishaviena, pseudonym (n)
dishela, diesel (n)
Disheperoshiuma, Dysprosium (n)
dita, list (n d:sequence)
ditapa, pool (n)
ditapeshoita, poolside (n)
ditapeshoitu, poolside (adj)
ditapo, pool (v)
ditha, currency (n)
dithoka, pixel (n)

dito, list (v d:sequence)
diuafa, voracity (n)
diuafiu, voraciously (adv)
diuafu, voracious (adj)
diufa, filter (n)
diufo, filter (v)
diufua, filterer (n doer)
diuga, keg (n)
diuipa, embarrassment (n)
diuipo, embarrass (v)
diuka, quiz (n)
diuko, quiz (v)
diuma, reel (n)
diumo, reel (v)
diuna, spy (n)
diunederinota, spyglass (n)
diuno, spy (v)
diupa, boast (n)
diupo, boast (v)
diupua, boaster (n doer)
diushoka, boost (n)
diushoko, boost (v)
diushokua, booster (n doer)
diuta, niche (n)
diutha, reed (n)
diuvata, vortex (n)
diverafeirana, ultraviolet (n)
diverafeiranu, ultraviolet (adj)
diverakarilu, ultranational (adj)
diverakarilua, ultranationalist (n doer)
diveraliukofitiu, ultraconservatively (adv)
diveraliukofitu, ultraconservative (adj)
diverazhanitana, ultrasound (n)
diverazhanitaniu, ultrasonically (adv)
diverazhanitanu, ultrasonic (adj)
diviula, today (n)
diviuliu, today (adv)
diviulu, today (adj)
divulo, mellow (v)
divulu, mellow (adj)
divura, melody (n)
divuru, melodic (adj)
divuta, adoption (n)
divuto, adopt (v)
divutu, adoptive (adj)
divutua, adopter (n doer)
dizha, thing (n)
doapa, chest (n d:torso)
doata, mouse (n)
doatethereipa, mousetrap (n)
doati, mice (n pl)
doato, mouse (v)
doatua, mouser (n doer)
dodu, then (adj/adv)
dofafa, pupil (n d:student)
dofita, button (n)
dofito, button (v)
dofitua, buttoner (n doer)
doiaka, poke (n d:push)

doiako, poke (v d:push)
doiaku, pokey (adj d:push)
doiakua, poker (n doer d:push)
doiara, table (n)
doiaredaupa, tabletop (n)
doiaredoripa, tablespoon (n)
doiarefelafa, tablecloth (n)
doiareshelefa, tableware (n)
doiaro, table (v)
doidana, lobby (n)
doidano, lobby (v)
doidanua, lobbyist (n doer)
doido, lob (v)
doifa, idol (n)
doifo, idolize (v)
doiga, margin (n)
doigiu, marginally (adv)
doigo, marginalize (v)
doigu, marginal (adj)
doikaka, harassment (n)
doikako, harass (v)
doikakua, harasser (n doer)
doikupa, bustle (n)
doikupo, bustle (v)
doilama, idiocy (n)
doilamiu, idiotically (adv)
doilamu, idiotic (adj)
doilamua, idiot (n doer)
doina, lobe (n)
doipa, squish (n)
doipo, squish (v)
doipu, squishy (adj)
doipua, squisher (n doer)
doishoka, bust (n d:burst)
doishoko, bust (v d:burst)
doishokua, buster (n doer d:burst)
doita, tablet (n)
doitha, page (n d:paper)
doithueta, pagination (n)
doithueto, paginate (v)
doitiara, tabloid (n)
doiva, fragment (n)
doivo, fragment (v)
doivu, fragile (adj)
doka, exit (n)
doko, exit (v)
dokua, exiter (n doer)
dola, readiness (n)
dolada, throat (n)
dolado, threaten (v)
dolama, idiom (n)
dolamo, idiomate (v)
dolamu, idiomatic (adj)
dolika, burglary (n)
doliko, burglarize (v)
doliko, burgle (v)
dolikua, burglar (n doer)
dolima, poll (n)
dolimo, poll (v)
dolimua, poller (n doer)
dolita, thread (n)
dolito, thread (v)

doliu, readily (adv)
dolo, ready (v)
dolu, ready (adj)
domulo, hallow (v)
dopeshelefa, cookware (n)
dopevonuda, cookbook (n)
dopipa, cookie (n)
dopo, cook (v)
dopua, cook (n doer)
dopuila, cookout (n)
doraifoka, pollutant (n)
doraika, pollution (n)
doraiko, pollute (v)
doraikua, polluter (n doer)
Dorana, EhoMonth07 (n)
doranika, carton (n)
dorebida, broadcast (n)
dorebidio, broadcast (v pa)
dorebido, broadcast (v)
dorebidua, broadcaster (n doer)
doreina, politeness (n)
doreinaku, impolite (adj)
doreiniu, politely (adv)
doreinu, polite (adj)
doriaka, bang (n d:collision)
doriako, bang (v d:collision)
doriakua, banger (n doer d:collision)
dorifa, gear (n d:equipment)
dorifemirofa, gearshift (n)
dorifeperenika, gearbox (n)
dorikaita, spice (n)
dorikaito, spice (v)
dorikaitu, spicy (adj)
dorikaitua, spicer (n doer)
dorikelatio, spent (v pa)
dorikelato, spend (v)
dorikelatu, spendable (adj)
dorikelatua, spender (n doer)
dorima, wear (n d:clothe)
dorimio, wore (v pa d:clothe)
dorimiu, wearably (adv d:clothe)
dorimo, wear (v d:clothe)
dorimu, wearable (adj d:clothe)
dorimua, wearer (n doer d:clothe)
doripa, spoon (n)
doripo, spoon (v)
doripu, spoonful (adj)
doripua, spooner (n doer)
dorisha, firm (n d:company)
dorishoka, policy (n)
dorishokata, police (n)
dorishokenagua, policymaker (n doer)
dorishokethorithua, policyholder (n doer)
dorishoko, police (v)
dorishokua, policeman (n doer)
doritha, poor (n d:low money)
dorithekiafa, poorhouse (n)
doruba, breadth (n)
dorubiu, broadly (adv)
dorubo, broaden (v)

dorubu, broad (adj)
dorubwaku, broadest (adj)
dorubwelu, broader (adj)
doruda, polity (n)
dorudara, politics (n)
dorudiu, politically (adv)
dorudo, politic (v)
dorudu, political (adj)
dorudua, politician (n doer)
doruga, gun (n)
dorugebiata, gunpowder (n)
dorugefeleva, gunship (n)
dorugepelona, gunman (n)
dorugepeloni, gunmen (n pl)
dorugeshekoba, gunboat (n)
dorugeshekoita, gunshot (n)
dorugetaifota, gunpoint (n)
dorugevauga, gunfight (n)
dorugiaula, gunfire (n)
dorugiaulao, shriauk (v prp)
dorugiaulio, giaul (v pa)
dorugo, gun (v)
dorugua, gunner (n doer)
dosheta, clarity (n)
dosheto, clarify (v)
doshiferepa, executable (n)
doshiferepiu, executably (adv)
doshiferepu, executable (adj)
doshika, execution (n d:perform)
doshikara, executive (n d:businessperson)
doshikiu, executively (adv d:perform)
doshiko, execute (v d:perform)
doshiku, executive (adj d:perform)
doshikua, executioner (n doer d:perform)
doshikua, executor (n doer)
doshipata, asbestos (n)
doshiuna, hallucination (n)
doshiuno, hallucinate (v)
dotaifa, vertex (n)
dotaika, vertical (n)
dotaikiu, vertically (adv)
dotaiku, vertical (adj)
dotaipa, vertebra (n)
dotaipi, vertebrae (n pl)
dotaitesha, vertigo (n)
dotharifa, traversal (n)
dotharifo, traverse (v)
dothoritha, threshold (n)
dotisha, pick (n)
dotishapa, pickle (n)
dotishapo, pickle (v)
dotishata, picket (n)
dotishato, picket (v)
dotishatua, picketer (n doer)
dotishelogafa, pickpocket (n)
dotishiveila, pickup (n)
dotisho, pick (v)
dotishu, picky (adj)
dotishua, picker (n doer)

dova, rap (n)
dovafa, rapport (n)
dovafo, rapport (v)
dovai, bravo (interj)
dovarita, report (n)
dovaritiu, reportedly (adv)
dovarito, report (v)
dovaritu, reportable (adj)
dovaritua, reporter (n doer)
dovata, tobacco (n)
dovenipa, exponent (n)
dovenipiu, exponentially (adv)
dovenipo, expone (v)
dovenipu, exponential (adj)
doviberautha, torrent (n)
doviberauthu, torrential (adj)
dovikutu, torrid (adj)
dovila, rapidity (n)
doviliu, rapidly (adv)
dovilu, rapid (adj)
dovina, wake (n d:trail)
dovita, travel (n)
dovito, travel (v)
dovitua, traveler (n doer)
dovitua, traveller (n doer)
dovo, rap (v)
dovua, rapper (n doer)
duafa, beam (n)
duafo, beam (v)
duafua, beamer (n doer)
duaifa, tightness (n)
duaifana, tights (n)
duaifevapa, tightrope (n)
duaifiu, tightly (adv)
duaifo, tighten (v)
duaifu, tight (adj)
duaifwaku, tightest (adj)
duaifwelu, tighter (adj)
duaika, chop (n)
duaikiu, choppily (adv)
duaiko, chop (v)
duaiku, choppy (adj)
duaikua, chopper (n doer)
duaikushineta, chopstick (n)
duakerita, gouge (n)
duakerito, gouge (v)
dualifa, beach (n)
dualifo, beach (v)
dualifua, beacher (n doer)
duama, anatomy (n)
duamu, anatomical (adj)
duapa, type (n d:kind)
duapiu, typically (adv d:kind)
duapo, type (v d:kind)
duapu, typical (adj d:kind)
duarika, beaker (n)
duasha, present (n d:give gift)
duashika, presentation (n)
duashikua, presenter (n doer)
duasho, present (v d:give gift)
duata, beak (n)
duatha, vent (n)
duathaga, ventilation (n)

duathago, ventilate (v)
duathagua, ventilator (n doer)
duatho, vent (v)
duathua, venter (n doer)
duavata, attic (n)
duavisha, FertilityStone (n)
dubana, bumble (n d:buzz)
dubano, bumble (v d:buzz)
dubata, ripeness (n)
dubato, ripen (v)
dubatu, ripe (adj)
dubelasha, oppression (n)
dubelashiu, oppressively (adv)
dubelasho, oppress (v)
dubelashu, oppressive (adj)
dubelashua, oppressor (n doer)
Dubeniuma, Dubnium (n)
dubielika, opportunity (n)
dubieliku, opportunistic (adj)
dubielikua, opportunist (n doer)
dudifa, puppy (n)
dueka, chip (n)
dueko, chip (v)
duekua, chipper (n doer)
dufala, odor (n)
dufalemenu, odorless (adj)
dufika, vengence (n)
dufiku, vengeful (adj)
dufita, criticism (n)
dufitara, criterion (n)
dufitari, criteria (n pl)
dufitiu, critically (adv)
dufito, criticize (v)
dufitu, critical (adj)
dufitua, critic (n doer)
duiafa, venom (n)
duiafu, venomous (adj)
duiaka, puck (n)
duiato, reap (v)
duiatua, reaper (n doer)
duida, pup (n)
duidaka, puppetry (n)
duidakua, puppeteer (n doer)
duidata, puppet (n)
duifa, softness (n)
duifeshelefa, softball (n)
duifiu, softly (adv)
duifo, soften (v)
duifu, soft (adj)
duifua, softener (n doer)
duika, bozo (n)
duila, leniency (n)
duiliu, leniently (adv)
duilu, lenient (adj)
duimoripa, swimsuit (n)
duina, swim (n)
duinio, swam (v pa)
duino, swim (v)
duinua, swimmer (n doer)
duiroga, kink (n)
duirogu, kinky (adj)
duishelefa, software (n)
duka, cog (n)

dukafo, vend (v)
dukafua, vendor (n doer)
dukapa, vendetta (n)
dukiaka, vindication (n)
dukiako, vindicate (v)
dukiakua, vindicator (n doer)
dukiakueta, vindictiveness (n)
dulana, drivel (n)
dulano, drivel (v)
dulano, drool (v)
Duliafa, EhoDay04 (n)
duliata, adventure (n)
duliatiu, adventurously (adv)
duliato, venture (v)
duliatu, adventurous (adj)
duliatua, adventurer (n doer)
dulika, cock (n)
dulikaifa, cocktail (n)
dulikata, cockiness (n)
dulikeluka, cockpit (n)
duliko, cock (v)
duliku, cocky (adj)
dulimiu, currently (adv d:now)
dulimu, current (adj d:now)
dulipa, bubble (n)
dulipo, bubble (v)
dulipu, bubbly (adj)
dulipua, bubbler (n doer)
dulitha, spool (n)
dulitho, spool (v)
dulufa, ooze (n)
dulufo, ooze (v)
duma, tween (n)
dunifa, opera (n)
dunina, ton (n)
duninoka, tonne (n)
dunipa, coop (n d:cage)
dunobeta, pump (n)
dunobeto, pump (v)
dunobetua, pumper (n doer)
dupafo, tailor (v)
dupafua, tailor (n doer)
dupako, madden (v d:angry)
dupaku, mad (adj d:angry)
dupakwelu, madder (adj d:angry)
duperana, capsule (n)
durai, voila (interj)
duredeiga, bridegroom (n)
durei, there (pron)
durekolora, bridesmaid (n)
durela, bill (n d:beak)
duriba, drone (n d:tone)
duribo, drone (v d:tone)
durifa, coast (n d:move)
durifo, coast (v d:move)
durifua, coaster (n doer d:move)
durisha, bride (n)
durishu, bridal (adj)
durita, operation (n)
duritana, operative (n)
duritiu, operationally (adv)
durito, operate (v)
duritu, operable (adj)

duritu, operational (adj)
duritua, operator (n doer)
duroga, knuckle (n)
durogo, knuckle (v)
durogua, knuckler (n doer)
duromafiu, therefore (adv)
duroviliu, thereafter (adv)
durovuniu, thereby (adv)
duru, there (adj/adv/interj)
dushata, desert (n d:wasteland)
dutaka, lawsuit (n)
dutako, sue (v)
duteka, washer (n d:spacer)
Dutesha, Dutch (n)
dutha, altar (n)
duthapa, season (n d:spice)
duthapo, season (v d:spice)
duvila, sponsorship (n)
duvilo, sponsor (v)
duvilua, sponsor (n doer)
duvoipa, sponge (n)
duvoipo, sponge (v)
e, (separator)
Efak, Bromine (n davoka)
Efap, Gallium (n davoka)
efelu, ever (adj/adv)
Efik, Krypton (n davoka)
Efip, Germanium (n davoka)
Efop, Arsenic (n davoka)
efubina, openness (n)
efubiniu, openly (adv)
efubino, open (v)
efubinu, open (adj)
efubinua, opener (n doer)
efueta, option (n)
efuetiu, optionally (adv)
efueto, opt (v)
efuetu, optional (adj)
Efup, Selenium (n davoka)
eikuita, dialog (n)
eikuita, dialogue (n)
Einesheteiniuma, Einsteinium (n)
eipora, diary (n)
eipota, dial (n)
eipoto, dial (v)
Ekak, Fluorine (n davoka)
Ekap, Boron (n davoka)
Ekik, Neon (n davoka)
ekip avekupat, carbon dioxide (n)
Ekip, Carbon (n davoka)
Ekop, Nitrogen (n davoka)
Ekup, Oxygen (n davoka)
ekupana, ozone (n)
ekupata, oxide (n)
ekupato, oxidize (v)
ekupatua, oxidizer (n doer)
ekupatueta, oxidation (n)
Elak, Iodine (n davoka)
Elap, Indium (n davoka)
elesha, earth (n)
eleshelova, earthling (n)
eleshiova, earthquake (n)
elesho, unearth (v)

eleshu, earthly (adj)
elfhem, Number_1e306
elfi, Es (let pl)
elialu, early (adj)
elialwaku, earliest (adj)
elialwelu, earlier (adj)
elifa, E (let sng)
Elip, Tin (n davoka)
Elop, Antimony (n davoka)
Elup, Tellurium (n davoka)
emodi, onto (prep)
Enak, Ununspetium (n davoka)
Enap, Ununtrium (n davoka)
engadafka, Number_1e4203
engahem, Number_1e4056
engala, Ng (let sng)
engali, Ngs (let pl)
Enik, Ununoctium (n davoka)
Enip, Ununquadium (n davoka)
enishota, inevitability (n)
enishotiu, inevitably (adv)
enishotu, inevitable (adj)
Enop, Ununpentium (n davoka)
Enup, Ununhexium (n davoka)
enutaka, eligibility (n)
enutaku, eligible (adj)
eposhilona, epsilon (n)
er, uh (interj)
Erak, Astatine (n davoka)
Erap, Thallium (n davoka)
eren, um (interj)
Erik, Radon (n davoka)
Erip, Lead (n davoka)
Erop, Bismuth (n davoka)
Erubiuma, Erbium (n)
Erup, Polonium (n davoka)
Etak, Chlorine (n davoka)
etana, eta (n)
Etap, Aluminum (n davoka)
Etik, Argon (n davoka)
Etip, Silicon (n davoka)
Etop, Phosphorus (n davoka)
Etup, Sulfur (n davoka)
Europiuma, Europium (n)
fabika, wheeze (n)
fabiko, wheeze (v)
fabofita, fusion (n)
fabota, fuse (n)
faboto, fuse (v)
fabotua, fuser (n doer)
fadifa, deer (n)
fadifi, deer (n pl)
fafata, fuzz (n)
fafato, fuzz (v)
fafatu, fuzz (adj)
fafita, civility (n)
fafitiu, civily (adv)
fafito, civilize (v)
fafitu, civil (adj)
fafitua, civilian (n doer)
fafitueta, civilization (n)
faiata, spike (n)
faiatio, spikes (v pa)

faiato, spike (v)
faifa, sigh (n)
faifo, sigh (v)
faika, spite (n)
faiko, spite (v)
faiku, spiteful (adj)
faitago, mangle (v)
faitesho, maul (v)
falafa, urine (n)
falafata, urinal (n)
falafekuita, urology (n)
falafekuitua, urologist (n doer)
falafika, urination (n)
falafiko, urinate (v)
falafikua, urinator (n doer)
falafu, urinary (adj)
falathu, seldom (adj/adv)
faleporugo, kidnap (v)
faleporugua, kidnapper (n doer)
faliapa, wheelbarrow (n)
falifa, steer (n d:cattle)
falika, rash (n)
falikiu, rashly (adv)
faliku, rash (adj)
falima, stream (n)
falimeroifo, streamline (v)
falimo, stream (v)
falimua, streamer (n doer)
falina, kid (n d:child)
falipa, urb (n)
falipo, urbanize (v)
falipu, urban (adj)
falipueta, urbanization (n)
falira, roll (n d:tumble)
falirafena, rollover (n)
falirevaka, rollback (n)
faliro, roll (v d:tumble)
falirua, roller (n doer d:tumble)
faliruila, rollout (n)
famesherana, bedroom (n)
fanafa, bag (n)
fanafara, baggage (n)
fanafaro, baggage (v)
fanafarua, baggager (n doer)
fanafiu, baggily (adv)
fanafo, bag (v)
fanafu, baggy (adj)
fanafua, bagger (n doer)
fanina, wood (n)
faninekiafa, woodhouse (n)
faninekioka, woodwork (n)
faninekioko, woodwork (v)
faninekiokua, woodworker (n
  doer)
faninepelona, woodman (n)
faninepelona, woodsman (n)
faninepeloni, woodmen (n pl)
faninepeloni, woodsmen (n pl)
fanineraupa, woodland (n)
fanineraupu, woodlands (adj)
faninethilofa, woodshed (n)
faninu, wooden (adj)
fanita, patron (n)

fanito, patronize (v)
fanitua, patronizer (n doer)
fanituna, patriot (n)
fanituniu, patriotically (adv)
fanitunu, patriotic (adj)
fapo, ask (v)
fapua, asker (n doer)
fareigaika, snakebite (n)
fareika, snake (n)
fareiko, snake (v)
fareiku, snakey (adj)
fareishika, serpent (n)
fareishiku, serpentine (adj)
farina, cinema (n)
fashika, faction (n)
fateta, mallet (n)
fatha, gap (n)
fatho, gap (v)
fatuka, cult (n)
fatupa, cultivation (n)
fatupo, cultivate (v)
fatupua, cultivator (n doer)
faudanapo, succumb (v)
faufa, buffer (n d:absorber)
faufo, buffer (v d:absorber)
fauina, virus (n)
fauini, virii (n pl)
fauini, viruses (n pl)
fauiniu, virally (adv)
fauinu, viral (adj)
fauinueta, virulence (n)
fauinuetiu, virulently (adv)
fauinuetu, virulent (adj)
faupo, suck (v)
faupua, sucker (n doer)
faupuano, sucker (v)
faupueta, suction (n)
faupueto, suction (v)
fausha, narcism (n)
fausha, narcissism (n)
taushoka, narcotic (n)
faushu, narcissistic (adj)
faushu, narcistic (adj)
faushua, narcissist (n doer)
faushua, narcist (n doer)
fazha, bur (n)
fefio, mumbles (v pa)
fefo, mumble (v)
fefua, mumbler (n doer)
feia, F (let sng)
feianiu, sparsely (adv)
feianu, sparse (adj)
feifa, show (n)
feifeberesha, showplace (n)
feifekelera, showgirl (n)
feifepelona, showman (n)
feifepelonefifa, showmanship (n)
feifepeloni, showmen (n pl)
feifeshekoba, showboat (n)
feifeshekobo, showboat (v)
feifesherana, showroom (n)
feifeshuata, showcase (n)
feifeshuato, showcase (v)

feifethetisha, showpiece (n)
feifethetisho, showpiece (v)
feifetiena, showdown (n)
feifiauna, clemency (n)
feifiaunu, clement (adj)
feifo, show (v)
feifu, showy (adj)
feigala, poker (n d:game)
feihem, Number_1e2106
feikada, vodka (n)
feili, Fs (let pl)
feirana, violet (n)
feiranu, violet (adj)
feiruga, ghost (n)
feirugo, ghost (v)
feirugu, ghostly (adj)
feisha, gust (n)
feisho, gust (v)
feishu, gusty (adj)
feitago, mingle (v)
feizhaka, murder (n)
feizhakiu, murderously (adv)
feizhako, murder (v)
feizhaku, murderous (adj)
feizhakua, murderer (n doer)
fekavata, platter (n)
fekiaku, vincible (adj)
fekilotu, negligible (adj)
fekita, neglect (n)
fekita, negligence (n)
fekitiu, neglectfully (adv)
fekitiu, negligently (adv)
fekito, neglect (v)
fekitu, neglectful (adj)
fekitu, negligent (adj)
felabikana, flack (n)
felada, clap (n)
felado, clap (v)
felafa, cloth (n)
felafiki, clothes (n pl)
felafo, clothe (v)
felaima, tunnel (n)
felaimo, tunnel (v)
felaimua, tunneler (n doer)
felaisha, worth (n)
felaishauku, worthwhile (adj)
felaishemenu, worthless (adj)
felaishu, worthy (adj)
felaitha, past (n)
felaneñfa, neighborhood (n)
felanefifa, nieghbourhood (n)
felanifa, album (n)
felanipa, bang (n d:hair)
felanisha, pane (n)
felanitiu, frankly (adv)
felanitu, frank (adj)
felanuda, neighbor (n)
felanuda, neighbour (n)
felanudo, neighbor (v)
felanudu, neighborly (adj)
felarima, dance (n)
felarimo, dance (v)

felarimua, dancer (n doer)
felarina, front (n)
felarinata, frontier (n)
felarineroifa, frontline (n)
felarino, front (v)
felaripa, aid (n)
felaripo, aid (v)
felaripua, aide (n doer)
felarita, aim (n)
felaritha, draft (n)
felaritho, draft (v)
felarithu, drafty (adj)
felarithua, drafter (n doer)
felarito, aim (v)
felaritomeniu, aimlessly (adv)
felaritomenu, aimless (adj)
felaruzha, bird (n)
felateka, bladder (n)
felatha, slate (n)
felatho, slate (v)
felaufa, frailty (n)
felauferifa, livestock (n)
felaufika, delivery (n)
felaufikara, deliverance (n)
felaufiko, deliver (v)
felaufikua, deliverer (n doer)
felaufitako, liven (v)
felaufiteferepiu, livably (adv)
felaufiteferepu, livable (adj)
felaufitefifa, livelihood (n)
felaufitiu, lively (adv)
felaufito, live (v)
felaufitu, live (adj)
felaufu, frail (adj)
felaugaitiu, lividly (adv)
felaugaitu, livid (adj)
felauka, smack (n)
felauko, smack (v)
felauma, dream (n)
felaumio, dreamt (v pa)
felaumiu, dreamily (adv)
felaumo, dream (v)
felaumu, dreamy (adj)
felaumua, dreamer (n doer)
felaupa, bong (n d:sound)
felaupo, bong (v d:sound)
felausha, life (n)
felaushebeleisha, lifespan (n)
felaushedauna, lifetime (n)
felausheferiafa, lifestyle (n)
felaushekoba, lifeboat (n)
felausheliroda, lifeblood (n)
felausherazhu, lifelong (adj)
felaushereiku, lifelike (adj)
felausheroifa, lifeline (n)
felaushevaifika, lifeguard (n)
felaushezhupo, lifesave (v)
felaushezhupua, lifesaver (n doer)
felaushu, life (adj)
felaushua, lifer (n doer)
felava, brag (n)
felavo, brag (v)
felebo, cope (v)

felefa, ease (n)
felefiu, easily (adv)
felefo, ease (v)
felefu, easy (adj)
felefwaku, easiest (adj)
felefwelu, easier (adj)
felega, lug (n)
felegara, luggage (n)
felego, lug (v)
felegua, lugger (n doer)
feleida, breed (n)
feleido, breed (v)
feleidua, breeder (n doer)
feleifa, breeze (n)
feleifana, prose (n)
feleifo, breeze (v)
feleifu, breezy (adj)
feleiga, glance (n)
feleigo, glance (v)
feleina, compassion (n)
feleinosha, compatibility (n)
feleinoshiu, compatibly (adv)
feleinoshu, compatible (adj)
feleinu, compassionate (adj)
feleisha, passion (n)
feleishiu, passionately (adv)
feleishu, passionate (adj)
feleita, shyness (n)
feleitha, vein (n)
feleithu, venous (adj)
feleito, shy (v)
feleitu, shy (adj)
feleivuta, property (n)
felekio, shut (v pa)
feleko, shut (v)
felekotiena, shutdown (n)
feleku, shut (adj)
felekuana, shutter (n)
felekuano, shutter (v)
felekuila, shutout (n)
felenekelofio, peacekept (v pa)
felenekelofo, peacekeep (v)
felenekelofua, peacekeeper (n
   doer)
felenipa, bluff (n)
felenipo, bluff (v)
felenipua, bluffer (n doer)
felenisha, credibility (n)
felenishu, credible (adj)
felenishueta, credential (n)
felenita, credit (n)
felenito, credit (v)
felenitua, creditor (n doer)
felenuda, peace (n)
felenudauna, peacetime (n)
felenudaunu, peacetime (adj)
felenudenagua, peacemaker (n
   doer)
felenudiu, peacefully (adv)
felenudu, peaceful (adj)
felepa, tub (n)
felesha, compartment (n)
felesho, compartmentalize (v)

feleta, wisp (n)
feletha, plasma (n)
feleto, wisp (v)
feleva, ship (n)
felevekarubaka, shipwreck (n)
felevekarubako, shipwreck (v)
felevelena, shipmate (n)
felevelurita, shipload (n)
felevepelona, shipman (n)
felevepeloni, shipmen (n pl)
felevethautha, shipyard (n)
felevetheifua, shipowner (n doer)
felevo, ship (v)
felevoritua, shipbuilder (n doer)
felevua, shipper (n doer)
felevueta, shipment (n)
feliafa, crawl (n)
feliafo, crawl (v)
feliafua, crawler (n doer)
feliaka, sweep (n)
feliakio, swept (v pa)
feliako, sweep (v)
feliakua, sweeper (n doer)
feliama, munchy (n)
feliamo, munch (v)
feliana, famile (n)
feliano, familiarize (v)
felianu, familiar (adj)
felianua, family (n doer)
feliasha, cleft (n d:split)
feliashio, clove (v pa d:split)
feliasho, cleave (v d:split)
feliashua, cleaver (n doer d:split)
feliata, tier (n)
feliatha, rose (n)
feliathepoapa, rosebud (n)
feliathu, rosy (adj)
feliato, tier (v)
feliaupa, swab (n)
feliaupo, swab (v)
feliaura, leisure (n)
feliauru, leisurely (adj)
felida, deed (n)
feliefa, whisper (n)
feliefo, whisper (v)
feliefua, whisperer (n doer)
feliega, swing (n)
feliegio, swung (v pa)
feliego, swing (v)
feliegua, swinger (n doer)
feliena, calm (n)
felieniu, calmly (adv)
felieno, calm (v)
felienu, calm (adj)
feliesho, slither (v)
felieta, whistle (n)
felieto, whistle (v)
felietua, whistler (n doer)
felifianu, fallopian (adj)
felifiu, slightly (adv)
felifo, slight (v)
felifopa, specie (n)
felifopana, specimen (n)

felifu, slight (adj)
felikafita, specific (n)
felikata, specification (n)
felikatiu, specifically (adv)
felikato, specify (v)
felikatu, specific (adj)
felila, tallness (n)
felilu, tall (adj)
felima, humor (n)
felimiu, humorously (adv)
felimo, humor (v)
felimu, humorous (adj)
felimua, humorist (n doer)
felina, brightness (n)
felinata, humility (n)
felinato, humiliate (v)
felinatueta, humiliation (n)
felinifa, gem (n)
felinifebarafa, gemstone (n)
feliniu, brightly (adv)
felino, brighten (v)
felinoka, slot (n)
felinoko, slot (v)
felinu, bright (adj)
felinua, brightener (n doer)
felinwaku, brightest (adj)
felinwelu, brighter (adj)
felioda, crew (n)
feliofa, proof (n)
feliofeliapio, proofread (v pa)
feliofeliapo, proof (v)
feliofeliapo, proofread (v)
feliofeliapua, proofreader (n doer)
feliofo, prove (v)
feliofu, provable (adj)
feliofua, prover (n doer)
felioma, cosmos (n)
feliomu, cosmic (adj)
feliomua, cosmopolitan (n doer)
feliona, crayon (n)
felipa, rasp (n)
felipo, rasp (v)
felipu, raspy (adj)
felira, story (n)
felirepelorika, storyboard (n)
felirepedetua, storyteller (n doer)
felirevonuda, storybook (n)
feliroifa, storyline (n)
felisha, grass (n)
felishasho, graze (v d:feed)
felishashua, grazer (n doer d:feed)
felisheraupa, grassland (n)
felishokiu, imminently (adv)
felishoku, imminent (adj)
felishwifuala, grasshopper (n)
felishwifualu, grassy (adj)
felitho, graze (v d:scrape)
felitio, brought (v pa)
felito, bring (v)
feliu, very (adv)
feliufa, prayer (n)
feliufo, pray (v)

feliufua, prayer (n doer)
feliuko, whittle (v)
feliukua, whittler (n doer)
feliunota, tribulation (n)
feliunoto, tribulate (v)
feliupa, fret (n d:strip)
feliupo, fret (v d:strip)
feliusha, tidiness (n)
feliushiu, tidily (adv)
feliusho, tidy (v)
feliushu, tidy (adj)
feliuta, praise (n)
feliutha, plume (n)
feliutho, plume (v)
feliuthueta, plumage (n)
feliuto, praise (v)
feliutua, praiser (n doer)
feliuvana, tribune (n)
feloiga, proximity (n)
feloigua, proxy (n doer)
feloika, ditch (n)
feloiko, ditch (v)
feloipa, frog (n)
feloita, pencil (n)
feloito, pencil (v)
felokiu, perhaps (adv)
felonapiu, humbly (adv)
felonapo, humble (v)
felonapu, humble (adj)
feloreta, aviation (n)
feloretu, aviatic (adj)
feloretua, aviator (n doer)
Feloridafa, Florida (n)
Felorina, Fluorine (n)
felosha, stray (n)
felosho, stray (v)
feloshu, stray (adj)
feluafiu, deliciously (adv)
feluafu, delicious (adj)
feluaika, creep (n)
feluaikio, crept (v pa)
feluaikiu, creepily (adv)
feluaiko, creep (v)
feluaiku, creepy (adj)
feluaikua, creeper (n doer)
feluaka, cripple (n)
feluako, cripple (v)
feluala, sail (n)
felualeshekoba, sailboat (n)
felualo, sail (v)
felualua, sailor (n doer)
feluana, light (n d:lumen)
feluanekiafa, lighthouse (n)
feluanio, lit (v pa d:lumen)
feluano, light (v d:lumen)
feluanua, lighter (n doer d:lumen)
feluasha, delight (n)
feluasho, delight (v)
feluashu, delightful (adj)
feluatha, illumination (n)
feluathiu, luminously (adv)
feluatho, illuminate (v)
feluathu, luminous (adj)

feluathua, illuminator (n doer)
felufa, chimney (n)
feluga, scum (n)
feluika, wisdom (n)
feluikiu, wisely (adv)
feluiko, wisen (v)
feluiku, wise (adj)
feluikua, wizard (n doer)
feluikuana, wizardry (n)
feluikuano, wizen (v)
feluikuniva, wiseguy (n)
feluikupelona, wiseman (n)
feluikupeloni, wisemen (n pl)
feluikutherapa, wisecrack (n)
feluma, shape (n)
felumegeruda, shepherd (n)
felumegerudi, shepherd (n pl)
felumegerudo, shepherd (v)
felumenu, shapeless (adj)
felumiu, shapely (adv)
felumo, shape (v)
felumua, shaper (n doer)
feluna, brilliance (n)
felunaka, lightning (n)
felunaku, lightning (adj)
felunita, shard (n)
feluniu, brilliantly (adv)
felunu, brilliant (adj)
felupa, chute (n)
felupo, chute (v)
feluripa, sculpture (n)
feluripiu, sculpturally (adv)
feluripo, sculpt (v)
feluripu, sculptural (adj)
feluripua, sculptor (n doer)
felurita, overload (n)
felurito, overload (v)
feluritua, overloader (n doer)
felutha, plum (n)
feluzha, cliff (n)
fenafita, harness (n)
fenafito, harness (v)
fenaiga, brain (n)
fenaigebiorita, brainpower (n)
fenaigefiausho, brainwash (v)
fenaigeluara, brainchild (n)
fenaigemenu, brainless (adj)
fenaigesha, brainwave (n)
fenaigu, brainy (adj)
fenaiguvata, brainstorm (n)
fenaiguvato, brainstorm (v)
fenaikika, frenzy (n)
fenaikikiu, frantically (adv)
fenaikiko, frenzy (v)
fenaikiku, frantic (adj)
fenaikiku, frenetic (adj)
fenaipa, brand (n)
fenaipo, brand (v)
fenaito, brandish (v)
fenaritho, scathe (v)
fenauka, wrong (n)
fenauketika, wrongdoing (n)
fenauketikua, wrongdoer (n doer)

fenaukiu, wrongfully (adv)
fenaukiu, wrongly (adv)
fenauko, wrong (v)
fenauku, wrong (adj)
fenauku, wrongful (adj)
fenaukueta, wrongness (n)
fenauna, blur (n)
fenauniu, blurrily (adv)
fenauno, blur (v)
fenaunu, blurry (adj)
fenautha, crouch (n)
fenautho, crouch (v)
fenauto, blurt (v)
feneiga, enemy (n)
feneipiu, bluntly (adv)
feneipo, blunt (v)
feneipu, blunt (adj)
fenifoka, splash (n)
fenifoko, splash (v)
fenifoku, splashy (adj)
fenifokua, splasher (n doer)
fenika, skip (n)
fenikao, skipped (v prp)
feniko, skip (v)
fenilota, skirt (n)
feniloto, skirt (v)
fenipa, mill (n)
fenipo, mill (v)
fenipua, miller (n doer)
fenirafa, snob (n)
fenirafo, snob (v)
fenirafu, snobby (adj)
fenirafueta, snobbery (n)
fenishiu, particularly (adv)
fenishu, particular (adj)
fenishula, particular (n)
fenito, scatter (v)
fenoila, trim (n)
fenoilo, trim (v)
fenoilua, trimmer (n doer)
fenoipa, blunder (n)
fenoipo, blunder (v)
fenorifa, pregnancy (n)
fenorifu, pregnant (adj)
fenorika, impregnation (n)
fenoriko, impregnate (v)
fenoruta, scalp (n)
fenorutata, scalpel (n)
fenoruto, scalp (v)
fenorutua, scalper (n doer)
tenupa, wrap (n)
fenupo, wrap (v)
fenupobelaitha, wraparound (n)
fenupua, wrapper (n doer)
fenuta, fork (n)
fenuterauka, forklift (n)
fenutiu, forkily (adv)
fenuto, fork (v)
fenutu, forky (adj)
fenutua, forker (n doer)
fepiga, stab (n)
fepigo, stab (v)
fepigua, stabber (n doer)

fepio, set (v pa d:place)
fepo, set (v d:place)
fepua, setter (n doer d:place)
feraba, trade (n)
ferabepelona, tradesman (n)
ferabepeloni, tradesmen (n pl)
ferabeshetata, trademark (n)
ferabeshetato, trademark (v)
ferabiu, tradably (adv)
ferabo, trade (v)
ferabu, tradable (adj)
ferabua, trader (n doer)
ferabunefa, tradeoff (n)
ferafa, bra (n)
feraifa, extreme (n)
feraifana, extremity (n)
feraifiu, extremely (adv)
feraifu, extreme (adj)
feraifua, extremist (n doer)
feraiga, plaster (n)
feraigo, plaster (v)
feraiguta, plastic (n)
feraiguto, plasticize (v)
feraigutua, plasticizer (n doer)
feraika, badness (n)
feraikeko, worst (v)
feraikeku, worst (adj)
feraikelo, worsen (v)
feraikelu, worse (adj)
feraikiu, badly (adv)
feraiku, bad (adj)
ferailoka, trend (n)
ferailoko, trend (v)
ferailoku, trendy (adj)
feraima, blond (n)
feraimu, blond (adj)
feraimua, blonde (n doer)
feraina, mockery (n)
ferainefelaruzha, mockingbird (n)
feraino, mock (v)
feraipa, worry (n)
feraipo, worry (v)
feraipu, worrisome (adj)
feraipua, worrier (n doer)
feraisha, excellence (n)
feraishiaka, extravagance (n)
feraishiakiu, extravagantly (adv)
feraishiaku, extravagant (adj)
feraishiakua, extrovert (n doer)
feraishiu, excellently (adv)
feraishu, excel (v)
feraishu, excellent (adj)
feraka, ugliness (n)
feraku, ugly (adj)
ferala, cell (n)
feralifota, democracy (n)
feralifotiu, democratically (adv)
feralifotu, democratic (adj)
feralifotua, democrat (n doer)
feralika, cellar (n)
feralina, blind (n)
feralino, blind (v)
feralipa, celebration (n)

feralipo, celebrate (v)
feralipua, celebrity (n doer)
feralisha, cement (n)
feralisho, cement (v)
feraliu, cellularly (adv)
feralu, cellular (adj)
feraluma, coalescence (n)
feralumo, coalesce (v)
feralumu, coalescent (adj)
feramina, coalition (n)
feramino, coalite (v)
Feranasha, French (n)
feranifa, burro (n)
feranifota, delay (n)
feranifoto, delay (v)
feranifotua, delayer (n doer)
Feranikofurita, Frankfurt (n)
Feranishafa, France (n)
feranita, lay (n d:place)
feranitara, layer (n)
feranitaro, layer (v)
feranitio, laid (v pa d:place)
feranito, lay (v d:place)
feranituila, layout (n)
feranitunifa, layoff (n)
Feranoshiuma, Francium (n)
ferashipa, cattle (n)
feraufa, mouth (n)
feraufethetisha, mouthpiece (n)
feraufiausha, mouthwash (n)
feraufiu, mouthfully (adv)
feraufo, mouth (v)
feraufu, mouthful (adj)
ferauga, fright (n)
feraugala, thrush (n)
feraugiu, frightfully (adv)
feraugo, frighten (v)
feraugu, frightful (adj)
feraugua, frightener (n doer)
ferauka, sag (n)
ferauko, sag (v)
ferauma, swarm (n)
feraumo, swarm (v)
feraupa, fry (n)
feraupo, fry (v)
feraupua, frier (n doer)
feraupua, fryer (n doer)
feraushekioshika, blowtorch (n)
feraushekioshiko, blowtorch (v)
feraushio, blew (v pa d:air)
fedaraushio, blow (v d:air)
feraushua, blower (n doer d:air)
ferauta, blurb (n)
ferauto, blurb (v)
ferava, tremble (n)
feravina, tremor (n)
feravino, tremor (v)
feravinokiu, tremendously (adv)
feravinoku, tremendous (adj)
feravo, tremble (v)
feravua, trembler (n doer)
feravuna, cortex (n)
ferazha, thaw (n)

ferazho, thaw (v)
ferefika, swiftness (n)
ferefikiu, swiftly (adv)
ferefiku, swift (adj)
fereiaufo, plop (v)
fereiaupo, plod (v)
fereifa, cape (n)
fereifua, caper (n doer)
fereigo, faze (v)
fereilasha, buddy (n)
fereipo, drench (v)
fereithio, felt (v pa)
fereitho, feel (v)
fereithu, feely (adj)
fereithua, feeler (n doer)
Fereiviula, Friday (n)
ferela, swirl (n)
ferelika, skillet (n)
ferelisha, swish (n)
ferelisho, swish (v)
ferelishua, swisher (n doer)
ferelo, swirl (v)
ferema, smoothness (n)
feremiu, smoothly (adv)
feremo, smooth (v)
feremu, smooth (adj)
feremua, smoother (n doer)
ferenika, pitcher (n d:container)
ferenita, native (n)
ferenitiu, natively (adv)
ferenitu, native (adj)
ferepa kodi, can (ndal d:ability)
ferepa kodi, could (ndal d:ability)
ferepa kodi, could have (ndal
   d:ability)
ferepa, ability (n)
ferepiu, ably (adv)
ferepo, enable (v)
ferepu, able (adj)
ferepua, enabler (n doer)
feriafa, style (n)
feriafana, stylus (n)
feriafani, styli (n pl)
feriafiu, stylishly (adv)
feriafo, style (v)
feriafu, stylish (adj)
feriafua, stylist (n doer)
feriaifa, sky (n)
feriaifekeladipua, skyscraper (n
   doer)
feriaifekeraika, skydive (n)
feriaifekeraiko, skydive (v)
feriaifekeraikua, skydiver (n doer)
feriaifeluana, skylight (n)
feriaiferoifa, skyline (n)
feriaifezhiarito, skyrocket (v)
feriaifiu, skywardly (adv)
feriaifo, sky (v)
feriaifu, skyward (adj)
feriaka, smut (n)
feriala, plea (n)
ferialo, plead (v)
ferialua, pleader (n doer)

ferianiko, skimp (v)
ferianiku, skimpy (adj)
feriano, skim (v)
ferianua, skimmer (n doer)
feriapa, fret (n d:worry)
feriapo, fret (v d:worry)
feriasho, kindle (v)
feriata, pamphlet (n)
feriaufa, maw (n)
feriauka, smirk (n)
feriauko, smirk (v)
feriava, divinity (n)
feriaviu, divinely (adv)
feriavo, divine (v)
feriavu, divine (adj)
feriazha, orgasm (n)
feriazhaka, orgy (n)
feriazhu, orgasmic (adj)
fericka, stinginess (n d:frugal)
ferieku, stingy (adj d:frugal)
feriemu, sleek (adj)
ferieta, slack (n d:pants)
ferietha, slough (n)
ferietho, slough (v)
ferifa, stock (n d:fill equity)
ferifana, stocking (n d:sock)
ferifekerolipua, stockbroker (n
   doer)
ferifenaipa, stockpile (n)
ferifenaipo, stockpile (v)
ferifepelona, stockman (n)
ferifepeloni, stockmen (n pl)
ferifesherana, stockroom (n)
ferifethorithua, stockholder (n
   doer)
ferifo, stock (v d:fill equity)
ferifu, stocky (adj d:fill equity)
ferifua, stocker (n doer d:fill
   equity)
feriga, swindle (n)
ferigo, swindle (v)
ferigua, swindler (n doer)
ferikata, staunch (n)
ferikato, staunch (v)
ferikatu, staunch (adj)
ferilaka, allowance (n)
ferilako, allow (v)
ferilaku, allowable (adj)
ferilopa, pleasure (n)
ferilopiu, pleasantly (adv)
ferilopo, please (v)
ferilopu, pleasant (adj)
ferilopua, pleaser (n doer)
ferilota, organization (n
   d:structure)
ferilotata, organism (n)
feriloto, organize (v d:structure)
ferilotu, organizational (adj
   d:structure)
ferilotua, organizer (n doer
   d:structure)
ferima, ally (n)
ferimara, alliance (n)

ferimo, ally (v)
ferina, smile (n)
ferinifa, hitch (n)
ferinifo, hitch (v)
ferinifua, hitcher (n doer)
ferinifwiasho, hitchhike (v)
ferinifwiashua, hitchhiker (n doer)
ferino, smile (v)
ferinua, smiley (n doer)
ferioka, witness (n)
ferioko, witness (v)
ferioma, gloom (n)
feriomiu, gloomily (adv)
feriomu, gloomy (adj)
feripa, storm (n)
feripo, storm (v)
feripu, stormy (adj)
ferisha, smudge (n)
ferisho, smudge (v)
ferishoka, immensity (n)
ferishokiu, immensely (adv)
ferishoku, immense (adj)
ferita, skit (n)
feritha, hit (n)
ferithio, hit (v pa)
feritho, hit (v)
ferithua, hitter (n doer)
feriugo, plunk (v)
feriukiu, chronically (adv)
feriuku, chronic (adj)
feriunaka, fugitive (n)
feriuno, flee (v)
feriunua, fleer (n doer)
feriusha, plunge (n)
feriusho, plunge (v)
feriushua, plunger (n doer)
ferodatha, autumn (n)
ferodatha, fall (n d:autumn)
ferodathu, autumnal (adj)
ferofu, organic (adj d:of life)
feroifa, sweat (n d:perspiration)
feroifelifada, sweatshirt (n)
feroifethofa, sweatshop (n)
feroifo, sweat (v d:perspiration)
feroifu, sweaty (adj d:perspiration)
feroika, swear (n)
feroikio, swore (v pa)
feroiko, swear (v)
ferolkua, swearer (n doer)
feroipa, pity (n)
feroipameniu, pitilessly (adv)
feroipamenu, pitiless (adj)
feroipara, pittance (n)
feroipiu, pitifully (adv)
feroipo, pity (v)
feroipu, pitiful (adj)
feroita, breech (n)
Feromiuma, Fermium (n)
feropa, organ (n d:body part)
ferota, chord (n)
feruama, snug (n)

feruamito, snuggle (v)
feruamiu, snugly (adv)
feruamo, snug (v)
feruamu, snug (adj)
feruata, plot (n)
feruato, plot (v)
feruatua, plotter (n doer)
feruba, rip (n)
ferubo, rip (v)
ferubua, ripper (n doer)
ferubunefa, ripoff (n)
ferufa, riff (n)
ferufita, rift (n)
feruga, pledge (n)
ferugo, pledge (v)
feruiberanita, playground (n)
feruifa, play (n)
feruifanitiu, ludicrously (adv)
feruifanitu, ludicrous (adj)
feruifebiuna, playboy (n)
feruifedizha, plaything (n)
feruifekiafa, playhouse (n)
feruifelena, playmate (n)
feruifenagua, playmaker (n doer)
feruiferepu, playable (adj)
feruifesherana, playroom (n)
feruifevaka, playback (n)
feruifevonuda, playbook (n)
feruifiu, playfully (adv)
feruifo, play (v)
feruifu, playful (adj)
feruifua, player (n doer)
feruifueta, playfulness (n)
feruifunefa, playoff (n)
feruina, display (n)
feruino, display (v)
feruinoka, dab (n)
feruinoko, dab (v)
feruinoriko, dabble (v)
feruinorikua, dabbler (n doer)
ferula, summer (n)
feruledauna, summertime (n)
feruma, blue (n)
ferumu, blue (adj)
feruna, rice (n)
ferunelipa, blueberry (n)
ferupa, sweetness (n)
ferupara, sweetie (n)
ferupedarala, sweetheart (n)
ferupiu, sweetly (adv)
ferupo, sweeten (v)
ferupu, sweet (adj)
ferupua, sweetener (n doer)
ferusha, river (n)
ferushefelarina, riverfront (n)
ferushekefita, riverhead (n)
ferushekoba, riverboat (n)
ferushepelara, riverbank (n)
ferushoita, riverside (n)
ferutha, blush (n)
ferutho, blush (v)
fesha, part (n)
feshana, portrait (n)

feshata, partial (n)
feshatiu, partially (adv)
feshatu, partial (adj)
fesheika, participle (n)
feshelika, participation (n)
fesheliko, participate (v)
feshelikua, participant (n doer)
feshetugo, parse (v)
feshetugua, parser (n doer)
feshiama, portrayal (n)
feshiamo, portray (v)
feshika, impartiality (n)
feshikiu, impartially (adv)
feshiko, impart (v)
feshiku, impartial (adj)
feshinata, partnership (n)
feshinato, partner (v)
feshinatua, partner (n doer)
feshipa, particle (n)
feshipa, particulate (n)
feshipo, particulate (v)
feshipu, particulate (n)
feshiu, partly (adv)
feshiufa, portfolio (n)
fesho, part (v)
feshota, departure (n)
feshoto, depart (v)
feshotua, departer (n doer)
feshueta, partition (n)
feshueto, partition (v)
fetagelurita, truckload (n)
fetaipa, entitlement (n)
fetaipo, entitle (v)
fetaipua, entitler (n doer)
fetipa, arrow (n)
fetiva, levitation (n)
fetiva, levity (n)
fetivo, levitate (v)
fetivua, levitator (n doer)
fezha, portion (n)
fiaba, peep (n)
fiabo, peep (v)
fiada, beauty (n)
fiadiu, beautifully (adv)
fiado, beautify (v)
fiadu, beautiful (adj)
fiafa, peer (n)
fiafo, peer (v)
fiaisha, vision (n)
fiaishana, visual (n)
fiaishaniu, visually (adv)
fiaishano, visualize (v)
fiaishanu, visual (adj)
fiaishanueta, visualization (n)
fiaishiu, visibly (adv)
fiaisho, envision (v)
fiaishu, visible (adj)
fiaishua, visionary (n doer)
fiaishueta, visibility (n)
fiaka, yard (n d:measurement)
fiakeshineta, yardstick (n)
fiakueta, yardage (n d:measurement)

fialita, sump (n)
fialitiu, sumptuously (adv)
fialitu, sumptuous (adj)
fialoifa, fiddle (n d:violin)
fialoifo, fiddle (v d:violin)
fialoifua, fiddler (n doer d:violin)
fiamo, kid (v d:joke)
Fianetha, EhoMonth06 (n)
fianipa, swamp (n)
fianipo, swamp (v)
fianipu, swampy (adj)
fianita, pattern (n)
fianito, pattern (v)
fiapa, peek (n)
fiapo, peek (v)
fiarepelona, freshman (n)
fiarepeloni, freshmen (n pl)
fiarifa, freshness (n)
fiarifeidona, freshwater (n)
fiarifeidonu, freshwater (adj)
fiarifiu, freshly (adv)
fiarifo, freshen (v)
fiarifu, fresh (adj)
fiarigo, vet (v d:examine)
fiasha, flame (n)
fiashekara, flair (n)
fiashekata, flagrancy (n)
fiashekatiu, flagrantly (adv)
fiashekatu, flagrant (adj)
fiasho, flame (v)
fiasho, inflame (v)
fiashu, flammable (adj)
fiashu, inflammable (adj)
fiashua, flamer (n doer)
fiashueta, inflamation (n)
fiashuetu, inflammatory (adj)
fiatako, pant (v d:breathe)
fiatha, flare (n)
fiatho, flare (v)
fiaumeniu, mercilessly (adv)
fiaumenu, merciless (adj)
fiauna, mercy (n)
fiauniu, mercifully (adv)
fiaunu, merciful (adj)
fiausha, wash (n d:clean)
fiaushefelafa, washcloth (n)
fiausheferepiu, washably (adv)
fiausheferepu, washable (adj)
fiaushepelorika, washboard (n)
fiausherana, washroom (n)
fiausho, wash (v d:clean)
fiaushu, washy (adj d:clean)
fiaushua, washer (n doer d:clean)
fiaushuila, washout (n)
fiava, vet (n d:veterinarian)
fiavata, veterinarian (n)
fiavatu, veterinary (adj)
fiduraka, philosophy (n)
fidurakua, philosopher (n doer)
fiefa, cat (n)
fiefu, catty (adj)
fiega, pang (n)
fielileta, stint (n)

fielileto, stint (v)
fielisha, scarlet (n)
fielishu, scarlet (adj)
fienara, loneliness (n)
fienaru, lonely (adj)
fienu, lone (adj)
fienua, loner (n doer)
fiesha, red (n)
fiesheiku, reddish (adj)
fieshekefita, redhead (n)
fiesheroifa, redline (n)
fiesheroifo, redline (v)
fieshethariba, redneck (n)
fiesho, redden (v)
fieshu, red (adj)
fieshueta, redness (n)
fietisha, stitch (n)
fietisho, stitch (v)
fifafa, kitty (n)
fifepa, ripple (n)
fifepo, ripple (v)
fifima, kitten (n)
fikafa, plate (n)
fikafo, plate (v)
fikafua, plater (n doer)
fikanika, cramp (n)
fikaniko, cramp (v)
fikavona, platform (n)
fikokeruga, protagony (n)
fikokerugo, protagonize (v)
fikokerugu, protagonistic (adj)
fikokerugua, protagonist (n doer)
fikoleta, screen (n)
fikoleteferuifa, screenplay (n)
fikoleteloidua, screenwriter (n doer)
fikoleto, screen (v)
fikoletua, screener (n doer)
fikuita, catalog (n)
fikuito, catalog (v)
fikuitua, cataloger (n doer)
fikuta, shuttle (n)
fikuto, shuttle (v)
filada, vamp (n)
Filadelofifa, Philadelphia (n)
filidarifa, polygraph (n)
filidarifu, polygraphic (adj)
filimesha, polymer (n)
filimesho, polymerize (v)
filimuka, polygon (n)
filimuki, polygon (n pl)
filimuku, polygonal (adj)
Filipifa, Philippine (n)
filiuyapa, polyphony (n)
filiuyapu, polyphonic (adj)
filivulana, polygamy (n)
filodaufa, vampire (n)
filofa, butter (n)
filofo, butter (v)
filofu, buttery (adj)
filotapa, kettle (n)
filuna, ballad (n)
filunua, balladeer (n doer)

filushoka, butterfly (n)
fimala, evening (n d:late daytime)
fimara, eve (n)
fina, phi (n)
finaka, spit (n)
finakio, spat (v pa)
finako, spit (v)
finakua, spitter (n doer)
finana, skinniness (n)
finanu, skinny (adj)
finapa, skin (n)
finapekefita, skinhead (n)
finapo, skin (v)
finapua, skinner (n doer)
Finelanuda, Finland (n)
Fineshoka, Phoenix (n)
fineta, stead (n)
finetezhaisha, steadfastness (n)
finetezhaishiu, steadfastly (adv)
finetezhaishu, steadfast (adj)
finetiu, steadily (adv)
fineto, steady (v)
finetu, steady (adj)
finetueta, steadiness (n)
finorika, scallop (n)
finoriko, scallop (v)
finuina, cello (n)
finuto, ream (v d:clear)
finutua, reamer (n doer d:clear)
fioba, oval (n)
fiobala, ellipse (n)
fiobalu, elliptical (adj)
fiofa, loyalty (n)
fiofiu, loyally (adv)
fiofonuda, frequency (n)
fiofonudiu, frequently (adv)
fiofonudo, frequent (v)
fiofonudu, frequent (adj)
fiofu, loyal (adj)
fioka, tool (n)
fiokapeluda, toolkit (n)
fiokeperenika, toolbox (n)
fioko, tool (v)
fioma, loom (n)
fiona, poem (n)
fionika, callus (n)
fiorika, freeze (n)
fiorikio, froze (v pa)
fioriko, freeze (v)
fiorikua, freezer (n doer)
fiorisha, calico (n)
fiorishu, calico (adj)
fiorita, frost (n)
fioritegaika, frostbite (n)
fioritiu, frostily (adv)
fiorito, frost (v)
fioritu, frosty (adj)
fioritua, froster (n doer)
fioruba, frustration (n)
fiorubo, frustrate (v)
fiosha, freedom (n)
fioshekapa, freehand (n)
fioshelurito, freeload (v)

fiosheluritua, freeloader (n doer)
fioshepeliola, freeway (n)
fioshevorina, freeform (n)
fioshevorinu, freeform (adj)
fioshiu, freely (adv)
fiosho, free (v)
fioshosha, freebie (n)
fioshu, free (adj)
fiota, poetry (n)
fiotu, poetic (adj)
fiotua, poet (n doer)
fipata, expulsion (n)
fipato, expel (v)
fipufa, stable (n d:barn)
firoda, event (n)
firodaika, eventuality (n)
firodaikiu, eventually (adv)
firodaiku, eventual (adj)
firodiu, eventfully (adv)
firodu, eventful (adj)
firoka, ridicule (n)
firokiu, ridiculously (adv)
firoko, ridicule (v)
firoku, ridiculous (adj)
firona, ballet (n)
firono, ballet (v)
fironua, ballerina (n doer)
firopa, riddance (n)
firopio, rid (v pa)
firopo, rid (v)
firopua, ridder (n doer)
firotesha, rifle (n)
firotesho, rifle (v)
firoteshua, rifler (n doer)
fishota, dinosaur (n)
fitaga, truck (n)
fitago, truck (v)
fitagua, trucker (n doer)
fitaka, arrest (n)
fitako, arrest (v)
fitaku, arrestive (adj)
fitakua, arrestor (n doer)
fitalota, arrival (n)
fitaloto, arrive (v)
fitapa, stability (n)
fitapo, stabilize (v)
fitapu, stabile (adj)
fitapua, stabilizer (n doer)
fitapueta, stabilization (n)
fitava, levy (n)
fitavo, levy (v)
fitisha, fission (n)
fitisho, fission (v)
fitishopa, fissure (n)
fituina, ski (n)
fituino, ski (v)
fituinua, skier (n doer)
fiuana, prom (n)
fiuasha, prostitution (n)
fiuasho, prostitute (v)
fiuashua, prostitute (n doer)
fiuba, probe (n)
fiubo, probe (v)

fiubofita, protrusion (n)
fiubofito, protrude (v)
fiubua, prober (n doer)
fiudafa, protein (n)
fiudaiba, prohibition (n)
fiudaibiu, prohibitively (adv)
fiudaibo, prohibit (v)
fiudaibu, prohibitive (adj)
fiudaibua, prohibitor (n doer)
fiudana, proverb (n d:saying)
fiudanu, proverbial (adj d:saying)
fiudokata, prosecution (n)
fiudokato, prosecute (v)
fiudokatu, prosecutable (adj)
fiudokatua, prosecutor (n doer)
fiufa, pro (n d:advantage)
fiufabota, profusion (n)
fiufabotiu, profusely (adv)
fiufabotu, profuse (adj)
fiufelausha, proliferation (n)
fiufelaushiu, prolifically (adv)
fiufelausho, proliferate (v)
fiufelaushu, prolific (adj)
fiufelaushua, proliferator (n doer)
fiuferepa, probability (n)
fiuferepiu, probably (adv)
fiuferepu, probable (adj)
fiufezha, proportion (n)
fiufezhiu, proportionally (adv)
fiufezhu, proportional (adj)
fiuga, probation (n)
fiugalita, protraction (n)
fiugalito, protract (v)
fiugalitua, protractor (n doer)
fiugana, propagation (n)
fiugano, propagate (v)
fiuganora, propaganda (n)
fiuganori, propaganda (n pl)
fiuganua, propagator (n doer)
fiuka, product (n)
fiukaga, promenade (n)
fiukago, promenade (v)
fiukana, produce (n)
fiukata, productivity (n)
fiukelipa, propriety (n)
fiukelipu, proprietary (adj)
fiukelipua, proprietor (n doer)
fiukeruga, prominence (n)
fiukerugiu, prominently (adv)
fiukerugu, prominent (adj)
fiukiu, productively (adv)
fiuko, produce (v)
fiuku, productive (adj)
fiukua, producer (n doer)
fiukueta, production (n)
fiukuita, prolog (n)
fiukuita, prologue (n)
fiukureitha, procrastination (n)
fiukureitho, procrastinate (v)
fiukureithua, procrastinator (n doer)
fiulekoika, fungicide (n)
fiulinika, proficiency (n)

fiulinikiu, proficiently (adv)
fiuliniku, proficient (adj)
fiuloipa, fungus (n)
fiuloipi, fungi (n pl)
fiuloipu, fungal (adj)
fiuloka, proposal (n)
fiuloka, proposition (n)
fiuloko, propose (v)
fiulokua, proposer (n doer)
fiulotela, prosperity (n)
fiuloteliu, prosperously (adv)
fiulotelo, prosper (v)
fiulotelu, prosperous (adj)
fiumala, proton (n)
fiumipa, prong (n)
fiumipo, prong (v)
fiuna, pro (n d:professional)
fiunana, prophecy (n)
fiunana, prophesy (n)
fiunanua, prophet (n doer)
fiunelika, program (n)
fiuneliko, program (v)
fiuneliku, programmable (adj)
fiunelikua, programmer (n doer)
fiunifeta, pronunciation (n)
fiunifeto, pronounce (v)
fiunika, profession (n)
fiunikiu, professionally (adv)
fiuniko, profess (v)
fiuniku, professional (adj)
fiunikua, professor (n doer)
fiunoarita, proclamation (n)
fiunoarito, proclaim (v)
fiunoka, promise (n)
fiunoko, promise (v)
fiunokua, promiser (n doer)
fiunotaka, professional (n)
fiunotako, professionalize (v)
fiunotakueta, professionalism (n)
fiunuyena, pronoun (n)
fiupada, propulsion (n)
fiupadana, propellant (n)
fiupado, propel (v)
fiupadua, propeller (n doer)
fiupafita, profit (n)
fiupafitepa, profitability (n)
fiupafitiu, profitably (adv)
fiupafito, profit (v)
fiupafitu, profitable (adj)
fiupafitua, profiteer (n doer)
fiupafituano, profiteer (v)
fiupaka, punt (n)
fiupako, punt (v)
fiupakua, punter (n doer)
fiupalitakiu, proactively (adv)
fiupalitaku, proactive (adj)
fiupeliuta, procreation (n)
fiupeliuto, procreate (v)
fiupeliutua, procreator (n doer)
fiurazha, prolongation (n)
fiurazho, prolong (v)
fiushaika, provocation (n)
fiushaikiu, provocatively (adv)

fiushaiko, provoke (v)
fiushaiku, provocative (adj)
fiushaikua, provoker (n doer)
fiushemana, prognosis (n)
fiushemano, prognosticate (v)
fiushemanua, prognosticator (n doer)
Fiushetipa, Protestant (n)
Fiushetipueta, Protestantism (n)
fiushetita, protest (n)
fiushetito, protest (v)
fiushetitua, protester (n doer)
fiushetitua, protestor (n doer)
fiushupiu, profoundly (adv)
fiushupu, profound (adj)
fiuta, problem (n)
fiutepa, projection (n d:thrust)
fiutepiu, projectively (adv d:thrust)
fiutepo, project (v d:thrust)
fiutepu, projective (adj d:thrust)
fiutepua, projector (n doer d:thrust)
fiutepuina, projectile (n)
fiuteshipa, project (n d:workplan)
fiuthiufa, profile (n)
fiuthiufo, profile (v)
fiuthiufua, profiler (n doer)
fiuthuka, prospect (n)
fiuthukiu, prospectively (adv)
fiuthuko, prospect (v)
fiuthuku, prospective (adj)
fiuthukua, prospector (n doer)
fiutianika, procurement (n)
fiutianiko, procure (v)
fiuvadava, promotion (n)
fiuvadavo, promote (v)
fiuvadavu, promotional (adj)
fiuvadavua, promoter (n doer)
fiuvefita, procession (n)
fiuveka, procedure (n)
fiuvekiu, procedurally (adv)
fiuveko, proceed (v)
fiuveku, procedural (adj)
fiuvelika, proceed (n)
fiuvelipa, proponent (n)
fiuveta, process (n)
fiuveto, process (v)
fiuvetua, processor (n doer)
fiuvoruga, progress (n)
fiuvorugiu, progressively (adv)
fiuvorugo, progress (v)
fiuvorugu, progressive (adj)
fiuvorugua, progressor (n doer)
fiuvorugueta, progression (n)
fivala, season (n d:climate)
fivaliu, seasonally (adv d:climate)
fivalu, seasonal (adj d:climate)
foariniu, loosely (adv)
foarino, loosen (v)
foarinu, loose (adj)
foidata, bacon (n)
foifa, fairy (n)

foiferaupa, fairyland (n)
foina, lace (n)
foinaka, divorce (n)
foinako, divorce (v)
foinakuina, divorcee (n)
foino, lace (v)
foinu, lacey (adj)
foisha, fair (n d:exhibition)
foisheberanita, fairground (n)
foita, vault (n d:arch)
foito, vault (v d:arch)
folelika, pitch (n d:sealant)
folito, crop (v d:narrow)
forelita, center (n)
forelitaifa, pivot (n)
forelitaifiu, pivotally (adv)
forelitaifo, pivot (v)
forelitaifu, pivotal (adj)
forelitaka, centralization (n)
forelitako, centralize (v)
forelitakua, centralizer (n doer)
forelitiu, centrally (adv)
forelito, center (v)
forelitu, central (adj)
forila, fragrance (n)
forilu, fragrant (adj)
forisha, sphere (n)
forishana, sphereoid (n)
forishiu, spherically (adv)
forishu, spherical (adj)
Foshiforusha, Phosphorus (n)
fuada, plough (n)
fuada, plow (n)
fuado, plow (v)
fuafo, saunter (v)
fualira, ghoul (n)
fualiru, ghoulish (adj)
fualu, via (prep)
fuarema, bed (n)
fuaremo, bed (v)
fuasha, oyster (n)
fuata, view (n)
fuataifota, viewpoint (n)
fuateshupua, viewfinder (n doer)
fuatha, sauna (n)
fuatiu, viewably (adv)
fuato, view (v)
fuatu, viewable (adj)
fuatua, viewer (n doer)
fufa, sauce (n)
fufapa, sausage (n)
fufatha, bowel (n)
fufemelika, saucepan (n)
fufo, sauce (v)
fufu, saucy (adj)
fuiaka, troll (n)
fuiako, troll (v)
fuifa, flight (n d:air travel)
fuifata, flyer (n)
fuifevuapi, flypaper (n pl)
fuifio, flew (v pa d:air travel)
fuifo, fly (v d:air travel)
fuifu, flighty (adj d:air travel)

fuifua, flier (n doer d:air travel)
fuisha, trolley (n)
fuita, idleness (n)
fuito, idle (v)
fuitu, idle (adj)
fulisha, plurality (n)
fulishu, plural (adj)
fumeilu, many (adj)
fumeiterava, manifold (n)
fumipa, canker (n)
fumipu, canker (adj)
fushipa, devastation (n)
fushipo, devastate (v)
fushishifa, fizz (n)
fushishifila, fizzle (n)
fushishifilo, fizzle (v)
fushishifo, fizz (v)
futaufa, spire (n)
futaufo, spire (v)
futauko, spiral (v)
futauku, spiral (adj)
futha, saucer (n)
gaberuba, colleague (n)
gadaka, collar (n)
gadaketoika, collarbone (n)
gadako, collar (v)
Gadoliniuma, Gadolinium (n)
gafana, gallon (n)
gafebarafa, gallstone (n)
gafelateka, gallbladder (n)
gafika, gall (n)
gafiko, gall (v)
gafikua, galler (n doer)
gafita, noise (n)
gafitiu, noisily (adv)
gafitu, noisy (adj)
gagalitha, hiccup (n)
gagalitho, hiccup (v)
gahem, Number_1e3756
gaiapa, coil (n)
gaiapo, coil (v)
gaiapua, coiler (n doer)
gaiba, helplessness (n)
gaibiu, helplessly (adv)
gaibu, helpless (adj)
gaifika, bitterness (n)
gaifikiu, bitterly (adv)
gaifiku, bitter (adj)
gaifotaga, rupture (n)
gaifotago, rupture (v)
gaigana, magnification (n)
gaigano, magnify (v)
gaiganua, magnifier (n doer)
gaigata, magnitude (n)
gaiguta, magnificence (n)
gaigutiu, magnificently (adv)
gaigutu, magnificent (adj)
gaika, bite (n d:chew)
gaikio, bit (v pa d:chew)
gaiko, bite (v d:chew)
gaikua, biter (n doer d:chew)
gaila, help (n)
gailo, help (v)

gailu, helpful (adj)
gailua, helper (n doer)
gaipa, buck (n)
gaipo, buck (v)
gaipua, buck (n doer)
gairifota, disruption (n)
gairifotiu, disruptively (adv)
gairifoto, disrupt (v)
gairifotu, disruptive (adj)
gairifotua, disrupter (n doer)
gaitha, roach (n)
gaithipa, beetle (n)
gaiva, tag (n)
gaivo, tag (v)
gaivua, tagger (n doer)
gala, G (let sng)
galeipa, eclipse (n)
galeipo, eclipse (v)
gali, Gs (let pl)
galika, dirt (n)
galikeshelefa, earthenware (n)
galikeshelefu, earthen (adj)
galikeyorina, earthworm (n)
galiko, dirty (v)
galiku, dirty (adj)
galikweku, dirtiest (adj)
galikwelu, dirtier (adj)
galisho, petrify (v)
galita, tract (n)
galiteta, traction (n)
galitha, cough (n)
galitho, cough (v)
galithua, cougher (n doer)
galitua, tractor (n doer)
Galiuma, Gallium (n)
galorina, maggot (n)
galuda, level (n)
galudo, level (v)
galudu, level (adj)
galudua, leveler (n doer)
galuga, curriculum (n)
Galutha, EhoMonth11 (n)
gamana, gamma (n)
ganikeka, ignition (n)
ganikeko, ignite (v)
ganikekua, igniter (n doer)
ganikena, engine (n)
ganikeno, engineer (v)
ganikenua, engineer (n doer)
ganipa, hammer (n)
ganipo, hammer (v)
ganisho, fasten (v)
ganishua, fastener (n doer)
ganolafa, ignorance (n)
ganolafo, ignore (v)
ganolafu, ignorant (adj)
ganuka, communism (n)
ganukua, communist (n doer)
ganupa, donkey (n)
garelago, gnaw (v)
gariko, collate (v)
gariluda, calculus (n)
garima, couch (n)

garimo, couch (v)
garina, coal (n)
garipa, collection (n)
garipiu, collectively (adv)
garipo, collect (v)
garipu, collective (adj)
garipua, collector (n doer)
garipuferepa, collectable (n)
garipuferepa, collectible (n)
garipuferepu, collectable (adj)
garipuferepu, collectible (adj)
garishata, collaboration (n)
garishatiu, collaboratively (adv)
garishato, collaborate (v)
garishatu, collaborative (adj)
garishatua, collaborator (n doer)
garishoka, collateral (n)
garodaka, calculation (n)
garodako, calculate (v)
garodakua, calculator (n doer)
garoshutiu, illicitly (adv)
garoshutu, illicit (adj)
garozhina, jersey (n)
gasha, trace (n)
gashipa, collapse (n)
gashipo, collapse (v)
gashipu, collapsible (adj)
gashiu, traceably (adv)
gasho, trace (v)
gashu, traceable (adj)
gashua, tracer (n doer)
gathana, squash (n d:fruit)
Gatholiga, Catholic (n)
gauapa, thunder (n)
gauapeferipa, thunderstorm (n)
gauapekiupa, thunderbolt (n)
gauapo, thunder (v)
gauba, chasm (n)
gaueta, canine (n)
gauetu, canine (adj)
gaufa, plague (n)
gaufita, argument (n)
gaufitiu, arguably (adv)
gaufito, argue (v)
gaufitu, arguable (adj)
gaufitua, arguer (n doer)
gaufo, plague (v)
gauiabiu, erratically (adv)
gauiabu, erratic (adj)
gauika, error (n)
gauikiu, erroneously (adv)
gauiko, err (v)
gauiku, errant (adj)
gauiku, erroneous (adj)
gauka, hound (n)
gauko, hound (v)
gaumerina, coconut (n)
gausha, notch (n)
gausho, notch (v)
gauvata, cocoa (n)
gaveta, agent (n)
gaviata, mafia (n)
gavuda, boldness (n d:make)

gavudiu, boldly (adv d:make)
gavudu, bold (adj d:make)
gavuga, jack (n d:lift)
gavugedaifa, jackpot (n)
gavugo, jack (v d:lift)
gavugua, jacker (n doer d:lift)
gebika, matter (n d:incident)
gebiko, matter (v d:incident)
gefipa, deferral (n)
gefipo, defer (v)
geipa, pat (n)
geipo, pat (v)
geiroda, dozen (n)
geitesha, twitch (n)
geitesho, twitch (v)
gelafa, vat (n)
gelafika, brew (n)
gelafiko, brew (v)
gelafikua, brewer (n doer)
gelafikuita, brewery (n)
gelaifa, fee (n)
gelaika, shank (n)
gelaiko, shank (v)
gelaita, bucket (n)
gelamisha, trawl (n)
gelamisho, trawl (v)
gelamishu, trawlers (adj)
gelanina, brook (n)
gelaninu, brooklike (adj)
gelanita, colloquium (n)
gelanitu, colloquial (adj)
gelaridiata, molestation (n)
gelaridiato, molest (v)
gelaridiatua, molester (n doer)
gelarika, mass (n)
gelarikiu, massively (adv)
gelariko, mass (v)
gelariku, massive (adj)
gelarina, cosmetic (n)
gelariniu, cosmetically (adv)
gelarinu, cosmetic (adj)
gelarinua, cosmetician (n doer)
gelaruda, trip (n d:journey)
gelaruga, contract (n
    d:agreement)
gelarugiu, contractually (adv
    d:agreement)
gelarugu, contractual (adj
    d:agreement)
gelarugua, contractor (n doer
    d:agreement)
gelasha, trail (n)
gelashekeraugua, trailblazer (n
    doer)
gelasho, trail (v)
gelashua, trailer (n doer)
gelata, bunt (n)
gelato, bunt (v)
gelaufa, complaint (n)
gelaufo, complain (v)
gelaufua, complainer (n doer)
gelauka, fake (n)
gelaukiuka, liberalism (n

d:political stance)
gelaukiuko, liberalize (v
    d:political stance)
gelaukiukua, liberal (n doer
    d:political stance)
gelaukiukueta, liberalization (n)
gelauko, fake (v)
gelaukua, faker (n doer)
gelausha, horse (n)
gelaushebiorita, horsepower (n)
gelaushekefa, horsehead (n)
gelaushemitha, horsetail (n)
gelaushepelona, horseman (n)
gelaushepeloni, horsemen (n pl)
gelaushetafana, horseshoe (n)
gelaushevaka, horseback (n)
gelausho, horse (v)
gelauta, brawl (n)
gelautha, brawn (n)
gelauto, brawl (v)
gelefa, leg (n)
gelefekioka, legwork (n)
gelefesherana, legroom (n)
gelefo, leg (v)
gelega, donation (n)
gelego, donate (v)
gelegua, donor (n doer)
geleiaka, broach (n)
geleiako, broach (v)
geleifo, purr (v)
geleita, secretion (n)
geleito, secrete (v)
geleiupa, brood (n)
geleiupo, brood (v)
geleka, knowledge (n)
gelekio, knew (v pa)
geleko, know (v)
gelekua, know-it-all (n doer)
gelemipa, bunk (n d:bed)
gelemipo, bunk (v d:bed)
gelepa, edit (n)
gelepana, editorial (n)
gelepara, edition (n)
gelepo, edit (v)
gelepu, editable (adj)
gelepua, editor (n doer)
gelesha, tie (n)
geleshepelikua, tiebreaker (n
    doer)
gelesho, tie (v)
geliafa, rawness (n)
geliafilafa, gauze (n)
geliafiu, rawly (adv)
geliafu, raw (adj)
geliapa, fruit (n)
geliapegurita, fruitcake (n)
geliapemenu, fruitless (adj)
geliapu, fruity (adj)
geliapueta, fruition (n)
geliapuetu, fruitful (adj)
geliasha, star (n d:celestial)
geliashefeleva, starship (n)
geliashefeluana, starlight (n)

geliashelesha, starfish (n)
geliashetiavo, stargaze (v)
geliashetiavua, stargazer (n doer)
geliashu, starry (adj d:celestial)
geliashu, stellar (adj d:celestial)
geliata, crutch (n)
geliazhika, breadwinner (n)
geliefa, scruff (n)
geliefu, scruffy (adj)
gelieka, winch (n)
gelieko, winch (v)
gelifa, perk (n)
gelifasha, deluge (n)
gelifasho, deluge (v)
gelifo, perk (v)
gelifoka, carrot (n)
gelifu, perky (adj)
gelika, twist (n)
geliko, twist (v)
geliku, twisty (adj)
gelikua, twister (n doer)
gelila, carriage (n)
gelimara, kidney (n)
gelina, calendar (n)
gelinoka, exemption (n)
gelinoko, exempt (v)
gelipa, crust (n)
gelipo, crust (v)
gelipu, crusty (adj)
gelisha, step (n)
gelisheluara, stepchild (n)
gelisheluari, stepchildren (n pl)
gelishelunora, stepdaughter (n)
gelishemalisha, stepmother (n)
gelisheterita, stepladder (n)
gelishevoteta, stepfather (n)
gelisho, step (v)
gelishu, step (adj)
gelishua, stepper (n doer)
gelita, tide (n)
geliteidona, tidewater (n)
gelitha, spider (n)
gelithu, spidery (adj)
gelito, tide (v)
gelitu, tidal (adj)
geliuka, flaw (n)
geliukemeniu, flawlessly (adv)
geliukemenu, flawless (adj)
geliuko, flaw (v)
geliupa, sickness (n)
geliupiu, sickly (adv)
geliupo, sicken (v)
geliupu, sick (adj)
geliutha, flask (n)
gelofa, steel (n)
gelofekioka, steelwork (n)
gelofekiokua, steelworker (n
    doer)
gelofenagio, steelmade (v pa)
gelofenago, steelmake (v)
gelofenagua, steelmaker (n doer)
gelofepelona, steelman (n)
gelofepeloni, steelmen (n pl)

gelofu, steely (adj)
geloikio, quit (v pa)
geloiko, quit (v)
geloikua, quitter (n doer)
geloipa, dumbness (n)
geloipo, dumb (v)
geloipu, dumb (adj)
geloipua, dummy (n doer)
geloirifa, charity (n)
geloirifiu, charitably (adv)
geloirifu, charitable (adj)
geloishiu, quite (adv)
geloita, charge (n)
geloito, charge (v)
geloitua, charger (n doer)
gelorifa, board (n d:Enter ship)
gelorifiu, aboard (adv d:Enter
    ship)
gelorifo, board (v d:Enter ship)
gelorifua, boarder (n doer d:Enter
    ship)
gelorina, dreariness (n)
gelorinu, dreary (adj)
geloritha, dread (n)
geloritho, dread (v)
gelorithu, dreadful (adj)
geloruga, reach (n)
gelorugo, reach (v)
gelorugu, reachable (adj)
gelorugua, reacher (n doer)
gelosha, crotch (n)
gelufa, guilt (n)
gelufipa, bonnet (n)
gelufiu, guiltily (adv)
gelufo, guilt (v)
gelufu, guilty (adj)
geluka, bunk (n d:nonsense)
gelumenita, carpentry (n)
gelumenitua, carpenter (n doer)
gelumeta, carpet (n)
gelumeto, carpet (v)
gelupa, burp (n)
gelupo, burp (v)
gelupua, burper (n doer)
gelurinu, dire (adj)
gelusha, jack (n d:toy)
gelutha, broth (n)
genai-, oct- (num 8 pref)
genaimuka, octagon (n)
geneth, eighth (num 8 ord)
genfk, octoquadragintillion (num
    1e147 card)
genft, octotrigintillion (num
    1e117 card)
geni, eight (num 8 card)
genialfhemka, Number_1e32556
genida, eighty (num 80 card)
genidai-, eighty- (num 80 pref)
genideth, eightieth (num 80 ord)
genipa, eighteen (num 18 card)
genipai-, eighteen- (num 18 pref)
genipeth, eighteenth (num 18

ord)
genka, octillion (num 1e27 card)
genkai-, xenna- (num 1e27 pref)
genketh, octillionth (num 1e27 ord)
genshk, octovigintillion (num 1e87 card)
genshkai-, cianta-
genshketh, octovigintillionth (num 1e87 ord)
gensht, octodecillion (num 1e57 card)
genshtai-, meikosi- (num 1e57 pref)
genshteth, octodecillionth (num 1e57 ord)
gerafipa, deference (n)
geraifa, fetch (n)
geraifita, cusp (n)
geraifo, fetch (v)
geraifua, fetcher (n doer)
geraigiu, sluggishly (adv d:slow)
geraigu, sluggish (adj d:slow)
geraiko, mug (v d:rob)
geraikua, mugger (n doer d:rob)
geraisha, etch (n)
geraishiu, etchily (adv)
geraisho, etch (v)
geraishu, etchy (adj)
geraishua, etcher (n doer)
geraita, stretch (n)
geraitho, strew (v)
geraito, stretch (v)
geraitu, stretchy (adj)
geraitua, stretcher (n doer)
geraizha, vastness (n)
geraizhiu, vastly (adv)
geraizhu, vast (adj)
geraka, anger (n)
gerakiu, angrily (adv)
gerako, anger (v)
geraku, angry (adj)
gerala, corn (n)
geralu, corny (adj)
geraluga, angst (n)
geraluga, anxiety (n)
geralugiu, anxiously (adv)
geralugu, anxious (adj)
geranika, flank (n)
gcraniku, flank (v)
geranilaka, flange (n)
gerarika, churn (n)
gerariko, churn (v)
gerarikua, churner (n doer)
gerasha, paint (n)
gerashekelusha, paintbrush (n)
gerasho, paint (v)
gerashua, painter (n doer)
gerashuelueta, pigmentation (n)
gerashueta, pigment (n)
gerata, bat (n d:stick)
gerataka, battery (n d:attack)

geratako, batter (v d:attack)
geratha, Eho9seconds (n)
gerato, bat (v d:stick)
geratua, batter (n doer d:stick)
geratupa, battle (n)
geratupo, battle (v)
geratupua, battler (n doer)
geraufa, roar (n)
geraufo, roar (v)
gerauga, enlargement (n)
geraugiasha, massacre (n)
geraugiasho, massacre (v)
geraugiu, largely (adv)
geraugo, enlarge (v)
geraugu, large (adj)
gerraugua, enlarger (n doer)
geraugwaku, largest (adj)
geraugwelu, larger (adj)
gerauka, halt (n)
geraukata, halter (n)
gerauko, halt (v)
gerauno, roam (v)
gerautho, roil (v)
geravuga, dissolution (n)
geravugo, dissolve (v)
gerazha, saw (n d:tool)
gerazhefenipa, sawmill (n)
gerazhekereisha, sawdust (n)
gerazho, saw (v d:tool)
geredisha, mustache (n)
gereiaga, mania (n)
gereiagu, maniacal (adj)
gereiagu, manic (adj)
gereiagua, maniac (n doer)
gereiaka, bunker (n)
gereibabila, granddaddy (n)
gereibelapa, grandpa (n)
gereidathifefa, grandparent (n)
gereifa, camel (n)
gereiga, smear (n)
gereigo, smear (v)
gereika, incarnation (n)
gereikaga, carnage (n)
gereiko, incarnate (v)
gereiku, carnal (adj)
gereiliu, grandly (adv)
gereilu, grand (adj)
gereiluara, grandchild (n)
gereiluari, grandchildren (n pl)
gereilunora, granddaughter (n)
gereilunoru, granddaughterly (adj)
gereima, grandma (n)
gereimalisha, grandmother (n)
gereimalisho, grandmother (v)
gereimalishu, grandmotherly (adj)
gereimelimala, grandmommy (n)
gereimetheiana, grandson (n)
gereiterelita, grandstand (n)
gereiterelito, grandstand (v)
gereithioka, grandmaster (n)
gereivoteta, grandfather (n)

gereivoteto, grandfather (v)
gereivotetu, grandfatherly (adj)
gerela, car (n)
gerelifa, carve (n)
gerelifio, carve (v pa)
gerelifo, carve (v)
gerelifua, carver (n doer)
gerelina, carryon (n)
gerelipa, slug (n d:animal)
gerelisha, gash (n)
gerelisho, gash (v)
gerelishua, gasher (n doer)
gerelita, stir (n)
gerelito, stir (v)
gerelitua, stirer (n doer)
gerelubielika, carport (n)
gerelukeluga, carsickness (n)
gerelukelugu, carsick (adj)
gereluvifa, cargo (n)
gereluvifo, cargo (v)
gerena, carry (n)
gerenama, cartoon (n)
gerenika, cart (n)
gereniko, cart (v)
gerenikua, carter (n doer)
gereno, carry (v)
gerenua, carrier (n doer)
gereshoka, cartel (n)
gereshota, closet (n)
gereta, closure (n)
geretata, closeness (n)
geretha, stiffness (n d:rigid)
gerethano, stiff (v d:cheat)
gerethato, stifle (v)
geretho, stiffen (v d:rigid)
gerethu, stiff (adj d:rigid)
geretiu, closely (adv)
gereto, close (v)
geretu, close (adj)
geretua, closer (n doer)
geretwaku, closest (adj)
geretwelu, closer (adj)
geriago, stagger (v)
geriaka, cowardice (n)
geriako, cower (v)
geriaku, cowardly (adj)
geriakua, coward (n doer)
geriapo, stalk (v d:pursue)
geriapua, stalker (n doer d:pursue)
geriasha, stagnation (n)
geriasho, stagnate (v)
geriashu, stagnant (adj)
geriata, stack (n)
geriato, stack (v)
geriatua, stacker (n doer)
geriauka, ghast (n)
geriauku, ghastly (adj)
gerieta, serration (n)
gerieto, serrate (v)
Gerifika, Greek (n)
gerika, sole (n)
gerikata, solitude (n)

gerikatu, solitary (adj)
gerikiu, solely (adv)
geriku, sole (adj)
gerilifa, frill (n)
gerilita, eerieness (n)
gerilitiu, eerily (adv)
gerilitu, eerie (adj)
gerilopa, treasure (n)
gerilopata, treasury (n)
gerilopo, treasure (v)
gerilopua, treasurer (n doer)
gerimana, burger (n)
gerinala, veneer (n)
geriofa, cuisine (n)
gerioka, jeer (n)
gerioko, jeer (v)
Gerisha, Greece (n)
gerishota, fringe (n)
gerita, might (n d:strength)
geritaka, soldier (n)
geritako, soldier (v)
geritha, salmon (n)
geritiu, mightily (adv d:strength)
geritu, mighty (adj d:strength)
geritweku, mightiest (adj)
geritwelu, mightier (adj)
geroga, roughness (n)
gerogepelona, roughneck (n)
gerogiu, roughly (adv)
gerogo, rough (v)
gerogu, rough (adj)
geroifa, starvation (n)
geroifo, starve (v)
geroiga, bong (n d:pipe)
gerola, measurement (n)
geroliu, measurably (adv)
gerolo, measure (v)
gerolu, measurable (adj)
gerolua, measurer (n doer)
Geromaniuma, Germanium (n)
geruapa, caliper (n)
geruasha, brush (n d:shrub)
geruba, boredom (n d:tiresome)
gerubo, bore (v d:tiresome)
gerubua, bore (n doer d:tiresome)
geruda, herd (n)
gerudo, herd (v)
gerudua, herder (n doer)
gerufipa, bearing (n d:metal ball)
gerufita, bearing (n d:direction)
gerufito, bear (v d:direction)
geruga, rear (n)
gerugo, rear (v)
gerugu, rear (adj)
gerukio, bore (v pa d:endure)
gerukiu, bearishly (adv d:endure)
geruko, bear (v d:endure)
geruku, bearish (adj d:endure)
gerukua, bearer (n doer d:endure)
gerulika, wound (n d:injury)
geruliko, wound (v d:injury)
gerulita, hunt (n)
gerulito, hunt (v)

gerulitua, hunter (n doer)
geruna, term (n d:word)
gerunekuita, terminology (n)
geruno, term (v d:word)
geruta, clue (n)
gerutemeniu, cluelessly (adv)
gerutemenu, clueless (adj)
gerutha, gift (n)
geruthio, gave (v pa)
gerutho, give (v)
geruthoka, ricochet (n)
geruthoko, ricochet (v)
geruthopeliola, giveaway (n)
geruthu, gifted (adj)
geruthua, giver (n doer)
gerutiafa, gavel (n)
geruto, clue (v)
geruva, mug (n d:cup)
geshota, host (n)
geshotara, hostess (n)
geshoto, host (v)
gethika, track (n)
gethiko, track (v)
gethikua, tracker (n doer)
getorala, lecture (n)
getoralo, lecture (v)
getoralua, lecturer (n doer)
gevasha, refuse (n d:garbage)
giafopa, decay (n)
giafopo, decay (v)
giagiasha, magic (n)
giagiashiu, magically (adv)
giagiashu, magical (adj)
giagiashua, magician (n doer)
giaka, pork (n)
gialipa, wince (n)
gialipo, wince (v)
gialofa, café (n)
gialofeta, cafeteria (n)
gialoka, bacterium (n)
gialoki, bacteria (n pl)
giamena, peanut (n)
giano, ram (v d:thrust)
gianoka, commodity (n)
gianua, rammer (n doer d:thrust)
giaripa, frown (n)
giaripo, frown (v)
giaripua, frowner (n doer)
giasho, heel (v d:tilt)
giashoka, curse (n)
giashoko, curse (v)
giata, boss (n)
giato, boss (v)
giatu, bossy (adj)
giauberesha, fireplace (n)
giaubiorita, firepower (n)
giaufanina, firewood (n)
giaufeliofo, fireproof (v)
giaufeliofu, fireproof (adj)
giauferipa, firestorm (n)
giaufika, bonfire (n)
giaukiafa, firehouse (n)
giaukioka, firewook (n)

giaula, fire (n)
giaulevauga, firefight (n)
giaulevaugua, firefighter (n doer)
giaulo, fire (v)
giaulu, fiery (adj)
giaumashipa, fireball (n)
giaunolitha, firewall (n)
giaushinena, firearm (n)
giaushipega, firefly (n)
giaushoita, fireside (n)
giauviluba, firebomb (n)
giena, courier (n)
giepa, romp (n)
giepo, romp (v)
gietha, cursor (n)
gifaka, impact (n)
gifako, impact (v)
gifakua, impacter (n doer)
gifana, pagan (n)
gifanueta, paganism (n)
gifiena, peasant (n)
gifopa, pact (n)
giketheiana, stepson (n)
gilipa, pluck (n)
gilipo, pluck (v)
gilipu, plucky (adj)
gilipua, plucker (n doer)
giloka, jig (n d:fixture)
gilota, ego (n)
gilotiu, egoistically (adv)
gilotiu, egotistically (adv)
gilotu, egoistic (adj)
gilotu, egotistic (adj)
gilotua, egoist (n doer)
gilotueta, egoism (n)
gilotueta, egotism (n)
gilufa, tweak (n)
ginata, military (n)
ginataka, militia (n)
ginato, militarize (v)
ginatua, militant (n doer)
gioba, tort (n)
giobata, torture (n)
giobato, torture (v)
giobatu, torturous (adj)
giodirifa, ramrod (n)
giodirifo, ramrod (v)
gioifa, rump (n)
gioika, quack (n)
gioikueta, quackery (n)
gioka, squeeze (n)
giokata, squeegee (n)
giokato, squeegee (v)
gioko, squeeze (v)
giokua, squeezer (n doer)
giopa, ramp (n)
giopo, ramp (v)
giopoika, rampage (n)
giopoiko, rampage (v)
giopoiku, rampant (adj)
giotha, porch (n)
gipashu, plush (adj)
gira, call (n)

giradarifa, calligraphy (n)
girena, ceil (n)
gireno, ceil (v)
girevafa, callback (n)
giro, call (v)
girogerazha, jigsaw (n)
giropa, turkey (n)
giru, callable (adj)
girua, caller (n doer)
gishoka, lesion (n)
gishoko, lesion (v)
githapa, plug (n)
githapo, plug (v)
githapua, plugger (n doer)
gituka, snag (n)
gituko, snag (v)
giufa, ham (n)
giuipa, dowel (n)
giuka, squad (n)
giukata, squadron (n)
giupa, coup (n)
giusha, dizziness (n)
giusho, dizzy (v)
giushu, dizzy (adj)
gizhapa, mechanism (n)
gizhapiu, mechanically (adv)
gizhapo, mechanize (v)
gizhapu, mechanical (adj)
gizhapua, mechanic (n doer)
gizhapueta, mechanization (n)
gizhauka, machine (n)
gizhaukara, machinery (n)
gizhauko, machine (v)
gizhaukua, machinist (n doer)
gofafa, lethargy (n)
gofafiu, lethargically (adv)
gofafu, lethargic (adj)
gofaifa, lethality (n)
gofaifiu, lethally (adv)
gofaifu, lethal (adj)
gofika, stake (n)
gofikethorithua, stakeholder (n
    doer)
gofiko, stake (v)
gofikuila, stakeout (n)
gofita, hesitation (n)
gofitiu, hesitantly (adv)
gofito, hesitate (v)
gofitu, hesitant (adj)
gogara, gland (n)
gogaru, glandular (adj)
goifena, tomato (n)
goifita, focus (n)
goifito, focus (v)
goifitu, focal (adj)
goifitua, focuser (n doer)
goiga, jug (n)
goika, crank (n)
goiko, crank (v)
goina, crane (n)
goino, crane (v)
goipa, wimp (n)
goipo, wimp (v)

goipu, wimpy (adj)
goito, cuss (v)
goka, take (n)
gokafena, takeover (n)
gokio, took (v pa)
goko, take (v)
gokua, taker (n doer)
gokuila, takeout (n)
gokunefa, takeoff (n)
Golada, Gold (n)
golisha, scar (n)
golisho, scar (v)
golita, concrete (n)
golito, concrete (v)
golitu, concrete (adj)
gorafa, tar (n)
gorafegaliko, tarnish (v)
gorafemarifa, tarmac (n)
gorafo, tar (v)
goralefenitha, goldsmith (n)
goralekeriga, goldmine (n)
goralipa, turbulence (n)
goralipu, turbulent (adj)
goralita, gold (n)
goraliteshelesha, goldfish (n)
goralitesheleshi, goldfish (n pl)
goralito, golden (v)
goralitu, gold (adj)
goranikeloipa, corkscrew (n)
goranipa, cork (n)
goranipo, cork (v)
goranipu, corky (adj)
goripa, contribution (n)
goripo, contribute (v)
goripua, contributor (n doer)
goropika, turbine (n)
goruda, volcano (n)
goshika, scare (n)
goshikeviaroka, scarecrow (n)
goshiko, scare (v)
goshiku, scary (adj)
goshikweku, scariest (adj)
goshikwelu, scarier (adj)
guaba, hoist (n)
guabo, hoist (v)
guafa, bail (n)
guafita, kind (n d:type)
guafo, bail (v)
guafuila, bailout (n)
guaka, hog (n)
guakefiausha, hogwash (n)
guako, hog (v)
guaniroko, trump (v)
guapa, toilet (n)
guapata, toiletry (n)
guauka, bigot (n)
guba, heave (n)
gubelasha, compression (n)
gubelashana, compress (n)
gubelasho, compress (v)
gubelashu, compressable (adj)
gubelashua, compressor (n doer)
guberaluma, compound (n

d:mixture)
guberalumo, compound (v
    d:mixture)
gubeshuisha, heavyweight (n)
gubiu, heavily (adv)
gubo, heave (v)
gubu, heavy (adj)
gubweku, heaviest (adj)
gubwelu, heavier (adj)
gufika, lust (n)
gufikiu, lustfully (adv)
gufiko, lust (v)
gufiku, lustful (adj)
gufipa, heel (n d:sole)
gufita, cane (n)
gufito, cane (v)
gugaita, magazine (n d:storage)
gugauga, vulgarity (n)
gugaugu, vulgar (adj)
gugifopa, compaction (n)
gugifopiu, compactly (adv)
gugifopo, compact (v)
gugifopu, compact (adj)
gugifopua, compactor (n doer)
guiama, spore (n)
guiamiu, sporadically (adv)
guiamu, sporadic (adj)
guiba, heist (n)
guifoka, nastiness (n)
guifokiu, nastily (adv)
guifoku, nasty (adj)
guifokweku, nastiest (adj)
guifokwelu, nastier (adj)
guisha, hiss (n)
guisho, hiss (v)
guishu, hissy (adj)
guishua, hisser (n doer)
gukafita, magnetic (n)
gukata, magnetism (n)
gukatiu, magnetically (adv)
gukato, magnetize (v)
gukatu, magnetic (adj)
gukatua, magnet (n doer)
gulina, communion (n)
gulino, commune (v)
gulinu, communal (adj)
gulita, buoyancy (n)
gulitiu, buoyantly (adv)
gulito, buoy (v)
gulitu, buoyant (adj)
gulitua, buoy (n doer)
guloba, heft (n)
gulobu, hefty (adj)
gulova, caffeine (n)
gumana, pudding (n)
gunaipa, compilation (n)
gunaipo, compile (v)
gunaipua, compiler (n doer)
gunaka, commune (n)
gunala, community (n)
guniana, communique (n)
guniata, communication (n)
guniato, communicate (v)

guniatua, communicator (n doer)
gupada, compulsion (n)
gupadiu, compulsory (adv)
gupado, compel (v)
gupadu, compulsive (adj)
gupadua, compeller (n doer)
gupapa, rudder (n)
gurapa, gulp (n)
gurapo, gulp (v)
gurapua, gulper (n doer)
guriberesha, commonplace (n)
guribereshu, commonplace (adj)
gurifa, current (n d:stream)
gurika, mood (n)
gurikaupa, commonwealth (n)
gurikiu, moodily (adv)
guriku, moody (adj)
gurina, commonality (n)
guriniu, commonly (adv)
gurino, commonize (v)
gurinu, common (adj)
gurinua, commoner (n doer)
gurishorifa, commonsense (n)
gurita, cake (n)
gurito, cake (v)
gushika, lure (n)
gushiko, lure (v)
gushikua, lurer (n doer)
gutesha, naught (n)
guteshu, naughty (adj)
gutha, moth (n)
guthemashipa, mothball (n)
guthemashipo, mothball (v)
gutomola, candy (n)
gutomolo, candy (v)
gutomolu, candy (adj)
guvaka, seizure (n)
guvako, seize (v)
guvata, invention (n)
guvatiu, inventively (adv)
guvato, invent (v)
guvatora, inventory (n)
guvatu, inventive (adj)
guvatua, inventor (n doer)
guvelipa, component (n)
guviusha, comprisal (n)
guviusho, comprise (v)
guviushu, comprisable (adj)
guzhepu, macho (adj)
Hafoniuma, Hafnium (n)
hakefei, whatever (pron)
hakefu, whatever (adj/interj)
hakei, what (pron)
hakezhaufelei, whatsoever (pron)
hakezhaufelu, whatsoever (adj)
haku, what (adj/adv/conj)
haloreta, world (n)
haloretakerashu, worldwide (adj)
haloretu, worldly (adj)
harfhem, Number_1e906
harfi, Hs (let pl)
harifa, H (let sng)
haripa, staff (n d:stick)

haripo, stave (v d:stick)
haruga, bat (n d:animal)
harugu, batty (adj d:animal)
Hashiuma, Hassium (n)
hausha, ward (n)
hausho, ward (v)
hautha, health (n)
hauthekeifa, healthcare (n)
hautho, heal (v)
hauthu, healthy (adj)
hauthua, healer (n doer)
hauthweku, healthiest (adj)
hauthwelu, healthier (adj)
havupa, well (n d:water)
heidona, water (n)
heidoneduaifa, watertightness (n)
heidoneduaifu, watertight (adj)
heidonefelarina, waterfront (n)
heidonefelarinu, waterfront (adj)
heidonefeliofo, waterproof (v)
heidonefeliofu, waterproof (adj)
heidonefuarema, waterbed (n)
heidonekiafa, waterhouse (n)
heidonekioka, waterwork (n)
heidonelirola, watercolor (n)
heidonemiuna, watertown (n)
heidonepeliola, waterway (n)
heidonepelona, waterman (n)
heidonepeloni, watermen (n pl)
heidoneshetata, watermark (n)
heidonethilofa, watershed (n)
heidonethilofu, watershed (adj)
heidonezhaila, waterfall (n)
heidono, water (v)
heidonu, watery (adj)
heidufitia, hypocracy (n)
heidufitiu, hypocritically (adv)
heidufitu, hypocritical (adj)
heidufitua, hypocrite (n doer)
heiguaka, boar (n)
hein, him (pron 3rd masc sng obj)
heipa, oak (n)
heish, his (pron 3rd masc sng pos obj)
heish, his (pron 3rd masc sng pos sub)
heishama, hypnosis (n)
heishamo, hypnotize (v)
heishfal, himself (pron 3rd masc sng refl)
heishoka, whiskey (n)
Heishota, AIDS (n)
Heliuma, Helium (n)
hemai-, mono- (num 1 pref)
hemaiata, monument (n)
hemaiatiu, monumentally (adv)
hemaiatu, monumental (adj)
hemaila, annual (n)
hemailiu, annually (adv)
hemailo, annualize (v)
hemailu, annual (adj)
hemaithara, anniversary (n)

hemalfhemka, Number_1e4206
heme, one (num 1 card)
hemedarifa, monograph (n)
hemedaunu, onetime (adj)
hemedorina, monopoly (n)
hemedorino, monopolize (v)
hemedorinu, monopolistic (adj)
hemedorinua, monopolist (n doer)
hemefa, once (n)
hemefu, once (adj/adv/conj)
hemekuita, monologue (n)
hemeluita, monorail (n)
hemenelika, monogram (n)
hemepereitha, monochrome (n)
hemepereithu, monochromatic (adj)
hemeru, only (adj/adv/conj)
hemeterila, monotone (n)
hemeterilata, monotony (n)
hemeth, first (num 1 ord)
hemethekapa, firsthand (n)
hemethereitha, monolith (n)
hemethereithu, monolithic (adj)
hemethi, firsts (n pl)
hemethiu, firstly (adv)
hemevalesha, firstborn (n)
hemifk, unquadragintillion (num 1e126 card)
hemift, untrigintillion (num 1e96 card)
hemiftai-, zantri-
hemifteth, untrigintillionth (num 1e96 ord)
hemka, million (num 1e6 card)
hemkadeth, millionth (num 1e6 ord)
hemkai-, mega- (num 1e6 pref)
hemoniapiu, unanimously (adv)
hemonlapu, unanimous (adj)
hempa, eleven (num 11 card)
hempai-, eleven- (num 11 pref)
hempeth, eleventh (num 11 ord)
hemshk, unvigintillion (num 1e66 card)
hemshkai-, jitri- (num 1e66 pref)
hemshketh, unvigintillionth (num 1e66 ord)
hemsht, undecillion (num 1e36 card)
hemshtai-, udeka- (num 1e36 pref)
hemshteth, undecillionth (num 1e36 ord)
hemthutesha, monotheism (n)
hemthuteshu, monotheistic (adj)
henata, wool (n)
henatu, wool (adj)
henatu, wooly (adj)
henieta, breakfast (n)
henieto, breakfast (v)

herifa, deposit (n)
herifeka, depot (n)
herifieka, depository (n)
herifo, deposit (v)
herifua, depositor (n doer)
hethefita, judiciary (n)
hetheta, judgement (n)
hetheta, judgment (n)
hethetefifa, judgeship (n)
hethetiu, judicially (adv)
hethetiu, judiciously (adv)
hetheto, judge (v)
hethetu, judicial (adj)
hethetu, judicious (adj)
hethetua, judge (n doer)
hethetueta, judgementalism (n)
hethetuetu, judgemental (adj)
hethieta, patient (n d:person)
hiafelu, however (adv/conj)
hiala, how (n)
hialu, how (adv/conj)
hiaroka, wolf (n)
hiaroko, wolf (v)
hiberatha, limb (n)
Hiderogena, Hydrogen (n)
hilorita, quotient (n)
hinafa, quotation (n)
hinafa, quote (n)
hinafo, quote (v)
hinafu, quotable (adj)
hinafua, quoter (n doer)
hinama, quota (n)
hinamo, quota (v)
hishefelei, whichever (pron)
hishefelu, whichever (adj)
hishei, which (pron)
hishu, which (adj)
hiu, why (adv/conj/interj)
hiua, why (n)
hofipa, deafness (n)
hofipo, deafen (v)
hofipu, deaf (adj)
hoina, jury (n)
hoinikata, jurisdiction (n)
hoinua, jurist (n doer)
hoinua, juror (n doer)
hoita, exile (n)
hoito, exile (v)
Holamiuma, Holmium (n)
honazhaimu, etc. (phrase)
nonazhaimu, etcetera (phrase)
Honuga Konuga, Hong Kong (n)
hua, wah (interj)
hui, he (pron 3rd masc sng sub)
ia, ah (interj)
ia, aye (interj)
iabofita, obtrusion (n)
iabofitiu, obtrusively (adv)
iabofito, obtrude (v)
iabofitu, obtrusive (adj)
iafuata, obvious (n)
iafuatiu, obviously (adv)
iafuatu, obvious (adj)

iagerika, obsolescence (n)
iagerikiu, obsoletely (adv)
iageriku, obsolete (adj)
iakelorika, obscurity (n)
iakeloriko, obscure (v)
iakofita, observation (n)
iakofitaka, observatory (n)
iakofitana, observance (n)
iakofitaniu, observantly (adv)
iakofitanu, observant (adj)
iakofitiu, observably (adv)
iakofito, observe (v)
iakofitu, observable (adj)
iakofitua, observer (n doer)
ialifoka, obedience (n)
ialifokiu, obediently (adv)
ialifoko, obey (v)
ialifoku, obedient (adj)
ialika, object (n d:thing)
ialikata, objective (n d:goal)
ialikatiu, objectively (adv d:goal)
ialikatu, objective (adj d:goal)
ialikueta, objectivity (n
    d:impartiality)
ialivatora, obliteration (n)
ialivatoro, obliterate (v)
ialopa, obsession (n)
ialopiu, obsessively (adv)
ialopo, obsess (v)
ialopu, obsessive (adj)
ialopua, obsessor (n doer)
iamikatiu, obnoxiously (adv)
iamikatu, obnoxious (adj)
ianeipa, obtuseness (n)
ianeipiu, obtusely (adv)
ianeipu, obtuse (adj)
iapifoto, obtain (v)
iapifotu, obtainable (adj)
iariloka, obstacle (n)
iasheleka, obstruction (n)
iashelekiu, obstructively (adv)
iasheleko, obstruct (v)
iasheleku, obstructive (adj)
iashelekua, obstructionist (n
    doer)
iashelekua, obstructor (n doer)
iatepa, objection (n d:protest)
iatepiu, objectionably (adv
    d:protest)
iatepo, object (v d:protest)
iatepu, objectionable (adj
    d:protest)
iatepua, objector (n doer
    d:protest)
iathulipa, obscenity (n)
iathulipiu, obscenely (adv)
iathulipu, obscene (adj)
ibafita, injunction (n)
ibara, infancy (n)
ibarekoika, infanticide (n)
ibarita, echo (n)
ibarito, echo (v)
ibarua, infant (n doer)

ibaufa, intuition (n)
ibaufiu, intuitively (adv)
ibaufo, intuit (v)
ibaufu, intuitive (adj)
ibelarifa, inflation (n)
ibelarifo, inflate (v)
ibelarifu, inflatable (adj)
ibelarifua, inflater (n doer)
ibelima, intimidation (n)
ibelimo, intimidate (v)
ibelimua, intimidator (n doer)
iberautha, inflow (n)
iberelika, incompleteness (n)
iberelikiu, incompletely (adv)
ibereliku, incomplete (adj)
iberolikiu, incomparably (adv)
iberoliku, incomparable (adj)
iberufitu, indispensable (adj)
iberunipa, independence (n)
iberunipiu, independently (adv)
iberunipu, independent (adj)
iberunipua, independent (n doer)
ibironita, endorsement (n)
ibironito, endorse (v)
ibironitua, endorser (n doer)
ibita, investment (n)
ibitaka, investigation (n)
ibitako, investigate (v)
ibitaku, investigational (adj)
ibitaku, investigative (adj)
ibitakua, investigator (n doer)
ibito, invest (v)
ibitua, investor (n doer)
idaiba, inhibition (n)
idaibo, inhibit (v)
idaibu, inhibitory (adj)
idaibua, inhibitor (n doer)
idainoka, inequality (n)
idainoka, inequity (n)
idainoku, inequitable (adj)
Idakofa, Idaho (n)
idauma, incubation (n)
idaumo, incubate (v)
idaumua, incubator (n doer)
ideferepa, incapability (n)
ideferepu, incapable (adj)
ideika, indictment (n)
ideiko, indict (v)
ideikua, indictor (n doer)
idelishoka, infraction (n)
ideruliku, incomprehensible (adj)
idethipa, incapacity (n)
idethipo, incapacitate (v)
idiafoka, intricacy (n)
idiafokiu, intricately (adv)
idiafoku, intricate (adj)
idiashika, intrigue (n)
idiashikiu, intriguingly (adv)
idiashiko, intrigue (v)
idiloshafu, inseparable (adj)
idu, at (prep)
idubieliku, inopportune (adj)
iduritu, inoperable (adj)

iduritu, inoperative (adj)
ienutaku, ineligible (adj)
ifabota, infusion (n)
ifaboto, infuse (v)
Ifak, Manganese (n davoka)
Ifap, Scandium (n davoka)
Ifat, Copper (n davoka)
ifeifiaunu, inclement (adj)
ifekiaka, invincibility (n)
ifekiaku, invincible (adj)
ifeleinosha, incompatibility (n)
ifeleinoshiu, incompatibly (adv)
ifeleinoshu, incompatible (adj)
iferepa, inability (n)
iferitha, entity (n)
ifiaisha, invisibility (n)
ifiaishiu, invisibly (adv)
ifiaishu, invisible (adj)
ifibeinuka, epitaph (n)
ifieshu, infrared (adj)
Ifik, Iron (n davoka)
ifikofa, epoch (n)
ifiofonudiu, infrequently (adv)
ifiofonudu, infrequent (adj)
Ifip, Titanium (n davoka)
ifipelona, epidemic (n)
Ifit, Zinc (n davoka)
ifitapa, instability (n)
Ifok, Cobalt (n davoka)
Ifop, Vanadium (n davoka)
iforelita, epicenter (n)
ifuaremo, embed (v)
ifudaufa, inspiration (n)
ifudaufiu, inspirationally (adv)
ifudaufo, inspire (v)
ifudaufu, inspirational (adj)
ifuifu, inflight (adj)
Ifuk, Nickel (n davoka)
Ifup, Chromium (n davoka)
igalifa, incursion (n)
igalifo, incur (v)
igefa, inference (n)
igefo, infer (v)
igepa, election (n)
igepana, electorate (n)
igepata, elective (n)
igepatiu, electively (adv)
igepatu, elective (adj)
igepeferepu, electable (adj)
Igepita, Egypt (n)
Igepitana, Egyptian (n)
igepo, elect (v)
igepu, electoral (adj)
igepua, elector (n doer)
igerishota, infringement (n)
igerishoto, infringe (v)
igeruta, inclusion (n)
igerutiu, inclusively (adv)
igeruto, include (v)
igerutu, inclusive (adj)
igeta, inflection (n)
igeto, inflect (v)
igetu, inflective (adj)

ihaushu, inward (adj)
ikathipa, invalidation (n)
ikathipo, invalidate (v)
ikathipu, invalid (adj)
ikaushiketa, insufficiency (n)
ikaushiketiu, insufficiently (adv)
ikaushiketu, insufficient (adj)
ikauvutiu, insufferably (adv)
ikauvutu, insufferable (adj)
ikemifa, involvement (n)
ikemifiu, involuntarily (adv)
ikemifo, involve (v)
ikemifu, involuntary (adj)
ikerakoferepa, invulnerability (n)
ikerakoferepu, invulnerable (adj)
ikeriuka, induction (n)
ikeriuko, induct (v)
ikeriukua, inductor (n doer)
ikeshopa, award (n)
ikeshopo, award (v)
ikiabaka, intoxication (n)
ikiabako, intoxicate (v)
ikiabakua, intoxicant (n doer)
ikiaga, ingestion (n)
ikiago, ingest (v)
ikiagua, ingester (n doer)
ikiaka, indication (n)
ikiakiu, indicatively (adv)
ikiako, indicate (v)
ikiaku, indicative (adj)
ikiakua, indicator (n doer)
ikifita, inertia (n)
ikifitu, inertial (adj)
ikifu, inert (adj)
ikika, infliction (n)
ikikiaga, indigestion (n)
ikiko, inflict (v)
ikiruetiu, inherently (adv)
ikiruetu, inherent (adj)
ikuafika, indirection (n)
ikuafikiu, indirectly (adv)
ikuafiku, indirect (adj)
iladanapu, incumbent (adj)
ilafarola, embassy (n)
ilafarolua, ambassador (n doer)
ilaiko, eureka (interj)
ilaila, inheritance (n)
ilailo, inherit (v)
Ilak, Technetium (n davoka)
ilalika, incest (n)
ilaliku, incestual (adj)
Ilanoifa, Illinois (n)
Ilap, Yttrium (n davoka)
ilaparima, ambulation (n)
ilaparimiu, ambulatorily (adv)
ilaparimo, ambulate (v)
ilaparimu, ambulatory (adj)
ilaparimua, ambulance (n doer)
ilapelutueta, ambition (n)
ilapelutuetiu, ambitiously (adv)
ilapelutuetu, ambitious (adj)
ilapeshika, ambush (n)
ilapeshiko, ambush (v)

Ilat, Silver (n davoka)
ileifara, inundation (n)
ileifaro, inundate (v)
ileka, intimacy (n)
ilekiu, intimately (adv)
ileko, intimate (v)
ileku, intimate (adj)
ilena, income (n)
ilfhem, Number_1e456
ilfi, Is (let pl)
ilianifa, incense (n d:smoke)
ilianifika, incendiary (n)
ilianifiku, incendiary (adj)
ilianita, incense (n d:anger)
ilianito, incense (v d:anger)
iliatesha, incineration (n)
iliatesho, incinerate (v)
iliateshua, incinerator (n doer)
iligerapa, insolvency (n)
iligerapu, insolvent (adj)
Ilik, Ruthenium (n davoka)
Ilip, Zirconium (n davoka)
ilipituapa, incoherence (n)
ilipituapiu, incoherently (adv)
ilipituapu, incoherent (adj)
ilishopa, indecency (n)
ilishopiu, indecently (adv)
ilishopu, indecent (adj)
Ilit, Cadmium (n davoka)
iliugerutiu, inconclusively (adv)
iliugerutu, inconclusive (adj)
iliukilata, incongruence (n)
iliukilata, incongruousness (n)
iliukilatiu, incongruently (adv)
iliukilatiu, incongruously (adv)
iliukilatu, incongruent (adj)
iliukilatu, incongruous (adj)
iliushipuferepiu, inconceivably
    (adv)
iliushipuferepu, inconceivable
    (adj)
iliuteloka, inconsistency (n)
iliutelokiu, inconsistently (adv)
iliuteloku, inconsistent (adj)
ilofa, I (let sng)
iloiga, indulgence (n)
iloigo, indulge (v)
Ilok, Rhodium (n davoka)
Ilop, Niobium (n davoka)
ilu, or (conj)
ilubereshu, irreplaceable (adj)
ilubishiu, irretrievably (adv)
ilubishu, irretrievable (adj)
ilubolikiu, irreparably (adv)
iluboliku, irreparable (adj)
iluduveka, irresponsibility (n)
iluduvekiu, irresponsibly (adv)
iluduveku, irresponsible (adj)
ilufabakiu, irrefutably (adv)
ilufabaku, irrefutable (adj)
Iluk, Palladium (n davoka)
Ilup, Molybdenum (n davoka)
ilurolama, irreconciliation (n)

ilurolamu, irreconcilable (adj)
ilushaikiu, irrevocably (adv)
ilushaiku, irrevocable (adj)
ilutelikiu, irresistibly (adv)
iluteliku, irresistible (adj)
ilutharifiu, irreversibly (adv)
ilutharifu, irreversible (adj)
iluthukiu, irrespectively (adv)
iluthuku, irrespective (adj)
iluvipa, irregularity (n)
iluvipiu, irregularly (adv)
iluvipu, irregular (adj)
imarota, influence (n)
imarotiu, influentially (adv)
imaroto, influence (v)
imarotu, influential (adj)
imarotua, influencer (n doer)
imashipa, eyeball (n)
imashipo, eyeball (v)
imiafa, innovation (n)
imiafiu, innovatively (adv)
imiafo, innovate (v)
imiafu, innovative (adj)
imiafua, innovator (n doer)
imikata, innocence (n)
imikatiu, innocently (adv)
imikatu, innocent (adj)
imoiva, irradiation (n)
imoivo, irradiate (v)
imolitha, inpatient (n)
inafika, infestation (n)
inafiko, infest (v)
Inak, Bohrium (n davoka)
Inap, Lawrencium (n davoka)
Inat, Roentgenium (n davoka)
inauka, emission (n)
inauko, emit (v)
inei, any (pron/adj/adv)
Inik, Hassium (n davoka)
Inip, Rutherfordium (n davoka)
Init, Ununbium (n davoka)
initha, eyelid (n)
iniva, infatuation (n)
inivo, infatuate (v)
inoberesha, anyplace (adv)
Inodiafa, India (n)
Inodiafana, Indian (n)
Inodianika, Indiana (n)
Inodianikapola, Indianapolis (n)
Inodiuma, Indium (n)
Inodizha, anything (n)
inohialu, anyhow (adv)
inohola, anywhere (n)
inoholu, anywhere (adv)
inoina, injury (n)
inoino, injure (v)
inoinua, injurer (n doer)
Inok, Meitnerium (n davoka)
inonei, anyone (pron)
Inop, Dubnium (n davoka)
inopeliola, anyway (adv)
inosheladei, anybody (n/pron)
inowelu, anymore (adv)

inuanika, indiscrimination (n)
inuanikiu, indiscriminately (adv)
inuaniku, indiscriminate (adj)
Inudonishiafa, Indonesia (n)
Inuk, Darmstadtium (n davoka)
Inup, Seaborgium (n davoka)
ioboritiu, inadvisably (adv)
ioboritu, inadvisable (adj)
Iodina, Iodine (n)
iofelikimiu, inappropriately (adv)
iofelikimu, inappropriate (adj)
iofika, ineptitude (n)
iofika, ineptness (n)
iofiku, inept (adj)
ioguveta, inaccessibility (n)
ioguvetu, inaccessible (adj)
iomudeniku, inanimate (adj)
iopifokueta, inattention (n)
iopifokuetiu, inattentively (adv)
iopifokuetu, inattentive (adj)
iorishekeiata, insubordination (n)
iorishekeiato, insubordinate (v)
iorishekeiatu, insubordinate (adj)
ioriterepiu, insubstantially (adv)
ioriterepu, insubstantial (adj)
iotana, iota (n)
iotharika, inadvertence (n)
iotharikiu, inadvertently (adv)
iothariku, inadvertent (adj)
Iowafa, Iowa (n)
ipaibu, intact (adj)
ipalitaka, inactivity (n)
ipalitako, inactivate (v)
ipalitaku, inactive (adj)
ipalitakueta, inactivation (n)
ipalitueta, inaction (n)
ipeikana, invigoration (n)
ipeikano, invigorate (v)
ipeka, bias (n)
ipeko, bias (v)
ipelamuna, insincereness (n)
ipelamuniu, insincerely (adv)
ipelamunu, insincere (adj)
ipelorita, eyebrow (n)
ipeludarita, correlation (n)
ipeludarito, correlate (v)
ipeludufipa, correspondence (n)
ipeludufipo, correspond (v)
ipeludufipua, correspondent (n
   doer)
iperalikiu, incorrectly (adv)
iperaliku, incorrect (adj)
ipeshipa, injustice (n)
ipi-, bi- (num 2 pref)
ipianu, binary (adj)
ipida, coop (n d:cooperative)
ipiderokirofa, costar (n)
ipiderokirofo, costar (v)
ipidilokata, bipolarity (n)
ipidilokato, bipolarize (v)
ipidilokatu, bipolar (adj)
ipidurita, cooperation (n d:agree)
ipiduritiu, cooperatively (adv

d:agree)
ipidurito, cooperate (v d:agree)
ipiduritu, cooperative (adj
   d:agree)
ipiduritua, cooperator (n doer
   d:agree)
ipidurituka, cooperative (n
   d:store)
ipifapa, intensity (n)
ipifapiu, intensely (adv)
ipifapiu, intensively (adv)
ipifapo, intensify (v)
ipifapu, intense (adj)
ipifapu, intensive (adj)
ipifiuvetuala, coprocessor (n)
ipifoka, intent (n)
ipifoka, intention (n)
ipifokiu, intentionally (adv)
ipifokiu, intently (adv)
ipifoko, intend (v)
ipifoku, intentional (adj)
ipikizhata, biotechnology (n)
ipimoimueta, copayment (n)
ipinarimiu, bilaterally (adv)
ipinarimu, bilateral (adj)
ipiropa, internal (n)
ipiropiu, internally (adv)
ipiropo, internalize (v)
ipiropu, internal (adj)
ipiropueta, internalization (n)
ipishateka, coincidence (n)
ipishatekiu, coincidentally (adv)
ipishateko, coincide (v)
ipishateku, coincident (adj)
ipishateku, coincidental (adj)
ipishelipa, corrosion (n)
ipishelipiu, corrosively (adv)
ipishelipo, corrode (v)
ipishelipu, corrosive (adj)
ipituapa, coherence (n)
ipituapu, coherent (adj)
ipituata, cohesion (n)
ipituatu, cohesive (adj)
ipituatueta, cohesiveness (n)
ipivairota, bicycle (n)
ipivairoto, bicycle (v)
ipivairotua, bicyclist (n doer)
ipoirata, indistinction (n)
ipoiratiu, indistinctly (adv)
ipoiratiu, indistinguishably (adv)
ipoiratu, indistinct (adj)
ipoiratu, indistinguishable (adj)
ipoita, instinct (n)
ipoitiu, instinctively (adv)
ipoitu, instinctive (adj)
Irafika, Iraq (n)
Irafikana, Iraqi (n)
irai-, tri- (num 3 pref)
iraimika, triangle (n)
iraimiko, triangulate (v)
iraimiku, triangular (adj)
iraimikueta, triangulation (n)
iraimoina, tripod (n)

irainarimu, trilateral (adj)
iraishata, triplet (n)
iraishoka, triple (n)
iraishoko, triple (v)
iraishoku, triple (adj)
iraitheranita, trimester (n)
Irak, Rhenium (n davoka)
iraliukiu, inaudibly (adv)
iraliuku, inaudible (adj)
Irana, Iran (n)
Iraniana, Iranian (n)
Irap, Lutetium (n davoka)
Irat, Gold (n davoka)
irathisha, insect (n)
iraupa, inland (n)
iraupu, inland (adj)
Irelanuda, Ireland (n)
Irelanudana, Irish (n)
ireth, third (num 3 ord)
iri, three (num 3 card)
irialfhemka, Number_1e12306
irida, thirty (num 30 card)
iridai-, thirty- (num 30 pref)
irideth, thirtieth (num 30 ord)
Iridiuma, Iridium (n)
irifk, tresquadragintillion (num
    1e132 card)
irift, trestrigintillion (num 1e102
    card)
Irik, Osmium (n davoka)
irika, trillion (num 1e12 card)
irikai-, tera- (num 1e12 pref)
iriketh, trillionth (num 1e12 ord)
Irip, Hafnium (n davoka)
iripa, thirteen (num 13 card)
iripai-, thirteen- (num 13 pref)
iripeth, thirteenth (num 13 ord)
irishk, trevigintillion (num 1e72
    card)
irishkai-, hienta-
irishketh, trevigintillionth (num
    1e72 ord)
irisht, tredecillion (num 1e42
    card)
irishtai-, sekata- (num 1e42 pref)
irishteth, tredecillionth (num
    1e42 ord)
Irit, Mercury (n davoka)
Irok, Ridium (n davoka)
Irona, Iron (n)
Irop, Tantalum (n davoka)
Iruk, Platinum (n davoka)
Irup, Tungsten (n davoka)
irushiu, elusively (adv)
irusho, elude (v)
irushu, elusive (adj)
iseperanida, infield (n)
iseperanidua, infielder (n doer)
ishai, shoo (interj)
ishaika, invocation (n)
ishaiko, invoke (v)

ishederaipu, inbound (adj)
ishefeleida, inbreed (n)
ishefeleido, inbreed (v)
ishegelorifu, inboard (adj)
ishegoka, intake (n)
isheifa, infertility (n)
isheifu, infertile (adj)
isheithu, inelastic (adj)
isheka, innard (n)
ishekiu, innerly (adv)
isheku, inner (adj)
Ishelama, Islam (n)
isheleka, instruction (n)
ishelekiu, instructionally (adv)
ishelekiu, instructively (adv)
isheleko, instruct (v)
isheleku, instructional (adj)
isheleku, instructive (adj)
ishelekua, instructor (n doer)
ishelena, inmate (n)
ishena, infamy (n)
isheniu, infamously (adv)
ishenu, infamous (adj)
ishepata, index (n)
ishepati, indices (n pl)
ishepato, index (v)
ishepatua, indexer (n doer)
Isherahila, Israel (n)
Isherahilana, Israeli (n)
ishereida, eyelash (n)
isherela, ensurance (n)
isherela, insurance (n)
isherelo, ensure (v)
isherelo, insure (v)
isherelua, insurer (n doer)
isheretiemiu, insidiously (adv)
isheretiemu, insidious (adj)
isherifokiu, indescribably (adv)
isherifoku, indescribable (adj)
isherolfu, inline (adj)
isheta, insertion (n)
ishetela, indoors (n)
ishetelu, indoor (adj)
isheteriago, instill (v)
isheto, insert (v)
ishetu, into (prep)
ishetua, inserter (n doer)
ishetuina, insert (n)
ishiafa, insanity (n)
ishiafiu, insanely (adv)
ishiafu, insane (adj)
ishiamipu, intangible (adj)
ishiata, inquest (n)
ishiatua, inquisitor (n doer)
ishiatueta, inquisition (n)
ishileka, infrastructure (n)
ishineta, instigation (n)
ishineto, instigate (v)
ishinetua, instigator (n doer)
ishiniuku, insurmountable (adj)
ishipa, inception (n)
ishoita, inside (n)
ishoitu, inside (adj/adv/prep)

ishoitua, insider (n doer)
ishopelita, institute (n)
ishopelito, institute (v)
ishopelitueta, institution (n)
ishopelituetiu, institutionally
    (adv)
ishopelitueto, institutionalize (v)
ishopelituetu, institutional (adj)
ishopeto, instate (v)
ishorifopa, insensitivity (n)
ishorifopu, insensitive (adj)
ishoteranaka, ingredient (n)
ishu, in (prep)
ishualifa, isolation (n)
ishualifara, isolationist (n)
ishualifo, isolate (v)
ishualifua, isolator (n doer)
ishualifueta, isolationism (n)
Italiana, Italian (n)
Italifa, Italy (n)
itatorifiu, inoffensively (adv)
itatorifu, inoffensive (adj)
itefudaida, inadequacy (n)
itefudaidiu, inadequately (adv)
itefudaidu, inadequate (adj)
iteira, installation (n)
iteira, installment (n)
iteiro, install (v)
iteirua, installer (n doer)
itelika, insistence (n)
itelikiu, insistently (adv)
iteliko, insist (v)
iteliku, insistent (adj)
itenika, inadmission (n)
iteniku, inadmissible (adj)
itepa, injection (n)
itepo, inject (v)
itepu, injectable (adj)
itepua, injector (n doer)
iterelisha, inroad (n)
iterifita, insinuation (n)
iterifito, insinuate (v)
iterinota, intolerance (n)
iterinotiu, intolerably (adv)
iterinotu, intolerable (adj)
Iteriuma, Yttrium (n)
Iterobiuma, Ytterbium (n)
ithaipa, invoice (n)
ithaipo, invoice (v)
itharika, inverse (n)
itharikiu, inversely (adv)
ithariko, invert (v)
ithariku, inverse (adj)
itharikua, inverter (n doer)
itharikueta, inversion (n)
itheriathu, inhospitable (adj)
ithima, episode (n)
ithimiu, episodally (adv)
ithimu, episodal (adj)
ithishaka, incision (n)
ithishakiu, incisively (adv)
ithishako, incise (v)
ithishaku, incisive (adj)

ithishakua, incisor (n doer)
ithishopa, indecision (n)
ithishopiu, indecisively (adv)
ithishopu, indecisive (adj)
ithoitiku, infeasible (adj)
ithoku, inapplicable (adj)
ithuata, emphasis (n)
ithuatio, emphasize (v pa)
ithuato, emphasize (v)
ithufishiu, irreverently (adv)
ithufishu, irreverent (adj)
ithuka, inspection (n)
ithuko, inspect (v)
ithukua, inspector (n doer)
ithumapa, invariant (n)
ithumapu, invariably (adj)
ithushota, irrationality (n)
ithushotiu, irrationally (adv)
ithushotu, irrational (adj)
ithutha, insight (n)
ithuthu, insightful (adj)
itieta, inflexibility (n)
itietu, inflexible (adj)
itiruika, irrelevance (n)
itiruika, irrelevancy (n)
itiruiku, irrelevant (adj)
itiufota, infinity (n)
itiufotiu, infinitely (adv)
itiufotu, infinite (adj)
itivisha, indiscretion (n)
itivishiu, indiscreetly (adv)
itivishu, indiscreet (adj)
itivoiku, indisputable (adj)
itorepa, instance (n)
itorepetoitiu, instantaneously (adv)
itorepetoitu, instantaneous (adj)
itorepiu, instantly (adv)
itorepo, instantiate (v)
itorepu, instant (adj)
itova, indifference (n)
itoviu, indifferently (adv)
itovu, indifferent (adj)
ituariko, inviolate (v)
ituariku, inviolate (adj)
ituberuniu, inexpensively (adv)
ituberunu, inexpensive (adj)
itugoitiu, inexcusably (adv)
ituguitu, inexcusable (adj)
itulifata, inaccuracy (n)
itulifatiu, inaccurately (adv)
itulifatu, inaccurate (adj)
itulifiu, incurably (adv)
itulifu, incurable (adj)
itulishiu, indeterminately (adv)
itulishu, indeterminate (adj)
itulishua, indeterminant (n doer)
itushatu, inexact (adj)
iumenu, unless (prep/conj)
iutaunu, until (prep/conj)
ivadava, emotion (n)

ivadaviu, emotionally (adv)
ivadavo, emote (v)
ivadavu, emotional (adj)
ivadavu, emotive (adj)
ivanipora, incompetence (n)
ivaniporiu, incompetently (adv)
ivaniporu, incompetent (adj)
ivaritufa, insecurity (n)
ivaritufiu, insecurely (adv)
ivaritufu, insecure (adj)
ivaupu, invaluable (adj)
iveidautu, upbeat (adj)
iveidieka, upright (n)
iveidiekiu, uprightly (adv)
iveidieku, upright (adj)
iveiduaifa, uptightness (n)
iveiduaifu, uptight (adj)
iveifalima, upstream (n)
iveifalimu, upstream (adj)
iveifelarinu, upfront (adj)
iveifeliega, upswing (n)
iveifepa, upset (n)
iveifepio, upset (v pa)
iveifepo, upset (v)
iveifepu, upset (adj)
iveigeraufa, uproar (n)
iveigoka, uptake (n)
iveiguba, upheaval (n)
iveihaushiu, upward (adv)
iveihaushiu, upwards (adv)
iveihaushu, upward (adj)
iveihaushu, upwards (adj)
iveikaima, upturn (n)
iveikelofa, upkeep (n)
iveilu, up (prep)
iveimiuna, uptown (n)
iveimiunu, uptown (adj)
iveiparinu, uphill (adj)
iveirauko, uplift (v)
iveishaiasha, upstate (n)
iveishaiashu, upstate (adj)
iveishekoita, upshot (n)
iveishoita, upside (n)
iveishokalita, upstart (n)
iveishokalitu, upstart (adj)
iveishoterana, upgrade (n)
iveishoterano, upgrade (v)
iveishuiku, upscale (adj)
iveita, up (n)
iveitaina, upstairs (n)
iveitainu, upstairs (adj)
iveithorithio, upheld (v pa)
iveithoritho, uphold (v)
iveitiu, upperly (adv)
iveito, up (v)
iveitolika, update (n)
iveitoliko, update (v)
iveitolikua, updater (n doer)
iveitu, upper (adj)
iveitueta, uppitiness (n)
iveituetu, uppity (adj)
iveitweku, uppermost (adj)
iveivoiga, upsurge (n)

iveiwefipo, uproot (v)
ivemu, upon (prep)
ivieraka, inferno (n)
ivieraku, infernal (adj)
ivirota, infection (n)
ivirothara, ineffectiveness (n)
ivirothara, inefficiency (n)
ivirothariu, ineffectively (adv)
ivirothariu, inefficiently (adv)
ivirotharu, ineffective (adj)
ivirotharu, inefficient (adj)
iviroto, infect (v)
ivirotu, infectious (adj)
ivirotu, infective (adj)
ivoiga, insurgency (n)
ivoigiu, insurgently (adv)
ivoigo, insurge (v)
ivoigu, insurgent (adj)
ivoigua, insurgent (n doer)
ivoikuata, insurrection (n)
ivoikuato, insurrect (v)
ivorina, information (n)
ivorinatiu, informally (adv)
ivorinatu, informal (adj)
ivoriniu, informatively (adv)
ivorino, inform (v)
ivorinu, informative (adj)
ivorinua, informer (n doer)
ivoshiakiu, inescapably (adv)
ivoshiaku, inescapable (adj)
ivuafitiu, indefinitely (adv)
ivuafitu, indefinite (adj)
ivugana, inferiority (n)
ivuganu, inferior (adj)
ivuta, input (n)
ivuto, input (v)
ivutua, inputer (n doer)
iwabaima, eyesore (n)
iwaderinota, eyeglass (n)
iwadorima, eyewear (n)
iwafa, eye (n)
iwafemenu, eyeless (adj)
iwaferioka, eyewitness (n)
iwafo, eye (v)
iwafoka, inhalant (n)
iwafoko, inhale (v)
iwafokua, inhaler (n doer)
iwafokueta, inhalation (n)
iwafua, ever (n doer)
iwaleka, eyelet (n)
iwaperulika, eyestrain (n)
iwaroifua, eyeliner (n doer)
iwathetisha, eyepiece (n)
iwathutha, eyesight (n)
iweifoka, insignificance (n)
iweifokiu, insignificantly (adv)
iweifoku, insignificant (adj)
izhaita, infallibility (n)
izhaitiu, infallibly (adv)
izhaitu, infallible (adj)
izhanika, invasion (n)
izhanikiu, invasively (adv)
izhaniko, invade (v)

izhaniku, invasive (adj)
izhanikua, invader (n doer)
izhuga, acid (n)
izhugo, acidify (v)
izhugu, acidic (adj)
izhurita, inexperience (n)
kabato, park (v d:stop)
kabika, sneeze (n)
kabiko, sneeze (v)
kabiku, sneezy (adj)
kabita, parlor (n)
kabito, parlor (v)
kabofita, intrusion (n)
kabofitiu, intrusively (adv)
kabofito, intrude (v)
kabofitu, intrusive (adj)
kabofitua, intruder (n doer)
kabofitueta, intrusiveness (n)
kada, cord (n)
kadaka, rudeness (n)
kadakiu, rudely (adv)
kadaku, rude (adj)
Kademiuma, Cadmium (n)
kado, cord (v)
kadorika, industry (n)
kadorikiu, industriously (adv)
kadoriko, industrialize (v)
kadoriku, industrial (adj)
kadoriku, industrious (adj)
kadorikua, industrialist (n doer)
kadorikueta, industrialization (n)
kafipa, craft (n)
kafipiu, craftily (adv)
kafipo, craft (v)
kafipu, crafty (adj)
kafipua, craftsman (n doer)
kafita, catch (n)
kafitio, caught (v pa)
kafito, catch (v)
kafitu, catchy (adj)
kafitua, catcher (n doer)
kai, yay (interj)
kaiapa, yap (n)
kaiapo, yap (v)
kaiapua, yapper (n doer)
kaiatha, wrath (n)
kaiathu, wrathful (adj)
kaibako, wrack (v)
kaifa, hate (n)
kaifa, hatred (n)
kaifiu, hatefully (adv)
kaifo, hate (v)
kaifoka, harshness (n)
kaifokiu, harshly (adv)
kaifoko, harshen (v)
kaifoku, harsh (adj)
kaifopa, jail (n)
kaifopekiafa, jailhouse (n)
kaifopo, jail (v)
kaifopua, jailer (n doer)
kaifu, hateful (adj)
kaifua, hater (n doer)
kaiga, hostage (n)

kaikala, StrontiumFood (n)
kaiko, raze (v)
kaikua, razor (n doer)
kail, you (pron 2nd sng obj)
kail, you (pron 2nd sng sub)
kaima, turn (n)
kaimafena, turnover (n)
kaimedoiara, turntable (n)
kaimegerafika, turncoat (n)
kaimepaiata, turnpike (n)
kaimeteriku, turnkey (adj)
kaimo, turn (v)
kaimobelaitha, turnaround (n)
kaimoveipa, turnabout (n)
kaimuila, turnout (n)
kaimunefa, turnoff (n)
kaina, chi (n)
kainupa, canard (n)
kair, you (pron 2nd pl obj)
kair, you (pron 2nd pl sub)
Kairofa, Cairo (n)
kairopa, mold (n d:form)
kairopo, mold (v d:form)
kairsh, your (pron 2nd pl pos sub)
kairsh, yours (pron 2nd pl pos obj)
kaish, your (pron 2nd sng pos sub)
kaish, yours (pron 2nd sng pos obj)
kaishfal, yourself (pron 2nd sng refl)
kaishfar, yourselves (pron 2nd pl refl)
kaitha, bouquet (n)
kaithepa, invalid (n d:person)
Kaitifa, Haiti (n)
kaiva, wag (n)
kaivapa, wagon (n)
kaivo, wag (v)
kaivua, wagger (n doer)
Kaleshiuma, Calcium (n)
kaleta, crick (n)
kaleto, crick (v)
kalifoka, crash (n)
kalifoko, crash (v)
kalifokua, crasher (n doer)
Kaliforeniuma, Californium (n)
Kaliforina, California (n)
kalika, cram (n)
kaliko, cram (v)
kalina, holly (n)
kalipa, crab (n)
kalipo, crab (v)
kalipu, crabby (adj)
kalishiu, lucratively (adv)
kalishu, lucrative (adj)
kalufa, stroll (n)
kalufo, stroll (v)
kalufua, stroller (n doer)
kalugo, crave (v)
kamafita, catalyst (n)

kamafito, catalyze (v)
kamafitu, catalytic (adj)
kamafitua, catalyzer (n doer)
kamisha, tissue (n)
Kamuberiga, Cambridge (n)
Kamubodiafa, Cambodia (n)
Kamubodiana, Cambodian (n)
Kanadafa, Canada (n)
Kanadiana, Canadian (n)
kanifa, chant (n)
kanifo, chant (v)
kanifopa, journey (n)
kanifopo, journey (v)
kanifota, journal (n)
kanifoto, journal (v)
kanifotu, journalistic (adj)
kanifotua, journalist (n doer)
kanifotueta, journalism (n)
kanifua, chanter (n doer)
kanika, gym (n)
kanikava, gymnasium (n)
Kanishasha, Kansas (n)
Kanukala, Hanukkah (n)
kapa, hand (n)
kapada, handle (n)
kapaderolata, handlebar (n)
kapado, handle (v)
kapadua, handler (n doer)
kapana, kappa (n)
kaparuga, handshake (n)
kaparugio, handshook (v pa)
kaparugo, handshake (v)
kapasha, parrot (n)
kapasho, parrot (v)
kapediefa, handcuff (n)
kapediefo, handcuff (v)
kapedoruga, handgun (n)
kapedotisho, handpick (v)
kapefipa, handicap (n)
kapefipo, handicap (v)
kapekafipo, handcraft (v)
kapeloafa, handkerchief (n)
kapeloidio, handwrote (v pa)
kapeloido, handwrite (v)
kapeloidua, handwriter (n doer)
kapeluga, fart (n)
kapelugo, fart (v)
kapeluita, handrail (n)
kapenafa, handbag (n)
kapenagio, handmade (v pa)
kapenago, handmake (v)
kapesha, handful (n)
kapesheriga, manuscript (n)
kapeterelita, handstand (n)
kapevonuda, handbook (n)
kapezhoda, handset (n)
kapo, hand (v)
kapozhiniu, handsomely (adv)
kapozhinu, handsome (adj)
kapu, handy (adj)
kapua, handyman (n doer)
kapuila, handout (n)
kapukioka, handiwork (n)

kapurita, maneuver (n)
kapuriteferepa, maneuverability (n)
kapurito, maneuver (v)
Karebona, Carbon (n)
kareka, crux (n)
Karibiana, Caribbean (n)
karifelualo, assail (v)
karifelualu, assailable (adj)
karifelualua, assailant (n doer)
karifoka, inducement (n)
karifokiu, inductively (adv)
karifoko, induce (v)
karifoku, inductive (adj)
karifokua, inducer (n doer)
karigaka, tournament (n)
karika, assassination (n)
kariko, assassinate (v)
karikua, assassin (n doer)
karila, nation (n)
karilana, nationality (n)
karilefifa, nationhood (n)
karilekerashu, nationwide (adj)
kariliu, nationally (adv)
karilo, nationalize (v)
karilota, attitude (n)
karilu, national (adj)
karilua, nationalist (n doer)
karilueta, nationalism (n)
karinafa, astronomy (n)
karinafiu, astronimically (adv)
karinafu, astronomical (adj)
karinafua, astronomer (n doer)
kariniata, astronavigation (n)
kariniato, astronavigate (v)
kariniatua, astronaut (n doer)
karisha, gulf (n)
karisho, engulf (v)
karitha, dose (n)
karitho, dose (v)
karithueta, dosage (n)
Karitoforuda, Hartford (n)
karodinala, cardinal (n)
Karokuaina, marijuana (n)
karubaka, wreck (n)
karubako, wreck (v)
karubakua, wrecker (n doer)
karubashika, wreckage (n)
kashina, casino (n)
kataka, rut (n)
kathalko, wield (v)
kathipa, validity (n)
kathipiu, validly (adv)
kathipo, validate (v)
kathipu, valid (adj)
kathipueta, validation (n)
kathiufa, valor (n)
kathiufu, valiant (adj)
katika, wage (n)
katiko, wage (v)
katisha, wager (n)
katisho, wager (v)
katufa, strobe (n)

katufo, strobe (v)
katuka, stroke (n)
katuko, stroke (v)
katukua, stroker (n doer)
kauaifa, wail (n)
kauaifo, wail (v)
kauaita, horror (n)
kauaitiu, horribly (adv)
kauaito, horrify (v)
kauaitu, horrible (adj)
kauaitu, horrific (adj)
kaudaiku, horrid (adj)
kaufuapa, hotdog (n)
kaufuapo, hotdog (v)
kaugaifu, horrendous (adj)
kaukatu, rank (adj d:rotten)
kaukiata, catapult (n)
kaukiato, catapult (v)
kauna, card (n)
kauno, card (v)
kaunupelorika, cardboard (n)
kaunupeloriku, cardboard (adj)
kaupa, wealth (n)
kaupu, wealthy (adj)
kaushefuarema, hotbed (n)
kaushegurita, hotcake (n)
kaushekefa, hothead (n)
kaushekoita, hotshot (n)
kausheroifa, hotline (n)
kaushi, hots (n pl)
kaushiketa, sufficiency (n)
kaushiketiu, sufficiently (adv)
kaushiketo, suffice (v)
kaushiketu, sufficient (adj)
kaushiu, hotly (adv)
kaushu, hot (adj)
kauvaipa, suffocation (n)
kauvaipo, suffocate (v)
kauvutiu, sufferably (adv)
kauvuto, suffer (v)
kauvutu, sufferable (adj)
kauvutua, sufferer (n doer)
Kauwifa, Hawaii (n)
kava, tug (n)
kavaika, hassle (n)
kavaiko, hassle (v)
kavaita, haste (n)
kavaitiu, hastily (adv)
kavaito, hasten (v)
kavaitu, hasty (adj)
kavalo, gather (v)
kavalua, gatherer (n doer)
kavata, mathematic (n)
kavatieno, haunt (v)
kavatiu, mathematically (adv)
kavatu, mathematical (adj)
kavatua, mathematician (n doer)
kavepa, basin (n)
kaveshekoba, tugboat (n)
kavilota, metropolis (n)
kavilotua, metropolitan (n doer)
kavita, math (n)
kavo, tug (v)

kazhiga, square (n)
kazhigiu, squarely (adv)
kazhigo, square (v)
Kebefika, Quebec (n)
kebeta, hobby (n)
kebetua, hobbyist (n doer)
kefebeluaga, headache (n)
kefeborifu, headstrong (adj)
kefedorifa, headgear (n)
kefegerulitua, headhunter (n doer)
kefeidona, headwater (n)
kefekarita, headquarters (n)
kefekarito, headquarter (v)
kefeluana, headlight (n)
kefepelesha, headdress (n)
kefepeleshua, headdresser (n doer)
kefepeliola, headway (n)
kefepelorika, headboard (n)
keferoifa, headline (n)
keferoifo, headline (v)
keferoifua, headliner (n doer)
kefesherana, headroom (n)
kefeshetaima, headband (n)
kefethelina, headwind (n)
kefethioka, headmaster (n)
kefezhoda, headset (n)
kefikeidona, meltwater (n)
kefiketiena, meltdown (n)
kefiko, melt (v)
kefita, head (n)
kefito, head (v)
kefitu, heady (adj)
kefitua, header (n doer)
kefyapa, headphone (n)
keia, K (let sng)
keianegufika, wanderlust (n)
keiano, wander (v)
keianua, wanderer (n doer)
keiapa, buckle (n)
keiapo, buckle (v)
keiapua, buckler (n doer)
keiba, visage (n)
keibata, visor (n)
keidana, hotel (n)
keiesho, wane (v)
keifa, care (n)
keifita, double (n)
keifitiu, doubly (adv)
keifito, double (v)
keifitu, double (adj)
keifitua, doubler (n doer)
keifo, care (v)
keifumena, carelessness (n)
keifumeniu, carelessly (adv)
keifumenu, careless (adj)
keifusha, carefulness (n)
keifushiu, carefully (adv)
keifushu, careful (adj)
keigiu, overwhelmingly (adv)
keigo, overwhelm (v)
keihem, Number_1e3906

keikuta, remark (n d:reply)
keikutiu, remarkably (adv d:reply)
keikuto, remark (v d:reply)
keikutu, remarkable (adj d:reply)
keili, Ks (let pl)
keilifa, viscera (n)
keilifiu, viscerally (adv)
keilifu, visceral (adj)
keilopa, consciousness (n)
keilopiu, consciously (adv)
keilopu, conscious (adj)
keinapa, nomad (n)
keinapu, nomadic (adj)
keinifa, gallery (n)
keipifota, patent (n)
keipifoto, patent (v)
keipipa, petal (n)
keisha, talent (n)
keisho, talent (v)
keita, lottery (n)
keitesha, wedge (n)
keitesho, wedge (v)
keitina, hyphen (n)
keitino, hyphenate (v)
keiuka, gag (n d:choke)
keiuko, gag (v d:choke)
keiuna, coo (n)
keiuno, coo (v)
keiva, nod (n)
keivo, nod (v)
keizhaka, x-ray (n)
keizhako, x-ray (v)
kelaba, stud (n)
kelabo, stud (v)
keladipa, scrape (n)
keladipo, scrape (v)
keladipua, scraper (n doer)
kelafa, scrap (n)
kelafegaitha, cockroach (n)
kelafevonuda, scrapbook (n)
kelafo, scrap (v)
kelafu, scrappy (adj)
kelafua, scrapper (n doer)
kelai, hooray (interj)
kelai, hurrah (interj)
kelai, hurray (interj)
kelaiafa, volley (n)
kelaiafo, volley (v)
kelaifa, greed (n)
kelaififa, kingdom (n)
kelaifiu, greedily (adv)
kelaifu, greedy (adj)
kelaika, strike (n)
kelaikio, struck (v pa)
kelaikiu, strikingly (adv)
kelaiko, strike (v)
kelaikua, striker (n doer)
kelaikuila, strikeout (n)
kelaipa, prick (n)
kelaipo, prick (v)
kelaishoka, scorch (n)
kelaishoko, scorch (v)

kelaishokua, scorcher (n doer)
kelaita, score (n)
kelaitekauna, scorecard (n)
kelaitemenu, scoreless (adj)
kelaitepelorika, scoreboard (n)
kelaito, score (v)
kelaitua, scorer (n doer)
kelaiva, swag (n)
kelaivata, swagger (n)
kelaivato, swagger (v)
kelaivo, swag (v)
kelala, laxity (n)
kelaliu, laxly (adv)
kelalo, lax (v)
kelalu, lax (adj)
kelamuta, scratch (n)
kelamuto, scratch (v)
kelamutu, scratchy (adj)
kelamutua, scratcher (n doer)
kelaniko, hamper (v d:hinder)
kelanipo, trample (v)
kelanita, tramp (n)
kelanito, tramp (v)
kelariga, attorney (n)
kelaripa, skull (n)
Kelasha, Christ (n)
Kelashamala, Christmas (n)
Kelashara, Christian (n)
kelashika, wack (n)
kelashiko, wack (v)
kelashiko, whack (v)
kelashiku, wacky (adj)
kelashiku, whacky (adj)
kelashikua, wacko (n doer)
kelashikua, whacko (n doer)
kelauapa, brunt (n)
kelaufa, horoscope (n)
kelaugo, gross (v d:disgusting)
kelaugu, gross (adj d:disgusting)
kelauka, greatness (n)
kelaukiu, greatly (adv)
kelauku, great (adj)
kelaukwaku, greatest (adj)
kelaukwelu, greater (adj)
kelaupa, wallop (n)
kelaupo, wallop (v)
kelautesha, brutality (n)
kelauteshiu, brutally (adv)
kelautesho, brutalize (v)
kelauteshu, brutal (adj)
kelauteshua, brute (n doer)
kelautha, bumble (n d:bungle)
kelautho, bumble (v d:bungle)
kelauthua, bumbler (n doer d:bungle)
kelavuga, craze (n)
kelavugiu, crazily (adv)
kelavugo, craze (v)
kelavugu, crazy (adj)
kelazho, trudge (v)
keleiaka, goof (n)
keleiako, goof (v)
keleiaku, goofy (adj)

keleida, rigidity (n)
keleidana, rigor (n)
keleidaniu, rigorously (adv)
keleidanu, rigorous (adj)
keleidiu, rigidly (adv)
keleidu, rigid (adj)
keleifa, principal (n)
keleika, deletion (n)
keleiko, delete (v)
keleipa, bulk (n)
keleipafu, bulky (adj)
keleipekefita, bulkhead (n)
keleipo, bulk (v)
keleipu, bulk (adj)
keleizha, reason (n)
keleizhiu, reasonably (adv)
keleizho, reason (v)
keleizhu, reasonable (adj)
keleizhua, reasoner (n doer)
kelenuda, chair (n d:seat)
kelera, girl (n)
keleru, girly (adj)
kelesha, replication (n)
keleshelefa, hardware (n)
kelesho, replicate (v)
keleshua, replicator (n doer)
keletha, chick (n)
keliaba, king (n)
Keliafa, EhoDay06 (n)
keliafa, scoop (n)
keliafeliukiu, crosswise (adv)
keliafeliuku, crosswise (adj)
keliafo, scoop (v)
keliafua, scooper (n doer)
keliagiaula, crossfire (n)
keliagurifa, crosscurrent (n)
keliaika, shriek (n)
keliaiko, shriek (v)
keliaikua, shrieker (n doer)
keliaka, cross (n)
keliakafena, crossover (n)
keliakediafa, crossbow (n)
keliako, cross (v)
kelialialita, crossword (n)
keliana, diplomacy (n)
kelianu, diplomatic (adj)
kelianua, diplomat (n doer)
keliapa, strife (n)
keliapio, strove (v pa)
keliapo, strive (v)
keliapua, strifer (n doer)
keliasha, countess (n)
keliashipalota, crosstalk (n)
keliata, guitar (n)
keliaterelisha, crossroad (n)
keliatha, tether (n)
keliatho, tether (v)
keliatua, guitarist (n doer)
keliaufa, scourge (n)
keliaufo, scourge (v)
keliauka, decimation (n)
keliauko, decimate (v)
keliaumo, tout (v)

keliausho, scour (v)
keliazha, scout (n)
keliazhethioka, scoutmaster (n)
keliazho, scout (v)
keliefo, scrimp (v)
keliega, wing (n)
keliegebeleisha, wingspan (n)
keliegepelona, wingman (n)
keliegepeloni, wingmen (n pl)
keliego, wing (v)
keliegua, winger (n doer)
kelieka, hawk (n)
kelieko, hawk (v)
keliekua, hawker (n doer)
kelieta, shrill (n)
kelietha, truss (n)
kelieto, shrill (v)
kelietu, shrill (adj)
kelifa, sip (n)
kelifata, siphon (n)
kelifato, siphon (v)
kelifiko, discard (v)
kelifo, sip (v)
kelifota, hardiness (n)
kelifotiu, hardily (adv)
kelifotu, hardy (adj)
kelifu, sippy (adj)
kelifua, sipper (n doer)
keliga, flea (n)
Keligata, VanAllenBelt (n)
kelika, visit (n)
kelikara, thatch (n)
kelikaro, thatch (v)
kelikarua, thatcher (n doer)
kelikata, university (n)
kelikioka, toil (n)
kelikioko, toil (v)
keliko, visit (v)
kelikua, visitor (n doer)
kelikueta, visitation (n)
kelinufa, turtle (n)
kelinufethariba, turtleneck (n)
kelinufetharibu, turtleneck (adj)
kelioisho, sear (v)
kelioka, duel (n)
kelioko, duel (v)
keliokua, dueler (n doer)
keliopa, quake (n)
keliopo, quake (v)
kelita, hardness (n)
kelitedalitha, hardcover (n)
kelitedalithu, hardcover (adj)
kelitedaupa, hardtop (n)
kelitefanina, hardwood (n)
kelitefifa, hardship (n)
kelitekirotu, hardcore (adj)
kelitemashipa, hardball (n)
keliteroifa, hardline (n)
keliteroifu, hardline (adj)
keliteroifua, hardliner (n doer)
kelitevaka, hardback (n)
kelitha, visa (n)
kelitiu, hard (adv)

kelito, harden (v)
kelitoiu, hardly (adv)
kelitu, hard (adj)
kelitwaku, hardest (adj)
kelitwelu, harder (adj)
keliupo, scrounge (v)
keliuta, putt (n)
keliutato, putter (v)
keliuto, putt (v)
keliutua, putter (n doer)
kelivatha, blubber (n)
kelivathu, blubbery (adj)
Kelivelanuda, Cleveland (n)
kelivuko, scurry (v)
keloako, pierce (v)
kelofa, keep (n)
kelofemoaka, keepsake (n)
kelofio, kept (v pa)
kelofo, keep (v)
kelofua, keeper (n doer)
keloiano, groom (v d:clean)
keloika, growth (n)
keloikio, grew (v pa)
keloiko, grow (v)
keloikua, grower (n doer)
keloina, tile (n)
keloino, tile (v)
keloinua, tiler (n doer)
keloipa, screw (n)
keloipediapua, screwdriver (n doer)
keloipo, screw (v)
keloipu, screwy (adj)
keloipua, screwer (n doer)
keloisho, scoff (v)
keloita, skepticism (n)
keloitiu, skeptically (adv)
keloitu, skeptical (adj)
keloitua, skeptic (n doer)
kelorika, dark (n)
kelorikesherana, darkroom (n)
kelorikesheranao, shranf (v prp)
kelorikesheranio, shran (v pa)
kelorikiu, darkly (adv)
keloriko, darken (v)
keloriku, dark (adj)
kelorikueta, darkness (n)
kelorikweku, darkest (adj)
kelorikwelu, darker (adj)
Kelorina, Chlorine (n)
keloripa, scorn (n)
keloripiu, scornfully (adv)
keloripo, scorn (v)
keloripu, scornful (adj)
keloripua, scorner (n doer)
keloritha, impulse (n)
kelorithiu, impulsively (adv)
kelorithu, impulsive (adj)
kelorito, scold (v)
kelosha, year (n)
keloshonuda, yearbook (n)
keloshu, yearly (adj)
keluafa, scope (n)

keluafo, scope (v)
keluafua, scoper (n doer)
keluaika, scepticism (n)
keluaiku, sceptical (adj)
keluaikua, sceptic (n doer)
keluaka, creak (n)
keluakiu, creakily (adv)
keluako, creak (v)
keluaku, creaky (adj)
keluakua, creaker (n doer)
keluapa, ovulation (n)
keluapo, ovulate (v)
keluapu, ovarian (adj)
keluapua, ovary (n doer)
keluautha, growl (n)
keluautho, growl (v)
keluba, counter (n d:d: shelf)
kelufota, brother (n)
kelufotefifa, brotherhood (n)
kelufotu, brotherly (adj)
keluga, loan (n)
kelugio, lent (v pa)
kelugo, lend (v)
kelugua, lender (n doer)
keluka, chicken (n)
kelukuta, chuckle (n d:laugh)
kelukuto, chuckle (v d:laugh)
kelumo, enfeeble (v)
kelumu, feeble (adj)
keluna, green (n)
kelunu, green (adj)
kelupa, ovum (n)
kelupi, ova (n pl)
keluripa, alleviation (n)
keluripo, alleviate (v)
kelurusha, collusion (n)
kelurusho, collude (v)
kelurushu, collusive (adj)
kelusha, brush (n d:bristle handle)
kelushika, collision (n)
kelushiko, collide (v)
kelushikua, collider (n doer)
kelusho, brush (v d:bristle handle)
kelushua, brusher (n doer d:bristle handle)
kemifu, vulldon (n)
kemifiu, voluntarily (adv)
kemifo, volunteer (v)
kemifu, voluntary (adj)
kemifua, volunteer (n doer)
kemikila, wannabe (n)
kemiko, wanna (v)
keminoka, ring (n d:sound)
keminokio, rang (v pa d:sound)
keminoko, ring (v d:sound)
keminokua, ringer (n doer d:sound)
kemipa, want (n)
kemipo, want (v)
kenatha, quicksand (n)
kenedauna, quicktime (n)

kenesharugena, quicksilver (n)
kenifa, revolution (n d:political change)
kenifo, revolutionize (v d:political change)
kenifu, revolutionary (adj d:political change)
kenifua, revolutionary (n doer d:political change)
kenika, revolt (n)
keniko, revolt (v)
kenikua, revolter (n doer)
kenota, quickness (n)
kenotiu, quickly (adv)
kenoto, quicken (v)
kenotu, quick (adj)
Kenotukifa, Kentucky (n)
kenotweku, quickest (adj)
kenotwelu, quicker (adj)
kepa, knee (n)
kepedefipa, kneecap (n)
kepefo, kneel (v)
kepefua, kneeling (n doer)
kepo, knee (v)
kerafika, task (n)
kerafiko, task (v)
kerafikua, tasker (n doer)
keraga, gear (n d:sprocket)
kerago, gear (v d:sprocket)
keraiapa, squabble (n)
keraiapo, squabble (v)
keraiapua, squabbler (n doer)
keraiba, club (n d:stick)
keraibo, club (v d:stick)
keraifota, negation (n)
keraifoto, negate (v)
keraiga, blast (n)
keraigo, blast (v)
keraigua, blaster (n doer)
keraika, dive (n)
keraikio, dove (v pa)
keraiko, dive (v)
keraikua, diver (n doer)
keraila, brass (n)
kerailakiu, brazenly (adv)
kerailaku, brazen (adj)
kerailu, brassy (adj)
keraina, clam (n)
kerainota, clamp (n)
kerainotheka, clamshell (n)
kerainotiena, clampdown (n)
kerainoto, clamp (v)
kerainotua, clamper (n doer)
keraishoka, shark (n)
keraita, negative (n)
keraitha, claw (n)
keraithieka, pounce (n d:catch)
keraithieko, pounce (v d:catch)
keraithiekua, pouncer (n doer d:catch)
keraitho, claw (v)
keraitiu, negatively (adv)
keraitu, negative (adj)

keraitueta, negativism (n)
keraka, weakness (n)
kerakiu, weakly (adv)
kerako, weaken (v)
kerakoferepa, vulnerability (n)
kerakoferepu, vulnerable (adj)
keraku, weak (adj)
kerakwaku, weakest (adj)
kerakwelu, weaker (adj)
keralika, scramble (n)
keraliko, scramble (v)
keralikua, scrambler (n doer)
keralipa, tarp (n)
keralishoka, cemetery (n)
kerana, gram (n)
keranifa, scroll (n)
keranifo, scroll (v)
keranikata, bandit (n)
kerasha, width (n)
Kerashata, Mister (n)
kerashethilopu, widespread (adj)
kerashiu, widely (adv)
kerasho, widen (v)
kerashu, wide (adj)
kerashua, widener (n doer)
kerashwaku, widest (adj)
kerashwelu, wider (adj)
kerata, wear (n d:erode, fatigue)
keratha, lot (n)
keratio, wore (v pa d:erode, fatigue)
keratiu, wearily (adv d:erode, fatigue)
kerato, wear (v d:erode, fatigue)
keratu, weary (adj d:erode, fatigue)
keratu, wearysome (adj d:fatigue)
keratueta, weariness (n d:fatigue)
kerauga, blaze (n)
keraugo, blaze (v)
kerauika, sneer (n)
kerauiko, sneer (v)
kerauka, junk (n)
kerauko, junk (v)
kerauku, junky (adj)
kerausho, shred (v)
keraushua, shredder (n doer)
kerefina, jewel (n)
kerefinoka, jewelry (n)
kerefinua, jeweler (n doer)
kerega, grunt (n)
kerego, grunt (v)
keregua, grunt (n doer)
kereida, clash (n)
kereido, clash (v)
kereifa, litter (n)
kereila, glory (n)
kereiliu, gloriously (adv)
kereilo, glorify (v)
kereilu, glorious (adj)
kereilueta, glorification (n)
kereinika, muck (n)
kereiniko, muck (v)

kereiniku, mucky (adj)
kereisha, dust (n)
kereishenupa, dustbin (n)
kereishiu, dustily (adv)
kereisho, dust (v)
kereishu, dusty (adj)
kereishua, duster (n doer)
kerela, grease (n)
kereliko, bludgeon (v)
kerelo, grease (v)
kerelu, greasy (adj)
kerena, lex (n)
kereniana, lexicon (n)
kerenianu, lexical (adj)
kerenika, logic (n)
kerenikata, logistic (n)
kerenikatiu, logistically (adv)
kerenikatu, logistical (adj)
kerenikiu, logically (adv)
kereniku, logical (adj)
kerenita, logo (n)
kereta, hat (n)
keriafa, qualification (n)
keriafo, qualify (v)
keriafota, quality (n)
keriafotu, quality (adj)
keriafua, qualifier (n doer)
keriako, shatter (v)
keriama, shrewdness (n)
keriamiu, shrewdly (adv)
keriamu, shrewd (adj)
keriana, yank (n)
keriano, yank (v)
keriasha, shroud (n)
keriasho, shroud (v)
keriata, negotiation (n)
keriatha, lingo (n)
keriato, negotiate (v)
keriatua, negotiator (n doer)
keriba, characterization (n d:person)
keribata, characteristic (n d:person)
keribiu, characteristically (adv d:person)
keribo, characterize (v d:person)
keribu, characteristic (adj d:person)
keribua, character (n doer d:person)
kerifa, edge (n)
kerifo, edge (v)
kerifu, edgy (adj)
kerifua, edger (n doer)
keriga, mine (n d:cave)
kerigara, mineral (n)
kerigo, mine (v d:cave)
kerigua, miner (n doer d:cave)
kerika, clip (n)
kerikepelorika, clipboard (n)
keriko, clip (v)
kerikua, clipper (n doer)
kerilafa, tavern (n)

kerilapo, borrow (v)
kerilapua, borrower (n doer)
keriloto, bash (v)
kerilotua, basher (n doer)
kerimofa, heap (n)
kerimofo, heap (v)
kerina, lip (n)
kerino, lip (v)
kerioka, nook (n)
keriomipo, flunk (v)
keriomipua, flunky (n doer)
keriopa, eddy (n)
keriopo, eddy (v)
keriora, eagle (n)
kerioro, eagle (v)
Keripetona, Krypton (n)
kerisha, breach (n)
kerishata, missile (n)
kerishineta, lipstick (n)
kerisho, breach (v)
kerita, bore (n d:hole)
keritesho, mow (v)
keriteshua, mower (n doer)
kerithika, punch (n d:hit)
kerithikeroifa, punchline (n)
kerithiko, punch (v d:hit)
kerithiku, punchy (adj d:hit)
kerithikua, puncher (n doer d:hit)
kerito, bore (v d:hole)
keritua, borer (n doer d:hole)
keriufo, grumble (v)
keriuga, grudge (n)
keriugo, begrudge (v)
keriuna, stool (n d:excrement)
keriuta, duct (n)
keriutha, whoop (n)
keriutho, whoop (v)
kerivuga, campaign (n)
kerivugo, campaign (v)
kerivugua, campaigner (n doer)
kerivupa, trip (n d:misstep)
kerivupo, trip (v d:misstep)
kerivupua, tripper (n doer
     d:misstep)
kerofika, incline (n)
kerofiko, incline (v)
kerofikueta, inclination (n)
keroiba, glob (n)
keroibo, glob (v)
keroibu, globular (adj)
keroifopa, decline (n)
keroifopo, decline (v)
keroifopua, decliner (n doer)
keroiforipa, declination (n)
keroiga, box (n d:fight)
keroigo, box (v d:fight)
keroigua, boxer (n doer d:fight)
keroila, brim (n)
keroilo, brim (v)
keroilua, brimmer (n doer)
keroima, horn (n)
keroimo, horn (v)
keroimu, horny (adj)

keroinieta, gobble (n)
keroinieto, gobble (v)
keroinietua, gobbler (n doer)
keroitha, globe (n)
keroithiu, globally (adv)
keroithu, global (adj)
keroithueta, globalization (n)
kerolipa, brokerage (n)
kerolipo, broker (v)
kerolipua, broker (n doer)
Keromiuma, Chromium (n)
kerosha, search (n)
keroshefeluana, searchlight (n)
kerosho, search (v)
keroshua, searcher (n doer)
keruanika, chunk (n)
keruaniku, chunky (adj)
keruasha, chuck (n d:throw)
keruasho, chuck (v d:throw)
kerufa, week (n)
kerufedaika, weekend (n)
kerufedaikua, weekender (n doer)
kerufemuana, weeknight (n)
keruferazhu, weeklong (adj)
kerufeviula, weekday (n)
kerufu, weekly (adj)
keruka, gore (n)
keruko, gore (v)
keruku, gory (adj)
kerunei, few (n/pron)
kerunu, few (adj)
kerunwaku, fewest (adj)
kerunwelu, fewer (adj)
kerupa, glut (n)
kerupu, gluttonous (adj)
kerupua, glutton (n doer)
kerupueta, gluttony (n)
kerusha, tusk (n)
keruzha, hearth (n)
keshina, xi (n)
keta, check (n d:review)
ketalika, garage (n)
ketefenika, checkmate (n)
ketefeniko, checkmate (v)
kethina, elegance (n)
kethiniu, elegantly (adv)
kethinu, elegant (adj)
ketisha, letter (n d:character)
ketisho, letter (v d:character)
keto, check (v d:review)
ketua, checker (n doer d:review)
ketudita, checklist (n)
kiaba, toxin (n)
kiabaka, toxicity (n)
kiabaku, toxic (adj)
kiabakuita, toxicology (n)
kiabakuitiu, toxicologically (adv)
kiabakuitu, toxicological (adj)
kiabakuitua, toxicologist (n doer)
kiada, tube (n)
kiado, tube (v)
kiadu, tubal (adj)
kiadu, tubular (adj)

kiafa, house (n)
kiafekelofio, housekept (v pa)
kiafekelofo, housekeep (v)
kiafekelofua, housekeeper (n
     doer)
kiafekioka, housework (n)
kiafeshekoba, houseboat (n)
kiafeshemo, houseclean (v)
kiafo, house (v)
kiafuana, hovel (n)
kiafuata, coroner (n)
kiaga, jest (n)
kiago, jest (v)
kiagua, jester (n doer)
kiaika, pest (n)
kiaiko, pester (v)
kiaikoika, pesticide (n)
kiaiku, pesky (adj)
kiaikueta, pestilence (n)
kiakioko, tinker (v)
kialipa, hack (n)
kialipegerazha, hacksaw (n)
kialipo, hack (v)
kialipua, hacker (n doer)
kialita, ace (n)
kialito, ace (v)
kialofika, bribery (n)
kialoka, bribe (n)
kialoko, bribe (v)
kialokua, briber (n doer)
kiana, video (n)
kianeifa, videotape (n)
kianeifo, videotape (v)
kianida, wand (n)
kianika, rink (n)
kianipa, stride (n)
kianofa, household (n)
kiapa, turbin (n)
kiarinu, gourmet (adj)
kiaruva, glue (n)
kiaruvo, glue (v)
kiasha, east (n)
kiasharofa, housewife (n)
kiashelada, corpse (n)
kiashoku, eastern (adj)
kiashota, chassis (n)
kiashu, east (adj)
kiata, death (n)
kiatefuarema, deathbed (n)
kiatha, hall (n)
kiathipa, hallway (n)
kiato, die (v)
kiauga, implosion (n)
kiaugiu, implosively (adv)
kiaugo, implode (v)
kiaugu, implosive (adj)
kiaugua, imploder (n doer)
kiauka, screech (n)
kiauko, screech (v)
kiaukua, screecher (n doer)
kiaula, turmoil (n)
kiaupa, howl (n)
kiaupo, howl (v)

kiaupua, howler (n doer)
kiausha, haze (n d:fog)
kiausho, haze (v d:fog)
kiaushu, hazy (adj d:fog)
kiauta, reform (n d:decorrupt)
kiauto, reform (v d:decorrupt)
kiautua, reformer (n doer d:decorrupt)
kiautua, reformist (n doer d:decorrupt)
kiaviaka, hazard (n)
kiaviako, hazard (v)
kiaviaku, hazardous (adj)
kibafika, axis (n)
kibaka, ax (n)
kibako, ax (v)
kibelishoku, impenetrable (adj)
kiberamipa, impoundment (n)
kiberamipo, impound (v)
kiberata, limbo (n)
kibereisha, impurity (n)
kibereishu, impure (adj)
kiberepa, implant (n)
kiberepo, implant (v)
kiberepueta, implantation (n)
kibereshiu, implicitly (adv)
kiberesho, imply (v)
kibereshu, implicit (adj)
kibereshueta, implication (n)
kibereshueto, implicate (v)
kibereshuetua, implicator (n doer)
kibielika, import (n)
kibieliko, import (v)
kibielikua, importer (n doer)
kibielikueta, importation (n)
kiboiga, impotence (n)
kiboigu, impotent (adj)
kidanita, immobility (n)
kidanita, immobilization (n)
kidanito, immobilize (v)
kidanitua, immobilizer (n doer)
Kiduna, Hindu (n)
Kidunueta, Hinduism (n)
kidurita, imperative (n)
kiduritu, imperative (adj)
kiedaisha, dichotomy (n)
kiefa, sink (n)
kiefekotha, sinkhole (n)
kiefio, sank (v pa)
kiefo, sink (v)
kiefua, sinker (n doer)
kiega, dilution (n)
kiego, dilute (v)
kiegu, dilute (adj)
kieitekafipa, hovercraft (n)
kieito, hover (v)
kieka, node (n)
kielata, dilation (n)
kielato, dilate (v)
kielatu, dilatory (adj)
kielatua, dilator (n doer)
kielofa, diploma (n)

kiepa, diet (n)
kiepo, diet (v)
kiepua, dieter (n doer)
kiesha, sib (n)
kieshika, sibling (n)
kieshikiu, siblings (adv)
kieshiku, sibling (adj)
kieta, jet (n)
kietaroifa, jetliner (n)
kieto, jet (v)
kievoruga, digression (n)
kievorugo, digress (v)
kifafa, article (n)
kifata, bend (n)
kifatio, bent (v pa)
kifatiu, bendably (adv)
kifato, bend (v)
kifatu, bendable (adj)
kifatua, bender (n doer)
kifeka, bench (n)
kifeko, bench (v)
kifelaruva, improvement (n)
kifelaruvo, improve (v)
kifelenishiu, incredibly (adv)
kifelenishu, incredible (adj)
kifepufita, folklore (n)
kifeshetata, benchmark (n)
kifiaisha, divide (n)
kifiaishapa, dividend (n)
kifiaishipa, divisiveness (n)
kifiaishipu, divisive (adj)
kifiaishipua, divisor (n doer)
kifiaisho, divide (v)
kifiaishu, divisible (adj)
kifiaishua, divider (n doer)
kifiaishueta, division (n)
kifiaishuetu, divisional (adj)
kifiata, skipper (n)
kifiuferepa, improbability (n)
kifiufereplu, improbably (adv)
kifiuferepu, improbable (adj)
kifopa, folk (n)
kifopereta, folktale (n)
kigala, artillery (n)
kigelaka, imposition (n)
kigelako, impose (v)
kigelakua, imposter (n doer)
kikelo, am (emphatic)
kikelo, be (inf, emphatic)
kikelo, is (emphatic)
kikero, are (emphatic)
kikiaga, digestion (n)
kikiago, digest (v)
kikiagu, digestive (adj)
kikiako, snicker (v)
kikiupu, snide (adj)
kikuta, gravity (n d:physics)
kikuto, gravitate (v d:physics)
kikutueta, gravitation (n)
kikutuetu, gravitational (adj)
kilafipo, immerge (v)
kilafita, immersion (n)
kilafito, immerse (v)

kilata, agreement (n)
kilatiu, agreebly (adv)
kilato, agree (v)
kilatu, agreeable (adj)
kiledumu, between (adv/prep)
kilega, traffic (n)
kilego, traffic (v)
kilegua, trafficker (n doer)
kilenio, became (v pa)
kileno, become (v)
kileshekashu, because (conj)
kiliaka, heroin (n)
kilikapiu, improperly (adv)
kilikapu, improper (adj)
kilisha, fetish (n)
kilitha, sniff (n)
kilitho, sniff (v)
kilithua, sniffer (n doer)
kilo, am (common)
kilo, be (inf, common)
kilo, is (common)
kilofu, several (adj)
kiloito, beseech (v)
kiloitua, beseecher (n doer)
kiloka, severance (n)
kilokata, severity (n)
kilokiu, severely (adv)
kiloko, sever (v)
kiloku, severe (adj)
kilopa, crib (n)
kiloshaka, impairment (n)
kiloshako, impair (v)
kiloshipa, imperception (n)
kiloshipiu, imperceptibly (adv)
kiloshipu, imperceptible (adj)
kilovirota, imperfection (n)
kilovirotiu, imperfectly (adv)
kilovirotu, imperfect (adj)
kilunita, impasse (n)
kilunitiu, impassably (adv)
kilunitu, impassable (adj)
kimatika, impracticality (n)
kimatiku, impractical (adj)
kimiokiu, immaculately (adv)
kimioku, immaculate (adj)
kimoida, impedance (n)
kimoido, impede (v)
kimoidueta, impediment (n)
kimoitesha, impeachment (n)
kimoitesho, impeach (v)
kimoiteshu, impeachable (adj)
kinabara, gender (n d:sexual identity)
kinafelafa, travesty (n)
kinai-, hex- (num 6 pref)
kinai-, sext- (num 6 pref)
kinaisha, mutilation (n)
kinaisho, mutilate (v)
kinaishua, mutilator (n doer)
kinaka, viscosity (n)
kinaku, viscous (adj)
kinala, imagination (n)
kinaleferepiu, imaginably (adv)

kinaleferepu, imaginable (adj)
kinalo, imagine (v)
kinalopu, imaginative (adj)
kinalu, imaginary (adj)
kinesha, dimension (n)
kinesho, dimension (v)
kineshu, dimensional (adj)
kineth, sixth (num 6 ord)
kinfk, sesquadragintillion (num 1e141 card)
kinft, sestrigintillion (num 1e111 card)
kini, six (num 6 card)
kinialfhemka, Number_1e24456
kinida, sixty (num 60 card)
kinidai-, sixty- (num 60 pref)
kinideth, sixtieth (num 60 ord)
kinipa, sixteen (num 16 card)
kinipai-, sixteen- (num 16 pref)
kinipeth, sixteenth (num 16 ord)
kiniupa, diminishment (n)
kiniupiu, diminutively (adv)
kiniupo, diminish (v)
kiniupu, diminutive (adj)
kinka, sextillion (num 1e21 card)
kinkai-, zetta- (num 1e21 pref)
kinketh, sextillionth (num 1e21 ord)
kinodata, imitation (n)
kinodato, imitate (v)
kinodatua, imitator (n doer)
kinofa, image (n)
kinofo, image (v)
kinofueta, imagery (n)
kinoina, mayhem (n)
kinoino, maim (v)
kinopa, graduation (n)
kinopiu, gradually (adv)
kinopo, graduate (v)
kinopu, gradual (adj)
kinopua, graduate (n doer)
kinota, vividness (n)
kinotiu, vividly (adv)
kinotu, vivid (adj)
kinshk, sexvigintillion (num 1e81 card)
kinshkai-, eikto-
kinshketh, sexvigintillionth (num 1e81 ord)
kinsht, sexdecillion (num 1e51 card)
kinshtai-, oshto- (num 1e51 pref)
kinshteth, sexdecillionth (num 1e51 ord)
kiofa, pace (n)
kiofata, pacifism (n)
kiofato, pacify (v)
kiofatu, pacific (adj)
kiofatua, pacifier (n doer)
kiofatua, pacifist (n doer)
kiofenagua, pacemaker (n doer)

kiofepua, pacesetter (n doer)
kiofita, cable (n)
kiofito, cable (v)
kiofitua, cabler (n doer)
kiofo, pace (v)
kiofua, pacer (n doer)
kioika, scream (n)
kioiko, scream (v)
kioikua, screamer (n doer)
kioka, work (n)
kiokagiana, workaholic (n)
kiokeberesha, workplace (n)
kiokeberona, workgroup (n)
kiokegelausha, workhorse (n)
kiokelurita, workload (n)
kiokepelona, workman (n)
kiokepelonefifa, workmanship (n)
kiokepeloni, workmen (n pl)
kiokesheluketa, workstation (n)
kioketaupa, worksheet (n)
kiokethusha, workspace (n)
kiokevithova, workshop (n)
kiokeviuka, workforce (n)
kiokeviula, workday (n)
kiokifeka, workbench (n)
kiokio, wrought (v pa)
kioko, work (v)
kioku, workable (adj)
kiokua, worker (n doer)
kiokuila, workout (n)
kioma, humidity (n)
kiomipa, funk (n d:fear/dejection)
kiomo, humidify (v)
kiomu, humid (adj)
kiona, cabin (n)
kiopa, cab (n)
kiopua, cabby (n doer)
kiora, fume (n)
kiorelueta, fumigation (n)
kiorelueto, fumigate (v)
kioreluetua, fumigator (n doer)
kiorena, cabinet (n)
kiorifoka, deadline (n)
kioriu, fumily (adv)
kioro, fume (v)
kioru, fumy (adj)
kiorua, fumer (n doer)
kioshadauta, deadbeat (n)
kioshata, dead (u)
kioshatiu, deadly (adv)
kioshatiuga, deadlock (n)
kioshatu, dead (adj)
kioshefanina, deadwood (n)
kioshika, torch (n)
kioshiko, torch (v)
kioshuisha, deadweight (n)
kiota, torque (n)
kiotesho, torment (v)
kioteshua, tormentor (n doer)
kiothipa, cabbage (n)
kioto, torque (v)
kipado, impel (v)

kipadua, impeller (n doer)
kipata, robot (n)
kipatiu, robotically (adv)
kipatu, robotic (adj)
kipeithu, impervious (adj)
kipeloniu, impersonally (adv)
kipelonu, impersonal (adj)
kipelonueta, impersonation (n)
kipelonueto, impersonate (v)
kipelonuetua, impersonator (n doer)
kiporita, artifact (n)
kira, here (n)
kirabako, wreak (v)
kirakitio, wrung (v pa)
kirakito, wring (v)
kirakitua, wringer (n doer)
kiralatha, wreath (n)
kirezhaupa, logjam (n)
kiro, are (common)
kirofa, art (n)
kirofika, deduction (n d:determination)
kirofiko, deduce (v d:determination)
kirofikua, deducer (n doer d:determination)
kirofiu, artistically (adv)
kirofu, artistic (adj)
kirofua, artist (n doer)
kiropa, robbery (n)
kiropo, rob (v)
kiropua, robber (n doer)
kirosha, physician (n)
kirota, core (n)
kiroto, core (v)
kirovila, hereafter (n)
kiru, here (adj/adv/interj)
kiruga, log (n d:tree)
kirugo, log (v d:tree)
kirugua, logger (n doer d:tree)
kiruthishaka, imprecision (n)
kiruthishakiu, imprecisely (adv)
kiruthishaku, imprecise (adj)
kishalikiu, implausibly (adv)
kishaliku, implausible (adj)
kishekita, copy (n)
kishekiteloidua, copywriter (n doer)
kishekiteruasha, copyright (n)
kishekiteruasho, copyright (v)
kishekito, copy (v)
kishekitua, copier (n doer)
kisheluaka, induration (n)
kisheluakiu, immutably (adv)
kisheluako, indurate (v)
kisheluaku, immutable (adj)
kisheluakua, indurator (n doer)
kishemotata, imbalance (n)
kishemotato, imbalance (v)
kisheta, hush (n)
kisheteriaga, distillation (n)
kisheteriagata, distillery (n)

kisheteriagata, still (n d:distillery)
kisheteriagato, still (v d:distillery)
kisheteriago, distill (v)
kisheteriagua, distiller (n doer)
kisheto, hush (v)
kishoketa, artifice (n)
kishoketiu, artificially (adv)
kishoketu, artificial (adj)
kishoketua, artificer (n doer)
Kishopanika, Hispanic (n)
kitafa, camp (n)
kitafeberanita, campground (n)
kitafegiaula, campfire (n)
kitafeniata, campsite (n)
kitafo, camp (v)
kitafua, camper (n doer)
kitaripa, campus (n)
kiterulisha, imprint (n)
kiterulisho, imprint (v)
kitesha, kill (n)
kitesho, kill (v)
kiteshua, killer (n doer)
kitha, pep (n)
kithailo, impale (v)
kithailua, impaler (n doer)
kitharika, diversion (n)
kithariko, divert (v)
kitharikua, diverter (n doer)
kithika, pepper (n)
kithiko, pepper (v)
kithiuna, immorality (n)
kithiuniu, immorally (adv)
kithiunu, immoral (adj)
Kitusha, EhoMonth12 (n)
kiufo, deem (v)
kiuga, tiger (n)
kiuka, liberation (n d:freedom)
kiukara, liberty (n)
kiukiu, liberally (adv d:freedom)
kiuko, liberate (v d:freedom)
kiuku, liberal (adj d:freedom)
kiukua, liberator (n doer d:freedom)
kiuloka, throat (n)
kiuloku, throaty (adj)
kiupa, bolt (n)
Kiuperiuna, Hebrew (n)
kiupo, bolt (v)
kiurita, accomplishment (n)
kiurito, accomplish (v)
kiuritua, accomplice (n doer)
kiusha, chaos (n)
kiushiu, chaotically (adv)
kiushu, chaotic (adj)
kiuta, bill (n d:document)
kiutepelorika, billboard (n)
kiutesha, tick (n d:insect)
kiutha, abyss (n)
kiuthiu, abysmally (adv)
kiuthu, abysmal (adj)
kiuto, bill (v d:document)
kiutoruka, billiard (n)
kiutoruku, billiard (adj)

kiutua, biller (n doer d:document)
kiviuga, importance (n)
kiviugiu, importantly (adv)
kiviugu, important (adj)
kivoanu, before (prep/conj)
kivoanukapu, beforehand (adj/adv)
kivuiuna, hurricane (n)
kivuka, hurry (n)
kivuko, hurry (v)
kizha, technique (n)
kizhata, technology (n)
kizhatiu, technologically (adv)
kizhatu, technological (adj)
kizhelialita, buzzword (n)
kizhepanika, tedium (n)
kizhepaniku, tedious (adj)
kizhiu, technically (adv)
kizhu, technical (adj)
kizhua, technician (n doer)
kizhumipo, imperil (v)
koatana, asteroid (n)
Kobalita, Cobalt (n)
kodi, have-to (ndal)
kofao, having (v prp)
kofika, bolster (n)
kofiko, bolster (v)
kofirato, deserve (v)
kofita, service (n)
kofitana, servitude (n)
kofitanua, servant (n doer)
kofitepelona, serviceman (n)
kofitepeloni, servicemen (n pl)
kofitha, oven (n)
kofito, serve (v)
kofitua, server (n doer)
kofitueto, service (v)
kofo, has (v sing)
kofo, have (v s)
koga, coca (n)
koiaka, worship (n)
koiako, worship (v)
koiaku, worshipful (adj)
koiakua, worshipper (n doer)
koiano, yearn (v)
koiata, stripe (n)
koiato, stripe (v)
koiatua, striper (n doer)
koiba, gob (n)
koidelina, supermarket (n)
koieka, streak (n)
koieko, streak (v)
koieku, streaky (adj)
koifa, emulation (n)
koifeleida, hybrid (n)
koifo, emulate (v)
koifu, emulous (adj)
koigavugo, hijack (v)
koigavugua, hijacker (n doer)
koila, height (n)
koila, heighth (n)
koilefeluana, highlight (n)
koilefeluano, highlight (v)

koilefeluanua, highlighter (n doer)
koilepeliola, highway (n)
koiliu, highly (adv)
koilo, heighten (v)
koilu, high (adj)
koilwaku, highest (adj)
koilwelu, higher (adj)
koipa, raise (n)
koipo, raise (v)
koisha, hype (n)
koishepalita, hyperactivity (n)
koishepalitiu, hyperactively (adv)
koishepalitu, hyperactive (adj)
koishibelarifa, hyperinflation (n)
koisho, hype (v)
koishorifopa, hypersensitivity (n)
koishorifopu, hypersensitive (adj)
koishu, hyper (adj)
koiteralita, hierarchy (n)
koiteralitu, hierarchical (adj)
koitiva, throne (n)
kokeio, will (pro-verb fu)
kokelo, was (emphatic)
kokelu, been (v pap sng emphatic)
kokero, were (emphatic)
kokeru, been (v pap pl emphatic)
kokeruga, antagony (n)
kokerugo, antagonize (v)
kokerugu, antagonistic (adj)
kokerugua, antagonist (n doer)
kokio, did/had (pro-verb pa)
koko, do/have (pro-verb pr)
kolana, welcome (n)
kolano, welcome (v)
kolata, quart (n)
kolatara, quarter (n)
kolatarethioka, quartermaster (n)
kolatariu, quarterly (adv)
kolathika, welfare (n)
koliava, heresy (n)
koliavu, heretical (adj)
koliavua, heretic (n doer)
kolifa, honor (n)
kolifo, honor (v)
kolifu, honorable (adj)
kolifu, honorary (adj)
kolima, gaiety (n d:happy)
kolima, happiness (n)
kolimiu, gaily (adv d:happy)
kolimiu, happily (adv)
kolimu, gay (adj d:happy)
kolimu, happy (adj)
kolimweku, happiest (adj)
kolimwelu, happier (adj)
kolipa, happenstance (n)
kolipo, happen (v)
kolishotala, cholesterol (n)
kolo, was (common)
kolomeniu, haplessly (adv)
kolomenu, hapless (adj)
Kolomubiafa, Colombia (n)

Kolomubiana, Colombian (n)
Kolorada, Colorado (n)
kolu, been (v pap sng common)
Kolumobiafa, Columbia (n)
Konadurasha, Honduras (n)
konafu, vascular (adj)
Konetikuta, Connecticut (n)
Koniterafa, Contra (n)
Konokausha, Holocaust (n)
kopaka, hoax (n)
kopaloka, hocus-pocus (n)
Kopera, Copper (n)
kora, wellness (n d:good)
koraviga, elimination (n)
koravigo, eliminate (v)
korefipa, category (n)
korefipiu, categorically (adv)
korefipo, categorize (v)
korefipu, categorical (adj)
korefipua, categorizer (n doer)
korekulauraa, wellbeing (n)
Koriafa, Korea (n)
Koriana, Korean (n)
koriga, ox (n)
korigi, oxen (n pl)
korilota, garlic (n)
korima, toll (n)
korimeturisha, tollbooth (n)
korimo, toll (v)
korinaka, slut (n)
korinoka, hunger (n)
korinokiu, hungrily (adv)
korinoko, hunger (v)
korinoku, hungry (adj)
koro, were (common)
koru, been (v pap pl common)
koru, well (adj d:good)
kosha, huff (n)
koshana, midge (n)
kosheta, keel (n)
Koshetafa Rikafa, Costa Rica (n)
kosheto, keel (v)
koshetua, keeler (n doer)
koshiatho, wean (v)
koshipa, content (n d:material)
kosho, huff (v)
kotha, hole (n)
kothara, bosom (n)
kotho, hole (v)
koto, had (v)
kovaka, havoc (n)
kovara, haven (n)
kovarila, heaven (n)
kovarilu, heavenly (adj)
koveio, have (v fut)
kovo, have (v pl)
kovuka, haze (n d:abuse)
kovuko, haze (v d:abuse)
kuaberivana, cobweb (n)
kuada, cob (n d:round)
kuadafa, cobble (n d:mend)
kuadafo, cobble (v d:mend)
kuadafua, cobbler (n doer

d:mend)
kuadaka, cobble (n d:roundstone)
kuadaka, cobblestone (n)
kuafa, paw (n)
kuafika, direction (n)
kuafikara, directory (n)
kuafikata, directive (n)
kuafikiu, directly (adv)
kuafiko, direct (v)
kuafiku, direct (adj)
kuafikua, director (n doer)
kuafo, paw (v)
kuaga, bummer (n)
kuago, bum (v)
kuagua, bum (n doer)
kuaifa, hail (n d:greeting)
kuaifo, hail (v d:greeting)
kuaipo, quash (v)
kuaka, yuck (n)
kuaku, yucky (adj)
kualiko, pamper (v)
kualipa, decoy (n)
kualipo, decoy (v)
kualu, coy (adj)
kuama, yummy (n)
kuana, gain (n)
kuanika, gong (n)
kuano, gain (v)
kuanua, gainer (n doer)
kuariko, sulk (v)
kuasha, coziness (n)
kuasho, cozy (v)
kuashu, cozy (adj)
kuba, bet (n)
Kubafa, Cuba (n)
Kubana, Cuban (n)
kubio, bet (v pa)
kubiuna, cowboy (n)
kubo, bet (v)
kuda, fig (n)
kuderika, decrease (n)
kuderiko, decrease (v)
kuderishoka, decrement (n)
kuderishokiu, decrementally
    (adv)
kuderishoko, decrement (v)
kuderishoku, decremental (adj)
kudueta, figment (n)
kuek, quack (interj)
kufa, good (n d:helpful)
kufaliau, goodbye (interj)
kufamufa, goodness (n)
kufelimena, goodmorning (interj)
kufemuana, goodnight (interj)
kufeweka, best (n)
kufewekio, best (v pa)
kufewekiu, best (adv)
kufeweko, best (v)
kufeweku, best (adj)
kufewelo, better (v)
kufewelu, better (adj)
kufiana, butler (n)
kufika, good (n d:product)

kufipa, ethic (n)
kufipatha, ethos (n)
kufipiu, ethically (adv)
kufipo, ethicate (v)
kufipu, ethical (adj)
kufita, ethnicity (n)
kufitu, ethnic (adj)
kufu, good (adj d:helpful)
kufuba, poop (n)
kufubo, poop (v)
kufubua, pooper (n doer)
kufyaka, goodwill (n)
kuiaka, weapon (n)
kuiakueta, weaponry (n)
kuiana, yawn (n)
kuiano, yawn (v)
kuiesho, quench (v)
kuieto, quell (v)
kuifopa, blink (n)
kuifopo, blink (v)
kuifopua, blinker (n doer)
kuika, toast (n d:cheer)
kuiko, toast (v d:cheer)
kuiku, toasty (adj d:cheer)
kuikua, toaster (n doer d:cheer)
kuilana, guerrilla (n)
kuilanu, guerrilla (adj)
kuisha, queasiness (n)
kuishu, queasy (adj)
kuita, log (n d:record)
kuitevonuda, logbook (n)
kuito, log (v d:record)
kuitua, logger (n doer d:record)
kukabika, allergy (n)
kukabiku, allergic (adj)
kukabikua, allergist (n doer)
kukani, goggles (n pl)
kukesho, shall (v)
kukesho, will (v emphat)
kukeshu, will-be (v fp emphatic)
kulaura, being (v prp common)
kulaurika, being (v prp emphatic)
kulenita, cricket (n)
kulifa, behavior (n)
kulifo, behave (v)
kulikefita, figurehead (n)
kuliko, be (imp, emphatic)
kulina, immunity (n)
kulinekulta, immunology (n)
kulinekuitu, immunological (adj)
kulinepeliashipa, immunotherapy
    (n)
kulinevubelasha,
    immunosuppression (n)
kulino, immunize (v)
kulinu, immune (adj)
kulinueta, immunization (n)
kulisha, dash (n d:sprint)
kulishepelorika, dashboard (n)
kulisho, dash (v d:sprint)
kulishua, dasher (n doer d:sprint)
kulita, figure (n)
kulitiu, figuratively (adv)

kulito, figure (v)
kulitoifa, figurine (n)
kulitu, figurative (adj)
kulo, be (imp, common)
kuluka, toot (n)
kuluko, toot (v)
kumipa, boulder (n)
Kunikariana, Hungarian (n)
Kunikarofa, Hungary (n)
kunio, began (v pa)
kuno, begin (v)
kunodu, behind (adj/adv/prep)
kunua, beginner (n doer)
kupafita, benefit (n)
kupafitiu, benefically (adv)
kupafito, benefit (v)
kupafitu, beneficial (adj)
kupafitua, beneficiary (n doer)
kupoga, debt (n)
kupogata, debenture (n)
kupogo, indebt (v)
kupogua, debtor (n doer)
kurazho, belong (v)
kureitha, tomorrow (n)
kureithiu, tomorrow (adv)
kurema, cow (n)
kuribana, tinder (n)
kuribaneperenika, tinderbox (n)
kuriga, nerd (n)
kurika, factory (n)
kuripa, timber (n)
Kuriuma, Curium (n)
Kushatona, Houston (n)
kusho, will (v common)
kushoitu, beside (adv/prep)
kushoitu, besides (adv/prep)
kushu, will-be (v fp common)
kuta, heat (n)
kutala, sword (n)
kutaleferuita, swordplay (n)
kutaleshelesha, swordfish (n)
kutalesheleshi, swordfish (n pl)
kutha, skeleton (n)
kuthu, skeletal (adj)
kutipa, deity (n)
kuto, heat (v)
kutua, heater (n doer)
kutuka, colon (n d:organ)
kuvada, goose (n)
kuvadi, geese (n pl)
kuvado, goose (v)
kuvezho, debug (v)
kuvezhua, debugger (n doer)
Kuwaita, Kuwait (n)
Kuwaitana, Kuwaiti (n)
kuyerulu, beyond (adv/prep)
kwaka, yuck (interj)
kwama, yum (interj)
kwami, yummy (interj)
labika, spade (n)
labiko, spade (v)
labolika, spare (n)
labolikiu, sparingly (adv)

laboliko, spare (v)
ladifiu, virtually (adv)
ladifu, virtual (adj)
lafika, merchandise (n)
lafikao, merchandized (v prp)
lafiko, merchandize (v)
lafikua, merchant (n doer)
lafima, venue (n)
lafimata, veneration (n)
lafimatiu, venerably (adv)
lafimato, venerate (v)
lafimatu, venerable (adj)
lafipa, merge (n)
lafipo, merge (v)
lafipua, merger (n doer)
lagala, ill (n)
lagala, illness (n)
lagalu, ill (adj)
lagarusha, illusion (n)
laiafa, saturation (n)
laiafo, saturate (v)
laiaka, satire (n)
laiako, satirize (v)
laiaku, satirical (adj)
laiakua, satirist (n doer)
laiatha, lash (n)
laiatho, lash (v)
laiathua, lasher (n doer)
laidaka, medium (n d:information flow)
laidaki, media (n pl d:information flow)
laidako, mediate (v d:information flow)
laidaku, medial (adj d:information flow)
laidakua, mediator (n doer d:information flow)
laidakueta, mediation (n)
laidachika, immediacy (n)
laidashikiu, immediately (adv)
laidashiku, immediate (adj)
laifiapa, emergency (n)
laifipa, emergence (n)
laifipo, emerge (v)
laigafa, disaster (n)
laigafiu, disastrously (adv)
laigafu, disastrous (adj)
laikalina, galaxy (n)
laila, heir (n)
laila, heiress (n)
lailethetisha, heirloom (n)
lailota, heredity (n)
lailotapa, heritage (n)
lailotu, hereditary (adj)
laipa, dimness (n)
laipiu, dimly (adv)
laipo, dim (v)
laipu, dim (adj)
laipua, dimmer (n doer)
laisha, joy (n)
laishineta, joystick (n)
laishiu, joyfully (adv)

laishu, joyful (adj)
laivuna, twine (n)
laizha, hell (n)
laizhegiaula, hellfire (n)
laizhu, hellish (adj)
lakana, garment (n)
lakirenoka, illogic (n)
lakirenoku, illogical (adj)
lakita, stove (n)
lalifoka, commerce (n)
lalifokana, commercial (n)
lalifokiu, commercially (adv)
lalifoku, commercial (adj)
lalipara, library (n)
laliparua, librarian (n doer)
lalirota, licence (n)
lalirota, license (n)
lalirotemenu, licentious (adj)
laliroto, license (v)
lalirotueta, licensure (n)
lalirotuina, licencee (n)
lalita, lead (n d:in front)
lalitafifa, leadership (n)
lalitemenu, leaderless (adj)
lalitera, liter (n)
lalito, lead (v d:in front)
lalitua, leader (n doer d:in front)
lalitunefa, leadoff (n)
lalitunefu, leadoff (adj)
lalivatora, illiteracy (n)
lalivatoru, illiterate (adj)
laluga, calorie (n)
Lamaila, May (n)
lamalita, original (n)
lamalitata, originality (n)
lamata, origin (n)
lamatiu, originally (adv)
lamato, originate (v)
lamatu, original (adj)
lamatua, originator (n doer)
lamatueta, origination (n)
lamudana, lambda (n)
Lanethanuma, Lanthanum (n)
lanifa, norm (n)
lanifiu, normally (adv)
lanifo, normalize (v)
lanifu, normal (adj)
lanifueta, normalization (n)
laniga, virtue (n)
lanigiu, virtuously (adv)
lanigu, virtuous (adj)
lanika, composition (n)
lanikara, composure (n)
lanikita, composite (n)
lanikitu, composite (adj)
laniko, compose (v)
lanikua, composer (n doer)
lanipa, nap (n)
lanipo, nap (v)
lanishoka, exposure (n)
lanishoko, expose (v)
lanishoku, expository (adj)
lanishokua, exposer (n doer)

lanishokueta, exposition (n)
lanita, gallantry (n)
lanitiu, gallantly (adv)
lanitu, gallant (adj)
lanudaka, HalfFaceSymbol (n)
lanuta, cameo (n)
lanutafika, illegitimacy (n)
lanutafiku, illegitimate (adj)
lanutaka, illegality (n)
lanutakiu, illegally (adv)
lanutaku, illegal (adj)
lanuva, irony (n)
lanuviu, ironically (adv)
lanuvu, ironic (adj)
laoma, run (n)
laomepeloila, runway (n)
laometiena, rundown (n)
laomio, ran (v pa)
laomo, run (v)
laomobelaitha, runaround (n)
laomopeliola, runaway (n)
laomu, runny (adj)
laomua, runner (n doer)
laomunefa, runoff (n)
Laparela, April (n)
lapueta, session (n)
laramika, burlap (n)
larana, rogation (n)
larano, rogate (v)
Larenoshiuma, Lawrencium (n)
larifa, roof (n)
larifedaupa, rooftop (n)
larifo, roof (v)
larifota, elephant (n)
larifotu, elephantic (adj)
larifua, roofer (n doer)
larigeraga, despot (n)
larigeragueta, despotism (n)
Larila, EhoMonth01 (n)
larina, fear (n)
larinafapa, lemonade (n)
larinana, lemon (n)
lariniu, fearfully (adv)
larino, fear (v)
larinu, fearful (adj)
larinumeniu, fearlessly (adv)
larinumenu, fearless (adj)
laripa, left (n d:direction)
laripekeliegu, leftwing (adj)
laripekeliegua, leftist (n doer)
laripu, left (adj d:direction)
laripua, lefty (n doer d:direction)
larisha, cassette (n)
Larishiala, Asia (n)
Larishiana, Asian (n)
larita, rule (n)
laritevonuda, rulebook (n)
larito, rule (v)
laritua, ruler (n doer)
larodaika, vehemence (n)
larodaikiu, vehemently (adv)
larodaiku, vehement (adj)
larodita, vehicle (n)

laroditu, vehicular (adj)
larudata, medal (n)
larudato, medal (v)
larudatua, medalist (n doer)
larukiu, intrinsically (adv)
laruku, intrinsic (adj)
Lash Veigasha, Las Vegas (n)
lashetafiku, illegible (adj)
lashika, cigar (n)
lashikefa, cigarette (n)
lashipa, breath (n)
lashipeferepu, breathable (adj)
lashipegokiu, breathtakingly
      (adv)
lashipegoku, breathtaking (adj)
lashipiu, breathily (adv)
lashipo, breathe (v)
lashipu, breathy (adj)
lashipua, breather (n doer)
latana, locum (n)
latha, roll (n d:bread)
lathipa, cache (n)
lathipo, cache (v)
Latinofa, Latin (n)
lauafa, satiation (n)
lauafo, satiate (v)
lauba, oddity (n d:different)
laubiu, oddly (adv d:different)
laubo, odden (v d:different)
laubu, odd (adj d:different)
laufaga, frigidity (n)
laufagu, frigid (adj)
laufo, bode (v)
lauita, satisfaction (n)
lauito, satisfy (v)
lauitu, satisfactory (adj)
lauka, planet (n)
lauku, planetary (adj)
Laukuta, August (n)
lauta, veil (n)
lauto, veil (v)
lavita, dissatisfaction (n)
lavito, dissatisfy (v)
lavufeluana, twilight (n)
lavuna, twin (n)
lazha, pride (n
      d:accomplishment)
lazhiu, proudly (adv
      d:accomplishment)
lazho, pride (v
      d:accomplishment)
Leada, Lead (n)
Lebanofa, Lebanon (n)
Lebanonifa, Lebanese (n)
lefeshethiu, everlastingly (adv)
lefeshethu, everlasting (adj)
lefugirana, concealment (n)
lefugirano, conceal (v)
lefugiranua, concealer (n doer)
leiama, oasis (n)
leiapa, leer (n)
leiapeliola, leeway (n)
leiapo, leer (v)

leiapu, leery (adj)
leida, nature (n)
leidiu, naturally (adv)
leidu, natural (adj)
leifa, pinky (n)
leifeliuta, flattery (n d:praise)
leifeliuto, flatter (v d:praise)
leikata, utility (n)
leikato, utilize (v)
leikatua, utilizer (n doer)
leikatueta, utilization (n)
leikatuetua, utilitarian (n doer)
leilata, utensil (n)
leinapa, pipe (n)
leinaperoifa, pipeline (n)
leinapo, pipe (v)
leinapua, piper (n doer)
leinishoita, intestine (n)
leinishoitu, intestinal (adj)
leinu, bland (adj)
leipa, pin (n)
leipata, pinch (n)
leipato, pinch (v)
leipatua, pincher (n doer)
leipauka, pinnacle (n)
leipekefita, pinhead (n)
leipekelaipa, pinprick (n)
leipekoiata, pinstripe (n)
leipekoiato, pinstripe (v)
leipemashipa, pinball (n)
leipetaifota, pinpoint (n)
leipetaifoto, pinpoint (v)
leipo, pin (v)
leiropa, pint (n)
leisha, extra (n)
leisheifa, exuberance (n)
leisheifiu, exuberantly (adv)
leisheifu, exuberant (adj)
leishiketaru, extraordinary (adj)
leishu, extra (adj)
leishugoka, extradition (n)
leishugoko, extradite (v)
leitha, moisture (n)
leithiu, moistly (adv)
leitho, moisten (v)
leitho, moisturize (v)
leithu, moist (adj)
leithua, moistener (n doer)
leithua, moisturizer (n doer)
leka, let (n)
leketiena, letdown (n)
lekio, let (v pa)
leko, let (v)
leluma, cereal (n)
lemuta, scarcity (n)
lemutoiu, scarcely (adv)
lemutu, scarce (adj)
leneshala, companionship (n)
leneshalua, companion (n doer)
leneshapa, company (n)
leneshapo, accompany (v)
lenetiluda, commencement (n)
lenetiludo, commence (v)

lenifoka, compass (n)
lenika, commitment (n)
lenikata, commission (n)
lenikato, commission (v)
lenikatua, commissioner (n doer)
leniko, commit (v)
lenikua, committee (n doer)
lenishekita, commotion (n)
lenishekito, commove (v)
lenisheluaka, commutation (n)
lenisheluako, commute (v)
lenisheluakua, commuter (n doer)
lenubereshota, complication (n)
lenubereshoto, complicate (v)
lepa, meet (n)
leparika, meteor (n)
leparikata, meteorite (n)
lepio, met (v pa)
lepo, meet (v)
lerfhem, Number_1e1056
lerfi, Ls (let pl)
lerifa, L (let sng)
lerifalizhei, everything (n/pron)
lerifeviula, everyday (n)
lerifeviulu, everyday (adj)
lerifitonei, everyone (pron)
lerifu, every (adj)
lerifusheladei, everybody (pron)
lerofital, everywhere (adv)
lesha, wave (n)
leshako, waver (v)
lesherazha, wavelength (n)
lesho, wave (v)
letherufa, sugar (n)
letherufo, sugar (v)
letherufu, sugary (adj)
liafoka, exhaust (n)
liafokiu, exhaustively (adv)
liafoko, exhaust (v)
liafoku, exhaustive (adj)
liaga, cold (n d:illness)
liaila, turret (n)
liaisha, trophy (n)
liaka, chore (n)
lialika, wink (n)
lialiko, wink (v)
lialita, word (n)
lialitefenitha, wordsmith (n)
lialito, word (v)
lialitu, wordy (adj)
liana, scan (n)
liano, scan (v)
lianoka, camouflage (n)
lianoko, camouflage (v)
lianua, scanner (n doer)
liapa, read (n)
liapio, read (v pa)
liapo, read (v)
liapu, readable (adj)
liapua, reader (n doer)
liapuafifa, readership (n)
liapuila, readout (n)
liarifoka, exhaustion (n)

liatha, scarf (n)
liatu, nautical (adj)
liau, bye (n/interj)
liauka, raid (n)
liauko, raid (v)
liaukua, raider (n doer)
liaunu, marine (adj)
liaunua, mariner (n doer)
liaupa, marina (n)
liausheneto, maroon (v)
liautha, marsh (n)
liautheraupa, marshland (n)
liauthu, marshy (adj)
liava, navy (n)
liavata, navigation (n)
liavato, navigate (v)
liavatua, navigator (n doer)
liavu, naval (adj)
liavuka, twinkle (n)
liavuko, twinkle (v)
libesha, settlement (n)
libesho, settle (v)
libeshua, settler (n doer)
Libiafa, Libya (n)
Libiana, Libyan (n)
libita, sediment (n)
libito, sedimentate (v)
libitu, sedimentary (adj)
libitueta, sedimentation (n)
lidiuta, nucleus (n)
lidiuti, nuclei (n pl)
lidiutu, nuclear (adj)
lidofa, era (n)
lidupa, obesity (n)
lidupiu, obesely (adv)
lidupu, obese (adj)
liebilefu, oncoming (adj)
liefepa, onset (n)
liefikoletu, onscreen (adj)
liegelorifu, onboard (adj)
liehushiu, onward (adv)
liemavifu, ongoing (adj)
liemu, on (prep)
lienosha, amnesty (n)
lienularitu, onshore (adj)
liereiginua, onlooker (n doer)
liesheriauta, onslaught (n)
lieta, idea (n)
lieteraka, onstage (n)
lieteraku, onstage (adj)
lietiu, ideally (adv)
lieto, idealize (v)
lietu, ideal (adj)
lifaba, stem (n)
lifabo, stem (v)
lifada, shirt (n)
lifezha, meagerness (n)
lifezhatu, measly (adj)
lifezhiu, meagerly (adv)
lifezhu, meager (adj)
lifoka, nutrient (n)
lifokueta, nutrition (n)
lifokuetiu, nutritionally (adv)

lifokuetu, nutritional (adj)
lifokuetua, nutritionist (n doer)
lifopa, discern (n)
lifopo, discern (v)
ligapa, solid (n)
ligapiu, solidly (adv)
ligapo, solidify (v)
ligapu, solid (adj)
ligeraga, solution (n)
ligerago, solve (v)
ligeragu, solvable (adj)
ligeragua, solver (n doer)
ligerapa, solvent (n)
ligerapu, soluble (adj)
ligerapueta, solvency (n)
ligerata, solute (n)
ligerika, consolation (n
    d:comfort)
ligeriko, console (v d:comfort)
ligula, string (n)
ligulio, strung (v pa)
ligulo, string (v)
ligulokiu, stringently (adv)
liguloku, stringent (adj)
likapiu, properly (adv)
likapu, proper (adj)
likima, prop (n)
likimo, prop (v)
lilakeluafa, microscope (n)
lilana, serenity (n)
lilaniu, serenely (adv)
lilanu, serene (adj)
liledeiora, microfilm (n)
lilemiekuita, microbiology (n)
lilemiekuitua, microbiologist (n
    doer)
lilesha, microwave (n)
lilesharishotuka, microsystem (n)
lilesho, microwave (v)
lilipa, sermon (n)
lilopa, final (n)
lilopiu, finally (adv)
lilopo, finalize (v)
lilopu, final (adj)
lilopua, finalist (n doer)
lilota, burrow (n)
liloto, burrow (v)
lilotua, burrower (n doer)
lilupa, microbe (n)
lilupu, microbial (adj)
liluyapa, microphone (n)
limafa, furniture (n)
limafo, furnish (v)
limaka, scandal (n)
limakiu, scandalously (adv)
limako, scandalize (v)
limaku, scandalous (adj)
limauka, raunchiness (n)
limauku, raunchy (adj)
limena, morning (n)
limeta, meter (n d:metric
    measurement)
limetha, min (n)

limifenilota, miniskirt (n)
limika, miniature (n)
limiko, miniaturize (v)
limiku, miniature (adj)
liminilofa, miniseries (n)
limisha, minimum (n)
limishiu, minimally (adv)
limisho, minimize (v)
limishu, minimal (adj)
limishua, minimalist (n doer)
limishueta, minimalism (n)
limishueta, minimalization (n)
limizhauna, minivan (n)
limoroka, ranch (n)
limoroko, ranch (v)
limorokua, rancher (n doer)
limusha, minus (n)
limushi, minuses (n pl)
limushu, minus (adj/prep)
linala, sheer (n d:clear)
linaliu, sheer (adv d:clear)
linalu, sheer (adj d:clear)
linapiu, fiscally (adv)
linapu, fiscal (adj)
linasha, trousers (n)
linofa, finance (n)
linofiu, financially (adv)
linofo, finance (v)
linofu, financial (adj)
linofua, financier (n doer)
linuna, note (n d:music)
lioila, woe (n)
lioiliu, woefully (adv)
lioilu, woeful (adj)
lioitha, moor (n d:marsh)
liopa, ruby (n)
lipeluta, orbit (n)
lipeluto, orbit (v)
lipelutu, orbital (adj)
lipelutua, orbiter (n doer)
lipina, bikini (n)
liraifopa, triumph (n)
liraifopiu, triumphantly (adv)
liraifopo, triumph (v)
liraifopu, triumphal (adj)
liraifopu, triumphant (adj)
liralimeta, centimeter (n)
lireta, cent (n)
liretata, century (n)
lirifa, scent (n)
lirifo, scent (v)
lirina, rum (n)
liroda, blood (n)
lirodiu, bloodily (adv)
lirodo, bleed (v)
lirodu, bloody (adj)
lirodua, bleeder (n doer)
lirola, color (n)
lirolata, publication (n)
lirolato, publish (v)
lirolatua, publisher (n doer)
liroliu, colorfully (adv)
lirolo, color (v)

lirolu, colorful (adj)
liropafa, republic (n)
liropafua, republican (n doer)
liropuka, publicity (n)
liropuko, publicize (v)
liroputa, public (n)
liroputiu, publicly (adv)
liroputu, public (adj)
lirosha, lily (n)
lishetana, tint (n)
lishetano, tint (v)
lisho, belittle (v)
lishopa, decency (n)
lishopiu, decently (adv)
lishopu, decent (adj)
lishu, little (adj)
litaga, obituary (n)
litana, plan (n)
litanika, plant (n d:factory)
litaniroka, plantation (n)
litano, plan (v)
litanua, planner (n doer)
Lithiuma, Lithium (n)
Lithuaniafa, Lithuania (n)
Lithuaniana, Lithuanian (n)
litika, dye (n)
litiko, dye (v)
litikua, dyer (n doer)
liubafika, constriction (n)
liubafiko, constrict (v)
liubafikua, constrictor (n doer)
liubafita, conjunction (n)
liubafito, conjoin (v)
liubaifa, conviction (n)
liubaifo, convict (v)
liubaifua, convict (n doer)
liubaipiu, convincingly (adv)
liubaipo, convince (v)
liubarikata, conductivity (n)
liuberefa, condensation (n)
liuberefita, condensate (n)
liuberefo, condense (v)
liuberefua, condenser (n doer)
liubiafafa, consecration (n)
liubiafafo, consecrate (v)
liubisha, contrivance (n)
liubisho, contrive (v)
liubota, confusion (n)
liubotiu, confusingly (adv)
liuboto, confuse (v)
liubupa, contentment (n
    d:satisfied)
liubupiu, contently (adv
    d:satisfied)
liubupu, content (adj d:satisfied)
liudereta, concentration (n)
liudereto, concentrate (v)
liuderetua, concentrator (n doer)
liuderoma, constellation (n)
liuderomo, constellate (v)
liudifota, contraption (n)
liudoshipa, concoction (n)
liudoshipo, concoct (v)

liufadaufa, conspiracy (n)
liufadaufo, conspire (v)
liufadaufu, conspiratorial (adj)
liufadaufua, conspirator (n doer)
liufadeka, consortium (n)
liufadeko, consort (v)
liufadekua, consort (n doer)
liufelarina, confrontation (n)
liufelarino, confront (v)
liufelarinu, confrontational (adj)
liufialota, consumption (n)
liufialoto, consume (v)
liufialotua, consumer (n doer)
liufima, convention (n)
liufimo, convene (v)
liufimu, conventional (adj)
liufirama, convenience (n)
liufiramiu, conveniently (adv)
liufiramu, convenient (adj)
liufoita, convex (n)
liufoitu, convex (adj)
liufopa, concern (n)
liufopo, concern (v)
liufuala, conveyance (n)
liufualika, convoy (n)
liufualo, convey (v)
liufualu, conveyable (adj)
liufualua, conveyor (n doer)
liugalifa, concurrence (n)
liugalifa, concurrency (n)
liugalifiu, concurrently (adv)
liugalifo, concur (v)
liugalifu, concurrent (adj)
liugalita, contraction (n d:shrink)
liugalito, contract (v d:shrink)
liugefa, conference (n)
liugefata, conferment (n)
liugefo, confer (v)
liugefua, conferor (n doer)
liugefuina, conferee (n)
liugego, condone (v)
liugelapa, conglomerate (n)
liugelapo, conglomerate (v)
liugeruta, conclusion (n)
liugerutiu, conclusively (adv)
liugeruto, conclude (v)
liugerutu, conclusive (adj)
liugoita, concussion (n)
liugoito, concuss (v)
liukaruga, contour (n)
liukarugo, contour (v)
liukavala, congregation (n)
liukavalo, congregate (v)
liukavalu, congregational (adj)
liukemifa, convolvement (n)
liukemifo, convolve (v)
liukemita, convolution (n)
liukemito, convolute (v)
liukeriuka, conduction (n)
liukeriuko, conduct (v)
liukeriuku, conductive (adj)
liukeriukua, conductor (n doer)
liukiaga, congestion (n)

liukiago, congest (v)
liukika, conflict (n)
liukiko, conflict (v)
liukilata, congruence (n)
liukilata, congruousness (n)
liukilatiu, congruently (adv)
liukilatiu, congruously (adv)
liukilatu, congruent (adj)
liukilatu, congruous (adj)
liukinopa, congratulation (n)
liukinopo, congratulate (v)
liukiota, contortion (n)
liukioto, contort (v)
liukiroko, conduce (v)
liukiroku, conducive (adj)
liukirokua, conducer (n doer)
liukofita, conservation (n)
liukofitana, conservative (n)
liukofitiu, conservatively (adv)
liukofito, conserve (v)
liukofitu, conservative (adj)
liukofitua, conservationist (n doer)
liukofitueta, conservatism (n)
liukorafita, conservatory (n)
liukulita, configuration (n)
liukulito, configure (v)
liukulitua, configurator (n doer)
liulaita, contrast (n)
liulaito, contrast (v)
liularika, consignment (n)
liulariko, consign (v)
liuliga, console (n d:cabinet)
liuligapa, consolidation (n)
liuligapo, consolidate (v)
liuligapua, consolidator (n doer)
liulinapa, confiscation (n)
liulinapo, confiscate (v)
liulinapu, confiscatory (adj)
liulofa, consent (n)
liulofata, consensus (n)
liulofo, consent (v)
liulofu, consensual (adj)
liuma, conceit (n)
liumarota, confluence (n)
liumarotu, confluent (adj)
liumeiga, convergence (n)
liumeigo, converge (v)
liumeigu, convergent (adj)
liumida, connotation (n)
liumido, connote (v)
liumiuga, contagion (n)
liumiugiu, contagious (adv)
liumiuka, contamination (n)
liumiuko, contaminate (v)
liumiukua, contaminant (n doer)
liumo, conceit (v)
liuna, confession (n)
liunana, confessional (n)
liuneipa, contusion (n)
liuneipo, contuse (v)
liuno, confess (v)
liunua, confessor (n doer)

liunuifa, confirmation (n)
liunuifo, confirm (v)
liupaiba, contact (n)
liupaibo, contact (v)
liupaibua, contact (n doer)
liupaiva, confederacy (n)
liupaiva, confederation (n)
liupaivo, confederate (v)
liupaivua, confederate (n doer)
liupauga, concave (n)
liupaugiu, concavely (adv)
liupaugo, concave (v)
liupaugu, concave (adj)
liupelaipo, construe (v)
liupelaipua, construer (n doer)
liupeluzha, condolence (n)
liupeluzho, condole (v)
liuperina, confidence (n)
liuperino, confide (v)
liuperinofiu, confidentially (adv)
liuperinofu, confidential (adj)
liuperinu, confident (adj)
liuperinua, confidant (n doer)
liuperulika, constraint (n)
liuperuliko, constrain (v)
liupifoka, contention (n d:challenge)
liupifoko, contend (v d:challenge)
liupifoku, contentious (adj d:challenge)
liupifokua, contender (n doer d:challenge)
liurilopa, consternation (n)
liurilopo, consternate (v)
liuroshipa, conception (n)
liushanita, consonant (n)
liusheleka, construction (n)
liusheleko, construct (v)
liusheleku, constructive (adj)
liushelekua, constructor (n doer)
liusheriga, conscription (n)
liusherigo, conscript (v)
liushetiba, context (n)
liushetita, contest (n)
liushetito, contest (v)
liushetitua, contestant (n doer)
liushipa, concept (n)
liushipiu, conceptually (adv)
liushipo, conceive (v)
liushipu, conceptual (adj)
liushipuferepiu, conceivably (adv)
liushipuferepu, conceivable (adj)
liushopelita, constitution (n)
liushopelitiu, constitutionally (adv)
liushopelito, constitute (v)
liushopelitu, constitutional (adj)
liushufitiu, consecutively (adv)
liushufito, consecute (v)
liushufitu, consecutive (adj)
liushulito, confound (v)
liutava, contrition (n)
liutaviu, contritely (adv)

liutavu, contrite (adj)
liutelika, consistency (n)
liutelikiu, consistently (adv)
liuteliko, consist (v)
liuteliku, consistent (adj)
liutepa, conjecture (n)
liutepo, conjecture (v)
liutereba, convulsion (n)
liuterebiu, convulsedly (adv)
liuterebo, convulse (v)
liuterebu, convulsible (adj)
liuterelika, constant (n)
liuterelikiu, constantly (adv)
liutereliku, constant (adj)
liuterelikueta, constancy (n)
liutharifa, conversation (n)
liutharifiu, conversationally (adv)
liutharifo, converse (v)
liutharifu, conversational (adj)
liutharifua, conversationalist (n doer)
liutharika, conversion (n)
liuthariko, convert (v)
liuthariku, convertible (adj)
liutharikua, converter (n doer)
liuthifita, convection (n)
liuthifito, convect (v)
liuthishakiu, concisely (adv)
liuthishaku, concise (adj)
liuthota, consideration (n)
liuthotaru, considerate (adj)
liuthotiu, considerably (adv)
liuthoto, consider (v)
liuthotu, considerable (adj)
liuthufika, conspectus (n)
liutifoka, condition (n)
liutifokiu, conditionally (adv)
liutifoko, condition (v)
liutifoku, conditional (adj)
liutifokua, conditioner (n doer)
liutiotha, contingency (n)
liutiothu, contingent (adj)
liutira, continuation (n)
liutiriu, continually (adv)
liutiriu, continuously (adv)
liutiro, continue (v)
liutiru, continual (adj)
liutiru, continuous (adj)
liuvafita, contempt (n)
liuvafitu, contemptable (adj)
liuvanita, consultation (n)
liuvanito, consult (v)
liuvanitua, consultant (n doer)
liuvarifoka, contemplation (n)
liuvarifoko, contemplate (v)
liuveka, concession (n)
liuveko, concede (v)
liuviaga, constipation (n)
liuviago, constipate (v)
liuviauka, condemnation (n)
liuviauko, condemn (v)
liuvirota, confection (n)
liuvirotara, confectionery (n)

liuviroto, confect (v)
liuvorina, conformity (n)
liuvorino, conform (v)
liuvorinua, conformer (n doer)
liuvorinua, conformist (n doer)
liuvorinueta, conformance (n)
liuvoruga, congress (n)
liuvorugu, congressional (adj)
liuvorugua, congressman (n doer)
liuvuata, confinement (n)
liuvuato, confine (v)
liuzhila, concert (n)
liuzhilo, concert (v)
livafita, literature (n)
livafitu, literary (adj)
livana, ivy (n)
livashota, literal (n)
livashotiu, literally (adv)
livashotu, literal (adj)
livata, literacy (n)
livatoru, literate (adj)
livienopa, phenomenon (n)
livienopi, phenomena (n pl)
livienopu, phenominal (adj)
livona, libel (n)
livono, libel (v)
livonu, libelous (adj)
lizhana, pizza (n)
loberiaka, perusal (n)
loberiako, peruse (v)
loberunitiu, perpendicularly (adv)
loberunitu, perpendicular (adj)
lobifeka, ordeal (n)
lobuka, support (n)
lobukiu, supportively (adv)
lobuko, support (v)
lobuku, supportable (adj)
lobuku, supportive (adj)
lobukua, supporter (n doer)
lodalipo, perturb (v)
lodokata, persecution (n)
lodokato, persecute (v)
lodokatua, persecutor (n doer)
lofama, orange (n d:color)
lofamu, orange (adj d:color)
lofana, curtain (n)
lofeko, curtail (v)
lofina, orchestra (n)
lofiniu, orchestrally (adv)
lofino, orchestrate (v)
lotinu, orchestral (adj)
lofinua, orchestrator (n doer)
lofinueta, orchestration (n)
lofipa, curve (n)
lofipara, curvature (n)
lofipo, curve (v)
lofipu, curvy (adj)
lofudaufa, perspiration (n)
lofudaufo, perspire (v)
logafa, pocket (n)
logafebiepa, pocketful (n)
logafevonuda, pocketbook (n)
logafo, pocket (v)

logafua, pocketer (n doer)
logatha, rabbit (n)
loidiana, perpetuation (n)
loidiana, perpetuity (n)
loidianiu, perpetually (adv)
loidiano, perpetuate (v)
loidianu, perpetual (adj)
loidio, wrote (v pa)
loido, write (v)
loidoipa, comedy (n)
loidoipiu, comically (adv)
loidoipu, comical (adj)
loidoipua, comedian (n doer)
loidoipua, comic (n doer)
loidua, writer (n doer)
loikana, shin (n)
loikauta, discord (n)
loinama, romance (n)
loinamiu, romatically (adv)
loinamo, romanticize (v)
loinamu, romantic (adj)
loinamua, romancer (n doer)
loipa, wrist (n)
loipeluka, wristwatch (n)
loipeshetaima, wristband (n)
loira kodi, ought (ndal d:desire)
loira, desire (n)
loiriu, desirably (adv)
loiro, desire (v)
loiru, desirable (adj)
loishapa, lobster (n)
loitha, sir (n)
loithika, sire (n)
loithiko, sire (v)
loithu, sir (adj)
loitiena, seepage (n)
loitieno, seep (v)
loitifo, seethe (v)
loitio, sought (v pa)
loito, seek (v)
loitua, seeker (n doer)
loiva, nerve (n)
loivekuita, neurology (n)
loivekuitu, neurological (adj)
loivekuitua, neurologist (n doer)
loivemofita, neurosurgery (n)
loivemofitua, neurosurgeon (n doer)
loiveraika, neurosis (n)
loiveraiku, neurotic (adj)
loiveshuasha, neuroscience (n)
loiveshuashua, neuroscientist (n doer)
loiveta, neuron (n)
loivethonoka, neurotransmission (n)
loivethonoko, neurotransmit (v)
loivethonokua, neurotransmitter (n doer)
loivetu, neural (adj)
loivipa, nervousness (n)
loivipiu, nervously (adv)
loivipu, nervous (adj)

loivo, nerve (v)
loivu, nervy (adj)
lokapo, poach (v)
lokapua, poacher (n doer)
lokiloka, perseverance (n)
lokiloko, persevere (v)
lokiora, perfume (n)
lokioro, perfume (v)
Lokitafa, October (n)
lolafa, kerchief (n)
lolifiu, dear (n)
lolifiu, dearly (adv)
lolifo, endear (v)
lolifu, dear (adj)
lolirota, percent (n)
lolirotata, percentage (n)
lomapa, gallop (n)
lomapo, gallop (v)
lonika, permit (n)
lonikata, permanence (n)
lonikatiu, permanently (adv)
lonikatu, permanent (adj)
loniki, permit (n pl)
loniko, permit (v)
lonuda, entrance (n)
lonuda, entry (n)
lonudepeliola, entryway (n)
lonudiusha, enterprise (n)
lonudiusho, enterprise (v)
lonudiushua, entrepreneur (n doer)
lonudo, enter (v)
Lonudona, London (n)
lonudua, entrant (n doer)
lopifoto, pertain (v)
lopifotu, pertinent (adj)
lorafa, twiddle (n)
lorafo, twiddle (v)
loraka, pejorative (n)
loredikefilu, altogether (adv)
lorehoishiu, always (adv)
loreifu, all (adj)
lorenoifa, maybe (n)
lorenoifiu, maybe (adv)
lorifa kodi, might (ndal d:possibility)
lorifa, possibility (n)
lorifiu, possibly (adv)
lorifu, possible (adj)
lorika, chorus (n)
loriko, choir (v)
lorikua, choir (n doer)
lorima, milk (n)
lorimo, milk (v)
lorimu, milky (adj)
lorimua, milker (n doer)
loripa, thumb (n)
loripetherina, thumbnail (n)
loripo, thumb (v)
lorisha, pulse (n)
lorisho, pulse (v)
lorishota, pulsation (n)
lorishoto, pulsate (v)

lorishotua, pulsator (n doer)
lorishua, pulser (n doer)
lorita, flavor (n)
lorito, flavor (v)
lorowaku, almost (adv)
lorudoliu, already (adv)
loruga, cracker (n d:saltine)
lorugeritu, almighty (adj)
Losha Anikelesha, Los Angeles (n)
losheluaka, permutation (n)
losheluako, permutate (v)
loshetu, rather (adv/interj)
Loshiafa, EhoDay01 (n)
loshipa, perception (n)
loshipiu, perceptively (adv)
loshipo, perceive (v)
loshipu, perceptive (adj)
loshipua, perceiver (n doer)
lotelika, persistence (n)
lotelikiu, persistently (adv)
loteliko, persist (v)
loteliku, persistent (adj)
lotharifa, perversion (n)
lotharifiu, perversely (adv)
lotharifo, perverse (v)
lotharifu, perverse (adj)
lotharifua, pervert (n doer)
lotharika, perversity (n)
lothariko, pervert (v)
lotherata, perforation (n)
lotherato, perforate (v)
lothuka, perspective (n)
lovirota, perfection (n)
lovirotiu, perfectly (adv)
loviroto, perfect (v)
lovirotu, perfect (adj)
lovora, darling (n)
lovorina, performance (n)
lovorino, perform (v)
lovorinua, performer (n doer)
lovoru, darling (adj)
lovoteta, perpetration (n)
lovoteto, perpetrate (v)
lovotetua, perpetrator (n doer)
lowangei, whose (pron)
lowefelei, whoever (pron)
lowei, who (pron)
lowei, whom (pron)
lozhanikiu, pervasively (adv)
lozhaniko, pervade (v)
lozhaniku, pervasive (adj)
luafika, education (n)
luafiko, educate (v)
luafiku, educational (adj)
luafikua, educator (n doer)
luaika, salute (n)
luaiko, salute (v)
luaikueta, salutation (n)
luaitha, salinity (n)
luaitho, salinate (v)
luaithu, saline (adj)
luaka, refuge (n)

luakuina, refugee (n)
luala, laugh (n)
lualara, laughter (n)
lualiu, laughably (adv)
lualo, laugh (v)
lualu, laughable (adj)
lualua, laugher (n doer)
luama, mire (n)
luamo, mire (v)
luapa, luster (n)
luapata, illustration (n)
luapatiu, illustratively (adv)
luapato, illustrate (v)
luapatu, illustrative (adj)
luapatua, illustrator (n doer)
luapo, luster (v)
luapu, lustrous (adj)
luara, child (n)
luari, children (n pl)
luariderupa, reinterpretation (n)
luariderupo, reinterpret (v)
luarikeifa, childcare (n)
luaritemota, kindergarten (n)
luaritemotua, kindergartener (n doer)
luarofifa, childhood (n)
luarokeriuka, reintroduction (n)
luarokeriuko, reintroduce (v)
luaru, childish (adj)
luaruvalesha, childbirth (n)
luasha, luxury (n)
luashiu, luxuriously (adv)
luashu, luxurious (adj)
luatha, salt (n)
luatheidona, saltwater (n)
luathiu, saltily (adv)
luatho, salt (v)
luathu, salty (adj)
luathua, salter (n doer)
lubafika, restriction (n)
lubafikiu, restrictively (adv)
lubafiko, restrict (v)
lubafiku, restrictive (adj)
lubafikua, restricter (n doer)
lubaifita, resource (n)
lubaifitiu, resourcefully (adv)
lubaifitu, resourceful (adj)
lubaifitueta, resourcefulness (n)
lubalifoka, recalibration (n)
lubalifoko, recalibrate (v)
lubeitata, repurchase (n)
lubeitato, repurchase (v)
lubeitha, reimbursement (n)
lubeitho, reimburse (v)
lubelaika, rebuttal (n)
lubelaiko, rebut (v)
lubelasha, repression (n)
lubelasho, repress (v)
lubelashu, repressive (adj)
lubelashua, repressor (n doer)
lubelega, reclassification (n)
lubelego, reclassify (v)
luberepo, replant (v)

luberesha, replacement (n)
luberesho, replace (v)
lubereshu, replaceable (adj)
lubereshua, replacer (n doer)
luberiako, reuse (v)
luberieno, rename (v)
luberono, regroup (v)
lubiaufo, redoubt (v)
lubiaufu, redoubtable (adj)
lubisha, retrieval (n)
lubisho, retrieve (v)
lubishua, retriever (n doer)
lubiuta, restatement (n)
lubiuto, restate (v)
lubolika, repair (n)
luboliko, repair (v)
luboliku, repairable (adj)
luboliku, reparable (adj)
lubolikua, repairer (n doer)
lubolikua, repairman (n doer)
lubuasha, rehearsal (n)
lubuasho, rehearse (v)
lubugato, repackage (v)
lubulesha, rebuff (n)
lubulesho, rebuff (v)
lubupa, refill (n)
lubupo, refill (v)
ludaiata, rescue (n)
ludaiato, rescue (v)
ludaiatua, rescuer (n doer)
ludairo, retype (v)
ludalitho, recover (v d:resurface)
ludalithu, recoverable (adj d:resurface)
ludana, reverberation (n)
ludano, reverberate (v)
ludarita, relation (n)
ludaritefifa, relationship (n)
ludaritefifiu, relationally (adv)
ludaritefifu, relational (adj)
ludaritiu, relatively (adv)
ludarito, relate (v)
ludaritu, relative (adj)
ludaritua, relative (n doer)
ludauto, rebuke (v)
ludefipa, recap (n)
ludefipo, recap (v)
ludeirota, redesign (n)
ludeiroto, redesign (v)
ludelika, recapitalization (n)
ludeliko, recapitalize (v)
ludelishika, refractory (n)
ludelishoka, refraction (n)
ludelishoko, refract (v)
ludelishoku, refractive (adj)
ludepio, rethought (v pa)
ludepo, rethink (v)
luderaba, restoration (n)
luderabiu, restoratively (adv)
luderabo, restore (v)
luderabu, restorative (adj)
luderabua, restorer (n doer)
luderaipa, rebound (n)

luderaipo, rebound (v)
luderata, repentance (n)
luderato, repent (v)
luderatu, repentant (adj)
luderauka, recruitment (n)
luderauko, recruit (v)
luderaukua, recruiter (n doer)
luderiko, recrease (v)
luderuka, reprehension (n)
luderuki, reprehension (n pl)
luderukiu, reprehensively (adv)
luderuko, reprehend (v)
luderuku, reprehensive (adj)
ludeshiaka, recapture (n)
ludeshiako, recapture (v)
ludiadaro, remodel (v)
ludiana, rediscovery (n)
ludiano, rediscover (v)
ludiato, rejoin (v)
ludiba, retry (n)
ludibaga, retrial (n)
ludibo, retry (v)
ludidana, resemblance (n)
ludidano, resemble (v)
ludiofa, retrenchment (n)
ludiofo, retrench (v)
ludorebida, rebroadcast (n)
ludorebidio, rebroadcast (v pa)
ludorebido, rebroadcast (v)
luduasha, representation (n)
luduasho, represent (v)
luduashu, representative (adj)
luduashua, representative (n
    doer)
ludufika, revenge (n)
ludufiko, revenge (v)
ludufipa, response (n)
ludufipiu, responsively (adv)
ludufipo, respond (v)
ludufipu, responsive (adj)
ludufipua, responder (n doer)
ludufipuina, respondent (n)
luduveka, responsibility (n)
luduvekiu, responsibly (adv)
luduveku, responsible (adj)
luefubino, reopen (v)
lueifa, ladle (n)
lueifo, ladle (v)
lueito, lade (v)
lueivezha, ladybug (n)
lufabaka, refutation (n)
lufabako, refute (v)
lufabota, refusion (n d:join again)
lufaboto, refuse (v d:join again)
lufadeko, resort (v d:sort again)
lufavena, nickname (n)
lufaveno, nickname (v)
lufelauda, reproach (n)
lufelaudo, reproach (v)
lufelaufito, relive (v)
lufeliotha, reprieve (n)
lufelumo, reshape (v)
lufepa, reset (n)

lufepio, reset (v pa)
lufepo, reset (v)
lufepua, resetter (n doer)
luferanito, relay (v d:place again)
luferiasho, rekindle (v)
luferifo, restock (v)
luferilota, reorganization (n)
luferiloto, reorganize (v)
luferilotua, reorganizer (n doer)
luferuifa, replay (n)
luferuifo, replay (v)
luferuifua, replayer (n doer)
luferuliko, refrain (v d:abstain)
lufiaisha, revision (n)
lufiaisho, revise (v)
lufiaishueta, revisionism (n)
lufiaishuetua, revisionist (n doer)
lufialita, resumption (n)
lufialito, resume (v)
lufialitua, resumer (n doer)
lufiarifa, refresh (n)
lufiarifiu, refreshingly (adv)
lufiarifo, refresh (v)
lufiarifota, refreshment (n)
lufiarifua, refresher (n doer)
lufioko, retool (v)
lufipa, nick (n)
lufipo, nick (v)
lufitapa, reestablishment (n)
lufitapo, reestablish (v)
lufiuneliko, reprogram (v)
lufiuveto, reprocess (v)
lufodaufa, respiration (n)
lufodaufo, respirate (v)
lufodaufu, respiratory (adj)
lufodaufua, respirator (n doer)
lufuama, revelation (n)
lufuamo, reveal (v)
lufuata, review (n)
lufuato, review (v)
lufuatu, rearview (adj)
lufuatua, reviewer (n doer)
lufurishemenu, relentless (adj)
lufurisho, relent (v)
lugaiapa, recoil (n)
lugaiapo, recoil (v)
lugalifa, recurrence (n)
lugalifiu, recurrently (adv)
lugalifo, recur (v)
lugalifu, recurrent (adj)
lugalita, retraction (n)
lugalito, retract (v)
lugalitu, retractable (adj)
lugaripa, recollection (n)
lugaripo, recollect (v)
lugarodaka, recalculation (n)
lugarodako, recalculate (v)
lugasho, retrace (v)
lugata, rebellion (n)
lugatiu, rebelliously (adv)
lugato, rebel (v)
lugatu, rebellious (adj)
lugatua, rebel (n doer)

lugefa, referral (n)
lugefo, refer (v)
lugefua, referer (n doer)
lugefuina, referee (n)
lugeloita, recharge (n)
lugeloito, recharge (v)
lugeloitu, rechargeable (adj)
lugeloitua, recharger (n doer)
lugeraga, resolution (n)
lugerago, resolve (v)
lugeragu, resolute (adj)
lugeragua, resolver (n doer)
lugerasho, repaint (v)
lugereika, reincarnation (n)
lugereiko, reincarnate (v)
lugeruta, recluse (n)
lugerutiu, reclusively (adv)
lugerutu, reclusive (adj)
lugesha, reference (n)
lugeshana, referendum (n)
lugeshani, referenda (n pl)
lugeshiu, referentially (adv)
lugesho, reference (v)
lugeshu, referential (adj)
lugeta, reflection (n)
lugetiu, reflectively (adv)
lugeto, reflect (v)
lugetu, reflective (adj)
lugetua, reflector (n doer)
lugiapa, rebate (n)
lugiapo, rebate (v)
lugiasha, recursal (n)
lugiashiu, recursively (adv)
lugiasho, recurse (v)
lugiashu, recursive (adj)
lugiashua, recurser (n doer)
lugira, recall (n)
lugiro, recall (v)
lugirua, recaller (n doer)
lugoifito, refocus (v)
lugoita, recusal (n)
lugoito, recuse (v)
lugokio, retook (v pa)
lugoko, retake (v)
luguvata, reinvention (n)
luguvato, reinvent (v)
luhausha, reward (n)
luhausho, reward (v)
luhaushua, rewarder (n doer)
luiafa, silo (n)
luiako, reckon (v)
luiasha, retardation (n)
luiasho, retard (v)
luiashu, retardant (adj)
luiatemena, recklessness (n)
luiatemeniu, recklessly (adv)
luiatemenu, reckless (adj)
luiato, reck (v)
luibita, reinvestment (n)
luibito, reinvest (v)
luifa, rein (n)
luifo, rein (v)
luigepa, reelection (n)

luigepo, reelect (v)
luika, rally (n)
luiko, rally (v)
luima, bust (n d:sculpture)
luina, sill (n)
luipeikano, reinvigorate (v)
luipeliola, railway (n)
luisha, rise (n)
luisherela, reinsurance (n)
luisherelo, reinsure (v)
luisherelua, reinsurer (n doer)
luisheta, reinsertion (n)
luisheto, reinsert (v)
Luishiafa, Louisiana (n)
luishio, rose (v pa)
luisho, rise (v)
luishopelita, reinstitution (n)
luishopelito, reinstitute (v)
luishua, riser (n doer)
luita, rail (n)
luitegerela, railcar (n)
luiteira, reinstallation (n)
luiteiro, reinstall (v)
luiterelisha, railroad (n)
luiterelisho, railroad (v)
luithuato, reemphasize (v)
luito, rail (v)
luiunu, retro (adj)
luiupafita, retrofit (n)
luiupafito, retrofit (v)
luiupalitaka, retroactivity (n)
luiupalitakiu, retroactively (adv)
luiupalitaku, retroactive (adj)
luiushoteranu, retrograde (adj)
luiuthuka, retrospect (n)
luiuthuku, retrospective (adj)
luka, watch (n d:clock)
lukaima, return (n)
lukaimo, return (v)
lukaimua, returner (n doer)
lukeifito, redouble (v)
lukelala, relaxation (n)
lukelalo, relax (v)
lukelika, revisitation (n)
lukeliko, revisit (v)
lukemifa, revolution (n d:journey around)
lukemifo, revolve (v d:journey around)
lukemifua, revolver (n doer d:journey around)
lukenagua, watchmaker (n doer)
lukeriafa, requalification (n)
lukeriafo, requalify (v)
lukeriafua, requalifier (n doer)
lukeriata, renegotiation (n)
lukeriato, renegotiate (v)
lukeroifa, reclination (n)
lukeroifo, recline (v)
lukeroifua, recliner (n doer)
lukerosha, research (n)
lukerosho, research (v)
lukeroshua, researcher (n doer)

luketo, recheck (v)
lukigelako, reimpose (v)
lukioko, rework (v)
lukiroka, reduction (n)
lukirokiu, reducibly (adv)
lukiroko, reduce (v)
lukiroku, reducible (adj)
lukirokua, reducer (n doer)
lukiufa, redemption (n)
lukiufo, redeem (v)
lukiufu, redeemable (adj)
lukiufu, redemptive (adj)
lukiufua, redeemer (n doer)
lukofata, reserve (n d:military)
lukofatua, reservist (n doer d:military)
lukofipa, reservoir (n)
lukofita, reserve (n d:storage)
lukofito, reserve (v d:storage)
lukofitua, reserver (n doer d:storage)
lukofitueta, reservation (n)
lukuafika, redirection (n)
lukuafiko, redirect (v)
lukuano, regain (v)
lulafima, revenue (n)
lulaida, remedy (n)
lulaidaka, remediation (n)
lulaidako, remediate (v)
lulaidakua, remediator (n doer)
lulaido, remedy (v)
lulaisho, rejoice (v)
lulaishua, rejoicer (n doer)
lulaomio, reran (v pa)
lulaomo, rerun (v)
lularika, resignation (n d:quit)
lulariko, resign (v d:quit)
lularikua, resigner (n doer d:quit)
lulato, miss (v d:regret absence)
lulaufa, fridge (n)
lulaufaga, refrigeration (n)
lulaufago, refrigerate (v)
lulaufagua, refrigerator (n doer)
lulaufaguata, refrigerant (n)
luleniko, recommit (v)
luliapio, reread (v pa)
luliapo, reread (v)
lulibesha, resettlement (n)
lulibesho, resettle (v)
lulinofo, refinance (v)
lulirolato, republish (v)
lulirotiu, recently (adv)
lulirotu, recent (adj)
luliufimo, reconvene (v)
luliukulita, reconfiguration (n)
luliukulito, reconfigure (v)
luliunuifa, reconfirmation (n)
luliunuifo, reconfirm (v)
luliusheleka, reconstruction (n)
luliusheleko, reconstruct (v)
luliusheleku, reconstructive (adj)
luliushopelita, reconstitution (n)
luliushopelito, reconstitute (v)

luliuthota, reconsideration (n)
luliuthoto, reconsider (v)
luliutifoko, recondition (v)
luloida, rewrite (n)
luloidio, rewrote (v pa)
luloido, rewrite (v)
luloidua, rewriter (n doer)
lulonuda, reentry (n)
lulonudo, reenter (v)
lulorisho, repulse (v)
lulorishu, repulsive (adj)
lululata, remission (n)
lululatiu, remissively (adv)
lululato, remiss (v)
lululatu, remissive (adj)
lulurito, reload (v)
lulutigata, reiteration (n)
lulutigato, reiterate (v)
luluvapa, reciprocation (n)
luluvapa, reciprocity (n)
luluvapo, reciprocate (v)
luluvapu, reciprocal (adj)
luma, hum (n)
lumaigifa, revitalization (n)
lumaigifo, revitalize (v)
lumarina, recourse (n)
lumarino, recourse (v)
lumarinua, recourser (n doer)
lumaromaka, regeneration (n)
lumaromako, regenerate (v)
lumaromakua, regenerator (n doer)
lumemifa, resuscitation (n)
lumemifo, resuscitate (v)
lumiafa, renovation (n)
lumiafo, renovate (v)
lumiafua, renovator (n doer)
lumiasha, reluctance (n)
lumiashiu, reluctantly (adv)
lumiashu, reluctant (adj)
lumiola, renewal (n)
lumiolo, renew (v)
lumiolu, renewable (adj)
lumiolua, renewer (n doer)
lumitha, retail (n)
lumitho, retail (v)
lumithua, retailer (n doer)
lumo, hum (v)
lumoima, repayment (n)
lumoimio, repaid (v pa)
lumoimo, repay (v)
lumoimua, repayer (n doer)
lumufito, renounce (v)
lumurita, redundancy (n)
lumuritiu, redundantly (adv)
lumuritu, redundant (adj)
lumutha, rematch (n)
lumutho, rematch (v)
lunaga, remake (n)
lunagio, remade (v pa)
lunago, remake (v)
lunagua, remaker (n doer)
lunata, revelry (n)

lunato, revel (v)
lunatu, revelatory (adj)
lunebielika, passport (n)
lunelialita, password (n)
luniapo, remind (v)
luniapua, reminder (n doer)
lunipa, cream (n)
lunipiu, creamily (adv)
lunipo, cream (v)
lunipu, creamy (adj)
lunipua, creamer (n doer)
lunita, pass (n)
lunitaka, passage (n)
lunitakua, passenger (n doer)
lunitiu, passively (adv)
lunito, pass (v)
lunitu, passive (adj)
lunitua, passer (n doer)
luniuna, replenishment (n)
luniuno, replenish (v)
lunoarita, reclamation (n)
lunoarito, reclaim (v)
lunoka, remittance (n)
lunoko, remit (v)
lunokua, remittor (n doer)
lunora, daughter (n)
lunuanueta, recrimination (n)
lunulipa, recombination (n)
lunulipo, recombine (v)
lunulipu, recombinant (adj)
lununa, release (n)
lununo, release (v)
lununua, releaser (n doer)
luolarika, reassignment (n)
luolariko, reassign (v)
luolashata, reassertion (n)
luolashato, reassert (v)
luolimota, rearrangement (n)
luolimoto, rearrange (v)
luolipa, reassurance (n)
luolipo, reassure (v)
luominopo, reawaken (v)
luopaika, reattachment (n)
luopaiko, reattach (v)
luopeliana, reappearance (n)
luopeliano, reappear (v)
luoraniufa, reaffirmation (n)
luoraniufo, reaffirm (v)
luorelapa, reassessment (n)
luorelapo, reassess (v)
luorishaipa, reallocation (n)
luorishaipo, reallocate (v)
luoroifa, realignment (n)
luoroifo, realign (v)
luotaifota, reappointment (n)
luotaifoto, reappoint (v)
luotherava, reassembly (n)
luotheravo, reassemble (v)
luotheta, reacquisition (n)
luotheto, reacquire (v)
lupada, repellant (n)
lupada, repellent (n)
lupado, repel (v)

lupadu, repellants (adj)
lupadu, repellent (adj)
lupadua, repeller (n doer)
lupafa, clown (n)
lupafita, refit (n)
lupafito, refit (v)
lupafo, clown (v)
lupalita, reaction (n)
lupalitaka, reactivation (n)
lupalitako, reactivate (v)
lupalitaku, reactive (adj)
lupalito, react (v)
lupalitu, reactionary (adj)
lupalitua, reactor (n doer)
lupalituna, reactionary (n)
lupana, retirement (n)
lupano, retire (v)
lupanua, retiree (n doer)
lupelata, regret (n)
lupelatiu, regretfully (adv)
lupelatiu, regrettably (adv)
lupelato, regret (v)
lupelatu, regretful (adj)
lupelatu, regrettable (adj)
lupelatua, regrettor (n doer)
lupeleika, reproduction (n)
lupeleikiu, reproductively (adv)
lupeleiko, reproduce (v)
lupeleiku, reproductive (adj)
lupeleikua, reproducer (n doer)
lupeliarika, reintegration (n)
lupeliariko, reintegrate (v)
lupeliuta, recreation (n d:remake)
lupeliuto, recreate (v d:remake)
lupeliutua, recreator (n doer
    d:remake)
luperaiko, reroute (v)
luperalifa, redecoration (n)
luperalifo, redecorate (v)
luperathio, redrew (v pa)
luperatho, redraw (v)
luperetio, retold (v pa)
lupereto, retell (v)
luperieta, resort (n d:rest, revert)
luperieto, resort (v d:rest, revert)
luperilapa, repossession (n)
luperilapo, repossess (v)
luperulika, restraint (n)
luperuliko, restrain (v)
luperulikua, restrainer (n doer)
luperupo, relinquish (v)
lupiaka, relegation (n)
lupiako, relegate (v)
lupietha, refurbishment (n)
lupietho, refurbish (v)
lupifota, retention (n)
lupifotiu, retentively (adv)
lupifoto, retain (v)
lupifotu, retentive (adj)
lupifotua, retainer (n doer)
lupoina, recount (n)
lupoino, recount (v)
lupoinua, recounter (n doer)

lureilota, rehabilitation (n)
lureiloto, rehabilitate (v)
luridafo, reschedule (v)
lurifa, herb (n)
lurifiu, herbally (adv)
lurifu, herbal (adj)
luripa, relief (n)
luripesherana, restroom (n)
luripo, relieve (v)
luripua, reliever (n doer)
lurita, load (n)
lurito, load (v)
luritua, loader (n doer)
lurolama, reconciliation (n)
lurolamo, reconcile (v)
Lushadora, Easter (n)
lushafa, recommendation (n)
lushafo, recommend (v)
lushaika, revocation (n)
lushaiko, revoke (v)
lushaiku, revocable (adj)
lushaipa, relocation (n)
lushaipo, relocate (v)
lushanita, resonance (n)
lushanito, resonate (v)
lushanitu, resonant (adj)
lushefinoka, resubmission (n)
lushefinoko, resubmit (v)
lushekita, removal (n)
lushekitiu, removably (adv)
lushekito, remove (v)
lushekitu, removable (adj)
lushekitua, remover (n doer)
lushelaitho, rescind (v)
lushelaufa, revival (n)
lushelaufo, revive (v)
lushelaufua, revivalist (n doer)
lushelaufua, reviver (n doer)
lusheloifita, redeployment (n)
lusheloifito, redeploy (v)
lusheluata, reply (n)
lusheluato, reply (v)
lusheluatua, replier (n doer)
lushenafa, reconnection (n)
lushenafo, reconnect (v)
lushenafua, reconnector (n doer)
lushenifo, rewire (v)
lusherita, redistribution (n)
lusherito, redistribute (v)
lusheroka, reflux (n)
lushethipa, resupply (n)
lushethipo, resupply (v)
lushiata, request (n)
lushiato, request (v)
lushiatua, requester (n doer)
lushiketo, reorder (v)
lushileko, restructure (v)
lushipeno, remap (v)
lushoika, remand (n)
lushoikauto, remanufacture (v)
lushoiko, remand (v)
lushoikua, remander (n doer)
lushoina, residence (n)

lushoino, reside (v)
lushoinu, residential (adj)
lushoinua, resident (n doer)
lushokalito, restart (v)
lushoriba, resentment (n
d:disdain)
lushoribo, resent (v d:disdain)
lushoribu, resentful (adj
d:disdain)
lushota, recipe (n)
lushotata, remark (n d:write
again)
lushotato, remark (v d:write
again)
lushuago, resize (v)
lutafino, revamp (v)
lutaluna, remembrance (n)
lutaluno, remember (v)
luteferapa, redevelopment (n)
luteferapo, redevelop (v)
lutefipesha, readjustment (n)
lutefipesho, readjust (v)
lutelika, resistance (n)
luteliko, resist (v)
luteliku, resistant (adj)
luteliku, resistible (adj)
lutelikua, resister (n doer)
lutelipa, repeal (n)
lutelipo, repeal (v)
lutelipua, repealer (n doer)
lutepa, reject (n)
lutepo, reject (v)
lutepua, rejector (n doer)
lutepueta, rejection (n)
lutereba, revulsion (n)
luterebo, revulse (v)
luterebu, revulsive (adj)
luterelifa, resale (n)
luterelifio, resold (v pa)
luterelifo, resell (v)
luterelifu, resale (adj)
luterelifua, reseller (n doer)
luteriloko, retrain (v)
luterulisha, reprint (n)
luterulisho, reprint (v)
Lutetiuma, Lutetium (n)
luthaitho, rehash (v)
lutharifa, reverse (n)
lutharifala, reversal (n)
lutharifo, reverse (v)
lutharifu, reversible (adj)
lutharika, reversion (n)
luthariko, revert (v)
lutharikua, reverter (n doer)
luthata, requirement (n)
luthatho, reshuffle (v)
luthato, require (v)
lutheraikio, rewound (v pa)
lutheraiko, rewind (v)
lutherefo, resurface (v)
lutherisha, reforestation (n)
lutherisho, reforest (v)
lutheriupa, retribution (n)

luthithoka, retaliation (n)
luthithoko, retaliate (v)
luthithoku, retaliatory (adj)
luthithokua, retaliator (n doer)
luthiufo, refile (v)
luthiufota, relapse (n)
luthiufoto, relapse (v)
luthoko, reapply (v)
luthonoka, retransmission (n)
luthonoko, retransmit (v)
luthuita, retreat (n)
luthuito, retreat (v)
luthuka, respect (n)
luthukilu, respectable (adj)
luthukiu, respectively (adv)
luthuko, respect (v)
luthuku, respective (adj)
luthukushiu, respectfully (adv)
luthukushu, respectful (adj)
luthunitana, recertification (n)
luthunitano, recertify (v)
lutibafiko, redistrict (v)
lutielika, resistor (n)
lutieta, reflex (n)
lutietu, reflexive (adj)
lutifoka, rendition (n)
lutifoko, render (v)
lutifokua, renderer (n doer)
lutigata, iteration (n)
lutigatiu, iteratively (adv)
lutigato, iterate (v)
lutigatu, iterative (adj)
lutikio, redid (v pa)
lutiko, redo (v)
lutimoka, refund (n)
lutimoko, refund (v)
lutimoku, refundable (adj)
lutimokua, refunder (n doer)
lutiogo, rehire (v)
lutiuto, refinish (v)
lutoipa, recitation (n)
lutoipata, recital (n)
lutoipo, recite (v)
lutukoiga, reexamination (n)
lutukoigo, reexamine (v)
lutulitio, recast (v pa)
lutulito, recast (v)
luuyanio, reheard (v pa)
luuyano, rehear (v)
luvadava, remote (n)
luvadaviu, remotely (adv)
luvadavu, remote (adj)
luvaika, regard (n)
luvaikamenu, regardless
(adj/adv)
luvaikemenu, irregardless (adj)
luvaikemenu, regardless (adj)
luvaiko, regard (v)
luvaikua, regarder (n doer)
luvairato, recycle (v)
luvairatua, recycler (n doer)
luvalesha, rebirth (n)
luvanita, result (n)

luvanito, result (v)
luvanitu, resultant (adj)
luvapa, repeat (n)
luvapiu, repeatedly (adv)
luvapo, repeat (v)
luvapu, repeatable (adj)
luvapu, repetitive (adj)
luvapua, repeater (n doer)
luvapueta, repetition (n)
luvapuetiu, repetitiously (adv)
luvapuetiu, repetitious (adj)
luvarafa, refrain (n d:verse)
luvarisho, rephrase (v)
luvaupa, revaluation (n)
luvaupo, revaluate (v)
luvausha, remainder (n)
luvausheta, remains (n)
luvausho, remain (v)
luveilina, reposition (n)
luveilino, reposition (v)
luveiloka, repository (n)
luveka, recess (n)
luveketa, recession (n)
luvekiu, recessively (adv)
luveko, recede (v)
luveku, recessive (adj)
luvekua, receder (n doer)
luvialota, recognition (n)
luvialotiu, recognizably (adv)
luvialoto, recognize (v)
luvialotu, recognizable (adj)
luvialotua, recognizer (n doer)
luvienoka, renomination (n)
luvienoko, renominate (v)
luvipa, regularity (n)
luvipiu, regularly (adv)
luvipo, regulate (v)
luvipu, regular (adj)
luvipua, regulator (n doer)
luvipueta, regulation (n)
luvipuetu, regulatory (adj)
luvipuna, regular (v)
luvoiga, resurgence (n)
luvoigo, resurge (v)
luvoigu, resurgent (adj)
luvoika, repute (n)
luvoikata, reputation (n)
luvoikato, repudiate (v)
luvoiko, repute (v)
luvopalita, reenactment (n)
luvopalito, reenact (v)
luvorieto, relearn (v)
luvorifa, recuperation (n)
luvorifo, recuperate (v)
luvorifu, recuperative (adj)
luvorina, reform (n d:form again)
luvorinaka, reformation (n)
luvorinako, reformat (v)
luvorinaku, reformatory (adj)
luvorinapa, reformulation (n)
luvorinapo, reformulate (v)
luvorino, reform (v d:form again)
luvorita, rebuild (n)

luvoritio, rebuilt (v pa)
luvorito, rebuild (v)
luvoruga, regression (n)
luvorugiu, regressively (adv)
luvorugo, regress (v)
luvorugu, regressive (adj)
luvorugua, regressor (n doer)
luvoshipeta, reinstatement (n)
luvoshipeto, reinstate (v)
luvovaupa, reevaluation (n)
luvovaupo, reevaluate (v)
luvoviuka, reinforcement (n)
luvoviuko, reinforce (v)
luvoviukua, reinforcer (n doer)
luvuafita, redefinition (n)
luvuafito, redefine (v)
luvuako, relaunch (v)
luvuanita, refinery (n)
luvuata, refinement (n)
luvuato, refine (v)
luvuatua, refiner (n doer)
luvulana, remarriage (n)
luvulano, remarry (v)
luweifo, re-sign (v d:sign again)
luwiona, silliness (n)
luwionu, silly (adj)
luyapa, phone (n)
luyapo, phone (v)
luyutaka, reunification (n)
luyutako, reunify (v)
luyutama, reunion (n)
luyutamo, reunite (v)
luzhaipio, resent (v pa d:send
    again)
luzhaipio, resend (v d:send again)
luzhaitho, revile (v)
luzhanitiu, resoundingly (adv)
luzhanito, resound (v)
luzhiapo, refuel (v)
luzhima, reissuance (n)
luzhimo, reissue (v)
luzhorika, remix (n)
luzhoriko, remix (v)
luzhumaka, rejuventation (n)
luzhumako, rejuvenate (v)
maa, ma (n)
Maderida, Madrid (n)
madika, olympics (n)
madlku, olymplc (adj)
madikua, olympian (n doer)
Madishota, Madison (n)
mafika, pert (n)
mafiku, pert (adj)
mafu, for (prep/conj)
Magoneshiuma, Magnesium (n)
mahila, now (n)
mahilu, now (adj/adv/conj)
mahiviula, nowadays (n)
mahiviuliu, nowadays (adv)
maia, M (let sng)
maiako, nix (v)
maiama, tan (n)
maiamo, tan (v)

maiamua, tanner (n doer)
maiapu, nope (interj)
maiata, goal (n)
maifa, valve (n)
maigama, vitamin (n)
maigifa, vitality (n)
maigifiu, vitally (adv)
maigifu, vital (adj)
maihem, Number_1e2256
maika, max (n)
maikata, maximum (n)
maikatiu, maximally (adv)
maikato, maximize (v)
maikatu, maximal (adj)
maiko, max (v)
mailena, mile (n)
mailenata, mileage (n)
maili, Ms (let pl)
Mainofa, Maine (n)
maipa, sock (n)
maipefa, socket (n)
maipo, sock (v)
maisha, mortar (n d:cement)
Maitaka, Marines (n)
maiva, narcotic (n)
maiwa, nay (interj)
Maknesi, Maknesi (n)
makoiu, never (adv)
malamita, mummification (n)
malamito, mummify (v)
malamitua, mummifier (n doer)
Malashiafa, Malaysia (n)
malifo, dote (v)
malifopa, maple (n)
malifua, dotard (n doer)
malika, lube (n)
malima, mummy (n)
malisha, mother (n)
malishepelorika, motherboard (n)
malisheraupa, motherland (n)
malisho, mother (v)
malishoka, lubrication (n)
malishoko, lubricate (v)
malishokua, lubricant (n doer)
malishu, motherly (adj)
maloshifa, motherhood (n)
manika, lump (n)
maniko, lump (v)
maniku, lumpy (adj)
manikua, lumper (n doer)
Manilofa, Manila (n)
Manisheshota, Manchester (n)
Manokatafa, Manhattan (n)
Manuganesha, Manganese (n)
mara, mama (n)
mara, mamma (n)
mariaita, genie (n)
marifa, mat (n)
marifana, mattress (n)
marifo, mat (v)
marila, lamb (n)
Marilanuda, Maryland (n)
marilo, lamb (v)

marimetha, generalization (n
    d:common)
marimethiu, generally (adv
    d:common)
marimetho, generalize (v
    d:common)
marimethu, general (adj
    d:common)
marina, course (n)
marino, course (v)
maripa, pig (n)
maripefinapa, pigskin (n)
maripo, pig (v)
maritiapa, genital (n)
maritiapi, genitalia (n pl)
maritiapu, genital (adj)
maromaita, genius (n)
maromaka, generation (n)
maromako, generate (v)
maromakua, generator (n doer)
maromala, generic (n)
maromalu, generic (adj)
maromana, geniality (n)
maromanu, genial (adj)
maromapa, generosity (n)
maromapiu, generously (adv)
maromapu, generous (adj)
maromitiu, genuinely (adv)
maromitu, genuine (adj)
marutha, cotton (n)
masharitei, neither (pron)
masharitu, neither (adj/conj)
Mashashutafa, Massachusetts (n)
mashiatha, botany (n)
mashiathu, botanical (adj)
mashipa, ball (n)
mashipo, ball (v)
matana, citizen (n)
matika, practice (n)
matikiu, practically (adv)
matiko, practice (v)
matiku, practical (adj)
matikua, practitioner (n doer)
mau, no (n/adj/adv)
maua, naw (interj)
mauakeniapa, nevermind (n)
mauakesheimiu, nevertheless
    (adv)
mauarigefa, noninterference (n)
maubusheleka, nondestruction
    (n)
maubushelekiu, nondestructively
    (adv)
maubusheleku, nondestructive
    (adj)
maufiufelausha, nonproliferation
    (n)
maufiunotaka, nonprofessional
    (n)
maufiupafitu, nonprofit (adj)
maugofaifu, nonlethal (adj)
mauhala, nowhere (n)
mauhalu, nowhere (adj/adv)

maukiabaku, nontoxic (adj)
maukizhu, nontechnical (adj)
maulalifoku, noncommercial (adj)
mauliroputu, nonpublic (adj)
mauliuvorinua, nonconformist (n doer)
maumeshuta, nonmember (n)
maumoimueta, nonpayment (n)
maunulita, nonexistence (n)
maunulitu, nonexistent (adj)
maupafika, nonfiction (n)
maupereiliafu, nontrivial (adj)
mauroifa, nonlinearity (n)
mauroifiu, nonlinearly (adv)
mauroifu, nonlinear (adj)
maushaipu, nonlocal (adj)
maushalirotu, nonessential (adj)
mausharua, nonbeliever (n doer)
mausheladei, nobody (n/pron)
mausheluanita, noncompliance (n)
maushetolifua, nonsmoker (n doer)
maushorifa, nonsense (n)
maushorifu, nonsensical (adj)
mautameniu, nonetheless (adv)
mautauku, nonstop (adj)
mautei, none (pron)
mauterabiru, nontraditional (adj)
mauterefiku, nonstandard (adj)
mauthiaku, nonfatal (adj)
mautigereta, nondisclosure (n)
mautu, none (adj/adv)
mautuarika, nonviolence (n)
mautuariku, nonviolent (adj)
mautuazhu, nonvolatile (adj)
mauyuanu, nonwhite (adj)
mauyutamanu, nonunion (adj)
mava, harm (n)
mavameniu, harmlessly (adv)
mavamenu, harmless (adj)
mavapa, kiss (n)
mavapo, kiss (v)
mavapua, kisser (n doer)
mavina, harmony (n)
mavinara, harmonic (n)
mavinelika, hologram (n)
mavineliku, holographic (adj)
mavino, harmonize (v)
mavinu, harmonic (adj)
mavo, harm (v)
mavuna, anonymity (n)
mavunu, anonymous (adj)
mavushiu, harmfully (adv)
mavushu, harmful (adj)
mawilu, nor (conj)
Mediteraniafa, Mediterranean (n)
mefa, pause (n)
mefitha, shallowness (n)
mefithu, shallow (adj)
mefo, pause (v)
meifa, socialization (n)
meifaka, society (n)

meifaku, societal (adj)
meifana, social (n)
meifara, socialism (n)
meifaru, socialistic (adj)
meifarua, socialist (n doer)
meifiu, socially (adv)
meifo, socialize (v)
meifu, sociable (adj)
meifu, social (adj)
meifua, socializer (n doer)
meiga, verge (n d:incline)
meigo, verge (v d:incline)
meilifa, bargain (n)
meilifo, bargain (v)
meirifa, role (n)
meishika, panic (n)
meishiko, panic (v)
meishiku, panicky (adj)
meishopa, expanse (n)
meishopa, expansion (n)
meishopiu, expansively (adv)
meishopo, expand (v)
meishopu, expandable (adj)
meishopu, expansive (adj)
meishopua, expander (n doer)
meishopua, expansionist (n doer)
meiva, numbness (n)
meivo, numb (v)
meivu, numb (adj)
mekani, pants (n pl d:clothing)
mela, rain (n)
melara, glamor (n)
melara, glamour (n)
melariu, glamorously (adv)
melaru, glamorous (adj)
meledaruga, raindrop (n)
melediafa, rainbow (n)
meleferipa, rainstorm (n)
meleidona, rainwater (n)
melenagua, rainmaker (n doer)
melerafika, raincoat (n)
meletherisha, rainforest (n)
melezhaila, rainfall (n)
melifa, panel (n)
melifo, panel (v)
melifua, panelist (n doer)
melika, pan (n)
melikato, pander (v)
melikegurita, pancake (n)
melikegurito, pancake (v)
meliko, pan (v)
melima, mom (n)
melimala, mommy (n)
melimela, murmur (n)
melimelo, murmur (v)
melimelu, murmurous (adj)
melimelua, murmurer (n doer)
melimo, mom (v)
melina, mare (n)
melinaka, marshal (n)
meliniko, marshal (v)
melipa, pride (n d:group)
melisha, tea (n)

melishedaifa, teapot (n)
melishedoripa, teaspoon (n)
melishevoripa, teacup (n)
melo, rain (v)
melu, rainy (adj)
meluila, rainout (n)
meluna, nut (n)
melunetheka, nutshell (n)
melunu, nutty (adj)
meluvana, marble (n)
memema, momma (n)
memepifeta, sustenance (n)
memepifeto, sustain (v)
memepifetu, sustainable (adj)
memeshipa, susceptibility (n)
memeshipu, susceptible (adj)
memiberuna, suspense (n)
memiberuno, suspend (v)
memiberunua, suspender (n doer)
memiberunueta, suspension (n)
memitana, pumpkin (n)
memithuka, suspicion (n)
memithukiu, suspiciously (adv)
memithuko, suspect (v)
memithuku, suspicious (adj)
memithukua, suspect (n doer)
Memofisha, Memphis (n)
Menadeleviuma, Mendelevium (n)
meno, lessen (v)
menu, less (adj)
mepa, pet (n)
mepo, pet (v)
Merakuria, Mercury (n)
merata, continent (n)
meratu, continental (adj)
Meshakifa, Mexico (n)
Meshakifana, Mexican (n)
meshefifa, membership (n)
meshika, hut (n)
meshuta, member (n)
meshutana, membrane (n)
meshutanu, membranous (adj)
methika, nephew (n)
Metoneriuma, Meitnerium (n)
mi, hi (interj)
miabo, mar (v)
miafa, nova (n)
miafana, novice (n)
miagerazha, chainsaw (n)
miagerazhu, chainsaw (v)
miaifa, prize (n)
miaifo, prize (v)
miaiko, pry (v)
miaka, chain (n)
miako, chain (v)
miala, flue (n)
Miamifa, Miami (n)
miana, fluid (n)
mianu, fluid (adj)
miapa, organ (n d:instrument)
miara, ocean (n)

miaredarifa, oceanography (n)
miaredarifu, oceanographic (adj)
miarefelarinu, oceanfront (adj)
miareshoita, oceanside (n)
miarota, fluency (n)
miarotiu, fluently (adv)
miarotu, fluent (adj)
miaru, oceanic (adj)
miashika, fluctuation (n)
miashiko, fluctuate (v)
miashikua, fluctuator (n doer)
miatha, alibi (n)
miauko, taunt (v)
mida, note (n d:text)
midata, notation (n)
midato, notate (v)
midebanifa, notepad (n)
midefelaishu, noteworthy (adj)
Midishata, Mideast (n)
midiu, notably (adv d:text)
midiuna, novelty (n)
midiunu, novel (adj)
mido, note (v d:text)
midoina, notion (n)
midota, noon (n)
midotedauna, noontime (n)
midotedaunu, noontime (adj)
midu, notable (adj d:text)
Miduesha, Midwest (n)
miduna, novel (n)
midunua, novelist (n doer)
miedarifa, biography (n)
miekuita, biology (n)
miekuitiu, biologically (adv)
miekuitu, biological (adj)
miela, dew (n)
miesha, fluff (n)
miesho, fluff (v)
mieshu, fluffy (adj)
mifota, colon (n d:character)
miga, barge (n d:boat)
migata, colonel (n)
mikara, angel (n)
mikariu, angelically (adv)
mikaru, angelic (adj)
mikatu, noxious (adj)
mikita, colony (n)
mikito, colonize (v)
mikitu, colonial (adj)
mikitua, colonist (n doer)
mikitua, colonizer (n doer)
mikitueta, colonization (n)
mila, tad (n)
milediloka, tadpole (n)
Miluakifa, Milwaukee (n)
milunu, beneath (adv/prep)
mima, dot (n)
mimana, range (n)
mimano, range (v)
mimanua, ranger (n doer)
mimo, dot (v)
minashu, lesser (adj)
Minekapola, Minneapolis (n)

Mineshota, Minnesota (n)
minopio, woke (v pa d:arise)
minopiveila, wakeup (n d:arise)
minopiveilu, wakeup (adj d:arise)
minopo, wake (v d:arise)
miobilefua, newcomer (n doer)
mioka, macula (n)
mioki, maculae (n pl)
mioko, maculate (v)
mioku, macular (adj)
Miola Kamoshira, New
    Hampshire (n)
Miola Orolinofa, New Orleans (n)
Miola Zhilanuda, New Zealand
    (n)
miola, newness (n)
mioliu, newly (adv)
miolu, new (adj)
miolwaku, newest (adj)
miolwelu, newer (adj)
miolyuva, newlywed (n)
miora, news (n)
miorashota, newsletter (n)
mioreberona, newsgroup (n)
miorediuma, newsreel (n)
miorefelaisha, newsworthiness
    (n)
miorefelaishu, newsworthy (adj)
miorenifopa, newsmagazine (n)
miorepelona, newsman (n)
miorepeloni, newsmen (n pl)
mioreshenifa, newswire (n)
mioresherana, newsroom (n)
mioreterelita, newsstand (n)
mioreterulisha, newsprint (n)
mioretulita, newscast (n)
mioretulitua, newscaster (n doer)
mioreviula, newsday (n)
miorevuapa, newspaper (n)
miorevuapelona, newspaperman
    (n)
miorevuapeloni, newspapermen
    (n pl)
mioriana, newshour (n)
mioripa, radio (n)
mioripalita, radioactivity (n)
mioripalitu, radioactive (adj)
mioripo, radio (v)
mioru, newsy (adj)
Mioruka, Major (n)
mioshupu, newfound (adj)
miovalesha, newborn (n)
mirana, canyon (n)
miremita, ivory (n)
miremitu, ivory (adj)
Miriafa, EhoDay03 (n)
miriakiu, sternly (adv d:firm)
miriaku, stern (adj d:firm)
Miriama, Miriam (n)
mirofa, shift (n)
mirofo, shift (v)
mirofu, shifty (adj)
mirofua, shifter (n doer)

miroka, angle (n)
mirokiu, angularly (adv)
miroko, angle (v)
miroku, angular (adj)
miropa, ankle (n)
Mishashipa, Mississippi (n)
mishefeluiku, otherwise
    (adj/adv/conj)
mishei, other (n/pron)
mishi, others (pron)
Mishigafa, Michigan (n)
mishu, other (adj/adv)
Mishurafa, Missouri (n)
mitesha, mulch (n)
mitesho, mulch (v)
mitha, tail (n)
mitheleinapa, tailpipe (n)
mitheperelika, tailgate (n)
mithepereliko, tailgate (v)
mitheshenapa, tailspin (n)
mitho, tail (v)
mithua, tailer (n doer)
mituma, cologne (n)
miufa, vase (n)
miufota, elbow (n)
miufoto, elbow (v)
miuko, taint (v)
miuna, town (n)
miunefifa, township (n)
miunekiafa, townhouse (n)
miunekifopa, townfolk (n)
miunekifopi, townsfolk (n pl)
miunepelona, townperson (n)
miunepeloni, townspeople (n pl)
miupa, lumber (n)
miupo, lumber (v)
miutha, flush (n)
miutho, flush (v)
miuthua, flusher (n doer)
mivana, leather (n)
mivanu, leathery (adj)
mivatha, noodle (n)
mivonuda, notebook (n)
moafa, fan (n d:move air)
moafo, fan (v d:move air)
moagana, caramel (n)
moaka, sake (n)
moakio, forsook (v pa)
moako, forsake (v)
mofita, surgery (n)
mofitiu, surgically (adv)
mofitu, surgical (adj)
mofitua, surgeon (n doer)
mogu, next (adj/adv/prep)
moi, hey (interj)
moiakiu, drastically (adv)
moiaku, drastic (adj)
moiama, farm (n)
moiamekapa, farmhand (n)
moiamekiafa, farmhouse (n)
moiameraupa, farmland (n)
moiamo, farm (v)
moiamua, farmer (n doer)

moiapa, suite (n)
moiba, bulb (n)
moida, pedal (n)
moidata, pedestrian (n)
moido, pedal (v)
moifa, swallow (n d:gulp)
moifo, swallow (v d:gulp)
moiga, bulge (n)
moigo, bulge (v)
moika, shield (n)
moikafa, radar (n)
moikafo, radar (v)
moikioka, network (n)
moikioko, network (v)
moiko, shield (v)
moilaubelutisha, omnipresence (n)
moilaubelutishu, omnipresent (adj)
moilauboiga, omnipotence (n)
moilauboigu, omnipotent (adj)
moilaudiuafu, omnivorous (adj)
moilaukuafiku, omnidirectional (adj)
moilaushuasha, omniscience (n)
moilaushuashu, omniscient (adj)
moima, pay (n)
moimelurita, payload (n)
moimepiroda, paycheck (n)
moimevaka, payback (n)
moimeviula, payday (n)
moimio, paid (v pa)
moimiu, payably (adv)
moimo, pay (v)
moimofalira, payroll (n)
moimu, payable (adj)
moimua, payer (n doer)
moimueta, payment (n)
moimuila, payout (n)
moimunefa, payoff (n)
moima, pod (n)
moipa, net (n)
moipo, net (v)
moiropa, label (n)
moiropo, label (v)
moiropua, labeler (n doer)
moishiana, MoissanRuby (n)
moishota, expedition (n)
moishoto, expedite (v)
moishotu, expedient (adj)
moishotueta, expedience (n)
moishotueta, expediency (n)
moishotuetiu, expeditiously (adv)
moishotuetu, expeditious (adj)
moita, orientation (n)
moitha, shine (n)
moithio, shone (v pa)
moitho, shine (v)
moithu, shiny (adj)
moithua, shiner (n doer)
moito, orient (v)
moiufa, suit (n d:apparel)
moiushuata, suitcase (n)

moiva, radiance (n)
moiva, radiation (n)
moivaka, radical (n)
moivakiu, radically (adv)
moivaku, radical (adj)
moivavu, geiger (adj)
moivo, radiate (v)
moivua, radiator (n doer)
mokarama, klutz (n)
mokasha, loot (n)
mokasho, loot (v)
mokashua, looter (n doer)
mokeshoito, lopside (v)
moko, lop (v)
Molibedenuma, Molybdenum (n)
molifasha, government (n)
molifasho, govern (v)
molifashua, governor (n doer)
molitha, patience (n d:endurance)
molithiu, patiently (adv d:endurance)
molithu, patient (adj d:endurance)
Monatanifa, Montana (n)
Moniteriala, Montreal (n)
Monitugorima, Montgomery (n)
moraga, fang (n)
morago, fangle (v)
morelifa, euphoria (n)
morelifu, euphoric (adj)
moremuana, honeymoon (n)
moremuanua, honeymooner (n doer)
morifa, honey (n)
moriferakada, honeycomb (n)
morifezhisha, honeybee (n)
morikata, muscle (n)
morikato, muscle (v)
morikatu, muscular (adj)
morilana, gill (n)
moripa, suit (n d:accord)
moripiu, suitably (adv d:accord)
moripo, suit (v d:accord)
moripu, suitable (adj d:accord)
moripua, suitor (n doer d:accord)
moripueta, suitability (n)
morithoka, impatience (n)
morithokiu, impatiently (adv)
morithoku, impatient (adj)
moriva, pear (n)
mosha, puff (n)
Moshikaufa, Moscow (n)
mosho, puff (v)
moshu, puffy (adj)
moshua, puffer (n doer)
motuyapa, saxophone (n)
moviula, holiday (n)
mua, huh (interj)
muada, voyage (n)
muado, voyage (v)
muadua, voyager (n doer)
muai-, non- (num 9 pref)
muana, night (n)

muanedauna, nighttime (n)
muanefelausha, nightlife (n)
muaneferaika, nightmare (n)
muanelifada, nightshirt (n)
muanetaida, nightclub (n)
muanezhaila, nightfall (n)
muanu, nightly (adj)
muara, lake (n)
muarenularita, lakeshore (n)
muareshoita, lakeside (n)
muariko, mope (v d:sad)
muata, shave (n)
muato, shave (v)
muatua, shaver (n doer)
mufiko, nestle (v)
mufipa, nest (n)
mufipo, nest (v)
mufipua, nester (n doer)
mui, nine (num 9 card)
muialfhemka, Number_1e36606
muiasha, prowl (n)
muiasho, prowl (v)
muiashua, prowler (n doer)
muiata, swell (n)
muiato, swell (v)
muida, ninety (num 90 card)
muidai-, ninety- (num 90 pref)
muideth, ninetieth (num 90 ord)
muifa, niceness (n)
muifa, nicety (n)
muifiu, nicely (adv)
muifk, novenquadragintillion (num 1e150 card)
muifo, nicen (v)
muift, noventrigintillion (num 1e120 card)
muifu, nice (adj)
muifweku, nicest (adj)
muifwelu, nicer (adj)
muika, nonillion (num 1e30 card)
muikai-, weka- (num 1e30 pref)
muiketh, nonillionth (num 1e30 ord)
muipa, nineteen (num 19 card)
muipai-, nineteen- (num 19 pref)
muipeth, nineteenth (num 19 ord)
muisha, mesa (n)
muishk, novemvigintillion (num 1e90 card)
muishkai-, bianten-
muishketh, novemvigintillionth (num 1e90 ord)
muisht, novemdecillion (num 1e60 card)
muishtai-, liena- (num 1e60 pref)
muishteth, novemdecillionth (num 1e60 ord)
muita, onion (n)
mukitak, pigeon (n)
Mulara, March (n)
muliona, ceramic (n)

mulionu, ceramic (adj)
mulita, element (n)
mulitu, elementary (adj)
mumatha, cushion (n)
mumatho, cushion (v)
mumathu, cushy (adj)
mumathua, cushioner (n doer)
mumela, lull (n)
mumeliaufa, lullaby (n)
mumelo, lull (v)
mumima, fumble (n)
mumimo, fumble (v)
muna, mu (n)
munana, midnight (n)
munapa, conscience (n)
munapu, conscionable (adj)
muniku, least (adj)
munoda, bay (n d:place)
mupa, stub (n)
mupana, stubble (n)
mupeka, stubbornness (n)
mupekiu, stubbornly (adv)
mupeku, stubborn (adj)
mupo, stub (v)
mureda, grime (n)
muredu, grimey (adj)
muridana, grimace (n)
muridano, grimace (v)
muridanu, grim (adj)
murifa, eloquence (n)
murifiu, eloquently (adv)
murifo, elocute (v)
murifu, eloquent (adj)
muriga, grunge (n)
murigu, grungy (adj)
murila, ceremony (n)
muriliu, ceremonially (adv)
murilu, ceremonial (adj)
murisha, sleet (n)
murisho, sleet (v)
murova, hollowness (n)
murovo, hollow (v)
murovu, hollow (adj)
Mushelima, Muslim (n)
mushika, patrol (n)
mushiko, patrol (v)
mushipa, mate (n)
mushipo, mate (v)
mutha, match (n d:selection)
muthatha, carnation (n)
muthemenu, matchless (adj
   d:selection)
muthenagio, matchmade (v pa
   d:make selection)
muthenago, matchmake (v
   d:make selection)
muthenagua, matchmaker (n
   doer d:make selection)
muthioka, carousel (n)
mutho, match (v d:selection)
muthorin, methane (n)
muthua, matcher (n doer
   d:selection)

mutika, jaw (n)
mutiketoika, jawbone (n)
mutiko, jaw (v)
muviana, carnival (n)
muyara, niece (n)
muyeth, ninth (num 9 ord)
muzha, fog (n)
muzhekeroima, foghorn (n)
muzhiu, foggily (adv)
muzho, fog (v)
muzhu, foggy (adj)
muzhua, fogger (n doer)
mwae, na (interj)
nabata, fuss (n)
nabato, fuss (v)
nabatu, fussy (adj)
nabita, harvest (n)
nabito, harvest (v)
nabitua, harvester (n doer)
nafiko, fester (v)
nafipa, mold (n d:microbe)
nafipu, moldy (adj d:microbe)
nafita, harbor (n)
nafita, harbour (n)
nafito, harbor (v)
nagaga, sogginess (n)
nagagu, soggy (adj)
nagiana, mosquito (n)
nagio, made (v pa)
nagiva, makeup (n)
nago, make (v)
nagua, maker (n doer)
naiapa, skewness (n)
naiapo, skew (v)
naigata, psychiatry (n)
naigatu, psychiatric (adj)
naigatua, psychiatrist (n doer)
naigetha, psychology (n)
naigethiu, psychologically (adv)
naigethu, psychological (adj)
naigethua, psychologist (n doer)
naika, psyche (n)
naikauka, psychosis (n)
naikauketha, psychopathology (n)
naikaukethua, psychopathologist
   (n doer)
naikauku, psychotic (adj)
naikaukua, psycho (n doer)
naikaukua, psychopath (n doer)
naikepeliashipa, psychotherapy
   (n)
naikepeliashipua, psychotherapist
   (n doer)
naiko, psych (v)
naikomafita, psychoanalysis (n)
naikomafitua, psychoanalyst (n
   doer)
naikua, psychic (n doer)
nailara, meadow (n)
nainofa, pilot (n)
nainofo, pilot (v)
naipa, pile (n)
naipiveila, pileup (n)

naipo, pile (v)
naisha, mess (n)
naisho, mess (v)
naishu, messy (adj)
naitho, sand (v d:abrasion)
naithua, sander (n doer
   d:abrasion)
nakipa, soak (n)
nakipo, soak (v)
nakipua, soaker (n doer)
nalana, mammal (n)
nalanarifota, mammography (n)
nalanelika, mammogram (n)
nalanu, mammalian (adj)
nalifa, shelf (n)
nalifo, shelve (v)
nalima, horizon (n)
nalimiu, horizontally (adv)
nalimu, horizontal (adj)
nalina, straw (n)
nalisho, deign (v)
nalitha, breast (n)
nalithefikafa, breastplate (n)
nalithepavo, breastfeed (v)
Namibiafa, Namibia (n)
namufeluana, moonlight (n)
namufeluano, moonlight (v)
namura, moon (n)
namurebarafa, moonstone (n)
namureduafa, moonbeam (n)
namuremoitha, moonshine (n)
Namuriviula, Monday (n)
nanisha, die (n d:number cube)
nanishi, dice (n pl d:number
   cube)
nanita, dexterity (n)
nanitiu, dexterously (adv)
nanitiu, dextrously (adv)
nanitu, dexterous (adj)
nanitu, dextrous (adj)
narano, sully (v)
narifo, loaf (v d:lounge)
narifua, loafer (n doer d:lounge)
narila, soap (n)
narileperenika, soapbox (n)
nariliu, soapily (adv)
narilo, soap (v)
narilu, soapy (adj)
narimiu, laterally (adv)
narimu, lateral (adj)
naripa, rug (n)
narisha, soil (n)
narisho, soil (v)
naritha, favor (n)
narithepa, favorite (n)
narithepiu, favorably (adv)
narithepu, favorable (adj)
naritho, favor (v)
narithu, favorite (adj)
narithueta, favoritism (n)
naromalita, latter (n)
naromalitu, latter (adj)
naromita, lattice (n)

naromuka, latitude (n)
nashiko, dice (v d:cube)
nashiku, dicey (adj d:cube)
Nashofila, Nashville (n)
natha, sand (n d:grains)
nathata, sandal (n)
nathebarafa, sandstone (n)
nathefanafa, sandbag (n)
natheferipa, sandstorm (n)
nathekeraigo, sandblast (v)
natheperenika, sandbox (n)
natherolata, sandbar (n)
nathevuapa, sandpaper (n)
nathu, sandy (adj d:grains)
nau, me (pron 1st sng obj)
naufa, muse (n)
naufara, museum (n)
naufika, dominance (n)
naufika, domination (n)
naufiko, dominate (v)
naufiku, dominant (adj)
naufikua, dominator (n doer)
naufo, muse (v)
nauka, mission (n)
naushika, foul (n)
naushiko, foul (v)
naushiku, foul (adj)
Neborashika, Nebraska (n)
nefita, domestication (n)
nefito, domesticate (v)
nefitu, domestic (adj)
nefitua, domesticator (n doer)
neiba, mop (n)
neibo, mop (v)
neida, lane (n)
neifa, tape (n)
neifo, tape (v)
neikafa, metaphor (n)
neikafu, metaphorical (adj)
neiku, meta (adj)
neilafa, marvel (n)
neilafiu, marvelously (adv)
neilafo, marvel (v)
neilafu, marvelous (adj)
neiluna, cadet (n)
neisha, pal (n)
Neitha, Miss (n)
neito, usher (v)
neitua, usher (n doer)
neivita, monitor (n)
neivito, monitor (v)
neiwifa, taper (n)
neiwifo, taper (v)
nelana, song (n)
nelaneloidua, songwriter (n doer)
nelanio, sang (v pa)
nelano, sing (v)
nelanua, singer (n doer)
nelenala, nanny (n)
nelenalo, nanny (v)
nelifa, calf (n)
nelifo, calve (v)
nelikara, grammar (n)

nelikariu, grammatically (adv)
nelikaru, grammatical (adj)
nelipa, berry (n)
nelisholu, elsewhere (adv)
nelishu, else (adj/adv)
nelitha, clutch (n d:hatch)
nenika, number (n)
nenikela, numeral (n)
nenikeliu, numerically (adv)
nenikelu, numeric (adj)
nenikelu, numerical (adj)
nenikelua, numerator (n doer)
nenikiu, numerously (adv)
neniko, number (v)
neniku, numerous (adj)
nenikuita, numerology (n)
Neodimiuma, Neodymium (n)
Neona, Neon (n)
nepa, tap (n)
nepo, tap (v)
Nepotuniuma, Neptunium (n)
nepua, tapper (n doer)
neshei, much (pron)
neshigafa, racket (n d:noise)
neshu, much (adj/adv)
Netherolanuda, Netherlands (n)
Nevadafa, Nevada (n)
nia, I (pron 1st sng sub)
niafa, naivete (n)
niafiu, naively (adv)
niafoka, miracle (n)
niafokiu, miraculously (adv)
niafoku, miraculous (adj)
niafu, naive (adj)
niai, we (pron 1st pl sub)
niaina, prism (n)
niaka, majority (n)
niako, major (v)
niaku, major (adj)
niala, music (n)
nialata, musical (n)
nialiu, musically (adv)
nialota, comment (n)
nialotara, commentary (n)
nialoto, comment (v)
nialotua, commentator (n doer)
nialu, musical (adj)
nialua, musician (n doer)
niama, smartness (n)
niamiu, smartly (adv)
niamo, smarten (v)
niamu, smart (adj)
niana, mirror (n)
nianata, mirage (n)
nianika, funk (n d:music/stench)
nianiku, funky (adj
  d:music/stench)
niano, mirror (v)
niapa, mind (n)
niapefepa, mindset (n)
niapefepa, mindset (n)
niapemeniu, mindlessly (adv)
niapemenu, mindless (adj)
niapiu, mindfully (adv)

niapo, mind (v)
niapu, mindful (adj)
niaroga, flu (n)
niarosha, laceration (n)
niarosho, lacerate (v)
niashederiada, tantrum (n)
niasheniuku, tantamount (adj)
niashiu, tanto (adv)
niata, site (n)
niatesha, tantalization (n)
niatesho, tantalize (v)
niateshua, tantalizer (n doer)
niatha, mint (n)
niathiu, mintly (adv)
niatho, mint (v)
niathu, mint (adj)
niathua, minter (n doer)
niaukizha, pyrotechnic (n)
niaupa, pyromaniac (n)
nielopa, tameness (n)
nielopo, tame (v)
nielopu, tame (adj)
niemo, tamper (v)
nieta, eat (n)
nietio, ate (v pa)
nieto, eat (v)
nietu, edible (adj)
nietua, eater (n doer)
nifoka, mash (n)
nifoko, mash (v)
nifokua, masher (n doer)
nifopa, magazine (n d:document)
nika, EhoSecond (n)
Nikaraguana, Nicaraguan (n)
Nikaragufa, Nicaragua (n)
Nikela, Nickel (n)
nikuta, laser (n)
nikuto, laser (v)
nilaka, termination (n)
nilakata, terminal (n)
nilakiu, terminally (adv)
nilako, terminate (v)
nilaku, terminal (adj)
nilakua, terminator (n doer)
nilebivoga, homosexuality (n)
nilebivogu, homosexual (adj)
nilebivogua, homosexual (n doer)
nilekoika, homicide (n)
nilekoiku, homicidal (adj)
nilesha, charm (n)
nilesho, charm (v)
nileshua, charmer (n doer)
nilishu, teeny (adj)
nilithu, teensy (adj)
nilofa, series (n)
nilofiu, serially (adv)
nilofu, serial (adj)
nilopa, sesame (n)
nilota, experiment (n)
nilotiu, experimentally (adv)
niloto, experiment (v)
nilotu, experimental (adj)
nilotua, experimenter (n doer)

nilubu, gay (adj d:homosexual)
nilufu, nifty (adj)
nimana, menu (n)
nimashiliu, minutely (adv d:small)
nimashilu, minute (adj d:small)
nimata, memo (n)
Nimsanta, Nimsant
nimufa, roast (n)
nimufo, roast (v)
nimufua, roaster (n doer)
ninato, tatter (v)
ninofa, fossil (n)
ninofo, fossilize (v)
Niobiuma, Niobium (n)
niofa, swap (n)
niofo, swap (v)
niofua, swaper (n doer)
nioka, meter (n d:device)
niokara, metric (n)
nioko, meter (v d:device)
niona, shrine (n)
niono, enshrine (v)
nionua, shriner (n doer)
niopa, rhyme (n)
niopata, rhythm (n)
niopatiu, rhythmically (adv)
niopatu, rhythmic (adj)
niopo, rhyme (v)
niopua, rhymer (n doer)
niota, shrug (n)
niotesha, swat (n)
niotesho, swat (v)
nioto, shrug (v)
nirota, address (n)
niroto, address (v)
nirotu, addressable (adj)
nirotua, addressor (n doer)
nirotuina, addressee (n)
nishoka kodi, had to (ndal d:need)
nishoka kodi, have to (ndal d:need)
nishoka kodi, must (ndal d:need)
nishoka, need (n)
nishokemeniu, needlessly (adv)
nishokemenu, needless (adj)
nishoko, need (v)
nishoku, needful (adj)
nishoku, needy (adj)
nishota, tininess (n)
nishotu, tiny (adj)
Niterogena, Nitrogen (n)
nitha, lid (n)
niudana, mound (n)
niudata, moat (n)
niufa, firmness (n d:steady)
niufeluana, flashlight (n)
niufiu, firmly (adv d:steady)
niufo, firm (v d:steady)
niufu, firm (adj d:steady)
niufweku, firmest (adj)
niufwelu, firmer (adj)

niugiuta, mountain (n)
niugiutedaupa, mountaintop (n)
niugiuteshoita, mountainside (n)
niugiutu, mountainous (adj)
niugiutua, mountaineer (n doer)
niuka, mount (n)
niuko, mount (v)
niulota, plenum (n)
niulotu, plenary (adj)
niumo, sow (v)
niuna, plenty (n)
niunifa, abundance (n)
niunifiu, abundantly (adv)
niunifu, abundant (adj)
niunu, plentiful (adj)
niupa, minority (n)
niupo, minor (v)
niupu, minor (adj)
niusha, flash (n)
niushevaka, flashback (n)
niushiu, flashily (adv)
niusho, flash (v)
niushu, flashy (adj)
niushua, flasher (n doer)
niuta, stadium (n)
niutha, snack (n)
niutho, snack (v)
niva, folly (n)
niva, foolishness (n)
Nivara, EhoMonth09 (n)
nivefeliofu, foolproof (adj)
nivekelifota, foolhardiness (n)
nivekelifotu, foolhardy (adj)
niviu, foolishly (adv)
niviva, moron (n)
nivivu, moronic (adj)
nivo, fool (v)
nivu, foolish (adj)
nivua, fool (n doer)
nizha, itch (n)
nizho, itch (v)
nizhu, itchy (adj)
noarita, claim (n)
noarito, claim (v)
noaritua, claimant (n doer)
noata, dib (n)
Nobeliuma, Nobelium (n)
noesha, loaf (n d:bread)
Nofefara, November (n)
nofita, ministry (n)
nofito, minister (v)
nofitua, minister (n doer)
noia, N (let sng)
noiaka, skewer (n)
noiako, skewer (v)
noifa kodi, may (ndal d:permission)
noifa, permission (n)
noihem, Number_1e3006
noika, lack (n)
noiko, lack (v)
noili, Ns (let pl)
noima, savage (n)

noimiu, savagely (adv)
noimu, savage (adj)
noipa, mayor (n)
noipu, mayoral (adj)
noiruna, nylon (n)
noisha, rinse (n)
noishika, rhetoric (n)
noishikiu, rhetorically (adv)
noishiku, rhetorical (adj)
noisho, rinse (v)
noishua, rinser (n doer)
noitha, race (n d:human)
noithata, racism (n)
noithatua, racist (n doer)
noithiu, racially (adv d:human)
noithiu, racial (adj d:human)
nolafa, fellow (n)
nolafifa, fellowship (n)
nolika, grain (n)
nolikiena, gravy (n)
noliku, grainy (adj)
nolitha, wall (n)
nolithevuapa, wallpaper (n)
nolithevuapo, wallpaper (v)
nolitho, wall (v)
nolithuana, wallflower (n)
nomaga, liver (n)
norevosha, courtship (n)
norifopa, jealousy (n)
norifopiu, jealously (adv)
norifopu, jealous (adj)
norika, rig (n)
norikata, sergeant (n)
noriko, rig (v)
norikua, rigger (n doer)
norila, court (n)
norilekiafa, courthouse (n)
norilesherana, courtroom (n)
norilethautha, courtyard (n)
norilo, court (v)
noriluena, courtesy (n)
norilueniu, courteously (adv)
noriluenu, courteous (adj)
norimaka, salvation (n)
norimako, salvage (v)
norinana, sandwich (n)
norinano, sandwich (v)
noripa, rag (n)
noripegaivu, ragtag (adj)
noripiu, raggedy (adv)
noripo, rag (v)
noripyuka, ragweed (n)
norisha, dawn (n)
norisho, dawn (v)
noruga, rack (n)
norugafa, racket (n d:bat, group)
norugafu, rackety (adj d:bat, group)
norugaito, racketeer (v)
norugaitua, racketeer (n doer)
norugo, rack (v)
norugua, racker (n doer)

Norwaifa, Norway (n)
Norwaifana, Norwegian (n)
nosha, man (n d:male)
noshetaiga, manure (n)
noshi, men (n pl d:male)
noshu, manly (adj d:male)
notha, muff (n)
nothato, muffle (v)
nothatua, muffler (n doer)
notho, muff (v)
novina, mole (n)
novineparina, molehill (n)
novino, mole (v)
nuaba, rival (n)
nuabaka, rivalry (n)
nuabo, rival (v)
nuafa, moss (n)
nuafu, mossy (adj)
nuaka, void (n)
nuako, void (v)
nuana, crime (n)
nuanika, discrimination (n)
nuaniko, discriminate (v)
nuanikua, discriminator (n doer)
nuanita, incrimination (n)
nuanito, incriminate (v)
nuano, criminalize (v)
nuanua, criminal (n doer)
Nuarika, Newark (n)
nuasha, rite (n)
nuatipa, ritual (n)
nuatipo, ritualize (v)
nuatipu, ritualistic (adj)
nufemashipa, mushroom (n)
nufenifa, mishmash (n)
nufika, mush (n)
nufikao, mushed (v prp)
nufiko, mush (v)
nufipa, ink (n)
nufipo, ink (v)
nufipu, inky (adj)
nufipua, inker (n doer)
nufita, lever (n)
nufitara, leverage (n)
nufitaro, leverage (v)
nufito, lever (v)
nufobietao, biet (v prp)
nufobietu, hetergeneous (adj)
nugana, lung (n)
nui, my (pron 1st sng pos sub)
nuibara, madam (n)
nuibara, madame (n)
nuifal, myself (pron 1st sng refl)
nuika, tank (n)
nuiko, tank (v)
nuikua, tanker (n doer)
nuime, mine (pron 1st sng pos obj)
nuish, our (pron 1st pl pos sub)
nukifa, physics (n)
nukifiu, physically (adv)
nukifu, physical (adj)
nulana, lease (n)

nulano, lease (v)
nulanua, leaser (n doer)
nulanua, lessor (n doer)
nulanuina, lessee (n)
nularita, shore (n)
nulariteroifa, shoreline (n)
nularito, shore (v)
nulifa, festival (n)
nulifu, festive (adj)
nulifueta, festivity (n)
nulika, leash (n)
nuliko, leash (v)
nulipa, combination (n)
nulipata, combine (n)
nulipo, combine (v)
nulipua, combiner (n doer)
nulita, existence (n)
nulito, exist (v)
nuloberuga, combustion (n)
nuloberugo, combust (v)
nuloberugu, combustible (adj)
nulogerata, combat (n)
nulogeratiu, combatively (adv)
nulogerato, combat (v)
nulogeratu, combative (adj)
nulogeratua, combatant (n doer)
numa, dullness (n)
numaka, javelin (n)
numata, plus (n)
numatu, plus (adj/prep)
numo, dull (v)
numu, dull (adj)
nuna, nu (n)
nunufa, taboo (n)
nunufu, taboo (adj)
nupa, bin (n)
nurabeilaku, multipurpose (adj)
nurabiazhu, multiparty (adj)
nuraferuifualu, multiplayer (adj)
nuraga, crap (n)
nuragaludu, multilevel (adj)
nurago, crap (v)
nuragu, crappy (adj)
nurakarila, multinational (n)
nurakarilu, multinational (adj)
nuralaidaka, multimedia (n)
nuralirolo, multicolor (v)
nuralirolu, multicolor (adj)
nuranoithu, multiracial (adj)
nuraperatu, multifunctional (adj)
nurashaiashu, multistate (adj)
nuratafiko, multiculture (v)
nuratafiku, multicultural (adj)
nuratuaroma, multichannel (n)
nuratueta, multitude (n)
nuratuetu, multitude (adj)
nuraviarithu, multilingual (adj)
nurilata, grit (n)
nurilato, grit (v)
nurilatu, gritty (adj)
nurina, grin (n)
nurino, grin (v)
nuroba, multiple (n)

nurobo, multiply (v)
nurobu, multiple (adj)
nurobua, multiplier (n doer)
nurobueta, multiplication (n)
nuru, nee (adj)
nuru, née (adj)
nushika, sneak (n)
nushikio, snuck (v pa)
nushikiu, sneakily (adv)
nushiko, sneak (v)
nushiku, sneaky (adj)
nushikua, sneaker (n doer)
nushipa, dusk (n)
nushitaka, allegation (n)
nushitako, allege (v)
nushitakua, alleger (n doer)
nutafa, legit (n)
nutafika, legitimacy (n)
nutafikiu, legitimately (adv)
nutafiko, legitimize (v)
nutafiku, legitimate (adj)
nutafu, legit (adj)
nutaka, legality (n)
nutakiu, legally (adv)
nutako, legalize (v)
nutaku, legal (adj)
nuterafa, yoke (n)
nuterafo, yoke (v)
nutesha, party (n d:group)
nutha, mitt (n)
nuthafa, mitten (n)
nuthiko, puke (v)
nuthikua, puker (n doer)
nuva, jar (n)
nuvo, jar (v)
nuyena, noun (n)
obeinaba, abdomen (n)
obelaithu, around (adv/prep)
obiabu, aloud (adv)
obiapa, alarm (n)
obiapo, alarm (v)
obiapua, alarmist (n doer)
obolipa, absorption (n)
obolipo, absorb (v)
obolipua, absorbant (n doer)
obolipua, absorber (n doer)
oborita, advice (n)
oboritana, advisory (n)
oboritiu, advisably (adv)
oborito, advise (v)
oboritu, advisable (adj)
oboritua, adviser (n doer)
oboritua, advisor (n doer)
obotafika, apathy (n)
obotafiku, apathetic (adj)
odalopiariu, asynchronously (adv)
odalopiaru, asynchronous (adj)
oderuketa, apprehension (n)
oderuketiu, apprehensively (adv)
oderuketo, apprehend (v)
oderuketu, apprehensive (adj)
odiama, adolescence (n)
odiamu, adolescent (adj)

odiamua, adolescent (n doer)
odiaufa, amazement (n)
odiaufo, amaze (v)
odoruba, abroad (n)
odorubiu, abroad (adv)
odufiko, avenge (v)
odufikua, avenger (n doer)
ofadelika, assortment (n)
ofadeliko, assort (v)
ofapueta, appetite (n)
ofapueto, appetize (v)
ofarina, aspirin (n)
ofelaruva, approval (n)
ofelaruvo, approve (v)
ofelaruvua, approver (n doer)
ofelauda, approach (n)
ofelaudo, approach (v)
ofelaudu, approachable (adj)
ofelaudua, approacher (n doer)
ofelikima, appropriation (n)
ofelikimiu, appropriately (adv)
ofelikimo, appropriate (v)
ofelikimu, appropriate (adj)
ofelikimua, appropriator (n doer)
ofeloigata, approximation (n)
ofeloigatiu, approximately (adv)
ofeloigato, approximate (v)
ofeloigatu, approximate (adj)
ofeloka, average (n)
ofeloka, mean (n d:average)
ofeloko, average (v)
ofeloku, average (adj)
ofialota, assumption (n)
ofialoto, assume (v)
ofienu, alone (adj/adv)
ofika, aptitude (n)
ofikiu, aptly (adv)
ofiku, apt (adj)
ofishaka, applause (n)
ofishako, applaud (v)
ofishakua, applauder (n doer)
ofoberuno, append (v)
ofudaufa, aspiration (n)
ofudaufo, aspire (v)
ogaifita, abruptness (n)
ogaifitiu, abruptly (adv)
ogaifitu, abrupt (adj)
ogalipa, attire (n)
ogalipo, attire (v)
ogalita, attraction (n)
ogalitiu, attractively (adv)
ogalito, attract (v)
ogalitu, attractive (adj)
ogalitua, attractor (n doer)
ogauika, aberration (n)
ogauiku, aberrant (adj)
ogavata, abolition (n)
ogavato, abolish (v)
ogavatua, abolitionist (n doer)
ogeleka, acknowledgment (n)
ogeleko, acknowledge (v)
ogerala, acorn (n)
ogeralita, abstract (n)

ogeraliti, abstract (n pl)
ogeralito, abstract (v)
ogeralitu, abstract (adj)
ogeralitua, abstractor (n doer)
ogianika, accommodation (n)
ogianikiu, accommodatively (adv)
ogianiko, accommodate (v)
ogianiku, accommodative (adj)
ogianikua, accommodator (n doer)
ogiapa, abatement (n)
ogiapo, abate (v)
ogiaulu, afire (adj)
oguveta, access (n)
oguveto, access (v)
oguvetu, accessible (adj)
oguvetua, accessory (n doer)
oi ferepa kodi, cannot (ndal d:ability)
oi, not (parcl)
oifo, oops (interj)
oilodanita, automobile (n)
oilodanitu, automotive (adj)
oilodarifa, autograph (n)
oilodarifo, autograph (v)
oilodenika, automation (n)
oilodenikiu, automatically (adv)
oilodeniko, automate (v)
oilodeniku, automatic (adj)
oilodenikua, automator (n doer)
oiloderonika, automatic (n)
oilonagua, automaker (n doer)
oiloviena, autonomy (n)
oipapa, alteration (n)
oipapo, alter (v)
oiparifopa, alternative (n)
oiparifopiu, alternatively (adv)
oiparifopo, alternate (v)
oiparifopu, alternative (adj)
oiparifopua, alternator (n doer)
okaka, ass (n)
okalifa, astonishment (n)
okalifio, astonish (v pa)
okalifo, astonish (v)
okalofata, agriculture (n)
okalofatu, agricultural (adj)
okauaita, abhorrence (n)
okauaito, abhor (v)
okauaitu, abhorrent (adj)
okefitiu, ahead (adv)
Okelakoma, Oklahoma (n)
Okelanuda, Oakland (n)
okelireta, accent (n)
okelireto, accent (v)
okelireto, accentuate (v)
okeraugu, ablaze (adj)
okeriafa, acquaintance (n)
okeriafo, acquaint (v)
okeriuka, abduction (n)
okeriuko, abduct (v)
okeriukua, abductor (n doer)
okeruga, agony (n)
okerugo, agonize (v)

Okigena, Oxygen (n)
Okiofa, Ohio (n)
okuaneku, against (prep)
okuanu, again (adv)
oladidana, assimilation (n)
oladidano, assimilate (v)
oladidanua, assimilator (n doer)
oladorida, apolity (n)
oladorideta, apology (n)
oladoridetiu, apologetically (adv)
oladorideto, apologize (v)
oladoridetu, apologetic (adj)
oladorido, apoliticize (v)
oladoridu, apolitical (adj)
olafeshalita, apartment (n)
olafeshofifa, apartheid (n)
olafeshu, apart (adj)
olafima, avenue (n)
olanifa, abnormality (n)
olanifiu, abnormally (adv)
olanifu, abnormal (adj)
olapa, assurance (n)
olapiu, assuratively (adv)
olapo, assure (v)
olapu, assurative (adj)
olapua, assurer (n doer)
olarika, assignment (n)
olariko, assign (v)
olarikua, assigner (n doer)
olashata, assertion (n)
olashatiu, assertively (adv)
olashato, assert (v)
olashatu, assertive (adj)
olaumu, among (prep)
olaumu, amongst (prep)
olazhoda, asset (n)
olenopa, arithmetic (n)
olenopua, arithmetician (n doer)
olimota, arrangement (n)
olimoto, arrange (v)
olimotua, arranger (n doer)
olipoila, array (n)
olipoilo, array (v)
olirika, ascent (n)
oliriko, ascend (v)
olirikua, ascender (n doer)
olirokueta, ascension (n)
oluishio, arose (v pa)
oluisho, arise (v)
omadoipa, anguish (n)
omadoipo, anguish (v)
omafita, analysis (n)
omafitiu, analytically (adv)
omafito, analyze (v)
omafitu, analytical (adj)
omafitua, analyst (n doer)
omafitua, analyzer (n doer)
omakelipa, antique (n)
omakelipara, antiquity (n)
omalalika, ancestry (n)
omalaliku, ancestral (adj)
omalalikua, ancestor (n doer)
omashelika, anticipation (n)

omasheliko, anticipate (v)
omashika, anecdote (n)
omashikiu, anecdotally (adv)
omashiku, anecdotal (adj)
omegana, omega (n)
omei, an (det)
omeifa, association (n)
omeifo, associate (v)
omeifua, associate (n doer)
omida, annotation (n)
omido, annotate (v)
omikadereifu, antitrust (adj)
omikamieka, antibiotic (n)
omikamoka, antidote (n)
omikanofa, antenna (n)
omikashelada, antibody (n)
omikaviena, antonym (n)
omikerona, omicron (n)
ominopio, awoke (v pa)
ominopo, awake (v)
ominopu, awake (adj)
omiopa, ancient (n)
omiopu, ancient (adj)
omishei, another (adj)
omudenika, animation (n)
omudeniko, animate (v)
omudenikua, animator (n doer)
omufeta, announcement (n)
omufeto, announce (v)
omufetua, announcer (n doer)
omugafa, annoyance (n)
omugafo, annoy (v)
omuna, animal (n)
ona, one (pron 3rd indefpers sng obj)
ona, one (pron 3rd indefpers sng sub)
Onaf, Mendelevium (n davoka)
Onak, Neptunium (n davoka)
onalipa, alert (n)
onalipaka, alertness (n)
onalipo, alert (v)
onalipua, alerter (n doer)
onamu, a.m. (adj)
Onap, Actinum (n davoka)
onar, them/people (pron 3rd indefpers pl obj)
onar, they/people (pron 3rd indefpers pl sub)
onash, one's (pron 3rd indefpers sng pos obj)
onash, one's (pron 3rd indefpers sng pos sub)
onash, people's (pron 3rd indefpers pl pos obj)
onash, people's (pron 3rd indefpers pl pos sub)
onashfal, oneself (pron 3rd indefpers sng refl)
onashfar, peopleselves (pron 3rd indefpers pl refl)
Onat, Berkelium (n davoka)

oneka, ark (n)
Onif, Nobelium (n davoka)
Onik, Plutonium (n davoka)
Onip, Thorium (n davoka)
Onit, Californium (n davoka)
Onitariofa, Ontario (n)
oniuka, amount (n)
oniuko, amount (v)
onoarita, acclaimation (n)
onoarito, acclaim (v)
Onok, Americium (n davoka)
Onop, Protactinium (n davoka)
Onot, Einsteinium (n davoka)
onuaka, avoidance (n)
onuakiu, avoidably (adv)
onuako, avoid (v)
onuaku, avoidable (adj)
Onuk, Curium (n davoka)
onularita, ashore (n)
Onup, Uranium (n davoka)
Onut, Fermium (n davoka)
opaika, attachment (n)
opaiko, attach (v)
opaita, attack (n)
opaito, attack (v)
opaitua, attacker (n doer)
opeifu, of (prep)
opeliana, appearance (n)
opelianiu, apparently (adv)
opeliano, appear (v)
opelianu, apparent (adj)
opelianua, apparition (n doer)
opelosho, abridge (v)
operushelu, asleep (adj)
opifoka, attendance (n)
opifoko, attend (v)
opifokua, attendant (n doer)
opifokueta, attention (n)
opifokuetiu, attentively (adv)
opifokuetu, attentive (adj)
opifota, attainment (n)
opifoto, attain (v)
opiolu, away (adj/adv)
opitelopa, appeal (n)
opitelopo, appeal (v)
oradorafiko, accustom (v)
Oraf, Thulium (n davoka)
orafelaufitu, alive (adj)
orafeliana, affiliate (n)
orafeliano, affiliate (v)
orafelianueta, affiliation (n)
oragoita, accusation (n)
oragoitiu, accusingly (adv)
oragoito, accuse (v)
oragoitua, accuser (n doer)
oragoituina, accused (n)
Orak, Promethium (n davoka)
orakada, accord (n)
orakadana, accordance (n)
orakadiu, accordingly (adv)
orakado, accord (v)
orakika, affliction (n)
orakiko, afflict (v)

orakiku, afflictive (adj)
orakuita, analog (n)
orakuitara, analogy (n)
oramiaruta, affluence (n)
oramiarutiu, affluently (adv)
oramiarutu, affluent (adj)
oraniala, amusement (n)
oranialo, amuse (v)
oraniufa, affirmation (n)
oraniufiu, affirmatively (adv)
oraniufo, affirm (v)
oraniufu, affirmative (adj)
oraniufua, affirmer (n doer)
Orap, Lanthanum (n davoka)
orapoina, account (n)
orapoino, account (v)
orapoinu, accountable (adj)
orapoinua, accountant (n doer)
orashikafa, amendment (n)
orashikafo, amend (v)
orashila, answer (n)
orashilo, answer (v)
orashipa, acceptance (n)
orashipiu, acceptably (adv)
orashipo, accept (v)
orashipu, acceptable (adj)
Orat, Terbium (n davoka)
oravishota, ashameness (n)
oravishoto, ashame (v)
orazhoitu, alongside (adv/prep)
orazhu, along (prep/adv)
orelapa, assessment (n)
orelapiu, assessively (adv)
orelapo, assess (v)
orelapu, assessive (adj)
orelapua, assessor (n doer)
oreshu, also (adv/conj)
orfhem, Number_1e606
orfi, Os (let pl)
oribelega, subclass (n)
oriberona, subgroup (n)
oribiuma, subpoena (n)
oridiathu, subacute (adj)
Orif, Ytterbium (n davoka)
orifa, O (let sng)
orifaiofu, subionic (adj)
orifalipa, suburb (n)
orifalipo, suburbanize (v)
orifalipu, suburban (adj)
orifalipueta, suburbanization (n)
orifepa, subset (n)
oriferuata, subplot (n)
origalita, subtraction (n)
origalito, subtract (v)
origalitua, subtractor (n doer)
origelaruga, subcontract (n)
origelarugua, subcontractor (n doer)
origizhauka, submachine (n)
origizhauku, submachine (adj)
Origona, Oregon (n)
origugifopa, subcompact (n)
origugifopu, subcompact (adj)

Orik, Samarium (n davoka)
orikadata, altitude (n)
orikeilopa, subconsciousness (n)
orikeilopu, subconscious (adj)
orikeratha, allotment (n)
orikeratho, allot (v)
orikifiaisha, subdivision (n)
orikifiaisho, subdivide (v)
orikifiaishua, subdivider (n doer)
orikiroko, subdue (v)
orikofitana, subservience (n)
orikofitaniu, subserviently (adv)
orikofitanu, subservient (adj)
orilafipa, submersion (n)
orilafipo, submerge (v)
orilafipu, submersible (adj)
orilafipula, submersible (n)
Orilanudofa, Orlando (n)
orilekio, sublet (v pa)
orileko, sublet (v)
oriliauna, submarine (n)
orilika, subject (n)
orilikueta, subjectivity (n)
orilikuetiu, subjectively (adv)
orilikuetu, subjective (adj)
orimerata, subcontinent (n)
orinava, amateur (n)
orinavu, amateurish (adj)
orinioka, altimeter (n)
orinoka, submission (n)
orinokiu, submissively (adv)
orinoko, submit (v)
orinoku, submissive (adj)
orinokua, submitter (n doer)
orinulana, sublease (n)
orinulano, sublease (v)
oriotherava, subassembly (n)
Orip, Cerium (n davoka)
oripelaipa, substrate (n)
oripelenikua, subcommittee (n doer)
oripeliola, subway (n)
orishaipa, allocation (n)
orishaipo, allocate (v)
orishaipua, allocator (n doer)
orisharishotuka, subsystem (n)
orishekeiata, subordination (n)
orishekeiato, subordinate (v)
orishekeiatua, subordinate (n doer)
orisheluketa, substation (n)
orisheluketo, substation (v)
orisheriga, subscription (n)
orisherigo, subscribe (v)
orisherigua, subscriber (n doer)
orishetaipa, subtitle (n)
orishetaipo, subtitle (v)
orishetiba, subtext (n)
orishetibo, subtext (v)
orishipelota, substitution (n)
orishipeloto, substitute (v)
orishipelotua, substitute (n doer)
orishoito, subside (v)

orishola, subhuman (n)
orishufita, subsequence (n)
orishufitiu, subsequently (adv)
orishufitu, subsequent (adj)
Orit, Dysprosium (n davoka)
oritafika, subculture (n)
oritelika, subsistence (n)
oriteliko, subsist (v)
oritepo, subject (v)
oriterepa, substance (n)
oriterepiu, substantially (adv)
oriterepiu, substantively (adv)
oriterepo, substantiate (v)
oriterepu, substantial (adj)
oriterepu, substantive (adj)
oritereputa, substantiation (n)
oritha, elf (n)
oritharifeta, subversion (n d:lower version)
oritharika, subversion (n d:undercut)
oritharikiu, subversively (adv d:undercut)
orit(h)ariko, subvert (v d:undercut)
orithariku, subversive (adj d:undercut)
oritharikula, subversive (n)
oritherefa, subsurface (n)
oritherefo, subsurface (v)
orithishala, subsection (n)
orithishalo, subsection (v)
oritilasha, subterra (n)
oritilashu, subterranean (adj)
oritimotu, subatomic (adj)
orivithiu, subliminally (adv)
orivitho, sublime (v)
orivithu, subliminal (adj)
oroduipa, alloy (n)
oroduipo, alloy (v)
orogushika, allure (n)
orogushiko, allure (v)
oroifa, alignment (n)
oroifo, align (v)
Orok, Europium (n davoka)
orokiu, o'clock (adv)
Orop, Praseodymium (n davoka)
Orot, Holmium (n davoka)
Oruk, Gadolinium (n davoka)
Orup, Neodymium (n davoka)
orusha, allusion (n)
orusho, allude (v)
Orut, Erbium (n davoka)
oshalifu, alike (adj/adv)
Oshamiuma, Osmium (n)
oshekelauku, across (prep/adj/adv)
oshelefa, awareness (n)
oshelefu, aware (adj)
oshenala, alias (n)
oshimana, agnosis (n)
oshimanu, agnostic (adj)
oshoita, aside (n)
oshoitiu, aside (adv)

otaifota, appointment (n)
otaifoto, appoint (v)
otaifotua, appointer (n doer)
otava, attrition (n)
otavo, attrite (v)
otavu, attritional (adj)
Otawafa, Ottawa (n)
otelika, assist (n)
oteliki, assistance (n pl)
otelikiu, assistively (adv)
oteliko, assist (v)
oteliku, assistive (adj)
otelikua, assistant (n doer)
otereilota, acclimation (n)
otereiloto, acclimate (v)
oteshanu, although (conj)
otharika, aversion (n)
othariko, avert (v)
otherava, assembly (n)
otheravo, assemble (v)
otheravua, assembler (n doer)
otheriupa, attribute (n)
otheriupiu, attributively (adv)
otheriupo, attribute (v)
otheriupu, attributive (adj)
otheriupua, attributor (n doer)
otheta, acquisition (n)
otheto, acquire (v)
othetua, acquirer (n doer)
othirela, affair (n)
othoita, abbreviation (n)
othoito, abbreviate (v)
othuka, aspect (n)
ovafita, attempt (n)
ovafito, attempt (v)
ovaita, achievement (n)
ovaito, achieve (v)
ovaitu, achievable (adj)
ovaitua, achiever (n doer)
ovata, apron (n)
oveipu, about (prep/adv/adj)
overamipa, abandonment (n)
overamipo, abandon (v)
ovilehaushu, afterward (adv)
ovilehaushu, afterwards (adv)
ovilu, after (prep/adj/adv)
ovimidota, afternoon (n)
ovimidotu, afternoon (adj)
oviripa, affection (n)
oviripiu, affectionately (adv)
oviripu, affectionate (adj)
ovirota, affect (n)
oviroto, affect (v)
ovoburifa, aggravation (n)
ovoburifo, aggravate (v)
ovoiburifa, agitation (n)
ovoiburifo, agitate (v)
ovoiburifua, agitator (n doer)
ovorata, acceleration (n)
ovorato, accelerate (v)
ovoratonioka, accelerometer (n)
ovoratua, accelerator (n doer)
ovoruga, aggression (n)

ovorugiu, aggressively (adv)
ovorugo, aggress (v)
ovorugu, aggressive (adj)
ovorugua, aggressor (n doer)
ovuka, abuse (n)
ovukiu, abusively (adv)
ovuko, abuse (v)
ovuku, abusive (adj)
ovukua, abuser (n doer)
oyalifo, await (v)
ozharu, amid (prep)
ozharu, amidst (prep)
padoripa, barrel (n)
padoripo, barrel (v)
pafa, fad (n)
pafika, fiction (n)
pafikiu, fictionally (adv)
pafiko, fictionalize (v)
pafiku, fictional (adj)
pafiku, fictitious (adj)
pafita, fit (n d:match)
pafito, fit (v d:match)
pafitua, fitter (n doer d:match)
pageloika, acquittal (n)
pageloiko, acquit (v)
paiata, pike (n)
paiato, pike (v)
paiba, tact (n)
paibaka, tactic (n)
paibakiu, tactically (adv)
paibaku, tactical (adj)
paibakua, tactician (n doer)
paibata, tactilation (n)
paibato, tactilate (v)
paibatu, tactile (adj)
paibiu, tactfully (adv)
paibu, tactful (adj)
paifa, coin (n)
paifo, coin (v)
pairona, bowl (n d:container, bend)
pairono, bowl (v d:container, bend)
paisha, vial (n)
paita, tack (n)
paitata, tackle (n)
paitato, tackle (v)
paitatua, tackler (n doer)
paitha, satellite (n)
paito, tack (v)
paitu, tacky (adj)
paiva, federation (n)
paiviu, federally (adv)
paivo, federate (v)
paivu, federal (adj)
paizha, beige (n)
paizhu, beige (adj)
paka, knock (n)
paketiena, knockdown (n)
Pakishotana, Pakistan (n)
pako, knock (v)
pakua, knocker (n doer)
pakuila, knockout (n)

Paladiuma, Palladium (n)
Paleshotifa, Palestine (n)
Paleshotina, Palestinian (n)
palika, brick (n)
paliko, brick (v)
palikua, bricklayer (n doer)
palita, act (n)
palitaka, activation (n)
palitakiu, actively (adv)
palitako, activate (v)
palitaku, active (adj)
palitakua, activist (n doer)
paliterola, activity (n)
palitiora, actuality (n)
palitioriu, actually (adv)
palitioro, actualize (v)
palitioru, actual (adj)
palito, act (v)
palitua, actor (n doer)
palitua, actress (n doer)
palitueta, action (n)
palofipa, bass (n d:fish)
paloka, fabric (n)
pama, pie (n)
Panama, Panama (n)
Panamana, Panamanian (n)
panerala, ribbon (n)
panifa, bishop (n)
panika, tiredness (n d:fatigue)
panikemenu, tireless (adj d:fatigueless)
paniko, tire (v d:fatigue)
paniku, tiresome (adj d:fatigue)
parelufa, palate (n)
parelufu, palatable (adj)
parepofita, symmetry (n)
parepofitiu, symmetrically (adv)
parepofitu, symmetrical (adj)
pariana, sleigh (n)
parifa, park (n d:playground)
parifepeliola, parkway (n)
parina, hill (n)
parinedaupa, hilltop (n)
parineshoita, hillside (n)
parinofa, chocolate (n)
parinofu, chocolate (adj)
parinu, hilly (adj)
paripa, drama (n)
paripara, dramatization (n)
paripiu, dramatically (adv)
paripo, dramatize (v)
paripu, dramatic (adj)
Parisha, Paris (n)
paritha, kitchen (n)
paritoina, symptom (n)
paritoinu, symptomatic (adj)
pariufa, slipper (n)
parolapa, sympathy (n)
parolapo, sympathize (v)
parolapu, sympathetic (adj)
parolapua, sympathizer (n doer)
parolita, symbol (n)
parolitiu, symbolically (adv)

parolito, symbolize (v)
parolitu, symbolic (adj)
parolitueta, symbolism (n)
paruyapa, symphony (n)
paruyapu, symphonic (adj)
pasha, food (n)
pashepeletha, foodstuff (n)
pashipa, feast (n)
pashipo, feast (v)
pashipua, feaster (n doer)
pashota, luck (n)
pashotemenu, luckless (adj)
pashotiu, luckily (adv)
pashoto, luck (v)
pashotu, lucky (adj)
pashotweku, luckiest (adj)
pashotwelu, luckier (adj)
pataka, stomach (n)
patesha, gotcha (interj)
pauaka, gargle (n)
pauako, gargle (v)
pauasha, gush (n)
pauasho, gush (v)
pauashua, gusher (n doer)
paufa, macro (n)
pauga, cave (n)
paugata, cavity (n)
paugila, cavern (n)
paugo, cave (v)
paugua, caver (n doer)
paugueta, cavitation (n)
paugueto, cavitate (v)
pauika, gag (n d:joke)
pauka, joke (n)
pauko, joke (v)
paukua, joker (n doer)
paumuba, bind (n d:constrain)
paumubio, bound (v pa d:constrain)
paumubo, bind (v d:constrain)
paumubu, bound (adj d:constrain)
paumubua, binder (n doer d:constrain)
paunifa, bounce (n)
paunifiu, bouncily (adv)
paunifo, bounce (v)
paunifu, bouncy (adj)
paunifua, bouncer (n doer)
pauorika, gurgle (n)
pauoriko, gurgle (v)
paupauka, juggle (n)
paupauko, juggle (v)
paupaukua, juggler (n doer)
paurimuba, bound (n d:limit)
paurimuba, boundary (n d:limit)
paurimubenu, boundless (adj)
pauripa, burial (n)
pauripo, bury (v)
pausho, douse (v)
pauta, gut (n)
pautemenu, gutless (adj)
pauto, gut (v)

pautu, gutsy (adj)
pautupa, gutter (n)
pava, feed (n)
pavaka, feedback (n)
pavo, feed (v)
pavua, feeder (n doer)
pavuapa, napkin (n)
pazha, buzz (n d:haircut)
pazho, buzz (v d:haircut)
pazhu, buzz (adj d:haircut)
pefa, bush (n)
pefika, dish (n)
pefikefiausha, dishwasher (n)
pefikefiausho, dishwash (v)
pefiko, dish (v)
pefita, bushel (n)
pefito, bushel (v)
pefu, bushy (adj)
peia, P (let sng)
peiaboko, knead (v)
peiamela, donut (n)
peiamela, doughnut (n)
peiana, dough (n)
peiato, rouse (v)
peifa, pink (n)
peiferepa, viability (n)
peiferepiu, viably (adv)
peiferepu, viable (adj)
peifu, pink (adj)
peiga, verge (n d:edge)
peigo, verge (v d:edge)
peihem, Number_1e1806
peikaka, virility (n)
peikaku, virile (adj)
peikana, vigor (n)
peikaniu, vigorously (adv)
peikanu, vigorous (adj)
peikapa, verve (n)
peikeriuka, viaduct (n)
peilafa, vine (n)
peilafo, vine (v)
peilanoka, vinegar (n)
peilatha, virgin (n)
peileraupa, vineland (n)
peilethautha, vineyard (n)
peili, Ps (let pl)
peipa, feint (n)
peipo, feign (v)
peipua, feigner (n doer)
peishei, both (pron)
peishu, both (adj/conj)
peita, rout (n d:defeat)
peithu, pervious (adj)
peito, rout (v d:defeat)
peiufa, taciturn (n)
peiufiu, tacitly (adv)
peiufu, tacit (adj)
pela, single (n)
pelaba, slab (n)
peladeika, contradiction (n)
peladeiko, contradict (v)
peladeiku, contradictory (adj)
pelafa, grace (n)

pelafeliapa, grapefruit (n)
pelafiga, quarry (n)
pelafigo, quarry (v)
pelafika, census (n)
pelafima, contravention (n)
pelafimo, contravene (v)
pelafipa, grape (n)
pelafipeilana, grapevine (n)
pelafiu, graciously (adv)
pelafo, grace (v)
pelafu, gracious (adj)
pelafueta, graciousness (n)
pelafushiu, gracefully (adv)
pelafushu, graceful (adj)
pelagata, quarrel (n)
pelagato, quarrel (v)
pelaifa, broom (n)
pelaika, strategy (n)
pelaikiu, strategically (adv)
pelaiku, strategic (adj)
pelaikua, strategist (n doer)
pelaipa, stratus (n)
pelaipi, strata (n pl)
pelaisha, proneness (n)
pelaishu, prone (adj)
pelaitha, grill (n)
pelaitho, grill (v)
pelaka, grate (n)
pelako, grate (v)
pelakua, grater (n doer)
pelamipa, hump (n)
pelamipevaka, humpback (n)
pelamipevaku, humpback (adj)
pelamipo, hump (v)
pelamuna, sincerity (n)
pelamuniu, sincerely (adv)
pelamunu, sincere (adj)
pelaripa, contrariness (n)
pelaripu, contrary (adj)
pelaroshipa, contraception (n)
pelaroshipua, contraceptive (n
    doer)
pelashota, censorship (n)
pelashoto, censor (v)
pelashotua, censor (n doer)
pelatha, controversy (n)
pelathu, controversial (adj)
Pelatinuma, Platinum (n)
pelatufekefa, moorhead (n)
pelatufo, moor (v d:secure)
pelatuka, speaker (n d:air cone)
pelaufa, cloud (n)
pelaufika, debris (n)
pelaufo, cloud (v)
pelaufu, cloudy (adj)
pelauga, crypt (n)
pelauka, bruise (n)
pelauko, bruise (v)
pelaukua, bruiser (n doer)
pelaveramipa, contraband (n)
pelazha, gratitude (n)
pelazhiu, gratefully (adv)
pelazho, gratify (v)

pelazhu, grateful (adj)
pelazhuda, gratuity (n)
pelazhueta, gratification (n)
pelefa, wish (n)
pelefetoika, wishbone (n)
pelefo, wish (v)
pelefu, wishful (adj)
pelefu, wishy (adj)
pelefua, wisher (n doer)
peleifa, moderation (n)
peleifara, module (n)
peleifarata, modularity (n)
peleifariu, modularly (adv)
peleifaro, modulate (v)
peleifaru, modular (adj)
peleifarua, modulator (n doer)
peleifarueta, modulation (n)
peleifiu, moderately (adv)
peleifo, moderate (v)
peleifoka, modification (n)
peleifoko, modify (v)
peleifokua, modifier (n doer)
peleifu, moderate (adj)
peleifua, moderator (n doer)
peleisha, waiver (n)
peleisho, waive (v)
pelenita, clerk (n)
pelepa, OvaCarrier (n)
pelesha, dress (n d:clothing)
peleshenagua, dressmaker (n
    doer)
peleshika, dresser (n d:cabinet)
pelesho, dress (v d:clothing)
peleshua, dresser (n doer
    d:clothing)
peletha, stuff (n)
peletho, stuff (v)
pelethu, stuffy (adj)
pelethua, stuffer (n doer)
peliafa, sprawl (n)
peliafo, sprawl (v)
peliaka, integer (n)
peliapo, bask (v)
peliashika, integration (n)
peliashikara, integrity (n)
peliashikiu, integrally (adv)
peliashiko, integrate (v)
peliashiku, integral (adj)
peliashikua, integrator (n doer)
peliashipa, therapy (n)
peliashipu, therapeutic (adj)
peliashipua, therapist (n doer)
peliata, recovery (n d:retrieve,
    heal)
peliato, recover (v d:retrieve,
    heal)
peliatu, recoverable (adj
    d:retrieve, heal)
peliatua, recoverer (n doer
    d:retrieve, heal)
peliauka, sprain (n)
peliauko, sprain (v)
peliauta, siren (n)

pelifoka, breakup (n)
pelifokio, brokeup (v pa)
pelifoko, breakup (v)
peligito, quibble (v)
pelika, break (n)
pelikara, breakage (n)
pelikeidona, breakwater (n)
peliketaifota, breakpoint (n)
pelikio, broke (v pa)
pelikiu, breakably (adv)
peliko, break (v)
pelikopiola, breakaway (n)
peliku, breakable (adj)
pelikua, breaker (n doer)
pelikuila, breakout (n)
pelima, chin (n)
pelimorika, franchise (n)
pelimoriko, enfranchise (v)
pelina, spree (n)
pelinana, omelet (n)
peliola, way (n)
pelioleshoita, wayside (n)
peliolu, wayward (adj)
pelipa, mail (n)
pelipana, mailer (n)
pelipefanafa, mailbag (n)
peliperenoka, mailbox (n)
pelipo, mail (v)
pelipua, mailman (n doer)
pelira, chill (n)
peliro, chill (v)
pelirota, elicitation (n)
peliroto, elicit (v)
peliru, chilly (adj)
pelirua, chiller (n doer)
pelisha, singularity (n)
pelishiu, singularly (adv)
pelishu, singular (adj)
pelita, item (n)
pelitcloohana, breakthrough (n)
pelithoka, velocity (n)
pelitiena, breakdown (n)
pelito, itemize (v)
pelitua, itemizer (n doer)
peliubu, jumbo (adj)
peliufa, spray (n)
peliufo, spray (v)
peliufua, sprayer (n doer)
peliuka, drain (n)
peliuko, drain (v)
peliukua, drainer (n doer)
peliukueta, drainage (n)
peliupa, jumble (n)
peliupo, jumble (v)
peliuta, creation (n)
peliutala, creature (n)
peliutiu, creatively (adv)
peliuto, create (v)
peliutu, creative (adj)
peliutua, creator (n doer)
peliutueta, creativity (n)
peliva, migration (n)
pelivaka, immigration (n)

pelivako, immigrate (v)
pelivakua, immigrant (n doer)
pelivo, migrate (v)
pelivu, migrant (adj)
pelivua, migrant (n doer)
pelivuga, emigration (n)
pelivugo, emigrate (v)
pelivugua, emigrant (n doer)
pelo, single (v)
pelofiena, monk (n)
pelofika, moniker (n)
peloifa, bracelet (n)
peloika, glitch (n)
peloisha, silk (n)
peloishefanina, silkwood (n)
peloishiu, silkily (adv)
peloishu, silky (adj)
peloishyorina, silkworm (n)
peloita, brace (n)
peloitaka, bracket (n)
peloitako, bracket (v)
peloito, brace (v)
peloitua, bracer (n doer)
peloka, lunge (n)
peloko, lunge (v)
pelokua, lunger (n doer)
pelona, person (n)
pelonaga, personification (n)
pelonago, personify (v)
pelonara, personnel (n)
pelonata, personality (n)
pelonegerulita, manhunt (n)
pelonekotha, manhole (n)
pelonesheriauta, manslaughter (n)
peloni, people (n pl)
pelonika, kernel (n)
peloniu, personally (adv)
pelono, personalize (v)
pelonu, personal (adj)
pelonueta, personalization (n)
pelonula, personal (n)
pelorifa, garb (n)
pelorika, board (n d:wood)
peloriko, board (v d:wood)
peloripa, bump (n)
peloripiu, bumpily (adv)
peloripo, bump (v)
peloripu, bumpy (adj)
peloripua, bumper (n doer)
pelorisha, mortar (n d:bowl)
pelorita, brow (n)
pelorito, brow (v)
pelosha, bridge (n)
pelosho, bridge (v)
pelovaka, rubbish (n)
pelovatha, rubber (n)
pelovathu, rubbery (adj)
pelu, single (adj)
peluaba, lamp (n)
peluabalita, lamppost (n)
peluafa, reality (n)
peluafiu, really (adv)

peluafu, real (adj)
peluafua, realist (n doer)
peluaka, grant (n)
peluako, grant (v)
peluakua, grantor (n doer)
peluana, realism (n)
peluaniu, realistically (adv)
peluano, realize (v)
peluanu, realistic (adj)
peluanueta, realization (n)
peluata, lantern (n)
peluatha, ovation (n)
pelubashalita, coauthority (n)
pelubashalitua, coauthor (n doer)
peluda, kit (n)
pelufei, enough (pron)
pelufu, enough (adj/adv)
peluika, hail (n d:precipitation)
peluiko, hail (v d:precipitation)
peluipa, piano (n)
pelukada, record (n)
pelukado, record (v)
pelukadu, recordable (adj)
pelukadua, recorder (n doer)
pelukeferipa, hailstorm (n)
pelukiota, distortion (n)
pelukioto, distort (v)
pelumaromaka, cogeneration (n)
pelumaromako, cogenerate (v)
pelumaromakua, cogenerator (n doer)
pelunipa, guest (n)
pelunisha, receipt (n)
pelunishaka, receptacle (n)
pelunishua, recipient (n doer)
pelunita, hint (n)
pelunito, hint (v)
pelunulita, coexistence (n)
pelunulito, coexist (v)
pelupa, guess (n)
pelupekioka, guesswork (n)
pelupeluta, tidbit (n)
pelupo, guess (v)
pelupua, guesser (n doer)
pelureishotueta, cohabitation (n)
pelureishotueto, cohabitate (v)
peluriga, sludge (n)
pelurika, improvisation (n)
peluriko, improvise (v)
pelushika, reception (n)
pelushikiu, receptively (adv)
pelushiku, receptive (adj)
pelushikua, receptor (n doer)
pelushipara, receptionist (n)
pelushipo, receive (v)
pelushipu, receivable (adj)
pelushipua, receiver (n doer)
pelushipuna, receivable (n)
pelushupato, cofound (v)
pelushupatua, cofounder (n doer)
peluta, bit (n d:part)
peluthuka, disrespect (n)
peluthuko, disrespect (v)

Pelutoniuma, Plutonium (n)
peluva, groan (n)
peluvaika, disregard (n)
peluvaiko, disregard (v)
peluvirothara, coefficient (n)
peluvo, groan (v)
peluvua, groaner (n doer)
peluzha, grief (n)
peluzhiu, grievously (adv)
peluzho, grieve (v)
peluzhu, grievous (adj)
peluzhua, griever (n doer)
peluzhueta, grievance (n)
pemudana, penny (n)
penoka, tongue (n)
penoko, tongue (v)
Penoshiluvaniafa, Pennsylvania (n)
perada, cradle (n)
perado, cradle (v)
perafibarafa, cornerstone (n)
perafiperanida, cornfield (n)
perafita, corner (n)
perafito, corner (v)
Peragafa, Prague (n)
perago, throb (v)
peraiaka, throe (n)
peraika, route (n d:path)
peraikata, routine (n)
peraikatiu, routinely (adv)
peraikatu, routine (adj)
peraiko, route (v d:path)
peraikua, router (n doer d:path)
peraina, foil (n d:prevent)
peraino, foil (v d:prevent)
peraisha, rarity (n)
peraishiu, rarely (adv)
peraisho, rarify (v)
peraishu, rare (adj)
peraita, theft (n)
peraitha, teller (n)
peraito, thieve (v)
peraitua, thief (n doer)
perala, knoll (n)
peralifa, decoration (n)
peralifara, decor (n)
peralifo, decorate (v)
peralifua, decorator (n doer)
peralika, correction (n)
peralikiu, correctly (adv)
peraliko, correct (v)
peraliku, correct (adj)
peralipa, corporation (n)
peralipo, incorporate (v)
peralipu, corporate (adj)
peralita, crate (n)
peralitapa, crater (n)
peralitapo, crater (v)
peralito, crate (v)
peramipo, encumber (v)
peramipu, cumbersome (adj)
peranida, field (n)
peranido, field (v)

peranidua, fielder (n doer)
peranisho, ramble (v)
peranishua, rambler (n doer)
Perasheodimiuma, Praseodymium (n)
perashika, rubble (n)
perata, function (n)
perataka, functionality (n)
peratha, draw (n d:pull, inscribe)
perathevaka, drawback (n)
perathio, drew (v pa d:pull, inscribe)
peratho, draw (v d:pull, inscribe)
perathua, drawer (n doer d:pull, inscribe)
peratisha, rabble (n)
peratisho, rabble (v)
peratishua, rabbler (n doer)
peratiu, functionally (adv)
perato, function (v)
peratu, functional (adj)
peratua, functioner (n doer)
peraufa, slop (n)
peraufo, slop (v)
peraufu, sloppy (adj)
peraufueta, sloppiness (n)
perauka, slob (n)
perauma, pelt (n d:fur)
peraupo, slobber (v)
perauta, blot (n)
perauto, blot (v)
perautua, blotter (n doer)
perazhana, dreg (n)
perazho, dredge (v)
peredizha, narration (n)
peredizhata, narrative (n)
peredizho, narrate (v)
peredizhu, narrative (adj)
peredizhua, narrator (n doer)
pereibida, telecast (n)
pereibido, telecast (v)
pereibieloka, teleport (n)
pereibieloko, teleport (v)
pereibielokua, teleporter (n doer)
pereibotesha, telepathy (n)
pereiboteshu, telepathic (adj)
pereiboteshua, telepath (n doer)
pereida, restaurant (n)
pereidarofa, telegraph (n)
pereidarofo, telegraph (v)
pereidifedarifa, telephotography (n)
pereidifedarifo, telephotograph (v)
pereidifedarifu, telephoto (adj)
pereifa, hope (n)
pereifa, hopefullness (n)
pereifena, hopelessness (n)
pereifeniu, hopelessly (adv)
pereifenu, hopeless (adj)
pereifiu, hopefully (adv)
pereifo, hope (v)
pereifu, hopeful (adj)

pereiguniata, telecommunication (n)
pereiguta, telecom (n)
pereika, spank (n)
pereiko, spank (v)
pereikua, spanker (n doer)
pereiliafa, trivium (n)
pereiliafi, trivia (n pl)
pereiliafo, trivialize (v)
pereiliafu, trivial (adj)
pereiliafueta, triviality (n)
pereiliugefa, teleconference (n)
pereiluafa, telescope (n)
pereiluafo, telescope (v)
pereiluafu, telescopic (adj)
pereinelika, telegram (n)
pereineliko, telegram (v)
pereipofita, telemetry (n)
pereisha, rest (n)
pereishiu, restfully (adv)
pereisho, rest (v)
pereishu, restful (adj)
pereishua, rester (n doer)
pereishumeniu, restlessy (adv)
pereishumenu, restless (adj)
pereitha, chroma (n)
pereithenota, telekinesis (n)
pereithenotu, telekinetic (adj)
pereithulida, television (n)
pereithulido, televise (v)
pereiyapa, telephone (n)
pereiyapo, telephone (v)
pereiyapu, telephonic (adj)
pereiyapueta, telephony (n)
perekutala, gladiator (n)
perelifiu, gladly (adv)
perelifo, gladden (v)
perelifora, glade (n)
perelifu, glad (adj)
perelika, gate (n)
perelikelofua, gatekeeper (n doer)
perelikipa, gateway (n)
pereliko, gate (v)
perelima, month (n)
perelimiu, monthly (adj)
perelufika, gait (n)
perenika, box (n d:cube)
pereniko, box (v d:cube)
pereniku, boxy (adj d:cube)
peresha, recreation (n d:rest)
pereshu, recreational (adj d:rest)
pereta, tale (n)
peretha, turf (n)
peretio, told (v pa)
peretiu, tellingly (adv)
pereto, tell (v)
peretoperetu, telltale (adj)
periafa, foil (n d:sheet)
periafo, foil (v d:sheet)
periaka, brittleness (n)
periako, brittle (v)
periaku, brittle (adj)
periama, prune (n d:fruit)

periana, jerk (n)
perianiu, jerkily (adv)
periano, jerk (v)
perianu, jerky (adj)
perianua, jerk (n doer)
periata, biscuit (n)
periauko, slouch (v)
periaukua, slouch (n doer)
perifa, hip (n)
perififa, cranny (n)
perifota, crop (n d:food)
perifotua, cropper (n doer d:food)
perilaka, pylon (n)
perilapa, possession (n)
perilapiu, possessively (adv)
perilapo, possess (v)
perilapu, possessive (adj)
perilapua, possessor (n doer)
perilika, silt (n)
periloma, blank (n)
perilomapa, blanket (n)
perilomapo, blanket (v)
perilomo, blank (v)
perinelita, faith (n)
perinelitiu, faithfully (adv)
perinelito, enfaith (v)
perinelitu, faithful (adj)
perinelitueta, faithfulness (n)
perinelomana, faithlessness (n)
perinelomaniu, faithlessly (adv)
perinelomanu, faithless (adj)
perineta, fidelity (n)
periofa, pore (n)
periofu, porous (adj)
peripa, braille (n)
perisha, fast (n d:starve)
perishemashipa, fastball (n)
perisho, fast (v d:starve)
perita, intelligence (n)
peritariu, intellectually (adv)
peritaru, intellectual (adj)
peritarua, intellectual (n doer)
periteferepiu, intelligibly (adv)
periteferepu, intelligible (adj)
peritho, mull (v)
peritiu, intelligently (adv)
peritu, intelligent (adj)
peritua, intellect (n doer)
periufa, luncheon (n)
periuma, dormancy (n)
periumu, dormant (adj)
periupa, robe (n)
periuta, lunch (n)
periutesherana, lunchroom (n)
periuto, lunch (v)
periutua, luncher (n doer)
peroida, knob (n)
peroka, dock (n)
perokefa, docket (n)
perokeshoita, dockside (n)
perokeshoitu, dockside (adj)
peroko, dock (v)
perolita, document (n)

perolitara, documentary (n)
peroliteta, documentation (n)
perolito, document (v)
perolitua, documenter (n doer)
Peromethiuma, Promethium (n)
peroshata, doctrine (n)
peroshato, indoctrinate (v)
Peroshiana, Persian (n)
Perotakotiniuma, Protactinium (n)
perothipa, doctor (n)
perothipo, doctor (v)
peruafa, vane (n)
Perufa, Peru (n)
perufita, blend (n)
perufito, blend (v)
perufitua, blender (n doer)
peruka, method (n)
perukiu, methodically (adv)
peruko, methodize (v)
peruku, methodical (adj)
perukuita, methodology (n)
perulika, strain (n)
peruliko, strain (v)
perulikua, strainer (n doer)
peruma, snail (n)
Peruna, EhoMonth04 (n)
perusha, sleep (n)
perushemenu, sleepless (adj)
perushezhoipo, sleepwalk (v)
perushezhoipua, sleepwalker (n doer)
perushio, slept (v pa)
perusho, sleep (v)
perushu, sleepy (adj)
perushua, sleeper (n doer)
perushueta, sleepiness (n)
peruta, blade (n)
perutesha, punk (n)
peruteshu, punky (adj)
peruzha, drudge (n)
peruzho, drudge (v)
peruzhu, drudgery (adj)
peruzhua, drudge (n doer)
peshina, psi (n)
peshipa, justice (n)
peshipeferepiu, justifiably (adv)
peshipeferepu, justifiable (adj)
peshipiu, justly (adv)
peshipo, justify (v)
peshipu, just (adj)
peshipueta, justification (n)
peshota, bottom (n)
peshoto, bottom (v)
piala, vice (n d:title)
pialifo, fiddle (v d:manipulate)
piapa, gib (n)
piapiapa, gibberish (n)
piapiapo, gibber (v)
piaritha, sieve (n)
piaritho, sieve (v)
piarodarifa, chronograph (n)
piarodarifiu, chronographically

(adv)
piarodarifo, chronograph (v)
piarodarifu, chronographical (adj)
piaroka, chronicle (n)
piaroko, chronicle (v)
piarokuita, chronology (n)
piarokuitiu, chronologically (adv)
piarokuitu, chronological (adj)
piata, cadence (n)
pietho, furbish (v)
pifa, tent (n d:housing)
pifalu, tenuous (adj)
pifana, tenderness (n)
pifaniu, tenderly (adv)
pifanu, tender (adj)
pifauka, tentacle (n)
pifelana, funeral (n)
pifoka, tendency (n)
pifokato, tender (v)
pifoko, tend (v)
pifotaniu, tentatively (adv)
pifotanu, tentative (adj)
pifotata, tension (n)
pifotatiu, tensely (adv)
pifotato, tensen (v)
pifotatu, tense (adj)
pikata, kite (n)
pilako, straggle (v)
pilakua, straggler (n doer)
pilama, friend (n)
pilamefifa, friendship (n)
pilamo, befriend (v)
pilamu, friendly (adj)
pilamua, friend (n doer)
pilamueta, friendliness (n)
pilefiuna, fiance (n)
pilefiuna, fiancee (n)
pileta, evenness (n d:distribute)
piletiu, evenly (adv d:distribute)
pileto, even (v d:distribute)
piletu, even (adj d:distribute)
pilika, mitigation (n)
piliko, mitigate (v)
pilisherana, comrade (n)
pilita, tweet (n)
pilito, tweet (v)
pilopa, bark (n d:tree skin)
piluava, coed (n)
pimafa, spouse (n)
pimafo, espouse (v)
pimafu, spousal (adj)
pina, pi (n)
pirama, ram (n d:animal)
pirana, plummet (n)
pirano, plummet (v)
piroda, check (n d:money)
piroika, obligation (n)
piroiko, oblige (v)
piroikueto, obligate (v)
piroikuetu, obligatory (adj)
pirotapa, exterior (n)
pirotapiu, externally (adv)

pirotapo, externalize (v)
pirotapu, external (adj)
pirotho, sift (v)
pirothua, sifter (n doer)
Piteshoburoga, Pittsburgh (n)
pithopa, tenancy (n)
pithopua, tenant (n doer)
piuagubidu, ungodly (adj)
piualotipu, unmentionable (adj)
piuanolaku, unalienable (adj)
piubashalipo, unauthorize (v)
piubelashikiu, unimpressively
    (adv)
piubelashiku, unimpressive (adj)
piubelego, unclassify (v)
piuberiakiu, unusually (adv)
piuberiakoferepu, unusable (adj)
piuberiaku, unusual (adj)
piuberianiko, unregister (v)
piuberietiu, undeniably (adv)
piuberietu, undeniable (adj)
piuberugo, unburn (v)
piubiaufiu, undoubtedly (adv)
piubinako, unoppose (v)
piubudolifu, undetectable (adj)
piubugapo, unpack (v)
piudainu, unequal (adj)
piudalitho, uncover (v)
piudaunu, untimely (adj)
piudautiu, unbeatably (adv)
piudautu, unbeatable (adj)
piudepiu, unthinkingly (adv)
piudepu, unthinkable (adj)
piudereifelaishu, untrustworthy
    (adj)
piudereilu, untrue (adj)
piudereisha, untruth (n)
piudereishiu, untruthfully (adv)
piudereishu, untruthful (adj)
piuderotu, unclear (adj)
piudhigoku, unmistakable (adj)
piudiako, unburden (v)
piudilanu, unholy (adj)
piudito, unlist (v)
piudofito, unbutton (v)
piuduapiu, untypically (adv)
piuduapu, untypical (adj)
piudufitiu, uncritically (adv)
piudufitu, uncritical (adj)
piuduthapiu, unseasonably (adv)
piuduthapu, unseasonable (adj)
piuefubino, unopen (v)
piufafitu, uncivil (adj)
piufanituniu, unpatriotically
    (adv)
piufanitunu, unpatriotic (adj)
piufelaishu, unworthy (adj)
piufelaufiteferepu, unlivable (adj)
piufelefa, unease (n)
piufelefiu, uneasily (adv)
piufelefu, uneasy (adj)
piufelefueta, uneasiness (n)
piufeliana, unfamiliarity (n)

piufelianu, unfamiliar (adj)
piufeliofo, unprove (v)
piufeliukiu, unwisely (adv)
piufeliuku, unwise (adj)
piufenaipo, unbrand (v)
piufenupo, unwrap (v)
piuferepa, unability (n)
piuferepekodu, uncanny (adj)
piuferepiu, unably (adv)
piuferepu, unable (adj)
piuferilopa, unpleasantness (n)
piuferilopiu, unpleasantly (adv)
piuferilopu, unpleasant (adj)
piuferiloto, unorganize (v)
piuferinifo, unhitch (v)
piuferitho, unidentify (v)
piufinetu, unsteady (adj)
piufirodu, uneventful (adj)
piufitapu, unstable (adj)
piufiukiu, unproductively (adv)
piufiuku, unproductive (adj)
piufiunikiu, unprofessionally
    (adv)
piufiuniku, unprofessional (adj)
piufiupafitiu, unprofitably (adv)
piufiupafitu, unprofitable (adj)
piufiushaiko, unprovoke (v)
piugailu, unhelpful (adj)
piugashu, untraceable (adj)
piugeleka, unknown (n)
piugelekiu, unknowingly (adv)
piugeleku, unknowable (adj)
piugelesho, untie (v)
piugeloirifu, uncharitable (adj)
piugelorugu, unreachable (adj)
piugerukiu, unbearably (adv)
piugeruku, unbearable (adj)
piugiro, uncall (v)
piugithapo, unplug (v)
piugoranipo, uncork (v)
piugurinu, uncommon (adj)
piuhauthu, unhealthy (adj)
piuhinafo, unquote (v)
piuiabofitiu, unobtrusively (adv)
piuiabofito, unobtrude (v)
piuiabofitu, unobtrusive (adj)
piuipeko, unbias (v)
piuipiduritiu, uncooperatively
    (adv)
piuipiduritu, uncooperative (adj)
piuipifokiu, unintentionally (adv)
piuipifoku, unintentional (adj)
piuivadavu, unemotional (adj)
piukarifelualu, unassailable (adj)
piukeikutiu, unremarkably (adv)
piukeikutu, unremarkable (adj)
piukeilopa, unconsciousness (n)
piukeilopiu, unconsciously (adv)
piukeilopu, unconscious (adj)
piukeleizhiu, unreasonably (adv)
piukeleizho, unreason (v)
piukeleizhu, unreasonable (adj)
piukeloipo, unscrew (v)

piukeraliko, unscramble (v)
piuketo, uncheck (v)
piukifatio, unbent (v pa)
piukifato, unbend (v)
piukilenio, unbecame (v pa)
piukileno, unbecome (v)
piukinaliu, unimaginably (adv)
piukinalu, unimaginable (adj)
piukioku, unworkable (adj)
piukirokiu, unduly (adv)
piukiroku, undue (adj)
piukiviugiu, unimportantly (adv)
piukiviugu, unimportant (adj)
piukolanu, unwelcome (adj)
piukolima, unhappiness (n)
piukolimiu, unhappily (adv)
piukolimu, unhappy (adj)
piukufipu, unethical (adj)
piulaliroto, unlicense (v)
piulauitu, unsatisfactory (adj)
piulauto, unveil (v)
piuleidiu, unnaturally (adv)
piuleidu, unnatural (adj)
piuleifara, undulation (n)
piuleifaro, undulate (v)
piuliapiu, unreadably (adv)
piuliapu, unreadable (adj)
piulibesho, unsettle (v)
piuligeragu, unsolvable (adj)
piulitano, unplan (v)
piuliufimu, unconventional (adj)
piuliushopelitiu,
    unconstitutionally (adv)
piuliushopelitu, unconstitutional
    (adj)
piuliutifokiu, unconditionally
    (adv)
piuliutifoku, unconditional (adj)
piulobuku, unsupportable (adj)
piuloiriu, undesirably (adv)
piuloiru, undesirable (adj)
piuluderatu, unrepentant (adj)
piuluduashu, unrepresentative
    (adj)
piuludufipu, unresponsive (adj)
piulurito, unload (v)
piuluvipo, unregulate (v)
piumemepifetiu, unsustainable
    (adv)
piumemithukiu, unsuspectingly
    (adv)
piumoimio, unpaid (v pa)
piumoimo, unpay (v)
piumoripiu, unsuitably (adv)
piumoripu, unsuitable (adj)
piumunapiu, unconscionably
    (adv)
piumunapu, unconscionable (adj)
piumutho, unmatch (v)
piunarithepu, unfavorable (adj)
piunepo, untap (v)
piunuliko, unleash (v)
piuofelaruvo, unapprove (v)

piuogalitiu, unattractively (adv)
piuogalitu, unattractive (adj)
piuogiapa, unabatement (n)
piuogiapo, unabate (v)
piuoipapiu, unalterably (adv)
piuoipapu, unalterable (adj)
piuonuakiu, unavoidably (adv)
piuonuaku, unavoidable (adj)
piuopelosha, unabridgement (n)
piuopelosho, unabridge (v)
piuorafeliano, unaffiliate (v)
piuorapoino, unaccount (v)
piuorapoinu, unaccountable (adj)
piuorashilu, unanswerable (adj)
piuorashipa, unacceptability (n)
piuorashipiu, unacceptably (adv)
piuorashipo, unaccept (v)
piuorashipu, unacceptable (adj)
piuoshelefu, unaware (adj)
piuparelufu, unpalatable (adj)
piuparolapu, unsympathetic (adj)
piupashotu, unlucky (adj)
piupaumubio, unbound (v pa)
piupaumubo, unbind (v)
piupelathu, uncontroversial (adj)
piupelesho, undress (v)
piupelikio, unbroke (v pa)
piupeliko, unbreak (v)
piupeliku, unbreakable (adj)
piupeluafa, unreality (n)
piupeluafu, unreal (adj)
piupeluaniu, unrealistically (adv)
piupeluanu, unrealistic (adj)
piupereisha, unrest (n)
piuperinelitiu, unfaithfully (adv)
piuperinelitu, unfaithful (adj)
piuperiteferepu, unintelligible (adj)
piupeshipiu, unjustly (adv)
piupeshipu, unjust (adj)
piupilamu, unfriendly (adj)
piupiletiu, unevenly (adv)
piupiletu, uneven (adj)
piureishotu, uninhabitable (adj)
piuridafo, unschedule (v)
piurigato, unravel (v)
piurudeika, unpredictability (n)
piurudeikiu, unpredictably (adv)
piurudeiku, unpredictable (adj)
piushalifu, unlike (prep/adj)
piushanifu, unlikely (adj/adv)
piushariu, unbelievably (adv)
piusharu, unbelievable (adj)
piusharua, unbeliever (n doer)
piushekito, unmove (v)
piushelaifu, unwary (adj)
piusheloita, unemployment (n)
piusheloito, unemploy (v)
piushelufu, uncool (adj)
piushemotato, unbalance (v)
piushemu, unclean (adj)
piushenaitho, unclutter (v)
piusheniko, untax (v)

piushereliu, unsure (adv)
piusherelu, unsure (adj)
piusheriko, unseat (v)
piushetato, unmark (v)
piushialu, untouchable (adj)
piushianu, unsanitary (adj)
piushineno, unarm (v)
piushiufipa, unavailability (n)
piushiufipu, unavailable (adj)
piushiupo, unavail (v)
piushiveshotiu, unnecessarily (adv)
piushiveshotu, unnecessary (adj)
piushotiatetiu, unquestionably (adv)
piushotiatetu, unquestionable (adj)
piushuashiu, unscientifically (adv)
piushuashu, unscientific (adj)
piutaigago, untangle (v)
piutalishiu, unspeakably (adv)
piutalishu, unspeakable (adj)
piutarofo, unhinge (v)
piutashikeliu, unofficially (adv)
piutashikelu, unofficial (adj)
piutaukiu, unstoppably (adv)
piutauku, unstoppable (adj)
piutebo, unrate (v)
piutefipesho, unadjust (v)
piuteranitiu, uncontrollably (adv)
piuteranitu, uncontrollable (adj)
piuteravo, unfold (v)
piuterema, unreliability (n)
piuteremiu, unreliably (adv)
piuteremu, unreliable (adj)
piuteriloku, untrainable (adj)
piuterulifo, unfurl (v)
piuterulishu, unprintable (adj)
piutharoiku, unverifiable (adj)
piutheralklo, unwound (v pa)
piutheraiko, unwind (v)
piutherauno, unbridle (v)
piutherela, unfairness (n)
piuthereliu, unfairly (adv)
piutherelu, unfair (adj)
piutheriutu, unscrupulous (adj)
piuthuitu, untreatable (adj)
piuthukelakiu, unspectacularly (adv)
piuthukelaku, unspectacular (adj)
piuthunu, unseemly (adj)
piutiagato, unhinder (v)
piutigereto, undisclose (v)
piutikio, undid (v pa)
piutiko, undo (v)
piutiugo, unlock (v)
piutuano, unchange (v)
piututhukiu, unexpectedly (adv)
piututhuku, unexpect (v)
piuvaigiu, unexplainably (adv)
piuvaigu, unexplainable (adj)
piuvalesha, unborn (n)

piuvanipu, uncompetitive (adj)
piuvaritufo, unsecure (v)
piuvaudiu, unlawfully (adv)
piuvaudu, unlawful (adj)
piuvelaruviu, uncomfortably (adv)
piuvelaruvu, uncomfortable (adj)
piuvelifu, unfit (adj)
piuvenikiu, uneconomically (adv)
piuveniku, uneconomical (adj)
piuveritiu, unexceptionally (adv)
piuveritu, unexceptional (adj)
piuvinoko, unbundle (v)
piuvitho, unlimit (v)
piuviuviatiu, unambiguously (adv)
piuviuviatu, unambiguous (adj)
piuvoamuniu, unfortunately (adv)
piuvoamunu, unfortunate (adj)
piuvoanethuthu, unforeseeable (adj)
piuvoatopu, unforgettable (adj)
piuvoiviushiu, unsurprisingly (adv)
piuvorida, unpopularity (n)
piuvoridiu, unpopularly (adv)
piuvoridu, unpopular (adj)
piuvosharo, unlove (v)
piuvoviuku, unenforceable (adj)
piuvulano, unmarry (v)
piuweifo, unsign (v)
piuyaka, unwillingness (n)
piuyakiu, unwillingly (adv)
piuzhatufu, unsound (adj)
piuzheifo, unzip (v)
piuzhilota, uncertainty (n)
piuzhilotu, uncertain (adj)
piuzhiunu, unselfish (adj)
piuzhiunueta, unselfishness (n)
piuzhoivo, unseal (v)
piuzhudu, unsafe (adj)
piuzhuvetushiu, unsuccessfully (adv)
piuzhuvetushu, unsuccessful (adj)
pivaka, tenacity (n)
pivaku, tenacious (adj)
pivatu, tenable (adj)
pivita, bike (n)
pivito, bike (v)
pivitua, biker (n doer)
poafa, clause (n)
poala, clay (n)
poapa, bud (n d:plant)
poapo, bud (v d:plant)
poefa, shade (n)
poefita, shadow (n)
poefito, shadow (v)
poefitu, shadowy (adj)
poefitua, shadower (n doer)
poefo, shade (v)
poefu, shady (adj)
poefua, shader (n doer)
pofiko, muddle (v)

pofipa, mud (n)
pofipeshukeraikio, mudslung (v pa)
pofipeshukeraiko, mudsling (v)
pofipiu, muddily (adv)
pofipo, muddy (v)
pofipu, muddy (adj)
pogaifa, hives (n d:skin eruption)
poidoipa, extinguishment (n)
poidoipo, extinguish (v)
poidoipua, extinguisher (n doer)
poifebakotueta, counterterrorism (n)
poifegaufita, counterargument (n)
poifegaufito, counterargue (v)
poifegerola, countermeasure (n)
poifekerithika, counterpunch (n)
poifekerithiko, counterpunch (v)
poifenoarita, counterclaim (n)
poifenoaritao, counterclaimed (v prp)
poifenoarito, counterclaim (v)
poifepaita, counterattack (n)
poifepaito, counterattack (v)
poifepalita, counteraction (n)
poifepalitiu, counteractively (adv)
poifepalito, counteract (v)
poifepalitu, counteractive (adj)
poifepalitua, counteractor (n doer)
poifepeimo, counterfeit (v)
poifepeimu, counterfeit (adj)
poifepeimua, counterfeiter (n doer)
poifeperita, counterintelligence (n)
poifesha, counterpart (n)
poifeshemotata, counterbalance (n)
poifeshemotato, counterbalance (v)
poifeshuisha, counterweight (n)
poifeshuisho, counterweigh (v)
poifetaifota, counterpoint (n)
poifiuku, counterproductive (adj)
poifiuloka, counterproposal (n)
poifo, counter (v d:d: oppose)
poika, tong (n)
poila, ray (n)
poina, count (n d:d: increment)
poinetiena, countdown (n)
poino, count (v d:d: increment)
poinua, counter (n doer d:d: increment)
poinuda, tennis (n)
poipa, fiber (n)
poipu, fibrous (adj)
poirata, distinction (n)
poiratiu, distinctly (adv)
poirato, distinguish (v)
poiratu, distinct (adj)
poiratu, distinctive (adj)
poishaka, count (n d:d: title)

poishota, extinction (n)
poishotu, extinct (adj)
poitha, absurdity (n)
poithiu, absurdly (adv)
poithu, absurd (adj)
pokitela, picture (n)
pokitelo, picture (v)
Polanuda, Poland (n)
polita, delicacy (n)
politiu, delicately (adv)
politu, delicate (adj)
Poloniuma, Polonium (n)
ponidena, pound (n d:weight)
ponifa, county (n)
ponika, coercion (n)
poniko, coerce (v)
poniku, coercive (adj)
ponikua, coercer (n doer)
ponita, bottle (n)
ponito, bottle (v)
ponitua, bottler (n doer)
porafa, beard (n)
porafo, beard (v)
porefita, factor (n)
porefito, factor (v)
porelana, period (n d:cycle)
porelaniu, periodically (adv d:cycle)
porelanu, periodic (adj d:cycle)
poreta, fact (n)
poretiu, factually (adv)
poretu, factual (adj)
porigethoila, knapsack (n)
porigo, nab (v)
porigua, nabber (n doer)
porila, hue (n)
Poritelanuda, Portland (n)
poritha, peripheral (n)
porithu, periperhal (adj)
Poritugala, Portugal (n)
posha, foot (n)
poshaka, football (n d:American)
poshata, honesty (n)
poshatiu, honestly (adv)
poshatu, honest (adj)
poshebotesha, footpath (n)
poshedorima, footwear (n)
poshefa, footstep (n)
poshekioka, footwork (n)
poshemida, footnote (n)
poshemido, footnote (v)
poshemola, football (n d:soccer)
posheparina, foothill (n)
posheterulisha, footprint (n)
poshezhaila, footfall (n)
poshi, feet (n pl)
posho, foot (v)
poshua, footer (n doer)
Potashiuma, Potassium (n)
pova, country (n)
povaipa, diner (n)
poveshoita, countryside (n)
puama, pawn (n)

puamethova, pawnshop (n)
puamo, pawn (v)
puata, barb (n)
puato, barb (v)
puatua, barber (n doer)
pulada, nudge (n)
pulado, nudge (v)
pulika, culpability (n)
puliku, culpable (adj)
pulikua, culprit (n doer)
pumufa, laziness (n)
pumufiu, lazily (adv)
pumufu, lazy (adj)
pumufweku, laziest (adj)
pumufwelu, lazier (adj)
punipa, helm (n d:helmet)
punipa, helmet (n)
puperusha, coma (n d:sleep)
puperushu, comatose (adj d:sleep)
purika, gross (n d:package)
putha, dune (n)
puvika, grog (n)
puviku, groggy (adj)
puvina, tear (n d:eyedrop)
puvino, tear (v d:eyedrop)
puvinu, tearful (adj)
puvinu, teary (adj d:eyedrop)
raba, tear (n d:rip)
rabio, tore (v pa d:rip)
rabo, tear (v d:rip)
Radiuma, Radium (n)
Radona, Radon (n)
rafika, coat (n)
rafiko, coat (v)
raifekioka, framework (n)
raifekioko, framework (v)
raifota, frame (n)
raifoto, frame (v)
raifotua, framer (n doer)
raizha, tease (n)
raizho, tease (v)
raizhua, teaser (n doer)
rakada, comb (n)
rakado, comb (v)
rakadua, comber (n doer)
rakaifa, loathness (n)
rakaifo, loathe (v)
rakaifu, loath (adj)
rakiu, meow (interj)
ralfka, audlt (u)
raliko, audit (v)
ralikua, auditor (n doer)
ralikueta, audition (n)
ralikueto, audition (v)
ralipa, fleece (n)
ralipo, fleece (v)
ralipua, fleecer (n doer)
ralisha, pettiness (n)
ralishiu, pettily (adv)
ralishu, petty (adj)
raliuka, audio (n)
raliukona, audience (n)

raliuku, audible (adj)
ramapa, banana (n)
ramesha, legend (n)
rameshu, legendary (adj)
ranena, mildness (n)
raneniu, mildly (adv)
ranenu, mild (adj)
ranenweku, mildest (adj)
ranenwelu, milder (adj)
raniapa, whale (n)
raniapo, whale (v)
ranipa, flesh (n)
ranipo, flesh (v)
ranipu, fleshy (adj)
rashala, coma (n d:oblong)
rasherila, comet (n)
rashota, letter (n d:message)
rashotekefita, letterhead (n)
rashotepelona, letterman (n)
rashotepeloni, lettermen (n pl)
rathaunu, lukewarm (adj)
rathiena, marathon (n)
rathienua, marathoner (n doer)
ratisha, meat (n)
ratishemashipa, meatball (n)
ratishemenu, meatless (adj)
ratishu, meaty (adj)
rau, us (pron 1st pl obj)
raubilara, landlady (n)
raubupa, landfill (n)
raufifa, feudalism (n)
raufifu, feudal (adj)
raufika, loft (n)
raufikiu, loftily (adv)
raufiko, loft (v)
raufiku, lofty (adj)
raugelarika, landmass (n)
rauka, lift (n)
rauko, lift (v)
raukua, lifter (n doer)
raukuncfa, liftoff (n)
raupa, land (n)
raupetheifua, landowner (n doer)
raupo, land (v)
raupua, lander (n doer)
raush, ours (pron 1st pl pos obj)
raushafipa, landlord (n)
raushelusha, landslide (n)
raushetata, landmark (n)
raushfal, ourself (pron 1st sing refl)
raushfar, ourselves (pron 1st pl refl)
raushiaka, landscape (n)
raushiako, landscape (v)
raushiakua, landscaper (n doer)
rautiuga, landlock (n)
rautiugo, landlock (v)
rauzha, lag (n)
rauzhaila, landfall (n)
rauzho, lag (v)
rauzhua, laggard (n doer)
rayu-rayu, bow-wow (interj)

razha, length (n)
razhadata, longitude (n)
razhaka, footage (n)
razhebarafa, milestone (n)
razhedaunu, longtime (adj)
razhekapa, longhand (n)
razheshekota, longshot (n)
razho, lengthen (v)
razhoila, longing (n d:desire)
razhoiliu, longingly (adv d:desire)
razhoilu, longing (adj d:desire)
razhu, lengthy (adj)
razhu, long (adj)
razhwaku, longest (adj)
razhwelu, lengthier (adj)
razhwelu, longer (adj)
refitiu, afforably (adv)
refito, afford (v)
refitu, affordable (adj)
reiapa, cheek (n)
reiaputoika, cheekbone (n)
reifa, elder (n)
reifiu, elderly (adv)
reifu, elder (adj)
reifweku, eldest (adj)
regina, look (n)
reigino, look (v)
reiginua, looker (n doer)
reiginuila, lookout (n)
reika, like (n)
reikeferepu, likeable (adj)
reikifu, like (prep)
reikiu, likely (adv)
reikiufifa, likelihood (n)
reiko, like (v)
reiku, like (adj)
reikueta, likeness (n)
reilafika, chemistry (n)
reilaka, chemical (n)
reilakiu, chemically (adv)
reilaku, chemical (adj)
reilakua, chemist (n doer)
Reilopa, Europe (n)
Reilopana, European (n)
reilota, habit (n)
reilotiu, habitually (adv)
reilotu, habitual (adj)
reinofa, par (n)
reinofo, par (v)
reinofu, par (adj)
reirota, cherry (n)
reirotu, cherry (adj)
reisho, rave (v)
reishota, habitat (n)
reishoto, inhabit (v)
reishotu, habitable (adj)
reishotua, inhabitant (n doer)
reishotueta, habitation (n)
reishua, raver (n doer)
reiuka, choke (n)
reiuko, choke (v)
reiukua, choker (n doer)
relana, merriment (n)

relaniu, merrily (adv)
relanu, merry (adj)
relanweku, merriest (adj)
relanwelu, merrier (adj)
relhem, Number_1e1356
relira, R (let sng)
relri, Rs (let pl)
rena, sun (n)
reneberuga, sunburn (n)
reneberugo, sunburn (v)
renedafika, sunbelt (n)
renedalifo, sunbathe (v)
renedalifua, sunbather (n doer)
renederinota, sunglass (n)
renederipa, sunspot (n)
reneduafa, sunbeam (n)
renefelarima, sundance (n)
renefelarimo, sundance (v)
renefeluana, sunlight (n)
renefeluanio, sunlit (v pa)
renefepa, sunset (n)
renefikoleta, sunscreen (n)
reneipota, sundial (n)
renelarifa, sunroof (n)
reneluisha, sunrise (n)
reneluishua, sunriser (n doer)
renemaiama, suntan (n)
renemoitha, sunshine (n)
renepoefa, sunshade (n)
reneshelesha, sunfish (n)
renesheleshi, sunfish (n pl)
renesherana, sunroom (n)
renethuana, sunflower (n)
renetiena, sundown (n)
reniu, sunnily (adv)
Reniuma, Rhenium (n)
reniveila, sunup (n)
renu, sunny (adj)
Renuviula, Sunday (n)
resha, right (n d:direction)
reshaushu, rightward (adj)
reshekapa, righty (n)
reshekeliegu, rightwing (adj)
reshu, right (adj d:direction)
retha, lie (n d:placement)
rethio, lay (v pa d:placement)
retho, lie (v d:placement)
retiena, joist (n)
riala, low (n)
rialeshikofa, lowercase (n)
rialiu, lowly (adv)
rialo, lower (v)
rialu, low (adj)
rialwaku, lowest (adj)
rialwelu, lower (adj)
riana, hour (n)
rianika, affray (n)
rianiko, affray (v)
rianikua, affrayer (n doer)
rianilofa, hourglass (n)
rianu, hourly (adj)
riaroka, acrobat (n)
riaroku, acrobatic (adj)

riaroviena, acronym (n)
riasha, massage (n)
riasho, massage (v)
riashua, massager (n doer)
riatha, owl (n)
riazho, linger (v)
ridafa, schedule (n)
ridafo, schedule (v)
ridafua, scheduler (n doer)
rideiga, groom (n d:bridegroom)
rifala, thanks (n)
rifalemenu, thankless (adj)
rifaliu, thankfully (adv)
rifalo, thank (v)
rifalu, thankful (adj)
Rifalugerufa, Thanksgiving (n)
rigato, ravel (v)
rilopa, spread (n)
rilopio, spread (v pa)
rilopo, spread (v)
rilopua, spreader (n doer)
rinagata, influenza (n)
rinini, meek (n pl)
rininiu, meekly (adv)
rininu, meek (adj)
riopa, pail (n)
riosha, aroma (n)
rioshiu, aromatically (adv)
rioshu, aromatic (adj)
rishada, teen (n)
rishedalita, teenager (n)
Rishemonuda, Richmond (n)
ritaro, loiter (v)
riterala, ring (n d:circle)
riteralita, ringleader (n)
riteralo, ring (v d:circle)
riteralua, ringer (n doer d:circle)
riterashoita, ringside (n)
riterashoitu, ringside (adj)
riterathioka, ringmaster (n)
ritha, smith (n)
riufa, rumble (n)
riufo, rumble (v)
riuka, lion (n)
riuma, hull (n)
riuna, boom (n)
riuno, boom (v)
rivuna, prestige (n)
rivunu, prestigious (adj)
Rodefa Ilanuda, Rhode Island (n)
Rodiuma, Rhodium (n)
Roenetugeniuma, Roentgenium (n)
rogalifa, occurrence (n)
rogalifo, occur (v)
rogalita, occasion (n)
rogalitiu, occasionally (adv)
rogalito, occasion (v)
rogalitu, occasional (adj)
roiaka, lien (n)
roifa, line (n)
roifipa, delineation (n)
roifipana, delinquence (n)

roifipanu, delinquent (adj)
roifipo, delineate (v)
roifipua, delineator (n doer)
roifiu, linearly (adv)
roifiveila, lineup (n)
roifo, line (v)
roifu, linear (adj)
roifua, liner (n doer)
roifueta, lineage (n)
roika, ligature (n)
roikafita, latch (n)
roikafito, latch (v)
roikata, ligament (n)
roiko, ligate (v)
roikueta, ligation (n)
roimeta, linen (n)
roina, lint (n)
roino, lint (v)
roinua, linter (n doer)
roisha, link (n)
roishiveila, linkup (n)
roisho, link (v)
roishua, linker (n doer)
roishueta, linkage (n)
roita, queue (n)
roitha, syllabus (n)
roithi, syllabi (n pl)
roito, queue (v)
rolama, council (n)
rolamo, conciliate (v)
rolata, bar (n d:rod)
rolato, bar (v d:rod)
rolifa, barrier (n)
rolipa, counsel (n)
rolipo, counsel (v)
rolipua, counselor (n doer)
Romafa, Rome (n)
Romafana, Roman (n)
Romiafa, Romania (n)
Romiana, Romanian (n)
rona, rho (n)
ronafa, vessel (n)
Roteshara, Rochester (n)
rotuto, pour (v)
rovaka, bake (n)
rovakara, bakery (n)
rovako, bake (v)
rovakua, baker (n doer)
rovoripa, occupation (n)
rovoripana, occupancy (n)
rovoripanua, occupant (n doer)
rovoripiu, occupationally (adv)
rovoripo, occupy (v)
rovoripu, occupational (adj)
rovoripua, occupier (n doer)
ruala, lyre (n)
rualipa, lyric (n)
rualipu, lyrical (adj)
ruanika, hunk (n)
ruaniko, hunker (v)
ruanikua, hunker (n doer)
ruasha, right (n d:ownership)
rubalivelariu, preposterously

(adv)
rubalivelaru, preposterous (adj)
Rubeka, EhoMonth02 (n)
Rubidiuma, Rubidium (n)
rubolika, preparation (n)
ruboliko, prepare (v)
rubolikua, preparer (n doer)
rubugato, prepackage (v)
rubushelana, predestination (n)
rubushelano, predestine (v)
rudeika, prediction (n)
rudeikiu, predictably (adv)
rudeiko, predict (v)
rudeiku, predictable (adj)
rudeiku, predictive (adj)
rudeikua, predictor (n doer)
ruderumaku, precancerous (adj)
rudibaga, pretrial (n)
ruduatha, prevention (n)
ruduathiu, preventably (adv)
ruduathiu, preventively (adv)
ruduatho, prevent (v)
ruduathu, preventable (adj)
ruduathu, preventive (adj)
ruduvaka, preservation (n)
rufapena, leftover (n)
rufekuka, legacy (n)
rufepa, preset (n)
rufepio, preset (v pa)
rufepo, preset (v)
rufialita, presumption (n)
rufialitiu, presumably (adv)
rufialitiu, presumptively (adv)
rufialito, presume (v)
rufialitu, presumable (adj)
rufialitu, presumptive (adj)
rufito, preach (v)
rufitu, preachy (adj)
rufitua, preacher (n doer)
rufivala, preseason (n)
rufuata, preview (n)
rufuato, preview (v)
rufuatua, previewer (n doer)
rugefa, preference (n)
rugefiu, preferably (adv)
rugefiu, preferentially (adv)
rugefo, prefer (v)
rugefu, preferable (adj)
rugefu, preferential (adj)
rugereniu, precariously (adv)
rugereniu, precarious (adj)
rugeruto, preclude (v)
rugineka, preemption (n)
ruginekiu, preemptively (adv)
rugineko, preempt (v)
rugineku, preemptive (adj)
ruheta, prejudice (n)
ruhetheta, prejudgement (n)
ruhetheto, prejudge (v)
ruheto, prejudice (v)
rukofita, preserve (n)
rukofito, preserve (v)
rukofitua, preserver (n doer)

rulenosha, gentleman (n)
rulenoshi, gentlemen (n pl)
rulezhimu, gingerly (adj)
ruliukulita, preconfiguration (n)
ruliukulito, preconfigure (v)
ruliushipa, preconception (n)
ruliushipo, preconceive (v)
ruliutifoka, precondition (n)
ruliutifoko, precondition (v)
ruluthata, prerequisite (n)
rumala, gentleness (n)
rumaliu, gently (adv)
rumalu, gentle (adj)
rumoima, prepayment (n)
rumoimio, prepaid (v pa)
rumoimo, prepay (v)
rumoimua, prepayer (n doer)
runaufika, predomination (n)
runaufikiu, predominantly (adv)
runaufiko, predominate (v)
runaufiku, predominant (adj)
runiatu, pristine (adj)
runisha, share (n)
runishethorithua, shareholder (n doer)
runisho, share (v)
runishua, sharer (n doer)
runoka, premise (n)
runoko, premise (v)
runulita, preexistence (n)
runulito, preexist (v)
ruola, prearrangement (n)
ruolo, prearrange (v)
rupa, leave (n d:departure)
rupelukado, prerecord (v)
rupifoka, pretense (n)
rupifoko, pretend (v)
rupifoku, pretentious (adj)
rupifokua, pretender (n doer)
rupio, left (v pa d:departure)
rupo, leave (v d:departure)
rurovoripa, preoccupation (n)
rurovoripo, preoccupy (v)
rurutesha, prelude (n)
rurutesho, prelude (v)
rusharitha, prehistory (n)
rusharithu, prehistoric (adj)
rusheleka, precipitation (n)
rusheleko, precipitate (v)
rushenika, pretax (n)
rusheniko, pretax (v)
rusheriga, prescription (n)
rusherigo, prescribe (v)
rushetiba, pretext (n)
Rushiafa, Russia (n)
Rushiana, Russian (n)
rushikashipa, precaution (n)
rushipesha, preschool (n)
rushipeshu, preschool (adj)
rushirofiu, prematurely (adv)
rushirofu, premature (adj)
rushiupa, prevalence (n)
rushiupo, prevail (v)

rushiupu, prevalent (adj)
rushuasha, prescience (n)
Rutheniuma, Ruthenium (n)
Rutheriforudiuma,
    Rutherfordium (n)
ruthishaka, precision (n)
ruthishakiu, precisely (adv)
ruthishaku, precise (adj)
ruthiu, preciously (adv)
ruthoisha, preface (n)
ruthoisho, preface (v)
ruthu, precious (adj)
rutilaka, predisposition (n)
rutilako, predispose (v)
rutulisha, predetermination (n)
rutulisho, predetermine (v)
ruvaushu, preliminary (adj)
ruveka, precession (n)
ruvekata, precedence (n)
ruvekata, precedent (n)
ruveko, precede (v)
ruvekua, predecessor (n doer)
ruvika, prefix (n)
ruviko, prefix (v)
ruvirota, prefecture (n)
ruvirotua, prefect (n doer)
ruviura, prewar (n)
ruvugelaka, presupposition (n)
ruvugelako, presuppose (v)
ruvulana, premarriage (n)
ruvulanu, premarital (adj)
ruzhiarofika, premeditation (n)
ruzhiarofiko, premeditate (v)
Sanau, Sanau (n)
seia, S (let sng)
seihem, Number_1e3306
seili, Ss (let pl)
Seranara, Seranara (n)
Serisa, Seris (n)
sha, she (pron 3rd fem sng sub)
shafikana, freckle (n)
shafilaka, trash (n)
shafilako, trash (v)
shafilaku, trashy (adj)
shafipa, lord (n)
shafipieita, dynasty (n)
shafipieitu, dynastic (adj)
shai, the (det)
shaiama, watch (n d:viewing)
shaiamederausha, watchdog (n)
shaiamepelona, watchman (n)
shaiamepeloni, watchmen (n pl)
shaiamiu, watchfully (adv
    d:viewing)
shaiamo, watch (v d:viewing)
shaiamu, watchful (adj d:viewing)
shaiamua, watcher (n doer
    d:viewing)
shaiasha, state (n d:region)
shaiashefifa, statehood (n)
shaiashekerashu, statewide (adj)
shaiashekiafa, statehouse (n)
shaiashepelona, statesman (n)

shaiashepelonefifa,
    statesmanship (n)
shaiashepeloni, statesmen (n pl)
shaiashoita, stateside (n)
shaiashoitu, stateside (adj)
shaifa, freak (n)
shaifo, freak (v)
shaifu, freaky (adj)
shailata, studio (n)
shaipa, locale (n)
shaipa, locality (n)
shaipa, location (n)
Shaiperusha, Cyprus (n)
shaipiu, locally (adv)
shaipo, locate (v)
shaipu, local (adj)
shaipua, locator (n doer)
shaipueta, localization (n)
shaipueto, localize (v)
shaitha, west (n)
shaithana, western (n d:film)
shaithaushu, westward (adj)
shaithederaipu, westbound (adj)
shaitho, westernize (v)
shaithu, west (adj)
shaithu, western (adj)
shaithua, westerner (n doer)
shaithweku, westernmost (adj)
Shaizhara, Caesar (n)
Shaizharu, Caesarean (adj)
Shakeramenita, Sacramento (n)
shakidoruga, shotgun (n)
shakita, shot (n)
shalifa, love (n d:pleasure)
shalifo, love (v d:pleasure)
shalifu, lovely (adj d:pleasure)
shalifua, lover (n doer d:pleasure)
shalikiu, plausibly (adv)
shaliko, plause (v)
shaliku, plausible (adj)
shalima, fur (n)
shalimo, fur (v)
shalimu, furry (adj)
shalina, simplicity (n)
shaliniu, simply (adv)
shalino, simplify (v)
shalinu, simple (adj)
shalinu, simplistic (adj)
shalinueta, simplification (n)
shalinwaku, simplest (adj)
shalinwelu, simpler (adj)
shalirota, essence (n)
shalirotiu, essentially (adv)
shaliroto, essentiate (v)
shalirotu, essential (adj)
Shamariuma, Samarium (n)
shamima, canoe (n)
shamimo, canoe (v)
shan, her (pron 3rd fem sng obj)
Shana Anitoniona, San Antonio
    (n)
Shana Diegofa, San Diego (n)
Shana Feranoshishaka, San

Francisco (n)
Shanikaifa, Shanghai (n)
Shanilana, January (n)
shanipa, example (n)
shanipo, exemplify (v)
Shanita Barubarafa, Santa
    Barbara (n)
Shanitafa Kelausha, Santa Claus
    (n)
Shapora, EhoMonth10 (n)
shara, belief (n)
sharadala, woman (n)
sharadali, women (n pl)
sharadoiaka, womanization (n)
sharadoiako, womanize (v)
sharadoiakua, womanizer (n
    doer)
sharala, midwife (n)
shareluima, robustness (n)
shareluimu, robust (adj)
sharena, situation (n)
shareniu, situationally (adv)
shareno, situate (v)
sharenu, situational (adj)
sharifa, wife (n)
sharigo, lodge (v d:stop)
sharilopa, sentiment (n)
sharilopu, sentimental (adj)
Sharilota, Charlotte (n)
sharima, cousin (n)
sharina, modernism (n)
sharina, modernization (n)
sharino, modernize (v)
sharinu, modern (adj)
sharinua, modernist (n doer)
sharitei, either (pron)
sharitha, history (n)
sharithiu, historically (adv)
sharithu, historic (adj)
sharithu, historical (adj)
sharithua, historian (n doer)
sharitu, either (adj/adv/conj)
shariu, believably (adv)
sharo, believe (v)
sharodaka, widow (n)
sharodako, widow (v)
sharodu, whether (conj)
sharolita, heroic (n)
sharolita, heroism (n)
sharolitiu, heroically (adv)
sharolitu, heroic (adj)
sharolitua, hero (n doer)
sharolitua, heroine (n doer)
sharu, believable (adj)
sharua, believer (n doer)
sharugena, silver (n)
sharuvaba, maternity (n)
sharuvabiu, maternally (adv)
sharuvabu, maternal (adj)
shash, her (pron 3rd fem sng pos
    sub)
shash, hers (pron 3rd fem sng pos
    obj)

shashfal, herself (pron 3rd fem
    sing refl)
shashika, management (n)
shashikiu, manageably (adv)
shashiko, manage (v)
shashiku, manageable (adj)
shashikua, manager (n doer)
shashikualu, managerial (adj)
shasho, man (v d:operate)
shateka, incident (n)
shatekiu, incidently (adv)
shateku, incidental (adj)
shatekueta, incidence (n)
shateta, inch (n)
shateto, inch (v)
shauana, whisker (n d:hair)
Shaudafa Arobana, Saudi Arabia
    (n)
Shaudana, Saudi (n)
shaufa, buffet (n d:strike)
shaufo, buffet (v d:strike)
shauka, estrangement (n)
shaukata, strangeness (n)
shaukiu, strangely (adv)
shauko, estrange (v)
shauku, strange (adj)
shaukua, stranger (n doer)
shaupa, asylum (n)
shaushutha, soybean (n)
shautha, trait (n)
shavana, gown (n)
Sheaboragiuma, Seaborgium (n)
shefira, subtlety (n)
shefiriu, subtly (adv)
shefiru, subtle (adj)
sheia, Sh (let sng)
sheiafa, fetus (n)
sheiafu, fetal (adj)
sheiama, theory (n)
sheiamiu, theoretically (adv)
sheiamo, theorize (v)
sheiamu, theoretical (adj)
sheiamua, theorist (n doer)
sheifa, fertility (n)
sheifita, veggie (n)
sheifo, fertilize (v)
sheifu, fertile (adj)
sheifua, fertilizer (n doer)
sheifueta, fertilization (n)
sheihem, Number_1e3606
sheilata, slogan (n)
sheili, Shs (let pl)
sheimaita, senility (n)
sheimaitu, senile (adj)
sheimata, senior (n)
sheimatu, senior (adj)
sheimatua, senior (n doer)
sheimatueta, seniority (n)
sheina, radius (n)
sheini, radii (n pl)
sheino, radius (v)
sheinofa, fountain (n)
sheironata, thesis (n)

sheisha, specialty (n)
sheishiu, especially (adv)
sheishiu, specially (adv)
sheisho, specialize (v)
sheishu, special (adj)
sheishua, specialist (n doer)
sheitha, elasticity (n)
sheithu, elastic (adj)
sheivana, vegetation (n)
sheivano, vegetate (v)
sheivanua, vegetator (n doer)
sheivota, vegetable (n)
sheivotuata, vegetarianism (n)
sheivotuatua, vegetarian (n doer)
shekaiauka, squawk (n)
shekaiauko, squawk (v)
shekaidana, igloo (n)
shekaina, cruise (n)
shekainaka, crusade (n)
shekainako, crusade (v)
shekainakua, crusader (n doer)
shekaino, cruise (v)
shekainua, cruiser (n doer)
shekaisha, smash (n)
shekaisho, smash (v)
shekaishua, smasher (n doer)
shekaita, ice (n)
shekaitaita, icicle (n)
shekaiteniuka, iceberg (n)
shekaitepelikua, icebreaker (n
    doer)
shekaitepelona, iceman (n)
shekaitepeloni, icemen (n pl)
shekaiteperenika, icebox (n)
shekaitiu, icily (adv)
shekaito, ice (v)
shekaitu, icy (adj)
shekaka, crack (n d:split)
shekakedaifa, crackpot (n)
shekaketiena, crackdown (n)
shekako, crack (v d:split)
shekakua, cracker (n doer d:split)
shekalaka, crackle (n)
shekalako, crackle (v)
shekalifota, crush (n)
shekalifoto, crush (v)
shekalifotua, crusher (n doer)
shekaluta, choice (n)
shekalutio, chose (v pa)
shekaluto, choose (v)
shekalutu, choosy (adj)
shekalutua, chooser (n doer)
shekama, strum (n)
shekamo, strum (v)
shekamua, strummer (n doer)
Shekanediuma, Scandium (n)
shekatho, strut (v)
shekaufu, stout (adj)
shekaupa, schism (n)
shekaupi, schism (n pl)
shekava, tussle (n)
shekavo, tussle (v)
shekeiata, ordination (n)

shekeiato, ordinate (v)
shekeika, squeak (n)
shekeikiu, squeakily (adv)
shekeiko, squeak (v)
shekeiku, squeaky (adj)
shekeitha, tuft (n)
shekeito, ordain (v)
shekekitarenagua, moviemaker (n doer)
shekelika, squeal (n)
shekeliko, squeal (v)
shekelipa, staple (n d:crimp)
shekelipo, staple (v d:crimp)
shekelipua, stapler (n doer d:crimp)
shekerisha, shim (n)
shekerisho, shim (v)
shekiaka, tuck (n)
shekiako, tuck (v)
shekiakua, tucker (n doer)
shekiata, stare (n)
shekiatho, scoot (v)
shekiathua, scooter (n doer)
shekiato, stare (v)
shekiauta, starkness (n)
shekiautu, stark (adj)
shekifu, indivisible (adj)
shekika, segment (n)
shekikena, mutiny (n)
shekikeno, mutiny (v)
shekikenua, mutineer (n doer)
shekiko, segment (v)
shekikueta, segmentation (n)
shekilopa, crimp (n)
shekilopo, crimp (v)
shekilopua, crimper (n doer)
shekilota, crinkle (n)
shekiloto, crinkle (v)
shekiota, squirt (n)
shekioto, squirt (v)
shekipa, individual (n)
shekipiu, individually (adv)
shekipo, individualize (v)
shekipu, individual (adj)
shekipueta, individualism (n)
shekipueta, individuality (n)
shekipuetu, individualistic (adj)
shekipuetua, individualist (n doer)
shekisha, piss (n)
shekisho, piss (v)
shekishua, pisser (n doer)
shekita, move (n)
shekitalita, movement (n)
shekitara, movie (n)
shekitha, match (n d:stick)
shekitheperenika, matchbox (n d:stickbox)
shekitiu, movably (adv)
shekito, move (v)
shekitu, movable (adj)
shekitua, mover (n doer)
shekiuko, skid (v)

shekoba, boat (n)
shekobo, boat (v)
shekobua, boater (n doer)
shekodaga, cottage (n)
shekoipa, slant (n)
shekoipo, slant (v)
shekoita, shot (n)
shekoraga, patch (n)
shekorago, patch (v)
shekoragu, patchy (adj)
shekoragua, patcher (n doer)
shekota, shoot (v)
Shekotelana, Scottish (n)
Shekotelanifa, Scotland (n)
shekotio, shot (v pa)
shekoto, shoot (v)
shekotua, shooter (n doer)
shekotuila, shootout (n)
shekubasha, squat (n)
shekubasho, squat (v)
shekubashua, squatter (n doer)
shekufebelaika, scuttlebutt (h)
shekufo, scuttle (v)
shekuka, stunt (n)
shekuko, stunt (v)
shekuniu, stunningly (adv)
shekuno, stun (v)
shelada, body (n)
sheladu, bodily (adj)
shelafa, commendation (n)
shelafo, commend (v)
shelaga, coarseness (n)
shelagiu, coarsely (adv)
shelagu, coarse (adj)
shelaiapa, splice (n)
shelaiapo, splice (v)
shelaibo, surround (v)
shelaifa, wariness (n)
shelaifiu, warily (adv)
shelaifu, wary (adj)
shelaiga, dragon (n)
shelaina, sway (n)
shelaino, sway (v)
shelaipa, martyr (n)
shelaipo, martyr (v)
shelaita, city (n)
shelaka, stealth (n)
shelakio, stole (v pa)
shelakiu, stealthily (adv)
shelako, steal (v)
shelaku, stealthy (adj)
shelakua, stealer (n doer)
shelanika, drawer (n d:compartment)
shelarepelorika, floorboard (n)
shelarina, floor (n)
shelarino, floor (v)
shelata, brink (n)
shelatha, swath (n)
shelatho, swathe (v)
shelauana, corsage (n)
shelauko, whisk (v d:swipe)
shelausho, slog (v)

shelaushua, slogger (n doer)
shelava, drag (n)
shelavo, drag (v)
shelefa, ware (n)
shelefekiafa, warehouse (n)
shelefekiafo, warehouse (v)
Shelefiana, Celsius (adj)
sheleiafiu, lavishly (adv)
sheleiafu, lavish (adj)
sheleifa, flag (n)
sheleifaripa, flagstaff (n)
sheleifaripi, flagstaves (n pl)
sheleifediloka, flagpole (n)
sheleifeleva, flagship (n)
sheleifo, flag (v)
sheleifua, flagger (n doer)
sheleina, lava (n)
sheleishuka, spasm (n)
sheleita, slyness (n)
sheleitha, sledge (n)
sheleitheganipa, sledgehammer (n)
sheleitho, sledge (v)
sheleitiu, slyly (adv)
sheleitu, sly (adj)
shelena, stillness (n d:calm)
sheleneidona, stillwater (n)
sheleniu, still (adv d:calm)
Sheleniuma, Selenium (n)
sheleno, still (v d:calm)
shelenu, still (adj d:calm)
shelesha, fish (n)
sheleshepelona, fisherman (n)
sheleshepeloni, fishermen (n pl)
sheleshetairoka, fishbowl (n)
sheleshi, fish (n pl)
sheleshi, fishes (n pl)
shelesho, fish (v)
sheleshu, fishy (adj)
sheleshua, fisher (n doer)
sheleshuata, fishery (n)
sheleta, stilt (n)
sheleto, stilt (v)
sheliaga, plunder (n)
sheliago, plunder (v)
sheliaka, split (n)
sheliakio, split (v pa)
sheliako, split (v)
sheliakua, splitter (n doer)
sheliama, swallow (n d:bird)
sheliasha, clinch (n)
sheliasho, clinch (v)
sheliashua, clincher (n doer)
sheliata, instrument (n)
sheliatu, instrumental (adj)
sheliatueta, instrumentation (n)
sheliba, ride (n)
shelibio, rode (v pa)
shelibo, ride (v)
shelibua, rider (n doer)
sheliesha, clench (n)
sheliesho, clench (v)
shelifa, ridge (n)

shelika, slice (n)
sheliko, slice (v)
shelikua, slicer (n doer)
shelina, slenderness (n)
shelinu, slender (adj)
shelipa, ballot (n)
shelira, flour (n)
shelisha, scissors (n)
shelisho, scissor (v)
shelithu, supple (adj)
sheliuna, splint (n)
sheliunaka, splinter (n)
sheliunako, splinter (v)
sheliusha, clutch (n d:grip)
sheliusho, clutch (v d:grip)
sheloata, slack (n d:loose)
sheloato, slack (v d:loose)
sheloatua, slacker (n doer
   d:loose)
sheloda, cheese (n)
shelodu, cheesy (adj)
shelofa, swerve (n)
shelofo, swerve (v)
sheloifita, deployment (n)
sheloifito, deploy (v)
sheloika, command (n)
sheloikata, commandment (n)
sheloiko, command (v)
sheloikua, commander (n doer)
sheloita, ploy (n)
shelorifa, impossibility (n)
shelorifiu, impossibly (adv)
shelorifu, impossible (adj)
shelota, cold (n d:temperature)
shelotu, cold (adj d:temperature)
shelotueta, coldness (n)
shelotwaku, coldest (adj)
shelotwelu, colder (adj)
sheluaka, mutation (n)
sheluakana, mutant (n)
sheluakiu, mutably (adv)
sheluako, mutate (v)
sheluaku, mutable (adj)
sheluakua, mutator (n doer)
sheluanita, compliance (n)
sheluanitapa, compliment (n)
sheluanitapiu, complimentarily
   (adv)
sheluanitapo, compliment (v)
sheluanitapu, complimentary
   (adj)
sheluanitapua, complimentor (n
   doer)
sheluanito, comply (v)
sheluanitu, compliant (adj)
sheluapa, haul (n)
sheluapo, haul (v)
sheluapua, hauler (n doer)
sheluata, ply (n)
sheluatefanina, plywood (n)
sheluato, ply (v)
sheluatu, pliable (adj)
sheluatua, plier (n doer)

shelubiu, facetiously (adv)
shelubu, facetious (adj)
sheluda, suddenness (n)
sheludiu, suddenly (adv)
sheludu, sudden (adj)
shelufa, coolness (n)
shelufita, coolant (n)
shelufiu, coolly (adv)
shelufo, cool (v)
shelufu, cool (adj)
shelufua, cooler (n doer)
shelufwaku, coolest (adj)
shelufwelu, cooler (adj)
sheluiata, swelter (n)
sheluiato, swelter (v)
sheluka, stay (n)
sheluketa, station (n)
sheluketo, station (v)
sheluketu, stationary (adj)
sheluko, stay (v)
shelukua, stayer (n doer)
shelumio, wept (v pa)
shelumo, weep (v)
shelumu, weepy (adj)
shelumua, weeper (n doer)
sheluna, sameness (n)
shelunika, bob (n)
sheluniko, bob (v)
shelunikua, bobber (n doer)
shelunu, same (adj)
shelupa, sled (n)
shelupo, sled (v)
shelusha, slide (n)
shelushio, slid (v pa)
shelusho, slide (v)
shelushua, slider (n doer)
shelutha, statistic (n)
sheluthu, statistical (adj)
shelutika, surrender (n)
shelutiko, surrender (v)
shelutikua, surrenderer (n doer)
shema, cleanliness (n)
shemafa, chance (n)
shemafo, chance (v)
shemafu, chance (adj)
shemalipa, snippet (n)
shemapa, snip (n)
shemapo, snip (v)
shematha, snoop (n)
shematho, snoop (v)
shemathu, snoopy (adj)
shemathua, snoop (n doer)
shemauka, snore (n)
shemauko, snore (v)
shemauta, snort (n)
shemauto, snort (v)
shemeifa, chancel (n)
shemeifo, chancel (v)
shemeifua, chancellor (n doer)
shemiaka, notoriety (n)
shemiakiu, notoriously (adv)
shemiaku, notorious (adj)
shemiapa, snout (n)

shemika, bough (n)
shemipa, snot (n)
shemipu, snotty (adj)
shemita, notice (n)
shemitaka, notification (n)
shemitako, notify (v)
shemitakua, notifier (n doer)
shemitiu, noticeably (adv)
shemito, notice (v)
shemitu, noticeable (adj)
shemiu, cleanly (adv)
shemiveila, cleanup (n)
shemo, clean (v)
shemoko, cleanse (v)
shemokua, cleanser (n doer)
shemonudaka, balloon (n)
shemonudako, balloon (v)
shemopa, baldness (n)
shemopo, bald (v)
shemopu, bald (adj)
shemota, balast (n)
shemotata, balance (n)
shemotato, balance (v)
shemoto, balast (v)
shemu, clean (adj)
shemua, cleaner (n doer)
shemuga, snooze (n)
shemugo, snooze (v)
shemugua, snoozer (n doer)
shemuna, tune (n)
shemuno, tune (v)
shemunua, tuner (n doer)
shena, fame (n)
shenago, flog (v)
shenaika, clot (n)
shenaiko, clot (v)
shenaina, lie (n d:deceit)
shenaino, lie (v d:deceit)
shenainua, liar (n doer d:deceit)
shenaita, spine (n)
shenaitemenu, spineless (adj)
shenaitha, clutter (n)
shenaitho, clutter (v)
shenaitu, spinal (adj)
shenaitu, spiny (adj)
shenaka, flick (n)
shenakata, flicker (n)
shenakato, flicker (v)
shenako, flick (v)
shenala, liaison (n)
shenalo, liaison (v)
shenapa, spin (n)
shenapana, spindle (n)
shenapio, spun (v pa)
shenapo, spin (v)
shenapua, spinner (n doer)
shenapunefa, spinoff (n)
shenata, spill (n)
shenatafena, spillover (n)
shenatepeliola, spillway (n)
shenatio, spilt (v pa)
shenato, spill (v)
shenatua, spiller (n doer)

shenatueta, spillage (n)
shenauka, snipe (n)
shenauko, snipe (v)
shenaukua, sniper (n doer)
shenaupa, snarl (n)
shenaupo, snarl (v)
sheneifa, flail (n)
sheneifo, flail (v)
sheneita, stash (n)
sheneito, stash (v)
sheneiuka, clog (n)
sheneiuko, clog (v)
sheneshu, since (adv/prep/conj)
sheniaka, skirmish (n)
sheniama, clump (n)
sheniamo, clump (v)
sheniamu, clumpy (adj)
shenianio, clung (v pa)
sheniano, cling (v)
shenianu, clingy (adj)
sheniatho, cleave (v d:stick)
shenifa, wire (n)
shenifemenu, wireless (adj)
shenifenepa, wiretap (n)
shenifenepo, wiretap (v)
shenifo, wire (v)
shenifu, wirey (adj)
shenika, tax (n)
sheniko, tax (v)
sheniku, taxable (adj)
shenikua, taxer (n doer)
shenikueta, taxation (n)
shenita, taxi (n)
shenitemoima, taxpayer (n)
shenito, taxi (v)
sheniu, famously (adv)
shenoika, stickiness (n d:adhere)
shenoikana, stickler (n)
shenoikio, stuck (v pa d:adhere)
shcnoiko, stick (v d:adhere)
shenoiku, sticky (adj d:adhere)
shenoikua, sticker (n doer
    d:adhere)
shenoipa, snatch (n)
shenoipo, snatch (v)
shenoipua, snatcher (n doer)
shenoito, spew (v)
shenorina, famine (n)
shenu, famous (adj)
shenuda, supper (n)
shenufa, cleverness (n)
shenufiu, cleverly (adv)
shenufu, clever (adj)
shenuka, ammunition (n)
shenusho, relish (v)
shepa, sub (n d:submarine)
shepaika, gripe (n)
shepaiko, gripe (v)
Shepaina, Spain (n)
Shepainana, Spanish (n)
shepelara, bank (n d:shore)
shepelaro, bank (v d:shore)
shepepefifa, scholarship (n)

shepepiu, scholarly (adv)
shepepu, scholastic (adj)
shepepua, scholar (n doer)
sheperufa, cost (n)
sheperufio, cost (v pa)
sheperufo, cost (v)
sheperufu, costly (adj)
shepesha, school (n)
shepeshebiuna, schoolboy (n)
shepeshedalisha, schoolteacher
    (n)
shepeshekelera, schoolgirl (n)
shepeshekiafa, schoolhouse (n)
shepeshelena, schoolmate (n)
shepesheluara, schoolchild (n)
shepesheluari, schoolchildren (n
    pl)
shepeshethautha, schoolyard (n)
shepeshevonuda, schoolbooks (n)
shepesho, school (v)
shepiofa, rant (n)
shepiofo, rant (v)
sheporako, spawn (v)
sheputereka, treadmill (n)
sheputha, tread (n)
sheputhio, trod (v pa)
sheputho, tread (v)
sheputo, stoke (v)
sheputua, stoker (n doer)
shera, hair (n)
sherabo, squander (v)
sherabu, squanderous (adj)
sherafa, miscellany (n)
sherafelika, mystique (n)
sherafelina, mystery (n)
sherafeliniu, mysteriously (adv)
sherafelino, mystify (v)
sherafelinu, mysterious (adj)
sherafelita, mysticism (n)
sherafelitu, mystical (adj)
sherafelitua, mystic (n doer)
sherafu, miscellaneous (adj)
sheraga, scab (n)
sheraiafa, scuff (n)
sheraiafo, scuff (v)
sheraiaka, slammer (n d:jail)
sheraiapa, scuffle (n)
sheraiapo, scuffle (v)
sheraika, scrub (n)
sheraiko, scrub (v)
sheraiku, scrubby (adj)
sheraikua, scrubber (n doer)
sheraila, whirl (n)
sheraileditapa, whirlpool (n)
sherailethelina, whirlwind (n)
sherailo, whirl (v)
sheraipa, slavery (n)
sheraipo, slave (v)
sheraipua, slave (n doer)
sheraisha, sketch (n)
sheraisho, sketch (v)
sheraishu, sketchy (adj)
sheraishua, sketcher (n doer)

sheraita, siege (n)
sheraitha, whir (n)
sheraitho, whir (v)
sheraito, siege (v)
sheraka, scale (n d:fish)
sherako, scale (v d:fish)
sherala, church (n)
sheralipa, college (n)
sheramo, slam (v d:hit)
sheramua, slammer (n doer d:hit)
sherana, room (n)
sheranelena, roommate (n)
sheraniepu, roomful (adj)
sherano, room (v)
sheranu, roomy (adj)
sherapa, slap (n)
sherapo, slap (v)
sherapua, slapper (n doer)
sherata, sharpness (n)
sheratana, sharp (n)
sherateshekota, sharpshooter (n)
sheratiu, sharply (adv)
sherato, sharpen (v)
sheratu, sharp (adj)
sheratua, sharpener (n doer)
sherava, struggle (n)
sheravo, struggle (v)
sherefa, bless (n)
shereferiafa, hairstyle (n)
sherefo, bless (v)
shereina, slime (n)
shereino, slime (v)
shereinu, slimy (adj)
shereipa, ensnarement (n d:trap)
shereipo, ensnare (v d:trap)
shereipo, snare (v d:trap)
shereipua, snare (n doer d:trap)
shereitha, myth (n)
shereithekuita, mythology (n)
shereithu, mythic (adj)
shereithu, mythical (adj)
sherela, surity (n)
shereleipa, hairpin (n)
shereliu, surely (adv)
sherelu, sure (adj)
sheremenu, hairless (adj)
sherepeleshua, hairdresser (n
    doer)
sherepeliufa, hairspray (n)
swhereroifa, hairline (n)
shereta, sit (n)
sheretika, hairdo (n)
sheretio, sat (v pa)
shereto, sit (v)
sheriaka, slat (n)
sheriako, slat (v)
sheriapa, sliver (n)
sheriasha, slowness (n)
sheriashetiena, slowdown (n)
sheriashiu, slowly (adv)
sheriasho, slow (v)
sheriashu, slow (adj)
sheriashwaku, slowest (adj)

sheriashwelu, slower (adj)
sheriata, slit (n)
sheriatio, slit (v pa)
sheriato, slit (v)
sheriauta, slaughter (n)
sheriautekiafa, slaughterhouse (n)
sheriauto, slaughter (v)
sheriavita, trek (n)
sheriavito, trek (v)
sheriavitua, trekker (n doer)
sheriepa, script (n)
sheriepata, scripture (n)
sheriepatu, scriptural (adj)
sheriepo, script (v)
sherifa, mist (n)
sherifiu, mistily (adv)
sherifo, mist (v)
sherifoka, description (n)
sherifokiu, descriptively (adv)
sherifoko, describe (v)
sherifoku, descriptive (adj)
sherifokua, descriptor (n doer)
sherifu, misty (adj)
sherifua, mister (n doer)
sheriga, scribble (n)
sherigo, scribble (v)
sherigua, scribe (n doer)
sherika, seat (n)
sherikadafika, seatbelt (n)
sheriko, seat (v)
sherilana, stipulation (n)
sherilano, stipulate (v)
sherilara, stipend (n)
sherioko, stow (v)
sheripo, slink (v)
sheripu, slinky (adj)
sherita, distribution (n)
sherito, distribute (v)
sheritua, distributor (n doer)
Sheriuma, Cerium (n)
sheriviena, nomenclature (n)
sheroigo, splurge (v)
sheroka, flux (n)
sheroko, flux (v)
sheru, hairy (adj)
sherudaisha, haircut (n)
sheruika, frivolity (n)
sheruikiu, frivolously (adv)
sheruiku, frivolous (adj)
sherupa, crumb (n)
sherupo, crumble (v)
sherupu, crumbly (adj)
sherutho, soothe (v)
sheshai, ok (interj)
sheshai, okay (interj)
Sheshiuma, Caesium (n)
shesho, okay (v)
sheshu, okay (adj)
shetafika, legibility (n)
shetafikiu, legibly (adv)
shetafiku, legible (adj)
shetafu, martial (adj)

shetaika, accident (n)
shetaikiu, accidentally (adv)
shetaikiu, accidently (adv)
shetaiku, accidental (adj)
shetaima, band (n d:strap)
shetaimaka, bandage (n)
shetaimako, bandage (v)
shetaimo, band (v d:strap)
shetaipa, title (n)
shetaipo, title (v)
shetaka, leger (n)
shetanita, dissonance (n)
shetanito, dissonate (v)
shetanitu, dissonant (adj)
shetata, mark (n)
shetatha, scale (n d:measure)
shetathara, scalar (n)
shetathu, scalable (adj d:measure)
shetatiena, markdown (n)
shetatiu, markedly (adv)
shetativeila, markup (n)
shetato, mark (v)
shetatu, marked (adj)
shetatua, marker (n doer)
shetauka, litigation (n)
shetauko, litigate (v)
shetaukua, litigator (n doer)
shetausha, endurance (n)
shetausho, endure (v)
shetefa, centigrade (n)
shetefu, centigrade (adj)
sheteifo, snuff (v)
shetela, door (n)
shetelediara, doorbell (n)
shetelegika, doorstep (n)
shetelemarifa, doormat (n)
shetelepeliola, doorway (n)
sheteleperoida, doorknob (n)
sheteropa, swipe (n)
sheteropo, swipe (v)
sheterupo, swoop (v)
sheterusha, swoon (n)
sheterusho, swoon (v)
shethipa, supply (n)
shethipeta, supplement (n)
shethipeto, supplement (v)
shethipetu, supplemental (adj)
shethipetu, supplementary (adj)
shethipetueta, supplementation (n)
shethipo, supply (v)
shethipua, supplier (n doer)
shetiaka, cage (n)
shetiakiu, cagily (adv)
shetiako, cage (v)
shetiaku, cagey (adj)
shetiakua, cager (n doer)
shetiba, text (n)
shetibo, text (v)
Shetironatiuma, Strontium (n)
shetisha, testimony (n)
shetisho, testify (v)

shetishueta, testimonial (n)
shetita, test (n)
shetitefuarema, testbed (n)
shetito, test (v)
shetitu, testy (adj)
shetitua, tester (n doer)
shetiuka, pit (n)
shetiukezhaila, pitfall (n)
shetiuko, pit (v)
shetivonuda, textbook (n)
shetobiufa, smolder (n)
shetobiufa, smoulder (n)
shetobiufo, smolder (v)
shetobiufo, smoulder (v)
shetoga, snow (n)
shetogebelashota, snowflake (n)
shetogedanita, snowmobile (n)
shetogeferipa, snowstorm (n)
shetogemashipa, snowball (n)
shetogemashipo, snowball (v)
shetogepelona, snowman (n)
shetogepeloni, snowmen (n pl)
shetogetafana, snowshoe (n)
shetogezhaila, snowfall (n)
shetogo, snow (v)
shetogu, snowy (adj)
shetoika, indentation (n)
shetoiko, indent (v)
Shetokolima, Stockholm (n)
shetolifa, smoke (n)
shetolifegeriata, smokestack (n)
shetolifemenu, smokeless (adj)
shetolifikoleta, smokescreen (n)
shetolifiu, smokily (adv)
shetolifo, smoke (v)
shetolifu, smoky (adj)
shetolifua, smoker (n doer)
shetorata, spatula (n)
shetorauka, spout (n)
shetorauko, spout (v)
shetorauta, spate (n d:flood)
shetoreipa, spat (n d:quarrel)
shetorina, spear (n)
shetorinekefito, spearhead (v)
shetorino, spear (v)
shetozha, smog (n)
shetozhu, smoggy (adj)
shetufa, enrichment (n)
shetufipa, rich (n)
shetufiu, richly (adv)
shetufo, enrich (v)
shetufu, rich (adj)
shetufua, enricher (n doer)
shetufueta, richness (n)
shetufweku, richest (adj)
shetufwelu, richer (adj)
shetuna, snub (n)
shetuno, snub (v)
shetutho, smother (v)
shevisha, secret (n)
shevishiu, secretively (adv)
shevishiu, secretly (adv)
shevishota, secrecy (n)

shevishu, secret (adj)
shevishu, secretive (adj)
shewenifu, during (prep)
shiafa, sanity (n)
shiafiu, sanely (adv)
shiafu, sane (adj)
shiaga, tangle (n)
shiago, tangle (v)
shiakebelieta, scapegoat (n)
shiala, touch (n)
shialebarafa, touchstone (n)
shialetiena, touchdown (n)
shialo, touch (v)
shialu, touchy (adj)
shiama, tangent (n)
shiamipa, tangible (n)
shiamipu, tangible (adj)
shiamiu, tangentially (adv)
shiamu, tangential (adj)
shiana, sanitation (n)
shiano, sanitize (v)
shianu, sanitary (adj)
shiapa, adept (n)
shiapu, adept (adj)
Shiarafa, Sierra (n)
shiarota, conquest (n)
shiaroto, conquer (v)
shiarotua, conqueror (n doer)
shiasha, fashion (n)
shiashiu, fashionably (adv)
shiasho, fashion (v)
shiashu, fashionable (adj)
Shiatala, Seattle (n)
shiauko, sap (v)
shiba, meal (n)
shibedauna, mealtime (n)
shibedaunu, mealtime (adj)
Shidunafa, Sydney (n)
shiemika, senate (n)
shiemikua, senator (n doer)
Shiena, Army (n)
shiga, spoke (n d:support)
shigemana, sigma (n)
shigo, spoke (v d:support)
shika, skill (n)
shikafo, mend (v)
shikaika, felony (n)
shikaikua, felon (n doer)
shikalipu, crude (adj)
shikapa, slash (n)
shikapo, slash (v)
shikapua, slasher (n doer)
shikasha, cause (n)
shikashipa, caution (n)
shikashipiu, cautiously (adv)
shikashipo, caution (v)
shikashipu, cautious (adj)
shikasho, cause (v)
shikashoka, casualty (n)
shikashokiu, casually (adv)
shikashoku, casual (adj)
shikashu, causal (adj)
shikelata, statute (n)

shikelatu, statutory (adj)
shikeleina, sea (n)
shikeleineberanifa, seacoast (n)
shikeleinebielika, seaport (n)
shikeleinefelarina, seafront (n)
shikeleinefuarema, seabed (n)
shikeleineidona, seawater (n)
shikeleinekelieka, seahawk (n)
shikeleinekiama, seagull (n)
shikeleinepasha, seafood (n)
shikeleinepeliola, seaway (n)
shikeleinepelona, seaman (n)
shikeleinepeloni, seamen (n pl)
shikeleineperelika, seagate (n)
shikeleineshoita, seaside (n)
shikeleineshoitu, seaside (adj)
shikeleinetheka, seashell (n)
shikeleinethiko, seafare (v)
shikeleinyuka, seaweed (n)
shikelivaga, meanness (n d:cruel)
shikelivagu, mean (adj d:cruel)
shikelivagweku, meanest (adj
  d:cruel)
shikelivagwelu, meaner (adj
  d:cruel)
shikepa, coordinate (n)
shikepeta, coordination (n)
shikepo, coordinate (v)
shikepua, coordinator (n doer)
shikerakio, slew (v pa)
shikerako, slay (v)
shikerakua, slayer (n doer)
shiketa, order (n)
shiketa, orderliness (n)
shiketariu, ordinarily (adv)
shiketaru, ordinary (adj)
shiketata, ordinance (n)
shiketo, order (v)
shiketu, orderly (adj)
shiketua, orderer (n doer)
shikiu, skillfully (adv)
shiko, skill (v)
shikofa, case (n d:investigation)
shikofelurita, caseload (n)
shikofo, case (v d:investigation)
shikoliaga, cruelty (n)
shikoliagiu, cruelly (adv)
shikoliagu, cruel (adj)
shikorika, slip (n)
shikoriko, slip (v)
shikoriku, slippery (adj)
shikorikueta, slippage (n)
shiku, skillful (adj)
shileka, structure (n)
shilekiu, structurally (adv)
shileko, structure (v)
shileku, structural (adj)
shilika, sap (n)
shilikapa, sapling (n)
Shilikona, Silicon (n)
Shilovera, Silver (n)
shilu, itty (adj)
shilufopa, picnic (n)

shilufopo, picnic (v)
shilufopua, picnicker (n doer)
shimana, gnosis (n)
shimanu, gnostic (adj)
shimena, tone (n d:quality)
shimeno, tone (v d:quality)
shimenua, toner (n doer
  d:quality)
shinafa, connection (n)
shinafata, connectivity (n)
shinaferepa, liability (n)
shinaferepiu, liably (adv)
shinaferepu, liable (adj)
shinafo, connect (v)
shinafua, connector (n doer)
shinefa, armor (n)
shinefo, armor (v)
shinena, arm (n)
shineno, arm (v)
shinenoka, army (n)
shinenua, armer (n doer)
shineta, stick (n d:twig, poke)
shinetio, stuck (v pa d:twig, poke)
shineto, stick (v d:twig, poke)
Shinokapora, Singapore (n)
Shinoshinata, Cincinnati (n)
shioba, hoop (n)
shiofa, texture (n)
shiofo, texturize (v)
shiofua, texturer (n doer)
shioiko, vanish (v)
shioikua, vanisher (n doer)
shiokeloina, textile (n)
Shiola, Seoul (n)
shiora, hook (n)
shioriveila, hookup (n)
shioro, hook (v)
shiorua, hooker (n doer)
shipaita, predicate (n)
shipaito, predicate (v)
shipaitueta, predicament (n)
shipalota, talk (n)
shipaloto, talk (v)
shipalotu, talkative (adj)
shipalotua, talker (n doer)
shipapa, rind (n)
shiparifa, stature (n)
shiparoka, statue (n)
shipefota, static (n)
shipefotu, static (adj)
shipega, fly (n d:insect)
shipena, map (n)
shipeno, map (v)
shiperata, parliament (n)
shiperatu, parliamentary (adj)
shiperena, iron (n d:clothes
  presser)
shipereno, iron (v d:clothes
  presser)
shipeta, state (n d:status)
shipetemenu, stateless (adj
  d:status)
shipetira, status (n)

shipoleka, difficulty (n)
shipolekiu, difficultly (adv)
shipoleko, difficult (v)
shipoleku, difficult (adj)
shiporaita, grind (n d:rip)
shiporaitio, ground (v pa d:rip)
shiporaito, grind (v d:rip)
shiporaitua, grinder (n doer d:rip)
shipuka, grip (n)
shipuko, grip (v)
shipukua, gripper (n doer)
shipusha, spell (n d:witchcraft)
shipushepaumubio, spellbound (v pa)
shipushepaumubo, spellbind (v)
Shiriafa, Syria (n)
Shiriana, Syrian (n)
shirofa, maturity (n)
shirofika, immaturity (n)
shirofikiu, immaturely (adv)
shirofiku, immature (adj)
shirofo, mature (v)
shirofu, mature (adj)
shirofueta, maturation (n)
shishi, these (pron)
shishu, these (adj)
shitho, lynch (v)
shiu, whew (interj)
shiuaifa, sizzle (n)
shiuaifo, sizzle (v)
shiufa, vanity (n)
shiufipa, availability (n)
shiufipu, available (adj)
shiufiu, vainly (adv)
shiufu, vain (adj)
shiuka, vaunt (n)
shiuko, vaunt (v)
shiuniku, lucent (adj)
shiuno, elucidate (v)
shiunu, lucid (adj)
shiupa, avail (n)
shiupo, avail (v)
shiusha, switch (n)
shiushafena, switchover (n)
shiushepelorika, switchboard (n)
shiusheperuta, switchblade (n)
shiusho, switch (v)
shiushu, switchy (adj)
shiushua, switcher (n doer)
shivata, knight (n)
shivato, knight (v)
shivatu, knightly (adj)
shiveshota, necessity (n)
shiveshotiu, necessarily (adv)
shiveshoto, necessitate (v)
shiveshotu, necessary (adj)
shoberautha, menstruation (n)
shoberautho, menstruate (v)
shoberauthu, menstrual (adj)
Shodiuma, Sodium (n)
shoidafika, satanism (n)
shoidafiko, satanize (v)
shoidafiku, satanic (adj)

shoidafikua, satanist (n doer)
Shoidaka, Satan (n)
shoifaka, manipulation (n)
shoifakiu, manipulatively (adv)
shoifako, manipulate (v)
shoifaku, manipulative (adj)
shoifakua, manipulator (n doer)
shoifana, mansion (n)
shoiga, shoulder (n)
shoigo, shoulder (v)
shoika, mandate (n)
shoikauto, manufacture (v)
shoikautua, manufacturer (n doer)
shoikelipa, manner (n)
shoiko, mandate (v)
shoiku, mandatory (adj)
shoikuka, manifest (n)
shoikuko, manifest (v)
shoipa, lick (n)
shoipo, lick (v)
shoipua, licker (n doer)
shoisha, manual (n)
shoishiu, manually (adv)
shoishu, manual (adj)
shoita, side (n)
shoitefeifa, sideshow (n)
shoitegelisha, sidestep (n)
shoitegelisho, sidestep (v)
shoitegethika, sidetrack (n)
shoitegethiko, sidetrack (v)
shoitepeliolu, sideways (adj/adv)
shoiteroifa, sideline (n)
shoiteroifo, sideline (v)
shoiterolata, sidebar (n)
shoiteshinena, sidearm (n)
shoitethiropa, sidekick (n)
shoito, side (v)
shoitua, sider (n doer)
shoizhoipa, sidewalk (n)
shokalita, start (n)
shokalitaka, startle (n)
shokalitako, startle (v)
shokalitiveila, startup (n)
shokalito, start (v)
shokalitua, starter (n doer)
shokenipa, optic (n)
shokenipiu, optically (adv)
shokenipu, optical (adj)
shokeroika, slope (n)
shokeroiko, slope (v)
shokiroka, seduction (n)
shokirokiu, seductively (adv)
shokiroko, seduce (v)
shokiroku, seductive (adj)
shokirokua, seducer (n doer)
shokiveva, thickness (n)
shokiveviu, thickly (adv)
shokivevo, thicken (v)
shokivevu, thick (adj)
shokivevua, thickener (n doer)
shola, human (n)
sholara, humanity (n)

sholarefifa, humankind (n)
sholarefifa, mankind (n)
sholariu, humanely (adv)
sholaru, humane (adj)
sholarua, humanitarian (n doer)
sholarueta, humanism (n)
sholaruetiu, humanistically (adv)
sholarueto, humanize (v)
sholaruetu, humanistic (adj)
sholaruetua, humanist (n doer)
sholebiorita, manpower (n)
sholenagu, manmade (adj)
sholiu, humanly (adv)
sholu, human (adj)
shomudoka, sentence (n d:words)
shopetoita, superstition (n)
shopetoitu, superstitious (adj)
shopiafita, deputization (n)
shopiata, deputy (n)
shopiato, deputize (v)
shopiatua, deputizer (n doer)
shoriana, stereo (n)
shorifa, sense (n)
shorifemeniu, senselessly (adv)
shorifemenu, senseless (adj)
shoriferepa, sensibility (n)
shoriferepiu, sensibly (adv)
shoriferepu, sensible (adj)
shorifita, sensation (n)
shorifitiu, sensationally (adv)
shorifitu, sensational (adj)
shorifitueta, sensationalism (n)
shorifitueto, sensationalize (v)
shorifiu, sensually (adv)
shorifiu, sensuously (adv)
shorifo, sense (v)
shorifopa, sensitivity (n)
shorifopiu, sensitively (adv)
shorifopo, sensitize (v)
shorifopu, sensitive (adj)
shorifu, sensual (adj)
shorifu, sensuous (adj)
shorifua, sensor (n doer)
shorifuanu, sensory (adj)
shorifuna, sensuality (n)
shoripu, rural (adj)
shoroda, containment (n)
shorodo, contain (v)
shorodua, container (n doer)
shoshi, those (pron)
shoshu, those (adj)
shotana, tin (n)
shotano, tin (v)
shoterana, grade (n)
shoteranaka, gradient (n)
shoterano, grade (v)
shoteranua, grader (n doer)
shotiafa, query (n)
shotiafo, query (v)
shotiata, quest (n)
shotiaterita, questionnaire (n)
shotiateta, question (n)
shotiatetiu, questionably (adv)

shotiateto, question (v)
shotiatetu, questionable (adj)
shotiatetua, questioner (n doer)
shotiato, bequest (v)
shotiufa, premier (n)
shotiufo, premier (v)
Shovieta, Soviet (n)
shuafa, female (n)
shuafo, effeminate (v)
shuafu, feminine (adj)
shuafua, feminist (n doer)
shuafueta, feminism (n)
shuaga, size (n)
shuagiu, sizably (adv)
shuago, size (v)
shuagu, sizable (adj)
shuagu, sizeable (adj)
shuagua, sizer (n doer)
shuaka, rank (n d:level, judge)
shuako, rank (v d:level, judge)
shuala, sol (n)
shualifa, solace (n)
shualifo, solace (v)
shualira, soul (n)
shualita, solemnity (n)
shualitu, solemn (adj)
shualo, solarize (v)
shualu, solar (adj)
shuana, theme (n)
shuapa, rake (n)
shuapo, rake (v)
shuapua, raker (n doer)
shuasha, science (n)
shuashiu, scientifically (adv)
shuashu, scientific (adj)
shuashua, scientist (n doer)
shuata, case (n d:container)
shuato, encase (v d:container)
shuausha, lesbian (n)
Shudavtula, Saturday (n)
shudolifa, protection (n)
shudolifiu, protectively (adv)
shudolifo, protect (v)
shudolifu, protective (adj)
shudolifua, protectionist (n doer)
shudolifu, protector (n doer)
shudolifueta, protectionism (n)
shuela, nearness (n)
shueliu, nearly (adv)
shuelo, near (v)
shuelu, near (adj)
shuelu, near (adj/adv/prep)
shueluvu, nearby (adj/adv)
shuelwaku, nearest (adj)
shuelwelu, nearer (adj)
shuesha, girlfriend (n)
shufa, lab (n)
shufetana, sequel (n)
shufiefa, bobcat (n)
shufiko, stump (v d:befuddle)
shufipa, stumble (n)
shufipo, stumble (v)
shufita, sequence (n)

shufitiu, sequentially (adv)
shufito, sequence (v)
shufitu, sequential (adj)
shufitua, sequencer (n doer)
shuiafo, shoo (v)
shuiana, icon (n)
shuiano, iconify (v)
Shuidafa, Sweden (n)
Shuidana, Swedish (n)
shuika, scale (n d:climb)
shuiko, scale (v d:climb)
shuisha, weight (n)
Shuishana, Swiss (n)
shuishemena, weightlessness (n)
shuishemenu, weightless (adj)
Shuisherolafa, Switzerland (n)
shuisho, weigh (v)   ǀ
shuishoko, weight (v)
shuishu, weighty (adj)
shuka, lens (n)
shukeraika, sling (n)
shukeraikeshekoita, slingshot (n)
shukeraikio, slung (v pa)
shukeraiko, sling (v)
shukeraikua, slinger (n doer)
shukerana, daze (n)
shukeranata, dazzle (n)
shukeranato, dazzle (v)
shukeranatua, dazzler (n doer)
shukerano, daze (v)
shukerifo, shimmer (v)
shuko, lens (v)
shulara, solo (n)
shularo, solo (v)
shularu, solo (adj)
shularua, soloist (n doer)
shulina, ounce (n)
shulita, foundary (n d:pour mold)
shulito, found (v d:pour mold)
Shulofura, Sulfur (n)
shumifa, vantage (n)
shumolifa, branch (n)
shumolifo, branch (v)
shumolifua, brancher (n doer)
shuna, comma (n)
shupa, find (n)
shupata, foundation (n d:begin)
shupato, found (v d:begin)
shupatua, founder (n doer d:begin)
shupereifa, cloak (n)
shupereifo, cloak (v)
shuperiko, thrash (v)
shuperikua, thrasher (n doer)
shupio, found (v pa)
shupo, find (v)
shupua, finder (n doer)
shushuta, solicitation (n)
shushuto, solicite (v)
shushutua, solicitor (n doer)
shut, zero (num 0 card)
shutai-, nul (num 0 pref)
shutaila, null (n)

shutailo, nullify (v)
shutailu, null (adj)
shutata, soccer (n)
shuterena, term (n d:timespan)
shuteth, zeroth (num 0 ord)
shutha, bean (n)
shutho, bean (v)
shuva, labor (n)
shuvashota, laboratory (n)
shuvo, labor (v)
shuvua, laborer (n doer)
shwaka, scat (interj)
shwi, whee (interj)
tafana, shoe (n)
tafanagua, shoemaker (n doer)
tafanefoina, shoelace (n)
tafanekeroima, shoehorn (n)
tafanekeroimo, shoehorn (v)
tafaneligula, shoestring (n)
tafanemoitha, shoeshine (n)
tafano, shoe (v)
tafika, culture (n)
tafiku, cultural (adj)
tafipa, golf (n)
tafipo, golf (v)
tafipua, golfer (n doer)
tafita, tote (n)
tafito, tote (v)
tagiana, alcoholic (n)
tagianueta, alcoholism (n)
tagina, alcohol (n)
taginu, alcoholic (adj)
tahofita, dehydration (n)
tahofito, dehydrate (v)
taiana, wobble (n)
taiano, wobble (v)
taianua, wobbler (n doer)
taibitiu, overtly (adv)
taibitu, overt (adj)
taida, club (n d:group)
taidekiafa, clubhouse (n)
taido, club (v d:group)
Taifa, Thai (n)
taifaupa, garble (n)
taifaupo, garble (v)
taifota, point (n)
taifotemenu, pointless (adj)
taifotiu, pointily (adv)
taifoto, point (v)
taifotu, pointy (adj)
taifotua, pointer (n doer)
taiga, garbage (n)
taigaga, tangle (n)
taigago, tangle (v)
taigagua, tangler (n doer)
taigo, garbage (v)
taigu, garbage (adj)
taikata, matrix (n)
Tailanuda, Thailand (n)
taina, stair (n)
tainavupa, stairwell (n)
tainepeliola, stairway (n)
taineshuata, staircase (n)

tairoka, bowl (n d:ball)
tairoko, bowl (v d:ball)
tairokua, bowler (n doer d:ball)
Taiwafa, Taiwan (n)
takalana, hallelujah (interj)
takiola, cocaine (n)
talata, datum (n)
talati, data (n pl)
talatuviasha, database (n)
talezhupa, souvenir (n)
taliguta, syllable (n)
talika, prince (n)
taliku, princely (adj)
talipa, corridor (n)
talisha, speech (n d:verbosity)
talishemenu, speechless (adj)
talishio, spoke (v pa d:verbosity)
talishiu, speakably (adv
    d:verbosity)
talisho, speak (v d:verbosity)
talishu, speakable (adj
    d:verbosity)
talishua, speaker (n doer
    d:verbosity)
talishua, spokesman (n doer)
talishua, spokesperson (n doer)
talishua, spokeswoman (n doer)
talitha, princess (n)
talithu, princessly (adj)
talofa, basket (n)
talofeshemonida, basketball (n)
taluna, memory (n)
talunana, memoir (n)
talunara, memorial (n)
talunaro, memorialize (v)
taluniu, memorably (adv)
taluno, memorize (v)
talunu, memorable (adj)
tama, fun (n)
tamafa, stool (n d:chair)
tamiama, funniness (n)
tamiamu, funny (adj)
tamiamweku, funniest (adj)
tamiamwelu, funnier (adj)
Tamipafa, Tampa (n)
tamu, fun (adj)
tanifa, tot (n)
tanifana, toddle (n)
tanifano, toddle (v)
tanifanua, toddler (n doer)
Tanitaluma, Tantalum (n)
tanuata, diamond (n)
Taraka, Tarak (n)
tarika, wax (n)
tariko, wax (v)
tariku, waxy (adj)
tarikua, waxer (n doer)
tarina, border (n)
tarineroifa, borderline (n)
tarino, border (v)
tarishoka, legislature (n)
taritha, throw (n)
tarithevaka, throwback (n)

tarithio, threw (v pa)
taritho, throw (v)
tarithua, thrower (n doer)
tarofa, hinge (n)
tarofo, hinge (v)
tarugafena, hangover (n)
tarugaga, dangle (n)
tarugago, dangle (v)
tarugio, hung (v pa)
tarugiveila, hangup (n)
tarugo, hang (v)
tarugua, hanger (n doer)
taruguila, hangout (n)
tash, hundred (num 100 card)
tasheth, hundredth (num 100 ord)
tashia-, hecto- (num 100 pref)
tashika, legislation (n)
tashikela, office (n)
tashikelefifua, officialdom (n
    doer)
tashikelethorithua, officeholder
    (n doer)
tashikeliu, officially (adv)
tashikelo, officiate (v)
tashikelu, official (adj)
tashikelua, officer (n doer)
tashikelua, official (n doer)
tashikiu, legislatively (adv)
tashiko, legislate (v)
tashiku, legislative (adj)
tashikua, legislator (n doer)
tathiata, casserole (n)
tathita, coffin (n)
tatorifa, offense (n)
tatorifiu, offensively (adv)
tatorifo, offend (v)
tatorifu, offensive (adj)
tatorifua, offender (n doer)
tatorifueta, offensiveness (n)
taufa, duck (n d:bird)
taufiata, cartilage (n)
tauga, liquid (n)
taugara, liquor (n)
taugaro, liquor (v)
taugata, liquidity (n)
taugo, liquidate (v)
taugueta, liquidation (n)
tauiana, weather (n)
tauianefeliofo, weatherproof (v)
tauianefeliufu, weatherproof (adj)
tauianepelona, weatherman (n)
tauianepeloni, weathermen (n pl)
tauiano, weather (v)
tauita, canopy (n)
tauka, stop (n)
taukafena, stopover (n)
taukedepa, dogma (n)
taukedepu, dogmatic (adj)
taukefatha, stopgap (n)
taukefathu, stopgap (adj)
taukefeluana, stoplight (n)
taukeluka, stopwatch (n)
tauko, stop (v)

taukua, stopper (n doer)
taukueta, stoppage (n)
taulika, circumference (n)
tauliku, circumferent (adj)
tauna, tau (n)
taupa, sheet (n)
tausha, durability (n)
taushiu, durably (adv)
taushota, duration (n)
taushu, durable (adj)
tautiaka, calamity (n)
tautiaku, calamitous (adj)
tava, triteness (n)
tavada, locomotion (n)
tavadua, locomotive (n doer)
taviu, tritely (adv)
tavu, trite (adj)
tavuka, adult (n)
tavuko, adulterate (v)
tavukofifa, adulthood (n)
tavuku, adult (adj)
tavukua, adulterer (n doer)
tazha, jog (n)
tazhaga, dodge (n)
tazhago, dodge (v)
tazhagu, dodgy (adj)
tazho, jog (v)
tazhua, jogger (n doer)
teba, rate (n)
tebika, ratification (n)
tebiko, ratify (v)
tebo, rate (v)
tefa, ad (n)
tefeika, addiction (n)
tefeiko, addict (v)
tefeiku, addictive (adj)
tefeikua, addict (n doer)
tefelirokiu, adjacently (adv)
tefeliroku, adjacent (adj)
tefelovita, administration (n)
tefelovito, administer (v)
tefelovitu, administrative (adj)
tefelovitua, administrator (n
    doer)
Tefenedala, December (n)
teferapa, development (n)
teferapo, develop (v)
teferapua, developer (n doer)
tefiata, adverb (n)
tefidota, advertisement (n)
tefidotiu, adversarially (adv)
tefidoto, advertise (v)
tefidotu, adversarial (adj)
tefidotua, advertiser (n doer)
tefika, offer (n)
tefiko, offer (v)
tefipesha, adjustment (n)
tefipesho, adjust (v)
tefipeshu, adjustable (adj)
tefipeshua, adjuster (n doer)
tefita, addition (n)
tefitaka, additive (n)
tefitema, add-on (n)

tefithaipa, advocation (n)
tefithaipo, advocate (v)
tefithaipua, advocate (n doer)
tefitiu, additionally (adv)
tefito, add (v)
tefitu, additional (adj)
tefitua, adder (n doer)
tefituaka, adhesive (n)
tefituapa, adherence (n)
tefituapo, adhere (v)
tefituapua, adherent (n doer)
tefituata, adhesion (n)
tefituatu, adhesive (adj)
tefotiropa, adjective (n)
tefudaida, adequation (n)
tefudaidiu, adequately (adv)
tefudaidu, adequate (adj)
tega, dig (n)
tegenata, degree (n)
tegeta, digit (n)
tegetiu, digitally (adv)
tegeto, digitize (v)
tegetu, digital (adj)
tegio, dug (v pa)
tegiouila, dugout (n)
tego, dig (v)
tegua, digger (n doer)
teia, T (let sng)
teiasha, drift (n)
teiashefanina, driftwood (n)
teiasho, drift (v)
teiashua, drifter (n doer)
teiata, tee (n)
teiatito, teeter (v)
teiato, tee (v)
teifa, cue (n)
teifita, temp (n)
teifitiu, temporarily (adv)
teifitu, temporary (adj)
teifo, cue (v)
teiga, lance (n)
teigo, lance (v)
teigua, lancer (n doer)
teihem, Number_1e2556
teika, stall (n d:wait)
teiko, stall (v d:wait)
teikua, staller (n doer d:wait)
teili, Ts (let pl)
teilota, contemporary (n)
teimu, keen (adj)
teisha, peach (n)
teishu, peachy (adj)
teita, tempo (n)
teitha, pessimism (n)
teithu, pessimistic (adj)
teitu, temporal (adj)
tekanifota, adjournment (n)
tekanifoto, adjourn (v)
Tekerafa, Tehran (n)
Tekonetiuma, Technetium (n)
telava, balm (n)
teleshanu, through
  (adj/adv/prep)

teleshanuilu, throughout
  (prep/adv)
teleshanuvuta, throughput (n)
teliforeta, interest (n d:desire)
teliforetiu, interestingly (adv
  d:desire)
teliforeto, interest (v d:desire)
teligata, throttle (n)
teligato, throttle (v)
telira, trill (n)
teliro, trill (v)
telirua, triller (n doer)
telita, peel (n)
telitha, hatch (n d:door)
telithevaka, hatchback (n)
telito, peel (v)
telitua, peeler (n doer)
telorika, forge (n)
teloriko, forge (v)
telorikua, forger (n doer)
telorikueta, forgery (n)
teluama, admiration (n)
teluamiu, admirably (adv)
teluamo, admire (v)
teluamu, admirable (adj)
teluamua, admirer (n doer)
Teluriuma, Tellurium (n)
temudala, garden (n)
temudalo, garden (v)
temudalua, gardener (n doer)
Teneshifa, Tennessee (n)
tenifa, insula (n)
tenifata, insularity (n)
tenifiu, insularly (adv)
tenifu, insular (adj)
tenifueta, insulation (n)
tenifuetiu, insulatively (adv)
tenifueto, insulate (v)
tenifuetu, insulative (adj)
tenifuetua, insulator (n doer)
tenika, admission (n)
tenikiu, admissibly (adv)
teniko, admit (v)
teniku, admissible (adj)
tenira, island (n)
tenira, isle (n)
tenirua, islander (n doer)
terabira, tradition (n)
terabiriu, traditionally (adv)
terabiru, traditional (adj)
terabirua, traditionalist (n doer)
terabiuka, traitor (n)
terafipa, archive (n)
terafipo, archive (v)
terafipu, archival (adj)
terafipua, archivist (n doer)
terafita, job (n)
terafitemena, joblessness (n)
terafitemenu, jobless (adj)
teraga, batch (n)
teraifa, fiend (n)
teraifiu, fiendishly (adv)
teraifu, fiendish (adj)

teraifuto, jab (v)
teraifutua, jabber (n doer)
teraipa, flap (n)
teraipo, flap (v)
teraipua, flapper (n doer)
teraisha, straightness (n)
teraishevoanaushiu,
  straightforwardly (adv)
teraishevoanaushu,
  straightforward (adj)
teraisho, straighten (v)
teraishu, straight (adj)
teraitha, strait (n)
teraithebifita, straitjacket (n)
teraka, stage (n)
terako, stage (v)
terala, arc (n)
teralemaka, matron (n)
teralemalisha, matriarch (n)
teralemalishu, matriarchal (adj)
teralemeta, monarchy (n)
teralemetha, monarch (n)
teralemetua, monarchist (n doer)
teralita, arch (n)
teralito, arch (v)
teralitua, archer (n doer)
teralo, arc (v)
teralofika, architecture (n)
teralofiko, architect (v)
teralofiku, architectural (adj)
teralofikua, architect (n doer)
terama, foam (n)
teramana, lather (n d:soap)
teramano, lather (v d:soap)
teramiu, foamily (adv)
teramo, foam (v)
teramu, foamy (adj)
teramua, foamer (n doer)
teranika, battery (n d:storage)
teranita, control (n)
teranito, control (v)
teranitu, controllable (adj)
teranitua, controller (n doer)
teratha, gray (n)
teratha, grey (n)
terathegauka, greyhound (n)
teratheiku, greyish (adj)
terathu, gray (adj)
terathu, grey (adj)
teraufa, blouse (n)
terauka, crown (n)
terauko, crown (v)
terauna, corona (n)
teraunata, coronation (n)
teraunato, coronate (v)
teraunatu, coronate (adj)
terava, fold (n)
teravo, fold (v)
teravua, folder (n doer)
tereba, pull (n)
terebana, pulley (n)
terebevaka, pullback (n)
terebo, pull (v)

terebua, puller (n doer)
terebuila, pullout (n)
terefika, standard (n)
terefiko, standardize (v)
terefikueta, standardization (n)
terefito, row (v d:paddle)
terefitua, rower (n doer d:paddle)
terefudava, boondocks (n)
tereiaka, academy (n)
tereiakani, academics (n pl)
tereiakiu, academically (adv)
tereiaku, academic (adj)
tereifa, grocery (n)
tereifua, grocer (n doer)
tereiga, castle (n)
tereigo, castle (v)
tereika, desertion (n d:flee)
tereiko, desert (v d:flee)
tereikua, deserter (n doer d:flee)
tereilafa, blossom (n)
tereilafo, blossom (v)
tereilota, climate (n)
tereima, client (n)
tereipa, climb (n)
tereipo, climb (v)
tereipua, climber (n doer)
tereisha, clinic (n)
tereishu, clinical (adj)
tereitho, rove (v)
tereithua, rover (n doer)
tereiuko, welch (v)
tereiuko, welsh (v)
tereiukua, welcher (n doer)
tereiukua, welsher (n doer)
terelatoita, boomerang (n)
terelevuta, standby (n)
terelevutu, standby (adj)
terelifa, sale (n)
terelifio, sold (v pa)
terelifo, sell (v)
terelifu, saleable (adj)
terelifua, salesman (n doer)
terelifua, salesperson (n doer)
terelifua, seller (n doer)
terelifuanefifa, salesmanship (n)
terelifuanefifa, salespersonship
    (n)
terelifuila, sellout (n)
terelisha, road (n)
terelishebelira, roadblock (n)
terelisheteifa, roadshow (n)
terelishekiafa, roadhouse (n)
terelishepeliola, roadway (n)
terelishoita, roadside (n)
terelita, stand (n)
terelitaifota, standpoint (n)
tereliteshelena, standstill (n)
terelitio, stood (v pa)
terelitiveila, standup (n)
terelitiveilu, standup (adj)
terelito, stand (v)
terelituila, standout (n)
terelitunefa, standoff (n)

terelofita, salary (n)
terema, reliability (n)
teremipa, reliance (n)
teremipu, reliant (adj)
teremiu, reliably (adv)
teremo, rely (v)
teremu, reliable (adj)
terepa, stance (n)
teretesha, reef (n)
teriafa, glow (n)
teriafo, glow (v)
teriafu, glowy (adj)
teriaka, rectification (n)
teriako, rectify (v)
teriakua, rectifier (n doer)
teriama, uterus (n)
teriana, staple (n d:commodity)
teriapa, chew (n)
teriapo, chew (v)
teriapua, chewer (n doer)
teriashekerifa, straightedge (n)
teriato, greet (v)
teriaufa, drought (n)
teriauika, rectum (n)
teriauikiu, rectally (adv)
teriauiku, rectal (adj)
teriausho, lurk (v)
teriaushua, lurker (n doer)
teriefa, bulletin (n)
terifa, neatness (n)
terifita, sinus (n)
terifitu, sinus (adj)
terifiu, neatly (adv)
terifu, neat (adj)
terika, key (n)
terikatuka, keystroke (n)
terikebanifa, keypad (n)
terikebarafa, keystone (n)
terikelialita, keyword (n)
terikelinuna, keynote (n)
terikemenu, keyless (adj)
teriko, key (v)
terikotha, keyhole (n)
terila, tone (n d:music)
terilana, scant (n)
terilaniu, scantily (adv)
terilano, scant (v)
terilanu, scanty (adj)
teriloko, train (v d:conditioning)
teriloku, trainable (adj
    d:conditioning)
terilokua, trainer (n doer
    d:conditioning)
terilokuina, trainee (n)
terilosha, intonation (n)
terilueta, tonality (n)
teriluko, scavenge (v)
terilukua, scavenger (n doer)
terina, pun (n)
terinota, tolerance (n)
terinoto, tolerate (v)
terinotu, tolerable (adj)
terinotu, tolerant (adj)

terinotueta, toleration (n)
terioripa, blooper (n)
terioripo, bloop (v)
terioripua, blooper (n doer)
teripata, wheat (n)
teripelorika, keyboard (n)
terishepa, dignity (n)
terishepo, dignify (v)
terishepua, dignitary (n doer)
terishoila, thesaurus (n)
terishoili, thesaurii (n pl)
terita, ladder (n)
teritha, wheel (n)
terithata, wheelie (n)
terithekelenuda, wheelchair (n)
terithekelenudo, wheelchair (v)
teritho, wheel (v)
terithua, wheeler (n doer)
teriuata, groove (n)
teriuato, groove (v)
teriuatu, groovy (adj)
teriufa, dryness (n)
teriufenolitha, drywall (n)
teriufo, dry (v)
teriufu, dry (adj)
teriufua, drier (n doer)
teriufua, dryer (n doer)
teriufweku, driest (adj)
teriufwelu, drier (adj)
teriugo, till (v)
teriugua, tiller (n doer)
teriuka, clout (n)
teriuko, clout (v)
teriukua, clouter (n doer)
teriuma, hive (n d:colony)
teriuna, bloom (n)
teriuno, bloom (v)
teriunua, bloomer (n doer)
teriupa, cheapness (n)
teriupiu, cheaply (adv)
teriupo, cheapen (v)
teriupu, cheap (adj)
teriupwaku, cheapest (adj)
teriupwelu, cheaper (adj)
teriusho, lurch (v)
teriutesho, parch (v)
teriuto, lean (v d:tilt)
teriutua, leaner (n doer d:tilt)
teriuzhaila, drizzle (n)
teriuzhailo, drizzle (v)
Teroba, EhoMonth08 (n)
Terobiuma, Terbium (n)
teroga, toughness (n)
terogo, toughen (v)
terogu, tough (adj)
terogwaku, toughest (adj)
terogwelu, tougher (adj)
teroiafo, wilt (v)
teroiaka, spar (n)
teroiako, spar (v)
teroika, spark (n)
teroikata, sparkle (n)
teroikato, sparkle (v)

teroikatu, sparkly (adj)
teroiko, spark (v)
teroiku, sparky (adj)
teroikua, sparker (n doer)
teroipa, flop (n)
teroipiu, floppily (adv)
teroipo, flop (v)
teroipu, floppy (adj)
teroipua, flopper (n doer)
teroita, salad (n)
terolifa, lesson (n)
terolita, husband (n)
teropa, wipe (n)
teropo, wipe (v)
teropua, wiper (n doer)
teropuila, wipeout (n)
terosha, chalk (n)
teroshepelorika, chalkboard (n)
terosho, chalk (v)
terotaka, widower (n)
terotakao, widowered (v prp)
terotako, widower (v)
terovata, husbandry (n)
teruatha, glove (n)
teruatho, glove (v)
terufipa, blame (n)
terufipo, blame (v)
teruifa, relay (n d:transceive)
teruita, premium (n)
teruitu, premium (adj)
teruka, cheat (n)
teruko, cheat (v)
terukua, cheater (n doer)
terulifo, furl (v)
terulisha, print (n)
terulisho, print (v)
terulishua, printer (n doer)
terusha, rung (n d:step)
teruta, desk (n)
terutauba, desktop (n)
tesh, their (pron 3rd fem-masc pl pos sub)
tesh, theirs (pron 3rd fem-masc pl pos obj)
teshaba, religion (n)
teshabiu, religiously (adv)
teshabu, religious (adj)
teshadei, that (pron)
teshadu, that (adj)
Teshamela, Juniper (n)
teshanu, though (adv/conj)
tesharafa, sister (n)
tesharafifa, sisterhood (n)
tesharafu, sisterly (adj)
tesharika, rock (n d:stone)
teshariku, rocky (adj d:stone)
Tesharolitona, Charleston (n)
teshatisha, tooth (n)
teshatishederafipa, toothpaste (n)
teshatishedotisha, toothpick (n)
teshatishekelusha, toothbrush (n)
teshatishi, teeth (n pl)
teshatisho, tooth (v)

teshatishu, toothy (adj)
Teshekoshelovaka, Czechoslovakia (n)
Tesherinobila, Chernobyl
teshfar, themselves (pron 3rd fem-masc pl pos)
Teshikafa, Texas (n)
Teshikaga, Chicago (n)
Teshila, Chile (n)
Teshinafa, China (n)
Teshinasha, Chinese (n)
teshomu, than (conj/prep)
teshufa, yeast (n)
teshufika, fermentation (n)
teshufiko, ferment (v)
teshufito, trounce (v)
teshunei, this (pron)
teshunu, this (adj)
teshutasho, teethe (v)
tethi, they (pron 3rd fem-masc pl sub)
tethin, them (pron 3rd fem-masc pl obj)
tevifoka, advantage (n)
tevifoku, advantageous (adj)
tezhigo, delve (v)
thadifa, nail (n d:metal pin)
thadifo, nail (v d:metal pin)
thafa, bread (n)
thafika, rent (n)
thafikala, rental (n)
thafiko, rent (v)
thafiku, rental (adj)
thafikua, renter (n doer)
thafipa, raft (n d:boat)
thafipo, raft (v d:boat)
thafipua, rafter (n doer d:boat)
thafita, enquiry (n)
thafita, inquiry (n)
thafito, enquire (v)
thafito, inquire (v)
thafitua, inquirer (n doer)
thafo, bread (v)
thagata, rafter (n d:roof support)
thaibara, vocabulary (n)
thaifa, chat (n)
thaifika, devotion (n)
thaifikana, devotional (n)
thaifikiu, devoutly (adv)
thaifiko, devote (v)
thaifiku, devout (adj)
thaifikua, devotee (n doer)
thaifo, chat (v)
thaifu, chatty (adj)
thaifua, chatter (n doer)
thaika, vote (n)
thaiko, vote (v)
thaikua, voter (n doer)
thaila, pale (n d:spike)
thaima, veto (n)
thaimo, veto (v)
thaina, fate (n)
thainiu, fatefully (adv)

thainu, fateful (adj)
thaipa, voice (n)
thaipaka, vocation (n)
thaipaku, vocational (adj)
thaipana, vocal (n)
thaipanu, vocal (adj)
thaipanua, vocalist (n doer)
thaipelipa, voicemail (n)
thaipo, voice (v)
thaisho, chafe (v)
thaita, bid (n)
thaitha, hash (n d:cut food)
thaithata, hatchet (n)
thaithiko, hatch (v d:create)
thaithikua, hatcher (n doer d:create)
thaithikueta, hatchery (n)
thaitho, hash (v d:cut food)
thaitio, bade (v pa)
thaitio, bid (v pa)
thaito, bid (v)
thaitua, bidder (n doer)
thalata, apple (n)
thalifa, gel (n)
thalifo, gel (v)
thalima, jam (n d:food)
thalipa, mast (n)
thalipekefita, masthead (n)
thalipo, mast (v)
Thaliuma, Thallium (n)
thama, brown (n)
thamo, brown (v)
thamu, brown (adj)
thanita, shack (n)
thanito, shack (v)
thanubera, sample (n)
thanubero, sample (v)
thanuberua, sampler (n doer)
thapa, hood (n)
thapo, hood (v)
thariata, veracity (n)
thariatu, veracious (adj)
thariba, neck (n)
tharibefoina, necklace (n)
tharibegelesha, necktie (n)
tharibo, neck (v)
tharifa, verse (n)
tharifeta, version (n)
tharifo, verse (v)
tharifoka, converse (n)
tharifokiu, conversely (adv)
tharifota, diversity (n)
tharifoteta, diversification (n)
tharifoto, diversify (v)
tharifotu, diverse (adj)
tharifotua, diversifier (n doer)
thariga, slang (n)
thariluka, convertible (n)
tharima, mane (n)
tharina, janitor (n)
tharishoka, convert (n)
tharita, adversity (n)
tharitha, shackle (n)

tharitho, shackle (v)
tharitiu, adversely (adv)
tharitu, adverse (adj)
tharitua, adversary (n doer)
tharo, spell (v d:character)
tharoika, verification (n)
tharoikiu, verifiably (adv)
tharoiko, verify (v)
tharoiku, verifiable (adj)
tharoita, verity (n)
tharoitu, veritable (adj)
tharomemu, versus (prep)
tharudeika, verdict (n)
thasha, toss (n)
thashika, ratchet (n)
thashiko, ratchet (v)
thashipa, gossip (n)
thashipo, gossip (v)
thashipu, gossipy (adj)
thashipua, gossiper (n doer)
thasho, toss (v)
thashua, tosser (n doer)
thatha, shuffle (n)
thatho, shuffle (v)
thaufa, reign (n)
thaufika, regime (n)
thaufo, reign (v)
thauka, acre (n)
thauna, warmth (n)
thauniu, warmly (adv)
thauniveila, warmup (n)
thauniveilu, warmup (adj)
thauno, warm (v)
thaunu, warm (adj)
thaupa, curiosity (n)
thaupiu, curiously (adv)
thaupu, curious (adj)
thautara, pharmacy (n)
thautarifa, pharmaceutical (n)
thautaru, pharmaceutical (adj)
thautha, yard (n d:field)
thava, gorge (n)
thaviu, gorgeously (adv)
thavo, gorge (v)
thavu, gorgeous (adj)
theia, Th (let sng)
theiana, son (n)
theifa, own (n)
theififa, ownership (n)
theifo, own (v)
theifu, own (adj)
theifua, owner (n doer)
theiguta, muffin (n)
theihem, Number_1e2856
theika, mask (n)
theikata, mascot (n)
theiko, mask (v)
theila, hay (n)
theili, Ths (let pl)
theima, shawl (n)
theinalipa, strawberry (n)
theiosha, mesh (n)
theiosho, mesh (v)

theipa, nip (n)
theipafa, nipple (n)
theipo, nip (v)
theipu, nippy (adj)
theiripa, shrimp (n)
theiripo, shrimp (v)
theiripua, shrimper (n doer)
theisha, smallness (n)
theishu, small (adj)
theishwaku, smallest (adj)
theishwelu, smaller (adj)
theitha, sash (n)
theka, shell (n)
thekeshelesha, shellfish (n)
thekesheleshi, shellfish (n pl)
theko, shell (v)
thekua, sheller (n doer)
thelifa, lotion (n)
thelina, wind (n d:air)
thelinaushu, windward (adj)
thelinefenipa, windmill (n)
thelinemoika, windshield (n)
thelinepelira, windchill (n)
thelinepeliru, windchill (adj)
thelinezhaila, windfall (n)
thelino, wind (v d:air)
thelinu, windy (adj d:air)
thelita, region (n)
thelitiu, regionally (adv)
thelitu, regional (adj)
thelofa, nothing (n)
thenata, kinesis (n)
thenatiu, kinetically (adv)
thenatu, kinetic (adj)
thepa, nib (n)
thepana, nibble (n)
thepano, nibble (v)
therafita, punctuation (n)
therafitiu, punctually (adv)
therafito, punctuate (v)
therafitu, punctual (adj)
theraidato, dwindle (v)
theraifa, smugness (n)
theraifiu, smugly (adv)
theraifu, smug (adj)
theraikio, wound (v pa
    d:energize)
theraiko, wind (v d:energize)
theraikua, winder (n doer
    d:energize)
theraila, dwell (n)
therailio, dwelt (v pa)
therailo, dwell (v)
therailua, dweller (n doer)
theraipo, smuggle (v)
theraipua, smuggler (n doer)
theraita, dwarf (n)
theraito, dwarf (v)
therakiu, hugely (adv)
theraku, huge (adj)
therama, thump (n)
theramo, thump (v)
theramua, thumper (n doer)

therana, oar (n)
theranika, punishment (n)
theranikiu, punitively (adv)
theraniko, punish (v)
theraniku, punishable (adj)
theraniku, punitive (adj)
theranikua, punisher (n doer)
theranita, semester (n)
therano, oar (v)
therapa, snap (n)
therapekoita, snapshot (n)
therapiu, snappily (adv)
therapo, snap (v)
therapu, snappy (adj)
therapua, snapper (n doer)
therata, puncture (n)
therato, puncture (v)
therauga, hug (n)
theraugo, hug (v)
theraugua, hugger (n doer)
therauka, scrutiny (n)
therauko, scrutinize (v)
therauna, bridle (n)
therauno, bridle (v)
theraupa, braid (n)
theraupo, braid (v)
theraupua, braider (n doer)
therausha, thrill (n)
therausho, thrill (v)
theraushua, thriller (n doer)
therauta, braiser (n)
therauto, braise (v)
therautua, braiser (n doer)
therava, semblance (n)
theraviaka, seminar (n)
therefa, surface (n)
therefo, surface (v)
thereipa, trap (n)
thereipeshetela, trapdoor (n)
thereipo, trap (v)
thereipua, trapper (n doer)
thereithedarifa, lithography (n)
thereka, athlete (n)
therekiu, athletically (adv)
thereku, athletic (adj)
therela, fairness (n d:good)
therelepeliola, fairway (n)
therelisha, fairing (n)
thereliu, fairly (adv d:good)
therelu, fair (adj d:good)
therelweku, fairest (adj d:best)
therelwelu, fairer (adj d:better)
therena, palm (n)
therenika, tariff (n)
thereno, palm (v)
thereta, spring (n d:coil, surprise)
theretepelorika, springboard (n)
theretio, sprang (v pa d:coil,
    surprise)
thereto, spring (v d:coil, surprise)
theretua, springer (n doer d:coil,
    surprise)
theriaka, hospital (n)

theriako, hospitalize (v)
theriasho, thrive (v)
theriatha, hospitality (n)
theriathiu, hospitably (adv)
theriathu, hospitable (adj)
therifa, sprinkle (n)
therifo, sprinkle (v)
therifua, sprinkler (n doer)
therima, slimness (n)
therimo, slim (v)
therimu, slim (adj)
therina, nail (n d:finger/toe tip)
theriopa, territory (n)
theriopu, territorial (adj)
theripa, tribe (n)
theripelona, tribesman (n)
theripeloni, tribesmen (n pl)
theripu, tribal (adj)
therisha, forest (n)
therisho, forest (v)
therishu, foresty (adj)
therishueta, forestry (n)
theriupa, tribute (n)
theriupata, tributary (n)
theriuta, scruple (n)
theriutiu, scrupulously (adv)
theriuto, scruple (v)
theriutu, scrupulous (adj)
therota, sheer (n d:divert)
theroto, sheer (v d:divert)
theruasha, shudder (n)
theruasho, shudder (v)
theruka, fleck (n)
theruko, fleck (v)
therupo, garner (v)
therutha, flute (n)
theruthua, flutist (n doer)
thesha, raffle (n)
thesho, raffle (v)
thetana, theta (n)
thetha, den (n)
thetisha, piece (n)
thetisho, piece (v)
thetishua, piecer (n doer)
thiada, hob (n)
thiadano, hobble (v)
thiadoitho, hobnob (v)
thiafa, tour (n)
thiafo, tour (v)
thiafua, tourist (n doer)
thiafueta, tourism (n)
thiaga, menace (n)
thiagiu, menacingly (adv)
thiago, menace (v)
thiaipo, heed (v)
thiaka, fatality (n)
thiakiu, fatally (adv)
thiaku, fatal (adj)
thiala, shortness (n)
thialebilefa, shortcoming (n)
thialedaisha, shortcut (n)
thialegurita, shortcake (n)
thialekapa, shorthand (n)

thialesha, shortwave (n)
thialeshu, shortwave (adj)
thialetauka, shortstop (n)
thialethutha, shortsightedness (n)
thialethuthu, shortsighted (adj)
thialetuano, shortchange (v)
thialezhaila, shortfall (n)
thialika, shorts (n d:clothing)
thialipa, shortage (n)
thialipo, short (v)
thialira, shorty (n)
thialiu, shortly (adv)
thialo, shorten (v)
thialu, short (adj)
thialweku, shortest (adj)
thialwelu, shorter (adj)
thiana, priest (n)
thiapo, appall (v)
thiareheidona, floodwater (n)
thiaroberala, floodplain (n)
thiarofeluana, floodlight (n)
thiaropa, flood (n)
thiaroperelika, floodgate (n)
thiaropo, flood (v)
thiaropua, flooder (n doer)
thiaruga, gruel (n)
thiasha, shear (n)
thiashika, fatigue (n)
thiashiko, fatigue (v)
thiasho, shear (v)
thiashua, shearer (n doer)
thiata, skate (n)
thiatepelorika, skateboard (n)
thiatepeloriko, skateboard (v)
thiatha, sheath (n)
thiatho, sheathe (v)
thiato, skate (v)
thiatua, skater (n doer)
thiauka, shuck (n)
thiauko, shuck (v)
thiauta, whole (n)
thiauterelifa, wholesale (n)
thiauterelifu, wholesale (adj)
thiauterelifua, wholesaler (n
    doer)
thiautiu, wholly (adv)
thiautu, whole (adj)
thiautueta, wholeness (n)
thiava, flock (n d:group)
thiavo, flock (v d:group)
thifita, vector (n)
thigata, mutterance (n)
thigato, mutter (v)
thika, fare (n)
thikelava, farce (n)
thikelavu, farcical (adj)
thikitha, ickiness (n)
thikithu, icky (adj)
thiko, fare (v)
thikora, farewell (v)
thikua, fare (n doer)
thilana, palette (n)
thileshaitha, northwest (n)

thileshaithu, northwest (adj)
thileshaithu, northwestern (adj)
thilethutha, farsightedness (n)
thilethuthu, farsighted (adj)
thiliwaku, furthest (adj)
thilofa, shed (n d:building)
thiloka, click (n)
thilokiasha, northeast (n)
thilokiashaushu, northeastward
    (adj)
thilokiashu, northeast (adj)
thilokiashu, northeasterly (adj)
thilokiashu, northeastern (adj)
thiloko, click (v)
thilokua, clicker (n doer)
thilopoimu, faraway (adj)
Thilosha Dakota, North Dakota
    (n)
Thilosha Karolina, North Carolina
    (n)
thilosha, north (n)
thiloshaushu, northward (adj)
thiloshederaipa, northbound (n)
thilosheraupa, northland (n)
thiloshu, north (adj)
thiloshu, northerly (adj)
thiloshu, northern (adj)
thiloshua, northerner (n doer)
thiloshwaku, northernmost (adj)
thilota, character (n d:symbol)
thilu, far (adj/adv)
thiluelifu, furthermore (adv)
thiluelu, farther (adj/adv)
thiluelu, further (adj/adv)
thinapa, estimate (n)
thinapo, estimate (v)
thinapua, estimator (n doer)
thioka, master (n)
thiokatuka, masterstroke (n)
thiokeniapa, mastermind (n)
thiokeniapo, mastermind (v)
thiokethetisha, masterpiece (n)
thiokiu, masterfully (adv)
thioko, master (v)
thioku, masterful (adj)
thiokueta, mastery (n)
thiona, pine (n)
thiorila, fjord (n)
thiosha, mistress (n)
thirofa, nobility (n)
thirofiu, nobly (adv)
thirofu, noble (adj)
thiropa, kick (n)
thiropevaka, kickback (n)
thiropo, kick (v)
thiropua, kicker (n doer)
thiropunefa, kickoff (n)
thirota, rumor (n)
thirota, rumour (n)
thiroto, rumor (v)
thiroto, rumour (v)
thisha, sect (n)
thishala, section (n)

thishalo, section (v)
thishalu, sectional (adj)
thishana, sectarianism (n)
thishanua, sectarian (n doer)
thishapa, sector (n)
thishianiu, secularly (adv)
thishianu, secular (adj)
thishianua, secularist (n doer)
thishopa, decision (n)
thishopiu, decisively (adv)
thishopo, decide (v)
thishopu, decisive (adj)
thitalita, period (n d:punctuation)
thitesha, twit (n)
thitha, tally (n)
thitho, tally (v)
thiuda, hub (n)
thiudefipa, hubcap (n)
thiufa, file (n d:storage)
thiufeshuata, briefcase (n)
thiufo, file (v d:storage)
thiufota, lapse (n)
thiufoto, lapse (v)
thiufua, filer (n doer d:storage)
thiuka, spectra (n)
thiukata, spectrum (n)
thiukeluafa, spectroscopy (n)
thiukeluafu, spectroscopic (adj)
thiukiu, spectrally (adv)
thiuku, spectral (adj)
thiula, royalty (n)
thiuliu, royally (adv)
thiulu, royal (adj)
thiuna, moral (n)
thiunata, morale (n)
thiuniu, morally (adv)
thiuno, moralize (v)
thiunu, moral (adj)
thiunua, moralist (n doer)
thiunueta, morality (n)
thiuta, lap (n)
thiutauba, laptop (n)
thiuto, lap (v)
thoama, paleness (n d:complexion)
thoamo, pale (v d:complexion)
thoamu, pale (adj d:complexion)
thoana, wine (n)
thoanina, winery (n)
thoano, wine (v)
thoanua, wino (n doer)
thofa, shop (n)
thofekelofua, shopkeeper (n doer)
thofeperaita, shoplifter (n)
thofipa, chap (n)
thofipo, chap (v)
thofo, shop (v)
thofua, shopper (n doer)
thoga, stress (n)
thogiu, stressfully (adv)
thogo, stressed (v)
thogu, stressful (adj)
thogua, stressor (n doer)

thoiata, tabulation (n)
thoiato, tabulate (v)
thoiatu, tabular (adj)
thoiatua, tabulator (n doer)
thoifata, sheriff (n)
thoifato, sheriff (v)
thoika, tab (n)
thoiko, tab (v)
thoila, sack (n)
thoilo, sack (v)
thoilua, sacker (n doer)
thoina, seal (n d:animal)
thoipo, veer (v)
thoisha, face (n)
thoishata, façade (n)
thoishefikafa, faceplate (n)
thoisherauka, facelift (n)
thoisherauko, facelift (v)
thoisho, face (v)
thoishoita, facet (n)
thoishu, facial (adj)
thoishua, facer (n doer)
thoishula, facial (n)
thoita, brief (n)
thoitara, brevity (n)
thoitika, feasibility (n)
thoitikiu, feasibly (adv)
thoitiku, feasible (adj)
thoitiu, briefly (adv)
thoito, brief (v)
thoitu, brief (adj)
thoka, application (n)
thokiu, applicably (adv)
thokiuna, tranquility (n)
thokiuno, tranquilize (v)
thokiunu, tranquil (adj)
thokiunua, tranquilizer (n doer)
thokiunueta, tranquilization (n)
thoko, apply (v)
thoku, applicable (adj)
thokua, applicator (n doer)
thokuinua, applicant (n doer)
tholava, harem (n)
thoratesha, weld (n)
thoratesho, weld (v)
thorateshua, welder (n doer)
thorida, chapter (n)
thorika, appliance (n)
thorila, ford (n)
thorilo, ford (v)
thoripa, trance (n)
thoripada, chapel (n)
thoritha, hold (n)
thorithafena, holdover (n)
thorithio, held (v pa)
thorithiviela, holdup (n)
thoritho, hold (v)
thorithua, holder (n doer)
Thoriuma, Thorium (n)
thoshelasha, decal (n)
thotelipa, trajectory (n)
thotepa, trajection (n)
thotepo, traject (v)

thotepua, trajector (n doer)
thuafa, mute (n)
thuafo, mute (v)
thuaka, mutuality (n)
thuakiu, mutually (adv)
thuaku, mutual (adj)
thualifa, palace (n)
thuamo, shun (v)
thuana, flower (n)
thuanedaifa, flowerpot (n)
thuanika, anchor (n)
thuaniko, anchor (v)
thuanita, shunt (n)
thuanito, shunt (v)
thuano, flower (v)
thuanu, flowery (adj)
thuara, flora (n)
thuaru, floral (adj)
thuarua, florist (n doer)
thuata, phase (n)
thuato, phase (v)
thuatua, phaser (n doer)
thuatuila, phaseout (n)
thufa, smell (n)
thufisha, reverence (n)
thufishiu, reverently (adv)
thufisho, revere (v)
thufishu, reverent (adj)
thufishua, reverend (n doer)
thufita, fever (n)
thufitiu, feverishly (adv)
thufito, fever (v)
thufitu, feverish (adj)
thufo, smell (v)
thufu, smelly (adj)
thuina, miser (n)
thuinu, miserly (adj)
thuita, treat (n)
thuitalita, treatment (n)
thuitana, treaty (n)
thuito, treat (v)
thuitu, treatable (adj)
thuka, speck (n)
thukasha, speculation (n)
thukashiu, speculatively (adv)
thukasho, speculate (v)
thukashu, speculative (adj)
thukashua, speculator (n doer)
thukelaka, spectacle (n)
thukelakiu, spectacularly (adv)
thukelako, spectate (v)
thukelaku, spectacular (adj)
thukelakua, spectator (n doer)
thulegerazha, seesaw (n)
thulegerazho, seesaw (v)
thuliapa, scenery (n)
thulika, ration (n)
thuliko, ration (v)
thulio, saw (v pa)
thulipa, scene (n)
thulipasha, scenario (n)
thulipu, scenic (adj)
Thuliuma, Thulium (n)

thulo, see (v)
thulua, seer (n doer)
thuma, variability (n)
thuma, variance (n)
thuma, variation (n)
thumaka, variety (n)
thumaku, varietal (adj)
thumapa, variable (n)
thumapa, variant (n)
thumapu, variable (adj)
thumapu, variant (adj)
thumiu, variously (adv)
thumo, vary (v)
thumu, various (adj)
thunaika, misery (n)
thunaikiu, miserably (adv)
thunaiku, miserable (adj)
thunitana, certificate (n)
thunitano, certify (v)
thunitanoka, certification (n)
thunitanua, certifier (n doer)
thuniu, seemingly (adv)
thuno, seem (v)
thupa, sud (n)
thurifiu, conspicuously (adv)
thurifu, conspicuous (adj)
thurisha, garnish (n)
thurisho, garnish (v)
thusha, space (n)
thushefeleva, spaceship (n)
thushekafopa, spacecraft (n)
thushepelona, spaceman (n)
thushepeloni, spacemen (n pl)
thushika kodi, should (ndal
    d:expectation)
thushiu, spatially (adv)
thusho, space (v)
thushota, rationality (n)
thushotiu, rationally (adv)
thushoto, rationalize (v)
thushotu, rational (adj)
thushu, spacious (adj)
thushu, spatial (adj)
thushua, spacer (n doer)
thutesha, theology (n)
thutha, sight (n)
thutho, sight (v)
thuthulio, sightsaw (v pa)
thuthulo, sightsee (v)
thutiana, ratio (n)
thuzha, scheme (n)
thuzhata, schema (n)
thuzho, scheme (v)
thuzhua, schemer (n doer)
thuzhuna, schematic (n)
thuzhunu, schematic (adj)
tiafa, shove (n)
tiafipa, privilege (n)
tiafipo, privilege (v)
tiafipu, privy (adj)
tiafo, shove (v)
tiafua, shover (n doer)
tiafuana, shovel (n)

tiafuano, shovel (v)
tiaga, hind (n)
tiagata, hindrance (n)
tiagato, hinder (v)
tiagethutha, hindsight (n)
tiaiata, tingle (n)
tiaiato, tingle (v)
tiaifa, lamina (n)
tiaifi, laminae (n pl)
tiaifiu, laminously (adv)
tiaifo, laminate (v)
tiaifu, laminous (adj)
tiaifua, laminator (n doer)
tiaiga, hem (n)
tiaigeroifa, hemline (n)
tiaigo, hem (v)
tiaika, lameness (n)
tiaikano, lament (v)
tiaikanu, lamentable (adj)
tiaikiu, lamely (adv)
tiaiku, lame (adj)
tiaina, latency (n)
tiainiu, latently (adv)
tiainu, latent (adj)
Tiakiafa, EhoDay05 (n)
tiala, boil (n d:evaporation)
tialo, boil (v d:evaporation)
tialua, boiler (n doer
    d:evaporation)
tiama, bow (n d:front)
tianatha, grapple (n)
tianatho, grapple (v)
tianathu, grapple (adj)
tianika, grab (n)
tianiko, grab (v)
tianikua, grabber (n doer)
tianipa, grasp (n)
tianipo, grasp (v)
tiapa, privacy (n)
tlapiu, privately (adv)
tiapo, privatize (v)
tiapu, private (adj)
tiapueta, privatization (n)
tiasha, glacier (n)
tiashiu, glacially (adv)
tiasho, glaciate (v)
tiashu, glacial (adj)
tiata, metal (n)
tiatha, rattle (n)
tiathefareika, rattlesnake (n)
tiintho, rattle (v)
tiatu, metallic (adj)
tiauga, envy (n)
tiaugiu, enviously (adv)
tiaugo, envy (v)
tiaugu, envious (adj)
tiaukiu, languidly (adv)
tiauko, languish (v)
tiauku, languid (adj)
tiaupa, hoard (n)
tiaupo, hoard (v)
tiautha, tart (n)
tiauthu, tart (adj)

tiava, gaze (n)
tiavo, gaze (v)
tiavua, gazer (n doer)
tiazha, pyramid (n)
tibafika, district (n)
tibafiko, district (v)
tibeitha, disbursement (n)
tibeitho, disburse (v)
tiberesha, displacement (n)
tiberesho, displace (v)
tiberiaka, disuse (n)
tiberiasho, disavow (v)
tibino, peddle (v)
tibinua, peddler (n doer)
tibita, divestment (n)
tibito, divest (v)
tidalima, dissuasion (n)
tidalimo, dissuade (v)
tidalipa, disturbance (n)
tidalipo, disturb (v)
tidaralo, dishearten (v)
tideiluda, disquiet (n)
tidereifa, distrust (n)
tidereifo, distrust (v)
tidereifu, distrustful (adj)
tidiasho, disjoint (v)
tidiruva, discouragement (n)
tidiruvo, discourage (v)
tieka, hide (n d:skin)
tiekopiola, hideaway (n)
tiekuila, hideout (n)
tielita, download (n)
tielito, download (v)
tielitua, downloader (n doer)
tiena, down (n)
tienedauna, downtime (n)
tienedauta, downbeat (n)
tienedautu, downbeat (adj)
tienediekiu, downright (adv)
tienefalima, downstream (n)
tienefeliega, downswing (v)
tieneferuifo, downplay (v)
tienekaima, downturn (n)
tienemiuna, downtown (n)
tieneparina, downhill (n)
tienerotuta, downpour (n)
tieneshoita, downside (n)
tieneshoterana, downgrade (n)
tieneshoterano, downgrade (v)
tieneshuago, downsize (v)
tienezhaila, downfall (n)
tienitaina, downstairs (n)
tienitainu, downstairs (adj)
tienu, down (adj/adv/prep)
tienuhaushu, downward
    (adj/adv)
tienuhaushu, downwardly (adv)
tiepu, lean (adj d:thin)
tieta, flex (n)
tietiu, flexibly (adv)
tieto, flex (v)
tietorepa, flexibility (n)
tietu, flexible (adj)

tifata, strand (n)
tifato, strand (v)
tifeisha, disgust (n)
tifeisho, disgust (v)
tifelaruva, disapproval (n)
tifelaruvo, disapprove (v)
tifelenita, discredit (n)
tifelenito, discredit (v)
tifeliofo, disprove (v)
tiferaikiu, dismally (adv)
tiferaiku, dismal (adj)
tiferepa, disability (n)
tiferepo, disable (v)
tiferepua, disabler (n doer)
tiferilako, disallow (v)
tiferilopa, displeasure (n)
tiferilopo, displease (v)
tiferilota, disorganization (n)
tiferiloto, disorganize (v)
tifiofa, disloyalty (n)
tifiofu, disloyal (adj)
tifopa, disc (n)
tifopa, disk (n)
tifopata, discus (n)
tifopefa, diskette (n)
tifuga, discipline (n)
tifugo, discipline (v)
tifugu, disciplinary (adj)
tifugua, disciplinarian (n doer)
tiga, peg (n)
tigaga, nag (n)
tigago, nag (v)
tigagu, naggy (adj)
tigalita, distraction (n)
tigalito, distract (v)
tigata, utterance (n)
tigatiu, utterly (adv)
tigato, utter (v)
tigatu, utter (adj)
tigaugo, divulge (v)
tigelaka, disposition (n)
tigelaku, dispositive (adj)
tigeloita, discharge (n)
tigeloito, discharge (v)
tigereta, disclosure (n)
tigereto, disclose (v)
tigo, peg (v)
tigoita, discussion (n)
tigoito, discuss (v)
tigota, discreteness (n)
tigotiu, discretely (adv)
tigotu, discrete (adj)
tiialifoka, disobedience (n)
tiialifokiu, disobediently (adv)
tiialifoko, disobey (v)
tiialifoku, disobedient (adj)
tiitoipa, disincentive (n)
tiivirota, disinfection (n)
tiiviroto, disinfect (v)
tiivirotua, disinfectant (n doer)
tiivorina, disinformation (n)
tikalo, get-lost (interj)
tikelata, disagreement (n)

tikelatana, discrepancy (n)
tikelataniu, discrepantly (adv)
tikelatanu, discrepant (adj)
tikelato, disagree (v)
tikelatu, disagreeable (adj)
tikerego, disgruntle (v)
tikeriafa, disqualification (n)
tikeriafo, disqualify (v)
tikeriafua, disqualifier (n doer)
tikio, did (v pa)
tiko, do (v)
tikoama, blemish (n)
tikoamo, blemish (v)
tikofita, disservice (n)
tikolifa, dishonor (n)
tiku, doable (adj)
tikua, doer (n doer)
tikulita, disfigurement (n)
tikulito, disfigure (v)
til, it (pron 3rd neut sng sub)
tilafesha, diligence (n)
tilafeshiu, diligently (adv)
tilafeshu, diligent (adj)
tilagarusha, disillusionment (n)
tilagarusho, disillusion (v)
tilaka, disposal (n)
tilako, dispose (v)
tilaku, disposable (adj)
tilasha, terra (n)
tilashanu, terrestrial (adj)
tilashata, terrain (n)
tilashika, terrace (n)
tilashu, terranean (adj)
tilata, straddle (n)
tilato, straddle (v)
tilen, it (pron 3rd neut sng obj)
tilesh, its (pron 3rd neut sng pos obj)
tilesh, its (pron 3rd neut sng pos sub)
tileshfal, itself (pron 3rd neut sng refl)
tilialita, discourse (n)
tilialito, discourse (v)
tilifa, tip (n)
tilifedilopa, tiptoe (n)
tilifedilopo, tiptoe (v)
tilifepelona, tipster (n)
tilifo, tip (v)
tilitu, tippy (adj)
tilifua, tipper (n doer)
tilifunefa, tipoff (n)
tilika, ire (n)
tilikiu, irascibly (adv)
tiliko, irk (v)
tiliku, irascible (adj)
tiliku, irate (adj)
tilita, needle (n)
tilitaifota, needlepoint (n)
tilitekioka, needlework (n)
tilito, needle (v)
tiliupifota, discontent (n)
tiliupifoto, discontent (v)

tiliutira, discontinuation (n)
tiliutira, discontinuity (n)
tiliutiro, discontinue (v)
tiloka, wit (n)
tilokiu, wittily (adv)
tiloku, witty (adj)
tilokuetiu, witlessly (adv)
tilokuetu, witless (adj)
tilotela, dispersal (n)
tilotela, dispersion (n)
tilotelo, disperse (v)
tilotelua, disperser (n doer)
tilubolika, disrepair (n)
tiluda, initiation (n)
tiludara, initiative (n)
tiludata, initial (n)
tiludiu, initially (adv)
tiludo, initiate (v)
tiludu, initial (adj)
tiludua, initiator (n doer)
tiluga, material (n)
tilugiu, materistically (adv)
tilugo, materialize (v)
tilugu, materialistic (adj)
tilugua, materialist (n doer)
tilugueta, materialism (n)
timavina, disharmony (n)
timeiga, divergence (n)
timeigo, diverge (v)
timeigu, divergent (adj)
timelata, funnel (n)
timelato, funnel (v)
timeshuta, dismemberment (n)
timeshuto, dismember (v)
timoita, disorientation (n)
timoito, disorient (v)
timoka, fund (n)
timokalita, fundamental (n)
timokalitiu, fundamentally (adv)
timokalitu, fundamental (adj)
timoko, fund (v)
timokua, funder (n doer)
timota, atom (n)
timotiu, atomically (adv)
timoto, atomize (v)
timotu, atomic (adj)
Tina, Tin (n)
tinalisha, disdain (n)
tinana, dime (n)
tinaritha, disfavor (n)
tinaritho, disfavor (v)
tinata, taste (n)
tinatemeniu, tastelessly (adv)
tinatemenu, tasteless (adj)
tinatiu, tastefully (adv)
tinato, taste (v)
tinatu, tasteful (adj)
tinatu, tasty (adj)
tinatua, taster (n doer)
tinita, irritation (n)
tinito, irritate (v)
tinitua, irritant (n doer)
tinoarita, disclaimer (n)

tinoarito, disclaim (v)
tinoifa, dismay (n)
tinoifo, dismay (v)
tinufa, dessert (n)
tinuko, neuter (v)
tiobaisha, mortgage (n)
tiobaisho, mortgage (v)
tiofa, mortality (n)
tioferaika, morbidity (n)
tioferaiku, morbid (adj)
tiofika, mortification (n)
tiofiko, mortify (v)
tiofipa, morgue (n)
tiofiu, mortally (adv)
tiofu, mortal (adj)
tiofua, mortal (n doer)
tioga, hire (n)
tiogo, hire (v)
tiogua, hirer (n doer)
tioka, stall (n d:compartment)
tiolipoila, disarray (n)
tiomeifa, disassociation (n)
tiomeifo, disassociate (v)
tiopa, nimbleness (n)
tiopiu, nimbly (adv)
tiopu, nimble (adj)
tiorofika, immortality (n)
tiorofiko, immortalize (v)
tiorofiku, immortal (adj)
tiorofikua, immortal (n doer)
tiota, message (n)
tiotha, tinge (n)
tiotheravo, disassemble (v)
tiotho, tinge (v)
tioto, message (v)
tiotua, messenger (n doer)
tioviripa, disaffection (n)
tioviripo, disaffect (v)
tipado, dispel (v)
tipadua, dispeller (n doer)
tipelafa, disgrace (n)
tipelafiu, disgracefully (adv)
tipelafo, disgrace (v)
tipelafu, disgraceful (adj)
tipeliana, disappearance (n)
tipeliano, disappear (v)
tipeliaroka, disintegration (n)
tipeliaroko, disintegrate (v)
tipeliarokua, disintegrator (n doer)
tiperata, dysfunction (n)
tiperatu, dysfunctional (adj)
tiperilapa, dispossession (n)
tiperilapo, dispossess (v)
tipifoka, distension (n)
tipifoko, distend (v)
tipoina, discount (n)
tipoino, discount (v)
tipoinua, discounter (n doer)
tiposhata, dishonesty (n)
tiposhatu, dishonest (adj)
tir, they (pron 3rd neut pl sub)
tiradha, disciple (n)

tirai-, pent- (num 5 pref)
tirai-, quint- (num 5 pref)
tiraimuka, pentagon (n)
tirasha, dismissal (n)
tirashiu, dismissively (adv)
tirasho, dismiss (v)
tirashu, dismissive (adj)
tiren, them (pron 3rd neut pl obj)
tiresh, their (pron 3rd neut pl pos sub)
tiresh, theirs (pron 3rd neut pl pos obj)
tireshfar, themselves (pron 3rd neut pl pos)
tireth, fifth (num 5 ord)
tiri, five (num 5 card)
tiriafa, ream (n d:paper)
tirialfhemka, Number_1e20406
tirida, fifty (num 50 card)
tiridai-, fifty- (num 50 pref)
tirideth, fiftieth (num 50 ord)
tirifk, quinquadragintillion (num 1e138 card)
tirift, quinquatrigintillion (num 1e108 card)
tirika, quintillion (num 1e18 card)
tirikai-, exa- (num 1e18 pref)
tiriketh, quintillionth (num 1e18 ord)
tiripa, fifteen (num 15 card)
tiripai-, fifteen- (num 15 pref)
tiripeth, fifteenth (num 15 ord)
tirishk, quinvigintillion (num 1e78 card)
tirishkai-, fiefta-
tirishketh, quinvigintillionth (num 1e78 ord)
tirisht, quindecillion (num 1e48 card)
tirishtai-, pafta- (num 1e48 pref)
tirishteth, quindecillionth (num 1e48 ord)
tirita, chirp (n)
tiritha, list (n d:tilt)
tiritho, list (v d:tilt)
tirito, chirp (v)
tiritua, chirper (n doer)
tiriusha, punch (n d:beverage)
tiroka, chart (n)
tiroko, chart (v)
tirokua, charter (n doer)
tirokula, charter (n)
tirokulo, charter (v)
tirolata, disbarment (n)
tirolato, disbar (v)
tiropa, price (n)
tiropemenu, priceless (adj)
tiropo, price (v)
tiropu, pricey (adj)
tiropua, pricer (n doer)
tiruika, relevance (n)

tiruika, relevancy (n)
tiruikiu, relevantly (adv)
tiruiku, relevant (adj)
tishaipa, dislocation (n)
tishaipo, dislocate (v)
tishalifa, dislike (n)
tishalifo, dislike (v)
tishara, disbelief (n)
tisharigo, dislodge (v)
tisharo, disbelieve (v)
tishata, pellet (n)
tishekorago, dispatch (v)
tishekoragua, dispatcher (n doer)
tishelika, dissipation (n)
tisheliko, dissipate (v)
tishiketa, disorder (n)
tishiketo, disorder (v)
tishinafa, disconnection (n)
tishinafo, disconnect (v)
tishinena, disarmament (n)
tishineno, disarm (v)
titaifota, disappointment (n)
titaifoto, disappoint (v)
titaka, simulation (n)
titako, simulate (v)
titakua, simulator (n doer)
Titaniuma, Titanium (n)
titeliforeta, disinterest (n)
titeliforeto, disinterest (v)
titheifo, disown (v)
tithisha, dissection (n)
tithisho, dissect (v)
tithoga, distress (n)
tithogo, distress (v)
tithogu, distraught (adj)
titinata, distaste (n)
titinatu, distasteful (adj)
tituifa, disguise (n)
tituifo, disguise (v)
tiufa, prime (n)
tiufana, primate (n)
tiufanu, primal (adj)
tiufedauna, primetime (n)
tiufedaunu, primetime (adj)
tiufita, primitive (n)
tiufitiu, primitively (adv)
tiufitu, primitive (adj)
tiufiu, primarily (adv)
tiufo, prime (v)
tiufopa, principle (n)
tiufopo, principle (v)
tiufota, finiteness (n)
tiufotiu, finitely (adv)
tiufotu, finite (adj)
tiufu, primary (adj)
tiufua, primer (n doer)
tiufula, primary (n)
tiuga, lock (n)
tiugeritha, locksmith (n)
tiugika, lockstep (n)
tiugiveila, lockup (n)
tiugo, lock (v)
tiugua, locker (n doer)

tiuguila, lockout (n)
tiuka, due (n)
tiukiu, due (adv)
tiuku, due (adj)
tiuma, neutrality (n)
tiumala, neutron (n)
tiumiu, neutrally (adv)
tiumo, neutralize (v)
tiumu, neutral (adj)
tiumua, neutralizer (n doer)
tiumueta, neutralization (n)
tiupa, curfew (n)
tiusha, priestess (n)
tiuta, finish (n)
tiuto, finish (v)
tiutua, finisher (n doer)
tivafika, distemper (n)
tivaga, strangulation (n)
tivagethoritha, stranglehold (n)
tivago, strangle (v)
tivaizha, dismantlement (n)
tivaizho, dismantle (v)
tivanita, insult (n)
tivanito, insult (v)
tivanitua, insulter (n doer)
tivapa, strap (n)
tivapo, strap (v)
tivapua, strapper (n doer)
tivefika, disadvantage (n)
tivefiko, disadvantage (v)
tivelaruva, discomfort (n)
tivelaruvo, discomfort (v)
tiveramipo, disband (v)
tivika, list (n d:strip)
tiviko, list (v d:strip)
tiviku, list (adj d:strip)
tivisha, discretion (n)
tivishiu, discreetly (adv)
tivishu, discreet (adj)
tivita, advance (n)
tivito, advance (v)
tivitueta, advancement (n)
tivobaika, disengagement (n)
tivobaiko, disengage (v)
tivoika, dispute (n)
tivoiko, dispute (v)
tivuka, strip (n)
tivukeraizha, striptease (n)
tivukeraizho, striptease (v)
tivuko, strip (v)
tivukua, stripper (n doer)
tiwaku, utmost (adj)
tizhako, pelt (v d:hit)
tizhauka, ultimatum (n)
tizhauki, ultimatum (n pl)
tizhaukiu, ultimately (adv)
tizhauku, ultimate (adj)
tizhualo, dispirit (v)
tofipa, kindness (n d:nice)
tofipiu, kindly (adv d:nice)
tofipu, kind (adj d:nice)
toiato, sass (v)
toifa, stain (n)

toifemena, stainless (n)
toifemenu, stainless (adj)
toifo, stain (v)
toifua, stainer (n doer)
toigaupa, sarcasm (n)
toigaupiu, sarcastically (adv)
toigaupu, sarcastic (adj)
toika, bone (n)
toikiu, bonily (adv)
toikomenu, boneless (adj)
toiku, bony (adj)
toima, ebony (n)
toipa, citation (n)
toipo, cite (v)
toipota, excitement (n)
toipotiu, excitably (adv)
toipoto, excite (v)
toipotu, excitable (adj)
toipotua, exciter (n doer)
toipotueta, excitation (n)
toira, boil (n d:infection)
toisha, incitation (n)
toisha, incitement (n)
toisho, incite (v)
toishua, inciter (n doer)
toita, simultaneity (n)
toitiu, simultaneously (adv)
toitu, simultaneous (adj)
toivata, oblivion (n)
toivatu, oblivious (adj)
Toiviula, Thursday (n)
Tokiofa, Tokyo (n)
tolafiga, dolphin (n)
tolefelu, wherever (adv/conj)
tolei, where (pron)
tolika, date (n d:time, meet)
toliko, date (v d:time, meet)
tolina, dollar (n)
tolipa, doll (n)
tolipaloka, fabrication (n)
tolipaloko, fabricate (v)
tolipalokua, fabricator (n doer)
tolipo, doll (v)
tolita, fax (n)
tolito, fax (v)
toloveipa, whereabout (n)
tolu, where (adv/conj)
toludidana, facsimile (n)
toluvu, whereby (conj/adv)
toluyosha, whereas (n)
toluyoshu, whereas (conj)
torama, hunch (n)
toramo, hunch (v)
toramua, huncher (n doer)
torefipa, distance (n)
torefipiu, distantly (adv)
torefipo, distance (v)
torefipu, distant (adj)
toribo, fend (v)
toribua, fender (n doer)
torifa, fence (n d:barrier)
torifo, fence (v d:barrier)
torifopa, defense (n)

torifopo, defend (v)
torifopu, defensive (adj)
torifopua, defendant (n doer)
torifopua, defender (n doer)
toripa, thrust (n)
toripio, thrust (v pa)
toripo, thrust (v)
toripua, thruster (n doer)
torisha, drip (n)
torisho, drip (v)
torishu, drippy (adj)
torishua, dripper (n doer)
Toronitofa, Toronto (n)
tosha, get (n)
toshio, got (v pa)
tosho, get (v)
toshopiola, getaway (n)
toshua, getter (n doer)
tova, difference (n)
tovabota, diffusion (n)
tovaboto, diffuse (v)
tovashika, differential (n)
tovashiko, differentiate (v)
tovelishoka, diffraction (n)
tovelishoko, diffract (v)
toviu, differently (adv)
tovo, differ (v)
tovu, different (adj)
tuaiata, expletive (n)
tuaika, exotic (n)
tuaiku, exotic (adj)
tuaka, circus (n)
tualita, circumstance (n)
tualitu, circumstantial (adj)
tuana, change (n)
tuanika, canal (n)
tuanita, exchange (n)
tuanito, exchange (v)
tuanitu, exchangeable (adj)
tuanitua, exchanger (n doer)
tuano, change (v)
tuanua, changer (n doer)
tuareshiana, ecstasy (n)
tuareshianiu, ecstatically (adv)
tuareshianu, ecstatic (adj)
tuarika, violence (n)
tuarikiu, violently (adv)
tuariko, violate (v)
tuariku, violent (adj)
tuarikua, violator (n doer)
tuarikueta, violation (n)
tuaroma, channel (n)
tuaromo, channel (v)
tuaromua, channeler (n doer)
tuatha, cash (n)
tuatho, cash (v)
tuathua, cashier (n doer)
tuaupa, warp (n)
tuaupo, warp (v)
tuazha, volatility (n)
tuazhu, volatile (adj)
tubelapeliola, expressway (n)
tubelasha, expression (n)

tubelashiu, expressively (adv)
tubelashiu, expressly (adv)
tubelasho, express (v)
tubelashu, expressive (adj)
tubelashua, expresser (n doer)
tubereshota, explication (n)
tubereshotiu, explicitly (adv)
tubereshoto, exply (v)
tubereshotu, explicit (adj)
tuberuna, expenditure (n)
tuberuna, expense (n)
tuberuneferepu, expendable (adj)
tuberuniu, expensively (adv)
tuberuno, expend (v)
tuberunu, expensive (adj)
tubielika, export (n)
tubieliko, export (v)
tubielikua, exporter (n doer)
tubofita, extrusion (n)
tubofito, extrude (v)
tudala, riddle (n)
tudalo, riddle (v)
tudarotha, ejaculation (n)
tudarotho, ejaculate (v)
tudata, gape (n)
tudato, gape (v)
tueifa, lathe (n d:machine)
tueifo, lathe (v d:machine)
tueifua, lather (n doer d:machine)
tufa, poof (interj)
tufana, curl (n)
tufano, curl (v)
tufanu, curly (adj)
tufanua, curler (n doer)
tufika, bus (n)
tufiki, buses (n pl)
tufiko, bus (v)
tufipa, knot (n)
tufipo, knot (v)
tufipu, knotty (adj)
tuforelita, eccentricity (n)
tuforelitu, eccentric (adj)
tugalita, extract (n)
tugalito, extract (v)
tugalituta, extractor (n doer)
tugalueta, extraction (n)
tugeruta, exclusion (n)
tugerutiu, exclusively (adv)
tugeruto, exclude (v)
tugerutu, exclusive (adj)
tugerutua, excluder (n doer)
tugilipa, excerpt (n)
tugilipo, excerpt (v)
tugoita, excuse (n)
tugoito, excuse (v)
tugoitu, excusable (adj)
tugoituta, excuser (n doer)
tugota, excrement (n)
tugota, excretion (n)
tugoto, excrete (v)
tugotu, excretive (adj)
tugotua, excreter (n doer)
tuguniata, excommunication (n)

tuguniato, excommunicate (v)
tuguniatua, excommunicator (n doer)
tuiafa, dynamo (n)
tuiafita, dynamic (n)
tuiafiu, dynamically (adv)
tuiafu, dynamic (adj)
tuiaka, trot (n)
tuiako, trot (v)
tuiakua, trotter (n doer)
tuiapa, stalk (n d:appendage)
tuifa, guise (n)
tuika, duty (n)
tuipa, guidance (n)
tuipebalita, guidepost (n)
tuiperoifa, guideline (n)
tuipevonuda, guidebook (n)
tuipo, guide (v)
tuipua, guide (n doer)
tuita, guy (n d:wire)
tuitiena, geyser (n)
tuitu, guy (adj d:wire)
tukiota, extortion (n)
tukioto, extort (v)
tukoiga, examination (n)
tukoigo, examine (v)
tukoigua, examiner (n doer)
tukora, exam (n)
tuledoripa, stereotype (n)
tuledoripo, stereotype (v)
tuledoripu, stereotypical (adj)
tuletherata, acupuncture (n)
tulifa, cure (n)
tulifata, accuracy (n)
tulifatiu, accurately (adv)
tulifatu, accurate (adj)
tulifo, cure (v)
tulifu, curable (adj)
tulifu, curative (adj)
tulifua, curer (n doer)
tulika, murk (n)
tulikiu, murkily (adv)
tuliku, murky (adj)
tulipa, curb (n)
tulipo, curb (v)
tulisha, determination (n)
tulisho, determine (v)
tulishu, determinative (adj)
tulishua, determinant (n doer)
tulita, cast (n)
tulitio, cast (v pa)
tulito, cast (v)
tulovaga, exaggeration (n)
tulovago, exaggerate (v)
tumarina, escort (n)
tumata, municipality (n)
tumatu, municipal (adj)
tunefeleba, helicopter (n)
tunilaka, extermination (n)
tunilako, exterminate (v)
tunilakua, exterminator (n doer)
tunita, helix (n)
tunitiu, helically (adv)

tunitu, helical (adj)
tunoarita, exclamation (n)
tunoarito, exclaim (v)
tunoaritu, exclamatory (adj)
Tunogishetena, Tungsten (n)
tuoripo, exert (v)
tupauga, excavation (n)
tupaugo, excavate (v)
tupaugua, excavator (n doer)
tupifoka, extent (n)
tupifokiu, extensively (adv)
tupifoko, extend (v)
tupifoku, extensive (adj)
tupifokua, extender (n doer)
tupifokueta, extension (n)
tupika, whiz (n)
tupiko, whiz (v)
turathishaka, exercise (n)
turathishako, exercise (v)
turathishakua, exerciser (n doer)
turederava, exploration (n)
turederavo, explore (v)
turederavu, exploratory (adj)
turederavua, explorer (n doer)
turisha, booth (n)
turita, boot (n)
turitha, drape (n)
turitho, drape (v)
turithua, draper (n doer)
turithueta, drapery (n)
turito, boot (v)
Turokifa, Turkey (n)
Turokifana, Turkish (n)
tushata, exactness (n)
tushatiu, exactly (adv)
tushato, exact (v)
tushatu, exact (adj)
tutata, chase (n)
tutato, chase (v)
tutatua, chaser (n doer)
tutereba, extrication (n)
tuterebo, extricate (v)
tuthafitiu, exquisitely (adv)
tuthafitu, exquisite (adj)
tuthishaka, excision (n)
tuthishako, excise (v)
tuthuka, expectation (n)
tuthuko, expect (v)
tuthukua, expectorant (n doer)
tutiku, crisp (adj)
tuvioisha, excruciation (n)
tuvioishiu, excruciatingly (adv)
tuvioisho, excruciate (v)
tuyana, harp (n)
tuyano, harp (v)
tuyanua, harper (n doer)
tuyata, harpoon (n)
ua, eh (interj)
uana, ear (n)
uanederiada, eardrum (n)
uanedoina, earlobe (n)
uaneriterala, earring (n)
uaneshekota, earshot (n)

uaneshetata, earmark (n)
uaneshetato, earmark (v)
uanetarika, earwax (n)
uanethetisha, earpiece (n)
uaneyapa, earphone (n)
udeika, edict (n)
udu, ago (adj/adv)
ufativa, elevation (n)
ufativo, elevate (v)
ufativua, elevator (n doer)
uferitha, identity (n)
uferithara, identification (n)
uferithiu, identically (adv)
uferitho, identify (v)
uferithu, identical (adj)
uferithua, identifier (n doer)
ufu, oomph (interj)
ui, oh (interj)
uila, out (n)
uilaomio, outran (v pa)
uilaomo, outrun (v)
uileberautha, outflow (n)
uileberautho, outflow (v)
uileberoifa, outcry (n)
uileberushota, outburst (n)
uilederaipa, outbound (n)
uilederaipu, outbound (adj)
uiledialita, outpost (n)
uiledieku, outright (adj)
uiledorugo, outgun (v)
uilefelaufito, outlive (v)
uilefenilota, outskirt (n)
uilefepa, outset (n)
uileferanita, outlay (n)
uileferanitio, outlaid (v pa)
uileferanito, outlie (v)
uilegelorifu, outboard (adj)
uilegeloruga, outreach (n)
uilegeraito, outstretch (v)
uilegeraniko, outflank (v)
uilehausha, outward (n)
uilehaushiu, outwardly (adv)
uilehaushu, outward (adj/adv)
uileka, outlet (n)
uilekeloika, outgrowth (n)
uilekeloikio, outgrew (v pa)
uilekeloiko, outgrow (v)
uilekiafa, outhouse (n)
uilekiofo, outpace (v)
uilemoithio, outshone (v pa)
uilemoitho, outshine (v)
uilemolitha, outpatient (n)
uilemolithu, outpatient (adj)
uileniamo, outsmart (v)
uilepelika, outbreak (n)
uileperanida, outfield (n)
uileperanidua, outfielder (n doer)
uilereiga, outlook (n)
uileroifa, outline (n)
uileroifo, outline (v)
uileroifua, outliner (n doer)
uilerotuta, outpour (n)
uilerotuto, outpour (v)

uileshetela, outdoors (n)
uileshetelu, outdoor (adj)
uileshoita, outside (n)
uileshoitu, outside
    (n/adj/adv/prep)
uileshoitua, outsider (n doer)
uileshuago, outsize (v)
uileshuisho, outweigh (v)
uiletalishu, outspoken (adj)
uileterelifio, outsold (v pa)
uileterelifo, outsell (v)
uilethaiko, outvote (v)
uilethaitio, outbid (v pa)
uilethaito, outbid (v)
uiletiloko, outwit (v)
uiletivuko, outstrip (v)
uilevaka, outback (n)
uilevuta, output (n)
uilevuto, output (v)
uilezhigata, outrage (n)
uilezhigatiu, outrageously (adv)
uilezhigato, outrage (v)
uilezhigatu, outrageous (adj)
uilobelefa, outcome (n)
uiloneniko, outnumber (v)
uilopafita, outfit (n)
uilopafito, outfit (v)
uilopafitua, outfitter (n doer)
uiloterelitu, outstanding (adj)
uilotulita, outcast (n)
uilovauda, outlaw (n)
uilovaudo, outlaw (v)
uilovifio, outwent (v pa)
uilovifo, outgo (v)
uilovifua, outgoer (n doer)
uilovorino, outperform (v)
uilu, out (adj/adv/prep/interj)
uilueta, outage (n)
uilweledorima, outerwear (n)
uilwelu, outer (adj)
uilwelwaku, outermost (adj)
Ukerainafa, Ukraine (n)
ul, hmm (interj)
ularita, elation (n)
ularito, elate (v)
ulidaufa, umpire (n)
ulu, if (conj)
unamu, p.m. (adj)
unauka, omission (n)
unauko, omit (v)
unaukua, omitter (n doer)
unefedautu, offbeat (adj)
unefefikoleta, offscreen (n)
unefefikoletu, offscreen (adj)
unefekapu, offhand (adj)
unefelurito, offload (v)
unefepa, offset (n)
unefepio, offset (v pa)
unefepo, offset (v)
uneferoifu, offline (adj)
unefeshekota, offshoot (n)
unefeshoita, offside (n)
unefeshoitu, offside (adj)

unefethereta, offspring (n)
unefu, off (prep)
unefularita, offshore (n)
unefularito, offshore (v)
Ununabiuma, Ununbium (n)
Ununahekiuma, Ununhexium (n)
Ununishepotiuma, Ununseptium
    (n)
Ununokatiuma, Ununoctium (n)
Ununokuadiuma, Ununquadium
    (n)
Ununopenetiuma, Ununpentium
    (n)
Ununoteriuma, Ununtrium (n)
upeshilona, upsilon (n)
Uraniuma, Uranium (n)
urfhem, Number_1e756
urfi, Us (let pl)
urifa, U (let sng)
Ushap, Unbiunium (n davoka)
usheko, oust (v)
ushekua, ouster (n doer)
ushepu, each (adj)
usheriga, enscription (n)
usheriga, inscription (n)
usherigo, enscribe (v)
usherigo, inscribe (v)
ushethiu, lastly (adv)
ushetho, last (v)
ushethu, last (adj)
Uship, Unbibium (n davoka)
ushutu, below (adv/prep)
ushuvada, elaboration (n)
ushuvado, elaborate (v)
ushuvadu, elaborate (adj)
Utafika, Utah (n)
utepa, ejection (n)
utepo, eject (v)
uthiufoto, elapse (v)
utiailata, understudy (n)
utiariboto, understaff (v)
utibelega, underclass (n)
utiberanita, underground (n)
utiberanitu, underground (adj)
utiberiako, underuse (v)
utibiorito, underpower (v)
utibiuta, understatement (n)
utidaisha, undercut (n)
utidaishio, undercut (v pa)
utidaisho, undercut (v)
utidalithu, undercover (adj)
utidalitu, underage (adj)
utidelagela, undersecretary (n)
utiderausha, underdog (n)
utidiaropa, underbelly (n)
utidopo, undercook (v)
utidovama, underwear (n)
utifanina, underwood (n)
utigeruasha, underbrush (n)
utigokio, undertook (v pa)
utigoko, undertake (v)
utigokua, undertaker (n doer)
utigurifa, undercurrent (n)

utihaloreta, underworld (n)
utiheidonu, underwater (adj)
utiisherelo, underinsure (v)
utikelaito, underscore (v)
utikeloika, undergrowth (n)
utikerigo, undermine (v)
utikina, undergrad (n)
utikinopu, undergraduate (adj)
utikinopua, undergraduate (n doer)
utilakana, undergarment (n)
utileipo, underpin (v)
utilifada, undershirt (n)
utiloidio, underwrote (v pa)
utiloido, underwrite (v)
utiloidua, underwriter (n doer)
utilunita, underpass (n)
utimekani, underpants (n pl)
utimoimio, underpaid (v pa)
utimoimo, underpay (v)
utiniluna, underneath (n)
utinilunu, underneath (adj/adv/prep)
utinu, under (adj/adv/prep)
utiovaitua, underachiever (n doer)
utipa, underling (n)
utipeliola, underway (n)
utipeliolu, underway (adj)
utipelono, underman (v)
utiretho, underlie (v)
utiroifa, underline (n)
utiroifo, underline (v)
utishikeleinu, undersea (adj)
utishinena, underarm (n)
utishinenu, underarm (adj)
utishoita, underside (n)
utishuisha, underweight (n)
utishuishu, underweight (adj)
utitebo, underrate (v)
utiteferapa, underdevelopment (n)
utiteferapo, underdevelop (v)
utiterelifio, undersold (v pa)
utiterelifo, undersell (v)
utiterelitio, understood (v pa)
utiterelitiu, understandably (adv)
utiterelito, understand (v)
utiterelitu, understandable (adj)
utiterila, undertone (n d:music, audio)
utithaita, underbid (n)
utithaitio, underbid (v pa)
utithaito, underbid (v)
utithinapa, underestimation (n)
utithinapo, underestimate (v)
utititiropo, underprice (v)
utivaupo, undervalue (v)
utivifio, underwent (v pa)
utivifo, undergo (v)
uvofu, above (prep/adv/adj)
uyanezhusha, hearsay (n)
uyanio, heard (v pa)

uyano, hear (v)
vaba, pop (n)
vabegerala, popcorn (n)
vabo, pop (v)
vabua, popper (n doer)
vadata, motive (n)
vadato, motivate (v)
vadatu, motivational (adj)
vadatua, motivator (n doer)
vadatueta, motivation (n)
vadava, motion (n)
vadavo, motion (v)
vafiaka, tempest (n)
vafika, temper (n)
vafikata, temperance (n)
vafikata, temperment (n)
vafikato, temperate (v)
vafikatu, temperate (adj)
vafiko, temper (v)
vafikueta, temperament (n)
vafikuetiu, temperamentally (adv)
vafipa, tepidity (n)
vafipiu, tepidly (adv)
vafipu, tepid (adj)
vafita, temptation (n)
vafito, tempt (v)
vafitua, tempter (n doer)
vagara, shake (n)
vagaretiena, shakedown (n)
vagario, shook (v pa)
vagariveila, shakeup (n)
vagaro, shake (v)
vagaru, shaky (adj)
vagarua, shaker (n doer)
vagaruila, shakeout (n)
vagata, rapture (n)
vagato, enrapture (v)
vagatu, rapt (adj)
vagauka, rape (n)
vagauko, rape (v)
vagaukua, rapist (n doer)
vahem, Number_1e1956
vaiaika, ferocity (n)
vaiaikiu, ferociously (adv)
vaiaiku, ferocious (adj)
vaiana, carnivore (n)
vaianiu, carnivorously (adv)
vaianu, carnivorous (adj)
vaiapa, girth (n)
vaiapara, girdle (n)
vaiapo, gird (v)
vaiapua, girder (n doer)
vaidotu, naked (adj)
vaifika, guard (n)
vaifikana, guardianship (n)
vaifikanua, guardian (n doer)
vaifikeluita, guardrail (n)
vaifiko, guard (v)
vaifopa, dinner (n)
vaifopedauna, dinnertime (n)
vaifopeshelefa, dinnerware (n)
vaifopo, dine (v)
vaifota, guarantee (n)

vaifoto, guarantee (v)
vaifotua, guarantor (n doer)
vaiga, explanation (n)
vaigauko, ravage (v)
vaigaukua, ravager (n doer)
vaigo, explain (v)
vailata, bounty (n)
vailatu, bountiful (adj)
vailoka, feist (n)
vailoko, feist (v)
vailoku, feist (adj)
vaima, plane (n d:flat)
vaimo, plane (v d:flat)
vairata, cycle (n)
vairatiu, cyclically (adv)
vairato, cycle (v)
vairatu, cyclic (adj)
vairatu, cyclical (adj)
vairatua, cycler (n doer)
vairopa, cylinder (n)
vaisha, chef (n)
vaita, chief (n)
vaitha, noose (n)
vaithaka, nuisance (n)
vaitho, noose (v)
vaitiu, chiefly (adv)
vaitu, chief (adj)
vaiwata, shelter (n)
vaiwato, shelter (v)
vaizha, mantle (n)
vaka, back (n)
vakaushu, backward (adj/adv)
vakeberanita, background (n)
vakethautha, backyard (n)
vaketoika, backbone (n)
vakiveila, backup (n)
vako, back (v)
vakua, backer (n doer)
vakuita, backlog (n)
vala, V (let sng)
valana, bonus (n)
valasha, gloss (n)
valasho, gloss (v)
valashu, glossy (adj)
valebara, connoisseur (n)
valekafelupa, parachute (n)
valekafelupo, parachute (v)
valekaito, parry (v)
valesha, birth (n)
valesheviula, birthday (n)
valesho, birth (v)
vali, Vs (let pl)
valiferata, parcel (n)
valiferato, parcel (v)
valikadarofa, paragraph (n)
valikafita, parasite (n)
valikafitu, parasitic (adj)
valikaiafa, parade (n)
valikaiafo, parade (v)
valikaiafua, parader (n doer)
valikaiaka, paranoia (n)
valikaiaku, paranoid (adj)
valikamafito, paralyze (v)

valikanina, parallel (n)
valikanino, parallel (v)
valikaninu, parallel (adj)
valikaninueta, parallelism (n)
valikanioka, parameter (n)
valikanioku, parametric (adj)
valikaniuku, paramount (adj)
valikaperena, paradox (n)
valikapereniu, paradoxically (adv)
valikaperenu, paradoxical (adj)
valikarena, parasol (n)
valikashaira, paradise (n)
valikavarosha, paraphrase (n)
valikavarosho, paraphrase (v)
valipafa, quantity (n)
valipafiu, quantitatively (adv)
valipafo, quantify (v)
valipafu, quantifiable (adj)
valipafu, quantitative (adj)
valipafueta, quantification (n)
valita, circle (n)
valitaiva, jeopardy (n)
valitaivo, jeopardize (v)
valitata, circulation (n)
valitato, circulate (v)
valitatua, circulator (n doer)
valitiu, circularly (adv)
valito, circle (v)
valitu, circular (adj)
valomeirifa, parole (n)
valotifoka, circuitry (n)
valotiga, pardon (n)
valotigo, pardon (v)
valotika, circuit (n)
valotiko, circuit (v)
Valuala, February (n)
valuripa, umbrella (n)
valusha, glide (n)
valusho, glide (v)
valushua, glider (n doer)
vama, soda (n)
Vanadiuma, Vanadium (n)
vanafa, couple (n)
vanafo, couple (v)
vanafua, coupler (n doer)
vanatha, caress (n)
vanatho, caress (v)
vanianu, cardiac (adj)
vanika, copulation (n)
vanikao, copulated (v prp)
vaniko, copulate (v)
Vanikuvifa, Vancouver (n)
vanipa, competition (n)
vanipata, competitiveness (n)
vanipiu, competitively (adv)
vanipo, compete (v)
vanipora, competence (n)
vaniporiu, competently (adv)
vaniporu, competent (adj)
vanipu, competitive (adj)
vanipua, competitor (n doer)
vanitara, sultan (n)
vanudu, sultry (adj)

vapa, rope (n)
vapo, rope (v)
vapua, roper (n doer)
vapueta, petition (n)
vapueto, petition (v)
vapuetua, petitioner (n doer)
Varemaina, Fahrenheit (adj)
vareta, pen (n d:ink device)
vareto, pen (v d:ink device)
varifoka, template (n)
varika, fort (n)
varikaliki, fortitude (n pl)
varikata, fortress (n)
varikiveila, followup (n)
varikiveila, follow-up (n)
varikiveilu, followup (adj)
varikiveilu, follow-up (adj)
variko, fortify (v)
varila, plane (n d:airplane)
varisha, phrase (n)
varisho, phrase (v)
varitesha, gulch (n)
varitha, language (n)
varitufa, security (n)
varitufiu, securely (adv)
varitufo, secure (v)
varitufu, secure (adj)
vashipa, bachelor (n)
vathipa, effort (n)
vathipemeniu, effortlessly (adv)
vathipemenu, effortless (adj)
Vatikana, Vatican (n)
vatuga, peak (n)
vatugo, peak (v)
vauda, law (n)
vaudemena, lawlessness (n)
vaudemeniu, lawlessly (adv)
vaudemenu, lawless (adj)
vaudenagua, lawmaker (n doer)
vaudepelikua, lawbreaker (n doer)
vaudepelona, lawman (n)
vaudepeloni, lawmen (n pl)
vauderolifa, vacillation (n)
vauderolifo, vacillate (v)
vauderolifu, vacillatory (adj)
vauderolifua, vacillator (n doer)
vaudiu, lawfully (adv)
vaudu, lawful (adj)
vaudua, lawyer (n doer)
vaufita, prison (n)
vaufito, imprison (v)
vaufitua, prisoner (n doer)
vaufitueta, imprisonment (n)
vauga, fight (n)
vaugio, fought (v pa)
vaugo, fight (v)
vaugua, fighter (n doer)
vauifa, vacuum (n)
vauifiu, vacuously (adv)
vauifo, vacuum (v)
vauifu, vacuous (adj)
vauiga, vagueness (n)

vauigiu, vaguely (adv)
vauigu, vague (adj)
vauika, vacancy (n)
vauiketa, vacation (n)
vauiketo, vacation (v)
vauiketua, vacationer (n doer)
vauikiu, vacantly (adv)
vauiko, vacate (v)
vauiku, vacant (adj)
vauikua, vacator (n doer)
vauka, urge (n)
vaukiu, urgently (adv)
vauko, urge (v)
vauku, urgent (adj)
vaukua, urger (n doer)
vaukueta, urgency (n)
vaula, valley (n)
vauna, spoil (n)
vauno, spoil (v)
vaunua, spoiler (n doer)
vaupa, value (n)
vaupifota, maintenance (n)
vaupifoto, maintain (v)
vaupifotua, maintainer (n doer)
vaupo, value (v)
vaupu, valuable (adj)
vaupueta, valuation (n)
vaupula, valuable (n)
vauriko, follow (v)
vaurikua, follower (n doer)
vaushefalimu, mainstream (adj)
vausheluka, mainstay (n)
vaushenoika, etiquette (n)
vausheraupa, mainland (n)
vausheroifa, mainline (n)
vaushiu, mainly (adv)
vaushu, main (adj)
vautha, domain (n)
vava, rub (n)
vavo, rub (v)
vazhada, bother (n)
vazhado, bother (v)
vazhima, fit (n d:spasm)
vazhimo, fit (v d:spasm)
vedu, but (adv/conj/prep)
vefelana, stationery (n)
vefipa, pond (n)
vefito, ponder (v)
veiakuita, gynecology (n)
veiakuitua, gynecologist (n doer)
veiata, nozzle (n)
veida, future (n)
veidu, futuristic (adj)
veidua, futurist (n doer)
veifota, positive (n)
veifotiu, positively (adv)
veifotu, positive (adj)
veikata, futility (n)
veikatu, futile (adj)
veilifa, splendor (n)
veilifiu, splendidly (adv)
veilifu, splendid (adj)
veilina, position (n)

veilino, position (v)
veilinua, positioner (n doer)
veilipa, poise (n)
veilipo, poise (v)
veilopa, pose (n)
veilopo, pose (v)
veilopua, poser (n doer)
veinena, pony (n)
veinenemitha, ponytail (n)
veineno, pony (v)
veipa, bout (n)
veisha, lawn (n)
veishekeriteshua, lawnmower (n doer)
veitha, olive (n)
veiuta, nuzzle (n)
veiuto, nuzzle (v)
veivoila, usurpation (n)
veivoilo, usurp (v)
veivoilua, usurper (n doer)
velarina, pasture (n)
velaruva, comfort (n)
velaruviu, comfortably (adv)
velaruvo, comfort (v)
velaruvu, comfortable (adj)
velaruvua, comforter (n doer)
veletolu, where-from (adv)
veletu, from (prep)
velifa, fitness (n d:healthy)
velifiu, fittingly (adv d:healthy)
velifu, fit (adj d:healthy)
velifweku, fittest (adj)
velifwelu, fitter (adj)
velika, budget (n)
veliko, budget (v)
veliku, budgetary (adj)
velina, summons (n)
velino, summon (v)
velipa, browse (n)
velipo, browse (v)
velipua, browser (n doer)
velira, entertainment (n)
veliro, entertain (v)
velirua, entertainer (n doer)
velisha, steam (n)
velishefaliro, steamroll (v)
velishefalirua, steamroller (n doer)
velishefeleva, steamship (n)
velishekoba, steamboat (n)
velisho, steam (v)
velishu, steamy (adj)
velishua, steamer (n doer)
veluda, budge (n)
veludo, budge (v)
vemiana, winter (n)
vemianedauna, wintertime (n)
vemiano, winterize (v)
vemianu, winter (adj)
vemianu, winterly (adj)
vemianu, wintry (adj)
venai-, hept- (num 7 pref)
venai-, sept- (num 7 pref)

veneth, seventh (num 7 ord)
Venezhuilafa, Venezuela (n)
venfk, septenquadragintillion (num 1e144 card)
venft, septentrigintillion (num 1e114 card)
veni, seven (num 7 card)
venialfhemka, Number_1e28506
venida, seventy (num 70 card)
venidai-, seventy- (num 70 pref)
venideth, seventieth (num 70 ord)
venika, economy (n)
venikara, economics (n)
venikaru, economic (adj)
venikiu, economically (adv)
veniko, economize (v)
veniku, economical (adj)
venikua, economist (n doer)
venipa, seventeen (num 17 card)
venipai-, seventeen- (num 17 pref)
venipeth, seventeenth (num 17 ord)
venka, septillion (num 1e24 card)
venkai-, yotta- (num 1e24 pref)
venketh, septillionth (num 1e24 ord)
venshk, septenvigintillion (num 1e84 card)
venshkai-, dieni-
venshketh, septenvigintillionth (num 1e84 ord)
vensht, septendecillion (num 1e54 card)
venshtai-, nekani- (num 1e54 pref)
venshteth, septendecillionth (num 1e54 ord)
veratita, deceleration (n)
verafito, decelerate (v)
verafitua, decelerator (n doer)
verago, fence (v d:spar)
verama, ban (n)
veramashika, banishment (n)
veramashiko, banish (v)
veramekerasha, bandwidth (n)
veramika, banality (n)
veramipa, band (n d:group)
veramipo, band (v d:group)
veramipu, bandy (adj d:group)
veramo, ban (v)
veramua, banner (n doer)
veranita, camera (n)
veranitua, cameraperson (n doer)
vereika, muzzle (n)
vereiko, muzzle (v)
verika, excess (n)
verikiu, excessively (adv)
veriko, exceed (v)
veriku, excessive (adj)
verit, except (prep/conj)

verita, exception (n)
veritiu, exceptionally (adv)
verito, except (v)
veritu, exceptional (adj)
veroka, block (n d:cube)
veroku, blocky (adj d:cube)
Verumonita, Vermont (n)
Veshaifara, September (n)
veshipa, pebble (n)
vetagiaula, cease-fire (n)
vetaka, agenda (n)
vetapa, agency (n)
vetaveta, cessation (n)
vetaveto, cease (v)
vetha, nose (n)
vethekeraika, nosedive (n)
vethelirodiota, nosebleed (n)
vetheraika, nausea (n)
vetheraiko, nauseate (v)
vetheraiku, nauseous (adj)
vethita, nostril (n)
vethiu, nasally (adv)
vetho, nosy (v)
vethu, nasal (adj)
vezha, bug (n)
vezho, bug (v)
vezhu, buggy (adj)
viafa, shower (n)
viafo, shower (v)
viaga, crowd (n)
viagara, shiver (n)
viagaro, shiver (v)
viago, crowd (v)
viagua, crowder (n doer)
viaha, gee (interj)
viaha, geez (interj)
viaina, swivel (n)
viaino, swivel (v)
viakelata, crowbar (n)
vialiafa, phantom (n)
vialita, cogitation (n)
vialitao, cogitated (v prp)
vialito, cogitate (v)
vialoifa, violin (n)
vialoifua, violinist (n doer)
viamo, pine (n)
vianika, pioneer (n)
vianiko, pioneer (v)
vianipa, fascination (n)
vianipo, fascinate (v)
viapa, cogency (n)
viapiu, cogently (adv)
viapu, cogent (adj)
viaritha, linguistics (n)
viarithiu, linguistically (adv)
viarithu, linguistic (adj)
viarithua, linguist (n doer)
viaroka, crow (n)
viaroko, crow (v)
viasha, base (n)
viashalita, basement (n)
viashemonida, baseball (n)
viasheta, basis (n)

viashiu, basically (adv)
viasho, base (v)
viashu, basic (adj)
viashua, baser (n doer)
viata, cognate (n)
viataka, cognition (n)
viataku, cognitive (adj)
viatakueta, cognizance (n)
viatakuetu, cognizant (adj)
viatesha, fece (n)
viatesho, defecate (v)
viateshu, fecal (adj)
viateshueta, defecation (n)
viatha, rev (n)
viatho, rev (v)
viauka, damn (n)
viauko, damn (v)
viauku, damn (adj)
viausha, sport (n)
viaushebidua, sportscaster (n doer)
viaushefelafa, sportswear (n)
viaushepelona, sportsman (n)
viaushepelonefifa, sportsmanship (n)
viaushepeloni, sportsmen (n pl)
viaushiu, sportily (adv)
viausho, sport (v)
viaushu, sporty (adj)
viaushua, sportster (n doer)
vibaka, bombardment (n)
vibako, bombard (v)
vidota, nudity (n)
vidotu, nude (adj)
vidotua, nude (n doer)
viena, nomen (n)
Vienafa, Vienna (n)
vienoka, nomination (n)
vienokiu, nominally (adv)
vienoko, nominate (v)
vienoku, nominal (adj)
vienokua, nominator (n doer)
vienokuina, nominee (n)
vieraka, fury (n)
vierakara, furor (n)
vierakiu, furiously (adv)
vierako, infuriate (v)
vieraku, furious (adj)
vierakua, infuriator (n doer)
vierofa, furnace (n)
vietha, brochure (n)
Vietonama, Vietnam (n)
Vietonamana, Vietnamese (n)
vifio, went (v pa)
vifo, go (v)
vifua, goer (n doer)
vigafa, giggle (n)
vigafo, giggle (v)
vigafua, giggler (n doer)
vigaka, shock (n)
vigakelesha, shockwave (n)
vigakiu, shockingly (adv)
vigako, shock (v)

vigakua, shocker (n doer)
vigauko, ravish (v)
vigito, vex (v)
vika, fix (n)
viketa, fixation (n)
viketo, fixate (v)
vikezhara, fixture (n)
vikiko, careen (v)
viko, fix (v)
viku, fixable (adj)
vikua, fixer (n doer)
vikuaka, chariot (n)
vilama, bond (n)
vilamaka, bondage (n)
vilamethorithua, bondholder (n doer)
vilamo, bond (v)
vilamua, bonder (n doer)
Vilana, EhoMonth05 (n)
viloka, fist (n)
viloko, fist (v)
viloku, fistful (adj)
viluba, bomb (n)
vilubo, bomb (v)
vilubua, bomber (n doer)
vimana, window (n)
vimanemenu, windowless (adj)
vimano, window (v)
vimanuano, eavesdrop (v)
vinada, coupon (n)
vinoka, bundle (n)
vinoko, bundle (v)
vinokua, bundler (n doer)
vinopa, bunch (n)
vinopo, bunch (v)
vinopu, bunchy (adj)
vinuina, cascade (n)
vinuino, cascade (v)
vioika, temple (n)
vioisha, crucifixion (n)
vioisho, crucify (v)
vioka, giant (n)
viokevioku, gigantic (adj)
viona, cruciality (n)
vioniu, crucially (adv)
vionu, crucial (adj)
Vioriafa, EhoDay02 (n)
Vipalapa, Bible (n)
vipoaka, caravan (n)
vipoako, caravan (v)
viputesha, carcass (n)
virasha, eagerness (n)
virashiu, eagerly (adv)
virashu, eager (adj)
virofata, defect (n)
virofatiu, defectively (adv)
virofato, defect (v)
virofatu, defective (adj)
virofatua, defector (n doer)
Viroginiafa, Virginia (n)
virotha, effect (n)
virothana, effectiveness (n)
virothara, efficiency (n)

virothariu, efficiently (adv)
virotharu, efficient (adj)
virothiu, effectively (adv)
virotho, effect (v)
virothu, effective (adj)
virothua, effector (n doer)
vishala, diva (n)
vishana, shampoo (n)
vishano, shampoo (v)
vishanua, shampooer (n doer)
vishikika, shamble (n)
vishikiko, shamble (v)
vishoka, sham (n)
vishota, shame (n)
vishotemeniu, shamelessly (adv)
vishotemenu, shameless (adj)
vishotiu, shamefully (adv)
vishoto, shame (v)
vishotu, shameful (adj)
vitarisha, gasoline (n)
vitesha, stump (n d:tree)
vitha, limit (n)
vithaifa, feline (n)
vithara, limitation (n)
vitho, limit (v)
vithopo, delimit (v)
vithopua, delimiter (n doer)
vithua, limiter (n doer)
viufika, warrant (n)
viufiko, warrant (v)
viugila, epic (n)
viugu, big (adj)
viugwaku, biggest (adj)
viugwelu, bigger (adj)
viuka, force (n)
viukiu, forcefully (adv)
viukiu, forcibly (adv)
viuko, force (v)
viuku, forceful (adj)
viuku, forcible (adj)
viukua, forcer (n doer)
viukuka, faucet (n)
viula, day (n)
viulu, daily (adj)
viuma, gulley (n)
viunefelauma, daydream (n)
viunefelaumo, daydream (v)
viunefeluana, daylight (n)
viunekeifa, daycare (n)
viunepelika, daybreak (n)
viunerazhu, daylong (adj)
viunodauna, daytime (n)
viupa, warranty (n)
viura, war (n)
viurebotesha, warpath (n)
viuredauna, wartime (n)
viurefeleva, warship (n)
viurekefita, warhead (n)
viurevarila, warplane (n)
viurifa, warfare (n)
viuro, war (v)
viuru, warlike (adj)
viurua, warrior (n doer)

viuto, warn (v)
viuviata, ambiguity (n)
viuviatiu, ambiguously (adv)
viuviatu, ambiguous (adj)
vivafa, mustard (n)
voagerutha, forgiveness (n)
voageruthio, forgave (v pa)
voagerutho, forgive (v)
voageruthu, forgivable (adj)
voageruthua, forgiver (n doer)
voaika, fierceness (n)
voaikiu, fiercely (adv)
voaiku, fierce (adj)
voalifa, forever (n)
voalifiu, forever (adv)
voamuna, fortune (n)
voamuniu, fortunately (adv)
voamunu, fortunate (adj)
voanariu, formerly (adv
   d:previous)
voanaru, former (adj d:previous)
voanausha, forward (n)
voanaushiu, forward (adv)
voanausho, forward (v)
voanaushu, forward (adj)
voaneberanita, foreground (n)
voanebida, forecast (n)
voanebido, forecast (v)
voanebidua, forecaster (n doer)
voanedepa, forethought (n)
voanedinana, forefinger (n)
voanefelarina, forefront (n)
voaneferuifa, foreplay (n)
voanegeleka, foreknowledge (n)
voanegereta, foreclosure (n)
voanegereto, foreclose (v)
voanegeruka, forbear (n
   d:ancestor)
voanegeruka, forbearer (n
   d:ancestor)
voanekapa, forehand (n)
voanelaomuala, forerunner (n)
voanelaufo, forebode (v)
voaneperetio, foretold (v pa)
voanepereto, foretell (v)
voanepoefita, foreshadow (n)
voanepoefito, foreshadow (v)
voaneshetausha, forbearance (n
   d:refrain)
voaneshetaushio, forbore (v pa
   d:refrain)
voaneshetausho, forbear (v
   d:refrain)
voaneshinena, forearm (n)
voaneteiko, forestall (v)
voanethutha, foresight (n)
voanethuthio, foresaw (v pa)
voanethuthiu, foreseeably (adv)
voanethutho, foresee (v)
voanethuthu, foreseeable (adj)
voanevifio, forewent (v pa)
voanevifo, forego (v)
voaneviuto, forewarn (v)

voanewaku, foremost (adj)
voanibilefio, forthcame (v pa)
voanibilefo, forthcome (v)
voanifiu, forth (adv)
voanikefita, forehead (n)
voanu, fore (adj)
voapeima, forfeiture (n)
voapeimo, forfeit (v)
voapeimua, forfeiter (n doer)
voapelona, foreman (n)
voapeloni, foremen (n pl)
voarifa, march (n)
voarifo, march (v)
voarifua, marcher (n doer)
voarino, forage (v)
voarinua, forager (n doer)
voasha, waste (n)
voasheidona, wastewater (n)
voasheraupa, wasteland (n)
voashetalofa, wastebasket (n)
voashevuapa, wastepaper (n)
voashiu, wastefully (adv)
voasho, waste (v)
voashu, wasteful (adj)
voashua, waster (n doer)
voashueta, wastefulness (n)
voatha, date (n d:fruit)
voathita, forbiddence (n)
voathitio, forbade (v pa)
voathito, forbid (v)
voathitua, forbidder (n doer)
voatopa, forgettance (n)
voatopio, forgot (v pa)
voatopiu, forgetfully (adv)
voatopo, forget (v)
voatopu, forgetful (adj)
voatopua, forgetter (n doer)
vobaifa, eviction (n)
vobaifo, evict (v)
vobaika, engagement (n)
vobaiko, engage (v)
vobala, medication (n)
vobala, medicine (n)
vobaliu, medically (adv)
vobalo, medicate (v)
vobalu, medical (adj)
vobalua, medic (n doer)
vobiufita, evaporation (n)
vobiufito, evaporate (v)
vobiufitua, evaporator (n doer)
vodeipa, equipment (n)
vodeipo, equip (v)
voferapa, envelope (n)
voferapo, envelop (v)
voferapua, enveloper (n doer)
vofeta, evidence (n)
vofetiu, evidently (adv)
vofeto, evidence (v)
vofetu, evident (adj)
vofitapa, establishment (n)
vofitapo, establish (v)
vofitapua, establisher (n doer)
vogaifota, eruption (n)

vogaifoto, erupt (v)
vogaifotua, eruptor (n doer)
vogalita, energy (n)
vogalito, energize (v)
vogalitu, energetic (adj)
vogalitua, energizer (n doer)
vogereta, enclosure (n)
vogereto, enclose (v)
voiafa, surf (n)
voiafepelorika, surfboard (n)
voiafo, surf (v)
voiafua, surfer (n doer)
voiberiena, surname (n)
voifa, navel (n)
voifelaufota, survival (n)
voifelaufoto, survive (v)
voifelaufotua, survivalist (n doer)
voifelaufotua, survivor (n doer)
voifelaufotueta, survivability (n)
voifuata, survey (n)
voifuataka, surveillance (n)
voifuato, survey (v)
voifuatua, surveyor (n doer)
voiga, surge (n)
voigeloita, surcharge (n)
voigo, surge (v)
voikuata, resurrection (n)
voikuato, resurrect (v)
voikuatua, resurrector (n doer)
voilarana, surrogation (n)
voilarano, surrogate (v)
voilaranu, surrogate (adj)
voilaranua, surrogate (n doer)
voilunito, surpass (v)
voina, knife (n)
voiniuko, surmount (v)
voino, knife (v)
voinua, knifer (n doer)
voinumata, surplus (n)
voipeluafa, surrealism (n)
voipeluatu, surreal (adj)
voisha, busyness (n)
voishenika, surtax (n)
voishika, business (n)
voishiku, businesslike (adj)
voishikua, businessman (n doer)
voishikua, businessperson (n
   doer)
voishiu, busily (adv)
voisho, busy (v)
voishu, busy (adj)
voitha, computation (n)
voithaka, computerization (n)
voithako, computerize (v)
voitho, compute (v)
voithu, computational (adj)
voithua, computer (n doer)
voitolipo, surmise (v)
voiva, gamble (n)
voivaka, gambit (n)
voiviusha, surprise (n)
voiviushiu, surprisingly (adv)
voiviusho, surprise (v)

voivo, gamble (v)
voivua, gambler (n doer)
vokaika, erasure (n)
vokaikaika, eradication (n)
vokaikaiko, eradicate (v)
vokaikaikua, eradicator (n doer)
vokaiko, erase (v)
vokaikua, eraser (n doer)
vokanifa, enchantment (n)
vokanifo, enchant (v)
vokanipa, enhancement (n)
vokanipo, enhance (v)
vokanipua, enhancer (n doer)
vokemifa, evolution (n)
vokemifo, evolve (v)
vokemifu, evolutionary (adj)
vokuapa, erotica (n)
vokuapu, erotic (adj)
vokuapueta, eroticism (n)
vokuata, erection (n)
vokuato, erect (v)
vokuatua, erector (n doer)
volaisha, enjoyment (n)
volaisho, enjoy (v)
volaishu, enjoyable (adj)
volanifa, enormity (n)
volanifiu, enormously (adv)
volanifu, enormous (adj)
volata, code (n)
volato, code (v)
volatua, coder (n doer)
volika, chest (n d:container)
vomaka, risk (n)
vomaka, riskiness (n)
vomakiu, riskily (adv)
vomako, risk (v)
vomaku, risky (adj)
vomoida, encyclopedia (n)
vomoidu, encyclopedic (adj)
vonelika, engram (n)
voneliko, engrain (v)
vonoliko, ingrain (v)
vonuda, book (n)
vonudaika, bookend (n)
vonudapa, booklet (n)
vonudathova, bookshop (n)
vonudathovua, bookshopper (n
    doer)
vonudekelofa, bookkeeping (n)
vonudekelofua, bookkeeper (n
    doer)
vonudenaga, bookmaking (n)
vonudenagua, bookmaker (n
    doer)
vonudenalifa, bookshelf (n)
vonuderapa, bookstore (n)
vonudeshuata, bookcase (n)
vonudo, book (v)
vonuterelifa, booksale (n)
vonuterelifua, bookseller (n doer)
vopalita, enaction (n)
vopalita, enactment (n)
vopalito, enact (v)

vopana, entirety (n)
vopaniu, entirely (adv)
vopanu, entire (adj)
vopiropa, eternity (n)
vopiropiu, eternally (adv)
vopiropo, eternalize (v)
vopiropu, eternal (adj)
vopiropua, eternalizer (n doer)
vopoifa, encounter (n)
vopoifo, encounter (v)
voreiba, errand (n)
vorepelorika, cupboard (n)
vorida, popularity (n)
voridiu, popularly (adv)
vorido, popularize (v)
voridu, popular (adj)
voridua, populace (n doer)
vorietio, learnt (v pa)
vorieto, learn (v)
vorietua, learner (n doer)
vorigurita, cupcake (n)
vorika, motor (n)
vorikato, motorize (v)
vorikegerela, motorcar (n)
vorikeida, motel (n)
vorikepivita, motorbike (n)
vorikeshekoba, motorboat (n)
vorikevairata, motorcycle (n)
vorikevairato, motorcycle (v)
vorikevairatua, motorcyclist (n
    doer)
voriko, motor (v)
vorikua, motorist (n doer)
vorila, spring (n d:season)
voriledauna, springtime (n)
vorilu, spring (adj d:season)
vorina, form (n d:shape)
vorinaka, format (n)
vorinako, format (v)
vorinakua, formatter (n doer)
vorinapa, formulation (n)
vorinapo, formulate (v)
vorinapua, formulator (n doer)
vorinaripa, formula (n)
vorinata, formal (n)
vorinatiu, formally (adv)
vorinato, formalize (v)
vorinatu, formal (adj)
vorinatueta, formality (n)
vorino, form (v d:shape)
vorinoka, deformation (n)
vorinokapu, formidable (adj)
vorinoko, deform (v)
vorinokua, deformer (n doer)
vorinua, former (n doer d:shape)
vorinueta, formation (n)
voripa, cup (n)
voripo, cup (v)
vorita, build (n)
voritha, forum (n)
voritio, built (v pa)
voritishu, builtin (adj)
voritiveila, buildup (n)

vorito, build (v)
voritua, builder (n doer)
voruva, population (n)
voruvo, populate (v)
voshaferepu, lovable (adj
    d:common)
voshaiko, evoke (v)
voshaka, scepter (n)
voshaka, sceptre (n)
voshara, love (n d:common)
vosharo, love (v d:common)
vosharu, lovely (adj d:common)
vosharua, lover (n doer
    d:common)
voshavova, love (n d:emphatic)
voshavovo, love (v d:emphatic)
voshavovu, lovely (adj
    d:emphatic)
voshavovua, lover (n doer
    d:emphatic)
voshelipa, erosion (n)
voshelipo, erode (v)
vosheta, column (n)
vosheto, columnate (v)
voshiaka, escape (n)
voshiakiapa, escapade (n)
voshiakipiu, escapably (adv)
voshiako, escape (v)
voshiaku, escapable (adj)
voshiakua, escapee (n doer)
voshiakueta, escapism (n)
voshika, shaft (n)
voshiko, shaft (v)
voshikua, shafter (n doer)
voshipeta, estate (n)
voshipeto, estate (v)
voshuika, escalation (n)
voshuiko, escalate (v)
voshuikua, escalator (n doer)
voteta, father (n)
votetefifa, fatherhood (n)
votetemenu, fatherless (adj)
voteteraupa, fatherland (n)
voteto, father (v)
votetu, fatherly (adj)
vothuta, esteem (n)
vothuto, esteem (v)
vovauifa, evacuation (n)
vovauifo, evacuate (v)
vovauifua, evacuator (n doer)
vovaupa, evaluation (n)
vovaupo, evaluate (v)
vovaupua, evaluator (n doer)
voviuka, enforcement (n)
voviuko, enforce (v)
voviuku, enforceable (adj)
voviukua, enforcer (n doer)
vozhaka, evil (n)
vozhakausha, arson (n)
vozhakausho, arson (v)
vozhakaushu, arsonous (adj)
vozhakaushua, arsonist (n doer)
vozhaku, evil (adj)

vozhakua, evildoer (n doer)
vozhanika, evasion (n)
vozhanikiu, evasively (adv)
vozhaniko, evade (v)
vozhaniku, evasive (adj)
vozhanikua, evader (n doer)
vozhufa, enthusiam (n)
vozhufiu, enthusiastically (adv)
vozhufo, enthuse (v)
vozhufu, enthusiastic (adj)
vozhufua, enthusiast (n doer)
vozhusha, essay (n)
vozhusho, essay (v)
vu, by (adj/adv/prep)
vuafita, definition (n)
vuafitiu, definitely (adv)
vuafito, define (v)
vuafitu, definite (adj)
vuafitu, definitive (adj)
vuaka, launch (n)
vuakebanifa, launchpad (n)
vuako, launch (v)
vuakua, launcher (n doer)
vuala, fine (n d:penalty)
vualo, fine (v d:penalty)
vualua, finer (n doer d:penalty)
vuama, laundry (n)
vuamita, laundromat (n)
vuamo, launder (v)
vuamua, launderer (n doer)
vuana, elite (n)
vuanu, elite (adj)
vuanua, elitist (n doer)
vuapa, paper (n)
vuapata, paperback (n)
vuapekioka, paperwork (n)
vuapelorika, paperboard (n)
vuapemenu, paperless (adj)
vuapeshuisha, paperweight (n)
vuapo, paper (v)
vuata, fineness (n d:small)
vuatiu, finely (adv d:small)
vuatu, fine (adj d:small)
vuaua, golly (interj)
vuausha, gosh (interj)
vuba, cub (n)
vubelasha, suppression (n)
vubelashana, suppressant (n)
vubelashiu, suppressively (adv)
vubelasho, suppress (v)
vubelashu, suppressive (adj)
vubelashua, suppressor (n doer)
vuberepo, supplant (v)
vuberesha, supplication (n)
vuberesho, supplicate (v)
vudauna, meantime (n)
vudauniu, meantime (adv)
vufiuka, byproduct (n)
vugaberautha, superflow (n)
vugaberautho, superflow (v)
vugaberauthu, superfluous (adj)
vugabiorita, superpower (n)
vugaderapa, superstore (n)

vugaderokirofa, superstar (n)
vugadiadara, supermodel (n)
vugafata, superficiality (n)
vugafatiu, superficially (adv)
vugafatu, superficial (adj)
vugafiaisha, supervision (n)
vugafiaisho, supervise (v)
vugafiaishu, supervisory (adj)
vugafiaishua, supervisor (n doer)
vugageloito, supercharge (v)
vugageloitua, supercharger (n doer)
vugagerena, superlative (n)
vugakigelako, superimpose (v)
vugakoilepeliola, superhighway (n)
vugakuto, superheat (v)
vugaleidiu, supernaturally (adv)
vugaleidu, supernatural (adj)
vugalipiu, superbly (adv)
vugalipu, superb (adj)
vugalu, super (adj)
vugamiafa, supernova (n)
vugana, superiority (n)
vuganu, superior (adj)
vuganua, superior (n doer)
vugapelona, superman (n)
vugapeloni, supermen (n pl)
vugasharolitua, superhero (n doer)
vugashelufo, supercool (v)
vugashelufu, supercool (adj)
vugashileka, superstructure (n)
vugasholu, superhuman (adj)
vugateruita, supremacy (n)
vugateruitiu, supremely (adv)
vugateruitu, supreme (adj)
vugateruitua, supremacist (n doer)
vugaveko, supercede (v)
vugaveko, supersede (v)
vugazhanitanu, supersonic (adj)
vugelaka, supposition (n)
vugelakiu, supposedly (adv)
vugelako, suppose (v)
vugelakua, supposer (n doer)
vugipifokana, superintendent (n)
vuiaufo, meander (v)
vuisha, friction (n)
vuishemenu, frictionless (adj)
vuishu, frictional (adj)
vuka, push (n)
vukafena, pushover (n)
vukida, puzzle (n)
vukido, puzzle (v)
vukidua, puzzler (n doer)
vukidueta, puzzlement (n)
vukiko, prod (v)
vukikua, prodder (n doer)
vuko, push (v)
vuku, pushy (adj)
vukua, pusher (n doer)
vulana, marriage (n)

vulano, marry (v)
vulanu, marital (adj)
vulasha, matrimony (n)
vulashu, matrimonial (adj)
vulika, quantum (n)
vuliku, quantum (adj)
vulunita, bypass (n)
vulunito, bypass (v)
vulunitua, bypasser (n doer)
vumaka, coffee (n)
vunahafa, cuddle (n)
vunahafo, cuddle (v)
vunopa, bark (n d:yelp)
vunopo, bark (v d:yelp)
vunopua, barker (n doer d:yelp)
vupana, mean (n)
vupauka, meanwhile (n)
vupaukiu, meanwhile (adv)
vupeliola, byway (n)
vupemena, meaninglessness (n)
vupemenu, meaningless (adj)
vupio, meant (v pa d:importance)
vupiu, meaningfully (adv d:importance)
vupo, mean (v d:importance)
vupu, meaningful (adj d:importance)
vureina, mucus (n)
vureinu, mucosal (adj)
vuroifa, byline (n)
vuta, put (n)
vuterelitua, bystander (n doer)
vutha, purge (n)
vuthiafa, purgatory (n)
vutho, purge (v)
vutio, put (v pa)
vuto, put (v)
vutolipa, demise (n)
vutolipo, demise (v)
vuvauda, bylaw (n)
vuvienoka, denomination (n)
vuvienoko, denominate (v)
vuvienoku, denominational (adj)
vuvienokua, denominator (n doer)
vuvifioa, bygone (n)
vuvifioi, bygones (n pl)
vuvifiou, bygone (adj)
wafipu, hence (adv)
wafiu, merely (adv)
wafu, mere (adj)
waiata, yell (n)
waiato, yell (v)
waiatua, yeller (n doer)
waiba, madness (n d:insane)
waibekiafa, madhouse (n)
waibepelona, madman (n)
waibepeloni, madmen (n pl)
waibu, mad (adj d:insane)
waibwelu, madder (adj d:insane)
waika, yikes (interj)
Waiominoka, Wyoming (n)
wakei, most (pron)

wakiu, mostly (adv)
waku, most (adj/adv)
walisha, youth (n)
walishu, young (adj)
walishu, youthful (adj)
walishueta, youngster (n)
walishwaku, youngest (adj)
walishwelu, younger (adj)
wapa, half (n)
wapeliolu, halfway (adj/adv)
wapo, halve (v)
wapu, half (adj)
warfhem, Number_1e1506
warfi, Ws (let pl)
warifa, W (let sng)
Waroshaufa, Warsaw (n)
washiku, yet (adv/conj)
Washinoketona, Washington (n)
watha, hen (n)
wathekiafa, henhouse (n)
wefana, wig (n)
wefika, rout (n d:dig)
wefiko, rout (v d:dig)
wefikua, router (n doer d:dig)
wefipa, root (n)
wefipo, root (v)
wei, yes (adv)
weia, yeah (adv)
weifa, sign (n)
weifebalita, signpost (n)
weifipa, signal (n)
weifipo, signal (v)
weifipua, signaler (n doer)
weifita, signature (n)
weifitua, signatory (n doer)
weifo, sign (v)
weifoka, significance (n)
weifokiu, significantly (adv)
weifoko, signify (v)
weifoku, significant (adj)
weifua, signer (n doer)
Weilosha, Wales (n)
weipu, yep (adv)
weipu, yup (adv)
weishekelosha, yesteryear (n)
weishekeloshiu, yesteryear (adv)
weishekeloshu, yesteryear (adj)
weisheviula, yesterday (n)
weisheviuliu, yesterday (adv)
weisheviulu, yesterday (adj)
welei, more (pron)
welifiu, moreover (adv)
welu, more (adj/adv)
wiafa, merit (n)
wiafo, merit (v)
wiapa, pilgramage (n)
wiapua, pilgrim (n doer)
wiasha, hike (n)
wiasho, hike (v)
wiashua, hiker (n doer)
wiato, owe (v)
wiatua, ower (n doer)
wiauka, odd (n d:probability)

wiaukemashipa, oddball (n)
wiena, home (n)
wienagio, homemade (v pa)
wienago, homemake (v)
wienagua, homemaker (n doer)
wienegeliupu, homesick (adj)
wienegiotu, homemade (adj)
wienelerina, homecoming (n)
wienemena, homelessness (n)
wienemeniu, homelessly (adv)
wienemenu, homeless (adj)
wienemiuna, hometown (n)
wieneraupa, homeland (n)
wienetheifo, homeown (v)
wienetheifua, homeowner (n
    doer)
wienevoritua, homebuilder (n
    doer)
wienika, homework (n)
wieno, home (v)
wienu, homey (adj)
wifa, hop (n)
wifo, hop (v)
wifopa, narrow (n)
wifopiu, narrowly (adv)
wifopo, narrow (v)
wifopu, narrow (adj)
wifopueta, narrowness (n)
wifopweku, narrowest (adj)
wifopwelu, narrower (adj)
wifua, hopper (n doer)
wikona, yogurt (n)
winofa, gum (n)
winofo, gum (v)
winofu, gummy (adj)
Wishakonisha, Wisconsin (n)
wiufo, hone (v)
wiusha, sewer (n d:waste conduit)
wiusha, sewerage (n)
wiusho, sewer (v d:waste conduit)
worofika, exhalation (n)
worofiko, exhale (v)
worofikua, exhaler (n doer)
ya, hah (interj)
yadita, yield (n)
yadito, yield (v)
yaditua, yielder (n doer)
yafefa, will (n d:inheritance)
yai, wow (interj)
vaifa, wafer (n)
yaifana, waffle (n)
yaifano, waffle (v)
yaigata, hostility (n)
yaigatu, hostile (adj)
yaila, foe (n)
yaita, verb (n)
yaivafitu, verbose (adj)
yaivata, verbiage (n)
yaivatiu, verbally (adv)
yaivatu, verbal (adj)
yaivuga, feud (n)
yaivugo, feud (v)
yaiya, wow (n)

yaiyo, wow (v)
yaka kodi, would (ndal d:will)
yaka, will (n d:determination)
yakebiorita, willpower (n)
yakiu, willfully (adv
    d:determination)
yakiu, willingly (adv)
yako, will (v d:determination)
yaku, willful (adj
    d:determination)
yakueta, willingness (n)
yalifa, wait (n)
yalifo, wait (v)
yalifua, waiter (n doer)
yalifua, waitress (n doer)
yalika, waddle (n)
yaliko, waddle (v)
yalipa, wad (n)
yalipo, wad (v)
yalusho, wallow (v)
yamefu, whenever (adv/conj)
yamei, when (pron)
yamika, quandary (n)
yamu, when (adv/conj)
yanu, amen (interj)
yariketala, algebra (n)
yariketaliu, algebraically (adv)
yariketalu, algebraic (adj)
yarikuta, algorithm (n)
yarikutiu, algorithmically (adv)
yarikutu, algorithmic (adj)
yarila, Y (let sng)
yaritu, foreign (adj)
yaritua, foreigner (n doer)
yarlhem, Number_1e1206
yarli, Ys (let pl)
yaroma, alumnus (n)
yaromi, alumni (n pl)
yasho, wade (v)
yashu, that (conj)
yashua, wader (n doer)
yatha, hoof (n)
yatho, hoof (v)
yathua, hoofer (n doer)
yaua, yow (interj)
yauaka, wretch (n)
yaufo, woo (v)
yauka, while (n)
yauku, while (conj)
youna, whimpei (n)
yauno, whimper (v)
yaupa, whip (n)
yaupelaiatha, whiplash (n)
yaupelaiatho, whiplash (v)
yaupo, whip (v)
yaupua, whipper (n doer)
yaushipu, awful (adj)
yaushoka, awkwardness (n)
yaushokiu, awkwardly (adv)
yaushoku, awkward (adj)
yaya, haha (interj)
yelifa, whim (n)
yelifa, whimsy (n)

yelifiu, whimsically (adv)
yelifu, whimsical (adj)
yelita, wetness (n)
yelitemoiufa, wetsuit (n)
yeliteraupa, wetland (n)
yelitio, wet (v pa)
yelito, wet (v)
yelitu, wet (adj)
yenausha, wonder (n)
yenausheraupa, wonderland (n)
yenaushiu, wonderfully (adv)
yenausho, wonder (v)
yenaushu, wonderful (adj)
yenaushu, wonderous (adj)
yenaushueta, wonderment (n)
yeriliu, yonder (adv)
yerilu, yonder (adj)
yesha, whiff (n)
yesho, whiff (v)
yilewapa, behalf (n)
yoi, whoa (interj)
yoiaka, wrench (n)
yoiako, wrench (v)
yoibako, wrangle (v)
yoibakua, wrangler (n doer)
yoikaniko, wrestle (v)
yoikanikua, wrestler (n doer)
yoikano, wrest (v)
yoilarika, WiggleTalk (n)
yoipa, whine (n)
yoipo, whine (v)
yoipu, whiney (adj)
yoipu, whiny (adj)
yoipua, whiner (n doer)
yoira, aisle (n)
yoitha, wiggle (n)
yoithata, wriggle (n)
yoithati, wriggler (n pl)
yoithato, wriggle (v)
yoitho, wiggle (v)
yoithua, wiggler (n doer)
yorina, worm (n)
yorino, worm (v)
yorinu, wormy (adj)
yoshu, as (adv/conj/prep)
yuaka, wick (n)
yuakata, wickedness (n)
yuakatu, wicked (adj)
yuana, white (n)
yuanefiausha, whitewash (n)
yuanefiausho, whitewash (v)
yuano, whiten (v)
yuanu, white (adj)
yufai-, quad- (num 4 pref)
yufai-, tetra- (num 4 pref)
yufaiaka, quadrant (n)
yufaimika, quadrangle (n)
yufeth, fourth (num 4 ord)
yufi, four (num 4 card)
yufialfhemka, Number_1e16356
yufida, forty (num 40 card)
yufidai-, forty- (num 40 pref)

yufidaka, quarantine (n)
yufidako, quarantine (v)
yufideth, fortieth (num 40 ord)
yufifk, quattuorquadragintillion (num 1e135 card)
yufift, quatturotrigintillion (num 1e105 card)
yufika, quadrillion (num 1e15 card)
yufikai-, peta- (num 1e15 pref)
yufiketh, quadrillionth (num 1e15 ord)
yufipa, fourteen (num 14 card)
yufipai-, fourteen- (num 14 pref)
yufipeth, fourteenth (num 14 ord)
yufishk, quattuorvigintillion (num 1e75 card)
yufishkai-, gieksi-
yufishketh, quattuorvigintillionth (num 1e75 ord)
yufisht, quattuordecillion (num 1e45 card)
yufishtai-, quaksi- (num 1e45 pref)
yufishteth, quattuordecillionth (num 1e45 ord)
Yugoshelava, Yugoslavia (n)
yuiana, suture (n)
yuiano, suture (v)
yuifoika, weirdness (n)
yuifoikiu, weirdly (adv)
yuifoiku, weird (adj)
yuifoikua, weirdo (n doer)
yuipa, awe (n)
yuipo, awe (v)
yuka, weed (n)
yuko, weed (v)
yuku, weedy (adj)
yukua, weeder (n doer)
yumata, waist (n)
yumateroifa, waistline (n)
yunipo, sew (v d:thread cloth)
yunipua, sewer (n doer d:thread cloth)
yupimiroka, rectangle (n)
yupimiroku, rectangular (adj)
yutabivanu, unisex (adj)
yutafonuda, uniqueness (n)
yutafonudiu, uniquely (adv)
yutafonudu, unique (adj)
yutaka, unification (n)
yutako, unify (v)
yutama, unit (n)
yutamana, union (n)
yutamano, unionize (v)
yutamanua, unionist (n doer)
yutamanueta, unionization (n)
yutamata, unity (n)
yutamo, unite (v)
yutamu, unitary (adj)
yutanarima, unilateralism (n)
yutanarimiu, unilaterally (adv)

yutanarimu, unilateral (adj)
yutasha, unison (n)
yutavorina, uniform (n)
yutavorino, uniform (v)
yutavorinu, uniformly (adj)
yutavorinueta, uniformity (n)
Yuteshuviula, Wednesday (n)
yutharifa, universe (n)
yutharifiu, universally (adv)
yutharifu, universal (adj)
yuvetiuga, wedlock (n)
yuvo, wed (v)
yuwana, vowel (n)
yuyau, wahoo (interj)
zahem, Number_1e3156
zala, Z (let sng)
zali, Zs (let pl)
zhaba, jump (n)
zhabiu, jumpily (adv)
zhabo, jump (v)
zhabu, jumpy (adj)
zhabua, jumper (n doer)
zhafa, zag (n)
zhafo, zag (v)
zhaguma, pajama (n)
zhahem, Number_1e3456
zhaiaga, hamburger (n)
zhaiaka, stimulation (n)
zhaiakana, stimulant (n)
zhaiakasha, stimulus (n)
zhaiakashi, stimuli (n pl)
zhaiako, stimulate (v)
zhaiakua, stimulator (n doer)
zhaidaisha, sentence (n d:punishment)
zhaidaisho, sentence (v d:punishment)
zhaifa, tragedy (n)
zhaifiu, tragically (adv)
zhaifu, tragic (adj)
zhaigaita, devil (n)
zhaigaitiu, devilishly (adv)
zhaigaito, bedevil (v)
zhaigaitu, devilish (adj)
zhaigiu, diabolically (adv)
zhaigu, diabolical (adj)
zhaika, vault (n d:leap)
zhaiko, vault (v d:leap)
zhaila, fall (n d:descent)
zhailio, fell (v pa d:descent)
zhailo, fall (v d:descent)
zhailuila, fallout (n)
zhaimo, flaunt (v)
zhaina, race (n d:competition)
zhainegelausha, racehorse (n)
zhainegethika, racetrack (n)
zhainepeliola, raceway (n)
zhaino, race (v d:competition)
zhainua, racer (n doer d:competition)
zhaipio, sent (v pa)
zhaipo, send (v)
zhaipota, fiasco (n)

zhaipua, sender (n doer)
zhairopa, dissent (n)
zhairopo, dissent (v)
zhairopua, dissenter (n doer)
zhairopua, dissident (n doer)
zhaishu, fast (adj d:speed)
zhaishwaku, fastest (adj)
zhaishwelu, faster (adj)
zhaita, failure (n)
zhaitazho, falter (v)
zhaithata, vilification (n)
zhaithato, vilify (v)
zhaithu, vile (adj)
zhaito, fail (v)
zhaitu, fallible (adj)
zhakata, villain (n)
zhala, Zh (let sng)
zhali, Zhs (let pl)
zhalideraipu, southbound (adj)
zhalikoika, suicide (n)
zhalikoiko, suicide (v)
zhalikoiku, suicidal (adj)
Zhalita Dakota, South Dakota (n)
Zhalita Karolina, South Carolina (n)
zhalita, south (n)
zhalitehaushu, southward (adj)
zhalitekuafa, southpaw (n)
zhaliteshaitha, southwest (n)
zhaliteshaithu, southwest (adj)
zhaliteshaithu, southwestern (adj)
zhalitokiasha, southeast (n)
zhalitokiashu, southeast (adj)
zhalitokiashu, southeastern (adj)
zhalitu, south (adj)
zhalitu, southern (adj)
zhalitua, southerner (n doer)
zhanifa, acoustics (n)
zhanifu, acoustic (adj)
zhanika, vandalism (n)
zhaniko, vandalize (v)
zhanikua, vandal (n doer)
zhanipa, dampness (n)
zhanipo, dampen (v)
zhanipu, damp (adj)
zhanipua, damper (n doer)
zhanita, sound (n d:audio)
zhanitafa, sonar (n)
zhanitana, sonance (n)
zhanitanelika, sonogram (n)
zhanitanu, sonic (adj)
zhanitegethika, soundtrack (n)
zhanito, sound (v d:audio)
zhanitua, sounder (n doer d:audio)
Zhapafa, Japan (n)
Zhapanifa, Japanese (n)
zharata, middle (n)
zharata, midst (n)
zharatepelona, middleman (n)
zharatu, middle (adj)
zharaula, midair (n)
zharefalima, midstream (n)

zhareferula, midsummer (n)
zharefivala, midseason (n)
zharekelosha, midyear (n)
zharekerufa, midweek (n)
zharelimena, midmorning (n)
zharemimana, midrange (n)
zharepeliola, midway (n)
zharetaifota, midpoint (n)
zharethishala, midsection (n)
zharevemipota, midwinter (n)
zharishotena, midterm (n)
zharishotenu, midterm (adj)
zharovimidota, midafternoon (n)
zharoviula, midday (n)
zhatufiu, sound (adv d:secure)
zhatufu, sound (adj d:secure)
zhau, so (adj/adv/conj/interj)
zhauba, danger (n)
zhaubo, endanger (v)
zhaubu, dangerous (adj)
zhaubueta, endangerment (n)
zhauei, so (pron)
zhaukaita, treachery (n)
zhaukaitiu, treacherously (adv)
zhaukaitu, treacherous (adj)
zhaukapa, treason (n)
zhauna, van (n)
zhaupa, jam (n d:bind)
zhauperufipa, vanquishment (n)
zhauperufipo, vanquish (v)
zhauperufipua, vanquisher (n doer)
zhaupo, jam (v d:bind)
zhaura, loss (n)
zhaurio, lost (v pa)
zhauro, lose (v)
zhaurua, loser (n doer)
zhauta, mine (n d:bomb)
zhauteperanida, minefield (n)
zhautha, zap (n)
zhautho, zap (v)
zhauto, mine (v d:bomb)
zhauvaifika, vanguard (n)
zhavaritesha, mediocrity (n)
zhavariteshu, mediocre (adj)
zhavatu, menial (adj)
zhazha, buzz (n d:hum)
zhazho, buzz (v d:hum)
zhazhu, buzzy (adj d:hum)
zhazhua, buzzer (n doer d:hum)
zheida, target (n)
zheido, target (v)
zheifiu, zippily (adv)
zheifo, zip (v)
zheifu, zippy (adj)
zheifua, zipper (n doer)
zheifuano, zipper (v)
zheikana, jungle (n)
Zheishusha, Jesus (n)
zheita, slick (n)
zheitu, slick (adj)
zheka, gas (n)
zheko, gas (v)

zheku, gaseous (adj)
zheleberepa, eggplant (n)
zheletheka, eggshell (n)
zhelipa, gasp (n)
zhelipo, gasp (v)
zheluga, egg (n)
zhelugo, egg (v)
Zheniva, Geneva (n)
Zhenona, Xenon (n)
Zheromana, German (n)
Zheromanifa, Germany (n)
Zherushaloma, Jerusalem (n)
zheshei, such (pron)
zheshu, such (adj/adv)
zheta, seriousness (n)
zhetana, zeta (n)
zhetiu, seriously (adv)
zhetu, serious (adj)
zhiafereilaku, electrochemical (adj)
zhiafiuba, electrode (n)
zhiafogukatu, electromagnetic (adj)
zhiafota, electricity (n)
zhiafotiu, electrically (adv)
zhiafoto, electrify (v)
zhiafotu, electric (adj)
zhiafotu, electrical (adj)
zhiafotua, electrician (n doer)
zhiafotueta, electrification (n)
zhiafuifa, plight (n)
zhiaga, pain (n)
zhiagemeniu, painlessly (adv)
zhiagemenu, painless (adj)
zhiagitesha, painkiller (n)
zhiagiu, painfully (adv)
zhiago, pain (v)
zhiagokio, painstook (v pa)
zhiagokiu, painstakingly (adv)
zhiagoko, painstake (v)
zhiagu, painful (adj)
zhiaka, electrocution (n)
zhiako, electrocute (v)
zhialima, meridian (n)
zhiama, medium (n d:middle)
zhiamu, medium (adj d:middle)
zhiano, rock (v d:sway)
zhianua, rocker (n doer d:sway)
zhiapa, fuel (n)
zhiapo, fuel (v)
zhiapua, fueler (n doer)
zhiarita, rocket (n)
zhiarito, rocket (v)
zhiarofika, meditation (n)
zhiarofiko, meditate (v)
zhiasha, electrics (n)
zhiasha, electronics (n)
zhiashipefota, electrostatic (n)
zhiashipefotu, electrostatic (adj)
zhiata, electron (n)
zhiatiu, electronically (adv)
zhiatu, electronic (adj)
zhiauka, zing (n)

zhiauko, zing (v)
zhiavigaka, electroshock (n)
zhiavigaku, electroshock (adj)
zhiazha, sin (n)
zhiazhiu, sinfully (adv)
zhiazho, sin (v)
zhiazhu, sinful (adj)
zhiazhua, sinner (n doer)
zhiberesha, someplace (n)
zhidauinu, sometimes (adj/adv)
zhidaunu, sometime (adj/adv)
zhidizha, something (n)
zhiena, zone (n)
zhieno, zone (v)
zhieta, game (n)
zhieto, game (v)
zhietua, gamer (n doer)
zhifa, zig (n)
zhifezhafa, zigzag (n)
zhifezhafo, zigzag (v)
zhifo, zig (v)
zhigaishoka, beast (n)
zhigashota, enragement (n)
zhigashoti, enragement (n pl)
zhigashoto, enrage (v)
zhigata, rage (n)
zhigato, rage (v)
zhika, win (n)
zhikio, won (v pa)
zhiko, win (v)
zhikua, winner (n doer)
zhilema, glimmer (n)
zhilemo, glimmer (v)
zhiletila, glitter (n)
zhiletilo, glitter (v)
zhiletilu, glittery (adj)
zhilika, glitz (n)
zhiliku, glitzy (adj)
zhilofa, glimpse (n)
zhilofo, glimpse (v)
zhilopa, glint (n)
zhilota, certainty (n)
zhilotiu, certainly (adv)
zhilotu, certain (adj)
zhima, issue (n)
zhimata, issuance (n)
zhimo, issue (v)
zhimua, issuer (n doer)
zhinakiu, somewhat (adv)
zhinei, some (pron)
zhinesha, jeans (n)
zhinialiu, somehow (adv)
Zhinoka, Zinc (n)
zhinola, somewhere (n)
zhinolu, somewhere (adv)
zhinonei, someone (pron)
zhinu, some (adj/adv)
zhiokio, hid (v pa d:obscure)
zhioko, hide (v d:obscure)
zhiopa, huddle (n)
zhiopo, huddle (v)
Zhioruzha, Georgia (n)
Zhirakoniuma, Zirconium (n)

zhisha, bee (n)
zhisheladei, somebody (n/pron)
Zhiufa, Jew (n)
Zhiufanu, Jewish (adj)
zhiumena, selflessness (n)
zhiumeniu, selflessly (adv)
zhiumenu, selfless (adj)
zhiuna, self (n)
zhiuniu, selfishly (adv)
zhiunu, selfish (adj)
zhiunueta, selfishness (n)
zhiuta, safe (n d:storage)
zhiva, jig (n d:dance)
zhiviuliu, someday (adv)
zhivo, jig (v d:dance)
zhizhala, ginger (n)
zhizhalethafa, gingerbread (n)
zhoda, set (n d:group)
zhodiveila, setup (n)
zhoduvaka, setback (n)
zhoiana, seam (n)
zhoianemeniu, seamlessly (adv)
zhoianemenu, seamless (adj)
zhoiano, seam (v)
zhoianoisha, seamstress (n)
zhoifa, silence (n)
zhoifiu, silently (adv)
zhoifo, silence (v)
zhoifu, silent (adj)
zhoifua, silencer (n doer)
zhoika, damage (n)
zhoiko, damage (v)
zhoipa, walk (n)
zhoipeliola, walkway (n)
zhoipiveila, walkup (n)
zhoipiveilu, walkup (adj)
zhoipo, walk (v)
zhoipua, walker (n doer)
zhoipuila, walkout (n)
zhoitha, wild (n)
zhoitheberesha, wilderness (n)
zhoithefelausha, wildlife (n)
zhoithefiefa, wildcat (n)
zhoithegiaula, wildfire (n)
zhoithekauna, wildcard (n)
zhoithiu, wildly (adv)
zhoithu, wild (adj)
zhoithuana, wildflower (n)
zhoithueta, wildness (n)
zhoiva, seal (n d:binding)
zhoivo, seal (v d:binding)
zhoivua, sealant (n
    d:binding)
zhokema, second (n d:time)
zhora, pill (n)
zhorana, pillow (n)
zhorano, pillow (v)
zhorela, beer (n)
zhorepana, median (n)
zhorepano, meddle (v)
zhorepanu, median (adj)
zhorepanua, meddler (n doer)
zhorika, mix (n)

zhorikara, mixture (n)
zhoriko, mix (v)
zhorikua, mixer (n doer)
zhorita, pillar (n)
zhoro, pill (v)
Zhorudana, Jordan (n)
zhuaborita, malice (n)
zhuaboritiu, maliciously (adv)
zhuaboritu, malicious (adj)
zhuaifa, spiff (n)
zhuaifo, spiff (v)
zhuaifu, spiffy (adj)
zhuaka, male (n)
zhuaka, masculinity (n)
zhuaku, male (adj)
zhuaku, masculine (adj)
zhuala, spirit (n)
zhualiu, spiritually (adv)
zhualiubupa, malcontent (n)
zhualo, spirit (v)
zhualu, spiritual (adj)
zhualueta, spirituality (n)
zhuana, malady (n)
zhuanoifa, malignancy (n)
zhuanoifo, malign (v)
zhuanoifu, malignant (adj)
zhuanueta, malaise (n)
zhuaperata, malfunction (n)
zhuaperato, malfunction (v)
zhuavorina, malformation (n)
zhuavorino, malform (v)
zhubaina, speed (n)
zhubainepeliola, speedway (n)
zhubaineshekoba, speedboat (n)
zhubainiu, speedily (adv)
zhubaino, speed (v)
zhubainu, speedy (adj)
zhubainua, speeder (n doer)
zhuda, safety (n d:trustworthy)
zhudana, drone (n d:bee)
zhudekelofio, safekept (v pa)
zhudekelofo, safekeep (v)
zhudiu, safely (adv d:trustworthy)
zhudo, safeguard (v
    d:trustworthy)
zhudu, safe (adj d:trustworthy)
zhudueta, safeguard (n)
zhudwaku, safest (adj)
zhudwelu, safer (adj)
zhugaita, poverty (n)
zhugaito, impoverish (v)
zhuiana, slander (n)
zhuiano, slander (v)
zhuianu, slanderous (adj)
zhuka, fox (n)
zhuko, outfox (v)
zhukotha, foxhole (n)
zhuku, foxy (adj)
Zhulaita, July (n)
zhulita, jelly (n)
zhuliteshelesha, jellyfish (n)
zhulitesheleshi, jellyfish (n pl)
zhulito, jell (v)

zhulitu, jellied (adj)
zhuma, juvenile (n)
zhumana, junior (n)
zhumanu, junior (adj)
zhumipa, peril (n)
zhumipiu, perilously (adv)
zhumipu, perilous (adj)
zhumu, juvenile (adj)
Zhuna, June (n)
zhupa, save (n)
zhupana, savior (n)
zhupana, saviours (n)
zhuparo, savor (v)
zhupata, savings (n)
zhupeisha, savvy (n)
zhupo, save (v)
zhupua, saver (n doer)
zhura, oil (n)

zhurashiashu, old-fashioned (adj)
zhurederita, oilseed (n)
zhurepelona, oilman (n)
zhurepeloni, oilmen (n pl)
zhureperanida, oilfield (n)
Zhurika, Zurich (n)
zhurita, experience (n)
zhuritana, expertise (n)
zhuritiu, expertly (adv)
zhurito, experience (v)
zhuritua, expert (n doer)
zhuro, oil (v)
zhuru, oily (adj)
zhurua, oiler (n doer)
zhusha, say (n)
zhushio, said (v pa)
zhusho, say (v)
zhushua, sayer (n doer)

zhuthiu, thus (adv)
zhutunipa, suggestion (n)
zhutunipiu, suggestibly (adv)
zhutunipiu, suggestively (adv)
zhutunipo, suggest (v)
zhutunipu, suggestible (adj)
zhutunipu, suggestive (adj)
zhuveta, success (n)
zhuvetiu, successively (adv)
zhuveto, succeed (v)
zhuvetu, successive (adj)
zhuvetua, successor (n doer)
zhuvetueta, succession (n)
zhuvetushiu, successfully (adv)
zhuvetushu, successful (adj)
zhuvika, suffix (n)

14

Nimiash to English Crossreference

The following crossreference, similar to the other Damiriak languages, is sorted by the English alphabet (and not the Noimil alphabet) for the convenience of Earth people.

Afap, Potassium (n davoka)
afblut, absence (n)
afblutiu, absently (adv)
afbluto, absent (v)
afblutu, absent (adj)
afblutua, absenter (n doer)
afebiorto, overpower (v)
afebiut, overstatement (n)
afebiuto, overstate (v)
afeblefiu, overcame (v pa)
afeblefo, overcome (v)
afebrauth, overflow (n)
afebrautho, overflow (v)
afebriak, overuse (n)
afebriako, overuse (v)
afedaun, overtime (n)
afedethp, overcapacity (n)
afediap, overdrive (n)
afedorklatio, overspent (v pa)
afedorklato, overspend (v)
afefiuk, overproduction (n)
afefiuko, overproduce (v)
afeflarth, overdraft (n)
afeflartho, overdraft (v)
afefraushio, overblew (v pa)
afefrausho, overblow (v)
afefrifo, overstock (v)
afefruif, overplay (n)
afefruifo, overplay (v)
afefuat, overview (n)
afefuato, overview (v)
afeglisho, overstep (v)
afegloit, overcharge (n)

afegloito, overcharge (v)
afeglorf, overboard (n)
afeglorgo, overreach (v)
afegokio, overtook (v pa)
afegoko, overtake (v)
afekaimo, overturn (v)
afekarth, overdose (n)
afekartho, overdose (v)
afekeft, overhead (n)
afekiok, overwork (n)
afekioko, overwork (v)
afekitsh, overkill (n)
afekriaf, overqualification (n)
afekriafo, overqualify (v)
afekuto, overheat (v)
afelaish, overjoy (n)
afelanshk, overexposure (n)
afelanshko, overexpose (v)
afelaomio, overran (v pa)
afelaomo, overrun (v)
afelarto, overrule (v)
afeliuprin, overconfidence (n)
afeliupriniu, overconfidently (adv)
afeliuprinu, overconfident (adj)
afeloidio, overwrote (v pa)
afeloido, overwrite (v)
afelor, overalls (n)
afeloriu, overall (adv)
afeloru, overall (adj)
afeluduash, overrepresentation (n)
afeluduasho, overrepresent (v)

afelunt, overpass (n)
afelupalt, overreaction (n)
afelupalto, overreact (v)
afemoim, overpayment (n)
afemoimio, overpaid (v pa)
afemoimo, overpay (v)
afemuan, overnight (n)
afemuaniu, overnight (adv)
afemuano, overnight (v)
afemuanu, overnight (adj)
afemuanua, overnighter (n doer)
afemutho, overmatch (v)
afen, over (n)
afenar, overture (n)
afenietio, overate (v pa)
afenieto, overeat (v)
afeniu, overly (adv)
afeniunf, overabundance (n)
afenorishrigo, oversubscribe (v)
afenreigo, overlook (v)
afenthauf, sovereignty (n)
afenthaufiu, sovereignly (adv)
afenthaufua, sovereign (n doer)
afenu, over (adv/adv/prep)
afepaltak, overactivity (n)
afepaltaku, overactive (adj)
afepavo, overfeed (v)
afepletho, overstuff (v)
afepoefto, overshadow (v)
afeprushio, overslept (v pa)
afeprusho, oversleep (v)
aferafk, overcoat (n)
aferant, overlay (n)

aferantio, overlaid (v pa)
aferanto, overlay (v)
aferaupu, overland (adj)
aferethio, overlay (v pa)
aferetho, overlie (v)
afeshaln, oversimplification (n)
afeshalno, oversimplify (v)
afeshenko, overtax (v)
afeshethp, oversupply (n)
afeshethpo, oversupply (v)
afeshklein, overseas (n)
afeshkleiniu, overseas (adv)
afeshkleinu, overseas (adj)
afeshkot, overshoot (n)
afeshkotio, overshot (v pa)
afeshkoto, overshoot (v)
afeshlesho, overfish (v)
afeshlib, override (n)
afeshlibio, overrode (v pa)
afeshlibo, override (v)
afeshluap, overhaul (n)
afeshluapo, overhaul (v)
afeshluapua, overhauler (n doer)
afeshuago, oversize (v)
afeshuish, overweight (n)
afetarg, overhang (n)
afetargio, overhung (v pa)
afetargo, overhang (v)
afetarth, overthrow (n)
afetarthio, overthrew (v pa)
afetartho, overthrow (v)
afetebo, overrate (v)
afethinp, overestimate (n)
afethinpo, overestimate (v)
afethiut, overlap (n)
afethiuto, overlap (v)
afethuth, oversight (n)
afethuthio, oversaw (v pa)
afethutho, oversee (v)
afethuthua, overseer (n doer)
afetikio, overdid (v pa)
afetiko, overdo (v)
afetirpo, overprice (v)
afetiuku, overdue (adj)
afetrelfio, oversold (v pa)
afetrelfo, oversell (v)
afetrem, overreliance (n)
afetremo, overrely (v)
afetril, overtone (n)
afetultu, overcast (adj)
afevaup, overvalue (n)
afevaupo, overvalue (v)
afeviago, overcrowd (v)
afevondo, overbook (v)
afevortio, overbuilt (v pa)
afevorto, overbuild (v)
afevorv, overpopulation (n)
afevorvo, overpopulate (v)
Afip, Calcium (n davoka)
Afkan, Afghan (n)
Afkanshan, Afghanistan (n)
afkiak, abdication (n)
afkiako, abdicate (v)

afkiakua, abdicator (n doer)
afligrag, absolution (n)
afligragiu, absolutely (adv)
afligrago, absolve (v)
afligragu, absolute (adj)
Afrik, Africa (n)
Afrikan, African (n)
afuyanio, overheard (v pa)
afuyano, overhear (v)
agubiashar, goddess (n)
agubid, god (n)
agubidmenu, godless (adj)
agubidu, godly (adj)
agubimalsh, godmother (n)
agubivotet, godfather (n)
agubizhaip, godsend (n)
aiko, vie (v)
ailt, study (n)
ailtiu, studiously (adv)
ailto, study (v)
ailtu, studious (adj)
ailtua, student (n doer)
ainduft, diacritic (n)
ainduftiu, diacritically (adv)
ainduftu, diacritical (adj)
ainelk, diagram (n)
ainelko, diagram (v)
ainelku, diagrammatic (adj)
ainmuk, diagonal (n)
ainmukiu, diagonally (adv)
ainmuku, diagonal (adj)
ainpin, diameter (n)
ainrit, dialect (n)
ainritu, dialectic (adj)
ainritu, dialectical (adj)
ainuan, diaper (n)
ainuano, diaper (v)
aiof, ion (n)
aiofo, ionize (v)
aiofu, ionic (adj)
aiofua, ionizer (n doer)
aishman, diagnosis (n)
aishmano, diagnose (v)
aishmant, diagnostic (n)
aishmanu, diagnostic (adj)
Akap, Lithium (n davoka)
Akip, Beryllium (n davoka)
Aktinium, Actinium (n)
Alap, Rubidium (n davoka)
Alham, Alabama (n)
Albertaf, Alberta (n)
aldor, yellow (n)
aldoreiku, yellowish (adj)
aldoro, yellow (v)
aldoru, yellow (adj)
alf, A (let sng)
alfan, alpha (n)
alfavuka, Number_1e159
alfdaka, Number_1e183
alfep, alphabet (n)
alfepiu, alphabetically (adv)
alfepo, alphabetize (v)
alfepu, alphabetic (adj)

alfgenka, Number_1e177
alfhemfk, Number_1e276
alfhemft, Number_1e246
alfhemka, Number_1e156
alfhemshk, Number_1e216
alfhemsht, Number_1e186
alfi, As (let pl)
alfirika, Number_1e162
alfkinka, Number_1e171
alfmuika, Number_1e180
alftirika, Number_1e168
alfvenka, Number_1e174
alfyufika, Number_1e165
Alik, Xenon (n davoka)
Alip, Strontium (n davoka)
alor, hello (interj)
alsh, emptiness (n)
Alshk, Alaska (n)
alsho, empty (v)
alshu, empty (adj)
altak, mentality (n)
altakiu, mentally (adv)
altaku, mental (adj)
altakuat, mentor (n)
altakuato, mentor (v)
altip, mention (n)
altipo, mention (v)
Aluminum, Aluminum (n)
Amerikium, Americium (n)
Amik, America (n)
Amikan, American (n)
amlazh, interest (n d:finance)
Amshterdam, Amsterdam (n)
Anap, Francium (n davoka)
anart, hangar (n)
anbek, amputation (n)
anbeko, amputate (v)
anbeniu, amply (adv)
anbenu, ample (adj)
anbet, amplification (n)
anbetan, amplitude (n)
anbeto, amplify (v)
anbetua, amplifier (n doer)
anbidal, embellishment (n)
anbidalo, embellish (v)
anbiort, empowerment (n)
anbiorto, empower (v)
anbotak, empathy (n)
anbotako, empathize (v)
anbriug, embroilment (n)
anbriugo, embroil (v)
anbrug, ember (n)
andiof, entrenchment (n)
andiofo, entrench (v)
andit, enlistment (n)
andito, enlist (v)
andreif, entrustment (n)
andreifo, entrust (v)
andupran, encapsulation (n)
anduprano, encapsulate (v)
andupranua, encapsulator (n
    doer)

andutako, ensue (v)
anegaifk, embitterment (n)
anegaifko, embitter (v)
anegiat, embossment (n)
anegiato, emboss (v)
anegushk, enticement (n)
anegushko, entice (v)
anenkel, enumeration (n)
anenkelo, enumerate (v)
anfalir, enrollment (n)
anfaliro, enroll (v)
anfalirua, enroller (n doer)
anfaliruin, enrollee (n)
anflaufto, enliven (v)
anfluan, enlightenment (n)
anfluano, enlighten (v)
anfual, envoy (n)
angai, ugh (interj)
Anip, Radium (n davoka)
Ankalsh, English (n)
ankenpiu, emphatically (adv)
ankenpu, emphatic (adj)
Anklan, England (n)
Ankolaf, Angola (n)
Ankorazh, Anchorage (n)
anlak, alien (n)
anlako, alienate (v)
anlaku, alienable (adj)
anlenfko, encompass (v)
anmig, embargo (n)
anmigo, embargo (v)
anmith, entailment (n)
anmitho, entail (v)
anovaft, empiricism (n)
anovaftiu, empirically (adv)
anovaftu, empiric (adj)
anovaftu, empirical (adj)
anovaftua, empiricist (n doer)
anpin, amp (n d:ampere)
anploit, embracement (n)
anploito, embrace (v)
anrauelk, emancipation (n)
anrauelko, emancipate (v)
anrauth, emanation (n)
anrautho, emanate (v)
anshkob, embarkation (n)
anshkobo, embark (v)
anshlad, embodiment (n)
anshlado, embody (v)
anshlak, embezzlement (n)
anshlako, embezzle (v)
anshplar, embankment (n)
anshplaro, embank (v)
anshraip, enslavement (n)
anshraipo, enslave (v)
anshraipua, enslaver (n doer)
antaigag, entanglement (n)
antaigago, entangle (v)
antelvo, embalm (v)
anthrav, ensemble (n)
anthreip, entrapment (n)
anthreipo, entrap (v)
antikoam, emblem (n)

antikoamu, emblematic (adj)
Antimoni, Antimony (n)
anuiat, embryo (n)
anuiatu, embryonic (adj)
anvalt, encirclement (n)
anvalto, encircle (v)
anvlato, encode (v)
anvlatua, encoder (n doer)
apafp, hydration (n)
apafpekip, hydrocarbon (n)
apafpo, hydrate (v)
apafpu, hydralic (adj)
apafpua, hydrater (n doer)
Apap, Hydrogen (n davoka)
Apip, Helium (n davoka)
Arap, Cesium (n davoka)
Arb, Arab (n)
arbot, staff (n d:people)
arboto, staff (v d:people)
arbotu, staff (adj d:people)
arbotua, staffer (n doer d:people)
Argentin, Argentina (n)
Argon, Argon (n)
aribrivakio, interwove (v pa)
aribrivako, interweave (v)
aribrunp, interdependence (n)
aribrunpiu, interdependently (adv)
aribrunpu, interdependent (adj)
aribruth, interleaf (n)
aribrutho, interleave (v)
aridap, interval (n)
aridromu, interstellar (adj)
aridrup, interpretation (n)
aridrupo, interpret (v)
aridrupu, interpretive (adj)
aridrupua, interpreter (n doer)
arifim, intervention (n)
arifimo, intervene (v)
arifoino, interlace (v)
arifruif, interplay (n)
arifuat, interview (n)
arifuato, interview (v)
arifuatua, interviewer (n doer)
arifuatuin, interviewee (n)
arigaift, interruption (n)
arigaifto, interrupt (v)
arigaiftu, interruptible (adj)
arigef, interference (n)
arigefo, interfere (v)
arikarliu, internationally (adv)
arikarlu, international (adj)
arilaidak, intermediacy (n)
arilaidako, intermediate (v)
arilaidakua, intermediary (n doer)
arilaifu, interim (adj)
arilaivuno, intertwine (v)
arilar, interior (n)
arilauku, interplanetary (adj)
arilotel, interspersion (n)
arilotelo, intersperse (v)
ariludart, interrelation (n)
ariludartfif, interrelationship (n)

ariludarto, interrelate (v)
arilushiat, interrogation (n)
arilushiato, interrogate (v)
arilushiatua, interrogator (n doer)
arimarn, intercourse (n)
arimoip, internet (n)
arinoithu, interracial (adj)
arinok, intermission (n)
arinokiu, intermittently (adv)
arinoko, intermit (v)
arinoku, intermittent (adj)
Arip, Barium (n davoka)
aripalt, interaction (n)
aripaltiu, interactively (adv)
aripalto, interact (v)
aripaltu, interactive (adj)
ariplonu, interpersonal (adj)
aiprineltu, interfaith (adj)
ariroish, interlink (n)
ariroisho, interlink (v)
arirush, interlude (n)
arishaiash, interstate (n)
arishaiashu, interstate (adj)
arishal, intersection (n)
arishalo, intersect (v)
ariship, interception (n)
arishipo, intercept (v)
arishipua, interceptor (n doer)
arishnaf, interconnection (n)
arishnafo, interconnect (v)
aritep, interjection (n)
aritepo, interject (v)
arithoish, interface (n)
arithoisho, interface (v)
aritiug, interlock (n)
arituan, interchange (n)
arituaniu, interchangeably (adv)
arituanu, interchangeable (adj)
arivek, intercession (n)
ariveko, intercede (v)
arivetap, interagency (n)
arivuln, intermarriage (n)
arivulno, intermarry (v)
Arizhon, Arizona (n)
arizhorko, intermix (v)
Arkansh, Arkansas (n)
Arlington, Arlington (n)
Armen, Armenia (n)
Armenan, Armenian (n)
arokriuk, introduction (n)
arokriuko, introduce (v)
arokriuku, introductory (adj)
arothark, introversion (n)
arotharko, introvert (v)
arotharkua, introvert (n doer)
arpo, eke (v)
arpua, eker (n doer)
Arshenik, Arsenic (n)
arthiam, street (n)
arthiamfluiku, streetwise (adj)
arthiamgrel, streetcar (n)
aruf, woof (interj)
arvu, old (adj)

arvwak, oldest (n)
arvwaku, oldest (adj)
arvwel, older (n)
arvwelu, older (adj)
Ashap, Ununennium (n davoka)
Aship, Unbinilium (n davoka)
ashloit, employment (n)
ashloito, employ (v)
ashloitu, employable (adj)
ashloitua, employer (n doer)
ashloituin, employee (n)
ashpedauniu, oftentimes (adv)
ashpiu, often (adv)
Ashtatin, Astatine (n)
Atap, Sodium (n davoka)
Atelant, Atlanta (n)
Atelantik, Atlantic (n)
Atelantish, Atlantis (n)
atheforsh, atmosphere (n)
atheforshiu, atmospherically
   (adv)
atheforshu, atmospheric (adj)
Atip, Magnesium (n davoka)
aua, ow (interj)
auk, ailment (n)
auko, ail (v)
aukua, ailer (n doer)
aul, air (n)
aulaku, aerobic (adj)
aulan, aerial (n)
aulanu, aerial (adj)
aulbielk, airport (n)
aulfnaf, airbag (n)
aulgrap, aerosol (n)
auliati, aeronautics (n pl)
auliatu, aeronautical (adj)
auliun, omen (n)
auliuniu, ominously (adv)
auliunu, ominous (adj)
aulkafp, aircraft (n)
aulkafpi, aircraft (n pl)
aulo, air (v)
aulpliol, airway (n)
aulprand, airfield (n)
aulroif, airline (n)
aulthik, airfare (n)
aultuiafi, aerodynamics (n pl)
aultuiafu, aerodynamic (adj)
aulu, airy (adj)
aulvarl, airplane (n)
aush, ash (n)
aushbiam, ashtray (n)
Aushimak, Admiral (n)
Aushtar, Austria (n)
Aushtarn, Austrian (n)
Aushtin, Austin (n)
Aushtral, Australia (n)
Aushtralan, Australian (n)
aushua, asher (n doer)
auta, ouch (inter)
authush, aerospace (n)
avaif, duality (n)
avaifat, duet (n)

avaifiu, dually (adv)
avaifu, dual (adj)
avain, boolean (n)
avainu, boolean (adj)
aveth, second (num 2 ord)
avethar, secondary (n)
avetharu, secondary (adj)
avethiu, secondly (adv d:count)
avethkapu, secondhand (adj)
aviuth, dilemma (n)
aviuthu, dilemmic (adj)
avu, two (num 2 card)
avualfhemka, Number_1e8256
avuda, twenty (num 20 card)
avudai-, twenty- (num 20 pref)
avudeth, twentieth (num 20 ord)
avufk, duoquadragintillion (num
   1e129 card)
avuft, duotrigintillion (num 1e99
   card)
avuftai-, yantesi-
avufteth, duotrigintillionth (num
   1e99 ord)
avugioko, tweeze (v)
avugiokua, tweezer (n doer)
avuikosh, tandem (n)
avuikoshu, tandem (adj)
avuka, billion (num 1e9 card)
avukai-, giga- (num 1e9 pref)
avuketh, billionth (num 1e9 ord)
avupa, twelve (num 12 card)
avupai-, twelv- (num 12 pref)
avupeth, twelfth (num 12 ord)
avushk, duovigintillion (num 1e69
   card)
avushkai-, itesa-
avushketh, duovigintillionth
   (num 1e69 ord)
avusht, duodecillion (num 1e39
   card)
avushtai-, tekatri- (num 1e39
   pref)
avushteth, duodecillionth (num
   1e39 ord)
avut, duet (n)
avuth, twice (adv)
Azherbaizhan, Azerbaijan (n)
ba, B (let sng)
bab, dad (n)
babil, daddy (n)
bafiak, cavalry (n)
bafk, strictness (n)
bafkiu, strictly (adv)
bafku, strict (adj)
bafpo, doze (v)
bafpua, dozer (n doer)
baft, junction (n)
baftu, junctional (adj)
Bagdad, Baghdad (n)
bahem, Number_1e1656
baial, sorcery (n)

baialua, sorcerer (n doer)
baif, victimization (n)
baifan, victim (n)
baifet, victory (n)
baifetiu, victoriously (adv)
baifetu, victorious (adj)
baifk, gadget (n)
baifku, gadgety (adj)
baifmeniu, victimlessly (adv)
baifmenu, victimless (adj)
baifo, victimize (v)
baift, source (n)
baifto, source (v)
baiftua, sourcer (n doer)
baifua, victor (n doer)
baig, sort (n)
baigo, sort (v)
baigua, sorter (n doer)
baim, sore (n)
baimat, sorrow (n)
baimatu, sorry (adj)
baimiu, sorely (adv)
baimu, sore (adj)
baish, gage (n)
baish, gauge (n)
baishk, abrasion (n)
baishkiu, abrasively (adv)
baishku, abrasive (adj)
baisho, gage (v)
baisho, gauge (v)
baith, byte (n)
baiuk, genesis (n)
baivat, sourness (n)
baivato, sour (v)
baivatu, sour (adj)
bakiat, tirade (n)
bakiniu, terrifically (adv)
bakinu, terrific (adj)
bakoshto, terrify (v)
bakot, terror (n)
bakotiu, terribly (adv)
bakoto, terrorize (v)
bakotu, terrible (adj)
bakotua, terrorist (n doer)
bakotuet, terrorism (n)
balf, caliber (n)
balf, calibre (n)
balfk, calibration (n)
balfko, calibrate (v)
balfkua, calibrator (n doer)
bali, Bs (let pl)
balishk, tutorial (n)
balishko, tutor (v)
balishkua, tutor (n doer)
baliuk, postulation (n)
baliuko, postulate (v)
balp, tardiness (n)
balpu, tardy (adj)
balsharnu, postmodern (adj)
balshrig, postscript (n)
balt, post (n d:pole)
baltar, posture (n)
baltaro, posture (v)

Baltik, Baltic (n)
Baltimor, Baltimore (n)
balto, post (v d:pole)
balvefk, postponement (n)
balvefko, postpone (v)
balvelar, posterior (n)
balviuru, postwar (adj)
bamiak, thorn (n)
bamiakiu, thornily (adv)
bamiako, thorn (v)
bamiaku, thorny (adj)
bamian, thirst (n)
bamianiu, thirstily (adv)
bamiano, thirst (v)
bamianu, thirsty (adj)
banf, pad (n)
banfat, paddle (n)
banfato, paddle (v)
banfo, pad (v)
bantiug, padlock (n)
bantiugo, padlock (v)
baraf, stone (n)
barafdaishio, stonecut (v pa)
barafdaisho, stonecut (v)
barafdaishua, stonecutter (n
    doer)
barafnoltho, stonewall (v)
barafo, stone (v)
barafshlef, stoneware (n)
barafu, stoney (adj)
barafua, stoner (n doer)
baraifan, stonehenge (n)
Barium, Barium (n)
barm, fan (n d:follower)
barmot, fanaticism (n)
barmotiu, fanatically (adv)
barmotu, fanatical (adj)
barmotua, fanatic (n doer)
barmthik, fanfare (n)
barmu, fanatic (adj d:follower)
barp, bastard (n)
barpo, bastardize (v)
barshk, conduit (n)
bartad, train (n d:locomotive)
bashalp, authorization (n)
bashalpiu, authoritatively (adv)
bashalpo, authorize (v)
bashalpu, authoritative (adj)
bashalt, authority (n)
bashaltua, author (n doer)
bashap, authentication (n)
bashapo, authenticate (v)
bashapu, authentic (adj)
bashk, feather (n)
bashko, feather (v)
bau, boo (interj)
bauf, tuition (n)
bauft, tower (n)
baufto, tower (v)
baug, fat (n)
baugo, fatten (v)
baugu, fat (adj)
baugu, fatty (adj)

bauin, stomp (n)
bauino, stomp (v)
bauinua, stomper (n doer)
bauk, boo (n)
bauko, boo (v)
baukua, booer (n doer)
baul, tow (n)
baulo, tow (v)
baulua, tower (n doer)
baun, stamp (n)
bauno, stamp (v)
baunoid, stampede (n)
baunua, stamper (n doer)
baurk, jangle (n)
baurko, jangle (v)
baush, towel (n)
bausho, towel (v)
bauth, menses (n)
bav, pair (n)
bavan, sheep (n)
bavani, sheep (n pl)
bavaniu, sheepishly (adv)
bavanu, sheepish (adj)
bavap, steepness (n)
bavapiu, steeply (adv)
bavapo, steep (v)
bavapu, steep (adj)
bavash, steeple (n)
bavashtutat, steeplechase (n)
bavat, steed (n)
bavo, pair (v)
bedior, petroleum (n)
bef, sod (n)
befnetiu, instead (adv)
beibukiu, purportedly (adv)
beibuko, purport (v)
beid, mutt (n)
beif, dub (n)
beifk, fling (n)
belfklo, flung (v pa)
beifko, fling (v)
beifku, flingy (adj)
beifkua, flinger (n doer)
beifo, dub (v)
beifp, flip (n)
beifpiu, flippily (adv)
beifpo, flip (v)
beifpu, flippy (adj)
beifpua, flipper (n doer)
beifua, dubber (n doer)
beilbak, dagger (n)
beilk, purpose (n)
beilkiu, purposely (adv)
beilko, purpose (v)
beilku, purposeful (adj)
beim, fin (n)
beinf, dome (n)
beink, tomb (n)
beinkbaraf, tombstone (n)
beinko, entomb (v)
beint, tumor (n)
beip, flinch (n)
beipo, flinch (v)

beipua, flincher (n doer)
beirn, career (n)
Beirut, Beirut (n)
beish, flirtation (n)
beishak, pursuit (n)
beishakiu, pursuantly (adv)
beishako, pursue (v)
beishaku, pursuant (adj)
beisho, flirt (v)
beishu, flirtatious (adj)
beishua, flirt (n doer)
beitat, purchase (n)
beitato, purchase (v)
beitatua, purchaser (n doer)
beith, purse (n)
beitho, purse (v)
beiuk, doom (n)
beiuko, doom (v)
beiukviul, doomsday (n)
Beizhing, Beijing (n)
Belgian, Belgian (n)
Belgium, Belgium (n)
beln, cone (n)
belnu, conical (adj)
benf, opinion (n)
benflide, indeed (adv/interj)
benfo, opine (v)
bentik, perch (n d:fish)
benufleithiu, intravenously (adv)
benufleithu, intravenous (adj)
Berilium, Beryllium (n)
Berkel, Berkeley (n)
Berkelium, Berkelium (n)
berkol, purple (n)
berkolu, purple (adj)
Berlin, Berlin (n)
betan, beta (n)
bev, dip (n)
Beverlif Hilsh, Beverly Hills (n)
bevo, dip (v)
bevua, dipper (n doer)
biabiu, loudly (adv)
biabu, loud (adj)
biabweku, loudest (adj)
biabwelu, louder (adj)
biafafu, sacred (adj)
biafak, sacrilege (n)
biafaku, sacriligous (adj)
biafp, toast (n d:bread)
biafpo, toast (v d:bread)
biafpu, toasty (adj d:bread)
biafpua, toaster (n doer d:bread)
biaft, sacrifice (n)
biaftiu, sacrificially (adv)
biafto, sacrifice (v)
biaftu, sacrificial (adj)
biaftua, sacrificer (n doer)
biag, sadness (n)
biagar, quiver (n)
biagaro, quiver (v)
biagiu, sadly (adv)
biago, sadden (v)
biagu, sad (adj)

biaibu, queer (adj)
biaibua, queer (n doer)
biak, drill (n)
biako, drill (v)
biakua, driller (n doer)
bial, vibe (n)
bialf, vibration (n)
bialfo, vibrate (v)
bialfu, vibrant (adj)
bialfua, vibrator (n doer)
bialfuet, vibrancy (n)
biam, tray (n)
bian, drug (n)
bianap, drugstore (n)
bianf, maid (n)
biano, drug (v)
Biansh, Atheism (n)
Bianshk, Atheist (n)
biant, compound (n d:place)
biaplatuk, loudspeaker (n)
biar, fanciness (n)
biargo, drown (v)
biariu, fancily (adv)
biarkian, fantasy (n)
biarkianiu, fantastically (adv)
biarkiano, fantasize (v)
biarkianu, fantastic (adj)
biaro, fancy (v)
biaru, fancy (adj)
biarweku, fanciest (adj)
biarwel, fancier (n)
biarwelu, fancier (adj)
biash, queen (n)
biashk, quill (n)
biasho, queen (v)
biat, powder (n)
biath, womb (n)
biato, powder (v)
biauf, doubt (n)
biaufo, doubt (v)
biaufu, doubtful (adj)
biaufua, doubter (n doer)
biauk, sabotage (n)
biauko, sabotage (v)
biaukua, saboteur (n doer)
biaupo, pout (v)
biaut, sadism (n)
biautu, sadistic (adj)
biautua, sadist (n doer)
biav, lounge (n)
biavo, lounge (v)
biazh, party (n d:celebration)
biazho, party (v d:celebration)
bibat, helm (n d:tiller)
bibato, helm (v d:tiller)
bibik, stutter (n)
bibiko, stutter (v)
bibuf, tattoo (n)
bibufo, tattoo (v)
bibut, total (n)
bibutan, totalitarianism (n)
bibutanua, totalitarian (n doer)
bibutiu, totally (adv)

bibuto, total (v)
bibutuet, totality (n)
bidaliu, prettily (adv)
bidalu, pretty (adj)
bidalweku, prettiest (adj)
bidalwelu, prettier (adj)
bidar, pupil (n d:eye)
bidaun, optimism (n)
bidaunal, optimum (n)
bidaunaliu, optimally (adv)
bidaunalu, optimal (adj)
bidauniu, optimistically (adv)
bidauno, optimize (v)
bidaunu, optimistic (adj)
bidaunua, optimist (n doer)
bidaunuet, optimization (n)
bidik, geek (n)
biebup, fulfillment (n)
biebupo, fulfill (v)
bief, polish (n)
biefo, polish (v)
biefua, polisher (n doer)
bieg, sting (n d:bite)
biegio, stung (v pa d:bite)
biego, sting (v d:bite)
biegu, stingy (adj d:bite)
biegua, stinger (n doer d:bite)
biek, stink (n)
biekio, stank (v pa)
bieko, stink (v)
bieku, stinky (adj)
biekua, stinker (n doer)
bielk, port (n)
bielkat, portal (n)
bielko, port (v)
bielkoth, porthole (n)
bielkrep, portability (n)
bielku, portable (adj)
bielkua, porter (n doer)
biendarf, geography (n)
biendarfiu, geographically (adv)
biendarfu, geographic (adj)
biendarfu, geographical (adj)
bienk, stoop (n d:porch)
bienkrent, geology (n)
bienkrentiu, geologically (adv)
bienkrentu, geologic (adj)
bienkrentu, geological (adj)
bienkrentua, geologist (n doer)
bienpoft, geometry (n)
bienpoftiu, geometrically (adv)
bienpoftu, geometric (adj)
bienpoftu, geometrical (adj)
biep, fullness (n)
biepdaun, fulltime (n)
biepdaunu, fulltime (adj)
biepiu, fully (adv)
biepu, full (adj)
biesh, environment (n)
bieshiu, environmentally (adv)
bieshu, environmental (adj)
bieshua, environmentalist (n
    doer)

biet, gene (n)
bieth, bristle (n)
bietho, bristle (v)
bietu, genetic (adj)
bietuet, genetics (n)
bietuetiu, genetically (adv)
bietuetu, genetical (adj)
bifit, jacket (n)
bifk, deal (n)
bifkio, dealt (v pa)
bifko, deal (v)
bifkua, dealer (n doer)
bifkuafif, dealership (n)
bift, leap (n)
biftefloip, leapfrog (n)
biftio, leapt (v pa)
bifto, leap (v)
biftua, leaper (n doer)
bigaift, corruption (n)
bigaiftiu, corruptly (adv)
bigaifto, corrupt (v)
bigaiftu, corrupt (adj)
bikiduap, prototype (n)
bikiduapo, prototype (v)
bikigir, protocol (n)
bil, am (common)
bil, be (inf, common)
bil, is (common)
bilbush, varnish (n)
bilbusho, varnish (v)
bildum, between (adv/prep)
bilenio, became (v pa)
bileno, become (v)
bilf, corps (n)
biloito, beseech (v)
biloitua, beseecher (n doer)
bilp, gang (n)
bilpo, gang (v)
bilpua, gangster (n doer)
bilsh, shrinkage (n)
bilshio, shrank (v pa)
bilshkash, because (conj)
bilsho, shrink (v)
bilshua, shrinker (n doer)
bilto, steer (v d:navigate)
biluashu, deluxe (adj)
biluk, caboose (n)
bimk, gnat (n)
bink, opposition (n)
binkar, opposite (n)
binkaru, opposite (adj)
binko, oppose (v)
binkua, opponent (n doer)
bint, moment (n)
bintap, momentum (n)
bintapu, momentous (adj)
bintiu, momentarily (adv)
bintu, momentary (adj)
binuf, ruth (n)
binufmen, ruthlessness (n)
binufmeniu, ruthlessly (adv)
binufmenu, ruthless (adj)
biodato, gawk (v)

biodatua, gawker (n doer)
biof, randomness (n)
biofiu, randomly (adv)
biofo, randomize (v)
biofu, random (adj)
biokato, stoop (v d:bend)
biol, cheer (n)
bioliu, cheerily (adv)
biolo, cheer (v)
biolu, cheery (adj)
bion, saddle (n)
bionfnaf, saddlebag (n)
bionk, troop (n)
bionko, troop (v)
bionkua, trooper (n doer)
biono, saddle (v)
biop, gesture (n)
biopo, gesture (v)
biork, trigger (n)
biorko, trigger (v)
biormen, cheerlessness (n)
biormeniu, cheerlessly (adv)
biormenu, cheerless (adj)
biorsh, drink (n d:beverage)
biorshio, drank (v pa d:beverage)
biorsho, drink (v d:beverage)
biorshua, drinker (n doer
    d:beverage)
biort, power (n)
biortebartad, powertrain (n)
biortelitank, powerplant (n)
biorth, quilt (n)
biortho, quilt (v)
biorthua, quilter (n doer)
biortiu, powerfully (adv)
biortkiaf, powerhouse (n)
biortmen, powerlessness (n)
biortmeniu, powerlessly (adv)
biortmenu, powerless (adj)
biorto, power (v)
biortsh, drunkenness (n
    d:intoxicated)
biortshkob, powerboat (n)
biortshu, drunk (adj
    d:intoxicated)
biortshua, drunk (n doer
    d:intoxicated)
biortshua, drunkard (n doer)
biortu, powerful (adj)
biorush, cheerfulness (n)
biorushiu, cheerfully (adv)
biorushu, cheerful (adj)
bioshaiku, stupendous (adj)
bioshk, stupidity (n)
bioshkat, stupor (n)
bioshkiu, stupidly (adv)
bioshko, stupify (v)
bioshku, stupid (adj)
biot, toy (n)
bioto, toy (v)
bir, are (common)
biralilp, semifinal (n)
biraliukriukua, semiconductor (n

doer)
biramift, semicolon (n)
birft, defeat (n)
birfto, defeat (v)
birftua, defeater (n doer)
birk, jingle (n)
birko, jingle (v)
Birmingam, Birmingham (n)
birnat, dorsum (n)
birnatu, dorsal (adj)
birt, feat (n)
birto, feature (v)
birtua, feature (n doer)
bishan, sturdiness (n)
bishaniu, sturdily (adv)
bishanu, sturdy (adj)
bishk, mite (n)
Bishmuth, Bismuth (n)
bishtak, token (n)
bishtako, tokenize (v)
bishtakua, tokenizer (n doer)
bithan, canary (n)
bitho, simmer (v)
biuauak, quirk (n)
biufirm, inconvenience (n)
biufirmiu, inconveniently (adv)
biufirmu, inconvenient (adj)
biuft, vapor (n)
biufto, vaporize (v)
biuftu, vapid (adj)
biuftua, vaporizer (n doer)
biuif, cypher (n)
biukan, boondoggle (n)
biukiu, poorly (adv d:unfortunate,
    bad)
biuku, poor (adj d:unfortunate,
    bad)
biult, crook (n)
biulto, crook (v)
bium, penalty (n)
biumo, penalize (v)
biumu, penal (adj)
biun, boy (n)
biunfif, boyhood (n)
biunt, boyfriend (n)
biunu, boyish (adj)
biup, jolt (n)
biupo, jolt (v)
biush, apparel (n)
biut, statement (n d:say)
biuth, boon (n)
biuto, state (v d:say)
biuzh, gig (n)
bivan, sex (n d:gender)
bivanmenu, sexless (adj)
bivanuet, sexism (n)
bivanuetu, sexist (adj)
bivanuetua, sexist (n doer)
bivel, am (emphatic)
bivel, be (inf, emphatic)
bivel, is (emphatic)
biver, are (emphatic)
bivik, sex (n d:intercourse)

bivikat, sexuality (n)
bivikatiu, sexually (adv)
bivikatu, sexual (adj)
biviko, sex (v d:intercourse)
biviku, sexy (adj d:intercourse)
bivoan, before (prep/conj)
bivoankapu, beforehand
    (adj/adv)
blafk, ledge (n)
blafp, pope (n)
blaft, prompt (n)
blaftiu, promptly (adv)
blafto, prompt (v)
blaftua, prompter (n doer)
blaiato, spurt (v)
blaif, volume (n)
blaik, butt (n d:strike)
blaiko, butt (v d:strike)
blaipo, spurn (v)
blaish, spur (n)
blaisho, spur (v)
blaishu, spurious (adj)
blaith, round (n)
blaithdoiar, roundtable (n)
blaithglardu, roundtrip (adj)
blaithiu, roundly (adv)
blaithiveil, roundup (n)
blaithkiaf, roundhouse (n)
blaitho, round (v)
blaithoveip, roundabout (n)
blaithoveipu, roundabout (adj)
blaithu, round (adj)
blaithuet, roundness (n)
blak, deposition (n)
blakako, thwart (v)
blako, depose (v)
blakua, deposer (n doer)
blamiak, bramble (n)
blamiako, bramble (v)
blanf, wallet (n)
blap, pa (n)
blapan, papa (n)
blar, lady (n)
blarf, flatness (n d:plain/plane)
blarfiu, flatly (adv d:plain/plane)
blarfo, flatten (v d:plain/plane)
blarfraup, flatland (n)
blarfu, flat (adj d:plain/plane)
blarfuarm, flatbed (n)
blarfuarmu, flatbed (adj)
blarg, shingle (n)
blargo, shingle (v)
blark, brake (n)
blarko, brake (v)
blash, press (n)
blashk, impression (n)
blashkfrepu, impressionable (adj)
blashkfrepua, impressionist (n
    doer)
blashkiu, impressively (adv)
blashko, impress (v)
blashku, impressive (adj)
blashkua, impresser (n doer)

blasho, press (v)
blashp, pressure (n)
blashpat, pressurization (n)
blashpato, pressurize (v)
blashpo, pressure (v)
blashpua, pressurizer (n doer)
blasht, flake (n)
blashtiu, flakily (adv)
blashto, flake (v)
blashtu, flakey (adj)
blashtua, flaker (n doer)
blashua, presser (n doer)
blat, lad (n d:boy)
blath, bran (n)
blauf, honk (n)
blaufo, honk (v)
blaufua, honker (n doer)
blaug, twang (n)
blaugo, twang (v)
blaum, bog (n)
blaumo, bog (v)
blautho, wither (v)
blef, come (n)
blefio, came (v pa)
blefo, come (v)
blefua, comer (n doer)
blefvak, comeback (n)
bleg, class (n)
blegat, classic (n)
blegatu, classical (adj)
bleglen, classmate (n)
blego, classify (v)
blegshran, classroom (n)
blegu, classy (adj)
bleifk, bleach (n)
bleifko, bleach (v)
bleinok, compromise (n)
bleinoko, compromise (v)
bleinokua, compromiser (n doer)
bleish, span (n)
bleisho, span (v)
bleishua, spanner (n doer)
bleith, truce (n)
blenk, ant (n)
blerg, classification (n)
bleth, staff (n d:plaster)
bleto, shed (v d:rid)
bletua, shedder (n doer d:rid)
bliaf, beef (n)
bliag, twinge (n)
bliago, twinge (v)
bliako, boggle (v)
blian, barn (n)
bliash, crunch (n)
bliasho, crunch (v)
bliashu, crunchy (adj)
bliashua, cruncher (n doer)
bliath, neigh (n)
bliatho, neigh (v)
bliaum, sprout (n)
bliaumo, sprout (v)
bliausho, scrunch (v)
bliet, goat (n)

blif, peninsula (n)
blifet, provision (n)
blifetar, providence (n)
blifeto, provide (v)
blifetua, provider (n doer)
blifk, province (n)
blifkiu, provincially (adv)
blifku, provincial (adj)
bligo, prune (v d:clip)
bligua, pruner (n doer d:clip)
blim, timidity (n)
blimiu, timidly (adv)
blimu, timid (adj)
blir, block (n d:barrier)
blirk, bloc (n)
bliro, block (v d:barrier)
blirua, blocker (n doer d:barrier)
blish, sleaze (n)
blishk, penetration (n)
blishko, penetrate (v)
blishkua, penetrator (n doer)
blishu, sleazy (adj)
blit, vest (n)
blith, sprint (n)
blitho, sprint (v)
blithua, sprinter (n doer)
blito, vest (v)
blitsh, vestige (n)
blitshiu, vestigially (adv)
blitshu, vestigial (adj)
bliuf, alley (n)
bliuku, bogus (adj)
blium, clone (n)
bliumo, clone (v)
bliumua, cloner (n doer)
bliun, prudence (n)
bliunu, prudent (adj)
bliunu, prudish (adj)
bliunua, prude (n doer)
bliup, putty (n)
bliush, ruse (n)
bliut, creed (n)
blofien, desolation (n)
blofieno, desolate (v)
bloiat, deviation (n)
bloiatiu, deviously (adv)
bloiato, deviate (v)
bloiatu, devious (adj)
bloiatua, deviant (n doer)
bloib, bead (n)
bloibo, bead (v)
bloif, chaff (n)
bloik, filth (n)
bloiko, filthy (v)
bloiku, filthy (adj)
bloin, row (n d:column)
bloip, boob (n)
bloisho, cringe (v)
bloith, pallet (n)
bloizh, bronze (n)
bloizho, bronze (v)
blomad, plumb (n)
blomado, plumb (v)

blomadu, plumb (adj)
blomadua, plumber (n doer)
blor, slum (n)
blorf, slumber (n)
blorfo, slumber (v)
blorfu, slumber (adj)
blork, bar (n d:pub)
blorko, bartend (v d:pub)
blorkua, bartender (n doer d:pub)
blorp, slump (n)
blorpiu, slumpily (adv)
blorpo, slump (v)
blorpu, slumpy (adj)
blorpua, slumper (n doer)
blorsh, slur (n)
blorshan, slurry (n)
blorsho, slur (v)
blort, device (n)
blortiu, devisively (adv)
blorto, devise (v)
blortu, devisive (adj)
blortua, deviser (n doer)
bluaf, adoration (n)
bluafiu, adorably (adv)
bluafo, adore (v)
bluafu, adorable (adj)
bluag, ache (n)
bluagiu, achily (adv)
bluago, ache (v)
bluagu, achy (adj)
bluako, slug (v d:hit)
bluakua, slugger (n doer d:hit)
bluam, femme (n)
bluan, dam (n)
bluap, cluster (n)
bluapo, cluster (v)
bluasho, soar (v)
bluat, adornment (n)
bluato, adorn (v)
blufk, rust (n)
blufkiu, rustily (adv)
blufko, rust (v)
blufku, rusty (adj)
blufp, pulp (n)
bluft, rush (n)
blufto, rush (v)
blug, thug (n)
bluguet, thuggery (n)
bluk, blow (n d:impact)
blukuil, blowout (n)
blun, prior (n)
blunf, priority (n)
blunfo, prioritize (v)
blunk, butt (n d:end/ rump)
blunk, buttocks (n d:end/ rump)
blunu, prior (adj)
blup, thud (n)
blusham, disease (n)
Blusham, EhoMonth03 (n)
blushamo, disease (v)
blushien, hermit (n)
blut, present (n d:now)
blutho, rustle (v)

bluthua, rustler (n doer)
blutip, pulpit (n)
blutiu, presently (adv d:now)
blutsh, presence (n d:existence)
bluviu, previously (adv)
bluvu, previous (adj)
bluzh, scam (n)
bluzho, scam (v)
bluzhua, scammer (n doer)
boan, fable (n)
boaniu, fabulously (adv)
boanu, fabulous (adj)
bodash, pathogen (n)
bodashu, pathogenic (adj)
boeko, faint (v d:pass out)
boekua, fainter (n doer d:pass out)
boelk, hurt (n)
boelkio, hurt (v pa)
boelkiu, hurtfully (adv)
boelko, hurt (v)
boelku, hurtful (adj)
boen, fade (n d:diminish)
boeniu, faintly (adv d:diminish)
boeno, fade (v d:diminish)
boenu, faint (adj d:diminish)
boenua, fader (n doer d:diminish)
boenweku, faintest (adj)
boenwelu, fainter (adj)
boht, dare (n)
bohto, dare (v)
bohtu, darish (adj)
boid, potato (n)
boif, bungie (n)
boifo, bungie (v)
boig, potency (n)
boigat, potential (n)
boigatiu, potentially (adv)
boigatu, potential (adj)
boigu, potent (adj)
boik, assault (n)
boikash, casket (n)
boiko, assault (v)
boilk, squiggle (n)
boilko, squiggle (v)
boin, dairy (n)
boinu, dairy (adj)
boip, bungle (n)
boipo, bungle (v)
boiran, squirrel (n)
boiranu, squirrely (adj)
boish, page (n d:person/contact)
boishat, pageant (n)
boisho, page (v d:person/contact)
boishua, pager (n doer d:person/contact)
boit, fault (n)
boitiu, faultily (adv)
boito, fault (v)
boitsh, cask (n)
boitu, faulty (adj)
bokat, bronco (n)
bokuit, ecology (n)

bokuit, ecosystem (n)
bokuitiu, ecologically (adv)
bokuitu, ecological (adj)
bokuitua, ecologist (n doer)
bol, been (v pap sng common)
bol, was (common)
bolf, dash (n d:line)
bolfo, dash (v d:line)
bolfua, dasher (n doer d:line)
bolkat, parity (n)
bolko, pare (v)
Bon, Bonn (n)
bonf, grave (n)
bonfbaraf, gravestone (n)
bonfo, engrave (v)
bonfshoit, graveside (n)
bonfthauth, graveyard (n)
bonfua, engraver (n doer)
bor, been (v pap pl common)
bor, were (common)
borf, strength (n)
borfiu, strongly (adv)
borfo, strengthen (v)
borfplon, strongman (n)
borfploni, strongmen (n pl)
borfthorth, stronghold (n)
borfu, strong (adj)
borfwaku, strongest (adj)
borfwelu, stronger (adj)
Borium, Bohrium (n)
borl, soup (n)
borlu, soupy (adj)
Boron, Boron (n)
bort, vice (n d:trap)
borth, resin (n)
borthk, residue (n)
borthku, residual (adj)
bortiu, viciously (adv d:trap)
bortu, vicious (adj d:trap)
bortuet, viciousness (n)
bosh, with (prep)
boshish, within (adv/prep)
boshish, within (n)
boshprath, withdrawal (n)
boshprathio, withdrew (v pa)
boshpratho, withdraw (v)
boshthorthio, withheld (v pa)
boshthortho, withhold (v)
Boshton, Boston (n)
boshtreltio, withstood (v pa)
boshtrelto, withstand (v)
boshuil, without (adv/prep)
boshuil, without (n)
botak, pathos (n)
botakiu, pathetically (adv)
botaku, pathetic (adj)
botsh, path (n)
botshpliol, pathway (n)
bovel, been (v pap sng emphatic)
bovel, was (emphatic)
bover, been (v pap pl emphatic)
bover, were (emphatic)
brab, sob (n)

brabo, sob (v)
brad, dentistry (n)
bradar, denture (n)
bradu, dental (adj)
bradua, dentist (n doer)
braf, fondness (n)
brafiu, fondly (adv)
brafk, ledger (n)
brafu, fond (adj)
braiak, callousness (n)
braiakiu, callously (adv)
braiaku, callous (adj)
braif, sobriety (n)
braifo, sober (v)
braifu, sober (adj)
braig, monster (n)
braigu, monstrous (adj)
braik, invitation (n)
braiko, invite (v)
braiku, invitational (adj)
braikua, invitor (n doer)
braikuin, invitee (n)
braish, char (n d:burn)
braisho, char (v d:burn)
braishu, chary (adj d:burn)
braith, jag (n)
braitho, jag (v)
braithua, jagger (n doer)
braizhgarn, charcoal (n)
brak, font (n)
bral, plain (n)
bralg, ding (n)
bralgo, ding (v)
braliu, plainly (adv)
bralk, prank (n)
bralkua, prankster (n doer)
bralp, dimple (n)
bralpo, dimple (v)
braltip, plaintiff (n)
bralu, plain (adj)
brampo, pound (v d:hit)
brampua, pounder (n doer d:hit)
branf, coast (n d:shore)
branfoip, coastline (n)
branfu, coastal (adj d:shore)
branin, till (n d:cash register)
brank, coach (n)
branko, coach (v)
brant, ground (n d:soil)
branto, ground (v d:soil)
brantua, grounder (n doer d:soil)
braug, bass (n d:sound)
brauk, dunk (n)
brauko, dunk (v)
braukua, dunker (n doer)
braup, area (n)
braush, plaza (n)
braut, arena (n)
brauth, flow (n)
brautho, flow (v)
bravilo, muster (v)
Brazhil, Brazil (n)
Brazhilan, Brazilian (n)

breb, hamper (n d:laundry)
bref, density (n)
brefiu, densely (adv)
brefk, demonstration (n)
brefko, demonstrate (v)
brefkua, demonstrator (n doer)
brefu, dense (adj)
brefweku, densest (adj)
brefwelu, denser (adj)
bregak, daemon (n)
bregak, demon (n)
bregako, daemonize (v)
bregako, demonize (v)
bregaku, demonic (adj)
breidon, irrigation (n)
breidono, irrigate (v)
breif, lightness (n d:weight)
breifiu, lightly (adv d:weight)
breifkeft, lightheadedness (n)
breifo, lighten (v d:weight)
breifshuish, lightweight (n)
breifshuishu, lightweight (adj)
breifu, light (adj d:weight)
breilt, MarbleRobot
breim, staleness (n)
breimfenk, stalemate (n)
breimu, stale (adj)
breish, purity (n)
breishfleid, purebreed (n)
breishfleidiot, purebred (n)
breishiu, purely (adv)
breisho, purify (v)
breishu, pure (adj)
breishua, purist (n doer)
breishuet, purification (n)
breishuetua, purifier (n doer)
breit, crest (n)
breith, slush (n)
breitho, slush (v)
breito, crest (v)
brekik, implement (n)
brekiko, implement (v)
brekikuet, implementation (n)
brelg, plank (n)
brelgo, plank (v)
brelk, completion (n)
brelkat, complement (n)
brelkato, complement (v)
brelkiu, completely (adv)
brelko, complete (v)
brelku, complete (adj)
brem, clumsiness (n)
bremiu, clumsily (adv)
bremu, clumsy (adj)
bren, ferry (n)
brend, money (n)
brendenagua, moneymaker (n
    doer)
brendiu, monetarily (adv)
brendu, monetary (adj)
brenk, chair (n d:meeting)
brenko, chair (v d:meeting)
brenkua, chairman (n doer

d:meeting)
brenkua, chairperson (n doer
    d:meeting)
breno, ferry (v)
brenshkob, ferryboat (n)
brentak, monkey (n)
brentako, monkey (v)
brep, plant (n d:life form, affix)
brepo, plant (v d:life form, affix)
brepua, planter (n doer d:life
    form, affix)
bresh, place (n)
breshk, complexity (n)
breshkat, complex (n)
breshku, complex (adj)
bresho, place (v)
breshpo, implore (v)
bresht, placation (n)
breshto, placate (v)
breshtua, placator (n doer)
breshua, placer (n doer)
breshuet, placement (n)
breshuish, freight (n)
breshuishroif, freightliner (n)
breshuishua, freighter (n doer)
bret, dent (n)
breto, dent (v)
briadit, roster (n)
briaf, dove (n d:bird)
briafmitho, dovetail (v)
briak, use (n)
briakab, usury (n)
briakat, usage (n)
briakfrep, useability (n)
briakfrepu, usable (adj)
briakiu, usually (adv)
briakmenu, useless (adj)
briako, use (v)
briaku, usual (adj)
briakua, user (n doer)
briakush, usefulness (n)
briakushiu, usefully (adv)
briakushu, useful (adj)
brialk, arbitration (n)
brialkiu, arbitrarily (adv)
brialko, arbitrate (v)
brialku, arbitrary (adj)
brialkua, arbitrator (n doer)
briam, vouch (n)
briamo, vouch (v)
briamua, voucher (n doer)
briank, registration (n)
brianko, register (v)
briankua, register (n doer)
briant, clank (n)
brianto, clank (v)
briantu, clanky (adj)
briantua, clanker (n doer)
briap, loop (n)
briapiu, loopily (adv)
briapkoth, loophole (n)
briapo, loop (v)
briapu, loopy (adj)

briapua, looper (n doer)
briash, vow (n)
briasho, vow (v)
briat, abortion (n)
briath, fleet (n)
briatho, fleet (v)
briato, abort (v)
briatua, abortionist (n doer)
briauk, riot (n)
briauko, riot (v)
briaukua, rioter (n doer)
briautsh, vomit (n)
briautsho, vomit (v)
bribako, bulldoze (v)
bribakua, bulldozer (n doer)
briel, mall (n)
brien, name (n)
brienfkaf, nameplate (n)
brieniu, namely (adv)
brienmenu, nameless (adj)
brienmoak, namesake (n)
brieno, name (v)
brient, clink (n)
briento, clink (v)
brientu, clinky (adj)
brientua, clinker (n doer)
brienua, namer (n doer)
briesh, stench (n)
briet, denial (n)
brieto, deny (v)
brik, black (n)
briko, blacken (v)
brikplork, blackboard (n)
briku, black (adj)
bril, inn (n)
brilp, thrift (n)
brilpu, thrifty (adj)
brilua, innkeeper (n doer)
briof, facility (n)
briofo, facilitate (v)
briofu, facile (adj)
briofua, facilitator (n doer)
briofuet, faculty (n)
briok, accumulation (n)
briokiu, cumulatively (adv)
brioko, accumulate (v)
brioku, cumulative (adj)
briokua, accumulator (n doer)
brion, peculiarity (n)
brioniu, peculiarly (adv)
briont, clonk (n)
brionto, clonk (v)
briontu, clonky (adj)
briontua, clonker (n doer)
brionu, peculiar (adj)
briop, thimble (n)
brishtiu, soon (adv)
brishtwakiu, soonest (adv)
brishtweliu, sooner (adv)
Britain, Britain (n)
British, British (n)
briuf, tumble (n)
briufo, tumble (v)

briufua, tumbler (n doer)
briugo, broil (v)
briugua, broiler (n doer)
briuk, leak (n)
briukat, leakage (n)
briukiu, leakily (adv)
briuko, leak (v)
briuku, leaky (adj)
briukua, leaker (n doer)
briump, bonk (n)
briumpo, bonk (v)
briun, Eho15minutes (n)
briupo, shrivel (v)
briush, leach (n)
briusho, leach (v)
briut, bleakness (n)
briutu, bleak (adj)
brivak, weave (n)
brivakio, wove (v pa)
brivako, weave (v)
brivakua, weaver (n doer)
brivan, web (n)
brivano, web (v)
brivut, stigma (n)
brivuto, stigmatize (v)
brizhan, buzzard (n)
Brodwain, Broadway (n)
broif, cry (n)
broifdeid, crybaby (n)
broifo, cry (v)
broifua, crier (n doer)
broig, abscess (n)
broigo, abscess (v)
broik, crisis (n)
broin, clunk (n)
broino, clunk (v)
broinu, clunky (adj)
broinua, clunker (n doer)
broisho, bicker (v)
broishua, bickerer (n doer)
broit, volt (n)
broituet, voltage (n)
brokiag, gestation (n)
brokiago, gestate (v)
brol, kin (n)
brolfif, kinship (n)
brolk, comparison (n)
brolkifp, kinfolk (n)
brolkiu, comparably (adv)
brolkiu, comparatively (adv)
brolko, compare (v)
brolku, comparable (adj)
brolku, comparative (adj)
brolkua, comparitor (n doer)
brolplon, kinsman (n)
brolreik, kindred (n)
brolreiku, kindred (adj)
Bromin, Bromine (n)
bron, group (n)
bronbar, gender (n d:group)
bronbaro, engender (v d:group)
brond, germ (n)
bronk, flock (n d:wool)

bronkoik, genocide (n)
bronkoiku, genocidal (adj)
bronlaf, genre (n)
brono, group (v)
bront, genus (n)
bronua, groupie (n doer)
broteir, crystal (n)
broteiro, crystalize (v)
broteiru, crystalline (adj)
broteiruet, crystalization (n)
broto, listen (v)
brotua, listener (n doer)
bruak, bluster (n)
bruako, bluster (v)
bruaku, blustery (adj)
brualfi, flutter (n pl)
brualfo, flutter (v)
bruano, flourish (v)
bruash, agility (n)
bruashu, agile (adj)
bruat, float (n)
bruato, float (v)
bruatua, floater (n doer)
bruatuet, flotation (n)
bruatuetu, flotation (adj)
brub, league (n)
brubua, leaguer (n doer)
brufet, pension (n)
bruft, dispensation (n)
brufto, dispense (v)
bruftu, dispensable (adj)
bruftua, dispenser (n doer)
brug, burn (n)
brugato, burnish (v)
brugio, burnt (v pa)
brugo, burn (v)
brugua, burner (n doer)
bruguil, burnout (n)
bruik, encryption (n)
bruikdarf, cryptography (n)
bruikdarfu, cryptic (adj)
bruiko, encrypt (v)
bruiku, cryptic (adj)
bruith, leech (n)
bruitho, leech (v)
bruk, tick (n d:increment)
brukap, ticket (n)
brukapo, ticket (v)
brukapua, ticketer (n doer)
brukat, tickle (n)
brukato, tickle (v)
brukatua, tickler (n doer)
Bruklin, Brooklyn (n)
bruko, tick (v d:increment)
brukua, ticker (n doer d:increment)
brulali, flurry (n pl)
brulf, compensation (n)
brulfo, compensate (v)
brulfua, compensator (n doer)
brulto, sputter (v)
brundan, pendulum (n)
brundat, pendant (n)

brunk, slug (n d:blank)
bruno, pend (v)
brunp, dependence (n)
brunp, dependency (n)
brunpiu, dependably (adv)
brunpo, depend (v)
brunpu, dependable (adj)
brunpua, dependant (n doer)
brunpua, dependent (n doer)
brup, ebb (n)
brupo, ebb (v)
Brushel, Brussels (n)
brusht, burst (n)
brushtio, burst (v pa)
brushto, burst (v)
bruth, leaf (n)
bruthap, leaflet (n)
brutho, leaf (v)
buait, poison (n)
buaito, poison (v)
buaitu, poisonous (adj)
buaitua, poisoner (n doer)
buak, harrow (n)
buako, harrow (v)
bual, trowel (n)
bualo, trowel (v)
bualua, troweler (n doer)
buank, dump (n)
buankap, dumpster (n)
buanko, dump (v)
buankua, dumper (n doer)
buant, defiance (n)
buantiu, defiantly (adv)
buanto, defy (v)
buantu, defiant (adj)
buash, hearse (n)
buasht, splatter (n)
buashto, splatter (v)
buat, splat (n)
buath, trough (n)
bubielk, deportation (n)
bubielko, deport (v)
bubielkua, deporter (n doer)
bubielkuin, deportee (n)
bublarf, deflation (n)
bublarfo, deflate (v)
bublarfu, deflationary (adj)
bublarfua, deflator (n doer)
bublash, depression (n)
bublashiu, depressively (adv)
bublasho, depress (v)
bublashu, depressive (adj)
bublashua, depressant (n doer)
bublashua, depressor (n doer)
bubleg, declassification (n)
bublego, declassify (v)
bubliut, decree (n)
bubliuto, decree (v)
buboit, default (n)
buboito, default (v)
bubroifo, decry (v)
bubruik, decryption (n)
bubruiko, decrypt (v)

bubrulif, decipherment (n)
bubrulifi, decipherments (n pl)
bubrulifo, decipher (v)
Budin, Buddha (n)
Budinua, Buddhist (n)
Budinuet, Buddhism (n)
budito, delist (v)
budiuafo, devour (v)
budolf, detection (n)
budolfat, detective (n)
budolfo, detect (v)
budolfu, detectable (adj)
budolfua, detector (n doer)
budufal, deodorization (n)
budufalo, deodorize (v)
budufalua, deodorent (n doer)
budufp, despondence (n)
budufpo, despond (v)
budufpua, desponder (n doer)
bufaboto, defuse (v)
bufaiko, despise (v)
bufaikua, despiser (n doer)
Bufalon, Buffalo (n)
bufapo, derogate (v)
bufapu, derogatory (adj)
bufiorto, defrost (v)
bufk, zoom (n)
bufko, zoom (v)
bufku, zoom (adj)
bufork, department (n)
buforkiu, departmentally (adv)
buforku, departmental (adj)
bufp, file (n d:tool)
bufpo, file (v d:tool)
bufpua, filer (n doer d:tool)
bufrilak, determent (n)
bufrilak, deterrence (n)
bufrilako, deter (v)
bufrilakua, deterrent (n doer)
bufrilakua, deterrer (n doer)
bufto, deplore (v)
buftu, deplorable (adj)
bugaft, packet (n)
bugalt, detraction (n)
bugalto, detract (v)
bugaltua, detractor (n doer)
bugap, pack (n)
bugapo, pack (v)
bugapua, packer (n doer)
bugat, package (n)
bugato, package (v)
bugatua, packager (n doer)
bugauroip, detonation (n)
bugauroipo, detonate (v)
bugauroipua, detonator (n doer)
buget, deflection (n)
bugeto, deflect (v)
bugetu, deflective (adj)
bugetua, deflector (n doer)
bugiap, debate (n)
bugiapo, debate (v)
bugiapua, debater (n doer)
bugluko, debunk (v)

bugrash, depiction (n)
bugrasho, depict (v)
bugublashan, decompression (n)
bugublashano, decompress (v)
buiasho, singe (v)
buiatu, sinister (adj)
buiauk, gloat (n)
buiauko, gloat (v)
buif, zoo (n)
buifp, debut (n)
buifpo, debut (v)
builar, deterioration (n)
builaro, deteriorate (v)
buisht, con (n d:consequence)
buisht, consequence (n)
buishtiu, consequentially (adv)
buishtiu, consequently (adv)
buishtu, conseqent (adj)
buishtu, consequential (adj)
buk, duck (n d:avoid)
bukeft, decapitation (n)
bukefto, decapitate (v)
bukemif, devolution (n)
bukemif, devolvement (n)
bukemifo, devolve (v)
bukiak, dedication (n)
bukiako, dedicate (v)
bukiakua, dedicator (n doer)
bukiuk, deliberation (n)
bukiukiu, deliberately (adv)
bukiuko, deliberate (v)
bukiuku, deliberate (adj)
buko, duck (v d:avoid)
bukoitivo, dethrone (v)
bukriuk, deductible (n d:subtraction)
bukriuk, deduction (n d:subtraction)
bukriuko, deduct (v d:subtraction)
bukriuku, deductible (adj d:subtraction)
bul, pen (n d:enclosure)
bulank, decomposition (n)
bulanko, decompose (v)
bulankua, decomposer (n doer)
bulenkat, decommission (n)
bulenkato, decommission (v)
bulf, rue (n)
bulfo, rue (v)
Bulgar, Bulgaria (n)
Bulgarian, Bulgarian (n)
buliag, demeanor (n)
bulink, deficiency (n)
bulinkiu, deficiently (adv)
bulinku, deficient (adj)
bulinp, deficit (n)
bulirk, descent (n)
bulirkat, descendant (n)
bulirkat, descendent (n)
bulirko, descend (v)
bulirkua, descender (n doer)
bulmot, derangement (n)

bulmoto, derange (v)
bulo, pen (v d:enclosure)
buloif, filament (n)
bulsh, buff (n d:rub)
bulsho, buff (v d:rub)
bulshua, buffer (n doer d:rub)
buluit, derailment (n)
buluito, derail (v)
buluvip, deregulation (n)
buluvipo, deregulate (v)
buluvipua, deregulator (n doer)
bulvat, boulevard (n)
bumarmak, degeneration (n)
bumarmako, degenerate (v)
bumarmaku, degenerative (adj)
bumid, denotation (n)
bumido, denote (v)
bumith, detail (n)
bumitho, detail (v)
bumithua, detailer (n doer)
bumuft, denouncement (n)
bumufto, denounce (v)
bumuftua, denouncer (n doer)
bup, fill (n)
bupaik, detachment (n)
bupaiko, detach (v)
bupaltak, deactivation (n)
bupaltako, deactivate (v)
bupaltakua, deactivator (n doer)
bupiak, delegation (n)
bupiako, delegate (v)
bupiakua, delegate (n doer)
bupift, detainment (n)
bupiftar, detention (n)
bupifto, detain (v)
bupiftua, detainor (n doer)
bupiftuin, detainee (n)
bupliuto, destroy (v)
bupliutua, destroyer (n doer)
bupo, fill (v)
bupua, filler (n doer)
burbolk, despair (n)
burbolkar, desperation (n)
burbolko, despair (v)
burbolku, desperate (adj)
burf, gravity (n d:serious)
burfaik, despite (prep)
burfiu, gravely (adv d:serious)
burtu, grave (adj d:serious)
burianko, defray (v)
burlat, gravel (n)
burlatu, gravelly (adj)
Burlington, Burlington (n)
burth, shrub (n)
burthuet, shrubbery (n)
burush, delusion (n)
burusho, delude (v)
burushu, delusional (adj)
busheif, sterility (n)
busheifiu, sterilely (adv)
busheifo, sterilize (v)
busheifu, sterile (adj)
busheifuet, sterilization (n)

bushk, depth (n)
bushklivago, demean (v)
bushlan, destiny (n)
bushlano, destine (v)
bushlant, destination (n)
bushlek, destruction (n)
bushleko, destruct (v)
bushleku, destructive (adj)
bushlib, derision (n)
bushlibo, deride (v)
bushoik, demand (n)
bushoiko, demand (v)
bushp, deep (n)
bushpiu, deeply (adv)
bushpo, deepen (v)
bushpu, deep (adj)
bushpwaku, deepest (adj)
bushpwelu, deeper (adj)
bushtito, detest (v)
bushtitu, detestable (adj)
bushtran, degradation (n)
bushtrano, degrade (v)
butelko, desist (v)
butep, dejection (n)
butepo, deject (v)
buthiaf, detour (n)
buthiafo, detour (v)
buthoisho, deface (v)
buthoito, debrief (v)
butiap, deprivation (n)
butiapo, deprive (v)
butrant, decontrol (n)
butranto, decontrol (v)
buvadav, demotion (n)
buvadavo, demote (v)
buvanfo, decouple (v)
buvathav, demolition (n)
buvathavo, demolish (v)
buvaup, devaluation (n)
buvaupo, devalue (v)
buvek, decease (n)
buveko, decease (v)
buvesh, shall (v)
buvesh, will (v emphat)
buvesh, will-be (v fp emphatic)
buvienk, denomination (n)
buvienko, denominate (v)
buvienku, denominational (adj)
buvienkua, denominator (n doer)
buvlato, decode (v)
buvlatua, decoder (n doer)
buvo, will (v common)
buvorv, depopulation (n)
buvorvo, depopulate (v)
buvu, will-be (v fp common)
buwelk, depletion (n)
buwelko, deplete (v)
buzhb, deceit (n)
buzhbet, deception (n)
buzhbetiu, deceptively (adv)
buzhbetu, deceptive (adj)
buzhbiu, deceitfully (adv)
buzhbo, deceive (v)

buzhbu, deceitful (adj)
buzhbua, deceiver (n doer)
buzheko, degas (v)
da, D (let sng)
dabit, theater (n)
dabit, theatre (n)
dabitu, theatrical (adj)
dabitul, theatric (n)
dafk, belt (n)
dafka, quinquagintillion (num
   1e153 card)
dafko, belt (v)
dafkua, belter (n doer)
dafp, championship (n)
dafpo, champion (v)
dafpua, champ (n doer)
dafpua, champion (n doer)
dafta, quadragintillion (num
   1e123 card)
dafumiu, suavely (adv)
dafumu, suave (adj)
dahem, Number_1e2406
Dahma, Dahma (n)
daiaf, tiff (n)
daiafo, tiff (v)
daiak, captain (n)
daiako, captain (v)
daian, uncle (n)
daiap, puddle (n)
daib, hibernation (n)
daibat, exhibit (n)
daibatet, exhibition (n)
daibatetua, exhibitionist (n doer)
daibato, exhibit (v)
daibatua, exhibitor (n doer)
daibo, hibernate (v)
daid, equation (n)
daido, equate (v)
daidua, equator (n doer)
dalf, pot (u)
daifaif, potty (n)
daifk, challenge (n)
daifko, challenge (v)
daifkoth, pothole (n)
daifkotho, pothole (v)
daifkua, challenger (n doer)
daifo, pot (v)
daifpasht, potluck (n)
daifshkoit, potshot (n)
daift, bravery (n)
daiftan, SplitWand (n)
daifto, brave (v)
daiftu, brave (adj)
daiftua, brave (n doer)
daifua, potter (n doer)
daig, fraud (n)
daigo, defraud (v)
daigua, defrauder (n doer)
daik, end (n)
daikiunf, equilibrium (n)
daikmeniu, endlessly (adv)
daikmenu, endless (adj)
daiko, end (v)

daiktaift, endpoint (n)
daikzhiet, endgame (n)
dailt, equivalence (n)
dailtu, equivalent (adj)
dain, equal (n)
dainiu, equally (adv)
daink, equality (n)
daink, equalization (n)
dainko, equalize (v)
dainkua, equalizer (n doer)
daino, equal (v)
daip, squash (n d:pressure)
daipo, squash (v d:pressure)
daipua, squasher (n doer
   d:pressure)
dairn, costume (n)
daish, cut (n)
daishio, cut (v pa)
daisho, cut (v)
daisht, equity (n)
daishua, cutter (n doer)
daishuil, cutout (n)
daishunf, cutoff (n)
daishvak, cutback (n)
daith, cuteness (n)
daithu, cute (adj)
Daiton, Dayton (n)
Daitonaf, Daytona (n)
daitsh, pouch (n)
daivg, ruin (n)
daivgo, ruin (v)
daka, decillion (num 1e33 card)
dakai-, vendeka- (num 1e33 pref)
dakaib, decade (n)
daketh, decillionth (num 1e33
   ord)
dakirn, decimal (n)
dakirnu, decimal (adj)
daklito, trickle (v)
dalag, syrup (n)
dalagu, syrupy (adj)
Dalash, Dallas (n)
dalduk, syntax (n)
dalel, aunt (n)
dalf, bath (n)
dalfo, bathe (v)
dalfshran, bathroom (n)
dalfua, bather (n doer)
dali, Ds (let pl)
dalid, bugle (n)
dalil, custom (n d:tradition)
dalilo, customize (v d:tradition)
dalilt, customs (n d:checkpoint)
dalilu, customary (adj d:tradition)
dalilua, customer (n doer
   d:tradition)
dalk, trick (n)
dalkiak, syndicate (n)
dalkiako, syndicate (v)
dalkiakua, syndicator (n doer)
dalkiakuet, syndication (n)
dalko, trick (v)
dalku, tricky (adj)

dalkua, trickster (n doer)
dalkuet, trickery (n)
dalm, persuasion (n)
dalmid, synopsis (n)
dalmiu, persuasively (adv)
dalmo, persuade (v)
dalmu, persuasive (adj)
daln, lodge (n d:building)
dalnag, synthesis (n)
dalnagiu, synthetically (adv)
dalnago, synthesize (v)
dalnagu, synthetic (adj)
dalnagua, synthesizer (n doer)
dalnagul, synthetic (n)
daloish, syringe (n)
dalparp, syndrome (n)
dalpiar, synchro (n)
dalpiariu, synchronously (adv)
dalpiaro, synchronize (v)
dalpiaru, synchronous (adj)
dalpiaruet, synchronization (n)
dalshio, taught (v pa)
dalsho, teach (v)
dalshua, teacher (n doer)
dalt, age (n)
dalth, cover (n)
dalthat, coverage (n)
dalthiveil, coverup (n)
daltho, cover (v)
dalto, age (v)
daltu, agey (adj)
daltua, ager (n doer)
daluk, system (n)
dalukat, systemization (n)
dalukatiu, systematically (adv)
dalukato, systemate (v)
dalukatu, systematic (adj)
daluko, systemize (v)
dalukrashu, systemwide (adj)
daluku, systemic (adj)
dalvien, synonym (n)
dalvieniu, synonymously (adv)
dalvienu, synonymous (adj)
dalvoglit, synergy (n)
dalvoglitu, synergistic (adj)
danat, cucumber (n)
dandan, bear (n d:animal)
danfp, mob (n)
danfpo, mob (v)
danfpua, mobster (n doer)
dank, butchery (n)
danko, butcher (v)
dankua, butcher (n doer)
danp, chamber (n)
dansh, tenure (n)
dansho, tenure (v)
dant, mobility (n)
dantat, mobile (n)
danto, mobilize (v)
dantu, mobile (adj)
dantuet, mobilization (n)
dapa, ten (num 10 card)
dapai-, dec- (num 10 pref)

dapalfhemka, Number_1e40656
dapeth, tenth (num 10 ord)
dapt, deck (n)
dapto, deck (v)
darf, graph (n)
darfet, graphic (n)
darfetiu, graphically (adv)
darfetu, graphical (adj)
darfil, graft (n)
darfilo, graft (v)
darfo, graph (v)
darfu, graphic (adj)
darg, drop (n)
dargapi, droplet (n pl)
dargo, drop (v)
dargua, dropper (n doer)
darguili, dropout (n pl)
darlf, juice (n)
darlfo, juice (v)
darlfu, juicy (adj)
darlfua, juicer (n doer)
darlian, potion (n)
darmik, minute (n d:time)
Darmshtat, Darmstadtium (n)
darnf, custody (n)
darnfua, custodian (n doer)
darshriash, drowsiness (n)
darshriashu, drowsy (adj)
darsht, lateness (n)
darshtblef, latecomer (n)
darshtiu, lately (adv)
darshtu, late (adj)
darshtwaku, latest (adj)
darshtwelu, later (adj)
Dart, Dart (n)
darth, dart (n)
dartho, dart (v)
darupo, droop (v)
darupu, droopy (adj)
dashk, cube (n)
dashka, trigintillion (num 1e93 card)
dashkai-, anto-
dashketh, trigintillionth (num 1e93 ord)
dashko, cube (v)
dashku, cubic (adj)
dashp, bareness (n)
dashpo, bare (v)
dashpoiu, barely (adv)
dashposhu, barefoot (adj)
dashpu, bare (adj)
dashta, vigintillion (num 1e63 card)
dashtai-, kido- (num 1e63 pref)
dashteth, vigintillionth (num 1e63 ord)
dath, villa (n)
dathan, village (n)
dathanua, villager (n doer)
dathfef, parent (n)
dathfefif, parenthood (n)

dathfefo, parent (v)
dathfefu, parental (adj)
dathiat, vicinity (n)
datiat, versatility (n)
datiatu, versatile (adj)
daua, pow (interj)
daufk, empire (n)
daufkua, emperor (n doer)
daufkuet, imperialism (n)
daufkuetu, imperial (adj)
daufkuetua, imperialist (n doer)
daufrauth, boycott (n)
daufrautho, boycott (v)
daufrauthua, boycotter (n doer)
dauft, expiration (n)
daufto, expire (v)
daugil, snare (n d:string)
dauiak, spook (n)
dauiako, spook (v)
dauiaku, spooky (adj)
dauit, vaccine (n)
dauito, vaccinate (v)
dauituet, vaccination (n)
dauk, type (n d:key)
daukdarf, typography (n)
daukdarfu, typographical (adj)
daukfepio, typeset (v pa)
daukfepo, typeset (v)
daukfepua, typesetter (n doer)
daukil, typo (n)
dauko, type (v d:key)
daukploidua, typewriter (n doer)
daukthoish, typeface (n)
daukua, typist (n doer d:key)
daulaviu, mournfully (adv)
daulavo, mourn (v)
daulavu, mournful (adj)
daulavua, mourner (n doer)
daun, time (n)
daundoiar, timetable (n)
daunmen, timelessness (n)
daunmenu, timeless (adj)
dauno, time (v)
daunroif, timeline (n)
daunthetsh, timepiece (n)
daunu, timely (adj)
daunua, timer (n doer)
daunuet, timeliness (n)
daunuil, timeout (n)
daup, top (n)
daupato, topple (v)
daupemenu, topless (adj)
daupik, topic (n)
daupiku, topical (adj)
daupinu, topsy (adj)
daupnarsh, topsoil (n)
daupo, top (v)
daupu, top (adj)
daupua, topper (n doer)
daush, falsity (n)
daushfif, falsehood (n)
daushiu, falsely (adv)
daushko, botch (v)

dausho, falsify (v)
daushu, false (adj)
daushuet, falsification (n)
daut, beat (n)
dautaf, piracy (n)
dautafo, pirate (v)
dautafua, pirate (n doer)
dauth, vet (n d:veteran)
dauthan, veteran (n)
dautio, beat (v pa)
dauto, beat (v)
dautu, beatable (adj)
dautua, beater (n doer)
dauv, moan (n)
dauvit, pavement (n)
dauvito, pave (v)
dauvitua, paver (n doer)
dauvo, moan (v)
davap, orange (n d:fruit)
dazh, jazz (n)
dazho, jazz (v)
dazhu, jazzy (adj)
defk, rat (n)
defko, rat (v)
defp, cap (n)
defpo, cap (v)
defrep, capability (n)
defrepu, capable (adj)
Deginak, General (n)
dehush, toward (prep)
deiaf, nourishment (n)
deiafo, nourish (v)
deian, witchcraft (n)
deiano, bewitch (v)
deianua, witch (n doer)
deiaup, piety (n)
deiaupu, pious (adj)
deid, baby (n)
deido, baby (v)
deif, bull (n)
deifian, bullion (n)
deiflur, daisy (n)
deifo, bull (v)
deifrashk, betrayal (n)
deifrashko, betray (v)
deift, bullet (n)
deiftfliofo, bulletproof (v)
deiftfliofu, bulletproof (adj)
deifu, bullish (adj)
deifua, bully (n doer)
deifuako, bully (v)
deig, guy (n d:male)
deigin, goggle (n)
deild, quiet (n)
deild, quietness (n)
deildiu, quietly (adv)
deildo, quiet (v)
deildu, quiet (adj)
deimako, linch (v)
deimuth, buffet (n d:food/ table)
deior, film (n)
deioro, film (v)
deiorshiu, flimsily (adv)

deiorshu, flimsy (adj)
deiorua, filmer (n doer)
deiot, tire (n d:wheel)
deip, quip (n)
deipo, quip (v)
deipua, quipper (n doer)
deiran, tulip (n)
deirfralt, bureaucracy (n)
deirfraltiu, bureaucratically (adv)
deirfraltu, bureaucratic (adj)
deirfraltua, bureaucrat (n doer)
deirn, bureau (n)
deirsh, diction (n)
deirt, design (n)
deirtak, designation (n)
deirtako, designate (v)
deirtakua, designator (n doer)
deirto, design (v)
deirtua, designer (n doer)
deish, dictation (n)
deisho, dictate (v)
deishu, dictatoral (adj)
deishua, dictator (n doer)
deishuafif, dictatorship (n)
deishvon, dictionary (n)
deith, modesty (n)
deithiu, modestly (adv)
deithu, modest (adj)
deiut, stern (n d:rear)
deizh, pitch (n d:throw)
deizho, pitch (v d:throw)
deizhua, pitcher (n doer d:throw)
delaif, tree (n)
delaifdaup, treetop (n)
delaifmenu, treeless (adj)
Delawar, Delaware (n)
delf, nursery (n)
delfko, nurture (v)
delfkua, nurturer (n doer)
delfo, nurse (v)
delfua, nurse (n doer)
delgel, secretary (n)
deliu, too (adv)
delk, capital (n)
delkar, capitalism (n)
delko, capitalize (v)
delm, candle (n)
delmfluan, candlelight (n)
delmshnet, candlestick (n)
delnabresh, marketplace (n)
delnat, market (n)
delnatfrep, marketability (n)
delnatfrepu, marketable (adj)
delnato, market (v)
delnatua, marketeer (n doer)
delnatua, marketer (n doer)
delp, knit (n)
delpedorim, knitwear (n)
delpo, knit (v)
delsh, fracture (n)
delshk, fraction (n)
delshkiu, fractionally (adv)
delshku, fractional (adj)

delsho, fracture (v)
deltan, delta (n)
delthiu, thoroughly (adv)
delthu, thorough (adj)
demb, cancellation (n)
dembo, cancel (v)
demgu, candid (adj)
dempan, candidate (n)
denan, ornament (n)
denaniu, ornamentally (adv)
denanu, ornamental (adj)
dend, temperature (n)
denfiu, ornately (adv)
denfu, ornate (adj)
denk, matter (n d:physics)
Denmak, Denmark (n)
denp, can (n d:container)
denpo, can (v d:container)
dentak, capitol (n)
Denver, Denver (n)
dep, thought (n)
depio, thought (v pa)
depiu, thoughtfully (adv)
depo, think (v)
depu, thoughtful (adj)
depua, thinker (n doer)
derft, canvas (n)
derfto, canvas (v)
deriagaift, bankruptcy (n)
deriagaifto, bankrupt (v)
dermak, cancer (n)
dermaku, cancerous (adj)
derp, spot (n)
derpefluan, spotlight (n)
derpemenu, spotless (adj)
derpo, spot (v)
derpu, spotty (adj)
derpua, spotter (n doer)
deshiafk, captivity (n)
deshiafko, captivate (v)
deshiak, capture (n)
deshiako, capture (v)
deshiakua, capturer (n doer)
deshp, caption (n)
deshpo, caption (v)
desht, presidency (n)
deshtiu, presidentially (adv)
deshto, preside (v)
deshtu, presidential (adj)
deshtua, president (n doer)
dethp, capacity (n)
Detroit, Detroit (n)
detsh, peck (n)
detsho, peck (v)
dha, Dh (let sng)
dhahem, Number_1e2706
dhai, was/will be (parcl d:passive
  voice)
dhak, and (conj)
dhali, Dhs (let pl)
dhauatelantiku, transatlantic
  (adj)
dhaubielk, transportation (n)

dhaubielko, transport (v)
dhaubielku, transportable (adj)
dhaubielkua, transporter (n doer)
dhaubivikat, transsexual (n)
dhaudart, translation (n)
dhaudarto, translate (v)
dhaudartua, translator (n doer)
dhaudauf, transpiration (n)
dhaudaufo, transpire (v)
dhaudufp, transponder (n)
dhaufabot, transfusion (n)
dhaufaboto, transfuse (v)
dhaufk, transit (n)
dhaufkuet, transition (n)
dhaufrep, transience (n)
dhaufrepiu, transiently (adv)
dhaufrepu, transient (adj)
dhaufrepua, transient (n doer)
dhauglak, transposition (n)
dhauglako, transpose (v)
dhauglakua, transposer (n doer)
dhaukarlu, transnational (adj)
dhaukiflaf, transvestite (n)
dhaukirk, transduction (n)
dhaukirko, transduce (v)
dhaukirkua, transducer (n doer)
dhaulirk, transcendence (n)
dhaulirko, transcend (v)
dhaulirku, transcendent (adj)
dhaulirkul, transcendent (n)
dhaulirkulu, transcendental (adj)
dhaulitank, transplant (n)
dhaulitanko, transplant (v)
dhaulitankuet, transplantation (n)
dhaulunto, trespass (v)
dhauluntua, trespasser (n doer)
dhaumertu, transcontinental (adj)
dhaumiaru, transocean (adj)
dhaunok, transmission (n)
dhaunok, transmittal (n)
dhaunoko, transmit (v)
dhaunokua, transmitter (n doer)
dhaupalt, transaction (n)
dhaupalto, transact (v)
dhaupaltua, transactor (n doer)
dhauplian, transparency (n)
dhauplianiu, transparently (adv)
dhauplianu, transparent (adj)
dhaush, transfer (v)
dhaushfrep, transferability (n)
dhaushiu, transferably (adv)
dhaushiunkiu, translucently (adv)
dhaushiunku, translucent (adj)
dhaushluak, transmutation (n)
dhaushluakiu, transmutably (adv)
dhaushluako, transmute (v)
dhaushluaku, transmutable (adj)
dhaushluakua, transmutor (n doer)
dhausho, transfer (v)
dhaushrig, transcript (n)

dhaushrigo, transcribe (v)
dhaushrigua, transcriber (n doer)
dhaushriguet, transcription (n)
dhaushu, transferable (adj)
dhaushuet, transference (n)
dhauthark, transverse (n)
dhautharko, transvert (v)
dhautharku, transverse (adj)
dhautielkua, transistor (n doer)
dhauviket, transfixation (n)
dhauviketo, transfixate (v)
dhauviko, transfix (v)
dhauvorg, transgression (n)
dhauvorgo, transgress (v)
dhauvorgua, transgressor (n doer)
dhauvorn, transformation (n)
dhauvorniu, transformationally (adv)
dhauvorno, transform (v)
dhauvornu, transformational (adj)
dhauvornua, transformer (n doer)
dheigrogo, roughen (v)
dhiaishman, misdiagnosis (n)
dhiaishmano, misdiagnose (v)
dhiaridrup, misinterpretation (n)
dhiaridrupo, misinterpret (v)
dhiash, miss (n d:avoid)
dhiasho, miss (v d:avoid)
dhibiut, misstatement (n)
dhibiuto, misstate (v)
dhibresh, misplacement (n)
dhibresho, misplace (v)
dhibriak, misuse (n)
dhibriako, misuse (v)
dhibuliag, misdemeanor (n)
dhidibag, mistrial (n)
dhidorklatio, misspent (v pa)
dhidorklato, misspend (v)
dhidreif, mistrust (n)
dhidreifo, mistrust (v)
dhiduliat, misadventure (n)
dhifiunfet, mispronunciation (n)
dhifiunfeto, mispronounce (v)
dhiflensh, miscredibility (n)
dhiflenshua, miscreant (n doer)
dhiflid, misdeed (n)
dhifruif, misplay (n)
dhifruifo, misplay (v)
dhigardak, miscalculation (n)
dhigardako, miscalculate (v)
dhigiaul, misfire (n)
dhigiaulo, misfire (v)
dhiglish, misstep (n)
dhiglisho, misstep (v)
dhigok, mistake (n)
dhigokio, mistook (v pa)
dhigokiu, mistakenly (adv)
dhigoko, mistake (v)
dhigren, miscarriage (n)
dhigreno, miscarry (v)
dhigruthio, misgave (v pa)

dhigrutho, misgive (v)
dhiguniat, miscommunication (n)
dhiguniato, miscommunicate (v)
dhihethet, misjudgement (n)
dhihethet, misjudgment (n)
dhihetheto, misjudge (v)
dhihinf, misquote (n)
dhihinfo, misquote (v)
dhiivorn, misinformation (n)
dhiivorno, misinform (v)
dhikapado, mishandle (v)
dhikolp, mishap (n)
dhikolpo, mishappen (v)
dhikuafk, misdirection (n)
dhikuafko, misdirect (v)
dhikulf, misbehavior (n)
dhikulfo, misbehave (v)
dhilaltiu, misleadingly (adv)
dhilalto, mislead (v)
dhilaltua, misleader (n doer)
dhilarto, misrule (v)
dhiliap, misread (n)
dhiliapio, misread (v pa)
dhiliapo, misread (v)
dhiliukriuk, misconduct (n)
dhiliukriuko, misconduct (v)
dhiliuplaipo, misconstrue (v)
dhiliushp, misconception (n)
dhiliushpo, misconceive (v)
dhiloship, misperception (n)
dhiloshipo, misperceive (v)
dhiluduash, misrepresentation (n)
dhiluduasho, misrepresent (v)
dhimuth, mismatch (n)
dhimutho, mismatch (v)
dhiodruket, misapprehension (n)
dhiodruketo, misapprehend (v)
dhioflikim, misappropriation (n)
dhioflikimo, misappropriate (v)
dhioroif, misalignment (n)
dhioroifo, misalign (v)
dhiorshaipi, misallocation (n pl)
dhiorshaipo, misallocate (v)
dhipaft, misfit (n)
dhishashk, mismanagement (n)
dhishashko, mismanage (v)
dhiteif, miscue (n)
dhiteifo, miscue (v)
dhitentio, misunderstood (v pa)
dhitento, misunderstand (v)
dhitharo, misspell (v)
dhithoki, misapplication (n pl)
dhithoko, misapply (v)
dhithuit, mistreatment (n)
dhithuito, mistreat (v)
dhitrulsh, misprint (n)
dhitrulsho, misprint (v)
dhituip, misguidance (n)
dhituipo, misguide (v)
dhiuferth, misidentification (n)
dhiufertho, misidentify (v)
dhiveian, misogyny (n)

dhivien, misnomer (n)
dhivit, mischief (n)
dhivitu, mischievous (adj)
dhivoamun, misfortune (n)
dho, a (det)
dhuf, goo (n)
dhufu, gooey (adj)
dhush, hose (n)
dhusho, hose (v)
dhushua, hoser (n doer)
dhushuet, hosiery (n)
di, to (prep)
diad, mode (n)
diadau, model (n)
diadaro, model (v)
diadiu, modally (adv)
diadu, modal (adj)
diaduet, modality (n)
diaf, bow (n d:bend)
diafo, bow (v d:bend)
diago, barge (v)
diagua, barger (n doer)
diak, burden (n)
diako, burden (v)
diaku, burdensome (adj)
dialk, trunk (n)
dialko, truncate (v)
dialsh, hurdle (n)
dialsho, hurdle (v)
dialt, post (n d:ad)
dialtar, postage (n)
dialtaru, postal (adj)
dialtarua, postman (n doer)
dialtaun, postcard (n)
dialtethiok, postmaster (n)
dialto, post (v d:ad)
dialtshtat, postmark (n)
dialtshtato, postmark (v)
dialtua, poster (n doer d:ad)
dialtuet, poster (n d:display)
dian, discovery (n)
diank, sanction (n)
dianko, sanction (v)
diano, discover (v)
diant, sanctity (n)
dianto, sanctify (v)
dianua, discoverer (n doer)
diap, drive (n)
diapio, drove (v pa)
diapliol, driveway (n)
diapo, drive (v)
diapua, driver (n doer)
diar, bell (n)
diariak, bellow (n)
diariako, bellow (v)
diarp, belly (n)
diarpo, belly (v)
diash, joint (n)
diashiu, jointly (adv)
diasho, joint (v)
diat, join (v)
diathiu, acutely (adv)
diathu, acute (adj)

diatiat, jitter (n)
diatiato, jitter (v)
diato, join (v)
diatraf, hurl (n)
diatrafo, hurl (v)
diatua, joiner (n doer)
diauf, maze (n)
diaug, explosion (n)
diaugiu, explosively (adv)
diaugo, explode (v)
diaugu, explosive (adj)
diaugua, explosive (n doer)
diauk, refusal (n d:decline)
diauko, refuse (v d:decline)
diazh, subsidy (n)
diazhan, subsidence (n)
diazhat, subsidiary (n)
diazho, subsidize (v)
dib, try (n)
dibag, trial (n)
dibal, melon (n)
dibo, try (v)
dibuil, tryout (n)
didan, similarity (n)
didaniu, similarly (adv)
didanu, similar (adj)
diduk, trouble (n)
diduko, trouble (v)
didukshkoto, troubleshoot (v)
didukshkotua, troubleshooter (n doer)
didukua, troublemaker (n doer)
didukzhinu, troublesome (adj)
dief, cuff (n)
diefo, cuff (v)
diek, right (n d:correct)
diekiepiu, rightfully (adv)
diekiepu, rightful (adj)
diekiu, rightly (adv d:correct)
dieko, right (v d:correct)
dieku, right (adj d:correct)
diekua, righter (n doer d:correct)
diekuet, righteousness (n)
diekuet, rightness (n)
diekuetiu, righteously (adv)
diekuetu, righteous (adj)
diekuetua, righteous (n doer)
dienk, cartridge (n)
diert, bay (n d:howl)
dierto, bay (v d:howl)
diertua, bayer (n doer d:howl)
diesh, apparatus (n)
dif, per (adv/prep)
difad, photo (n)
difdarf, photograph (n)
difdarfo, photograph (v)
difdarft, photography (n)
difdarfua, photographer (n doer)
difk, beg (n)
difkish, photocopy (n)
difkisho, photocopy (v)
difkishua, photocopier (n doer)
difko, beg (v)

difkua, beggar (n doer)
dift, adaptation (n)
diftiu, adaptably (adv)
diftiu, adaptively (adv)
difto, adapt (v)
diftu, adaptable (adj)
diftu, adaptive (adj)
diftua, adapter (n doer)
diftua, adaptor (n doer)
diholu, where-to (adv)
diholu, whither (adv/conj)
dikiuk, toggle (n)
dikiuko, toggle (v)
dikosh, togetherness (n)
dikoshiu, together (adv)
dilath, boutique (n)
dilf, limp (n)
dilfo, limp (v)
dilfu, limp (adj)
dilk, pole (n)
dilkat, polarity (n)
dilkato, polarize (v)
dilkatu, polar (adj)
dilkatuet, polarization (n)
diln, holiness (n)
dilnu, holy (adj)
diloik, molecule (n)
diloiku, molecular (adj)
dilorn, sweater (n d:clothing)
dilp, toe (n)
dilpthrin, toenail (n)
dilshaf, separation (n)
dilshafiu, separately (adv)
dilshafo, separate (v)
dilshafu, separate (adj)
dilshafua, separator (n doer)
dimuan, tonight (n)
dimuaniu, tonight (adv)
dinal, thinness (n)
dinaliu, thinly (adv)
dinalo, thin (v)
dinalu, thin (adj)
dinan, finger (n)
dinano, finger (v)
dinanthrin, fingernail (n)
dinantilf, fingertip (n)
dinantrulsh, fingerprint (n)
dinantrulsho, fingerprint (v)
dinkran, kilogram (n)
dinlimet, kilometer (n)
dint, thousand (num 1000 card)
dintai-, kilo- (num 1000 pref)
dintatu, myraid (adj)
dinteth, thousandth (num 1000 ord)
diof, trench (n)
diofo, trench (v)
diok, auction (n)
dioko, auction (v)
diokua, auctioneer (n doer)
dioniok, thermometer (n)
diorm, cannon (n)
diorp, buy (n)

diorpio, bought (v pa)
diorpo, buy (v)
diorpua, buyer (n doer)
diorpuil, buyout (n)
diort, rotation (n)
diortar, rotor (n)
diorth, perch (n d:pole)
diortho, perch (v d:pole)
diorto, rotate (v)
diortu, rotary (adj)
diortu, rotational (adj)
diortua, rotator (n doer)
diosh, therm (n)
dioshu, thermal (adj)
Dioshviul, Tuesday (n)
diotano, jot (v)
dioth, spoof (n)
diotho, spoof (v)
dirb, hormone (n)
dirf, rod (n)
dirk, oratory (n)
dirko, orate (v)
dirkua, orator (n doer)
dirm, tilt (n)
dirmo, tilt (v)
dirniu, orally (adv)
dirnu, oral (adj)
dirp, rot (n)
dirpo, rot (v)
dirv, courage (n)
dirvat, encouragement (n)
dirviu, courageously (adv)
dirvo, encourage (v)
dirvu, courageous (adj)
dishavien, pseudonym (n)
dishel, diesel (n)
Dishproshium, Dysprosium (n)
dit, list (n d:sequence)
ditap, pool (n)
ditapo, pool (v)
ditapshoit, poolside (n)
ditapshoitu, poolside (adj)
dith, currency (n)
dithk, pixel (n)
dito, list (v d:sequence)
diuaf, voracity (n)
diuafiu, voraciously (adv)
diuafu, voracious (adj)
diuf, filter (n)
diufo, filter (v)
diufua, filterer (n doer)
diug, keg (n)
diuip, embarrassment (n)
diuipo, embarrass (v)
diuk, quiz (n)
diuko, quiz (v)
dium, reel (n)
diumo, reel (v)
diun, spy (n)
diundrint, spyglass (n)
diuno, spy (v)
diup, boast (n)
diupo, boast (v)

diupua, boaster (n doer)
diushk, boost (n)
diushko, boost (v)
diushkua, booster (n doer)
diut, niche (n)
diuth, reed (n)
diuvat, vortex (n)
diviul, today (n)
diviuliu, today (adv)
diviulu, today (adj)
divrafeiran, ultraviolet (n)
divrafeiranu, ultraviolet (adj)
divrakarlu, ultranational (adj)
divrakarlua, ultranationalist (n
    doer)
divraliukoftiu, ultraconservatively
    (adv)
divraliukoftu, ultraconservative
    (adj)
divrazhantan, ultrasound (n)
divrazhantaniu, ultrasonically
    (adv)
divrazhantanu, ultrasonic (adj)
divulo, mellow (v)
divulu, mellow (adj)
divur, melody (n)
divuru, melodic (adj)
divut, adoption (n)
divuto, adopt (v)
divutu, adoptive (adj)
divutua, adopter (n doer)
dizh, thing (n)
doap, chest (n d:torso)
doat, mouse (n)
doatethreip, mousetrap (n)
doati, mice (n pl)
doato, mouse (v)
doatua, mouser (n doer)
dod, then (adj/adv)
dofaf, pupil (n d:student)
doft, button (n)
dofto, button (v)
doftua, buttoner (n doer)
doiak, poke (n d:push)
doiako, poke (v d:push)
doiaku, pokey (adj d:push)
doiakua, poker (n doer d:push)
doiar, table (n)
doiardaup, tabletop (n)
doiardorp, tablespoon (n)
doiarflaf, tablecloth (n)
doiaro, table (v)
doiarshlef, tableware (n)
doidan, lobby (n)
doidano, lobby (v)
doidanua, lobbyist (n doer)
doido, lob (v)
doif, idol (n)
doifo, idolize (v)
doig, margin (n)
doigiu, marginally (adv)
doigo, marginalize (v)
doigu, marginal (adj)

doikak, harassment (n)
doikako, harass (v)
doikakua, harasser (n doer)
doikup, bustle (n)
doikupo, bustle (v)
doilam, idiocy (n)
doilamiu, idiotically (adv)
doilamu, idiotic (adj)
doilamua, idiot (n doer)
doin, lobe (n)
doip, squish (n)
doipo, squish (v)
doipu, squishy (adj)
doipua, squisher (n doer)
doishk, bust (n d:burst)
doishko, bust (v d:burst)
doishkua, buster (n doer d:burst)
doit, tablet (n)
doith, page (n d:paper)
doithuet, pagination (n)
doithueto, paginate (v)
doitiar, tabloid (n)
doiv, fragment (n)
doivo, fragment (v)
doivu, fragile (adj)
dok, exit (n)
doko, exit (v)
dokua, exiter (n doer)
dol, readiness (n)
dolad, threat (n)
dolado, threaten (v)
dolam, idiom (n)
dolamo, idiomate (v)
dolamu, idiomatic (adj)
doliu, readily (adv)
dolk, burglary (n)
dolko, burglarize (v)
dolko, burgle (v)
dolkua, burglar (n doer)
dolm, poll (n)
dolmo, poll (v)
dolmua, poller (n doer)
dolo, ready (v)
dolt, thread (n)
dolto, thread (v)
dolu, ready (adj)
domulo, hallow (v)
dopip, cookie (n)
dopo, cook (v)
dopshlef, cookware (n)
dopua, cook (n doer)
dopuil, cookout (n)
dopvond, cookbook (n)
doraifk, pollutant (n)
doraik, pollution (n)
doraiko, pollute (v)
doraikua, polluter (n doer)
Doran, EhoMonth07 (n)
dorb, breadth (n)
dorbid, broadcast (n)
dorbidio, broadcast (v pa)
dorbido, broadcast (v)
dorbidua, broadcaster (n doer)

dorbiu, broadly (adv)
dorbo, broaden (v)
dorbu, broad (adj)
dorbwaku, broadest (adj)
dorbwelu, broader (adj)
dord, polity (n)
dordar, politics (n)
dordiu, politically (adv)
dordo, politic (v)
dordu, political (adj)
dordua, politician (n doer)
dorein, politeness (n)
doreiniu, politely (adv)
doreinku, impolite (adj)
doreinu, polite (adj)
dorf, gear (n d:equipment)
dorfmirf, gearshift (n)
dorfprenk, gearbox (n)
dorg, gun (n)
dorgbiat, gunpowder (n)
dorgeflev, gunship (n)
dorgeshkob, gunboat (n)
dorgeshkoit, gunshot (n)
dorgetaift, gunpoint (n)
dorgiaul, gunfire (n)
dorgiaulao, shriauk (v prp)
dorgiaulio, giaul (v pa)
dorgo, gun (v)
dorgplon, gunman (n)
dorgploni, gunmen (n pl)
dorgua, gunner (n doer)
dorgvaug, gunfight (n)
dorim, wear (n d:clothe)
dorimio, wore (v pa d:clothe)
dorimiu, wearably (adv d:clothe)
dorimo, wear (v d:clothe)
dorimu, wearable (adj d:clothe)
dorimua, wearer (n doer d:clothe)
dorkait, spice (n)
dorkaito, spice (v)
dorkaitu, spicy (adj)
dorkaitua, spicer (n doer)
dorklatio, spent (v pa)
dorklato, spend (v)
dorklatu, spendable (adj)
dorklatua, spender (n doer)
dornk, carton (n)
dorp, spoon (n)
dorpo, spoon (v)
dorpu, spoonful (adj)
dorpua, spooner (n doer)
dorsh, firm (n d:company)
dorshk, policy (n)
dorshkat, police (n)
dorshknagua, policymaker (n doer)
dorshko, police (v)
dorshkthorthua, policyholder (n doer)
dorshkua, policeman (n doer)
dorth, poor (n d:low money)
dorthkiaf, poorhouse (n)
doshfrep, executable (n)

doshfrepiu, executably (adv)
doshfrepu, executable (adj)
doshiun, hallucination (n)
doshiuno, hallucinate (v)
doshk, execution (n d:perform)
doshkar, executive (n d:businessperson)
doshkiu, executively (adv d:perform)
doshko, execute (v d:perform)
doshku, executive (adj d:perform)
doshkua, executioner (n doer d:perform)
doshkua, executor (n doer)
doshpat, asbestos (n)
dosht, clarity (n)
doshto, clarify (v)
dotaif, vertex (n)
dotaik, vertical (n)
dotaikiu, vertically (adv)
dotaiku, vertical (adj)
dotaip, vertebra (n)
dotaipi, vertebrae (n pl)
dotaitsh, vertigo (n)
dotharf, traversal (n)
dotharfo, traverse (v)
dothorth, threshold (n)
dotsh, pick (n)
dotshap, pickle (n)
dotshapo, pickle (v)
dotshat, picket (n)
dotshato, picket (v)
dotshatua, picketer (n doer)
dotshiveil, pickup (n)
dotshlogaf, pickpocket (n)
dotsho, pick (v)
dotshu, picky (adj)
dotshua, picker (n doer)
dov, rap (n)
dovaf, rapport (n)
dovafo, rapport (v)
dovai, bravo (interj)
dovart, report (n)
dovartiu, reportedly (adv)
dovarto, report (v)
dovartu, reportable (adj)
dovartua, reporter (n doer)
dovat, tobacco (n)
dovenp, exponent (n)
dovenpiu, exponentially (adv)
dovenpo, expone (v)
dovenpu, exponential (adj)
dovibrauth, torrent (n)
dovibrauthu, torrential (adj)
dovikutu, torrid (adj)
dovil, rapidity (n)
doviliu, rapidly (adv)
dovilu, rapid (adj)
dovin, wake (n d:trail)
dovit, travel (n)
dovito, travel (v)
dovitua, traveler (n doer)
dovitua, traveller (n doer)

dovo, rap (v)
dovua, rapper (n doer)
draf, team (n)
drafish, pastry (n)
drafkiok, teamwork (n)
draflen, teammate (n)
drafo, team (v)
drafp, paste (n)
drafpo, paste (v)
drafpu, pasty (adj)
drafpua, paster (n doer)
draig, brat (n)
draik, shout (n)
draiko, shout (v)
draikua, shouter (n doer)
drailk, summit (n)
drailko, summit (v)
draim, summary (n)
draimo, summarize (v)
draipo, bound (v d:move)
draipu, bound (adj d:move)
drait, sum (n)
draith, grid (n)
draito, sum (v)
drakeln, sophomore (n)
drakit, sophistication (n)
drakito, sophisticate (v)
dral, heart (n)
dralbluag, heartache (n)
dralbrug, heartburn (n)
draldaut, heartbeat (n)
dralf, pastel (n)
draliu, heartily (adv)
dralk, steak (n)
dralkiaf, steakhouse (n)
dralmenu, heartless (adj)
dralplik, heartbreak (n)
dralplikio, heartbroke (v pa)
dralpliko, heartbreak (v)
dralraup, heartland (n)
dralu, hearty (adj)
dran, bun (n)
drap, store (n)
drapat, storage (n)
drapflarn, storefront (n)
drapkiaf, storehouse (n)
drapklofua, storekeeper (n doer)
drapo, store (v)
drapua, storer (n doer)
drashk, exploit (n)
drashkat, exploitation (n)
drashkiu, exploitively (adv)
drashko, exploit (v)
drashku, exploitive (adj)
drashkua, exploiter (n doer)
draub, kennel (n)
drauf, brashness (n)
draufiu, brashly (adv)
draufu, brash (adj)
draugag, cynicism (n)
draugagiu, cynically (adv)
draugagu, cynical (adj)
draugagua, cynic (n doer)

draukuin, recruit (n)
draush, dog (n)
draushfanin, dogwood (n)
draushkiaf, doghouse (n)
drausho, dog (v)
draushvaug, dogfight (n)
drei, true (adj)
dreif, trust (n)
dreiflaish, trustworthiness (n)
dreiflaishu, trustworthy (adj)
dreifo, trust (v)
dreifu, trustful (adj)
dreifu, trusty (adj)
dreifuet, trustfulness (n)
dreifuin, trustee (n)
dreilu, truly (adv)
dreish, truth (n)
dreishiu, truthfully (adv)
dreishu, truthful (adj)
dreishuet, truism (n)
dreivoshar, truelove (n)
drel, pearl (n)
drelf, stew (n)
drelfo, stew (v)
dresh, duplicate (n)
dresho, duplicate (v)
dreshua, duplicator (n doer)
dreshuet, duplication (n)
driad, drum (n)
driadaut, drumbeat (n)
driado, drum (v)
driadua, drummer (n doer)
driafo, teem (v)
driag, bank (n d:storage)
driago, bank (v d:storage)
driagua, banker (n doer
     d:storage)
driak, bang (n d:collision)
driako, bang (v d:collision)
driakua, banger (n doer
     d:collision)
driap, earnestness (n)
driapiu, earnestly (adv)
driapo, earn (v)
driapu, earnest (adj)
driapua, earner (n doer)
driash, anointment (n)
driasho, anoint (v)
driat, quaintness (n)
driatho, perish (v)
driathtiug, gridlock (n)
driathu, perishable (adj)
driatiu, quaintly (adv)
driatu, quaint (adj)
drien, grove (n)
driento, grovel (v)
drifu, seismic (adj)
driget, selection (n)
drigetiu, selectively (adv)
drigeto, select (v)
drigetu, selective (adj)
drigetua, selector (n doer)
drigetuet, selectivity (n)

drigrut, seclusion (n)
drigruto, seclude (v)
drik, crease (n)
drikat, sedation (n)
drikatiu, sedatively (adv)
drikato, sedate (v)
drikatu, sedative (adj)
drikatua, sedative (n doer)
drikin, glean (n)
drikino, glean (v)
drikinp, segregation (n)
drikinpo, segregate (v)
drikinpua, segregationist (n doer)
driko, crease (v)
drikua, creaser (n doer)
drilan, bunny (n)
drilauk, bullhorn (n)
drilk, increase (n)
drilkiu, increasingly (adv)
drilko, increase (v)
drilsh, glass (n d:quartz)
drilshlef, glassware (n)
drilt, wrinkle (n)
drilto, wrinkle (v)
driltu, wrinkly (adj)
driltua, wrinkler (n doer)
drint, glass (n d:spectacles)
drishk, increment (n)
drishkiu, incrementally (adv)
drishko, increment (v)
drishku, incremental (adj)
drit, seed (n)
dritar, glare (n)
dritaro, glare (v)
drith, glee (n)
drithiu, gleefully (adv)
drithu, gleeful (adj)
dritip, seedling (n)
drito, seed (v)
dritu, seedy (adj)
dritua, seeder (n doer)
driuk, creek (n)
driup, beep (n)
driupo, beep (v)
driupua, beeper (n doer)
drivek, secession (n)
driveko, secede (v)
drizh, glaze (n)
drizhauk, sedition (n)
drizho, glaze (v)
drofliku, counterclockwise (adj)
droft, declaration (n)
drofto, declare (v)
droftu, declaratory (adj)
droftua, declarer (n doer)
droif, rib (n)
droifo, rib (v)
droil, rim (n)
drok, clock (n)
drokirf, star (n d:celebrity)
drokirfo, star (v d:celebrity)
droko, clock (v)
droku, clockwise (adj)

drolf, oscillation (n)
drolfo, oscillate (v)
drolfua, oscillator (n doer)
dronip, tropic (n)
dronipiu, tropically (adv)
dronipu, tropical (adj)
drosht, clarification (n)
drot, clearness (n)
drotan, clearance (n)
drotiu, clearly (adv)
droto, clear (v)
drotu, clear (adj)
druaf, gleam (n)
druafo, gleam (v)
druf, sleeve (n)
drufmenu, sleeveless (adj)
drufo, sleeve (v)
drufp, depreciation (n)
drufpo, depreciate (v)
druk, prey (n)
drukat, predation (n)
drukato, predate (v)
drukatu, predatory (adj)
drukatua, predator (n doer)
druko, prey (v)
drulk, comprehension (n)
drulkiu, comprehensively (adv)
drulko, comprehend (v)
drulku, comprehensive (adj)
drulp, appreciation (n)
drulpiu, appreciatively (adv)
drulpo, appreciate (v)
drulpu, appreciative (adj)
drush, derivation (n)
drusho, derive (v)
drushu, derivative (adj)
duaf, beam (n)
duafo, beam (v)
duafua, beamer (n doer)
duaif, tightness (n)
duaifan, tights (n)
duaifiu, tightly (adv)
duaifo, tighten (v)
duaifu, tight (adj)
duaifvap, tightrope (n)
duaifwaku, tightest (adj)
duaifwelu, tighter (adj)
duaik, chop (n)
duaikiu, choppily (adv)
duaiko, chop (v)
duaiku, choppy (adj)
duaikua, chopper (n doer)
duakrit, gouge (n)
duakrito, gouge (v)
dualf, beach (n)
dualfo, beach (v)
dualfua, beacher (n doer)
duam, anatomy (n)
duamu, anatomical (adj)
duap, type (n d:kind)
duapiu, typically (adv d:kind)
duapo, type (v d:kind)
duapu, typical (adj d:kind)

duark, beaker (n)
duash, present (n d:give gift)
duashk, presentation (n)
duashkua, presenter (n doer)
duasho, present (v d:give gift)
duat, beak (n)
duath, vent (n)
duathag, ventilation (n)
duathago, ventilate (v)
duathagua, ventilator (n doer)
duatho, vent (v)
duathua, venter (n doer)
duavat, attic (n)
duavit, FertilityStone (n)
duban, bumble (n d:buzz)
dubano, bumble (v d:buzz)
dubat, ripeness (n)
dubato, ripen (v)
dubatu, ripe (adj)
dubielk, opportunity (n)
dubielku, opportunistic (adj)
dubielkua, opportunist (n doer)
dublash, oppression (n)
dublashiu, oppressively (adv)
dublasho, oppress (v)
dublashu, oppressive (adj)
dublashua, oppressor (n doer)
Dubnium, Dubnium (n)
dudif, puppy (n)
duek, chip (n)
dueko, chip (v)
duekua, chipper (n doer)
dufal, odor (n)
dufalmenu, odorless (adj)
dufk, vengence (n)
dufku, vengeful (adj)
duft, criticism (n)
duftar, criterion (n)
duftari, criteria (n pl)
duftiu, critically (adv)
dufto, criticize (v)
duftu, critical (adj)
duftua, critic (n doer)
duiaf, venom (n)
duiafu, venomous (adj)
duiaikshnet, chopstick (n)
duiak, puck (n)
duiato, reap (v)
duiatua, reaper (n doer)
duid, pup (n)
duidak, puppetry (n)
duidakua, puppeteer (n doer)
duidat, puppet (n)
duif, softness (n)
duifiu, softly (adv)
duifo, soften (v)
duifshlef, softball (n)
duifu, soft (adj)
duifua, softener (n doer)
duik, bozo (n)
duil, leniency (n)
duiliu, leniently (adv)
duilu, lenient (adj)

duimorp, swimsuit (n)
duin, swim (n)
duinio, swam (v pa)
duino, swim (v)
duinua, swimmer (n doer)
duirg, kink (n)
duirgu, kinky (adj)
duishlef, software (n)
duk, cog (n)
dukafo, vend (v)
dukafua, vendor (n doer)
dukap, vendetta (n)
dukiak, vindication (n)
dukiako, vindicate (v)
dukiakua, vindicator (n doer)
dukiakuet, vindictiveness (n)
dulan, drivel (n)
dulano, drivel (v)
dulano, drool (v)
dulf, ooze (n)
dulfo, ooze (v)
Duliaf, EhoDay04 (n)
duliat, adventure (n)
duliatiu, adventurously (adv)
duliato, venture (v)
duliatu, adventurous (adj)
duliatua, adventurer (n doer)
dulith, spool (n)
dulitho, spool (v)
dulk, cock (n)
dulkaif, cocktail (n)
dulkat, cockiness (n)
dulkluk, cockpit (n)
dulko, cock (v)
dulku, cocky (adj)
dulmiu, currently (adv d:now)
dulmu, current (adj d:now)
dulp, bubble (n)
dulpo, bubble (v)
dulpu, bubbly (adj)
dulpua, bubbler (n doer)
dum, tween (n)
dunbet, pump (n)
dunbeto, pump (v)
dunbetua, pumper (n doer)
dunf, opera (n)
dunin, ton (n)
dunink, tonne (n)
dunp, coop (n d:cage)
dupafo, tailor (v)
dupafua, tailor (n doer)
dupako, madden (v d:angry)
dupaku, mad (adj d:angry)
dupakwelu, madder (adj d:angry)
dupran, capsule (n)
dur, there (adj/adv/interj)
dur, there (pron)
durai, voila (interj)
durb, drone (n d:tone)
durbo, drone (v d:tone)
durdeig, bridegroom (n)
durf, coast (n d:move)
durfo, coast (v d:move)

durfua, coaster (n doer d:move)
durg, knuckle (n)
durgo, knuckle (v)
durgua, knuckler (n doer)
durkeler, bridesmaid (n)
durl, bill (n d:beak)
durmafiu, therefore (adv)
duroviliu, thereafter (adv)
dursh, bride (n)
durshu, bridal (adj)
durt, operation (n)
durtan, operative (n)
durtiu, operationally (adv)
durto, operate (v)
durtu, operable (adj)
durtu, operational (adj)
durtua, operator (n doer)
durvuniu, thereby (adv)
dusht, desert (n d:wasteland)
dutak, lawsuit (n)
dutako, sue (v)
dutek, washer (n d:spacer)
duth, altar (n)
duthap, season (n d:spice)
duthapo, season (v d:spice)
Dutsh, Dutch (n)
duvil, sponsorship (n)
duvilo, sponsor (v)
duvilua, sponsor (n doer)
duvoip, sponge (n)
duvoipo, sponge (v)
e, (separator)
Efak, Bromine (n davoka)
Efap, Gallium (n davoka)
efbin, openness (n)
efbiniu, openly (adv)
efbino, open (v)
efbinu, open (adj)
efbinua, opener (n doer)
efel , ever (adj/adv)
Efik, Krypton (n davoka)
Efip, Germanium (n davoka)
Efop, Arsenic (n davoka)
efuet, option (n)
efuetiu, optionally (adv)
efueto, opt (v)
efuetu, optional (adj)
Efup, Selenium (n davoka)
eikuit, dialog (n)
eikuit, dialogue (n)
Einshteinium, Einsteinium (n)
eipor, diary (n)
eipot, dial (n)
eipoto, dial (v)
Ekak, Fluorine (n davoka)
Ekap, Boron (n davoka)
Ekik, Neon (n davoka)
ekip avekupat, carbon dioxide (n)
Ekip, Carbon (n davoka)
Ekop, Nitrogen (n davoka)
Ekup, Oxygen (n davoka)
ekupan, ozone (n)
ekupat, oxide (n)

ekupato, oxidize (v)
ekupatua, oxidizer (n doer)
ekupatuet, oxidation (n)
Elak, Iodine (n davoka)
Elap, Indium (n davoka)
elesh, earth (n)
eleshiov, earthquake (n)
eleshlov, earthling (n)
elesho, unearth (v)
eleshu, earthly (adj)
elf, E (let sng)
elfhem, Number_1e306
elfi, Es (let pl)
elialu, early (adj)
elialwaku, earliest (adj)
elialwelu, earlier (adj)
Elip, Tin (n davoka)
Elop, Antimony (n davoka)
Elup, Tellurium (n davoka)
emdi, onto (prep)
Enak, Ununspetium (n davoka)
Enap, Ununtrium (n davoka)
enga, Ng (let sng)
engadafka, Number_1e4203
engahem, Number_1e4056
engali, Ngs (let pl)
Enik, Ununoctium (n davoka)
Enip, Ununquadium (n davoka)
Enop, Ununpentium (n davoka)
ensht, inevitability (n)
enshtiu, inevitably (adv)
enshtu, inevitable (adj)
Enup, Ununhexium (n davoka)
enutak, eligibility (n)
enutaku, eligible (adj)
epshilon, epsilon (n)
er, uh (interj)
Erak, Astatine (n davoka)
Erap, Thallium (n davoka)
Erbium, Erbium (n)
Erik, Radon (n davoka)
Erip, Lead (n davoka)
ern, um (interj)
Erop, Bismuth (n davoka)
Erup, Polonium (n davoka)
Etak, Chlorine (n davoka)
etan, eta (n)
Etap, Aluminum (n davoka)
Etik, Argon (n davoka)
Etip, Silicon (n davoka)
Etop, Phosphorus (n davoka)
Etup, Sulfur (n davoka)
Europium, Europium (n)
fabik, wheeze (n)
fabiko, wheeze (v)
faboft, fusion (n)
fabot, fuse (n)
faboto, fuse (v)
fabotua, fuser (n doer)
fafat, fuzz (n)
fafato, fuzz (v)
fafatu, fuzz (adj)
faft, civility (n)

faftiu, civily (adv)
fafto, civilize (v)
faftu, civil (adj)
faftua, civilian (n doer)
faftuet, civilization (n)
faiat, spike (n)
faiatio, spikes (v pa)
faiato, spike (v)
faif, sigh (n)
faifo, sigh (v)
faik, spite (n)
faiko, spite (v)
faiku, spiteful (adj)
faitago, mangle (v)
faitsho, maul (v)
falaf, urine (n)
falafat, urinal (n)
falafk, urination (n)
falafko, urinate (v)
falafkua, urinator (n doer)
falafkuit, urology (n)
falafkuitua, urologist (n doer)
falafu, urinary (adj)
falath, seldom (adj/adv)
falf, steer (n d:cattle)
faliap, wheelbarrow (n)
falir, roll (n d:tumble)
falirafen, rollover (n)
faliro, roll (v d:tumble)
falirua, roller (n doer d:tumble)
faliruil, rollout (n)
falirvak, rollback (n)
falk, rash (n)
falkiu, rashly (adv)
falku, rash (adj)
falm, stream (n)
falmo, stream (v)
falmroifo, streamline (v)
falmua, streamer (n doer)
faln, kid (n d:child)
falp, urb (n)
falpo, urbanize (v)
falporgo, kidnap (v)
falporgua, kidnapper (n doer)
falpu, urban (adj)
falpuet, urbanization (n)
famshran, bedroom (n)
fanin, wood (n)
faninkiaf, woodhouse (n)
faninkiok, woodwork (n)
faninkioko, woodwork (v)
faninkiokua, woodworker (n doer)
faninplon, woodman (n)
faninplon, woodsman (n)
faninploni, woodmen (n pl)
faninploni, woodsmen (n pl)
faninraup, woodland (n)
faninraupu, woodlands (adj)
faninthilf, woodshed (n)
faninu, wooden (adj)
fant, patron (n)
fanto, patronize (v)

fantua, patronizer (n doer)
fantun, patriot (n)
fantuniu, patriotically (adv)
fantunu, patriotic (adj)
fapo, ask (v)
fapua, asker (n doer)
fareishk, serpent (n)
fareishku, serpentine (adj)
farn, cinema (n)
fashk, faction (n)
fatet, mallet (n)
fath, gap (n)
fatho, gap (v)
fatuk, cult (n)
fatup, cultivation (n)
fatupo, cultivate (v)
fatupua, cultivator (n doer)
faudanapo, succumb (v)
fauf, buffer (n d:absorber)
faufo, buffer (v d:absorber)
fauin, virus (n)
fauini, virii (n pl)
fauini, viruses (n pl)
fauiniu, virally (adv)
fauinu, viral (adj)
fauinuet, virulence (n)
fauinuetiu, virulently (adv)
fauinuetu, virulent (adj)
faupo, suck (v)
faupua, sucker (n doer)
faupuano, sucker (v)
faupuet, suction (n)
faupueto, suction (v)
faush, narcism (n)
faush, narcissism (n)
faushk, narcotic (n)
faushu, narcissistic (adj)
faushu, narcistic (adj)
faushua, narcissist (n doer)
faushua, narcist (n doer)
fazh, bur (n)
fefefio, mumbles (v pa)
fefefo, mumble (v)
fefefua, mumbler (n doer)
fei, F (let sng)
feianiu, sparsely (adv)
feianu, sparse (adj)
feif, show (n)
feifbresh, showplace (n)
feifiaun, clemency (n)
feiflaunu, clement (adj)
feifkeler, showgirl (n)
feifo, show (v)
feifplon, showman (n)
feifplonfif, showmanship (n)
feifploni, showmen (n pl)
feifshkob, showboat (n)
feifshkobo, showboat (v)
feifshran, showroom (n)
feifshuat, showcase (n)
feifshuato, showcase (v)
feifthetsh, showpiece (n)
feifthetsho, showpiece (v)

feiftien, showdown (n)
feifu, showy (adj)
feigal, poker (n d:game)
feihem, Number_1e2106
feikad, vodka (n)
feili, Fs (let pl)
feiran, violet (n)
feiranu, violet (adj)
feirg, ghost (n)
feirgo, ghost (v)
feirgu, ghostly (adj)
feish, gust (n)
feisho, gust (v)
feishu, gusty (adj)
feitago, mingle (v)
feizhak, murder (n)
feizhakiu, murderously (adv)
feizhako, murder (v)
feizhaku, murderous (adj)
feizhakua, murderer (n doer)
fekiaku, vincible (adj)
felifianu, fallopian (adj)
feliu, very (adv)
felm, humor (n)
felmiu, humorously (adv)
felmo, humor (v)
felmu, humorous (adj)
felmua, humorist (n doer)
felnapiu, humbly (adv)
felnapo, humble (v)
felnapu, humble (adj)
felnat, humility (n)
felnato, humiliate (v)
felnatuet, humiliation (n)
felp, rasp (n)
felpo, rasp (v)
felpu, raspy (adj)
felsh, compartment (n)
felsho, compartmentalize (v)
fenp, mill (n)
fenpo, mill (v)
fenpua, miller (n doer)
fenshiu, particularly (adv)
fenshu, particular (adj)
fenshul, particular (n)
fento, scatter (v)
fepio, set (v pa d:place)
fepo, set (v d:place)
fepua, setter (n doer d:place)
Fermium, Fermium (n)
fesh, part (n)
feshan, portrait (n)
feshat, partial (n)
feshatiu, partially (adv)
feshatu, partial (adj)
fesheik, participle (n)
feshelk, participation (n)
feshelko, participate (v)
feshelkua, participant (n doer)
feshiam, portrayal (n)
feshiamo, portray (v)
feshiu, partly (adv)
feshiuf, portfolio (n)

feshk, impartiality (n)
feshkiu, impartially (adv)
feshko, impart (v)
feshku, impartial (adj)
feshnat, partnership (n)
feshnato, partner (v)
feshnatua, partner (n doer)
fesho, part (v)
feshp, particle (n)
feshp, particulate (n)
feshpo, particulate (v)
feshpu, particulate (adj)
fesht, departure (n)
feshto, depart (v)
feshtua, departer (n doer)
feshtugo, parse (v)
feshtugua, parser (n doer)
feshuet, partition (n)
feshueto, partition (v)
fezh, portion (n)
fiab, peep (n)
fiabo, peep (v)
fiad, beauty (n)
fiadiu, beautifully (adv)
fiado, beautify (v)
fiadu, beautiful (adj)
fiaf, peer (n)
fiafo, peer (v)
fiaish, vision (n)
fiaishan, visual (n)
fiaishaniu, visually (adv)
fiaishano, visualize (v)
fiaishanu, visual (adj)
fiaishanuet, visualization (n)
fiaishiu, visibly (adv)
fiaisho, envision (v)
fiaishu, visible (adj)
fiaishua, visionary (n doer)
fiaishuet, visibility (n)
fiak, yard (n d:measurement)
fiakshnet, yardstick (n)
fiakuet, yardage (n
   d:measurement)
fialoif, fiddle (n d:violin)
fialoifo, fiddle (v d:violin)
fialoifua, fiddler (n doer d:violin)
fialt, sump (n)
fialtiu, sumptuously (adv)
fialtu, sumptuous (adj)
fiamo, kid (v d:joke)
fianp, swamp (n)
fianpo, swamp (v)
fianpu, swampy (adj)
fiant, pattern (n)
Fianth, EhoMonth06 (n)
fianto, pattern (v)
fiap, peek (n)
fiapo, peek (v)
fiarf, freshness (n)
fiarfheidon, freshwater (n)
fiarfheidonu, freshwater (adj)
fiarfiu, freshly (adv)
fiarfo, freshen (v)

fiarfu, fresh (adj)
fiargo, vet (v d:examine)
fiarplon, freshman (n)
fiarploni, freshmen (n pl)
fiash, flame (n)
fiashkar, flair (n)
fiashkat, flagrancy (n)
fiashkatiu, flagrantly (adv)
fiashkatu, flagrant (adj)
fiasho, flame (v)
fiashu, inflame (v)
fiashu, flammable (adj)
fiashu, inflammable (adj)
fiashua, flamer (n doer)
fiashuet, inflamation (n)
fiashuetu, inflammatory (adj)
fiatako, pant (v d:breathe)
fiath, flare (n)
fiatho, flare (v)
fiaumeniu, mercilessly (adv)
fiaumenu, merciless (adj)
fiaun, mercy (n)
fiauniu, mercifully (adv)
fiaunu, merciful (adj)
fiaush, wash (n d:clean)
fiaushflaf, washcloth (n)
fiaushfrepiu, washably (adv)
fiaushfrepu, washable (adj)
fiausho, wash (v d:clean)
fiaushplork, washboard (n)
fiaushran, washroom (n)
fiaushu, washy (adj d:clean)
fiaushua, washer (n doer d:clean)
fiaushuil, washout (n)
fiav, vet (n d:veterinarian)
fiavat, veterinarian (n)
fiavatu, veterinary (adj)
fidurk, philosophy (n)
fidurkua, philosopher (n doer)
fief, cat (n)
fiefu, catty (adj)
fieg, pang (n)
fielsh, scarlet (n)
fielshu, scarlet (adj)
fielt, stint (n)
fielto, stint (v)
fienar, loneliness (n)
fienaru, lonely (adj)
fienu, lone (adj)
fienua, loner (n doer)
fiesh, red (n)
fiesheiku, reddish (adj)
fieshkeft, redhead (n)
fiesho, redden (v)
fieshroif, redline (n)
fieshroifo, redline (v)
fieshtharb, redneck (n)
fieshu, red (adj)
fieshuet, redness (n)
fietsh, stitch (n)
fietsho, stitch (v)
fifaf, kitty (n)
fifim, kitten (n)

fifp, ripple (n)
fifpo, ripple (v)
fikokrug, protagony (n)
fikokrugo, protagonize (v)
fikokrugu, protagonistic (adj)
fikokrugua, protagonist (n doer)
filad, vamp (n)
Filadelfif, Philadelphia (n)
fildauf, vampire (n)
filf, butter (n)
filfo, butter (v)
filfu, buttery (adj)
filidarf, polygraph (n)
filidarfu, polygraphic (adj)
filimesh, polymer (n)
filimesho, polymerize (v)
filimuk, polygon (n)
filimuki, polygon (n pl)
filimuku, polygonal (adj)
Filipif, Philippine (n)
filiuyap, polyphony (n)
filiuyapu, polyphonic (adj)
filivuln, polygamy (n)
filn, ballad (n)
filnua, balladeer (n doer)
filtap, kettle (n)
fimal, evening (n d:late daytime)
fimar, eve (n)
fin, phi (n)
Fineshk, Phoenix (n)
Finland, Finland (n)
finork, scallop (n)
finorko, scallop (v)
finto, ream (v d:clear)
fintua, reamer (n doer d:clear)
finuin, cello (n)
fiob, oval (n)
fiobal, ellipse (n)
fiobalu, elliptical (adj)
fiof, loyalty (n)
fiofiu, loyally (adv)
fiofond, frequency (n)
fiofondiu, frequently (adv)
fiofondo, frequent (v)
fiofondu, frequent (adj)
fiofu, loyal (adj)
fiok, tool (n)
fioko, tool (v)
fiokplud, toolkit (n)
fiokprenk, toolbox (n)
fiom, loom (n)
fion, poem (n)
fionk, callus (n)
fiorb, frustration (n)
fiorbo, frustrate (v)
fiorish, calico (n)
fiorishu, calico (adj)
fiork, freeze (n)
fiorkio, froze (v pa)
fiorko, freeze (v)
fiorkua, freezer (n doer)
fiort, frost (n)
fiortgaik, frostbite (n)

fiortiu, frostily (adv)
fiorto, frost (v)
fiortu, frosty (adj)
fiortua, froster (n doer)
fiosh, freedom (n)
fioshiu, freely (adv)
fioshkap, freehand (n)
fioshlurto, freeload (v)
fioshlurtua, freeloader (n doer)
fiosho, free (v)
fioshosh, freebie (n)
fioshpliol, freeway (n)
fioshu, free (adj)
fioshvorn, freeform (n)
fioshvornu, freeform (adj)
fiot, poetry (n)
fiotu, poetic (adj)
fiotua, poet (n doer)
fird, event (n)
firdaik, eventuality (n)
firdaikiu, eventually (adv)
firdaiku, eventual (adj)
firdiu, eventfully (adv)
firdu, eventful (adj)
firk, ridicule (n)
firkiu, ridiculously (adv)
firko, ridicule (v)
firku, ridiculous (adj)
firn, ballet (n)
firno, ballet (v)
firnua, ballerina (n doer)
firp, riddance (n)
firpio, rid (v pa)
firpo, rid (v)
firpua, ridder (n doer)
firtsh, rifle (n)
firtsho, rifle (v)
firtshua, rifler (n doer)
fisht, dinosaur (n)
fitav, levy (n)
fitavo, levy (v)
fitish, fission (n)
fitisho, fission (v)
fitishp, fissure (n)
fiuan, prom (n)
fiuash, prostitution (n)
fiuasho, prostitute (v)
fiuashua, prostitute (n doer)
fiub, probe (n)
fiubo, probe (v)
fiuboft, protrusion (n)
fiubofto, protrude (v)
fiubua, prober (n doer)
fiudaf, protein (n)
fiudaib, prohibition (n)
fiudaibiu, prohibitively (adv)
fiudaibo, prohibit (v)
fiudaibu, prohibitive (adj)
fiudaibua, prohibitor (n doer)
fiudan, proverb (n d:saying)
fiudanu, proverbial (adj d:saying)
fiudokat, prosecution (n)
fiudokato, prosecute (v)

fiudokatu, prosecutable (adj)
fiudokatua, prosecutor (n doer)
fiuf, pro (n d:advantage)
fiufabot, profusion (n)
fiufabotiu, profusely (adv)
fiufabotu, profuse (adj)
fiufezh, proportion (n)
fiufezhiu, proportionally (adv)
fiufezhu, proportional (adj)
fiuflaush, proliferation (n)
fiuflaushiu, prolifically (adv)
fiuflausho, proliferate (v)
fiuflaushu, prolific (adj)
fiuflaushua, proliferator (n doer)
fiufrep, probability (n)
fiufrepiu, probably (adv)
fiufrepu, probable (adj)
fiufvuapi, flypaper (n pl)
fiug, probation (n)
fiugalt, protraction (n)
fiugalto, protract (v)
fiugaltua, protractor (n doer)
fiugan, propagation (n)
fiugano, propagate (v)
fiuganor, propaganda (n)
fiuganori, propaganda (n pl)
fiuganua, propagator (n doer)
fiuk, product (n)
fiukag, promenade (n)
fiukago, promenade (v)
fiukan, produce (n)
fiukat, productivity (n)
fiukiu, productively (adv)
fiuklip, propriety (n)
fiuklipu, proprietary (adj)
fiuklipua, proprietor (n doer)
fiuko, produce (v)
fiukreith, procrastination (n)
fiukreitho, procrastinate (v)
fiukreithua, procrastinator (n doer)
fiukrig, prominence (n)
fiukrigiu, prominently (adv)
fiukrigu, prominent (adj)
fiuku, productive (adj)
fiukua, producer (n doer)
fiukuet, production (n)
fiukuit, prolog (n)
fiukuit, prologue (n)
fiulink, proficiency (n)
fiulinkiu, proficiently (adv)
fiulinku, proficient (adj)
fiulk, proposal (n)
fiulk, proposition (n)
fiulko, propose (v)
fiulkoik, fungicide (n)
fiulkua, proposer (n doer)
fiuloip, fungus (n)
fiuloipi, fungi (n pl)
fiuloipu, fungal (adj)
fiulotel, prosperity (n)
fiuloteliu, prosperously (adv)
fiulotelo, prosper (v)

fiulotelu, prosperous (adj)
fiumal, proton (n)
fiump, prong (n)
fiumpo, prong (v)
fiun, pro (n d:professional)
fiunan, prophecy (n)
fiunan, prophesy (n)
fiunanua, prophet (n doer)
fiunelk, program (n)
fiunelko, program (v)
fiunelku, programmable (adj)
fiunelkua, programmer (n doer)
fiunfet, pronunciation (n)
fiunfeto, pronounce (v)
fiunk, profession (n)
fiunkiu, professionally (adv)
fiunko, profess (v)
fiunku, professional (adj)
fiunkua, professor (n doer)
fiunoart, proclamation (n)
fiunoarto, proclaim (v)
fiunok, promise (n)
fiunoko, promise (v)
fiunokua, promiser (n doer)
fiuntak, professional (n)
fiuntako, professionalize (v)
fiuntakuet, professionalism (n)
fiunuyen, pronoun (n)
fiupad, propulsion (n)
fiupadan, propellant (n)
fiupado, propel (v)
fiupadua, propeller (n doer)
fiupaft, profit (n)
fiupaftep, profitability (n)
fiupaftiu, profitably (adv)
fiupafto, profit (v)
fiupaftu, profitable (adj)
fiupaftua, profiteer (n doer)
fiupaftuano, profiteer (v)
fiupak, punt (n)
fiupako, punt (v)
fiupakua, punter (n doer)
fiupaltakiu, proactively (adv)
fiupaltaku, proactive (adj)
fiupliut, procreation (n)
fiupliuto, procreate (v)
fiupliutua, procreator (n doer)
fiurazh, prolongation (n)
fiurazho, prolong (v)
fiushaik, provocation (n)
fiushaikiu, provocatively (adv)
fiushaiko, provoke (v)
fiushaiku, provocative (adj)
fiushaikua, provoker (n doer)
fiushman, prognosis (n)
fiushmano, prognosticate (v)
fiushmanua, prognosticator (n doer)
fiushpiu, profoundly (adv)
fiushpu, profound (adj)
Fiushtip, Protestant (n)
Fiushtipuet, Protestantism (n)
fiushtit, protest (n)

fiushtito, protest (v)
fiushtitua, protester (n doer)
fiushtitua, protestor (n doer)
fiut, problem (n)
fiutep, projection (n d:thrust)
fiutepiu, projectively (adv d:thrust)
fiutepo, project (v d:thrust)
fiutepu, projective (adj d:thrust)
fiutepua, projector (n doer d:thrust)
fiutepuin, projectile (n)
fiuteshp, project (n d:workplan)
fiuthiuf, profile (n)
fiuthiufo, profile (v)
fiuthiufua, profiler (n doer)
fiuthuk, prospect (n)
fiuthukiu, prospectively (adv)
fiuthuko, prospect (v)
fiuthuku, prospective (adj)
fiuthukua, prospector (n doer)
fiutiank, procurement (n)
fiutianko, procure (v)
fiuvadav, promotion (n)
fiuvadavo, promote (v)
fiuvadavu, promotional (adj)
fiuvadavua, promoter (n doer)
fiuveft, procession (n)
fiuvek, procedure (n)
fiuvekiu, procedurally (adv)
fiuveko, proceed (v)
fiuveku, procedural (adj)
fiuvelk, proceed (n)
fiuvelp, proponent (n)
fiuvet, process (n)
fiuveto, process (v)
fiuvetua, processor (n doer)
fiuvorg, progress (n)
fiuvorgiu, progressively (adv)
fiuvorgo, progress (v)
fiuvorgu, progressive (adj)
fiuvorgua, progressor (n doer)
fiuvorguet, progression (n)
fival, season (n d:climate)
fivaliu, seasonally (adv d:climate)
fivalu, seasonal (adj d:climate)
fkaf, plate (n)
fkafo, plate (v)
fkafua, plater (n doer)
fkank, cramp (n)
fkanko, cramp (v)
fkavat, platter (n)
fkavon, platform (n)
fkiltu, negligible (adj)
fkit, neglect (n)
fkit, negligence (n)
fkitiu, neglectfully (adv)
fkitiu, negligently (adv)
fkito, neglect (v)
fkitu, neglectful (adj)
fkitu, negligent (adj)
fklet, screen (n)
fkletfruif, screenplay (n)

fkletloidua, screenwriter (n doer)
fkleto, screen (v)
fkletua, screener (n doer)
fkuit, catalog (n)
fkuito, catalog (v)
fkuitua, cataloger (n doer)
fkut, shuttle (n)
fkuto, shuttle (v)
flabkan, flack (n)
flad, clap (n)
flado, clap (v)
flaf, cloth (n)
flafki, clothes (n pl)
flafo, clothe (v)
flaim, tunnel (n)
flaimo, tunnel (v)
flaimua, tunneler (n doer)
flaish, worth (n)
flaishauku, worthwhile (adj)
flaishmenu, worthless (adj)
flaishu, worthy (adj)
flaishuet, worthiness (n)
flaith, past (n)
fland, neighbor (n)
fland, neighbour (n)
flando, neighbor (v)
flandu, neighborly (adj)
flanf, album (n)
flanfif, neighborhood (n)
flanfif, nieghbourhood (n)
flanp, bang (n d:hair)
flansh, pane (n)
flantiu, frankly (adv)
flantu, frank (adj)
flarm, dance (n)
flarmo, dance (v)
flarmua, dancer (n doer)
flarn, front (n)
flarnat, frontier (n)
flarno, front (v)
flarnroif, frontline (n)
flarp, aid (n)
flarpo, aid (v)
flarpua, aide (n doer)
flart, aim (n)
flarth, draft (n)
flartho, draft (v)
flarthu, drafty (adj)
flarthua, drafter (n doer)
flartmeniu, aimlessly (adv)
flartmenu, aimless (adj)
flarto, aim (v)
flarzh, bird (n)
flatek, bladder (n)
flath, slate (n)
flatho, slate (v)
flauf, frailty (n)
flaufk, delivery (n)
flaufkar, deliverance (n)
flaufko, deliver (v)
flaufkua, deliverer (n doer)
flaufrif, livestock (n)
flauftako, liven (v)

flauftfif, livelihood (n)
flauftfrepiu, livably (adv)
flauftfrepu, livable (adj)
flauftiu, lively (adv)
flaufto, live (v)
flauftu, live (adj)
flaufu, frail (adj)
flaugaitiu, lividly (adv)
flaugaitu, livid (adj)
flauk, smack (n)
flauko, smack (v)
flaum, dream (n)
flaumio, dreamt (v pa)
flaumiu, dreamily (adv)
flaumo, dream (v)
flaumu, dreamy (adj)
flaumua, dreamer (n doer)
flaup, bong (n d:sound)
flaupo, bong (v d:sound)
flaush, life (n)
flaushbleish, lifespan (n)
flaushdaun, lifetime (n)
flaushezhupo, lifesave (v)
flaushezhupua, lifesaver (n doer)
flaushfriaf, lifestyle (n)
flaushkob, lifeboat (n)
flaushlird, lifeblood (n)
flaushrazhu, lifelong (adj)
flaushreiku, lifelike (adj)
flaushroif, lifeline (n)
flaushu, life (adj)
flaushua, lifer (n doer)
flaushvaifk, lifeguard (n)
flav, brag (n)
flavo, brag (v)
flebo, cope (v)
flef, ease (n)
flefiu, easily (adv)
flefo, ease (v)
flefu, easy (adj)
flefwaku, easiest (adj)
flefwelu, easier (adj)
fleg, lug (n)
flegar, luggage (n)
flego, lug (v)
flegua, lugger (n doer)
fleid, breed (n)
fleido, breed (v)
fleidua, breeder (n doer)
fleif, breeze (n)
tleifan, prose (n)
fleifo, breeze (v)
fleifu, breezy (adj)
fleig, glance (n)
fleigo, glance (v)
flein, compassion (n)
fleinsh, compatibility (n)
fleinshiu, compatibly (adv)
fleinshu, compatible (adj)
fleinu, compassionate (adj)
fleish, passion (n)
fleishiu, passionately (adv)
fleishu, passionate (adj)

fleit, shyness (n)
fleith, vein (n)
fleithu, venous (adj)
fleito, shy (v)
fleitu, shy (adj)
fleivut, property (n)
flekio, shut (v pa)
fleko, shut (v)
flektien, shutdown (n)
fleku, shut (adj)
flekuan, shutter (n)
flekuano, shutter (v)
flekuil, shutout (n)
flelk, pitch (n d:sealant)
flend, peace (n)
flendaun, peacetime (n)
flendaunu, peacetime (adj)
flendenagua, peacemaker (n doer)
flendiu, peacefully (adv)
flendu, peaceful (adj)
flenklofio, peacekept (v pa)
flenklofo, peacekeep (v)
flenklofua, peacekeeper (n doer)
flenp, bluff (n)
flenpo, bluff (v)
flenpua, bluffer (n doer)
flensh, credibility (n)
flenshu, credible (adj)
flenshuet, credential (n)
flent, credit (n)
flento, credit (v)
flentua, creditor (n doer)
flep, tub (n)
flet, wisp (n)
fleth, plasma (n)
fleto, wisp (v)
flev, ship (n)
flevkarbak, shipwreck (n)
flevkarbako, shipwreck (v)
flevlen, shipmate (n)
flevlurt, shipload (n)
flevo, ship (v)
flevortua, shipbuilder (n doer)
flevplon, shipman (n)
flevploni, shipmen (n pl)
flevthauth, shipyard (n)
flevtheifua, shipowner (n doer)
flevua, shipper (n doer)
flevuet, shipment (n)
fliaf, crawl (n)
fliafo, crawl (v)
fliafua, crawler (n doer)
fliak, sweep (n)
fliakio, swept (v pa)
fliako, sweep (v)
fliakua, sweeper (n doer)
fliam, munchy (n)
fliamo, munch (v)
flian, famile (n)
fliano, familiarize (v)
flianu, familiar (adj)
flianua, family (n doer)
fliash, cleft (n d:split)

fliashio, clove (v pa d:split)
fliasho, cleave (v d:split)
fliashua, cleaver (n doer d:split)
fliat, tier (n)
fliath, rose (n)
fliathpoap, rosebud (n)
fliathu, rosy (adj)
fliato, tier (v)
fliaup, swab (n)
fliaupo, swab (v)
fliaur, leisure (n)
fliauru, leisurely (adj)
flid, deed (n)
flief, whisper (n)
fliefo, whisper (v)
fliefua, whisperer (n doer)
flieg, swing (n)
fliegio, swung (v pa)
fliego, swing (v)
fliegua, swinger (n doer)
flien, calm (n)
flieniu, calmly (adv)
flieno, calm (v)
flienu, calm (adj)
fliesho, slither (v)
fliet, whistle (n)
flieto, whistle (v)
flietua, whistler (n doer)
flifiu, slightly (adv)
flifo, slight (v)
flifp, specie (n)
flifpan, specimen (n)
flifu, slight (adj)
flikaft, specific (n)
flikat, specification (n)
flikatiu, specifically (adv)
flikato, specify (v)
flikatu, specific (adj)
flil, tallness (n)
flilu, tall (adj)
flin, brightness (n)
flinf, gem (n)
flinfbaraf, gemstone (n)
fliniu, brightly (adv)
flink, slot (n)
flinko, slot (v)
flino, brighten (v)
flinu, bright (adj)
flinua, brightener (n doer)
flinwaku, brightest (adj)
flinwelu, brighter (adj)
fliod, crew (n)
fliof, proof (n)
fliofliapio, proofread (v pa)
fliofliapo, proof (v)
fliofliapo, proofread (v)
fliofliapua, proofreader (n doer)
fliofo, prove (v)
fliofu, provable (adj)
fliofua, prover (n doer)
fliom, cosmos (n)
fliomu, cosmic (adj)
fliomua, cosmopolitan (n doer)

flion, crayon (n)
flir, story (n)
fliroif, storyline (n)
flirplork, storyboard (n)
flirpretua, storyteller (n doer)
flirvond, storybook (n)
flish, grass (n)
flishasho, graze (v d:feed)
flishashua, grazer (n doer d:feed)
flishkiu, imminently (adv)
flishku, imminent (adj)
flishraup, grassland (n)
flishwifual, grasshopper (n)
flishwifualu, grassy (adj)
flitho, graze (v d:scrape)
flitio, brought (v pa)
flito, bring (v)
fliuf, prayer (n)
fliufo, pray (v)
fliufua, prayer (n doer)
fliuko, whittle (v)
fliukua, whittler (n doer)
fliunt, tribulation (n)
fliunto, tribulate (v)
fliup, fret (n d:strip)
fliupo, fret (v d:strip)
fliush, tidiness (n)
fliushiu, tidily (adv)
fliusho, tidy (v)
fliushu, tidy (adj)
fliut, praise (n)
fliuth, plume (n)
fliutho, plume (v)
fliuthuet, plumage (n)
fliuto, praise (v)
fliutua, praiser (n doer)
fliuvan, tribune (n)
floig, proximity (n)
floigua, proxy (n doer)
floik, ditch (n)
floiko, ditch (v)
floip, frog (n)
floit, pencil (n)
floito, pencil (v)
flokiu, perhaps (adv)
floret, aviation (n)
floretu, aviatic (adj)
floretua, aviator (n doer)
Floridaf, Florida (n)
Florin, Fluorine (n)
flosh, stray (n)
flosho, stray (v)
floshu, stray (adj)
fluafiu, deliciously (adv)
fluafu, delicious (adj)
fluaik, creep (n)
fluaikio, crept (v pa)
fluaikiu, creepily (adv)
fluaiko, creep (v)
fluaiku, creepy (adj)
fluaikua, creeper (n doer)
fluak, cripple (n)
fluako, cripple (v)

flual, sail (n)
flualo, sail (v)
flualshkob, sailboat (n)
flualua, sailor (n doer)
fluan, light (n d:lumen)
fluanio, lit (v pa d:lumen)
fluank, lightning (n)
fluankiaf, lighthouse (n)
fluanku, lightning (adj)
fluano, light (v d:lumen)
fluanua, lighter (n doer d:lumen)
fluash, delight (n)
fluasho, delight (v)
fluashu, delightful (adj)
fluath, illumination (n)
fluathiu, luminously (adv)
fluatho, illuminate (v)
fluathu, luminous (adj)
fluathua, illuminator (n doer)
fluf, chimney (n)
flug, scum (n)
fluik, wisdom (n)
fluikiu, wisely (adv)
fluiko, wisen (v)
fluiku, wise (adj)
fluikua, wizard (n doer)
fluikuan, wizardry (n)
fluikuano, wizen (v)
fluikuniv, wiseguy (n)
fluikuplon, wiseman (n)
fluikuploni, wisemen (n pl)
fluikuthrap, wisecrack (n)
flum, shape (n)
flumenu, shapeless (adj)
flumgrud, shepherd (n)
flumgrudi, shepherd (n pl)
flumgrudo, shepherd (v)
flumiu, shapely (adv)
flumo, shape (v)
flumua, shaper (n doer)
flun, brilliance (n)
fluniu, brilliantly (adv)
flunt, shard (n)
flunu, brilliant (adj)
flup, chute (n)
flupo, chute (v)
flurp, sculpture (n)
flurpiu, sculpturally (adv)
flurpo, sculpt (v)
flurpu, sculptural (adj)
flurpua, sculptor (n doer)
flurt, overload (n)
flurto, overload (v)
flurtua, overloader (n doer)
flushk, butterfly (n)
fluth, plum (n)
fluthu, plum (adj)
fluzh, cliff (n)
fnaf, bag (n)
fnafar, baggage (n)
fnafaro, baggage (v)
fnafarua, baggager (n doer)
fnafiu, baggily (adv)
fnafo, bag (v)

fnaft, harness (n)
fnafto, harness (v)
fnafu, baggy (adj)
fnafua, bagger (n doer)
fnaig, brain (n)
fnaigbiort, brainpower (n)
fnaigefiausho, brainwash (v)
fnaiglesh, brainwave (n)
fnaigluar, brainchild (n)
fnaigmenu, brainless (adj)
fnaigu, brainy (adj)
fnaiguvat, brainstorm (n)
fnaiguvato, brainstorm (v)
fnaikik, frenzy (n)
fnaikikiu, frantically (adv)
fnaikiko, frenzy (v)
fnaikiku, frantic (adj)
fnaikiku, frenetic (adj)
fnaip, brand (n)
fnaipo, brand (v)
fnaito, brandish (v)
fnak, spit (n)
fnakio, spat (v pa)
fnako, spit (v)
fnakua, spitter (n doer)
fnan, skinniness (n)
fnanu, skinny (adj)
fnap, skin (n)
fnapkeft, skinhead (n)
fnapo, skin (v)
fnapua, skinner (n doer)
fnartho, scathe (v)
fnauk, wrong (n)
fnauketik, wrongdoing (n)
fnauketikua, wrongdoer (n doer)
fnaukiu, wrongfully (adv)
fnaukiu, wrongly (adv)
fnauko, wrong (v)
fnauku, wrong (adj)
fnauku, wrongful (adj)
fnaukuet, wrongness (n)
fnaun, blur (n)
fnauniu, blurrily (adv)
fnauno, blur (v)
fnaunu, blurry (adj)
fnauth, crouch (n)
fnautho, crouch (v)
fnauto, blurt (v)
fneig, enemy (n)
fneipiu, bluntly (adv)
fneipo, blunt (v)
fneipu, blunt (adj)
fnet, stead (n)
fnetezhaish, steadfastness (n)
fnetezhaishiu, steadfastly (adv)
fnetezhaishu, steadfast (adj)
fnetiu, steadily (adv)
fneto, steady (v)
fnetu, steady (adj)
fnetuet, steadiness (n)
fnifk, splash (n)
fnifko, splash (v)
fnifku, splashy (adj)

fnifkua, splasher (n doer)
fnik, skip (n)
fnikao, skipped (v prp)
fniko, skip (v)
fnilt, skirt (n)
fnilto, skirt (v)
fnirf, snob (n)
fnirfo, snob (v)
fnirfu, snobby (adj)
fnirfuet, snobbery (n)
fnoil, trim (n)
fnoilo, trim (v)
fnoilua, trimmer (n doer)
fnoip, blunder (n)
fnoipo, blunder (v)
fnorf, pregnancy (n)
fnorfu, pregnant (adj)
fnork, impregnation (n)
fnorko, impregnate (v)
fnort, scalp (n)
fnortat, scalpel (n)
fnorto, scalp (v)
fnortua, scalper (n doer)
fnup, wrap (n)
fnupo, wrap (v)
fnupoblaith, wraparound (n)
fnupua, wrapper (n doer)
fnut, fork (n)
fnutiu, forkily (adv)
fnuto, fork (v)
fnutrauk, forklift (n)
fnutu, forky (adj)
fnutua, forker (n doer)
foarniu, loosely (adv)
foarno, loosen (v)
foarnu, loose (adj)
foft, deer (n)
fofti, deer (n pl)
foidat, bacon (n)
foif, fairy (n)
foifraup, fairyland (n)
foin, lace (n)
foink, divorce (n)
foinko, divorce (v)
foinkuin, divorcee (n)
foino, lace (v)
foinu, lacey (adj)
foish, fair (n d:exhibition)
foishbrant, fairground (n)
foit, vault (n d:arch)
folto, vault (v d:arch)
folto, crop (v d:narrow)
forl, fragrance (n)
forlu, fragrant (adj)
forsh, sphere (n)
forshan, sphereoid (n)
forshiu, spherically (adv)
forshu, spherical (adj)
Foshforush, Phosphorus (n)
fpat, expulsion (n)
fpato, expel (v)
fpig, stab (n)
fpigo, stab (v)

fpigua, stabber (n doer)
fpuf, stable (n d:barn)
frab, trade (n)
frabeplon, tradesman (n)
frabeploni, tradesmen (n pl)
frabiu, tradably (adv)
frabo, trade (v)
frabshtat, trademark (n)
frabshtato, trademark (v)
frabu, tradable (adj)
frabua, trader (n doer)
frabunf, tradeoff (n)
fraf, bra (n)
fraif, extreme (n)
fraifan, extremity (n)
fraifiu, extremely (adv)
fraifu, extreme (adj)
fraifua, extremist (n doer)
fraig, plaster (n)
fraigo, plaster (v)
fraigut, plastic (n)
fraiguto, plasticize (v)
fraigutua, plasticizer (n doer)
fraik, badness (n)
fraikeko, worst (v)
fraikeku, worst (adj)
fraikelo, worsen (v)
fraikelu, worse (adj)
fraikiu, badly (adv)
fraiku, bad (adj)
frailk, trend (n)
frailko, trend (v)
frailku, trendy (adj)
fraim, blond (n)
fraimu, blond (adj)
fraimua, blonde (n doer)
frain, mockery (n)
frainflarzh, mockingbird (n)
fraino, mock (v)
fraip, worry (n)
fraipo, worry (v)
fraipu, worrisome (adj)
fraipua, worrier (n doer)
fraish, excellence (n)
fraishiak, extravagance (n)
fraishiakiu, extravagantly (adv)
fraishiaku, extravagant (adj)
fraishiakua, extrovert (n doer)
fraishiu, excellently (adv)
fraisho, excel (v)
fraishu, excellent (adj)
frak, ugliness (n)
fraku, ugly (adj)
fral, cell (n)
fralft, democracy (n)
fralftiu, democratically (adv)
fralftu, democratic (adj)
fralftua, democrat (n doer)
fraliu, cellularly (adv)
fralk, cellar (n)
fralm, coalescence (n)
fralmo, coalesce (v)
fralmu, coalescent (adj)

fraln, blind (n)
fralno, blind (v)
fralp, celebration (n)
fralpo, celebrate (v)
fralpua, celebrity (n doer)
fralsh, cement (n)
fralsho, cement (v)
fralu, cellular (adj)
framin, coalition (n)
framino, coalite (v)
Franash, French (n)
franf, burro (n)
franft, delay (n)
franfto, delay (v)
franftua, delayer (n doer)
Frankfurt, Frankfurt (n)
Franshaf, France (n)
Franshium, Francium (n)
frant, lay (n d:place)
frantar, layer (n)
frantaro, layer (v)
frantio, laid (v pa d:place)
franto, lay (v d:place)
frantuil, layout (n)
frantunf, layoff (n)
frashp, cattle (n)
frauf, mouth (n)
fraufiaush, mouthwash (n)
fraufiu, mouthfully (adv)
fraufo, mouth (v)
fraufthetsh, mouthpiece (n)
fraufu, mouthful (adj)
fraug, fright (n)
fraugal, thrush (n)
fraugiu, frightfully (adv)
fraugo, frighten (v)
fraugu, frightful (adj)
fraugua, frightener (n doer)
frauk, sag (n)
frauko, sag (v)
fraum, swarm (n)
fraumo, swarm (v)
fraup, fry (n)
fraupo, fry (v)
fraupua, frier (n doer)
fraupua, fryer (n doer)
fraushio, blew (v pa d:air)
fraushkioshk, blowtorch (n)
fraushkioshko, blowtorch (v)
frausho, blow (v d:air)
fraushua, blower (n doer d:air)
fraut, blurb (n)
frauto, blurb (v)
frav, tremble (n)
fravin, tremor (n)
fravinkiu, tremendously (adv)
fravinku, tremendous (adj)
fravino, tremor (v)
fravo, tremble (v)
fravua, trembler (n doer)
fravun, cortex (n)
frazh, thaw (n)
frazho, thaw (v)

frefk, swiftness (n)
frefkiu, swiftly (adv)
frefku, swift (adj)
freiaufo, plop (v)
freiaupo, plod (v)
freif, cape (n)
freifua, caper (n doer)
freigaik, snakebite (n)
freigo, faze (v)
freik, snake (n)
freiko, snake (v)
freiku, snakey (adj)
freilash, buddy (n)
freipo, drench (v)
freithio, felt (v pa)
freitho, feel (v)
freithu, feely (adj)
freithua, feeler (n doer)
Freiviul, Friday (n)
frel, swirl (n)
frelk, skillet (n)
frelo, swirl (v)
frelsh, swish (n)
frelsho, swish (v)
frelshua, swisher (n doer)
frelt, center (n)
freltaif, pivot (n)
freltaifiu, pivotally (adv)
freltaifo, pivot (v)
freltaifu, pivotal (adj)
freltak, centralization (n)
freltako, centralize (v)
freltakua, centralizer (n doer)
freltiu, centrally (adv)
frelto, center (v)
freltu, central (adj)
frem, smoothness (n)
fremiu, smoothly (adv)
fremo, smooth (v)
fremu, smooth (adj)
fremua, smoother (n doer)
frenk, pitcher (n d:container)
frent, native (n)
frentiu, natively (adv)
frentu, native (adj)
frep kodi, can (ndal d:ability)
frep kodi, could (ndal d:ability)
frep kodi, could have (ndal
 d:ability)
frep, ability (n)
frepiu, ably (adv)
frepo, enable (v)
frepu, able (adj)
frepua, enabler (n doer)
friaf, style (n)
friafan, stylus (n)
friafani, styli (n pl)
friafiu, stylishly (adv)
friafo, style (v)
friafu, stylish (adj)
friafua, stylist (n doer)
friaif, sky (n)
friaifiu, skywardly (adv)

friaifkladipua, skyscraper (n doer)
friaifkraik, skydive (n)
friaifkraiko, skydive (v)
friaifkraikua, skydiver (n doer)
friaifluan, skylight (n)
friaifo, sky (v)
friaifroif, skyline (n)
friaifu, skyward (adj)
friaifzhiarto, skyrocket (v)
friak, smut (n)
frial, plea (n)
frialo, plead (v)
frialua, pleader (n doer)
frianko, skimp (v)
frianku, skimpy (adj)
friano, skim (v)
frianua, skimmer (n doer)
friap, fret (n d:worry)
friapo, fret (v d:worry)
friasho, kindle (v)
friat, pamphlet (n)
friauf, maw (n)
friauk, smirk (n)
friauko, smirk (v)
friav, divinity (n)
friaviu, divinely (adv)
friavo, divine (v)
friavu, divine (adj)
friazh, orgasm (n)
friazhak, orgy (n)
friazhu, orgasmic (adj)
friek, stinginess (n d:frugal)
frieku, stingy (adj d:frugal)
friemu, sleek (adj)
friet, slack (n d:pants)
frieth, slough (n)
frietho, slough (v)
frif, stock (n d:fill equity)
frifan, stocking (n d:sock)
frifkrolpua, stockbroker (n doer)
frifnaip, stockpile (n)
frifnaipo, stockpile (v)
frifo, stock (v d:fill equity)
frifplon, stockman (n)
frifploni, stockmen (n pl)
frifshran, stockroom (n)
frifthorthua, stockholder (n doer)
frifu, stocky (adj d:fill equity)
frifua, stocker (n doer d:fill
 equity)
frig, swindle (n)
frigo, swindle (v)
frigua, swindler (n doer)
frikat, staunch (n)
frikato, staunch (v)
frikatu, staunch (adj)
frilak, allowance (n)
frilako, allow (v)
frilaku, allowable (adj)
frilp, pleasure (n)
frilpiu, pleasantly (adv)
frilpo, please (v)
frilpu, pleasant (adj)

frilpua, pleaser (n doer)
frilt, organization (n d:structure)
friltat, organism (n)
frilto, organize (v d:structure)
friltu, organizational (adj
 d:structure)
friltua, organizer (n doer
 d:structure)
frim, ally (n)
frimar, alliance (n)
frimo, ally (v)
frin, smile (n)
frinf, hitch (n)
frinfo, hitch (v)
frinfua, hitcher (n doer)
frinfwiasho, hitchhike (v)
frinfwiashua, hitchhiker (n doer)
frino, smile (v)
frinua, smiley (n doer)
friok, witness (n)
frioko, witness (v)
friom, gloom (n)
friomiu, gloomily (adv)
friomu, gloomy (adj)
frip, storm (n)
fripo, storm (v)
fripu, stormy (adj)
frish, smudge (n)
frishk, immensity (n)
frishkiu, immensely (adv)
frishku, immense (adj)
frisho, smudge (v)
frit, skit (n)
frith, hit (n)
frithio, hit (v pa)
fritho, hit (v)
frithua, hitter (n doer)
friugo, plunk (v)
friukiu, chronically (adv)
friuku, chronic (adj)
friunak, fugitive (n)
friuno, flee (v)
friunua, fleer (n doer)
friush, plunge (n)
friusho, plunge (v)
friushua, plunger (n doer)
frodath, autumn (n)
frodath, fall (n d:autumn)
frodathu, autumnal (adj)
frofu, organic (adj d:of life)
froif, sweat (n d:perspiration)
froiflifad, sweatshirt (n)
froifo, sweat (v d:perspiration)
froifthof, sweatshop (n)
froifu, sweaty (adj d:perspiration)
froik, swear (n)
froikio, swore (v pa)
froiko, swear (v)
froikua, swearer (n doer)
froip, pity (n)
froipar, pittance (n)
froipiu, pitifully (adv)
froipmeniu, pitilessly (adv)

froipmenu, pitiless (adj)
froipo, pity (v)
froipu, pitiful (adj)
froit, breech (n)
frop, organ (n d:body part)
frot, chord (n)
fruam, snug (n)
fruamito, snuggle (v)
fruamiu, snugly (adv)
fruamo, snug (v)
fruamu, snug (adj)
fruat, plot (n)
fruato, plot (v)
fruatua, plotter (n doer)
frub, rip (n)
frubo, rip (v)
frubua, ripper (n doer)
frubunf, ripoff (n)
fruf, riff (n)
fruft, rift (n)
frug, pledge (n)
frugo, pledge (v)
fruibrant, playground (n)
fruif, play (n)
fruifantiu, ludicrously (adv)
fruifantu, ludicrous (adj)
fruifbiun, playboy (n)
fruifdizh, plaything (n)
fruifevak, playback (n)
fruifevond, playbook (n)
fruifiu, playfully (adv)
fruifkiaf, playhouse (n)
fruiflen, playmate (n)
fruifnagua, playmaker (n doer)
fruifo, play (v)
fruifrepu, playable (adj)
fruifshran, playroom (n)
fruifu, playful (adj)
fruifua, player (n doer)
fruifuet, playfulness (n)
fruifunf, playoff (n)
fruin, display (n)
fruink, dab (n)
fruinko, dab (v)
fruino, display (v)
fruinorko, dabble (v)
fruinorkua, dabbler (n doer)
frul, summer (n)
fruldaun, summertime (n)
frum, blue (n)
frumiu, blue (adj)
frun, rice (n)
frunelp, blueberry (n)
frup, sweetness (n)
frupar, sweetie (n)
frupedral, sweetheart (n)
frupiu, sweetly (adv)
frupo, sweeten (v)
frupu, sweet (adj)
frupua, sweetener (n doer)
frush, river (n)
frushflarn, riverfront (n)
frushkeft, riverhead (n)

frushkob, riverboat (n)
frushoit, riverside (n)
frushplar, riverbank (n)
fruth, blush (n)
frutho, blush (v)
fshishf, fizz (n)
fshishfil, fizzle (n)
fshishfilo, fizzle (v)
fshishfo, fizz (v)
ftag, truck (n)
ftaglurt, truckload (n)
ftago, truck (v)
ftagua, trucker (n doer)
ftaip, entitlement (n)
ftaipo, entitle (v)
ftaipua, entitler (n doer)
ftak, arrest (n)
ftako, arrest (v)
ftaku, arrestive (adj)
ftakua, arrestor (n doer)
ftalt, arrival (n)
ftalto, arrive (v)
ftap, stability (n)
ftapo, stabilize (v)
ftapu, stabile (adj)
ftapua, stabilizer (n doer)
ftapuet, stabilization (n)
ftauf, spire (n)
ftaufo, spire (v)
ftauko, spiral (v)
ftauku, spiral (adj)
ftip, arrow (n)
ftiv, levitation (n)
ftiv, levity (n)
ftivo, levitate (v)
ftivua, levitator (n doer)
ftuin, ski (n)
ftuino, ski (v)
ftuinua, skier (n doer)
fuad, plough (n)
fuad, plow (n)
fuado, plow (v)
fuafo, saunter (v)
fual, via (prep)
fualir, ghoul (n)
fualiru, ghoulish (adj)
fuarm, bed (n)
fuarmo, bed (v)
fuash, oyster (n)
fuat, view (n)
fuataift, viewpoint (n)
fuath, sauna (n)
fuatiu, viewably (adv)
fuato, view (v)
fuatshupua, viewfinder (n doer)
fuatu, viewable (adj)
fuatua, viewer (n doer)
fuf, sauce (n)
fufap, sausage (n)
fufath, bowel (n)
fufmelk, saucepan (n)
fufo, sauce (v)
fufu, saucy (adj)

fuiak, troll (n)
fuiako, troll (v)
fuif, flight (n d:air travel)
fuifat, flyer (n)
fuifio, flew (v pa d:air travel)
fuifo, fly (v d:air travel)
fuifu, flighty (adj d:air travel)
fuifua, flier (n doer d:air travel)
fuish, trolley (v)
fuit, idleness (n)
fuito, idle (v)
fuitu, idle (adj)
fulsh, plurality (n)
fulshu, plural (adj)
fumeilu, many (adj)
fumeitrav, manifold (n)
fump, canker (n)
fumpu, canker (adj)
fushp, devastation (n)
fushpo, devastate (v)
futh, saucer (n)
ga, G (let sng)
gabrub, colleague (n)
gadak, collar (n)
gadako, collar (v)
gadaktoik, collarbone (n)
Gadolinium, Gadolinium (n)
gafan, gallon (n)
gafbaraf, gallstone (n)
gafk, gall (n)
gafko, gall (v)
gafkua, galler (n doer)
gaflatek, gallbladder (n)
gaft, noise (n)
gaftiu, noisily (adv)
gaftu, noisy (adj)
gagalth, hiccup (n)
gagaltho, hiccup (v)
gahem, Number_1e3756
gaiap, coil (n)
gaiapo, coil (v)
gaiapua, coiler (n doer)
gaib, helplessness (n)
gaibiu, helplessly (adv)
gaibu, helpless (adj)
gaifk, bitterness (n)
gaifkiu, bitterly (adv)
gaifku, bitter (adj)
gaiftag, rupture (n)
gaiftago, rupture (v)
gaigan, magnification (n)
gaigano, magnify (v)
gaiganua, magnifier (n doer)
gaigat, magnitude (n)
gaigut, magnificence (n)
gaigutiu, magnificently (adv)
gaigutu, magnificent (adj)
gaik, bite (n d:chew)
gaikio, bit (v pa d:chew)
gaiko, bite (v d:chew)
gaikua, biter (n doer d:chew)
gail, help (n)
gailo, help (v)

gailu, helpful (adj)
gailua, helper (n doer)
gaip, buck (n)
gaipo, buck (v)
gaipua, buck (n doer)
gairft, disruption (n)
gairftiu, disruptively (adv)
gairfto, disrupt (v)
gairftu, disruptive (adj)
gairftua, disrupter (n doer)
gaith, roach (n)
gaithp, beetle (n)
gaiv, tag (n)
gaivo, tag (v)
gaivua, tagger (n doer)
gald, level (n)
galdo, level (v)
galdu, level (adj)
galdua, leveler (n doer)
galg, curriculum (n)
gali, Gs (let pl)
Galium, Gallium (n)
galk, dirt (n)
galko, dirty (v)
galkshlef, earthenware (n)
galkshlefu, earthen (adj)
galku, dirty (adj)
galkweku, dirtiest (adj)
galkwelu, dirtier (adj)
galkyorn, earthworm (n)
galorn, maggot (n)
galsho, petrify (v)
galt, tract (n)
galtet, traction (n)
galth, cough (n)
galtho, cough (v)
galthua, cougher (n doer)
galtua, tractor (n doer)
Galuth, EhoMonth11 (n)
gaman, gamma (n)
gankek, ignition (n)
gankeko, ignite (v)
gankekua, igniter (n doer)
ganken, engine (n)
gankeno, engineer (v)
gankenua, engineer (n doer)
ganlaf, ignorance (n)
ganlafo, ignore (v)
ganlafu, ignorant (adj)
ganp, hammer (n)
ganpo, hammer (v)
gansho, fasten (v)
ganshua, fastener (n doer)
ganuk, communism (n)
ganukua, communist (n doer)
ganup, donkey (n)
gardak, calculation (n)
gardako, calculate (v)
gardakua, calculator (n doer)
garko, collate (v)
garlago, gnaw (v)
garld, calculus (n)
garm, couch (n)

garmo, couch (v)
garn, coal (n)
garp, collection (n)
garpfrep, collectable (n)
garpfrep, collectible (n)
garpfrepu, collectable (adj)
garpfrepu, collectible (adj)
garpiu, collectively (adv)
garpo, collect (v)
garpu, collective (adj)
garpua, collector (n doer)
garshk, collateral (n)
garsht, collaboration (n)
garshtiu, collaboratively (adv)
garshto, collaborate (v)
garshtu, collaborative (adj)
garshtua, collaborator (n doer)
garshutiu, illicitly (adv)
garshutu, illicit (adj)
garzhin, jersey (n)
gash, trace (n)
gashiu, traceably (adv)
gasho, trace (v)
gashp, collapse (n)
gashpo, collapse (v)
gashpu, collapsible (adj)
gashu, traceable (adj)
gashua, tracer (n doer)
gathan, squash (n d:fruit)
Gatholig, Catholic (n)
gauap, thunder (n)
gauapfrip, thunderstorm (n)
gauapkiup, thunderbolt (n)
gauapo, thunder (v)
gaub, chasm (n)
gauet, canine (n)
gauetu, canine (adj)
gauf, plague (n)
gaufo, plague (v)
gauft, argument (n)
gauftiu, arguably (adv)
gaufto, argue (v)
gauftu, arguable (adj)
gauftua, arguer (n doer)
gauiabiu, erratically (adv)
gauiabu, erratic (adj)
gauik, error (n)
gauikiu, erroneously (adv)
gauiko, err (v)
gauiku, errant (adj)
gauiku, erroneous (adj)
gauk, hound (n)
gauko, hound (v)
gaumern, coconut (n)
gaush, notch (n)
gausho, notch (v)
gauvat, cocoa (n)
gavd, boldness (n d:make)
gavdiu, boldly (adv d:make)
gavdu, bold (adj d:make)
gavet, agent (n)
gavg, jack (n d:lift)
gavgedaif, jackpot (n)

gavgo, jack (v d:lift)
gavgua, jacker (n doer d:lift)
gaviat, mafia (n)
gebik, matter (n d:incident)
gebiko, matter (v d:incident)
gefp, deferral (n)
gefpo, defer (v)
geip, pat (n)
geipo, pat (v)
geird, dozen (n)
geitsh, twitch (n)
geitsho, twitch (v)
gelfk, brew (n)
gelfko, brew (v)
gelfkua, brewer (n doer)
gelfkuit, brewery (n)
gelil, carriage (n)
gelk, twist (n)
gelko, twist (v)
gelku, twisty (adj)
gelkua, twister (n doer)
gelmar, kidney (n)
gelment, carpentry (n)
gelmentua, carpenter (n doer)
gelmet, carpet (n)
gelmeto, carpet (v)
geln, calendar (n)
genai-, oct- (num 8 pref)
genaimuk, octagon (n)
geneth, eighth (num 8 ord)
genfk, octoquadragintillion (num
    1e147 card)
genft, octotrigintillion (num
    1e117 card)
geni, eight (num 8 card)
genialfhemka, Number_1e32556
genida, eighty (num 80 card)
genidai-, eighty- (num 80 pref)
genideth, eightieth (num 80 ord)
genipa, eighteen (num 18 card)
genipai-, eighteen- (num 18 pref)
genipeth, eighteenth (num 18
    ord)
genka, octillion (num 1e27 card)
genkai-, xenna- (num 1e27 pref)
genketh, octillionth (num 1e27
    ord)
genshk, octovigintillion (num
    1e87 card)
genshkai-, cianta-
genshkketh, octovigintillionth
    (num 1e87 ord)
gensht, octodecillion (num 1e57
    card)
genshtai-, meikosi- (num 1e57
    pref)
genshteth, octodecillionth (num
    1e57 ord)
gerb, boredom (n d:tiresome)
gerbo, bore (v d:tiresome)
gerbua, bore (n doer d:tiresome)

gerfp, deference (n)
Germanium, Germanium (n)
gert, might (n d:strength)
gertiu, mightily (adv d:strength)
gertu, mighty (adj d:strength)
gertweku, mightiest (adj)
gertwelu, mightier (adj)
gesht, host (n)
geshtar, hostess (n)
geshto, host (v)
gethk, track (n)
gethko, track (v)
gethkua, tracker (n doer)
getral, lecture (n)
getralo, lecture (v)
getralua, lecturer (n doer)
gevash, refuse (n d:garbage)
giafp, decay (n)
giafpo, decay (v)
giagiash, magic (n)
giagiashiu, magically (adv)
giagiashu, magical (adj)
giagiashua, magician (n doer)
giak, pork (n)
gialf, café (n)
gialfet, cafeteria (n)
gialk, bacterium (n)
gialki, bacteria (n pl)
gialp, wince (n)
gialpo, wince (v)
giamen, peanut (n)
giank, commodity (n)
giano, ram (v d:thrust)
gianua, rammer (n doer d:thrust)
giarp, frown (n)
giarpo, frown (v)
giarpua, frowner (n doer)
giashk, curse (n)
giashko, curse (v)
giasho, heel (v d:tilt)
giat, boss (n)
giato, boss (v)
giatu, bossy (adj)
giaubiort, firepower (n)
giaubresh, fireplace (n)
giaufanin, firewood (n)
giaufk, bonfire (n)
giaufliofo, fireproof (v)
giaufliofu, fireproof (adj)
giaufrip, firestorm (n)
giaukiaf, firehouse (n)
giaukiok, firewook (n)
giaul, fire (n)
giaulo, fire (v)
giaulu, fiery (adj)
giaumashp, fireball (n)
giaunolth, firewall (n)
giaushnen, firearm (n)
giaushoit, fireside (n)
giaushpeg, firefly (n)
giauvaug, firefight (n)
giauvaugua, firefighter (n doer)
giauvilb, firebomb (n)

gien, courier (n)
giep, romp (n)
giepo, romp (v)
gieth, cursor (n)
gifan, pagan (n)
gifanuet, paganism (n)
gifien, peasant (n)
gifk, impact (n)
gifko, impact (v)
gifkua, impacter (n doer)
gifp, pact (n)
giktheian, stepson (n)
gilf, tweak (n)
gilk, jig (n d:fixture)
gilp, pluck (n)
gilpo, pluck (v)
gilpu, plucky (adj)
gilpua, plucker (n doer)
gilt, ego (n)
giltiu, egoistically (adv)
giltiu, egotistically (adv)
giltu, egoistic (adj)
giltu, egotistic (adj)
giltua, egoist (n doer)
giltuet, egoism (n)
giltuet, egotism (n)
gint, military (n)
gintak, militia (n)
ginto, militarize (v)
gintua, militant (n doer)
giob, tort (n)
giobat, torture (n)
giobato, torture (v)
giobatu, torturous (adj)
giodirf, ramrod (n)
giodirfo, ramrod (v)
gioif, rump (n)
gioik, quack (n)
gioikuet, quackery (n)
giok, squeeze (n)
giokat, squeegee (n)
giokato, squeegee (v)
gioko, squeeze (v)
giokua, squeezer (n doer)
giop, ramp (n)
giopo, ramp (v)
giopoik, rampage (n)
giopoiko, rampage (v)
giopoiku, rampant (adj)
gioth, porch (n)
gipashu, plush (adj)
gir, call (n)
girgrazh, jigsaw (n)
girn, ceil (n)
girno, ceil (v)
giro, call (v)
girp, turkey (n)
giru, callable (adj)
girua, caller (n doer)
girvak, callback (n)
gishk, lesion (n)
gishko, lesion (v)
githp, plug (n)

githpo, plug (v)
githpua, plugger (n doer)
gituk, snag (n)
gituko, snag (v)
giuf, ham (n)
giuip, dowel (n)
giuk, squad (n)
giukat, squadron (n)
giup, coup (n)
giush, dizziness (n)
giusho, dizzy (v)
giushu, dizzy (adj)
gizhap, mechanism (n)
gizhapiu, mechanically (adv)
gizhapo, mechanize (v)
gizhapu, mechanical (adj)
gizhapua, mechanic (n doer)
gizhapuet, mechanization (n)
gizhauk, machine (n)
gizhaukar, machinery (n)
gizhauko, machine (v)
gizhaukua, machinist (n doer)
glaf, vat (n)
glaif, fee (n)
glaik, shank (n)
glaiko, shank (v)
glait, bucket (n)
glamsh, trawl (n)
glamsho, trawl (v)
glamshu, trawlers (adj)
glanin, brook (n)
glaninu, brooklike (adj)
glant, colloquium (n)
glantu, colloquial (adj)
glard, trip (n d:journey)
glardiat, molestation (n)
glardiato, molest (v)
glardiatua, molester (n doer)
glarg, contract (n d:agreement)
glargiu, contractually (adv
    d:agreement)
glargu, contractual (adj
    d:agreement)
glargua, contractor (n doer
    d:agreement)
glark, mass (n)
glarkiu, massively (adv)
glarko, mass (v)
glarku, massive (adj)
glarn, cosmetic (n)
glarniu, cosmetically (adv)
glarnu, cosmetic (adj)
glarnua, cosmetician (n doer)
glash, trail (n)
glashkraugua, trailblazer (n doer)
glasho, trail (v)
glashua, trailer (n doer)
glat, bunt (n)
glato, bunt (v)
glauf, complaint (n)
glaufo, complain (v)
glaufua, complainer (n doer)
glauk, fake (n)

glaukiuk, liberalism (n d:political stance)
glaukiuko, liberalize (v d:political stance)
glaukiukua, liberal (n doer d:political stance)
glaukiukuet, liberalization (n)
glauko, fake (v)
glaukua, faker (n doer)
glaush, horse (n)
glaushbiort, horsepower (n)
glaushkef, horsehead (n)
glaushmith, horsetail (n)
glausho, horse (v)
glaushplon, horseman (n)
glaushploni, horsemen (n pl)
glaushtafan, horseshoe (n)
glaushvak, horseback (n)
glaut, brawl (n)
glauth, brawn (n)
glauto, brawl (v)
glef, leg (n)
glefkiok, legwork (n)
glefo, leg (v)
glefshran, legroom (n)
gleg, donation (n)
glego, donate (v)
glegua, donor (n doer)
gleiak, broach (n)
gleiako, broach (v)
gleifo, purr (v)
gleik, winch (n)
gleiko, winch (v)
gleip, eclipse (n)
gleipo, eclipse (v)
gleit, secretion (n)
gleito, secrete (v)
gleiup, brood (n)
gleiupo, brood (v)
glek, knowledge (n)
glekio, knew (v pa)
gleko, know (v)
glekua, know-it-all (n doer)
glemp, bunk (n d:bed)
glempo, bunk (v d:bed)
glep, edit (n)
glepan, editorial (n)
glepar, edition (n)
glepo, edit (v)
glepu, editable (adj)
glepua, editor (n doer)
glesh, tie (n)
glesho, tie (v)
gleshplikua, tiebreaker (n doer)
gliaf, rawness (n)
gliafiu, rawly (adv)
gliaflaf, gauze (n)
gliafu, raw (adj)
gliap, fruit (n)
gliapgurt, fruitcake (n)
gliapmenu, fruitless (adj)
gliapu, fruity (adj)
gliapuet, fruition (n)

gliapuetu, fruitful (adj)
gliash, star (n d:celestial)
gliashflev, starship (n)
gliashfluan, starlight (n)
gliashlesh, starfish (n)
gliashtiavo, stargaze (v)
gliashtiavua, stargazer (n doer)
gliashu, starry (adj d:celestial)
gliashu, stellar (adj d:celestial)
gliat, crutch (n)
gliazhik, breadwinner (n)
glief, scruff (n)
gliefu, scruffy (adj)
glif, perk (n)
glifash, deluge (n)
glifasho, deluge (v)
glifk, carrot (n)
glifo, perk (v)
glifu, perky (adj)
glink, exemption (n)
glinko, exempt (v)
glip, crust (n)
glipo, crust (v)
glipu, crusty (adj)
glish, step (n)
glishluar, stepchild (n)
glishluari, stepchildren (n pl)
glishlurn, stepdaughter (n)
glishmalsh, stepmother (n)
glisho, step (v)
glishtrit, stepladder (n)
glishu, step (adj)
glishua, stepper (n doer)
glishvotet, stepfather (n)
glit, tide (n)
gliteidon, tidewater (n)
glith, spider (n)
glithu, spidery (adj)
glito, tide (v)
glitu, tidal (adj)
gliuk, flaw (n)
gliukmeniu, flawlessly (adv)
gliukmenu, flawless (adj)
gliuko, flaw (v)
gliup, sickness (n)
gliupiu, sickly (adv)
gliupo, sicken (v)
gliupu, sick (adj)
gliuth, flask (n)
glof, steel (n)
glofkiok, steelwork (n)
glofkiokua, steelworker (n doer)
glofnagio, steelmade (v pa)
glofnago, steelmake (v)
glofnagua, steelmaker (n doer)
glofplon, steelman (n)
glofploni, steelmen (n pl)
glofu, steely (adj)
gloikio, quit (v pa)
gloiko, quit (v)
gloikua, quitter (n doer)
gloip, dumbness (n)
gloipo, dumb (v)

gloipu, dumb (adj)
gloipua, dummy (n doer)
gloirf, charity (n)
gloirfiu, charitably (adv)
gloirfu, charitable (adj)
gloishiu, quite (adv)
gloit, charge (n)
gloito, charge (v)
gloitua, charger (n doer)
glorf, board (n d:Enter ship)
glorfiu, aboard (adv d:Enter ship)
glorfo, board (v d:Enter ship)
glorfua, boarder (n doer d:Enter ship)
glorg, reach (n)
glorgo, reach (v)
glorgu, reachable (adj)
glorgua, reacher (n doer)
glorn, dreariness (n)
glornu, dreary (adj)
glorth, dread (n)
glortho, dread (v)
glorthu, dreadful (adj)
glosh, crotch (n)
gluf, guilt (n)
glufiu, guiltily (adv)
glufo, guilt (v)
glufp, bonnet (n)
glufu, guilty (adj)
gluk, bunk (n d:nonsense)
glup, burp (n)
glupo, burp (v)
glupua, burper (n doer)
glurnu, dire (adj)
glush, jack (n d:toy)
gluth, broth (n)
gofaf, lethargy (n)
gofafiu, lethargically (adv)
gofafu, lethargic (adj)
gofaif, lethality (n)
gofaifiu, lethally (adv)
gofaifu, lethal (adj)
gofk, stake (n)
gofko, stake (v)
gofkthorthua, stakeholder (n doer)
gofkuil, stakeout (n)
goft, hesitation (n)
goftiu, hesitantly (adv)
gofto, hesitate (v)
goftu, hesitant (adj)
gogar, gland (n)
gogaru, glandular (adj)
goifen, tomato (n)
goift, focus (n)
goifto, focus (v)
goiftu, focal (adj)
goiftua, focuser (n doer)
goig, jug (n)
goik, crank (n)
goiko, crank (v)
goin, crane (n)
goino, crane (v)

goip, wimp (n)
goipo, wimp (v)
goipu, wimpy (adj)
goito, cuss (v)
gok, take (n)
gokafen, takeover (n)
gokio, took (v pa)
goko, take (v)
gokua, taker (n doer)
gokuil, takeout (n)
gokunf, takeoff (n)
Gold, Gold (n)
golsh, scar (n)
golsho, scar (v)
golt, concrete (n)
golto, concrete (v)
goltu, concrete (adj)
goralfnith, goldsmith (n)
goralkrig, goldmine (n)
goralt, gold (n)
goralto, golden (v)
goraltshlesh, goldfish (n)
goraltshleshi, goldfish (n pl)
goraltu, gold (adj)
gord, volcano (n)
gorf, tar (n)
gorfgalko, tarnish (v)
gorfmarf, tarmac (n)
gorfo, tar (v)
gorlp, turbulence (n)
gorlpu, turbulent (adj)
gorp, contribution (n)
gorpik, turbine (n)
gorpo, contribute (v)
gorpua, contributor (n doer)
goshk, scare (n)
goshko, scare (v)
goshku, scary (adj)
goshkviark, scarecrow (n)
goshkweku, scariest (adj)
goshkwelu, scarier (adj)
gradarf, calligraphy (n)
graif, fetch (n)
graifo, fetch (v)
graift, cusp (n)
graifua, fetcher (n doer)
graigiu, sluggishly (adv d:slow)
graigu, sluggish (adj d:slow)
graiko, mug (v d:rob)
graikua, mugger (n doer d:rob)
graish, etch (n)
graishiu, etchily (adv)
graisho, etch (v)
graishu, etchy (adj)
graishua, etcher (n doer)
grait, stretch (n)
graitho, strew (v)
graito, stretch (v)
graitu, stretchy (adj)
graitua, stretcher (n doer)
graizh, vastness (n)
graizhiu, vastly (adv)
graizhu, vast (adj)

grak, anger (n)
grakiu, angrily (adv)
grako, anger (v)
graku, angry (adj)
gral, corn (n)
gralg, angst (n)
gralg, anxiety (n)
gralgiu, anxiously (adv)
gralgu, anxious (adj)
gralu, corny (adj)
grank, flank (n)
grankloip, corkscrew (n)
granko, flank (v)
granlak, flange (n)
granp, cork (n)
granpo, cork (v)
granpu, corky (adj)
grark, churn (n)
grarko, churn (v)
grarkua, churner (n doer)
grash, paint (n)
grashklush, paintbrush (n)
grasho, paint (v)
grashua, painter (n doer)
grashueluet, pigmentation (n)
grashuet, pigment (n)
grat, bat (n d:stick)
gratak, battery (n d:attack)
gratako, batter (v d:attack)
grath, Eho9seconds (n)
grato, bat (v d:stick)
gratua, batter (n doer d:stick)
gratup, battle (n)
gratupo, battle (v)
gratupua, battler (n doer)
grauf, roar (n)
graufo, roar (v)
graug, enlargement (n)
graugiash, massacre (n)
graugiasho, massacre (v)
graugiu, largely (adv)
graugo, enlarge (v)
graugu, large (adj)
graugua, enlarger (n doer)
graugwaku, largest (adj)
graugwelu, larger (adj)
grauk, halt (n)
graukat, halter (n)
grauko, halt (v)
grauno, roam (v)
grautho, roil (v)
gravg, dissolution (n)
gravgo, dissolve (v)
grazh, saw (n d:tool)
grazhfenp, sawmill (n)
grazhkreish, sawdust (n)
grazho, saw (v d:tool)
gredish, mustache (n)
greiag, mania (n)
greiagu, maniacal (adj)
greiagu, manic (adj)
greiagua, maniac (n doer)
greiak, bunker (n)

greibabil, granddaddy (n)
greiblap, grandpa (n)
greidathfef, grandparent (n)
greif, camel (n)
greig, smear (n)
greigo, smear (v)
greik, incarnation (n)
greikag, carnage (n)
greiko, incarnate (v)
greiku, carnal (adj)
greiliu, grandly (adv)
greilu, grand (adj)
greiluar, grandchild (n)
greiluari, grandchildren (n pl)
greilurn, granddaughter (n)
greilurnu, granddaughterly (adj)
greim, grandma (n)
greimalsh, grandmother (n)
greimalsho, grandmother (v)
greimalshu, grandmotherly (adj)
greimelmal, grandmommy (n)
greimtheian, grandson (n)
greithiok, grandmaster (n)
greitrelt, grandstand (n)
greitrelto, grandstand (v)
greivotet, grandfather (n)
greivoteto, grandfather (v)
greivotetu, grandfatherly (adj)
grel, car (n)
grelbielk, carport (n)
grelf, carve (n)
grelfio, carve (v pa)
grelfo, carve (v)
grelfua, carver (n doer)
grelkelg, carsickness (n)
grelkelgu, carsick (adj)
greln, carryon (n)
grelp, slug (n d:animal)
grelsh, gash (n)
grelsho, gash (v)
grelshua, gasher (n doer)
grelt, stir (n)
grelto, stir (v)
greltua, stirer (n doer)
grelvif, cargo (n)
grelvifo, cargo (v)
gren, carry (n)
grenam, cartoon (n)
grenk, cart (n)
grenko, cart (v)
grenkua, carter (n doer)
greno, carry (v)
grenua, carrier (n doer)
greshk, cartel (n)
gresht, closet (n)
gret, closure (n)
gretat, closeness (n)
greth, stiffness (n d:rigid)
grethano, stiff (v d:cheat)
grethato, stifle (v)
gretho, stiffen (v d:rigid)
grethu, stiff (adj d:rigid)
gretiu, closely (adv)

greto, close (v)
gretu, close (adj)
gretua, closer (n doer)
gretwaku, closest (adj)
gretwelu, closer (adj)
griago, stagger (v)
griak, cowardice (n)
griako, cower (v)
griaku, cowardly (adj)
griakua, coward (n doer)
griapo, stalk (v d:pursue)
griapua, stalker (n doer d:pursue)
griash, stagnation (n)
griasho, stagnate (v)
griashu, stagnant (adj)
griat, stack (n)
griato, stack (v)
griatua, stacker (n doer)
griauk, ghast (n)
griauku, ghastly (adj)
griet, serration (n)
grieto, serrate (v)
Grifk, Greek (n)
grik, sole (n)
grikat, solitude (n)
grikatu, solitary (adj)
grikiu, solely (adv)
griku, sole (adj)
grilf, frill (n)
grilit, eerieness (n)
grilitiu, eerily (adv)
grilitu, eerie (adj)
grilp, treasure (n)
grilpat, treasury (n)
grilpo, treasure (v)
grilpua, treasurer (n doer)
griman, burger (n)
grinal, veneer (n)
griof, cuisine (n)
griok, jeer (n)
grioko, jeer (v)
Grish, Greece (n)
grisht, fringe (n)
gritak, soldier (n)
gritako, soldier (v)
grith, salmon (n)
grog, roughness (n)
grogiu, roughly (adv)
grogo, rough (v)
grogplon, roughneck (n)
grogu, rough (adj)
groif, starvation (n)
groifo, starve (v)
groig, bong (n d:pipe)
grol, measurement (n)
groliu, measurably (adv)
grolo, measure (v)
grolu, measurable (adj)
grolua, measurer (n doer)
gruap, caliper (n)
gruash, brush (n d:shrub)
grud, herd (n)
grudo, herd (v)

grudua, herder (n doer)
grufp, bearing (n d:metal ball)
gruft, bearing (n d:direction)
grufto, bear (v d:direction)
grug, rear (n)
grugo, rear (v)
grugu, rear (adj)
grukio, bore (v pa d:endure)
grukiu, bearishly (adv d:endure)
gruko, bear (v d:endure)
gruku, bearish (adj d:endure)
grukua, bearer (n doer d:endure)
grulk, wound (n d:injury)
grulko, wound (v d:injury)
grult, hunt (n)
grulto, hunt (v)
grultua, hunter (n doer)
grun, term (n d:word)
grunkuit, terminology (n)
gruno, term (v d:word)
grut, clue (n)
gruth, gift (n)
gruthio, gave (v pa)
grutho, give (v)
gruthok, ricochet (n)
gruthoko, ricochet (v)
gruthopliol, giveaway (n)
gruthu, gifted (adj)
gruthua, giver (n doer)
grutiaf, gavel (n)
grutmeniu, cluelessly (adv)
grutmenu, clueless (adj)
gruto, clue (v)
gruv, mug (n d:cup)
guab, hoist (n)
guabo, hoist (v)
guaf, bail (n)
guafo, bail (v)
guaft, kind (n d:type)
guafuil, bailout (n)
guak, hog (n)
guakfiaush, hogwash (n)
guako, hog (v)
guanko, trump (v)
guap, toilet (n)
guapat, toiletry (n)
guauk, bigot (n)
gub, heave (n)
gubiu, heavily (adv)
gublash, compression (n)
gublashan, compress (n)
gublasho, compress (v)
gublashu, compressable (adj)
gublashua, compressor (n doer)
gubo, heave (v)
gubralm, compound (n
    d:mixture)
gubralmo, compound (v
    d:mixture)
gubshuish, heavyweight (n)
gubu, heavy (adj)
gubweku, heaviest (adj)
gubwelu, heavier (adj)

gufk, lust (n)
gufkiu, lustfully (adv)
gufko, lust (v)
gufku, lustful (adj)
gufp, heel (n d:sole)
guft, cane (n)
gufto, cane (v)
gugait, magazine (n d:storage)
gugaug, vulgarity (n)
gugaugu, vulgar (adj)
gugifp, compaction (n)
gugifpiu, compactly (adv)
gugifpo, compact (v)
gugifpu, compact (adj)
gugifpua, compactor (n doer)
guiam, spore (n)
guiamiu, sporadically (adv)
guiamu, sporadic (adj)
guib, heist (n)
guifk, nastiness (n)
guifkiu, nastily (adv)
guifku, nasty (adj)
guifkwelu, nastier (adj)
guifkweku, nastiest (adj)
guish, hiss (n)
guisho, hiss (v)
guishu, hissy (adj)
guishua, hisser (n doer)
gukaft, magnetic (n)
gukat, magnetism (n)
gukatiu, magnetically (adv)
gukato, magnetize (v)
gukatu, magnetic (adj)
gukatua, magnet (n doer)
gulb, heft (n)
gulbu, hefty (adj)
guln, communion (n)
gulno, commune (v)
gulnu, communal (adj)
gult, buoyancy (n)
gultiu, buoyantly (adv)
gulto, buoy (v)
gultu, buoyant (adj)
gultua, buoy (n doer)
gulv, caffeine (n)
guman, pudding (n)
gunaip, compilation (n)
gunaipo, compile (v)
gunaipua, compiler (n doer)
gunak, commune (n)
gunal, community (n)
gunian, communique (n)
guniat, communication (n)
guniato, communicate (v)
guniatua, communicator (n doer)
gupad, compulsion (n)
gupadiu, compulsory (adv)
gupado, compel (v)
gupadu, compulsive (adj)
gupadua, compeller (n doer)
gupap, rudder (n)
gurf, current (n d:stream)
gurk, mood (n)

gurkiu, moodily (adv)
gurku, moody (adj)
gurn, commonality (n)
gurnbresh, commonplace (n)
gurnbreshu, commonplace (adj)
gurniu, commonly (adv)
gurnkaup, commonwealth (n)
gurno, commonize (v)
gurnshorf, commonsense (n)
gurnu, common (adj)
gurnua, commoner (n doer)
gurp, gulp (n)
gurpo, gulp (v)
gurpua, gulper (n doer)
gurt, cake (n)
gurto, cake (v)
gushk, lure (n)
gushko, lure (v)
gushkua, lurer (n doer)
guth, moth (n)
guthmashp, mothball (n)
guthmashpo, mothball (v)
gutmol, candy (n)
gutmolo, candy (v)
gutmolu, candy (adj)
gutsh, naught (n)
gutshu, naughty (adj)
guvak, seizure (n)
guvako, seize (v)
guvat, invention (n)
guvatiu, inventively (adv)
guvato, invent (v)
guvator, inventory (n)
guvatu, inventive (adj)
guvatua, inventor (n doer)
guvelp, component (n)
guviush, comprisal (n)
guviusho, comprise (v)
guviushu, comprisable (adj)
guzhepu, macho (adj)
Hafnium, Hafnium (n)
hak, what (adj/adv/conj)
hak, what (pron)
hakef, whatever (adj/interj)
hakef, whatever (pron)
hakzhaufel, whatsoever (adj)
hakzhaufel, whatsoever (pron)
halret, world (n)
halretakrashu, worldwide (adj)
halretu, worldly (adj)
harf, H (let ong)
harfhem, Number_1e906
harfi, Hs (let pl)
harg, bat (n d:animal)
hargu, batty (adj d:animal)
harip, staff (n d:stick)
haripo, stave (v d:stick)
Hashium, Hassium (n)
haush, ward (n)
hausho, ward (v)
hauth, health (n)
hauthkeif, healthcare (n)
hautho, heal (v)

hauthu, healthy (adj)
hauthua, healer (n doer)
hauthweku, healthiest (adj)
hauthwelu, healthier (adj)
havup, well (n d:water)
heidon, water (n)
heidonduaif, watertightness (n)
heidonduaifu, watertight (adj)
heidonflarn, waterfront (n)
heidonflarnu, waterfront (adj)
heidonfliofo, waterproof (v)
heidonfliofu, waterproof (adj)
heidonfuarm, waterbed (n)
heidonkiaf, waterhouse (n)
heidonkiok, waterwork (n)
heidonlirol, watercolor (n)
heidonmiun, watertown (n)
heidono, water (v)
heidonpliol, waterway (n)
heidonplon, waterman (n)
heidonploni, watermen (n pl)
heidonshtat, watermark (n)
heidonthilf, watershed (n)
heidonthilfu, watershed (adj)
heidonu, watery (adj)
heidonzhail, waterfall (n)
heiduft, hypocracy (n)
heiduftiu, hypocritically (adv)
heiduftu, hypocritical (adj)
heiduftua, hypocrite (n doer)
heiguak, boar (n)
hein, him (pron 3rd masc sng obj)
heip, oak (n)
heish, his (pron 3rd masc sng pos obj)
heish, his (pron 3rd masc sng pos sub)
heisham, hypnosis (n)
heishamo, hypnotize (v)
heishfal, himself (pron 3rd masc sng refl)
heishk, whiskey (n)
Heisht, AIDS (n)
Helium, Helium (n)
hemai-, mono- (num 1 pref)
hemaiat, monument (n)
hemaiatiu, monumentally (adv)
hemaiatu, monumental (adj)
hemail, annual (n)
hemailiu, annually (adv)
hemailo, annualize (v)
hemailu, annual (adj)
hemaithar, anniversary (n)
hemalfhemka, Number_1e4206
hemdarf, monograph (n)
hemdaunu, onetime (adj)
hemdorn, monopoly (n)
hemdorno, monopolize (v)
hemdornu, monopolistic (adj)
hemdornua, monopolist (n doer)
heme, one (num 1 card)
hemeru, only (adj/adv/conj)

hemeth, first (num 1 ord)
hemethi, firsts (n pl)
hemethiu, firstly (adv)
hemethkap, firsthand (n)
hemevalsh, firstborn (n)
hemf, once (adj/adv/conj)
hemf, once (n)
hemifk, unquadragintillion (num 1e126 card)
hemift, untrigintillion (num 1e96 card)
hemiftai-, zantri-
hemifteth, untrigintillionth (num 1e96 ord)
hemka, million (num 1e6 card)
hemkadeth, millionth (num 1e6 ord)
hemkai-, mega- (num 1e6 pref)
hemkuit, monologue (n)
hemluit, monorail (n)
hemnelk, monogram (n)
hemniapiu, unanimously (adv)
hemniapu, unanimous (adj)
hempa, eleven (num 11 card)
hempai-, eleven- (num 11 pref)
hempeth, eleventh (num 11 ord)
hempreith, monochrome (n)
hempreithu, monochromatic (adj)
hemshk, unvigintillion (num 1e66 card)
hemshkai-, jitri- (num 1e66 pref)
hemshketh, unvigintillionth (num 1e66 ord)
hemsht, undecillion (num 1e36 card)
hemshtai-, udeka- (num 1e36 pref)
hemshteth, undecillionth (num 1e36 ord)
hemthreith, monolith (n)
hemthreithu, monolithic (adj)
hemthutsh, monotheism (n)
hemthutshu, monotheistic (adj)
hemtril, monotone (n)
hemtrilat, monotony (n)
hemat, wool (n)
henatu, wool (adj)
henatu, wooly (adj)
heniet, breakfast (n)
henieto, breakfast (v)
herf, deposit (n)
herfiek, depository (n)
herfk, depot (n)
herfo, deposit (v)
herfua, depositor (n doer)
hetheft, judiciary (n)
hethet, judgement (n)
hethet, judgment (n)
hethetfif, judgeship (n)
hethetiu, judicially (adv)
hethetiu, judiciously (adv)

hetheto, judge (v)
hethetu, judicial (adj)
hethetu, judicious (adj)
hethetua, judge (n doer)
hethetuet, judgementalism (n)
hethetuetu, judgemental (adj)
hetht, patient (n d:person)
hia, how (adv/conj)
hia, how (n)
hiafel, however (adv/conj)
hiark, wolf (n)
hiarko, wolf (v)
hibrath, limb (n)
Hidrogen, Hydrogen (n)
hilort, quotient (n)
hinam, quota (n)
hinamo, quota (v)
hinf, quotation (n)
hinf, quote (n)
hinfo, quote (v)
hinfu, quotable (adj)
hinfua, quoter (n doer)
hish, which (pron)
hishefel, whichever (adj)
hishefel, whichever (pron)
hishu, which (adj)
hiu, why (adv/conj/interj)
hiu, why (n)
hofp, deafness (n)
hofpo, deafen (v)
hofpu, deaf (adj)
hoin, jury (n)
hoinkat, jurisdiction (n)
hoinua, jurist (n doer)
hoinua, juror (n doer)
hoit, exile (n)
hoito, exile (v)
Holmium, Holmium (n)
Honug Konug, Hong Kong (n)
honzhaim, etc. (phrase)
honzhaim, etcetera (phrase)
hua, wah (interj)
hui, he (pron 3rd masc sng sub)
ia, ah (interj)
ia, aye (interj)
iaboft, obtrusion (n)
iaboftiu, obtrusively (adv)
iabofto, obtrude (v)
iaboftu, obtrusive (adj)
iafuat, obvious (n)
iafuatiu, obviously (adv)
iafuatu, obvious (adj)
iagrik, obsolescence (n)
iagrikiu, obsoletely (adv)
iagriku, obsolete (adj)
iaklork, obscurity (n)
iaklorko, obscure (v)
iakoft, observation (n)
iakoftak, observatory (n)
iakoftan, observance (n)
iakoftaniu, observantly (adv)
iakoftanu, observant (adj)
iakoftiu, observably (adv)

iakofto, observe (v)
iakoftu, observable (adj)
iakoftua, observer (n doer)
ialfk, obedience (n)
ialfkiu, obediently (adv)
ialfko, obey (v)
ialfku, obedient (adj)
ialivator, obliteration (n)
ialivatoro, obliterate (v)
ialk, object (n d:thing)
ialkat, objective (n d:goal)
ialkatiu, objectively (adv d:goal)
ialkatu, objective (adj d:goal)
ialkuet, objectivity (n
   d:impartiality)
ialp, obsession (n)
ialpiu, obsessively (adv)
ialpo, obsess (v)
ialpu, obsessive (adj)
ialpua, obsessor (n doer)
iamikatiu, obnoxiously (adv)
iamikatu, obnoxious (adj)
ianeip, obtuseness (n)
ianeipiu, obtusely (adv)
ianeipu, obtuse (adj)
iapifto, obtain (v)
iapiftu, obtainable (adj)
iarlk, obstacle (n)
iaroik, obligation (n)
iaroiko, oblige (v)
iaroikueto, obligate (v)
iaroikuetu, obligatory (adj)
iashlek, obstruction (n)
iashlekiu, obstructively (adv)
iashleko, obstruct (v)
iashleku, obstructive (adj)
iashlekua, obstructionist (n doer)
iashlekua, obstructor (n doer)
iatep, objection (n d:protest)
iatepiu, objectionably (adv
   d:protest)
iatepo, object (v d:protest)
iatepu, objectionable (adj
   d:protest)
iatepua, objector (n doer
   d:protest)
iathulp, obscenity (n)
iathulpiu, obscenely (adv)
iathulpu, obscene (adj)
ibaft, injunction (n)
ibar, infancy (n)
ibarkoik, infanticide (n)
ibart, echo (n)
ibarto, echo (v)
ibarua, infant (n doer)
ibauf, intuition (n)
ibaufiu, intuitively (adv)
ibaufo, intuit (v)
ibaufu, intuitive (adj)
ibirnt, endorsement (n)
ibirnto, endorse (v)
ibirntua, endorser (n doer)
ibit, investment (n)

ibitak, investigation (n)
ibitako, investigate (v)
ibitaku, investigational (adj)
ibitaku, investigative (adj)
ibitakua, investigator (n doer)
ibito, invest (v)
ibitua, investor (n doer)
iblarf, inflation (n)
iblarfo, inflate (v)
iblarfu, inflatable (adj)
iblarfua, inflater (n doer)
iblim, intimidation (n)
iblimo, intimidate (v)
iblimua, intimidator (n doer)
ibrauth, inflow (n)
ibrelk, incompleteness (n)
ibrelkiu, incompletely (adv)
ibrelku, incomplete (adj)
ibrolkiu, incomparably (adv)
ibrolku, incomparable (adj)
ibruftiu, indispensable (adj)
ibrunp, independence (n)
ibrunpiu, independently (adv)
ibrunpu, independent (adj)
ibrunpua, independent (n doer)
id, at (prep)
idaib, inhibition (n)
idaibo, inhibit (v)
idaibu, inhibitory (adj)
idaibua, inhibitor (n doer)
idaink, inequality (n)
idaink, inequity (n)
idainku, inequitable (adj)
Idakof, Idaho (n)
idaum, incubation (n)
idaumo, incubate (v)
idaumua, incubator (n doer)
idefrep, incapability (n)
idefrepu, incapable (adj)
ideik, indictment (n)
ideiko, indict (v)
ideikua, indictor (n doer)
idelshk, infraction (n)
idethp, incapacity (n)
idethpo, incapacitate (v)
idiafk, intricacy (n)
idiafkiu, intricately (adv)
idiafku, intricate (adj)
idiashk, intrigue (n)
idiashkiu, intriguingly (adv)
idiashko, intrigue (v)
idilshafu, inseparable (adj)
idrulku, incomprehensible (adj)
idubielku, inopportune (adj)
idurtu, inoperable (adj)
idurtu, inoperative (adj)
ienutaku, ineligible (adj)
ifabot, infusion (n)
ifaboto, infuse (v)
Ifak, Manganese (n davoka)
Ifap, Scandium (n davoka)
Ifat, Copper (n davoka)
ifdauf, inspiration (n)

ifdaufiu, inspirationally (adv)
ifdaufo, inspire (v)
ifdaufu, inspirational (adj)
ifeifiaunu, inclement (adj)
ifekiak, invincibility (n)
ifekiaku, invincible (adj)
iferth, entity (n)
ifiaish, invisibility (n)
ifiaishiu, invisibly (adv)
ifiaishu, invisible (adj)
ifibeink, epitaph (n)
ifieshu, infrared (adj)
Ifik, Iron (n davoka)
ifikof, epoch (n)
ifiofondiu, infrequently (adv)
ifiofondu, infrequent (adj)
Ifip, Titanium (n davoka)
ifiplon, epidemic (n)
Ifit, Zinc (n davoka)
ifleinsh, incompatibility (n)
ifleinshiu, incompatibly (adv)
ifleinshu, incompatible (adj)
Ifok, Cobalt (n davoka)
Ifop, Vanadium (n davoka)
ifrelt, epicenter (n)
ifrep, inability (n)
iftap, instability (n)
ifuarmo, embed (v)
ifuifu, inflight (adj)
Ifuk, Nickel (n davoka)
Ifup, Chromium (n davoka)
igalf, incursion (n)
igalfo, incur (v)
igef, inference (n)
igefo, infer (v)
igep, election (n)
igepan, electorate (n)
igepat, elective (n)
igepatiu, electively (adv)
igepatu, elective (adj)
igepfrepu, electable (adj)
igepo, elect (v)
Igept, Egypt (n)
Igeptan, Egyptian (n)
igepu, electoral (adj)
igepua, elector (n doer)
iget, inflection (n)
igeto, inflect (v)
igetu, inflective (adj)
igrisht, infringement (n)
igrishto, infringe (v)
igrut, inclusion (n)
igrutiu, inclusively (adv)
igruto, include (v)
igrutu, inclusive (adj)
ihaushu, inward (adj)
ikathp, invalidation (n)
ikathpo, invalidate (v)
ikathpu, invalid (adj)
ikaushket, insufficiency (n)
ikaushketiu, insufficiently (adv)
ikaushketu, insufficient (adj)
ikauvutiu, insufferably (adv)

ikauvutu, insufferable (adj)
ikemif, involvement (n)
ikemifiu, involuntarily (adv)
ikemifo, involve (v)
ikemifu, involuntary (adj)
ikiabak, intoxication (n)
ikiabako, intoxicate (v)
ikiabakua, intoxicant (n doer)
ikiag, ingestation (n)
ikiago, ingest (v)
ikiagua, ingester (n doer)
ikiak, indication (n)
ikiakiu, indicatively (adv)
ikiako, indicate (v)
ikiaku, indicative (adj)
ikiakua, indicator (n doer)
ikifit, inertia (n)
ikifitu, inertial (adj)
ikifu, inert (adj)
ikik, infliction (n)
ikikiag, indigestion (n)
ikiko, inflict (v)
ikiruetiu, inherently (adv)
ikiruetu, inherent (adj)
ikrakfrep, invulnerability (n)
ikrakfrepu, invulnerable (adj)
ikriuk, induction (n)
ikriuko, induct (v)
ikriukua, inductor (n doer)
ikshop, award (n)
ikshopo, award (v)
ikuafk, indirection (n)
ikuafkiu, indirectly (adv)
ikuafku, indirect (adj)
il, or (conj)
ilaiko, eureka (interj)
ilail, inheritance (n)
ilailo, inherit (v)
Ilak, Technetium (n davoka)
ilalk, incest (n)
ilalku, incestual (adj)
Ilanoif, Illinois (n)
Ilap, Yttrium (n davoka)
Ilat, Silver (n davoka)
ildanapu, incumbent (adj)
ileifar, inundation (n)
ileifaro, inundate (v)
ilek, intimacy (n)
ilekiu, intimately (adv)
ileko, intimate (v)
ileku, intimate (adj)
ilen, income (n)
ilf, I (let sng)
ilfarl, embassy (n)
ilfarlua, ambassador (n doer)
ilfhem, Number_1e456
ilfi, Is (let pl)
ilianf, incense (n d:smoke)
ilianfk, incendiary (n)
ilianfku, incendiary (adj)
iliant, incense (n d:anger)
ilianto, incense (v d:anger)
iliatsh, incineration (n)

iliatsho, incinerate (v)
iliatshua, incinerator (n doer)
iligrap, insolvency (n)
iligrapu, insolvent (adj)
Ilik, Ruthenium (n davoka)
Ilip, Zirconium (n davoka)
ilipituap, incoherence (n)
ilipituapiu, incoherently (adv)
ilipituapu, incoherent (adj)
ilishp, indecency (n)
ilishpiu, indecently (adv)
ilishpu, indecent (adj)
Ilit, Cadmium (n davoka)
iliugrutiu, inconclusively (adv)
iliugrutu, inconclusive (adj)
iliuklat, incongruence (n)
iliuklatiu, incongruously (adv)
iliuklatiu, incongruently (adv)
iliuklatu, incongruent (adj)
iliuklatu, incongruous (adj)
iliushpfrepiu, inconceivably (adv)
iliushpfrepu, inconceivable (adj)
iliutelk, inconsistency (n)
iliutelkiu, inconsistently (adv)
iliutelku, inconsistent (adj)
iloig, indulgence (n)
iloigo, indulge (v)
Ilok, Rhodium (n davoka)
Ilop, Niobium (n davoka)
ilparm, ambulation (n)
ilparmiu, ambulatorily (adv)
ilparmo, ambulate (v)
ilparmu, ambulatory (adj)
ilparmua, ambulance (n doer)
ilpeshk, ambush (n)
ilpeshko, ambush (v)
ilplutuet, ambition (n)
ilplutuetiu, ambitiously (adv)
ilplutuetu, ambitious (adj)
ilubishiu, irretrievably (adv)
ilubishu, irretrievable (adj)
ilubolkiu, irreparably (adv)
ilubolku, irreparable (adj)
ilubreshu, irreplaceable (adj)
iluduvek, irresponsibility (n)
iluduvekiu, irresponsibly (adv)
iluduveku, irresponsible (adj)
ilufabakiu, irrefutably (adv)
ilufabaku, irrefutable (adj)
Iluk, Palladium (n davoka)
Ilup, Molybdenum (n davoka)
ilurolm, irreconciliation (n)
ilurolmu, irreconcilable (adj)
ilushaikiu, irrevocably (adv)
ilushaiku, irrevocable (adj)
ilutelkiu, irresistibly (adv)
ilutelku, irresistible (adj)
ilutharfiu, irreversibly (adv)
ilutharfu, irreversible (adj)
iluthukiu, irrespectively (adv)
iluthuku, irrespective (adj)
iluvip, irregularity (n)

iluvipiu, irregularly (adv)
iluvipu, irregular (adj)
imashp, eyeball (n)
imashpo, eyeball (v)
imiaf, innovation (n)
imiafiu, innovatively (adv)
imiafo, innovate (v)
imiafu, innovative (adj)
imiafua, innovator (n doer)
imiart, influence (n)
imiartiu, influentially (adv)
imiarto, influence (v)
imiartu, influential (adj)
imiartua, influencer (n doer)
imikat, innocence (n)
imikatiu, innocently (adv)
imikatu, innocent (adj)
imoiv, irradiation (n)
imoivo, irradiate (v)
imolth, inpatient (n)
inafk, infestation (n)
inafko, infest (v)
Inak, Bohrium (n davoka)
Inap, Lawrencium (n davoka)
Inat, Roentgenium (n davoka)
inauk, emission (n)
inauko, emit (v)
Indiaf, India (n)
Indiafan, Indian (n)
Indiank, Indiana (n)
Indiankapol, Indianapolis (n)
Indium, Indium (n)
Indonishiaf, Indonesia (n)
Inik, Hassium (n davoka)
Inip, Rutherfordium (n davoka)
Init, Ununbium (n davoka)
inith, eyelid (n)
iniv, infatuation (n)
inivo, infatuate (v)
ino, any (pron/adj/adv)
inobrcsh, anyplace (adv)
inodizh, anything (n)
inohia, anyhow (adv)
inohol, anywhere (n)
inoholu, anywhere (adv)
inoin, injury (n)
inoino, injure (v)
inoinua, injurer (n doer)
Inok, Meitnerium (n davoka)
inona, anyone (pron)
Inop, Dubnium (n davoka)
inoplio, anyway (adv)
inoshlad, anybody (n/pron)
inowel, anymore (adv)
inuank, indiscrimination (n)
inuankiu, indiscriminately (adv)
inuanku, indiscriminate (adj)
Inuk, Darmstadtium (n davoka)
Inup, Seaborgium (n davoka)
iobortiu, inadvisably (adv)
iobortu, inadvisable (adj)
Iodin, Iodine (n)
iofk, ineptitude (n)

iofk, ineptness (n)
iofku, inept (adj)
ioflikimiu, inappropriately (adv)
ioflikimu, inappropriate (adj)
iogvet, inaccessibility (n)
iogvetu, inaccessible (adj)
iomudenku, inanimate (adj)
iopifkuet, inattention (n)
iopifkuetiu, inattentively (adv)
iopifkuetu, inattentive (adj)
iorishkeiat, insubordination (n)
iorishkeiato, insubordinate (v)
iorishkeiatu, insubordinate (adj)
ioritrepiu, insubstantially (adv)
ioritrepu, insubstantial (adj)
iotan, iota (n)
iothark, inadvertence (n)
iotharkiu, inadvertently (adv)
iotharku, inadvertent (adj)
Iowaf, Iowa (n)
ipaibu, intact (adj)
ipaltak, inactivity (n)
ipaltako, inactivate (v)
ipaltaku, inactive (adj)
ipaltakuet, inactivation (n)
ipaltuet, inaction (n)
ipeikan, invigoration (n)
ipeikano, invigorate (v)
ipelmun, insincereness (n)
ipelmuniu, insincerely (adv)
ipelmunu, insincere (adj)
ipeshp, injustice (n)
ipi-, bi- (num 2 pref)
ipianu, binary (adj)
ipid, coop (n d:cooperative)
ipidilkat, bipolarity (n)
ipidilkato, bipolarize (v)
ipidilkatu, bipolar (adj)
ipidrokirf, costar (n)
ipidrokirfo, costar (v)
Ipldurt, cooperation (n d:agree)
ipidurtiu, cooperatively (adv
   d:agree)
ipidurto, cooperate (v d:agree)
ipidurtu, cooperative (adj
   d:agree)
ipidurtua, cooperator (n doer
   d:agree)
ipidurtuk, cooperative (n d:store)
ipifiuvetual, coprocessor (n)
ipifk, intent (n)
ipifk, intention (n)
ipifkiu, intentionally (adv)
ipifkiu, intently (adv)
ipifko, intend (v)
ipifku, intentional (adj)
ipifp, intensity (n)
ipifpiu, intensely (adv)
ipifpiu, intensively (adv)
ipifpo, intensify (v)
ipifpu, intense (adj)
ipifpu, intensive (adj)
ipikizhat, biotechnology (n)

ipimoimuet, copayment (n)
ipinarmiu, bilaterally (adv)
ipinarmu, bilateral (adj)
ipirp, internal (n)
ipirpiu, internally (adv)
ipirpo, internalize (v)
ipirpu, internal (adj)
ipirpuet, internalization (n)
ipishlip, corrosion (n)
ipishlipiu, corrosively (adv)
ipishlipo, corrode (v)
ipishlipu, corrosive (adj)
ipishtek, coincidence (n)
ipishtekiu, coincidentally (adv)
ipishteko, coincide (v)
ipishteku, coincident (adj)
ipishteku, coincidental (adj)
ipituap, coherence (n)
ipituapu, coherent (adj)
ipituat, cohesion (n)
ipituatu, cohesive (adj)
ipituatuet, cohesiveness (n)
ipivairt, bicycle (n)
ipivairto, bicycle (v)
ipivairtua, bicyclist (n doer)
ipk, bias (n)
ipko, bias (v)
iplort, eyebrow (n)
ipludart, correlation (n)
ipludarto, correlate (v)
ipludufp, correspondence (n)
ipludufpo, correspond (v)
ipludufpua, correspondent (n
   doer)
ipoirt, indistinction (n)
ipoirtiu, indistinctly (adv)
ipoirtiu, indistinguishably (adv)
ipoirtu, indistinct (adj)
ipoirtu, indistinguishable (adj)
ipoit, instinct (n)
ipoitiu, instinctively (adv)
ipoitu, instinctive (adj)
ipralkiu, incorrectly (adv)
ipralku, incorrect (adj)
Irafk, Iraq (n)
Irafkan, Iraqi (n)
irai-, tri- (num 3 pref)
iraimik, triangle (n)
iraimiko, triangulate (v)
iraimiku, triangular (adj)
iraimikuet, triangulation (n)
iraimoin, tripod (n)
irainarmu, trilateral (adj)
iraishk, triple (n)
iraishko, triple (v)
iraishku, triple (adj)
iraisht, triplet (n)
iraithrant, trimester (n)
Irak, Rhenium (n davoka)
iraliukiu, inaudibly (adv)
iraliuku, inaudible (adj)
Iran, Iran (n)
Iranian, Iranian (n)

Irap, Lutetium (n davoka)
Irat, Gold (n davoka)
iraup, inland (n)
iraupu, inland (adj)
Ireland, Ireland (n)
Irelandan, Irish (n)
ireth, third (num 3 ord)
iri, three (num 3 card)
irialfhemka, Number_1e12306
irida, thirty (num 30 card)
iridai-, thirty- (num 30 pref)
irideth, thirtieth (num 30 ord)
Iridium, Iridium (n)
irifk, tresquadragintillion (num 1e132 card)
irift, trestrigintillion (num 1e102 card)
Irik, Osmium (n davoka)
irika, trillion (num 1e12 card)
irikai-, tera- (num 1e12 pref)
iriketh, trillionth (num 1e12 ord)
Irip, Hafnium (n davoka)
iripa, thirteen (num 13 card)
iripai-, thirteen- (num 13 pref)
iripeth, thirteenth (num 13 ord)
irishk, trevigintillion (num 1e72 card)
irishkai-, hienta-
irishketh, trevigintillionth (num 1e72 ord)
irisht, tredecillion (num 1e42 card)
irishtai-, sekata- (num 1e42 pref)
irishteth, tredecillionth (num 1e42 ord)
Irit, Mercury (n davoka)
Irok, Ridium (n davoka)
Iron, Iron (n)
Irop, Tantalum (n davoka)
irthish, insect (n)
Iruk, Platinum (n davoka)
Irup, Tungsten (n davoka)
irushiu, elusively (adv)
irusho, elude (v)
irushu, elusive (adj)
ishai, shoo (interj)
ishaik, invocation (n)
ishaiko, invoke (v)
ishe, in (prep)
ishedraipu, inbound (adj)
ishefleid, inbreed (n)
ishefleido, inbreed (v)
isheglorfu, inboard (adj)
ishegok, intake (n)
isheif, infertility (n)
isheifu, infertile (adj)
isheithu, inelastic (adj)
ishen, infamy (n)
isheniu, infamously (adv)
ishenu, infamous (adj)
isheprand, infield (n)

isheprandua, infielder (n doer)
isheroifu, inline (adj)
ishet, insertion (n)
isheto, insert (v)
ishetriago, instill (v)
ishetua, inserter (n doer)
ishetuin, insert (n)
ishiaf, insanity (n)
ishiafiu, insanely (adv)
ishiafu, insane (adj)
ishiampu, intangible (adj)
ishiat, inquest (n)
ishiatua, inquisitor (n doer)
ishiatuet, inquisition (n)
ishiniuku, insurmountable (adj)
iship, inception (n)
ishk, innard (n)
ishkiu, innerly (adv)
ishku, inner (adj)
Ishlam, Islam (n)
ishlek, infrastructure (n)
ishlek, instruction (n)
ishlekiu, instructionally (adv)
ishlekiu, instructively (adv)
ishleko, instruct (v)
ishleku, instructional (adj)
ishleku, instructive (adj)
ishlekua, instructor (n doer)
ishlen, inmate (n)
ishnet, instigation (n)
ishneto, instigate (v)
ishnetua, instigator (n doer)
ishoit, inside (adj/adv/prep)
ishoit, inside (n)
ishoitua, insider (n doer)
ishorfp, insensitivity (n)
ishorfpu, insensitive (adj)
ishpat, index (n)
ishpati, indices (n pl)
ishpato, index (v)
ishpatua, indexer (n doer)
ishpelt, institute (n)
ishpelto, institute (v)
ishpeltuet, institution (n)
ishpeltuetiu, institutionally (adv)
ishpeltueto, institutionalize (v)
ishpeltuetu, institutional (adj)
ishpeto, instate (v)
Ishrahil, Israel (n)
Ishrahiln, Israeli (n)
ishreid, eyelash (n)
ishrel, ensurance (n)
ishrel, insurance (n)
ishrelo, ensure (v)
ishrelo, insure (v)
ishrelua, insurer (n doer)
ishretiemiu, insidiously (adv)
ishretiemu, insidious (adj)
ishrifkiu, indescribably (adv)
ishrifku, indescribable (adj)
ishtel, indoors (n)
ishtelu, indoor (adj)
ishtrank, ingredient (n)

ishtu, into (prep)
ishualf, isolation (n)
ishualfar, isolationist (n)
ishualfo, isolate (v)
ishualfua, isolator (n doer)
ishualfuet, isolationism (n)
Italian, Italian (n)
Italif, Italy (n)
itatorfiu, inoffensively (adv)
itatorfu, inoffensive (adj)
itefdaid, inadequacy (n)
itefdaidiu, inadequately (adv)
itefdaidu, inadequate (adj)
iteir, installation (n)
iteir, installment (n)
iteiro, install (v)
iteirua, installer (n doer)
itelk, insistence (n)
itelkiu, insistently (adv)
itelko, insist (v)
itelku, insistent (adj)
itenk, inadmission (n)
itenku, inadmissible (adj)
itep, injection (n)
itepo, inject (v)
itepu, injectable (adj)
itepua, injector (n doer)
Iterbium, Ytterbium (n)
ithaip, invoice (n)
ithaipo, invoice (v)
ithark, inverse (n)
itharkiu, inversely (adv)
itharko, invert (v)
itharku, inverse (adj)
itharkua, inverter (n doer)
itharkuet, inversion (n)
ithim, episode (n)
ithimiu, episodally (adv)
ithimu, episodal (adj)
ithishk, incision (n)
ithishkiu, incisively (adv)
ithishko, incise (v)
ithishku, incisive (adj)
ithishkua, incisor (n doer)
ithishp, indecision (n)
ithishpiu, indecisively (adv)
ithishpu, indecisive (adj)
ithoitiku, infeasible (adj)
ithoku, inapplicable (adj)
ithriathu, inhospitable (adj)
ithuat, emphasis (n)
ithuatio, emphasize (v pa)
ithuato, emphasize (v)
ithufishiu, irreverently (adv)
ithufishu, irreverent (adj)
ithuk, inspection (n)
ithuko, inspect (v)
ithukua, inspector (n doer)
ithumap, invariant (n)
ithumapu, invariably (adj)
ithusht, irrationality (n)
ithushtiu, irrationally (adv)
ithushtu, irrational (adj)

ithuth, insight (n)
ithuthu, insightful (adj)
itiet, inflexibility (n)
itietu, inflexible (adj)
itiuft, infinity (n)
itiuftiu, infinitely (adv)
itiuftu, infinite (adj)
itivish, indiscretion (n)
itivishiu, indiscreetly (adv)
itivishu, indiscreet (adj)
itivoikiu, indisputably (adv)
itivoiku, indisputable (adj)
itoip, incentive (n)
itov, indifference (n)
itoviu, indifferently (adv)
itovu, indifferent (adj)
itrelsh, inroad (n)
itrep, instance (n)
itrepiu, instantly (adv)
itrepo, instantiate (v)
itreptoitiu, instantaneously (adv)
itreptoitu, instantaneous (adj)
itrepu, instant (adj)
itrift, insinuation (n)
itrifto, insinuate (v)
itrint, intolerance (n)
itrintiu, intolerably (adv)
itrintu, intolerable (adj)
Itrium, Yttrium (n)
itruik, irrelevance (n)
itruik, irrelevancy (n)
itruiku, irrelevant (adj)
ituarko, inviolate (v)
ituarku, inviolate (adj)
itubruniu, inexpensively (adv)
itubrunu, inexpensive (adj)
itugoitiu, inexcusably (adv)
itugoitu, inexcusable (adj)
itulfat, inaccuracy (n)
itulfatiu, inaccurately (adv)
itulfatu, inaccurate (adj)
itulfiu, incurably (adv)
itulfu, incurable (adj)
itulshiu, indeterminately (adv)
itulshu, indeterminate (adj)
itulshua, indeterminant (n doer)
itushtu, inexact (adj)
iumen, unless (prep/conj)
iutaun, until (prep/conj)
ivadav, emotion (n)
ivadaviu, emotionally (adv)
ivadavo, emote (v)
ivadavu, emotional (adj)
ivadavu, emotive (adj)
ivanpor, incompetence (n)
ivanporiu, incompetently (adv)
ivanporu, incompetent (adj)
ivartuf, insecurity (n)
ivartufiu, insecurely (adv)
ivartufu, insecure (adj)
ivaupu, invaluable (adj)
ivei, up (prep)
iveidautu, upbeat (adj)

iveidiek, upright (n)
iveidiekiu, uprightly (adv)
iveidieku, upright (adj)
iveiduaif, uptightness (n)
iveiduaifu, uptight (adj)
iveifalm, upstream (n)
iveifalmu, upstream (adj)
iveifep, upset (n)
iveifepio, upset (v pa)
iveifepo, upset (v)
iveifepu, upset (adj)
iveiflarnu, upfront (adj)
iveiflieg, upswing (n)
iveigok, uptake (n)
iveigrauf, uproar (n)
iveigub, upheaval (n)
iveihaushiu, upward (adv)
iveihaushiu, upwards (adv)
iveihaushu, upward (adj)
iveihaushu, upwards (adj)
iveikaim, upturn (n)
iveiklof, upkeep (n)
iveimiun, uptown (n)
iveimiunu, uptown (adj)
iveiparnu, uphill (adj)
iveirauko, uplift (v)
iveishaiash, upstate (n)
iveishaiashu, upstate (adj)
iveishkalt, upstart (n)
iveishkaltu, upstart (adj)
iveishkoit, upshot (n)
iveishoit, upside (n)
iveishtran, upgrade (n)
iveishtrano, upgrade (v)
iveishuiku, upscale (adj)
iveit, up (n)
iveitain, upstairs (n)
iveitainu, upstairs (adj)
iveithorthio, upheld (v pa)
iveithortho, uphold (v)
iveitiu, upperly (adv)
iveito, up (v)
iveitolk, update (n)
iveitolko, update (v)
iveitolkua, updater (n doer)
iveitu, upperly (adv)
iveituet, uppiness (n)
iveituetu, uppity (adj)
iveitweku, uppermost (adj)
iveivoig, upsurge (n)
iveiwefpo, uproot (v)
ivem, upon (prep)
ivierk, inferno (n)
ivierku, infernal (adj)
ivirt, infection (n)
ivirthar, ineffectiveness (n)
ivirthar, inefficiency (n)
ivirthariu, ineffectively (adv)
ivirthariu, inefficiently (adv)
ivirtharu, ineffective (adj)
ivirtharu, inefficient (adj)
ivirto, infect (v)
ivirtu, infectious (adj)

ivirtu, infective (adj)
ivoig, insurgency (n)
ivoigiu, insurgently (adv)
ivoigo, insurge (v)
ivoigu, insurgent (adj)
ivoigua, insurgent (n doer)
ivoikuat, insurrection (n)
ivoikuato, insurrect (v)
ivorn, information (n)
ivornatiu, informally (adv)
ivornatu, informal (adj)
ivorniu, informatively (adv)
ivorno, inform (v)
ivornu, informative (adj)
ivornua, informer (n doer)
ivoshiakiu, inescapably (adv)
ivoshiaku, inescapable (adj)
ivuaftiu, indefinitely (adv)
ivuaftu, indefinite (adj)
ivugan, inferiority (n)
ivuganu, inferior (adj)
ivut, input (n)
ivuto, input (v)
ivutua, inputer (n doer)
iwabaim, eyesore (n)
iwadorim, eyewear (n)
iwadrint, eyeglass (n)
iwaf, eye (n)
iwafk, inhalant (n)
iwafko, inhale (v)
iwafkua, inhaler (n doer)
iwafkuet, inhalation (n)
iwafmenu, eyeless (adj)
iwafo, eye (v)
iwafriok, eyewitness (n)
iwafua, eyer (n doer)
iwalek, eyelet (n)
iwaprulk, eyestrain (n)
iwaroifua, eyeliner (n doer)
iwathetsh, eyepiece (n)
iwathuth, eyesight (n)
iweifk, insignificance (n)
iweifkiu, insignificantly (adv)
iweifku, insignificant (adj)
izhait, infallibility (n)
izhaitiu, infallibly (adv)
izhaitu, infallible (adj)
izhank, invasion (n)
izhankiu, invasively (adv)
izhanko, invade (v)
izhanku, invasive (adj)
izhankua, invader (n doer)
izhg, acid (n)
izhgo, acidify (v)
izhgu, acidic (adj)
izhurt, inexperience (n)
kabato, park (v d:stop)
kabik, sneeze (n)
kabiko, sneeze (v)
kabiku, sneezy (adj)
kabit, parlor (n)
kabito, parlor (v)
kaboft, intrusion (n)

kaboftiu, intrusively (adv)
kabofto, intrude (v)
kaboftu, intrusive (adj)
kaboftua, intruder (n doer)
kaboftuet, intrusiveness (n)
kad, cord (n)
kadak, rudeness (n)
kadakiu, rudely (adv)
kadaku, rude (adj)
Kadmium, Cadmium (n)
kado, cord (v)
kadork, industry (n)
kadorkiu, industriously (adv)
kadorko, industrialize (v)
kadorku, industrial (adj)
kadorku, industrious (adj)
kadorkua, industrialist (n doer)
kadorkuet, industrialization (n)
kafp, craft (n)
kafpiu, craftily (adv)
kafpo, craft (v)
kafpu, crafty (adj)
kafpua, craftsman (n doer)
kaft, catch (n)
kaftio, caught (v pa)
kafto, catch (v)
kaftu, catchy (adj)
kaftua, catcher (n doer)
kai, yay (interj)
kaiap, yap (n)
kaiapo, yap (v)
kaiapua, yapper (n doer)
kaiath, wrath (n)
kaiathu, wrathful (adj)
kaibako, wrack (v)
kaif, hate (n)
kaif, hatred (n)
kaifiu, hatefully (adv)
kaifk, harshness (n)
kaifkiu, harshly (adv)
kaifko, harshen (v)
kaifku, harsh (adj)
kaifo, hate (v)
kaifp, jail (n)
kaifpekiaf, jailhouse (n)
kaifpo, jail (v)
kaifpua, jailer (n doer)
kaifu, hateful (adj)
kaifua, hater (n doer)
kaig, hostage (n)
kaiko, raze (v)
kaikua, razor (n doer)
kail, you (pron 2nd sng obj)
kail, you (pron 2nd sng sub)
kailk, StrontiumFood (n)
kaim, turn (n)
kaimafen, turnover (n)
kaimdoiar, turntable (n)
kaimgrafk, turncoat (n)
kaimo, turn (v)
kaimoblaith, turnaround (n)
kaimoveip, turnabout (n)
kaimpaiat, turnpike (n)

kaimtriku, turnkey (adj)
kaimuil, turnout (n)
kaimunf, turnoff (n)
kain, chi (n)
kainup, canard (n)
kair, you (pron 2nd pl obj)
kair, you (pron 2nd pl sub)
Kairof, Cairo (n)
kairp, mold (n d:form)
kairpo, mold (v d:form)
kairsh, your (pron 2nd pl pos sub)
kairsh, yours (pron 2nd pl pos obj)
kaish, your (pron 2nd sng pos sub)
kaish, yours (pron 2nd sng pos obj)
kaishfal, yourself (pron 2nd sng refl)
kaishfar, yourselves (pron 2nd pl refl)
kaith, bouquet (n)
kaithp, invalid (n d:person)
Kaitif, Haiti (n)
kaiv, wag (n)
kaivap, wagon (n)
kaivo, wag (v)
kaivua, wagger (n doer)
kalfk, crash (n)
kalfko, crash (v)
kalfkua, crasher (n doer)
kalgo, crave (v)
Kaliforn, California (n)
Kalifornium, Californium (n)
kalk, cram (n)
kalko, cram (v)
kaln, holly (n)
kalp, crab (n)
kalpo, crab (v)
kalpu, crabby (adj)
kalshiu, lucratively (adv)
Kalshium, Calcium (n)
kalshu, lucrative (adj)
kaluf, stroll (n)
kalufo, stroll (v)
kalufua, stroller (n doer)
kamaft, catalyst (n)
kamafto, catalyze (v)
kamaftu, catalytic (adj)
kamaftua, catalyzer (n doer)
Kambodiaf, Cambodia (n)
Kambodian, Cambodian (n)
Kambrig, Cambridge (n)
kamsh, tissue (n)
Kanadaf, Canada (n)
Kanadian, Canadian (n)
kanf, chant (n)
kanfo, chant (v)
kanfua, chanter (n doer)
kanifp, journey (n)
kanifpo, journey (v)
kanift, journal (n)

kanifto, journal (v)
kaniftu, journalistic (adj)
kaniftua, journalist (n doer)
kaniftuet, journalism (n)
kank, gym (n)
Kankal, Hanukkah (n)
kankav, gymnasium (n)
Kanshash, Kansas (n)
kap, hand (n)
kapad, handle (n)
kapado, handle (v)
kapadrolt, handlebar (n)
kapadua, handler (n doer)
kapan, kappa (n)
kaparg, handshake (n)
kapargio, handshook (v pa)
kapargo, handshake (v)
kapash, parrot (n)
kapasho, parrot (v)
kapedief, handcuff (n)
kapediefo, handcuff (v)
kapedorg, handgun (n)
kapedotsho, handpick (v)
kapefp, handicap (n)
kapefpo, handicap (v)
kapesh, handful (n)
kapevond, handbook (n)
kapezhod, handset (n)
kapkafpo, handcraft (v)
kaploaf, handkerchief (n)
kaploidio, handwrote (v pa)
kaploido, handwrite (v)
kaploidua, handwriter (n doer)
kaplug, fart (n)
kaplugo, fart (v)
kapluit, handrail (n)
kapnaf, handbag (n)
kapnagio, handmade (v pa)
kapnago, handmake (v)
kapo, hand (v)
kapshrig, manuscript (n)
kaptrelt, handstand (n)
kapu, handy (adj)
kapua, handyman (n doer)
kapuil, handout (n)
kapukiok, handiwork (n)
kapurt, maneuver (n)
kapurtfrep, maneuverability (n)
kapurto, maneuver (v)
kapzhiniu, handsomely (adv)
kapzhinu, handsome (adj)
karbak, wreck (n)
karbako, wreck (v)
karbakua, wrecker (n doer)
karbashk, wreckage (n)
Karbon, Carbon (n)
kardinal, cardinal (n)
karfk, inducement (n)
karfkiu, inductively (adv)
karfko, induce (v)
karfku, inductive (adj)
karfkua, inducer (n doer)
karflualo, assail (v)

karflualu, assailable (adj)
karflualua, assailant (n doer)
kargak, tournament (n)
Karibian, Caribbean (n)
kark, assassination (n)
karko, assassinate (v)
karkua, assassin (n doer)
Karkuain, marijuana (n)
karl, nation (n)
karlan, nationality (n)
karlfif, nationhood (n)
karliu, nationally (adv)
karlkrashu, nationwide (adj)
karlo, nationalize (v)
karlt, attitude (n)
karlu, national (adj)
karlua, nationalist (n doer)
karluet, nationalism (n)
karnaf, astronomy (n)
karnafiu, astronimically (adv)
karnafu, astronomical (adj)
karnafua, astronomer (n doer)
karniat, astronavigation (n)
karniato, astronavigate (v)
karniatua, astronaut (n doer)
karsh, gulf (n)
karsho, engulf (v)
Kartford, Hartford (n)
karth, dose (n)
kartho, dose (v)
karthuet, dosage (n)
kashin, casino (n)
katak, rut (n)
kathaiko, wield (v)
kathiuf, valor (n)
kathiufu, valiant (adj)
kathp, validity (n)
kathpiu, validly (adv)
kathpo, validate (v)
kathpu, valid (adj)
kathpuct, validation (n)
katik, wage (n)
katiko, wage (v)
katish, wager (n)
katisho, wager (v)
katuf, strobe (n)
katufo, strobe (v)
katuk, stroke (n)
katuko, stroke (v)
katukua, stroker (n doer)
kauaif, wail (n)
kauaifo, wail (v)
kauait, horror (n)
kauaitiu, horribly (adv)
kauaito, horrify (v)
kauaitu, horrible (adj)
kauaitu, horrific (adj)
kaudaiku, horrid (adj)
kaufuap, hotdog (n)
kaufuapo, hotdog (v)
kaugaifu, horrendous (adj)
kaukatu, rank (adj d:rotten)
kaukiat, catapult (n)

kaukiato, catapult (v)
kaun, card (n)
kauno, card (v)
kaunplork, cardboard (n)
kaunplorku, cardboard (adj)
kaup, wealth (n)
kaupu, wealthy (adj)
kaushfuarm, hotbed (n)
kaushgurt, hotcake (n)
kaushi, hots (n pl)
kaushiu, hotly (adv)
kaushkef, hothead (n)
kaushket, sufficiency (n)
kaushketiu, sufficiently (adv)
kaushketo, suffice (v)
kaushketu, sufficient (adj)
kaushkoit, hotshot (n)
kaushroif, hotline (n)
kaushu, hot (adj)
kauvaip, suffocation (n)
kauvaipo, suffocate (v)
kauvutiu, sufferably (adv)
kauvuto, suffer (v)
kauvutu, sufferable (adj)
kauvutua, sufferer (n doer)
Kauwif, Hawii (n)
kav, tug (n)
kavaik, hassle (n)
kavaiko, hassle (v)
kavait, haste (n)
kavaitiu, hastily (adv)
kavaito, hasten (v)
kavaitu, hasty (adj)
kavalo, gather (v)
kavalua, gatherer (n doer)
kavat, mathematic (n)
kavatieno, haunt (v)
kavatiu, mathematically (adv)
kavatu, mathematical (adj)
kavatua, mathematician (n doer)
kavep, basin (n)
kavilt, metropolis (n)
kaviltua, metropolitan (n doer)
kavit, math (n)
kavo, tug (v)
kavshkob, tugboat (n)
kazhig, square (n)
kazhigiu, squarely (adv)
kazhigo, square (v)
Kebefk, Quebec (n)
kebet, hobby (n)
kebetua, hobbyist (n doer)
kefbluag, headache (n)
kefborfu, headstrong (adj)
kefdorf, headgear (n)
kefeidon, headwater (n)
kefezhod, headset (n)
kefgrultua, headhunter (n doer)
kefkarit, headquarters (n)
kefkarito, headquarter (v)
kefkeidon, meltwater (n)
kefketien, meltdown (n)
kefko, melt (v)

kefluan, headlight (n)
kefplesh, headdress (n)
kefpleshua, headdresser (n doer)
kefpliol, headway (n)
kefplork, headboard (n)
kefroif, headline (n)
kefroifo, headline (v)
kefroifua, headliner (n doer)
kefshran, headroom (n)
kefshtaim, headband (n)
keft, head (n)
keftheln, headwind (n)
kefthiok, headmaster (n)
kefto, head (v)
keftu, heady (adj)
keftua, header (n doer)
kefyap, headphone (n)
kei, K (let sng)
keianegufk, wanderlust (n)
keiano, wander (v)
keianua, wanderer (n doer)
keiap, buckle (n)
keiapo, buckle (v)
keiapua, buckler (n doer)
keib, visage (n)
keibat, visor (n)
keidan, hotel (n)
keiesho, wane (v)
keif, care (n)
keifmen, carelessness (n)
keifmeniu, carelessly (adv)
keifmenu, careless (adj)
keifo, care (v)
keift, double (n)
keiftiu, doubly (adv)
keifto, double (v)
keiftu, double (adj)
keiftua, doubler (n doer)
keifush, carefulness (n)
keifushiu, carefully (adv)
keitushu, careful (adj)
keigiu, overwhelmingly (adv)
keigo, overwhelm (v)
keihem, Number_1e3906
keikut, remark (n d:reply)
keikutiu, remarkably (adv
   d:reply)
keikuto, remark (v d:reply)
keikutu, remarkable (adj d:reply)
keilf, viscera (n)
keilfiu, viscerally (adv)
keilfu, visceral (adj)
keili, Ks (let pl)
keilp, consciousness (n)
keilpiu, consciously (adv)
keilpu, conscious (adj)
keinap, nomad (n)
keinapu, nomadic (adj)
keinf, gallery (n)
keipift, patent (n)
keipifto, patent (v)
keipip, petal (n)
keish, talent (n)

keisho, talent (v)
keit, lottery (n)
keitin, hyphen (n)
keitino, hyphenate (v)
keitsh, wedge (n)
keitsho, wedge (v)
keiuk, gag (n d:choke)
keiuko, gag (v d:choke)
keiun, coo (n)
keiuno, coo (v)
keiv, nod (n)
keivo, nod (v)
keizhak, x-ray (n)
keizhako, x-ray (v)
kelai, hooray (interj)
kelai, hurrah (interj)
kelai, hurray (interj)
kelb, counter (n d:d: shelf)
keler, girl (n)
keleru, girly (adj)
kelft, hardiness (n)
kelftiu, hardily (adv)
kelftu, hardy (adj)
Keliaf, EhoDay06 (n)
kelk, visit (n)
kelkat, university (n)
kelkiok, toil (n)
kelkioko, toil (v)
kelko, visit (v)
kelkua, visitor (n doer)
kelkuet, visitation (n)
kelshlef, hardware (n)
kelt, hardness (n)
keltedalth, hardcover (n)
keltedalthu, hardcover (adj)
keltedaup, hardtop (n)
keltevak, hardback (n)
keltfanin, hardwood (n)
keltfif, hardship (n)
kelth, visa (n)
keltiu, hard (adv)
keltkirtu, hardcore (adj)
keltmashp, hardball (n)
kelto, harden (v)
keltoiu, hardly (adv)
keltroif, hardline (n)
keltroifu, hardline (adj)
keltroifua, hardliner (n doer)
keltu, hard (adj)
keltwadu, hardest (adj)
keltwelu, harder (adj)
kembil, wannabe (n)
kemif, volition (n)
kemifiu, voluntarily (adv)
kemifo, volunteer (v)
kemifu, voluntary (adj)
kemifua, volunteer (n doer)
kemink, ring (n d:sound)
keminkio, rang (v pa d:sound)
keminko, ring (v d:sound)
keminkua, ringer (n doer
    d:sound)
kemko, wanna (v)

kemp, want (n)
kempo, want (v)
kenath, quicksand (n)
kendaun, quicktime (n)
kenf, revolution (n d:political
    change)
kenfo, revolutionize (v d:political
    change)
kenfu, revolutionary (adj
    d:political change)
kenfua, revolutionary (n doer
    d:political change)
kenk, revolt (n)
kenko, revolt (v)
kenkua, revolter (n doer)
kenshargen, quicksilver (n)
kent, quickness (n)
kentiu, quickly (adv)
kento, quicken (v)
kentu, quick (adj)
Kentukif, Kentucky (n)
kenweku, quickest (adj)
kenwelu, quicker (adj)
kep, knee (n)
kepedefp, kneecap (n)
kepefo, kneel (v)
kepefua, kneeling (n doer)
kepo, knee (v)
kerf, edge (n)
kerfo, edge (v)
kerfu, edgy (adj)
kerfua, edger (n doer)
keshin, xi (n)
ket, check (n d:review)
ketalk, garage (n)
ketfenk, checkmate (n)
ketfenko, checkmate (v)
kethin, elegance (n)
kethiniu, elegantly (adv)
kethinu, elegant (adj)
keto, check (v d:review)
ketsh, letter (n d:character)
ketsho, letter (v d:character)
ketua, checker (n doer d:review)
ketudit, checklist (n)
kiab, toxin (n)
kiabak, toxicity (n)
kiabaku, toxic (adj)
kiabakuit, toxicology (n)
kiabakuitiu, toxicologically (adv)
kiabakuitu, toxicological (adj)
kiabakuitua, toxicologist (n doer)
kiad, tube (n)
kiado, tube (v)
kiadu, tubal (adj)
kiadu, tubular (adj)
kiaf, house (n)
kiafkiok, housework (n)
kiafklofio, housekept (v pa)
kiafklofo, housekeep (v)
kiafklofua, housekeeper (n doer)
kiafo, house (v)
kiafshemo, houseclean (v)

kiafshkob, houseboat (n)
kiafuan, hovel (n)
kiafuat, coroner (n)
kiag, jest (n)
kiago, jest (v)
kiagua, jester (n doer)
kiaik, pest (n)
kiaiko, pester (v)
kiaikoik, pesticide (n)
kiaiku, pesky (adj)
kiaikuet, pestilence (n)
kiakioko, tinker (v)
kialfk, bribery (n)
kialk, bribe (n)
kialko, bribe (v)
kialkua, briber (n doer)
kialp, hack (n)
kialpegrazh, hacksaw (n)
kialpo, hack (v)
kialpua, hacker (n doer)
kialt, ace (n)
kialto, ace (v)
kian, video (n)
kiand, wand (n)
kianeif, videotape (n)
kianeifo, videotape (v)
kianf, household (n)
kiank, rink (n)
kianp, stride (n)
kiap, turbin (n)
kiarnu, gourmet (adj)
kiarv, glue (n)
kiarvo, glue (v)
kiash, east (n)
kiasharf, housewife (n)
kiashku, eastern (adj)
kiashlad, corpse (n)
kiasht, chassis (n)
kiashu, east (adj)
kiat, death (n)
kiatfuarm, deathbed (n)
kiath, hall (n)
kiathip, hallway (n)
kiato, die (v)
kiaug, implosion (n)
kiaugiu, implosively (adv)
kiaugo, implode (v)
kiaugu, implosive (adj)
kiaugua, imploder (n doer)
kiauk, screech (n)
kiauko, screech (v)
kiaukua, screecher (n doer)
kiaul, turmoil (n)
kiaup, howl (n)
kiaupo, howl (v)
kiaupua, howler (n doer)
kiaush, haze (n d:fog)
kiausho, haze (v d:fog)
kiaushu, hazy (adj d:fog)
kiaut, reform (n d:decorrupt)
kiauto, reform (v d:decorrupt)
kiautua, reformer (n doer
    d:decorrupt)

kiautua, reformist (n doer d:decorrupt)
kiaviak, hazard (n)
kiaviako, hazard (v)
kiaviaku, hazardous (adj)
kibafk, axis (n)
kibaft, axle (n)
kibak, ax (n)
kibako, ax (v)
kibielk, import (n)
kibielko, import (v)
kibielkua, importer (n doer)
kibielkuet, importation (n)
kiblishku, impenetrable (adj)
kiboig, impotence (n)
kiboigu, impotent (adj)
kibramp, impoundment (n)
kibrampo, impound (v)
kibrat, limbo (n)
kibreish, impurity (n)
kibreishu, impure (adj)
kibrep, implant (n)
kibrepo, implant (v)
kibrepuet, implantation (n)
kibreshiu, implicitly (adv)
kibresho, imply (v)
kibreshu, implicit (adj)
kibreshuet, implication (n)
kibreshueto, implicate (v)
kibreshuetua, implicator (n doer)
kidant, immobility (n)
kidant, immobilization (n)
kidanto, immobilize (v)
kidantua, immobilizer (n doer)
Kidun, Hindu (n)
Kidunuet, Hinduism (n)
kidurt, imperative (n)
kidurtu, imperative (adj)
kiedaish, dichotomy (n)
kief, sink (n)
kiefio, sank (v pa)
kiefkoth, sinkhole (n)
kiefo, sink (v)
kiefua, sinker (n doer)
kieg, dilution (n)
kiego, dilute (v)
kiegu, dilute (adj)
kieitkafp, hovercraft (n)
kieito, hover (v)
kiek, node (n)
kielf, diploma (n)
kielt, dilation (n)
kielto, dilate (v)
kieltu, dilatory (adj)
kieltua, dilator (n doer)
kiep, diet (n)
kiepo, diet (v)
kiepua, dieter (n doer)
kiesh, sib (n)
kieshk, sibling (n)
kieshkiu, siblings (adv)
kieshku, sibling (adj)
kiet, jet (n)

kieto, jet (v)
kietroif, jetliner (n)
kievorg, digression (n)
kievorgo, digress (v)
kifaf, article (n)
kifiaish, divide (n)
kifiaishap, dividend (n)
kifiaiship, divisiveness (n)
kifiaishipu, divisive (adj)
kifiaishipua, divisor (n doer)
kifiaisho, divide (v)
kifiaishu, divisible (adj)
kifiaishua, divider (n doer)
kifiaishuet, division (n)
kifiaishuetu, divisional (adj)
kifiat, skipper (n)
kifiufrep, improbability (n)
kifiufrepiu, improbably (adv)
kifiufrepu, improbable (adj)
kifk, bench (n)
kifko, bench (v)
kiflarv, improvement (n)
kiflarvo, improve (v)
kiflenshiu, incredibly (adv)
kiflenshu, incredible (adj)
kifp, folk (n)
kifpret, folktale (n)
kifpuft, folklore (n)
kifshtat, benchmark (n)
kift, bend (n)
kiftio, bent (v pa)
kiftiu, bendably (adv)
kifto, bend (v)
kiftu, bendable (adj)
kiftua, bender (n doer)
kigal, artillery (n)
kiglak, imposition (n)
kiglako, impose (v)
kiglakua, imposter (n doer)
kikiag, digestion (n)
kikiago, digest (v)
kikiagu, digestive (adj)
kikiako, snicker (v)
kikiupu, snide (adj)
kikut, gravity (n d:physics)
kikuto, gravitate (v d:physics)
kikutuet, gravitation (n)
kikutuetu, gravitational (adj)
kilafpo, immerge (v)
kilaft, immersion (n)
kilafto, immerse (v)
kilfu, several (adj)
kiliak, heroin (n)
kilikapiu, improperly (adv)
kilikapu, improper (adj)
kilk, severance (n)
kilkat, severity (n)
kilkiu, severely (adv)
kilko, sever (v)
kilku, severe (adj)
kiloshak, impairment (n)
kiloshako, impair (v)
kiloship, imperception (n)

kiloshipiu, imperceptibly (adv)
kiloshipu, imperceptible (adj)
kilovirt, imperfection (n)
kilovirtiu, imperfectly (adv)
kilovirtu, imperfect (adj)
kilp, crib (n)
kilsh, fetish (n)
kilth, sniff (n)
kiltho, sniff (v)
kilthua, sniffer (n doer)
kilunt, impasse (n)
kiluntiu, impassably (adv)
kiluntu, impassable (adj)
kimatik, impracticality (n)
kimatiku, impractical (adj)
kimiokiu, immaculately (adv)
kimioku, immaculate (adj)
kimoid, impedance (n)
kimoido, impede (v)
kimoiduet, impediment (n)
kimoitsh, impeachment (n)
kimoitsho, impeach (v)
kimoitshu, impeachable (adj)
kinaflaf, travesty (n)
kinai-, hex- (num 6 pref)
kinai-, sext- (num 6 pref)
kinaish, mutilation (n)
kinaisho, mutilate (v)
kinaishua, mutilator (n doer)
kinak, viscosity (n)
kinaku, viscous (adj)
kinal, imagination (n)
kinalfrepiu, imaginably (adv)
kinalfrepu, imaginable (adj)
kinalo, imagine (v)
kinalpu, imaginative (adj)
kinalu, imaginary (adj)
kinbar, gender (n d:sexual identity)
kindat, imitation (n)
kindato, imitate (v)
kindatua, imitator (n doer)
kinesh, dimension (n)
kinesho, dimension (v)
kineshu, dimensional (adj)
kineth, sixth (num 6 ord)
kinf, image (n)
kinfk, sesquadragintillion (num 1e141 card)
kinfo, image (v)
kinft, sestrigintillion (num 1e111 card)
kinfuet, imagery (n)
kini, six (num 6 card)
kinialfhemka, Number_1e24456
kinida, sixty (num 60 card)
kinidai-, sixty- (num 60 pref)
kinideth, sixtieth (num 60 ord)
kinipa, sixteen (num 16 card)
kinipai-, sixteen- (num 16 pref)
kinipeth, sixteenth (num 16 ord)
kiniup, diminishment (n)

kiniupiu, diminutively (adv)
kiniupo, diminish (v)
kiniupu, diminutive (adj)
kinka, sextillion (num 1e21 card)
kinkai-, zetta- (num 1e21 pref)
kinketh, sextillionth (num 1e21 ord)
kinoin, mayhem (n)
kinoino, maim (v)
kinp, graduation (n)
kinpiu, gradually (adv)
kinpo, graduate (v)
kinpu, gradual (adj)
kinpua, graduate (n doer)
kinshk, sexvigintillion (num 1e81 card)
kinshkai-, eikto-
kinshketh, sexvigintillionth (num 1e81 ord)
kinsht, sexdecillion (num 1e51 card)
kinshtai-, oshto- (num 1e51 pref)
kinshteth, sexdecillionth (num 1e51 ord)
kint, vividness (n)
kintiu, vividly (adv)
kintu, vivid (adj)
kiof, pace (n)
kiofat, pacifism (n)
kiofato, pacify (v)
kiofatu, pacific (adj)
kiofatua, pacifier (n doer)
kiofatua, pacifist (n doer)
kiofepua, pacesetter (n doer)
kiofnagua, pacemaker (n doer)
kiofo, pace (v)
kioft, cable (n)
kiofto, cable (v)
kioftua, cabler (n doer)
kiofua, pacer (n doer)
kioik, scream (n)
kioiko, scream (v)
kioikua, screamer (n doer)
kiok, work (n)
kiokabresh, workplace (n)
kiokagian, workaholic (n)
kiokathov, workshop (n)
kiokbron, workgroup (n)
kiokeglaush, workhorse (n)
kiokitk, workbench (n)
kiokio, wrought (v pa)
kioklurt, workload (n)
kioko, work (v)
kiokplon, workman (n)
kiokplonfif, workmanship (n)
kiokploni, workmen (n pl)
kiokshluket, workstation (n)
kioktaup, worksheet (n)
kiokthush, workspace (n)
kioku, workable (adj)
kiokua, worker (n doer)
kiokuil, workout (n)

kiokviuk, workforce (n)
kiokviul, workday (n)
kiom, humidity (n)
kiomo, humidify (v)
kiomp, funk (n d:fear/dejection)
kiomu, humid (adj)
kion, cabin (n)
kiop, cab (n)
kiopua, cabby (n doer)
kior, fume (n)
kiorfk, deadline (n)
kioriu, fumily (adv)
kiorluet, fumigation (n)
kiorlueto, fumigate (v)
kiorluetua, fumigator (n doer)
kiorn, cabinet (n)
kioro, fume (v)
kioru, fumy (adj)
kiorua, fumer (n doer)
kioshdaut, deadbeat (n)
kioshfanin, deadwood (n)
kioshk, torch (n)
kioshko, torch (v)
kiosht, dead (n)
kioshtiu, deadly (adv)
kioshtiug, deadlock (n)
kioshtu, dead (adj)
kioshuish, deadweight (n)
kiot, torque (n)
kiothp, cabbage (n)
kioto, torque (v)
kiotsho, torment (v)
kiotshua, tormentor (n doer)
kipado, impel (v)
kipadua, impeller (n doer)
kipat, robot (n)
kipatiu, robotically (adv)
kipatu, robotic (adj)
kipeithu, impervious (adj)
kiploniu, impersonally (adv)
kiplonu, impersonal (adj)
kiplonuet, impersonation (n)
kiplonueto, impersonate (v)
kiplonuetua, impersonator (n doer)
kiport, artifact (n)
kir, here (adj/adv/interj)
kir, here (n)
kirbako, wreak (v)
kirf, art (n)
kirfiu, artistically (adv)
kirfk, deduction (n d:determination)
kirfko, deduce (v d:determination)
kirfkua, deducer (n doer d:determination)
kirfu, artistic (adj)
kirfua, artist (n doer)
kirg, log (n d:tree)
kirgo, log (v d:tree)
kirgua, logger (n doer d:tree)
kirkitio, wrung (v pa)

kirkito, wring (v)
kirkitua, wringer (n doer)
kirlath, wreath (n)
kirovil, hereafter (n)
kirp, robbery (n)
kirpo, rob (v)
kirpua, robber (n doer)
kirsh, physician (n)
kirt, core (n)
kirto, core (v)
kiruthishk, imprecision (n)
kiruthishkiu, imprecisely (adv)
kiruthishku, imprecise (adj)
kirzhaup, logjam (n)
kishalkiu, implausibly (adv)
kishalku, implausible (adj)
kishetriag, distillation (n)
kishetriagat, distillery (n)
kishetriagat, still (n d:distillery)
kishetriagato, still (v d:distillery)
kishetriago, distill (v)
kishetriagua, distiller (n doer)
kishket, artifice (n)
kishketiu, artificially (adv)
kishketu, artificial (adj)
kishketua, artificer (n doer)
kishkit, copy (n)
kishkitloidua, copywriter (n doer)
kishkito, copy (v)
kishkitruash, copyright (n)
kishkitruasho, copyright (v)
kishkitua, copier (n doer)
kishluak, induration (n)
kishluakiu, immutably (adv)
kishluako, indurate (v)
kishluaku, immutable (adj)
kishluakua, indurator (n doer)
kishmotat, imbalance (n)
kishmotato, imbalance (v)
Kishpanik, Hispanic (n)
kisht, hush (n)
kishto, hush (v)
kitaf, camp (n)
kitafbrant, campground (n)
kitafgiaul, campfire (n)
kitafniat, campsite (n)
kitafo, camp (v)
kitafua, camper (n doer)
kitarp, campus (n)
kith, pep (n)
kithallo, impale (v)
kithailua, impaler (n doer)
kithark, diversion (n)
kitharko, divert (v)
kitharkua, diverter (n doer)
kithiun, immorality (n)
kithiuniu, immorally (adv)
kithiunu, immoral (adj)
kithk, pepper (n)
kithko, pepper (v)
kitrulsh, imprint (n)
kitrulsho, imprint (v)
kitsh, kill (n)

kitsho, kill (v)
kitshua, killer (n doer)
Kitush, EhoMonth12 (n)
kiufo, deem (v)
kiug, tiger (n)
kiuk, liberation (n d:freedom)
kiukar, liberty (n)
kiukiu, liberally (adv d:freedom)
kiuko, liberate (v d:freedom)
kiuku, liberal (adj d:freedom)
kiukua, liberator (n doer
    d:freedom)
kiulk, throat (n)
kiulku, throaty (adj)
kiup, bolt (n)
kiupo, bolt (v)
Kiupriun, Hebrew (n)
kiurt, accomplishment (n)
kiurto, accomplish (v)
kiurtua, accomplice (n doer)
kiush, chaos (n)
kiushiu, chaotically (adv)
kiushu, chaotic (adj)
kiut, bill (n d:document)
kiuth, abyss (n)
kiuthiu, abysmally (adv)
kiuthu, abysmal (adj)
kiuto, bill (v d:document)
kiutork, billiard (n)
kiutorku, billiard (adj)
kiutplork, billboard (n)
kiutsh, tick (n d:insect)
kiutua, biller (n doer d:document)
kiviug, importance (n)
kiviugiu, importantly (adv)
kiviugu, important (adj)
kivugif, hurricane (n)
kivuk, hurry (n)
kivuko, hurry (v)
kizh, technique (n)
kizhat, technology (n)
kizhatiu, technologically (adv)
kizhatu, technological (adj)
kizhiu, technically (adv)
kizhlialt, buzzword (n)
kizhpank, tedium (n)
kizhpanku, tedious (adj)
kizhu, technical (adj)
kizhua, technician (n doer)
kizhumpo, imperil (v)
klab, stud (n)
klabo, stud (v)
kladip, scrape (n)
kladipo, scrape (v)
kladipua, scraper (n doer)
klaf, scrap (n)
klafevond, scrapbook (n)
klafgaith, cockroach (n)
klafo, scrap (v)
klafu, scrappy (adj)
klafua, scrapper (n doer)
klaiaf, volley (n)
klaiafo, volley (v)

klaib, king (n)
klaif, greed (n)
klaifif, kingdom (n)
klaifiu, greedily (adv)
klaifu, greedy (adj)
klaik, strike (n)
klaikio, struck (v pa)
klaikiu, strikingly (adv)
klaiko, strike (v)
klaikua, striker (n doer)
klaikuil, strikeout (n)
klaip, prick (n)
klaipo, prick (v)
klaishk, scorch (n)
klaishko, scorch (v)
klaishkua, scorcher (n doer)
klait, score (n)
klaitkaun, scorecard (n)
klaitmenu, scoreless (adj)
klaito, score (v)
klaitplork, scoreboard (n)
klaitua, scorer (n doer)
klaiv, swag (n)
klaivat, swagger (n)
klaivato, swagger (v)
klaivo, swag (v)
klal, laxity (n)
klaliu, laxly (adv)
klalo, lax (v)
klalu, lax (adj)
klamut, scratch (n)
klamuto, scratch (v)
klamutu, scratchy (adj)
klamutua, scratcher (n doer)
klanko, hamper (v d:hinder)
klanpo, trample (v)
klant, tramp (n)
klanto, tramp (v)
klarg, attorney (n)
klarp, skull (n)
Klarsh, Christian (n)
Klash, Christ (n)
klashk, wack (n)
klashko, wack (v)
klashko, whack (v)
klashku, wacky (adj)
klashku, whacky (adj)
klashkua, wacko (n doer)
klashkua, whacko (n doer)
Klashmal, Christmas (n)
klat, agreement (n)
klatiu, agreeably (adv)
klato, agree (v)
klatu, agreeable (adj)
klauap, brunt (n)
klauf, horoscope (n)
klaugo, gross (v d:disgusting)
klaugu, gross (adj d:disgusting)
klauk, greatness (n)
klaukiu, greatly (adv)
klauku, great (adj)
klaukwaku, greatest (adj)
klaukwelu, greater (adj)

klaup, wallop (n)
klaupo, wallop (v)
klauth, bumble (n d:bungle)
klautho, bumble (v d:bungle)
klauthua, bumbler (n doer
    d:bungle)
klautsh, brutality (n)
klautshiu, brutally (adv)
klautsho, brutalize (v)
klautshu, brutal (adj)
klautshua, brute (n doer)
klavg, craze (n)
klavgiu, crazily (adv)
klavgo, craze (v)
klavgu, crazy (adj)
klazho, trudge (v)
kleg, traffic (n)
klego, traffic (v)
klegua, trafficker (n doer)
kleiak, goof (n)
kleiako, goof (v)
kleiaku, goofy (adj)
kleid, rigidity (n)
kleidan, rigor (n)
kleidaniu, rigorously (adv)
kleidanu, rigorous (adj)
kleidiu, rigidly (adv)
kleidu, rigid (adj)
kleif, principal (n)
kleik, deletion (n)
kleiko, delete (v)
kleip, bulk (n)
kleipafu, bulky (adj)
kleipkeft, bulkhead (n)
kleipo, bulk (v)
kleipu, bulk (adj)
kleith, truss (n)
kleizh, reason (n)
kleizhiu, reasonably (adv)
kleizho, reason (v)
kleizhu, reasonable (adj)
kleizhua, reasoner (n doer)
klend, chair (n d:seat)
klent, cricket (n)
klesh, replication (n)
klesho, replicate (v)
kleshua, replicator (n doer)
klet, crick (n)
kleth, chick (n)
kleto, crick (v)
kliaf, scoop (n)
kliafo, scoop (v)
kliafua, scooper (n doer)
kliagiaul, crossfire (n)
kliagurf, crosscurrent (n)
kliaik, shriek (n)
kliaiko, shriek (v)
kliaikua, shrieker (n doer)
kliak, cross (n)
kliakafen, crossover (n)
kliakdiaf, crossbow (n)
kliakfluikiu, crosswise (adv)
kliakfluiku, crosswise (adj)

kliaklialt, crossword (n)
kliako, cross (v)
kliakshpalt, crosstalk (n)
kliaktrelsh, crossroad (n)
klian, diplomacy (n)
klianu, diplomatic (adj)
klianua, diplomat (n doer)
kliap, strife (n)
kliapio, strove (v pa)
kliapo, strive (v)
kliapua, strifer (n doer)
kliash, countess (n)
kliat, guitar (n)
kliath, tether (n)
kliatho, tether (v)
kliatua, guitarist (n doer)
kliauf, scourge (n)
kliaufo, scourge (v)
kliauk, decimation (n)
kliauko, decimate (v)
kliaumo, tout (v)
kliausho, scour (v)
kliazh, scout (n)
kliazho, scout (v)
kliazhthiok, scoutmaster (n)
kliefo, scrimp (v)
klieg, wing (n)
kliegbleish, wingspan (n)
kliego, wing (v)
kliegplon, wingman (n)
kliegploni, wingmen (n pl)
kliegua, winger (n doer)
kliek, hawk (n)
klieko, hawk (v)
kliekua, hawker (n doer)
kliet, shrill (n)
klieto, shrill (v)
klietu, shrill (adj)
klif, sip (n)
klifat, siphon (n)
klifato, siphon (v)
klifko, discard (v)
klifo, sip (v)
klifu, sippy (adj)
klifua, sipper (n doer)
klig, flea (n)
Kligat, VanAllenBelt (n)
klikar, thatch (n)
klikaro, thatch (v)
klikarua, thatcher (n doer)
klinut, turtle (n)
klinuftharb, turtleneck (n)
klinuftharbu, turtleneck (adj)
klioisho, sear (v)
kliok, duel (n)
klioko, duel (v)
kliokua, dueler (n doer)
kliop, quake (n)
kliopo, quake (v)
klish, dash (n d:sprint)
klisho, dash (v d:sprint)
klishplork, dashboard (n)
klishua, dasher (n doer d:sprint)

kliupo, scrounge (v)
kliut, putt (n)
kliutato, putter (v)
kliuto, putt (v)
kliutua, putter (n doer)
klivath, blubber (n)
klivathu, blubbery (adj)
Klivland, Cleveland (n)
klivuko, scurry (v)
kloako, pierce (v)
klof, keep (n)
klofio, kept (v pa)
klofmoak, keepsake (n)
klofo, keep (v)
klofua, keeper (n doer)
kloiano, groom (v d:clean)
kloik, growth (n)
kloikio, grew (v pa)
kloiko, grow (v)
kloikua, grower (n doer)
kloin, tile (n)
kloino, tile (v)
kloinua, tiler (n doer)
kloip, screw (n)
kloipdiapua, screwdriver (n doer)
kloipo, screw (v)
kloipu, screwy (adj)
kloipua, screwer (n doer)
kloisho, scoff (v)
kloit, skepticism (n)
kloitiu, skeptically (adv)
kloitu, skeptical (adj)
kloitua, skeptic (n doer)
Klorin, Chlorine (n)
klork, dark (n)
klorkiu, darkly (adv)
klorko, darken (v)
klorkshran, darkroom (n)
klorkshranao, shranf (v prp)
klorkshranio, shran (v pa)
klorku, dark (adj)
klorkuet, darkness (n)
klorkweku, darkest (adj)
klorkwelu, darker (adj)
klorp, scorn (n)
klorpiu, scornfully (adv)
klorpo, scorn (v)
klorpu, scornful (adj)
klorpua, scorner (n doer)
klorth, impulse (n)
klorthiu, impulsively (adv)
klorthu, impulsive (adj)
klorto, scold (v)
klosh, year (n)
kloshond, yearbook (n)
kloshu, yearly (adj)
kluaf, scope (n)
kluafo, scope (v)
kluafua, scoper (n doer)
kluaik, scepticism (n)
kluaiku, sceptical (adj)
kluaikua, sceptic (n doer)
kluak, creak (n)

kluakiu, creakily (adv)
kluako, creak (v)
kluaku, creaky (adj)
kluakua, creaker (n doer)
kluap, ovulation (n)
kluapo, ovulate (v)
kluapu, ovarian (adj)
kluapua, ovary (n doer)
kluauth, growl (n)
kluautho, growl (v)
kluft, brother (n)
kluftfif, brotherhood (n)
kluftu, brotherly (adj)
klug, loan (n)
klugio, lent (v pa)
klugo, lend (v)
klugua, lender (n doer)
kluk, chicken (n)
klukut, chuckle (n d:laugh)
klukuto, chuckle (v d:laugh)
klumo, enfeeble (v)
klumu, feeble (adj)
klun, green (n)
klunu, green (adj)
klup, ovum (n)
klupi, ova (n pl)
klurp, alleviation (n)
klurpo, alleviate (v)
klurush, collusion (n)
klurusho, collude (v)
klurushu, collusive (adj)
klush, brush (n d:bristle handle)
klushk, collision (n)
klushko, collide (v)
klushkua, collider (n doer)
klusho, brush (v d:bristle handle)
klushua, brusher (n doer d:bristle
    handle)
koatan, asteroid (n)
Kobalt, Cobalt (n)
kodi, have-to (ndal)
kofao, having (v prp)
kofirto, deserve (v)
kofith, oven (n)
kofk, bolster (n)
kofko, bolster (v)
kofo, has (v sing)
kofo, have (v s)
koft, service (n)
koftan, servitude (n)
koftanua, servant (n doer)
kofto, serve (v)
koftplon, serviceman (n)
koftploni, servicemen (n pl)
koftua, server (n doer)
koftueto, service (v)
kog, coca (n)
koiak, worship (n)
koiako, worship (v)
koiaku, worshipful (adj)
koiakua, worshipper (n doer)
koiano, yearn (v)
koiat, stripe (n)

koiato, stripe (v)
koiatua, striper (n doer)
koib, gob (n)
koideln, supermarket (n)
koiek, streak (n)
koieko, streak (v)
koieku, streaky (adj)
koif, emulation (n)
koifleid, hybrid (n)
koifo, emulate (v)
koifu, emulous (adj)
koigavgo, hijack (v)
koigavgua, hijacker (n doer)
koil, height (n)
koil, heighth (n)
koilfluan, highlight (n)
koilfluano, highlight (v)
koilfluanua, highlighter (n doer)
koiliu, highly (adv)
koilo, heighten (v)
koilpliol, highway (n)
koilu, high (adj)
koilwaku, highest (adj)
koilwelu, higher (adj)
koip, raise (n)
koipo, raise (v)
koish, hype (n)
koishiblarf, hyperinflation (n)
koisho, hype (v)
koishorfp, hypersensitivity (n)
koishorfpu, hypersensitive (adj)
koishpalt, hyperactivity (n)
koishpaltiu, hyperactively (adv)
koishpaltu, hyperactive (adj)
koishu, hyper (adj)
koitiv, throne (n)
koitralt, hierarchy (n)
koitraltu, hierarchical (adj)
kokeio, will (pro-verb fu)
kokio, did/had (pro-verb pa)
koko, do/have (pro-verb pr)
kokrug, antagony (n)
kokrugo, antagonize (v)
kokrugu, antagonistic (adj)
kokrugua, antagonist (n doer)
kolan, welcome (n)
kolano, welcome (v)
kolf, honor (n)
kolfo, honor (v)
kolfu, honorable (adj)
kolfu, honorary (adj)
koliav, heresy (n)
koliavu, heretical (adj)
koliavua, heretic (n doer)
kolishtal, cholesterol (n)
kolm, gaiety (n d:happy)
kolm, happiness (n)
kolmeniu, haplessly (adv)
kolmenu, hapless (adj)
kolmiu, gaily (adv d:happy)
kolmiu, happily (adv)
kolmu, gay (adj d:happy)
kolmu, happy (adj)

kolmweku, happiest (adj)
kolmwelu, happier (adj)
Kolombiaf, Colombia (n)
Kolombian, Colombian (n)
Kolorad, Colorado (n)
kolp, happenstance (n)
kolpo, happen (v)
kolt, quart (n)
koltar, quarter (n)
koltariu, quarterly (adv)
koltarthiok, quartermaster (n)
kolthik, welfare (n)
Kolumbiaf, Columbia (n)
konafu, vascular (adj)
Kondurash, Honduras (n)
Konetikut, Connecticut (n)
Konokaush, Holocaust (n)
Kontraf, Contra (n)
kopak, hoax (n)
kopalok, hocus-pocus (n)
Koper, Copper (n)
kor, wellness (n d:good)
korg, ox (n)
korgi, oxen (n pl)
Koriaf, Korea (n)
Korian, Korean (n)
korifkuet, inclination (n)
korkulaur, wellbeing (n)
korlt, garlic (n)
korm, toll (n)
kormo, toll (v)
kormtursh, tollbooth (n)
kornak, slut (n)
kornk, hunger (n)
kornkiu, hungrily (adv)
kornko, hunger (v)
kornku, hungry (adj)
koru, well (adj d:good)
korvig, elimination (n)
korvigo, eliminate (v)
kosh, huff (n)
koshan, midge (n)
koshiatho, wean (v)
kosho, huff (v)
koshp, content (n d:material)
kosht, keel (n)
Koshtaf Rikaf, Costa Rica (n)
koshto, keel (v)
koshtua, keeler (n doer)
koth, hole (n)
kothar, bosom (n)
kotho, hole (v)
koto, had (v)
kovak, havoc (n)
kovar, haven (n)
kovarl, heaven (n)
kovarlu, heavenly (adj)
koveio, have (v fut)
kovo, have (v pl)
kovuk, haze (n d:abuse)
kovuko, haze (v d:abuse)
krafk, task (n)
krafko, task (v)

krafkua, tasker (n doer)
krag, gear (n d:sprocket)
krago, gear (v d:sprocket)
kraiap, squabble (n)
kraiapo, squabble (v)
kraiapua, squabbler (n doer)
kraib, club (n d:stick)
kraibo, club (v d:stick)
kraift, negation (n)
kraifto, negate (v)
kraig, blast (n)
kraigo, blast (v)
kraigua, blaster (n doer)
kraik, dive (n)
kraikio, dove (v pa)
kraiko, dive (v)
kraikua, diver (n doer)
krail, brass (n)
krailkiu, brazenly (adv)
krailku, brazen (adj)
krailu, brassy (adj)
krain, clam (n)
kraint, clamp (n)
krainthek, clamshell (n)
kraintien, clampdown (n)
krainto, clamp (v)
kraintua, clamper (n doer)
kraishk, shark (n)
krait, negative (n)
kraith, claw (n)
kraithiek, pounce (n d:catch)
kraithieko, pounce (v d:catch)
kraithiekua, pouncer (n doer d:catch)
kraitho, claw (v)
kraitiu, negatively (adv)
kraitu, negative (adj)
kraituet, negativism (n)
krak, weakness (n)
krakfrep, vulnerability (n)
krakfrepu, vulnerable (adj)
krakiu, weakly (adv)
krako, weaken (v)
kraku, weak (adj)
krakwaku, weakest (adj)
krakwelu, weaker (adj)
kralk, scramble (n)
kralko, scramble (v)
kralkua, scrambler (n doer)
kralp, tarp (n)
kralshk, cemetery (n)
kran, gram (n)
kranf, scroll (n)
kranfo, scroll (v)
krankat, bandit (n)
krash, width (n)
Krashat, Mister (n)
krashiu, widely (adv)
krasho, widen (v)
krashthilpu, widespread (adj)
krashu, wide (adj)
krashua, widener (n doer)
krashwaku, widest (adj)

krashwelu, wider (adj)
krat, wear (n d:erode, fatigue)
krath, lot (n)
kratio, wore (v pa d:erode, fatigue)
kratiu, wearily (adv d:erode, fatigue)
krato, wear (v d:erode, fatigue)
kratu, weary (adj d:erode, fatigue)
kratu, wearysome (adj d:fatigue)
kratuet, weariness (n d:fatigue)
kraug, blaze (n)
kraugo, blaze (v)
krauik, sneer (n)
krauiko, sneer (v)
krauk, junk (n)
krauko, junk (v)
krauku, junky (adj)
krausho, shred (v)
kraushua, shredder (n doer)
krazho, belong (v)
krefin, jewel (n)
krefink, jewelry (n)
krefinua, jeweler (n doer)
krefp, category (n)
krefpiu, categorically (adv)
krefpo, categorize (v)
krefpu, categorical (adj)
krefpua, categorizer (n doer)
kreg, grunt (n)
krego, grunt (v)
kregua, grunt (n doer)
kreid, clash (n)
kreido, clash (v)
kreif, litter (n)
kreil, glory (n)
kreiliu, gloriously (adv)
kreilo, glorify (v)
kreilu, glorious (adj)
kreiluet, glorification (n)
kreink, muck (n)
kreinko, muck (v)
kreinku, mucky (adj)
kreish, dust (n)
kreishiu, dustily (adv)
kreishnup, dustbin (n)
kreisho, dust (v)
kreishu, dusty (adj)
kreishua, duster (n doer)
kreith, tomorrow (n)
kreithiu, tomorrow (adv)
krek, crux (n)
krel, grease (n)
krelko, bludgeon (v)
krelo, grease (v)
krelu, greasy (adj)
kren, lex (n)
krenian, lexicon (n)
krenianu, lexical (adj)
krenk, logic (n)
krenkat, logistic (n)
krenkatiu, logistically (adv)
krenkatu, logistical (adj)

krenkiu, logically (adv)
krenku, logical (adj)
krent, logo (n)
kret, hat (n)
kriaf, qualification (n)
kriafo, qualify (v)
kriaft, quality (n)
kriaftu, quality (adj)
kriafua, qualifier (n doer)
kriako, shatter (v)
kriam, shrewdness (n)
kriamiu, shrewdly (adv)
kriamu, shrewd (adj)
krian, yank (n)
kriano, yank (v)
kriash, shroud (n)
kriasho, shroud (v)
kriat, negotiation (n)
kriath, lingo (n)
kriato, negotiate (v)
kriatua, negotiator (n doer)
krib, characterization (n d:person)
kribat, characteristic (n d:person)
kribiu, characteristically (adv d:person)
kribo, characterize (v d:person)
kribu, characteristic (adj d:person)
kribua, character (n doer d:person)
krig, mine (n d:cave)
krigar, mineral (n)
krigo, mine (v d:cave)
krigua, miner (n doer d:cave)
krik, clip (n)
kriko, clip (v)
krikplork, clipboard (n)
krikua, clipper (n doer)
krilf, tavern (n)
krilpo, borrow (v)
krilpua, borrower (n doer)
krilto, bash (v)
kriltua, basher (n doer)
krimf, heap (n)
krimfo, heap (v)
krin, lip (n)
krino, lip (v)
kriok, nook (n)
kriompo, flunk (v)
kriompua, flunky (n doer)
kriop, eddy (n)
kriopo, eddy (v)
krior, eagle (n)
krioro, eagle (v)
Kripton, Krypton (n)
krish, breach (n)
krishat, missile (n)
krishnet, lipstick (n)
krisho, breach (v)
krit, bore (n d:hole)
krithk, punch (n d:hit)
krithko, punch (v d:hit)

krithkroif, punchline (n)
krithku, punchy (adj d:hit)
krithkua, puncher (n doer d:hit)
krito, bore (v d:hole)
kritsho, mow (v)
kritshua, mower (n doer)
kritua, borer (n doer d:hole)
kriufo, grumble (v)
kriug, grudge (n)
kriugo, begrudge (v)
kriun, stool (n d:excrement)
kriut, duct (n)
kriuth, whoop (n)
kriutho, whoop (v)
krivg, campaign (n)
krivgo, campaign (v)
krivgua, campaigner (n doer)
krivup, trip (n d:misstep)
krivupo, trip (v d:misstep)
krivupua, tripper (n doer d:misstep)
kroib, glob (n)
kroibo, glob (v)
kroibu, globular (adj)
kroifk, incline (n)
kroifko, incline (v)
kroiforp, declination (n)
kroifp, decline (n)
kroifpo, decline (v)
kroifpua, decliner (n doer)
kroig, box (n d:fight)
kroigo, box (v d:fight)
kroigua, boxer (n doer d:fight)
kroil, brim (n)
kroilo, brim (v)
kroilua, brimmer (n doer)
kroim, horn (n)
kroimo, horn (v)
kroimu, horny (adj)
kroiniet, gobble (n)
kroinieto, gobble (v)
kroinietua, gobbler (n doer)
kroith, globe (n)
kroithiu, globally (adv)
kroithu, global (adj)
kroithuet, globalization (n)
krolp, brokerage (n)
krolpo, broker (v)
krolpua, broker (n doer)
Vromium, Chromium (n)
krosh, search (n)
kroshfluan, searchlight (n)
krosho, search (v)
kroshua, searcher (n doer)
kruank, chunk (n)
kruanku, chunky (adj)
kruash, chuck (n d:throw)
kruasho, chuck (v d:throw)
kruf, week (n)
krufdaik, weekend (n)
krufdaikua, weekender (n doer)
krufmuan, weeknight (n)
krufrazhu, weeklong (adj)

krufu, weekly (adj)
krufviul, weekday (n)
kruk, gore (n)
kruko, gore (v)
kruku, gory (adj)
krun, few (n/pron)
krunu, few (adj)
krunwaku, fewest (adj)
krunwelu, fewer (adj)
krup, glut (n)
krupu, gluttonous (adj)
krupua, glutton (n doer)
krupuet, gluttony (n)
krush, tusk (n)
kruzh, hearth (n)
kuabrivan, cobweb (n)
kuad, cob (n d:round)
kuadaf, cobble (n d:mend)
kuadafo, cobble (v d:mend)
kuadafua, cobbler (n doer
    d:mend)
kuadak, cobble (n d:roundstone)
kuadak, cobblestone (n)
kuaf, paw (n)
kuafk, direction (n)
kuafkar, directory (n)
kuafkat, directive (n)
kuafkiu, directly (adv)
kuafko, direct (v)
kuafku, direct (adj)
kuafkua, director (n doer)
kuafo, paw (v)
kuag, bummer (n)
kuago, bum (v)
kuagua, bum (n doer)
kuaif, hail (n d:greeting)
kuaifo, hail (v d:greeting)
kuaipo, quash (v)
kuak, yuck (n)
kuaku, yucky (adj)
kualko, pamper (v)
kualp, decoy (n)
kualpo, decoy (v)
kualu, coy (adj)
kuam, yummy (n)
kuan, gain (n)
kuank, gong (n)
kuano, gain (v)
kuanua, gainer (n doer)
kuarko, sulk (v)
kuash, coziness (n)
kuasho, cozy (v)
kuashu, cozy (adj)
kub, bet (n)
Kubaf, Cuba (n)
Kuban, Cuban (n)
kubio, bet (v pa)
kubiun, cowboy (n)
kubo, bet (v)
kud, fig (n)
kudrik, decrease (n)
kudriko, decrease (v)
kudrishk, decrement (n)

kudrishkiu, decrementally (adv)
kudrishko, decrement (v)
kudrishku, decremental (adj)
kuduet, figment (n)
kuek, quack (interj)
kuf, good (n d:helpful)
kufian, butler (n)
kufk, good (n d:product)
kufliau, goodbye (interj)
kuflimen, goodmorning (interj)
kufmuan, goodnight (interj)
kufmuf, goodness (n)
kufp, ethic (n)
kufpath, ethos (n)
kufpiu, ethically (adv)
kufpo, ethicate (v)
kufpu, ethical (adj)
kuft, ethnicity (n)
kuftu, ethnic (adj)
kufu, good (adj d:helpful)
kufub, poop (n)
kufubo, poop (v)
kufubua, pooper (n doer)
kufwek, best (n)
kufwekio, best (v pa)
kufwekiu, best (adv)
kufweko, best (v)
kufweku, best (adj)
kufwelo, better (v)
kufwelu, better (adj)
kufyak, goodwill (n)
kuiak, weapon (n)
kuiakuet, weaponry (n)
kuian, yawn (n)
kuiano, yawn (v)
kuiesho, quench (v)
kuieto, quell (v)
kuifp, blink (n)
kuifpo, blink (v)
kuifpua, blinker (n doer)
kuik, toast (n d:cheer)
kuiko, toast (v d:cheer)
kuiku, toasty (adj d:cheer)
kuikua, toaster (n doer d:cheer)
kuilan, guerrilla (n)
kuilanu, guerrilla (adj)
kuish, queasiness (n)
kuishu, queasy (adj)
kuit, log (n d:record)
kuito, log (v d:record)
kuitua, logger (n doer d:record)
kuitvond, logbook (n)
kukabik, allergy (n)
kukabiku, allergic (adj)
kukabikua, allergist (n doer)
kukani, goggles (n pl)
kul, be (imp, common)
kulaur, being (v prp common)
kulaurk, being (v prp emphatic)
kulf, behavior (n)
kulfo, behave (v)
kulko, be (imp, emphatic)
kuln, immunity (n)

kulnepliashp, immunotherapy (n)
kulnevublash,
    immunosuppression (n)
kulnkuit, immunology (n)
kulnkuitu, immunological (adj)
kulno, immunize (v)
kulnu, immune (adj)
kulnuet, immunization (n)
kult, figure (n)
kultiu, figuratively (adv)
kultkeft, figurehead (n)
kulto, figure (v)
kultoif, figurine (n)
kultu, figurative (adj)
kuluk, toot (n)
kuluko, toot (v)
kump, boulder (n)
kund, behind (adj/adv/prep)
kunio, began (v pa)
Kunkarf, Hungary (n)
Kunkarian, Hungarian (n)
kuno, begin (v)
kunua, beginner (n doer)
kupaft, benefit (n)
kupaftiu, benefically (adv)
kupafto, benefit (v)
kupaftu, beneficial (adj)
kupaftua, beneficiary (n doer)
kupog, debt (n)
kupogat, debenture (n)
kupogo, indebt (v)
kupogua, debtor (n doer)
kurban, tinder (n)
kurbanprenk, tinderbox (n)
kurg, nerd (n)
Kurium, Curium (n)
kurk, factory (n)
kurm, cow (n)
kurp, timber (n)
kushoit, beside (adv/prep)
kushoit, besides (adv/prep)
Kushton, Houston (n)
kut, heat (n)
kutal, sword (n)
kutalfruif, swordplay (n)
kutalshlesh, swordfish (n)
kutalshleshi, swordfish (n pl)
kuth, skeleton (n)
kuthu, skeletal (adj)
kuto, heat (v)
kutsh, deity (n)
kutua, heater (n doer)
kutuk, colon (n d:organ)
kuvad, goose (n)
kuvadi, geese (n pl)
kuvado, goose (v)
kuvezho, debug (v)
kuvezhua, debugger (n doer)
Kuwait, Kuwait (n)
Kuwaitan, Kuwaiti (n)
kuyerl, beyond (adv/prep)
kwak, yuck (interj)
kwam, yum (interj)

kwami, yummy (interj)
labik, spade (n)
labiko, spade (v)
labolk, spare (n)
labolkiu, sparingly (adv)
labolko, spare (v)
ladifiu, virtually (adv)
ladifu, virtual (adj)
lafim, venue (n)
lafk, merchandise (n)
lafkao, merchandized (v prp)
lafko, merchandize (v)
lafkua, merchant (n doer)
lafmat, veneration (n)
lafmatiu, venerably (adv)
lafmato, venerate (v)
lafmatu, venerable (adj)
lafp, merge (n)
lafpo, merge (v)
lafpua, merger (n doer)
lagal, ill (n)
lagal, illness (n)
lagalu, ill (adj)
lagrush, illusion (n)
laiaf, saturation (n)
laiafo, saturate (v)
laiak, satire (n)
laiako, satirize (v)
laiaku, satirical (adj)
laiakua, satirist (n doer)
laiath, lash (n)
laiatho, lash (v)
laiathua, lasher (n doer)
laidak, medium (n d:information flow)
laidaki, media (n pl d:information flow)
laidako, mediate (v d:information flow)
laidaku, medial (adj d:information flow)
laidakua, mediator (n doer d:information flow)
laidakuet, mediation (n)
laidashk, immediacy (n)
laidashkiu, immediately (adv)
laidashku, immediate (adj)
laifiap, emergency (n)
laifp, emergence (n)
laifpo, emerge (v)
laigaf, disaster (n)
laigafiu, disastrously (adv)
laigafu, disastrous (adj)
laikaln, galaxy (n)
lail, heir (n)
lail, heiress (n)
lailt, heredity (n)
lailtap, heritage (n)
lailthetsh, heirloom (n)
lailtu, hereditary (adj)
laip, dimness (n)
laipiu, dimly (adv)
laipo, dim (v)

laipu, dim (adj)
laipua, dimmer (n doer)
laish, joy (n)
laishiu, joyfully (adv)
laishnet, joystick (n)
laishu, joyful (adj)
laivun, twine (n)
laizh, hell (n)
laizhgiaul, hellfire (n)
laizhu, hellish (adj)
lakan, garment (n)
lakit, stove (n)
lakrenk, illogic (n)
lakrenku, illogical (adj)
lalfk, commerce (n)
lalfkan, commercial (n)
lalfkiu, commercially (adv)
lalfku, commercial (adj)
lalg, calorie (n)
lalirt, licence (n)
lalirt, license (n)
lalirtmenu, licentious (adj)
lalirto, license (v)
lalirtuet, licensure (n)
lalirtuin, licencee (n)
laliter, liter (n)
lalivator, illiteracy (n)
lalivatoru, illiterate (adj)
lalpar, library (n)
lalparua, librarian (n doer)
lalt, lead (n d:in front)
laltemenu, leaderless (adj)
laltfif, leadership (n)
lalto, lead (v d:in front)
laltua, leader (n doer d:in front)
laltunf, leadoff (n)
laltunfu, leadoff (adj)
Lamail, May (n)
lamalt, original (n)
lamaltat, originality (n)
lamat, origin (n)
lamatiu, originally (adv)
lamato, originate (v)
lamatu, original (adj)
lamatua, originator (n doer)
lamatuet, origination (n)
lamdan, lambda (n)
landark, HalfFaceSymbol (n)
lanf, norm (n)
lanfiu, normally (adv)
lanfo, normalize (v)
lanfu, normal (adj)
lanfuet, normalization (n)
lanig, virtue (n)
lanigiu, virtuously (adv)
lanigu, virtuous (adj)
lank, composition (n)
lankar, composure (n)
lankit, composite (n)
lankitu, composite (adj)
lanko, compose (v)
lankua, composer (n doer)
lanp, nap (n)

lanpo, nap (v)
lanshk, exposure (n)
lanshko, expose (v)
lanshku, expository (adj)
lanshkua, exposer (n doer)
lanshkuet, exposition (n)
lant, gallantry (n)
Lanthanum, Lanthanum (n)
lantiu, gallantly (adv)
lantu, gallant (adj)
lanut, cameo (n)
lanutafk, illegitimacy (n)
lanutafku, illegitimate (adj)
lanutak, illegality (n)
lanutakiu, illegally (adv)
lanutaku, illegal (adj)
lanv, irony (n)
lanviu, ironically (adv)
lanvu, ironic (adj)
laom, run (n)
laomio, ran (v pa)
laomo, run (v)
laomoblaith, runaround (n)
laomopliol, runaway (n)
laompliol, runway (n)
laomtien, rundown (n)
laomu, runny (adj)
laomua, runner (n doer)
laomunf, runoff (n)
Laprel, April (n)
lapuet, session (n)
laran, rogation (n)
larano, rogate (v)
lardaik, vehemence (n)
lardaikiu, vehemently (adv)
lardaiku, vehement (adj)
lardat, medal (n)
lardato, medal (v)
lardatua, medalist (n doer)
lardit, vehicle (n)
larditu, vehicular (adj)
Larenshium, Lawrencium (n)
larf, roof (n)
larfdaup, rooftop (n)
larfo, roof (v)
larft, elephant (n)
larftu, elephantic (adj)
larfua, roofer (n doer)
largrag, despot (n)
largraguet, despotism (n)
Laril, EhoMonth01 (n)
larmeniu, fearlessly (adv)
larmenu, fearless (adj)
larmik, burlap (n)
larn, fear (n)
larnafap, lemonade (n)
larnan, lemon (n)
larniu, fearfully (adv)
larno, fear (v)
larnu, fearful (adj)
larp, left (n d:direction)
larpekliegu, leftwing (adj)
larpekliegua, leftist (n doer)

larpu, left (adj d:direction)
larpua, lefty (n doer d:direction)
larsh, cassette (n)
Larshial, Asia (n)
Larshian, Asian (n)
lart, rule (n)
larto, rule (v)
lartua, ruler (n doer)
lartvond, rulebook (n)
larukiu, intrinsically (adv)
laruku, intrinsic (adj)
Lash Veigash, Las Vegas (n)
lashk, cigar (n)
lashkef, cigarette (n)
lashp, breath (n)
lashpfrepu, breathable (adj)
lashpgokiu, breathtakingly (adv)
lashpgoku, breathtaking (adj)
lashpiu, breathily (adv)
lashpo, breathe (v)
lashpu, breathy (adj)
lashpua, breather (n doer)
lashtafku, illegible (adj)
latan, locum (n)
lath, roll (n d:bread)
lathp, cache (n)
lathpo, cache (v)
Latinf, Latin (n)
lauaf, satiation (n)
lauafo, satiate (v)
laub, oddity (n d:different)
laubiu, oddly (adv d:different)
laubo, odden (v d:different)
laubu, odd (adj d:different)
laufag, frigidity (n)
laufagu, frigid (adj)
laufo, bode (v)
lauit, satisfaction (n)
lauito, satisfy (v)
lauitu, satisfactory (adj)
lauk, planet (n)
lauku, planetary (adj)
Laukut, August (n)
laut, veil (n)
lauto, veil (v)
lavit, dissatisfaction (n)
lavito, dissatisfy (v)
lavufluan, twilight (n)
lavun, twin (n)
lazh, pride (n d:accomplishment)
lazhiu, proudly (adv
    d:accomplishment)
lazho, pride (v
    d:accomplishment)
Lead, Lead (n)
Lebanof, Lebanon (n)
Lebanonf, Lebanese (n)
lefgirn, concealment (n)
lefgirno, conceal (v)
lefgirnua, concealer (n doer)
lefshethiu, everlastingly (adv)
lefshethu, everlasting (adj)
leiam, oasis (n)

leiap, leer (n)
leiapliol, leeway (n)
leiapo, leer (v)
leiapu, leery (adj)
leid, nature (n)
leidiu, naturally (adv)
leidu, natural (adj)
leif, pinky (n)
leifliut, flattery (n d:praise)
leifliuto, flatter (v d:praise)
leikat, utility (n)
leikato, utilize (v)
leikatua, utilizer (n doer)
leikatuet, utilization (n)
leikatuetua, utilitarian (n doer)
leilat, utensil (n)
leinishoit, intestine (n)
leinishoitu, intestinal (adj)
leinp, pipe (n)
leinpo, pipe (v)
leinproif, pipeline (n)
leinpua, piper (n doer)
leinu, bland (adj)
leip, pin (n)
leipat, pinch (n)
leipato, pinch (v)
leipatua, pincher (n doer)
leipauk, pinnacle (n)
leipekeft, pinhead (n)
leipeklaip, pinprick (n)
leipekoiat, pinstripe (n)
leipekoiato, pinstripe (v)
leipemashp, pinball (n)
leipetaift, pinpoint (n)
leipetaifto, pinpoint (v)
leipo, pin (v)
leirp, pint (n)
leish, extra (n)
leisheif, exuberance (n)
leisheifiu, exuberantly (adv)
leisheifu, exuberant (adj)
leishgok, extradition (n)
leishgoko, extradite (v)
leishketaru, extraordinary (adj)
leishu, extra (adj)
leith, moisture (n)
leithiu, moistly (adv)
leitho, moisten (v)
leitho, moisturize (v)
leithu, moist (adj)
lcithua, moistener (n doer)
leithua, moisturizer (n doer)
lek, let (n)
lekio, let (v pa)
leko, let (v)
lektien, letdown (n)
lelm, cereal (n)
lemut, scarcity (n)
lemutoiu, scarcely (adv)
lemutu, scarce (adj)
lenbresh, complication (n)
lenbresho, complicate (v)
lenfk, compass (n)

lenk, commitment (n)
lenkat, commission (n)
lenkato, commission (v)
lenkatua, commissioner (n doer)
lenko, commit (v)
lenkua, committee (n doer)
lenshal, companionship (n)
lenshalua, companion (n doer)
lenshap, company (n)
lenshapo, accompany (v)
lenshkit, commotion (n)
lenshkito, commove (v)
lenshluak, commutation (n)
lenshluako, commute (v)
lenshluakua, commuter (n doer)
lentild, commencement (n)
lentildo, commence (v)
lep, meet (n)
lepark, meteor (n)
leparkat, meteorite (n)
lepio, met (v pa)
lepo, meet (v)
lerf, L (let sng)
lerfhem, Number_1e1056
lerfi, Ls (let pl)
lerfital, everywhere (adv)
lerflizh, everything (n/pron)
lerfshlad, everybody (pron)
lerfton, everyone (pron)
lerfu, every (adj)
lerfviul, everyday (n)
lerfviulu, everyday (adj)
lesh, wave (n)
leshko, waver (v)
lesho, wave (v)
leshrazh, wavelength (n)
lethruf, sugar (n)
lethrufo, sugar (v)
lethrufu, sugary (adj)
liafk, exhaust (n)
liafkiu, exhaustively (adv)
liafko, exhaust (v)
liafku, exhaustive (adj)
liag, cold (n d:illness)
liail, turret (n)
liaish, trophy (n)
liak, chore (n)
lialk, wink (n)
lialko, wink (v)
lialt, word (n)
lialtfnith, wordsmith (n)
lialto, word (v)
lialtu, wordy (adj)
lian, scan (n)
liank, camouflage (n)
lianko, camouflage (v)
liano, scan (v)
lianua, scanner (n doer)
liap, read (n)
liapio, read (v pa)
liapo, read (v)
liapu, readable (adj)
liapua, reader (n doer)

liapuafif, readership (n)
liapuil, readout (n)
liarfk, exhaustion (n)
liath, scarf (n)
liatu, nautical (adj)
liau, bye (n/interj)
liauk, raid (n)
liauko, raid (v)
liaukua, raider (n doer)
liaunu, marine (adj)
liaunua, mariner (n doer)
liaup, marina (n)
liaushneto, maroon (v)
liauth, marsh (n)
liauthraup, marshland (n)
liauthu, marshy (adj)
liav, navy (n)
liavat, navigation (n)
liavato, navigate (v)
liavatua, navigator (n doer)
liavu, naval (adj)
liavuk, twinkle (n)
liavuko, twinkle (v)
libesh, settlement (n)
libesho, settle (v)
libeshua, settler (n doer)
Libiaf, Libya (n)
Libian, Libyan (n)
libit, sediment (n)
libito, sedimentate (v)
libitu, sedimentary (adj)
libituet, sedimentation (n)
lidiut, nucleus (n)
lidiuti, nuclei (n pl)
lidiutu, nuclear (adj)
lidof, era (n)
lidup, obesity (n)
lidupiu, obesely (adv)
lidupu, obese (adj)
lieblefu, oncoming (adj)
liefep, onset (n)
liefkletu, onscreen (adj)
lieglorfu, onboard (adj)
liehushiu, onward (adv)
liem, on (prep)
liemavifu, ongoing (adj)
liensh, amnesty (n)
lienulartu, onshore (adj)
liereiginua, onlooker (n doer)
lieshriaut, onslaught (n)
llet, idea (n)
lietiu, ideally (adv)
lieto, idealize (v)
lietrak, onstage (n)
lietraku, onstage (adj)
lietu, ideal (adj)
lifab, stem (n)
lifabo, stem (v)
lifad, shirt (n)
lifezh, meagerness (n)
lifezhatu, measly (adj)
lifezhiu, meagerly (adv)
lifezhu, meager (adj)

lifk, nutrient (n)
lifkuet, nutrition (n)
lifkuetiu, nutritionally (adv)
lifkuetu, nutritional (adj)
lifkuetua, nutritionist (n doer)
lifp, discern (n)
lifpo, discern (v)
ligap, solid (n)
ligapiu, solidly (adv)
ligapo, solidify (v)
ligapu, solid (adj)
ligrag, solution (n)
ligrago, solve (v)
ligragu, solvable (adj)
ligragua, solver (n doer)
ligrap, solvent (n)
ligrapu, soluble (adj)
ligrapuet, solvency (n)
ligrat, solute (n)
ligul, string (n)
ligulio, strung (v pa)
ligulkiu, stringently (adv)
ligulku, stringent (adj)
ligulo, string (v)
likapiu, properly (adv)
likapu, proper (adj)
likim, prop (n)
likimo, prop (v)
lilakluaf, microscope (n)
lilan, serenity (n)
lilaniu, serenely (adv)
lilanu, serene (adj)
lildeior, microfilm (n)
lilesh, microwave (n)
lilesho, microwave (v)
lilip, sermon (n)
lilmiekuit, microbiology (n)
lilmiekuitua, microbiologist (n
    doer)
lilp, final (n)
lilpiu, finally (adv)
lilpo, finalize (v)
lilpu, final (adj)
lilpua, finalist (n doer)
lilsharshtuk, microsystem (n)
lilt, burrow (n)
lilto, burrow (v)
liltua, burrower (n doer)
lilup, microbe (n)
lilupu, microbial (adj)
liluyap, microphone (n)
limaf, furniture (n)
limafo, furnish (v)
limak, scandal (n)
limakiu, scandalously (adv)
limako, scandalize (v)
limaku, scandalous (adj)
limauk, raunchiness (n)
limauku, raunchy (adj)
limen, morning (n)
limet, meter (n d:metric
    measurement)
limfnilt, miniskirt (n)

limk, miniature (n)
limko, miniaturize (v)
limku, miniature (adj)
limnilf, miniseries (n)
limork, ranch (n)
limorko, ranch (v)
limorkua, rancher (n doer)
limsh, minimum (n)
limshiu, minimally (adv)
limsho, minimize (v)
limshu, minimal (adj)
limshua, minimalist (n doer)
limshuet, minimalism (n)
limshuet, minimalization (n)
limth, min (n)
limush, minus (adj/prep)
limush, minus (v)
limushi, minuses (n pl)
limzhaun, minivan (n)
linal, sheer (n d:clear)
linaliu, sheer (adv d:clear)
linalu, sheer (adj d:clear)
linash, trousers (n)
linf, finance (n)
linfiu, financially (adv)
linfo, finance (v)
linfu, financial (adj)
linfua, financier (n doer)
linpiu, fiscally (adv)
linpu, fiscal (adj)
linun, note (n d:music)
lioil, woe (n)
lioiliu, woefully (adv)
lioilu, woeful (adj)
lioith, moor (n d:marsh)
liop, ruby (n)
lipin, bikini (n)
liplut, orbit (n)
lipluto, orbit (v)
liplutu, orbital (adj)
liplutua, orbiter (n doer)
liraifp, triumph (n)
liraifpiu, triumphantly (adv)
liraifpo, triumph (v)
liraifpu, triumphal (adj)
liraifpu, triumphant (adj)
lird, blood (n)
lirdiu, bloodily (adv)
lirdo, bleed (v)
lirdu, bloody (adj)
lirdua, bleeder (n doer)
lirf, scent (n)
lirfo, scent (v)
lirlat, publication (n)
lirlato, publish (v)
lirlatua, publisher (n doer)
lirlimet, centimeter (n)
lirn, rum (n)
lirol, color (n)
liroliu, colorfully (adv)
lirolo, color (v)
lirolu, colorful (adj)
lirpaf, republic (n)

lirpafua, republican (n doer)
lirpuk, publicity (n)
lirpuko, publicize (v)
lirput, public (n)
lirputiu, publicly (adv)
lirputu, public (adj)
lirsh, lily (n)
lirt, cent (n)
lirtat, century (n)
lisho, belittle (v)
lishp, decency (n)
lishpiu, decently (adv)
lishpu, decent (adj)
lishtan, tint (n)
lishtano, tint (v)
lishu, little (adj)
litag, obituary (n)
litan, plan (n)
litanirk, plantation (n)
litank, plant (n d:factory)
litano, plan (v)
litanua, planner (n doer)
Lithium, Lithium (n)
Lithuaniaf, Lithuania (n)
Lithuanian, Lithuanian (n)
litik, dye (n)
litiko, dye (v)
litikua, dyer (n doer)
liubafk, constriction (n)
liubafko, constrict (v)
liubafkua, constrictor (n doer)
liubaft, conjunction (n)
liubafto, conjoin (v)
liubaif, conviction (n)
liubaifo, convict (v)
liubaifua, convict (n doer)
liubaipiu, convincingly (adv)
liubaipo, convince (v)
liubarkat, conductivity (n)
liubiafaf, consecration (n)
liubiafafo, consecrate (v)
liubish, contrivance (n)
liubisho, contrive (v)
liubot, confusion (n)
liubotiu, confusingly (adv)
liuboto, confuse (v)
liubref, condensation (n)
liubrefit, condensate (n)
liubrefo, condense (v)
liubrefua, condenser (n doer)
liubup, contentment (n
    d:satisfied)
liubupiu, contently (adv
    d:satisfied)
liubupu, content (adj d:satisfied)
liudift, contraption (n)
liudoshp, concoction (n)
liudoshpo, concoct (v)
liudret, concentration (n)
liudreto, concentrate (v)
liudretua, concentrator (n doer)
liudrom, constellation (n)
liudromo, constellate (v)

liufadek, consortium (n)
liufadeko, consort (v)
liufadekua, consort (n doer)
liufdauf, conspiracy (n)
liufdaufo, conspire (v)
liufdaufu, conspiratorial (adj)
liufdaufua, conspirator (n doer)
liufialt, consumption (n)
liufialto, consume (v)
liufialtua, consumer (n doer)
liufim, convention (n)
liufimo, convene (v)
liufimu, conventional (adj)
liufirm, convenience (n)
liufirmiu, conveniently (adv)
liufirmu, convenient (adj)
liuflarn, confrontation (n)
liuflarno, confront (v)
liuflarnu, confrontational (adj)
liufoit, convex (n)
liufoitu, convex (adj)
liufp, concern (n)
liufpo, concern (v)
liufual, conveyance (n)
liufualk, convoy (n)
liufualo, convey (v)
liufualu, conveyable (adj)
liufualua, conveyor (n doer)
liugalf, concurrence (n)
liugalf, concurrency (n)
liugalfiu, concurrently (adv)
liugalfo, concur (v)
liugalfu, concurrent (adj)
liugalt, contraction (n d:shrink)
liugalto, contract (v d:shrink)
liugef, conference (n)
liugefo, confer (v)
liugeft, conferment (n)
liugefua, conferor (n doer)
liugefuin, conferee (n)
liugego, condone (v)
liuglap, conglomerate (n)
liuglapo, conglomerate (v)
liugoit, concussion (n)
liugoito, concuss (v)
liugrik, consolation (n d:comfort)
liugriko, console (v d:comfort)
liugrut, conclusion (n)
liugrutiu, conclusively (adv)
liugruto, conclude (v)
liugrutu, conclusive (adj)
liukarg, contour (n)
liukargo, contour (v)
liukaval, congregation (n)
liukavalo, congregate (v)
liukavalu, congregational (adj)
liukemif, convolvement (n)
liukemifo, convolve (v)
liukemt, convolution (n)
liukemto, convolute (v)
liukiag, congestion (n)
liukiago, congest (v)
liukik, conflict (n)

liukiko, conflict (v)
liukinp, congratulation (n)
liukinpo, congratulate (v)
liukiot, contortion (n)
liukioto, contort (v)
liukirko, conduce (v)
liukirku, conducive (adj)
liukirkua, conducer (n doer)
liuklat, congruence (n)
liuklat, congruousness (n)
liuklatiu, congruently (adv)
liuklatiu, congruously (adv)
liuklatu, congruent (adj)
liuklatu, congruous (adj)
liukoft, conservation (n)
liukoftan, conservative (n)
liukoftiu, conservatively (adv)
liukofto, conserve (v)
liukoftu, conservative (adj)
liukoftua, conservationist (n doer)
liukoftuet, conservatism (n)
liukorft, conservatory (n)
liukriuk, conduction (n)
liukriuko, conduct (v)
liukriuku, conductive (adj)
liukriukua, conductor (n doer)
liukult, configuration (n)
liukulto, configure (v)
liukultua, configurator (n doer)
liulait, contrast (n)
liulaito, contrast (v)
liulark, consignment (n)
liularko, consign (v)
liulf, consent (n)
liulfat, consensus (n)
liulfo, consent (v)
liulfu, consensual (adj)
liulig, console (n d:cabinet)
liuligap, consolidation (n)
liuligapo, consolidate (v)
liuligapua, consolidator (n doer)
liulinp, confiscation (n)
liulinpo, confiscate (v)
liulinpu, confiscatory (adj)
lium, conceit (n)
liumeig, convergence (n)
liumeigo, converge (v)
liumeigu, convergent (adj)
liumiart, confluence (n)
liumiartu, confluent (adj)
liumid, connotation (n)
liumido, connote (v)
liumiug, contagion (n)
liumiugiu, contagious (adv)
liumiuk, contamination (n)
liumiuko, contaminate (v)
liumiukua, contaminant (n doer)
liumo, conceit (v)
liun, confession (n)
liunan, confessional (n)
liuneip, contusion (n)
liuneipo, contuse (v)
liuno, confess (v)

liunua, confessor (n doer)
liunuif, confirmation (n)
liunuifo, confirm (v)
liupaib, contact (n)
liupaibo, contact (v)
liupaibua, contact (n doer)
liupaiv, confederacy (n)
liupaiv, confederation (n)
liupaivo, confederate (v)
liupaivua, confederate (n doer)
liupaug, concave (n)
liupaugiu, concavely (adv)
liupaugo, concave (v)
liupaugu, concave (adj)
liupifk, contention (n d:challenge)
liupifko, contend (v d:challenge)
liupifku, contentious (adj
    d:challenge)
liupifkua, contender (n doer
    d:challenge)
liuplaipo, construe (v)
liuplaipua, construer (n doer)
liupluzh, condolence (n)
liupluzho, condole (v)
liuprin, confidence (n)
liuprinfiu, confidentially (adv)
liuprinfu, confidential (adj)
liuprino, confide (v)
liuprinu, confident (adj)
liuprinua, confidant (n doer)
liuprulk, constraint (n)
liuprulko, constrain (v)
liurilp, consternation (n)
liurilpo, consternate (v)
liurshp, conception (n)
liushant, consonant (n)
liushlek, construction (n)
liushleko, construct (v)
liushleku, constructive (adj)
liushlekua, constructor (n doer)
liushp, concept (n)
liushpelt, constitution (n)
liushpeltiu, constitutionally (adv)
liushpelto, constitute (v)
liushpeltu, constitutional (adj)
liushpfrepiu, conceivably (adv)
liushpfrepu, conceivable (adj)
liushpiu, conceptually (adv)
liushpo, conceive (v)
liushpu, conceptual (adj)
liushrig, conscription (n)
liushrigo, conscript (v)
liushtib, context (n)
liushtit, contest (n)
liushtito, contest (v)
liushtitua, contestant (n doer)
liushuftiu, consecutively (adv)
liushufto, consecute (v)
liushuftu, consecutive (adj)
liushulto, confound (v)
liutav, contrition (n)
liutaviu, contritely (adv)
liutavu, contrite (adj)

liutelk, consistency (n)
liutelkiu, consistently (adv)
liutelko, consist (v)
liutelku, consistent (adj)
liutep, conjecture (n)
liutepo, conjecture (v)
liutharf, conversation (n)
liutharfiu, conversationally (adv)
liutharfo, converse (v)
liutharfu, conversational (adj)
liutharfua, conversationalist (n
    doer)
liuthark, conversion (n)
liutharko, convert (v)
liutharku, convertible (adj)
liutharkua, converter (n doer)
liuthift, convection (n)
liuthifto, convect (v)
liuthishkiu, concisely (adv)
liuthishku, concise (adj)
liuthot, consideration (n)
liuthotaru, considerate (adj)
liuthotiu, considerably (adv)
liuthoto, consider (v)
liuthotu, considerable (adj)
liuthufk, conspectus (n)
liutifk, condition (n)
liutifkiu, conditionally (adv)
liutifko, condition (v)
liutifku, conditional (adj)
liutifkua, conditioner (n doer)
liutioth, contingency (n)
liutiothu, contingent (adj)
liutir, continuation (n)
liutiriu, continually (adv)
liutiriu, continuously (adv)
liutiro, continue (v)
liutiru, continual (adj)
liutiru, continuous (adj)
liutreb, convulsion (n)
liutrebiu, convulsedly (adv)
liutrebo, convulse (v)
liutrebu, convulsible (adj)
liutrelk, constant (n)
liutrelkiu, constantly (adv)
liutrelku, constant (adj)
liutrelkuet, constancy (n)
liuvaft, contempt (n)
liuvaftu, contemptable (adj)
liuvant, consultation (n)
liuvanto, consult (v)
liuvantua, consultant (n doer)
liuvarfk, contemplation (n)
liuvarfko, contemplate (v)
liuvek, concession (n)
liuveko, concede (v)
liuviag, constipation (n)
liuviago, constipate (v)
liuviauk, condemnation (n)
liuviauko, condemn (v)
liuvirt, confection (n)
liuvirtar, confectionery (n)
liuvirto, confect (v)

liuvorg, congress (n)
liuvorgu, congressional (adj)
liuvorgua, congressman (n doer)
liuvorn, conformity (n)
liuvorno, conform (v)
liuvornua, conformer (n doer)
liuvornua, conformist (n doer)
liuvornuet, conformance (n)
liuvuat, confinement (n)
liuvuato, confine (v)
liuzhil, concert (n)
liuzhilo, concert (v)
livaft, literature (n)
livaftu, literary (adj)
livan, ivy (n)
livasht, literal (n)
livashtiu, literally (adv)
livashtu, literal (adj)
livat, literacy (n)
livatoru, literate (adj)
livienp, phenomenon (n)
livienpi, phenomena (n pl)
livienpu, phenominal (adj)
livon, libel (n)
livono, libel (v)
livonu, libelous (adj)
lizhan, pizza (n)
lobifk, ordeal (n)
lobriak, perusal (n)
lobriako, peruse (v)
lobruntiu, perpendicularly (adv)
lobruntu, perpendicular (adj)
lobuk, support (n)
lobukiu, supportively (adv)
lobuko, support (v)
lobuku, supportable (adj)
lobuku, supportive (adj)
lobukua, supporter (n doer)
lodalpo, perturb (v)
lodokat, persecution (n)
lodokato, persecute (v)
lodokatua, persecutor (n doer)
lofam, orange (n d:color)
lofamu, orange (adj d:color)
lofan, curtain (n)
lofdauf, perspiration (n)
lofdaufo, perspire (v)
lofin, orchestra (n)
lofiniu, orchestrally (adv)
lofino, orchestrate (v)
lofinu, orchestral (adj)
lofinua, orchestrator (n doer)
lofinuet, orchestration (n)
lofko, curtail (v)
lofp, curve (n)
lofpar, curvature (n)
lofpo, curve (v)
lofpu, curvy (adj)
logaf, pocket (n)
logafbiep, pocketful (n)
logafevond, pocketbook (n)
logafo, pocket (v)
logafua, pocketer (n doer)

logath, rabbit (n)
loidian, perpetuation (n)
loidian, perpetuity (n)
loidianiu, perpetually (adv)
loidiano, perpetuate (v)
loidianu, perpetual (adj)
loidio, wrote (v pa)
loido, write (v)
loidoip, comedy (n)
loidoipiu, comically (adv)
loidoipu, comical (adj)
loidoipua, comedian (n doer)
loidoipua, comic (n doer)
loidua, writer (n doer)
loikan, shin (n)
loikaut, discord (n)
loinam, romance (n)
loinamiu, romatically (adv)
loinamo, romanticize (v)
loinamu, romantic (adj)
loinamua, romancer (n doer)
loip, wrist (n)
loipluk, wristwatch (n)
loipshtaim, wristband (n)
loir kodi, ought (ndal d:desire)
loir, desire (n)
loiriu, desirably (adv)
loiro, desire (v)
loiru, desirable (adj)
loishp, lobster (n)
loith, sir (n)
loithk, sire (n)
loithko, sire (v)
loithu, sir (adj)
loitien, seepage (n)
loitieno, seep (v)
loitifo, seethe (v)
loitio, sought (v pa)
loito, seek (v)
loitua, seeker (n doer)
loiv, nerve (n)
loivekuit, neurology (n)
loivekuitu, neurological (adj)
loivekuitua, neurologist (n doer)
loivemoft, neurosurgery (n)
loivemoftua, neurosurgeon (n
    doer)
loiveshuash, neuroscience (n)
loiveshuashua, neuroscientist (n
    doer)
loivet, neuron (n)
loivethonok, neurotransmission
    (n)
loivethonoko, neurotransmit (v)
loivethonokua, neurotransmitter
    (n doer)
loivetu, neural (adj)
loivip, nervousness (n)
loivipiu, nervously (adv)
loivipu, nervous (adj)
loivo, nerve (v)
loivraik, neurosis (n)
loivraiku, neurotic (adj)

loivu, nervy (adj)
lokapo, poach (v)
lokapua, poacher (n doer)
lokilk, perseverance (n)
lokilko, persevere (v)
lokior, perfume (n)
lokioro, perfume (v)
Loktaf, October (n)
lolaf, kerchief (n)
lolf, dear (n)
lolfiu, dearly (adv)
lolfo, endear (v)
lolfu, dear (adj)
lolirt, percent (n)
lolirtat, percentage (n)
lomap, gallop (n)
lomapo, gallop (v)
lond, entrance (n)
lond, entry (n)
londiush, enterprise (n)
londiusho, enterprise (v)
londiushua, entrepreneur (n
    doer)
londo, enter (v)
London, London (n)
londpliol, entryway (n)
londua, entrant (n doer)
lonk, permit (n)
lonkat, permanence (n)
lonkatiu, permanently (adv)
lonkatu, permanent (adj)
lonki, permit (n pl)
lonko, permit (v)
lopifto, pertain (v)
lopiftu, pertinent (adj)
lor, all (adj)
loraf, twiddle (n)
lorafo, twiddle (v)
lorak, pejorative (n)
lordikefil, altogether (adv)
lordolu, already (adv)
lorf kodi, might (ndal
    d:possibility)
lorf, possibility (n)
lorfiu, possibly (adv)
lorfu, possible (adj)
lorg, cracker (n d:saltine)
lorgertu, almighty (adj)
lorhoish, always (adv)
lork, chorus (n)
lorko, choir (v)
lorkua, choir (n doer)
lorm, milk (n)
lormo, milk (v)
lormu, milky (adj)
lormua, milker (n doer)
lornoif, maybe (n)
lornoifiu, maybe (adv)
lorp, thumb (n)
lorpo, thumb (v)
lorpthrin, thumbnail (n)
lorsh, pulse (n)
lorsho, pulse (v)

lorsht, pulsation (n)
lorshto, pulsate (v)
lorshtua, pulsator (n doer)
lorshua, pulser (n doer)
lort, flavor (n)
lorto, flavor (v)
lorv, darling (n)
lorvu, darling (adj)
lorwak, almost (adv)
Losh Ankelesh, Los Angeles (n)
Loshiaf, EhoDay01 (n)
loship, perception (n)
loshipiu, perceptively (adv)
loshipo, perceive (v)
loshipu, perceptive (adj)
loshipua, perceiver (n doer)
loshluak, permutation (n)
loshluako, permutate (v)
losht, rather (adv/interj)
lotelk, persistence (n)
lotelkiu, persistently (adv)
lotelko, persist (v)
lotelku, persistent (adj)
lotharf, perversion (n)
lotharfiu, perversely (adv)
lotharfo, perverse (v)
lotharfu, perverse (adj)
lotharfua, pervert (n doer)
lothark, perversity (n)
lotharko, pervert (v)
lothrat, perforation (n)
lothrato, perforate (v)
lothuk, perspective (n)
lovirt, perfection (n)
lovirtiu, perfectly (adv)
lovirto, perfect (v)
lovirtu, perfect (adj)
lovorn, performance (n)
lovorno, perform (v)
lovornua, performer (n doer)
lovotet, perpetration (n)
lovoteto, perpetrate (v)
lovotetua, perpetrator (n doer)
lowang, whose (pron)
lowefel, whoever (pron)
lowei, who (pron)
lowei, whom (pron)
lozhankiu, pervasively (adv)
lozhanko, pervade (v)
lozhanku, pervasive (adj)
luafk, education (n)
luafko, educate (v)
luafku, educational (adj)
luafkua, educator (n doer)
luaftap, reestablishment (n)
luaftapo, reestablish (v)
luaik, salute (n)
luaiko, salute (v)
luaikuet, salutation (n)
luaith, salinity (n)
luaitho, salinate (v)
luaithu, saline (adj)
luak, refuge (n)

luakuin, refugee (n)
lual, laugh (n)
lualar, laughter (n)
lualiu, laughably (adv)
lualo, laugh (v)
lualu, laughable (adj)
lualua, laugher (n doer)
luam, mire (n)
luamo, mire (v)
luap, luster (n)
luapat, illustration (n)
luapatiu, illustratively (adv)
luapato, illustrate (v)
luapatu, illustrative (adj)
luapatua, illustrator (n doer)
luapo, luster (v)
luapu, lustrous (adj)
luar, child (n)
luarfif, childhood (n)
luari, children (n pl)
luaridrup, reinterpretation (n)
luaridrupo, reinterpret (v)
luarkeif, childcare (n)
luarokriuk, reintroduction (n)
luarokriuko, reintroduce (v)
luartemt, kindergarten (n)
luartemtua, kindergartener (n
    doer)
luaru, childish (adj)
luarvalsh, childbirth (n)
luash, luxury (n)
luashiu, luxuriously (adv)
luashu, luxurious (adj)
luath, salt (n)
luatheidon, saltwater (n)
luathiu, saltily (adv)
luatho, salt (v)
luathu, salty (adj)
luathua, salter (n doer)
lubafk, restriction (n)
lubafkiu, restrictively (adv)
lubafko, restrict (v)
lubafku, restrictive (adj)
lubafkua, restricter (n doer)
lubaift, resource (n)
lubaiftiu, resourcefully (adv)
lubaiftu, resourceful (adj)
lubaiftuet, resourcefulness (n)
lubalfk, recalibration (n)
lubalfko, recalibrate (v)
lubeitat, repurchase (n)
lubeitato, repurchase (v)
lubeith, reimbursement (n)
lubeitho, reimburse (v)
lubiaufo, redoubt (v)
lubiaufu, redoubtable (adj)
lubish, retrieval (n)
lubisho, retrieve (v)
lubishua, retriever (n doer)
lubiut, restatement (n)
lubiuto, restate (v)
lublaik, rebuttal (n)
lublaiko, rebut (v)

lublash, repression (n)
lublasho, repress (v)
lublashu, repressive (adj)
lublashua, repressor (n doer)
lubleg, reclassification (n)
lublego, reclassify (v)
lubolk, repair (n)
lubolko, repair (v)
lubolku, repairable (adj)
lubolku, reparable (adj)
lubolkua, repairer (n doer)
lubolkua, repairman (n doer)
lubrepo, replant (v)
lubresh, replacement (n)
lubresho, replace (v)
lubreshu, replaceable (adj)
lubreshua, replacer (n doer)
lubriako, reuse (v)
lubrieno, rename (v)
lubrono, regroup (v)
lubuash, rehearsal (n)
lubuasho, rehearse (v)
lubugato, repackage (v)
lubulsh, rebuff (n)
lubulsho, rebuff (v)
lubup, refill (n)
lubupo, refill (v)
ludaiat, rescue (n)
ludaiato, rescue (v)
ludaiatua, rescuer (n doer)
ludairo, retype (v)
ludaltho, recover (v d:resurface)
ludalthu, recoverable (adj
    d:resurface)
ludan, reverberation (n)
ludano, reverberate (v)
ludart, relation (n)
ludartfif, relationship (n)
ludartfifiu, relationally (adv)
ludartfifu, relational (adj)
ludartiu, relatively (adv)
ludarto, relate (v)
ludartu, relative (adj)
ludartua, relative (n doer)
ludauto, rebuke (v)
ludefp, recap (n)
ludefpo, recap (v)
ludeirt, redesign (n)
ludeirto, redesign (v)
ludolk, recapitalization (n)
ludelko, recapitalize (v)
ludelshik, refractory (adj)
ludelshk, refraction (n)
ludelshko, refract (v)
ludelshku, refractive (adj)
ludepio, rethought (v pa)
ludepo, rethink (v)
ludeshiak, recapture (n)
ludeshiako, recapture (v)
ludiadaro, remodel (v)
ludian, rediscovery (n)
ludiano, rediscover (v)
ludiato, rejoin (v)

ludib, retry (n)
ludibag, retrial (n)
ludibo, retry (v)
ludidan, resemblance (n)
ludidano, resemble (v)
ludiof, retrenchment (n)
ludiofo, retrench (v)
ludorbid, rebroadcast (n)
ludorbidio, rebroadcast (v pa)
ludorbido, rebroadcast (v)
ludrab, restoration (n)
ludrabiu, restoratively (adv)
ludrabo, restore (v)
ludrabu, restorative (adj)
ludrabua, restorer (n doer)
ludraip, rebound (n)
ludraipo, rebound (v)
ludrat, repentance (n)
ludrato, repent (v)
ludratu, repentant (adj)
ludrauk, recruitment (n)
ludrauko, recruit (v)
ludraukua, recruiter (n doer)
ludriko, recrease (v)
ludruk, reprehension (n)
ludruki, reprehension (n pl)
ludrukiu, reprehensively (adv)
ludruko, reprehend (v)
ludruku, reprehensive (adj)
luduash, representation (n)
luduasho, represent (v)
luduashiu, representative (adj)
luduashua, representative (n
    doer)
ludufk, revenge (n)
ludufko, revenge (v)
ludufp, response (n)
ludufpiu, responsively (adv)
ludufpo, respond (v)
ludufpu, responsive (adj)
ludufpua, responder (n doer)
ludufpuin, respondent (n)
luduvek, responsibility (n)
luduvekiu, responsibly (adv)
luduveku, responsible (adj)
luefbino, reopen (v)
lueif, ladle (n)
lueifo, ladle (v)
lueito, ladle (v)
lueivezh, ladybug (n)
lufabak, refutation (n)
lufabako, refute (v)
lufabot, refusion (n d:join again)
lufaboto, refuse (v d:join again)
lufadeko, resort (v d:sort again)
lufaven, nickname (n)
lufaveno, nickname (v)
lufdauf, respiration (n)
lufdaufo, respirate (v)
lufdaufu, respiratory (adj)
lufdaufua, respirator (n doer)
lufep, reset (n)
lufepio, reset (v pa)

lufepo, reset (v)
lufepua, resetter (n doer)
lufiaish, revision (n)
lufiaisho, revise (v)
lufiaishuet, revisionism (n)
lufiaishuetua, revisionist (n doer)
lufialt, resumption (n)
lufialto, resume (v)
lufialtua, resumer (n doer)
lufiarf, refresh (n)
lufiarfiu, refreshingly (adv)
lufiarfo, refresh (v)
lufiarft, refreshment (n)
lufiarfua, refresher (n doer)
lufioko, retool (v)
lufiunelko, reprogram (v)
lufiuveto, reprocess (v)
luflaud, reproach (n)
luflaudo, reproach (v)
luflaufto, relive (v)
luflioth, reprieve (n)
luflumo, reshape (v)
lufp, nick (n)
lufpo, nick (v)
lufranto, relay (v d:place again)
lufriasho, rekindle (v)
lufrifo, restock (v)
lufrilt, reorganization (n)
lufrilto, reorganize (v)
lufriltua, reorganizer (n doer)
lufruif, replay (n)
lufruifo, replay (v)
lufruifua, replayer (n doer)
lufrulko, refrain (v d:abstain)
lufuam, revelation (n)
lufuamo, reveal (v)
lufuat, review (n)
lufuato, review (v)
lufuatu, rearview (adj)
lufuatua, reviewer (n doer)
lufurshmenu, relentless (adj)
lufursho, relent (v)
lugaiap, recoil (n)
lugaiapo, recoil (v)
lugalf, recurrence (n)
lugalfiu, recurrently (adv)
lugalfo, recur (v)
lugalfu, recurrent (adj)
lugalt, retraction (n)
lugalto, retract (v)
lugaltu, retractable (adj)
lugardak, recalculation (n)
lugardako, recalculate (v)
lugarp, recollection (n)
lugarpo, recollect (v)
lugasho, retrace (v)
lugat, rebellion (n)
lugatiu, rebelliously (adv)
lugato, rebel (v)
lugatu, rebellious (adj)
lugatua, rebel (n doer)
lugef, referral (n)
lugefo, refer (v)

lugefua, referer (n doer)
lugefuin, referee (n)
lugesh, reference (n)
lugeshan, referendum (n)
lugeshani, referenda (n pl)
lugeshiu, referentially (adv)
lugesho, reference (v)
lugeshu, referential (adj)
luget, reflection (n)
lugetiu, reflectively (adv)
lugeto, reflect (v)
lugetu, reflective (adj)
lugetua, reflector (n doer)
lugiap, rebate (n)
lugiapo, rebate (v)
lugiash, recursal (n)
lugiashiu, recursively (adv)
lugiasho, recurse (v)
lugiashu, recursive (adj)
lugiashua, recurser (n doer)
lugir, recall (n)
lugiro, recall (v)
lugirua, recaller (n doer)
lugloit, recharge (n)
lugloito, recharge (v)
lugloitu, rechargeable (adj)
lugloitua, recharger (n doer)
lugoifto, refocus (v)
lugoit, recusal (n)
lugoito, recuse (v)
lugokio, retook (v pa)
lugoko, retake (v)
lugrag, resolution (n)
lugrago, resolve (v)
lugragu, resolute (adj)
lugragua, resolver (n doer)
lugrasho, repaint (v)
lugreik, reincarnation (n)
lugreiko, reincarnate (v)
lugrut, recluse (n)
lugrutiu, reclusively (adv)
lugrutu, reclusive (adj)
luguvat, reinvention (n)
luguvato, reinvent (v)
luhaush, reward (n)
luhausho, reward (v)
luhaushua, rewarder (n doer)
luiaf, silo (n)
luiako, reckon (v)
luiash, retardation (n)
luiasho, retard (v)
luiashu, retardant (adj)
luiatmen, recklessness (n)
luiatmeniu, recklessly (adv)
luiatmenu, reckless (adj)
luiato, reck (v)
luibit, reinvestment (n)
luibito, reinvest (v)
luif, rein (n)
luifo, rein (v)
luigep, reelection (n)
luigepo, reelect (v)
luik, rally (n)

luiko, rally (v)
luim, bust (n d:sculpture)
luin, sill (n)
luipeikano, reinvigorate (v)
luipliol, railway (n)
luish, rise (n)
luishet, reinsertion (n)
luisheto, reinsert (v)
Luishiaf, Louisiana (n)
luishio, rose (v pa)
luisho, rise (v)
luishpelt, reinstitution (n)
luishpelto, reinstitute (v)
luishrel, reinsurance (n)
luishrelo, reinsure (v)
luishrelua, reinsurer (n doer)
luishua, riser (n doer)
luit, rail (n)
luitegrel, railcar (n)
luiteir, reinstallation (n)
luiteiro, reinstall (v)
luithuato, reemphasize (v)
luito, rail (v)
luitrelsh, railroad (n)
luitrelsho, railroad (v)
luiunu, retro (adj)
luiupaft, retrofit (n)
luiupafto, retrofit (v)
luiupaltak, retroactivity (n)
luiupaltakiu, retroactively (adv)
luiupaltaku, retroactive (adj)
luiushtranu, retrograde (adj)
luiuthuk, retrospect (n)
luiuthuku, retrospective (adj)
luk, watch (n d:clock)
lukaim, return (n)
lukaimo, return (v)
lukaimua, returner (n doer)
lukeifto, redouble (v)
lukelk, revisitation (n)
lukelko, revisit (v)
lukemif, revolution (n d:journey
   around)
lukemifo, revolve (v d:journey
   around)
lukemifua, revolver (n doer
   d:journey around)
luketo, recheck (v)
lukiglako, reimpose (v)
lukioko, rework (v)
lukirk, reduction (n)
lukirkiu, reducibly (adv)
lukirko, reduce (v)
lukirku, reducible (adj)
lukirkua, reducer (n doer)
lukiuf, redemption (n)
lukiufo, redeem (v)
lukiufu, redeemable (adj)
lukiufu, redemptive (adj)
lukiufua, redeemer (n doer)
luklal, relaxation (n)
luklalo, relax (v)
luknagua, watchmaker (n doer)

lukofat, reserve (n d:military)
lukofatua, reservist (n doer d:military)
lukofp, reservoir (n)
lukoft, reserve (n d:storage)
lukofto, reserve (v d:storage)
lukoftua, reserver (n doer d:storage)
lukoftuet, reservation (n)
lukriaf, requalification (n)
lukriafo, requalify (v)
lukriafua, requalifier (n doer)
lukriat, renegotiation (n)
lukriato, renegotiate (v)
lukroif, reclination (n)
lukroifo, recline (v)
lukroifua, recliner (n doer)
lukrosh, research (n)
lukrosho, research (v)
lukroshua, researcher (n doer)
lukuafk, redirection (n)
lukuafko, redirect (v)
lukuano, regain (v)
lulaid, remedy (n)
lulaidak, remediation (n)
lulaidako, remediate (v)
lulaidakua, remediator (n doer)
lulaido, remedy (v)
lulaisho, rejoice (v)
lulaishua, rejoicer (n doer)
lulaomio, reran (v pa)
lulaomo, rerun (v)
lulark, resignation (n d:quit)
lularko, resign (v d:quit)
lularkua, resigner (n doer d:quit)
lulauf, fridge (n)
lulaufag, refrigeration (n)
lulaufago, refrigerate (v)
lulaufagua, refrigerator (n doer)
lulaufaguat, refrigerant (n)
lulenko, recommit (v)
lulfim, revenue (n)
luliapio, reread (v pa)
luliapo, reread (v)
lulibesh, resettlement (n)
lulibesho, resettle (v)
lulinfo, refinance (v)
lulirlato, republish (v)
lulirtiu, recently (adv)
lulirtu, recent (adj)
luliuflmo, reconvene (v)
luliukult, reconfiguration (n)
luliukulto, reconfigure (v)
luliunuif, reconfirmation (n)
luliunuifo, reconfirm (v)
luliushlek, reconstruction (n)
luliushleko, reconstruct (v)
luliushleku, reconstructive (adj)
luliushpelt, reconstitution (n)
luliushpelto, reconstitute (v)
luliuthot, reconsideration (n)
luliuthoto, reconsider (v)
luliutifko, recondition (v)

luloid, rewrite (n)
luloidio, rewrote (v pa)
luloido, rewrite (v)
luloidua, rewriter (n doer)
lulond, reentry (n)
lulondo, reenter (v)
lulorsho, repulse (v)
lulorshu, repulsive (adj)
lulto, miss (v d:regret absence)
lulult, remission (n)
lulultiu, remissively (adv)
lululto, remiss (v)
lulultu, remissive (adj)
lulurto, reload (v)
lulutigat, reiteration (n)
lulutigato, reiterate (v)
luluvap, reciprocation (n)
luluvap, reciprocity (n)
luluvapo, reciprocate (v)
luluvapu, reciprocal (adj)
lum, hum (n)
lumaigif, revitalization (n)
lumaigifo, revitalize (v)
lumarmak, regeneration (n)
lumarmako, regenerate (v)
lumarmakua, regenerator (n doer)
lumarn, recourse (n)
lumarno, recourse (v)
lumarnua, recourser (n doer)
lumemif, resuscitation (n)
lumemifo, resuscitate (v)
lumiaf, renovation (n)
lumiafo, renovate (v)
lumiafua, renovator (n doer)
lumiash, reluctance (n)
lumiashiu, reluctantly (adv)
lumiashu, reluctant (adj)
lumiol, renewal (n)
lumiolo, renew (v)
lumiolu, renewable (adj)
lumiolua, renewer (n doer)
lumith, retail (n)
lumitho, retail (v)
lumithua, retailer (n doer)
lumo, hum (v)
lumoim, repayment (n)
lumoimio, repaid (v pa)
lumoimo, repay (v)
lumoimua, repayer (n doer)
lumufto, renounce (v)
lumurt, redundancy (n)
lumurtiu, redundantly (adv)
lumurtu, redundant (adj)
lumuth, rematch (n)
lumutho, rematch (v)
lunag, remake (n)
lunagio, remade (v pa)
lunago, remake (v)
lunagua, remaker (n doer)
lunat, revelry (n)
lunato, revel (v)
lunatu, revelatory (adj)

lunbielk, passport (n)
luniapo, remind (v)
luniapua, reminder (n doer)
luniun, replenishment (n)
luniuno, replenish (v)
lunk, remittance (n)
lunko, remit (v)
lunkua, remittor (n doer)
lunlialt, password (n)
lunoart, reclamation (n)
lunoarto, reclaim (v)
lunp, cream (n)
lunpiu, creamily (adv)
lunpo, cream (v)
lunpu, creamy (adj)
lunpua, creamer (n doer)
lunt, pass (n)
luntak, passage (n)
luntakua, passenger (n doer)
luntiu, passively (adv)
lunto, pass (v)
luntu, passive (adj)
luntua, passer (n doer)
lunuanuet, recrimination (n)
lunulp, recombination (n)
lunulpo, recombine (v)
lunulpu, recombinant (adj)
lunun, release (n)
lununo, release (v)
lununua, releaser (n doer)
luolark, reassignment (n)
luolarko, reassign (v)
luolmot, rearrangement (n)
luolmoto, rearrange (v)
luolp, reassurance (n)
luolpo, reassure (v)
luolshat, reassertion (n)
luolshato, reassert (v)
luominpo, reawaken (v)
luopaik, reattachment (n)
luopaiko, reattach (v)
luoplian, reappearance (n)
luopliano, reappear (v)
luorlap, reassessment (n)
luorlapo, reassess (v)
luorniuf, reaffirmation (n)
luorniufo, reaffirm (v)
luoroif, realignment (n)
luoroifo, realign (v)
luorshaip, reallocation (n)
luorshaipo, reallocate (v)
luotaift, reappointment (n)
luotaifto, reappoint (v)
luothet, reacquisition (n)
luotheto, reacquire (v)
luothrav, reassembly (n)
luothravo, reassemble (v)
lupad, repellant (n)
lupad, repellent (n)
lupado, repel (v)
lupadu, repellants (adj)
lupadu, repellent (adj)
lupadua, repeller (n doer)

lupaf, clown (n)
lupafo, clown (v)
lupaft, refit (n)
lupafto, refit (v)
lupalt, reaction (n)
lupaltak, reactivation (n)
lupaltako, reactivate (v)
lupaltaku, reactive (adj)
lupalto, react (v)
lupaltu, reactionary (adj)
lupaltua, reactor (n doer)
lupaltun, reactionary (n)
lupan, retirement (n)
lupano, retire (v)
lupanua, retiree (n doer)
lupiak, relegation (n)
lupiako, relegate (v)
lupieth, refurbishment (n)
lupietho, refurbish (v)
lupift, retention (n)
lupiftiu, retentively (adv)
lupifto, retain (v)
lupiftu, retentive (adj)
lupiftua, retainer (n doer)
luplat, regret (n)
luplatiu, regretfully (adv)
luplatiu, regrettably (adv)
luplato, regret (v)
luplatu, regretful (adj)
luplatu, regrettable (adj)
luplatua, regrettor (n doer)
lupleik, reproduction (n)
lupleikiu, reproductively (adv)
lupleiko, reproduce (v)
lupleiku, reproductive (adj)
lupleikua, reproducer (n doer)
lupliark, reintegration (n)
lupliarko, reintegrate (v)
lupliut, recreation (n d:remake)
lupliuto, recreate (v d:remake)
lupliutua, recreator (n doer
    d:remake)
lupoin, recount (n)
lupoino, recount (v)
lupoinua, recounter (n doer)
lupraiko, reroute (v)
lupralf, redecoration (n)
lupralfo, redecorate (v)
luprathio, redrew (v pa)
lupratho, redraw (v)
lupretio, retold (v pa)
lupreto, retell (v)
lupriet, resort (n d:rest, revert)
luprieto, resort (v d:rest, revert)
luprilp, repossession (n)
luprilpo, repossess (v)
luprulk, restraint (n)
luprulko, restrain (v)
luprulkua, restrainer (n doer)
luprupo, relinquish (v)
lureilt, rehabilitation (n)
lureilto, rehabilitate (v)
lurf, herb (n)

lurfiu, herbally (adv)
lurfu, herbal (adj)
luridafo, reschedule (v)
lurn, daughter (n)
lurolm, reconciliation (n)
lurolmo, reconcile (v)
lurp, relief (n)
lurpo, relieve (v)
lurpshran, restroom (n)
lurpua, reliever (n doer)
lurt, load (n)
lurto, load (v)
lurtua, loader (n doer)
lushaf, recommendation (n)
lushafo, recommend (v)
lushaik, revocation (n)
lushaiko, revoke (v)
lushaiku, revocable (adj)
lushaip, relocation (n)
lushaipo, relocate (v)
lushant, resonance (n)
lushanto, resonate (v)
lushantu, resonant (adj)
Lushdor, Easter (n)
lushefnok, resubmission (n)
lushefnoko, resubmit (v)
lushethp, resupply (n)
lushethpo, resupply (v)
lushiat, request (n)
lushiato, request (v)
lushiatua, requester (n doer)
lushkalto, restart (v)
lushketo, reorder (v)
lushkit, removal (n)
lushkitiu, removably (adv)
lushkito, remove (v)
lushkitu, removable (adj)
lushkitua, remover (n doer)
lushlaitho, rescind (v)
lushlauf, revival (n)
lushlaufo, revive (v)
lushlaufua, revivalist (n doer)
lushlaufua, reviver (n doer)
lushleko, restructure (v)
lushloift, redeployment (n)
lushloifto, redeploy (v)
lushluat, reply (n)
lushluato, reply (v)
lushluatua, replier (n doer)
lushnaf, reconnection (n)
lushnafo, reconnect (v)
lushnafua, reconnector (n doer)
lushnifo, rewire (v)
lushoik, remand (n)
lushoikauto, remanufacture (v)
lushoiko, remand (v)
lushoikua, remander (n doer)
lushoin, residence (n)
lushoino, reside (v)
lushoinu, residential (adj)
lushoinua, resident (n doer)
lushorb, resentment (n d:disdain)
lushorbo, resent (v d:disdain)

lushorbu, resentful (adj
    d:disdain)
lushpeno, remap (v)
lushrit, redistribution (n)
lushrito, redistribute (v)
lushrok, reflux (n)
lusht, recipe (n)
lushtat, remark (n d:write again)
lushtato, remark (v d:write again)
lushuago, resize (v)
lutafino, revamp (v)
lutaln, remembrance (n)
lutalno, remember (v)
lutefpesh, readjustment (n)
lutefpesho, readjust (v)
lutefrap, redevelopment (n)
lutefrapo, redevelop (v)
lutelk, resistance (n)
lutelko, resist (v)
lutelku, resistant (adj)
lutelku, resistible (adj)
lutelkua, resister (n doer)
lutelp, repeal (n)
lutelpo, repeal (v)
lutelpua, repealer (n doer)
lutep, reject (n)
lutepo, reject (v)
lutepua, rejector (n doer)
lutepuet, rejection (n)
Lutetium, Lutetium (n)
luthaitho, rehash (v)
lutharf, reverse (n)
lutharfal, reversal (n)
lutharfo, reverse (v)
lutharfu, reversible (adj)
luthark, reversion (n)
lutharko, revert (v)
lutharkua, reverter (n doer)
luthat, requirement (n)
luthatho, reshuffle (v)
luthato, require (v)
luthithk, retaliation (n)
luthithko, retaliate (v)
luthithku, retaliatory (adj)
luthithkua, retaliator (n doer)
luthiufo, refile (v)
luthiuft, relapse (n)
luthiufto, relapse (v)
luthoko, reapply (v)
luthonok, retransmission (n)
luthonoko, retransmit (v)
luthraikio, rewound (v pa)
luthraiko, rewind (v)
luthrefo, resurface (v)
luthrish, reforestation (n)
luthrisho, reforest (v)
luthriup, retribution (n)
luthuit, retreat (n)
luthuito, retreat (v)
luthuk, respect (n)
luthukilu, respectable (adj)
luthukiu, respectively (adv)
luthuko, respect (v)

luthuku, respective (adj)
luthukushiu, respectfully (adv)
luthukushu, respectful (adj)
luthuntan, recertification (n)
luthuntano, recertify (v)
lutibafko, redistrict (v)
lutielk, resistor (n)
lutiet, reflex (n)
lutietu, reflexive (adj)
lutifk, rendition (n)
lutifko, render (v)
lutifkua, renderer (n doer)
lutigat, iteration (n)
lutigatiu, iteratively (adv)
lutigato, iterate (v)
lutigatu, iterative (adj)
lutikio, redid (v pa)
lutiko, redo (v)
lutimk, refund (n)
lutimko, refund (v)
lutimku, refundable (adj)
lutimkua, refunder (n doer)
lutiogo, rehire (v)
lutiuto, refinish (v)
lutoip, recitation (n)
lutoipat, recital (n)
lutoipo, recite (v)
lutreb, revulsion (n)
lutrebo, revulse (v)
lutrebu, revulsive (adj)
lutrelf, resale (n)
lutrelfio, resold (v pa)
lutrelfo, resell (v)
lutrelfu, resale (adj)
lutrelfua, reseller (n doer)
lutrilko, retrain (v)
lutrulsh, reprint (n)
lutrulsho, reprint (v)
lutukoig, reexamination (n)
lutukoigo, reexamine (v)
lutultio, recast (v pa)
lutulto, recast (v)
luuyanio, reheard (v pa)
luuyano, rehear (v)
luvadav, remote (n)
luvadaviu, remotely (adv)
luvadavu, remote (adj)
luvaik, regard (n)
luvaikmen, regardless (adj/adv)
luvaikmenu, irregardless (adj)
luvaikmenu, regardless (adj)
luvaiko, regard (v)
luvaikua, regarder (n doer)
luvairto, recycle (v)
luvairtua, recycler (n doer)
luvalsh, rebirth (n)
luvant, result (n)
luvanto, result (v)
luvantu, resultant (adj)
luvap, repeat (n)
luvapiu, repeatedly (adv)
luvapo, repeat (v)
luvapu, repeatable (adj)

luvapu, repetitive (adj)
luvapua, repeater (n doer)
luvapuet, repetition (n)
luvapuetiu, repetitiously (adv)
luvapuetu, repetitious (adj)
luvaraf, refrain (n d:verse)
luvarsho, rephrase (v)
luvaup, revaluation (n)
luvaupo, revaluate (v)
luvaush, remainder (n)
luvausho, remain (v)
luvausht, remains (n)
luveilk, repository (n)
luveiln, reposition (n)
luveilno, reposition (v)
luvek, recess (n)
luveket, recession (n)
luvekiu, recessively (adv)
luveko, recede (v)
luveku, recessive (adj)
luvekua, receder (n doer)
luvialt, recognition (n)
luvialtiu, recognizably (adv)
luvialto, recognize (v)
luvialtu, recognizable (adj)
luvialtua, recognizer (n doer)
luvienk, renomination (n)
luvienko, renominate (v)
luvip, regularity (n)
luvipiu, regularly (adv)
luvipo, regulate (v)
luvipu, regular (adj)
luvipua, regulator (n doer)
luvipuet, regulation (n)
luvipuetu, regulatory (adj)
luvipun, regular (n)
luvoig, resurgence (n)
luvoigo, resurge (v)
luvoigu, resurgent (adj)
luvoik, repute (n)
luvoikat, reputation (n)
luvoikato, repudiate (v)
luvoiko, repute (v)
luvopalt, reenactment (n)
luvopalto, reenact (v)
luvorf, recuperation (n)
luvorfo, recuperate (v)
luvorfu, recuperative (adj)
luvorg, regression (n)
luvorgiu, regressively (adv)
luvorgo, regress (v)
luvorgu, regressive (adj)
luvorgua, regressor (n doer)
luvorn, reform (n d:form again)
luvornak, reformation (n)
luvornako, reformat (v)
luvornaku, reformatory (adj)
luvornap, reformulation (n)
luvornapo, reformulate (v)
luvorno, reform (v d:form again)
luvort, rebuild (n)
luvortio, rebuilt (v pa)
luvorto, rebuild (v)

luvoshpet, reinstatement (n)
luvoshpeto, reinstate (v)
luvovaup, reevaluation (n)
luvovaupo, reevaluate (v)
luvoviuk, reinforcement (n)
luvoviuko, reinforce (v)
luvoviukua, reinforcer (n doer)
luvrieto, relearn (v)
luvuaft, redefinition (n)
luvuafto, redefine (v)
luvuako, relaunch (v)
luvuant, refinery (n)
luvuat, refinement (n)
luvuato, refine (v)
luvuatua, refiner (n doer)
luvuln, remarriage (n)
luvulno, remarry (v)
luweifo, re-sign (v d:sign again)
luwion, silliness (n)
luwionu, silly (adj)
luyap, phone (n)
luyapo, phone (v)
luyutak, reunification (n)
luyutako, reunify (v)
luyutam, reunion (n)
luyutamo, reunite (v)
luzhaipio, resent (v pa d:send
     again)
luzhaipo, resend (v d:send again)
luzhaitho, revile (v)
luzhantiu, resoundingly (adv)
luzhanto, resound (v)
luzhiapo, refuel (v)
luzhim, reissuance (n)
luzhimo, reissue (v)
luzhork, remix (n)
luzhorko, remix (v)
luzhumak, rejuventation (n)
luzhumako, rejuvenate (v)
ma, ma (n)
madik, olympics (n)
madiku, olympic (adj)
madikua, olympian (n doer)
Madishof, Madison (n)
Madrid, Madrid (n)
maf, for (prep/conj)
mafk, pert (n)
mafku, pert (adj)
Magneshium, Magnesium (n)
mahi, now (adj/adv/conj)
mahi, now (n)
mahiviul, nowadays (n)
mahiviuliu, nowadays (adv)
mai, M (let sng)
maiako, nix (v)
maiam, tan (n)
maiamo, tan (v)
maiamua, tanner (n doer)
maiap, nope (interj)
maiat, goal (n)
maif, valve (n)
maigam, vitamin (n)
maigif, vitality (n)

maigifiu, vitally (adv)
maigifu, vital (adj)
maihem, Number_1e2256
maik, max (n)
maikat, maximum (n)
maikatiu, maximally (adv)
maikato, maximize (v)
maikatu, maximal (adj)
maiko, max (v)
mailen, mile (n)
mailenat, mileage (n)
maili, Ms (let pl)
Mainf, Maine (n)
maip, sock (n)
maipef, socket (n)
maipo, sock (v)
maish, mortar (n d:cement)
Maitak, Marines (n)
maiv, narcotic (n)
maiwa, nay (interj)
Maknesi, Maknesi (n)
Malashiaf, Malaysia (n)
malfo, dote (v)
malfp, maple (n)
malfua, dotard (n doer)
malk, lube (n)
malm, mummy (n)
malmit, mummification (n)
malmito, mummify (v)
malmitua, mummifier (n doer)
malsh, mother (n)
malshif, motherhood (n)
malshk, lubrication (n)
malshko, lubricate (v)
malshkua, lubricant (n doer)
malsho, mother (v)
malshplork, motherboard (n)
malshraup, motherland (n)
malshu, motherly (adj)
Manganesh, Manganese (n)
Manilf, Manila (n)
mank, lump (n)
Mankataf, Manhattan (n)
manko, lump (v)
manku, lumpy (adj)
mankua, lumper (n doer)
Manshesht, Manchester (n)
mar, mama (n)
mar, mamma (n)
marf, mat (n)
marfan, mattress (n)
marfo, mat (v)
mariait, genie (n)
Mariland, Maryland (n)
marl, lamb (n)
marlo, lamb (v)
marmait, genius (n)
marmak, generation (n)
marmako, generate (v)
marmakua, generator (n doer)
marmal, generic (n)
marmalu, generic (adj)
marman, geniality (n)

marmanu, genial (adj)
marmeth, generalization (n
   d:common)
marmethiu, generally (adv
   d:common)
marmetho, generalize (v
   d:common)
marmethu, general (adj
   d:common)
marmitiu, genuinely (adv)
marmitu, genuine (adj)
marmp, generosity (n)
marmpiu, generously (adv)
marmpu, generous (adj)
marn, course (n)
marno, course (v)
marp, pig (n)
marpefnap, pigskin (n)
marpo, pig (v)
marth, cotton (n)
martiap, genital (n)
martiapi, genitalia (n pl)
martiapu, genital (adj)
mashart, neither (pron)
mashartu, neither (adj/conj)
Mashashutaf, Massachusetts (n)
mashiath, botany (n)
mashiathu, botanical (adj)
mashp, ball (n)
mashpo, ball (v)
matan, citizen (n)
matik, practice (n)
matikiu, practically (adv)
matiko, practice (v)
matiku, practical (adj)
matikua, practitioner (n doer)
mau, no (n/adj/adv)
maua, naw (interj)
mauak, never (adv)
mauakniap, nevermind (n)
mauaksheimiu, nevertheless
   (adv)
mauarigef, noninterference (n)
maubushlek, nondestruction (n)
maubushlekiu, nondestructively
   (adv)
maubushleku, nondestructive
   (adj)
maufiuflaush, nonproliferation
   (n)
maufiuntak, nonprofessional (n)
maufiupaftu, nonprofit (adj)
maugofaifu, nonlethal (adj)
mauhal, nowhere (adj/adv)
mauhal, nowhere (n)
maukiabaku, nontoxic (adj)
maukizhu, nontechnical (adj)
maulalfku, noncommercial (adj)
maulirputu, nonpublic (adj)
mauliuvornua, nonconformist (n
   doer)
maumesht, nonmember (n)
maumoimuet, nonpayment (n)

maunult, nonexistence (n)
maunultu, nonexistent (adj)
maupafk, nonfiction (n)
maupreiliafu, nontrivial (adj)
mauroif, nonlinearity (n)
mauroifiu, nonlinearly (adv)
mauroifu, nonlinear (adj)
maushaipu, nonlocal (adj)
maushalirtu, nonessential (adj)
maushrua, nonbeliever (n doer)
maushlad, nobody (n/pron)
maushluant, noncompliance (n)
maushorf, nonsense (n)
maushorfu, nonsensical (adj)
maushtolfua, nonsmoker (n doer)
maut, none (pron)
mautauku, nonstop (adj)
mauthiaku, nonfatal (adj)
mautigret, nondisclosure (n)
mautmeniu, nonetheless (adv)
mautrabiru, nontraditional (adj)
mautrefku, nonstandard (adj)
mautu, none (adj/adv)
mautuark, nonviolence (n)
mautuarku, nonviolent (adj)
mautuazhu, nonvolatile (adj)
mauyuanu, nonwhite (adj)
mauyutamanu, nonunion (adj)
mav, harm (n)
mavap, kiss (n)
mavapo, kiss (v)
mavapua, kisser (n doer)
mavin, harmony (n)
mavinar, harmonic (n)
mavinelk, hologram (n)
mavinelku, holographic (adj)
mavino, harmonize (v)
mavinu, harmonic (adj)
mavmeniu, harmlessly (adv)
mavmenu, harmless (adj)
mavo, harm (v)
mavun, anonymity (n)
mavunu, anonymous (adj)
mavushiu, harmfully (adv)
mavushu, harmful (adj)
mawil, nor (conj)
Mediteranf, Mediterranean (n)
mef, pause (n)
mefo, pause (v)
mefth, shallowness (n)
mefthu, shallow (adj)
meif, socialization (n)
meifak, society (n)
meifaku, societal (adj)
meifan, social (n)
meifar, socialism (n)
meifaru, socialistic (adj)
meifarua, socialist (n doer)
meifiu, socially (adv)
meifo, socialize (v)
meifu, sociable (adj)
meifu, social (adj)
meifua, socializer (n doer)

meig, verge (n d:incline)
meigo, verge (v d:incline)
meilf, bargain (n)
meilfo, bargain (v)
meirf, role (n)
meishk, panic (n)
meishko, panic (v)
meishku, panicky (adj)
meishp, expanse (n)
meishp, expansion (n)
meishpiu, expansively (adv)
meishpo, expand (v)
meishpu, expandable (adj)
meishpu, expansive (adj)
meishpua, expander (n doer)
meishpua, expansionist (n doer)
meiv, numbness (n)
meivo, numb (v)
meivu, numb (adj)
mekani, pants (n pl d:clothing)
mel, rain (n)
melar, glamor (n)
melar, glamour (n)
melariu, glamorously (adv)
melaru, glamorous (adj)
meldarg, raindrop (n)
meldiaf, rainbow (n)
melf, panel (n)
melfo, panel (v)
melfrip, rainstorm (n)
melfua, panelist (n doer)
melheidon, rainwater (n)
melin, mare (n)
melink, marshal (n)
melinko, marshal (v)
melk, pan (n)
melkato, pander (v)
melkegurt, pancake (n)
melkegurto, pancake (v)
melko, pan (v)
melm, mom (n)
melmal, mommy (n)
melmel, murmur (n)
melmelo, murmur (v)
melmelu, murmurous (adj)
melmelua, murmurer (n doer)
melmo, mom (v)
meln, nut (n)
melnagua, rainmaker (n doer)
melnthek, nutshell (n)
melnu, nutty (adj)
melo, rain (v)
melp, pride (n d:group)
melrafk, raincoat (n)
melsh, tea (n)
melshdaif, teapot (n)
melshdorp, teaspoon (n)
melshvorp, teacup (n)
melthrish, rainforest (n)
melu, rainy (adj)
meluil, rainout (n)
melvan, marble (n)
melzhail, rainfall (n)

membrun, suspense (n)
membruno, suspend (v)
membrunua, suspender (n doer)
membrunuet, suspension (n)
memem, momma (n)
Memfish, Memphis (n)
mempift, sustenance (n)
mempifto, sustain (v)
mempiftu, sustainable (adj)
memship, susceptibility (n)
memshipu, susceptible (adj)
memthuk, suspicion (n)
memthukiu, suspiciously (adv)
memthuko, suspect (v)
memthuku, suspicious (adj)
memthukua, suspect (n doer)
men, less (adj)
Mendelevium, Mendelevium (n)
meno, lessen (v)
mentan, pumpkin (n)
mep, pet (n)
mepo, pet (v)
Merkuri, Mercury (n)
mert, continent (n)
mertu, continental (adj)
meshfif, membership (n)
meshk, hut (n)
Meshkif, Mexico (n)
Meshkifan, Mexican (n)
mesht, member (n)
meshtan, membrane (n)
meshtanu, membranous (adj)
methk, nephew (n)
Metnerium, Meitnerium (n)
mi, hi (interj)
miabo, mar (v)
miaf, nova (n)
miafan, novice (n)
miagrazh, chainsaw (n)
miagrazho, chainsaw (v)
miaif, prize (n)
miaifo, prize (v)
miaiko, pry (v)
miak, chain (n)
miako, chain (v)
mial, flue (n)
Miamif, Miami (n)
mian, fluid (n)
mianu, fluid (adj)
miap, organ (n d:instrument)
miar, ocean (n)
miardarf, oceanography (n)
miardarfu, oceanographic (adj)
miarflarnu, oceanfront (adj)
miarshoit, oceanside (n)
miart, fluency (n)
miartiu, fluently (adv)
miartu, fluent (adj)
miaru, oceanic (adj)
miashk, fluctuation (n)
miashko, fluctuate (v)
miashkua, fluctuator (n doer)
miath, alibi (n)

miauko, taunt (v)
mid, note (n d:text)
midat, notation (n)
midato, notate (v)
midebanf, notepad (n)
mideflaishu, noteworthy (adj)
Midisht, Mideast (n)
midiu, notably (adv d:text)
midiun, novelty (n)
midiunu, novel (adj)
mido, note (v d:text)
midoin, notion (n)
midot, noon (n)
midotedaun, noontime (n)
midotedaunu, noontime (adj)
midu, notable (adj d:text)
Miduesh, Midwest (n)
midun, novel (n)
midunua, novelist (n doer)
miedarf, biography (n)
miekuit, biology (n)
miekuitiu, biologically (adv)
miekuitu, biological (adj)
miel, dew (n)
miesh, fluff (n)
miesho, fluff (v)
mieshu, fluffy (adj)
mift, colon (n d:character)
mig, barge (n d:boat)
migat, colonel (n)
mikar, angel (n)
mikariu, angelically (adv)
mikaru, angelic (adj)
mikatu, noxious (adj)
mikit, colony (n)
mikito, colonize (v)
mikitu, colonial (adj)
mikitua, colonist (n doer)
mikitua, colonizer (n doer)
mikituet, colonization (n)
mil, tad (n)
mildilk, tadpole (n)
Miluakif, Milwaukee (n)
milun, beneath (adv/prep)
mim, dot (n)
miman, range (n)
mimano, range (v)
mimanua, ranger (n doer)
mimo, dot (v)
minash, lesser (adj)
Minkapol, Minneapolis (n)
minpio, woke (v pa d:arise)
minpiveil, wakeup (n d:arise)
minpiveilu, wakeup (adj d:arise)
minpo, wake (v d:arise)
Minshot, Minnesota (n)
mioblefua, newcomer (n doer)
miok, macula (n)
mioki, maculae (n pl)
mioko, maculate (v)
mioku, macular (adj)
Miol Kamshir, New Hampshire (n)

Miol Orlinf, New Orleans (n)
Miol Zhilanud, New Zealand (n)
miol, newness (n)
mioliu, newly (adv)
miolu, new (adj)
miolwaku, newest (adj)
miolwelu, newer (adj)
miolyuv, newlywed (n)
mior, news (n)
miorasht, newsletter (n)
miorbron, newsgroup (n)
miordium, newsreel (n)
miorflaish, newsworthiness (n)
miorflaishu, newsworthy (adj)
miorian, newshour (n)
Miork, Major (n)
miornifp, newsmagazine (n)
miorp, radio (n)
miorpalt, radioactivity (n)
miorpaltu, radioactive (adj)
miorplon, newsman (n)
miorploni, newsmen (n pl)
miorpo, radio (v)
miorshnif, newswire (n)
miorshran, newsroom (n)
miortrelt, newsstand (n)
miortrulsh, newsprint (n)
miortult, newscast (n)
miortultua, newscaster (n doer)
mioru, newsy (adj)
miorviul, newsday (n)
miorvuap, newspaper (n)
miorvuaplon, newspaperman (n)
miorvuaploni, newspapermen (n pl)
mioshupu, newfound (adj)
miovalsh, newborn (n)
mirf, shift (n)
mirfo, shift (v)
mirfu, shifty (adj)
mirfua, shifter (n doer)
Miriaf, EhoDay03 (n)
miriakiu, sternly (adv d:firm)
miriaku, stern (adj d:firm)
Miriam, Miriam (n)
mirk, angle (n)
mirkiu, angularly (adv)
mirko, angle (v)
mirku, angular (adj)
mirmit, ivory (n)
mirmitu, ivory (adj)
mirn, canyon (n)
mirp, ankle (n)
mish, other (n/pron)
Mishaship, Mississippi (n)
mishfluik, otherwise
   (adj/adv/conj)
mishi, others (pron)
Mishigaf, Michigan (n)
mishu, other (adj/adv)
Mishurf, Missouri (n)
mith, tail (n)
mithleinp, tailpipe (n)

mitho, tail (v)
mithprelk, tailgate (n)
mithprelko, tailgate (v)
mithshnap, tailspin (n)
mithua, tailer (n doer)
mitsh, mulch (n)
mitsho, mulch (v)
mitum, cologne (n)
miuf, vase (n)
miuft, elbow (n)
miufto, elbow (v)
miuko, taint (v)
miun, town (n)
miunfif, township (n)
miunkiaf, townhouse (n)
miunkifp, townfolk (n)
miunkifpi, townsfolk (n pl)
miunplon, townperson (n)
miunploni, townspeople (n pl)
miup, lumber (n)
miupo, lumber (v)
miuth, flush (n)
miutho, flush (v)
miuthua, flusher (n doer)
mivan, leather (n)
mivanu, leathery (adj)
mivath, noodle (n)
mivond, notebook (n)
moaf, fan (n d:move air)
moafo, fan (v d:move air)
moagan, caramel (n)
moak, sake (n)
moakio, forsook (v pa)
moako, forsake (v)
moft, surgery (n)
moftiu, surgically (adv)
moftu, surgical (adj)
moftua, surgeon (n doer)
mog, next (adj/adv/prep)
moi, hey (interj)
moiakiu, drastically (adv)
moiaku, drastic (adj)
moiam, farm (n)
moiamkap, farmhand (n)
moiamkiaf, farmhouse (n)
moiamo, farm (v)
moiamraup, farmland (n)
moiamua, farmer (n doer)
moiap, suite (n)
moib, bulb (n)
moid, pedal (n)
moidat, pedestrian (n)
moido, pedal (v)
moif, swallow (n d:gulp)
moifo, swallow (v d:gulp)
moig, bulge (n)
moigo, bulge (v)
moik, shield (n)
moikaf, radar (n)
moikafo, radar (v)
moikiok, network (n)
moikioko, network (v)
moiko, shield (v)

moilaublutsh, omnipresence (n)
moilaublutshu, omnipresent (adj)
moilauboig, omnipotence (n)
moilauboigu, omnipotent (adj)
moilaudiuafu, omnivorous (adj)
moilaukuafku, omnidirectional
   (adj)
moilaushuash, omniscience (n)
moilaushuashu, omniscient (adj)
moim, pay (n)
moimeviul, payday (n)
moimfalir, payroll (n)
moimio, paid (v pa)
moimiu, payably (adv)
moimlurt, payload (n)
moimo, pay (v)
moimpird, paycheck (n)
moimu, payable (adj)
moimua, payer (n doer)
moimuet, payment (n)
moimuil, payout (n)
moimunf, payoff (n)
moimvak, payback (n)
moin, pod (n)
moip, net (n)
moipo, net (v)
moirp, label (n)
moirpo, label (v)
moirpua, labeler (n doer)
moishan, MoissanRuby (n)
moisht, expedition (n)
moishto, expedite (v)
moishtu, expedient (adj)
moishtuet, expedience (n)
moishtuet, expediency (n)
moishtuetiu, expeditiously (adv)
moishtuetu, expeditious (adj)
moit, orientation (n)
moith, shine (n)
moithio, shone (v pa)
moitho, shine (v)
moithu, shiny (adj)
moithua, shiner (n doer)
moito, orient (v)
moiuf, suit (n d:apparel)
moiushuat, suitcase (n)
moiv, radiance (n)
moiv, radiation (n)
moivak, radical (n)
moivakiu, radically (adv)
moivaku, radical (adj)
moivavu, geiger (adj)
moivo, radiate (v)
moivua, radiator (n doer)
mokash, loot (n)
mokasho, loot (v)
mokashua, looter (n doer)
moko, lop (v)
mokram, klutz (n)
mokshoito, lopside (v)
molfash, government (n)
molfasho, govern (v)
molfashua, governor (n doer)

Molibdenum, Molybdenum (n)
molth, patience (n d:endurance)
molthiu, patiently (adv
d:endurance)
molthu, patient (adj d:endurance)
molv, pear (n)
Montanf, Montana (n)
Montrial, Montreal (n)
Montugorm, Montgomery (n)
morf, honey (n)
morfrakad, honeycomb (n)
morfzhish, honeybee (n)
morkat, muscle (n)
morkato, muscle (v)
morkatu, muscular (adj)
morlan, gill (n)
morlif, euphoria (n)
morlifu, euphoric (adj)
mormuan, honeymoon (n)
mormuanua, honeymooner (n
doer)
morp, suit (n d:accord)
morpiu, suitably (adv d:accord)
morpo, suit (v d:accord)
morpu, suitable (adj d:accord)
morpua, suitor (n doer d:accord)
morpuet, suitability (n)
morthk, impatience (n)
morthkiu, impatiently (adv)
morthku, impatient (adj)
mosh, puff (n)
Moshkauf, Moscow (n)
mosho, puff (v)
moshu, puffy (adj)
moshua, puffer (n doer)
motuyap, saxophone (n)
moviul, holiday (n)
mrag, fang (n)
mrago, fangle (v)
mua, huh (interj)
muad, voyage (n)
muado, voyage (v)
muadua, voyager (n doer)
muai-, non- (num 9 pref)
muan, night (n)
muandaun, nighttime (n)
muanflaush, nightlife (n)
muanfraik, nightmare (n)
muanlifad, nightshirt (n)
muantaid, nightclub (n)
nuainu, nightly (adj)
muanzhail, nightfall (n)
muar, lake (n)
muarko, mope (v d:sad)
muarnulart, lakeshore (n)
muarshoit, lakeside (n)
muat, shave (n)
muato, shave (v)
muatua, shaver (n doer)
mufko, nestle (v)
mufp, nest (n)
mufpo, nest (v)
mufpua, nester (n doer)

mui, nine (num 9 card)
muialfhemka, Number_1e36606
muiash, prowl (n)
muiasho, prowl (v)
muiashua, prowler (n doer)
muiat, swell (n)
muiato, swell (v)
muida, ninety (num 90 card)
muidai-, ninety- (num 90 pref)
muideth, ninetieth (num 90 ord)
muif, niceness (n)
muif, nicety (n)
muifiu, nicely (adv)
muifk, novenquadragintillion
(num 1e150 card)
muifo, nicen (v)
muift, noventrigintillion (num
1e120 card)
muifu, nice (adj)
muifweku, nicest (adj)
muifwelu, nicer (adj)
muika, nonillion (num 1e30 card)
muikai-, weka- (num 1e30 pref)
muiketh, nonillionth (num 1e30
ord)
muipa, nineteen (num 19 card)
muipai-, nineteen- (num 19 pref)
muipeth, nineteenth (num 19 ord)
muish, mesa (n)
muishk, novemvigintillion (num
1e90 card)
muishkai-, bianten-
muishketh, novemvigintillionth
(num 1e90 ord)
muisht, novemdecillion (num
1e60 card)
muishtai-, liena- (num 1e60 pref)
muishteth, novemdecillionth
(num 1e60 ord)
muit, onion (n)
muktak, pigeon (n)
Mular, March (n)
mulion, ceramic (n)
mulionu, ceramic (adj)
mult, element (n)
multu, elementary (adj)
mumath, cushion (n)
mumatho, cushion (v)
mumathu, cushy (adj)
mumathua, cushioner (n doer)
mumel, lull (n)
mumeliauf, lullaby (n)
mumelo, lull (v)
mumim, fumble (n)
mumimo, fumble (v)
mun, mu (n)
munan, midnight (n)
mund, bay (n d:place)
munk, least (adj)
munp, conscience (n)
munpu, conscionable (adj)

mup, stub (n)
mupan, stubble (n)
mupek, stubbornness (n)
mupekiu, stubbornly (adv)
mupeku, stubborn (adj)
mupo, stub (v)
murd, grime (n)
murdan, grimace (n)
murdano, grimace (v)
murdanu, grim (adj)
murdu, grimey (adj)
murf, eloquence (n)
murfiu, eloquently (adv)
murfo, elocute (v)
murfu, eloquent (adj)
murg, grunge (n)
murgu, grungy (adj)
murl, ceremony (n)
murliu, ceremonially (adv)
murlu, ceremonial (adj)
mursh, sleet (n)
mursho, sleet (v)
murv, hollowness (n)
murvo, hollow (v)
murvu, hollow (adj)
mushk, patrol (n)
mushko, patrol (v)
Mushlim, Muslim (n)
mushp, mate (n)
mushpo, mate (v)
muth, match (n d:selection)
muthath, carnation (n)
muthiok, carousel (n)
muthmenu, matchless (adj
d:selection)
muthnagio, matchmade (v pa
d:make selection)
muthnago, matchmake (v d:make
selection)
muthnagua, matchmaker (n doer
d:make selection)
mutho, match (v d:selection)
muthorn, methane (n)
muthua, matcher (n doer
d:selection)
mutik, jaw (n)
mutiko, jaw (v)
mutiktoik, jawbone (n)
nuuvlan, carnival (n)
muyar, niece (n)
muyeth, ninth (num 9 ord)
muzh, fog (n)
muzhiu, foggily (adv)
muzhkroim, foghorn (n)
muzho, fog (v)
muzhu, foggy (adj)
muzhua, fogger (n doer)
mwae, na (interj)
nabat, fuss (n)
nabato, fuss (v)
nabatu, fussy (adj)
nabit, harvest (n)
nabito, harvest (v)

nabitua, harvester (n doer)
nafko, fester (v)
nafp, mold (n d:microbe)
nafpu, moldy (adj d:microbe)
naft, harbor (n)
naft, harbour (n)
nafto, harbor (v)
nagag, sogginess (n)
nagagu, soggy (adj)
nagian, mosquito (n)
nagio, made (v pa)
nagiv, makeup (n)
nago, make (v)
nagua, maker (n doer)
naiap, skewness (n)
naiapo, skew (v)
naigat, psychiatry (n)
naigatu, psychiatric (adj)
naigatua, psychiatrist (n doer)
naigeth, psychology (n)
naigethiu, psychologically (adv)
naigethu, psychological (adj)
naigethua, psychologist (n doer)
naik, psyche (n)
naikauk, psychosis (n)
naikauketh, psychopathology (n)
naikaukethua, psychopathologist
    (n doer)
naikauku, psychotic (adj)
naikaukua, psycho (n doer)
naikaukua, psychopath (n doer)
naiko, psych (v)
naikomaft, psychoanalysis (n)
naikomaftua, psychoanalyst (n
    doer)
naikpliashp, psychotherapy (n)
naikpliashpua, psychotherapist (n
    doer)
naikua, psychic (n doer)
nailar, meadow (n)
nainf, pilot (n)
nainfo, pilot (v)
naip, pile (n)
naipiveil, pileup (n)
naipo, pile (v)
naish, mess (n)
naisho, mess (v)
naishu, messy (adj)
naitho, sand (v d:abrasion)
naithua, sander (n doer
    d:abrasion)
nakip, soak (n)
nakipo, soak (v)
nakipua, soaker (n doer)
nalan, mammal (n)
nalanarft, mammography (n)
nalanelk, mammogram (n)
nalanu, mammalian (adj)
nalf, shelf (n)
nalfo, shelve (v)
nalm, horizon (n)
nalmiu, horizontally (adv)
nalmu, horizontal (adj)

naln, straw (n)
nalsho, deign (v)
nalth, breast (n)
nalthfkaf, breastplate (n)
nalthpavo, breastfeed (v)
Namibiaf, Namibia (n)
namufluan, moonlight (n)
namufluano, moonlight (v)
namur, moon (n)
namurbaraf, moonstone (n)
namurduaf, moonbeam (n)
namurmoith, moonshine (n)
Namurviul, Monday (n)
nansh, die (n d:number cube)
nanshi, dice (n pl d:number cube)
nant, dexterity (n)
nantiu, dexterously (adv)
nantiu, dextrously (adv)
nantu, dexterous (adj)
nantu, dextrous (adj)
narano, sully (v)
narfo, loaf (v d:lounge)
narfua, loafer (n doer d:lounge)
narl, soap (n)
narliu, soapily (adv)
narlo, soap (v)
narlprenk, soapbox (n)
narlu, soapy (adj)
narmalt, latter (n)
narmaltu, latter (adj)
narmit, lattice (n)
narmiu, laterally (adv)
narmu, lateral (adj)
narmuk, latitude (n)
narp, rug (n)
narsh, soil (n)
narsho, soil (v)
narth, favor (n)
narthep, favorite (n)
narthepiu, favorably (adv)
narthepu, favorable (adj)
nartho, favor (v)
narthu, favorite (adj)
narthuet, favoritism (n)
Nashfil, Nashville (n)
nashko, dice (v d:cube)
nashku, dicey (adj d:cube)
nath, sand (n d:grains)
nathat, sandal (n)
nathbaraf, sandstone (n)
nathfnaf, sandbag (n)
nathfrip, sandstorm (n)
nathkraigo, sandblast (v)
nathprenk, sandbox (n)
nathrolt, sandbar (n)
nathu, sandy (adj d:grains)
nathvuap, sandpaper (n)
nau, me (pron 1st sng obj)
nauf, muse (n)
naufar, museum (n)
naufk, dominance (n)
naufk, domination (n)
naufko, dominate (v)

naufku, dominant (adj)
naufkua, dominator (n doer)
naufo, muse (v)
nauk, mission (n)
naushk, foul (n)
naushko, foul (v)
naushku, foul (adj)
Nebrashk, Nebraska (n)
neft, domestication (n)
nefto, domesticate (v)
neftu, domestic (adj)
neftua, domesticator (n doer)
neib, mop (n)
neibo, mop (v)
neid, lane (n)
neif, tape (n)
neifo, tape (v)
neikaf, metaphor (n)
neikafu, metaphorical (adj)
neiku, meta (adj)
neilf, marvel (n)
neilfiu, marvelously (adv)
neilfo, marvel (v)
neilfu, marvelous (adj)
neilun, cadet (n)
neish, pal (n)
Neith, Miss (n)
neito, usher (v)
neitua, usher (n doer)
neivit, monitor (n)
neivito, monitor (v)
neiwif, taper (n)
neiwifo, taper (v)
nelf, calf (n)
nelfo, calve (v)
neliloidua, songwriter (n doer)
nelkar, grammar (n)
nelkariu, grammatically (adv)
nelkaru, grammatical (adj)
neln, song (n)
nelnal, nanny (n)
nelnalo, nanny (v)
nelnio, sang (v pa)
nelno, sing (v)
nelnua, singer (n doer)
nelp, berry (n)
nelsh, else (adj/adv)
nelsholu, elsewhere (adv)
nelth, clutch (n d:hatch)
nenk, number (n)
nenkel, numeral (n)
nenkeliu, numerically (adv)
nenkelu, numeric (adj)
nenkelu, numerical (adj)
nenkelua, numerator (n doer)
nenkiu, numerously (adv)
nenko, number (v)
nenku, numerous (adj)
nenkuit, numerology (n)
Neodimium, Neodymium (n)
Neon, Neon (n)
nep, tap (n)
nepo, tap (v)

Neptunium, Neptunium (n)
nepua, tapper (n doer)
nesh, much (adj/adv)
nesh, much (pron)
neshgaf, racket (n d:noise)
Netherlanud, Netherlands (n)
Nevadaf, Nevada (n)
nia, I (pron 1st sng sub)
niaf, naivete (n)
niafiu, naively (adv)
niafk, miracle (n)
niafkiu, miraculously (adv)
niafku, miraculous (adj)
niafu, naive (adj)
niai, we (pron 1st pl sub)
niain, prism (n)
niak, majority (n)
niako, major (v)
niaku, major (adj)
nial, music (n)
nialat, musical (n)
nialiu, musically (adv)
nialt, comment (n)
nialtar, commentary (n)
nialto, comment (v)
nialtua, commentator (n doer)
nialu, musical (adj)
nialua, musician (n doer)
niam, smartness (n)
niamiu, smartly (adv)
niamo, smarten (v)
niamu, smart (adj)
nian, mirror (n)
nianat, mirage (n)
niank, funk (n d:music/stench)
nianku, funky (adj
      d:music/stench)
niano, mirror (v)
niap, mind (n)
niapefep, mindset (n)
niapemeniu, mindlessly (adv)
niapemenu, mindless (adj)
niapiu, mindfully (adv)
niapo, mind (v)
niapu, mindful (adj)
niarg, flu (n)
niarsh, laceration (n)
niarsho, lacerate (v)
niashdriad, tantrum (n)
niashiu, tanto (adv)
niashinluku, tantamount (adj)
niat, site (n)
niath, mint (n)
niathiu, mintly (adv)
niatho, mint (v)
niathu, mint (adj)
niathua, minter (n doer)
niatsh, tantalization (n)
niatsho, tantalize (v)
niatshua, tantalizer (n doer)
niaukizh, pyrotechnic (n)
niaup, pyromaniac (n)
nielp, tameness (n)

nielpo, tame (v)
nielpu, tame (adj)
niemo, tamper (v)
niet, eat (n)
nietio, ate (v pa)
nieto, eat (v)
nietu, edible (adj)
nietua, eater (n doer)
nifk, mash (n)
nifko, mash (v)
nifkua, masher (n doer)
nifp, magazine (n d:document)
nik, EhoSecond (n)
Nikaraguan, Nicaraguan (n)
Nikaraguf, Nicaragua (n)
Nikel, Nickel (n)
nikut, laser (n)
nikuto, laser (v)
nilbivg, homosexuality (n)
nilbivgu, homosexual (adj)
nilbivgua, homosexual (n doer)
nilbu, gay (adj d:homosexual)
nilf, series (n)
nilfiu, serially (adv)
nilfu, serial (adj)
nilishu, teeny (adj)
nilithu, teensy (adj)
nilk, termination (n)
nilkat, terminal (n)
nilkiu, terminally (adv)
nilko, terminate (v)
nilkoik, homicide (n)
nilkoiku, homicidal (adj)
nilku, terminal (adj)
nilkua, terminator (n doer)
nilp, sesame (n)
nilsh, charm (n)
nilsho, charm (v)
nilshua, charmer (n doer)
nilt, experiment (n)
niltiu, experimentally (adv)
nilto, experiment (v)
niltu, experimental (adj)
niltua, experimenter (n doer)
nilufu, nifty (adj)
niman, menu (n)
nimat, memo (n)
Nimsant, Nimsant
nimshiliu, minutely (adv d·small)
nimshillu, minute (adj d:small)
nimuf, roast (n)
nimufo, roast (v)
nimufua, roaster (n doer)
ninato, tatter (v)
ninf, fossil (n)
ninfo, fossilize (v)
Niobium, Niobium (n)
niof, swap (n)
niofo, swap (v)
niofua, swaper (n doer)
niok, meter (n d:device)
niokar, metric (n)
nioko, meter (v d:device)

nion, shrine (n)
niono, enshrine (v)
nionua, shriner (n doer)
niop, rhyme (n)
niopat, rhythm (n)
niopatiu, rhythmically (adv)
niopatu, rhythmic (adj)
niopo, rhyme (v)
niopua, rhymer (n doer)
niot, shrug (n)
nioto, shrug (v)
niotsh, swat (n)
niotsho, swat (v)
nirt, address (n)
nirto, address (v)
nirtu, addressable (adj)
nirtua, addressor (n doer)
nirtuin, addressee (n)
nishk, need (n)
nishke kodi, had to (ndal d:need)
nishke kodi, have to (ndal d:need)
nishke kodi, must (ndal d:need)
nishkmeniu, needlessly (adv)
nishkmenu, needless (adj)
nishko, need (v)
nishku, needful (adj)
nishku, needy (adj)
nisht, tininess (n)
nishtu, tiny (adj)
nith, lid (n)
Nitrogen, Nitrogen (n)
niudan, mound (n)
niudat, moat (n)
niuf, firmness (n d:steady)
niufiu, firmly (adv d:steady)
niufluan, flashlight (n)
niufo, firm (v d:steady)
niufu, firm (adj d:steady)
niufweku, firmest (adj)
niufwelu, firmer (adj)
niugiut, mountain (n)
niugiutshoit, mountainside (n)
niugiutu, mountainous (adj)
niugiutua, mountaineer (n doer)
niuiutedaup, mountaintop (n)
niuk, mount (n)
niuko, mount (v)
niult, plenum (n)
niultu, plenary (adj)
niumo, sow (v)
niun, plenty (n)
niunf, abundance (n)
niunfiu, abundantly (adv)
niunfu, abundant (adj)
niunu, plentiful (adj)
niup, minority (n)
niupo, minor (v)
niupu, minor (adj)
niush, flash (n)
niushiu, flashily (adv)
niusho, flash (v)
niushu, flashy (adj)
niushua, flasher (n doer)

niushvak, flashback (n)
niut, stadium (n)
niuth, snack (n)
niutho, snack (v)
niv, folly (n)
niv, foolishness (n)
Nivar, EhoMonth09 (n)
nivefliofu, foolproof (adj)
niviu, foolishly (adv)
niviv, moron (n)
nivivu, moronic (adj)
nivkelft, foolhardiness (n)
nivkelftu, foolhardy (adj)
nivo, fool (v)
nivu, foolish (adj)
nivua, fool (n doer)
nizh, itch (n)
nizho, itch (v)
nizhu, itchy (adj)
noart, claim (n)
noarto, claim (v)
noartua, claimant (n doer)
noat, dib (n)
Nobelium, Nobelium (n)
noesh, loaf (n d:bread)
Nofefar, November (n)
noft, ministry (n)
nofto, minister (v)
noftua, minister (n doer)
noi, N (let sng)
noiak, skewer (n)
noiako, skewer (v)
noif kodi, may (ndal
    d:permission)
noif, permission (n)
noihem, Number_1e3006
noik, lack (n)
noiko, lack (v)
noili, Ns (let pl)
noim, savage (n)
noimiu, savagely (adv)
noimu, savage (adj)
noip, mayor (n)
noipu, mayoral (adj)
noirn, nylon (n)
noish, rinse (n)
noishk, rhetoric (n)
noishkiu, rhetorically (adv)
noishku, rhetorical (adj)
noisho, rinse (v)
noishua, rinser (n doer)
noith, race (n d:human)
noithat, racism (n)
noithatua, racist (n doer)
noithiu, racially (adv d:human)
noithu, racial (adj d:human)
nolf, fellow (n)
nolfif, fellowship (n)
nolk, grain (n)
nolkien, gravy (n)
nolku, grainy (adj)
nolth, wall (n)
noltho, wall (v)

nolthuan, wallflower (n)
nolthvuap, wallpaper (n)
nolthvuapo, wallpaper (v)
nomag, liver (n)
norfp, jealousy (n)
norfpiu, jealously (adv)
norfpu, jealous (adj)
norg, rack (n)
norgaf, racket (n d:bat, group)
norgaf, racquet (n)
norgafu, rackety (adj d:bat,
    group)
norgaito, racketeer (v)
norgaitua, racketeer (n doer)
norgo, rack (v)
norgua, racker (n doer)
nork, rig (n)
norkat, sergeant (n)
norko, rig (v)
norkua, rigger (n doer)
norl, court (n)
norlkiaf, courthouse (n)
norlo, court (v)
norlshran, courtroom (n)
norlthauth, courtyard (n)
norluen, courtesy (n)
norlueniu, courteously (adv)
norluenu, courteous (adj)
normak, salvation (n)
normako, salvage (v)
nornan, sandwich (n)
nornano, sandwich (v)
norp, rag (n)
norpegaivu, ragtag (adj)
norpiu, raggedy (adv)
norpo, rag (v)
norpyuk, ragweed (n)
norsh, dawn (n)
norsho, dawn (v)
norvosh, courtship (n)
Norwaif, Norway (n)
Norwaifan, Norwegian (n)
nosh, man (n d:male)
noshi, men (n pl d:male)
noshtaig, manure (n)
noshu, manly (adj d:male)
noth, muff (n)
nothato, muffle (v)
nothatua, muffler (n doer)
notho, muff (v)
novin, mole (n)
novino, mole (v)
novinparn, molehill (n)
nuab, rival (n)
nuabak, rivalry (n)
nuabo, rival (v)
nuaf, moss (n)
nuafu, mossy (adj)
nuak, void (n)
nuako, void (v)
nuan, crime (n)
nuank, discrimination (n)
nuanko, discriminate (v)

nuankua, discriminator (n doer)
nuano, criminalize (v)
nuant, incrimination (n)
nuanto, incriminate (v)
nuanua, criminal (n doer)
Nuark, Newark (n)
nuash, rite (n)
nuatip, ritual (n)
nuatipo, ritualize (v)
nuatipu, ritualistic (adj)
nufk, mush (n)
nufkao, mushed (v prp)
nufko, mush (v)
nufmashp, mushroom (n)
nufnif, mishmash (n)
nufobietao, hetergeneous (v prp)
nufobietu, hetergeneous (adj)
nufp, ink (n)
nufpo, ink (v)
nufpu, inky (adj)
nufpua, inker (n doer)
nuft, lever (n)
nuftar, leverage (n)
nuftaro, leverage (v)
nufto, lever (v)
nugan, lung (n)
nui, my (pron 1st sng pos sub)
nuibar, madam (n)
nuibar, madame (n)
nuifal, myself (pron 1st sng refl)
nuik, tank (n)
nuiko, tank (v)
nuikua, tanker (n doer)
nuime, mine (pron 1st sng pos
    obj)
nuish, our (pron 1st pl pos sub)
nukif, physics (n)
nukifiu, physically (adv)
nukifu, physical (adj)
nulart, shore (n)
nularto, shore (v)
nulartroif, shoreline (n)
nulbrug, combustion (n)
nulbrugo, combust (v)
nulbrugu, combustible (adj)
nulf, festival (n)
nulfu, festive (adj)
nulfuet, festivity (n)
nulgrat, combat (n)
nulgratiu, combatively (adv)
nulgrato, combat (v)
nulgratu, combative (adj)
nulgratua, combatant (n doer)
nulk, leash (n)
nulko, leash (v)
nuln, lease (n)
nulno, lease (v)
nulnua, leaser (n doer)
nulnua, lessor (n doer)
nulnuin, lessee (n)
nulp, combination (n)
nulpat, combine (n)
nulpo, combine (v)

nulpua, combiner (n doer)
nult, existence (n)
nulto, exist (v)
num, dullness (n)
numak, javelin (n)
numat, plus (adj/prep)
numat, plus (n)
numo, dull (v)
numu, dull (adj)
nun, nu (n)
nunuf, taboo (n)
nunufu, taboo (adj)
nup, bin (n)
nurabeilku, multipurpose (adj)
nurabiazhu, multiparty (adj)
nuragaldu, multilevel (adj)
nurakarl, multinational (n)
nurakarlu, multinational (adj)
nuralaidak, multimedia (n)
nuralfruifualu, multiplayer (adj)
nuralirolo, multicolor (v)
nuralirolu, multicolor (adj)
nuranoithu, multiracial (adj)
nurapratu, multifunctional (adj)
nurashaiashu, multistate (adj)
nuratafko, multiculture (v)
nuratafku, multicultural (adj)
nuratuarm, multichannel (n)
nuratuet, multitude (n)
nuratuetu, multitude (adj)
nuraviarthu, multilingual (adj)
nurb, multiple (n)
nurbo, multiply (v)
nurbu, multiple (adj)
nurbua, multiplier (n doer)
nurbuet, multiplication (n)
nurg, crap (n)
nurgo, crap (v)
nurgu, crappy (adj)
nurlat, grit (n)
nurlato, grit (v)
nurlatu, gritty (adj)
nurn, grin (n)
nurno, grin (v)
nuru, nee (adj)
nuru, née (adj)
nushk, sneak (n)
nushkio, snuck (v pa)
nushkiu, sneakily (adv)
nushko, sneak (v)
nushku, sneaky (adj)
nushkua, sneaker (n doer)
nushp, dusk (n)
nushtak, allegation (n)
nushtako, allege (v)
nushtakua, alleger (n doer)
nutaf, legit (n)
nutafk, legitimacy (n)
nutafkiu, legitimately (adv)
nutafko, legitimize (v)
nutafku, legitimate (adj)
nutafu, legit (adj)
nutak, legality (n)

nutakiu, legally (adv)
nutako, legalize (v)
nutaku, legal (adj)
nuth, mitt (n)
nuthaf, mitten (n)
nuthko, puke (v)
nuthkua, puker (n doer)
nutraf, yoke (n)
nutrafo, yoke (v)
nutsh, party (n d:group)
nuv, jar (n)
nuvo, jar (v)
nuyen, noun (n)
obeinab, abdomen (n)
obiab, aloud (adv)
obiap, alarm (n)
obiapo, alarm (v)
obiapua, alarmist (n doer)
oblaithu, around (adv/prep)
obolp, absorption (n)
obolpo, absorb (v)
obolpua, absorbant (n doer)
obolpua, absorber (n doer)
obort, advice (n)
obortan, advisory (n)
obortiu, advisably (adv)
oborto, advise (v)
obortu, advisable (adj)
obortua, adviser (n doer)
obortua, advisor (n doer)
obotafk, apathy (n)
obotafku, apathetic (adj)
odalpiariu, asynchronously (adv)
odalpiaru, asynchronous (adj)
odiam, adolescence (n)
odiamu, adolescent (adj)
odiamua, adolescent (n doer)
odiauf, amazement (n)
odiaufo, amaze (v)
odorb, abroad (n)
odorbiu, abroad (adv)
odruket, apprehension (n)
odruketiu, apprehensively (adv)
odruketo, apprehend (v)
odruketu, apprehensive (adj)
odufko, avenge (v)
odufkua, avenger (n doer)
ofadelk, assortment (n)
ofadelko, assort (v)
ofarn, aspirin (n)
ofbruno, append (v)
ofdauf, aspiration (n)
ofdaufo, aspire (v)
ofelk, average (n)
ofelko, average (v)
ofelku, average (adj)
ofialt, assumption (n)
ofialto, assume (v)
ofien, alone (adj/adv)
ofk, aptitude (n)
ofkiu, aptly (adv)
ofku, apt (adj)
oflarv, approval (n)

oflarvo, approve (v)
oflarvua, approver (n doer)
oflaud, approach (n)
oflaudo, approach (v)
oflaudu, approachable (adj)
oflaudua, approacher (n doer)
oflikim, appropriation (n)
oflikimiu, appropriately (adv)
oflikimo, appropriate (v)
oflikimu, appropriate (adj)
oflikimua, appropriator (n doer)
ofloigat, approximation (n)
ofloigatiu, approximately (adv)
ofloigato, approximate (v)
ofloigatu, approximate (adj)
oflok, mean (n d:average)
ofpuet, appetite (n)
ofpueto, appetize (v)
ofshak, applause (n)
ofshako, applaud (v)
ofshakua, applauder (n doer)
ogaift, abruptness (n)
ogaiftiu, abruptly (adv)
ogaiftu, abrupt (adj)
ogalp, attire (n)
ogalpo, attire (v)
ogalt, attraction (n)
ogaltiu, attractively (adv)
ogalto, attract (v)
ogaltu, attractive (adj)
ogaltua, attractor (n doer)
ogauik, aberration (n)
ogauiku, aberrant (adj)
ogavat, abolition (n)
ogavato, abolish (v)
ogavatua, abolitionist (n doer)
ogiank, accommodation (n)
ogiankiu, accommodatively (adv)
ogianko, accommodate (v)
ogianku, accommodative (adj)
ogiankua, accommodator (n doer)
ogiap, abatement (n)
ogiapo, abate (v)
ogiaulu, afire (adj)
oglek, acknowledgment (n)
ogleko, acknowledge (v)
ogral, acorn (n)
ogralt, abstract (n)
ogralti, abstract (n pl)
ogralto, abstract (v)
ograltu, abstract (adj)
ograltua, abstractor (n doer)
ogvet, access (n)
ogveto, access (v)
ogvetu, accessible (adj)
ogvetua, accessory (n doer)
oi frep kodi, cannot (ndal
    d:ability)
oi, not (parcl)
oif, oops (interj)
oilodant, automobile (n)
oilodantu, automotive (adj)
oilodarf, autograph (n)

oilodarfo, autograph (v)
oilodenk, automation (n)
oilodenkiu, automatically (adv)
oilodenko, automate (v)
oilodenku, automatic (adj)
oilodenkua, automator (n doer)
oilodernk, automatic (n)
oilonagua, automaker (n doer)
oilovien, autonomy (n)
oipap, alteration (n)
oipapo, alter (v)
oiparfp, alternative (n)
oiparfpiu, alternatively (adv)
oiparfpo, alternate (v)
oiparfpu, alternative (adj)
oiparfpua, alternator (n doer)
okak, ass (n)
okalf, astonishment (n)
okalfio, astonish (v pa)
okalfo, astonish (v)
okauait, abhorrence (n)
okauaito, abhor (v)
okauaitu, abhorrent (adj)
okeftru, ahead (adv)
Okigen, Oxygen (n)
Okiof, Ohio (n)
Oklakom, Oklahoma (n)
Okland, Oakland (n)
oklirt, accent (n)
oklirto, accent (v)
oklirto, accentuate (v)
oklofat, agriculture (n)
oklofatu, agricultural (adj)
okraugu, ablaze (adj)
okriaf, acquaintance (n)
okriafo, acquaint (v)
okriuk, abduction (n)
okriuko, abduct (v)
okriukua, abductor (n doer)
okrug, agony (n)
okrugo, agonize (v)
okuan, again (adv)
okuank, against (prep)
olanf, abnormality (n)
olanfiu, abnormally (adv)
olanfu, abnormal (adj)
olap, assurance (n)
olapiu, assuratively (adv)
olapo, assure (v)
olapu, assurative (adj)
olapua, assurer (n doer)
olark, assignment (n)
olarko, assign (v)
olarkua, assigner (n doer)
olaum, among (prep)
olaum, amongst (prep)
oldidan, assimilation (n)
oldidano, assimilate (v)
oldidanua, assimilator (n doer)
oldord, apology (n)
oldordet, apology (n)
oldordetiu, apologetically (adv)
oldordeto, apologize (v)

oldordetu, apologetic (adj)
oldordo, apoliticize (v)
oldordu, apolitical (adj)
olenp, arithmetic (n)
olenpua, arithmetician (n doer)
olfeshalt, apartment (n)
olfeshfif, apartheid (n)
olfeshu, apart (adj)
olfim, avenue (n)
olirk, ascent (n)
olirko, ascend (v)
olirkua, ascender (n doer)
olirkuet, ascension (n)
olmot, arrangement (n)
olmoto, arrange (v)
olmotua, arranger (n doer)
olpoil, array (n)
olpoilo, array (v)
olshat, assertion (n)
olshatiu, assertively (adv)
olshato, assert (v)
olshatu, assertive (adj)
oluishio, arose (v pa)
oluisho, arise (v)
olzhod, asset (n)
om, an (det)
omaft, analysis (n)
omaftiu, analytically (adv)
omafto, analyze (v)
omaftu, analytical (adj)
omaftua, analyst (n doer)
omaftua, analyzer (n doer)
omashk, anecdote (n)
omashkiu, anecdotally (adv)
omashku, anecdotal (adj)
omdoip, anguish (n)
omdoipo, anguish (v)
omegan, omega (n)
omeif, association (n)
omcifo, associate (v)
omeifua, associate (n doer)
omgaf, annoyance (n)
omgafo, annoy (v)
omid, annotation (n)
omido, annotate (v)
omikron, omicron (n)
ominpio, awoke (v pa)
ominpo, awake (v)
ominpu, awake (adj)
omiop, ancient (n)
omiopu, ancient (adj)
omishu, another (adj)
omkadreifu, antitrust (adj)
omkamiek, antibiotic (n)
omkamk, antidote (n)
omkanf, antenna (n)
omkashlad, antibody (n)
omkavien, antonym (n)
omklap, antique (n)
omklapar, antiquity (n)
omlalk, ancestry (n)
omlalku, ancestral (adj)
omlalkua, ancestor (n doer)

omshelk, anticipation (n)
omshelko, anticipate (v)
omudenk, animation (n)
omudenko, animate (v)
omudenkua, animator (n doer)
omuft, announcement (n)
omufto, announce (v)
omuftua, announcer (n doer)
omun, animal (n)
ona, one (pron 3rd indefpers sng obj)
ona, one (pron 3rd indefpers sng sub)
Onaf, Mendelevium (n davoka)
Onak, Neptunium (n davoka)
onalp, alert (n)
onalpak, alertness (n)
onalpo, alert (v)
onalpua, alerter (n doer)
onam, a.m. (adj)
Onap, Actinum (n davoka)
onar, them/people (pron 3rd indefpers pl obj)
onar, they/people (pron 3rd indefpers pl sub)
onash, one's (pron 3rd indefpers sng pos obj)
onash, one's (pron 3rd indefpers sng pos sub)
onash, people's (pron 3rd indefpers pl pos obj)
onash, people's (pron 3rd indefpers pl pos sub)
onashfal, oneself (pron 3rd indefpers sng refl)
onashfar, peopleselves (pron 3rd indefpers pl refl)
Onat, Berkelium (n davoka)
Onif, Nobelium (n davoka)
Onik, Plutonium (n davoka)
Onip, Thorium (n davoka)
Onit, Californium (n davoka)
oniuk, amount (n)
oniuko, amount (v)
onk, ark (n)
onoart, acclaimation (n)
onoarto, acclaim (v)
Onok, Americium (n davoka)
Onop, Protactinium (n davoka)
Onot, Einsteinium (n davoka)
Ontariof, Ontario (n)
onuak, avoidance (n)
onuakiu, avoidably (adv)
onuako, avoid (v)
onuaku, avoidable (adj)
Onuk, Curium (n davoka)
onulart, ashore (n)
Onup, Uranium (n davoka)
Onut, Fermium (n davoka)
op, of (prep)
opaik, attachment (n)
opaiko, attach (v)

opait, attack (n)
opaito, attack (v)
opaitua, attacker (n doer)
opifk, attendance (n)
opifko, attend (v)
opifkua, attendant (n doer)
opifkuet, attention (n)
opifkuetiu, attentively (adv)
opifkuetu, attentive (adj)
opift, attainment (n)
opifto, attain (v)
opiol, away (adj/adv)
oplian, appearance (n)
oplianiu, apparently (adv)
opliano, appear (v)
oplianu, apparent (adj)
oplianua, apparition (n doer)
oplosho, abridge (v)
oprushel, asleep (adj)
optelp, appeal (n)
optelpo, appeal (v)
Oraf, Thulium (n davoka)
Orak, Promethium (n davoka)
Orap, Lanthanum (n davoka)
Orat, Terbium (n davoka)
orazh, along (prep/adv)
orazhoit, alongside (adv/prep)
ordorfko, accustom (v)
orduip, alloy (n)
orduipo, alloy (v)
orf, O (let sng)
orfhem, Number_1e606
orfi, Os (let pl)
orflauft, alive (adj)
orflian, affiliate (n)
orfliano, affiliate (v)
orflianuet, affiliation (n)
orgoit, accusation (n)
orgoitiu, accusingly (adv)
orgoito, accuse (v)
orgoitua, accuser (n doer)
orgoituin, accused (n)
orgushk, allure (n)
orgushko, allure (v)
oribium, subpoena (n)
oribleg, subclass (n)
oribron, subgroup (n)
oridiathu, subacute (adj)
Orif, Ytterbium (n davoka)
orifaiofu, subionic (adj)
orifalp, suburb (n)
orifalpo, suburbanize (v)
orifalpu, suburban (adj)
orifalpuet, suburbanization (n)
orifep, subset (n)
orifruat, subplot (n)
origalt, subtraction (n)
origalto, subtract (v)
origaltua, subtractor (n doer)
origizhauk, submachine (n)
origizhauku, submachine (adj)
origlarg, subcontract (n)
origlargua, subcontractor (n doer)

Origon, Oregon (n)
origugifp, subcompact (n)
origugifpu, subcompact (adj)
Orik, Samarium (n davoka)
orikeilp, subconsciousness (n)
orikeilpu, subconscious (adj)
orikifiaish, subdivision (n)
orikifiaisho, subdivide (v)
orikifiaishua, subdivider (n doer)
orikirko, subdue (v)
orikoftan, subservience (n)
orikoftaniu, subserviently (adv)
orikoftanu, subservient (adj)
orilafp, submersion (n)
orilafpo, submerge (v)
orilafpu, submersible (adj)
orilafpul, submersible (n)
orilekio, sublet (v pa)
orileko, sublet (v)
oriliaun, submarine (n)
orilk, subject (n)
orilkuet, subjectivity (n)
orilkuetiu, subjectively (adv)
orilkuetu, subjective (adj)
orimert, subcontinent (n)
orinok, submission (n)
orinokiu, submissively (adv)
orinoko, submit (v)
orinoku, submissive (adj)
orinokua, submitter (n doer)
orinuln, sublease (n)
orinulno, sublease (v)
oriothrav, subassembly (n)
Orip, Cerium (n davoka)
oriplaip, substrate (n)
oriplenkua, subcommittee (n doer)
oripliol, subway (n)
orisharshtuk, subsystem (n)
orishkeiat, subordination (n)
orishkeiato, subordinate (v)
orishkeiatua, subordinate (n doer)
orishluket, substation (n)
orishluketo, substation (v)
orishoito, subside (v)
orishol, subhuman (n)
orishpelt, substitution (n)
orishpelto, substitute (v)
orishpeltua, substitute (n doer)
orishrig, subscription (n)
orishrigo, subscribe (v)
orishrigua, subscriber (n doer)
orishtaip, subtitle (n)
orishtaipo, subtitle (v)
orishtib, subtext (n)
orishtibo, subtext (v)
orishuft, subsequence (n)
orishuftiu, subsequently (adv)
orishuftu, subsequent (adj)
Orit, Dysprosium (n davoka)
oritafk, subculture (n)
oritelk, subsistence (n)

oritelko, subsist (v)
oritepo, subject (v)
oritharfet, subversion (n d:lower version)
orithark, subversion (n d:undercut)
oritharkiu, subversively (adv d:undercut)
oritharko, subvert (v d:undercut)
oritharku, subversive (adj d:undercut)
oritharkul, subversive (n)
orithishal, subsection (n)
orithishalo, subsection (v)
orithref, subsurface (n)
orithrefo, subsurface (v)
oritilash, subterra (n)
oritilashu, subterranean (adj)
oritimotu, subatomic (adj)
oritrep, substance (n)
oritrepiu, substantially (adv)
oritrepiu, substantively (adv)
oritrepo, substantiate (v)
oritrepu, substantial (adj)
oritrepu, substantive (adj)
oritrepuet, substantiation (n)
orivithiu, subliminally (adv)
orivitho, sublime (v)
orivithu, subliminal (adj)
orkad, accord (n)
orkadan, accordance (n)
orkadat, altitude (n)
orkadiu, accordingly (adv)
orkado, accord (v)
orkik, affliction (n)
orkiko, afflict (v)
orkiku, afflictive (adj)
orkrath, allotment (n)
orkratho, allot (v)
orkuit, analog (n)
orkuitar, analogy (n)
Orlandof, Orlando (n)
orlap, assessment (n)
orlapiu, assessively (adv)
orlapo, assess (v)
orlapu, assessive (adj)
orlapua, assessor (n doer)
ormiart, affluence (n)
ormiartiu, affluently (adv)
ormiartu, affluent (adj)
ornav, amateur (n)
ornavu, amateurish (adj)
ornial, amusement (n)
ornialo, amuse (v)
orniok, altimeter (n)
orniuf, affirmation (n)
orniufiu, affirmatively (adv)
orniufo, affirm (v)
orniufu, affirmative (adj)
orniufua, affirmer (n doer)
oroif, alignment (n)
oroifo, align (v)
Orok, Europium (n davoka)

orokiu, o'clock (adv)
Orop, Praseodymium (n davoka)
Orot, Holmium (n davoka)
orpoin, account (n)
orpoino, account (v)
orpoinu, accountable (adj)
orpoinua, accountant (n doer)
orsh, also (adv/conj)
orshaip, allocation (n)
orshaipo, allocate (v)
orshaipua, allocator (n doer)
orshil, answer (n)
orshilo, answer (v)
orship, acceptance (n)
orshipiu, acceptably (adv)
orshipo, accept (v)
orshipu, acceptable (adj)
orshkaf, amendment (n)
orshkafo, amend (v)
orth, elf (n)
Oruk, Gadolinium (n davoka)
Orup, Neodymium (n davoka)
orush, allusion (n)
orusho, allude (v)
Orut, Erbium (n davoka)
orvisht, ashameness (n)
orvishto, ashame (v)
oshalf, alike (adj/adv)
oshklauk, across (prep/adj/adv)
oshlef, awareness (n)
oshlefu, aware (adj)
oshman, agnosis (n)
oshmanu, agnostic (adj)
Oshmium, Osmium (n)
oshnal, alias (n)
oshoit, aside (n)
oshoitiu, aside (adv)
otaift, appointment (n)
otaifto, appoint (v)
otaiftua, appointer (n doer)
otav, attrition (n)
otavo, attrite (v)
otavu, attritional (adj)
Otawaf, Ottawa (n)
otelk, assist (n)
otelki, assistance (n pl)
otelkiu, assistively (adv)
otelko, assist (v)
otelku, assistive (adj)
otelkua, assistant (n doer)
othark, aversion (n)
otharko, avert (v)
othet, acquisition (n)
otheto, acquire (v)
othetua, acquirer (n doer)
othoit, abbreviation (n)
othoito, abbreviate (v)
othrav, assembly (n)
othravo, assemble (v)
othravua, assembler (n doer)
othrel, affair (n)
othriup, attribute (n)
othriupiu, attributively (adv)

othriupo, attribute (v)
othriupu, attributive (adj)
othriupua, attributor (n doer)
othuk, aspect (n)
otreilt, acclimation (n)
otreilto, acclimate (v)
otshan, although (conj)
ovaft, attempt (n)
ovafto, attempt (v)
ovait, achievement (n)
ovaito, achieve (v)
ovaitu, achievable (adj)
ovaitua, achiever (n doer)
ovat, apron (n)
oveip, about (prep/adv/adj)
ovil, after (prep/adj/adv)
ovilhaush, afterward (adv)
ovilhaush, afterwards (adv)
ovimidot, afternoon (n)
ovimidotu, afternoon (adj)
ovirp, affection (n)
ovirpiu, affectionately (adv)
ovirpu, affectionate (adj)
ovirt, affect (n)
ovirto, affect (v)
ovoburf, aggravation (n)
ovoburfo, aggravate (v)
ovoiburf, agitation (n)
ovoiburfo, agitate (v)
ovoiburfua, agitator (n doer)
ovorg, aggression (n)
ovorgiu, aggressively (adv)
ovorgo, aggress (v)
ovorgu, aggressive (adj)
ovorgua, aggressor (n doer)
ovramp, abandonment (n)
ovrampo, abandon (v)
ovrat, acceleration (n)
ovratniok, accelerometer (n)
ovrato, accelerate (v)
ovratua, accelerator (n doer)
ovuk, abuse (n)
ovukiu, abusively (adv)
ovuko, abuse (v)
ovuku, abusive (adj)
ovukua, abuser (n doer)
oyalfo, await (v)
ozhar, amid (prep)
ozhar, amidst (prep)
padorp, barrel (n)
padorpo, barrel (v)
paf, fad (n)
pafk, fiction (n)
pafkiu, fictionally (adv)
pafko, fictionalize (v)
pafku, fictional (adj)
pafku, fictitious (adj)
paft, fit (n d:match)
pafto, fit (v d:match)
paftua, fitter (n doer d:match)
pagloik, acquittal (n)
pagloiko, acquit (v)
paiat, pike (n)

paiato, pike (v)
paib, tact (n)
paibak, tactic (n)
paibakiu, tactically (adv)
paibaku, tactical (adj)
paibakua, tactician (n doer)
paibat, tactilation (n)
paibato, tactilate (v)
paibatu, tactile (adj)
paibiu, tactfully (adv)
paibu, tactful (adj)
paif, coin (n)
paifo, coin (v)
pairn, bowl (n d:container, bend)
pairno, bowl (v d:container, bend)
paish, vial (n)
pait, tack (n)
paitat, tackle (n)
paitato, tackle (v)
paitatua, tackler (n doer)
paith, satellite (n)
paito, tack (v)
paitu, tacky (adj)
paiv, federation (n)
paiviu, federally (adv)
paivo, federate (v)
paivu, federal (adj)
paizh, beige (n)
paizhu, beige (adj)
pak, knock (n)
Pakishtan, Pakistan (n)
pako, knock (v)
paktien, knockdown (n)
pakua, knocker (n doer)
pakuil, knockout (n)
Paladium, Palladium (n)
Paleshtif, Palestine (n)
Paleshtin, Palestinian (n)
palfp, bass (n d:fish)
palk, brick (n)
palko, brick (v)
palkua, bricklayer (n doer)
palok, fabric (n)
palt, act (n)
paltak, activation (n)
paltakiu, actively (adv)
paltako, activate (v)
paltaku, active (adj)
paltakua, activist (n doer)
paltior, actuality (n)
paltioriu, actually (adv)
paltioro, actualize (v)
paltioru, actual (adj)
palto, act (v)
paltrol, activity (n)
paltua, actor (n doer)
paltua, actress (n doer)
paltuet, action (n)
pam, pie (n)
Panam, Panama (n)
Panaman, Panamanian (n)
panf, bishop (n)

pank, tiredness (n d:fatigue)
pankmenu, tireless (adj d:fatigueless)
panko, tire (v d:fatigue)
panku, tiresome (adj d:fatigue)
panral, ribbon (n)
parf, park (n d:playground)
parfpliol, parkway (n)
parian, sleigh (n)
Parish, Paris (n)
pariuf, slipper (n)
parlap, sympathy (n)
parlapo, sympathize (v)
parlapu, sympathetic (adj)
parlapua, sympathizer (n doer)
parlit, symbol (n)
parlitiu, symbolically (adv)
parlito, symbolize (v)
parlitu, symbolic (adj)
parlituet, symbolism (n)
parluf, palate (n)
parlufu, palatable (adj)
parn, hill (n)
parndaup, hilltop (n)
parnf, chocolate (n)
parnfu, chocolate (adj)
parnshoit, hillside (n)
parnu, hilly (adj)
parp, drama (n)
parpar, dramatization (n)
parpiu, dramatically (adv)
parpo, dramatize (v)
parpoft, symmetry (n)
parpoftiu, symmetrically (adv)
parpoftu, symmetrical (adj)
parpu, dramatic (adj)
parth, kitchen (n)
partoin, symptom (n)
partoinu, symptomatic (adj)
paruyap, symphony (n)
paruyapu, symphonic (adj)
pash, food (n)
pashp, feast (n)
pashpleth, foodstuff (n)
pashpo, feast (v)
pashpua, feaster (n doer)
pasht, luck (n)
pashtiu, luckily (adv)
pashtmenu, luckless (adj)
pashto, luck (v)
pashtu, lucky (adj)
pashtweku, luckiest (adj)
pashtwelu, luckier (adj)
patak, stomach (n)
patsha, gotcha (interj)
pauak, gargle (n)
pauako, gargle (v)
pauash, gush (n)
pauasho, gush (v)
pauashua, gusher (n doer)
pauf, macro (n)
paug, cave (n)
paugat, cavity (n)

paugil, cavern (n)
paugo, cave (v)
paugua, caver (n doer)
pauguet, cavitation (n)
paugueto, cavitate (v)
pauik, gag (n d:joke)
pauk, joke (n)
pauko, joke (v)
paukua, joker (n doer)
paumb, bind (n d:constrain)
paumbio, bound (v pa d:constrain)
paumbo, bind (v d:constrain)
paumbu, bound (adj d:constrain)
paumbua, binder (n doer d:constrain)
paunf, bounce (n)
paunfiu, bouncily (adv)
paunfo, bounce (v)
paunfu, bouncy (adj)
paunfua, bouncer (n doer)
pauork, gurgle (n)
pauorko, gurgle (v)
paupauk, juggle (n)
paupauko, juggle (v)
paupaukua, juggler (n doer)
paurmb, bound (n d:limit)
paurmb, boundary (n d:limit)
paurmbenu, boundless (adj)
paurp, burial (n)
paurpo, bury (v)
pausho, douse (v)
paut, gut (n)
pautmenu, gutless (adj)
pauto, gut (v)
pautu, gutsy (adj)
pautup, gutter (n)
pav, feed (n)
pavak, feedback (n)
pavo, feed (v)
pavua, feeder (n doer)
pavuap, napkin (n)
pazh, buzz (n d:haircut)
pazho, buzz (v d:haircut)
pazhu, buzz (adj d:haircut)
pef, bush (n)
pefk, dish (n)
pefkfiaush, dishwasher (n)
pefkfiausho, dishwash (v)
pefko, dish (v)
peft, bushel (n)
pefto, bushel (v)
pefu, bushy (adj)
pei, P (let sng)
peiaboko, knead (v)
peiamel, donut (n)
peiamel, doughnut (n)
peian, dough (n)
peiato, rouse (v)
peif, pink (n)
peifrep, viability (n)
peifrepiu, viably (adv)
peifrepu, viable (adj)

peifu, pink (adj)
peig, verge (n d:edge)
peigo, verge (v d:edge)
peihem, Number_1e1806
peikak, virility (n)
peikaku, virile (adj)
peikan, vigor (n)
peikaniu, vigorously (adv)
peikanu, vigorous (adj)
peikap, verve (n)
peikriuk, viaduct (n)
peilath, virgin (n)
peilf, vine (n)
peilfo, vine (v)
peili, Ps (let pl)
peilnok, vinegar (n)
peilraup, vineland (n)
peilthauth, vineyard (n)
peip, feint (n)
peipo, feign (v)
peipua, feigner (n doer)
peish, both (adj/conj)
peish, both (pron)
peit, rout (n d:defeat)
peithu, pervious (adj)
peito, rout (v d:defeat)
peiuf, taciturn (n)
peiufiu, tacitly (adv)
peiufu, tacit (adj)
pel, single (n)
pelk, lunge (n)
pelko, lunge (v)
pelkua, lunger (n doer)
pelmun, sincerity (n)
pelmuniu, sincerely (adv)
pelmunu, sincere (adj)
pelnan, omelet (n)
pelo, single (v)
pelp, mail (n)
pelpan, mailer (n)
pelpefnaf, mailbag (n)
pelpo, mail (v)
pelprenk, mailbox (n)
pelpua, mailman (n doer)
pelsh, singularity (n)
pelshiu, singularly (adv)
pelshu, singular (adj)
pelu, single (adj)
pemdan, penny (n)
penk, tongue (n)
penko, tongue (v)
Penshilvaniaf, Pennsylvania (n)
Pershian, Persian (n)
Peruf, Peru (n)
Perun, EhoMonth04 (n)
peshin, psi (n)
peshp, justice (n)
peshpefrepiu, justifiably (adv)
peshpefrepu, justifiable (adj)
peshpiu, justly (adv)
peshpo, justify (v)
peshpu, just (adj)
peshpuet, justification (n)

pesht, bottom (n)
peshto, bottom (v)
pial, vice (n d:title)
pialfo, fiddle (v d:manipulate)
piap, gib (n)
piapiap, gibberish (n)
piapiapo, gibber (v)
piardarf, chronograph (n)
piardarfiu, chronographically (adv)
piardarfo, chronograph (v)
piardarfu, chronographical (adj)
piark, chronicle (n)
piarko, chronicle (v)
piarkuit, chronology (n)
piarkuitiu, chronologically (adv)
piarkuitu, chronological (adj)
piarth, sieve (n)
piartho, sieve (v)
piat, cadence (n)
pietho, furbish (v)
pif, tent (n d:housing)
pifalu, tenuous (adj)
pifan, tenderness (n)
pifaniu, tenderly (adv)
pifanu, tender (adj)
pifauk, tentacle (n)
pifk, tendency (n)
pifkato, tender (v)
pifko, tend (v)
piflan, funeral (n)
piftaniu, tentatively (adv)
piftanu, tentative (adj)
piftat, tension (n)
piftatiu, tensely (adv)
piftato, tensen (v)
piftatu, tense (adj)
pikat, kite (n)
pilako, straggle (v)
pilakua, straggler (n doer)
pilfiun, fiance (n)
pilfiun, fiancee (n)
pilk, mitigation (n)
pilko, mitigate (v)
pilm, friend (n)
pilmfif, friendship (n)
pilmo, befriend (v)
pilmu, friendly (adj)
pilmua, friend (n doer)
pilmuet, friendliness (n)
pilp, bark (n d:tree skin)
pilshran, comrade (n)
pilt, tweet (n)
pilto, tweet (v)
pimaf, spouse (n)
pimafo, espouse (v)
pimafu, spousal (adj)
pin, pi (n)
piran, plummet (n)
pirano, plummet (v)
pird, check (n d:money)
pirtap, exterior (n)
pirtapiu, externally (adv)

pirtapo, externalize (v)
pirtapu, external (adj)
pirtho, sift (v)
pirthua, sifter (n doer)
pithp, tenancy (n)
pithpua, tenant (n doer)
Pitshburg, Pittsburgh (n)
piuagubidu, ungodly (adj)
piualtipu, unmentionable (adj)
piuanlaku, unalienable (adj)
piubashalpo, unauthorize (v)
piubiaufiu, undoubtedly (adv)
piubilenio, unbecame (v pa)
piubileno, unbecome (v)
piubinko, unoppose (v)
piublashkiu, unimpressively (adv)
piublashku, unimpressive (adj)
piublego, unclassify (v)
piubriakfrepu, unusable (adj)
piubriakiu, unusually (adv)
piubriaku, unusual (adj)
piubrianko, unregister (v)
piubrietiu, undeniably (adv)
piubrietu, undeniable (adj)
piubrugo, unburn (v)
piubudolfu, undetectable (adj)
piubugapo, unpack (v)
piudainu, unequal (adj)
piudaltho, uncover (v)
piudaunu, untimely (adj)
piudautiu, unbeatably (adv)
piudautu, unbeatable (adj)
piudepiu, unthinkingly (adv)
piudepu, unthinkable (adj)
piudhigoku, unmistakable (adj)
piudiako, unburden (v)
piudilnu, unholy (adj)
piudito, unlist (v)
piudofto, unbutton (v)
piudreiflaishu, untrustworthy (adj)
piudreilu, untrue (adj)
piudreish, untruth (n)
piudreishiu, untruthfully (adv)
piudreishu, untruthful (adj)
piudrotu, unclear (adj)
piuduapiu, untypically (adv)
piuduapu, untypical (adj)
piuduftiu, uncritically (adv)
piuduftu, uncritical (adj)
piuduthapiu, unseasonably (adv)
piuduthapu, unseasonable (adj)
piuefbino, unopen (v)
piufaftu, uncivil (adj)
piufantuniu, unpatriotically (adv)
piufantunu, unpatriotic (adj)
piufertho, unidentify (v)
piufirdu, uneventful (adj)
piufiukiu, unproductively (adv)
piufiuku, unproductive (adj)
piufiunkiu, unprofessionally (adv)
piufiunku, unprofessional (adj)
piufiupaftiu, unprofitably (adv)

piufiupaftu, unprofitable (adj)
piufiushaiko, unprovoke (v)
piuflaishu, unworthy (adj)
piuflauftfrepu, unlivable (adj)
piuflef, unease (n)
piuflefiu, uneasily (adv)
piuflefu, uneasy (adj)
piuflefuet, uneasiness (n)
piuflian, unfamiliarity (n)
piuflianu, unfamiliar (adj)
piufliofo, unprove (v)
piufluikiu, unwisely (adv)
piufluiku, unwise (adj)
piufnaipo, unbrand (v)
piufnetu, unsteady (adj)
piufnupo, unwrap (v)
piufrep, unability (n)
piufrepiu, unably (adv)
piufrepkodu, uncanny (adj)
piufrepu, unable (adj)
piufrilp, unpleasantness (n)
piufrilpiu, unpleasantly (adv)
piufrilpu, unpleasant (adj)
piufrilto, unorganize (v)
piufrinfo, unhitch (v)
piuftapu, unstable (adj)
piugailu, unhelpful (adj)
piugashu, untraceable (adj)
piugiro, uncall (v)
piugithpo, unplug (v)
piuglek, unknown (n)
piuglekiu, unknowingly (adv)
piugleku, unknowable (adj)
piuglesho, untie (v)
piugloirfu, uncharitable (adj)
piuglorgu, unreachable (adj)
piugranpo, uncork (v)
piugrukiu, unbearably (adv)
piugruku, unbearable (adj)
piugurnu, uncommon (adj)
piuhauthu, unhealthy (adj)
piuhinfo, unquote (v)
piuiaboftiu, unobtrusively (adv)
piuiabofto, unobtrude (v)
piuiaboftu, unobtrusive (adj)
piuipidurtiu, uncooperatively (adv)
piuipidurtu, uncooperative (adj)
piuipifkiu, unintentionally (adv)
piuipifku, unintentional (adj)
piuipko, unbias (v)
piuivadavu, unemotional (adj)
piukarflualu, unassailable (adj)
piukeikutiu, unremarkably (adv)
piukeikutu, unremarkable (adj)
piukeilp, unconsciousness (n)
piukeilpiu, unconsciously (adv)
piukeilpu, unconscious (adj)
piuketo, uncheck (v)
piukiftio, unbent (v pa)
piukifto, unbend (v)
piukinaliu, unimaginably (adv)
piukinalu, unimaginable (adj)

piukioku, unworkable (adj)
piukirkiu, unduly (adv)
piukirku, undue (adj)
piukiviugiu, unimportantly (adv)
piukiviugu, unimportant (adj)
piukleizhiu, unreasonably (adv)
piukleizho, unreason (v)
piukleizhu, unreasonable (adj)
piukloipo, unscrew (v)
piukolanu, unwelcome (adj)
piukolm, unhappiness (n)
piukolmiu, unhappily (adv)
piukolmu, unhappy (adj)
piukralko, unscramble (v)
piukufpu, unethical (adj)
piulalirto, unlicense (v)
piulauitu, unsatisfactory (adj)
piulauto, unveil (v)
piuleidiu, unnaturally (adv)
piuleidu, unnatural (adj)
piuleifar, undulation (n)
piuleifaro, undulate (v)
piuliapiu, unreadably (adv)
piuliapu, unreadable (adj)
piulibesho, unsettle (v)
piuligragu, unsolvable (adj)
piulitano, unplan (v)
piuliufimu, unconventional (adj)
piuliushpeltiu, unconstitutionally
    (adv)
piuliushpeltu, unconstitutional
    (adj)
piuliutifkiu, unconditionally (adv)
piuliutifku, unconditional (adj)
piulobuku, unsupportable (adj)
piuloiriu, undesirably (adv)
piuloiru, undesirable (adj)
piuludratu, unrepentant (adj)
piuluduashu, unrepresentative
    (adj)
piuludufpu, unresponsive (adj)
piulurto, unload (v)
piuluvipo, unregulate (v)
piumempiftiu, unsustainable
    (adv)
piumemthukiu, unsuspectingly
    (adv)
piumoimio, unpaid (v pa)
piumoimo, unpay (v)
piumorpiu, unsuitably (adv)
piumorpu, unsuitable (adj)
piumunpiu, unconscionably (adv)
piumunpu, unconscionable (adj)
piumutho, unmatch (v)
piunarthepu, unfavorable (adj)
piunepo, untap (v)
piunulko, unleash (v)
piuoflarvo, unapprove (v)
piuogaltiu, unattractively (adv)
piuogaltu, unattractive (adj)
piuogiap, unabatement (n)
piuogiapo, unabate (v)
piuoipapiu, unalterably (adv)

piuoipapu, unalterable (adj)
piuonuakiu, unavoidably (adv)
piuonuaku, unavoidable (adj)
piuoplosh, unabridgement (n)
piuoplosho, unabridge (v)
piuorfliano, unaffiliate (v)
piuorpoino, unaccount (v)
piuorpoinu, unaccountable (adj)
piuorshilu, unanswerable (adj)
piuorship, unacceptability (n)
piuorshipiu, unacceptably (adv)
piuorshipo, unaccept (v)
piuorshipu, unacceptable (adj)
piuoshlefu, unaware (adj)
piuparlapu, unsympathetic (adj)
piuparlufu, unpalatable (adj)
piupashtu, unlucky (adj)
piupaumbio, unbound (v pa)
piupaumbo, unbind (v)
piupeshpiu, unjustly (adv)
piupeshpu, unjust (adj)
piupilmu, unfriendly (adj)
piuplathu, uncontroversial (adj)
piuplesho, undress (v)
piupletiu, unevenly (adv)
piupletu, uneven (adj)
piuplikio, unbroke (v pa)
piupliko, unbreak (v)
piupliku, unbreakable (adj)
piupluaf, unreality (n)
piupluafu, unreal (adj)
piupluaniu, unrealistically (adv)
piupluanu, unrealistic (adj)
piupreish, unrest (n)
piupreitfrepu, unintelligible (adj)
piuprineltiu, unfaithfully (adv)
piuprineltu, unfaithful (adj)
piureishtu, uninhabitable (adj)
piuridafo, unschedule (v)
piurigato, unravel (v)
piurudeik, unpredictability (n)
piurudeikiu, unpredictably (adv)
piurudeiku, unpredictable (adj)
piushalf, unlike (prep/adj)
piushanf, unlikely (adj/adv)
piushariu, unbelievably (adv)
piusharu, unbelievable (adj)
piusharua, unbeliever (n doer)
piushemu, unclean (adj)
piushenko, untax (v)
piushialu, untouchable (adj)
piushianu, unsanitary (adj)
piushiufp, unavailability (n)
piushiufpu, unavailable (adj)
piushiupo, unavail (v)
piushiveshtiu, unnecessarily (adv)
piushiveshtu, unnecessary (adj)
piushkito, unmove (v)
piushlaifu, unwary (adj)
piushloit, unemployment (n)
piushloito, unemploy (v)
piushlufu, uncool (adj)
piushmotato, unbalance (v)

piushnaitho, unclutter (v)
piushneno, unarm (v)
piushreliu, unsure (adv)
piushrelu, unsure (adj)
piushriko, unseat (v)
piushtato, unmark (v)
piushtiatetiu, unquestionably
    (adv)
piushtiatetu, unquestionable (adj)
piushuashiu, unscientifically
    (adv)
piushuashu, unscientific (adj)
piutaigago, untangle (v)
piutalshiu, unspeakably (adv)
piutalshu, unspeakable (adj)
piutarfo, unhinge (v)
piutashkeliu, unofficially (adv)
piutashkelu, unofficial (adj)
piutaukiu, unstoppably (adv)
piutauku, unstoppable (adj)
piutebo, unrate (v)
piutefpesho, unadjust (v)
piutharoiku, unverifiable (adj)
piuthraikio, unwound (v pa)
piuthraiko, unwind (v)
piuthrauno, unbridle (v)
piuthrel, unfairness (n)
piuthreliu, unfairly (adv)
piuthrelu, unfair (adj)
piuthriutu, unscrupulous (adj)
piuthuitu, untreatable (adj)
piuthuklakiu, unspectacularly
    (adv)
piuthuklaku, unspectacular (adj)
piuthunu, unseemly (adj)
piutigagato, unhinder (v)
piutigreto, undisclose (v)
piutikio, undid (v pa)
piutiko, undo (v)
piutiugo, unlock (v)
piutrantiu, uncontrollably (adv)
piutrantu, uncontrollable (adj)
piutravo, unfold (v)
piutrem, unreliability (n)
piutremiu, unreliably (adv)
piutremu, unreliable (adj)
piutrilku, untrainable (adj)
piutrulfo, unfurl (v)
piutrulshu, unprintable (adj)
piututuano, unchange (v)
piututhukiu, unexpectedly (adv)
piututhuko, unexpect (v)
piuvaigiu, unexplainably (adv)
piuvaigu, unexplainable (adj)
piuvalsh, unborn (n)
piuvanpu, uncompetitive (adj)
piuvartufo, unsecure (v)
piuvaudiu, unlawfully (adv)
piuvaudu, unlawful (adj)
piuvelfu, unfit (adj)
piuvenkiu, uneconomically (adv)
piuvenku, uneconomical (adj)
piuvertiu, unexceptionally (adv)

piuvertu, unexceptional (adj)
piuvinko, unbundle (v)
piuvitho, unlimit (v)
piuviuviatiu, unambiguously (adv)
piuviuviatu, unambiguous (adj)
piuvlarviu, uncomfortably (adv)
piuvlarvu, uncomfortable (adj)
piuvoamuniu, unfortunately (adv)
piuvoamunu, unfortunate (adj)
piuvoanthuthu, unforeseeable (adj)
piuvoatopu, unforgettable (adj)
piuvoiviushiu, unsurprisingly (adv)
piuvord, unpopularity (n)
piuvordiu, unpopularly (adv)
piuvordu, unpopular (adj)
piuvosharo, unlove (v)
piuvoviuku, unenforceable (adj)
piuvulno, unmarry (v)
piuweifo, unsign (v)
piuyak, unwillingness (n)
piuyakiu, unwillingly (adv)
piuzhatufu, unsound (adj)
piuzheifo, unzip (v)
piuzhilt, uncertainty (n)
piuzhiltu, uncertain (adj)
piuzhiunu, unselfish (adj)
piuzhiunuet, unselfishness (n)
piuzhoivo, unseal (v)
piuzhudu, unsafe (adj)
piuzhuvetushiu, unsuccessfully (adv)
piuzhuvetushu, unsuccessful (adj)
pivak, tenacity (n)
pivaku, tenacious (adj)
pivatu, tenable (adj)
pivit, bike (n)
pivito, bike (v)
pivitua, biker (n doer)
plab, slab (n)
pladeik, contradiction (n)
pladeiko, contradict (v)
pladeiku, contradictory (adj)
plaf, grace (n)
plafig, quarry (n)
plafigo, quarry (v)
plafim, contravention (n)
plafimo, contravene (v)
plafiu, graciously (adv)
plafk, census (n)
plafliap, grapefruit (n)
plafo, grace (v)
plafp, grape (n)
plafpeilan, grapevine (n)
plafu, gracious (adj)
plafuet, graciousness (n)
plafushiu, gracefully (adv)
plafushu, graceful (adj)
plagat, quarrel (n)
plagato, quarrel (v)
plaif, broom (n)

plaik, strategy (n)
plaikiu, strategically (adv)
plaiku, strategic (adj)
plaikua, strategist (n doer)
plaip, stratus (n)
plaipi, strata (n pl)
plaish, proneness (n)
plaishu, prone (adj)
plaith, grill (n)
plaitho, grill (v)
plak, grate (n)
plako, grate (v)
plakua, grater (n doer)
plamp, hump (n)
plampevak, humpback (n)
plampevaku, humpback (adj)
plampo, hump (v)
plarp, contrariness (n)
plarpu, contrary (adj)
plarshp, contraception (n)
plarshpua, contraceptive (n doer)
plasht, censorship (n)
plashto, censor (v)
plashtua, censor (n doer)
plath, controversy (n)
plathu, controversial (adj)
Platinum, Platinum (n)
platufkef, moorhead (n)
platufo, moor (v d:secure)
platuk, speaker (n d:air cone)
plauf, cloud (n)
plaufk, debris (n)
plaufo, cloud (v)
plaufu, cloudy (adj)
plaug, crypt (n)
plauk, bruise (n)
plauko, bruise (v)
plaukua, bruiser (n doer)
plavramp, contraband (n)
plazh, gratitude (n)
plazhd, gratuity (n)
plazhiu, gratefully (adv)
plazho, gratify (v)
plazhu, grateful (adj)
plazhuet, gratification (n)
plef, wish (n)
plefo, wish (v)
pleftoik, wishbone (n)
plefu, wishful (adj)
plefu, wishy (adj)
plefua, wisher (n doer)
pleif, moderation (n)
pleifar, module (n)
pleifarat, modularity (n)
pleifariu, modularly (adv)
pleifaro, modulate (v)
pleifaru, modular (adj)
pleifarua, modulator (n doer)
pleifaruet, modulation (n)
pleifiu, moderately (adv)
pleifk, modification (n)
pleifko, modify (v)
pleifkua, modifier (n doer)

pleifo, moderate (v)
pleifu, moderate (adj)
pleifua, moderator (n doer)
pleish, waiver (n)
pleisho, waive (v)
plent, clerk (n)
plep, OvaCarrier (n)
plesh, dress (n d:clothing)
pleshk, dresser (n d:cabinet)
pleshnagua, dressmaker (n doer)
plesho, dress (v d:clothing)
pleshua, dresser (n doer d:clothing)
plet, evenness (n d:distribute)
pleth, stuff (n)
pletho, stuff (v)
plethu, stuffy (adj)
plethua, stuffer (n doer)
pletiu, evenly (adv d:distribute)
pleto, even (v d:distribute)
pletu, even (adj d:distribute)
pliaf, sprawl (n)
pliafo, sprawl (v)
pliak, integer (n)
pliapo, bask (v)
pliashk, integration (n)
pliashkar, integrity (n)
pliashkiu, integrally (adv)
pliashko, integrate (v)
pliashku, integral (adj)
pliashkua, integrator (n doer)
pliashp, therapy (n)
pliashpu, therapeutic (adj)
pliashpua, therapist (n doer)
pliat, recovery (n d:retrieve, heal)
pliato, recover (v d:retrieve, heal)
pliatu, recoverable (adj d:retrieve, heal)
pliatua, recoverer (n doer d:retrieve, heal)
pliauk, sprain (n)
pliauko, sprain (v)
pliaut, siren (n)
plifk, breakup (n)
plifkio, brokeup (v pa)
plifko, breakup (v)
pligito, quibble (v)
plik, break (n)
plikar, breakage (n)
plikeidon, breakwater (n)
plikio, broke (v pa)
plikiu, breakably (adv)
pliko, break (v)
plikopiol, breakaway (n)
pliktaift, breakpoint (n)
pliku, breakable (adj)
plikua, breaker (n doer)
plikuil, breakout (n)
plim, chin (n)
plimork, franchise (n)
plimorko, enfranchise (v)
plin, spree (n)
pliol, way (n)

pliolshoit, wayside (n)
pliolu, wayward (adj)
plir, chill (n)
pliro, chill (v)
plirt, elicitation (n)
plirto, elicit (v)
pliru, chilly (adj)
plirua, chiller (n doer)
plit, item (n)
plitelshan, breakthrough (n)
plithk, velocity (n)
plitien, breakdown (n)
plito, itemize (v)
plitua, itemizer (n doer)
pliubu, jumbo (adj)
pliuf, spray (n)
pliufo, spray (v)
pliufua, sprayer (n doer)
pliuk, drain (n)
pliuko, drain (v)
pliukua, drainer (n doer)
pliukuet, drainage (n)
pliup, jumble (n)
pliupo, jumble (v)
pliut, creation (n)
pliutal, creature (n)
pliutiu, creatively (adv)
pliuto, create (v)
pliutu, creative (adj)
pliutua, creator (n doer)
pliutuet, creativity (n)
pliv, migration (n)
plivak, immigration (n)
plivako, immigrate (v)
plivakua, immigrant (n doer)
plivg, emigration (n)
plivgo, emigrate (v)
plivgua, emigrant (n doer)
plivo, migrate (v)
plivu, migrant (adj)
plivua, migrant (n doer)
plofien, monk (n)
plofk, moniker (n)
ploif, bracelet (n)
ploik, glitch (n)
ploish, silk (n)
ploishfanin, silkwood (n)
ploishiu, silkily (adv)
ploishu, silky (adj)
ploishyorn, silkworm (n)
ploit, brace (n)
ploitak, bracket (n)
ploitako, bracket (v)
ploito, brace (v)
ploitua, bracer (n doer)
plon, person (n)
plonag, personification (n)
plonago, personify (v)
plonar, personnel (n)
plonegrult, manhunt (n)
ploni, people (n pl)
ploniu, personally (adv)
plonk, kernel (n)

plonkoth, manhole (n)
plono, personalize (v)
plonshriaut, manslaughter (n)
plont, personality (n)
plonu, personal (adj)
plonuet, personalization (n)
plonul, personal (n)
plorf, garb (n)
plork, board (n d:wood)
plorko, board (v d:wood)
plorp, bump (n)
plorpiu, bumpily (adv)
plorpo, bump (v)
plorpu, bumpy (adj)
plorpua, bumper (n doer)
plorsh, mortar (n d:bowl)
plort, brow (n)
plorto, brow (v)
plosh, bridge (n)
plosho, bridge (v)
plovak, rubbish (n)
plovath, rubber (n)
plovathu, rubbery (adj)
pluab, lamp (n)
pluabalt, lamppost (n)
pluaf, reality (n)
pluafiu, really (adv)
pluafu, real (adj)
pluafua, realist (n doer)
pluak, grant (n)
pluako, grant (v)
pluakua, grantor (n doer)
pluan, realism (n)
pluaniu, realistically (adv)
pluano, realize (v)
pluanu, realistic (adj)
pluanuet, realization (n)
pluat, lantern (n)
pluath, ovation (n)
pluav, coed (n)
plubashalt, coauthority (n)
plubashaltua, coauthor (n doer)
plud, kit (n)
pluf, enough (adj/adv)
pluf, enough (pron)
pluik, hail (n d:precipitation)
pluikfrip, hailstorm (n)
pluiko, hail (v d:precipitation)
pluip, piano (n)
plukad, record (n)
plukado, record (v)
plukadu, recordable (adj)
plukadua, recorder (n doer)
plukiot, distortion (n)
plukioto, distort (v)
plumarmak, cogeneration (n)
plumarmako, cogenerate (v)
plumarmakua, cogenerator (n
   doer)
plunp, guest (n)
plunsh, receipt (n)
plunshak, receptacle (n)
plunshua, recipient (n doer)

plunt, hint (n)
plunto, hint (v)
plunult, coexistence (n)
plunulto, coexist (v)
plup, guess (n)
plupkiok, guesswork (n)
pluplut, tidbit (n)
plupo, guess (v)
plupua, guesser (n doer)
plureishtuet, cohabitation (n)
plureishtueto, cohabitate (v)
plurg, sludge (n)
plurk, improvisation (n)
plurko, improvise (v)
plushik, reception (n)
plushikiu, receptively (adv)
plushiku, receptive (adj)
plushikua, receptor (n doer)
plushipar, receptionist (n)
plushipo, receive (v)
plushipu, receivable (adj)
plushipua, receiver (n doer)
plushipun, receivable (n)
plushupato, cofound (v)
plushupatua, cofounder (n doer)
plut, bit (n d:part)
pluthuk, disrespect (n)
pluthuko, disrespect (v)
Plutonium, Plutonium (n)
pluv, groan (n)
pluvaik, disregard (n)
pluvaiko, disregard (v)
pluvirthar, coefficient (n)
pluvo, groan (v)
pluvua, groaner (n doer)
pluzh, grief (n)
pluzhiu, grievously (adv)
pluzho, grieve (v)
pluzhu, grievous (adj)
pluzhua, griever (n doer)
pluzhuet, grievance (n)
poaf, clause (n)
poal, clay (n)
poap, bud (n d:plant)
poapo, bud (v d:plant)
poef, shade (n)
poefo, shade (v)
poeft, shadow (n)
poefto, shadow (v)
poeftu, shadowy (adj)
poeftua, shadower (n doer)
poefu, shady (adj)
poefua, shader (n doer)
pofko, muddle (v)
pofp, mud (n)
pofpeshkraikio, mudslung (v pa)
pofpeshkraiko, mudsling (v)
pofpiu, muddily (adv)
pofpo, muddy (v)
pofpu, muddy (adj)
pogaif, hives (n d:skin eruption)
poidoip, extinguishment (n)
poidoipo, extinguish (v)

poidoipua, extinguisher (n doer)
poifbakotuet, counterterrorism (n)
poifesh, counterpart (n)
poifgauft, counterargument (n)
poifgaufto, counterargue (v)
poifgrol, countermeasure (n)
poifiuku, counterproductive (adj)
poifiulk, counterproposal (n)
poifkrithk, counterpunch (n)
poifkrithko, counterpunch (v)
poifnoart, counterclaim (n)
poifnoartao, counterclaimed (v prp)
poifnoarto, counterclaim (v)
poifo, counter (v d:d: oppose)
poifopait, counterattack (n)
poifopaito, counterattack (v)
poifpalt, counteraction (n)
poifpaltiu, counteractively (adv)
poifpalto, counteract (v)
poifpaltu, counteractive (adj)
poifpaltua, counteractor (n doer)
poifpeimo, counterfeit (v)
poifpeimu, counterfeit (adj)
poifpeimua, counterfeiter (n doer)
poifpreit, counterintelligence (n)
poifshmotat, counterbalance (n)
poifshmotato, counterbalance (v)
poifshuish, counterweight (n)
poifshuisho, counterweigh (v)
poiftaift, counterpoint (n)
poik, tong (n)
poil, ray (n)
poin, count (n d:d: increment)
poind, tennis (n)
poino, count (v d:d: increment)
pointien, countdown (n)
poinua, counter (n doer d:d: increment)
poip, fiber (n)
poipu, fibrous (adj)
poirt, distinction (n)
poirtiu, distinctly (adv)
poirto, distinguish (v)
poirtu, distinct (adj)
poirtu, distinctive (adj)
poishk, count (n d:d: title)
poisht, extinction (n)
poishtu, extinct (adj)
poith, absurdity (n)
poithiu, absurdly (adv)
poithu, absurd (adj)
poktel, picture (n)
poktelo, picture (v)
Polanud, Poland (n)
Polonium, Polonium (n)
polt, delicacy (n)
poltiu, delicately (adv)
poltu, delicate (adj)
ponden, pound (n d:weight)
ponf, county (n)

ponk, coercion (n)
ponko, coerce (v)
ponku, coercive (adj)
ponkua, coercer (n doer)
pont, bottle (n)
ponto, bottle (v)
pontua, bottler (n doer)
poreft, factor (n)
porefto, factor (v)
poret, fact (n)
poretiu, factually (adv)
poretu, factual (adj)
porf, beard (n)
porfo, beard (v)
porgo, nab (v)
porgthoil, knapsack (n)
porgua, nabber (n doer)
porlan, period (n d:cycle)
porlaniu, periodically (adv d:cycle)
porlanu, periodic (adj d:cycle)
Portelanud, Portland (n)
porth, peripheral (n)
porthu, periperhal (adj)
Portugal, Portugal (n)
posh, foot (n)
poshak, football (n d:American)
poshbotsh, footpath (n)
poshdorim, footwear (n)
poshef, footstep (n)
poshezhail, footfall (n)
poshi, feet (n pl)
poshkiok, footwork (n)
poshmid, footnote (n)
poshmido, footnote (v)
poshmol, football (n d:soccer)
posho, foot (v)
poshparn, foothill (n)
posht, honesty (n)
poshtiu, honestly (adv)
poshtrulsh, footprint (n)
poshtu, honest (adj)
poshua, footer (n doer)
Potashium, Potassium (n)
pov, country (n)
povaip, diner (n)
povshoit, countryside (n)
prad, cradle (n)
prado, cradle (v)
praft, corner (n)
praftbaraf, cornerstone (n)
prafto, corner (v)
praftprand, cornfield (n)
Pragaf, Prague (n)
prago, throb (v)
praiak, throe (n)
praik, route (n d:path)
praikat, routine (n)
praikatiu, routinely (adv)
praikatu, routine (adj)
praiko, route (v d:path)
praikua, router (n doer d:path)
prain, foil (n d:prevent)

praino, foil (v d:prevent)
praish, rarity (n)
praishiu, rarely (adv)
praisho, rarify (v)
praishu, rare (adj)
prait, theft (n)
praith, teller (n)
praito, thieve (v)
praitua, thief (n doer)
pral, knoll (n)
pralf, decoration (n)
pralfar, decor (n)
pralfo, decorate (v)
pralfua, decorator (n doer)
pralk, correction (n)
pralkiu, correctly (adv)
pralko, correct (v)
pralku, correct (adj)
pralp, corporation (n)
pralpo, incorporate (v)
pralpu, corporate (adj)
pralt, crate (n)
praltap, crater (n)
praltapo, crater (v)
pralto, crate (v)
pram, ram (n d:animal)
prampo, encumber (v)
prampu, cumbersome (adj)
prand, field (n)
prando, field (v)
prandua, fielder (n doer)
pransho, ramble (v)
pranshua, rambler (n doer)
Prasheodimium, Praseodymium (n)
prashk, rubble (n)
prat, function (n)
pratak, functionality (n)
prath, draw (n d:pull, inscribe)
prathio, drew (v pa d:pull, inscribe)
pratho, draw (v d:pull, inscribe)
prathua, drawer (n doer d:pull, inscribe)
prathvak, drawback (n)
pratiu, functionally (adv)
prato, function (v)
pratsh, rabble (n)
pratsho, rabble (v)
pratshua, rabbler (n doer)
pratu, functional (adj)
pratua, functioner (n doer)
prauf, slop (n)
praufo, slop (v)
praufu, sloppy (adj)
praufuet, sloppiness (n)
prauk, slob (n)
praum, pelt (n d:fur)
praupo, slobber (v)
praut, blot (n)
prauto, blot (v)
prautua, blotter (n doer)
prazhan, dreg (n)

prazho, dredge (v)
predizh, narration (n)
predizhat, narrative (n)
predizho, narrate (v)
predizhu, narrative (adj)
predizhua, narrator (n doer)
preibid, telecast (n)
preibido, telecast (v)
preibielk, teleport (n)
preibielko, teleport (v)
preibielkua, teleporter (n doer)
preibotsh, telepathy (n)
preibotshu, telepathic (adj)
preibotshua, telepath (n doer)
preid, restaurant (n)
preidarf, telegraph (n)
preidarfo, telegraph (v)
preidifdarf, telephotography (n)
preidifdarfo, telephotograph (v)
preidifdarfu, telephoto (adj)
preif, hope (n)
preif, hopefullness (n)
preifen, hopelessness (n)
preifeniu, hopelessly (adv)
preifenu, hopeless (adj)
preifiu, hopefully (adv)
preifo, hope (v)
preifu, hopeful (adj)
preiguniat, telecommunication (n)
preigut, telecom (n)
preik, spank (n)
preiko, spank (v)
preikua, spanker (n doer)
preiliaf, trivium (n)
preiliafi, trivia (n pl)
preiliafo, trivialize (v)
preiliafu, trivial (adj)
preiliafuet, triviality (n)
preiliugef, teleconference (n)
preiluaf, telescope (n)
preiluafo, telescope (v)
preiluafu, telescopic (adj)
preinelk, telegram (n)
preinelko, telegram (v)
preipoft, telemetry (n)
preish, rest (n)
preishiu, restfully (adv)
preishmeniu, restlessy (adv)
preishmenu, restless (adj)
preisho, rest (v)
preishu, restful (adj)
preishua, rester (n doer)
preit, intelligence (n)
preitariu, intellectually (adv)
preitaru, intellectual (adj)
preitarua, intellectual (n doer)
preitfrepiu, intelligibly (adv)
preitfrepu, intelligible (adj)
preith, chroma (n)
preithent, telekinesis (n)
preithentu, telekinetic (adj)
preithulid, television (n)

preithulido, televise (v)
preitiu, intelligently (adv)
preitu, intelligent (adj)
preitua, intellect (n doer)
preiyap, telephone (n)
preiyapo, telephone (v)
preiyapu, telephonic (adj)
preiyapuet, telephony (n)
prekutal, gladiator (n)
prelfiu, gladly (adv)
prelfk, gait (n)
prelfo, gladden (v)
prelfor, glade (n)
prelfu, glad (adj)
prelk, gate (n)
prelkip, gateway (n)
prelklofua, gatekeeper (n doer)
prelko, gate (v)
prelm, month (n)
prelmu, monthly (adj)
prenk, box (n d:cube)
prenko, box (v d:cube)
prenku, boxy (adj d:cube)
presh, recreation (n d:rest)
preshu, recreational (adj d:rest)
pret, tale (n)
preth, turf (n)
pretio, told (v pa)
pretiu, tellingly (adv)
preto, tell (v)
pretopretu, telltale (adj)
priaf, foil (n d:sheet)
priafo, foil (v d:sheet)
priak, brittleness (n)
priako, brittle (v)
priaku, brittle (adj)
priam, prune (n d:fruit)
prian, jerk (n)
prianiu, jerkily (adv)
priano, jerk (v)
prianu, jerky (adj)
prianua, jerk (n doer)
priat, biscuit (n)
priauko, slouch (v)
priaukua, slouch (n doer)
prif, hip (n)
prifif, cranny (n)
prift, crop (n d:food)
priftua, cropper (n doer d:food)
pill, hue (n)
prilak, pylon (n)
prilk, silt (n)
prilm, blank (n)
prilmap, blanket (n)
prilmapo, blanket (v)
prilmo, blank (v)
prilp, possession (n)
prilpiu, possessively (adv)
prilpo, possess (v)
prilpu, possessive (adj)
prilpua, possessor (n doer)
prinelmen, faithlessness (n)
prinelmeniu, faithlessly (adv)

prinelmenu, faithless (adj)
prinelt, faith (n)
prineltiu, faithfully (adv)
prinelto, enfaith (v)
prineltu, faithful (adj)
prineltuet, faithfulness (n)
prinet, fidelity (n)
priof, pore (n)
priofu, porous (adj)
prip, braille (n)
prish, fast (n d:starve)
prishmashp, fastball (n)
prisho, fast (v d:starve)
pritho, mull (v)
priuf, luncheon (n)
prium, dormancy (n)
priumu, dormant (adj)
priup, robe (n)
priut, lunch (n)
priuto, lunch (v)
priutshran, lunchroom (n)
priutua, luncher (n doer)
proid, knob (n)
prok, dock (n)
prokef, docket (n)
proko, dock (v)
prokshoit, dockside (n)
prokshoitu, dockside (adj)
prolt, document (n)
proltar, documentary (n)
proltet, documentation (n)
prolto, document (v)
proltua, documenter (n doer)
Promethium, Promethium (n)
prosht, doctrine (n)
proshto, indoctrinate (v)
Protaktinium, Protactinium (n)
prothp, doctor (n)
prothpo, doctor (v)
pruaf, vane (n)
pruat, blade (n)
pruft, blend (n)
prufto, blend (v)
pruftua, blender (n doer)
pruk, method (n)
prukiu, methodically (adv)
pruko, methodize (v)
pruku, methodical (adj)
prukuit, methodology (n)
prulk, strain (n)
prulko, strain (v)
prulkua, strainer (n doer)
prum, snail (n)
prush, sleep (n)
prushio, slept (v pa)
prushmenu, sleepless (adj)
prusho, sleep (v)
prushu, sleepy (adj)
prushua, sleeper (n doer)
prushuet, sleepiness (n)
prushzhoipo, sleepwalk (v)
prushzhoipua, sleepwalker (n doer)

prutsh, punk (n)
prutshu, punky (adj)
pruzh, drudge (n)
pruzho, drudge (v)
pruzhu, drudgery (adj)
pruzhua, drudge (n doer)
puam, pawn (n)
puamo, pawn (v)
puamthov, pawnshop (n)
puat, barb (n)
puato, barb (v)
puatua, barber (n doer)
puld, nudge (n)
puldo, nudge (v)
pulk, culpability (n)
pulku, culpable (adj)
pulkua, culprit (n doer)
pumuf, laziness (n)
pumufiu, lazily (adv)
pumufu, lazy (adj)
pumufweku, laziest (adj)
pumufwelu, lazier (adj)
punp, helm (n d:helmet)
punp, helmet (n)
puprush, coma (n d:sleep)
puprushu, comatose (adj d:sleep)
purk, gross (n d:package)
puth, dune (n)
puvik, grog (n)
puviku, groggy (adj)
puvin, tear (n d:eyedrop)
puvino, tear (v d:eyedrop)
puvinu, tearful (adj)
puvinu, teary (adj d:eyedrop)
rab, tear (n d:rip)
rabio, tore (v pa d:rip)
rabo, tear (v d:rip)
Radium, Radium (n)
Radon, Radon (n)
rafk, coat (n)
rafko, coat (v)
raifkiok, framework (n)
raifkioko, framework (v)
raift, frame (n)
raifto, frame (v)
raiftua, framer (n doer)
raizh, tease (n)
raizho, tease (v)
raizhua, teaser (n doer)
rakad, comb (n)
rakado, comb (v)
rakadua, comber (n doer)
rakaif, loathness (n)
rakaifo, loathe (v)
rakaifu, loath (adj)
rakiu, meow (interj)
raliuk, audio (n)
raliukon, audience (n)
raliuku, audible (adj)
ralk, audit (n)
ralko, audit (v)
ralkua, auditor (n doer)
ralkuet, audition (n)

ralkueto, audition (v)
ralp, fleece (n)
ralpo, fleece (v)
ralpua, fleecer (n doer)
ralsh, pettiness (n)
ralshiu, pettily (adv)
ralshu, petty (adj)
ramap, banana (n)
ramsh, legend (n)
ramshu, legendary (adj)
ranen, mildness (n)
raneniu, mildly (adv)
ranenu, mild (adj)
ranenweku, mildest (adj)
ranenwelu, milder (adj)
raniap, whale (n)
raniapo, whale (v)
ranp, flesh (n)
ranpo, flesh (v)
ranpu, fleshy (adj)
rashal, coma (n d:oblong)
rasherl, comet (n)
rasht, letter (n d:message)
rashtkeft, letterhead (n)
rashtplon, letterman (n)
rashtploni, lettermen (n pl)
rathaunu, lukewarm (adj)
rathien, marathon (n)
rathienua, marathoner (n doer)
ratsh, meat (n)
ratshmashp, meatball (n)
ratshmenu, meatless (adj)
ratshu, meaty (adj)
rau, us (pron 1st pl obj)
raublar, landlady (n)
raubup, landfill (n)
raufif, feudalism (n)
raufifu, feudal (adj)
raufk, loft (n)
rautkiu, loftlly (adv)
raufko, loft (v)
raufku, lofty (adj)
rauglark, landmass (n)
rauk, lift (n)
rauko, lift (v)
raukua, lifter (n doer)
raukunf, liftoff (n)
raup, land (n)
raupo, land (v)
rauptheifua, landowner (n doer)
raupua, lander (n doer)
raush, ours (pron 1st pl pos obj)
raushafp, landlord (n)
raushfal, ourself (pron 1st sing refl)
raushfar, ourselves (pron 1st pl refl)
raushiak, landscape (n)
raushiako, landscape (v)
raushiakua, landscaper (n doer)
raushlush, landslide (n)
raushtat, landmark (n)
rautiug, landlock (n)

rautiugo, landlock (v)
rauzh, lag (n)
rauzhail, landfall (n)
rauzho, lag (v)
rauzhua, laggard (n doer)
rayu-rayu, bow-wow (interj)
razh, length (n)
razhak, footage (n)
razhbaraf, milestone (n)
razhdat, longitude (n)
razhdaunu, longtime (adj)
razheshkot, longshot (n)
razhkap, longhand (n)
razho, lengthen (v)
razhoil, longing (n d:desire)
razhoiliu, longingly (adv d:desire)
razhoilu, longing (adj d:desire)
razhu, lengthy (adj)
razhu, long (adj)
razhwaku, longest (adj)
razhwelu, lengthier (adj)
razhwelu, longer (adj)
reftiu, afforably (adv)
refto, afford (v)
reftu, affordable (adj)
reiap, cheek (n)
reiaptoik, cheekbone (n)
reif, elder (n)
reifiu, elderly (adv)
reifu, elder (adj)
reifweku, eldest (adj)
reigin, look (n)
reigino, look (v)
reiginua, looker (n doer)
reiginuil, lookout (n)
reik, like (n)
reikfrepu, likeable (adj)
reikif, like (prep)
reikiu, likely (adv)
reikiufif, likelihood (n)
reiko, like (v)
reiku, like (adj)
reikuet, likeness (n)
reilafk, chemistry (n)
reilak, chemical (n)
reilakiu, chemically (adv)
reilaku, chemical (adj)
reilakua, chemist (n doer)
Reilop, Europe (n)
Reilopan, European (n)
reilt, habit (n)
reiltiu, habitually (adv)
reiltu, habitual (adj)
reinf, par (n)
reinfo, par (v)
reinfu, par (adj)
reirt, cherry (n)
reirtu, cherry (adj)
reisho, rave (v)
reisht, habitat (n)
reishto, inhabit (v)
reishtu, habitable (adj)
reishtua, inhabitant (n doer)

reishtuet, habitation (n)
reishua, raver (n doer)
reiuk, choke (n)
reiuko, choke (v)
reiukua, choker (n doer)
rel, R (let sng)
relhem, Number_1e1356
reln, merriment (n)
relniu, merrily (adv)
relnu, merry (adj)
relnweku, merriest (adj)
relnwelu, merrier (adj)
relri, Rs (let pl)
ren, sun (n)
renbrug, sunburn (n)
renbrugo, sunburn (v)
rendafk, sunbelt (n)
rendalfo, sunbathe (v)
rendalfua, sunbather (n doer)
renderp, sunspot (n)
rendrint, sunglass (n)
renduaf, sunbeam (n)
reneipot, sundial (n)
renfep, sunset (n)
renfklet, sunscreen (n)
renflarm, sundance (n)
renflarmo, sundance (v)
renfluan, sunlight (n)
renfluanio, sunlit (v pa)
reniu, sunnily (adv)
Renium, Rhenium (n)
reniveil, sunup (n)
renlarf, sunroof (n)
renluish, sunrise (n)
renluishua, sunriser (n doer)
renmaiam, suntan (n)
renmoith, sunshine (n)
renpoef, sunshade (n)
renshlesh, sunfish (n)
renshleshi, sunfish (n pl)
renshran, sunroom (n)
renthuan, sunflower (n)
rentien, sundown (n)
renu, sunny (adj)
Renviul, Sunday (n)
resh, right (n d:direction)
reshaushu, rightward (adj)
reshkap, righty (n)
reshkliegu, rightwing (adj)
reshu, right (adj d:direction)
reth, lie (n d:placement)
rethio, lay (v pa d:placement)
retho, lie (v d:placement)
retien, joist (n)
rial, low (n)
rialiu, lowly (adv)
rialo, lower (v)
rialshkof, lowercase (n)
rialu, low (adj)
rialwaku, lowest (adj)
rialwelu, lower (adj)
rian, hour (n)
rianilf, hourglass (n)

riank, affray (n)
rianko, affray (v)
riankua, affrayer (n doer)
rianu, hourly (adj)
riark, acrobat (n)
riarku, acrobatic (adj)
riarvien, acronym (n)
riash, massage (n)
riasho, massage (v)
riashua, massager (n doer)
riath, owl (n)
riazho, linger (v)
ridaf, schedule (n)
ridafo, schedule (v)
ridafua, scheduler (n doer)
rideig, groom (n d:bridegroom)
rifal, thanks (n)
Rifalgruf, Thanksgiving (n)
rifaliu, thankfully (adv)
rifalmenu, thankless (adj)
rifalo, thank (v)
rifalu, thankful (adj)
rigato, ravel (v)
rilp, spread (n)
rilpio, spread (v pa)
rilpo, spread (v)
rilpua, spreader (n doer)
rinagat, influenza (n)
rinini, meek (n pl)
rininiu, meekly (adv)
rininu, meek (adj)
riop, pail (n)
riosh, aroma (n)
rioshiu, aromatically (adv)
rioshu, aromatic (adj)
rishad, teen (n)
rishdalt, teenager (n)
Rishmonud, Richmond (n)
ritaro, loiter (v)
rith, smith (n)
ritral, ring (n d:circle)
ritralo, ring (v d:circle)
ritralt, ringleader (n)
ritralua, ringer (n doer d:circle)
ritrashoit, ringside (n)
ritrashoitu, ringside (adj)
ritrathiok, ringmaster (n)
riuf, rumble (n)
riufo, rumble (v)
riuk, lion (n)
rium, hull (n)
riun, boom (n)
riuno, boom (v)
rivun, prestige (n)
rivunu, prestigious (adj)
Rodef Ilanud, Rhode Island (n)
Rodium, Rhodium (n)
Roentgenium, Roentgenium (n)
rogalf, occurrence (n)
rogalfo, occur (v)
rogalt, occasion (n)
rogaltiu, occasionally (adv)
rogalto, occasion (v)

rogaltu, occasional (adj)
roiak, lien (n)
roif, line (n)
roifiu, linearly (adv)
roifiveil, lineup (n)
roifo, line (v)
roifp, delineation (n)
roifpan, delinquence (n)
roifpanu, delinquent (adj)
roifpo, delineate (v)
roifpua, delineator (n doer)
roifu, linear (adj)
roifua, liner (n doer)
roifuet, lineage (n)
roik, ligature (n)
roikaft, latch (n)
roikafto, latch (v)
roikat, ligament (n)
roiko, ligate (v)
roikuet, ligation (n)
roimet, linen (n)
roin, lint (n)
roino, lint (v)
roinua, linter (n doer)
roish, link (n)
roishiveil, linkup (n)
roisho, link (v)
roishua, linker (n doer)
roishuet, linkage (n)
roit, queue (n)
roith, syllabus (n)
roithi, syllabi (n pl)
roito, queue (v)
rolf, barrier (n)
rolm, council (n)
rolmo, conciliate (v)
rolp, counsel (n)
rolpo, counsel (v)
rolpua, counselor (n doer)
rolt, bar (n d:rod)
rolto, bar (v d:rod)
Romaf, Rome (n)
Romafan, Roman (n)
Romiaf, Romania (n)
Romian, Romanian (n)
ron, rho (n)
ronaf, vessel (n)
Roteshar, Rochester (n)
rotuto, pour (v)
rovak, bake (n)
rovakar, bakery (n)
rovako, bake (v)
rovakua, baker (n doer)
rovorp, occupation (n)
rovorpan, occupancy (n)
rovorpanua, occupant (n doer)
rovorpiu, occupationally (adv)
rovorpo, occupy (v)
rovorpu, occupational (adj)
rovorpua, occupier (n doer)
rual, lyre (n)
rualp, lyric (n)
rualpu, lyrical (adj)

ruank, hunk (n)
ruanko, hunker (v)
ruankua, hunker (n doer)
ruash, right (n d:ownership)
rubalvelariu, preposterously (adv)
rubalvelaru, preposterous (adj)
Rubek, EhoMonth02 (n)
Rubidium, Rubidium (n)
rubolk, preparation (n)
rubolko, prepare (v)
rubolkua, preparer (n doer)
rubugato, prepackage (v)
rubushlan, predestination (n)
rubushlano, predestine (v)
rudeik, prediction (n)
rudeikiu, predictably (adv)
rudeiko, predict (v)
rudeiku, predictable (adj)
rudeiku, predictive (adj)
rudeikua, predictor (n doer)
rudermaku, precancerous (adj)
rudibag, pretrial (n)
ruduath, prevention (n)
ruduathiu, preventably (adv)
ruduathiu, preventively (adv)
ruduatho, prevent (v)
ruduathu, preventable (adj)
ruduathu, preventive (adj)
ruduvak, preservation (n)
rufep, preset (n)
rufepio, preset (v pa)
rufepo, preset (v)
rufialt, presumption (n)
rufialtiu, presumably (adv)
rufialtiu, presumptively (adv)
rufialto, presume (v)
rufialtu, presumable (adj)
rufialtu, presumptive (adj)
rufival, preseason (n)
rufkuk, legacy (n)
rufpen, leftover (n)
rufto, preach (v)
ruftu, preachy (adj)
ruftua, preacher (n doer)
rufuat, preview (n)
rufuato, preview (v)
rufuatua, previewer (n doer)
rugef, preference (n)
rugefiu, preferably (adv)
rugefiu, preferentially (adv)
rugefo, prefer (v)
rugefu, preferable (adj)
rugefu, preferential (adj)
rugink, preemption (n)
ruginkiu, preemptively (adv)
ruginko, preempt (v)
ruginku, preemptive (adj)
rugreniu, precariously (adv)
rugrenu, precarious (adj)
rugruto, preclude (v)
ruhet, prejudice (n)
ruhethet, prejudgement (n)
ruhetheto, prejudge (v)

ruheto, prejudice (v)
rukoft, preserve (n)
rukofto, preserve (v)
rukoftua, preserver (n doer)
ruliukult, preconfiguration (n)
ruliukulto, preconfigure (v)
ruliushp, preconception (n)
ruliushpo, preconceive (v)
ruliutifk, precondition (n)
ruliutifko, precondition (v)
rulm, gentleness (n)
rulmiu, gently (adv)
rulmu, gentle (adj)
rulnosh, gentleman (n)
rulnoshi, gentlemen (n pl)
ruluthat, prerequisite (n)
rulzhimu, gingerly (adj)
rumoim, prepayment (n)
rumoimio, prepaid (v pa)
rumoimo, prepay (v)
rumoimua, prepayer (n doer)
runaufk, predomination (n)
runaufkiu, predominantly (adv)
runaufko, predominate (v)
runaufku, predominant (adj)
runiatu, pristine (adj)
runok, premise (n)
runoko, premise (v)
runsh, share (n)
runsho, share (v)
runshthorthua, shareholder (n doer)
runshua, sharer (n doer)
runult, preexistence (n)
runulto, preexist (v)
ruol, prearrangement (n)
ruolo, prearrange (v)
rup, leave (n d:departure)
rupifk, pretense (n)
rupifko, pretend (v)
rupifku, pretentious (adj)
rupifkua, pretender (n doer)
rupio, left (v pa d:departure)
ruplukado, prerecord (v)
rupo, leave (v d:departure)
rurovorp, preoccupation (n)
rurovorpo, preoccupy (v)
rurutsh, prelude (n)
rurutsho, prelude (v)
rusharth, prehistory (n)
rusharthu, prehistoric (adj)
rushenk, pretax (n)
rushenko, pretax (v)
Rushiaf, Russia (n)
Rushian, Russian (n)
rushirfiu, prematurely (adv)
rushirfu, premature (adj)
rushiup, prevalence (n)
rushiupo, prevail (v)
rushiupu, prevalent (adj)
rushkashp, precaution (n)
rushlek, precipitation (n)
rushleko, precipitate (v)

rushpesh, preschool (n)
rushpeshu, preschool (adj)
rushrig, prescription (n)
rushrigo, prescribe (v)
rushtib, pretext (n)
rushuash, prescience (n)
Ruthenium, Ruthenium (n)
Rutherfordium, Rutherfordium (n)
ruthishk, precision (n)
ruthishkiu, precisely (adv)
ruthishku, precise (adj)
ruthiu, preciously (adv)
ruthoish, preface (n)
ruthoisho, preface (v)
ruthu, precious (adj)
rutilak, predisposition (n)
rutilako, predispose (v)
rutulsh, predetermination (n)
rutulsho, predetermine (v)
ruvaushu, preliminary (adj)
ruvek, precession (n)
ruvekat, precedence (n)
ruvekat, precedent (n)
ruveko, precede (v)
ruvekua, predecessor (n doer)
ruvik, prefix (n)
ruviko, prefix (v)
ruvirt, prefecture (n)
ruvirtua, prefect (n doer)
ruviur, prewar (n)
ruvuglak, presupposition (n)
ruvuglako, presuppose (v)
ruvuln, premarriage (n)
ruvulnu, premarital (adj)
ruzhiarfk, premeditation (n)
ruzhiarfko, premeditate (v)
Sanau, Sanau (n)
sei, S (let sng)
seihem, Number_1e3306
seili, Ss (let pl)
Seranara, Seranara (n)
Seris, Seris (n)
sha, she (pron 3rd fem sng sub)
shafkan, freckle (n)
shaflak, trash (n)
shaflako, trash (v)
shaflaku, trashy (adj)
shafp, lord (n)
shafpieit, dynasty (n)
shafpieitu, dynastic (adj)
shai, the (det)
shaiam, watch (n d:viewing)
shaiamdraush, watchdog (n)
shaiamiu, watchfully (adv d:viewing)
shaiamo, watch (v d:viewing)
shaiamplon, watchman (n)
shaiamploni, watchmen (n pl)
shaiamu, watchful (adj d:viewing)
shaiamua, watcher (n doer d:viewing)
shaiash, state (n d:region)

shaiashfif, statehood (n)
shaiashkiaf, statehouse (n)
shaiashkrashu, statewide (adj)
shaiashoit, stateside (n)
shaiashoitu, stateside (adj)
shaiashplon, statesman (n)
shaiashplonfif, statesmanship (n)
shaiashploni, statesmen (n pl)
shaif, freak (n)
shaifo, freak (v)
shaifu, freaky (adj)
shailt, studio (n)
shaip, locale (n)
shaip, locality (n)
shaip, location (n)
shaipiu, locally (adv)
shaipo, locate (v)
Shaiprush, Cyprus (n)
shaipu, local (adj)
shaipua, locator (n doer)
shaipuet, localization (n)
shaipueto, localize (v)
shaith, west (n)
shaithan, western (n d:film)
shaithaushu, westward (adj)
shaithdraipu, westbound (adj)
shaitho, westernize (v)
shaithu, west (adj)
shaithu, western (adj)
shaithua, westerner (n doer)
shaithweku, westernmost (adj)
Shaizhar, Caesar (n)
Shaizharu, Caesarean (adj)
shakidorg, shotgun (n)
shakit, shot (n)
Shakrament, Sacramento (n)
shalf, love (n d:pleasure)
shalfo, love (v d:pleasure)
shalfu, lovely (adj d:pleasure)
shalfua, lover (n doer d:pleasure)
shalirt, essence (n)
shalirtiu, essentially (adv)
shalirto, essentiate (v)
shalirtu, essential (adj)
shalkiu, plausibly (adv)
shalko, plause (v)
shalku, plausible (adj)
shalm, fur (n)
shalmo, fur (v)
shalmu, furry (adj)
shaln, simplicity (n)
shalniu, simply (adv)
shalno, simplify (v)
shalnu, simple (adj)
shalnu, simplistic (adj)
shalnuet, simplification (n)
shalnwaku, simplest (adj)
shalnwelu, simpler (adj)
Shamarium, Samarium (n)
shamim, canoe (n)
shamimo, canoe (v)
Shan Antonion, San Antonio (n)
Shan Diegof, San Diego (n)

Shan Franshishk, San Francisco (n)
shan, her (pron 3rd fem sng obj)
Shanilan, January (n)
Shankaif, Shanghai (n)
shanp, example (n)
shanpo, exemplify (v)
Shant Barbaraf, Santa Barbara (n)
Shantaf Klaush, Santa Claus (n)
Shapor, EhoMonth10 (n)
shar, belief (n)
sharal, midwife (n)
shardak, widow (n)
shardako, widow (v)
shardal, woman (n)
shardali, women (n pl)
shardoiak, womanization (n)
shardoiako, womanize (v)
shardoiakua, womanizer (n doer)
shardu, whether (conj)
sharf, wife (n)
shargen, silver (n)
shargo, lodge (v d:stop)
shariu, believably (adv)
Sharlot, Charlotte (n)
sharlp, sentiment (n)
sharlpu, sentimental (adj)
sharlt, heroic (n)
sharlt, heroism (n)
sharltiu, heroically (adv)
sharltu, heroic (adj)
sharltua, hero (n doer)
sharltua, heroine (n doer)
sharluim, robustness (n)
sharluimu, robust (adj)
sharn, modernism (n)
sharn, modernization (n)
sharno, modernize (v)
sharnu, modern (adj)
sharnua, modernist (n doer)
sharo, believe (v)
shart, either (pron)
sharth, history (n)
sharthiu, historically (adv)
sharthu, historic (adj)
sharthu, historical (adj)
sharthua, historian (n doer)
shartu, either (adj/adv/conj)
sharu, believable (adj)
sharua, believer (n doer)
sharvab, maternity (n)
sharvabiu, maternally (adv)
sharvabu, maternal (adj)
shash, her (pron 3rd fem sng pos sub)
shash, hers (pron 3rd fem sng pos obj)
shashfal, herself (pron 3rd fem sing refl)
shashk, management (n)
shashkiu, manageably (adv)
shashko, manage (v)
shashku, manageable (adj)

shashkua, manager (n doer)
shashkualu, managerial (adj)
shasho, man (v d:operate)
shauan, whisker (n d:hair)
Shaudaf Arban, Saudi Arabia (n)
Shaudan, Saudi (n)
shauf, buffet (n d:strike)
shaufo, buffet (v d:strike)
shauk, estrangement (n)
shaukat, strangeness (n)
shaukiu, strangely (adv)
shauko, estrange (v)
shauku, strange (adj)
shaukua, stranger (n doer)
shaup, asylum (n)
shaushuth, soybean (n)
shauth, trait (n)
shavan, gown (n)
shdolf, protection (n)
shdolfiu, protectively (adv)
shdolfo, protect (v)
shdolfu, protective (adj)
shdolfua, protectionist (n doer)
shdolfua, protector (n doer)
shdolfuet, protectionism (n)
Sheaborgium, Seaborgium (n)
shefir, subtlety (n)
shefiriu, subtly (adv)
shefiru, subtle (adj)
shei, Sh (let sng)
sheiaf, fetus (n)
sheiafu, fetal (adj)
sheiam, theory (n)
sheiamiu, theoretically (adv)
sheiamo, theorize (v)
sheiamu, theoretical (adj)
sheiamua, theorist (n doer)
sheif, fertility (n)
sheifit, veggie (n)
sheifo, fertilize (v)
sheifu, fertile (adj)
sheifua, fertilizer (n doer)
sheifuet, fertilization (n)
sheihem, Number_1e3606
sheili, Shs (let pl)
sheilt, slogan (n)
sheimait, senility (n)
sheimaitu, senile (adj)
sheimat, sonior (n)
sheimatu, senior (adj)
sheimatua, senior (n doer)
sheimatuet, seniority (n)
shein, radius (n)
sheinf, fountain (n)
sheini, radii (n pl)
sheino, radius (v)
sheirnat, thesis (n)
sheish, specialty (n)
sheishiu, especially (adv)
sheishiu, specially (adv)
sheisho, specialize (v)
sheishu, special (adj)
sheishua, specialist (n doer)

sheith, elasticity (n)
sheithu, elastic (adj)
sheivan, vegetation (n)
sheivano, vegetate (v)
sheivanua, vegetator (n doer)
sheivot, vegetable (n)
sheivotuat, vegetarianism (n)
sheivotuatua, vegetarian (n doer)
Shelenium, Selenium (n)
Shelfian, Celsius (adj)
shelthu, supple (adj)
shem, cleanliness (n)
shemiu, cleanly (adv)
shemiveil, cleanup (n)
shemo, clean (v)
shemu, clean (adj)
shemua, cleaner (n doer)
shen, fame (n)
shend, supper (n)
sheniu, famously (adv)
shenk, tax (n)
shenko, tax (v)
shenku, taxable (adj)
shenkua, taxer (n doer)
shenkuet, taxation (n)
shent, taxi (n)
shentmoim, taxpayer (n)
shento, taxi (v)
shenu, famous (adj)
shep, sub (n d:submarine)
sher, hair (n)
sherdaish, haircut (n)
sherfriaf, hairstyle (n)
Sherium, Cerium (n)
sherleip, hairpin (n)
shermenu, hairless (adj)
sheroif, hairline (n)
sherpleshua, hairdresser (n doer)
sherpliuf, hairspray (n)
shertik, hairdo (n)
sheru, hairy (adj)
sheshai, ok (interj)
sheshai, okay (interj)
Sheshium, Caesium (n)
shesho, okay (v)
sheshu, okay (adj)
shethp, supply (n)
shethpet, supplement (n)
shethpeto, supplement (v)
shethpetu, supplemental (adj)
shethpetu, supplementary (adj)
shethpetuet, supplementation (n)
shethpo, supply (v)
shethpua, supplier (n doer)
shevish, secret (n)
shevishiu, secretively (adv)
shevishiu, secretly (adv)
shevisht, secrecy (n)
shevishu, secret (adj)
shevishu, secretive (adj)
shiaf, sanity (n)
shiafiu, sanely (adv)
shiafu, sane (adj)

shiag, tangle (n)
shiago, tangle (v)
shiakbliet, scapegoat (n)
shial, touch (n)
shialbaraf, touchstone (n)
shialo, touch (v)
shialtien, touchdown (n)
shialu, touchy (adj)
shiam, tangent (n)
shiamiu, tangentially (adv)
shiamp, tangible (n)
shiampu, tangible (adj)
shiamu, tangential (adj)
shian, sanitation (n)
shiano, sanitize (v)
shianu, sanitary (adj)
shiap, adept (n)
shiapu, adept (adj)
Shiaraf, Sierra (n)
shiart, conquest (n)
shiarto, conquer (v)
shiartua, conqueror (n doer)
shiash, fashion (n)
shiashiu, fashionably (adv)
shiasho, fashion (v)
shiashu, fashionable (adj)
Shiatal, Seattle (n)
shiauko, sap (v)
shib, meal (n)
shibedaun, mealtime (n)
shibedaunu, mealtime (adj)
Shidunaf, Sydney (n)
shiemk, senate (n)
shiemkua, senator (n doer)
Shien, Army (n)
shig, spoke (n d:support)
shigman, sigma (n)
shigo, spoke (v d:support)
shik, skill (n)
shikiu, skillfully (adv)
shiko, skill (v)
shiku, skillful (adj)
Shilikon, Silicon (n)
shilk, sap (n)
shilkap, sapling (n)
shilu, itty (adj)
Shilver, Silver (n)
Shinkapor, Singapore (n)
Shinshinat, Cincinnati (n)
shiob, hoop (n)
shiof, texture (n)
shiofo, texturize (v)
shiofua, texturer (n doer)
shioiko, vanish (v)
shioikua, vanisher (n doer)
shiokloin, textile (n)
Shiol, Seoul (n)
shior, hook (n)
shioriveil, hookup (n)
shioro, hook (v)
shiorua, hooker (n doer)
shirf, maturity (n)
shirfk, immaturity (n)

shirfkiu, immaturely (adv)
shirfku, immature (adj)
shirfo, mature (v)
shirfu, mature (adj)
shirfuet, maturation (n)
Shiriaf, Syria (n)
Shirian, Syrian (n)
shish, these (pron)
shishu, these (adj)
shitho, lynch (v)
shiu, whew (interj)
shiuaif, sizzle (n)
shiuaifo, sizzle (v)
shiuf, vanity (n)
shiufiu, vainly (adv)
shiufp, availability (n)
shiufpu, available (adj)
shiufu, vain (adj)
shiuk, vaunt (n)
shiuko, vaunt (v)
shiunku, lucent (adj)
shiuno, elucidate (v)
shiunu, lucid (adj)
shiup, avail (n)
shiupo, avail (v)
shiush, switch (n)
shiushafen, switchover (n)
shiusho, switch (v)
shiushplork, switchboard (n)
shiushpruat, switchblade (n)
shiushu, switchy (adj)
shiushua, switcher (n doer)
shivat, knight (n)
shivato, knight (v)
shivatu, knightly (adj)
shivesht, necessity (n)
shiveshtiu, necessarily (adv)
shivesho, necessitate (v)
shiveshtu, necessary (adj)
shkafo, mend (v)
shkaiauk, squawk (n)
shkaiauko, squawk (v)
shkaidan, igloo (n)
shkaik, felony (n)
shkaikua, felon (n doer)
shkain, cruise (n)
shkainak, crusade (n)
shkainako, crusade (v)
shkainakua, crusader (n doer)
shkaino, cruise (v)
shkainua, cruiser (n doer)
shkaish, smash (n)
shkaisho, smash (v)
shkaishua, smasher (n doer)
shkait, ice (n)
shkaitait, icicle (n)
shkaitiu, icily (adv)
shkaitniuk, iceberg (n)
shkaito, ice (v)
shkaitplikua, icebreaker (n doer)
shkaitplon, iceman (n)
shkaitploni, icemen (n pl)
shkaitprenk, icebox (n)

shkaitu, icy (adj)
shkak, crack (n d:split)
shkakdarb, crackpot (n)
shkako, crack (v d:split)
shkaktien, crackdown (n)
shkakua, cracker (n doer d:split)
shkalak, crackle (n)
shkalako, crackle (v)
shkalt, start (n)
shkaltak, startle (n)
shkaltako, startle (v)
shkaltiveil, startup (n)
shkalto, start (v)
shkaltua, starter (n doer)
shkam, strum (n)
shkamo, strum (v)
shkamua, strummer (n doer)
Shkandium, Scandium (n)
shkap, slash (n)
shkapo, slash (v)
shkapua, slasher (n doer)
shkash, cause (n)
shkashk, casualty (n)
shkashkiu, casually (adv)
shkashku, casual (adj)
shkasho, cause (v)
shkashp, caution (n)
shkashpiu, cautiously (adv)
shkashpo, caution (v)
shkashpu, cautious (adj)
shkashu, causal (adj)
shkatho, strut (v)
shkaufu, stout (adj)
shkaup, schism (n)
shkaupi, schism (n pl)
shkaush, arson (n)
shkausho, arson (v)
shkaushu, arsonous (adj)
shkaushua, arsonist (n doer)
shkav, tussle (n)
shkavo, tussle (v)
shkeiat, ordination (n)
shkeiato, ordinate (v)
shkeik, squeak (n)
shkeikiu, squeakily (adv)
shkeiko, squeak (v)
shkeiku, squeaky (adj)
shkeith, tuft (n)
shkeito, ordain (v)
shkelk, squeal (n)
shkelko, squeal (v)
shkelp, staple (n d:crimp)
shkelpo, staple (v d:crimp)
shkelpua, stapler (n doer d:crimp)
shkenp, optic (n)
shkenpiu, optically (adv)
shkenpu, optical (adj)
shkep, coordinate (n)
shkepet, coordination (n)
shkepo, coordinate (v)
shkepua, coordinator (n doer)
shket, order (n)
shket, orderliness (n)

shketariu, ordinarily (adv)
shketaru, ordinary (adj)
shketat, ordinance (n)
shketo, order (v)
shketu, orderly (adj)
shketua, orderer (n doer)
shkiak, tuck (n)
shkiako, tuck (v)
shkiakua, tucker (n doer)
shkiat, stare (n)
shkiatho, scoot (v)
shkiathua, scooter (n doer)
shkiato, stare (v)
shkiaut, starkness (n)
shkiautu, stark (adj)
shkifu, indivisible (adj)
shkik, segment (n)
shkiken, mutiny (n)
shkikeno, mutiny (v)
shkikenua, mutineer (n doer)
shkiko, segment (v)
shkikuet, segmentation (n)
shkilp, crimp (n)
shkilpo, crimp (v)
shkilpua, crimper (n doer)
shkilt, crinkle (n)
shkilto, crinkle (v)
shkiot, squirt (n)
shkioto, squirt (v)
shkip, individual (n)
shkipiu, individually (adv)
shkipo, individualize (v)
shkipu, individual (adj)
shkipuet, individualism (n)
shkipuet, individuality (n)
shkipuetu, individualistic (adj)
shkipuetua, individualist (n doer)
shkirk, seduction (n)
shkirkiu, seductively (adv)
shkirko, seduce (v)
shkirku, seductive (adj)
shkirkua, seducer (n doer)
shkish, piss (n)
shkisho, piss (v)
shkishua, pisser (n doer)
shkit, move (n)
shkitalt, movement (n)
shkitar, movie (n)
shkitarnagua, moviemaker (n
    doer)
shkitiu, movably (adv)
shkito, move (v)
shkitu, movable (adj)
shkitua, mover (n doer)
shkiuko, skid (v)
shkivev, thickness (n)
shkiveviu, thickly (adv)
shkivevo, thicken (v)
shkivevu, thick (adj)
shkivevua, thickener (n doer)

shklat, statute (n)
shklatu, statutory (adj)
shklein, sea (n)
shkleinbielk, seaport (n)
shkleinbranf, seacoast (n)
shkleineidon, seawater (n)
shkleinflarn, seafront (n)
shkleinfuarm, seabed (n)
shkleinkiam, seagull (n)
shkleinkliek, seahawk (n)
shkleinpash, seafood (n)
shkleinpliol, seaway (n)
shkleinplon, seaman (n)
shkleinploni, seamen (n pl)
shkleinprelk, seagate (n)
shkleinshoit, seaside (n)
shkleinshoitu, seaside (adj)
shkleinthek, seashell (n)
shkleinthiko, seafare (v)
shkleinyuk, seaweed (n)
shkliag, cruelty (n)
shkliagiu, cruelly (adv)
shkliagu, cruel (adj)
shklift, crush (n)
shklifto, crush (v)
shkliftua, crusher (n doer)
shklipu, crude (adj)
shklivag, meanness (n d:cruel)
shklivagu, mean (adj d:cruel)
shklivagweku, meanest (adj
    d:cruel)
shklivagwelu, meaner (adj
    d:cruel)
shklut, choice (n)
shklutio, chose (v pa)
shkluto, choose (v)
shklutu, choosy (adj)
shklutua, chooser (n doer)
shkob, boat (n)
shkobo, boat (v)
shkobua, boater (n doer)
shkodag, cottage (n)
shkof, case (n d:investigation)
shkoflurt, caseload (n)
shkofo, case (v d:investigation)
shkoip, slant (n)
shkoipo, slant (v)
shkoit, shot (n)
shkot, shoot (n)
shkotio, shot (v pa)
Shkotlan, Scottish (n)
Shkotlanf, Scotland (n)
shkoto, shoot (v)
shkotua, shooter (n doer)
shkotuil, shootout (n)
shkrag, patch (n)
shkrago, patch (v)
shkragu, patchy (adj)
shkragua, patcher (n doer)
shkraik, sling (n)
shkraikio, slung (v pa)
shkraiko, sling (v)
shkraikshkoit, slingshot (n)

shkraikua, slinger (n doer)
shkrakio, slew (v pa)
shkrako, slay (v)
shkrakua, slayer (n doer)
shkran, daze (n)
shkranat, dazzle (n)
shkranato, dazzle (v)
shkranatua, dazzler (n doer)
shkrano, daze (v)
shkrifo, shimmer (v)
shkrik, slip (n)
shkriko, slip (v)
shkriku, slippery (adj)
shkrikuet, slippage (n)
shkrish, shim (n)
shkrisho, shim (v)
shkroik, slope (n)
shkroiko, slope (v)
shkubash, squat (n)
shkubasho, squat (v)
shkubashua, squatter (n doer)
shkufblaik, scuttlebutt (n)
shkufo, scuttle (v)
shkuk, stunt (n)
shkuko, stunt (v)
shkuniu, stunningly (adv)
shkuno, stun (v)
shlad, body (n)
shladu, bodily (adj)
shlaf, commendation (n)
shlafo, commend (v)
shlag, coarseness (n)
shlagiu, coarsely (adv)
shlagu, coarse (adj)
shlaiap, splice (n)
shlaiapo, splice (v)
shlaibo, surround (v)
shlaif, wariness (n)
shlaifiu, warily (adv)
shlaifu, wary (adj)
shlaig, dragon (n)
shlaik, split (n)
shlaikio, split (v pa)
shlaiko, split (v)
shlaikua, splitter (n doer)
shlain, sway (n)
shlaino, sway (v)
shlaip, martyr (n)
shlaipo, martyr (v)
shlait, city (n)
shlak, stealth (n)
shlakio, stole (v pa)
shlakiu, stealthily (adv)
shlako, steal (v)
shlaku, stealthy (adj)
shlakua, stealer (n doer)
shlank, drawer (n
   d:compartment)
shlarn, floor (n)
shlarno, floor (v)
shlarnplork, floorboard (n)
shlat, brink (n)
shlath, swath (n)

shlatho, swathe (v)
shlauan, corsage (n)
shlauko, whisk (v d:swipe)
shlausho, slog (v)
shlaushua, slogger (n doer)
shlav, drag (n)
shlavo, drag (v)
shlef, ware (n)
shlefkiaf, warehouse (n)
shlefkiafo, warehouse (v)
shleiafiu, lavishly (adv)
shleiafu, lavish (adj)
shleif, flag (n)
shleifarip, flagstaff (n)
shleifaripi, flagstaves (n pl)
shleifdilk, flagpole (n)
shleiflev, flagship (n)
shleifo, flag (v)
shleifua, flagger (n doer)
shlein, lava (n)
shleishk, spasm (n)
shleit, slyness (n)
shleith, sledge (n)
shleithganp, sledgehammer (n)
shleitho, sledge (v)
shleitiu, slyly (adv)
shleitu, sly (adj)
shlek, structure (n)
shlekiu, structurally (adv)
shleko, structure (v)
shleku, structural (adj)
shlen, stillness (n d:calm)
shleneidon, stillwater (n)
shleniu, still (adv d:calm)
shleno, still (v d:calm)
shlenu, still (adj d:calm)
shlesh, fish (n)
shleshi, fish (n pl)
shleshi, fishes (n pl)
shlesho, fish (v)
shleshplon, fisherman (n)
shleshploni, fishermen (n pl)
shleshtairk, fishbowl (n)
shleshu, fishy (adj)
shleshua, fisher (n doer)
shleshuat, fishery (n)
shlet, stilt (n)
shleto, stilt (v)
shliag, plunder (n)
shliago, plunder (v)
shliam, swallow (n d:bird)
shliash, clinch (n)
shliasho, clinch (v)
shliashua, clincher (n doer)
shliat, instrument (n)
shliatu, instrumental (adj)
shliatuet, instrumentation (n)
shlib, ride (n)
shlibio, rode (v pa)
shlibo, ride (v)
shlibua, rider (n doer)
shliesh, clench (n)
shliesho, clench (v)

shlif, ridge (n)
shlik, slice (n)
shliko, slice (v)
shlikua, slicer (n doer)
shlin, slenderness (n)
shlinu, slender (adj)
shlip, ballot (n)
shlir, flour (n)
shlish, scissors (n)
shlisho, scissor (v)
shliun, splint (n)
shliunk, splinter (n)
shliunko, splinter (v)
shliush, clutch (n d:grip)
shliusho, clutch (v d:grip)
shloat, slack (n d:loose)
shloato, slack (v d:loose)
shloatua, slacker (n doer d:loose)
shlod, cheese (n)
shlodu, cheesy (adj)
shlof, swerve (n)
shlofo, swerve (v)
shloift, deployment (n)
shloifto, deploy (v)
shloik, command (n)
shloikat, commandment (n)
shloiko, command (v)
shloikua, commander (n doer)
shloit, ploy (n)
shlorf, impossibility (n)
shlorfiu, impossibly (adv)
shlorfu, impossible (adj)
shlot, cold (n d:temperature)
shlotu, cold (adj d:temperature)
shlotuet, coldness (n)
shlotwaku, coldest (adj)
shlotwelu, colder (adj)
shluak, mutation (n)
shluakan, mutant (n)
shluakiu, mutably (adv)
shluako, mutate (v)
shluaku, mutable (adj)
shluakua, mutator (n doer)
shluant, compliance (n)
shluantap, compliment (n)
shluantapiu, complimentarily
   (adv)
shluantapo, compliment (v)
shluantapu, complimentary (adj)
shluantapua, complimentor (n
   doer)
shluanto, comply (v)
shluantu, compliant (adj)
shluap, haul (n)
shluapo, haul (v)
shluapua, hauler (n doer)
shluat, ply (n)
shluatfanin, plywood (n)
shluato, ply (v)
shluatu, pliable (adj)
shluatua, plier (n doer)
shlubiu, facetiously (adv)
shlubu, facetious (adj)

shlud, suddenness (n)
shludiu, suddenly (adv)
shludu, sudden (adj)
shluf, coolness (n)
shlufit, coolant (n)
shlufiu, coolly (adv)
shlufo, cool (v)
shlufp, picnic (n)
shlufpo, picnic (v)
shlufpua, picnicker (n doer)
shlufu, cool (adj)
shlufua, cooler (n doer)
shlufwaku, coolest (adj)
shlufwelu, cooler (adj)
shluiat, swelter (n)
shluiato, swelter (v)
shluk, stay (n)
shluket, station (n)
shluketo, station (v)
shluketu, stationary (adj)
shluko, stay (v)
shlukua, stayer (n doer)
shlumio, wept (v pa)
shlumo, weep (v)
shlumu, weepy (adj)
shlumua, weeper (n doer)
shlun, sameness (n)
shlunk, bob (n)
shlunko, bob (v)
shlunkua, bobber (n doer)
shlunu, same (adj)
shlup, sled (n)
shlupo, sled (v)
shlush, slide (n)
shlushio, slid (v pa)
shlusho, slide (v)
shlushua, slider (n doer)
shluth, statistic (n)
shluthu, statistical (adj)
shlutik, surrender (n)
shlutiko, surrender (v)
shlutikua, surrenderer (n doer)
shmaf, chance (n)
shmafo, chance (v)
shmafu, chance (adj)
shmalp, snippet (n)
shman, gnosis (n)
shmanu, gnostic (adj)
shmap, snip (n)
shmapo, snip (v)
shmath, snoop (n)
shmatho, snoop (v)
shmathu, snoopy (adj)
shmathua, snoop (n doer)
shmauk, snore (n)
shmauko, snore (v)
shmaut, snort (n)
shmauto, snort (v)
shmeif, chancel (n)
shmeifo, chancel (v)
shmeifua, chancellor (n doer)
shmen, tone (n d:quality)
shmeno, tone (v d:quality)

shmenua, toner (n doer d:quality)
shmiak, notoriety (n)
shmiakiu, notoriously (adv)
shmiaku, notorious (adj)
shmiap, snout (n)
shmik, bough (n)
shmip, snot (n)
shmipu, snotty (adj)
shmit, notice (n)
shmitak, notification (n)
shmitako, notify (v)
shmitakua, notifier (n doer)
shmitiu, noticeably (adv)
shmito, notice (v)
shmitu, noticeable (adj)
shmoko, cleanse (v)
shmokua, cleanser (n doer)
shmolf, branch (n)
shmolfo, branch (v)
shmolfua, brancher (n doer)
shmondak, balloon (n)
shmondako, balloon (v)
shmop, baldness (n)
shmopo, bald (v)
shmopu, bald (adj)
shmot, balast (n)
shmotat, balance (n)
shmotato, balance (v)
shmoto, balast (v)
shmug, snooze (n)
shmugo, snooze (v)
shmugua, snoozer (n doer)
shmun, tune (n)
shmuno, tune (v)
shmunua, tuner (n doer)
shnaf, connection (n)
shnafat, connectivity (n)
shnafo, connect (v)
shnafrep, liability (n)
shnafrepiu, liably (adv)
shnafrepu, liable (adj)
shnafua, connector (n doer)
shnago, flog (v)
shnaik, clot (n)
shnaiko, clot (v)
shnain, lie (n d:deceit)
shnaino, lie (v d:deceit)
shnainua, liar (n doer d:deceit)
shnait, spine (n)
shnaith, clutter (n)
shnaitho, clutter (v)
shnaitmenu, spineless (adj)
shnaitu, spinal (adj)
shnaitu, spiny (adj)
shnak, flick (n)
shnakat, flicker (n)
shnakato, flicker (v)
shnako, flick (v)
shnal, liaison (n)
shnalo, liaison (v)
shnap, spin (n)
shnapan, spindle (n)
shnapio, spun (v pa)

shnapo, spin (v)
shnapua, spinner (n doer)
shnapunf, spinoff (n)
shnat, spill (n)
shnatafen, spillover (n)
shnatio, spilt (v pa)
shnato, spill (v)
shnatpliol, spillway (n)
shnatua, spiller (n doer)
shnatuet, spillage (n)
shnauk, snipe (n)
shnauko, snipe (v)
shnaukua, sniper (n doer)
shnaup, snarl (n)
shnaupo, snarl (v)
shnef, armor (n)
shnefo, armor (v)
shneif, flail (n)
shneifo, flail (v)
shneit, stash (n)
shneito, stash (v)
shneiuk, clog (n)
shneiuko, clog (v)
shnen, arm (n)
shnenk, army (n)
shneno, arm (v)
shnenua, armer (n doer)
shnesh, since (adv/prep/conj)
shnet, stick (n d:twig, poke)
shnetio, stuck (v pa d:twig, poke)
shneto, stick (v d:twig, poke)
shniak, skirmish (n)
shniam, clump (n)
shniamo, clump (v)
shniamu, clumpy (adj)
shnianio, clung (v pa)
shniano, cling (v)
shnianu, clingy (adj)
shniatho, cleave (v d:stick)
shnif, wire (n)
shnifmenu, wireless (adj)
shnifnep, wiretap (n)
shnifnepo, wiretap (v)
shnifo, wire (v)
shnifu, wirey (adj)
shnoik, stickiness (n d:adhere)
shnoikan, stickler (n)
shnoikio, stuck (v pa d:adhere)
shnoiko, stick (v d:adhere)
shnoiku, sticky (adj d:adhere)
shnoikua, sticker (n doer
    d:adhere)
shnoip, snatch (n)
shnoipo, snatch (v)
shnoipua, snatcher (n doer)
shnoito, spew (v)
shnorn, famine (n)
shnuf, cleverness (n)
shnufiu, cleverly (adv)
shnufu, clever (adj)
shnuk, ammunition (n)
shnusho, relish (v)
shobrauth, menstruation (n)

shobrautho, menstruate (v)
shobrauthu, menstrual (adj)
Shodium, Sodium (n)
shoidafk, satanism (n)
shoidafko, satanize (v)
shoidafku, satanic (adj)
shoidafkua, satanist (n doer)
Shoidak, Satan (n)
shoifan, mansion (n)
shoifk, manipulation (n)
shoifkiu, manipulatively (adv)
shoifko, manipulate (v)
shoifku, manipulative (adj)
shoifkua, manipulator (n doer)
shoig, shoulder (n)
shoigo, shoulder (v)
shoik, mandate (n)
shoikauto, manufacture (v)
shoikautua, manufacturer (n doer)
shoiklip, manner (n)
shoiko, mandate (v)
shoiku, mandatory (adj)
shoikuk, manifest (n)
shoikuko, manifest (v)
shoip, lick (n)
shoipo, lick (v)
shoipua, licker (n doer)
shoish, manual (n)
shoishiu, manually (adv)
shoishu, manual (adj)
shoit, side (n)
shoitethirp, sidekick (n)
shoitfeif, sideshow (n)
shoitgethk, sidetrack (n)
shoitgethko, sidetrack (v)
shoitglish, sidestep (n)
shoitglisho, sidestep (v)
shoito, side (v)
shoitpliol, sideways (adj/adv)
shoitroif, sideline (n)
shoitroifo, sideline (v)
shoitrolt, sidebar (n)
shoitshnen, sidearm (n)
shoitua, sider (n doer)
shoizhoip, sidewalk (n)
shol, human (n)
sholar, humanity (n)
sholarfif, humankind (n)
sholarfif, mankind (n)
sholariu, humanely (adv)
sholaru, humane (adj)
sholarua, humanitarian (n doer)
sholaruet, humanism (n)
sholaruetiu, humanistically (adv)
sholarueto, humanize (v)
sholaruetu, humanistic (adj)
sholaruetua, humanist (n doer)
sholbiort, manpower (n)
sholiu, humanly (adv)
sholnagu, manmade (adj)
sholu, human (adj)
shomdok, sentence (n d:words)

shord, containment (n)
shordo, contain (v)
shordua, container (n doer)
shorf, sense (n)
shorfiu, sensually (adv)
shorfiu, sensuously (adv)
shorfmeniu, senselessly (adv)
shorfmenu, senseless (adj)
shorfo, sense (v)
shorfp, sensitivity (n)
shorfpiu, sensitively (adv)
shorfpo, sensitize (v)
shorfpu, sensitive (adj)
shorfrep, sensibility (n)
shorfrepiu, sensibly (adv)
shorfrepu, sensible (adj)
shorft, sensation (n)
shorftiu, sensationally (adv)
shorftu, sensational (adj)
shorftuet, sensationalism (n)
shorftueto, sensationalize (v)
shorfu, sensual (adj)
shorfu, sensuous (adj)
shorfua, sensor (n doer)
shorfuanu, sensory (adj)
shorfun, sensuality (n)
shorian, stereo (n)
shorpu, rural (adj)
shosh, those (pron)
shoshu, those (adj)
Shoviet, Soviet (n)
shpaik, gripe (n)
shpaiko, gripe (v)
Shpain, Spain (n)
Shpainan, Spanish (n)
shpait, predicate (n)
shpaito, predicate (v)
shpaituet, predicament (n)
shpalt, talk (n)
shpalto, talk (v)
shpaltu, talkative (adj)
shpaltua, talker (n doer)
shpap, rind (n)
shparf, stature (n)
shpark, statue (n)
shpeft, static (n)
shpeftu, static (adj)
shpeg, fly (n d:insect)
shpen, map (n)
shpeno, map (v)
shpepfif, scholarship (n)
shpepiu, scholarly (adv)
shpepu, scholastic (adj)
shpepua, scholar (n doer)
shpesh, school (n)
shpeshbiun, schoolboy (n)
shpeshdalsh, schoolteacher (n)
shpeshkeler, schoolgirl (n)
shpeshkiaf, schoolhouse (n)
shpeshlen, schoolmate (n)
shpeshluar, schoolchild (n)
shpeshluari, schoolchildren (n pl)
shpesho, school (v)

shpeshthauth, schoolyard (n)
shpeshvond, schoolbooks (n)
shpet, state (n d:status)
shpetir, status (n)
shpetmenu, stateless (adj d:status)
shpetoit, superstition (n)
shpetoitu, superstitious (adj)
shpiaft, deputization (n)
shpiat, deputy (n)
shpiato, deputize (v)
shpiatua, deputizer (n doer)
shpiof, rant (n)
shpiofo, rant (v)
shplar, bank (n d:shore)
shplaro, bank (v d:shore)
shplek, difficulty (n)
shplekiu, difficultly (adv)
shpleko, difficult (v)
shpleku, difficult (adj)
shprait, grind (n d:rip)
shpraitio, ground (v pa d:rip)
shpraito, grind (v d:rip)
shpraitua, grinder (n doer d:rip)
shprako, spawn (v)
shprat, parliament (n)
shpratu, parliamentary (adj)
shpreif, cloak (n)
shpreifo, cloak (v)
shpren, iron (n d:clothes presser)
shpreno, iron (v d:clothes presser)
shpriko, thrash (v)
shprikua, thrasher (n doer)
shpruf, cost (n)
shprufio, cost (v pa)
shprufo, cost (v)
shprufu, costly (adj)
shpuk, grip (n)
shpuko, grip (v)
shpukua, gripper (n doer)
shpush, spell (n d:witchcraft)
shpushpaumbio, spellbound (v pa)
shpushpaumbo, spellbind (v)
shputh, tread (n)
shputhio, trod (v pa)
shputho, tread (v)
shputo, stoke (v)
shputrek, treadmill (n)
shputua, stoker (n doer)
shrabo, squander (v)
shrabu, squanderous (adj)
shraf, miscellany (n)
shraflik, mystique (n)
shraflin, mystery (n)
shrafliniu, mysteriously (adv)
shraflino, mystify (v)
shraflinu, mysterious (adj)
shraflit, mysticism (n)
shraflitu, mystical (adj)
shraflitua, mystic (n doer)
shrafu, miscellaneous (adj)

shrag, scab (n)
shraiaf, scuff (n)
shraiafo, scuff (v)
shraiak, slammer (n d:jail)
shraiap, scuffle (n)
shraiapo, scuffle (v)
shraik, scrub (n)
shraiko, scrub (v)
shraiku, scrubby (adj)
shraikua, scrubber (n doer)
shrail, whirl (n)
shrailditap, whirlpool (n)
shrailo, whirl (v)
shrailtheln, whirlwind (n)
shraip, slavery (n)
shraipo, slave (v)
shraipua, slave (n doer)
shraish, sketch (n)
shraisho, sketch (v)
shraishu, sketchy (adj)
shraishua, sketcher (n doer)
shrait, siege (n)
shraith, whir (n)
shraitho, whir (v)
shraito, siege (v)
shrak, scale (n d:fish)
shrako, scale (v d:fish)
shral, church (n)
shralp, college (n)
shramo, slam (v d:hit)
shramua, slammer (n doer d:hit)
shran, room (n)
shraniepu, roomful (adj)
shranlen, roommate (n)
shrano, room (v)
shranu, roomy (adj)
shrap, slap (n)
shrapo, slap (v)
shrapua, slapper (n doer)
shrat, sharpness (n)
shratan, sharp (n)
shratiu, sharply (adv)
shrato, sharpen (v)
shratshkot, sharpshooter (n)
shratu, sharp (adj)
shratua, sharpener (n doer)
shrav, struggle (n)
shravo, struggle (v)
shref, bless (n)
shrefo, bless (v)
shrein, slime (n)
shreino, slime (v)
shreinu, slimy (adj)
shreip, ensnarement (n d:trap)
shreipo, ensnare (v d:trap)
shreipo, snare (v d:trap)
shreipua, snare (n doer d:trap)
shreith, myth (n)
shreithkuit, mythology (n)
shreithu, mythic (adj)
shreithu, mythical (adj)
shrel, surity (n)
shreliu, surely (adv)

shrelu, sure (adj)
shren, situation (n)
shreniu, situationally (adv)
shreno, situate (v)
shrenu, situational (adj)
shret, sit (n)
shretio, sat (v pa)
shreto, sit (v)
shriak, slat (n)
shriako, slat (v)
shriap, sliver (n)
shriash, slowness (n)
shriashiu, slowly (adv)
shriasho, slow (v)
shriashtien, slowdown (n)
shriashu, slow (adj)
shriashwaku, slowest (adj)
shriashwelu, slower (adj)
shriat, slit (n)
shriatio, slit (v pa)
shriato, slit (v)
shriaut, slaughter (n)
shriautkiaf, slaughterhouse (n)
shriauto, slaughter (v)
shriavit, trek (n)
shriavito, trek (v)
shriavitua, trekker (n doer)
shriep, script (n)
shriepat, scripture (n)
shriepatu, scriptural (adj)
shriepo, script (v)
shrif, mist (n)
shrifiu, mistily (adv)
shrifk, description (n)
shrifkiu, descriptively (adv)
shrifko, describe (v)
shrifku, descriptive (adj)
shrifkua, descriptor (n doer)
shrifo, mist (v)
shrifu, misty (adj)
shrifua, mister (n doer)
shrig, scribble (n)
shrigo, scribble (v)
shrigua, scribe (n doer)
shrik, seat (n)
shrikdafk, seatbelt (n)
shriko, seat (v)
shrilan, stipulation (n)
shrilano, stipulate (v)
shrillar, stipend (n)
shrim, cousin (n)
shrioko, stow (v)
shripo, slink (v)
shripu, slinky (adj)
shrit, distribution (n)
shrito, distribute (v)
shritua, distributor (n doer)
shrivien, nomenclature (n)
shroigo, splurge (v)
shrok, flux (n)
shroko, flux (v)
shruik, frivolity (n)
shruikiu, frivolously (adv)

shruiku, frivolous (adj)
shrup, crumb (n)
shrupo, crumble (v)
shrupu, crumbly (adj)
shrutho, soothe (v)
shtafk, legibility (n)
shtafkiu, legibly (adv)
shtafku, legible (adj)
shtafu, martial (adj)
shtaik, accident (n)
shtaikiu, accidentally (adv)
shtaikiu, accidently (adv)
shtaiku, accidental (adj)
shtaim, band (n d:strap)
shtaimak, bandage (n)
shtaimako, bandage (v)
shtaimo, band (v d:strap)
shtaip, title (n)
shtaipo, title (v)
shtak, leger (n)
shtan, tin (n)
shtano, tin (v)
shtant, dissonance (n)
shtanto, dissonate (v)
shtantu, dissonant (adj)
shtat, mark (n)
shtath, scale (n d:measure)
shtathar, scalar (n)
shtathu, scalable (adj d:measure)
shtatien, markdown (n)
shtatiu, markedly (adv)
shtativeil, markup (n)
shtato, mark (v)
shtatu, marked (adj)
shtatua, marker (n doer)
shtauk, litigation (n)
shtauko, litigate (v)
shtaukua, litigator (n doer)
shtaush, endurance (n)
shtausho, endure (v)
shtef, centigrade (n)
shtefu, centigrade (adj)
shteifo, snuff (v)
shtek, incident (n)
shtekiu, incidently (adv)
shteku, incidental (adj)
shtekuet, incidence (n)
shtel, door (n)
shteldiar, doorbell (n)
shtelgik, doorstep (n)
shtelmarf, doormat (n)
shtelpliol, doorway (n)
shtelproid, doorknob (n)
shtet, inch (n)
shteto, inch (v)
shtiaf, query (n)
shtiafo, query (v)
shtiak, cage (n)
shtiakiu, cagily (adv)
shtiako, cage (v)
shtiaku, cagey (adj)
shtiakua, cager (n doer)
shtiat, quest (n)

shtiatert, questionnaire (n)
shtiatet, question (n)
shtiatetiu, questionably (adv)
shtiateto, question (v)
shtiatetu, questionable (adj)
shtiatetua, questioner (n doer)
shtiato, bequest (v)
shtib, text (n)
shtibo, text (v)
shtish, testimony (n)
shtisho, testify (v)
shtishuet, testimonial (n)
shtit, test (n)
shtitfuarm, testbed (n)
shtito, test (v)
shtitu, testy (adj)
shtitua, tester (n doer)
shtiuf, premier (n)
shtiufo, premier (v)
shtiuk, pit (n)
shtiukezhail, pitfall (n)
shtiuko, pit (v)
shtivond, textbook (n)
shtobiuf, smolder (n)
shtobiuf, smoulder (n)
shtobiufo, smolder (v)
shtobiufo, smoulder (v)
shtog, snow (n)
shtogblasht, snowflake (n)
shtogdant, snowmobile (n)
shtogfrip, snowstorm (n)
shtogmashp, snowball (n)
shtogmashpo, snowball (v)
shtogo, snow (v)
shtogplon, snowman (n)
shtogploni, snowmen (n pl)
shtogtafan, snowshoe (n)
shtogu, snowy (adj)
shtogzhail, snowfall (n)
shtoik, indentation (n)
shtoiko, indent (v)
Shtokolm, Stockholm (n)
shtolf, smoke (n)
shtolfgriat, smokestack (n)
shtolfiu, smokily (adv)
shtolfklet, smokescreen (n)
shtolfmenu, smokeless (adj)
shtolfo, smoke (v)
shtolfu, smoky (adj)
shtolfua, smoker (n doer)
shtozh, smog (n)
shtozhu, smoggy (adj)
shtran, grade (n)
shtrank, gradient (n)
shtrano, grade (v)
shtranua, grader (n doer)
shtrat, spatula (n)
shtrauk, spout (n)
shtrauko, spout (v)
shtraut, spate (n d:flood)
shtreip, spat (n d:quarrel)
shtren, term (n d:timespan)
shtrin, spear (n)

shtrinkefto, spearhead (v)
shtrino, spear (v)
Shtrontium, Strontium (n)
shtrop, swipe (n)
shtropo, swipe (v)
shtrupo, swoop (v)
shtrush, swoon (n)
shtrusho, swoon (v)
shtuf, enrichment (n)
shtufiu, richly (adv)
shtufo, enrich (v)
shtufp, rich (n)
shtufu, rich (adj)
shtufua, enricher (n doer)
shtufuet, richness (n)
shtufweku, richest (adj)
shtufwelu, richer (adj)
shtun, snub (n)
shtuno, snub (v)
shtutho, smother (v)
shuaf, female (n)
shuafo, effeminate (v)
shuafu, feminine (adj)
shuafua, feminist (n doer)
shuafuet, feminism (n)
shuag, size (n)
shuagiu, sizably (adv)
shuago, size (v)
shuagu, sizable (adj)
shuagu, sizeable (adj)
shuagua, sizer (n doer)
shuak, rank (n d:level, judge)
shuako, rank (v d:level, judge)
shual, sol (n)
shualf, solace (n)
shualfo, solace (v)
shualir, soul (n)
shualo, solarize (v)
shualt, solemnity (n)
shualtu, solemn (adj)
shualu, solar (adj)
shuan, theme (n)
shuap, rake (n)
shuapo, rake (v)
shuapua, raker (n doer)
shuash, science (n)
shuashiu, scientifically (adv)
shuashu, scientific (adj)
shuashua, scientist (n doer)
shuat, case (n d:container)
shuato, encase (v d:container)
shuaush, lesbian (n)
Shudaviul, Saturday (n)
shuel, near (adj/adv/prep)
shuel, nearness (n)
shueliu, nearly (adv)
shuelo, near (v)
shuelu, near (adj)
shuelvu, nearby (adj/adv)
shuelwaku, nearest (adj)
shuelwelu, nearer (adj)
shuesh, girlfriend (n)
shuf, lab (n)

shufief, bobcat (n)
shufko, stump (v d:befuddle)
shufp, stumble (n)
shufpo, stumble (v)
shuft, sequence (n)
shuftan, sequel (n)
shuftiu, sequentially (adv)
shufto, sequence (v)
shuftu, sequential (adj)
shuftua, sequencer (n doer)
shuiafo, shoo (v)
shuian, icon (n)
shuiano, iconify (v)
Shuidaf, Sweden (n)
Shuidan, Swedish (n)
shuik, scale (n d:climb)
shuiko, scale (v d:climb)
shuish, weight (n)
Shuishan, Swiss (n)
Shuisherlaf, Switzerland (n)
shuishko, weight (v)
shuishmen, weightlessness (n)
shuishmenu, weightless (adj)
shuisho, weigh (v)
shuishu, weighty (adj)
shuk, lens (n)
shuko, lens (v)
shular, solo (n)
shularo, solo (v)
shularu, solo (adj)
shularua, soloist (n doer)
Shulfur, Sulfur (n)
shuln, ounce (n)
shult, foundary (n d:pour mold)
shulto, found (v d:pour mold)
shumif, vantage (n)
shun, comma (n)
shup, find (n)
shupat, foundation (n d:begin)
shupato, found (v d:begin)
shupatua, founder (n doer
    d:begin)
shupio, found (v pa)
shupo, find (v)
shupua, finder (n doer)
shushut, solicitation (n)
shushuto, solicite (v)
shushutua, solicitor (n doer)
shut, zero (num 0 card)
shutai-, nul (num 0 pref)
shutail, null (n)
shutailo, nullify (v)
shutailu, null (adj)
shutat, soccer (n)
shuteth, zeroth (num 0 ord)
shuth, bean (n)
shutho, bean (v)
shuv, labor (n)
shuvasht, laboratory (n)
shuvo, labor (v)
shuvua, laborer (n doer)
shwak, scat (interj)
shwenf, during (prep)

shwi, whee (interj)
tafan, shoe (n)
tafanagua, shoemaker (n doer)
tafanfoin, shoelace (n)
tafankroim, shoehorn (n)
tafankroimo, shoehorn (v)
tafanligul, shoestring (n)
tafanmoith, shoeshine (n)
tafano, shoe (v)
tafk, culture (n)
tafku, cultural (adj)
tafp, golf (n)
tafpo, golf (v)
tafpua, golfer (n doer)
taft, tote (n)
tafto, tote (v)
tagian, alcoholic (n)
tagianuet, alcoholism (n)
tagin, alcohol (n)
taginu, alcoholic (adj)
tahft, dehydration (n)
tahfto, dehydrate (v)
taian, wobble (n)
taiano, wobble (v)
taianua, wobbler (n doer)
taibitiu, overtly (adv)
taibitu, overt (adj)
taid, club (n d:group)
taidkiaf, clubhouse (n)
taido, club (v d:group)
Taif, Thai (n)
taifaug, garble (n)
taifaugo, garble (v)
taift, point (n)
taiftiu, pointily (adv)
taifto, point (v)
taiftu, pointy (adj)
taiftua, pointer (n doer)
taig, garbage (n)
taigag, tangle (n)
taigago, tangle (v)
taigagua, tangler (n doer)
taigo, garbage (v)
taigu, garbage (adj)
taikat, matrix (n)
Tailanud, Thailand (n)
tain, stair (n)
tainavup, stairwell (n)
tainpliol, stairway (n)
tainshuat, staircase (n)
tairk, bowl (n d:ball)
tairko, bowl (v d:ball)
tairkua, bowler (n doer d:ball)
Taiwaf, Taiwan (n)
takalan, hallelujah (interj)
takiol, cocaine (n)
talf, basket (n)
talfshmond, basketball (n)
talgut, syllable (n)
talik, prince (n)
taliku, princely (adj)
taln, memory (n)
talnan, memoir (n)

talnar, memorial (n)
talnaro, memorialize (v)
talniu, memorably (adv)
talno, memorize (v)
talnu, memorable (adj)
talp, corridor (n)
talsh, speech (n d:verbosity)
talshio, spoke (v pa d:verbosity)
talshiu, speakably (adv
    d:verbosity)
talshmenu, speechless (adj)
talsho, speak (v d:verbosity)
talshu, speakable (adj
    d:verbosity)
talshua, speaker (n doer
    d:verbosity)
talshua, spokesman (n doer)
talshua, spokesperson (n doer)
talshua, spokeswoman (n doer)
talt, datum (n)
talth, princess (n)
talthu, princessly (adj)
talti, data (n pl)
taltviash, database (n)
talzhup, souvenir (n)
tam, fun (n)
tamaf, stool (n d:chair)
tamiam, funniness (n)
tamiamu, funny (adj)
tamiamweku, funniest (adj)
tamiamwelu, funnier (adj)
Tampaf, Tampa (n)
tamu, fun (adj)
tanf, tot (n)
tanfan, toddle (n)
tanfano, toddle (v)
tanfanua, toddler (n doer)
Tantalum, Tantalum (n)
tanuat, diamond (n)
Tarak, Tarak (n)
tarf, hinge (n)
tarfo, hinge (v)
targafen, hangover (n)
targag, dangle (n)
targago, dangle (v)
targio, hung (v pa)
targiveil, hangup (n)
targo, hang (v)
targua, hanger (n doer)
targuil, hangout (n)
tark, wax (n)
tarko, wax (v)
tarku, waxy (adj)
tarkua, waxer (n doer)
tarn, border (n)
tarno, border (v)
tarnroif, borderline (n)
tarshk, legislature (n)
tarth, throw (n)
tarthio, threw (v pa)
tartho, throw (v)
tarthua, thrower (n doer)
tarthvak, throwback (n)

tash, hundred (num 100 card)
tasheth, hundredth (num 100 ord)
tashia-, hecto- (num 100 pref)
tashk, legislation (n)
tashkel, office (n)
tashkelfifua, officialdom (n doer)
tashkeliu, officially (adv)
tashkelo, officiate (v)
tashkelthorthua, officeholder (n
    doer)
tashkelu, official (adj)
tashkelua, officer (n doer)
tashkelua, official (n doer)
tashkiu, legislatively (adv)
tashko, legislate (v)
tashku, legislative (adj)
tashkua, legislator (n doer)
tathiat, casserole (n)
tatht, coffin (n)
tatorf, offense (n)
tatorfiu, offensively (adv)
tatorfo, offend (v)
tatorfu, offensive (adj)
tatorfua, offender (n doer)
tatorfuet, offensiveness (n)
tauf, duck (n d:bird)
taufiat, cartilage (n)
taug, liquid (n)
taugar, liquor (n)
taugaro, liquor (v)
taugat, liquidity (n)
taugo, liquidate (v)
tauguet, liquidation (n)
tauian, weather (n)
tauianfliofo, weatherproof (v)
tauianfliofu, weatherproof (adj)
tauiano, weather (v)
tauianplon, weatherman (n)
tauianploni, weathermen (n pl)
tauit, canopy (n)
tauk, stop (n)
taukafen, stopover (n)
taukdep, dogma (n)
taukdepu, dogmatic (adj)
taukfath, stopgap (n)
taukfathu, stopgap (adj)
taukfluan, stoplight (n)
taukluk, stopwatch (n)
tauko, stop (v)
taukua, stopper (n doer)
taukuet, stoppage (n)
taun, tau (n)
taup, sheet (n)
taush, durability (n)
taushiu, durably (adv)
tausht, duration (n)
taushu, durable (adj)
tautiak, calamity (n)
tautiaku, calamitous (adj)
tav, triteness (n)
tavad, locomotion (n)
tavadua, locomotive (n doer)
taviu, tritely (adv)

tavu, trite (adj)
tavuk, adult (n)
tavukfif, adulthood (n)
tavuko, adulterate (v)
tavuku, adult (adj)
tavukua, adulterer (n doer)
tazh, jog (n)
tazhg, dodge (n)
tazhgo, dodge (v)
tazhgu, dodgy (adj)
tazho, jog (v)
tazhua, jogger (n doer)
teb, rate (n)
tebik, ratification (n)
tebiko, ratify (v)
tebo, rate (v)
tef, ad (n)
tefdaid, adequation (n)
tefdaidiu, adequately (adv)
tefdaidu, adequate (adj)
tefdot, advertisement (n)
tefdotiu, adversarially (adv)
tefdoto, advertise (v)
tefdotu, adversarial (adj)
tefdotua, advertiser (n doer)
tefeik, addiction (n)
tefeiko, addict (v)
tefeiku, addictive (adj)
tefeikua, addict (n doer)
Tefendal, December (n)
tefk, offer (n)
tefko, offer (v)
teflirkiu, adjacently (adv)
teflirku, adjacent (adj)
teflovit, administration (n)
teflovito, administer (v)
teflovitu, administrative (adj)
teflovitua, administrator (n doer)
tefpcoh, adjustment (n)
tefpesho, adjust (v)
tefpeshu, adjustable (adj)
tefpeshua, adjuster (n doer)
tefrap, development (n)
tefrapo, develop (v)
tefrapua, developer (n doer)
teft, addition (n)
teftat, additive (n)
teftem, add-on (n)
tefthaip, advocation (n)
tefthaipo, advocate (v)
tefthaipua, advocate (n doer)
teftirp, adjective (n)
teftiu, additionally (adv)
tefto, add (v)
teftu, additional (adj)
teftua, adder (n doer)
teftuak, adhesive (n)
teftuap, adherence (n)
teftuapo, adhere (v)
teftuapua, adherent (n doer)
teftuat, adhesion (n)
teftuatu, adhesive (adj)
tefyait, adverb (n)

teg, dig (n)
teget, digit (n)
tegetiu, digitally (adv)
tegeto, digitize (v)
tegetu, digital (adj)
tegio, dug (v pa)
tegiouil, dugout (n)
tegnat, degree (n)
tego, dig (v)
tegua, digger (n doer)
tei, T (let sng)
teiash, drift (n)
teiashfanin, driftwood (n)
teiasho, drift (v)
teiashua, drifter (n doer)
teiat, tee (n)
teiatito, teeter (v)
teiato, tee (v)
teif, cue (n)
teifo, cue (v)
teift, temp (n)
teiftiu, temporarily (adv)
teiftu, temporary (adj)
teig, lance (n)
teigo, lance (v)
teigua, lancer (n doer)
teihem, Number_1e2556
teik, stall (n d:wait)
teiko, stall (v d:wait)
teikua, staller (n doer d:wait)
teili, Ts (let pl)
teilt, contemporary (n)
teimu, keen (adj)
teish, peach (n)
teishu, peachy (adj)
teit, tempo (n)
teith, pessimism (n)
teithu, pessimistic (adj)
teitu, temporal (adj)
tekanift, adjournment (n)
tekanifto, adjourn (v)
Teknetium, Technetium (n)
Tekraf, Tehran (n)
telfret, interest (n d:desire)
telfretiu, interestingly (adv d:desire)
telfreto, interest (v d:desire)
telgat, throttle (n)
telgato, throttle (v)
telir, trill (n)
teliro, trill (v)
telirua, triller (n doer)
telork, forge (n)
telorko, forge (v)
telorkua, forger (n doer)
telorkuet, forgery (n)
telshan, through (adj/adv/prep)
telshanuil, throughout (prep/adv)
telshanvut, throughput (n)
telshkiaf, roadhouse (n)
telt, peel (n)
telth, hatch (n d:door)
telthvak, hatchback (n)

telto, peel (v)
teltua, peeler (n doer)
teluam, admiration (n)
teluamiu, admirably (adv)
teluamo, admire (v)
teluamu, admirable (adj)
teluamua, admirer (n doer)
Telurium, Tellurium (n)
telv, balm (n)
temdal, garden (n)
temdalo, garden (v)
temdalua, gardener (n doer)
Teneshif, Tennessee (n)
tenf, insula (n)
tenfat, insularity (n)
tenfiu, insularly (adv)
tenfu, insular (adj)
tenfuet, insulation (n)
tenfuetiu, insulatively (adv)
tenfueto, insulate (v)
tenfuetu, insulative (adj)
tenfuetua, insulator (n doer)
tenir, island (n)
tenir, isle (n)
tenirua, islander (n doer)
tenk, admission (n)
tenkiu, admissibly (adv)
tenko, admit (v)
tenku, admissible (adj)
Terbium, Terbium (n)
Terob, EhoMonth08 (n)
tesh, their (pron 3rd fem-masc pl
    pos sub)
tesh, theirs (pron 3rd fem-masc pl
    pos obj)
teshab, religion (n)
teshabiu, religiously (adv)
teshabu, religious (adj)
teshfar, themselves (pron 3rd
    fem-masc pl pos)
Teshkaf, Texas (n)
teshraf, sister (n)
teshrafif, sisterhood (n)
teshrafu, sisterly (adj)
tethi, they (pron 3rd fem-masc pl
    sub)
tethin, them (pron 3rd fem-masc
    pl obj)
tevifk, advantage (n)
tevifku, advantageous (adj)
tezhgo, delve (v)
thadif, nail (n d:metal pin)
thadifo, nail (v d:metal pin)
thaf, bread (n)
thafk, rent (n)
thafkal, rental (n)
thafko, rent (v)
thafku, rental (adj)
thafkua, renter (n doer)
thafo, bread (v)
thafp, raft (n d:boat)
thafpo, raft (v d:boat)

thafpua, rafter (n doer d:boat)
thaft, enquiry (n)
thaft, inquiry (n)
thafto, enquire (v)
thafto, inquire (v)
thaftua, inquirer (n doer)
thagat, rafter (n d:roof support)
thaibar, vocabulary (n)
thaidano, hobble (v)
thaif, chat (n)
thaifk, devotion (n)
thaifkan, devotional (n)
thaifkiu, devoutly (adv)
thaifko, devote (v)
thaifku, devout (adj)
thaifkua, devotee (n doer)
thaifo, chat (v)
thaifu, chatty (adj)
thaifua, chatter (n doer)
thaik, vote (n)
thaiko, vote (v)
thaikua, voter (n doer)
thail, pale (n d:spike)
thaim, veto (n)
thaimo, veto (v)
thain, fate (n)
thainiu, fatefully (adv)
thainu, fateful (adj)
thaip, voice (n)
thaipak, vocation (n)
thaipaku, vocational (adj)
thaipan, vocal (n)
thaipanu, vocal (adj)
thaipanua, vocalist (n doer)
thaipelp, voicemail (n)
thaipo, voice (v)
thaisho, chafe (v)
thait, bid (n)
thaith, hash (n d:cut food)
thaithat, hatchet (n)
thaithko, hatch (v d:create)
thaithkua, hatcher (n doer
    d:create)
thaithkuet, hatchery (n)
thaitho, hash (v d:cut food)
thaitio, bade (v pa)
thaitio, bid (v pa)
thaito, bid (v)
thaitua, bidder (n doer)
thalf, gel (n)
thalfo, gel (v)
Thalium, Thallium (n)
thalm, jam (n d:food)
thalp, mast (n)
thalpekeft, masthead (n)
thalpo, mast (v)
thalt, apple (n)
tham, brown (n)
thamo, brown (v)
thamu, brown (adj)
thanber, sample (n)
thanbero, sample (v)
thanberua, sampler (n doer)

thant, shack (n)
thanto, shack (v)
thap, hood (n)
thapo, hood (v)
tharb, neck (n)
tharbefoin, necklace (n)
tharbeglesh, necktie (n)
tharbo, neck (v)
thardeik, verdict (n)
tharf, verse (n)
tharfet, version (n)
tharfk, converse (n)
tharfkiu, conversely (adv)
tharfo, verse (v)
tharft, diversity (n)
tharftet, diversification (n)
tharfto, diversify (v)
tharftu, diverse (adj)
tharftua, diversifier (n doer)
tharg, slang (n)
thariat, veracity (n)
thariatu, veracious (adj)
tharluk, convertible (n)
tharm, mane (n)
tharmem, versus (prep)
tharn, janitor (n)
tharo, spell (v d:character)
tharoik, verification (n)
tharoikiu, verifiably (adv)
tharoiko, verify (v)
tharoiku, verifiable (adj)
tharoit, verity (n)
tharoitu, veritable (adj)
tharshk, convert (n)
thart, adversity (n)
tharth, shackle (n)
thartho, shackle (v)
thartiu, adversely (adv)
thartu, adverse (adj)
thartua, adversary (n doer)
thash, toss (n)
thashk, ratchet (n)
thashko, ratchet (v)
thasho, toss (v)
thashp, gossip (n)
thashpo, gossip (v)
thashpu, gossipy (adj)
thashpua, gossiper (n doer)
thashua, tosser (n doer)
thath, shuffle (n)
thatho, shuffle (v)
thauf, reign (n)
thaufk, regime (n)
thaufo, reign (v)
thauk, acre (n)
thaun, warmth (n)
thauniu, warmly (adv)
thauniveil, warmup (n)
thauniveilu, warmup (adj)
thauno, warm (v)
thaunu, warm (adj)
thaup, curiosity (n)
thaupiu, curiously (adv)

thaupu, curious (adj)
thautar, pharmacy (n)
thautarf, pharmaceutical (n)
thautaru, pharmaceutical (adj)
thauth, yard (n d:field)
thav, gorge (n)
thaviu, gorgeously (adv)
thavo, gorge (v)
thavu, gorgeous (adj)
thei, Th (let sng)
theian, son (n)
theif, own (n)
theifif, ownership (n)
theifo, own (v)
theifu, own (adj)
theifua, owner (n doer)
theigut, muffin (n)
theihem, Number_1e2856
theik, mask (n)
theikat, mascot (n)
theiko, mask (v)
theil, hay (n)
theili, Ths (let pl)
theim, shawl (n)
theinalp, strawberry (n)
theiosh, mesh (n)
theiosho, mesh (v)
theip, nip (n)
theipaf, nipple (n)
theipo, nip (v)
theipu, nippy (adj)
theirp, shrimp (n)
theirpo, shrimp (v)
theirpua, shrimper (n doer)
theish, smallness (n)
theishu, small (adj)
theishwaku, smallest (adj)
theishwelu, smaller (adj)
theith, sash (n)
thek, shell (n)
theko, shell (v)
thekshlesh, shellfish (n)
thekshleshi, shellfish (n pl)
thekua, sheller (n doer)
thelf, lotion (n)
theln, wind (n d:air)
thelnaushu, windward (adj)
thelnfenp, windmill (n)
thelnmoik, windshield (n)
thelno, wind (v d:air)
thelnplir, windchill (n)
thelnpliru, windchill (adj)
thelnu, windy (adj d:air)
thelnzhail, windfall (n)
thelt, region (n)
theltiu, regionally (adv)
theltu, regional (adj)
thep, nib (n)
thepan, nibble (n)
thepano, nibble (v)
thesh, raffle (n)
thesho, raffle (v)
thetan, theta (n)

theth, den (n)
thetsh, piece (n)
thetsho, piece (v)
thetshua, piecer (n doer)
thiad, hob (n)
thiadoitho, hobnob (v)
thiaf, tour (n)
thiafo, tour (v)
thiafua, tourist (n doer)
thiafuet, tourism (n)
thiag, menace (n)
thiagiu, menacingly (adv)
thiago, menace (v)
thiaipo, heed (v)
thiak, fatality (n)
thiakiu, fatally (adv)
thiaku, fatal (adj)
thial, shortness (n)
thialblef, shortcoming (n)
thialdaish, shortcut (n)
thialesh, shortwave (n)
thialeshu, shortwave (adj)
thialgurt, shortcake (n)
thialir, shorty (n)
thialiu, shortly (adv)
thialk, shorts (n d:clothing)
thialkap, shorthand (n)
thialo, shorten (v)
thialp, shortage (n)
thialpo, short (v)
thialtauk, shortstop (n)
thialthuth, shortsightedness (n)
thialthuthu, shortsighted (adj)
thialtuano, shortchange (v)
thialu, short (adj)
thialweku, shortest (adj)
thialwelu, shorter (adj)
thialzhail, shortfall (n)
thian, priest (n)
thiapo, appall (v)
thiarbral, floodplain (n)
thiarfluan, floodlight (n)
thiarg, gruel (n)
thiarheidon, floodwater (n)
thiarp, flood (n)
thiarpo, flood (v)
thiarprelk, floodgate (n)
thiarpua, flooder (n doer)
thiash, shear (n)
thiashk, fatigue (n)
thiashko, fatigue (v)
thiasho, shear (v)
thiashua, shearer (n doer)
thiat, skate (n)
thiath, sheath (n)
thiatho, sheathe (v)
thiato, skate (v)
thiatplork, skateboard (n)
thiatplorko, skateboard (v)
thiatua, skater (n doer)
thiauk, shuck (n)
thiauko, shuck (v)
thiaut, whole (n)

thiautiu, wholly (adv)
thiautrelf, wholesale (n)
thiautrelfu, wholesale (adj)
thiautrelfua, wholesaler (n doer)
thiautu, whole (adj)
thiautuet, wholeness (n)
thiav, flock (n d:group)
thiavo, flock (v d:group)
thift, vector (n)
thigat, mutterance (n)
thigato, mutter (v)
thik, fare (n)
thikith, ickiness (n)
thikithu, icky (adj)
thiklav, farce (n)
thiklavu, farcical (adj)
thiko, fare (v)
thikor, farewell (n)
thikua, fare (n doer)
thil, far (adj/adv)
thilan, palette (n)
thilf, shed (n d:building)
thilk, click (n)
thilkiash, northeast (n)
thilkiashaushu, northeastward
   (adj)
thilkiashu, northeast (adj)
thilkiashu, northeasterly (adj)
thilkiashu, northeastern (adj)
thilko, click (v)
thilkua, clicker (n doer)
thilpoimu, faraway (adj)
Thilsh Dakot, North Dakota (n)
Thilsh Karolin, North Carolina
   (n)
thilsh, north (n)
thilshaith, northwest (n)
thilshaithu, northwest (adj)
thilshaithu, northwestern (adj)
thilshaushu, northward (adj)
thilshdraip, northbound (n)
thilshraup, northland (n)
thilshu, north (adj)
thilshu, northerly (adj)
thilshu, northern (adj)
thilshua, northerner (n doer)
thilshwaku, northernmost (adj)
thilt, character (n d:symbol)
thilthuth, farsightedness (n)
thilthuthu, farsighted (adj)
thiluel, farther (adj/adv)
thiluel, further (adj/adv)
thiluelf, furthermore (adv)
thilwak, furthest (adj)
thinp, estimate (n)
thinpo, estimate (v)
thinpua, estimator (n doer)
thiok, master (n)
thiokatuk, masterstroke (n)
thiokiu, masterfully (adv)
thiokniap, mastermind (n)
thiokniapo, mastermind (v)
thioko, master (v)

thiokthetsh, masterpiece (n)
thioku, masterful (adj)
thiokuet, mastery (n)
thion, pine (n)
thiorl, fjord (n)
thiosh, mistress (n)
thirf, nobility (n)
thirfiu, nobly (adv)
thirfu, noble (adj)
thirp, kick (n)
thirpevak, kickback (n)
thirpo, kick (v)
thirpua, kicker (n doer)
thirpunf, kickoff (n)
thirt, rumor (n)
thirt, rumour (n)
thirto, rumor (v)
thirto, rumour (v)
thish, sect (n)
thishal, section (n)
thishalo, section (v)
thishalu, sectional (adj)
thishan, sectarianism (n)
thishanua, sectarian (n doer)
thishap, sector (n)
thishianiu, secularly (adv)
thishianu, secular (adj)
thishianua, secularist (n doer)
thishp, decision (n)
thishpiu, decisively (adv)
thishpo, decide (v)
thishpu, decisive (adj)
thitalt, period (n d:punctuation)
thith, tally (n)
thitho, tally (v)
thitsh, twit (n)
thiud, hub (n)
thiudefp, hubcap (n)
thiuf, file (n d:storage)
thiufo, file (v d:storage)
thiufshuat, briefcase (n)
thiuft, lapse (n)
thiufto, lapse (v)
thiufua, filer (n doer d:storage)
thiuk, spectra (n)
thiukat, spectrum (n)
thiukiu, spectrally (adv)
thiukluaf, spectroscopy (n)
thiukluafu, spectroscopic (adj)
thiuku, spectral (adj)
thiul, royalty (n)
thiuliu, royally (adv)
thiulu, royal (adj)
thiun, moral (n)
thiunat, morale (n)
thiuniu, morally (adv)
thiuno, moralize (v)
thiunu, moral (adj)
thiunua, moralist (n doer)
thiunuet, morality (n)
thiut, lap (n)
thiutaub, laptop (n)
thiuto, lap (v)

thlof, nothing (n)
thnat, kinesis (n)
thnatiu, kinetically (adv)
thnatu, kinetic (adj)
thoam, paleness (n d:complexion)
thoamo, pale (v d:complexion)
thoamu, pale (adj d:complexion)
thoan, wine (n)
thoanin, winery (n)
thoano, wine (v)
thoanua, wino (n doer)
thof, shop (n)
thofklofua, shopkeeper (n doer)
thofo, shop (v)
thofp, chap (n)
thofpo, chap (v)
thofprait, shoplifter (n)
thofua, shopper (n doer)
thog, stress (n)
thogiu, stressfully (adv)
thogo, stressed (v)
thogu, stressful (adj)
thogua, stressor (n doer)
thoiat, tabulation (n)
thoiato, tabulate (v)
thoiatu, tabular (adj)
thoiatua, tabulator (n doer)
thoift, sheriff (n)
thoifto, sheriff (v)
thoik, tab (n)
thoiko, tab (v)
thoil, sack (n)
thoilo, sack (v)
thoilua, sacker (n doer)
thoin, seal (n d:animal)
thoipo, veer (v)
thoish, face (n)
thoishat, façade (n)
thoishfkaf, faceplate (n)
thoisho, face (v)
thoishoit, facet (n)
thoishrauk, facelift (n)
thoishrauko, facelift (v)
thoishu, facial (adj)
thoishua, facer (n doer)
thoishul, facial (n)
thoit, brief (n)
thoitar, brevity (n)
thoitik, feasibility (n)
thoitikiu, feasibly (adv)
thoitiku, feasible (adj)
thoitiu, briefly (adv)
thoito, brief (v)
thoitu, brief (adj)
thok, application (n)
thokiu, applicably (adv)
thokiun, tranquility (n)
thokiuno, tranquilize (v)
thokiunu, tranquil (adj)
thokiunua, tranquilizer (n doer)
thokiunuet, tranquilization (n)
thoko, apply (v)
thoku, applicable (adj)

thokua, applicator (n doer)
thokuinua, applicant (n doer)
tholav, harem (n)
thord, chapter (n)
Thorium, Thorium (n)
thork, appliance (n)
thorl, ford (n)
thorlo, ford (v)
thorp, trance (n)
thorpad, chapel (n)
thorth, hold (n)
thorthafen, holdover (n)
thorthio, held (v pa)
thorthiveil, holdup (n)
thortho, hold (v)
thorthua, holder (n doer)
thortsh, weld (n)
thortsho, weld (v)
thortshua, welder (n doer)
thoshlash, decal (n)
thotelp, trajectory (n)
thotep, trajection (n)
thotepo, traject (v)
thotepua, trajector (n doer)
thraft, punctuation (n)
thraftiu, punctually (adv)
thrafto, punctuate (v)
thraftu, punctual (adj)
thraidato, dwindle (v)
thraif, smugness (n)
thraifiu, smugly (adv)
thraifu, smug (adj)
thraikio, wound (v pa d:energize)
thraiko, wind (v d:energize)
thraikua, winder (n doer
    d:energize)
thrail, dwell (n)
thrailio, dwelt (v pa)
thrailo, dwell (v)
thrailua, dweller (n doer)
thraipo, smuggle (v)
thraipua, smuggler (n doer)
thraisho, thrive (v)
thrait, dwarf (n)
thraito, dwarf (v)
thrakiu, hugely (adv)
thraku, huge (adj)
thram, thump (n)
thramo, thump (v)
thramua, thumper (n doer)
thran, oar (n)
thrank, punishment (n)
thrankiu, punitively (adv)
thranko, punish (v)
thranku, punishable (adj)
thranku, punitive (adj)
thrankua, punisher (n doer)
thrano, oar (v)
thrant, semester (n)
thrap, snap (n)
thrapiu, snappily (adv)
thrapkoit, snapshot (n)
thrapo, snap (v)

thrapu, snappy (adj)
thrapua, snapper (n doer)
thrat, puncture (n)
thrato, puncture (v)
thraug, hug (n)
thraugo, hug (v)
thraugua, hugger (n doer)
thrauk, scrutiny (n)
thrauko, scrutinize (v)
thraun, bridle (n)
thrauno, bridle (v)
thraup, braid (n)
thraupo, braid (v)
thraupua, braider (n doer)
thraush, thrill (n)
thrausho, thrill (v)
thraushua, thriller (n doer)
thraut, braiser (n)
thrauto, braise (v)
thrautua, braiser (n doer)
thrav, semblance (n)
thraviak, seminar (n)
thref, surface (n)
threfo, surface (v)
threip, trap (n)
threipo, trap (v)
threipshtel, trapdoor (n)
threipua, trapper (n doer)
threithdarf, lithography (n)
threk, athlete (n)
threkiu, athletically (adv)
threku, athletic (adj)
threl, fairness (n d:good)
threliu, fairly (adv d:good)
threlpliol, fairway (n)
threlsh, fairing (n)
threlu, fair (adj d:good)
threlweku, fairest (adj d:best)
threlwelu, fairer (adj d:better)
thren, palm (n)
threnk, tariff (n)
threno, palm (v)
thret, spring (n d:coil, surprise)
thretio, sprang (v pa d:coil,
    surprise)
threto, spring (v d:coil, surprise)
thretplork, springboard (n)
thretua, springer (n doer d:coil,
    surprise)
thriak, hospital (n)
thriako, hospitalize (v)
thriath, hospitality (n)
thriathiu, hospitably (adv)
thriathu, hospitable (adj)
thrif, sprinkle (n)
thrifo, sprinkle (v)
thrifua, sprinkler (n doer)
thrim, slimness (n)
thrimo, slim (v)
thrimu, slim (adj)
thrin, nail (n d:finger/toe tip)
thriop, territory (n)
thriopu, territorial (adj)

thrip, tribe (n)
thriplon, tribesman (n)
thriploni, tribesmen (n pl)
thripu, tribal (adj)
thrish, forest (n)
thrisho, forest (v)
thrishu, foresty (adj)
thrishuet, forestry (n)
thriup, tribute (n)
thriupat, tributary (n)
thriut, scruple (n)
thriutiu, scrupulously (adv)
thriuto, scruple (v)
thriutu, scrupulous (adj)
throt, sheer (n d:divert)
throto, sheer (v d:divert)
thruash, shudder (n)
thruasho, shudder (v)
thruk, fleck (n)
thruko, fleck (v)
thrupo, garner (v)
thruth, flute (n)
thruthua, flutist (n doer)
thuaf, mute (n)
thuafo, mute (v)
thuak, mutuality (n)
thuakiu, mutually (adv)
thuaku, mutual (adj)
thualf, palace (n)
thuamo, shun (v)
thuan, flower (n)
thuandaif, flowerpot (n)
thuank, anchor (n)
thuanko, anchor (v)
thuano, flower (v)
thuant, shunt (n)
thuanto, shunt (v)
thuanu, flowery (adj)
thuar, flora (n)
thuaru, floral (adj)
thuarua, florist (n doer)
thuat, phase (n)
thuato, phase (v)
thuatua, phaser (n doer)
thuatuil, phaseout (n)
thuf, smell (n)
thufish, reverence (n)
thufishiu, reverently (adv)
thufisho, revere (v)
thufishu, reverent (adj)
thufishua, reverend (n doer)
thufo, smell (v)
thuft, fever (n)
thuftiu, feverishly (adv)
thufto, fever (v)
thuftu, feverish (adj)
thufu, smelly (adj)
thuin, miser (n)
thuinu, miserly (adj)
thuit, treat (n)
thuitalt, treatment (n)
thuitan, treaty (n)
thuito, treat (v)

thuitu, treatable (adj)
thuk, speck (n)
thukash, speculation (n)
thukashiu, speculatively (adv)
thukasho, speculate (v)
thukashu, speculative (adj)
thukashua, speculator (n doer)
thuklak, spectacle (n)
thuklakiu, spectacularly (adv)
thuklako, spectate (v)
thuklaku, spectacular (adj)
thuklakua, spectator (n doer)
thulgrazh, seesaw (n)
thulgrazho, seesaw (v)
thuliap, scenery (n)
thulio, saw (v pa)
Thulium, Thulium (n)
thulk, ration (n)
thulko, ration (v)
thulo, see (v)
thulp, scene (n)
thulpash, scenario (n)
thulpu, scenic (adj)
thulua, seer (n doer)
thum, variability (n)
thum, variance (n)
thum, variation (n)
thumak, variety (n)
thumaku, varietal (adj)
thumap, variable (n)
thumap, variant (n)
thumapu, variable (adj)
thumapu, variant (adj)
thumiu, variously (adv)
thumo, vary (v)
thumu, various (adj)
thunaik, misery (n)
thunaikiu, miserably (adv)
thunaiku, miserable (adj)
thuniu, seemingly (adv)
thuno, seem (v)
thuntan, certificate (n)
thuntank, certification (n)
thuntano, certify (v)
thuntanua, certifier (n doer)
thup, sud (n)
thurfiu, conspicuously (adv)
thurfu, conspicuous (adj)
thursh, garnish (n)
thursho, garnish (v)
thush, space (n)
thushflev, spaceship (n)
thushiu, spatially (adv)
thushkafp, spacecraft (n)
thushke kodi, should (ndal
    d:expectation)
thusho, space (v)
thushplon, spaceman (n)
thushploni, spacemen (n pl)
thusht, rationality (n)
thushtiu, rationally (adv)
thushto, rationalize (v)
thushtu, rational (adj)

thushu, spacious (adj)
thushu, spatial (adj)
thushua, spacer (n doer)
thuth, sight (n)
thutho, sight (v)
thuthulio, sightsaw (v pa)
thuthulo, sightsee (v)
thutian, ratio (n)
thutsh, theology (n)
thuzh, scheme (n)
thuzhat, schema (n)
thuzho, scheme (v)
thuzhua, schemer (n doer)
thuzhun, schematic (n)
thuzhunu, schematic (adj)
tiaf, shove (n)
tiafo, shove (v)
tiafp, privilege (n)
tiafpo, privilege (v)
tiafpu, privy (adj)
tiaftmenu, pointless (adj)
tiafua, shover (n doer)
tiafuan, shovel (n)
tiafuano, shovel (v)
tiag, hind (n)
tiagat, hindrance (n)
tiagato, hinder (v)
tiagthuth, hindsight (n)
tiaiat, tingle (n)
tiaiato, tingle (v)
tiaif, lamina (n)
tiaifi, laminae (n pl)
tiaifiu, laminously (adv)
tiaifo, laminate (v)
tiaifu, laminous (adj)
tiaifua, laminator (n doer)
tiaig, hem (n)
tiaigo, hem (v)
tiaigroif, hemline (n)
tiaik, lameness (n)
tiaikano, lament (n)
tiaikanu, lamentable (adj)
tiaikiu, lamely (adv)
tiaiku, lame (adj)
tiain, latency (n)
tiainiu, latently (adv)
tiainu, latent (adj)
Tiakiaf, EhoDay05 (n)
tial, boil (n d:evaporation)
tialo, boil (v d:evaporation)
tialua, boiler (n doer
    d:evaporation)
tiam, bow (n d:front)
tiank, grab (n)
tianko, grab (v)
tiankua, grabber (n doer)
tianp, grasp (n)
tianpo, grasp (v)
tianth, grapple (n)
tiantho, grapple (v)
tianthu, grapple (adj)
tiap, privacy (n)
tiapiu, privately (adv)

tiapo, privatize (v)
tiapu, private (adj)
tiapuet, privatization (n)
tiash, glacier (n)
tiashiu, glacially (adv)
tiasho, glaciate (v)
tiashu, glacial (adj)
tiat, metal (n)
tiath, rattle (n)
tiathfreik, rattlesnake (n)
tiatho, rattle (v)
tiatu, metallic (adj)
tiaug, envy (n)
tiaugiu, enviously (adv)
tiaugo, envy (v)
tiaugu, envious (adj)
tiaukiu, languidly (adv)
tiauko, languish (v)
tiauku, languid (adj)
tiaup, hoard (n)
tiaupo, hoard (v)
tiauth, tart (n)
tiauthu, tart (adj)
tiav, gaze (n)
tiavo, gaze (v)
tiavua, gazer (n doer)
tiazh, pyramid (n)
tibafk, district (n)
tibafko, district (v)
tibeith, disbursement (n)
tibeitho, disburse (v)
tibino, peddle (v)
tibinua, peddler (n doer)
tibit, divestment (n)
tibito, divest (v)
tibresh, displacement (n)
tibresho, displace (v)
tibriak, disuse (n)
tibriasho, disavow (v)
tidalm, dissuasion (n)
tidalmo, dissuade (v)
tidalp, disturbance (n)
tidalpo, disturb (v)
tideild, disquiet (n)
tidiasho, disjoint (v)
tidirv, discouragement (n)
tidirvo, discourage (v)
tidralo, dishearten (v)
tidreif, distrust (n)
tidreifo, distrust (v)
tidreifua, distrustful (adj)
tiek, hide (n d:skin)
tiekopiol, hideaway (n)
tiekuil, hideout (n)
tielt, download (n)
tielto, download (v)
tieltua, downloader (n doer)
tien, down (adj/adv/prep)
tien, down (n)
tiendaun, downtime (n)
tiendaut, downbeat (n)
tiendautu, downbeat (adj)
tiendiekiu, downright (adv)

tienfalm, downstream (n)
tienflieg, downswing (n)
tienfruifo, downplay (v)
tienhaush, downward (adj/adv)
tienhaush, downwardly (adv)
tienkaim, downturn (n)
tienmiun, downtown (n)
tienparn, downhill (n)
tienrotut, downpour (n)
tienshoit, downside (n)
tienshtran, downgrade (n)
tienshtrano, downgrade (v)
tienshuago, downsize (v)
tientain, downstairs (n)
tientainu, downstairs (adj)
tienzhail, downfall (n)
tiepu, lean (adj d:thin)
tiet, flex (n)
tietiu, flexibly (adv)
tieto, flex (v)
tietrep, flexibility (n)
tietu, flexible (adj)
tifat, strand (n)
tifato, strand (v)
tifeish, disgust (n)
tifeisho, disgust (v)
tifiof, disloyalty (n)
tifiofu, disloyal (adj)
tiflarv, disapproval (n)
tiflarvo, disapprove (v)
tiflent, discredit (n)
tiflento, discredit (v)
tifliofo, disprove (v)
tifp, disc (n)
tifp, disk (n)
tifpat, discus (n)
tifpef, diskette (n)
tifraikiu, dismally (adv)
tifraiku, dismal (adj)
tifrep, disability (n)
tifrepo, disable (v)
tifrepua, disabler (n doer)
tifrilako, disallow (v)
tifrilp, displeasure (n)
tifrilpo, displease (v)
tifrilt, disorganization (n)
tifrilto, disorganize (v)
tifug, discipline (n)
tifugo, discipline (v)
tifugu, disciplinary (adj)
tifugua, disciplinarian (n doer)
tig, peg (n)
tigag, nag (n)
tigago, nag (v)
tigagu, naggy (adj)
tigalt, distraction (n)
tigalto, distract (v)
tigat, utterance (n)
tigatiu, utterly (adv)
tigato, utter (v)
tigatu, utter (adj)
tigaugo, divulge (v)
tiglak, disposition (n)

tiglaku, dispositive (adj)
tigloit, discharge (n)
tigloito, discharge (v)
tigo, peg (v)
tigoit, discussion (n)
tigoito, discuss (v)
tigot, discreteness (n)
tigotiu, discretely (adv)
tigotu, discrete (adj)
tigret, disclosure (n)
tigreto, disclose (v)
tiialfk, disobedience (n)
tiialfkiu, disobediently (adv)
tiialfko, disobey (v)
tiialfku, disobedient (adj)
tiitoip, disincentive (n)
tiivirt, disinfection (n)
tiivirto, disinfect (v)
tiivirtua, disinfectant (n doer)
tiivorn, disinformation (n)
tikio, did (v pa)
tiklat, disagreement (n)
tiklatan, discrepancy (n)
tiklataniu, discrepantly (adv)
tiklatanu, discrepant (adj)
tiklato, disagree (v)
tiklatu, disagreeable (adj)
tiklo, get-lost (interj)
tiko, do (v)
tikoam, blemish (n)
tikoamo, blemish (v)
tikoft, disservice (n)
tikolf, dishonor (n)
tikrego, disgruntle (v)
tikriaf, disqualification (n)
tikriafo, disqualify (v)
tikriafua, disqualifier (n doer)
tiku, doable (adj)
tikua, doer (n doer)
tikult, disfigurement (n)
tikulto, disfigure (v)
til, it (pron 3rd neut sng sub)
tilagrush, disillusionment (n)
tilagrusho, disillusion (v)
tilak, disposal (n)
tilako, dispose (v)
tilaku, disposable (adj)
tilash, terra (n)
tilashanu, terrestrial (adj)
tilashat, terrain (n)
tilashk, terrace (n)
tilashu, terranean (adj)
tilat, straddle (n)
tilato, straddle (v)
tild, initiation (n)
tildar, initiative (n)
tildat, initial (n)
tildiu, initially (adv)
tildo, initiate (v)
tildu, initial (adj)
tildua, initiator (n doer)
tilen, it (pron 3rd neut sng obj)
tilesh, its (pron 3rd neut sng pos

obj)

tilesh, its (pron 3rd neut sng pos sub)

tileshfal, itself (pron 3rd neut sng refl)

tilf, tip (n)

tilfdilp, tiptoe (n)

tilfdilpo, tiptoe (v)

tilfesh, diligence (n)

tilfeshiu, diligently (adv)

tilfeshu, diligent (adj)

tilfo, tip (v)

tilfplon, tipster (n)

tilfu, tippy (adj)

tilfua, tipper (n doer)

tilfunf, tipoff (n)

tilg, material (n)

tilgiu, materistically (adv)

tilgo, materialize (v)

tilgu, materialistic (adj)

tilgua, materialist (n doer)

tilguet, materialism (n)

tilialt, discourse (n)

tilialto, discourse (v)

tilik, ire (n)

tilikiu, irascibly (adv)

tiliko, irk (v)

tiliku, irascible (adj)

tiliku, irate (adj)

tilit, needle (n)

tilitaift, needlepoint (n)

tilitkiok, needlework (n)

tilito, needle (v)

tiliupift, discontent (n)

tiliupifto, discontent (v)

tiliutir, discontinuation (n)

tiliutir, discontinuity (n)

tiliutiro, discontinue (v)

tilk, wit (n)

tilkiu, wittily (adv)

tilku, witty (adj)

tilkuetiu, witlessly (adv)

tilkuetu, witless (adj)

tilotel, dispersal (n)

tilotel, dispersion (n)

tilotelo, disperse (v)

tilotelua, disperser (n doer)

tilubolk, disrepair (n)

timavin, disharmony (n)

timeig, divergence (n)

timeigo, diverge (v)

timeigu, divergent (adj)

timesht, dismemberment (n)

timeshto, dismember (v)

timk, fund (n)

timkalt, fundamental (n)

timkaltiu, fundamentally (adv)

timkaltu, fundamental (adj)

timko, fund (v)

timkua, funder (n doer)

timlat, funnel (n)

timlato, funnel (v)

timoit, disorientation (n)

timoito, disorient (v)

timot, atom (n)

timotiu, atomically (adv)

timoto, atomize (v)

timotu, atomic (adj)

Tin, Tin (n)

tinalsh, disdain (n)

tinan, dime (n)

tinarth, disfavor (n)

tinartho, disfavor (v)

tinat, taste (n)

tinatiu, tastefully (adv)

tinatmeniu, tastelessly (adv)

tinatmenu, tasteless (adj)

tinato, taste (v)

tinatu, tasteful (adj)

tinatu, tasty (adj)

tinatua, taster (n doer)

tinf, dessert (n)

tinit, irritation (n)

tinito, irritate (v)

tinitua, irritant (n doer)

tinko, neuter (v)

tinoart, disclaimer (n)

tinoarto, disclaim (v)

tinoif, dismay (n)

tinoifo, dismay (v)

tiobaish, mortgage (n)

tiobaisho, mortgage (v)

tiof, mortality (n)

tiofiu, mortally (adv)

tiofk, mortification (n)

tiofko, mortify (v)

tiofp, morgue (n)

tiofraik, morbidity (n)

tiofraiku, morbid (adj)

tiofu, mortal (adj)

tiofua, mortal (n doer)

tiog, hire (n)

tlogo, hire (v)

tiogua, hirer (n doer)

tiok, stall (n d:compartment)

tiolpoil, disarray (n)

tiomeif, disassociation (n)

tiomeifo, disassociate (v)

tiop, nimbleness (n)

tiopiu, nimbly (adv)

tiopu, nimble (adj)

tiorfk, immortality (n)

tiorfko, immortalize (v)

tiorfku, immortal (adj)

tiorfkua, immortal (n doer)

tiot, message (n)

tioth, tinge (n)

tiotho, tinge (v)

tiothravo, disassemble (v)

tioto, message (v)

tiotua, messenger (n doer)

tiovirp, disaffection (n)

tiovirpo, disaffect (v)

tipado, dispel (v)

tipadua, dispeller (n doer)

tipifk, distension (n)

tipifko, distend (v)

tiplaf, disgrace (n)

tiplafiu, disgracefully (adv)

tiplafo, disgrace (v)

tiplafu, disgraceful (adj)

tiplian, disappearance (n)

tipliano, disappear (v)

tipliark, disintegration (n)

tipliarko, disintegrate (v)

tipliarkua, disintegrator (n doer)

tipoin, discount (n)

tipoino, discount (v)

tipoinua, discounter (n doer)

tiposht, dishonesty (n)

tiposhtu, dishonest (adj)

tiprat, dysfunction (n)

tipratu, dysfunctional (adj)

tiprilp, dispossession (n)

tiprilpo, dispossess (v)

tir, they (pron 3rd neut pl sub)

tiradh, disciple (n)

tirai-, pent- (num 5 pref)

tirai-, quint- (num 5 pref)

tirash, dismissal (n)

tirashiu, dismissively (adv)

tirasho, dismiss (v)

tirashu, dismissive (adj)

tiren, them (pron 3rd neut pl obj)

tiresh, their (pron 3rd neut pl pos sub)

tiresh, theirs (pron 3rd neut pl pos obj)

tireshfar, themselves (pron 3rd neut pl pos)

tireth, fifth (num 5 ord)

tiri, five (num 5 card)

tiriaf, ream (n d:paper)

tirialfhemka, Number_1e20406

tirida, fifty (num 50 card)

tiridai-, fifty- (num 50 pref)

tirideth, fiftieth (num 50 ord)

tirifk, quinquadragintillion (num 1e138 card)

tirift, quinquatrigintillion (num 1e108 card)

tirika, quintillion (num 1e18 card)

tirikai-, exa- (num 1e18 pref)

tiriketh, quintillionth (num 1e18 ord)

tiripa, fifteen (num 15 card)

tiripai-, fifteen- (num 15 pref)

tiripeth, fifteenth (num 15 ord)

tirishk, quinvigintillion (num 1e78 card)

tirishkai-, fiefta-

tirishketh, quinvigintillionth (num 1e78 ord)

tirisht, quindecillion (num 1e48 card)

tirishtai-, pafta- (num 1e48 pref)

tirishteth, quindecillionth (num

1e48 ord)
tiriush, punch (n d:beverage)
tirk, chart (n)
tirko, chart (v)
tirkua, charter (n doer)
tirkul, charter (n)
tirkulo, charter (v)
tirolt, disbarment (n)
tirolto, disbar (v)
tirp, price (n)
tirpmenu, priceless (adj)
tirpo, price (v)
tirpu, pricey (adj)
tirpua, pricer (n doer)
tirt, chirp (n)
tirth, list (n d:tilt)
tirtho, list (v d:tilt)
tirto, chirp (v)
tirtua, chirper (n doer)
tishaip, dislocation (n)
tishaipo, dislocate (v)
tishalf, dislike (n)
tishalfo, dislike (v)
tishar, disbelief (n)
tishargo, dislodge (v)
tisharo, disbelieve (v)
tishat, pellet (n)
tishelk, dissipation (n)
tishelko, dissipate (v)
tishket, disorder (n)
tishketo, disorder (v)
tishkrago, dispatch (v)
tishkragua, dispatcher (n doer)
tishnaf, disconnection (n)
tishnafo, disconnect (v)
tishnen, disarmament (n)
tishneno, disarm (v)
titaift, disappointment (n)
titaifto, disappoint (v)
titak, simulation (n)
titako, simulate (v)
titakua, simulator (n doer)
Titanium, Titanium (n)
titelfret, disinterest (n)
titelfreto, disinterest (v)
titheifo, disown (v)
tithish, dissection (n)
tithisho, dissect (v)
tithog, distress (n)
tithogo, distress (v)
tithogu, distraught (adj)
titinat, distaste (n)
titinatu, distasteful (adj)
tituif, disguise (n)
tituifo, disguise (v)
tiuf, prime (n)
tiufan, primate (n)
tiufanu, primal (adj)
tiufdaun, primetime (n)
tiufdaunu, primetime (adj)
tiufit, primitive (n)
tiufitiu, primitively (adv)
tiufitu, primitive (adj)

tiufiu, primarily (adv)
tiufo, prime (v)
tiufp, principle (n)
tiufpo, principle (v)
tiuft, finiteness (n)
tiuftiu, finitely (adv)
tiuftu, finite (adj)
tiufu, primary (adj)
tiufua, primer (n doer)
tiuful, primary (n)
tiug, lock (n)
tiugik, lockstep (n)
tiugiveil, lockup (n)
tiugo, lock (v)
tiugrith, locksmith (n)
tiugua, locker (n doer)
tiuguil, lockout (n)
tiuk, due (n)
tiukiu, due (adv)
tiuku, due (adj)
tium, neutrality (n)
tiumal, neutron (n)
tiumiu, neutrally (adv)
tiumo, neutralize (v)
tiumu, neutral (adj)
tiumua, neutralizer (n doer)
tiumuet, neutralization (n)
tiup, curfew (n)
tiush, priestess (n)
tiut, finish (n)
tiuto, finish (v)
tiutua, finisher (n doer)
tivafk, distemper (n)
tivag, strangulation (n)
tivago, strangle (v)
tivagthorth, stranglehold (n)
tivaizh, dismantlement (n)
tivaizho, dismantle (v)
tivant, insult (n)
tivanto, insult (v)
tivantua, insulter (n doer)
tivap, strap (n)
tivapo, strap (v)
tivapua, strapper (n doer)
tivefk, disadvantage (n)
tivefko, disadvantage (v)
tivik, list (n d:strip)
tiviko, list (v d:strip)
tiviku, list (adj d:strip)
tivish, discretion (n)
tivishiu, discreetly (adv)
tivishu, discreet (adj)
tivit, advance (n)
tivito, advance (v)
tivituet, advancement (n)
tivlarv, discomfort (n)
tivlarvo, discomfort (v)
tivobaik, disengagement (n)
tivobaiko, disengage (v)
tivoik, dispute (n)
tivoiko, dispute (v)
tivramepo, disband (v)
tivuk, strip (n)

tivuko, strip (v)
tivukraizh, striptease (n)
tivukraizho, striptease (v)
tivukua, stripper (n doer)
tiwaku, utmost (adj)
tizhako, pelt (v d:hit)
tizhauk, ultimatum (n)
tizhauki, ultimatum (n pl)
tizhaukiu, ultimately (adv)
tizhauku, ultimate (adj)
tizhualo, dispirit (v)
tofp, kindness (n d:nice)
tofpiu, kindly (adv d:nice)
tofpu, kind (adj d:nice)
toiato, sass (v)
toif, stain (n)
toifmen, stainless (n)
toifmenu, stainless (adj)
toifo, stain (v)
toifua, stainer (n doer)
toigaup, sarcasm (n)
toigaupiu, sarcastically (adv)
toigaupu, sarcastic (adj)
toik, bone (n)
toikiu, bonily (adv)
toikmenu, boneless (adj)
toiku, bony (adj)
toim, ebony (n)
toip, citation (n)
toipo, cite (v)
toipot, excitement (n)
toipotiu, excitably (adv)
toipoto, excite (v)
toipotu, excitable (adj)
toipotua, exciter (n doer)
toiptuet, excitation (n)
toir, boil (n d:infection)
toish, incitation (n)
toish, incitement (n)
toisho, incite (v)
toishua, inciter (n doer)
toit, simultaneity (n)
toitiu, simultaneously (adv)
toitu, simultaneous (adj)
toivat, oblivion (n)
toivatu, oblivious (adj)
Toiviul, Thursday (n)
Tokiof, Tokyo (n)
tol, where (pron)
toldidan, facsimile (n)
tolefel, wherever (adv/conj)
tolfig, dolphin (n)
tolk, date (n d:time, meet)
tolko, date (v d:time, meet)
toln, dollar (n)
toloveip, whereabout (n)
tolp, doll (n)
tolpalk, fabrication (n)
tolpalko, fabricate (v)
tolpalkua, fabricator (n doer)
tolpo, doll (v)
tolt, fax (n)
tolto, fax (v)

tolu, where (adv/conj)
toluvu, whereby (conj/adv)
toluyosh, whereas (conj)
toluyosh, whereas (n)
torbo, fend (v)
torbua, fender (n doer)
torf, fence (n d:barrier)
torfo, fence (v d:barrier)
torfp, defense (n)
torfpo, defend (v)
torfpu, defensive (adj)
torfpua, defendant (n doer)
torfpua, defender (n doer)
torm, hunch (n)
tormo, hunch (v)
tormua, huncher (n doer)
Torontof, Toronto (n)
torp, thrust (n)
torpio, thrust (v pa)
torpo, thrust (v)
torpua, thruster (n doer)
torsh, drip (n)
torsho, drip (v)
torshu, drippy (adj)
torshua, dripper (n doer)
tosh, get (n)
toshio, got (v pa)
tosho, get (v)
toshopiol, getaway (n)
toshua, getter (n doer)
tov, difference (n)
tovabot, diffusion (n)
tovaboto, diffuse (v)
tovashk, differential (n)
tovashko, differentiate (v)
tovelshk, diffraction (n)
tovelshko, diffract (v)
toviu, differently (adv)
tovo, differ (v)
tovu, different (adj)
trabir, tradition (n)
trabiriu, traditionally (adv)
trabiru, traditional (adj)
trabirua, traditionalist (n doer)
trabiuk, traitor (n)
trafp, archive (n)
trafpo, archive (v)
trafpu, archival (adj)
trafpua, archivist (n doer)
traft, job (n)
traftmen, joblessness (n)
traftmenu, jobless (adj)
trag, batch (n)
traif, fiend (n)
traifiu, fiendishly (adv)
traifto, jab (v)
traiftua, jabber (n doer)
traifu, fiendish (adj)
traimuk, pentagon (n)
traip, flap (n)
traipo, flap (v)
traipua, flapper (n doer)
traish, straightness (n)

traishkerf, straightedge (n)
traisho, straighten (v)
traishu, straight (adj)
traishvoanaushiu,
    straightforwardly (adv)
traishvoanaushu, straightforward
    (adj)
traith, strait (n)
traithbifit, straitjacket (n)
trak, stage (n)
trako, stage (v)
tral, arc (n)
tralfk, architecture (n)
tralfko, architect (v)
tralfku, architectural (adj)
tralfkua, architect (n doer)
tralmak, matron (n)
tralmalsh, matriarch (n)
tralmalshu, matriarchal (adj)
tralmet, monarchy (n)
tralmeth, monarch (n)
tralmetua, monarchist (n doer)
tralo, arc (v)
tralt, arch (n)
tralto, arch (v)
traltua, archer (n doer)
tram, foam (n)
traman, lather (n d:soap)
tramano, lather (v d:soap)
tramiu, foamily (adv)
tramo, foam (v)
tramu, foamy (adj)
tramua, foamer (n doer)
trank, battery (n d:storage)
trant, control (n)
tranto, control (v)
trantu, controllable (adj)
trantua, controller (n doer)
trath, gray (n)
trath, grey (n)
tratheiku, greyish (adj)
trathgauk, greyhound (n)
trathu, gray (adj)
trathu, grey (adj)
trauf, blouse (n)
trauk, crown (n)
trauko, crown (v)
traun, corona (n)
traunat, coronation (n)
traunato, coronate (v)
traunatu, coronate (adj)
trav, fold (n)
travo, fold (v)
travua, folder (n doer)
treb, pull (n)
treban, pulley (n)
trebevak, pullback (n)
trebo, pull (v)
trebua, puller (n doer)
trebuil, pullout (n)
trefdav, boondocks (n)
trefk, standard (n)
trefko, standardize (v)

trefkuet, standardization (n)
trefp, distance (n)
trefpiu, distantly (adv)
trefpo, distance (v)
trefpu, distant (adj)
trefto, row (v d:paddle)
treftua, rower (n doer d:paddle)
treiak, academy (n)
treiakani, academics (n pl)
treiakiu, academically (adv)
treiaku, academic (adj)
treif, grocery (n)
treifua, grocer (n doer)
treig, castle (n)
treigo, castle (v)
treik, desertion (n d:flee)
treiko, desert (v d:flee)
treikua, deserter (n doer d:flee)
treilf, blossom (n)
treilfo, blossom (v)
treilt, climate (n)
treim, client (n)
treip, climb (n)
treipo, climb (v)
treipua, climber (n doer)
treish, clinic (n)
treishu, clinical (adj)
treitho, rove (v)
treithua, rover (n doer)
treiuko, welch (v)
treiuko, welsh (v)
treiukua, welcher (n doer)
treiukua, welsher (n doer)
trelf, sale (n)
trelfio, sold (v pa)
trelfit, salary (n)
trelfo, sell (v)
trelfu, saleable (adj)
trelfua, salesman (n doer)
trelfua, salesperson (n doer)
trelfua, seller (n doer)
trelfuanfif, salesmanship (n)
trelfuanfif, salespersonship (n)
trelfuil, sellout (n)
trelsh, road (n)
trelshblir, roadblock (n)
trelshfeif, roadshow (n)
trelshoit, roadside (n)
trelshpliol, roadway (n)
trelt, stand (n)
treltaift, standpoint (n)
treltio, stood (v pa)
treltiveil, standup (n)
treltiveilu, standup (adj)
trelto, stand (v)
treltoit, boomerang (n)
treltshlen, standstill (n)
treltuil, standout (n)
treltunf, standoff (n)
trelvut, standby (n)
trelvutu, standby (adj)
trem, reliability (n)
tremiu, reliably (adv)

tremo, rely (v)
tremp, reliance (n)
trempu, reliant (adj)
tremu, reliable (adj)
trep, stance (n)
tretsh, reef (n)
triaf, glow (n)
triafo, glow (v)
triafu, glowy (adj)
triak, rectification (n)
triako, rectify (v)
triakua, rectifier (n doer)
triam, uterus (n)
trian, staple (n d:commodity)
triap, chew (n)
triapo, chew (v)
triapua, chewer (n doer)
triato, greet (v)
triauf, drought (n)
triauik, rectum (n)
triauikiu, rectally (adv)
triauiku, rectal (adj)
triausho, lurk (v)
triaushua, lurker (n doer)
trief, bulletin (n)
trif, neatness (n)
trifiu, neatly (adv)
trift, sinus (n)
triftu, sinus (adj)
trifu, neat (adj)
trik, key (n)
trikatuk, keystroke (n)
trikebanf, keypad (n)
trikebaraf, keystone (n)
triklialt, keyword (n)
triklinun, keynote (n)
trikmenu, keyless (adj)
triko, key (v)
trikoth, keyhole (n)
tril, tone (n d:music)
trilan, scant (n)
trilaniu, scantily (adv)
trilano, scant (v)
trilanu, scanty (adj)
trilko, train (v d:conditioning)
trilku, trainable (adj
    d:conditioning)
trilkua, trainer (n doer
    d:conditioning)
trilkuin, trainee (n)
trilsh, intonation (n)
triluet, tonality (n)
triluko, scavenge (v)
trilukua, scavenger (n doer)
trin, pun (n)
trint, tolerance (n)
trinto, tolerate (v)
trintu, tolerable (adj)
trintu, tolerant (adj)
trintuet, toleration (n)
triorp, blooper (n)
triorpo, bloop (v)
triorpua, blooper (n doer)

tripat, wheat (n)
triplork, keyboard (n)
trishoil, thesaurus (n)
trishoili, thesaurii (n pl)
trishp, dignity (n)
trishpo, dignify (v)
trishpua, dignitary (n doer)
trit, ladder (n)
trith, wheel (n)
trithat, wheelie (n)
trithklend, wheelchair (n)
trithklendo, wheelchair (v)
tritho, wheel (v)
trithua, wheeler (n doer)
triuat, groove (n)
triuato, groove (v)
triuatu, groovy (adj)
triuf, dryness (n)
triufnolth, drywall (n)
triufo, dry (v)
triufu, dry (adj)
triufua, drier (n doer)
triufua, dryer (n doer)
triufweku, driest (adj)
triufwelu, drier (adj)
triugo, till (v)
triugua, tiller (n doer)
triuk, clout (n)
triuko, clout (v)
triukua, clouter (n doer)
trium, hive (n d:colony)
triun, bloom (n)
triuno, bloom (v)
triunua, bloomer (n doer)
triup, cheapness (n)
triupiu, cheaply (adv)
triupo, cheapen (v)
triupu, cheap (adj)
triupwaku, cheapest (adj)
triupwelu, cheaper (adj)
triusho, lurch (v)
triuto, lean (v d:tilt)
triutsho, parch (v)
triutua, leaner (n doer d:tilt)
triuzhail, drizzle (n)
triuzhailo, drizzle (v)
trog, toughness (n)
trogo, toughen (v)
trogu, tough (adj)
trogwaku, toughest (adj)
trogwelu, tougher (adj)
troiafo, wilt (v)
troiak, spar (n)
troiako, spar (v)
troik, spark (n)
troikat, sparkle (n)
troikato, sparkle (v)
troikatu, sparkly (adj)
troiko, spark (v)
troiku, sparky (adj)
troikua, sparker (n doer)
troip, flop (n)
troipiu, floppily (adv)

troipo, flop (v)
troipu, floppy (adj)
troipua, flopper (n doer)
troit, salad (n)
trolf, lesson (n)
trolt, husband (n)
trop, wipe (n)
tropo, wipe (v)
tropua, wiper (n doer)
tropuil, wipeout (n)
trosh, chalk (n)
trosho, chalk (v)
troshplork, chalkboard (n)
trotak, widower (n)
trotakao, widowered (v prp)
trotako, widower (v)
trovat, husbandry (n)
truath, glove (n)
truatho, glove (v)
trufp, blame (n)
trufpo, blame (v)
truif, relay (n d:transceive)
truik, relevance (n)
truik, relevancy (n)
truikiu, relevantly (adv)
truiku, relevant (adj)
truit, premium (n)
truitu, premium (adj)
truk, cheat (n)
truko, cheat (v)
trukua, cheater (n doer)
trulfo, furl (v)
trulsh, print (n)
trulsho, print (v)
trulshua, printer (n doer)
trush, rung (n d:step)
trut, desk (n)
trutaub, desktop (n)
tshad, that (pron)
tshadu, that (adj)
Tshamel, Juniper (n)
tshan, though (adv/conj)
tshark, rock (n d:stone)
tsharku, rocky (adj d:stone)
Tsharlton, Charleston (n)
tshatsh, tooth (n)
tshatshdotsh, toothpick (n)
tshatshdrafp, toothpaste (n)
tshatshi, teeth (n pl)
tshatshklush, toothbrush (n)
tshatsho, tooth (v)
tshatshu, toothy (adj)
Tshekoshlovak, Czechoslovakia
    (n)
Tshernobil, Chernobyl
Tshikag, Chicago (n)
Tshil, Chile (n)
Tshinaf, China (n)
Tshinash, Chinese (n)
tshom, than (conj/prep)
tshuf, yeast (n)
tshufk, fermentation (n)
tshufko, ferment (v)

tshufto, trounce (v)
tshun, this (pron)
tshunu, this (adj)
tshutsho, teethe (v)
tuaiat, expletive (n)
tuaik, exotic (n)
tuaiku, exotic (adj)
tuak, circus (n)
tualk, circumference (n)
tualku, circumferent (adj)
tualt, circumstance (n)
tualtu, circumstantial (adj)
tuan, change (n)
tuank, canal (n)
tuano, change (v)
tuant, exchange (n)
tuanto, exchange (v)
tuantu, exchangeable (adj)
tuantua, exchanger (n doer)
tuanua, changer (n doer)
tuark, violence (n)
tuarkiu, violently (adv)
tuarko, violate (v)
tuarku, violent (adj)
tuarkua, violator (n doer)
tuarkuet, violation (n)
tuarm, channel (n)
tuarmo, channel (v)
tuarmua, channeler (n doer)
tuarshian, ecstasy (n)
tuarshianiu, ecstatically (adv)
tuarshianu, ecstatic (adj)
tuath, cash (n)
tuatho, cash (v)
tuathua, cashier (n doer)
tuaup, warp (n)
tuaupo, warp (v)
tuazh, volatility (n)
tuazhu, volatile (adj)
tubielk, export (n)
tubielko, export (v)
tubielkua, exporter (n doer)
tublapliol, expressway (n)
tublash, expression (n)
tublashiu, expressively (adv)
tublashiu, expressly (adv)
tublasho, express (v)
tublashu, expressive (adj)
tublashua, expresser (n doer)
tuboft, extrusion (n)
tubofto, extrude (v)
tubresht, explication (n)
tubreshtiu, explicitly (adv)
tubreshto, exply (v)
tubreshtu, explicit (adj)
tubrun, expenditure (n)
tubrun, expense (n)
tubrunfrepu, expendable (adj)
tubruniu, expensively (adv)
tubruno, expend (v)
tubrunu, expensive (adj)
tudal, riddle (n)
tudalo, riddle (v)

tudarth, ejaculation (n)
tudartho, ejaculate (v)
tudat, gape (n)
tudato, gape (v)
tudrav, exploration (n)
tudravo, explore (v)
tudravu, exploratory (adj)
tudravua, explorer (n doer)
tueif, lathe (n d:machine)
tueifo, lathe (v d:machine)
tueifua, lather (n doer d:machine)
tuf, poof (interj)
tufan, curl (n)
tufano, curl (v)
tufanu, curly (adj)
tufanua, curler (n doer)
tufk, buses (n)
tufki, buses (n pl)
tufko, bus (v)
tufp, knot (n)
tufpo, knot (v)
tufpu, knotty (adj)
tufrelt, eccentricity (n)
tufreltu, eccentric (adj)
tugalt, extract (n)
tugalto, extract (v)
tugaltua, extractor (n doer)
tugaluet, extraction (n)
tugilp, excerpt (n)
tugilpo, excerpt (v)
tugoit, excuse (n)
tugoito, excuse (v)
tugoitu, excusable (adj)
tugoitua, excuser (n doer)
tugot, excrement (n)
tugot, excretion (n)
tugoto, excrete (v)
tugotu, excretive (adj)
tugotua, excreter (n doer)
tugrut, exclusion (n)
tugrutiu, exclusively (adv)
tugruto, exclude (v)
tugrutu, exclusive (adj)
tugrutua, excluder (n doer)
tuguniat, excommunication (n)
tuguniato, excommunicate (v)
tuguniatua, excommunicator (n doer)
tuiaf, dynamo (n)
tuiafiu, dynamically (adv)
tuiaft, dynamic (n)
tuiafu, dynamic (adj)
tuiak, trot (n)
tuiako, trot (v)
tuiakua, trotter (n doer)
tuiap, stalk (n d:appendage)
tuif, guise (n)
tuik, duty (n)
tuip, guidance (n)
tuipebalt, guidepost (n)
tuipo, guide (v)
tuiproif, guideline (n)
tuipua, guide (n doer)

tuipvond, guidebook (n)
tuit, guy (n d:wire)
tuitien, geyser (n)
tuitu, guy (adj d:wire)
tukiot, extortion (n)
tukioto, extort (v)
tukoig, examination (n)
tukoigo, examine (v)
tukoigua, examiner (n doer)
tukor, exam (n)
tuldorp, stereotype (n)
tuldorpo, stereotype (v)
tuldorpu, stereotypical (adj)
tulf, cure (n)
tulfat, accuracy (n)
tulfatiu, accurately (adv)
tulfatu, accurate (adj)
tulfo, cure (v)
tulfu, curable (adj)
tulfu, curative (adj)
tulfua, curer (n doer)
tulk, murk (n)
tulkiu, murkily (adv)
tulku, murky (adj)
tulovg, exaggeration (n)
tulovgo, exaggerate (v)
tulp, curb (n)
tulpo, curb (v)
tulsh, determination (n)
tulsho, determine (v)
tulshu, determinative (adj)
tulshua, determinant (n doer)
tult, cast (n)
tulthrat, acupuncture (n)
tultio, cast (v pa)
tulto, cast (v)
tumarn, escort (n)
tumat, municipality (n)
tumatu, municipal (adj)
tunfleb, helicopter (n)
Tungshten, Tungsten (n)
tunilk, extermination (n)
tunilko, exterminate (v)
tunilkua, exterminator (n doer)
tunoart, exclamation (n)
tunoarto, exclaim (v)
tunoartu, exclamatory (adj)
tunt, helix (n)
tuntiu, helically (adv)
tuntu, helical (adj)
tuorpo, exert (v)
tupaug, excavation (n)
tupaugo, excavate (v)
tupaugua, excavator (n doer)
tupifk, extent (n)
tupifkiu, extensively (adv)
tupifko, extend (v)
tupifku, extensive (adj)
tupifkua, extender (n doer)
tupifkuet, extension (n)
tupik, whiz (n)
tupiko, whiz (v)
turathishk, exercise (n)

turathishko, exercise (v)
turathishkua, exerciser (n doer)
Turkif, Turkey (n)
Turkifan, Turkish (n)
tursh, booth (n)
turt, boot (n)
turth, drape (n)
turtho, drape (v)
turthua, draper (n doer)
turthuet, drapery (n)
turto, boot (v)
tusht, exactness (n)
tushtiu, exactly (adv)
tushto, exact (v)
tushtu, exact (adj)
tutat, chase (n)
tutato, chase (v)
tutatua, chaser (n doer)
tuthaftiu, exquisitely (adv)
tuthaftu, exquisite (adj)
tuthishk, excision (n)
tuthishko, excise (v)
tuthuk, expectation (n)
tuthuko, expect (v)
tuthukua, expectorant (n doer)
tutiku, crisp (adj)
tutreb, extrication (n)
tutrebo, extricate (v)
tuvioish, excruciation (n)
tuvioishiu, excruciatingly (adv)
tuvioisho, excruciate (v)
tuyan, harp (n)
tuyano, harp (v)
tuyanua, harper (n doer)
tuyat, harpoon (n)
ua, eh (interj)
uan, ear (n)
uandoin, earlobe (n)
uandriad, eardrum (n)
uanritral, earring (n)
uanshkot, earshot (n)
uanshtat, earmark (n)
uanshtato, earmark (v)
uantark, earwax (n)
uanthetsh, earpiece (n)
uanyap, earphone (n)
ud, ago (adj/adv)
udeik, edict (n)
uf, oomph (interj)
uferth, identity (n)
uferthar, identification (n)
uferthiu, identically (adv)
ufertho, identify (v)
uferthu, identical (adj)
uferthua, identifier (n doer)
uftiv, elevation (n)
uftivo, elevate (v)
uftivua, elevator (n doer)
ui, oh (interj)
uil, out (adj/adv/prep/interj)
uil, out (n)
uilaomio, outran (v pa)
uilaomo, outrun (v)

uilblef, outcome (n)
uilbrauth, outflow (n)
uilbrautho, outflow (v)
uilbroif, outcry (n)
uilbrusht, outburst (n)
uildialt, outpost (n)
uildieku, outright (adj)
uildorgo, outgun (v)
uildraip, outbound (n)
uildraipu, outbound (adj)
uilek, outlet (n)
uilfep, outset (n)
uilflaufto, outlive (v)
uilfnilt, outskirt (n)
uilfrant, outlay (n)
uilfrantio, outlaid (v pa)
uilfranto, outlie (v)
uilglorfu, outboard (adj)
uilglorg, outreach (n)
uilgraito, outstretch (v)
uilgranko, outflank (v)
uilhaush, outward (n)
uilhaushiu, outwardly (adv)
uilhaushu, outward (adj/adv)
uilkiaf, outhouse (n)
uilkiofo, outpace (v)
uilkloik, outgrowth (n)
uilkloikio, outgrew (v pa)
uilkloiko, outgrow (v)
uilmoithio, outshone (v pa)
uilmoitho, outshine (v)
uilmolth, outpatient (n)
uilmolthu, outpatient (adj)
uilnenko, outnumber (v)
uilniamo, outsmart (v)
uilovorno, outperform (v)
uilpaft, outfit (n)
uilpafto, outfit (v)
uilpaftua, outfitter (n doer)
uilplik, outbreak (n)
uilprand, outfield (n)
uilprandua, outfielder (n doer)
uilreig, outlook (n)
uilroif, outline (n)
uilroifo, outline (v)
uilroifua, outliner (n doer)
uilrotut, outpour (n)
uilrotuto, outpour (v)
uilshoit, outside (n)
uilshoit, outside (n/adj/adv/prep)
uilshoitua, outsider (n doer)
uilshtel, outdoors (n)
uilshtelu, outdoor (adj)
uilshuago, outsize (v)
uilshuisho, outweigh (v)
uiltalshu, outspoken (adj)
uilthaiko, outvote (v)
uilthaitio, outbid (v pa)
uilthaito, outbid (v)
uiltilko, outwit (v)
uiltivuko, outstrip (v)
uiltrelfio, outsold (v pa)
uiltrelfo, outsell (v)

uiltreltu, outstanding (adj)
uiltult, outcast (n)
uiluet, outage (n)
uilvak, outback (n)
uilvaud, outlaw (n)
uilvaudo, outlaw (v)
uilvifio, outwent (v pa)
uilvifo, outgo (v)
uilvifua, outgoer (n doer)
uilvut, output (n)
uilvuto, output (v)
uilweldorim, outerwear (n)
uilwelu, outer (adj)
uilwelwaku, outermost (adj)
uilzhigat, outrage (n)
uilzhigatiu, outrageously (adv)
uilzhigato, outrage (v)
uilzhigatu, outrageous (adj)
Ukrainaf, Ukraine (n)
ulart, elation (n)
ularto, elate (v)
uldauf, umpire (n)
uli, if (conj)
um, hmm (interj)
unam, p.m. (adj)
unauk, omission (n)
unauko, omit (v)
unaukua, omitter (n doer)
unf, off (prep)
unfdautu, offbeat (adj)
unfefklet, offscreen (n)
unfefkletu, offscreen (adj)
unfep, offset (n)
unfepio, offset (v pa)
unfepo, offset (v)
unfkapu, offhand (adj)
unflurto, offload (v)
unfroifu, offline (adj)
unfshkot, offshoot (n)
unfshoit, offside (n)
unfshoitu, offside (adj)
unfthret, offspring (n)
unfulart, offshore (n)
unfularto, offshore (v)
Ununbium, Ununbium (n)
Ununhekium, Ununhexium (n)
Ununkuadium, Ununquadium (n)
Ununoktium, Ununoctium (n)
Ununpentium, Ununpentium (n)
Ununsheptium, Ununseptium (n)
Ununtrium, Ununtrium (n)
upshilon, upsilon (n)
Uranium, Uranium (n)
urf, U (let sng)
urfhem, Number_1e756
urfi, Us (let pl)
Ushap, Unbiunium (n davoka)
ushethiu, lastly (adv)
ushetho, last (v)
ushethu, last (adj)
Uship, Unbibium (n davoka)
ushko, oust (v)
ushkua, ouster (n doer)

ushpu, each (adj)
ushrig, enscription (n)
ushrig, inscription (n)
ushrigo, enscribe (v)
ushrigo, inscribe (v)
ushut, below (adv/prep)
ushuvd, elaboration (n)
ushuvdo, elaborate (v)
ushuvdu, elaborate (adj)
Utafk, Utah (n)
utep, ejection (n)
utepo, eject (v)
uthiufto, elapse (v)
utiailt, understudy (n)
utiarboto, understaff (v)
utibiorto, underpower (v)
utibiut, understatement (n)
utibleg, underclass (n)
utibrant, underground (n)
utibrantu, underground (adj)
utibriako, underuse (v)
utidaish, undercut (n)
utidaishio, undercut (v pa)
utidaisho, undercut (v)
utidalthu, undercover (adj)
utidaltu, underage (adj)
utidelgel, undersecretary (n)
utidiarp, underbelly (n)
utidopo, undercook (v)
utidovam, underwear (n)
utidraush, underdog (n)
utifanin, underwood (n)
utigokio, undertook (v pa)
utigoko, undertake (v)
utigokua, undertaker (n doer)
utigruash, underbrush (n)
utigurf, undercurrent (n)
utihalret, underworld (n)
utiheidonu, underwater (adj)
utiishrelo, underinsure (v)
utikin, undergrad (n)
utikinpu, undergraduate (adj)
utikinpua, undergraduate (n doer)
utiklaito, underscore (v)
utikloik, undergrowth (n)
utikrigo, undermine (v)
utilakan, undergarment (n)
utileipo, underpin (v)
utilifad, undershirt (n)
utiloidio, underwrote (v pa)
utiloido, underwrite (v)
utiloidua, underwriter (n doer)
utilunt, underpass (n)
utimekani, underpants (n pl)
utimoimio, underpaid (v pa)
utimoimo, underpay (v)
utin, under (adj/adv/prep)
utinilun, underneath (adj/adv/prep)
utinilun, underneath (n)
utiovaitua, underachiever (n doer)

utip, underling (n)
utipliol, underway (n)
utipliolu, underway (adj)
utiplono, underman (v)
utiretho, underlie (v)
utiroif, underline (n)
utiroifo, underline (v)
utishkleinu, undersea (adj)
utishnen, underarm (n)
utishnenu, underarm (adj)
utishoit, underside (n)
utishuish, underweight (n)
utishuishu, underweight (adj)
utitebo, underrate (v)
utitefrap, underdevelopment (n)
utitefrapo, underdevelop (v)
utithait, underbid (n)
utithaitio, underbid (v pa)
utithaito, underbid (v)
utithinp, underestimation (n)
utithinpo, underestimate (v)
utitirpo, underprice (v)
utitrelfio, undersold (v pa)
utitrelfo, undersell (v)
utitreltio, understood (v pa)
utitreltiu, understandably (adv)
utitrelto, understand (v)
utitreltu, understandable (adj)
utitril, undertone (n d:music, audio)
utivaupo, undervalue (v)
utivifio, underwent (v pa)
utivifo, undergo (v)
uvof, above (prep/adv/adj)
uyanio, heard (v pa)
uyano, hear (v)
uyanzhush, hearsay (n)
va, V (let sng)
vab, pop (n)
vabegral, popcorn (n)
vabo, pop (v)
vabua, popper (n doer)
vadat, motive (n)
vadato, motivate (v)
vadatu, motivational (adj)
vadatua, motivator (n doer)
vadatuet, motivation (n)
vadav, motion (n)
vadavo, motion (v)
vafiak, tempest (n)
vafk, temper (n)
vafkat, temperance (n)
vafkat, temperment (n)
vafkato, temperate (v)
vafkatu, temperate (adj)
vafko, temper (v)
vafkuet, temperament (n)
vafkuetiu, temperamentally (adv)
vafp, tepidity (n)
vafpiu, tepidly (adv)
vafpu, tepid (adj)
vaft, temptation (n)
vafto, tempt (v)

vaftua, tempter (n doer)
vagar, shake (n)
vagario, shook (v pa)
vagariveil, shakeup (n)
vagaro, shake (v)
vagartien, shakedown (n)
vagaru, shaky (adj)
vagarua, shaker (n doer)
vagaruil, shakeout (n)
vagat, rapture (n)
vagato, enrapture (v)
vagatu, rapt (adj)
vagauk, rape (n)
vagauko, rape (v)
vagaukua, rapist (n doer)
vahem, Number_1e1956
vaiaik, ferocity (n)
vaiaikiu, ferociously (adv)
vaiaiku, ferocious (adj)
vaian, carnivore (n)
vaianiu, carnivorously (adv)
vaianu, carnivorous (adj)
vaiap, girth (n)
vaiapar, girdle (n)
vaiapo, gird (v)
vaiapua, girder (n doer)
vaidotu, naked (adj)
vaifk, guard (n)
vaifkan, guardianship (n)
vaifkanua, guardian (n doer)
vaifkluit, guardrail (n)
vaifko, guard (v)
vaifp, dinner (n)
vaifpedaun, dinnertime (n)
vaifpo, dine (v)
vaifpshlef, dinnerware (n)
vaift, guarantee (n)
vaifto, guarantee (v)
vaiftua, guarantor (n doer)
vaig, explanation (n)
vaigauko, ravage (v)
vaigaukua, ravager (n doer)
vaigo, explain (v)
vailk, feist (n)
vailko, feist (v)
vailku, feist (adj)
vailt, bounty (n)
vailtu, bountiful (adj)
vaim, plane (n d:flat)
vaimo, plane (v d:flat)
vairp, cylinder (n)
vairt, cycle (n)
vairtiu, cyclically (adv)
vairto, cycle (v)
vairtu, cyclic (adj)
vairtu, cyclical (adj)
vairtua, cycler (n doer)
vaish, chef (n)
vait, chief (n)
vaith, noose (n)
vaithak, nuisance (n)
vaitho, noose (v)
vaitiu, chiefly (adv)

vaitu, chief (adj)
vaiwat, shelter (n)
vaiwato, shelter (v)
vaizh, mantle (n)
vak, back (n)
vakaush, backward (adj/adv)
vakbrant, background (n)
vakiveil, backup (n)
vako, back (v)
vakthauth, backyard (n)
vaktoik, backbone (n)
vakua, backer (n doer)
vakuit, backlog (n)
valash, gloss (n)
valasho, gloss (v)
valashu, glossy (adj)
valbar, connoisseur (n)
valfrat, parcel (n)
valfrato, parcel (v)
vali, Vs (let pl)
valkadarf, paragraph (n)
valkaflup, parachute (n)
valkaflupo, parachute (v)
valkaft, parasite (n)
valkaftu, parasitic (adj)
valkaiaf, parade (n)
valkaiafo, parade (v)
valkaiafua, parader (n doer)
valkaiak, paranoia (n)
valkaiaku, paranoid (adj)
valkaito, parry (v)
valkamafto, paralyze (v)
valkanin, parallel (n)
valkanino, parallel (v)
valkaninu, parallel (adj)
valkaninuet, parallelism (n)
valkaniok, parameter (n)
valkanioku, parametric (adj)
valkaniuku, paramount (adj)
valkapren, paradox (n)
valkapreniu, paradoxically (adv)
valkaprenu, paradoxical (adj)
valkaren, parasol (n)
valkashair, paradise (n)
valkavarsh, paraphrase (n)
valkavarsho, paraphrase (v)
valmeirf, parole (n)
valn, bonus (n)
valpaf, quantity (n)
valpafiu, quantitatively (adv)
valpafo, quantify (v)
valpafu, quantifiable (adj)
valpafu, quantitative (adj)
valpafuet, quantification (n)
valsh, birth (n)
valsho, birth (v)
valshviul, birthday (n)
valt, circle (n)
valtaiv, jeopardy (n)
valtaivo, jeopardize (v)
valtat, circulation (n)
valtato, circulate (v)
valtatua, circulator (n doer)

valtifk, circuitry (n)
valtig, pardon (n)
valtigo, pardon (v)
valtik, circuit (n)
valtiko, circuit (v)
valtiu, circularly (adv)
valto, circle (v)
valtu, circular (adj)
Valual, February (n)
valurp, umbrella (n)
valush, glide (n)
valusho, glide (v)
valushua, glider (n doer)
vam, soda (n)
Vanadium, Vanadium (n)
vanf, couple (n)
vanfo, couple (v)
vanfua, coupler (n doer)
vanianu, cardiac (adj)
vank, copulation (n)
vankao, copulated (v prp)
vanko, copulate (v)
Vankuvif, Vancouver (n)
vanp, competition (n)
vanpat, competitiveness (n)
vanpiu, competitively (adv)
vanpo, compete (v)
vanpor, competence (n)
vanporiu, competently (adv)
vanporu, competent (adj)
vanpu, competitive (adj)
vanpua, competitor (n doer)
vantar, sultan (n)
vanth, caress (n)
vantho, caress (v)
vanudu, sultry (adj)
vap, rope (n)
vapo, rope (v)
vapua, roper (n doer)
vapuet, petition (n)
vapueto, petition (v)
vapuetua, petitioner (n doer)
Varemain, Fahrenheit (adj)
varfk, template (n)
vark, fort (n)
varkalki, fortitude (n pl)
varkat, fortress (n)
varko, fortify (v)
varl, plane (n d:airplane)
varoh, phrase (n)
varsho, phrase (v)
varth, language (n)
vartsh, gulch (n)
vartuf, security (n)
vartufiu, securely (adv)
vartufo, secure (v)
vartufu, secure (adj)
vashp, bachelor (n)
vathp, effort (n)
vathpemeniu, effortlessly (adv)
vathpemenu, effortless (adj)
Vatikan, Vatican (n)
vatug, peak (n)

vatugo, peak (v)
vaud, law (n)
vaudenagua, lawmaker (n doer)
vaudeplikua, lawbreaker (n doer)
vaudeplon, lawman (n)
vaudeploni, lawmen (n pl)
vaudiu, lawfully (adv)
vaudmen, lawlessness (n)
vaudmeniu, lawlessly (adv)
vaudmenu, lawless (adj)
vaudrolf, vacillation (n)
vaudrolfo, vacillate (v)
vaudrolfu, vacillatory (adj)
vaudrolfua, vacillator (n doer)
vaudu, lawful (adj)
vaudua, lawyer (n doer)
vauft, prison (n)
vaufto, imprison (v)
vauftua, prisoner (n doer)
vauftuet, imprisonment (n)
vaug, fight (n)
vaugio, fought (v pa)
vaugo, fight (v)
vaugua, fighter (n doer)
vauif, vacuum (n)
vauifiu, vacuously (adv)
vauifo, vacuum (v)
vauifu, vacuous (adj)
vauig, vagueness (n)
vauigiu, vaguely (adv)
vauigu, vague (adj)
vauik, vacancy (n)
vauiket, vacation (n)
vauiketo, vacation (v)
vauiketua, vacationer (n doer)
vauikiu, vacantly (adv)
vauiko, vacate (v)
vauiku, vacant (adj)
vauikua, vacator (n doer)
vauk, urge (n)
vaukiu, urgently (adv)
vauko, urge (v)
vauku, urgent (adj)
vaukua, urger (n doer)
vaukuet, urgency (n)
vaul, valley (n)
vaun, spoil (n)
vauno, spoil (v)
vaunua, spoiler (n doer)
vaup, value (n)
vaupift, maintenance (n)
vaupifto, maintain (v)
vaupiftua, maintainer (n doer)
vaupo, value (v)
vaupu, valuable (adj)
vaupuet, valuation (n)
vaupul, valuable (n)
vaurkiveil, followup (n)
vaurkiveil, follow-up (n)
vaurkiveilu, followup (adj)
vaurkiveilu, follow-up (adj)
vaurko, follow (v)
vaurkua, follower (n doer)

vaushfalmu, mainstream (adj)
vaushiu, mainly (adv)
vaushluk, mainstay (n)
vaushnoik, etiquette (n)
vaushraup, mainland (n)
vaushroif, mainline (n)
vaushu, main (adj)
vauth, domain (n)
vav, rub (n)
vavo, rub (v)
vazhd, bother (n)
vazhdo, bother (v)
vazhim, fit (n d:spasm)
vazhimo, fit (v d:spasm)
ved, but (adv/conj/prep)
veflan, stationery (n)
vefp, pond (n)
vefto, ponder (v)
veiakuit, gynecology (n)
veiakuitua, gynecologist (n doer)
veiat, nozzle (n)
veid, future (n)
veidu, futuristic (adj)
veidua, futurist (n doer)
veift, positive (n)
veiftiu, positively (adv)
veiftu, positive (adj)
veikat, futility (n)
veikatu, futile (adj)
veilf, splendor (n)
veilfiu, splendidly (adv)
veilfu, splendid (adj)
veilip, poise (n)
veilipo, poise (v)
veiln, position (n)
veilno, position (v)
veilnua, positioner (n doer)
veilp, pose (n)
veilpo, pose (v)
veilpua, poser (n doer)
veinen, pony (n)
veinenmith, ponytail (n)
veineno, pony (v)
veip, bout (n)
veish, lawn (n)
veith, olive (n)
veithkraik, nosedive (n)
veiut, nuzzle (n)
veiuto, nuzzle (v)
veivoil, usurpation (n)
veivoilo, usurp (v)
veivoilua, usurper (n doer)
veld, budge (n)
veldo, budge (v)
velf, fitness (n d:healthy)
velfiu, fittingly (adv d:healthy)
velfu, fit (adj d:healthy)
velfweku, fittest (adj)
velfwelu, fitter (adj)
velk, budget (n)
velko, budget (v)
velku, budgetary (adj)
veln, summons (n)

velno, summon (v)
velp, browse (n)
velpo, browse (v)
velpua, browser (n doer)
velt, from (prep)
veltolu, where-from (adv)
vemian, winter (n)
vemiandaun, wintertime (n)
vemiano, winterize (v)
vemianu, winter (adj)
vemianu, winterly (adj)
vemianu, wintry (adj)
venai-, hept- (num 7 pref)
venai-, sept- (num 7 pref)
veneth, seventh (num 7 ord)
venfk, septenquadragintillion
　(num 1e144 card)
venft, septentrigintillion (num
　1e114 card)
veni, seven (num 7 card)
venialfhemka, Number_1e28506
venida, seventy (num 70 card)
venidai-, seventy- (num 70 pref)
venideth, seventieth (num 70 ord)
venipa, seventeen (num 17 card)
venipai-, seventeen- (num 17
　pref)
venipeth, seventeenth (num 17
　ord)
venk, economy (n)
venka, septillion (num 1e24 card)
venkai-, yotta- (num 1e24 pref)
venkar, economics (n)
venkaru, economic (adj)
venketh, septillionth (num 1e24
　ord)
venkiu, economically (adv)
venko, economize (v)
venku, economical (adj)
venkua, economist (n doer)
venshk, septenvigintillion (num
　1e84 card)
venshkai-, dieni-
venshketh, septenvigintillionth
　(num 1e84 ord)
vensht, septendecillion (num 1e54
　card)
venshtai-, nekani- (num 1e54
　pref)
venshteth, septendecillionth
　(num 1e54 ord)
Venzhuilaf, Venezuela (n)
verk, excess (n)
verkiu, excessively (adv)
verko, exceed (v)
verku, excessive (adj)
Vermont, Vermont (n)
vert, except (prep/conj)
vert, exception (n)
vertiu, exceptionally (adv)
verto, except (v)

vertu, exceptional (adj)
Veshaifar, September (n)
veshp, pebble (n)
vetagiaul, cease-fire (n)
vetak, agenda (n)
vetap, agency (n)
vetavet, cessation (n)
vetaveto, cease (v)
veth, nose (n)
vethit, nostril (n)
vethiu, nasally (adv)
vethlirdiot, nosebleed (n)
vetho, nosy (v)
vethraik, nausea (n)
vethraiko, nauseate (v)
vethraiku, nauseous (adj)
vethu, nasal (adj)
vezh, bug (n)
vezho, bug (v)
vezhu, buggy (adj)
viaf, shower (n)
viafo, shower (v)
viag, crowd (n)
viagar, shiver (n)
viagaro, shiver (v)
viago, crowd (v)
viagua, crowder (n doer)
viah, gee (interj)
viah, geez (interj)
viain, swivel (n)
viaino, swivel (v)
viakrolt, crowbar (n)
vialiaf, phantom (n)
vialoif, violin (n)
vialoifua, violinist (n doer)
vialt, cogitation (n)
vialtao, cogitated (v prp)
vialto, cogitate (v)
viamo, pine (v)
viank, pioneer (n)
vianko, pioneer (v)
vianp, fascination (n)
vianpo, fascinate (v)
viap, cogency (n)
viapiu, cogently (adv)
viapu, cogent (adj)
viark, crow (n)
viarko, crow (v)
viarth, linguistics (n)
viarthiu, linguistically (adv)
viarthu, linguistic (adj)
viarthua, linguist (n doer)
viash, base (n)
viashet, basis (n)
viashiu, basically (adv)
viashmond, baseball (n)
viasho, base (v)
viashu, basic (adj)
viashua, baser (n doer)
viashyalt, basement (n)
viat, cognate (n)
viatak, cognition (n)
viataku, cognitive (adj)

viatakuet, cognizance (n)
viatakuetu, cognizant (adj)
viath, rev (n)
viatho, rev (v)
viatsh, fece (n)
viatsho, defecate (v)
viatshu, fecal (adj)
viatshuet, defecation (n)
viauk, damn (n)
viauko, damn (v)
viauku, damn (adj)
viaush, sport (n)
viaushbidua, sportscaster (n doer)
viaushflaf, sportswear (n)
viaushiu, sportily (adv)
viausho, sport (v)
viaushplon, sportsman (n)
viaushplonfif, sportsmanship (n)
viaushploni, sportsmen (n pl)
viaushu, sporty (adj)
viaushua, sportster (n doer)
vibak, bombardment (n)
vibako, bombard (v)
vidot, nudity (n)
vidotu, nude (adj)
vidotua, nude (n doer)
vien, nomen (n)
Vienaf, Vienna (n)
vienk, nomination (n)
vienkiu, nominally (adv)
vienko, nominate (v)
vienku, nominal (adj)
vienkua, nominator (n doer)
vienkuin, nominee (n)
vierf, furnace (n)
vierk, fury (n)
vierkar, furor (n)
vierkiu, furiously (adv)
vierko, infuriate (v)
vierku, furious (adj)
vierkua, infuriator (n doer)
vieshkritshua, lawnmower (n doer)
vieth, brochure (n)
Vietnam, Vietnam (n)
Vietnaman, Vietnamese (n)
vifio, went (v pa)
vifo, go (v)
vifua, goer (n doer)
vigaf, giggle (n)
vigafo, giggle (v)
vigafua, giggler (n doer)
vigak, shock (n)
vigakiu, shockingly (adv)
vigaklesh, shockwave (n)
vigako, shock (v)
vigakua, shocker (n doer)
vigauko, ravish (v)
vigito, vex (v)
vik, fix (n)
viket, fixation (n)
viketo, fixate (v)

vikiko, careen (v)
viko, fix (v)
viku, fixable (adj)
vikua, fixer (n doer)
vikuak, chariot (n)
vikzhar, fixture (n)
Vilan, EhoMonth05 (n)
vilb, bomb (n)
vilbo, bomb (v)
vilbua, bomber (n doer)
vilk, fist (n)
vilko, fist (v)
vilku, fistful (adj)
vilm, bond (n)
vilmak, bondage (n)
vilmo, bond (v)
vilmthorthua, bondholder (n doer)
vilmua, bonder (n doer)
viman, window (n)
vimanmenu, windowless (adj)
vimano, window (v)
vimanuano, eavesdrop (v)
vind, coupon (n)
vink, bundle (n)
vinko, bundle (v)
vinkua, bundler (n doer)
vinp, bunch (n)
vinpo, bunch (v)
vinpu, bunchy (adj)
vinuin, cascade (n)
vinuino, cascade (v)
vioik, temple (n)
vioish, crucifixion (n)
vioisho, crucify (v)
viok, giant (n)
viokvioku, gigantic (adj)
vion, cruciality (n)
vioniu, crucially (adv)
vionu, crucial (adj)
Vioriaf, EhoDay02 (n)
Vipalp, Bible (n)
vipoak, caravan (n)
vipoako, caravan (v)
viputsh, carcass (n)
virft, defect (n)
virftiu, defectively (adv)
virfto, defect (v)
virftu, defective (adj)
virftua, defector (n doer)
Virginiaf, Virginia (n)
virsh, eagerness (n)
virshiu, eagerly (adv)
virshu, eager (adj)
virth, effect (n)
virthan, effectiveness (n)
virthar, efficiency (n)
virthariu, efficiently (adv)
virtharu, efficient (adj)
virthiu, effectively (adv)
virtho, effect (v)
virthu, effective (adj)
virthua, effector (n doer)

vishal, diva (n)
vishan, shampoo (n)
vishano, shampoo (v)
vishanua, shampooer (n doer)
vishk, sham (n)
vishkik, shamble (n)
vishkiko, shamble (v)
visht, shame (n)
vishtiu, shamefully (adv)
vishtmeniu, shamelessly (adv)
vishtmenu, shameless (adj)
vishto, shame (v)
vishtu, shameful (adj)
vitarsh, gasoline (n)
vith, limit (n)
vithaif, feline (n)
vithar, limitation (n)
vitho, limit (v)
vithpo, delimit (v)
vithpua, delimiter (n doer)
vithua, limiter (n doer)
vitsh, stump (n d:tree)
viufk, warrant (n)
viufko, warrant (v)
viugil, epic (n)
viugu, big (adj)
viugwaku, biggest (adj)
viugwelu, bigger (adj)
viuk, force (n)
viukiu, forcefully (adv)
viukiu, forcibly (adv)
viuko, force (v)
viuku, forceful (adj)
viuku, forcible (adj)
viukua, forcer (n doer)
viukuk, faucet (n)
viul, day (n)
viulu, daily (adj)
vium, gulley (n)
viund, daytime (n)
viunf, daylight (n)
viunflaum, daydream (n)
viunflaumo, daydream (v)
viunkeif, daycare (n)
viunplik, daybreak (n)
viunrazhu, daylong (adj)
viup, warranty (n)
viur, war (n)
viurbotsh, warpath (n)
viurdaun, wartime (n)
viurf, warfare (n)
viurflev, warship (n)
viurkeft, warhead (n)
viuro, war (v)
viuru, warlike (adj)
viurua, warrior (n doer)
viurvarl, warplane (n)
viuto, warn (v)
viuviat, ambiguity (n)
viuviatiu, ambiguously (adv)
viuviatu, ambiguous (adj)
vivaf, mustard (n)
vlarn, pasture (n)

vlarv, comfort (n)
vlarviu, comfortably (adv)
vlarvo, comfort (v)
vlarvu, comfortable (adj)
vlarvua, comforter (n doer)
vlat, code (n)
vlato, code (v)
vlatua, coder (n doer)
vlir, entertainment (n)
vliro, entertain (v)
vlirua, entertainer (n doer)
vlish, steam (n)
vlishfaliro, steamroll (v)
vlishfalirua, steamroller (n doer)
vlishflev, steamship (n)
vlishkob, steamboat (n)
vlisho, steam (v)
vlishu, steamy (adj)
vlishua, steamer (n doer)
voagruth, forgiveness (n)
voagruthio, forgave (v pa)
voagrutho, forgive (v)
voagruthu, forgivable (adj)
voagruthua, forgiver (n doer)
voaik, fierceness (n)
voaikiu, fiercely (adv)
voaiku, fierce (adj)
voalf, forever (n)
voalfiu, forever (adv)
voamun, fortune (n)
voamuniu, fortunately (adv)
voamunu, fortunate (adj)
voanariu, formerly (adv
    d:previous)
voanaru, former (adj d:previous)
voanaush, forward (n)
voanaushiu, forward (adv)
voanausho, forward (v)
voanaushu, forward (adj)
voanbid, forecast (n)
voanbido, forecast (v)
voanbidua, forecaster (n doer)
voanblefio, forthcame (v pa)
voanblefo, forthcome (v)
voanbrant, foreground (n)
voandep, forethought (n)
voandinan, forefinger (n)
voaneglek, foreknowledge (n)
voanegret, foreclosure (n)
voanegreto, foreclose (v)
voanegruk, forbear (n d:ancestor)
voanegruk, forbearer (n
    d:ancestor)
voanfiu, forth (adv)
voanflarn, forefront (n)
voanfruif, foreplay (n)
voankap, forehand (n)
voankeft, forehead (n)
voanlaomual, forerunner (n)
voanlaufo, forebode (v)
voanpoeft, foreshadow (n)
voanpoefto, foreshadow (v)
voanpretio, foretold (v pa)

voanpreto, foretell (v)
voanshnen, forearm (n)
voanshtaush, forbearance (n
    d:refrain)
voanshtaushio, forbore (v pa
    d:refrain)
voanshtausho, forbear (v
    d:refrain)
voanteiko, forestall (v)
voanthuth, foresight (n)
voanthuthio, foresaw (v pa)
voanthuthiu, foreseeably (adv)
voanthutho, foresee (v)
voanthuthu, foreseeable (adj)
voanu, fore (adj)
voanvifio, forewent (v pa)
voanvifo, forego (v)
voanviuto, forewarn (v)
voanwaku, foremost (adj)
voapeim, forfeiture (n)
voapeimo, forfeit (v)
voapeimua, forfeiter (n doer)
voaplon, foreman (n)
voaploni, foremen (n pl)
voarf, march (n)
voarfo, march (v)
voarfua, marcher (n doer)
voarno, forage (v)
voarnua, forager (n doer)
voash, waste (n)
voasheidon, wastewater (n)
voashiu, wastefully (adv)
voasho, waste (v)
voashraup, wasteland (n)
voashtalf, wastebasket (n)
voashu, wasteful (adj)
voashua, waster (n doer)
voashuet, wastefulness (n)
voashvuap, wastepaper (n)
voath, date (n d.fruit)
voatht, forbiddence (n)
voathtio, forbade (v pa)
voathto, forbid (v)
voathtua, forbidder (n doer)
voatop, forgettance (n)
voatopio, forgot (v pa)
voatopiu, forgetfully (adv)
voatopo, forget (v)
voatopu, forgetful (adj)
voatopua, forgetter (n doer)
vobaif, eviction (n)
vobaifo, evict (v)
vobaik, engagement (n)
vobaiko, engage (v)
vobal, medication (n)
vobal, medicine (n)
vobaliu, medically (adv)
vobalo, medicate (v)
vobalu, medical (adj)
vobalua, medic (n doer)
vobiuft, evaporation (n)
vobiufto, evaporate (v)
vobiuftua, evaporator (n doer)

vodeip, equipment (n)
vodeipo, equip (v)
vofrap, envelope (n)
vofrapo, envelop (v)
vofrapua, enveloper (n doer)
voft, evidence (n)
voftap, establishment (n)
voftapo, establish (v)
voftapua, establisher (n doer)
voftiu, evidently (adv)
vofto, evidence (v)
voftu, evident (adj)
vogaift, eruption (n)
vogaifto, erupt (v)
vogaiftua, eruptor (n doer)
voglit, energy (n)
voglito, energize (v)
voglitu, energetic (adj)
voglitua, energizer (n doer)
vogret, enclosure (n)
vogreto, enclose (v)
voiaf, surf (n)
voiafo, surf (v)
voiafplork, surfboard (n)
voiafua, surfer (n doer)
voibrien, surname (n)
voif, navel (n)
voiflauft, survival (n)
voiflaufto, survive (v)
voiflauftua, survivalist (n doer)
voiflauftua, survivor (n doer)
voiflauftuet, survivability (n)
voifuat, survey (n)
voifuatak, surveillance (n)
voifuato, survey (v)
voifuatua, surveyor (n doer)
voig, surge (n)
voigloit, surcharge (n)
voigo, surge (v)
voikuat, resurrection (n)
voikuato, resurrect (v)
voikuatua, resurrector (n doer)
voilaran, surrogation (n)
voilarano, surrogate (v)
voilaranu, surrogate (adj)
voilaranua, surrogate (n doer)
voilunto, surpass (v)
voin, knife (n)
voiniuko, surmount (v)
voino, knife (v)
voinua, knifer (n doer)
voinumat, surplus (n)
voipluaf, surrealism (n)
voipluafu, surreal (adj)
voish, busyness (n)
voishenk, surtax (n)
voishiu, busily (adv)
voishk, business (n)
voishku, businesslike (adj)
voishkua, businessman (n doer)
voishkua, businessperson (n
    doer)
voisho, busy (v)

voishu, busy (adj)
voith, computation (n)
voithak, computerization (n)
voithako, computerize (v)
voitho, compute (v)
voithu, computational (adj)
voithua, computer (n doer)
voitolpo, surmise (v)
voiv, gamble (n)
voivak, gambit (n)
voiviush, surprise (n)
voiviushiu, surprisingly (adv)
voiviusho, surprise (v)
voivo, gamble (v)
voivua, gambler (n doer)
vokaik, erasure (n)
vokaikiak, eradication (n)
vokaikiako, eradicate (v)
vokaikiakua, eradicator (n doer)
vokaiko, erase (v)
vokaikua, eraser (n doer)
vokanf, enchantment (n)
vokanfo, enchant (v)
vokanp, enhancement (n)
vokanpo, enhance (v)
vokanpua, enhancer (n doer)
vokmif, evolution (n)
vokmifo, evolve (v)
vokmifu, evolutionary (adj)
vokuap, erotica (n)
vokuapu, erotic (adj)
vokuapuet, eroticism (n)
vokuat, erection (n)
vokuato, erect (v)
vokuatua, erector (n doer)
volaish, enjoyment (n)
volaisho, enjoy (v)
volaishu, enjoyable (adj)
volanf, enormity (n)
volanfiu, enormously (adv)
volanfu, enormous (adj)
volk, chest (n d:container)
vomak, risk (n)
vomak, riskiness (n)
vomakiu, riskily (adv)
vomako, risk (v)
vomaku, risky (adj)
vomoid, encyclopedia (n)
vomoidu, encyclopedic (adj)
vond, book (n)
vondaik, bookend (n)
vondap, booklet (n)
vondathov, bookshop (n)
vondathovua, bookshopper (n doer)
vondenag, bookmaking (n)
vondenagua, bookmaker (n doer)
vondenalf, bookshelf (n)
vondklof, bookkeeping (n)
vondklofua, bookkeeper (n doer)
vondo, book (v)
vondrap, bookstore (n)
vondshuat, bookcase (n)

vonelk, engram (n)
vonelko, engrain (v)
vonolko, ingrain (v)
vontrelf, booksale (n)
vontrelfua, bookseller (n doer)
vopalt, enaction (n)
vopalt, enactment (n)
vopalto, enact (v)
vopan, entirety (n)
vopaniu, entirely (adv)
vopanu, entire (adj)
vopirp, eternity (n)
vopirpiu, eternally (adv)
vopirpo, eternalize (v)
vopirpu, eternal (adj)
vopirpua, eternalizer (n doer)
vopoif, encounter (n)
vopoifo, encounter (v)
vord, popularity (n)
vordiu, popularly (adv)
vordo, popularize (v)
vordu, popular (adj)
vordua, populace (n doer)
voreib, errand (n)
vork, motor (n)
vorkato, motorize (v)
vorkegrel, motorcar (n)
vorkeid, motel (n)
vorkepivit, motorbike (n)
vorkevairt, motorcycle (n)
vorkevairto, motorcycle (v)
vorkevairtua, motorcyclist (n doer)
vorko, motor (v)
vorkshkob, motorboat (n)
vorkua, motorist (n doer)
vorl, spring (n d:season)
vorldaun, springtime (n)
vorlu, spring (adj d:season)
vorn, form (n d:shape)
vornak, format (n)
vornako, format (v)
vornakua, formatter (n doer)
vornap, formulation (n)
vornapo, formulate (v)
vornapua, formulator (n doer)
vornarp, formula (n)
vornat, formal (n)
vornatiu, formally (adv)
vornato, formalize (v)
vornatu, formal (adj)
vornatuet, formality (n)
vornk, deformation (n)
vornkapu, formidable (adj)
vornko, deform (v)
vornkua, deformer (n doer)
vorno, form (v d:shape)
vornua, former (n doer d:shape)
vornuet, formation (n)
vorp, cup (n)
vorpgurt, cupcake (n)
vorplork, cupboard (n)
vorpo, cup (v)

vort, build (n)
vorth, forum (n)
vortio, built (v pa)
vortishu, builtin (adj)
vortiveil, buildup (n)
vorto, build (v)
vortua, builder (n doer)
vorv, population (n)
vorvo, populate (v)
voshafrepu, lovable (adj d:common)
voshaiko, evoke (v)
voshak, scepter (n)
voshak, sceptre (n)
voshar, love (n d:common)
vosharo, love (v d:common)
vosharu, lovely (adj d:common)
vosharua, lover (n doer d:common)
voshav, love (n d:emphatic)
voshavo, love (v d:emphatic)
voshavu, lovely (adj d:emphatic)
voshavua, lover (n doer d:emphatic)
voshiak, escape (n)
voshiakiap, escapade (n)
voshiakiu, escapably (adv)
voshiako, escape (v)
voshiaku, escapable (adj)
voshiakua, escapee (n doer)
voshiakuet, escapism (n)
voshk, shaft (n)
voshko, shaft (v)
voshkua, shafter (n doer)
voshlip, erosion (n)
voshlipo, erode (v)
voshpet, estate (n)
voshpeto, estate (v)
vosht, column (n)
voshto, columnate (v)
voshuik, escalation (n)
voshuiko, escalate (v)
voshuikua, escalator (n doer)
votet, father (n)
votetfif, fatherhood (n)
votetmenu, fatherless (adj)
voteto, father (v)
votetraup, fatherland (n)
votetu, fatherly (adj)
vothut, esteem (n)
vothuto, esteem (v)
vovauif, evacuation (n)
vovauifo, evacuate (v)
vovauifua, evacuator (n doer)
vovaup, evaluation (n)
vovaupo, evaluate (v)
vovaupua, evaluator (n doer)
voviuk, enforcement (n)
voviuko, enforce (v)
voviuku, enforceable (adj)
voviukua, enforcer (n doer)
vozhak, evil (n)
vozhaku, evil (adj)

vozhakua, evildoer (n doer)
vozhank, evasion (n)
vozhankiu, evasively (adv)
vozhanko, evade (v)
vozhanku, evasive (adj)
vozhankua, evader (n doer)
vozhuf, enthusiam (n)
vozhufiu, enthusiastically (adv)
vozhufo, enthuse (v)
vozhufu, enthusiastic (adj)
vozhufua, enthusiast (n doer)
vozhush, essay (n)
vozhusho, essay (v)
vraft, deceleration (n)
vrafto, decelerate (v)
vraftua, decelerator (n doer)
vrago, fence (v d:spar)
vram, ban (n)
vramashk, banishment (n)
vramashko, banish (v)
vramep, band (n d:group)
vramepo, band (v d:group)
vramepu, bandy (adj d:group)
vramk, banality (n)
vramkrash, bandwidth (n)
vramo, ban (v)
vramua, banner (n doer)
vrant, camera (n)
vrantua, cameraperson (n doer)
vreik, muzzle (n)
vreiko, muzzle (v)
vrein, mucus (n)
vreinu, mucosal (adj)
vret, pen (n d:ink device)
vreto, pen (v d:ink device)
vrietio, learnt (v pa)
vrieto, learn (v)
vrietua, learner (n doer)
vrok, block (n d:cube)
vroku, blocky (adj d:cube)
vu, by (adj/adv/prep)
vuaft, definition (n)
vuaftiu, definitely (adv)
vuafto, define (v)
vuaftu, definite (adj)
vuaftu, definitive (adj)
vuak, launch (n)
vuakbanf, launchpad (n)
vuako, launch (v)
vuakua, launcher (n doer)
vual, fine (n d:penalty)
vualo, fine (v d:penalty)
vualua, finer (n doer d:penalty)
vuam, laundry (n)
vuamit, laundromat (n)
vuamo, launder (v)
vuamua, launderer (n doer)
vuan, elite (n)
vuanu, elite (adj)
vuanua, elitist (n doer)
vuap, paper (n)
vuapat, paperback (n)
vuapemenu, paperless (adj)

vuapkiok, paperwork (n)
vuaplork, paperboard (n)
vuapo, paper (v)
vuapshuish, paperweight (n)
vuat, fineness (n d:small)
vuatiu, finely (adv d:small)
vuatu, fine (adj d:small)
vuau, golly (interj)
vuaush, gosh (interj)
vub, cub (n)
vublash, suppression (n)
vublashan, suppressant (n)
vublashiu, suppressively (adv)
vublasho, suppress (v)
vublashu, suppressive (adj)
vublashua, suppressor (n doer)
vubrepo, supplant (v)
vubresh, supplication (n)
vubresho, supplicate (v)
vudaun, meantime (n)
vudauniu, meantime (adv)
vufiuk, byproduct (n)
vugabiort, superpower (n)
vugabrauth, superflow (n)
vugabrautho, superflow (v)
vugabrauthu, superfluous (adj)
vugadiadar, supermodel (n)
vugadrap, superstore (n)
vugadrokirf, superstar (n)
vugafiaish, supervision (n)
vugafiaisho, supervise (v)
vugafiaishu, supervisory (adj)
vugafiaishua, supervisor (n doer)
vugaft, superficiality (n)
vugaftiu, superficially (adv)
vugaftu, superficial (adj)
vugagloito, supercharge (v)
vugagloitua, supercharger (n doer)
vugagren, superlative (n)
vugakiglako, superimpose (v)
vugakoilpliol, superhighway (n)
vugakuto, superheat (v)
vugaleidiu, supernaturally (adv)
vugaleidu, supernatural (adj)
vugalpiu, superbly (adv)
vugalpu, superb (adj)
vugalu, super (adj)
vugamiaf, supernova (n)
vugan, superiority (n)
vuganu, superior (adj)
vuganua, superior (n doer)
vugaplon, superman (n)
vugaploni, supermen (n pl)
vugasharltua, superhero (n doer)
vugashlek, superstructure (n)
vugashlufo, supercool (v)
vugashlufu, supercool (adj)
vugasholu, superhuman (adj)
vugatruit, supremacy (n)
vugatruitiu, supremely (adv)
vugatruitu, supreme (adj)
vugatruitua, supremacist (n doer)

vugaveko, supercede (v)
vugaveko, supersede (v)
vugazhantanu, supersonic (adj)
vugipifkan, superintendent (n)
vuglak, supposition (n)
vuglakiu, supposedly (adv)
vuglako, suppose (v)
vuglakua, supposer (n doer)
vuiaufo, meander (v)
vuish, friction (n)
vuishmenu, frictionless (adj)
vuishu, frictional (adj)
vuk, push (n)
vukafen, pushover (n)
vukid, puzzle (n)
vukido, puzzle (v)
vukidua, puzzler (n doer)
vukiduet, puzzlement (n)
vukiko, prod (v)
vukikua, prodder (n doer)
vuko, push (v)
vuku, pushy (adj)
vukua, pusher (n doer)
vulash, matrimony (n)
vulashu, matrimonial (adj)
vulk, quantum (n)
vulku, quantum (adj)
vuln, marriage (n)
vulno, marry (v)
vulnu, marital (adj)
vulunt, bypass (n)
vulunto, bypass (v)
vuluntua, bypasser (n doer)
vumak, coffee (n)
vunhaf, cuddle (n)
vunhafo, cuddle (v)
vunp, bark (n d:yelp)
vunpo, bark (v d:yelp)
vunpua, barker (n doer d:yelp)
vupan, mean (n)
vupauk, meanwhile (n)
vupaukiu, meanwhile (adv)
vupemen, meaninglessness (n)
vupemenu, meaningless (adj)
vupio, meant (v pa d:importance)
vupiu, meaningfully (adv
    d:importance)
vupliol, byway (n)
vupo, mean (v d:importance)
vupu, meaningful (adj
    d:importance)
vuroif, byline (n)
vut, put (n)
vuth, purge (n)
vuthiaf, purgatory (n)
vutho, purge (v)
vutio, put (v pa)
vuto, put (v)
vutolp, demise (n)
vutolpo, demise (v)
vutreltua, bystander (n doer)
vuvaud, bylaw (n)
vuvifioa, bygone (n)

vuvifioi, bygones (n pl)
vuvifiou, bygone (adj)
wafiu, merely (adv)
wafp, hence (adv)
wafu, mere (adj)
waiat, yell (n)
waiato, yell (v)
waiatua, yeller (n doer)
waib, madness (n d:insane)
waibekiaf, madhouse (n)
waibeplon, madman (n)
waibeploni, madmen (n pl)
waibu, mad (adj d:insane)
waibwelu, madder (adj d:insane)
waik, yikes (interj)
Waiomink, Wyoming (n)
wak, most (adj/adv)
wak, most (pron)
wakiu, mostly (adv)
walsh, youth (n)
walshu, young (adj)
walshu, youthful (adj)
walshuet, youngster (n)
walshwaku, youngest (adj)
walshwelu, younger (adj)
wap, half (n)
wapliol, halfway (adj/adv)
wapo, halve (v)
wapu, half (adj)
warf, W (let sng)
warfhem, Number_1e1506
warfi, Ws (let pl)
Warshauf, Warsaw (n)
Washinkton, Washington (n)
washk, yet (adv/conj)
wath, hen (n)
wathkiaf, henhouse (n)
wefan, wig (n)
wefk, rout (n d:dig)
wefko, rout (v d:dig)
wefkua, router (n doer d:dig)
wefp, root (n)
wefpo, root (v)
wei, yes (adv)
weia, yeah (adv)
weif, sign (n)
weifbalt, signpost (n)
weifk, significance (n)
weifkiu, significantly (adv)
weifko, signify (v)
weifku, significant (adj)
weifo, sign (v)
weifp, signal (n)
weifpo, signal (v)
weifpua, signaler (n doer)
weift, signature (n)
weiftua, signatory (n doer)
weifua, signer (n doer)
Weilsh, Wales (n)
weip, yep (adv)
weip, yup (adv)
weishklosh, yesteryear (n)
weishkloshiu, yesteryear (adv)

weishkloshu, yesteryear (adj)
weishviul, yesterday (n)
weishviuliu, yesterday (adv)
weishviulu, yesterday (adj)
wel, more (adj/adv)
wel, more (pron)
welfiu, moreover (adv)
wiaf, merit (n)
wiafo, merit (v)
wiap, pilgramage (n)
wiapua, pilgrim (n doer)
wiash, hike (n)
wiasho, hike (v)
wiashua, hiker (n doer)
wiato, owe (v)
wiatua, ower (n doer)
wiauk, odd (n d:probability)
wiaukmashp, oddball (n)
wien, home (n)
wienagio, homemade (v pa)
wienago, homemake (v)
wienagua, homemaker (n doer)
wienegiotu, homemade (adj)
wienegliupu, homesick (adj)
wienk, homework (n)
wienlern, homecoming (n)
wienmen, homelessness (n)
wienmeniu, homelessly (adv)
wienmenu, homeless (adj)
wienmiun, hometown (n)
wieno, home (v)
wienraup, homeland (n)
wientheifo, homeown (v)
wientheifua, homeowner (n doer)
wienu, homey (adj)
wienvortua, homebuilder (n doer)
wif, hop (n)
wifo, hop (v)
wifp, narrow (n)
wifpiu, narrowly (adv)
wifpo, narrow (v)
wifpu, narrow (adj)
wifpuet, narrowness (n)
wifpweku, narrowest (adj)
wifpwelu, narrower (adj)
wifua, hopper (n doer)
wikon, yogurt (n)
winf, gum (n)
winfo, gum (v)
winfu, gummy (adj)
Wishkonsh, Wisconsin (n)
wiufo, hone (v)
wiush, sewer (n d:waste conduit)
wiush, sewerage (n)
wiusho, sewer (v d:waste conduit)
worfk, exhalation (n)
worfko, exhale (v)
worfkua, exhaler (n doer)
ya, hah (interj)
yadit, yield (n)
yadito, yield (v)
yaditua, yielder (n doer)
yafef, will (n d:inheritance)

yai, wow (interj)
yaif, wafer (n)
yaifan, waffle (n)
yaifano, waffle (v)
yaigat, hostility (n)
yaigatu, hostile (adj)
yail, foe (n)
yait, verb (n)
yaivaftu, verbose (adj)
yaivat, verbiage (n)
yaivatiu, verbally (adv)
yaivatu, verbal (adj)
yaivug, feud (n)
yaivugo, feud (v)
yaiy, wow (n)
yaiyo, wow (v)
yak, will (n d:determination)
yakbiort, willpower (n)
yake kodi, would (ndal d:will)
yakiu, willfully (adv
    d:determination)
yakiu, willingly (adv)
yako, will (v d:determination)
yaku, willful (adj
    d:determination)
yakuet, willingness (n)
yalf, wait (n)
yalfo, wait (v)
yalfua, waiter (n doer)
yalfua, waitress (n doer)
yalk, waddle (n)
yalko, waddle (v)
yalp, wad (n)
yalpo, wad (v)
yalsho, wallow (v)
yam, when (adv/conj)
yam, when (pron)
yamef, whenever (adv/conj)
yamik, quandary (n)
yanu, amen (interj)
yarketal, algebra (n)
yarketaliu, algebraically (adv)
yarketalu, algebraic (adj)
yarkut, algorithm (n)
yarkutiu, algorithmically (adv)
yarkutu, algorithmic (adj)
yarl, Y (let sng)
yarlhem, Number_1e1206
yarli, Ys (let pl)
yarm, alumnus (n)
yarmi, alumni (n pl)
yartu, foreign (adj)
yartua, foreigner (n doer)
yash, that (conj)
yasho, wade (v)
yashua, wader (n doer)
yath, hoof (n)
yatho, hoof (v)
yathua, hoofer (n doer)
yaua, yow (interj)
yauak, wretch (n)
yaufo, woo (v)
yauk, while (conj)

yauk, while (n)
yaun, whimper (n)
yauno, whimper (v)
yaup, whip (n)
yauplaiath, whiplash (n)
yauplaiatho, whiplash (v)
yaupo, whip (v)
yaupua, whipper (n doer)
yaushk, awkwardness (n)
yaushkiu, awkwardly (adv)
yaushku, awkward (adj)
yaushpu, awful (adj)
yaya, haha (interj)
yelf, whim (n)
yelf, whimsy (n)
yelfiu, whimsically (adv)
yelfu, whimsical (adj)
yelt, wetness (n)
yeltio, wet (v pa)
yeltmoiuf, wetsuit (n)
yelto, wet (v)
yeltraup, wetland (n)
yeltu, wet (adj)
yenaush, wonder (n)
yenaushiu, wonderfully (adv)
yenausho, wonder (v)
yenaushraup, wonderland (n)
yenaushu, wonderful (adj)
yenaushu, wonderous (adj)
yenaushuet, wonderment (n)
yerliu, yonder (adv)
yerlu, yonder (adj)
yesh, whiff (n)
yesho, whiff (v)
yilwap, behalf (n)
yoi, whoa (interj)
yoiak, wrench (n)
yoiako, wrench (v)
yoibako, wrangle (v)
yoibakua, wrangler (n doer)
yoikanko, wrestle (v)
yoikankua, wrestler (n doer)
yoikano, wrest (v)
yoilark, WiggleTalk (n)
yoip, whine (n)
yoipo, whine (v)
yoipu, whiney (adj)
yoipu, whiny (adj)
yoipua, whiner (n doer)
yoir, aisle (n)
yoith, wiggle (n)
yoithat, wriggle (n)
yoithati, wriggler (n pl)
yoithato, wriggle (v)
yoitho, wiggle (v)
yoithua, wiggler (n doer)
yorn, worm (n)
yorno, worm (v)
yornu, wormy (adj)
yosh, as (adv/conj/prep)
yuak, wick (n)
yuakat, wickedness (n)
yuakatu, wicked (adj)

yuan, white (n)
yuanfiaush, whitewash (n)
yuanfiausho, whitewash (v)
yuano, whiten (v)
yuanu, white (adj)
yufai-, quad- (num 4 pref)
yufai-, tetra- (num 4 pref)
yufaiak, quadrant (n)
yufaimik, quadrangle (n)
yufeth, fourth (num 4 ord)
yufi, four (num 4 card)
yufialfhemka, Number_1e16356
yufida, forty (num 40 card)
yufidai-, forty- (num 40 pref)
yufidak, quarantine (n)
yufidako, quarantine (v)
yufideth, fortieth (num 40 ord)
yufifk, quattuorquadragintillion
    (num 1e135 card)
yufift, quattuorotrigintillion (num
    1e105 card)
yufika, quadrillion (num 1e15
    card)
yufikai-, peta- (num 1e15 pref)
yufiketh, quadrillionth (num 1e15
    ord)
yufipa, fourteen (num 14 card)
yufipai-, fourteen- (num 14 pref)
yufipeth, fourteenth (num 14 ord)
yufishk, quattuorvigintillion (num
    1e75 card)
yufishkai-, gieksi-
yufishketh, quattuorvigintillionth
    (num 1e75 ord)
yufisht, quattuordecillion (num
    1e45 card)
yufishtai-, quaksi- (num 1e45
    pref)
yufishteth, quattuordecillionth
    (num 1e45 ord)
Yugoshlav, Yugoslavia (n)
yuian, suture (n)
yuiano, suture (v)
yuifoik, weirdness (n)
yuifoikiu, weirdly (adv)
yuifoiku, weird (adj)
yuifoikua, weirdo (n doer)
yuip, awe (n)
yuipo, awe (v)
yuk, weed (n)
yuko, weed (v)
yuku, weedy (adj)
yukua, weeder (n doer)
yumat, waist (n)
yumatroif, waistline (n)
yunpo, sew (v d:thread cloth)
yunpua, sewer (n doer d:thread
    cloth)
yupimirk, rectangle (n)
yupimirku, rectangular (adj)
yutabivanu, unisex (adj)

yutafond, uniqueness (n)
yutafondiu, uniquely (adv)
yutafondu, unique (adj)
yutak, unification (n)
yutako, unify (v)
yutam, unit (n)
yutaman, union (n)
yutamano, unionize (v)
yutamanua, unionist (n doer)
yutamanuet, unionization (n)
yutamat, unity (n)
yutamo, unite (v)
yutamu, unitary (adj)
yutanarm, unilateralism (n)
yutanarmiu, unilaterally (adv)
yutanarmu, unilateral (adj)
yutash, unison (n)
yutavorn, uniform (n)
yutavorno, uniform (v)
yutavornu, uniformly (adj)
yutavornuet, uniformity (n)
Yuteshviul, Wednesday (n)
yutharf, universe (n)
yutharfiu, universally (adv)
yutharfu, universal (adj)
yuvo, wed (v)
yuvtiug, wedlock (n)
yuwan, vowel (n)
yuyau, wahoo (interj)
za, Z (let sng)
zahem, Number_1e3156
zali, Zs (let pl)
zha, Zh (let sng)
zhab, jump (n)
zhabiu, jumpily (adv)
zhabo, jump (v)
zhabu, jumpy (adj)
zhabua, jumper (n doer)
zhaf, zag (n)
zhafo, zag (v)
zhagum, pajama (n)
zhahem, Number_1e3456
zhaiag, hamburger (n)
zhaiak, stimulation (n)
zhaiakan, stimulant (n)
zhaiakash, stimulus (n)
zhaiakashi, stimuli (n pl)
zhaiako, stimulate (v)
zhaiakua, stimulator (n doer)
zhaidaish, sentence (n
    d:punishment)
zhaidaisho, sentence (v
    d:punishment)
zhaif, tragedy (n)
zhaifiu, tragically (adv)
zhaifu, tragic (adj)
zhaigait, devil (n)
zhaigaitiu, devilishly (adv)
zhaigaito, bedevil (v)
zhaigaitu, devilish (adj)
zhaigiu, diabolically (adv)
zhaigu, diabolical (adj)
zhaik, vault (n d:leap)

zhaiko, vault (v d:leap)
zhail, fall (n d:descent)
zhailio, fell (v pa d:descent)
zhailo, fall (v d:descent)
zhailuil, fallout (n)
zhaimo, flaunt (v)
zhain, race (n d:competition)
zhainegethk, racetrack (n)
zhaineglaush, racehorse (n)
zhaino, race (v d:competition)
zhainpliol, raceway (n)
zhainua, racer (n doer
    d:competition)
zhaipio, sent (v pa)
zhaipo, send (v)
zhaipot, fiasco (n)
zhaipua, sender (n doer)
zhairp, dissent (n)
zhairpo, dissent (v)
zhairpua, dissenter (n doer)
zhairpua, dissident (n doer)
zhaishu, fast (adj d:speed)
zhaishwaku, fastest (adj)
zhaishwelu, faster (adj)
zhait, failure (n)
zhaitazho, falter (v)
zhaitht, vilification (n)
zhaithto, vilify (v)
zhaithu, vile (adj)
zhaito, fail (v)
zhaitu, fallible (adj)
zhakat, villain (n)
zhaldraipu, southbound (adj)
zhali, Zhs (let pl)
zhalkoik, suicide (n)
zhalkoiko, suicide (v)
zhalkoiku, suicidal (adj)
Zhalt Dakot, South Dakota (n)
Zhalt Karolin, South Carolina (n)
zhalt, south (n)
zhaltehaushu, southward (adj)
zhalteshaith, southwest (n)
zhalteshaithu, southwest (adj)
zhalteshaithu, southwestern (adj)
zhaltkiash, southeast (n)
zhaltkiashu, southeast (adj)
zhaltkiashu, southeastern (adj)
zhaltkuaf, southpaw (n)
zhaltu, south (adj)
zhaltu, southern (adj)
zhaltua, southerner (n doer)
zhanf, acoustics (n)
zhanfu, acoustic (adj)
zhank, vandalism (n)
zhanko, vandalize (v)
zhankua, vandal (n doer)
zhanp, dampness (n)
zhanpo, dampen (v)
zhanpu, damp (adj)
zhanpua, damper (n doer)
zhant, sound (n d:audio)
zhantaf, sonar (n)
zhantan, sonance (n)

zhantanelk, sonogram (n)
zhantanu, sonic (adj)
zhantgethk, soundtrack (n)
zhanto, sound (v d:audio)
zhantua, sounder (n doer
    d:audio)
Zhapaf, Japan (n)
Zhapanf, Japanese (n)
zharaul, midair (n)
zharfalm, midstream (n)
zharfival, midseason (n)
zharfrul, midsummer (n)
zharklosh, midyear (n)
zharkruf, midweek (n)
zharlimen, midmorning (n)
zharmiman, midrange (n)
zharovimidot, midafternoon (n)
zharpliol, midway (n)
zharshten, midterm (n)
zharshtenu, midterm (adj)
zhart, middle (n)
zhart, midst (n)
zhartaift, midpoint (n)
zharthishal, midsection (n)
zhartplon, middleman (n)
zhartu, middle (adj)
zharvempot, midwinter (n)
zharviul, midday (n)
zhatufiu, sound (adv d:secure)
zhatufu, sound (adj d:secure)
zhau, so (adj/adv/conj/interj)
zhau, so (pron)
zhaub, danger (n)
zhaubo, endanger (v)
zhaubu, dangerous (adj)
zhaubuet, endangerment (n)
zhaukait, treachery (n)
zhaukaitiu, treacherously (adv)
zhaukaitu, treacherous (adj)
zhaukap, treason (n)
zhaun, van (n)
zhaup, jam (n d:bind)
zhaupo, jam (v d:bind)
zhauprufp, vanquishment (n)
zhauprufpo, vanquish (v)
zhauprufpua, vanquisher (n doer)
zhaur, loss (n)
zhaurio, lost (v pa)
zhauro, lose (v)
zhauttua, loser (n doer)
zhaut, mine (n d:bomb)
zhauteprand, minefield (n)
zhauth, zap (n)
zhautho, zap (v)
zhauto, mine (v d:bomb)
zhauvaifk, vanguard (n)
zhavartsh, mediocrity (n)
zhavartshu, mediocre (adj)
zhavatu, menial (adj)
zhazh, buzz (n d:hum)
zhazho, buzz (v d:hum)
zhazhu, buzzy (adj d:hum)
zhazhua, buzzer (n doer d:hum)

zhbain, speed (n)
zhbainiu, speedily (adv)
zhbaino, speed (v)
zhbainpliol, speedway (n)
zhbainshkob, speedboat (n)
zhbainu, speedy (adj)
zhbainua, speeder (n doer)
zheid, target (n)
zheido, target (v)
zheifiu, zippily (adv)
zheifo, zip (v)
zheifu, zippy (adj)
zheifua, zipper (n doer)
zheifuano, zipper (v)
zheikan, jungle (n)
Zheishush, Jesus (n)
zheit, slick (v)
zheitu, slick (adj)
zhek, gas (n)
zheko, gas (v)
zheku, gaseous (adj)
zhelbrep, eggplant (n)
zhelg, egg (n)
zhelgo, egg (v)
zhelp, gasp (n)
zhelpo, gasp (v)
zhelthek, eggshell (n)
Zheniv, Geneva (n)
Zhenon, Xenon (n)
Zherman, German (n)
Zhermanf, Germany (n)
Zherushalom, Jerusalem (n)
zhesh, such (adj/adv)
zhesh, such (pron)
zhet, seriousness (n)
zhetan, zeta (n)
zhetiu, seriously (adv)
zhetu, serious (adj)
zhiafgukatu, electromagnetic
    (adj)
zhiafiub, electrode (n)
zhiafreilaku, electrochemical (adj)
zhiaft, electricity (n)
zhiaftiu, electrically (adv)
zhiafto, electrify (v)
zhiaftu, electric (adj)
zhiaftu, electrical (adj)
zhiaftua, electrician (n doer)
zhiaftuet, electrification (n)
zhiafuif, plight (n)
zhiag, pain (n)
zhiagitsh, painkiller (n)
zhiagiu, painfully (adv)
zhiagmeniu, painlessly (adv)
zhiagmenu, painless (adj)
zhiago, pain (v)
zhiagokio, painstook (v pa)
zhiagokiu, painstakingly (adv)
zhiagoko, painstake (v)
zhiagu, painful (adj)
zhiak, electrocution (n)
zhiako, electrocute (v)
zhialm, meridian (n)

zhiam, medium (n d:middle)
zhiamat, median (n)
zhiamatu, median (adj)
zhiamu, medium (adj d:middle)
zhiano, rock (v d:sway)
zhianua, rocker (n doer d:sway)
zhiap, fuel (n)
zhiapo, fuel (v)
zhiapua, fueler (n doer)
zhiarfk, meditation (n)
zhiarfko, meditate (v)
zhiart, rocket (n)
zhiarto, rocket (v)
zhiash, electrics (n)
zhiash, electronics (n)
zhiashpeft, electrostatic (n)
zhiashpeftu, electrostatic (adj)
zhiat, electron (n)
zhiatiu, electronically (adv)
zhiatu, electronic (adj)
zhiauk, zing (n)
zhiauko, zing (v)
zhiavigak, electroshock (n)
zhiavigaku, electroshock (adj)
zhiazh, sin (n)
zhiazhiu, sinfully (adv)
zhiazho, sin (v)
zhiazhu, sinful (adj)
zhiazhua, sinner (n doer)
zhibresh, someplace (n)
zhidauin, sometimes (adj/adv)
zhidaun, sometime (adj/adv)
zhidizh, something (n)
zhien, zone (n)
zhieno, zone (v)
zhiet, game (n)
zhieto, game (v)
zhietua, gamer (n doer)
zhif, zig (n)
zhifo, zig (v)
zhifzhaf, zigzag (n)
zhifzhafo, zigzag (v)
zhigaishk, beast (n)
zhigasht, enragement (n)
zhigashti, enragement (n pl)
zhigasho, enrage (v)
zhigat, rage (n)
zhigato, rage (v)
zhik, win (n)
zhikio, won (v pa)
zhiko, win (v)
zhikua, winner (n doer)
zhilf, glimpse (n)
zhilfo, glimpse (v)
zhilk, glitz (n)
zhilku, glitzy (adj)
zhilm, glimmer (n)
zhilmo, glimmer (v)
zhilp, glint (n)
zhilt, certainty (n)
zhiltil, glitter (n)
zhiltilo, glitter (v)
zhiltilu, glittery (adj)

zhiltiu, certainly (adv)
zhiltu, certain (adj)
zhim, issue (n)
zhimat, issuance (n)
zhimo, issue (v)
zhimua, issuer (n doer)
zhin, some (adj/adv)
zhin, some (pron)
zhinakiu, somewhat (adv)
zhinesh, jeans (n)
zhinialiu, somehow (adv)
Zhink, Zinc (n)
zhinol, somewhere (adv)
zhinol, somewhere (n)
zhinon, someone (pron)
zhiokio, hid (v pa d:obscure)
zhioko, hide (v d:obscure)
zhiop, huddle (n)
zhiopo, huddle (v)
Zhiorzh, Georgia (n)
Zhirkonium, Zirconium (n)
zhish, bee (n)
zhishlad, somebody (n/pron)
Zhiuf, Jew (n)
Zhiufan, Jewish (adj)
zhiumen, selflessness (n)
zhiumeniu, selflessly (adv)
zhiumenu, selfless (adj)
zhiun, self (n)
zhiuniu, selfishly (adv)
zhiunu, selfish (adj)
zhiunuet, selfishness (n)
zhiut, safe (n d:storage)
zhiv, jig (n d:dance)
zhiviuliu, someday (adv)
zhivo, jig (v d:dance)
zhizhal, ginger (n)
zhizhalthaf, gingerbread (n)
zhod, set (n d:group)
zhodiveil, setup (n)
zhodvak, setback (n)
zhoian, seam (n)
zhoianmeniu, seamlessly (adv)
zhoianmenu, seamless (adj)
zhoiano, seam (v)
zhoianoish, seamstress (n)
zhoif, silence (n)
zhoifiu, silently (adv)
zhoifo, silence (v)
zhoifu, silent (adj)
zhoifua, silencer (n doer)
zhoik, damage (n)
zhoiko, damage (v)
zhoip, walk (n)
zhoipiveil, walkup (n)
zhoipiveilu, walkup (adj)
zhoipliol, walkway (n)
zhoipo, walk (v)
zhoipua, walker (n doer)
zhoipuil, walkout (n)
zhoith, wild (v)
zhoithbresh, wilderness (n)
zhoithfief, wildcat (n)

zhoithflaush, wildlife (n)
zhoithgiaul, wildfire (n)
zhoithiu, wildly (adv)
zhoithkaun, wildcard (n)
zhoithu, wild (adj)
zhoithuan, wildflower (n)
zhoithuet, wildness (n)
zhoiv, seal (n d:binding)
zhoivo, seal (v d:binding)
zhoivua, sealant (n doer
     d:binding)
zhokem, second (n d:time)
zhor, pill (n)
Zhordan, Jordan (n)
zhork, mix (n)
zhorkar, mixture (n)
zhorko, mix (v)
zhorkua, mixer (n doer)
zhorl, beer (n)
zhorn, pillow (n)
zhorno, pillow (v)
zhoro, pill (v)
zhorpano, meddle (v)
zhorpanua, meddler (n doer)
zhort, pillar (n)
zhuabort, malice (n)
zhuabortiu, maliciously (adv)
zhuabortu, malicious (adj)
zhuaif, spiff (n)
zhuaifo, spiff (v)
zhuaifu, spiffy (adj)
zhuak, male (n)
zhuak, masculinity (n)
zhuaku, male (adj)
zhuaku, masculine (adj)
zhual, spirit (n)
zhualiu, spiritually (adv)
zhualiubup, malcontent (n)
zhualo, spirit (v)
zhualu, spiritual (adj)
zhualuet, spirituality (n)
zhuan, malady (n)
zhuanoif, malignancy (n)
zhuanoifo, malign (v)
zhuanoifu, malignant (adj)
zhuanuet, malaise (n)
zhuaprat, malfunction (n)
zhuaprato, malfunction (v)
zhuavorn, malformation (n)
zhuavorno, malform (v)
zhud, safety (n d:trustworthy)
zhudan, drone (n d:bee)
zhudeklofio, safekept (v pa)
zhudeklofo, safekeep (v)
zhudiu, safely (adv d:trustworthy)
zhudo, safeguard (v
     d:trustworthy)
zhudu, safe (adj d:trustworthy)
zhuduet, safeguard (n)
zhudwaku, safest (adj)
zhudwelu, safer (adj)
zhugait, poverty (n)
zhugaito, impoverish (v)

zhuian, slander (n)
zhuiano, slander (v)
zhuianu, slanderous (adj)
zhuk, fox (n)
zhuko, outfox (v)
zhukoth, foxhole (n)
zhuku, foxy (adj)
Zhulait, July (n)
zhult, jelly (n)
zhulteshlesh, jellyfish (n)
zhulteshleshi, jellyfish (n pl)
zhulto, jell (v)
zhultu, jellied (adj)
zhum, juvenile (n)
zhuman, junior (n)
zhumanu, junior (adj)
zhump, peril (n)
zhumpiu, perilously (adv)
zhumpu, perilous (adj)
zhumu, juvenile (adj)
Zhun, June (n)
zhup, save (n)

zhupan, savior (n)
zhupan, saviours (n)
zhuparo, savor (v)
zhupat, savings (n)
zhupeish, savvy (n)
zhupo, save (v)
zhupua, saver (n doer)
zhur, oil (n)
zhurdrit, oilseed (n)
Zhurik, Zurich (n)
zhuro, oil (v)
zhurplon, oilman (n)
zhurploni, oilmen (n pl)
zhurprand, oilfield (n)
zhurshiashu, old-fashioned (adj)
zhurt, experience (n)
zhurtan, expertise (n)
zhurtiu, expertly (adv)
zhurto, experience (v)
zhurtua, expert (n doer)
zhuru, oily (adj)
zhurua, oiler (n doer)

zhush, say (n)
zhushio, said (v pa)
zhusho, say (v)
zhushua, sayer (n doer)
zhuthiu, thus (adv)
zhutunp, suggestion (n)
zhutunpiu, suggestibly (adv)
zhutunpiu, suggestively (adv)
zhutunpo, suggest (v)
zhutunpu, suggestible (adj)
zhutunpu, suggestive (adj)
zhuvet, success (n)
zhuvetiu, successively (adv)
zhuveto, succeed (v)
zhuvetu, successive (adj)
zhuvetua, successor (n doer)
zhuvetuet, succession (n)
zhuvetushiu, successfully (adv)
zhuvetushu, successful (adj)
zhuvik, suffix (n)

www.ingramcontent.com/pod-product-compliance
Lightning Source LLC
Chambersburg PA
CBHW071330020726
47502CB00001B/43